image comics presents

THE WALKING DEAD

COMPENDIUM THREE

ROBERT KIRKMAN
creator, writer

CHARLIE ADLARD
penciler, inker (chapters 17-19)

STEFANO GAUDIANO
inker (chapters 20-24)

CLIFF RATHBURN
gray tones

RUS WOOTON
letterer

SEAN MACKIEWICZ
editor

CHARLIE ADLARD & DAVE STEWART
cover

For SKYBOUND ENTERTAINMENT

Robert Kirkman - CEO
David Alpert - President
Sean Mackiewicz - Editorial Director
Shawn Kirkham - Director of Business Development
Brian Huntington - Online Editorial Director
June Alian - Publicity Director
Rachel Skidmore - Director of Media Development
Michael Williamson - Assistant Editor
Dan Petersen - Operations Manager
Sarah Effinger - Office Manager
Nick Palmer - Operations Coordinator
Genevieve Jones - Production Coordinator
Andres Juarez - Graphic Designer
Stephan Murillo - Administrative Assistant

International inquiries: foreign@skybound.com
Licensing inquiries: contact@skybound.com

WWW.SKYBOUND.COM

IMAGE COMICS, INC.
Robert Kirkman – Chief Operating Officer
Erik Larsen – Chief Financial Officer
Todd McFarlane – President
Marc Silvestri – Chief Executive Officer
Jim Valentino – Vice-President

Eric Stephenson – Publisher
Corey Murphy – Director of Sales
Jeremy Sullivan – Director of Digital Sales
Kat Salazar – Director of PR & Marketing
Emily Miller – Director of Operations
Branwyn Bigglestone – Senior Accounts Manager
Sarah Mello – Accounts Manager
Drew Gill – Art Director
Jonathan Chan – Production Manager
Meredith Wallace – Print Manager
Randy Okamura – Marketing Production Designer
David Brothers – Content Manager
Addison Duke – Production Artist
Vincent Kukua – Production Artist
Sasha Head – Production Artist
Tricia Ramos – Production Artist
Emilio Bautista – Sales Assistant
Jessica Ambriz – Administrative Assistant
IMAGECOMICS.COM

PRINTED IN THE U.S.A.

ISBN: 978-1-63215-456-9

Chapter Seventeen: Something to Fear

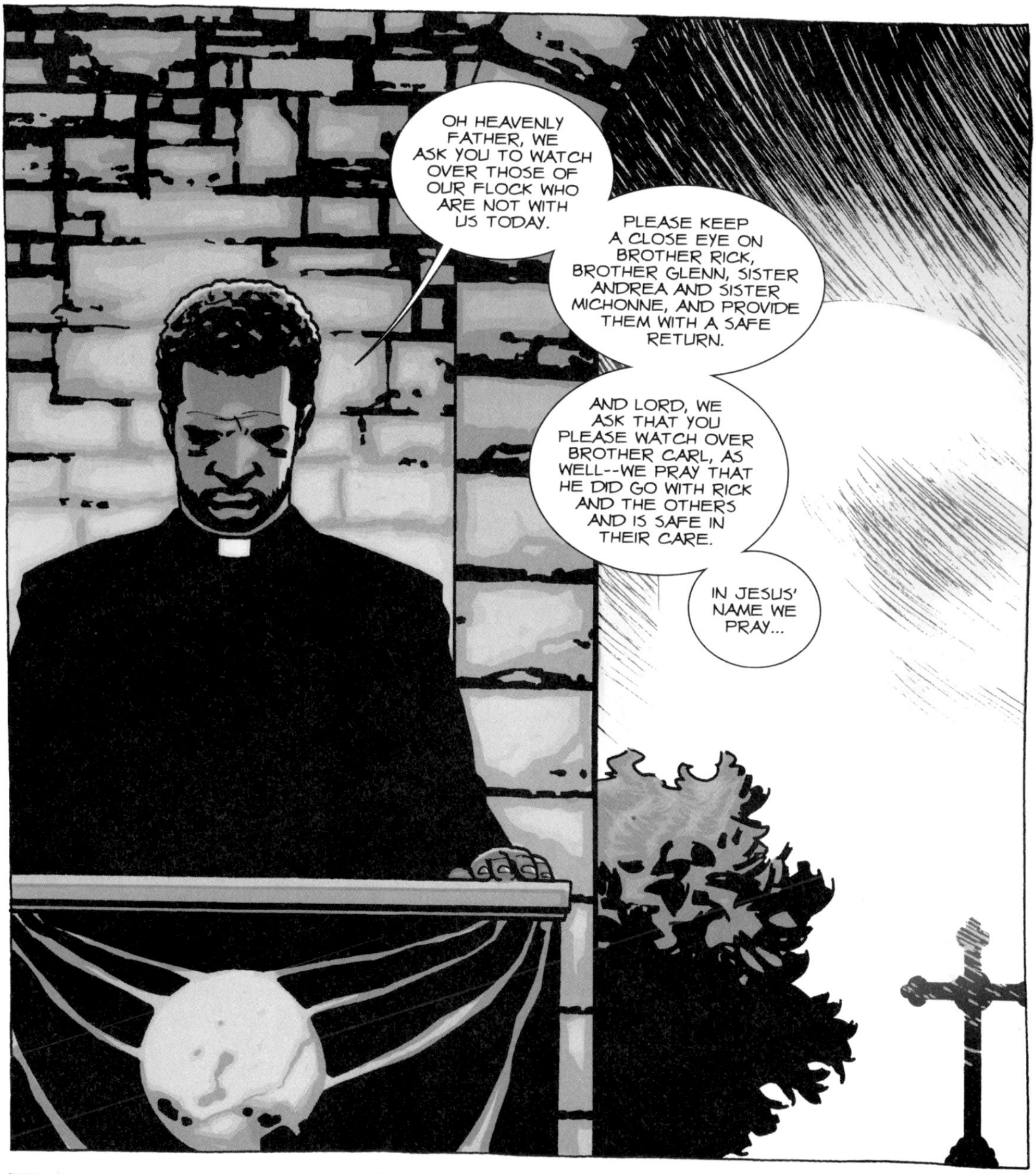
OH HEAVENLY FATHER, WE ASK YOU TO WATCH OVER THOSE OF OUR FLOCK WHO ARE NOT WITH US TODAY.
PLEASE KEEP A CLOSE EYE ON BROTHER RICK, BROTHER GLENN, SISTER ANDREA AND SISTER MICHONNE, AND PROVIDE THEM WITH A SAFE RETURN.
AND LORD, WE ASK THAT YOU PLEASE WATCH OVER BROTHER CARL, AS WELL--WE PRAY THAT HE DID GO WITH RICK AND THE OTHERS AND IS SAFE IN THEIR CARE.
IN JESUS' NAME WE PRAY...

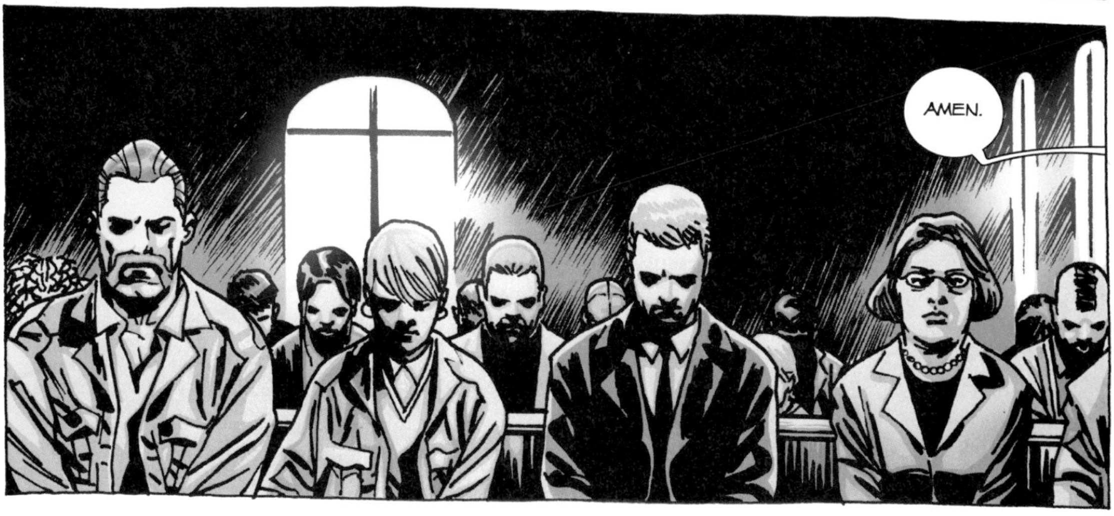
AMEN.

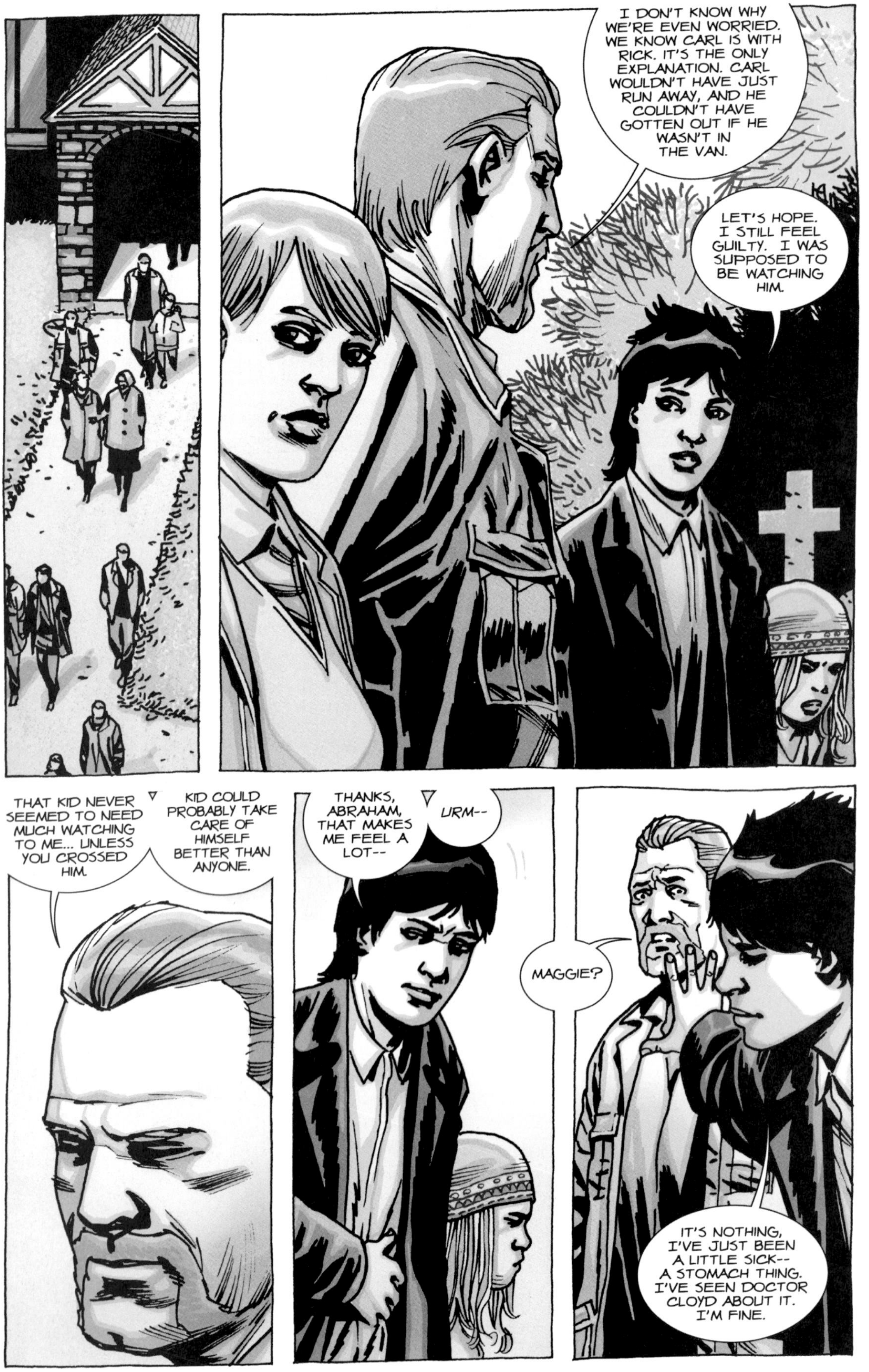
I DON'T KNOW WHY WE'RE EVEN WORRIED. WE KNOW CARL IS WITH RICK. IT'S THE ONLY EXPLANATION. CARL WOULDN'T HAVE JUST RUN AWAY, AND HE COULDN'T HAVE GOTTEN OUT IF HE WASN'T IN THE VAN.
LET'S HOPE. I STILL FEEL GUILTY. I WAS SUPPOSED TO BE WATCHING HIM.
THAT KID NEVER SEEMED TO NEED MUCH WATCHING TO ME... UNLESS YOU CROSSED HIM.
KID COULD PROBABLY TAKE CARE OF HIMSELF BETTER THAN ANYONE.
THANKS, ABRAHAM, THAT MAKES ME FEEL A LOT--
URM--
MAGGIE?
IT'S NOTHING, I'VE JUST BEEN A LITTLE SICK-- A STOMACH THING. I'VE SEEN DOCTOR CLOYD ABOUT IT. I'M FINE.

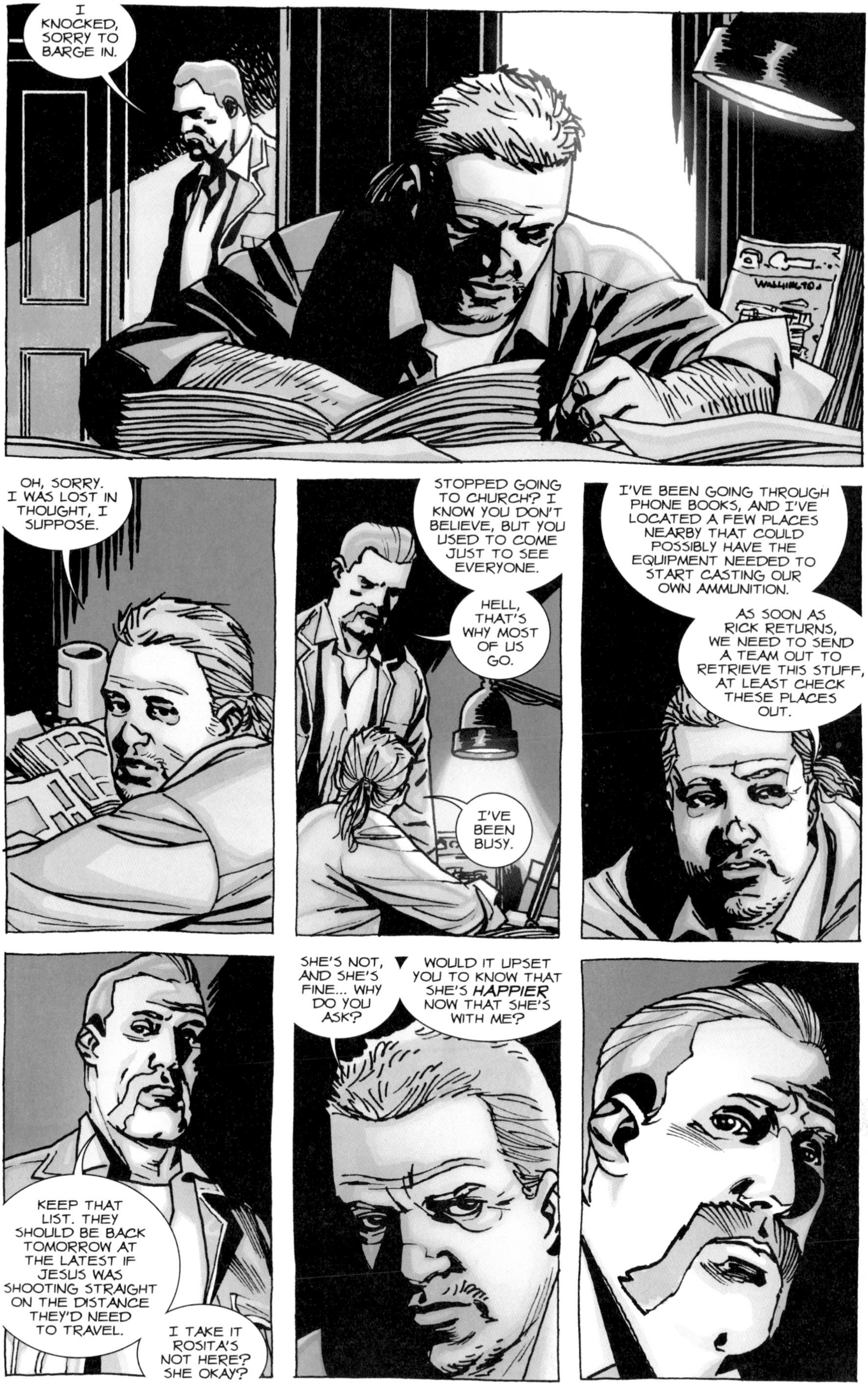
I KNOCKED, SORRY TO BARGE IN.
OH, SORRY. I WAS LOST IN THOUGHT, I SUPPOSE.
STOPPED GOING TO CHURCH? I KNOW YOU DON'T BELIEVE, BUT YOU USED TO COME JUST TO SEE EVERYONE.
HELL, THAT'S WHY MOST OF US GO.
I'VE BEEN BUSY.
I'VE BEEN GOING THROUGH PHONE BOOKS, AND I'VE LOCATED A FEW PLACES NEARBY THAT COULD POSSIBLY HAVE THE EQUIPMENT NEEDED TO START CASTING OUR OWN AMMUNITION.
AS SOON AS RICK RETURNS, WE NEED TO SEND A TEAM OUT TO RETRIEVE THIS STUFF, AT LEAST CHECK THESE PLACES OUT.
KEEP THAT LIST. THEY SHOULD BE BACK TOMORROW AT THE LATEST IF JESUS WAS SHOOTING STRAIGHT ON THE DISTANCE THEY'D NEED TO TRAVEL.
I TAKE IT ROSITA'S NOT HERE? SHE OKAY?
SHE'S NOT, AND SHE'S FINE... WHY DO YOU ASK?
WOULD IT UPSET YOU TO KNOW THAT SHE'S *HAPPIER* NOW THAT SHE'S WITH ME?

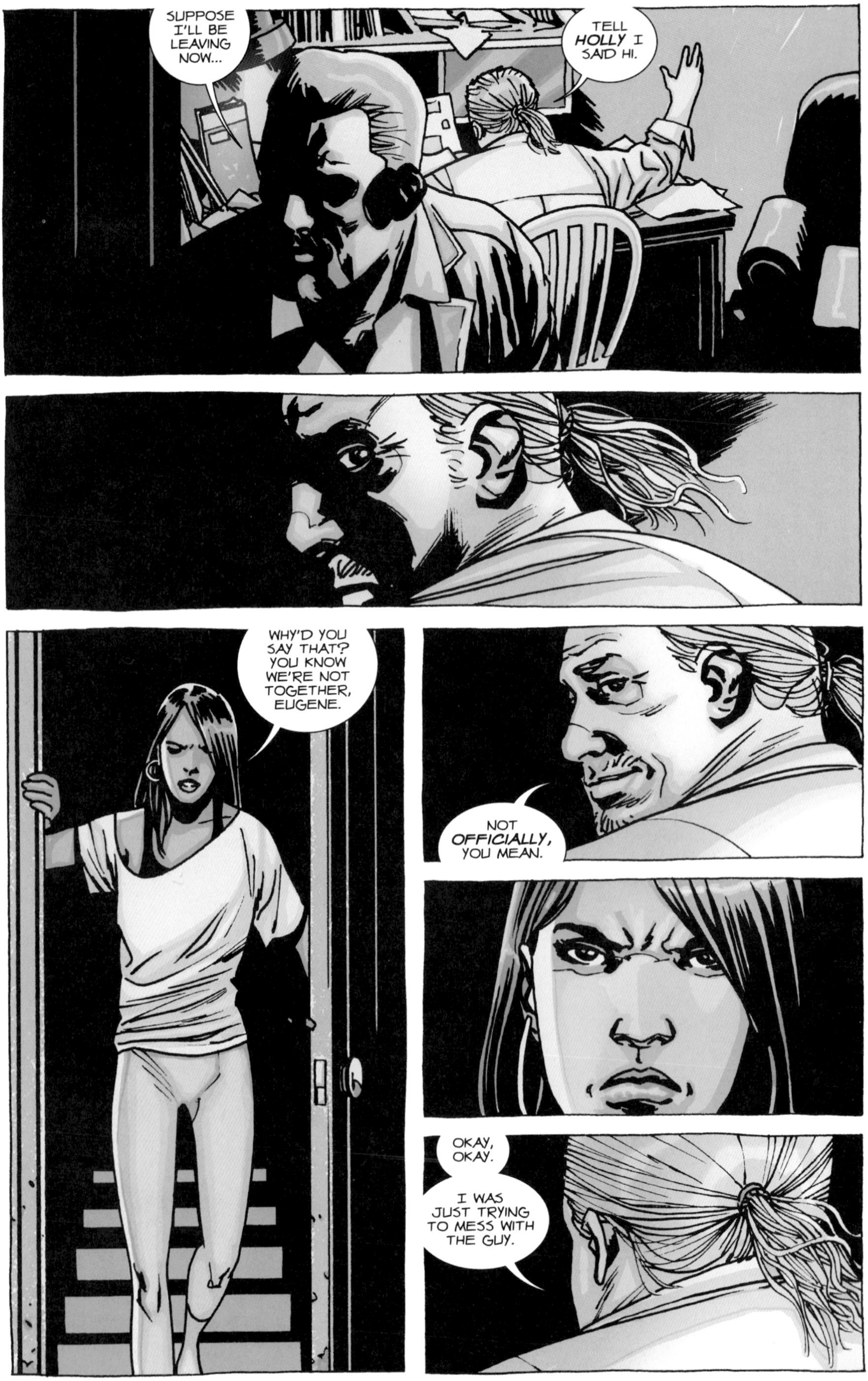
SUPPOSE I'LL BE LEAVING NOW...
TELL HOLLY I SAID HI.
WHY'D YOU SAY THAT? YOU KNOW WE'RE NOT TOGETHER, EUGENE.
NOT OFFICIALLY, YOU MEAN.
OKAY, OKAY.
I WAS JUST TRYING TO MESS WITH THE GUY.

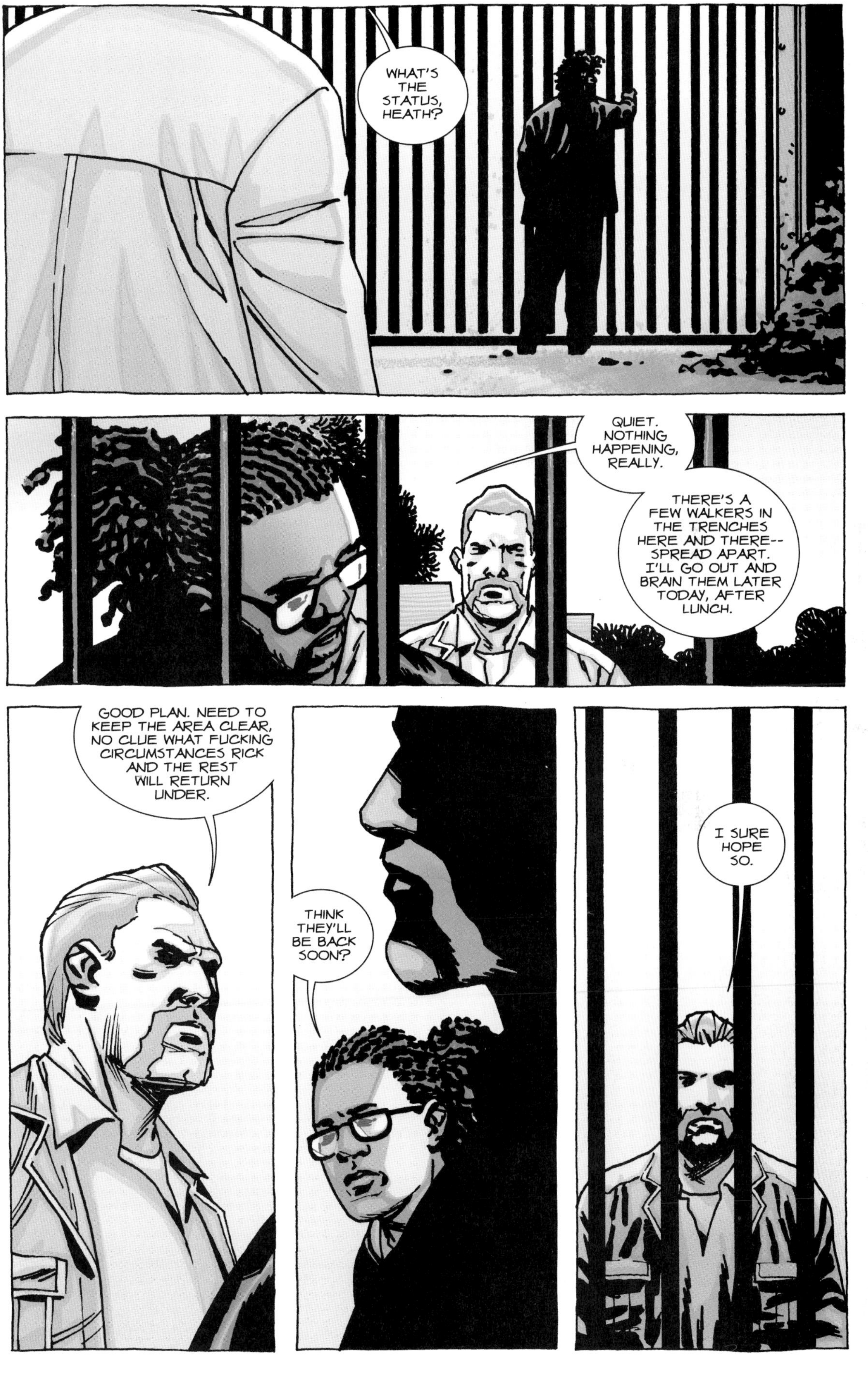
WHAT'S THE STATUS, HEATH?
QUIET. NOTHING HAPPENING, REALLY.
THERE'S A FEW WALKERS IN THE TRENCHES HERE AND THERE-- SPREAD APART. I'LL GO OUT AND BRAIN THEM LATER TODAY, AFTER LUNCH.
GOOD PLAN. NEED TO KEEP THE AREA CLEAR, NO CLUE WHAT FUCKING CIRCUMSTANCES RICK AND THE REST WILL RETURN UNDER.
THINK THEY'LL BE BACK SOON?
I SURE HOPE SO.

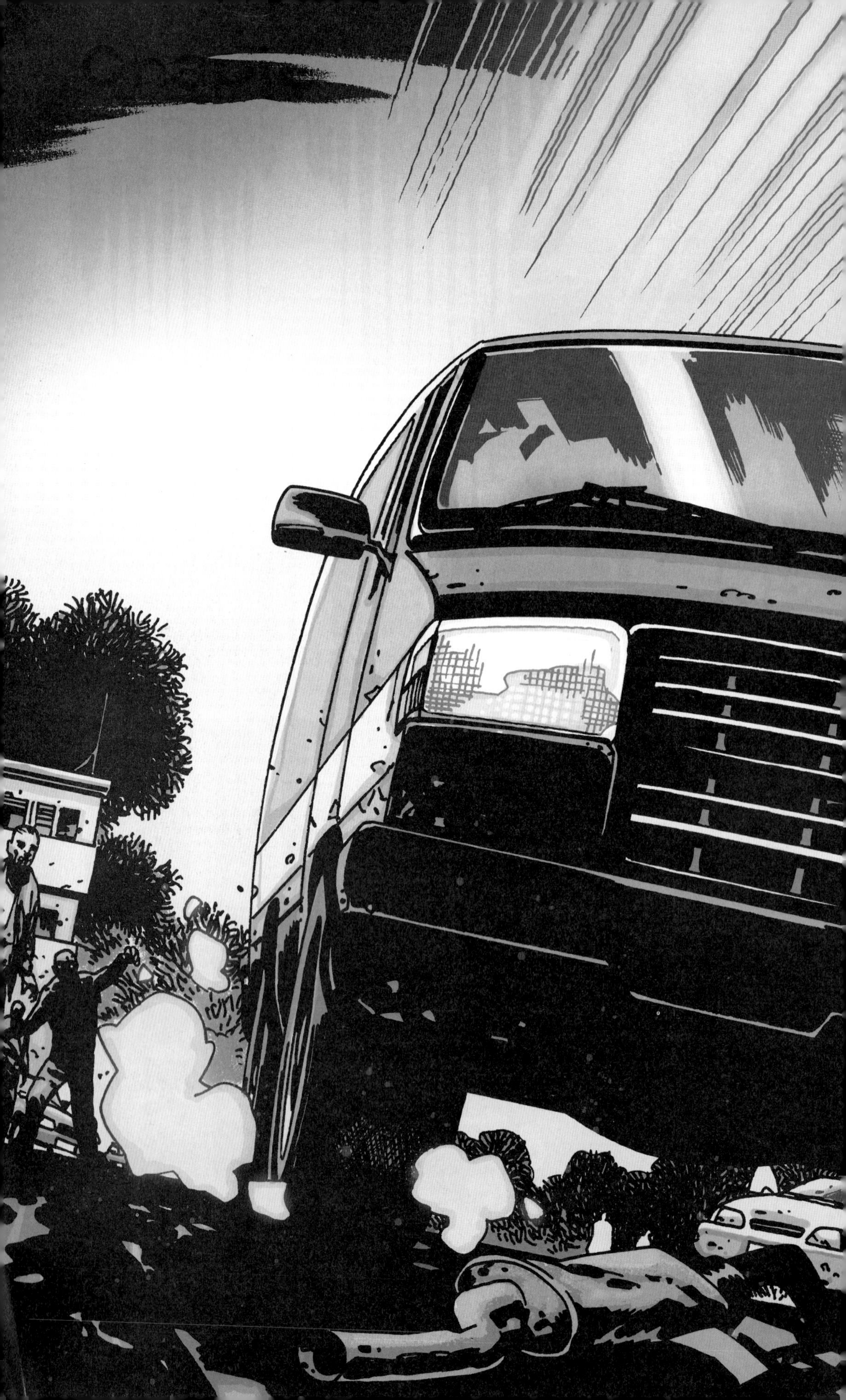

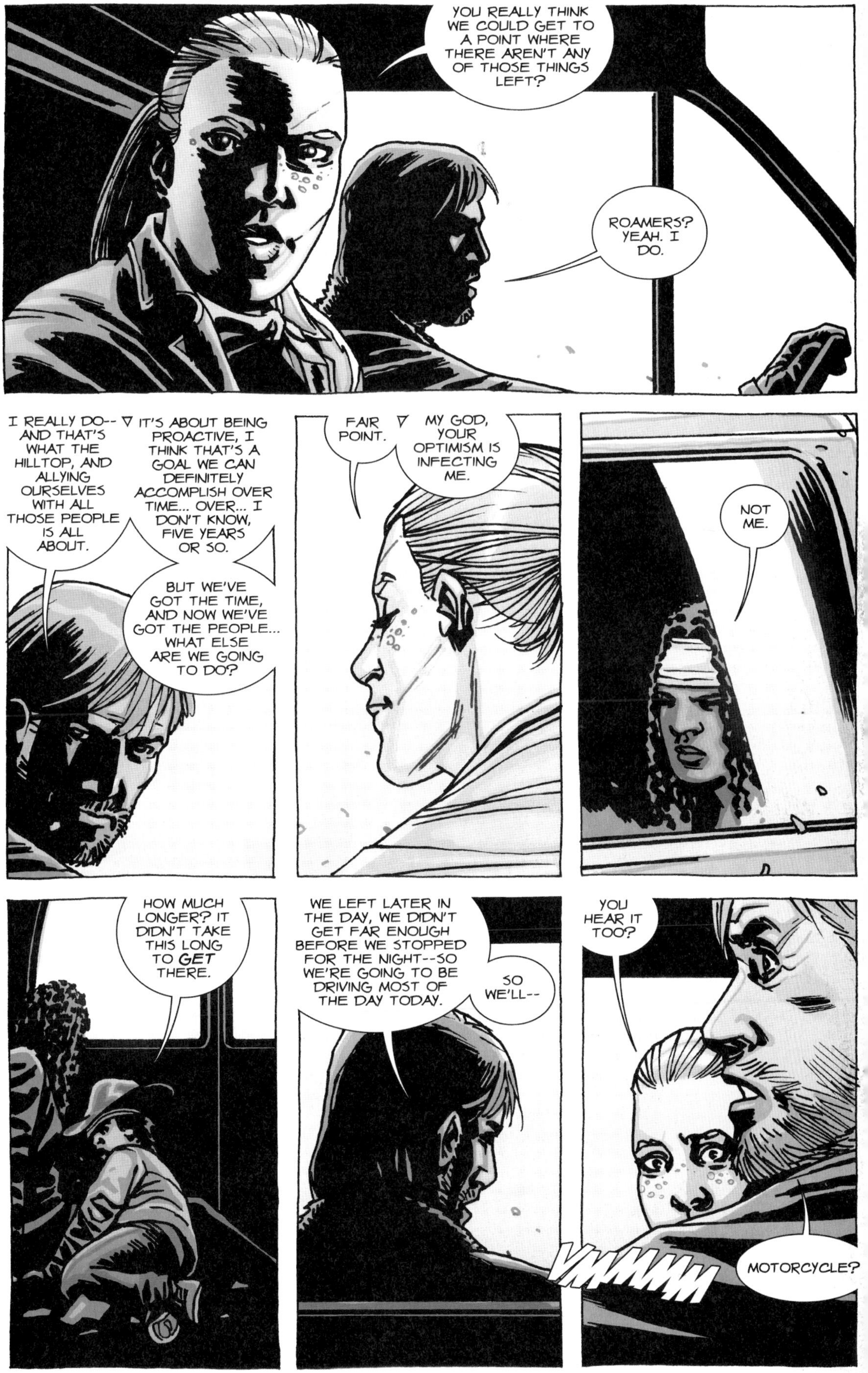

YOU REALLY THINK WE COULD GET TO A POINT WHERE THERE AREN'T ANY OF THOSE THINGS LEFT?
ROAMERS? YEAH. I DO.
I REALLY DO-- AND THAT'S WHAT THE HILLTOP, AND ALLYING OURSELVES WITH ALL THOSE PEOPLE IS ALL ABOUT.
IT'S ABOUT BEING PROACTIVE, I THINK THAT'S A GOAL WE CAN DEFINITELY ACCOMPLISH OVER TIME... OVER... I DON'T KNOW, FIVE YEARS OR SO.
BUT WE'VE GOT THE TIME, AND NOW WE'VE GOT THE PEOPLE... WHAT ELSE ARE WE GOING TO DO?
FAIR POINT.
MY GOD, YOUR OPTIMISM IS INFECTING ME.
NOT ME.
HOW MUCH LONGER? IT DIDN'T TAKE THIS LONG TO **GET** THERE.
WE LEFT LATER IN THE DAY, WE DIDN'T GET FAR ENOUGH BEFORE WE STOPPED FOR THE NIGHT--SO WE'RE GOING TO BE DRIVING MOST OF THE DAY TODAY.
SO WE'LL--
YOU HEAR IT TOO?
VMMMMM
MOTORCYCLE?

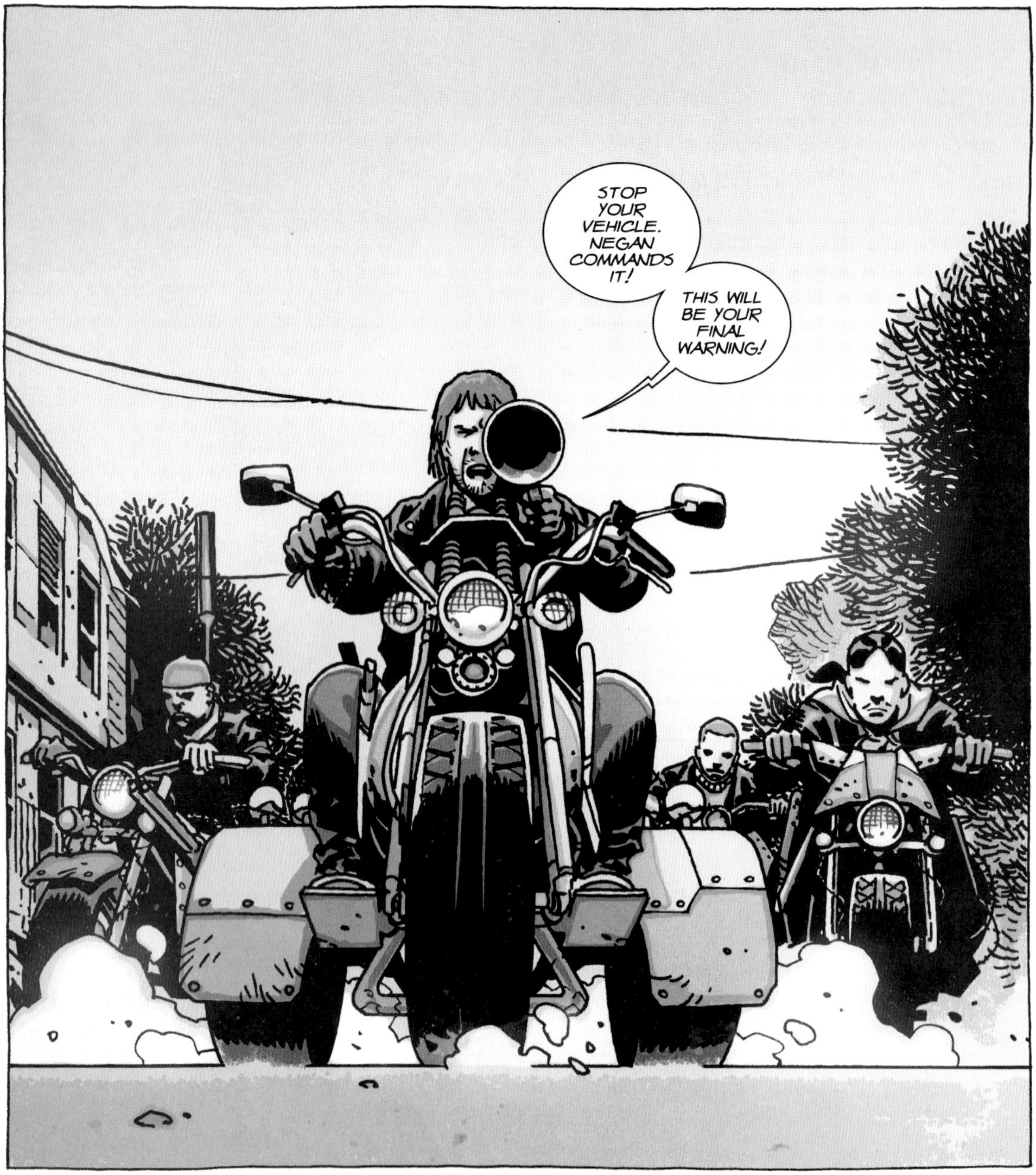
STOP YOUR VEHICLE. NEGAN COMMANDS IT!
THIS WILL BE YOUR FINAL WARNING!

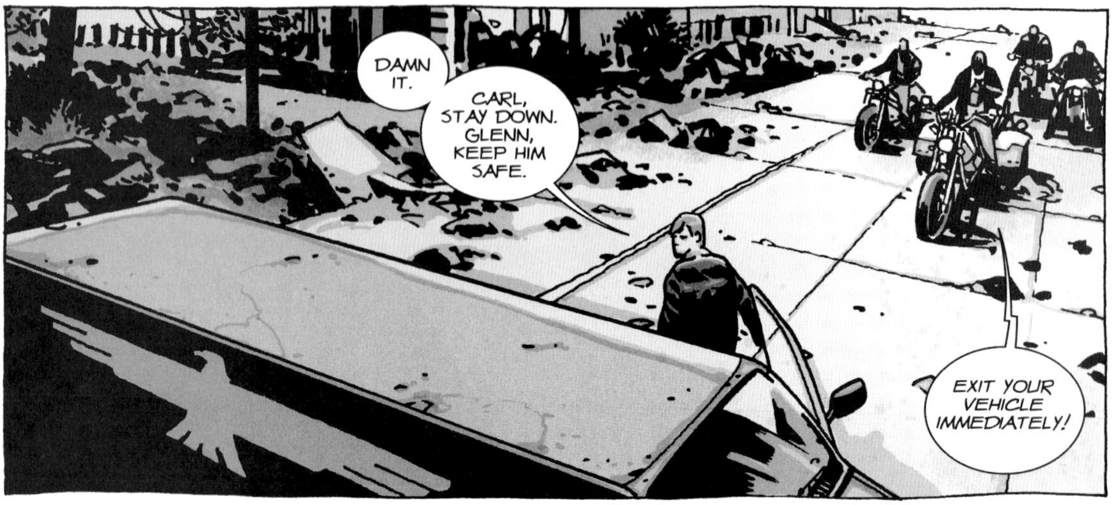
DAMN IT.
CARL, STAY DOWN. GLENN, KEEP HIM SAFE.
EXIT YOUR VEHICLE IMMEDIATELY!

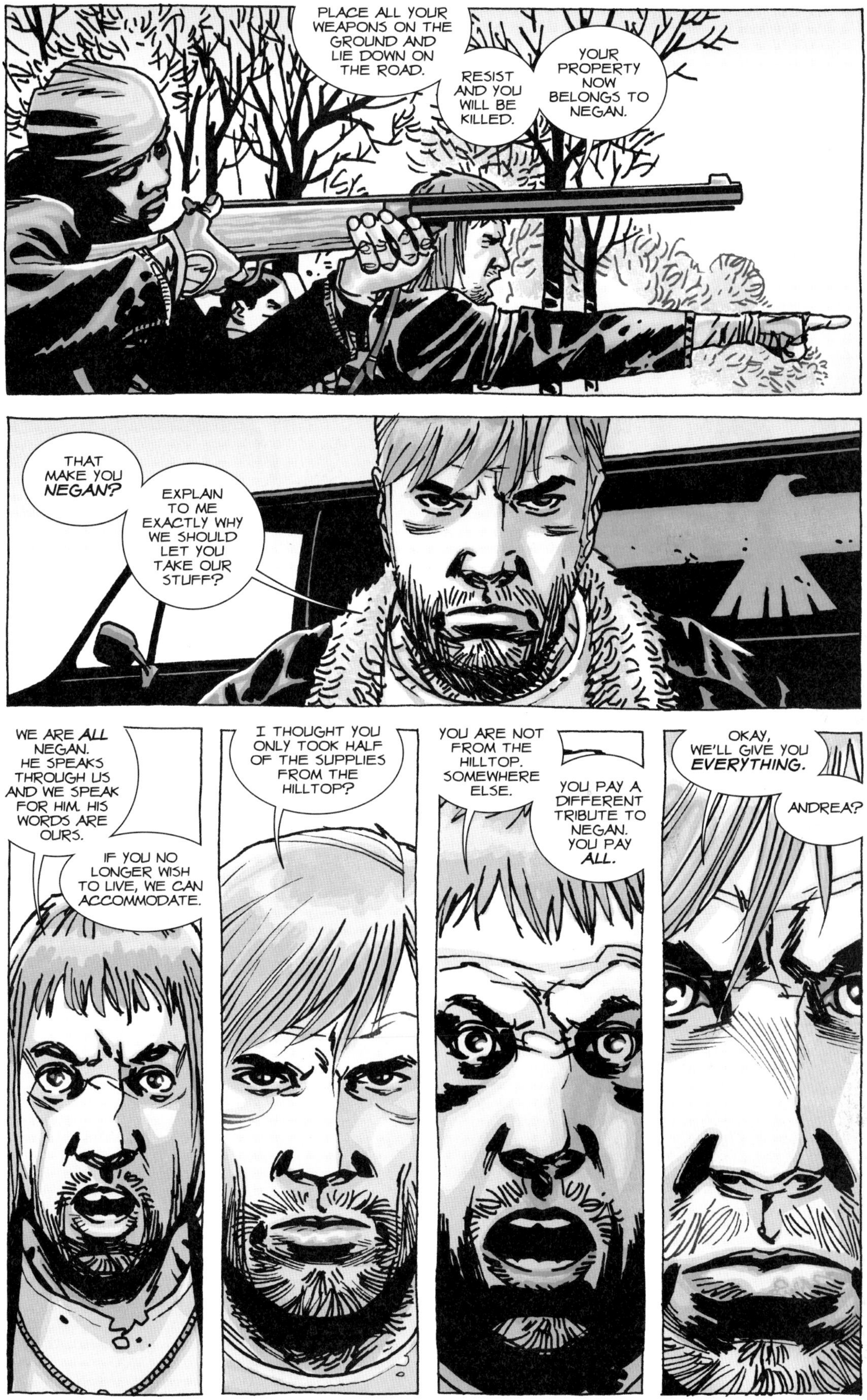
PLACE ALL YOUR WEAPONS ON THE GROUND AND LIE DOWN ON THE ROAD.
RESIST AND YOU WILL BE KILLED.
YOUR PROPERTY NOW BELONGS TO NEGAN.
THAT MAKE YOU *NEGAN?*
EXPLAIN TO ME EXACTLY WHY WE SHOULD LET YOU TAKE OUR STUFF?
WE ARE *ALL* NEGAN. HE SPEAKS THROUGH US AND WE SPEAK FOR HIM. HIS WORDS ARE OURS.
IF YOU NO LONGER WISH TO LIVE, WE CAN ACCOMMODATE.
I THOUGHT YOU ONLY TOOK HALF OF THE SUPPLIES FROM THE HILLTOP?
YOU ARE NOT FROM THE HILLTOP. SOMEWHERE ELSE.
YOU PAY A DIFFERENT TRIBUTE TO NEGAN. YOU PAY *ALL.*
OKAY, WE'LL GIVE YOU *EVERYTHING.*
ANDREA?

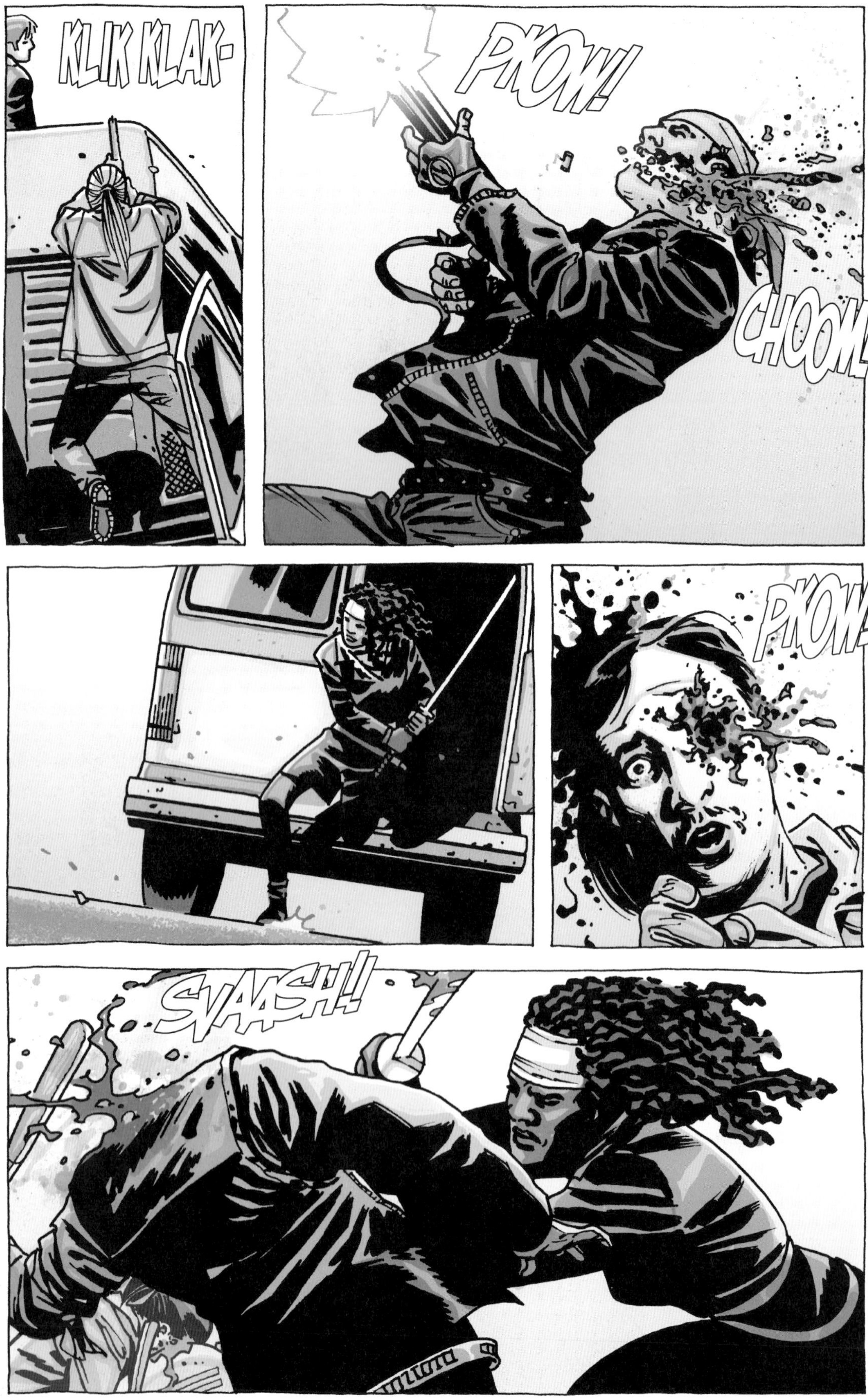
KLIK KLAK-
PKOW!
CHOOM!
PKOW!
SVAASH!!

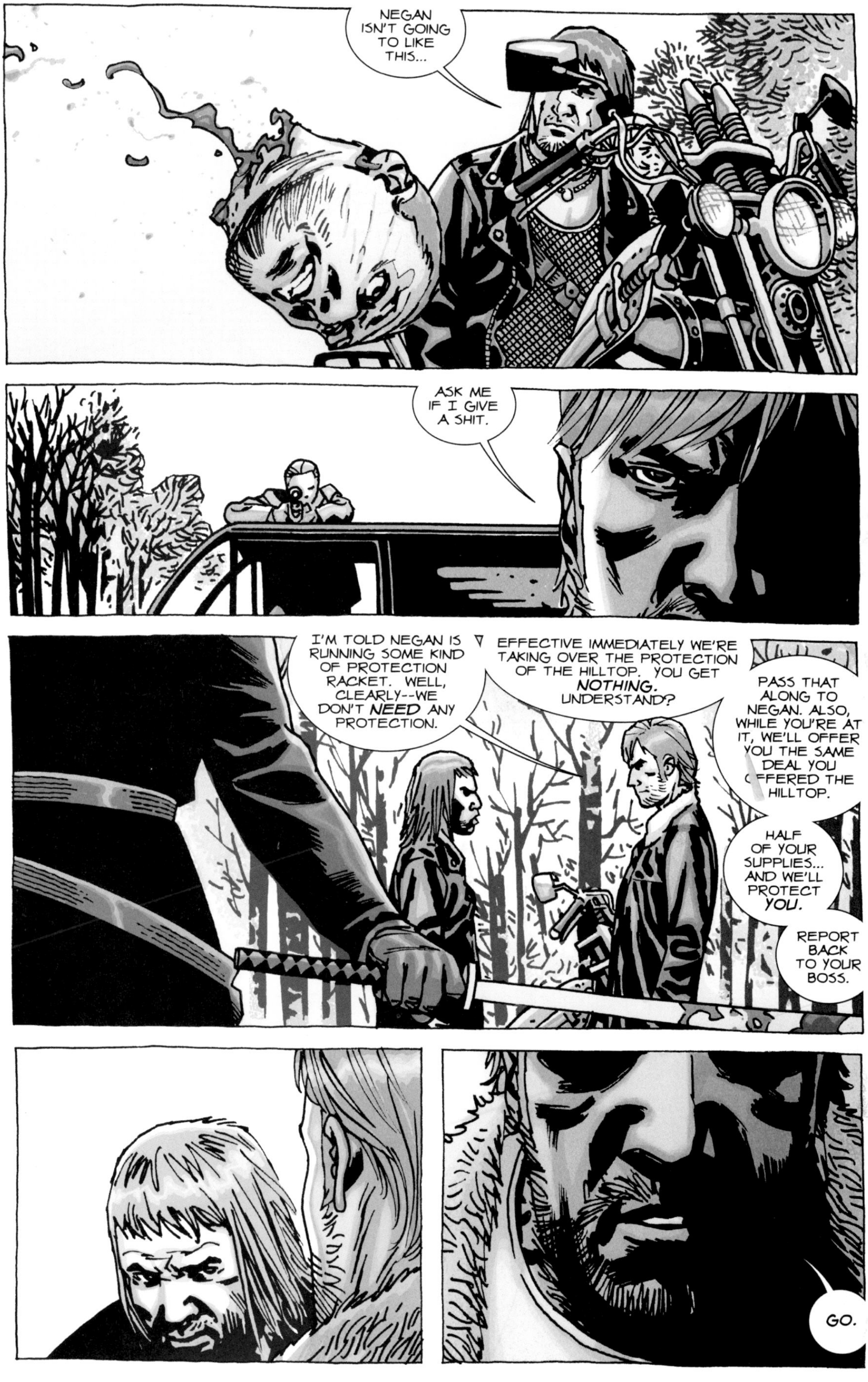
NEGAN ISN'T GOING TO LIKE THIS...
ASK ME IF I GIVE A SHIT.
I'M TOLD NEGAN IS RUNNING SOME KIND OF PROTECTION RACKET. WELL, CLEARLY--WE DON'T NEED ANY PROTECTION.
EFFECTIVE IMMEDIATELY WE'RE TAKING OVER THE PROTECTION OF THE HILLTOP. YOU GET NOTHING. UNDERSTAND?
PASS THAT ALONG TO NEGAN. ALSO, WHILE YOU'RE AT IT, WE'LL OFFER YOU THE SAME DEAL YOU OFFERED THE HILLTOP.
HALF OF YOUR SUPPLIES... AND WE'LL PROTECT YOU.
REPORT BACK TO YOUR BOSS.
GO.

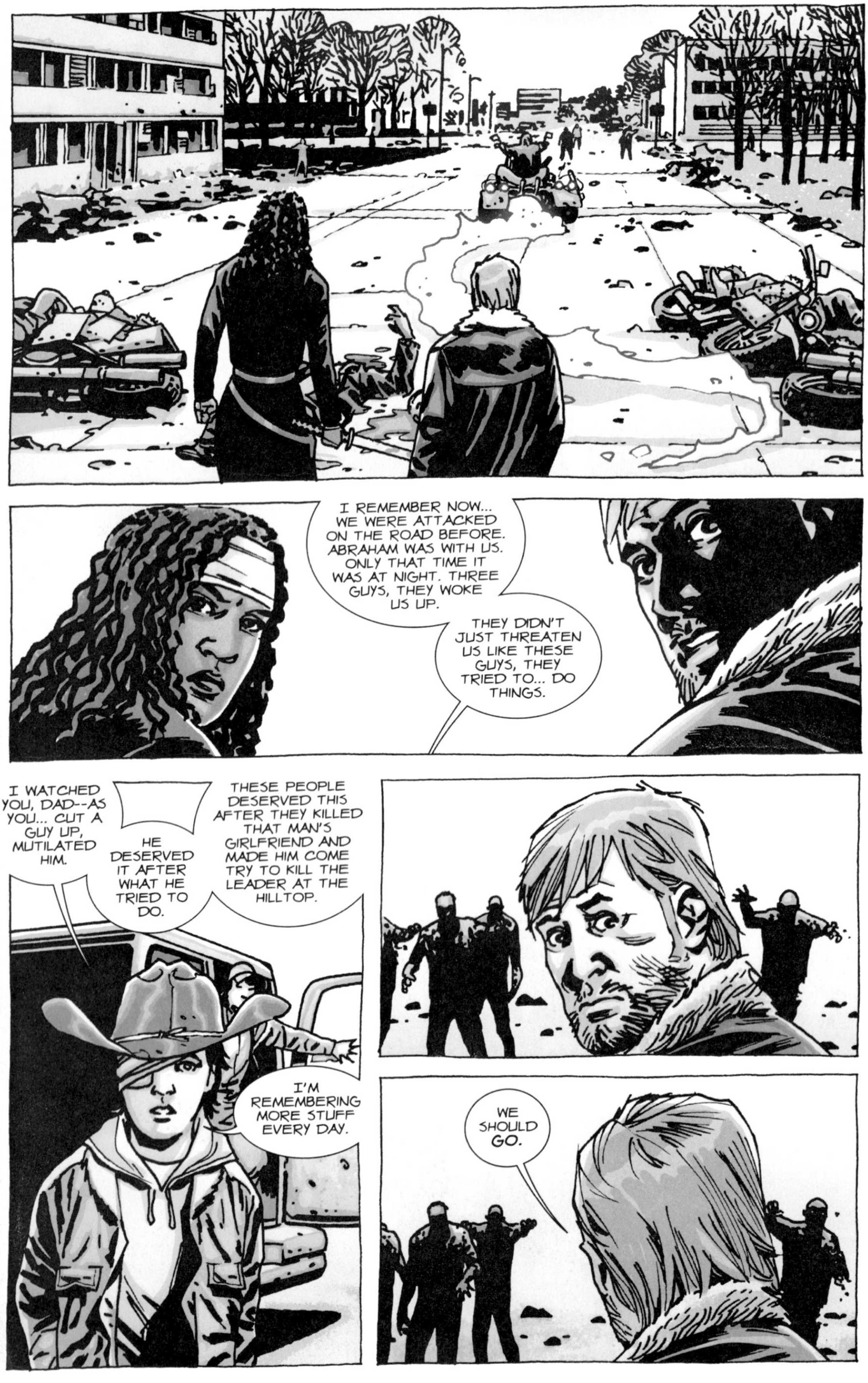
I REMEMBER NOW... WE WERE ATTACKED ON THE ROAD BEFORE. ABRAHAM WAS WITH US. ONLY THAT TIME IT WAS AT NIGHT. THREE GUYS, THEY WOKE US UP.
THEY DIDN'T JUST THREATEN US LIKE THESE GUYS, THEY TRIED TO... DO THINGS.
I WATCHED YOU, DAD--AS YOU... CUT A GUY UP, MUTILATED HIM.
HE DESERVED IT AFTER WHAT HE TRIED TO DO.
THESE PEOPLE DESERVED THIS AFTER THEY KILLED THAT MAN'S GIRLFRIEND AND MADE HIM COME TRY TO KILL THE LEADER AT THE HILLTOP.
I'M REMEMBERING MORE STUFF EVERY DAY.
WE SHOULD GO.

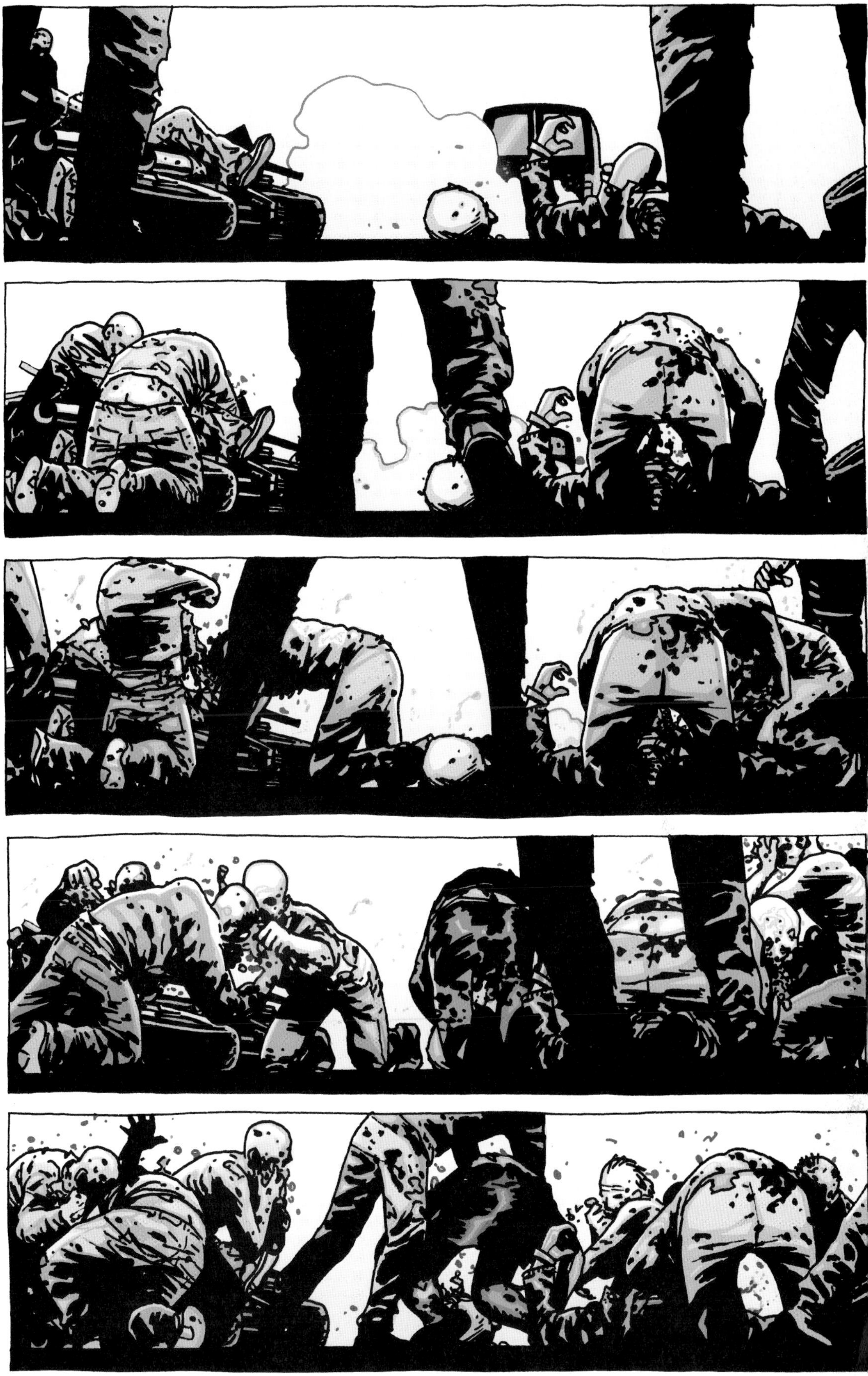

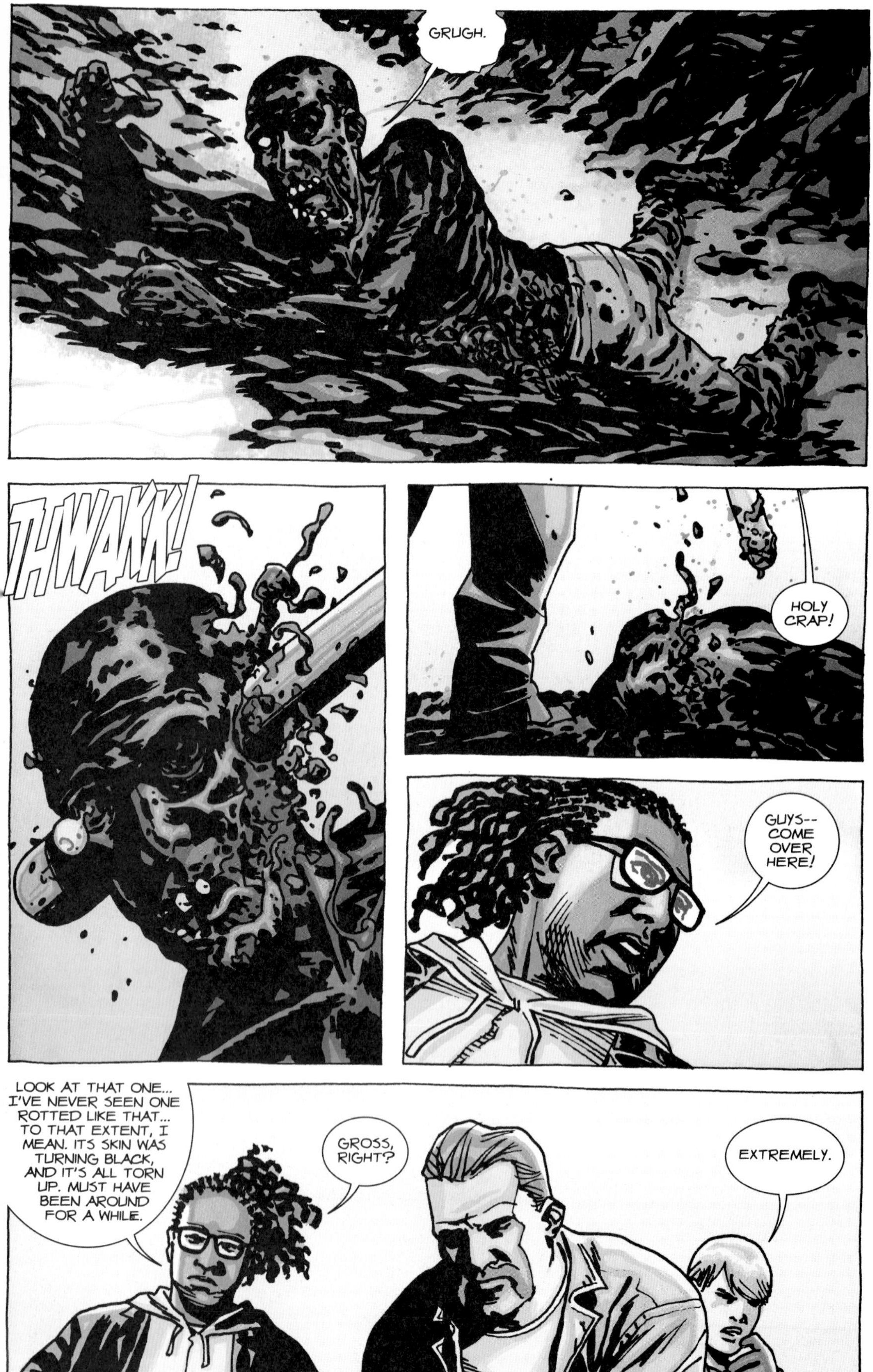
GRUGH.
THWAKK!
HOLY CRAP!
GUYS-- COME OVER HERE!
LOOK AT THAT ONE... I'VE NEVER SEEN ONE ROTTED LIKE THAT... TO THAT EXTENT, I MEAN. ITS SKIN WAS TURNING BLACK, AND IT'S ALL TORN UP. MUST HAVE BEEN AROUND FOR A WHILE.
GROSS, RIGHT?
EXTREMELY.

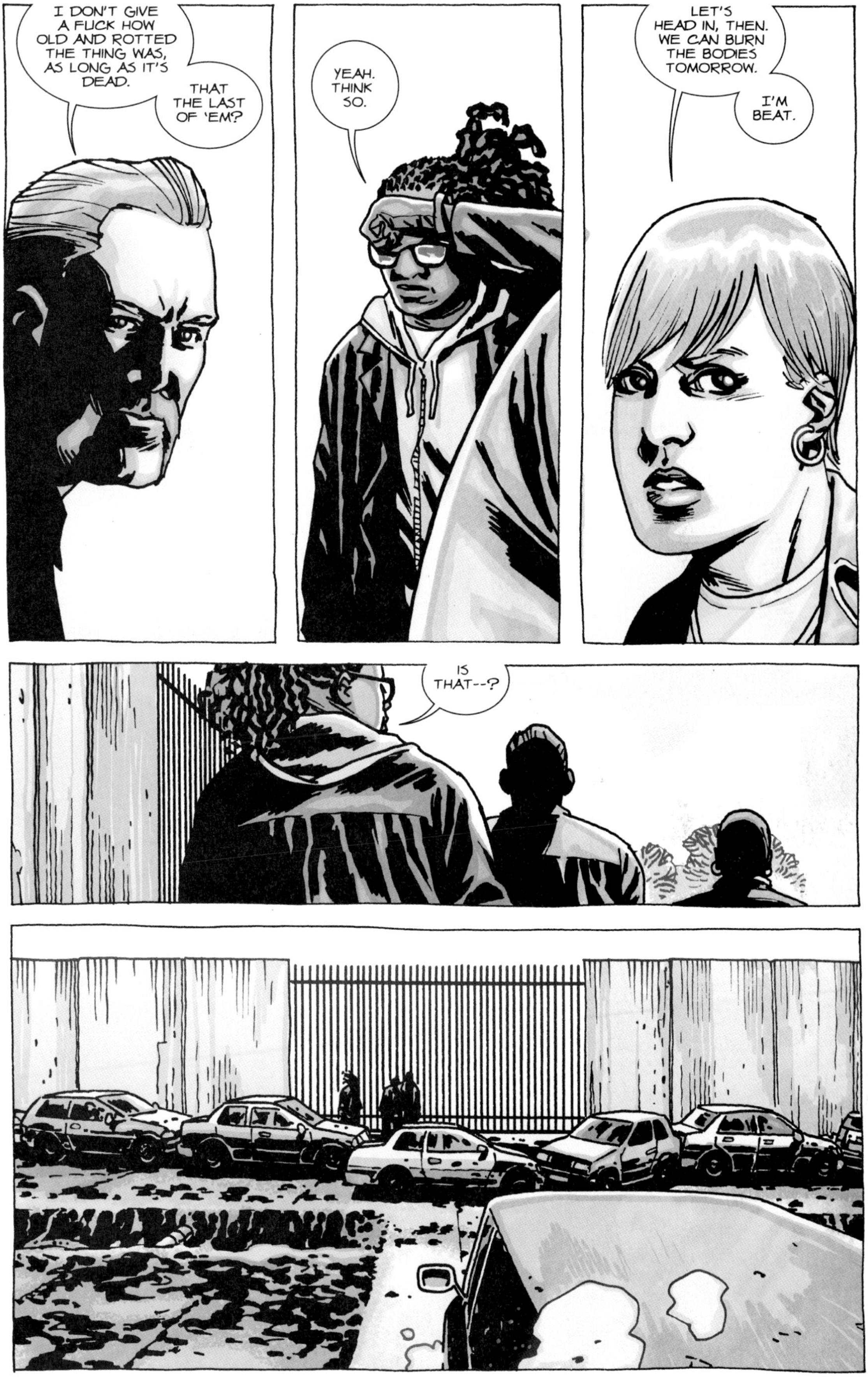
I DON'T GIVE A FUCK HOW OLD AND ROTTED THE THING WAS, AS LONG AS IT'S DEAD.
THAT THE LAST OF 'EM?
YEAH. THINK SO.
LET'S HEAD IN, THEN. WE CAN BURN THE BODIES TOMORROW.
I'M BEAT.
IS THAT--?

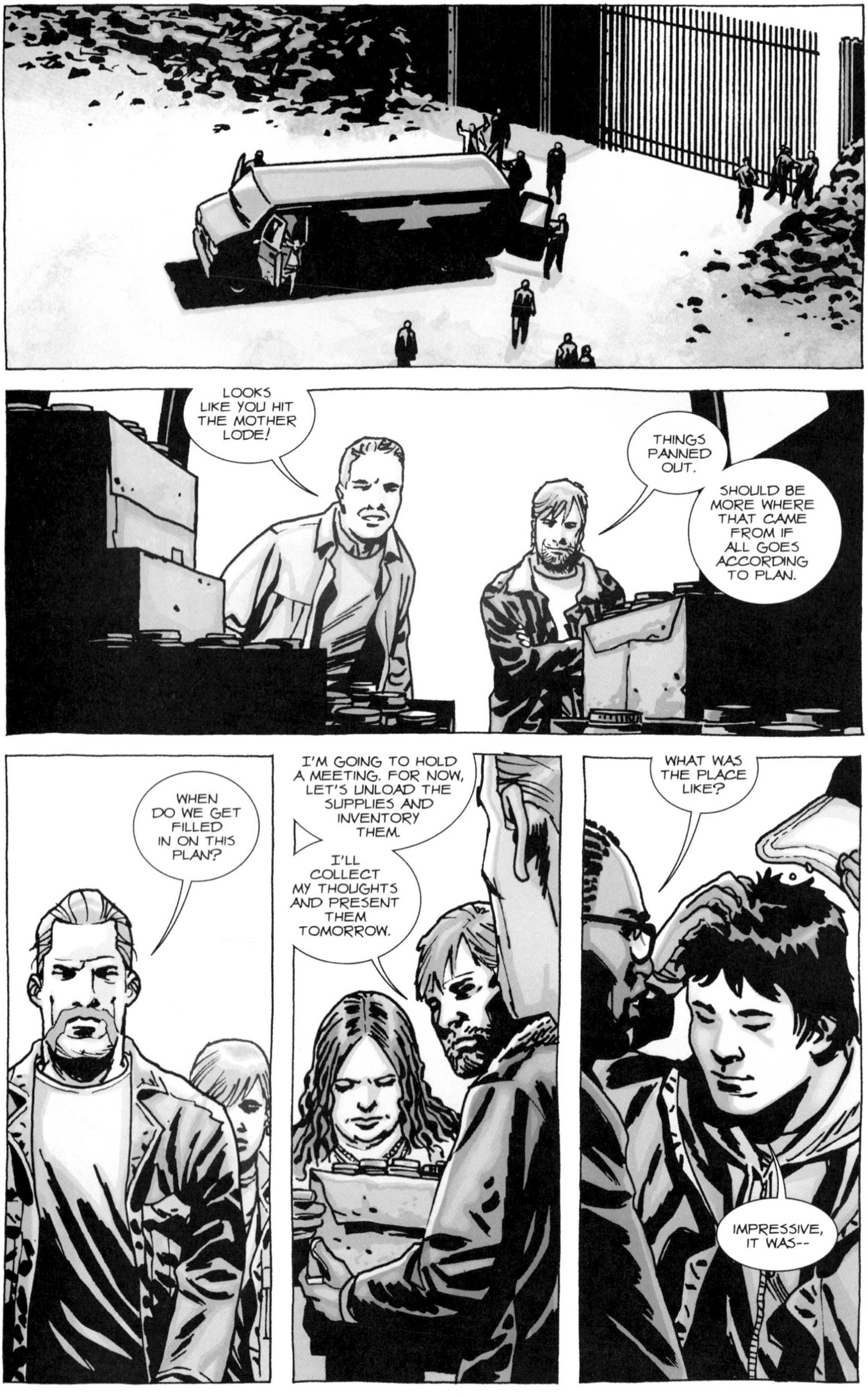
LOOKS LIKE YOU HIT THE MOTHER LODE!
THINGS PANNED OUT.
SHOULD BE MORE WHERE THAT CAME FROM IF ALL GOES ACCORDING TO PLAN.
WHEN DO WE GET FILLED IN ON THIS PLAN?
I'M GOING TO HOLD A MEETING. FOR NOW, LET'S UNLOAD THE SUPPLIES AND INVENTORY THEM.
I'LL COLLECT MY THOUGHTS AND PRESENT THEM TOMORROW.
WHAT WAS THE PLACE LIKE?
IMPRESSIVE, IT WAS--

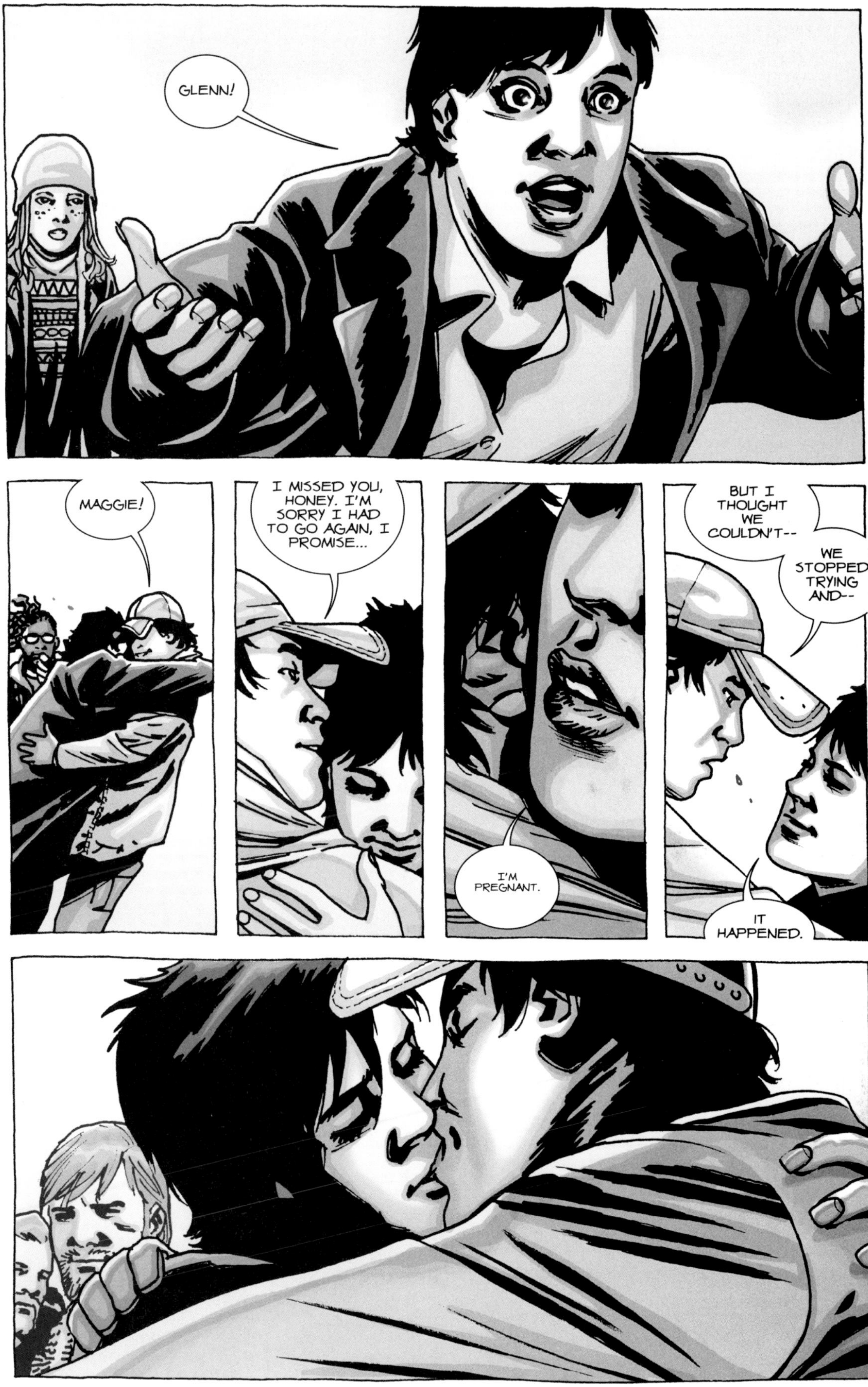
GLENN!
MAGGIE!
I MISSED YOU, HONEY. I'M SORRY I HAD TO GO AGAIN, I PROMISE...
I'M PREGNANT.
BUT I THOUGHT WE COULDN'T--
WE STOPPED TRYING AND--
IT HAPPENED.

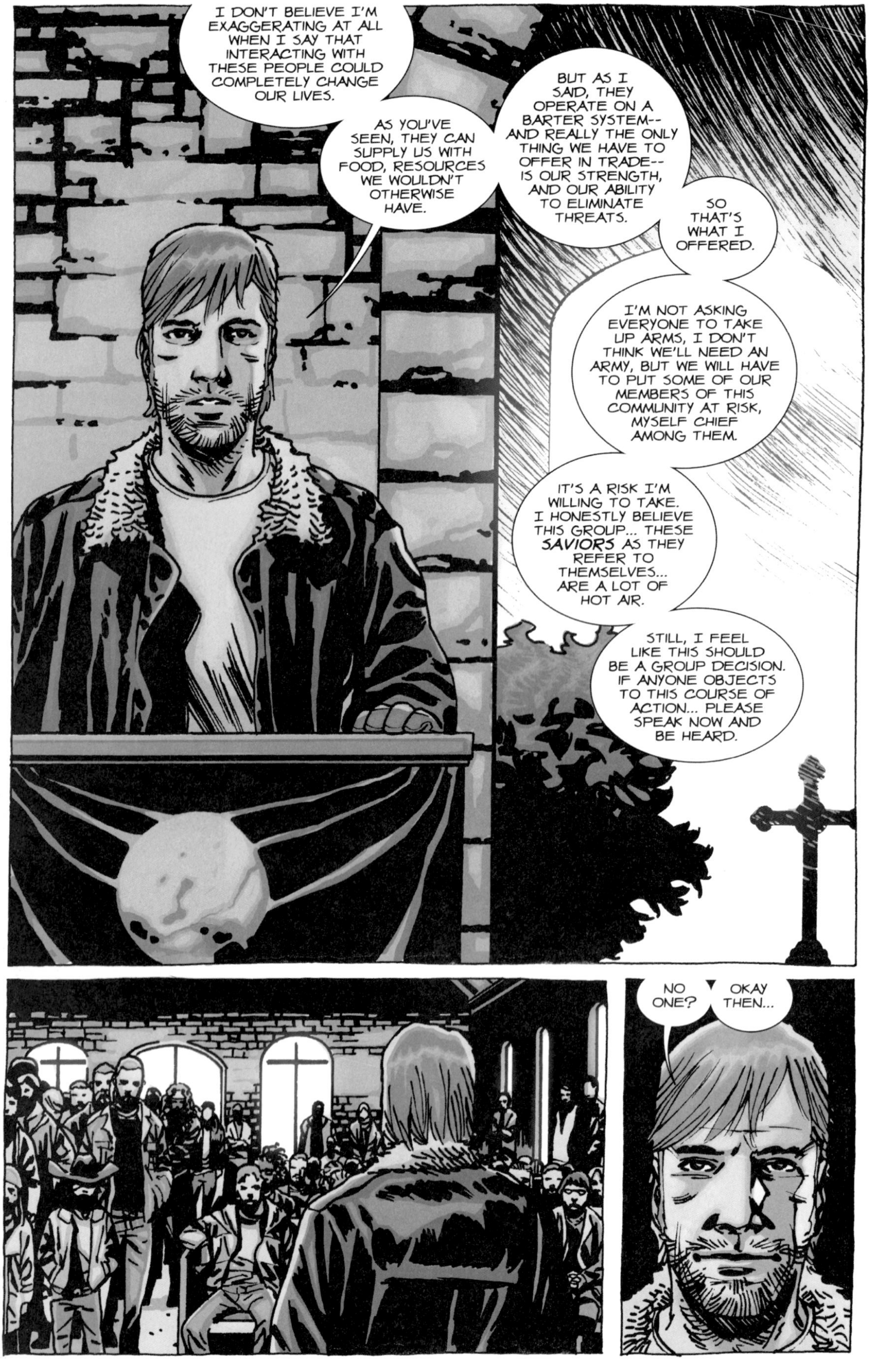
I DON'T BELIEVE I'M EXAGGERATING AT ALL WHEN I SAY THAT INTERACTING WITH THESE PEOPLE COULD COMPLETELY CHANGE OUR LIVES.
AS YOU'VE SEEN, THEY CAN SUPPLY US WITH FOOD, RESOURCES WE WOULDN'T OTHERWISE HAVE.
BUT AS I SAID, THEY OPERATE ON A BARTER SYSTEM-- AND REALLY THE ONLY THING WE HAVE TO OFFER IN TRADE-- IS OUR STRENGTH, AND OUR ABILITY TO ELIMINATE THREATS.
SO THAT'S WHAT I OFFERED.
I'M NOT ASKING EVERYONE TO TAKE UP ARMS, I DON'T THINK WE'LL NEED AN ARMY, BUT WE WILL HAVE TO PUT SOME OF OUR MEMBERS OF THIS COMMUNITY AT RISK, MYSELF CHIEF AMONG THEM.
IT'S A RISK I'M WILLING TO TAKE. I HONESTLY BELIEVE THIS GROUP... THESE SAVIORS AS THEY REFER TO THEMSELVES... ARE A LOT OF HOT AIR.
STILL, I FEEL LIKE THIS SHOULD BE A GROUP DECISION. IF ANYONE OBJECTS TO THIS COURSE OF ACTION... PLEASE SPEAK NOW AND BE HEARD.
NO ONE?
OKAY THEN...

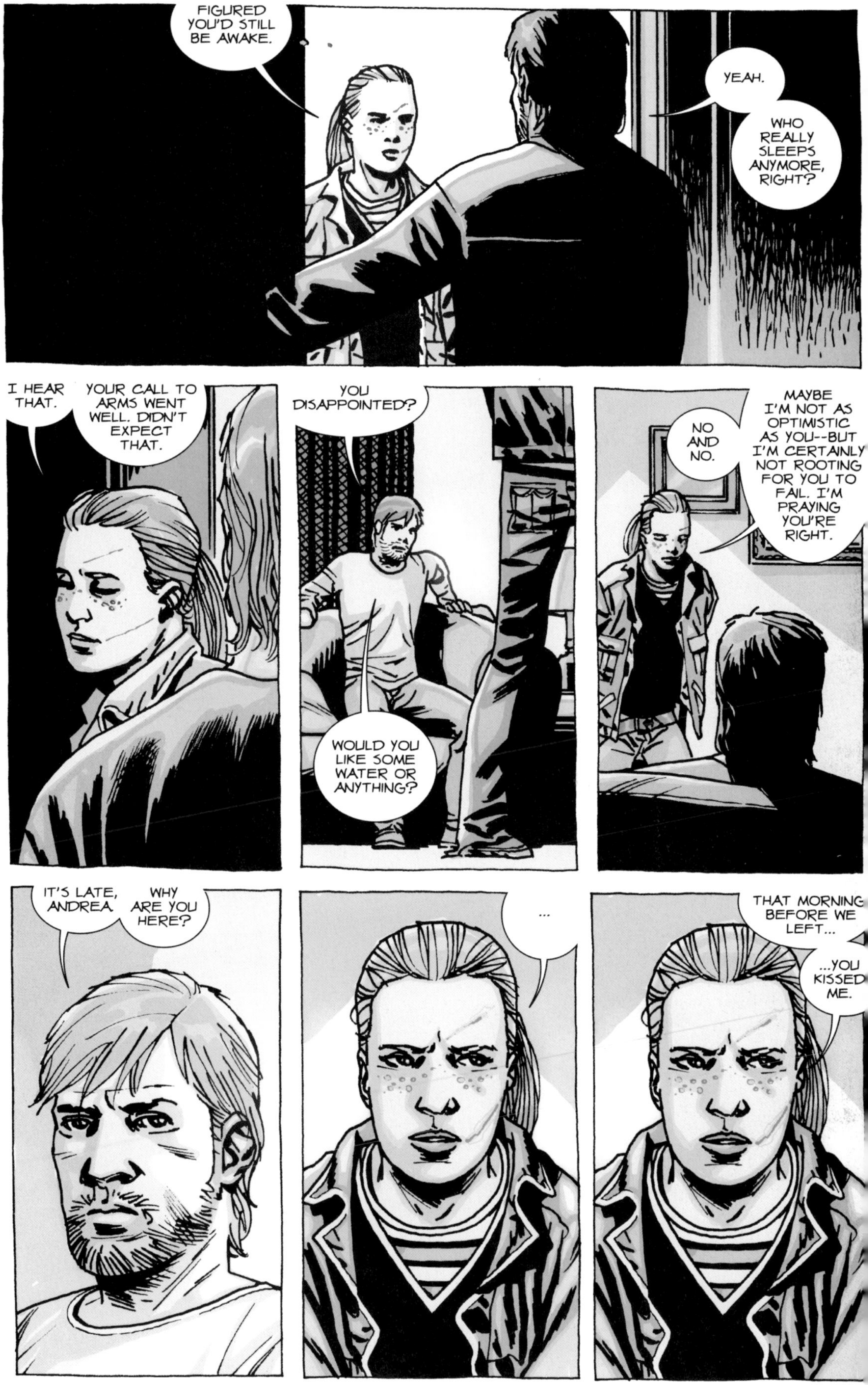
FIGURED YOU'D STILL BE AWAKE.
YEAH.
WHO REALLY SLEEPS ANYMORE, RIGHT?
I HEAR THAT.
YOUR CALL TO ARMS WENT WELL. DIDN'T EXPECT THAT.
YOU DISAPPOINTED?
WOULD YOU LIKE SOME WATER OR ANYTHING?
NO AND NO.
MAYBE I'M NOT AS OPTIMISTIC AS YOU--BUT I'M CERTAINLY NOT ROOTING FOR YOU TO FAIL. I'M PRAYING YOU'RE RIGHT.
IT'S LATE, ANDREA.
WHY ARE YOU HERE?
...
THAT MORNING BEFORE WE LEFT...
...YOU KISSED ME.

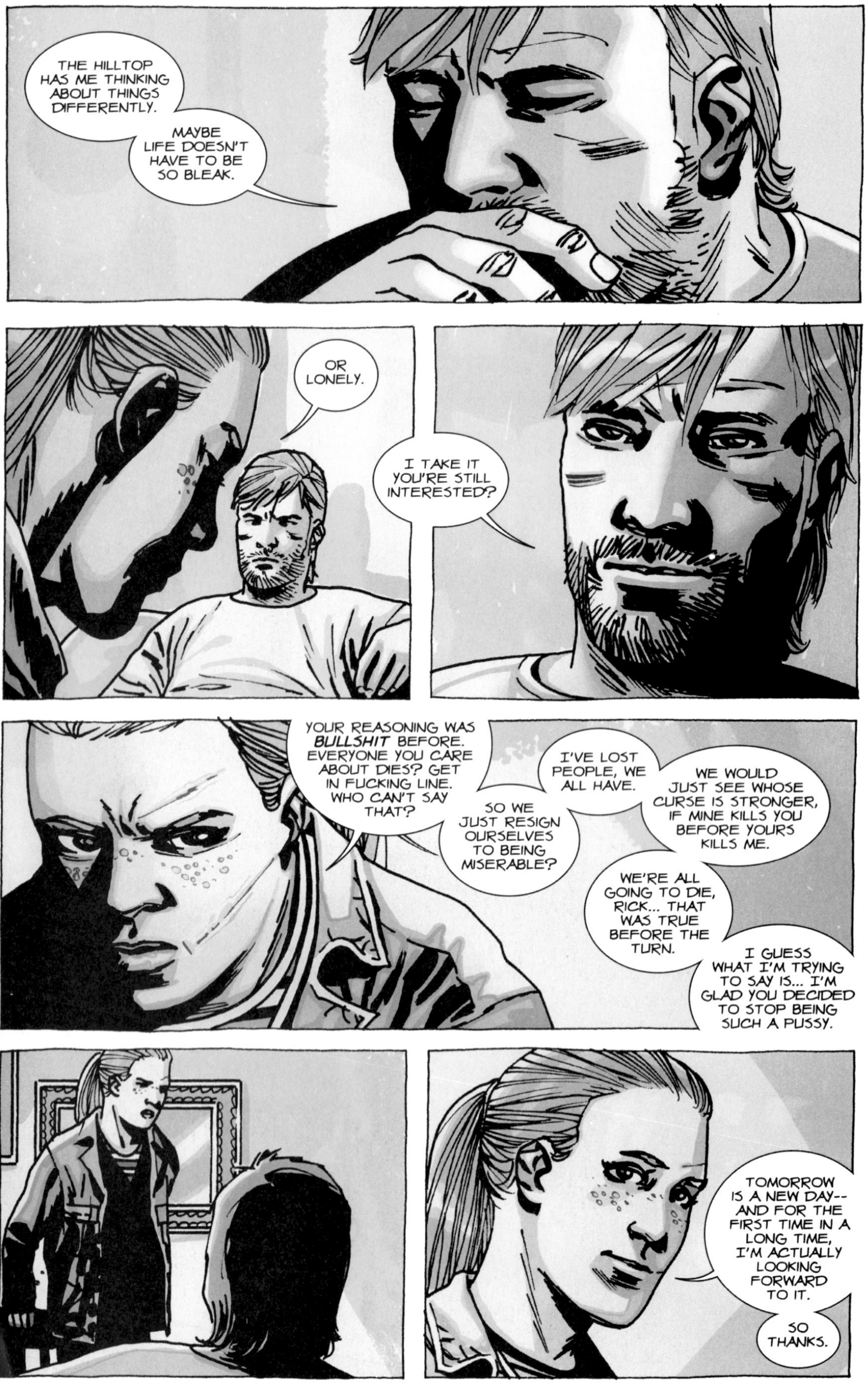
THE HILLTOP HAS ME THINKING ABOUT THINGS DIFFERENTLY.
MAYBE LIFE DOESN'T HAVE TO BE SO BLEAK.
OR LONELY.
I TAKE IT YOU'RE STILL INTERESTED?
YOUR REASONING WAS BULLSHIT BEFORE. EVERYONE YOU CARE ABOUT DIES? GET IN FUCKING LINE. WHO CAN'T SAY THAT?
SO WE JUST RESIGN OURSELVES TO BEING MISERABLE?
I'VE LOST PEOPLE, WE ALL HAVE.
WE WOULD JUST SEE WHOSE CURSE IS STRONGER, IF MINE KILLS YOU BEFORE YOURS KILLS ME.
WE'RE ALL GOING TO DIE, RICK... THAT WAS TRUE BEFORE THE TURN.
I GUESS WHAT I'M TRYING TO SAY IS... I'M GLAD YOU DECIDED TO STOP BEING SUCH A PUSSY.
TOMORROW IS A NEW DAY-- AND FOR THE FIRST TIME IN A LONG TIME, I'M ACTUALLY LOOKING FORWARD TO IT.
SO THANKS.

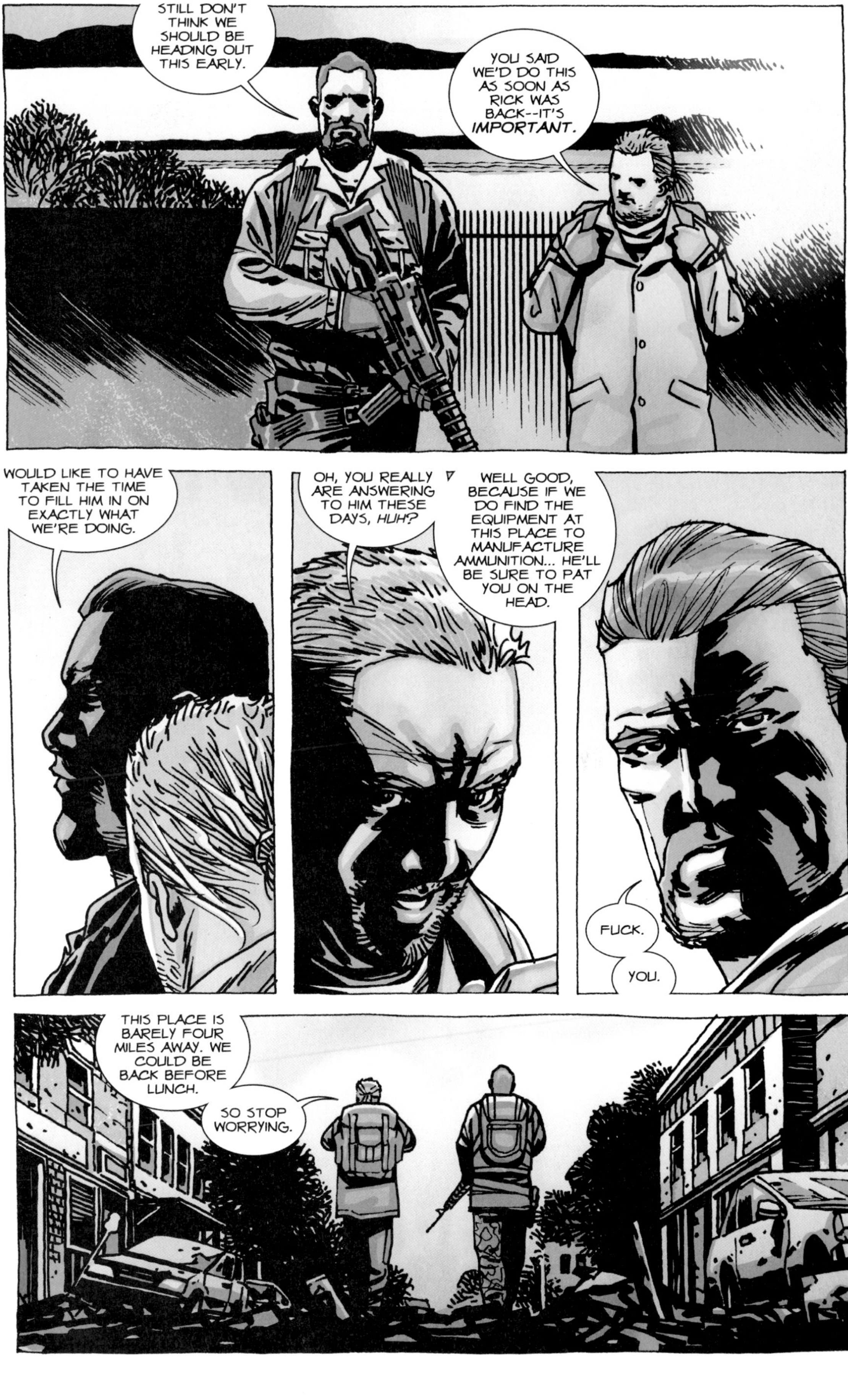
STILL DON'T THINK WE SHOULD BE HEADING OUT THIS EARLY.
YOU SAID WE'D DO THIS AS SOON AS RICK WAS BACK--IT'S *IMPORTANT*.
WOULD LIKE TO HAVE TAKEN THE TIME TO FILL HIM IN ON EXACTLY WHAT WE'RE DOING.
OH, YOU REALLY ARE ANSWERING TO HIM THESE DAYS, *HUH?*
WELL GOOD, BECAUSE IF WE DO FIND THE EQUIPMENT AT THIS PLACE TO MANUFACTURE AMMUNITION... HE'LL BE SURE TO PAT YOU ON THE HEAD.
FUCK.
YOU.
THIS PLACE IS BARELY FOUR MILES AWAY. WE COULD BE BACK BEFORE LUNCH.
SO STOP WORRYING.

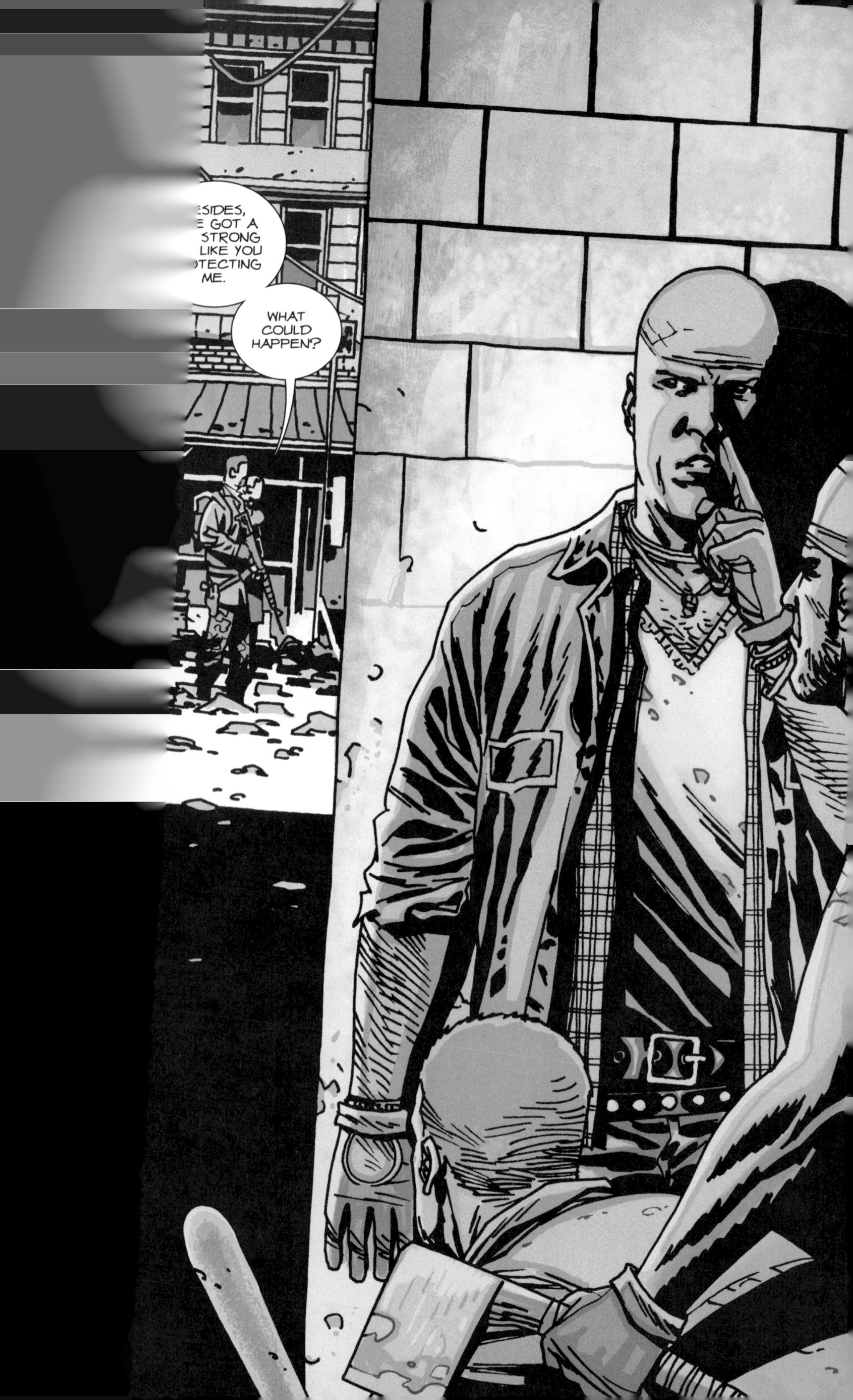
ESIDES, E GOT A STRONG LIKE YOU OTECTING ME.
WHAT COULD HAPPEN?

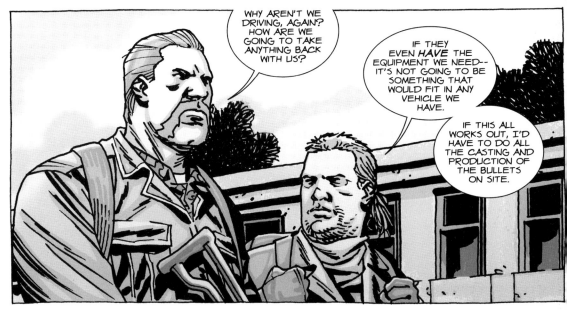

WHY AREN'T WE DRIVING, AGAIN? HOW ARE WE GOING TO TAKE ANYTHING BACK WITH US?

IF THEY EVEN *HAVE* THE EQUIPMENT WE NEED-- IT'S NOT GOING TO BE SOMETHING THAT WOULD FIT IN ANY VEHICLE WE HAVE.

IF THIS ALL WORKS OUT, I'D HAVE TO DO ALL THE CASTING AND PRODUCTION OF THE BULLETS ON SITE.

AND YOU'RE TRYING TO TRIM DOWN FOR ROSITA, RIGHT?

I'VE NOTICED YOU'VE DROPPED A FEW POUNDS.

I'M *TRYING*... BUT I JUST DON'T THINK SHE'LL EVER *REALLY* LOOK AT ME IN THAT WAY.

I REALLY CARE ABOUT HER, ALWAYS HAVE-- EVEN WHEN YOU GUYS WERE TOGETHER.

CARED ENOUGH TO WATCH US WHILE WE--

PLEASE DON'T BRING THAT UP.

JUST... BEING ALONE... LONELY... IT DRIVES YOU TO DO THINGS, RIGHT? OR MAYBE I'M JUST A WEIRDO.

SHE'S *ALWAYS* JUST GOING TO LOOK AT ME LIKE A WEIRDO.

PROBABLY... BUT IT'S NOT LIKE THERE'S A LOT OF FUCKING OPTIONS OUT THERE FOR HER.

YOU REALLY JUST NEED TO BE LESS OF A WEIRDO THAN WHATEVER OTHER WEIRDOS TRY TO GET IN HER PANTS.

UM... *THANKS?*

ANYWAY, I'M SORRY I THREW IT IN YOUR FACE YESTERDAY... US LIVING TOGETHER. WE'RE *CLEARLY* NOT THE COUPLE I MADE US OUT TO BE.

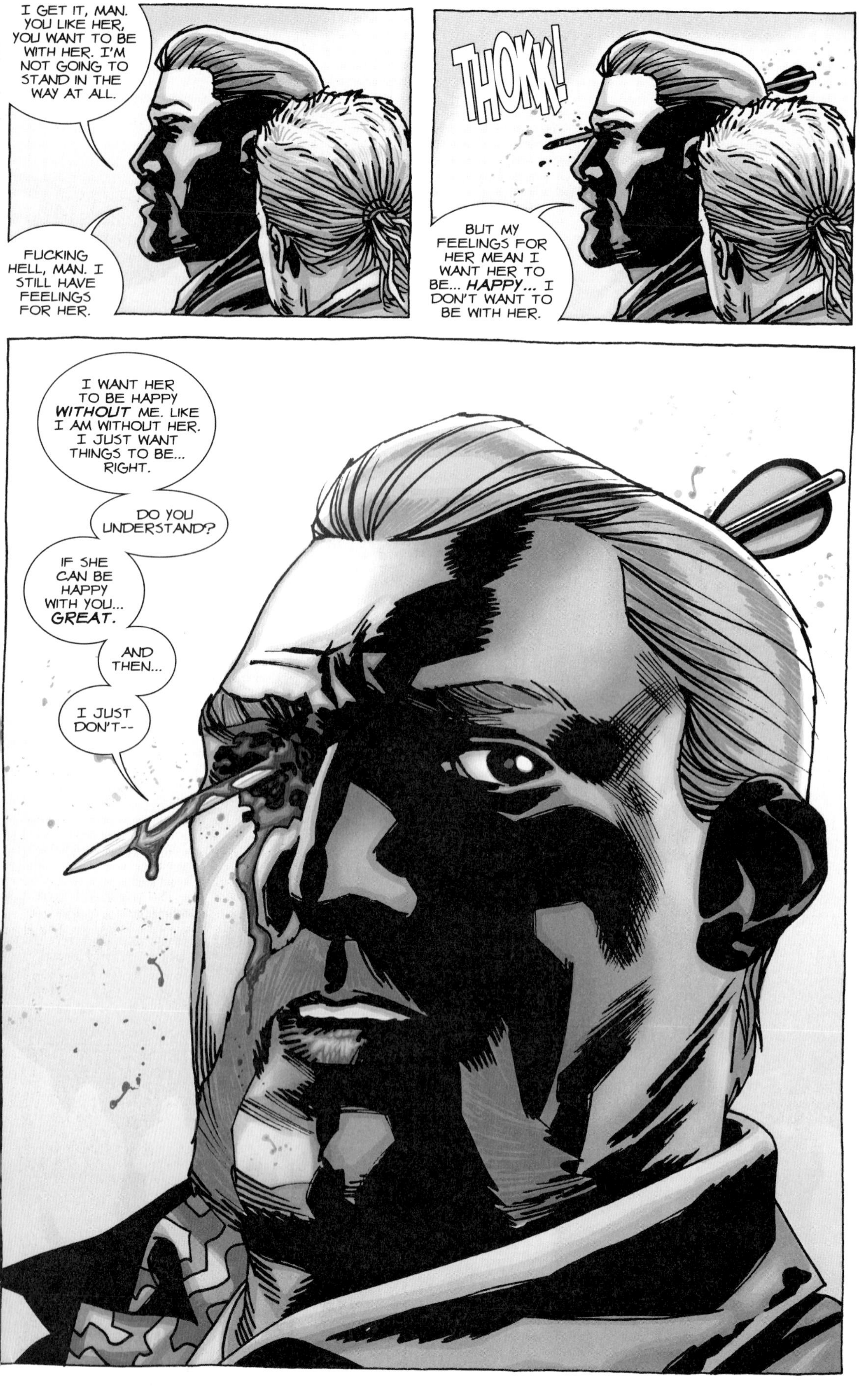
I GET IT, MAN. YOU LIKE HER, YOU WANT TO BE WITH HER. I'M NOT GOING TO STAND IN THE WAY AT ALL.
FUCKING HELL, MAN. I STILL HAVE FEELINGS FOR HER.
THOKK!
BUT MY FEELINGS FOR HER MEAN I WANT HER TO BE... HAPPY... I DON'T WANT TO BE WITH HER.
I WANT HER TO BE HAPPY WITHOUT ME. LIKE I AM WITHOUT HER. I JUST WANT THINGS TO BE... RIGHT.
DO YOU UNDERSTAND?
IF SHE CAN BE HAPPY WITH YOU... GREAT.
AND THEN...
I JUST DON'T--

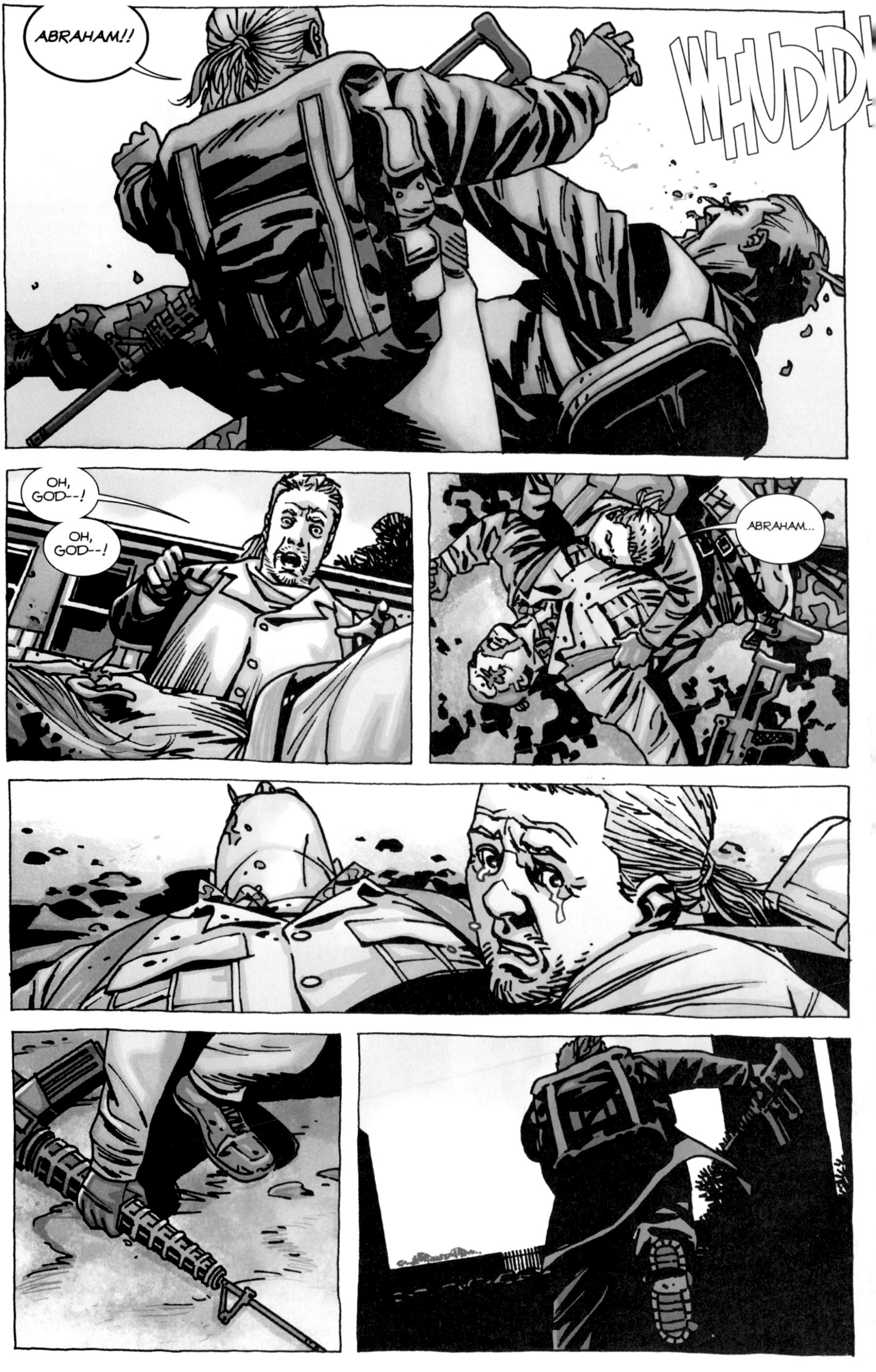
ABRAHAM!!
WHUDD!
OH, GOD--!
OH, GOD--!
ABRAHAM...

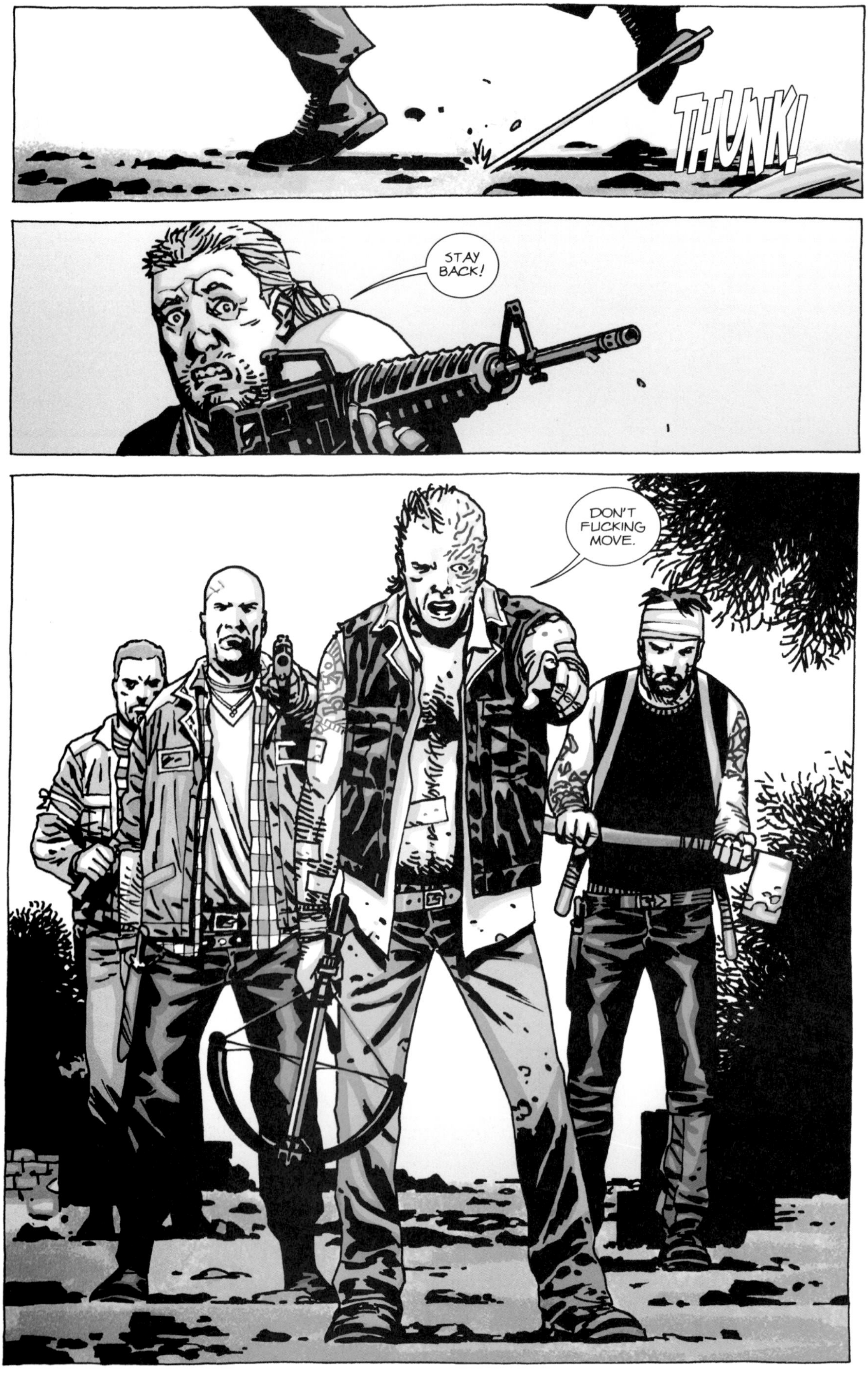
THUNK!
STAY BACK!
DON'T FUCKING MOVE.

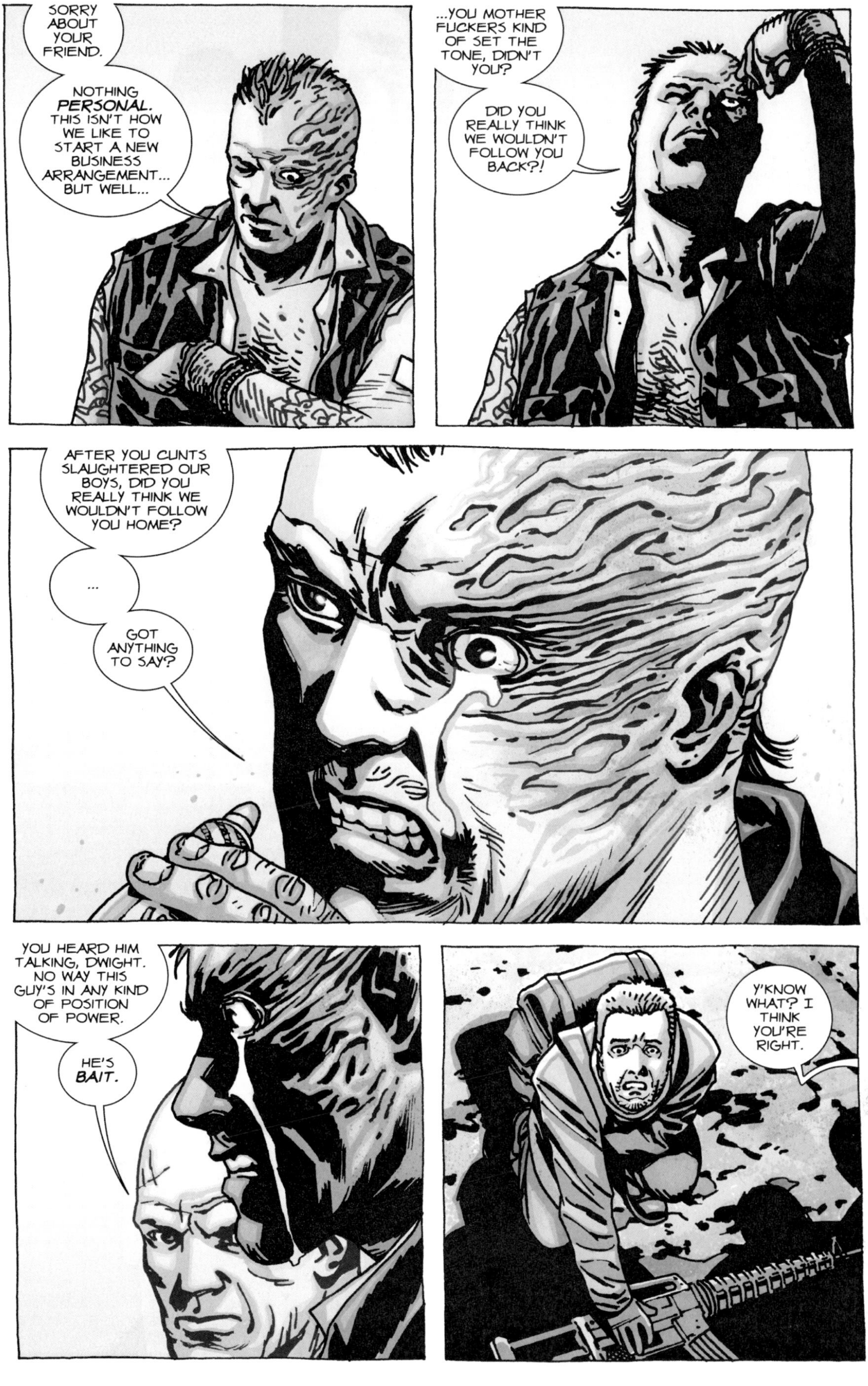
SORRY ABOUT YOUR FRIEND.
NOTHING PERSONAL. THIS ISN'T HOW WE LIKE TO START A NEW BUSINESS ARRANGEMENT... BUT WELL...
...YOU MOTHER FUCKERS KIND OF SET THE TONE, DIDN'T YOU?
DID YOU REALLY THINK WE WOULDN'T FOLLOW YOU BACK?!
AFTER YOU CUNTS SLAUGHTERED OUR BOYS, DID YOU REALLY THINK WE WOULDN'T FOLLOW YOU HOME?
...
GOT ANYTHING TO SAY?
YOU HEARD HIM TALKING, DWIGHT. NO WAY THIS GUY'S IN ANY KIND OF POSITION OF POWER.
HE'S BAIT.
Y'KNOW WHAT? I THINK YOU'RE RIGHT.

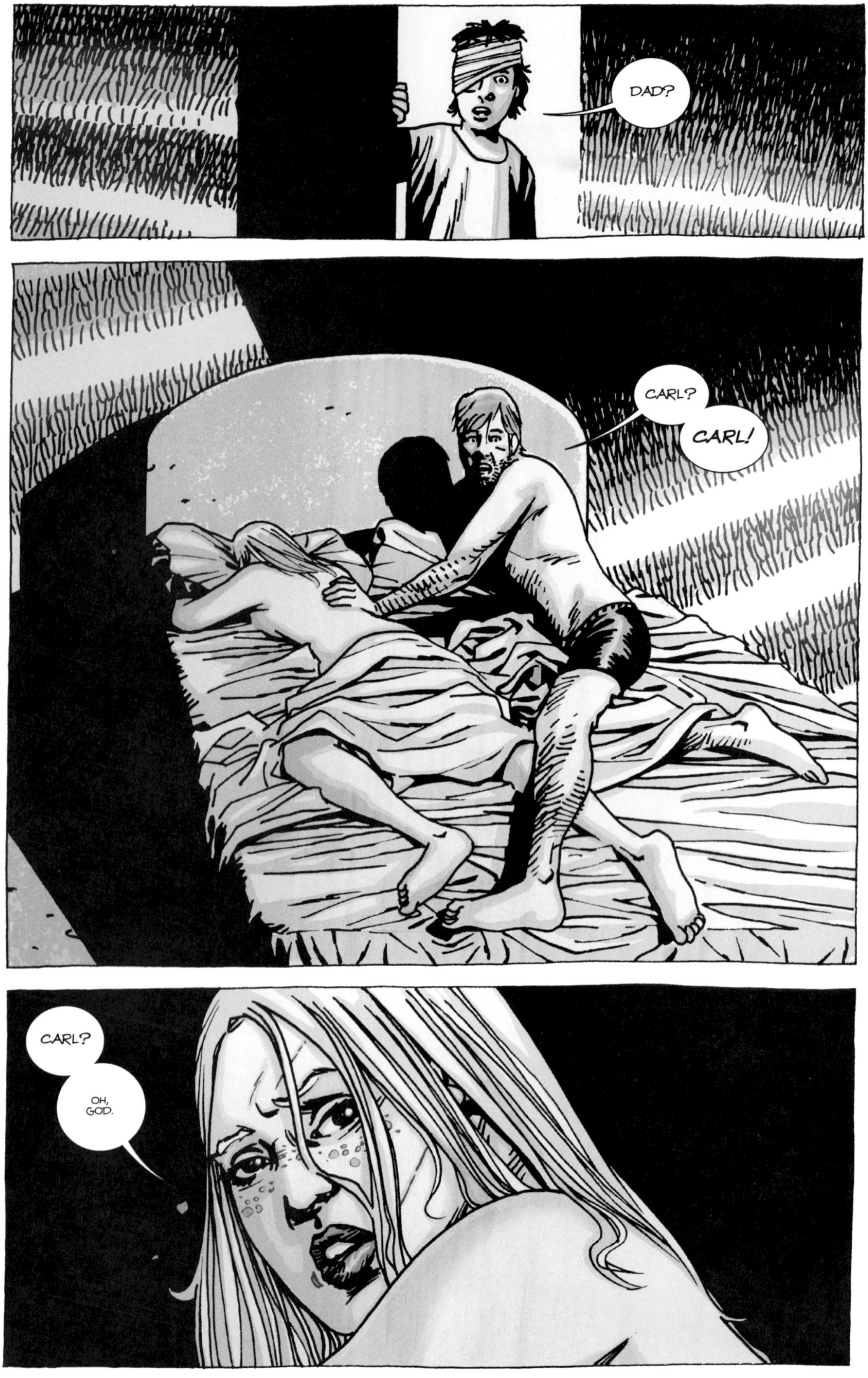
DAD?
CARL?
CARL!
CARL?
OH, GOD.

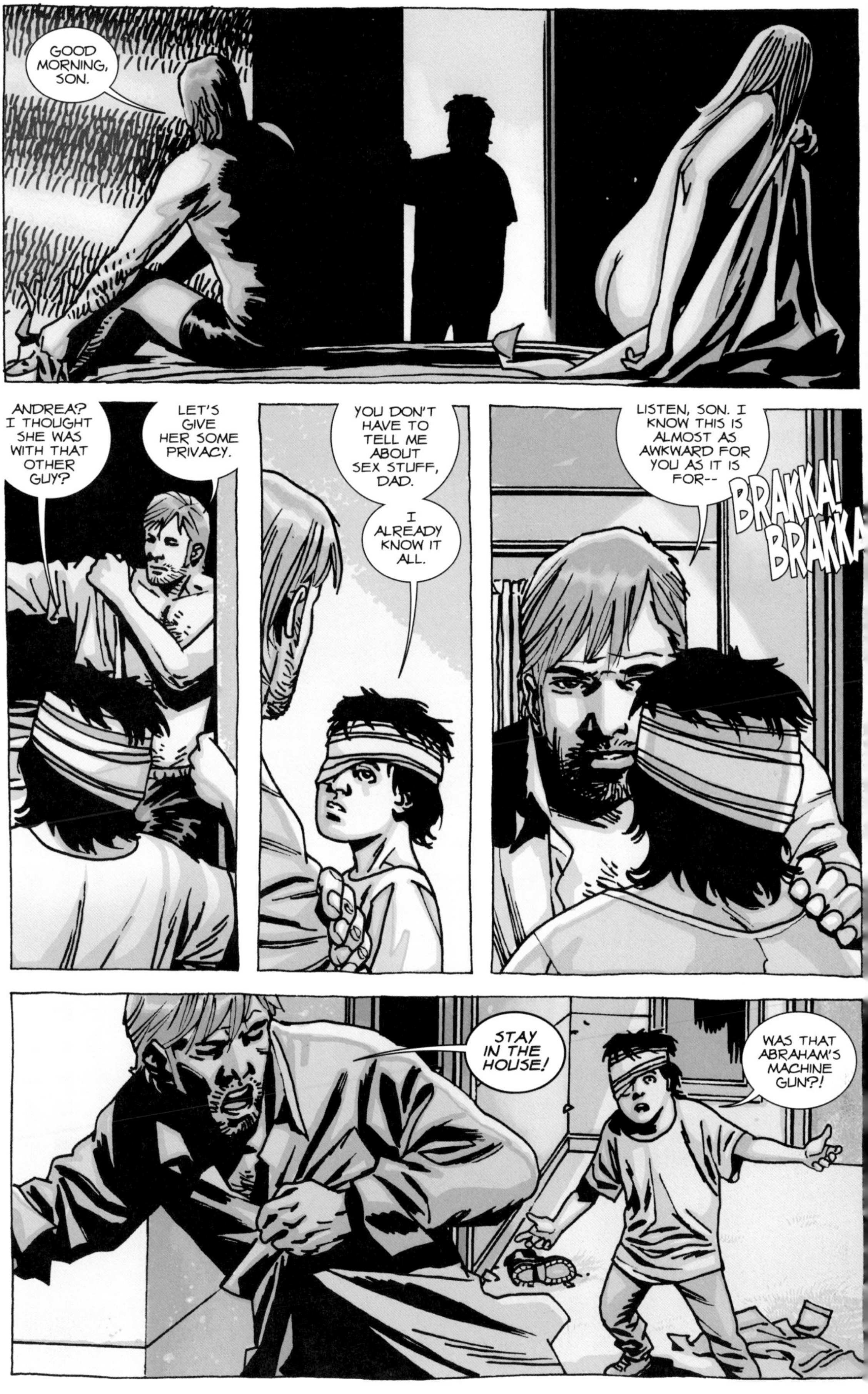

GOOD MORNING, SON.
ANDREA? I THOUGHT SHE WAS WITH THAT OTHER GUY?
LET'S GIVE HER SOME PRIVACY.
YOU DON'T HAVE TO TELL ME ABOUT SEX STUFF, DAD.
I ALREADY KNOW IT ALL.
LISTEN, SON. I KNOW THIS IS ALMOST AS AWKWARD FOR YOU AS IT IS FOR--
BRAKKA! BRAKKA
STAY IN THE HOUSE!
WAS THAT ABRAHAM'S MACHINE GUN?!

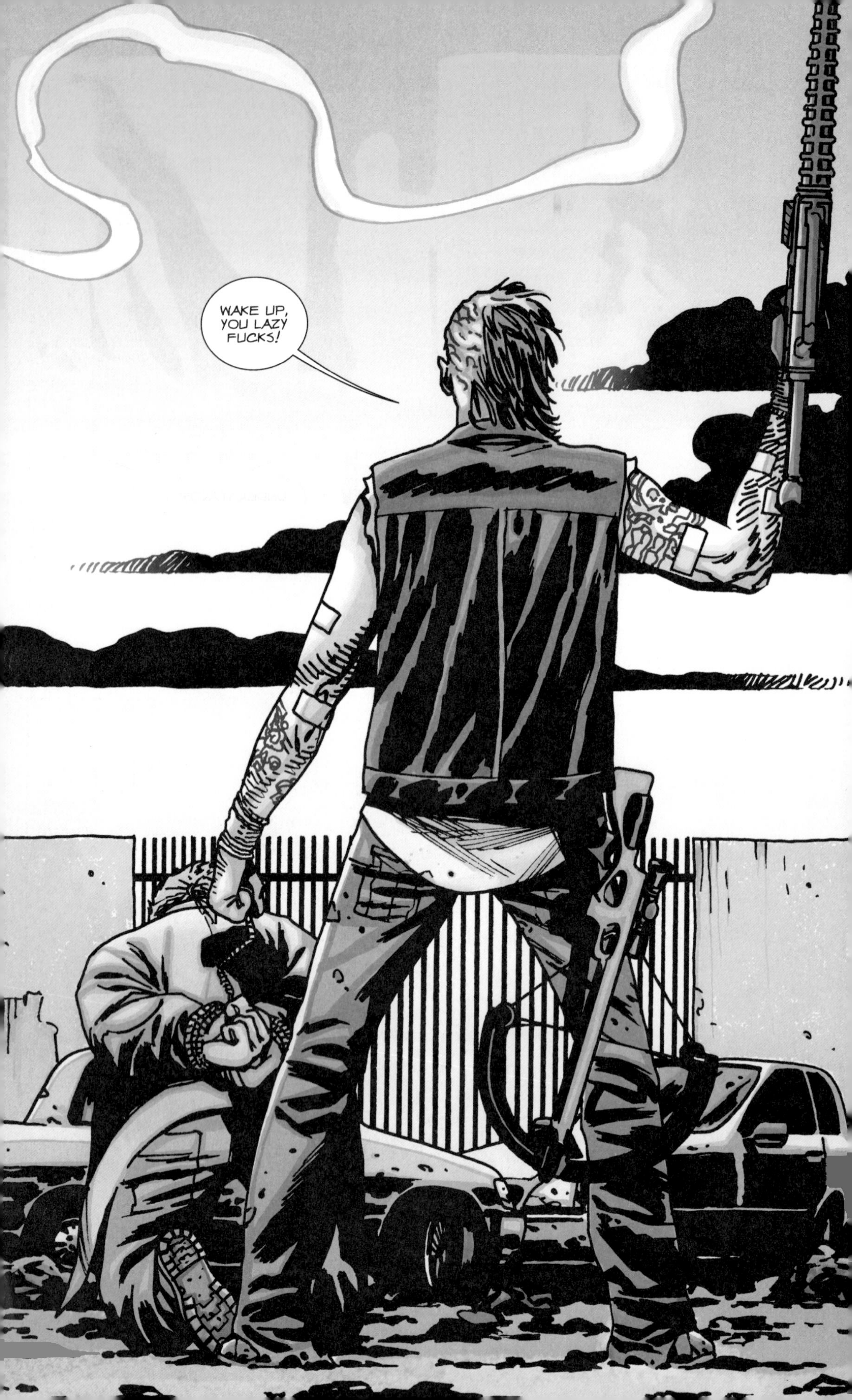
WAKE UP, YOU LAZY FUCKS!

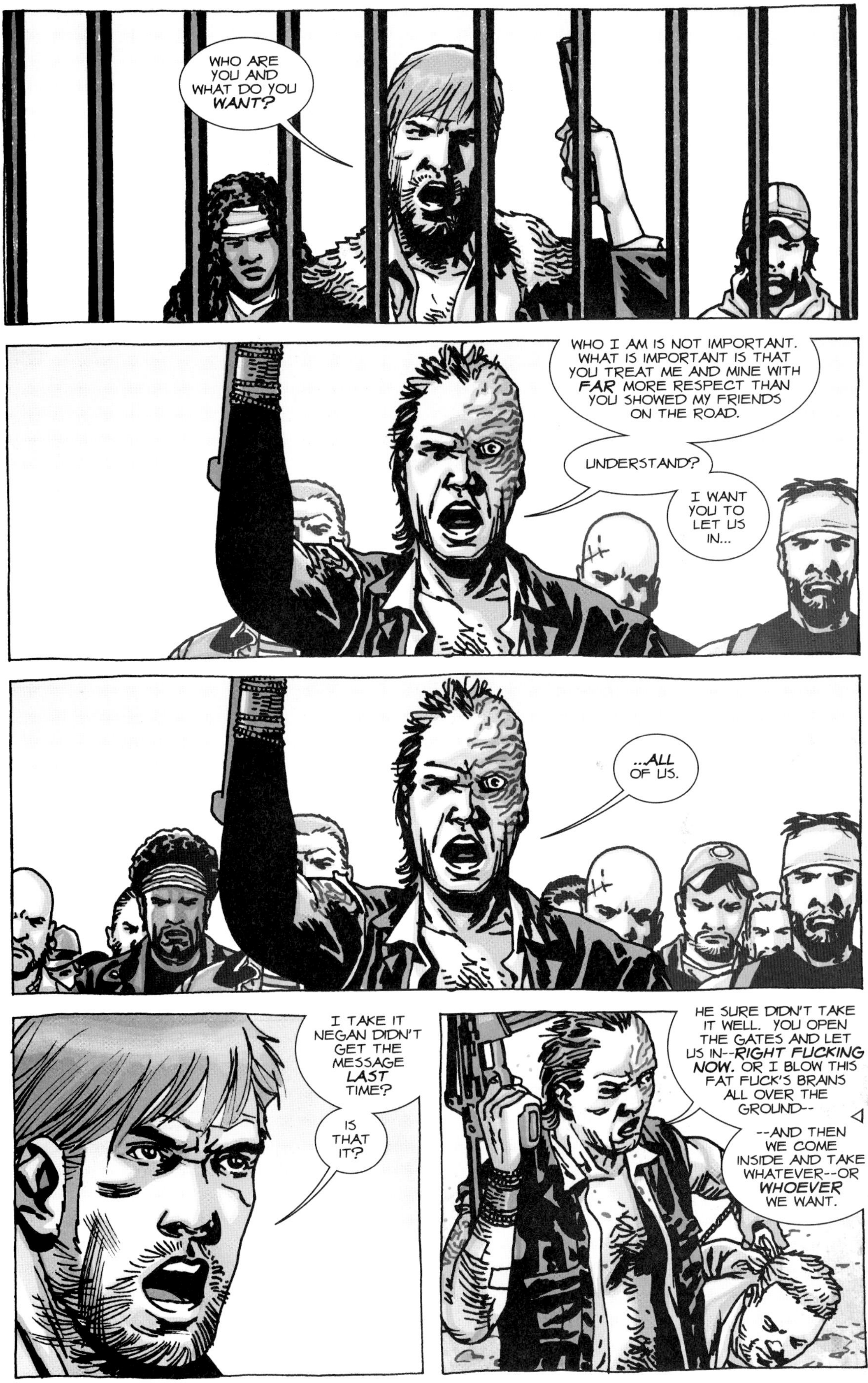
WHO ARE YOU AND WHAT DO YOU WANT?
WHO I AM IS NOT IMPORTANT. WHAT IS IMPORTANT IS THAT YOU TREAT ME AND MINE WITH FAR MORE RESPECT THAN YOU SHOWED MY FRIENDS ON THE ROAD.
UNDERSTAND?
I WANT YOU TO LET US IN...
...ALL OF US.
I TAKE IT NEGAN DIDN'T GET THE MESSAGE LAST TIME?
IS THAT IT?
HE SURE DIDN'T TAKE IT WELL. YOU OPEN THE GATES AND LET US IN--RIGHT FUCKING NOW. OR I BLOW THIS FAT FUCK'S BRAINS ALL OVER THE GROUND--
--AND THEN WE COME INSIDE AND TAKE WHATEVER--OR WHOEVER WE WANT.

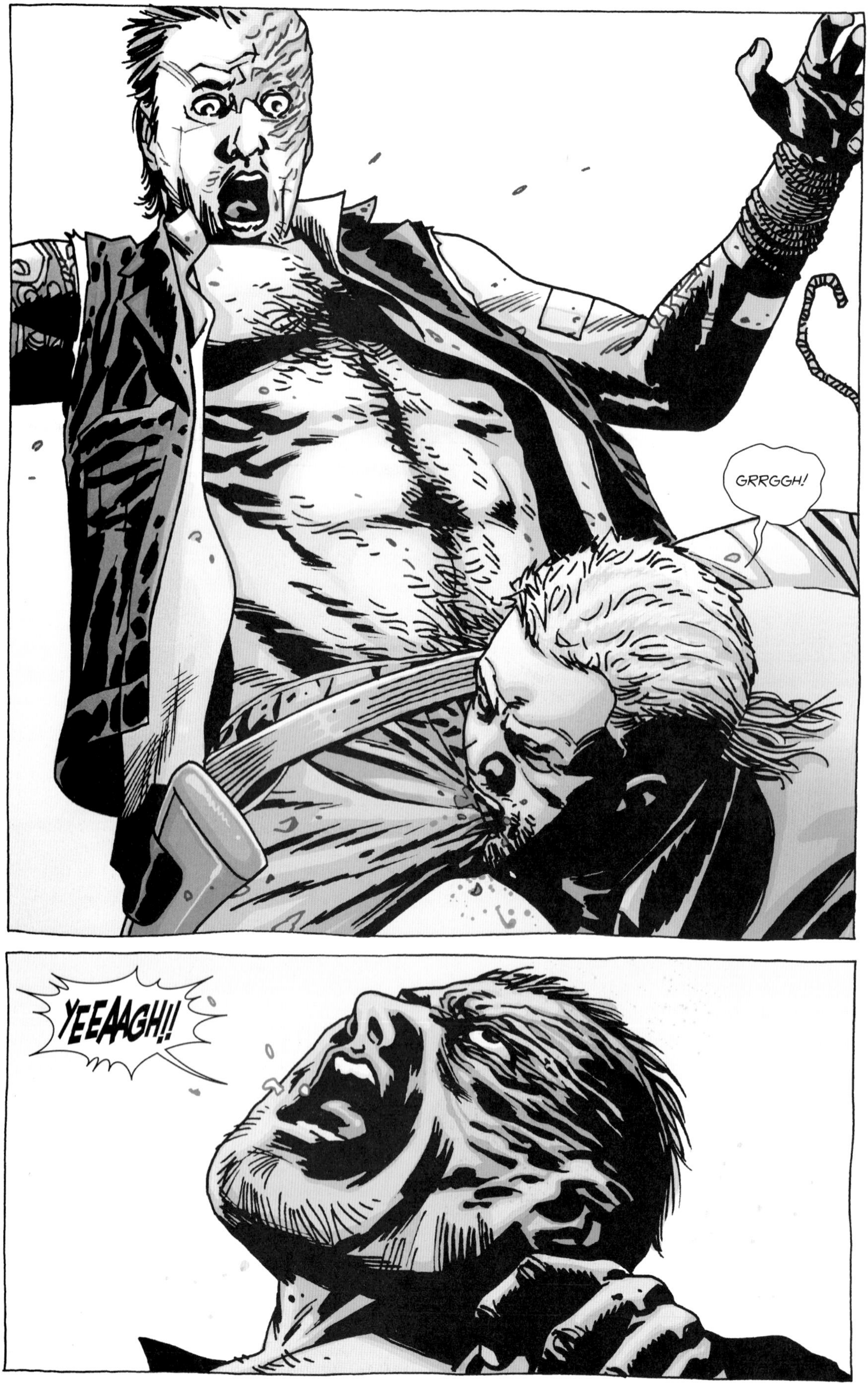
GRRGGH!
YEEAAGH!!

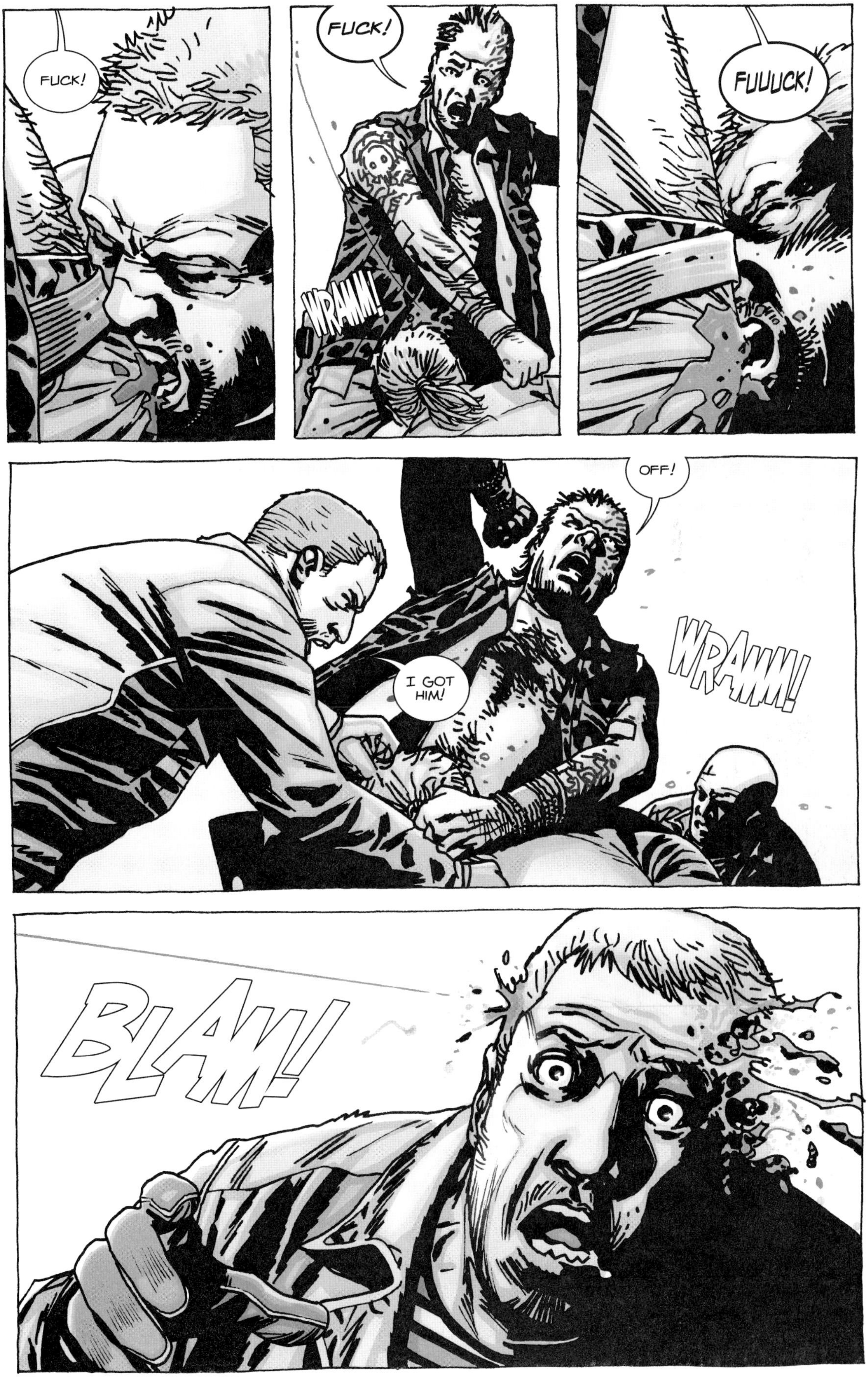
FUCK!
FUCK!
WRAMM!
FUUUCK!
OFF!
I GOT HIM!
WRAMM!
BLAM!

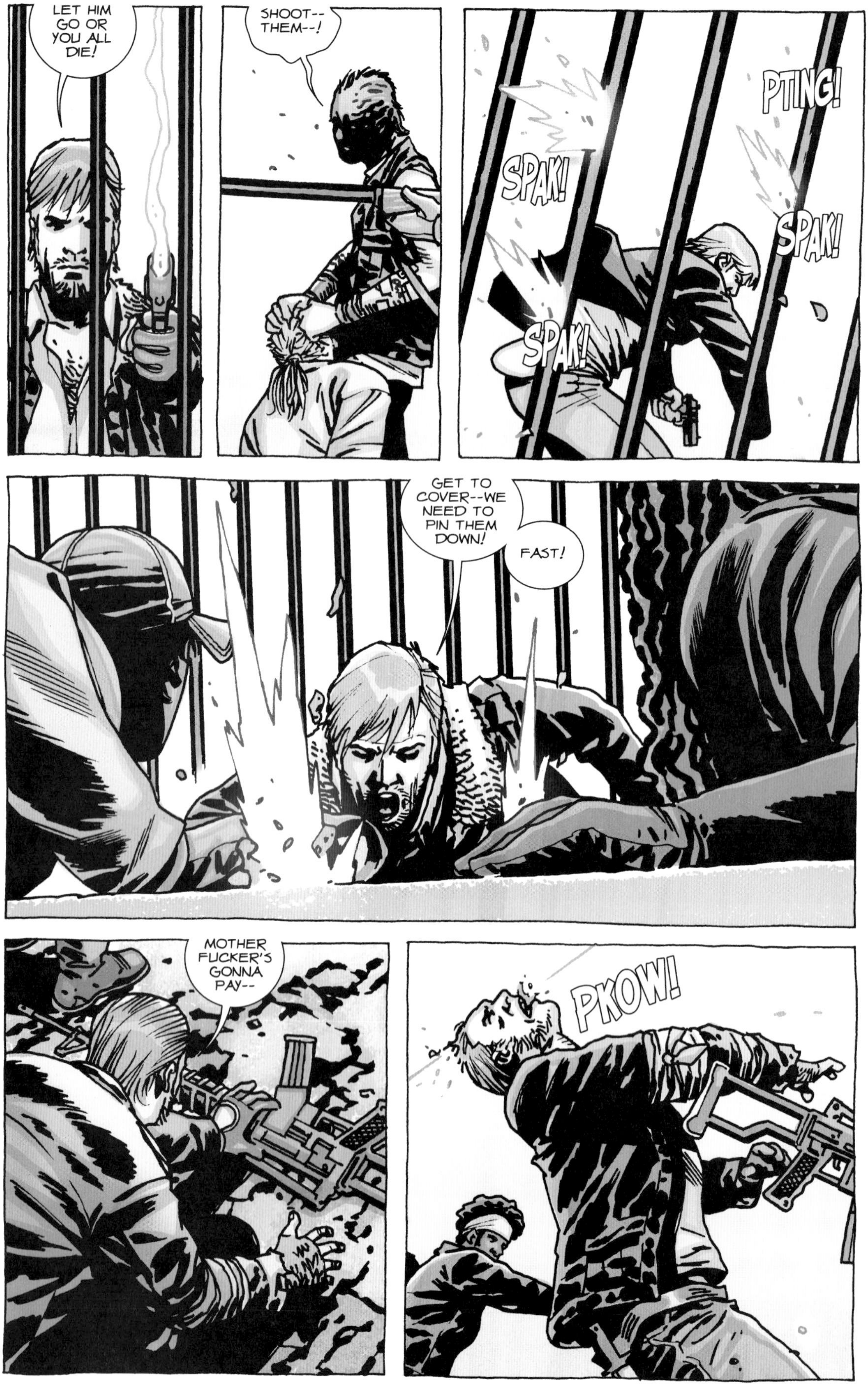
LET HIM GO OR YOU ALL DIE!
SHOOT-- THEM--!
PTING!
SPAK!
SPAK!
SPAK!
GET TO COVER--WE NEED TO PIN THEM DOWN!
FAST!
MOTHER FUCKER'S GONNA PAY--
PKOW!

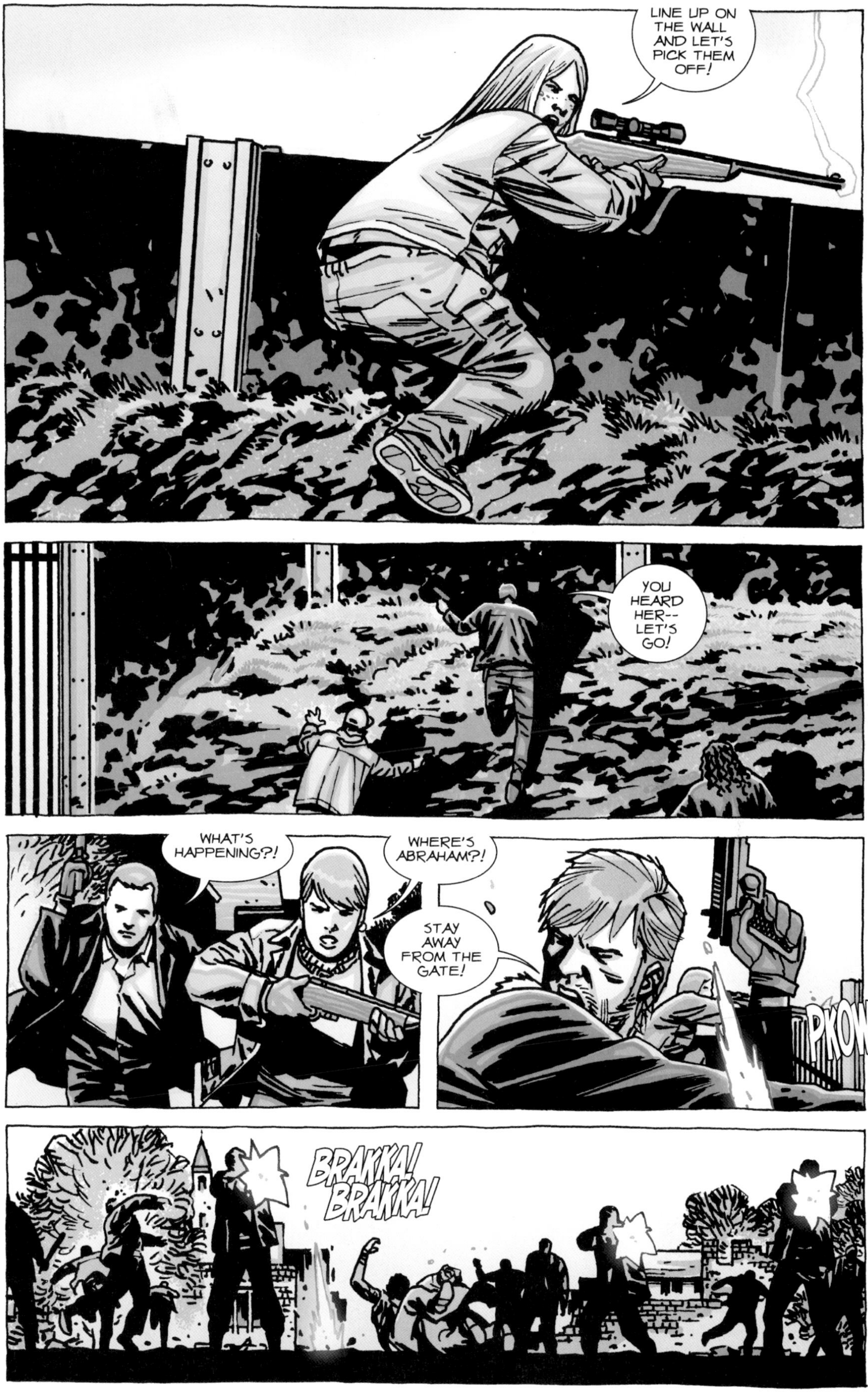
LINE UP ON THE WALL AND LET'S PICK THEM OFF!
YOU HEARD HER-- LET'S GO!
WHAT'S HAPPENING?!
WHERE'S ABRAHAM?!
STAY AWAY FROM THE GATE!
PKOW!
BRAKKA! BRAKKA!

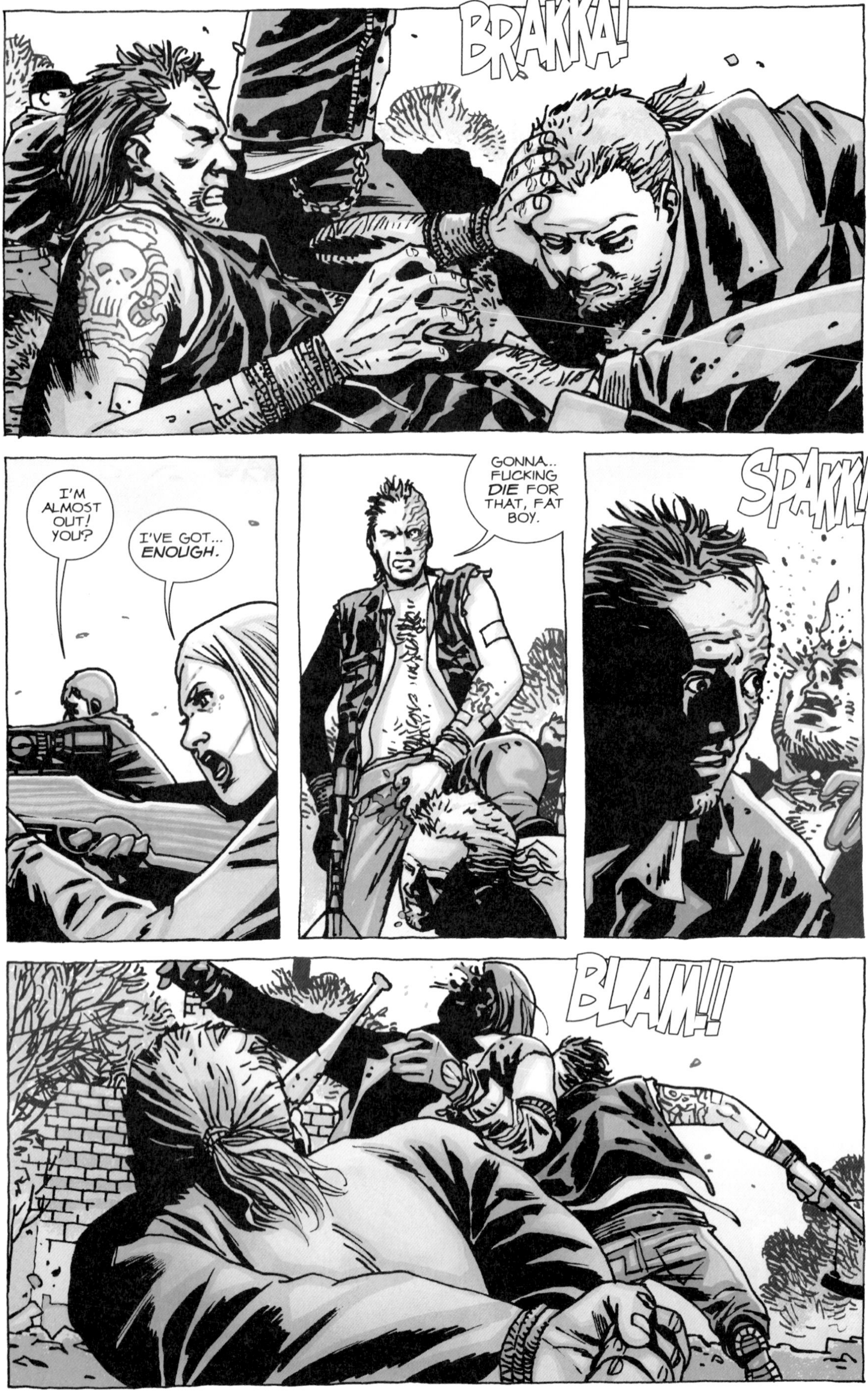
BRAKKA!
I'M ALMOST OUT! YOU?
I'VE GOT... ENOUGH.
GONNA... FUCKING DIE FOR THAT, FAT BOY.
SPAKK!
BLAM!!

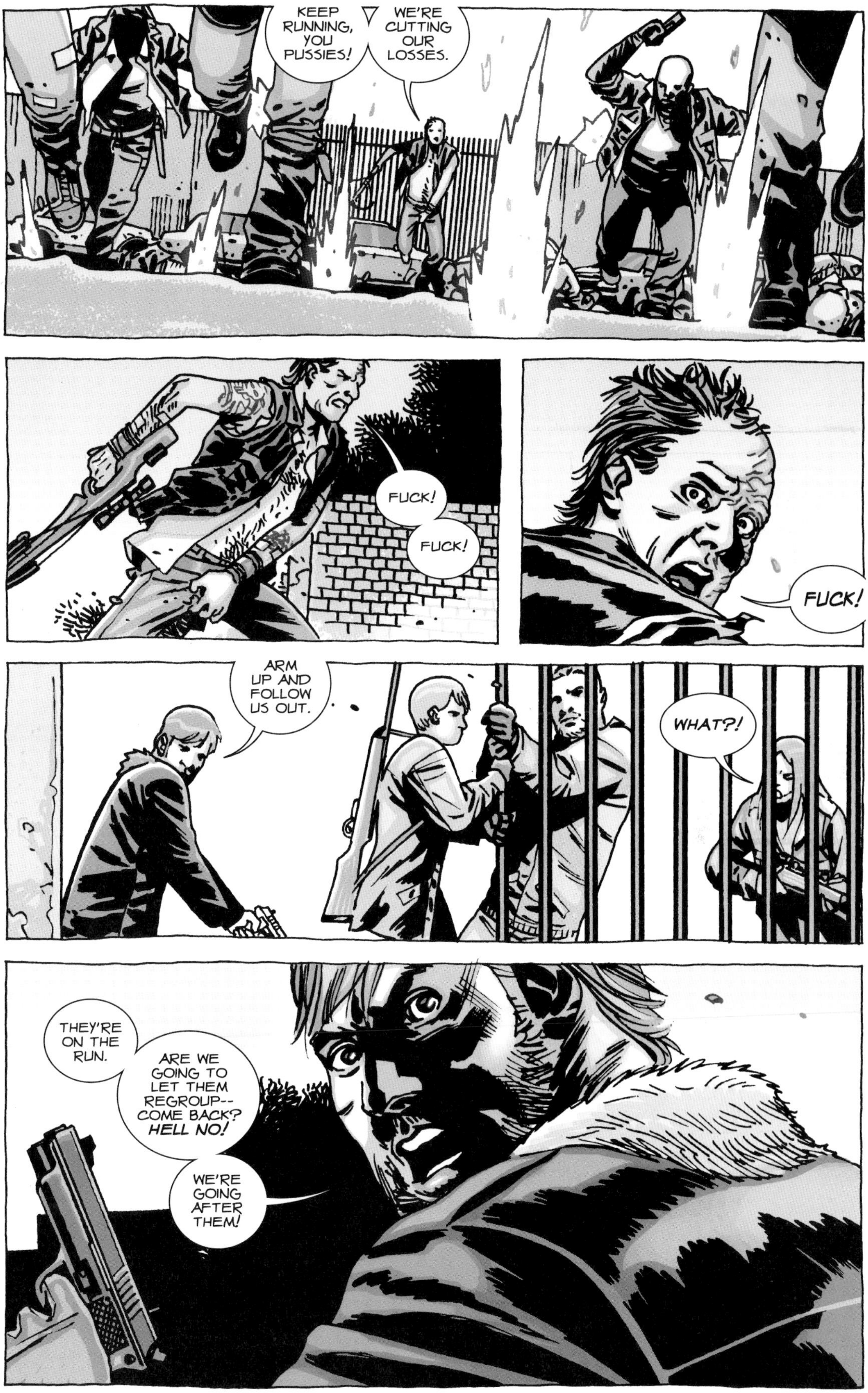
KEEP RUNNING, YOU PUSSIES!
WE'RE CUTTING OUR LOSSES.
FUCK!
FUCK!
FUCK!
ARM UP AND FOLLOW US OUT.
WHAT?!
THEY'RE ON THE RUN.
ARE WE GOING TO LET THEM REGROUP-- COME BACK? HELL NO!
WE'RE GOING AFTER THEM!

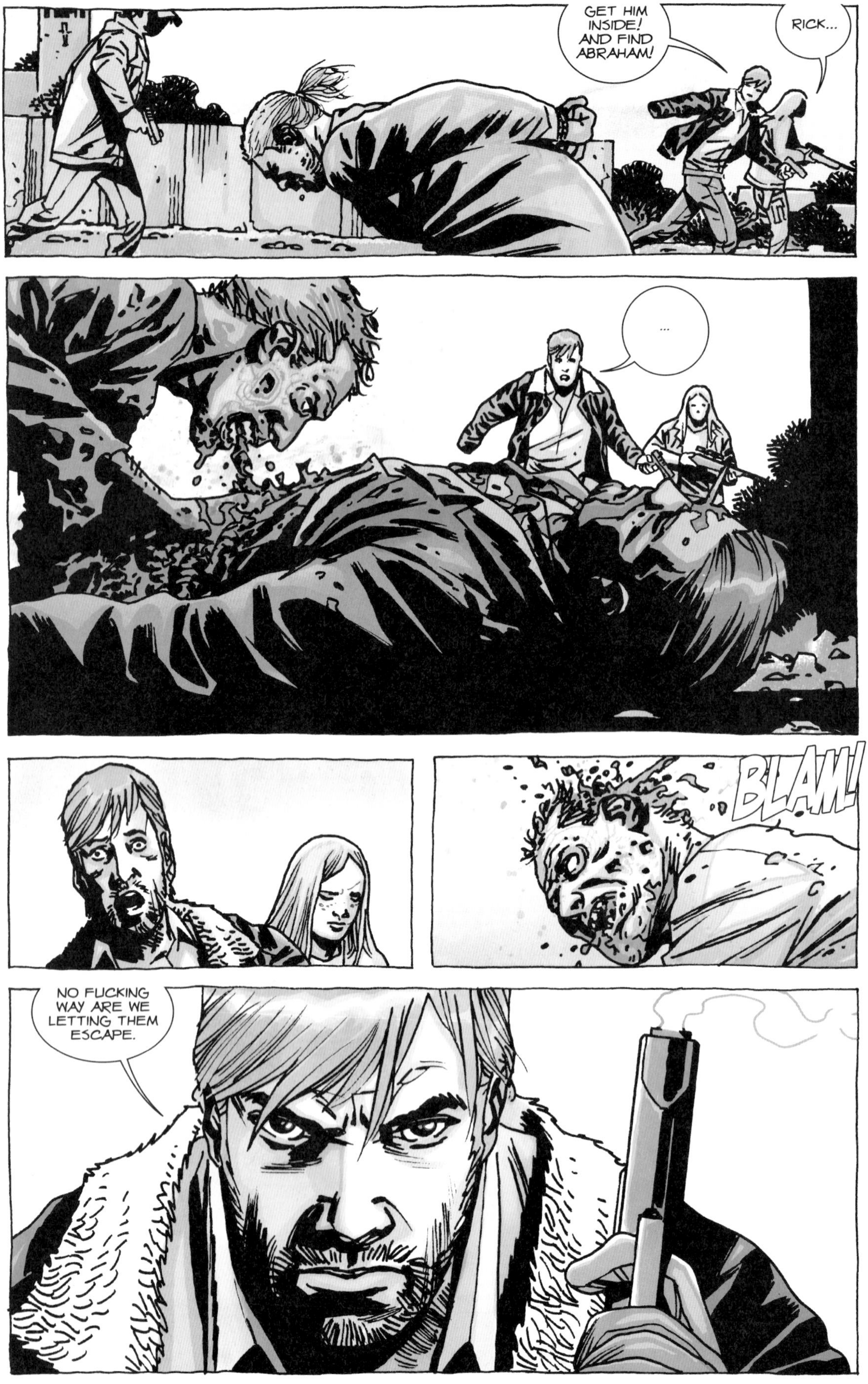
GET HIM INSIDE! AND FIND ABRAHAM!
RICK...
...
BLAM!
NO FUCKING WAY ARE WE LETTING THEM ESCAPE.

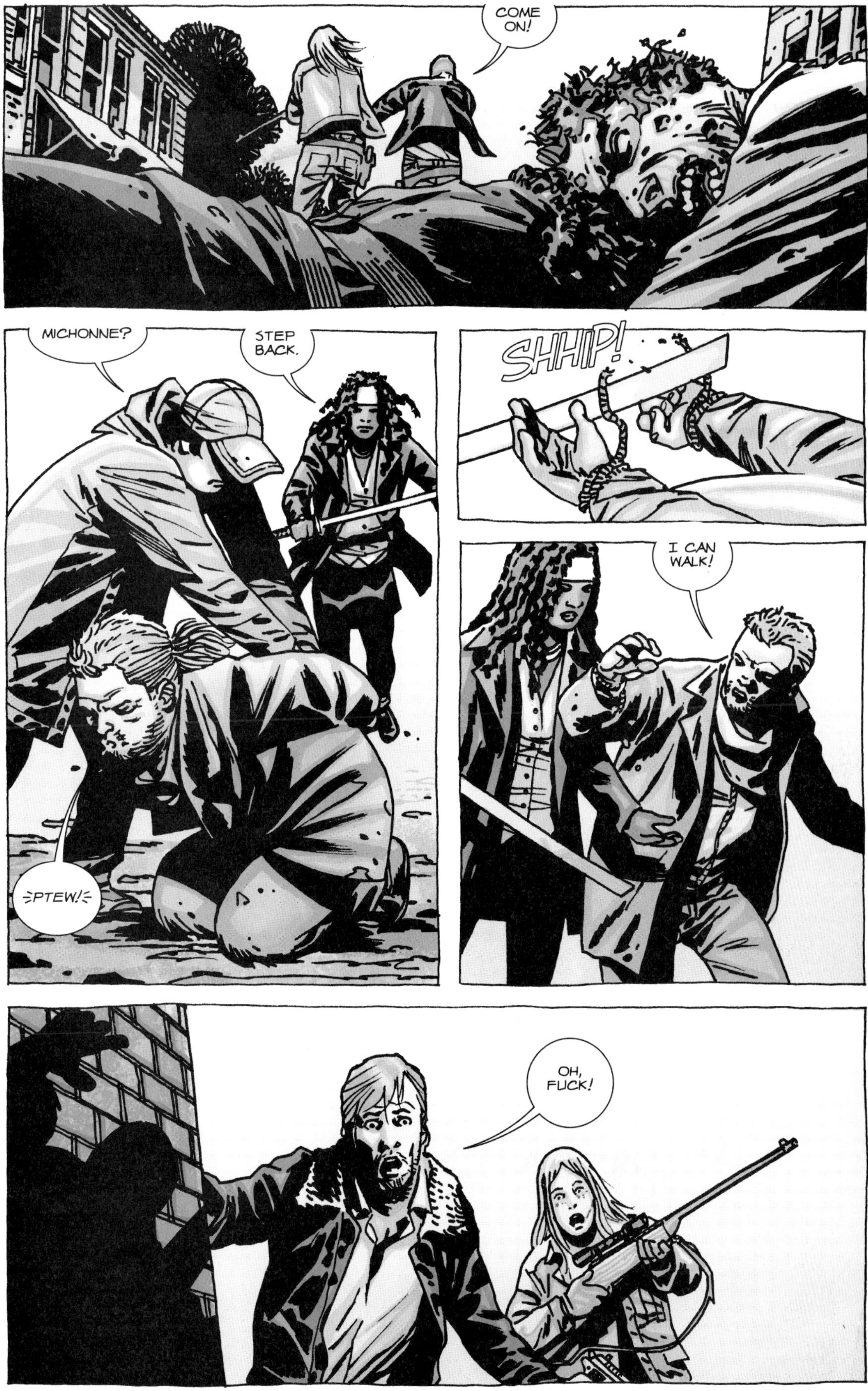
COME ON!
MICHONNE?
STEP BACK.
=PTEW!=
SHHIP!
I CAN WALK!
OH, FUCK!

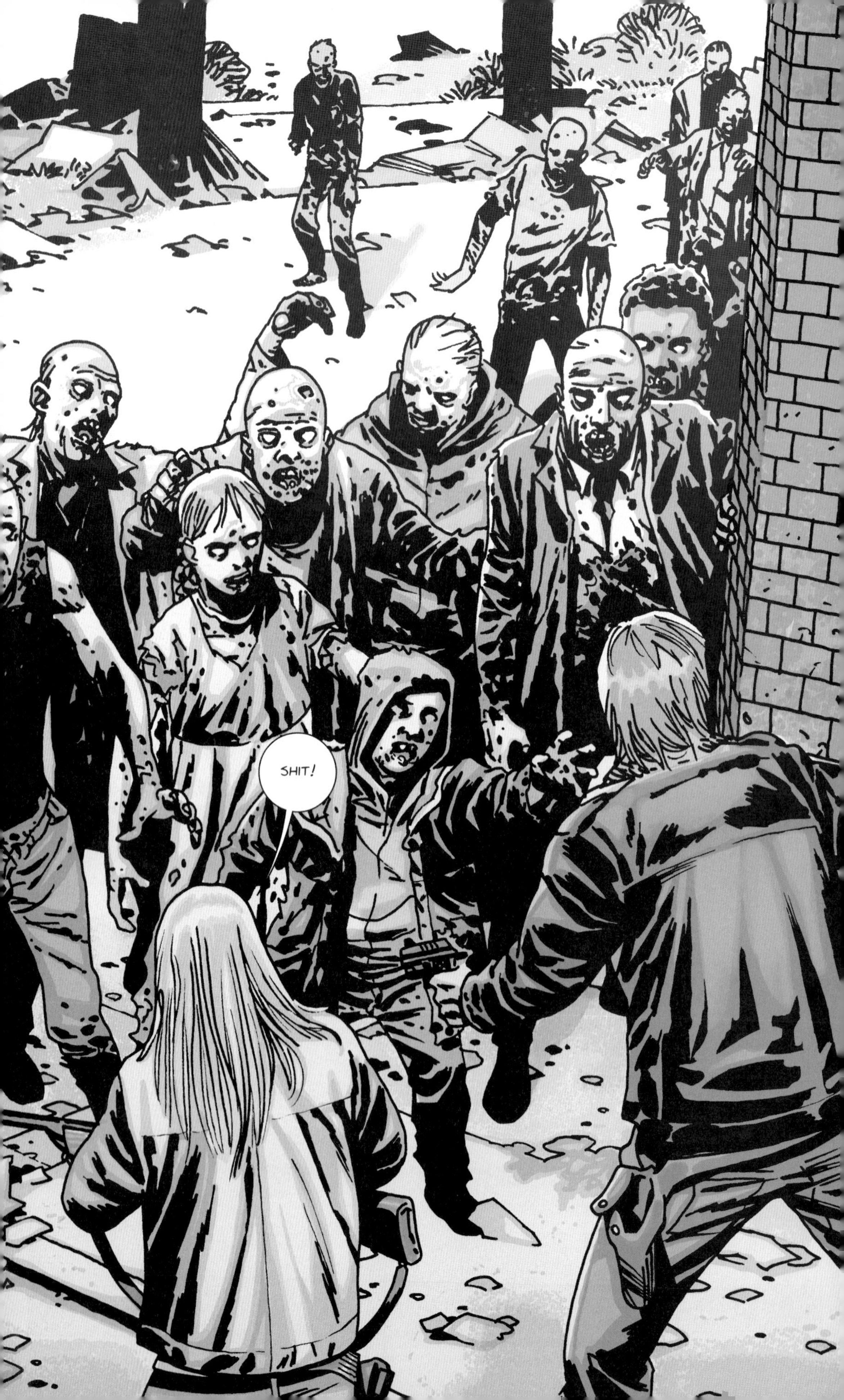
SHIT!

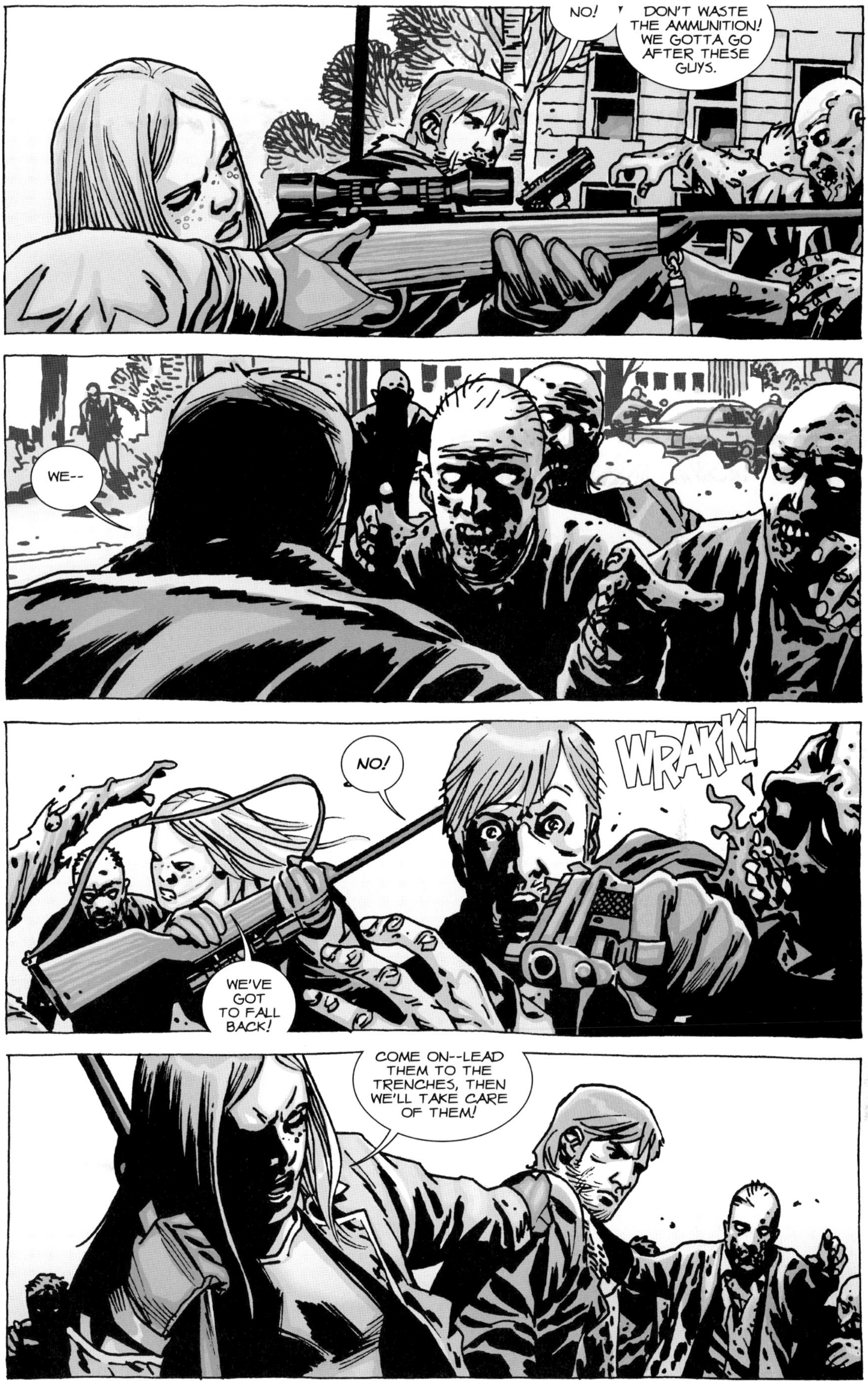
NO!
DON'T WASTE THE AMMUNITION! WE GOTTA GO AFTER THESE GUYS.
WE--
NO!
WRAKK!
WE'VE GOT TO FALL BACK!
COME ON--LEAD THEM TO THE TRENCHES, THEN WE'LL TAKE CARE OF THEM!

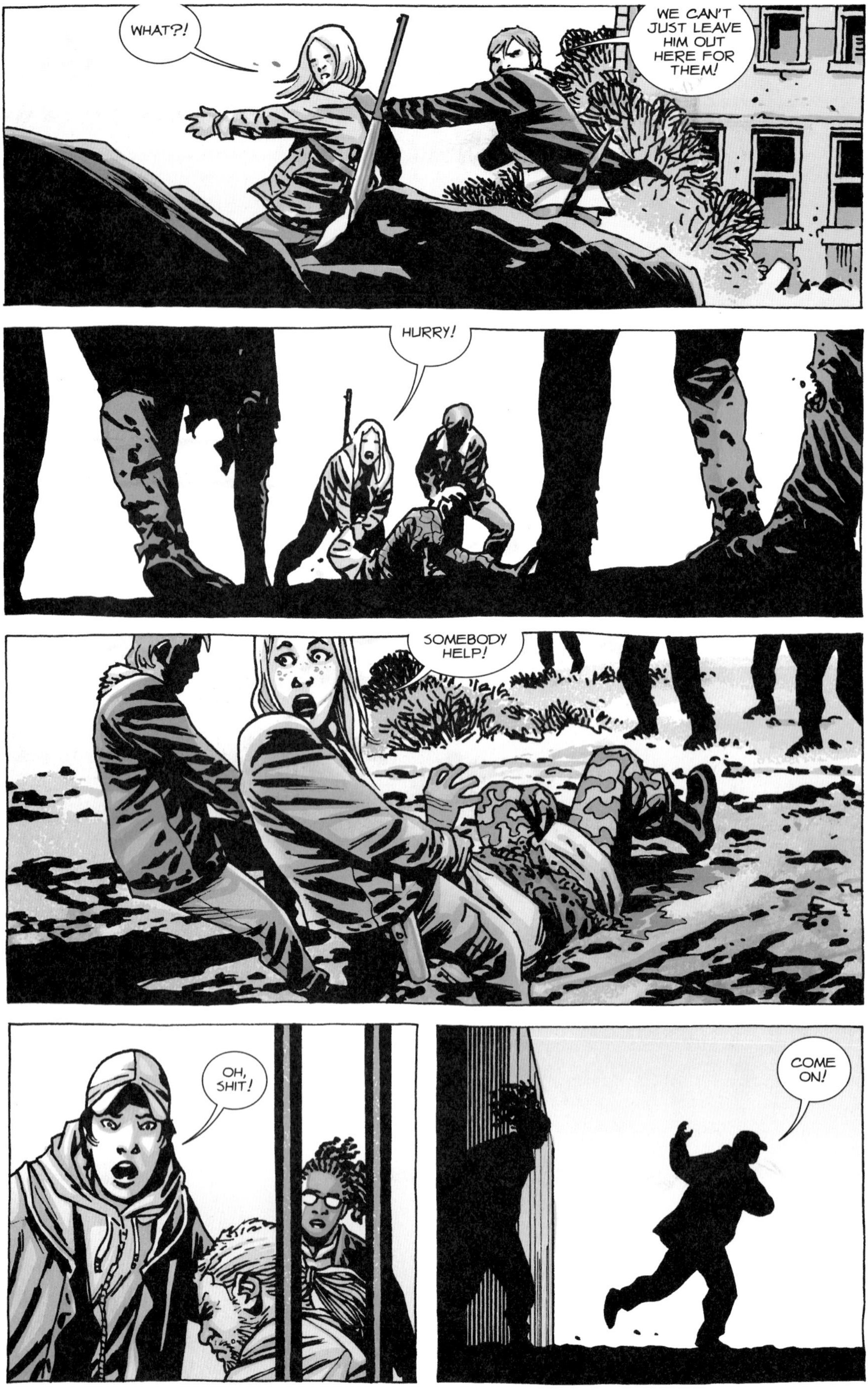
WHAT?!
WE CAN'T JUST LEAVE HIM OUT HERE FOR THEM!
HURRY!
SOMEBODY HELP!
OH, SHIT!
COME ON!

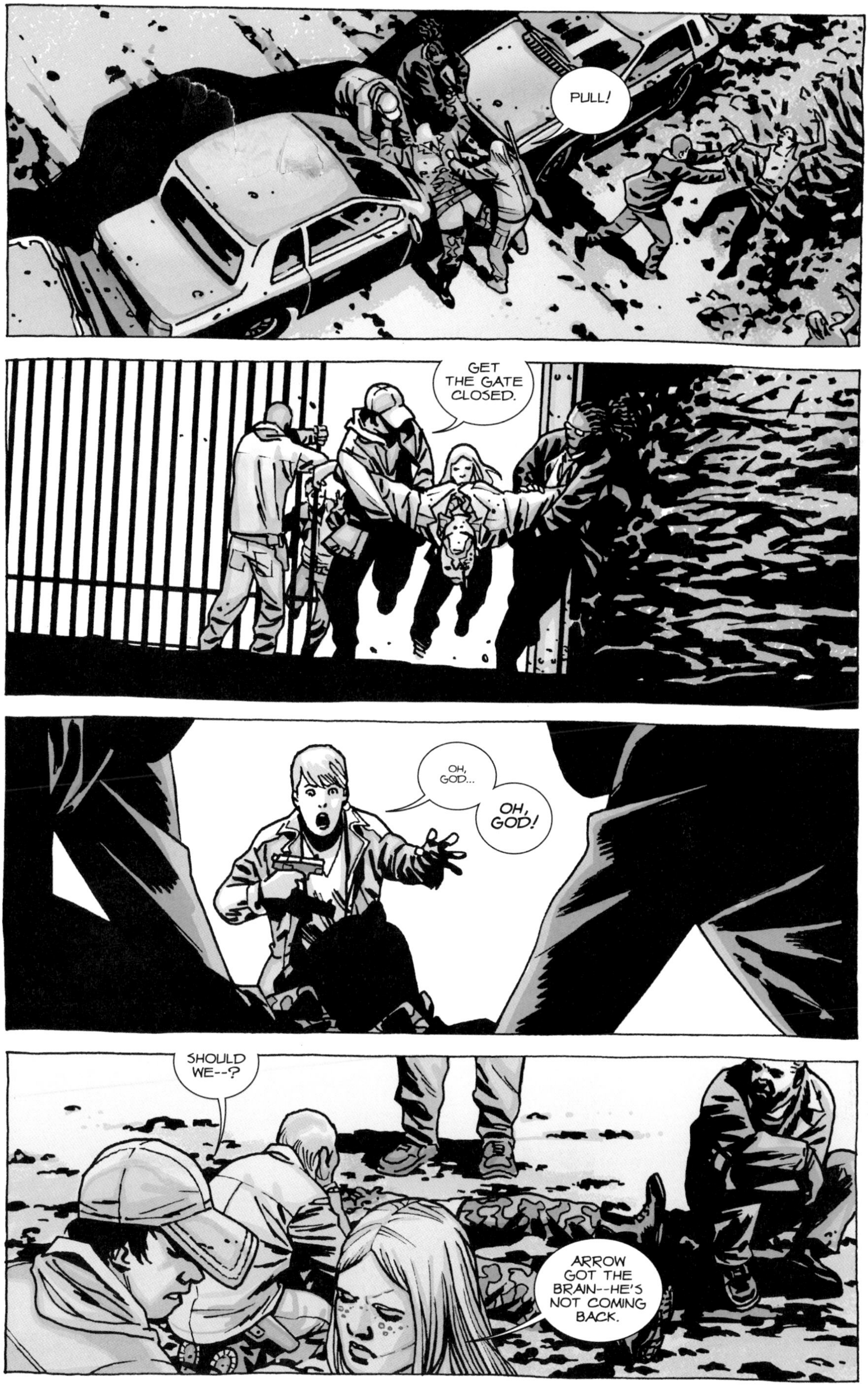
PULL!
GET THE GATE CLOSED.
OH, GOD...
OH, GOD!
SHOULD WE--?
ARROW GOT THE BRAIN--HE'S NOT COMING BACK.

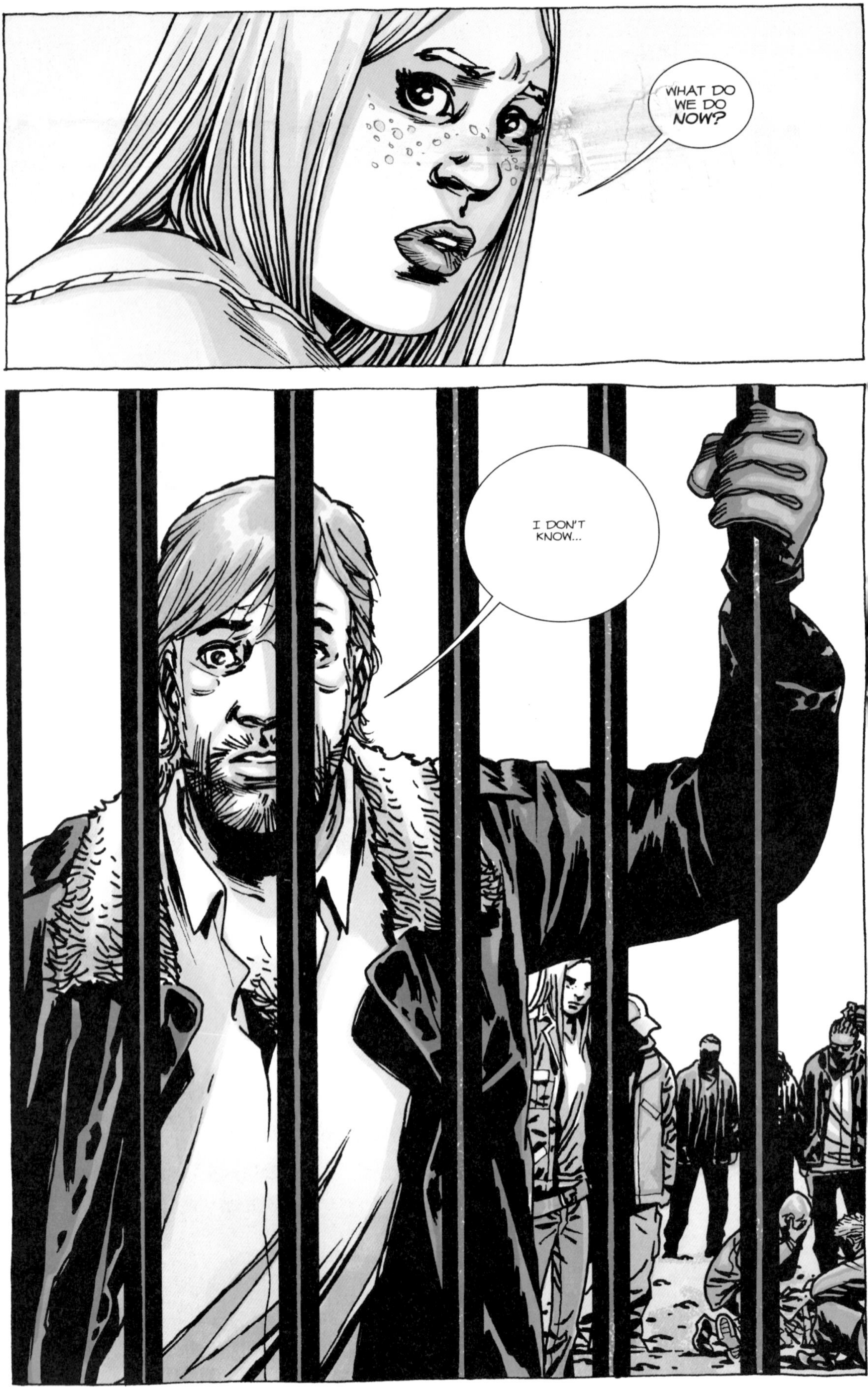
WHAT DO WE DO NOW?
I DON'T KNOW...

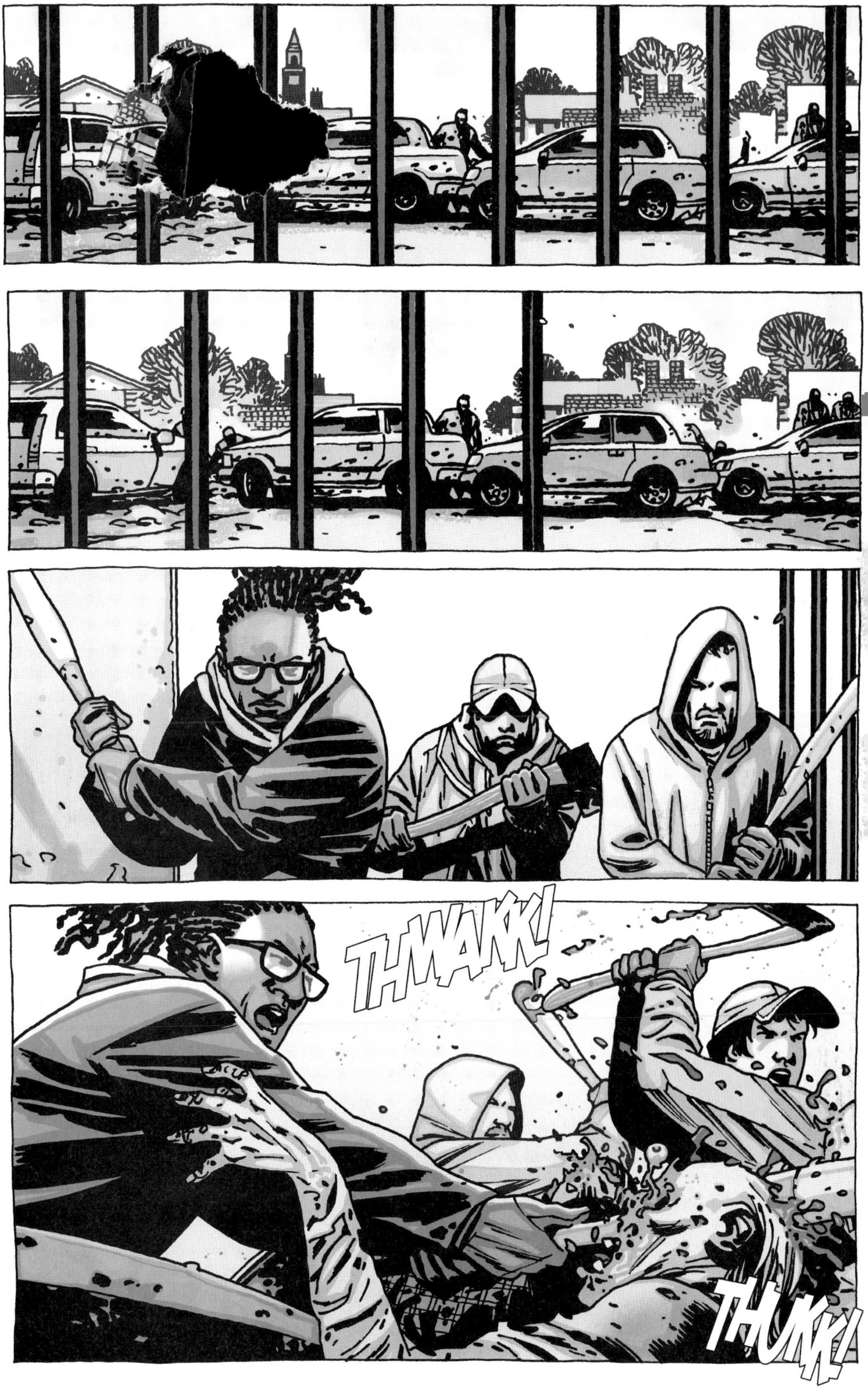
THWAKK!
THUKK!

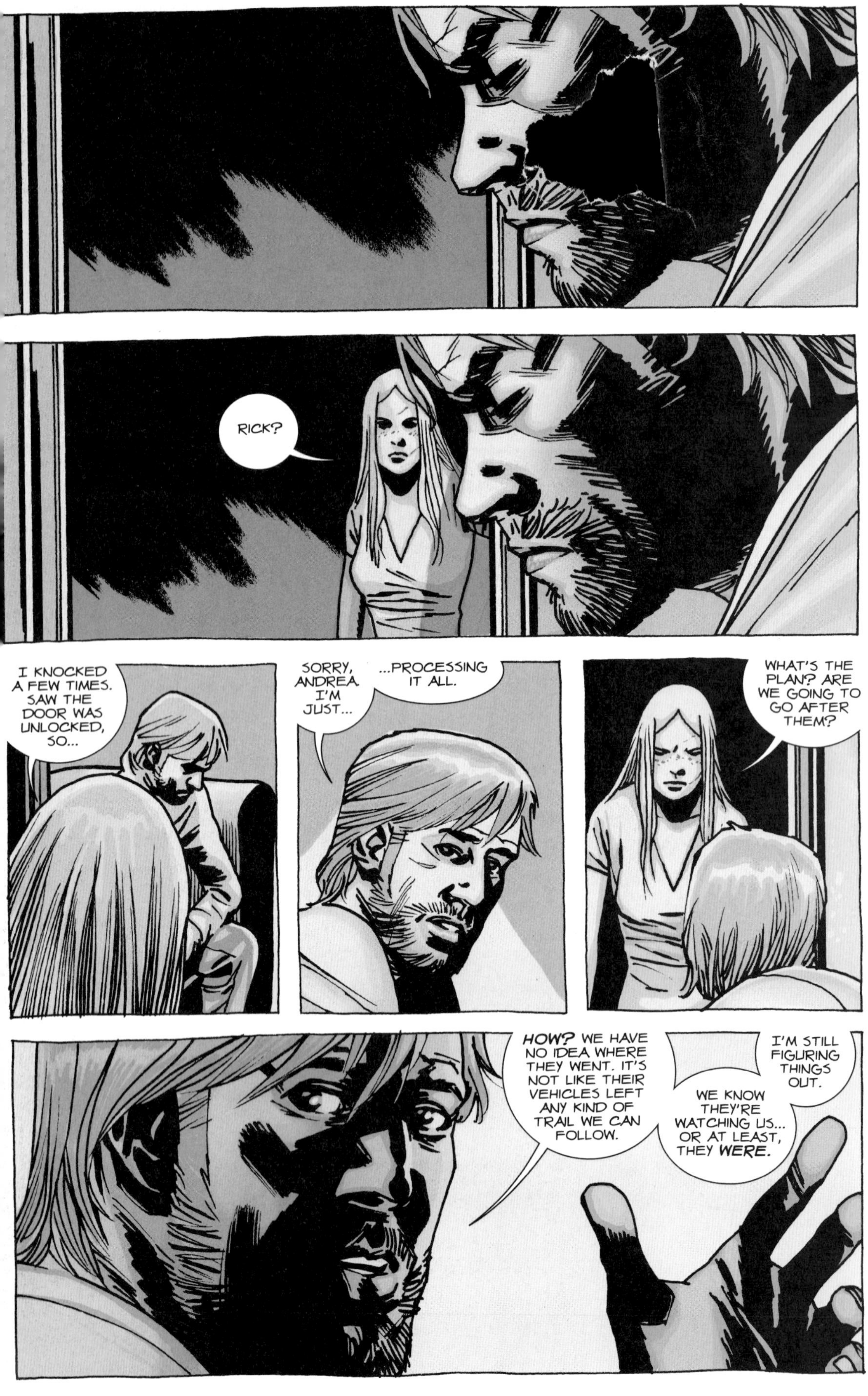
RICK?
I KNOCKED A FEW TIMES. SAW THE DOOR WAS UNLOCKED, SO...
SORRY, ANDREA. I'M JUST...
...PROCESSING IT ALL.
WHAT'S THE PLAN? ARE WE GOING TO GO AFTER THEM?
HOW? WE HAVE NO IDEA WHERE THEY WENT. IT'S NOT LIKE THEIR VEHICLES LEFT ANY KIND OF TRAIL WE CAN FOLLOW.
I'M STILL FIGURING THINGS OUT.
WE KNOW THEY'RE WATCHING US... OR AT LEAST, THEY WERE.

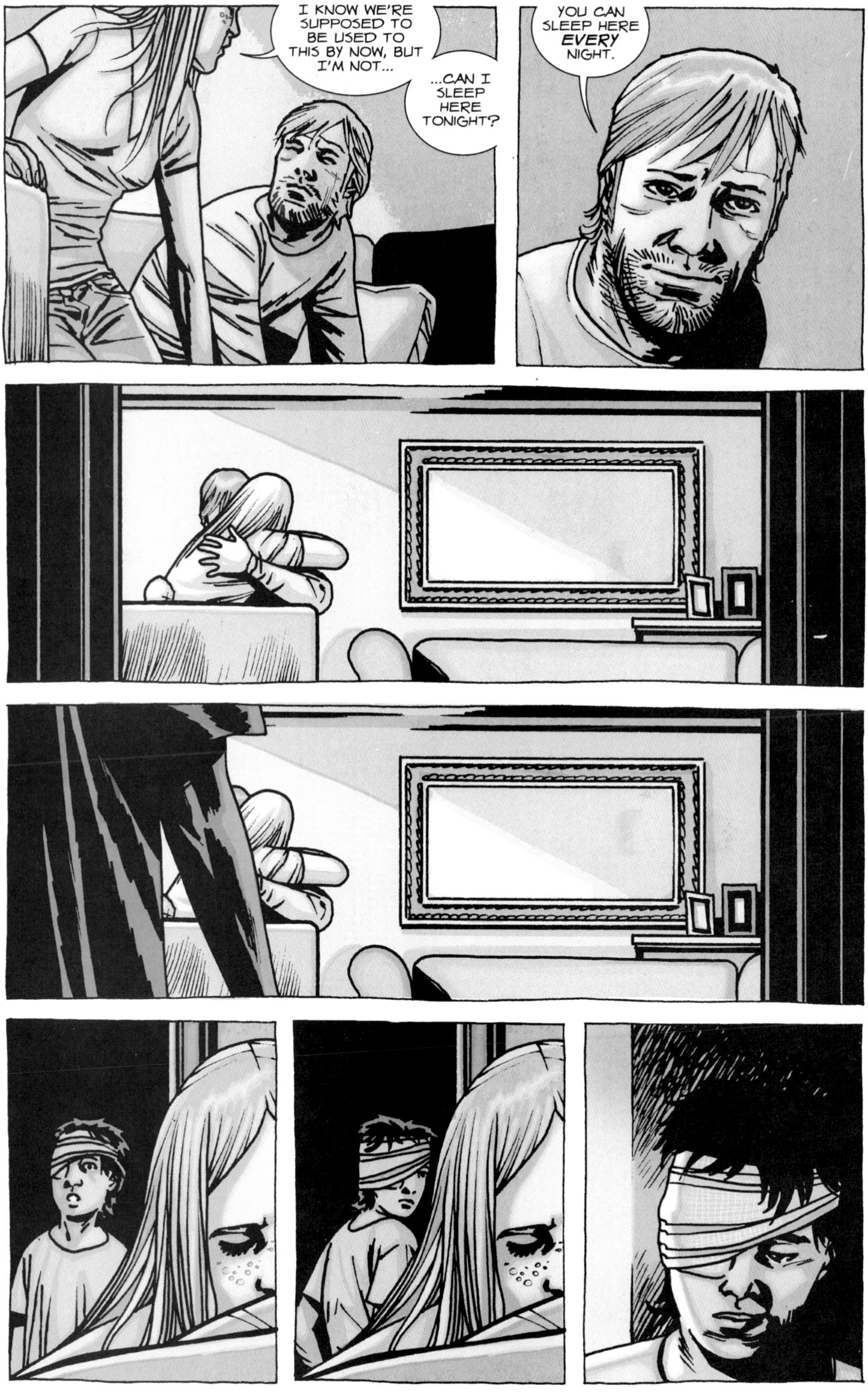
I KNOW WE'RE SUPPOSED TO BE USED TO THIS BY NOW, BUT I'M NOT...
...CAN I SLEEP HERE TONIGHT?
YOU CAN SLEEP HERE EVERY NIGHT.

I WANT TO LEAVE.

SOPHIA, DEAR-- GO PLAY IN THE LIVING ROOM.

THOSE PEOPLE ARE OUT THERE. I'M NOT GOING *ANYWHERE*.

WHY ARE YOU DOING THAT? SHE'S GOING TO FIND OUT ABRAHAM DIED. THE GUNFIRE WAS TRAINING? HOW LONG IS SHE GOING TO BUY THAT?

HELL, *CARL* WILL PROBABLY TELL HER WE WERE ATTACKED.

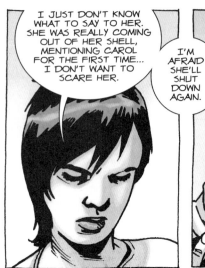

I JUST DON'T KNOW WHAT TO SAY TO HER. SHE WAS REALLY COMING OUT OF HER SHELL, MENTIONING CAROL FOR THE FIRST TIME... I DON'T WANT TO SCARE HER.

I'M AFRAID SHE'LL SHUT DOWN AGAIN.

YOU WANT HER OUT OF HER SHELL, LIVING A HAPPY LIFE--THEN WE NEED TO MOVE TO THE HILLTOP.

TRUST ME.

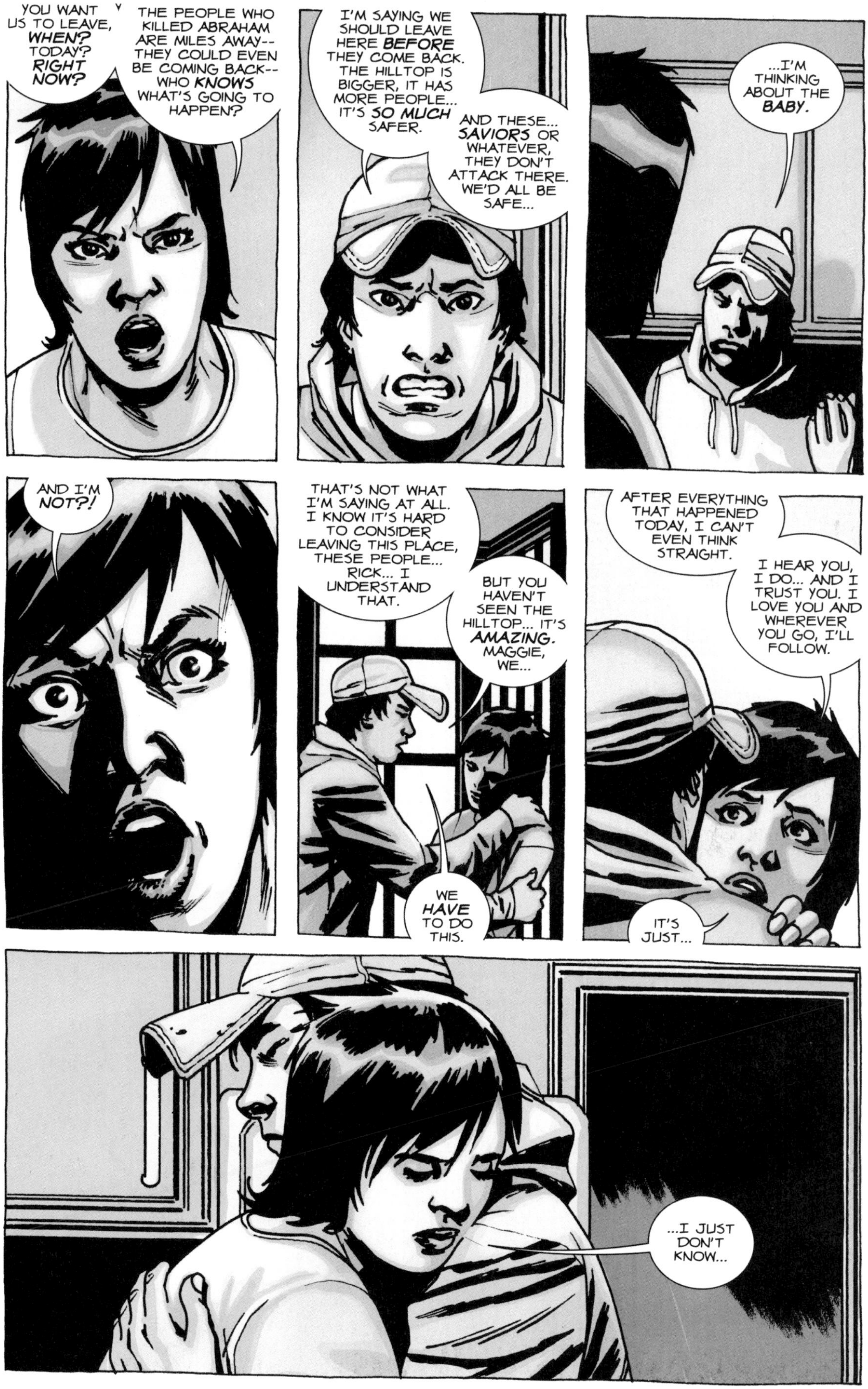
YOU WANT US TO LEAVE, WHEN? TODAY? RIGHT NOW?
THE PEOPLE WHO KILLED ABRAHAM ARE MILES AWAY-- THEY COULD EVEN BE COMING BACK-- WHO KNOWS WHAT'S GOING TO HAPPEN?
I'M SAYING WE SHOULD LEAVE HERE BEFORE THEY COME BACK. THE HILLTOP IS BIGGER, IT HAS MORE PEOPLE... IT'S SO MUCH SAFER.
AND THESE... SAVIORS OR WHATEVER, THEY DON'T ATTACK THERE. WE'D ALL BE SAFE...
...I'M THINKING ABOUT THE BABY.
AND I'M NOT?!
THAT'S NOT WHAT I'M SAYING AT ALL. I KNOW IT'S HARD TO CONSIDER LEAVING THIS PLACE, THESE PEOPLE... RICK... I UNDERSTAND THAT.
BUT YOU HAVEN'T SEEN THE HILLTOP... IT'S AMAZING. MAGGIE, WE...
WE HAVE TO DO THIS.
AFTER EVERYTHING THAT HAPPENED TODAY, I CAN'T EVEN THINK STRAIGHT.
I HEAR YOU, I DO... AND I TRUST YOU. I LOVE YOU AND WHEREVER YOU GO, I'LL FOLLOW.
IT'S JUST...
...I JUST DON'T KNOW...

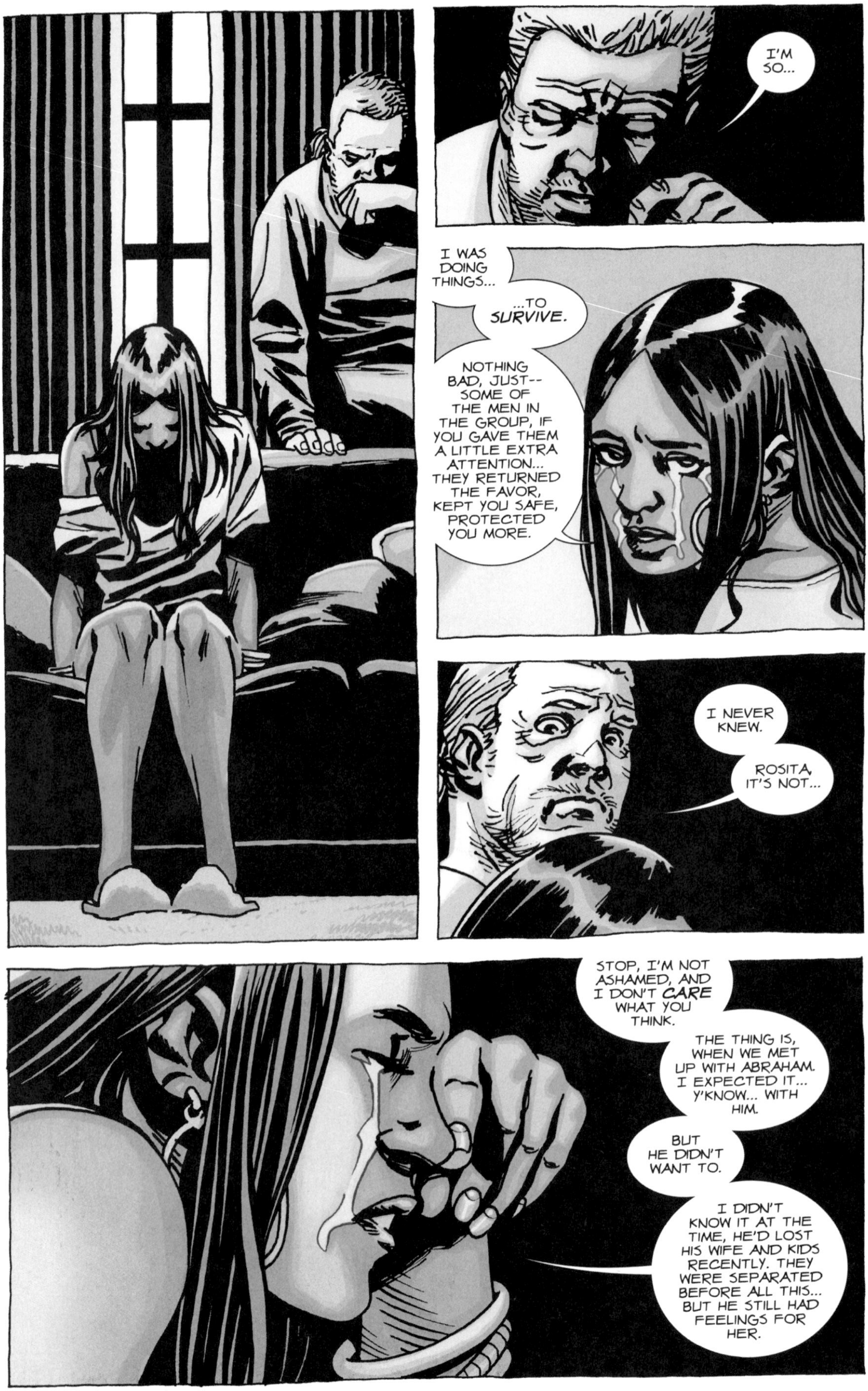
I'M SO...
I WAS DOING THINGS...
...TO SURVIVE.
NOTHING BAD, JUST-- SOME OF THE MEN IN THE GROUP, IF YOU GAVE THEM A LITTLE EXTRA ATTENTION... THEY RETURNED THE FAVOR, KEPT YOU SAFE, PROTECTED YOU MORE.
I NEVER KNEW.
ROSITA, IT'S NOT...
STOP, I'M NOT ASHAMED, AND I DON'T CARE WHAT YOU THINK.
THE THING IS, WHEN WE MET UP WITH ABRAHAM. I EXPECTED IT... Y'KNOW... WITH HIM.
BUT HE DIDN'T WANT TO.
I DIDN'T KNOW IT AT THE TIME, HE'D LOST HIS WIFE AND KIDS RECENTLY. THEY WERE SEPARATED BEFORE ALL THIS... BUT HE STILL HAD FEELINGS FOR HER.

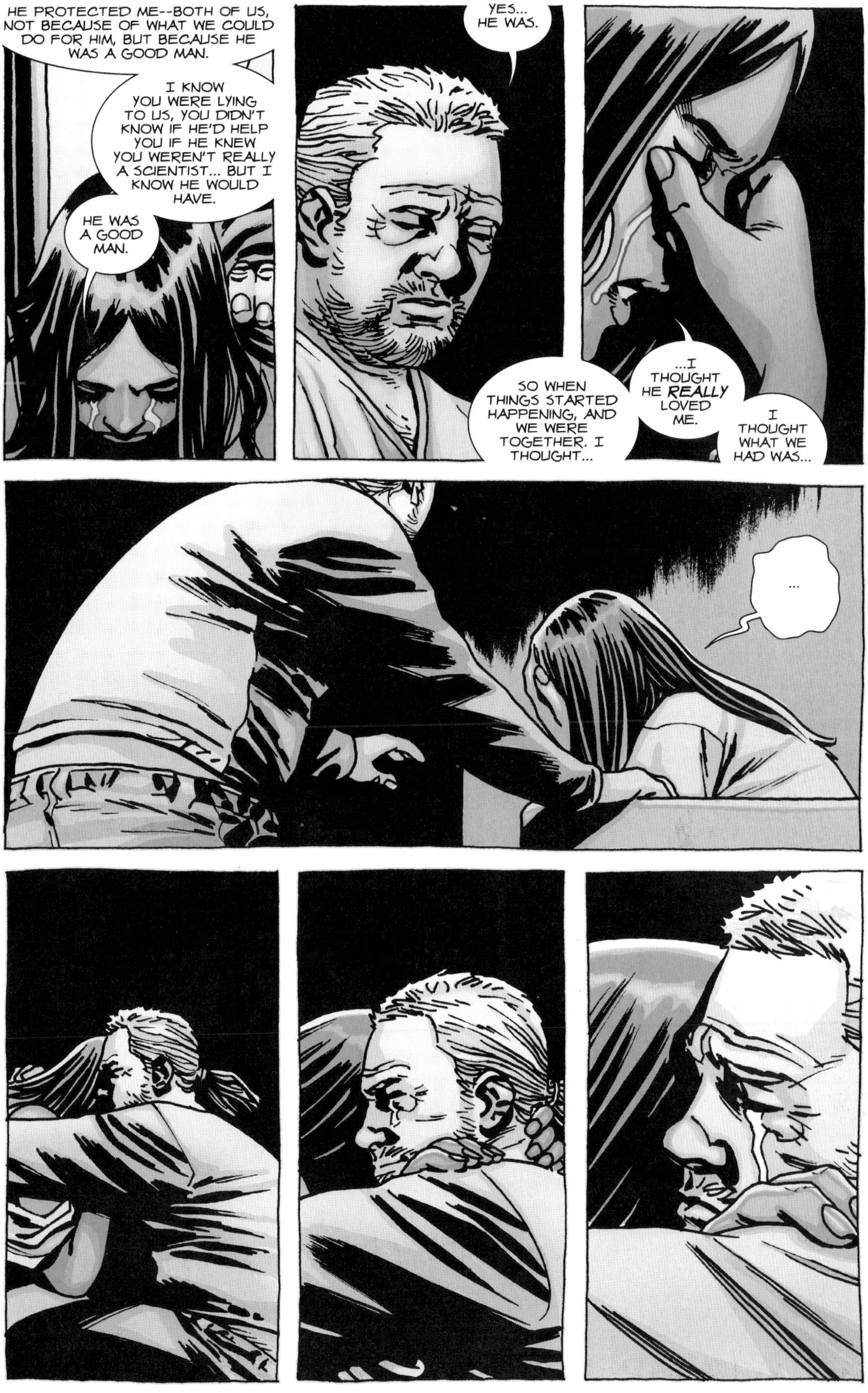
HE PROTECTED ME--BOTH OF US, NOT BECAUSE OF WHAT WE COULD DO FOR HIM, BUT BECAUSE HE WAS A GOOD MAN.
I KNOW YOU WERE LYING TO US, YOU DIDN'T KNOW IF HE'D HELP YOU IF HE KNEW YOU WEREN'T REALLY A SCIENTIST... BUT I KNOW HE WOULD HAVE.
HE WAS A GOOD MAN.
YES... HE WAS.
SO WHEN THINGS STARTED HAPPENING, AND WE WERE TOGETHER. I THOUGHT...
...I THOUGHT HE REALLY LOVED ME.
I THOUGHT WHAT WE HAD WAS...
...

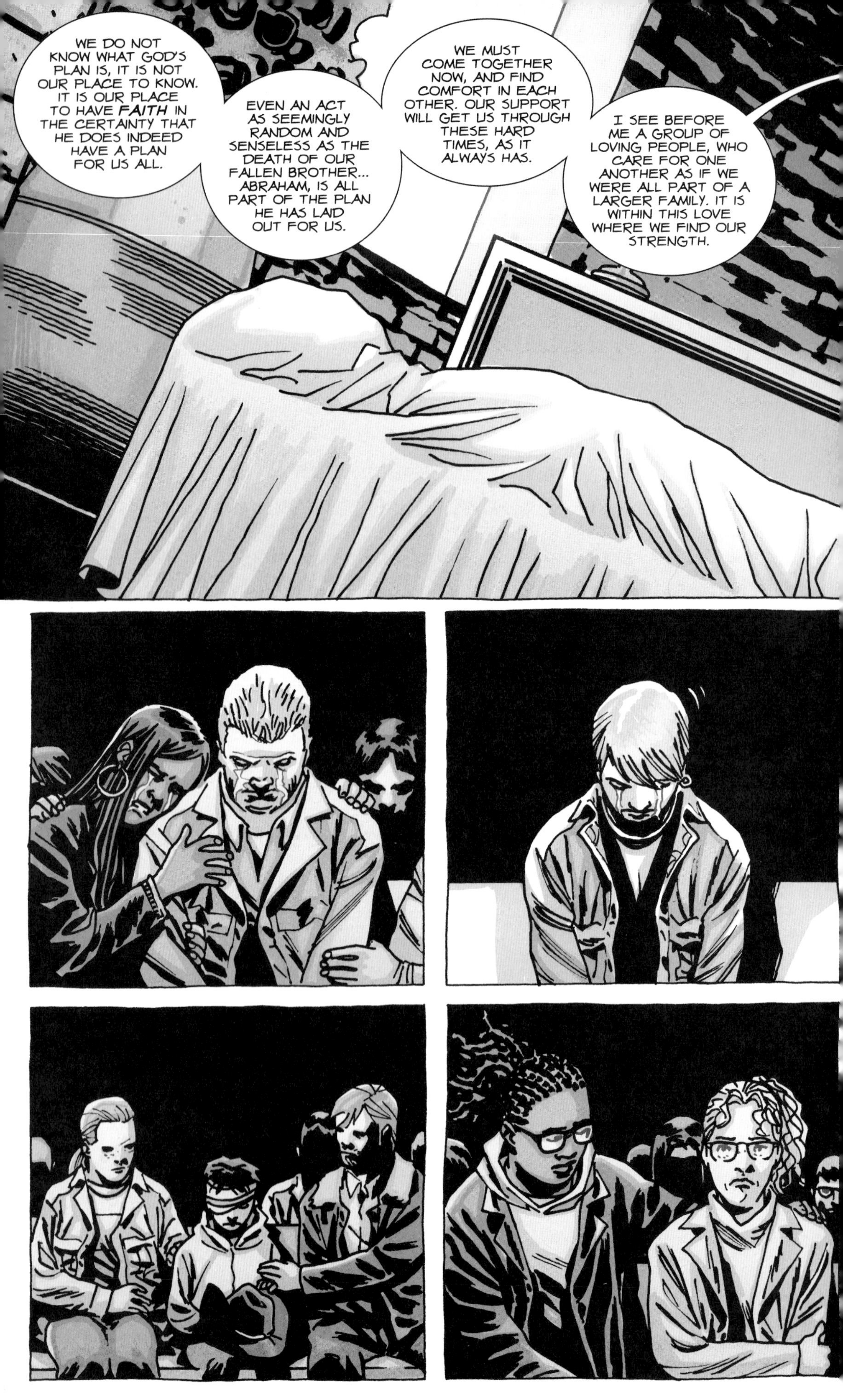
WE DO NOT KNOW WHAT GOD'S PLAN IS, IT IS NOT OUR PLACE TO KNOW. IT IS OUR PLACE TO HAVE **FAITH** IN THE CERTAINTY THAT HE DOES INDEED HAVE A PLAN FOR US ALL.
EVEN AN ACT AS SEEMINGLY RANDOM AND SENSELESS AS THE DEATH OF OUR FALLEN BROTHER... ABRAHAM, IS ALL PART OF THE PLAN HE HAS LAID OUT FOR US.
WE MUST COME TOGETHER NOW, AND FIND COMFORT IN EACH OTHER. OUR SUPPORT WILL GET US THROUGH THESE HARD TIMES, AS IT ALWAYS HAS.
I SEE BEFORE ME A GROUP OF LOVING PEOPLE, WHO CARE FOR ONE ANOTHER AS IF WE WERE ALL PART OF A LARGER FAMILY. IT IS WITHIN THIS LOVE WHERE WE FIND OUR STRENGTH.

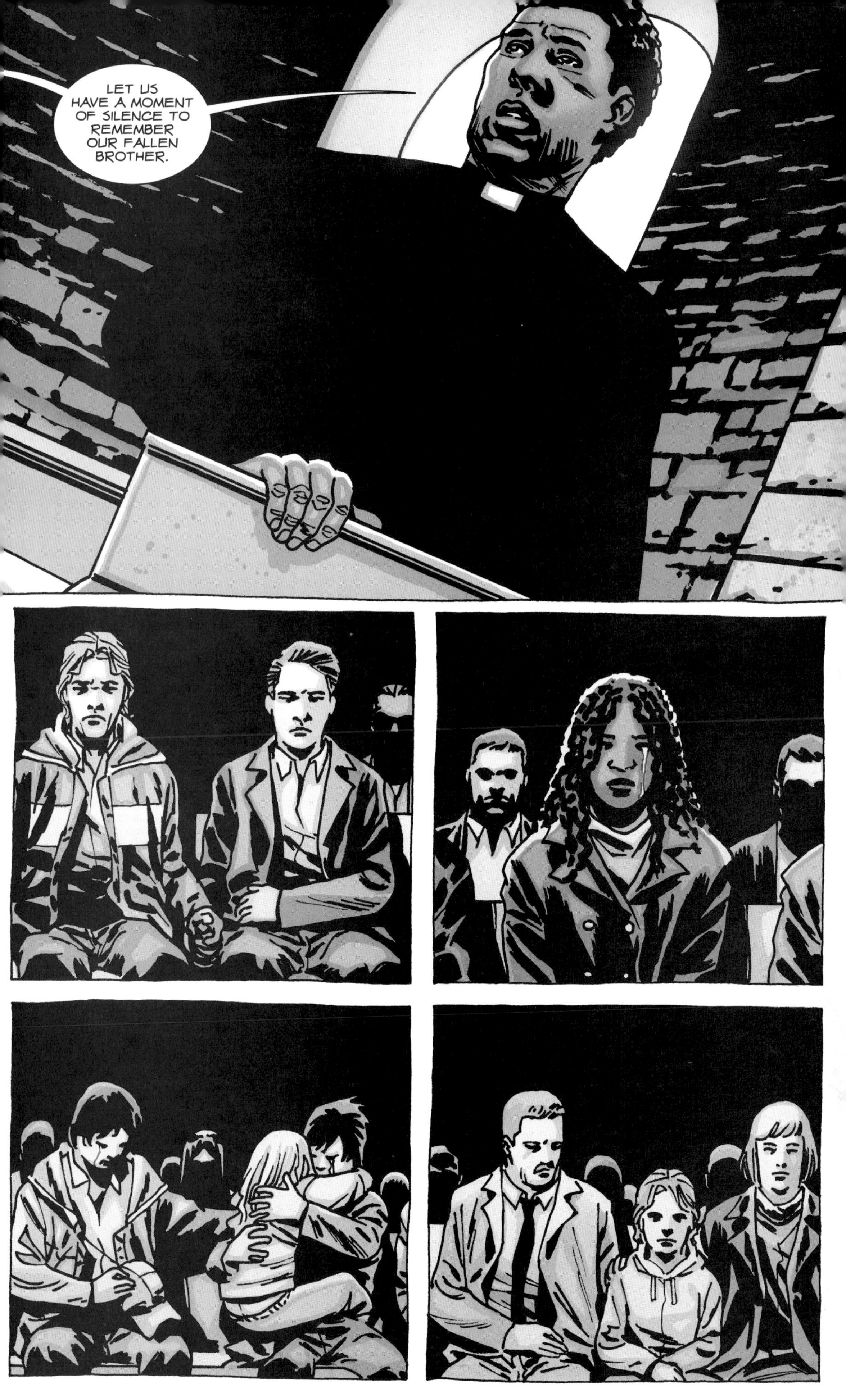
LET US HAVE A MOMENT OF SILENCE TO REMEMBER OUR FALLEN BROTHER.

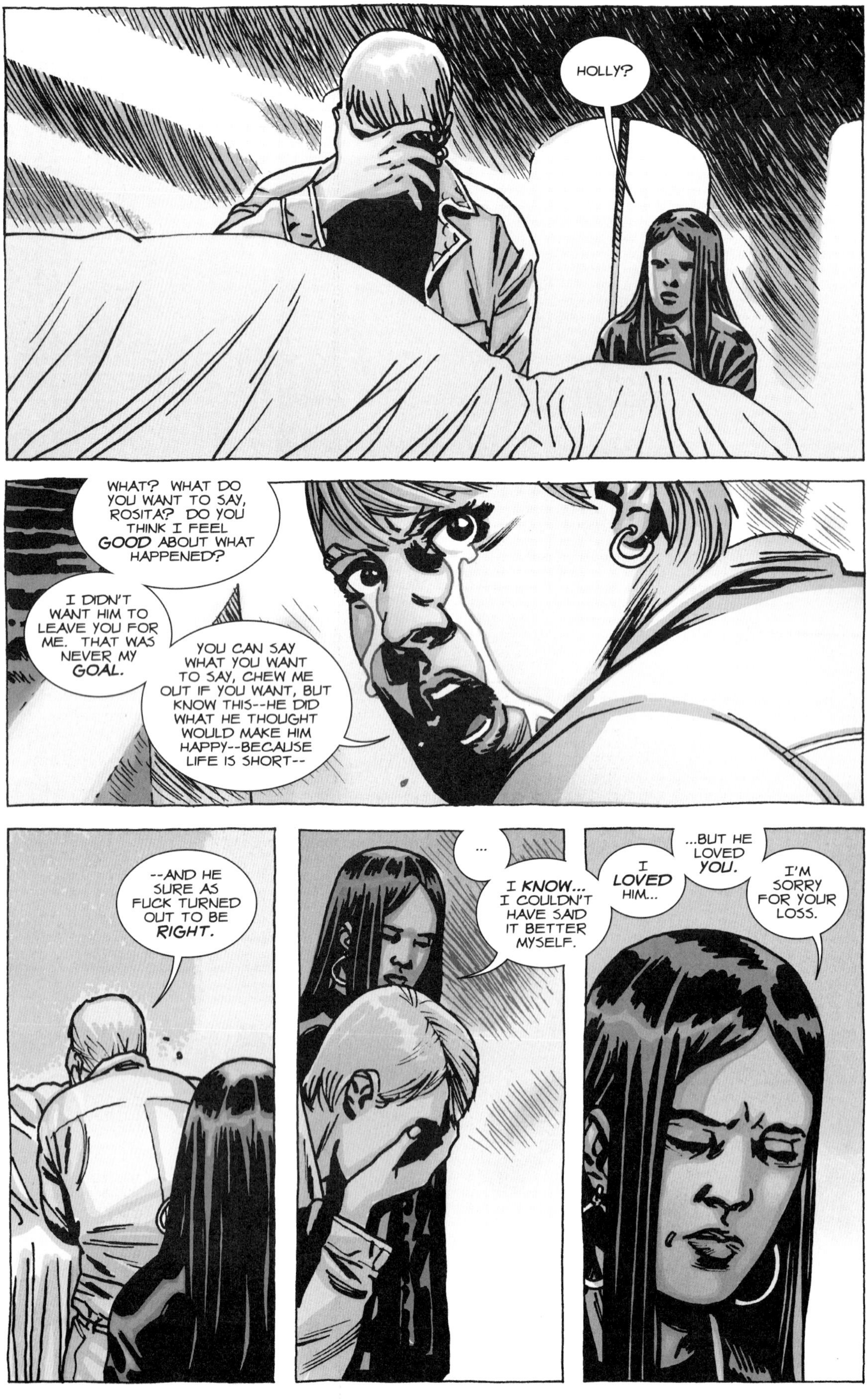
HOLLY?
WHAT? WHAT DO YOU WANT TO SAY, ROSITA? DO YOU THINK I FEEL GOOD ABOUT WHAT HAPPENED?
I DIDN'T WANT HIM TO LEAVE YOU FOR ME. THAT WAS NEVER MY GOAL.
YOU CAN SAY WHAT YOU WANT TO SAY, CHEW ME OUT IF YOU WANT, BUT KNOW THIS--HE DID WHAT HE THOUGHT WOULD MAKE HIM HAPPY--BECAUSE LIFE IS SHORT--
--AND HE SURE AS FUCK TURNED OUT TO BE RIGHT.
...
I KNOW... I COULDN'T HAVE SAID IT BETTER MYSELF.
I LOVED HIM...
...BUT HE LOVED YOU.
I'M SORRY FOR YOUR LOSS.

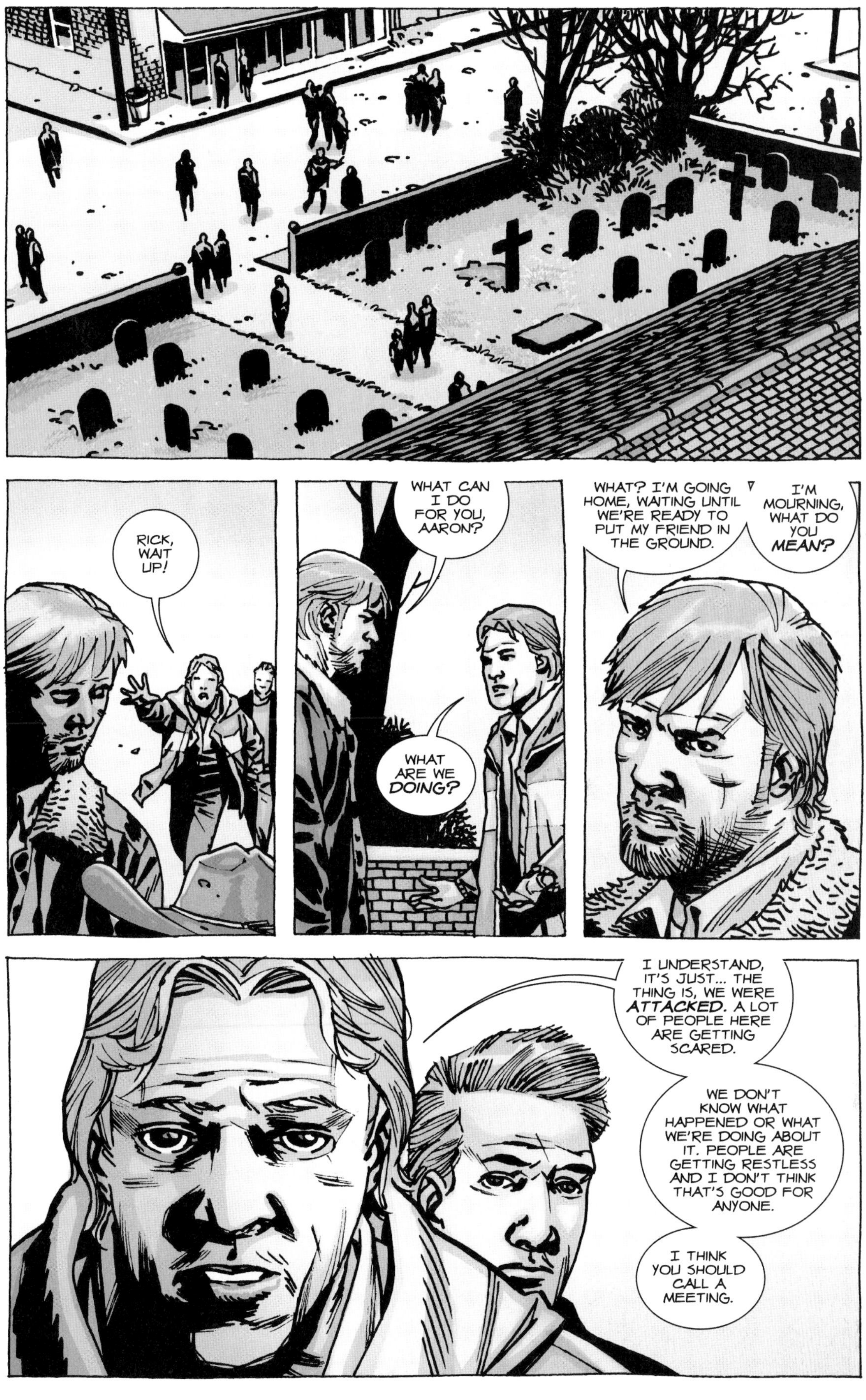
RICK, WAIT UP!
WHAT CAN I DO FOR YOU, AARON?
WHAT ARE WE DOING?
WHAT? I'M GOING HOME, WAITING UNTIL WE'RE READY TO PUT MY FRIEND IN THE GROUND.
I'M MOURNING, WHAT DO YOU MEAN?
I UNDERSTAND, IT'S JUST... THE THING IS, WE WERE ATTACKED. A LOT OF PEOPLE HERE ARE GETTING SCARED.
WE DON'T KNOW WHAT HAPPENED OR WHAT WE'RE DOING ABOUT IT. PEOPLE ARE GETTING RESTLESS AND I DON'T THINK THAT'S GOOD FOR ANYONE.
I THINK YOU SHOULD CALL A MEETING.

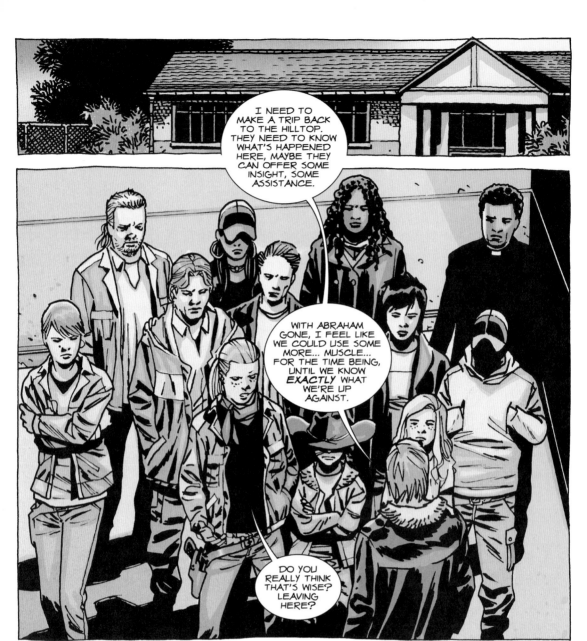

I NEED TO MAKE A TRIP BACK TO THE HILLTOP. THEY NEED TO KNOW WHAT'S HAPPENED HERE, MAYBE THEY CAN OFFER SOME INSIGHT, SOME ASSISTANCE.

WITH ABRAHAM GONE, I FEEL LIKE WE COULD USE SOME MORE... MUSCLE... FOR THE TIME BEING, UNTIL WE KNOW *EXACTLY* WHAT WE'RE UP AGAINST.

DO YOU REALLY THINK THAT'S WISE? LEAVING HERE?

WE'VE KILLED A LOT OF THESE PEOPLE. A FEW ON THE ROAD, NEARLY A DOZEN YESTERDAY.

THEY HAVE TO BE FEELING THAT.

I DON'T FEEL LIKE THEY'RE GOING TO BE STAGING ANOTHER ATTACK ON US RIGHT AWAY. WE'VE GOT SOME TIME.

DOESN'T MAKE SENSE TO ME-- LEAVING THIS PLACE WITH FEWER PEOPLE TO DEFEND THE WALLS.

IT'S GOING TO BE AN OVERNIGHT TRIP. COULD BE OUR LAST CHANCE TO GET HELP FROM THE HILLTOP BEFORE THEY ATTACK AGAIN.

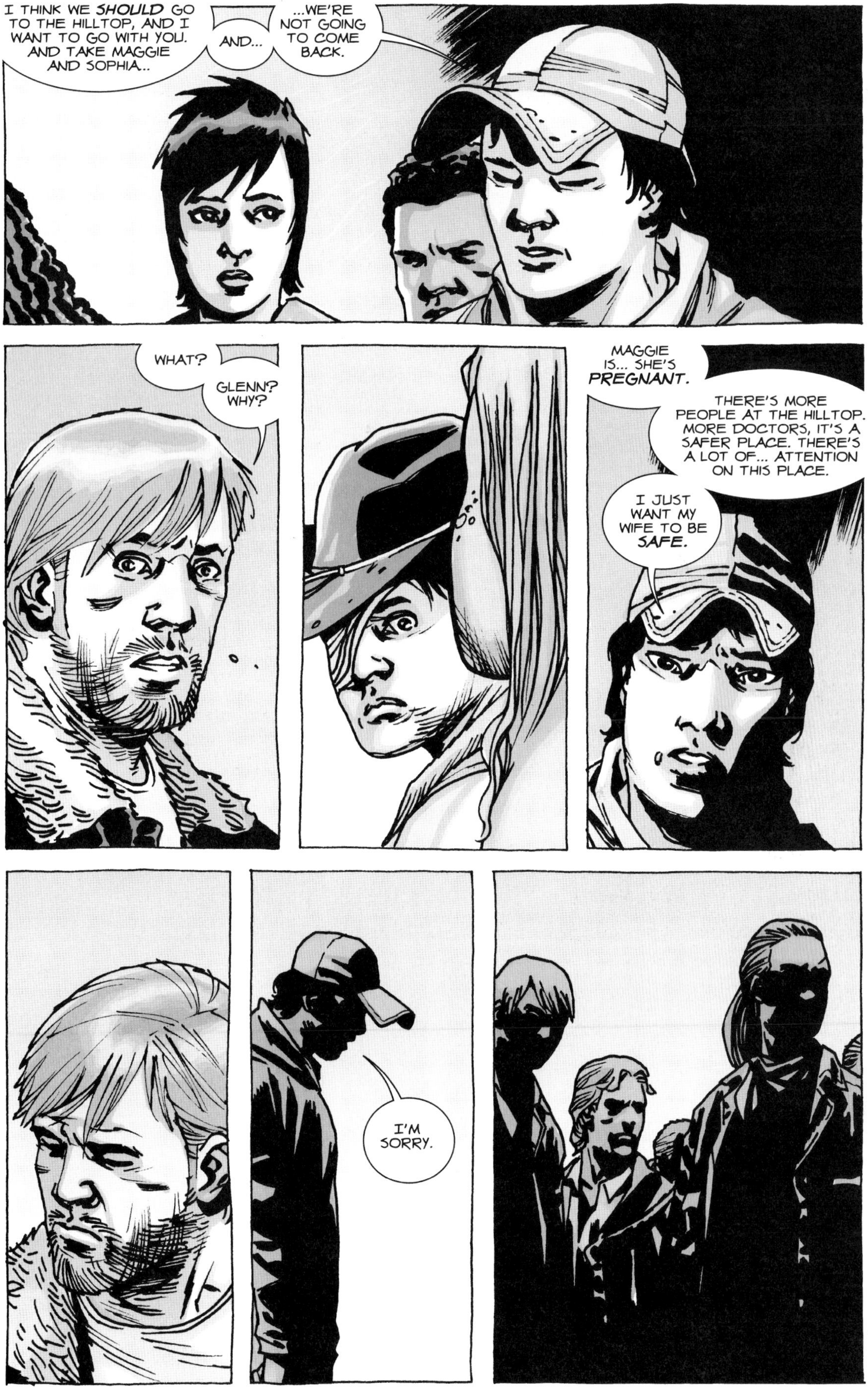

I THINK WE SHOULD GO TO THE HILLTOP, AND I WANT TO GO WITH YOU. AND TAKE MAGGIE AND SOPHIA...
AND...
...WE'RE NOT GOING TO COME BACK.
WHAT?
GLENN? WHY?
MAGGIE IS... SHE'S PREGNANT.
THERE'S MORE PEOPLE AT THE HILLTOP. MORE DOCTORS, IT'S A SAFER PLACE. THERE'S A LOT OF... ATTENTION ON THIS PLACE.
I JUST WANT MY WIFE TO BE SAFE.
I'M SORRY.

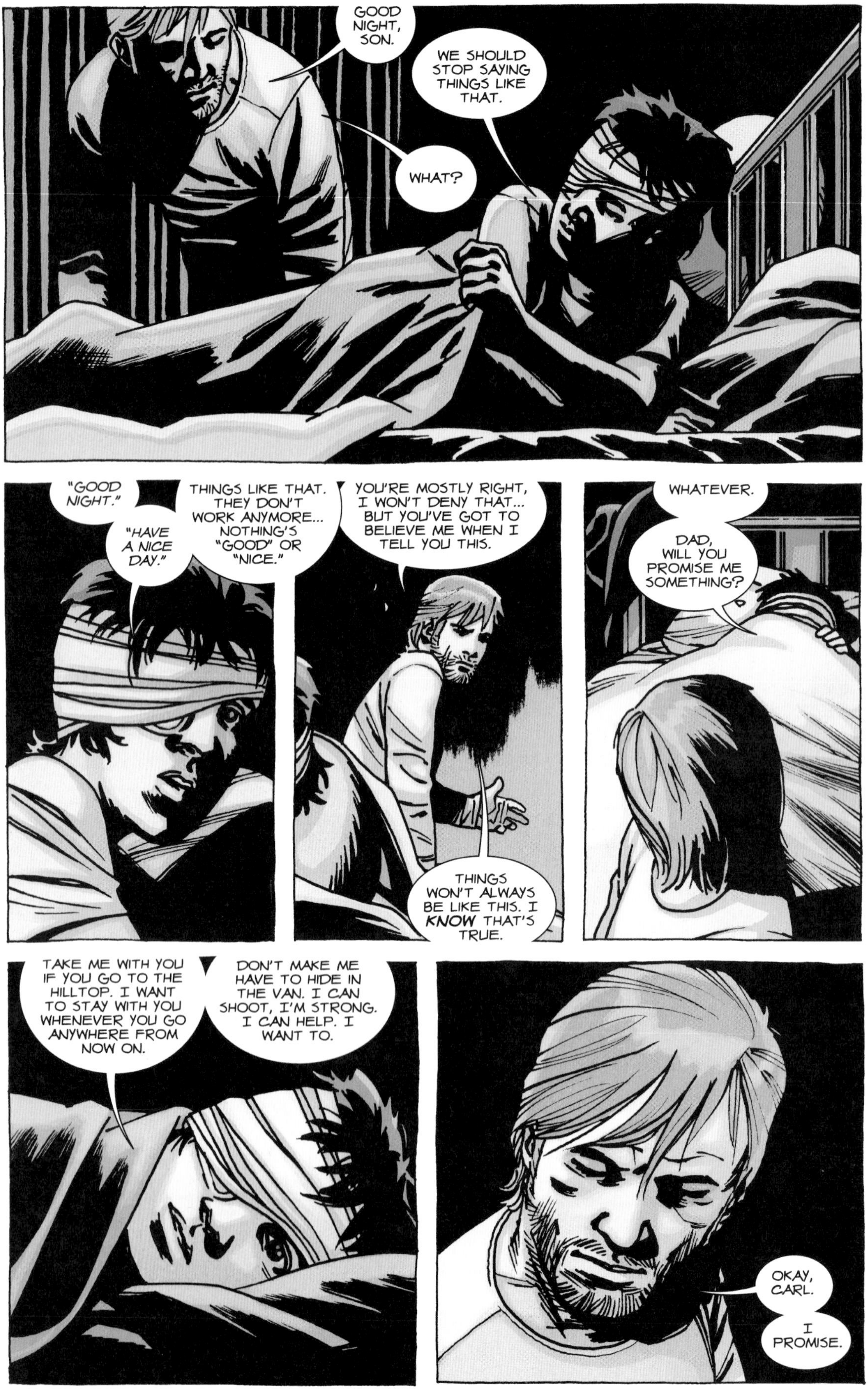
GOOD NIGHT, SON.
WE SHOULD STOP SAYING THINGS LIKE THAT.
WHAT?
"GOOD NIGHT."
"HAVE A NICE DAY."
THINGS LIKE THAT. THEY DON'T WORK ANYMORE... NOTHING'S "GOOD" OR "NICE."
YOU'RE MOSTLY RIGHT, I WON'T DENY THAT... BUT YOU'VE GOT TO BELIEVE ME WHEN I TELL YOU THIS.
THINGS WON'T ALWAYS BE LIKE THIS. I *KNOW* THAT'S TRUE.
WHATEVER.
DAD, WILL YOU PROMISE ME SOMETHING?
TAKE ME WITH YOU IF YOU GO TO THE HILLTOP. I WANT TO STAY WITH YOU WHENEVER YOU GO ANYWHERE FROM NOW ON.
DON'T MAKE ME HAVE TO HIDE IN THE VAN. I CAN SHOOT, I'M STRONG. I CAN HELP. I WANT TO.
OKAY, CARL.
I PROMISE.

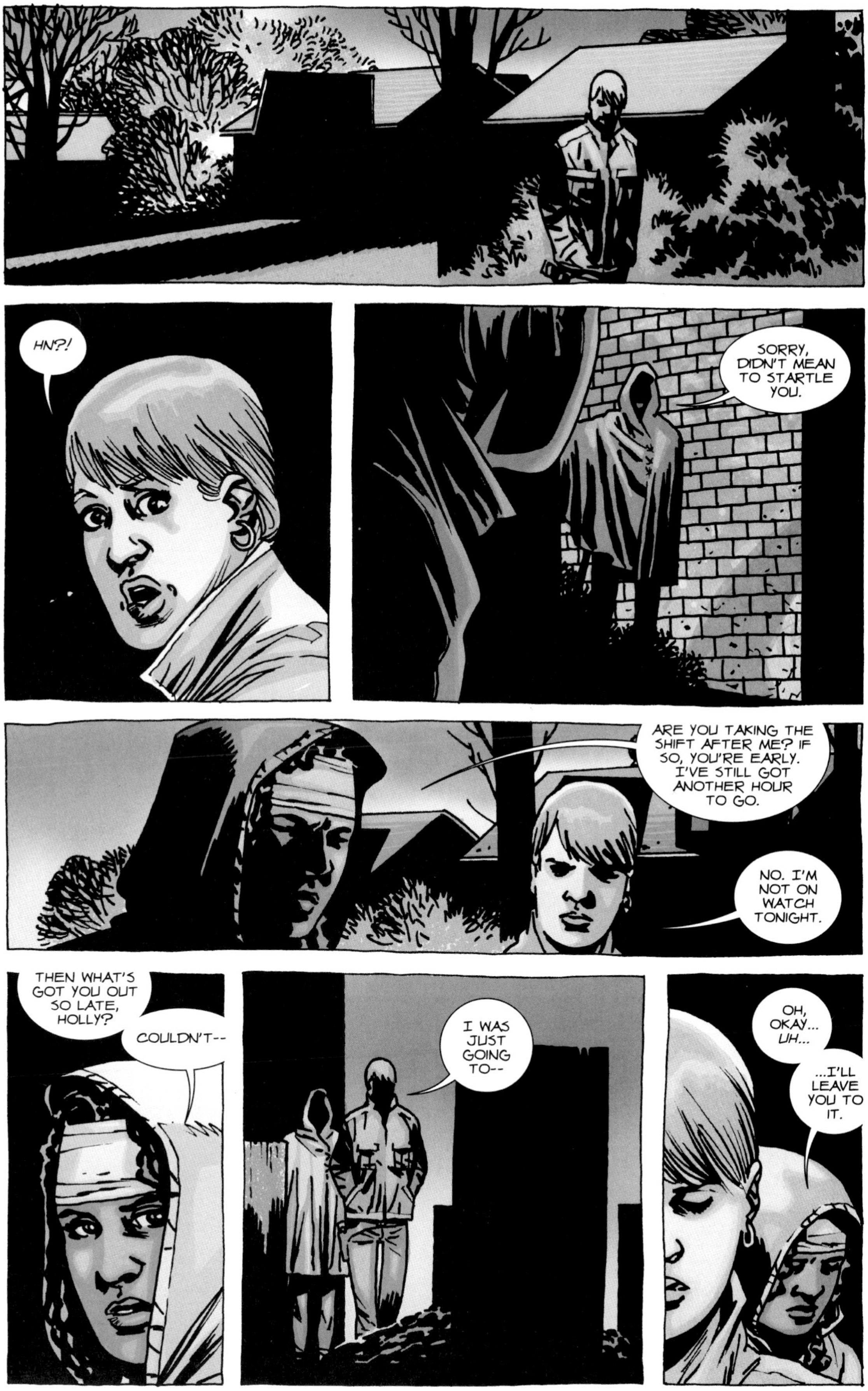
HN?!
SORRY, DIDN'T MEAN TO STARTLE YOU.
ARE YOU TAKING THE SHIFT AFTER ME? IF SO, YOU'RE EARLY. I'VE STILL GOT ANOTHER HOUR TO GO.
NO. I'M NOT ON WATCH TONIGHT.
THEN WHAT'S GOT YOU OUT SO LATE, HOLLY?
COULDN'T--
I WAS JUST GOING TO--
OH, OKAY... UH...
...I'LL LEAVE YOU TO IT.

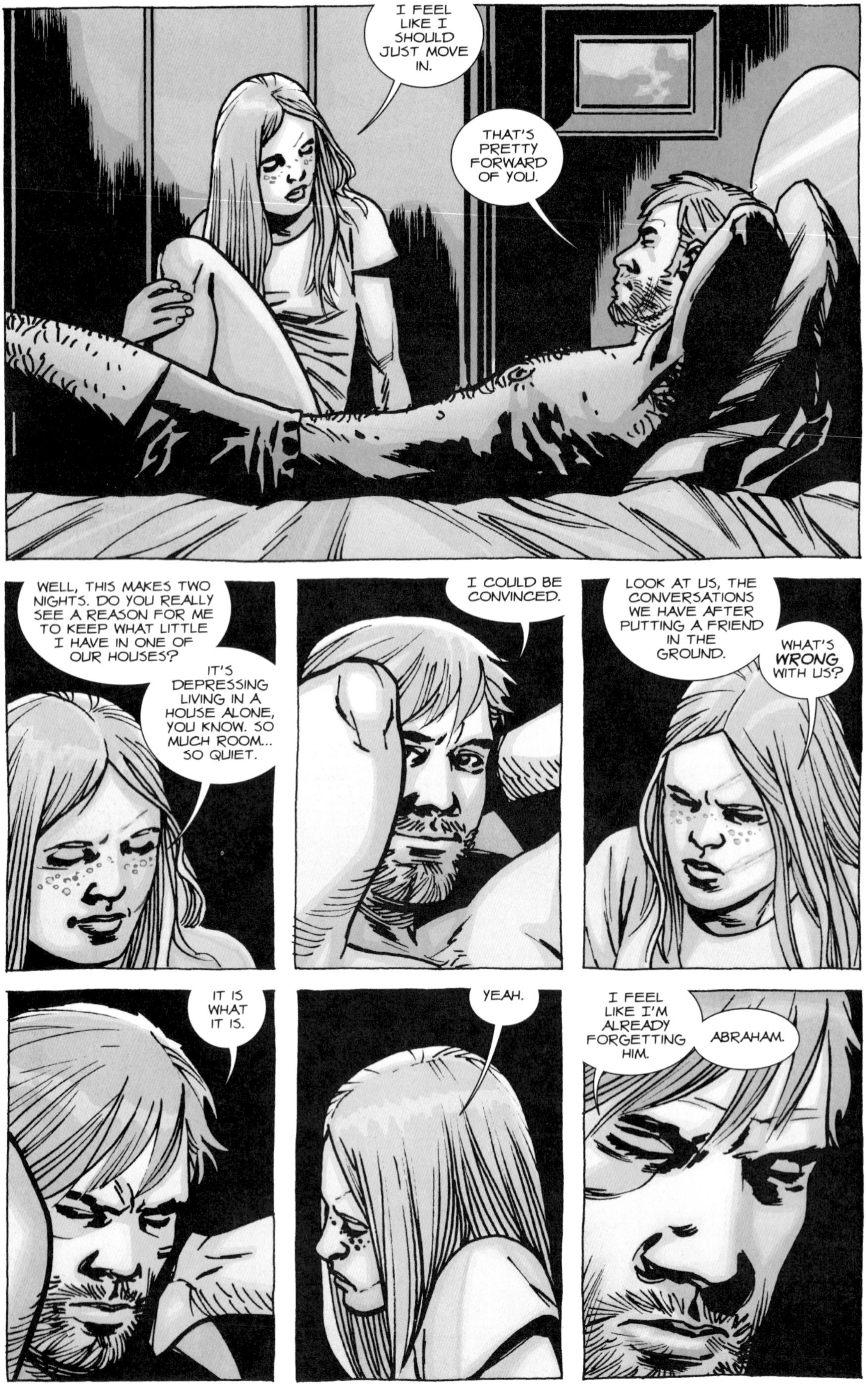
I FEEL LIKE I SHOULD JUST MOVE IN.
THAT'S PRETTY FORWARD OF YOU.
WELL, THIS MAKES TWO NIGHTS. DO YOU REALLY SEE A REASON FOR ME TO KEEP WHAT LITTLE I HAVE IN ONE OF OUR HOUSES?
IT'S DEPRESSING LIVING IN A HOUSE ALONE, YOU KNOW. SO MUCH ROOM... SO QUIET.
I COULD BE CONVINCED.
LOOK AT US, THE CONVERSATIONS WE HAVE AFTER PUTTING A FRIEND IN THE GROUND.
WHAT'S WRONG WITH US?
IT IS WHAT IT IS.
YEAH.
I FEEL LIKE I'M ALREADY FORGETTING HIM.
ABRAHAM.

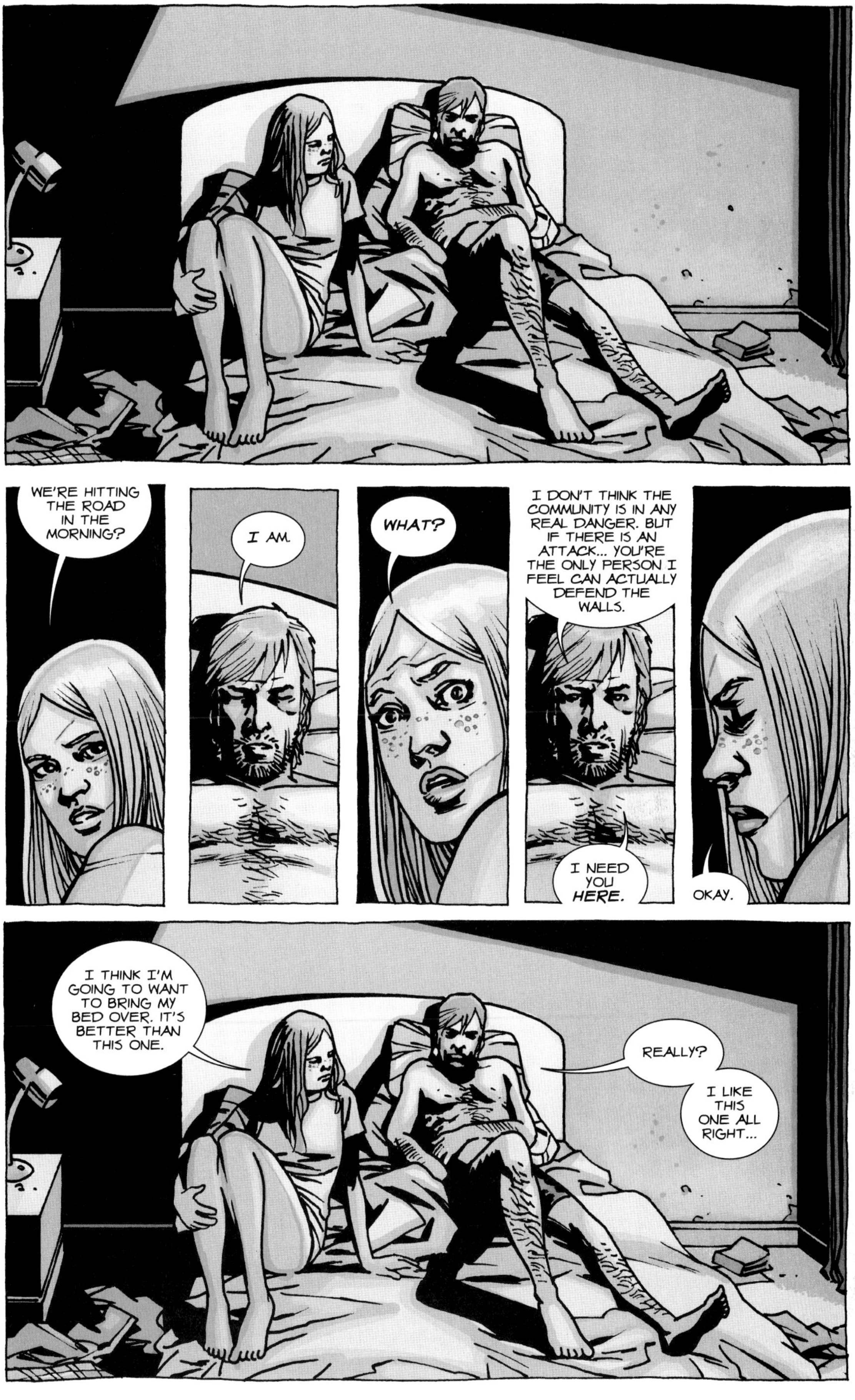
WE'RE HITTING THE ROAD IN THE MORNING?
I AM.
WHAT?
I DON'T THINK THE COMMUNITY IS IN ANY REAL DANGER. BUT IF THERE IS AN ATTACK... YOU'RE THE ONLY PERSON I FEEL CAN ACTUALLY DEFEND THE WALLS.
I NEED YOU HERE.
OKAY.
I THINK I'M GOING TO WANT TO BRING MY BED OVER. IT'S BETTER THAN THIS ONE.
REALLY?
I LIKE THIS ONE ALL RIGHT...

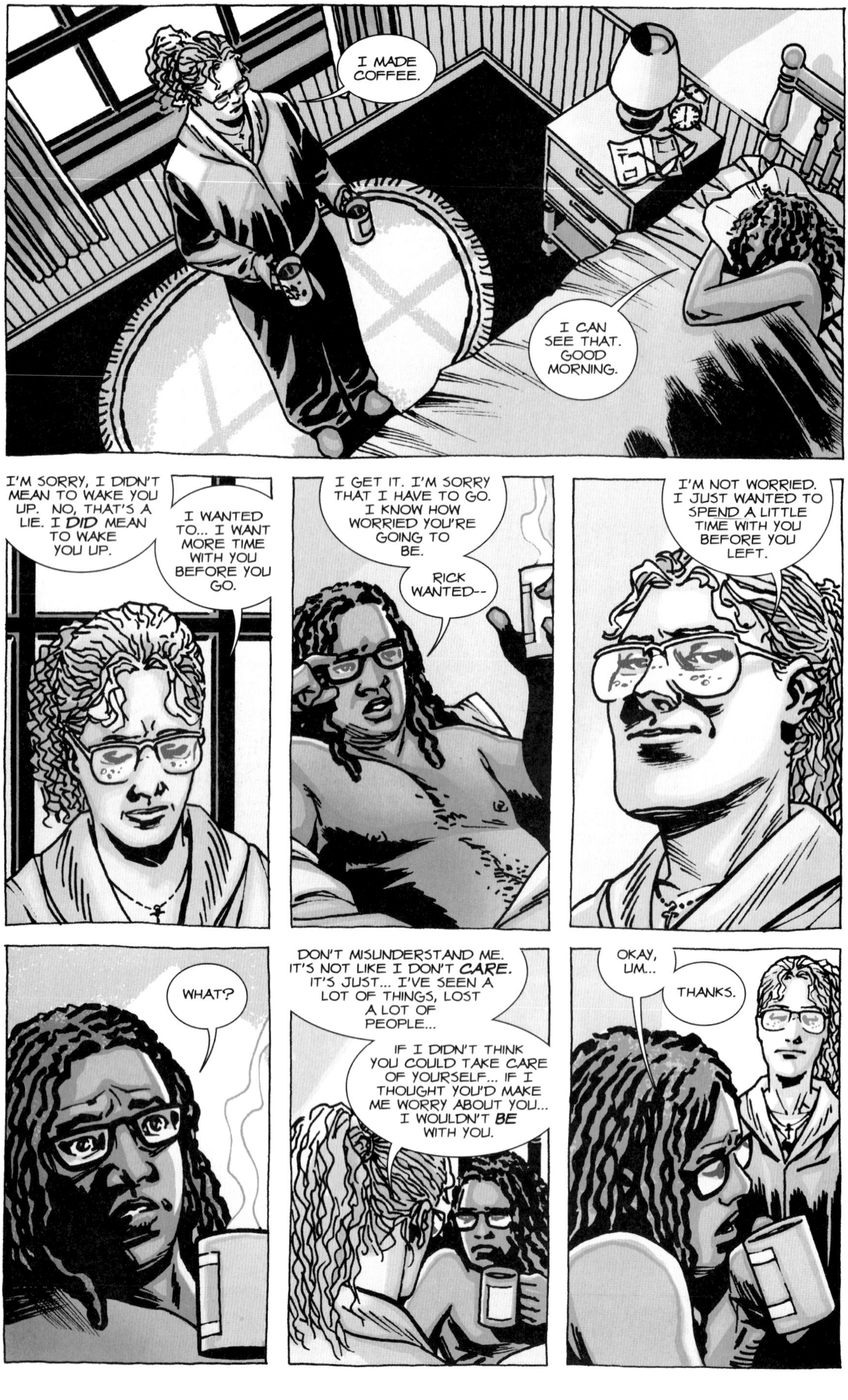
I MADE COFFEE.
I CAN SEE THAT. GOOD MORNING.
I'M SORRY, I DIDN'T MEAN TO WAKE YOU UP. NO, THAT'S A LIE. I *DID* MEAN TO WAKE YOU UP.
I WANTED TO... I WANT MORE TIME WITH YOU BEFORE YOU GO.
I GET IT. I'M SORRY THAT I HAVE TO GO. I KNOW HOW WORRIED YOU'RE GOING TO BE.
RICK WANTED--
I'M NOT WORRIED. I JUST WANTED TO SPEND A LITTLE TIME WITH YOU BEFORE YOU LEFT.
WHAT?
DON'T MISUNDERSTAND ME. IT'S NOT LIKE I DON'T *CARE.* IT'S JUST... I'VE SEEN A LOT OF THINGS, LOST A LOT OF PEOPLE...
IF I DIDN'T THINK YOU COULD TAKE CARE OF YOURSELF... IF I THOUGHT YOU'D MAKE ME WORRY ABOUT YOU... I WOULDN'T *BE* WITH YOU.
OKAY, UM...
THANKS.

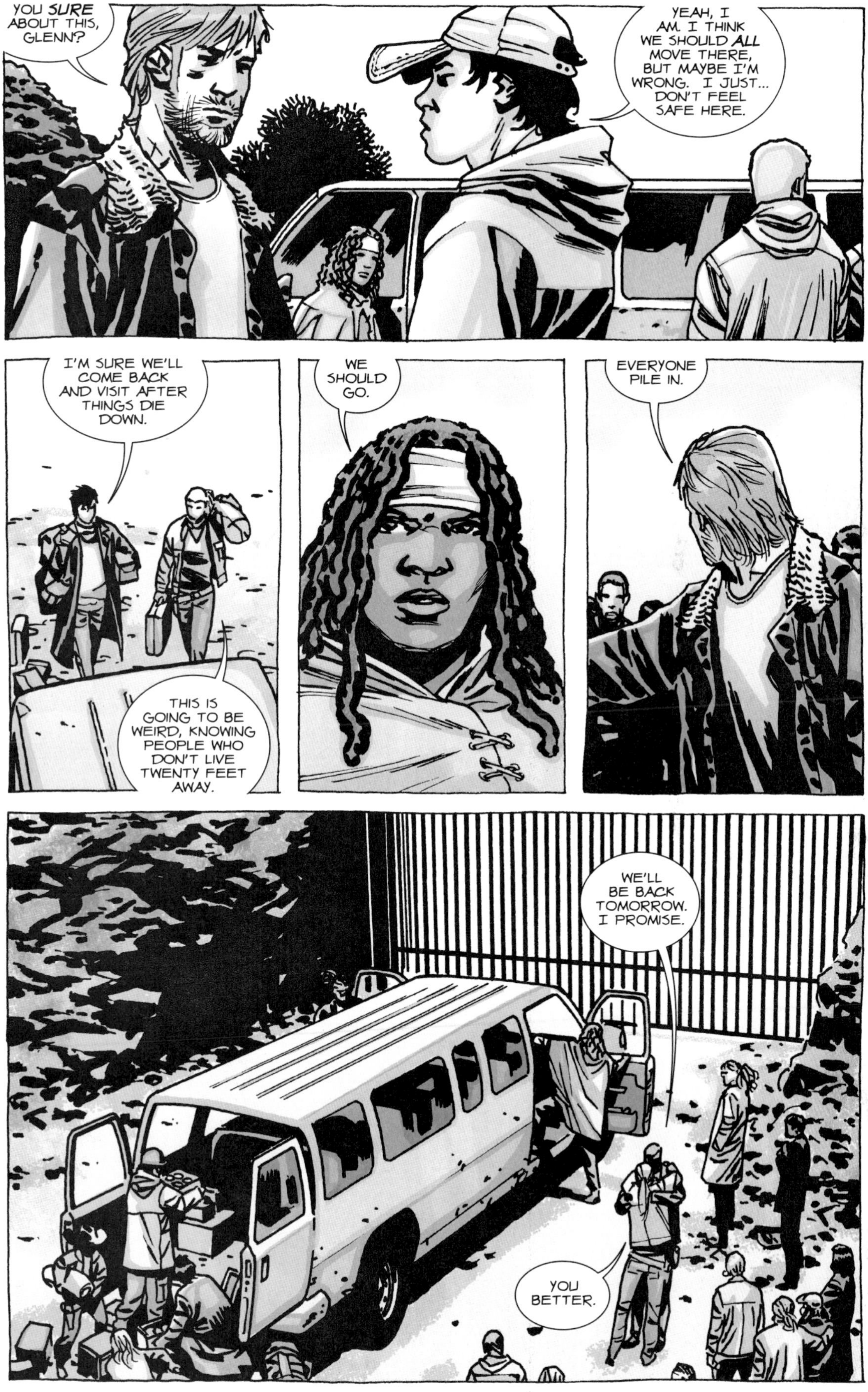

YOU SURE ABOUT THIS, GLENN?
YEAH, I AM. I THINK WE SHOULD ALL MOVE THERE, BUT MAYBE I'M WRONG. I JUST... DON'T FEEL SAFE HERE.
I'M SURE WE'LL COME BACK AND VISIT AFTER THINGS DIE DOWN.
THIS IS GOING TO BE WEIRD, KNOWING PEOPLE WHO DON'T LIVE TWENTY FEET AWAY.
WE SHOULD GO.
EVERYONE PILE IN.
WE'LL BE BACK TOMORROW. I PROMISE.
YOU BETTER.

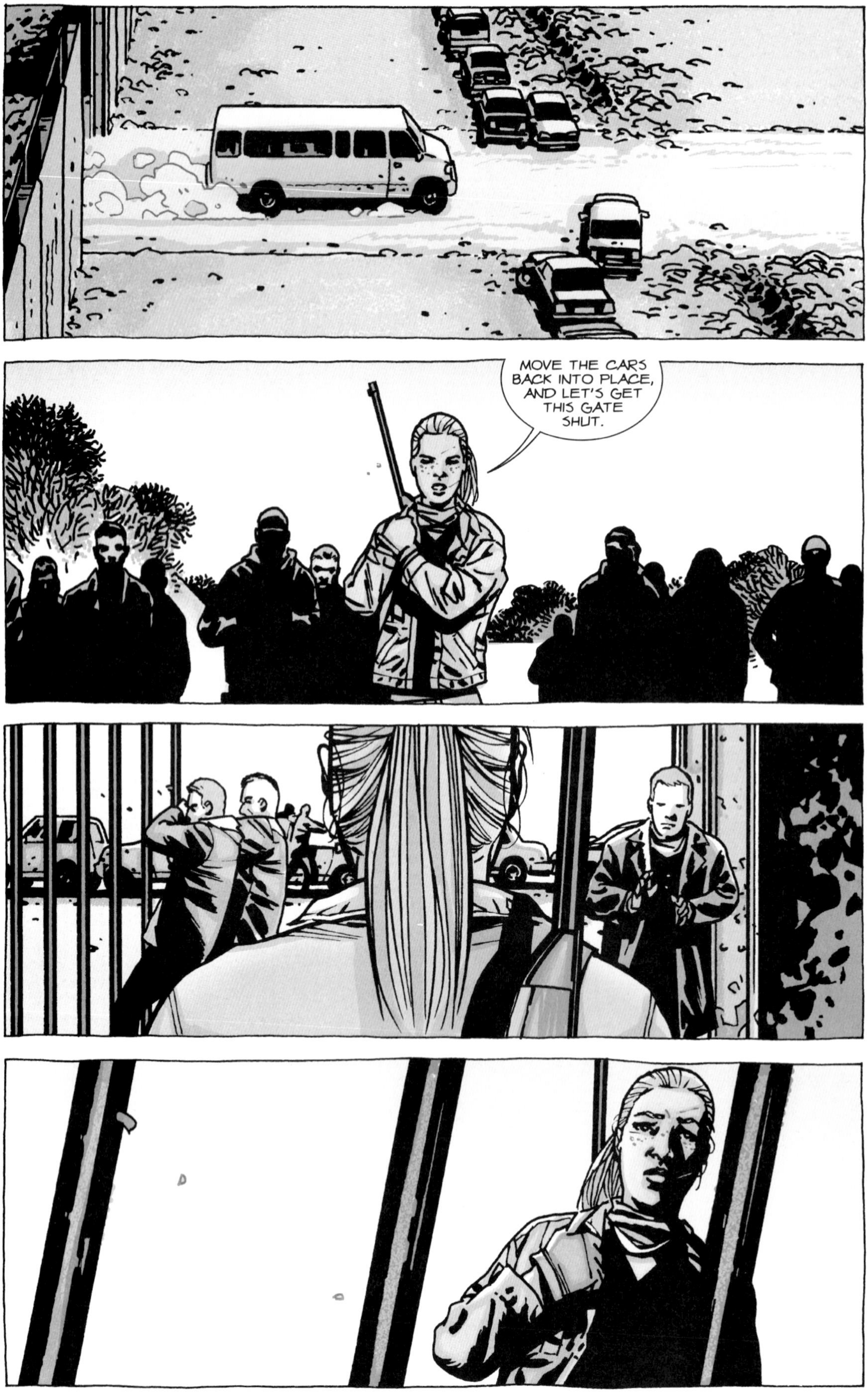
MOVE THE CARS BACK INTO PLACE, AND LET'S GET THIS GATE SHUT.

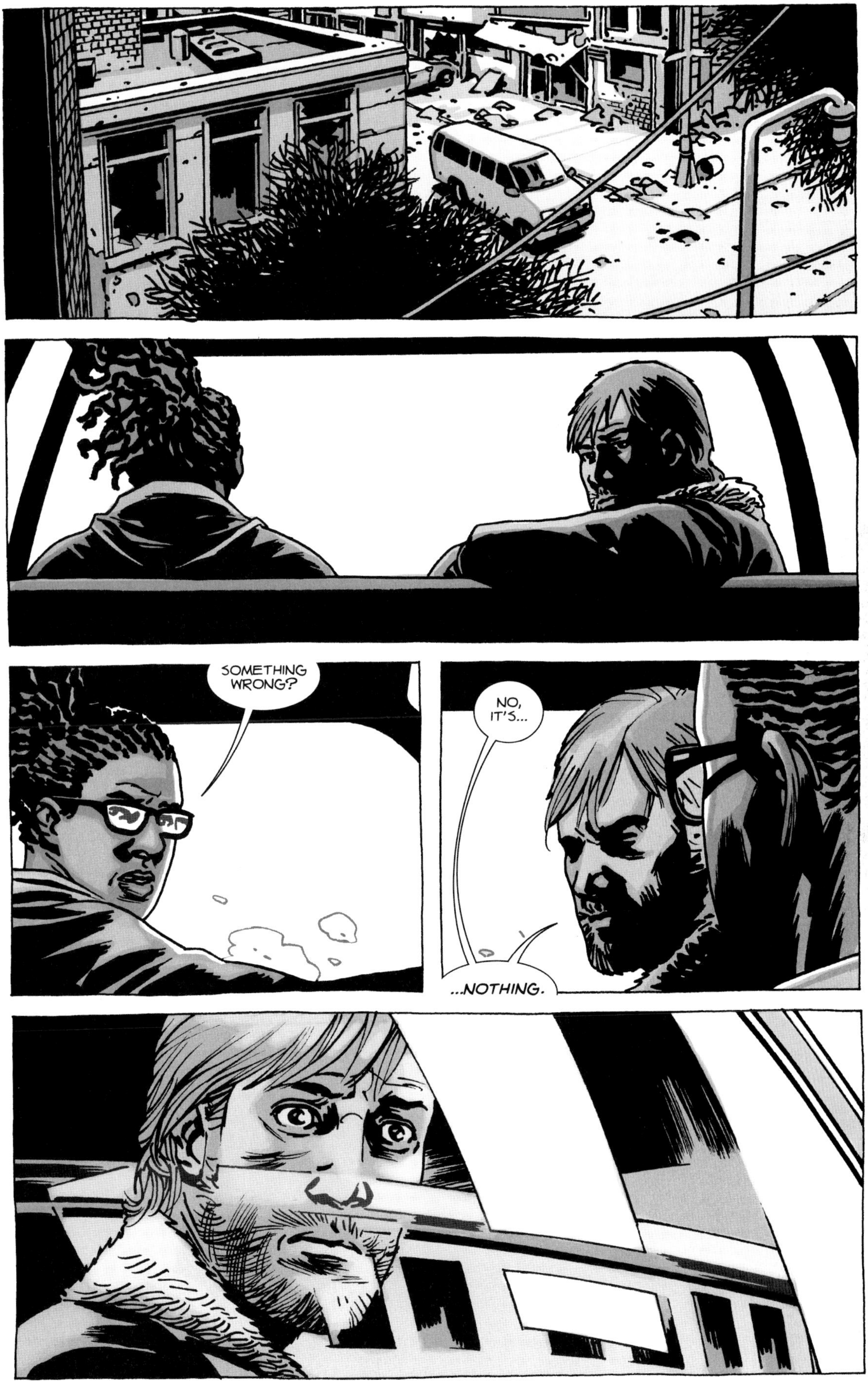
SOMETHING WRONG?
NO, IT'S...
...NOTHING.

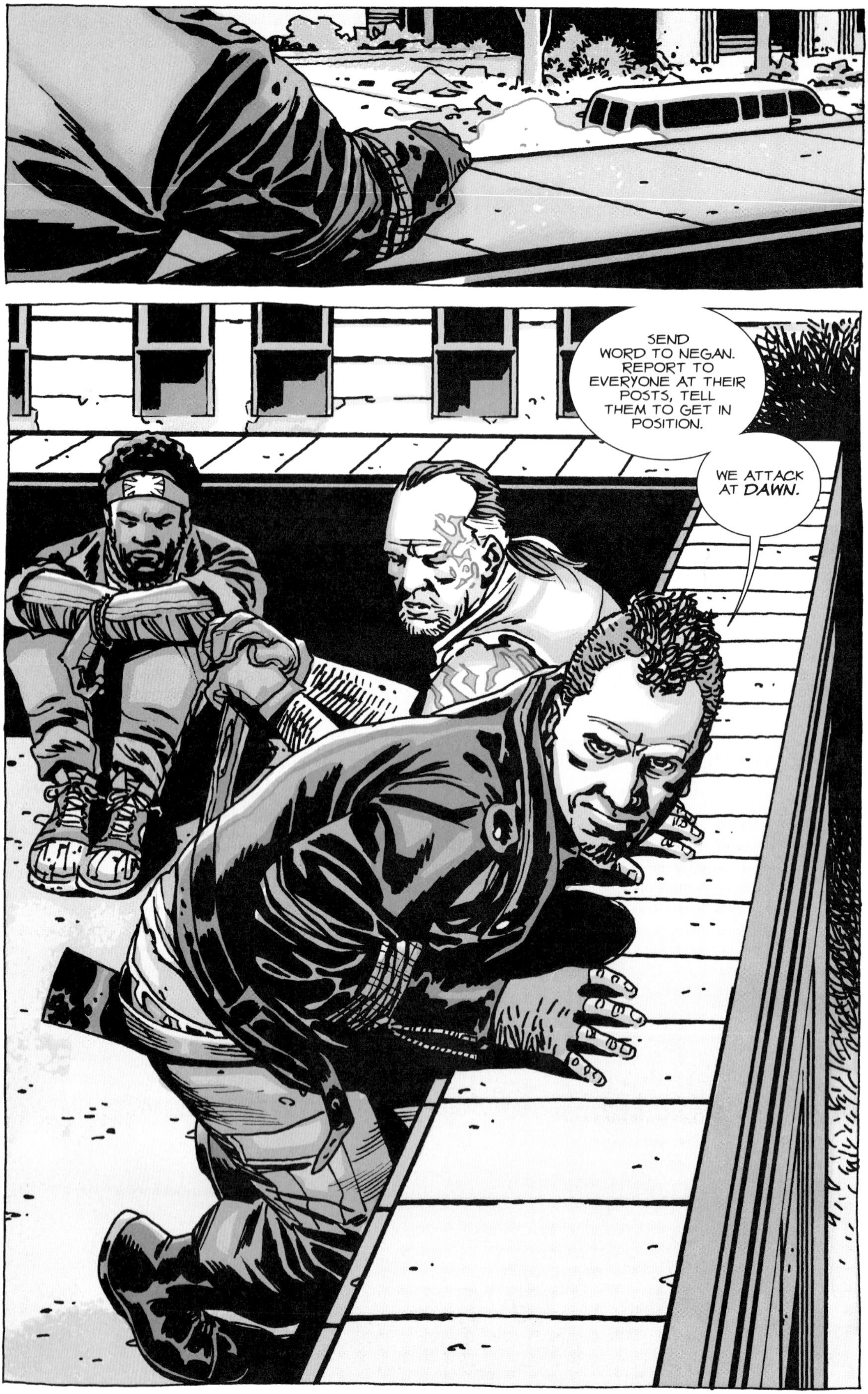
SEND WORD TO NEGAN. REPORT TO EVERYONE AT THEIR POSTS, TELL THEM TO GET IN POSITION.
WE ATTACK AT DAWN.

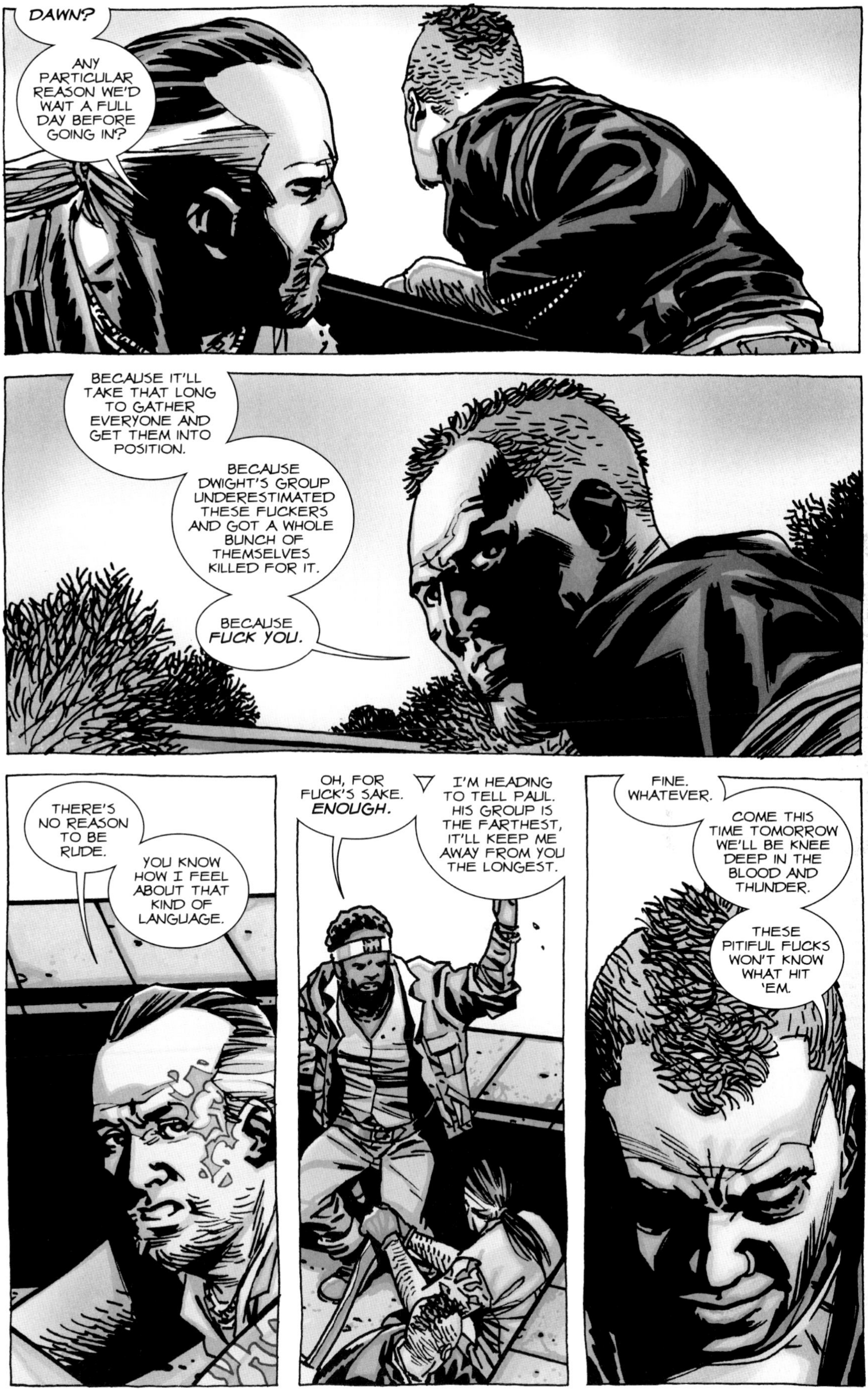
DAWN?
ANY PARTICULAR REASON WE'D WAIT A FULL DAY BEFORE GOING IN?
BECAUSE IT'LL TAKE THAT LONG TO GATHER EVERYONE AND GET THEM INTO POSITION.
BECAUSE DWIGHT'S GROUP UNDERESTIMATED THESE FUCKERS AND GOT A WHOLE BUNCH OF THEMSELVES KILLED FOR IT.
BECAUSE *FUCK YOU.*
THERE'S NO REASON TO BE RUDE.
YOU KNOW HOW I FEEL ABOUT THAT KIND OF LANGUAGE.
OH, FOR FUCK'S SAKE. *ENOUGH.*
I'M HEADING TO TELL PAUL. HIS GROUP IS THE FARTHEST, IT'LL KEEP ME AWAY FROM YOU THE LONGEST.
FINE. WHATEVER.
COME THIS TIME TOMORROW WE'LL BE KNEE DEEP IN THE BLOOD AND THUNDER.
THESE PITIFUL FUCKS WON'T KNOW WHAT HIT 'EM.

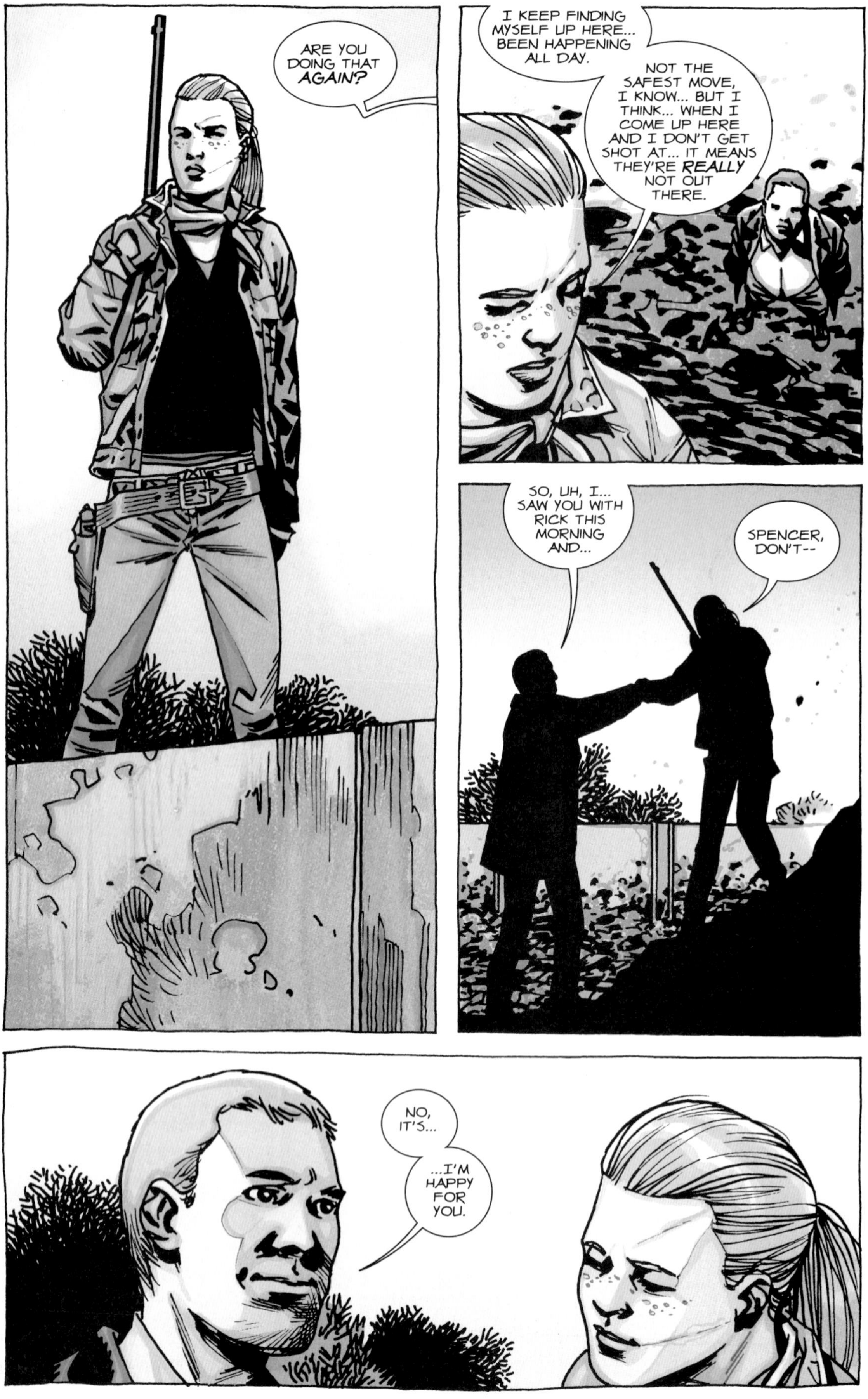
ARE YOU DOING THAT *AGAIN?*
I KEEP FINDING MYSELF UP HERE... BEEN HAPPENING ALL DAY.
NOT THE SAFEST MOVE, I KNOW... BUT I THINK... WHEN I COME UP HERE AND I DON'T GET SHOT AT... IT MEANS THEY'RE *REALLY* NOT OUT THERE.
SO, UH, I... SAW YOU WITH RICK THIS MORNING AND...
SPENCER, DON'T--
NO, IT'S...
...I'M HAPPY FOR YOU.

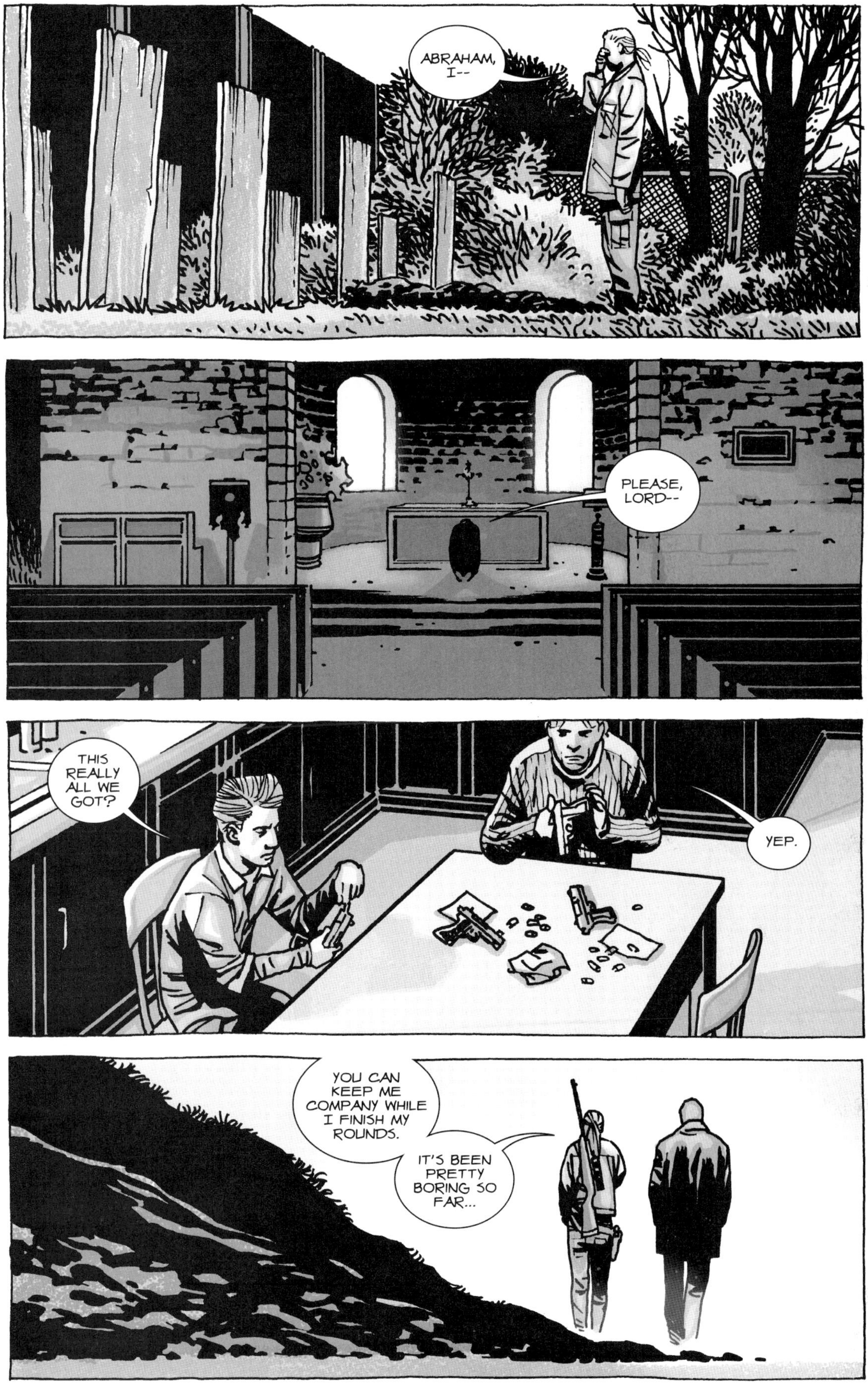
ABRAHAM, I--
PLEASE, LORD--
THIS REALLY ALL WE GOT?
YEP.
YOU CAN KEEP ME COMPANY WHILE I FINISH MY ROUNDS.
IT'S BEEN PRETTY BORING SO FAR...

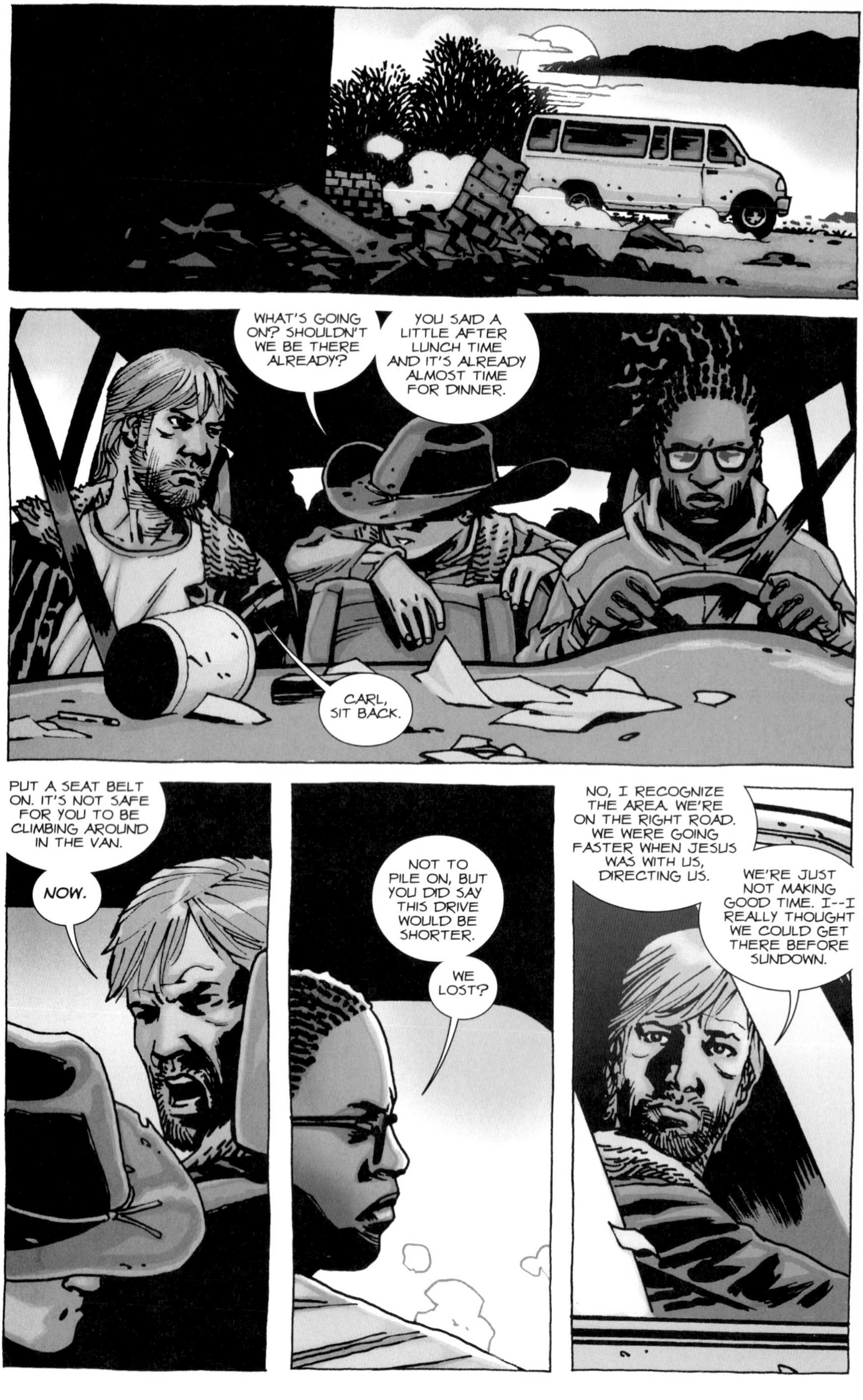
WHAT'S GOING ON? SHOULDN'T WE BE THERE ALREADY?
YOU SAID A LITTLE AFTER LUNCH TIME AND IT'S ALREADY ALMOST TIME FOR DINNER.
CARL, SIT BACK.
PUT A SEAT BELT ON. IT'S NOT SAFE FOR YOU TO BE CLIMBING AROUND IN THE VAN.
NOW.
NOT TO PILE ON, BUT YOU DID SAY THIS DRIVE WOULD BE SHORTER.
WE LOST?
NO, I RECOGNIZE THE AREA. WE'RE ON THE RIGHT ROAD. WE WERE GOING FASTER WHEN JESUS WAS WITH US, DIRECTING US.
WE'RE JUST NOT MAKING GOOD TIME. I--I REALLY THOUGHT WE COULD GET THERE BEFORE SUNDOWN.

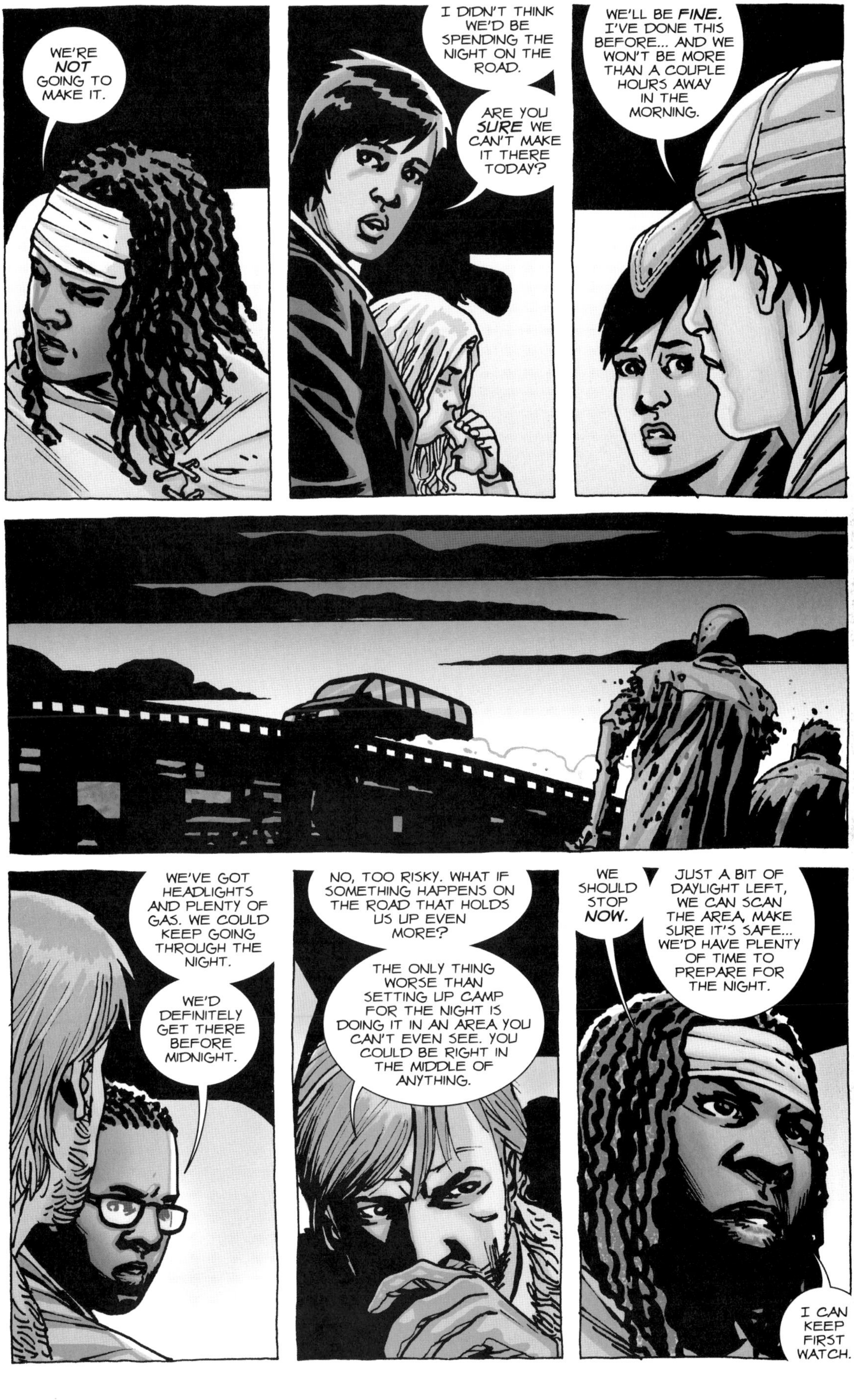
WE'RE NOT GOING TO MAKE IT.
I DIDN'T THINK WE'D BE SPENDING THE NIGHT ON THE ROAD.
ARE YOU SURE WE CAN'T MAKE IT THERE TODAY?
WE'LL BE FINE. I'VE DONE THIS BEFORE... AND WE WON'T BE MORE THAN A COUPLE HOURS AWAY IN THE MORNING.
WE'VE GOT HEADLIGHTS AND PLENTY OF GAS. WE COULD KEEP GOING THROUGH THE NIGHT.
WE'D DEFINITELY GET THERE BEFORE MIDNIGHT.
NO, TOO RISKY. WHAT IF SOMETHING HAPPENS ON THE ROAD THAT HOLDS US UP EVEN MORE?
THE ONLY THING WORSE THAN SETTING UP CAMP FOR THE NIGHT IS DOING IT IN AN AREA YOU CAN'T EVEN SEE. YOU COULD BE RIGHT IN THE MIDDLE OF ANYTHING.
WE SHOULD STOP NOW.
JUST A BIT OF DAYLIGHT LEFT, WE CAN SCAN THE AREA, MAKE SURE IT'S SAFE... WE'D HAVE PLENTY OF TIME TO PREPARE FOR THE NIGHT.
I CAN KEEP FIRST WATCH.

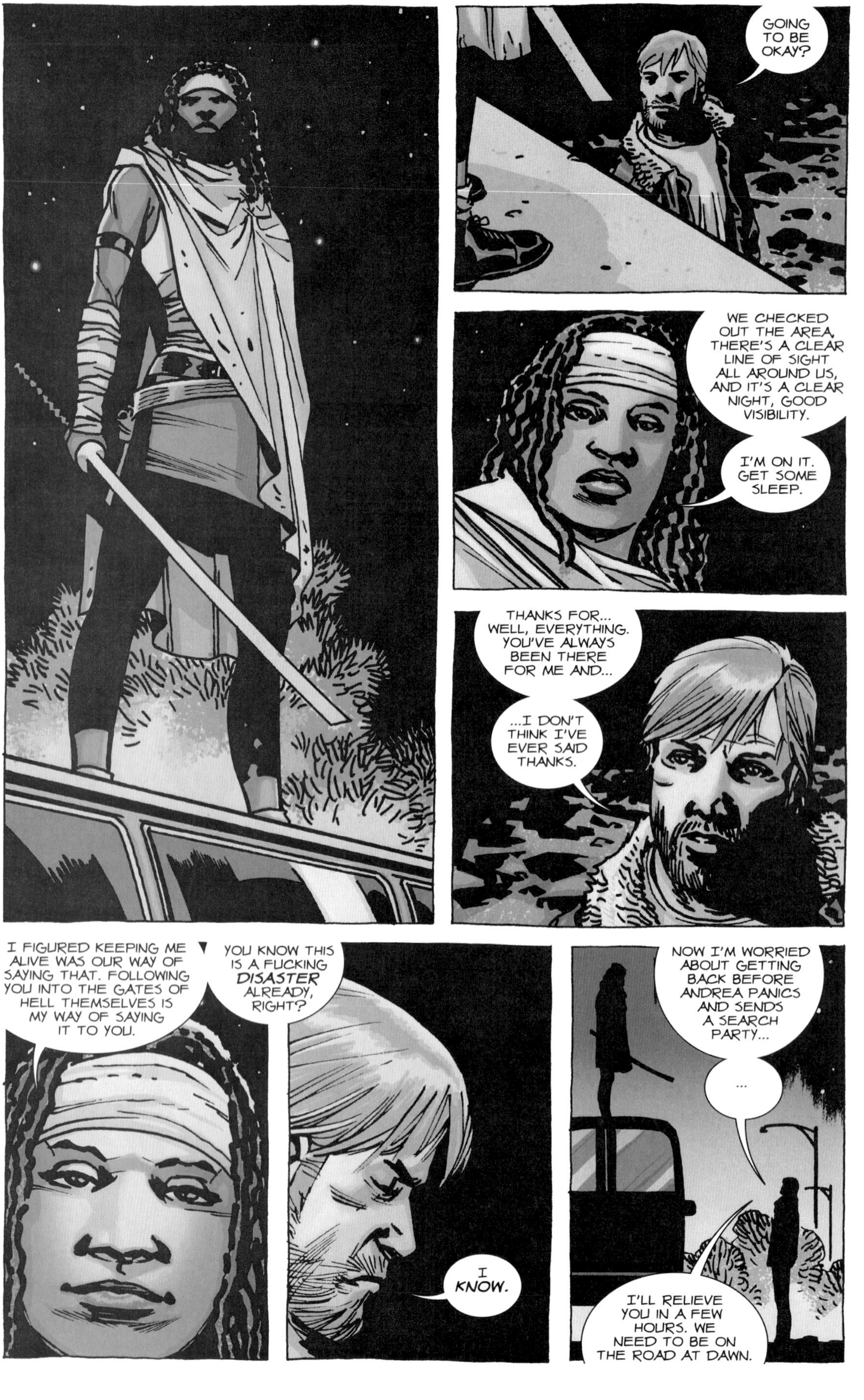
GOING TO BE OKAY?
WE CHECKED OUT THE AREA, THERE'S A CLEAR LINE OF SIGHT ALL AROUND US, AND IT'S A CLEAR NIGHT, GOOD VISIBILITY.
I'M ON IT. GET SOME SLEEP.
THANKS FOR... WELL, EVERYTHING. YOU'VE ALWAYS BEEN THERE FOR ME AND...
...I DON'T THINK I'VE EVER SAID THANKS.
I FIGURED KEEPING ME ALIVE WAS OUR WAY OF SAYING THAT. FOLLOWING YOU INTO THE GATES OF HELL THEMSELVES IS MY WAY OF SAYING IT TO YOU.
YOU KNOW THIS IS A FUCKING *DISASTER* ALREADY, RIGHT?
I *KNOW.*
NOW I'M WORRIED ABOUT GETTING BACK BEFORE ANDREA PANICS AND SENDS A SEARCH PARTY...
...
I'LL RELIEVE YOU IN A FEW HOURS. WE NEED TO BE ON THE ROAD AT DAWN.

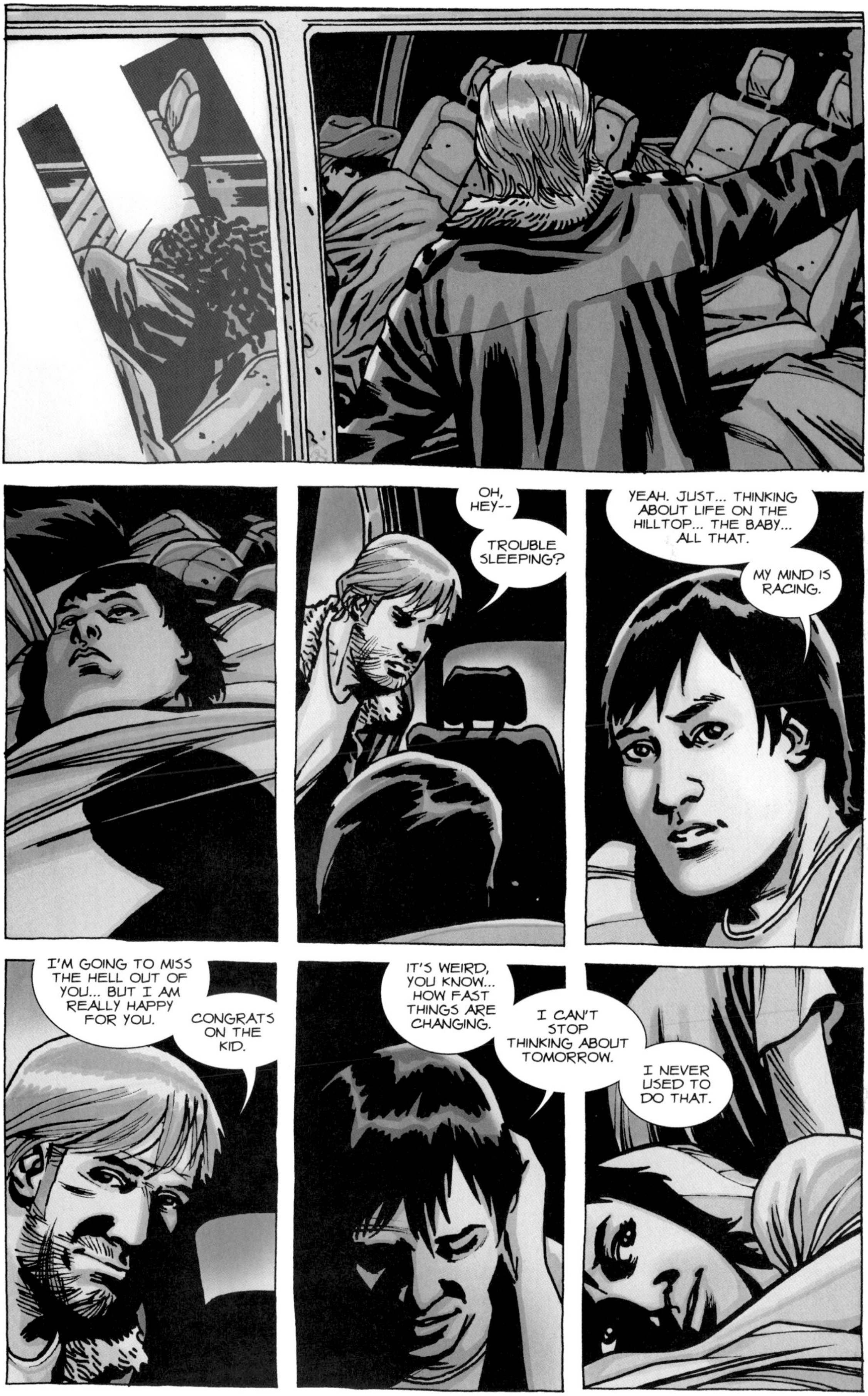
OH, HEY--
TROUBLE SLEEPING?
YEAH. JUST... THINKING ABOUT LIFE ON THE HILLTOP... THE BABY... ALL THAT.
MY MIND IS RACING.
I'M GOING TO MISS THE HELL OUT OF YOU... BUT I AM REALLY HAPPY FOR YOU.
CONGRATS ON THE KID.
IT'S WEIRD, YOU KNOW... HOW FAST THINGS ARE CHANGING.
I CAN'T STOP THINKING ABOUT TOMORROW.
I NEVER USED TO DO THAT.

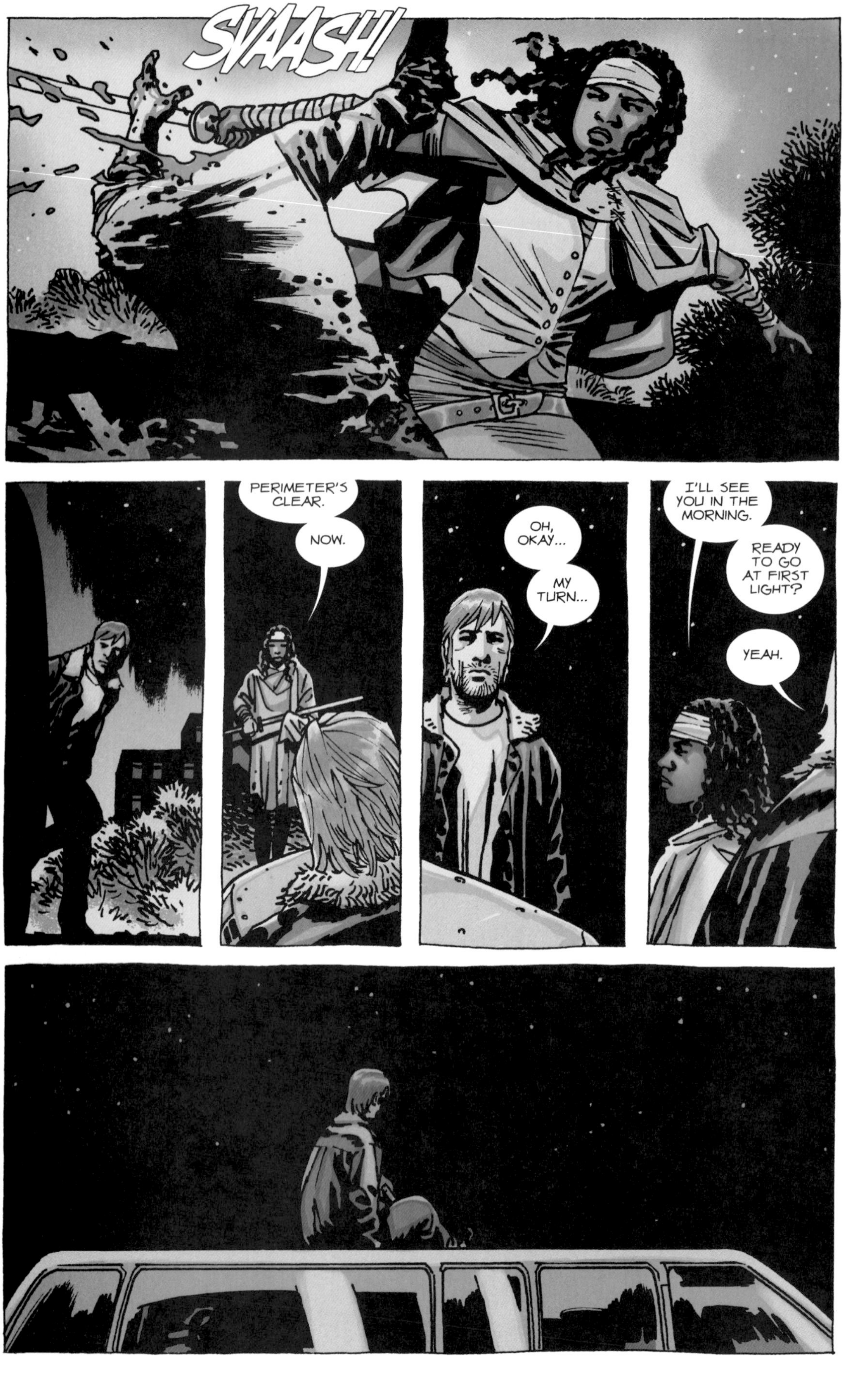
SVAASH!
PERIMETER'S CLEAR.
NOW.
OH, OKAY...
MY TURN...
I'LL SEE YOU IN THE MORNING.
READY TO GO AT FIRST LIGHT?
YEAH.

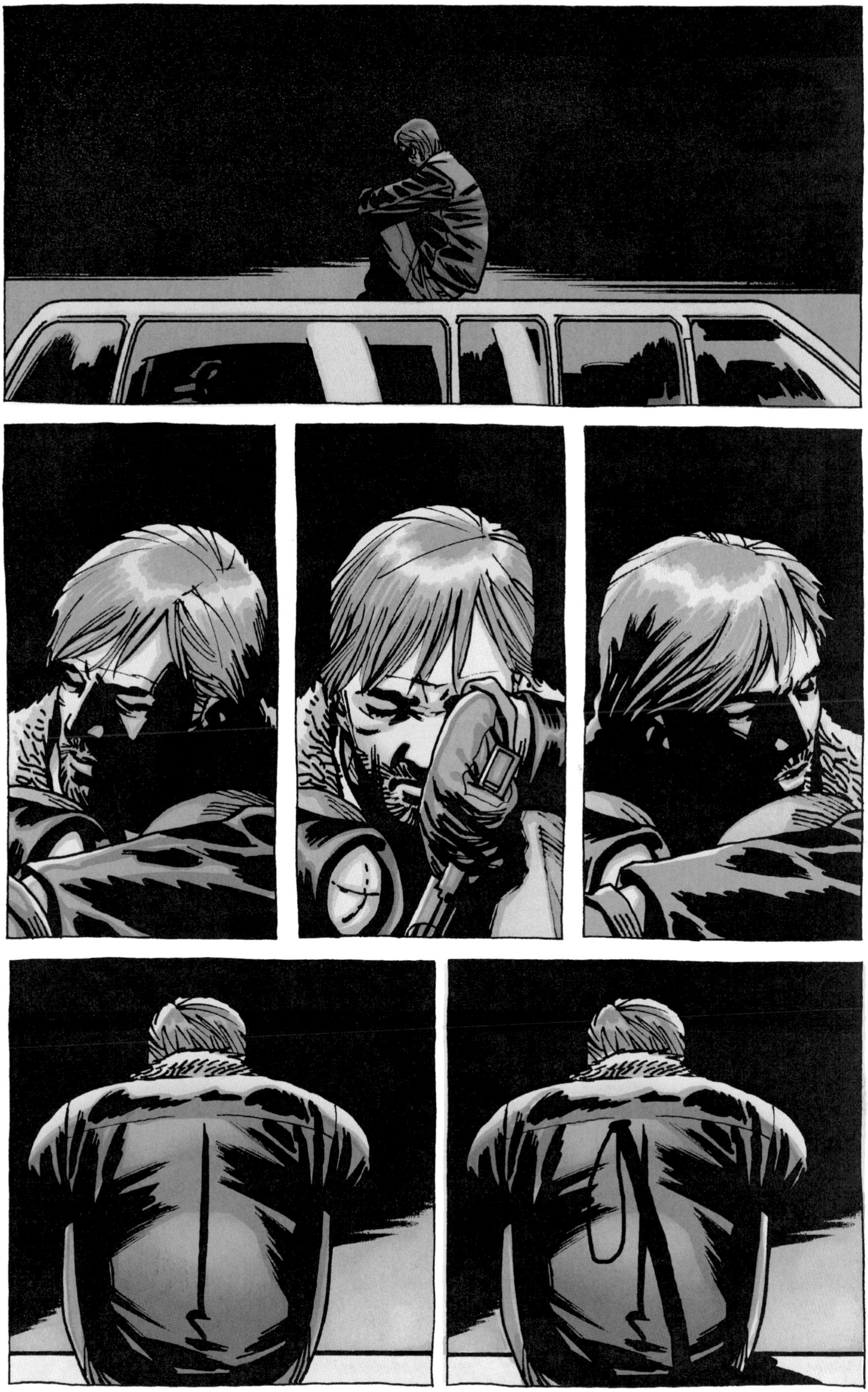

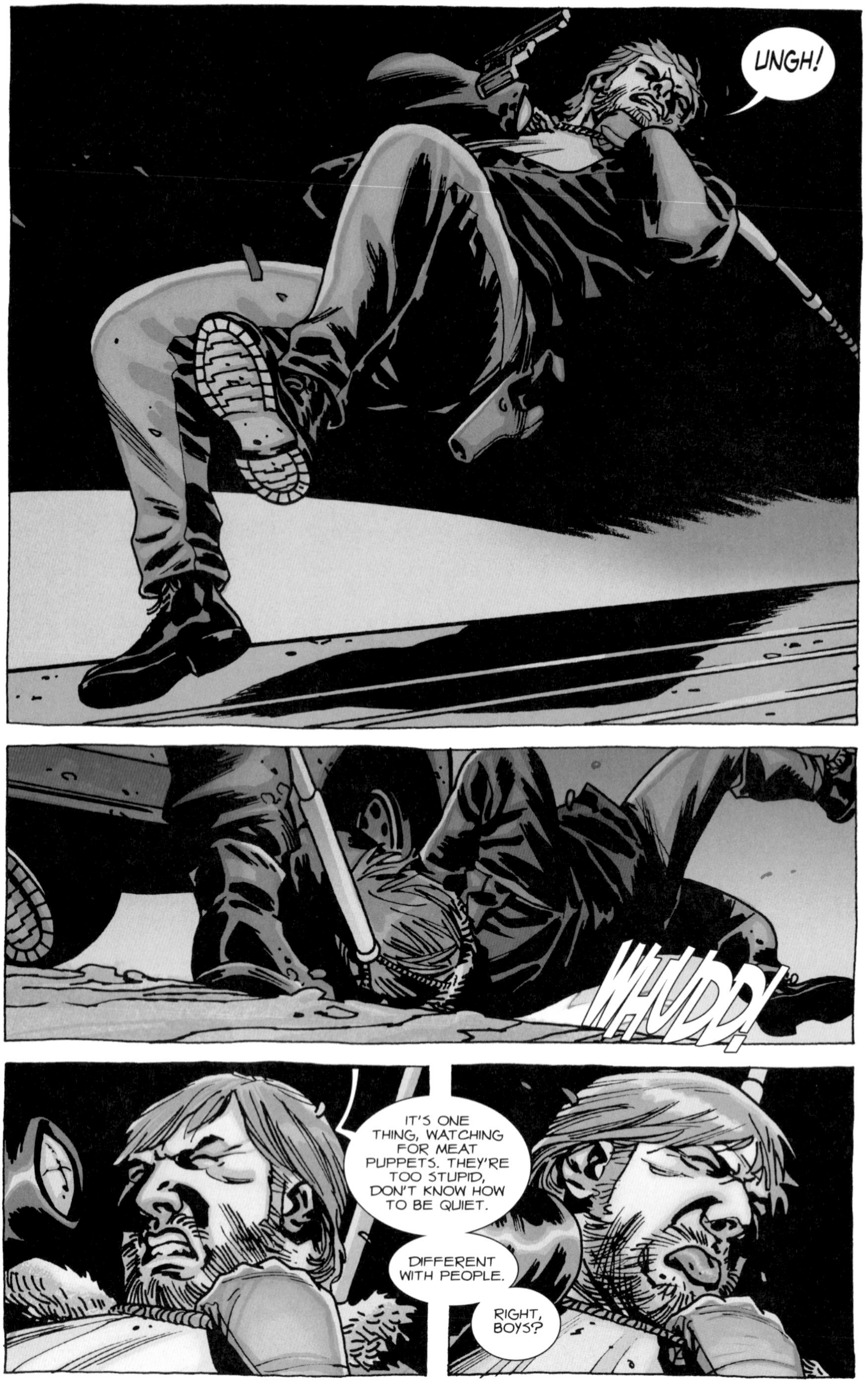
UNGH!
WHUDD!
IT'S ONE THING, WATCHING FOR MEAT PUPPETS. THEY'RE TOO STUPID, DON'T KNOW HOW TO BE QUIET.
DIFFERENT WITH PEOPLE.
RIGHT, BOYS?

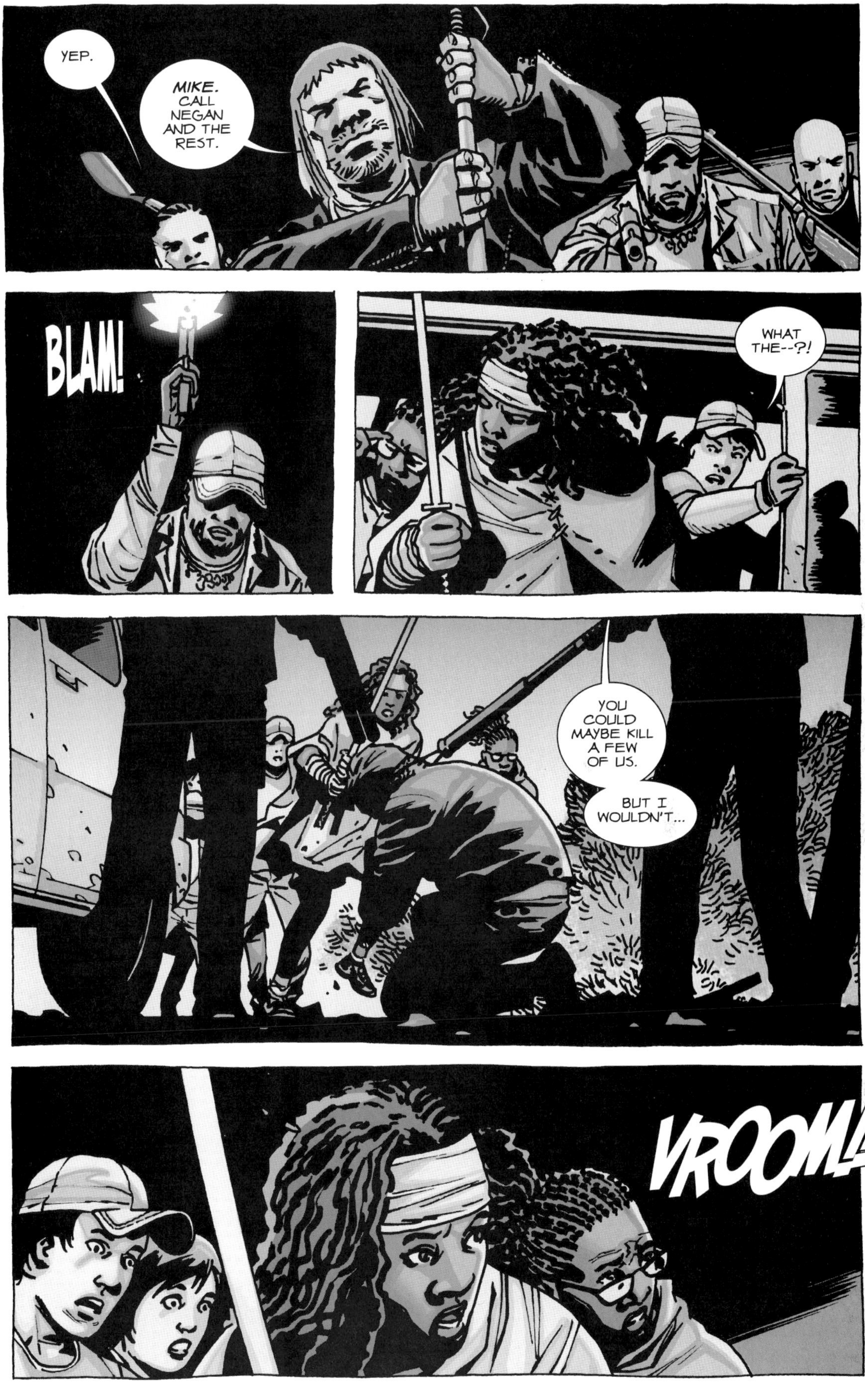

YEP.
MIKE. CALL NEGAN AND THE REST.
BLAM!
WHAT THE--?!
YOU COULD MAYBE KILL A FEW OF US.
BUT I WOULDN'T...
VROOM!!

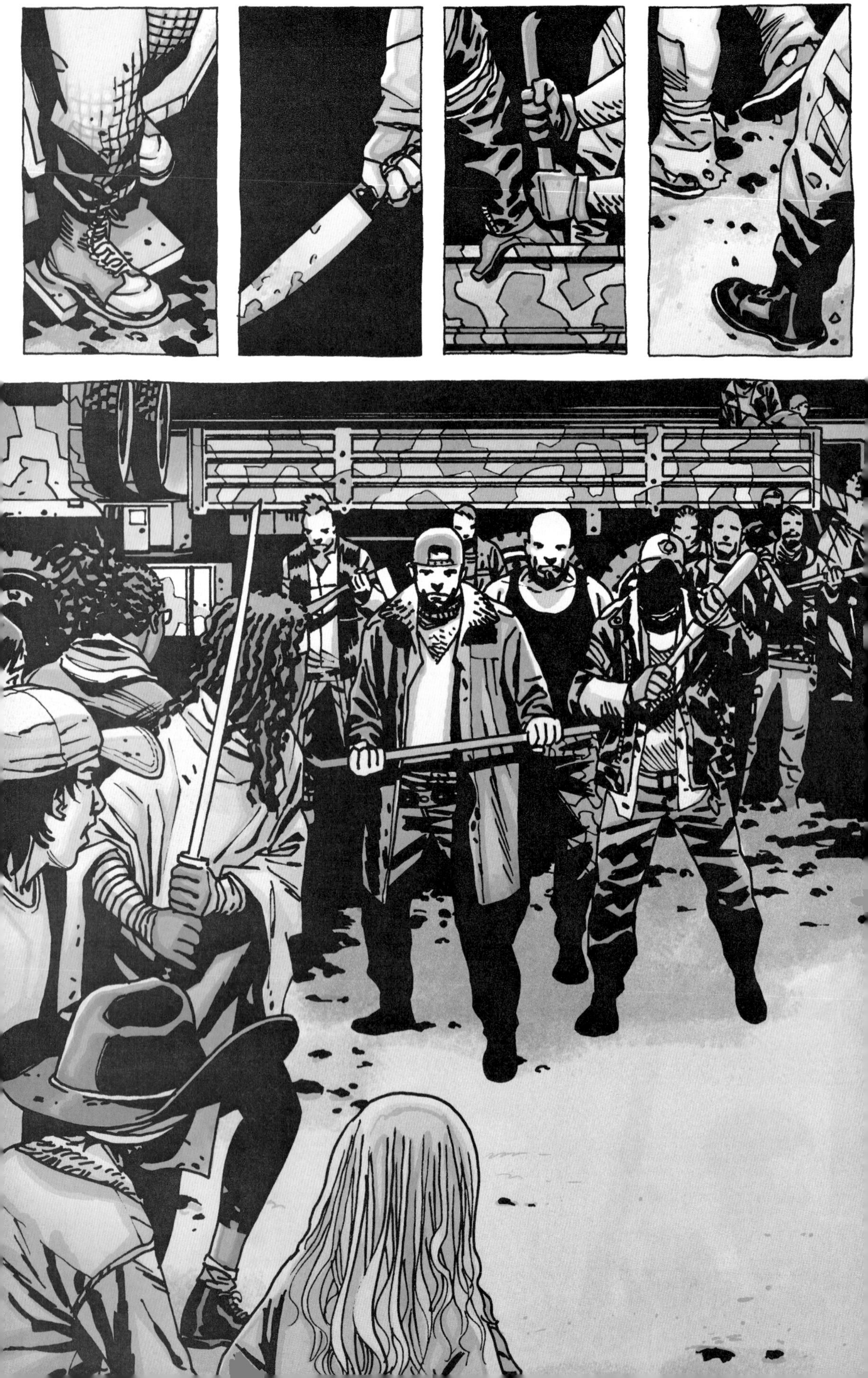

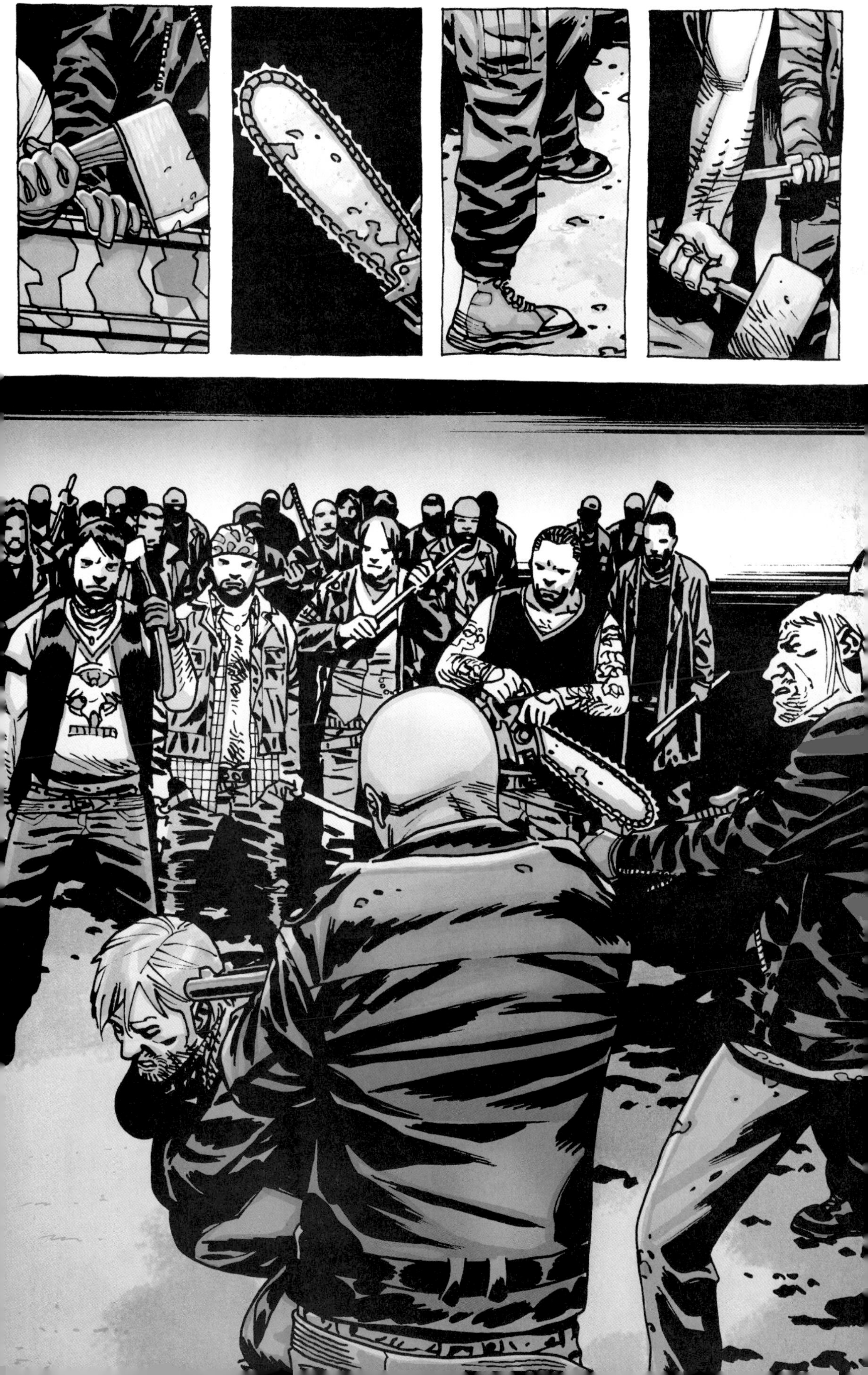

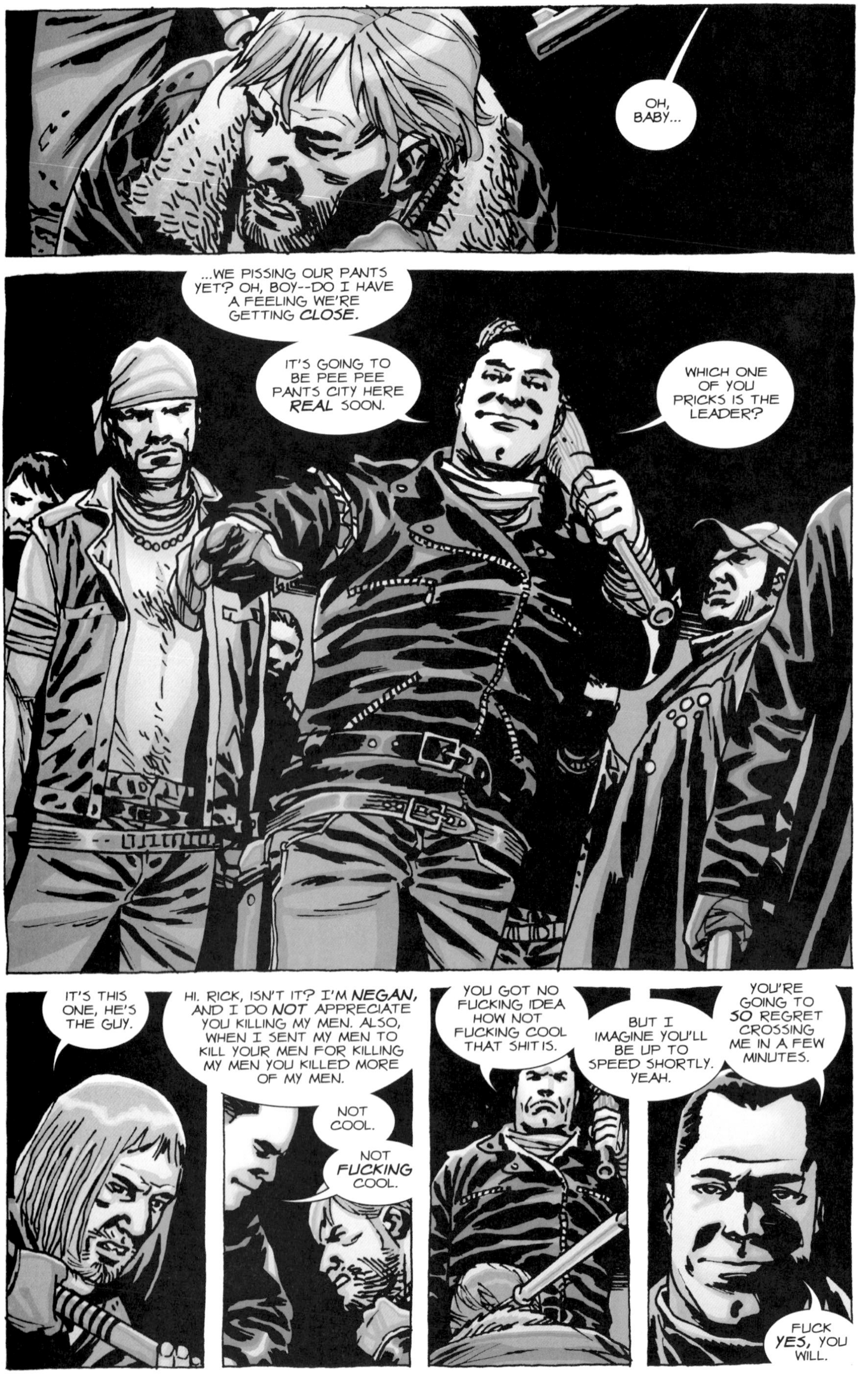
OH, BABY...
...WE PISSING OUR PANTS YET? OH, BOY--DO I HAVE A FEELING WE'RE GETTING CLOSE.
IT'S GOING TO BE PEE PEE PANTS CITY HERE REAL SOON.
WHICH ONE OF YOU PRICKS IS THE LEADER?
IT'S THIS ONE, HE'S THE GUY.
HI. RICK, ISN'T IT? I'M NEGAN, AND I DO NOT APPRECIATE YOU KILLING MY MEN. ALSO, WHEN I SENT MY MEN TO KILL YOUR MEN FOR KILLING MY MEN YOU KILLED MORE OF MY MEN.
NOT COOL.
NOT FUCKING COOL.
YOU GOT NO FUCKING IDEA HOW NOT FUCKING COOL THAT SHIT IS.
BUT I IMAGINE YOU'LL BE UP TO SPEED SHORTLY. YEAH.
YOU'RE GOING TO SO REGRET CROSSING ME IN A FEW MINUTES.
FUCK YES, YOU WILL.

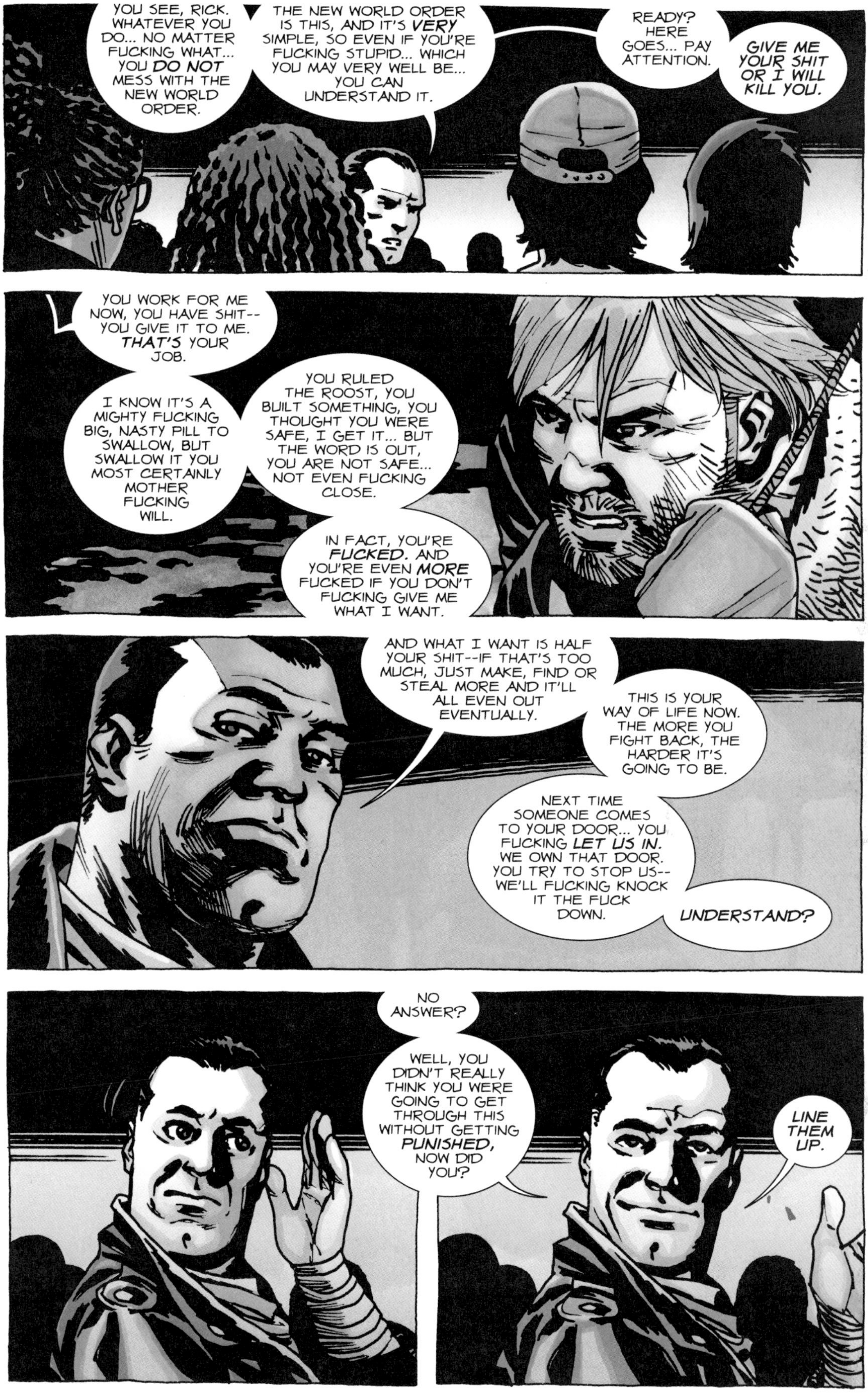

YOU SEE, RICK. WHATEVER YOU DO... NO MATTER FUCKING WHAT... YOU DO NOT MESS WITH THE NEW WORLD ORDER.
THE NEW WORLD ORDER IS THIS, AND IT'S VERY SIMPLE, SO EVEN IF YOU'RE FUCKING STUPID... WHICH YOU MAY VERY WELL BE... YOU CAN UNDERSTAND IT.
READY? HERE GOES... PAY ATTENTION.
GIVE ME YOUR SHIT OR I WILL KILL YOU.
YOU WORK FOR ME NOW, YOU HAVE SHIT-- YOU GIVE IT TO ME. THAT'S YOUR JOB.
I KNOW IT'S A MIGHTY FUCKING BIG, NASTY PILL TO SWALLOW, BUT SWALLOW IT YOU MOST CERTAINLY MOTHER FUCKING WILL.
YOU RULED THE ROOST, YOU BUILT SOMETHING, YOU THOUGHT YOU WERE SAFE, I GET IT... BUT THE WORD IS OUT, YOU ARE NOT SAFE... NOT EVEN FUCKING CLOSE.
IN FACT, YOU'RE FUCKED. AND YOU'RE EVEN MORE FUCKED IF YOU DON'T FUCKING GIVE ME WHAT I WANT.
AND WHAT I WANT IS HALF YOUR SHIT--IF THAT'S TOO MUCH, JUST MAKE, FIND OR STEAL MORE AND IT'LL ALL EVEN OUT EVENTUALLY.
THIS IS YOUR WAY OF LIFE NOW. THE MORE YOU FIGHT BACK, THE HARDER IT'S GOING TO BE.
NEXT TIME SOMEONE COMES TO YOUR DOOR... YOU FUCKING LET US IN. WE OWN THAT DOOR. YOU TRY TO STOP US-- WE'LL FUCKING KNOCK IT THE FUCK DOWN.
UNDERSTAND?
NO ANSWER?
WELL, YOU DIDN'T REALLY THINK YOU WERE GOING TO GET THROUGH THIS WITHOUT GETTING PUNISHED, NOW DID YOU?
LINE THEM UP.

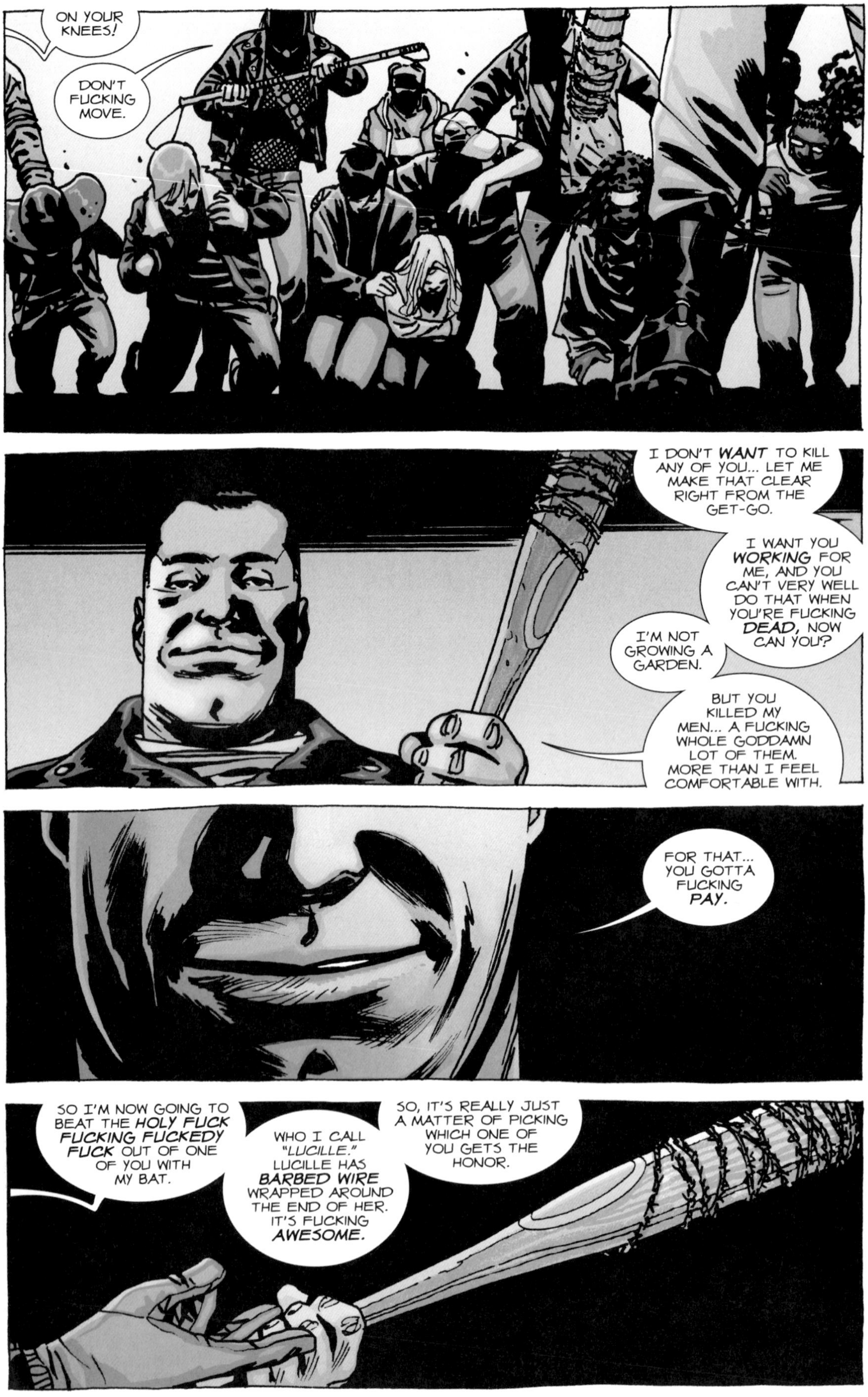

ON YOUR KNEES!
DON'T FUCKING MOVE.
I DON'T WANT TO KILL ANY OF YOU... LET ME MAKE THAT CLEAR RIGHT FROM THE GET-GO.
I WANT YOU WORKING FOR ME, AND YOU CAN'T VERY WELL DO THAT WHEN YOU'RE FUCKING DEAD, NOW CAN YOU?
I'M NOT GROWING A GARDEN.
BUT YOU KILLED MY MEN... A FUCKING WHOLE GODDAMN LOT OF THEM. MORE THAN I FEEL COMFORTABLE WITH.
FOR THAT... YOU GOTTA FUCKING PAY.
SO I'M NOW GOING TO BEAT THE HOLY FUCK FUCKING FUCKEDY FUCK OUT OF ONE OF YOU WITH MY BAT.
WHO I CALL "LUCILLE." LUCILLE HAS BARBED WIRE WRAPPED AROUND THE END OF HER. IT'S FUCKING AWESOME.
SO, IT'S REALLY JUST A MATTER OF PICKING WHICH ONE OF YOU GETS THE HONOR.

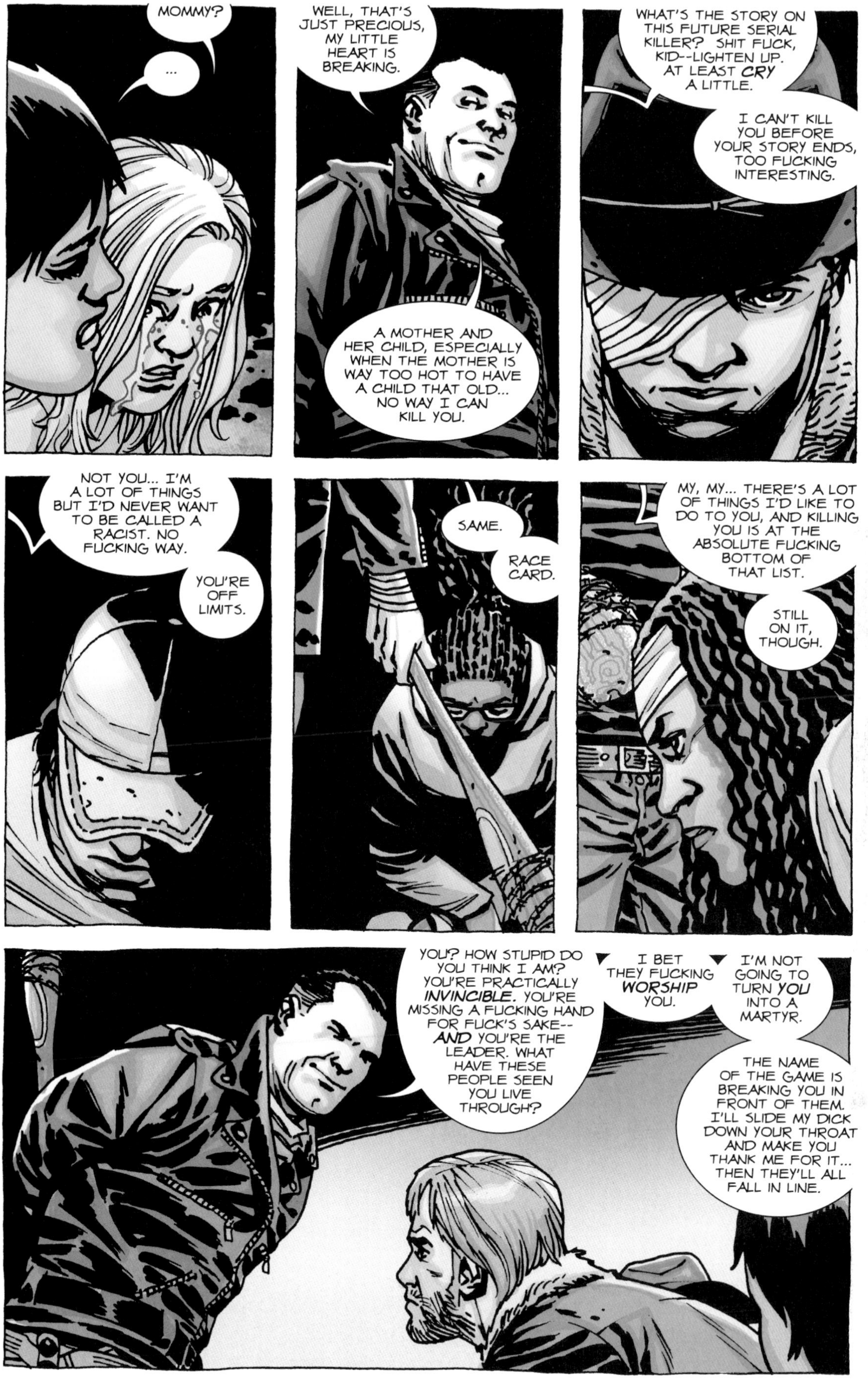
MOMMY?
...
WELL, THAT'S JUST PRECIOUS, MY LITTLE HEART IS BREAKING.
A MOTHER AND HER CHILD, ESPECIALLY WHEN THE MOTHER IS WAY TOO HOT TO HAVE A CHILD THAT OLD... NO WAY I CAN KILL YOU.
WHAT'S THE STORY ON THIS FUTURE SERIAL KILLER? SHIT FUCK, KID--LIGHTEN UP. AT LEAST CRY A LITTLE.
I CAN'T KILL YOU BEFORE YOUR STORY ENDS, TOO FUCKING INTERESTING.
NOT YOU... I'M A LOT OF THINGS BUT I'D NEVER WANT TO BE CALLED A RACIST. NO FUCKING WAY.
YOU'RE OFF LIMITS.
SAME.
RACE CARD.
MY, MY... THERE'S A LOT OF THINGS I'D LIKE TO DO TO YOU, AND KILLING YOU IS AT THE ABSOLUTE FUCKING BOTTOM OF THAT LIST.
STILL ON IT, THOUGH.
YOU? HOW STUPID DO YOU THINK I AM? YOU'RE PRACTICALLY INVINCIBLE. YOU'RE MISSING A FUCKING HAND FOR FUCK'S SAKE-- AND YOU'RE THE LEADER. WHAT HAVE THESE PEOPLE SEEN YOU LIVE THROUGH?
I BET THEY FUCKING WORSHIP YOU.
I'M NOT GOING TO TURN YOU INTO A MARTYR.
THE NAME OF THE GAME IS BREAKING YOU IN FRONT OF THEM. I'LL SLIDE MY DICK DOWN YOUR THROAT AND MAKE YOU THANK ME FOR IT... THEN THEY'LL ALL FALL IN LINE.

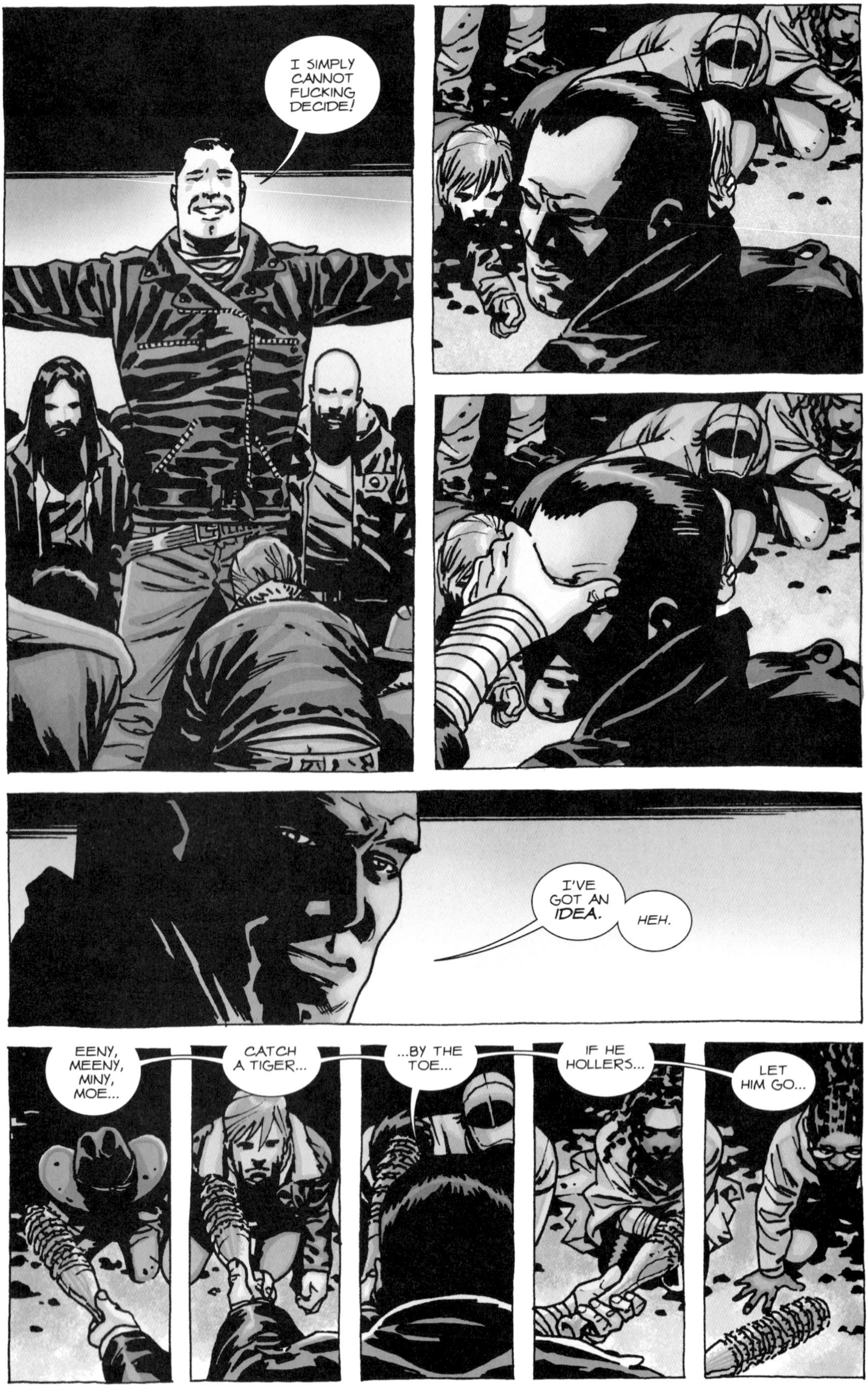
I SIMPLY CANNOT FUCKING DECIDE!
I'VE GOT AN *IDEA.*
HEH.
EENY, MEENY, MINY, MOE...
CATCH A TIGER...
...BY THE TOE...
IF HE HOLLERS...
LET HIM GO...

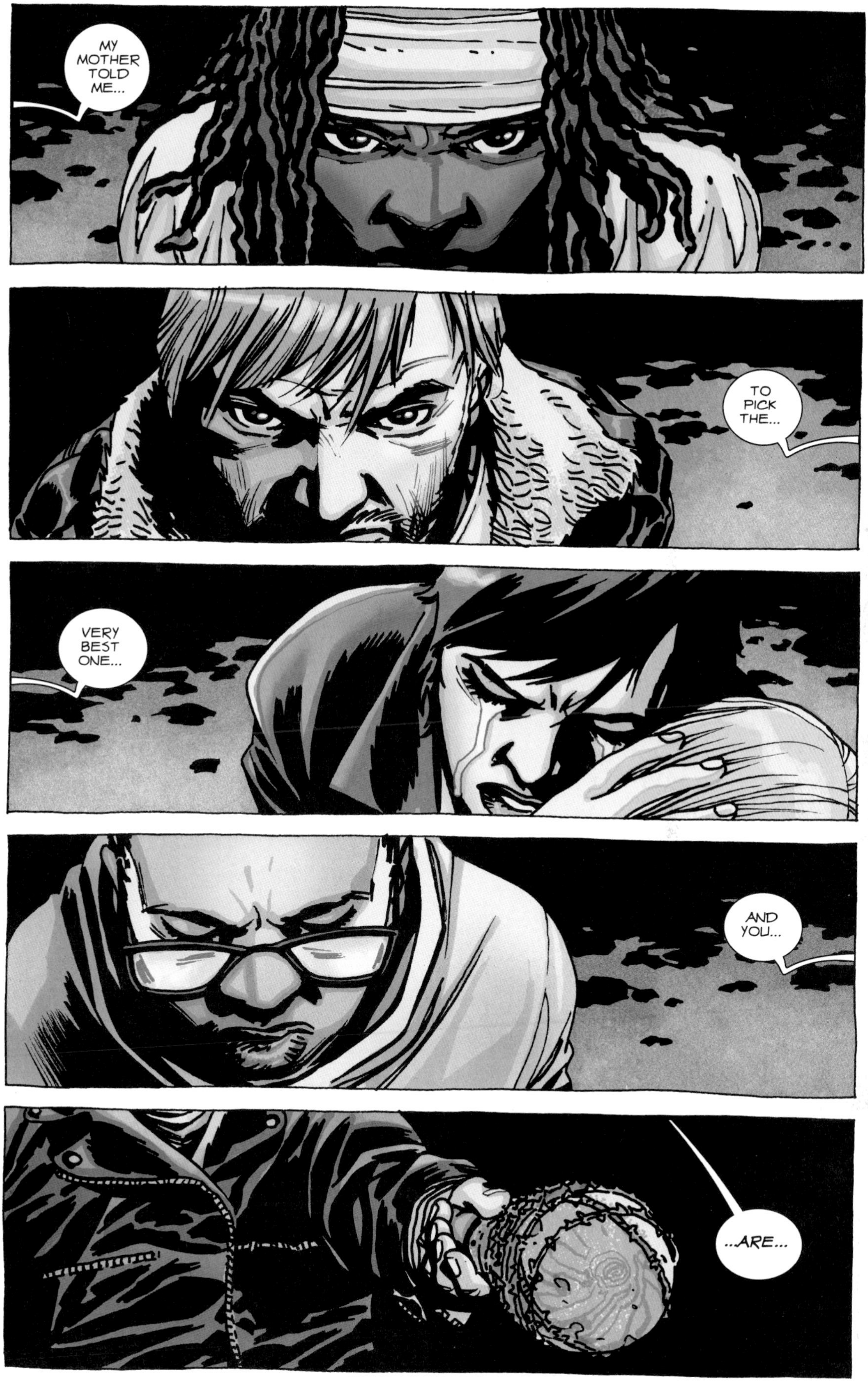
MY MOTHER TOLD ME...
TO PICK THE...
VERY BEST ONE...
AND YOU...
...ARE...

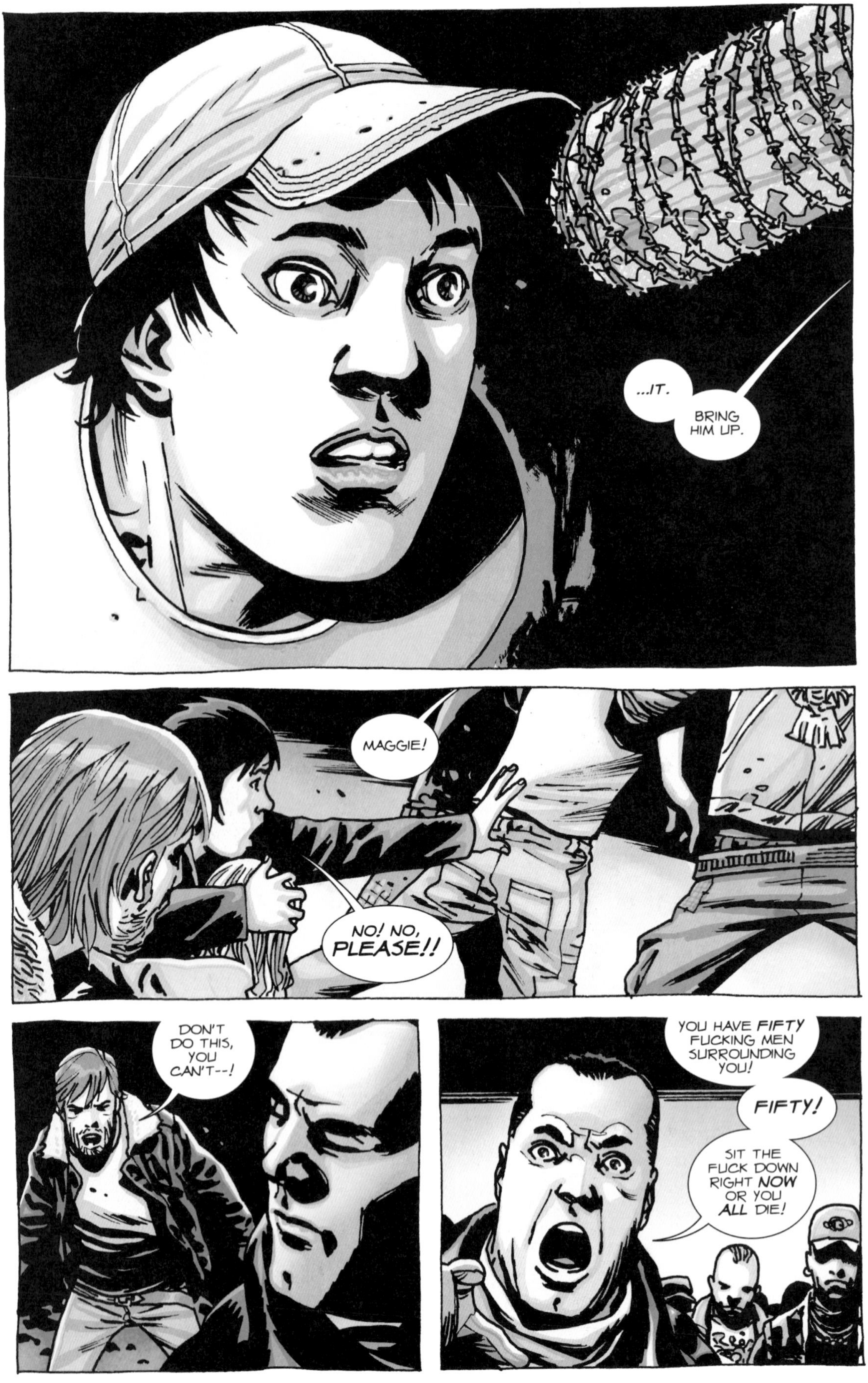

...IT.
BRING HIM UP.
MAGGIE!
NO! NO, PLEASE!!
DON'T DO THIS, YOU CAN'T--!
YOU HAVE FIFTY FUCKING MEN SURROUNDING YOU!
FIFTY!
SIT THE FUCK DOWN RIGHT NOW OR YOU ALL DIE!

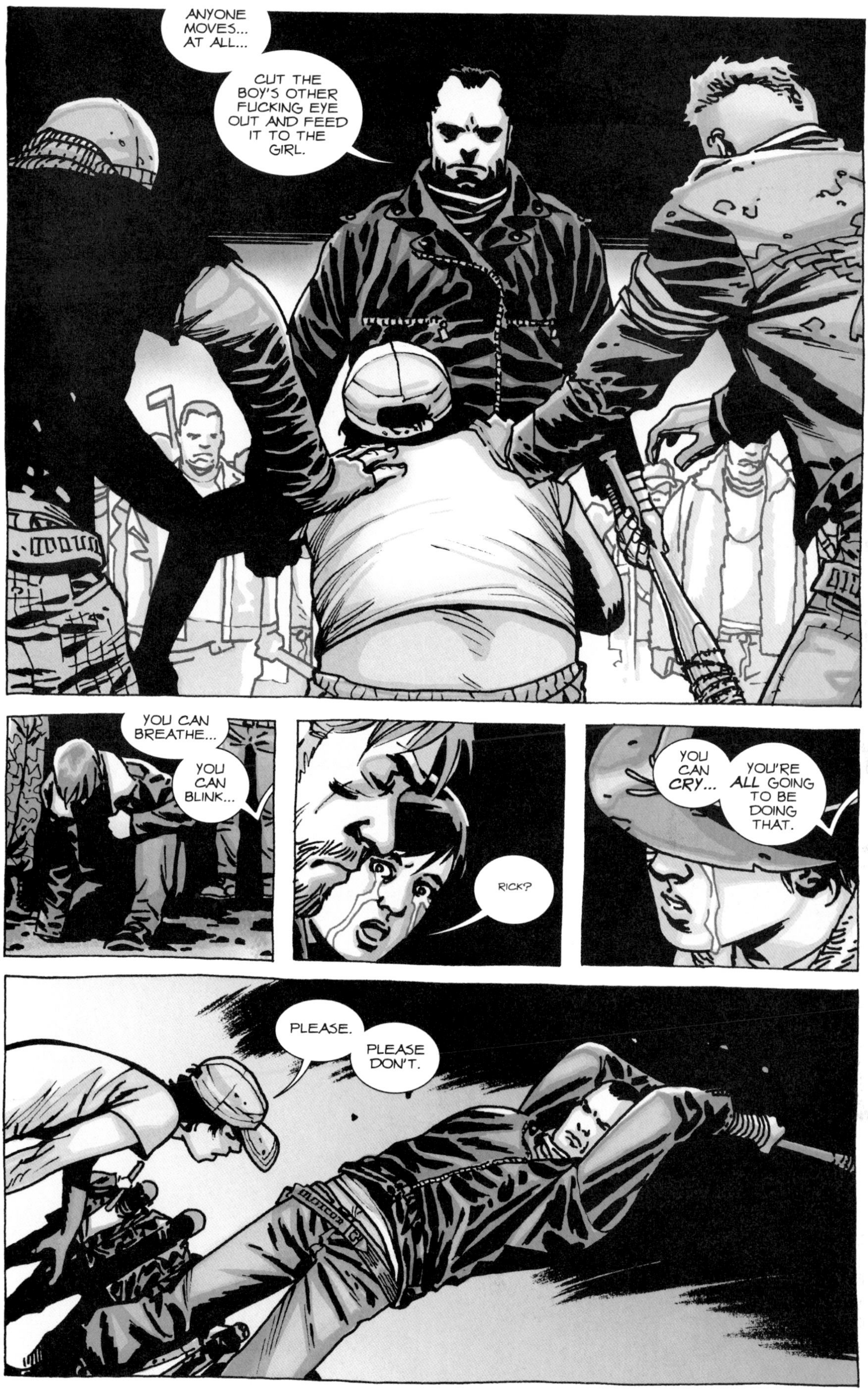
ANYONE MOVES... AT ALL...
CUT THE BOY'S OTHER FUCKING EYE OUT AND FEED IT TO THE GIRL.
YOU CAN BREATHE...
YOU CAN BLINK...
RICK?
YOU CAN CRY...
YOU'RE ALL GOING TO BE DOING THAT.
PLEASE.
PLEASE DON'T.

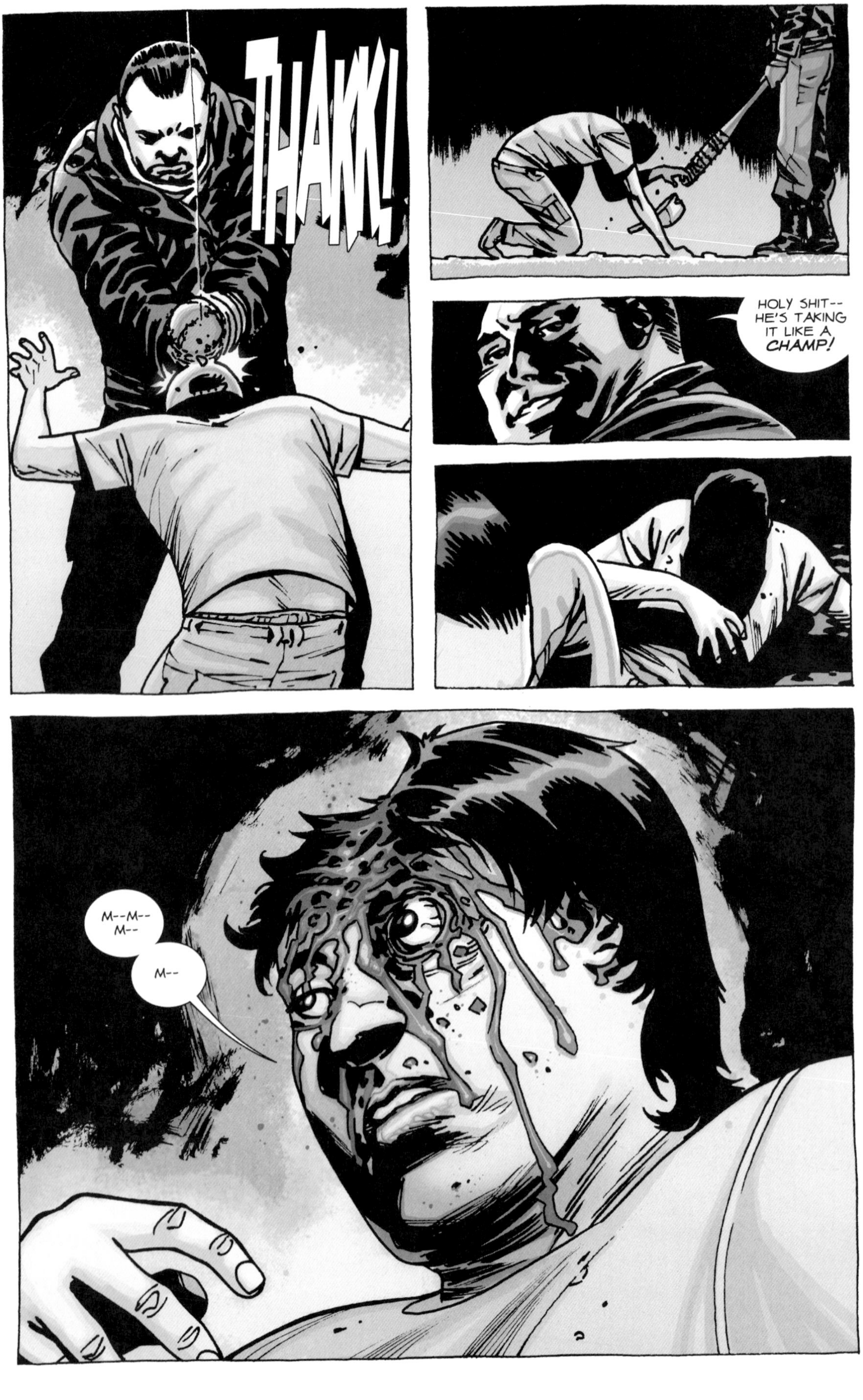
THAKK!
HOLY SHIT-- HE'S TAKING IT LIKE A CHAMP!
M--M-- M--
M--

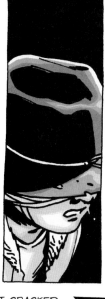

YOU IN THERE, BUDDY? I JUST DON'T KNOW. SEEMS LIKE YOU'RE TRYING TO SPEAK, BUT YOU JUST TOOK A *HELL* OF A HIT.

I CRACKED YOUR SKULL SO MUCH THAT YOUR FUCKING *EYE* POPPED OUT. IT'S GROSS AS SHIT.

I DON'T THINK--

MAG--!

MAGGIE!

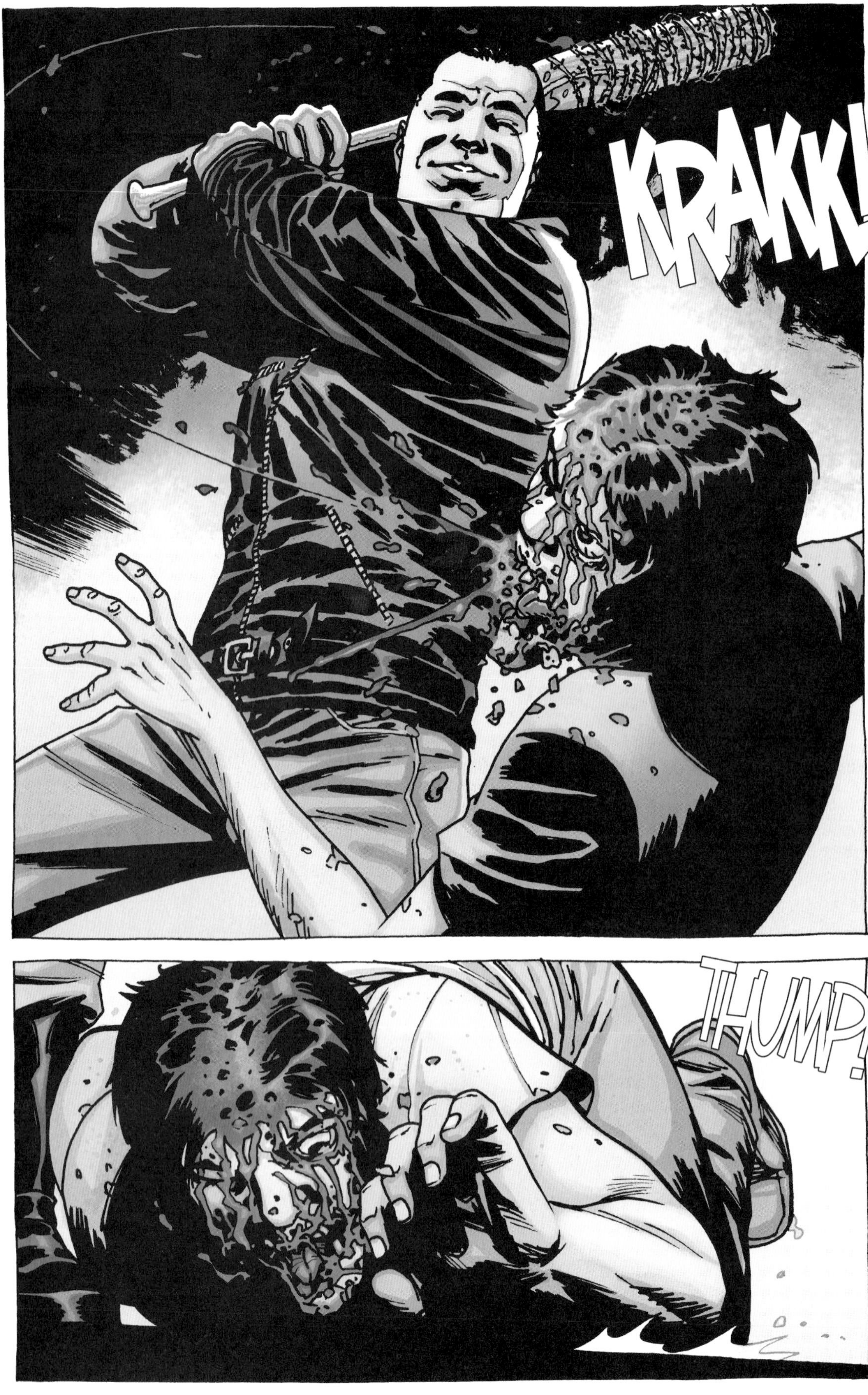
KRAKK!
THUMP!

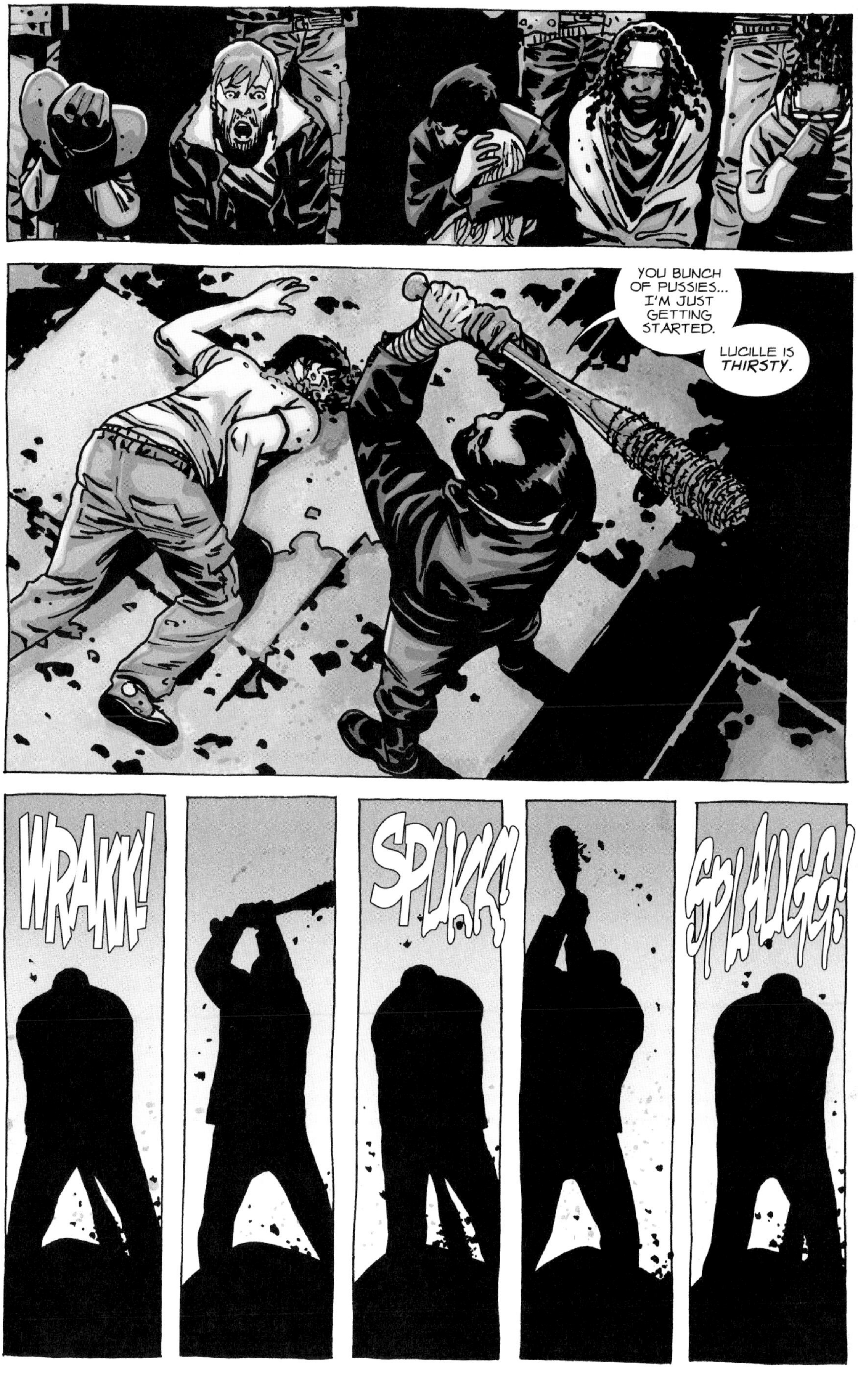
YOU BUNCH OF PUSSIES... I'M JUST GETTING STARTED.
LUCILLE IS *THIRSTY*.
WRAKK!
SPLUKK!
SPLAUGG!

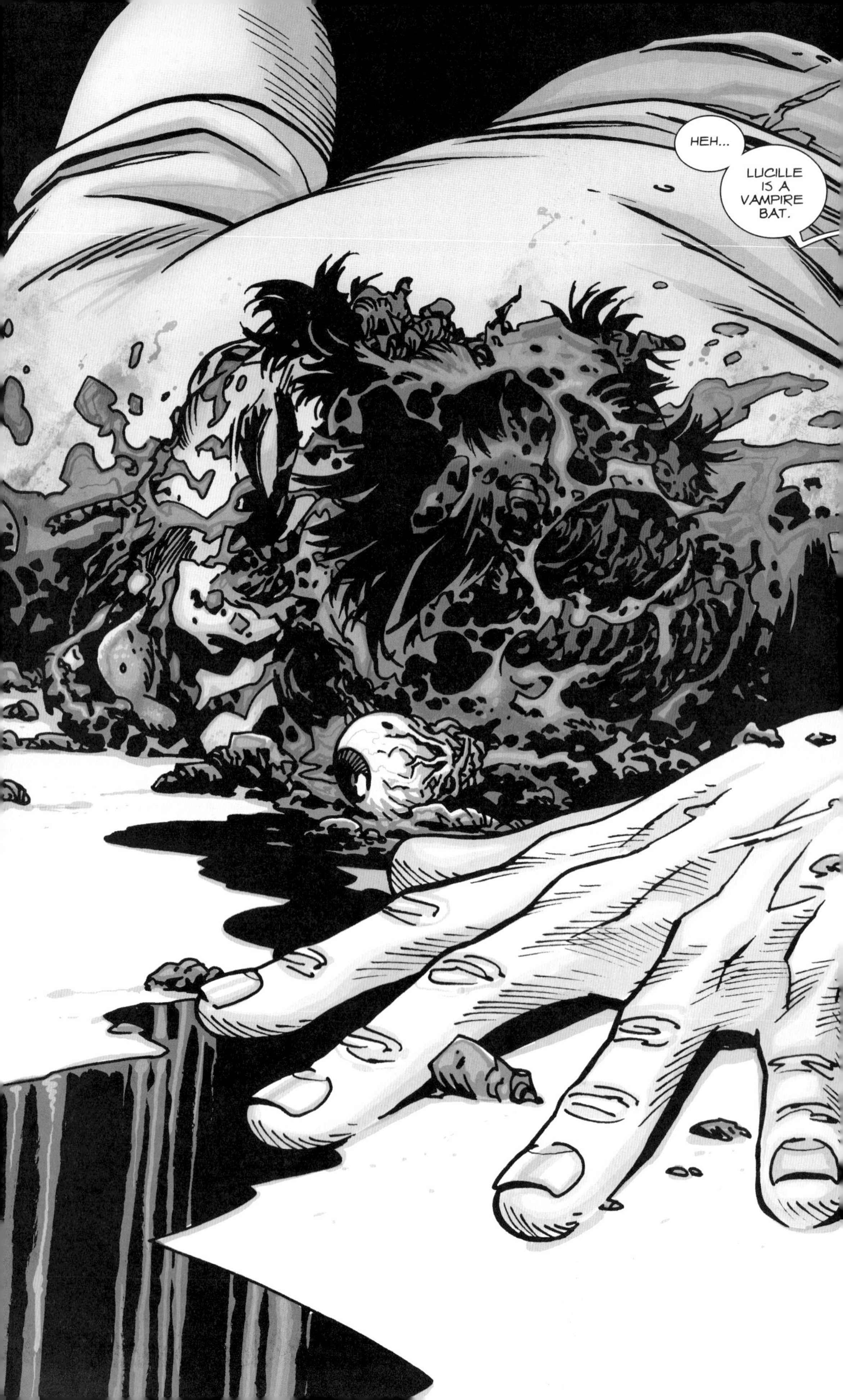
HEH...
LUCILLE IS A VAMPIRE BAT.

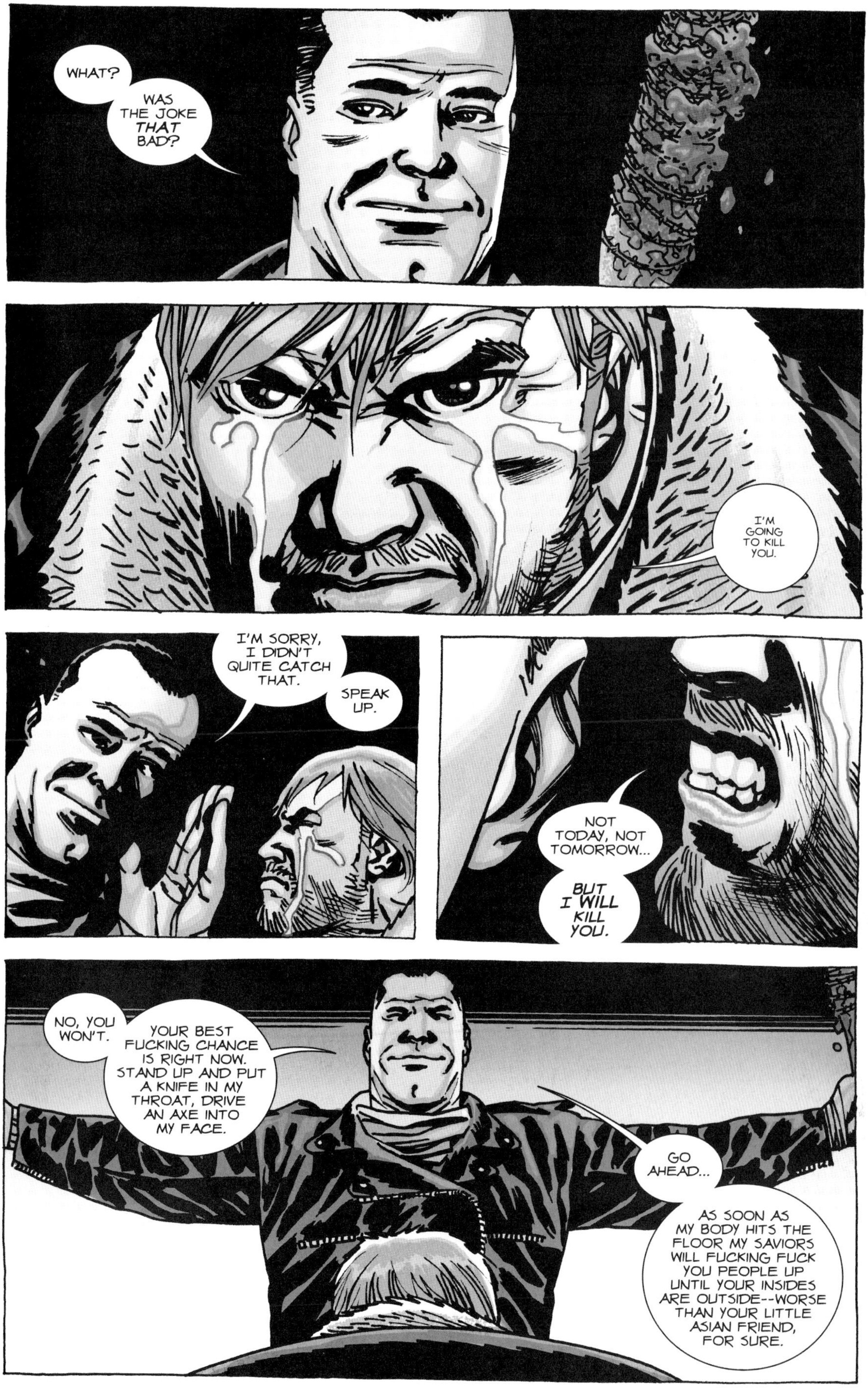
WHAT?
WAS THE JOKE THAT BAD?
I'M GOING TO KILL YOU.
I'M SORRY, I DIDN'T QUITE CATCH THAT.
SPEAK UP.
NOT TODAY, NOT TOMORROW...
BUT I WILL KILL YOU.
NO, YOU WON'T.
YOUR BEST FUCKING CHANCE IS RIGHT NOW. STAND UP AND PUT A KNIFE IN MY THROAT, DRIVE AN AXE INTO MY FACE.
GO AHEAD...
AS SOON AS MY BODY HITS THE FLOOR MY SAVIORS WILL FUCKING FUCK YOU PEOPLE UP UNTIL YOUR INSIDES ARE OUTSIDE--WORSE THAN YOUR LITTLE ASIAN FRIEND, FOR SURE.

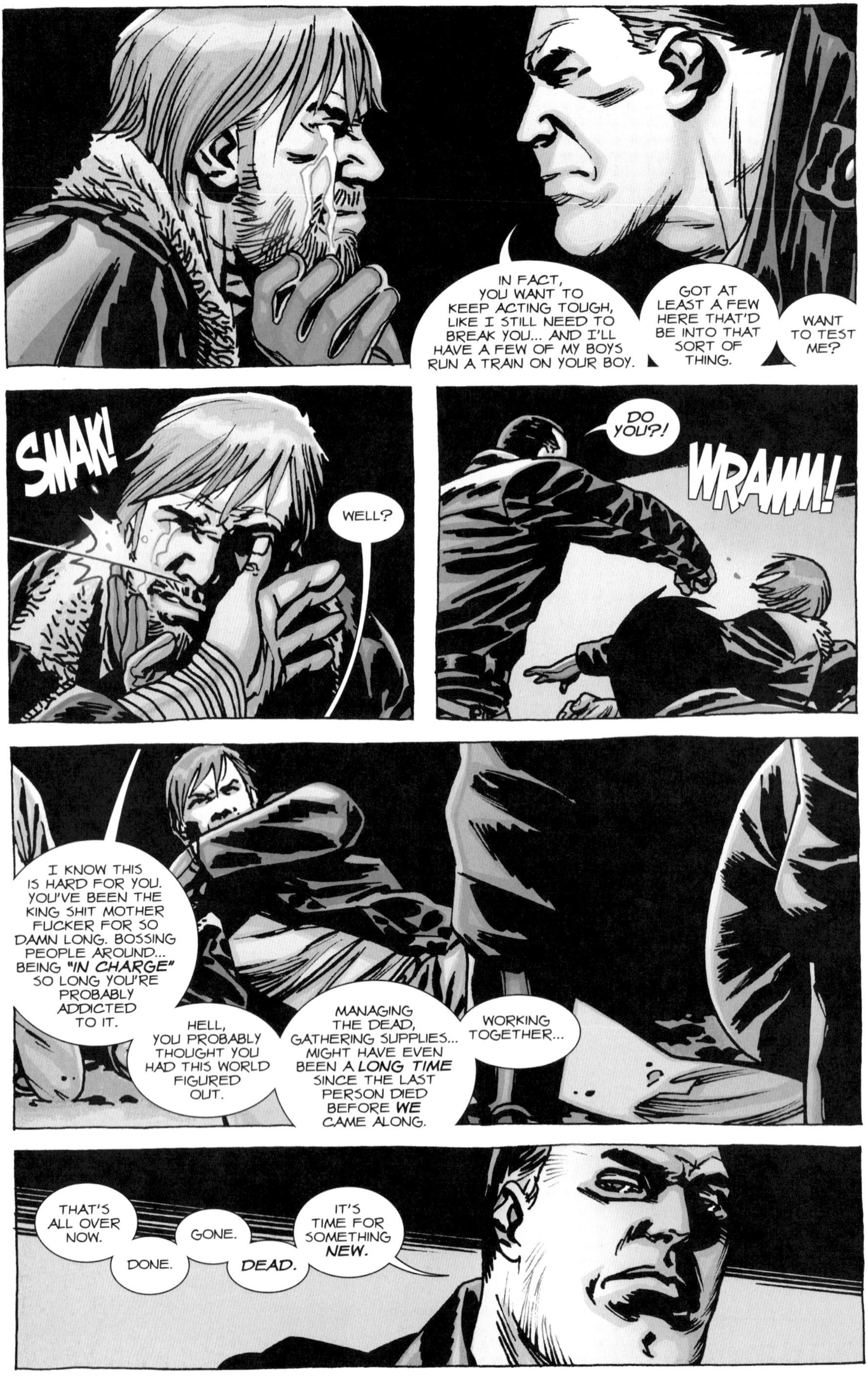
IN FACT, YOU WANT TO KEEP ACTING TOUGH, LIKE I STILL NEED TO BREAK YOU... AND I'LL HAVE A FEW OF MY BOYS RUN A TRAIN ON YOUR BOY.
GOT AT LEAST A FEW HERE THAT'D BE INTO THAT SORT OF THING.
WANT TO TEST ME?
SMAK!
WELL?
DO YOU?!
WRAMM!
I KNOW THIS IS HARD FOR YOU. YOU'VE BEEN THE KING SHIT MOTHER FUCKER FOR SO DAMN LONG. BOSSING PEOPLE AROUND... BEING "IN CHARGE" SO LONG YOU'RE PROBABLY ADDICTED TO IT.
HELL, YOU PROBABLY THOUGHT YOU HAD THIS WORLD FIGURED OUT.
MANAGING THE DEAD, GATHERING SUPPLIES... MIGHT HAVE EVEN BEEN A LONG TIME SINCE THE LAST PERSON DIED BEFORE WE CAME ALONG.
WORKING TOGETHER...
THAT'S ALL OVER NOW.
DONE.
GONE.
DEAD.
IT'S TIME FOR SOMETHING NEW.

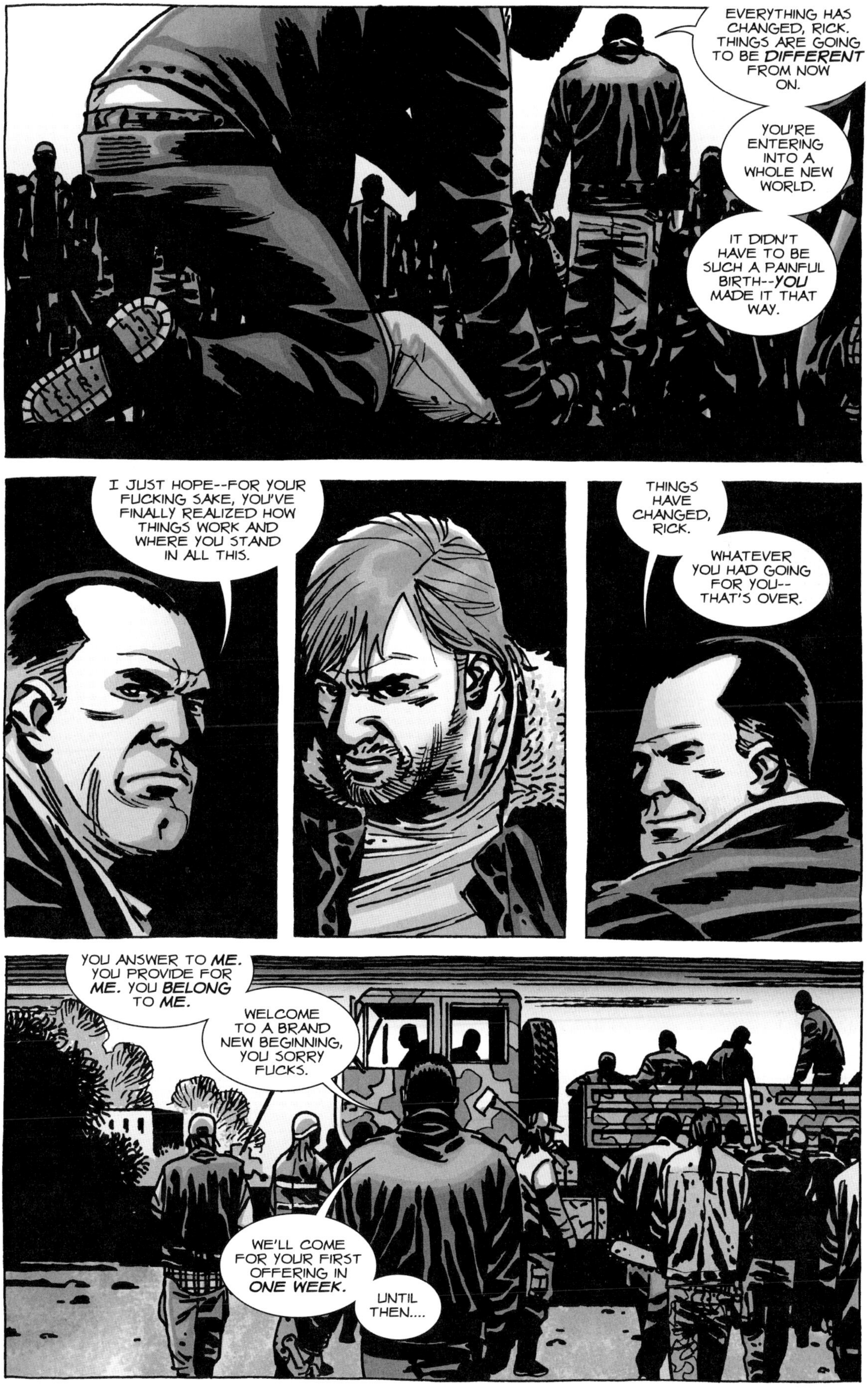
EVERYTHING HAS CHANGED, RICK. THINGS ARE GOING TO BE DIFFERENT FROM NOW ON.
YOU'RE ENTERING INTO A WHOLE NEW WORLD.
IT DIDN'T HAVE TO BE SUCH A PAINFUL BIRTH--YOU MADE IT THAT WAY.
I JUST HOPE--FOR YOUR FUCKING SAKE, YOU'VE FINALLY REALIZED HOW THINGS WORK AND WHERE YOU STAND IN ALL THIS.
THINGS HAVE CHANGED, RICK.
WHATEVER YOU HAD GOING FOR YOU--THAT'S OVER.
YOU ANSWER TO ME. YOU PROVIDE FOR ME. YOU BELONG TO ME.
WELCOME TO A BRAND NEW BEGINNING, YOU SORRY FUCKS.
WE'LL COME FOR YOUR FIRST OFFERING IN ONE WEEK.
UNTIL THEN....

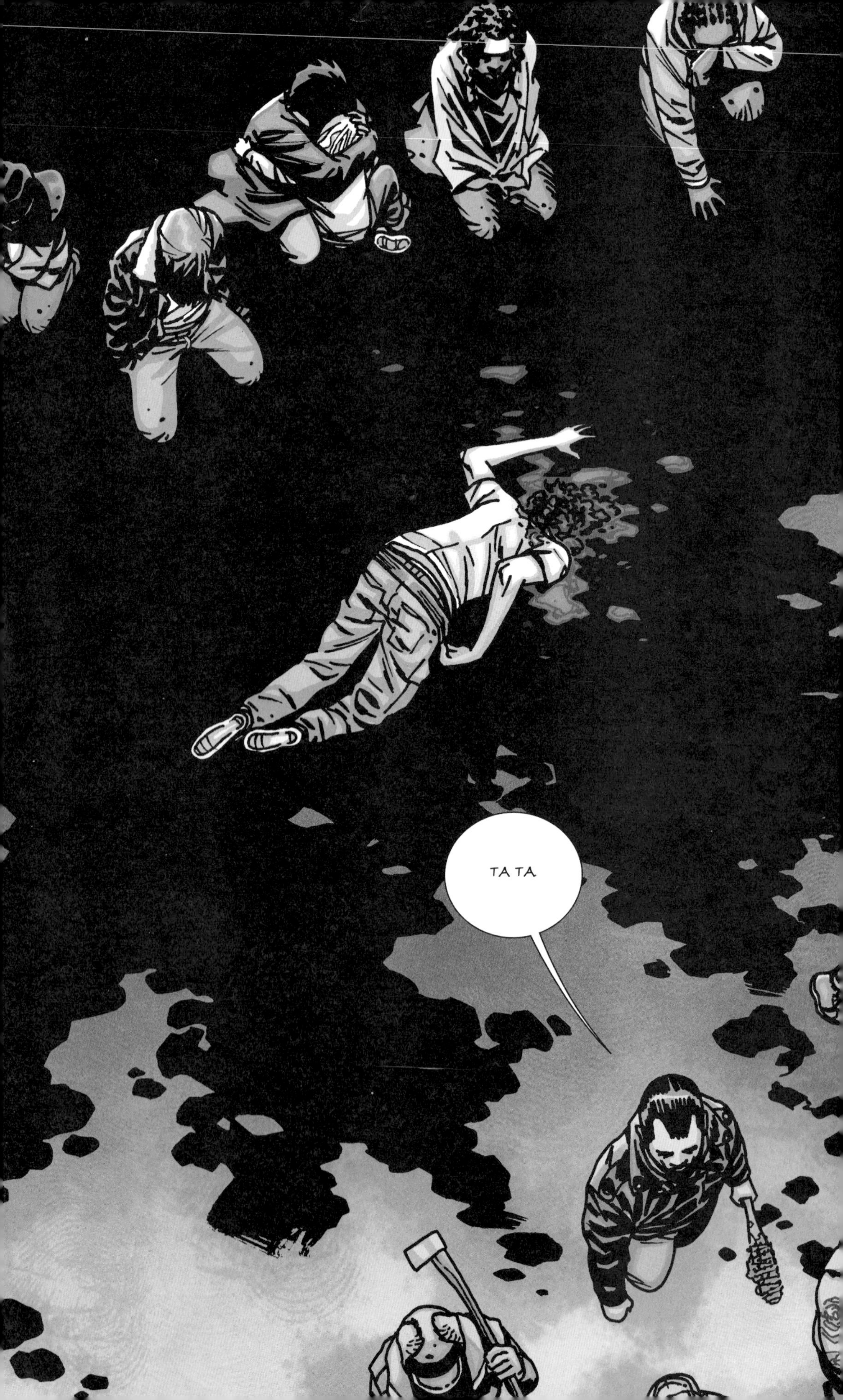
TA TA

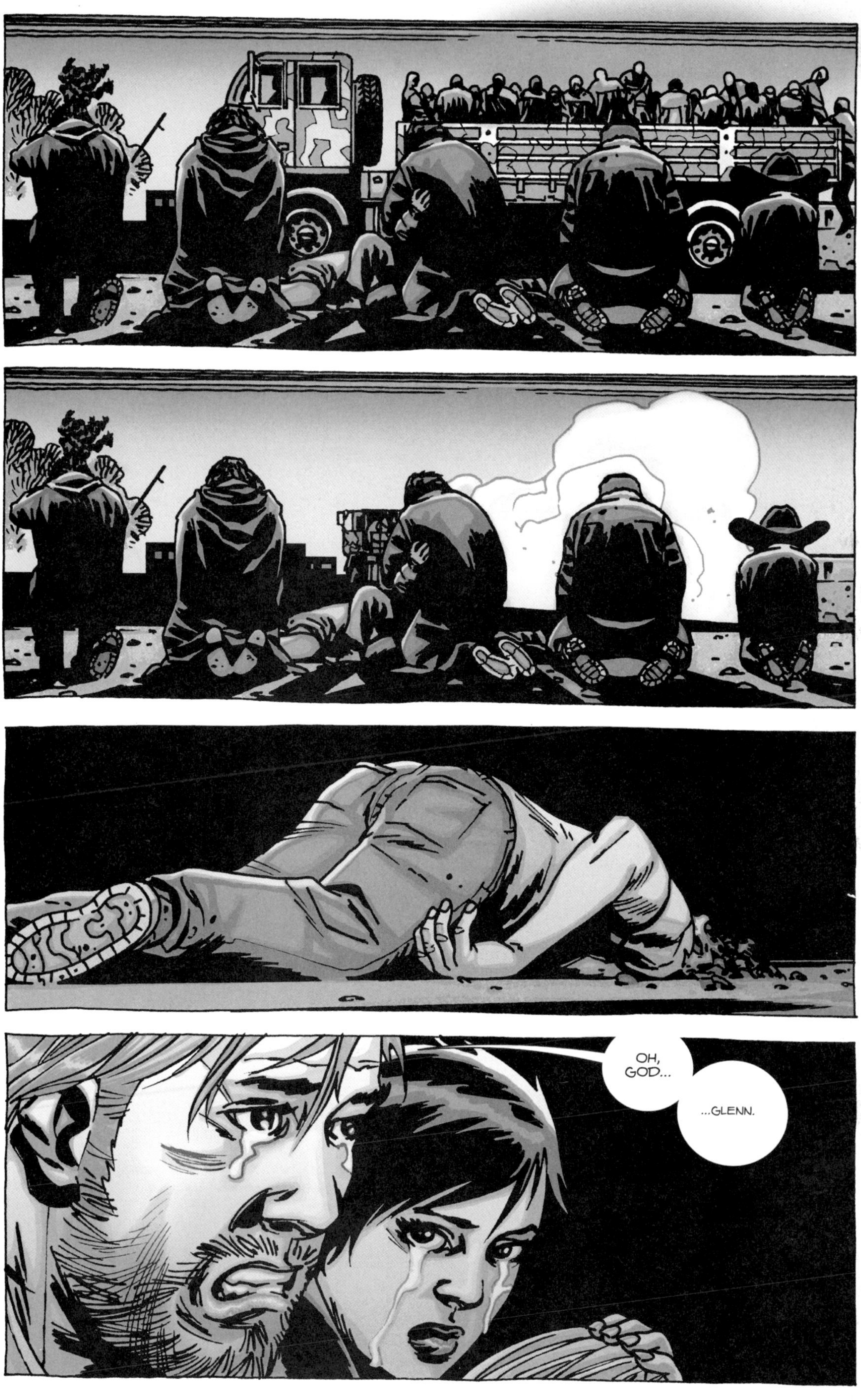
OH, GOD...
...GLENN.

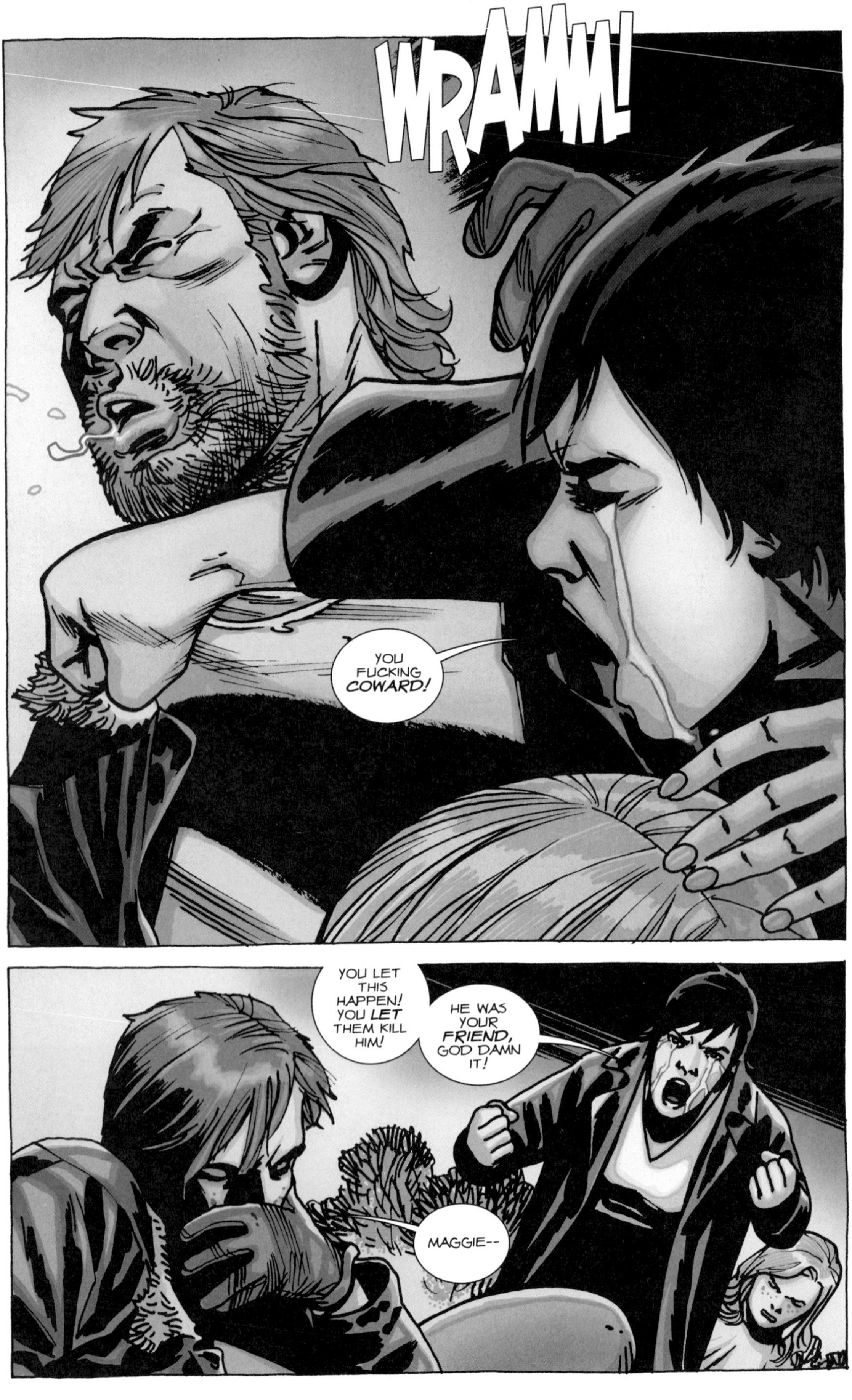
WRAMM!
YOU FUCKING COWARD!
YOU LET THIS HAPPEN! YOU LET THEM KILL HIM!
HE WAS YOUR FRIEND, GOD DAMN IT!
MAGGIE--

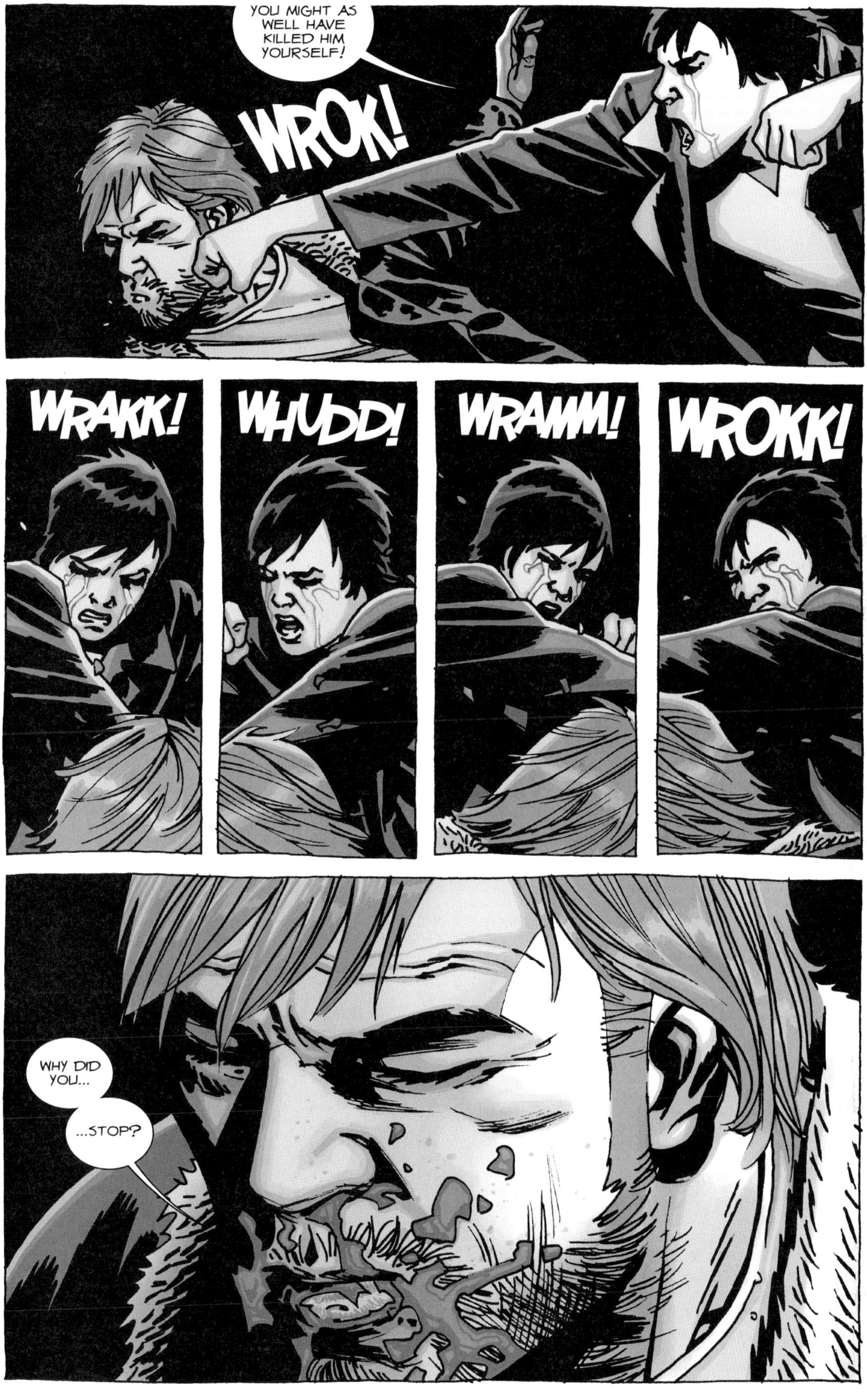
YOU MIGHT AS WELL HAVE KILLED HIM YOURSELF!
WROK!
WRAKK!
WHUDD!
WRAMM!
WROKK!
WHY DID YOU...
...STOP?

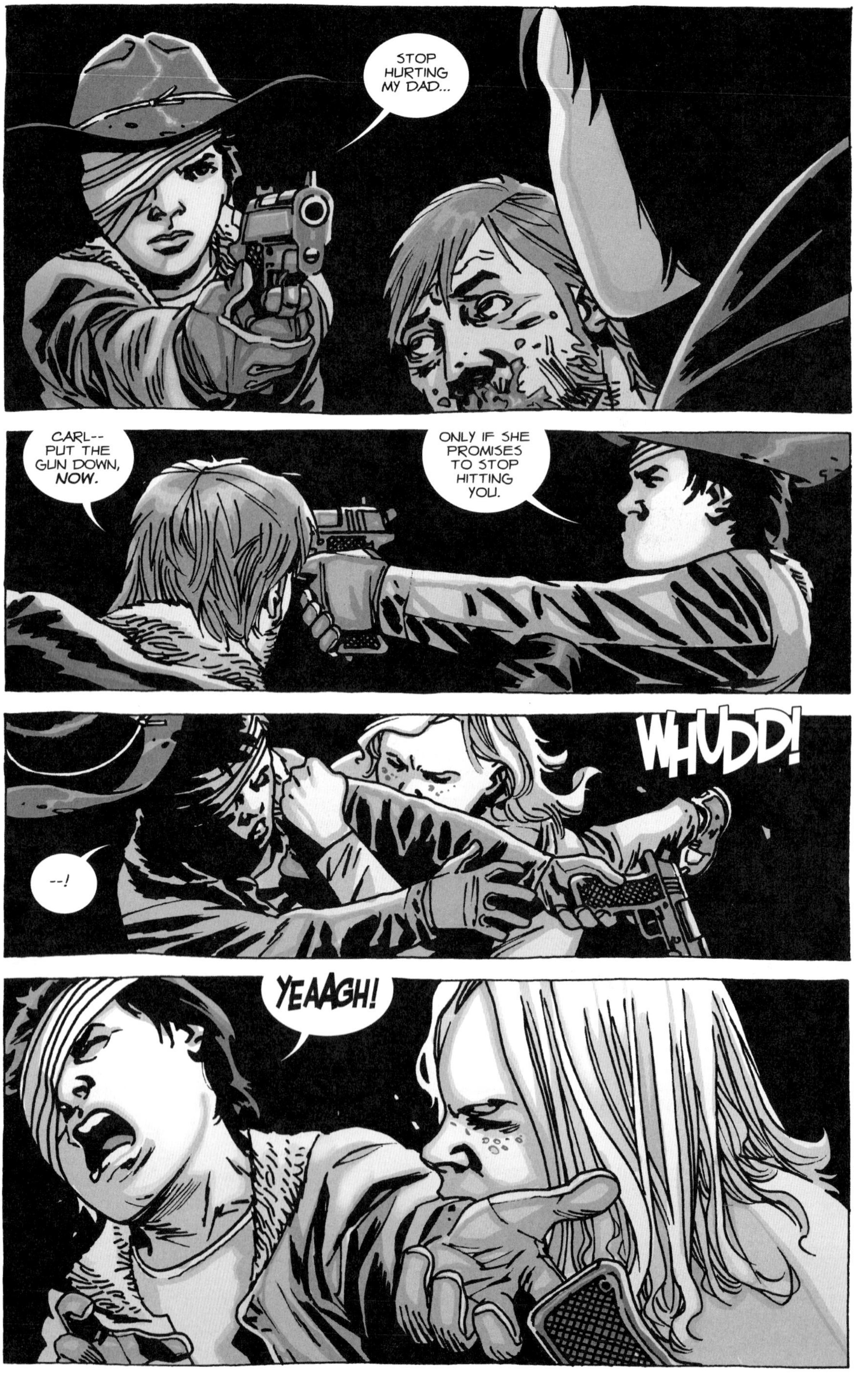
STOP HURTING MY DAD...
CARL-- PUT THE GUN DOWN, NOW.
ONLY IF SHE PROMISES TO STOP HITTING YOU.
WHUDD!
--!
YEAAGH!

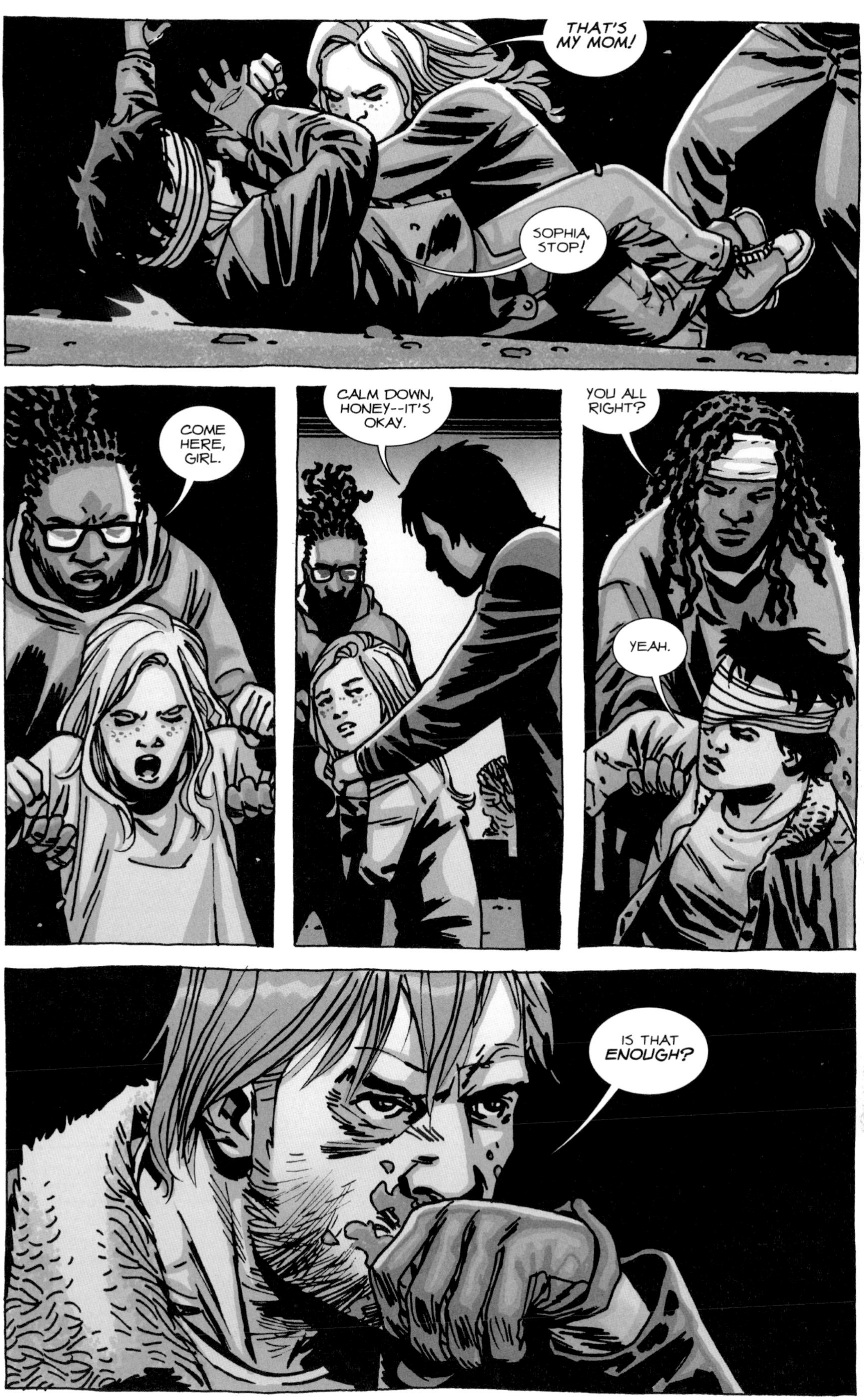
THAT'S MY MOM!
SOPHIA, STOP!
COME HERE, GIRL.
CALM DOWN, HONEY--IT'S OKAY.
YOU ALL RIGHT?
YEAH.
IS THAT ENOUGH?

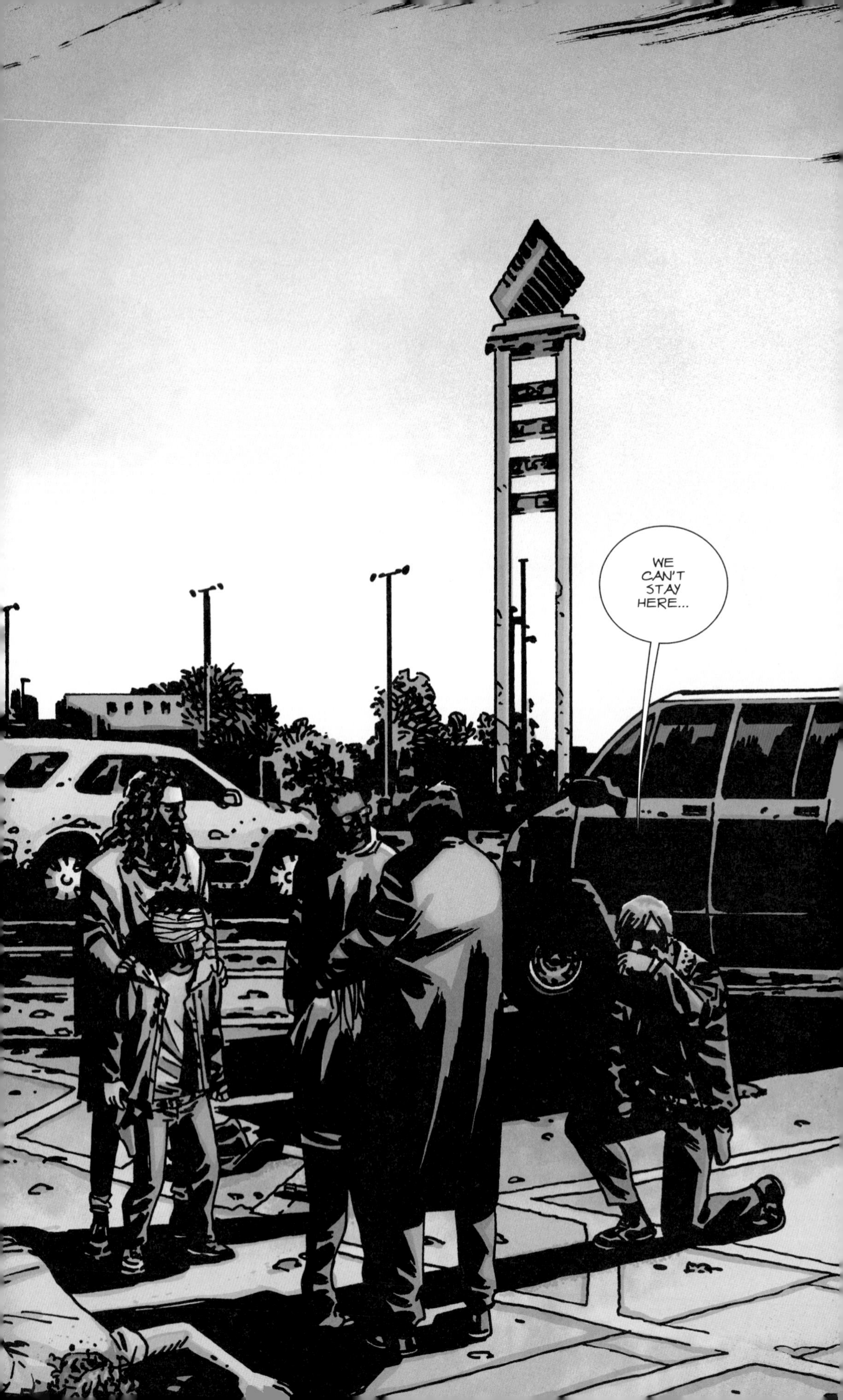
WE CAN'T STAY HERE...

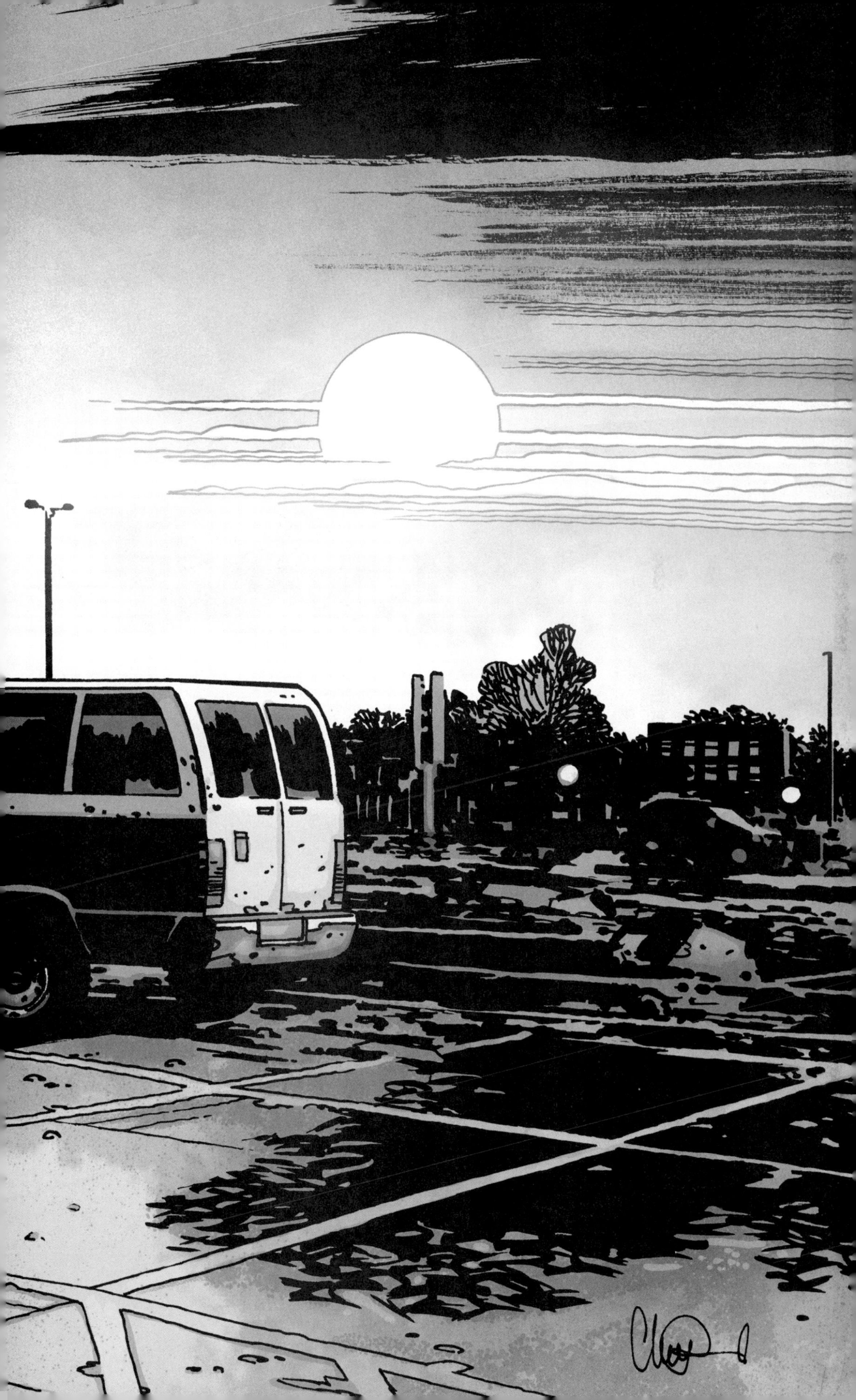

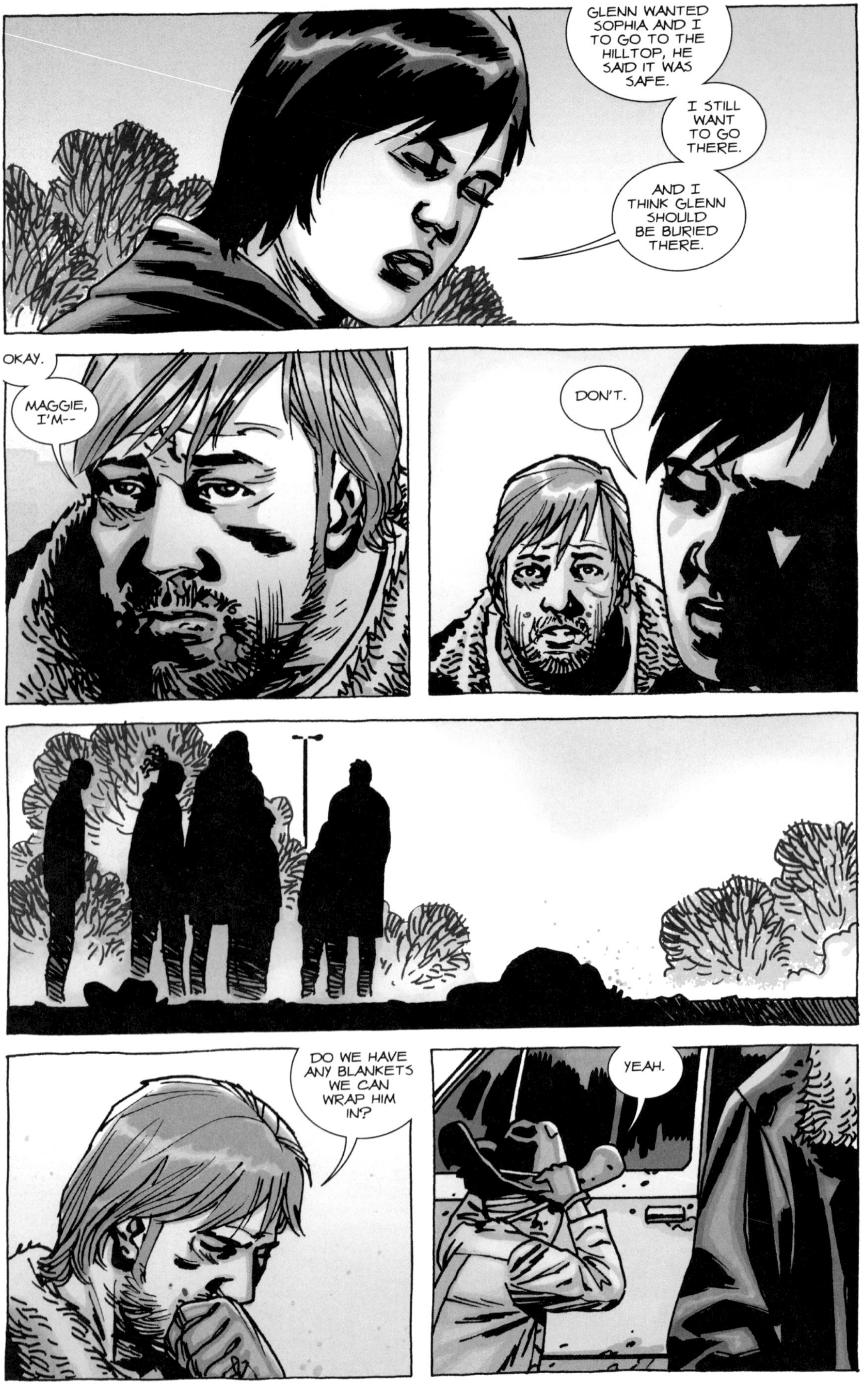
GLENN WANTED SOPHIA AND I TO GO TO THE HILLTOP, HE SAID IT WAS SAFE.
I STILL WANT TO GO THERE.
AND I THINK GLENN SHOULD BE BURIED THERE.
OKAY.
MAGGIE, I'M--
DON'T.
DO WE HAVE ANY BLANKETS WE CAN WRAP HIM IN?
YEAH.

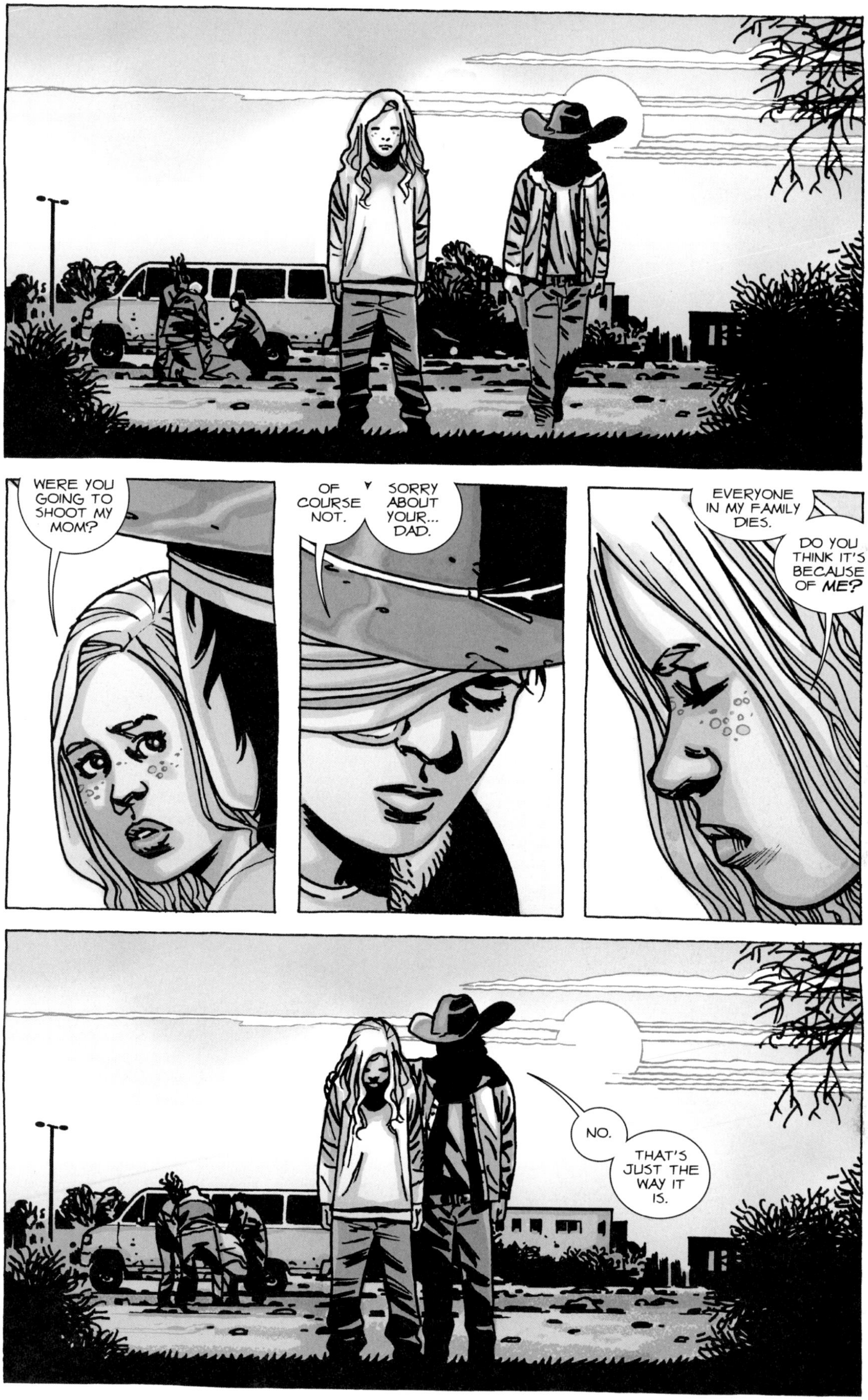
WERE YOU GOING TO SHOOT MY MOM?
OF COURSE NOT.
SORRY ABOUT YOUR... DAD.
EVERYONE IN MY FAMILY DIES.
DO YOU THINK IT'S BECAUSE OF ME?
NO.
THAT'S JUST THE WAY IT IS.

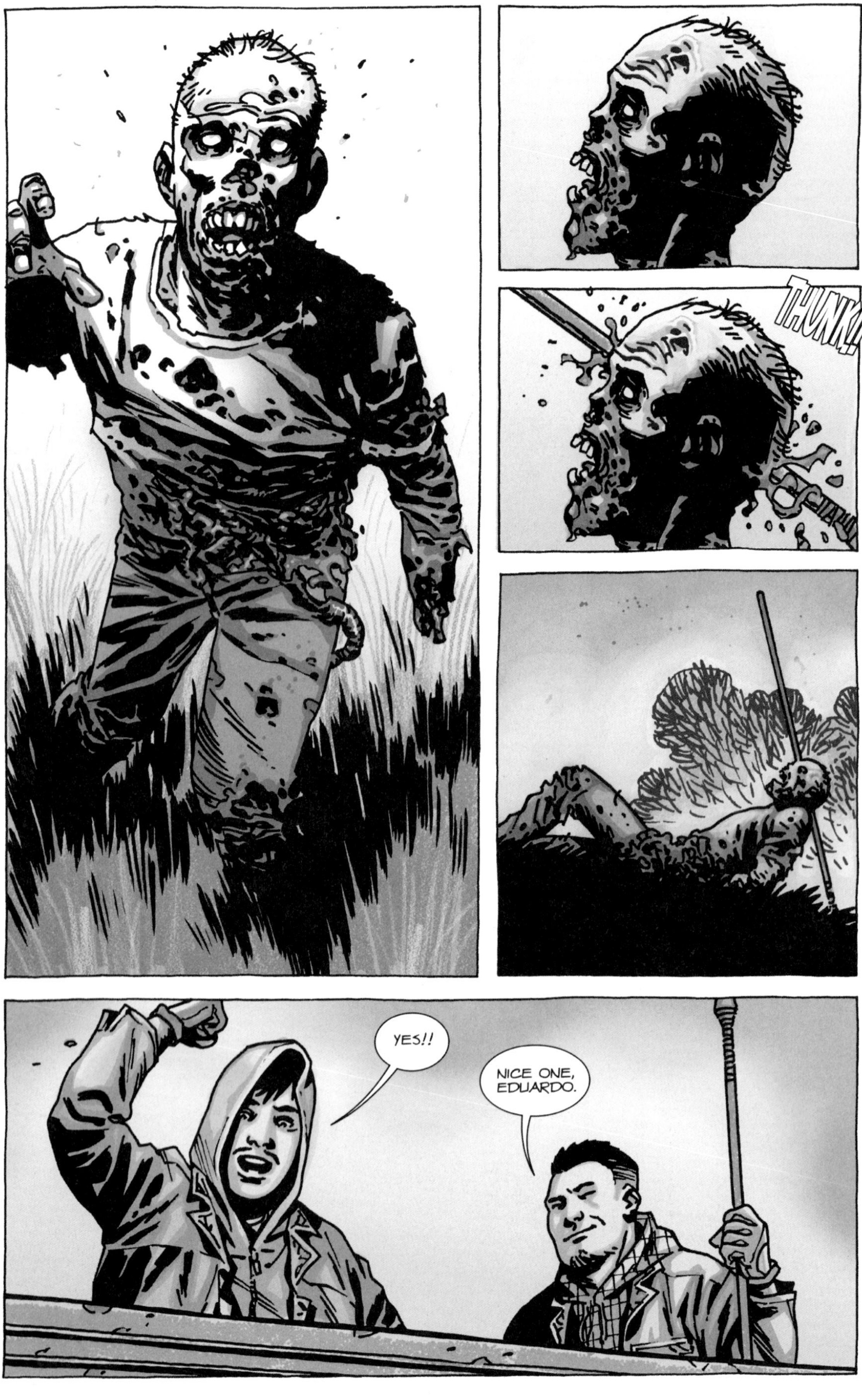
THUNK!!
YES!!
NICE ONE, EDUARDO.

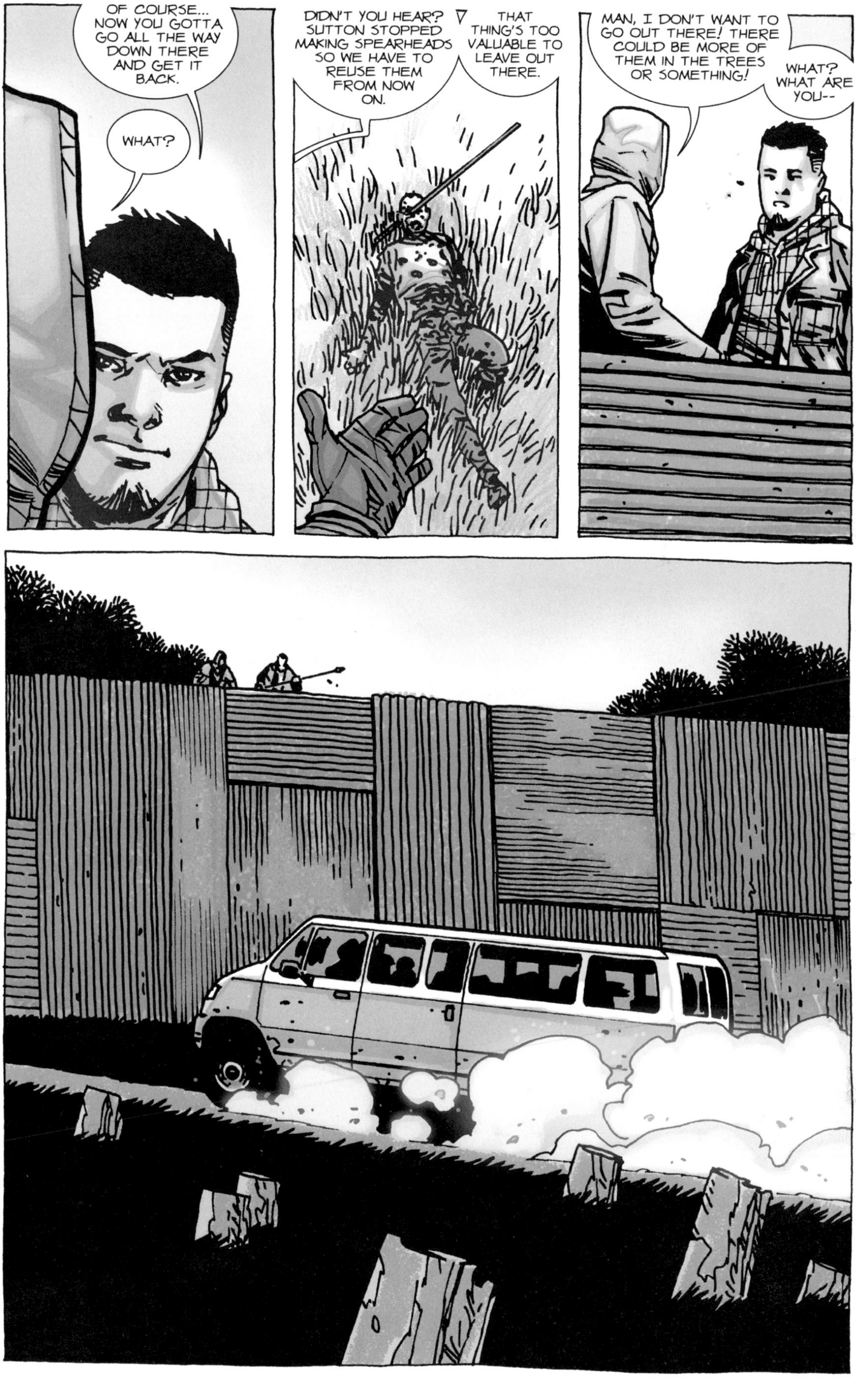

OF COURSE... NOW YOU GOTTA GO ALL THE WAY DOWN THERE AND GET IT BACK.
WHAT?
DIDN'T YOU HEAR? SUTTON STOPPED MAKING SPEARHEADS SO WE HAVE TO REUSE THEM FROM NOW ON.
THAT THING'S TOO VALUABLE TO LEAVE OUT THERE.
MAN, I DON'T WANT TO GO OUT THERE! THERE COULD BE MORE OF THEM IN THE TREES OR SOMETHING!
WHAT? WHAT ARE YOU--

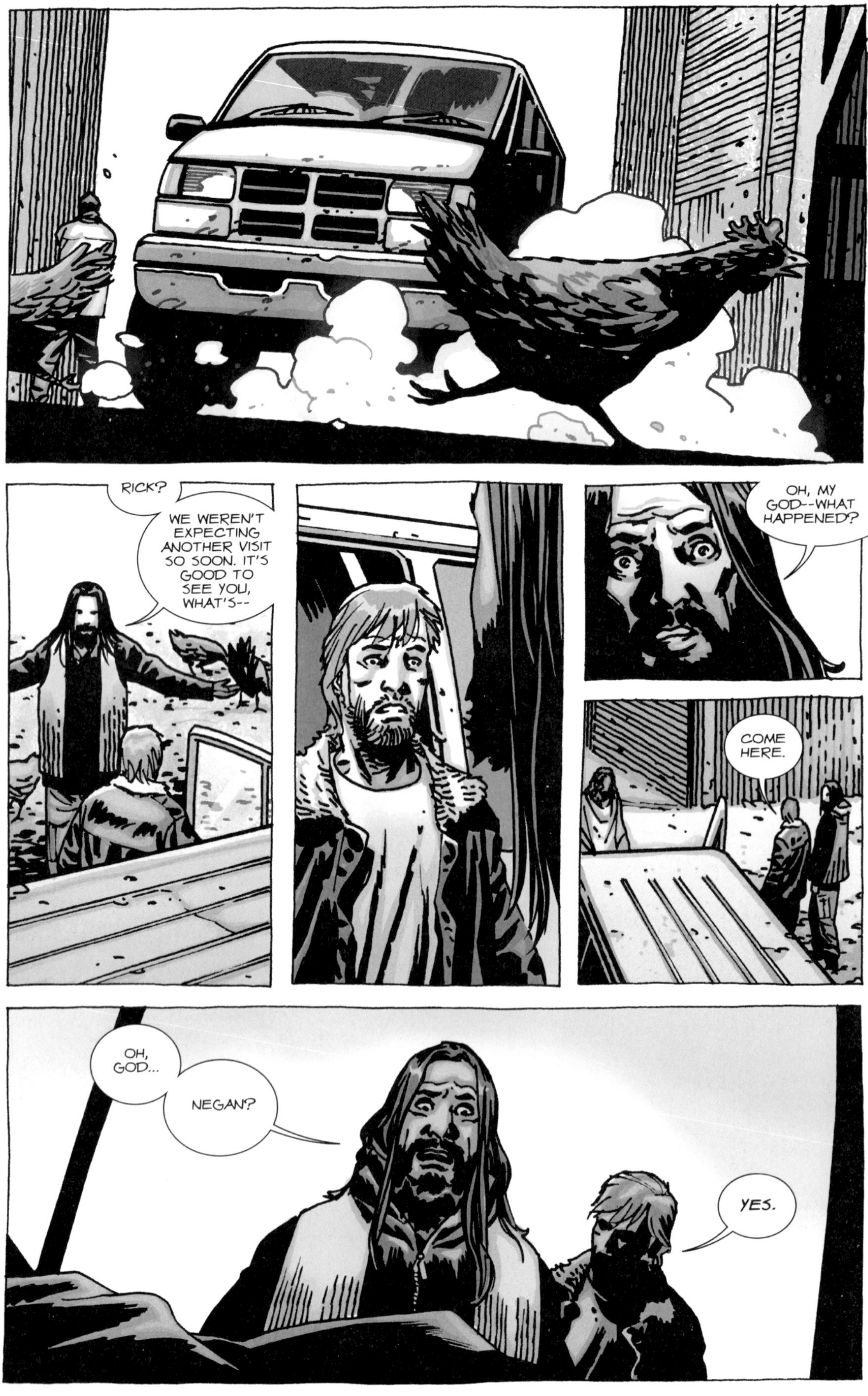
RICK?
WE WEREN'T EXPECTING ANOTHER VISIT SO SOON. IT'S GOOD TO SEE YOU, WHAT'S--
OH, MY GOD--WHAT HAPPENED?
COME HERE.
OH, GOD...
NEGAN?
YES.

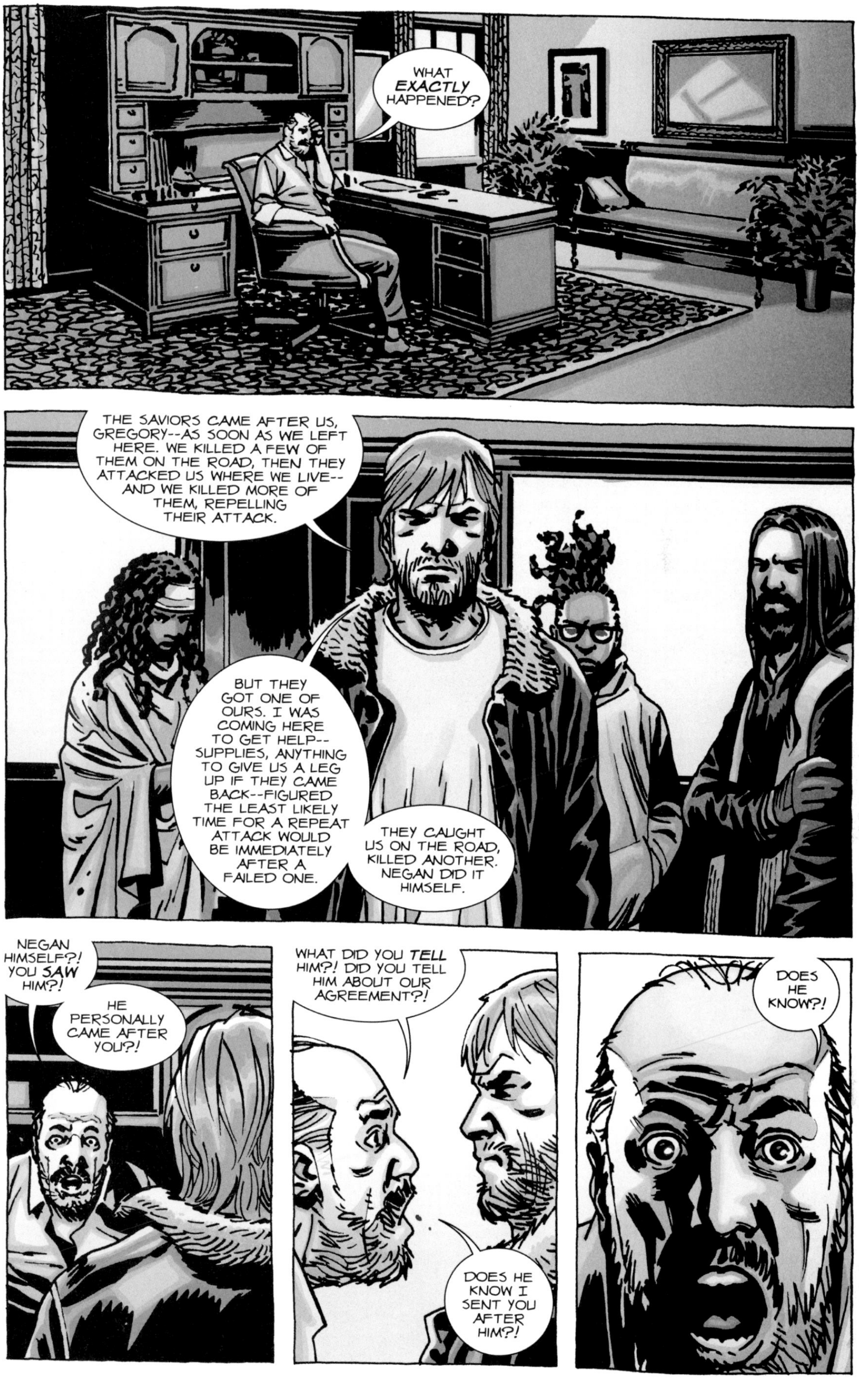

WHAT EXACTLY HAPPENED?
THE SAVIORS CAME AFTER US, GREGORY--AS SOON AS WE LEFT HERE. WE KILLED A FEW OF THEM ON THE ROAD, THEN THEY ATTACKED US WHERE WE LIVE--AND WE KILLED MORE OF THEM, REPELLING THEIR ATTACK.
BUT THEY GOT ONE OF OURS. I WAS COMING HERE TO GET HELP--SUPPLIES, ANYTHING TO GIVE US A LEG UP IF THEY CAME BACK--FIGURED THE LEAST LIKELY TIME FOR A REPEAT ATTACK WOULD BE IMMEDIATELY AFTER A FAILED ONE.
THEY CAUGHT US ON THE ROAD, KILLED ANOTHER. NEGAN DID IT HIMSELF.
NEGAN HIMSELF?! YOU SAW HIM?!
HE PERSONALLY CAME AFTER YOU?!
WHAT DID YOU TELL HIM?! DID YOU TELL HIM ABOUT OUR AGREEMENT?!
DOES HE KNOW I SENT YOU AFTER HIM?!
DOES HE KNOW?!

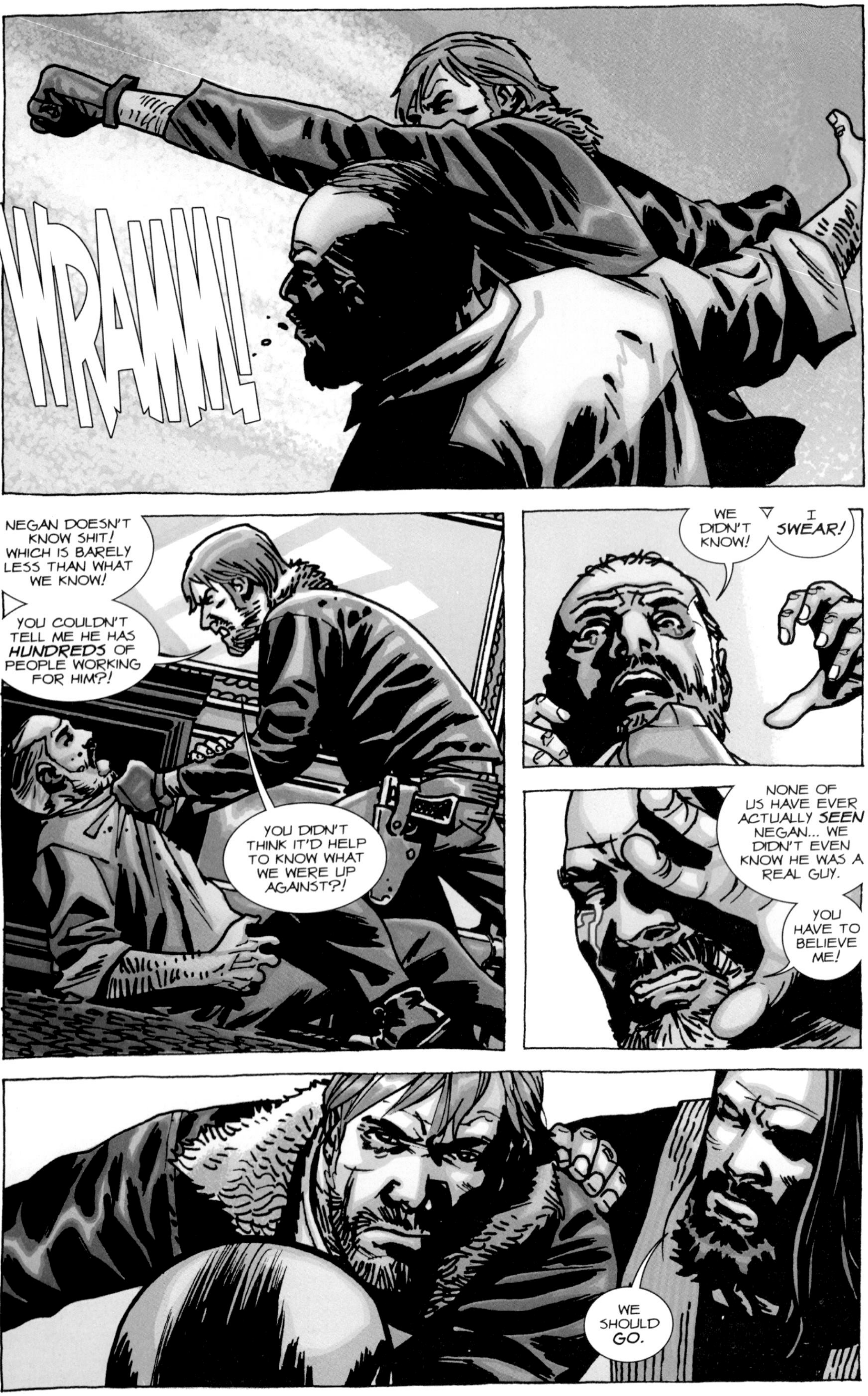
WRAMMM!
NEGAN DOESN'T KNOW SHIT! WHICH IS BARELY LESS THAN WHAT WE KNOW!
YOU COULDN'T TELL ME HE HAS HUNDREDS OF PEOPLE WORKING FOR HIM?!
YOU DIDN'T THINK IT'D HELP TO KNOW WHAT WE WERE UP AGAINST?!
WE DIDN'T KNOW!
I SWEAR!
NONE OF US HAVE EVER ACTUALLY SEEN NEGAN... WE DIDN'T EVEN KNOW HE WAS A REAL GUY.
YOU HAVE TO BELIEVE ME!
WE SHOULD GO.

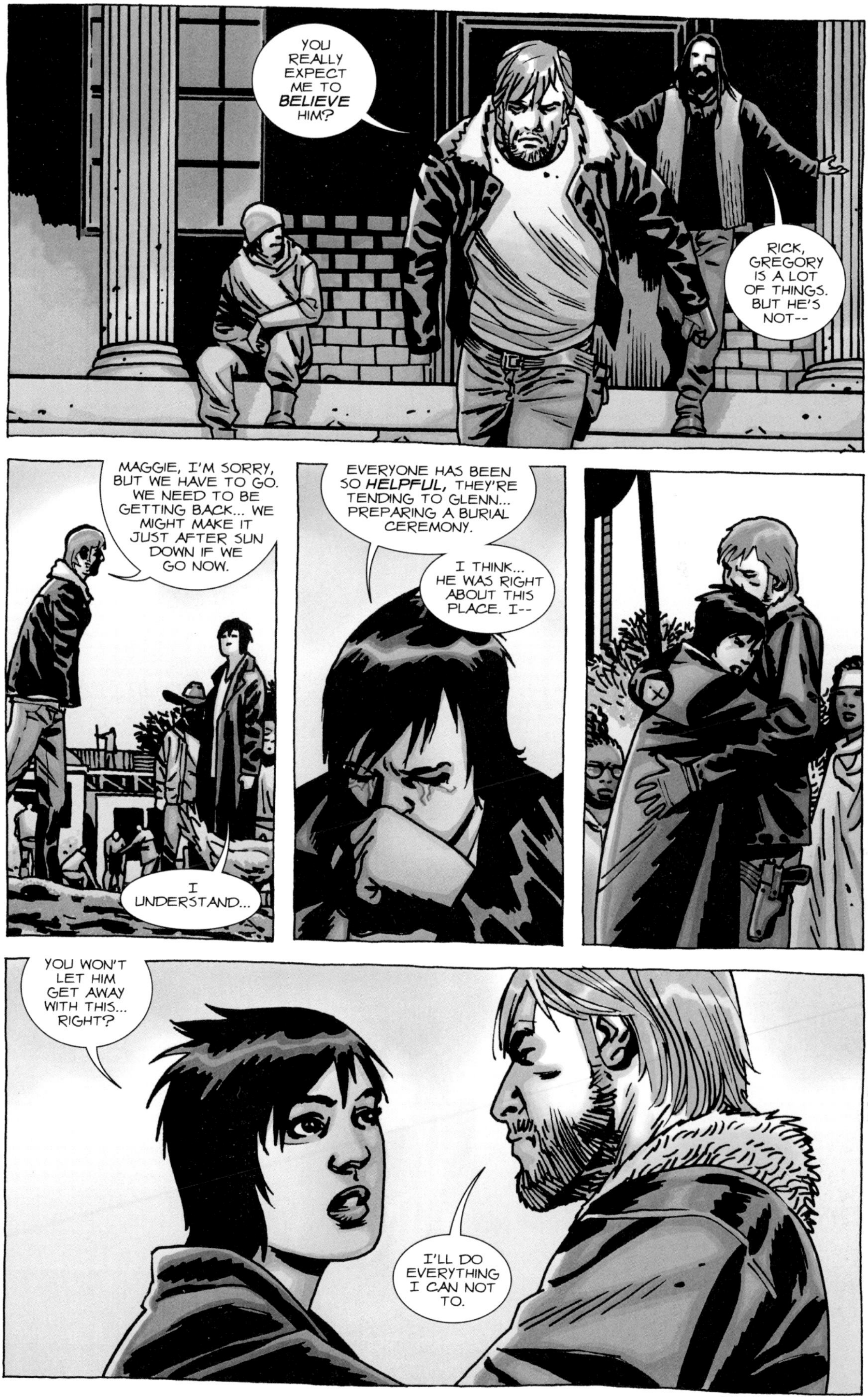
YOU REALLY EXPECT ME TO BELIEVE HIM?
RICK, GREGORY IS A LOT OF THINGS. BUT HE'S NOT--
MAGGIE, I'M SORRY, BUT WE HAVE TO GO. WE NEED TO BE GETTING BACK... WE MIGHT MAKE IT JUST AFTER SUN DOWN IF WE GO NOW.
I UNDERSTAND...
EVERYONE HAS BEEN SO HELPFUL, THEY'RE TENDING TO GLENN... PREPARING A BURIAL CEREMONY.
I THINK... HE WAS RIGHT ABOUT THIS PLACE. I--
YOU WON'T LET HIM GET AWAY WITH THIS... RIGHT?
I'LL DO EVERYTHING I CAN NOT TO.

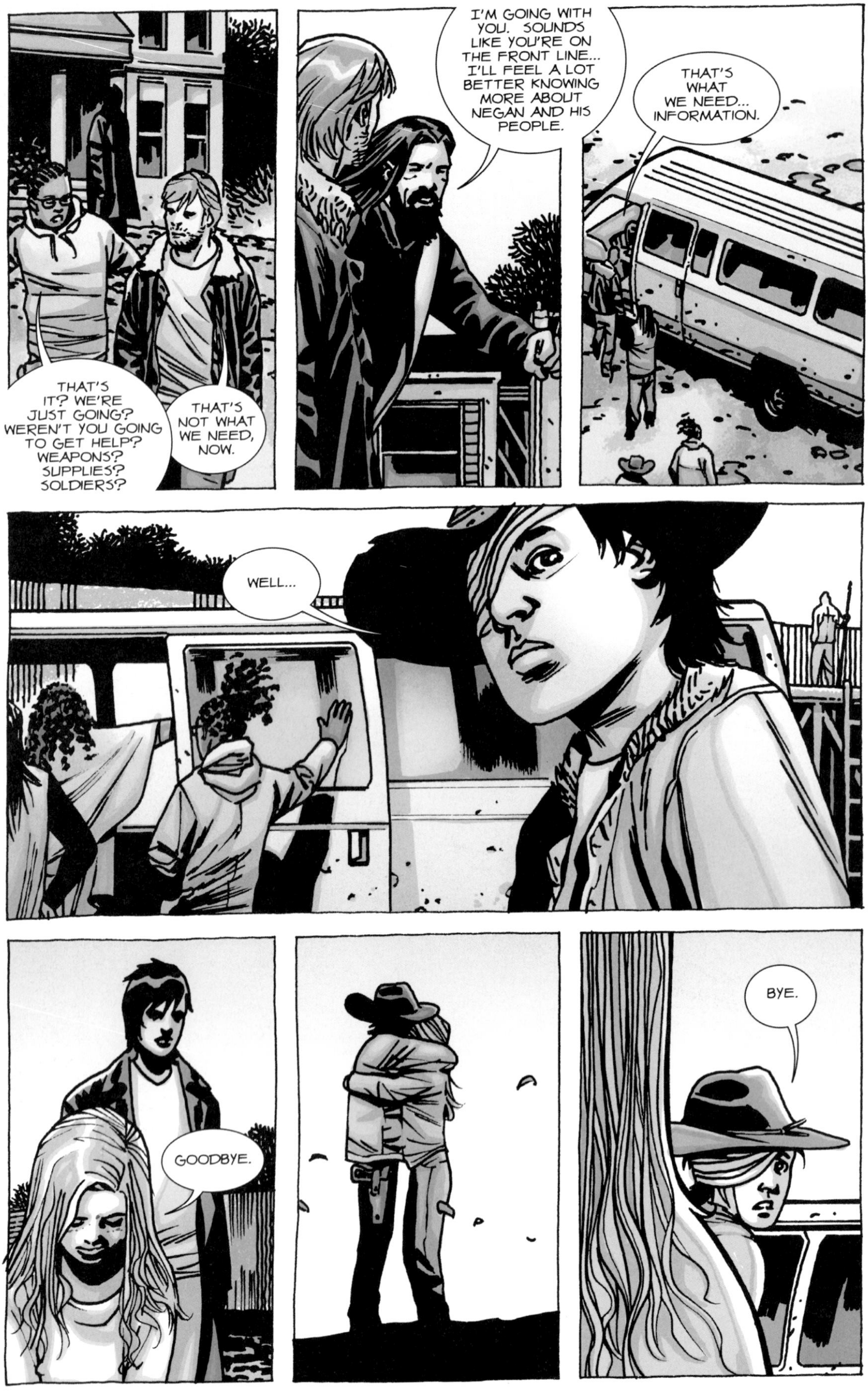
THAT'S IT? WE'RE JUST GOING? WEREN'T YOU GOING TO GET HELP? WEAPONS? SUPPLIES? SOLDIERS?
THAT'S NOT WHAT WE NEED, NOW.
I'M GOING WITH YOU. SOUNDS LIKE YOU'RE ON THE FRONT LINE... I'LL FEEL A LOT BETTER KNOWING MORE ABOUT NEGAN AND HIS PEOPLE.
THAT'S WHAT WE NEED... INFORMATION.
WELL...
GOODBYE.
BYE.

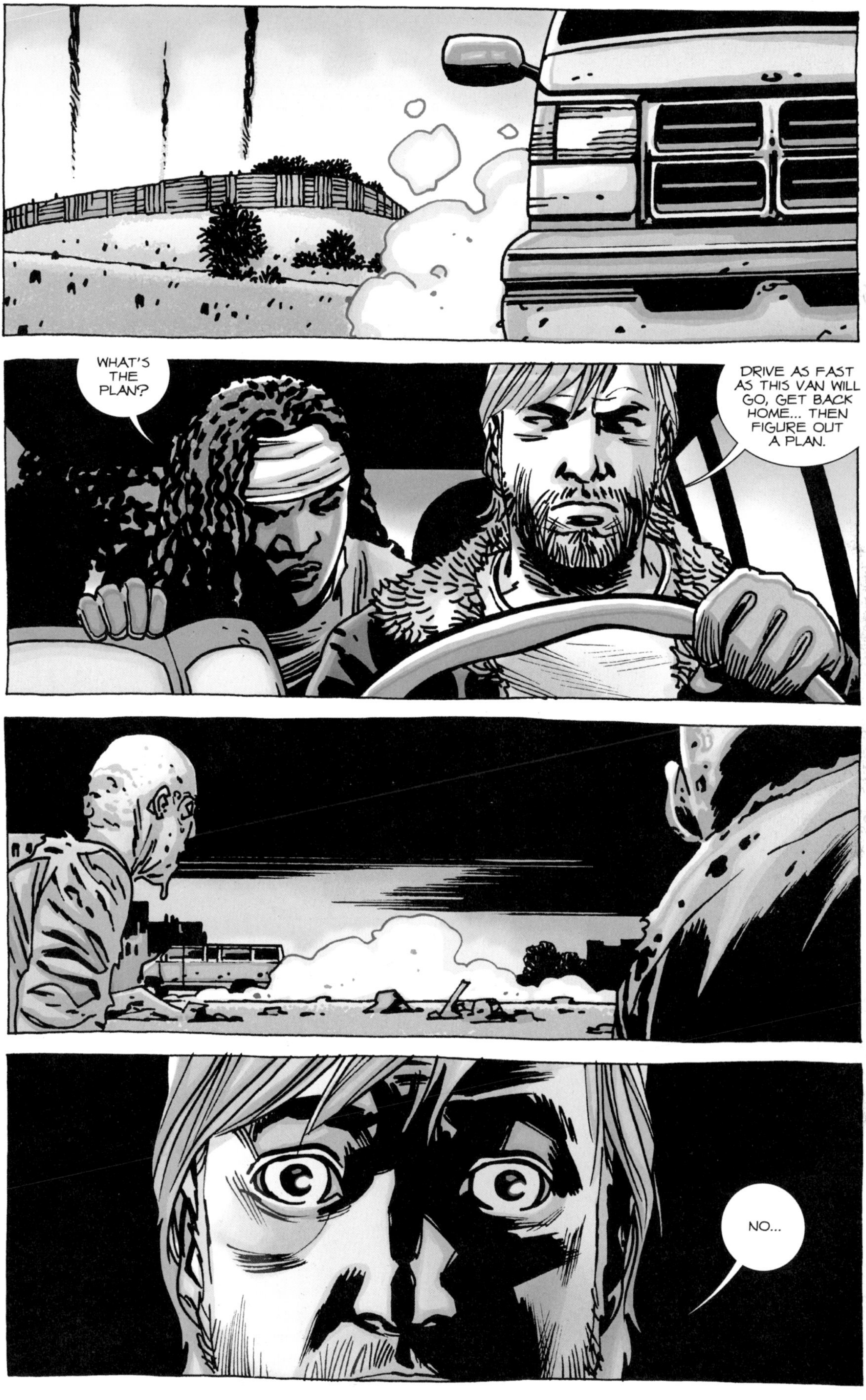
WHAT'S THE PLAN?
DRIVE AS FAST AS THIS VAN WILL GO, GET BACK HOME... THEN FIGURE OUT A PLAN.
NO...

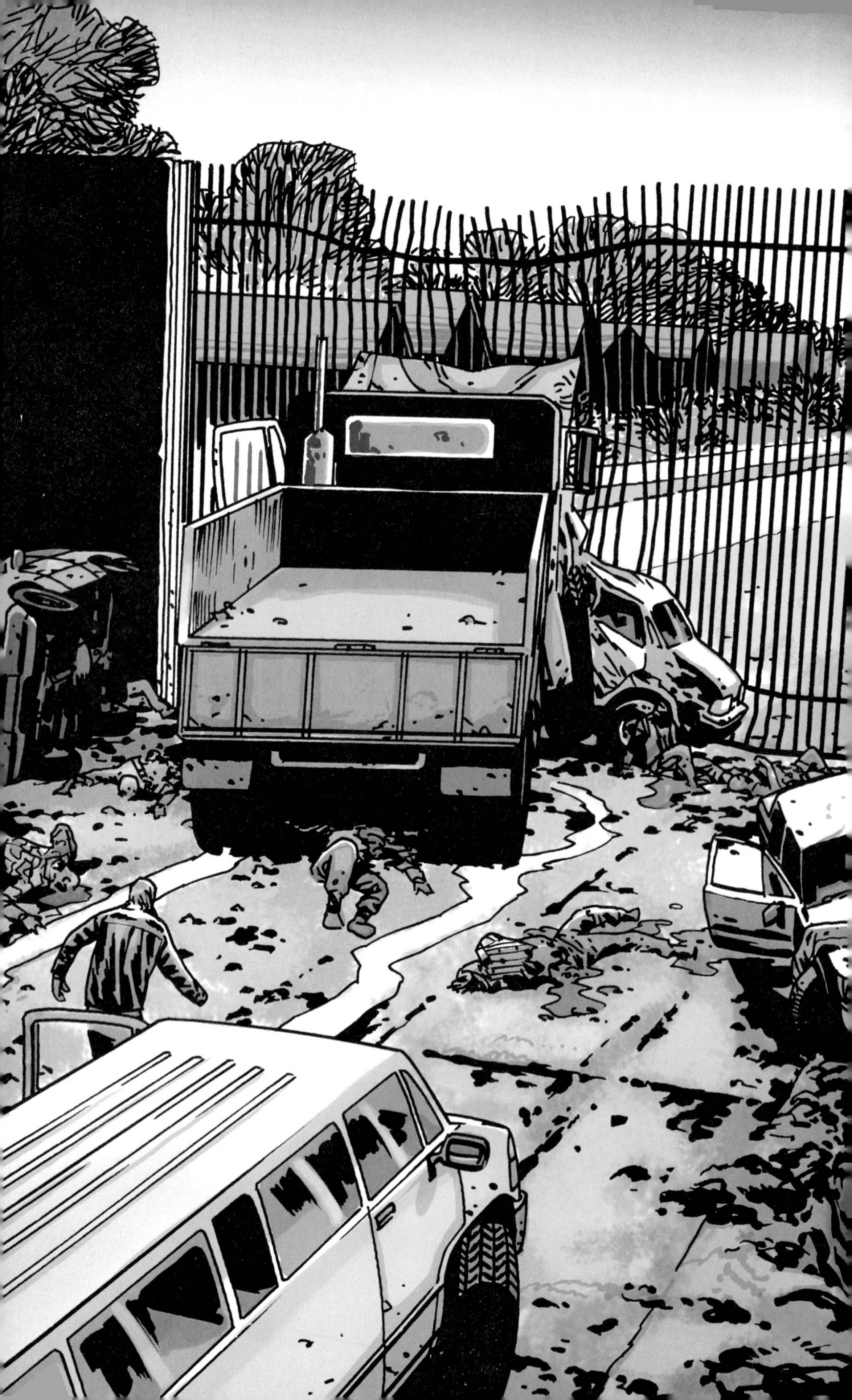

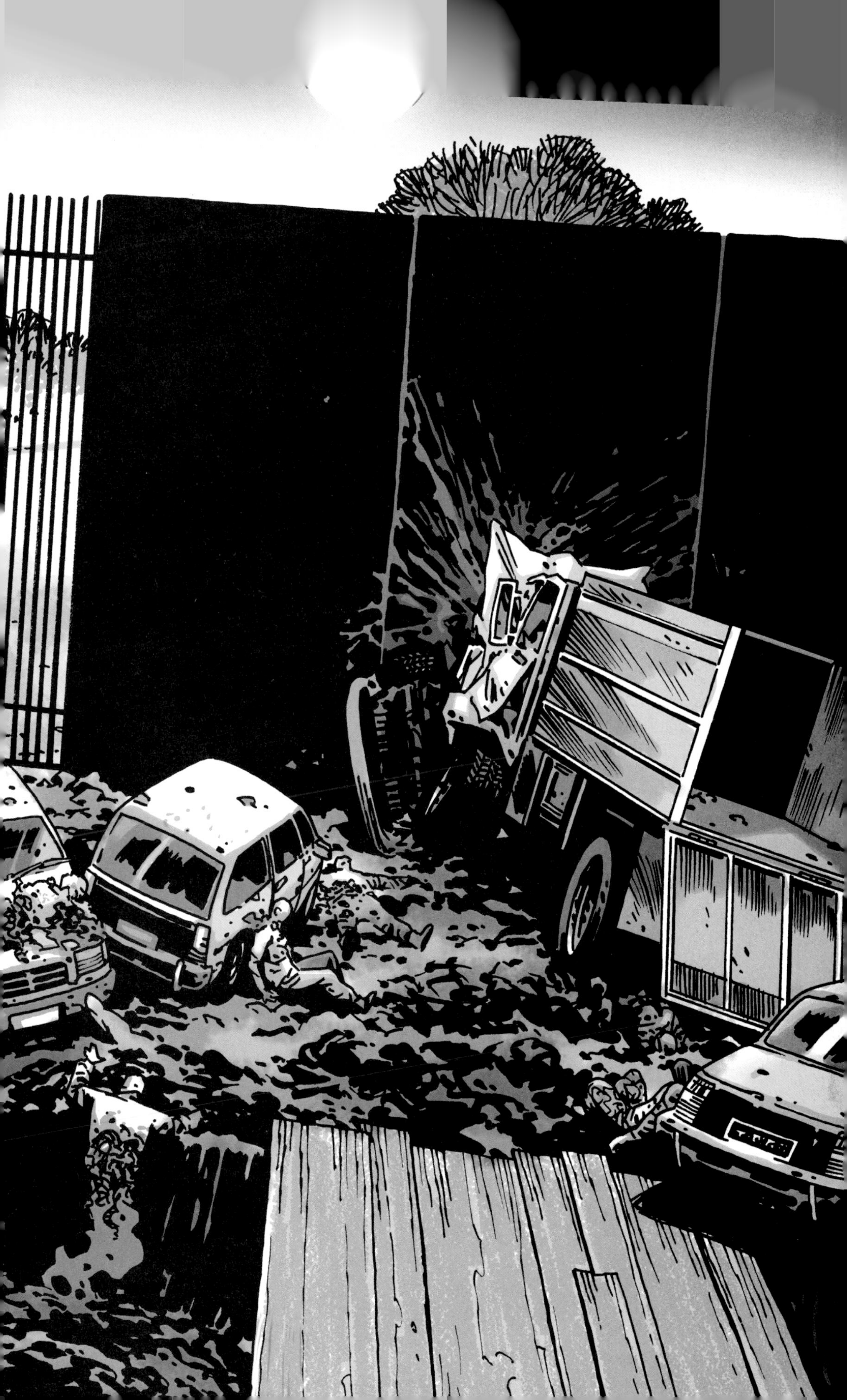

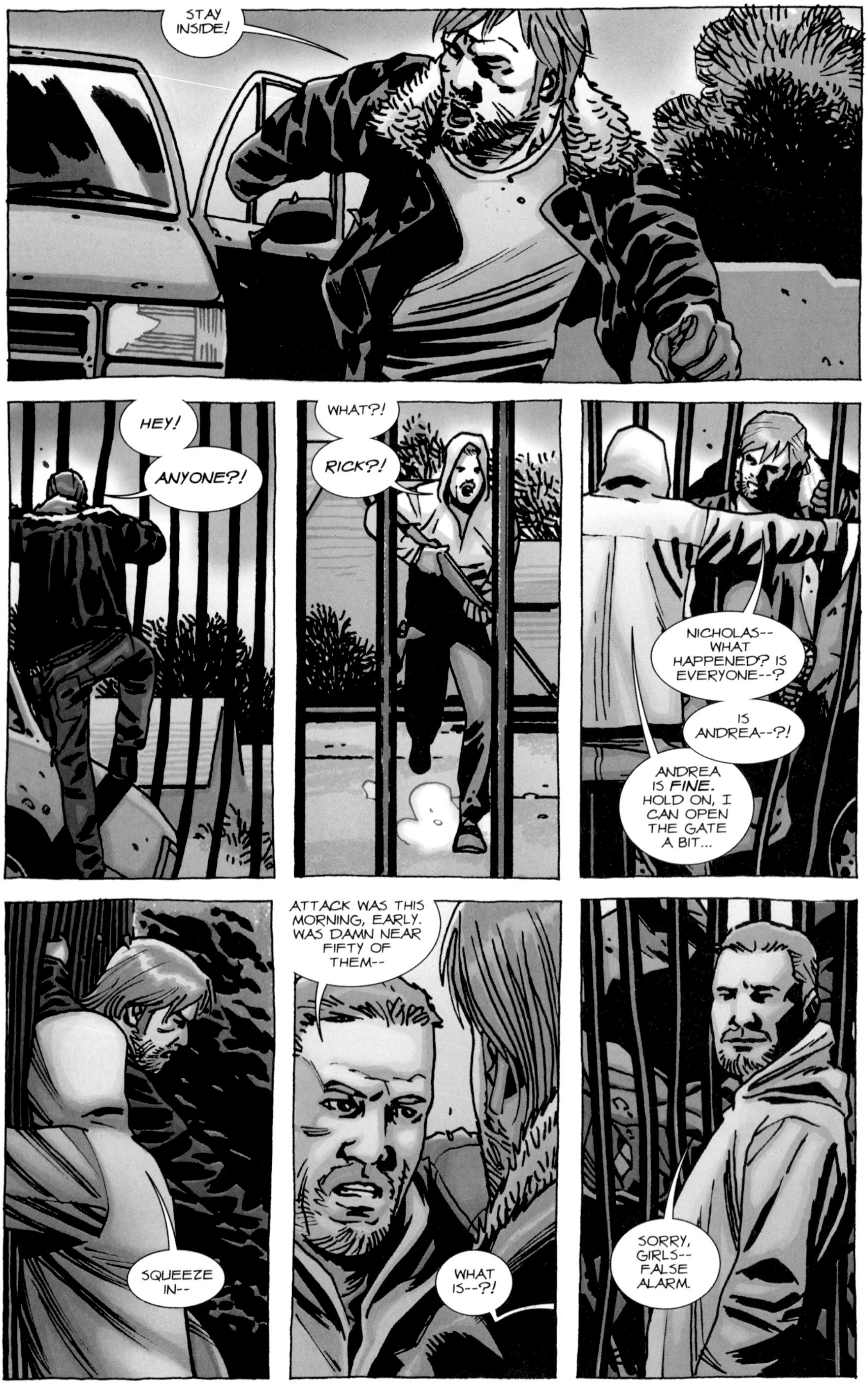
STAY INSIDE!
HEY!
ANYONE?!
WHAT?!
RICK?!
NICHOLAS-- WHAT HAPPENED? IS EVERYONE--?
IS ANDREA--?!
ANDREA IS FINE. HOLD ON, I CAN OPEN THE GATE A BIT...
SQUEEZE IN--
ATTACK WAS THIS MORNING, EARLY. WAS DAMN NEAR FIFTY OF THEM--
WHAT IS--?!
SORRY, GIRLS-- FALSE ALARM.

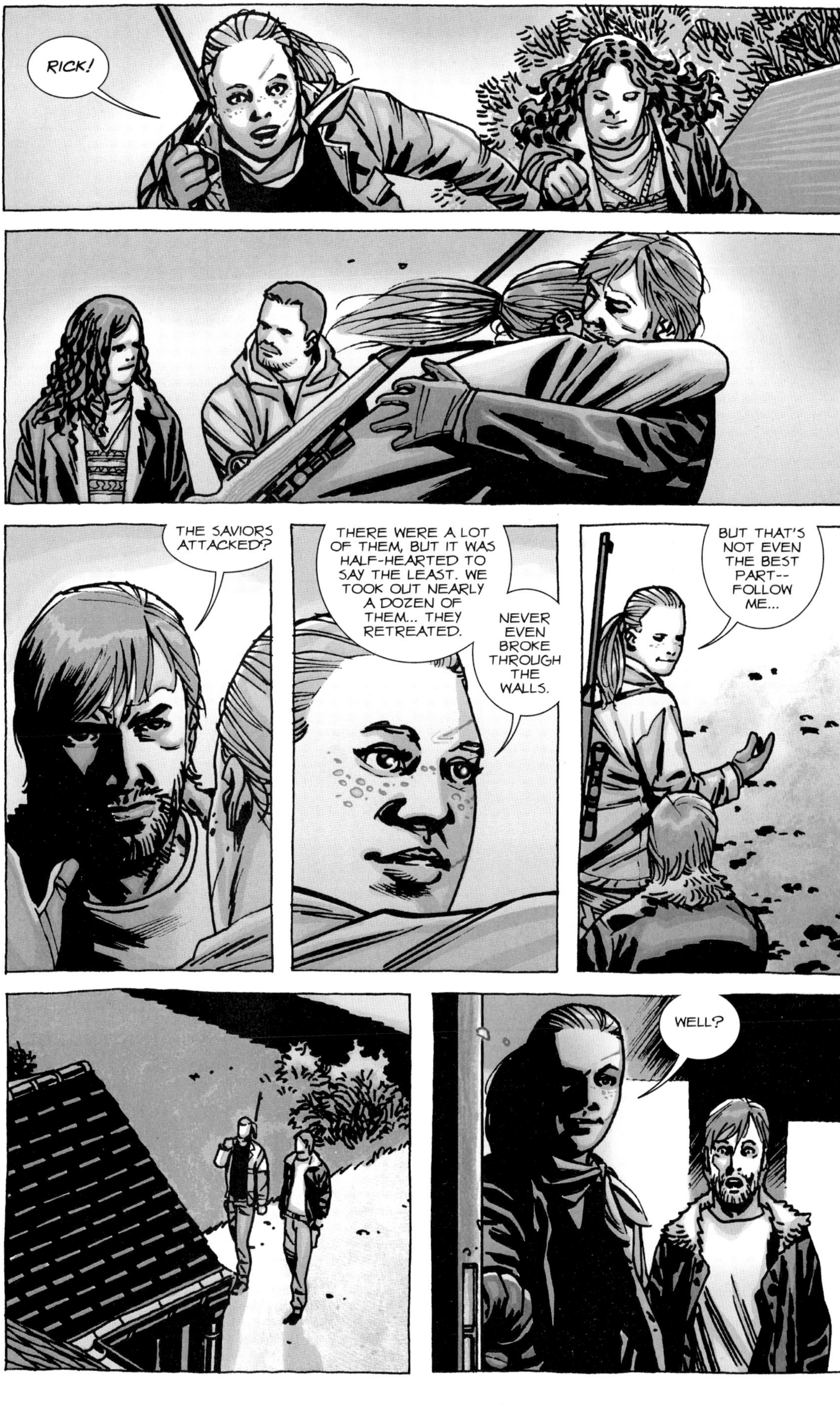
RICK!
THE SAVIORS ATTACKED?
THERE WERE A LOT OF THEM, BUT IT WAS HALF-HEARTED TO SAY THE LEAST. WE TOOK OUT NEARLY A DOZEN OF THEM... THEY RETREATED.
NEVER EVEN BROKE THROUGH THE WALLS.
BUT THAT'S NOT EVEN THE BEST PART-- FOLLOW ME...
WELL?

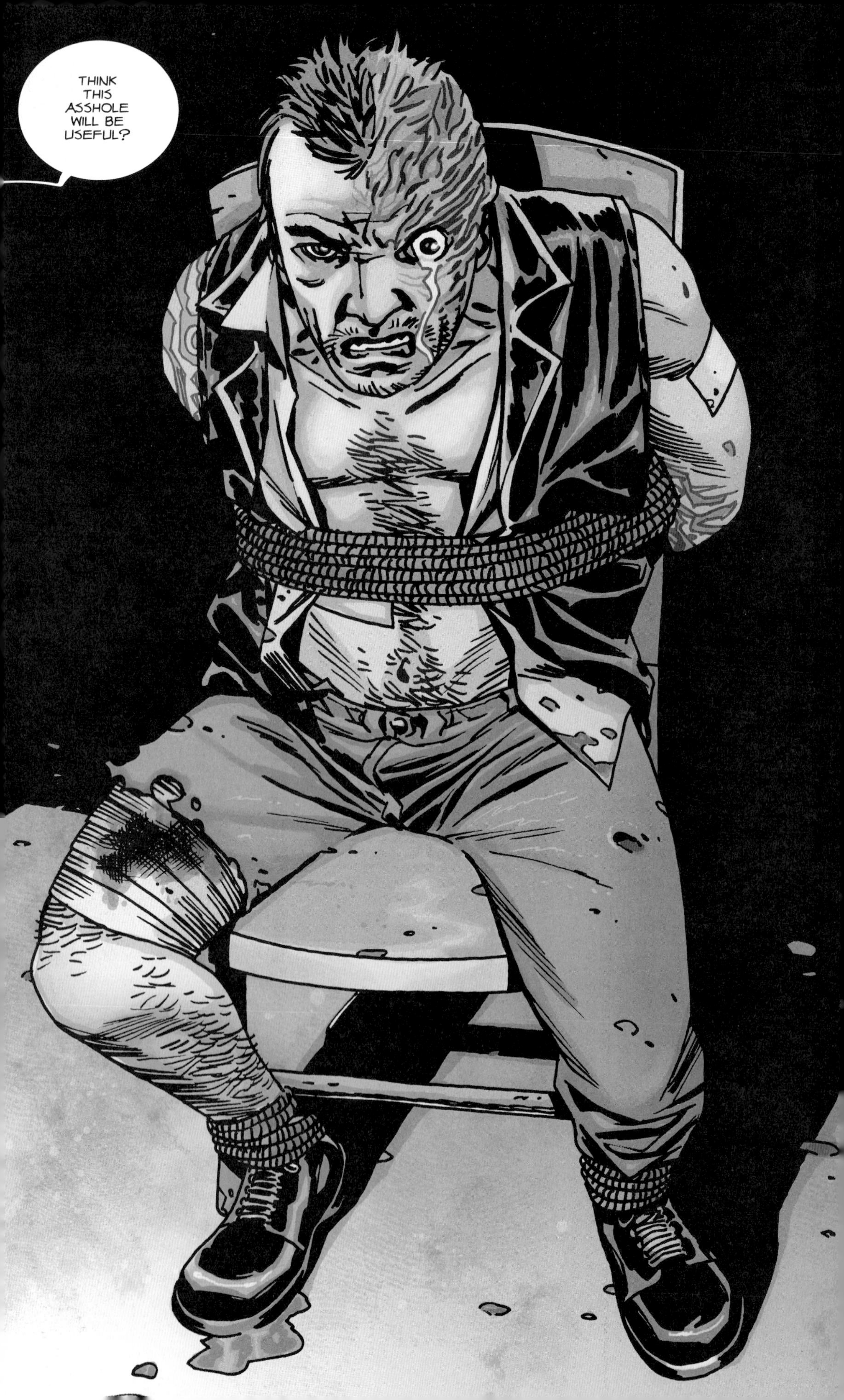
THINK THIS ASSHOLE WILL BE USEFUL?

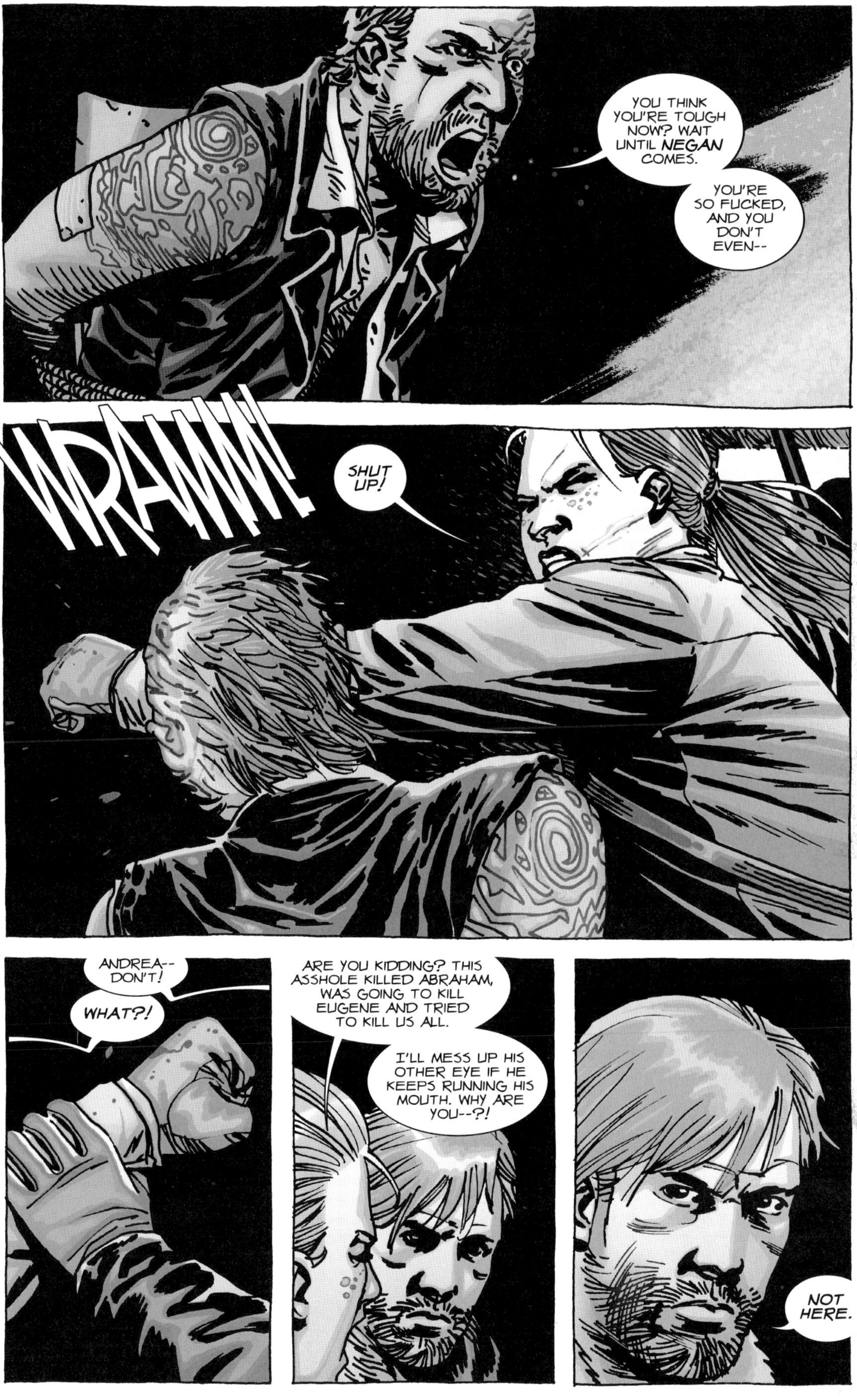
YOU THINK YOU'RE TOUGH NOW? WAIT UNTIL NEGAN COMES.
YOU'RE SO FUCKED, AND YOU DON'T EVEN--
WRAMM!
SHUT UP!
ANDREA-- DON'T!
WHAT?!
ARE YOU KIDDING? THIS ASSHOLE KILLED ABRAHAM, WAS GOING TO KILL EUGENE AND TRIED TO KILL US ALL.
I'LL MESS UP HIS OTHER EYE IF HE KEEPS RUNNING HIS MOUTH. WHY ARE YOU--?!
NOT HERE.

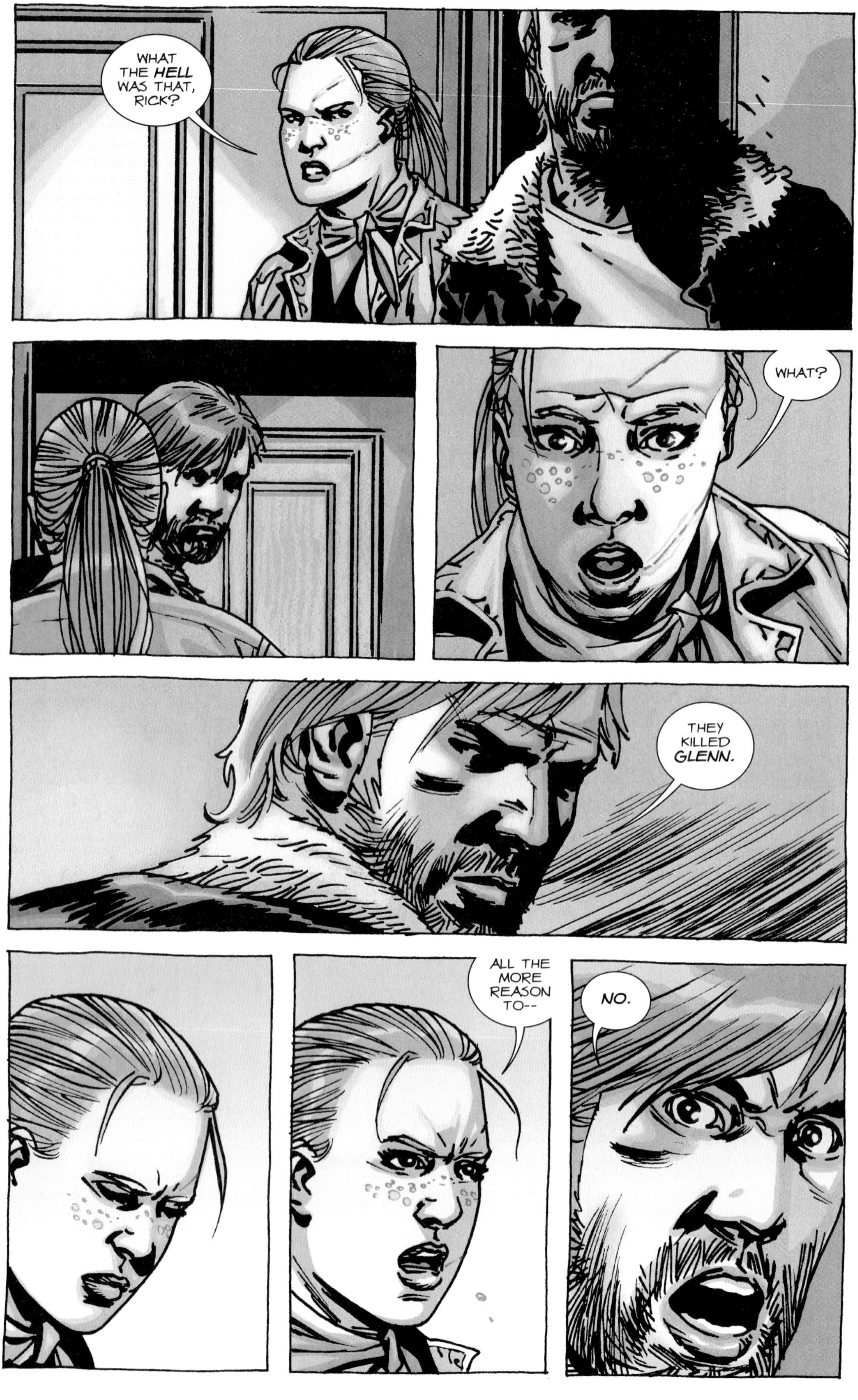

WHAT THE HELL WAS THAT, RICK?
WHAT?
THEY KILLED GLENN.
ALL THE MORE REASON TO--
NO.

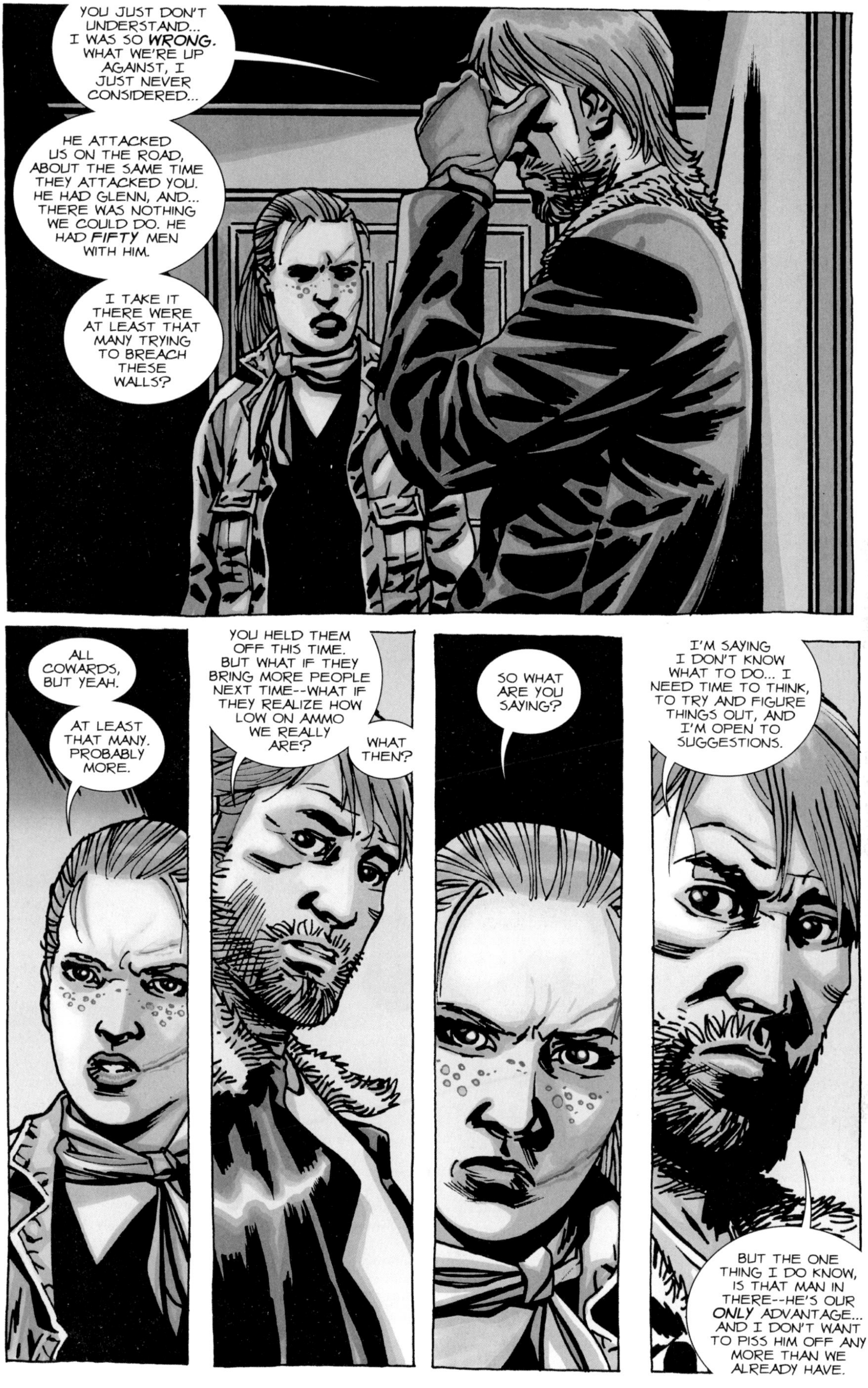
YOU JUST DON'T UNDERSTAND... I WAS SO WRONG. WHAT WE'RE UP AGAINST, I JUST NEVER CONSIDERED...
HE ATTACKED US ON THE ROAD, ABOUT THE SAME TIME THEY ATTACKED YOU. HE HAD GLENN, AND... THERE WAS NOTHING WE COULD DO. HE HAD FIFTY MEN WITH HIM.
I TAKE IT THERE WERE AT LEAST THAT MANY TRYING TO BREACH THESE WALLS?
ALL COWARDS, BUT YEAH.
AT LEAST THAT MANY. PROBABLY MORE.
YOU HELD THEM OFF THIS TIME. BUT WHAT IF THEY BRING MORE PEOPLE NEXT TIME--WHAT IF THEY REALIZE HOW LOW ON AMMO WE REALLY ARE?
WHAT THEN?
SO WHAT ARE YOU SAYING?
I'M SAYING I DON'T KNOW WHAT TO DO... I NEED TIME TO THINK, TO TRY AND FIGURE THINGS OUT, AND I'M OPEN TO SUGGESTIONS.
BUT THE ONE THING I DO KNOW, IS THAT MAN IN THERE--HE'S OUR ONLY ADVANTAGE... AND I DON'T WANT TO PISS HIM OFF ANY MORE THAN WE ALREADY HAVE.

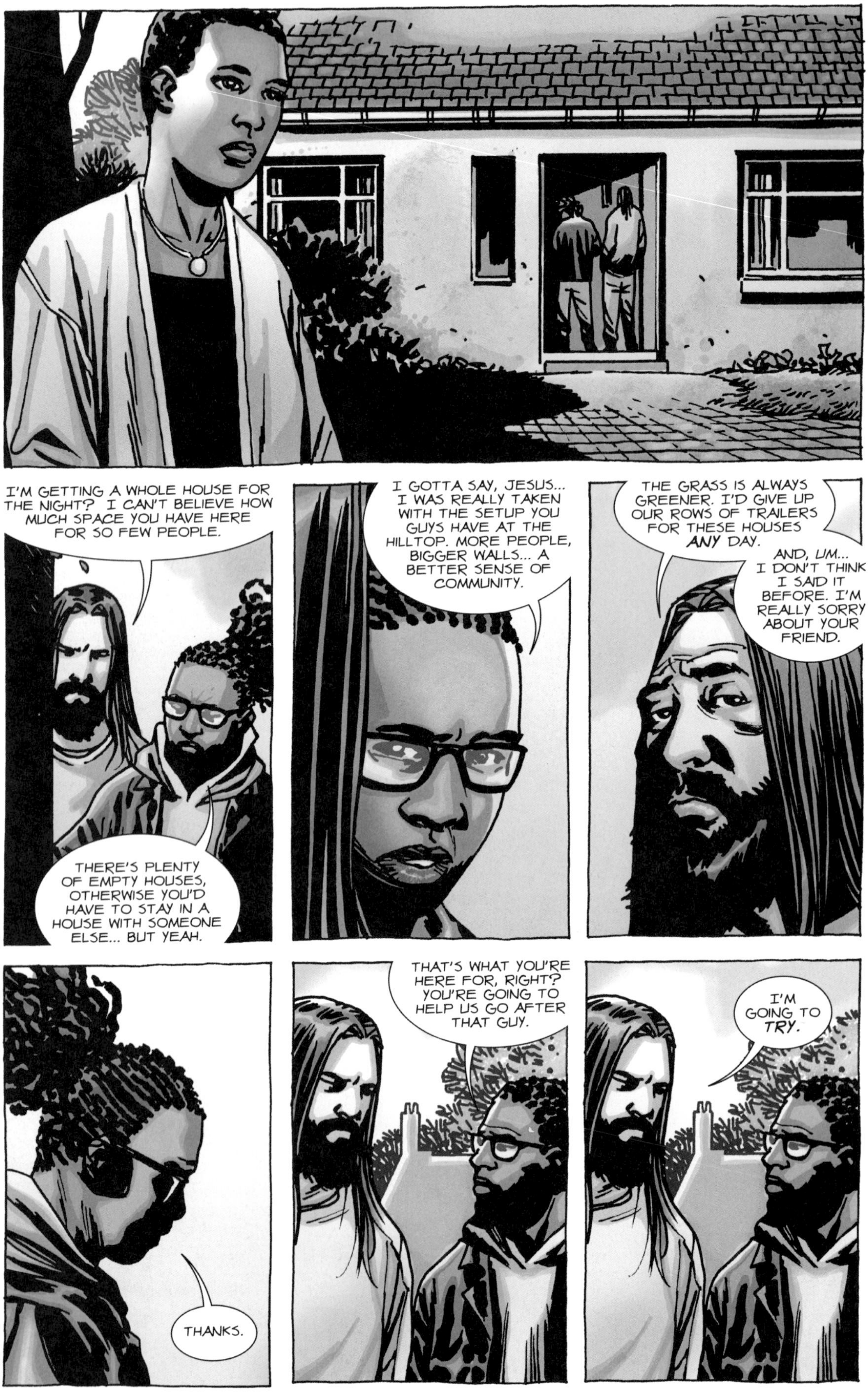

I'M GETTING A WHOLE HOUSE FOR THE NIGHT? I CAN'T BELIEVE HOW MUCH SPACE YOU HAVE HERE FOR SO FEW PEOPLE.
THERE'S PLENTY OF EMPTY HOUSES, OTHERWISE YOU'D HAVE TO STAY IN A HOUSE WITH SOMEONE ELSE... BUT YEAH.
I GOTTA SAY, JESUS... I WAS REALLY TAKEN WITH THE SETUP YOU GUYS HAVE AT THE HILLTOP. MORE PEOPLE, BIGGER WALLS... A BETTER SENSE OF COMMUNITY.
THE GRASS IS ALWAYS GREENER. I'D GIVE UP OUR ROWS OF TRAILERS FOR THESE HOUSES ANY DAY.
AND, UM... I DON'T THINK I SAID IT BEFORE. I'M REALLY SORRY ABOUT YOUR FRIEND.
THANKS.
THAT'S WHAT YOU'RE HERE FOR, RIGHT? YOU'RE GOING TO HELP US GO AFTER THAT GUY.
I'M GOING TO TRY.

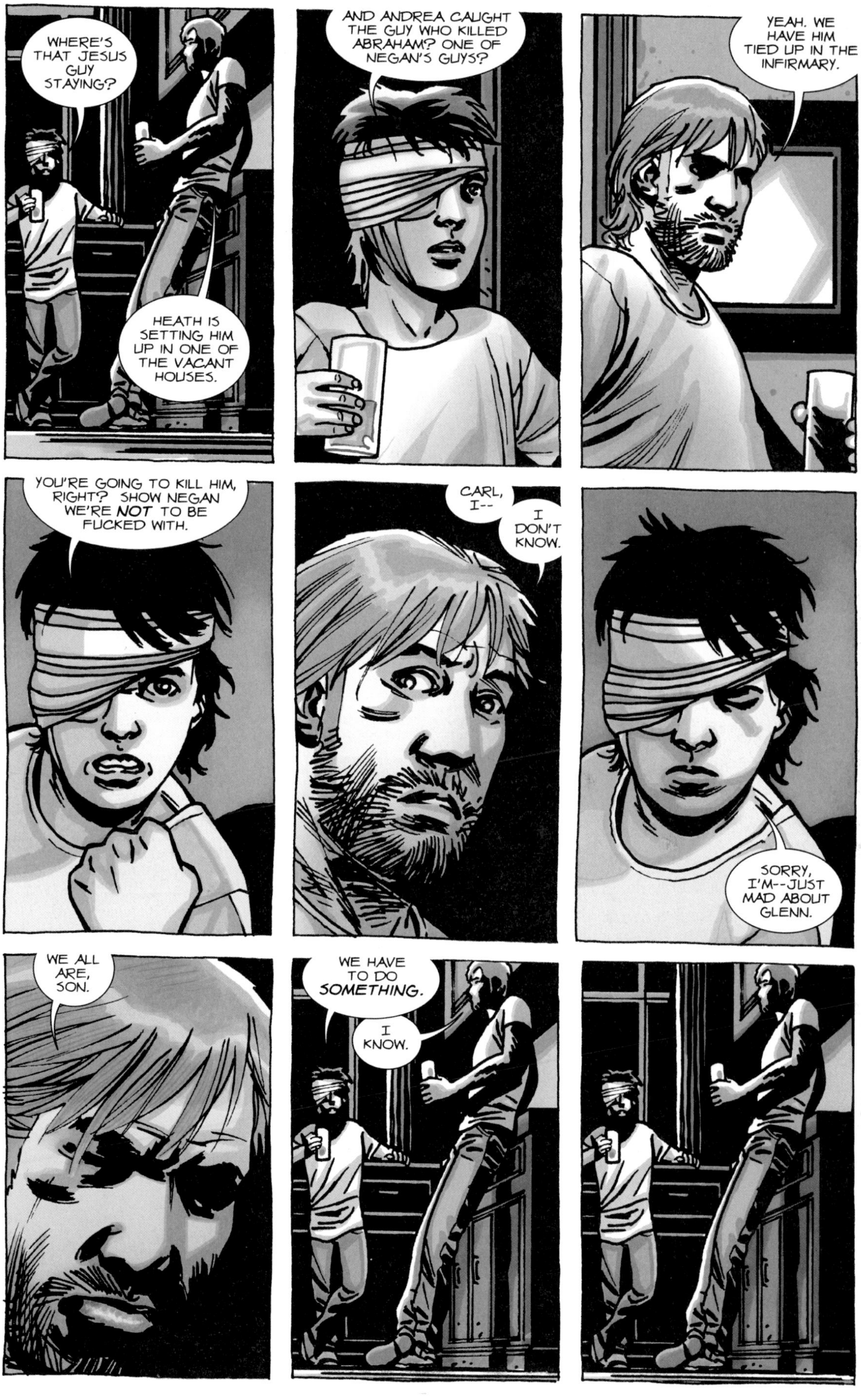

WHERE'S THAT JESUS GUY STAYING?
HEATH IS SETTING HIM UP IN ONE OF THE VACANT HOUSES.
AND ANDREA CAUGHT THE GUY WHO KILLED ABRAHAM? ONE OF NEGAN'S GUYS?
YEAH. WE HAVE HIM TIED UP IN THE INFIRMARY.
YOU'RE GOING TO KILL HIM, RIGHT? SHOW NEGAN WE'RE NOT TO BE FUCKED WITH.
CARL, I--
I DON'T KNOW.
SORRY, I'M--JUST MAD ABOUT GLENN.
WE ALL ARE, SON.
WE HAVE TO DO SOMETHING.
I KNOW.

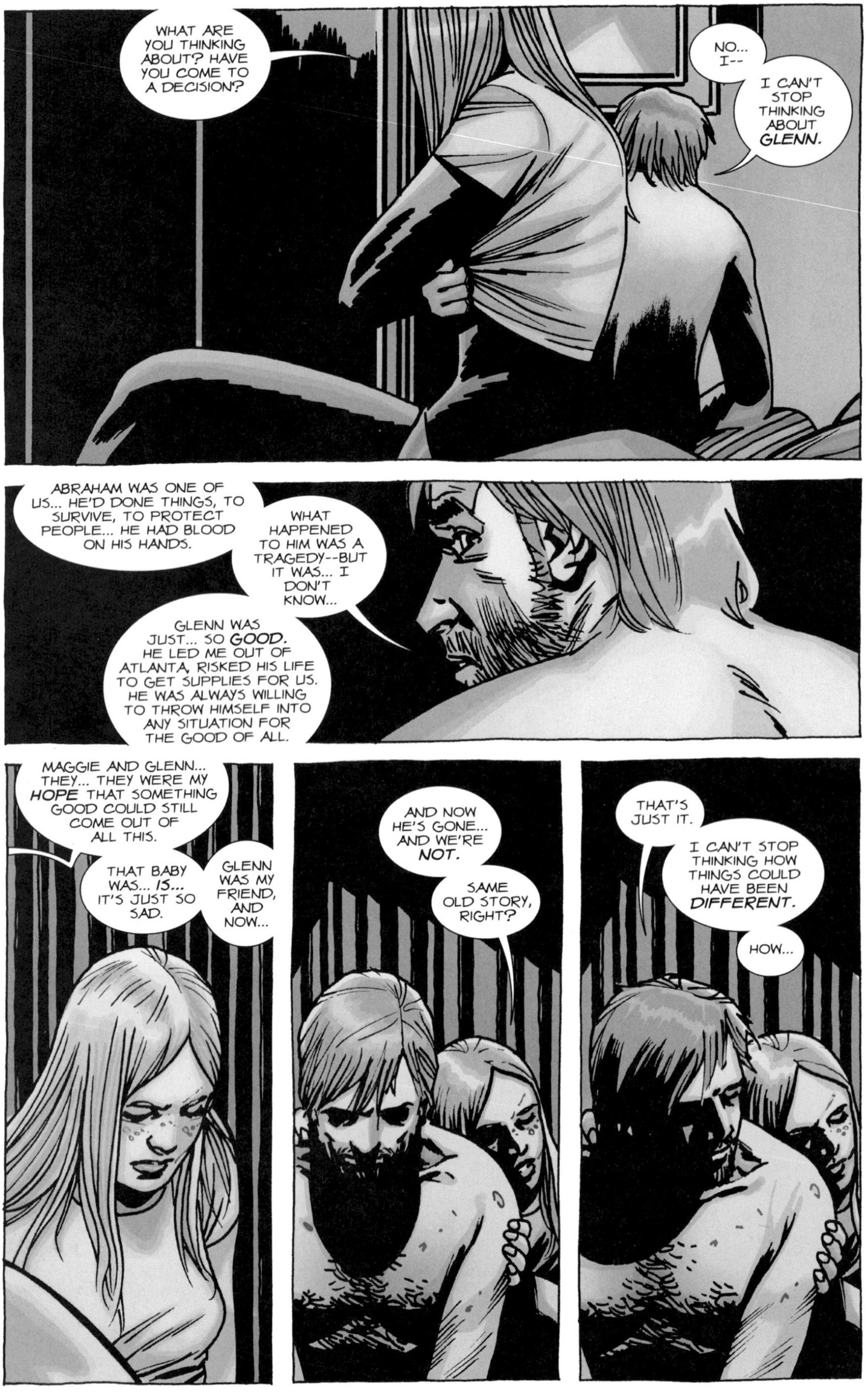

WHAT ARE YOU THINKING ABOUT? HAVE YOU COME TO A DECISION?
NO... I--
I CAN'T STOP THINKING ABOUT GLENN.
ABRAHAM WAS ONE OF US... HE'D DONE THINGS, TO SURVIVE, TO PROTECT PEOPLE... HE HAD BLOOD ON HIS HANDS.
WHAT HAPPENED TO HIM WAS A TRAGEDY--BUT IT WAS... I DON'T KNOW...
GLENN WAS JUST... SO GOOD. HE LED ME OUT OF ATLANTA, RISKED HIS LIFE TO GET SUPPLIES FOR US. HE WAS ALWAYS WILLING TO THROW HIMSELF INTO ANY SITUATION FOR THE GOOD OF ALL.
MAGGIE AND GLENN... THEY... THEY WERE MY HOPE THAT SOMETHING GOOD COULD STILL COME OUT OF ALL THIS.
THAT BABY WAS... IS... IT'S JUST SO SAD.
GLENN WAS MY FRIEND, AND NOW...
AND NOW HE'S GONE... AND WE'RE NOT.
SAME OLD STORY, RIGHT?
THAT'S JUST IT.
I CAN'T STOP THINKING HOW THINGS COULD HAVE BEEN DIFFERENT.
HOW...

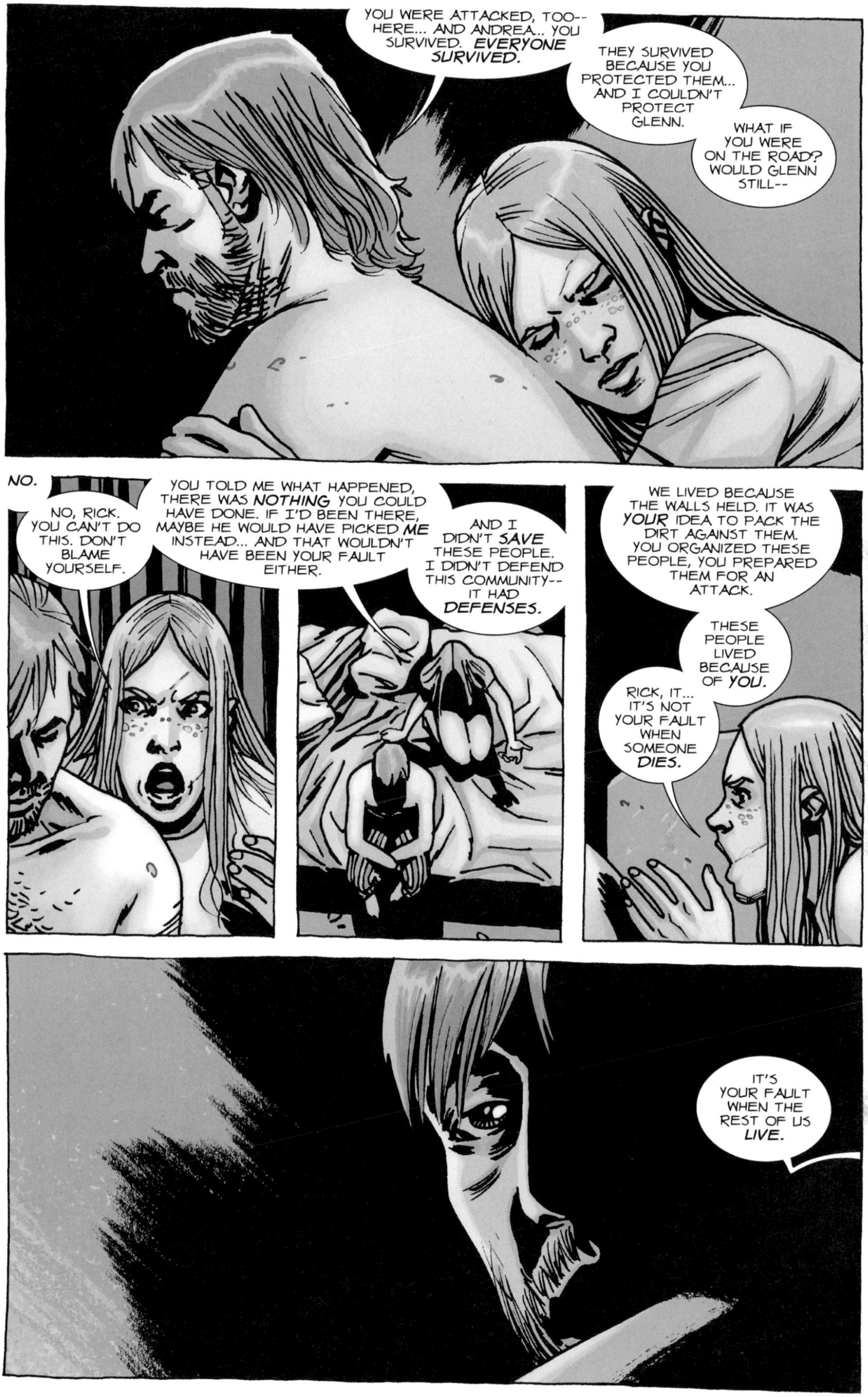

YOU WERE ATTACKED, TOO-- HERE... AND ANDREA... YOU SURVIVED. EVERYONE SURVIVED.
THEY SURVIVED BECAUSE YOU PROTECTED THEM... AND I COULDN'T PROTECT GLENN.
WHAT IF YOU WERE ON THE ROAD? WOULD GLENN STILL--
NO.
NO, RICK. YOU CAN'T DO THIS. DON'T BLAME YOURSELF.
YOU TOLD ME WHAT HAPPENED, THERE WAS NOTHING YOU COULD HAVE DONE. IF I'D BEEN THERE, MAYBE HE WOULD HAVE PICKED ME INSTEAD... AND THAT WOULDN'T HAVE BEEN YOUR FAULT EITHER.
AND I DIDN'T SAVE THESE PEOPLE. I DIDN'T DEFEND THIS COMMUNITY-- IT HAD DEFENSES.
WE LIVED BECAUSE THE WALLS HELD. IT WAS YOUR IDEA TO PACK THE DIRT AGAINST THEM. YOU ORGANIZED THESE PEOPLE, YOU PREPARED THEM FOR AN ATTACK.
THESE PEOPLE LIVED BECAUSE OF YOU.
RICK, IT... IT'S NOT YOUR FAULT WHEN SOMEONE DIES.
IT'S YOUR FAULT WHEN THE REST OF US LIVE.

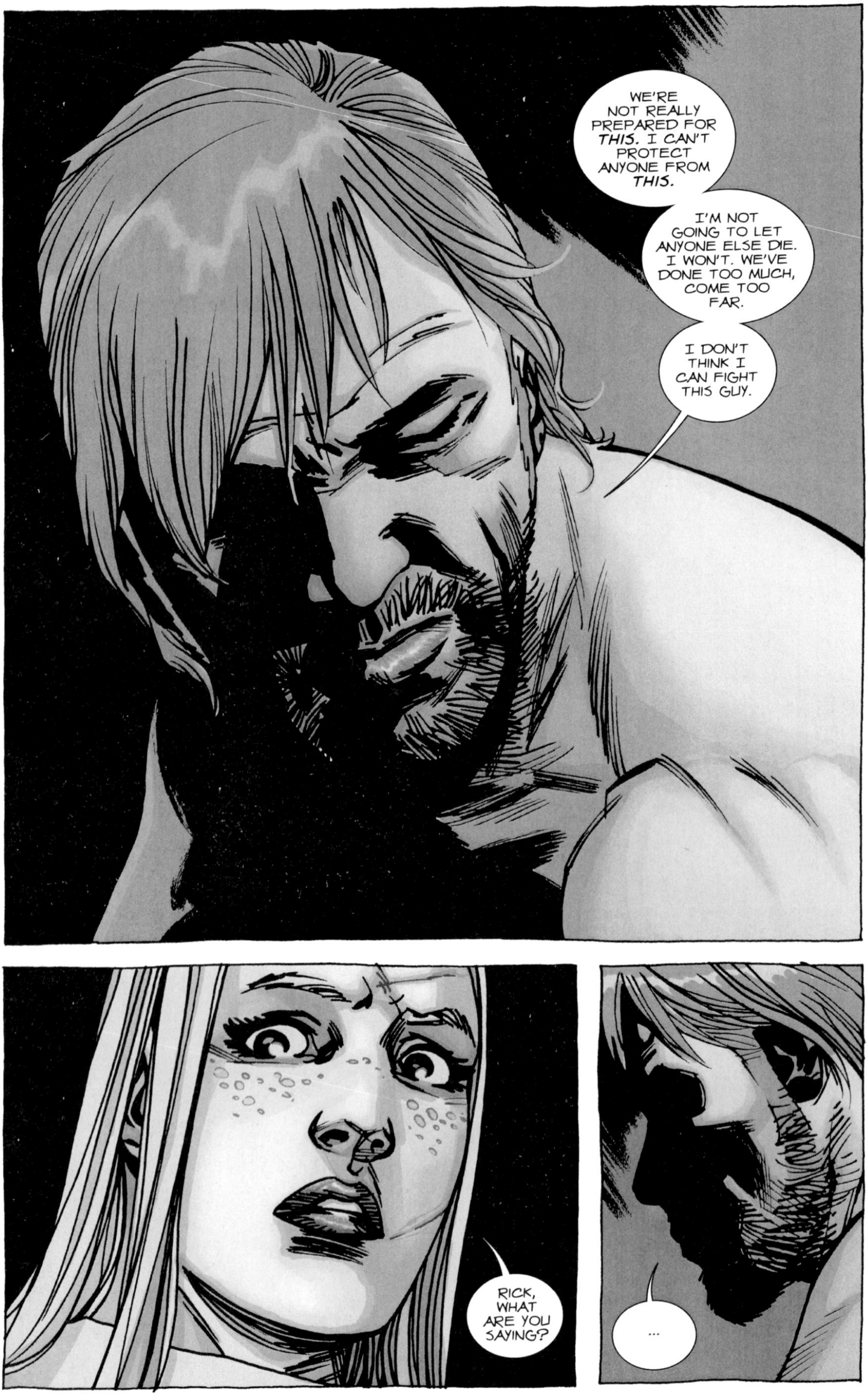
WE'RE NOT REALLY PREPARED FOR THIS. I CAN'T PROTECT ANYONE FROM THIS.
I'M NOT GOING TO LET ANYONE ELSE DIE. I WON'T. WE'VE DONE TOO MUCH, COME TOO FAR.
I DON'T THINK I CAN FIGHT THIS GUY.
RICK, WHAT ARE YOU SAYING?
...

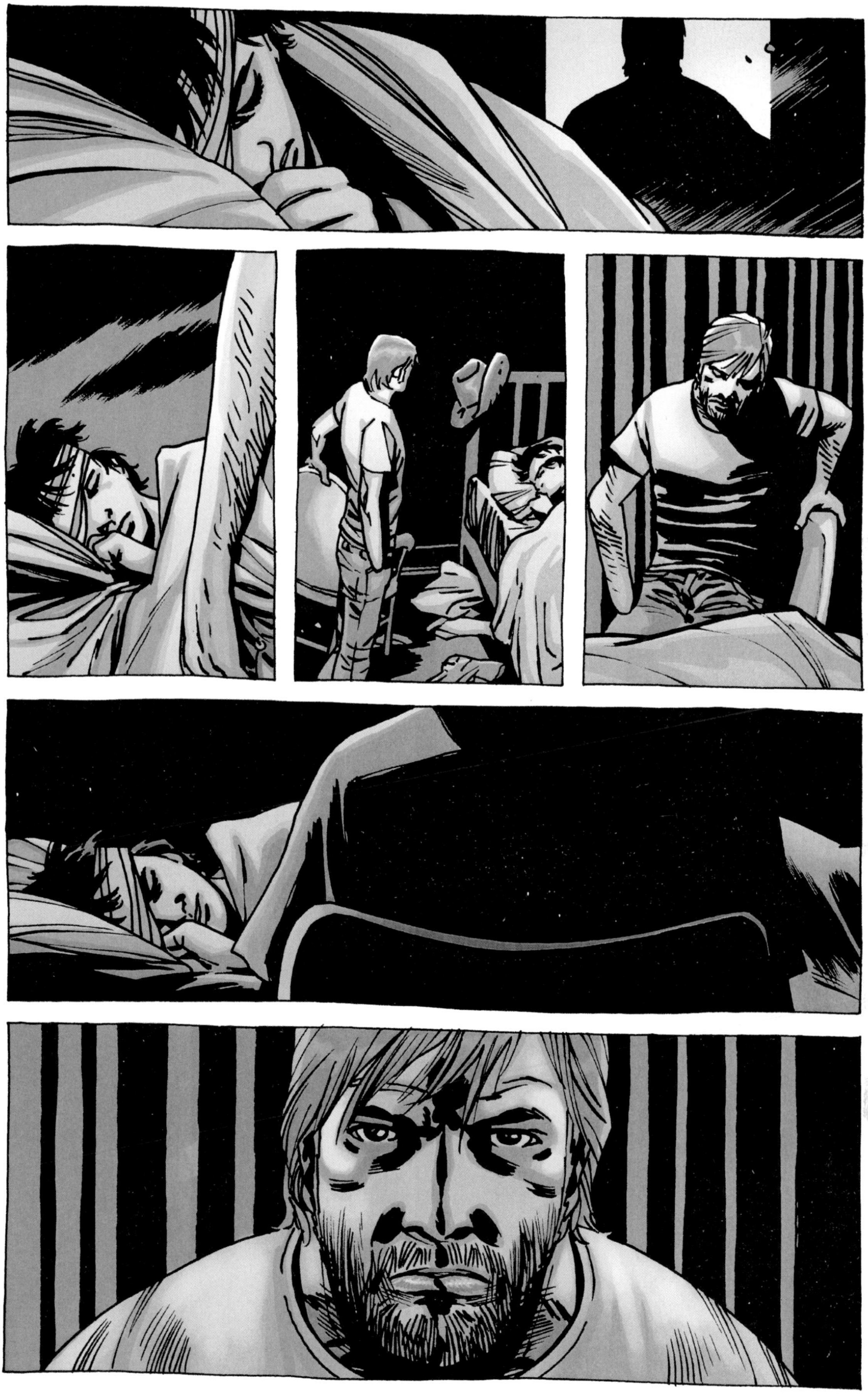

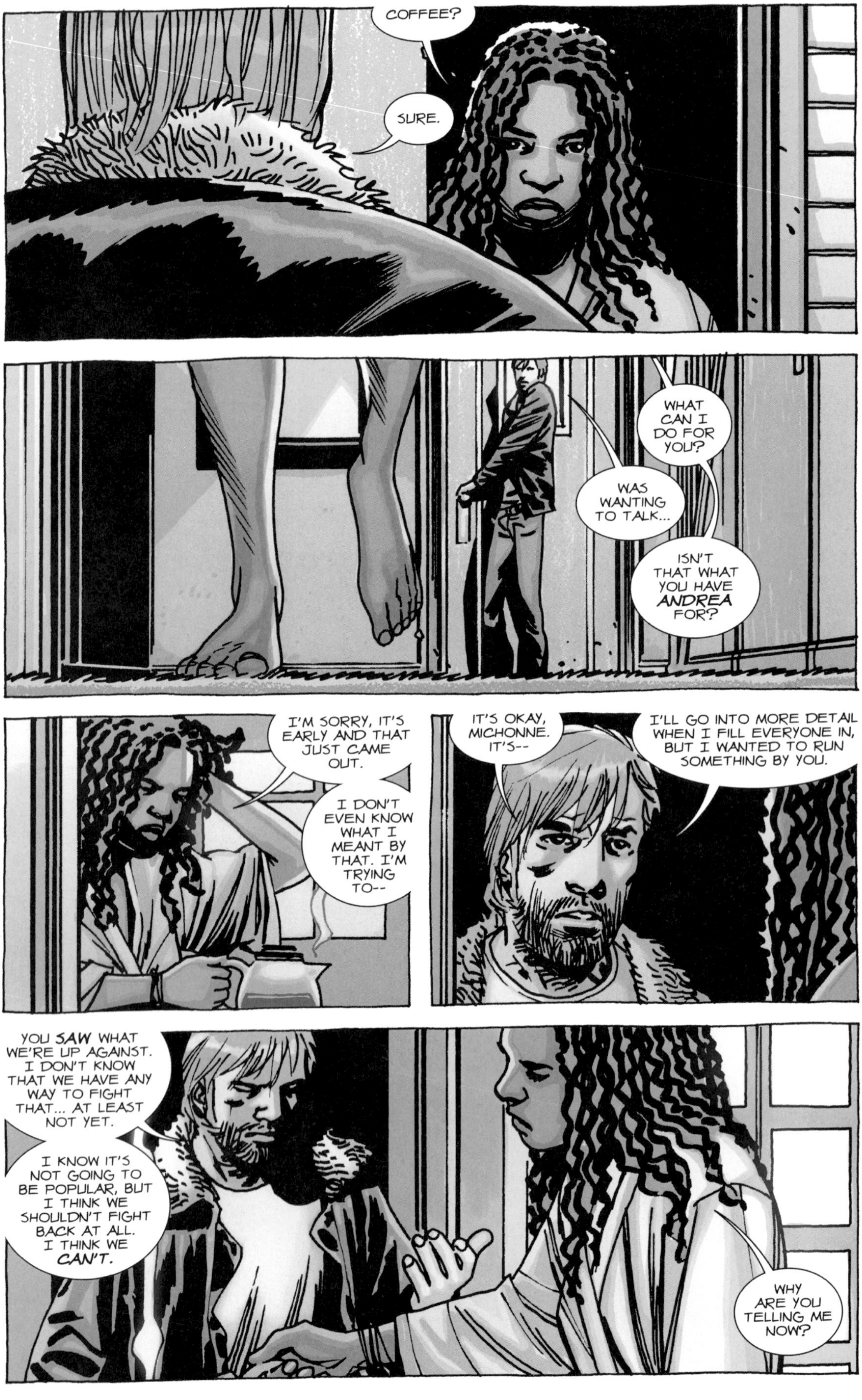

COFFEE?
SURE.
WHAT CAN I DO FOR YOU?
WAS WANTING TO TALK...
ISN'T THAT WHAT YOU HAVE ANDREA FOR?
I'M SORRY, IT'S EARLY AND THAT JUST CAME OUT.
I DON'T EVEN KNOW WHAT I MEANT BY THAT. I'M TRYING TO--
IT'S OKAY, MICHONNE. IT'S--
I'LL GO INTO MORE DETAIL WHEN I FILL EVERYONE IN, BUT I WANTED TO RUN SOMETHING BY YOU.
YOU SAW WHAT WE'RE UP AGAINST. I DON'T KNOW THAT WE HAVE ANY WAY TO FIGHT THAT... AT LEAST NOT YET.
I KNOW IT'S NOT GOING TO BE POPULAR, BUT I THINK WE SHOULDN'T FIGHT BACK AT ALL. I THINK WE CAN'T.
WHY ARE YOU TELLING ME NOW?

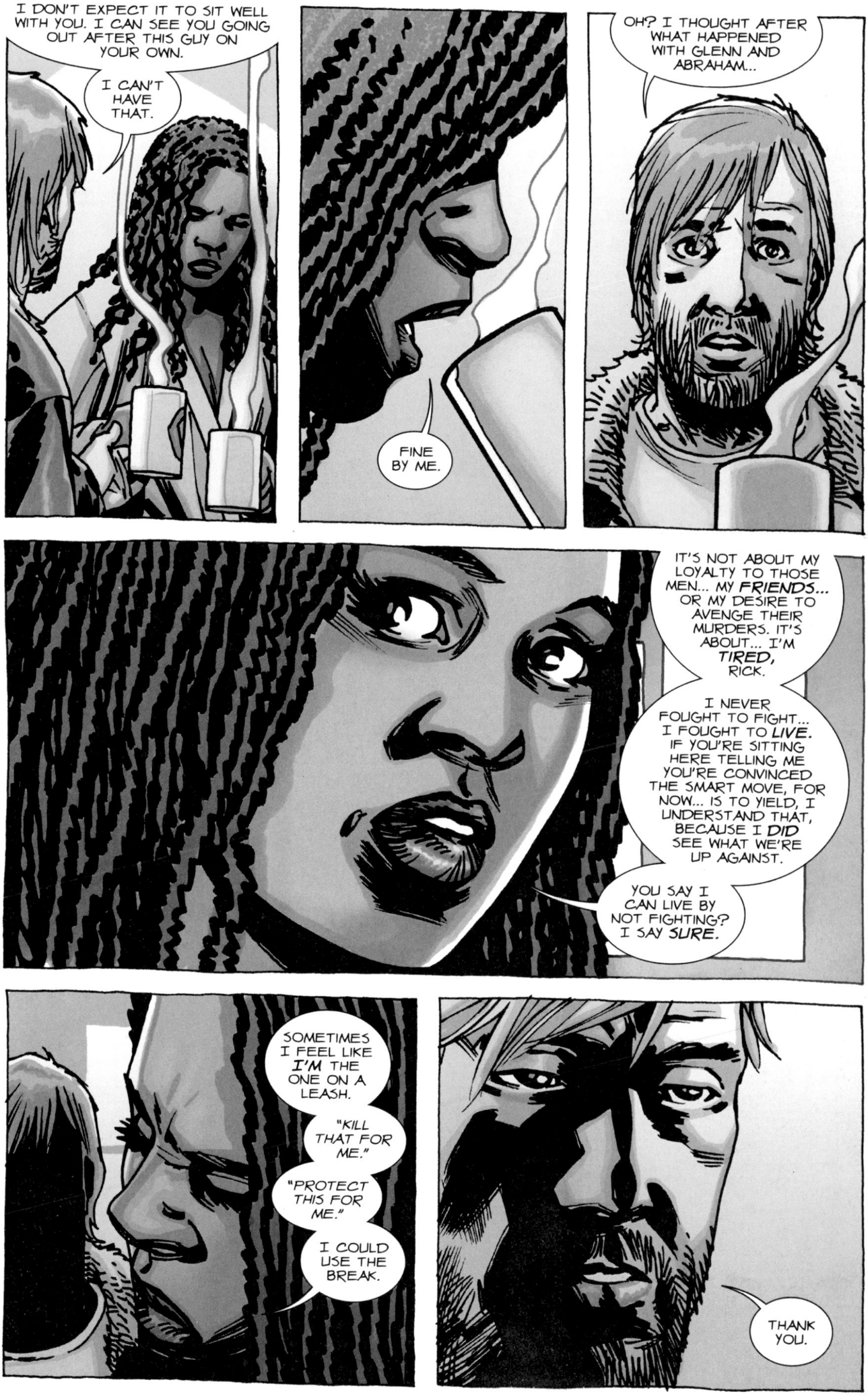
I DON'T EXPECT IT TO SIT WELL WITH YOU. I CAN SEE YOU GOING OUT AFTER THIS GUY ON YOUR OWN.
I CAN'T HAVE THAT.
FINE BY ME.
OH? I THOUGHT AFTER WHAT HAPPENED WITH GLENN AND ABRAHAM...
IT'S NOT ABOUT MY LOYALTY TO THOSE MEN... MY FRIENDS... OR MY DESIRE TO AVENGE THEIR MURDERS. IT'S ABOUT... I'M TIRED, RICK.
I NEVER FOUGHT TO FIGHT... I FOUGHT TO LIVE. IF YOU'RE SITTING HERE TELLING ME YOU'RE CONVINCED THE SMART MOVE, FOR NOW... IS TO YIELD, I UNDERSTAND THAT, BECAUSE I DID SEE WHAT WE'RE UP AGAINST.
YOU SAY I CAN LIVE BY NOT FIGHTING? I SAY SURE.
SOMETIMES I FEEL LIKE I'M THE ONE ON A LEASH.
"KILL THAT FOR ME."
"PROTECT THIS FOR ME."
I COULD USE THE BREAK.
THANK YOU.

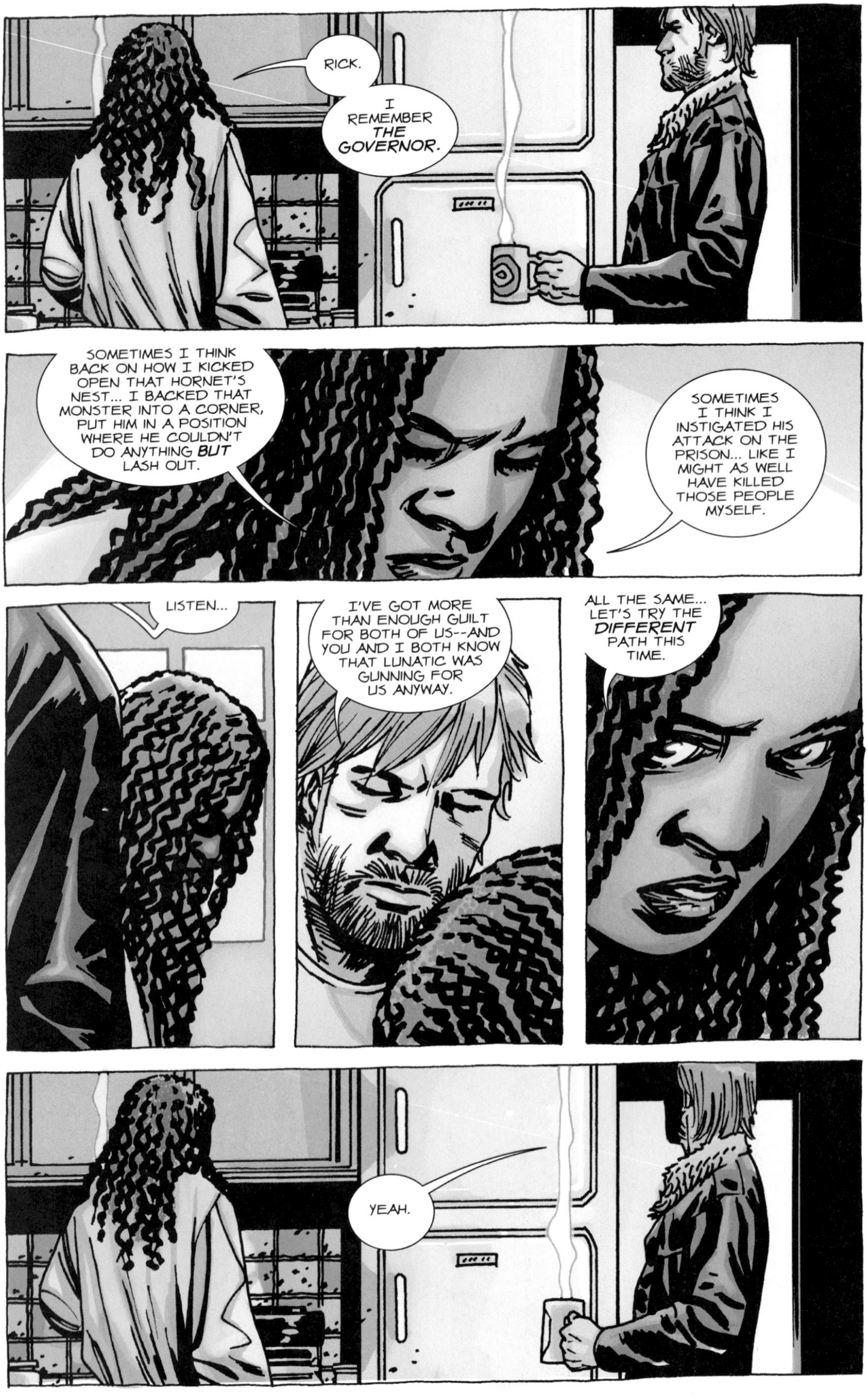
RICK.
I REMEMBER THE GOVERNOR.
SOMETIMES I THINK BACK ON HOW I KICKED OPEN THAT HORNET'S NEST... I BACKED THAT MONSTER INTO A CORNER, PUT HIM IN A POSITION WHERE HE COULDN'T DO ANYTHING BUT LASH OUT.
SOMETIMES I THINK I INSTIGATED HIS ATTACK ON THE PRISON... LIKE I MIGHT AS WELL HAVE KILLED THOSE PEOPLE MYSELF.
LISTEN...
I'VE GOT MORE THAN ENOUGH GUILT FOR BOTH OF US--AND YOU AND I BOTH KNOW THAT LUNATIC WAS GUNNING FOR US ANYWAY.
ALL THE SAME... LET'S TRY THE DIFFERENT PATH THIS TIME.
YEAH.

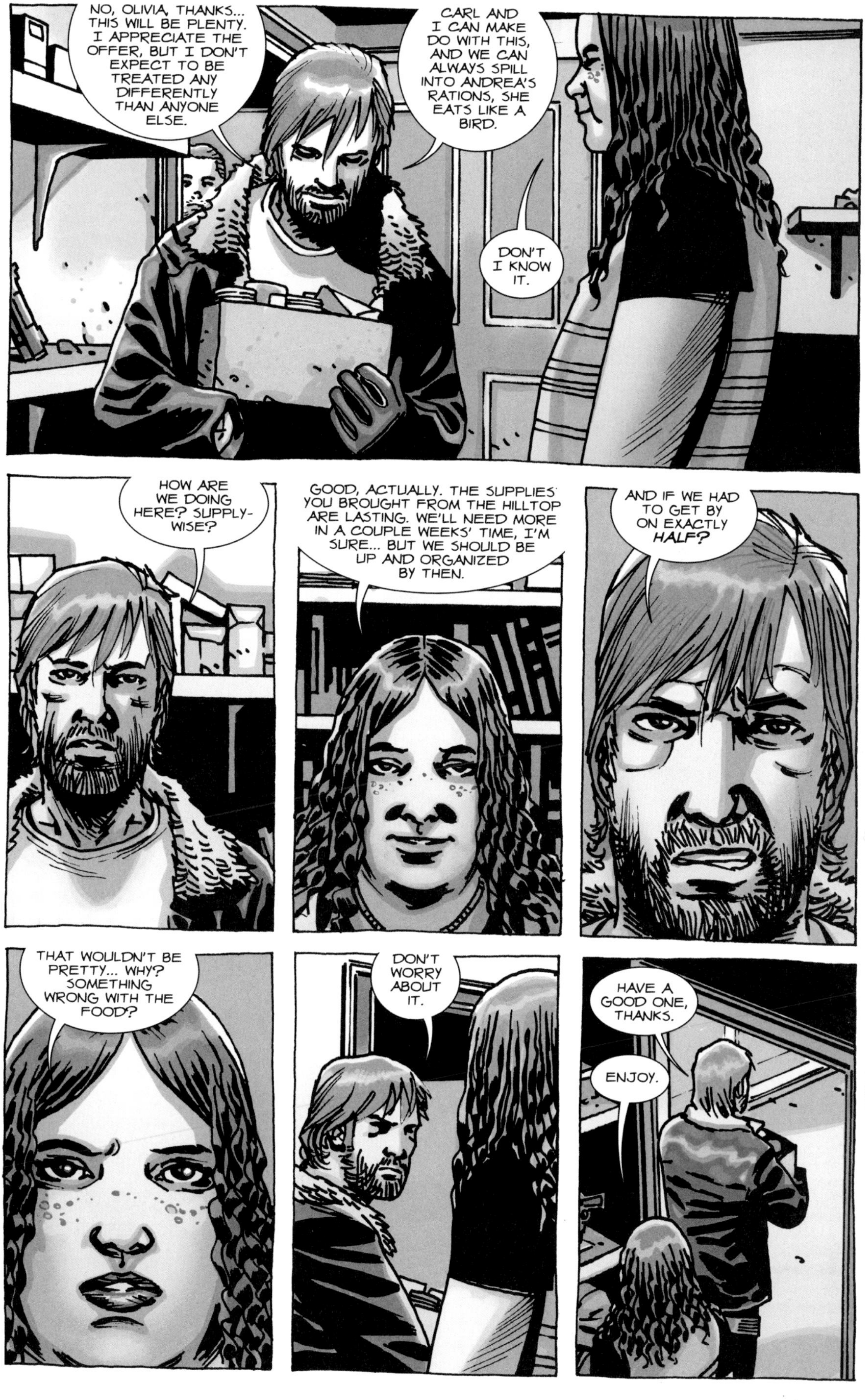

NO, OLIVIA, THANKS... THIS WILL BE PLENTY. I APPRECIATE THE OFFER, BUT I DON'T EXPECT TO BE TREATED ANY DIFFERENTLY THAN ANYONE ELSE.
CARL AND I CAN MAKE DO WITH THIS, AND WE CAN ALWAYS SPILL INTO ANDREA'S RATIONS, SHE EATS LIKE A BIRD.
DON'T I KNOW IT.
HOW ARE WE DOING HERE? SUPPLY-WISE?
GOOD, ACTUALLY. THE SUPPLIES YOU BROUGHT FROM THE HILLTOP ARE LASTING. WE'LL NEED MORE IN A COUPLE WEEKS' TIME, I'M SURE... BUT WE SHOULD BE UP AND ORGANIZED BY THEN.
AND IF WE HAD TO GET BY ON EXACTLY ***HALF?***
THAT WOULDN'T BE PRETTY... WHY? SOMETHING WRONG WITH THE FOOD?
DON'T WORRY ABOUT IT.
HAVE A GOOD ONE, THANKS.
ENJOY.

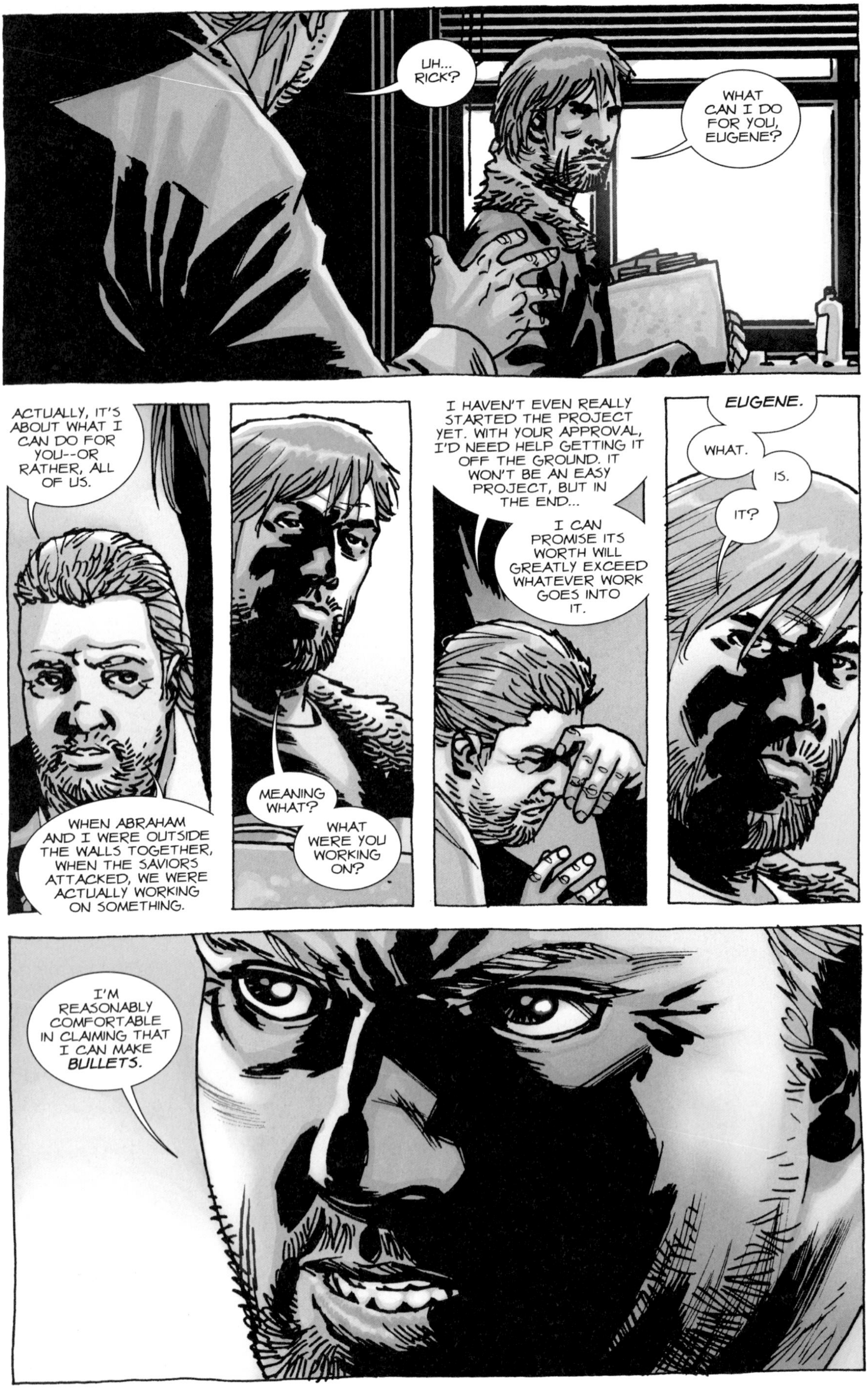
UH... RICK?
WHAT CAN I DO FOR YOU, EUGENE?
ACTUALLY, IT'S ABOUT WHAT I CAN DO FOR YOU--OR RATHER, ALL OF US.
WHEN ABRAHAM AND I WERE OUTSIDE THE WALLS TOGETHER, WHEN THE SAVIORS ATTACKED, WE WERE ACTUALLY WORKING ON SOMETHING.
MEANING WHAT?
WHAT WERE YOU WORKING ON?
I HAVEN'T EVEN REALLY STARTED THE PROJECT YET. WITH YOUR APPROVAL, I'D NEED HELP GETTING IT OFF THE GROUND. IT WON'T BE AN EASY PROJECT, BUT IN THE END...
I CAN PROMISE ITS WORTH WILL GREATLY EXCEED WHATEVER WORK GOES INTO IT.
EUGENE.
WHAT.
IS.
IT?
I'M REASONABLY COMFORTABLE IN CLAIMING THAT I CAN MAKE BULLETS.

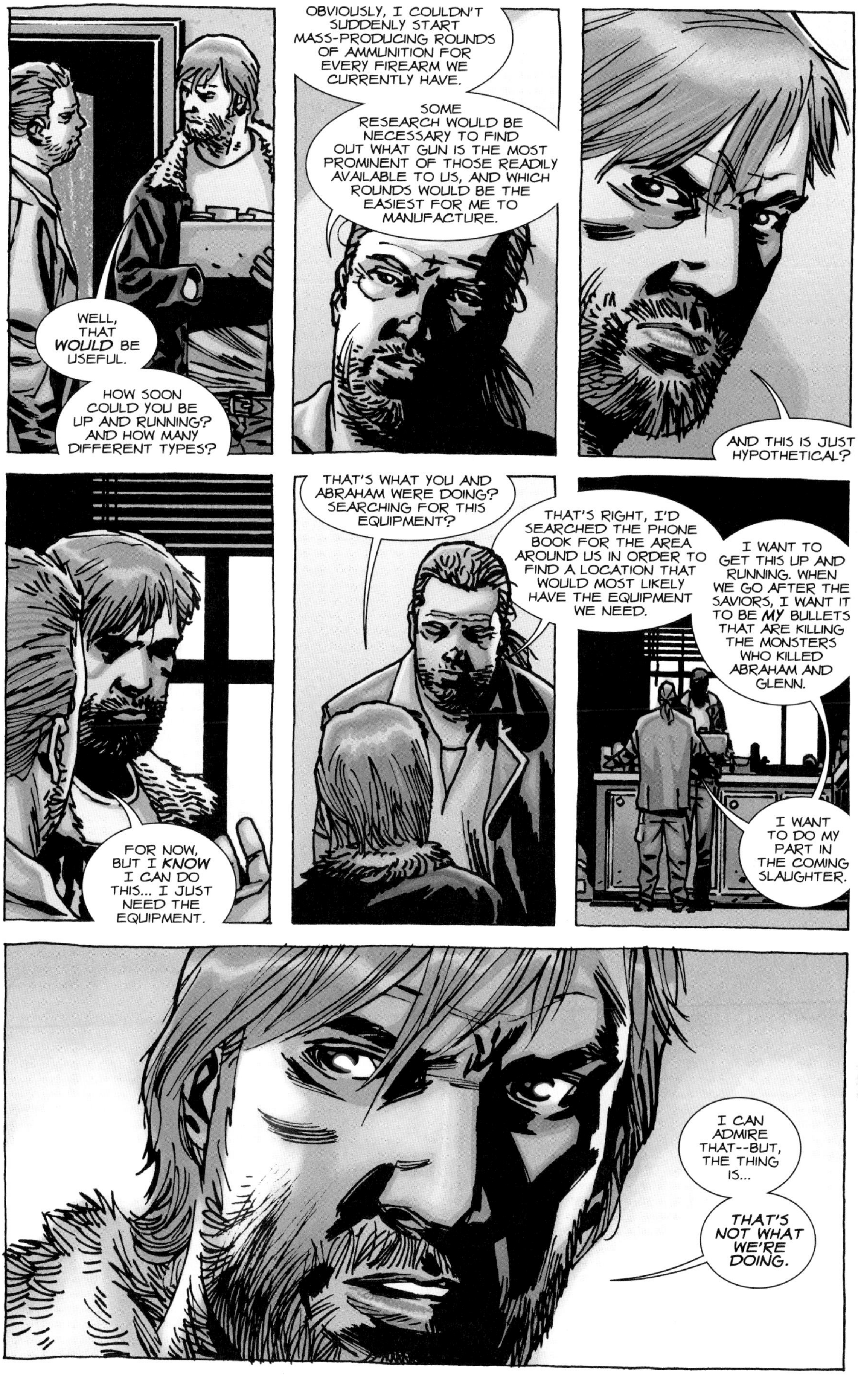
OBVIOUSLY, I COULDN'T SUDDENLY START MASS-PRODUCING ROUNDS OF AMMUNITION FOR EVERY FIREARM WE CURRENTLY HAVE.
SOME RESEARCH WOULD BE NECESSARY TO FIND OUT WHAT GUN IS THE MOST PROMINENT OF THOSE READILY AVAILABLE TO US, AND WHICH ROUNDS WOULD BE THE EASIEST FOR ME TO MANUFACTURE.
WELL, THAT *WOULD* BE USEFUL.
HOW SOON COULD YOU BE UP AND RUNNING? AND HOW MANY DIFFERENT TYPES?
AND THIS IS JUST HYPOTHETICAL?
FOR NOW, BUT I *KNOW* I CAN DO THIS... I JUST NEED THE EQUIPMENT.
THAT'S WHAT YOU AND ABRAHAM WERE DOING? SEARCHING FOR THIS EQUIPMENT?
THAT'S RIGHT, I'D SEARCHED THE PHONE BOOK FOR THE AREA AROUND US IN ORDER TO FIND A LOCATION THAT WOULD MOST LIKELY HAVE THE EQUIPMENT WE NEED.
I WANT TO GET THIS UP AND RUNNING. WHEN WE GO AFTER THE SAVIORS, I WANT IT TO BE *MY* BULLETS THAT ARE KILLING THE MONSTERS WHO KILLED ABRAHAM AND GLENN.
I WANT TO DO MY PART IN THE COMING SLAUGHTER.
I CAN ADMIRE THAT--BUT, THE THING IS...
THAT'S NOT WHAT WE'RE DOING.

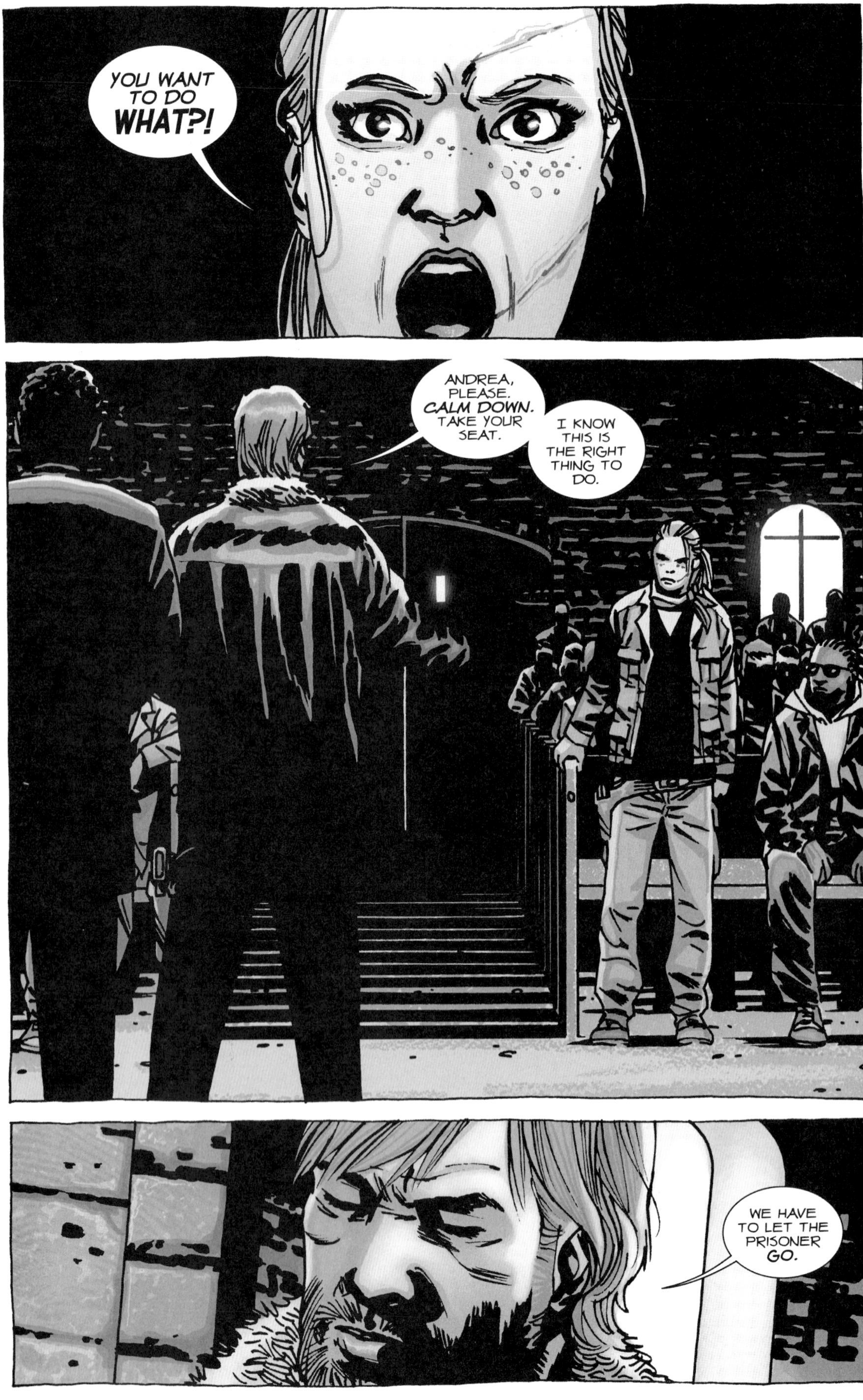
YOU WANT TO DO **WHAT?!**
ANDREA, PLEASE. ***CALM DOWN.*** TAKE YOUR SEAT.
I KNOW THIS IS THE RIGHT THING TO DO.
WE HAVE TO LET THE PRISONER ***GO.***

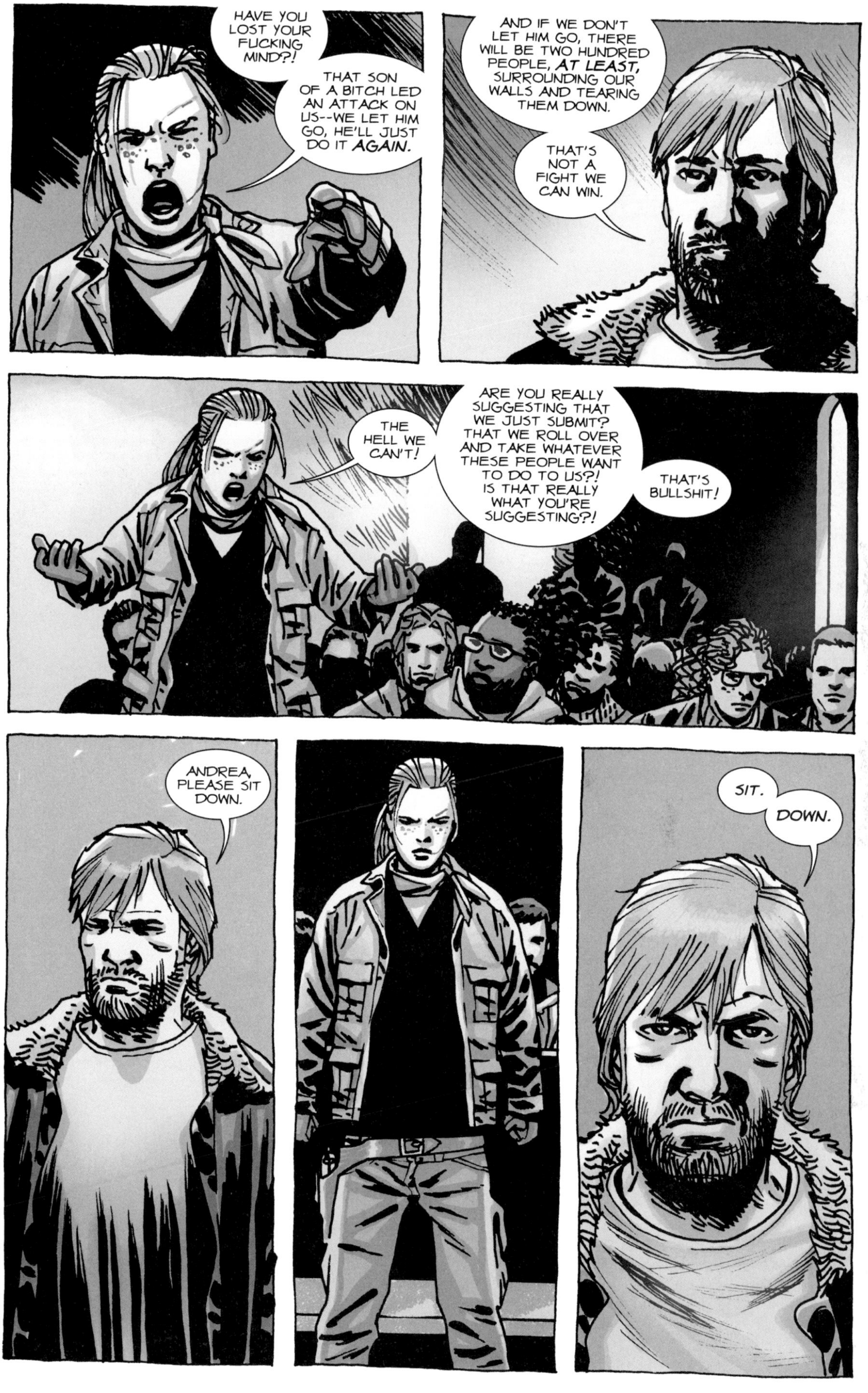
HAVE YOU LOST YOUR FUCKING MIND?!
THAT SON OF A BITCH LED AN ATTACK ON US--WE LET HIM GO, HE'LL JUST DO IT AGAIN.
AND IF WE DON'T LET HIM GO, THERE WILL BE TWO HUNDRED PEOPLE, AT LEAST, SURROUNDING OUR WALLS AND TEARING THEM DOWN.
THAT'S NOT A FIGHT WE CAN WIN.
THE HELL WE CAN'T!
ARE YOU REALLY SUGGESTING THAT WE JUST SUBMIT? THAT WE ROLL OVER AND TAKE WHATEVER THESE PEOPLE WANT TO DO TO US?! IS THAT REALLY WHAT YOU'RE SUGGESTING?!
THAT'S BULLSHIT!
ANDREA, PLEASE SIT DOWN.
SIT.
DOWN.

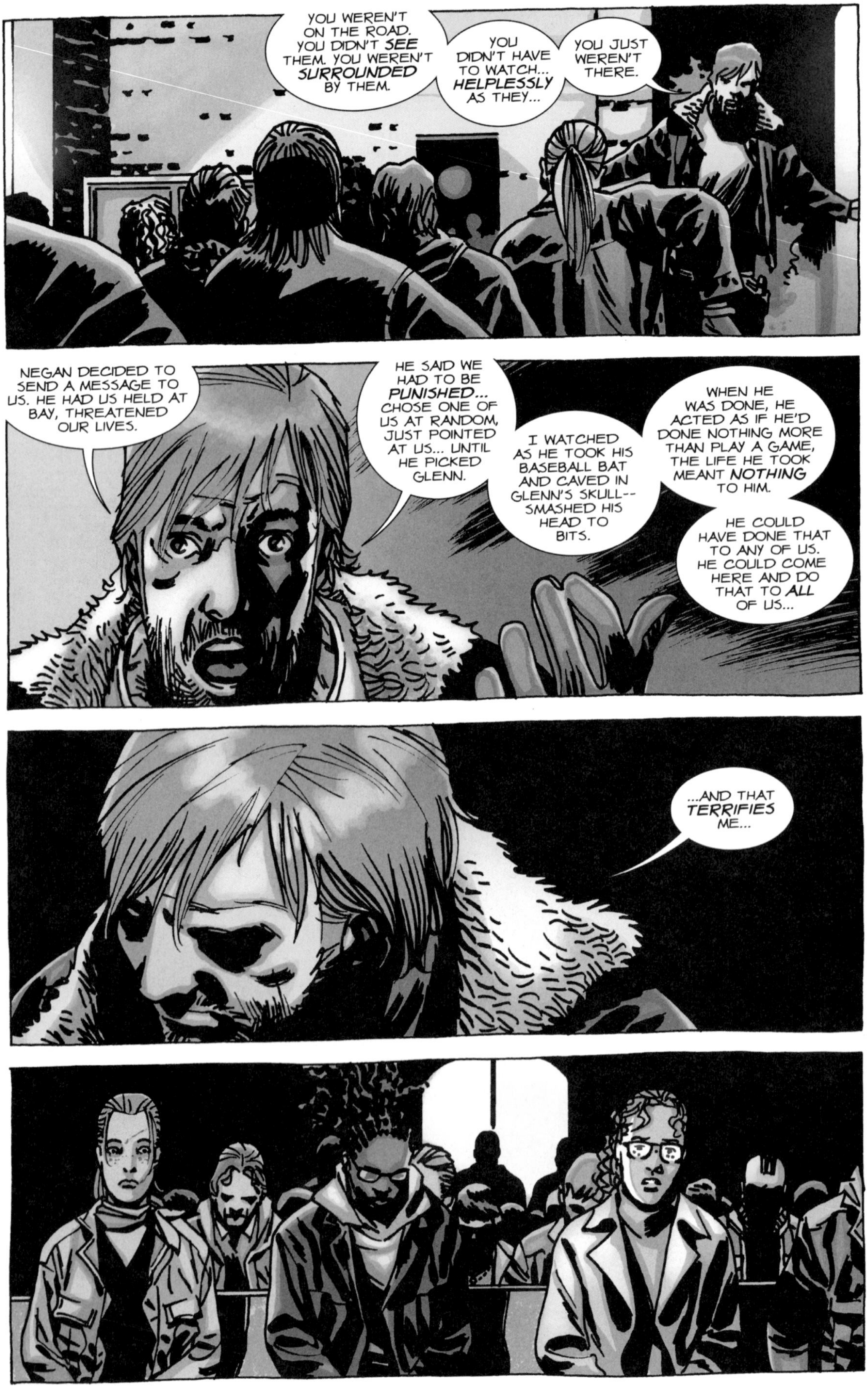
YOU WEREN'T ON THE ROAD. YOU DIDN'T SEE THEM. YOU WEREN'T SURROUNDED BY THEM.
YOU DIDN'T HAVE TO WATCH... HELPLESSLY AS THEY...
YOU JUST WEREN'T THERE.
NEGAN DECIDED TO SEND A MESSAGE TO US. HE HAD US HELD AT BAY, THREATENED OUR LIVES.
HE SAID WE HAD TO BE PUNISHED... CHOSE ONE OF US AT RANDOM, JUST POINTED AT US... UNTIL HE PICKED GLENN.
I WATCHED AS HE TOOK HIS BASEBALL BAT AND CAVED IN GLENN'S SKULL-- SMASHED HIS HEAD TO BITS.
WHEN HE WAS DONE, HE ACTED AS IF HE'D DONE NOTHING MORE THAN PLAY A GAME, THE LIFE HE TOOK MEANT NOTHING TO HIM.
HE COULD HAVE DONE THAT TO ANY OF US. HE COULD COME HERE AND DO THAT TO ALL OF US...
...AND THAT TERRIFIES ME...

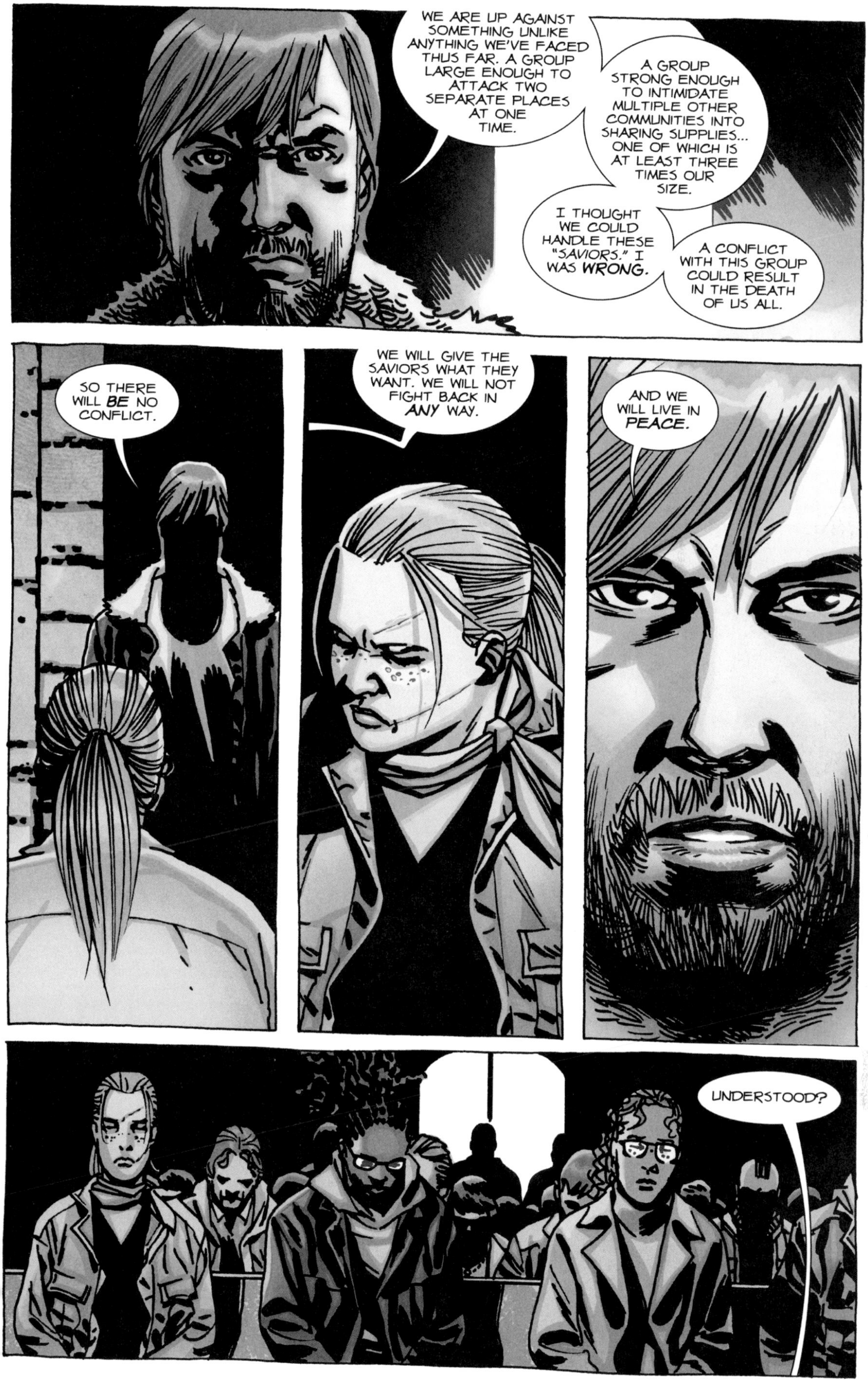
WE ARE UP AGAINST SOMETHING UNLIKE ANYTHING WE'VE FACED THUS FAR. A GROUP LARGE ENOUGH TO ATTACK TWO SEPARATE PLACES AT ONE TIME.
A GROUP STRONG ENOUGH TO INTIMIDATE MULTIPLE OTHER COMMUNITIES INTO SHARING SUPPLIES... ONE OF WHICH IS AT LEAST THREE TIMES OUR SIZE.
I THOUGHT WE COULD HANDLE THESE "SAVIORS." I WAS **WRONG.**
A CONFLICT WITH THIS GROUP COULD RESULT IN THE DEATH OF US ALL.
SO THERE WILL **BE** NO CONFLICT.
WE WILL GIVE THE SAVIORS WHAT THEY WANT. WE WILL NOT FIGHT BACK IN **ANY** WAY.
AND WE WILL LIVE IN **PEACE.**
UNDERSTOOD?

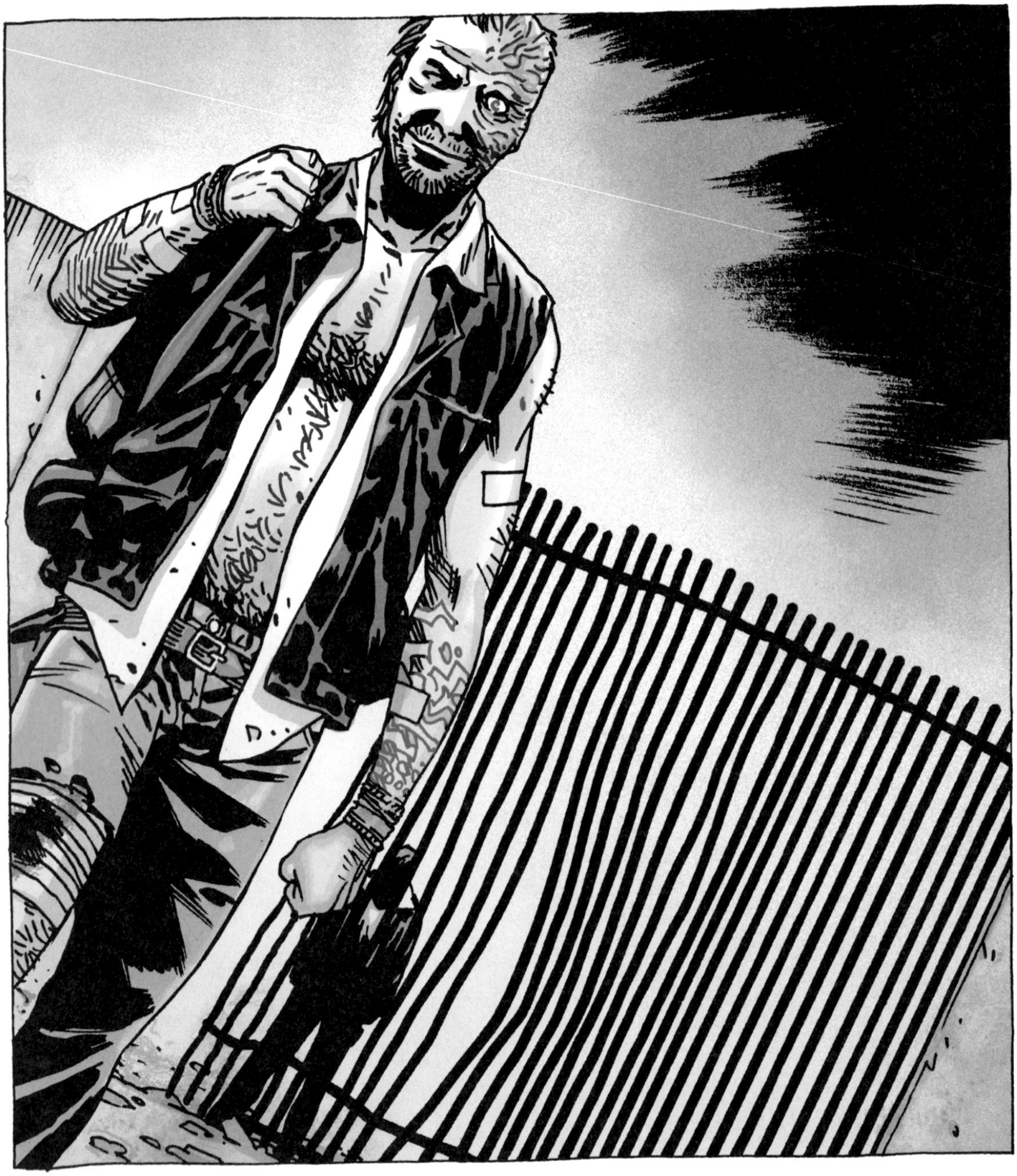
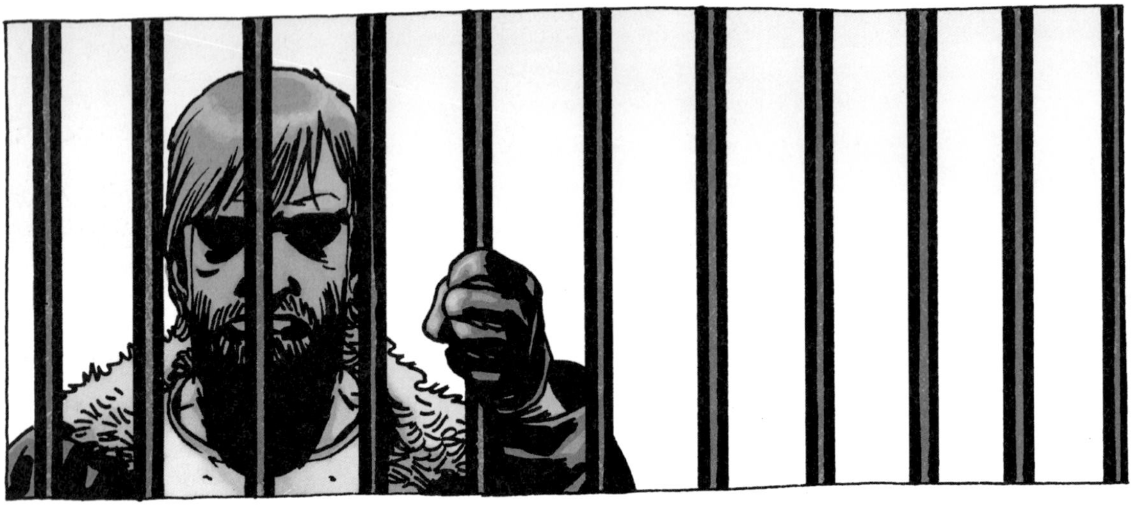

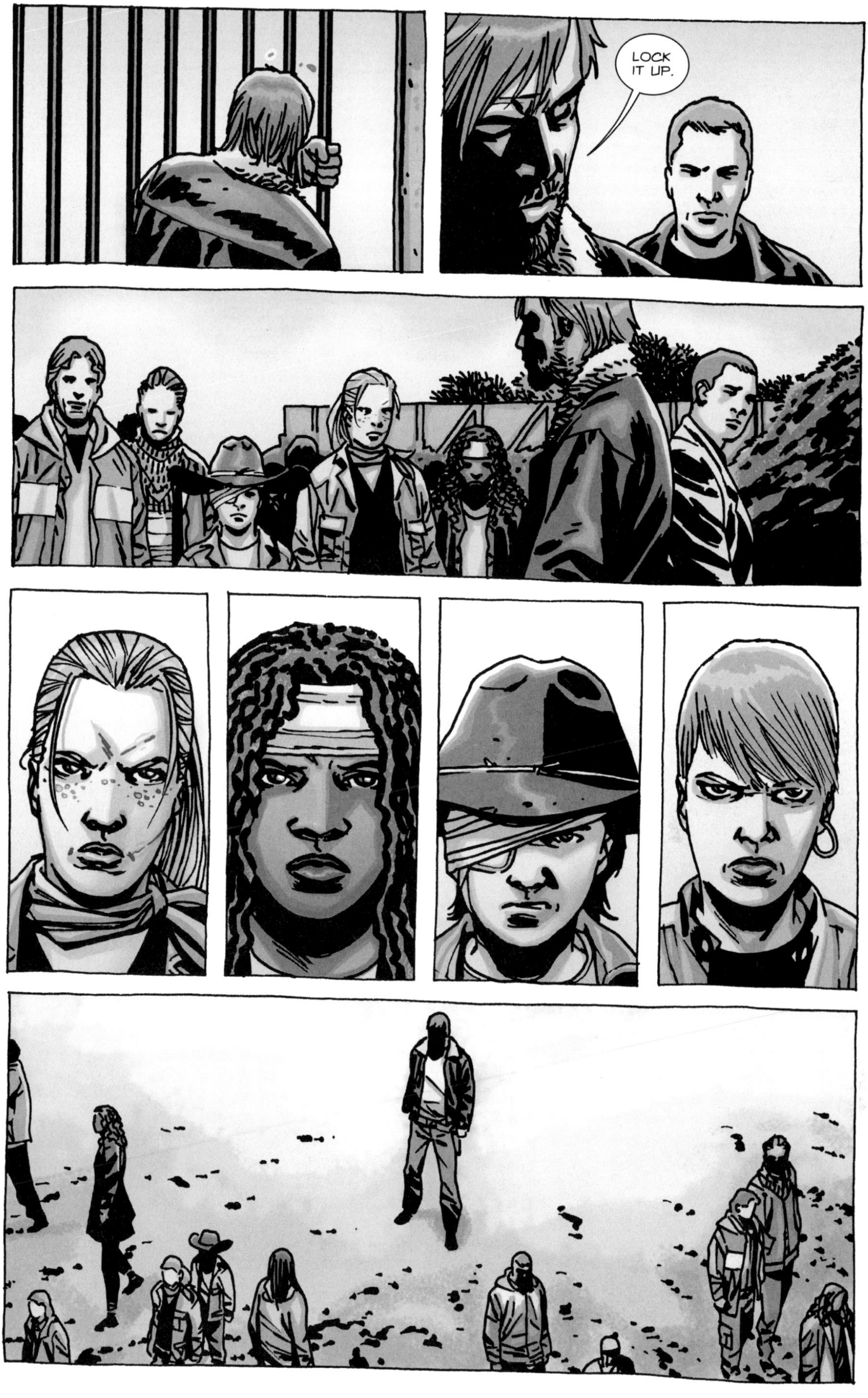
LOCK IT UP.

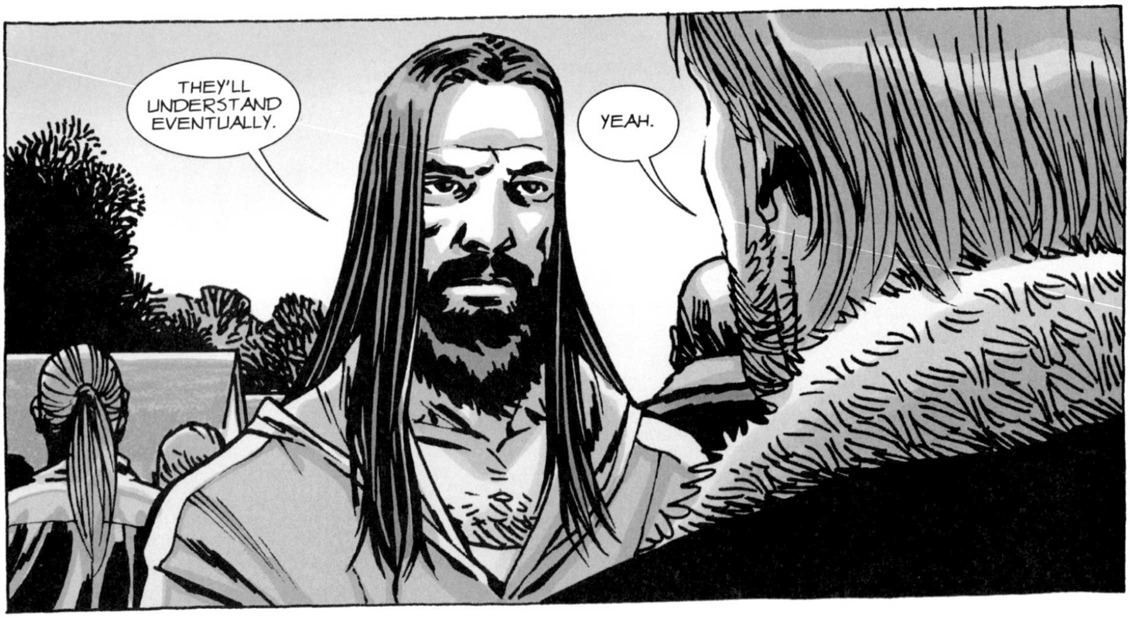
THEY'LL UNDERSTAND EVENTUALLY.
YEAH.
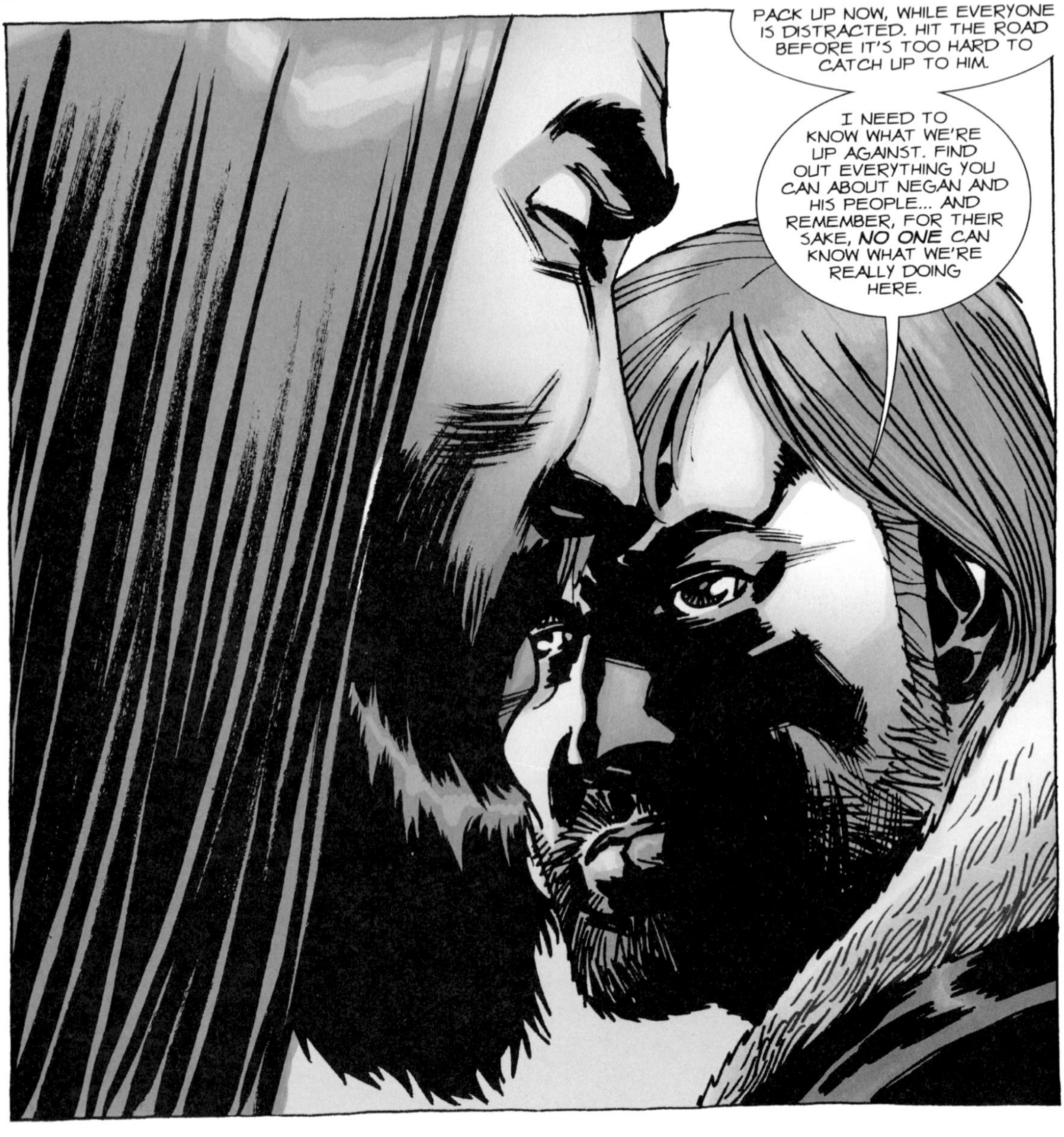
PACK UP NOW, WHILE EVERYONE IS DISTRACTED. HIT THE ROAD BEFORE IT'S TOO HARD TO CATCH UP TO HIM.
I NEED TO KNOW WHAT WE'RE UP AGAINST. FIND OUT EVERYTHING YOU CAN ABOUT NEGAN AND HIS PEOPLE... AND REMEMBER, FOR THEIR SAKE, ***NO ONE*** CAN KNOW WHAT WE'RE REALLY DOING HERE.

Chapter Eighteen:
What Comes After

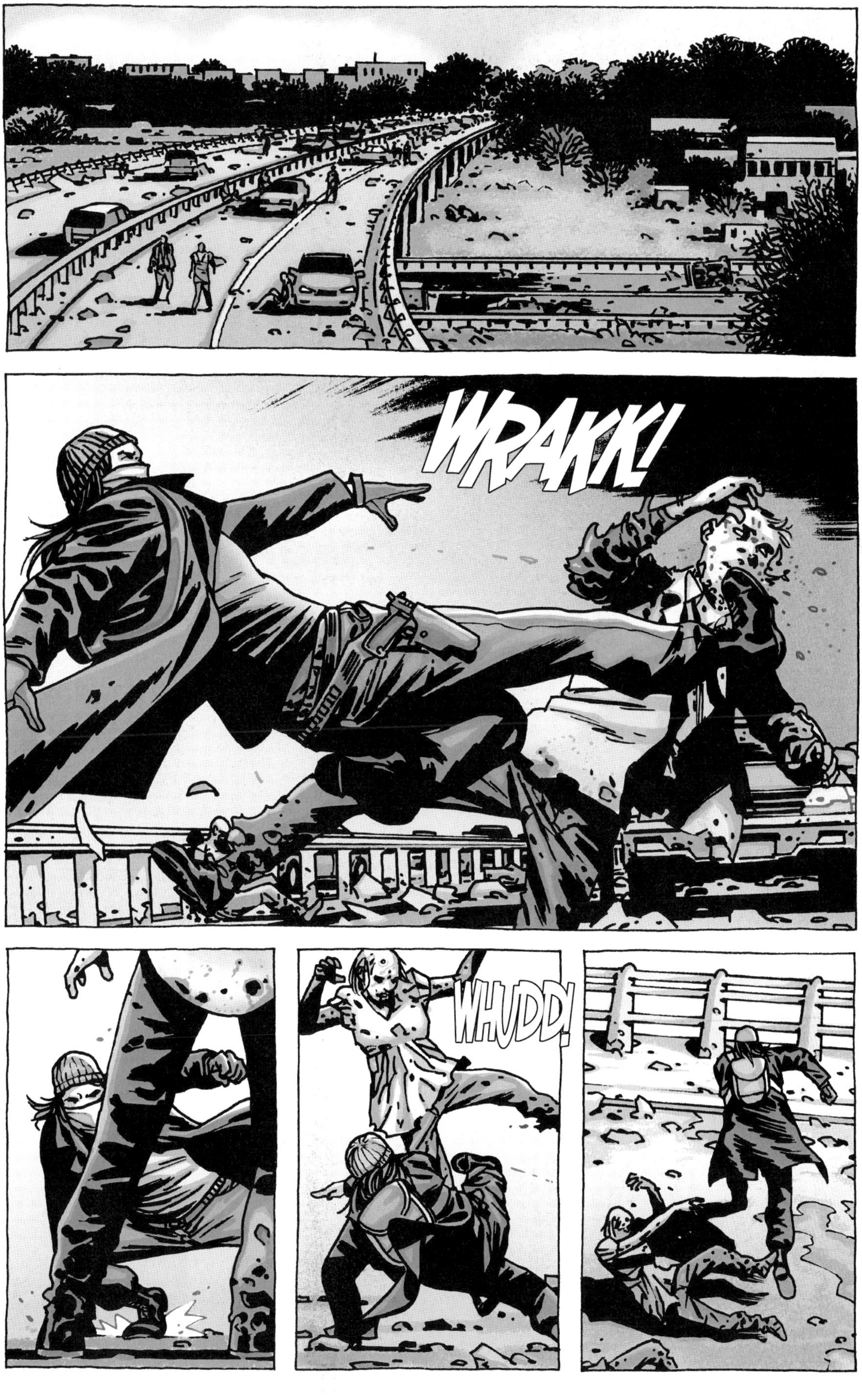
WRAKK!
WHUDD!

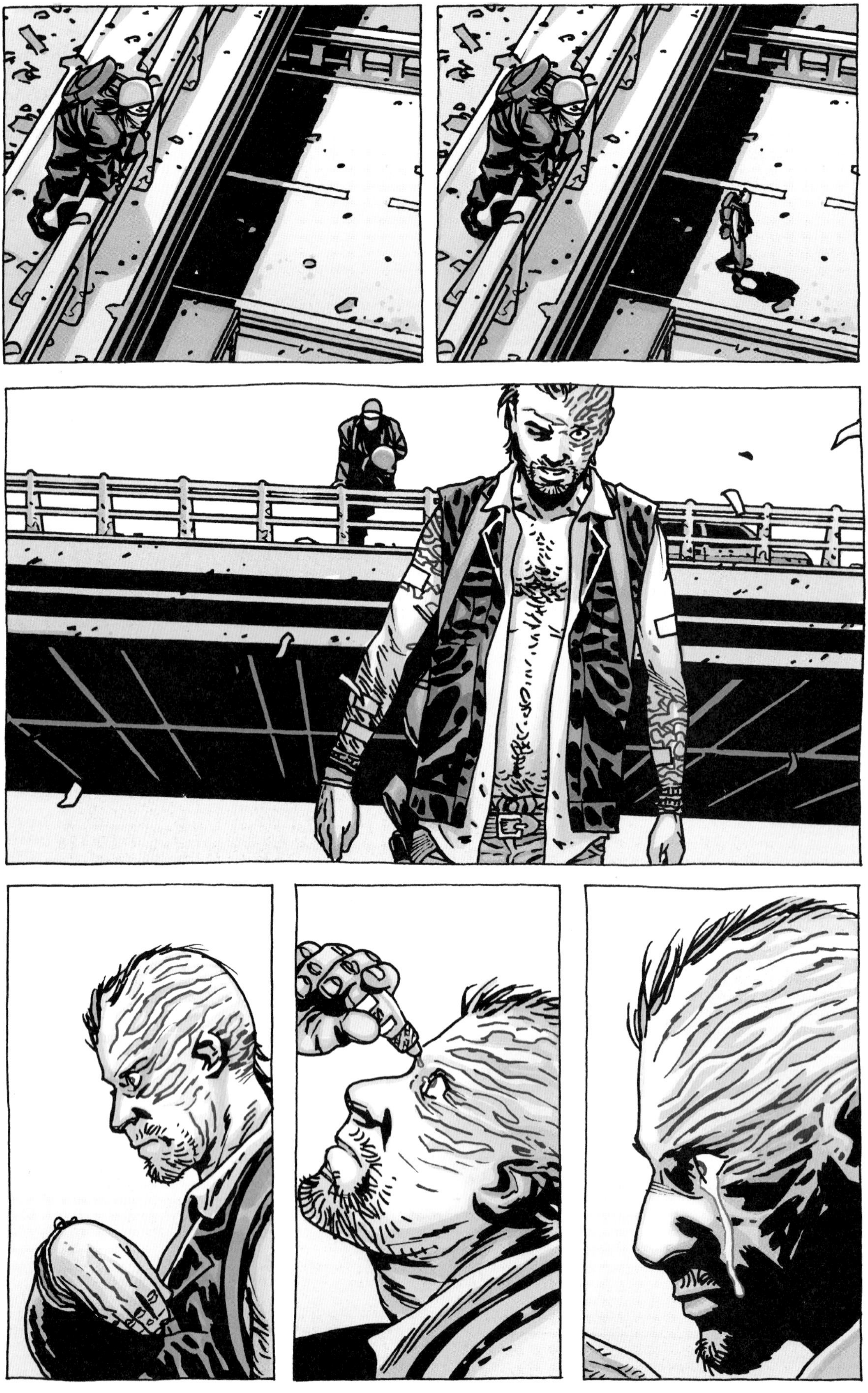

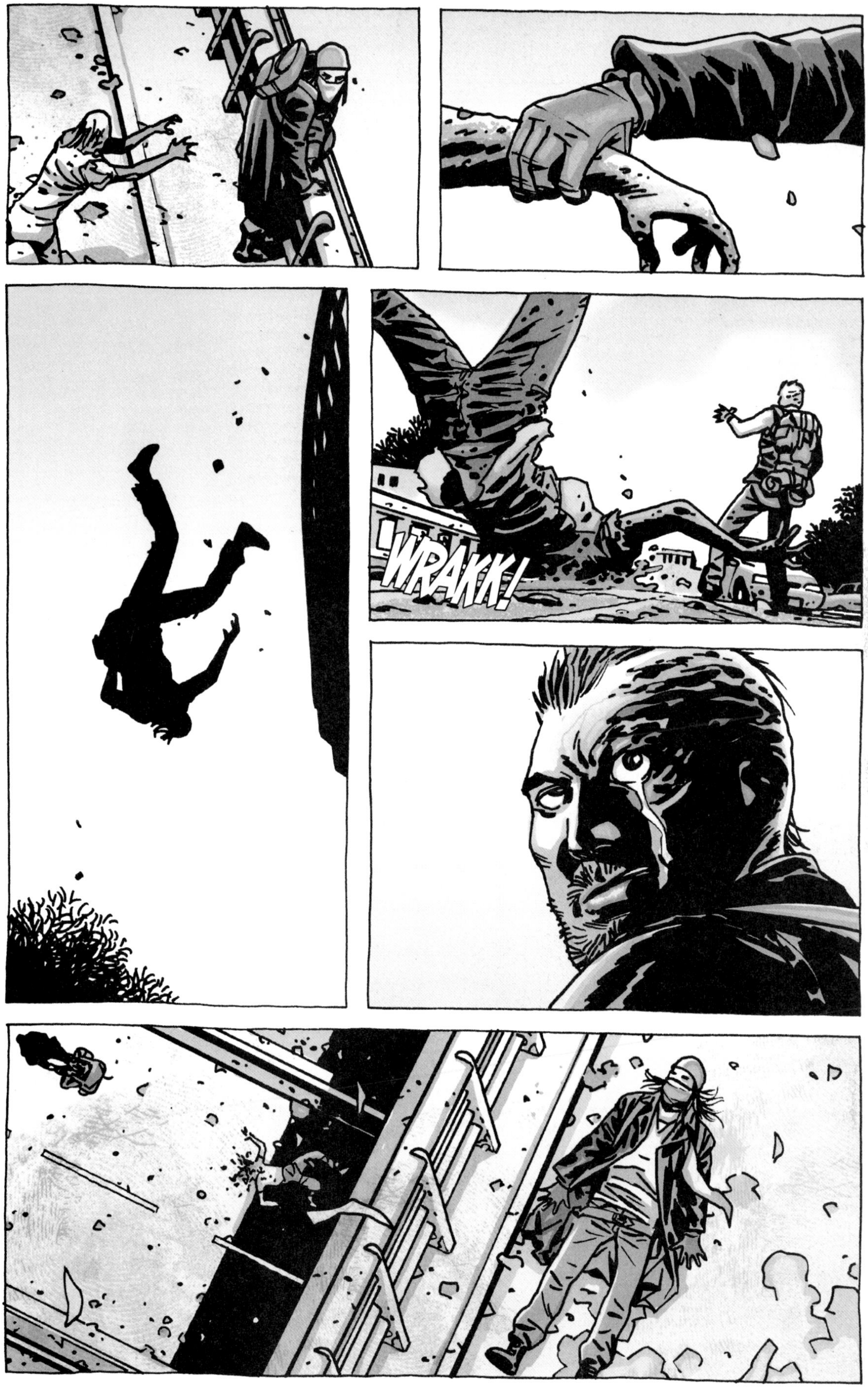
WRAKK!

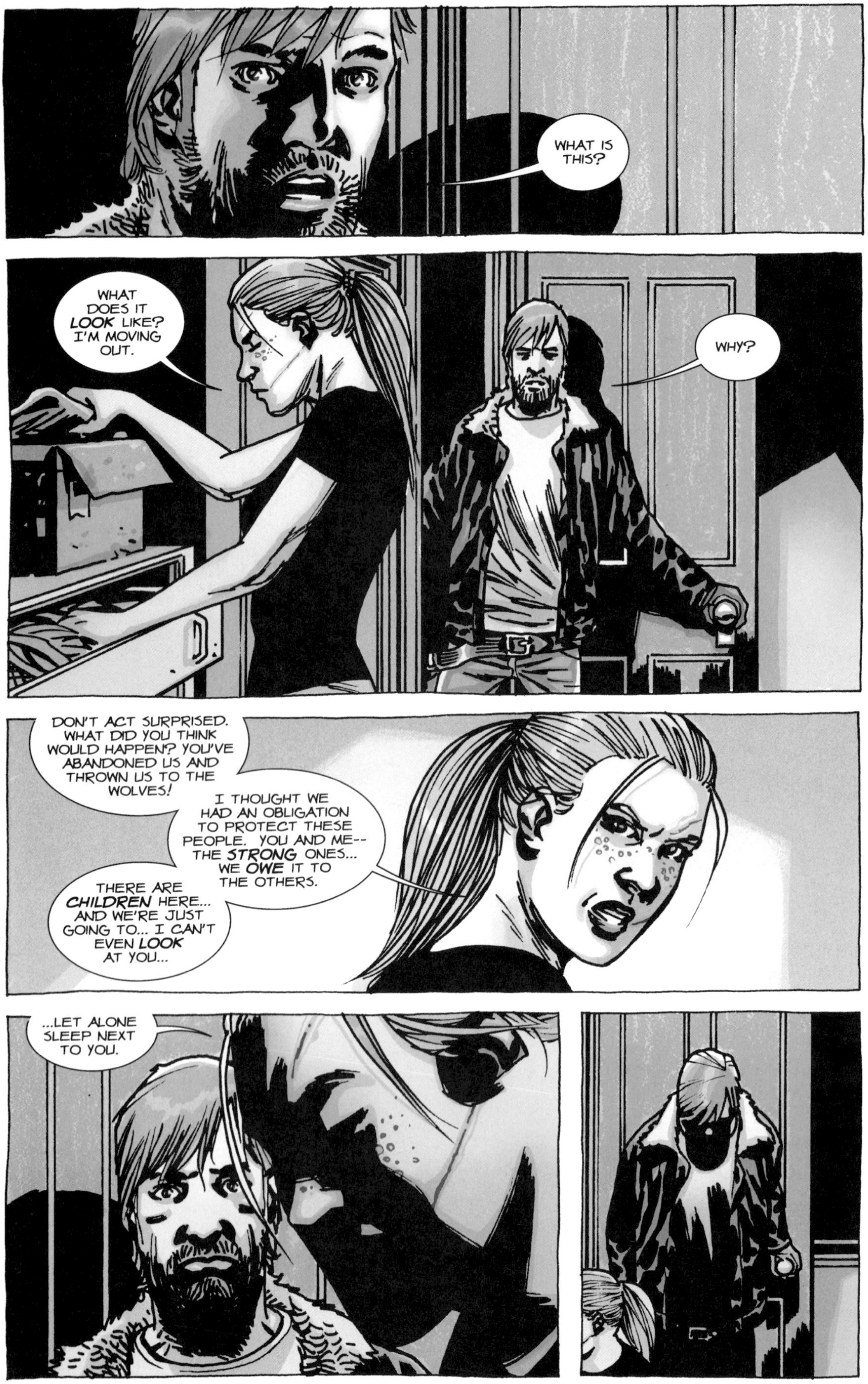
WHAT IS THIS?
WHAT DOES IT LOOK LIKE? I'M MOVING OUT.
WHY?
DON'T ACT SURPRISED. WHAT DID YOU THINK WOULD HAPPEN? YOU'VE ABANDONED US AND THROWN US TO THE WOLVES!
I THOUGHT WE HAD AN OBLIGATION TO PROTECT THESE PEOPLE. YOU AND ME-- THE STRONG ONES... WE OWE IT TO THE OTHERS.
THERE ARE CHILDREN HERE... AND WE'RE JUST GOING TO... I CAN'T EVEN LOOK AT YOU...
...LET ALONE SLEEP NEXT TO YOU.

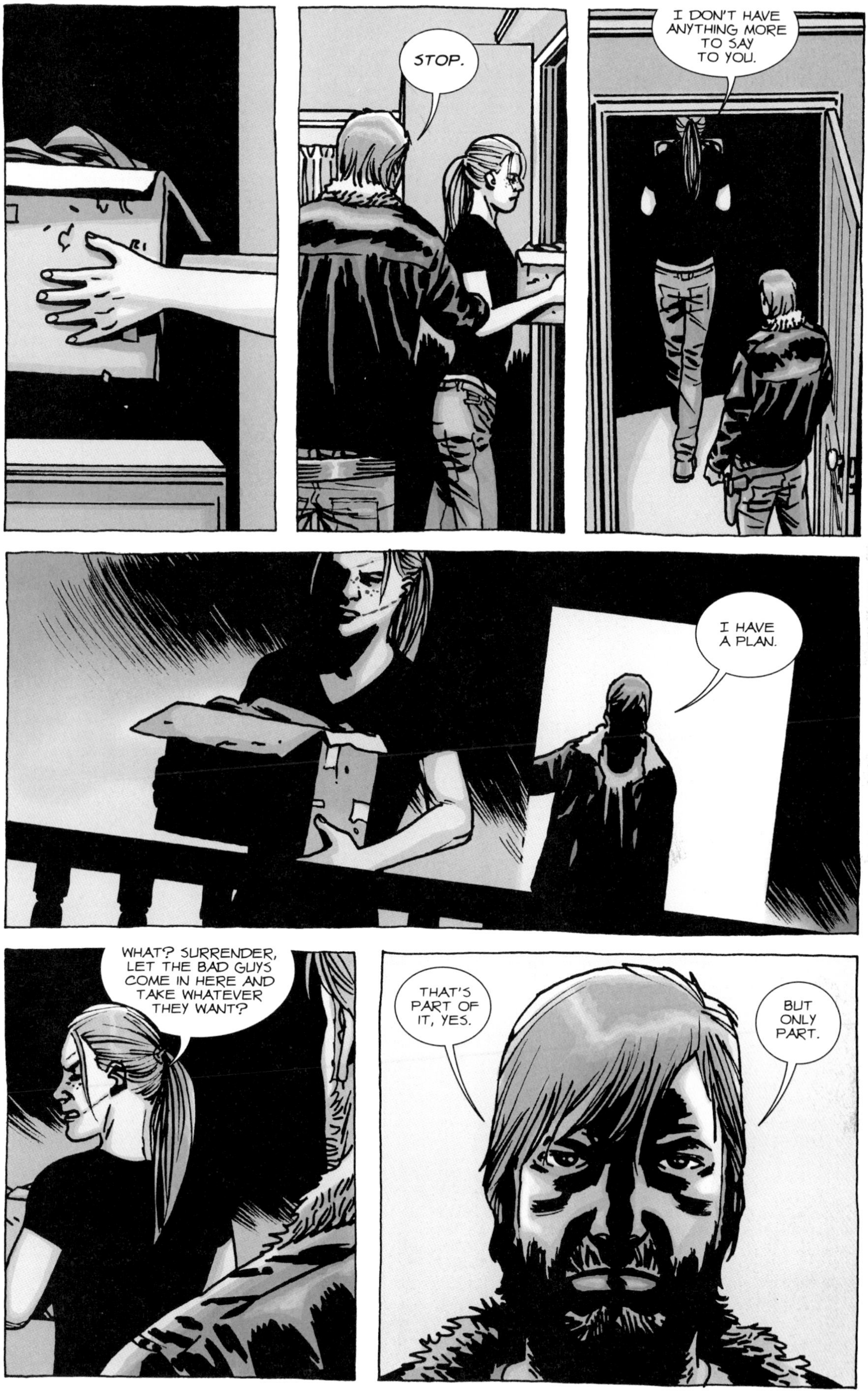
STOP.
I DON'T HAVE ANYTHING MORE TO SAY TO YOU.
I HAVE A PLAN.
WHAT? SURRENDER, LET THE BAD GUYS COME IN HERE AND TAKE WHATEVER THEY WANT?
THAT'S PART OF IT, YES.
BUT ONLY PART.

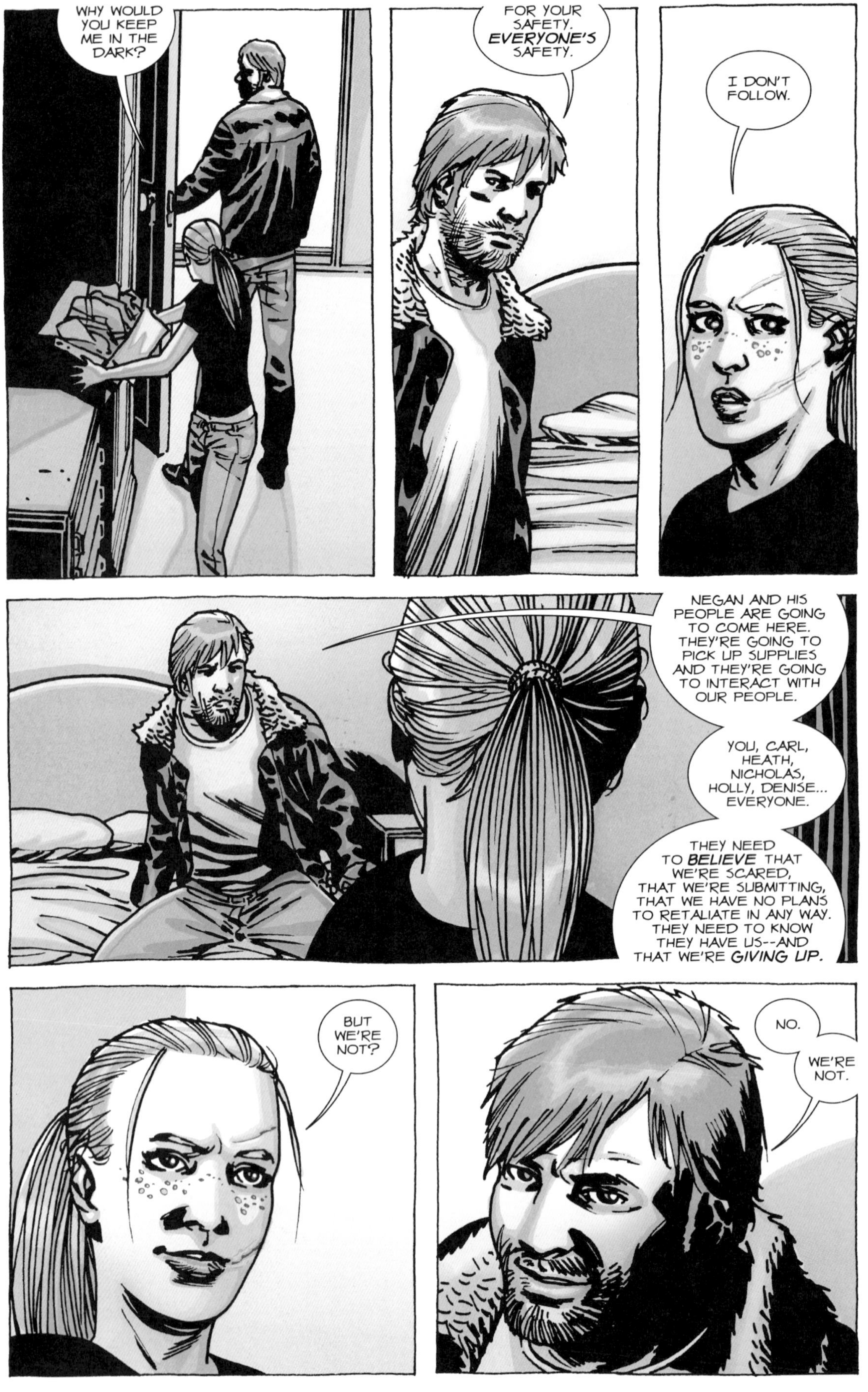
WHY WOULD YOU KEEP ME IN THE DARK?
FOR YOUR SAFETY. EVERYONE'S SAFETY.
I DON'T FOLLOW.
NEGAN AND HIS PEOPLE ARE GOING TO COME HERE. THEY'RE GOING TO PICK UP SUPPLIES AND THEY'RE GOING TO INTERACT WITH OUR PEOPLE.
YOU, CARL, HEATH, NICHOLAS, HOLLY, DENISE... EVERYONE.
THEY NEED TO BELIEVE THAT WE'RE SCARED, THAT WE'RE SUBMITTING, THAT WE HAVE NO PLANS TO RETALIATE IN ANY WAY. THEY NEED TO KNOW THEY HAVE US--AND THAT WE'RE GIVING UP.
BUT WE'RE NOT?
NO.
WE'RE NOT.

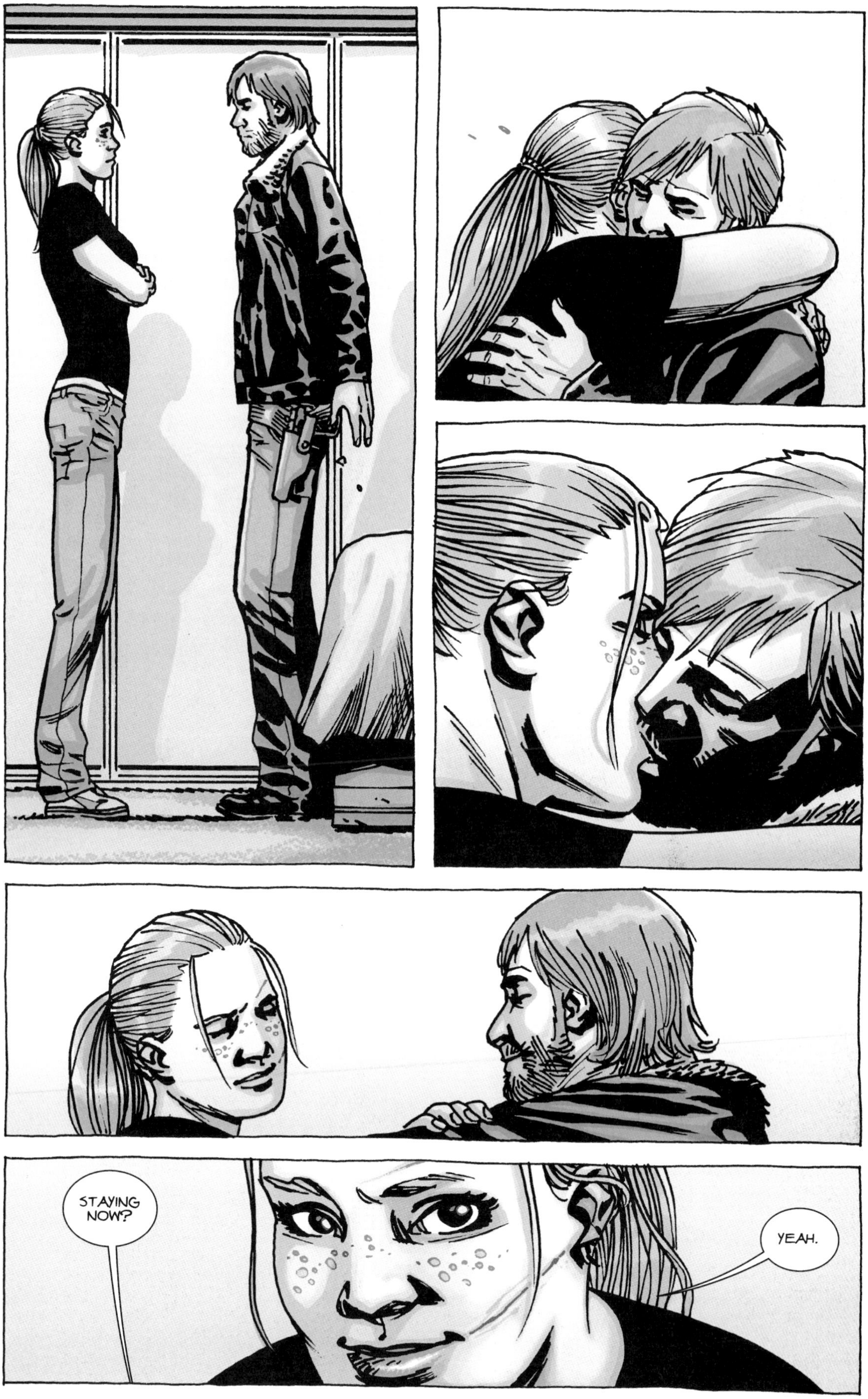
STAYING NOW?
YEAH.

I'M MAKING LUNCH.

YOU WANT A SANDWICH?

CARL?

DAMN IT, CARL.

LOOK AT ME.

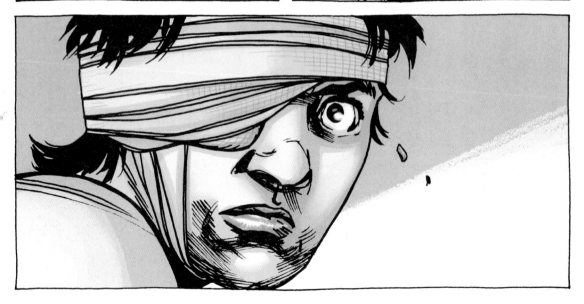

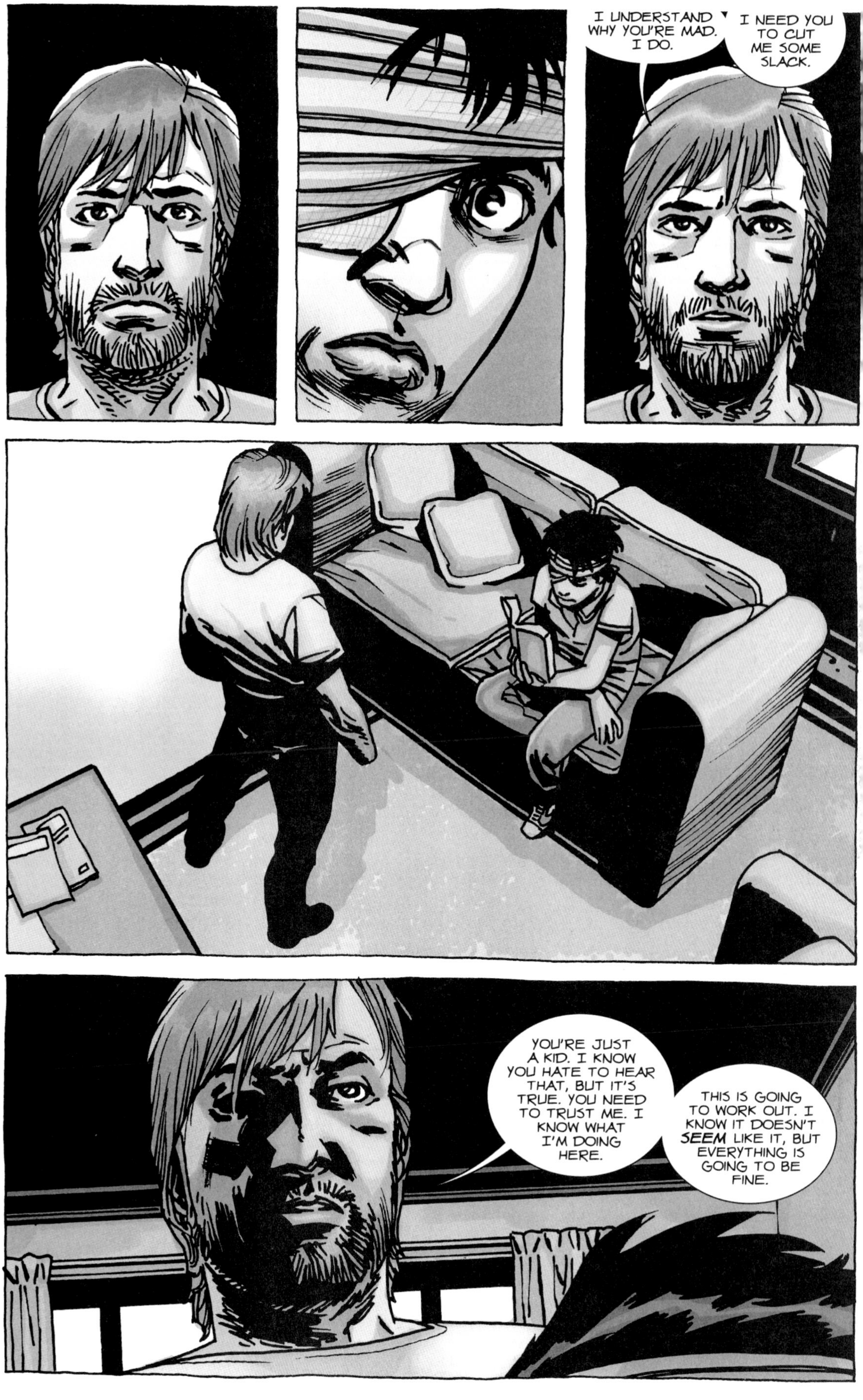

I UNDERSTAND WHY YOU'RE MAD. I DO.
I NEED YOU TO CUT ME SOME SLACK.
YOU'RE JUST A KID. I KNOW YOU HATE TO HEAR THAT, BUT IT'S TRUE. YOU NEED TO TRUST ME. I KNOW WHAT I'M DOING HERE.
THIS IS GOING TO WORK OUT. I KNOW IT DOESN'T SEEM LIKE IT, BUT EVERYTHING IS GOING TO BE FINE.

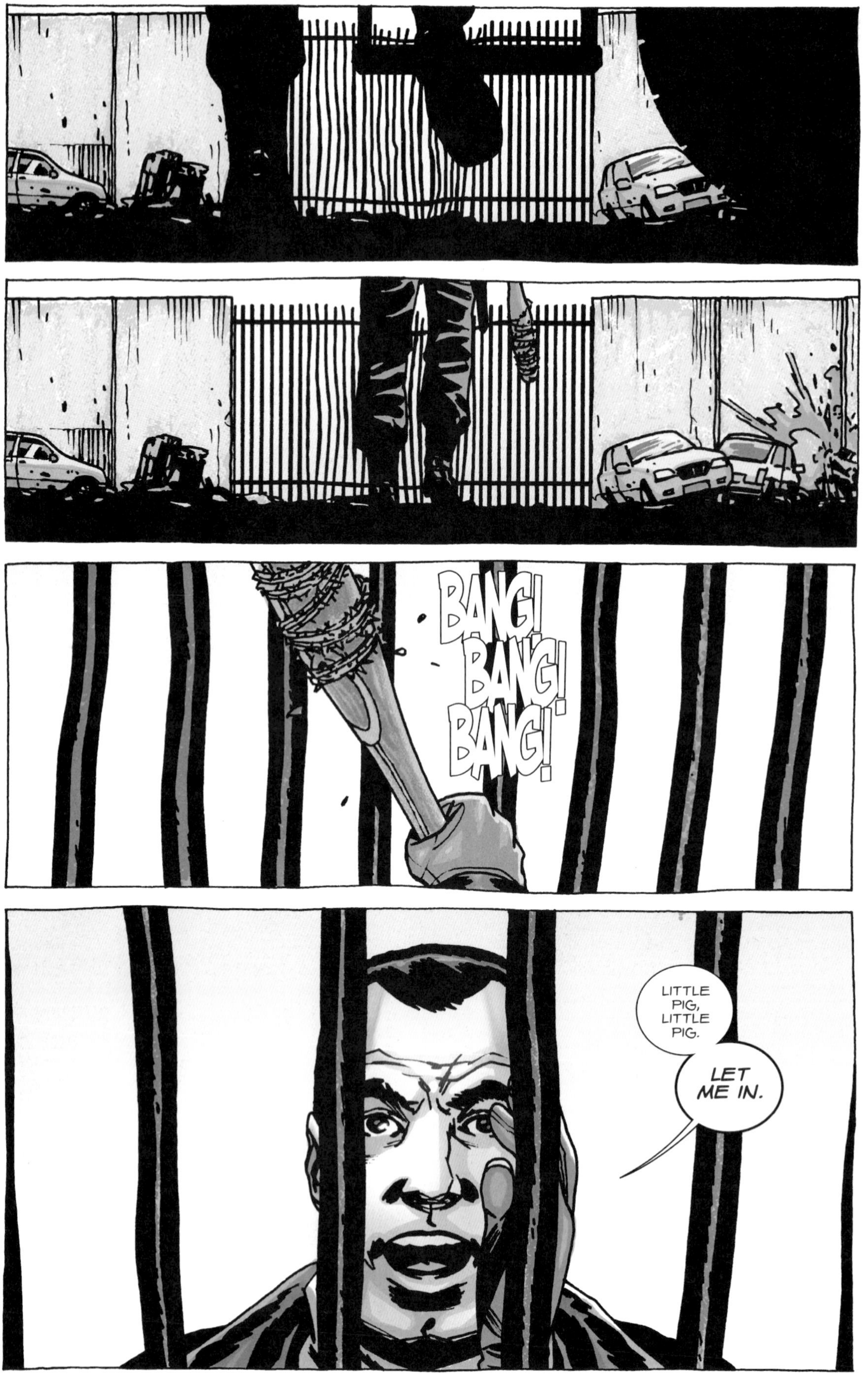
BANG! BANG! BANG!
LITTLE PIG, LITTLE PIG.
LET ME IN.

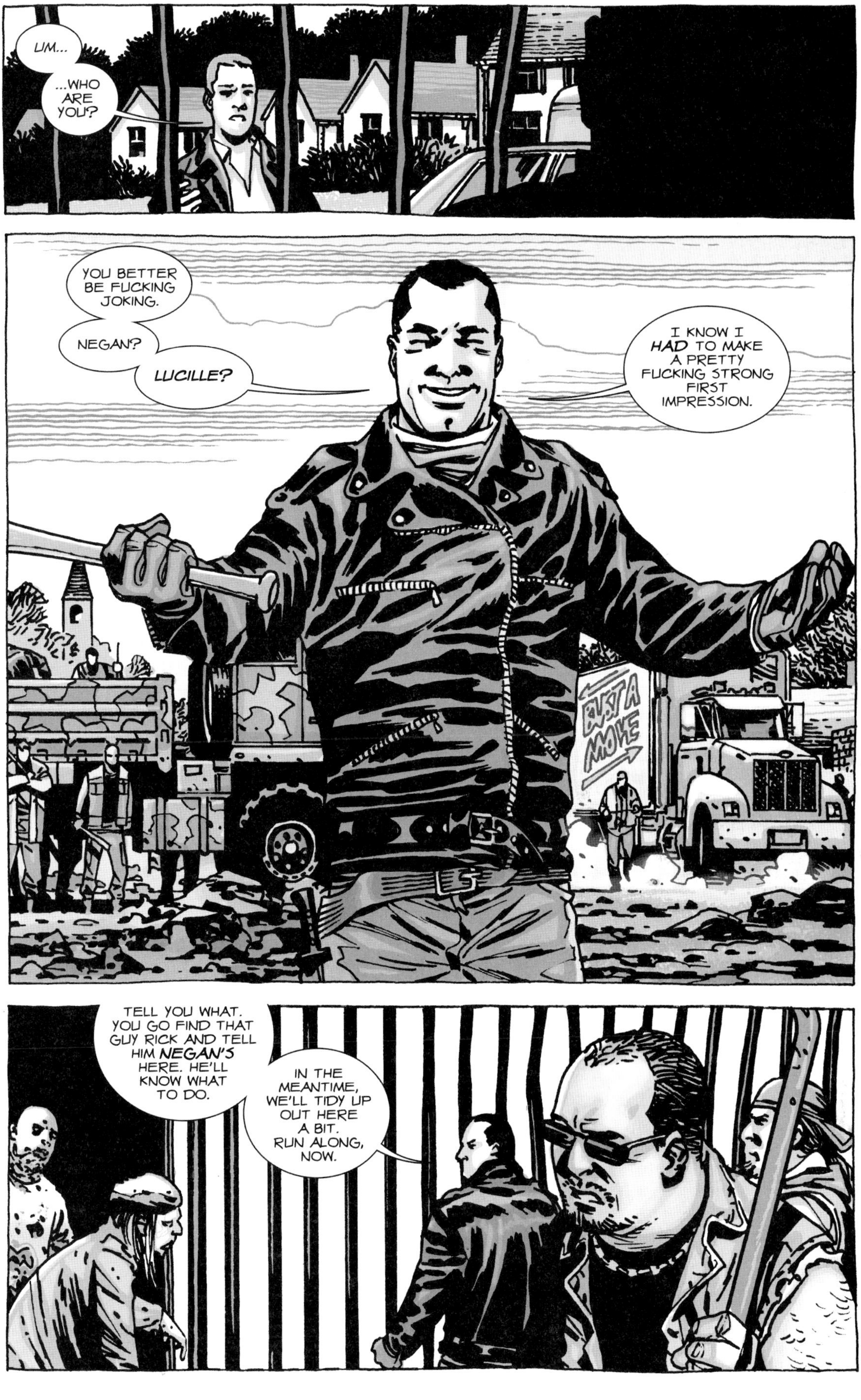
UM...
...WHO ARE YOU?
YOU BETTER BE FUCKING JOKING.
NEGAN?
LUCILLE?
I KNOW I HAD TO MAKE A PRETTY FUCKING STRONG FIRST IMPRESSION.
BUST A MOVE
TELL YOU WHAT. YOU GO FIND THAT GUY RICK AND TELL HIM NEGAN'S HERE. HE'LL KNOW WHAT TO DO.
IN THE MEANTIME, WE'LL TIDY UP OUT HERE A BIT. RUN ALONG, NOW.

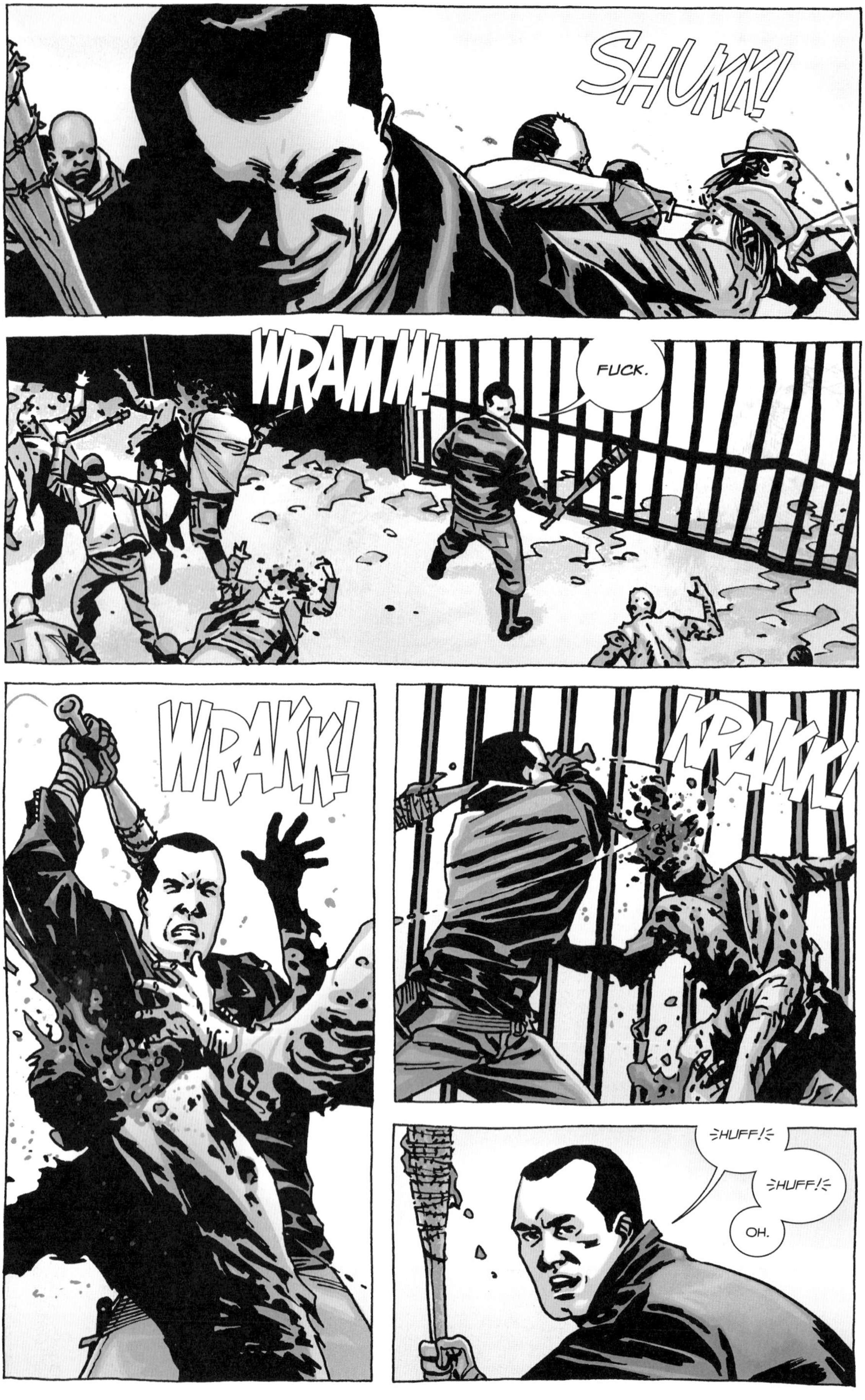
SHUKK!
WRAMM!
FUCK.
WRAKK!
KRAKK!
HUFF!
HUFF!
OH.

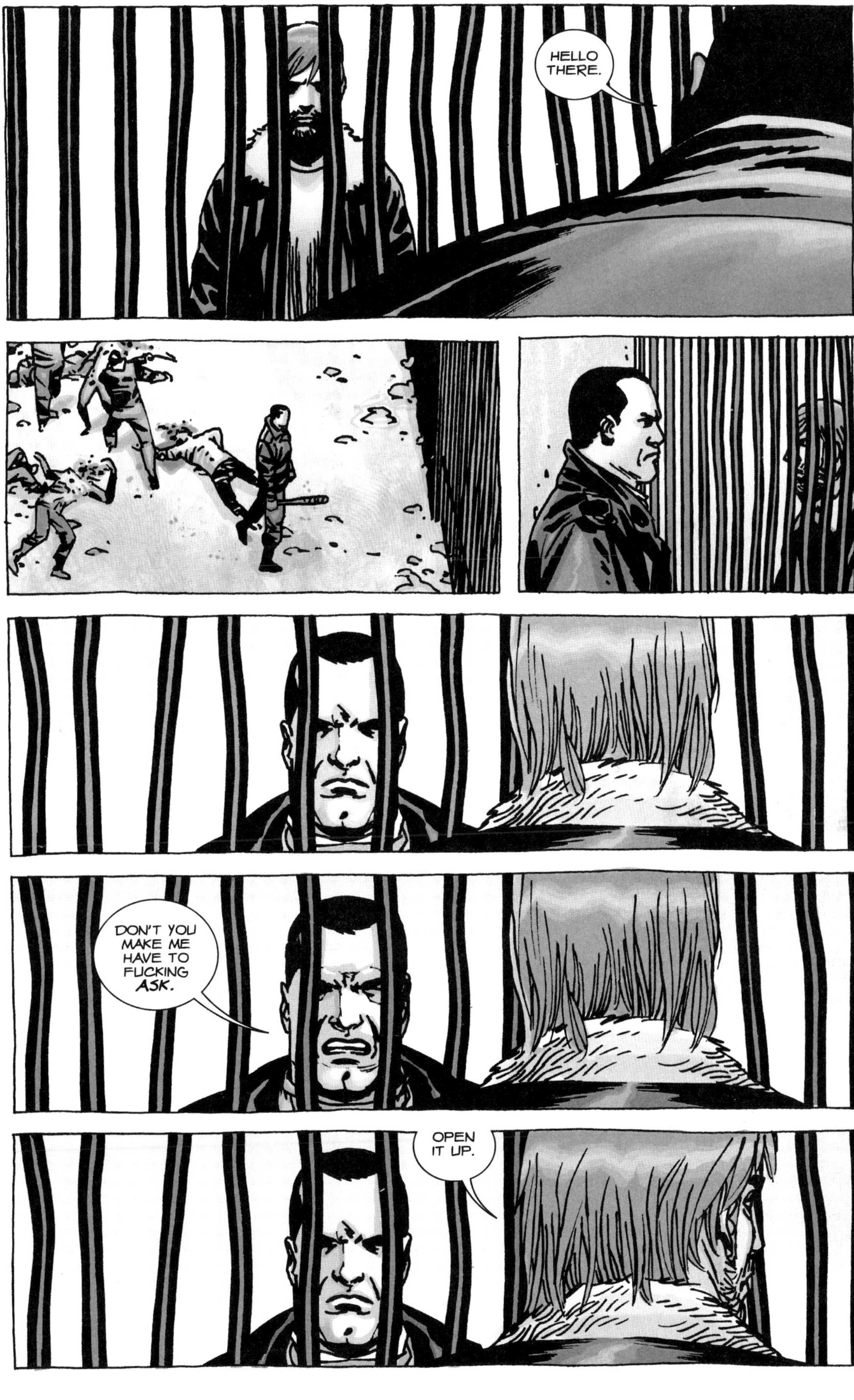
HELLO THERE.
DON'T YOU MAKE ME HAVE TO FUCKING ASK.
OPEN IT UP.

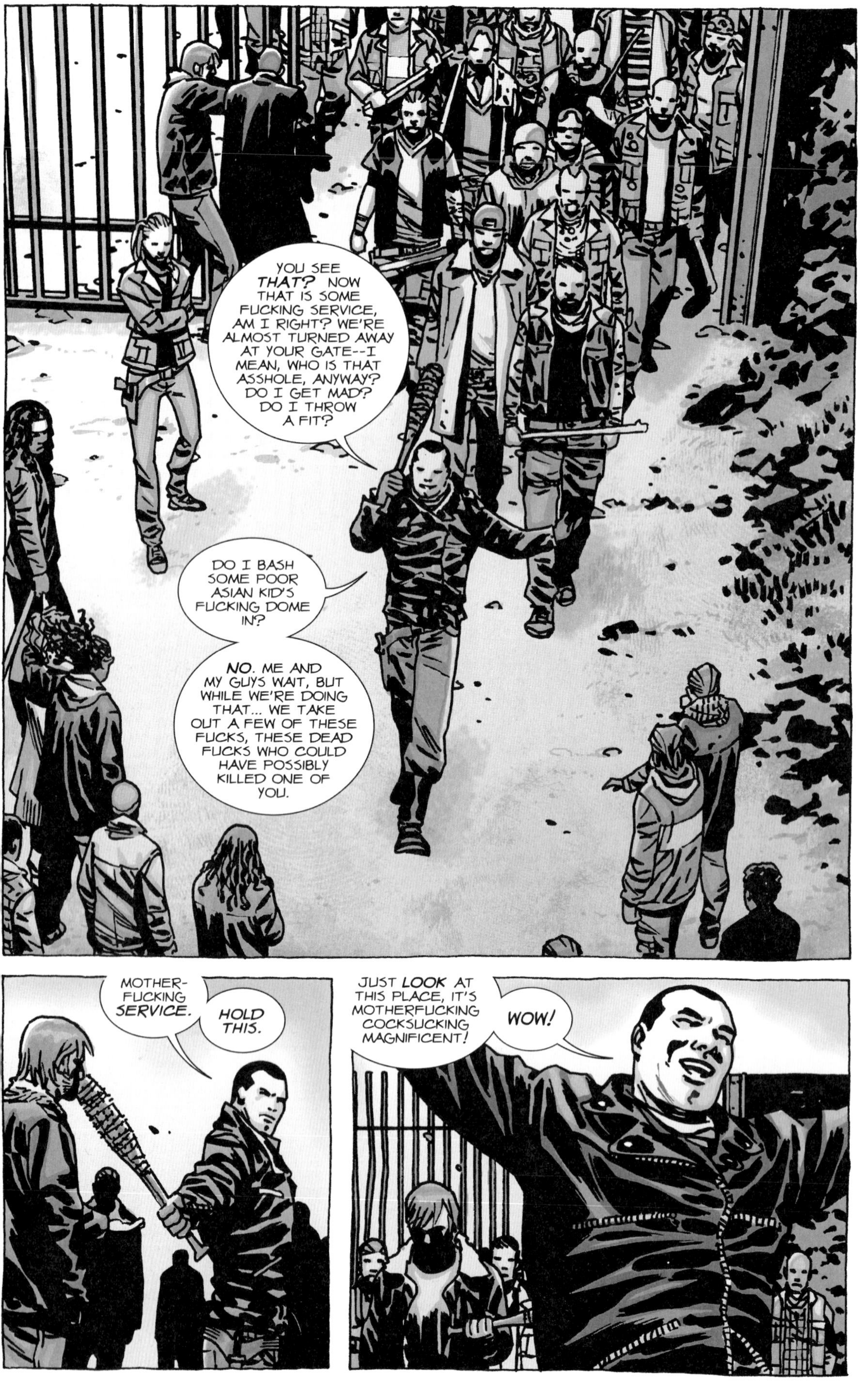
YOU SEE THAT? NOW THAT IS SOME FUCKING SERVICE, AM I RIGHT? WE'RE ALMOST TURNED AWAY AT YOUR GATE--I MEAN, WHO IS THAT ASSHOLE, ANYWAY? DO I GET MAD? DO I THROW A FIT?
DO I BASH SOME POOR ASIAN KID'S FUCKING DOME IN?
NO. ME AND MY GUYS WAIT, BUT WHILE WE'RE DOING THAT... WE TAKE OUT A FEW OF THESE FUCKS, THESE DEAD FUCKS WHO COULD HAVE POSSIBLY KILLED ONE OF YOU.
MOTHER-FUCKING SERVICE.
HOLD THIS.
JUST LOOK AT THIS PLACE, IT'S MOTHERFUCKING COCKSUCKING MAGNIFICENT!
WOW!

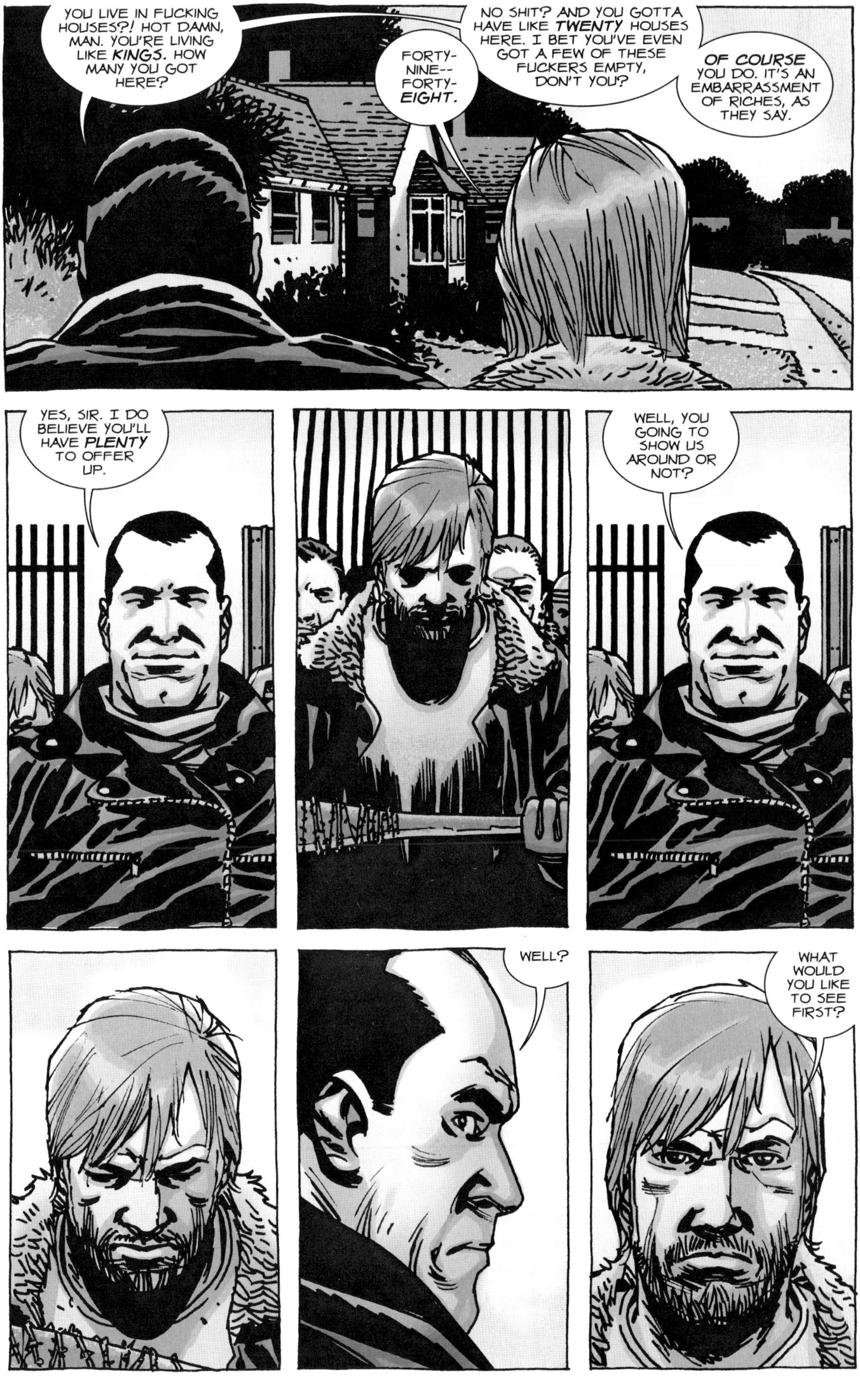
YOU LIVE IN FUCKING HOUSES?! HOT DAMN, MAN. YOU'RE LIVING LIKE KINGS. HOW MANY YOU GOT HERE?
FORTY-NINE--FORTY-EIGHT.
NO SHIT? AND YOU GOTTA HAVE LIKE TWENTY HOUSES HERE. I BET YOU'VE EVEN GOT A FEW OF THESE FUCKERS EMPTY, DON'T YOU?
OF COURSE YOU DO. IT'S AN EMBARRASSMENT OF RICHES, AS THEY SAY.
YES, SIR. I DO BELIEVE YOU'LL HAVE PLENTY TO OFFER UP.
WELL, YOU GOING TO SHOW US AROUND OR NOT?
WELL?
WHAT WOULD YOU LIKE TO SEE FIRST?

MY MEN ARE GOING TO SPLIT UP, SEARCH THE HOUSES A BIT, SPEED THIS PROCESS ALONG.

WHILE THEY'RE AT IT, I JUST WANT TO POINT OUT THAT WE'RE NOT TAKING A *SCRAP* OF YOUR FOOD. IT'S SLIM PICKENS IN THERE...

...AND I CAN'T BE THE ONLY ONE TO NOTICE YOU'VE GOT THE FAT LADY IN CHARGE OF KEEPING TRACK OF RATIONS, CAN I?

REGARDLESS, IF YOU GUYS STARVE TO DEATH, I DON'T GET SHIT. SO FOR NOW, YOUR FOOD STAYS WITH YOU.

WHAT DO YOU WANT ME TO SAY?

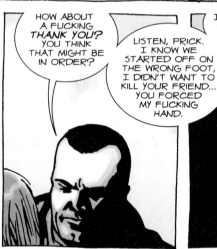

HOW ABOUT A FUCKING *THANK YOU?* YOU THINK THAT MIGHT BE IN ORDER?

LISTEN, PRICK. I KNOW WE STARTED OFF ON THE WRONG FOOT, I DIDN'T WANT TO KILL YOUR FRIEND... YOU FORCED MY FUCKING HAND.

I'M ACTUALLY *QUITE* REASONABLE IF YOU JUST FUCKING COOPERATE.

I'LL BELIEVE IT WHEN I SEE IT.

YOU SHOULD ALL GO HOME...

...BEFORE YOU LEARN JUST HOW *DANGEROUS* WE ALL ARE.

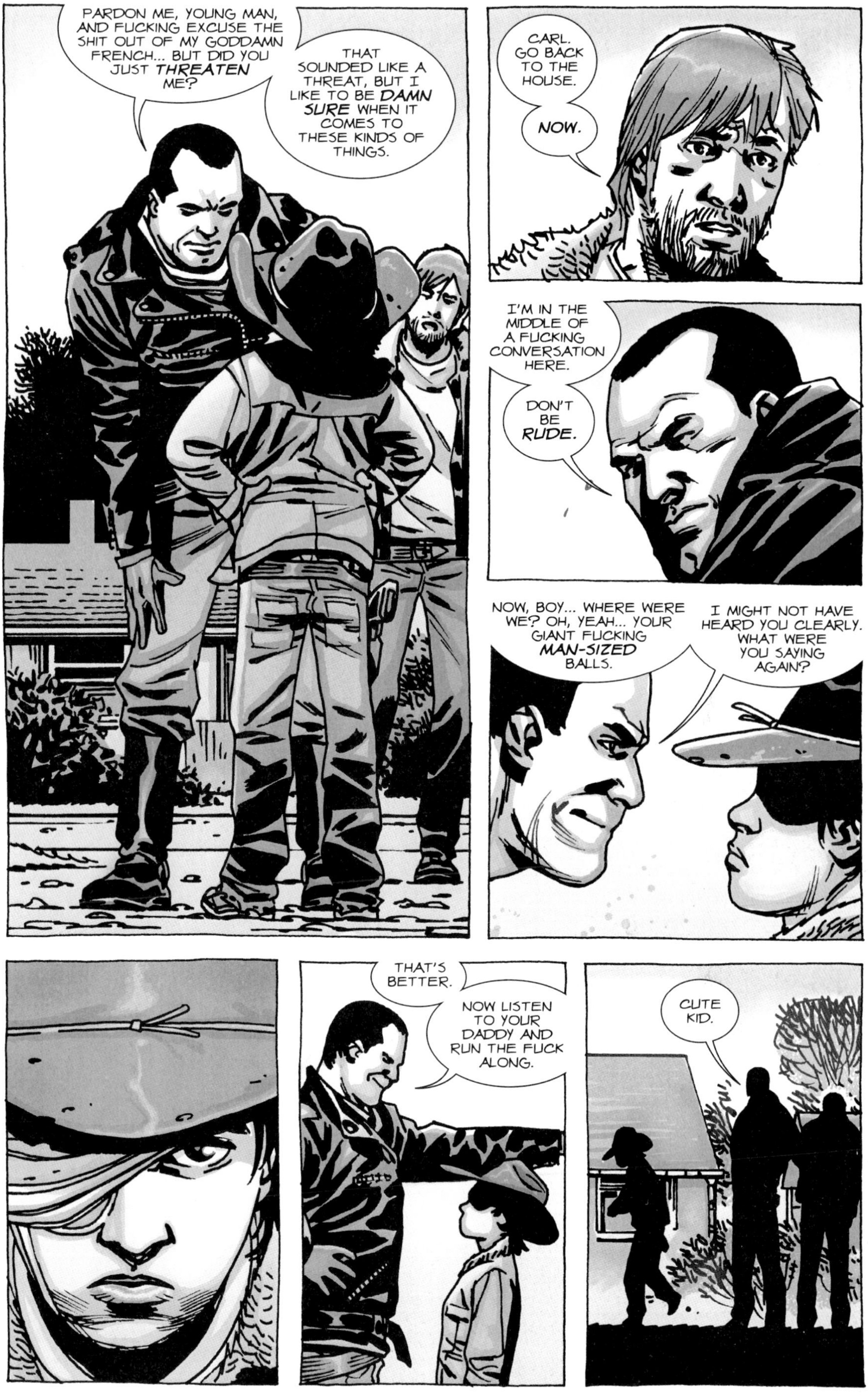
PARDON ME, YOUNG MAN, AND FUCKING EXCUSE THE SHIT OUT OF MY GODDAMN FRENCH... BUT DID YOU JUST THREATEN ME?
THAT SOUNDED LIKE A THREAT, BUT I LIKE TO BE DAMN SURE WHEN IT COMES TO THESE KINDS OF THINGS.
CARL. GO BACK TO THE HOUSE.
NOW.
I'M IN THE MIDDLE OF A FUCKING CONVERSATION HERE.
DON'T BE RUDE.
NOW, BOY... WHERE WERE WE? OH, YEAH... YOUR GIANT FUCKING MAN-SIZED BALLS.
I MIGHT NOT HAVE HEARD YOU CLEARLY. WHAT WERE YOU SAYING AGAIN?
THAT'S BETTER.
NOW LISTEN TO YOUR DADDY AND RUN THE FUCK ALONG.
CUTE KID.

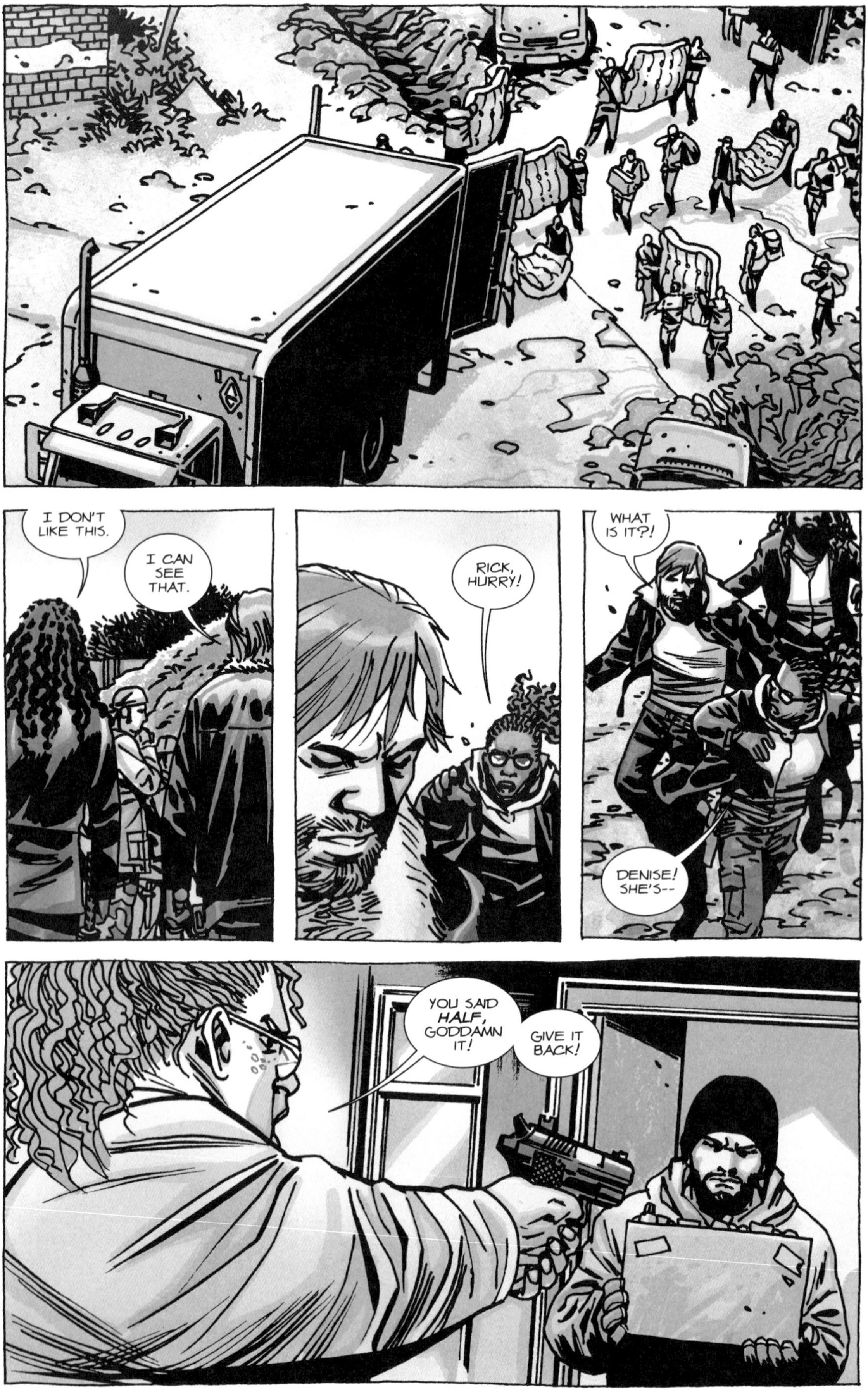

I DON'T LIKE THIS.
I CAN SEE THAT.
RICK, HURRY!
WHAT IS IT?!
DENISE! SHE'S--
YOU SAID **HALF**, GODDAMN IT!
GIVE IT BACK!

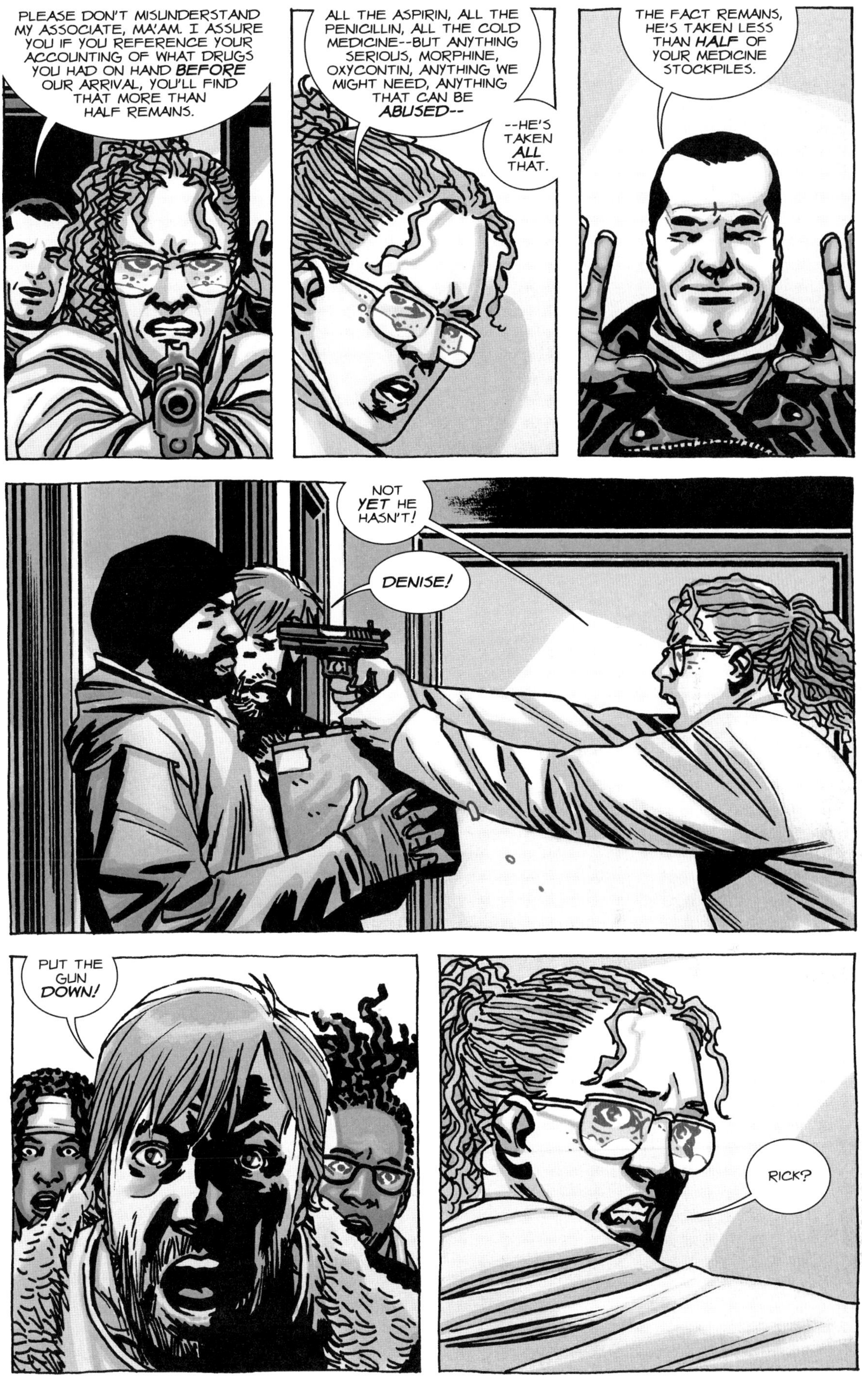
PLEASE DON'T MISUNDERSTAND MY ASSOCIATE, MA'AM. I ASSURE YOU IF YOU REFERENCE YOUR ACCOUNTING OF WHAT DRUGS YOU HAD ON HAND BEFORE OUR ARRIVAL, YOU'LL FIND THAT MORE THAN HALF REMAINS.
ALL THE ASPIRIN, ALL THE PENICILLIN, ALL THE COLD MEDICINE--BUT ANYTHING SERIOUS, MORPHINE, OXYCONTIN, ANYTHING WE MIGHT NEED, ANYTHING THAT CAN BE ABUSED--
--HE'S TAKEN ALL THAT.
THE FACT REMAINS, HE'S TAKEN LESS THAN HALF OF YOUR MEDICINE STOCKPILES.
NOT YET HE HASN'T!
DENISE!
PUT THE GUN DOWN!
RICK?

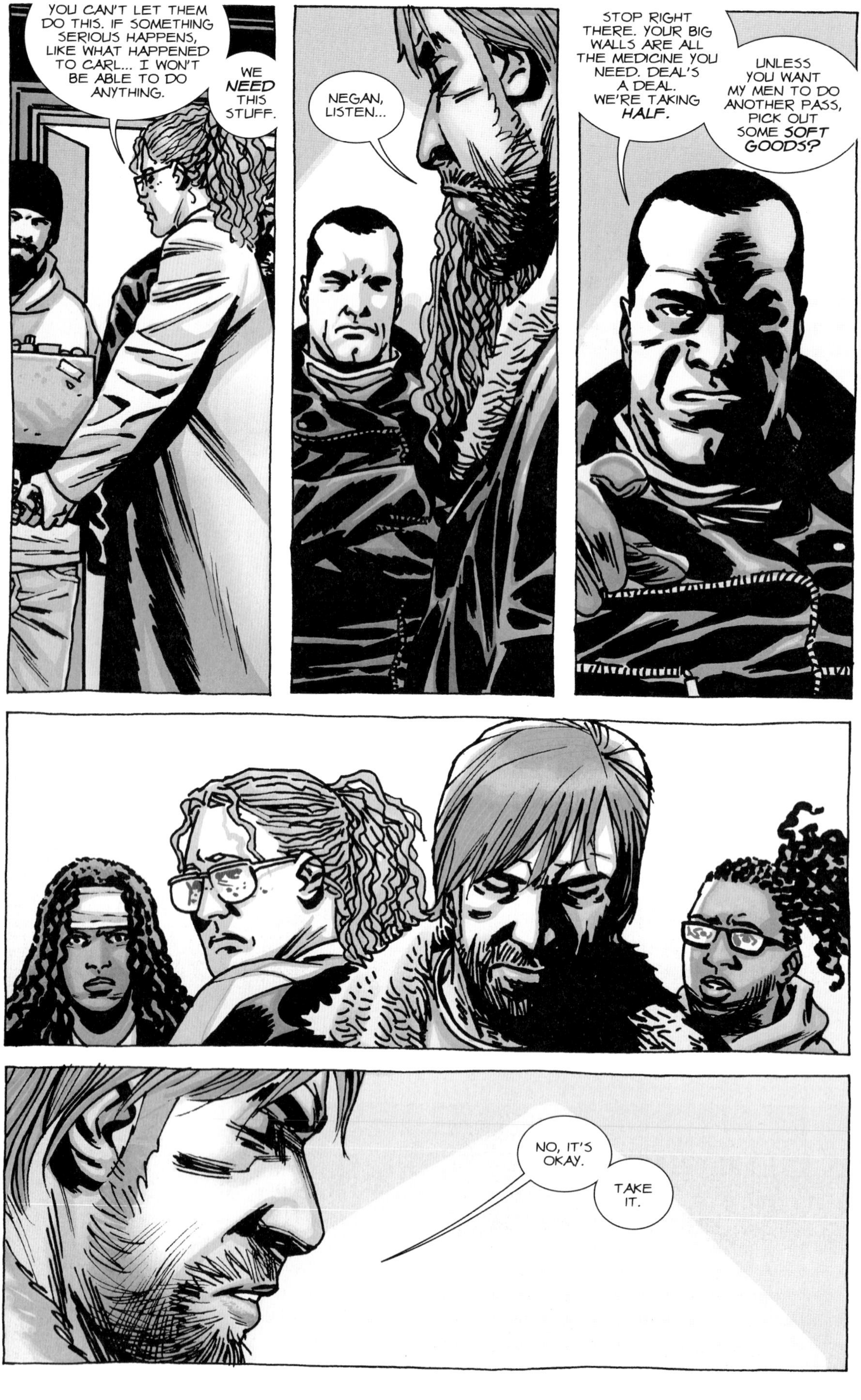

YOU CAN'T LET THEM DO THIS. IF SOMETHING SERIOUS HAPPENS, LIKE WHAT HAPPENED TO CARL... I WON'T BE ABLE TO DO ANYTHING.
WE **NEED** THIS STUFF.
NEGAN, LISTEN...
STOP RIGHT THERE. YOUR BIG WALLS ARE ALL THE MEDICINE YOU NEED. DEAL'S A DEAL. WE'RE TAKING **HALF.**
UNLESS YOU WANT MY MEN TO DO ANOTHER PASS, PICK OUT SOME **SOFT GOODS?**
NO, IT'S OKAY.
TAKE IT.

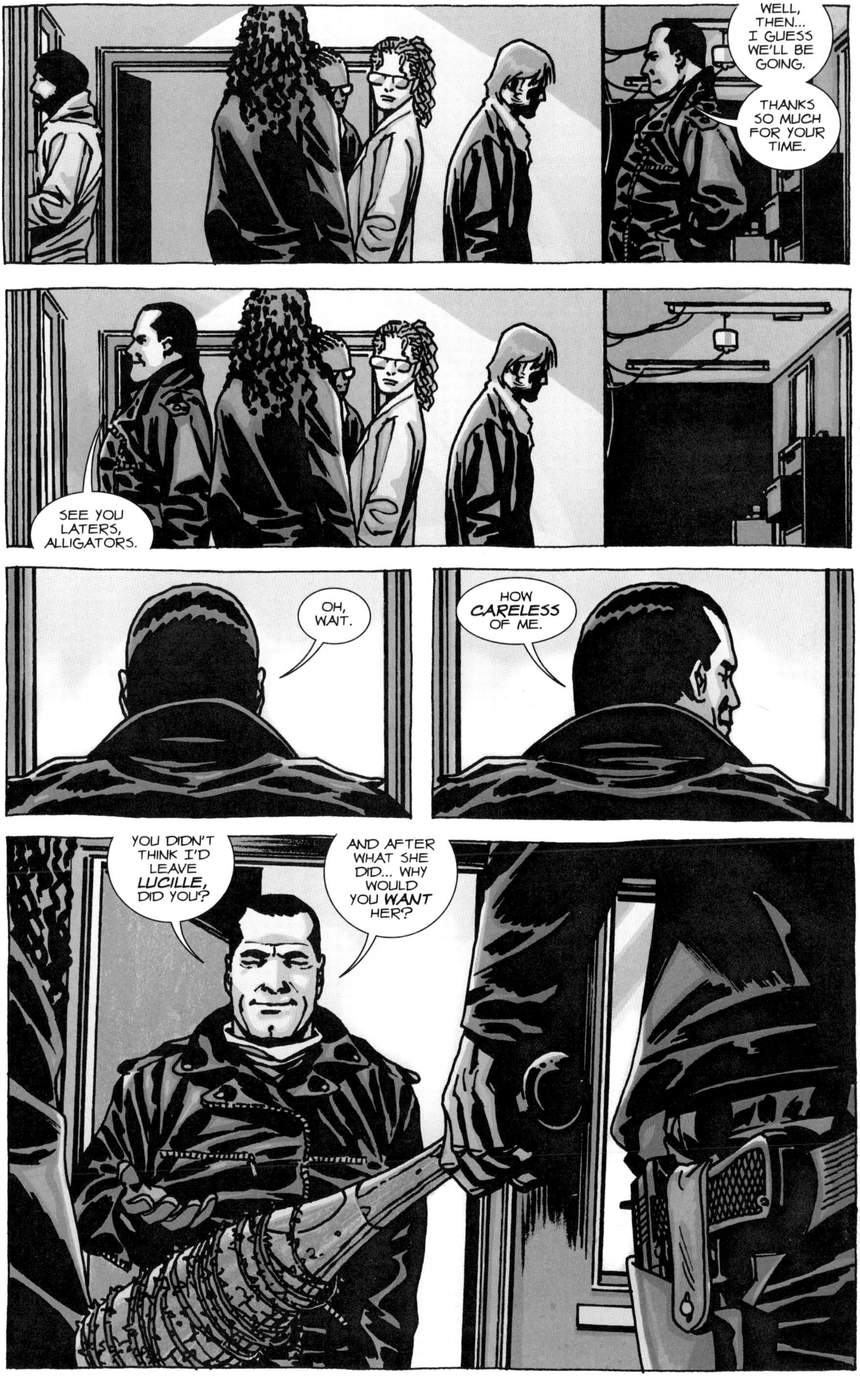
WELL, THEN... I GUESS WE'LL BE GOING.
THANKS SO MUCH FOR YOUR TIME.
SEE YOU LATERS, ALLIGATORS.
OH, WAIT.
HOW *CARELESS* OF ME.
YOU DIDN'T THINK I'D LEAVE *LUCILLE,* DID YOU?
AND AFTER WHAT SHE DID... WHY WOULD YOU *WANT* HER?

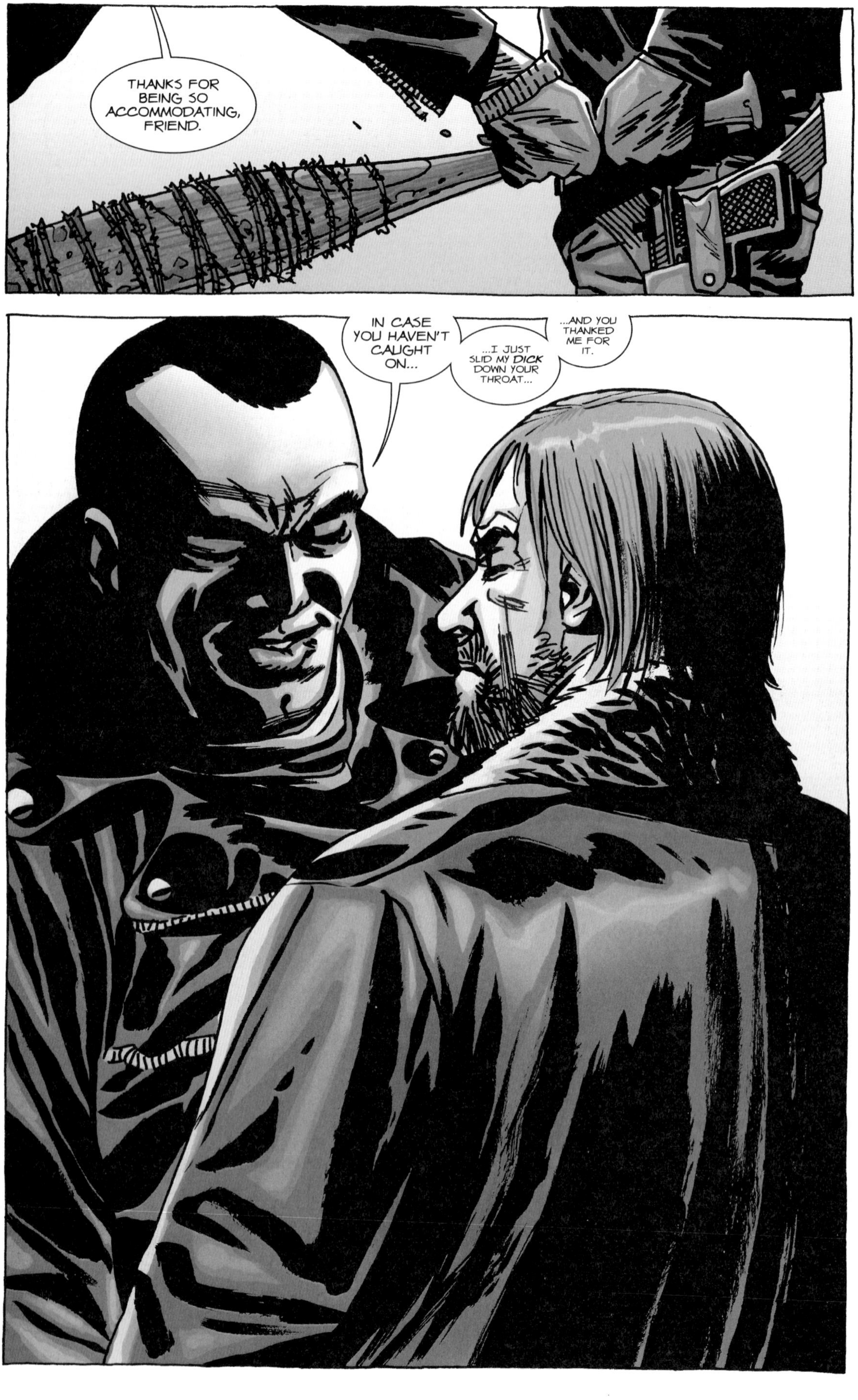
THANKS FOR BEING SO ACCOMMODATING, FRIEND.
IN CASE YOU HAVEN'T CAUGHT ON...
...I JUST SLID MY *DICK* DOWN YOUR THROAT...
...AND YOU THANKED ME FOR IT.

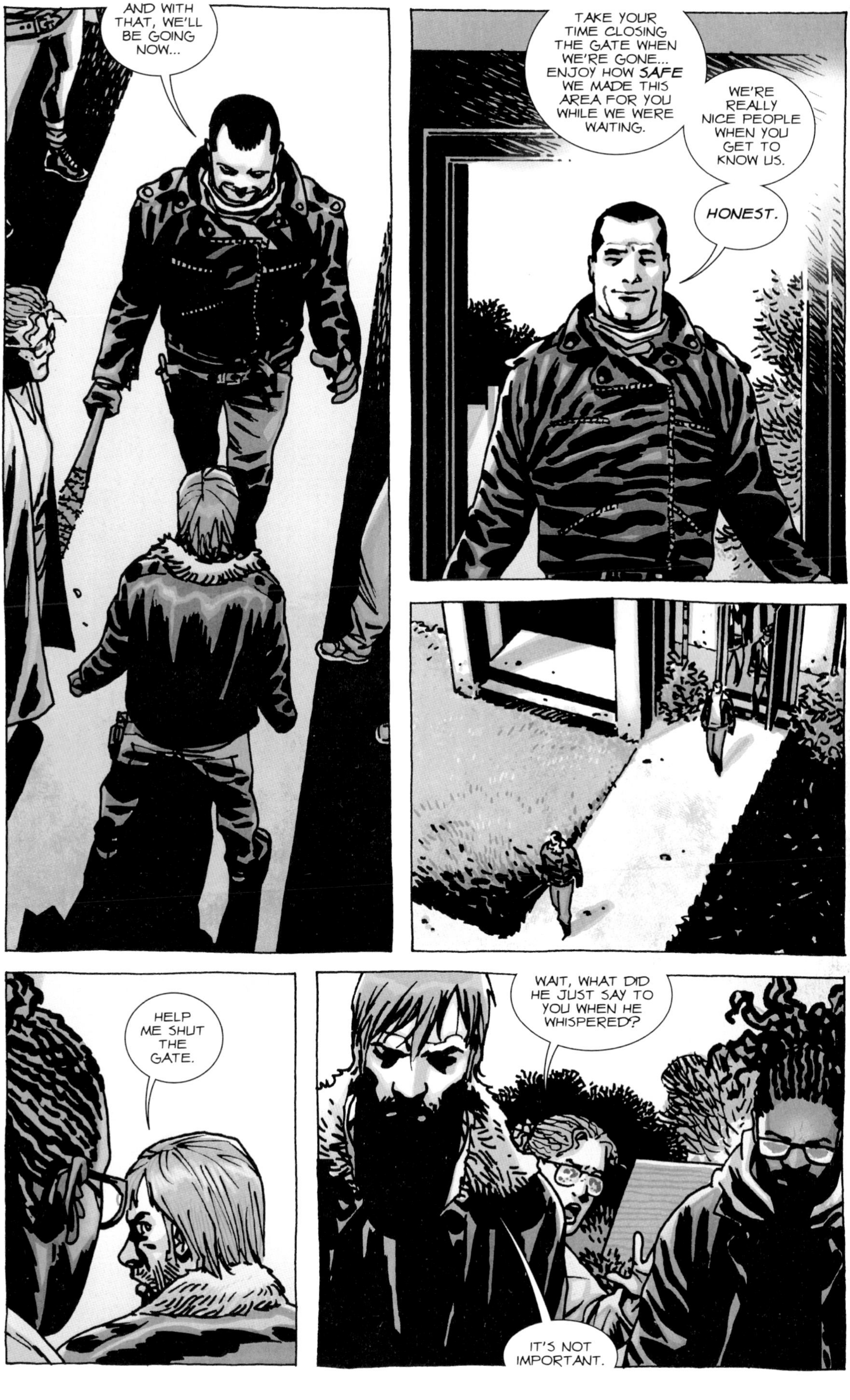
AND WITH THAT, WE'LL BE GOING NOW...
TAKE YOUR TIME CLOSING THE GATE WHEN WE'RE GONE... ENJOY HOW SAFE WE MADE THIS AREA FOR YOU WHILE WE WERE WAITING.
WE'RE REALLY NICE PEOPLE WHEN YOU GET TO KNOW US.
HONEST.
HELP ME SHUT THE GATE.
WAIT, WHAT DID HE JUST SAY TO YOU WHEN HE WHISPERED?
IT'S NOT IMPORTANT.

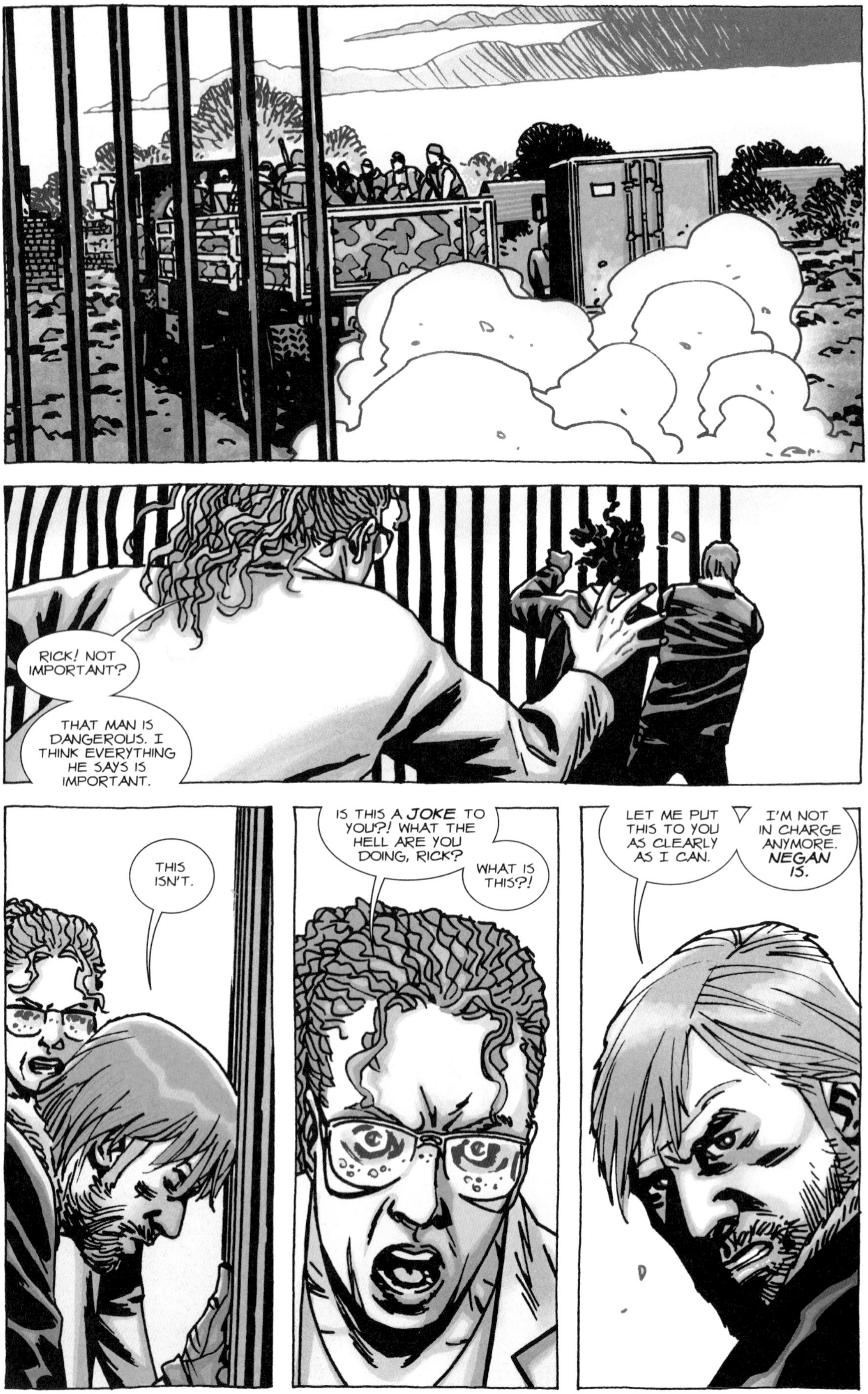

RICK! NOT IMPORTANT?
THAT MAN IS DANGEROUS. I THINK EVERYTHING HE SAYS IS IMPORTANT.
THIS ISN'T.
IS THIS A JOKE TO YOU?! WHAT THE HELL ARE YOU DOING, RICK?
WHAT IS THIS?!
LET ME PUT THIS TO YOU AS CLEARLY AS I CAN.
I'M NOT IN CHARGE ANYMORE. NEGAN IS.

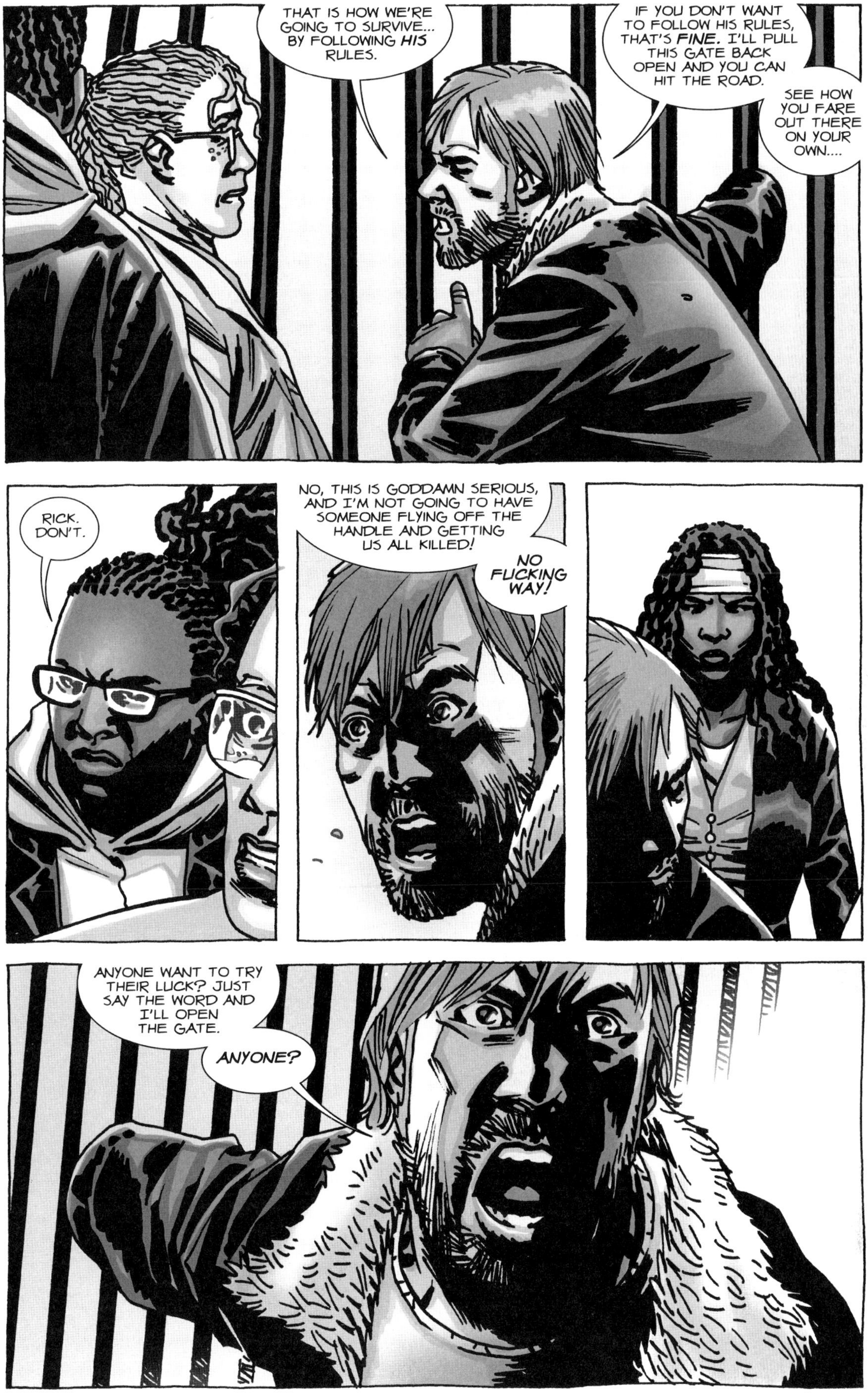
THAT IS HOW WE'RE GOING TO SURVIVE... BY FOLLOWING *HIS* RULES.
IF YOU DON'T WANT TO FOLLOW HIS RULES, THAT'S *FINE.* I'LL PULL THIS GATE BACK OPEN AND YOU CAN HIT THE ROAD.
SEE HOW YOU FARE OUT THERE ON YOUR OWN....
RICK. DON'T.
NO, THIS IS GODDAMN SERIOUS, AND I'M NOT GOING TO HAVE SOMEONE FLYING OFF THE HANDLE AND GETTING US ALL KILLED!
NO FUCKING WAY!
ANYONE WANT TO TRY THEIR LUCK? JUST SAY THE WORD AND I'LL OPEN THE GATE.
ANYONE?

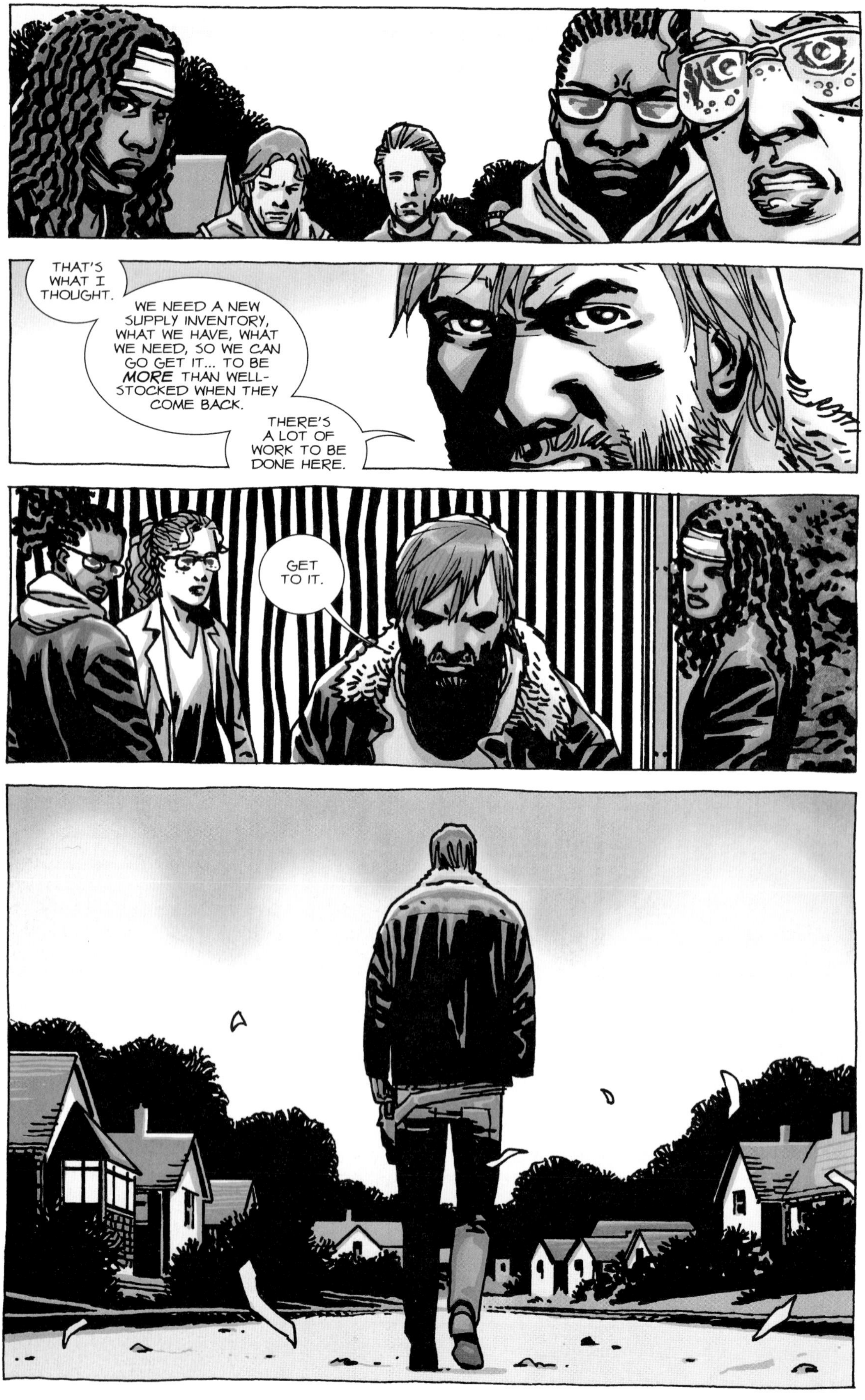
THAT'S WHAT I THOUGHT.
WE NEED A NEW SUPPLY INVENTORY, WHAT WE HAVE, WHAT WE NEED, SO WE CAN GO GET IT... TO BE MORE THAN WELL-STOCKED WHEN THEY COME BACK.
THERE'S A LOT OF WORK TO BE DONE HERE.
GET TO IT.

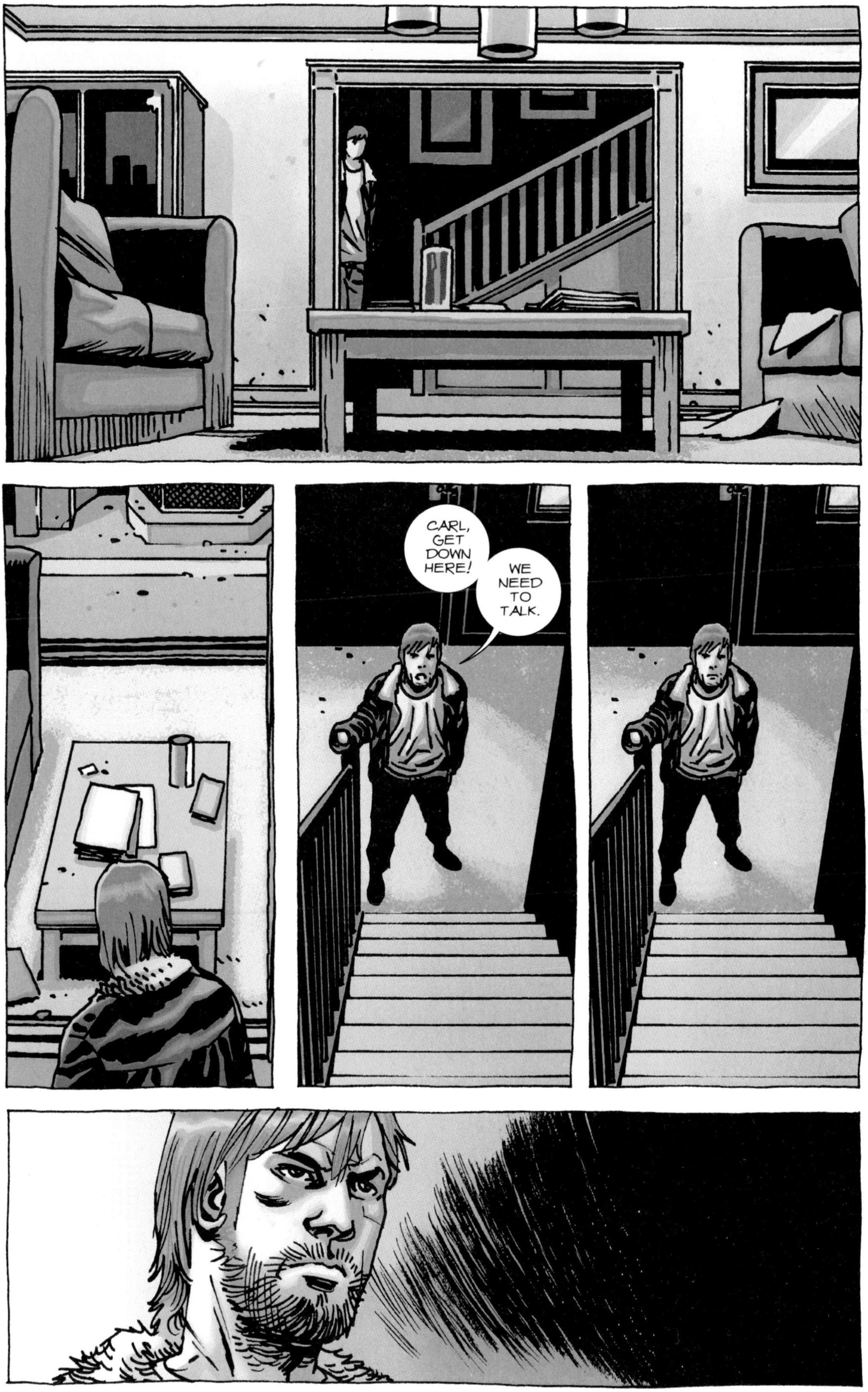
CARL, GET DOWN HERE!
WE NEED TO TALK.

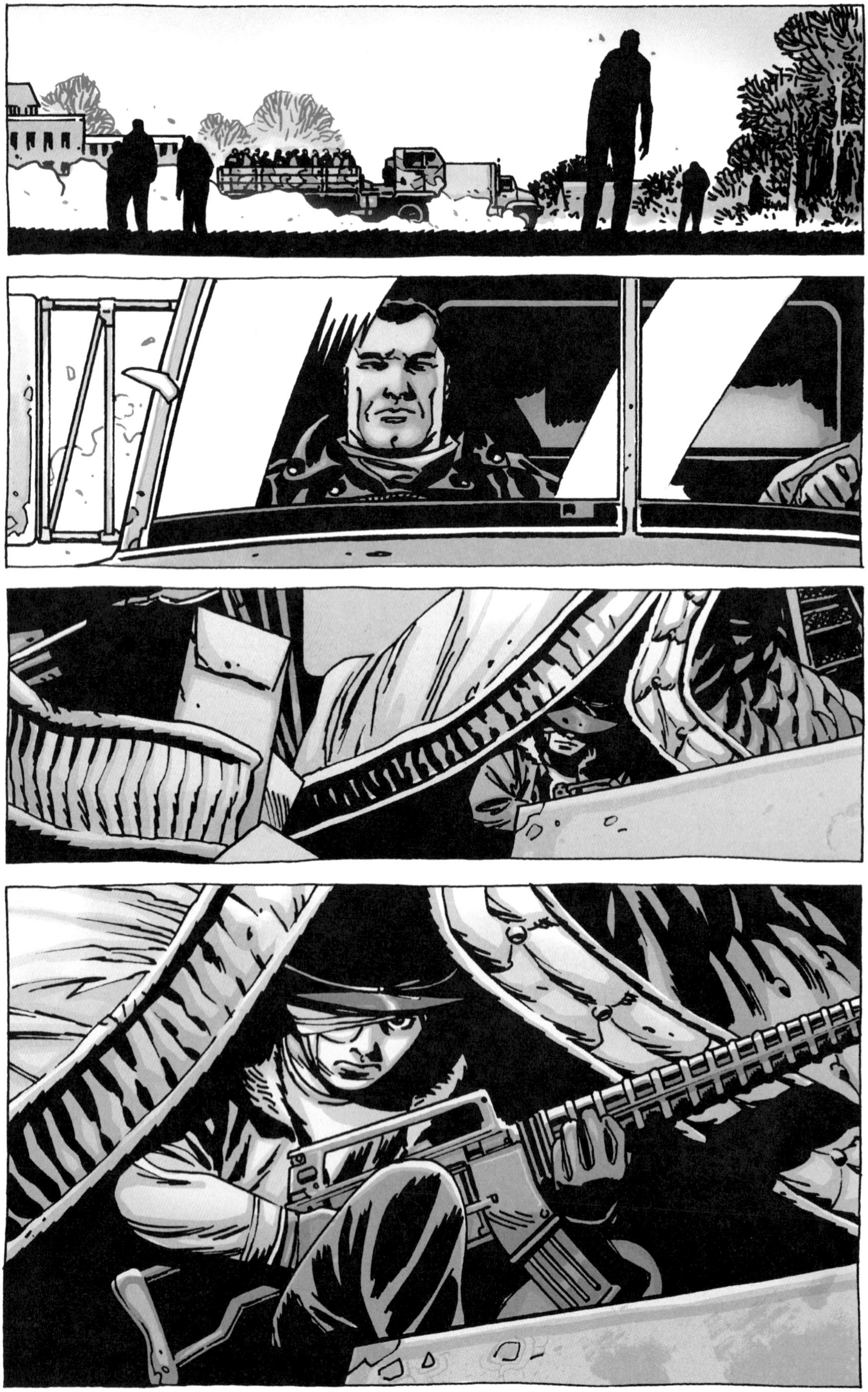

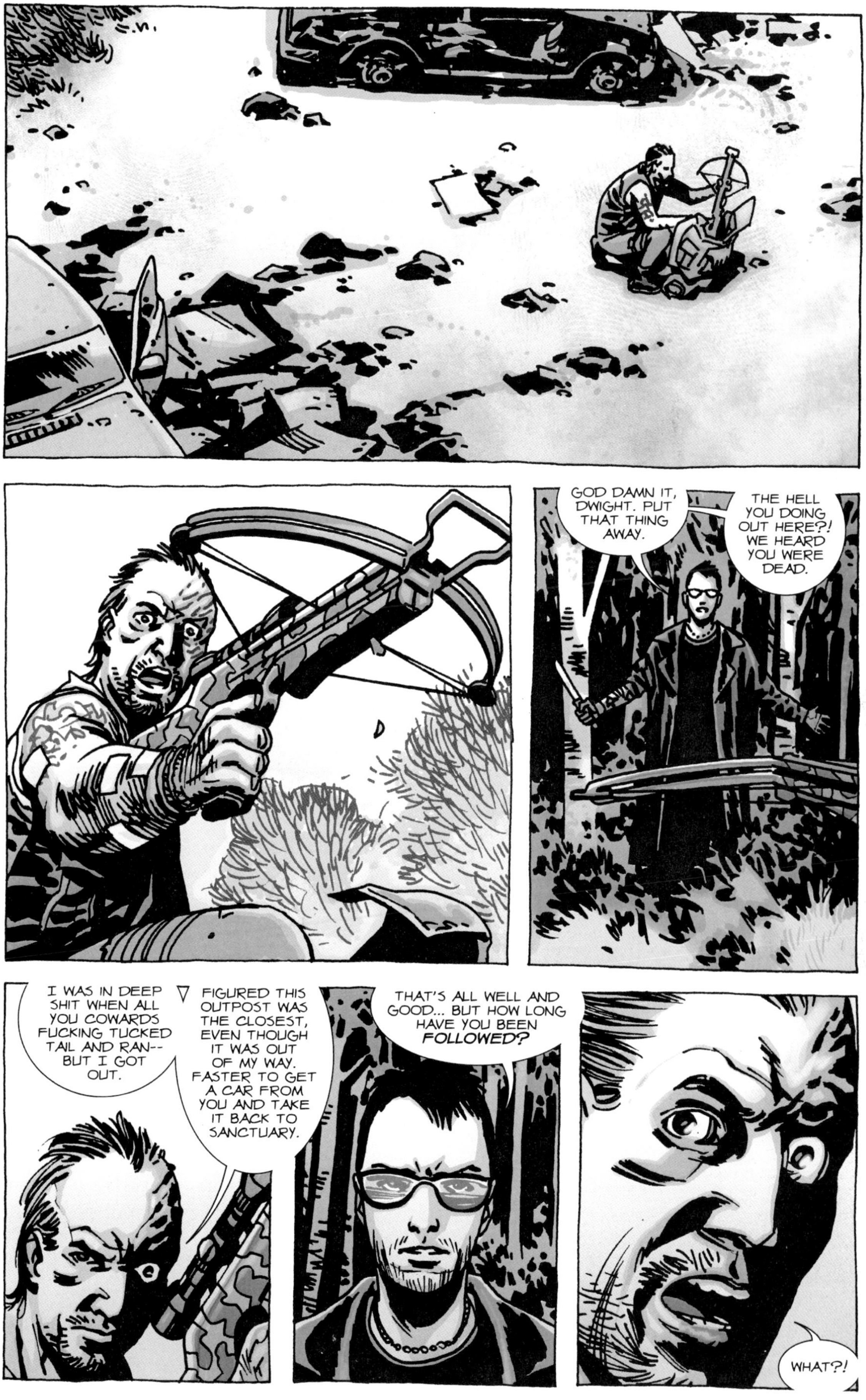
GOD DAMN IT, DWIGHT. PUT THAT THING AWAY.
THE HELL YOU DOING OUT HERE?! WE HEARD YOU WERE DEAD.
I WAS IN DEEP SHIT WHEN ALL YOU COWARDS FUCKING TUCKED TAIL AND RAN-- BUT I GOT OUT.
FIGURED THIS OUTPOST WAS THE CLOSEST, EVEN THOUGH IT WAS OUT OF MY WAY. FASTER TO GET A CAR FROM YOU AND TAKE IT BACK TO SANCTUARY.
THAT'S ALL WELL AND GOOD... BUT HOW LONG HAVE YOU BEEN FOLLOWED?
WHAT?!

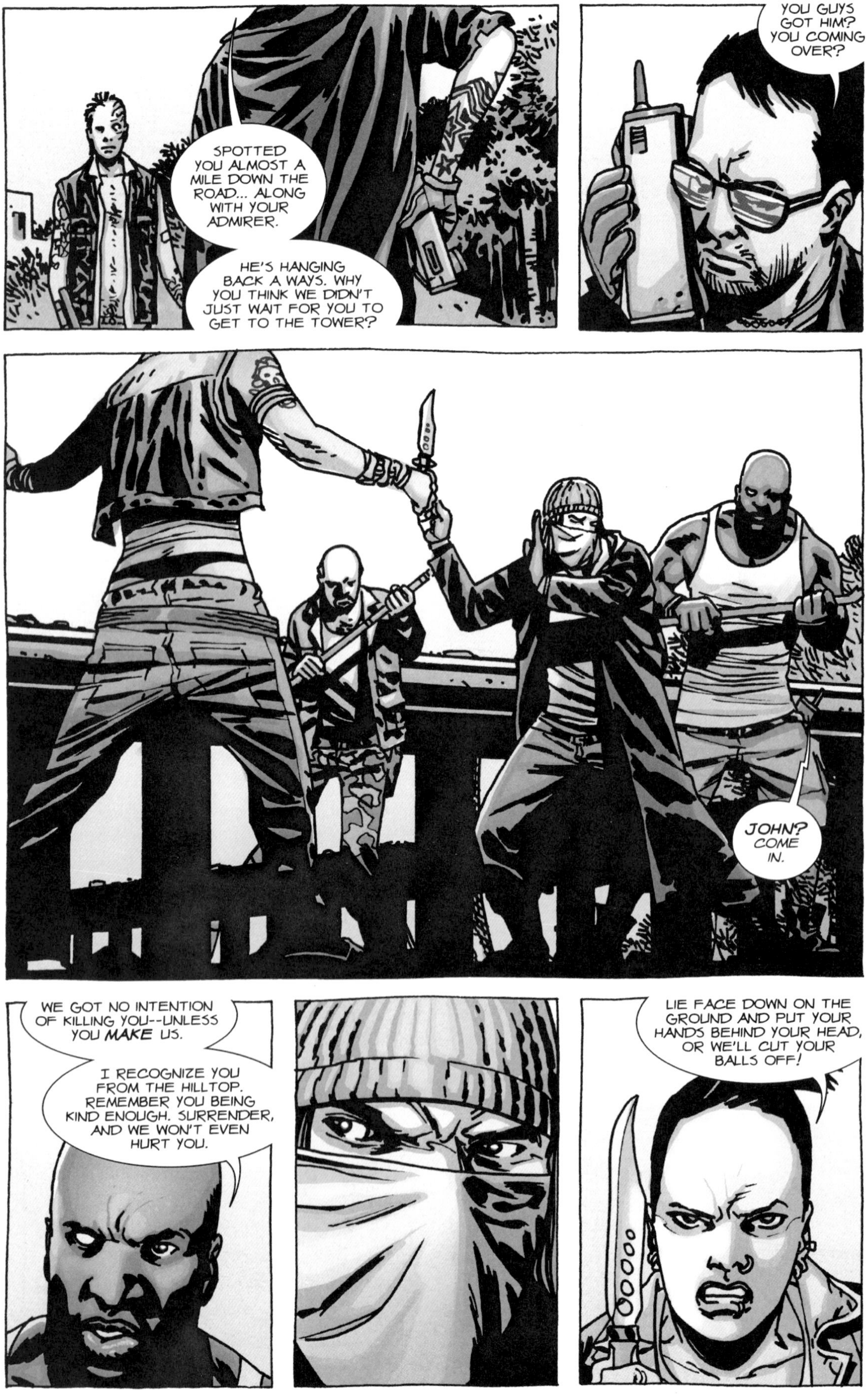
SPOTTED YOU ALMOST A MILE DOWN THE ROAD... ALONG WITH YOUR ADMIRER.
HE'S HANGING BACK A WAYS. WHY YOU THINK WE DIDN'T JUST WAIT FOR YOU TO GET TO THE TOWER?
YOU GUYS GOT HIM? YOU COMING OVER?
JOHN? COME IN.
WE GOT NO INTENTION OF KILLING YOU--UNLESS YOU MAKE US.
I RECOGNIZE YOU FROM THE HILLTOP. REMEMBER YOU BEING KIND ENOUGH. SURRENDER, AND WE WON'T EVEN HURT YOU.
LIE FACE DOWN ON THE GROUND AND PUT YOUR HANDS BEHIND YOUR HEAD, OR WE'LL CUT YOUR BALLS OFF!

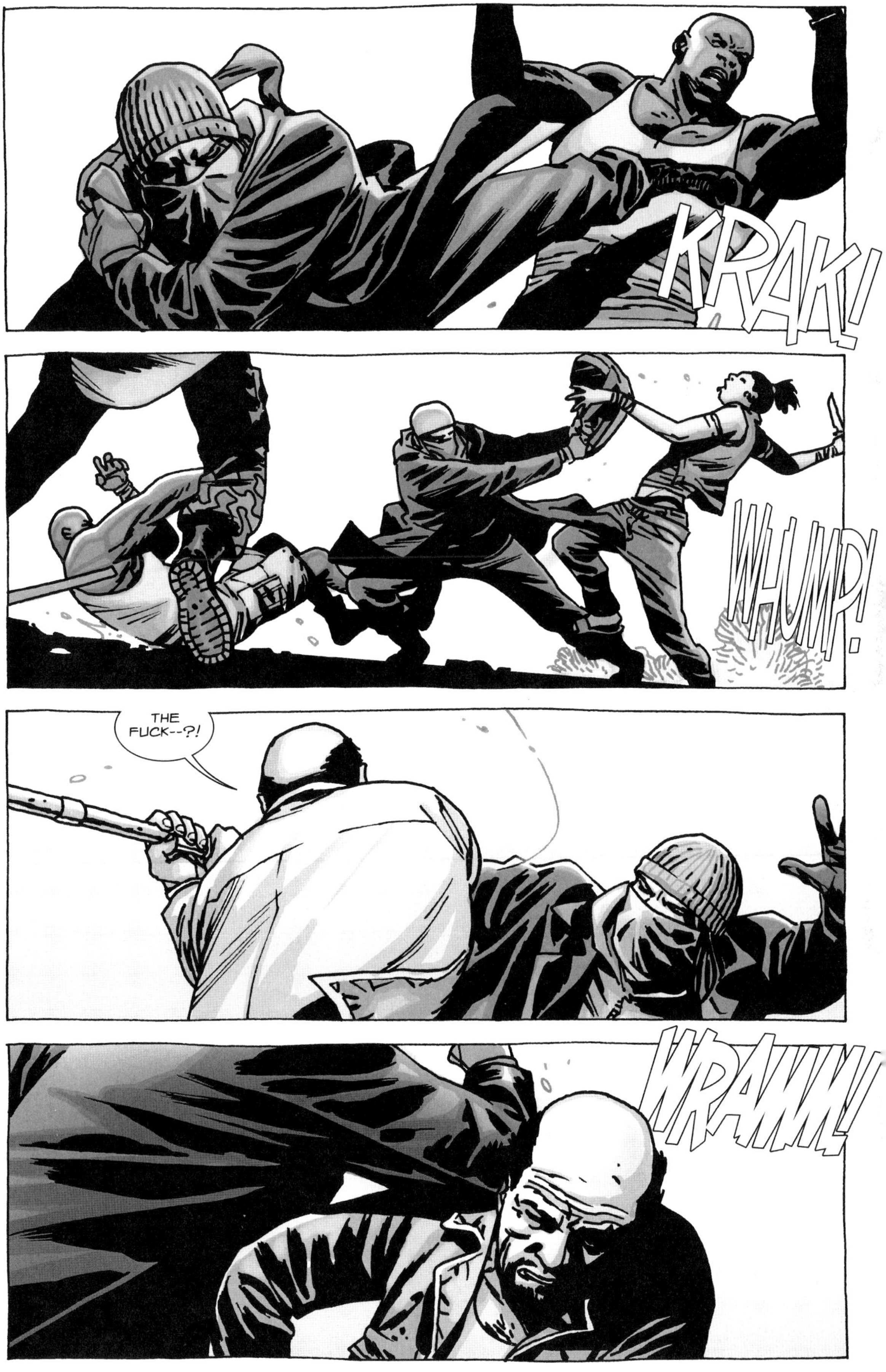
KRAK!
WHUMP!
THE FUCK--?!
WRAMM!

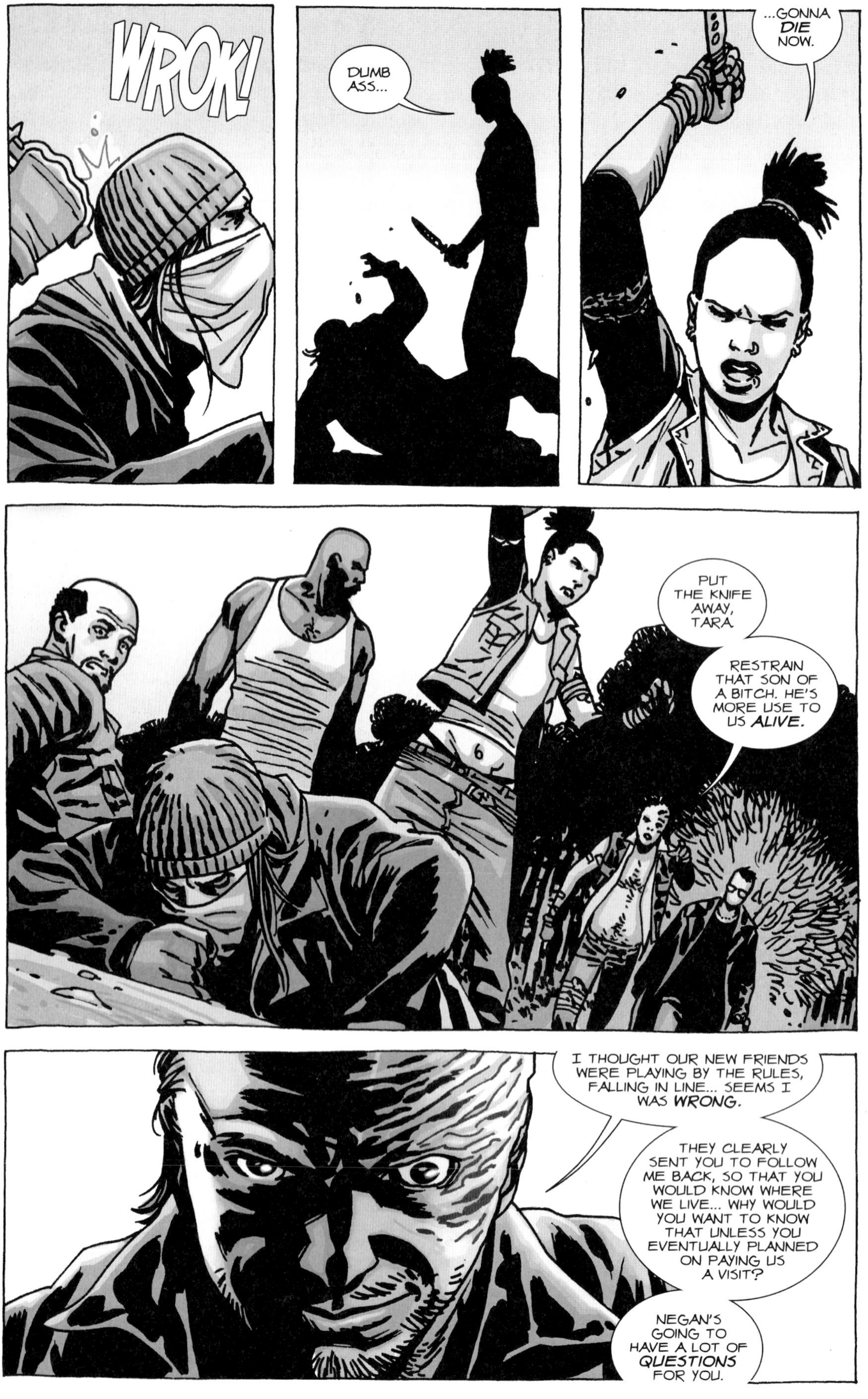
WROK!
DUMB ASS...
...GONNA DIE NOW.
PUT THE KNIFE AWAY, TARA.
RESTRAIN THAT SON OF A BITCH. HE'S MORE USE TO US ALIVE.
I THOUGHT OUR NEW FRIENDS WERE PLAYING BY THE RULES, FALLING IN LINE... SEEMS I WAS WRONG.
THEY CLEARLY SENT YOU TO FOLLOW ME BACK, SO THAT YOU WOULD KNOW WHERE WE LIVE... WHY WOULD YOU WANT TO KNOW THAT UNLESS YOU EVENTUALLY PLANNED ON PAYING US A VISIT?
NEGAN'S GOING TO HAVE A LOT OF QUESTIONS FOR YOU.

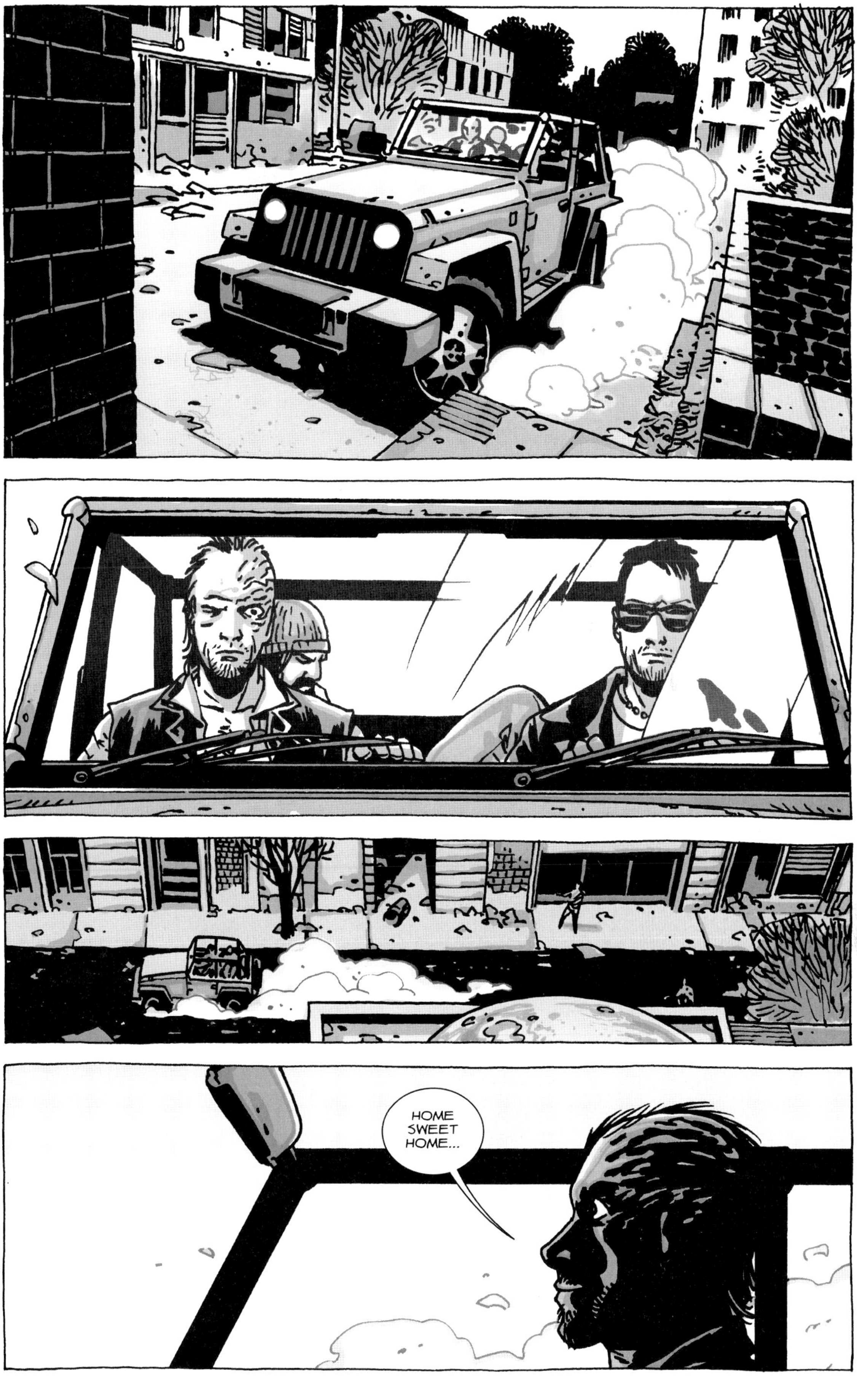
HOME SWEET HOME...

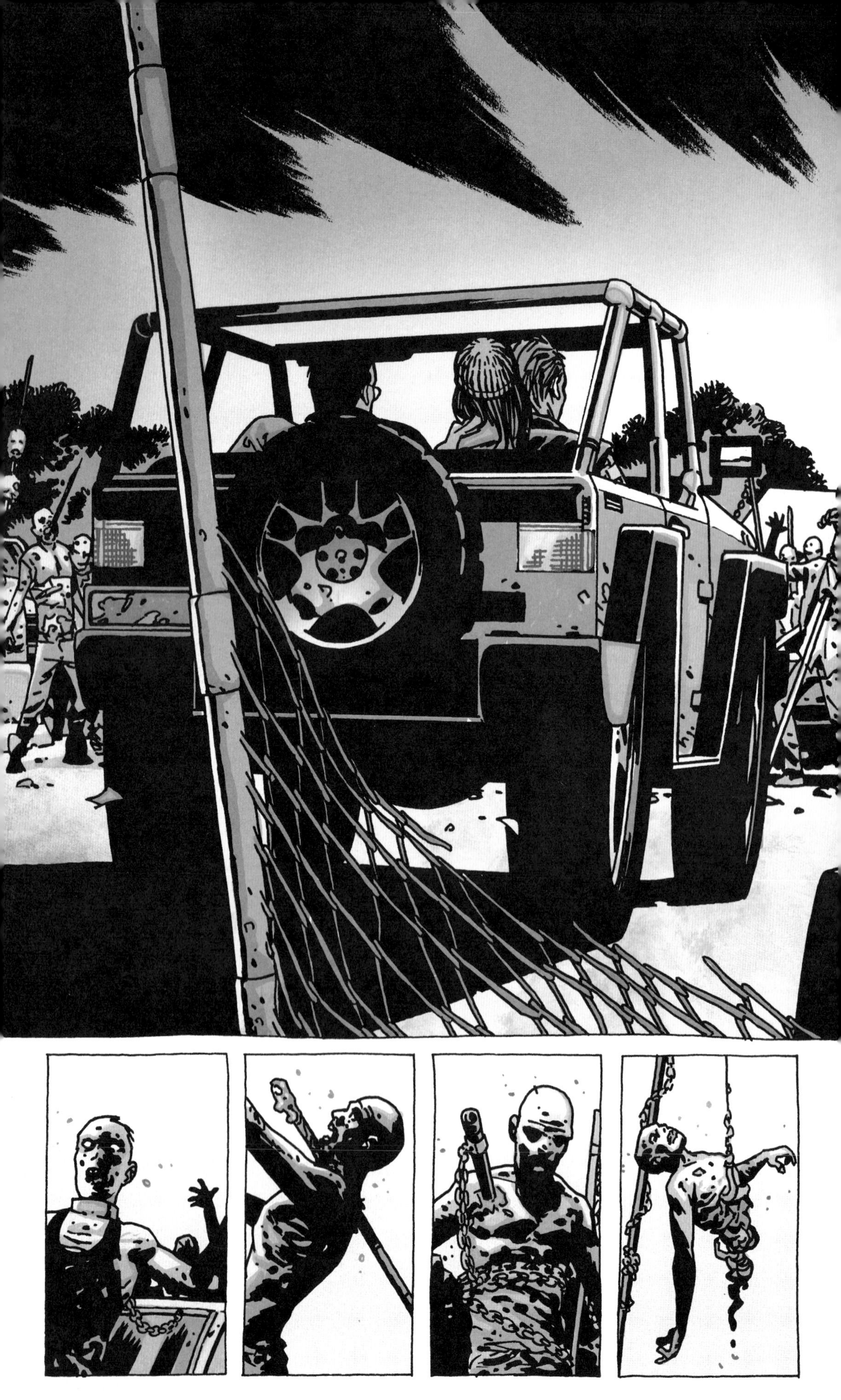

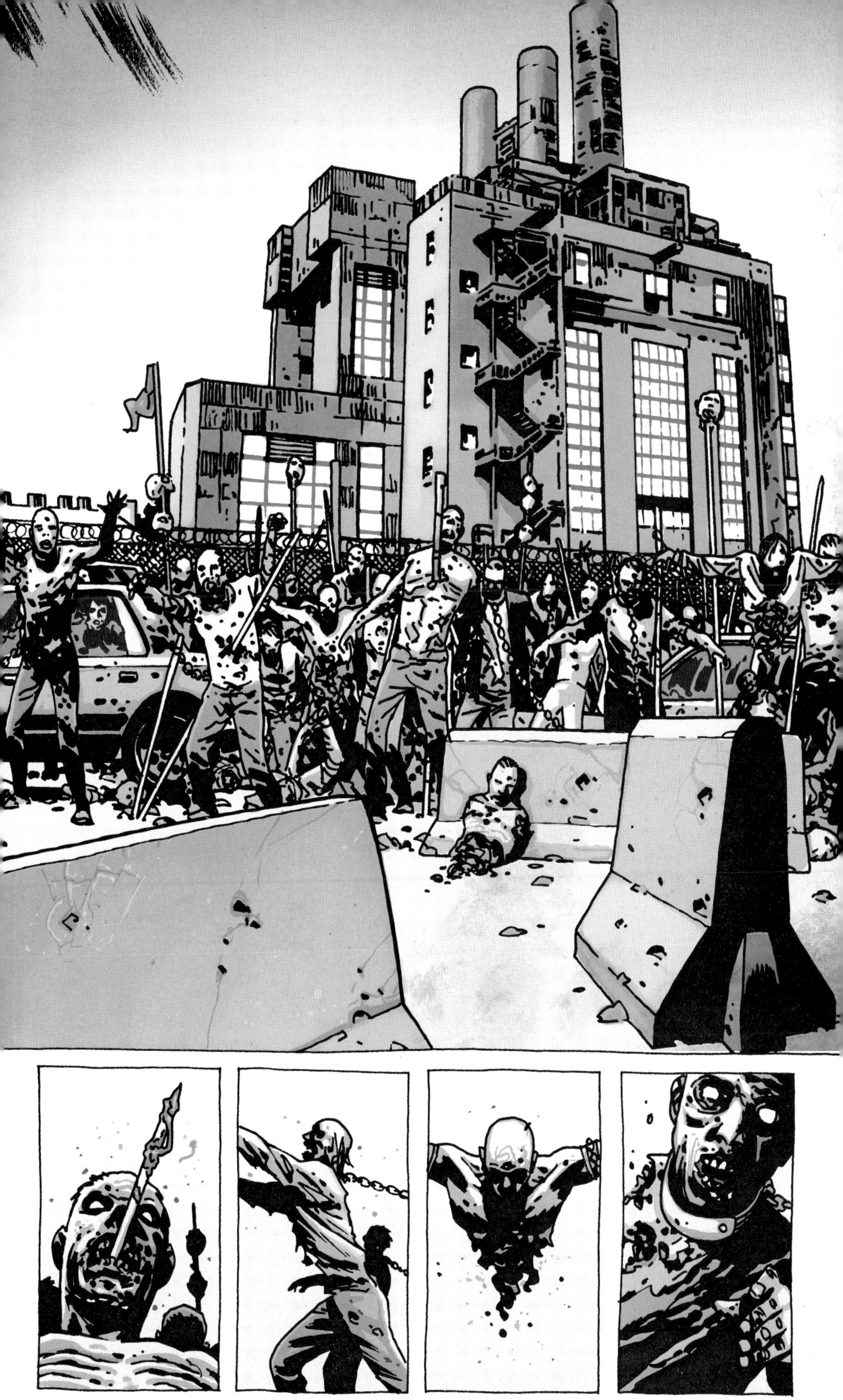

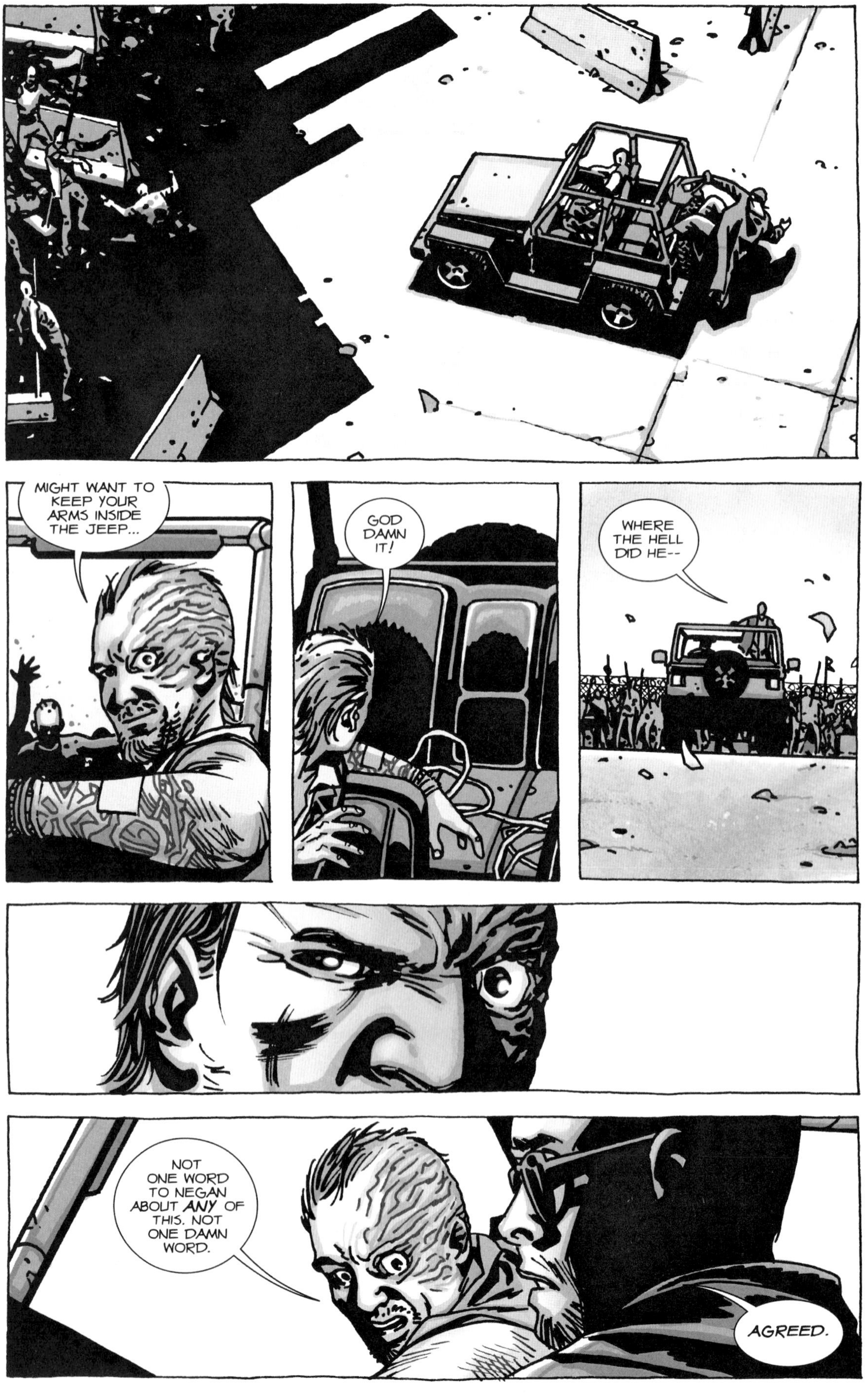
MIGHT WANT TO KEEP YOUR ARMS INSIDE THE JEEP...
GOD DAMN IT!
WHERE THE HELL DID HE--
NOT ONE WORD TO NEGAN ABOUT *ANY* OF THIS. NOT ONE DAMN WORD.
AGREED.

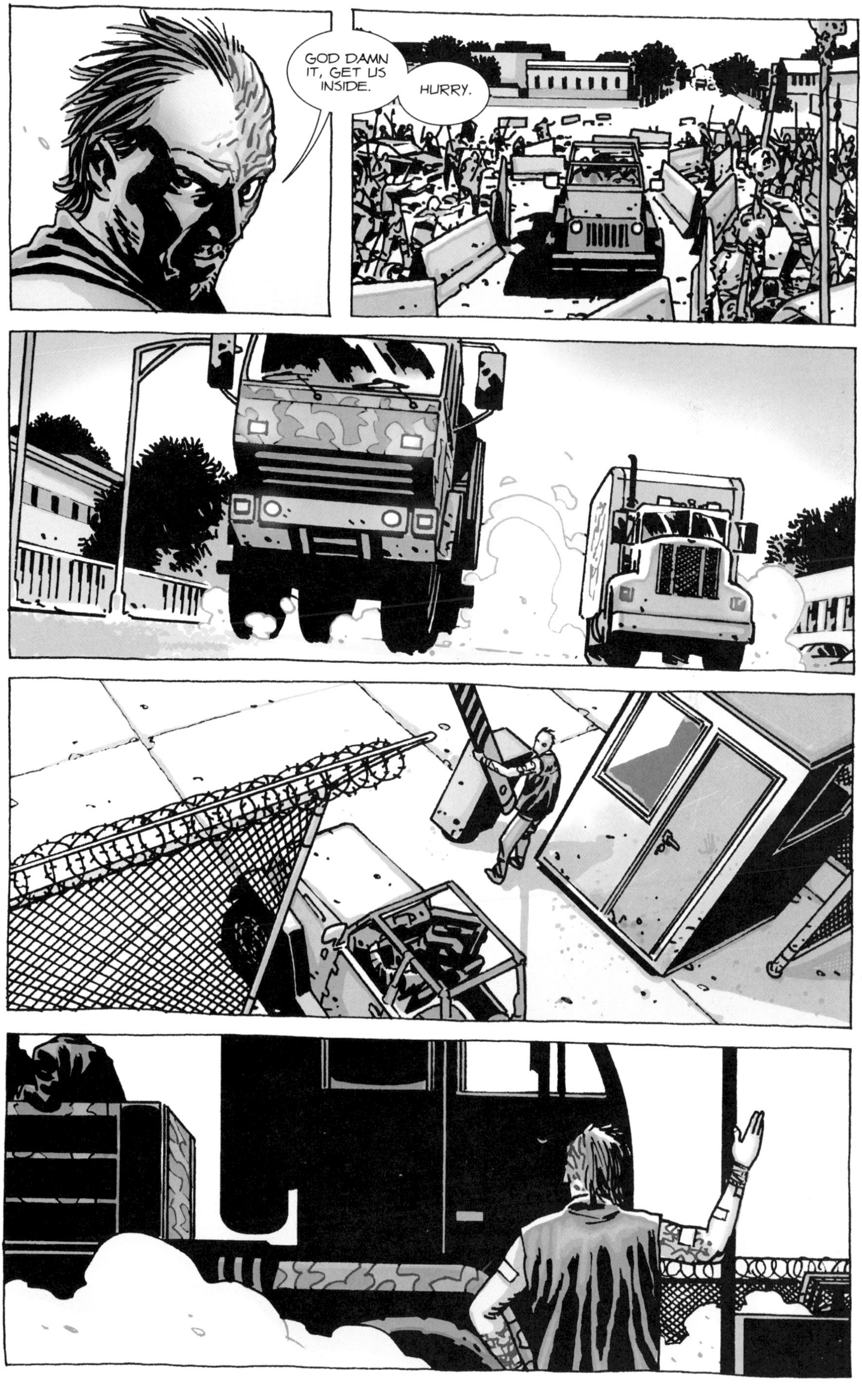
GOD DAMN IT, GET US INSIDE.
HURRY.

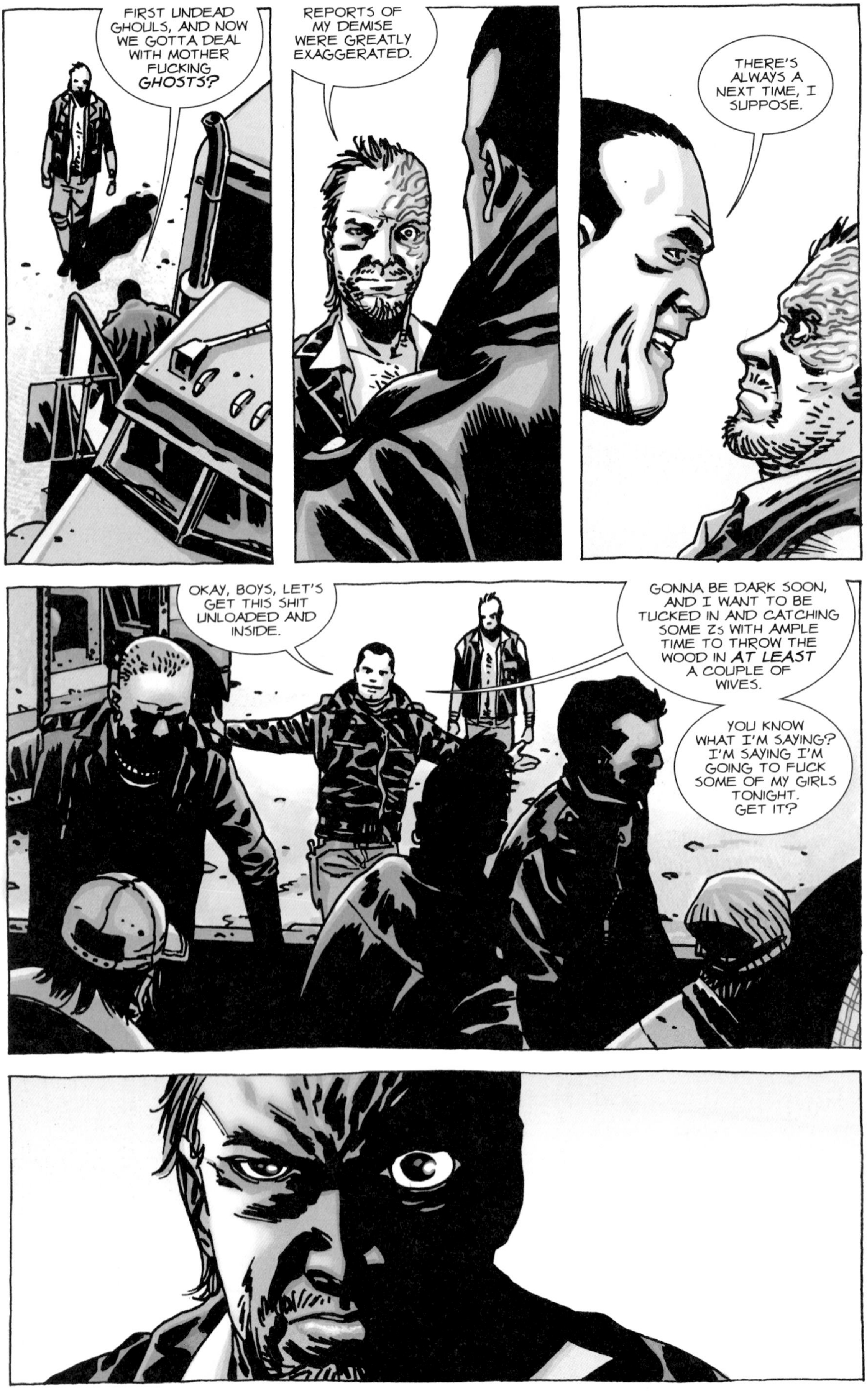
FIRST UNDEAD GHOULS, AND NOW WE GOTTA DEAL WITH MOTHER FUCKING GHOSTS?
REPORTS OF MY DEMISE WERE GREATLY EXAGGERATED.
THERE'S ALWAYS A NEXT TIME, I SUPPOSE.
OKAY, BOYS, LET'S GET THIS SHIT UNLOADED AND INSIDE.
GONNA BE DARK SOON, AND I WANT TO BE TUCKED IN AND CATCHING SOME Zs WITH AMPLE TIME TO THROW THE WOOD IN AT LEAST A COUPLE OF WIVES.
YOU KNOW WHAT I'M SAYING? I'M SAYING I'M GOING TO FUCK SOME OF MY GIRLS TONIGHT. GET IT?

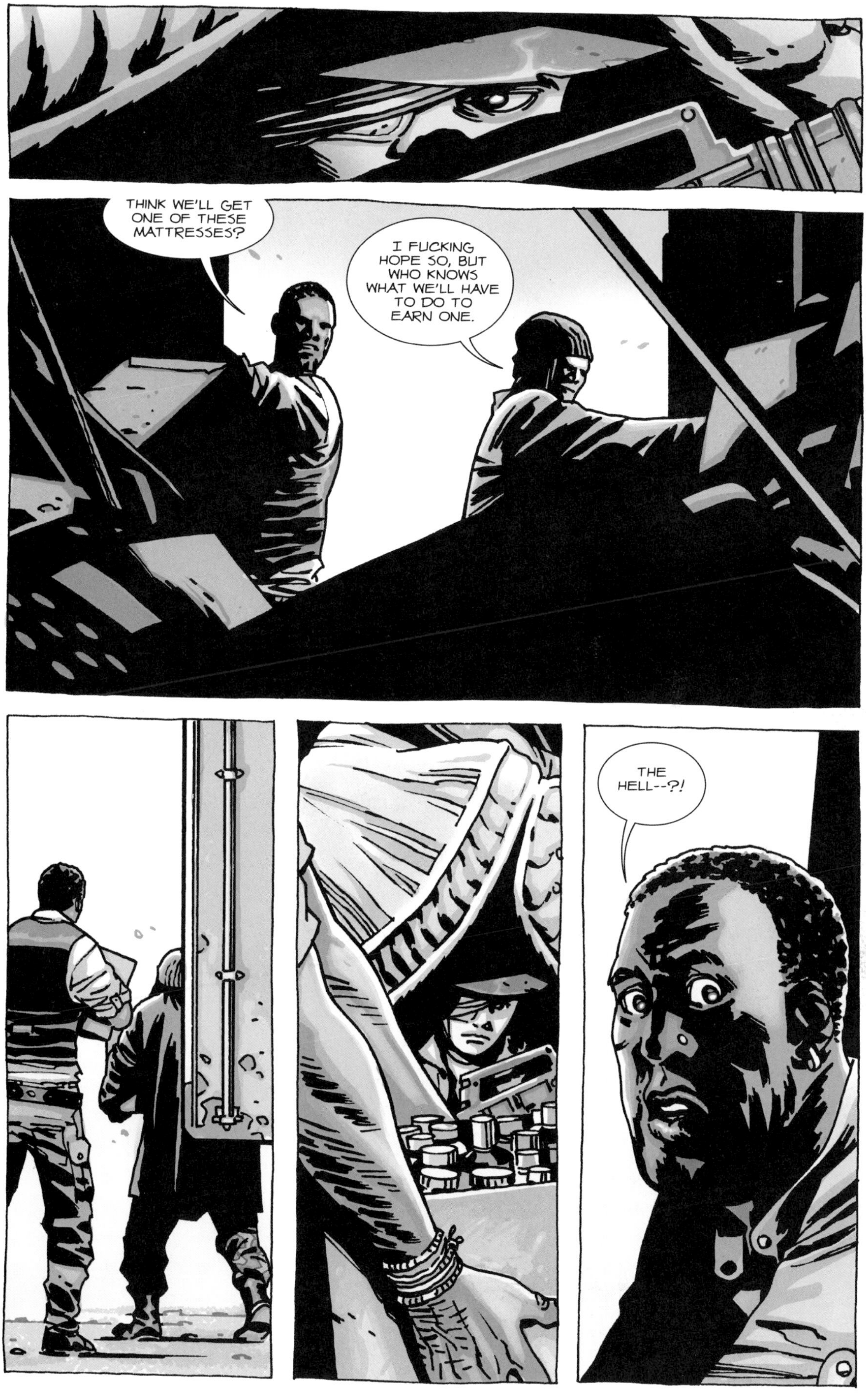
THINK WE'LL GET ONE OF THESE MATTRESSES?
I FUCKING HOPE SO, BUT WHO KNOWS WHAT WE'LL HAVE TO DO TO EARN ONE.
THE HELL--?!

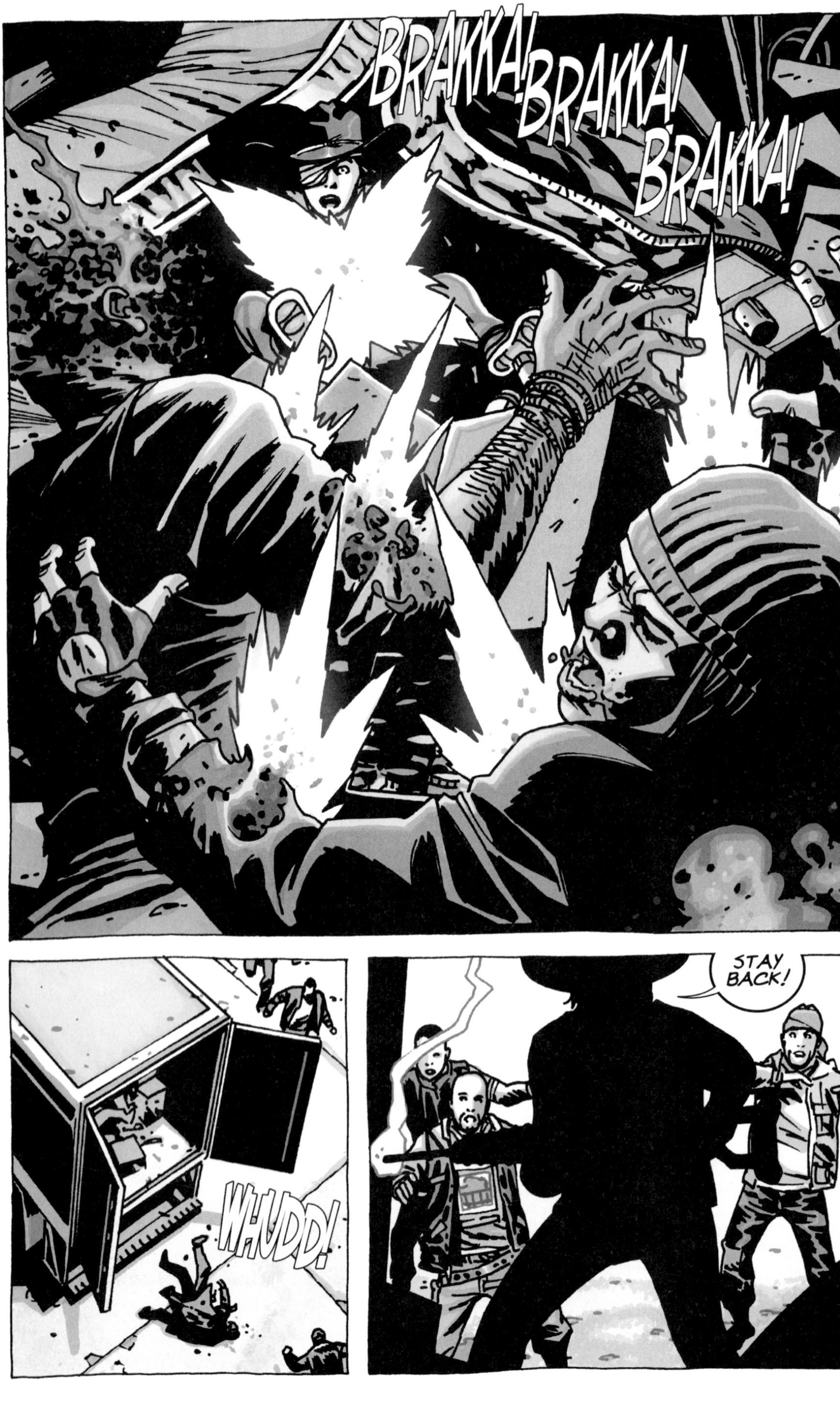
BRAKKA! BRAKKA! BRAKKA!
WHUDD!
STAY BACK!

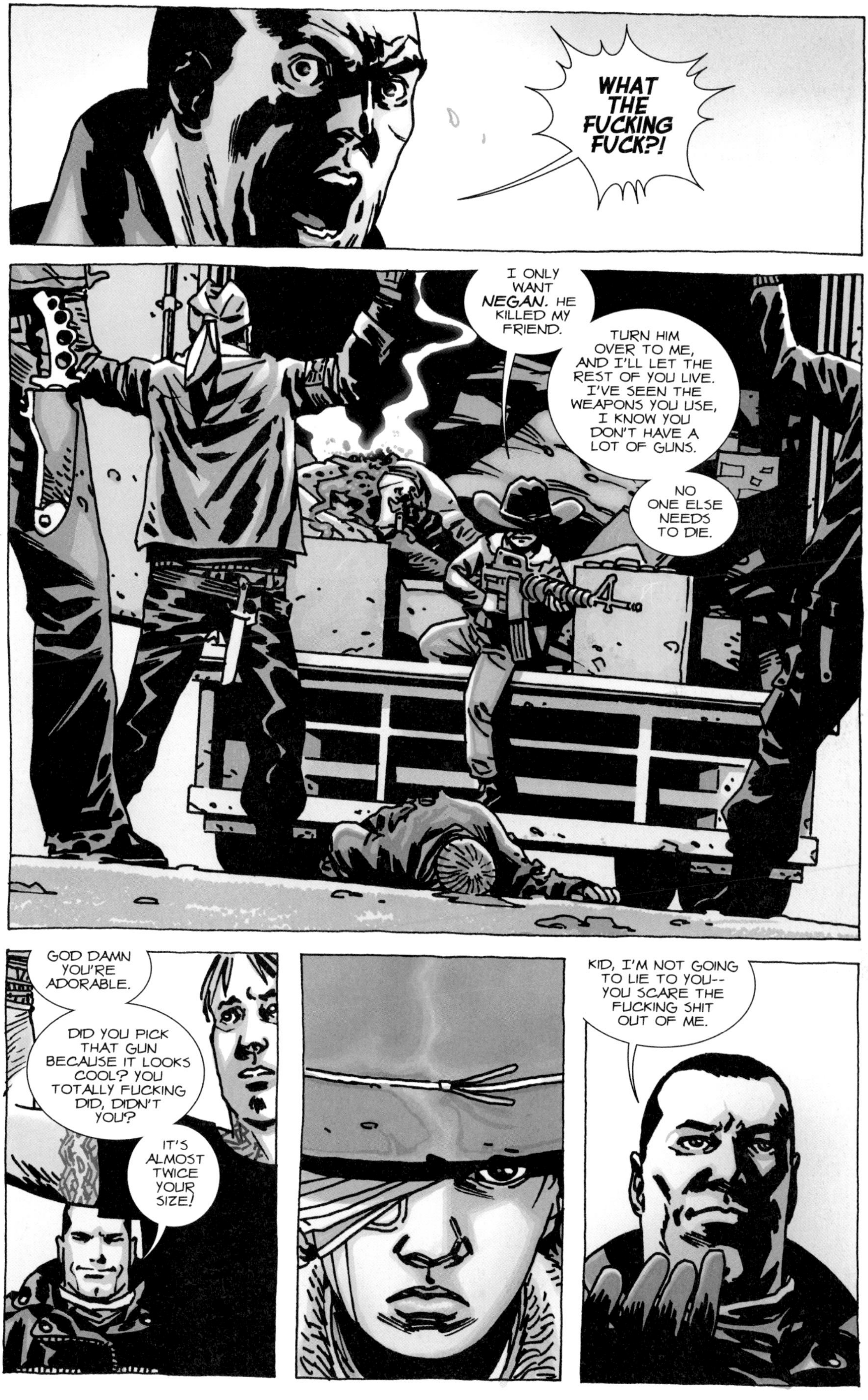
WHAT THE FUCKING FUCK?!
I ONLY WANT NEGAN. HE KILLED MY FRIEND.
TURN HIM OVER TO ME, AND I'LL LET THE REST OF YOU LIVE. I'VE SEEN THE WEAPONS YOU USE, I KNOW YOU DON'T HAVE A LOT OF GUNS.
NO ONE ELSE NEEDS TO DIE.
GOD DAMN YOU'RE ADORABLE.
DID YOU PICK THAT GUN BECAUSE IT LOOKS COOL? YOU TOTALLY FUCKING DID, DIDN'T YOU?
IT'S ALMOST TWICE YOUR SIZE!
KID, I'M NOT GOING TO LIE TO YOU-- YOU SCARE THE FUCKING SHIT OUT OF ME.

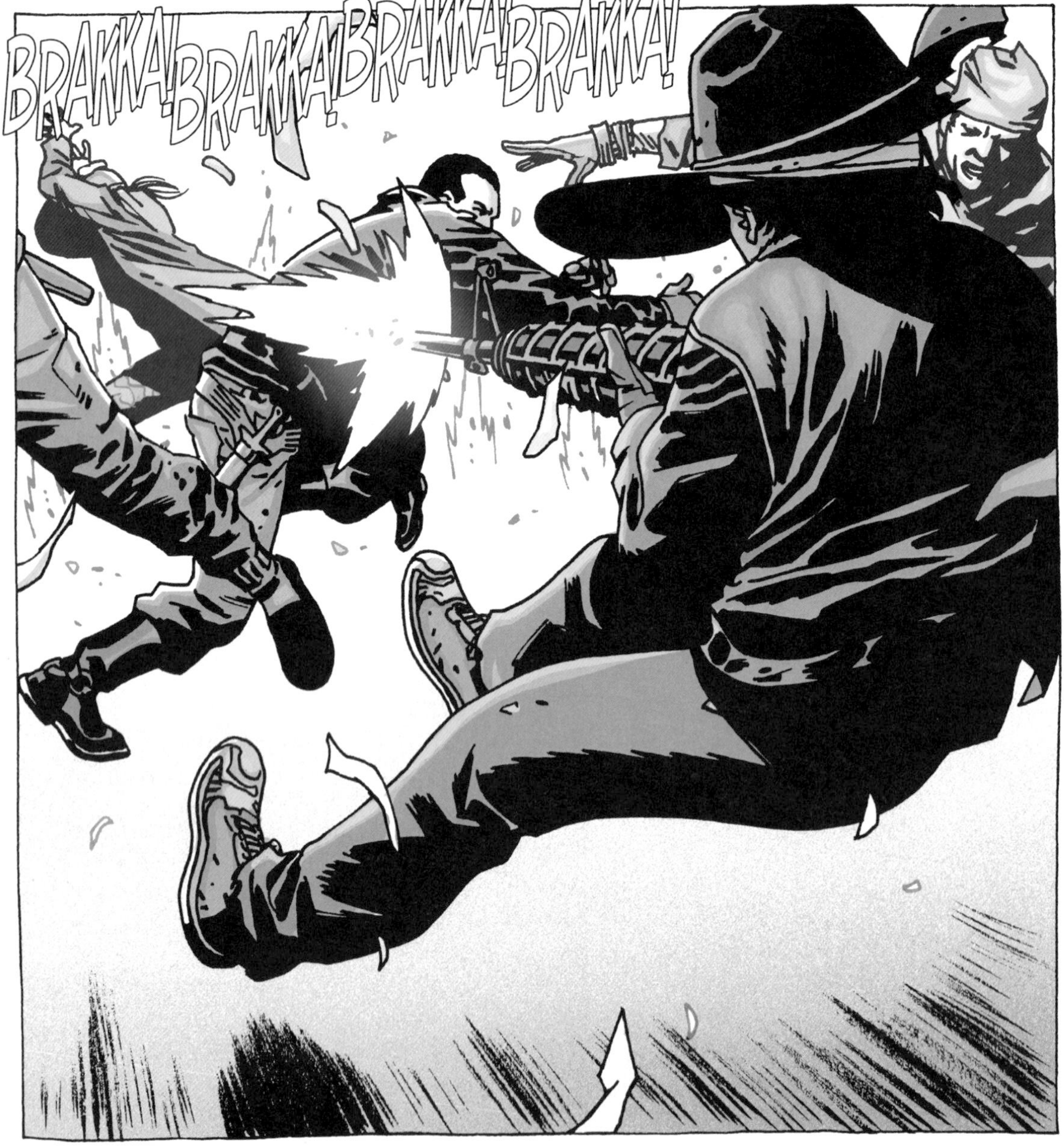
BRAKKA! BRAKKA! BRAKKA! BRAKKA!

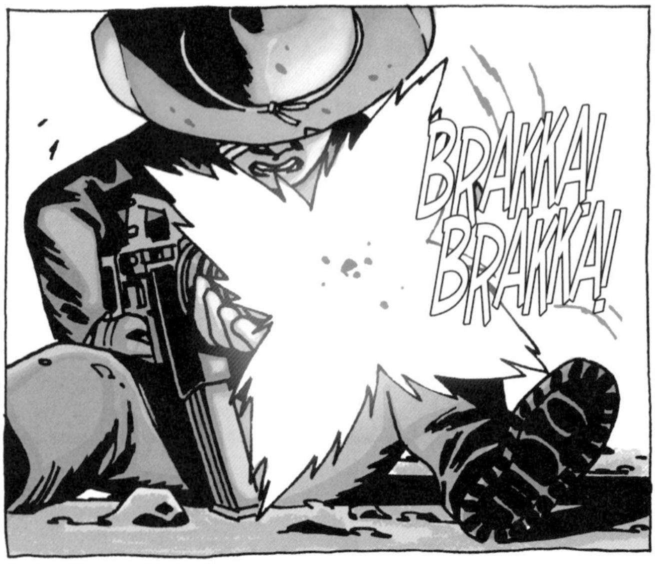
BRAKKA!
BRAKKA!

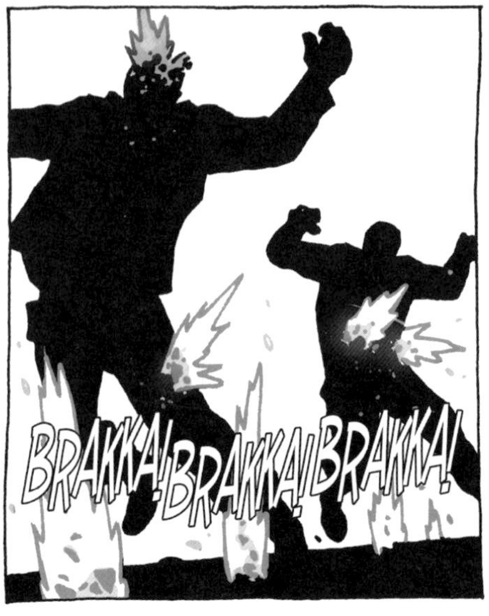
BRAKKA! BRAKKA! BRAKKA!

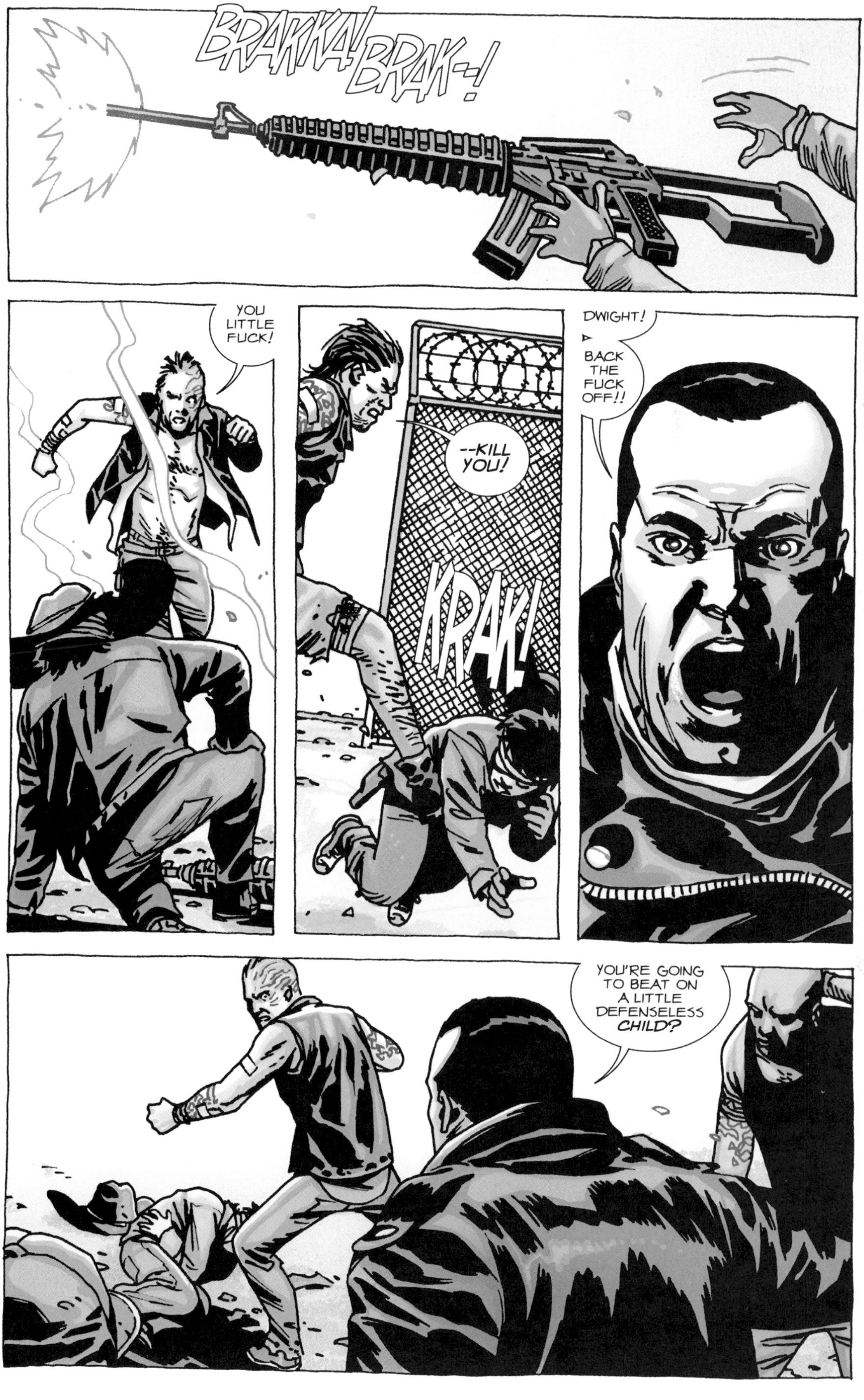
BRAKKA! BRAK--!
YOU LITTLE FUCK!
--KILL YOU!
KRAK!
DWIGHT!
BACK THE FUCK OFF!!
YOU'RE GOING TO BEAT ON A LITTLE DEFENSELESS *CHILD?*

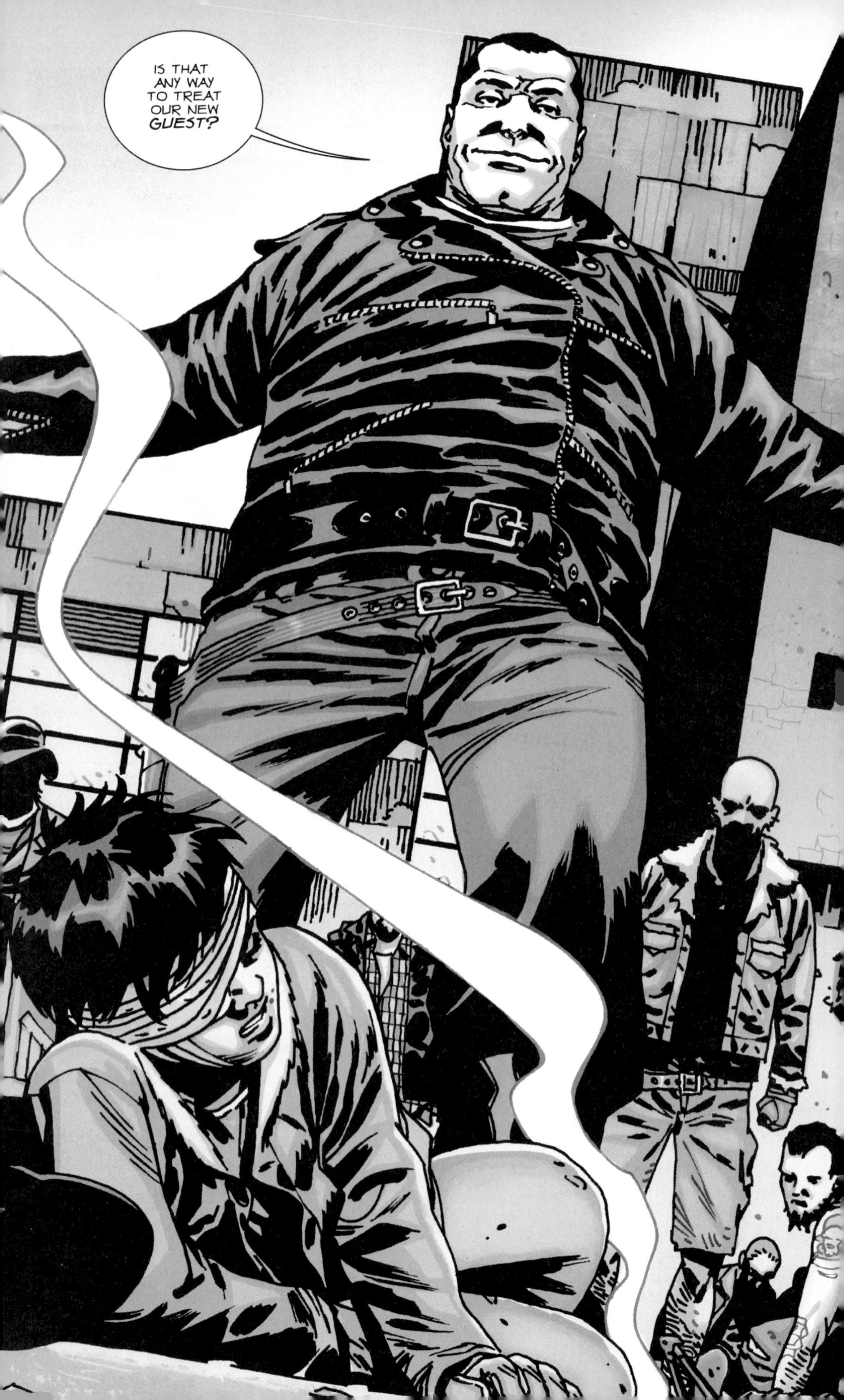
IS THAT ANY WAY TO TREAT OUR NEW GUEST?

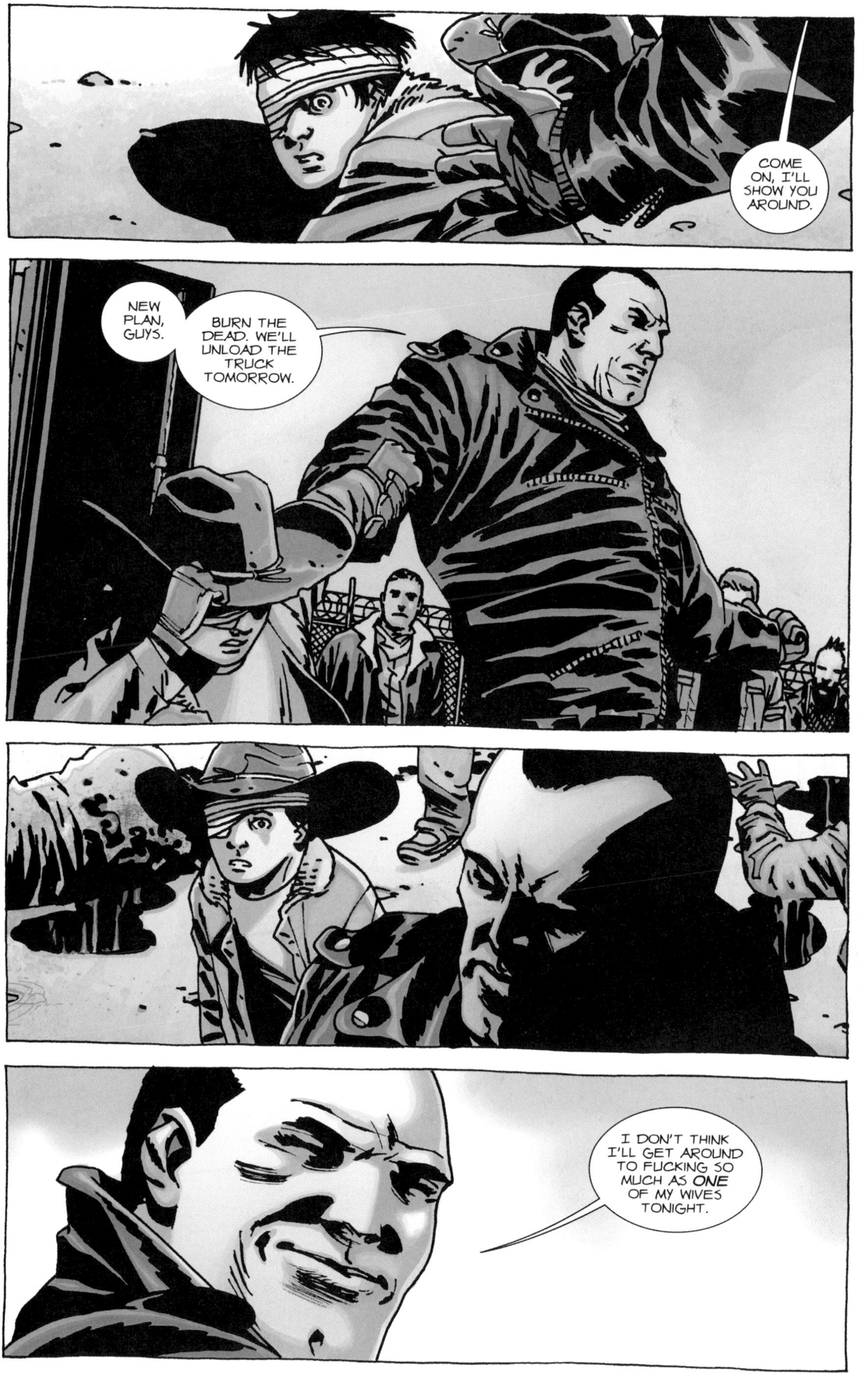
COME ON, I'LL SHOW YOU AROUND.
NEW PLAN, GUYS.
BURN THE DEAD. WE'LL UNLOAD THE TRUCK TOMORROW.
I DON'T THINK I'LL GET AROUND TO FUCKING SO MUCH AS *ONE* OF MY WIVES TONIGHT.

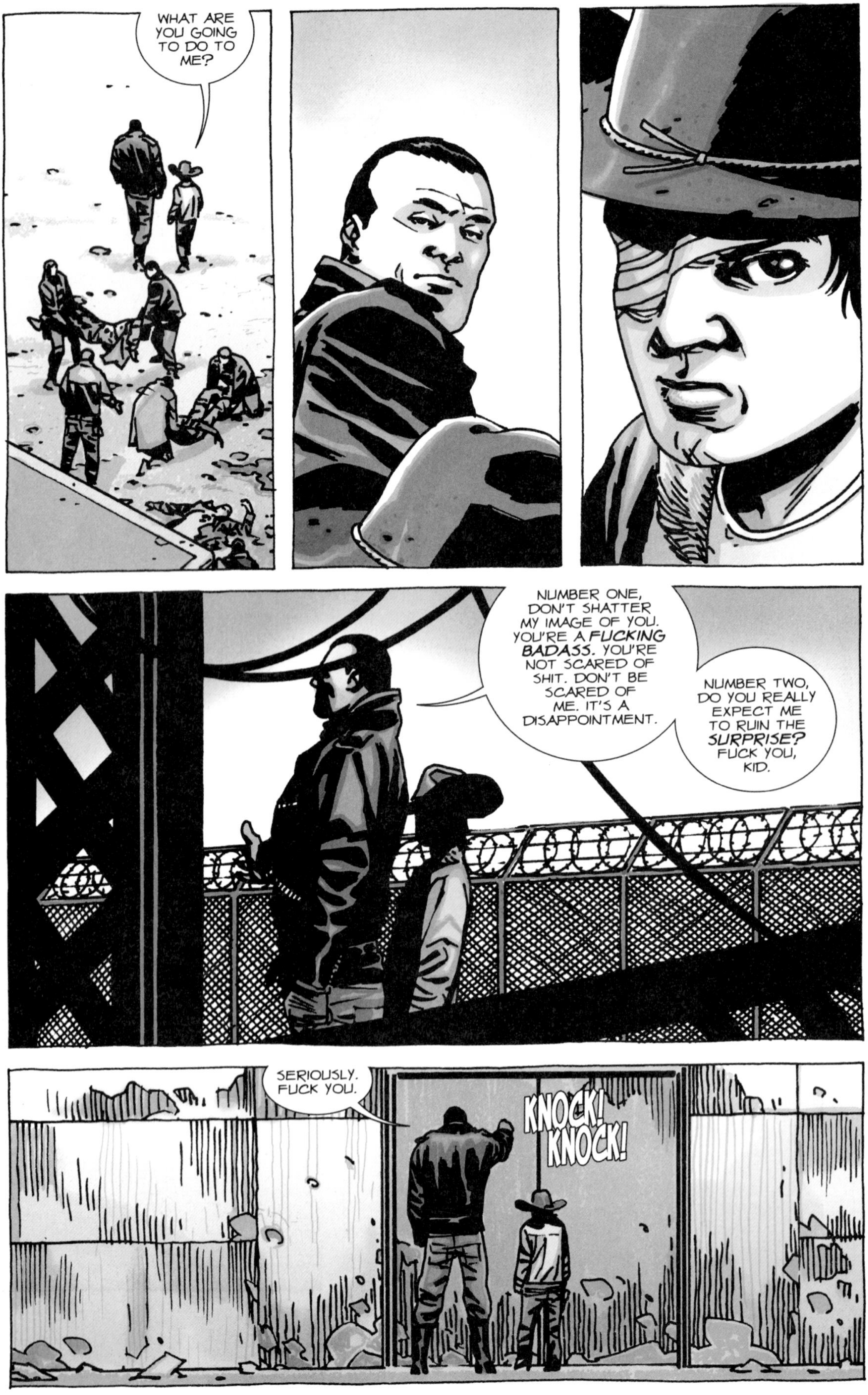
WHAT ARE YOU GOING TO DO TO ME?
NUMBER ONE, DON'T SHATTER MY IMAGE OF YOU. YOU'RE A FUCKING BADASS. YOU'RE NOT SCARED OF SHIT. DON'T BE SCARED OF ME. IT'S A DISAPPOINTMENT.
NUMBER TWO, DO YOU REALLY EXPECT ME TO RUIN THE SURPRISE? FUCK YOU, KID.
SERIOUSLY. FUCK YOU.
KNOCK! KNOCK!

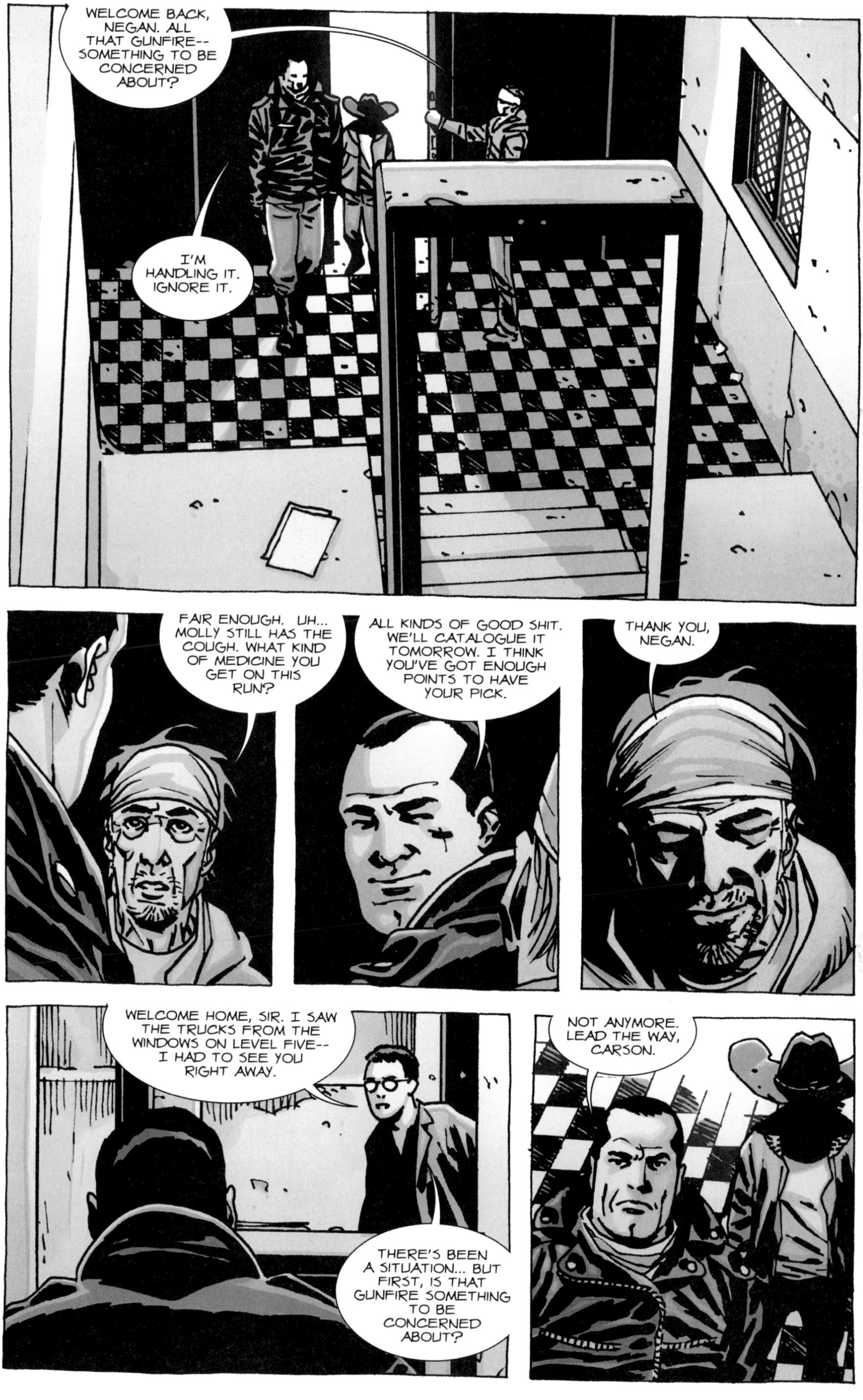
WELCOME BACK, NEGAN. ALL THAT GUNFIRE-- SOMETHING TO BE CONCERNED ABOUT?
I'M HANDLING IT. IGNORE IT.
FAIR ENOUGH. UH... MOLLY STILL HAS THE COUGH. WHAT KIND OF MEDICINE YOU GET ON THIS RUN?
ALL KINDS OF GOOD SHIT. WE'LL CATALOGUE IT TOMORROW. I THINK YOU'VE GOT ENOUGH POINTS TO HAVE YOUR PICK.
THANK YOU, NEGAN.
WELCOME HOME, SIR. I SAW THE TRUCKS FROM THE WINDOWS ON LEVEL FIVE-- I HAD TO SEE YOU RIGHT AWAY.
THERE'S BEEN A SITUATION... BUT FIRST, IS THAT GUNFIRE SOMETHING TO BE CONCERNED ABOUT?
NOT ANYMORE. LEAD THE WAY, CARSON.

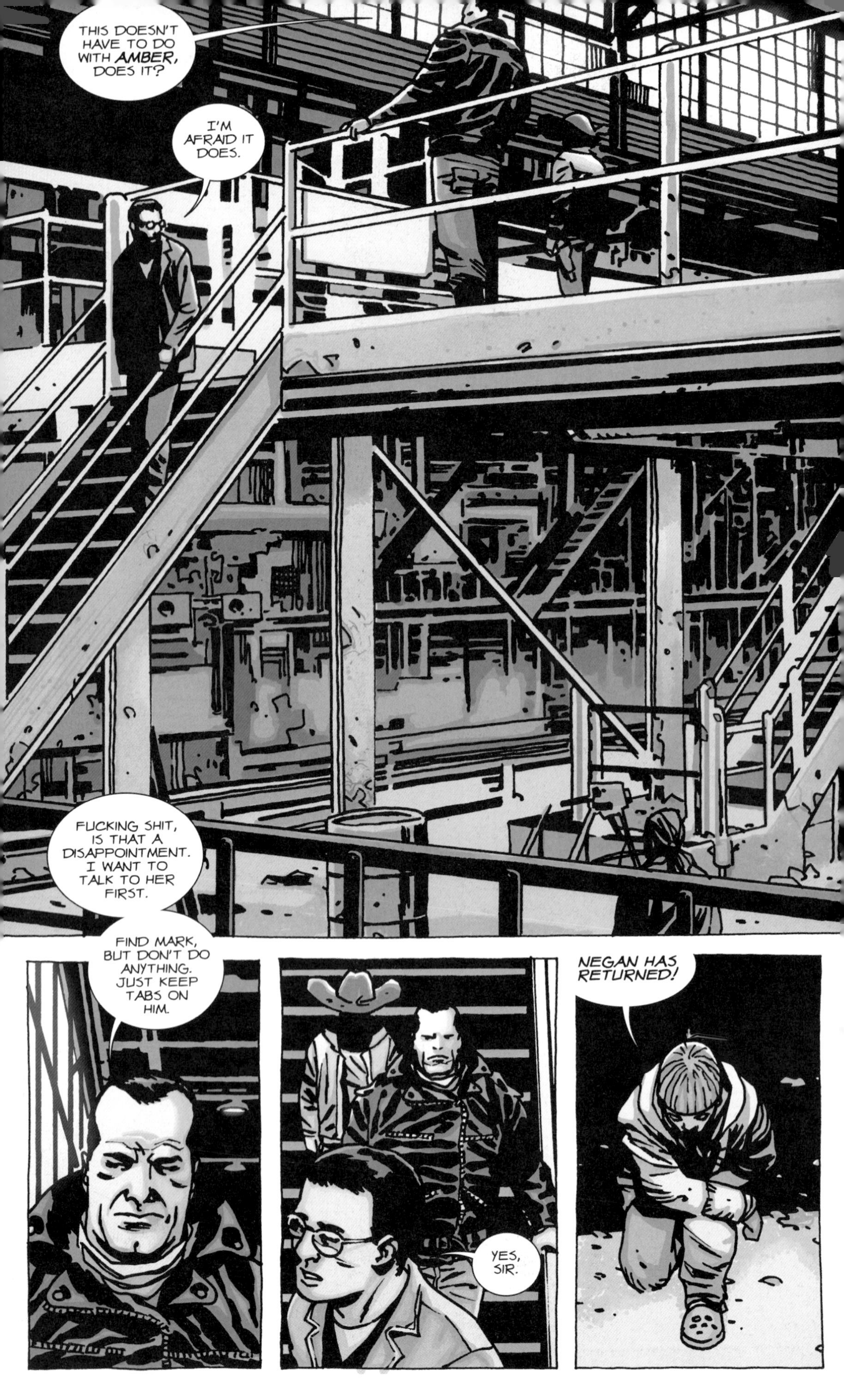
THIS DOESN'T HAVE TO DO WITH AMBER, DOES IT?
I'M AFRAID IT DOES.
FUCKING SHIT, IS THAT A DISAPPOINTMENT. I WANT TO TALK TO HER FIRST.
FIND MARK, BUT DON'T DO ANYTHING. JUST KEEP TABS ON HIM.
YES, SIR.
NEGAN HAS RETURNED!

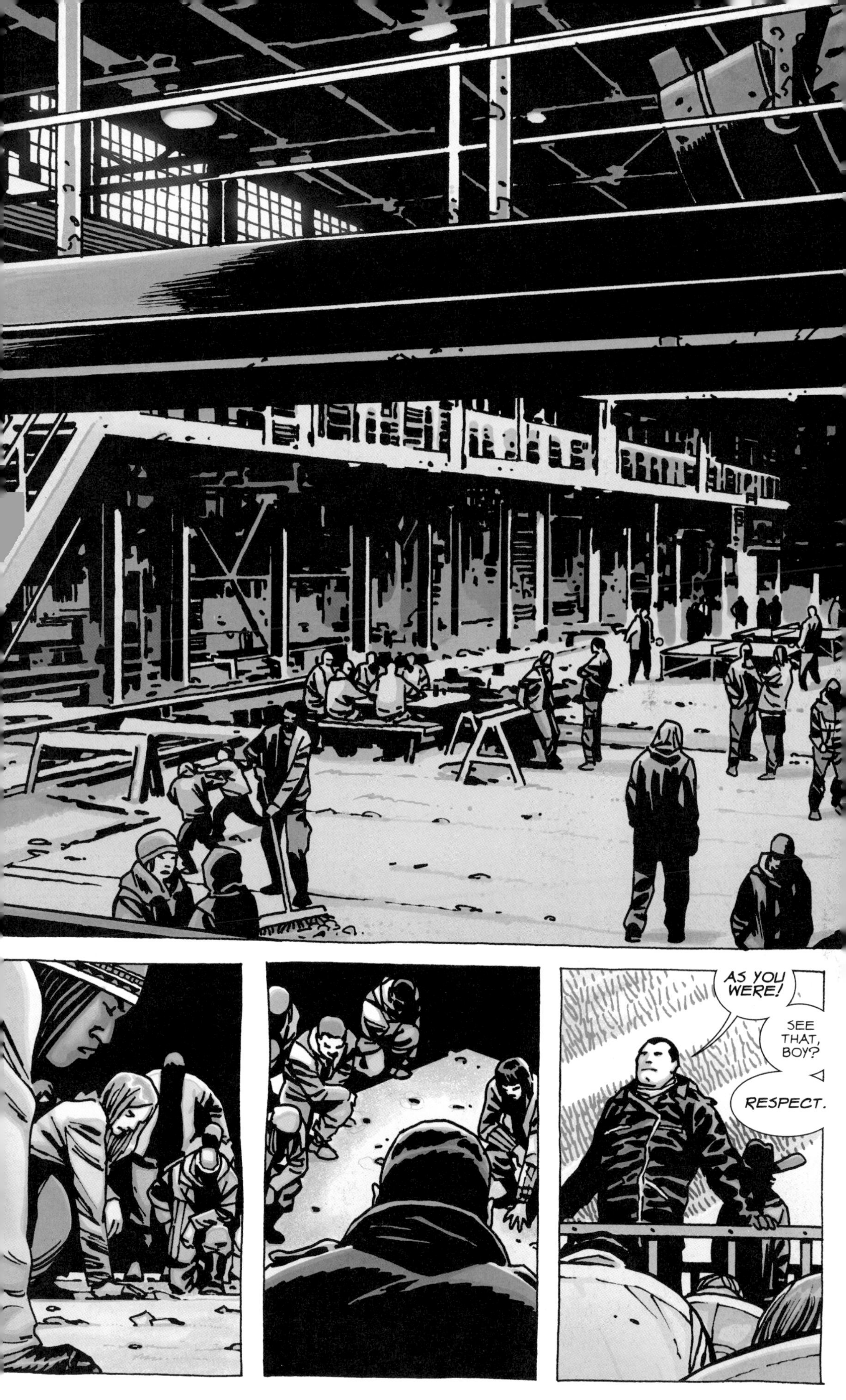
AS YOU WERE!
SEE THAT, BOY?
RESPECT.

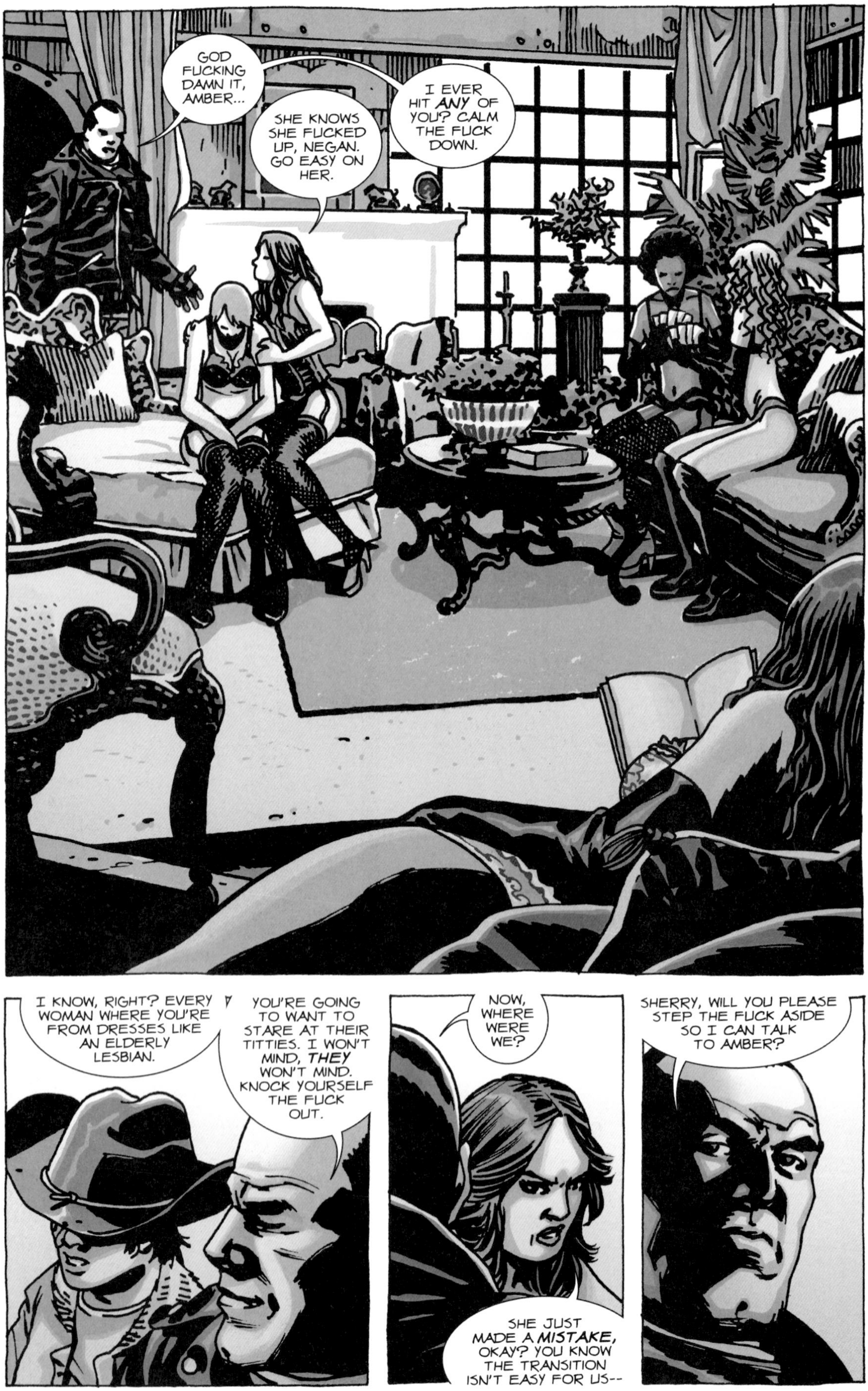
GOD FUCKING DAMN IT, AMBER...
SHE KNOWS SHE FUCKED UP, NEGAN. GO EASY ON HER.
I EVER HIT ANY OF YOU? CALM THE FUCK DOWN.
I KNOW, RIGHT? EVERY WOMAN WHERE YOU'RE FROM DRESSES LIKE AN ELDERLY LESBIAN.
YOU'RE GOING TO WANT TO STARE AT THEIR TITTIES. I WON'T MIND, THEY WON'T MIND. KNOCK YOURSELF THE FUCK OUT.
NOW, WHERE WERE WE?
SHE JUST MADE A MISTAKE, OKAY? YOU KNOW THE TRANSITION ISN'T EASY FOR US--
SHERRY, WILL YOU PLEASE STEP THE FUCK ASIDE SO I CAN TALK TO AMBER?

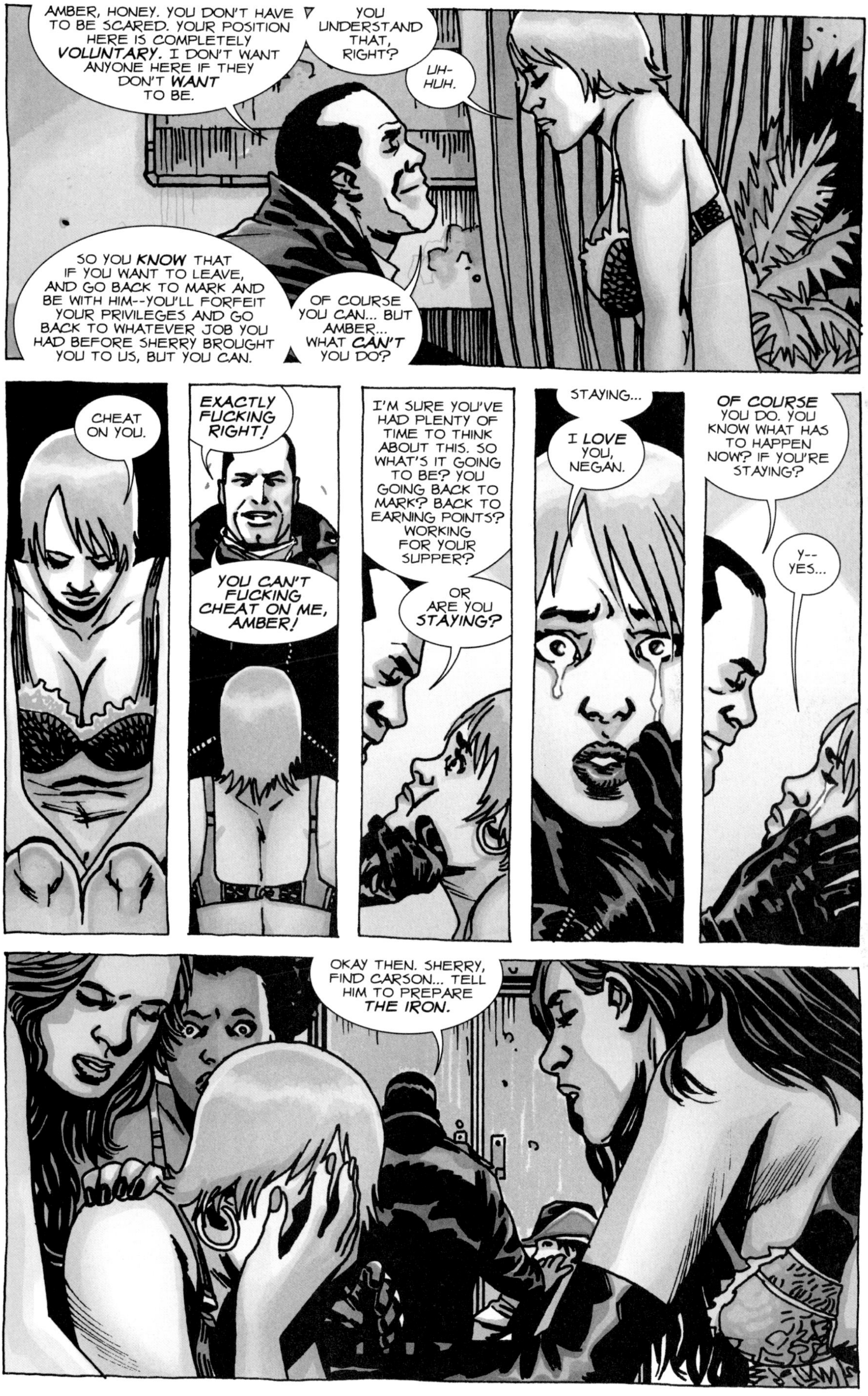
AMBER, HONEY. YOU DON'T HAVE TO BE SCARED. YOUR POSITION HERE IS COMPLETELY VOLUNTARY. I DON'T WANT ANYONE HERE IF THEY DON'T WANT TO BE.
YOU UNDERSTAND THAT, RIGHT?
UH-HUH.
SO YOU KNOW THAT IF YOU WANT TO LEAVE, AND GO BACK TO MARK AND BE WITH HIM--YOU'LL FORFEIT YOUR PRIVILEGES AND GO BACK TO WHATEVER JOB YOU HAD BEFORE SHERRY BROUGHT YOU TO US, BUT YOU CAN.
OF COURSE YOU CAN... BUT AMBER... WHAT CAN'T YOU DO?
CHEAT ON YOU.
EXACTLY FUCKING RIGHT!
YOU CAN'T FUCKING CHEAT ON ME, AMBER!
I'M SURE YOU'VE HAD PLENTY OF TIME TO THINK ABOUT THIS. SO WHAT'S IT GOING TO BE? YOU GOING BACK TO MARK? BACK TO EARNING POINTS? WORKING FOR YOUR SUPPER?
OR ARE YOU STAYING?
STAYING...
I LOVE YOU, NEGAN.
OF COURSE YOU DO. YOU KNOW WHAT HAS TO HAPPEN NOW? IF YOU'RE STAYING?
Y-- YES...
OKAY THEN. SHERRY, FIND CARSON... TELL HIM TO PREPARE THE IRON.

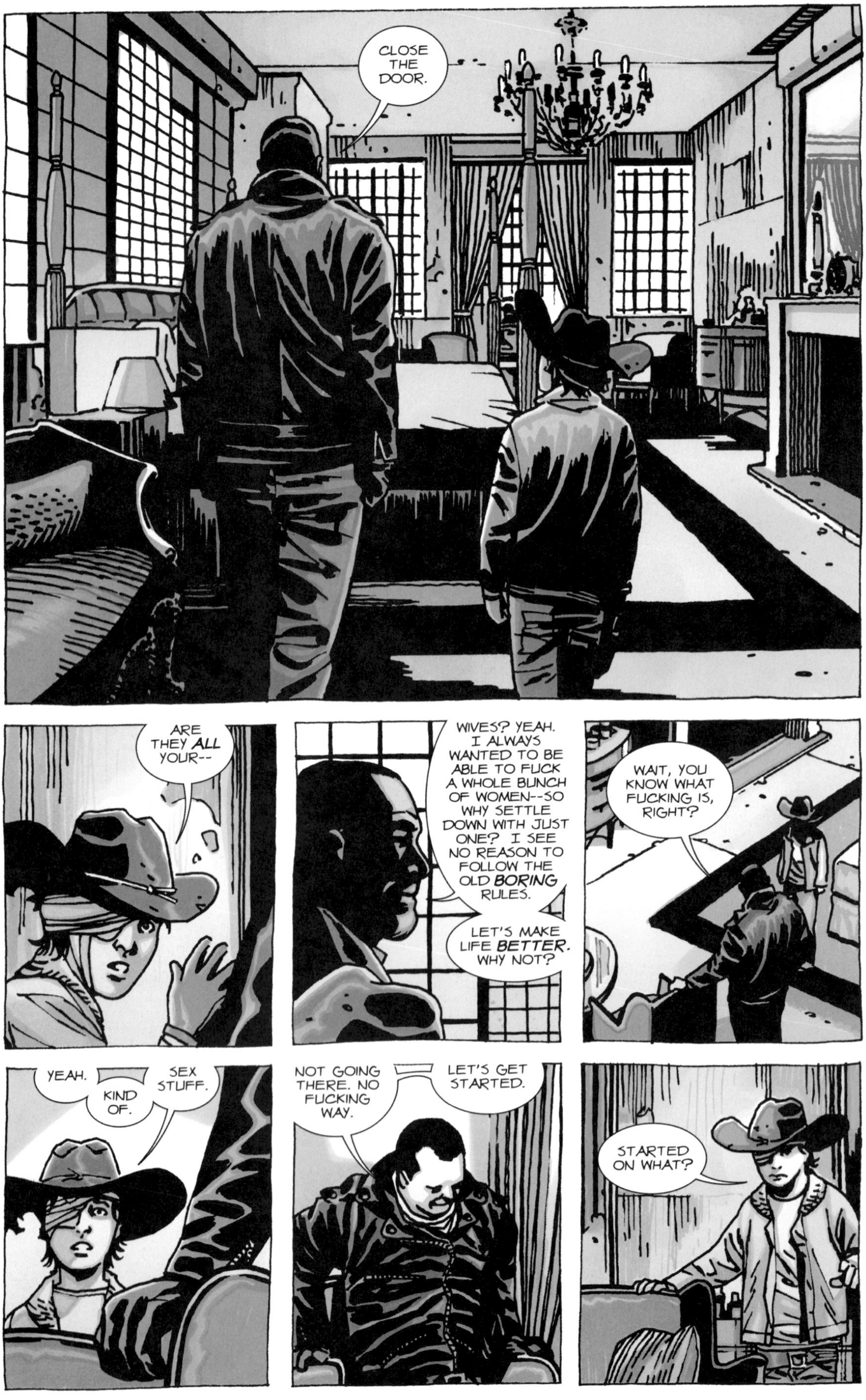
CLOSE THE DOOR.
ARE THEY ALL YOUR--
WIVES? YEAH. I ALWAYS WANTED TO BE ABLE TO FUCK A WHOLE BUNCH OF WOMEN--SO WHY SETTLE DOWN WITH JUST ONE? I SEE NO REASON TO FOLLOW THE OLD BORING RULES.
LET'S MAKE LIFE BETTER. WHY NOT?
WAIT, YOU KNOW WHAT FUCKING IS, RIGHT?
YEAH.
KIND OF.
SEX STUFF.
NOT GOING THERE. NO FUCKING WAY.
LET'S GET STARTED.
STARTED ON WHAT?

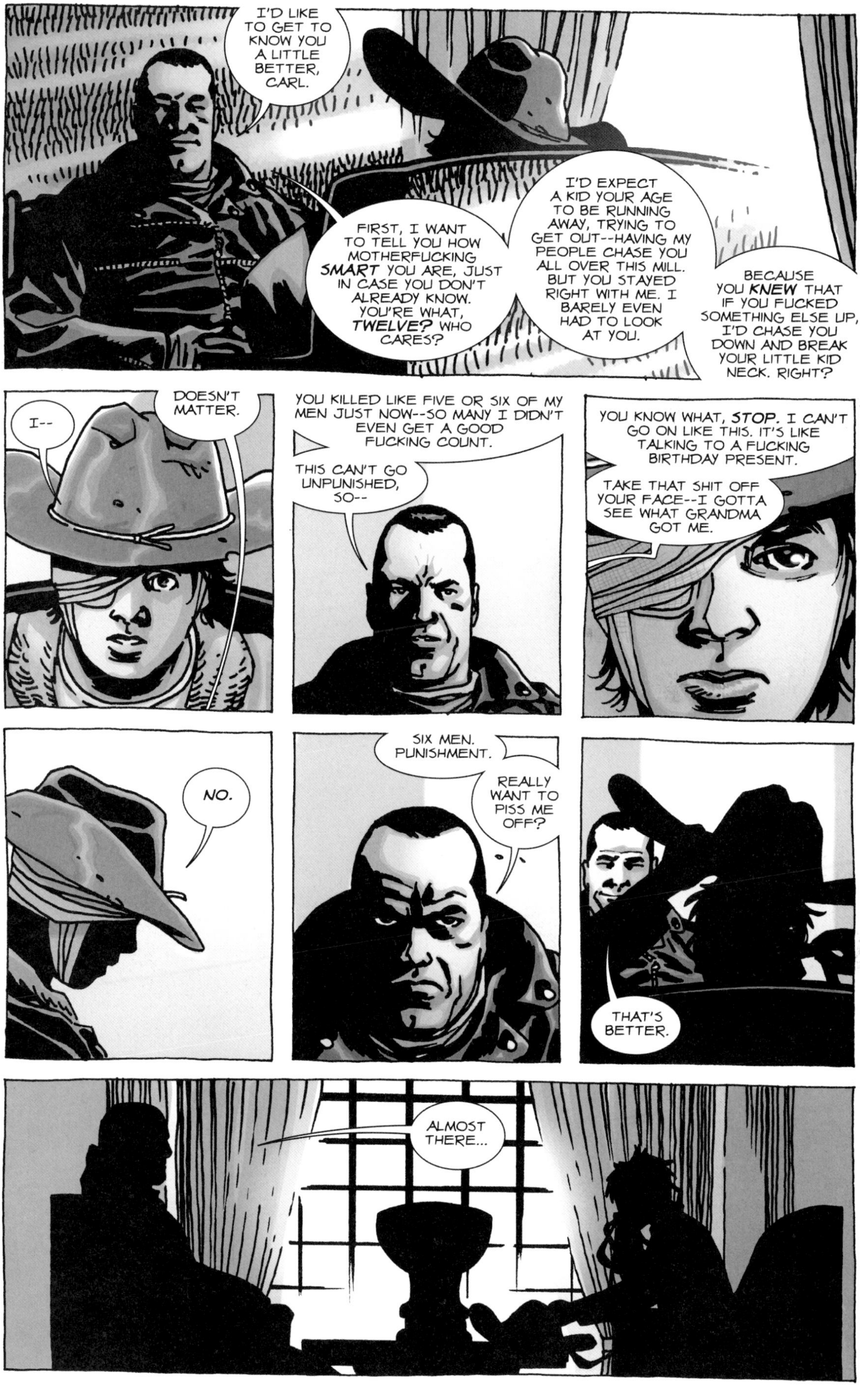
I'D LIKE TO GET TO KNOW YOU A LITTLE BETTER, CARL.
FIRST, I WANT TO TELL YOU HOW MOTHERFUCKING SMART YOU ARE, JUST IN CASE YOU DON'T ALREADY KNOW. YOU'RE WHAT, TWELVE? WHO CARES?
I'D EXPECT A KID YOUR AGE TO BE RUNNING AWAY, TRYING TO GET OUT--HAVING MY PEOPLE CHASE YOU ALL OVER THIS MILL. BUT YOU STAYED RIGHT WITH ME. I BARELY EVEN HAD TO LOOK AT YOU.
BECAUSE YOU KNEW THAT IF YOU FUCKED SOMETHING ELSE UP, I'D CHASE YOU DOWN AND BREAK YOUR LITTLE KID NECK. RIGHT?
I--
DOESN'T MATTER.
YOU KILLED LIKE FIVE OR SIX OF MY MEN JUST NOW--SO MANY I DIDN'T EVEN GET A GOOD FUCKING COUNT.
THIS CAN'T GO UNPUNISHED, SO--
YOU KNOW WHAT, STOP. I CAN'T GO ON LIKE THIS. IT'S LIKE TALKING TO A FUCKING BIRTHDAY PRESENT.
TAKE THAT SHIT OFF YOUR FACE--I GOTTA SEE WHAT GRANDMA GOT ME.
NO.
SIX MEN. PUNISHMENT.
REALLY WANT TO PISS ME OFF?
THAT'S BETTER.
ALMOST THERE...

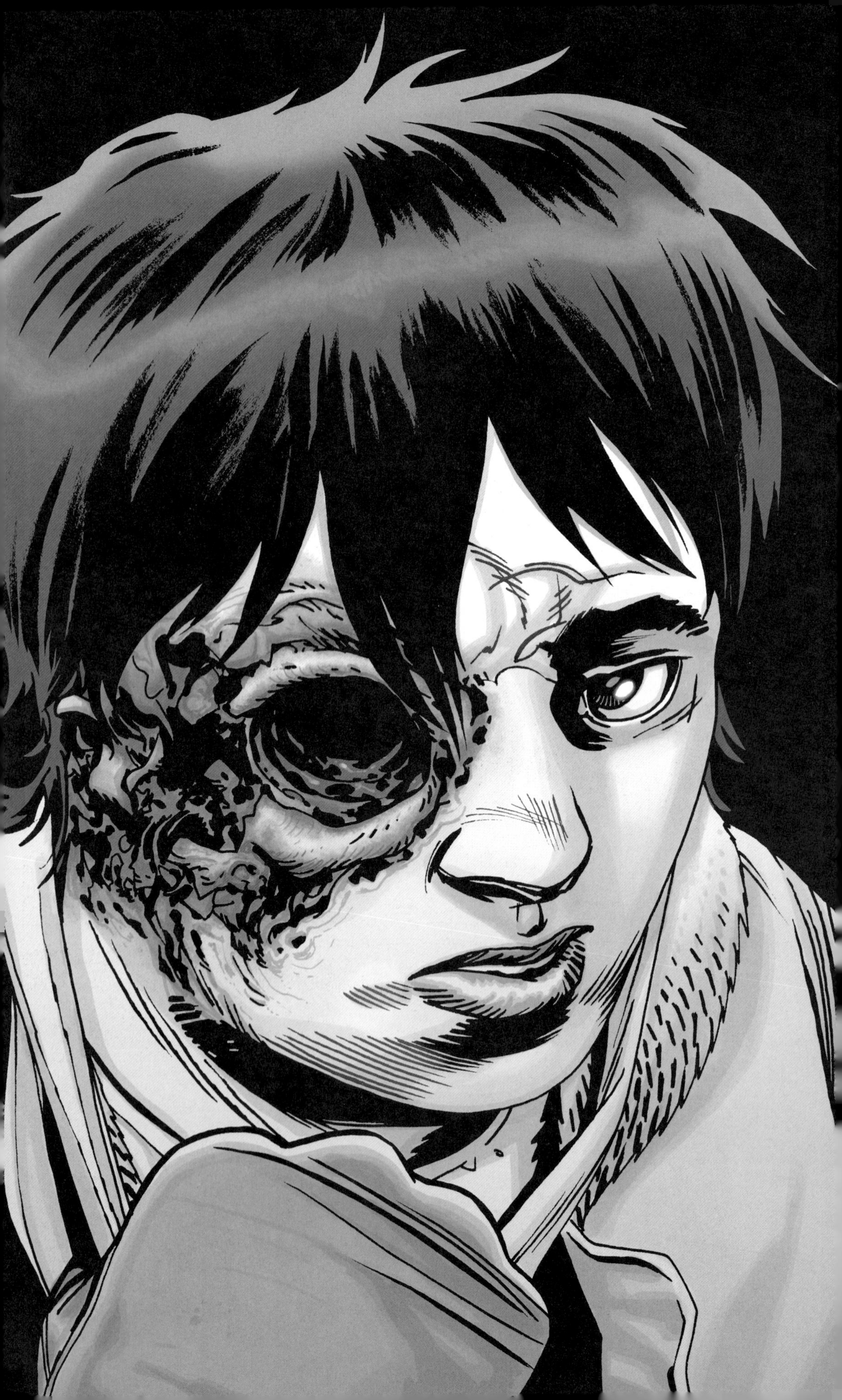

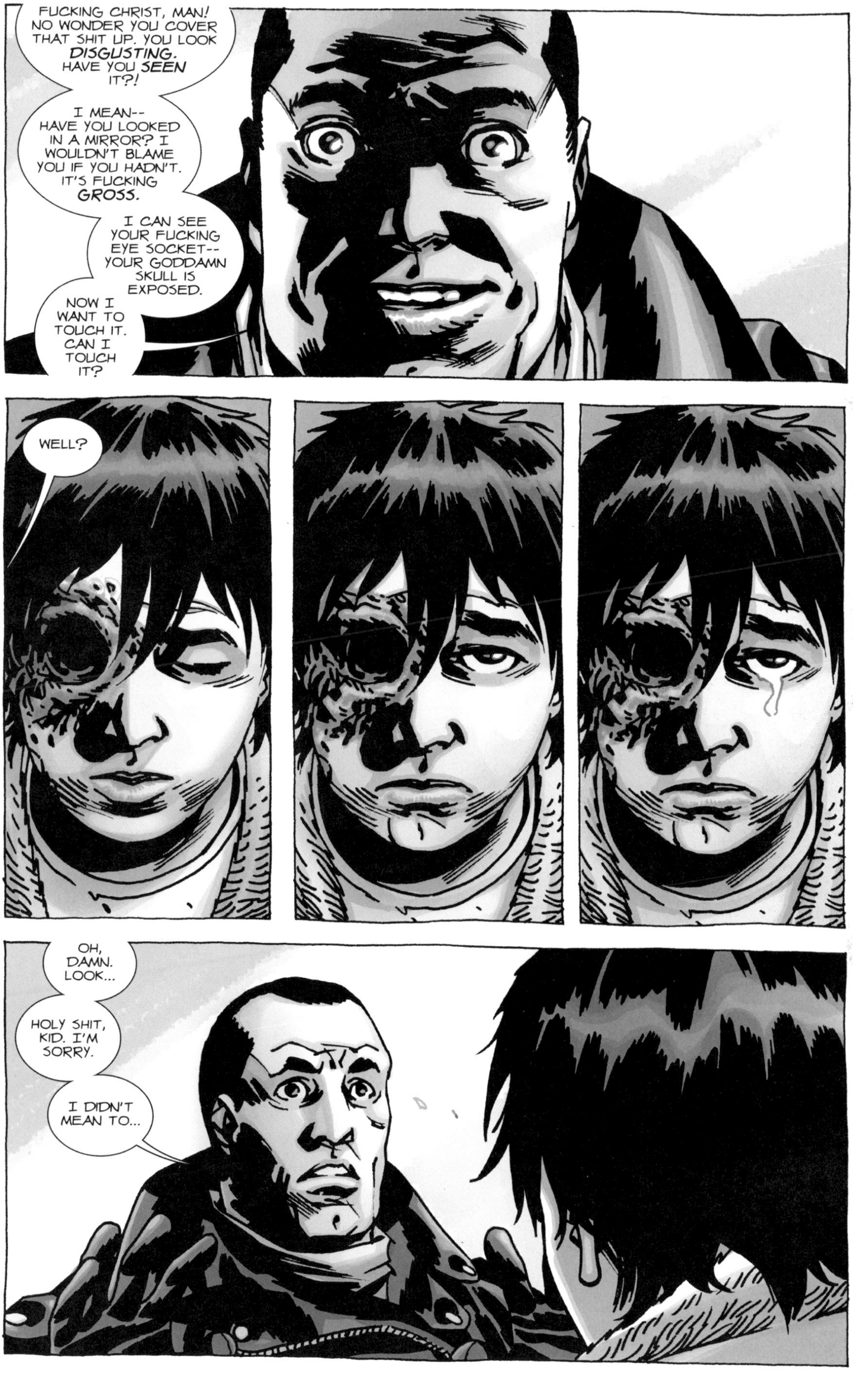
FUCKING CHRIST, MAN! NO WONDER YOU COVER THAT SHIT UP. YOU LOOK DISGUSTING. HAVE YOU SEEN IT?!
I MEAN-- HAVE YOU LOOKED IN A MIRROR? I WOULDN'T BLAME YOU IF YOU HADN'T. IT'S FUCKING GROSS.
I CAN SEE YOUR FUCKING EYE SOCKET-- YOUR GODDAMN SKULL IS EXPOSED.
NOW I WANT TO TOUCH IT. CAN I TOUCH IT?
WELL?
OH, DAMN. LOOK...
HOLY SHIT, KID. I'M SORRY.
I DIDN'T MEAN TO...

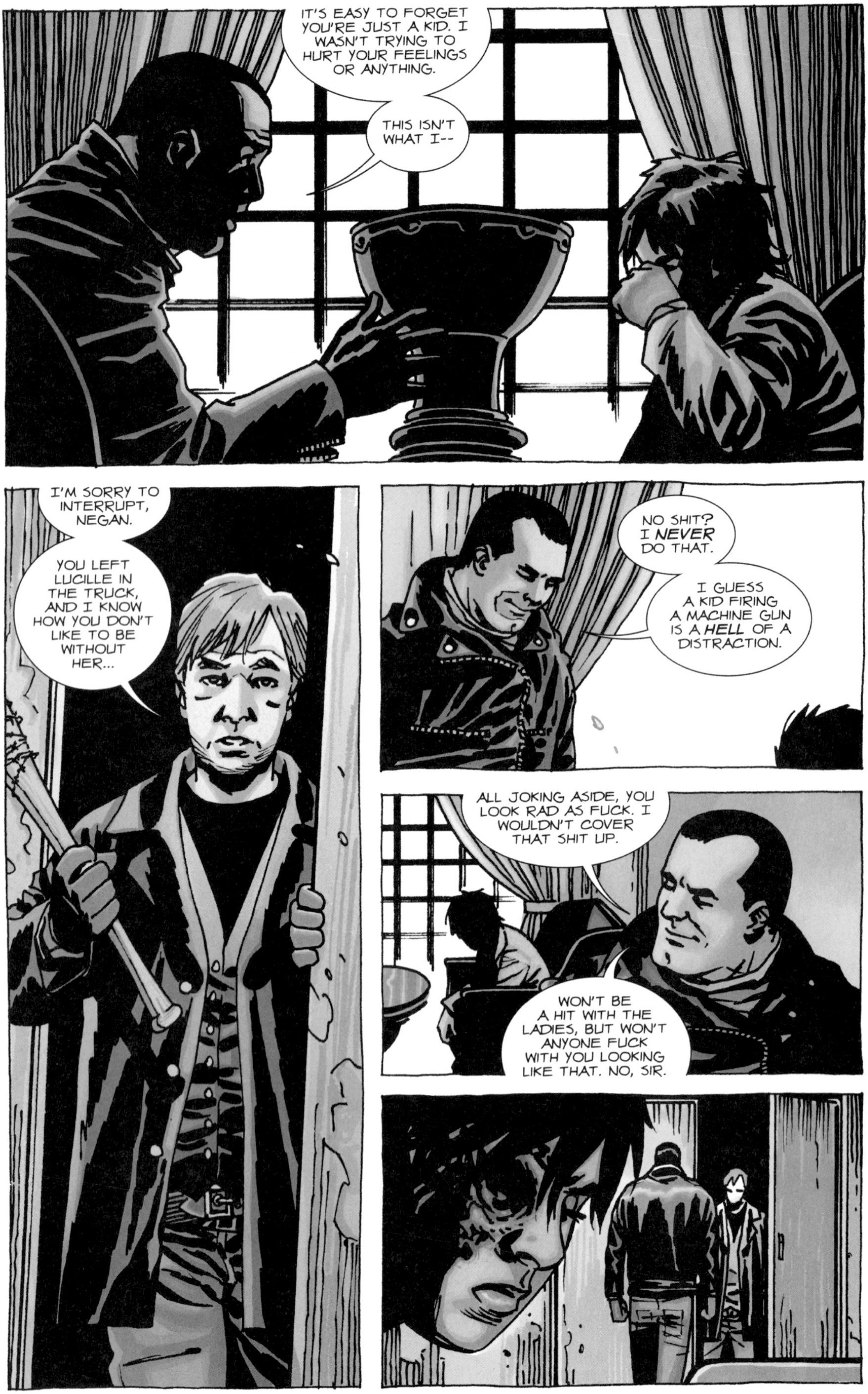

IT'S EASY TO FORGET YOU'RE JUST A KID. I WASN'T TRYING TO HURT YOUR FEELINGS OR ANYTHING.
THIS ISN'T WHAT I--
I'M SORRY TO INTERRUPT, NEGAN.
YOU LEFT LUCILLE IN THE TRUCK, AND I KNOW HOW YOU DON'T LIKE TO BE WITHOUT HER...
NO SHIT? I NEVER DO THAT.
I GUESS A KID FIRING A MACHINE GUN IS A HELL OF A DISTRACTION.
ALL JOKING ASIDE, YOU LOOK RAD AS FUCK. I WOULDN'T COVER THAT SHIT UP.
WON'T BE A HIT WITH THE LADIES, BUT WON'T ANYONE FUCK WITH YOU LOOKING LIKE THAT. NO, SIR.

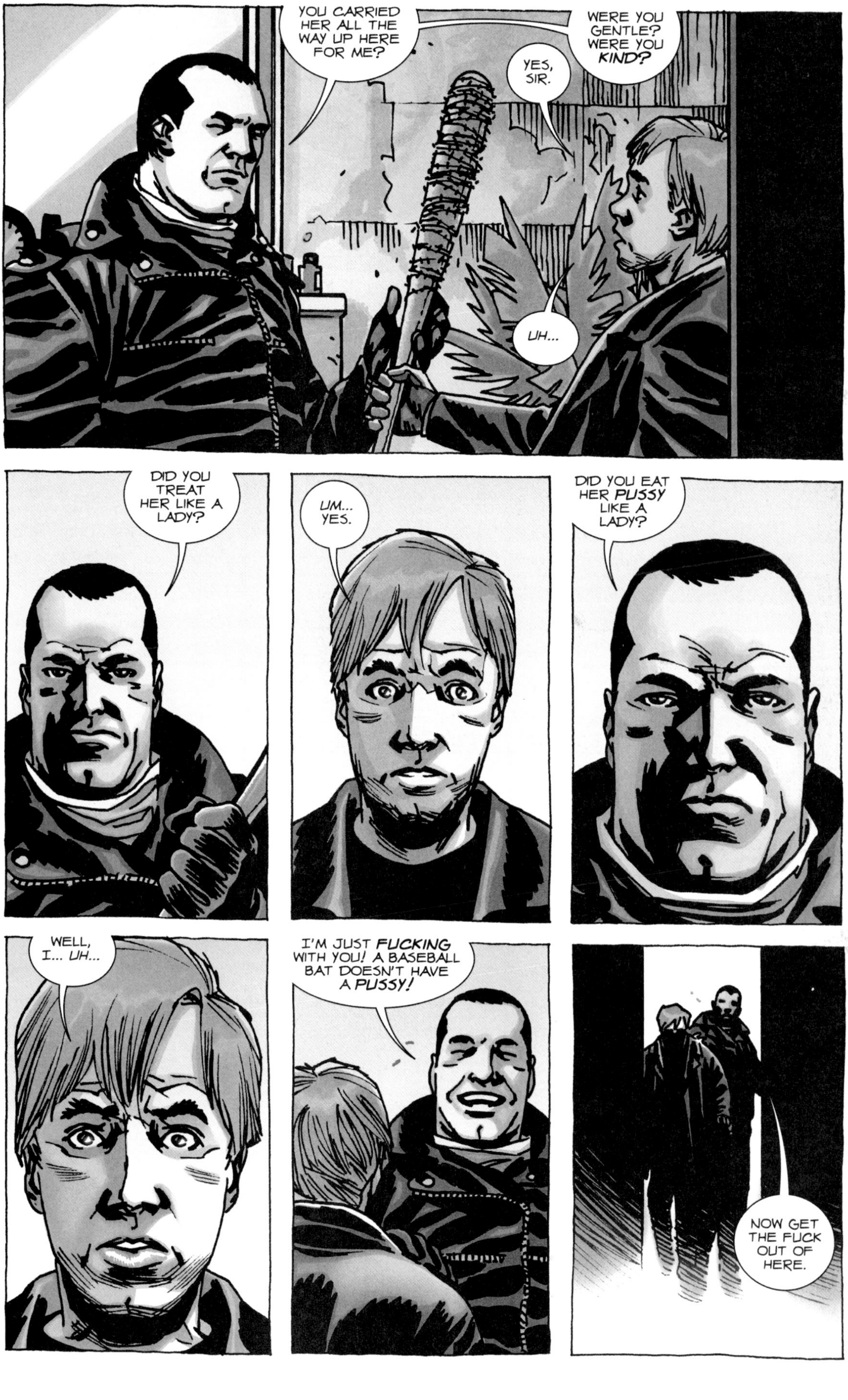
YOU CARRIED HER ALL THE WAY UP HERE FOR ME?
WERE YOU GENTLE? WERE YOU KIND?
YES, SIR.
UH...
DID YOU TREAT HER LIKE A LADY?
UM... YES.
DID YOU EAT HER PUSSY LIKE A LADY?
WELL, I... UH...
I'M JUST FUCKING WITH YOU! A BASEBALL BAT DOESN'T HAVE A PUSSY!
NOW GET THE FUCK OUT OF HERE.

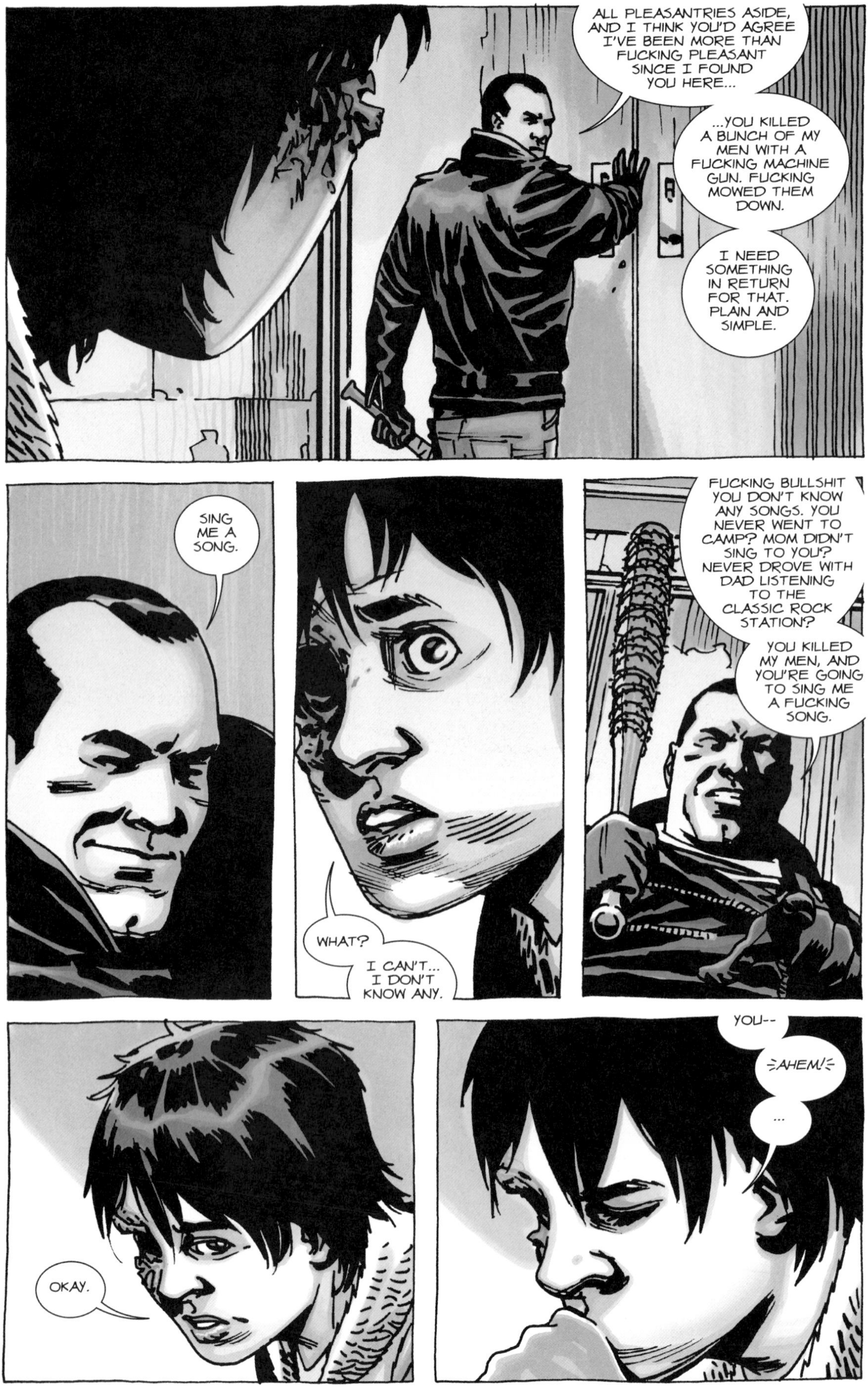
ALL PLEASANTRIES ASIDE, AND I THINK YOU'D AGREE I'VE BEEN MORE THAN FUCKING PLEASANT SINCE I FOUND YOU HERE...
...YOU KILLED A BUNCH OF MY MEN WITH A FUCKING MACHINE GUN. FUCKING MOWED THEM DOWN.
I NEED SOMETHING IN RETURN FOR THAT. PLAIN AND SIMPLE.
SING ME A SONG.
WHAT?
I CAN'T... I DON'T KNOW ANY.
FUCKING BULLSHIT YOU DON'T KNOW ANY SONGS. YOU NEVER WENT TO CAMP? MOM DIDN'T SING TO YOU? NEVER DROVE WITH DAD LISTENING TO THE CLASSIC ROCK STATION?
YOU KILLED MY MEN, AND YOU'RE GOING TO SING ME A FUCKING SONG.
OKAY.
YOU--
AHEM!
...

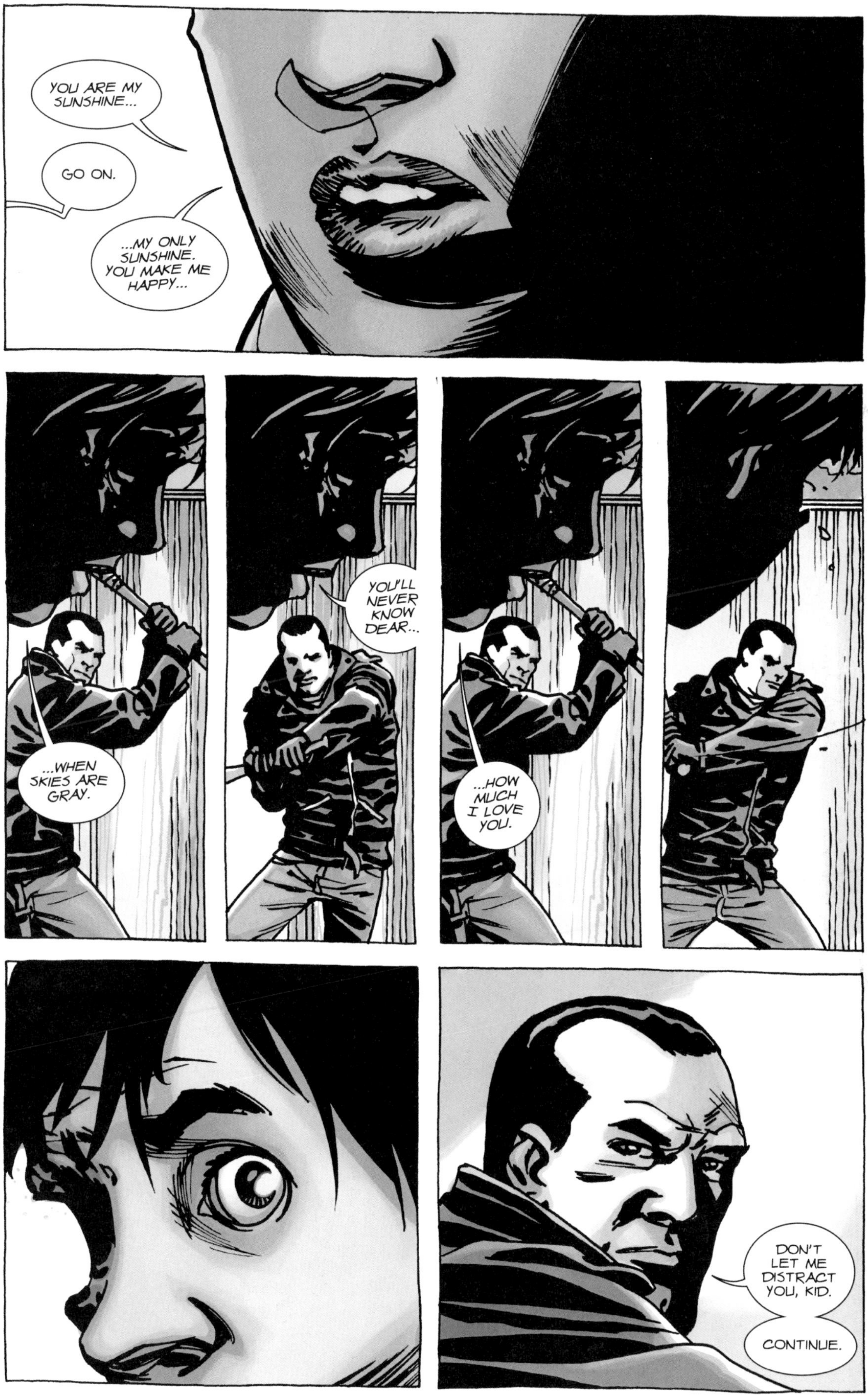

YOU ARE MY SUNSHINE...
GO ON.
...MY ONLY SUNSHINE. YOU MAKE ME HAPPY...
...WHEN SKIES ARE GRAY.
YOU'LL NEVER KNOW DEAR...
...HOW MUCH I LOVE YOU.
DON'T LET ME DISTRACT YOU, KID.
CONTINUE.

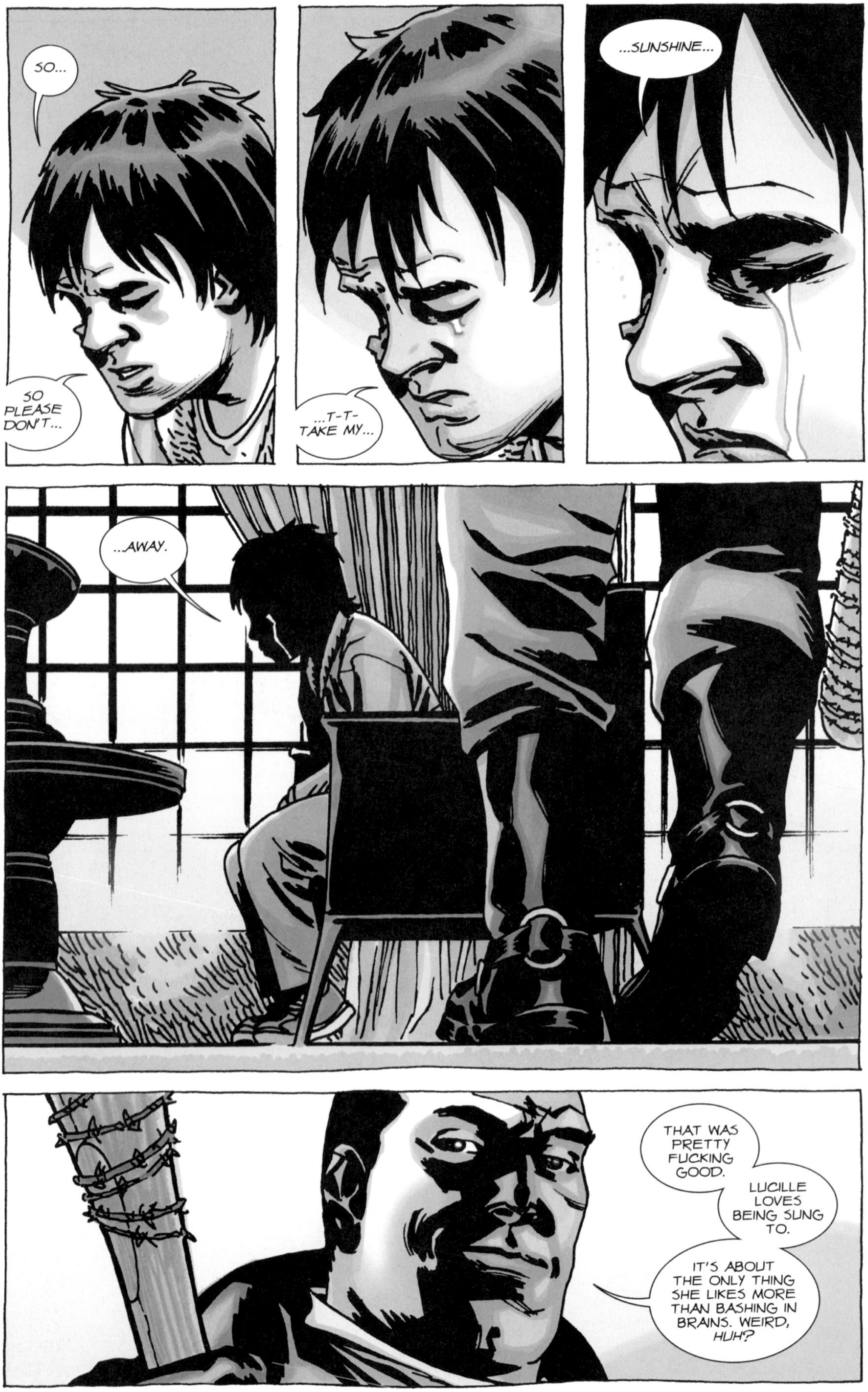
SO...
SO PLEASE DON'T...
...T-T-TAKE MY...
...SUNSHINE...
...AWAY.
THAT WAS PRETTY FUCKING GOOD.
LUCILLE LOVES BEING SUNG TO.
IT'S ABOUT THE ONLY THING SHE LIKES MORE THAN BASHING IN BRAINS. WEIRD, HUH?

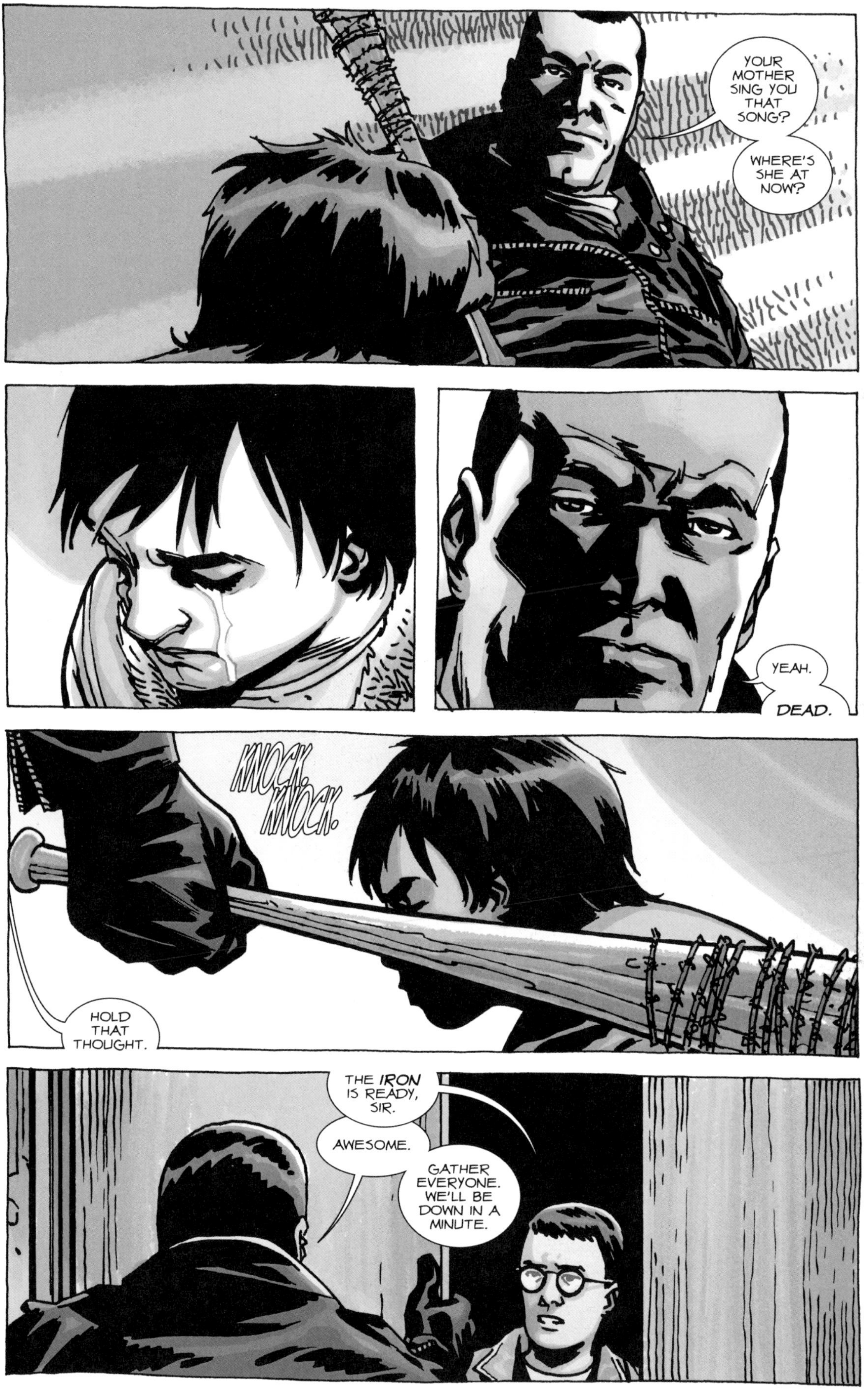
YOUR MOTHER SING YOU THAT SONG?
WHERE'S SHE AT NOW?
YEAH.
DEAD.
KNOCK. KNOCK.
HOLD THAT THOUGHT.
THE *IRON* IS READY, SIR.
AWESOME.
GATHER EVERYONE. WE'LL BE DOWN IN A MINUTE.

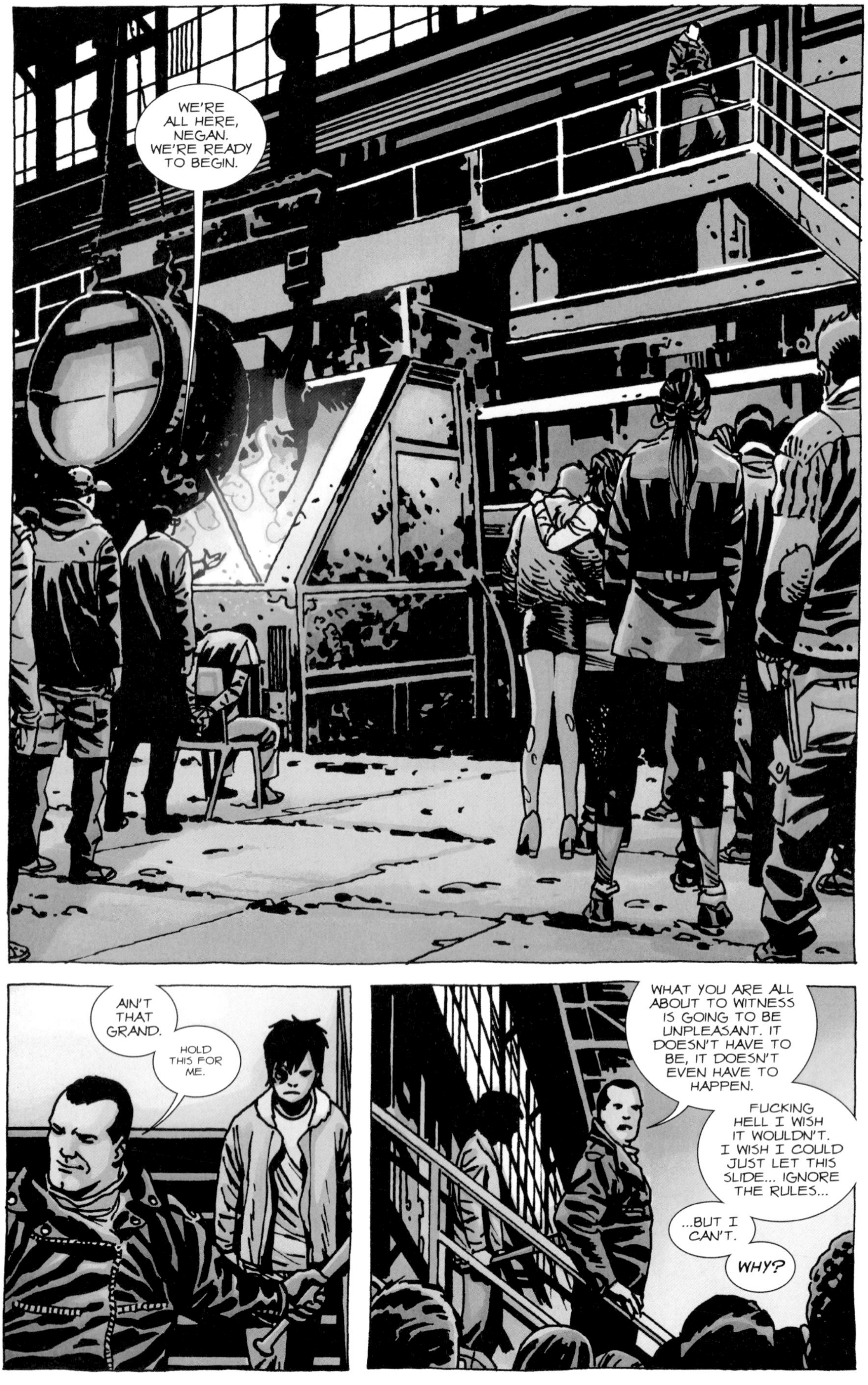
WE'RE ALL HERE, NEGAN. WE'RE READY TO BEGIN.
AIN'T THAT GRAND.
HOLD THIS FOR ME.
WHAT YOU ARE ALL ABOUT TO WITNESS IS GOING TO BE UNPLEASANT. IT DOESN'T HAVE TO BE, IT DOESN'T EVEN HAVE TO HAPPEN.
FUCKING HELL I WISH IT WOULDN'T. I WISH I COULD JUST LET THIS SLIDE... IGNORE THE RULES...
...BUT I CAN'T.
WHY?

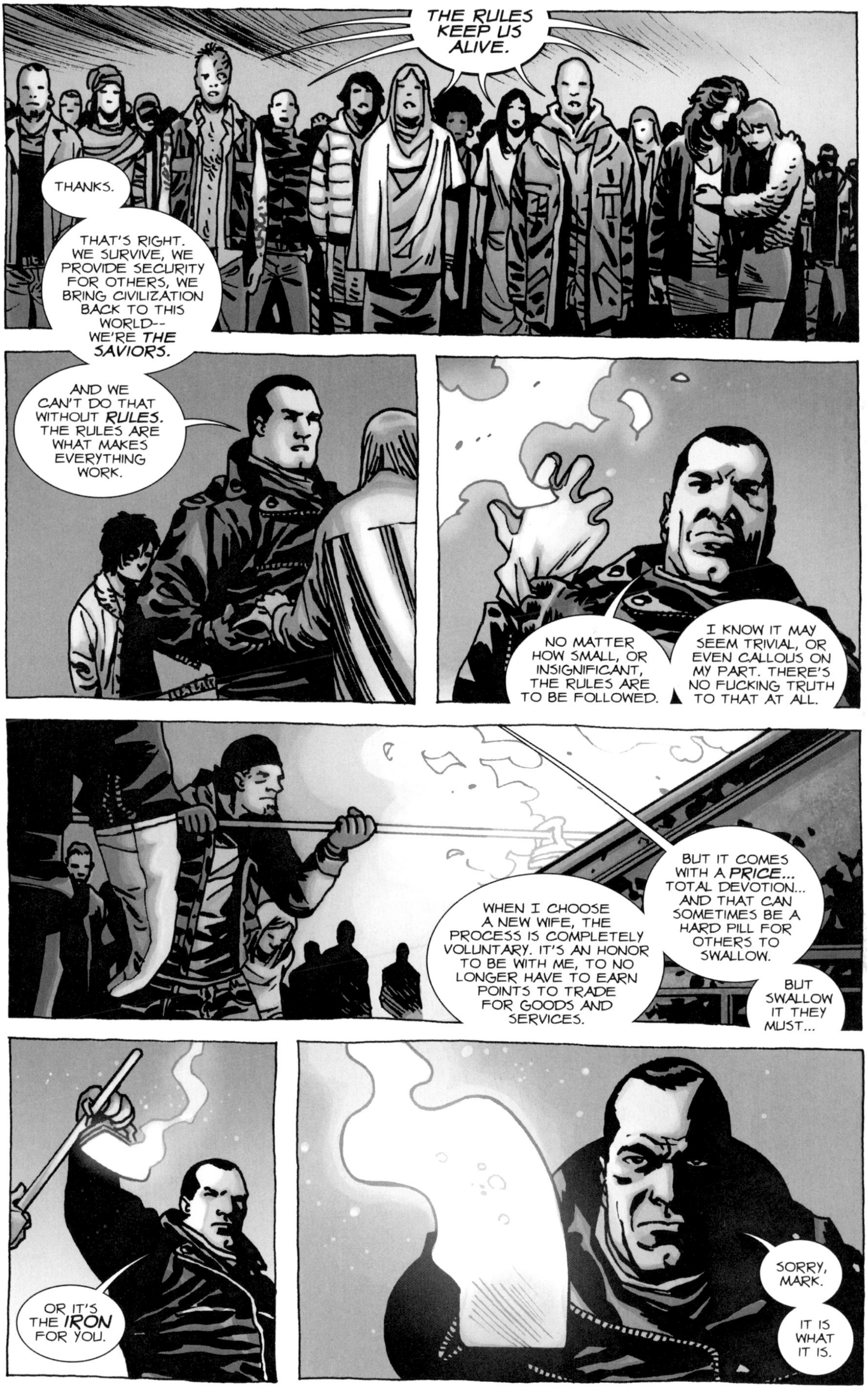
THE RULES KEEP US ALIVE.
THANKS.
THAT'S RIGHT. WE SURVIVE, WE PROVIDE SECURITY FOR OTHERS, WE BRING CIVILIZATION BACK TO THIS WORLD-- WE'RE THE SAVIORS.
AND WE CAN'T DO THAT WITHOUT RULES. THE RULES ARE WHAT MAKES EVERYTHING WORK.
NO MATTER HOW SMALL, OR INSIGNIFICANT, THE RULES ARE TO BE FOLLOWED.
I KNOW IT MAY SEEM TRIVIAL, OR EVEN CALLOUS ON MY PART. THERE'S NO FUCKING TRUTH TO THAT AT ALL.
WHEN I CHOOSE A NEW WIFE, THE PROCESS IS COMPLETELY VOLUNTARY. IT'S AN HONOR TO BE WITH ME, TO NO LONGER HAVE TO EARN POINTS TO TRADE FOR GOODS AND SERVICES.
BUT IT COMES WITH A PRICE... TOTAL DEVOTION... AND THAT CAN SOMETIMES BE A HARD PILL FOR OTHERS TO SWALLOW.
BUT SWALLOW IT THEY MUST...
OR IT'S THE IRON FOR YOU.
SORRY, MARK.
IT IS WHAT IT IS.

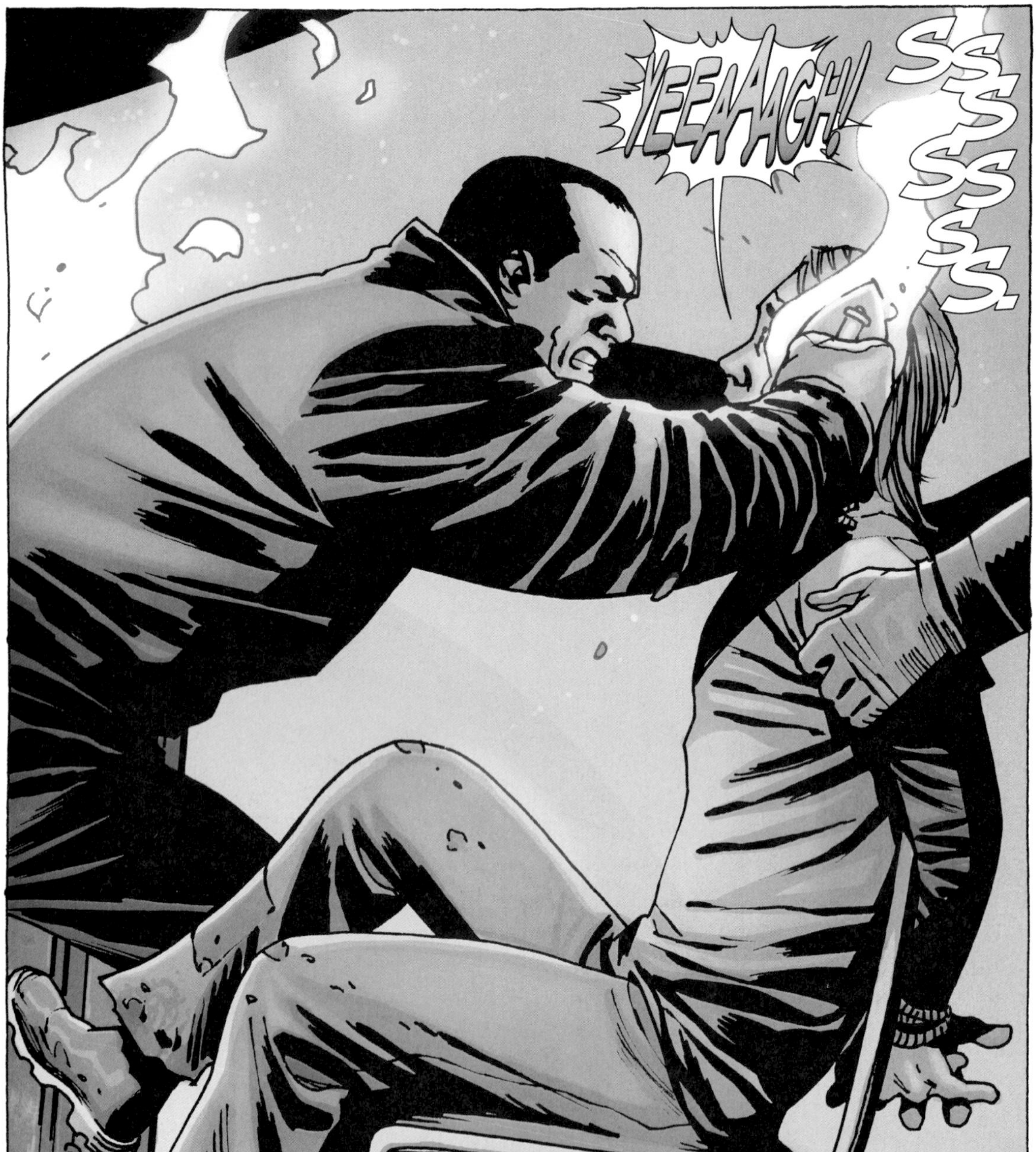
YEEAAAGH!!
SSSSSS

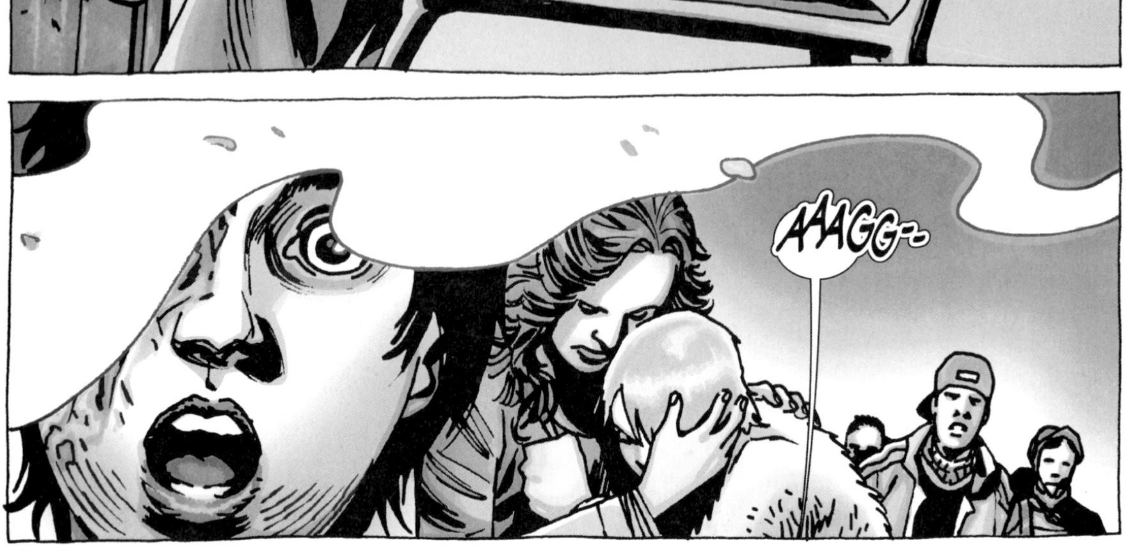
AAAGG--

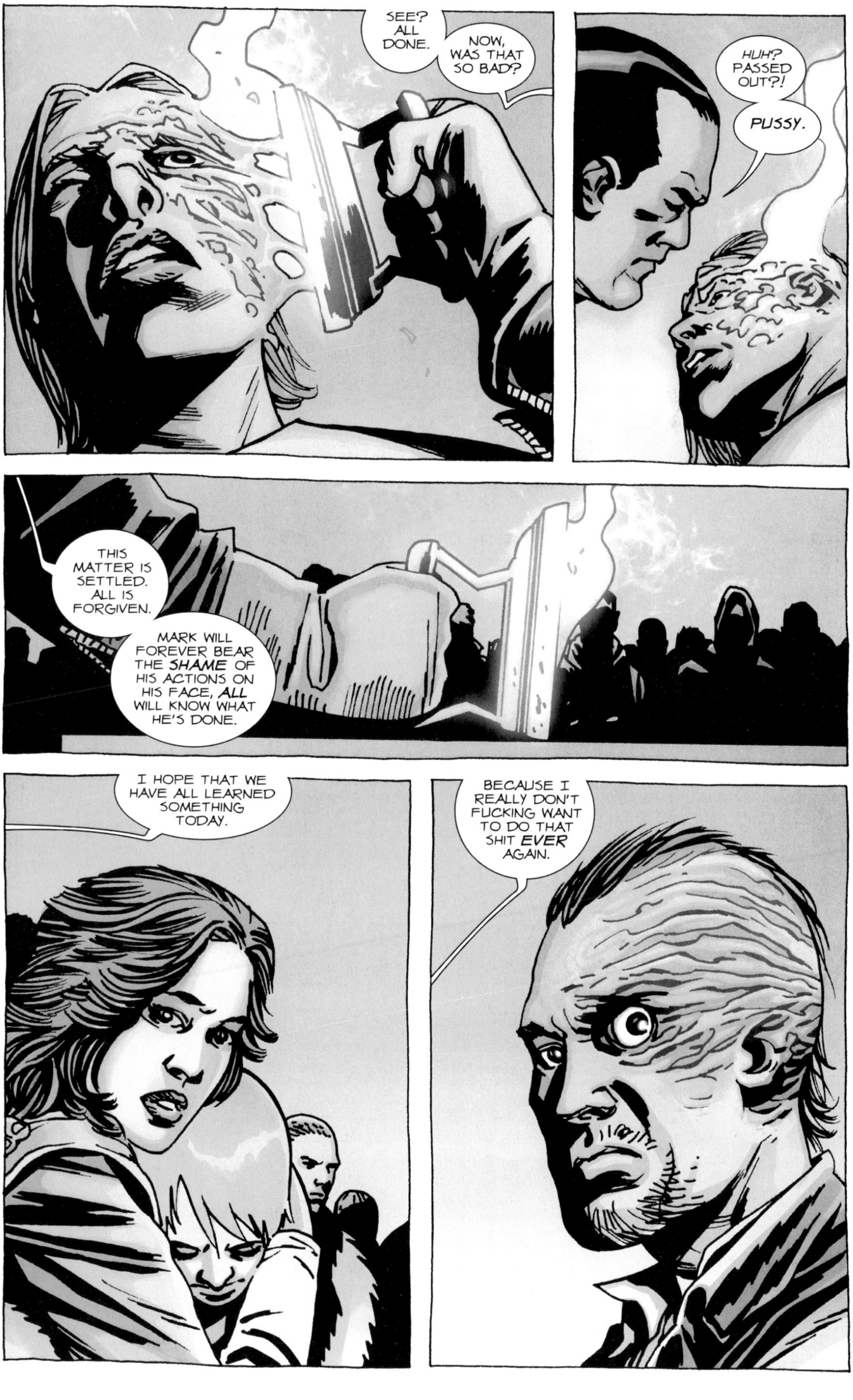

SEE? ALL DONE.
NOW, WAS THAT SO BAD?
HUH? PASSED OUT?!
PUSSY.
THIS MATTER IS SETTLED. ALL IS FORGIVEN.
MARK WILL FOREVER BEAR THE SHAME OF HIS ACTIONS ON HIS FACE, ALL WILL KNOW WHAT HE'S DONE.
I HOPE THAT WE HAVE ALL LEARNED SOMETHING TODAY.
BECAUSE I REALLY DON'T FUCKING WANT TO DO THAT SHIT EVER AGAIN.

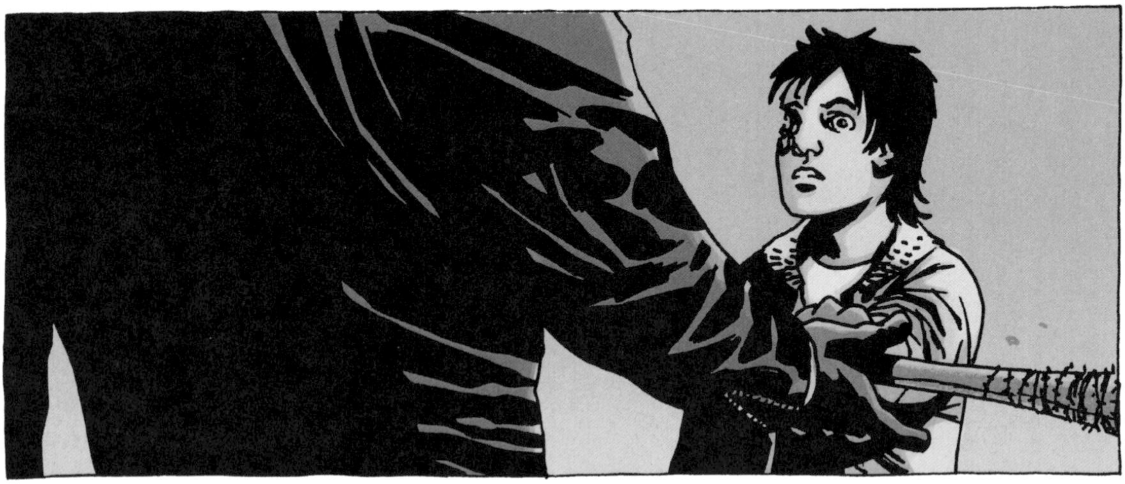

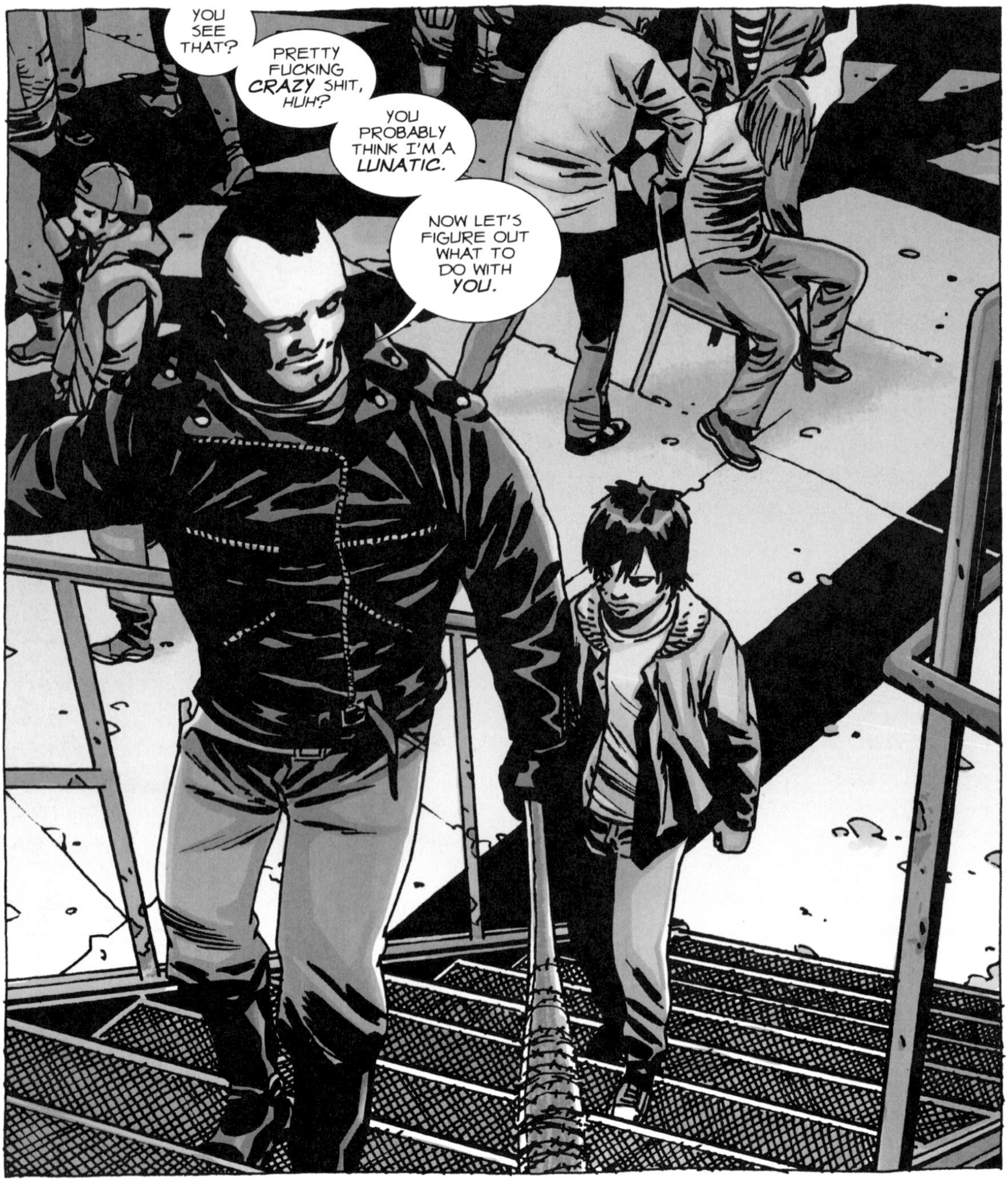
YOU SEE THAT?
PRETTY FUCKING CRAZY SHIT, HUH?
YOU PROBABLY THINK I'M A LUNATIC.
NOW LET'S FIGURE OUT WHAT TO DO WITH YOU.

MARK?

I'M SO SORRY-- I--

DON'T.

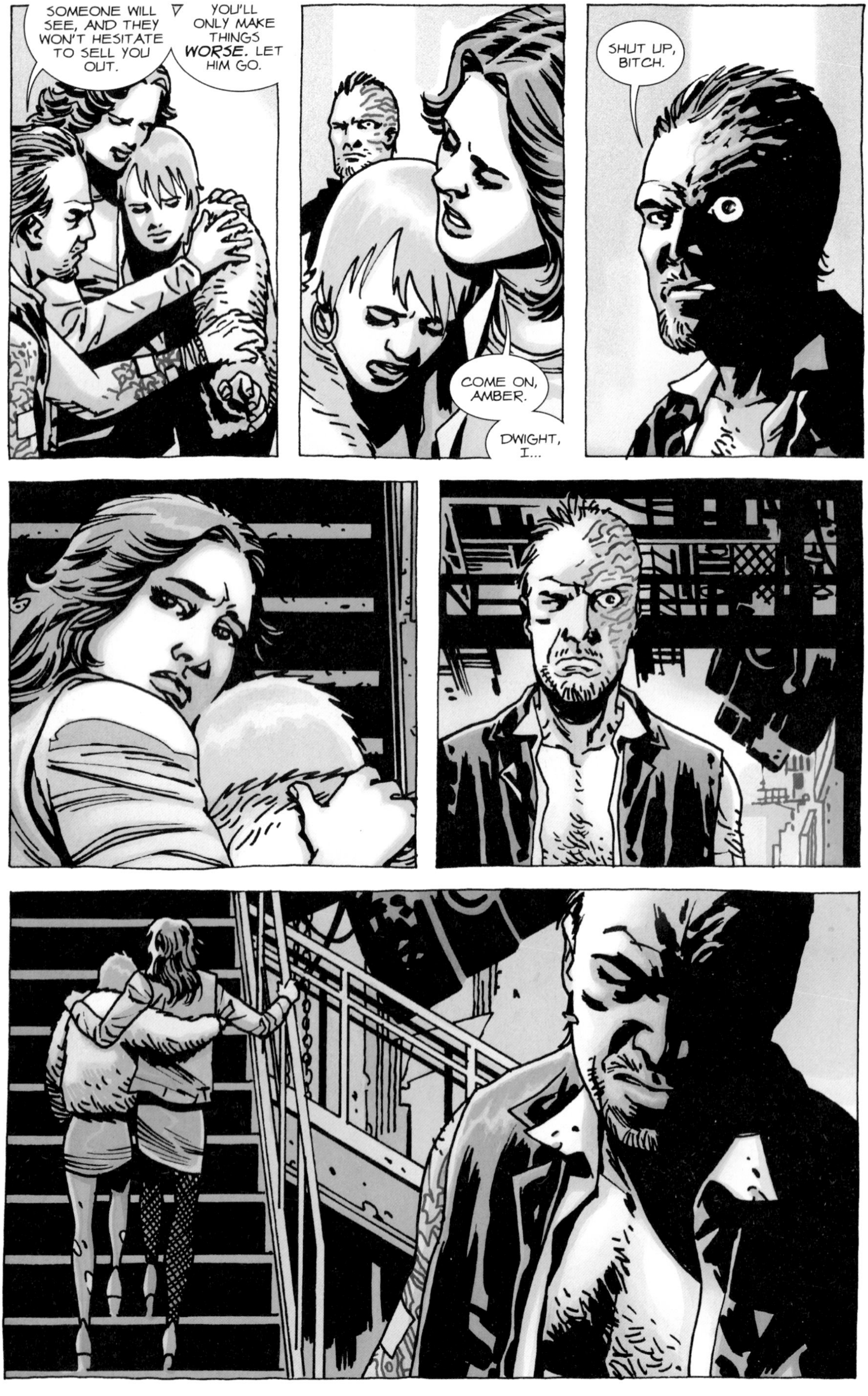
SOMEONE WILL SEE, AND THEY WON'T HESITATE TO SELL YOU OUT.
YOU'LL ONLY MAKE THINGS WORSE. LET HIM GO.
COME ON, AMBER.
DWIGHT, I...
SHUT UP, BITCH.

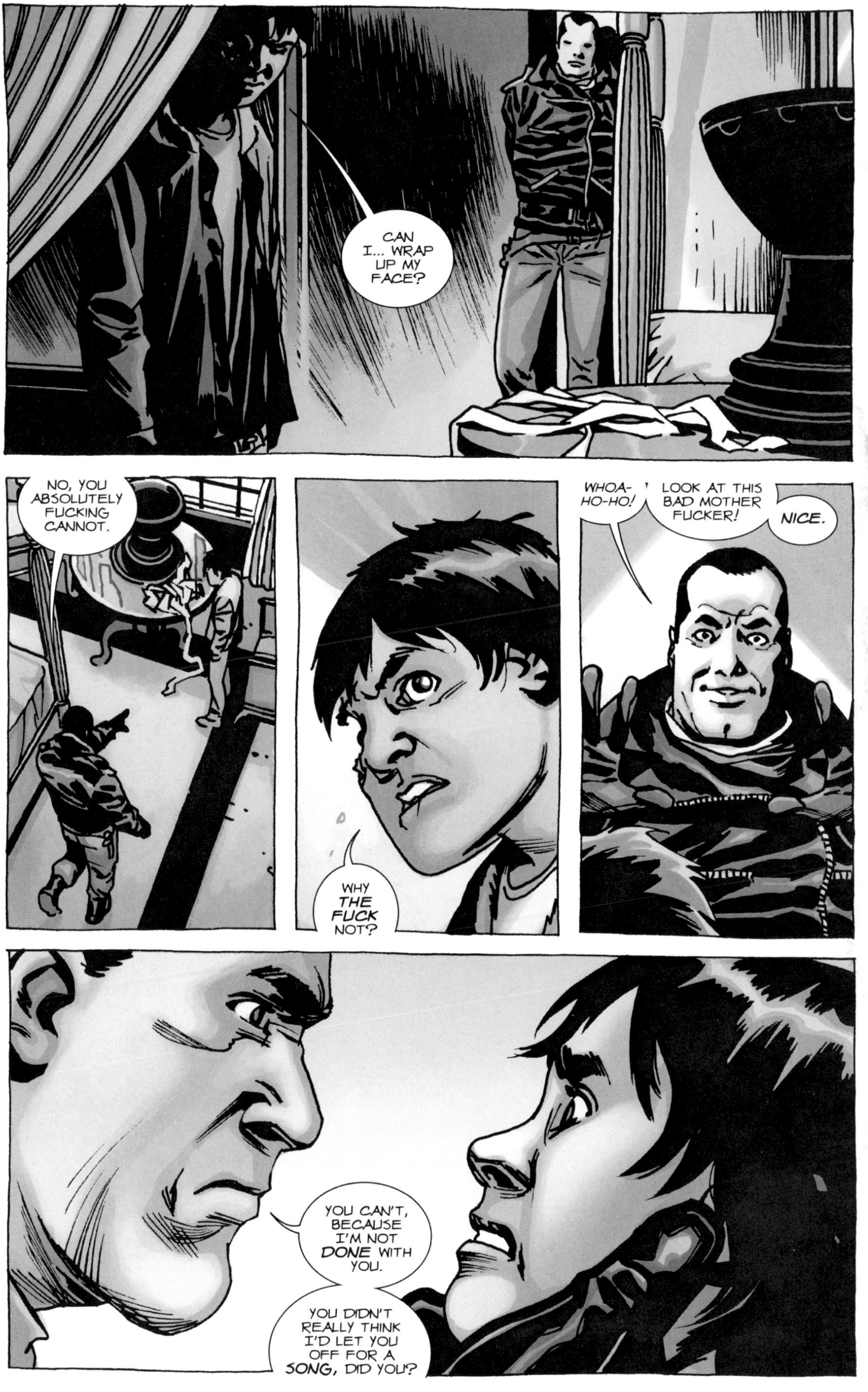
CAN I... WRAP UP MY FACE?
NO, YOU ABSOLUTELY FUCKING CANNOT.
WHY THE FUCK NOT?
WHOA-HO-HO!
LOOK AT THIS BAD MOTHER FUCKER!
NICE.
YOU CAN'T, BECAUSE I'M NOT DONE WITH YOU.
YOU DIDN'T REALLY THINK I'D LET YOU OFF FOR A SONG, DID YOU?

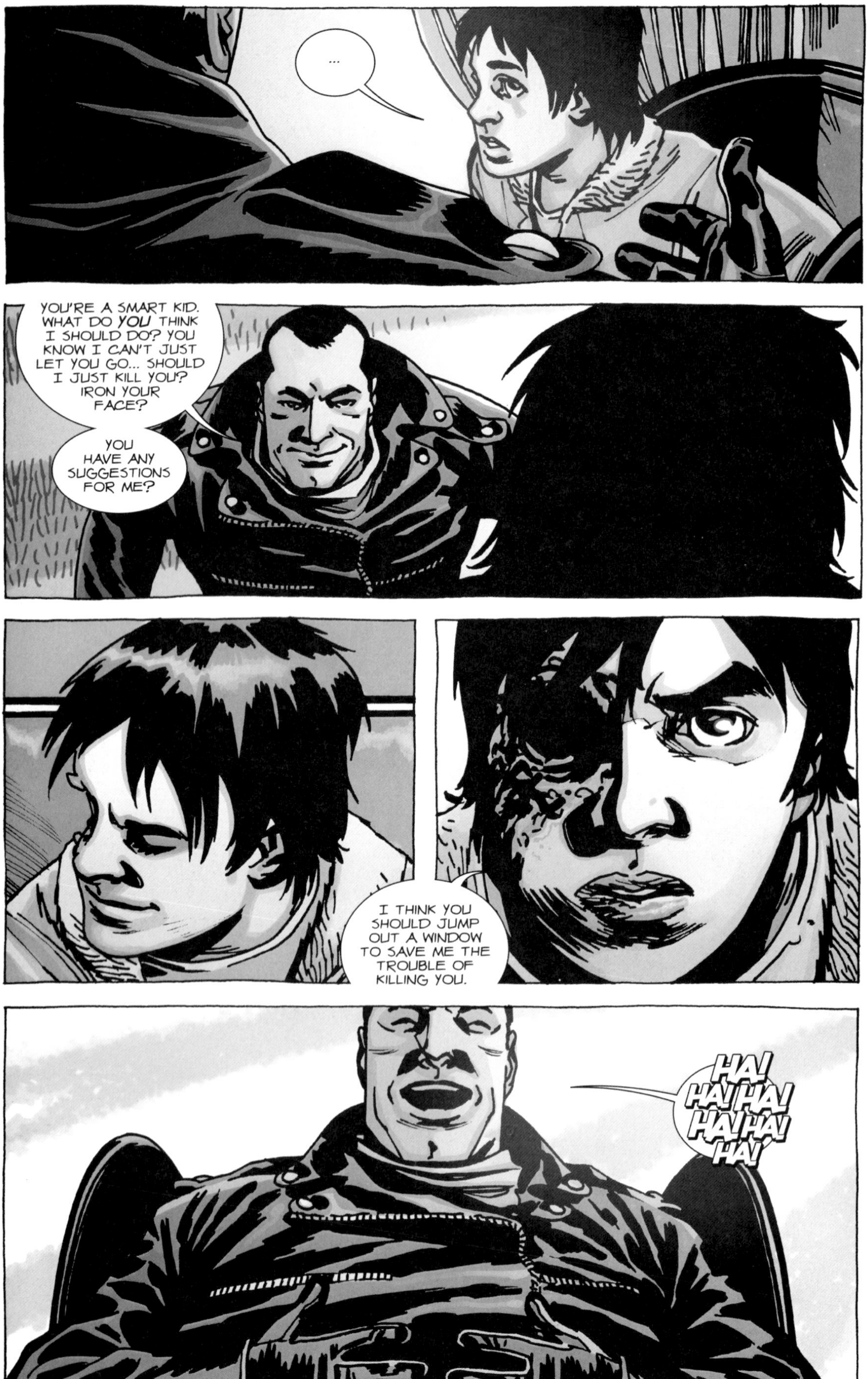
...
YOU'RE A SMART KID. WHAT DO YOU THINK I SHOULD DO? YOU KNOW I CAN'T JUST LET YOU GO... SHOULD I JUST KILL YOU? IRON YOUR FACE?
YOU HAVE ANY SUGGESTIONS FOR ME?
I THINK YOU SHOULD JUMP OUT A WINDOW TO SAVE ME THE TROUBLE OF KILLING YOU.
HA! HA! HA! HA! HA! HA!

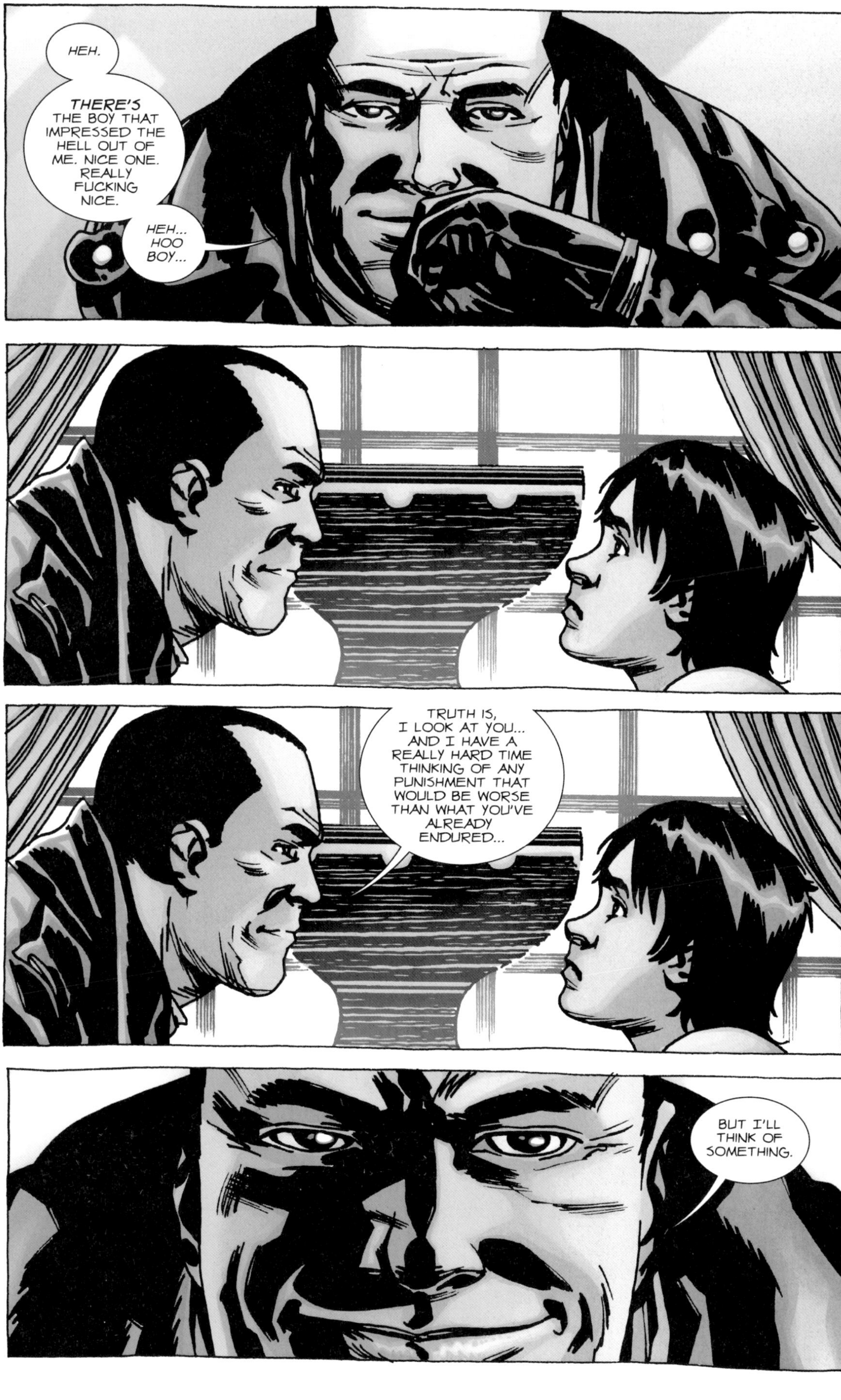
HEH.
THERE'S THE BOY THAT IMPRESSED THE HELL OUT OF ME. NICE ONE. REALLY FUCKING NICE.
HEH... HOO BOY...
TRUTH IS, I LOOK AT YOU... AND I HAVE A REALLY HARD TIME THINKING OF ANY PUNISHMENT THAT WOULD BE WORSE THAN WHAT YOU'VE ALREADY ENDURED...
BUT I'LL THINK OF SOMETHING.

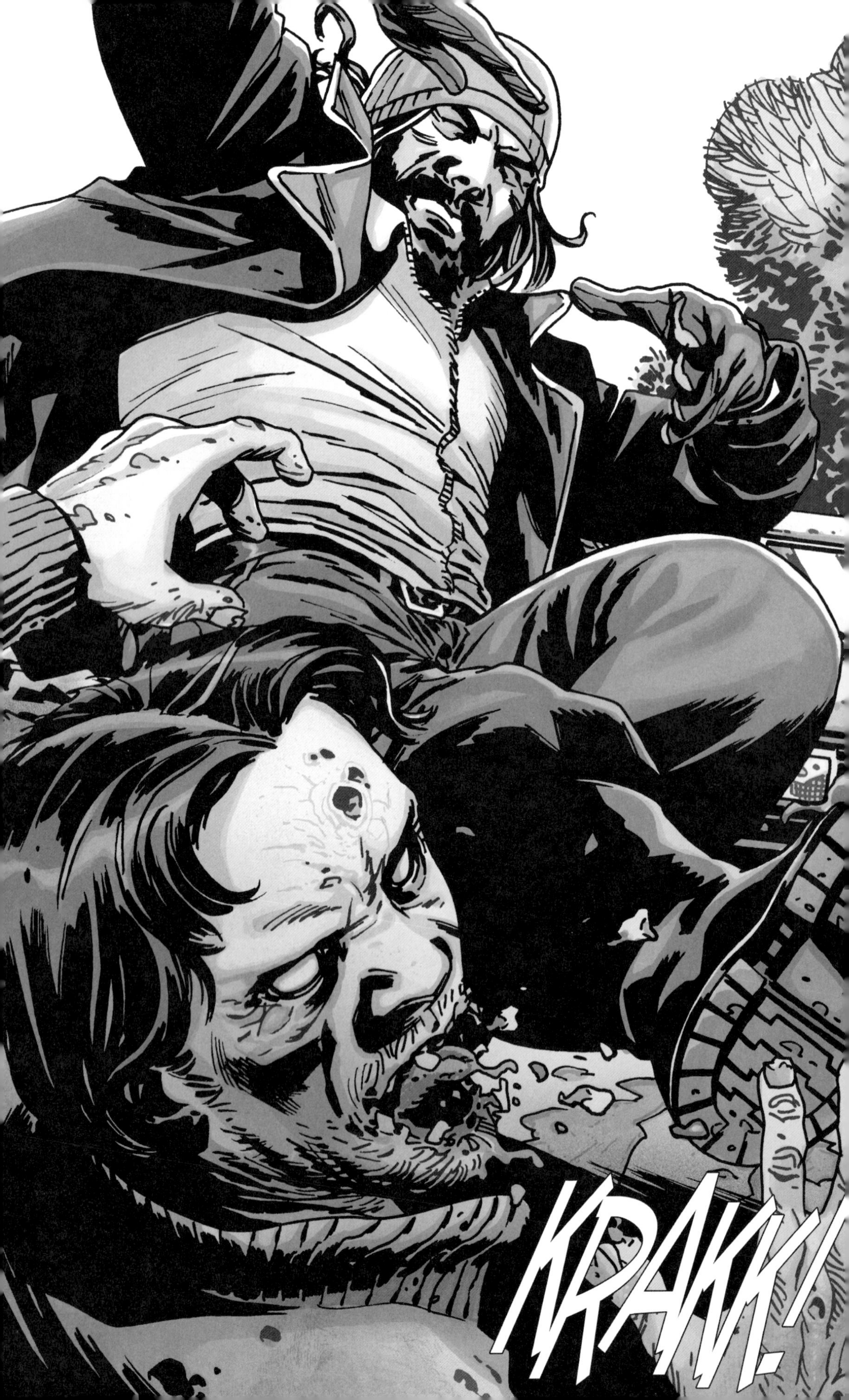
KRAKK!

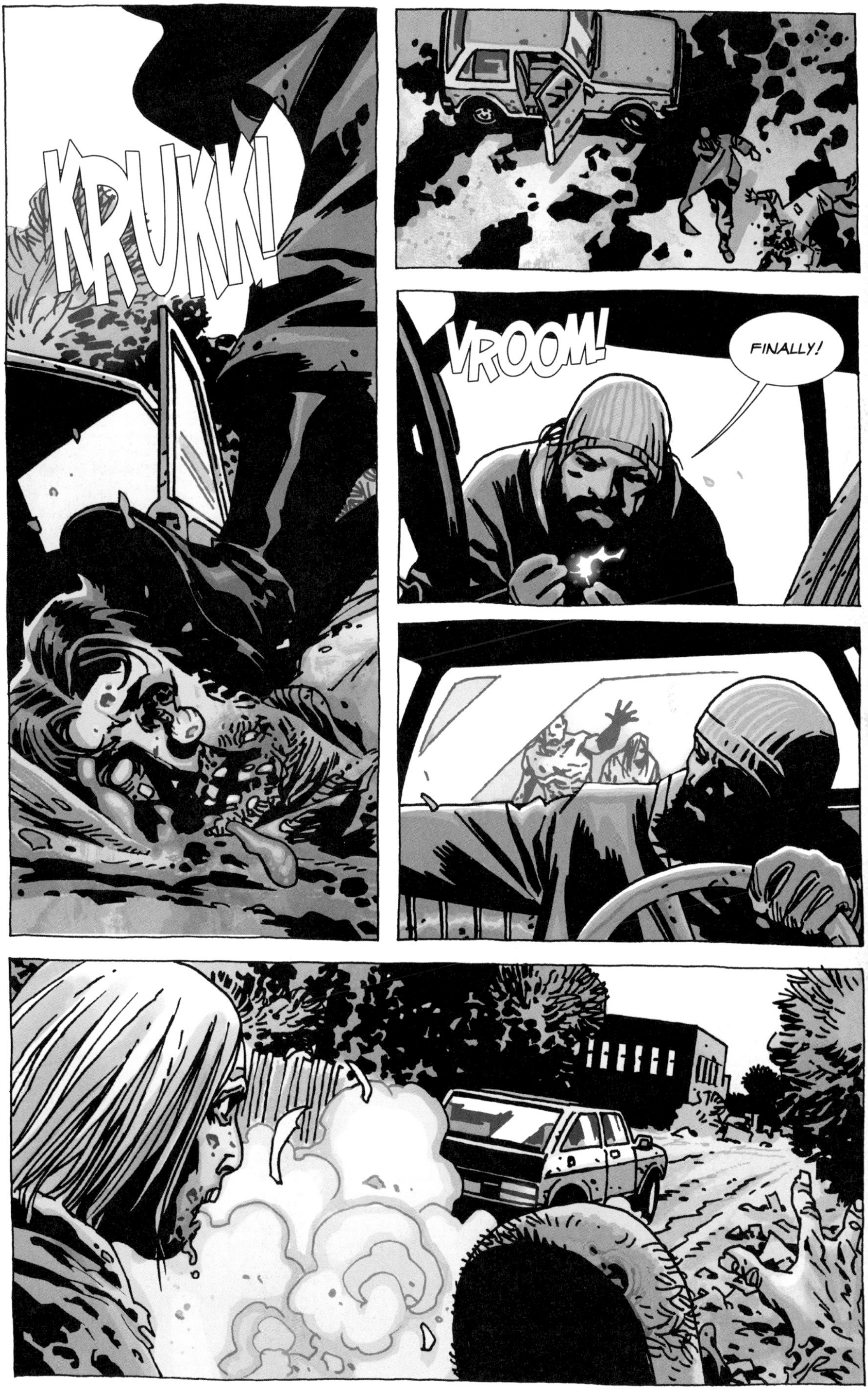

KRUKK!
VROOM!
FINALLY!

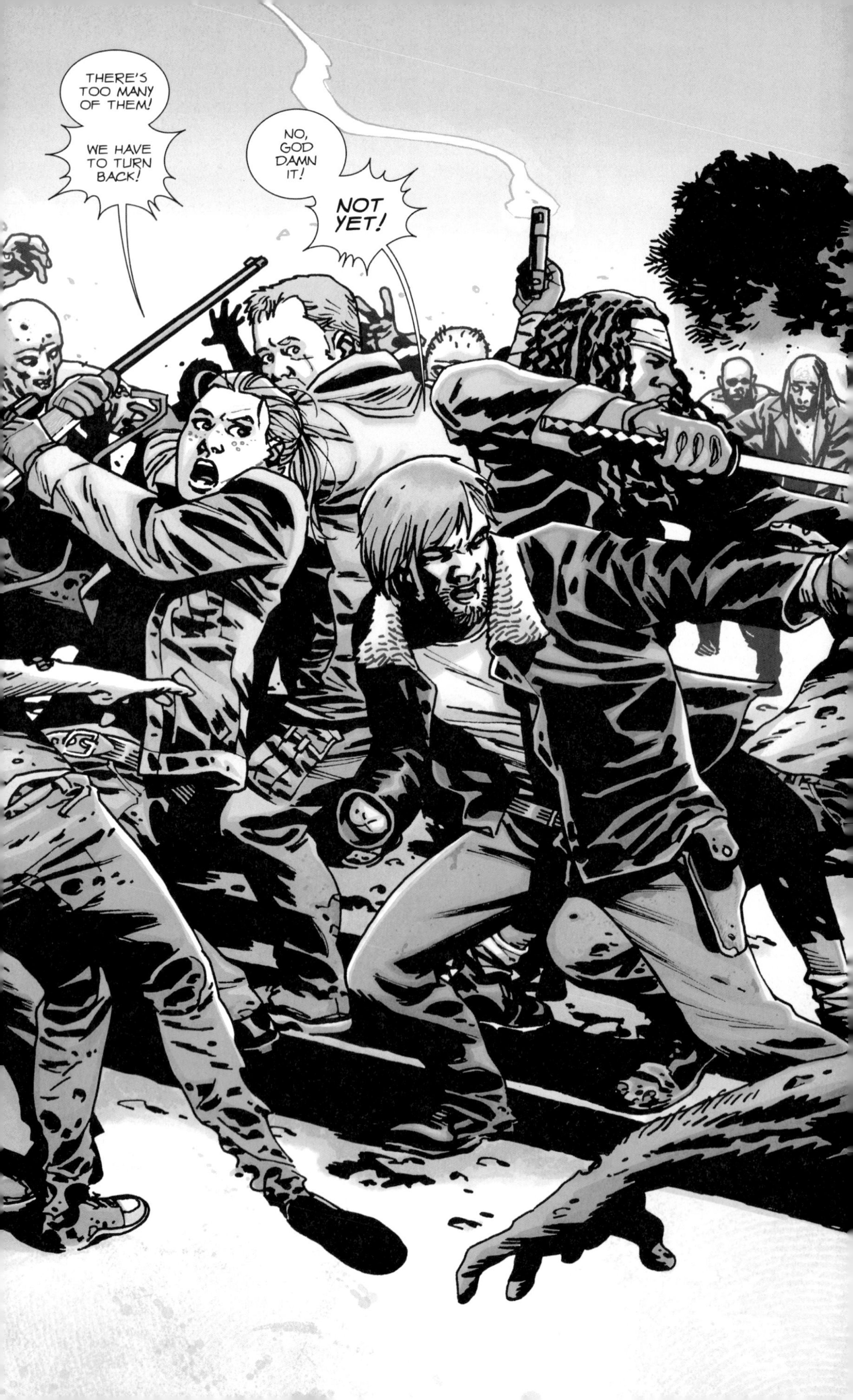

THERE'S TOO MANY OF THEM!
WE HAVE TO TURN BACK!
NO, GOD DAMN IT!
NOT YET!

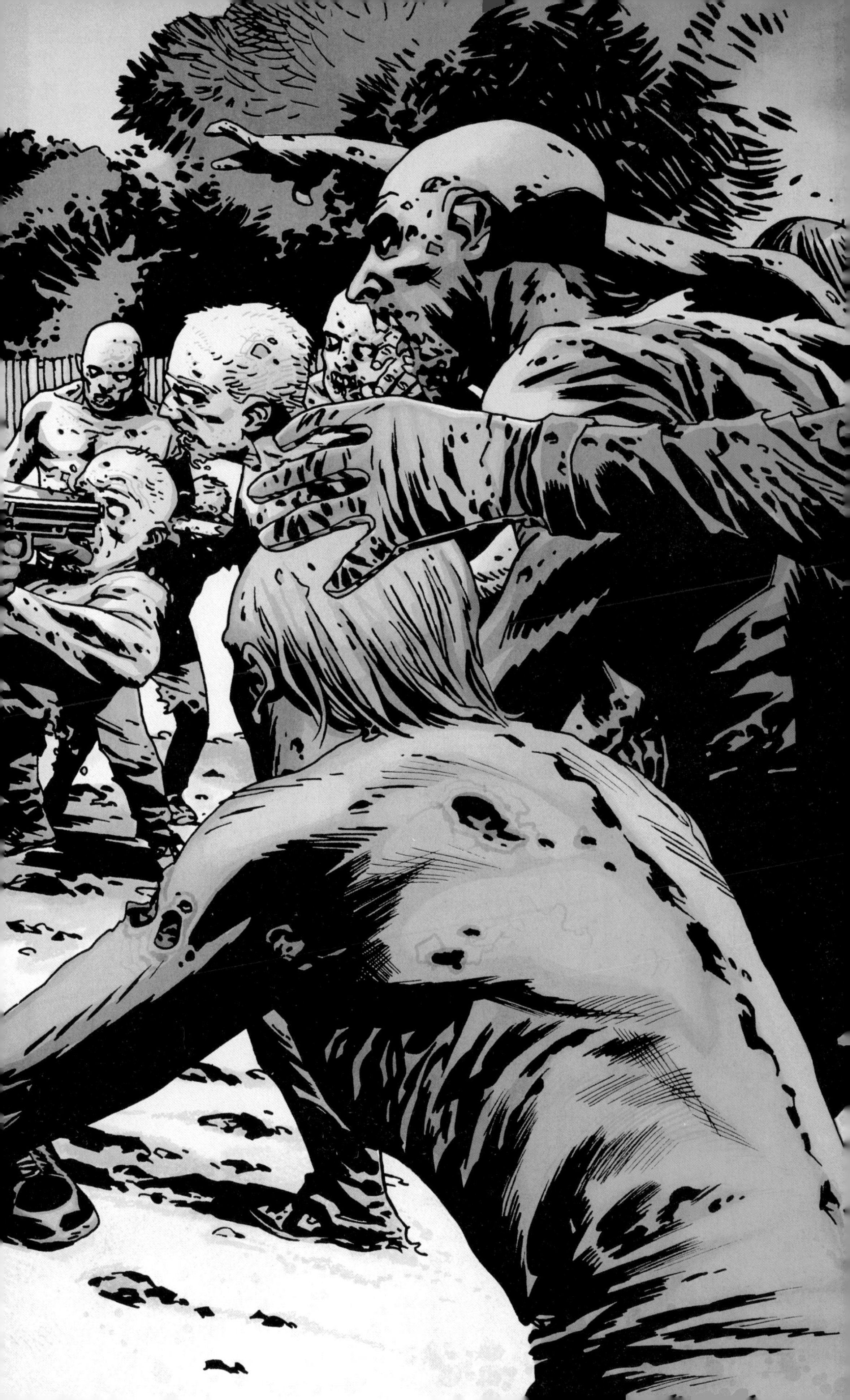

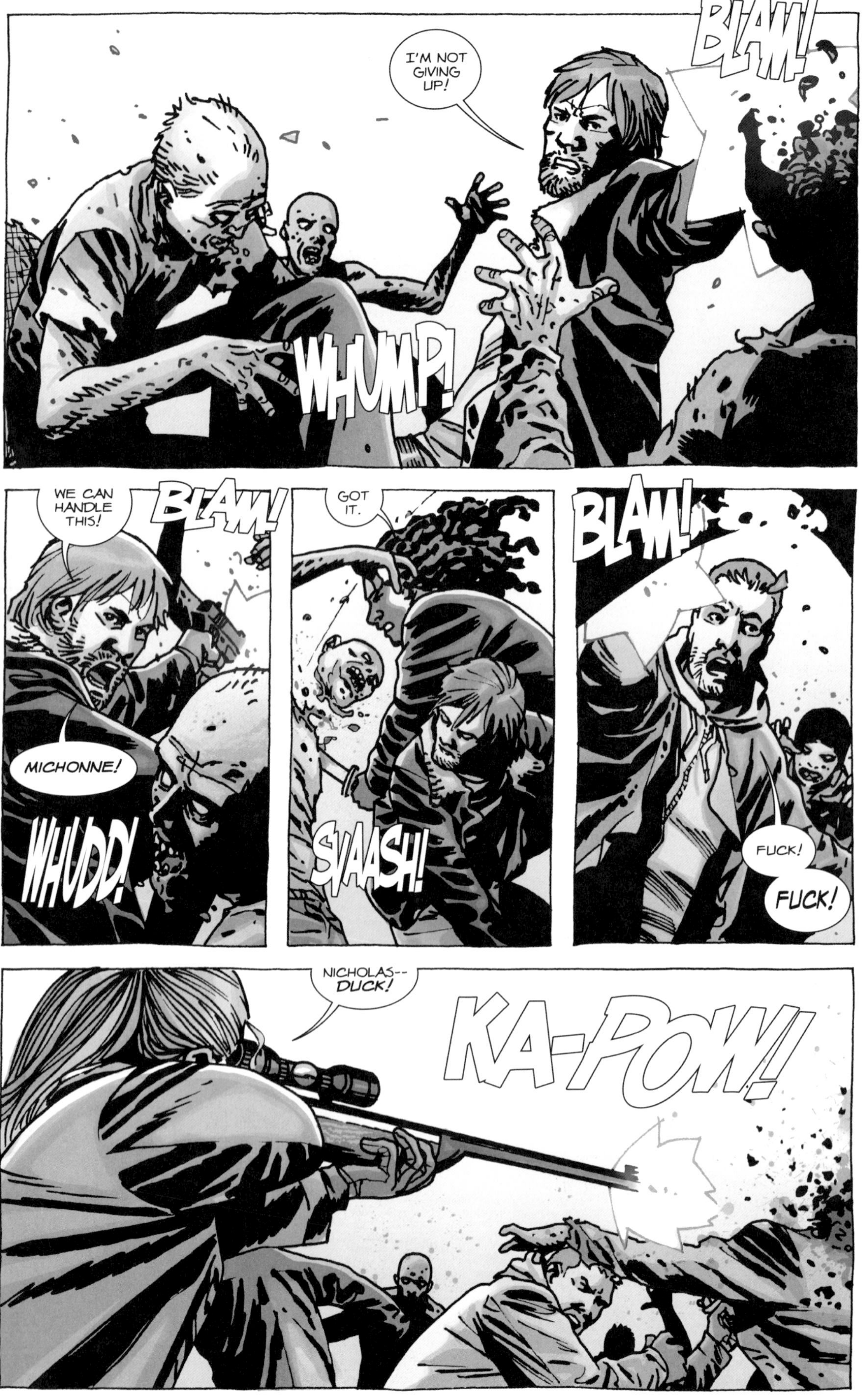
I'M NOT GIVING UP!
BLAM!
WHUMP!
WE CAN HANDLE THIS!
BLAM!
MICHONNE!
WHUDD!
GOT IT.
SVAASH!
BLAM!
FUCK!
FUCK!
NICHOLAS-- DUCK!
KA-POW!

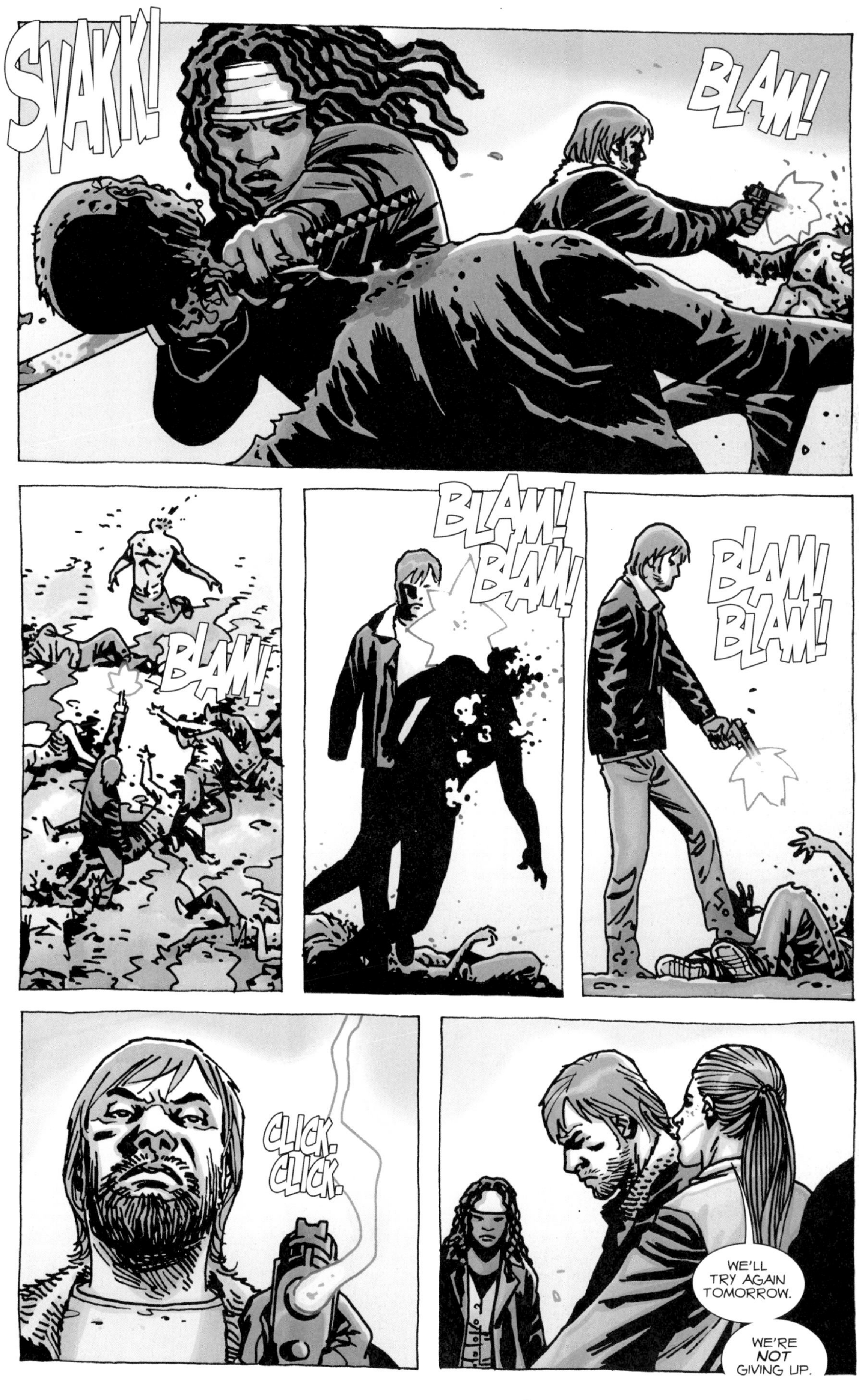
SHAKK!
BLAM!
BLAM!
BLAM!
BLAM!
BLAM!
BLAM!
CLICK.
CLICK.
WE'LL TRY AGAIN TOMORROW.
WE'RE NOT GIVING UP.

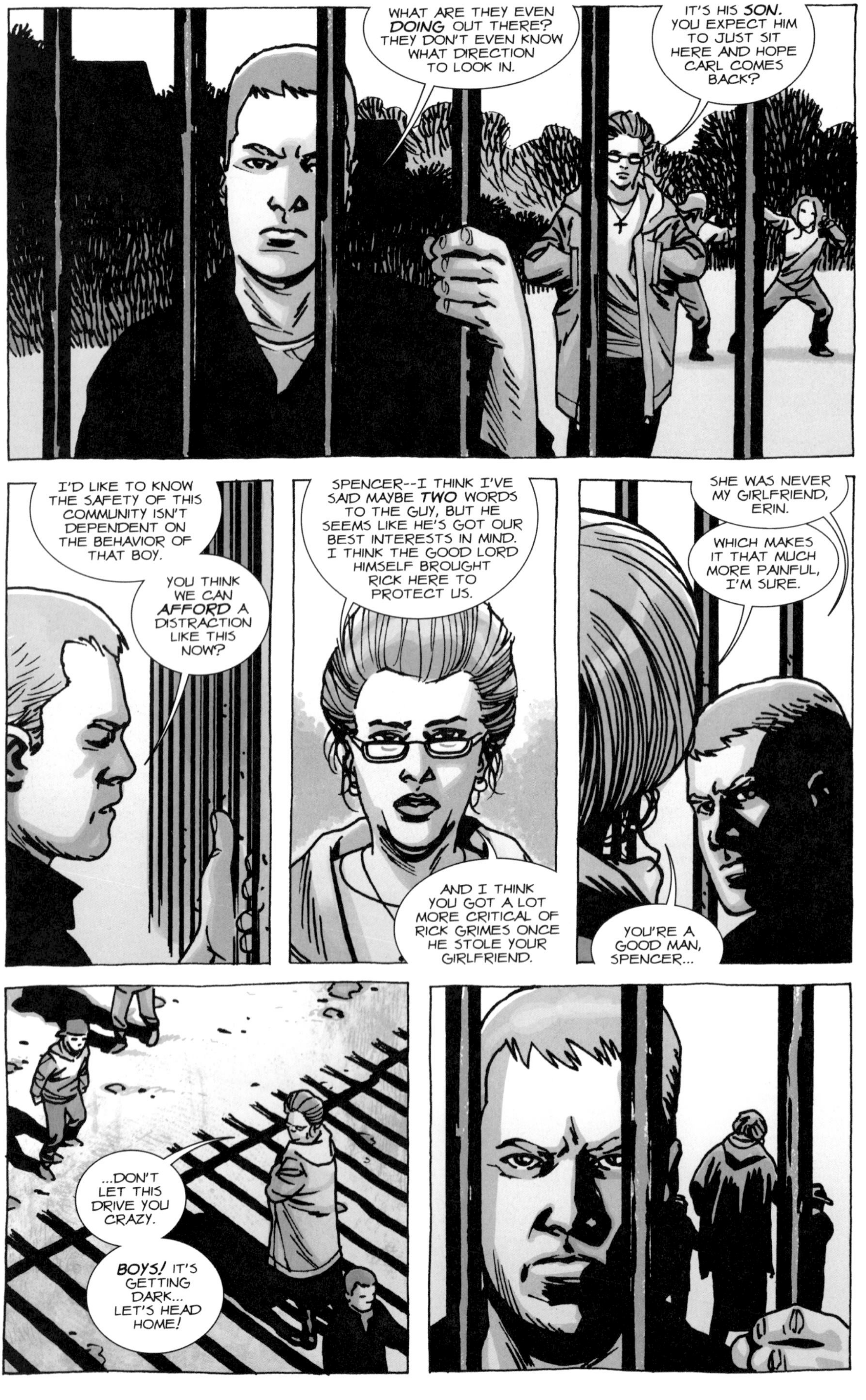
WHAT ARE THEY EVEN DOING OUT THERE? THEY DON'T EVEN KNOW WHAT DIRECTION TO LOOK IN.
IT'S HIS SON. YOU EXPECT HIM TO JUST SIT HERE AND HOPE CARL COMES BACK?
I'D LIKE TO KNOW THE SAFETY OF THIS COMMUNITY ISN'T DEPENDENT ON THE BEHAVIOR OF THAT BOY.
YOU THINK WE CAN AFFORD A DISTRACTION LIKE THIS NOW?
SPENCER--I THINK I'VE SAID MAYBE TWO WORDS TO THE GUY, BUT HE SEEMS LIKE HE'S GOT OUR BEST INTERESTS IN MIND. I THINK THE GOOD LORD HIMSELF BROUGHT RICK HERE TO PROTECT US.
AND I THINK YOU GOT A LOT MORE CRITICAL OF RICK GRIMES ONCE HE STOLE YOUR GIRLFRIEND.
SHE WAS NEVER MY GIRLFRIEND, ERIN.
WHICH MAKES IT THAT MUCH MORE PAINFUL, I'M SURE.
YOU'RE A GOOD MAN, SPENCER...
...DON'T LET THIS DRIVE YOU CRAZY.
BOYS! IT'S GETTING DARK... LET'S HEAD HOME!

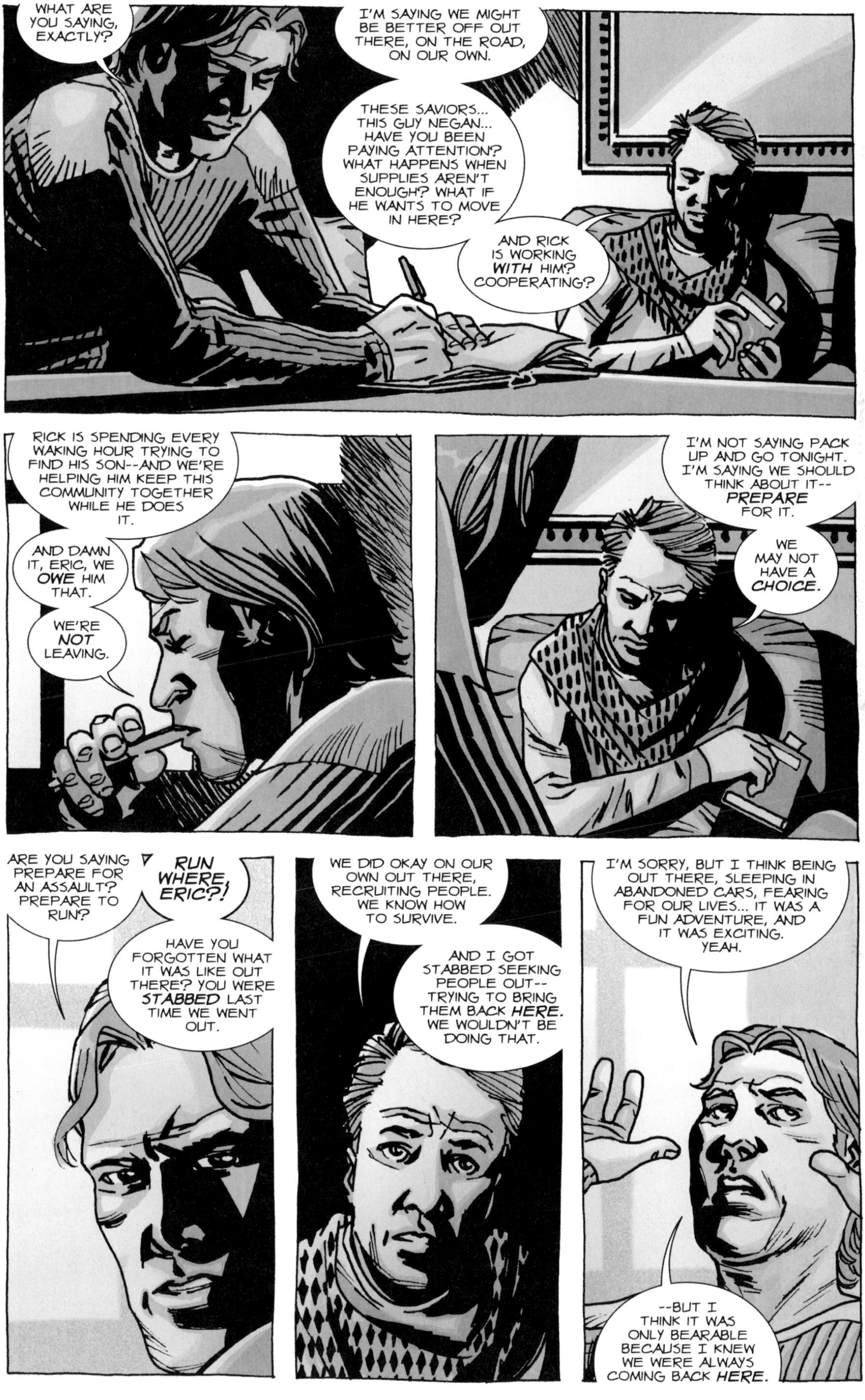
WHAT ARE YOU SAYING, EXACTLY?
I'M SAYING WE MIGHT BE BETTER OFF OUT THERE, ON THE ROAD, ON OUR OWN.
THESE SAVIORS... THIS GUY NEGAN... HAVE YOU BEEN PAYING ATTENTION? WHAT HAPPENS WHEN SUPPLIES AREN'T ENOUGH? WHAT IF HE WANTS TO MOVE IN HERE?
AND RICK IS WORKING WITH HIM? COOPERATING?
RICK IS SPENDING EVERY WAKING HOUR TRYING TO FIND HIS SON--AND WE'RE HELPING HIM KEEP THIS COMMUNITY TOGETHER WHILE HE DOES IT.
AND DAMN IT, ERIC, WE OWE HIM THAT.
WE'RE NOT LEAVING.
I'M NOT SAYING PACK UP AND GO TONIGHT. I'M SAYING WE SHOULD THINK ABOUT IT-- PREPARE FOR IT.
WE MAY NOT HAVE A CHOICE.
ARE YOU SAYING PREPARE FOR AN ASSAULT? PREPARE TO RUN?
RUN WHERE, ERIC?!
HAVE YOU FORGOTTEN WHAT IT WAS LIKE OUT THERE? YOU WERE STABBED LAST TIME WE WENT OUT.
WE DID OKAY ON OUR OWN OUT THERE, RECRUITING PEOPLE. WE KNOW HOW TO SURVIVE.
AND I GOT STABBED SEEKING PEOPLE OUT-- TRYING TO BRING THEM BACK HERE. WE WOULDN'T BE DOING THAT.
I'M SORRY, BUT I THINK BEING OUT THERE, SLEEPING IN ABANDONED CARS, FEARING FOR OUR LIVES... IT WAS A FUN ADVENTURE, AND IT WAS EXCITING. YEAH.
--BUT I THINK IT WAS ONLY BEARABLE BECAUSE I KNEW WE WERE ALWAYS COMING BACK HERE.

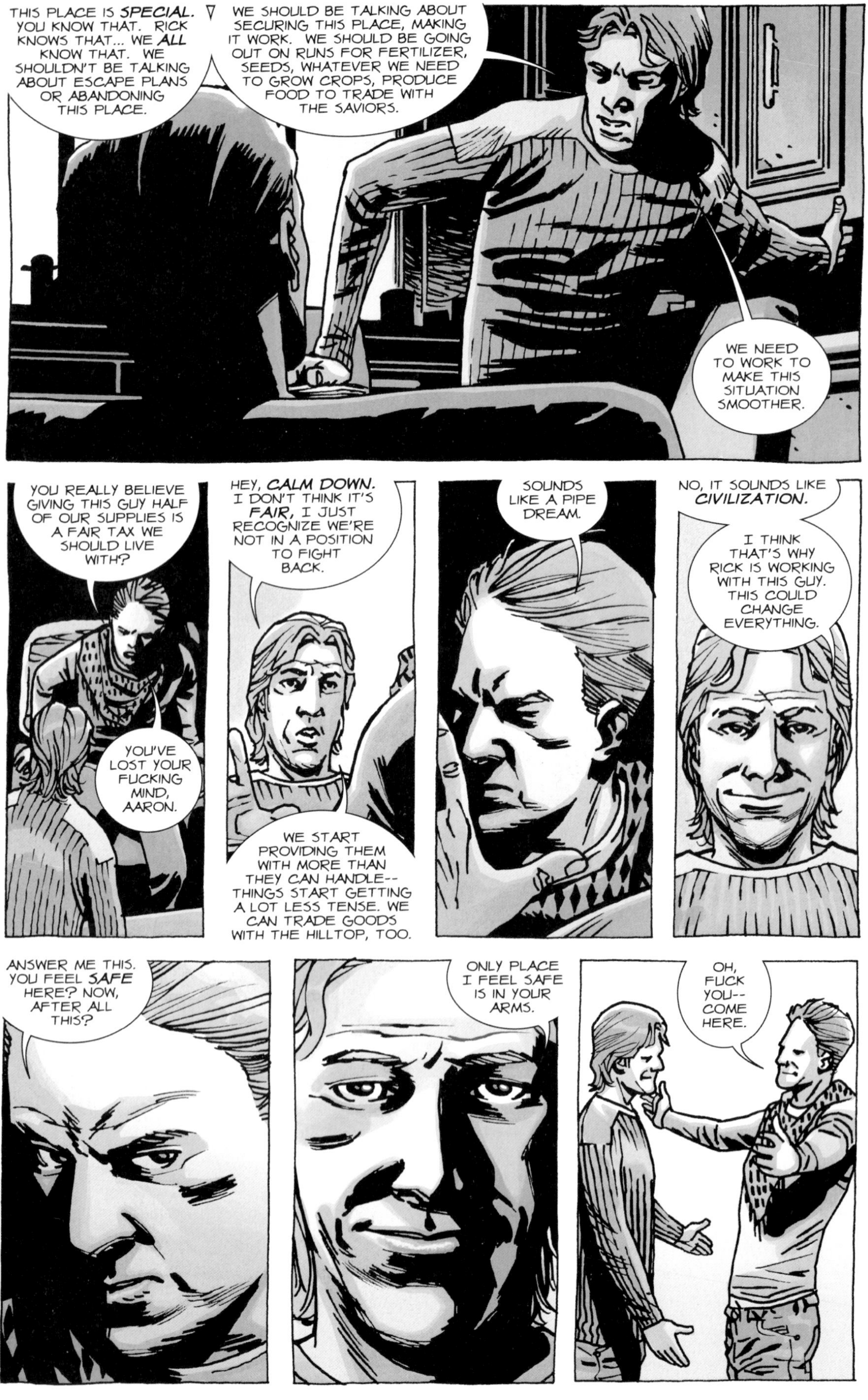
THIS PLACE IS SPECIAL. YOU KNOW THAT. RICK KNOWS THAT... WE ALL KNOW THAT. WE SHOULDN'T BE TALKING ABOUT ESCAPE PLANS OR ABANDONING THIS PLACE.
WE SHOULD BE TALKING ABOUT SECURING THIS PLACE, MAKING IT WORK. WE SHOULD BE GOING OUT ON RUNS FOR FERTILIZER, SEEDS, WHATEVER WE NEED TO GROW CROPS, PRODUCE FOOD TO TRADE WITH THE SAVIORS.
WE NEED TO WORK TO MAKE THIS SITUATION SMOOTHER.
YOU REALLY BELIEVE GIVING THIS GUY HALF OF OUR SUPPLIES IS A FAIR TAX WE SHOULD LIVE WITH?
YOU'VE LOST YOUR FUCKING MIND, AARON.
HEY, CALM DOWN. I DON'T THINK IT'S FAIR, I JUST RECOGNIZE WE'RE NOT IN A POSITION TO FIGHT BACK.
WE START PROVIDING THEM WITH MORE THAN THEY CAN HANDLE-- THINGS START GETTING A LOT LESS TENSE. WE CAN TRADE GOODS WITH THE HILLTOP, TOO.
SOUNDS LIKE A PIPE DREAM.
NO, IT SOUNDS LIKE CIVILIZATION.
I THINK THAT'S WHY RICK IS WORKING WITH THIS GUY. THIS COULD CHANGE EVERYTHING.
ANSWER ME THIS. YOU FEEL SAFE HERE? NOW, AFTER ALL THIS?
ONLY PLACE I FEEL SAFE IS IN YOUR ARMS.
OH, FUCK YOU-- COME HERE.

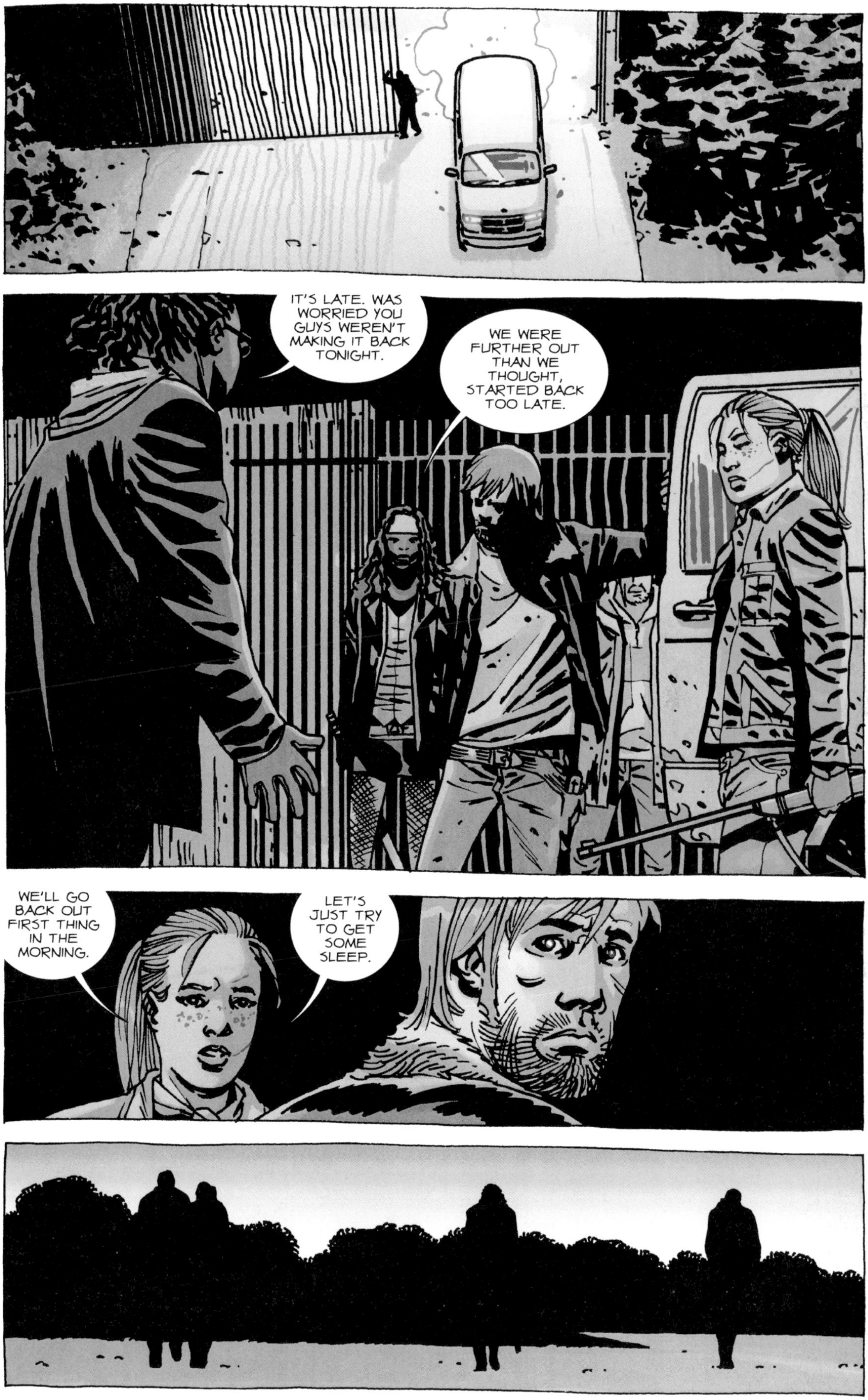
IT'S LATE. WAS WORRIED YOU GUYS WEREN'T MAKING IT BACK TONIGHT.
WE WERE FURTHER OUT THAN WE THOUGHT, STARTED BACK TOO LATE.
WE'LL GO BACK OUT FIRST THING IN THE MORNING.
LET'S JUST TRY TO GET SOME SLEEP.

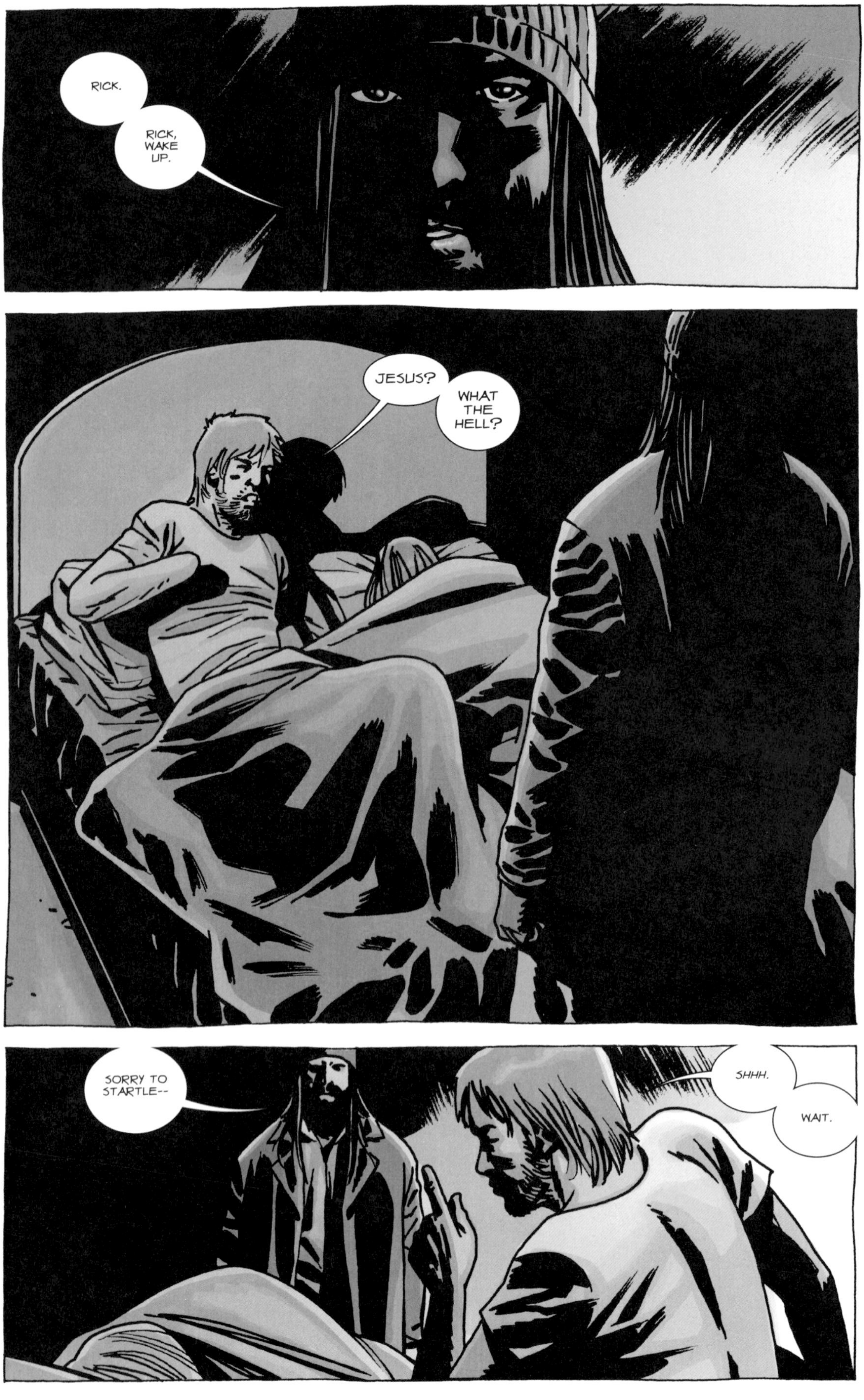
RICK.
RICK, WAKE UP.
JESUS?
WHAT THE HELL?
SORRY TO STARTLE--
SHHH.
WAIT.

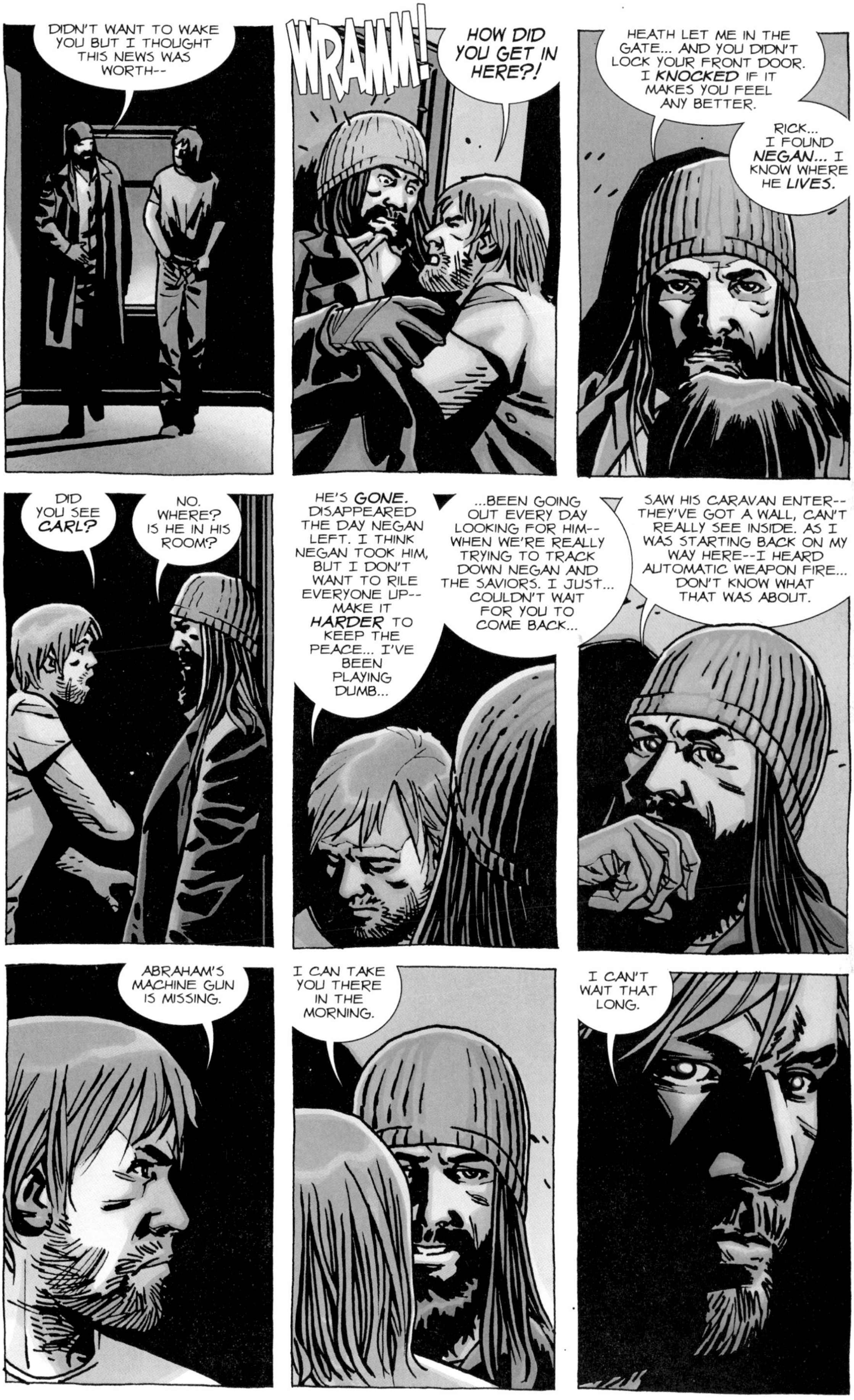
DIDN'T WANT TO WAKE YOU BUT I THOUGHT THIS NEWS WAS WORTH--
WRAMM!
HOW DID YOU GET IN HERE?!
HEATH LET ME IN THE GATE... AND YOU DIDN'T LOCK YOUR FRONT DOOR. I KNOCKED IF IT MAKES YOU FEEL ANY BETTER.
RICK... I FOUND NEGAN... I KNOW WHERE HE LIVES.
DID YOU SEE CARL?
NO. WHERE? IS HE IN HIS ROOM?
HE'S GONE. DISAPPEARED THE DAY NEGAN LEFT. I THINK NEGAN TOOK HIM, BUT I DON'T WANT TO RILE EVERYONE UP-- MAKE IT HARDER TO KEEP THE PEACE... I'VE BEEN PLAYING DUMB...
...BEEN GOING OUT EVERY DAY LOOKING FOR HIM-- WHEN WE'RE REALLY TRYING TO TRACK DOWN NEGAN AND THE SAVIORS. I JUST... COULDN'T WAIT FOR YOU TO COME BACK...
SAW HIS CARAVAN ENTER-- THEY'VE GOT A WALL, CAN'T REALLY SEE INSIDE. AS I WAS STARTING BACK ON MY WAY HERE--I HEARD AUTOMATIC WEAPON FIRE... DON'T KNOW WHAT THAT WAS ABOUT.
ABRAHAM'S MACHINE GUN IS MISSING.
I CAN TAKE YOU THERE IN THE MORNING.
I CAN'T WAIT THAT LONG.

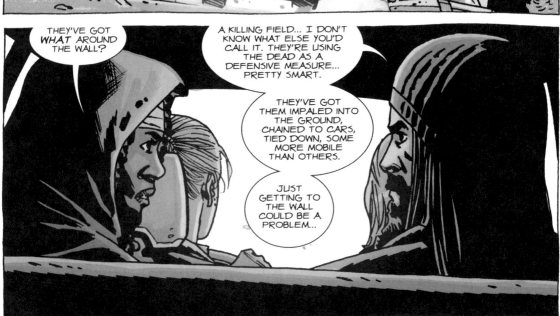

THEY'VE GOT *WHAT* AROUND THE WALL?

A KILLING FIELD... I DON'T KNOW WHAT ELSE YOU'D CALL IT. THEY'RE USING THE DEAD AS A DEFENSIVE MEASURE... PRETTY SMART.

THEY'VE GOT THEM IMPALED INTO THE GROUND, CHAINED TO CARS, TIED DOWN, SOME MORE MOBILE THAN OTHERS.

JUST GETTING TO THE WALL COULD BE A PROBLEM...

I KNOW A WAY.

ROAMERS WON'T EVEN NOTICE US.

AND ONCE WE'RE INSIDE--HOW DO WE FIND HIM? YOU SAID THIS PLACE HAS HOW MANY FLOORS?

I DON'T KNOW... A BUNCH. TEN? IT'S A HUGE PLACE.

THAT DOESN'T SOUND PROMISING.

THERE A PLACE NEARBY WHERE I COULD SET UP, WATCH THEM THROUGH MY SCOPE? IT'D BE BEST TO KNOW WHAT WE'RE RUNNING INTO-- MAYBE I'D SEE CARL.

SOME TALL TREES NEARBY--DON'T KNOW HOW CLEAR A VIEW YOU COULD GET WITHOUT RISK OF BEING SPOTTED.

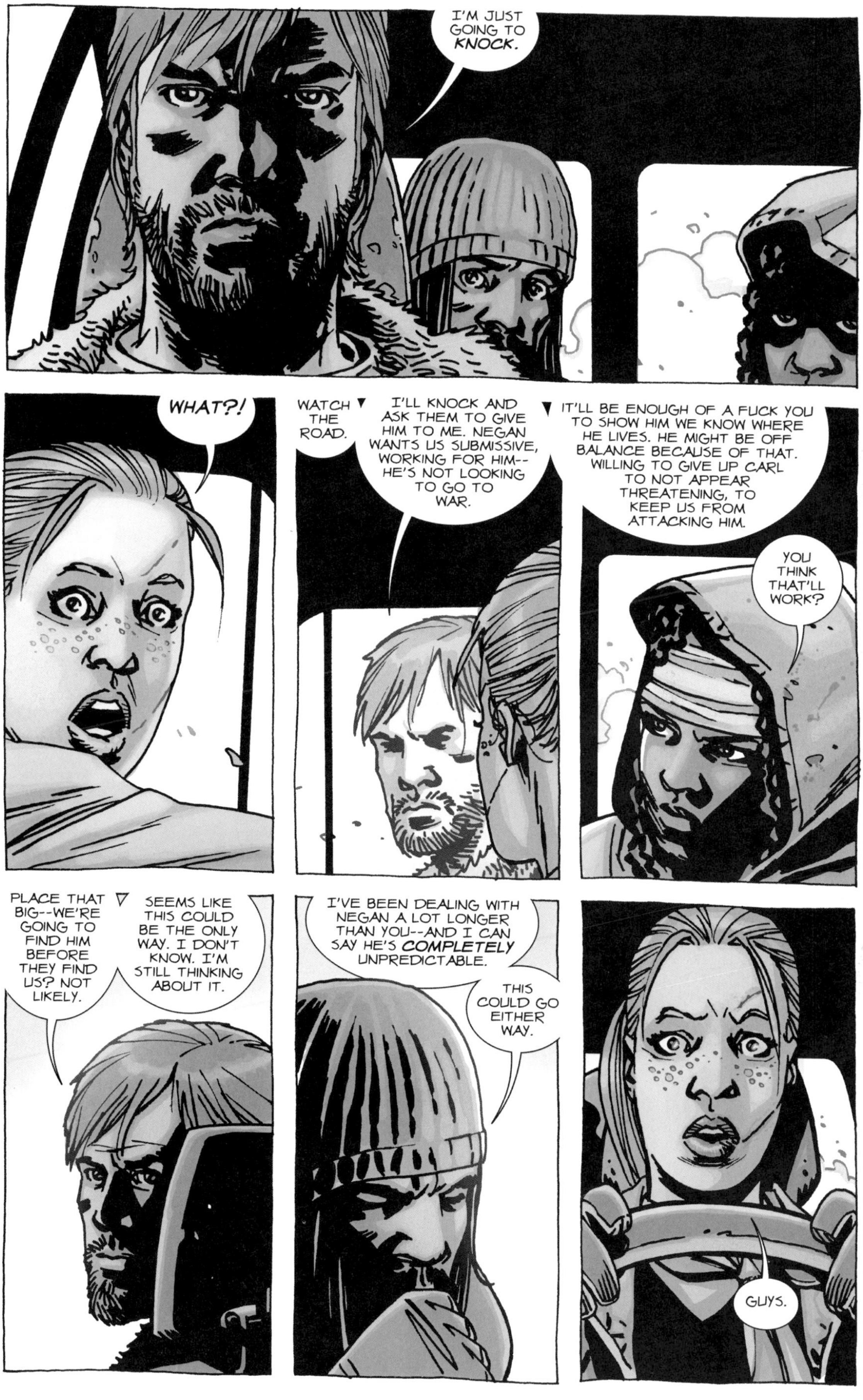
I'M JUST GOING TO KNOCK.
WHAT?!
WATCH THE ROAD.
I'LL KNOCK AND ASK THEM TO GIVE HIM TO ME. NEGAN WANTS US SUBMISSIVE, WORKING FOR HIM-- HE'S NOT LOOKING TO GO TO WAR.
IT'LL BE ENOUGH OF A FUCK YOU TO SHOW HIM WE KNOW WHERE HE LIVES. HE MIGHT BE OFF BALANCE BECAUSE OF THAT. WILLING TO GIVE UP CARL TO NOT APPEAR THREATENING, TO KEEP US FROM ATTACKING HIM.
YOU THINK THAT'LL WORK?
PLACE THAT BIG--WE'RE GOING TO FIND HIM BEFORE THEY FIND US? NOT LIKELY.
SEEMS LIKE THIS COULD BE THE ONLY WAY. I DON'T KNOW. I'M STILL THINKING ABOUT IT.
I'VE BEEN DEALING WITH NEGAN A LOT LONGER THAN YOU--AND I CAN SAY HE'S COMPLETELY UNPREDICTABLE.
THIS COULD GO EITHER WAY.
GUYS.

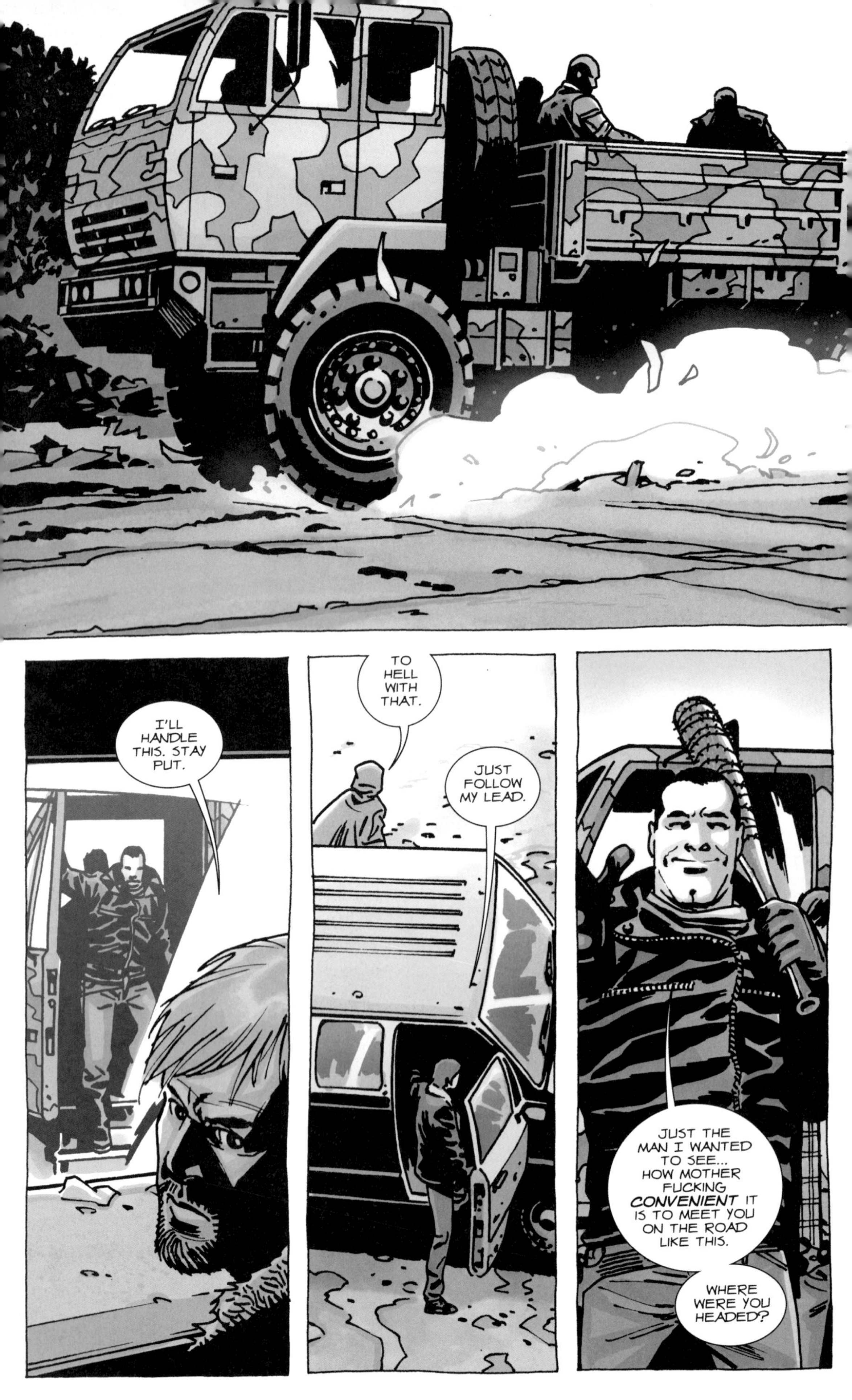
I'LL HANDLE THIS. STAY PUT.
TO HELL WITH THAT.
JUST FOLLOW MY LEAD.
JUST THE MAN I WANTED TO SEE... HOW MOTHER FUCKING *CONVENIENT* IT IS TO MEET YOU ON THE ROAD LIKE THIS.
WHERE WERE YOU HEADED?

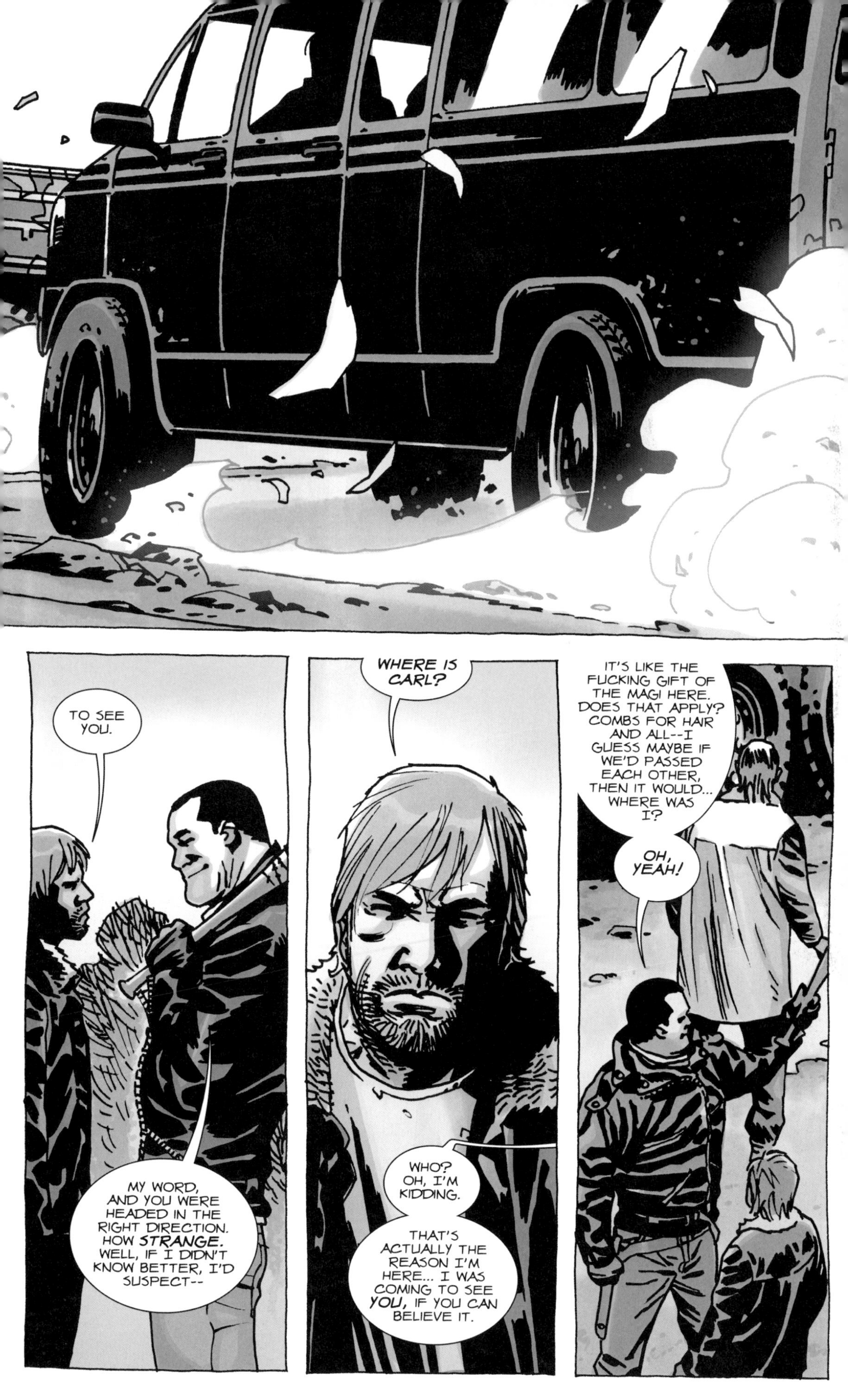

TO SEE YOU.
MY WORD, AND YOU WERE HEADED IN THE RIGHT DIRECTION. HOW STRANGE. WELL, IF I DIDN'T KNOW BETTER, I'D SUSPECT--
WHERE IS CARL?
WHO? OH, I'M KIDDING.
THAT'S ACTUALLY THE REASON I'M HERE... I WAS COMING TO SEE YOU, IF YOU CAN BELIEVE IT.
IT'S LIKE THE FUCKING GIFT OF THE MAGI HERE. DOES THAT APPLY? COMBS FOR HAIR AND ALL--I GUESS MAYBE IF WE'D PASSED EACH OTHER, THEN IT WOULD... WHERE WAS I?
OH, YEAH!

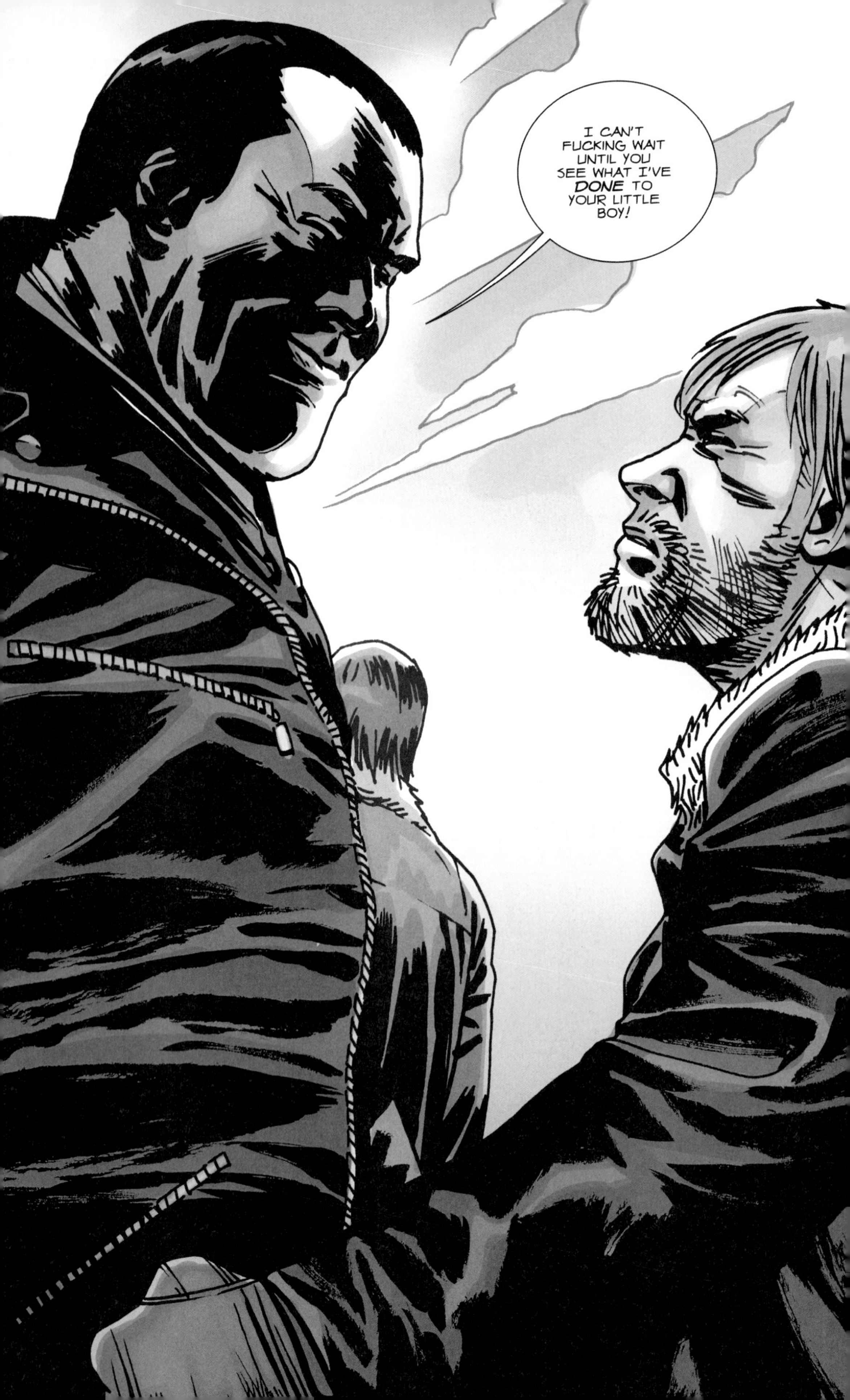
I CAN'T FUCKING WAIT UNTIL YOU SEE WHAT I'VE DONE TO YOUR LITTLE BOY!

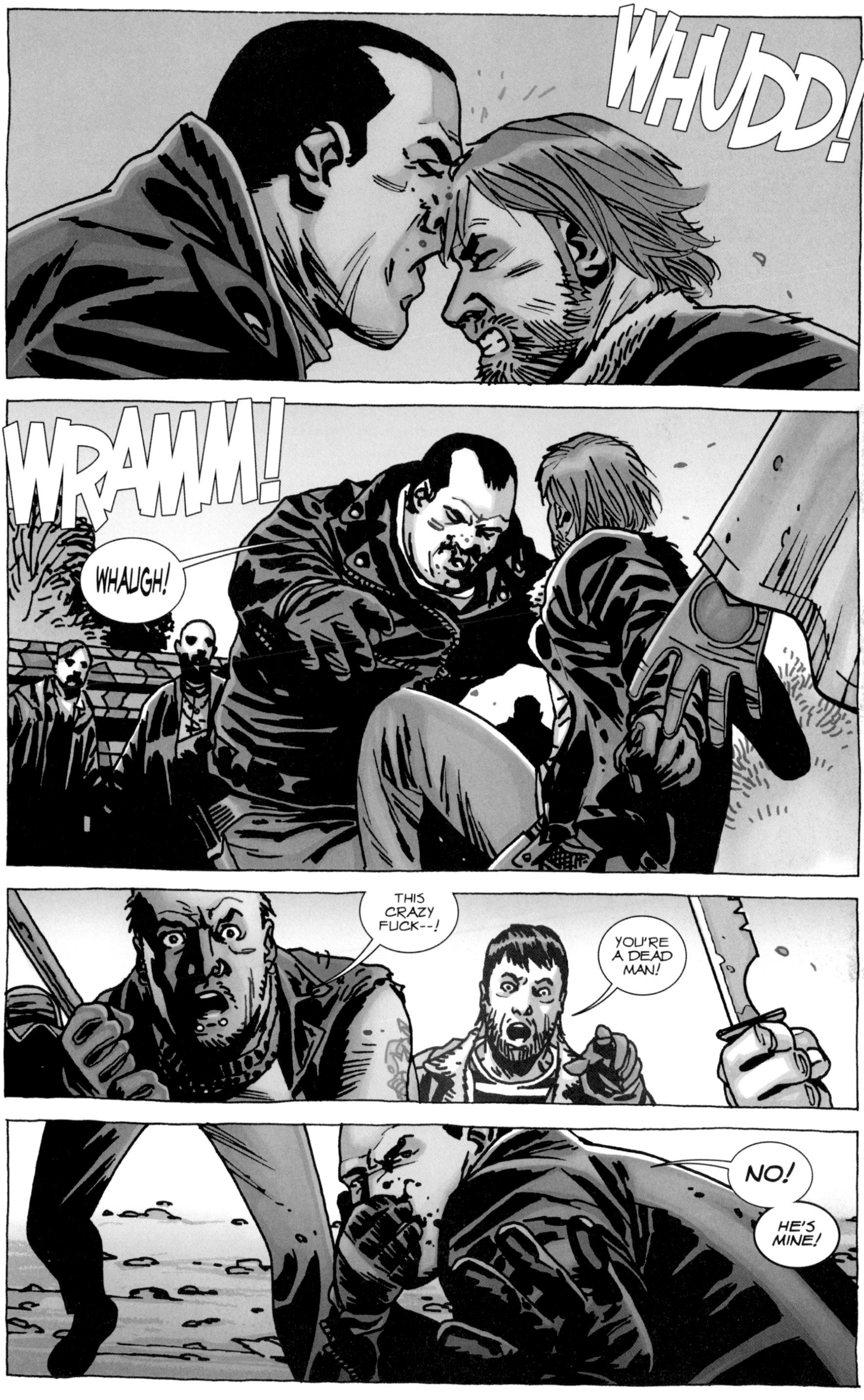
WHUDD!
WRAMM!
WHAUGH!
THIS CRAZY FUCK--!
YOU'RE A DEAD MAN!
NO!
HE'S MINE!

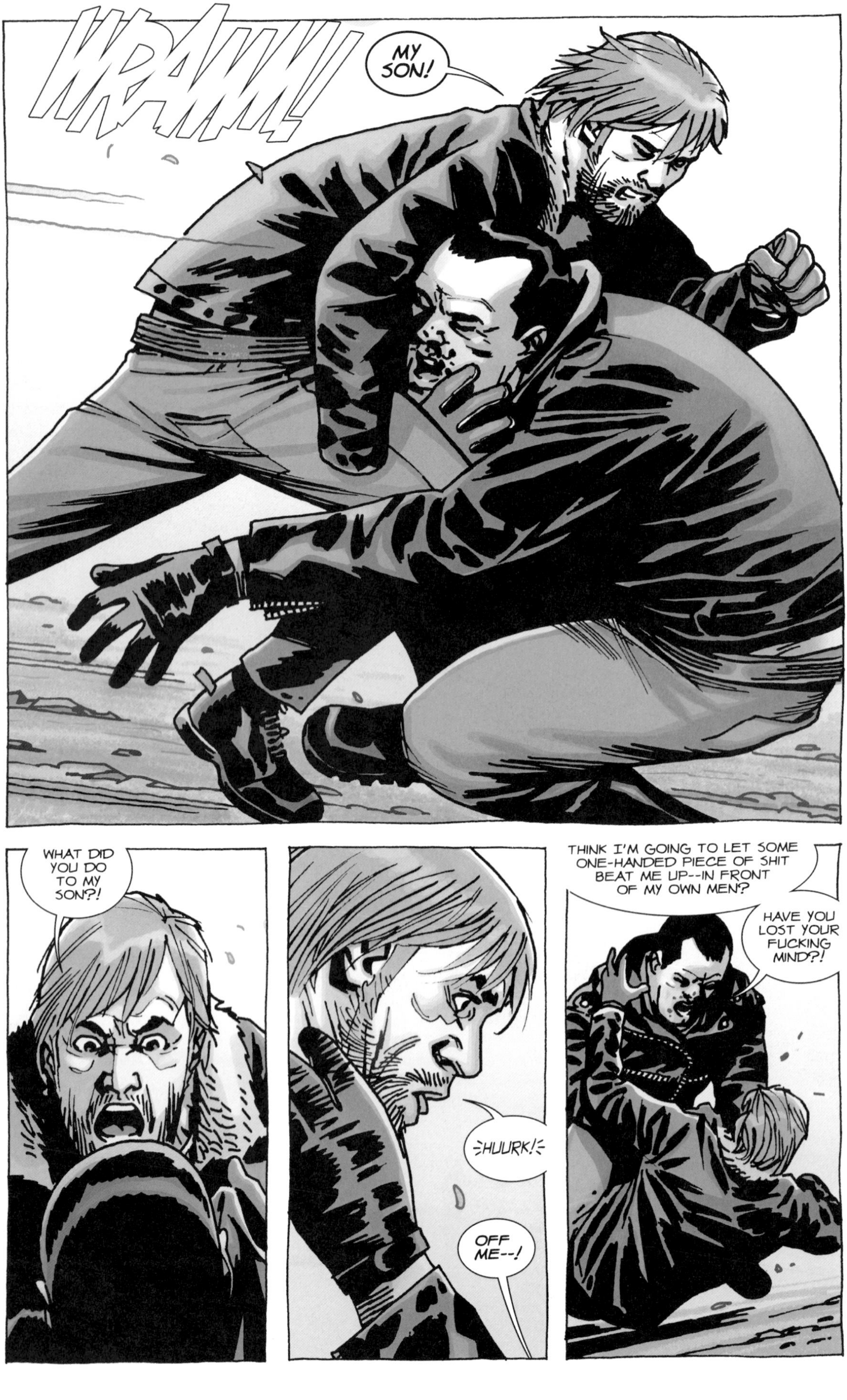
WRAMM!
MY SON!
WHAT DID YOU DO TO MY SON?!
HUURK!
OFF ME--!
THINK I'M GOING TO LET SOME ONE-HANDED PIECE OF SHIT BEAT ME UP--IN FRONT OF MY OWN MEN?
HAVE YOU LOST YOUR FUCKING MIND?!

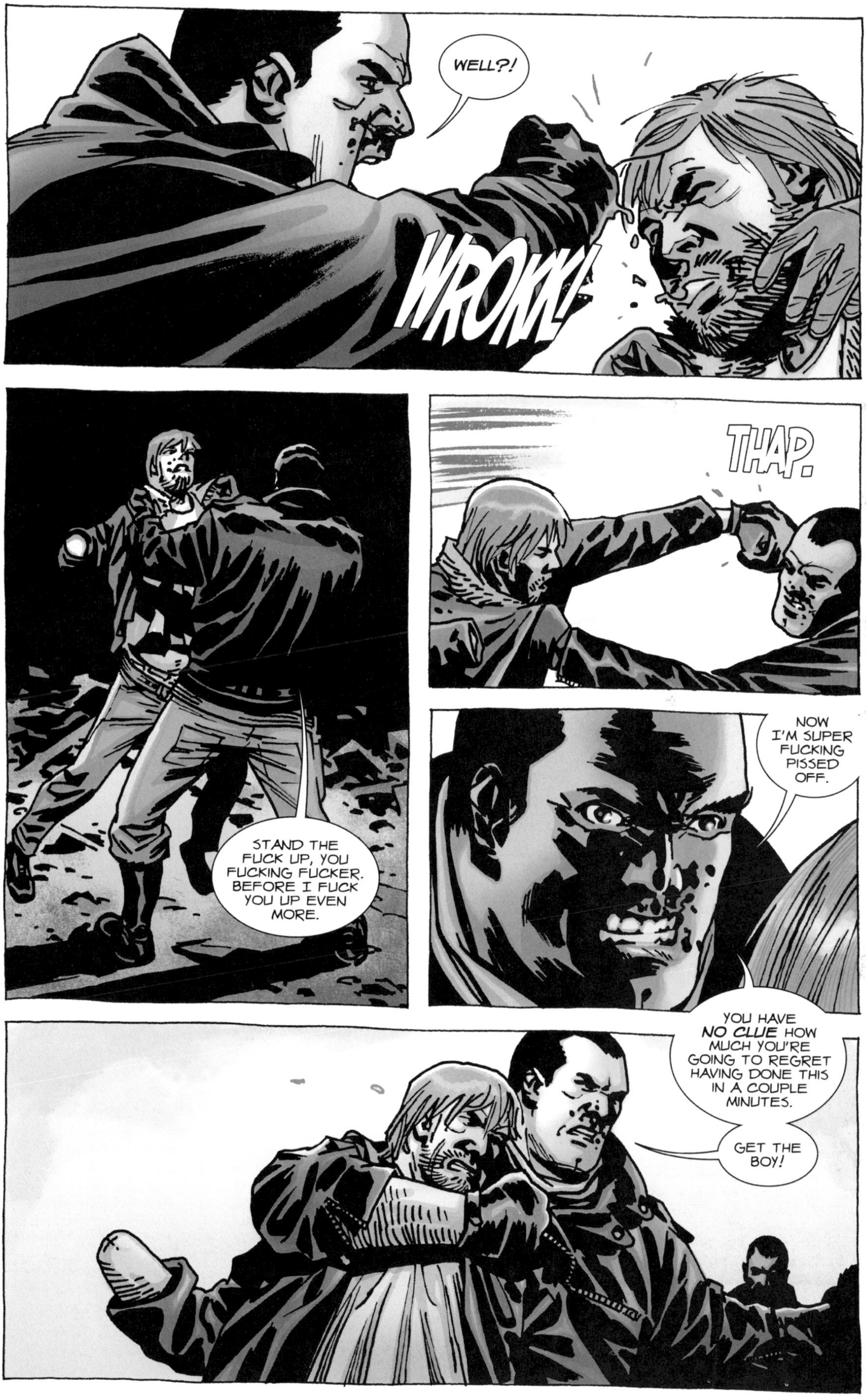
WELL?!
WRONK!
STAND THE FUCK UP, YOU FUCKING FUCKER. BEFORE I FUCK YOU UP EVEN MORE.
THAP.
NOW I'M SUPER FUCKING PISSED OFF.
YOU HAVE NO CLUE HOW MUCH YOU'RE GOING TO REGRET HAVING DONE THIS IN A COUPLE MINUTES.
GET THE BOY!

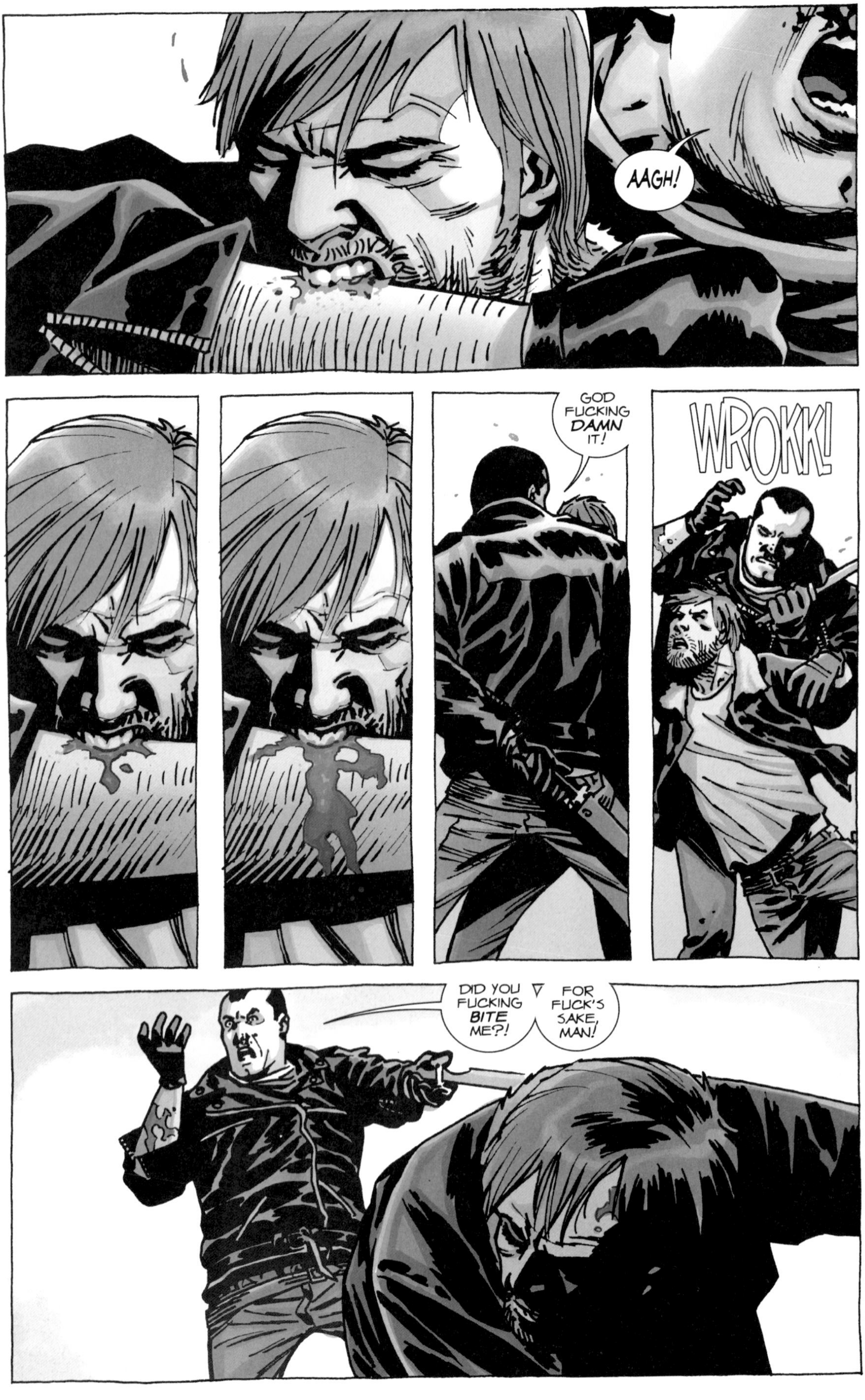
AAGH!
GOD FUCKING DAMN IT!
WROKK!
DID YOU FUCKING BITE ME?!
FOR FUCK'S SAKE, MAN!

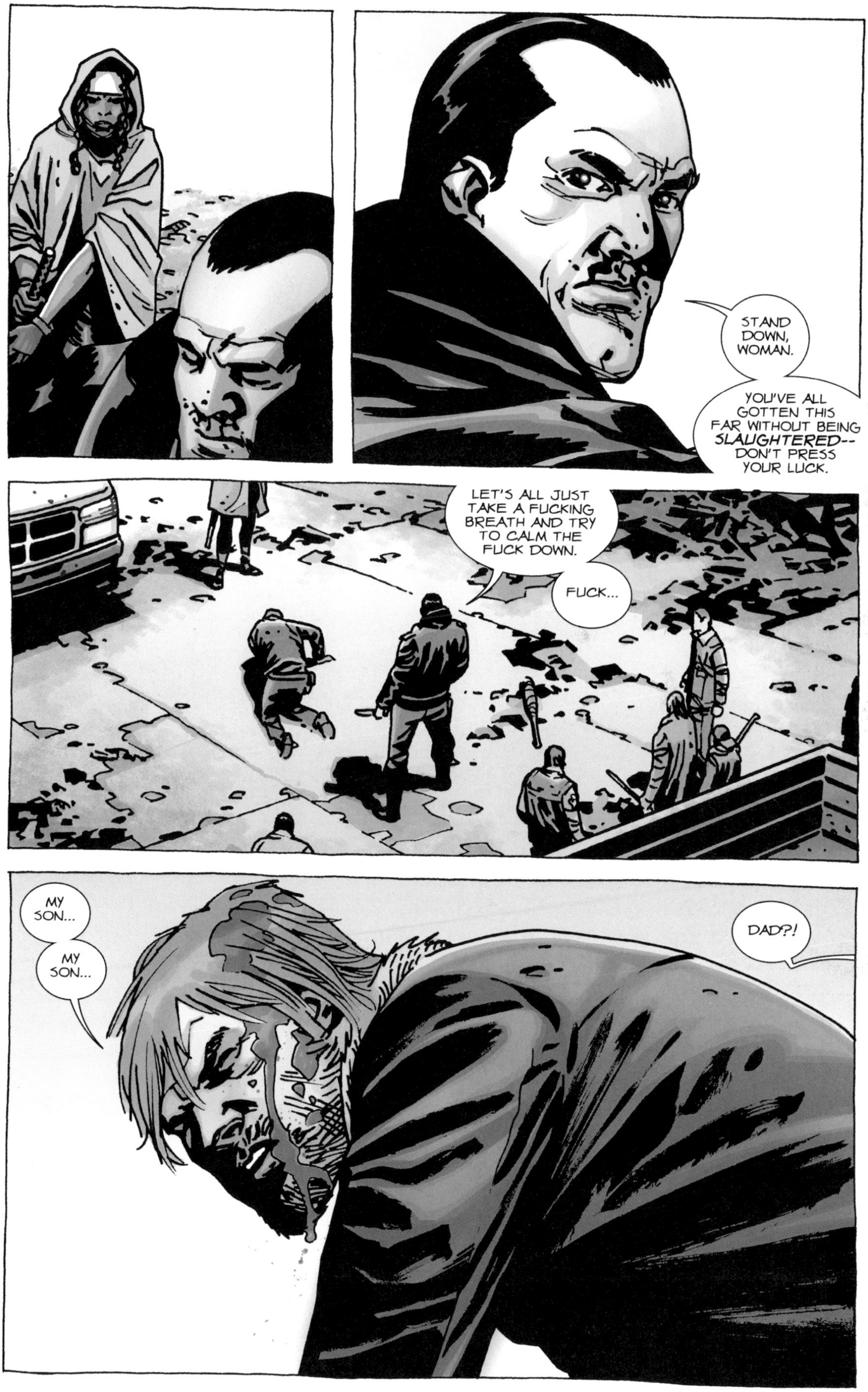

STAND DOWN, WOMAN.
YOU'VE ALL GOTTEN THIS FAR WITHOUT BEING SLAUGHTERED-- DON'T PRESS YOUR LUCK.
LET'S ALL JUST TAKE A FUCKING BREATH AND TRY TO CALM THE FUCK DOWN.
FUCK...
MY SON...
MY SON...
DAD?!

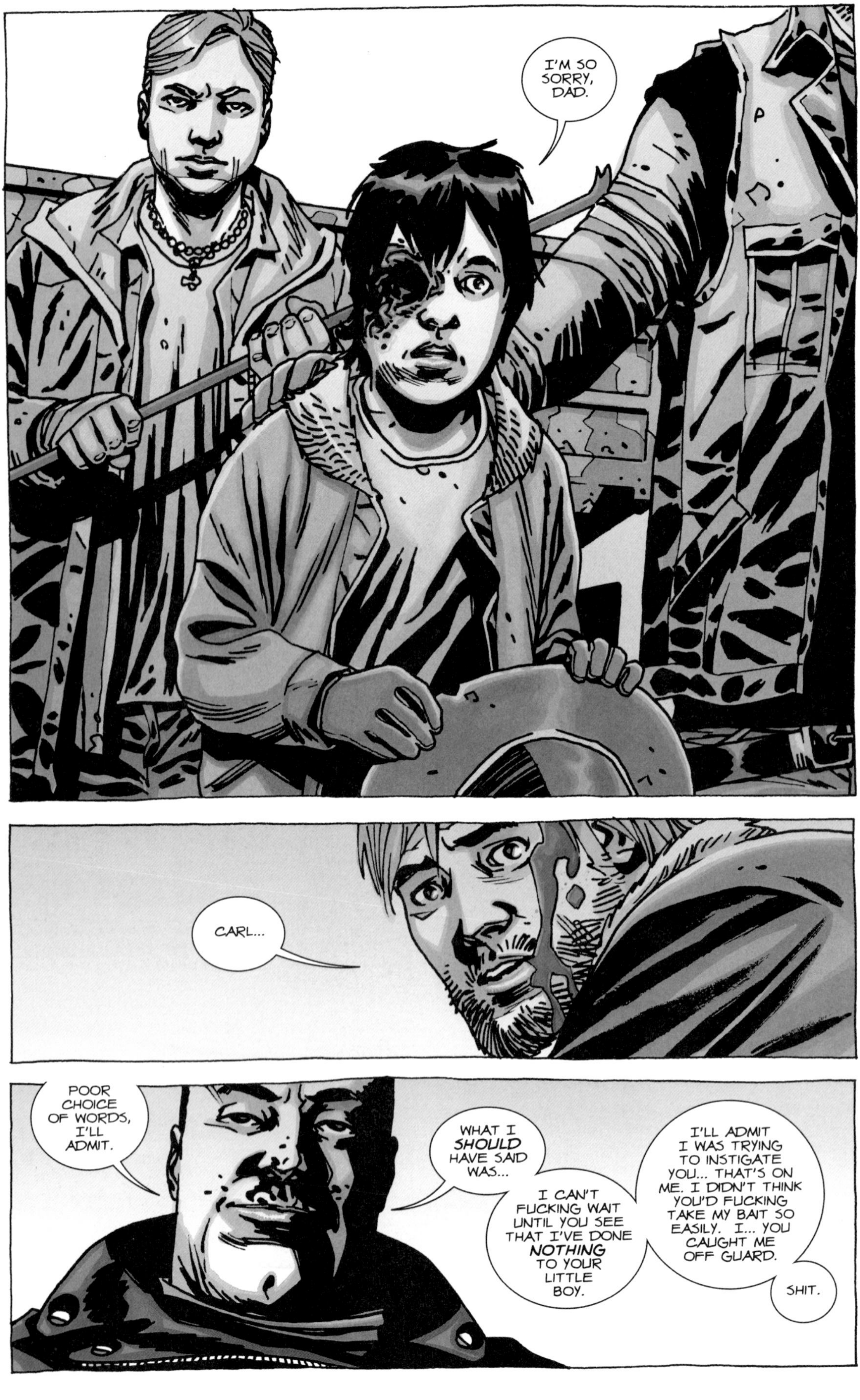
I'M SO SORRY, DAD.
CARL...
POOR CHOICE OF WORDS, I'LL ADMIT.
WHAT I *SHOULD* HAVE SAID WAS...
I CAN'T FUCKING WAIT UNTIL YOU SEE THAT I'VE DONE *NOTHING* TO YOUR LITTLE BOY.
I'LL ADMIT I WAS TRYING TO INSTIGATE YOU... THAT'S ON ME. I DIDN'T THINK YOU'D FUCKING TAKE MY BAIT SO EASILY. I... YOU CAUGHT ME OFF GUARD.
SHIT.

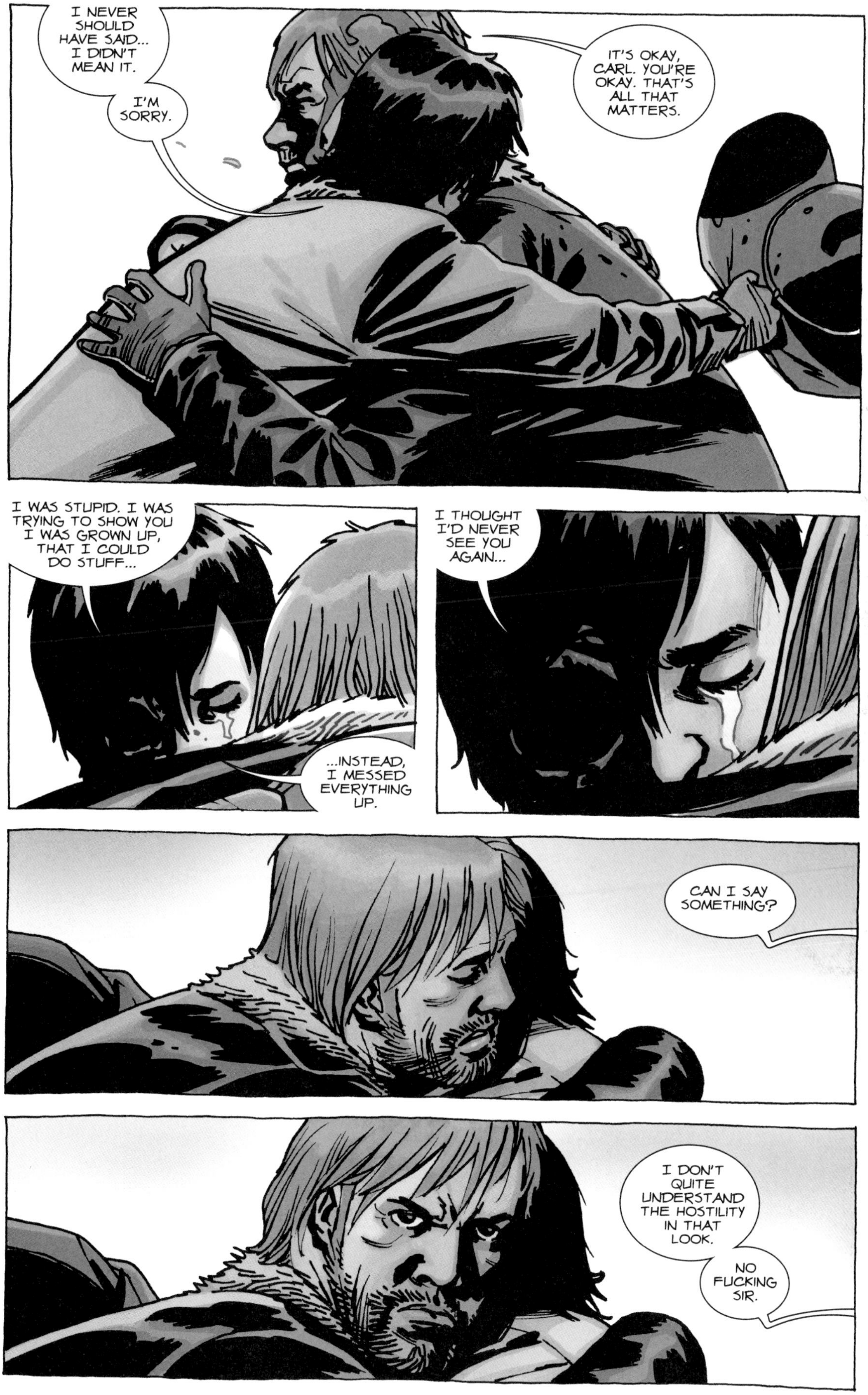
I NEVER SHOULD HAVE SAID... I DIDN'T MEAN IT.
I'M SORRY.
IT'S OKAY, CARL. YOU'RE OKAY. THAT'S ALL THAT MATTERS.
I WAS STUPID. I WAS TRYING TO SHOW YOU I WAS GROWN UP, THAT I COULD DO STUFF...
...INSTEAD, I MESSED EVERYTHING UP.
I THOUGHT I'D NEVER SEE YOU AGAIN...
CAN I SAY SOMETHING?
I DON'T QUITE UNDERSTAND THE HOSTILITY IN THAT LOOK.
NO FUCKING SIR.

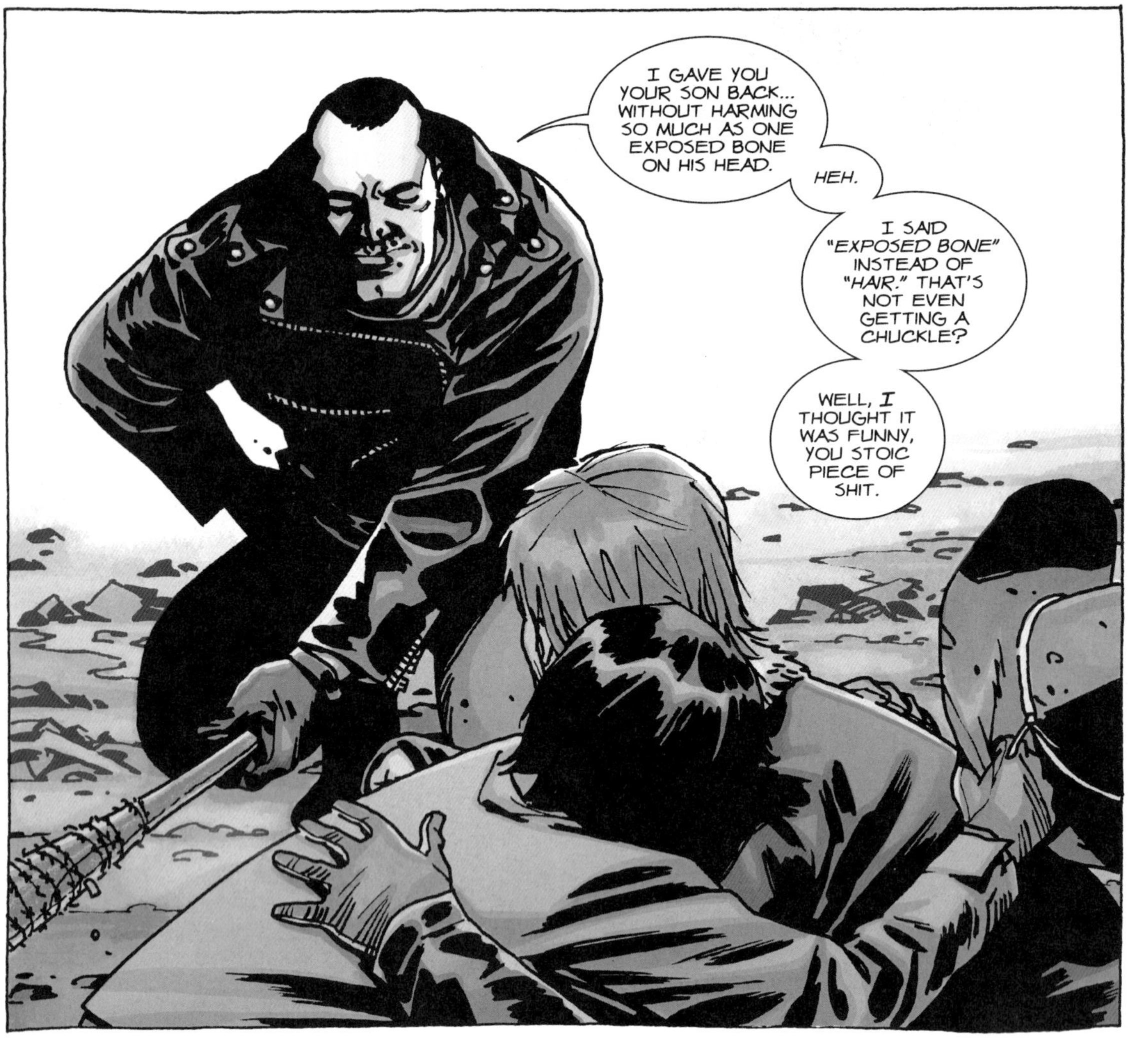
I GAVE YOU YOUR SON BACK... WITHOUT HARMING SO MUCH AS ONE EXPOSED BONE ON HIS HEAD.
HEH.
I SAID "EXPOSED BONE" INSTEAD OF "HAIR." THAT'S NOT EVEN GETTING A CHUCKLE?
WELL, I THOUGHT IT WAS FUNNY, YOU STOIC PIECE OF SHIT.

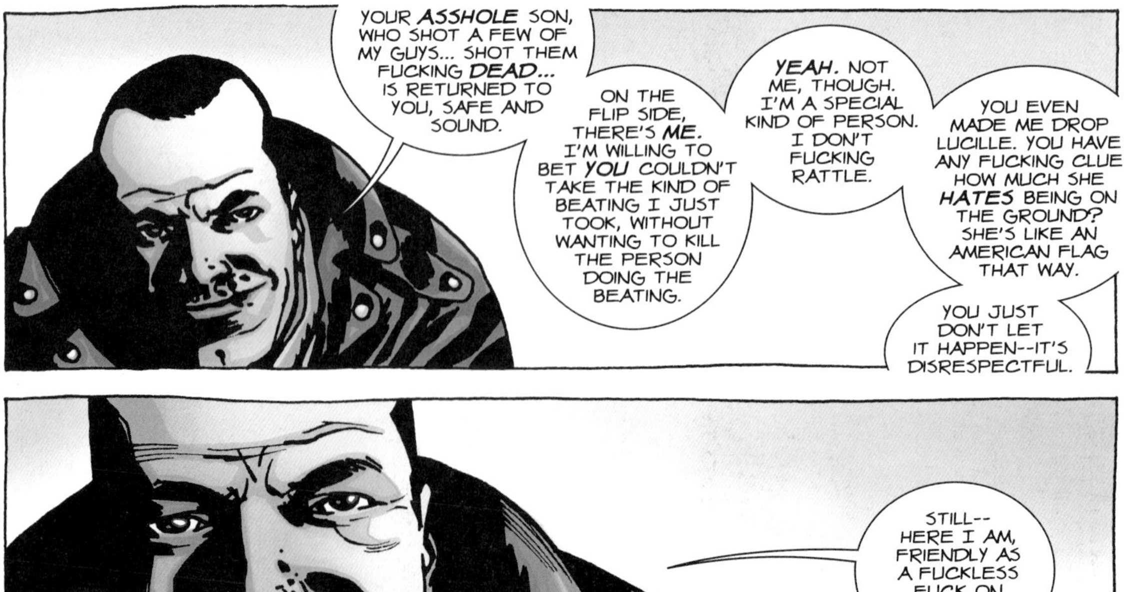
YOUR ASSHOLE SON, WHO SHOT A FEW OF MY GUYS... SHOT THEM FUCKING DEAD... IS RETURNED TO YOU, SAFE AND SOUND.
ON THE FLIP SIDE, THERE'S ME. I'M WILLING TO BET YOU COULDN'T TAKE THE KIND OF BEATING I JUST TOOK, WITHOUT WANTING TO KILL THE PERSON DOING THE BEATING.
YEAH. NOT ME, THOUGH. I'M A SPECIAL KIND OF PERSON. I DON'T FUCKING RATTLE.
YOU EVEN MADE ME DROP LUCILLE. YOU HAVE ANY FUCKING CLUE HOW MUCH SHE HATES BEING ON THE GROUND? SHE'S LIKE AN AMERICAN FLAG THAT WAY.
YOU JUST DON'T LET IT HAPPEN--IT'S DISRESPECTFUL.

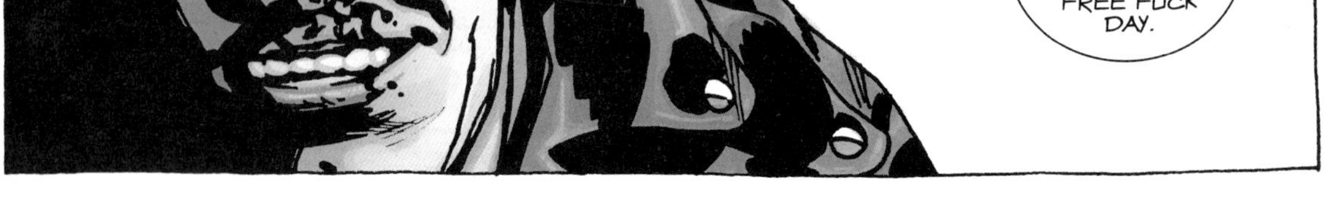
STILL-- HERE I AM, FRIENDLY AS A FUCKLESS FUCK ON FREE FUCK DAY.

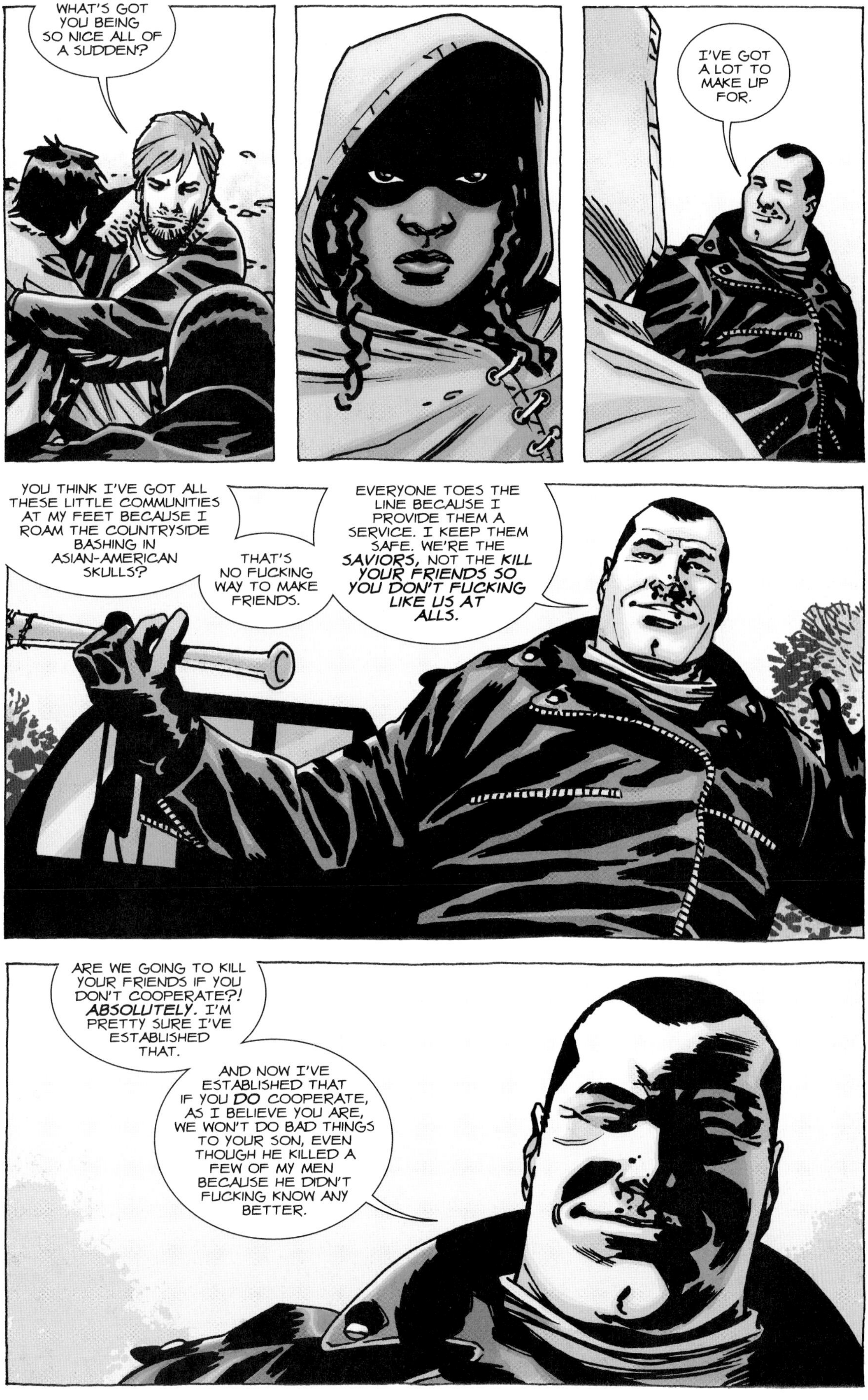
WHAT'S GOT YOU BEING SO NICE ALL OF A SUDDEN?
I'VE GOT A LOT TO MAKE UP FOR.
YOU THINK I'VE GOT ALL THESE LITTLE COMMUNITIES AT MY FEET BECAUSE I ROAM THE COUNTRYSIDE BASHING IN ASIAN-AMERICAN SKULLS?
THAT'S NO FUCKING WAY TO MAKE FRIENDS.
EVERYONE TOES THE LINE BECAUSE I PROVIDE THEM A SERVICE. I KEEP THEM SAFE. WE'RE THE SAVIORS, NOT THE KILL YOUR FRIENDS SO YOU DON'T FUCKING LIKE US AT ALLS.
ARE WE GOING TO KILL YOUR FRIENDS IF YOU DON'T COOPERATE?! ABSOLUTELY. I'M PRETTY SURE I'VE ESTABLISHED THAT.
AND NOW I'VE ESTABLISHED THAT IF YOU DO COOPERATE, AS I BELIEVE YOU ARE, WE WON'T DO BAD THINGS TO YOUR SON, EVEN THOUGH HE KILLED A FEW OF MY MEN BECAUSE HE DIDN'T FUCKING KNOW ANY BETTER.

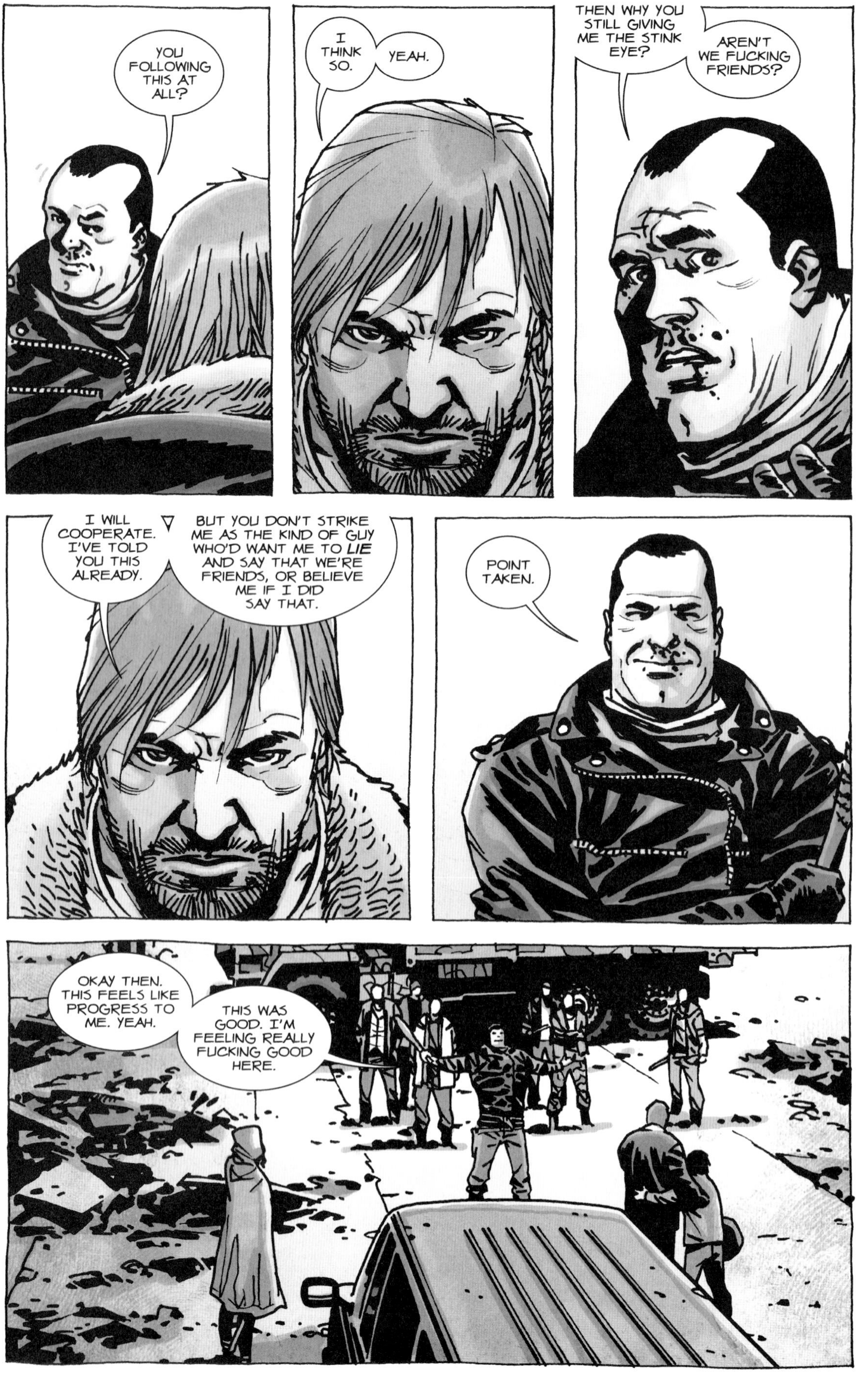
YOU FOLLOWING THIS AT ALL?
I THINK SO.
YEAH.
THEN WHY YOU STILL GIVING ME THE STINK EYE?
AREN'T WE FUCKING FRIENDS?
I WILL COOPERATE. I'VE TOLD YOU THIS ALREADY.
BUT YOU DON'T STRIKE ME AS THE KIND OF GUY WHO'D WANT ME TO *LIE* AND SAY THAT WE'RE FRIENDS, OR BELIEVE ME IF I DID SAY THAT.
POINT TAKEN.
OKAY THEN. THIS FEELS LIKE PROGRESS TO ME. YEAH.
THIS WAS GOOD. I'M FEELING REALLY FUCKING GOOD HERE.

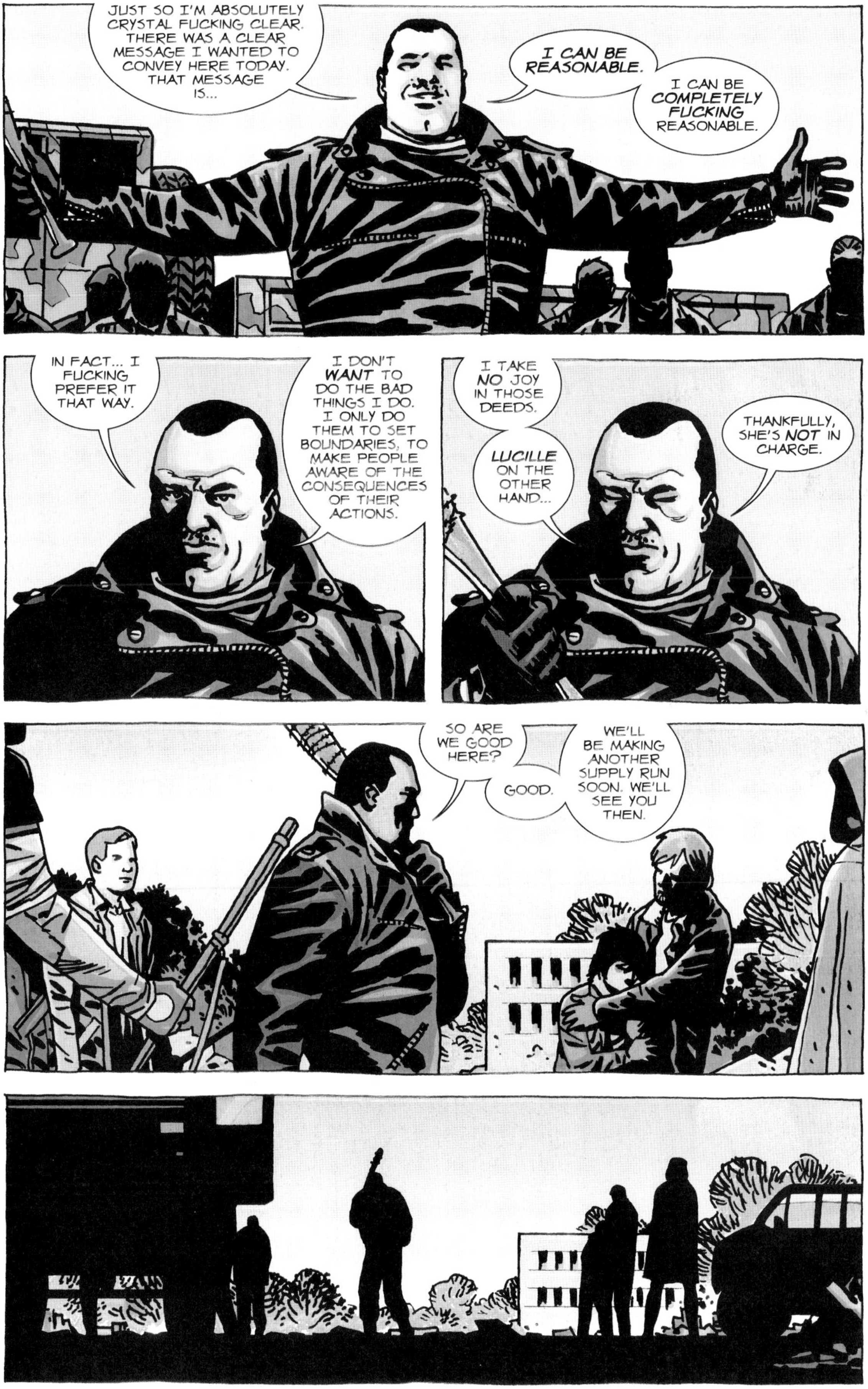
JUST SO I'M ABSOLUTELY CRYSTAL FUCKING CLEAR. THERE WAS A CLEAR MESSAGE I WANTED TO CONVEY HERE TODAY. THAT MESSAGE IS...
I CAN BE REASONABLE.
I CAN BE COMPLETELY FUCKING REASONABLE.
IN FACT... I FUCKING PREFER IT THAT WAY.
I DON'T WANT TO DO THE BAD THINGS I DO. I ONLY DO THEM TO SET BOUNDARIES, TO MAKE PEOPLE AWARE OF THE CONSEQUENCES OF THEIR ACTIONS.
I TAKE NO JOY IN THOSE DEEDS.
LUCILLE ON THE OTHER HAND...
THANKFULLY, SHE'S NOT IN CHARGE.
SO ARE WE GOOD HERE?
GOOD.
WE'LL BE MAKING ANOTHER SUPPLY RUN SOON. WE'LL SEE YOU THEN.

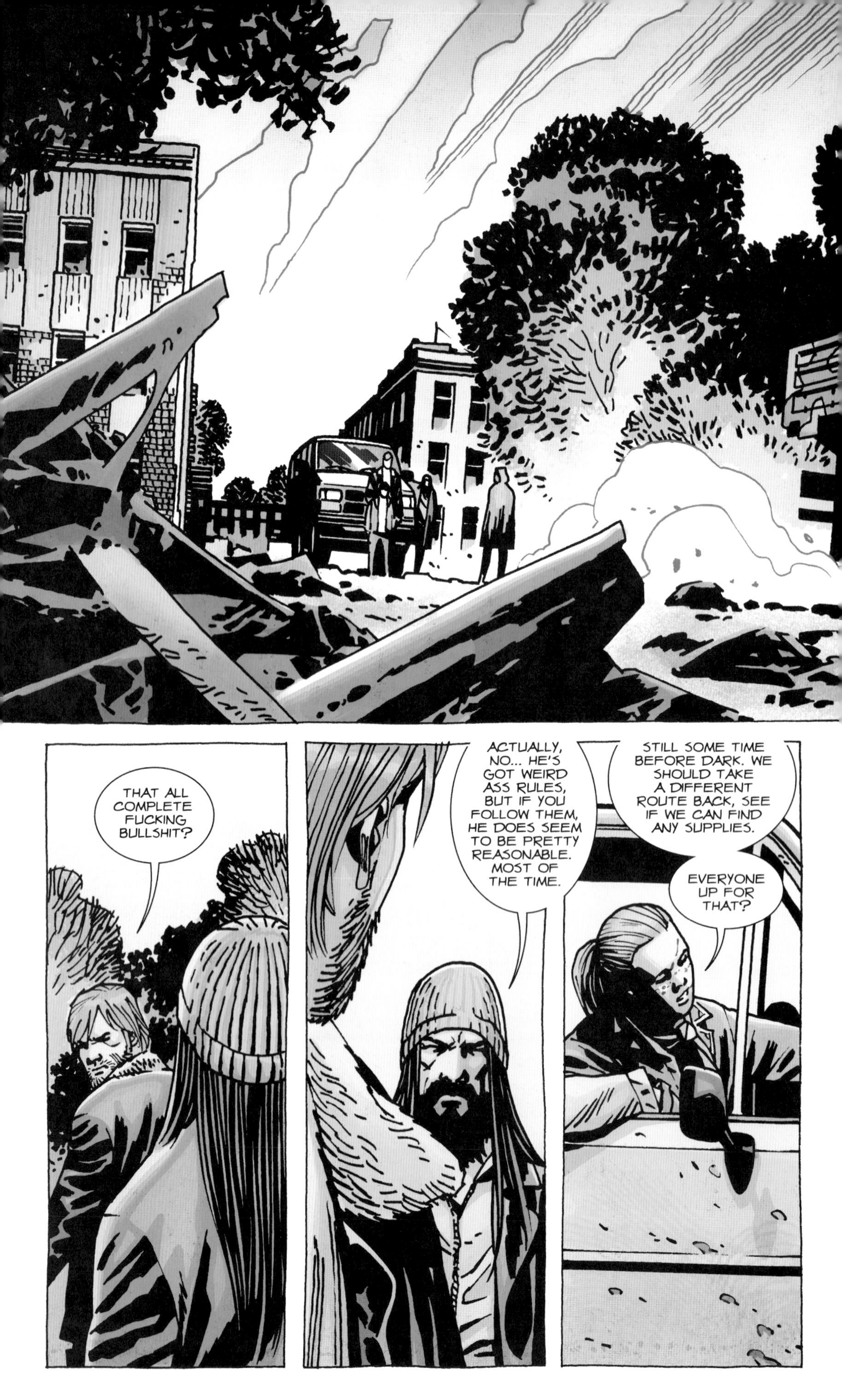
THAT ALL COMPLETE FUCKING BULLSHIT?
ACTUALLY, NO... HE'S GOT WEIRD ASS RULES, BUT IF YOU FOLLOW THEM, HE DOES SEEM TO BE PRETTY REASONABLE. MOST OF THE TIME.
STILL SOME TIME BEFORE DARK. WE SHOULD TAKE A DIFFERENT ROUTE BACK, SEE IF WE CAN FIND ANY SUPPLIES.
EVERYONE UP FOR THAT?

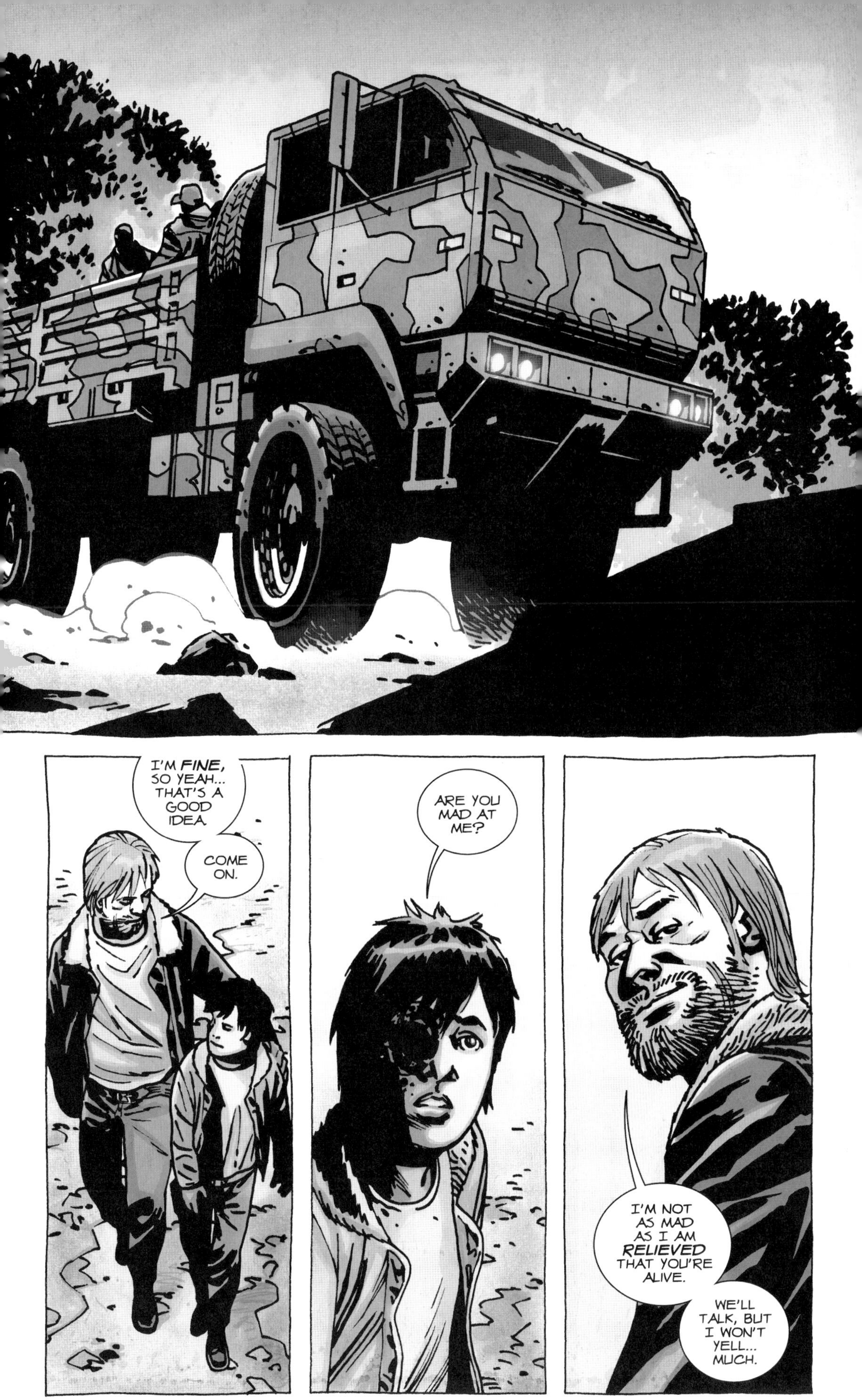
I'M FINE, SO YEAH... THAT'S A GOOD IDEA.
COME ON.
ARE YOU MAD AT ME?
I'M NOT AS MAD AS I AM RELIEVED THAT YOU'RE ALIVE.
WE'LL TALK, BUT I WON'T YELL... MUCH.

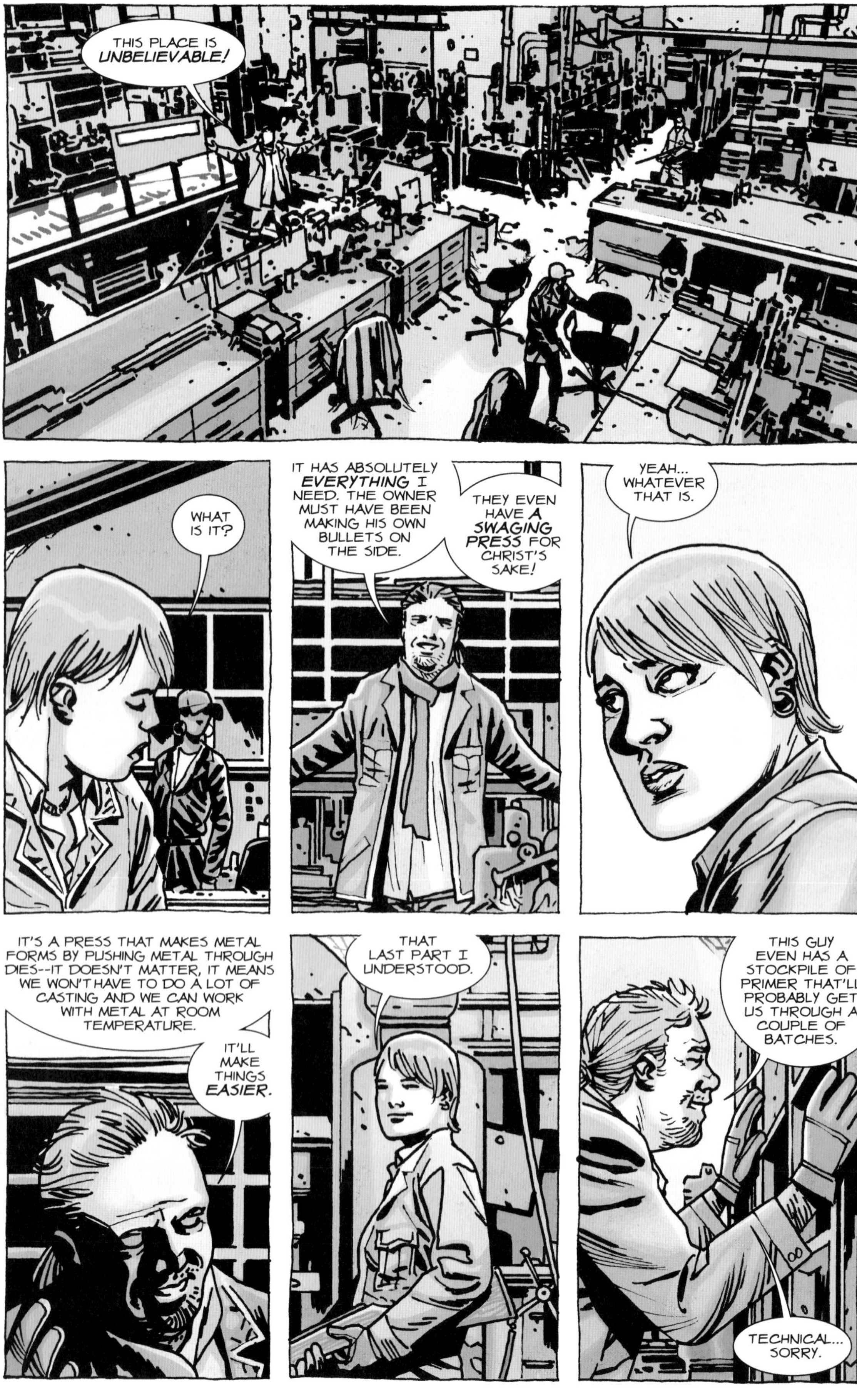

THIS PLACE IS *UNBELIEVABLE!*
WHAT IS IT?
IT HAS ABSOLUTELY *EVERYTHING* I NEED. THE OWNER MUST HAVE BEEN MAKING HIS OWN BULLETS ON THE SIDE.
THEY EVEN HAVE *A SWAGING PRESS* FOR CHRIST'S SAKE!
YEAH... WHATEVER THAT IS.
IT'S A PRESS THAT MAKES METAL FORMS BY PUSHING METAL THROUGH DIES--IT DOESN'T MATTER, IT MEANS WE WON'T HAVE TO DO A LOT OF CASTING AND WE CAN WORK WITH METAL AT ROOM TEMPERATURE.
IT'LL MAKE THINGS *EASIER*.
THAT LAST PART I UNDERSTOOD.
THIS GUY EVEN HAS A STOCKPILE OF PRIMER THAT'LL PROBABLY GET US THROUGH A COUPLE OF BATCHES.
TECHNICAL... SORRY.

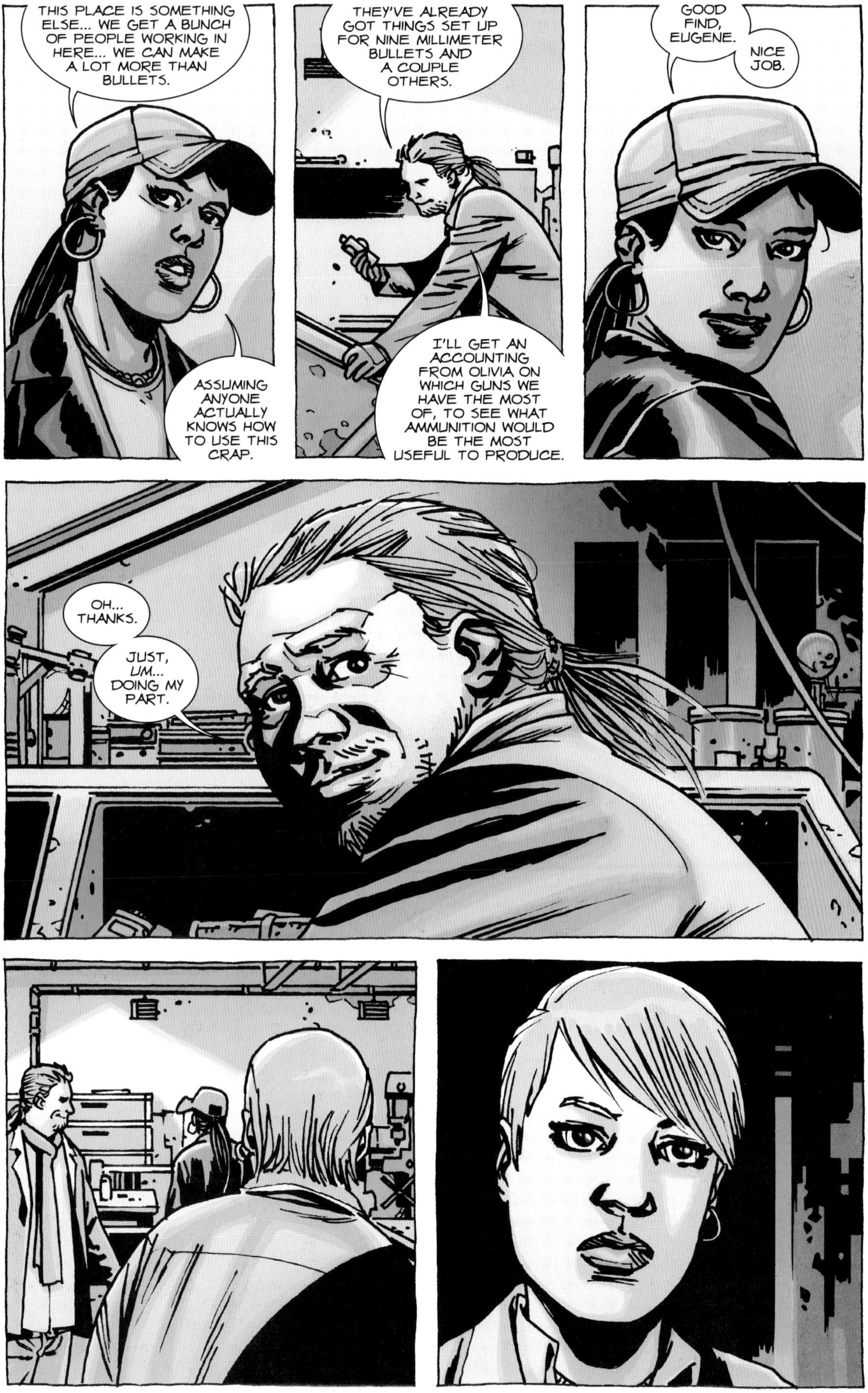
THIS PLACE IS SOMETHING ELSE... WE GET A BUNCH OF PEOPLE WORKING IN HERE... WE CAN MAKE A LOT MORE THAN BULLETS.
ASSUMING ANYONE ACTUALLY KNOWS HOW TO USE THIS CRAP.
THEY'VE ALREADY GOT THINGS SET UP FOR NINE MILLIMETER BULLETS AND A COUPLE OTHERS.
I'LL GET AN ACCOUNTING FROM OLIVIA ON WHICH GUNS WE HAVE THE MOST OF, TO SEE WHAT AMMUNITION WOULD BE THE MOST USEFUL TO PRODUCE.
GOOD FIND, EUGENE.
NICE JOB.
OH... THANKS.
JUST, UM... DOING MY PART.

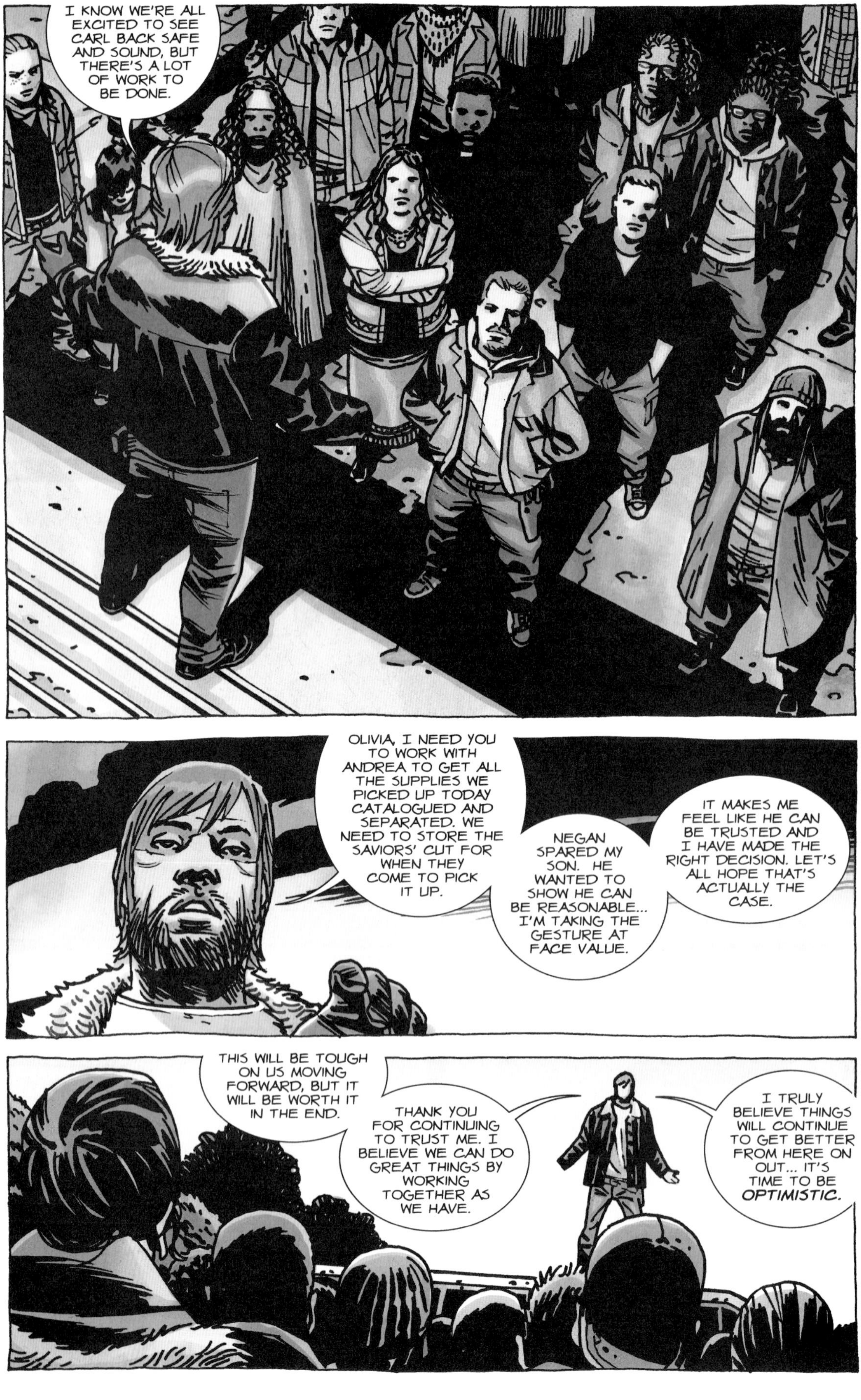
I KNOW WE'RE ALL EXCITED TO SEE CARL BACK SAFE AND SOUND, BUT THERE'S A LOT OF WORK TO BE DONE.
OLIVIA, I NEED YOU TO WORK WITH ANDREA TO GET ALL THE SUPPLIES WE PICKED UP TODAY CATALOGUED AND SEPARATED. WE NEED TO STORE THE SAVIORS' CUT FOR WHEN THEY COME TO PICK IT UP.
NEGAN SPARED MY SON. HE WANTED TO SHOW HE CAN BE REASONABLE... I'M TAKING THE GESTURE AT FACE VALUE.
IT MAKES ME FEEL LIKE HE CAN BE TRUSTED AND I HAVE MADE THE RIGHT DECISION. LET'S ALL HOPE THAT'S ACTUALLY THE CASE.
THIS WILL BE TOUGH ON US MOVING FORWARD, BUT IT WILL BE WORTH IT IN THE END.
THANK YOU FOR CONTINUING TO TRUST ME. I BELIEVE WE CAN DO GREAT THINGS BY WORKING TOGETHER AS WE HAVE.
I TRULY BELIEVE THINGS WILL CONTINUE TO GET BETTER FROM HERE ON OUT... IT'S TIME TO BE *OPTIMISTIC.*

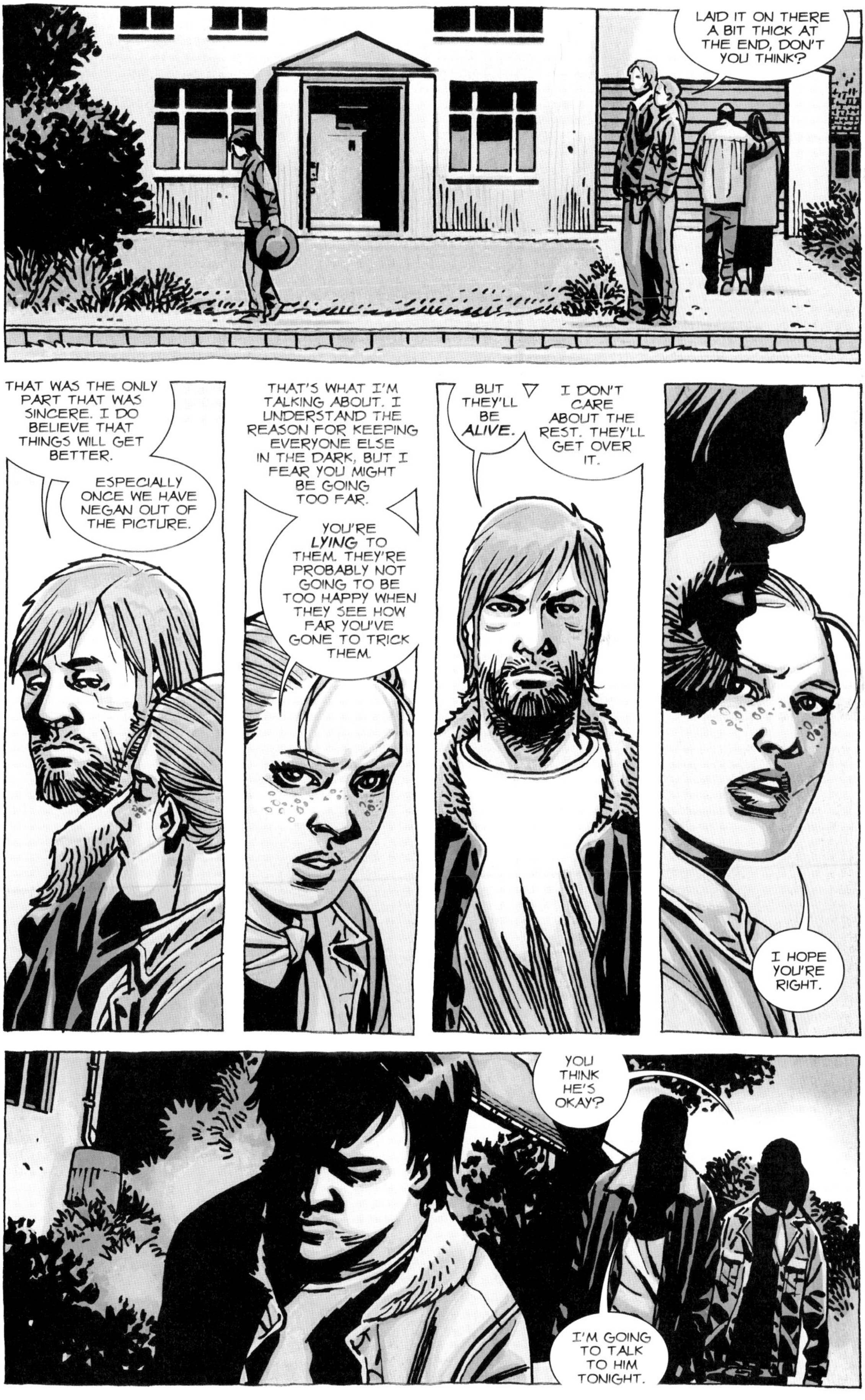

LAID IT ON THERE A BIT THICK AT THE END, DON'T YOU THINK?
THAT WAS THE ONLY PART THAT WAS SINCERE. I DO BELIEVE THAT THINGS WILL GET BETTER.
ESPECIALLY ONCE WE HAVE NEGAN OUT OF THE PICTURE.
THAT'S WHAT I'M TALKING ABOUT. I UNDERSTAND THE REASON FOR KEEPING EVERYONE ELSE IN THE DARK, BUT I FEAR YOU MIGHT BE GOING TOO FAR.
YOU'RE LYING TO THEM. THEY'RE PROBABLY NOT GOING TO BE TOO HAPPY WHEN THEY SEE HOW FAR YOU'VE GONE TO TRICK THEM.
I DON'T CARE ABOUT THE REST. THEY'LL GET OVER IT.
BUT THEY'LL BE ALIVE.
I HOPE YOU'RE RIGHT.
YOU THINK HE'S OKAY?
I'M GOING TO TALK TO HIM TONIGHT.

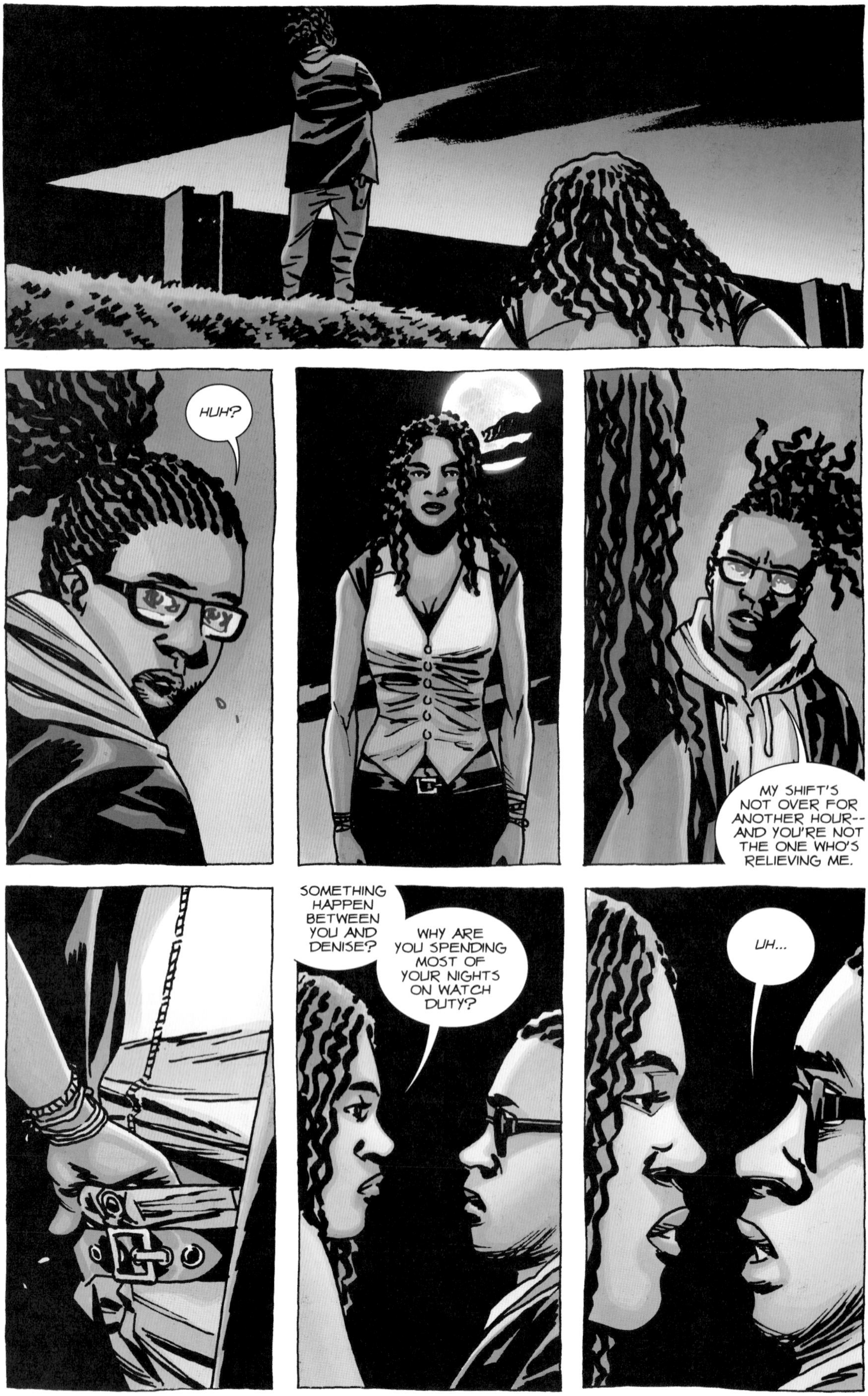

HUH?
MY SHIFT'S NOT OVER FOR ANOTHER HOUR-- AND YOU'RE NOT THE ONE WHO'S RELIEVING ME.
SOMETHING HAPPEN BETWEEN YOU AND DENISE?
WHY ARE YOU SPENDING MOST OF YOUR NIGHTS ON WATCH DUTY?
UH...

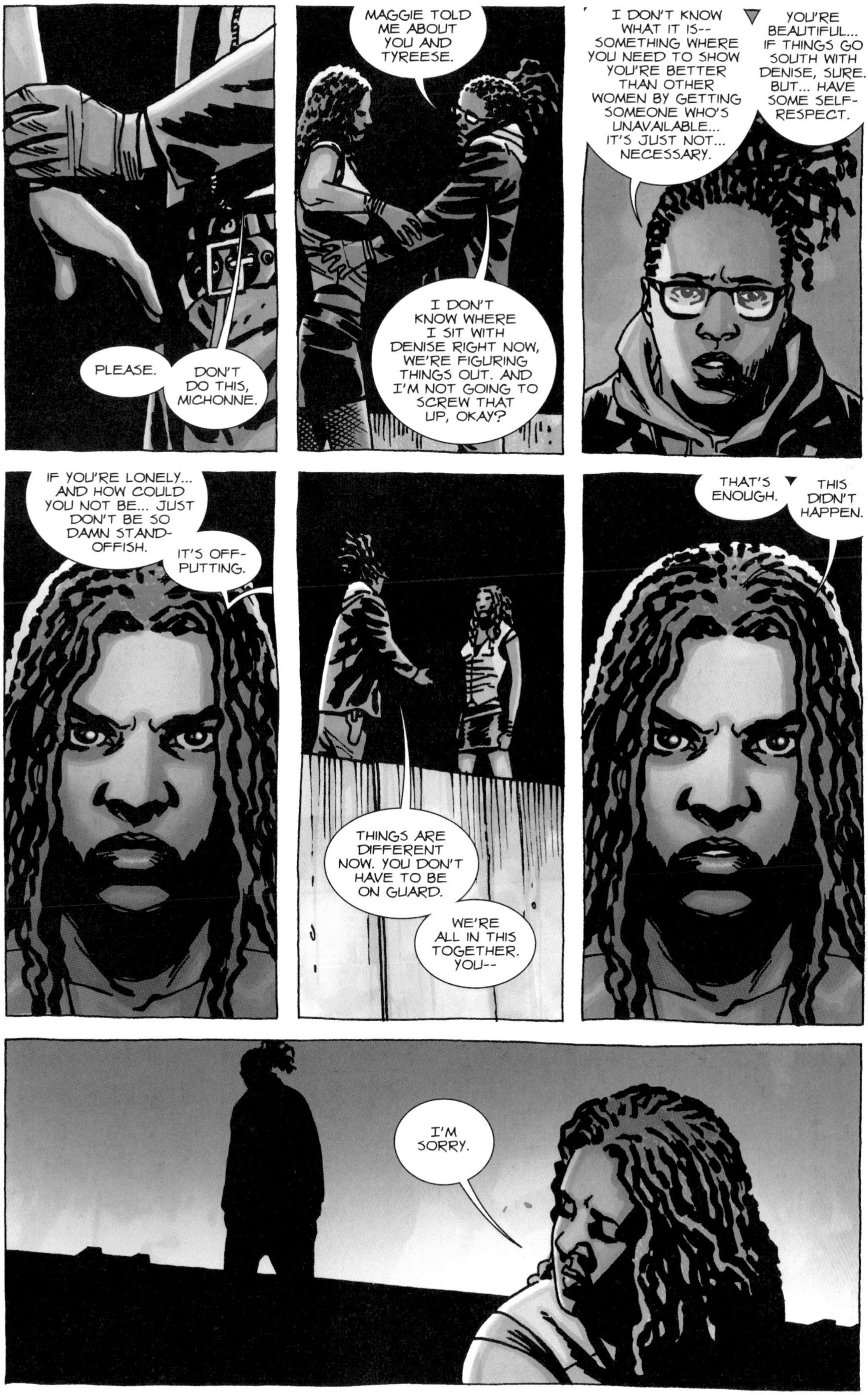
PLEASE.
DON'T DO THIS, MICHONNE.
MAGGIE TOLD ME ABOUT YOU AND TYREESE.
I DON'T KNOW WHERE I SIT WITH DENISE RIGHT NOW, WE'RE FIGURING THINGS OUT. AND I'M NOT GOING TO SCREW THAT UP, OKAY?
I DON'T KNOW WHAT IT IS-- SOMETHING WHERE YOU NEED TO SHOW YOU'RE BETTER THAN OTHER WOMEN BY GETTING SOMEONE WHO'S UNAVAILABLE... IT'S JUST NOT... NECESSARY.
YOU'RE BEAUTIFUL... IF THINGS GO SOUTH WITH DENISE, SURE. BUT... HAVE SOME SELF-RESPECT.
IF YOU'RE LONELY... AND HOW COULD YOU NOT BE... JUST DON'T BE SO DAMN STAND-OFFISH.
IT'S OFF-PUTTING.
THINGS ARE DIFFERENT NOW. YOU DON'T HAVE TO BE ON GUARD.
WE'RE ALL IN THIS TOGETHER. YOU--
THAT'S ENOUGH.
THIS DIDN'T HAPPEN.
I'M SORRY.

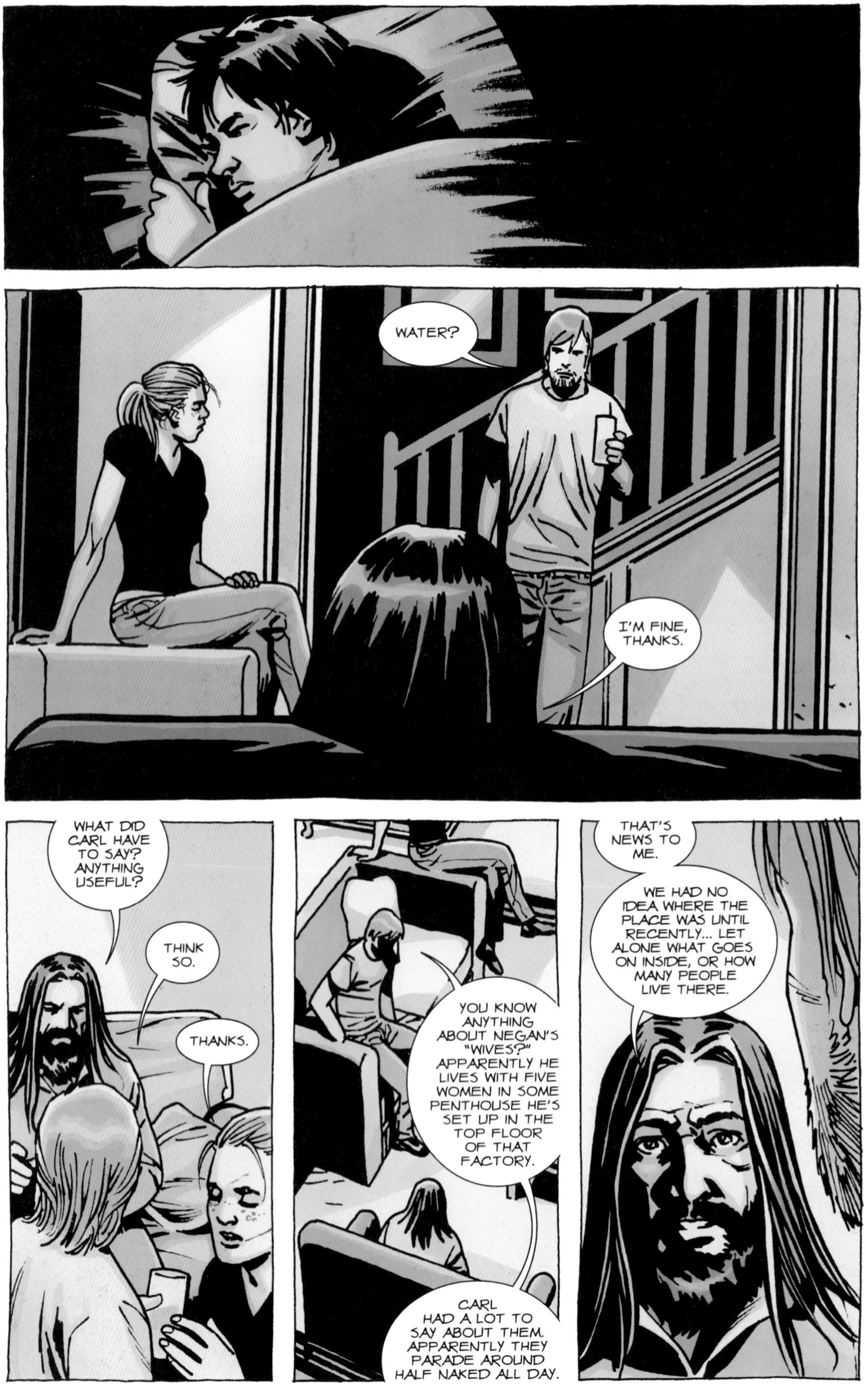
WATER?
I'M FINE, THANKS.
WHAT DID CARL HAVE TO SAY? ANYTHING USEFUL?
THINK SO.
THANKS.
YOU KNOW ANYTHING ABOUT NEGAN'S "WIVES?" APPARENTLY HE LIVES WITH FIVE WOMEN IN SOME PENTHOUSE HE'S SET UP IN THE TOP FLOOR OF THAT FACTORY.
CARL HAD A LOT TO SAY ABOUT THEM. APPARENTLY THEY PARADE AROUND HALF NAKED ALL DAY.
THAT'S NEWS TO ME.
WE HAD NO IDEA WHERE THE PLACE WAS UNTIL RECENTLY... LET ALONE WHAT GOES ON INSIDE, OR HOW MANY PEOPLE LIVE THERE.

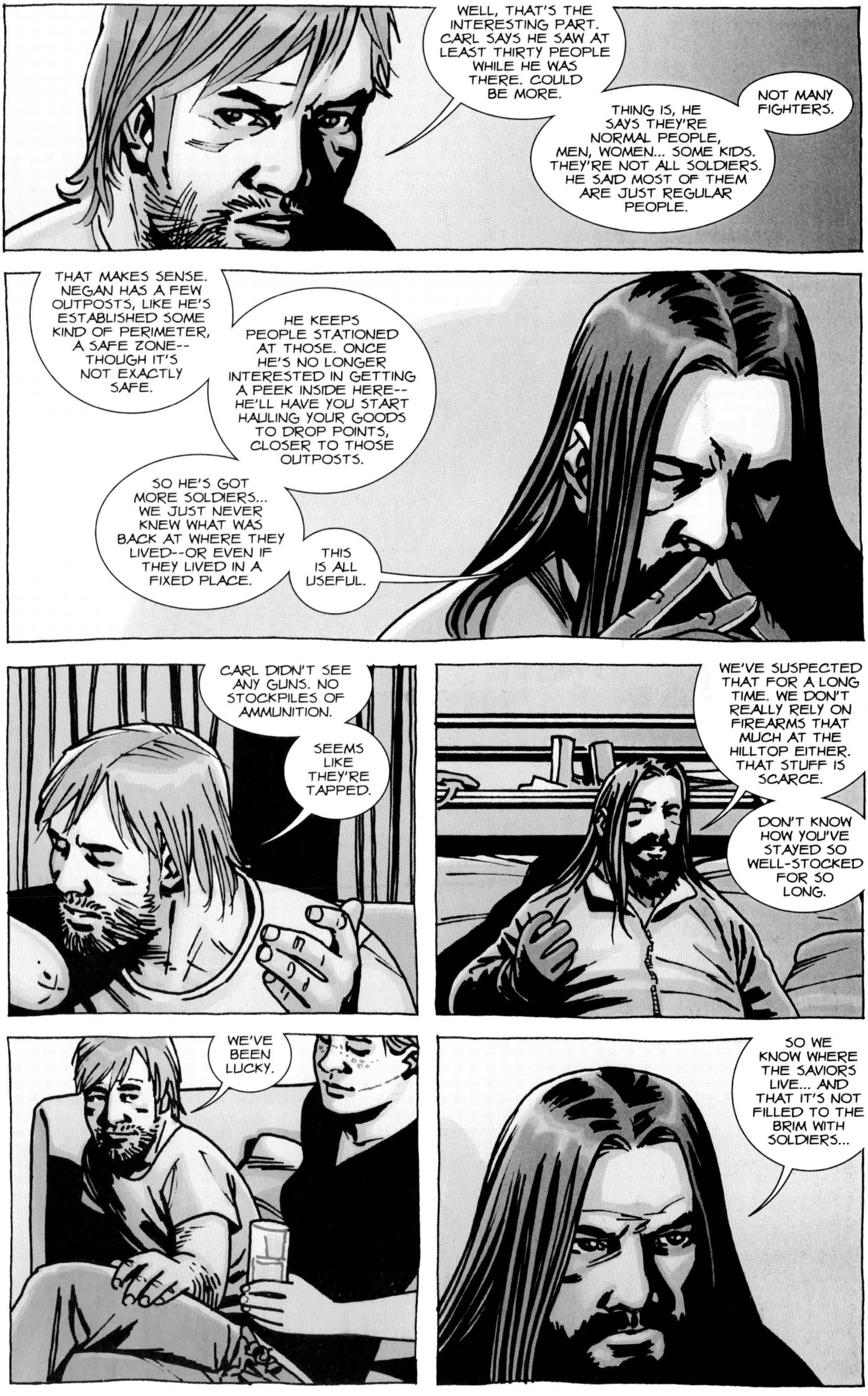
WELL, THAT'S THE INTERESTING PART. CARL SAYS HE SAW AT LEAST THIRTY PEOPLE WHILE HE WAS THERE. COULD BE MORE.
THING IS, HE SAYS THEY'RE NORMAL PEOPLE, MEN, WOMEN... SOME KIDS. THEY'RE NOT ALL SOLDIERS. HE SAID MOST OF THEM ARE JUST REGULAR PEOPLE.
NOT MANY FIGHTERS.
THAT MAKES SENSE. NEGAN HAS A FEW OUTPOSTS, LIKE HE'S ESTABLISHED SOME KIND OF PERIMETER, A SAFE ZONE-- THOUGH IT'S NOT EXACTLY SAFE.
HE KEEPS PEOPLE STATIONED AT THOSE. ONCE HE'S NO LONGER INTERESTED IN GETTING A PEEK INSIDE HERE-- HE'LL HAVE YOU START HAULING YOUR GOODS TO DROP POINTS, CLOSER TO THOSE OUTPOSTS.
SO HE'S GOT MORE SOLDIERS... WE JUST NEVER KNEW WHAT WAS BACK AT WHERE THEY LIVED--OR EVEN IF THEY LIVED IN A FIXED PLACE.
THIS IS ALL USEFUL.
CARL DIDN'T SEE ANY GUNS. NO STOCKPILES OF AMMUNITION.
SEEMS LIKE THEY'RE TAPPED.
WE'VE SUSPECTED THAT FOR A LONG TIME. WE DON'T REALLY RELY ON FIREARMS THAT MUCH AT THE HILLTOP EITHER. THAT STUFF IS SCARCE.
DON'T KNOW HOW YOU'VE STAYED SO WELL-STOCKED FOR SO LONG.
WE'VE BEEN LUCKY.
SO WE KNOW WHERE THE SAVIORS LIVE... AND THAT IT'S NOT FILLED TO THE BRIM WITH SOLDIERS...

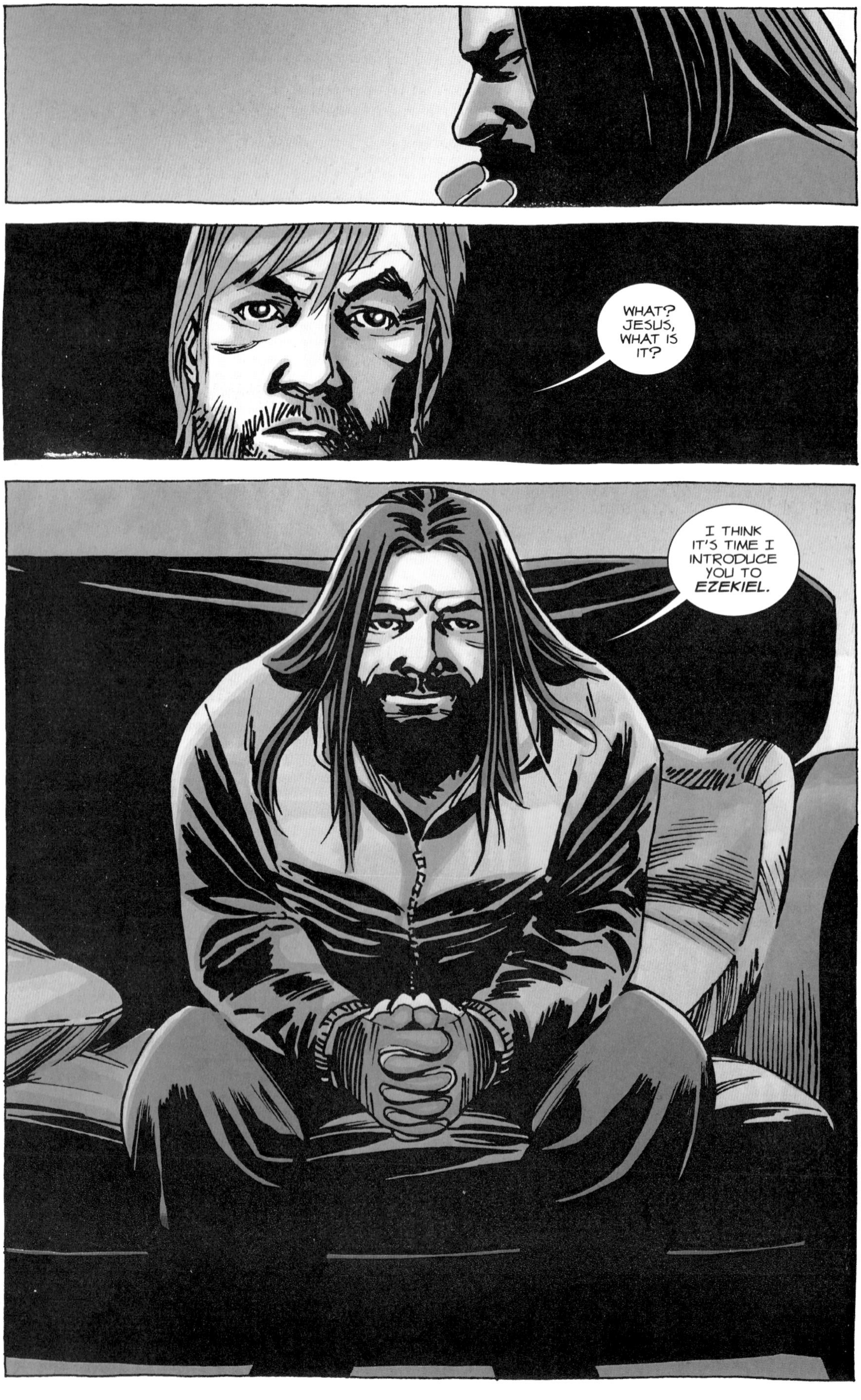
WHAT? JESUS, WHAT IS IT?
I THINK IT'S TIME I INTRODUCE YOU TO *EZEKIEL.*

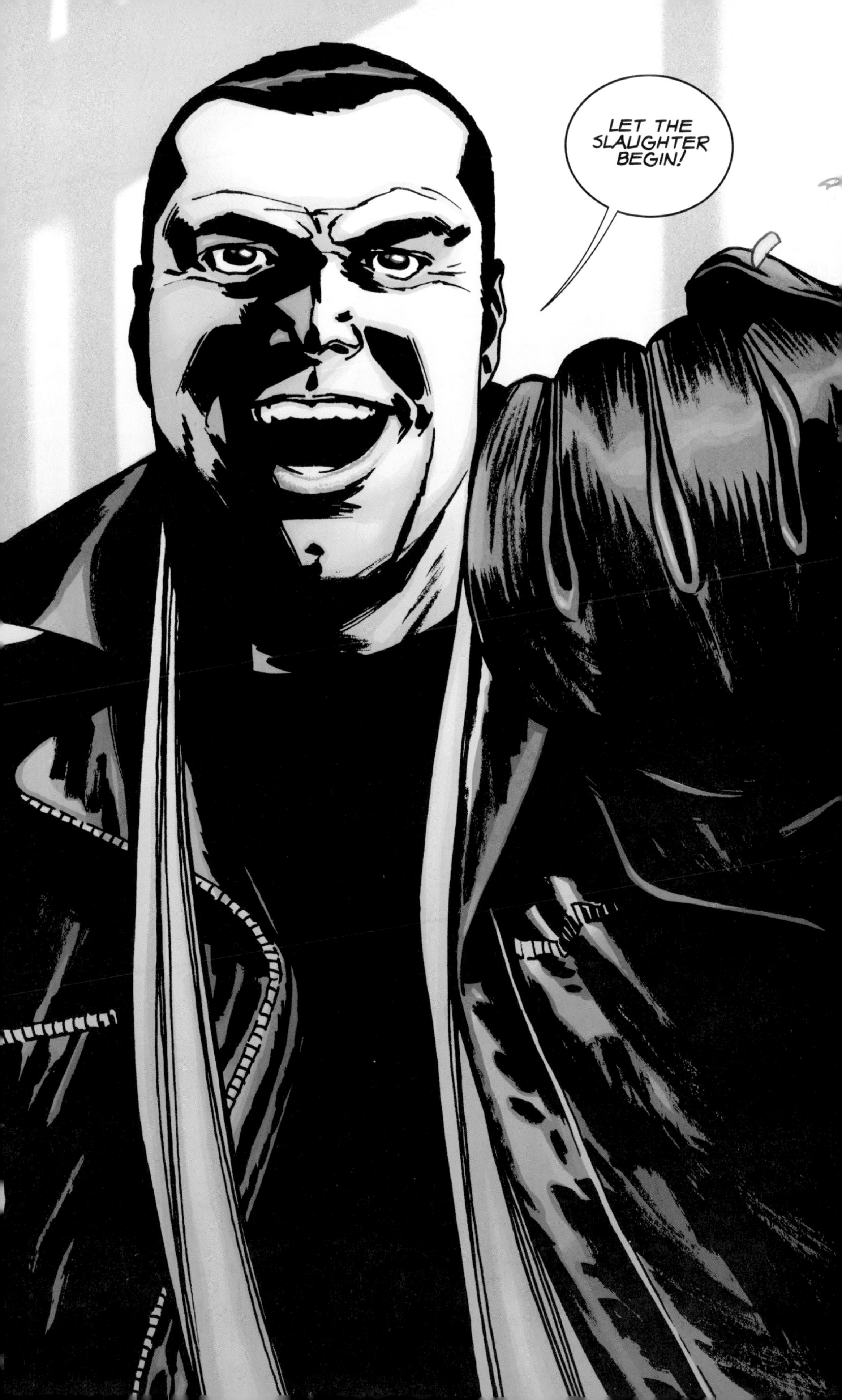
LET THE SLAUGHTER BEGIN!

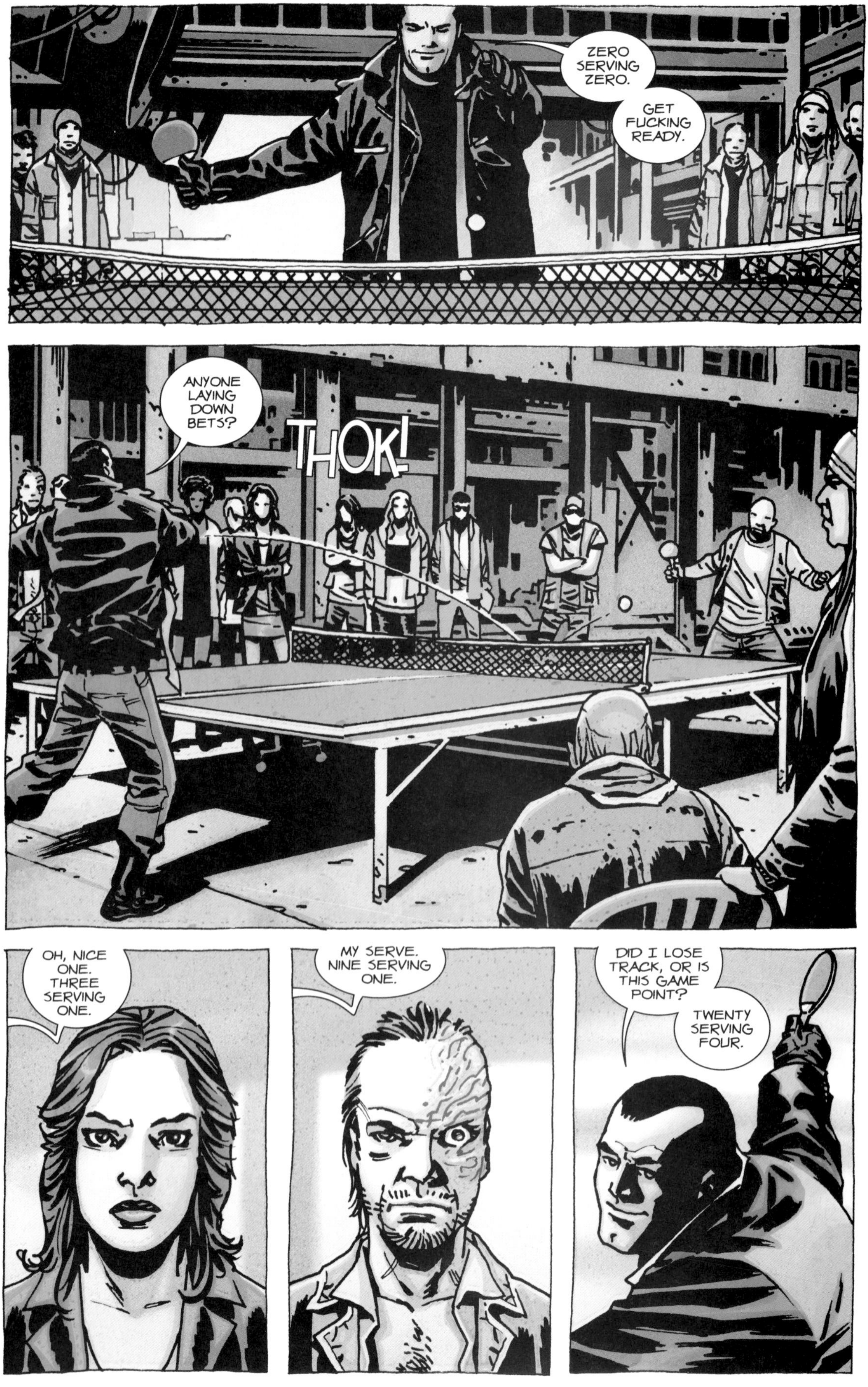
ZERO SERVING ZERO.
GET FUCKING READY.
ANYONE LAYING DOWN BETS?
THOK!
OH, NICE ONE. THREE SERVING ONE.
MY SERVE. NINE SERVING ONE.
DID I LOSE TRACK, OR IS THIS GAME POINT?
TWENTY SERVING FOUR.

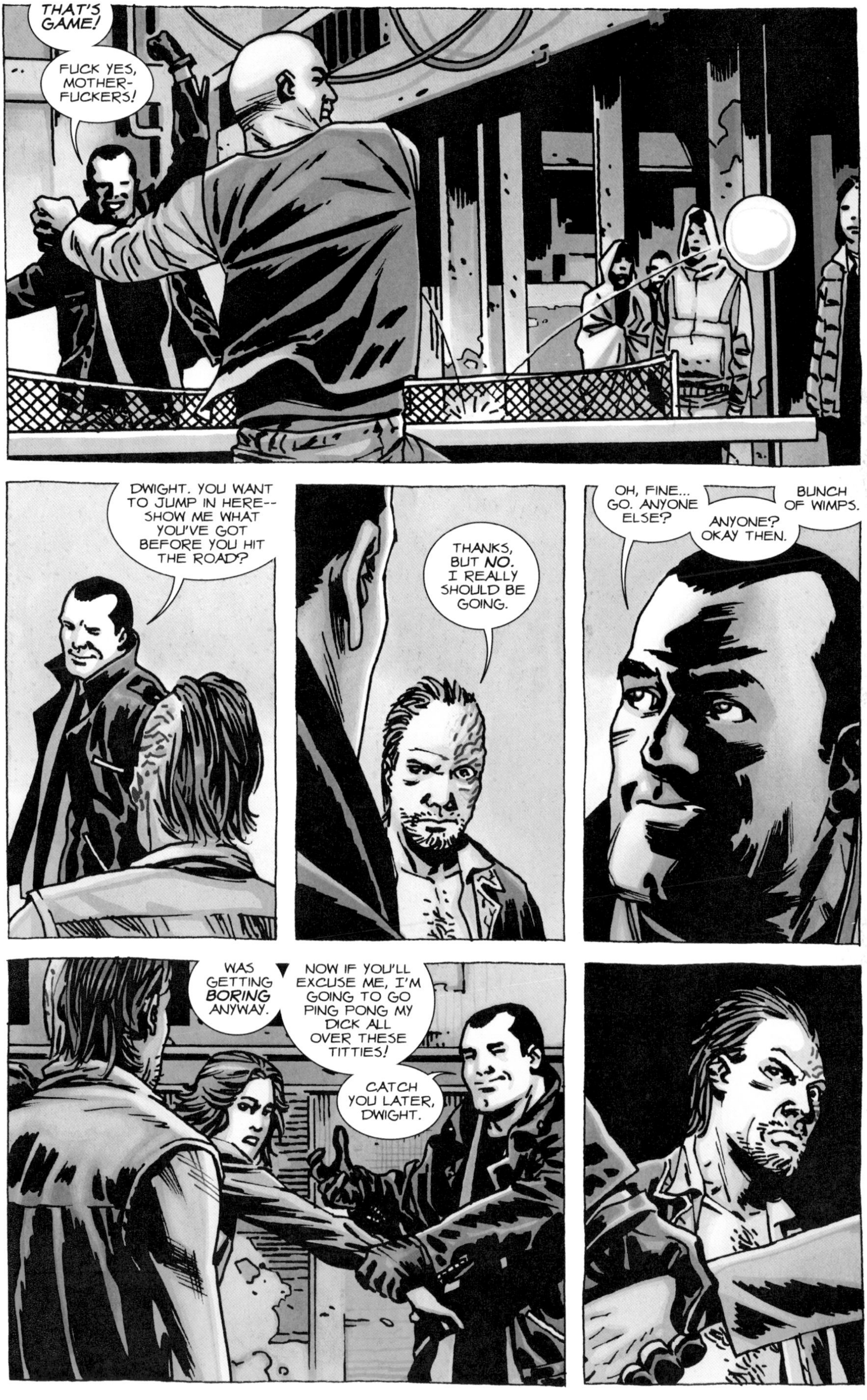
THAT'S GAME!
FUCK YES, MOTHER-FUCKERS!
DWIGHT. YOU WANT TO JUMP IN HERE-- SHOW ME WHAT YOU'VE GOT BEFORE YOU HIT THE ROAD?
THANKS, BUT **NO.** I REALLY SHOULD BE GOING.
OH, FINE... GO. ANYONE ELSE?
ANYONE? OKAY THEN.
BUNCH OF WIMPS.
WAS GETTING ***BORING*** ANYWAY.
NOW IF YOU'LL EXCUSE ME, I'M GOING TO GO PING PONG MY DICK ALL OVER THESE TITTIES!
CATCH YOU LATER, DWIGHT.

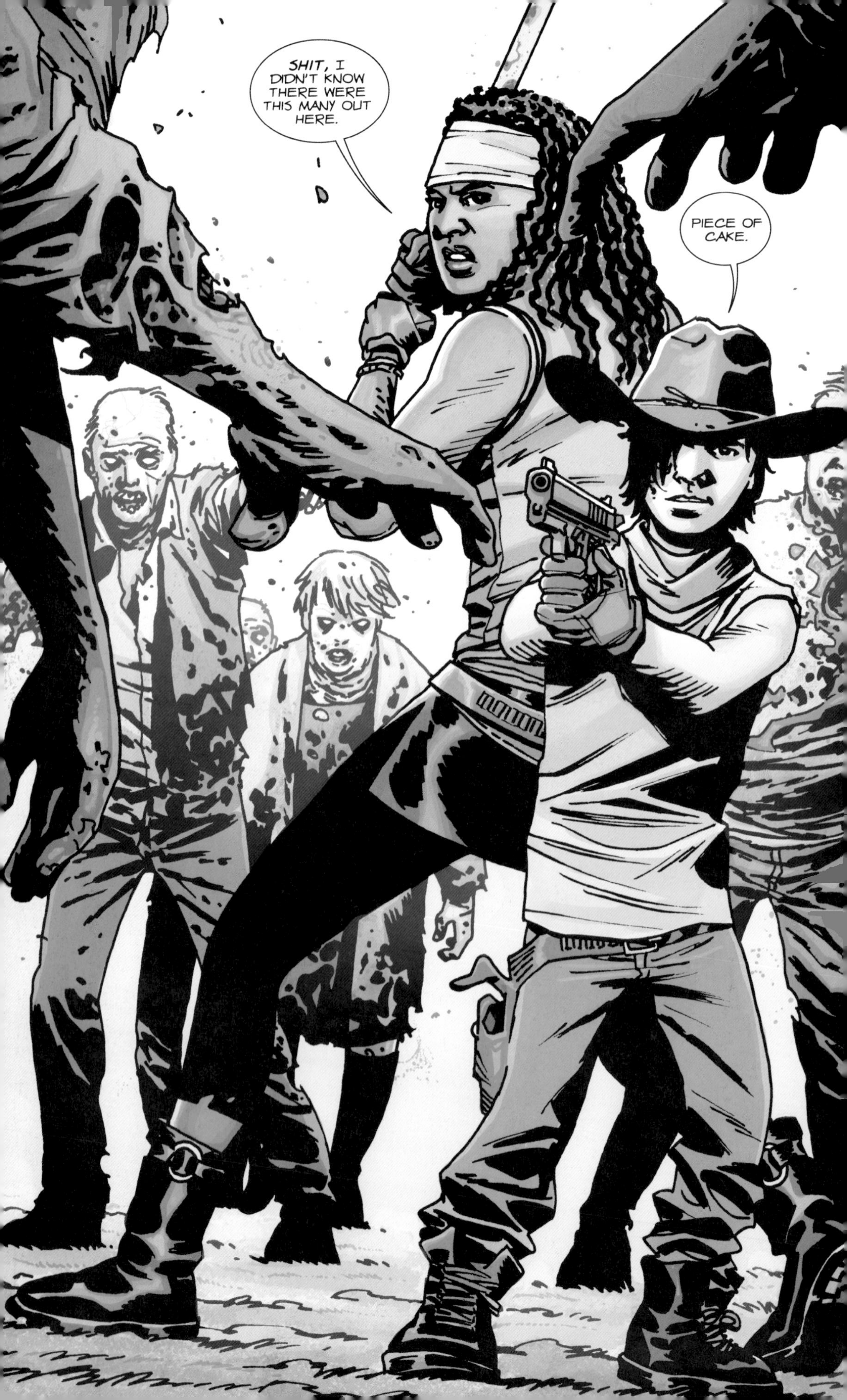
SHIT, I DIDN'T KNOW THERE WERE THIS MANY OUT HERE.
PIECE OF CAKE.

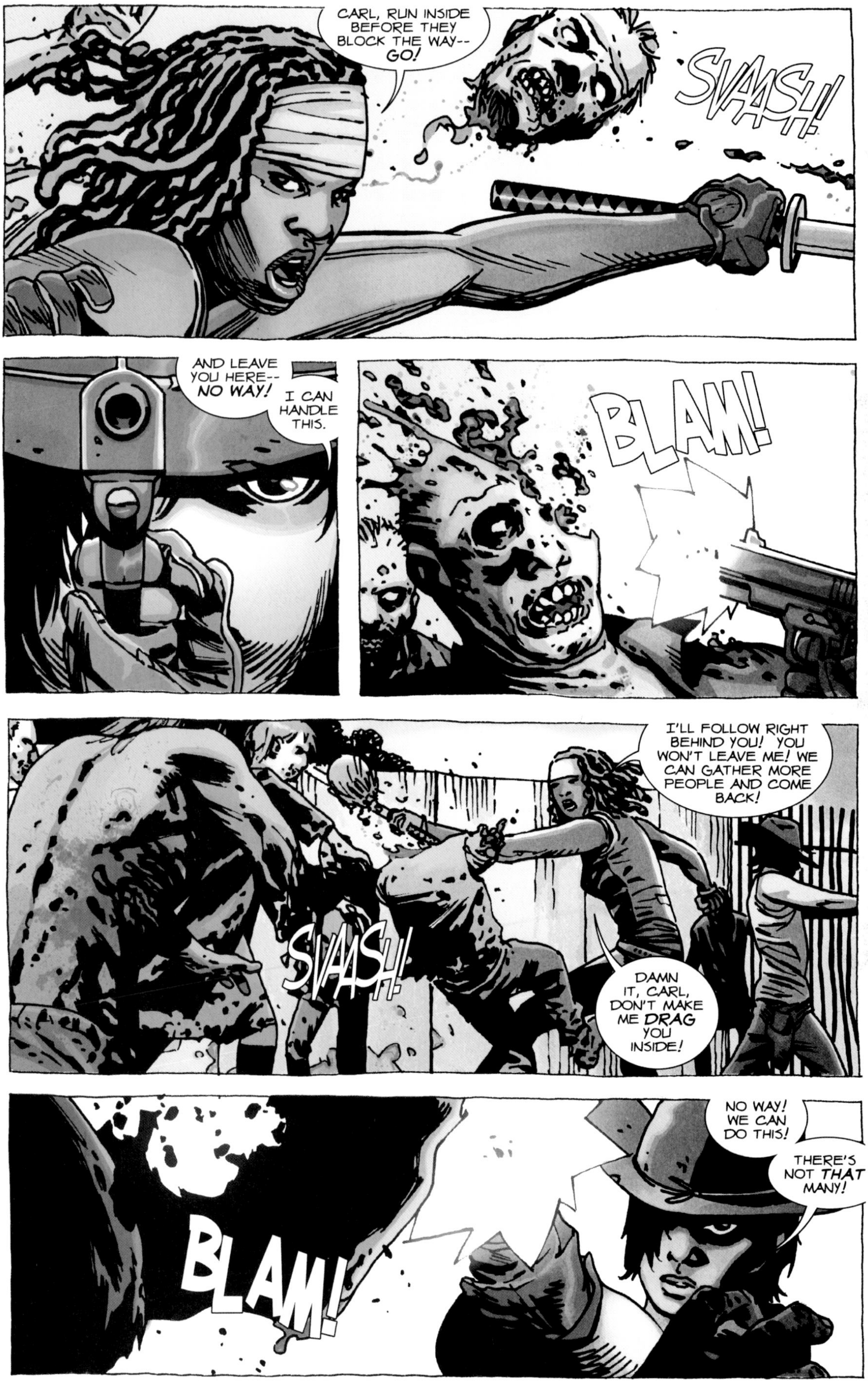

CARL, RUN INSIDE BEFORE THEY BLOCK THE WAY-- GO!
SVAASH!
AND LEAVE YOU HERE-- NO WAY!
I CAN HANDLE THIS.
BLAM!
I'LL FOLLOW RIGHT BEHIND YOU! YOU WON'T LEAVE ME! WE CAN GATHER MORE PEOPLE AND COME BACK!
SVAASH!
DAMN IT, CARL, DON'T MAKE ME DRAG YOU INSIDE!
BLAM!
NO WAY! WE CAN DO THIS!
THERE'S NOT THAT MANY!

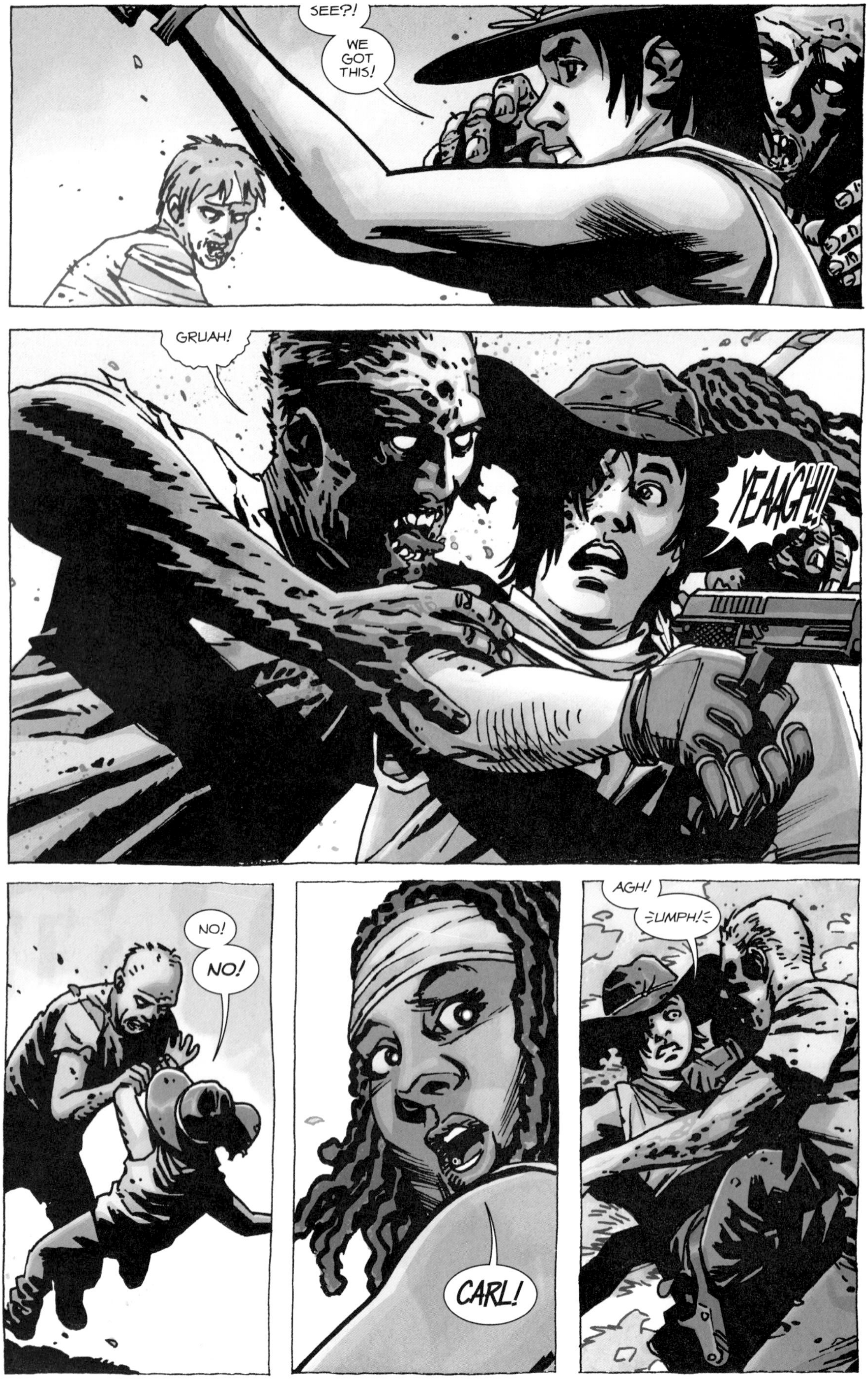
SEE?!
WE GOT THIS!
GRUAH!
YEAAGH!!
NO!
NO!
CARL!
AGH!
UMPH!

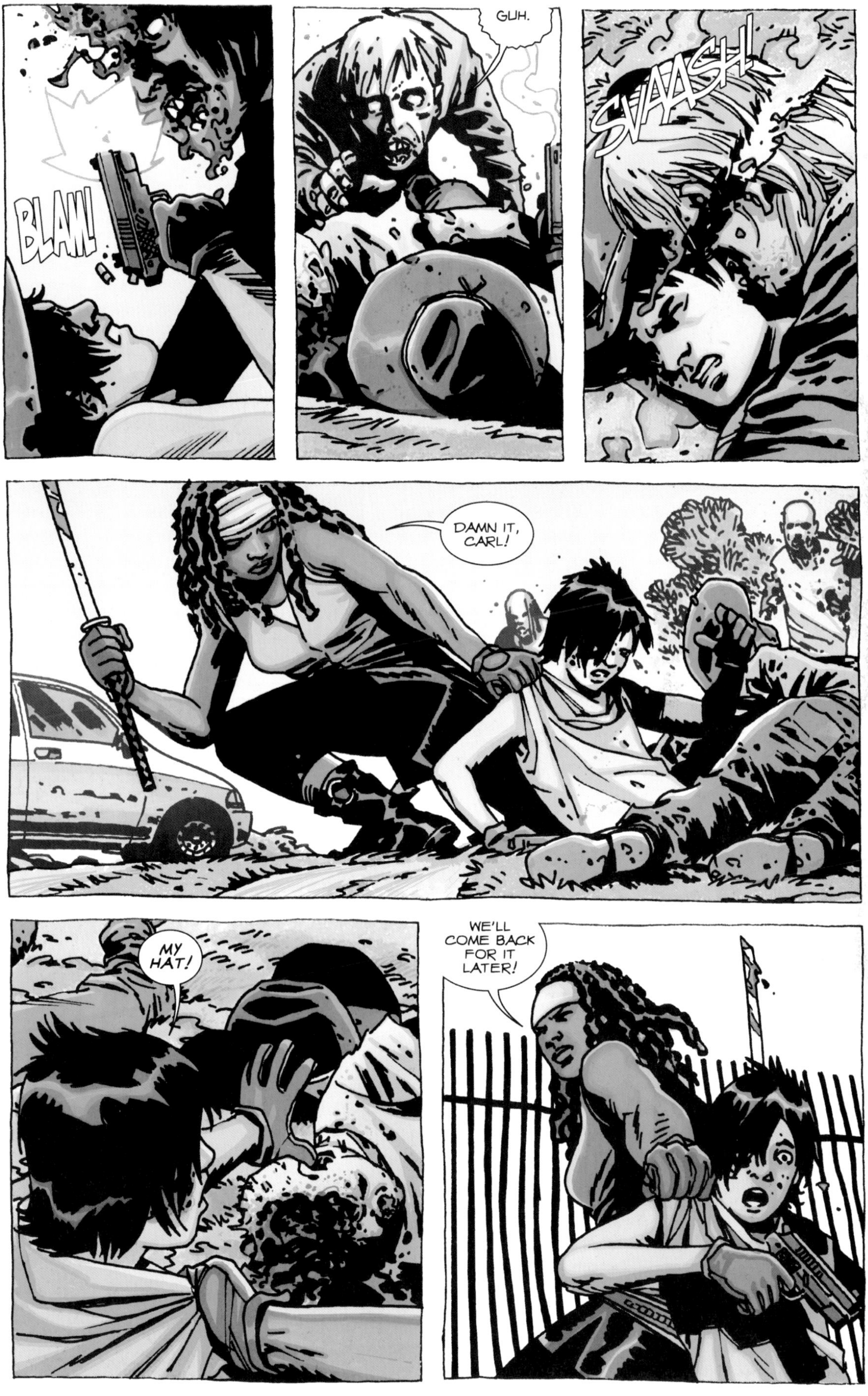
BLAM!
GUH.
SVAASH!
DAMN IT, CARL!
MY HAT!
WE'LL COME BACK FOR IT LATER!

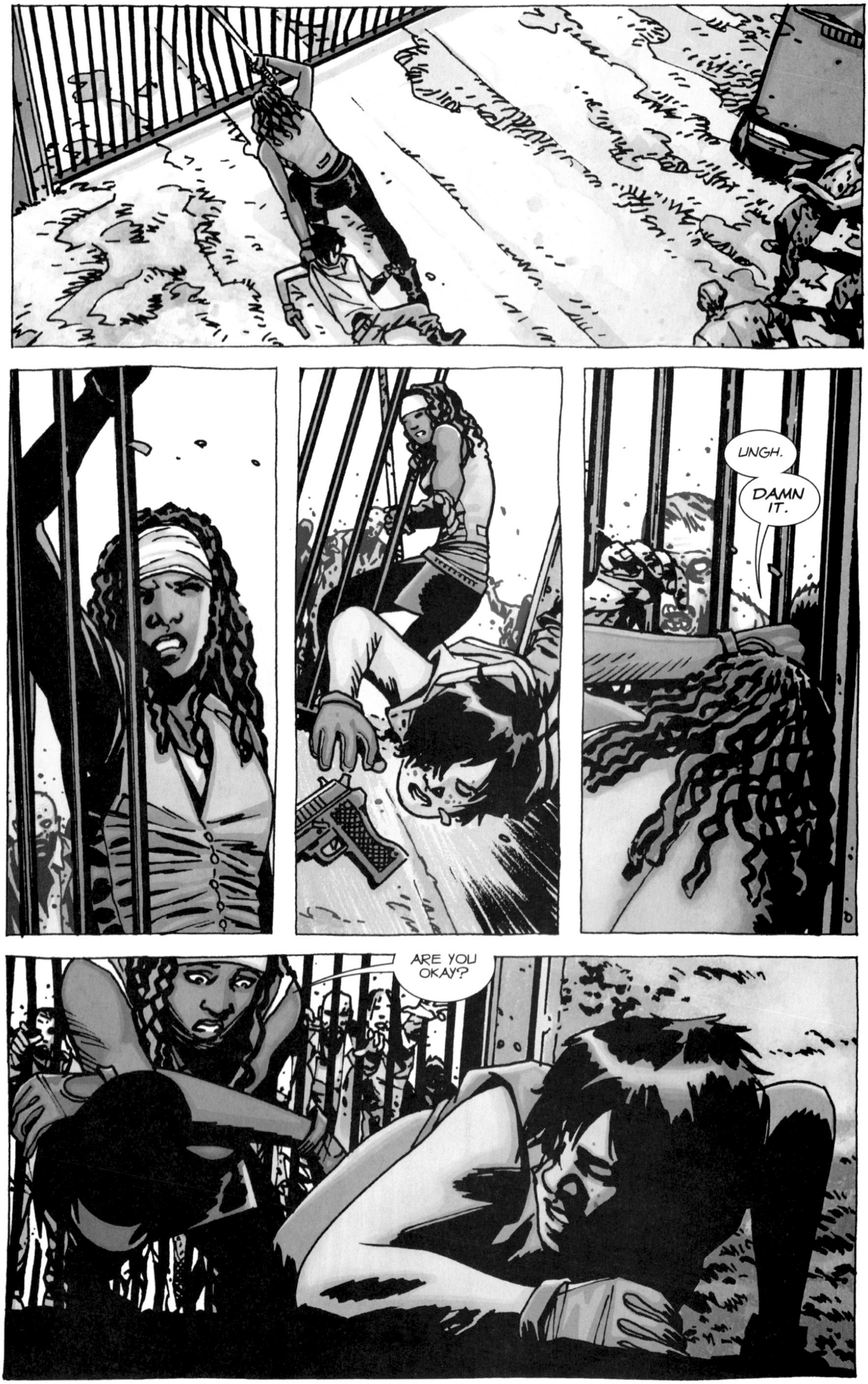

UNGH.
DAMN IT.
ARE YOU OKAY?

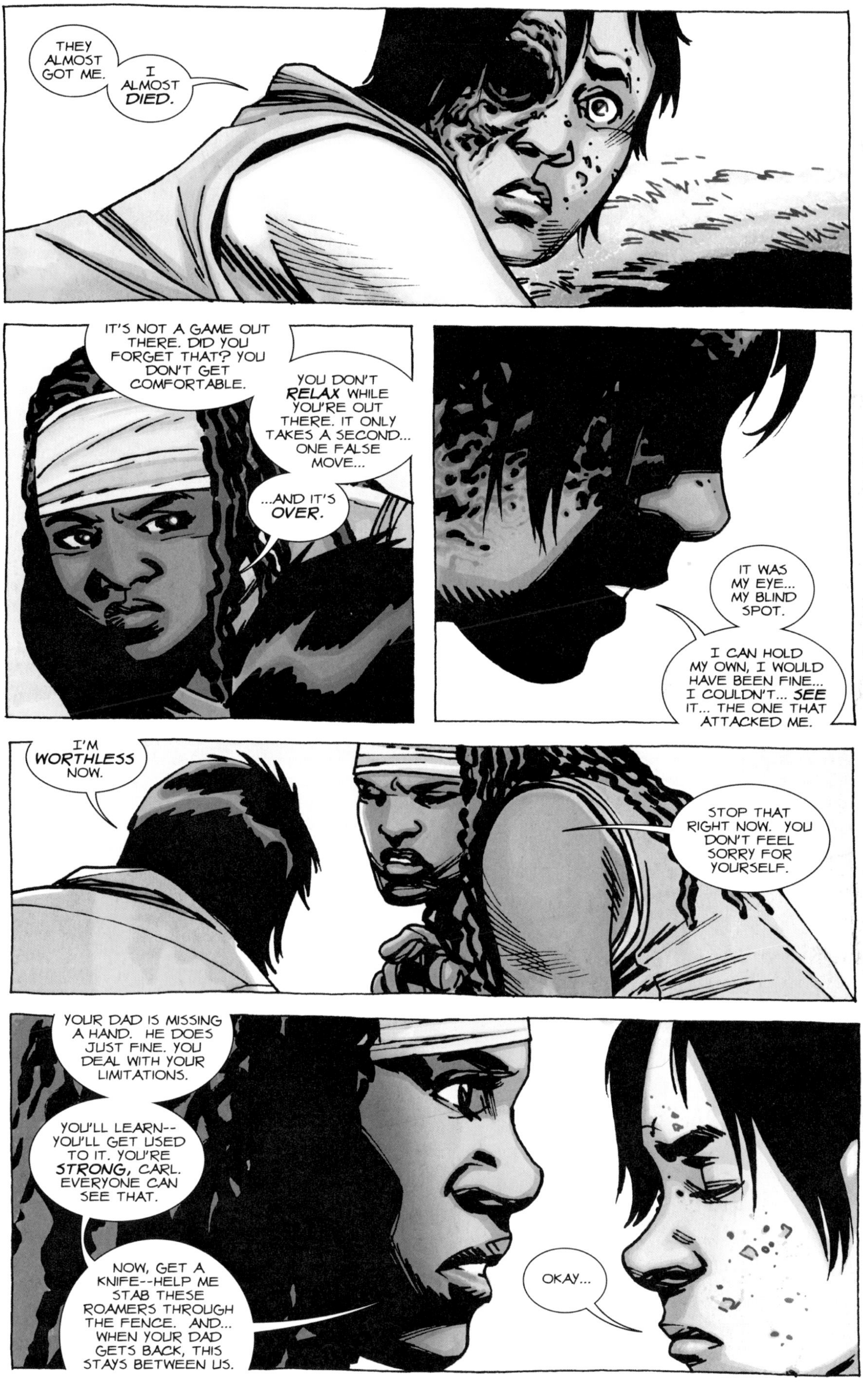
THEY ALMOST GOT ME.
I ALMOST *DIED.*
IT'S NOT A GAME OUT THERE. DID YOU FORGET THAT? YOU DON'T GET COMFORTABLE.
YOU DON'T *RELAX* WHILE YOU'RE OUT THERE. IT ONLY TAKES A SECOND... ONE FALSE MOVE...
...AND IT'S *OVER.*
IT WAS MY EYE... MY BLIND SPOT.
I CAN HOLD MY OWN, I WOULD HAVE BEEN FINE... I COULDN'T... *SEE* IT... THE ONE THAT ATTACKED ME.
I'M *WORTHLESS* NOW.
STOP THAT RIGHT NOW. YOU DON'T FEEL SORRY FOR YOURSELF.
YOUR DAD IS MISSING A HAND. HE DOES JUST FINE. YOU DEAL WITH YOUR LIMITATIONS.
YOU'LL LEARN-- YOU'LL GET USED TO IT. YOU'RE *STRONG,* CARL. EVERYONE CAN SEE THAT.
NOW, GET A KNIFE--HELP ME STAB THESE ROAMERS THROUGH THE FENCE. AND... WHEN YOUR DAD GETS BACK, THIS STAYS BETWEEN US.
OKAY...

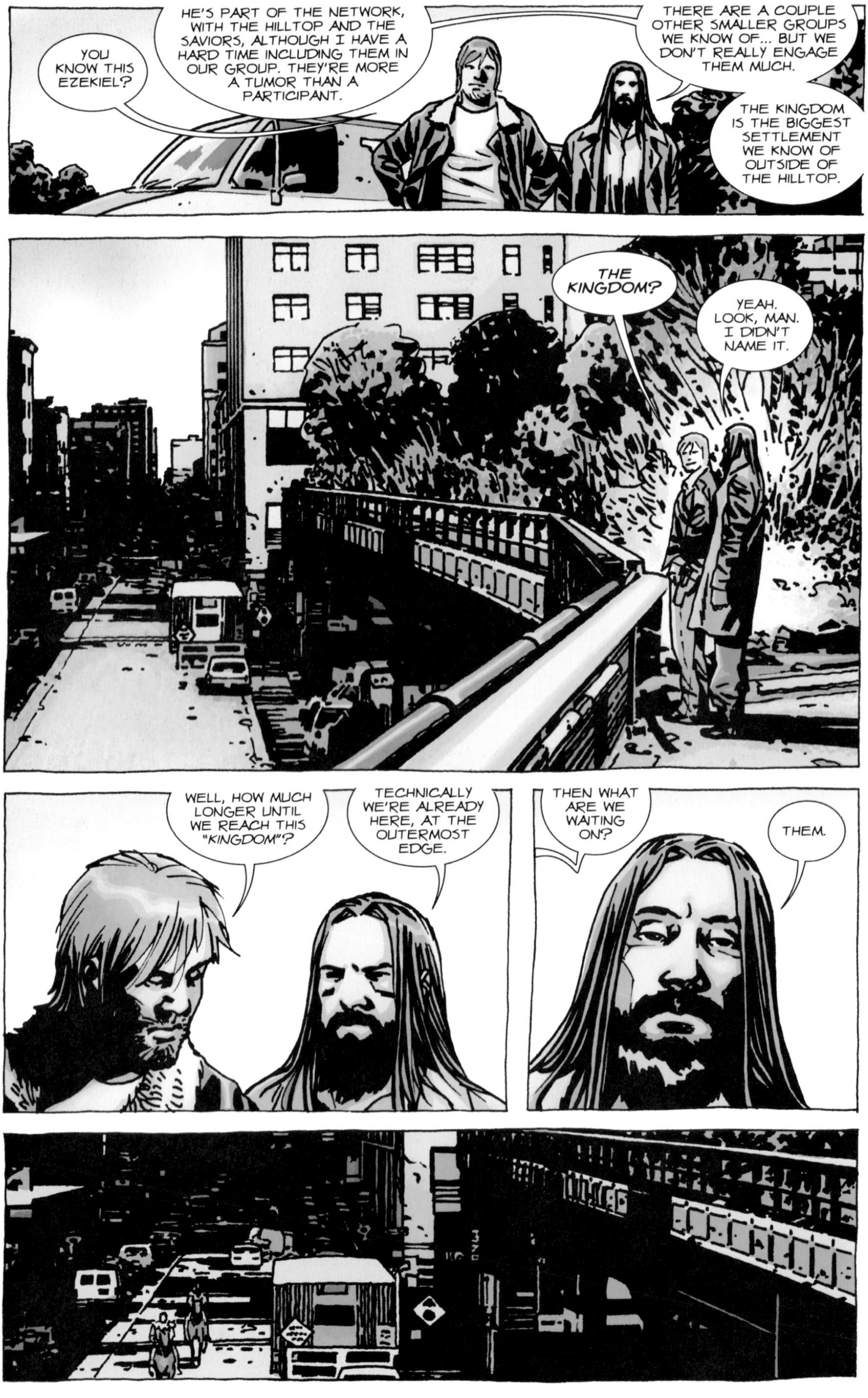
YOU KNOW THIS EZEKIEL?
HE'S PART OF THE NETWORK, WITH THE HILLTOP AND THE SAVIORS, ALTHOUGH I HAVE A HARD TIME INCLUDING THEM IN OUR GROUP. THEY'RE MORE A TUMOR THAN A PARTICIPANT.
THERE ARE A COUPLE OTHER SMALLER GROUPS WE KNOW OF... BUT WE DON'T REALLY ENGAGE THEM MUCH.
THE KINGDOM IS THE BIGGEST SETTLEMENT WE KNOW OF OUTSIDE OF THE HILLTOP.
THE KINGDOM?
YEAH. LOOK, MAN. I DIDN'T NAME IT.
WELL, HOW MUCH LONGER UNTIL WE REACH THIS "KINGDOM"?
TECHNICALLY WE'RE ALREADY HERE, AT THE OUTERMOST EDGE.
THEN WHAT ARE WE WAITING ON?
THEM.

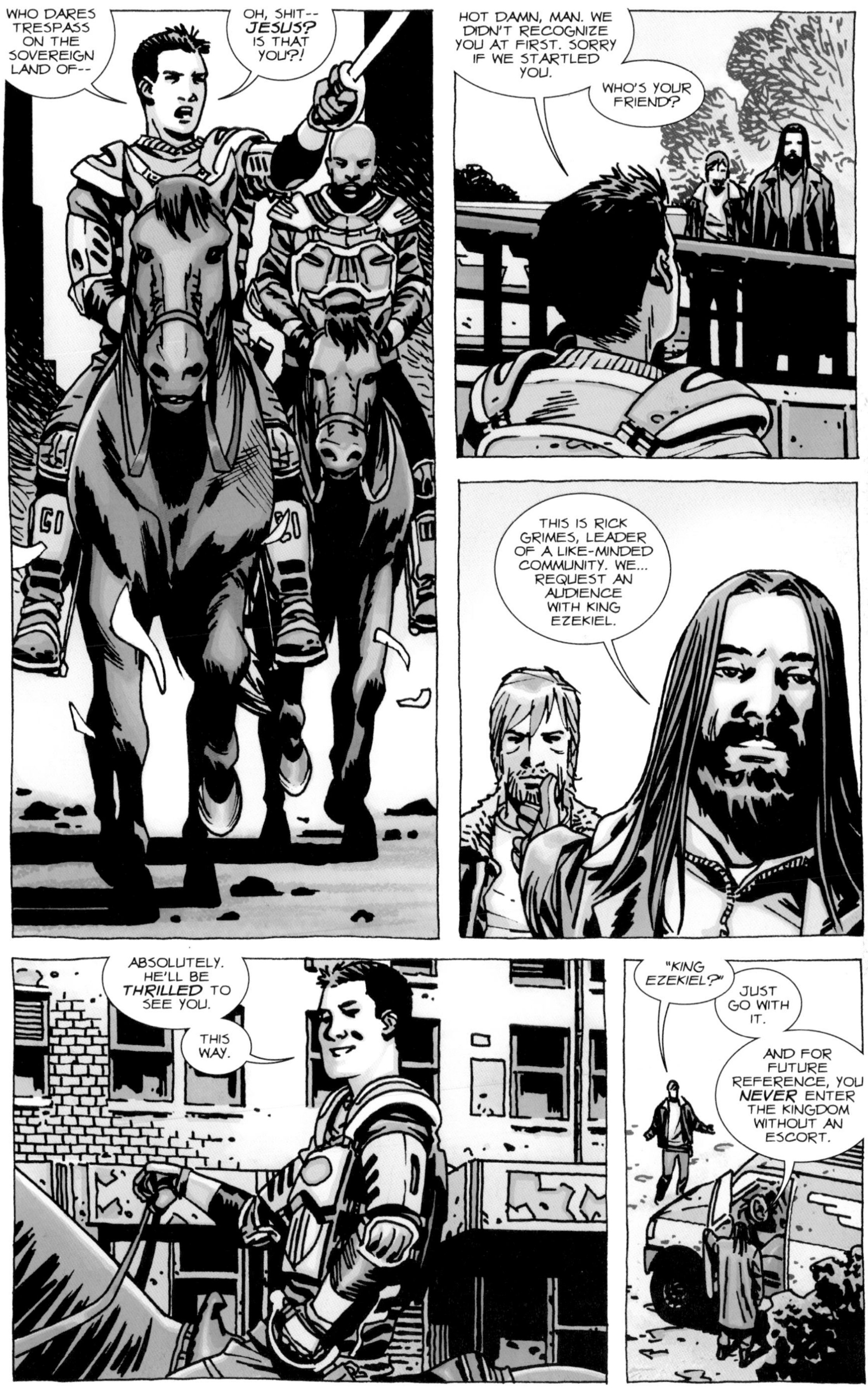

WHO DARES TRESPASS ON THE SOVEREIGN LAND OF--
OH, SHIT-- *JESUS?* IS THAT YOU?!
HOT DAMN, MAN. WE DIDN'T RECOGNIZE YOU AT FIRST. SORRY IF WE STARTLED YOU.
WHO'S YOUR FRIEND?
THIS IS RICK GRIMES, LEADER OF A LIKE-MINDED COMMUNITY. WE... REQUEST AN *AUDIENCE* WITH KING EZEKIEL.
ABSOLUTELY. HE'LL BE *THRILLED* TO SEE YOU.
THIS WAY.
"KING EZEKIEL?"
JUST GO WITH IT.
AND FOR FUTURE REFERENCE, YOU *NEVER* ENTER THE KINGDOM WITHOUT AN ESCORT.

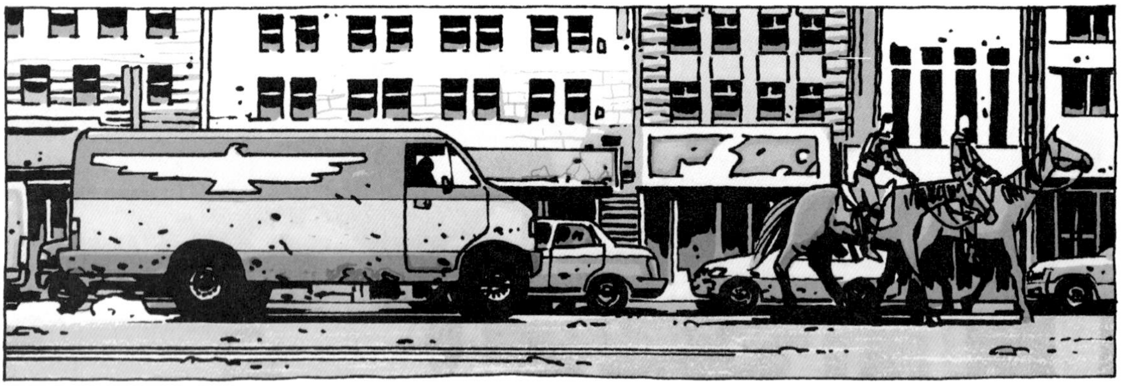

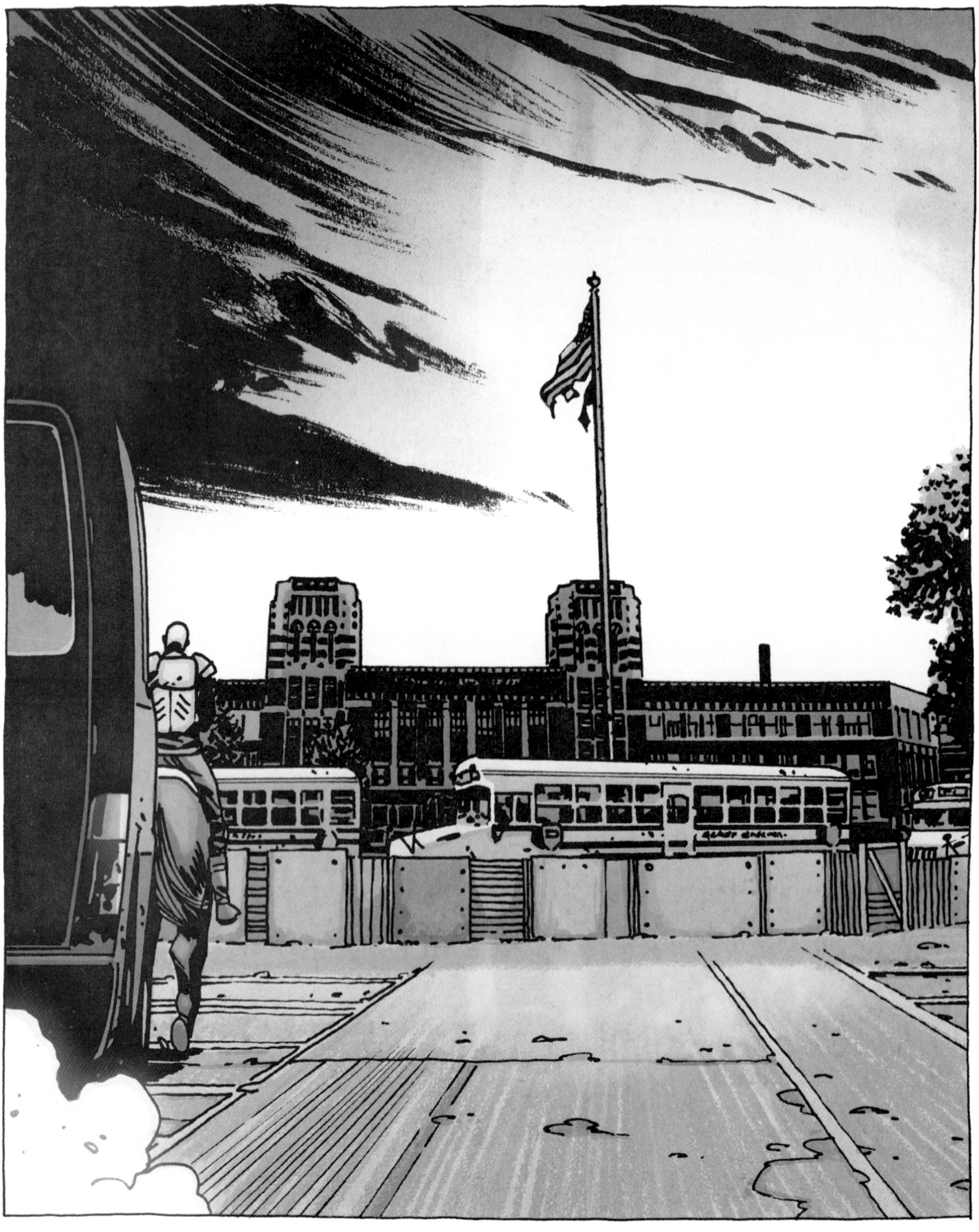

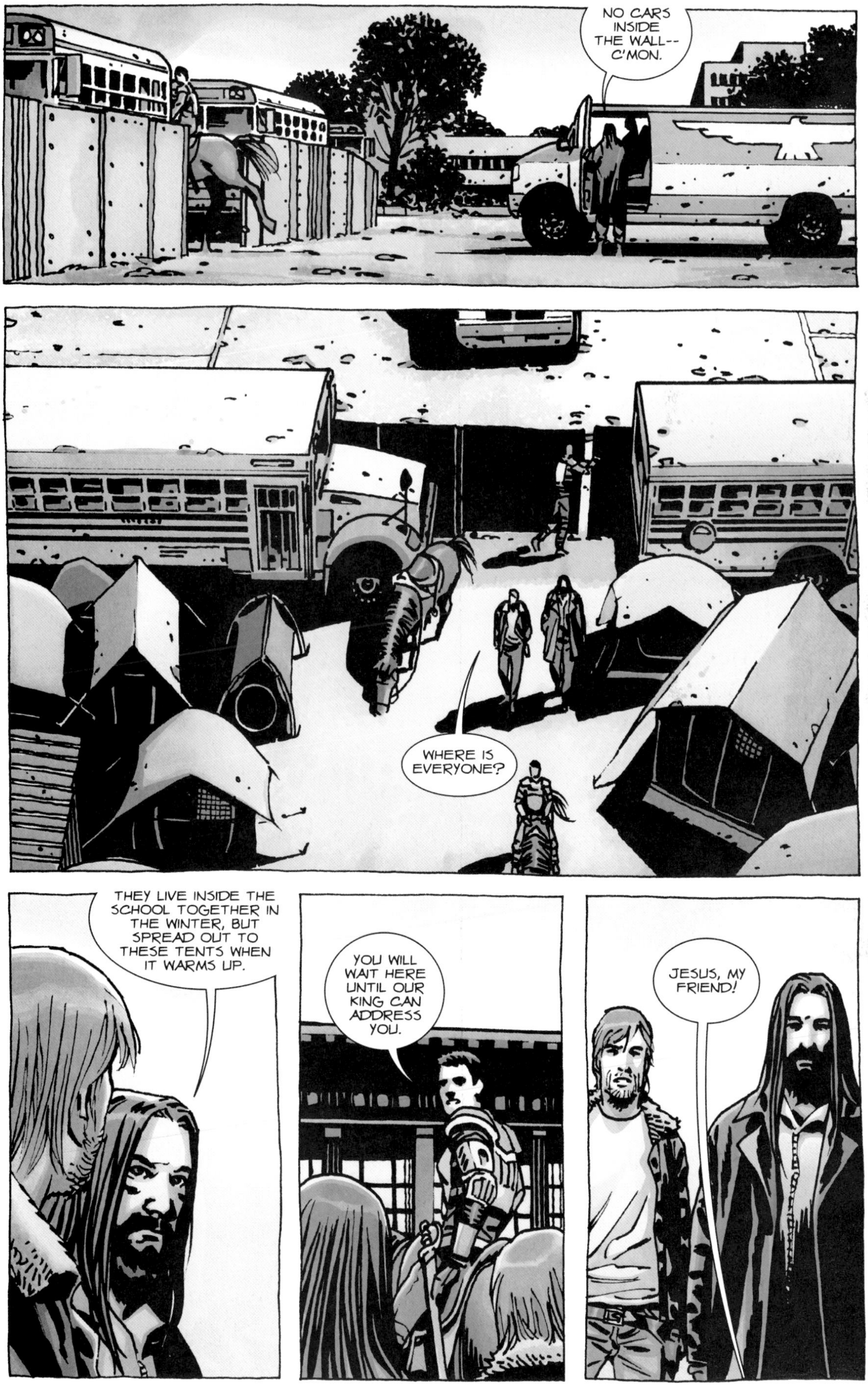

NO CARS INSIDE THE WALL-- C'MON.
WHERE IS EVERYONE?
THEY LIVE INSIDE THE SCHOOL TOGETHER IN THE WINTER, BUT SPREAD OUT TO THESE TENTS WHEN IT WARMS UP.
YOU WILL WAIT HERE UNTIL OUR KING CAN ADDRESS YOU.
JESUS, MY FRIEND!

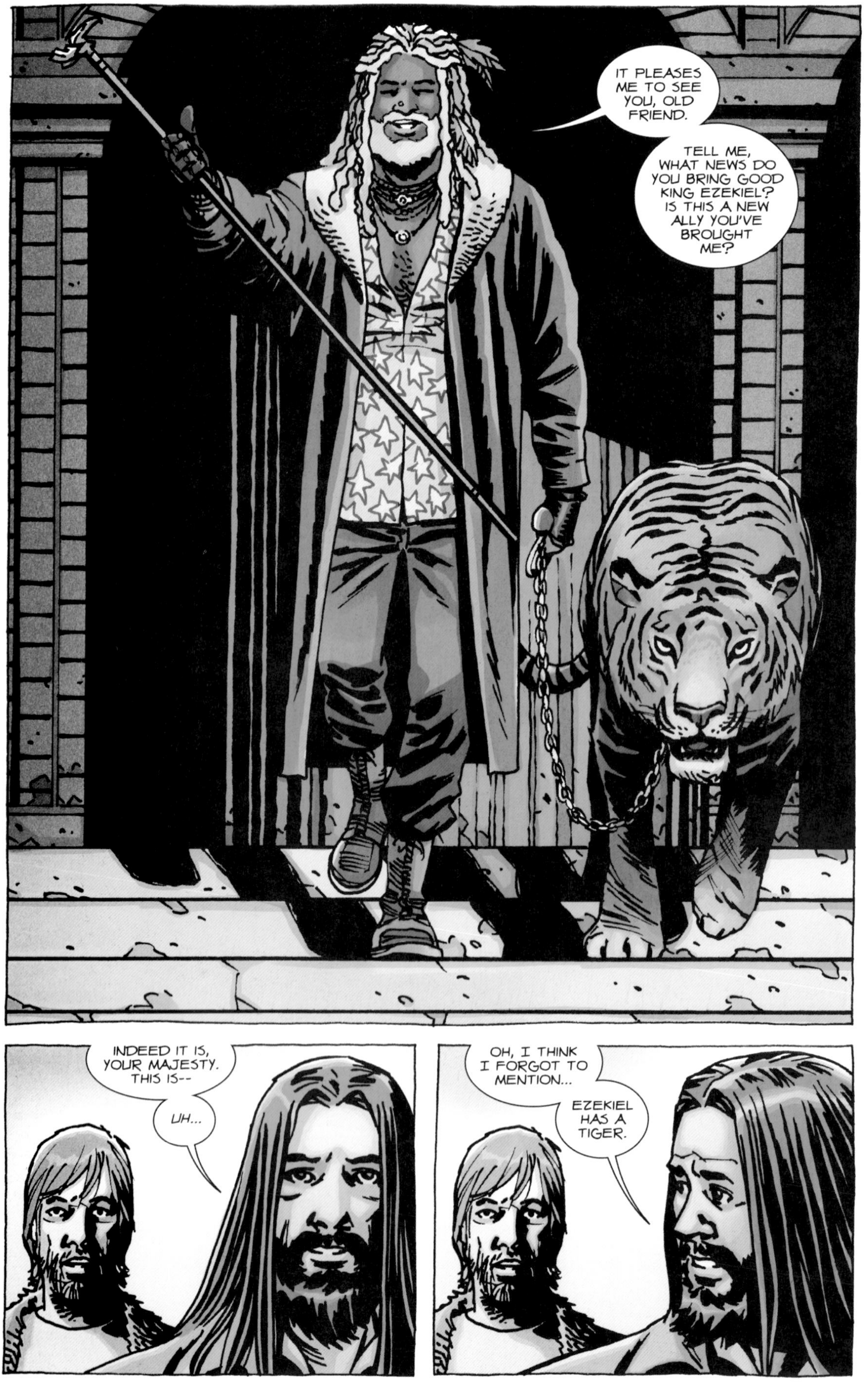
IT PLEASES ME TO SEE YOU, OLD FRIEND.
TELL ME, WHAT NEWS DO YOU BRING GOOD KING EZEKIEL? IS THIS A NEW ALLY YOU'VE BROUGHT ME?
INDEED IT IS, YOUR MAJESTY. THIS IS--
UH...
OH, I THINK I FORGOT TO MENTION...
EZEKIEL HAS A TIGER.

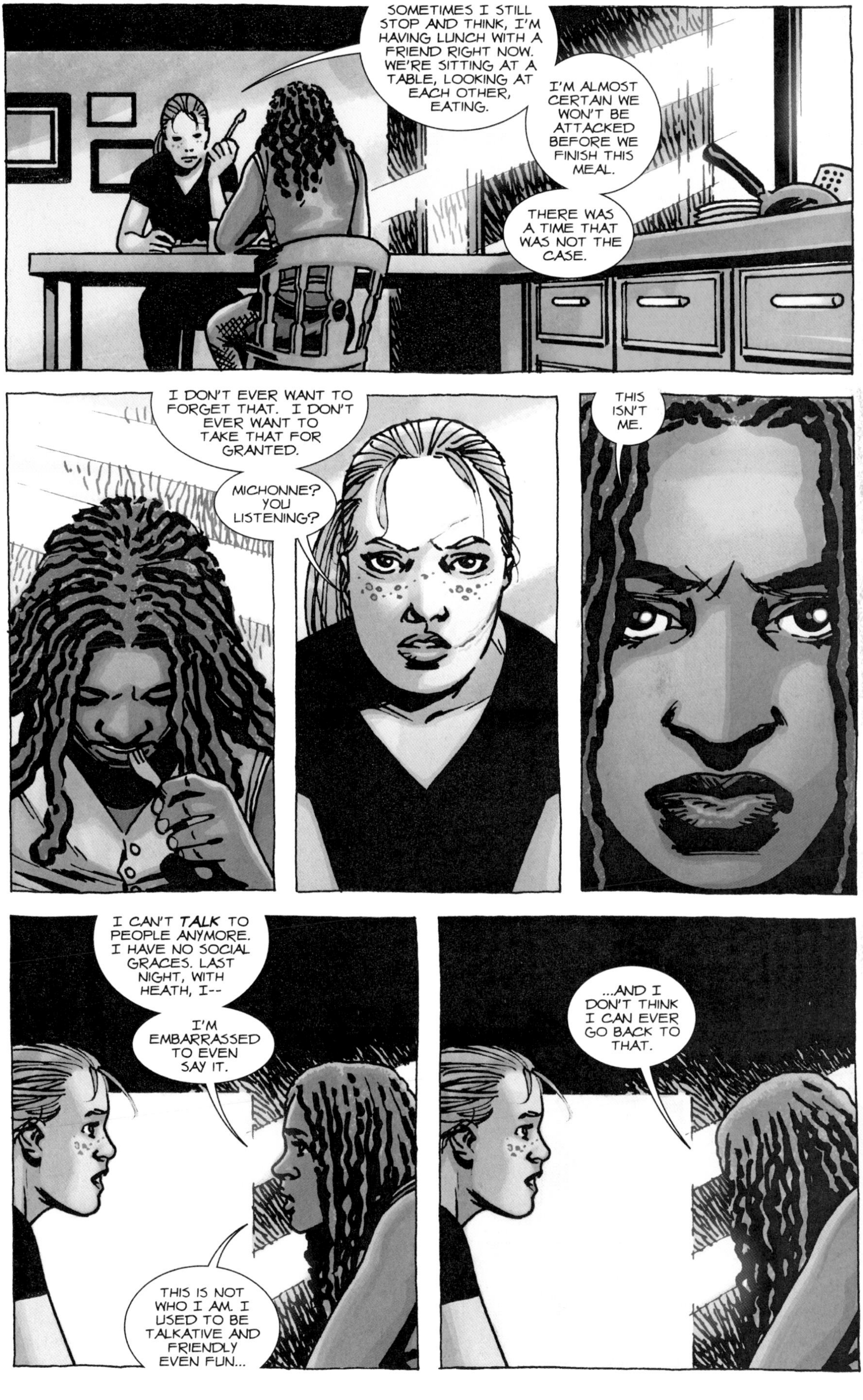

SOMETIMES I STILL STOP AND THINK, I'M HAVING LUNCH WITH A FRIEND RIGHT NOW. WE'RE SITTING AT A TABLE, LOOKING AT EACH OTHER, EATING.
I'M ALMOST CERTAIN WE WON'T BE ATTACKED BEFORE WE FINISH THIS MEAL.
THERE WAS A TIME THAT WAS NOT THE CASE.
I DON'T EVER WANT TO FORGET THAT. I DON'T EVER WANT TO TAKE THAT FOR GRANTED.
MICHONNE? YOU LISTENING?
THIS ISN'T ME.
I CAN'T *TALK* TO PEOPLE ANYMORE. I HAVE NO SOCIAL GRACES. LAST NIGHT, WITH HEATH, I--
I'M EMBARRASSED TO EVEN SAY IT.
THIS IS NOT WHO I AM. I USED TO BE TALKATIVE AND FRIENDLY EVEN FUN...
...AND I DON'T THINK I CAN EVER GO BACK TO THAT.

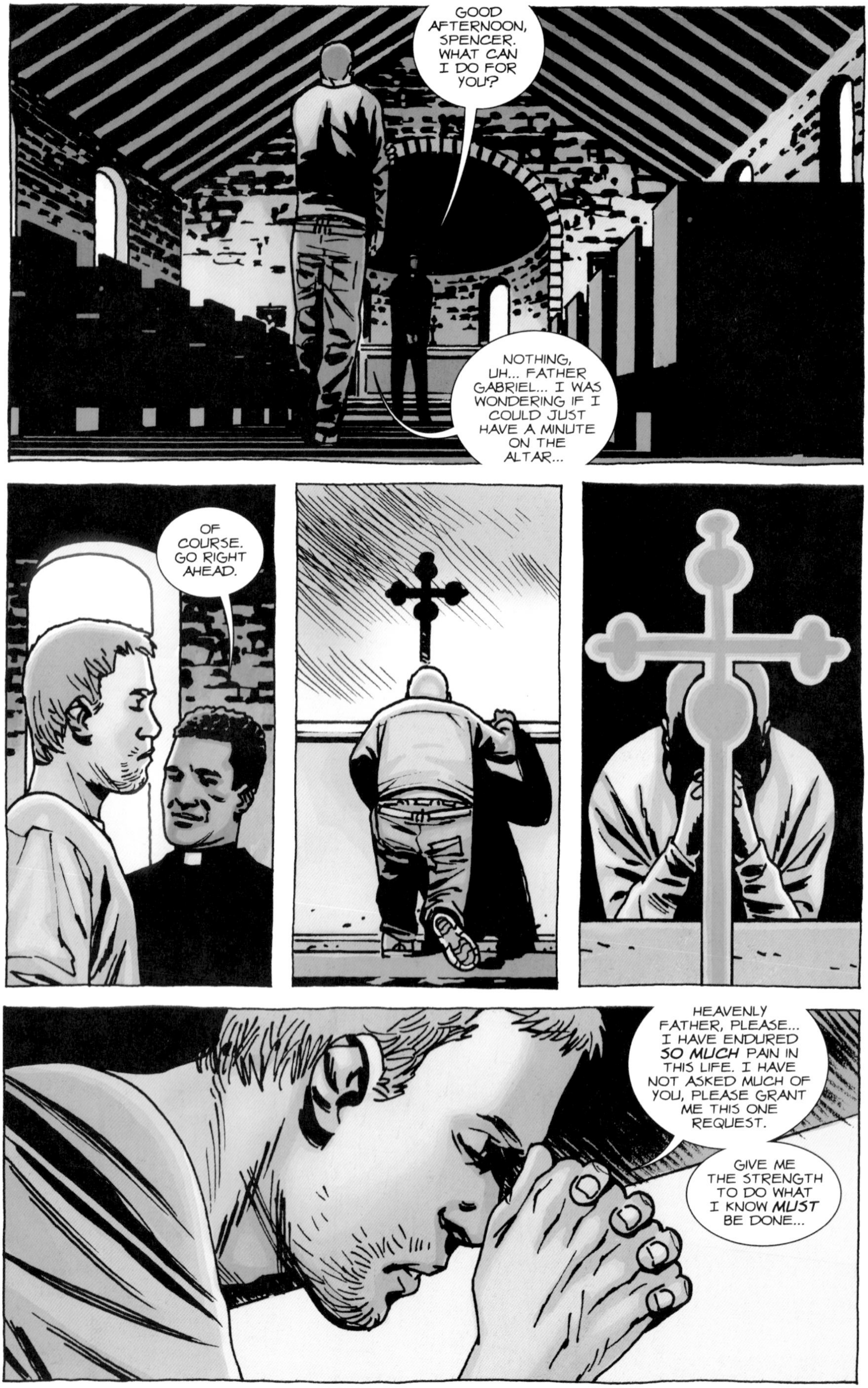
GOOD AFTERNOON, SPENCER. WHAT CAN I DO FOR YOU?
NOTHING, UH... FATHER GABRIEL... I WAS WONDERING IF I COULD JUST HAVE A MINUTE ON THE ALTAR...
OF COURSE. GO RIGHT AHEAD.
HEAVENLY FATHER, PLEASE... I HAVE ENDURED SO MUCH PAIN IN THIS LIFE. I HAVE NOT ASKED MUCH OF YOU, PLEASE GRANT ME THIS ONE REQUEST.
GIVE ME THE STRENGTH TO DO WHAT I KNOW MUST BE DONE...

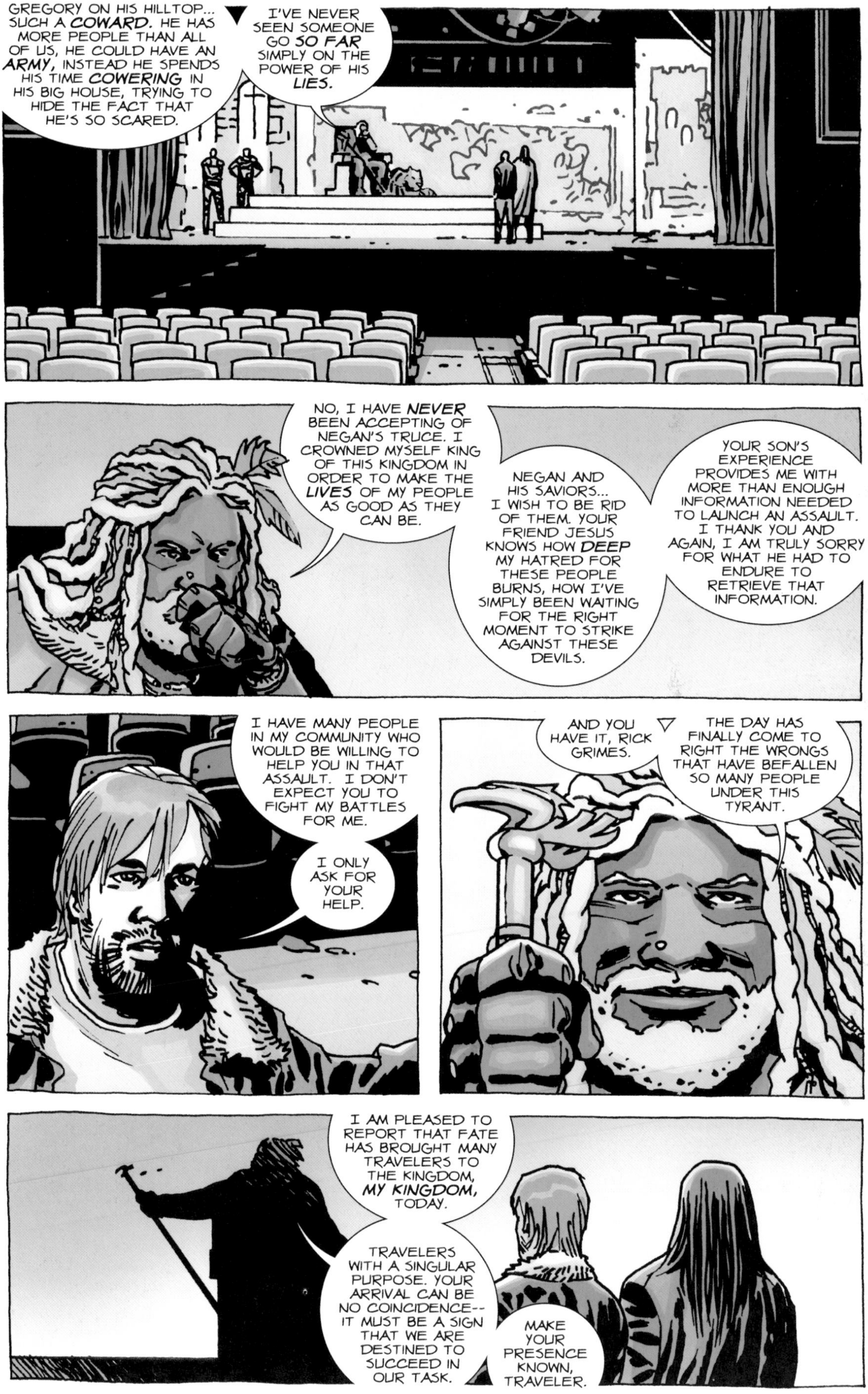

GREGORY ON HIS HILLTOP... SUCH A COWARD. HE HAS MORE PEOPLE THAN ALL OF US, HE COULD HAVE AN ARMY, INSTEAD HE SPENDS HIS TIME COWERING IN HIS BIG HOUSE, TRYING TO HIDE THE FACT THAT HE'S SO SCARED.
I'VE NEVER SEEN SOMEONE GO SO FAR SIMPLY ON THE POWER OF HIS LIES.
NO, I HAVE NEVER BEEN ACCEPTING OF NEGAN'S TRUCE. I CROWNED MYSELF KING OF THIS KINGDOM IN ORDER TO MAKE THE LIVES OF MY PEOPLE AS GOOD AS THEY CAN BE.
NEGAN AND HIS SAVIORS... I WISH TO BE RID OF THEM. YOUR FRIEND JESUS KNOWS HOW DEEP MY HATRED FOR THESE PEOPLE BURNS, HOW I'VE SIMPLY BEEN WAITING FOR THE RIGHT MOMENT TO STRIKE AGAINST THESE DEVILS.
YOUR SON'S EXPERIENCE PROVIDES ME WITH MORE THAN ENOUGH INFORMATION NEEDED TO LAUNCH AN ASSAULT. I THANK YOU AND AGAIN, I AM TRULY SORRY FOR WHAT HE HAD TO ENDURE TO RETRIEVE THAT INFORMATION.
I HAVE MANY PEOPLE IN MY COMMUNITY WHO WOULD BE WILLING TO HELP YOU IN THAT ASSAULT. I DON'T EXPECT YOU TO FIGHT MY BATTLES FOR ME.
I ONLY ASK FOR YOUR HELP.
AND YOU HAVE IT, RICK GRIMES.
THE DAY HAS FINALLY COME TO RIGHT THE WRONGS THAT HAVE BEFALLEN SO MANY PEOPLE UNDER THIS TYRANT.
I AM PLEASED TO REPORT THAT FATE HAS BROUGHT MANY TRAVELERS TO THE KINGDOM, MY KINGDOM, TODAY.
TRAVELERS WITH A SINGULAR PURPOSE. YOUR ARRIVAL CAN BE NO COINCIDENCE-- IT MUST BE A SIGN THAT WE ARE DESTINED TO SUCCEED IN OUR TASK.
MAKE YOUR PRESENCE KNOWN, TRAVELER.

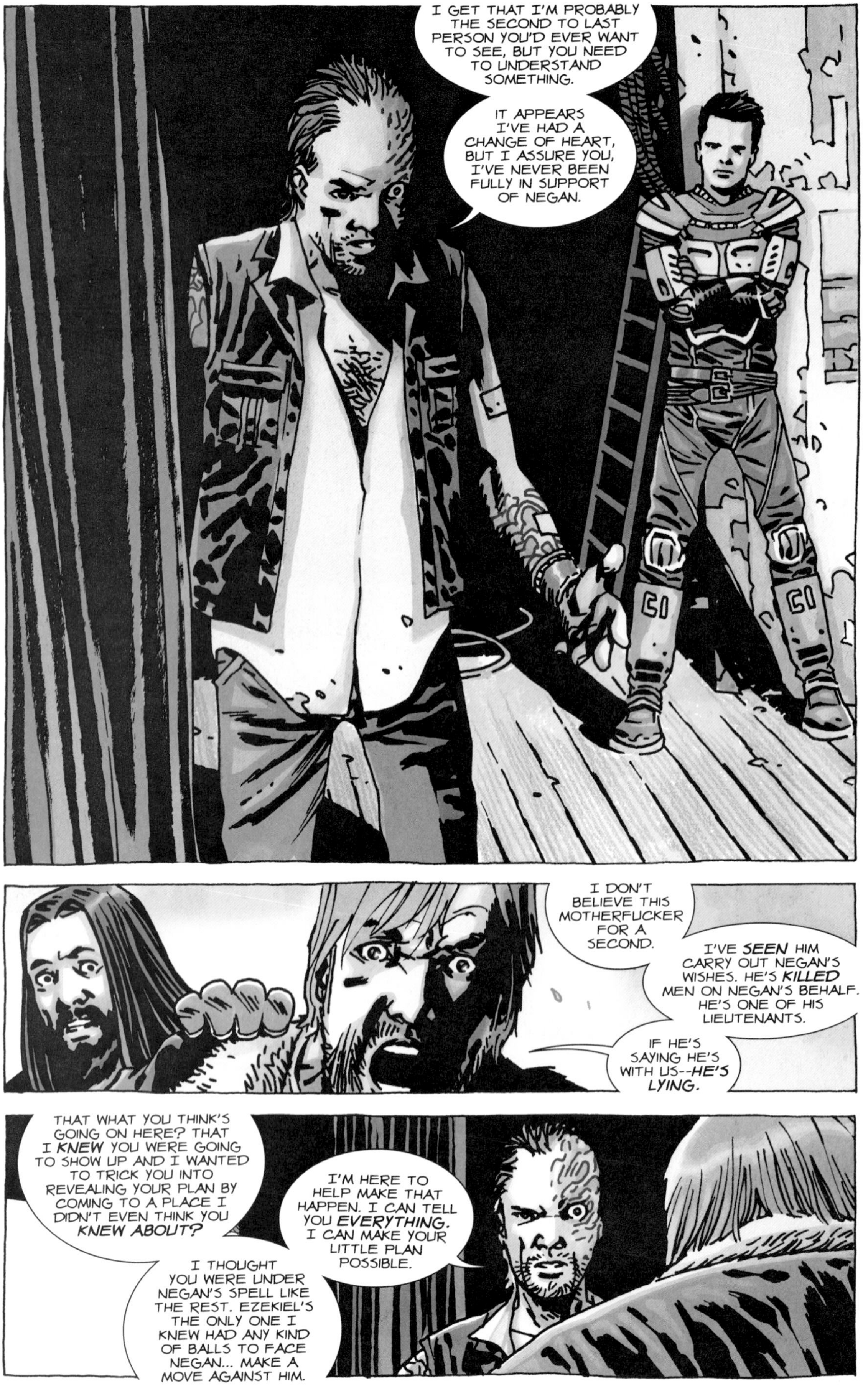
I GET THAT I'M PROBABLY THE SECOND TO LAST PERSON YOU'D EVER WANT TO SEE, BUT YOU NEED TO UNDERSTAND SOMETHING.
IT APPEARS I'VE HAD A CHANGE OF HEART, BUT I ASSURE YOU, I'VE NEVER BEEN FULLY IN SUPPORT OF NEGAN.
I DON'T BELIEVE THIS MOTHERFUCKER FOR A SECOND.
I'VE SEEN HIM CARRY OUT NEGAN'S WISHES. HE'S KILLED MEN ON NEGAN'S BEHALF. HE'S ONE OF HIS LIEUTENANTS.
IF HE'S SAYING HE'S WITH US--HE'S LYING.
THAT WHAT YOU THINK'S GOING ON HERE? THAT I KNEW YOU WERE GOING TO SHOW UP AND I WANTED TO TRICK YOU INTO REVEALING YOUR PLAN BY COMING TO A PLACE I DIDN'T EVEN THINK YOU KNEW ABOUT?
I THOUGHT YOU WERE UNDER NEGAN'S SPELL LIKE THE REST. EZEKIEL'S THE ONLY ONE I KNEW HAD ANY KIND OF BALLS TO FACE NEGAN... MAKE A MOVE AGAINST HIM.
I'M HERE TO HELP MAKE THAT HAPPEN. I CAN TELL YOU EVERYTHING. I CAN MAKE YOUR LITTLE PLAN POSSIBLE.

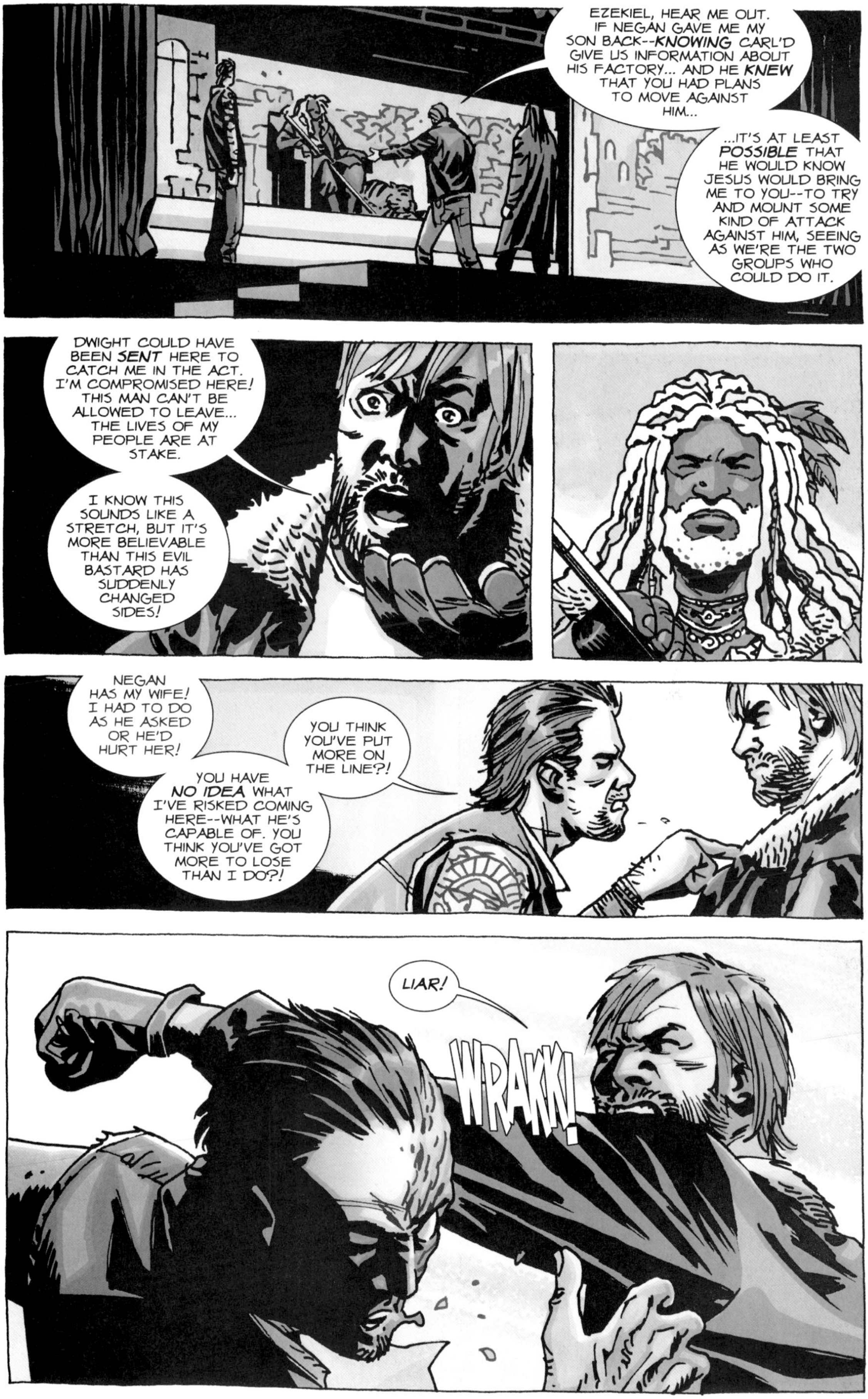
EZEKIEL, HEAR ME OUT. IF NEGAN GAVE ME MY SON BACK--KNOWING CARL'D GIVE US INFORMATION ABOUT HIS FACTORY... AND HE KNEW THAT YOU HAD PLANS TO MOVE AGAINST HIM...
...IT'S AT LEAST POSSIBLE THAT HE WOULD KNOW JESUS WOULD BRING ME TO YOU--TO TRY AND MOUNT SOME KIND OF ATTACK AGAINST HIM, SEEING AS WE'RE THE TWO GROUPS WHO COULD DO IT.
DWIGHT COULD HAVE BEEN SENT HERE TO CATCH ME IN THE ACT. I'M COMPROMISED HERE! THIS MAN CAN'T BE ALLOWED TO LEAVE... THE LIVES OF MY PEOPLE ARE AT STAKE.
I KNOW THIS SOUNDS LIKE A STRETCH, BUT IT'S MORE BELIEVABLE THAN THIS EVIL BASTARD HAS SUDDENLY CHANGED SIDES!
NEGAN HAS MY WIFE! I HAD TO DO AS HE ASKED OR HE'D HURT HER!
YOU THINK YOU'VE PUT MORE ON THE LINE?!
YOU HAVE NO IDEA WHAT I'VE RISKED COMING HERE--WHAT HE'S CAPABLE OF. YOU THINK YOU'VE GOT MORE TO LOSE THAN I DO?!
LIAR!
WRAKK!

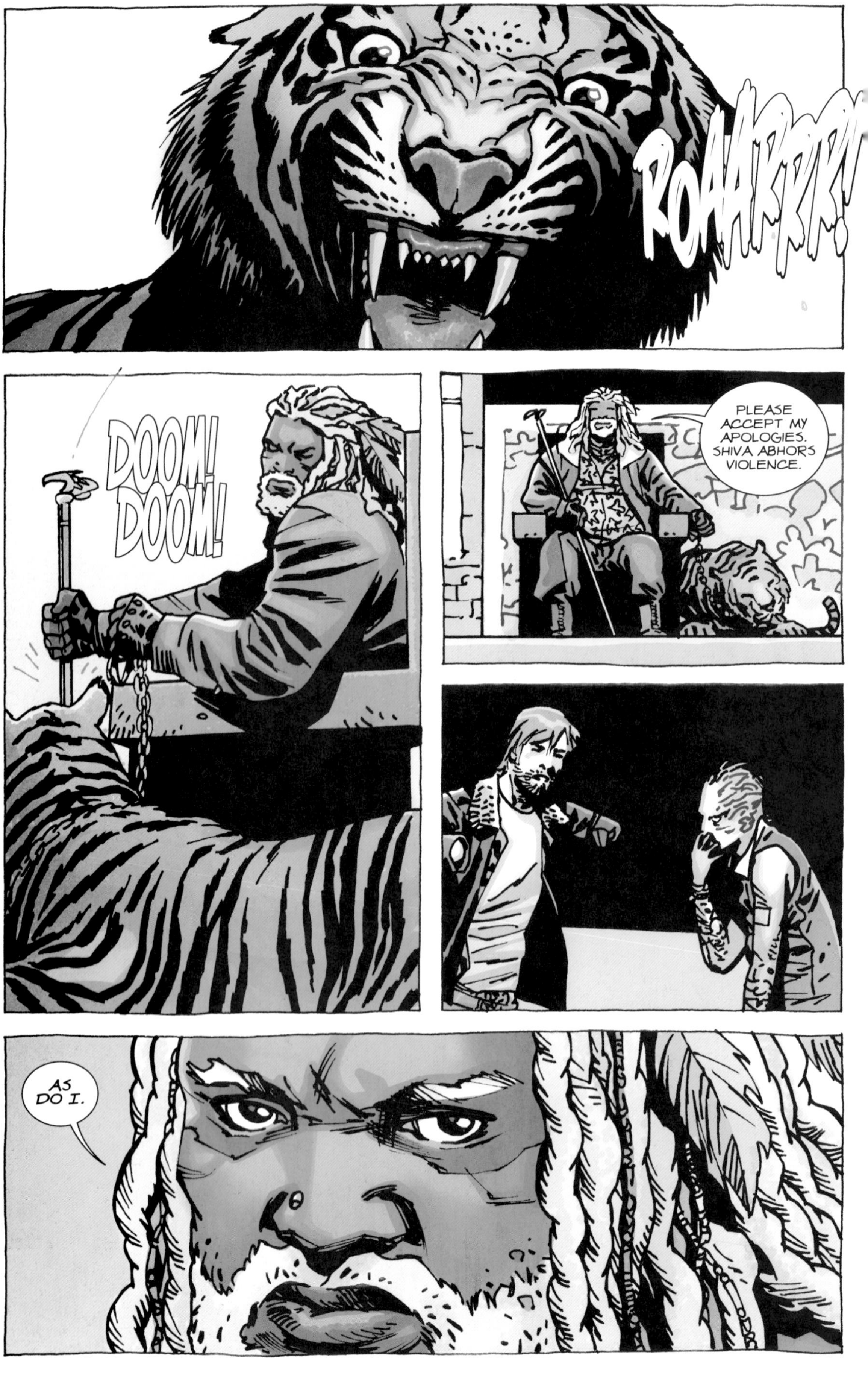
ROAARRR!
DOOM! DOOM!
PLEASE ACCEPT MY APOLOGIES. SHIVA ABHORS VIOLENCE.
AS DO I.

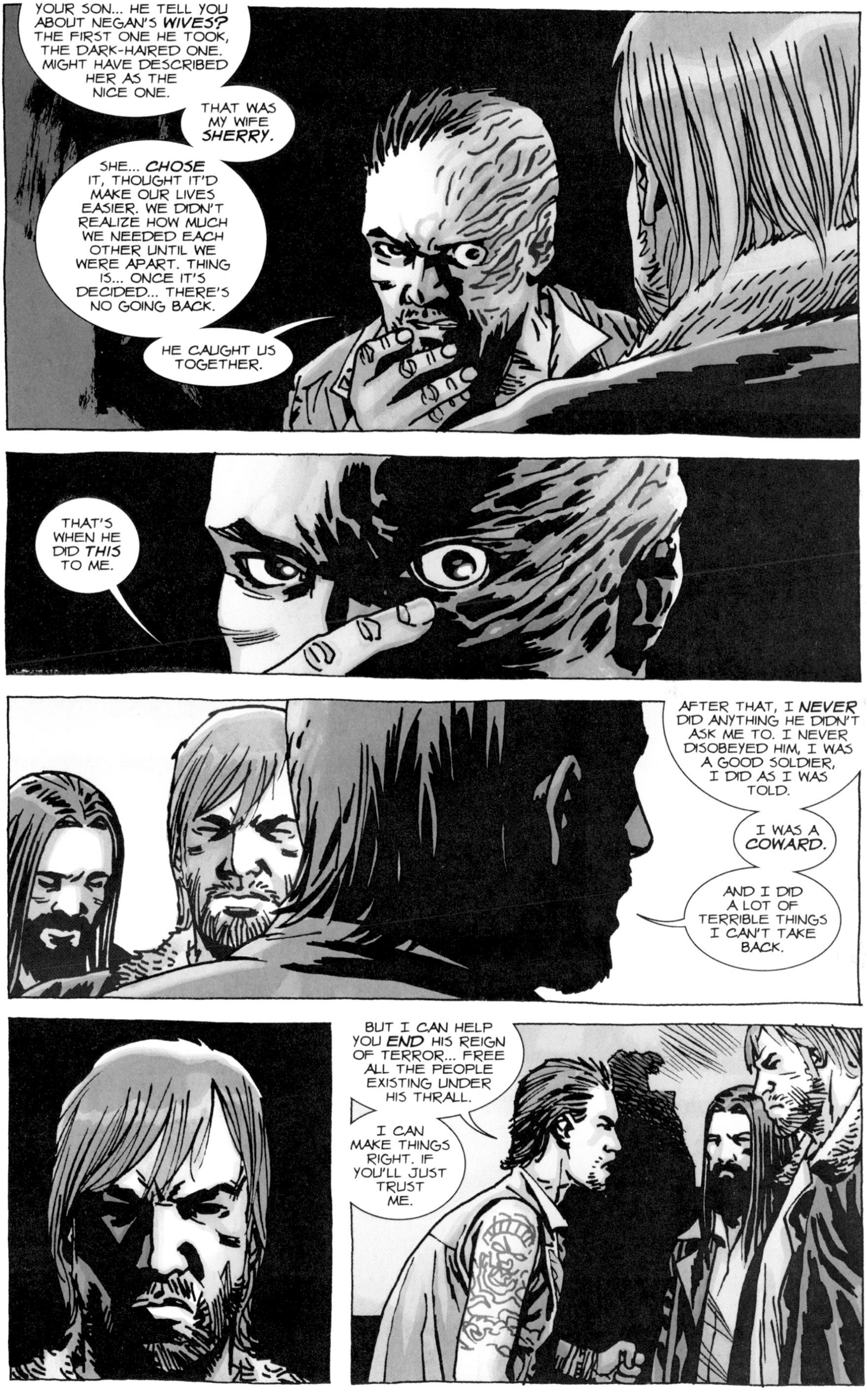
YOUR SON... HE TELL YOU ABOUT NEGAN'S WIVES? THE FIRST ONE HE TOOK, THE DARK-HAIRED ONE. MIGHT HAVE DESCRIBED HER AS THE NICE ONE.
THAT WAS MY WIFE SHERRY.
SHE... CHOSE IT, THOUGHT IT'D MAKE OUR LIVES EASIER. WE DIDN'T REALIZE HOW MUCH WE NEEDED EACH OTHER UNTIL WE WERE APART. THING IS... ONCE IT'S DECIDED... THERE'S NO GOING BACK.
HE CAUGHT US TOGETHER.
THAT'S WHEN HE DID THIS TO ME.
AFTER THAT, I NEVER DID ANYTHING HE DIDN'T ASK ME TO. I NEVER DISOBEYED HIM, I WAS A GOOD SOLDIER, I DID AS I WAS TOLD.
I WAS A COWARD.
AND I DID A LOT OF TERRIBLE THINGS I CAN'T TAKE BACK.
BUT I CAN HELP YOU END HIS REIGN OF TERROR... FREE ALL THE PEOPLE EXISTING UNDER HIS THRALL.
I CAN MAKE THINGS RIGHT. IF YOU'LL JUST TRUST ME.

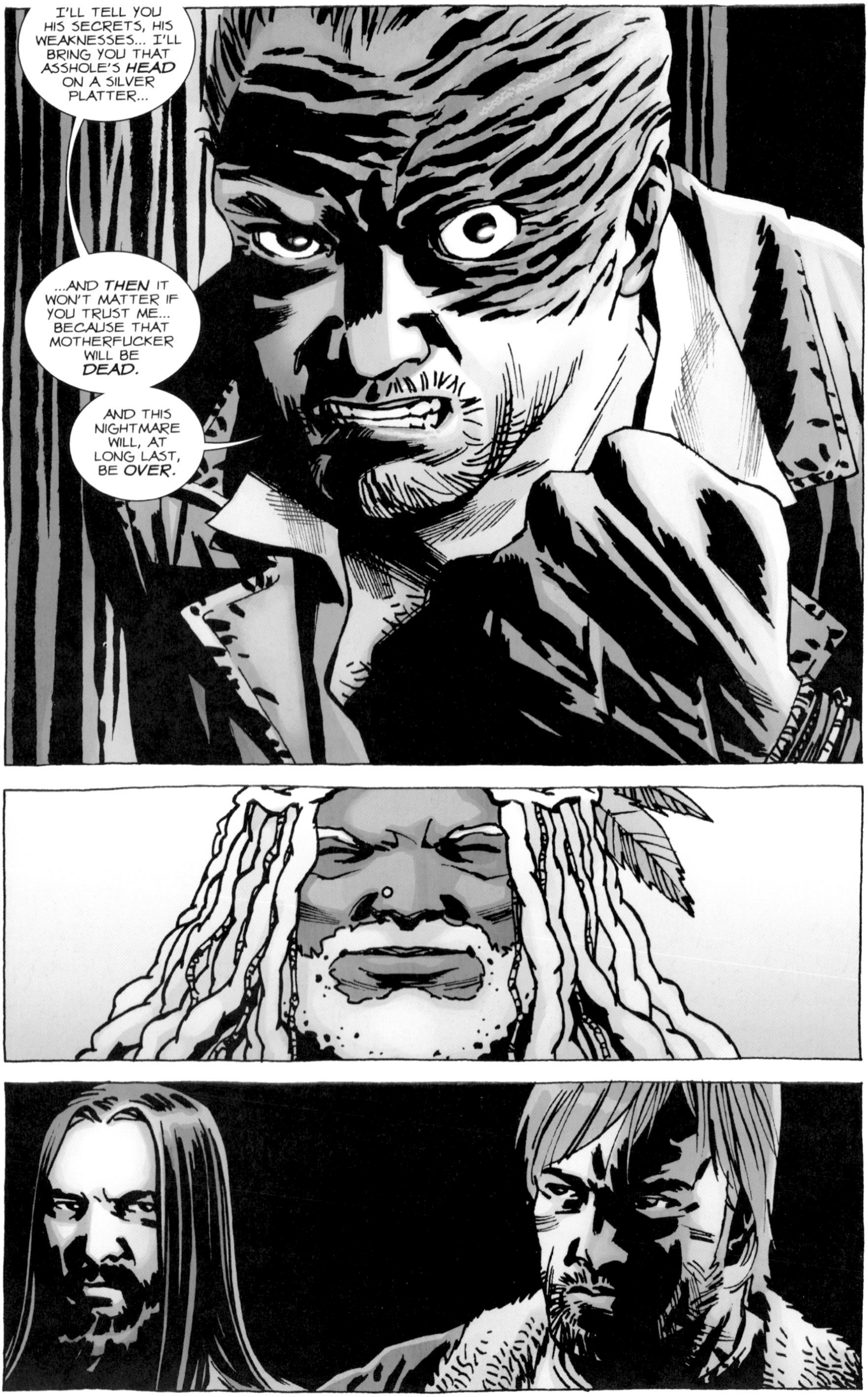
I'LL TELL YOU HIS SECRETS, HIS WEAKNESSES... I'LL BRING YOU THAT ASSHOLE'S HEAD ON A SILVER PLATTER...
...AND THEN IT WON'T MATTER IF YOU TRUST ME... BECAUSE THAT MOTHERFUCKER WILL BE DEAD.
AND THIS NIGHTMARE WILL, AT LONG LAST, BE OVER.

Chapter Nineteen: March to War

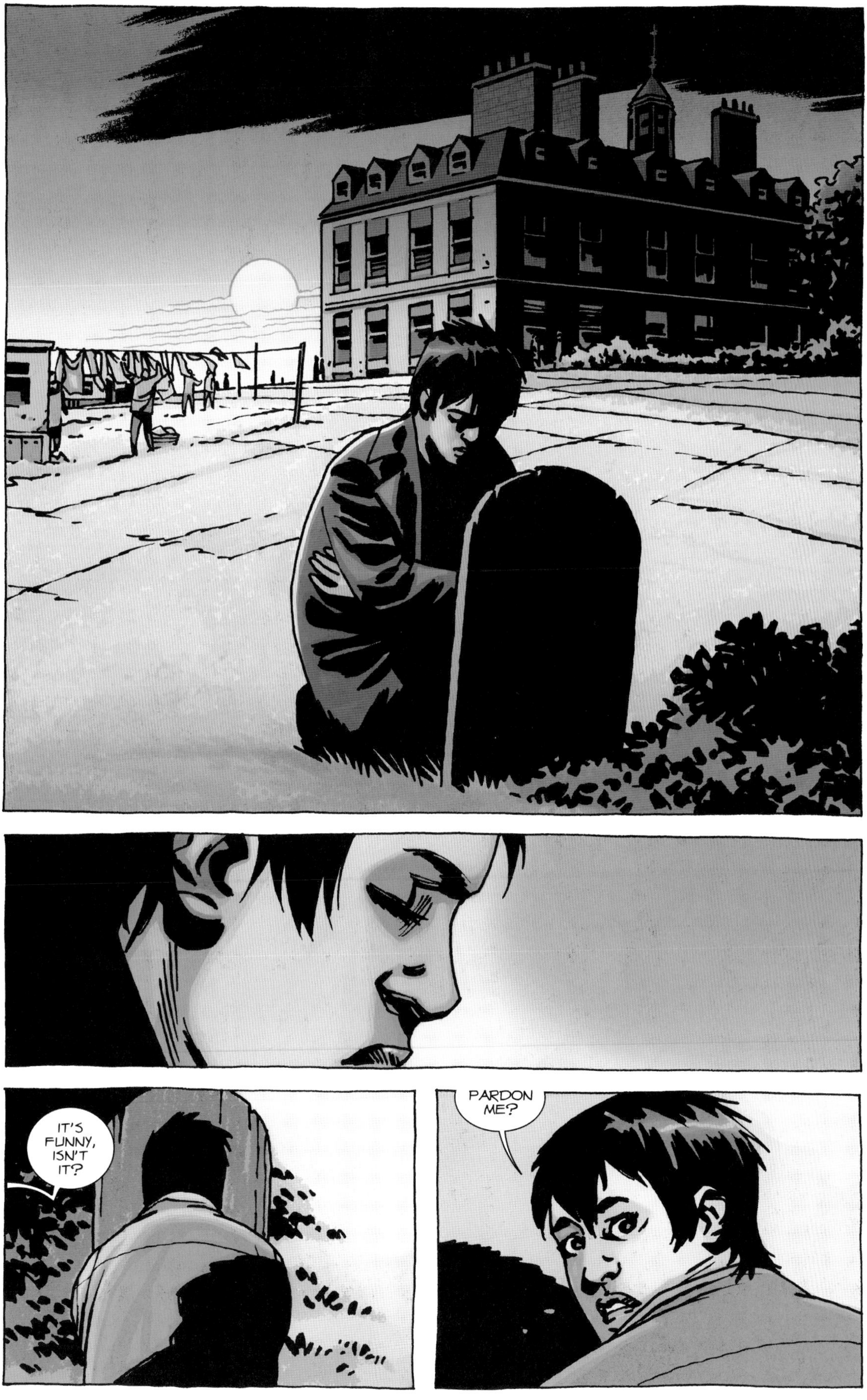
IT'S FUNNY, ISN'T IT?
PARDON ME?

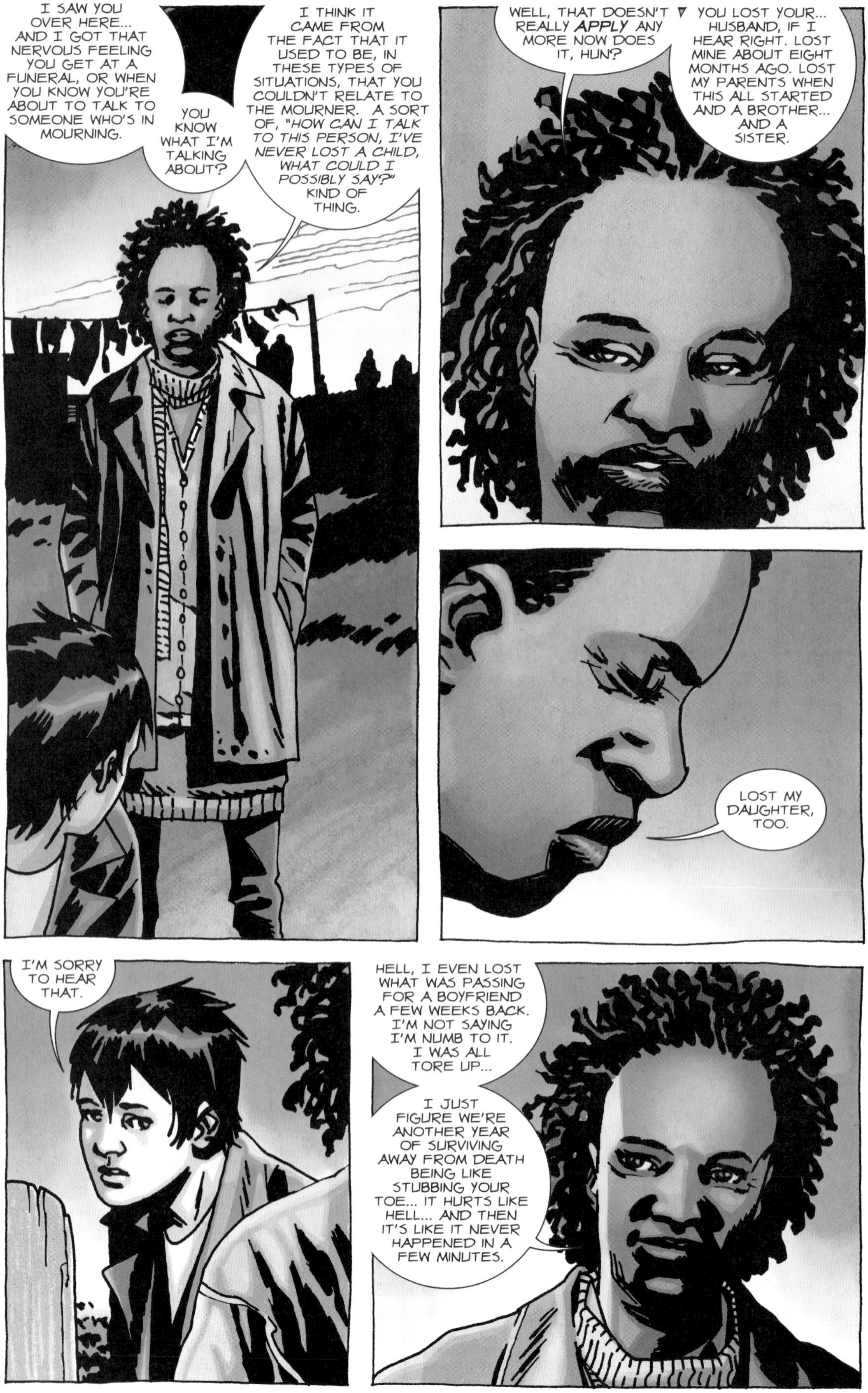
I SAW YOU OVER HERE... AND I GOT THAT NERVOUS FEELING YOU GET AT A FUNERAL, OR WHEN YOU KNOW YOU'RE ABOUT TO TALK TO SOMEONE WHO'S IN MOURNING.
YOU KNOW WHAT I'M TALKING ABOUT?
I THINK IT CAME FROM THE FACT THAT IT USED TO BE, IN THESE TYPES OF SITUATIONS, THAT YOU COULDN'T RELATE TO THE MOURNER. A SORT OF, "HOW CAN I TALK TO THIS PERSON, I'VE NEVER LOST A CHILD, WHAT COULD I POSSIBLY SAY?" KIND OF THING.
WELL, THAT DOESN'T REALLY APPLY ANY MORE NOW DOES IT, HUN?
YOU LOST YOUR... HUSBAND, IF I HEAR RIGHT. LOST MINE ABOUT EIGHT MONTHS AGO. LOST MY PARENTS WHEN THIS ALL STARTED AND A BROTHER... AND A SISTER.
LOST MY DAUGHTER, TOO.
I'M SORRY TO HEAR THAT.
HELL, I EVEN LOST WHAT WAS PASSING FOR A BOYFRIEND A FEW WEEKS BACK. I'M NOT SAYING I'M NUMB TO IT. I WAS ALL TORE UP...
I JUST FIGURE WE'RE ANOTHER YEAR OF SURVIVING AWAY FROM DEATH BEING LIKE STUBBING YOUR TOE... IT HURTS LIKE HELL... AND THEN IT'S LIKE IT NEVER HAPPENED IN A FEW MINUTES.

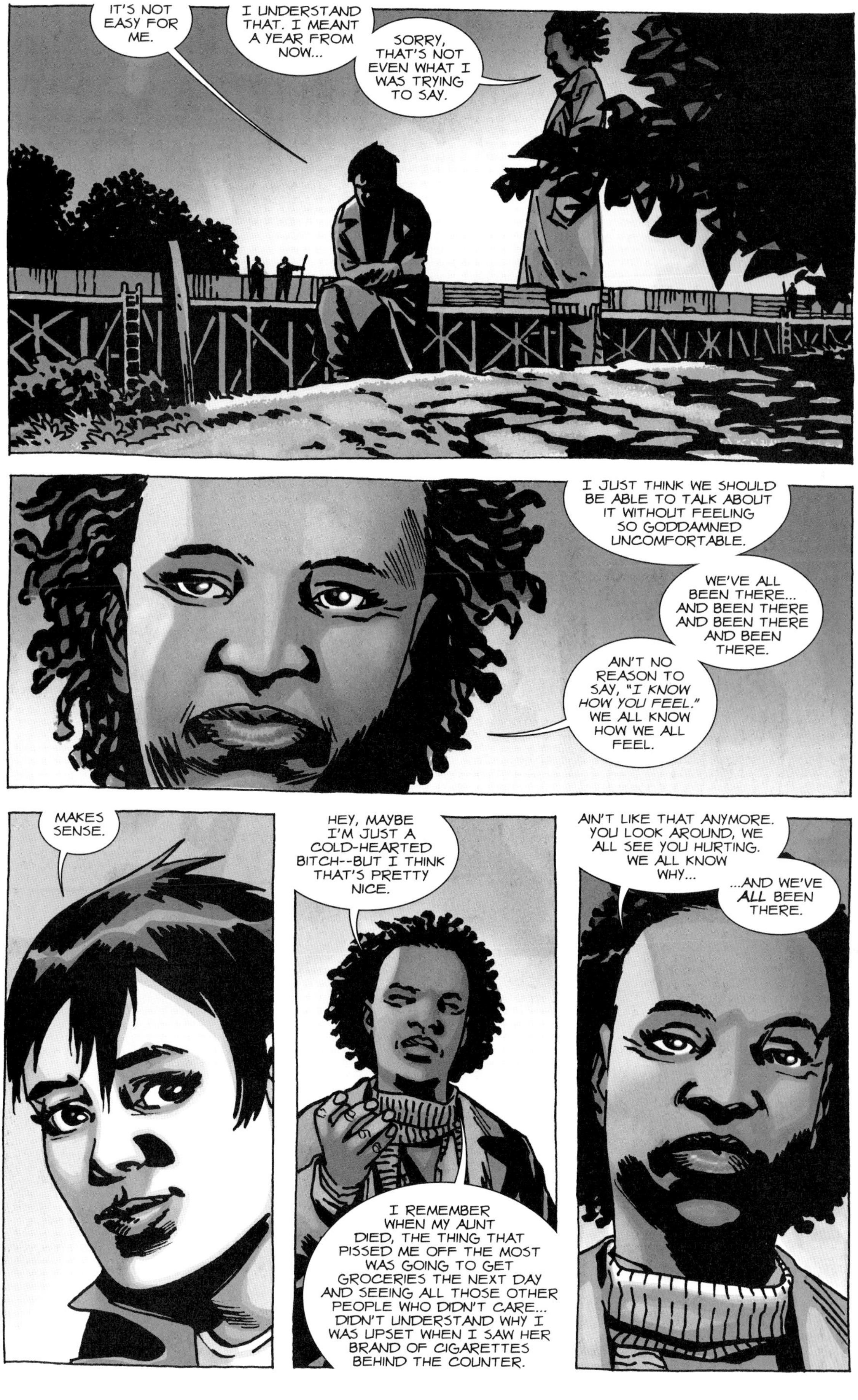
IT'S NOT EASY FOR ME.
I UNDERSTAND THAT. I MEANT A YEAR FROM NOW...
SORRY, THAT'S NOT EVEN WHAT I WAS TRYING TO SAY.
I JUST THINK WE SHOULD BE ABLE TO TALK ABOUT IT WITHOUT FEELING SO GODDAMNED UNCOMFORTABLE.
WE'VE ALL BEEN THERE... AND BEEN THERE AND BEEN THERE AND BEEN THERE.
AIN'T NO REASON TO SAY, *"I KNOW HOW YOU FEEL."* WE ALL KNOW HOW WE ALL FEEL.
MAKES SENSE.
HEY, MAYBE I'M JUST A COLD-HEARTED BITCH--BUT I THINK THAT'S PRETTY NICE.
I REMEMBER WHEN MY AUNT DIED, THE THING THAT PISSED ME OFF THE MOST WAS GOING TO GET GROCERIES THE NEXT DAY AND SEEING ALL THOSE OTHER PEOPLE WHO DIDN'T CARE... DIDN'T UNDERSTAND WHY I WAS UPSET WHEN I SAW HER BRAND OF CIGARETTES BEHIND THE COUNTER.
AIN'T LIKE THAT ANYMORE. YOU LOOK AROUND, WE ALL SEE YOU HURTING. WE ALL KNOW WHY...
...AND WE'VE ***ALL*** BEEN THERE.

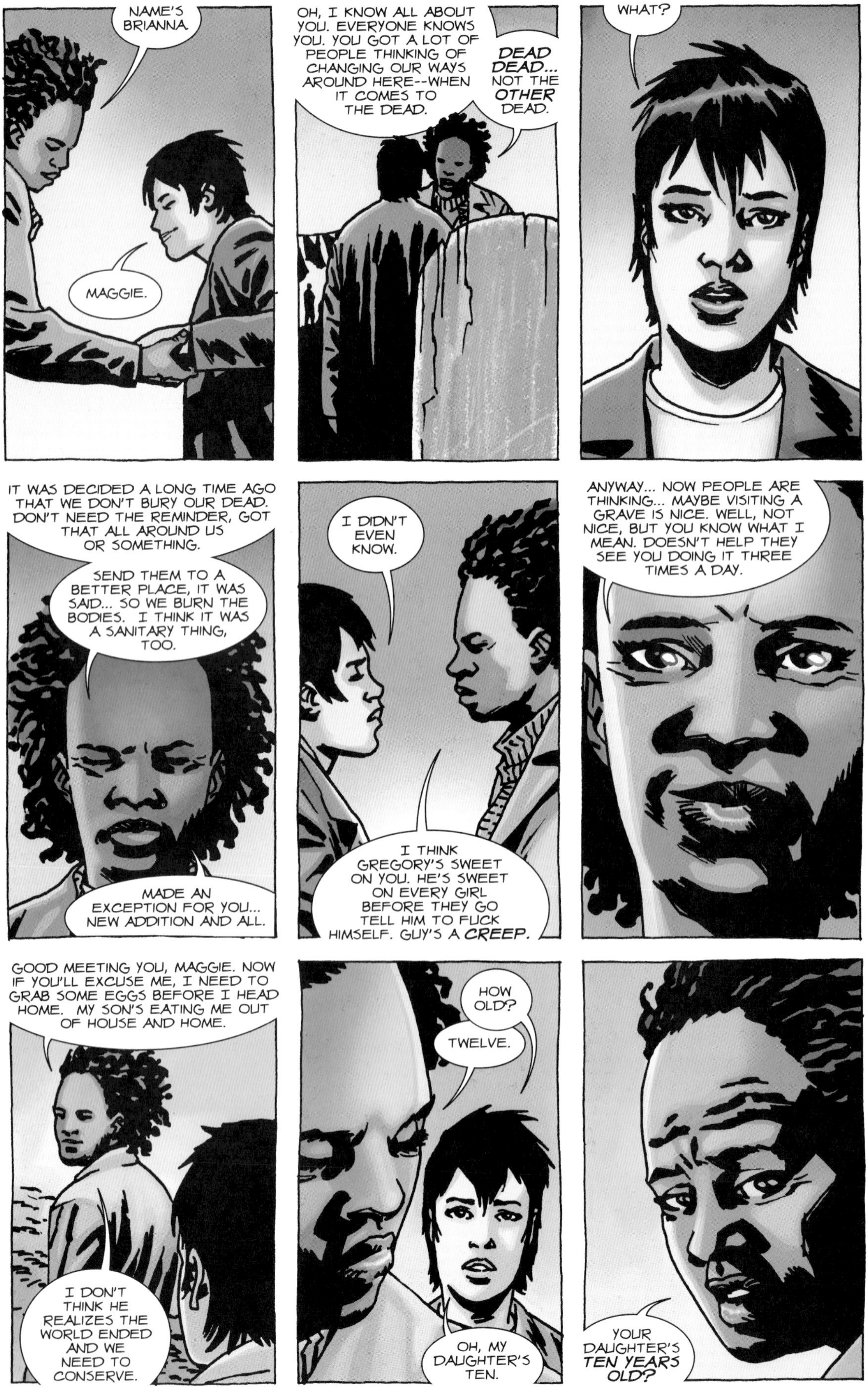
NAME'S BRIANNA.
MAGGIE.
OH, I KNOW ALL ABOUT YOU. EVERYONE KNOWS YOU. YOU GOT A LOT OF PEOPLE THINKING OF CHANGING OUR WAYS AROUND HERE--WHEN IT COMES TO THE DEAD.
DEAD DEAD... NOT THE OTHER DEAD.
WHAT?
IT WAS DECIDED A LONG TIME AGO THAT WE DON'T BURY OUR DEAD. DON'T NEED THE REMINDER, GOT THAT ALL AROUND US OR SOMETHING.
SEND THEM TO A BETTER PLACE, IT WAS SAID... SO WE BURN THE BODIES. I THINK IT WAS A SANITARY THING, TOO.
MADE AN EXCEPTION FOR YOU... NEW ADDITION AND ALL.
I DIDN'T EVEN KNOW.
I THINK GREGORY'S SWEET ON YOU. HE'S SWEET ON EVERY GIRL BEFORE THEY GO TELL HIM TO FUCK HIMSELF. GUY'S A CREEP.
ANYWAY... NOW PEOPLE ARE THINKING... MAYBE VISITING A GRAVE IS NICE. WELL, NOT NICE, BUT YOU KNOW WHAT I MEAN. DOESN'T HELP THEY SEE YOU DOING IT THREE TIMES A DAY.
GOOD MEETING YOU, MAGGIE. NOW IF YOU'LL EXCUSE ME, I NEED TO GRAB SOME EGGS BEFORE I HEAD HOME. MY SON'S EATING ME OUT OF HOUSE AND HOME.
I DON'T THINK HE REALIZES THE WORLD ENDED AND WE NEED TO CONSERVE.
HOW OLD?
TWELVE.
OH, MY DAUGHTER'S TEN.
YOUR DAUGHTER'S TEN YEARS OLD?

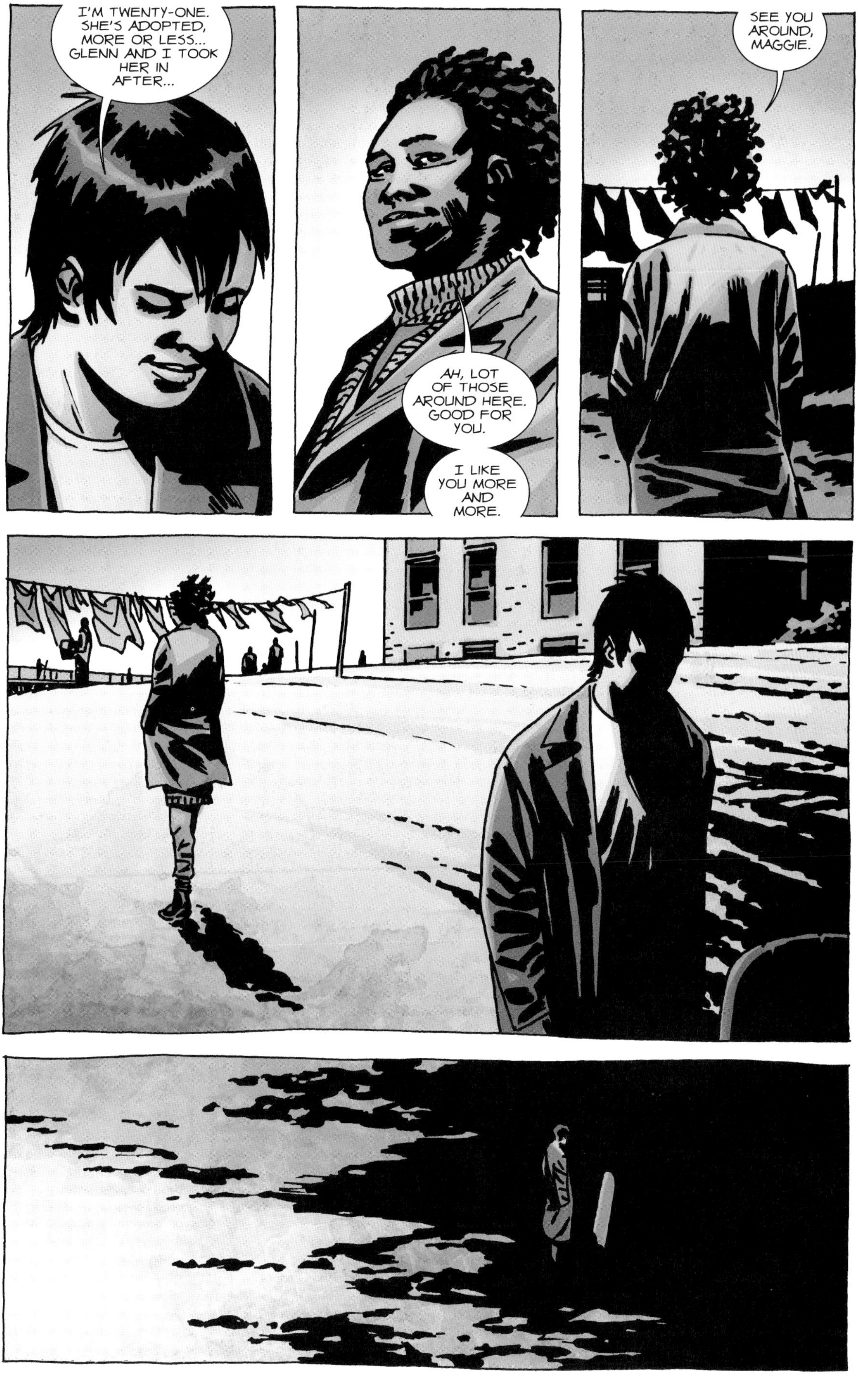
I'M TWENTY-ONE. SHE'S ADOPTED, MORE OR LESS... GLENN AND I TOOK HER IN AFTER...
AH, LOT OF THOSE AROUND HERE. GOOD FOR YOU.
I LIKE YOU MORE AND MORE.
SEE YOU AROUND, MAGGIE.

EVERYTHING LOOKS TO BE PROCEEDING EXACTLY HOW IT SHOULD BE.

NO NEWS IS GOOD NEWS. NATURE'S DOING ITS THING.

CONGRATULATIONS.

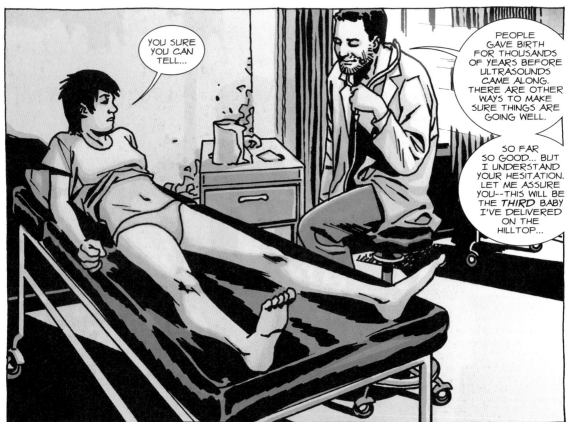

YOU SURE YOU CAN TELL...

PEOPLE GAVE BIRTH FOR THOUSANDS OF YEARS BEFORE ULTRASOUNDS CAME ALONG. THERE ARE OTHER WAYS TO MAKE SURE THINGS ARE GOING WELL.

SO FAR SO GOOD... BUT I UNDERSTAND YOUR HESITATION. LET ME ASSURE YOU--THIS WILL BE THE *THIRD* BABY I'VE DELIVERED ON THE HILLTOP...

WE KNOW WHAT WE'RE DOING.

I CAN VOUCH FOR THAT.

UH...

GREGORY, PLEASE.

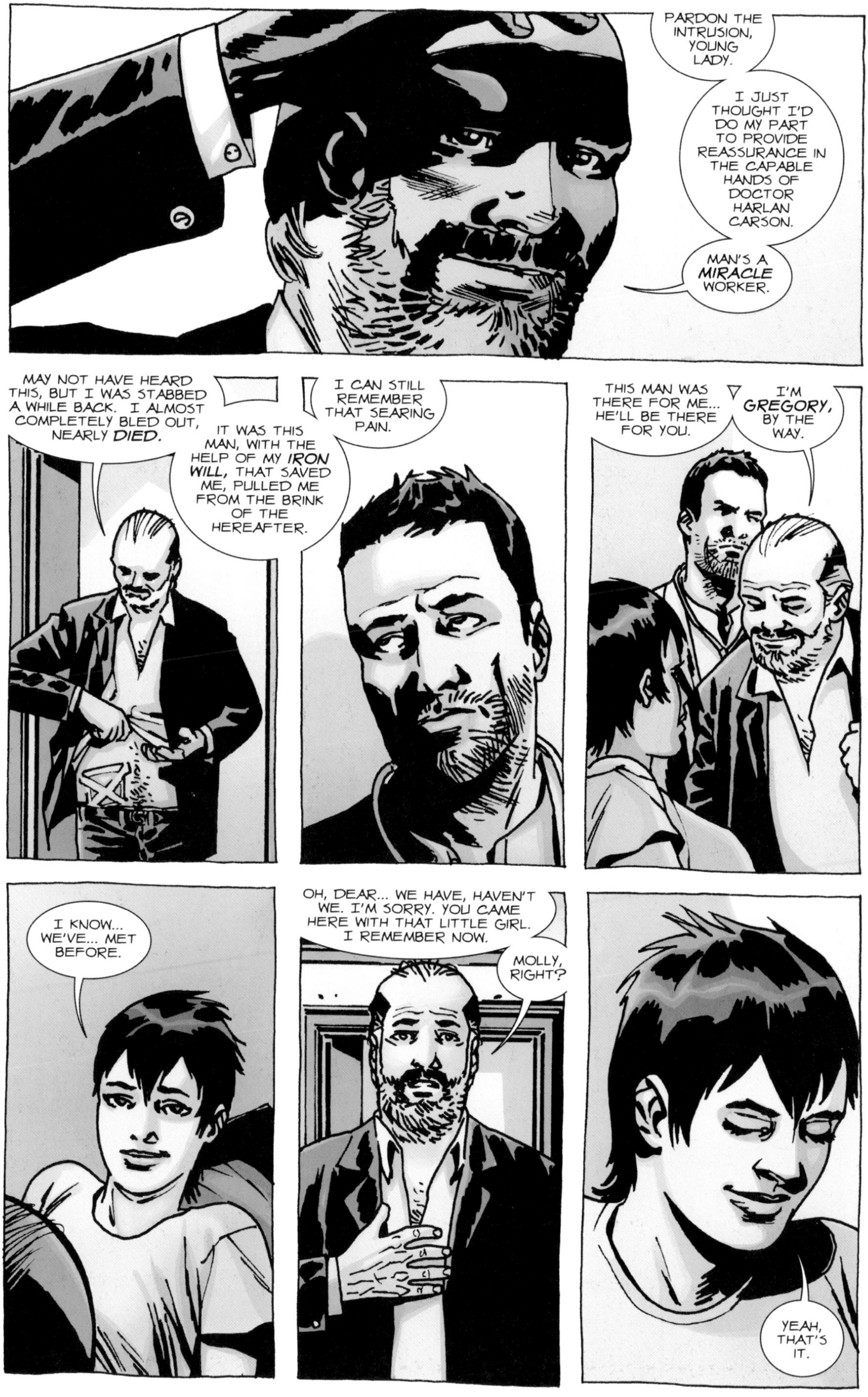
PARDON THE INTRUSION, YOUNG LADY.
I JUST THOUGHT I'D DO MY PART TO PROVIDE REASSURANCE IN THE CAPABLE HANDS OF DOCTOR HARLAN CARSON.
MAN'S A MIRACLE WORKER.
MAY NOT HAVE HEARD THIS, BUT I WAS STABBED A WHILE BACK. I ALMOST COMPLETELY BLED OUT, NEARLY DIED.
IT WAS THIS MAN, WITH THE HELP OF MY IRON WILL, THAT SAVED ME, PULLED ME FROM THE BRINK OF THE HEREAFTER.
I CAN STILL REMEMBER THAT SEARING PAIN.
THIS MAN WAS THERE FOR ME... HE'LL BE THERE FOR YOU.
I'M GREGORY, BY THE WAY.
I KNOW... WE'VE... MET BEFORE.
OH, DEAR... WE HAVE, HAVEN'T WE. I'M SORRY. YOU CAME HERE WITH THAT LITTLE GIRL. I REMEMBER NOW.
MOLLY, RIGHT?
YEAH, THAT'S IT.

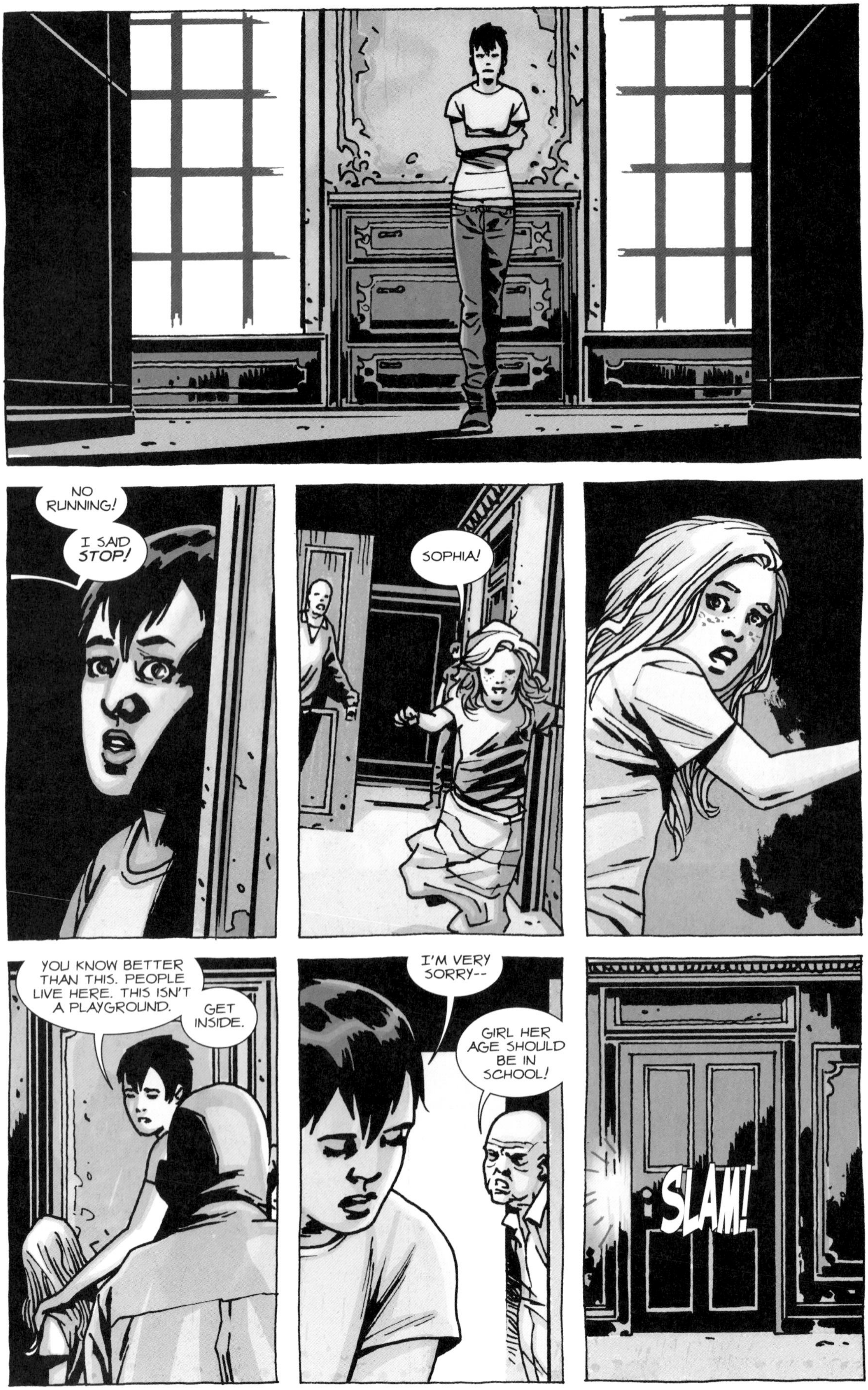
NO RUNNING!
I SAID STOP!
SOPHIA!
YOU KNOW BETTER THAN THIS. PEOPLE LIVE HERE. THIS ISN'T A PLAYGROUND.
GET INSIDE.
I'M VERY SORRY--
GIRL HER AGE SHOULD BE IN SCHOOL!
SLAM!

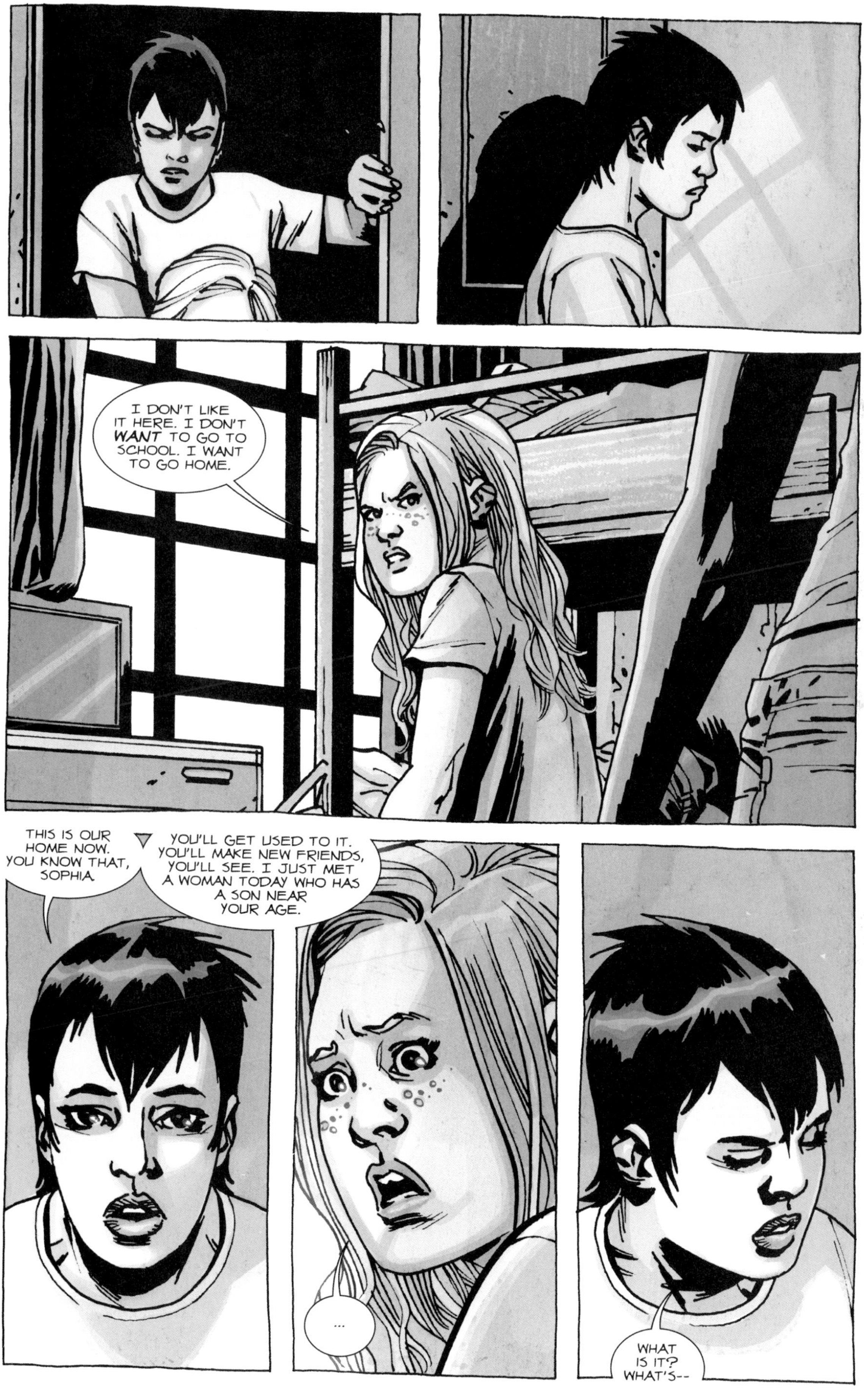
I DON'T LIKE IT HERE. I DON'T WANT TO GO TO SCHOOL. I WANT TO GO HOME.
THIS IS OUR HOME NOW. YOU KNOW THAT, SOPHIA.
YOU'LL GET USED TO IT. YOU'LL MAKE NEW FRIENDS, YOU'LL SEE. I JUST MET A WOMAN TODAY WHO HAS A SON NEAR YOUR AGE.
...
WHAT IS IT? WHAT'S--

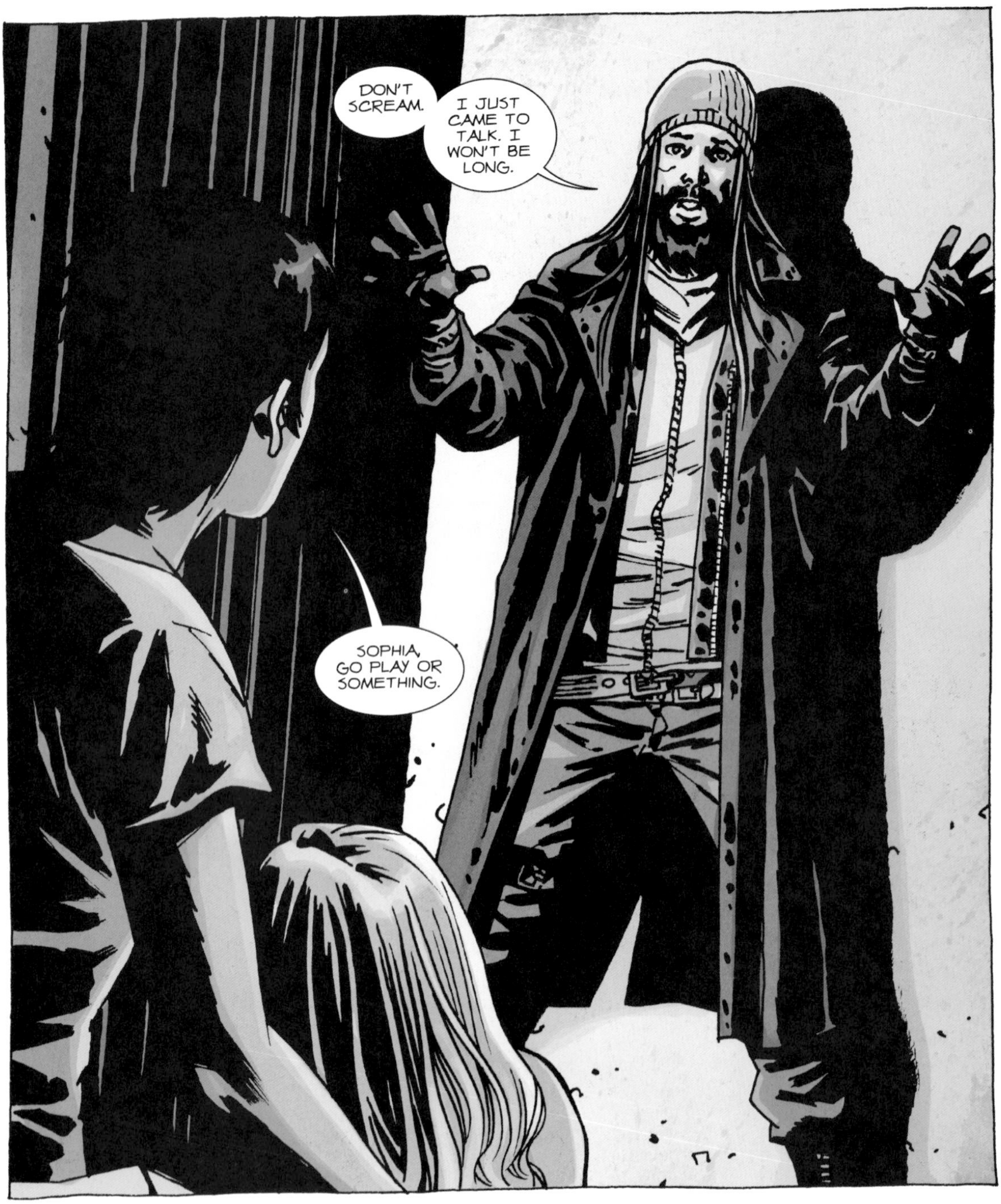
DON'T SCREAM.
I JUST CAME TO TALK. I WON'T BE LONG.
SOPHIA, GO PLAY OR SOMETHING.
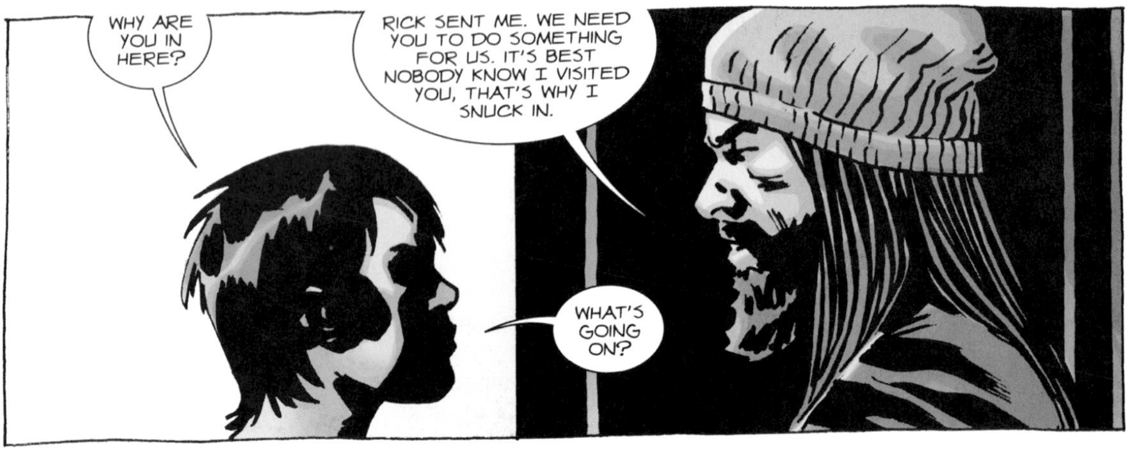
WHY ARE YOU IN HERE?
RICK SENT ME. WE NEED YOU TO DO SOMETHING FOR US. IT'S BEST NOBODY KNOW I VISITED YOU, THAT'S WHY I SNUCK IN.
WHAT'S GOING ON?

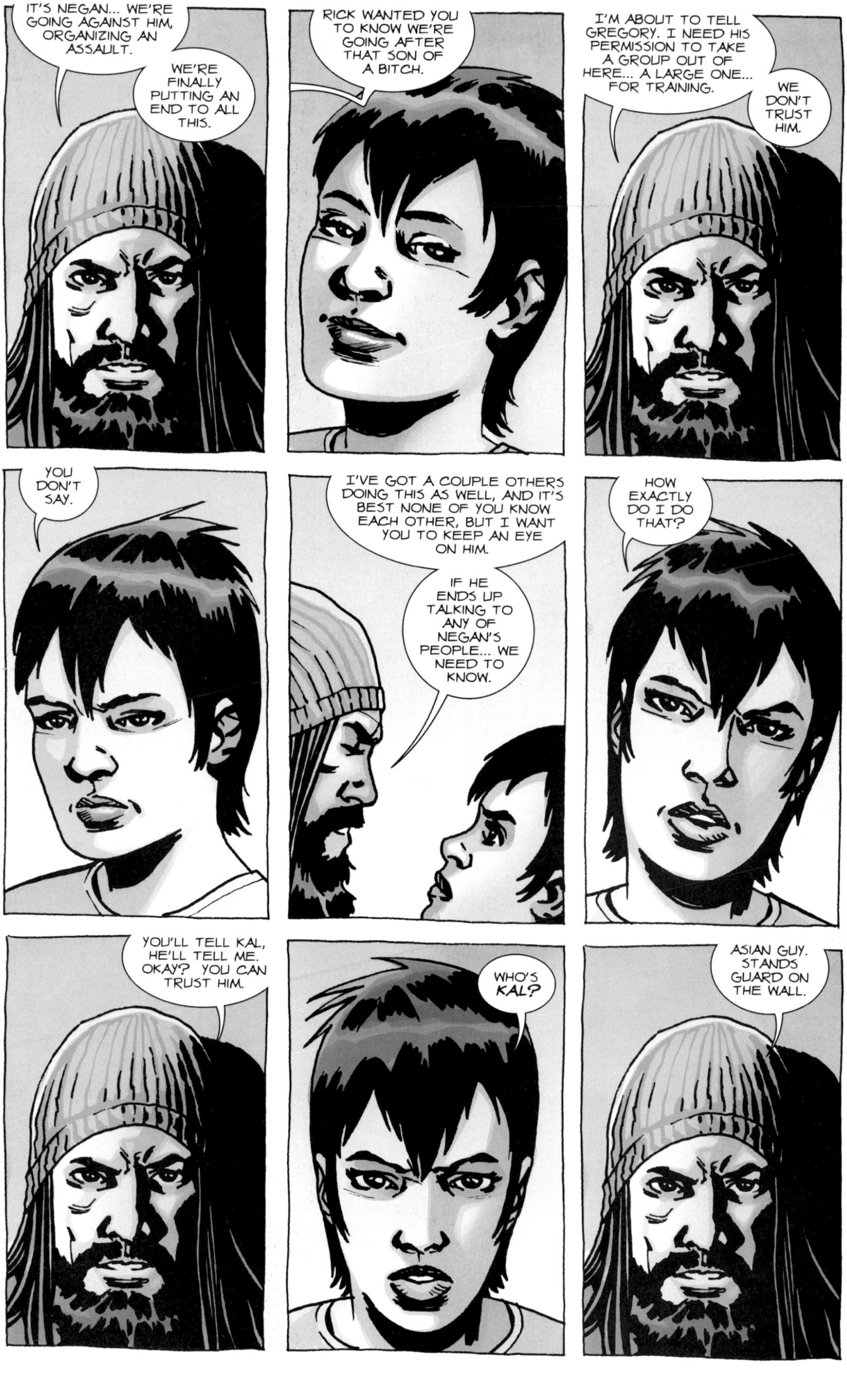
IT'S NEGAN... WE'RE GOING AGAINST HIM, ORGANIZING AN ASSAULT.
WE'RE FINALLY PUTTING AN END TO ALL THIS.
RICK WANTED YOU TO KNOW WE'RE GOING AFTER THAT SON OF A BITCH.
I'M ABOUT TO TELL GREGORY. I NEED HIS PERMISSION TO TAKE A GROUP OUT OF HERE... A LARGE ONE... FOR TRAINING.
WE DON'T TRUST HIM.
YOU DON'T SAY.
I'VE GOT A COUPLE OTHERS DOING THIS AS WELL, AND IT'S BEST NONE OF YOU KNOW EACH OTHER, BUT I WANT YOU TO KEEP AN EYE ON HIM.
IF HE ENDS UP TALKING TO ANY OF NEGAN'S PEOPLE... WE NEED TO KNOW.
HOW EXACTLY DO I DO THAT?
YOU'LL TELL KAL, HE'LL TELL ME. OKAY? YOU CAN TRUST HIM.
WHO'S *KAL?*
ASIAN GUY. STANDS GUARD ON THE WALL.

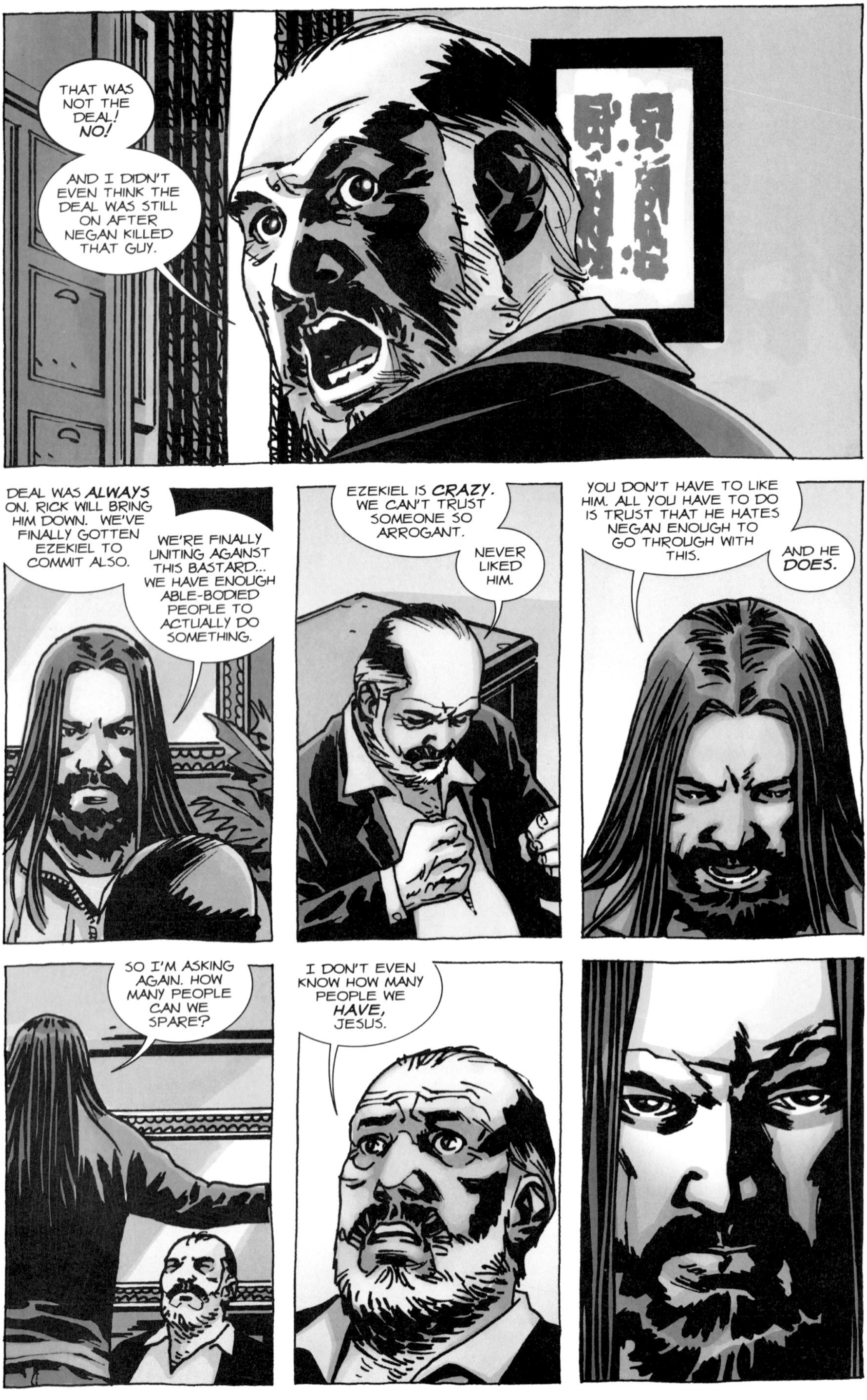
THAT WAS NOT THE DEAL! NO!
AND I DIDN'T EVEN THINK THE DEAL WAS STILL ON AFTER NEGAN KILLED THAT GUY.
DEAL WAS ALWAYS ON. RICK WILL BRING HIM DOWN. WE'VE FINALLY GOTTEN EZEKIEL TO COMMIT ALSO.
WE'RE FINALLY UNITING AGAINST THIS BASTARD... WE HAVE ENOUGH ABLE-BODIED PEOPLE TO ACTUALLY DO SOMETHING.
EZEKIEL IS CRAZY. WE CAN'T TRUST SOMEONE SO ARROGANT.
NEVER LIKED HIM.
YOU DON'T HAVE TO LIKE HIM. ALL YOU HAVE TO DO IS TRUST THAT HE HATES NEGAN ENOUGH TO GO THROUGH WITH THIS.
AND HE DOES.
SO I'M ASKING AGAIN. HOW MANY PEOPLE CAN WE SPARE?
I DON'T EVEN KNOW HOW MANY PEOPLE WE HAVE, JESUS.

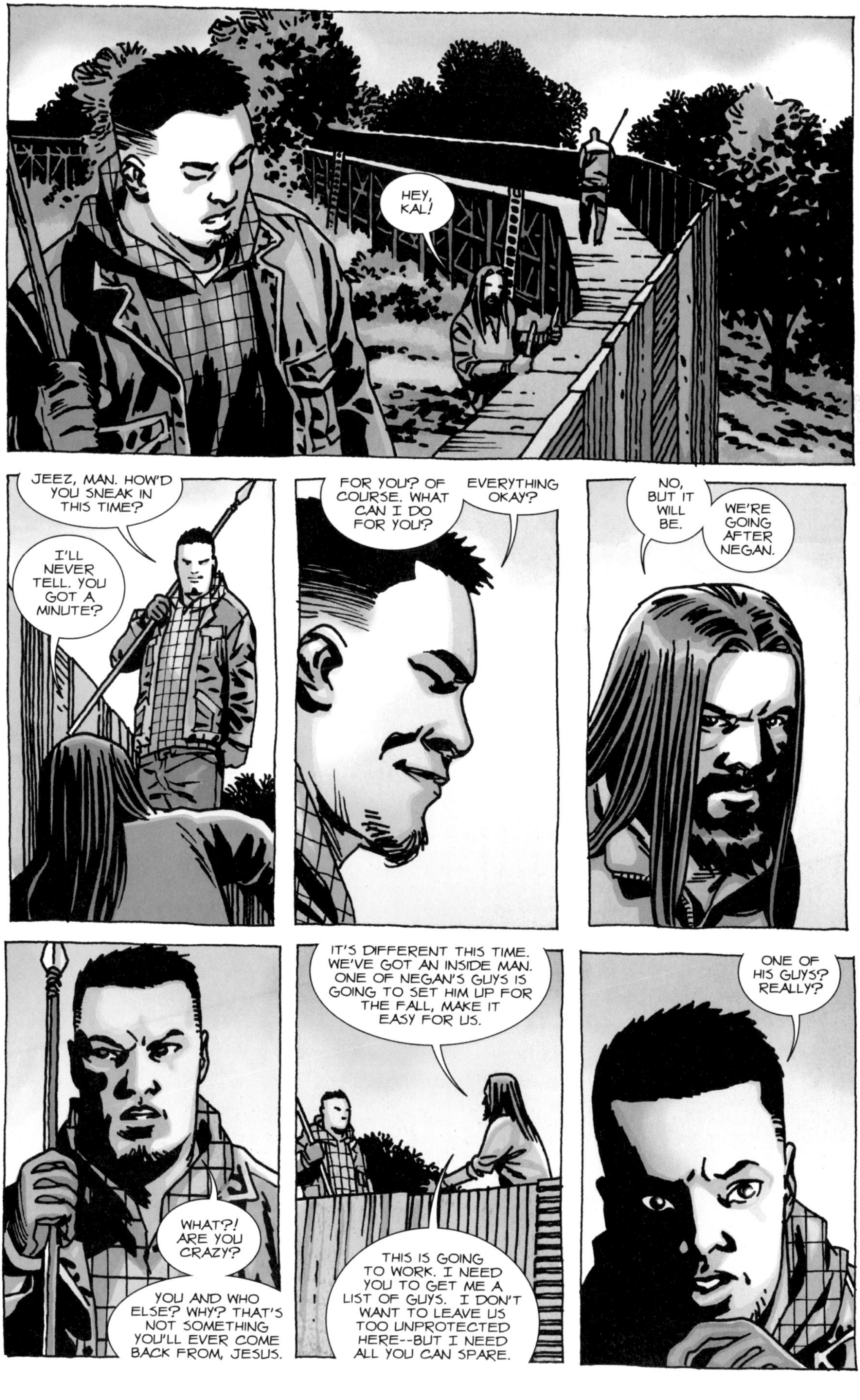
HEY, KAL!
JEEZ, MAN. HOW'D YOU SNEAK IN THIS TIME?
I'LL NEVER TELL. YOU GOT A MINUTE?
FOR YOU? OF COURSE. WHAT CAN I DO FOR YOU?
EVERYTHING OKAY?
NO, BUT IT WILL BE.
WE'RE GOING AFTER NEGAN.
WHAT?! ARE YOU CRAZY?
YOU AND WHO ELSE? WHY? THAT'S NOT SOMETHING YOU'LL EVER COME BACK FROM, JESUS.
IT'S DIFFERENT THIS TIME. WE'VE GOT AN INSIDE MAN. ONE OF NEGAN'S GUYS IS GOING TO SET HIM UP FOR THE FALL, MAKE IT EASY FOR US.
THIS IS GOING TO WORK. I NEED YOU TO GET ME A LIST OF GUYS. I DON'T WANT TO LEAVE US TOO UNPROTECTED HERE--BUT I NEED ALL YOU CAN SPARE.
ONE OF HIS GUYS? REALLY?

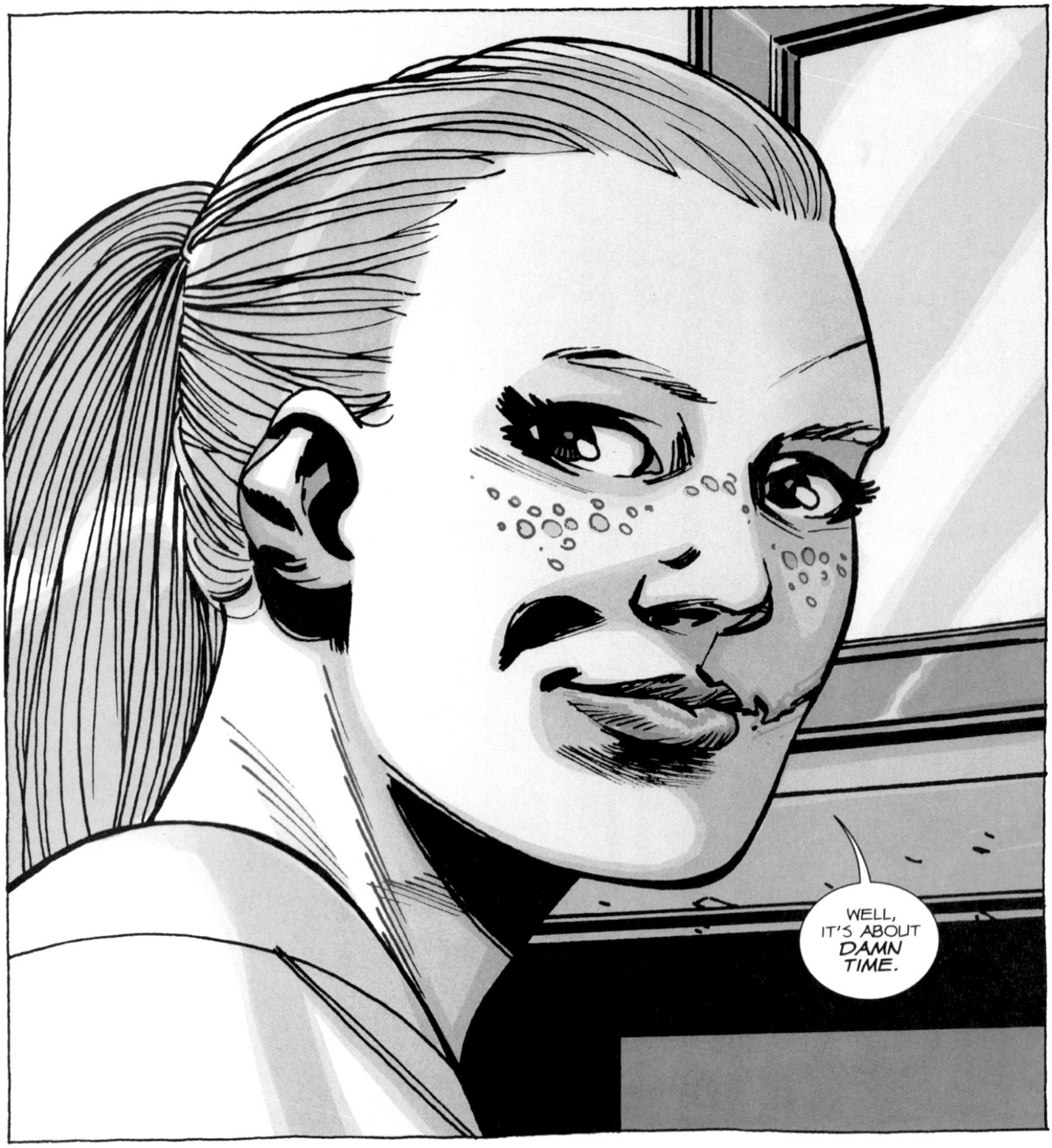
WELL, IT'S ABOUT DAMN TIME.

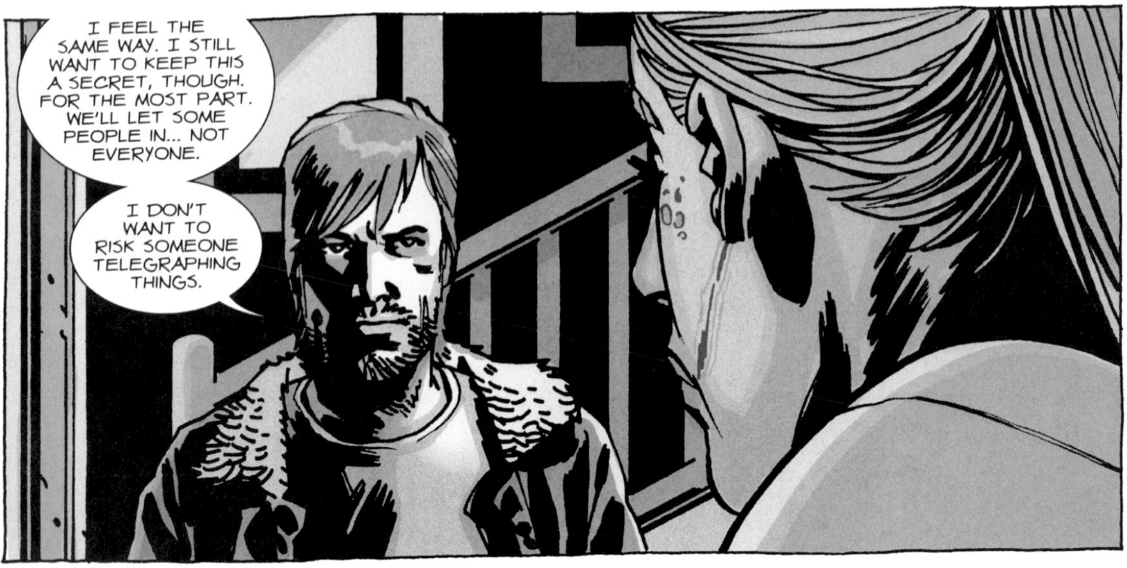
I FEEL THE SAME WAY. I STILL WANT TO KEEP THIS A SECRET, THOUGH. FOR THE MOST PART. WE'LL LET SOME PEOPLE IN... NOT EVERYONE.
I DON'T WANT TO RISK SOMEONE TELEGRAPHING THINGS.

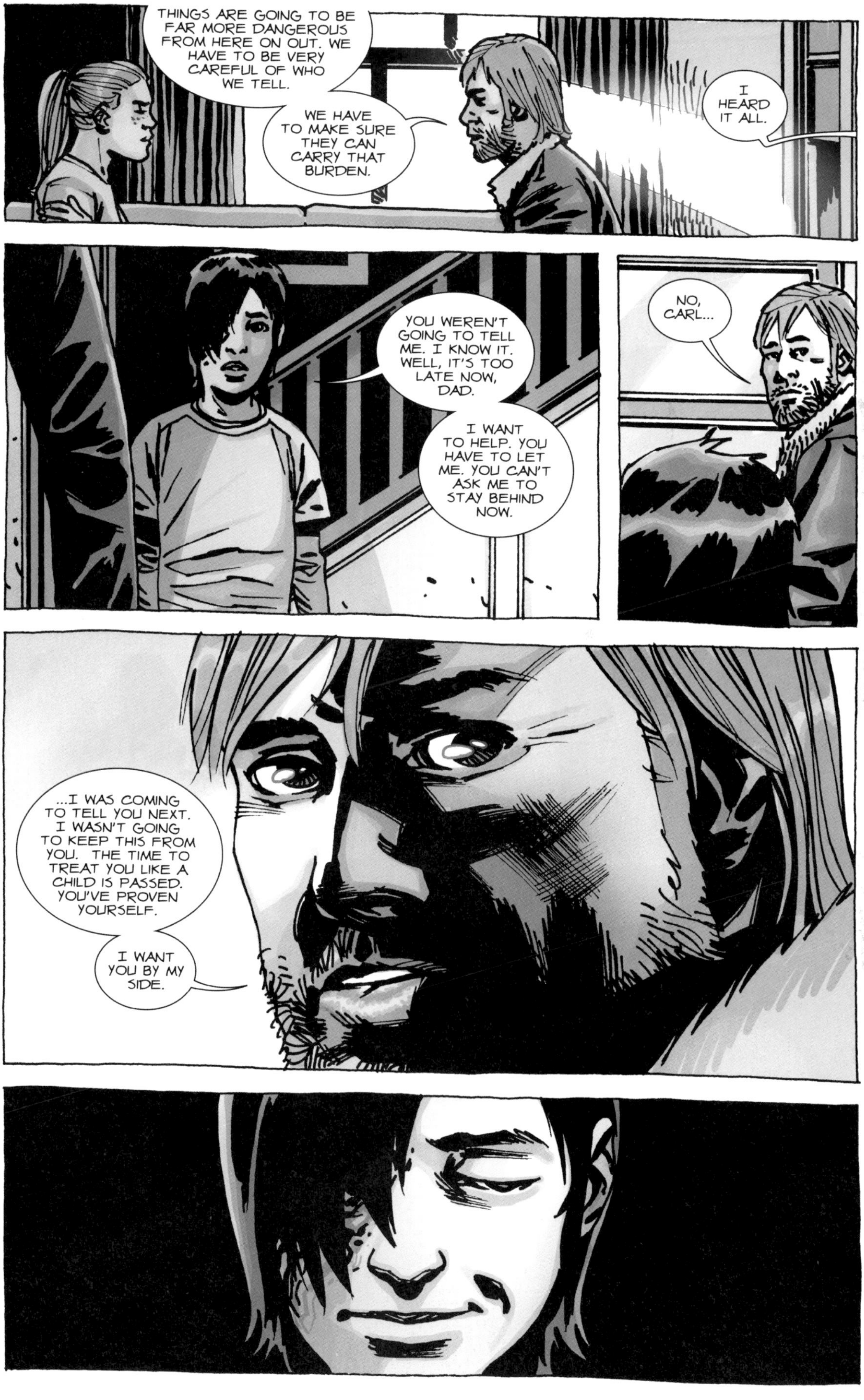
THINGS ARE GOING TO BE FAR MORE DANGEROUS FROM HERE ON OUT. WE HAVE TO BE VERY CAREFUL OF WHO WE TELL.
WE HAVE TO MAKE SURE THEY CAN CARRY THAT BURDEN.
I HEARD IT ALL.
YOU WEREN'T GOING TO TELL ME. I KNOW IT. WELL, IT'S TOO LATE NOW, DAD.
I WANT TO HELP. YOU HAVE TO LET ME. YOU CAN'T ASK ME TO STAY BEHIND NOW.
NO, CARL...
...I WAS COMING TO TELL YOU NEXT. I WASN'T GOING TO KEEP THIS FROM YOU. THE TIME TO TREAT YOU LIKE A CHILD IS PASSED. YOU'VE PROVEN YOURSELF.
I WANT YOU BY MY SIDE.

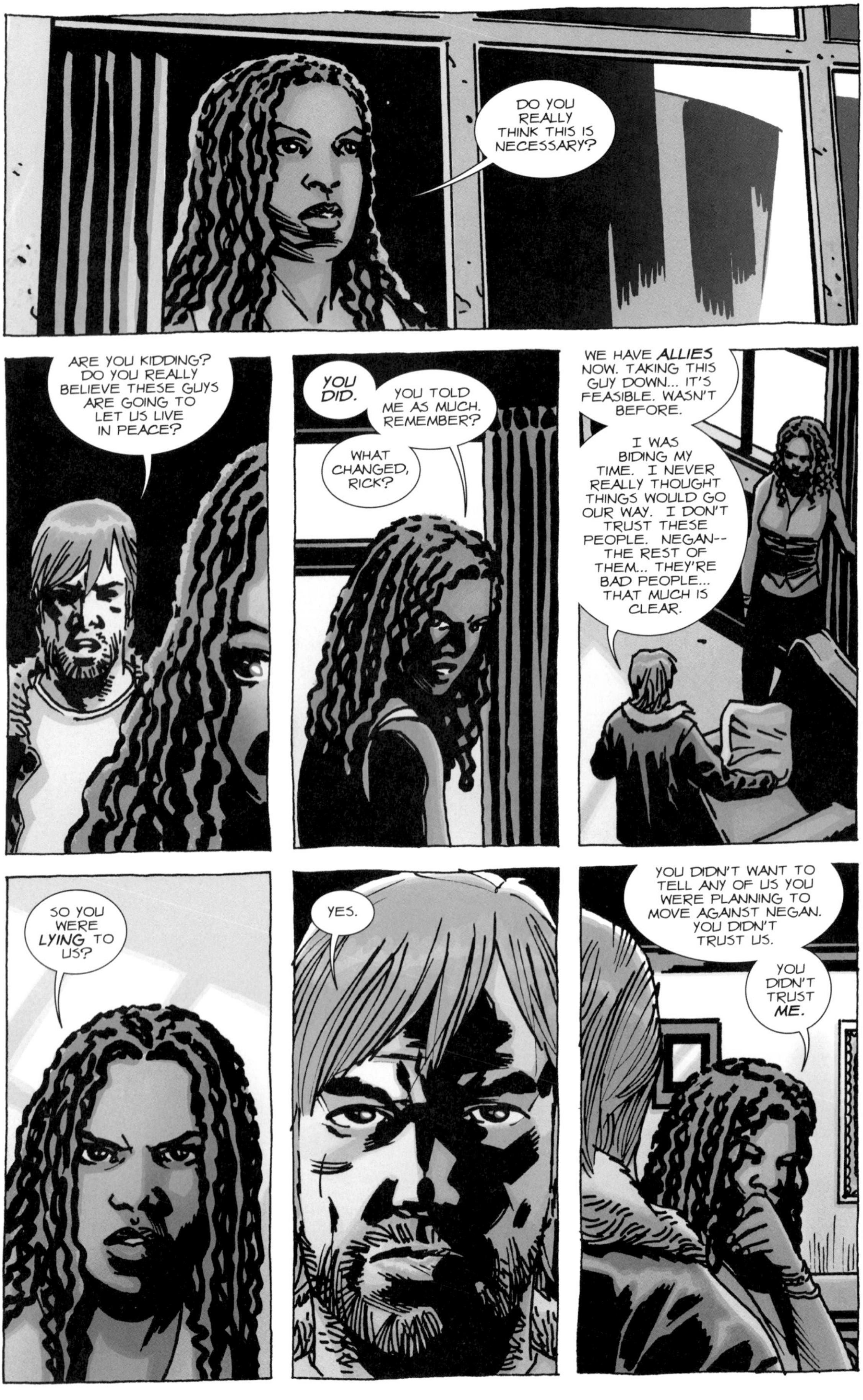

DO YOU REALLY THINK THIS IS NECESSARY?
ARE YOU KIDDING? DO YOU REALLY BELIEVE THESE GUYS ARE GOING TO LET US LIVE IN PEACE?
YOU DID.
YOU TOLD ME AS MUCH. REMEMBER?
WHAT CHANGED, RICK?
WE HAVE ALLIES NOW. TAKING THIS GUY DOWN... IT'S FEASIBLE. WASN'T BEFORE.
I WAS BIDING MY TIME. I NEVER REALLY THOUGHT THINGS WOULD GO OUR WAY. I DON'T TRUST THESE PEOPLE. NEGAN-- THE REST OF THEM... THEY'RE BAD PEOPLE... THAT MUCH IS CLEAR.
SO YOU WERE LYING TO US?
YES.
YOU DIDN'T WANT TO TELL ANY OF US YOU WERE PLANNING TO MOVE AGAINST NEGAN. YOU DIDN'T TRUST US.
YOU DIDN'T TRUST ME.

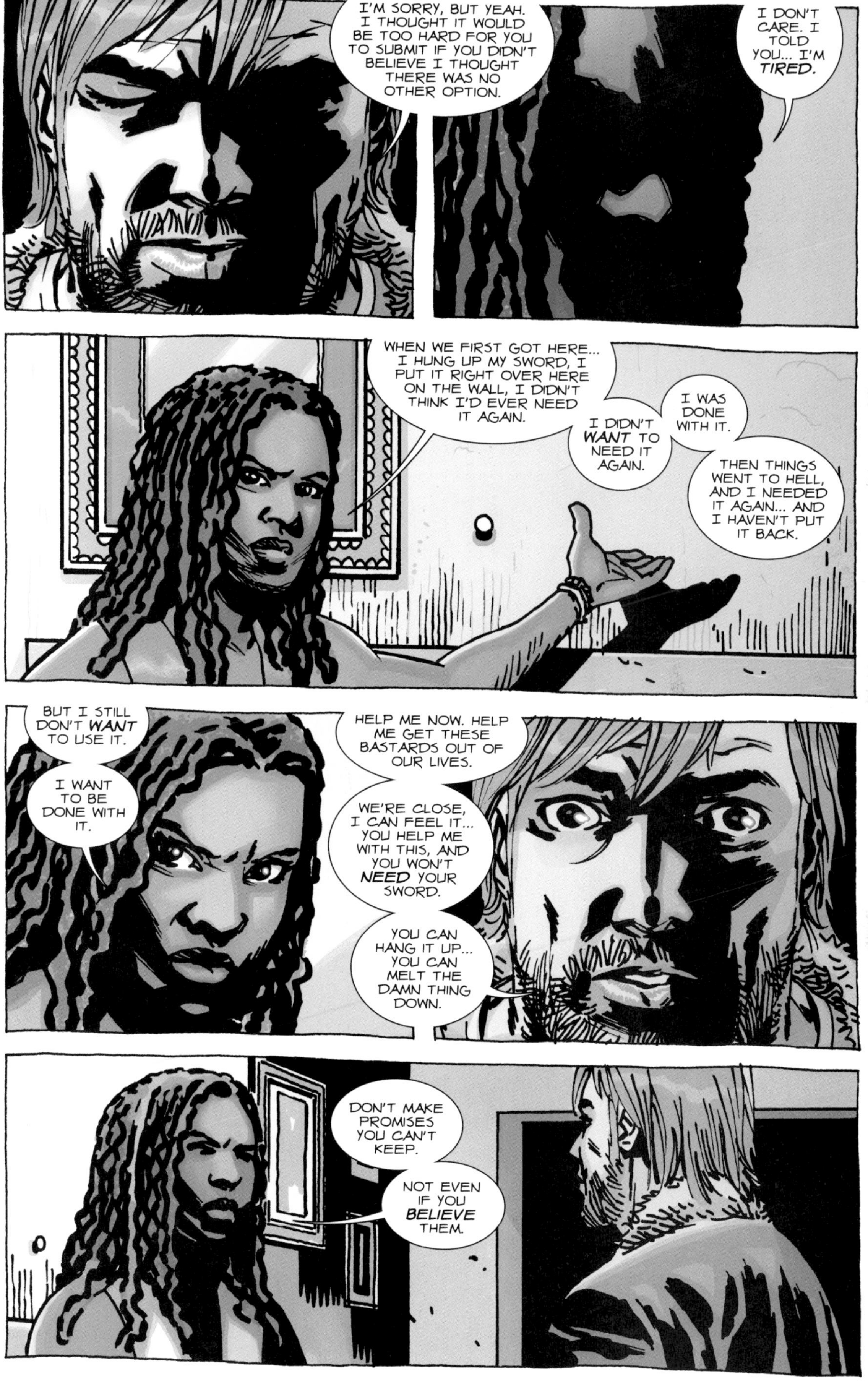

I'M SORRY, BUT YEAH. I THOUGHT IT WOULD BE TOO HARD FOR YOU TO SUBMIT IF YOU DIDN'T BELIEVE I THOUGHT THERE WAS NO OTHER OPTION.
I DON'T CARE. I TOLD YOU... I'M *TIRED.*
WHEN WE FIRST GOT HERE... I HUNG UP MY SWORD, I PUT IT RIGHT OVER HERE ON THE WALL, I DIDN'T THINK I'D EVER NEED IT AGAIN.
I DIDN'T *WANT* TO NEED IT AGAIN.
I WAS DONE WITH IT.
THEN THINGS WENT TO HELL, AND I NEEDED IT AGAIN... AND I HAVEN'T PUT IT BACK.
BUT I STILL DON'T *WANT* TO USE IT.
I WANT TO BE DONE WITH IT.
HELP ME NOW. HELP ME GET THESE BASTARDS OUT OF OUR LIVES.
WE'RE CLOSE, I CAN FEEL IT... YOU HELP ME WITH THIS, AND YOU WON'T **NEED** YOUR SWORD.
YOU CAN HANG IT UP... YOU CAN MELT THE DAMN THING DOWN.
DON'T MAKE PROMISES YOU CAN'T KEEP.
NOT EVEN IF YOU *BELIEVE* THEM.

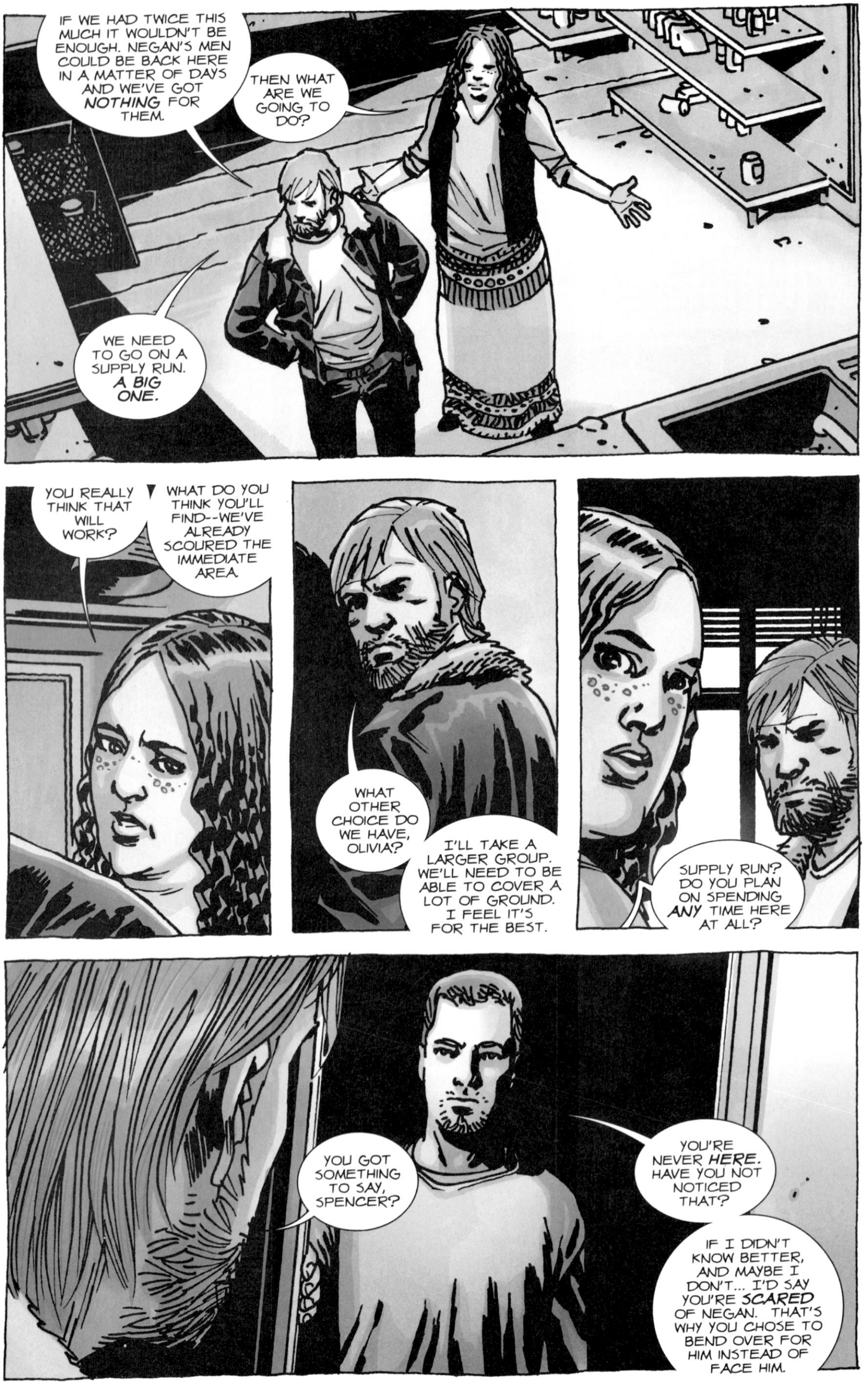
IF WE HAD TWICE THIS MUCH IT WOULDN'T BE ENOUGH. NEGAN'S MEN COULD BE BACK HERE IN A MATTER OF DAYS AND WE'VE GOT NOTHING FOR THEM.
THEN WHAT ARE WE GOING TO DO?
WE NEED TO GO ON A SUPPLY RUN. A BIG ONE.
YOU REALLY THINK THAT WILL WORK?
WHAT DO YOU THINK YOU'LL FIND--WE'VE ALREADY SCOURED THE IMMEDIATE AREA.
WHAT OTHER CHOICE DO WE HAVE, OLIVIA?
I'LL TAKE A LARGER GROUP. WE'LL NEED TO BE ABLE TO COVER A LOT OF GROUND. I FEEL IT'S FOR THE BEST.
SUPPLY RUN? DO YOU PLAN ON SPENDING ANY TIME HERE AT ALL?
YOU GOT SOMETHING TO SAY, SPENCER?
YOU'RE NEVER HERE. HAVE YOU NOT NOTICED THAT?
IF I DIDN'T KNOW BETTER, AND MAYBE I DON'T... I'D SAY YOU'RE SCARED OF NEGAN. THAT'S WHY YOU CHOSE TO BEND OVER FOR HIM INSTEAD OF FACE HIM.

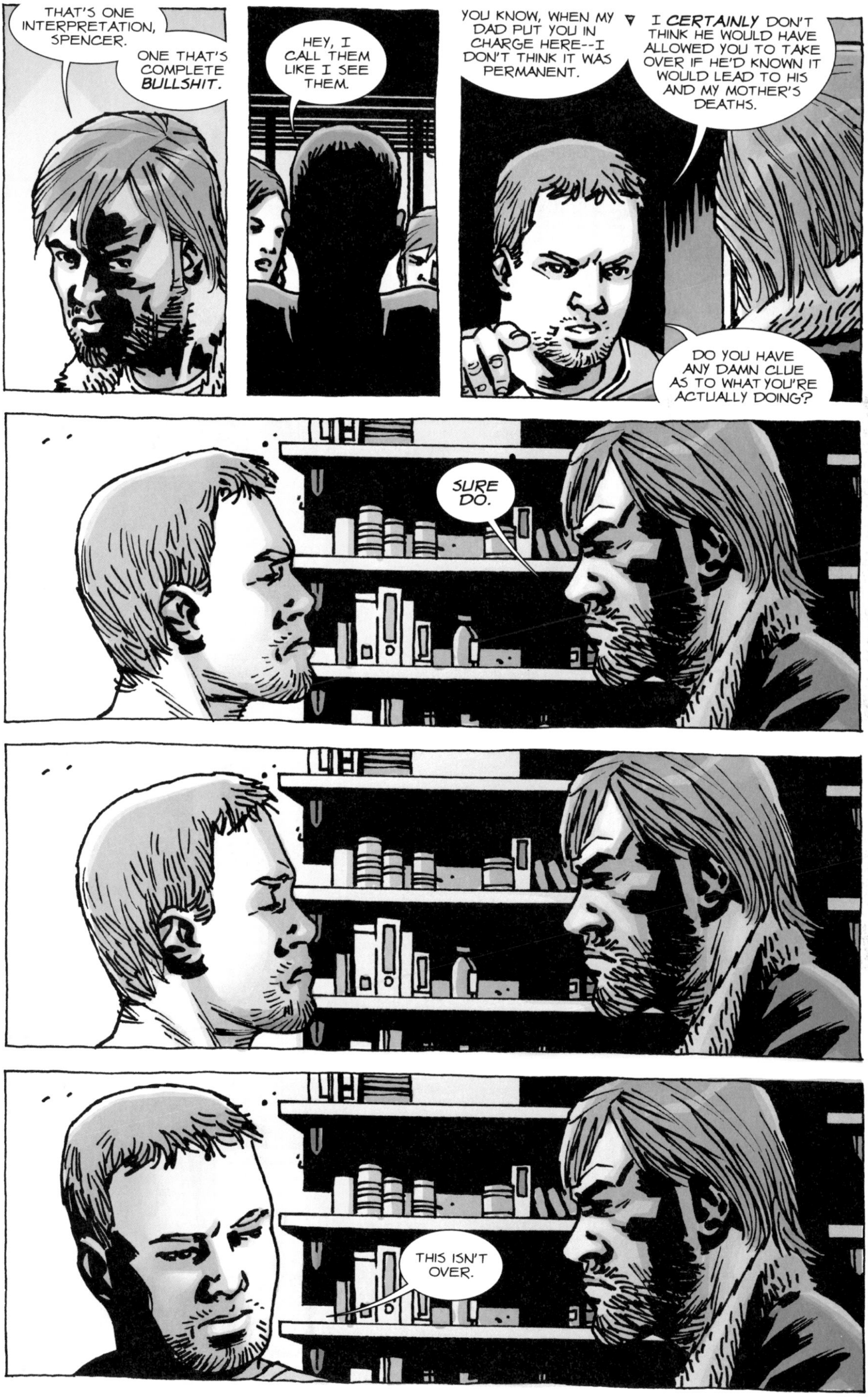

THAT'S ONE INTERPRETATION, SPENCER.
ONE THAT'S COMPLETE BULLSHIT.
HEY, I CALL THEM LIKE I SEE THEM.
YOU KNOW, WHEN MY DAD PUT YOU IN CHARGE HERE--I DON'T THINK IT WAS PERMANENT.
I CERTAINLY DON'T THINK HE WOULD HAVE ALLOWED YOU TO TAKE OVER IF HE'D KNOWN IT WOULD LEAD TO HIS AND MY MOTHER'S DEATHS.
DO YOU HAVE ANY DAMN CLUE AS TO WHAT YOU'RE ACTUALLY DOING?
SURE DO.
THIS ISN'T OVER.

FWOOSH!

FWOOSH!

EARL!

EARL!

EARL SUTTON!

HUH?!

MORNING, PAUL. I DIDN'T HEAR YOU THERE.

SSSSSSSSSSSS!

EARL HERE IS PRETTY MUCH THE ONLY ONE AT THE HILLTOP WHO DOESN'T CALL ME BY MY NICKNAME.

UNDERSTANDABLE.

IT'S A STUPID NICKNAME-- DISRESPECTFUL, FRANKLY. YOU LOOK LIKE CERTAIN DEPICTIONS OF THE GUY, BUT IT SEEMS LIKE YOU THINK PRETTY HIGHLY OF YOURSELF THAT YOU'VE LET THE NICKNAME STICK.

IT DOESN'T BOTHER ME, BUT I GET WHAT YOU'RE SAYING. MY FATHER SURE WOULDN'T HAVE BEEN A FAN.

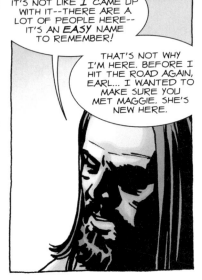

IT'S NOT LIKE I CAME UP WITH IT--THERE ARE A LOT OF PEOPLE HERE-- IT'S AN EASY NAME TO REMEMBER!

THAT'S NOT WHY I'M HERE. BEFORE I HIT THE ROAD AGAIN, EARL... I WANTED TO MAKE SURE YOU MET MAGGIE. SHE'S NEW HERE.

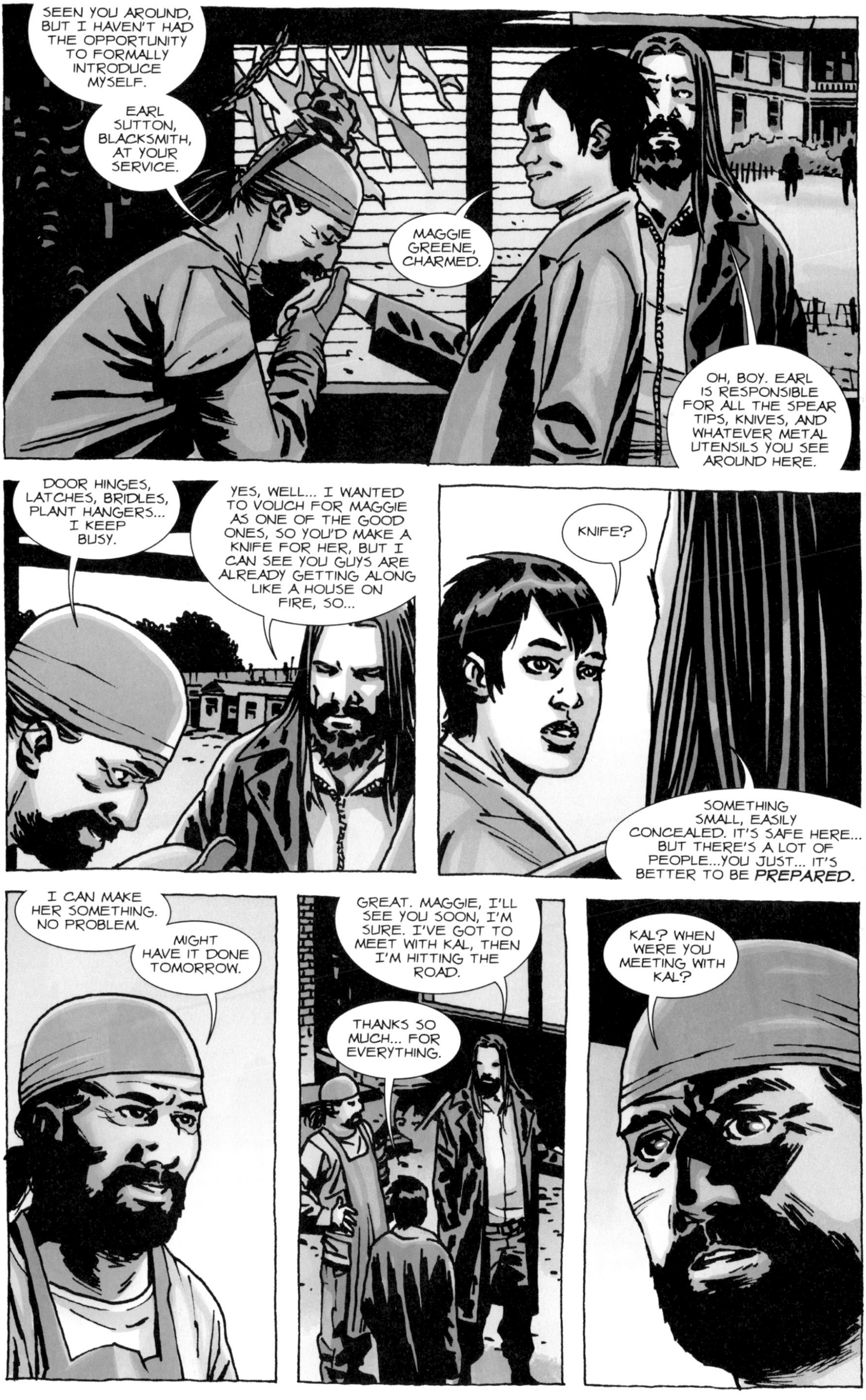
SEEN YOU AROUND, BUT I HAVEN'T HAD THE OPPORTUNITY TO FORMALLY INTRODUCE MYSELF.
EARL SUTTON, BLACKSMITH, AT YOUR SERVICE.
MAGGIE GREENE, CHARMED.
OH, BOY. EARL IS RESPONSIBLE FOR ALL THE SPEAR TIPS, KNIVES, AND WHATEVER METAL UTENSILS YOU SEE AROUND HERE.
DOOR HINGES, LATCHES, BRIDLES, PLANT HANGERS... I KEEP BUSY.
YES, WELL... I WANTED TO VOUCH FOR MAGGIE AS ONE OF THE GOOD ONES, SO YOU'D MAKE A KNIFE FOR HER, BUT I CAN SEE YOU GUYS ARE ALREADY GETTING ALONG LIKE A HOUSE ON FIRE, SO...
KNIFE?
SOMETHING SMALL, EASILY CONCEALED. IT'S SAFE HERE... BUT THERE'S A LOT OF PEOPLE...YOU JUST... IT'S BETTER TO BE PREPARED.
I CAN MAKE HER SOMETHING. NO PROBLEM.
MIGHT HAVE IT DONE TOMORROW.
GREAT. MAGGIE, I'LL SEE YOU SOON, I'M SURE. I'VE GOT TO MEET WITH KAL, THEN I'M HITTING THE ROAD.
THANKS SO MUCH... FOR EVERYTHING.
KAL? WHEN WERE YOU MEETING WITH KAL?

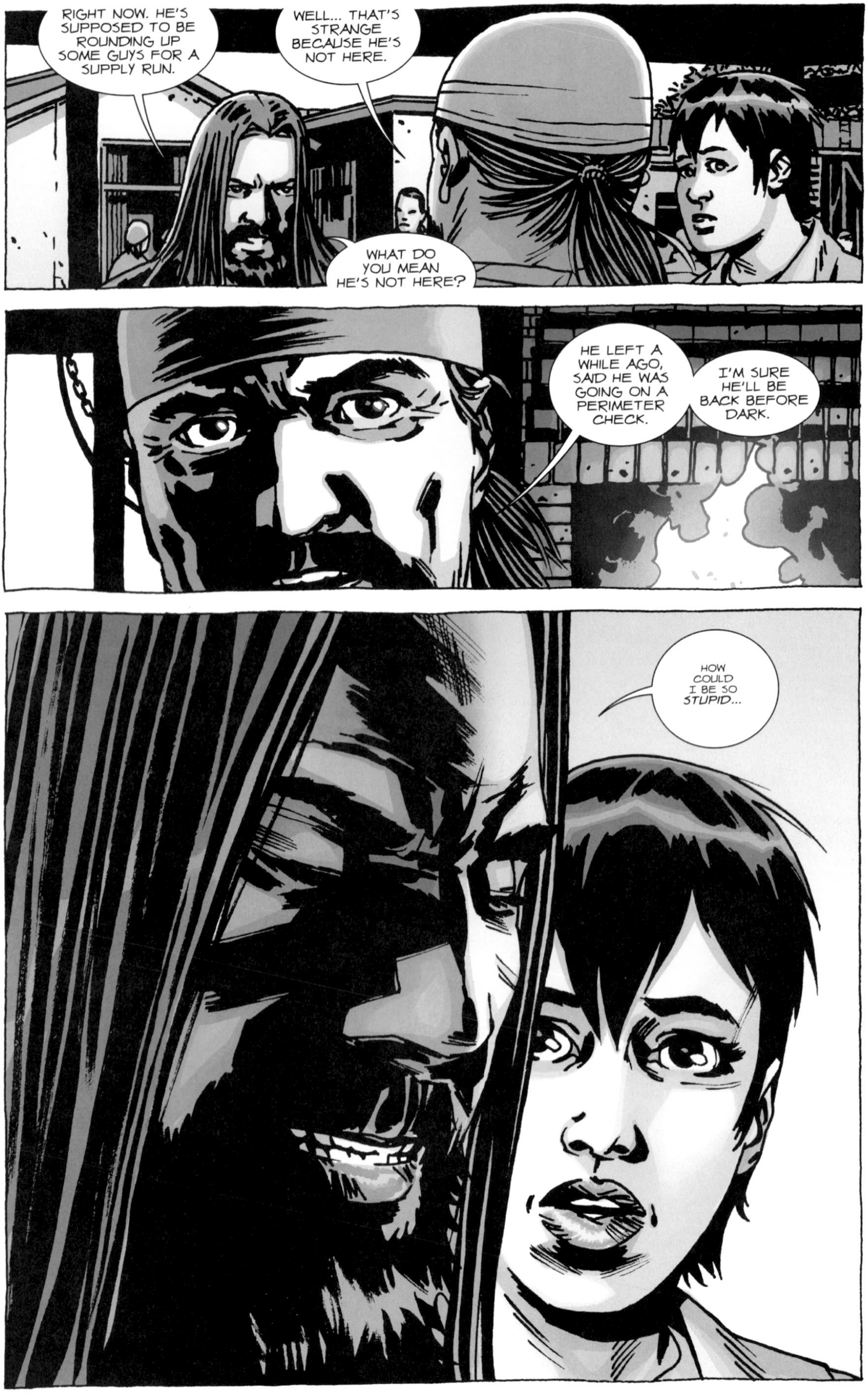
RIGHT NOW. HE'S SUPPOSED TO BE ROUNDING UP SOME GUYS FOR A SUPPLY RUN.
WELL... THAT'S STRANGE BECAUSE HE'S NOT HERE.
WHAT DO YOU MEAN HE'S NOT HERE?
HE LEFT A WHILE AGO, SAID HE WAS GOING ON A PERIMETER CHECK.
I'M SURE HE'LL BE BACK BEFORE DARK.
HOW COULD I BE SO *STUPID*...

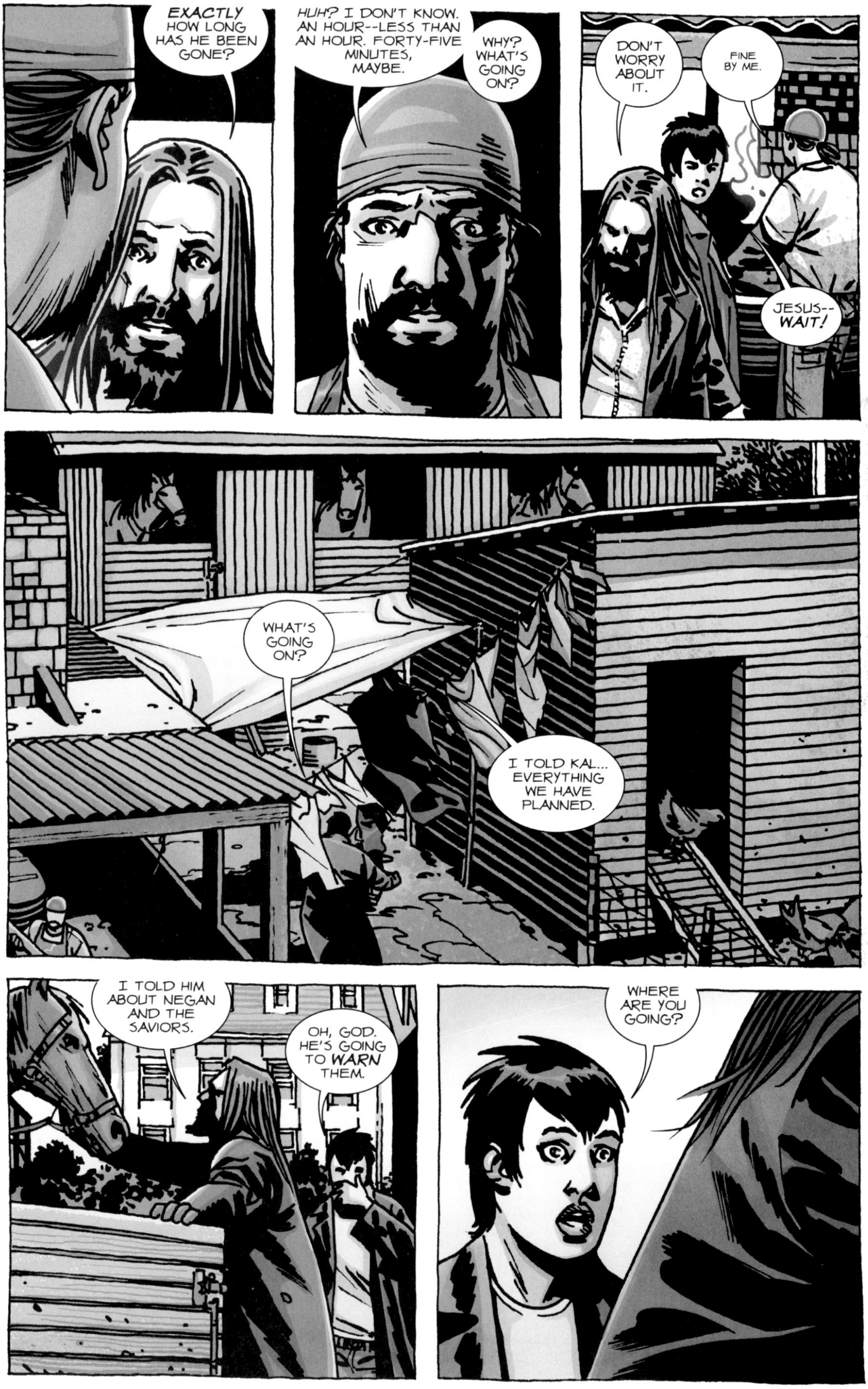
EXACTLY HOW LONG HAS HE BEEN GONE?
HUH? I DON'T KNOW. AN HOUR--LESS THAN AN HOUR. FORTY-FIVE MINUTES, MAYBE.
WHY? WHAT'S GOING ON?
DON'T WORRY ABOUT IT.
FINE BY ME.
JESUS-- WAIT!
WHAT'S GOING ON?
I TOLD KAL... EVERYTHING WE HAVE PLANNED.
I TOLD HIM ABOUT NEGAN AND THE SAVIORS.
OH, GOD. HE'S GOING TO WARN THEM.
WHERE ARE YOU GOING?

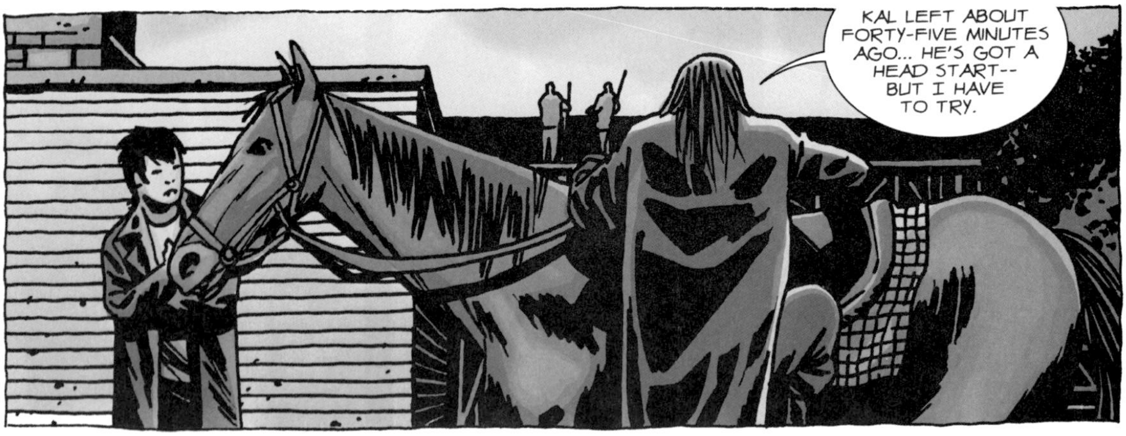
KAL LEFT ABOUT FORTY-FIVE MINUTES AGO... HE'S GOT A HEAD START-- BUT I HAVE TO TRY.
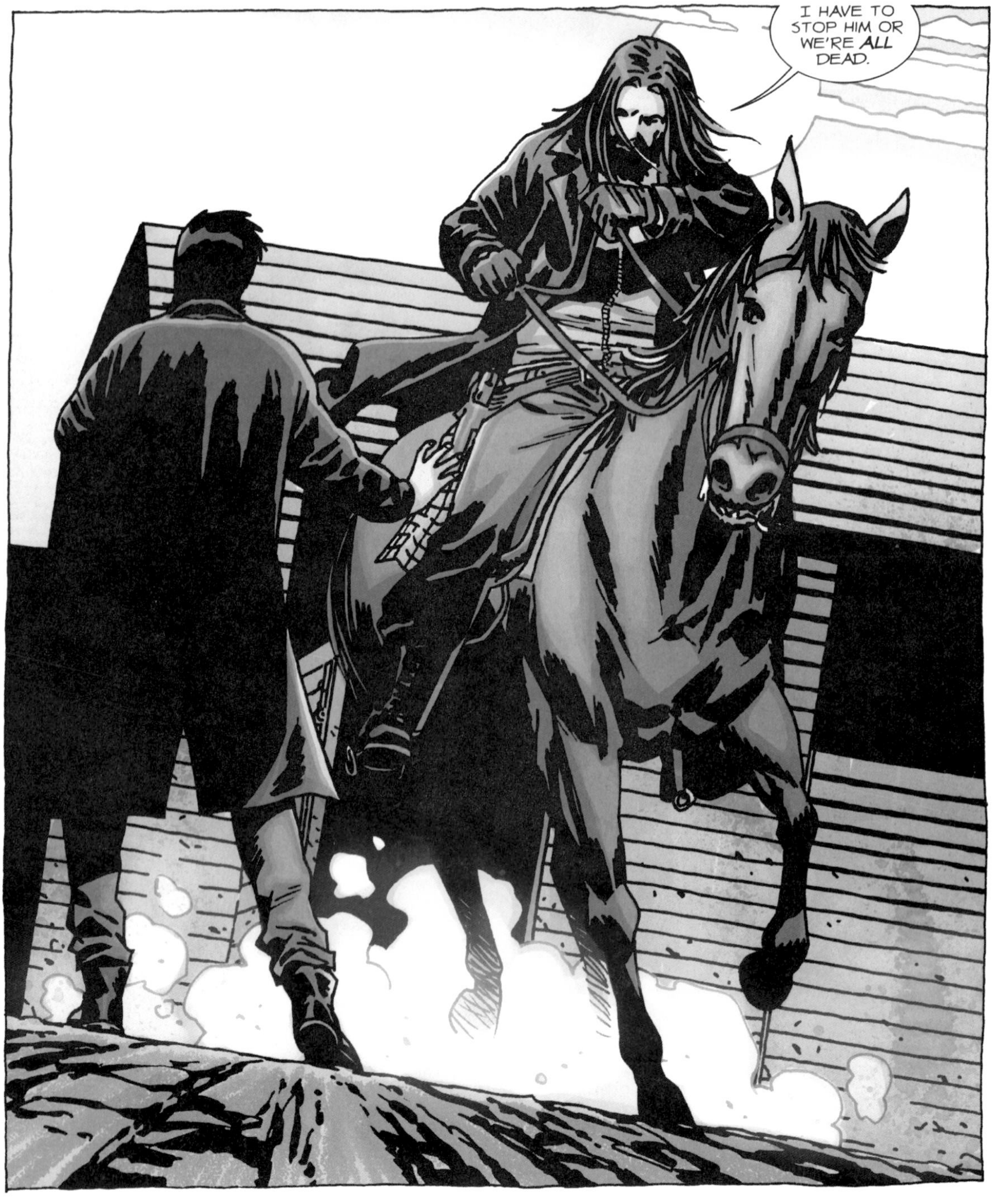
I HAVE TO STOP HIM OR WE'RE *ALL* DEAD.

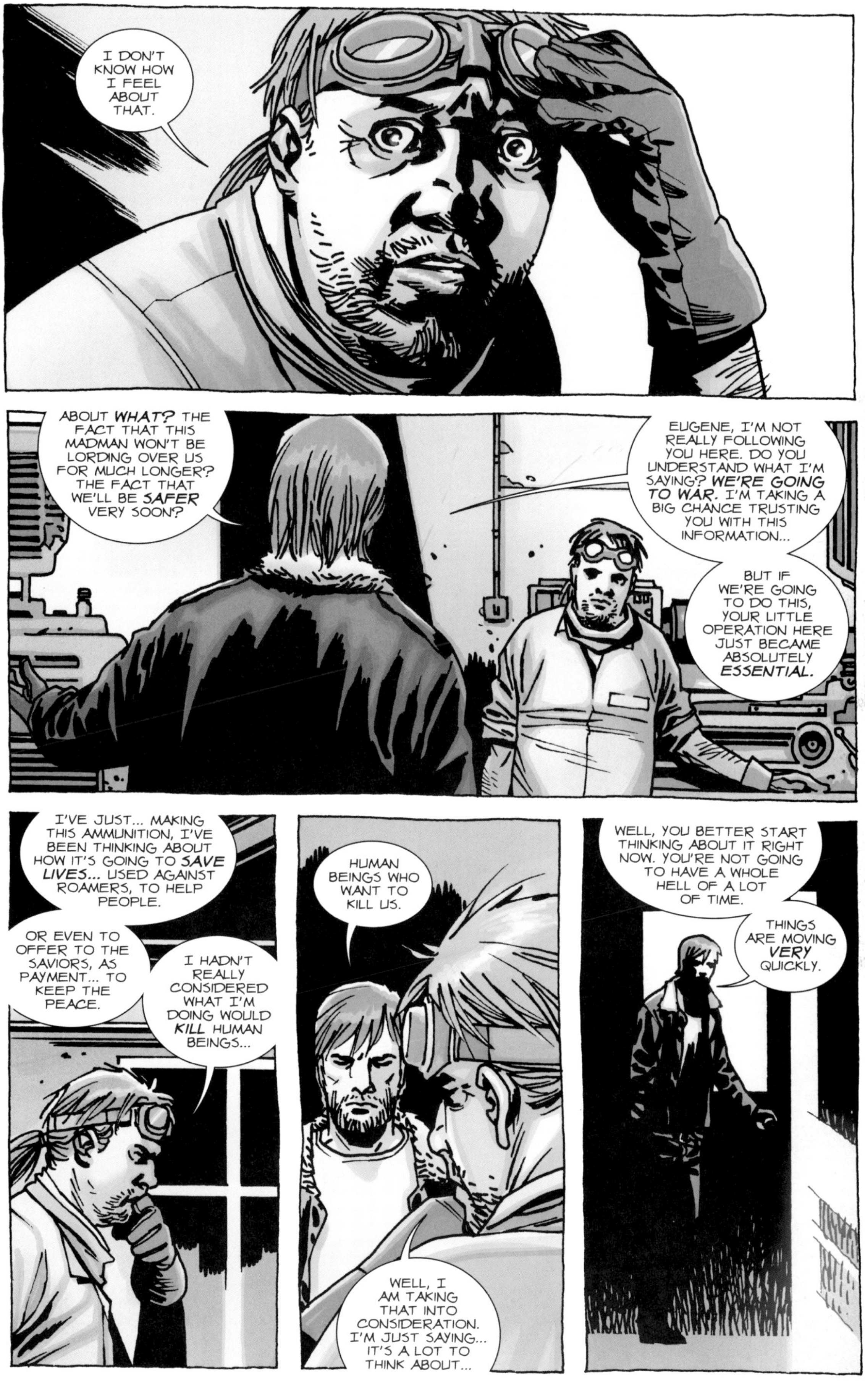

I DON'T KNOW HOW I FEEL ABOUT THAT.
ABOUT WHAT? THE FACT THAT THIS MADMAN WON'T BE LORDING OVER US FOR MUCH LONGER? THE FACT THAT WE'LL BE SAFER VERY SOON?
EUGENE, I'M NOT REALLY FOLLOWING YOU HERE. DO YOU UNDERSTAND WHAT I'M SAYING? WE'RE GOING TO WAR. I'M TAKING A BIG CHANCE TRUSTING YOU WITH THIS INFORMATION...
BUT IF WE'RE GOING TO DO THIS, YOUR LITTLE OPERATION HERE JUST BECAME ABSOLUTELY ESSENTIAL.
I'VE JUST... MAKING THIS AMMUNITION, I'VE BEEN THINKING ABOUT HOW IT'S GOING TO SAVE LIVES... USED AGAINST ROAMERS, TO HELP PEOPLE.
OR EVEN TO OFFER TO THE SAVIORS, AS PAYMENT... TO KEEP THE PEACE.
I HADN'T REALLY CONSIDERED WHAT I'M DOING WOULD KILL HUMAN BEINGS...
HUMAN BEINGS WHO WANT TO KILL US.
WELL, I AM TAKING THAT INTO CONSIDERATION. I'M JUST SAYING... IT'S A LOT TO THINK ABOUT...
WELL, YOU BETTER START THINKING ABOUT IT RIGHT NOW. YOU'RE NOT GOING TO HAVE A WHOLE HELL OF A LOT OF TIME.
THINGS ARE MOVING VERY QUICKLY.

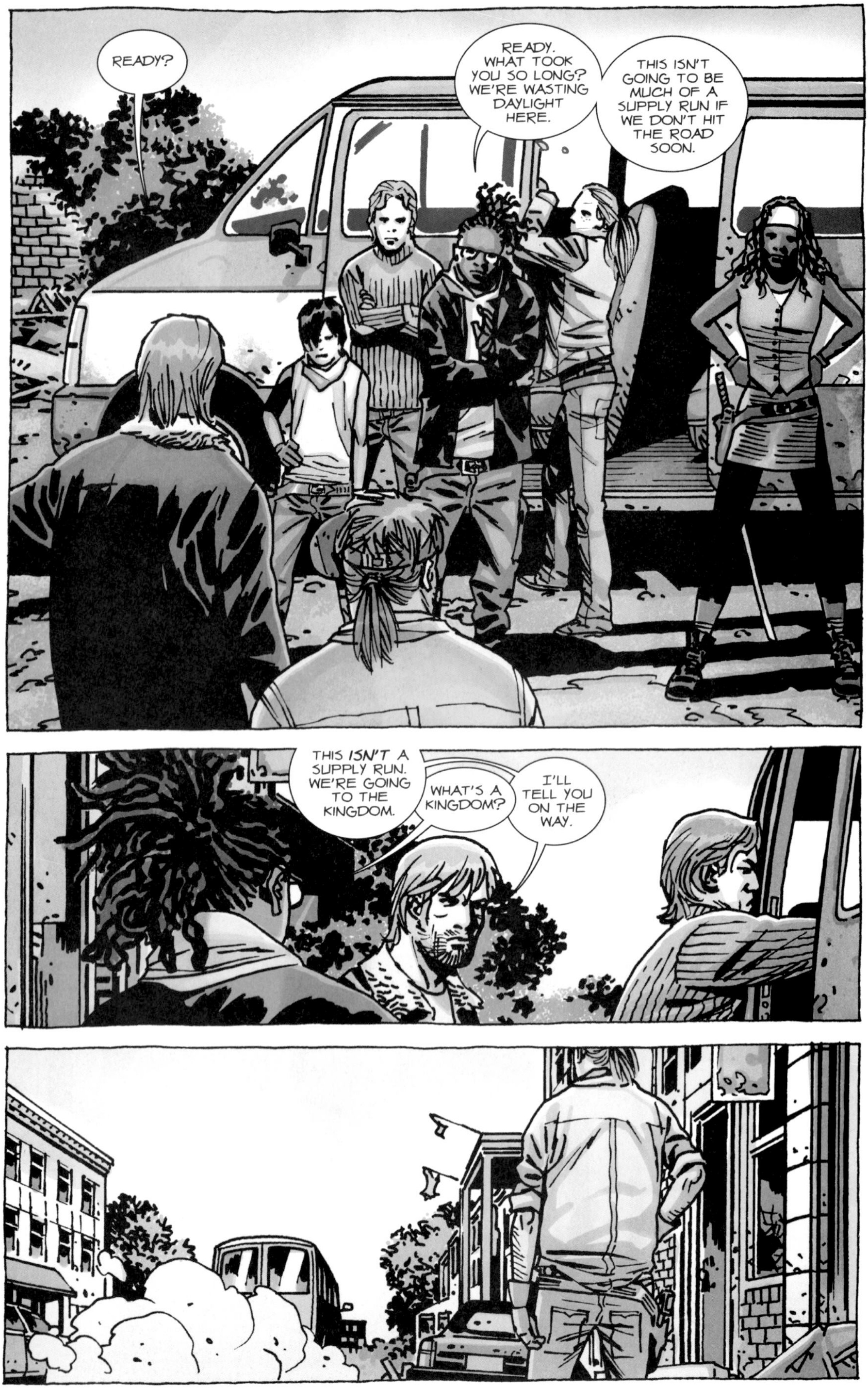
READY?
READY. WHAT TOOK YOU SO LONG? WE'RE WASTING DAYLIGHT HERE.
THIS ISN'T GOING TO BE MUCH OF A SUPPLY RUN IF WE DON'T HIT THE ROAD SOON.
THIS *ISN'T* A SUPPLY RUN. WE'RE GOING TO THE KINGDOM.
WHAT'S A KINGDOM?
I'LL TELL YOU ON THE WAY.

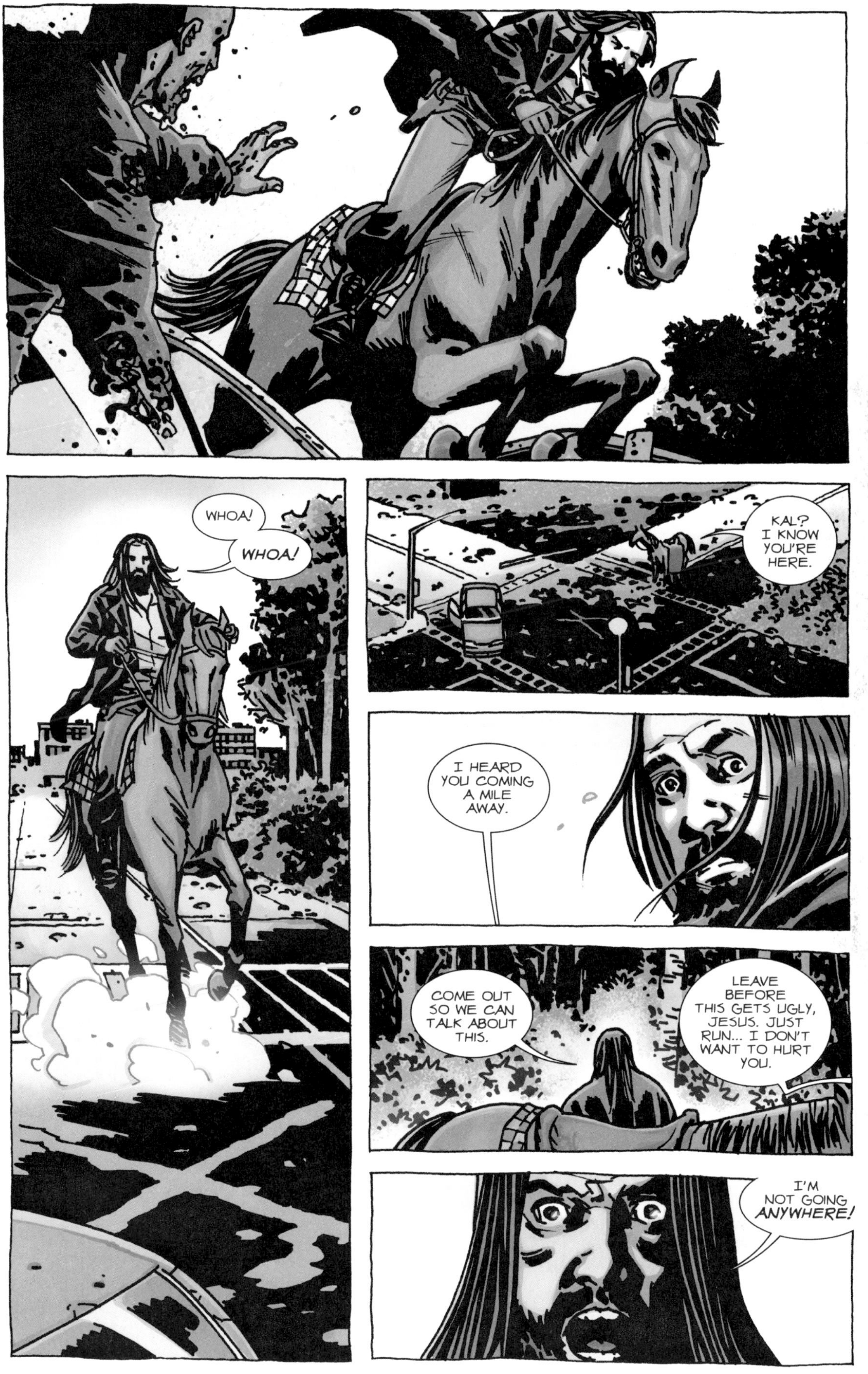

WHOA!
WHOA!
KAL? I KNOW YOU'RE HERE.
I HEARD YOU COMING A MILE AWAY.
COME OUT SO WE CAN TALK ABOUT THIS.
LEAVE BEFORE THIS GETS UGLY, JESUS. JUST RUN... I DON'T WANT TO HURT YOU.
I'M NOT GOING ANYWHERE!

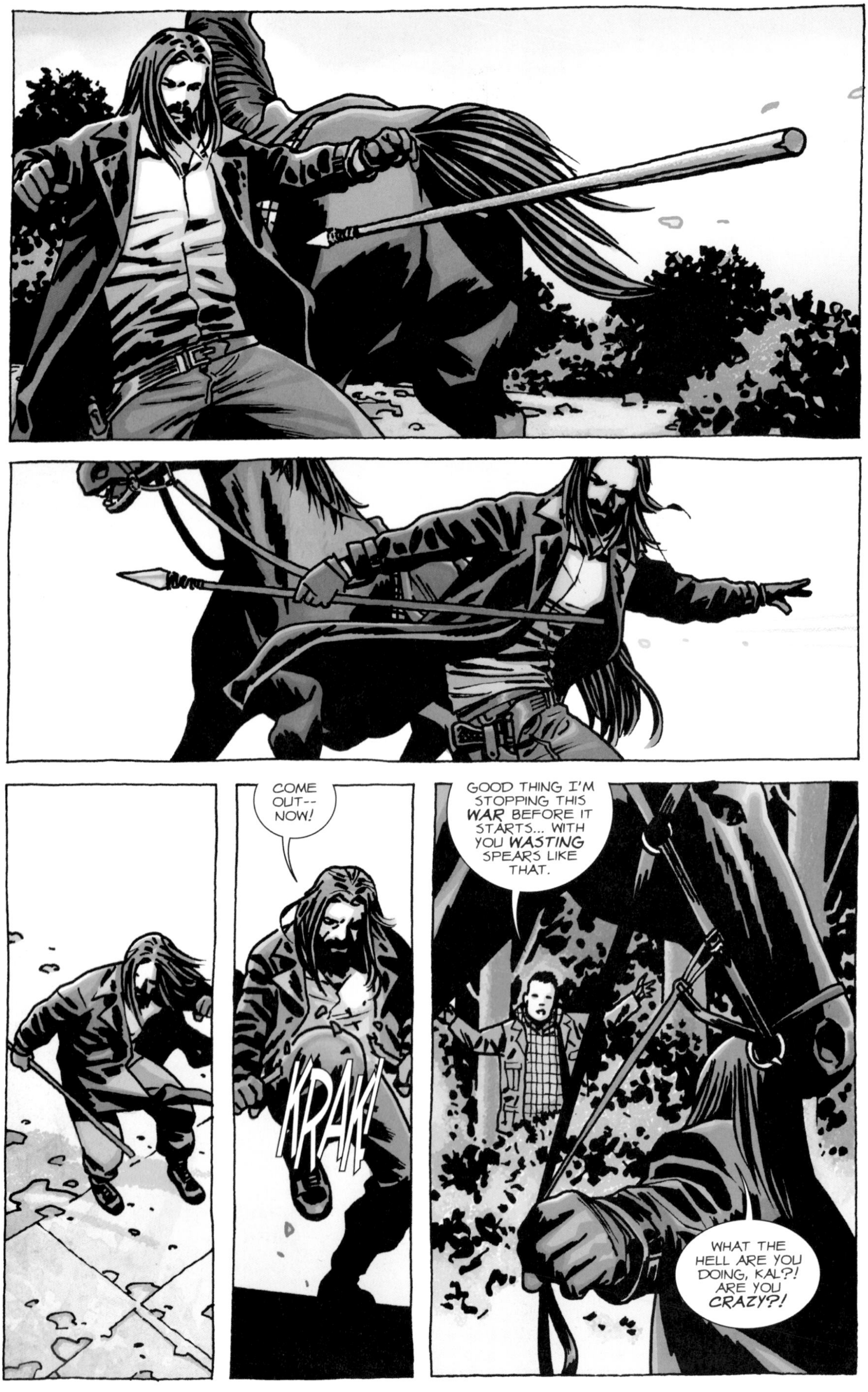
COME OUT-- NOW!
KRAK!
GOOD THING I'M STOPPING THIS WAR BEFORE IT STARTS... WITH YOU WASTING SPEARS LIKE THAT.
WHAT THE HELL ARE YOU DOING, KAL?! ARE YOU CRAZY?!

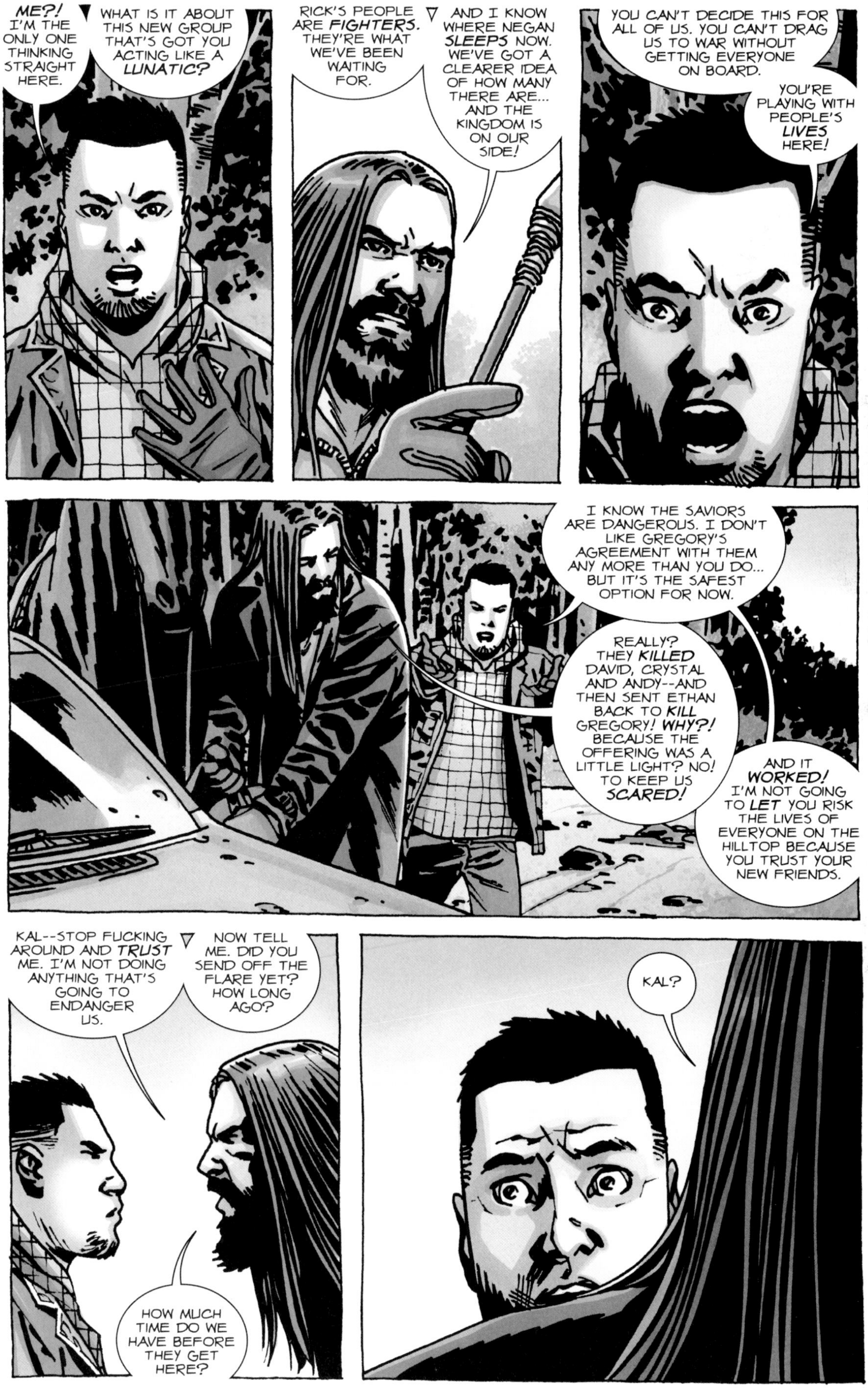
ME?! I'M THE ONLY ONE THINKING STRAIGHT HERE.
WHAT IS IT ABOUT THIS NEW GROUP THAT'S GOT YOU ACTING LIKE A LUNATIC?
RICK'S PEOPLE ARE FIGHTERS. THEY'RE WHAT WE'VE BEEN WAITING FOR.
AND I KNOW WHERE NEGAN SLEEPS NOW. WE'VE GOT A CLEARER IDEA OF HOW MANY THERE ARE... AND THE KINGDOM IS ON OUR SIDE!
YOU CAN'T DECIDE THIS FOR ALL OF US. YOU CAN'T DRAG US TO WAR WITHOUT GETTING EVERYONE ON BOARD.
YOU'RE PLAYING WITH PEOPLE'S LIVES HERE!
I KNOW THE SAVIORS ARE DANGEROUS. I DON'T LIKE GREGORY'S AGREEMENT WITH THEM ANY MORE THAN YOU DO... BUT IT'S THE SAFEST OPTION FOR NOW.
REALLY? THEY KILLED DAVID, CRYSTAL AND ANDY--AND THEN SENT ETHAN BACK TO KILL GREGORY! WHY?! BECAUSE THE OFFERING WAS A LITTLE LIGHT? NO! TO KEEP US SCARED!
AND IT WORKED! I'M NOT GOING TO LET YOU RISK THE LIVES OF EVERYONE ON THE HILLTOP BECAUSE YOU TRUST YOUR NEW FRIENDS.
KAL--STOP FUCKING AROUND AND TRUST ME. I'M NOT DOING ANYTHING THAT'S GOING TO ENDANGER US.
NOW TELL ME. DID YOU SEND OFF THE FLARE YET? HOW LONG AGO?
HOW MUCH TIME DO WE HAVE BEFORE THEY GET HERE?
KAL?

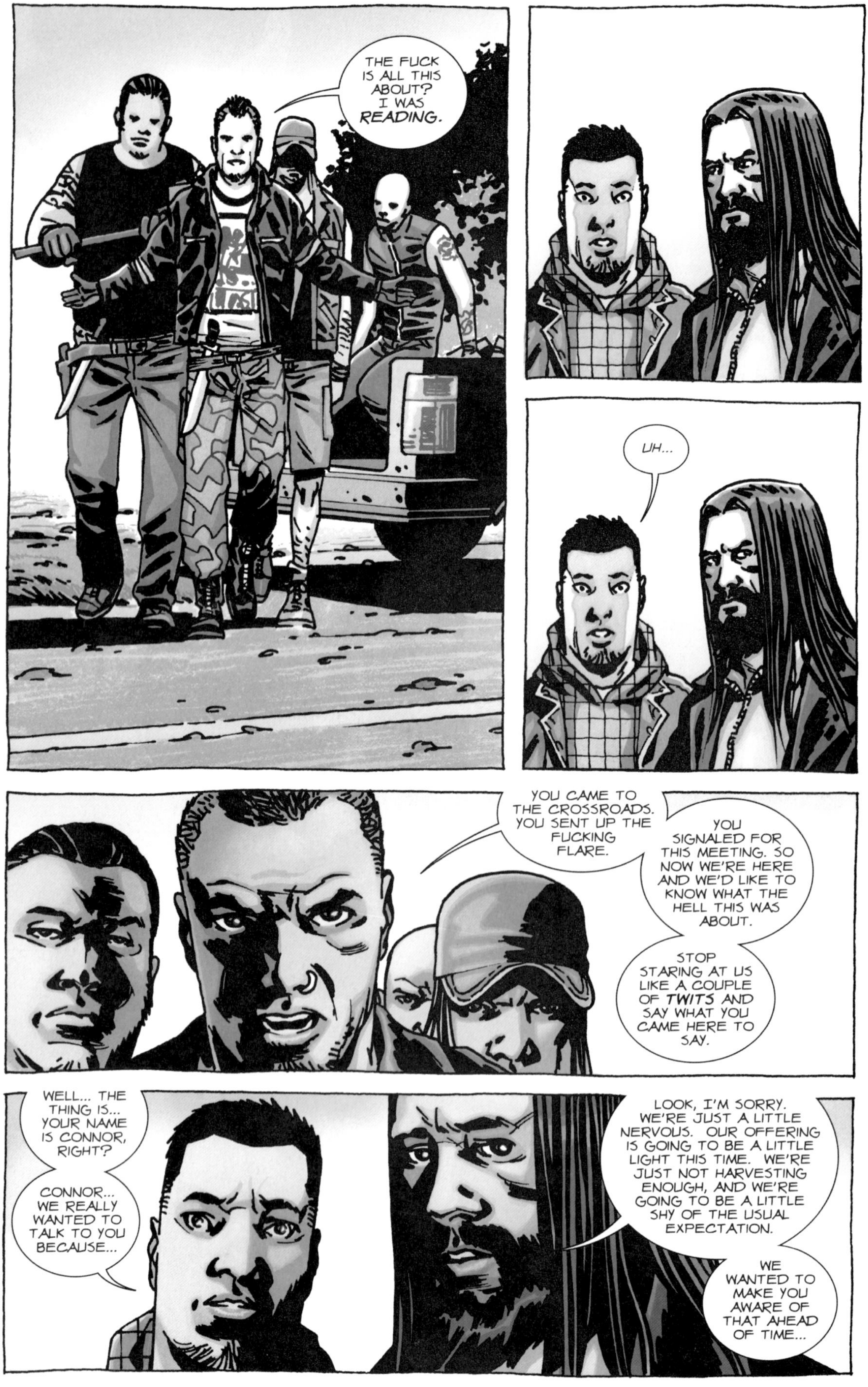
THE FUCK IS ALL THIS ABOUT? I WAS *READING.*
UH...
YOU CAME TO THE CROSSROADS. YOU SENT UP THE FUCKING FLARE.
YOU SIGNALED FOR THIS MEETING. SO NOW WE'RE HERE AND WE'D LIKE TO KNOW WHAT THE HELL THIS WAS ABOUT.
STOP STARING AT US LIKE A COUPLE OF *TWITS* AND SAY WHAT YOU CAME HERE TO SAY.
WELL... THE THING IS... YOUR NAME IS CONNOR, RIGHT?
CONNOR... WE REALLY WANTED TO TALK TO YOU BECAUSE...
LOOK, I'M SORRY. WE'RE JUST A LITTLE NERVOUS. OUR OFFERING IS GOING TO BE A LITTLE LIGHT THIS TIME. WE'RE JUST NOT HARVESTING ENOUGH, AND WE'RE GOING TO BE A LITTLE SHY OF THE USUAL EXPECTATION.
WE WANTED TO MAKE YOU AWARE OF THAT AHEAD OF TIME...

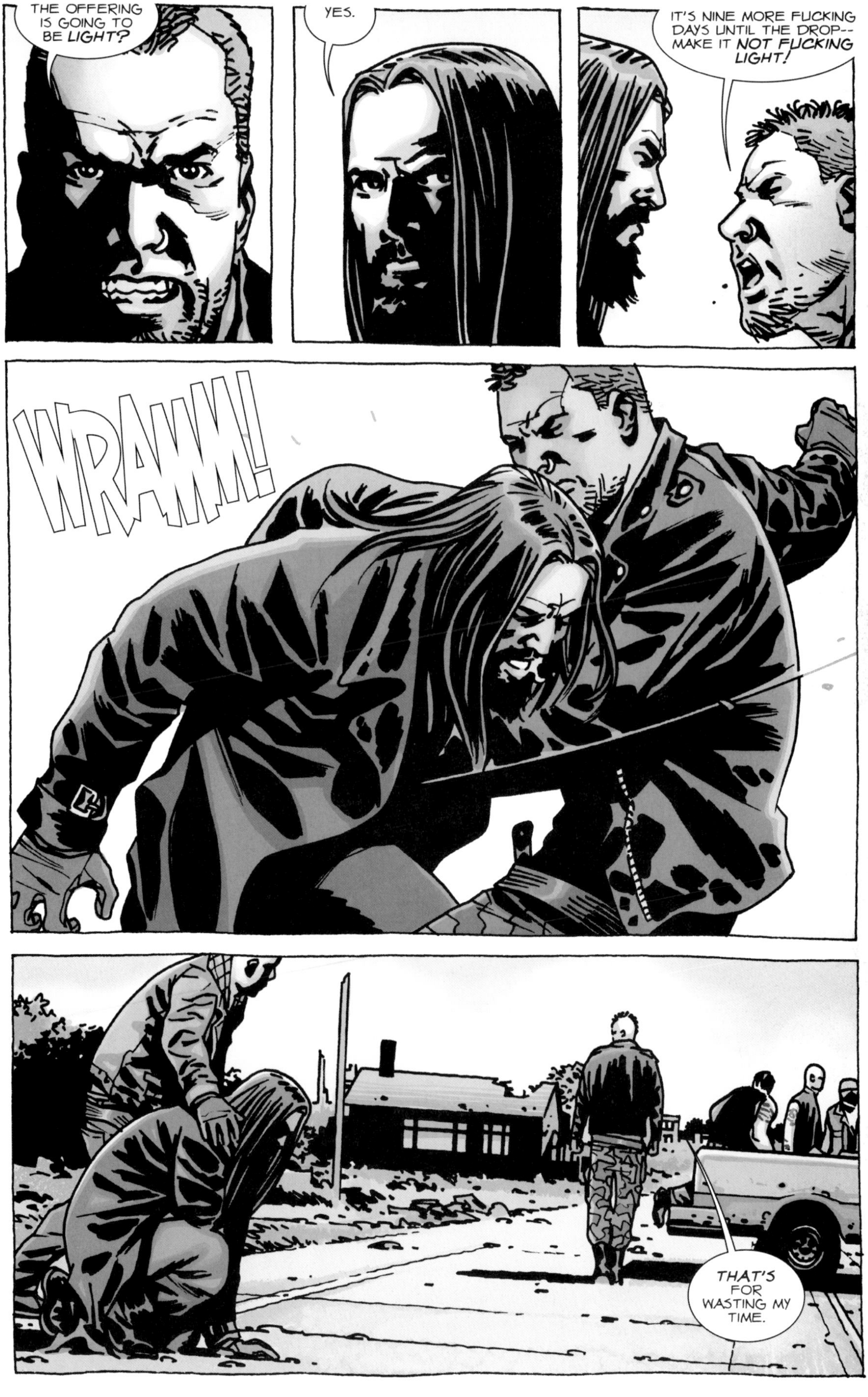

THE OFFERING IS GOING TO BE *LIGHT?*
YES.
IT'S NINE MORE FUCKING DAYS UNTIL THE DROP-- MAKE IT *NOT FUCKING LIGHT!*
WRAMM!
THAT'S FOR WASTING MY TIME.

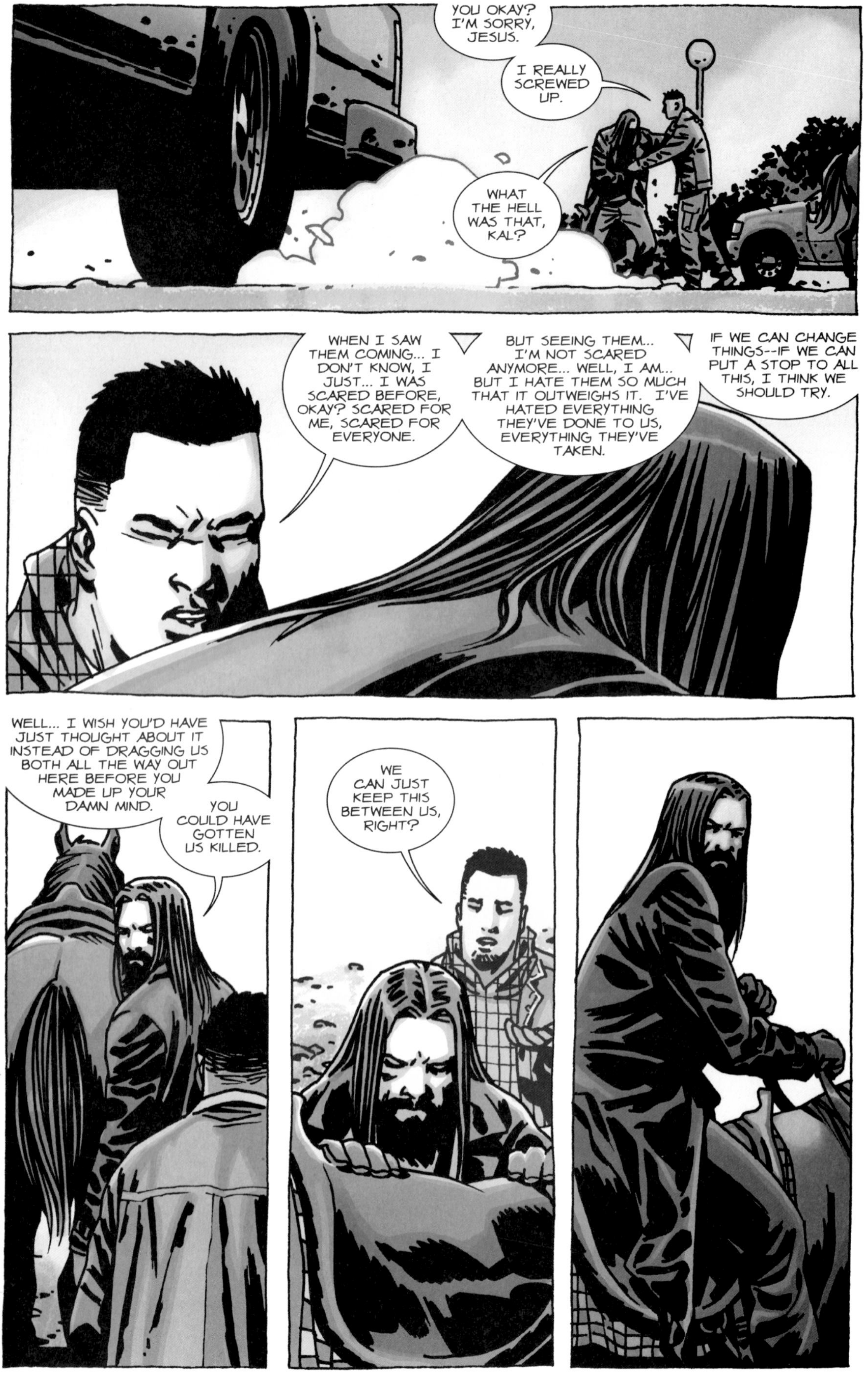

YOU OKAY? I'M SORRY, JESUS.
I REALLY SCREWED UP.
WHAT THE HELL WAS THAT, KAL?
WHEN I SAW THEM COMING... I DON'T KNOW, I JUST... I WAS SCARED BEFORE, OKAY? SCARED FOR ME, SCARED FOR EVERYONE.
BUT SEEING THEM... I'M NOT SCARED ANYMORE... WELL, I AM... BUT I HATE THEM SO MUCH THAT IT OUTWEIGHS IT. I'VE HATED EVERYTHING THEY'VE DONE TO US, EVERYTHING THEY'VE TAKEN.
IF WE CAN CHANGE THINGS--IF WE CAN PUT A STOP TO ALL THIS, I THINK WE SHOULD TRY.
WELL... I WISH YOU'D HAVE JUST THOUGHT ABOUT IT INSTEAD OF DRAGGING US BOTH ALL THE WAY OUT HERE BEFORE YOU MADE UP YOUR DAMN MIND.
YOU COULD HAVE GOTTEN US KILLED.
WE CAN JUST KEEP THIS BETWEEN US, RIGHT?

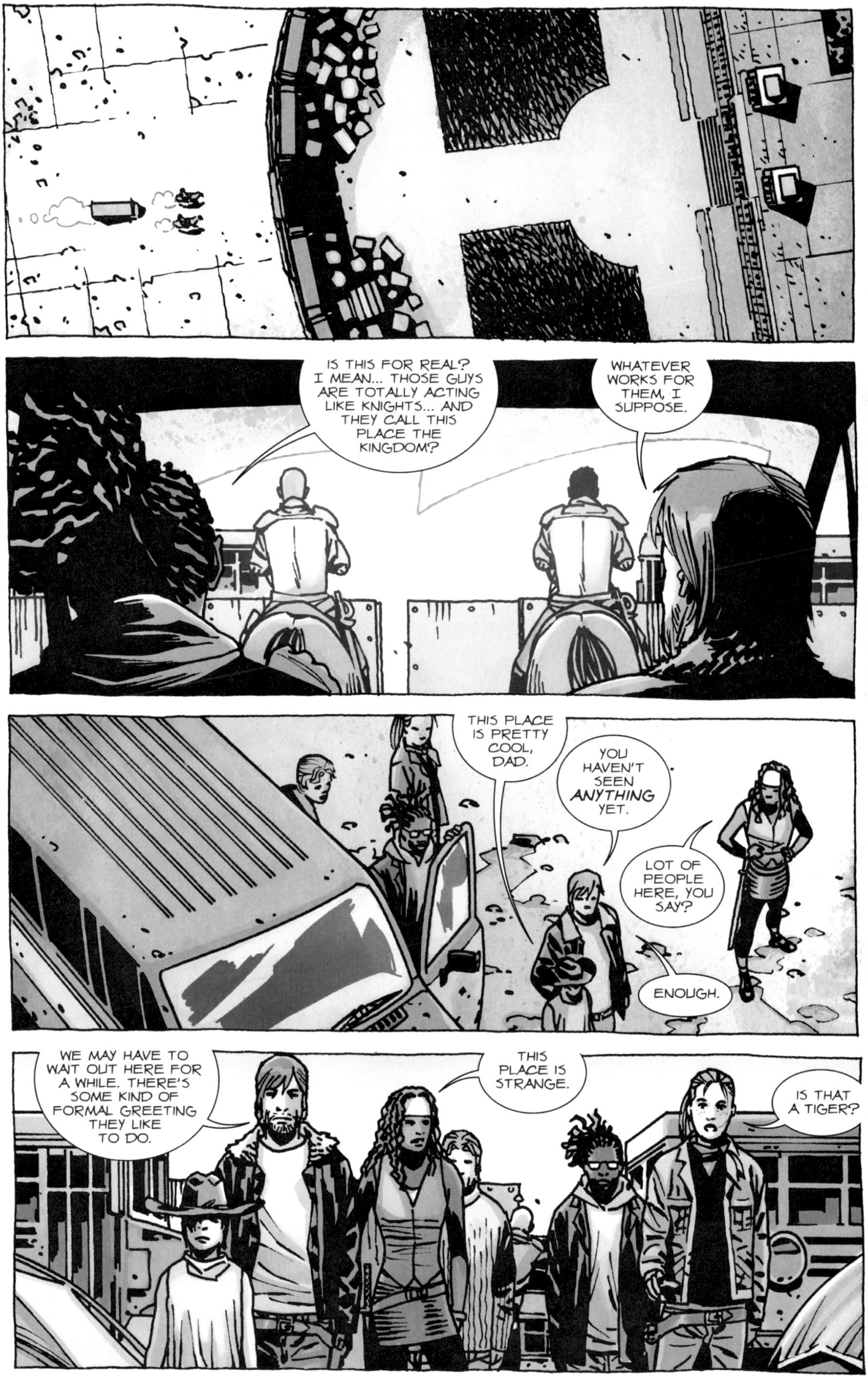
IS THIS FOR REAL? I MEAN... THOSE GUYS ARE TOTALLY ACTING LIKE KNIGHTS... AND THEY CALL THIS PLACE THE KINGDOM?
WHATEVER WORKS FOR THEM, I SUPPOSE.
THIS PLACE IS PRETTY COOL, DAD.
YOU HAVEN'T SEEN ANYTHING YET.
LOT OF PEOPLE HERE, YOU SAY?
ENOUGH.
WE MAY HAVE TO WAIT OUT HERE FOR A WHILE. THERE'S SOME KIND OF FORMAL GREETING THEY LIKE TO DO.
THIS PLACE IS STRANGE.
IS THAT A TIGER?

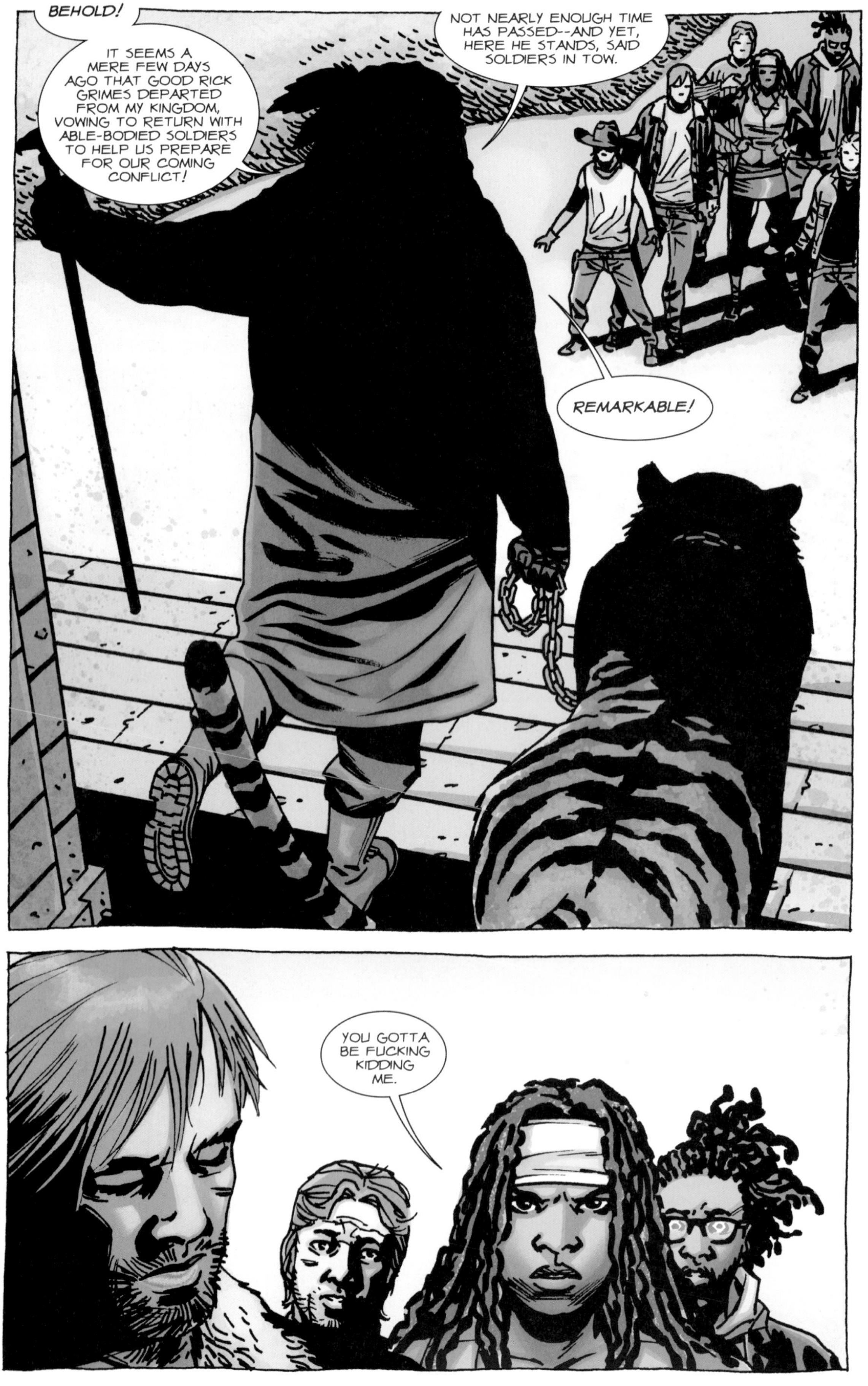
BEHOLD!
IT SEEMS A MERE FEW DAYS AGO THAT GOOD RICK GRIMES DEPARTED FROM MY KINGDOM, VOWING TO RETURN WITH ABLE-BODIED SOLDIERS TO HELP US PREPARE FOR OUR COMING CONFLICT!
NOT NEARLY ENOUGH TIME HAS PASSED--AND YET, HERE HE STANDS, SAID SOLDIERS IN TOW.
REMARKABLE!
YOU GOTTA BE FUCKING KIDDING ME.

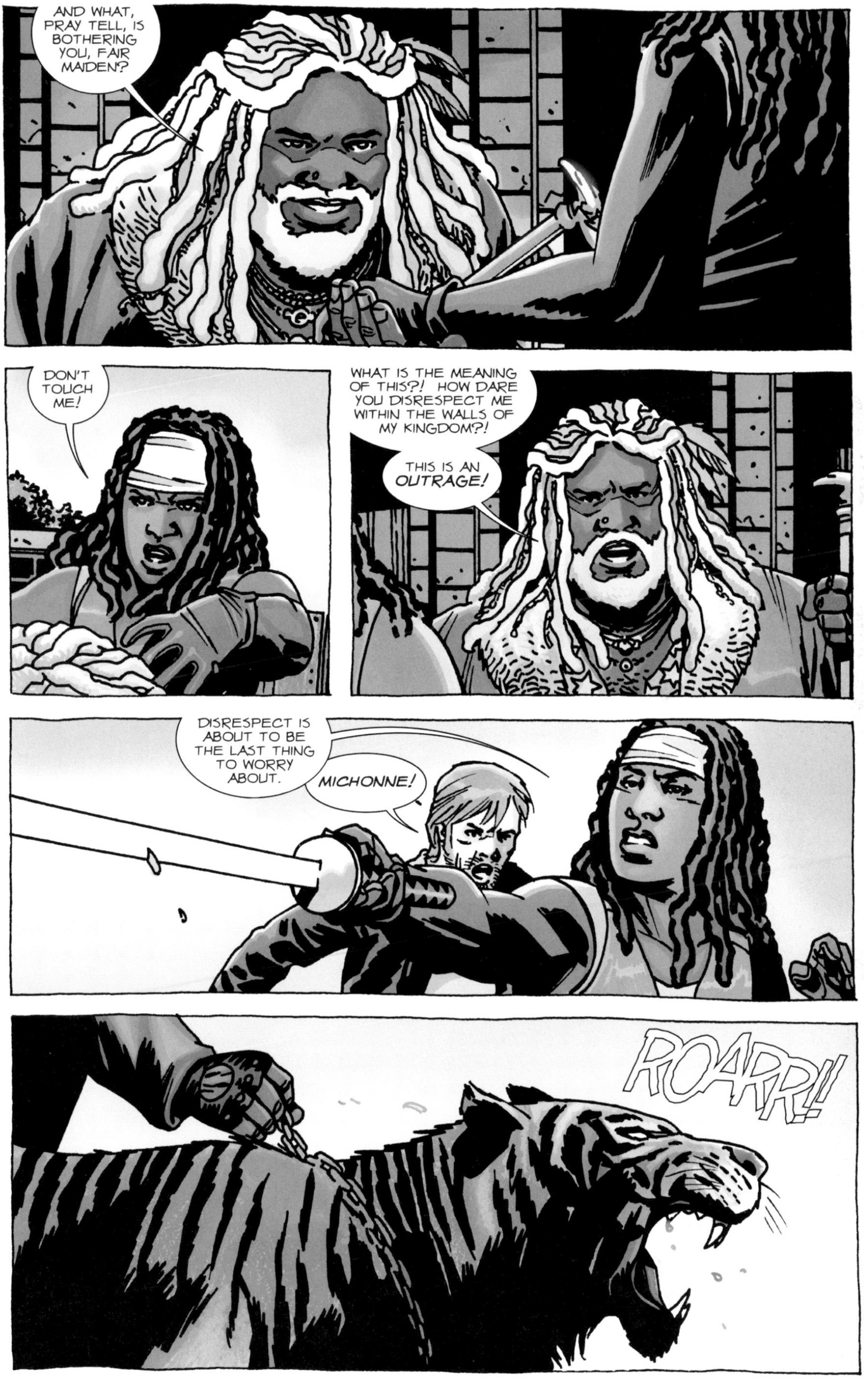
AND WHAT, PRAY TELL, IS BOTHERING YOU, FAIR MAIDEN?
DON'T TOUCH ME!
WHAT IS THE MEANING OF THIS?! HOW DARE YOU DISRESPECT ME WITHIN THE WALLS OF MY KINGDOM?!
THIS IS AN OUTRAGE!
DISRESPECT IS ABOUT TO BE THE LAST THING TO WORRY ABOUT.
MICHONNE!
ROARR!!

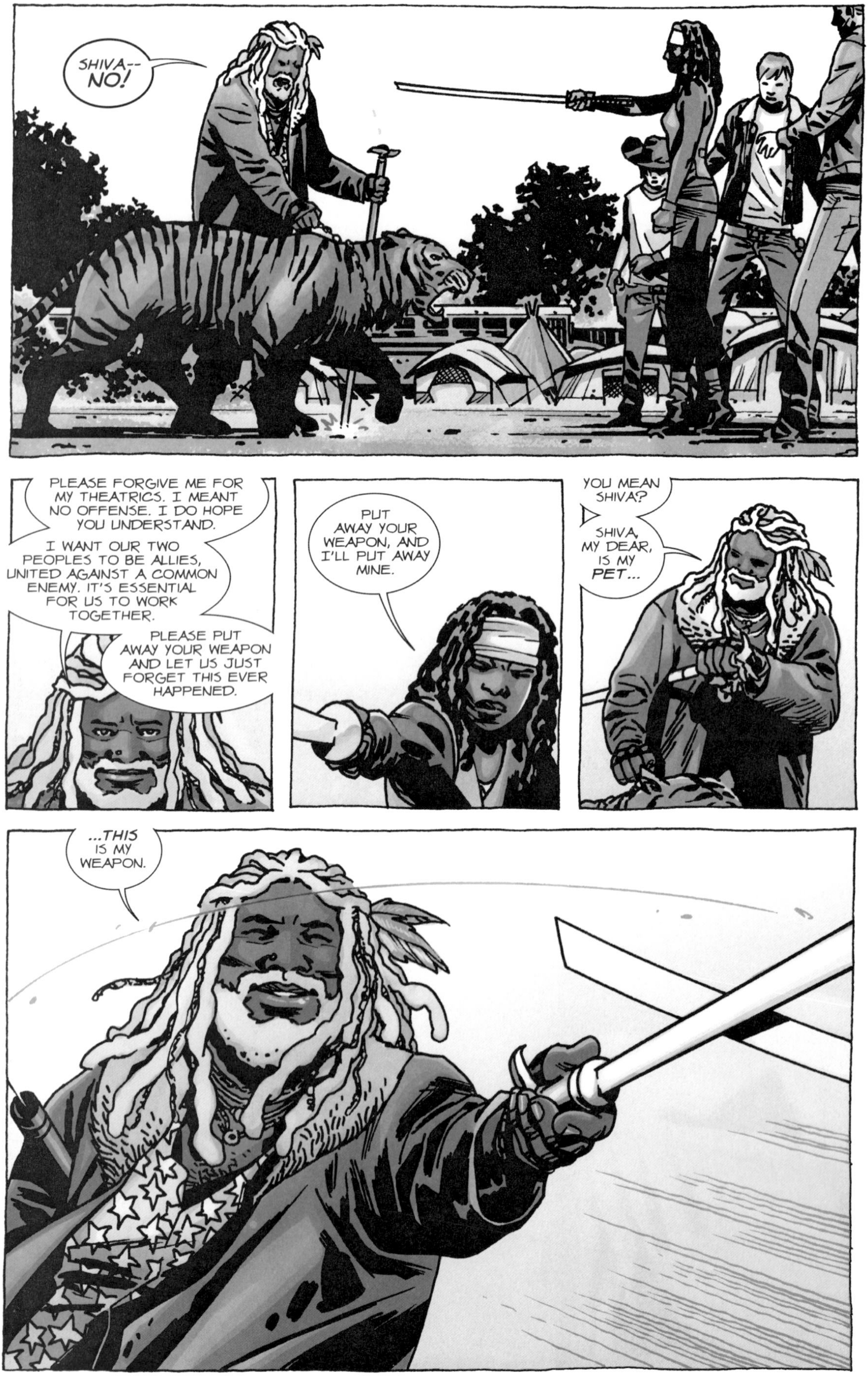
SHIVA-- NO!
PLEASE FORGIVE ME FOR MY THEATRICS. I MEANT NO OFFENSE. I DO HOPE YOU UNDERSTAND.
I WANT OUR TWO PEOPLES TO BE ALLIES, UNITED AGAINST A COMMON ENEMY. IT'S ESSENTIAL FOR US TO WORK TOGETHER.
PLEASE PUT AWAY YOUR WEAPON AND LET US JUST FORGET THIS EVER HAPPENED.
PUT AWAY YOUR WEAPON, AND I'LL PUT AWAY MINE.
YOU MEAN SHIVA?
SHIVA, MY DEAR, IS MY PET...
...THIS IS MY WEAPON.

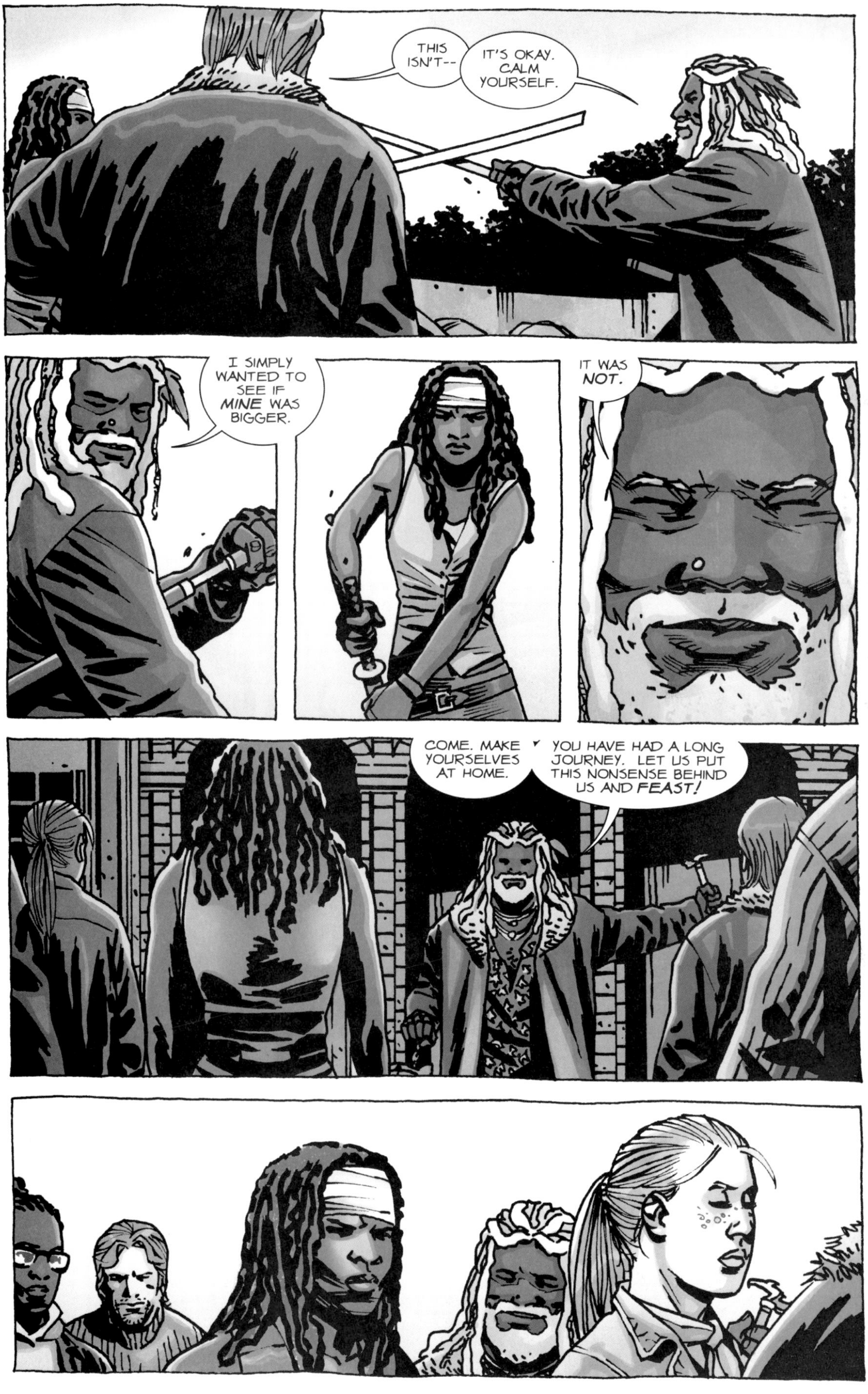
THIS ISN'T--
IT'S OKAY. CALM YOURSELF.
I SIMPLY WANTED TO SEE IF MINE WAS BIGGER.
IT WAS NOT.
COME. MAKE YOURSELVES AT HOME.
YOU HAVE HAD A LONG JOURNEY. LET US PUT THIS NONSENSE BEHIND US AND FEAST!

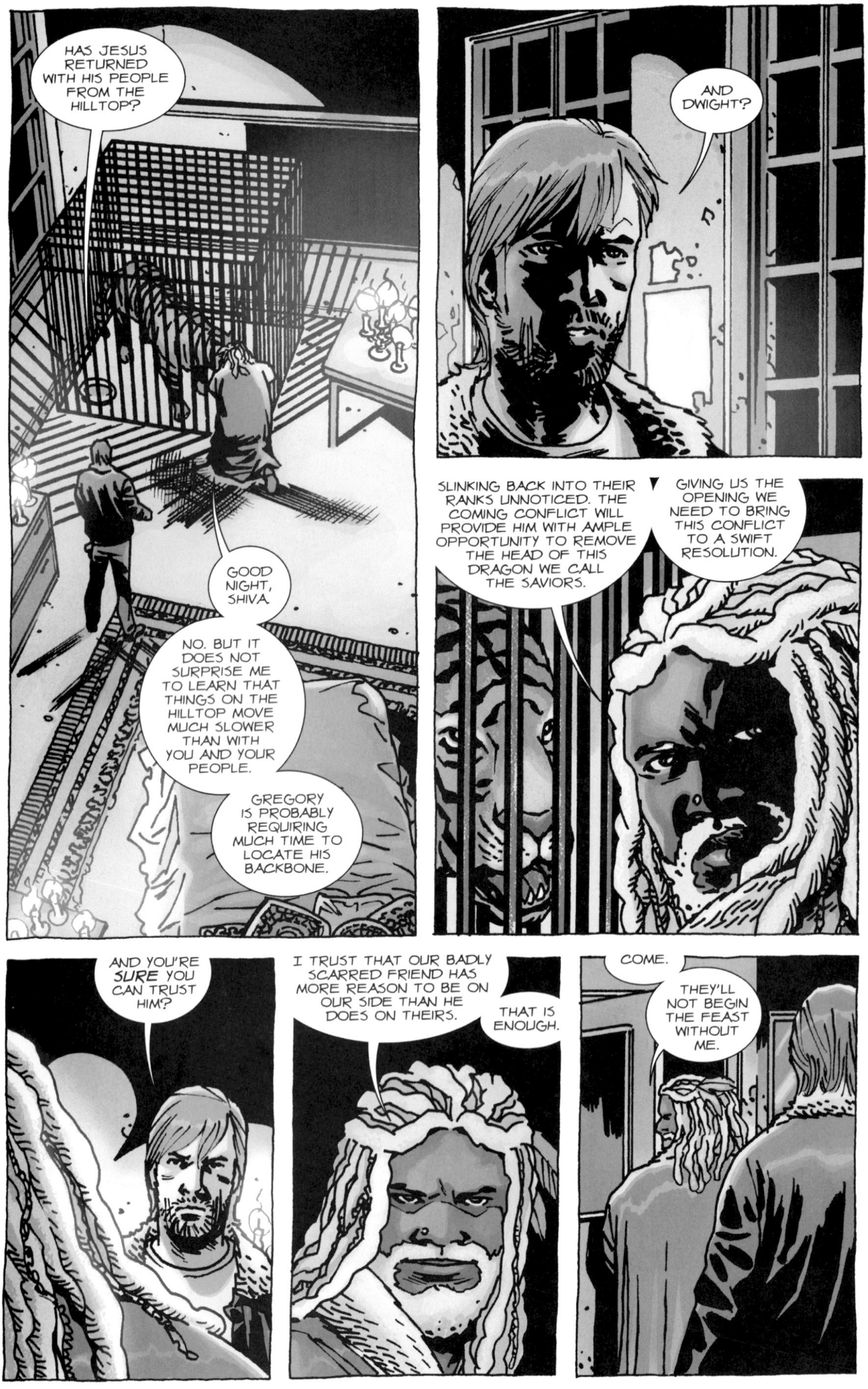
HAS JESUS RETURNED WITH HIS PEOPLE FROM THE HILLTOP?
NO. BUT IT DOES NOT SURPRISE ME TO LEARN THAT THINGS ON THE HILLTOP MOVE MUCH SLOWER THAN WITH YOU AND YOUR PEOPLE.
GREGORY IS PROBABLY REQUIRING MUCH TIME TO LOCATE HIS BACKBONE.
GOOD NIGHT, SHIVA.
AND DWIGHT?
SLINKING BACK INTO THEIR RANKS UNNOTICED. THE COMING CONFLICT WILL PROVIDE HIM WITH AMPLE OPPORTUNITY TO REMOVE THE HEAD OF THIS DRAGON WE CALL THE SAVIORS.
GIVING US THE OPENING WE NEED TO BRING THIS CONFLICT TO A SWIFT RESOLUTION.
AND YOU'RE *SURE* YOU CAN TRUST HIM?
I TRUST THAT OUR BADLY SCARRED FRIEND HAS MORE REASON TO BE ON OUR SIDE THAN HE DOES ON THEIRS.
THAT IS ENOUGH.
COME.
THEY'LL NOT BEGIN THE FEAST WITHOUT ME.

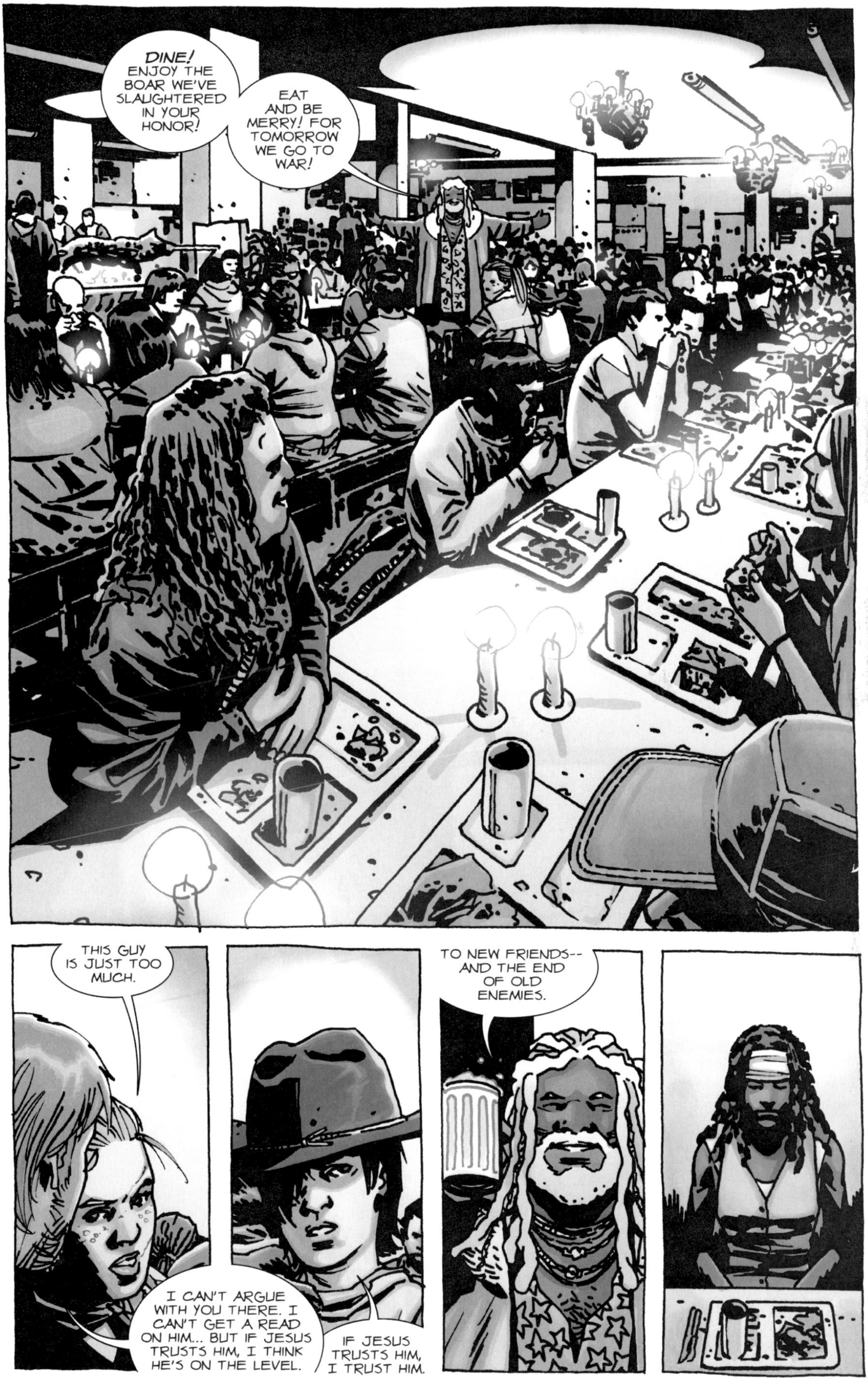

DINE! ENJOY THE BOAR WE'VE SLAUGHTERED IN YOUR HONOR!
EAT AND BE MERRY! FOR TOMORROW WE GO TO WAR!
THIS GUY IS JUST TOO MUCH.
I CAN'T ARGUE WITH YOU THERE. I CAN'T GET A READ ON HIM... BUT IF JESUS TRUSTS HIM, I THINK HE'S ON THE LEVEL.
IF JESUS TRUSTS HIM, I TRUST HIM.
TO NEW FRIENDS-- AND THE END OF OLD ENEMIES.

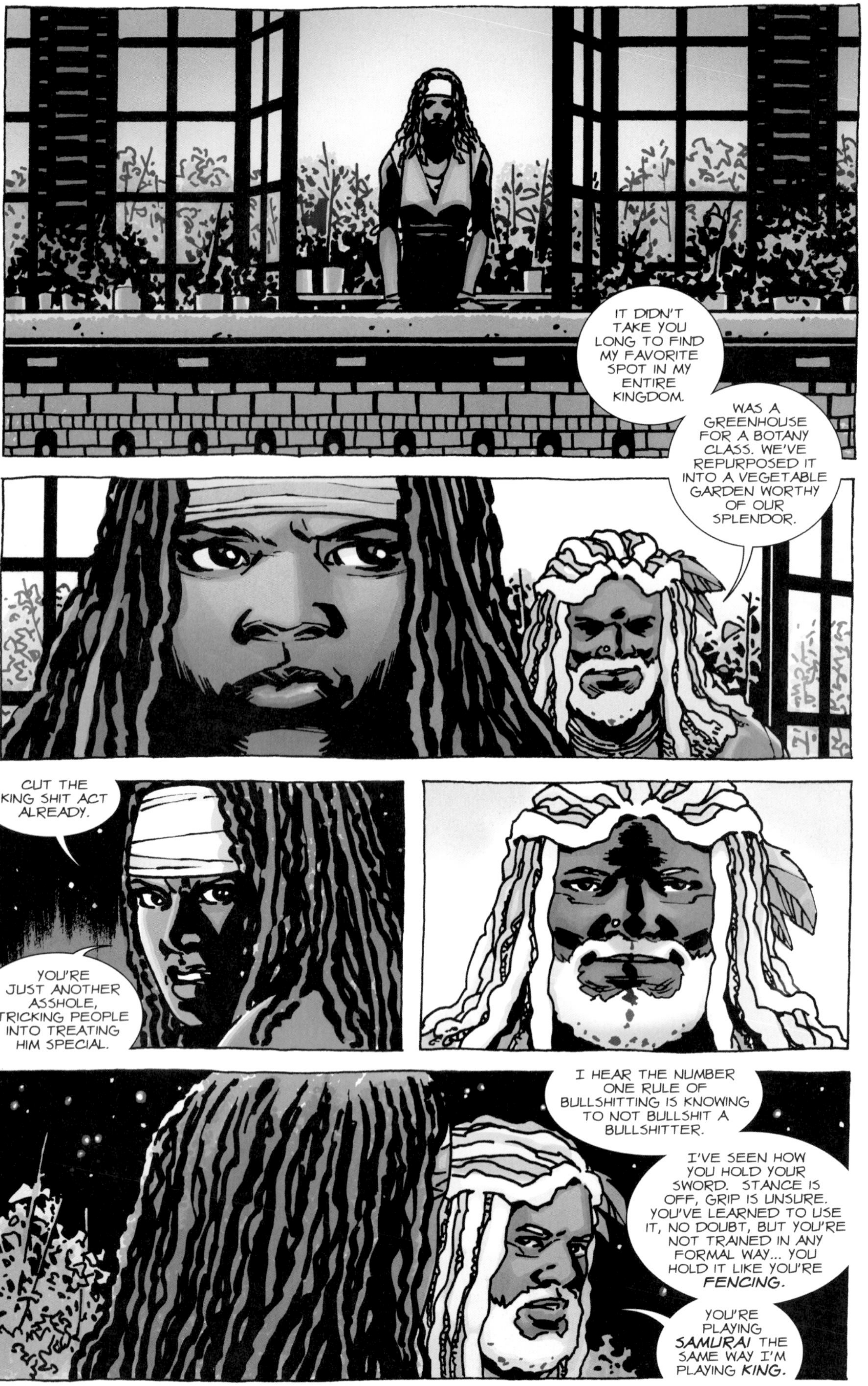
IT DIDN'T TAKE YOU LONG TO FIND MY FAVORITE SPOT IN MY ENTIRE KINGDOM.
WAS A GREENHOUSE FOR A BOTANY CLASS. WE'VE REPURPOSED IT INTO A VEGETABLE GARDEN WORTHY OF OUR SPLENDOR.
CUT THE KING SHIT ACT ALREADY.
YOU'RE JUST ANOTHER ASSHOLE, TRICKING PEOPLE INTO TREATING HIM SPECIAL.
I HEAR THE NUMBER ONE RULE OF BULLSHITTING IS KNOWING TO NOT BULLSHIT A BULLSHITTER.
I'VE SEEN HOW YOU HOLD YOUR SWORD. STANCE IS OFF, GRIP IS UNSURE. YOU'VE LEARNED TO USE IT, NO DOUBT, BUT YOU'RE NOT TRAINED IN ANY FORMAL WAY... YOU HOLD IT LIKE YOU'RE FENCING.
YOU'RE PLAYING SAMURAI THE SAME WAY I'M PLAYING KING.

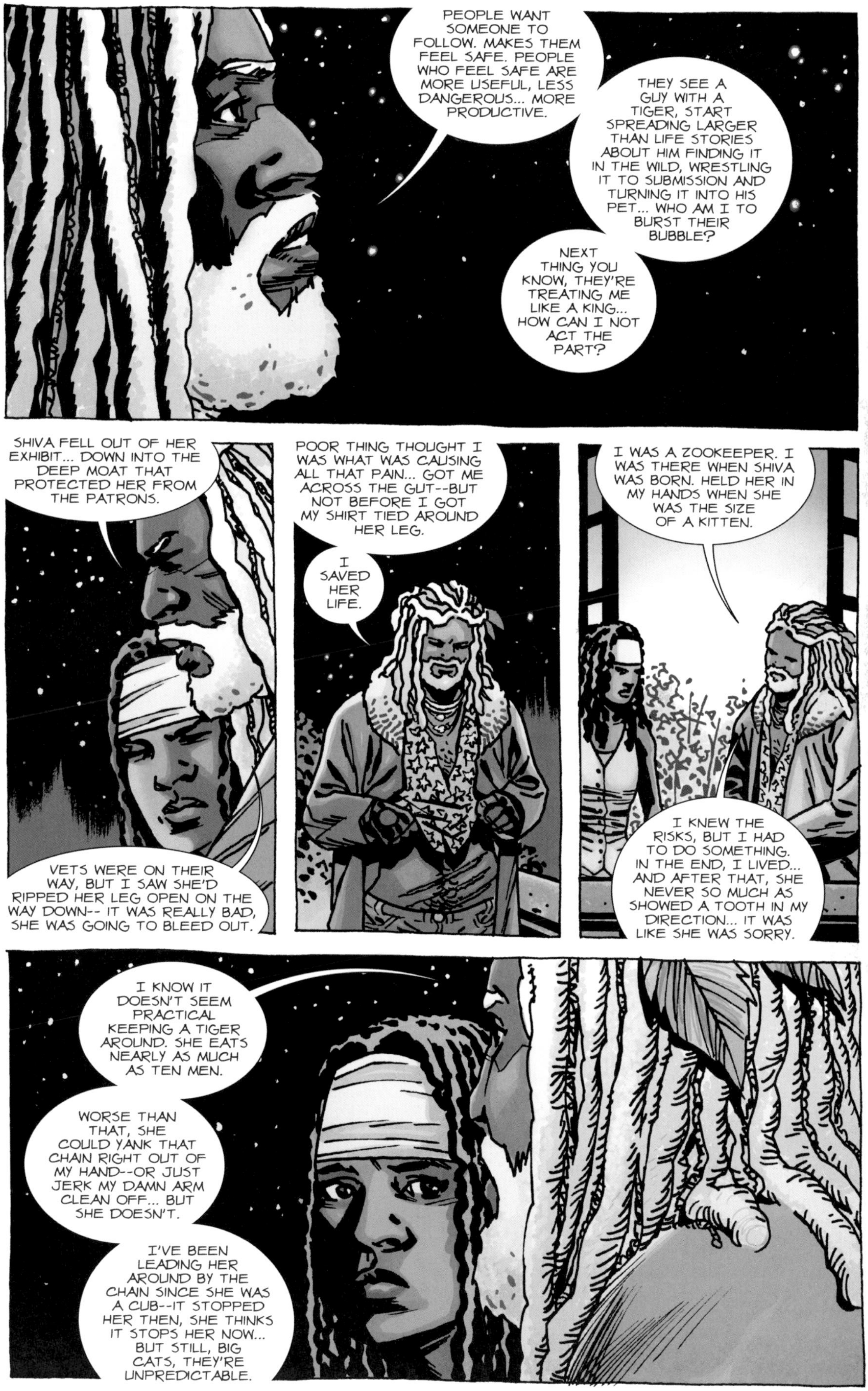
PEOPLE WANT SOMEONE TO FOLLOW. MAKES THEM FEEL SAFE. PEOPLE WHO FEEL SAFE ARE MORE USEFUL, LESS DANGEROUS... MORE PRODUCTIVE.
THEY SEE A GUY WITH A TIGER, START SPREADING LARGER THAN LIFE STORIES ABOUT HIM FINDING IT IN THE WILD, WRESTLING IT TO SUBMISSION AND TURNING IT INTO HIS PET... WHO AM I TO BURST THEIR BUBBLE?
NEXT THING YOU KNOW, THEY'RE TREATING ME LIKE A KING... HOW CAN I NOT ACT THE PART?
SHIVA FELL OUT OF HER EXHIBIT... DOWN INTO THE DEEP MOAT THAT PROTECTED HER FROM THE PATRONS.
VETS WERE ON THEIR WAY, BUT I SAW SHE'D RIPPED HER LEG OPEN ON THE WAY DOWN-- IT WAS REALLY BAD, SHE WAS GOING TO BLEED OUT.
POOR THING THOUGHT I WAS WHAT WAS CAUSING ALL THAT PAIN... GOT ME ACROSS THE GUT--BUT NOT BEFORE I GOT MY SHIRT TIED AROUND HER LEG.
I SAVED HER LIFE.
I WAS A ZOOKEEPER. I WAS THERE WHEN SHIVA WAS BORN. HELD HER IN MY HANDS WHEN SHE WAS THE SIZE OF A KITTEN.
I KNEW THE RISKS, BUT I HAD TO DO SOMETHING. IN THE END, I LIVED... AND AFTER THAT, SHE NEVER SO MUCH AS SHOWED A TOOTH IN MY DIRECTION... IT WAS LIKE SHE WAS SORRY.
I KNOW IT DOESN'T SEEM PRACTICAL KEEPING A TIGER AROUND. SHE EATS NEARLY AS MUCH AS TEN MEN.
WORSE THAN THAT, SHE COULD YANK THAT CHAIN RIGHT OUT OF MY HAND--OR JUST JERK MY DAMN ARM CLEAN OFF... BUT SHE DOESN'T.
I'VE BEEN LEADING HER AROUND BY THE CHAIN SINCE SHE WAS A CUB--IT STOPPED HER THEN, SHE THINKS IT STOPS HER NOW... BUT STILL, BIG CATS, THEY'RE UNPREDICTABLE.

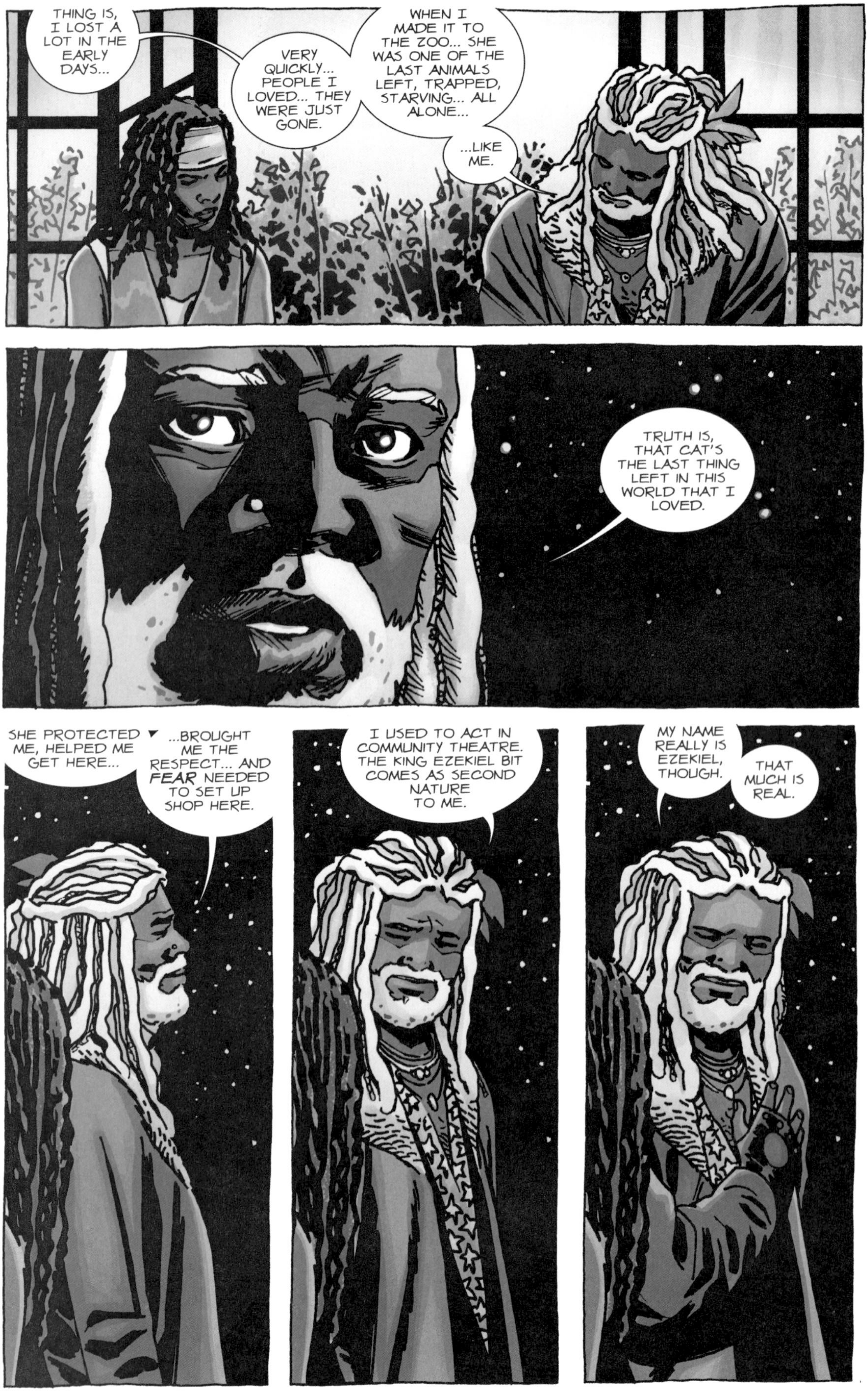
THING IS, I LOST A LOT IN THE EARLY DAYS...
VERY QUICKLY... PEOPLE I LOVED... THEY WERE JUST GONE.
WHEN I MADE IT TO THE ZOO... SHE WAS ONE OF THE LAST ANIMALS LEFT, TRAPPED, STARVING... ALL ALONE...
...LIKE ME.
TRUTH IS, THAT CAT'S THE LAST THING LEFT IN THIS WORLD THAT I LOVED.
SHE PROTECTED ME, HELPED ME GET HERE...
...BROUGHT ME THE RESPECT... AND FEAR NEEDED TO SET UP SHOP HERE.
I USED TO ACT IN COMMUNITY THEATRE. THE KING EZEKIEL BIT COMES AS SECOND NATURE TO ME.
MY NAME REALLY IS EZEKIEL, THOUGH.
THAT MUCH IS REAL.

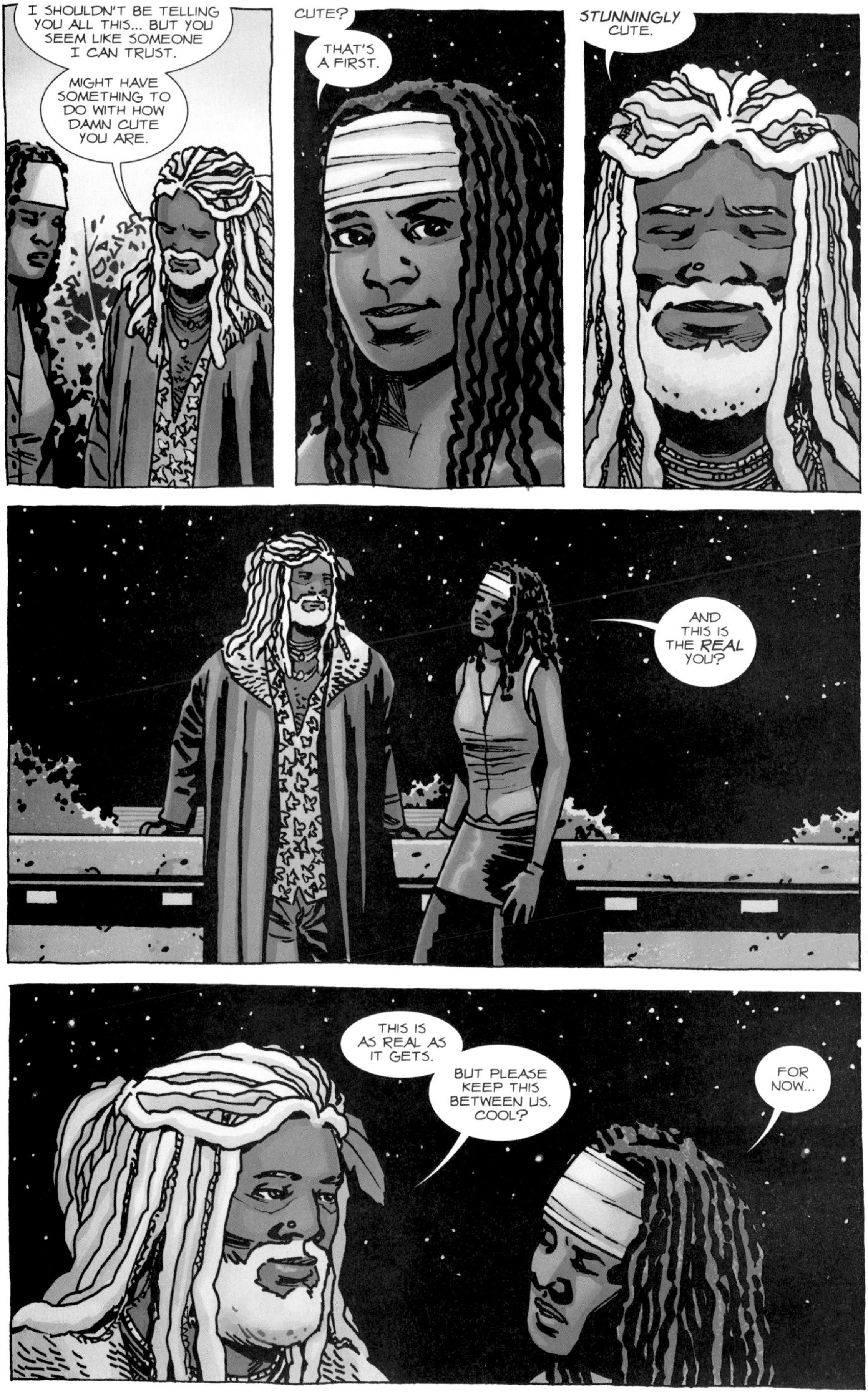

I SHOULDN'T BE TELLING YOU ALL THIS... BUT YOU SEEM LIKE SOMEONE I CAN TRUST.
MIGHT HAVE SOMETHING TO DO WITH HOW DAMN CUTE YOU ARE.
CUTE?
THAT'S A FIRST.
STUNNINGLY CUTE.
AND THIS IS THE REAL YOU?
THIS IS AS REAL AS IT GETS.
BUT PLEASE KEEP THIS BETWEEN US. COOL?
FOR NOW...

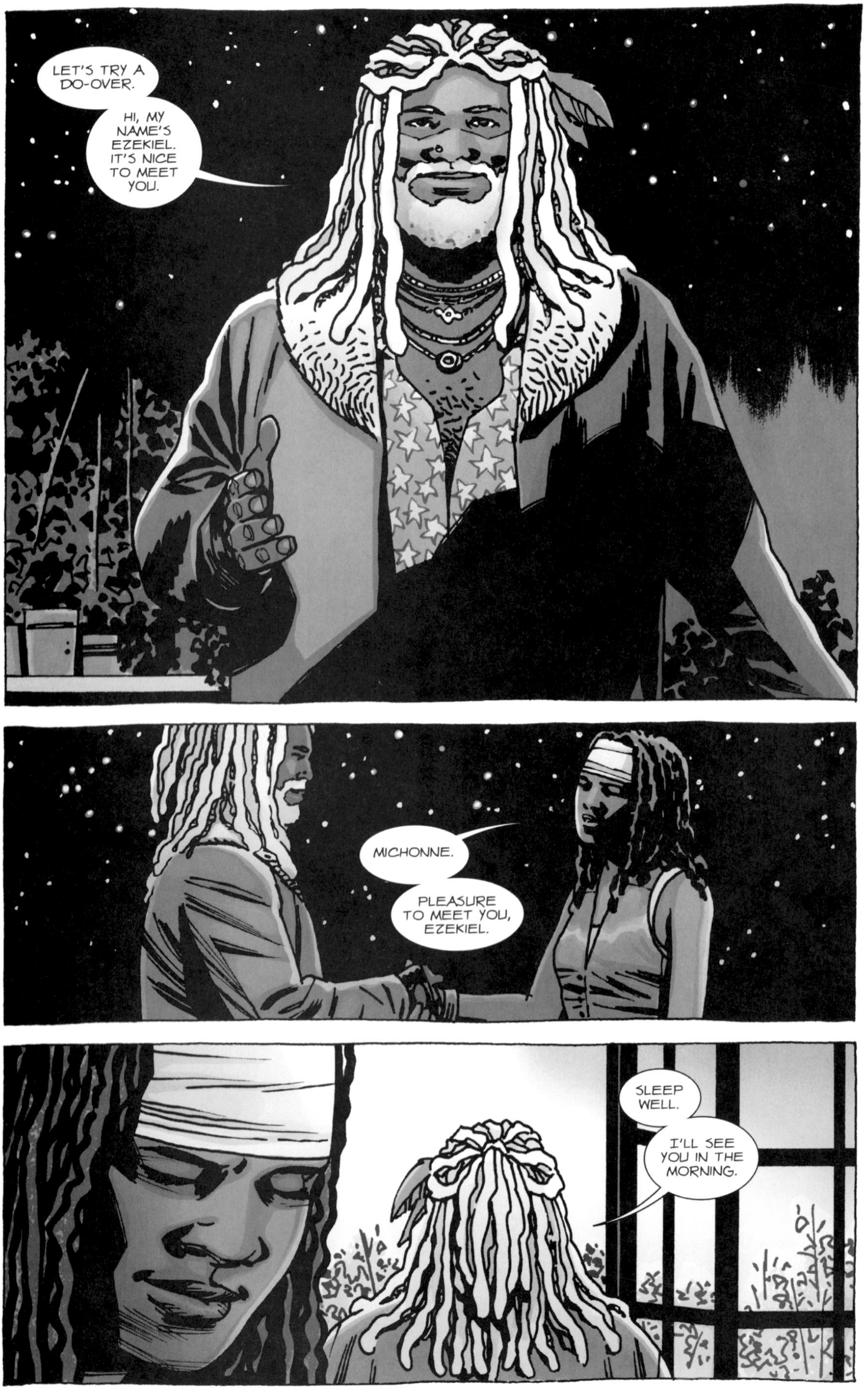
LET'S TRY A DO-OVER.
HI, MY NAME'S EZEKIEL. IT'S NICE TO MEET YOU.
MICHONNE.
PLEASURE TO MEET YOU, EZEKIEL.
SLEEP WELL.
I'LL SEE YOU IN THE MORNING.

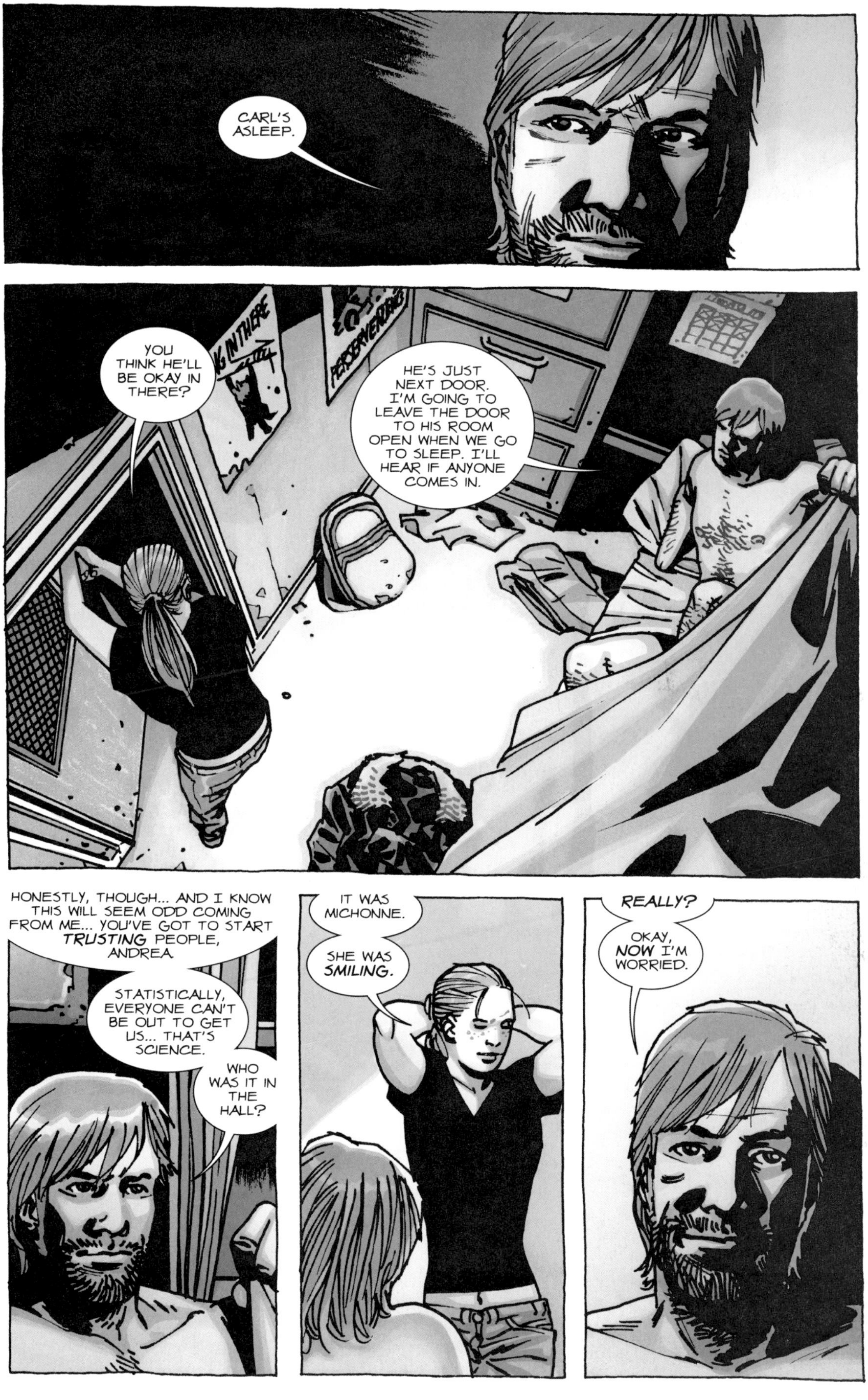
CARL'S ASLEEP.
YOU THINK HE'LL BE OKAY IN THERE?
HE'S JUST NEXT DOOR. I'M GOING TO LEAVE THE DOOR TO HIS ROOM OPEN WHEN WE GO TO SLEEP. I'LL HEAR IF ANYONE COMES IN.
HONESTLY, THOUGH... AND I KNOW THIS WILL SEEM ODD COMING FROM ME... YOU'VE GOT TO START TRUSTING PEOPLE, ANDREA.
STATISTICALLY, EVERYONE CAN'T BE OUT TO GET US... THAT'S SCIENCE.
WHO WAS IT IN THE HALL?
IT WAS MICHONNE.
SHE WAS SMILING.
REALLY?
OKAY, NOW I'M WORRIED.

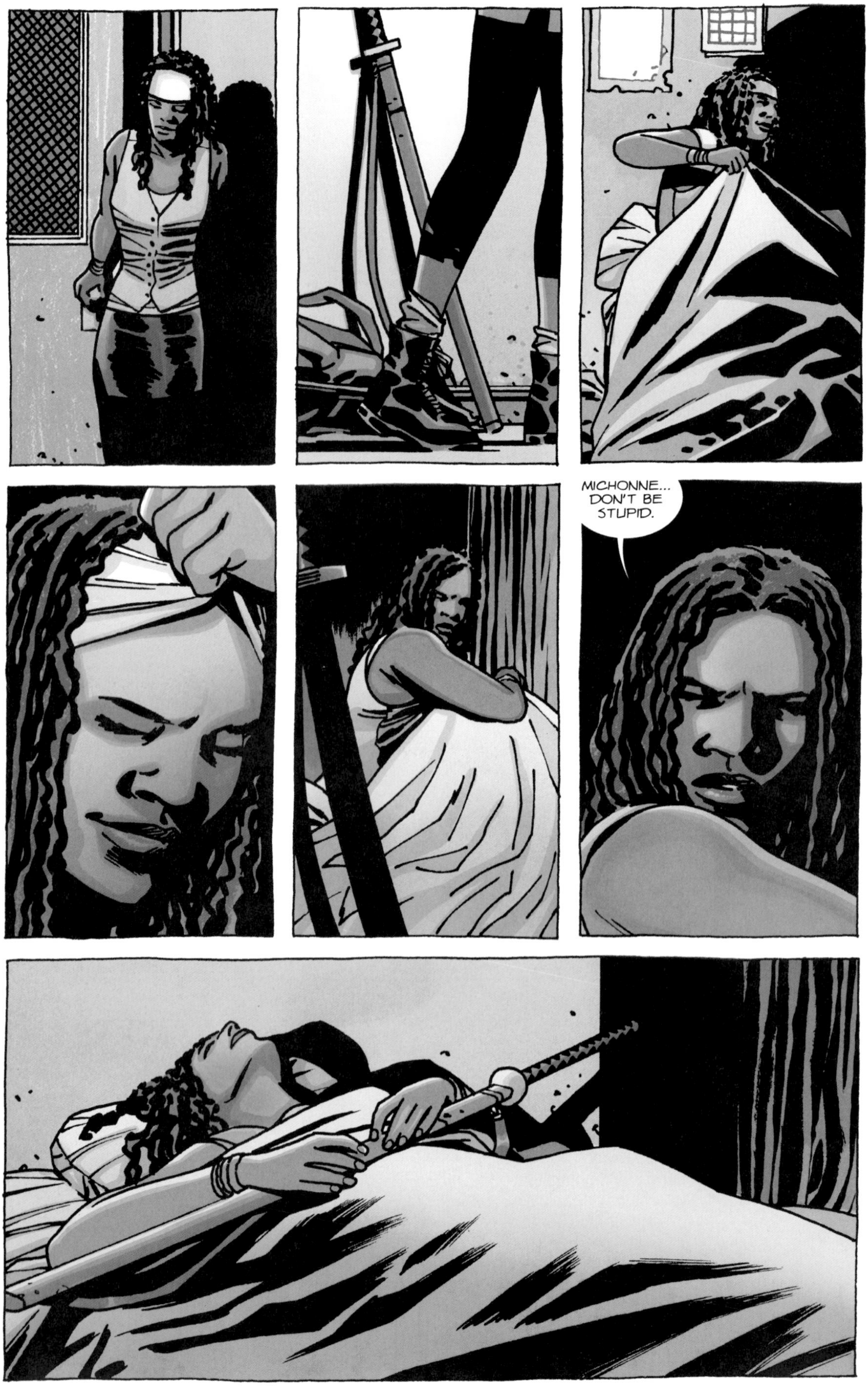
MICHONNE... DON'T BE STUPID.

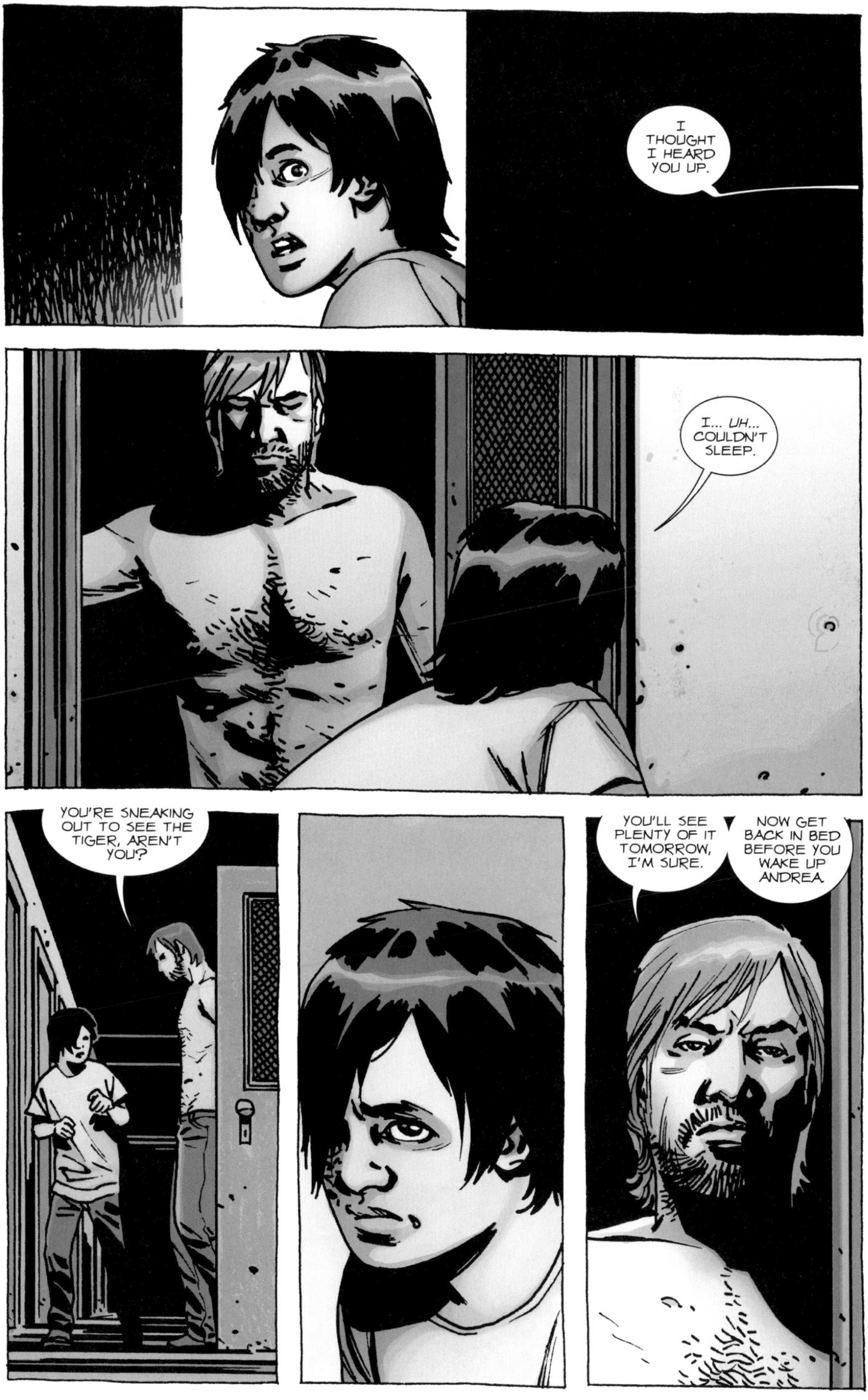
I THOUGHT I HEARD YOU UP.
I... UH... COULDN'T SLEEP.
YOU'RE SNEAKING OUT TO SEE THE TIGER, AREN'T YOU?
YOU'LL SEE PLENTY OF IT TOMORROW, I'M SURE.
NOW GET BACK IN BED BEFORE YOU WAKE UP ANDREA.

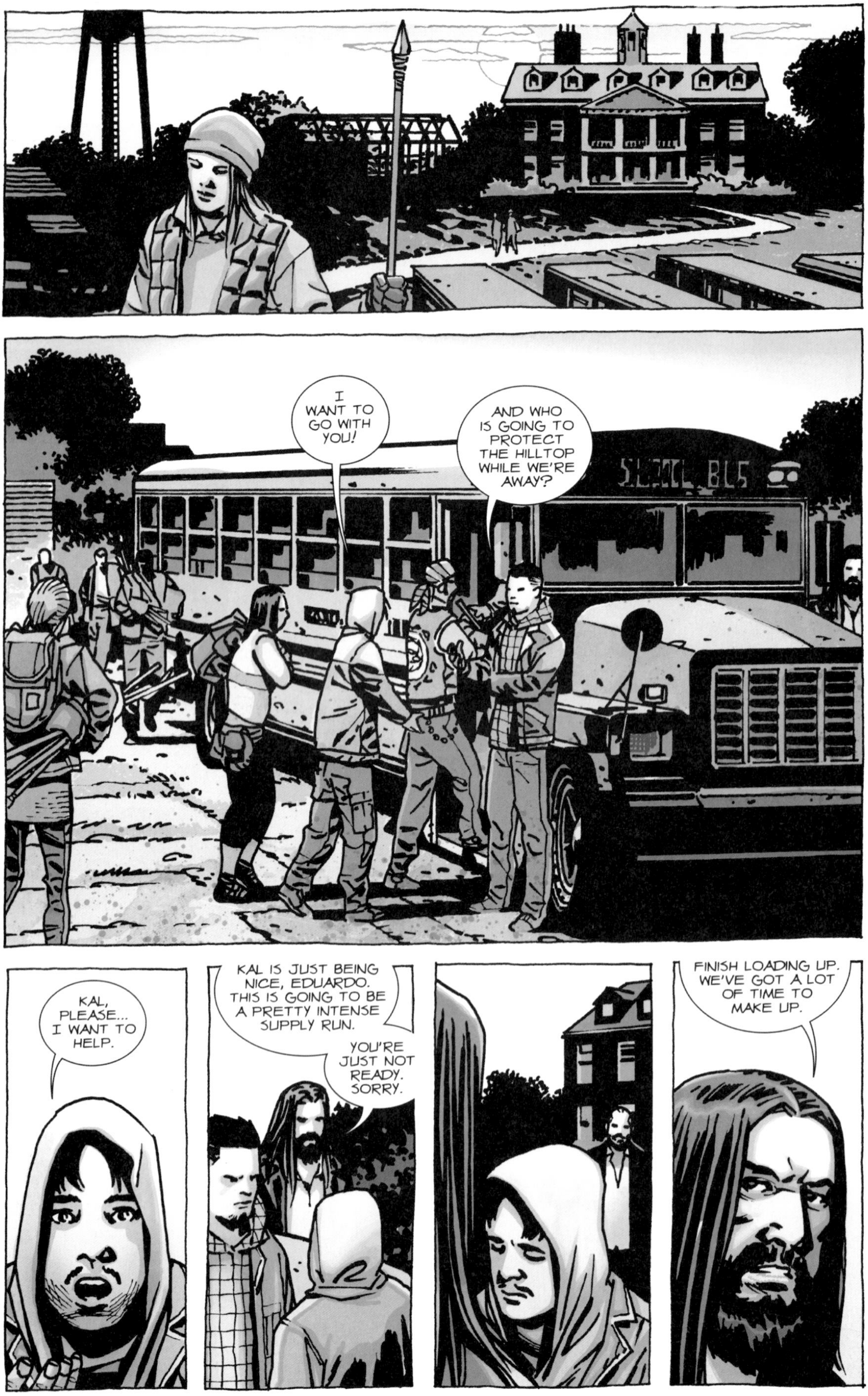

I WANT TO GO WITH YOU!
AND WHO IS GOING TO PROTECT THE HILLTOP WHILE WE'RE AWAY?
SCHOOL BUS
KAL, PLEASE... I WANT TO HELP.
KAL IS JUST BEING NICE, EDUARDO. THIS IS GOING TO BE A PRETTY INTENSE SUPPLY RUN.
YOU'RE JUST NOT READY. SORRY.
FINISH LOADING UP. WE'VE GOT A LOT OF TIME TO MAKE UP.

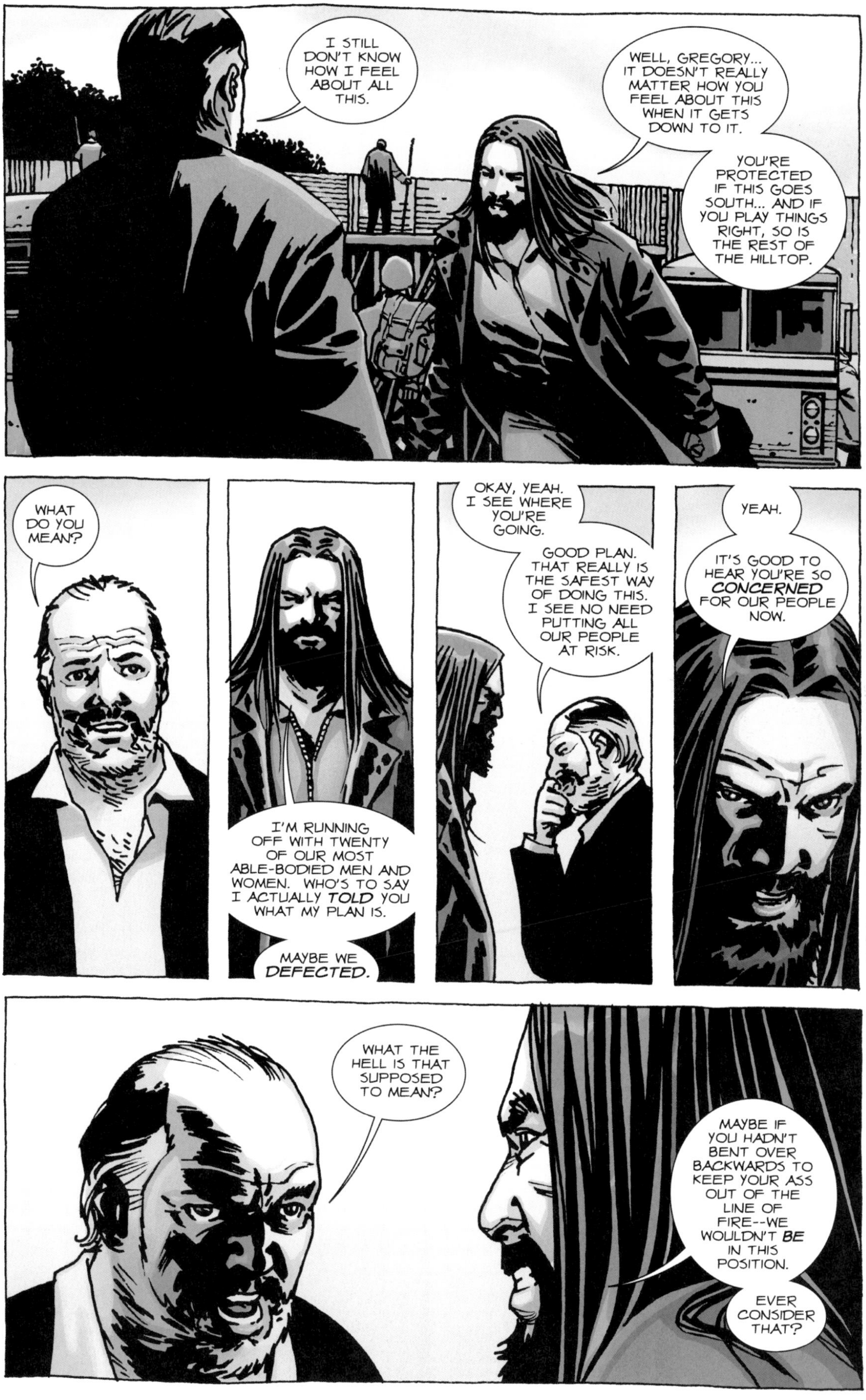
I STILL DON'T KNOW HOW I FEEL ABOUT ALL THIS.
WELL, GREGORY... IT DOESN'T REALLY MATTER HOW YOU FEEL ABOUT THIS WHEN IT GETS DOWN TO IT.
YOU'RE PROTECTED IF THIS GOES SOUTH... AND IF YOU PLAY THINGS RIGHT, SO IS THE REST OF THE HILLTOP.
WHAT DO YOU MEAN?
I'M RUNNING OFF WITH TWENTY OF OUR MOST ABLE-BODIED MEN AND WOMEN. WHO'S TO SAY I ACTUALLY TOLD YOU WHAT MY PLAN IS.
MAYBE WE DEFECTED.
OKAY, YEAH. I SEE WHERE YOU'RE GOING.
GOOD PLAN. THAT REALLY IS THE SAFEST WAY OF DOING THIS. I SEE NO NEED PUTTING ALL OUR PEOPLE AT RISK.
YEAH.
IT'S GOOD TO HEAR YOU'RE SO CONCERNED FOR OUR PEOPLE NOW.
WHAT THE HELL IS THAT SUPPOSED TO MEAN?
MAYBE IF YOU HADN'T BENT OVER BACKWARDS TO KEEP YOUR ASS OUT OF THE LINE OF FIRE--WE WOULDN'T BE IN THIS POSITION.
EVER CONSIDER THAT?

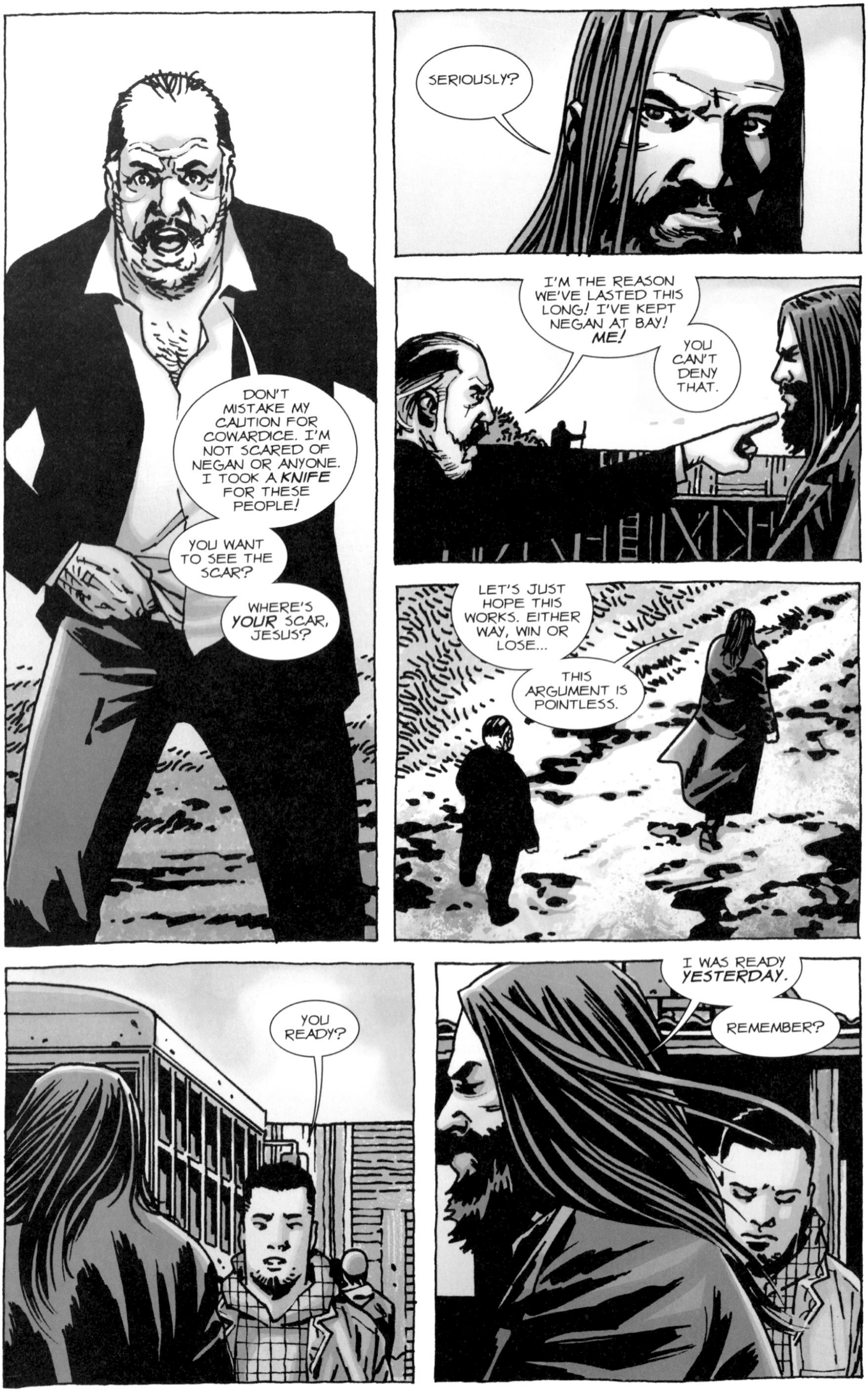
DON'T MISTAKE MY CAUTION FOR COWARDICE. I'M NOT SCARED OF NEGAN OR ANYONE. I TOOK A KNIFE FOR THESE PEOPLE!
YOU WANT TO SEE THE SCAR?
WHERE'S YOUR SCAR, JESUS?
SERIOUSLY?
I'M THE REASON WE'VE LASTED THIS LONG! I'VE KEPT NEGAN AT BAY! ME!
YOU CAN'T DENY THAT.
LET'S JUST HOPE THIS WORKS. EITHER WAY, WIN OR LOSE...
THIS ARGUMENT IS POINTLESS.
YOU READY?
I WAS READY YESTERDAY.
REMEMBER?

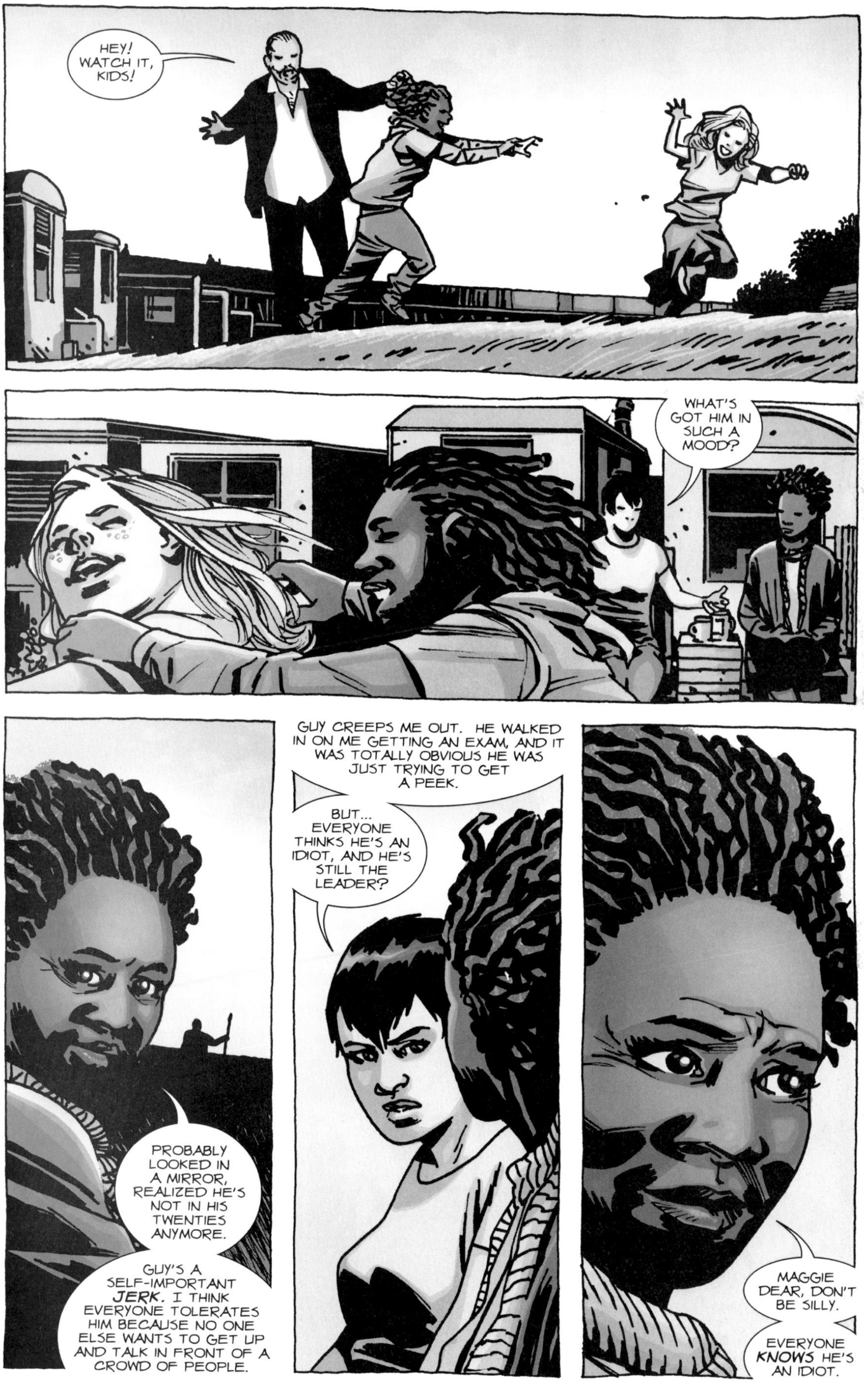
HEY! WATCH IT, KIDS!
WHAT'S GOT HIM IN SUCH A MOOD?
PROBABLY LOOKED IN A MIRROR, REALIZED HE'S NOT IN HIS TWENTIES ANYMORE.
GUY'S A SELF-IMPORTANT JERK. I THINK EVERYONE TOLERATES HIM BECAUSE NO ONE ELSE WANTS TO GET UP AND TALK IN FRONT OF A CROWD OF PEOPLE.
GUY CREEPS ME OUT. HE WALKED IN ON ME GETTING AN EXAM, AND IT WAS TOTALLY OBVIOUS HE WAS JUST TRYING TO GET A PEEK.
BUT... EVERYONE THINKS HE'S AN IDIOT, AND HE'S STILL THE LEADER?
MAGGIE DEAR, DON'T BE SILLY.
EVERYONE KNOWS HE'S AN IDIOT.

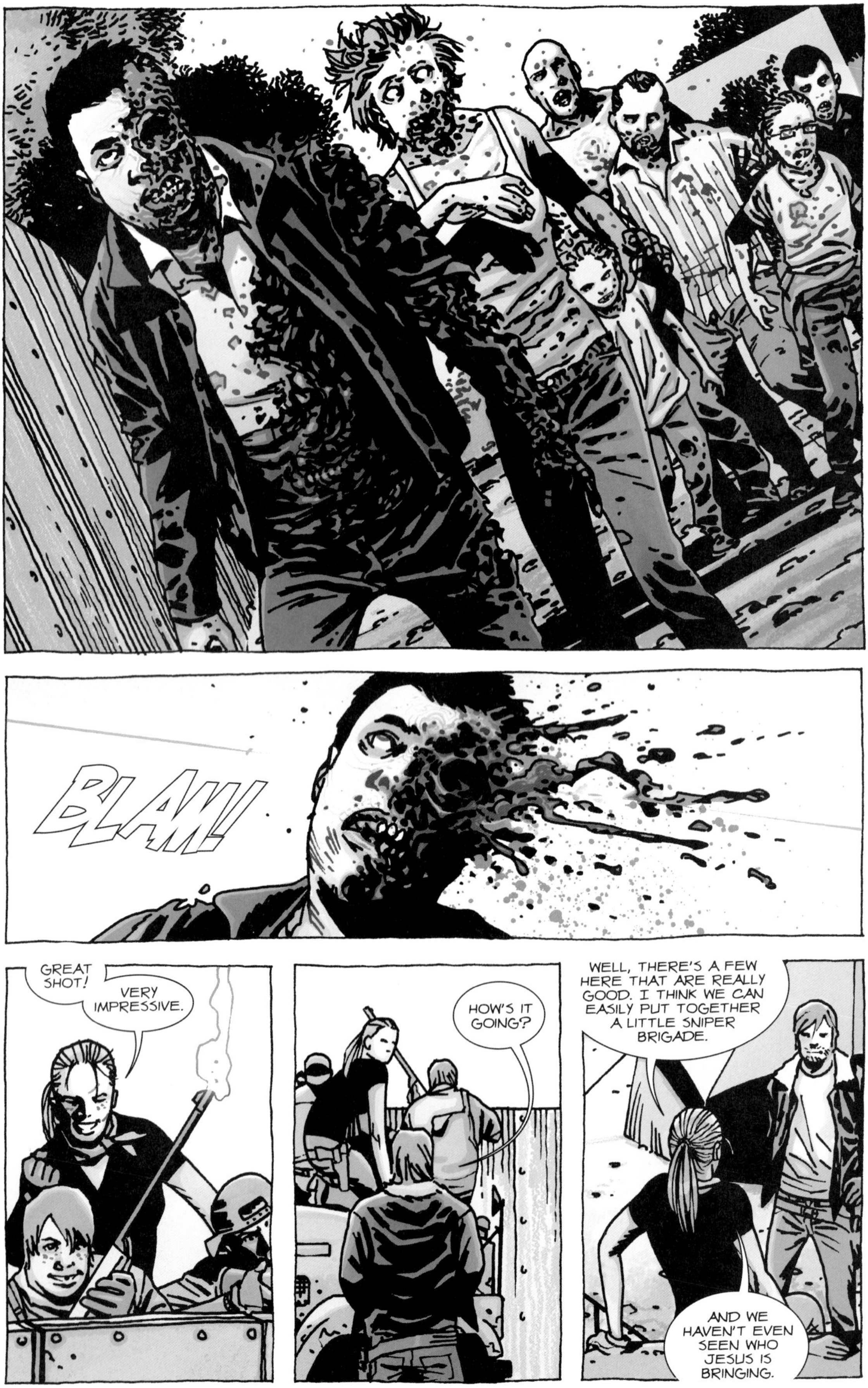
BLAM!
GREAT SHOT!
VERY IMPRESSIVE.
HOW'S IT GOING?
WELL, THERE'S A FEW HERE THAT ARE REALLY GOOD. I THINK WE CAN EASILY PUT TOGETHER A LITTLE SNIPER BRIGADE.
AND WE HAVEN'T EVEN SEEN WHO JESUS IS BRINGING.

HOW ARE THINGS ON YOUR END?

GOOD. THERE'S A LOT OF STRENGTH, SOME GOOD HAND-TO-HAND FIGHTERS. EZEKIEL'S NUMBERS ARE ACTUALLY IMPRESSIVE. HE'S GOT AT LEAST THIRTY PEOPLE THAT ARE IN FIGHTING SHAPE.

MORE THAN US OR THE HILLTOP.

WHAT'S THAT PUTTING OUR TOTAL FORCES AT?

ALMOST FIFTY, WITHOUT WHOEVER JESUS IS BRINGING. HE THOUGHT HE'D BE ABLE TO GET CLOSE TO *TWENTY*.

WE'LL SEE.

STILL THINK WE'RE UNDER WHERE WE NEED TO BE?

I DON'T KNOW. I'M NO STRATEGIST. COULD HAVE REALLY USED ABRAHAM FOR THIS.

NUMBERS WISE... I THINK JESUS ESTIMATED THE SAVIORS HAVE LIKE SIXTY PEOPLE AT THEIR PLACE... BUT HE STILL HAS NO IDEA HOW MANY PEOPLE THEY KEEP AT THEIR OUTPOSTS, OR HOW MANY OUTPOSTS THEY HAVE.

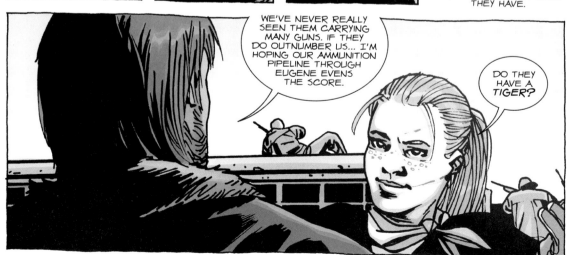

WE'VE NEVER REALLY SEEN THEM CARRYING MANY GUNS. IF THEY DO OUTNUMBER US... I'M HOPING OUR AMMUNITION PIPELINE THROUGH EUGENE EVENS THE SCORE.

DO THEY HAVE A *TIGER*?

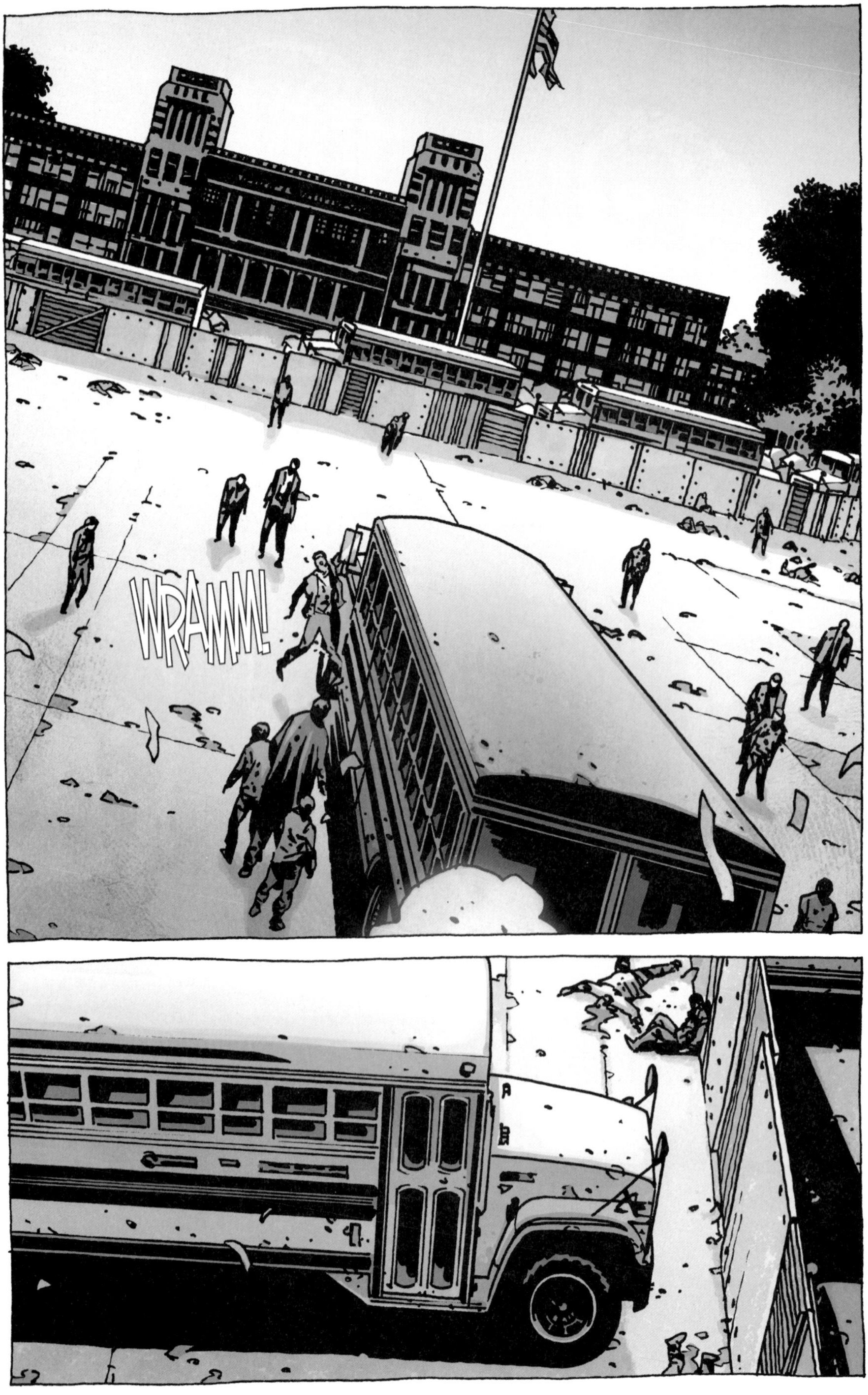
WRAMM!

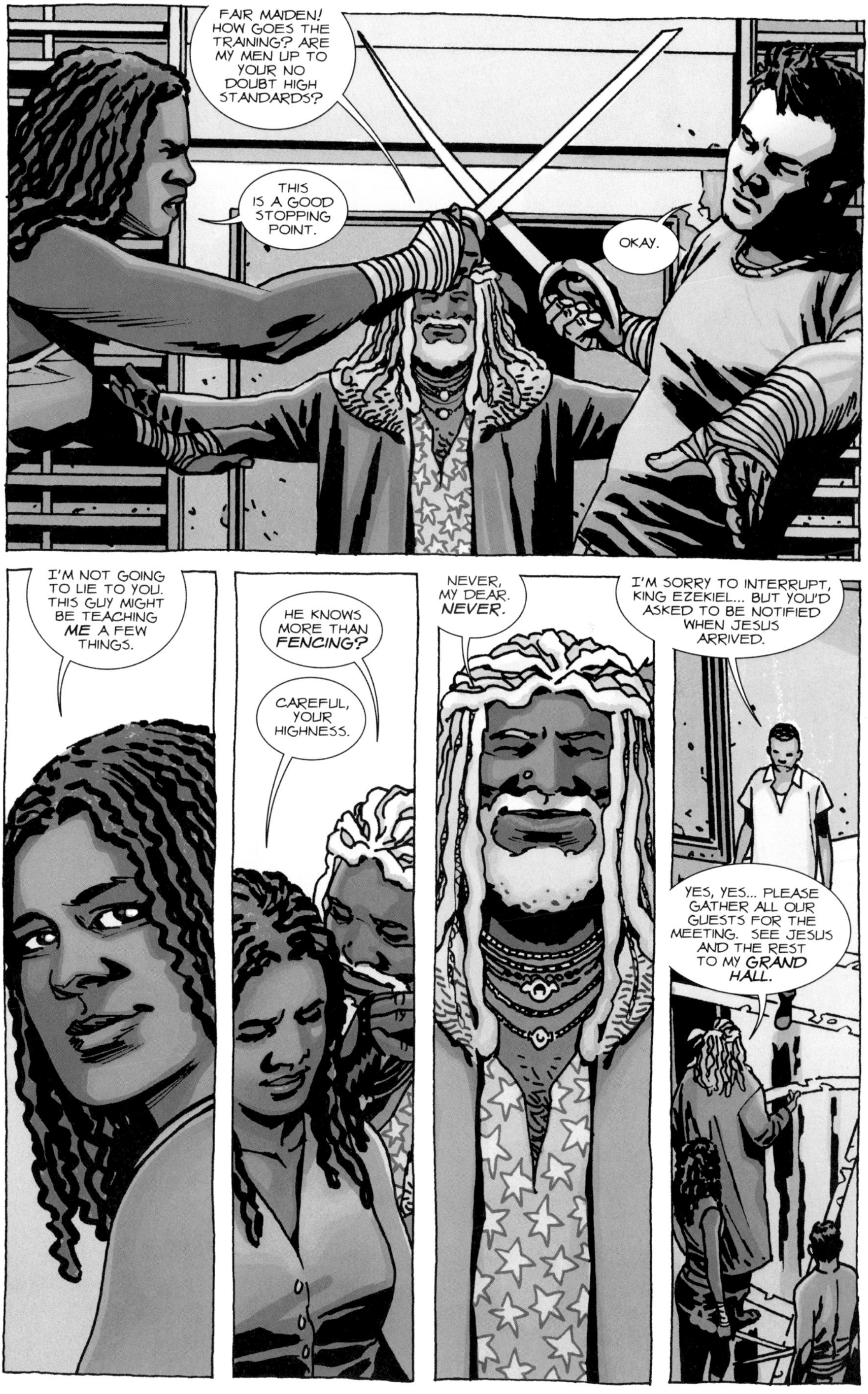

FAIR MAIDEN! HOW GOES THE TRAINING? ARE MY MEN UP TO YOUR NO DOUBT HIGH STANDARDS?
THIS IS A GOOD STOPPING POINT.
OKAY.
I'M NOT GOING TO LIE TO YOU. THIS GUY MIGHT BE TEACHING ME A FEW THINGS.
HE KNOWS MORE THAN FENCING?
CAREFUL, YOUR HIGHNESS.
NEVER, MY DEAR. NEVER.
I'M SORRY TO INTERRUPT, KING EZEKIEL... BUT YOU'D ASKED TO BE NOTIFIED WHEN JESUS ARRIVED.
YES, YES... PLEASE GATHER ALL OUR GUESTS FOR THE MEETING. SEE JESUS AND THE REST TO MY GRAND HALL.

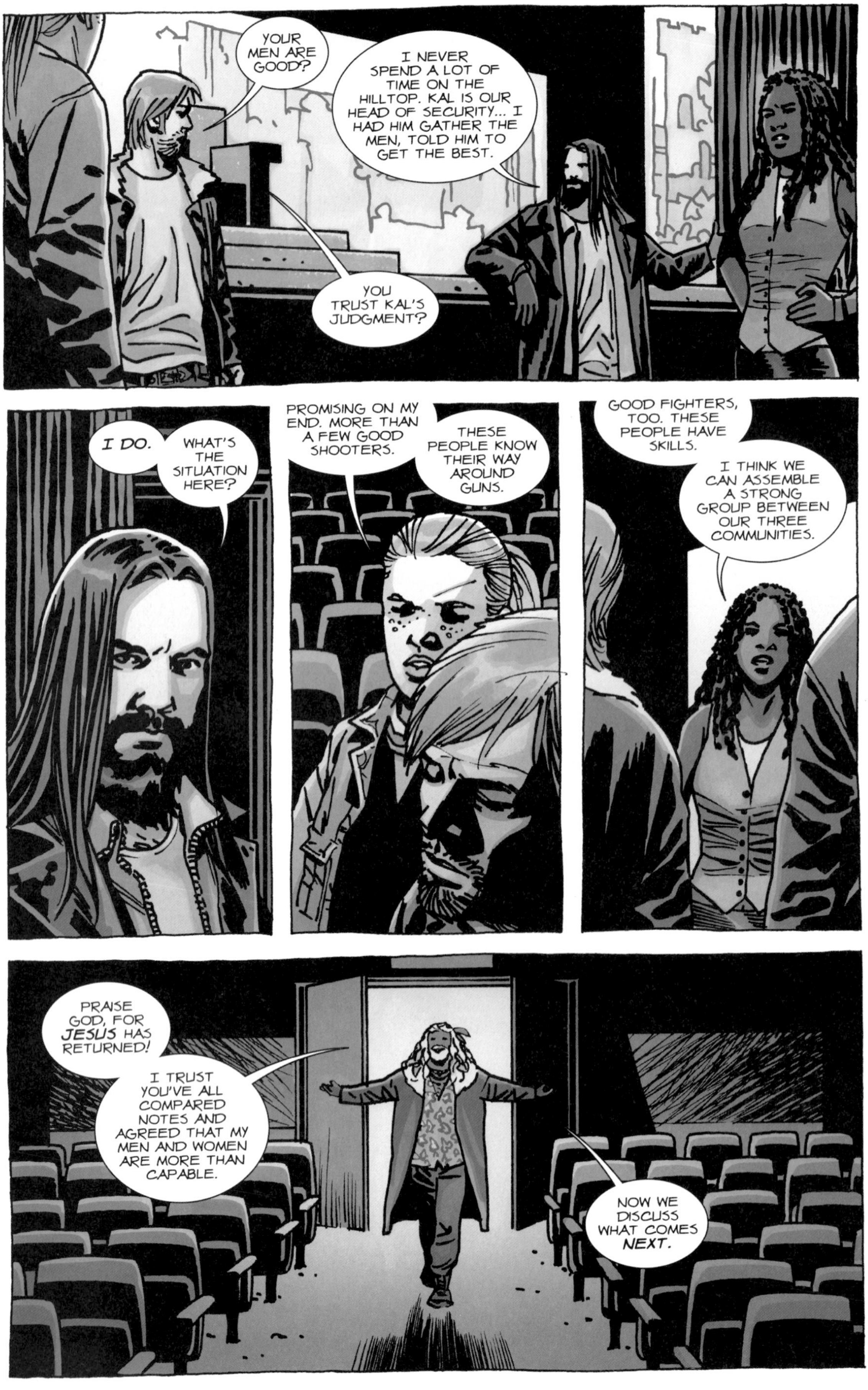
YOUR MEN ARE GOOD?
I NEVER SPEND A LOT OF TIME ON THE HILLTOP. KAL IS OUR HEAD OF SECURITY... I HAD HIM GATHER THE MEN, TOLD HIM TO GET THE BEST.
YOU TRUST KAL'S JUDGMENT?
I DO.
WHAT'S THE SITUATION HERE?
PROMISING ON MY END. MORE THAN A FEW GOOD SHOOTERS.
THESE PEOPLE KNOW THEIR WAY AROUND GUNS.
GOOD FIGHTERS, TOO. THESE PEOPLE HAVE SKILLS.
I THINK WE CAN ASSEMBLE A STRONG GROUP BETWEEN OUR THREE COMMUNITIES.
PRAISE GOD, FOR JESUS HAS RETURNED!
I TRUST YOU'VE ALL COMPARED NOTES AND AGREED THAT MY MEN AND WOMEN ARE MORE THAN CAPABLE.
NOW WE DISCUSS WHAT COMES NEXT.

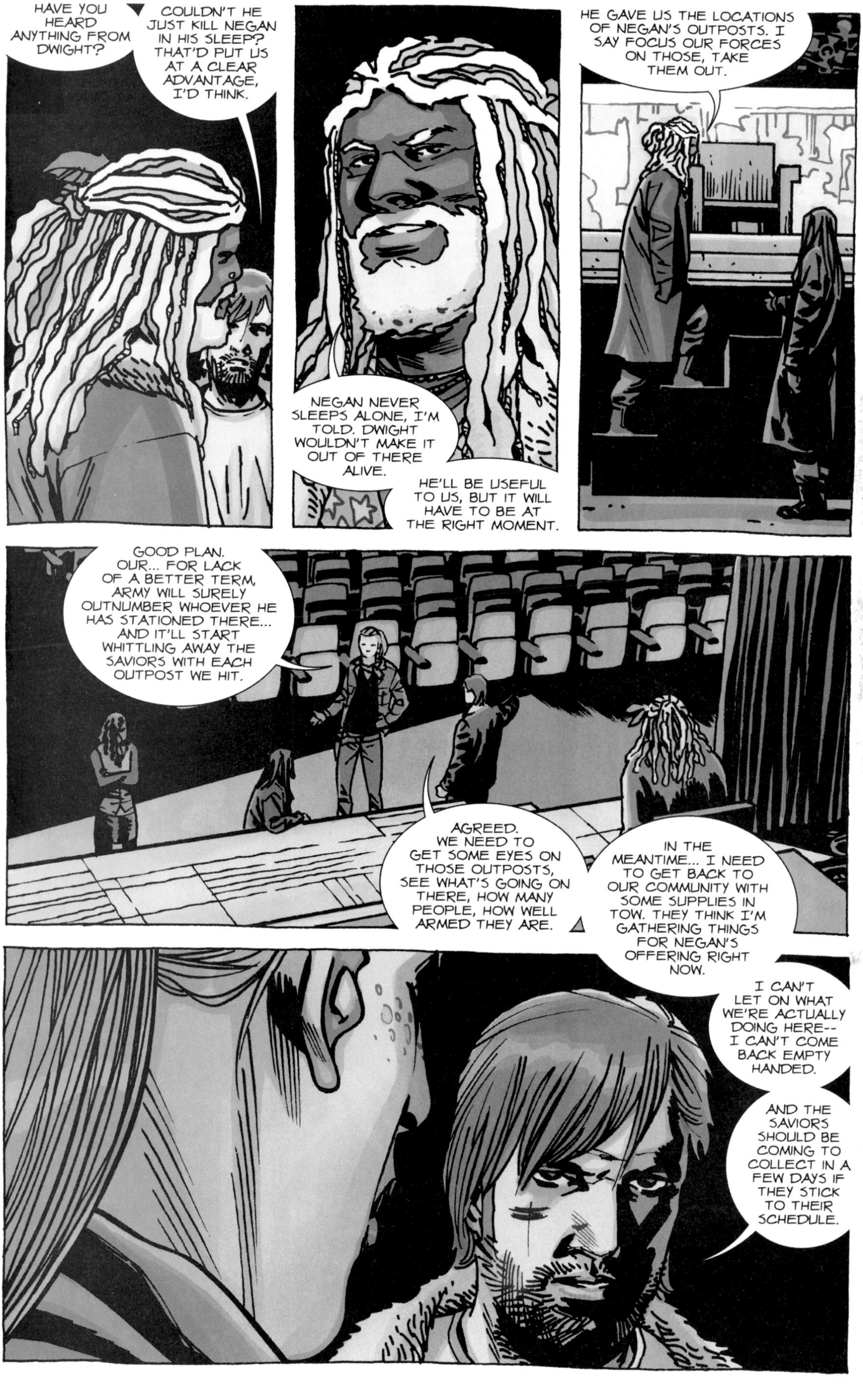
HAVE YOU HEARD ANYTHING FROM DWIGHT?
COULDN'T HE JUST KILL NEGAN IN HIS SLEEP? THAT'D PUT US AT A CLEAR ADVANTAGE, I'D THINK.
NEGAN NEVER SLEEPS ALONE, I'M TOLD. DWIGHT WOULDN'T MAKE IT OUT OF THERE ALIVE.
HE'LL BE USEFUL TO US, BUT IT WILL HAVE TO BE AT THE RIGHT MOMENT.
HE GAVE US THE LOCATIONS OF NEGAN'S OUTPOSTS. I SAY FOCUS OUR FORCES ON THOSE, TAKE THEM OUT.
GOOD PLAN. OUR... FOR LACK OF A BETTER TERM, ARMY WILL SURELY OUTNUMBER WHOEVER HE HAS STATIONED THERE... AND IT'LL START WHITTLING AWAY THE SAVIORS WITH EACH OUTPOST WE HIT.
AGREED. WE NEED TO GET SOME EYES ON THOSE OUTPOSTS, SEE WHAT'S GOING ON THERE, HOW MANY PEOPLE, HOW WELL ARMED THEY ARE.
IN THE MEANTIME... I NEED TO GET BACK TO OUR COMMUNITY WITH SOME SUPPLIES IN TOW. THEY THINK I'M GATHERING THINGS FOR NEGAN'S OFFERING RIGHT NOW.
I CAN'T LET ON WHAT WE'RE ACTUALLY DOING HERE-- I CAN'T COME BACK EMPTY HANDED.
AND THE SAVIORS SHOULD BE COMING TO COLLECT IN A FEW DAYS IF THEY STICK TO THEIR SCHEDULE.

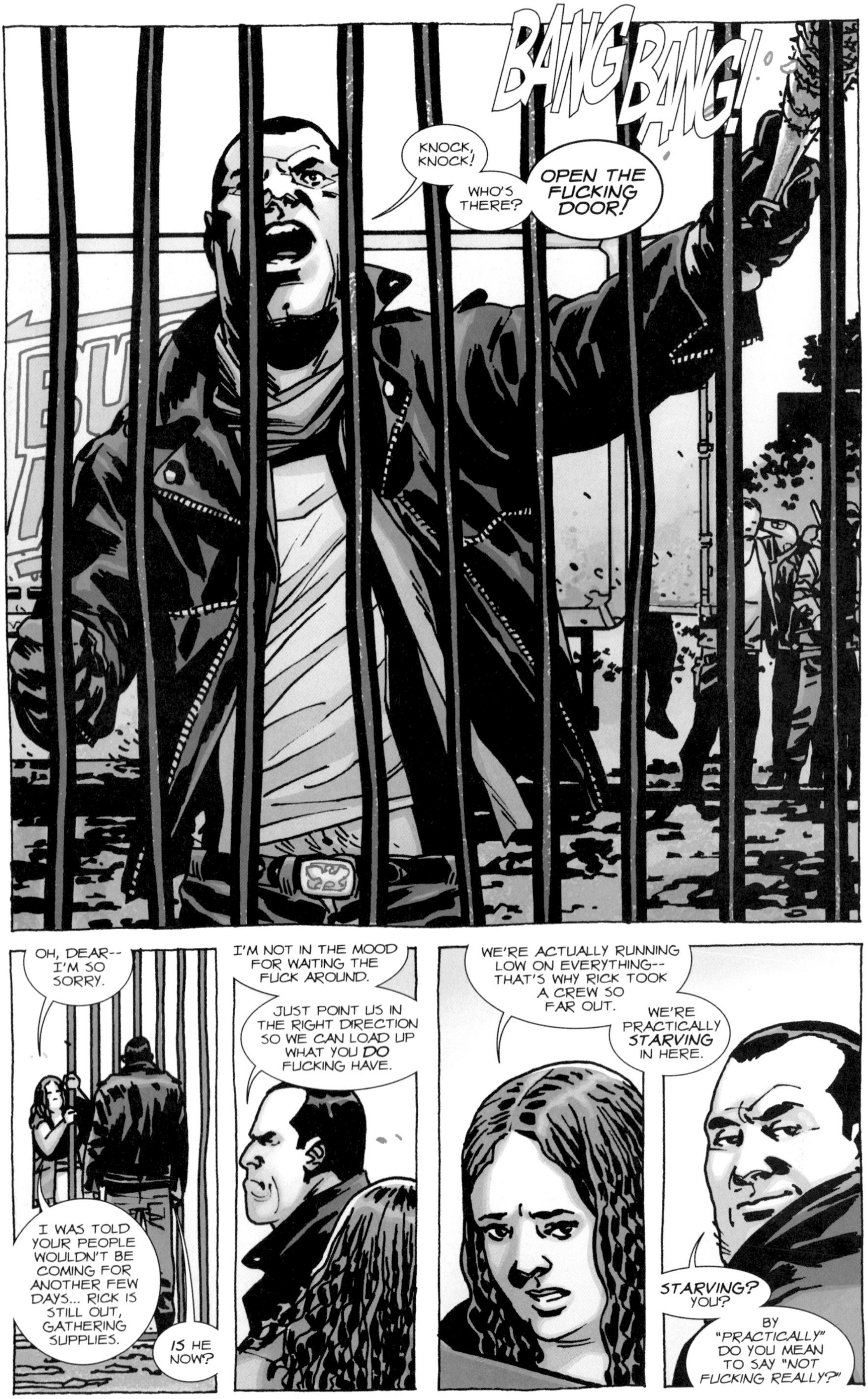

BANG BANG!
KNOCK, KNOCK!
WHO'S THERE?
OPEN THE FUCKING DOOR!
OH, DEAR-- I'M SO SORRY.
I WAS TOLD YOUR PEOPLE WOULDN'T BE COMING FOR ANOTHER FEW DAYS... RICK IS STILL OUT, GATHERING SUPPLIES.
IS HE NOW?
I'M NOT IN THE MOOD FOR WAITING THE FUCK AROUND.
JUST POINT US IN THE RIGHT DIRECTION SO WE CAN LOAD UP WHAT YOU DO FUCKING HAVE.
WE'RE ACTUALLY RUNNING LOW ON EVERYTHING-- THAT'S WHY RICK TOOK A CREW SO FAR OUT.
WE'RE PRACTICALLY STARVING IN HERE.
STARVING? YOU?
BY "PRACTICALLY" DO YOU MEAN TO SAY "NOT FUCKING REALLY?"

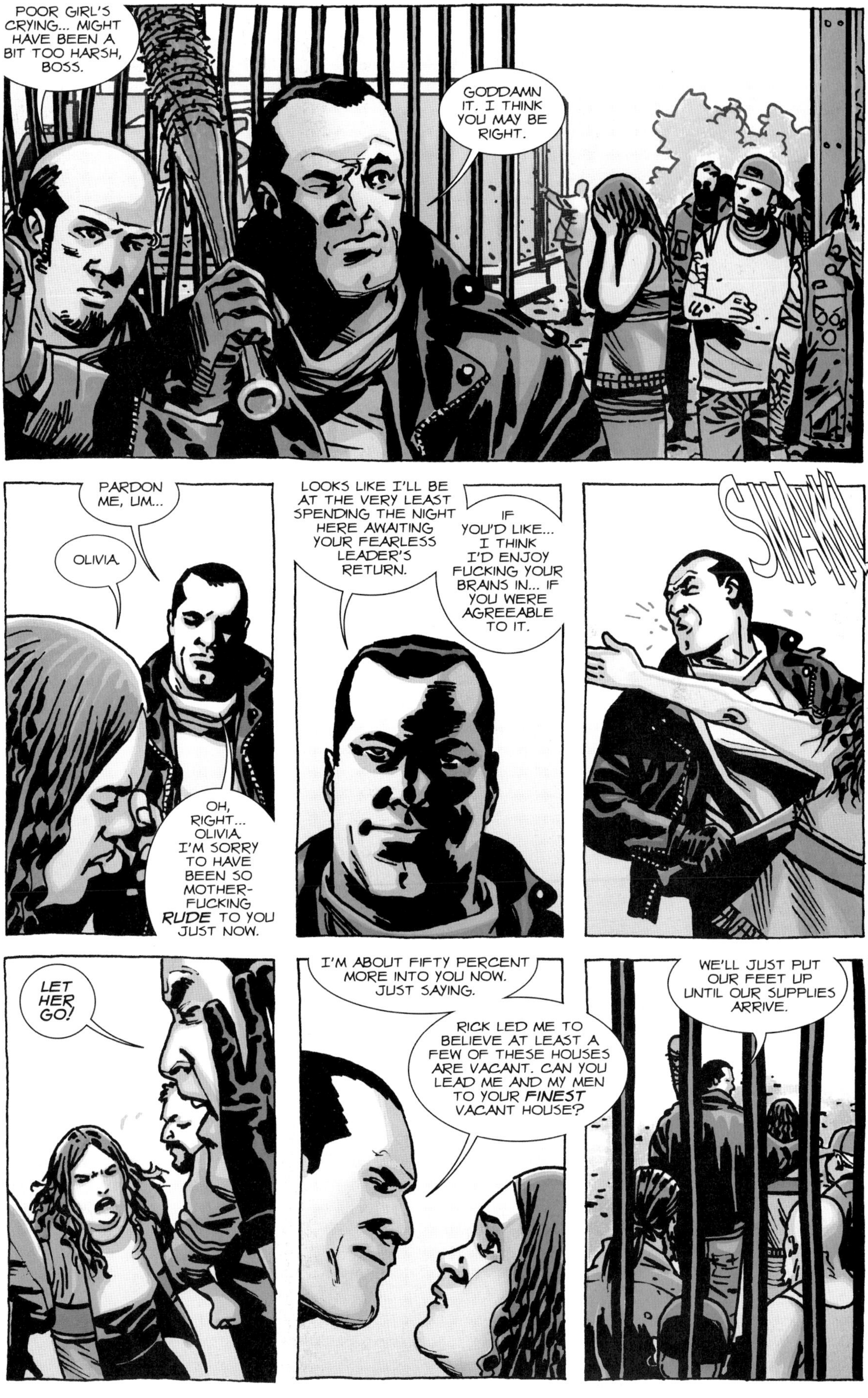
POOR GIRL'S CRYING... MIGHT HAVE BEEN A BIT TOO HARSH, BOSS.
GODDAMN IT. I THINK YOU MAY BE RIGHT.
PARDON ME, UM...
OLIVIA.
OH, RIGHT... OLIVIA. I'M SORRY TO HAVE BEEN SO MOTHER-FUCKING RUDE TO YOU JUST NOW.
LOOKS LIKE I'LL BE AT THE VERY LEAST SPENDING THE NIGHT HERE AWAITING YOUR FEARLESS LEADER'S RETURN.
IF YOU'D LIKE... I THINK I'D ENJOY FUCKING YOUR BRAINS IN... IF YOU WERE AGREEABLE TO IT.
SMAKK!
LET HER GO!
I'M ABOUT FIFTY PERCENT MORE INTO YOU NOW. JUST SAYING.
RICK LED ME TO BELIEVE AT LEAST A FEW OF THESE HOUSES ARE VACANT. CAN YOU LEAD ME AND MY MEN TO YOUR FINEST VACANT HOUSE?
WE'LL JUST PUT OUR FEET UP UNTIL OUR SUPPLIES ARRIVE.

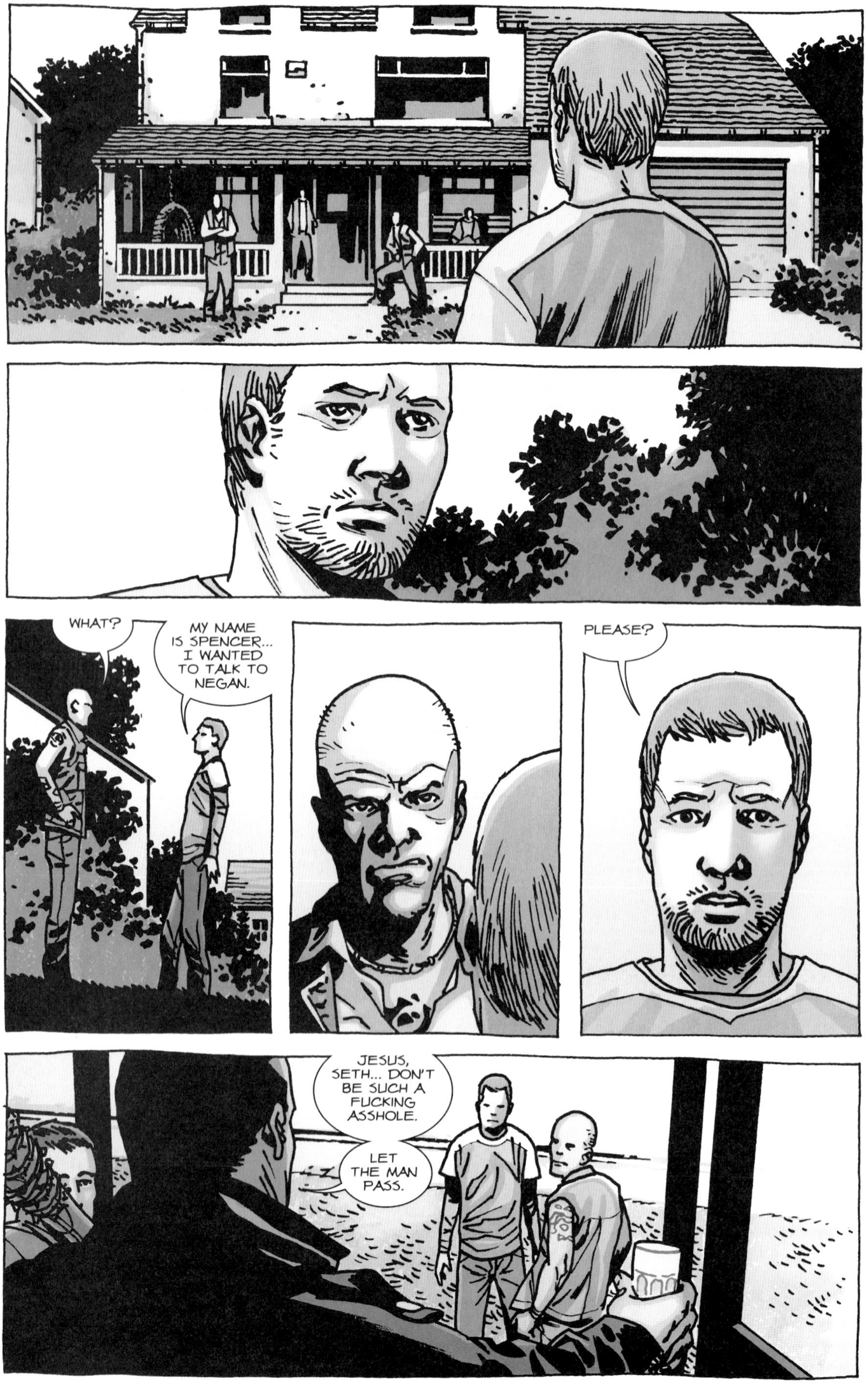
WHAT?
MY NAME IS SPENCER... I WANTED TO TALK TO NEGAN.
PLEASE?
JESUS, SETH... DON'T BE SUCH A FUCKING ASSHOLE.
LET THE MAN PASS.

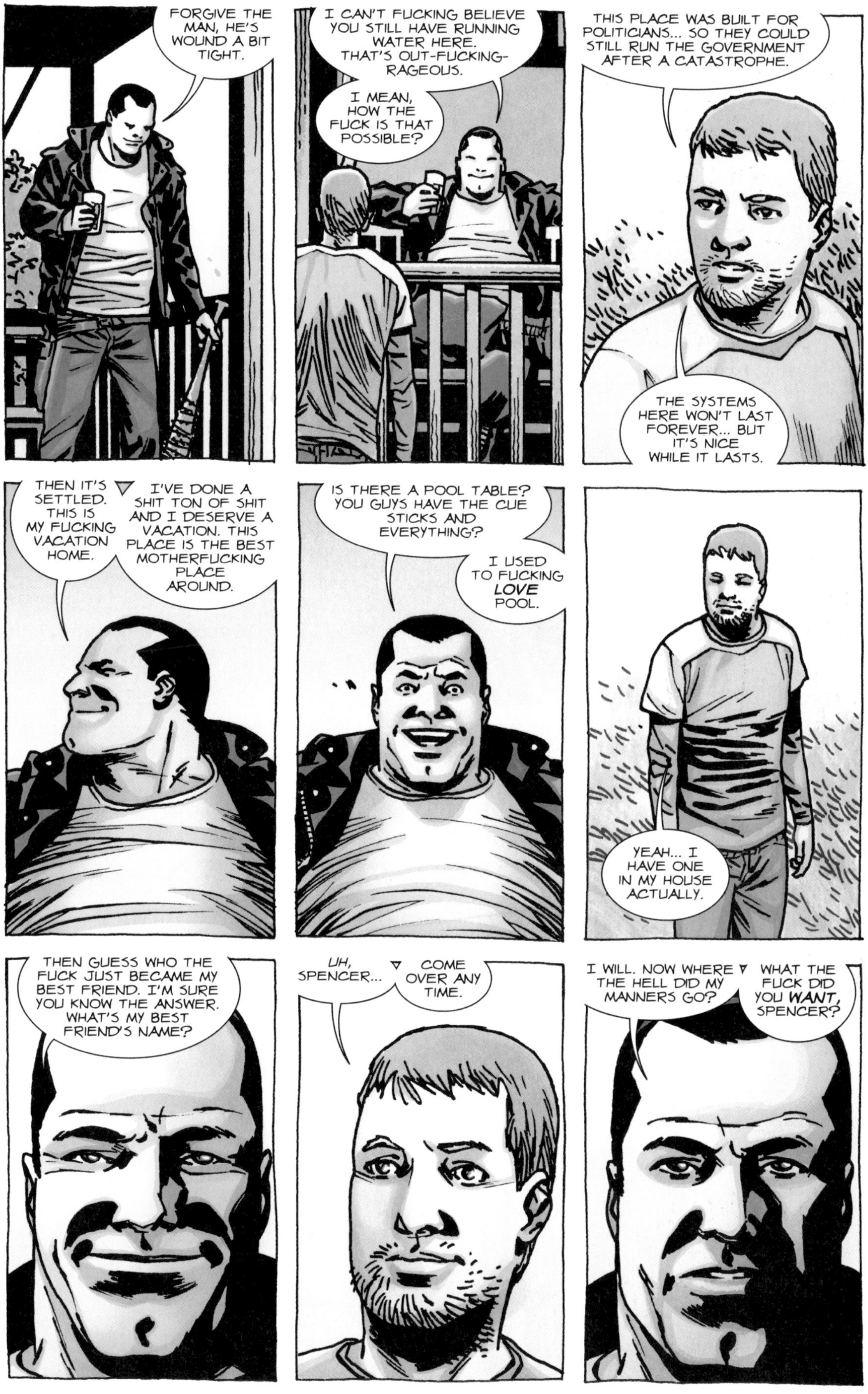
FORGIVE THE MAN, HE'S WOUND A BIT TIGHT.
I CAN'T FUCKING BELIEVE YOU STILL HAVE RUNNING WATER HERE. THAT'S OUT-FUCKING-RAGEOUS.
I MEAN, HOW THE FUCK IS THAT POSSIBLE?
THIS PLACE WAS BUILT FOR POLITICIANS... SO THEY COULD STILL RUN THE GOVERNMENT AFTER A CATASTROPHE.
THE SYSTEMS HERE WON'T LAST FOREVER... BUT IT'S NICE WHILE IT LASTS.
THEN IT'S SETTLED. THIS IS MY FUCKING VACATION HOME.
I'VE DONE A SHIT TON OF SHIT AND I DESERVE A VACATION. THIS PLACE IS THE BEST MOTHERFUCKING PLACE AROUND.
IS THERE A POOL TABLE? YOU GUYS HAVE THE CUE STICKS AND EVERYTHING?
I USED TO FUCKING *LOVE* POOL.
YEAH... I HAVE ONE IN MY HOUSE ACTUALLY.
THEN GUESS WHO THE FUCK JUST BECAME MY BEST FRIEND. I'M SURE YOU KNOW THE ANSWER. WHAT'S MY BEST FRIEND'S NAME?
UH, SPENCER...
COME OVER ANY TIME.
I WILL. NOW WHERE THE HELL DID MY MANNERS GO?
WHAT THE FUCK DID YOU *WANT,* SPENCER?

ACTUALLY... I WANTED TO TALK TO YOU ABOUT RICK.

WHAT ABOUT HIM?

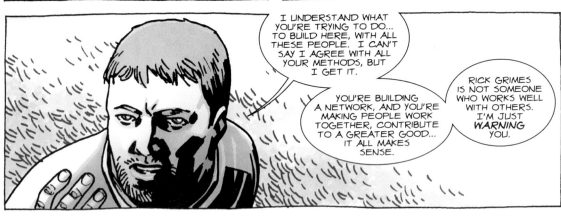

I UNDERSTAND WHAT YOU'RE TRYING TO DO... TO BUILD HERE, WITH ALL THESE PEOPLE. I CAN'T SAY I AGREE WITH ALL YOUR METHODS, BUT I GET IT.

YOU'RE BUILDING A NETWORK, AND YOU'RE MAKING PEOPLE WORK TOGETHER, CONTRIBUTE TO A GREATER GOOD... IT ALL MAKES SENSE.

RICK GRIMES IS NOT SOMEONE WHO WORKS WELL WITH OTHERS. I'M JUST *WARNING* YOU.

RICK WASN'T ORIGINALLY THE LEADER HERE... IT WAS MY FATHER AND HE WAS DOING A MUCH BETTER JOB OF IT.

RICK CAME ALONG, WITH HIS GROUP, AND REALLY WRECKED THINGS FOR US HERE. HE'S... WELL... *HE'S A MANIAC.* THAT'S THE BEST WAY TO PUT IT.

HE MAY EVEN WANT TO WORK WITH YOU, BUT I'M TELLING YOU... THIS GUY *CAN'T NOT* BE THE BOSS. HE'S GOTTA BE IN CHARGE... OTHERWISE HIS EGO DRIVES HIM NUTS.

IS THAT SO?

WELL, WHAT DO YOU PROPOSE?

WELL... I AM MY FATHER'S SON.

I THINK I CAN BE THE LEADER HE WAS... I THINK THAT'S WHAT WE NEED... WHAT *YOU* NEED.

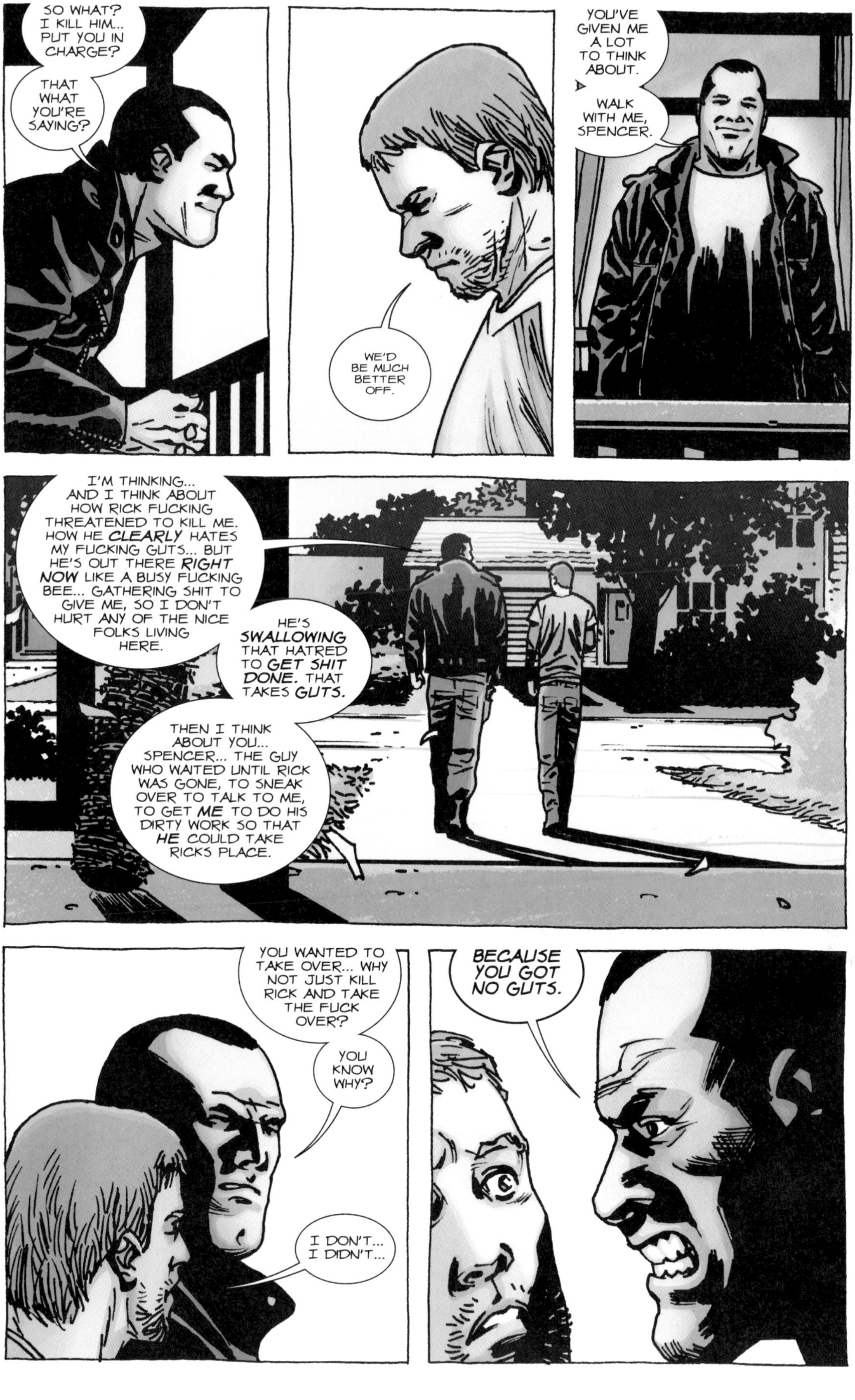
SO WHAT? I KILL HIM... PUT YOU IN CHARGE?
THAT WHAT YOU'RE SAYING?
WE'D BE MUCH BETTER OFF.
YOU'VE GIVEN ME A LOT TO THINK ABOUT.
WALK WITH ME, SPENCER.
I'M THINKING... AND I THINK ABOUT HOW RICK FUCKING THREATENED TO KILL ME. HOW HE CLEARLY HATES MY FUCKING GUTS... BUT HE'S OUT THERE RIGHT NOW LIKE A BUSY FUCKING BEE... GATHERING SHIT TO GIVE ME, SO I DON'T HURT ANY OF THE NICE FOLKS LIVING HERE.
HE'S SWALLOWING THAT HATRED TO GET SHIT DONE. THAT TAKES GUTS.
THEN I THINK ABOUT YOU... SPENCER... THE GUY WHO WAITED UNTIL RICK WAS GONE, TO SNEAK OVER TO TALK TO ME, TO GET ME TO DO HIS DIRTY WORK SO THAT HE COULD TAKE RICKS PLACE.
YOU WANTED TO TAKE OVER... WHY NOT JUST KILL RICK AND TAKE THE FUCK OVER?
YOU KNOW WHY?
I DON'T... I DIDN'T...
BECAUSE YOU GOT NO GUTS.

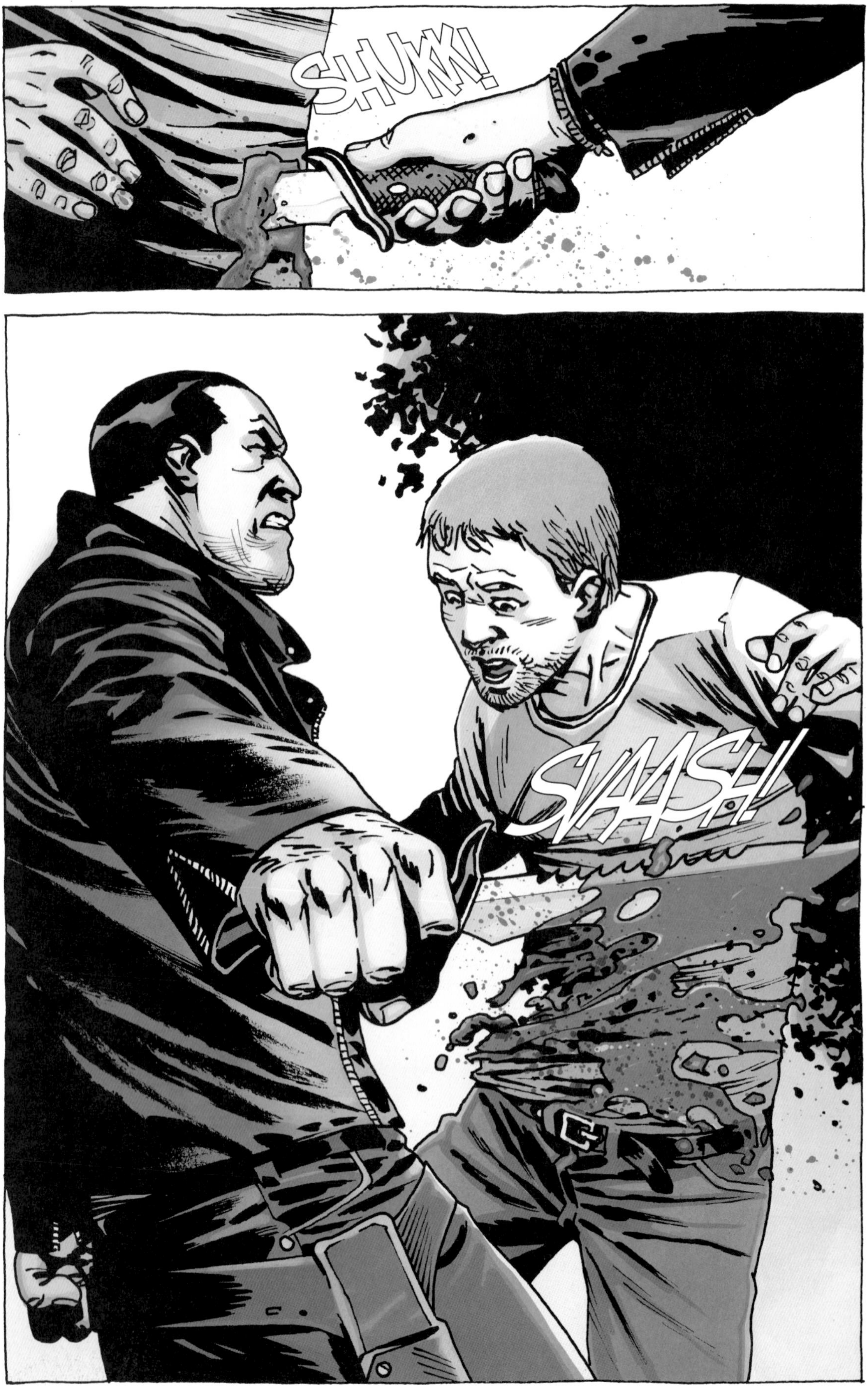
SHUKK!
SVAASH!

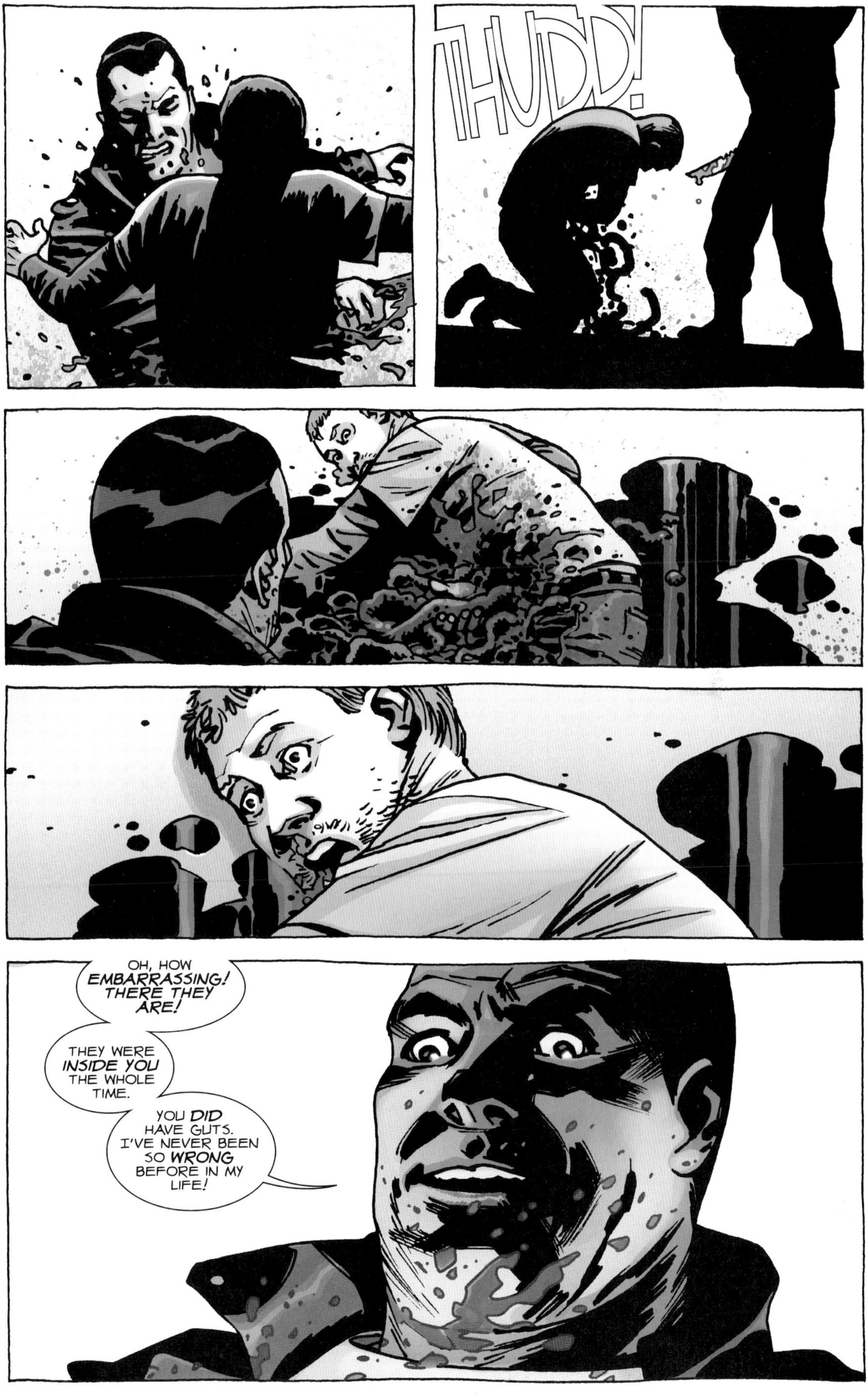
THUDD!
OH, HOW EMBARRASSING! THERE THEY ARE!
THEY WERE INSIDE YOU THE WHOLE TIME.
YOU DID HAVE GUTS. I'VE NEVER BEEN SO WRONG BEFORE IN MY LIFE!

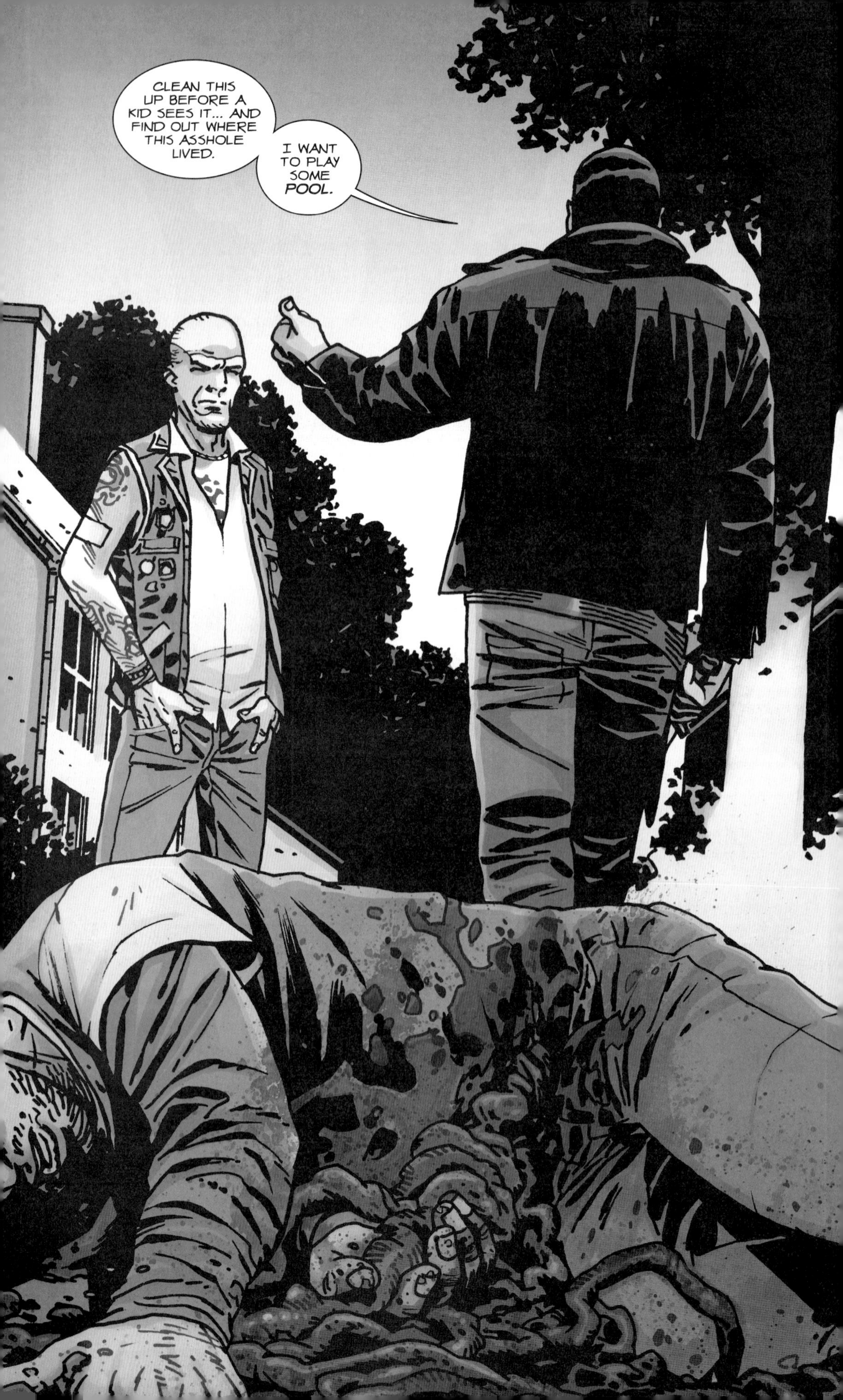
CLEAN THIS UP BEFORE A KID SEES IT... AND FIND OUT WHERE THIS ASSHOLE LIVED.
I WANT TO PLAY SOME *POOL.*

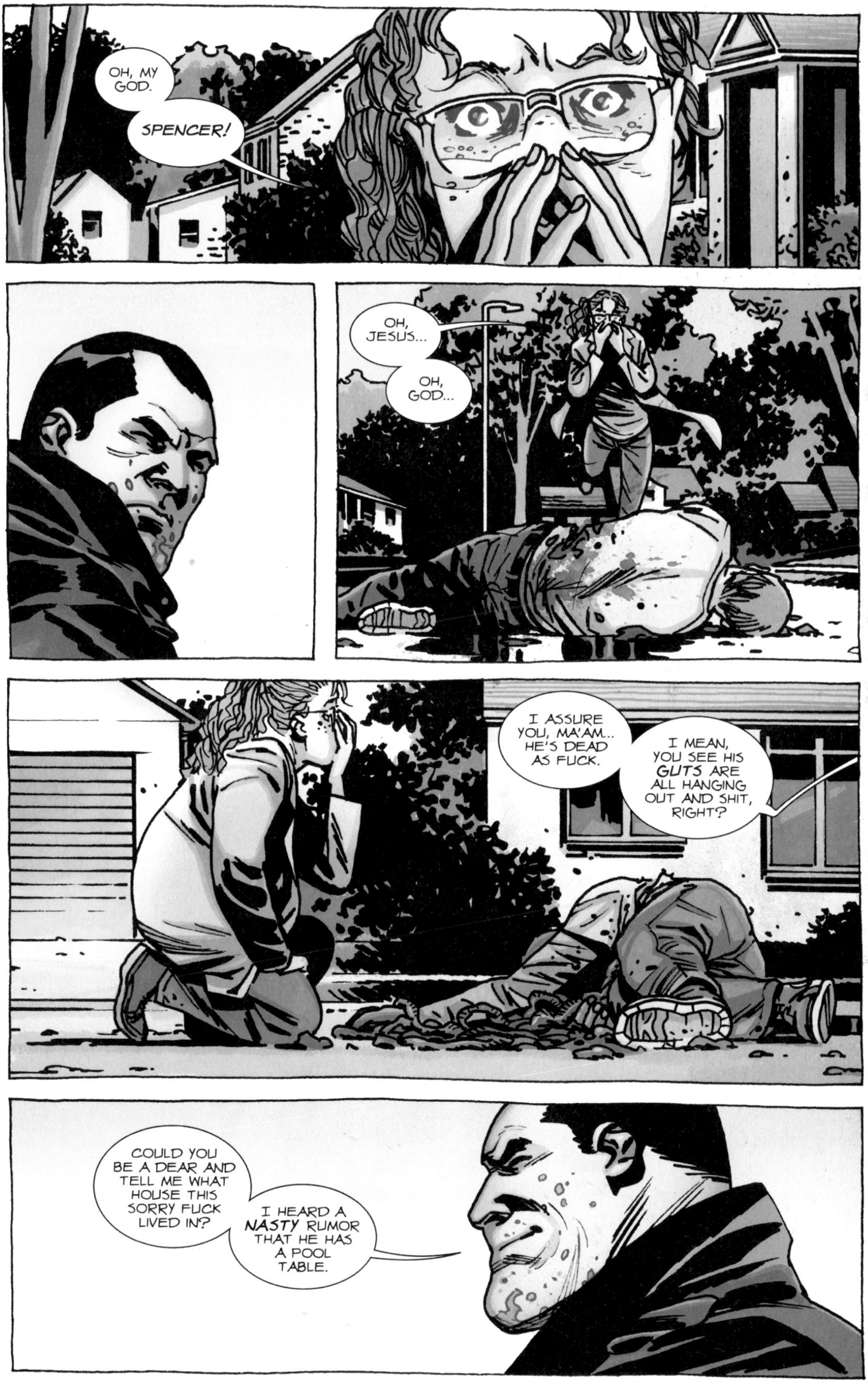

OH, MY GOD.
SPENCER!
OH, JESUS...
OH, GOD...
I ASSURE YOU, MA'AM... HE'S DEAD AS FUCK.
I MEAN, YOU SEE HIS GUTS ARE ALL HANGING OUT AND SHIT, RIGHT?
COULD YOU BE A DEAR AND TELL ME WHAT HOUSE THIS SORRY FUCK LIVED IN?
I HEARD A NASTY RUMOR THAT HE HAS A POOL TABLE.

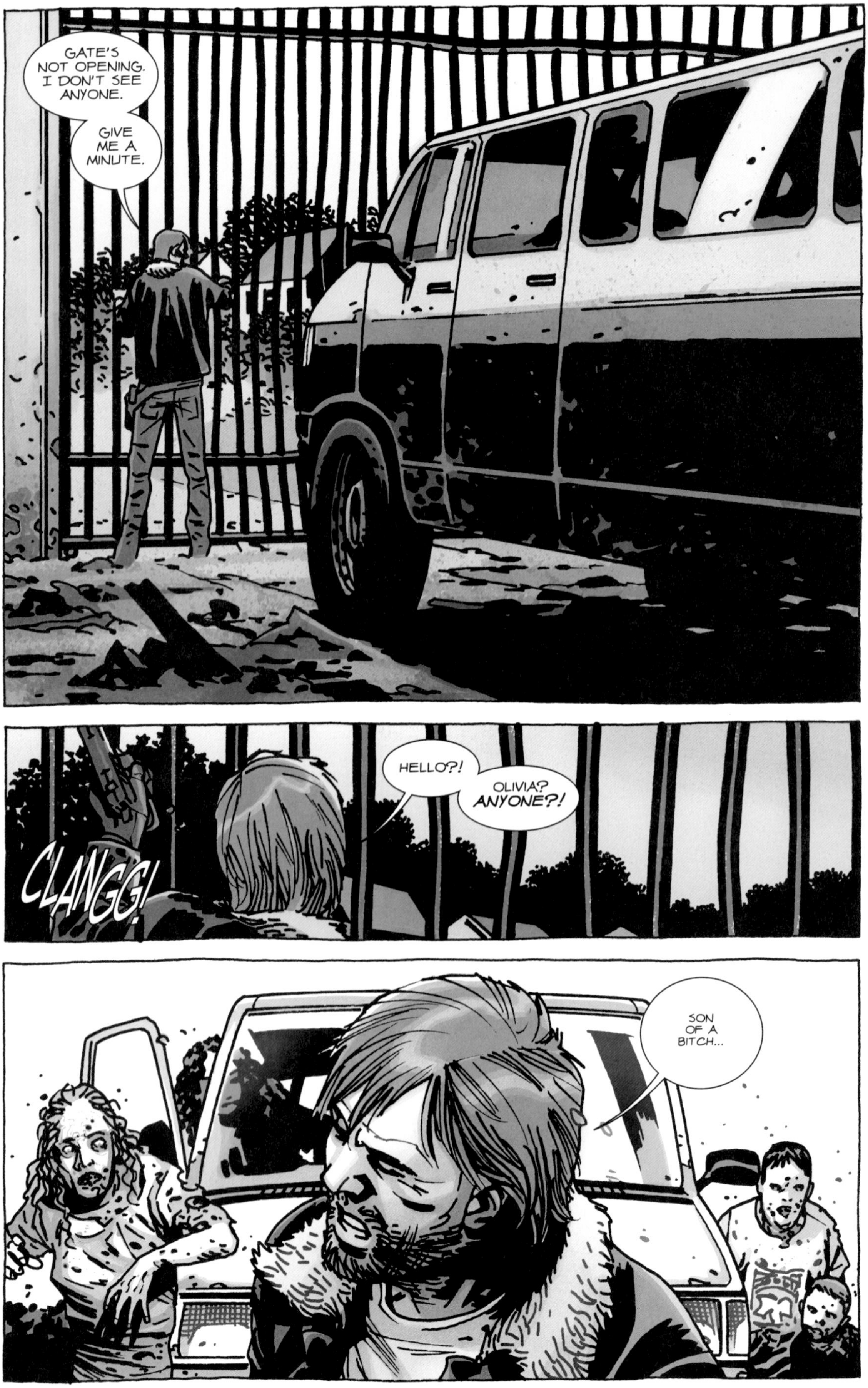
GATE'S NOT OPENING. I DON'T SEE ANYONE.
GIVE ME A MINUTE.
CLANGG!
HELLO?!
OLIVIA? ANYONE?!
SON OF A BITCH...

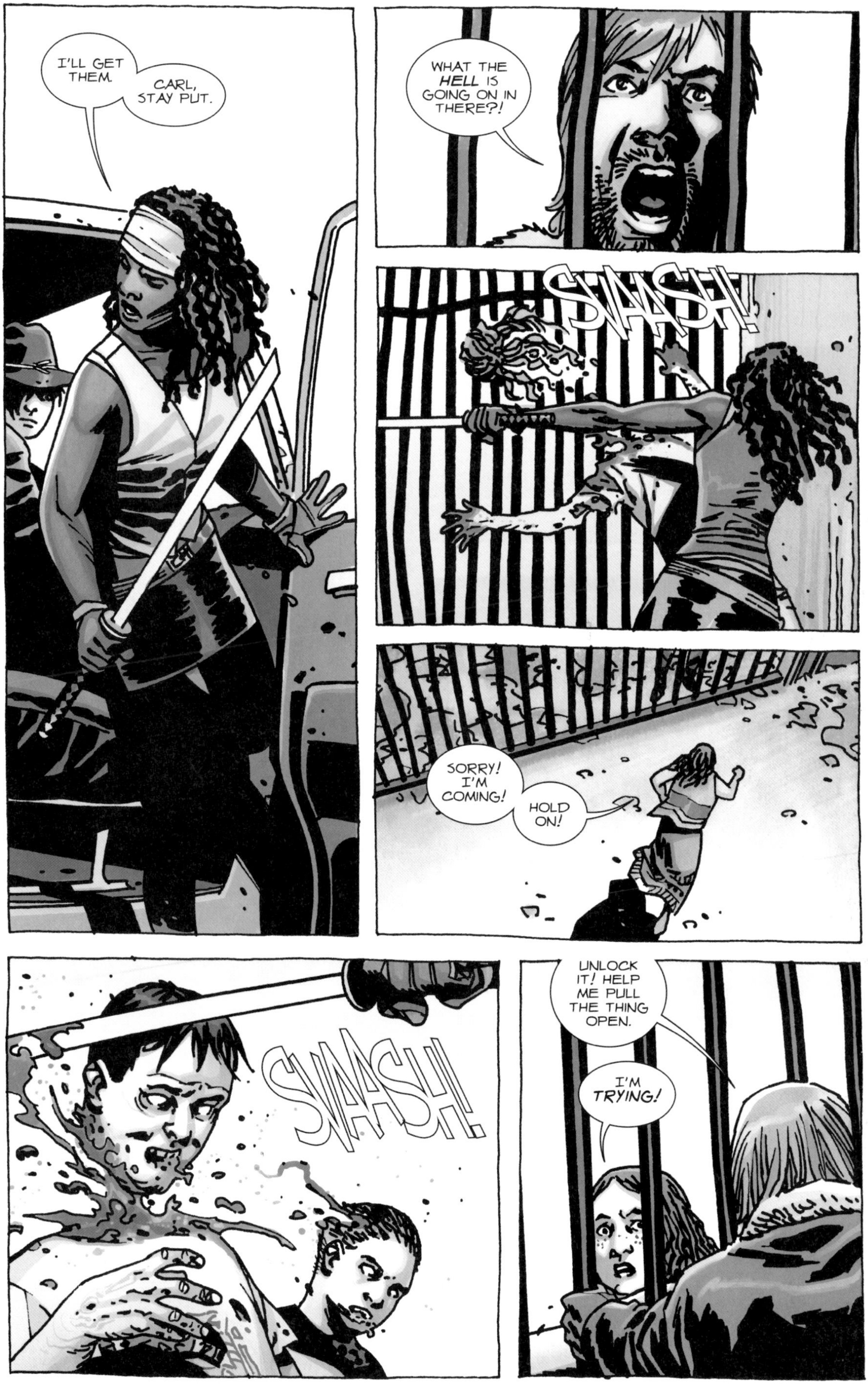

I'LL GET THEM.
CARL, STAY PUT.
WHAT THE HELL IS GOING ON IN THERE?!
SWASH!
SORRY! I'M COMING!
HOLD ON!
SWASH!
UNLOCK IT! HELP ME PULL THE THING OPEN.
I'M TRYING!

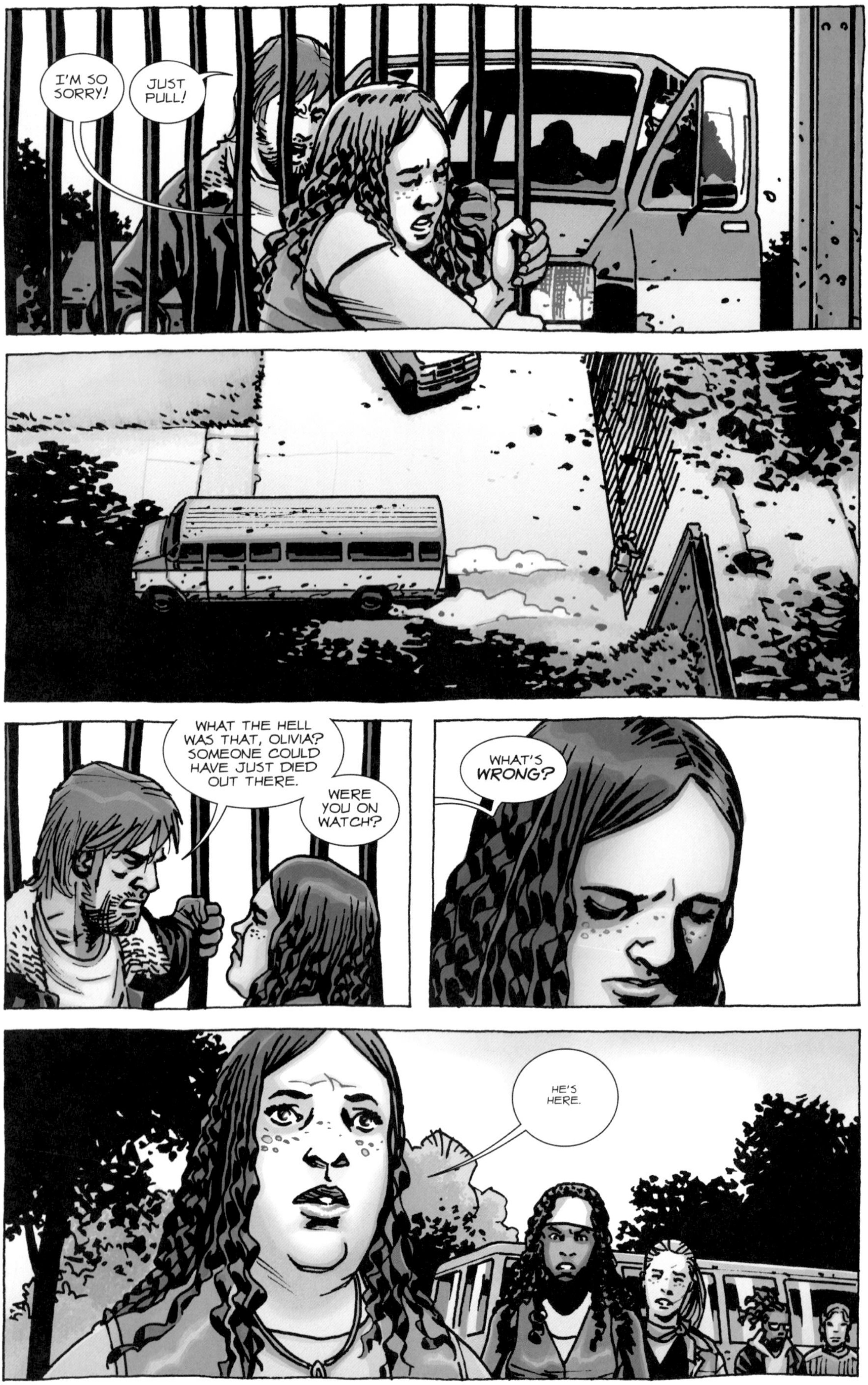

I'M SO SORRY!
JUST PULL!
WHAT THE HELL WAS THAT, OLIVIA? SOMEONE COULD HAVE JUST DIED OUT THERE.
WERE YOU ON WATCH?
WHAT'S WRONG?
HE'S HERE.

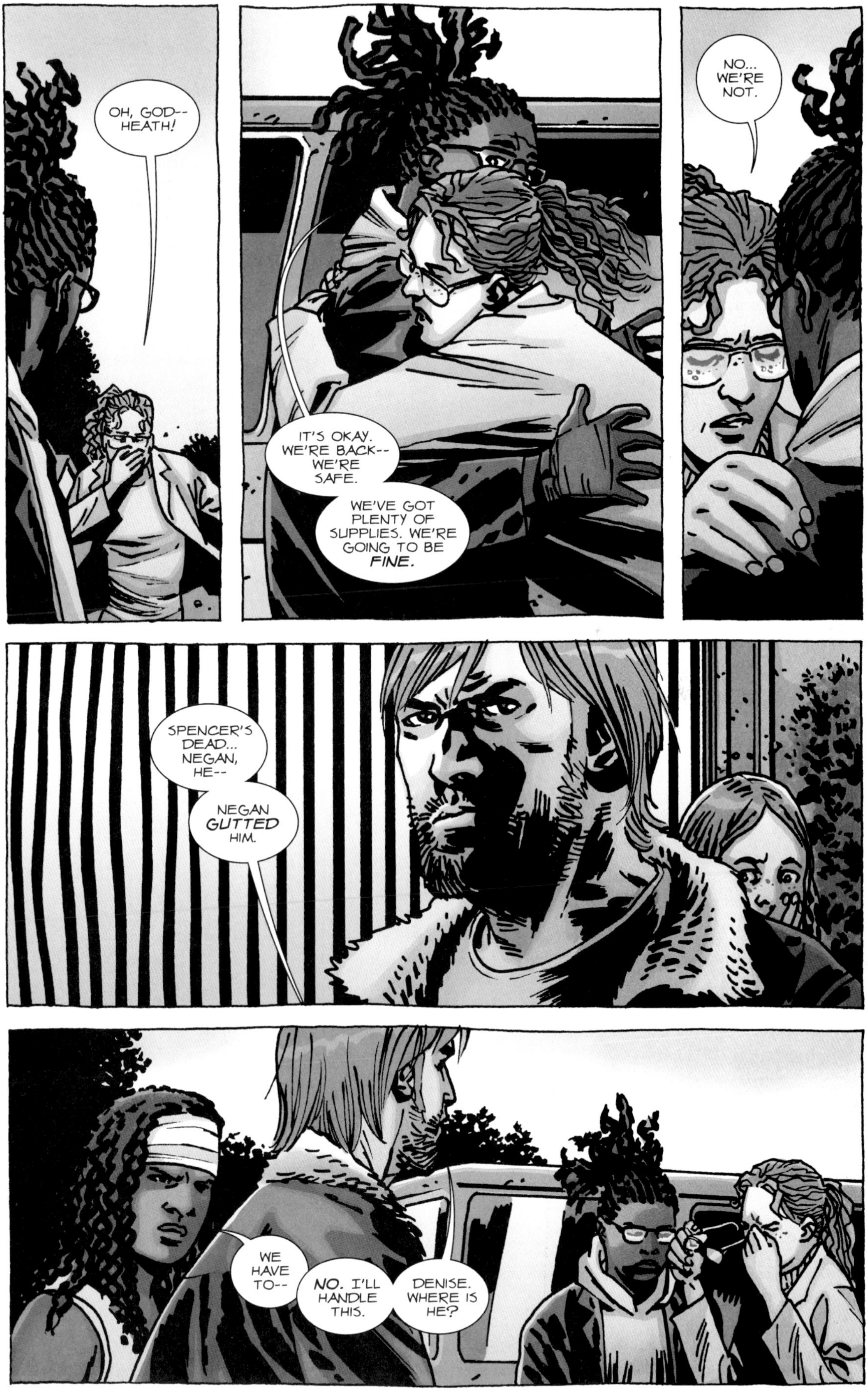

OH, GOD--
HEATH!
IT'S OKAY. WE'RE BACK-- WE'RE SAFE.
WE'VE GOT PLENTY OF SUPPLIES. WE'RE GOING TO BE *FINE.*
NO... WE'RE NOT.
SPENCER'S DEAD... NEGAN, HE--
NEGAN *GUTTED* HIM.
DENISE. WHERE IS HE?
NO. I'LL HANDLE THIS.
WE HAVE TO--

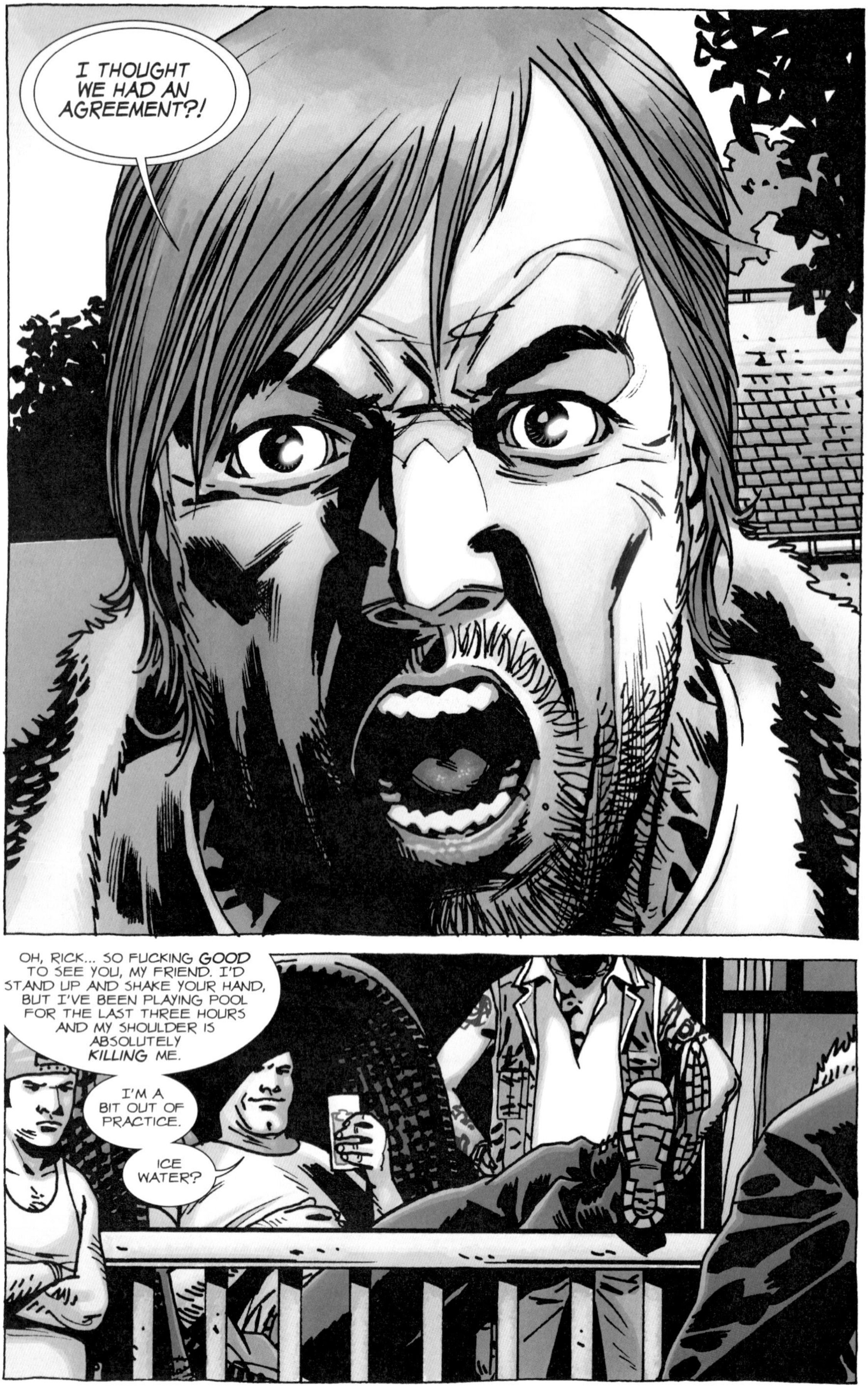
I THOUGHT WE HAD AN AGREEMENT?!
OH, RICK... SO FUCKING GOOD TO SEE YOU, MY FRIEND. I'D STAND UP AND SHAKE YOUR HAND, BUT I'VE BEEN PLAYING POOL FOR THE LAST THREE HOURS AND MY SHOULDER IS ABSOLUTELY KILLING ME.
I'M A BIT OUT OF PRACTICE.
ICE WATER?

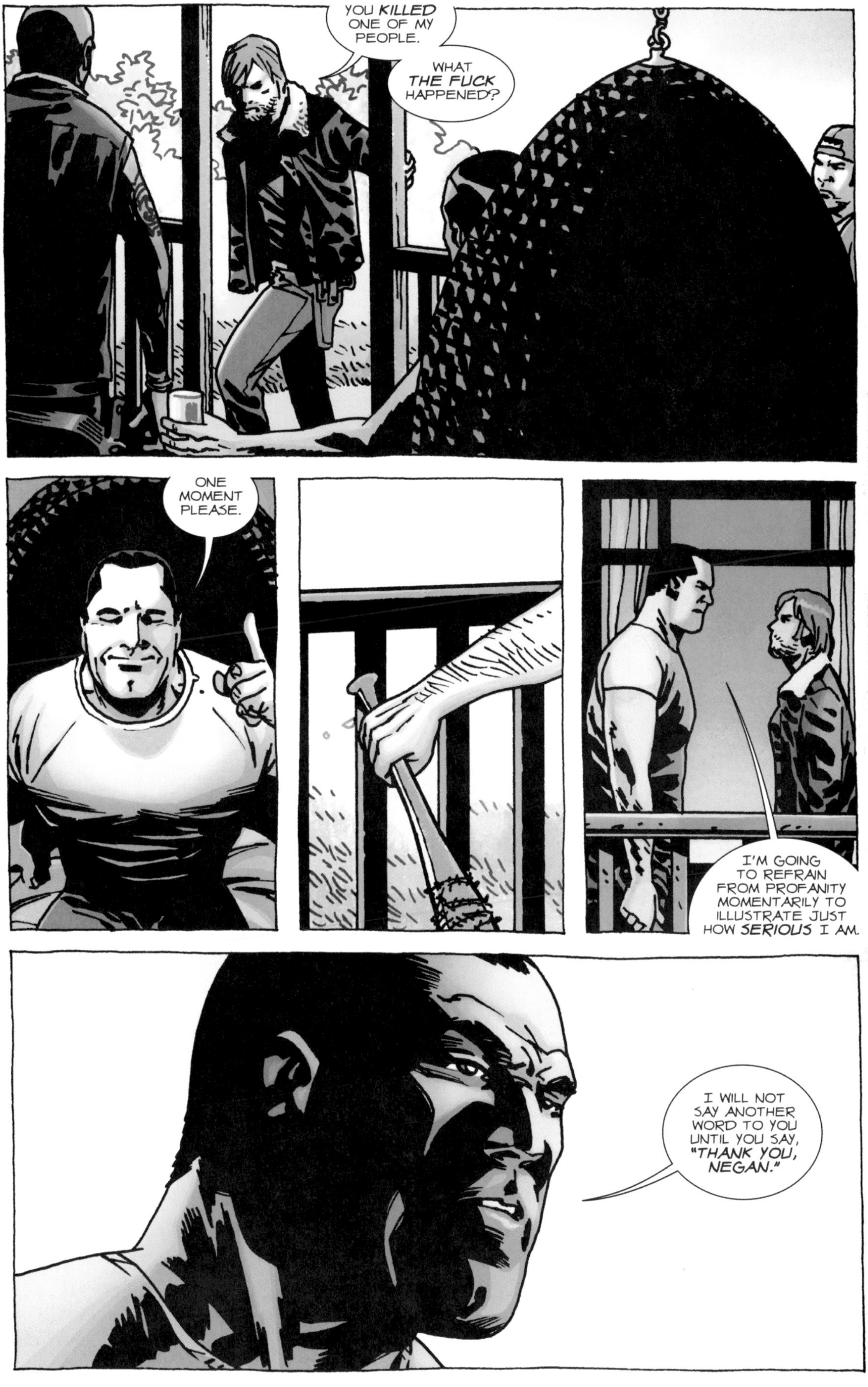

YOU KILLED ONE OF MY PEOPLE.
WHAT THE FUCK HAPPENED?
ONE MOMENT PLEASE.
I'M GOING TO REFRAIN FROM PROFANITY MOMENTARILY TO ILLUSTRATE JUST HOW SERIOUS I AM.
I WILL NOT SAY ANOTHER WORD TO YOU UNTIL YOU SAY, "THANK YOU, NEGAN."

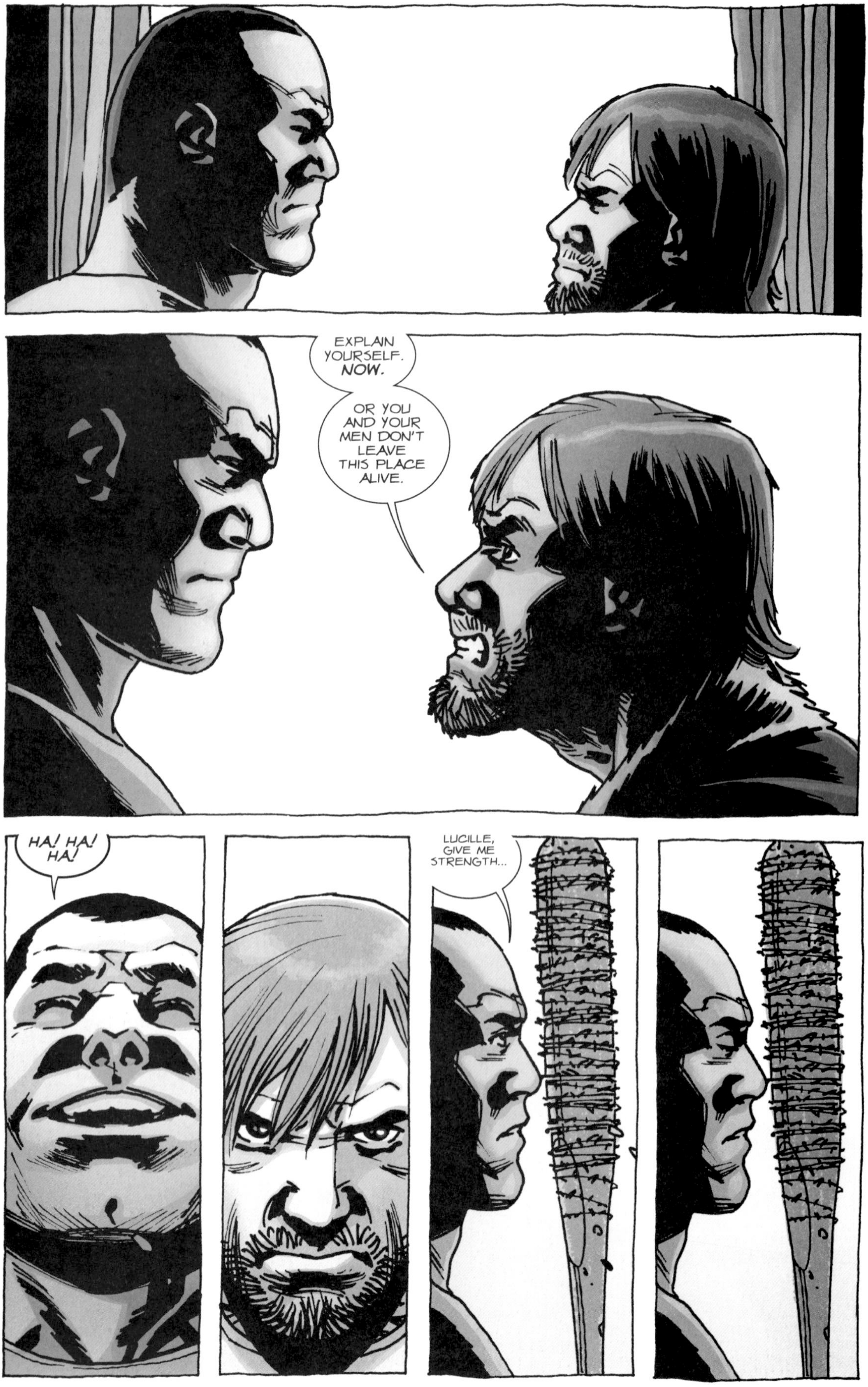
EXPLAIN YOURSELF. NOW.
OR YOU AND YOUR MEN DON'T LEAVE THIS PLACE ALIVE.
HA! HA! HA!
LUCILLE, GIVE ME STRENGTH...

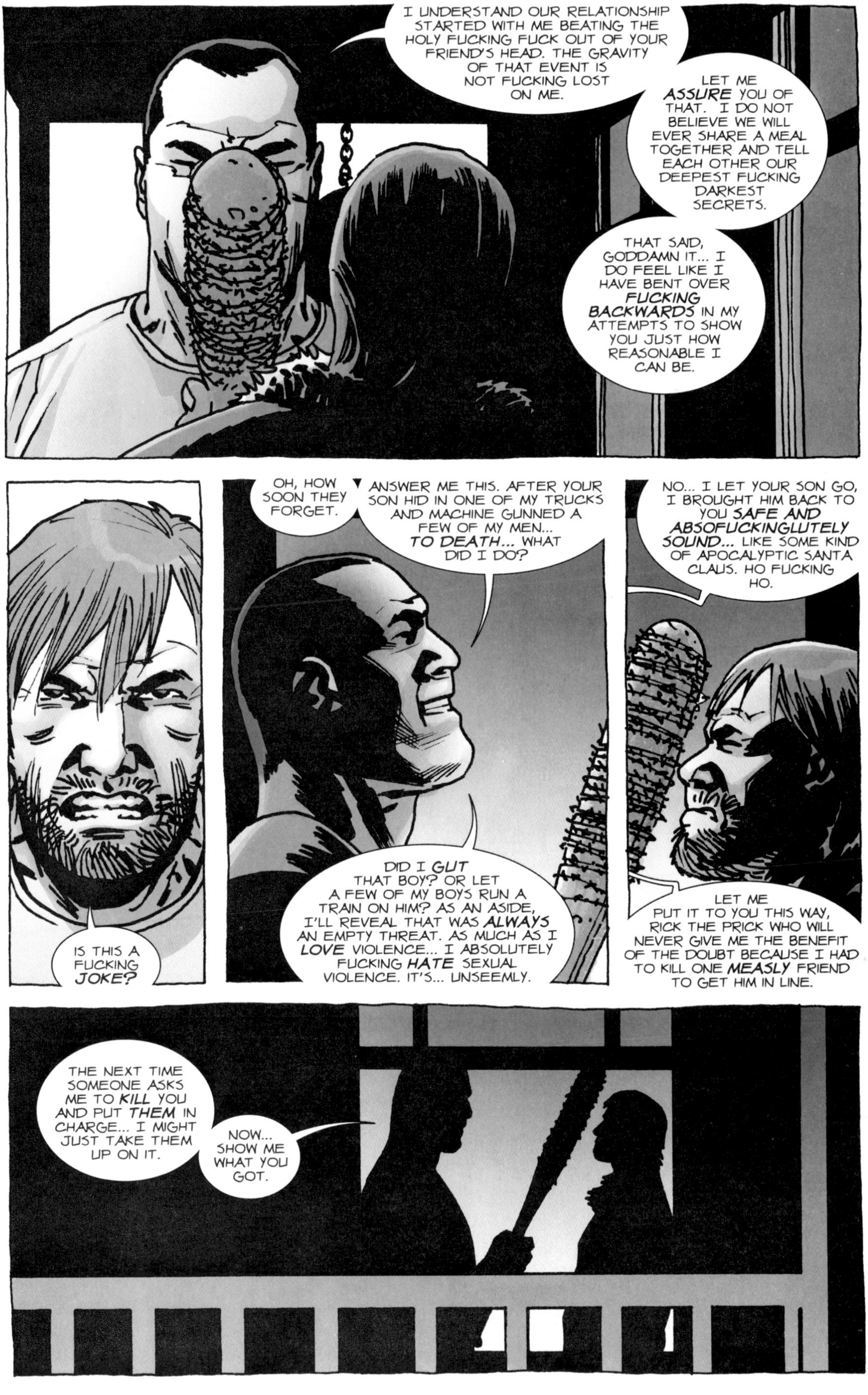
I UNDERSTAND OUR RELATIONSHIP STARTED WITH ME BEATING THE HOLY FUCKING FUCK OUT OF YOUR FRIEND'S HEAD. THE GRAVITY OF THAT EVENT IS NOT FUCKING LOST ON ME.
LET ME ASSURE YOU OF THAT. I DO NOT BELIEVE WE WILL EVER SHARE A MEAL TOGETHER AND TELL EACH OTHER OUR DEEPEST FUCKING DARKEST SECRETS.
THAT SAID, GODDAMN IT... I DO FEEL LIKE I HAVE BENT OVER FUCKING BACKWARDS IN MY ATTEMPTS TO SHOW YOU JUST HOW REASONABLE I CAN BE.
IS THIS A FUCKING JOKE?
OH, HOW SOON THEY FORGET.
ANSWER ME THIS. AFTER YOUR SON HID IN ONE OF MY TRUCKS AND MACHINE GUNNED A FEW OF MY MEN... TO DEATH... WHAT DID I DO?
DID I GUT THAT BOY? OR LET A FEW OF MY BOYS RUN A TRAIN ON HIM? AS AN ASIDE, I'LL REVEAL THAT WAS ALWAYS AN EMPTY THREAT. AS MUCH AS I LOVE VIOLENCE... I ABSOLUTELY FUCKING HATE SEXUAL VIOLENCE. IT'S... UNSEEMLY.
NO... I LET YOUR SON GO, I BROUGHT HIM BACK TO YOU SAFE AND ABSOFUCKINGLUTELY SOUND... LIKE SOME KIND OF APOCALYPTIC SANTA CLAUS. HO FUCKING HO.
LET ME PUT IT TO YOU THIS WAY, RICK THE PRICK WHO WILL NEVER GIVE ME THE BENEFIT OF THE DOUBT BECAUSE I HAD TO KILL ONE MEASLY FRIEND TO GET HIM IN LINE.
THE NEXT TIME SOMEONE ASKS ME TO KILL YOU AND PUT THEM IN CHARGE... I MIGHT JUST TAKE THEM UP ON IT.
NOW... SHOW ME WHAT YOU GOT.

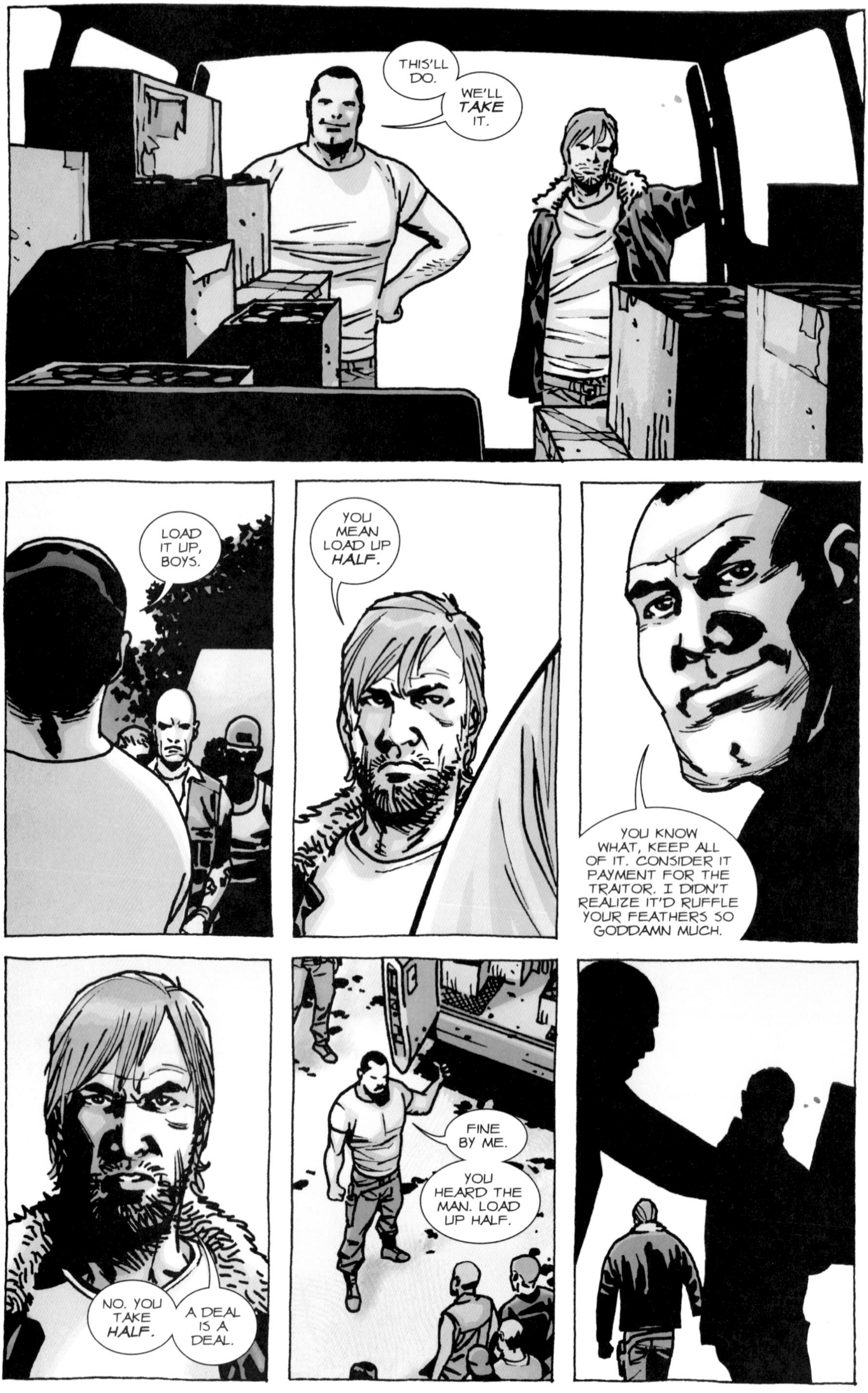

THIS'LL DO.
WE'LL *TAKE* IT.
LOAD IT UP, BOYS.
YOU MEAN LOAD UP *HALF.*
YOU KNOW WHAT, KEEP ALL OF IT. CONSIDER IT PAYMENT FOR THE TRAITOR. I DIDN'T REALIZE IT'D RUFFLE YOUR FEATHERS SO GODDAMN MUCH.
NO. YOU TAKE *HALF.*
A DEAL IS A DEAL.
FINE BY ME.
YOU HEARD THE MAN. LOAD UP HALF.

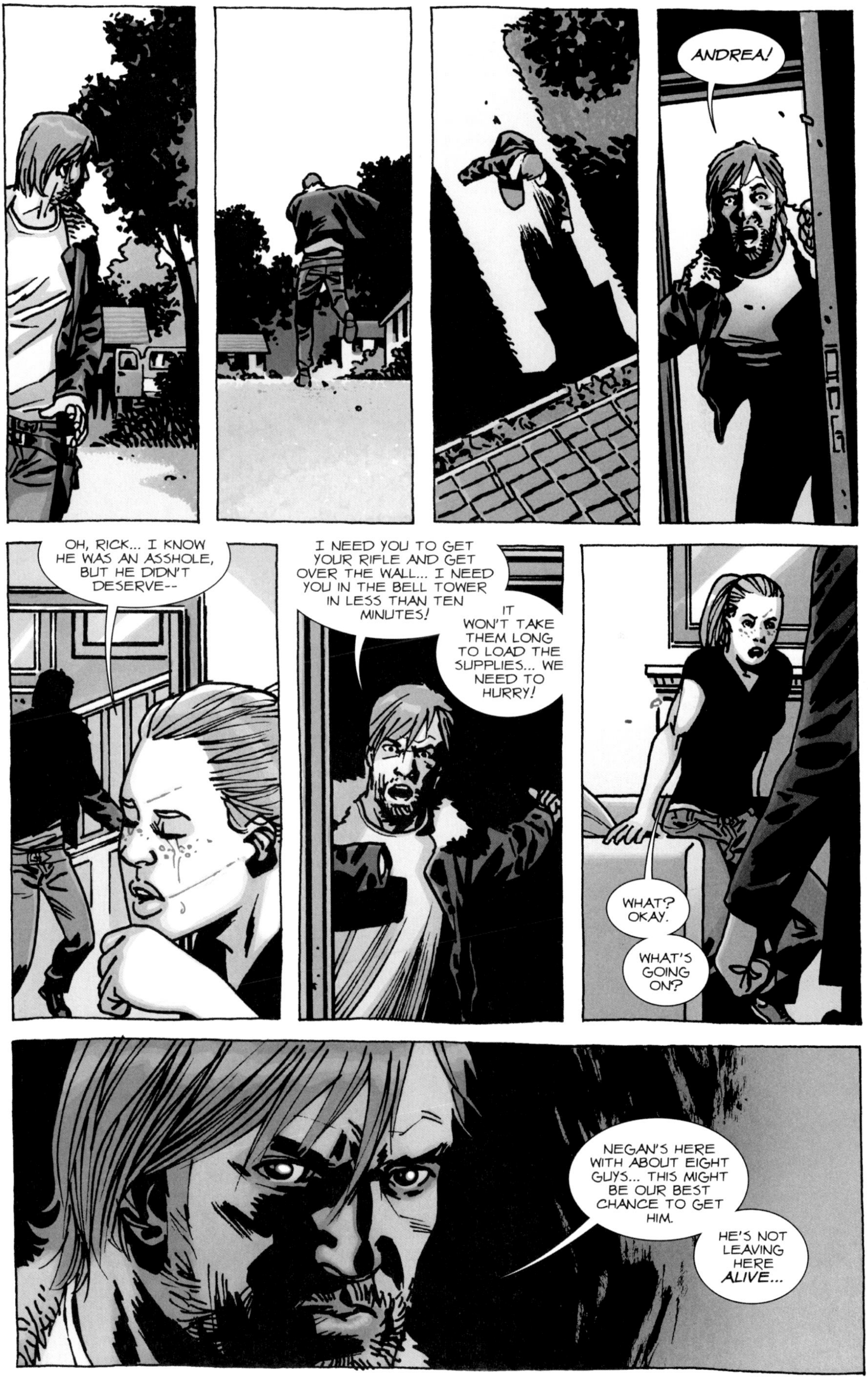
ANDREA!
OH, RICK... I KNOW HE WAS AN ASSHOLE, BUT HE DIDN'T DESERVE--
I NEED YOU TO GET YOUR RIFLE AND GET OVER THE WALL... I NEED YOU IN THE BELL TOWER IN LESS THAN TEN MINUTES!
IT WON'T TAKE THEM LONG TO LOAD THE SUPPLIES... WE NEED TO HURRY!
WHAT? OKAY.
WHAT'S GOING ON?
NEGAN'S HERE WITH ABOUT EIGHT GUYS... THIS MIGHT BE OUR BEST CHANCE TO GET HIM.
HE'S NOT LEAVING HERE ALIVE...

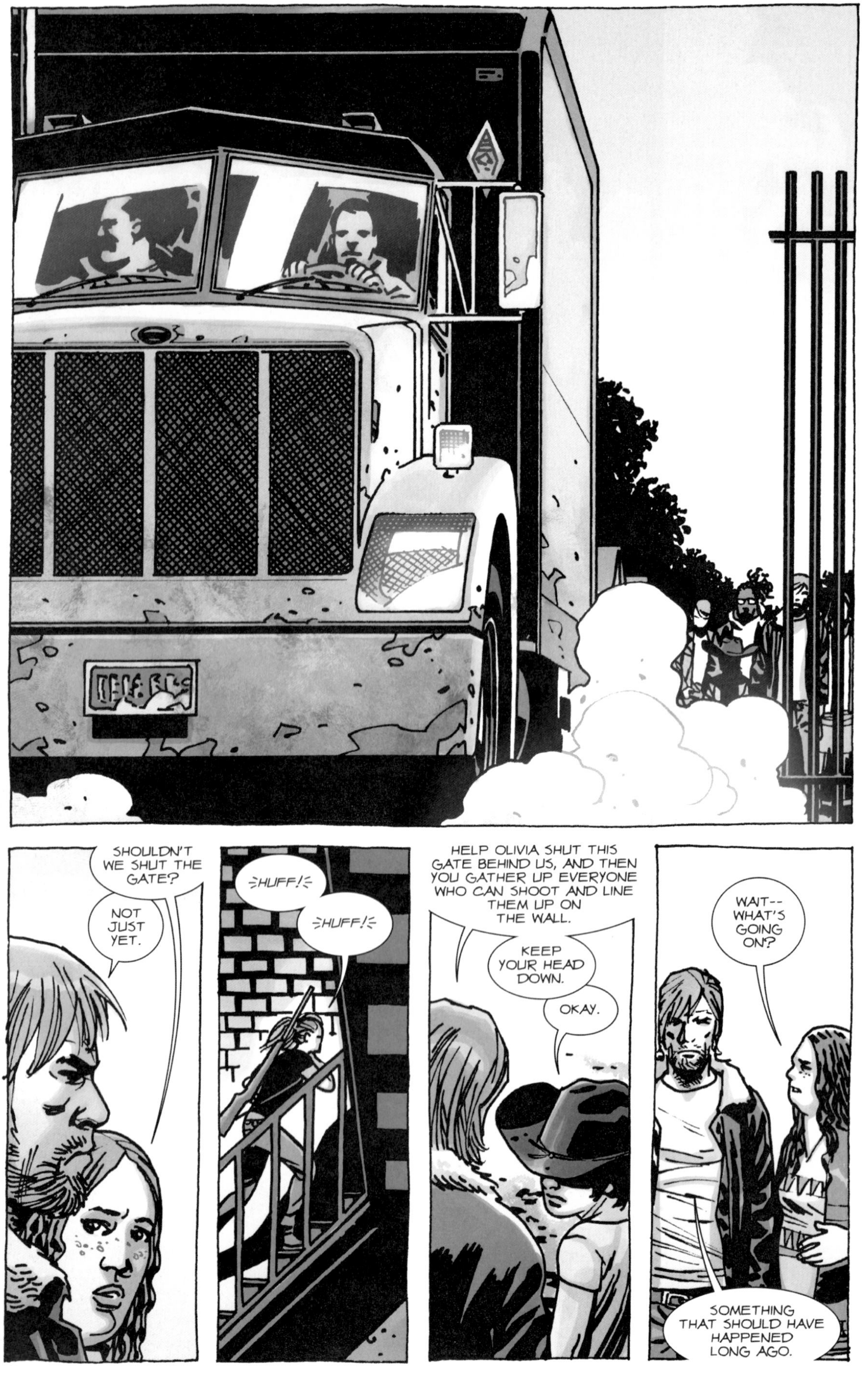
SHOULDN'T WE SHUT THE GATE?
NOT JUST YET.
≈HUFF!≈
≈HUFF!≈
HELP OLIVIA SHUT THIS GATE BEHIND US, AND THEN YOU GATHER UP EVERYONE WHO CAN SHOOT AND LINE THEM UP ON THE WALL.
KEEP YOUR HEAD DOWN.
OKAY.
WAIT-- WHAT'S GOING ON?
SOMETHING THAT SHOULD HAVE HAPPENED LONG AGO.

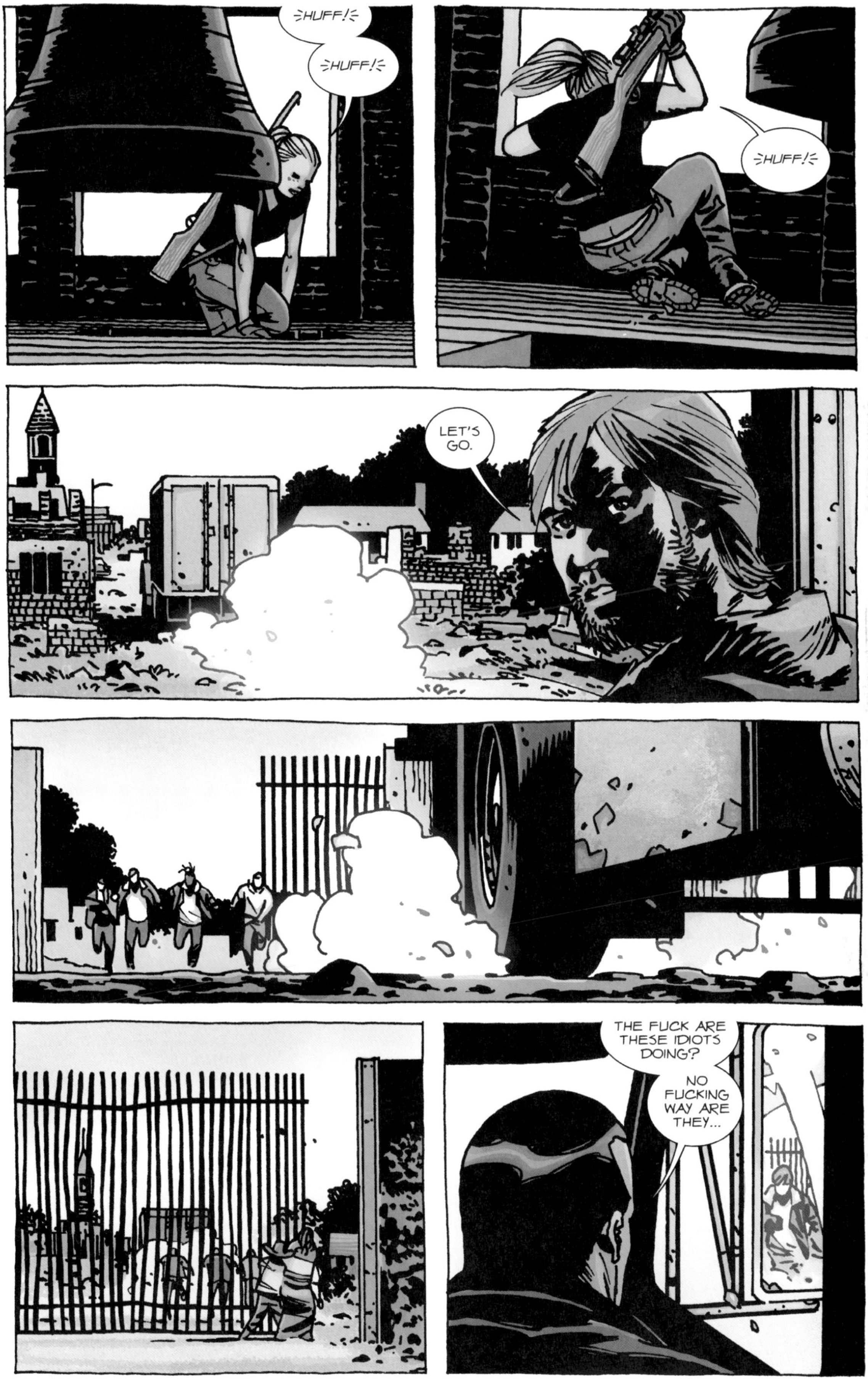

HUFF!
HUFF!
HUFF!
LET'S GO.
THE FUCK ARE THESE IDIOTS DOING?
NO FUCKING WAY ARE THEY...

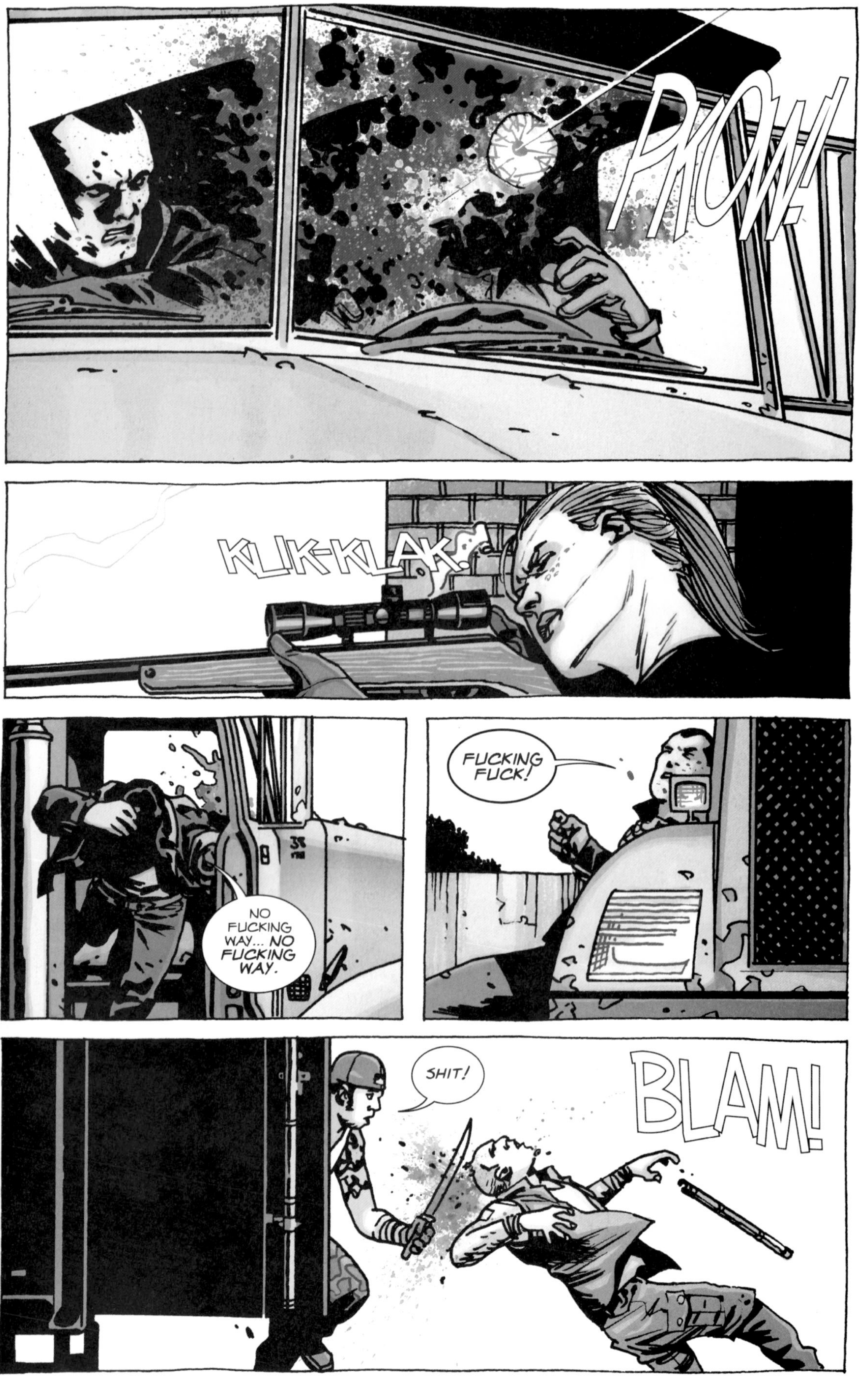
PKOW!
KLIK-KLAK!
NO FUCKING WAY... NO FUCKING WAY.
FUCKING FUCK!
SHIT!
BLAM!

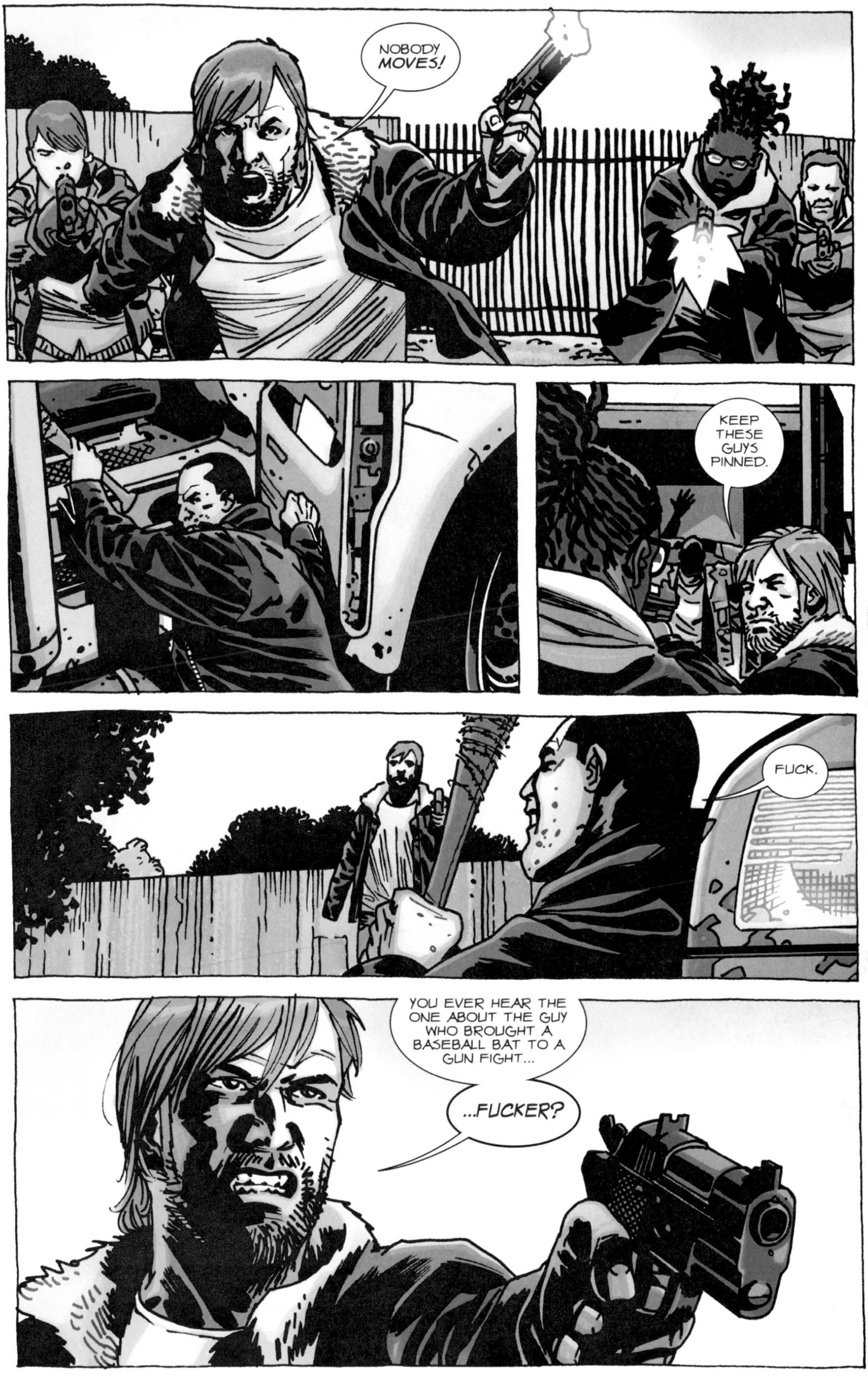
NOBODY MOVES!
KEEP THESE GUYS PINNED.
FUCK.
YOU EVER HEAR THE ONE ABOUT THE GUY WHO BROUGHT A BASEBALL BAT TO A GUN FIGHT...
...FUCKER?

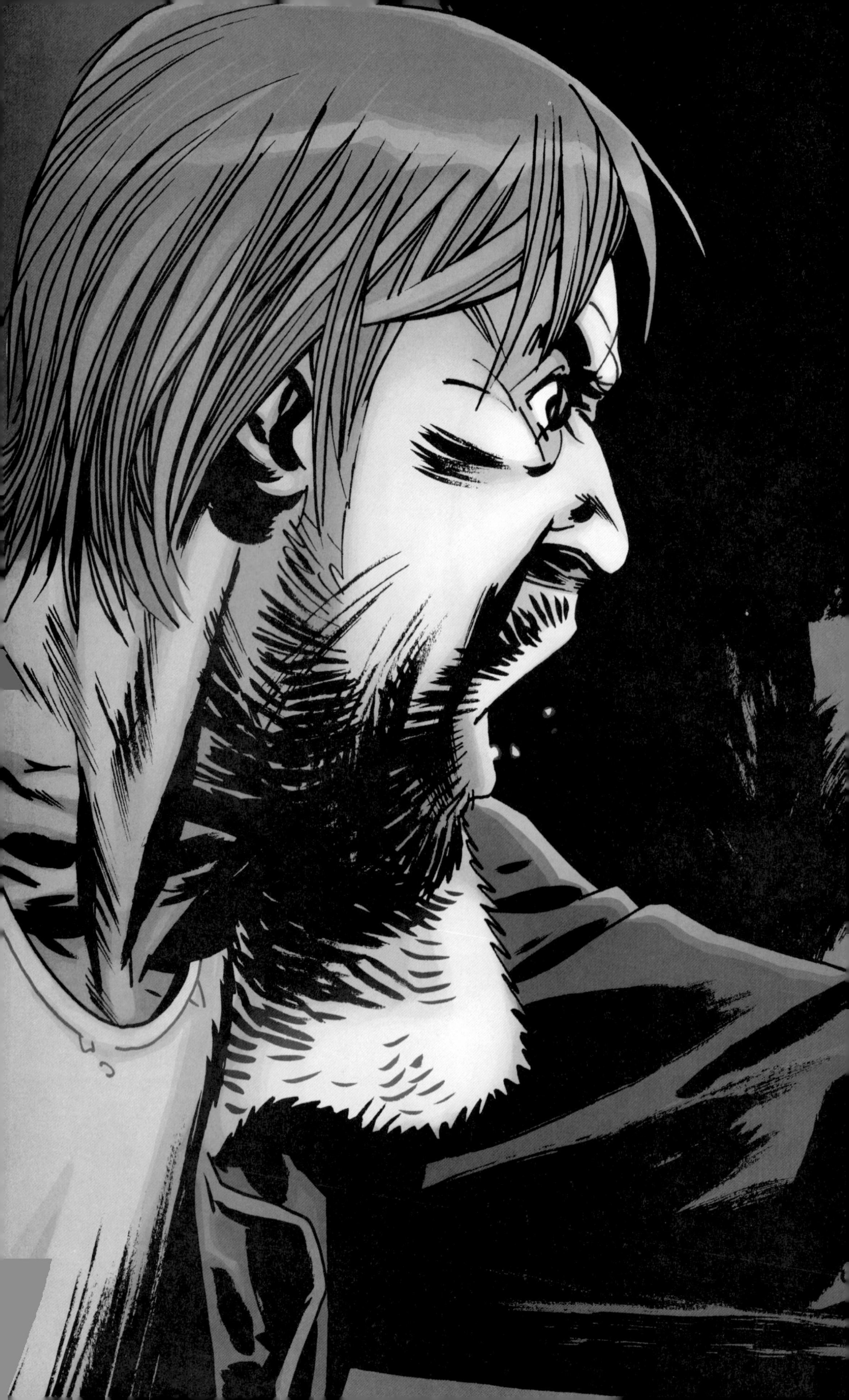

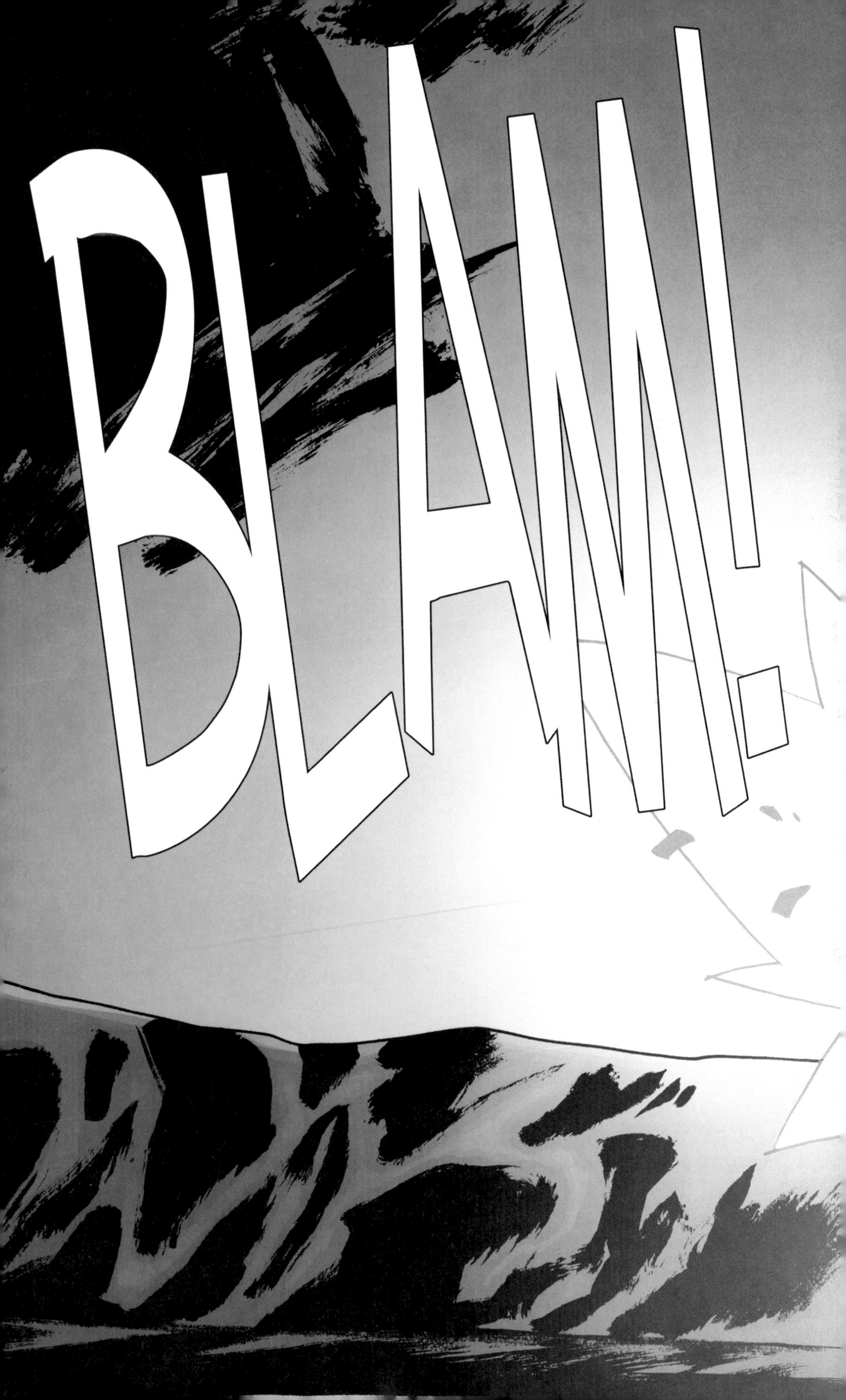
BLAM!

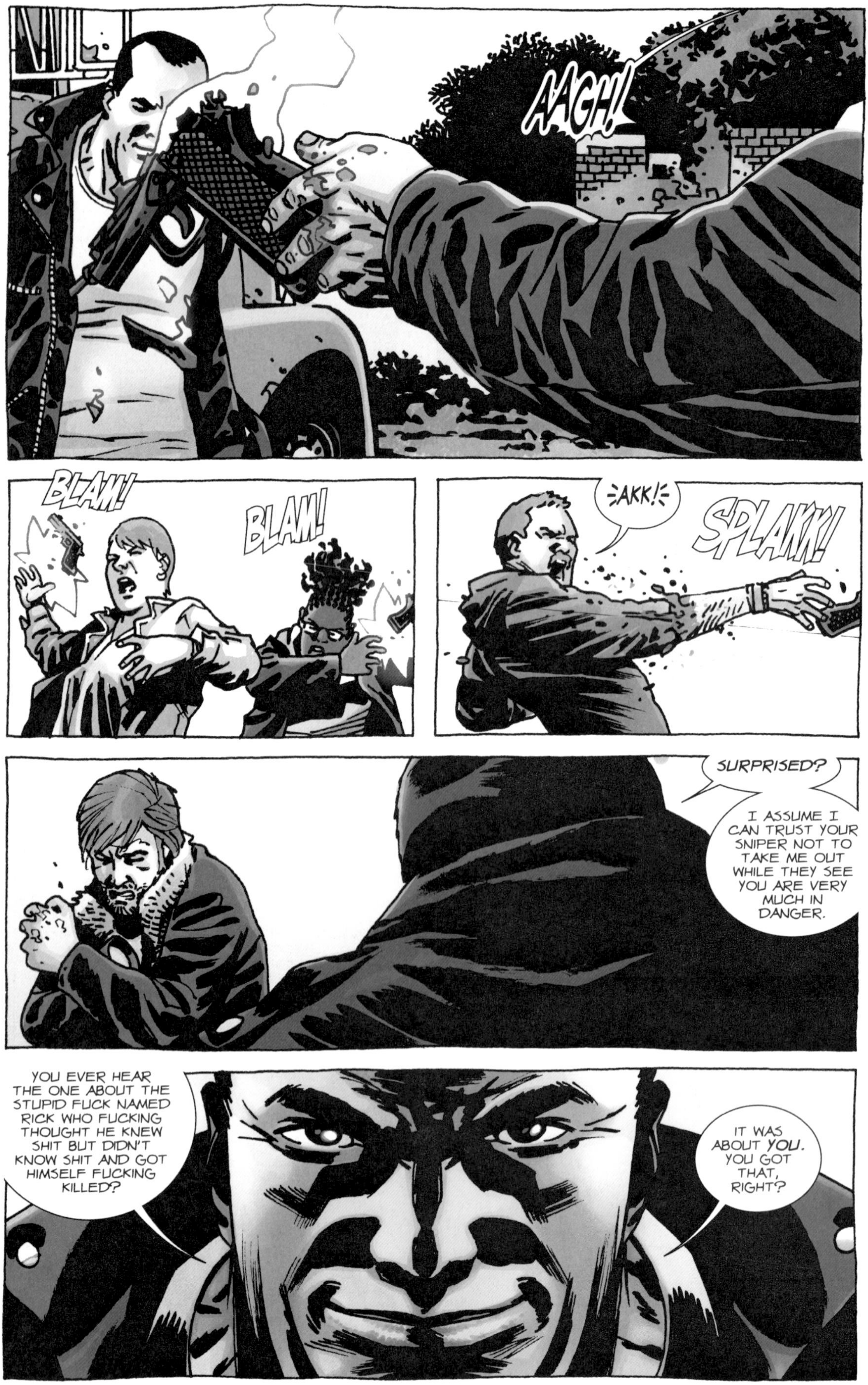
AAGH!
BLAM!
BLAM!
AKK!
SPLAKK!
SURPRISED?
I ASSUME I CAN TRUST YOUR SNIPER NOT TO TAKE ME OUT WHILE THEY SEE YOU ARE VERY MUCH IN DANGER.
YOU EVER HEAR THE ONE ABOUT THE STUPID FUCK NAMED RICK WHO FUCKING THOUGHT HE KNEW SHIT BUT DIDN'T KNOW SHIT AND GOT HIMSELF FUCKING KILLED?
IT WAS ABOUT YOU. YOU GOT THAT, RIGHT?

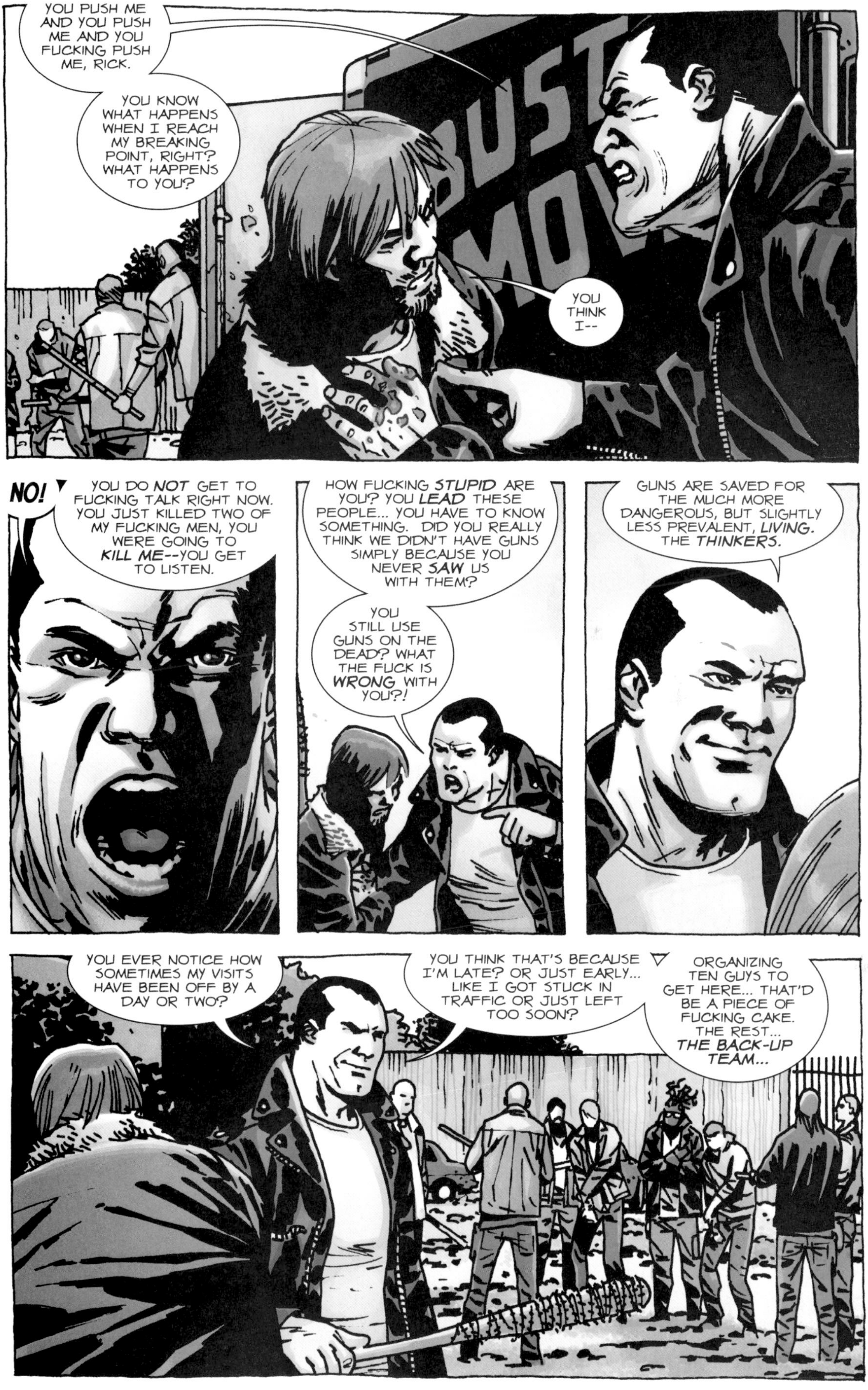
YOU PUSH ME AND YOU PUSH ME AND YOU FUCKING PUSH ME, RICK.
YOU KNOW WHAT HAPPENS WHEN I REACH MY BREAKING POINT, RIGHT? WHAT HAPPENS TO YOU?
BUST MOV
YOU THINK I--
NO!
YOU DO NOT GET TO FUCKING TALK RIGHT NOW. YOU JUST KILLED TWO OF MY FUCKING MEN, YOU WERE GOING TO KILL ME--YOU GET TO LISTEN.
HOW FUCKING STUPID ARE YOU? YOU LEAD THESE PEOPLE... YOU HAVE TO KNOW SOMETHING. DID YOU REALLY THINK WE DIDN'T HAVE GUNS SIMPLY BECAUSE YOU NEVER SAW US WITH THEM?
YOU STILL USE GUNS ON THE DEAD? WHAT THE FUCK IS WRONG WITH YOU?!
GUNS ARE SAVED FOR THE MUCH MORE DANGEROUS, BUT SLIGHTLY LESS PREVALENT, LIVING. THE THINKERS.
YOU EVER NOTICE HOW SOMETIMES MY VISITS HAVE BEEN OFF BY A DAY OR TWO?
YOU THINK THAT'S BECAUSE I'M LATE? OR JUST EARLY... LIKE I GOT STUCK IN TRAFFIC OR JUST LEFT TOO SOON?
ORGANIZING TEN GUYS TO GET HERE... THAT'D BE A PIECE OF FUCKING CAKE. THE REST... THE BACK-UP TEAM...

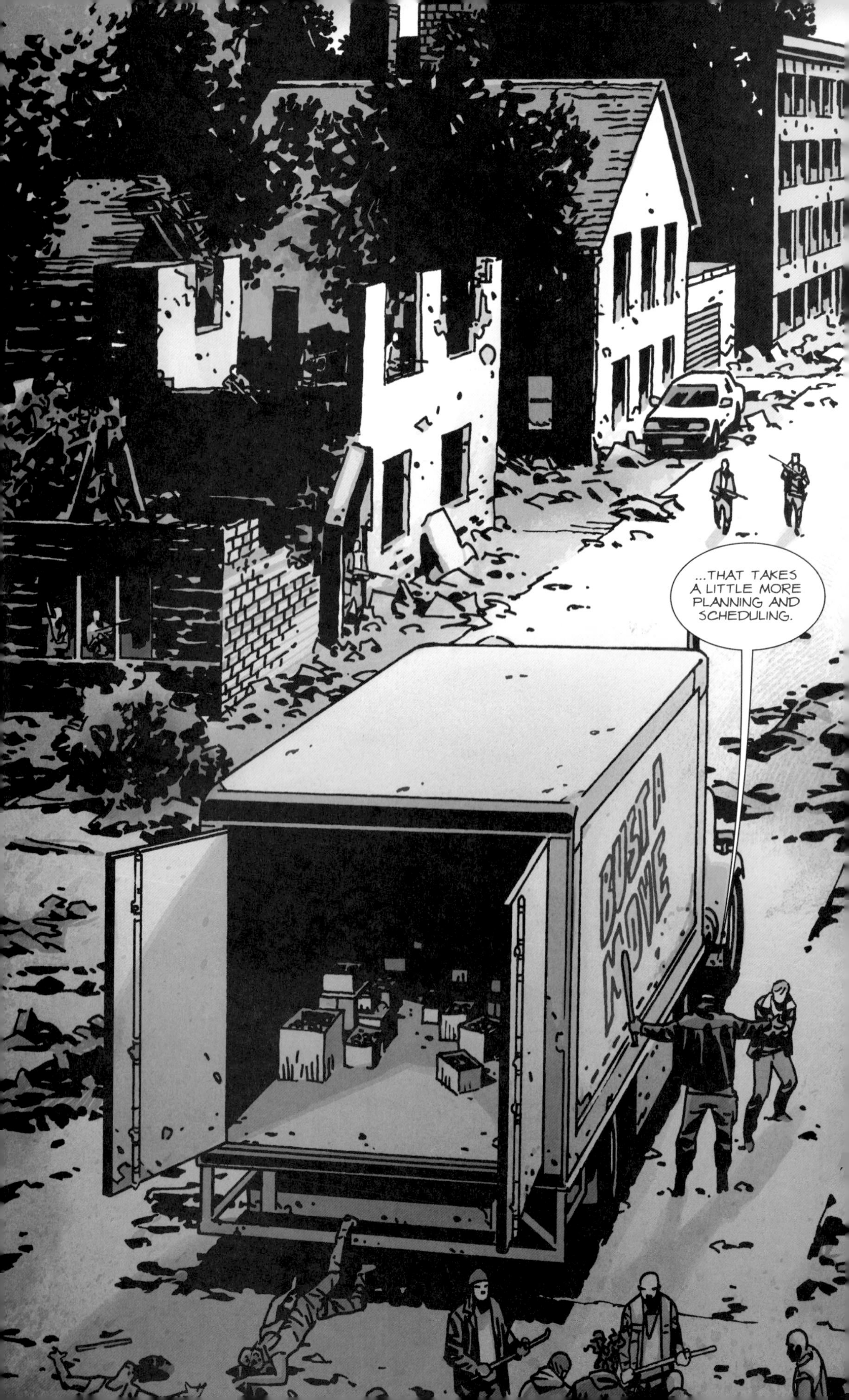
...THAT TAKES A LITTLE MORE PLANNING AND SCHEDULING.
BUST A MOVE

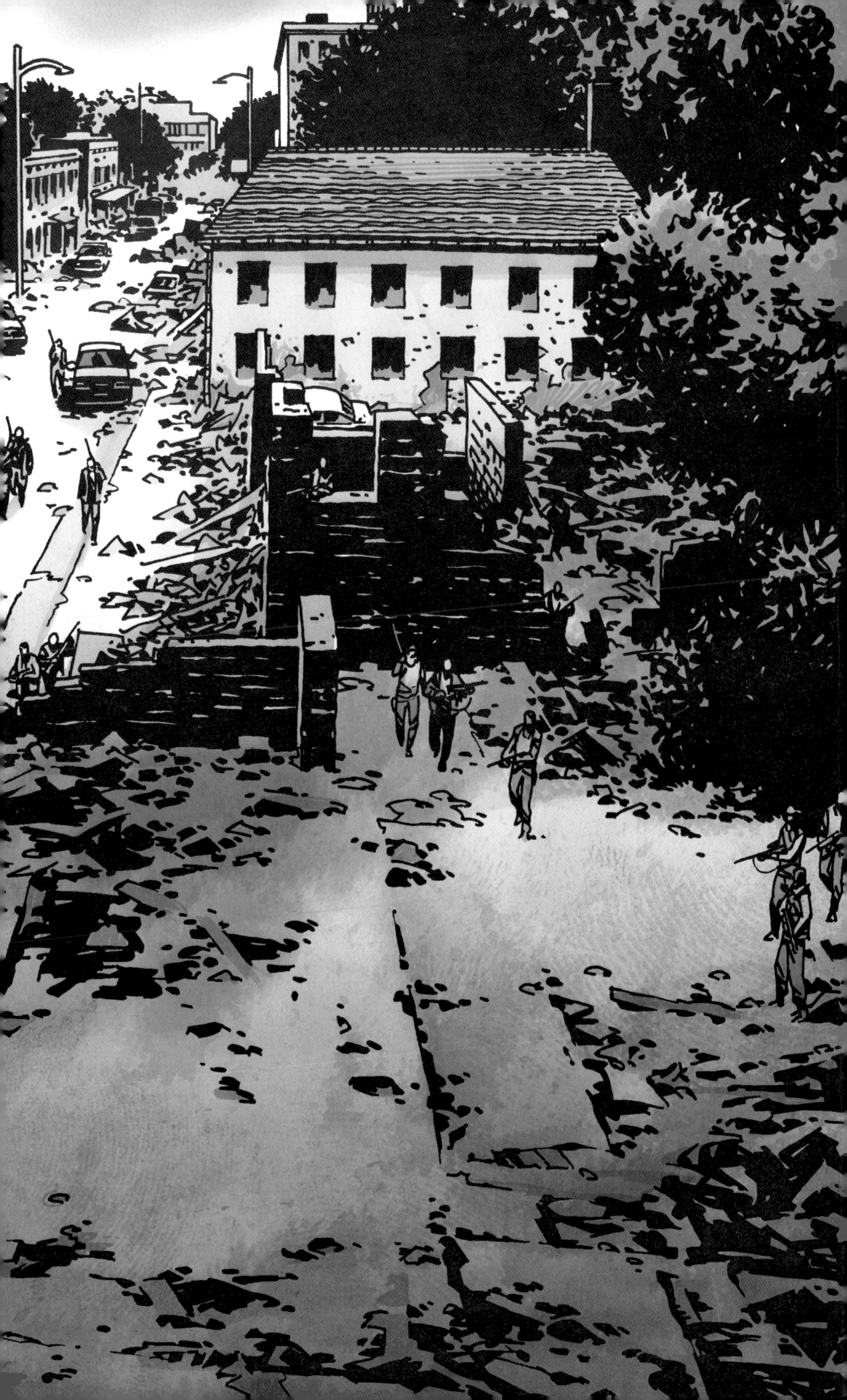

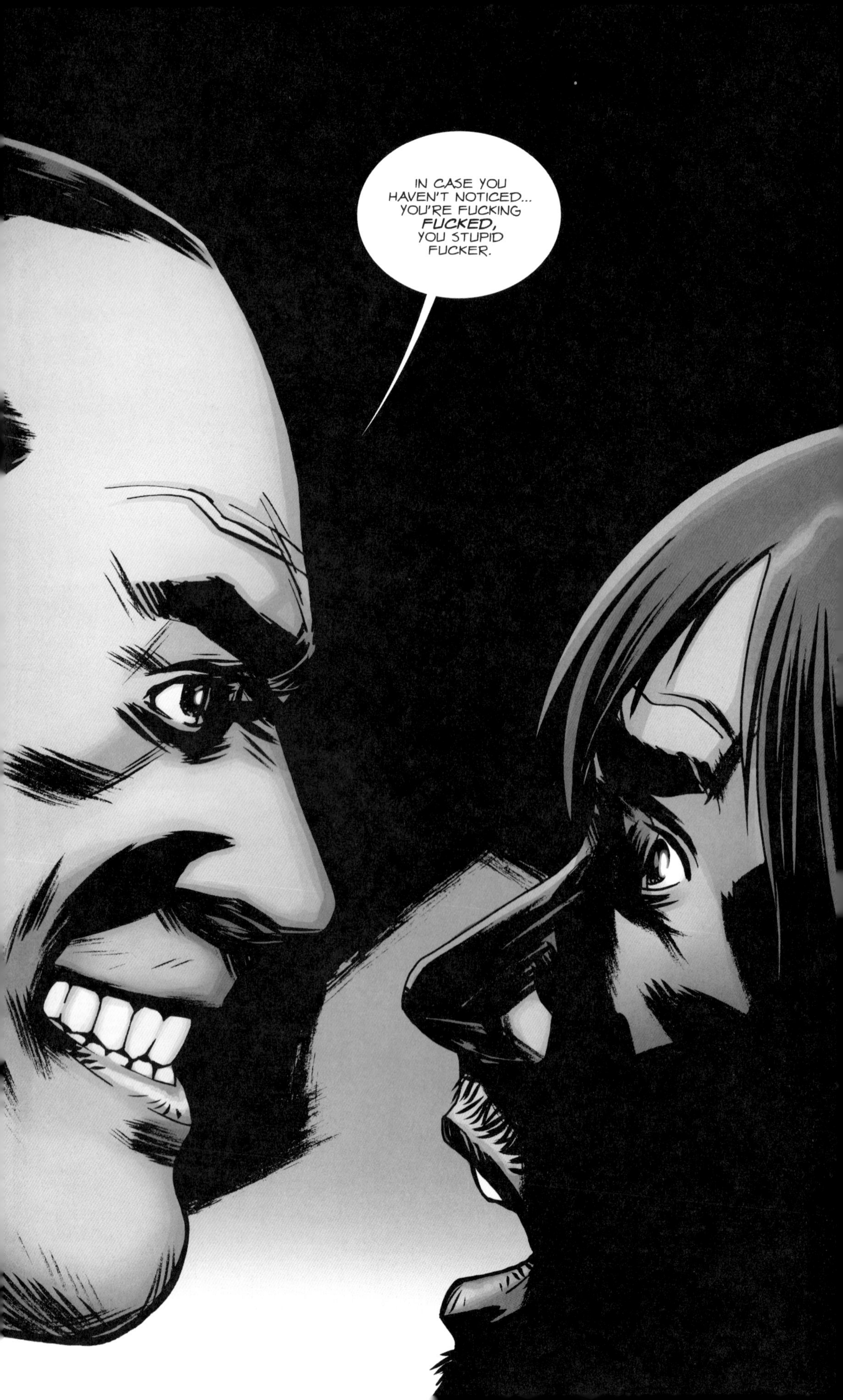
IN CASE YOU HAVEN'T NOTICED... YOU'RE FUCKING FUCKED, YOU STUPID FUCKER.

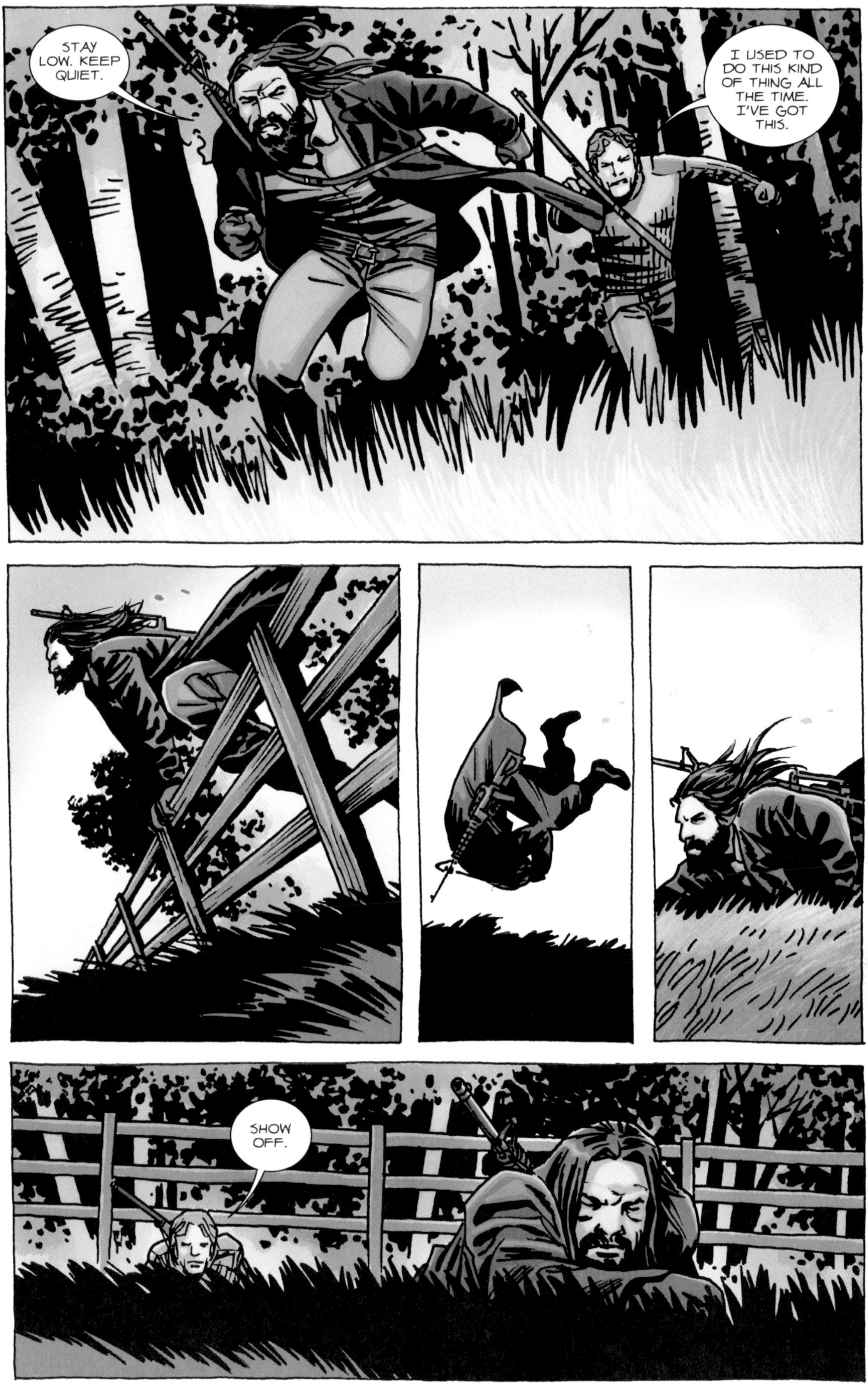
STAY LOW. KEEP QUIET.
I USED TO DO THIS KIND OF THING ALL THE TIME. I'VE GOT THIS.
SHOW OFF.

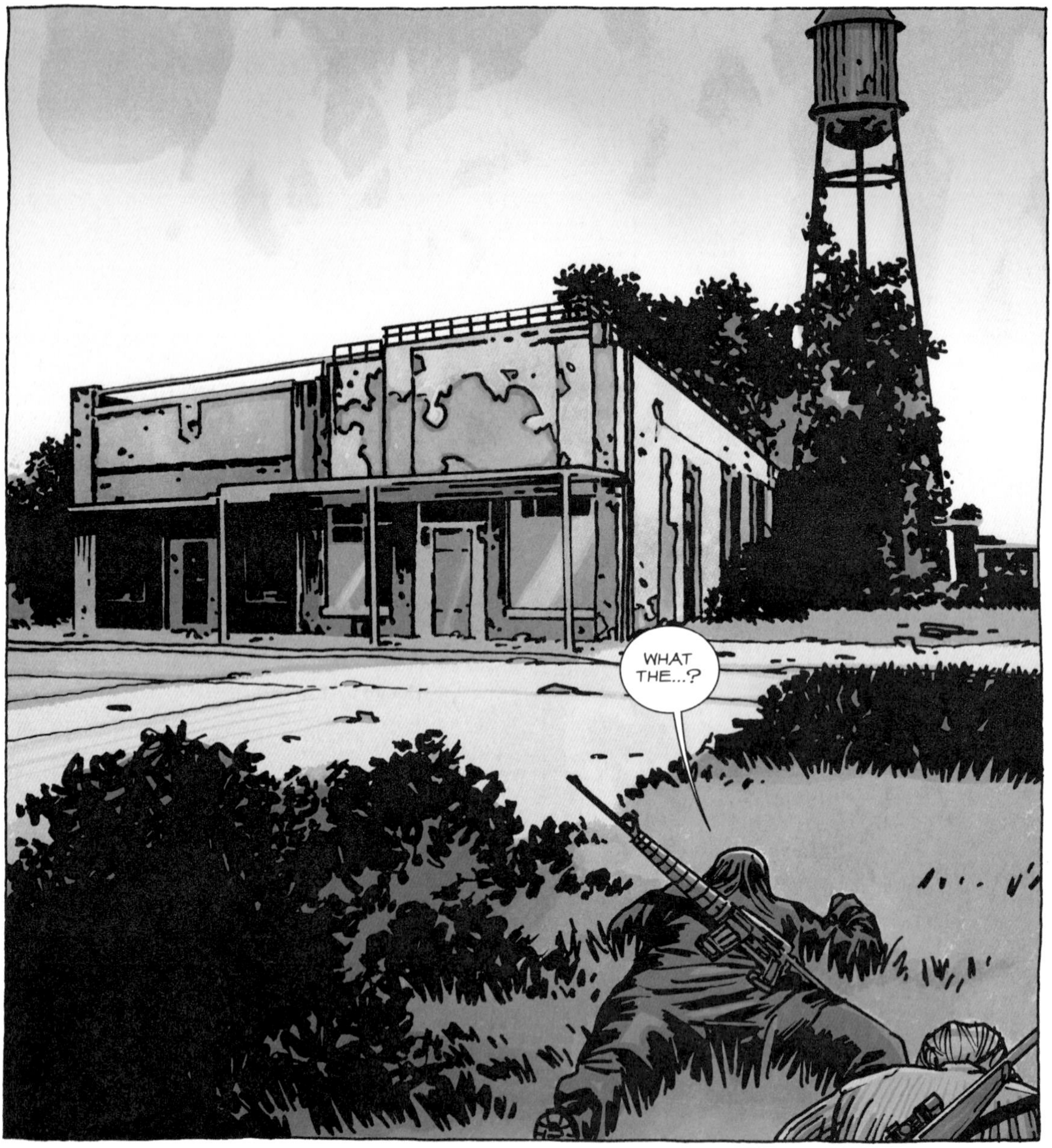
WHAT THE...?

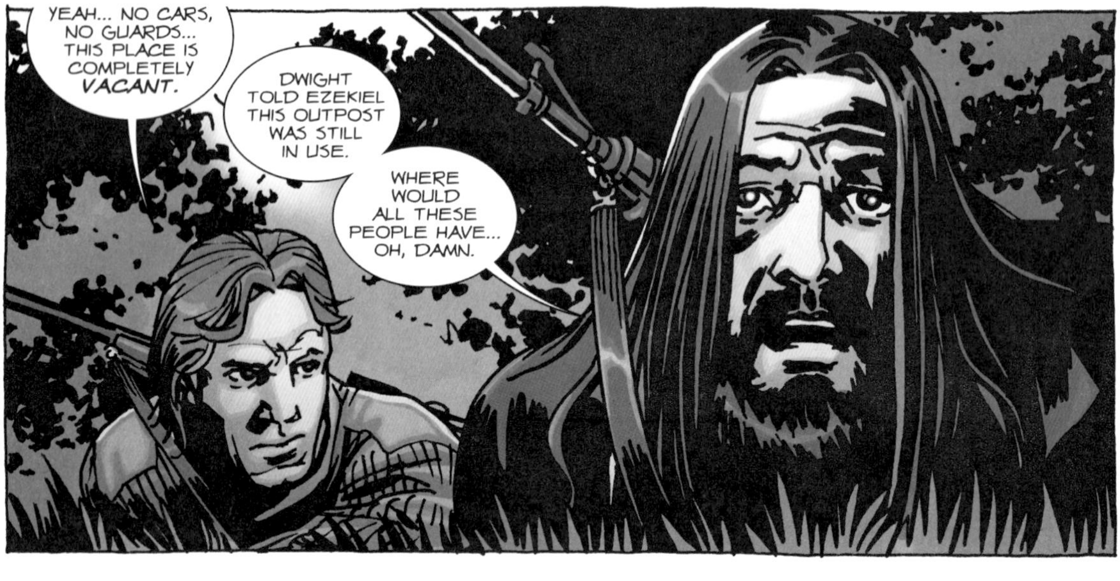
YEAH... NO CARS, NO GUARDS... THIS PLACE IS COMPLETELY *VACANT.*
DWIGHT TOLD EZEKIEL THIS OUTPOST WAS STILL IN USE.
WHERE WOULD ALL THESE PEOPLE HAVE... OH, DAMN.

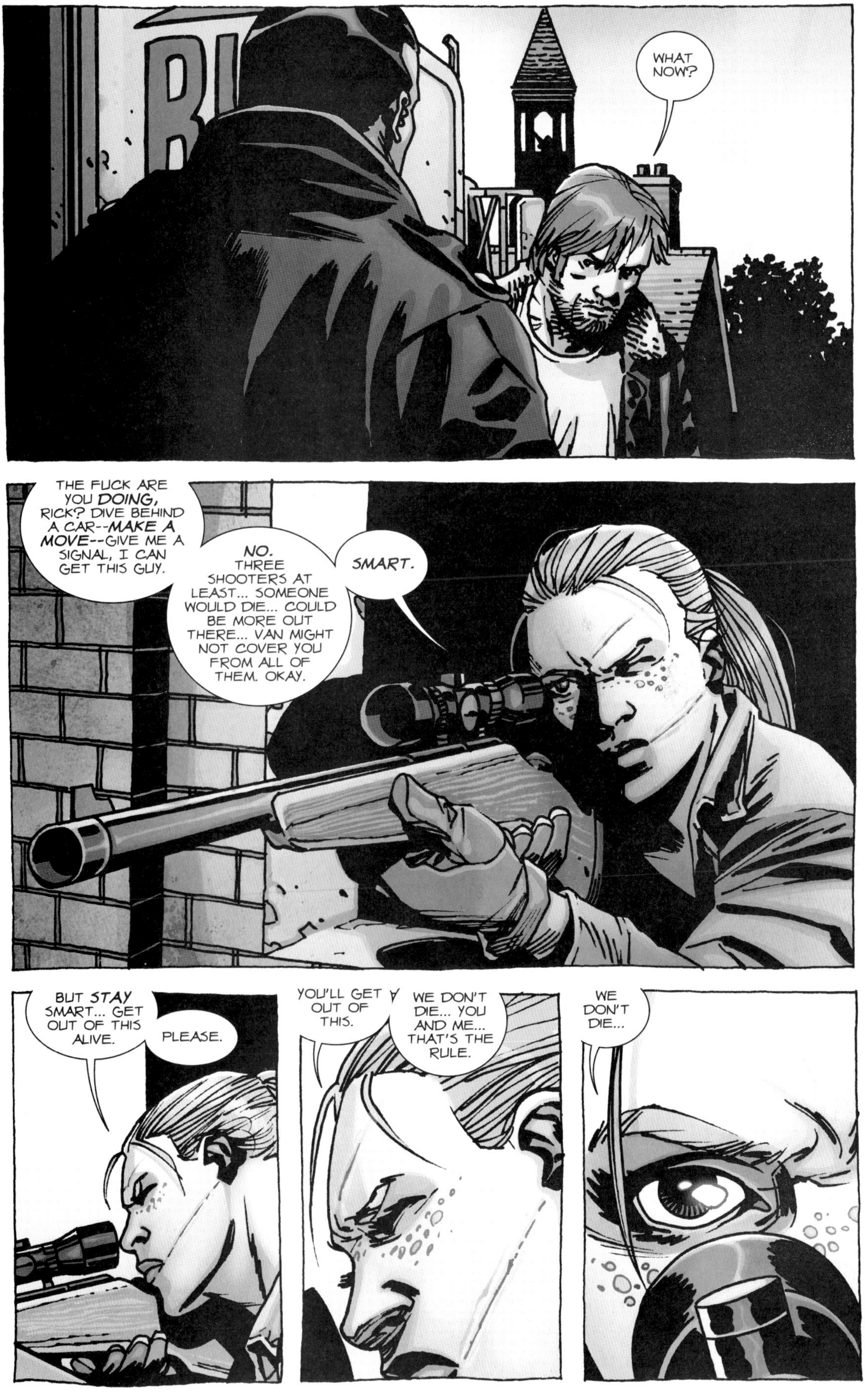
WHAT NOW?
THE FUCK ARE YOU DOING, RICK? DIVE BEHIND A CAR--MAKE A MOVE--GIVE ME A SIGNAL, I CAN GET THIS GUY.
NO. THREE SHOOTERS AT LEAST... SOMEONE WOULD DIE... COULD BE MORE OUT THERE... VAN MIGHT NOT COVER YOU FROM ALL OF THEM. OKAY.
SMART.
BUT STAY SMART... GET OUT OF THIS ALIVE.
PLEASE.
YOU'LL GET OUT OF THIS.
WE DON'T DIE... YOU AND ME... THAT'S THE RULE.
WE DON'T DIE...

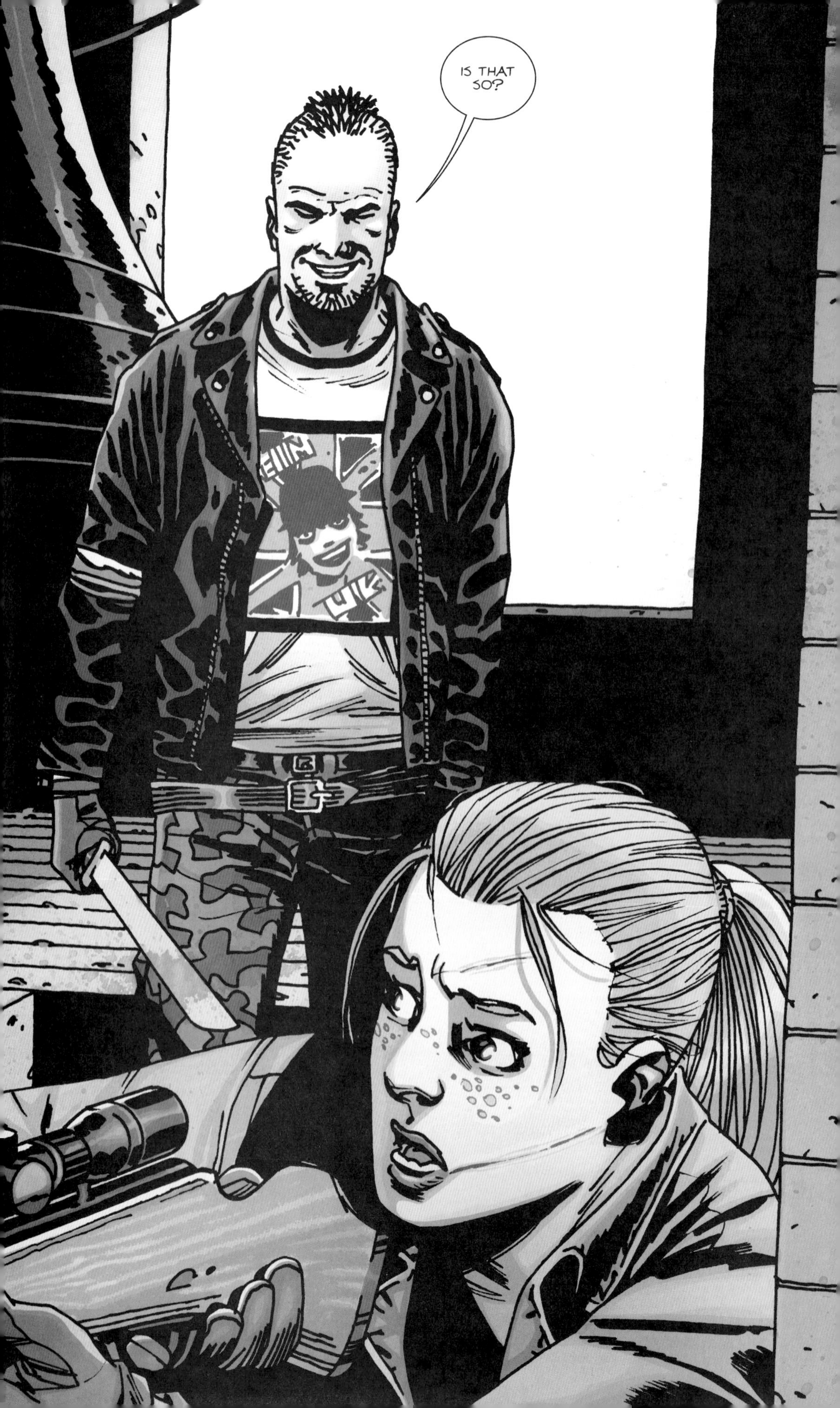
IS THAT SO?

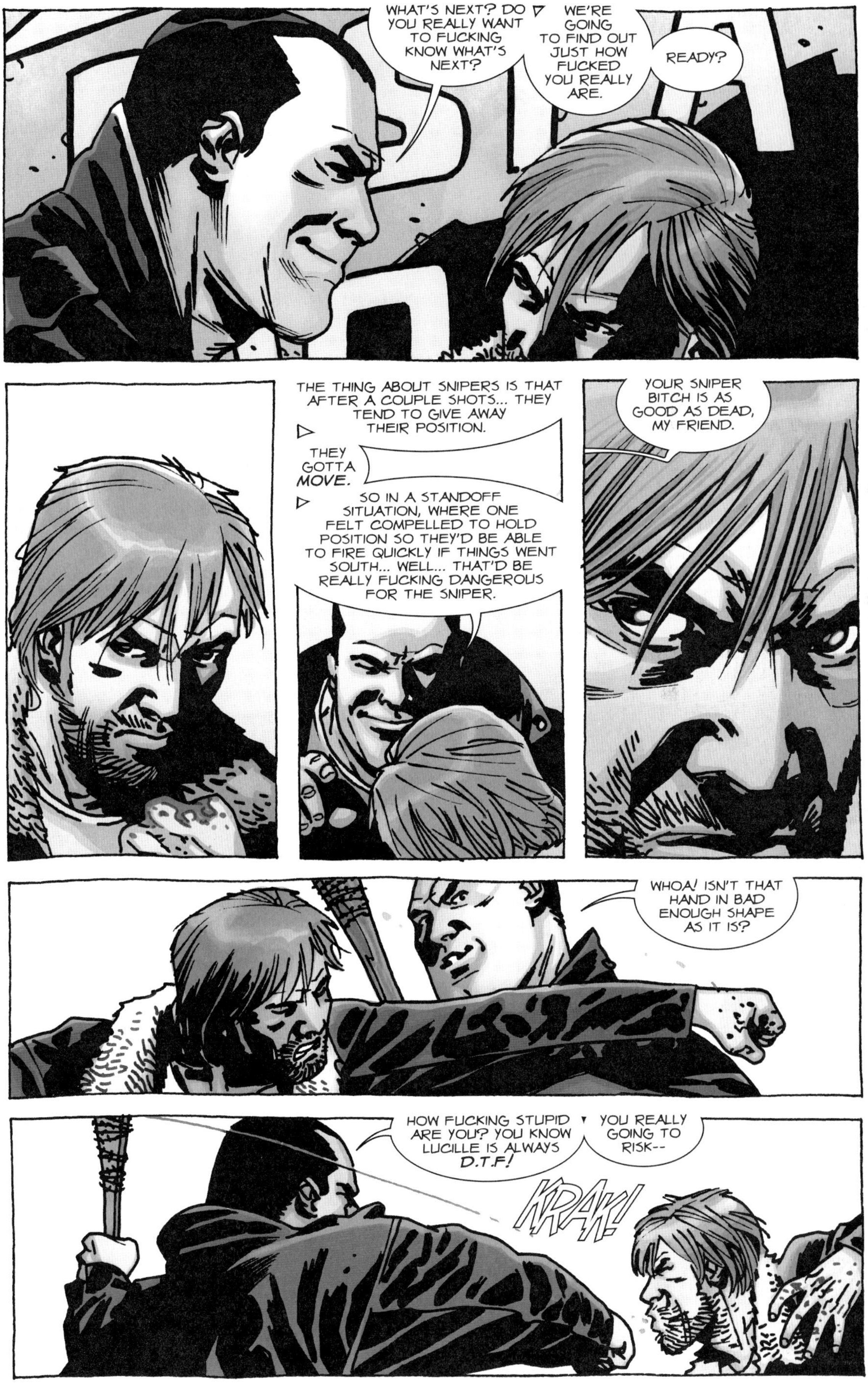
WHAT'S NEXT? DO YOU REALLY WANT TO FUCKING KNOW WHAT'S NEXT?
WE'RE GOING TO FIND OUT JUST HOW FUCKED YOU REALLY ARE.
READY?
THE THING ABOUT SNIPERS IS THAT AFTER A COUPLE SHOTS... THEY TEND TO GIVE AWAY THEIR POSITION.
THEY GOTTA *MOVE.*
SO IN A STANDOFF SITUATION, WHERE ONE FELT COMPELLED TO HOLD POSITION SO THEY'D BE ABLE TO FIRE QUICKLY IF THINGS WENT SOUTH... WELL... THAT'D BE REALLY FUCKING DANGEROUS FOR THE SNIPER.
YOUR SNIPER BITCH IS AS GOOD AS DEAD, MY FRIEND.
WHOA! ISN'T THAT HAND IN BAD ENOUGH SHAPE AS IT IS?
HOW FUCKING STUPID ARE YOU? YOU KNOW LUCILLE IS ALWAYS *D.T.F!*
YOU REALLY GOING TO RISK--
KRAK!

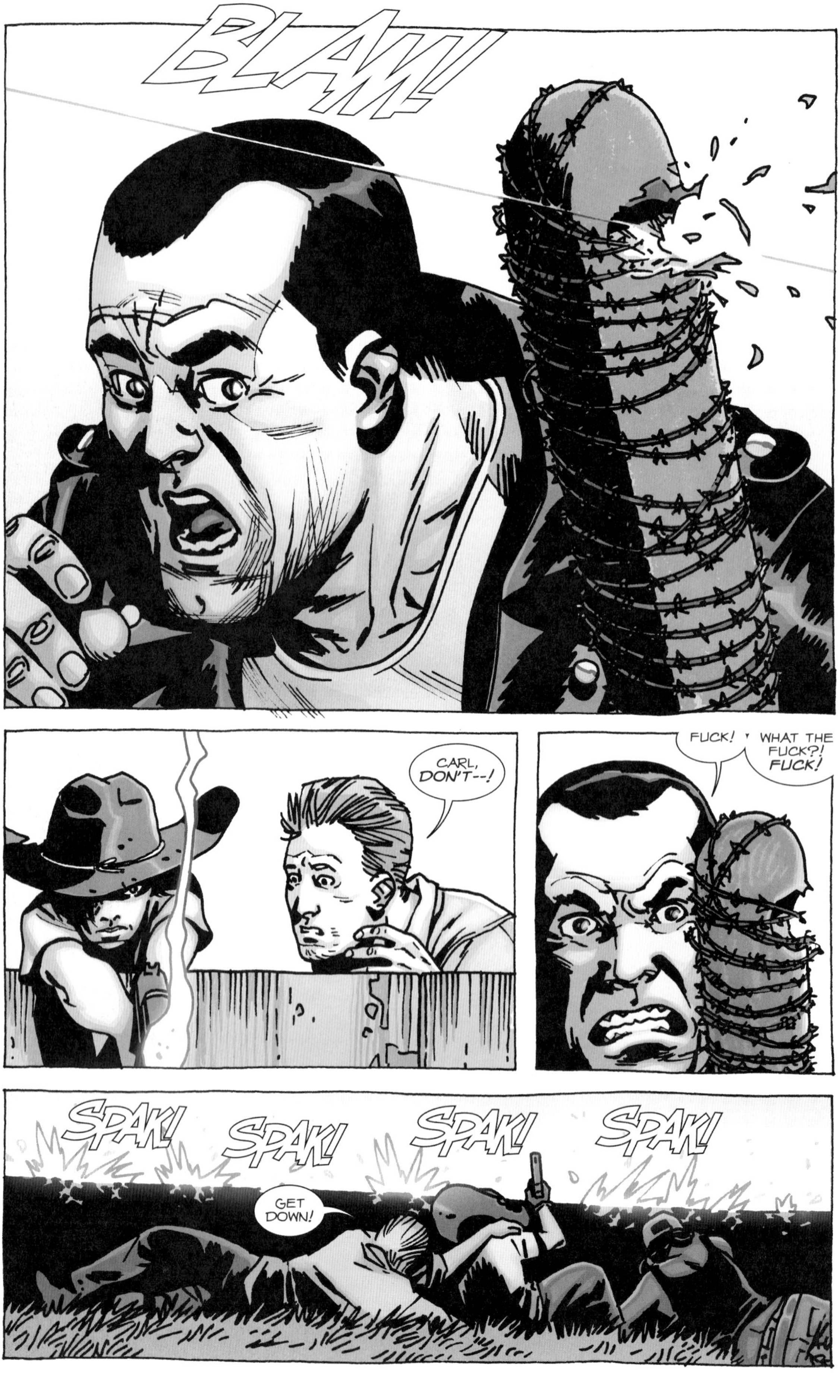
BLAM!
CARL, DON'T--!
FUCK!
WHAT THE FUCK?! FUCK!
SPAK!
SPAK!
SPAK!
SPAK!
GET DOWN!

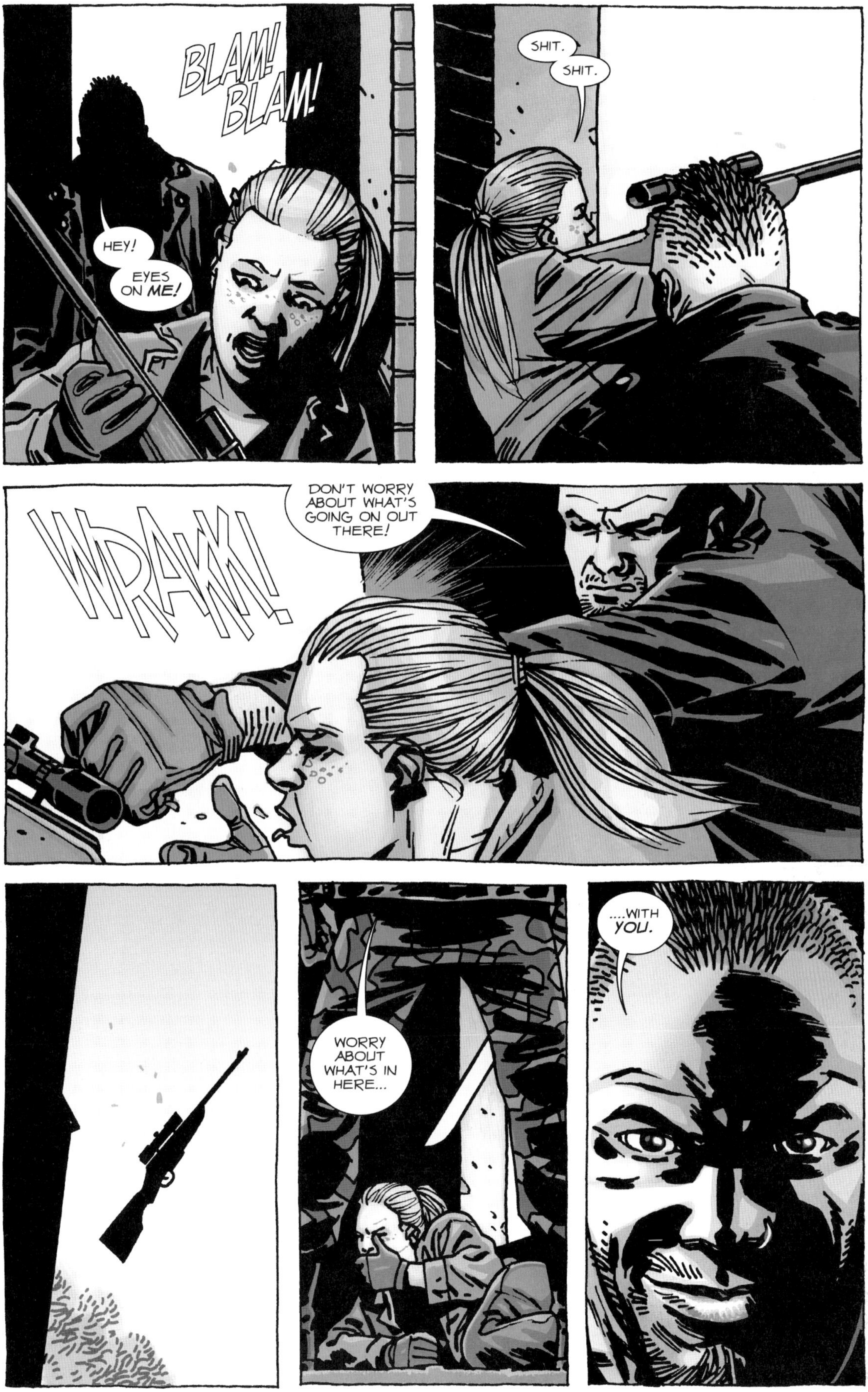
BLAM! BLAM!
HEY!
EYES ON ME!
SHIT.
SHIT.
WRAKK!
DON'T WORRY ABOUT WHAT'S GOING ON OUT THERE!
WORRY ABOUT WHAT'S IN HERE...
...WITH YOU.

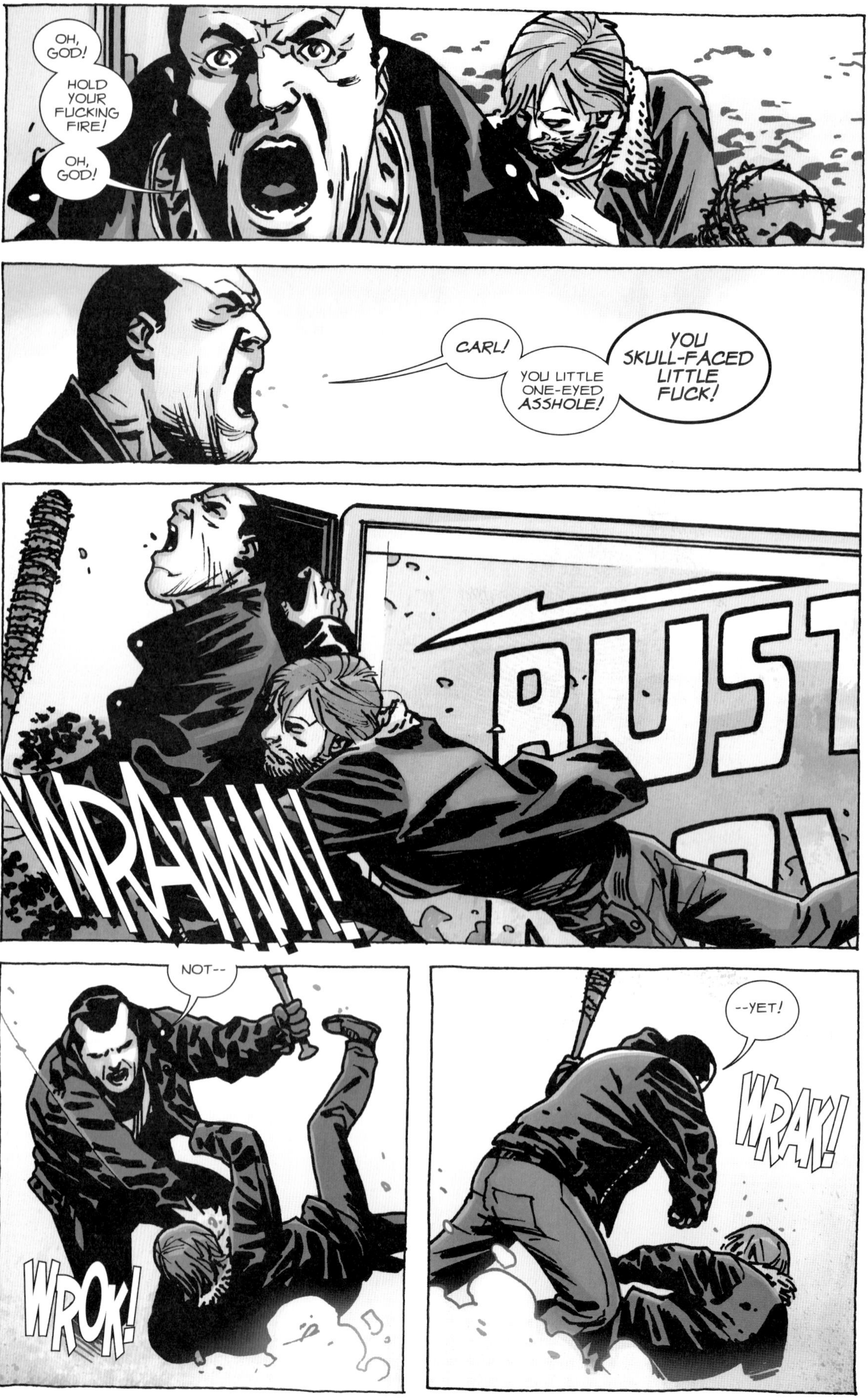

OH, GOD!
HOLD YOUR FUCKING FIRE!
OH, GOD!
CARL!
YOU LITTLE ONE-EYED ASSHOLE!
YOU SKULL-FACED LITTLE FUCK!
BUST
WRAMM!
NOT--
WROK!
--YET!
WRAK!

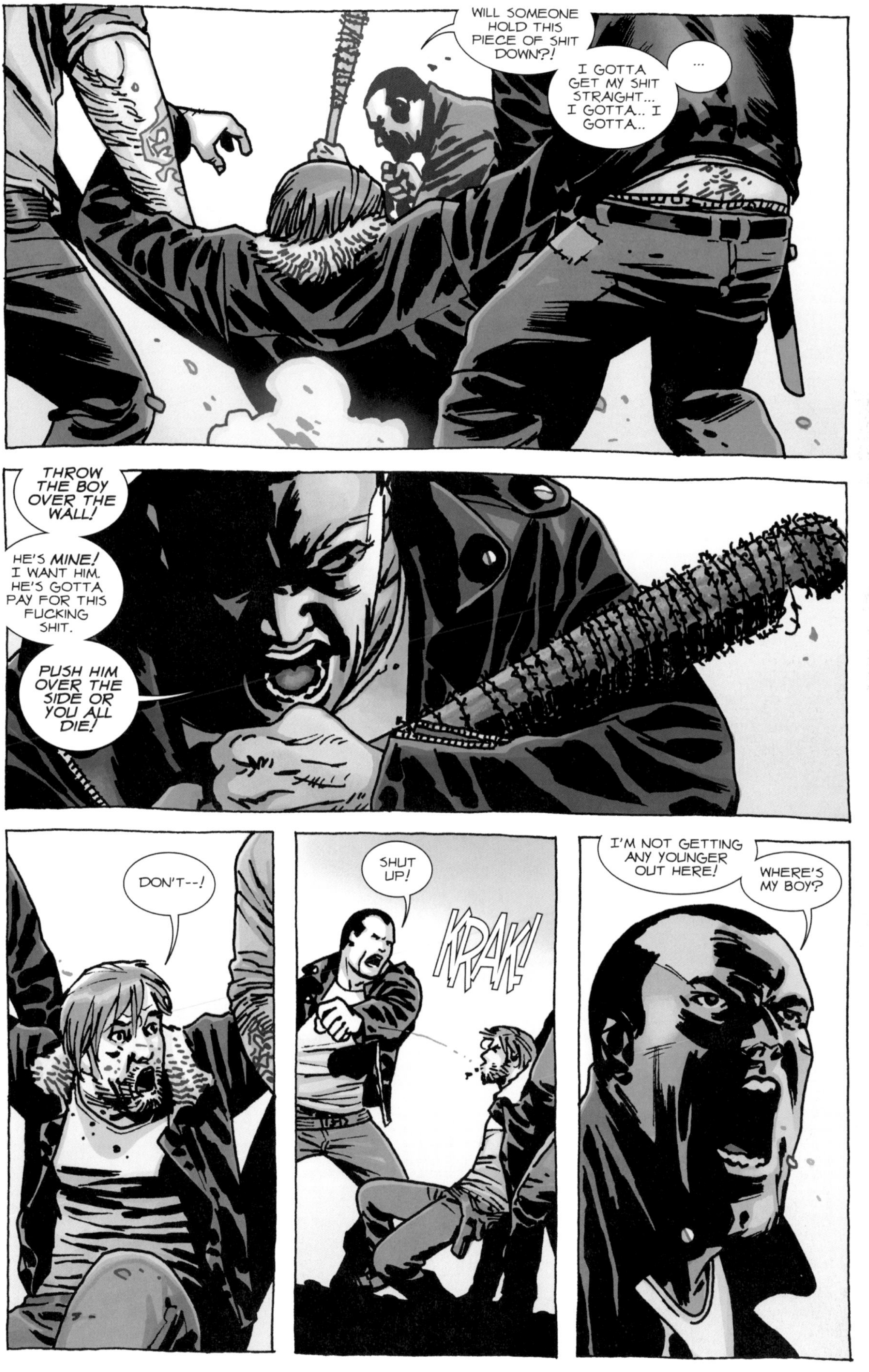
WILL SOMEONE HOLD THIS PIECE OF SHIT DOWN?!
I GOTTA GET MY SHIT STRAIGHT... I GOTTA.. I GOTTA..
...
THROW THE BOY OVER THE WALL!
HE'S MINE! I WANT HIM. HE'S GOTTA PAY FOR THIS FUCKING SHIT.
PUSH HIM OVER THE SIDE OR YOU ALL DIE!
DON'T--!
SHUT UP!
KRAK!
I'M NOT GETTING ANY YOUNGER OUT HERE!
WHERE'S MY BOY?

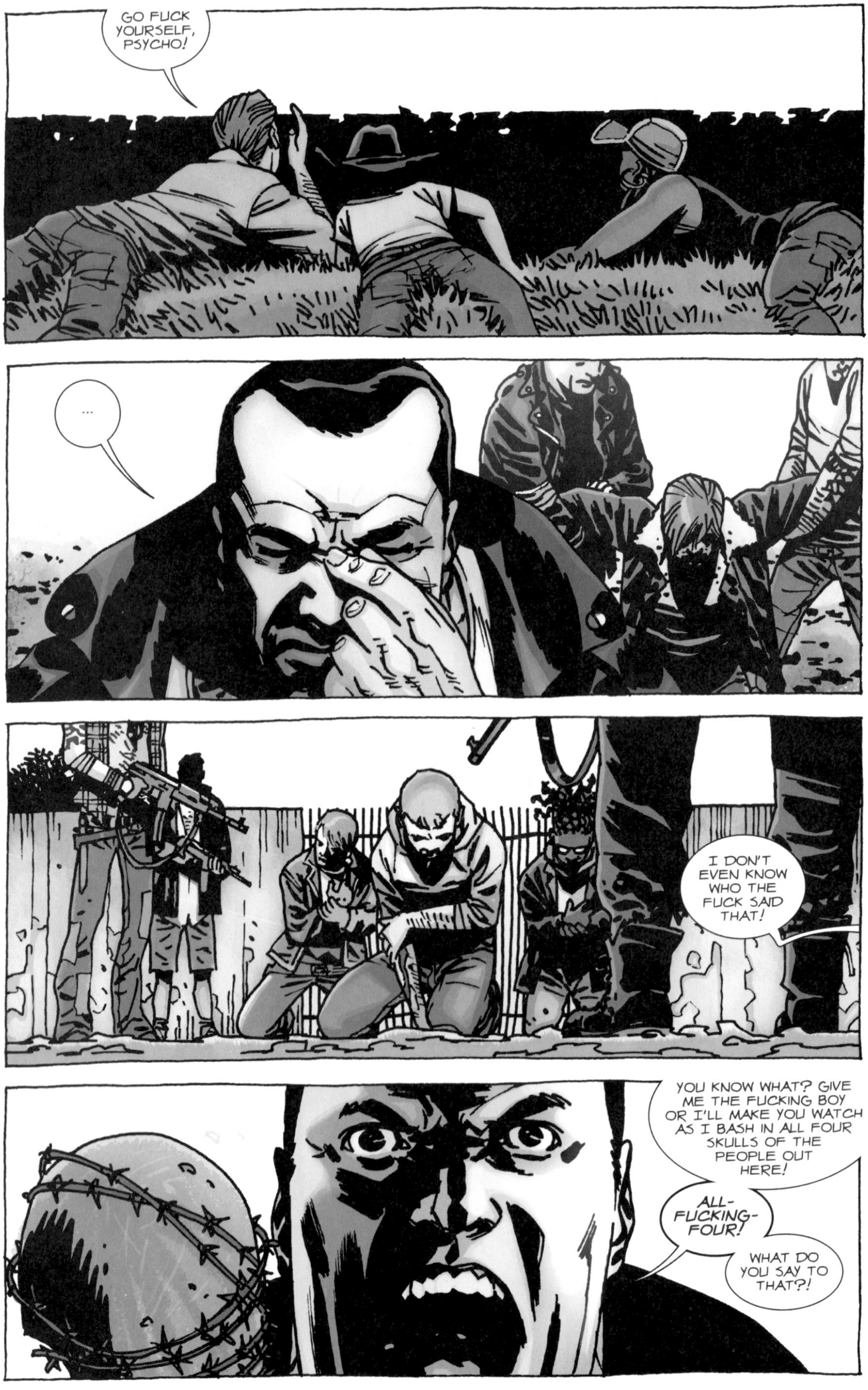
GO FUCK YOURSELF, PSYCHO!
...
I DON'T EVEN KNOW WHO THE FUCK SAID THAT!
YOU KNOW WHAT? GIVE ME THE FUCKING BOY OR I'LL MAKE YOU WATCH AS I BASH IN ALL FOUR SKULLS OF THE PEOPLE OUT HERE!
ALL-FUCKING-FOUR!
WHAT DO YOU SAY TO THAT?!

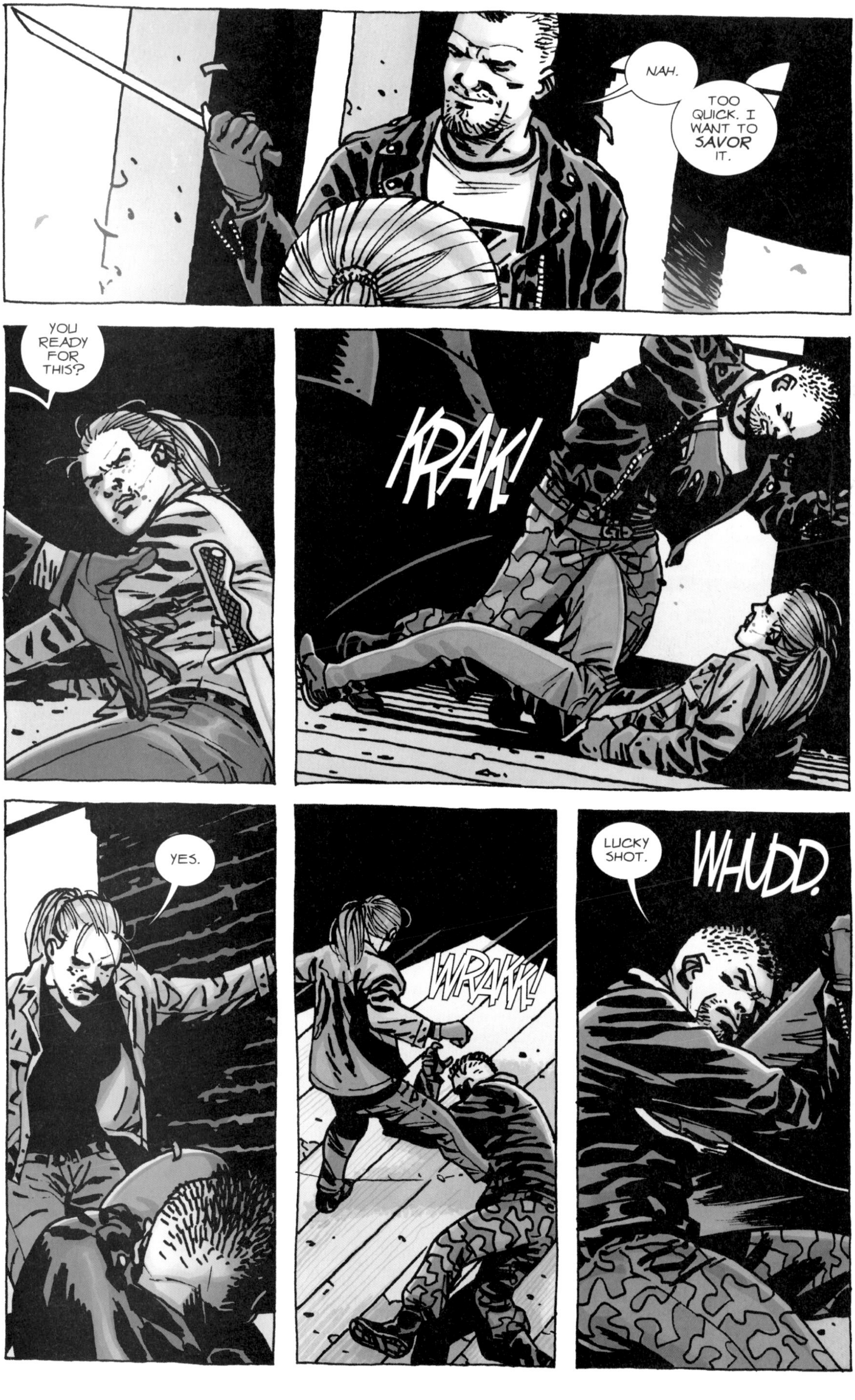
NAH.
TOO QUICK. I WANT TO SAVOR IT.
YOU READY FOR THIS?
KRAK!
YES.
WRAKK!
LUCKY SHOT.
WHUDD.

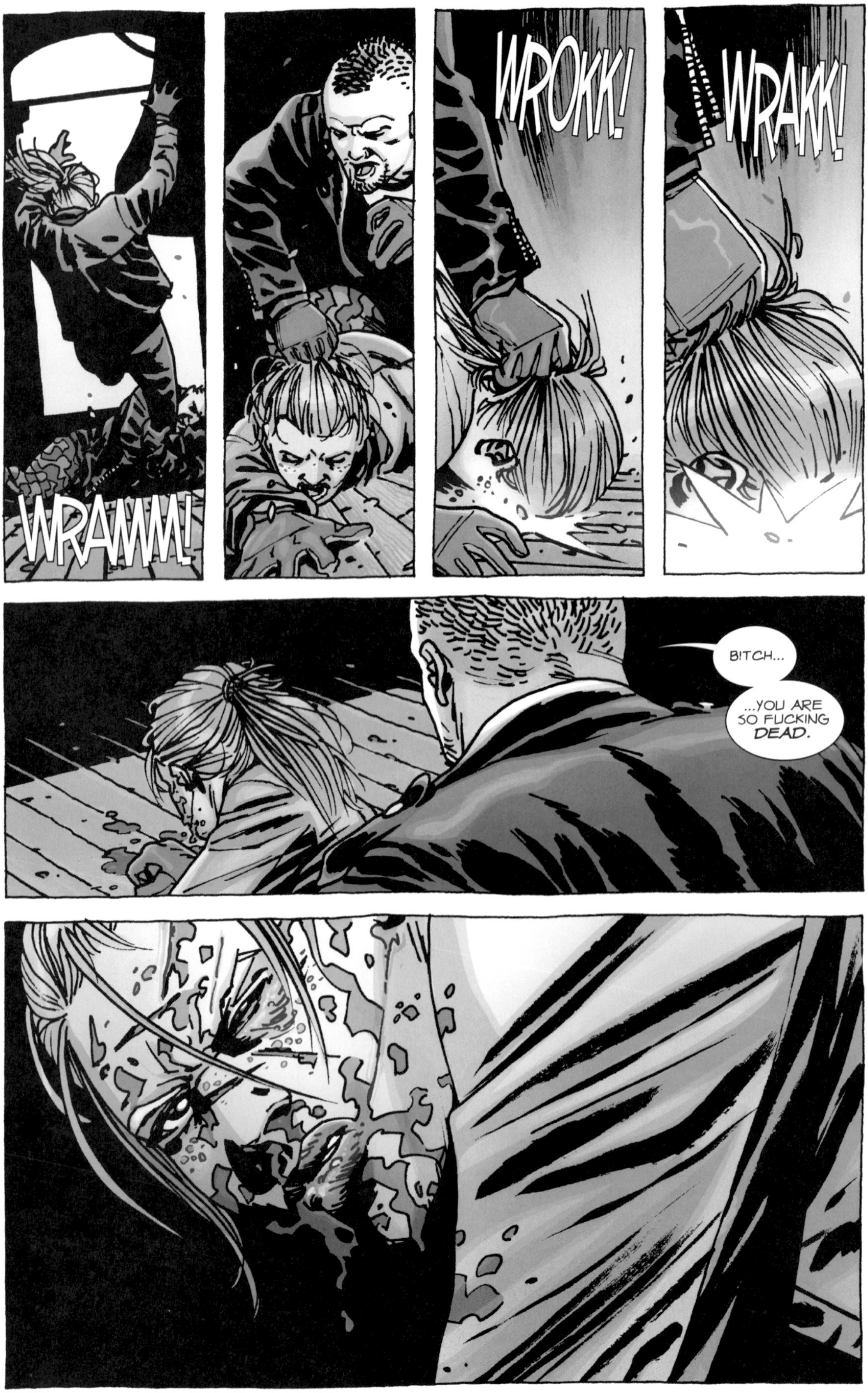
WRAMMM!
WROKK!
WRAKK!
BITCH...
...YOU ARE SO FUCKING DEAD.

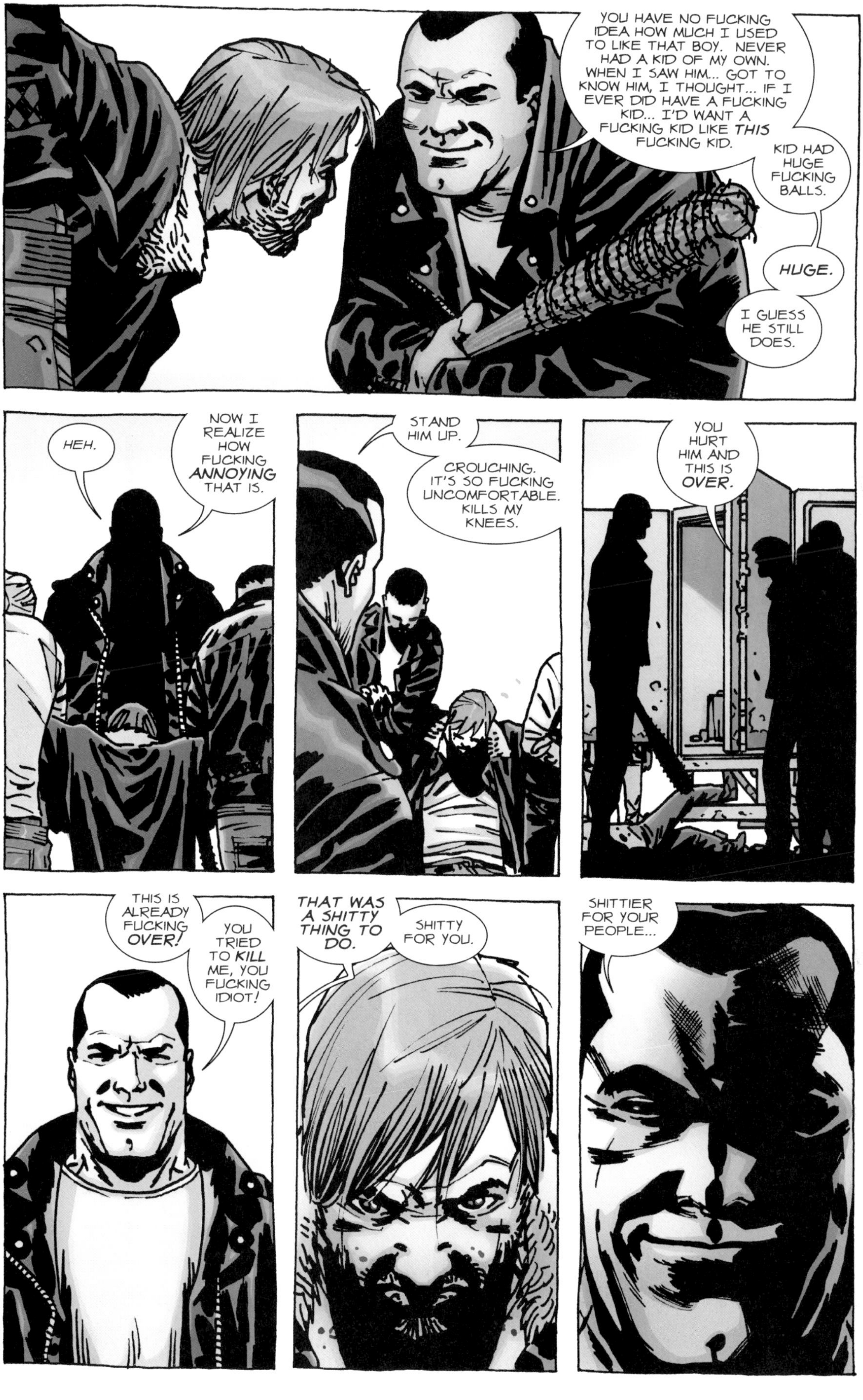
YOU HAVE NO FUCKING IDEA HOW MUCH I USED TO LIKE THAT BOY. NEVER HAD A KID OF MY OWN. WHEN I SAW HIM... GOT TO KNOW HIM, I THOUGHT... IF I EVER DID HAVE A FUCKING KID... I'D WANT A FUCKING KID LIKE *THIS* FUCKING KID.
KID HAD HUGE FUCKING BALLS.
HUGE.
I GUESS HE STILL DOES.
HEH.
NOW I REALIZE HOW FUCKING *ANNOYING* THAT IS.
STAND HIM UP.
CROUCHING. IT'S SO FUCKING UNCOMFORTABLE. KILLS MY KNEES.
YOU HURT HIM AND THIS IS *OVER.*
THIS IS ALREADY FUCKING *OVER!*
YOU TRIED TO *KILL* ME, YOU FUCKING IDIOT!
THAT WAS A SHITTY THING TO DO.
SHITTY FOR YOU.
SHITTIER FOR YOUR PEOPLE...

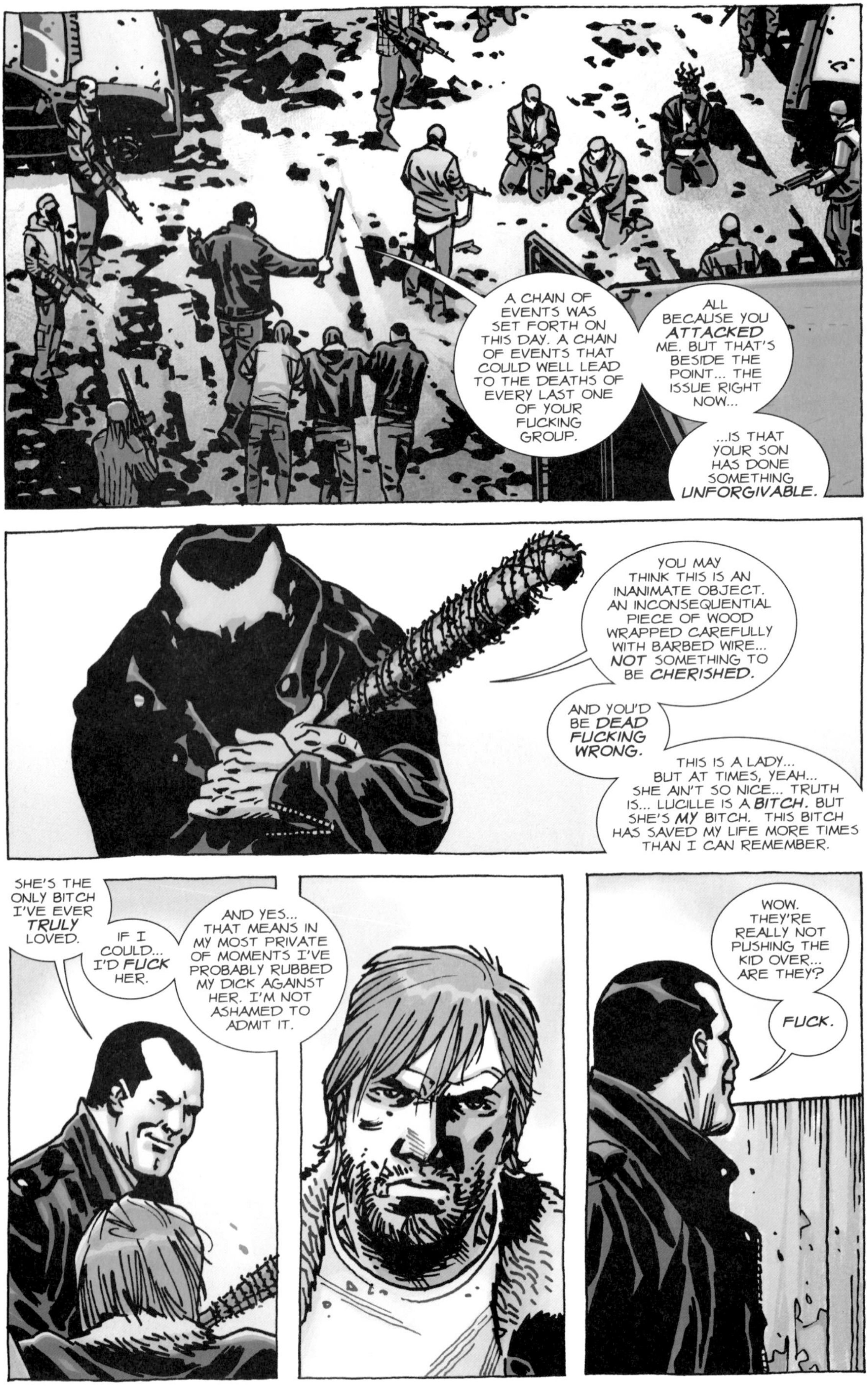

A CHAIN OF EVENTS WAS SET FORTH ON THIS DAY. A CHAIN OF EVENTS THAT COULD WELL LEAD TO THE DEATHS OF EVERY LAST ONE OF YOUR FUCKING GROUP.
ALL BECAUSE YOU ATTACKED ME. BUT THAT'S BESIDE THE POINT... THE ISSUE RIGHT NOW...
...IS THAT YOUR SON HAS DONE SOMETHING UNFORGIVABLE.
YOU MAY THINK THIS IS AN INANIMATE OBJECT. AN INCONSEQUENTIAL PIECE OF WOOD WRAPPED CAREFULLY WITH BARBED WIRE... NOT SOMETHING TO BE CHERISHED.
AND YOU'D BE DEAD FUCKING WRONG.
THIS IS A LADY... BUT AT TIMES, YEAH... SHE AIN'T SO NICE... TRUTH IS... LUCILLE IS A BITCH. BUT SHE'S MY BITCH. THIS BITCH HAS SAVED MY LIFE MORE TIMES THAN I CAN REMEMBER.
SHE'S THE ONLY BITCH I'VE EVER TRULY LOVED.
IF I COULD... I'D FUCK HER.
AND YES... THAT MEANS IN MY MOST PRIVATE OF MOMENTS I'VE PROBABLY RUBBED MY DICK AGAINST HER. I'M NOT ASHAMED TO ADMIT IT.
WOW. THEY'RE REALLY NOT PUSHING THE KID OVER... ARE THEY?
FUCK.

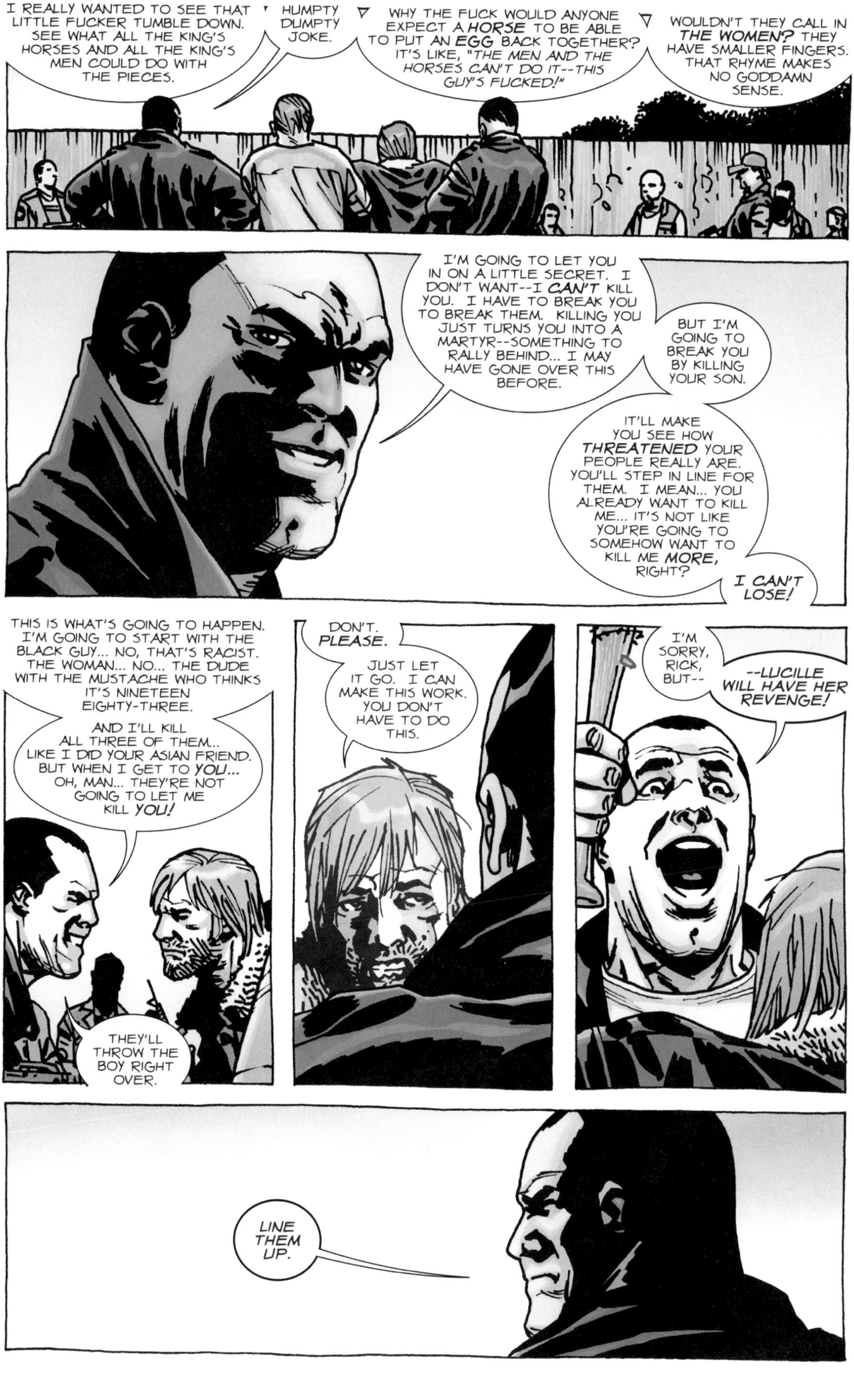
I REALLY WANTED TO SEE THAT LITTLE FUCKER TUMBLE DOWN. SEE WHAT ALL THE KING'S HORSES AND ALL THE KING'S MEN COULD DO WITH THE PIECES.
HUMPTY DUMPTY JOKE.
WHY THE FUCK WOULD ANYONE EXPECT A HORSE TO BE ABLE TO PUT AN EGG BACK TOGETHER? IT'S LIKE, "THE MEN AND THE HORSES CAN'T DO IT--THIS GUY'S FUCKED!"
WOULDN'T THEY CALL IN THE WOMEN? THEY HAVE SMALLER FINGERS. THAT RHYME MAKES NO GODDAMN SENSE.
I'M GOING TO LET YOU IN ON A LITTLE SECRET. I DON'T WANT--I CAN'T KILL YOU. I HAVE TO BREAK YOU TO BREAK THEM. KILLING YOU JUST TURNS YOU INTO A MARTYR--SOMETHING TO RALLY BEHIND... I MAY HAVE GONE OVER THIS BEFORE.
BUT I'M GOING TO BREAK YOU BY KILLING YOUR SON.
IT'LL MAKE YOU SEE HOW THREATENED YOUR PEOPLE REALLY ARE. YOU'LL STEP IN LINE FOR THEM. I MEAN... YOU ALREADY WANT TO KILL ME... IT'S NOT LIKE YOU'RE GOING TO SOMEHOW WANT TO KILL ME MORE, RIGHT?
I CAN'T LOSE!
THIS IS WHAT'S GOING TO HAPPEN. I'M GOING TO START WITH THE BLACK GUY... NO, THAT'S RACIST. THE WOMAN... NO... THE DUDE WITH THE MUSTACHE WHO THINKS IT'S NINETEEN EIGHTY-THREE.
AND I'LL KILL ALL THREE OF THEM... LIKE I DID YOUR ASIAN FRIEND. BUT WHEN I GET TO YOU... OH, MAN... THEY'RE NOT GOING TO LET ME KILL YOU!
THEY'LL THROW THE BOY RIGHT OVER.
DON'T. PLEASE.
JUST LET IT GO. I CAN MAKE THIS WORK. YOU DON'T HAVE TO DO THIS.
I'M SORRY, RICK, BUT--
--LUCILLE WILL HAVE HER REVENGE!
LINE THEM UP.

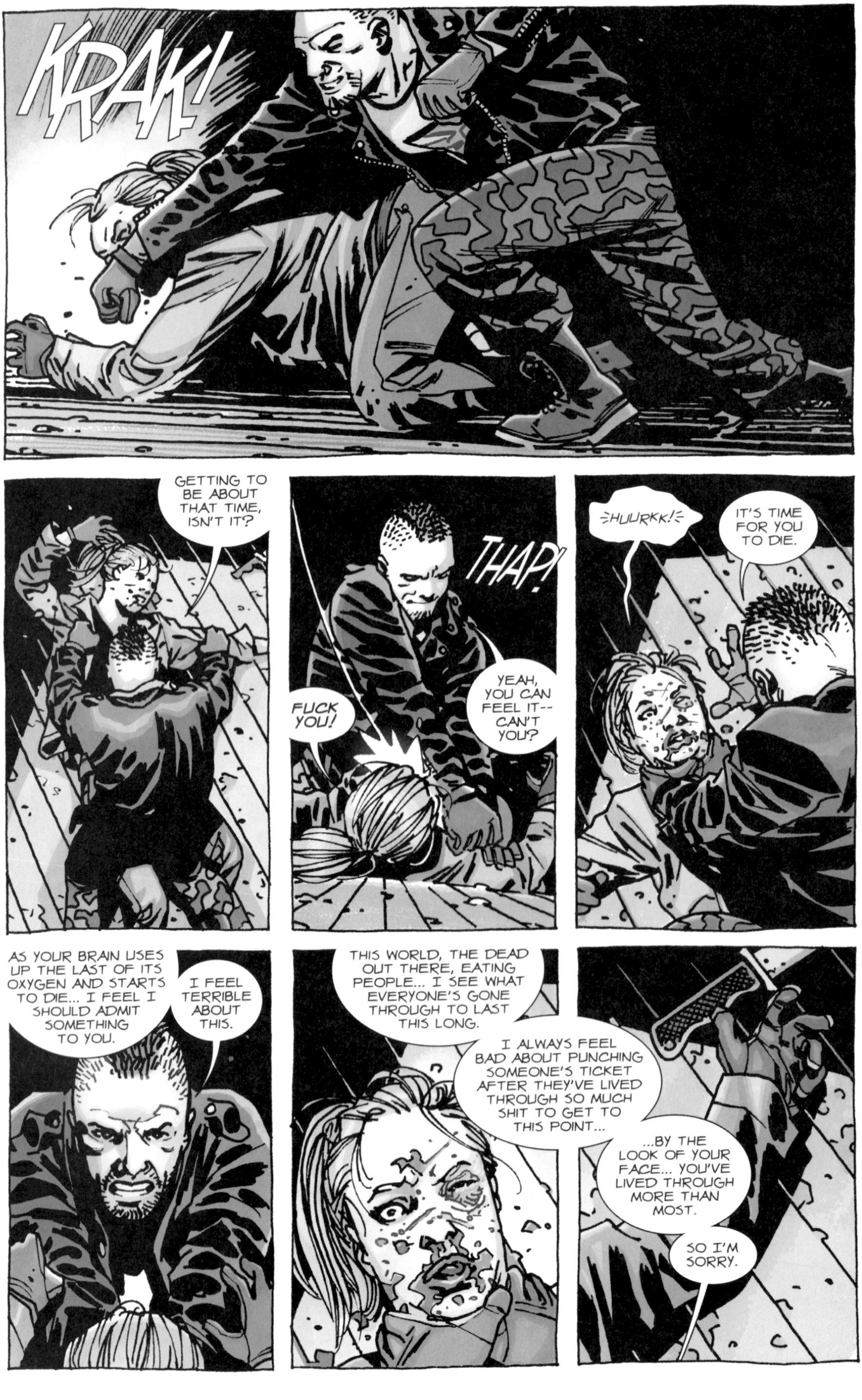
KRAK!
GETTING TO BE ABOUT THAT TIME, ISN'T IT?
THAP!
FUCK YOU!
YEAH, YOU CAN FEEL IT-- CAN'T YOU?
HUURKK!
IT'S TIME FOR YOU TO DIE.
AS YOUR BRAIN USES UP THE LAST OF ITS OXYGEN AND STARTS TO DIE... I FEEL I SHOULD ADMIT SOMETHING TO YOU.
I FEEL TERRIBLE ABOUT THIS.
THIS WORLD, THE DEAD OUT THERE, EATING PEOPLE... I SEE WHAT EVERYONE'S GONE THROUGH TO LAST THIS LONG.
I ALWAYS FEEL BAD ABOUT PUNCHING SOMEONE'S TICKET AFTER THEY'VE LIVED THROUGH SO MUCH SHIT TO GET TO THIS POINT...
...BY THE LOOK OF YOUR FACE... YOU'VE LIVED THROUGH MORE THAN MOST.
SO I'M SORRY.

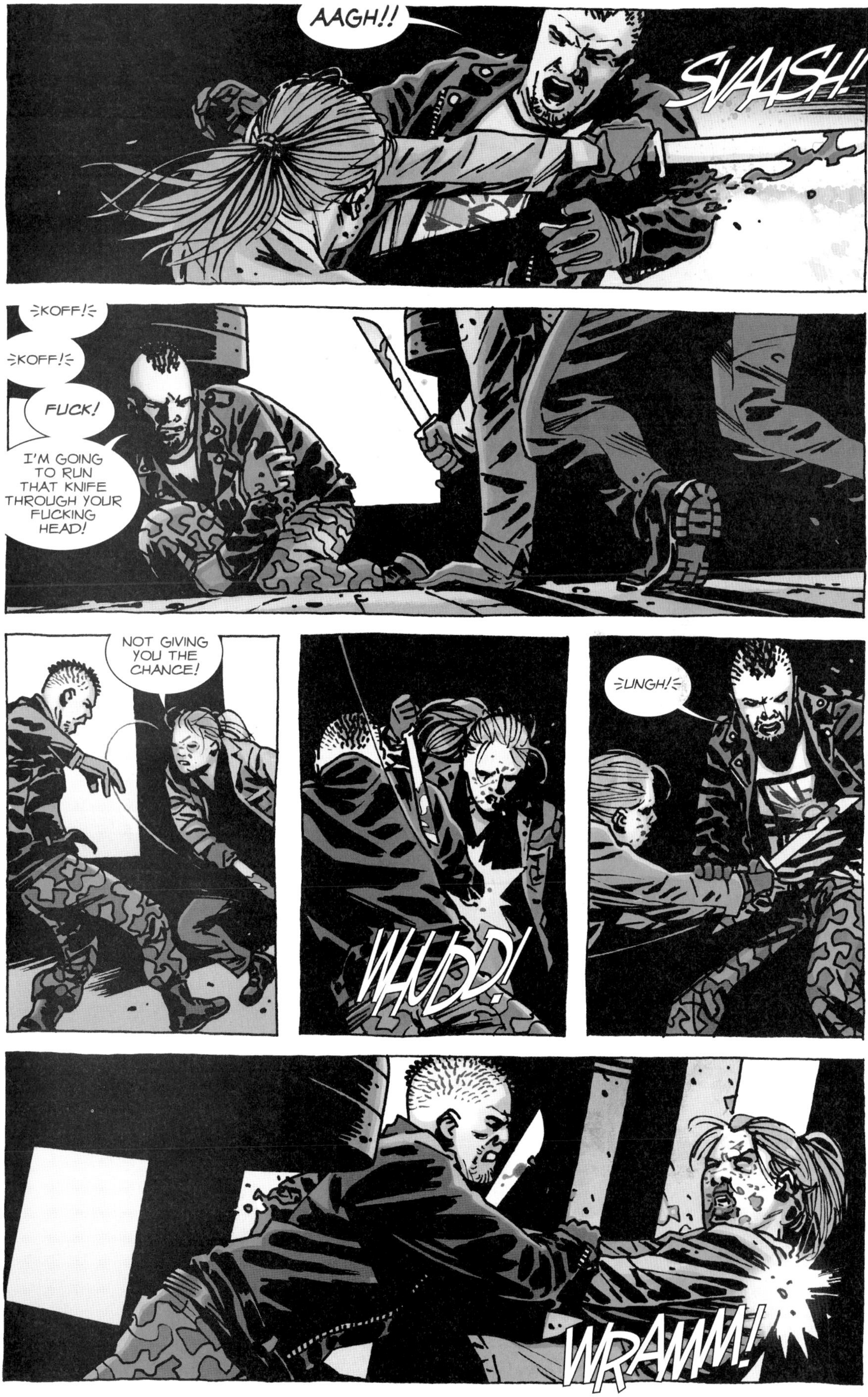
AAGH!!
SVAASH!
KOFF!
KOFF!
FUCK!
I'M GOING TO RUN THAT KNIFE THROUGH YOUR FUCKING HEAD!
NOT GIVING YOU THE CHANCE!
WHUDD!
UNGH!
WRAMM!

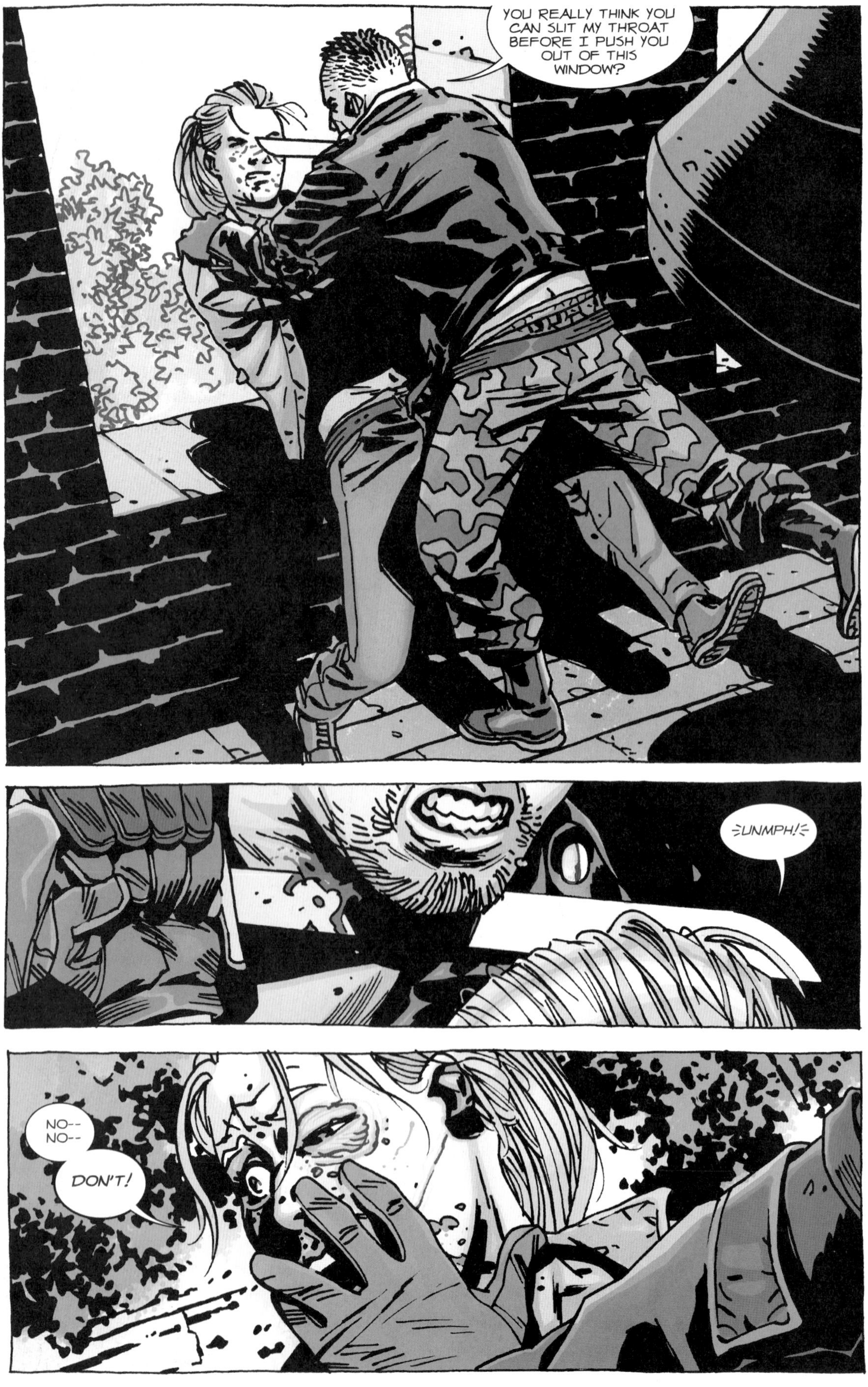

YOU REALLY THINK YOU CAN SLIT MY THROAT BEFORE I PUSH YOU OUT OF THIS WINDOW?
UNMPH!
NO-- NO--
DON'T!

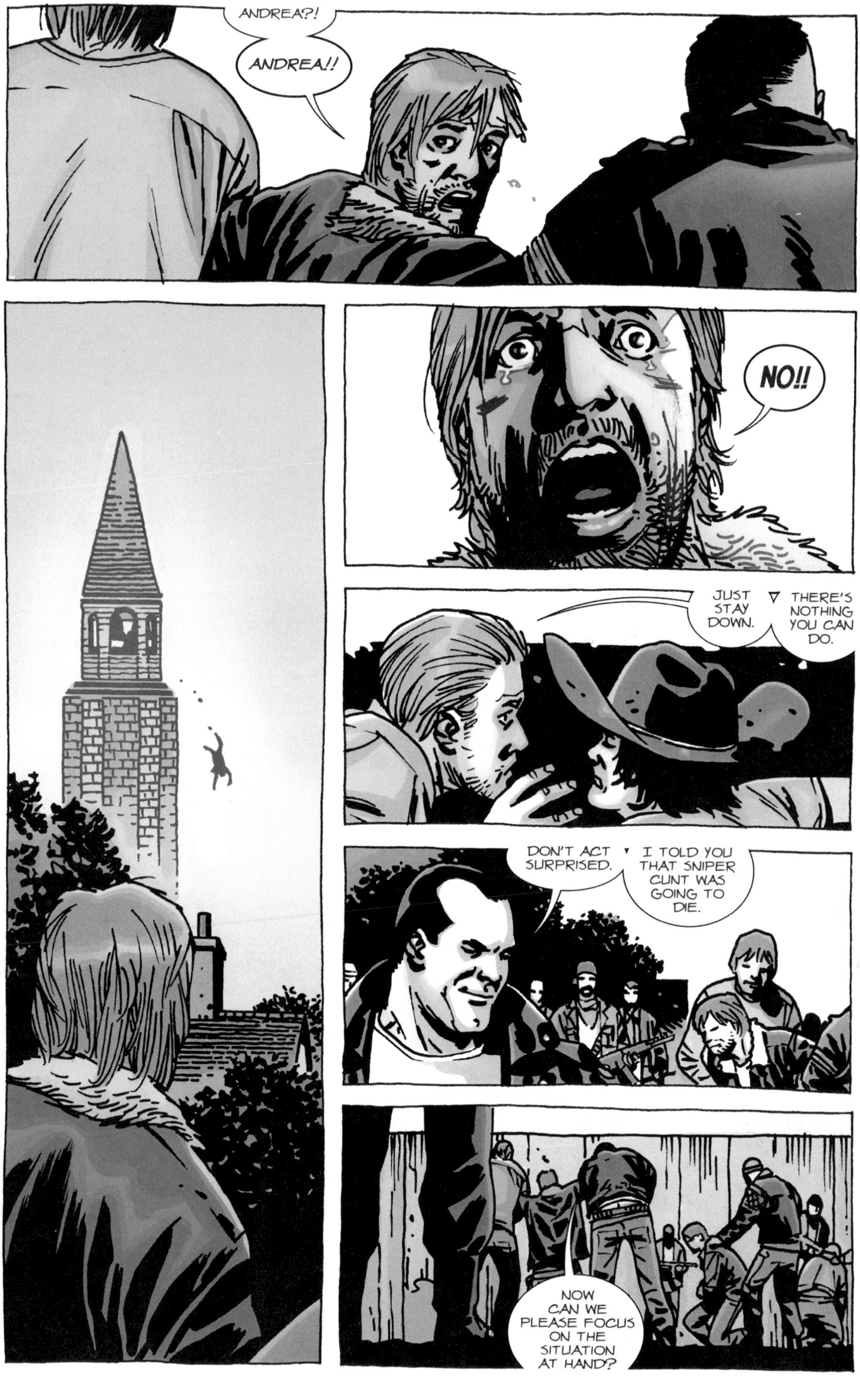
ANDREA?!
ANDREA!!
NO!!
JUST STAY DOWN.
THERE'S NOTHING YOU CAN DO.
DON'T ACT SURPRISED.
I TOLD YOU THAT SNIPER CUNT WAS GOING TO DIE.
NOW CAN WE PLEASE FOCUS ON THE SITUATION AT HAND?

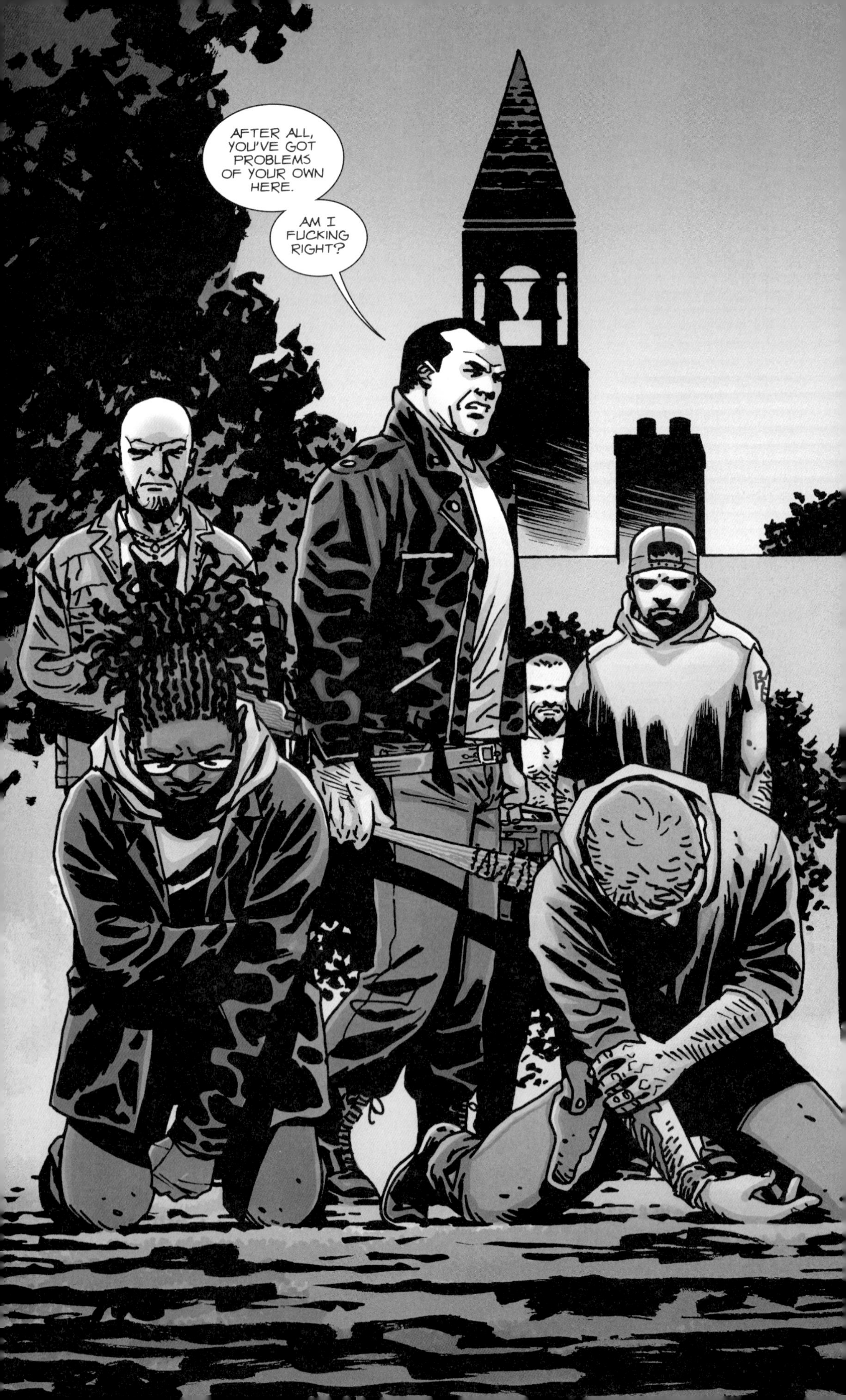
AFTER ALL, YOU'VE GOT PROBLEMS OF YOUR OWN HERE.
AM I FUCKING RIGHT?

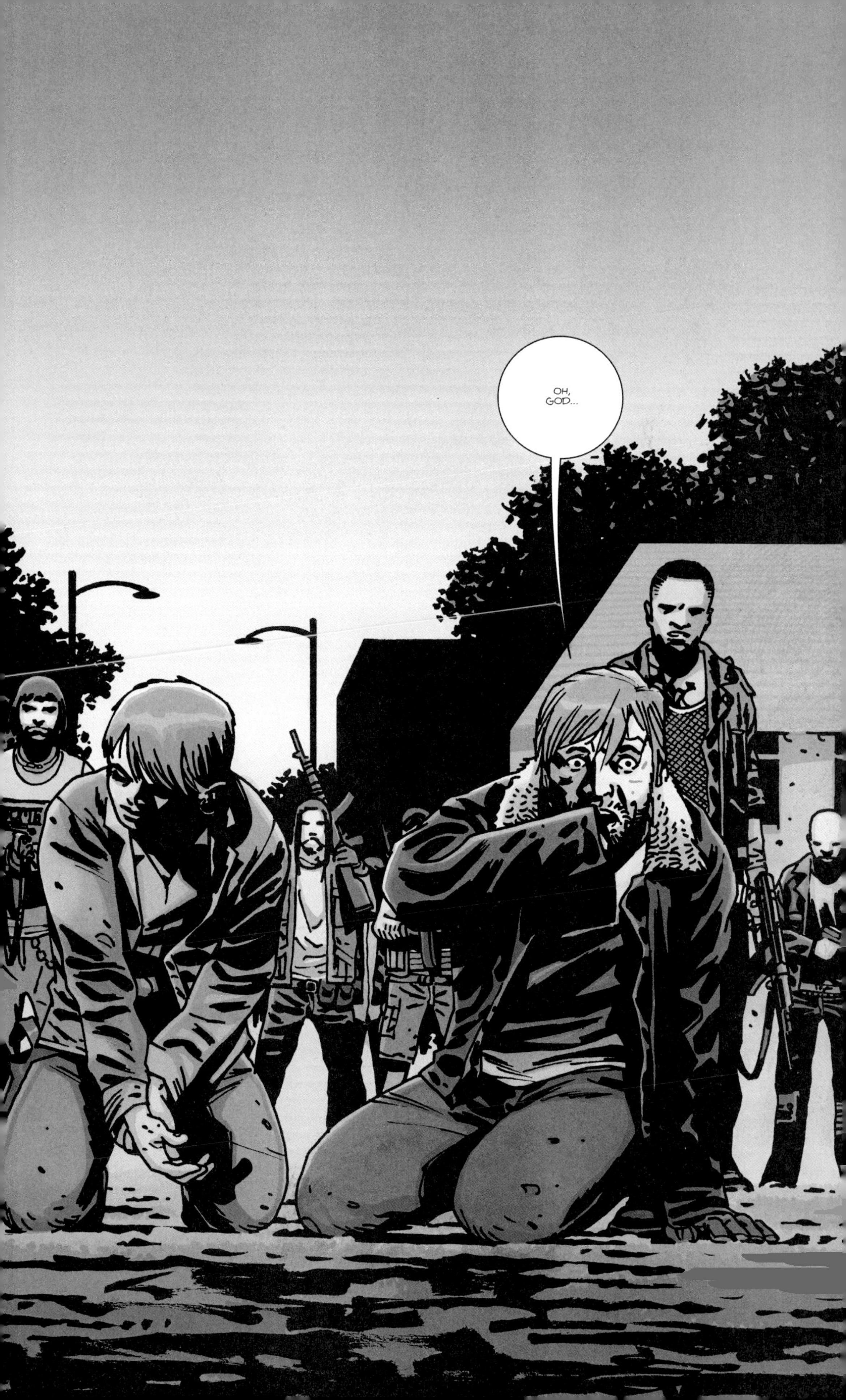
OH, GOD...

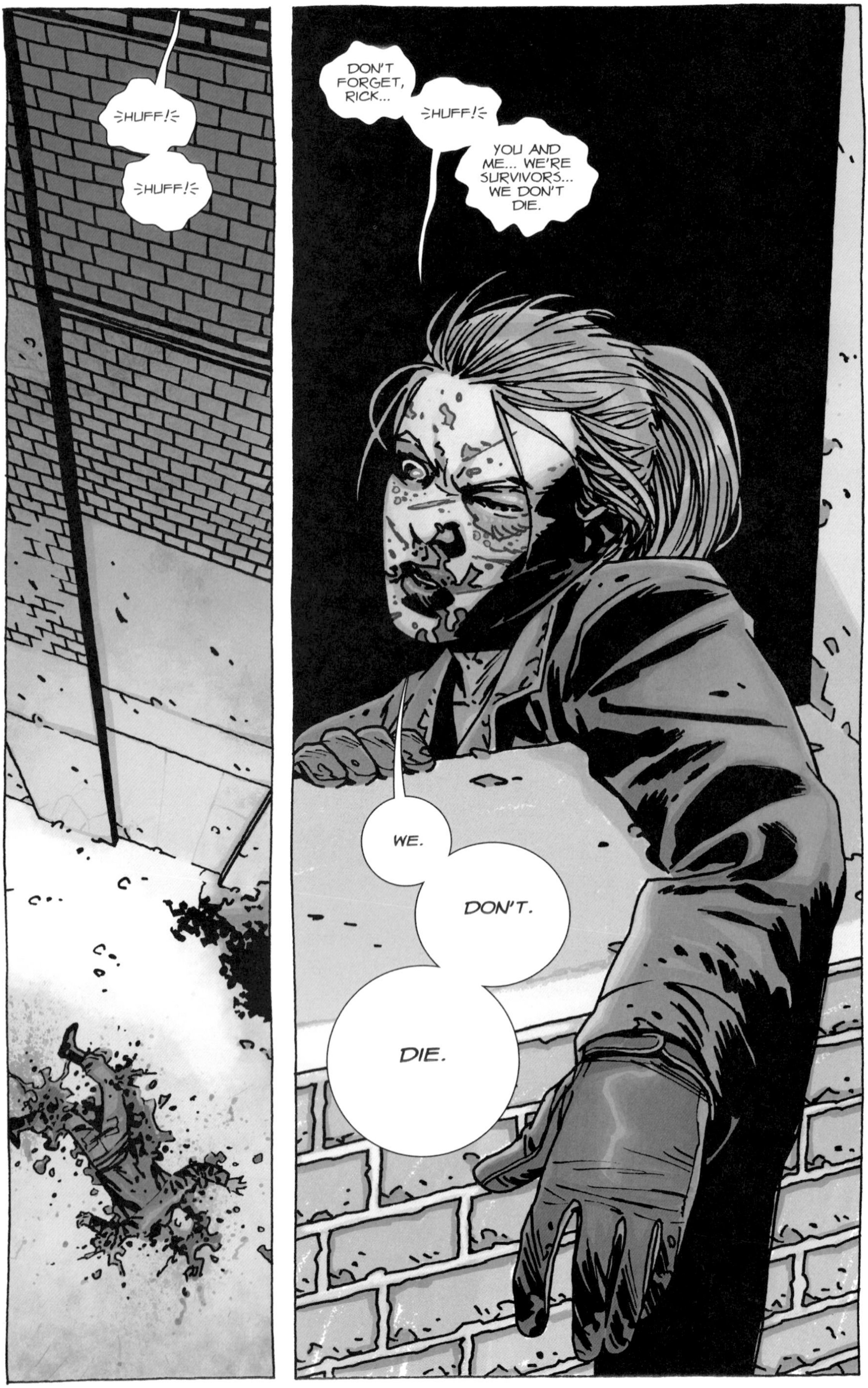
HUFF!
HUFF!
DON'T FORGET, RICK...
HUFF!
YOU AND ME... WE'RE SURVIVORS... WE DON'T DIE.
WE.
DON'T.
DIE.

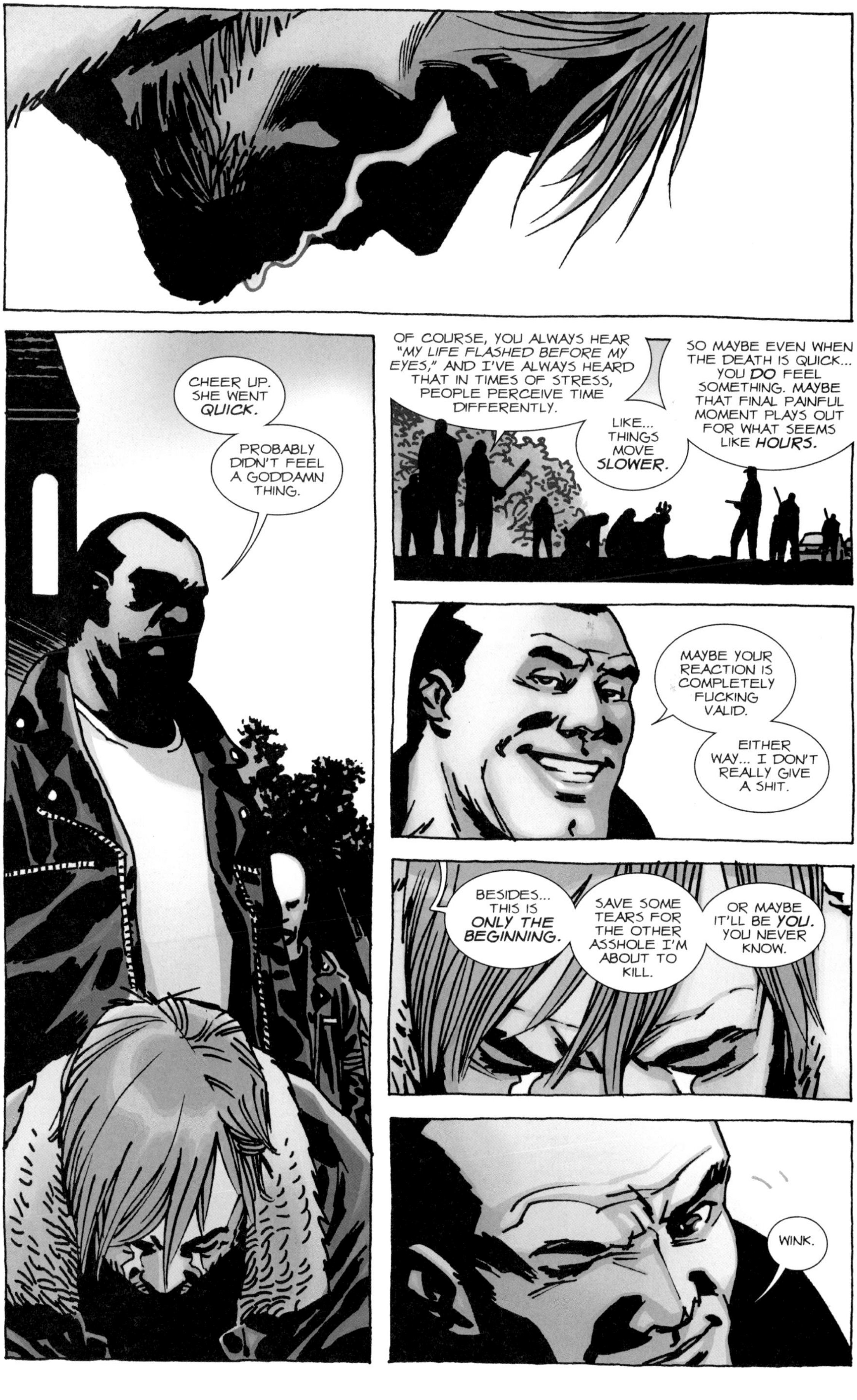

CHEER UP. SHE WENT QUICK.
PROBABLY DIDN'T FEEL A GODDAMN THING.
OF COURSE, YOU ALWAYS HEAR "MY LIFE FLASHED BEFORE MY EYES," AND I'VE ALWAYS HEARD THAT IN TIMES OF STRESS, PEOPLE PERCEIVE TIME DIFFERENTLY.
LIKE... THINGS MOVE SLOWER.
SO MAYBE EVEN WHEN THE DEATH IS QUICK... YOU DO FEEL SOMETHING. MAYBE THAT FINAL PAINFUL MOMENT PLAYS OUT FOR WHAT SEEMS LIKE HOURS.
MAYBE YOUR REACTION IS COMPLETELY FUCKING VALID.
EITHER WAY... I DON'T REALLY GIVE A SHIT.
BESIDES... THIS IS ONLY THE BEGINNING.
SAVE SOME TEARS FOR THE OTHER ASSHOLE I'M ABOUT TO KILL.
OR MAYBE IT'LL BE YOU. YOU NEVER KNOW.
WINK.

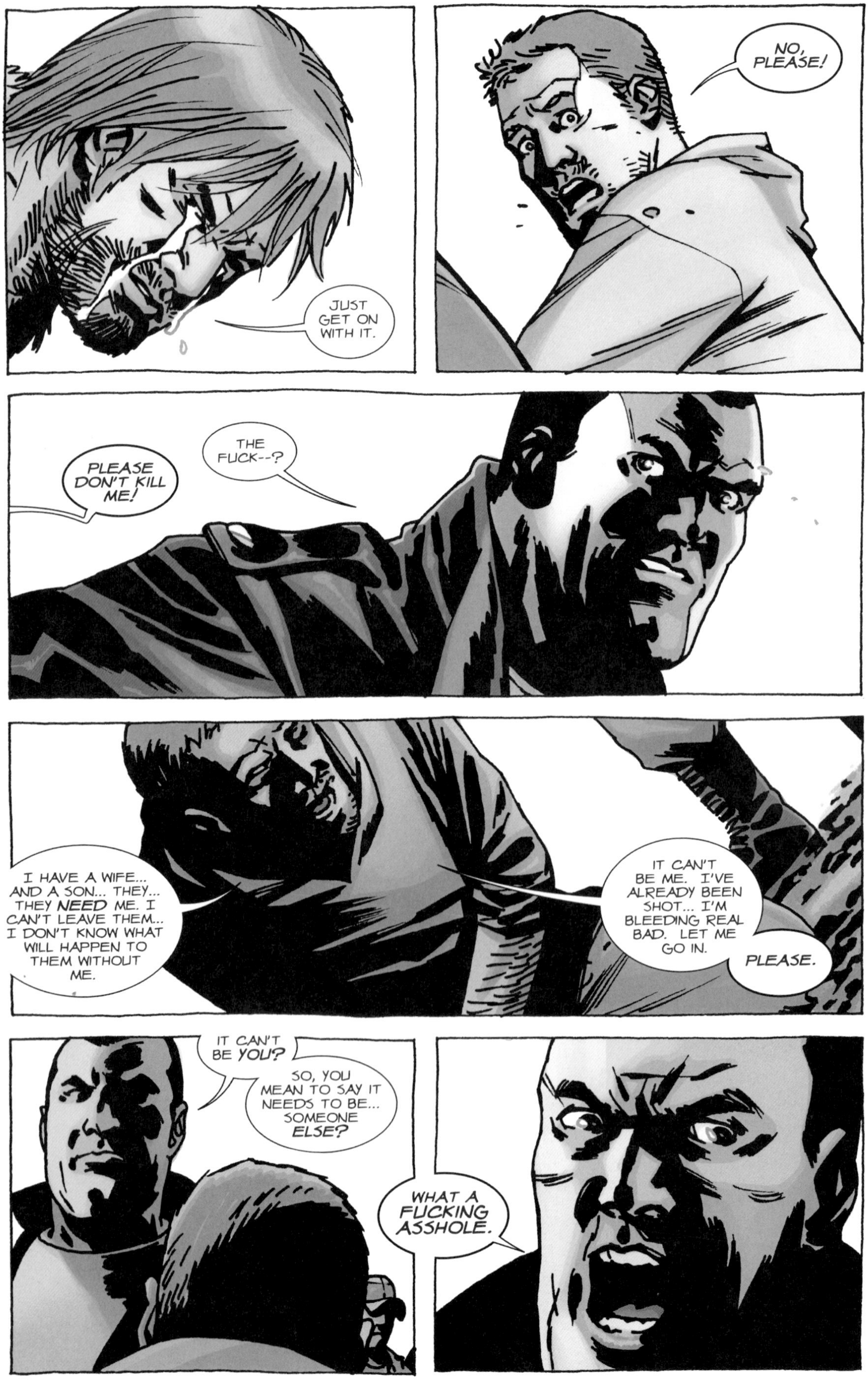
JUST GET ON WITH IT.
NO, PLEASE!
PLEASE DON'T KILL ME!
THE FUCK--?
I HAVE A WIFE... AND A SON... THEY... THEY NEED ME. I CAN'T LEAVE THEM... I DON'T KNOW WHAT WILL HAPPEN TO THEM WITHOUT ME.
IT CAN'T BE ME. I'VE ALREADY BEEN SHOT... I'M BLEEDING REAL BAD. LET ME GO IN.
PLEASE.
IT CAN'T BE YOU?
SO, YOU MEAN TO SAY IT NEEDS TO BE... SOMEONE ELSE?
WHAT A FUCKING ASSHOLE.

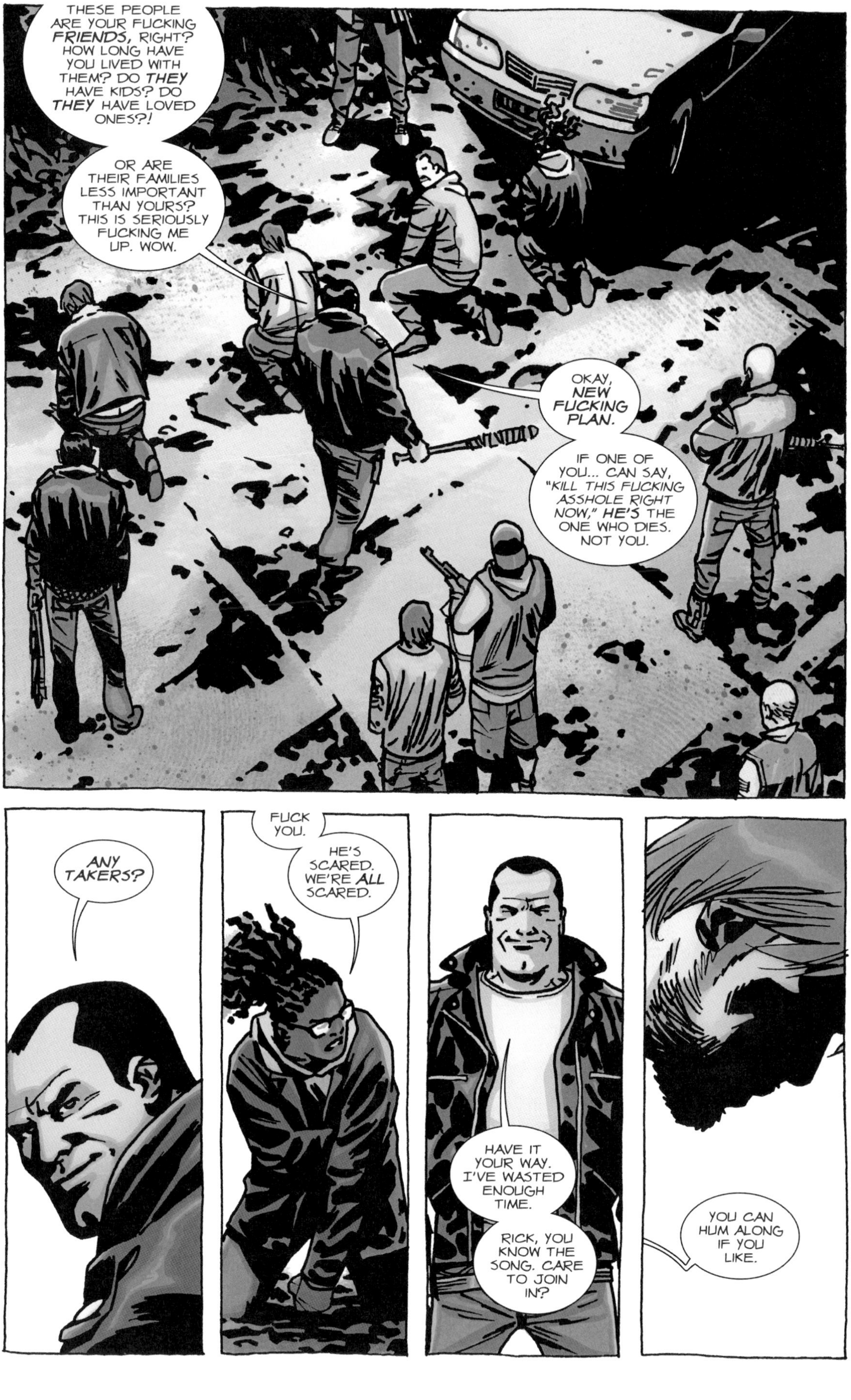
THESE PEOPLE ARE YOUR FUCKING FRIENDS, RIGHT? HOW LONG HAVE YOU LIVED WITH THEM? DO THEY HAVE KIDS? DO THEY HAVE LOVED ONES?!
OR ARE THEIR FAMILIES LESS IMPORTANT THAN YOURS? THIS IS SERIOUSLY FUCKING ME UP. WOW.
OKAY, NEW FUCKING PLAN.
IF ONE OF YOU... CAN SAY, "KILL THIS FUCKING ASSHOLE RIGHT NOW," HE'S THE ONE WHO DIES. NOT YOU.
ANY TAKERS?
FUCK YOU.
HE'S SCARED. WE'RE ALL SCARED.
HAVE IT YOUR WAY. I'VE WASTED ENOUGH TIME.
RICK, YOU KNOW THE SONG. CARE TO JOIN IN?
YOU CAN HUM ALONG IF YOU LIKE.

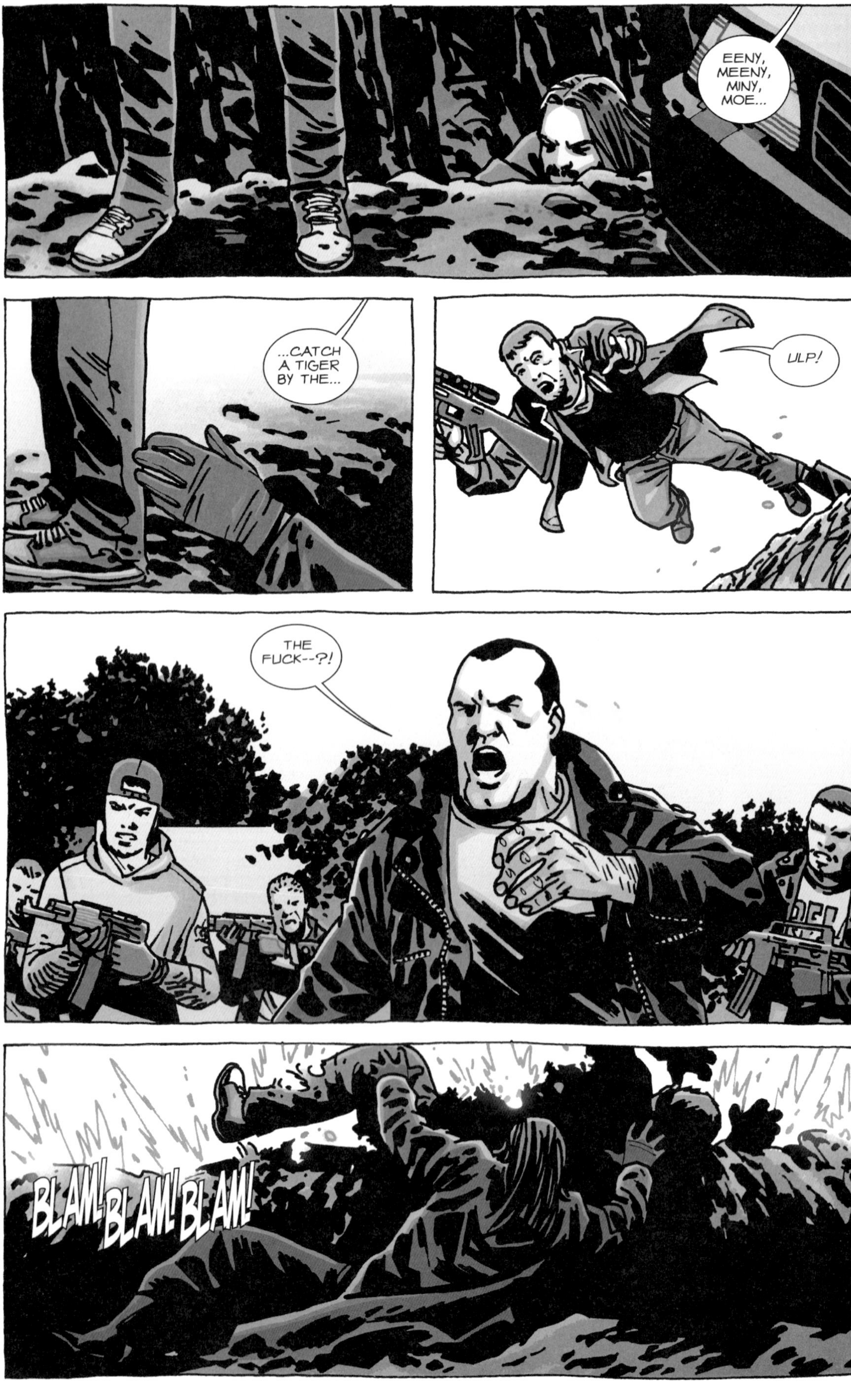
EENY, MEENY, MINY, MOE...
...CATCH A TIGER BY THE...
ULP!
THE FUCK--?!
BLAM! BLAM! BLAM!

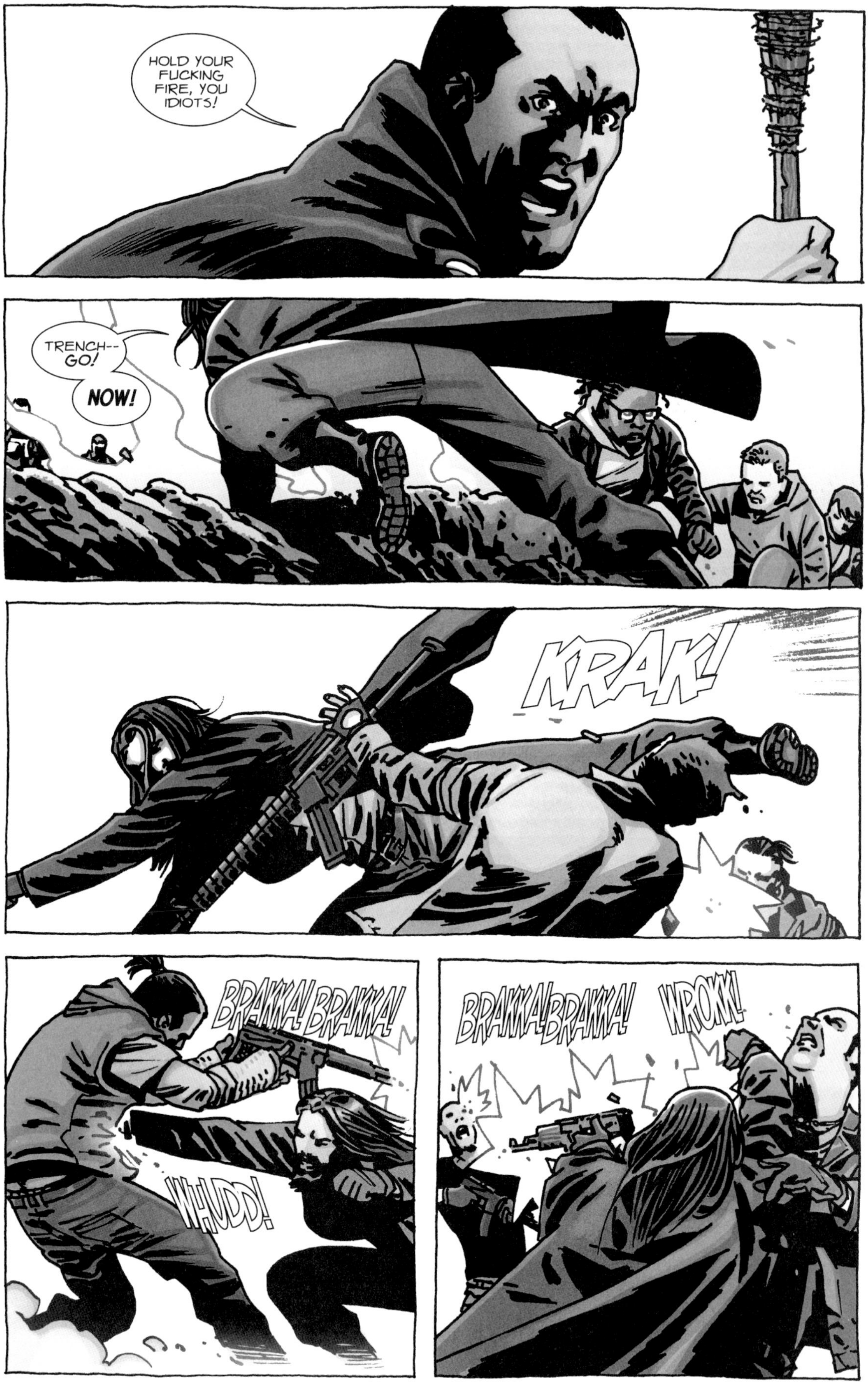
HOLD YOUR FUCKING FIRE, YOU IDIOTS!
TRENCH-- GO!
NOW!
KRAK!
BRAKKA! BRAKKA!
WHUDD!
BRAKKA! BRAKKA!
WROKK!

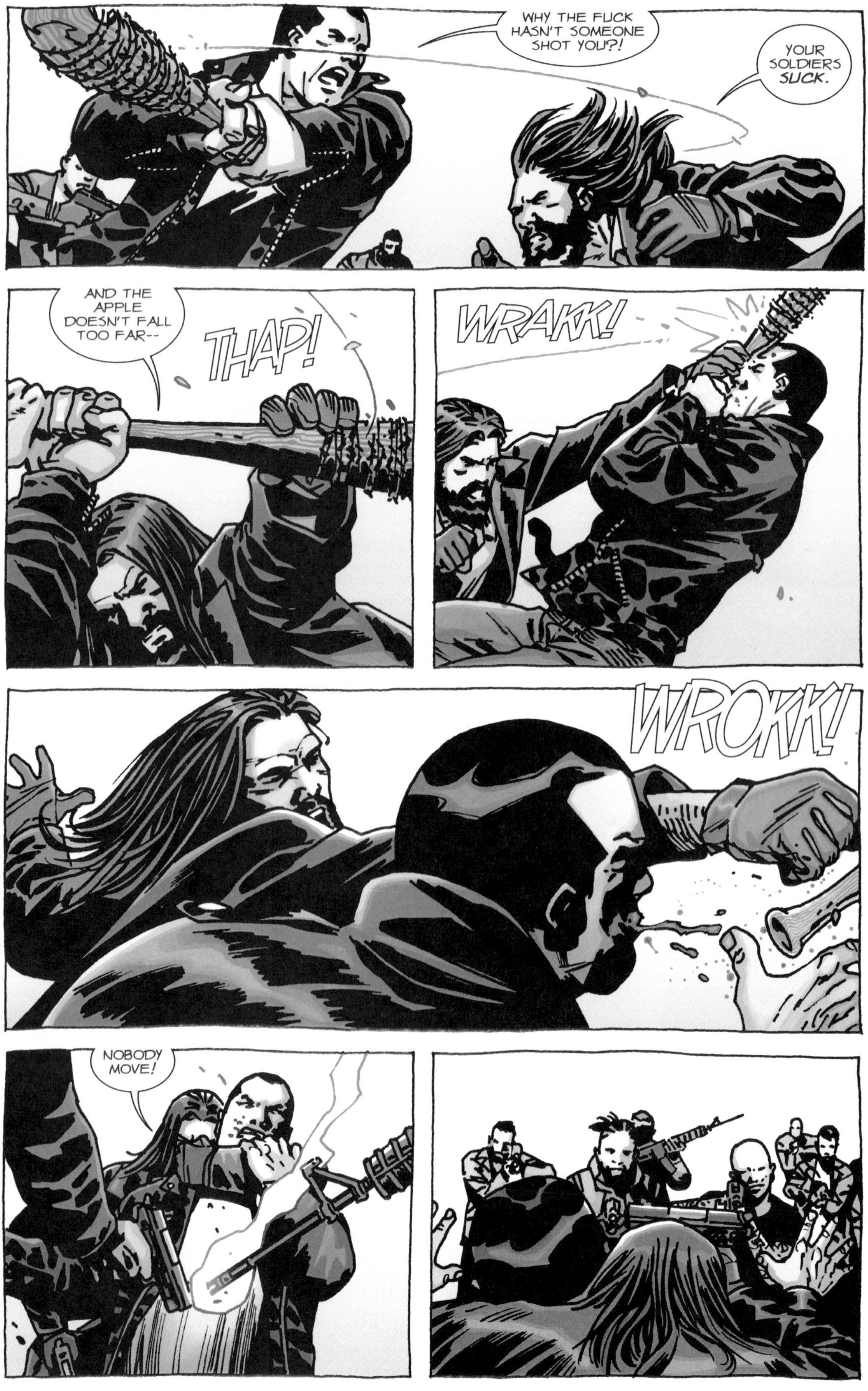

WHY THE FUCK HASN'T SOMEONE SHOT YOU?!
YOUR SOLDIERS SUCK.
AND THE APPLE DOESN'T FALL TOO FAR--
THAP!
WRAKK!
WROKK!
NOBODY MOVE!

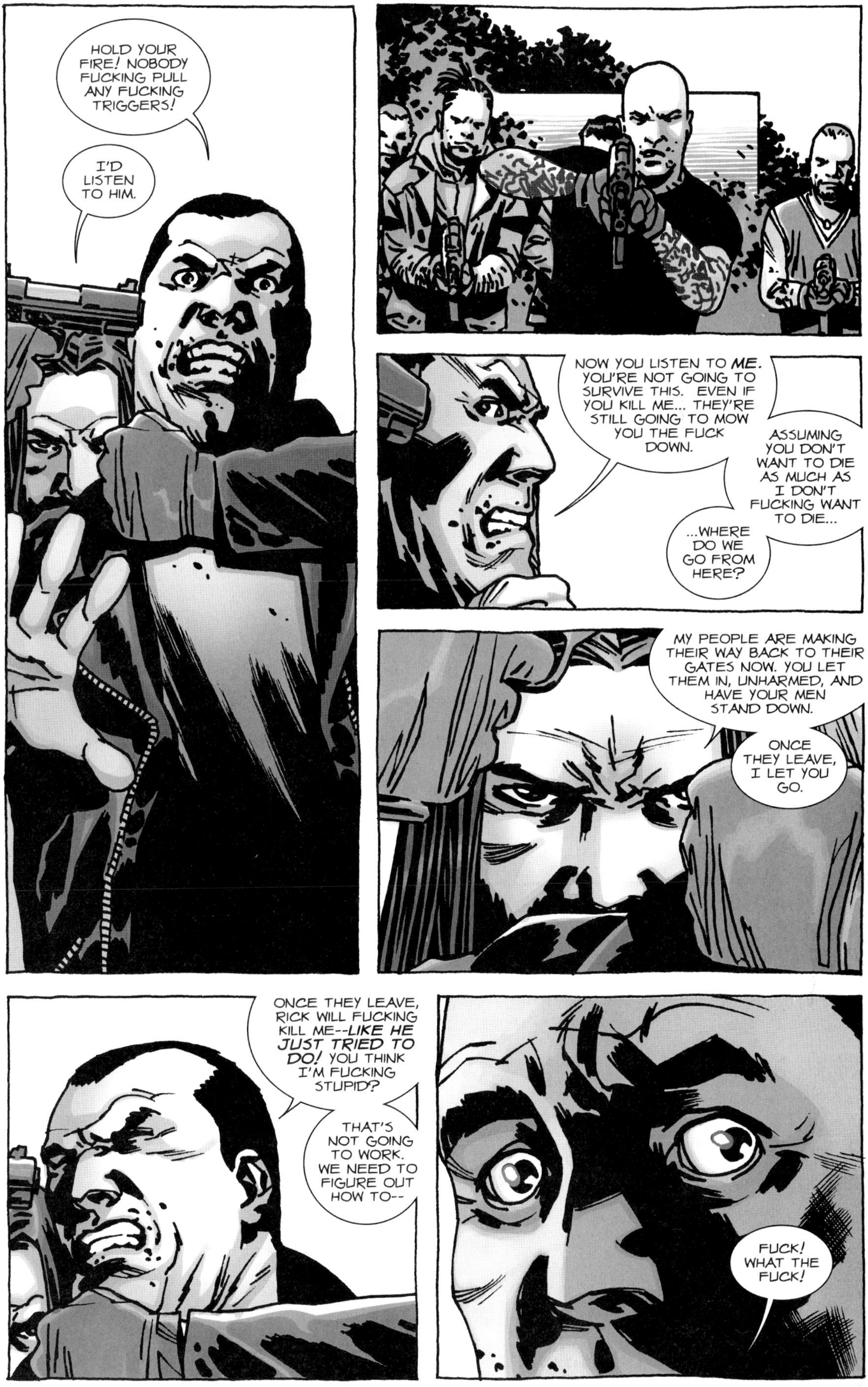
HOLD YOUR FIRE! NOBODY FUCKING PULL ANY FUCKING TRIGGERS!
I'D LISTEN TO HIM.
NOW YOU LISTEN TO ME. YOU'RE NOT GOING TO SURVIVE THIS. EVEN IF YOU KILL ME... THEY'RE STILL GOING TO MOW YOU THE FUCK DOWN.
ASSUMING YOU DON'T WANT TO DIE AS MUCH AS I DON'T FUCKING WANT TO DIE...
...WHERE DO WE GO FROM HERE?
MY PEOPLE ARE MAKING THEIR WAY BACK TO THEIR GATES NOW. YOU LET THEM IN, UNHARMED, AND HAVE YOUR MEN STAND DOWN.
ONCE THEY LEAVE, I LET YOU GO.
ONCE THEY LEAVE, RICK WILL FUCKING KILL ME--LIKE HE JUST TRIED TO DO! YOU THINK I'M FUCKING STUPID?
THAT'S NOT GOING TO WORK. WE NEED TO FIGURE OUT HOW TO--
FUCK! WHAT THE FUCK!

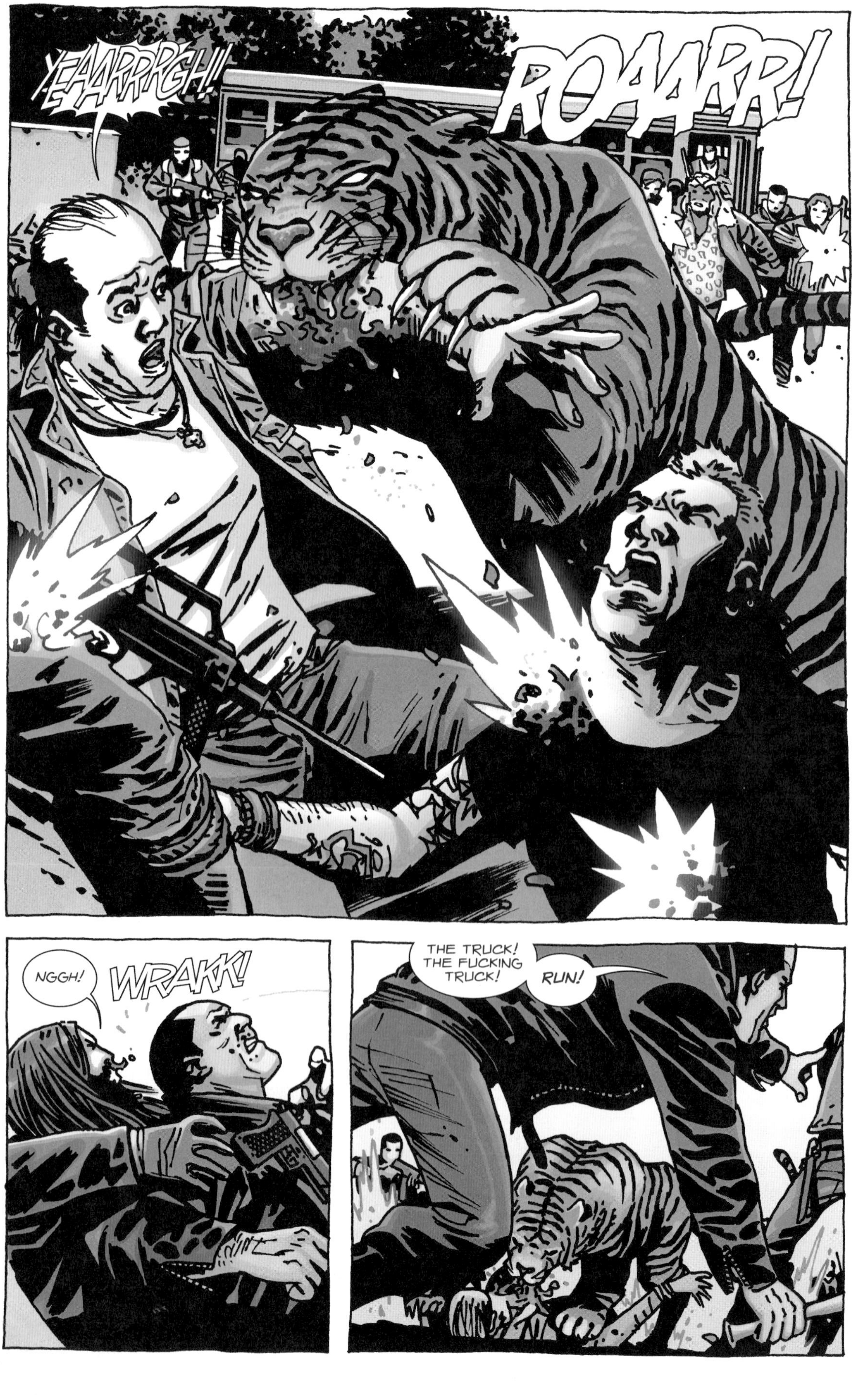
YEAARRRGH!!
ROAARR!
NGGH!
WRAKK!
THE TRUCK! THE FUCKING TRUCK!
RUN!

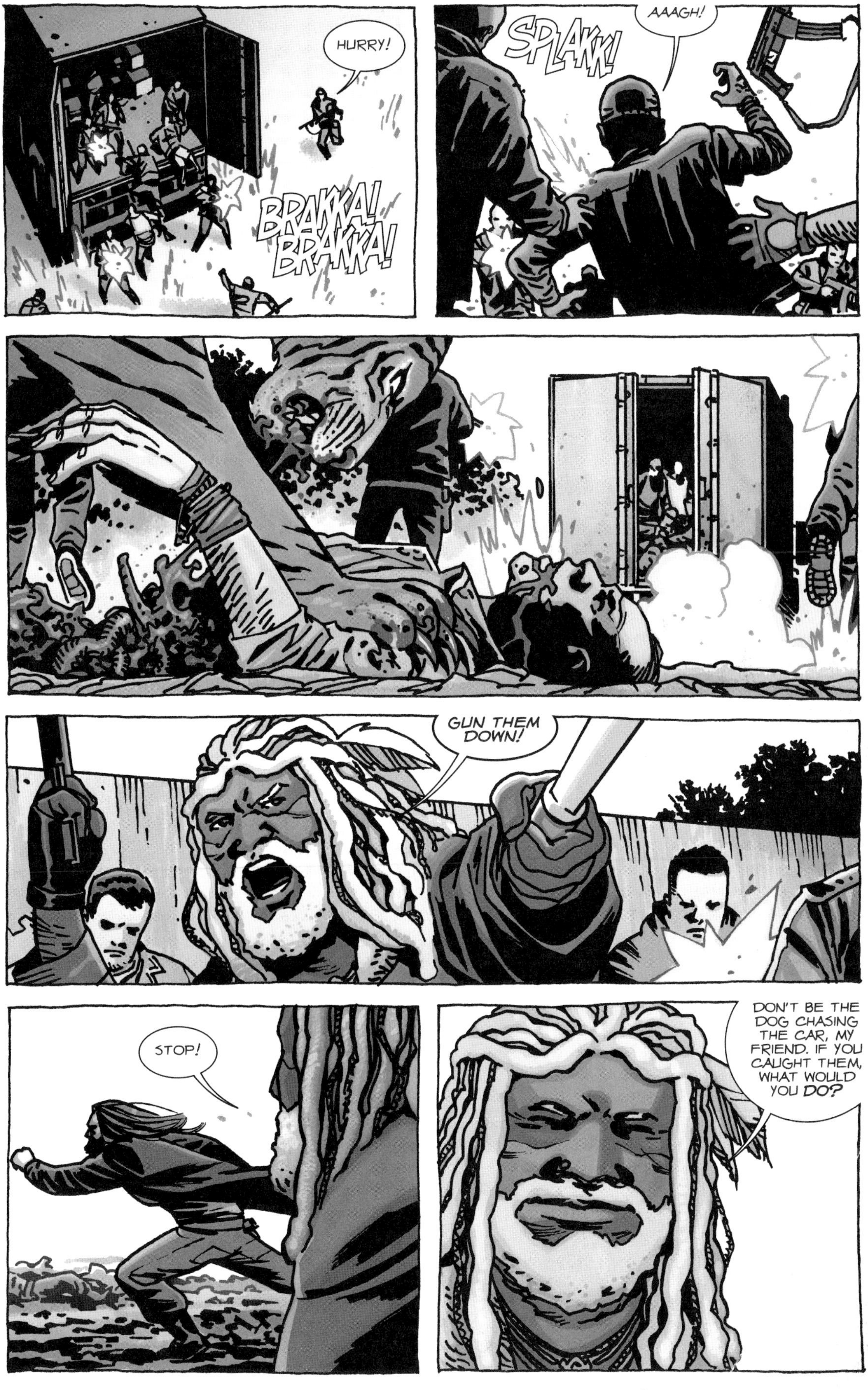
HURRY!
BRAKKA! BRAKKA!
SPLAKK!
AAAGH!
GUN THEM DOWN!
STOP!
DON'T BE THE DOG CHASING THE CAR, MY FRIEND. IF YOU CAUGHT THEM, WHAT WOULD YOU DO?

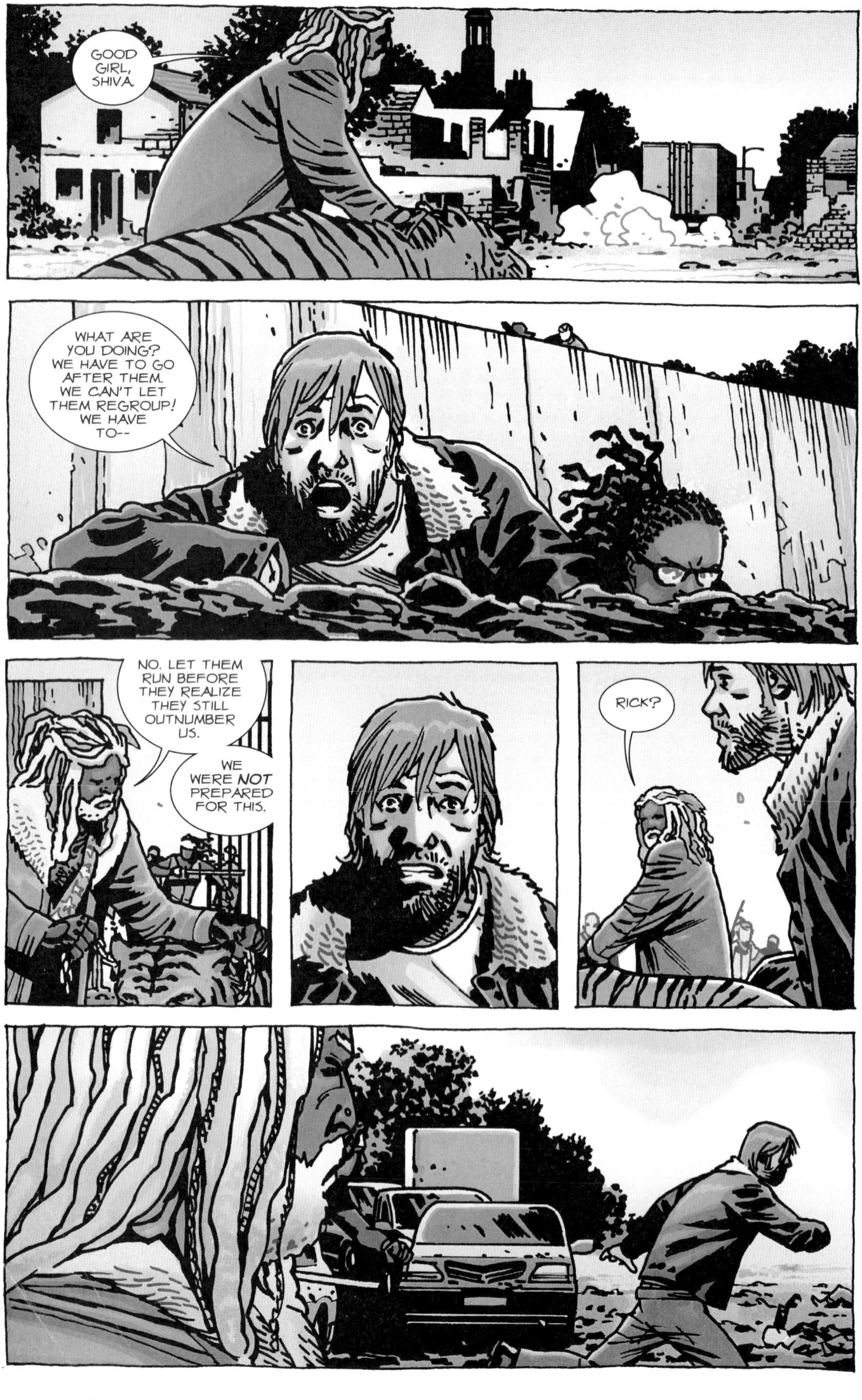
GOOD GIRL, SHIVA.
WHAT ARE YOU DOING? WE HAVE TO GO AFTER THEM. WE CAN'T LET THEM REGROUP! WE HAVE TO--
NO. LET THEM RUN BEFORE THEY REALIZE THEY STILL OUTNUMBER US.
WE WERE NOT PREPARED FOR THIS.
RICK?

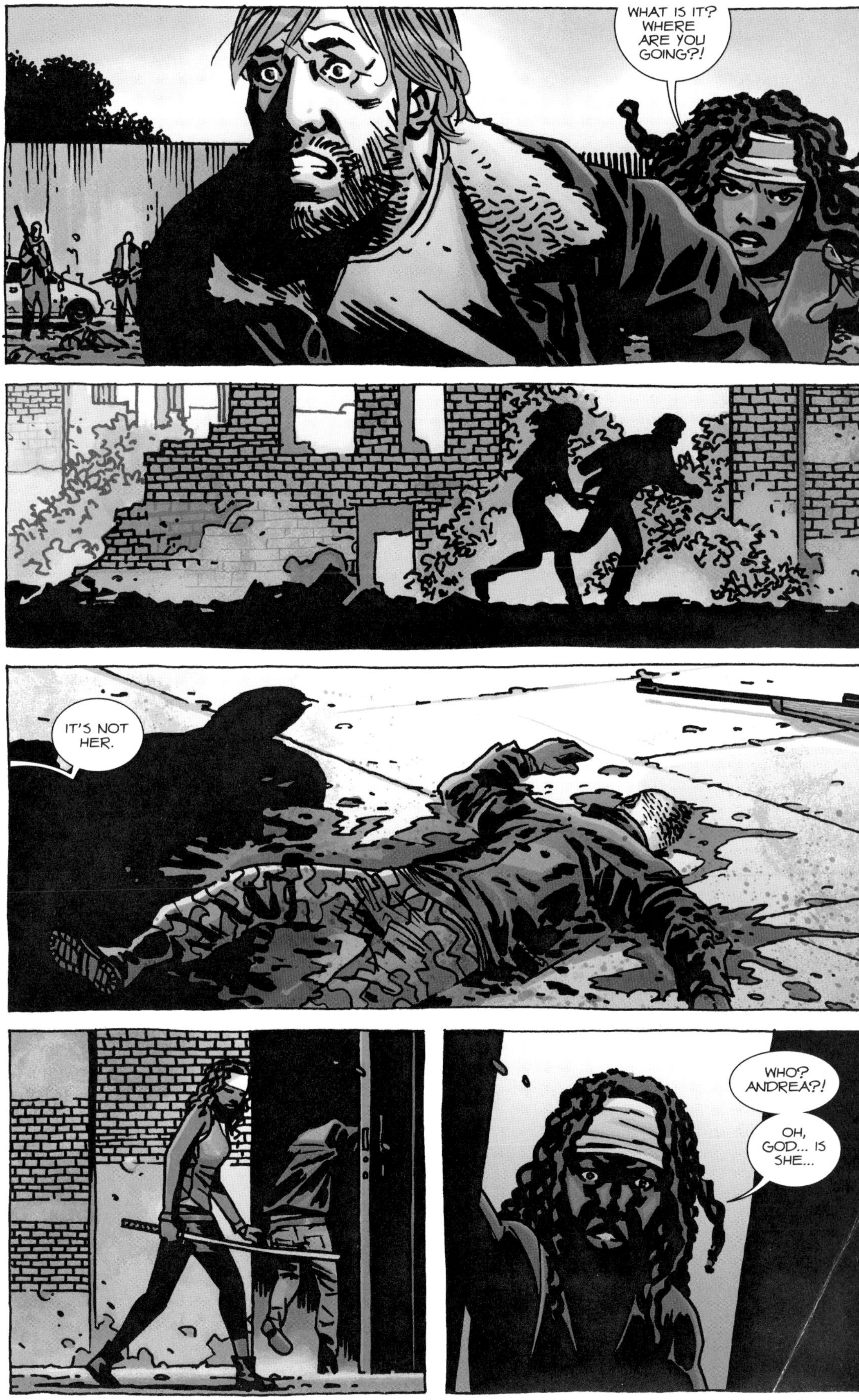
WHAT IS IT? WHERE ARE YOU GOING?!
IT'S NOT HER.
WHO? ANDREA?!
OH, GOD... IS SHE...

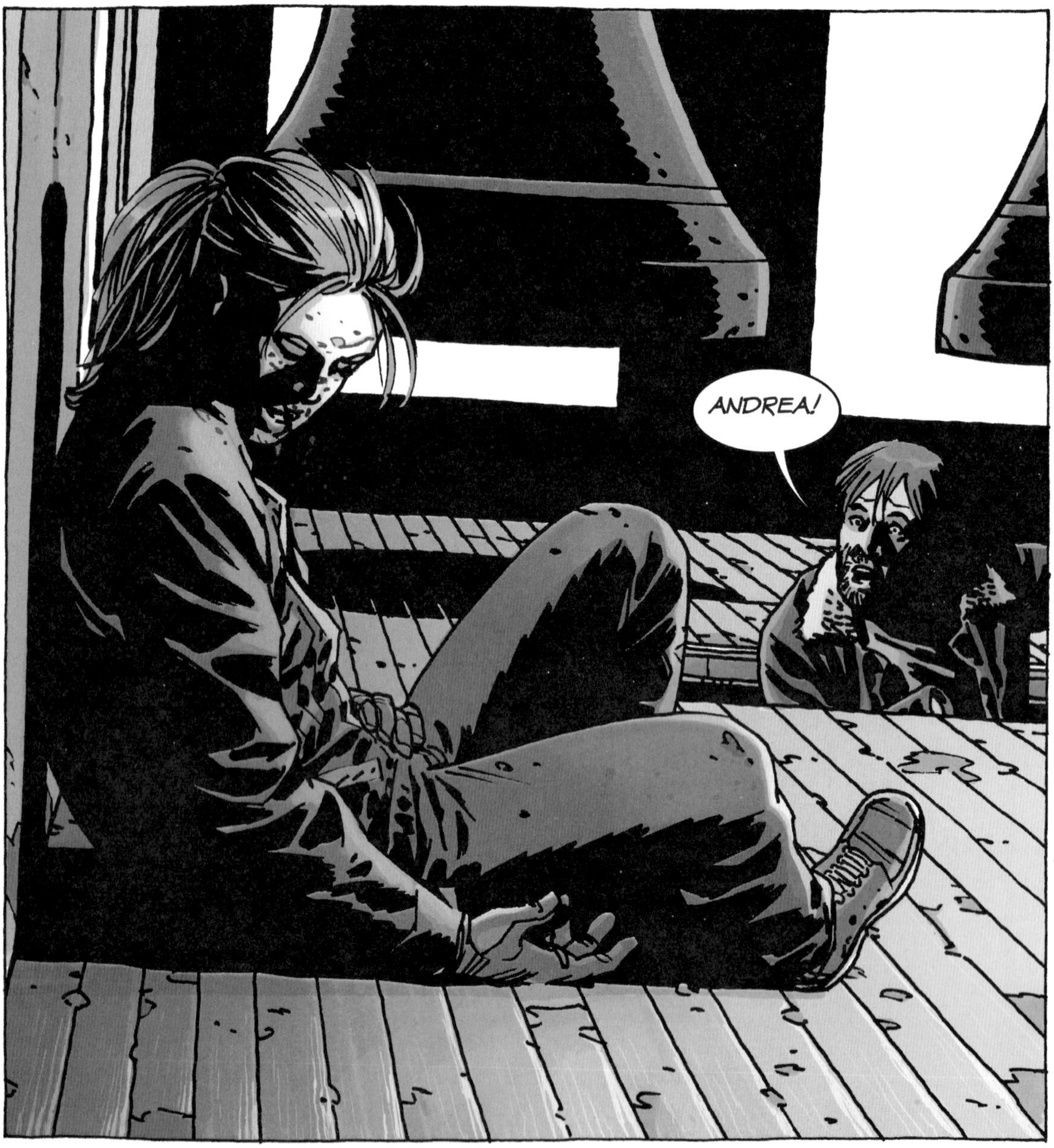
ANDREA!

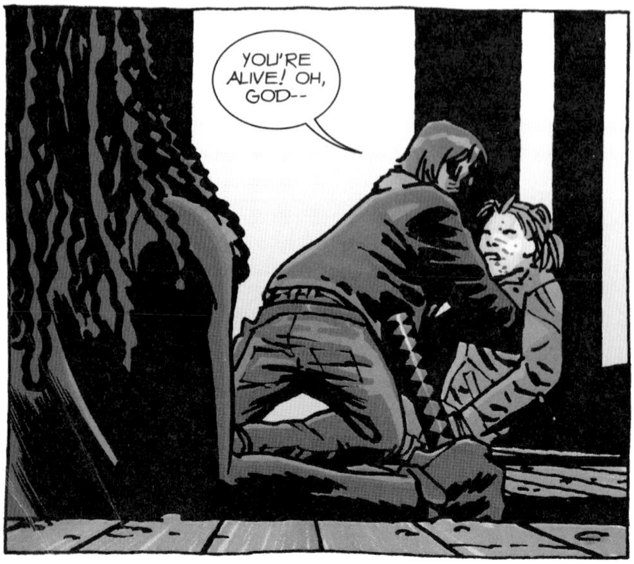
YOU'RE ALIVE! OH, GOD--

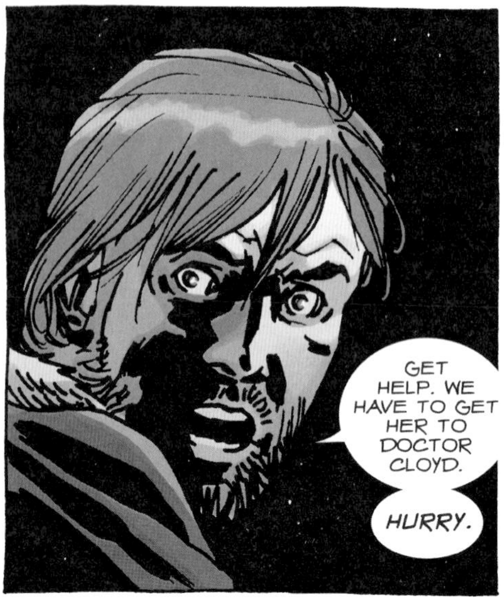
GET HELP. WE HAVE TO GET HER TO DOCTOR CLOYD.
HURRY.

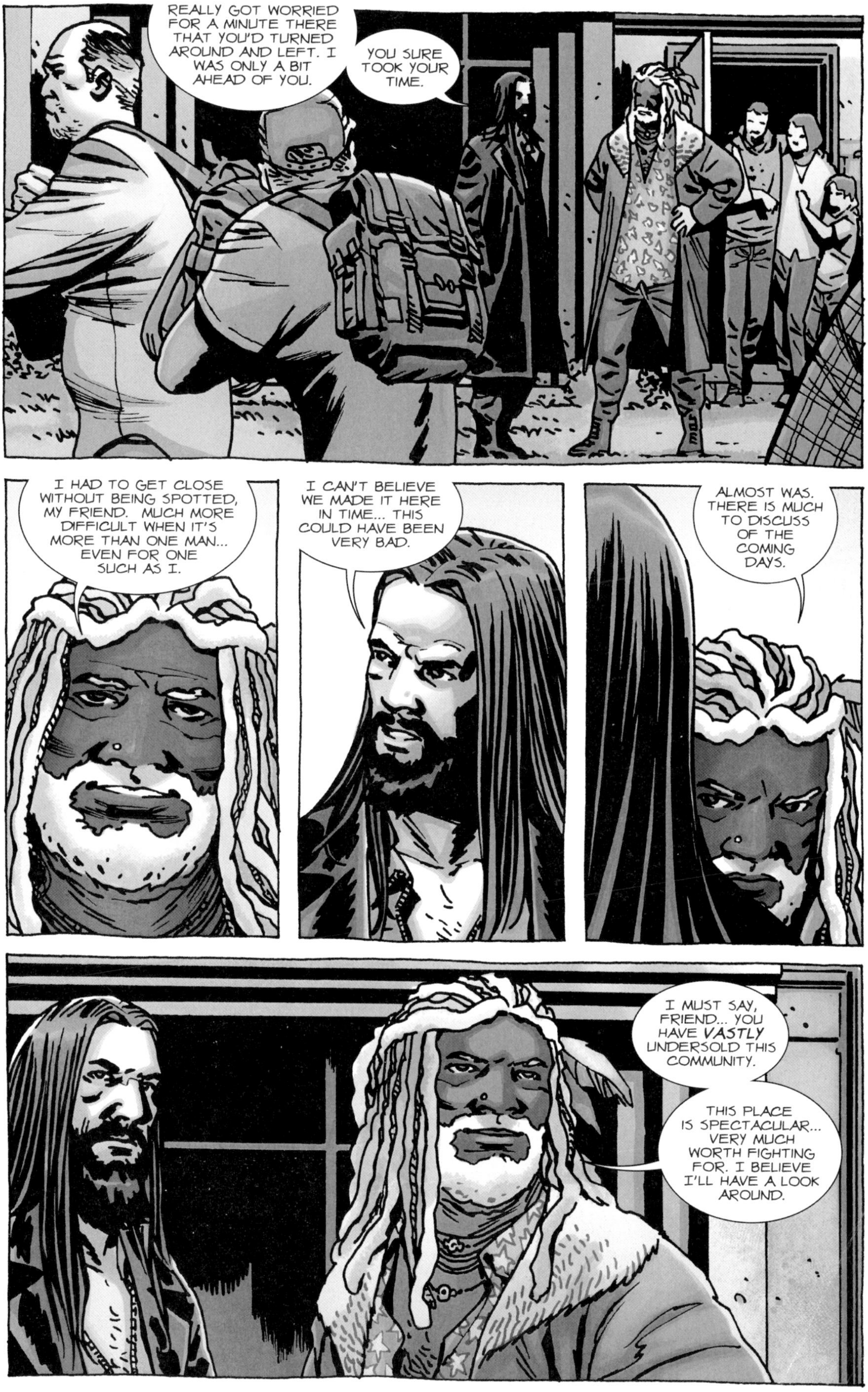
REALLY GOT WORRIED FOR A MINUTE THERE THAT YOU'D TURNED AROUND AND LEFT. I WAS ONLY A BIT AHEAD OF YOU.
YOU SURE TOOK YOUR TIME.
I HAD TO GET CLOSE WITHOUT BEING SPOTTED, MY FRIEND. MUCH MORE DIFFICULT WHEN IT'S MORE THAN ONE MAN... EVEN FOR ONE SUCH AS I.
I CAN'T BELIEVE WE MADE IT HERE IN TIME... THIS COULD HAVE BEEN VERY BAD.
ALMOST WAS. THERE IS MUCH TO DISCUSS OF THE COMING DAYS.
I MUST SAY, FRIEND... YOU HAVE VASTLY UNDERSOLD THIS COMMUNITY.
THIS PLACE IS SPECTACULAR... VERY MUCH WORTH FIGHTING FOR. I BELIEVE I'LL HAVE A LOOK AROUND.

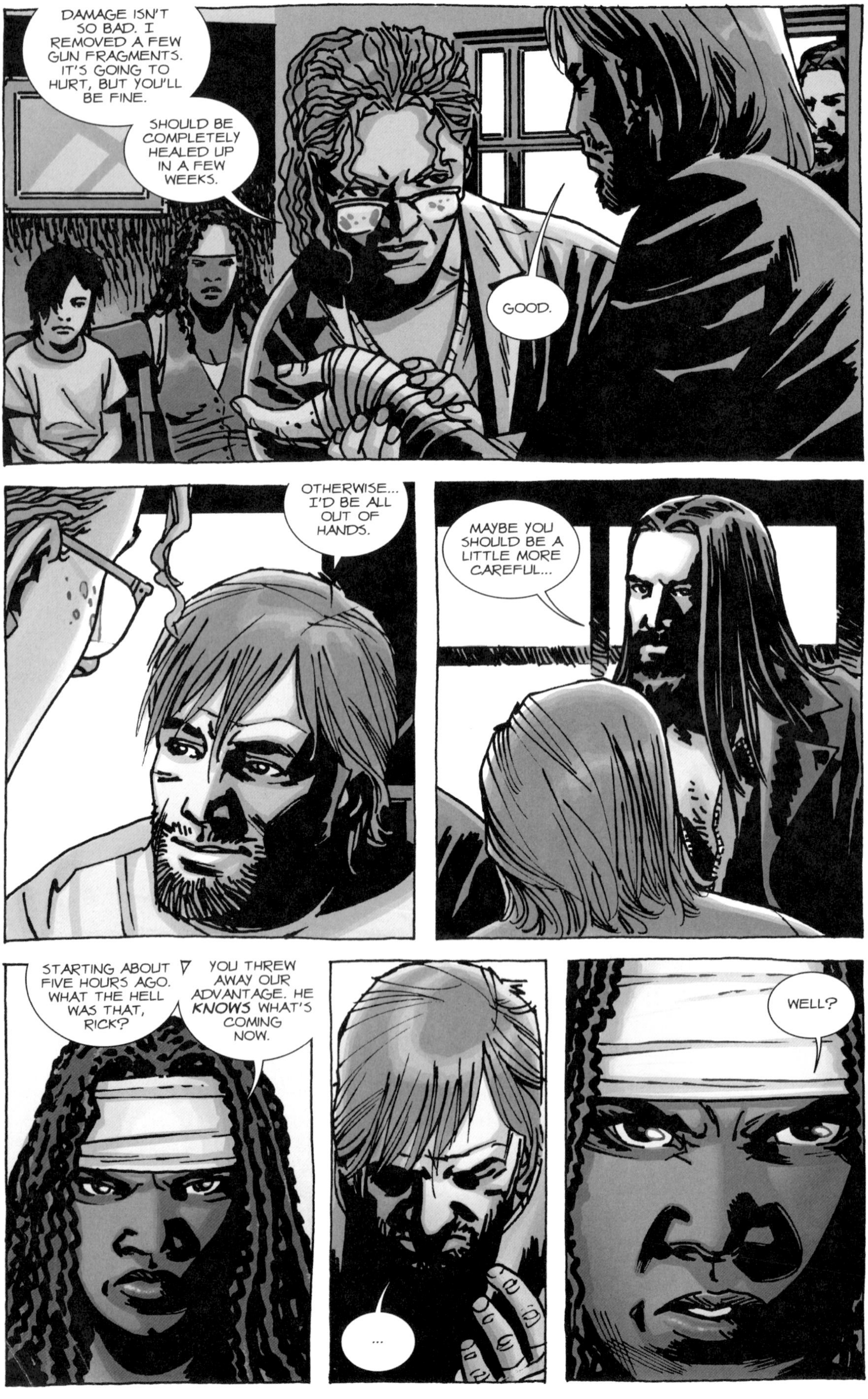
DAMAGE ISN'T SO BAD. I REMOVED A FEW GUN FRAGMENTS. IT'S GOING TO HURT, BUT YOU'LL BE FINE.
SHOULD BE COMPLETELY HEALED UP IN A FEW WEEKS.
GOOD.
OTHERWISE... I'D BE ALL OUT OF HANDS.
MAYBE YOU SHOULD BE A LITTLE MORE CAREFUL...
STARTING ABOUT FIVE HOURS AGO. WHAT THE HELL WAS THAT, RICK?
YOU THREW AWAY OUR ADVANTAGE. HE KNOWS WHAT'S COMING NOW.
...
WELL?

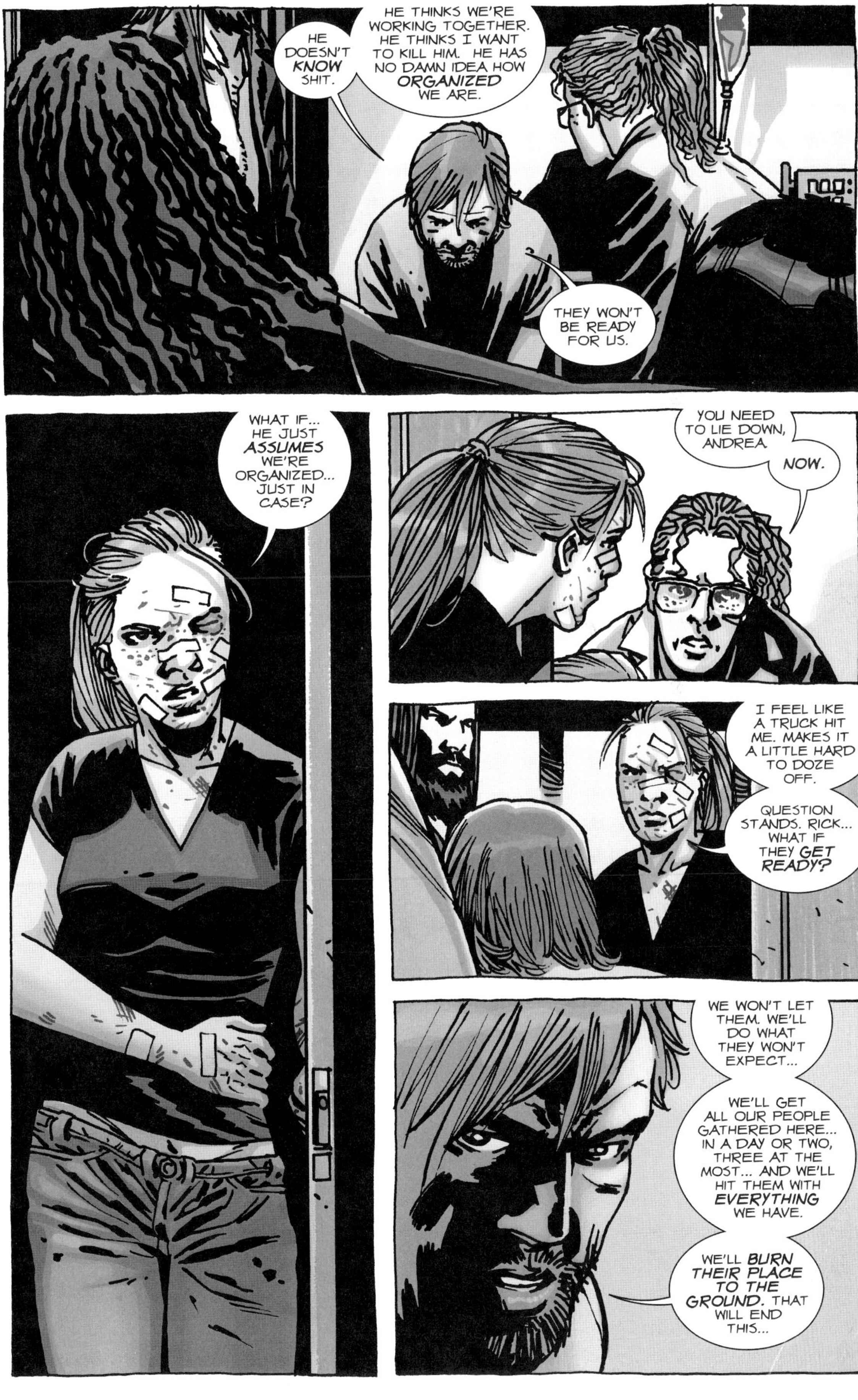
HE DOESN'T KNOW SHIT.
HE THINKS WE'RE WORKING TOGETHER. HE THINKS I WANT TO KILL HIM. HE HAS NO DAMN IDEA HOW ORGANIZED WE ARE.
THEY WON'T BE READY FOR US.
WHAT IF... HE JUST ASSUMES WE'RE ORGANIZED... JUST IN CASE?
YOU NEED TO LIE DOWN, ANDREA
NOW.
I FEEL LIKE A TRUCK HIT ME. MAKES IT A LITTLE HARD TO DOZE OFF.
QUESTION STANDS. RICK... WHAT IF THEY GET READY?
WE WON'T LET THEM. WE'LL DO WHAT THEY WON'T EXPECT...
WE'LL GET ALL OUR PEOPLE GATHERED HERE... IN A DAY OR TWO, THREE AT THE MOST... AND WE'LL HIT THEM WITH EVERYTHING WE HAVE.
WE'LL BURN THEIR PLACE TO THE GROUND. THAT WILL END THIS...

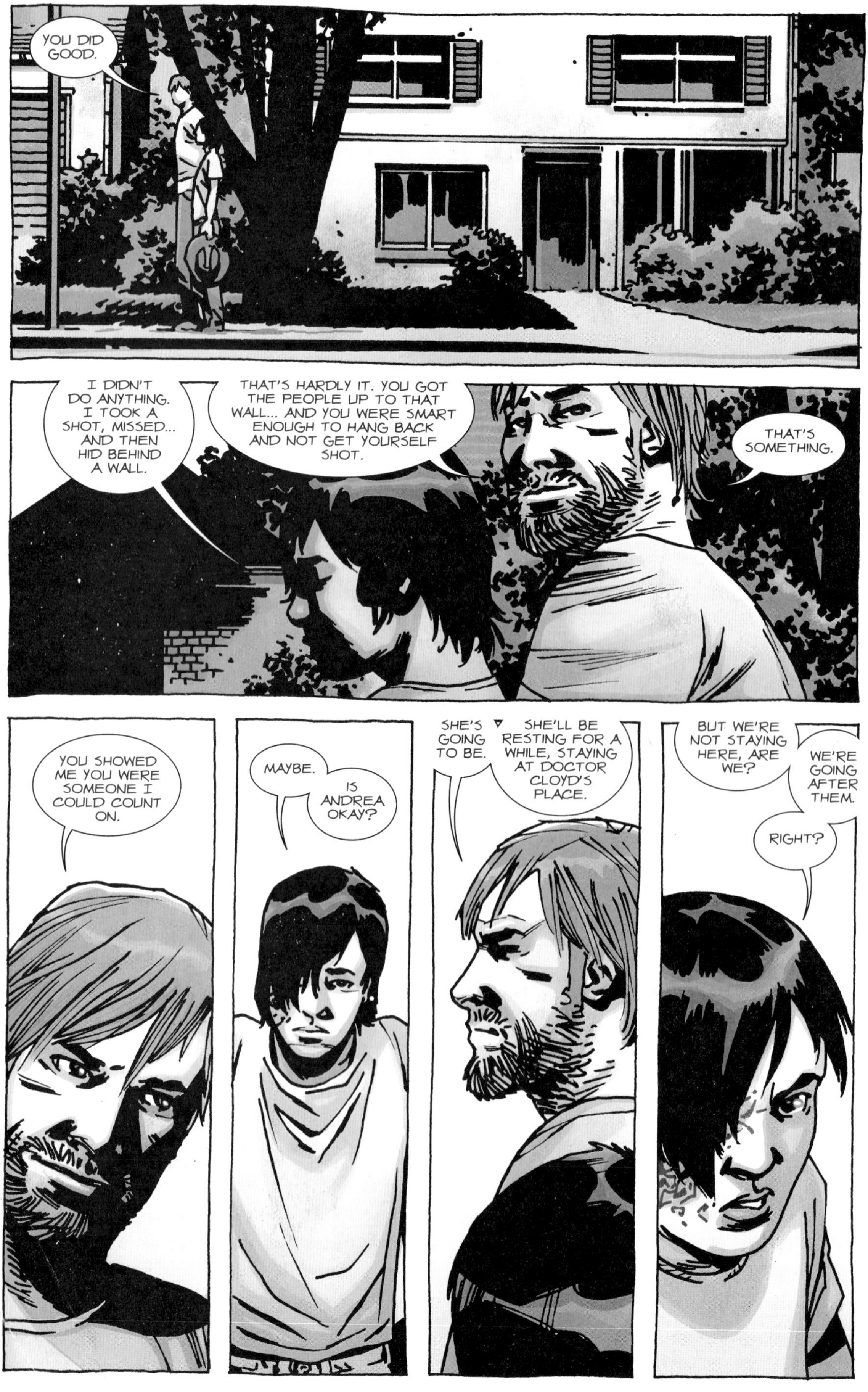
YOU DID GOOD.
I DIDN'T DO ANYTHING. I TOOK A SHOT, MISSED... AND THEN HID BEHIND A WALL.
THAT'S HARDLY IT. YOU GOT THE PEOPLE UP TO THAT WALL... AND YOU WERE SMART ENOUGH TO HANG BACK AND NOT GET YOURSELF SHOT.
THAT'S SOMETHING.
YOU SHOWED ME YOU WERE SOMEONE I COULD COUNT ON.
MAYBE.
IS ANDREA OKAY?
SHE'S GOING TO BE.
SHE'LL BE RESTING FOR A WHILE, STAYING AT DOCTOR CLOYD'S PLACE.
BUT WE'RE NOT STAYING HERE, ARE WE?
WE'RE GOING AFTER THEM.
RIGHT?

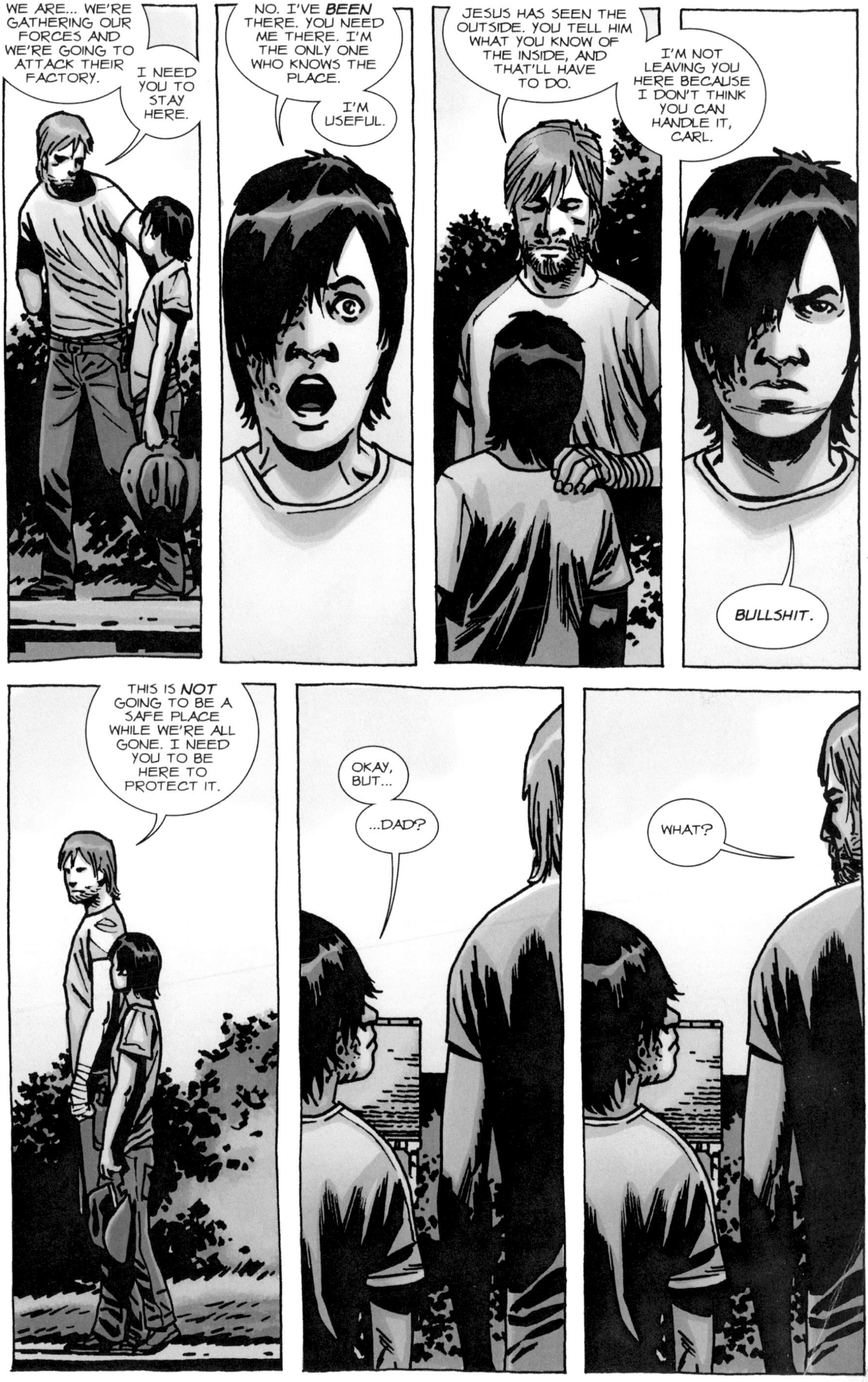
WE ARE... WE'RE GATHERING OUR FORCES AND WE'RE GOING TO ATTACK THEIR FACTORY.
I NEED YOU TO STAY HERE.
NO. I'VE BEEN THERE. YOU NEED ME THERE. I'M THE ONLY ONE WHO KNOWS THE PLACE.
I'M USEFUL.
JESUS HAS SEEN THE OUTSIDE. YOU TELL HIM WHAT YOU KNOW OF THE INSIDE, AND THAT'LL HAVE TO DO.
I'M NOT LEAVING YOU HERE BECAUSE I DON'T THINK YOU CAN HANDLE IT, CARL.
BULLSHIT.
THIS IS NOT GOING TO BE A SAFE PLACE WHILE WE'RE ALL GONE. I NEED YOU TO BE HERE TO PROTECT IT.
OKAY, BUT...
...DAD?
WHAT?

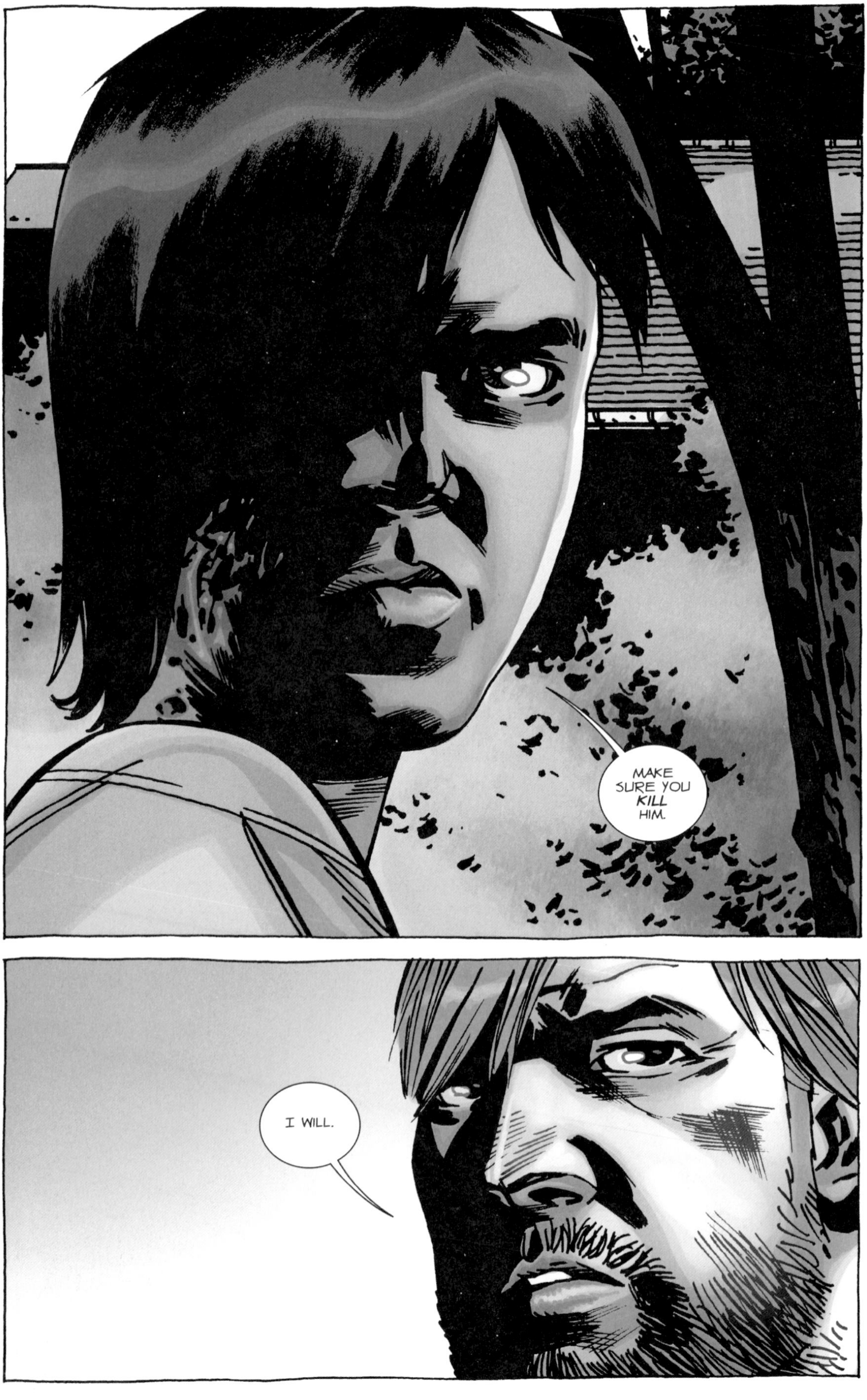
MAKE SURE YOU KILL HIM.
I WILL.

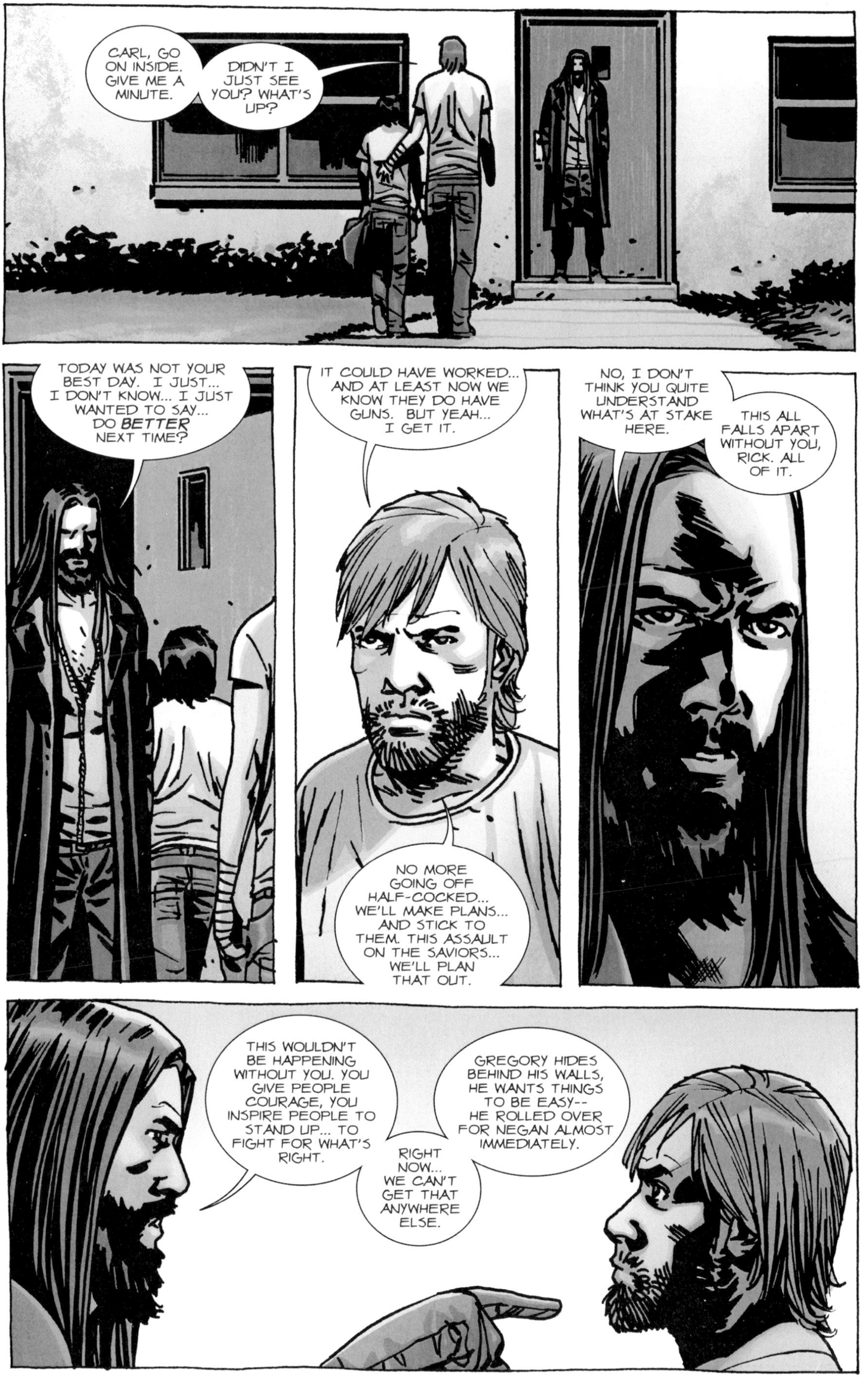
CARL, GO ON INSIDE. GIVE ME A MINUTE.
DIDN'T I JUST SEE YOU? WHAT'S UP?
TODAY WAS NOT YOUR BEST DAY. I JUST... I DON'T KNOW... I JUST WANTED TO SAY... DO BETTER NEXT TIME?
IT COULD HAVE WORKED... AND AT LEAST NOW WE KNOW THEY DO HAVE GUNS. BUT YEAH... I GET IT.
NO MORE GOING OFF HALF-COCKED... WE'LL MAKE PLANS... AND STICK TO THEM. THIS ASSAULT ON THE SAVIORS... WE'LL PLAN THAT OUT.
NO, I DON'T THINK YOU QUITE UNDERSTAND WHAT'S AT STAKE HERE.
THIS ALL FALLS APART WITHOUT YOU, RICK. ALL OF IT.
THIS WOULDN'T BE HAPPENING WITHOUT YOU. YOU GIVE PEOPLE COURAGE, YOU INSPIRE PEOPLE TO STAND UP... TO FIGHT FOR WHAT'S RIGHT.
GREGORY HIDES BEHIND HIS WALLS, HE WANTS THINGS TO BE EASY-- HE ROLLED OVER FOR NEGAN ALMOST IMMEDIATELY.
RIGHT NOW... WE CAN'T GET THAT ANYWHERE ELSE.

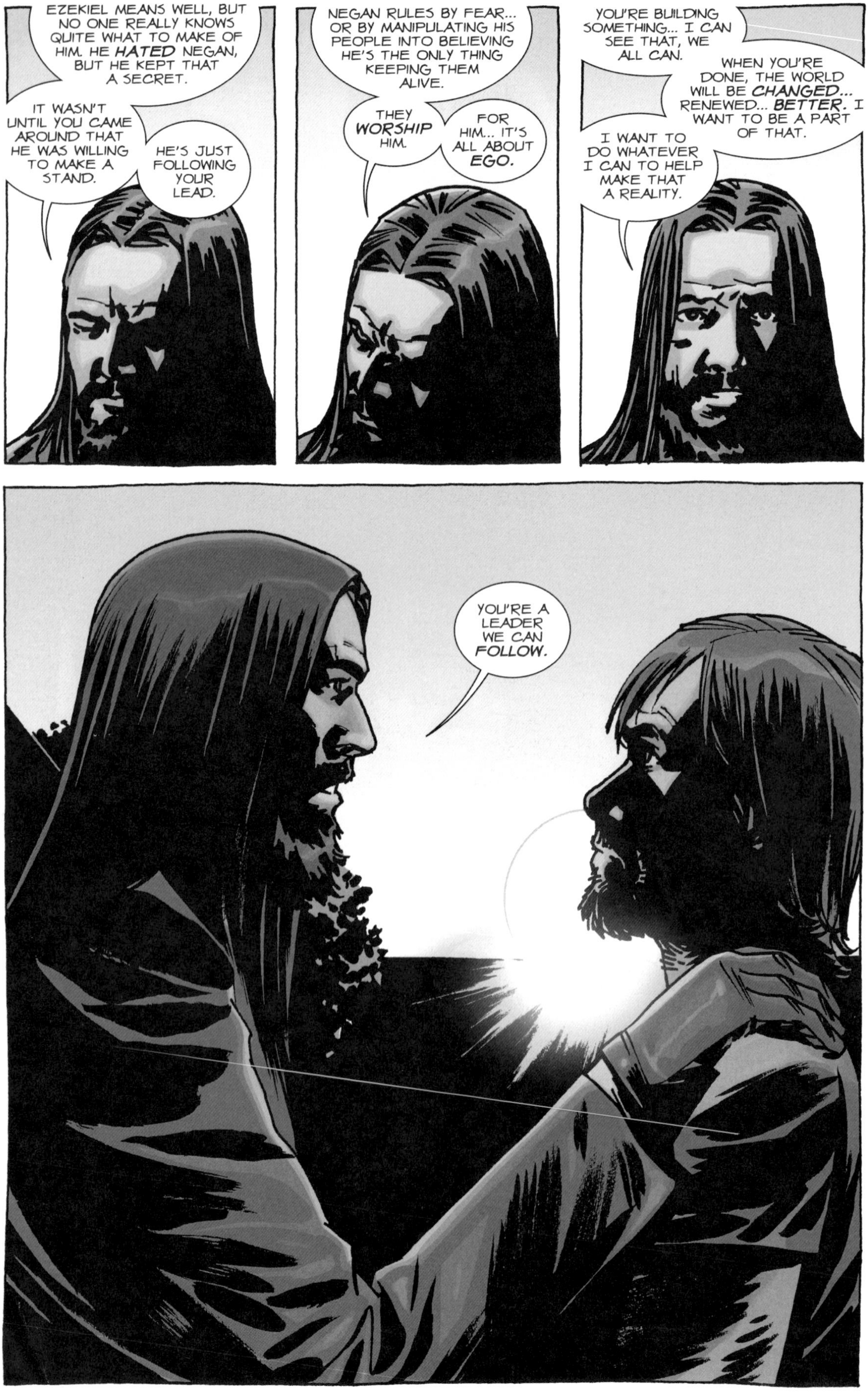

EZEKIEL MEANS WELL, BUT NO ONE REALLY KNOWS QUITE WHAT TO MAKE OF HIM. HE HATED NEGAN, BUT HE KEPT THAT A SECRET.
IT WASN'T UNTIL YOU CAME AROUND THAT HE WAS WILLING TO MAKE A STAND.
HE'S JUST FOLLOWING YOUR LEAD.
NEGAN RULES BY FEAR... OR BY MANIPULATING HIS PEOPLE INTO BELIEVING HE'S THE ONLY THING KEEPING THEM ALIVE.
THEY WORSHIP HIM.
FOR HIM... IT'S ALL ABOUT EGO.
YOU'RE BUILDING SOMETHING... I CAN SEE THAT, WE ALL CAN.
WHEN YOU'RE DONE, THE WORLD WILL BE CHANGED... RENEWED... BETTER. I WANT TO BE A PART OF THAT.
I WANT TO DO WHATEVER I CAN TO HELP MAKE THAT A REALITY.
YOU'RE A LEADER WE CAN FOLLOW.

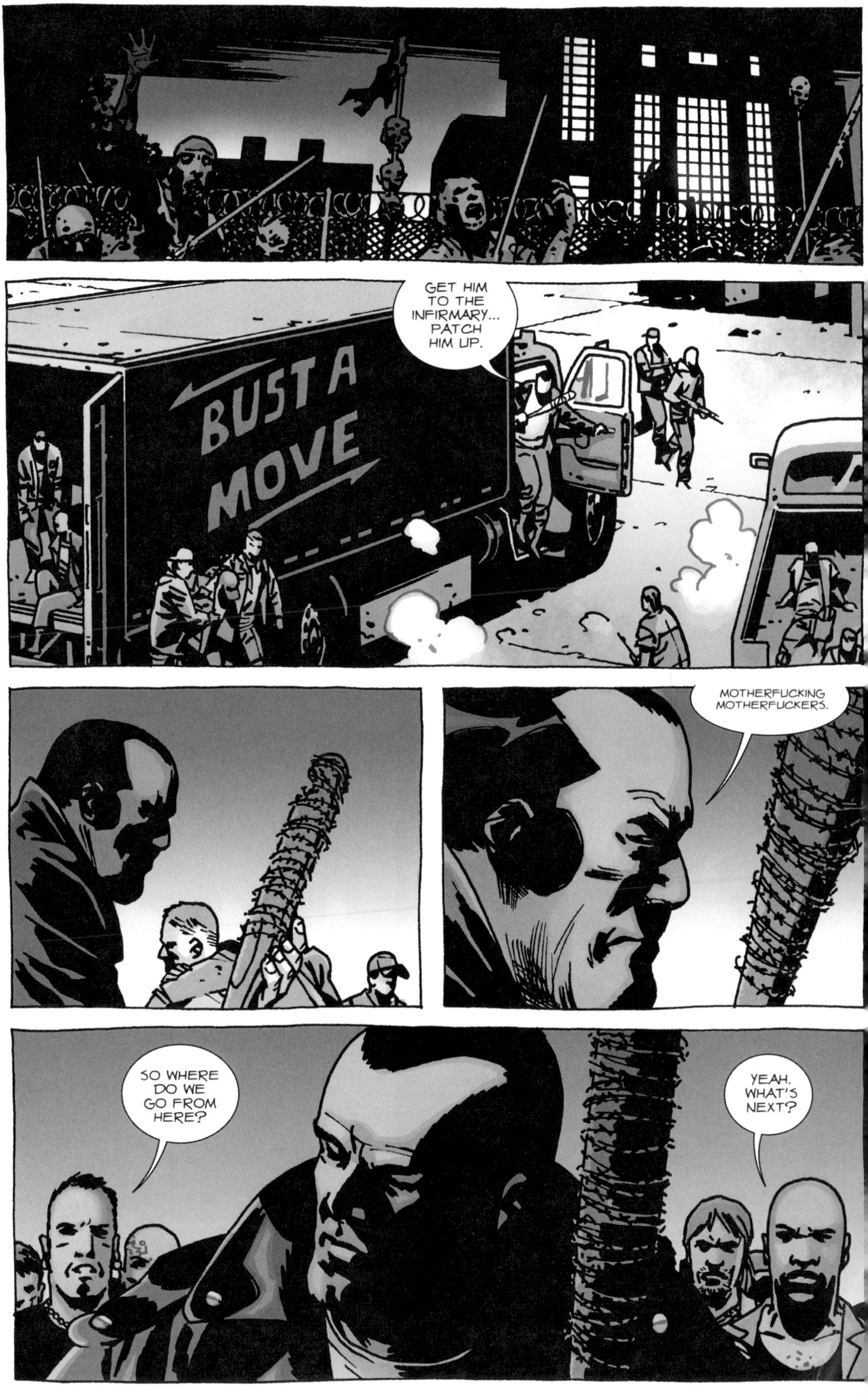

BUST A MOVE
GET HIM TO THE INFIRMARY... PATCH HIM UP.
MOTHERFUCKING MOTHERFUCKERS.
SO WHERE DO WE GO FROM HERE?
YEAH. WHAT'S NEXT?

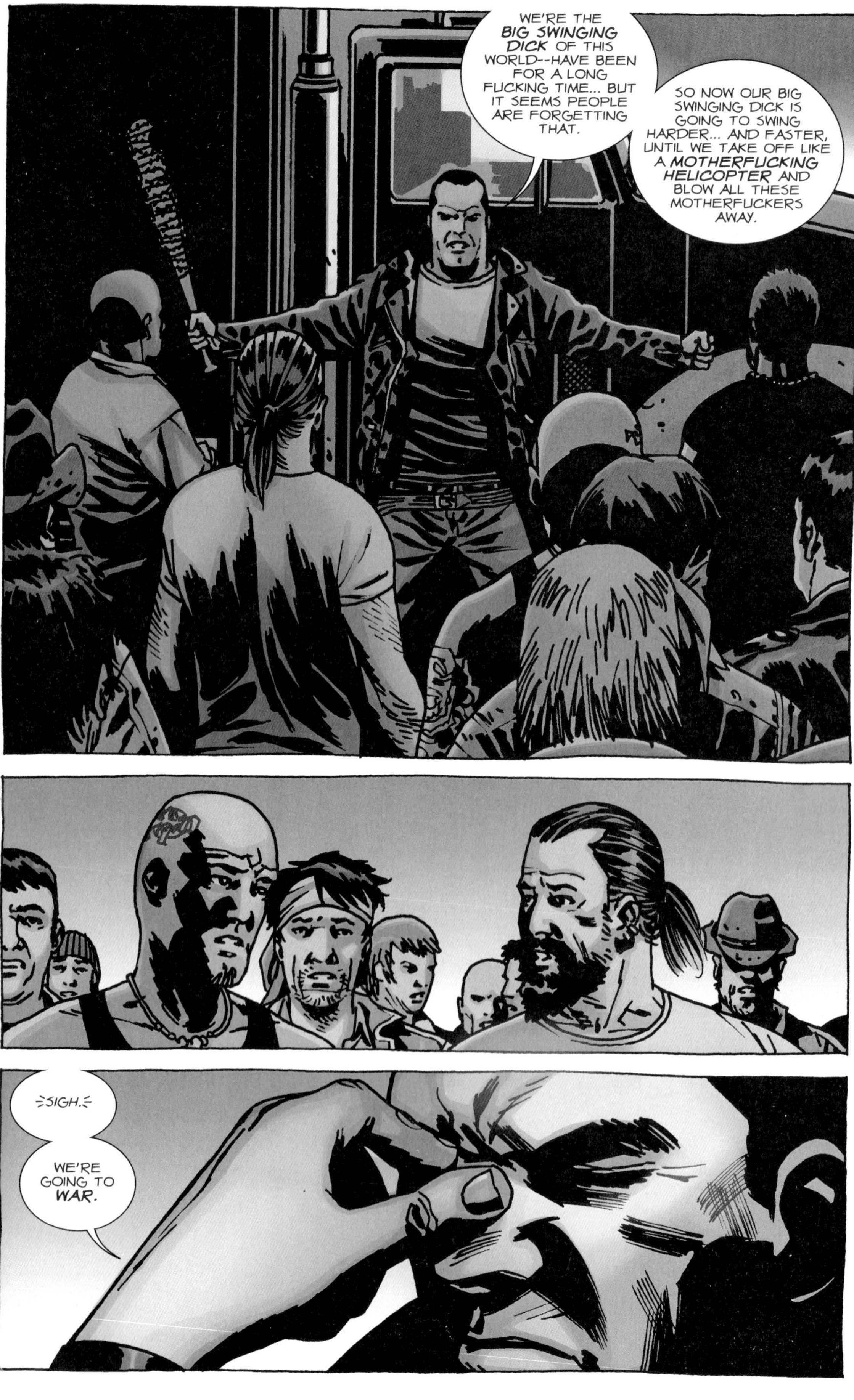
WE'RE THE BIG SWINGING DICK OF THIS WORLD--HAVE BEEN FOR A LONG FUCKING TIME... BUT IT SEEMS PEOPLE ARE FORGETTING THAT.
SO NOW OUR BIG SWINGING DICK IS GOING TO SWING HARDER... AND FASTER, UNTIL WE TAKE OFF LIKE A MOTHERFUCKING HELICOPTER AND BLOW ALL THESE MOTHERFUCKERS AWAY.
=SIGH.=
WE'RE GOING TO WAR.

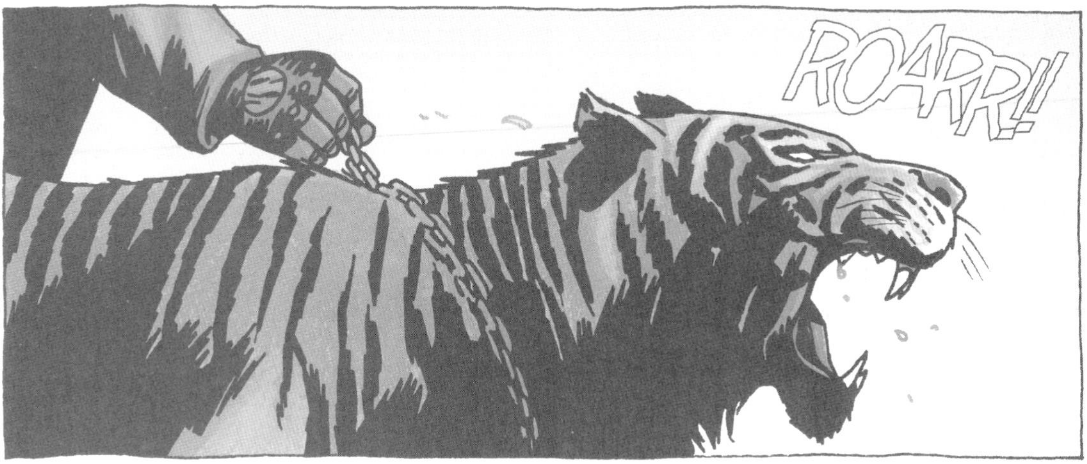
ROARR!!

Chapter Twenty:
All Out War Part One

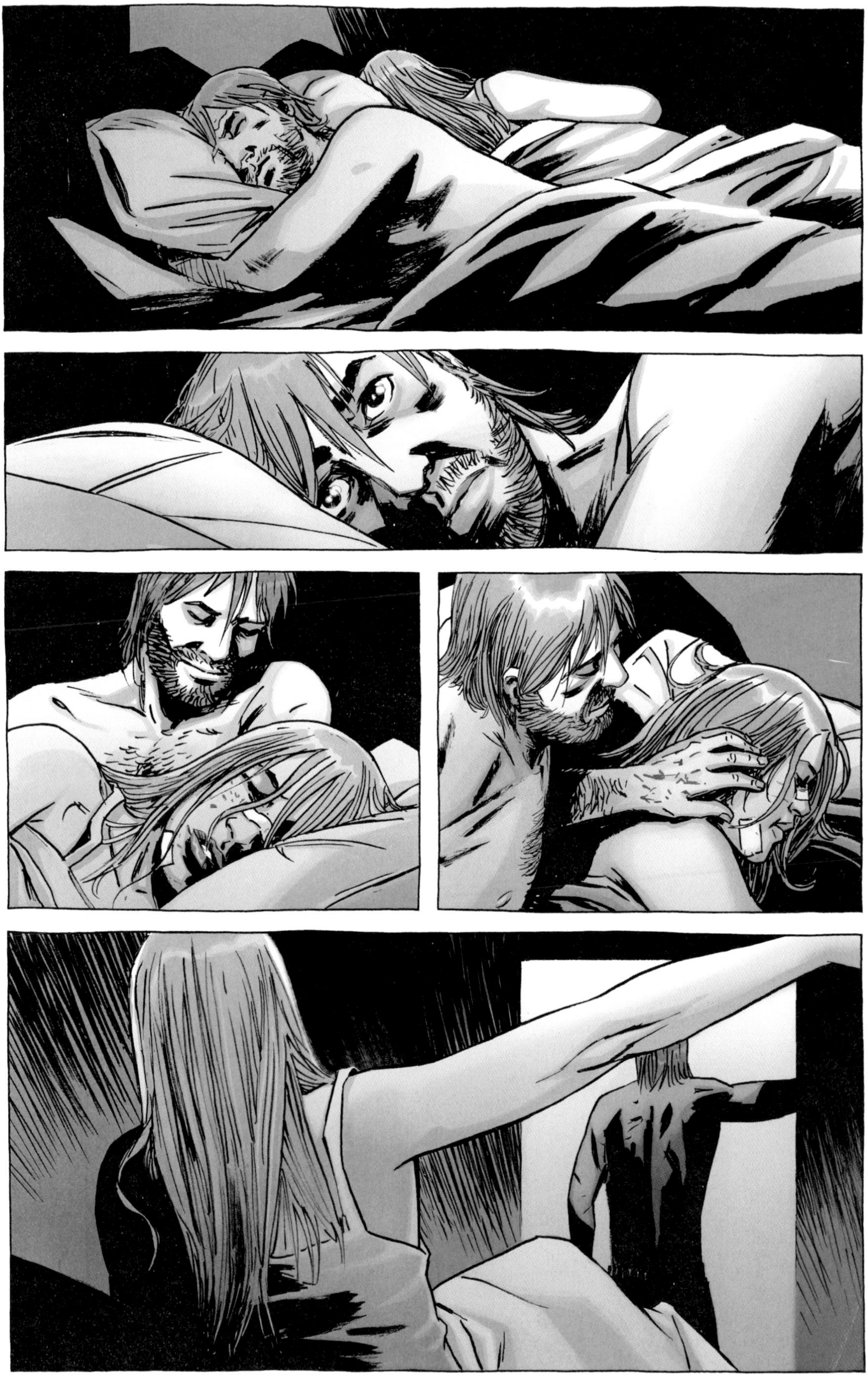

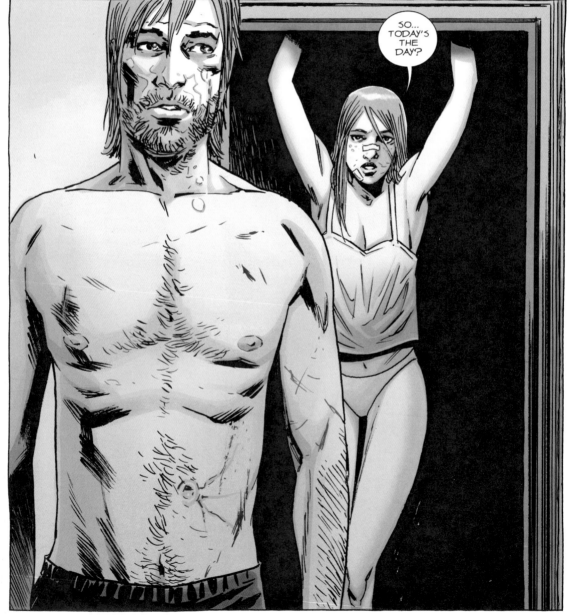

SO... TODAY'S THE DAY?

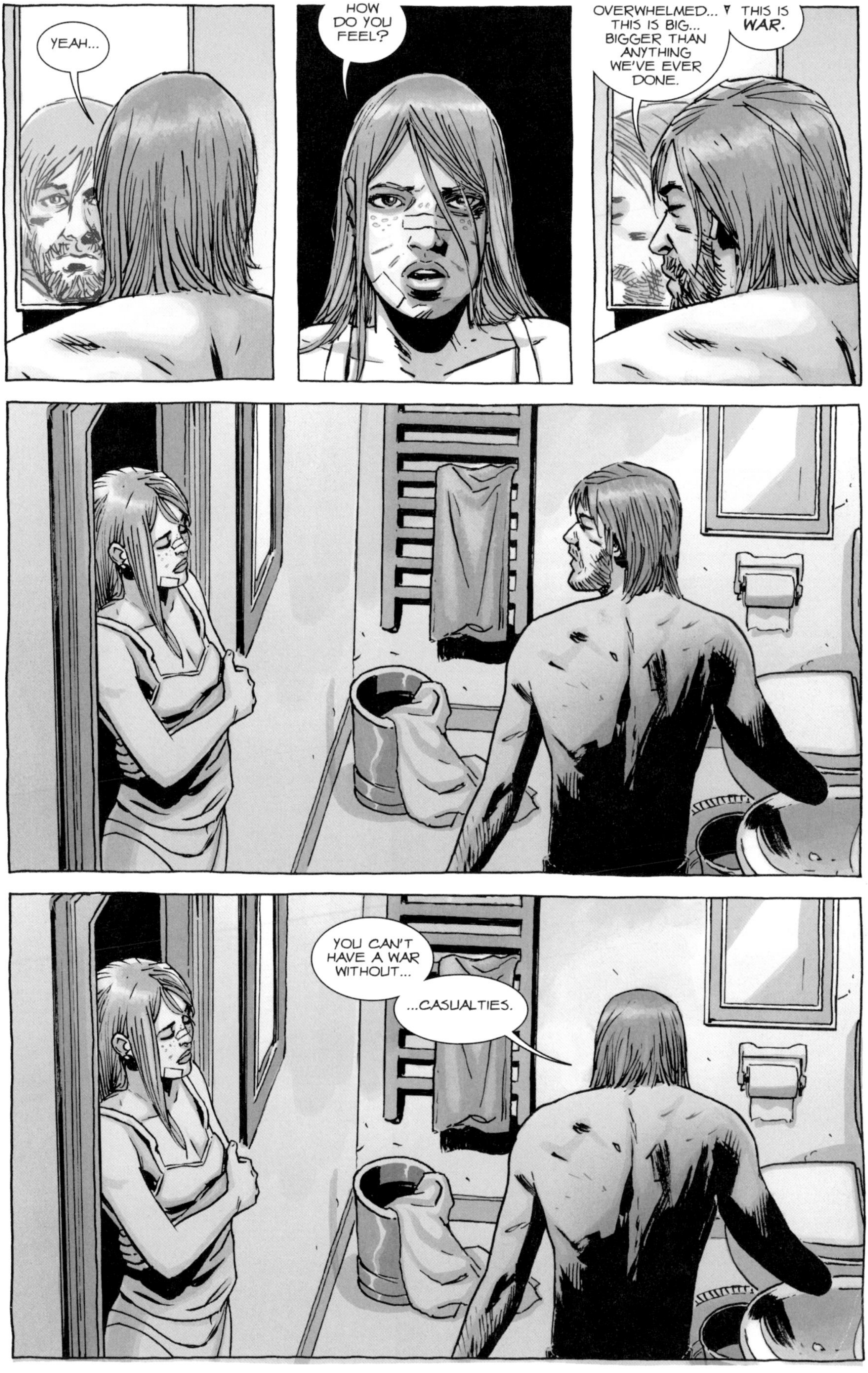
YEAH...
HOW DO YOU FEEL?
OVERWHELMED... THIS IS BIG... BIGGER THAN ANYTHING WE'VE EVER DONE.
THIS IS WAR.
YOU CAN'T HAVE A WAR WITHOUT...
...CASUALTIES.

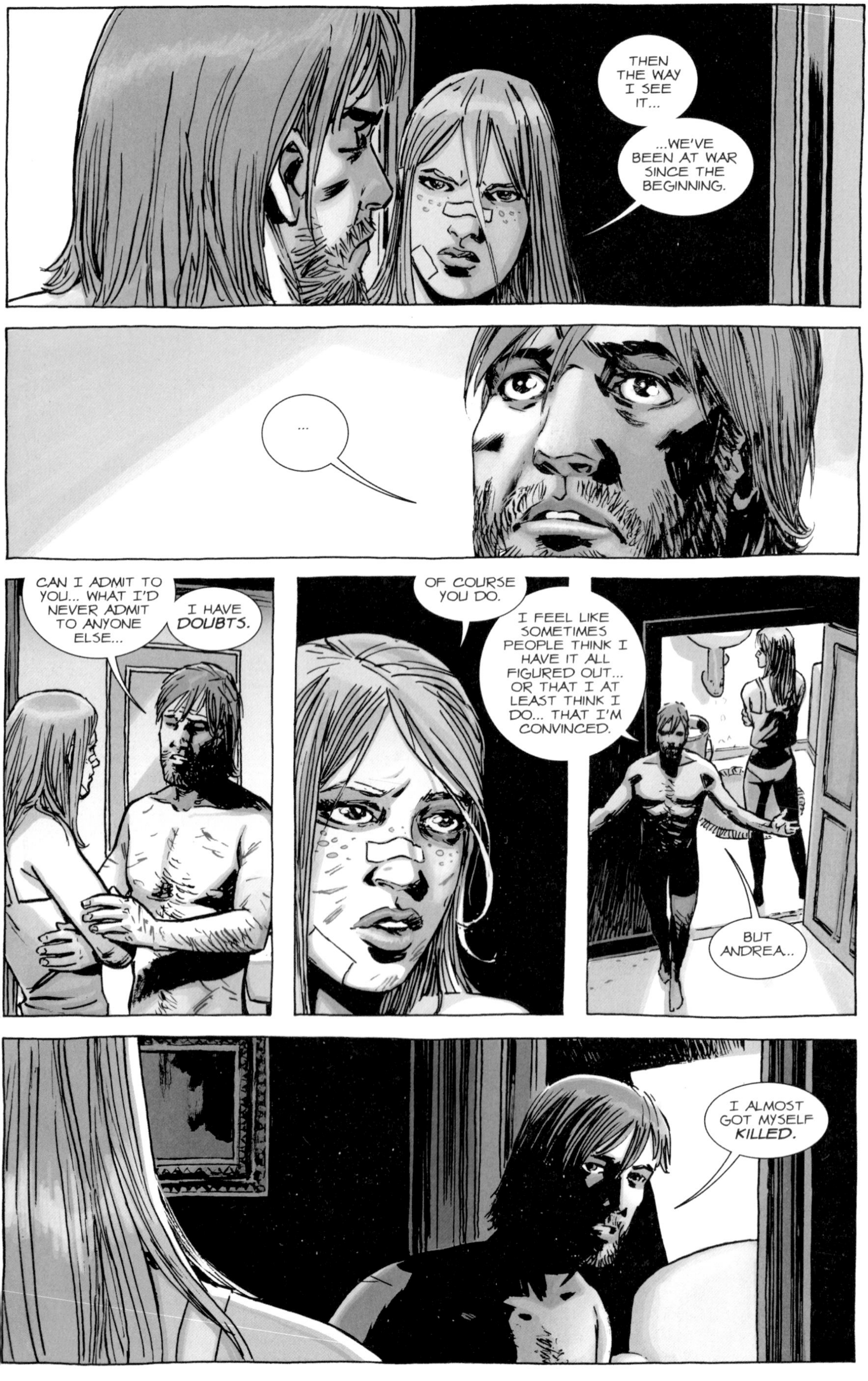
THEN THE WAY I SEE IT...
...WE'VE BEEN AT WAR SINCE THE BEGINNING.
...
CAN I ADMIT TO YOU... WHAT I'D NEVER ADMIT TO ANYONE ELSE...
I HAVE DOUBTS.
OF COURSE YOU DO.
I FEEL LIKE SOMETIMES PEOPLE THINK I HAVE IT ALL FIGURED OUT... OR THAT I AT LEAST THINK I DO... THAT I'M CONVINCED.
BUT ANDREA...
I ALMOST GOT MYSELF KILLED.

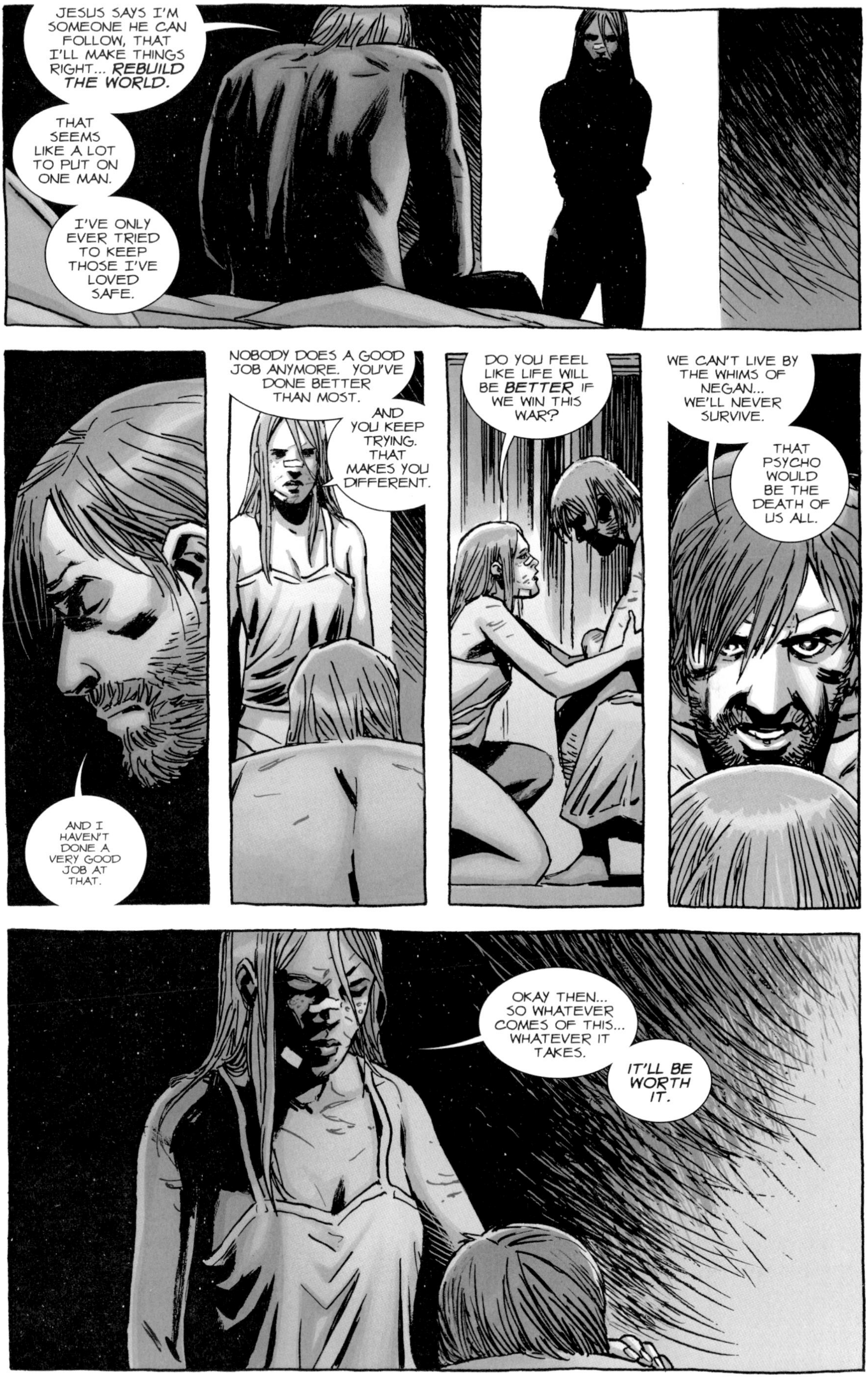

JESUS SAYS I'M SOMEONE HE CAN FOLLOW, THAT I'LL MAKE THINGS RIGHT... *REBUILD THE WORLD.*
THAT SEEMS LIKE A LOT TO PUT ON ONE MAN.
I'VE ONLY EVER TRIED TO KEEP THOSE I'VE LOVED SAFE.
AND I HAVEN'T DONE A VERY GOOD JOB AT THAT.
NOBODY DOES A GOOD JOB ANYMORE. YOU'VE DONE BETTER THAN MOST.
AND YOU KEEP TRYING. THAT MAKES YOU DIFFERENT.
DO YOU FEEL LIKE LIFE WILL BE *BETTER* IF WE WIN THIS WAR?
WE CAN'T LIVE BY THE WHIMS OF NEGAN... WE'LL NEVER SURVIVE.
THAT PSYCHO WOULD BE THE DEATH OF US ALL.
OKAY THEN... SO WHATEVER COMES OF THIS... WHATEVER IT TAKES.
IT'LL BE WORTH IT.

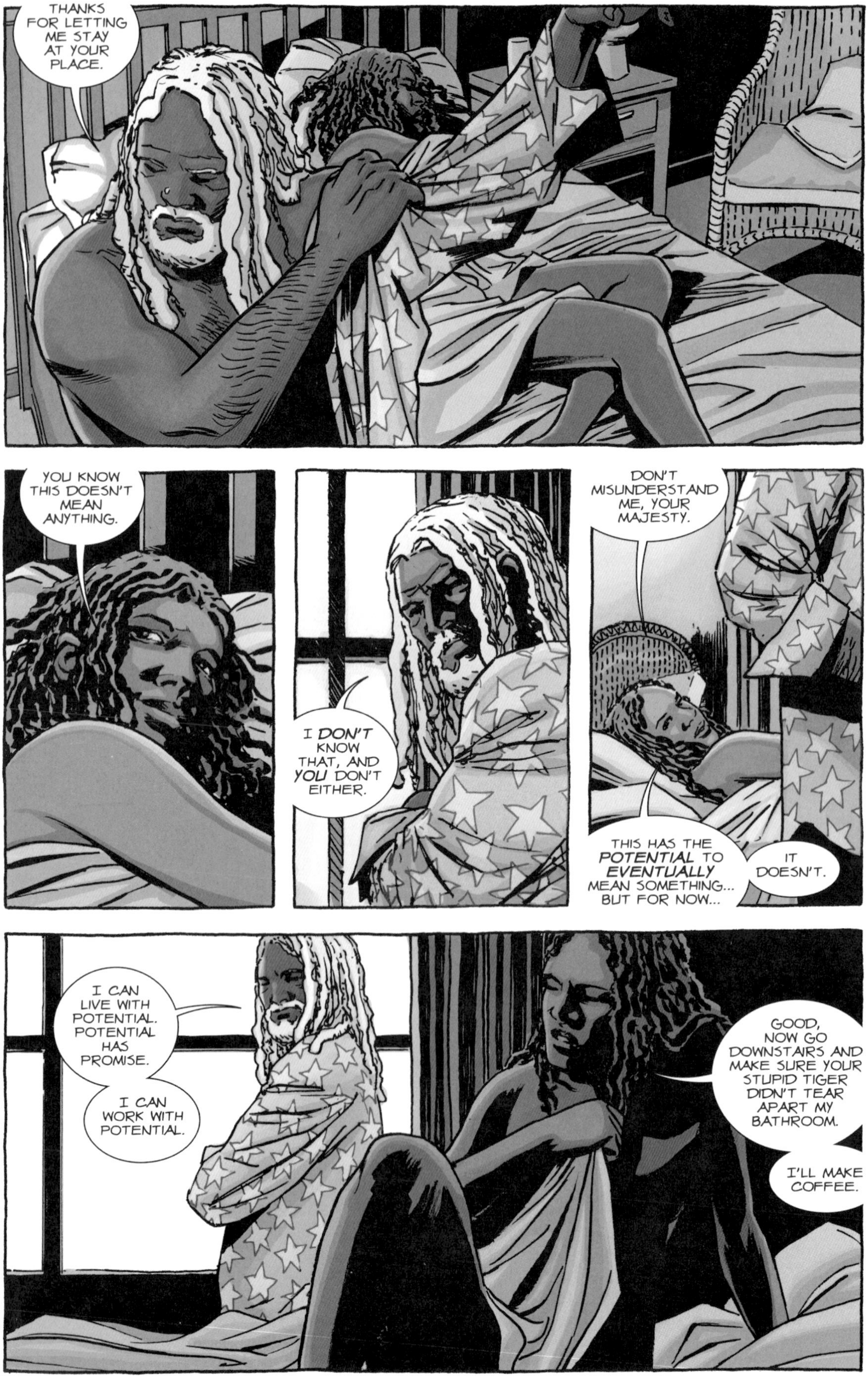
THANKS FOR LETTING ME STAY AT YOUR PLACE.
YOU KNOW THIS DOESN'T MEAN ANYTHING.
I *DON'T* KNOW THAT, AND *YOU* DON'T EITHER.
DON'T MISUNDERSTAND ME, YOUR MAJESTY.
THIS HAS THE *POTENTIAL* TO *EVENTUALLY* MEAN SOMETHING... BUT FOR NOW...
IT DOESN'T.
I CAN LIVE WITH POTENTIAL. POTENTIAL HAS PROMISE.
I CAN WORK WITH POTENTIAL.
GOOD, NOW GO DOWNSTAIRS AND MAKE SURE YOUR STUPID TIGER DIDN'T TEAR APART MY BATHROOM.
I'LL MAKE COFFEE.

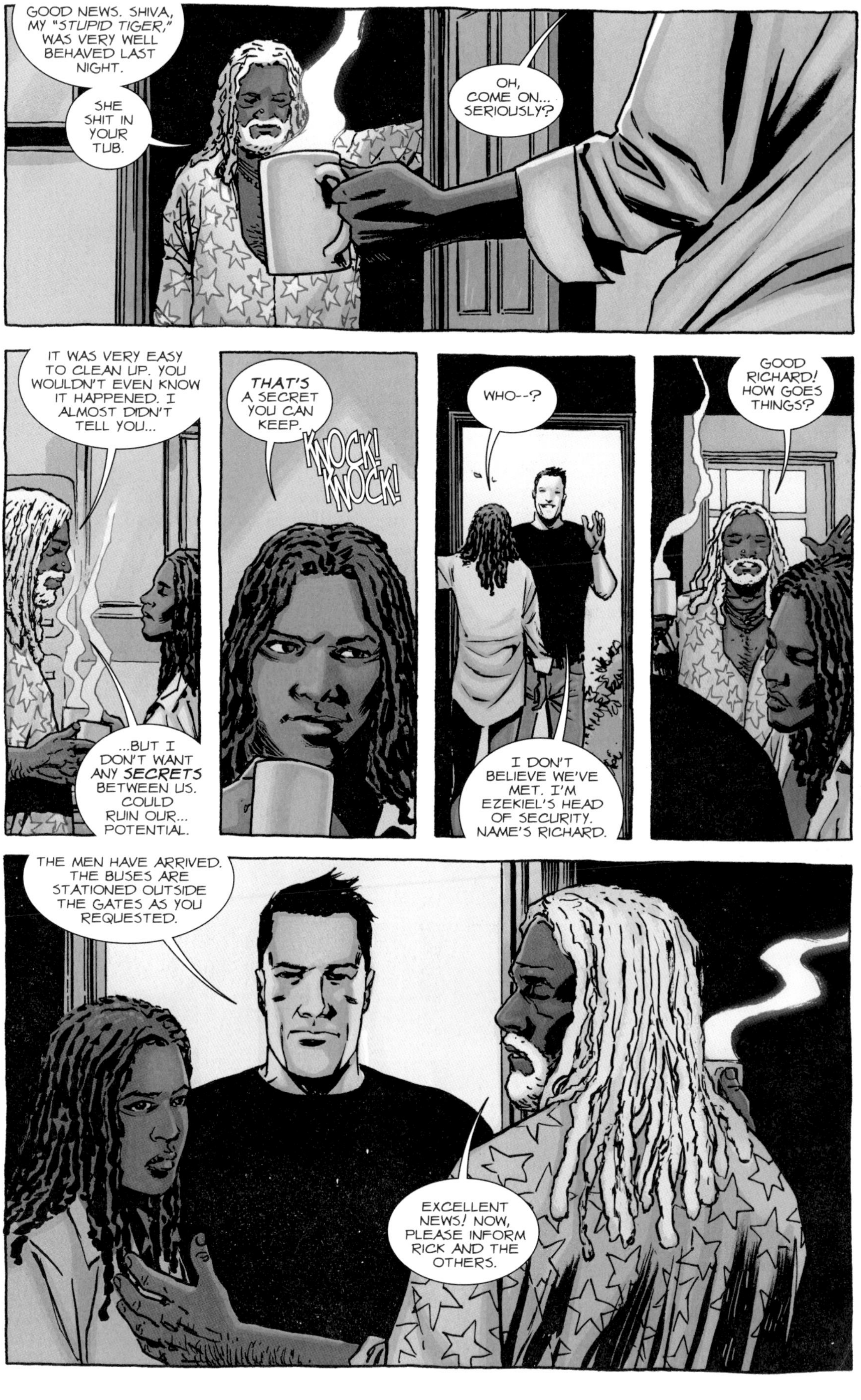
GOOD NEWS. SHIVA, MY "STUPID TIGER," WAS VERY WELL BEHAVED LAST NIGHT.
SHE SHIT IN YOUR TUB.
OH, COME ON... SERIOUSLY?
IT WAS VERY EASY TO CLEAN UP. YOU WOULDN'T EVEN KNOW IT HAPPENED. I ALMOST DIDN'T TELL YOU...
...BUT I DON'T WANT ANY SECRETS BETWEEN US. COULD RUIN OUR... POTENTIAL.
THAT'S A SECRET YOU CAN KEEP.
KNOCK! KNOCK!
WHO--?
I DON'T BELIEVE WE'VE MET. I'M EZEKIEL'S HEAD OF SECURITY. NAME'S RICHARD.
GOOD RICHARD! HOW GOES THINGS?
THE MEN HAVE ARRIVED. THE BUSES ARE STATIONED OUTSIDE THE GATES AS YOU REQUESTED.
EXCELLENT NEWS! NOW, PLEASE INFORM RICK AND THE OTHERS.

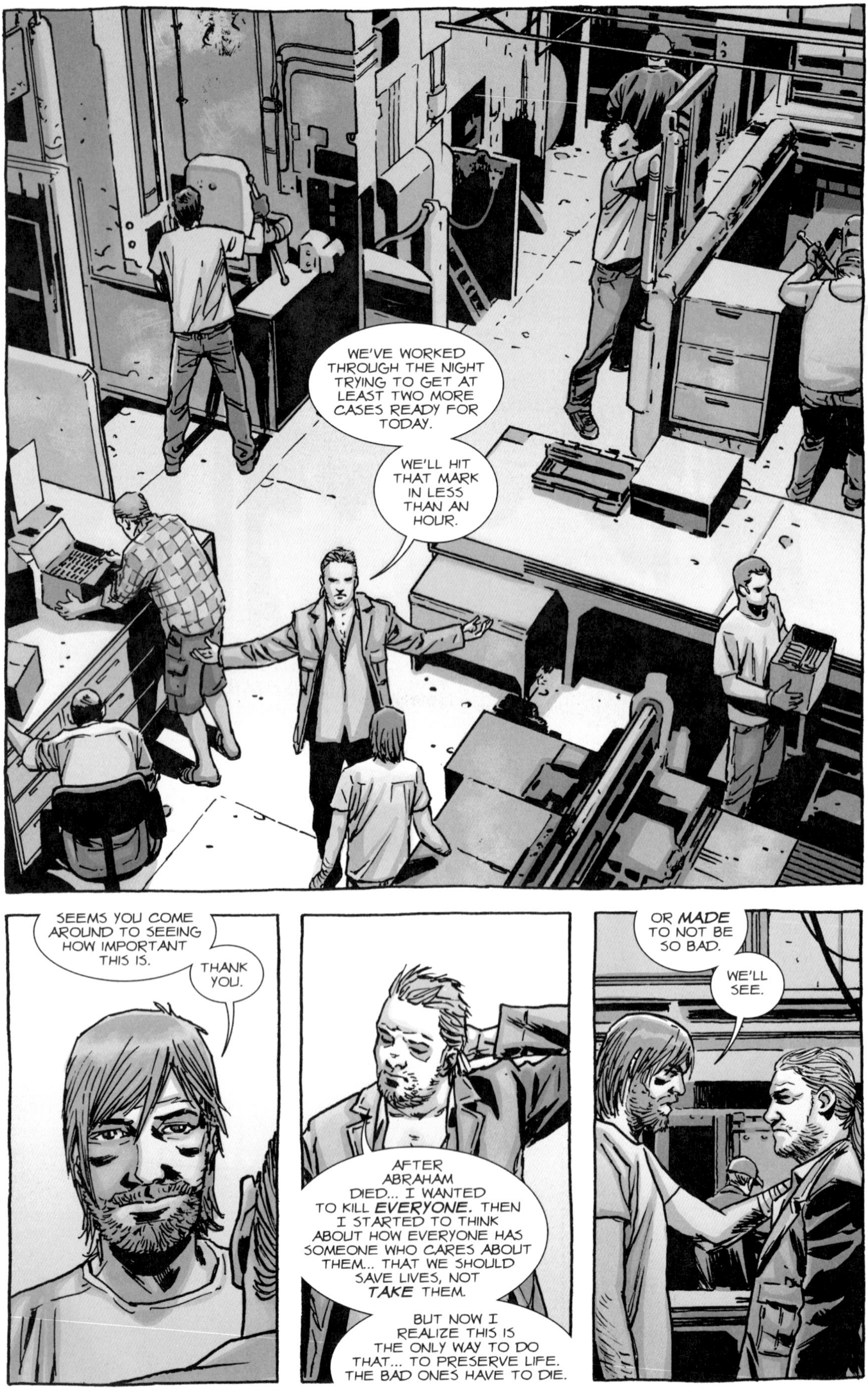
WE'VE WORKED THROUGH THE NIGHT TRYING TO GET AT LEAST TWO MORE CASES READY FOR TODAY.
WE'LL HIT THAT MARK IN LESS THAN AN HOUR.
SEEMS YOU COME AROUND TO SEEING HOW IMPORTANT THIS IS.
THANK YOU.
AFTER ABRAHAM DIED... I WANTED TO KILL EVERYONE. THEN I STARTED TO THINK ABOUT HOW EVERYONE HAS SOMEONE WHO CARES ABOUT THEM... THAT WE SHOULD SAVE LIVES, NOT TAKE THEM.
BUT NOW I REALIZE THIS IS THE ONLY WAY TO DO THAT... TO PRESERVE LIFE. THE BAD ONES HAVE TO DIE.
OR MADE TO NOT BE SO BAD.
WE'LL SEE.

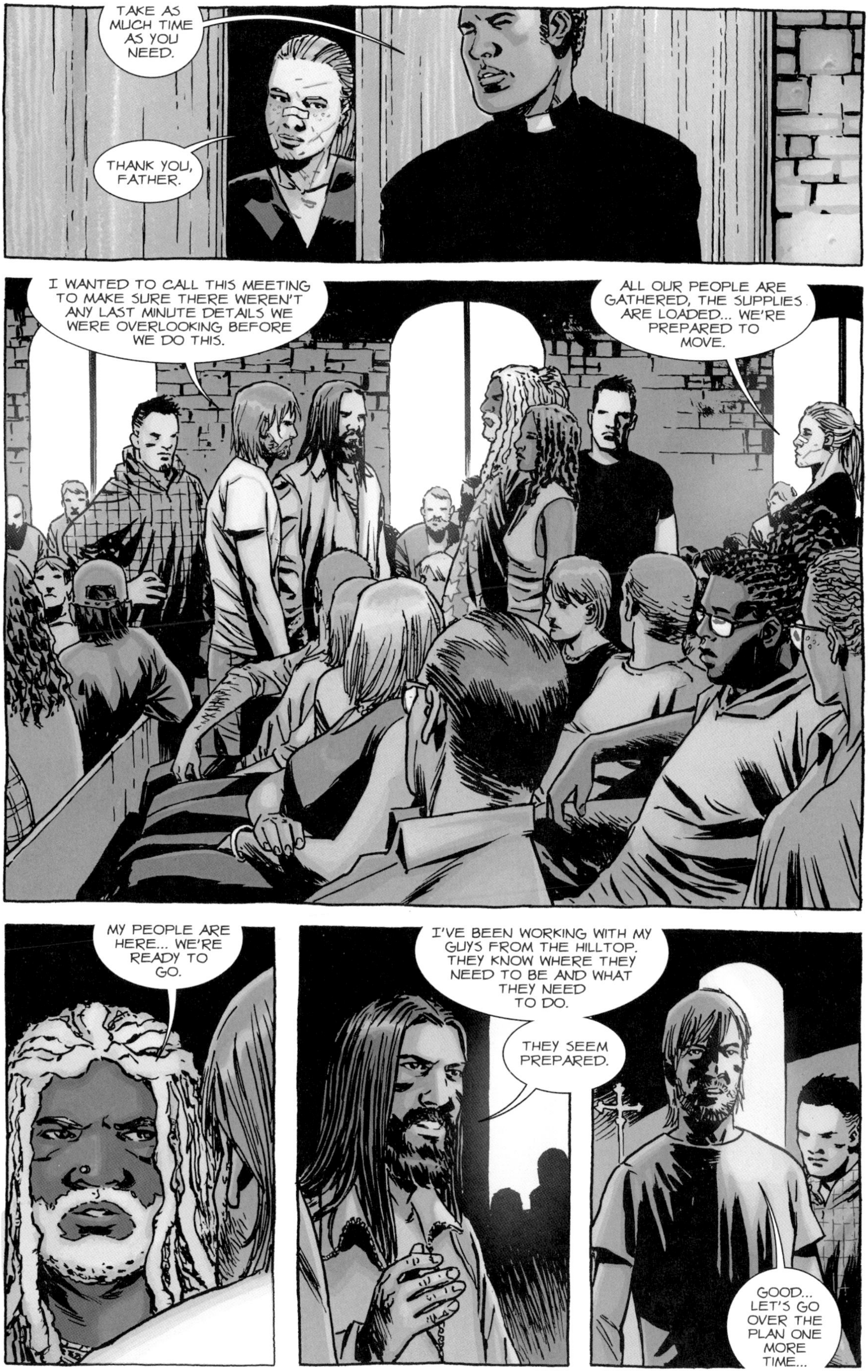

TAKE AS MUCH TIME AS YOU NEED.
THANK YOU, FATHER.
I WANTED TO CALL THIS MEETING TO MAKE SURE THERE WEREN'T ANY LAST MINUTE DETAILS WE WERE OVERLOOKING BEFORE WE DO THIS.
ALL OUR PEOPLE ARE GATHERED, THE SUPPLIES ARE LOADED... WE'RE PREPARED TO MOVE.
MY PEOPLE ARE HERE... WE'RE READY TO GO.
I'VE BEEN WORKING WITH MY GUYS FROM THE HILLTOP. THEY KNOW WHERE THEY NEED TO BE AND WHAT THEY NEED TO DO.
THEY SEEM PREPARED.
GOOD... LET'S GO OVER THE PLAN ONE MORE TIME...

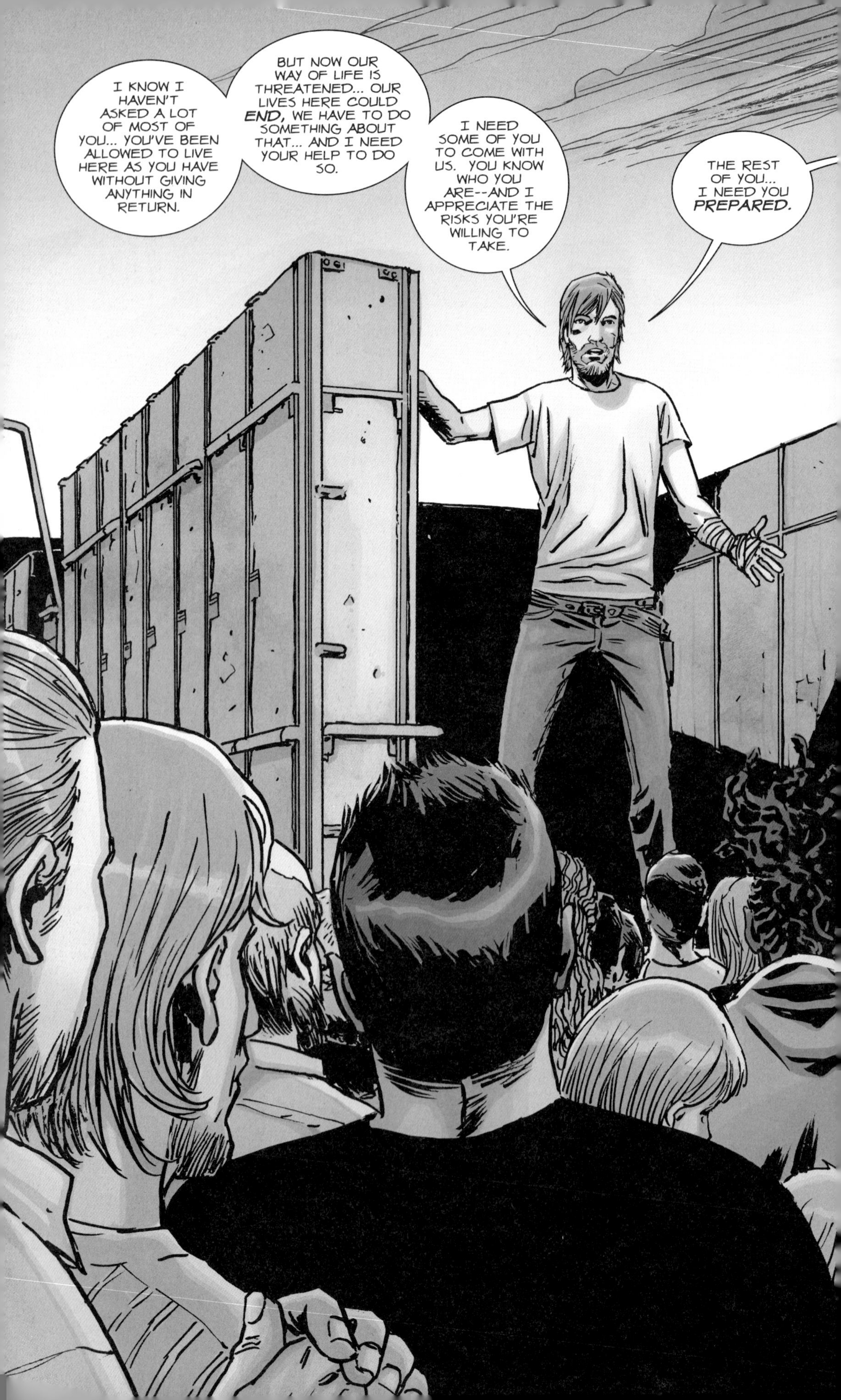
I KNOW I HAVEN'T ASKED A LOT OF MOST OF YOU... YOU'VE BEEN ALLOWED TO LIVE HERE AS YOU HAVE WITHOUT GIVING ANYTHING IN RETURN.
BUT NOW OUR WAY OF LIFE IS THREATENED... OUR LIVES HERE COULD *END,* WE HAVE TO DO SOMETHING ABOUT THAT... AND I NEED YOUR HELP TO DO SO.
I NEED SOME OF YOU TO COME WITH US. YOU KNOW WHO YOU ARE--AND I APPRECIATE THE RISKS YOU'RE WILLING TO TAKE.
THE REST OF YOU... I NEED YOU *PREPARED.*

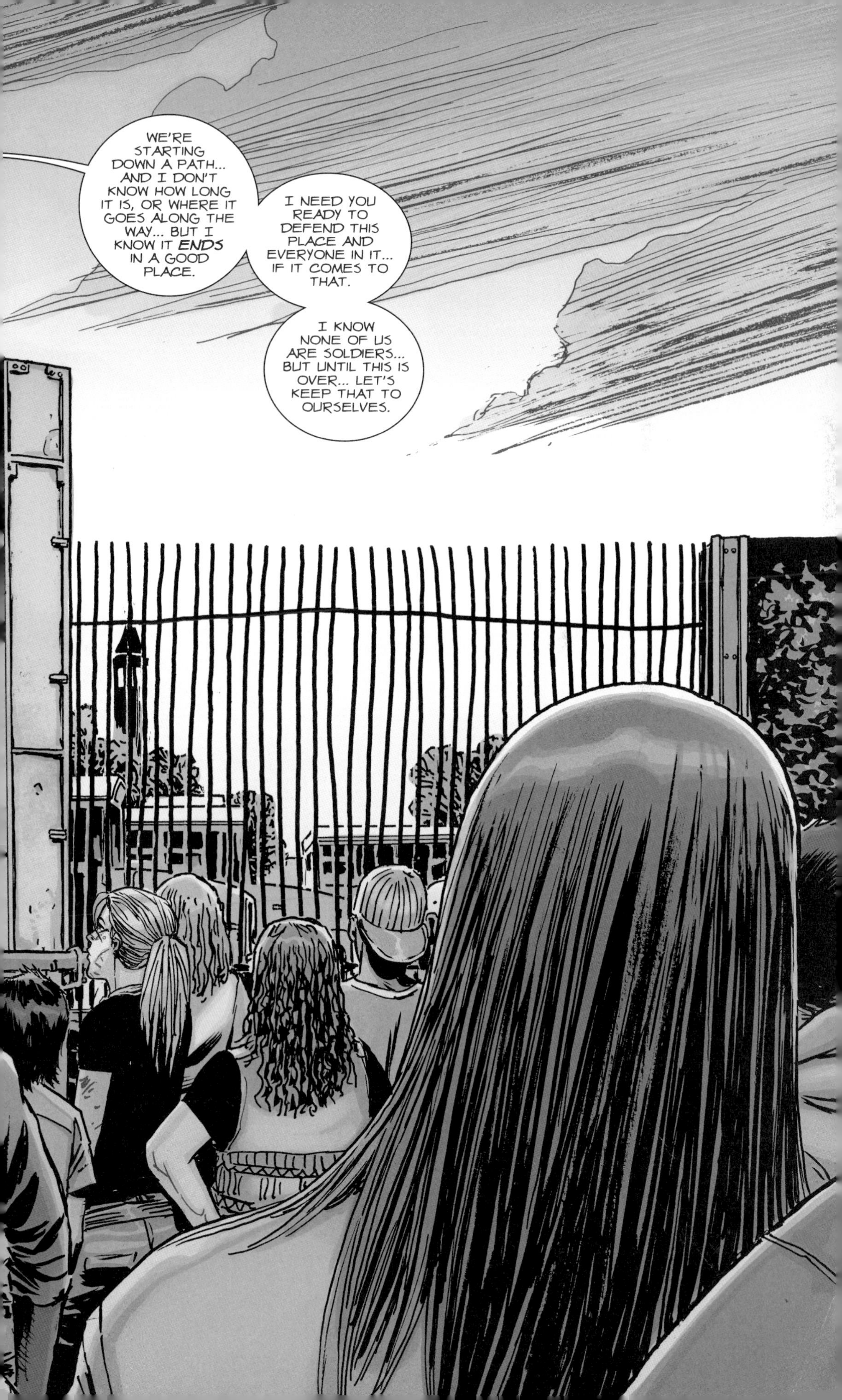
WE'RE STARTING DOWN A PATH... AND I DON'T KNOW HOW LONG IT IS, OR WHERE IT GOES ALONG THE WAY... BUT I KNOW IT **ENDS** IN A GOOD PLACE.
I NEED YOU READY TO DEFEND THIS PLACE AND EVERYONE IN IT... IF IT COMES TO THAT.
I KNOW NONE OF US ARE SOLDIERS... BUT UNTIL THIS IS OVER... LET'S KEEP THAT TO OURSELVES.

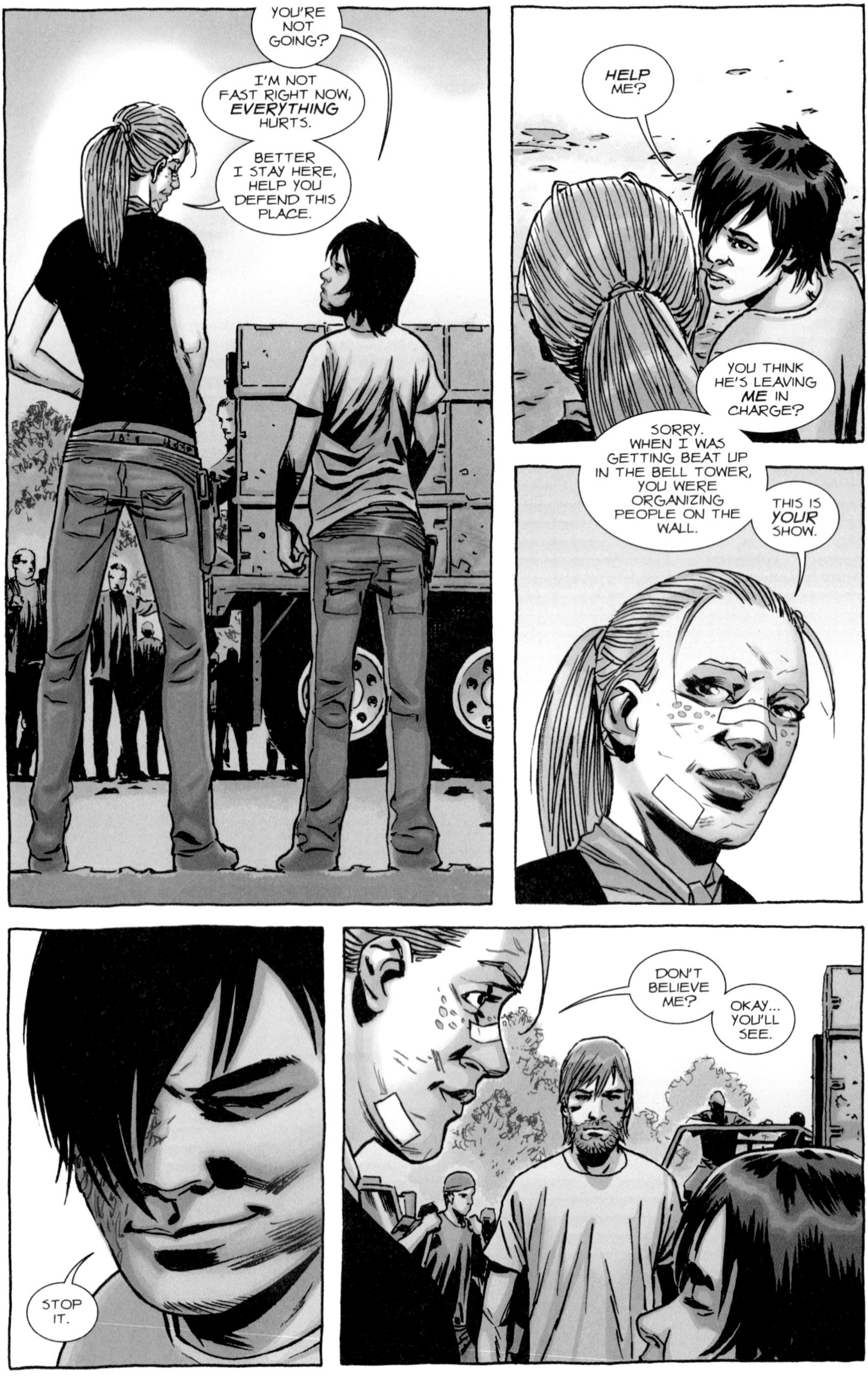
YOU'RE NOT GOING?
I'M NOT FAST RIGHT NOW, EVERYTHING HURTS.
BETTER I STAY HERE, HELP YOU DEFEND THIS PLACE.
HELP ME?
YOU THINK HE'S LEAVING ME IN CHARGE?
SORRY. WHEN I WAS GETTING BEAT UP IN THE BELL TOWER, YOU WERE ORGANIZING PEOPLE ON THE WALL.
THIS IS YOUR SHOW.
STOP IT.
DON'T BELIEVE ME?
OKAY... YOU'LL SEE.

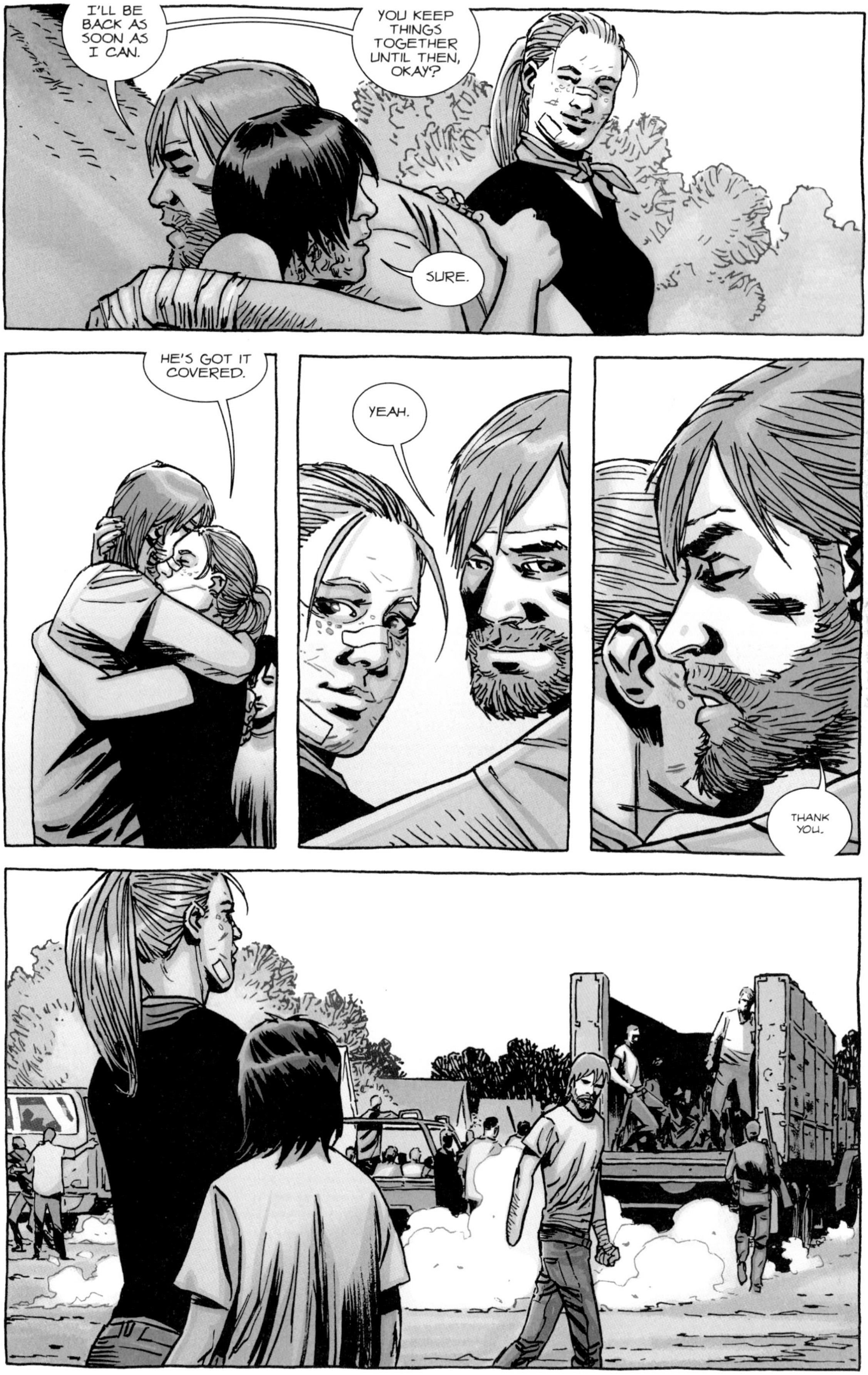
I'LL BE BACK AS SOON AS I CAN.
YOU KEEP THINGS TOGETHER UNTIL THEN, OKAY?
SURE.
HE'S GOT IT COVERED.
YEAH.
THANK YOU.

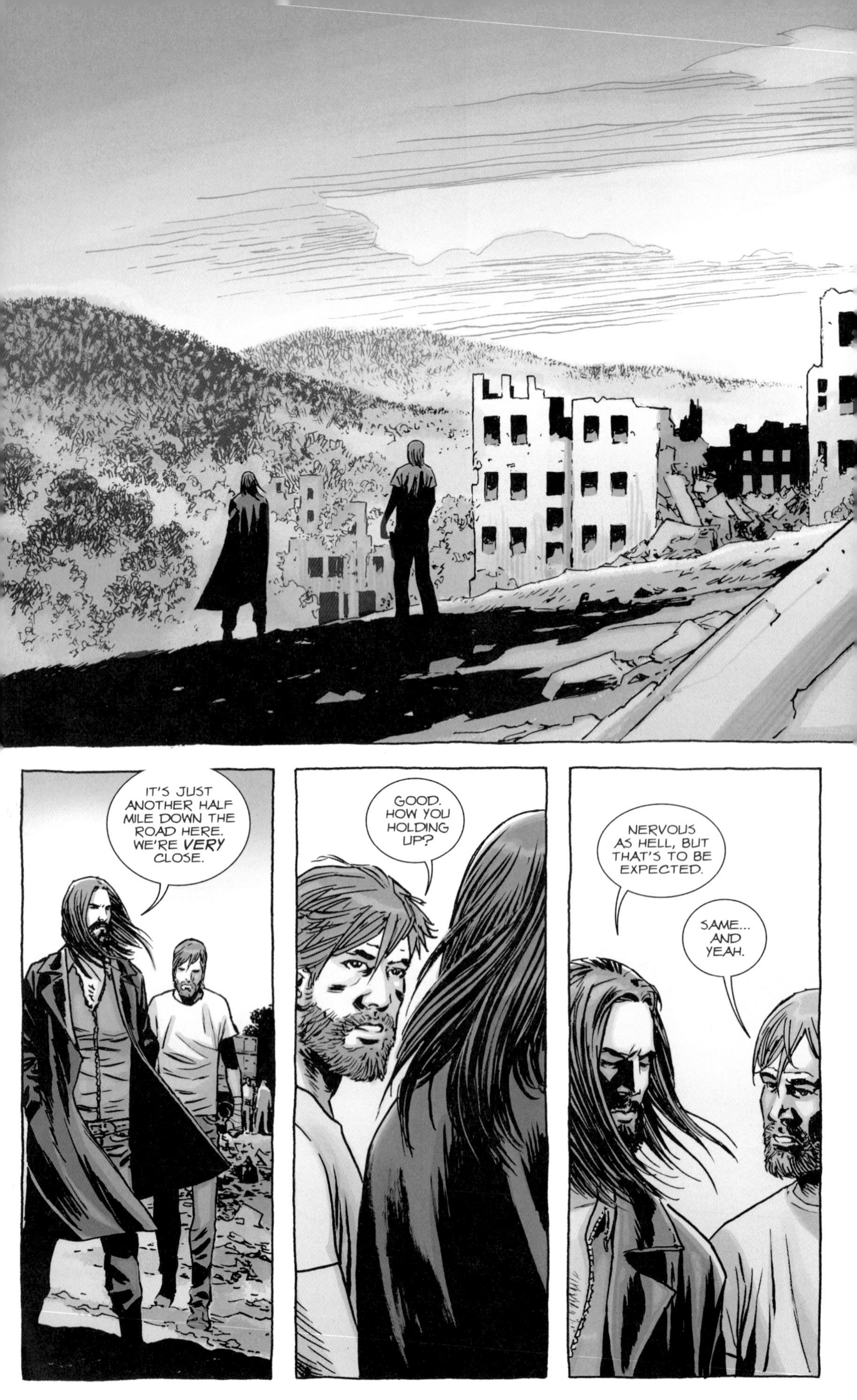

IT'S JUST ANOTHER HALF MILE DOWN THE ROAD HERE. WE'RE **VERY** CLOSE.
GOOD. HOW YOU HOLDING UP?
NERVOUS AS HELL, BUT THAT'S TO BE EXPECTED.
SAME... AND YEAH.

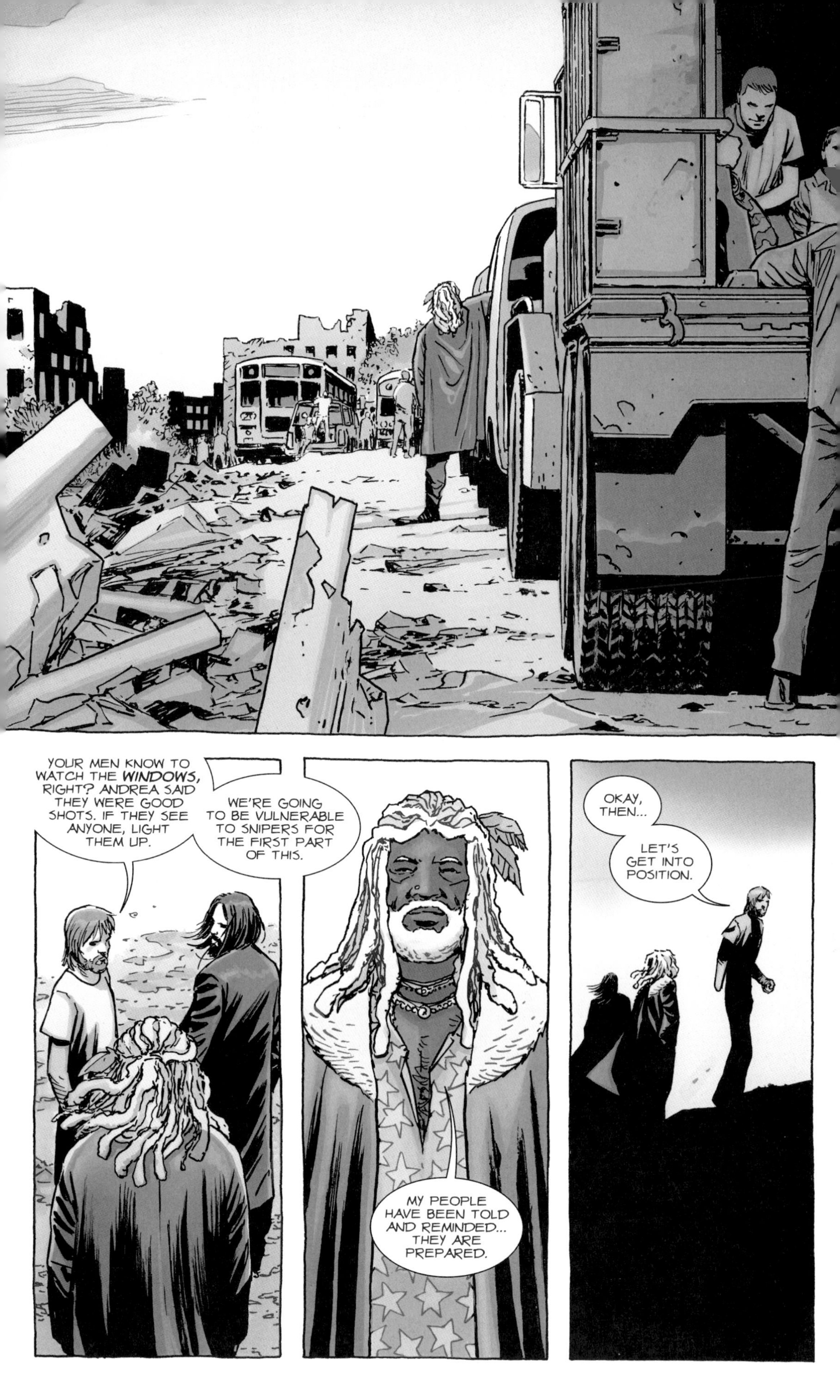
YOUR MEN KNOW TO WATCH THE WINDOWS, RIGHT? ANDREA SAID THEY WERE GOOD SHOTS. IF THEY SEE ANYONE, LIGHT THEM UP.
WE'RE GOING TO BE VULNERABLE TO SNIPERS FOR THE FIRST PART OF THIS.
MY PEOPLE HAVE BEEN TOLD AND REMINDED... THEY ARE PREPARED.
OKAY, THEN...
LET'S GET INTO POSITION.

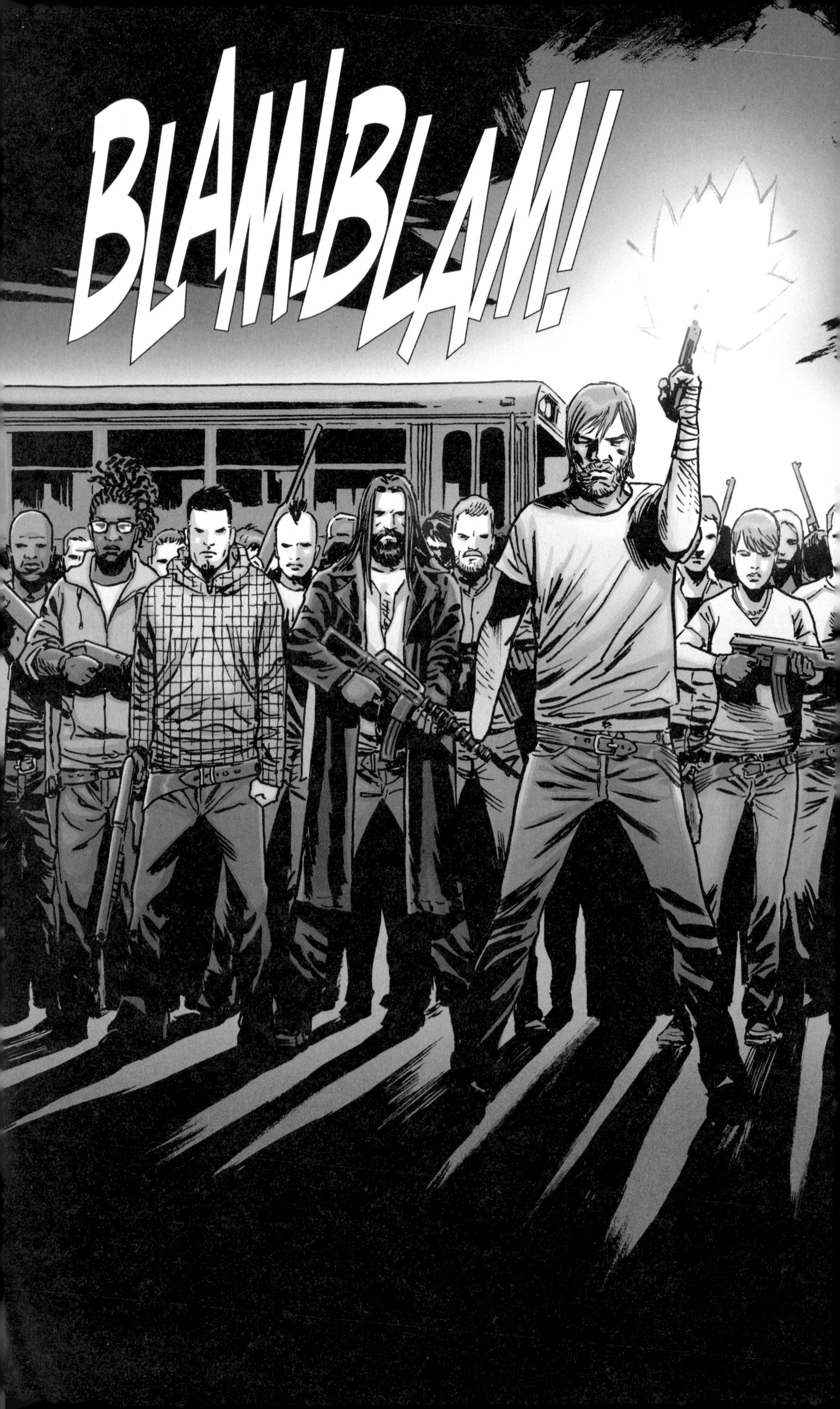
BLAM! BLAM!

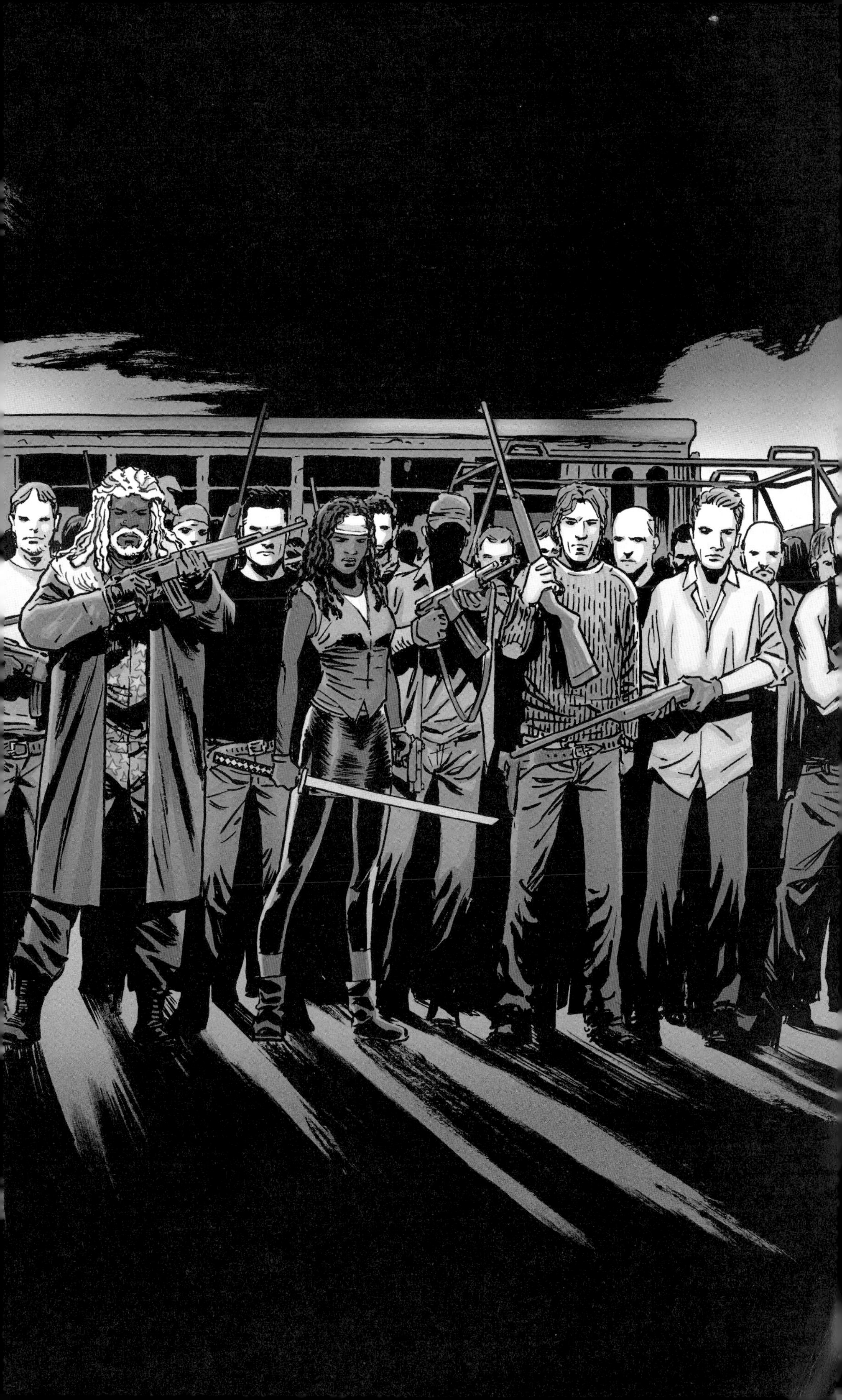

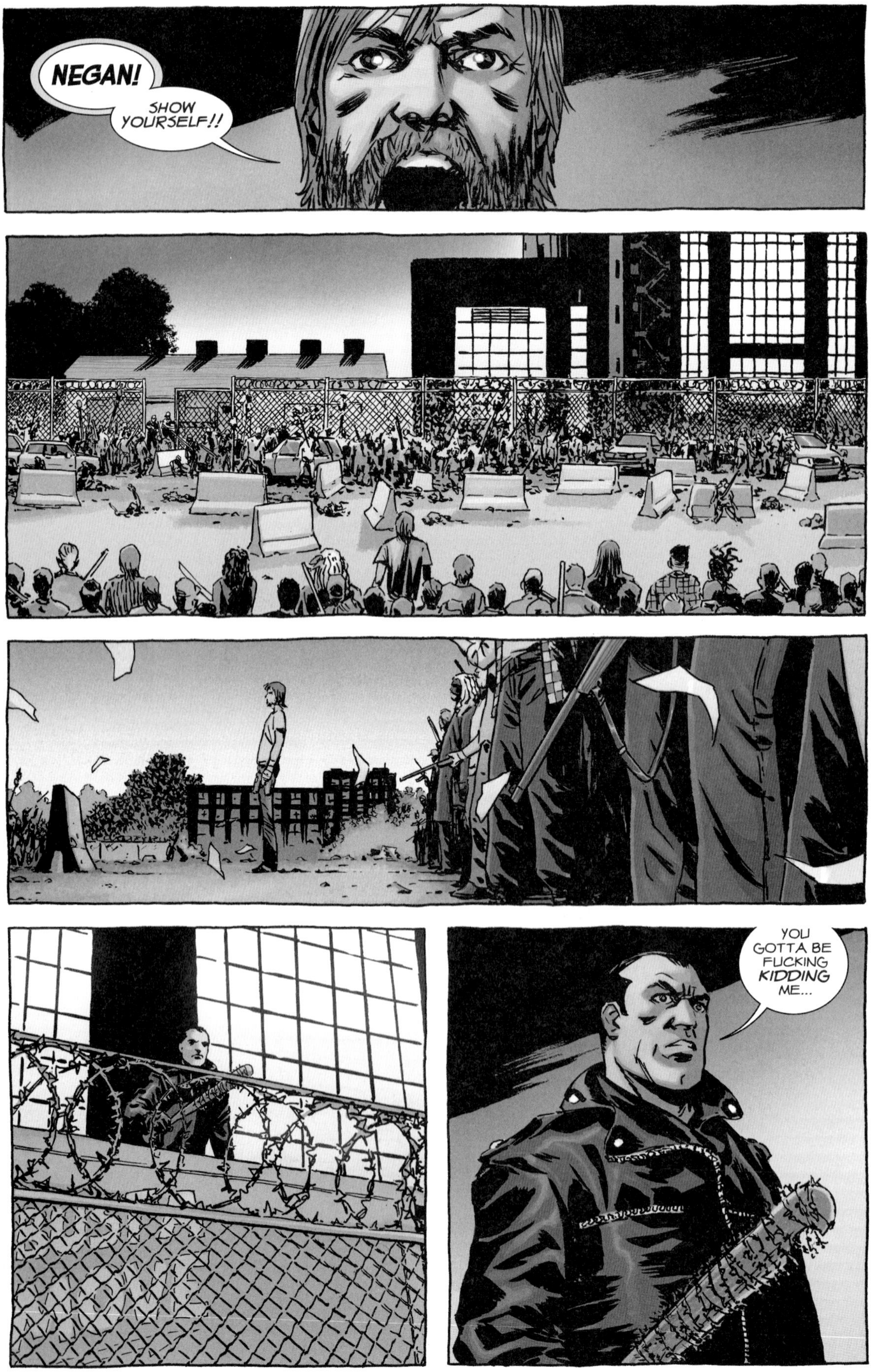
NEGAN!
SHOW YOURSELF!!
YOU GOTTA BE FUCKING KIDDING ME...

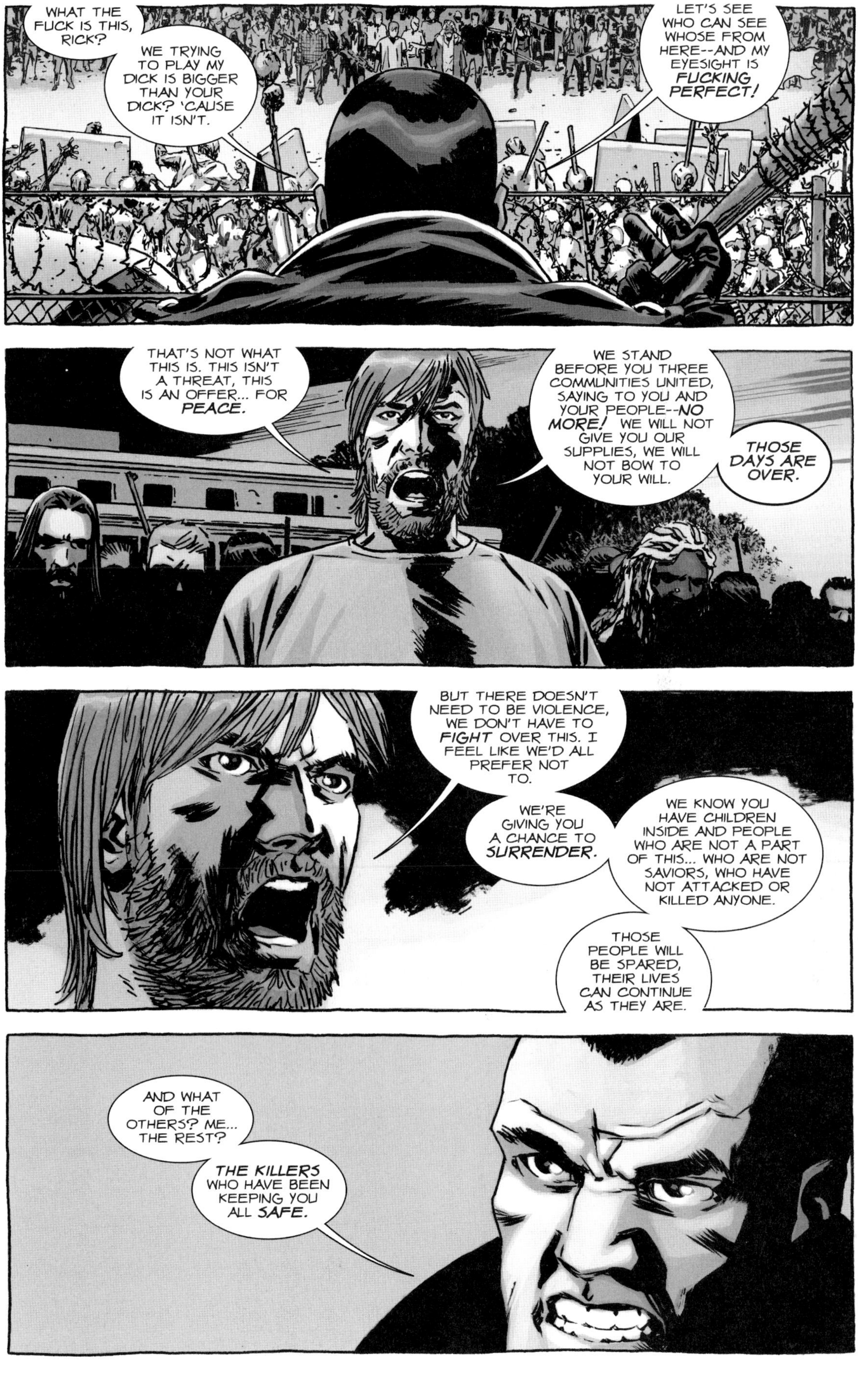
WHAT THE FUCK IS THIS, RICK?
WE TRYING TO PLAY MY DICK IS BIGGER THAN YOUR DICK? 'CAUSE IT ISN'T.
LET'S SEE WHO CAN SEE WHOSE FROM HERE--AND MY EYESIGHT IS FUCKING PERFECT!
THAT'S NOT WHAT THIS IS. THIS ISN'T A THREAT, THIS IS AN OFFER... FOR PEACE.
WE STAND BEFORE YOU THREE COMMUNITIES UNITED, SAYING TO YOU AND YOUR PEOPLE--NO MORE! WE WILL NOT GIVE YOU OUR SUPPLIES, WE WILL NOT BOW TO YOUR WILL.
THOSE DAYS ARE OVER.
BUT THERE DOESN'T NEED TO BE VIOLENCE, WE DON'T HAVE TO FIGHT OVER THIS. I FEEL LIKE WE'D ALL PREFER NOT TO.
WE'RE GIVING YOU A CHANCE TO SURRENDER.
WE KNOW YOU HAVE CHILDREN INSIDE AND PEOPLE WHO ARE NOT A PART OF THIS... WHO ARE NOT SAVIORS, WHO HAVE NOT ATTACKED OR KILLED ANYONE.
THOSE PEOPLE WILL BE SPARED, THEIR LIVES CAN CONTINUE AS THEY ARE.
AND WHAT OF THE OTHERS? ME... THE REST?
THE KILLERS WHO HAVE BEEN KEEPING YOU ALL SAFE.

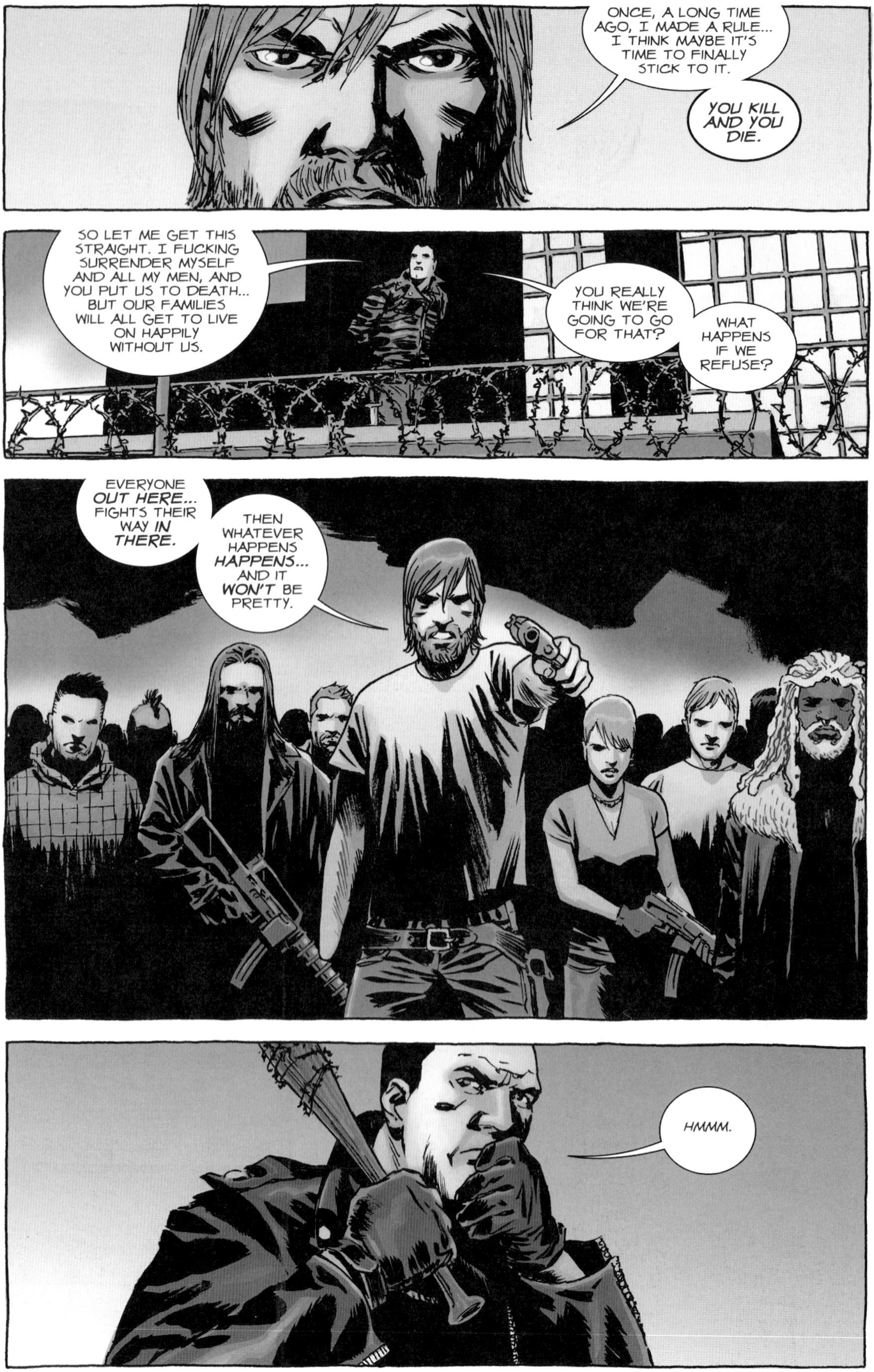
ONCE, A LONG TIME AGO, I MADE A RULE... I THINK MAYBE IT'S TIME TO FINALLY STICK TO IT.
YOU KILL AND YOU DIE.
SO LET ME GET THIS STRAIGHT. I FUCKING SURRENDER MYSELF AND ALL MY MEN, AND YOU PUT US TO DEATH... BUT OUR FAMILIES WILL ALL GET TO LIVE ON HAPPILY WITHOUT US.
YOU REALLY THINK WE'RE GOING TO GO FOR THAT?
WHAT HAPPENS IF WE REFUSE?
EVERYONE OUT HERE... FIGHTS THEIR WAY IN THERE.
THEN WHATEVER HAPPENS HAPPENS... AND IT WON'T BE PRETTY.
HMMM.

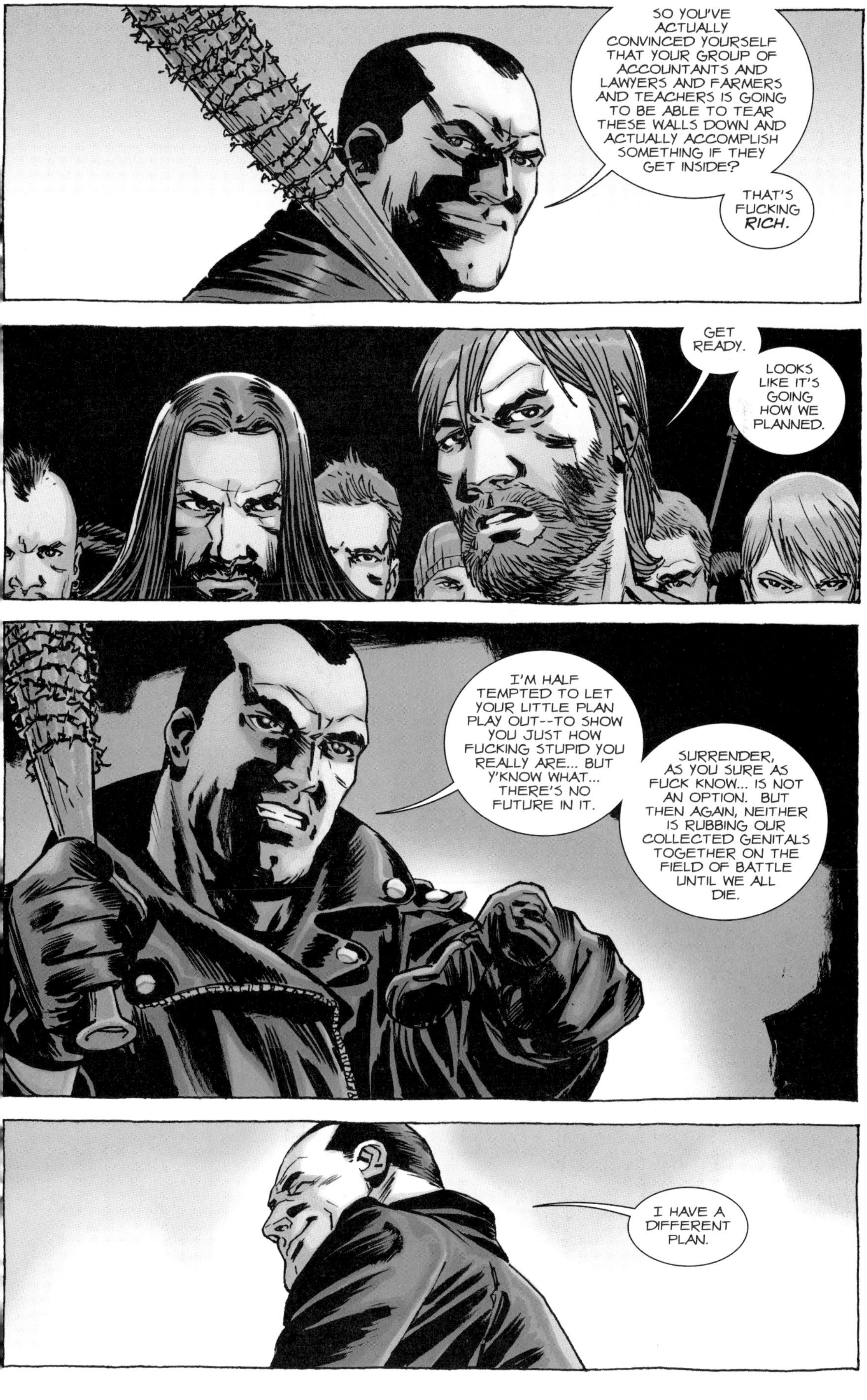
SO YOU'VE ACTUALLY CONVINCED YOURSELF THAT YOUR GROUP OF ACCOUNTANTS AND LAWYERS AND FARMERS AND TEACHERS IS GOING TO BE ABLE TO TEAR THESE WALLS DOWN AND ACTUALLY ACCOMPLISH SOMETHING IF THEY GET INSIDE?
THAT'S FUCKING *RICH.*
GET READY.
LOOKS LIKE IT'S GOING HOW WE PLANNED.
I'M HALF TEMPTED TO LET YOUR LITTLE PLAN PLAY OUT--TO SHOW YOU JUST HOW FUCKING STUPID YOU REALLY ARE... BUT Y'KNOW WHAT... THERE'S NO FUTURE IN IT.
SURRENDER, AS YOU SURE AS FUCK KNOW... IS NOT AN OPTION. BUT THEN AGAIN, NEITHER IS RUBBING OUR COLLECTED GENITALS TOGETHER ON THE FIELD OF BATTLE UNTIL WE ALL DIE.
I HAVE A DIFFERENT PLAN.

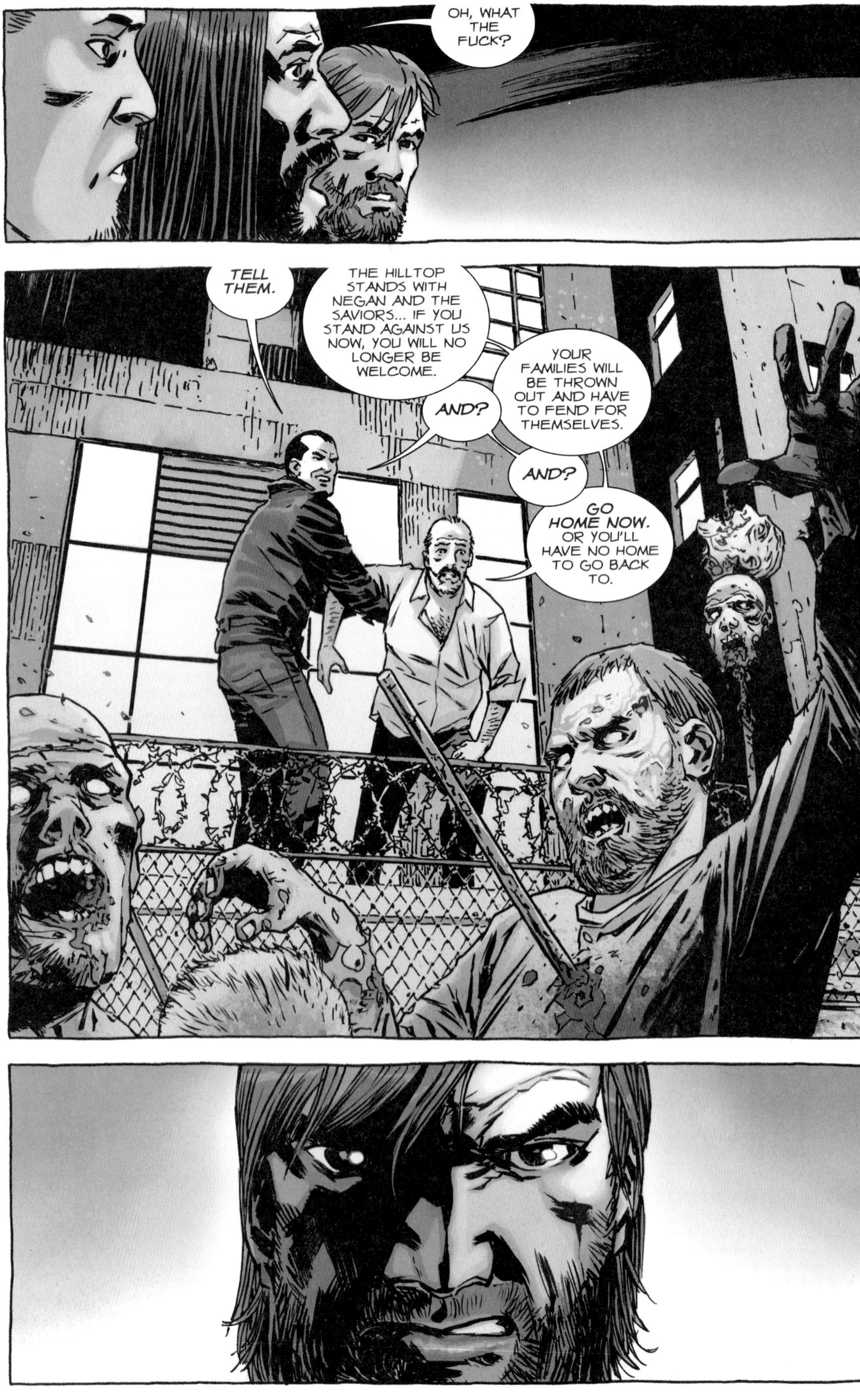
OH, WHAT THE FUCK?
TELL THEM.
THE HILLTOP STANDS WITH NEGAN AND THE SAVIORS... IF YOU STAND AGAINST US NOW, YOU WILL NO LONGER BE WELCOME.
AND?
YOUR FAMILIES WILL BE THROWN OUT AND HAVE TO FEND FOR THEMSELVES.
AND?
GO HOME NOW. OR YOU'LL HAVE NO HOME TO GO BACK TO.

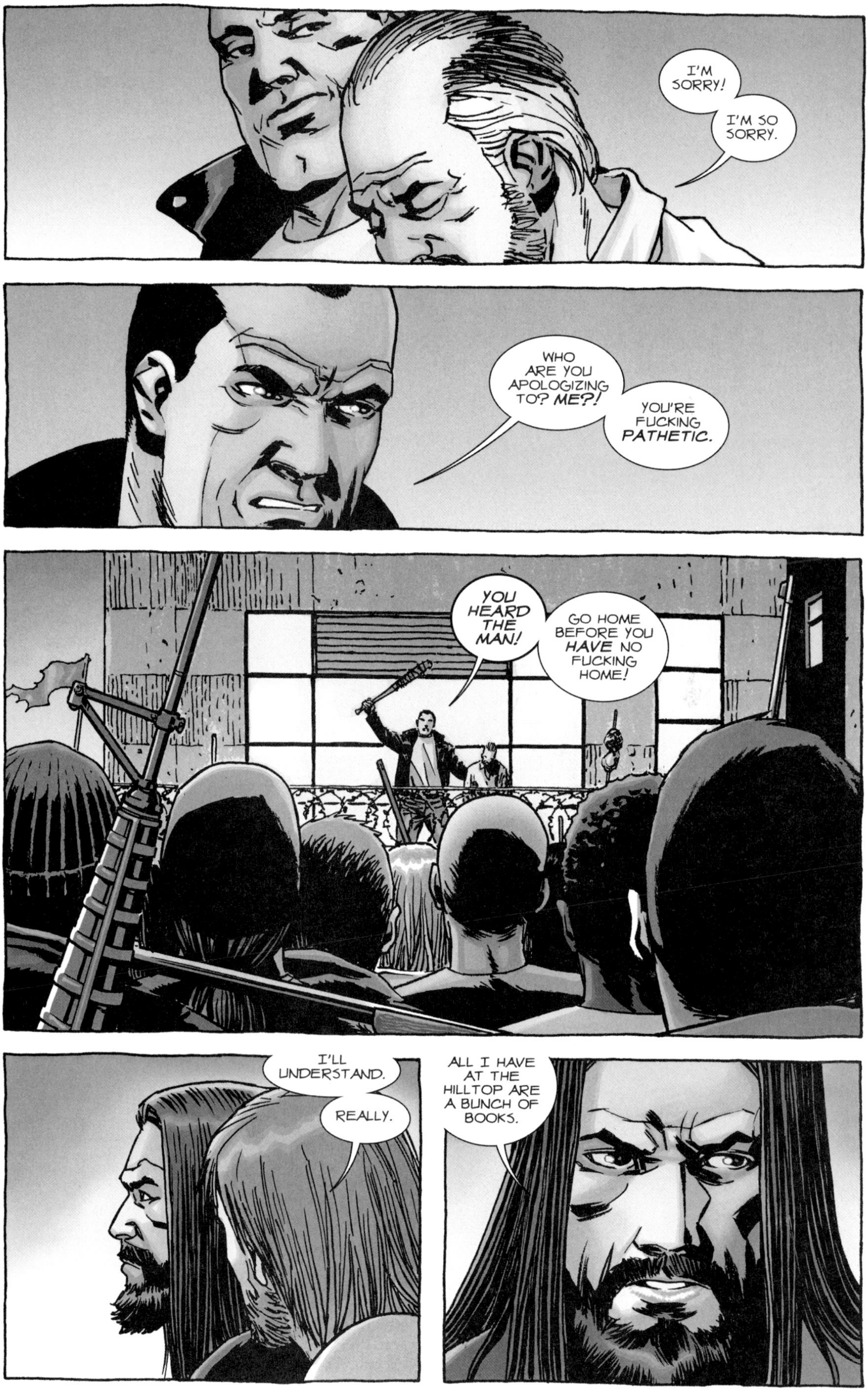
I'M SORRY!
I'M SO SORRY.
WHO ARE YOU APOLOGIZING TO? ME?!
YOU'RE FUCKING PATHETIC.
YOU HEARD THE MAN!
GO HOME BEFORE YOU HAVE NO FUCKING HOME!
I'LL UNDERSTAND.
REALLY.
ALL I HAVE AT THE HILLTOP ARE A BUNCH OF BOOKS.

I'M SORRY, JESUS.

I CAN'T... I GOTTA...

THE FUCK?!

I COUNT *EIGHT* GUYS.

FUCKING EIGHT!

I DIDN'T KNOW... I'M SORRY!

YOU SAID IT WAS *HALF* THEIR FUCKING ARMY!

YOU DIDN'T KNOW HOW MANY FUCKING PEOPLE LEFT YOUR PLACE?! YOU THOUGHT IT WAS MORE THAN EIGHT?!

I THOUGHT IT WAS MORE.

PATHETIC.

WRAMM!

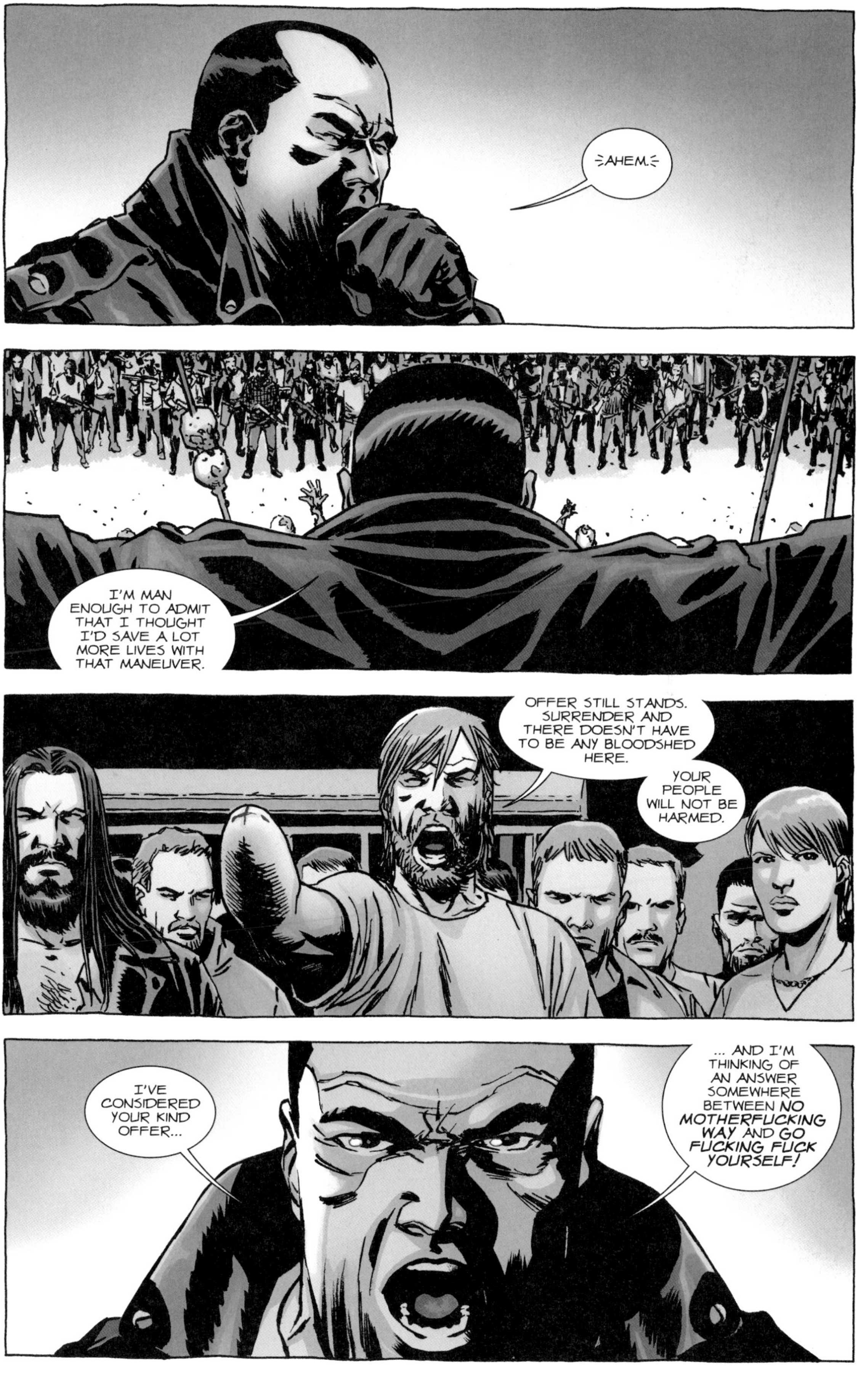
AHEM.
I'M MAN ENOUGH TO ADMIT THAT I THOUGHT I'D SAVE A LOT MORE LIVES WITH THAT MANEUVER.
OFFER STILL STANDS. SURRENDER AND THERE DOESN'T HAVE TO BE ANY BLOODSHED HERE.
YOUR PEOPLE WILL NOT BE HARMED.
I'VE CONSIDERED YOUR KIND OFFER...
... AND I'M THINKING OF AN ANSWER SOMEWHERE BETWEEN NO MOTHERFUCKING WAY AND GO FUCKING FUCK YOURSELF!

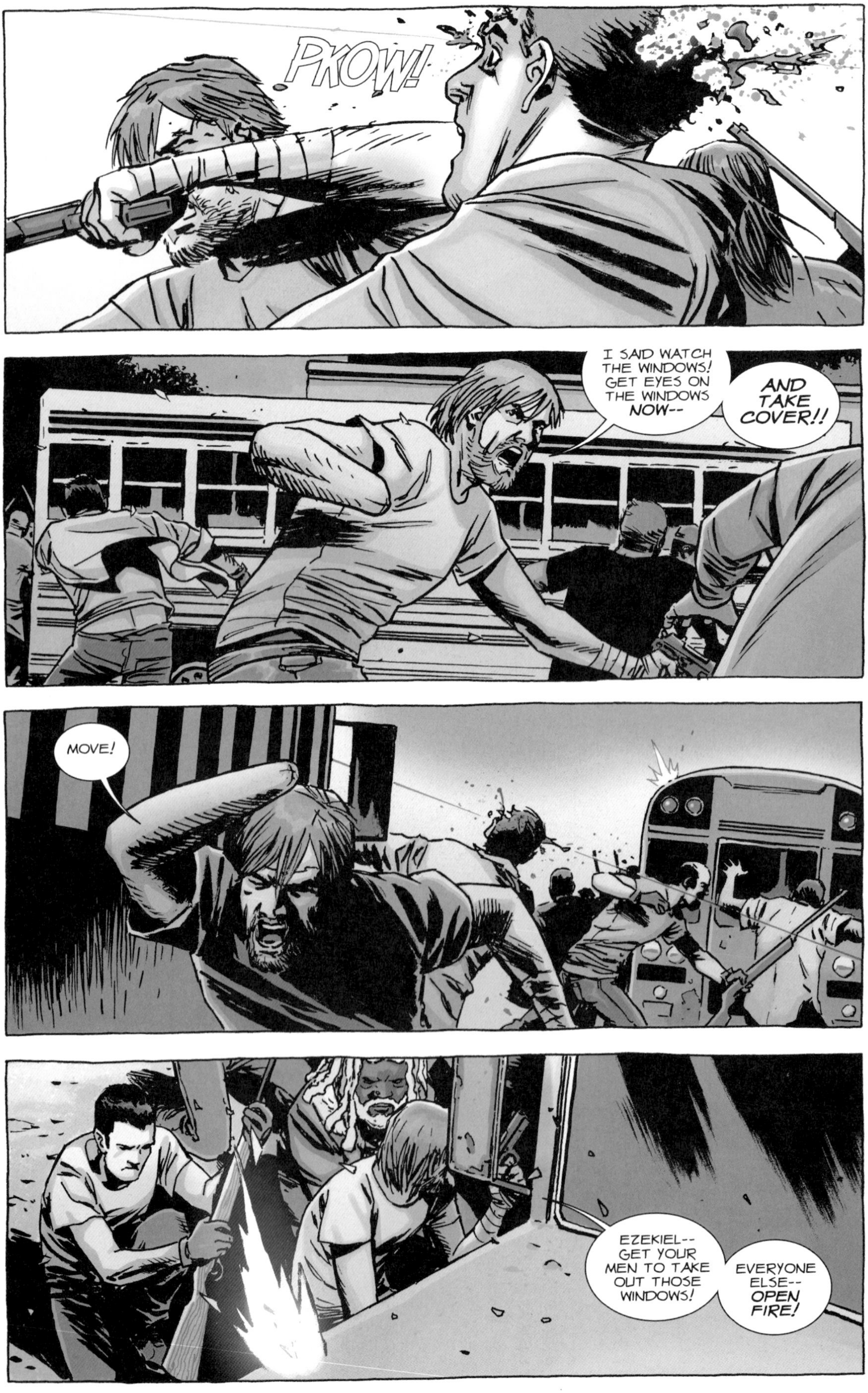
PKOW!
I SAID WATCH THE WINDOWS! GET EYES ON THE WINDOWS NOW--
AND TAKE COVER!!
MOVE!
EZEKIEL-- GET YOUR MEN TO TAKE OUT THOSE WINDOWS!
EVERYONE ELSE-- OPEN FIRE!

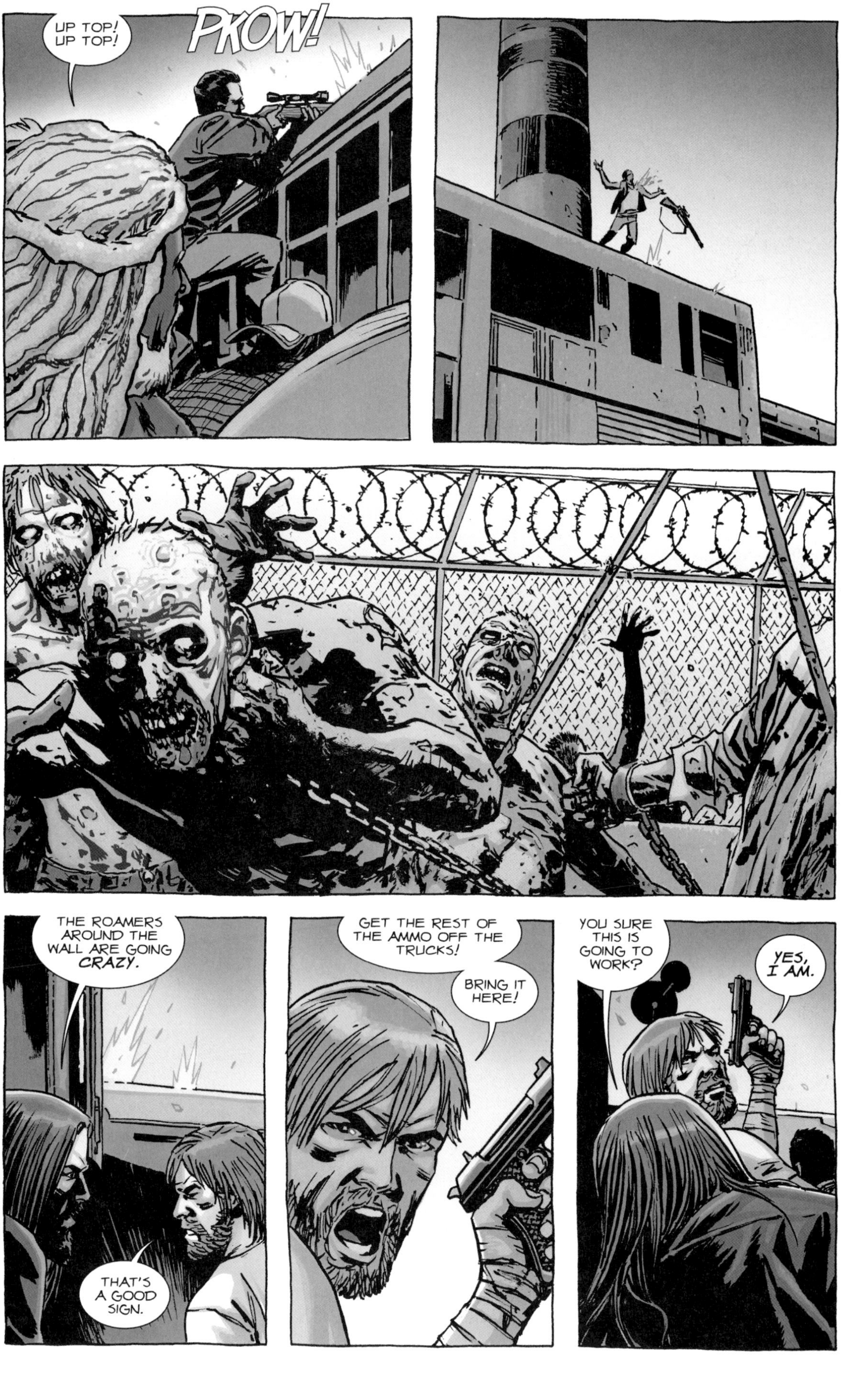
UP TOP! UP TOP!
PKOW!
THE ROAMERS AROUND THE WALL ARE GOING CRAZY.
THAT'S A GOOD SIGN.
GET THE REST OF THE AMMO OFF THE TRUCKS!
BRING IT HERE!
YOU SURE THIS IS GOING TO WORK?
YES, I AM.

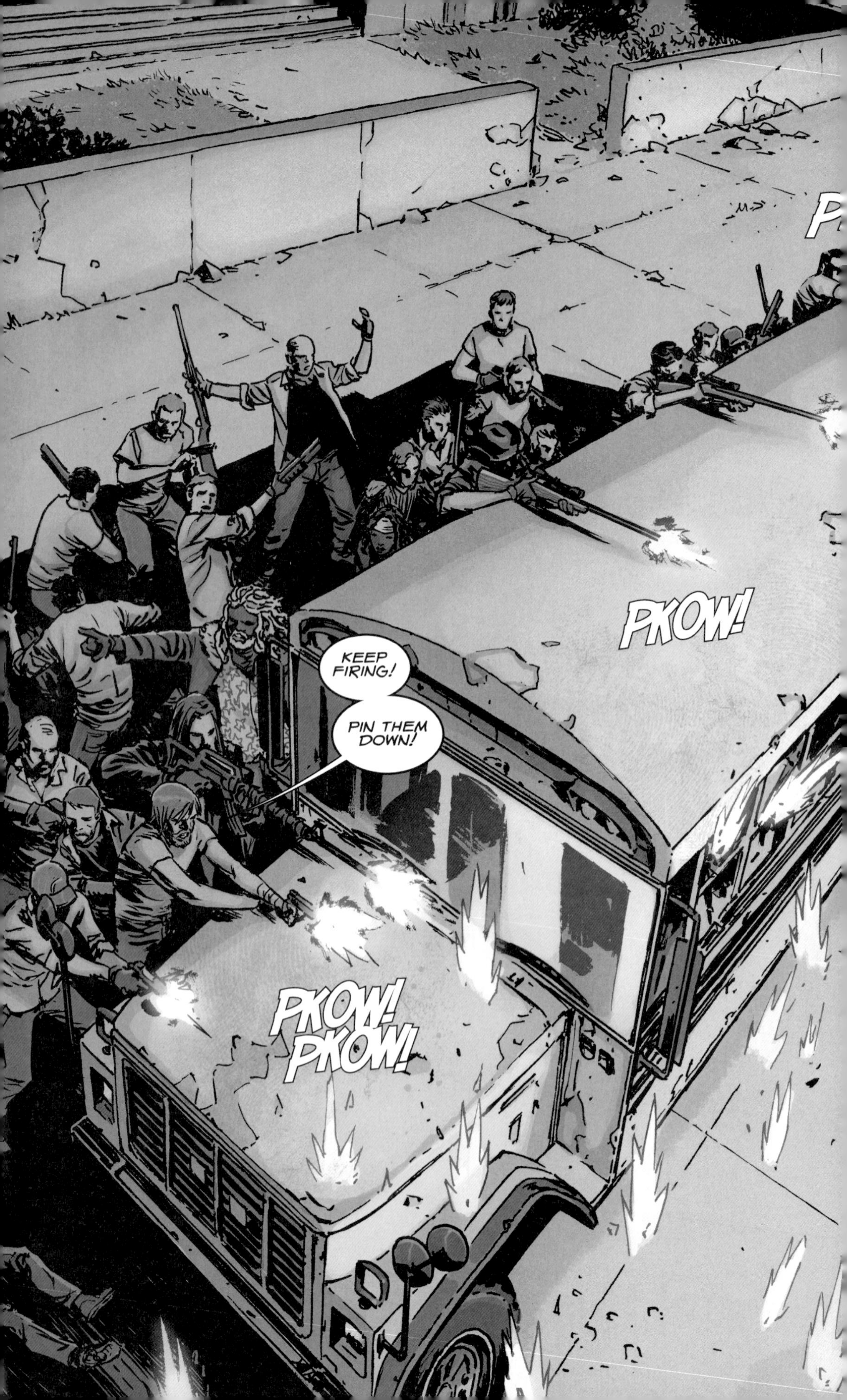
PKOW!
KEEP FIRING!
PIN THEM DOWN!
PKOW! PKOW!

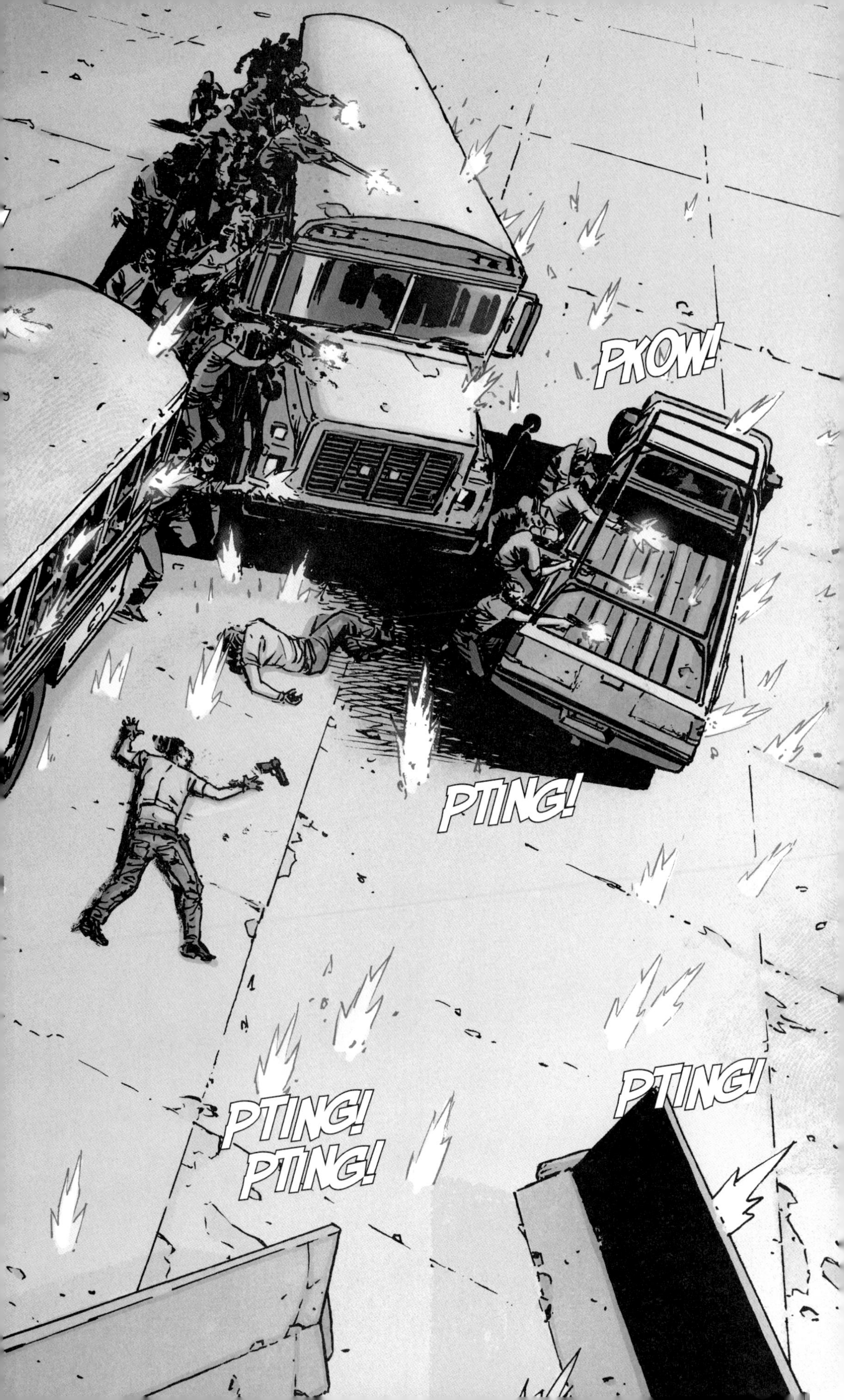
PKOW!
PTING!
PTING!
PTING!
PTING!

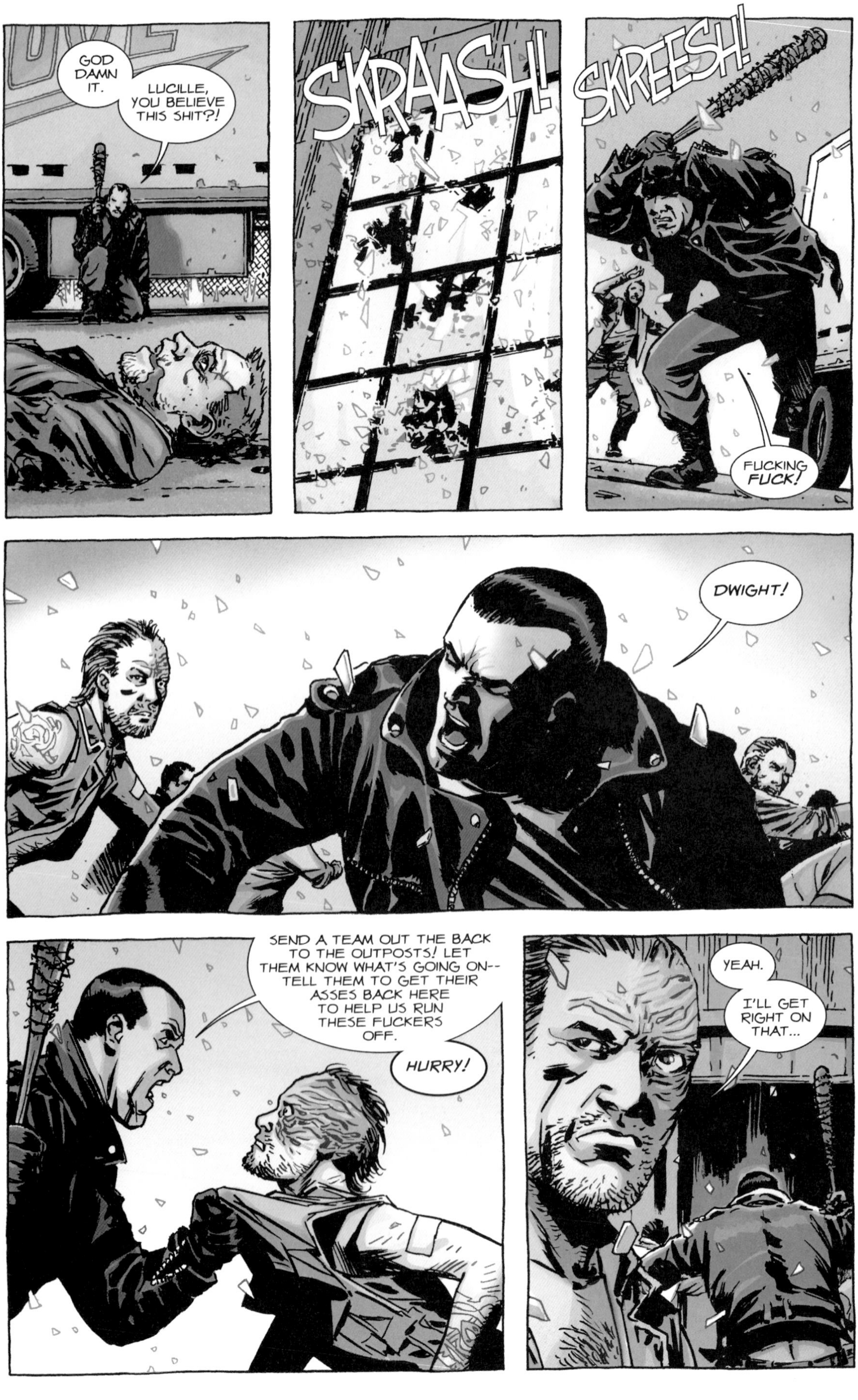
GOD DAMN IT.
LUCILLE, YOU BELIEVE THIS SHIT?!
SKRAASH!
SKREESH!
FUCKING FUCK!
DWIGHT!
SEND A TEAM OUT THE BACK TO THE OUTPOSTS! LET THEM KNOW WHAT'S GOING ON-- TELL THEM TO GET THEIR ASSES BACK HERE TO HELP US RUN THESE FUCKERS OFF.
HURRY!
YEAH.
I'LL GET RIGHT ON THAT...

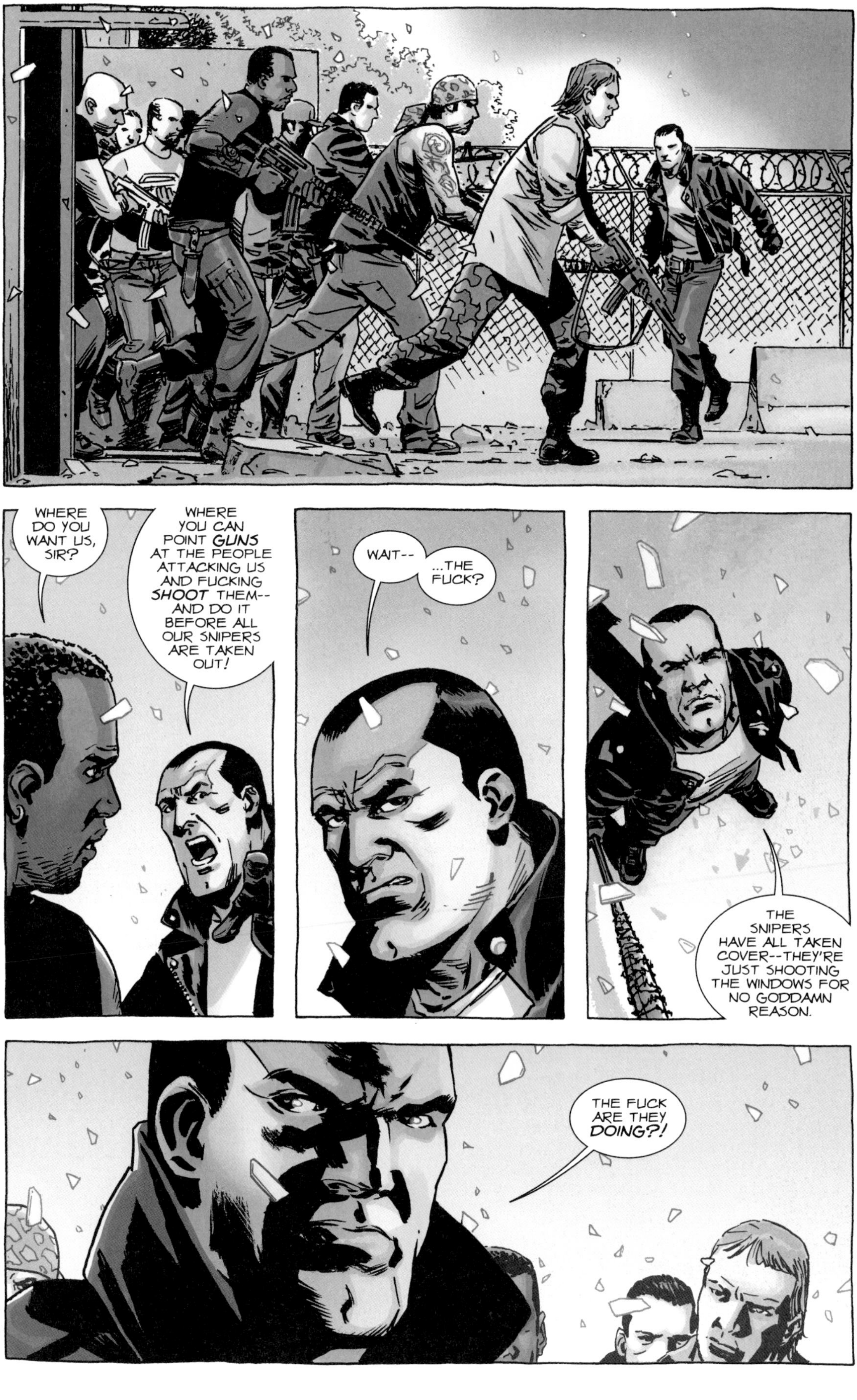

WHERE DO YOU WANT US, SIR?
WHERE YOU CAN POINT GUNS AT THE PEOPLE ATTACKING US AND FUCKING SHOOT THEM-- AND DO IT BEFORE ALL OUR SNIPERS ARE TAKEN OUT!
WAIT--
...THE FUCK?
THE SNIPERS HAVE ALL TAKEN COVER--THEY'RE JUST SHOOTING THE WINDOWS FOR NO GODDAMN REASON.
THE FUCK ARE THEY DOING?!

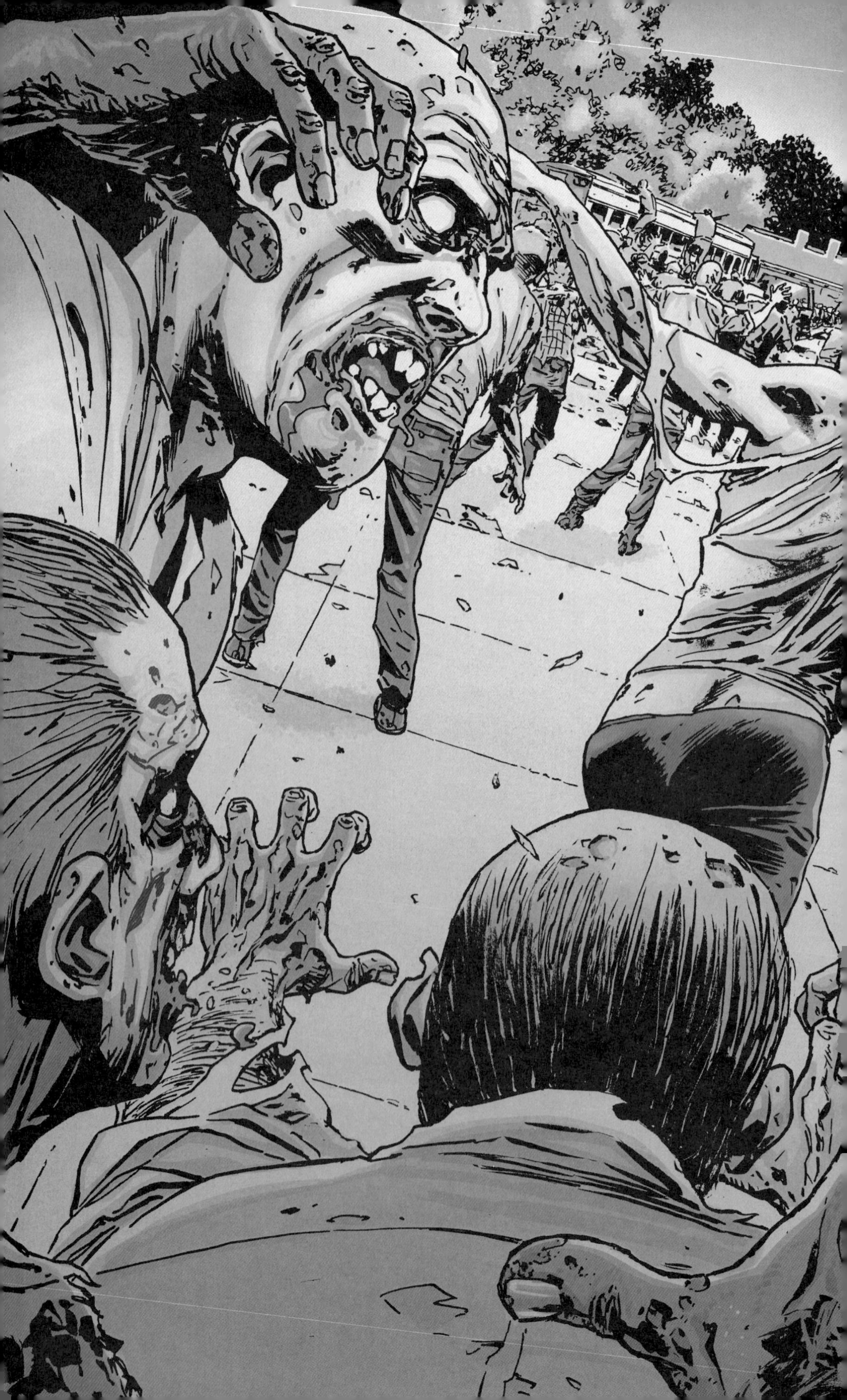

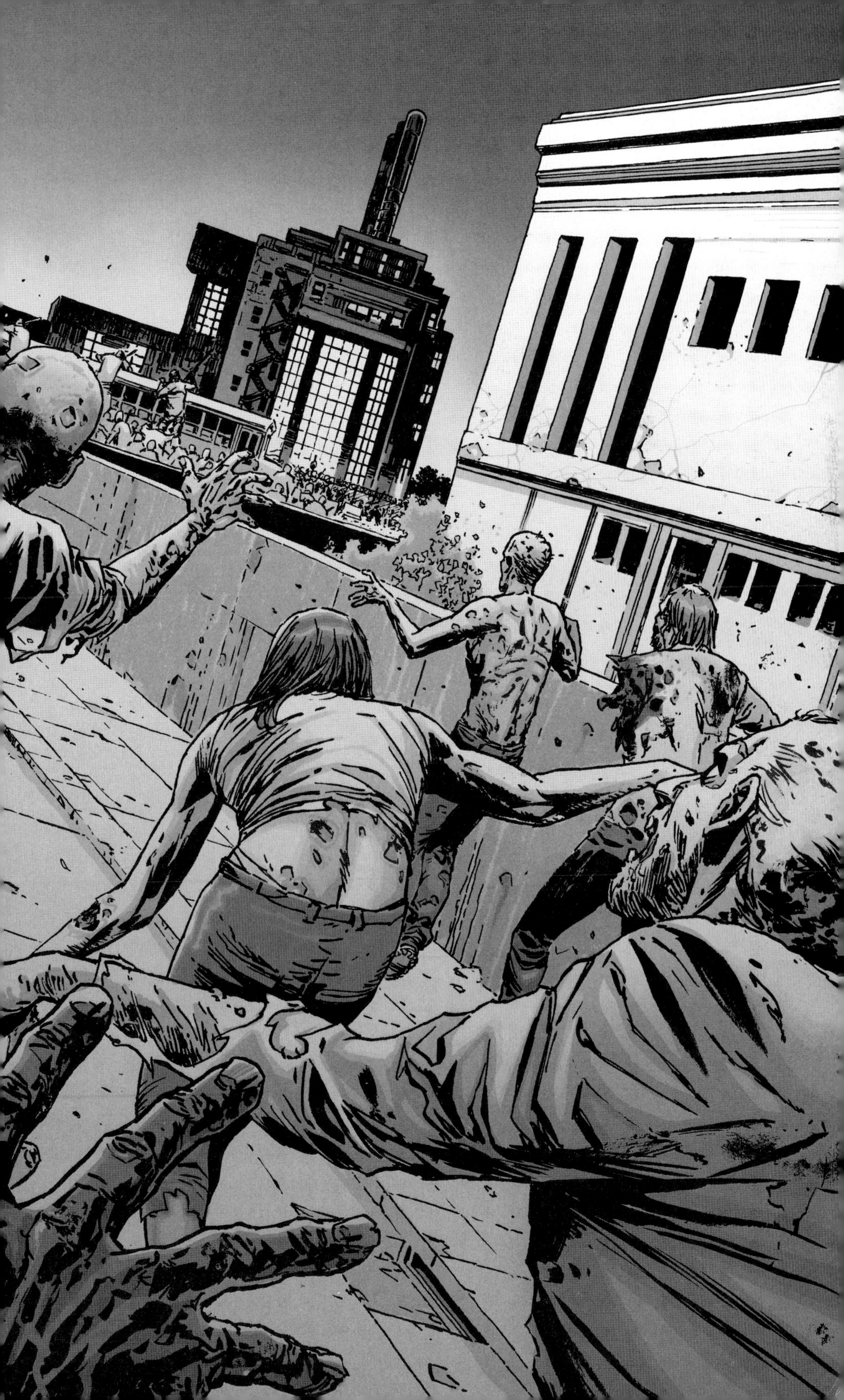

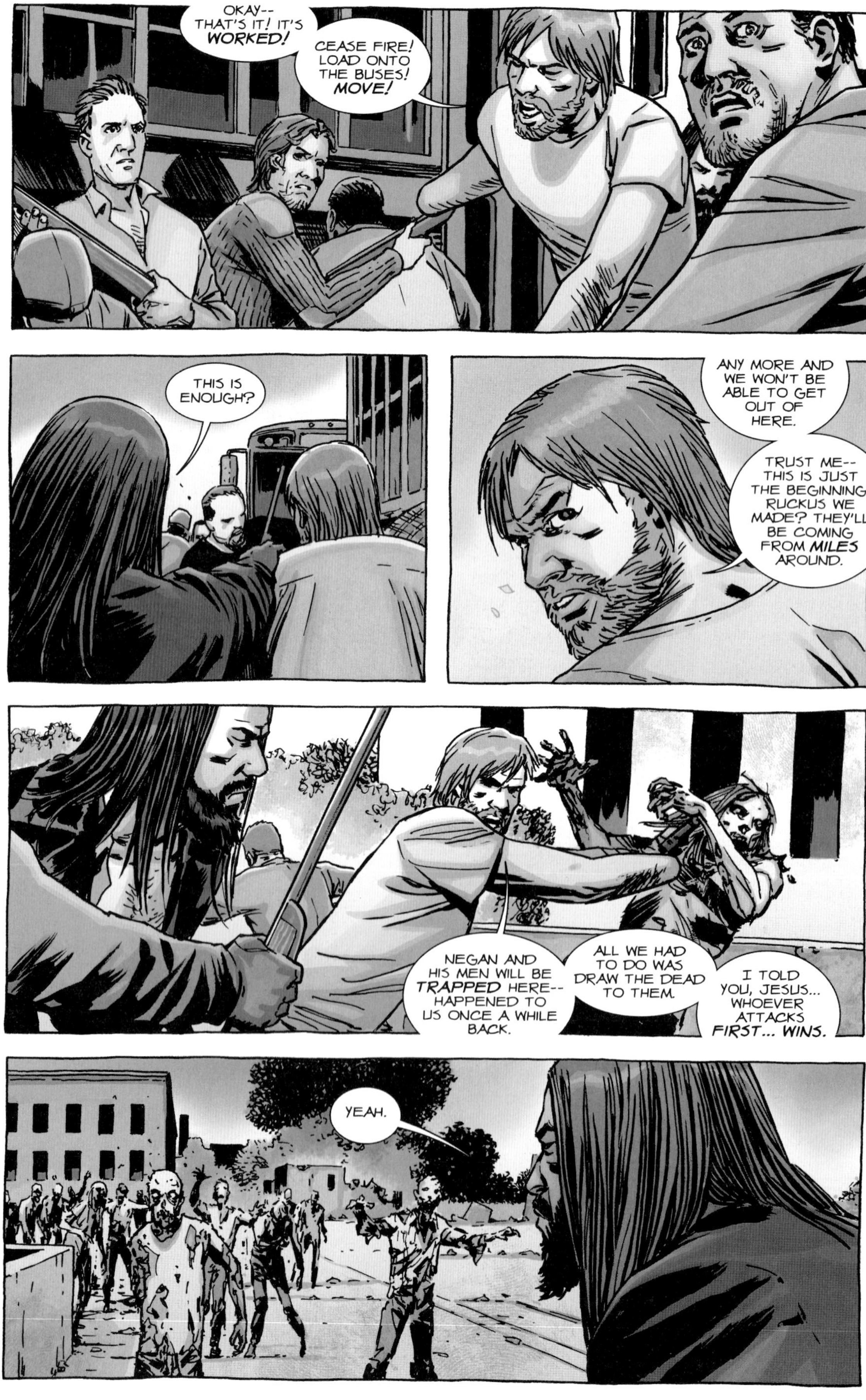
OKAY-- THAT'S IT! IT'S WORKED!
CEASE FIRE! LOAD ONTO THE BUSES! MOVE!
THIS IS ENOUGH?
ANY MORE AND WE WON'T BE ABLE TO GET OUT OF HERE.
TRUST ME-- THIS IS JUST THE BEGINNING. RUCKUS WE MADE? THEY'LL BE COMING FROM MILES AROUND.
NEGAN AND HIS MEN WILL BE TRAPPED HERE-- HAPPENED TO US ONCE A WHILE BACK.
ALL WE HAD TO DO WAS DRAW THE DEAD TO THEM.
I TOLD YOU, JESUS... WHOEVER ATTACKS FIRST... WINS.
YEAH.

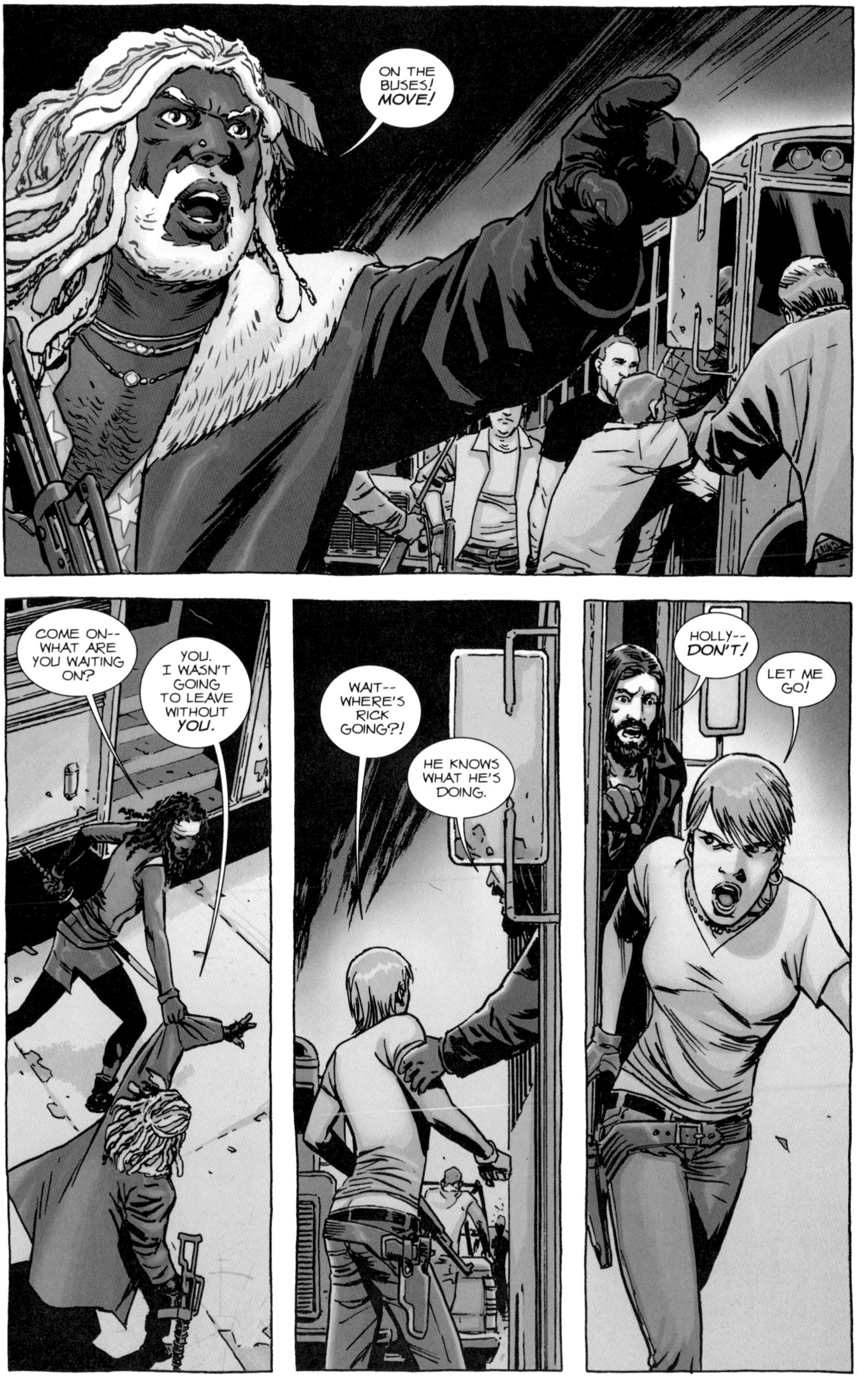

ON THE BUSES! *MOVE!*
COME ON-- WHAT ARE YOU WAITING ON?
YOU. I WASN'T GOING TO LEAVE WITHOUT *YOU*.
WAIT-- WHERE'S RICK GOING?!
HE KNOWS WHAT HE'S DOING.
HOLLY-- *DON'T!*
LET ME GO!

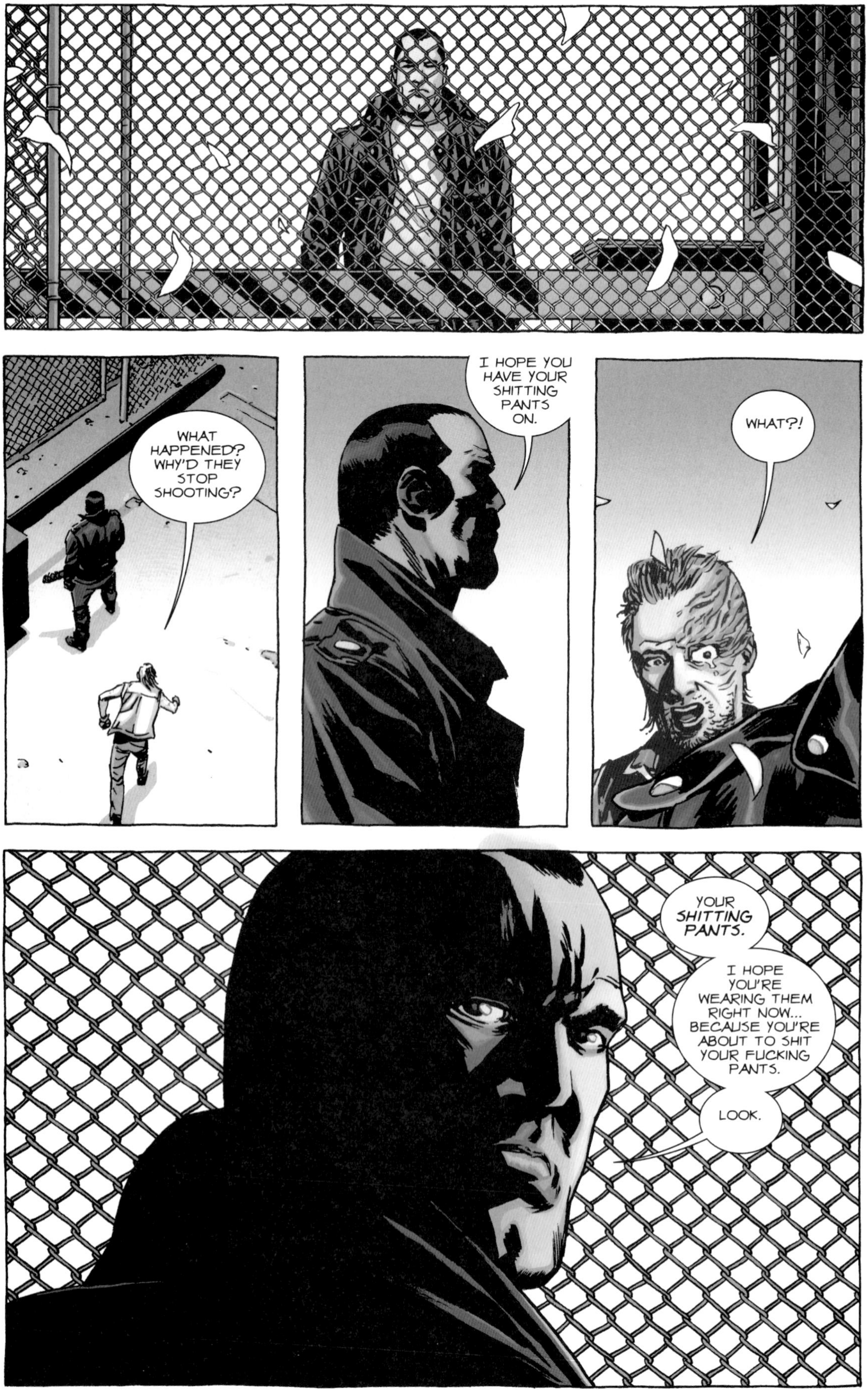
WHAT HAPPENED? WHY'D THEY STOP SHOOTING?
I HOPE YOU HAVE YOUR SHITTING PANTS ON.
WHAT?!
YOUR SHITTING PANTS.
I HOPE YOU'RE WEARING THEM RIGHT NOW... BECAUSE YOU'RE ABOUT TO SHIT YOUR FUCKING PANTS.
LOOK.

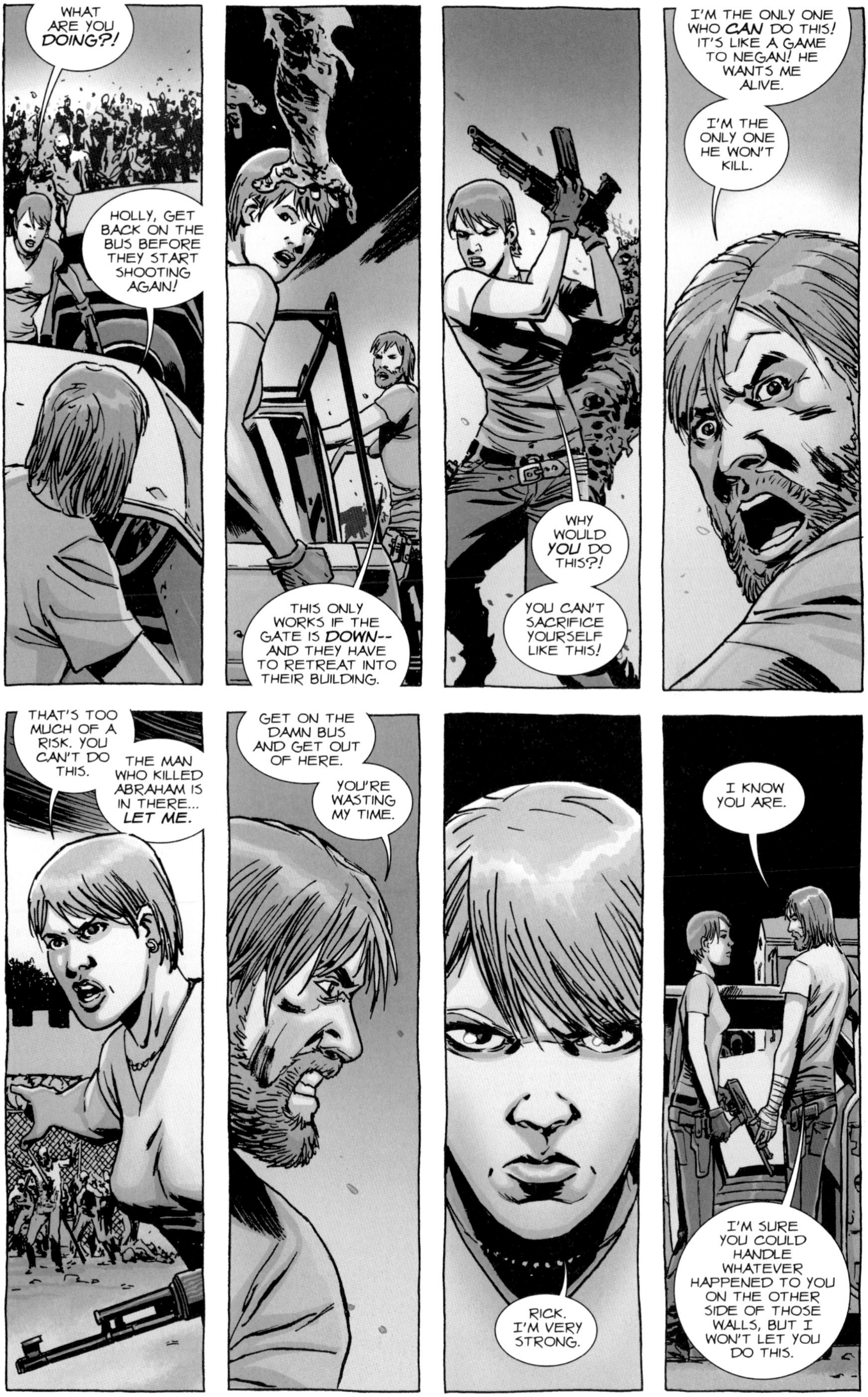

WHAT ARE YOU DOING?!
HOLLY, GET BACK ON THE BUS BEFORE THEY START SHOOTING AGAIN!
THIS ONLY WORKS IF THE GATE IS DOWN-- AND THEY HAVE TO RETREAT INTO THEIR BUILDING.
WHY WOULD YOU DO THIS?!
YOU CAN'T SACRIFICE YOURSELF LIKE THIS!
I'M THE ONLY ONE WHO CAN DO THIS! IT'S LIKE A GAME TO NEGAN! HE WANTS ME ALIVE.
I'M THE ONLY ONE HE WON'T KILL.
THAT'S TOO MUCH OF A RISK. YOU CAN'T DO THIS.
THE MAN WHO KILLED ABRAHAM IS IN THERE... LET ME.
GET ON THE DAMN BUS AND GET OUT OF HERE.
YOU'RE WASTING MY TIME.
RICK. I'M VERY STRONG.
I KNOW YOU ARE.
I'M SURE YOU COULD HANDLE WHATEVER HAPPENED TO YOU ON THE OTHER SIDE OF THOSE WALLS, BUT I WON'T LET YOU DO THIS.

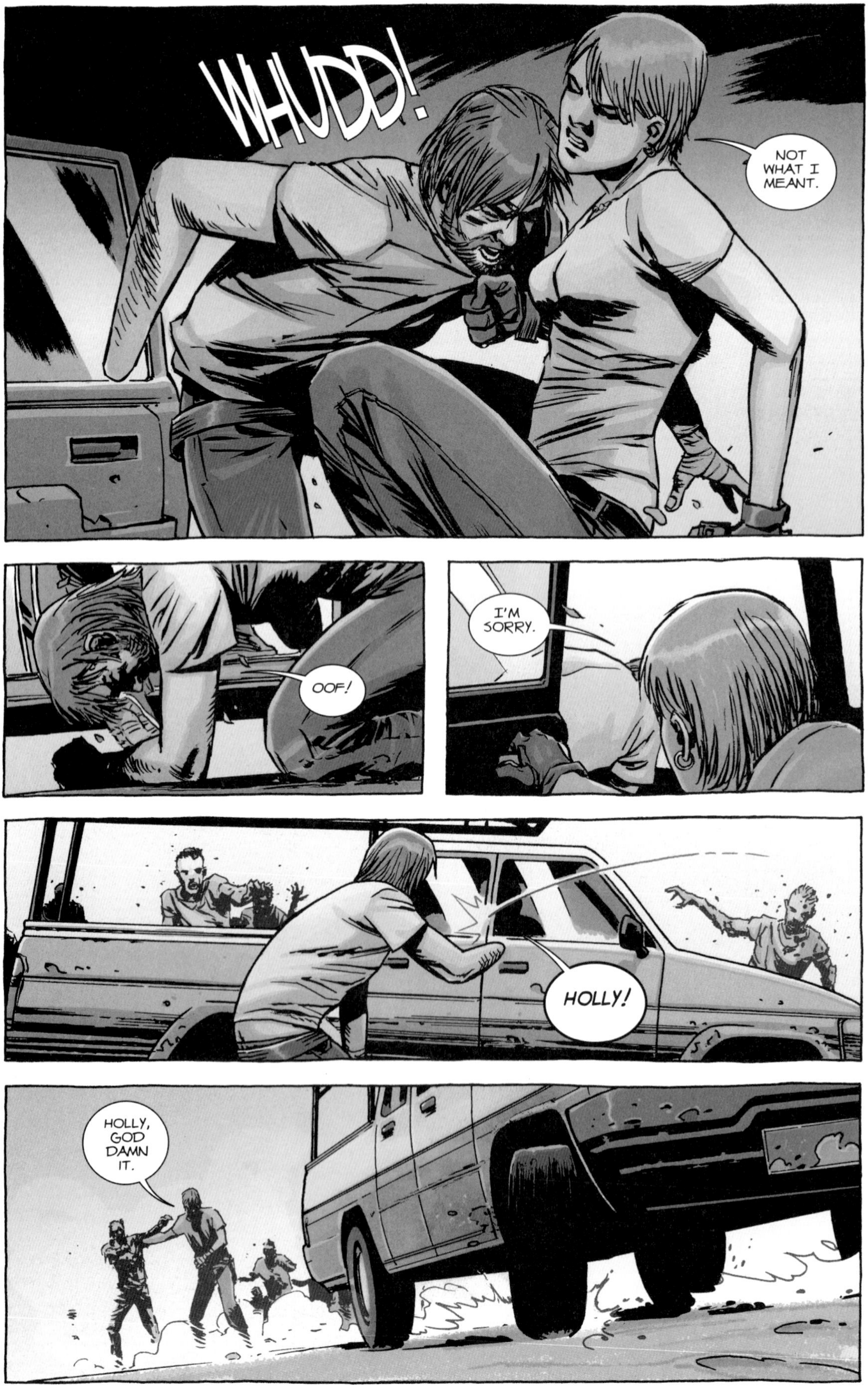
WHUDD!
NOT WHAT I MEANT.
OOF!
I'M SORRY.
HOLLY!
HOLLY, GOD DAMN IT.

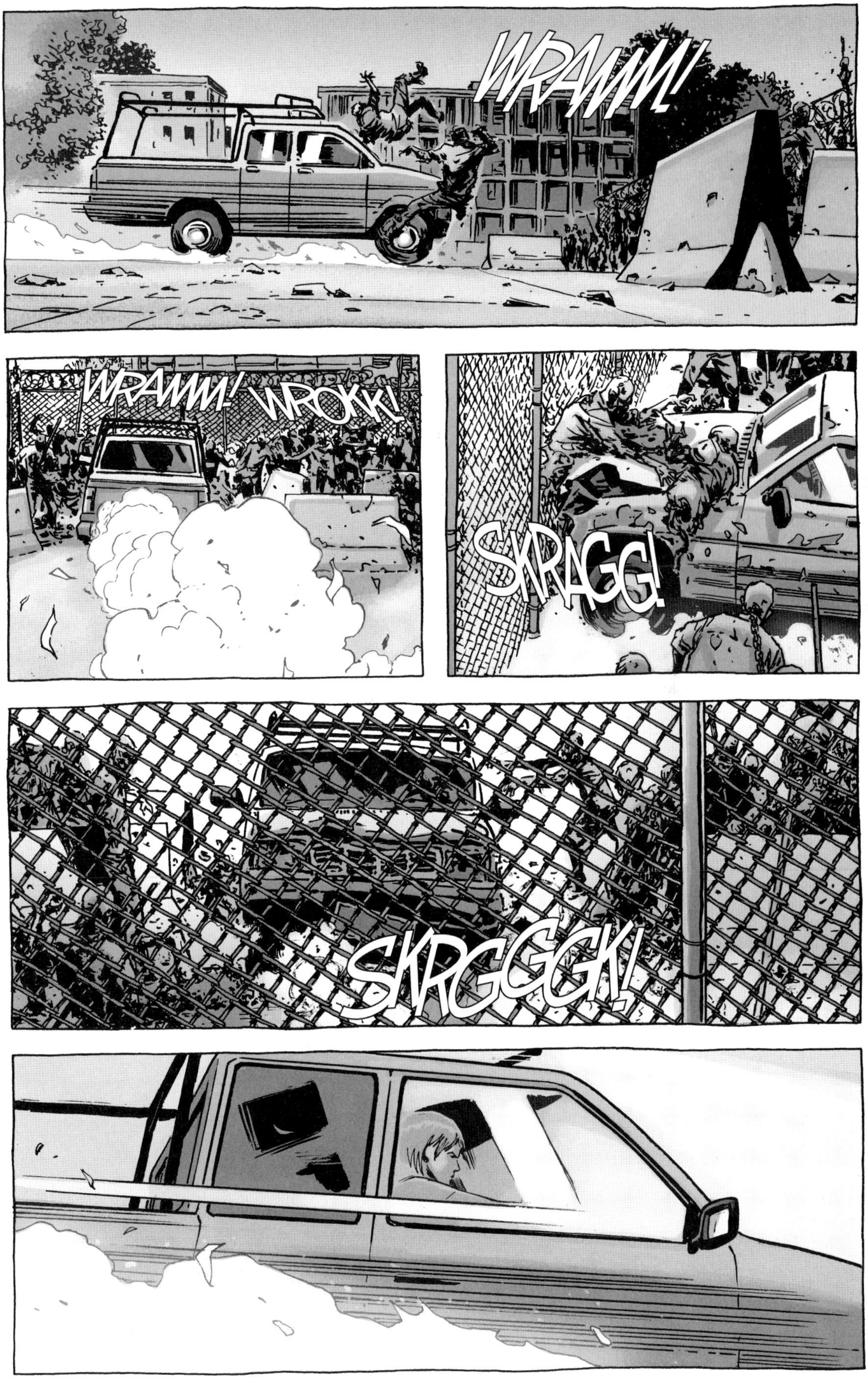
WRAMM!
WRAMM!
WROKK!
SKRAGG!
SKRGGGK!

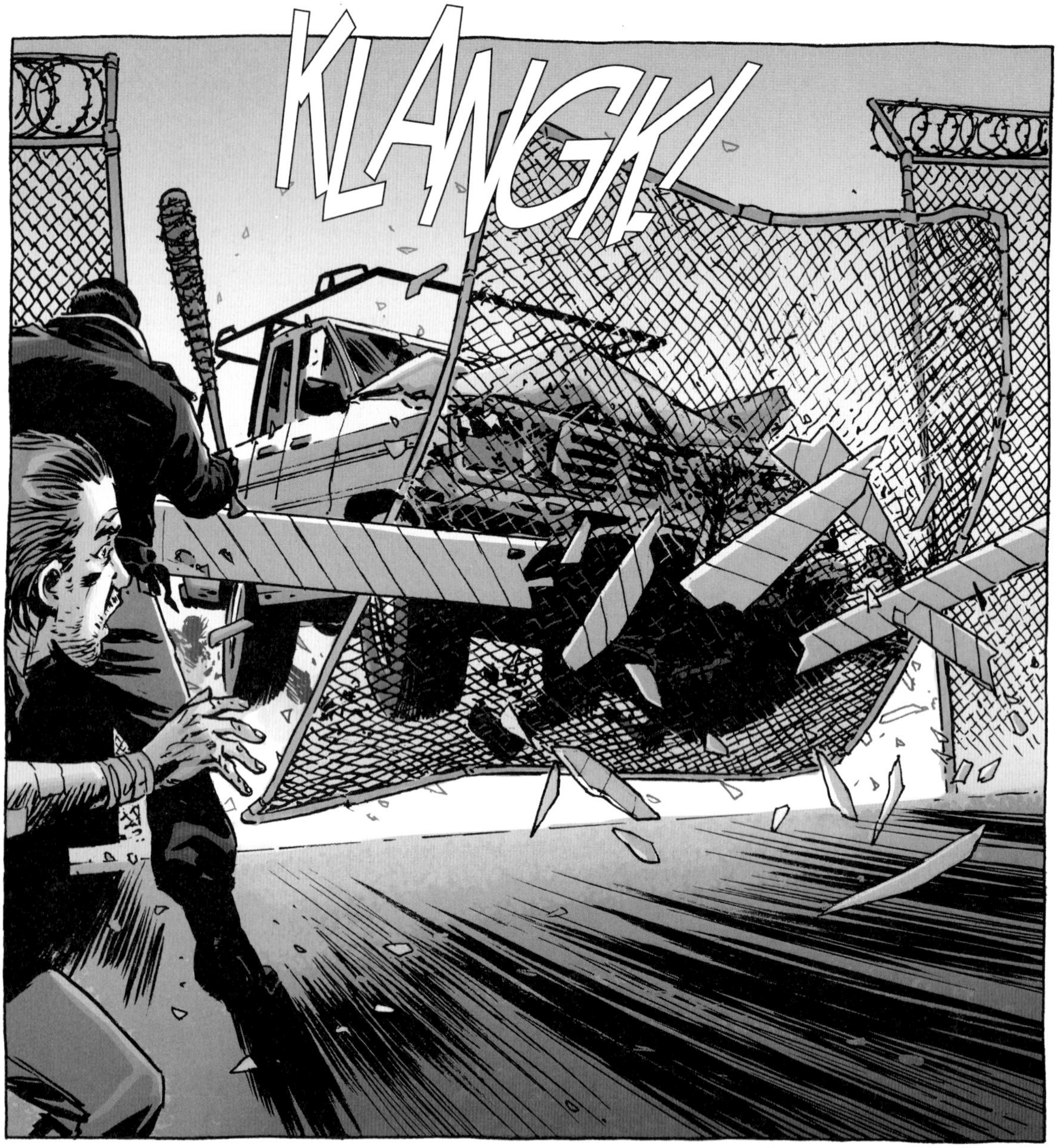
KLANGK!

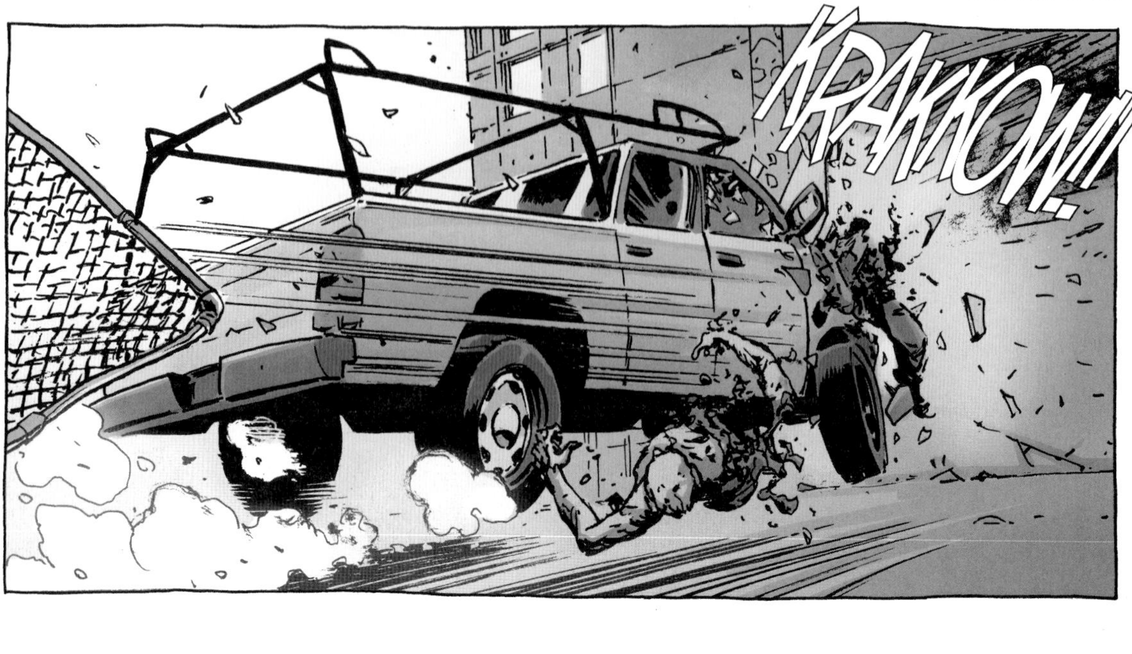
KRAKKOW!!

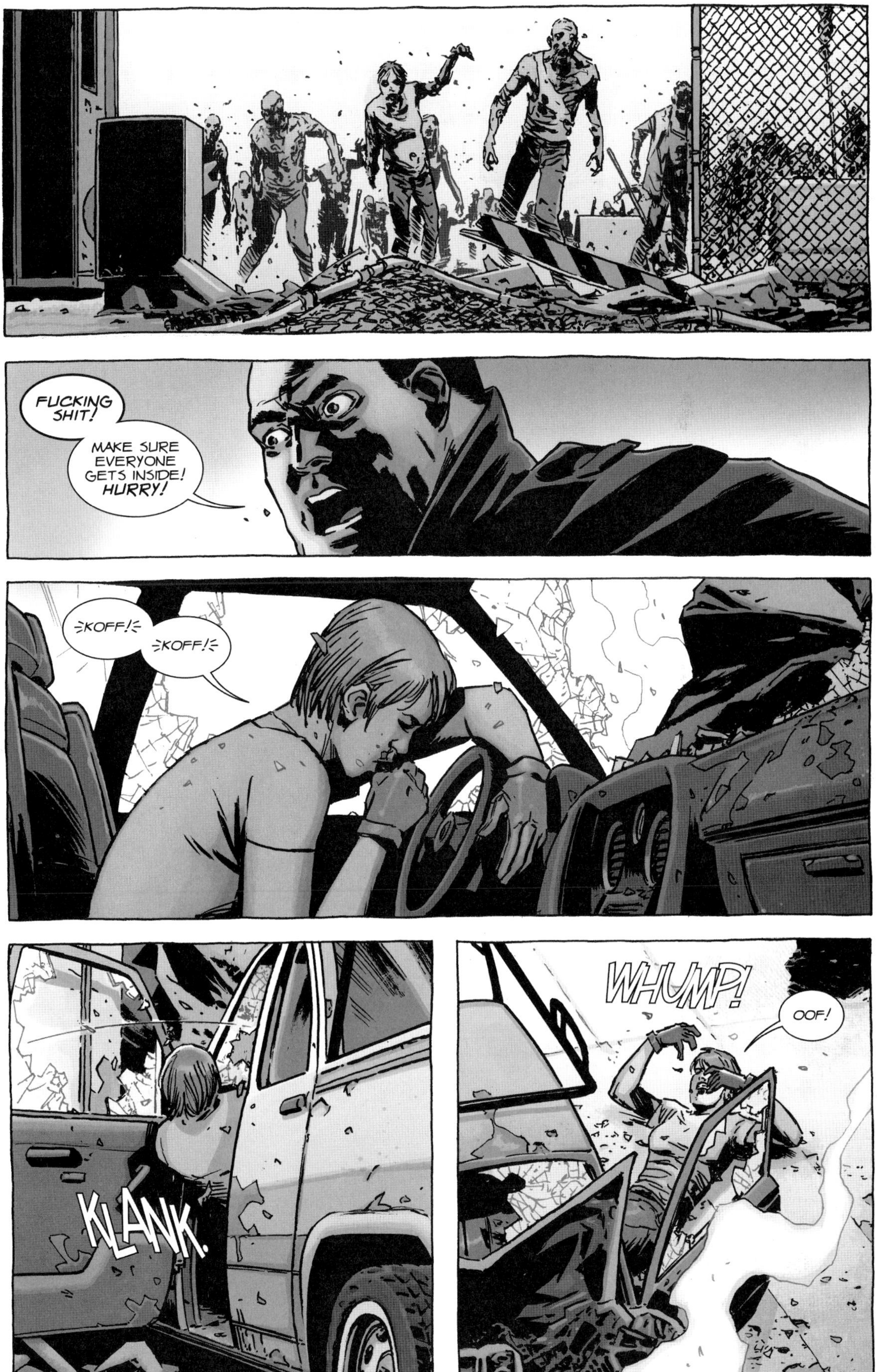

FUCKING SHIT!
MAKE SURE EVERYONE GETS INSIDE! HURRY!
KOFF!
KOFF!
KLANK.
WHUMP!
OOF!

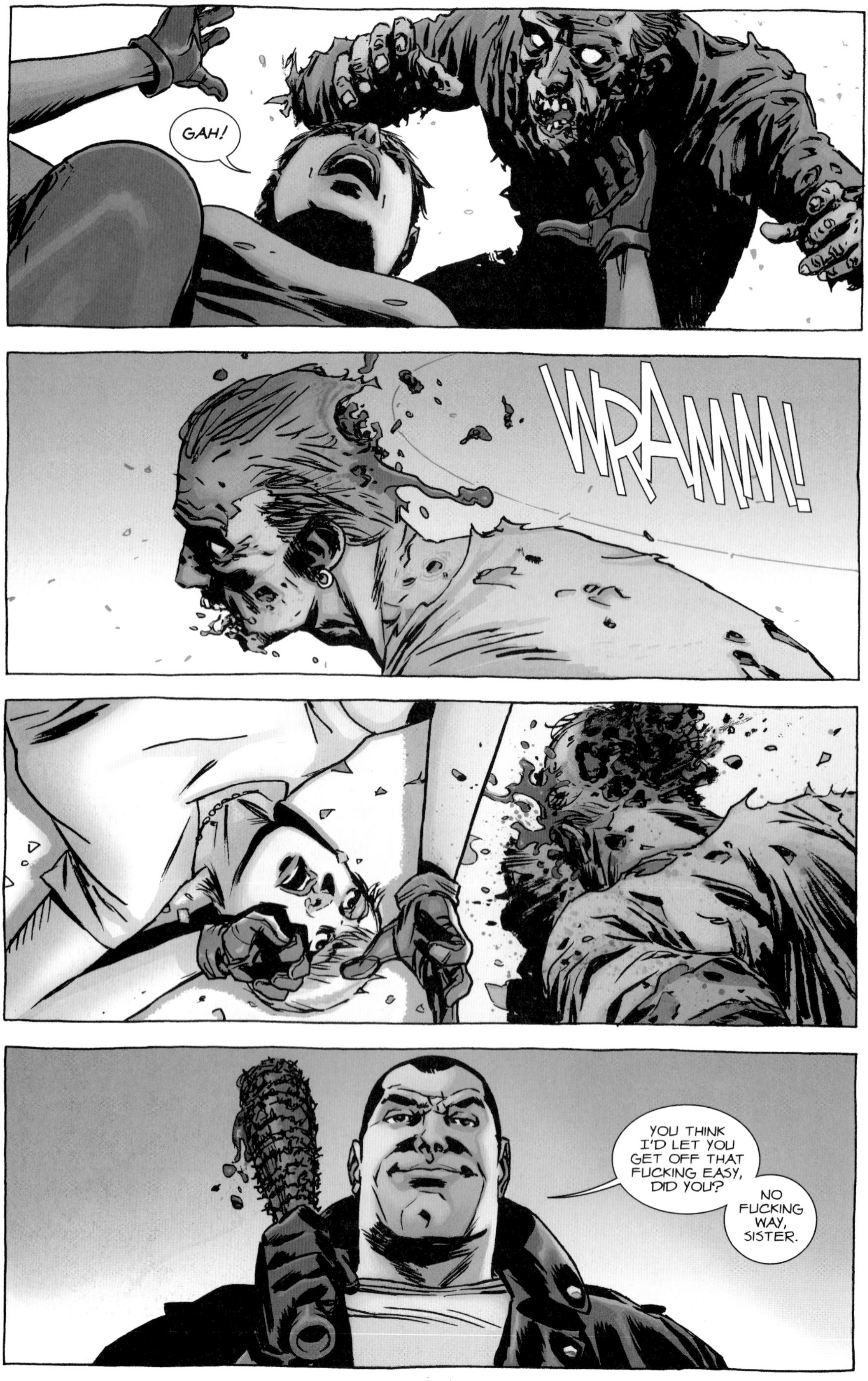
GAH!
WRAMM!
YOU THINK I'D LET YOU GET OFF THAT FUCKING EASY, DID YOU?
NO FUCKING WAY, SISTER.

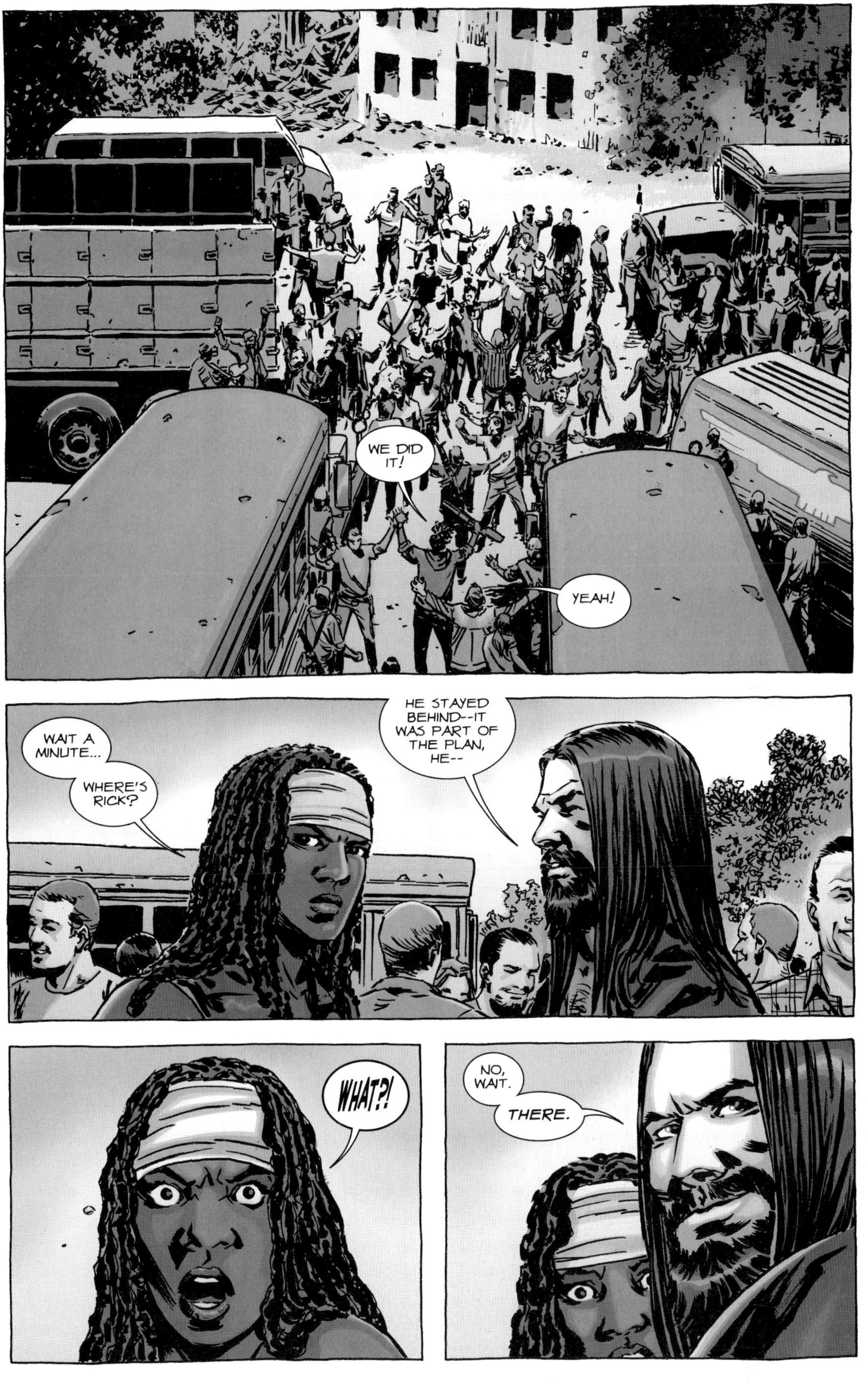
WE DID IT!
YEAH!
WAIT A MINUTE...
WHERE'S RICK?
HE STAYED BEHIND--IT WAS PART OF THE PLAN, HE--
WHAT?!
NO, WAIT.
THERE.

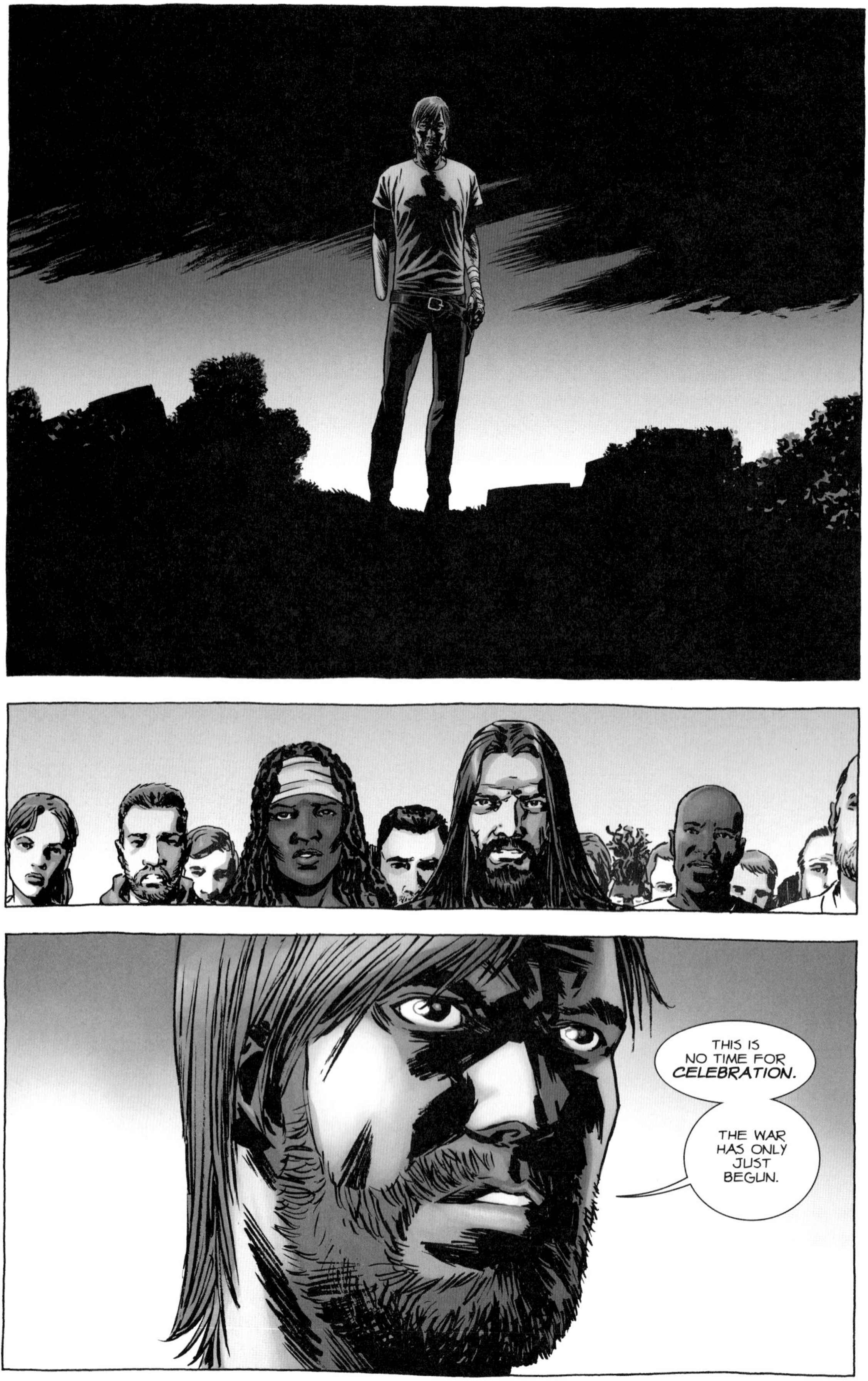
THIS IS NO TIME FOR CELEBRATION.
THE WAR HAS ONLY JUST BEGUN.

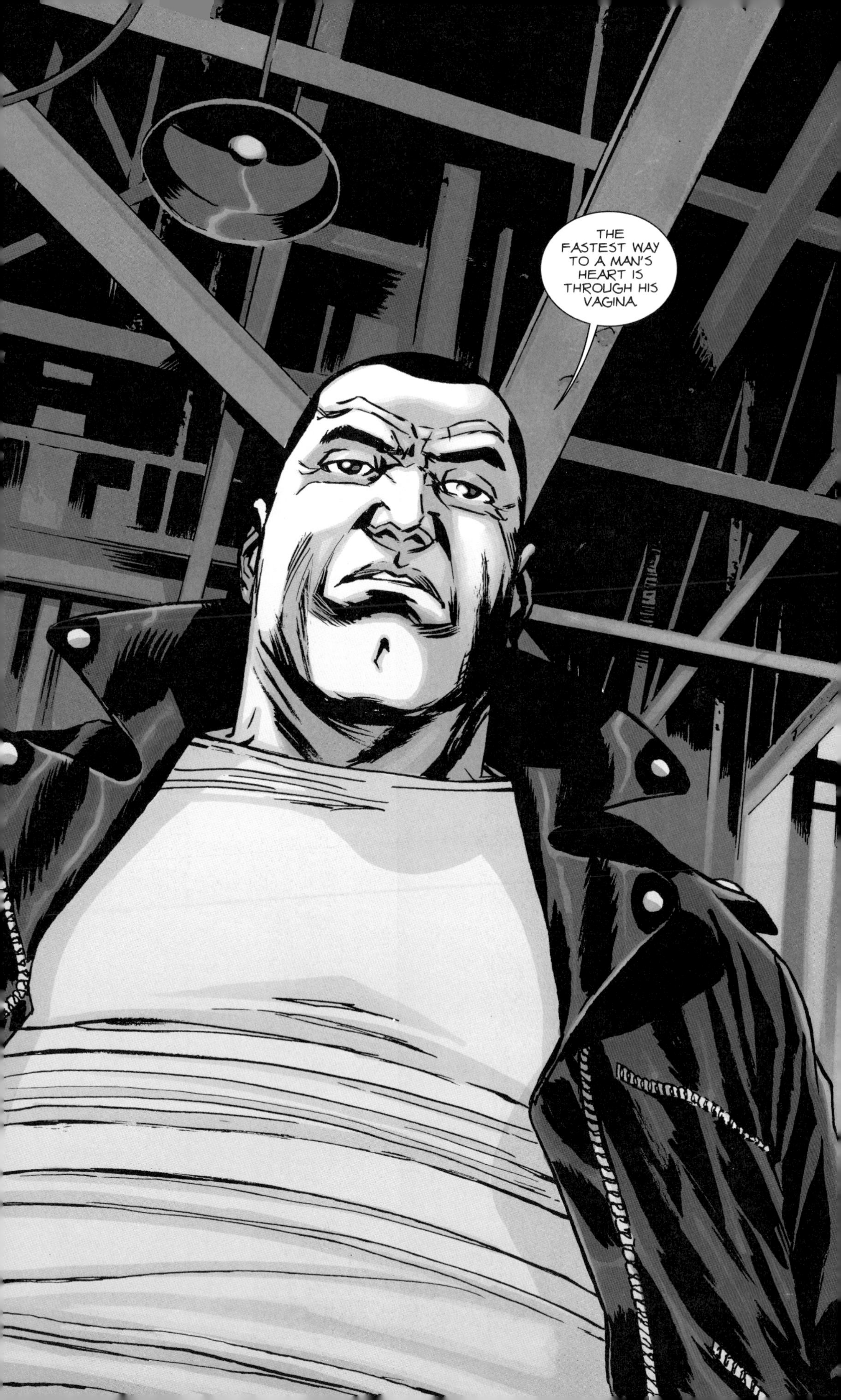
THE FASTEST WAY TO A MAN'S HEART IS THROUGH HIS VAGINA.

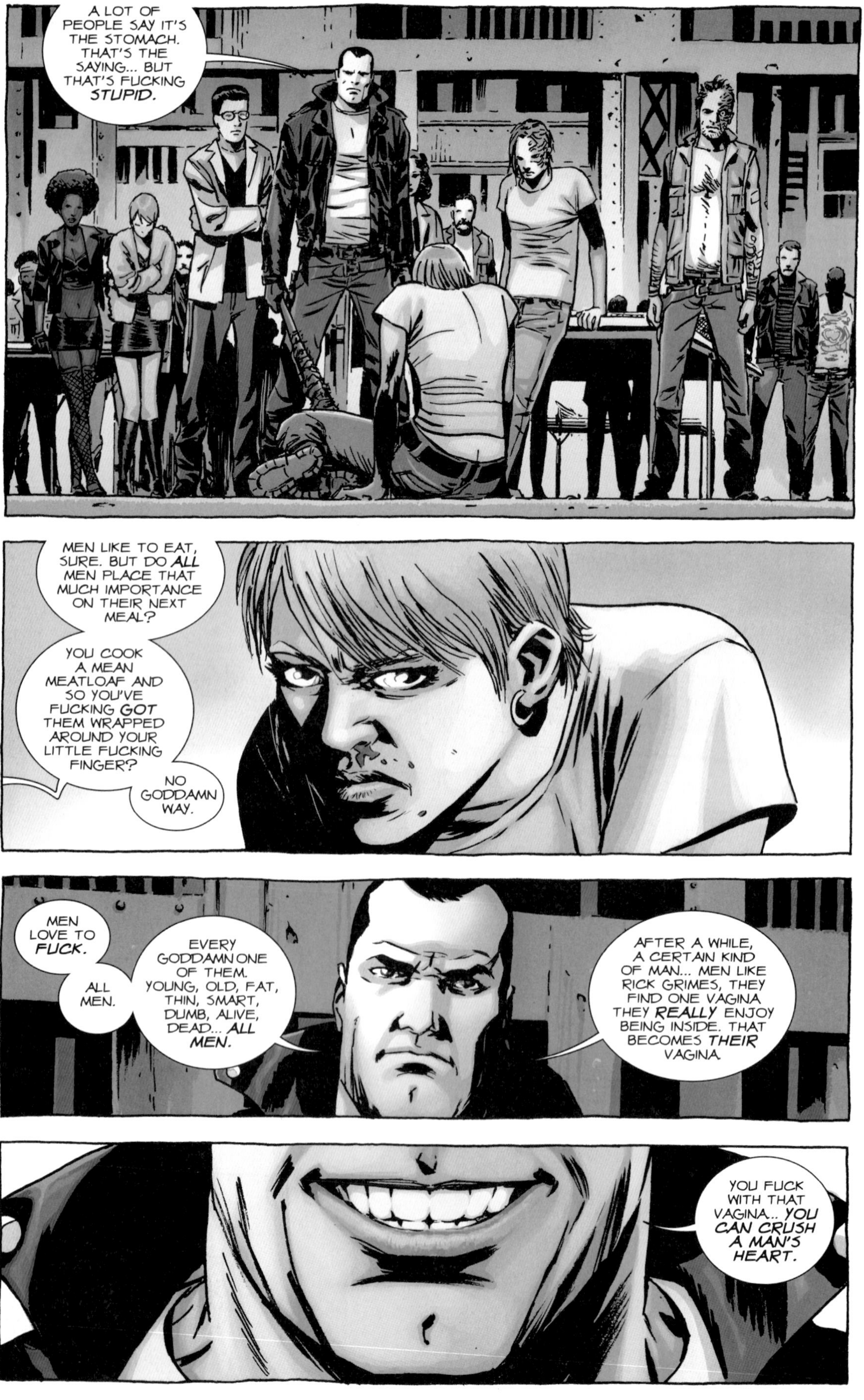
A LOT OF PEOPLE SAY IT'S THE STOMACH. THAT'S THE SAYING... BUT THAT'S FUCKING STUPID.
MEN LIKE TO EAT, SURE. BUT DO ALL MEN PLACE THAT MUCH IMPORTANCE ON THEIR NEXT MEAL?
YOU COOK A MEAN MEATLOAF AND SO YOU'VE FUCKING GOT THEM WRAPPED AROUND YOUR LITTLE FUCKING FINGER?
NO GODDAMN WAY.
MEN LOVE TO FUCK.
ALL MEN.
EVERY GODDAMN ONE OF THEM. YOUNG, OLD, FAT, THIN, SMART, DUMB, ALIVE, DEAD... ALL MEN.
AFTER A WHILE, A CERTAIN KIND OF MAN... MEN LIKE RICK GRIMES, THEY FIND ONE VAGINA THEY REALLY ENJOY BEING INSIDE. THAT BECOMES THEIR VAGINA.
YOU FUCK WITH THAT VAGINA.. YOU CAN CRUSH A MAN'S HEART.

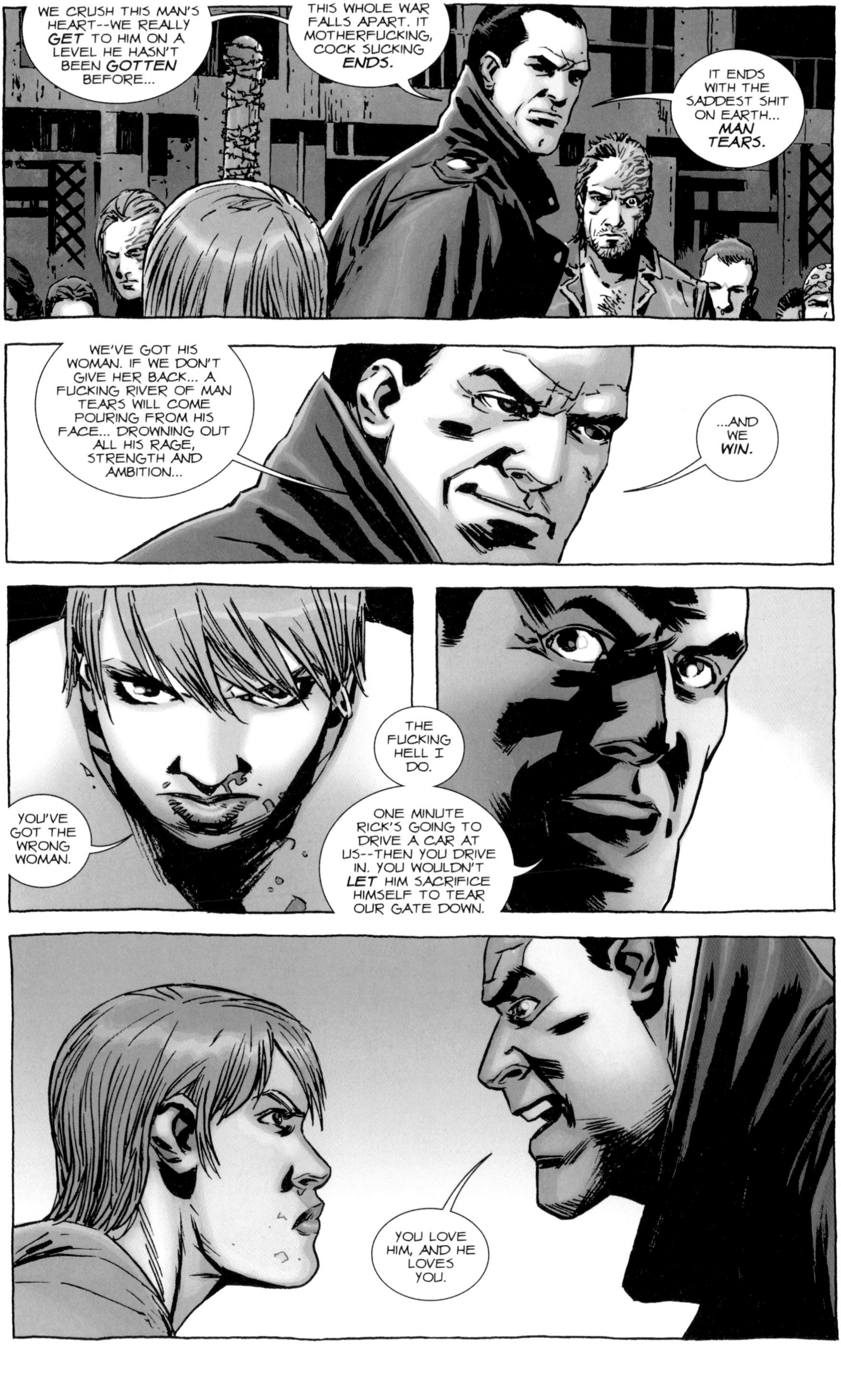

WE CRUSH THIS MAN'S HEART--WE REALLY GET TO HIM ON A LEVEL HE HASN'T BEEN GOTTEN BEFORE...
THIS WHOLE WAR FALLS APART. IT MOTHERFUCKING, COCK SUCKING ENDS.
IT ENDS WITH THE SADDEST SHIT ON EARTH... MAN TEARS.
WE'VE GOT HIS WOMAN. IF WE DON'T GIVE HER BACK... A FUCKING RIVER OF MAN TEARS WILL COME POURING FROM HIS FACE... DROWNING OUT ALL HIS RAGE, STRENGTH AND AMBITION...
...AND WE WIN.
YOU'VE GOT THE WRONG WOMAN.
THE FUCKING HELL I DO.
ONE MINUTE RICK'S GOING TO DRIVE A CAR AT US--THEN YOU DRIVE IN. YOU WOULDN'T LET HIM SACRIFICE HIMSELF TO TEAR OUR GATE DOWN.
YOU LOVE HIM, AND HE LOVES YOU.

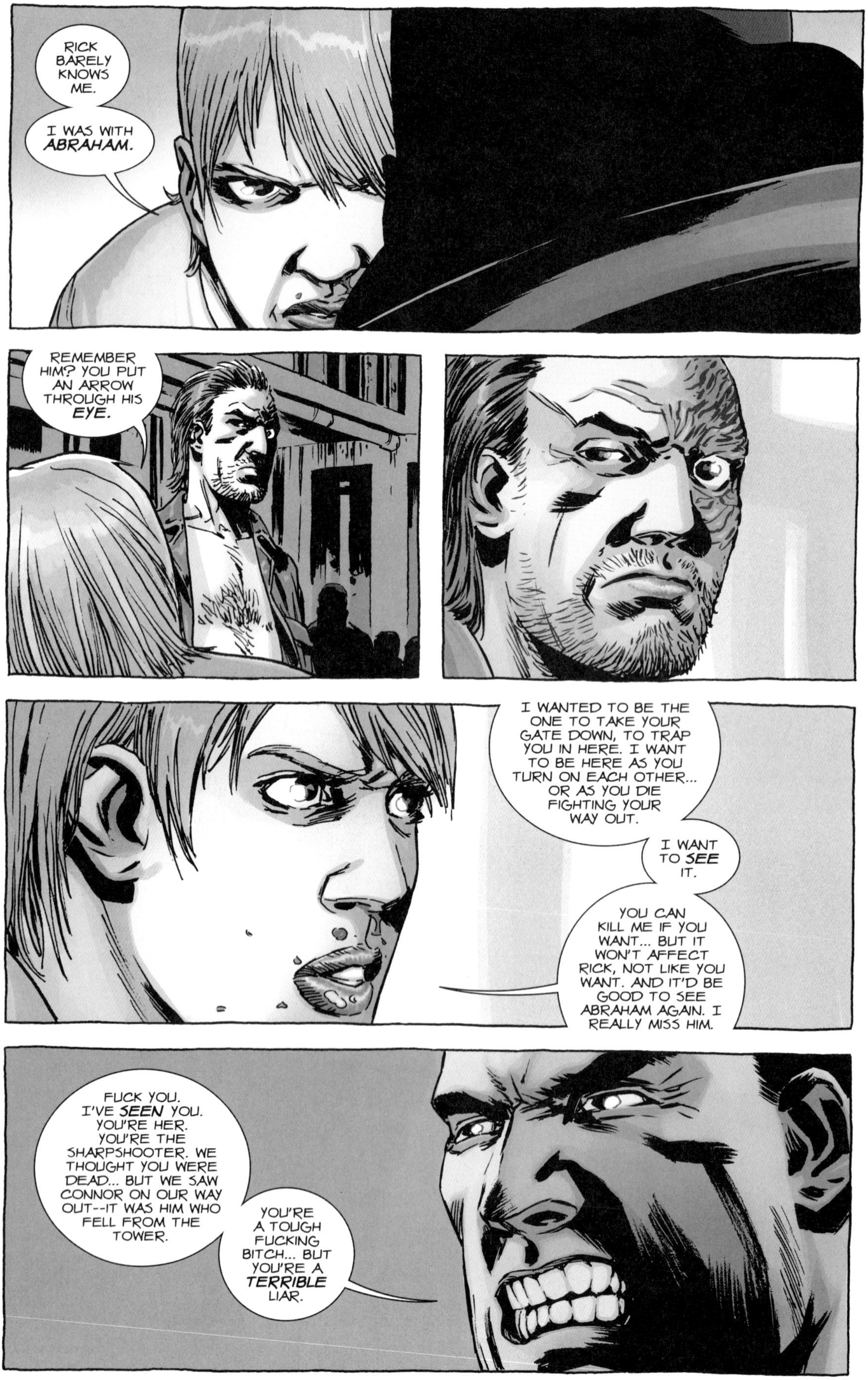
RICK BARELY KNOWS ME.
I WAS WITH ABRAHAM.
REMEMBER HIM? YOU PUT AN ARROW THROUGH HIS EYE.
I WANTED TO BE THE ONE TO TAKE YOUR GATE DOWN, TO TRAP YOU IN HERE. I WANT TO BE HERE AS YOU TURN ON EACH OTHER... OR AS YOU DIE FIGHTING YOUR WAY OUT.
I WANT TO SEE IT.
YOU CAN KILL ME IF YOU WANT... BUT IT WON'T AFFECT RICK, NOT LIKE YOU WANT. AND IT'D BE GOOD TO SEE ABRAHAM AGAIN. I REALLY MISS HIM.
FUCK YOU. I'VE SEEN YOU. YOU'RE HER. YOU'RE THE SHARPSHOOTER. WE THOUGHT YOU WERE DEAD... BUT WE SAW CONNOR ON OUR WAY OUT--IT WAS HIM WHO FELL FROM THE TOWER.
YOU'RE A TOUGH FUCKING BITCH... BUT YOU'RE A TERRIBLE LIAR.

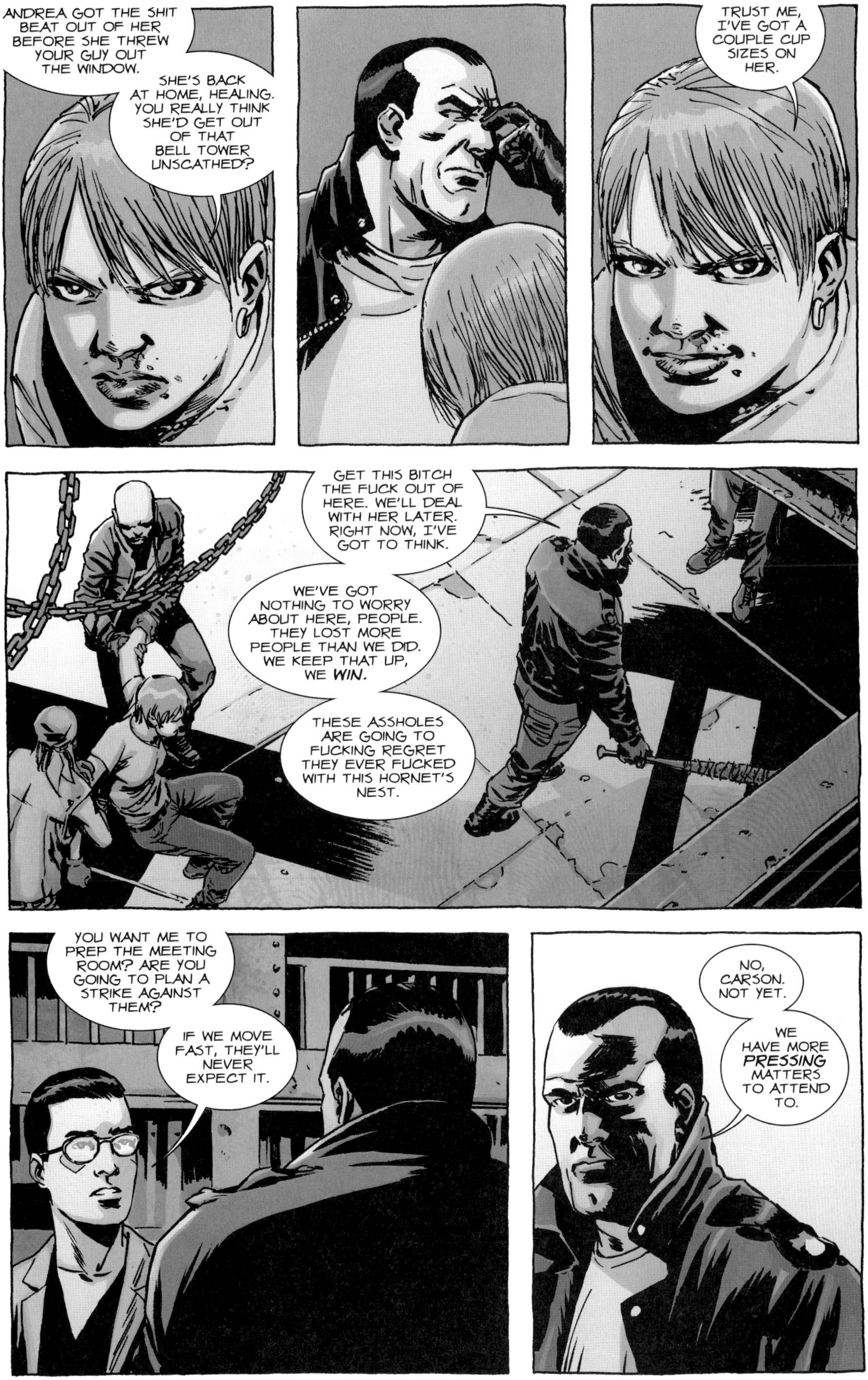
ANDREA GOT THE SHIT BEAT OUT OF HER BEFORE SHE THREW YOUR GUY OUT THE WINDOW.
SHE'S BACK AT HOME, HEALING. YOU REALLY THINK SHE'D GET OUT OF THAT BELL TOWER UNSCATHED?
TRUST ME, I'VE GOT A COUPLE CUP SIZES ON HER.
GET THIS BITCH THE FUCK OUT OF HERE. WE'LL DEAL WITH HER LATER. RIGHT NOW, I'VE GOT TO THINK.
WE'VE GOT NOTHING TO WORRY ABOUT HERE, PEOPLE. THEY LOST MORE PEOPLE THAN WE DID. WE KEEP THAT UP, WE *WIN.*
THESE ASSHOLES ARE GOING TO FUCKING REGRET THEY EVER FUCKED WITH THIS HORNET'S NEST.
YOU WANT ME TO PREP THE MEETING ROOM? ARE YOU GOING TO PLAN A STRIKE AGAINST THEM?
IF WE MOVE FAST, THEY'LL NEVER EXPECT IT.
NO, CARSON. NOT YET.
WE HAVE MORE ***PRESSING*** MATTERS TO ATTEND TO.

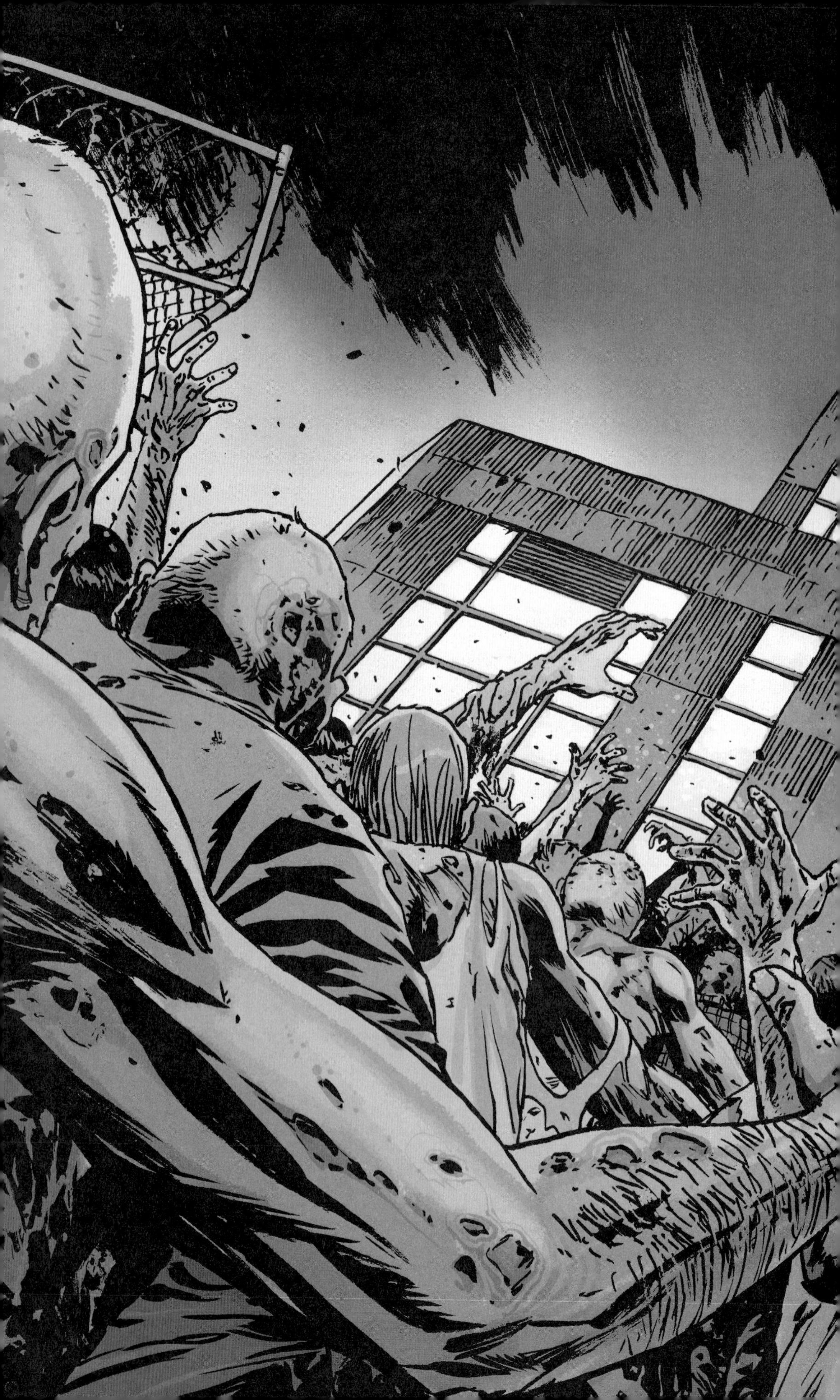

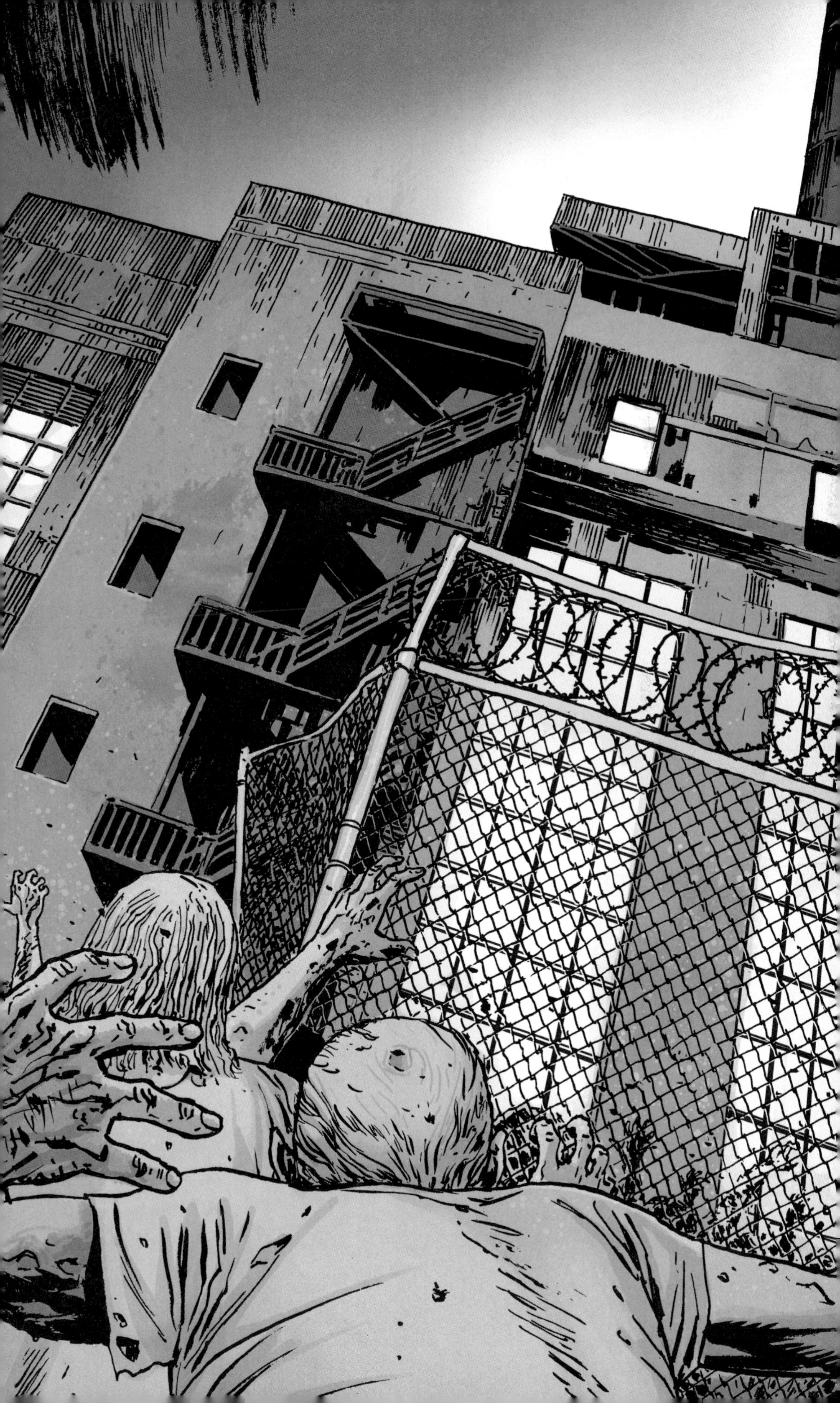

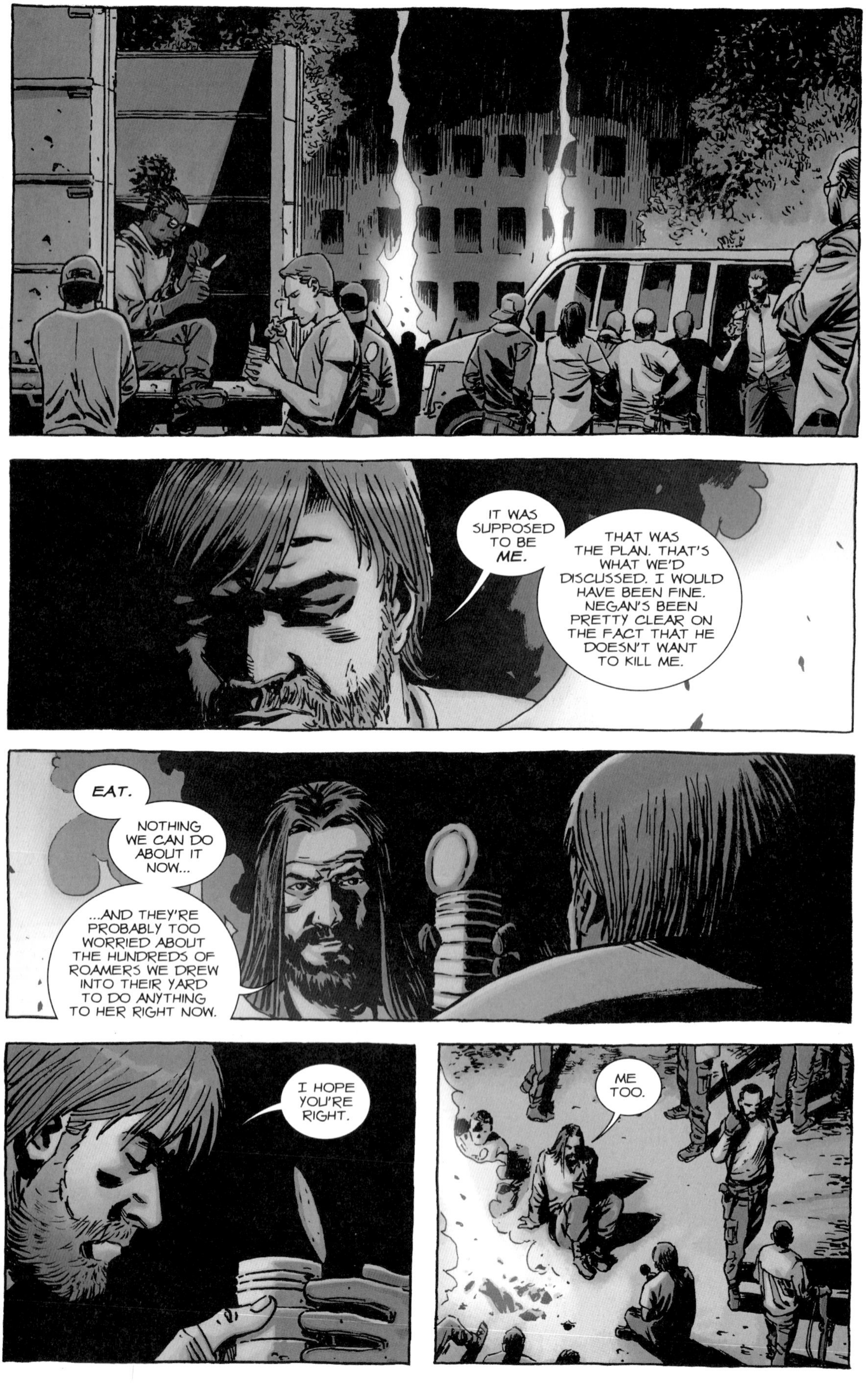
IT WAS SUPPOSED TO BE *ME.*
THAT WAS THE PLAN. THAT'S WHAT WE'D DISCUSSED. I WOULD HAVE BEEN FINE. NEGAN'S BEEN PRETTY CLEAR ON THE FACT THAT HE DOESN'T WANT TO KILL ME.
EAT.
NOTHING WE CAN DO ABOUT IT NOW...
...AND THEY'RE PROBABLY TOO WORRIED ABOUT THE HUNDREDS OF ROAMERS WE DREW INTO THEIR YARD TO DO ANYTHING TO HER RIGHT NOW.
I HOPE YOU'RE RIGHT.
ME TOO.

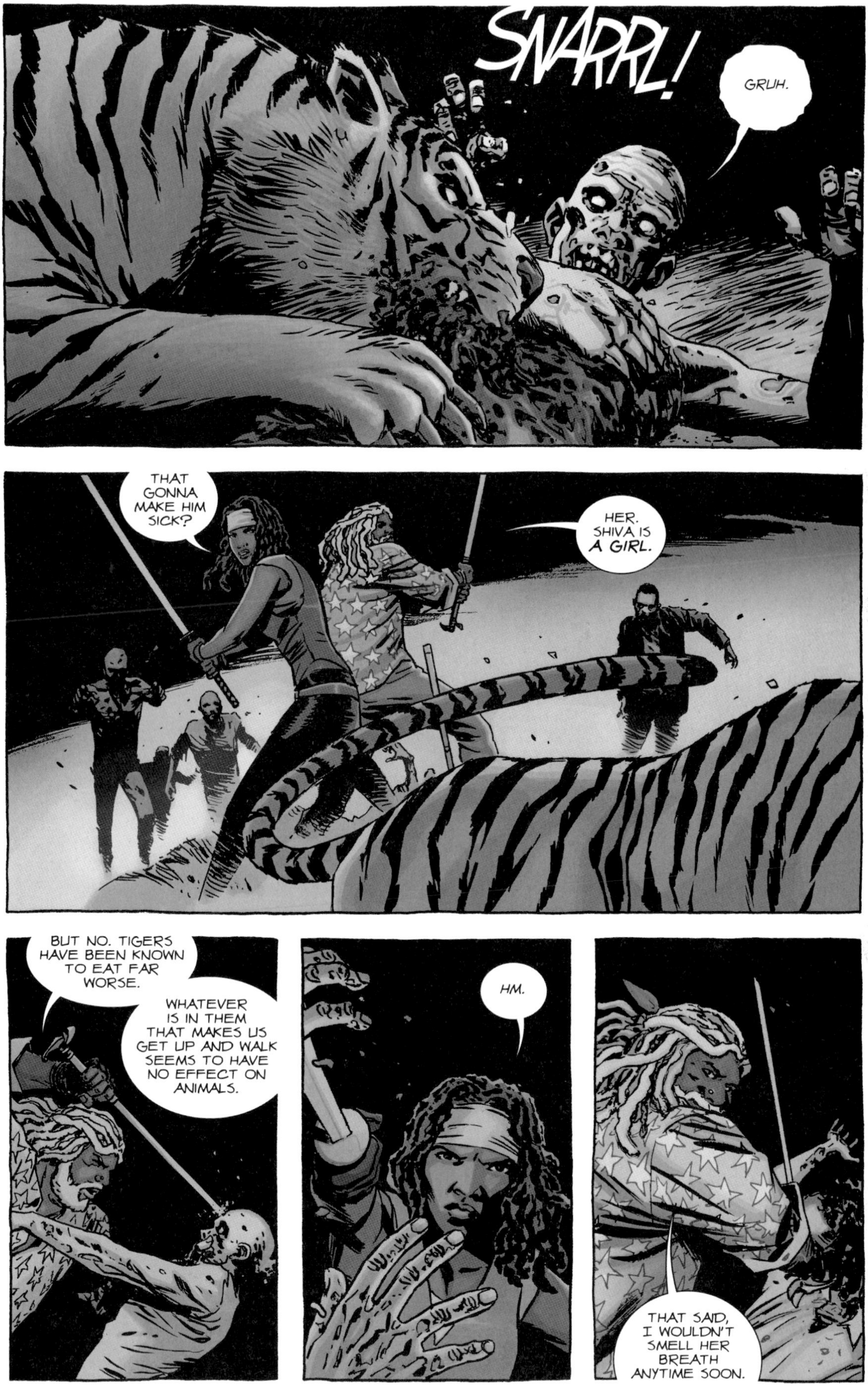
SNARRL!
GRUH.
THAT GONNA MAKE HIM SICK?
HER. SHIVA IS A GIRL.
BUT NO. TIGERS HAVE BEEN KNOWN TO EAT FAR WORSE.
WHATEVER IS IN THEM THAT MAKES US GET UP AND WALK SEEMS TO HAVE NO EFFECT ON ANIMALS.
HM.
THAT SAID, I WOULDN'T SMELL HER BREATH ANYTIME SOON.

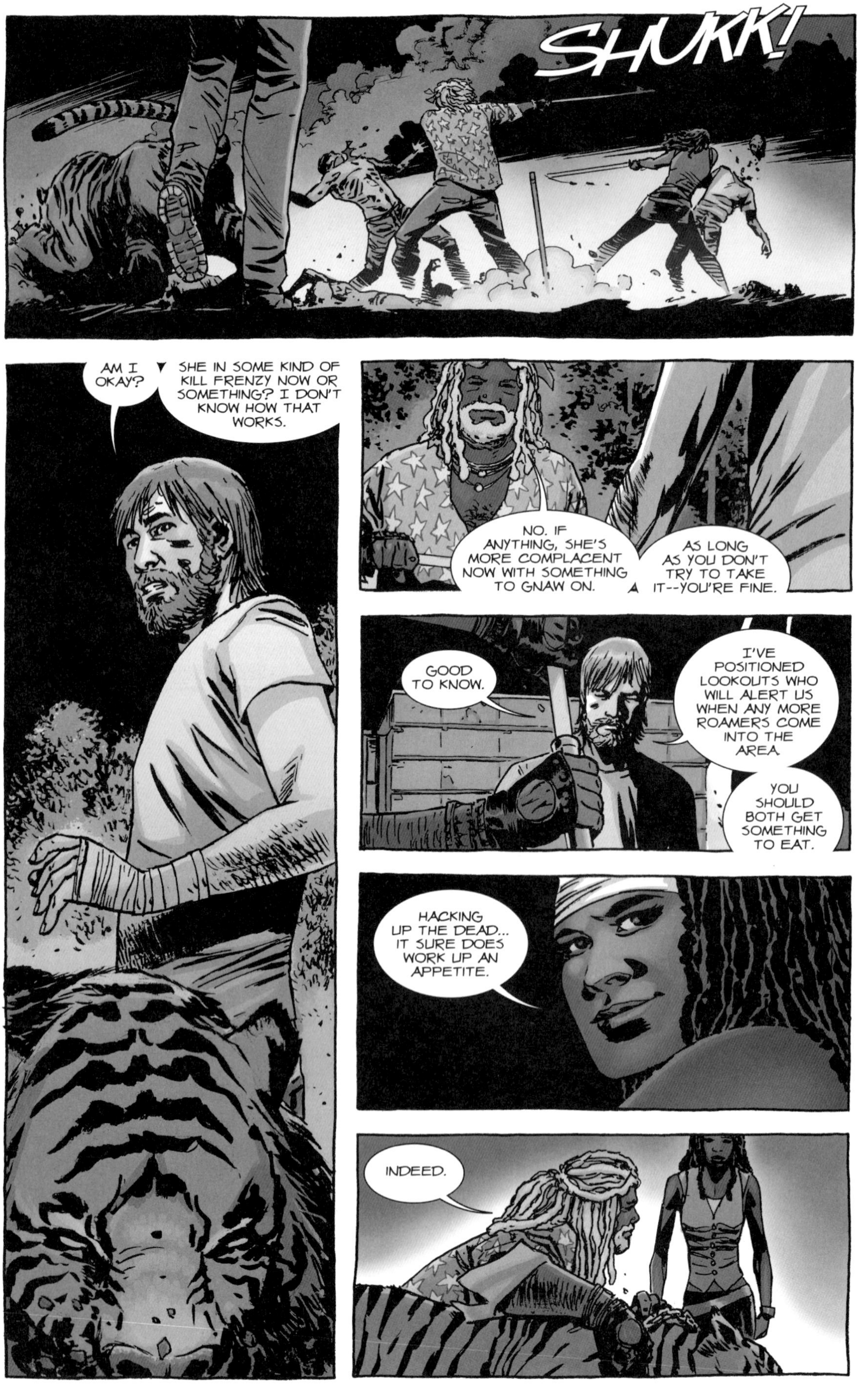
SHUKK!
AM I OKAY?
SHE IN SOME KIND OF KILL FRENZY NOW OR SOMETHING? I DON'T KNOW HOW THAT WORKS.
NO. IF ANYTHING, SHE'S MORE COMPLACENT NOW WITH SOMETHING TO GNAW ON.
AS LONG AS YOU DON'T TRY TO TAKE IT--YOU'RE FINE.
GOOD TO KNOW.
I'VE POSITIONED LOOKOUTS WHO WILL ALERT US WHEN ANY MORE ROAMERS COME INTO THE AREA.
YOU SHOULD BOTH GET SOMETHING TO EAT.
HACKING UP THE DEAD... IT SURE DOES WORK UP AN APPETITE.
INDEED.

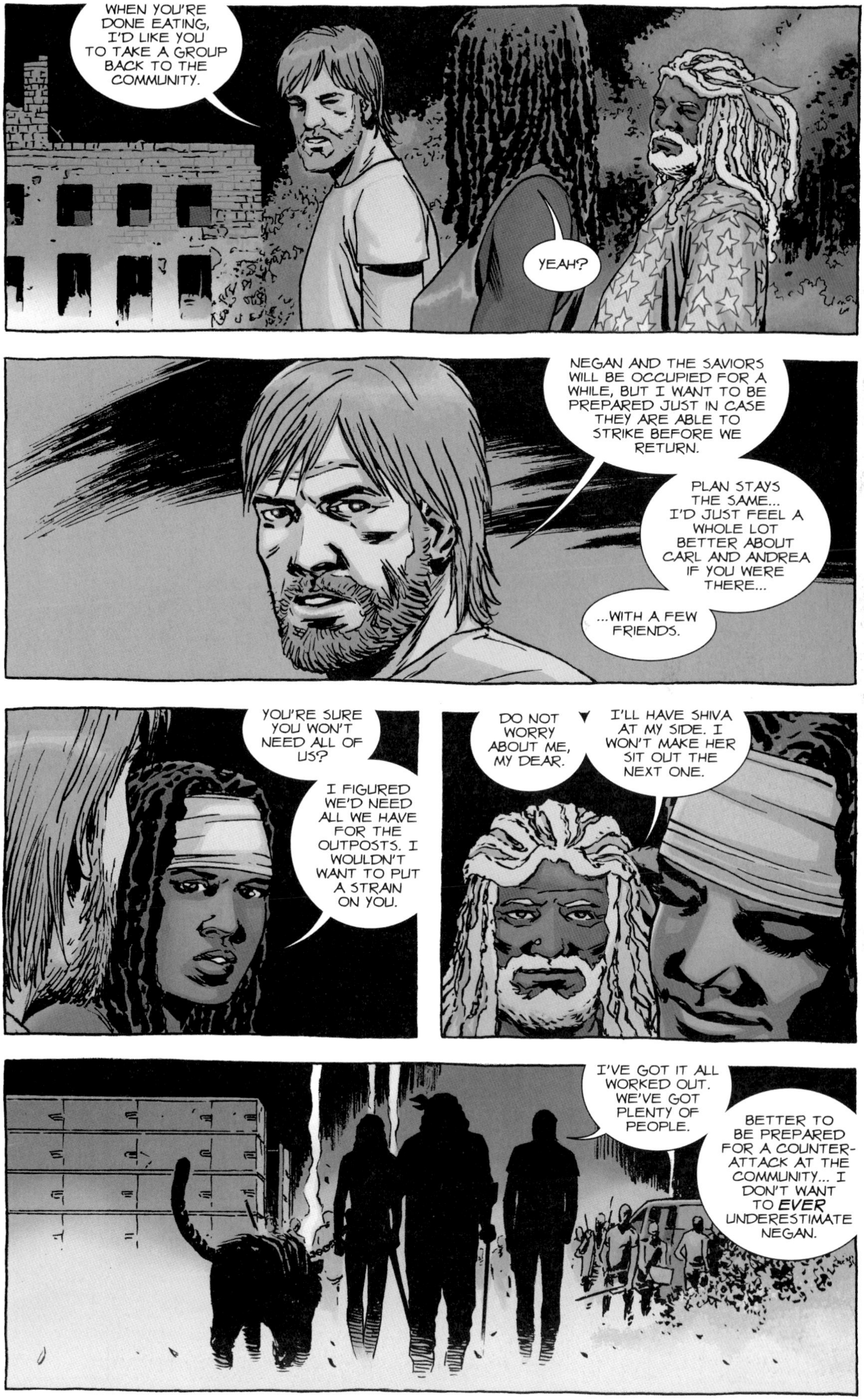
WHEN YOU'RE DONE EATING, I'D LIKE YOU TO TAKE A GROUP BACK TO THE COMMUNITY.
YEAH?
NEGAN AND THE SAVIORS WILL BE OCCUPIED FOR A WHILE, BUT I WANT TO BE PREPARED JUST IN CASE THEY ARE ABLE TO STRIKE BEFORE WE RETURN.
PLAN STAYS THE SAME... I'D JUST FEEL A WHOLE LOT BETTER ABOUT CARL AND ANDREA IF YOU WERE THERE...
...WITH A FEW FRIENDS.
YOU'RE SURE YOU WON'T NEED ALL OF US?
I FIGURED WE'D NEED ALL WE HAVE FOR THE OUTPOSTS. I WOULDN'T WANT TO PUT A STRAIN ON YOU.
DO NOT WORRY ABOUT ME, MY DEAR.
I'LL HAVE SHIVA AT MY SIDE. I WON'T MAKE HER SIT OUT THE NEXT ONE.
I'VE GOT IT ALL WORKED OUT. WE'VE GOT PLENTY OF PEOPLE.
BETTER TO BE PREPARED FOR A COUNTER-ATTACK AT THE COMMUNITY... I DON'T WANT TO *EVER* UNDERESTIMATE NEGAN.

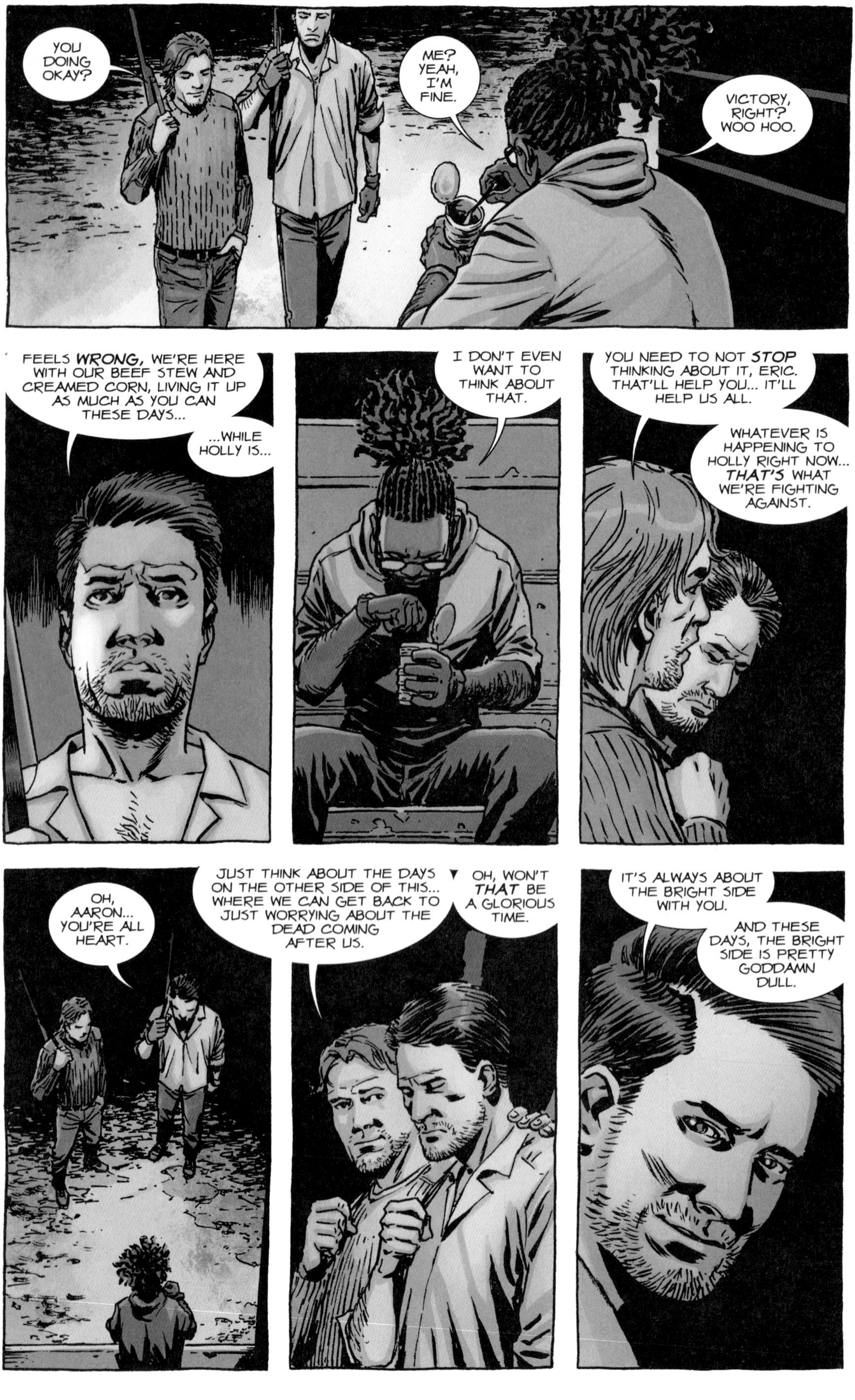
YOU DOING OKAY?
ME? YEAH, I'M FINE.
VICTORY, RIGHT? WOO HOO.
FEELS WRONG, WE'RE HERE WITH OUR BEEF STEW AND CREAMED CORN, LIVING IT UP AS MUCH AS YOU CAN THESE DAYS...
...WHILE HOLLY IS...
I DON'T EVEN WANT TO THINK ABOUT THAT.
YOU NEED TO NOT STOP THINKING ABOUT IT, ERIC. THAT'LL HELP YOU... IT'LL HELP US ALL.
WHATEVER IS HAPPENING TO HOLLY RIGHT NOW... THAT'S WHAT WE'RE FIGHTING AGAINST.
OH, AARON... YOU'RE ALL HEART.
JUST THINK ABOUT THE DAYS ON THE OTHER SIDE OF THIS... WHERE WE CAN GET BACK TO JUST WORRYING ABOUT THE DEAD COMING AFTER US.
OH, WON'T THAT BE A GLORIOUS TIME.
IT'S ALWAYS ABOUT THE BRIGHT SIDE WITH YOU.
AND THESE DAYS, THE BRIGHT SIDE IS PRETTY GODDAMN DULL.

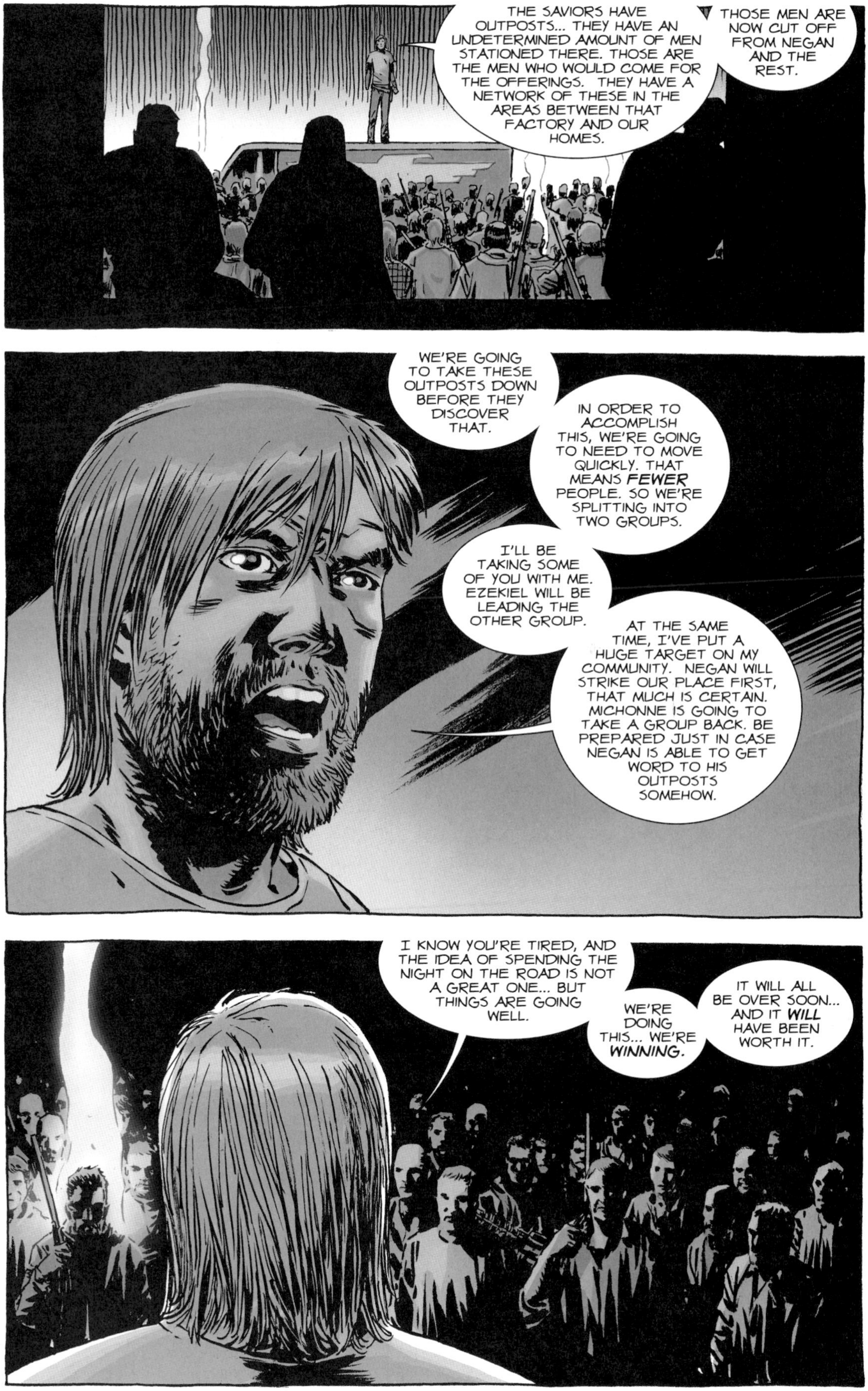
THE SAVIORS HAVE OUTPOSTS... THEY HAVE AN UNDETERMINED AMOUNT OF MEN STATIONED THERE. THOSE ARE THE MEN WHO WOULD COME FOR THE OFFERINGS. THEY HAVE A NETWORK OF THESE IN THE AREAS BETWEEN THAT FACTORY AND OUR HOMES.
THOSE MEN ARE NOW CUT OFF FROM NEGAN AND THE REST.
WE'RE GOING TO TAKE THESE OUTPOSTS DOWN BEFORE THEY DISCOVER THAT.
IN ORDER TO ACCOMPLISH THIS, WE'RE GOING TO NEED TO MOVE QUICKLY. THAT MEANS **FEWER** PEOPLE. SO WE'RE SPLITTING INTO TWO GROUPS.
I'LL BE TAKING SOME OF YOU WITH ME. EZEKIEL WILL BE LEADING THE OTHER GROUP.
AT THE SAME TIME, I'VE PUT A HUGE TARGET ON MY COMMUNITY. NEGAN WILL STRIKE OUR PLACE FIRST, THAT MUCH IS CERTAIN. MICHONNE IS GOING TO TAKE A GROUP BACK. BE PREPARED JUST IN CASE NEGAN IS ABLE TO GET WORD TO HIS OUTPOSTS SOMEHOW.
I KNOW YOU'RE TIRED, AND THE IDEA OF SPENDING THE NIGHT ON THE ROAD IS NOT A GREAT ONE... BUT THINGS ARE GOING WELL.
WE'RE DOING THIS... WE'RE ***WINNING.***
IT WILL ALL BE OVER SOON... AND IT ***WILL*** HAVE BEEN WORTH IT.

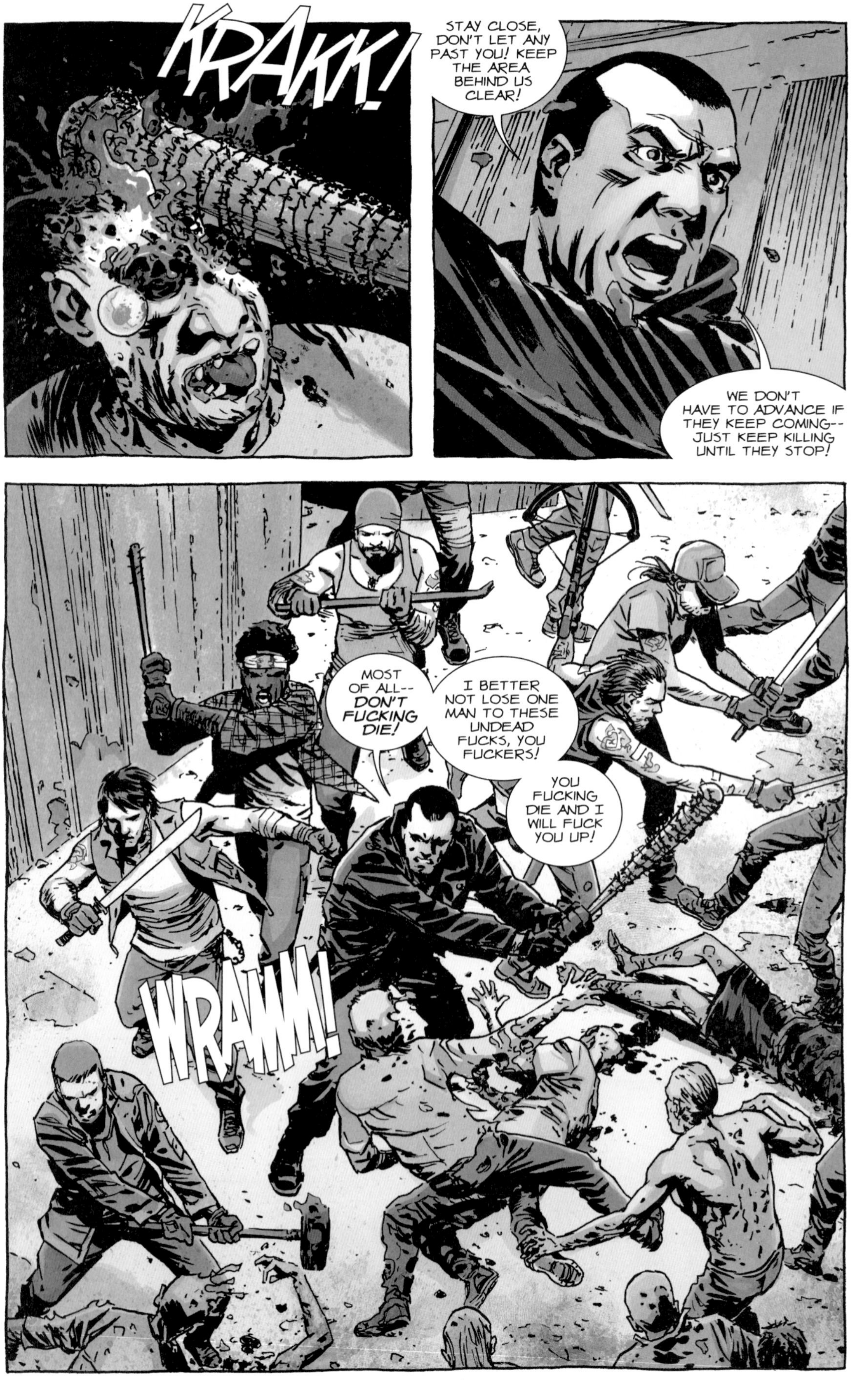
KRAKK!
STAY CLOSE, DON'T LET ANY PAST YOU! KEEP THE AREA BEHIND US CLEAR!
WE DON'T HAVE TO ADVANCE IF THEY KEEP COMING-- JUST KEEP KILLING UNTIL THEY STOP!
MOST OF ALL-- DON'T FUCKING DIE!
I BETTER NOT LOSE ONE MAN TO THESE UNDEAD FUCKS, YOU FUCKERS!
YOU FUCKING DIE AND I WILL FUCK YOU UP!
WRAMM!

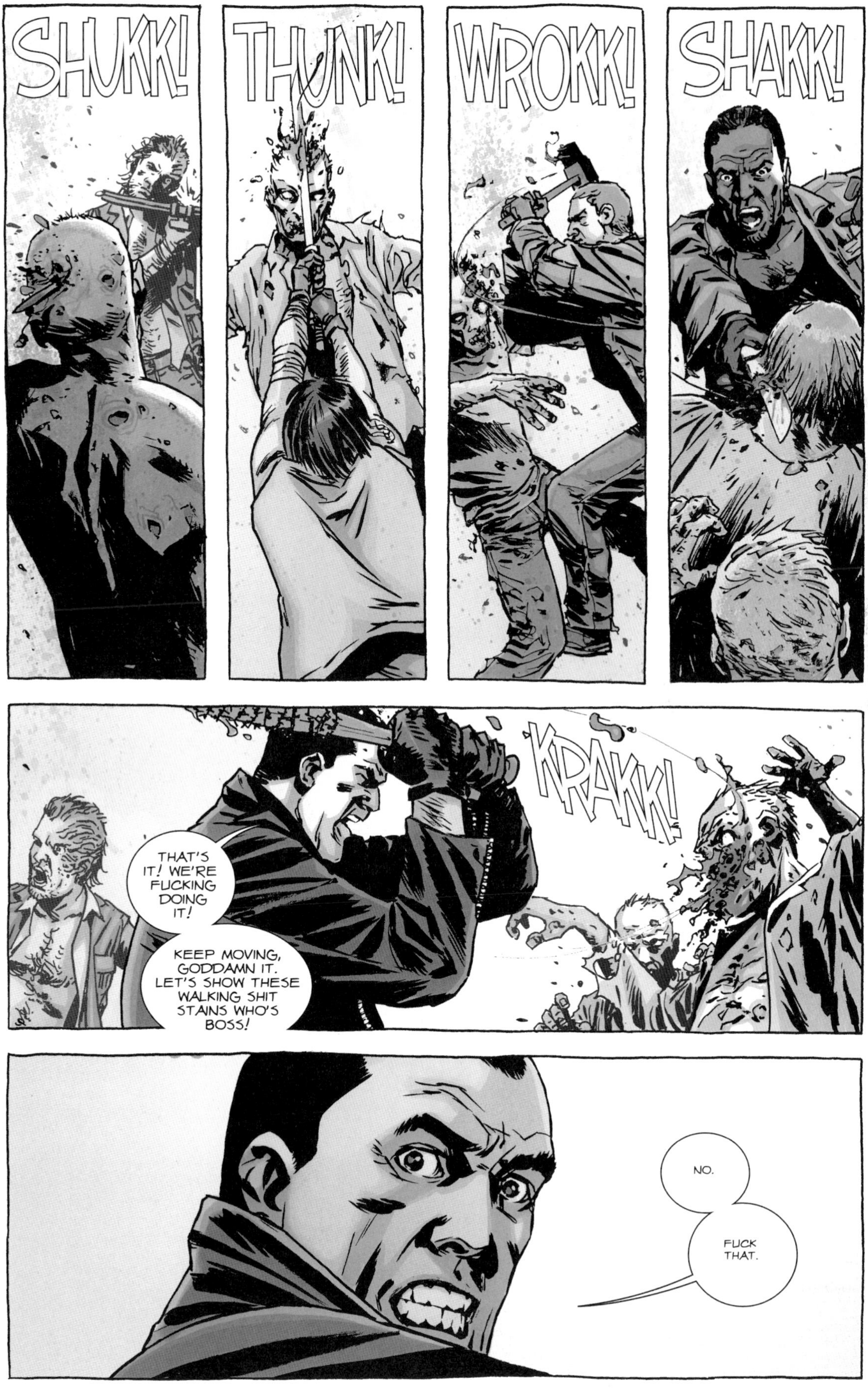
SHUKK!
THUNK!
WROKK!
SHAKK!
KRAKK!
THAT'S IT! WE'RE FUCKING DOING IT!
KEEP MOVING, GODDAMN IT. LET'S SHOW THESE WALKING SHIT STAINS WHO'S BOSS!
NO.
FUCK THAT.

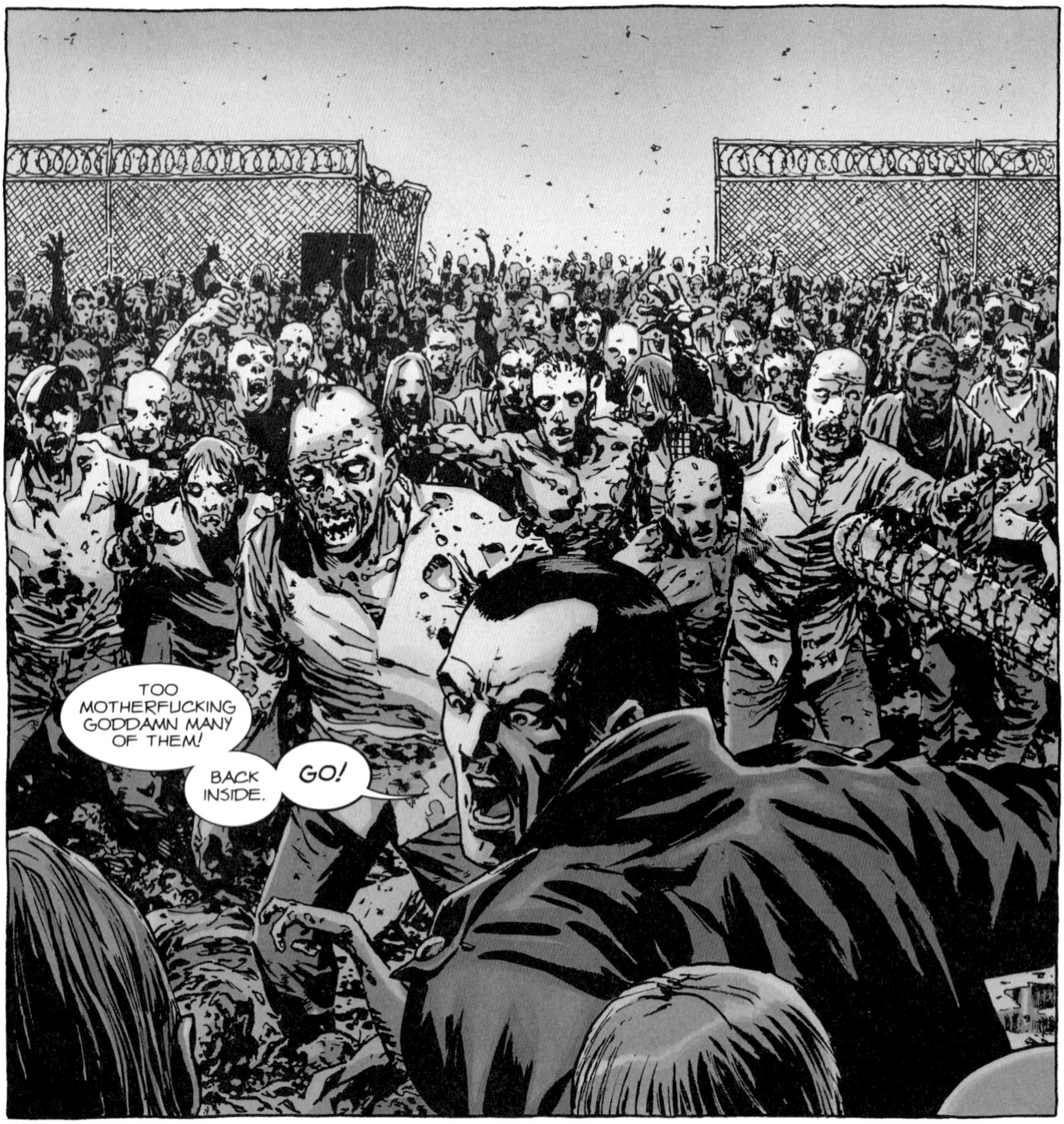
TOO MOTHERFUCKING GODDAMN MANY OF THEM!
BACK INSIDE.
GO!

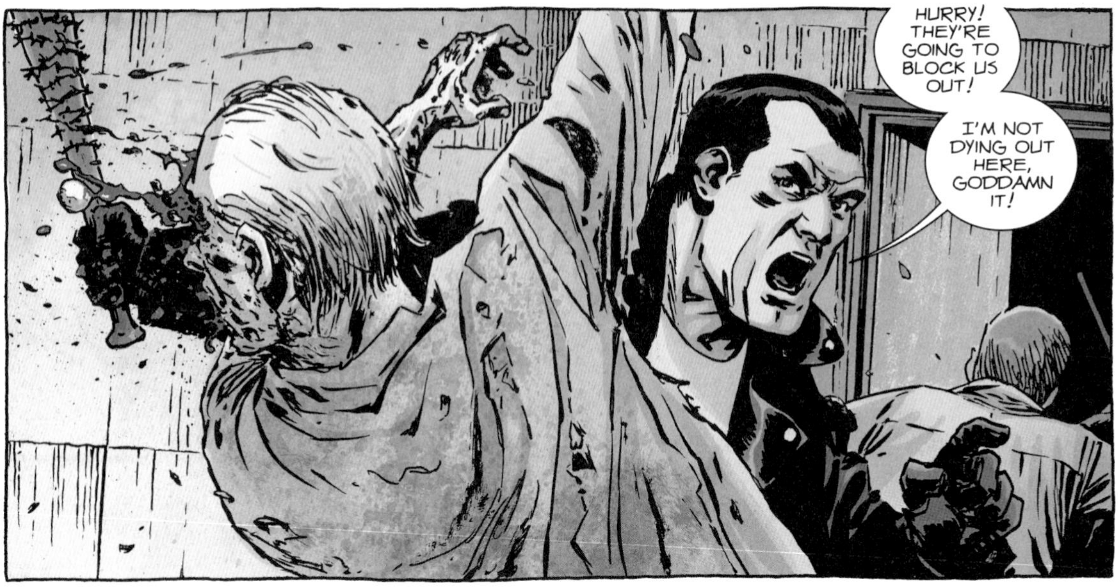
HURRY! THEY'RE GOING TO BLOCK US OUT!
I'M NOT DYING OUT HERE, GODDAMN IT!

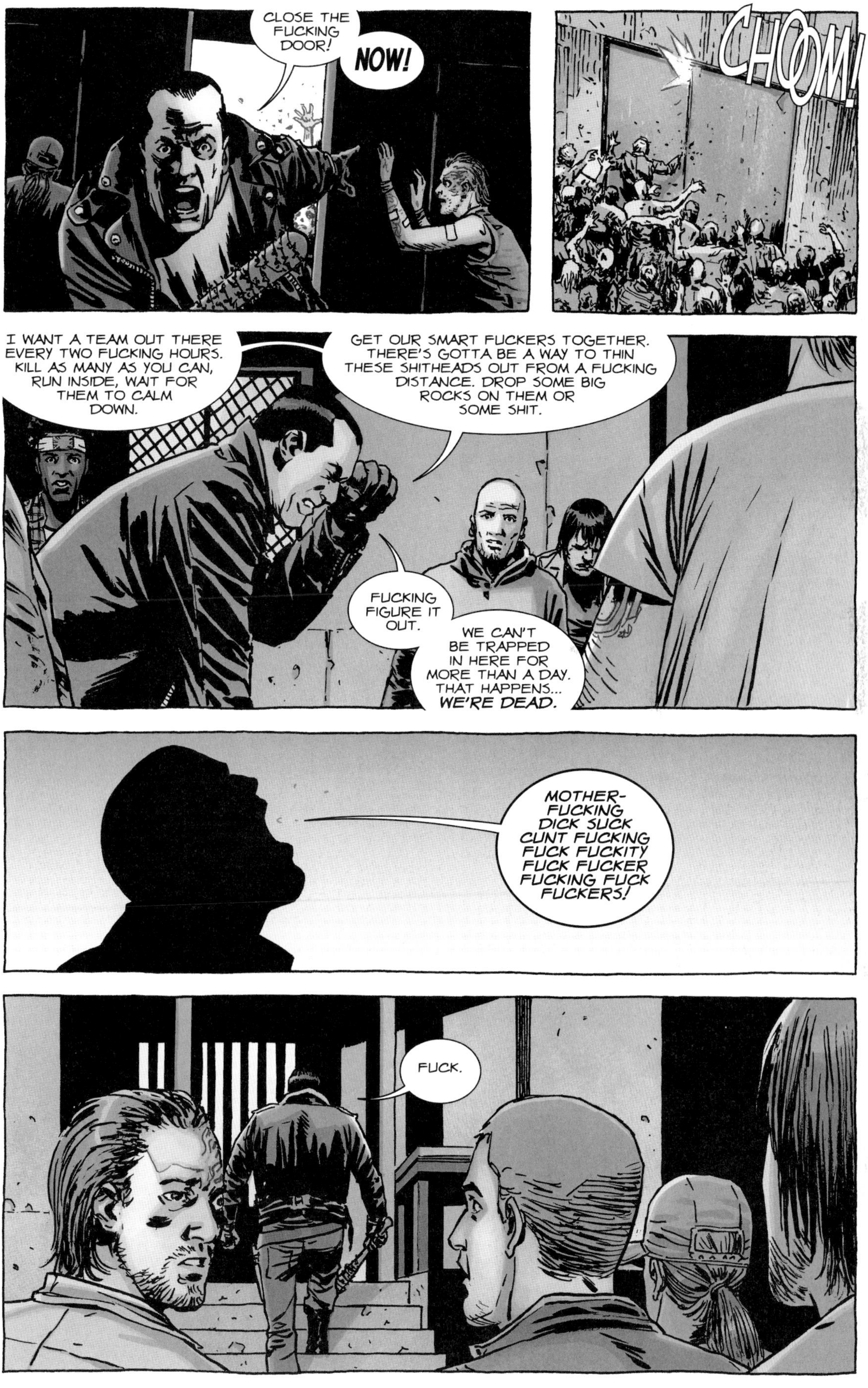
CLOSE THE FUCKING DOOR!
NOW!
CHOOM!
I WANT A TEAM OUT THERE EVERY TWO FUCKING HOURS. KILL AS MANY AS YOU CAN, RUN INSIDE, WAIT FOR THEM TO CALM DOWN.
GET OUR SMART FUCKERS TOGETHER. THERE'S GOTTA BE A WAY TO THIN THESE SHITHEADS OUT FROM A FUCKING DISTANCE. DROP SOME BIG ROCKS ON THEM OR SOME SHIT.
FUCKING FIGURE IT OUT.
WE CAN'T BE TRAPPED IN HERE FOR MORE THAN A DAY. THAT HAPPENS... WE'RE DEAD.
MOTHER-FUCKING DICK SUCK CUNT FUCKING FUCK FUCKITY FUCK FUCKER FUCKING FUCK FUCKERS!
FUCK.

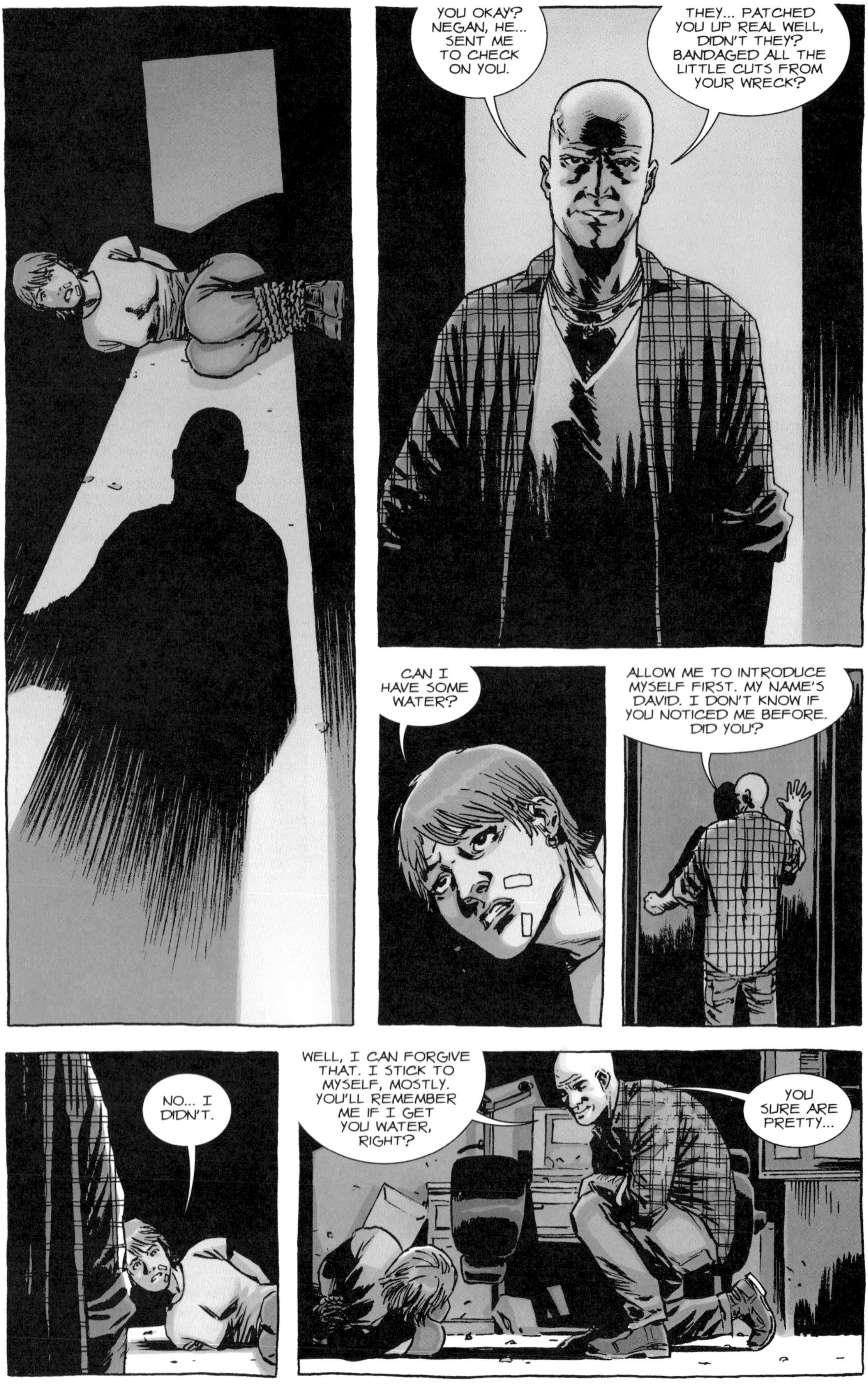
YOU OKAY? NEGAN, HE... SENT ME TO CHECK ON YOU.
THEY... PATCHED YOU UP REAL WELL, DIDN'T THEY? BANDAGED ALL THE LITTLE CUTS FROM YOUR WRECK?
CAN I HAVE SOME WATER?
ALLOW ME TO INTRODUCE MYSELF FIRST. MY NAME'S DAVID. I DON'T KNOW IF YOU NOTICED ME BEFORE. DID YOU?
NO... I DIDN'T.
WELL, I CAN FORGIVE THAT. I STICK TO MYSELF, MOSTLY. YOU'LL REMEMBER ME IF I GET YOU WATER, RIGHT?
YOU SURE ARE PRETTY...

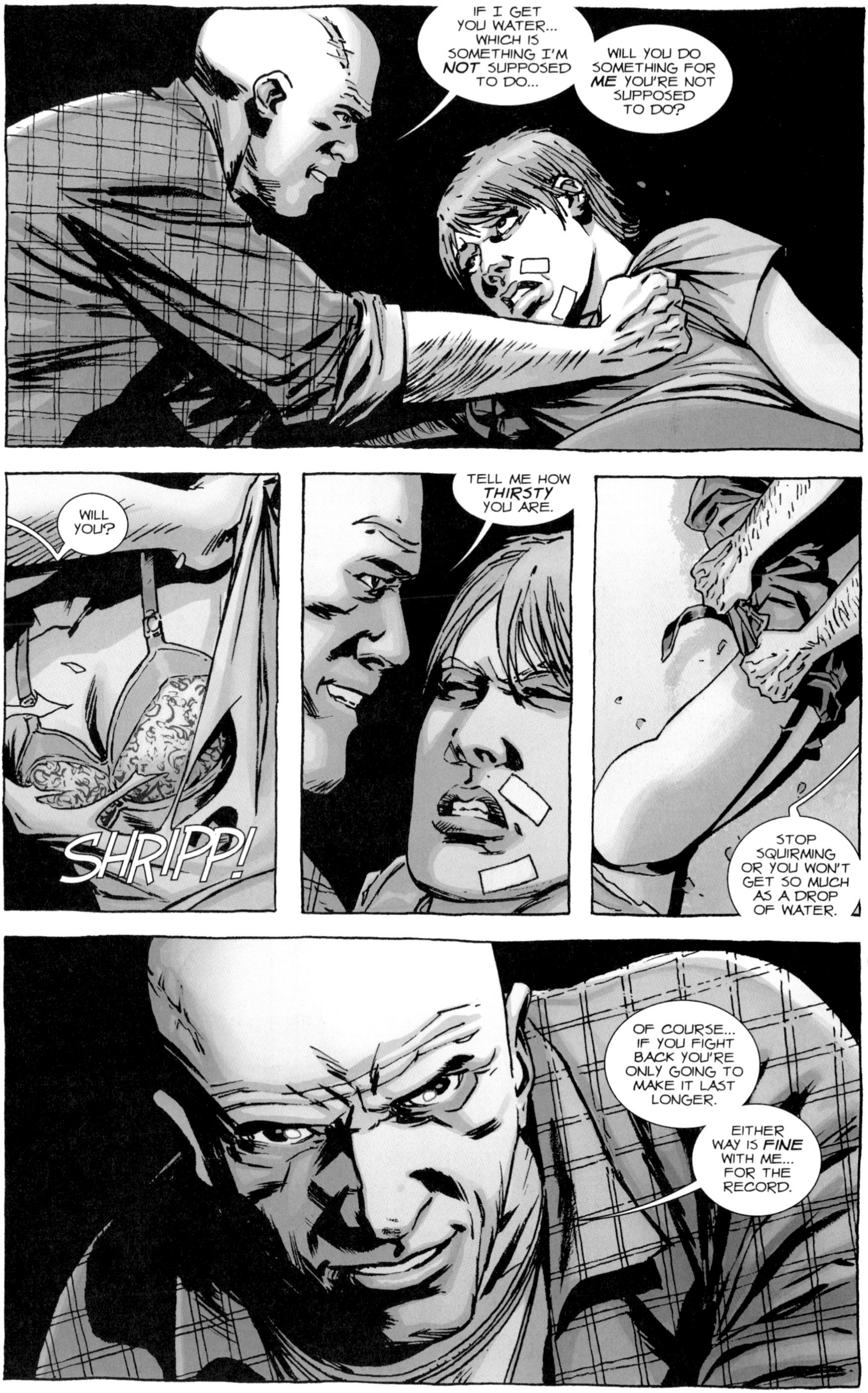
IF I GET YOU WATER... WHICH IS SOMETHING I'M NOT SUPPOSED TO DO...
WILL YOU DO SOMETHING FOR ME YOU'RE NOT SUPPOSED TO DO?
WILL YOU?
SHRIPP!
TELL ME HOW THIRSTY YOU ARE.
STOP SQUIRMING OR YOU WON'T GET SO MUCH AS A DROP OF WATER.
OF COURSE... IF YOU FIGHT BACK YOU'RE ONLY GOING TO MAKE IT LAST LONGER.
EITHER WAY IS FINE WITH ME... FOR THE RECORD.

DAVID!

WHAT THE FUCKING FUCK ARE YOU DOING IN HERE?!

NEGAN, SIR--

I--

DO YOU REALLY THINK I NEED YOU TO ANSWER THAT? I CAN FUCKING SEE YOU'RE TRYING TO *RAPE* THIS WOMAN.

YOU WERE GOING TO FUCKING RAPE THIS WOMAN, WEREN'T YOU?!

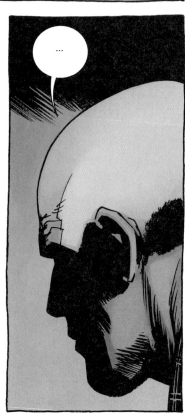

...

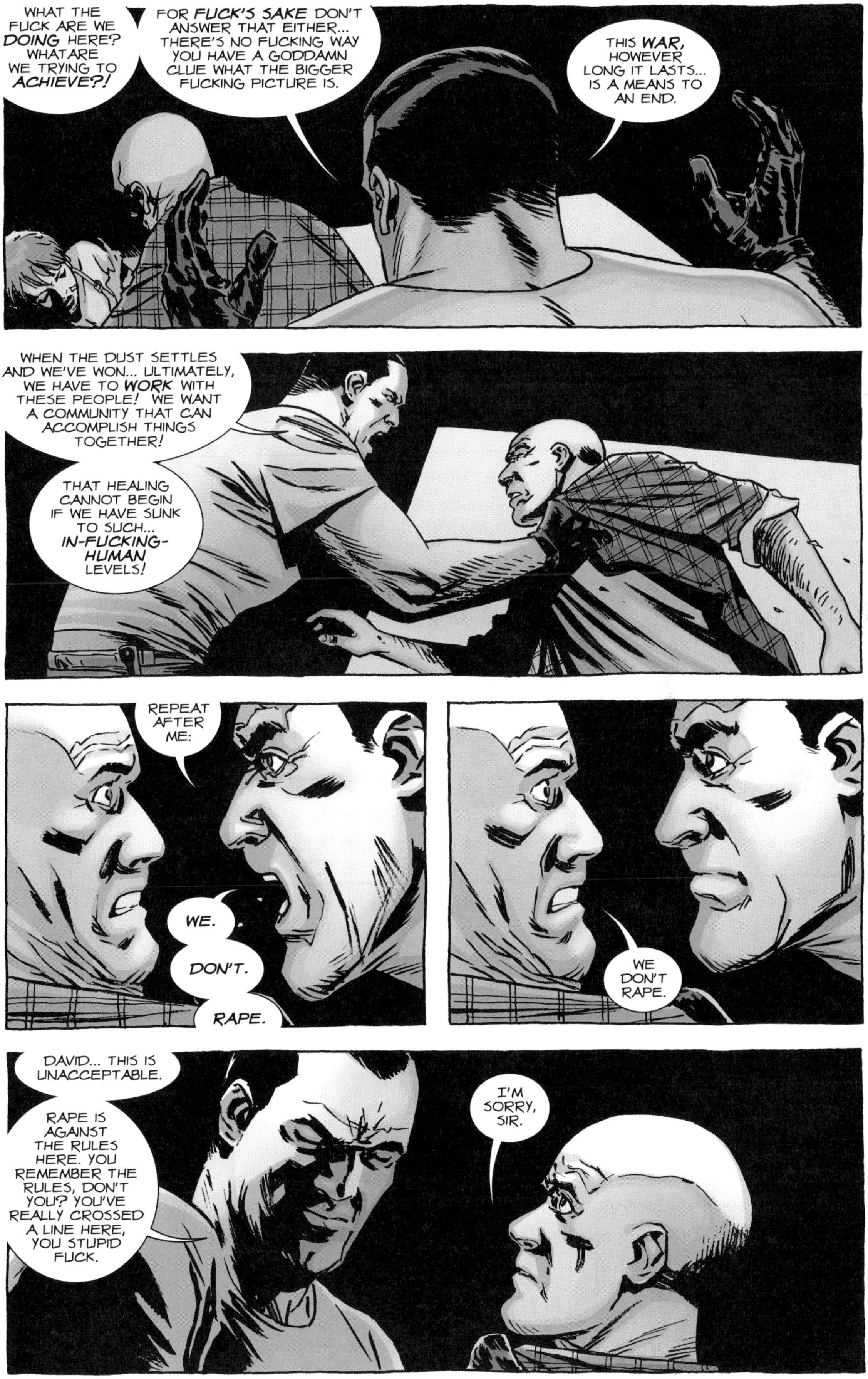

WHAT THE FUCK ARE WE DOING HERE? WHATARE WE TRYING TO ACHIEVE?!
FOR FUCK'S SAKE DON'T ANSWER THAT EITHER... THERE'S NO FUCKING WAY YOU HAVE A GODDAMN CLUE WHAT THE BIGGER FUCKING PICTURE IS.
THIS WAR, HOWEVER LONG IT LASTS... IS A MEANS TO AN END.
WHEN THE DUST SETTLES AND WE'VE WON... ULTIMATELY, WE HAVE TO WORK WITH THESE PEOPLE! WE WANT A COMMUNITY THAT CAN ACCOMPLISH THINGS TOGETHER!
THAT HEALING CANNOT BEGIN IF WE HAVE SUNK TO SUCH... IN-FUCKING-HUMAN LEVELS!
REPEAT AFTER ME:
WE.
DON'T.
RAPE.
WE DON'T RAPE.
DAVID... THIS IS UNACCEPTABLE.
RAPE IS AGAINST THE RULES HERE. YOU REMEMBER THE RULES, DON'T YOU? YOU'VE REALLY CROSSED A LINE HERE, YOU STUPID FUCK.
I'M SORRY, SIR.

SHUKK!

I'M SORRY YOU HAD TO SEE THAT. I REALLY WANT YOU TO UNDERSTAND...

...WE'RE NOT MONSTERS.

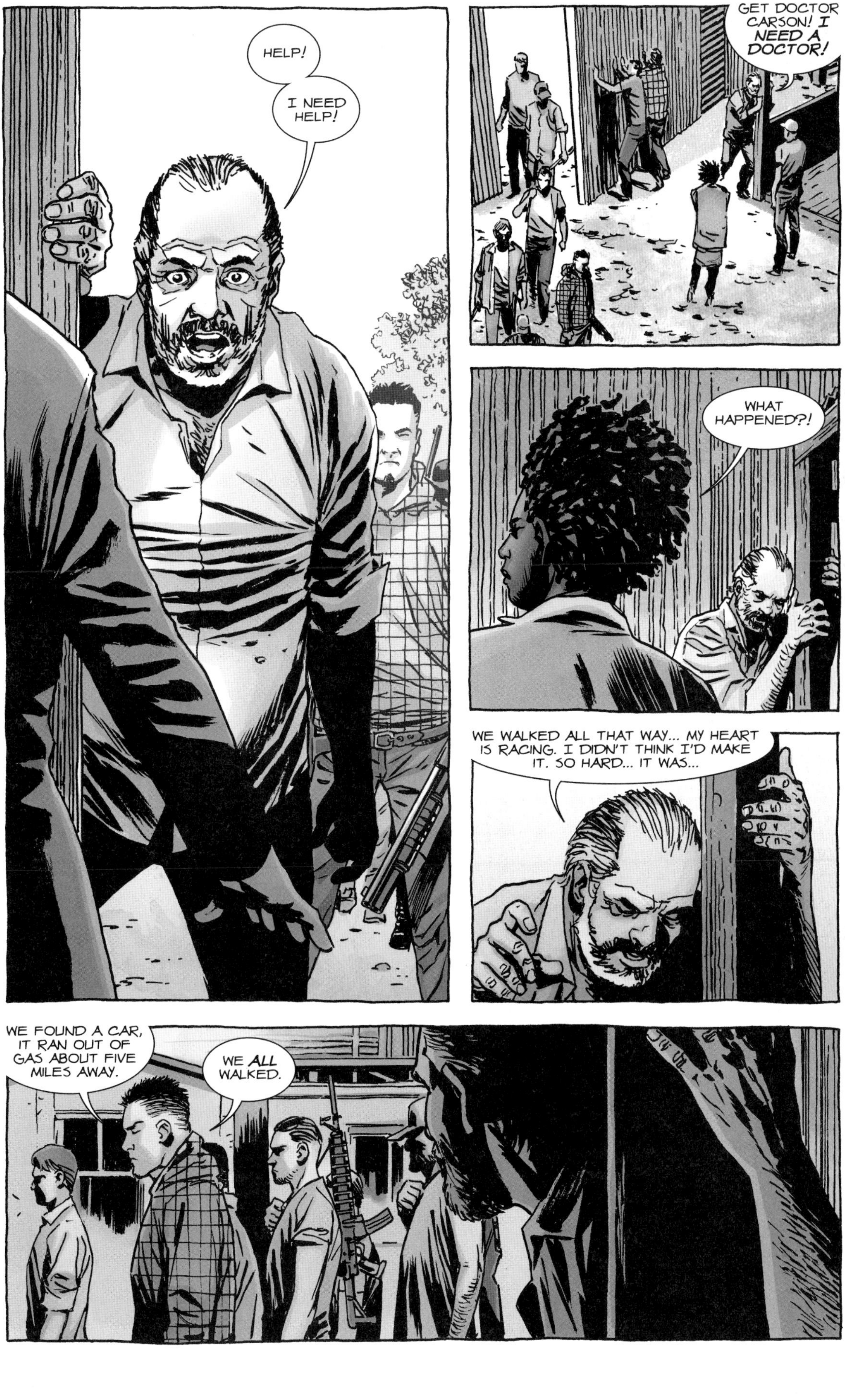

HELP!
I NEED HELP!
GET DOCTOR CARSON! I NEED A DOCTOR!
WHAT HAPPENED?!
WE WALKED ALL THAT WAY... MY HEART IS RACING. I DIDN'T THINK I'D MAKE IT. SO HARD... IT WAS...
WE FOUND A CAR, IT RAN OUT OF GAS ABOUT FIVE MILES AWAY.
WE ALL WALKED.

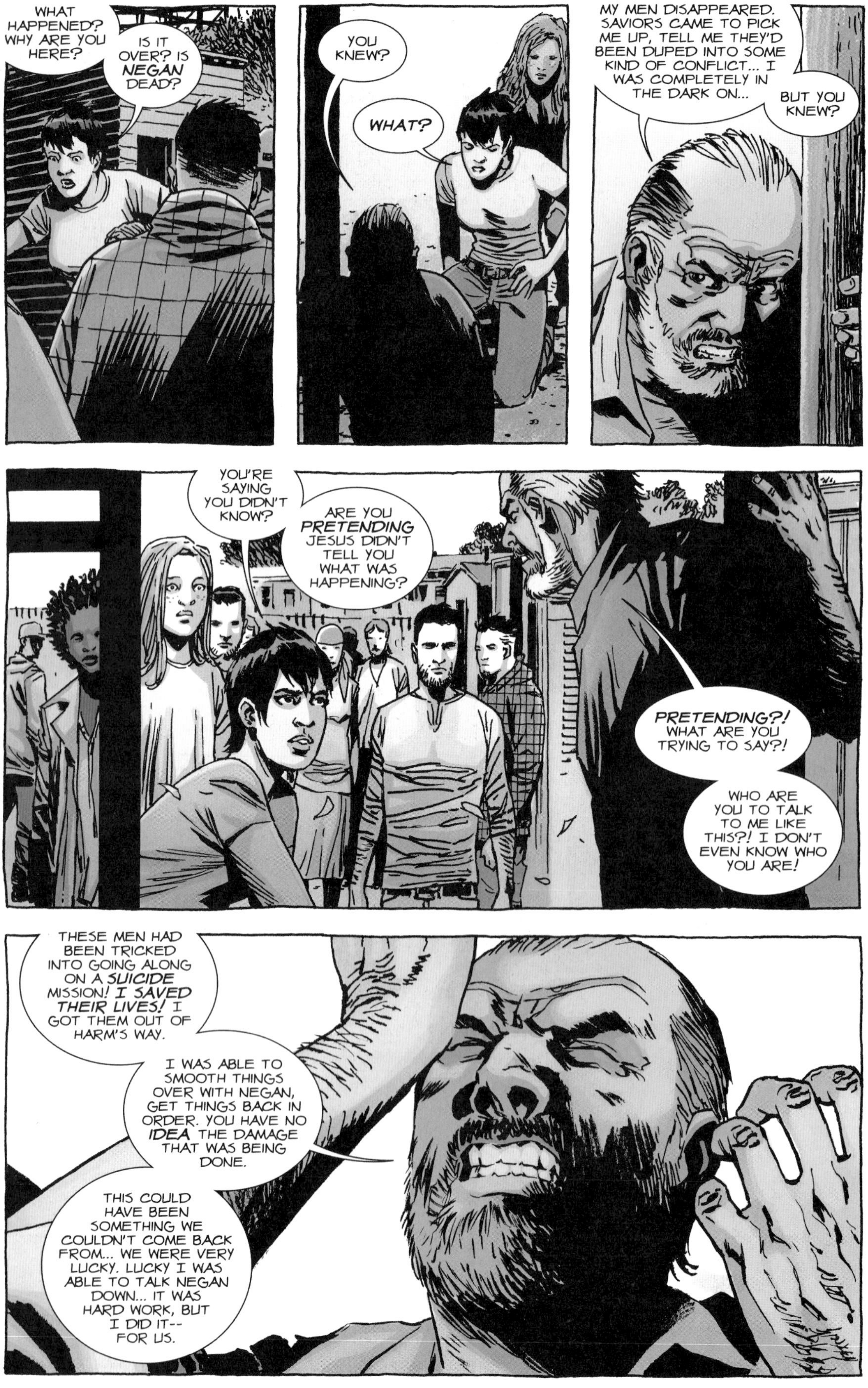
WHAT HAPPENED? WHY ARE YOU HERE?
IS IT OVER? IS NEGAN DEAD?
YOU KNEW?
WHAT?
MY MEN DISAPPEARED. SAVIORS CAME TO PICK ME UP, TELL ME THEY'D BEEN DUPED INTO SOME KIND OF CONFLICT... I WAS COMPLETELY IN THE DARK ON...
BUT YOU KNEW?
YOU'RE SAYING YOU DIDN'T KNOW?
ARE YOU PRETENDING JESUS DIDN'T TELL YOU WHAT WAS HAPPENING?
PRETENDING?! WHAT ARE YOU TRYING TO SAY?!
WHO ARE YOU TO TALK TO ME LIKE THIS?! I DON'T EVEN KNOW WHO YOU ARE!
THESE MEN HAD BEEN TRICKED INTO GOING ALONG ON A SUICIDE MISSION! I SAVED THEIR LIVES! I GOT THEM OUT OF HARM'S WAY.
I WAS ABLE TO SMOOTH THINGS OVER WITH NEGAN, GET THINGS BACK IN ORDER. YOU HAVE NO IDEA THE DAMAGE THAT WAS BEING DONE.
THIS COULD HAVE BEEN SOMETHING WE COULDN'T COME BACK FROM... WE WERE VERY LUCKY. LUCKY I WAS ABLE TO TALK NEGAN DOWN... IT WAS HARD WORK, BUT I DID IT-- FOR US.

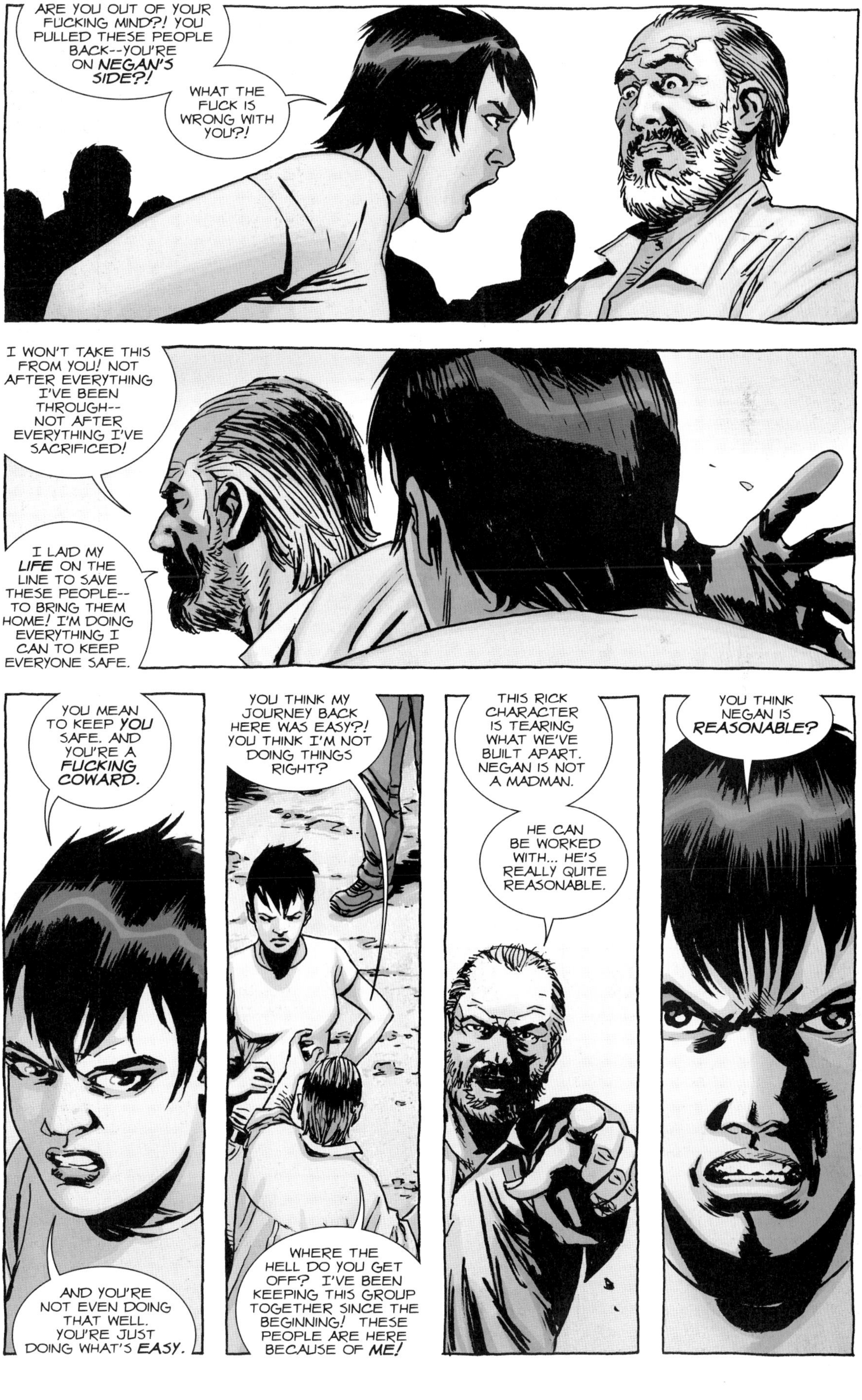
ARE YOU OUT OF YOUR FUCKING MIND?! YOU PULLED THESE PEOPLE BACK--YOU'RE ON NEGAN'S SIDE?!
WHAT THE FUCK IS WRONG WITH YOU?!
I WON'T TAKE THIS FROM YOU! NOT AFTER EVERYTHING I'VE BEEN THROUGH-- NOT AFTER EVERYTHING I'VE SACRIFICED!
I LAID MY LIFE ON THE LINE TO SAVE THESE PEOPLE-- TO BRING THEM HOME! I'M DOING EVERYTHING I CAN TO KEEP EVERYONE SAFE.
YOU MEAN TO KEEP YOU SAFE. AND YOU'RE A FUCKING COWARD.
AND YOU'RE NOT EVEN DOING THAT WELL. YOU'RE JUST DOING WHAT'S EASY.
YOU THINK MY JOURNEY BACK HERE WAS EASY?! YOU THINK I'M NOT DOING THINGS RIGHT?
WHERE THE HELL DO YOU GET OFF? I'VE BEEN KEEPING THIS GROUP TOGETHER SINCE THE BEGINNING! THESE PEOPLE ARE HERE BECAUSE OF ME!
THIS RICK CHARACTER IS TEARING WHAT WE'VE BUILT APART. NEGAN IS NOT A MADMAN.
HE CAN BE WORKED WITH... HE'S REALLY QUITE REASONABLE.
YOU THINK NEGAN IS REASONABLE?

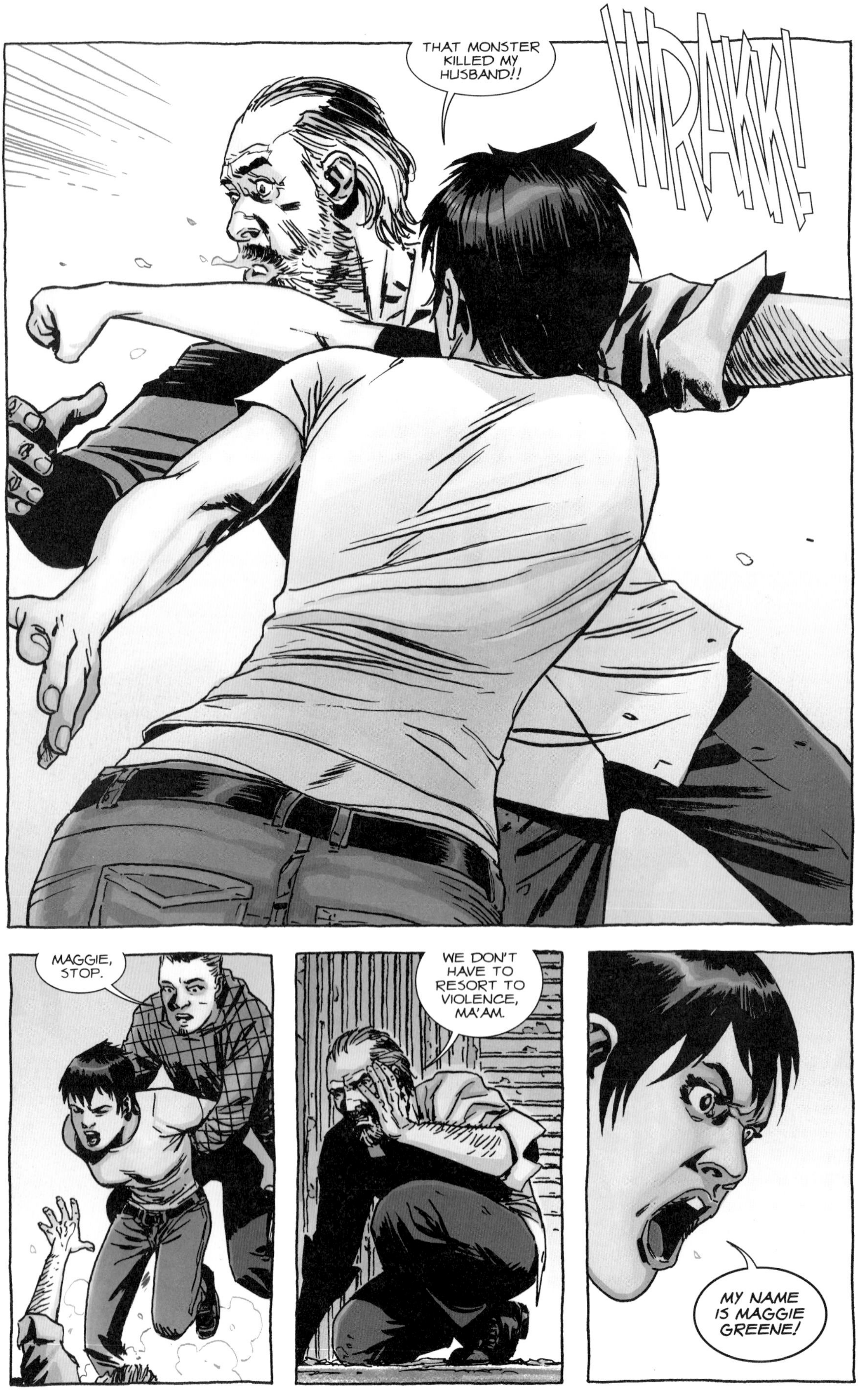
THAT MONSTER KILLED MY HUSBAND!!
WRAKK!
MAGGIE, STOP.
WE DON'T HAVE TO RESORT TO VIOLENCE, MA'AM.
MY NAME IS MAGGIE GREENE!

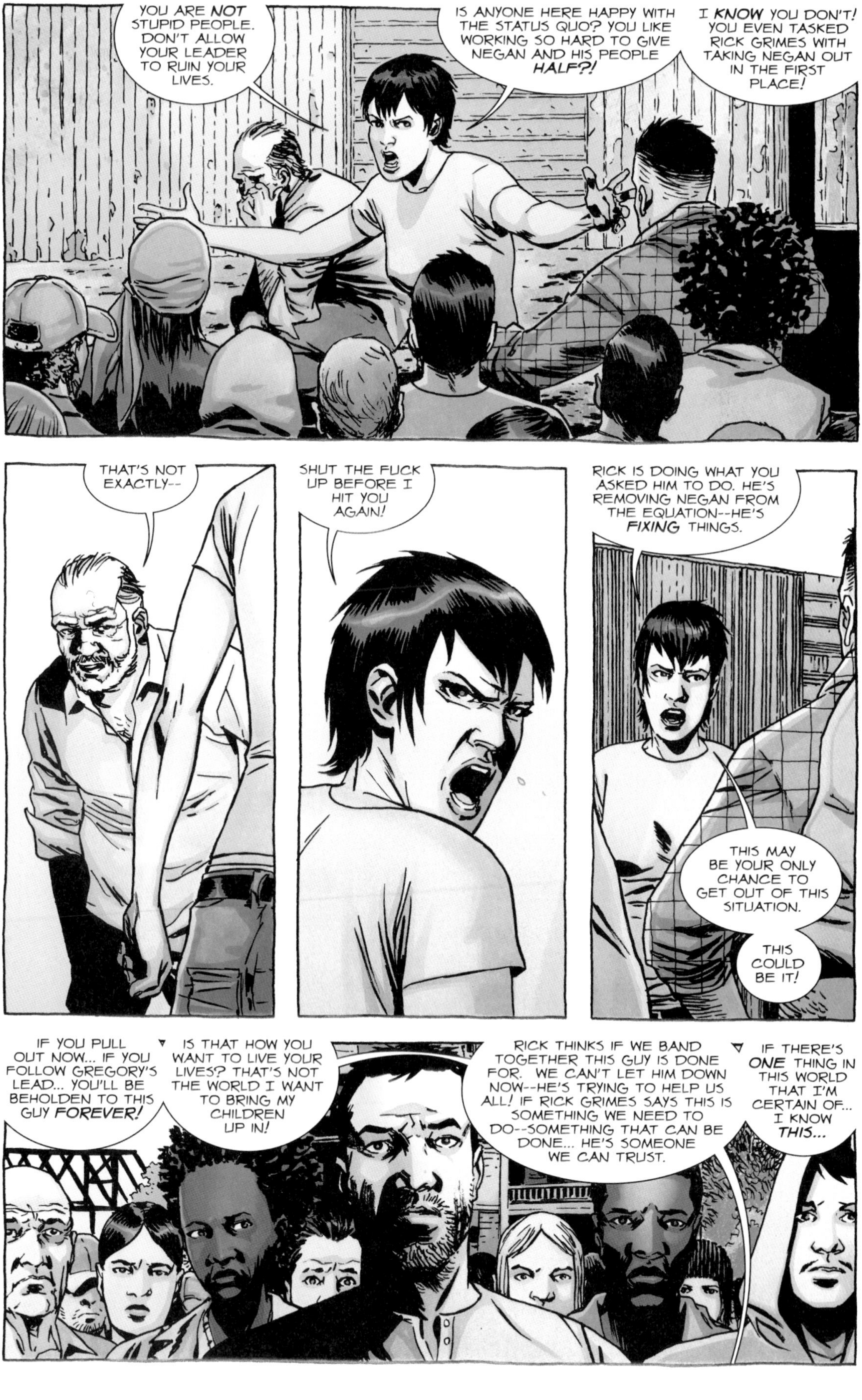
YOU ARE NOT STUPID PEOPLE. DON'T ALLOW YOUR LEADER TO RUIN YOUR LIVES.
IS ANYONE HERE HAPPY WITH THE STATUS QUO? YOU LIKE WORKING SO HARD TO GIVE NEGAN AND HIS PEOPLE HALF?!
I KNOW YOU DON'T! YOU EVEN TASKED RICK GRIMES WITH TAKING NEGAN OUT IN THE FIRST PLACE!
THAT'S NOT EXACTLY--
SHUT THE FUCK UP BEFORE I HIT YOU AGAIN!
RICK IS DOING WHAT YOU ASKED HIM TO DO. HE'S REMOVING NEGAN FROM THE EQUATION--HE'S FIXING THINGS.
THIS MAY BE YOUR ONLY CHANCE TO GET OUT OF THIS SITUATION.
THIS COULD BE IT!
IF YOU PULL OUT NOW... IF YOU FOLLOW GREGORY'S LEAD... YOU'LL BE BEHOLDEN TO THIS GUY FOREVER!
IS THAT HOW YOU WANT TO LIVE YOUR LIVES? THAT'S NOT THE WORLD I WANT TO BRING MY CHILDREN UP IN!
RICK THINKS IF WE BAND TOGETHER THIS GUY IS DONE FOR. WE CAN'T LET HIM DOWN NOW--HE'S TRYING TO HELP US ALL! IF RICK GRIMES SAYS THIS IS SOMETHING WE NEED TO DO--SOMETHING THAT CAN BE DONE... HE'S SOMEONE WE CAN TRUST.
IF THERE'S ONE THING IN THIS WORLD THAT I'M CERTAIN OF... I KNOW THIS...

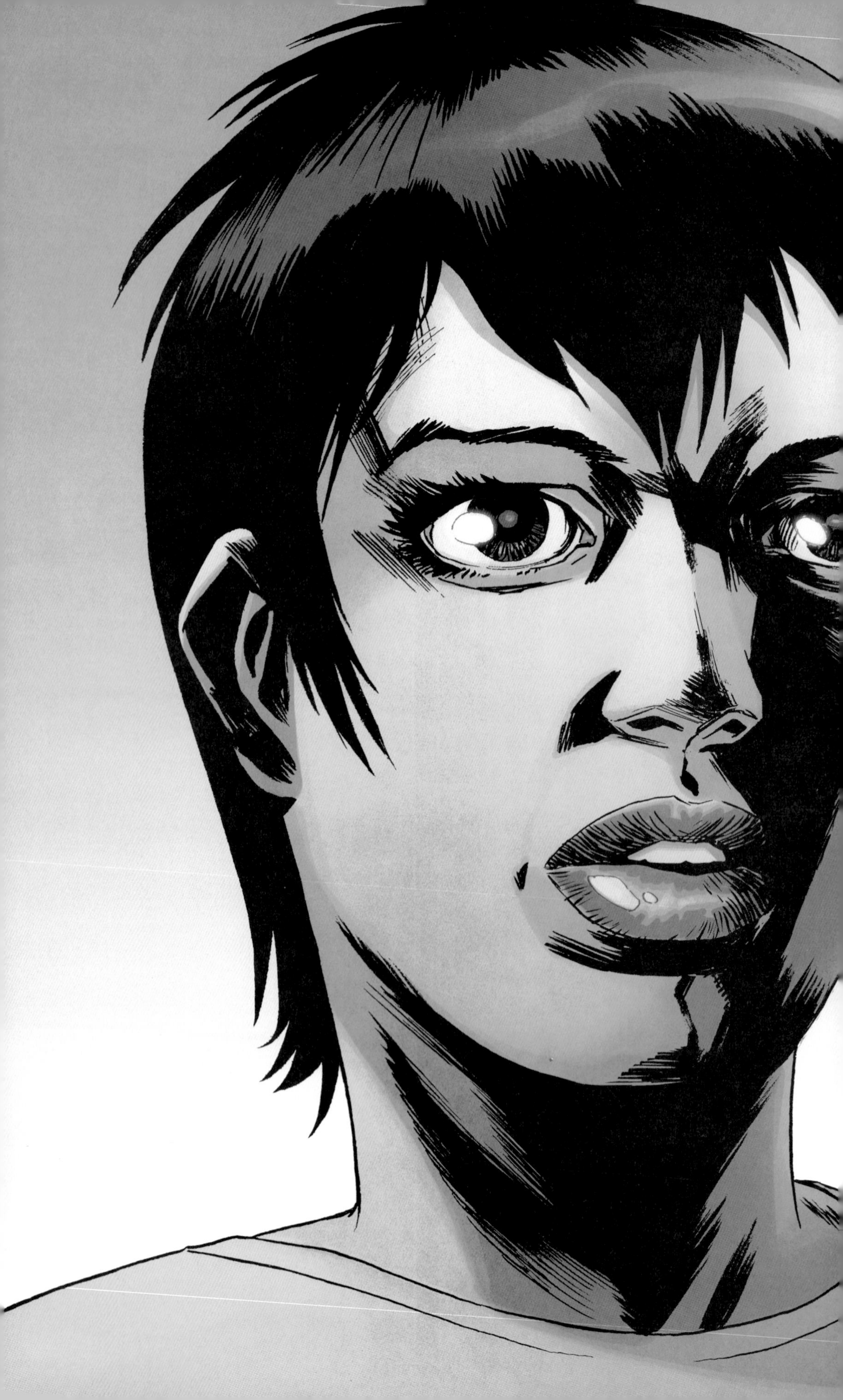

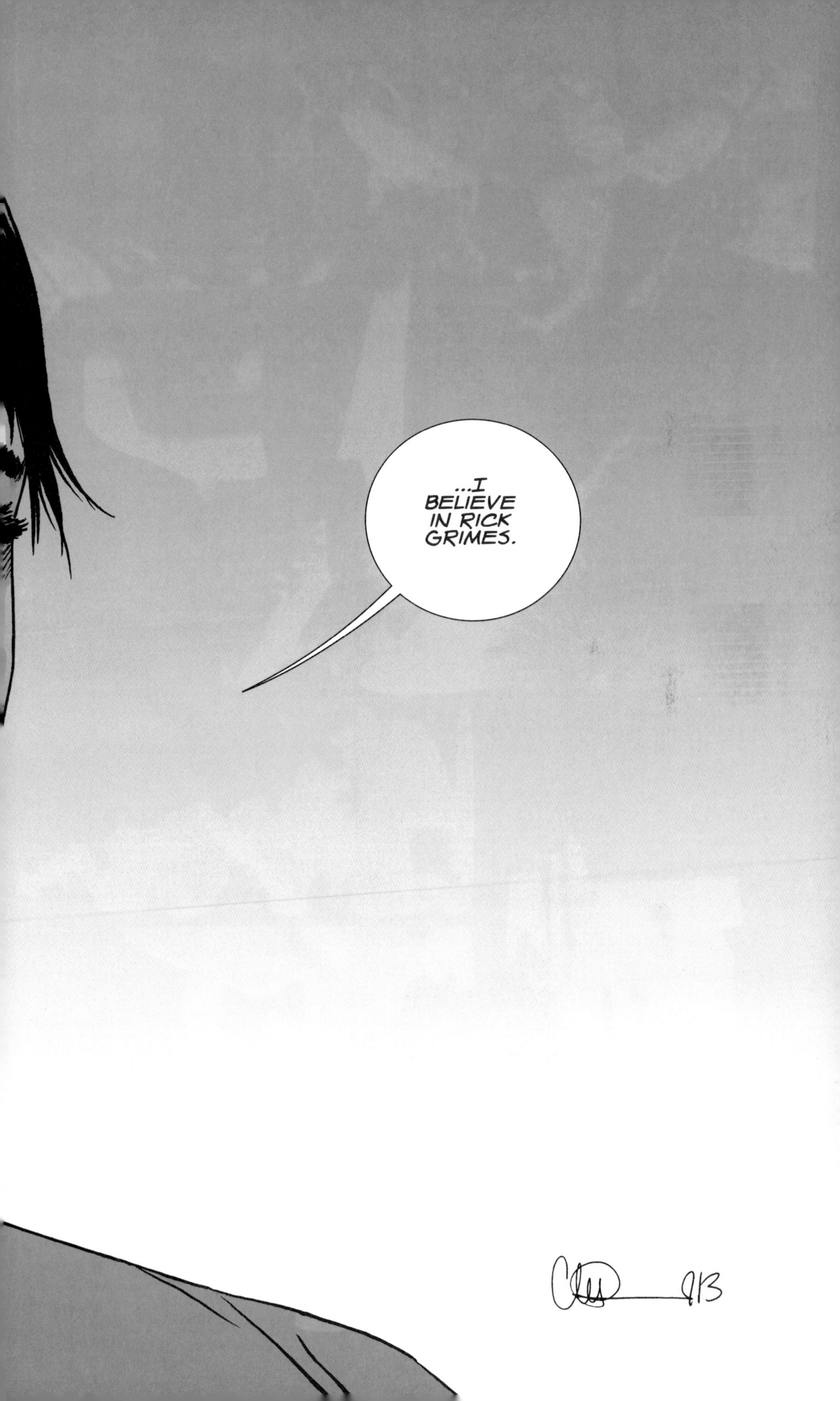
...I BELIEVE IN RICK GRIMES.

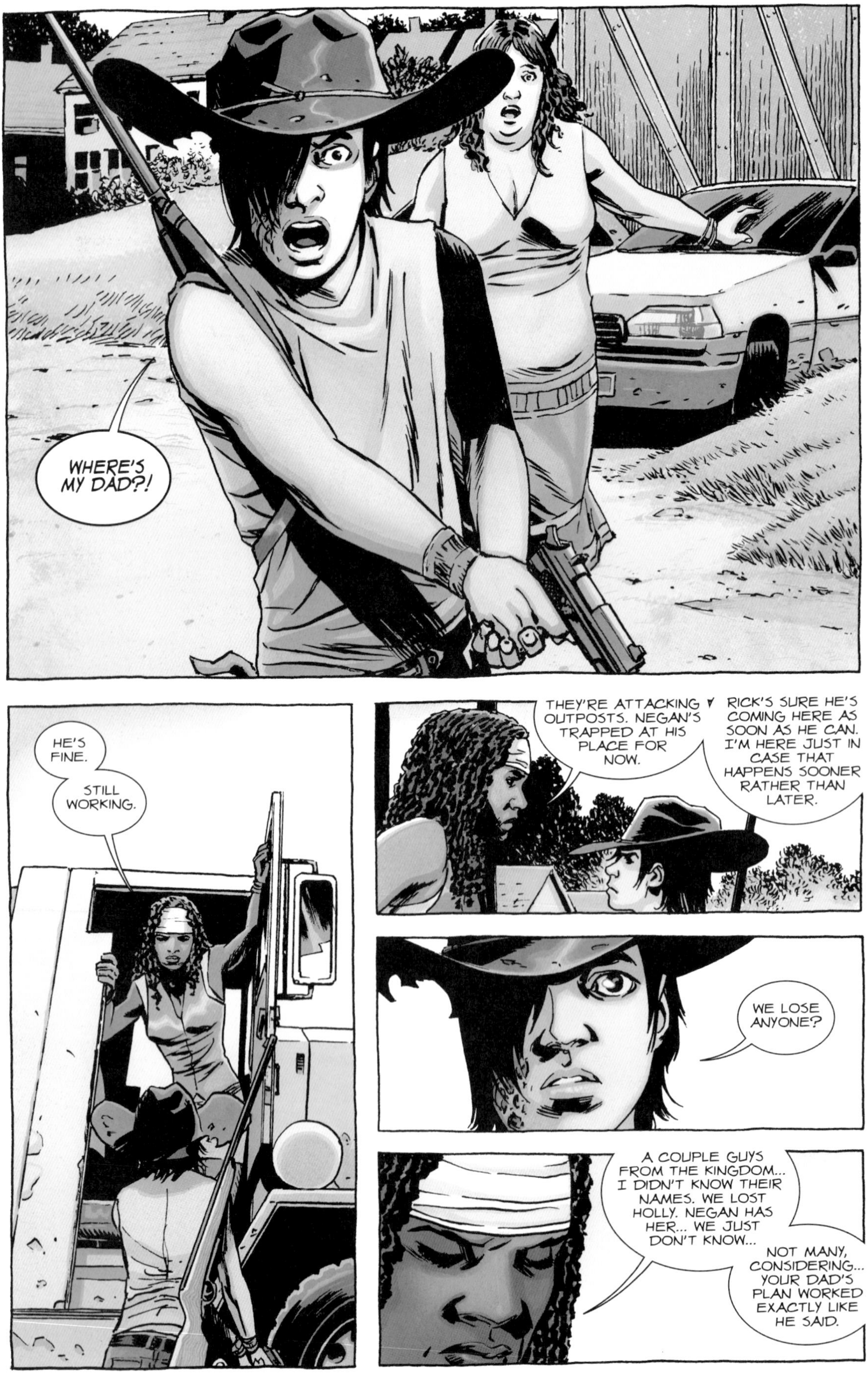
WHERE'S MY DAD?!
HE'S FINE.
STILL WORKING.
THEY'RE ATTACKING OUTPOSTS. NEGAN'S TRAPPED AT HIS PLACE FOR NOW.
RICK'S SURE HE'S COMING HERE AS SOON AS HE CAN. I'M HERE JUST IN CASE THAT HAPPENS SOONER RATHER THAN LATER.
WE LOSE ANYONE?
A COUPLE GUYS FROM THE KINGDOM... I DIDN'T KNOW THEIR NAMES. WE LOST HOLLY. NEGAN HAS HER... WE JUST DON'T KNOW...
NOT MANY, CONSIDERING... YOUR DAD'S PLAN WORKED EXACTLY LIKE HE SAID.

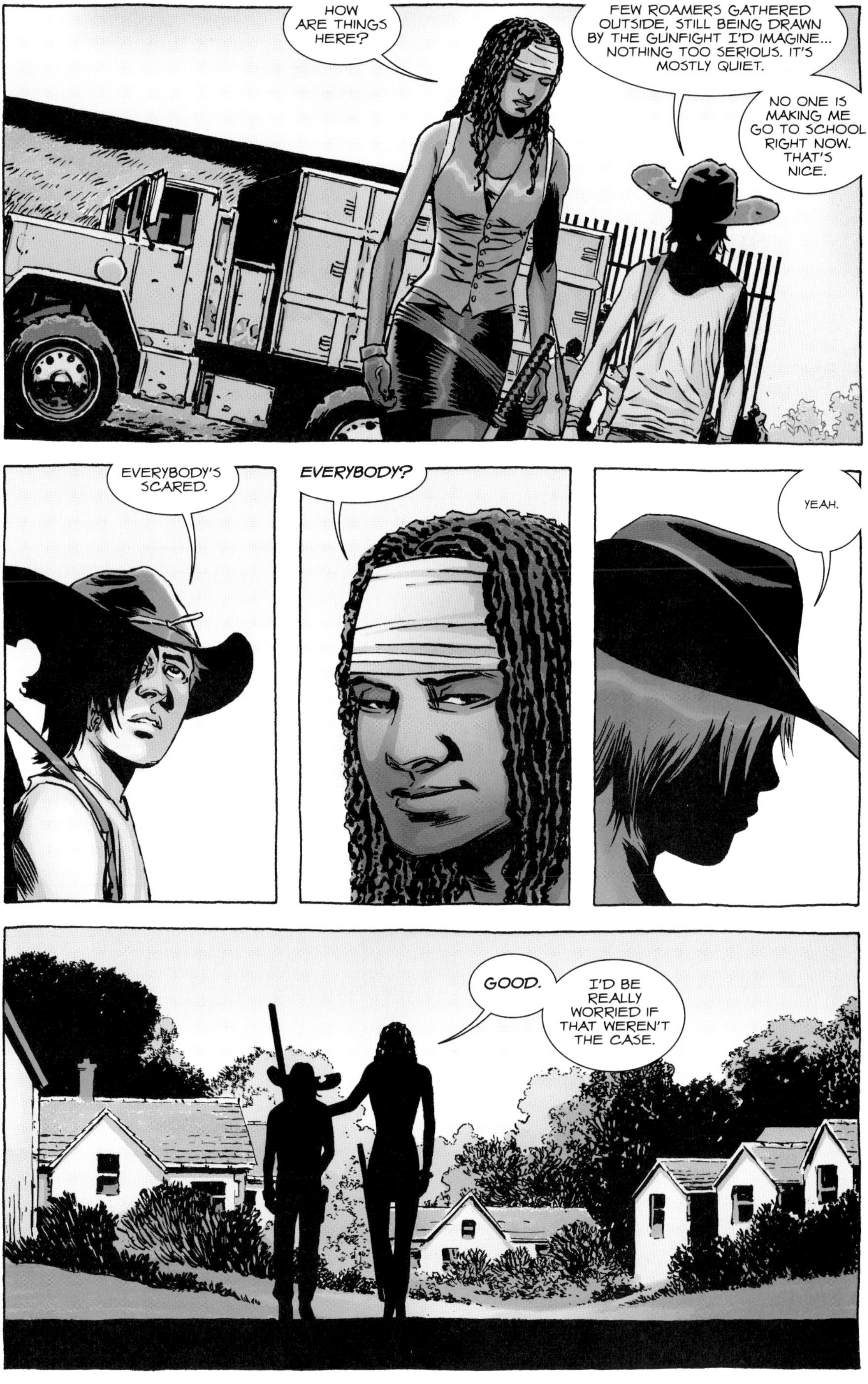
HOW ARE THINGS HERE?
FEW ROAMERS GATHERED OUTSIDE, STILL BEING DRAWN BY THE GUNFIGHT I'D IMAGINE... NOTHING TOO SERIOUS. IT'S MOSTLY QUIET.
NO ONE IS MAKING ME GO TO SCHOOL RIGHT NOW. THAT'S NICE.
EVERYBODY'S SCARED.
EVERYBODY?
YEAH.
GOOD.
I'D BE REALLY WORRIED IF THAT WEREN'T THE CASE.

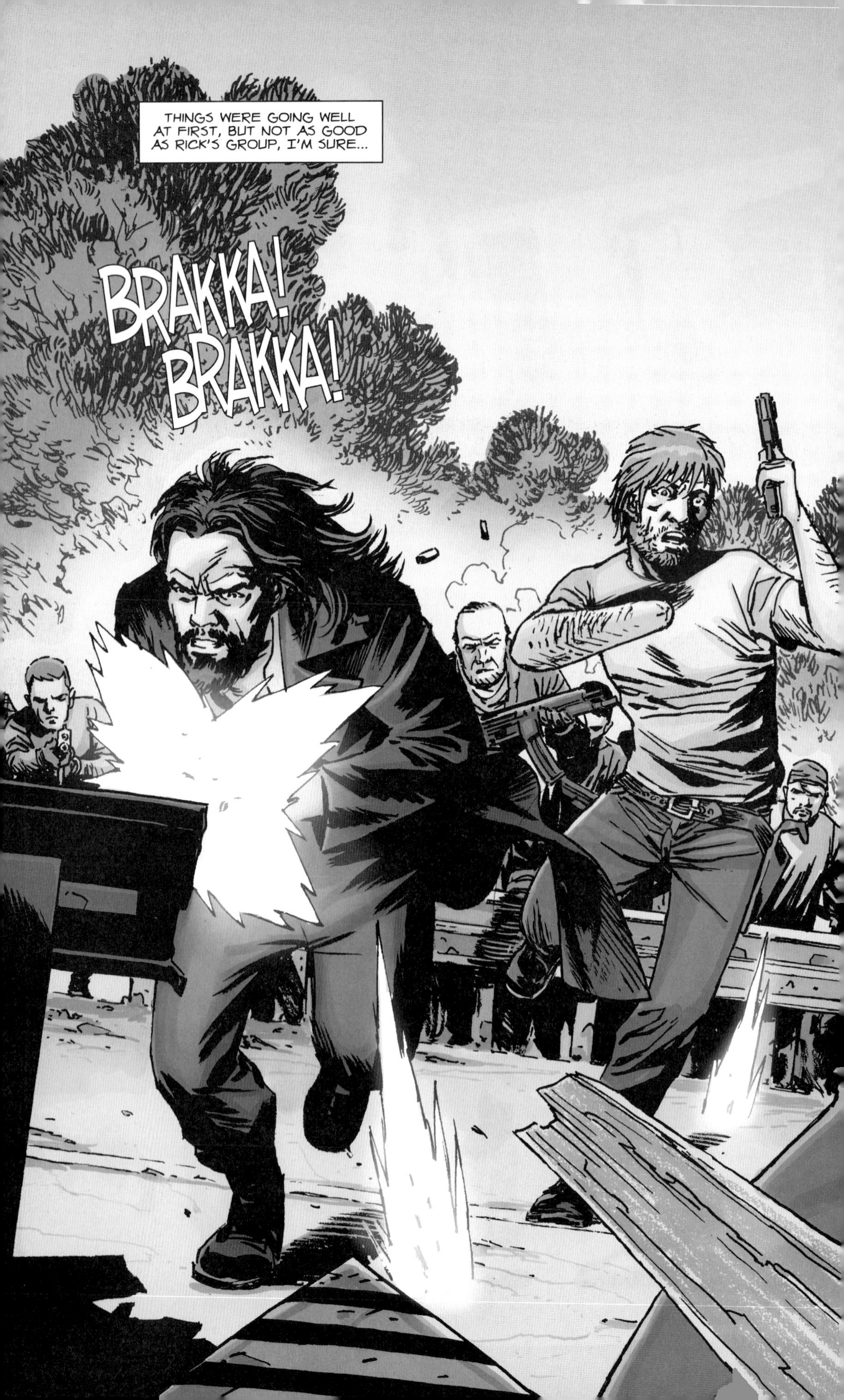
THINGS WERE GOING WELL AT FIRST, BUT NOT AS GOOD AS RICK'S GROUP, I'M SURE...
BRAKKA! BRAKKA!

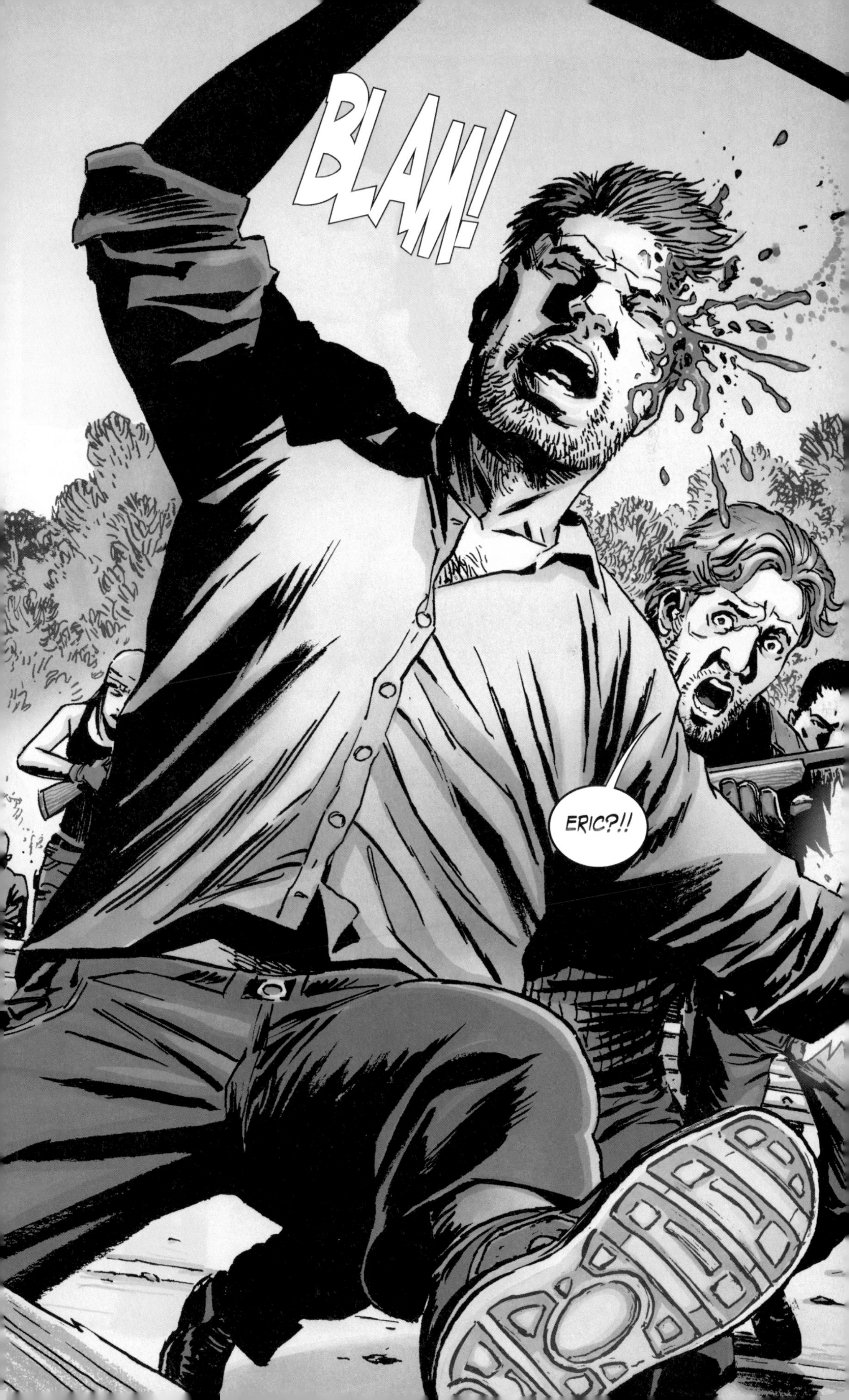
BLAM!
ERIC?!!

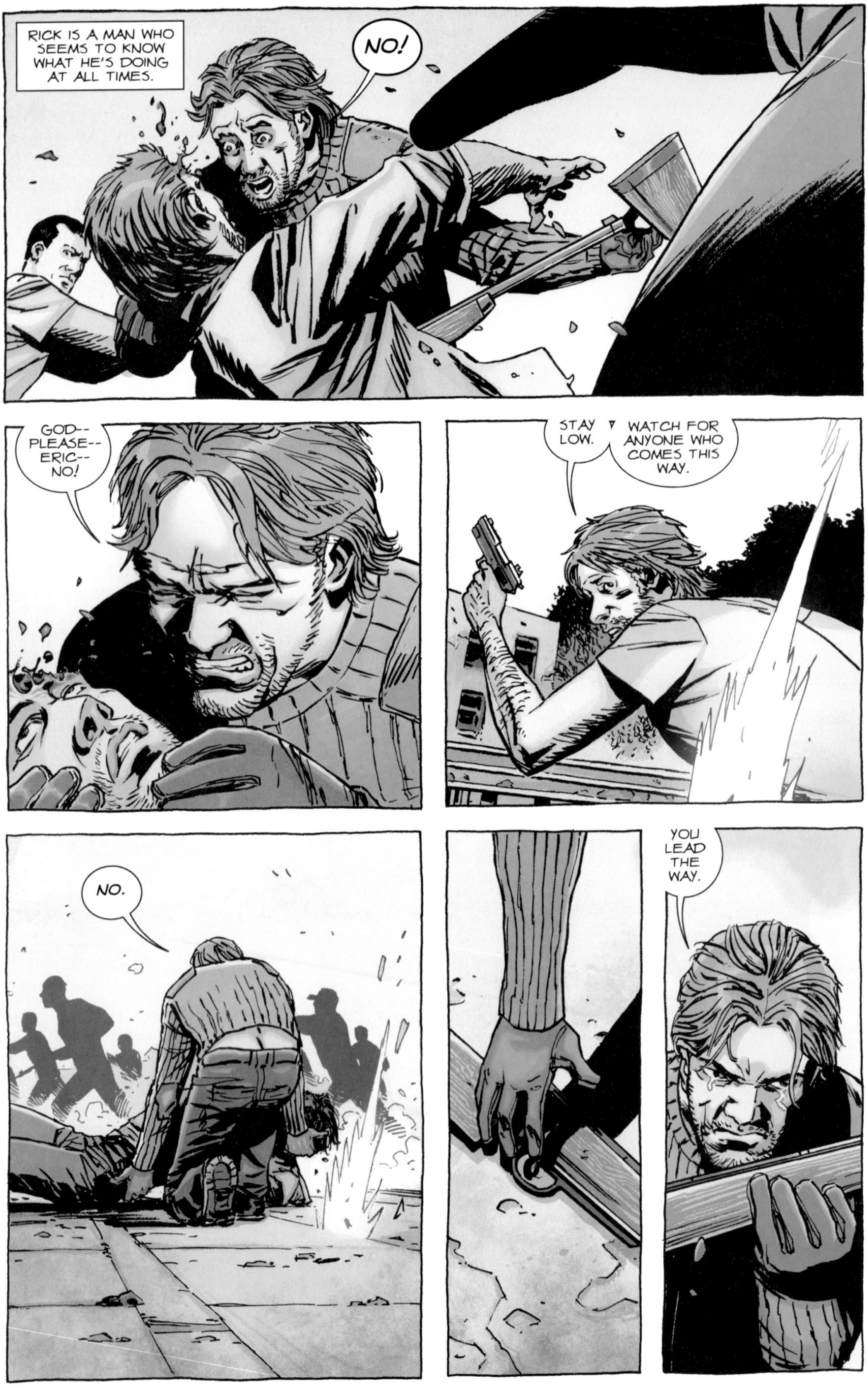
RICK IS A MAN WHO SEEMS TO KNOW WHAT HE'S DOING AT ALL TIMES.
NO!
GOD-- PLEASE-- ERIC-- NO!
STAY LOW.
WATCH FOR ANYONE WHO COMES THIS WAY.
NO.
YOU LEAD THE WAY.

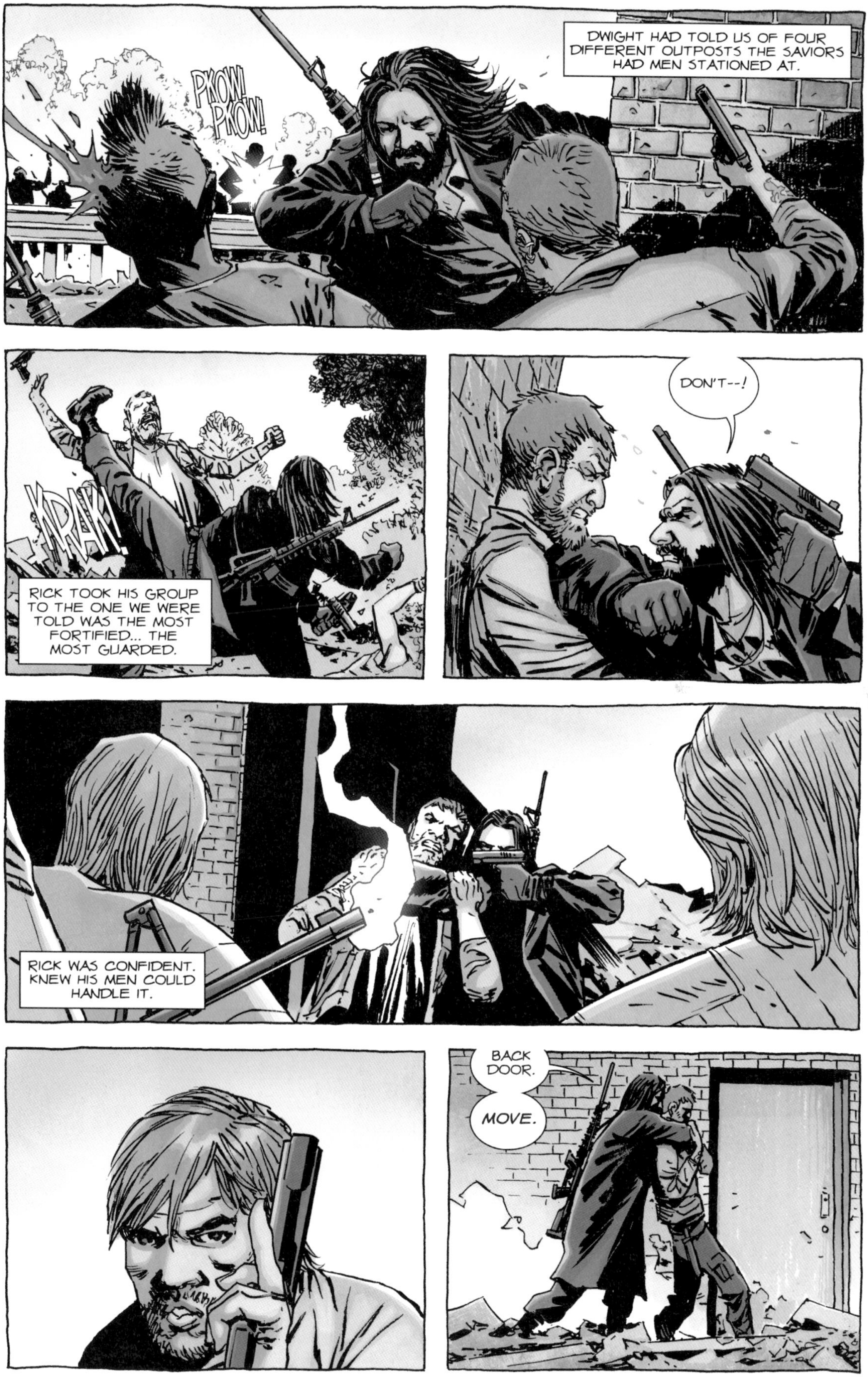
DWIGHT HAD TOLD US OF FOUR DIFFERENT OUTPOSTS THE SAVIORS HAD MEN STATIONED AT.
PKOW! PKOW!
KRAK!
RICK TOOK HIS GROUP TO THE ONE WE WERE TOLD WAS THE MOST FORTIFIED... THE MOST GUARDED.
DON'T--!
RICK WAS CONFIDENT. KNEW HIS MEN COULD HANDLE IT.
BACK DOOR.
MOVE.

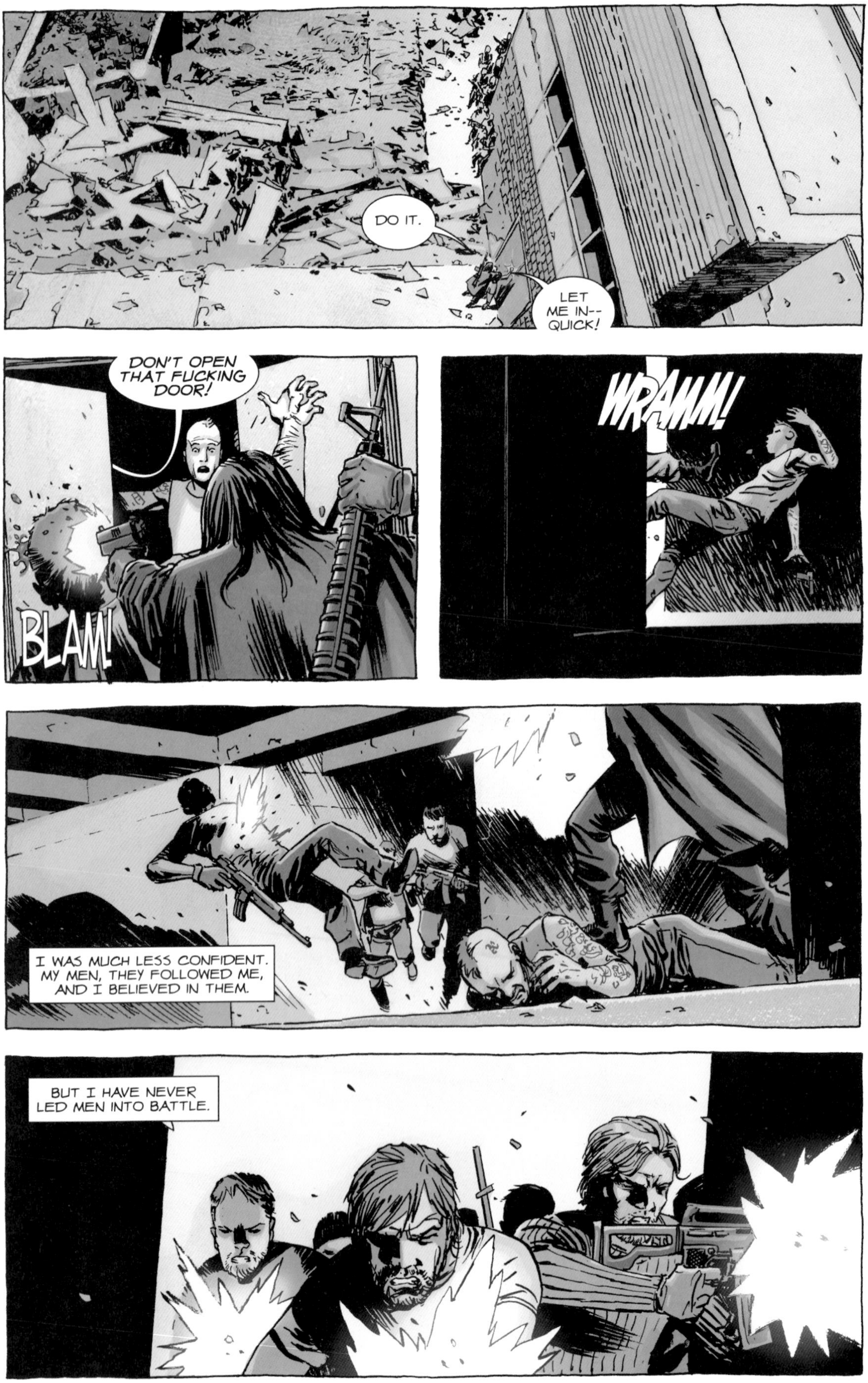
DO IT.
LET ME IN-- QUICK!
DON'T OPEN THAT FUCKING DOOR!
BLAM!
WRAMM!
I WAS MUCH LESS CONFIDENT. MY MEN, THEY FOLLOWED ME, AND I BELIEVED IN THEM.
BUT I HAVE NEVER LED MEN INTO BATTLE.

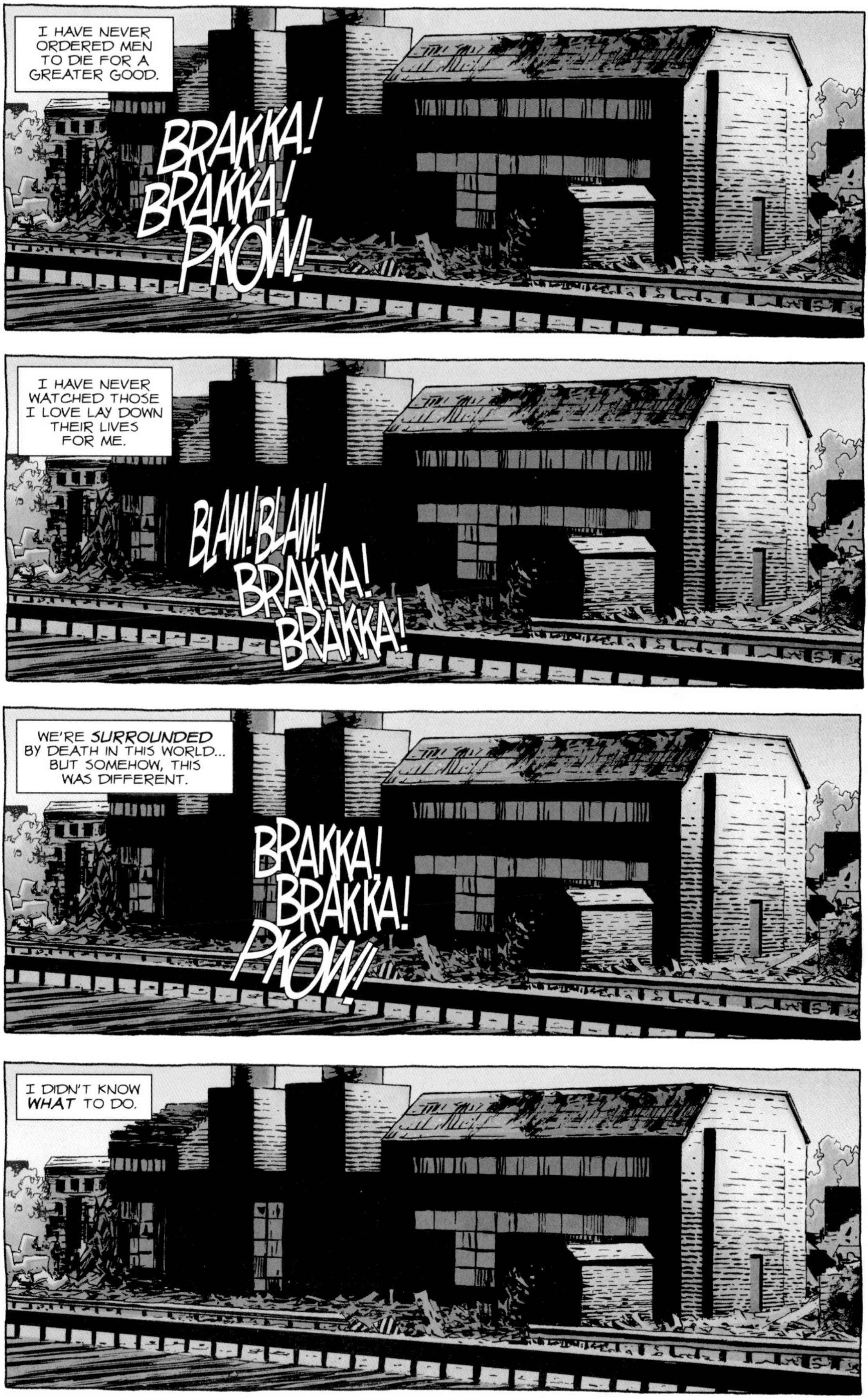
I HAVE NEVER ORDERED MEN TO DIE FOR A GREATER GOOD.
BRAKKA! BRAKKA! PKOW!
I HAVE NEVER WATCHED THOSE I LOVE LAY DOWN THEIR LIVES FOR ME.
BLAM! BLAM! BRAKKA! BRAKKA!
WE'RE SURROUNDED BY DEATH IN THIS WORLD... BUT SOMEHOW, THIS WAS DIFFERENT.
BRAKKA! BRAKKA! PKOW!
I DIDN'T KNOW WHAT TO DO.

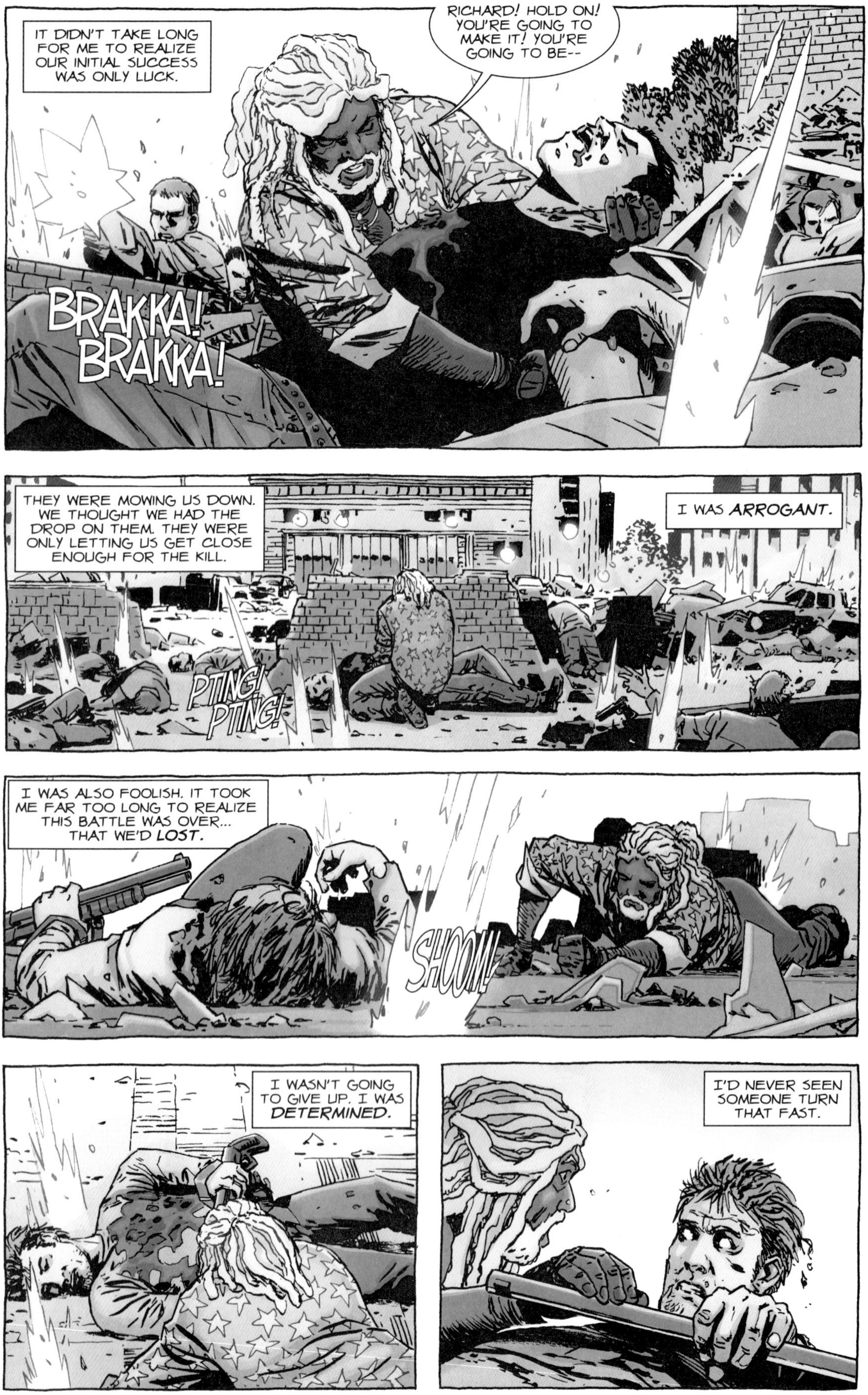
IT DIDN'T TAKE LONG FOR ME TO REALIZE OUR INITIAL SUCCESS WAS ONLY LUCK.
RICHARD! HOLD ON! YOU'RE GOING TO MAKE IT! YOU'RE GOING TO BE--
BRAKKA! BRAKKA!
THEY WERE MOWING US DOWN. WE THOUGHT WE HAD THE DROP ON THEM. THEY WERE ONLY LETTING US GET CLOSE ENOUGH FOR THE KILL.
I WAS ARROGANT.
PTING! PTING!
I WAS ALSO FOOLISH. IT TOOK ME FAR TOO LONG TO REALIZE THIS BATTLE WAS OVER... THAT WE'D LOST.
SHOOM!
I WASN'T GOING TO GIVE UP. I WAS DETERMINED.
I'D NEVER SEEN SOMEONE TURN THAT FAST.

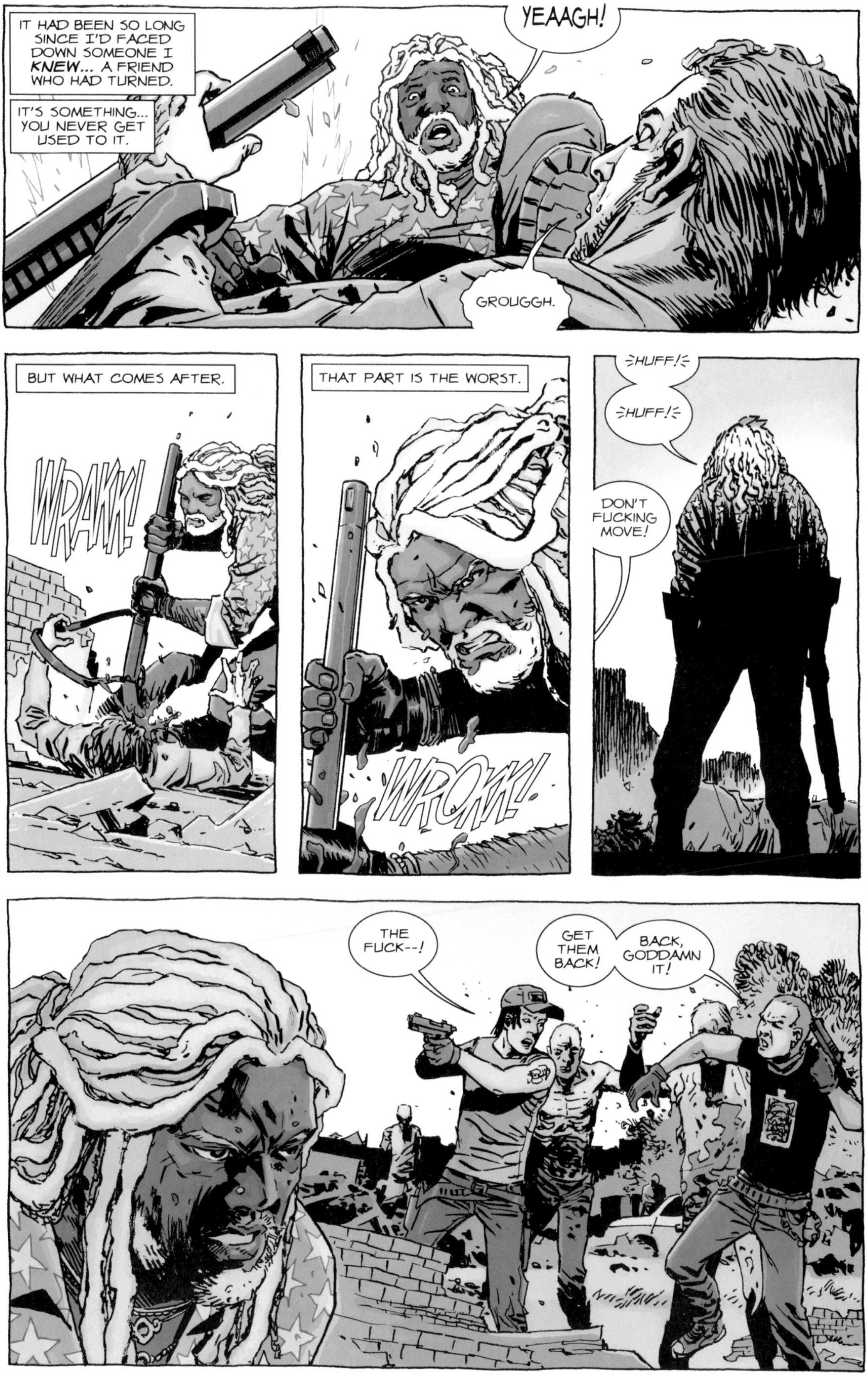
IT HAD BEEN SO LONG SINCE I'D FACED DOWN SOMEONE I KNEW... A FRIEND WHO HAD TURNED.
IT'S SOMETHING... YOU NEVER GET USED TO IT.
YEAAGH!
GROUGGH.
BUT WHAT COMES AFTER.
WRAKK!
THAT PART IS THE WORST.
WROKK!
HUFF!
HUFF!
DON'T FUCKING MOVE!
THE FUCK--!
GET THEM BACK!
BACK, GODDAMN IT!

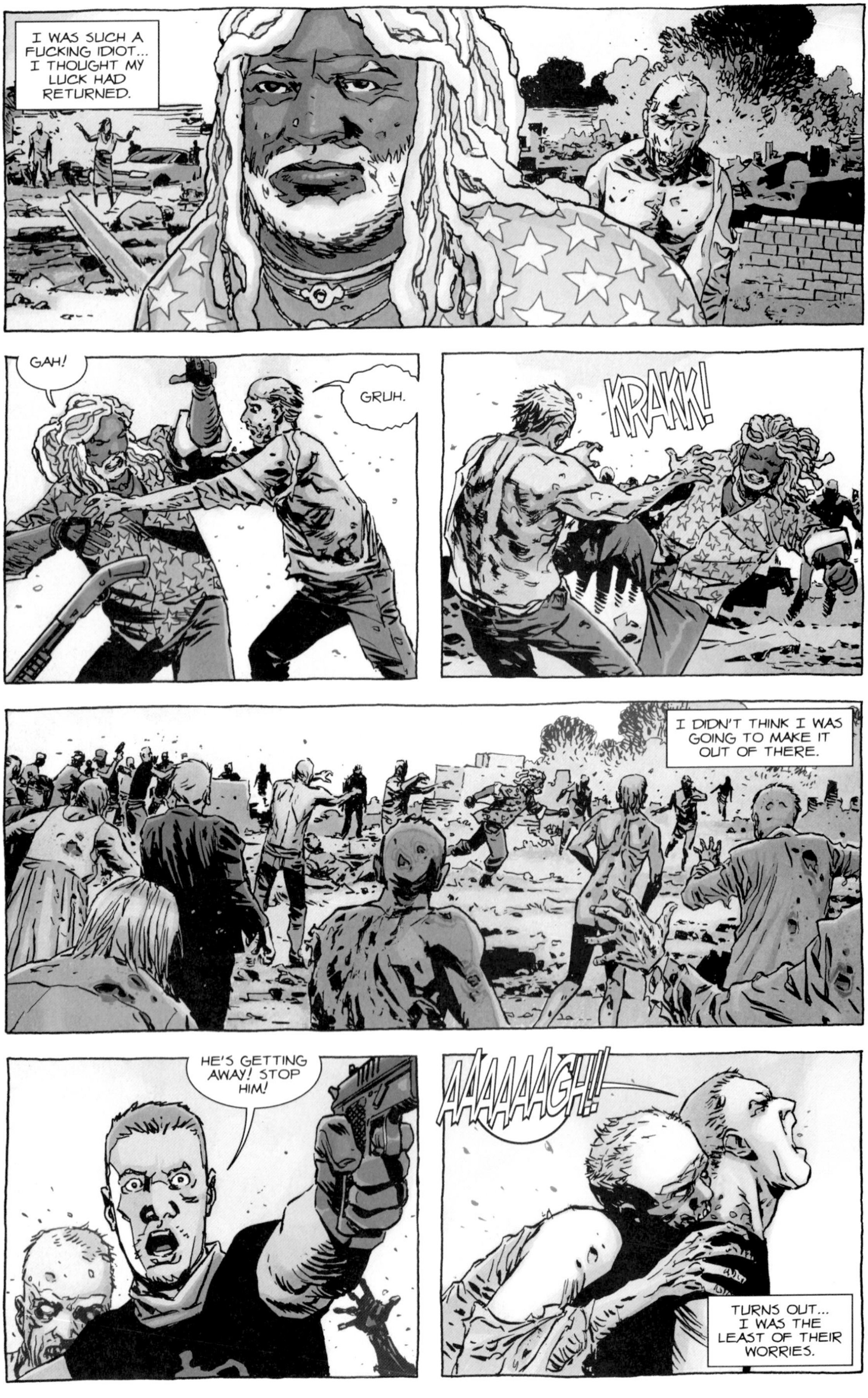
I WAS SUCH A FUCKING IDIOT... I THOUGHT MY LUCK HAD RETURNED.
GAH!
GRUH.
KRAKK!
I DIDN'T THINK I WAS GOING TO MAKE IT OUT OF THERE.
HE'S GETTING AWAY! STOP HIM!
AAAAAAGH!!
TURNS OUT... I WAS THE LEAST OF THEIR WORRIES.

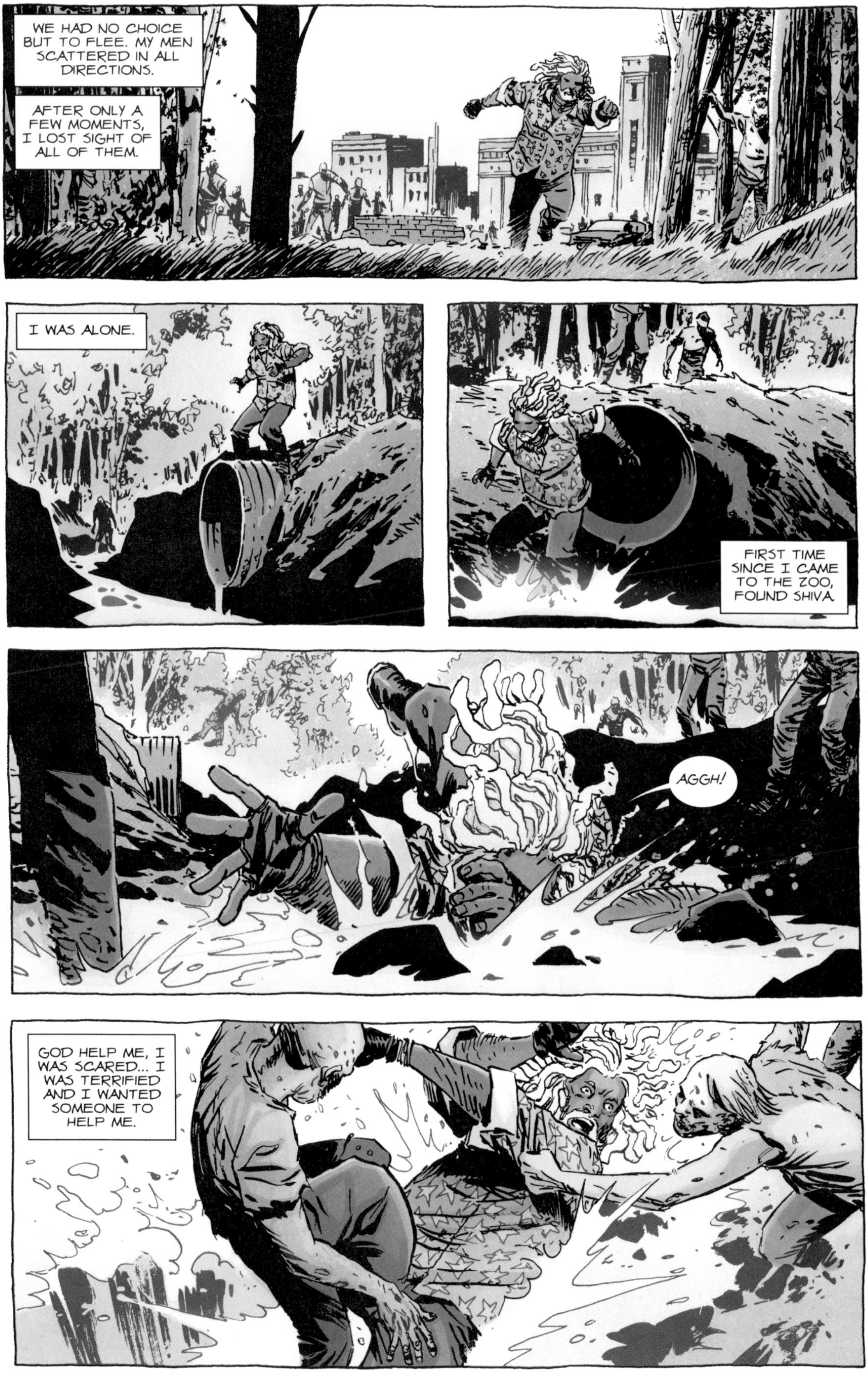

WE HAD NO CHOICE BUT TO FLEE. MY MEN SCATTERED IN ALL DIRECTIONS.
AFTER ONLY A FEW MOMENTS, I LOST SIGHT OF ALL OF THEM.
I WAS ALONE.
FIRST TIME SINCE I CAME TO THE ZOO, FOUND SHIVA.
AGGH!
GOD HELP ME, I WAS SCARED... I WAS TERRIFIED AND I WANTED SOMEONE TO HELP ME.

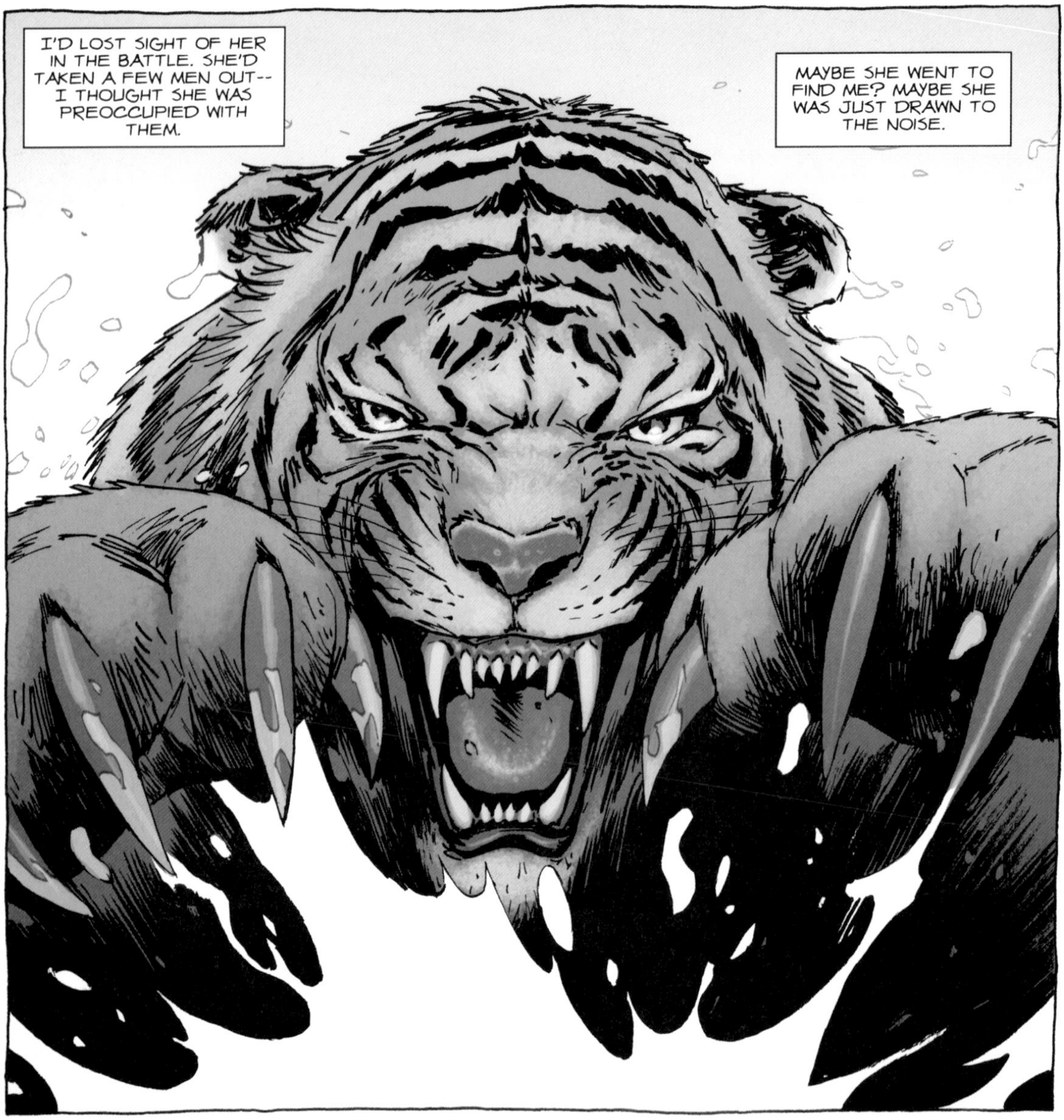
I'D LOST SIGHT OF HER IN THE BATTLE. SHE'D TAKEN A FEW MEN OUT-- I THOUGHT SHE WAS PREOCCUPIED WITH THEM.
MAYBE SHE WENT TO FIND ME? MAYBE SHE WAS JUST DRAWN TO THE NOISE.
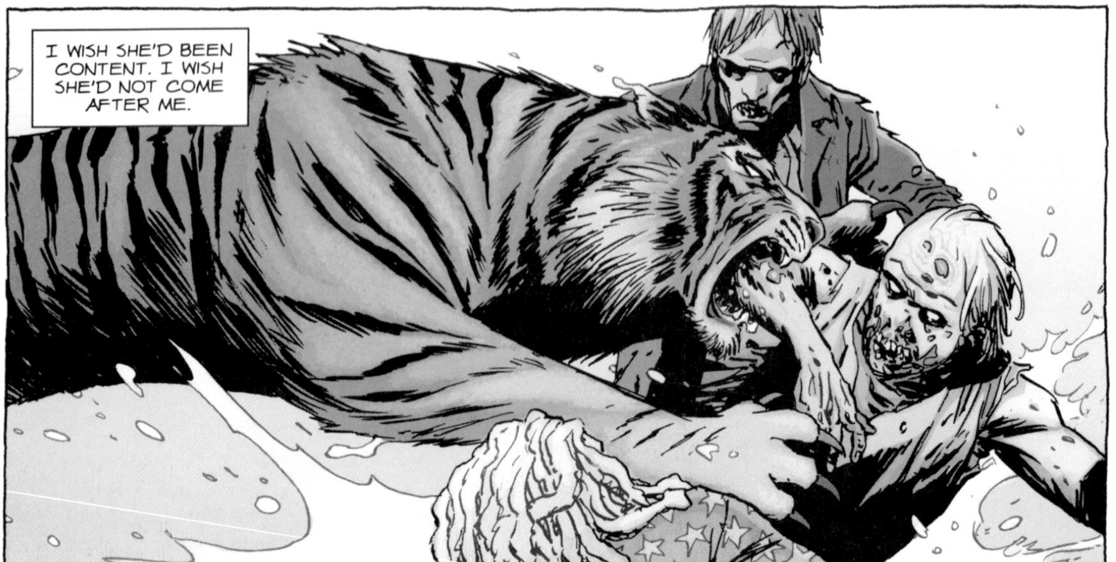
I WISH SHE'D BEEN CONTENT. I WISH SHE'D NOT COME AFTER ME.

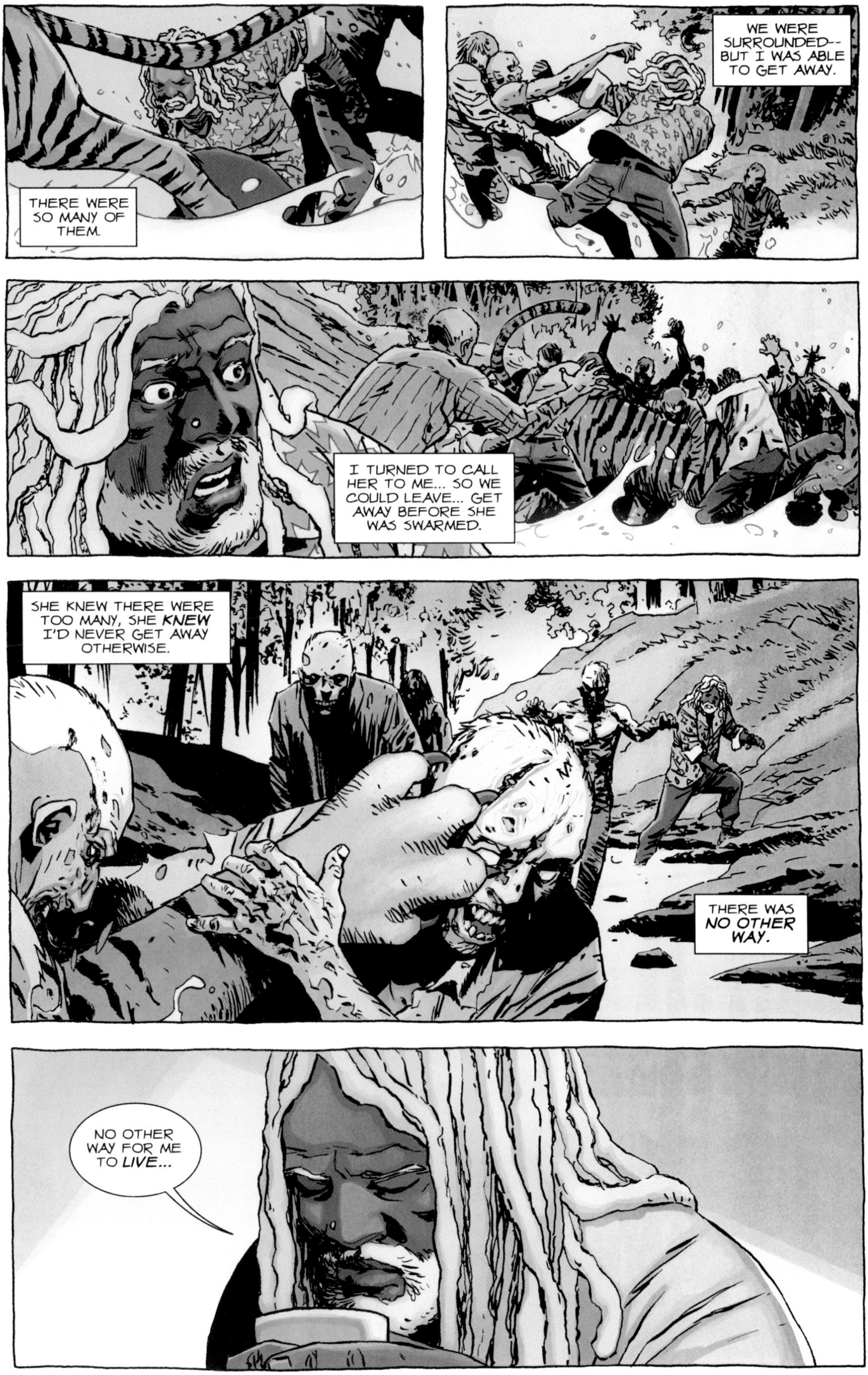
THERE WERE SO MANY OF THEM.
WE WERE SURROUNDED-- BUT I WAS ABLE TO GET AWAY.
I TURNED TO CALL HER TO ME... SO WE COULD LEAVE... GET AWAY BEFORE SHE WAS SWARMED.
SHE KNEW THERE WERE TOO MANY, SHE KNEW I'D NEVER GET AWAY OTHERWISE.
THERE WAS NO OTHER WAY.
NO OTHER WAY FOR ME TO LIVE...

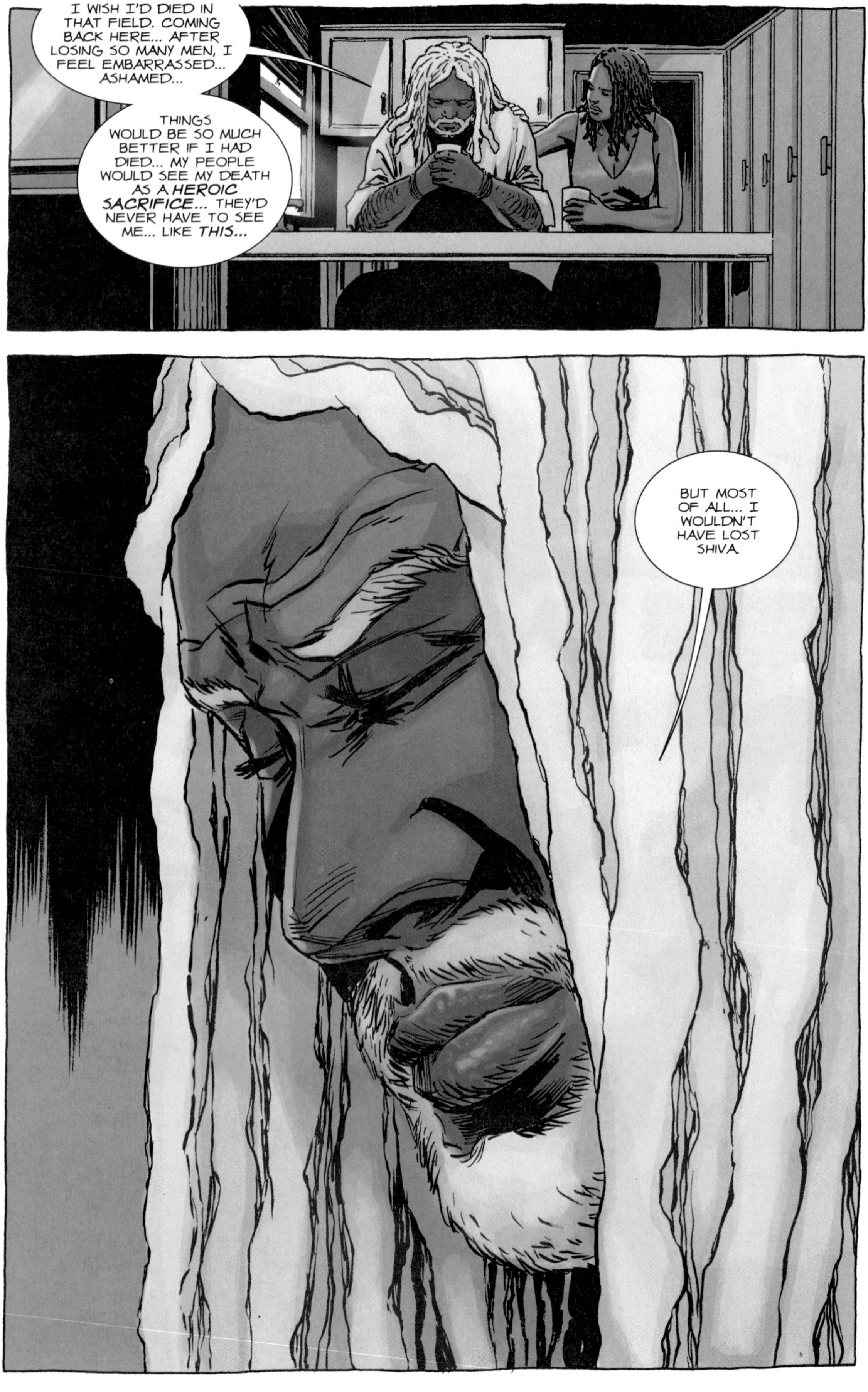
I WISH I'D DIED IN THAT FIELD. COMING BACK HERE... AFTER LOSING SO MANY MEN, I FEEL EMBARRASSED... ASHAMED...
THINGS WOULD BE SO MUCH BETTER IF I HAD DIED... MY PEOPLE WOULD SEE MY DEATH AS A HEROIC SACRIFICE... THEY'D NEVER HAVE TO SEE ME... LIKE THIS...
BUT MOST OF ALL... I WOULDN'T HAVE LOST SHIVA.

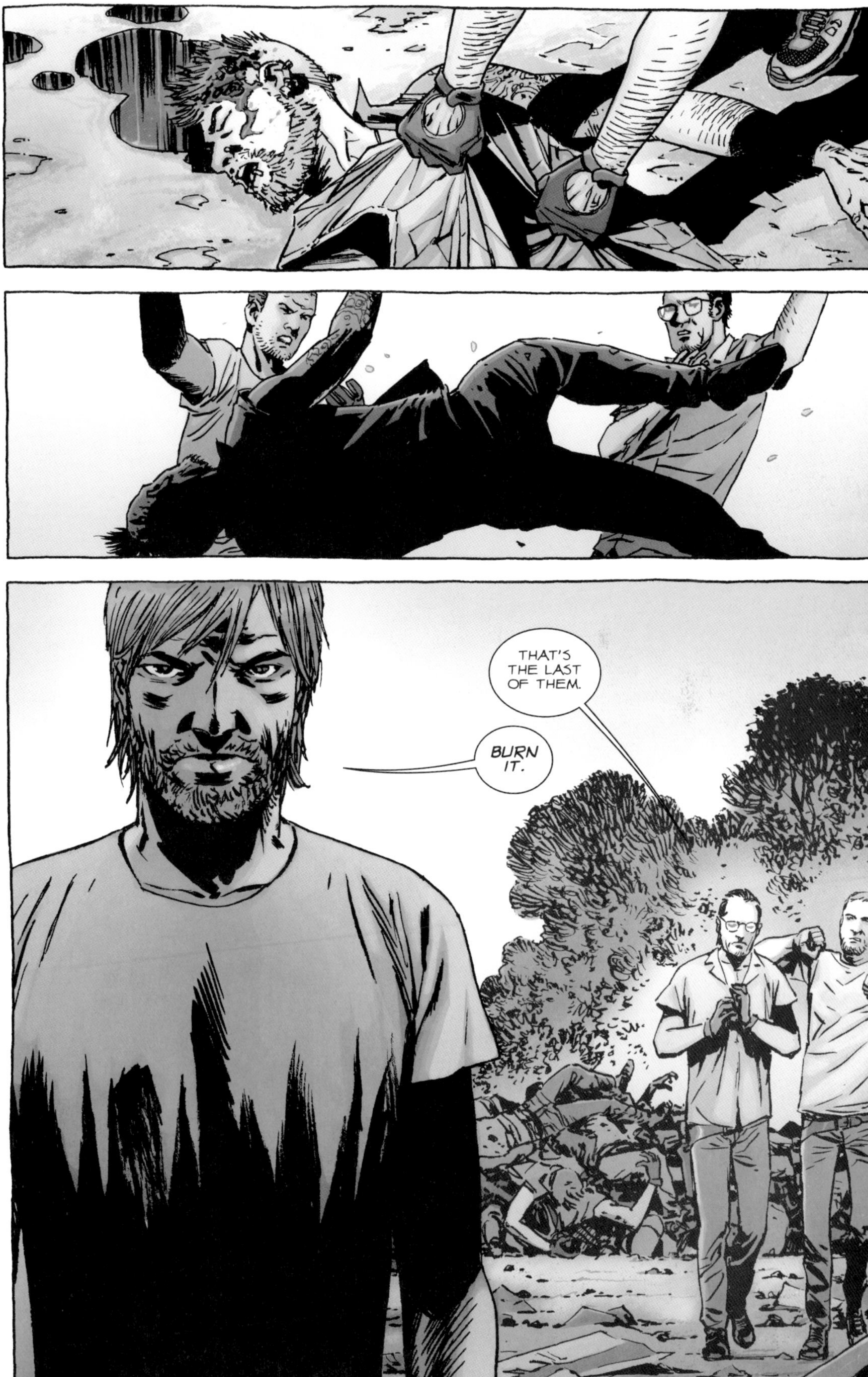
THAT'S THE LAST OF THEM.
BURN IT.

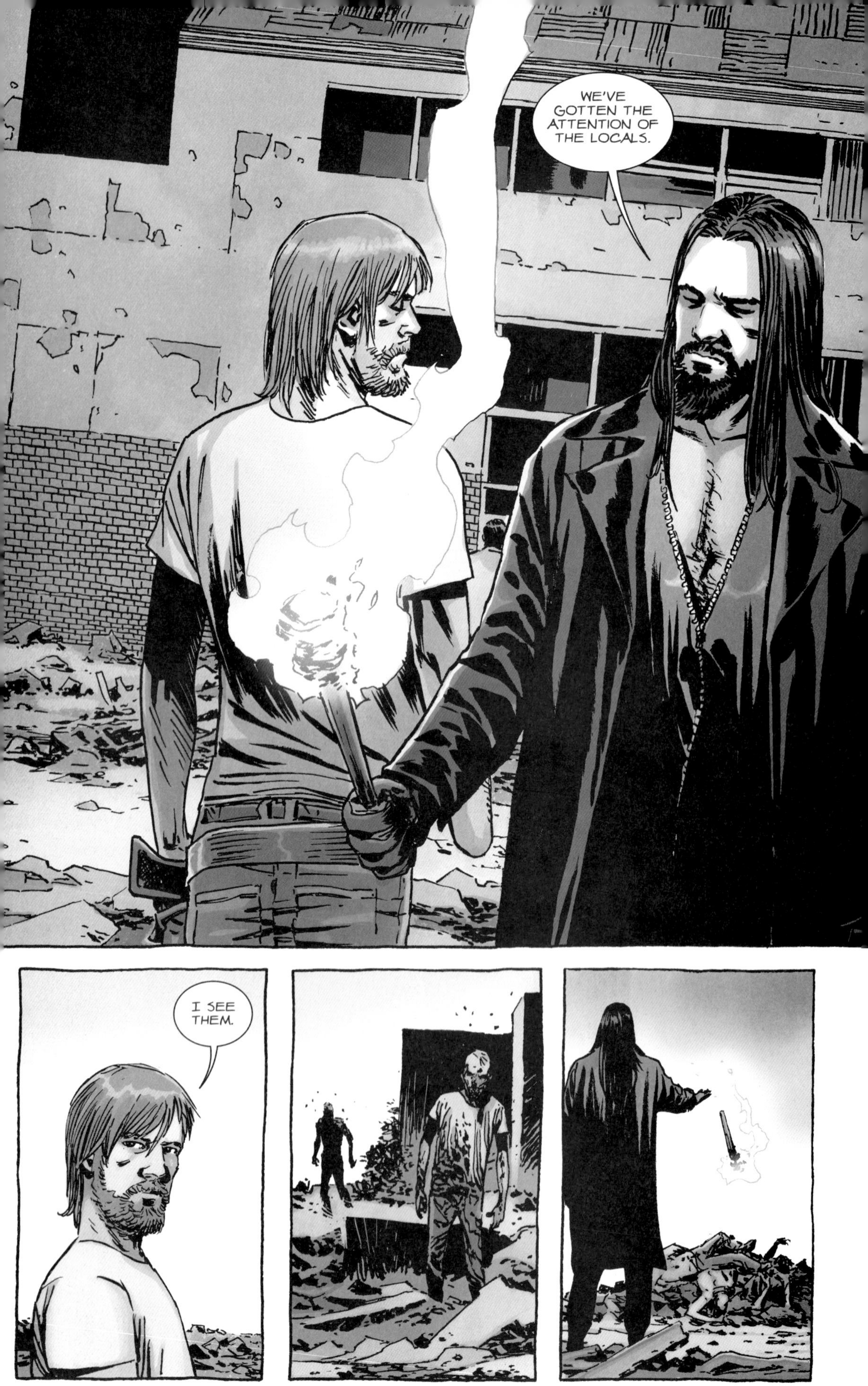
WE'VE GOTTEN THE ATTENTION OF THE LOCALS.
I SEE THEM.

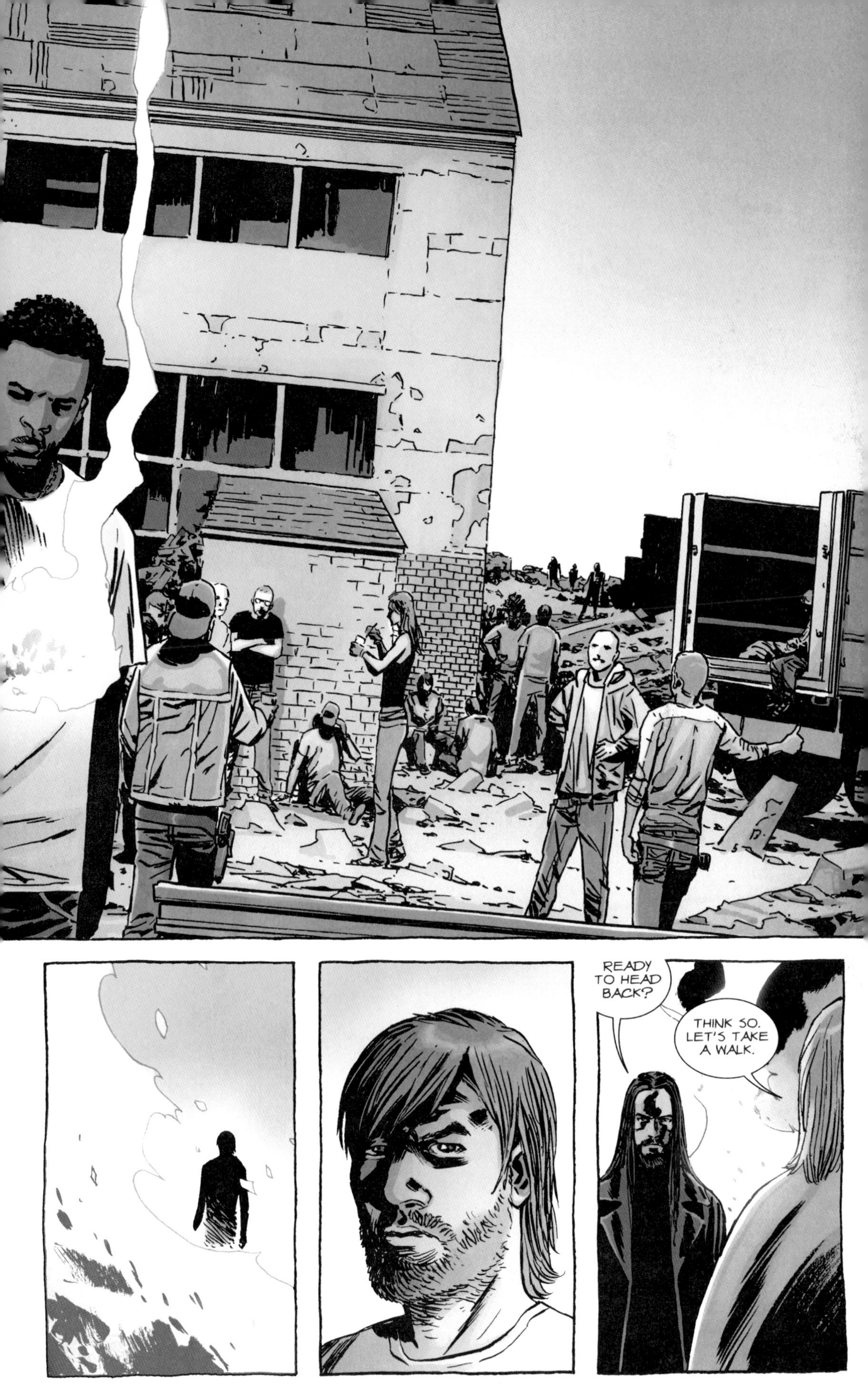
READY TO HEAD BACK?
THINK SO. LET'S TAKE A WALK.

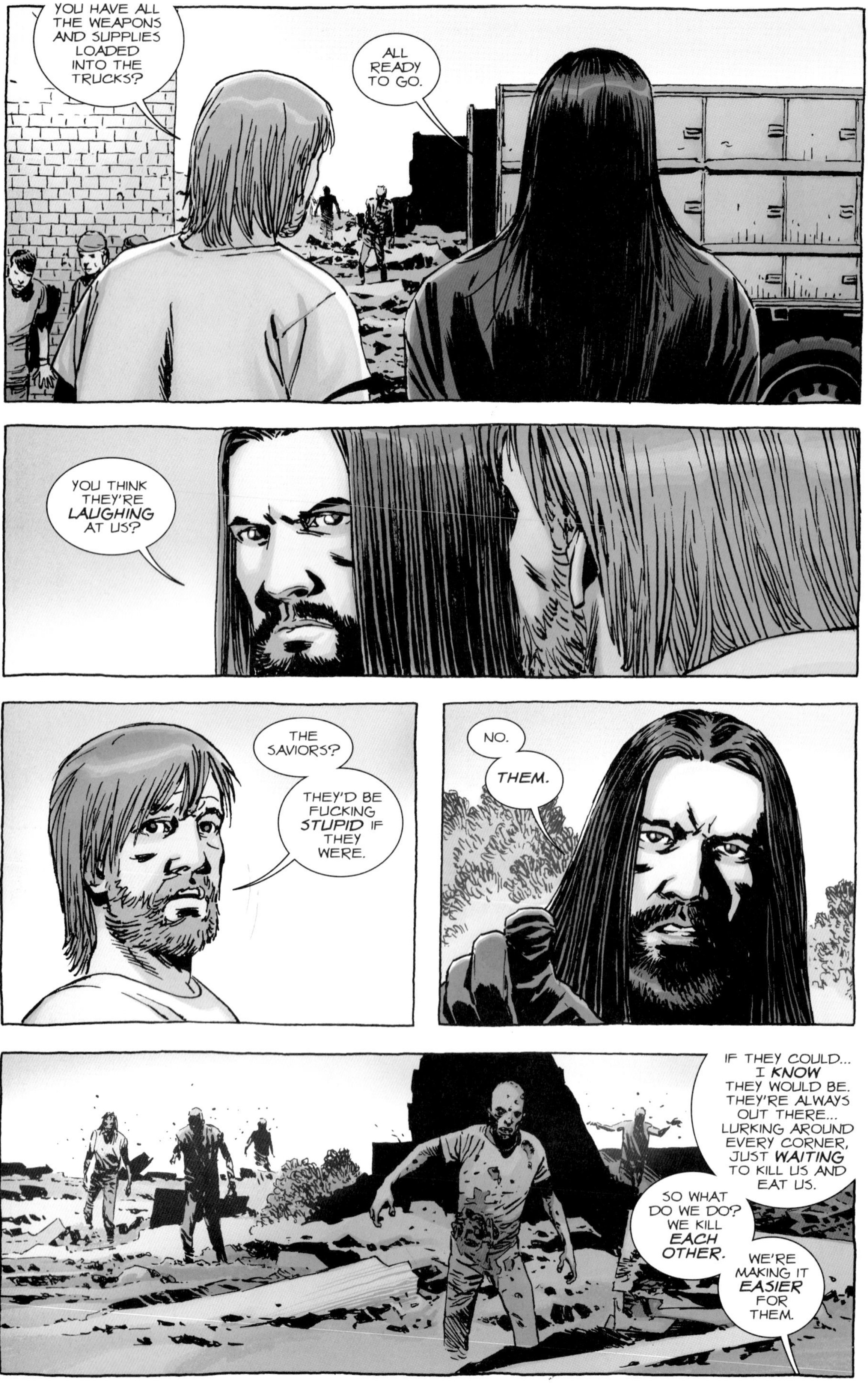
YOU HAVE ALL THE WEAPONS AND SUPPLIES LOADED INTO THE TRUCKS?
ALL READY TO GO.
YOU THINK THEY'RE *LAUGHING* AT US?
THE SAVIORS?
THEY'D BE FUCKING *STUPID* IF THEY WERE.
NO.
THEM.
IF THEY COULD... I *KNOW* THEY WOULD BE. THEY'RE ALWAYS OUT THERE... LURKING AROUND EVERY CORNER, JUST *WAITING* TO KILL US AND EAT US.
SO WHAT DO WE DO? WE KILL *EACH OTHER.*
WE'RE MAKING IT *EASIER* FOR THEM.

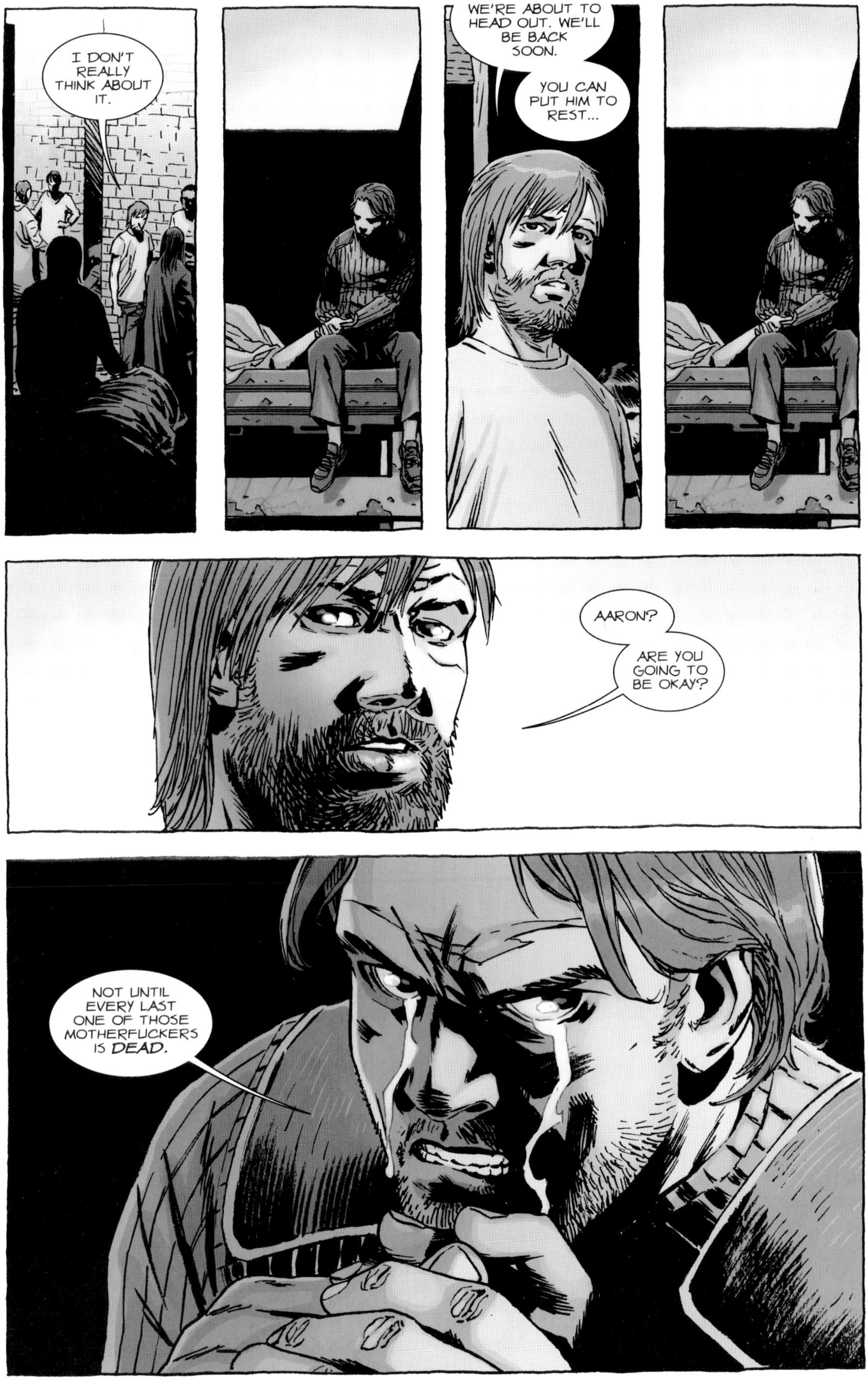
I DON'T REALLY THINK ABOUT IT.
WE'RE ABOUT TO HEAD OUT. WE'LL BE BACK SOON.
YOU CAN PUT HIM TO REST...
AARON?
ARE YOU GOING TO BE OKAY?
NOT UNTIL EVERY LAST ONE OF THOSE MOTHERFUCKERS IS *DEAD.*

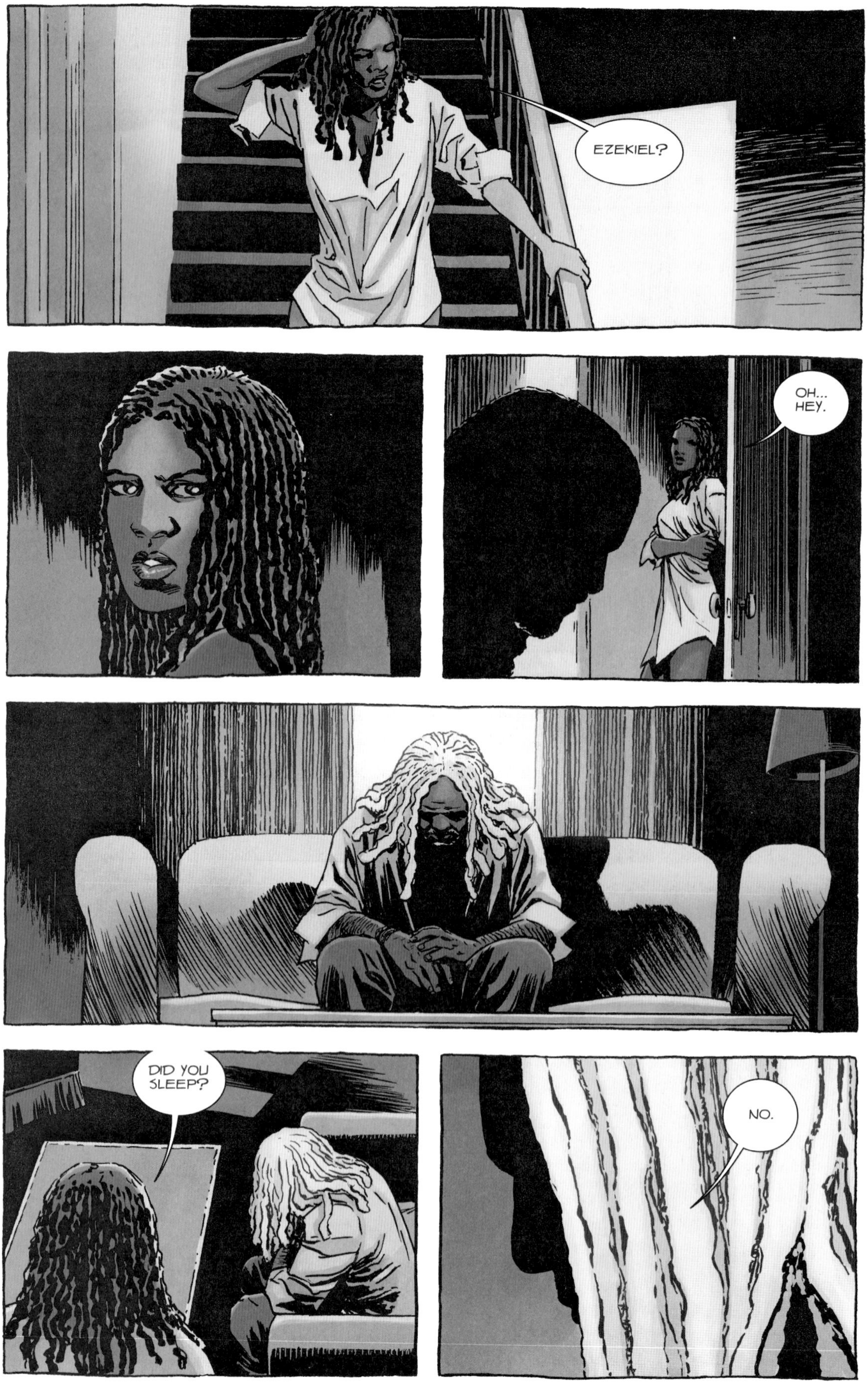
EZEKIEL?
OH... HEY.
DID YOU SLEEP?
NO.

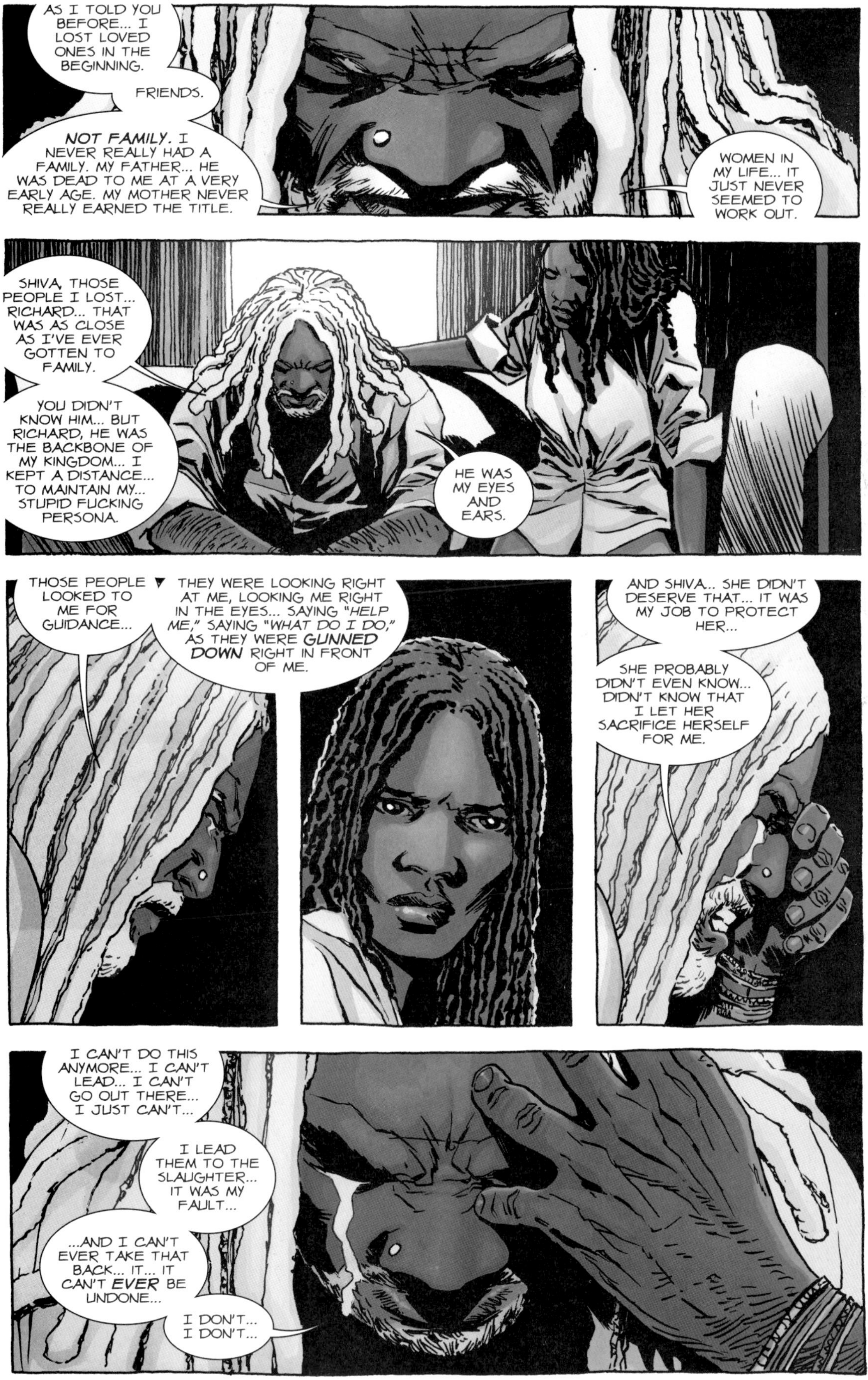

AS I TOLD YOU BEFORE... I LOST LOVED ONES IN THE BEGINNING.
FRIENDS.
NOT FAMILY. I NEVER REALLY HAD A FAMILY. MY FATHER... HE WAS DEAD TO ME AT A VERY EARLY AGE. MY MOTHER NEVER REALLY EARNED THE TITLE.
WOMEN IN MY LIFE... IT JUST NEVER SEEMED TO WORK OUT.
SHIVA, THOSE PEOPLE I LOST... RICHARD... THAT WAS AS CLOSE AS I'VE EVER GOTTEN TO FAMILY.
YOU DIDN'T KNOW HIM... BUT RICHARD, HE WAS THE BACKBONE OF MY KINGDOM... I KEPT A DISTANCE... TO MAINTAIN MY... STUPID FUCKING PERSONA.
HE WAS MY EYES AND EARS.
THOSE PEOPLE LOOKED TO ME FOR GUIDANCE...
THEY WERE LOOKING RIGHT AT ME, LOOKING ME RIGHT IN THE EYES... SAYING "HELP ME," SAYING "WHAT DO I DO," AS THEY WERE GUNNED DOWN RIGHT IN FRONT OF ME.
AND SHIVA... SHE DIDN'T DESERVE THAT... IT WAS MY JOB TO PROTECT HER...
SHE PROBABLY DIDN'T EVEN KNOW... DIDN'T KNOW THAT I LET HER SACRIFICE HERSELF FOR ME.
I CAN'T DO THIS ANYMORE... I CAN'T LEAD... I CAN'T GO OUT THERE... I JUST CAN'T...
I LEAD THEM TO THE SLAUGHTER... IT WAS MY FAULT...
...AND I CAN'T EVER TAKE THAT BACK... IT... IT CAN'T EVER BE UNDONE...
I DON'T... I DON'T...

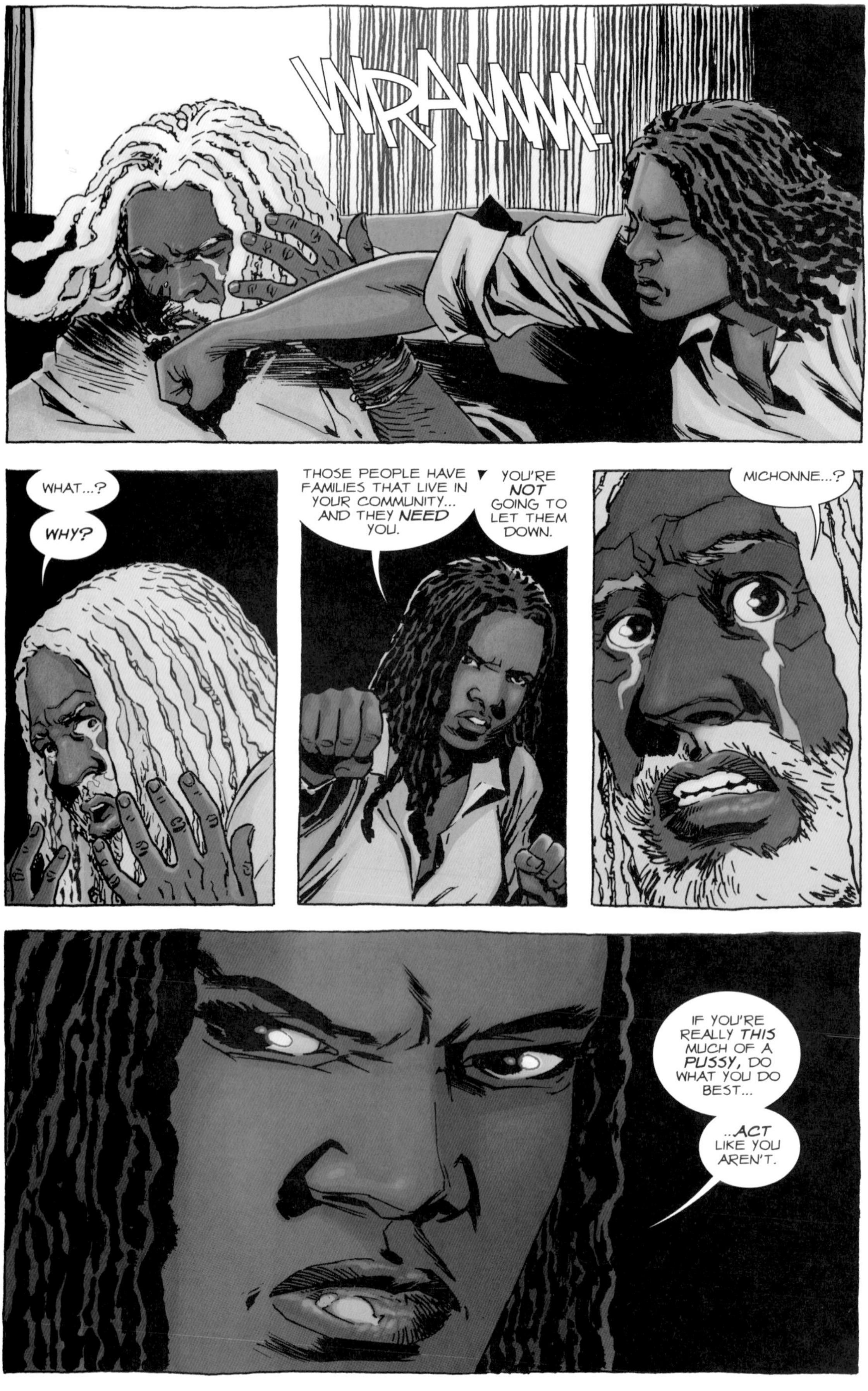
WRAMM!
WHAT...?
WHY?
THOSE PEOPLE HAVE FAMILIES THAT LIVE IN YOUR COMMUNITY... AND THEY NEED YOU.
YOU'RE NOT GOING TO LET THEM DOWN.
MICHONNE...?
IF YOU'RE REALLY THIS MUCH OF A PUSSY, DO WHAT YOU DO BEST...
...ACT LIKE YOU AREN'T.

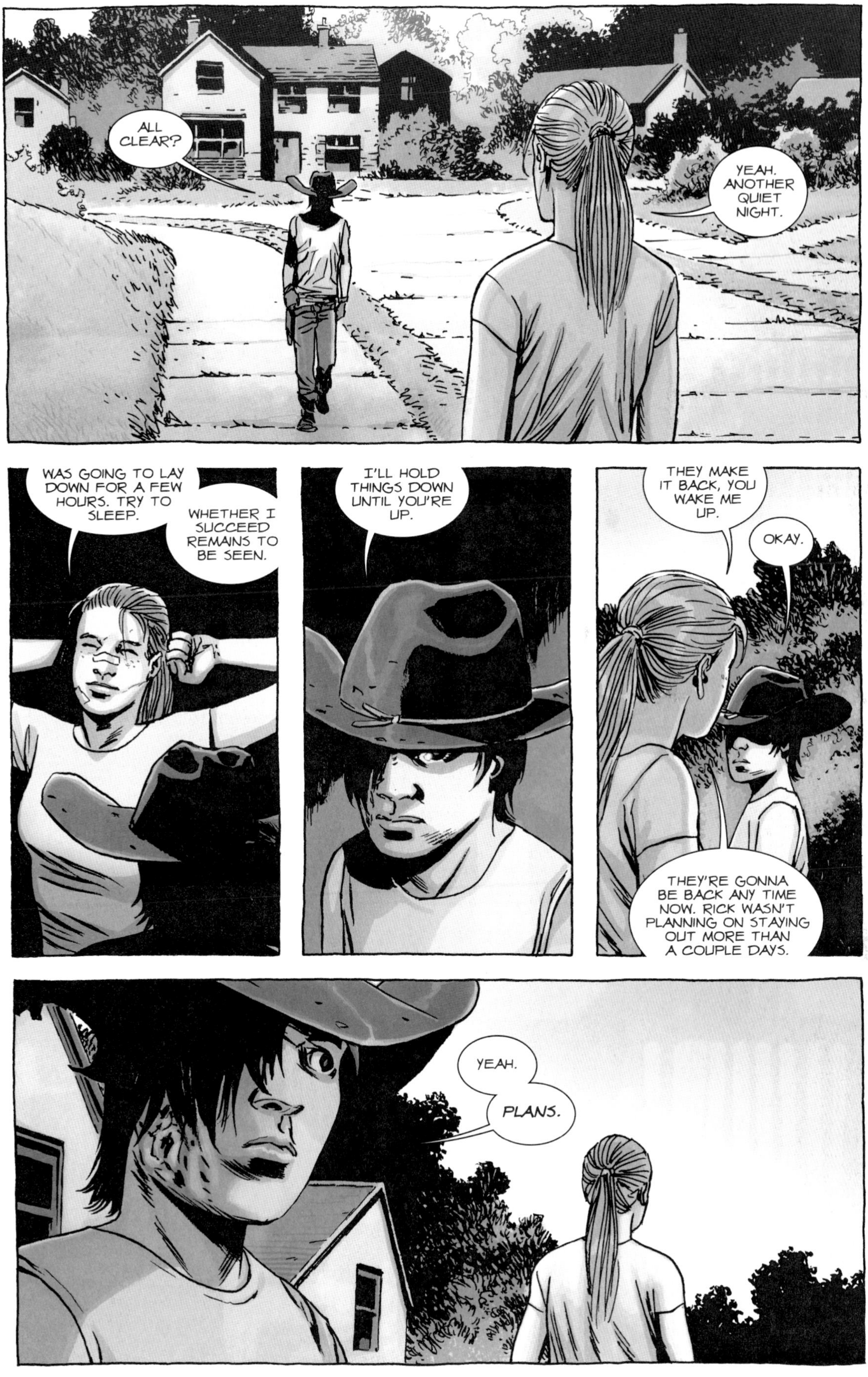
ALL CLEAR?
YEAH. ANOTHER QUIET NIGHT.
WAS GOING TO LAY DOWN FOR A FEW HOURS. TRY TO SLEEP.
WHETHER I SUCCEED REMAINS TO BE SEEN.
I'LL HOLD THINGS DOWN UNTIL YOU'RE UP.
THEY MAKE IT BACK, YOU WAKE ME UP.
OKAY.
THEY'RE GONNA BE BACK ANY TIME NOW. RICK WASN'T PLANNING ON STAYING OUT MORE THAN A COUPLE DAYS.
YEAH.
PLANS.

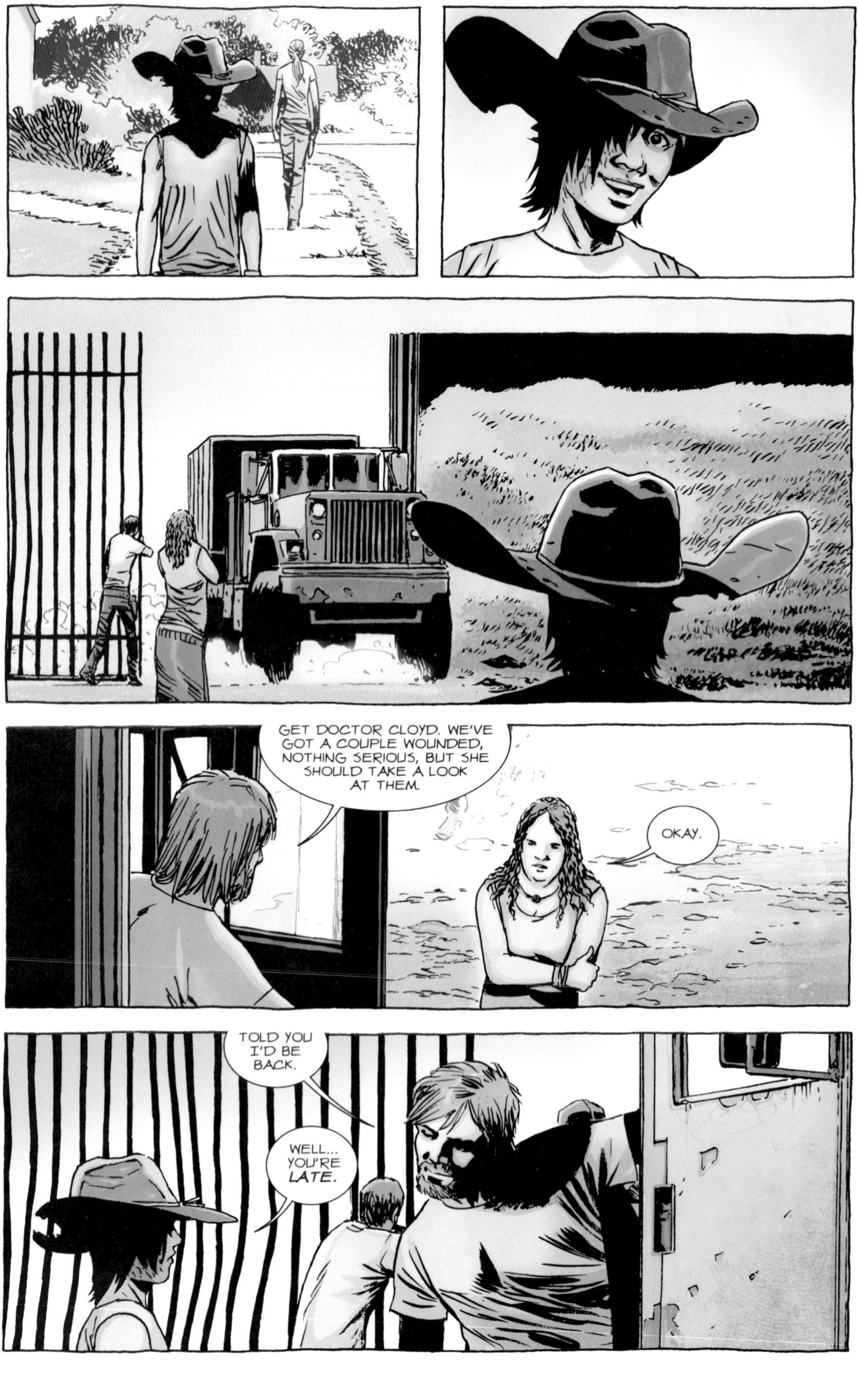
GET DOCTOR CLOYD. WE'VE GOT A COUPLE WOUNDED, NOTHING SERIOUS, BUT SHE SHOULD TAKE A LOOK AT THEM.
OKAY.
TOLD YOU I'D BE BACK.
WELL... YOU'RE *LATE*.

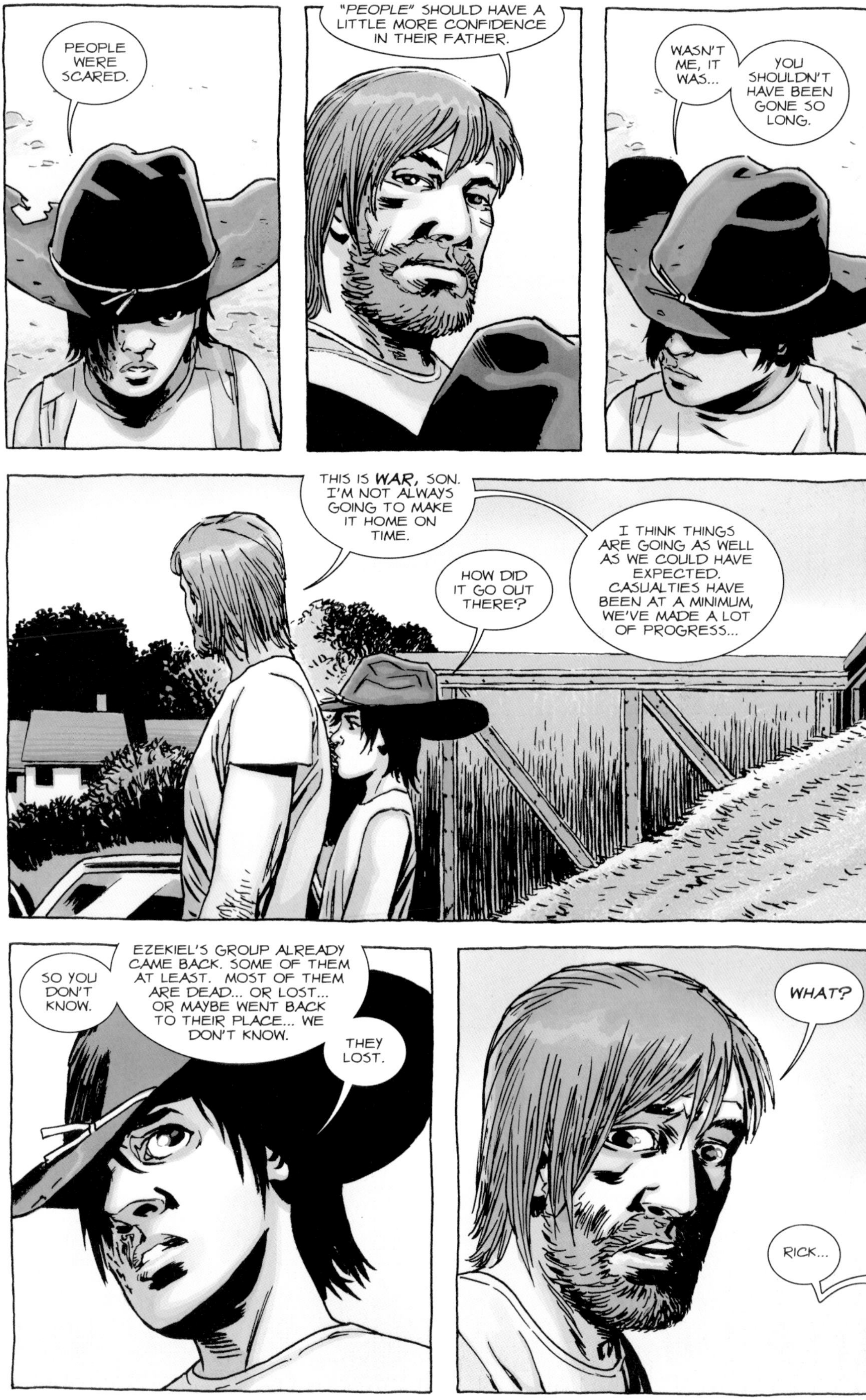
PEOPLE WERE SCARED.
"PEOPLE" SHOULD HAVE A LITTLE MORE CONFIDENCE IN THEIR FATHER.
WASN'T ME, IT WAS...
YOU SHOULDN'T HAVE BEEN GONE SO LONG.
THIS IS WAR, SON. I'M NOT ALWAYS GOING TO MAKE IT HOME ON TIME.
HOW DID IT GO OUT THERE?
I THINK THINGS ARE GOING AS WELL AS WE COULD HAVE EXPECTED. CASUALTIES HAVE BEEN AT A MINIMUM, WE'VE MADE A LOT OF PROGRESS...
SO YOU DON'T KNOW.
EZEKIEL'S GROUP ALREADY CAME BACK. SOME OF THEM AT LEAST. MOST OF THEM ARE DEAD... OR LOST... OR MAYBE WENT BACK TO THEIR PLACE... WE DON'T KNOW.
THEY LOST.
WHAT?
RICK...

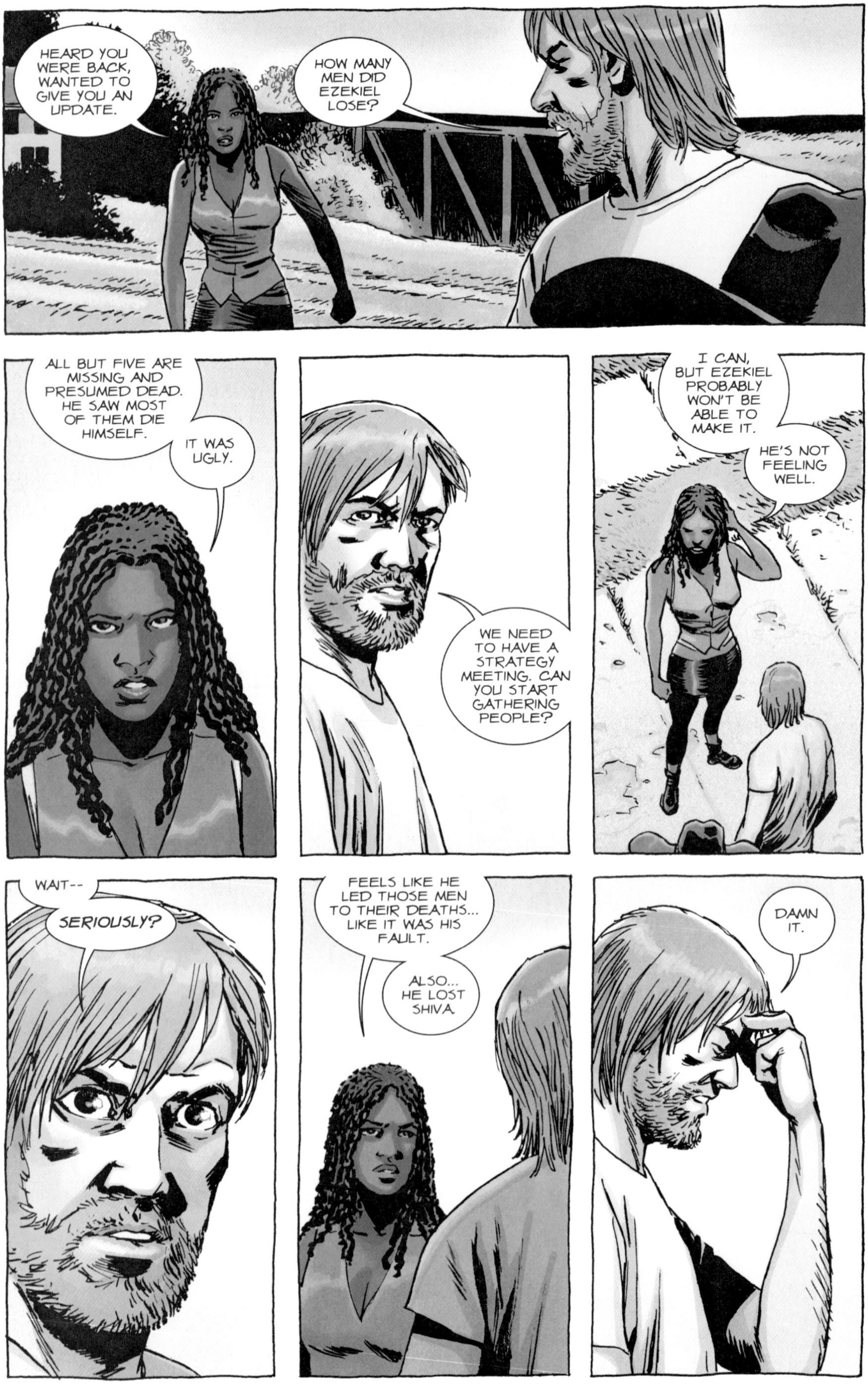
HEARD YOU WERE BACK, WANTED TO GIVE YOU AN UPDATE.
HOW MANY MEN DID EZEKIEL LOSE?
ALL BUT FIVE ARE MISSING AND PRESUMED DEAD. HE SAW MOST OF THEM DIE HIMSELF.
IT WAS UGLY.
WE NEED TO HAVE A STRATEGY MEETING. CAN YOU START GATHERING PEOPLE?
I CAN, BUT EZEKIEL PROBABLY WON'T BE ABLE TO MAKE IT.
HE'S NOT FEELING WELL.
WAIT--
SERIOUSLY?
FEELS LIKE HE LED THOSE MEN TO THEIR DEATHS... LIKE IT WAS HIS FAULT.
ALSO... HE LOST SHIVA.
DAMN IT.

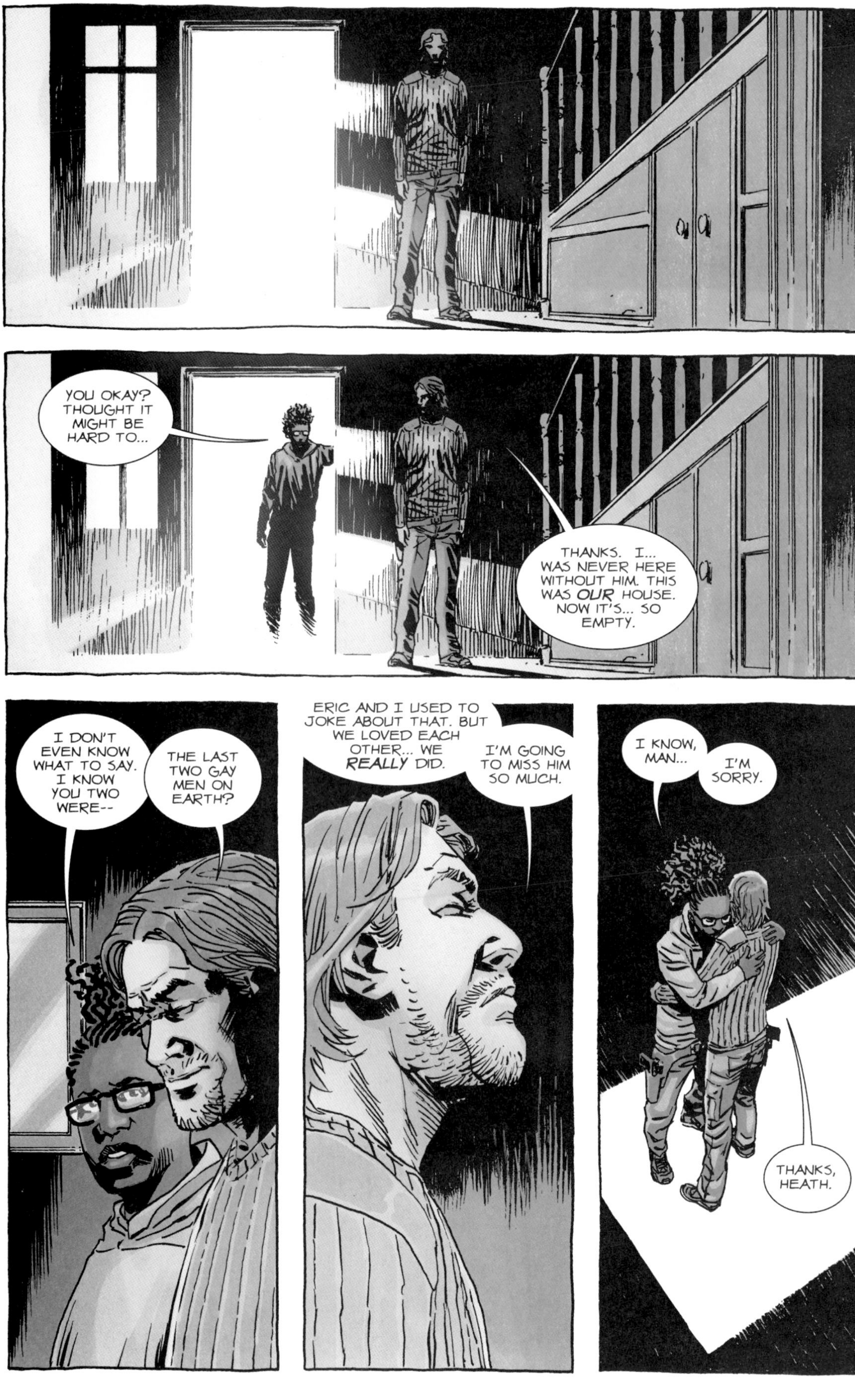

YOU OKAY? THOUGHT IT MIGHT BE HARD TO...
THANKS. I... WAS NEVER HERE WITHOUT HIM. THIS WAS OUR HOUSE. NOW IT'S... SO EMPTY.
I DON'T EVEN KNOW WHAT TO SAY. I KNOW YOU TWO WERE--
THE LAST TWO GAY MEN ON EARTH?
ERIC AND I USED TO JOKE ABOUT THAT. BUT WE LOVED EACH OTHER... WE REALLY DID.
I'M GOING TO MISS HIM SO MUCH.
I KNOW, MAN...
I'M SORRY.
THANKS, HEATH.

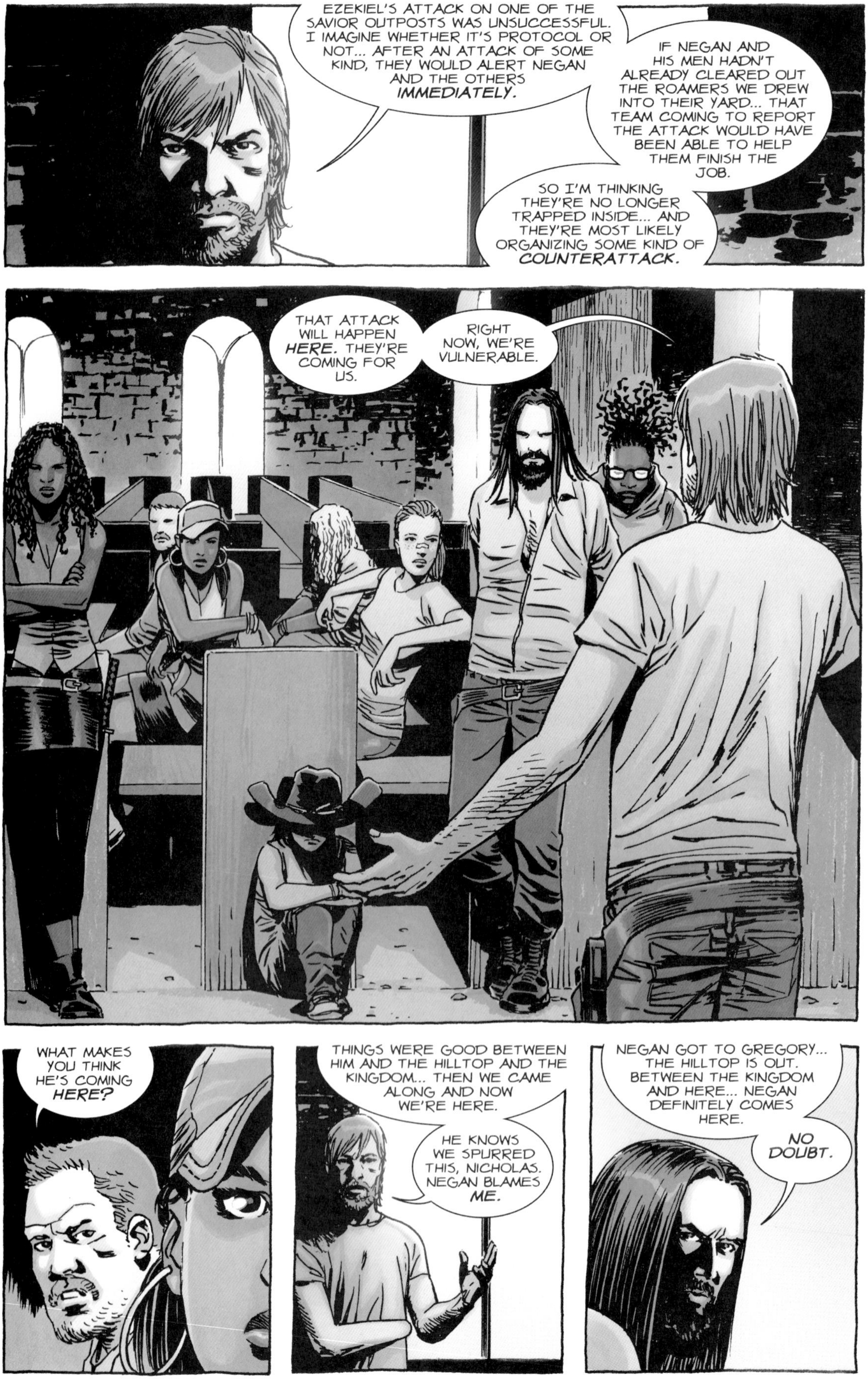
EZEKIEL'S ATTACK ON ONE OF THE SAVIOR OUTPOSTS WAS UNSUCCESSFUL. I IMAGINE WHETHER IT'S PROTOCOL OR NOT... AFTER AN ATTACK OF SOME KIND, THEY WOULD ALERT NEGAN AND THE OTHERS *IMMEDIATELY.*
IF NEGAN AND HIS MEN HADN'T ALREADY CLEARED OUT THE ROAMERS WE DREW INTO THEIR YARD... THAT TEAM COMING TO REPORT THE ATTACK WOULD HAVE BEEN ABLE TO HELP THEM FINISH THE JOB.
SO I'M THINKING THEY'RE NO LONGER TRAPPED INSIDE... AND THEY'RE MOST LIKELY ORGANIZING SOME KIND OF *COUNTERATTACK.*
THAT ATTACK WILL HAPPEN *HERE.* THEY'RE COMING FOR US.
RIGHT NOW, WE'RE VULNERABLE.
WHAT MAKES YOU THINK HE'S COMING *HERE?*
THINGS WERE GOOD BETWEEN HIM AND THE HILLTOP AND THE KINGDOM... THEN WE CAME ALONG AND NOW WE'RE HERE.
HE KNOWS WE SPURRED THIS, NICHOLAS. NEGAN BLAMES *ME.*
NEGAN GOT TO GREGORY... THE HILLTOP IS OUT. BETWEEN THE KINGDOM AND HERE... NEGAN DEFINITELY COMES HERE.
NO DOUBT.

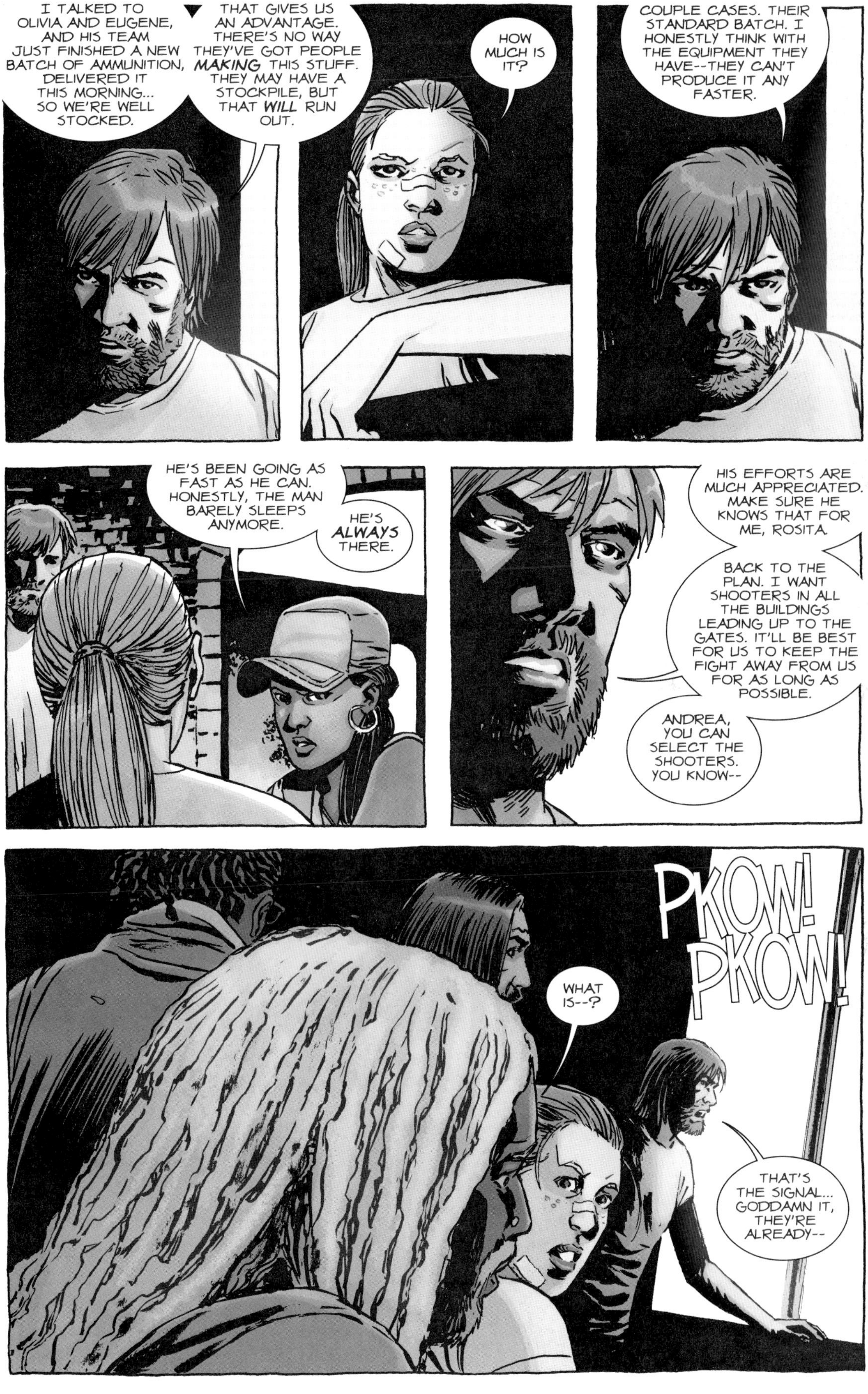

I TALKED TO OLIVIA AND EUGENE, AND HIS TEAM JUST FINISHED A NEW BATCH OF AMMUNITION, DELIVERED IT THIS MORNING... SO WE'RE WELL STOCKED.
THAT GIVES US AN ADVANTAGE. THERE'S NO WAY THEY'VE GOT PEOPLE *MAKING* THIS STUFF. THEY MAY HAVE A STOCKPILE, BUT THAT *WILL* RUN OUT.
HOW MUCH IS IT?
COUPLE CASES. THEIR STANDARD BATCH. I HONESTLY THINK WITH THE EQUIPMENT THEY HAVE--THEY CAN'T PRODUCE IT ANY FASTER.
HE'S BEEN GOING AS FAST AS HE CAN. HONESTLY, THE MAN BARELY SLEEPS ANYMORE.
HE'S *ALWAYS* THERE.
HIS EFFORTS ARE MUCH APPRECIATED. MAKE SURE HE KNOWS THAT FOR ME, ROSITA.
BACK TO THE PLAN. I WANT SHOOTERS IN ALL THE BUILDINGS LEADING UP TO THE GATES. IT'LL BE BEST FOR US TO KEEP THE FIGHT AWAY FROM US FOR AS LONG AS POSSIBLE.
ANDREA, YOU CAN SELECT THE SHOOTERS. YOU KNOW--
PKOW! PKOW!
WHAT IS--?
THAT'S THE SIGNAL... GODDAMN IT, THEY'RE ALREADY--

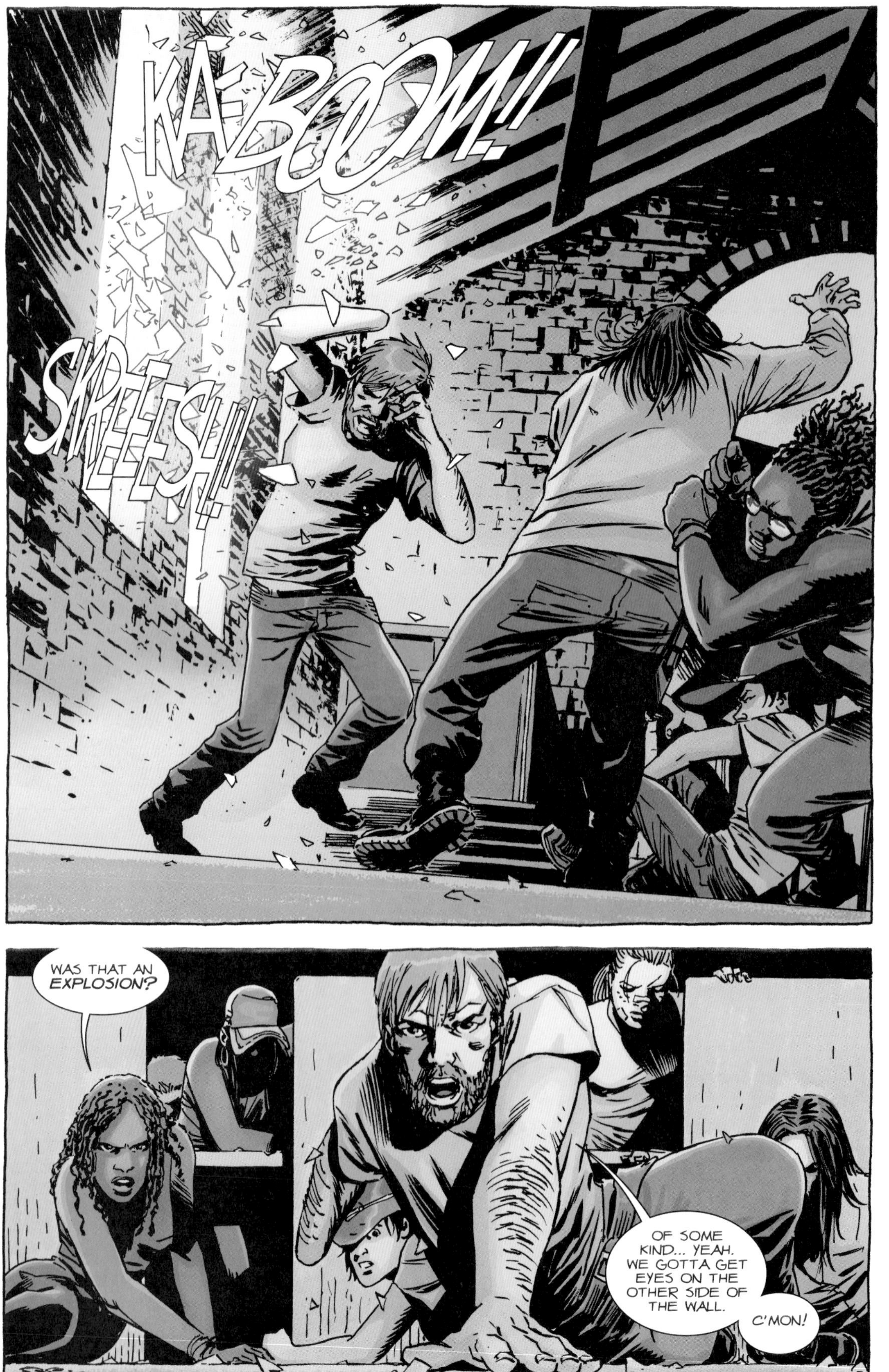
KA-BOOM!!
SKREEESH!!
WAS THAT AN EXPLOSION?
OF SOME KIND... YEAH. WE GOTTA GET EYES ON THE OTHER SIDE OF THE WALL.
C'MON!

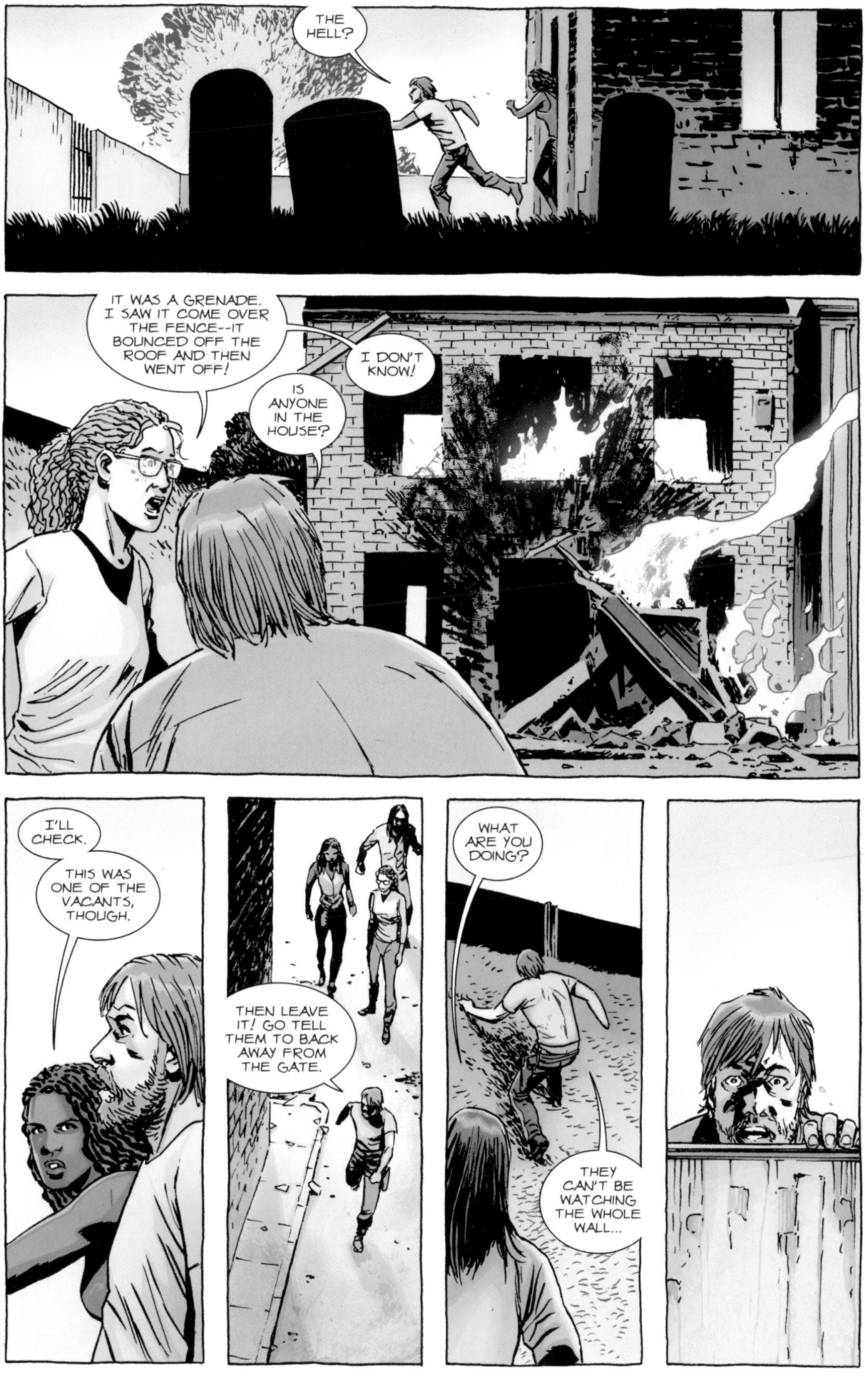
THE HELL?
IT WAS A GRENADE. I SAW IT COME OVER THE FENCE--IT BOUNCED OFF THE ROOF AND THEN WENT OFF!
IS ANYONE IN THE HOUSE?
I DON'T KNOW!
I'LL CHECK.
THIS WAS ONE OF THE VACANTS, THOUGH.
THEN LEAVE IT! GO TELL THEM TO BACK AWAY FROM THE GATE.
WHAT ARE YOU DOING?
THEY CAN'T BE WATCHING THE WHOLE WALL...

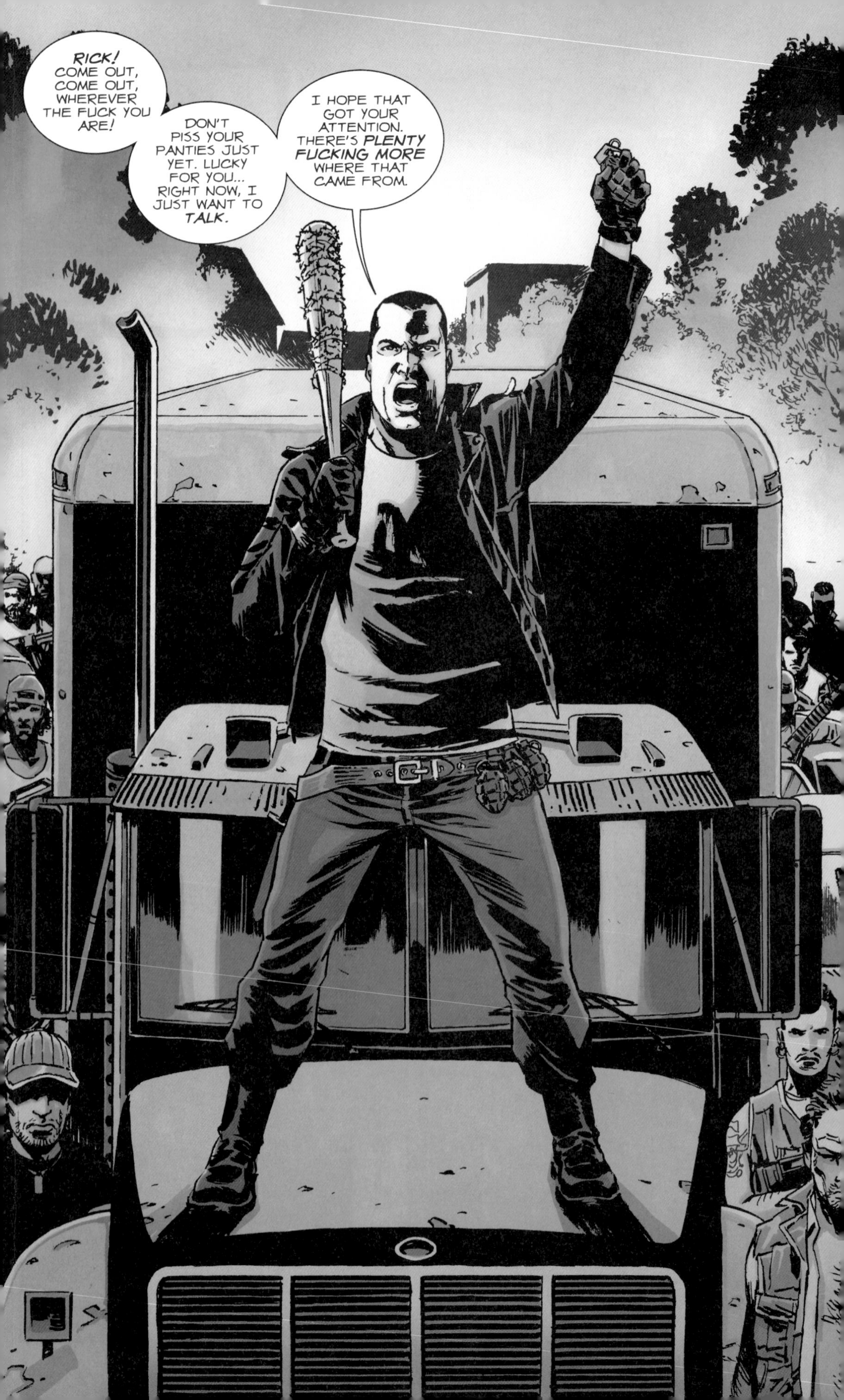
RICK! COME OUT, COME OUT, WHEREVER THE FUCK YOU ARE!
DON'T PISS YOUR PANTIES JUST YET. LUCKY FOR YOU... RIGHT NOW, I JUST WANT TO TALK.
I HOPE THAT GOT YOUR ATTENTION. THERE'S PLENTY FUCKING MORE WHERE THAT CAME FROM.

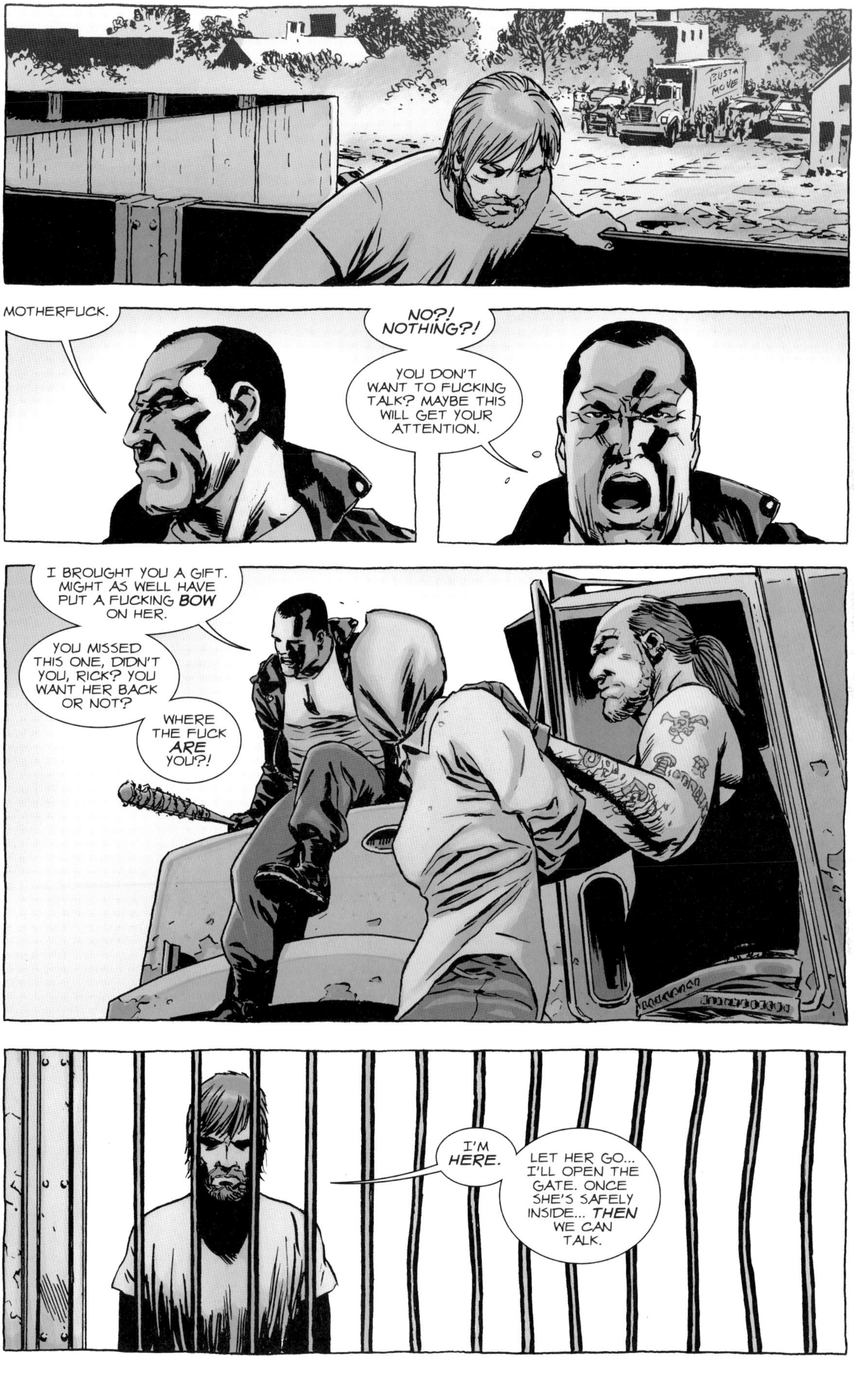

BUSTA MOVE
MOTHERFUCK.
NO?! NOTHING?!
YOU DON'T WANT TO FUCKING TALK? MAYBE THIS WILL GET YOUR ATTENTION.
I BROUGHT YOU A GIFT. MIGHT AS WELL HAVE PUT A FUCKING BOW ON HER.
YOU MISSED THIS ONE, DIDN'T YOU, RICK? YOU WANT HER BACK OR NOT?
WHERE THE FUCK ARE YOU?!
I'M HERE.
LET HER GO... I'LL OPEN THE GATE. ONCE SHE'S SAFELY INSIDE... THEN WE CAN TALK.

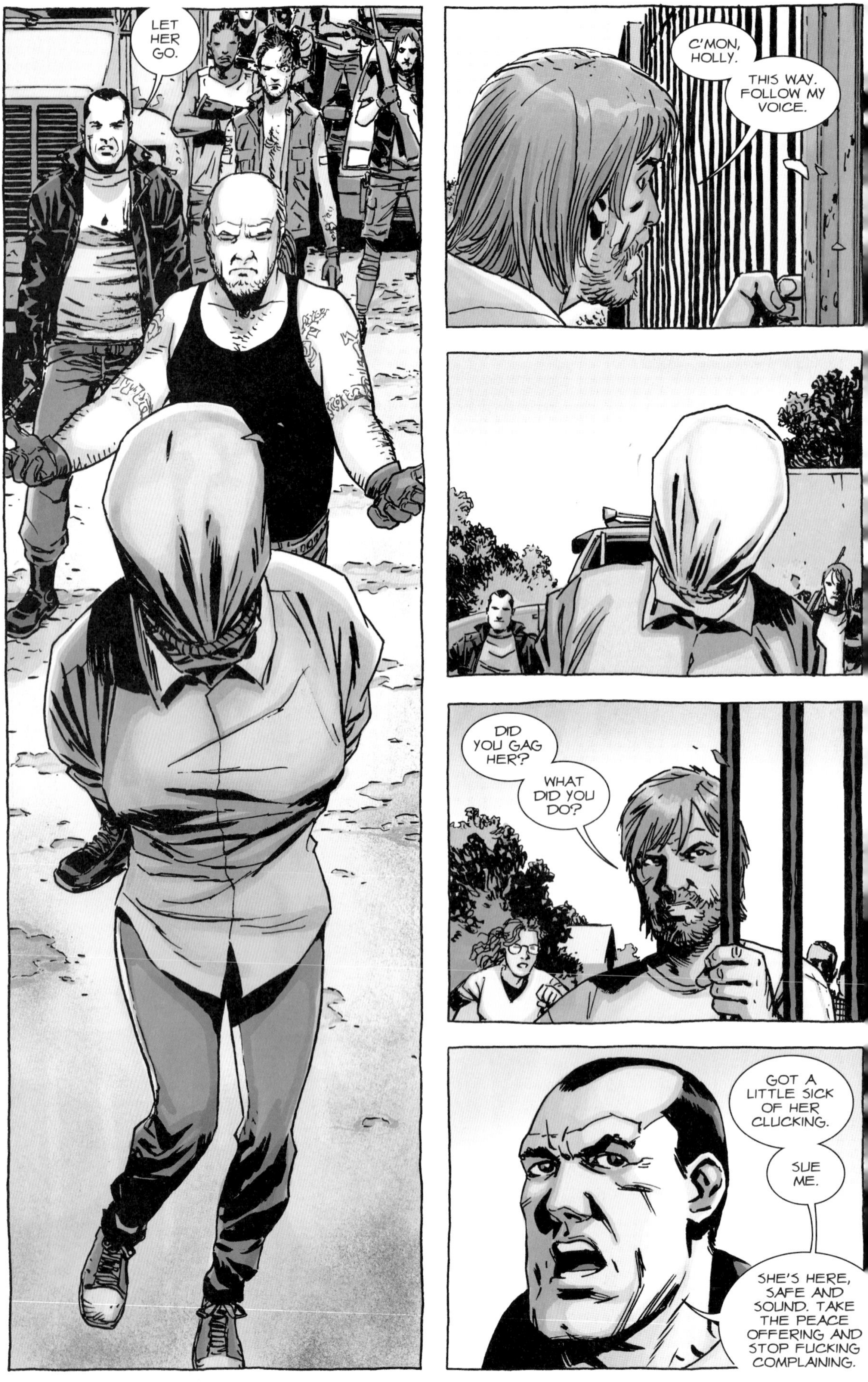
LET HER GO.
C'MON, HOLLY.
THIS WAY. FOLLOW MY VOICE.
DID YOU GAG HER?
WHAT DID YOU DO?
GOT A LITTLE SICK OF HER CLUCKING.
SUE ME.
SHE'S HERE, SAFE AND SOUND. TAKE THE PEACE OFFERING AND STOP FUCKING COMPLAINING.

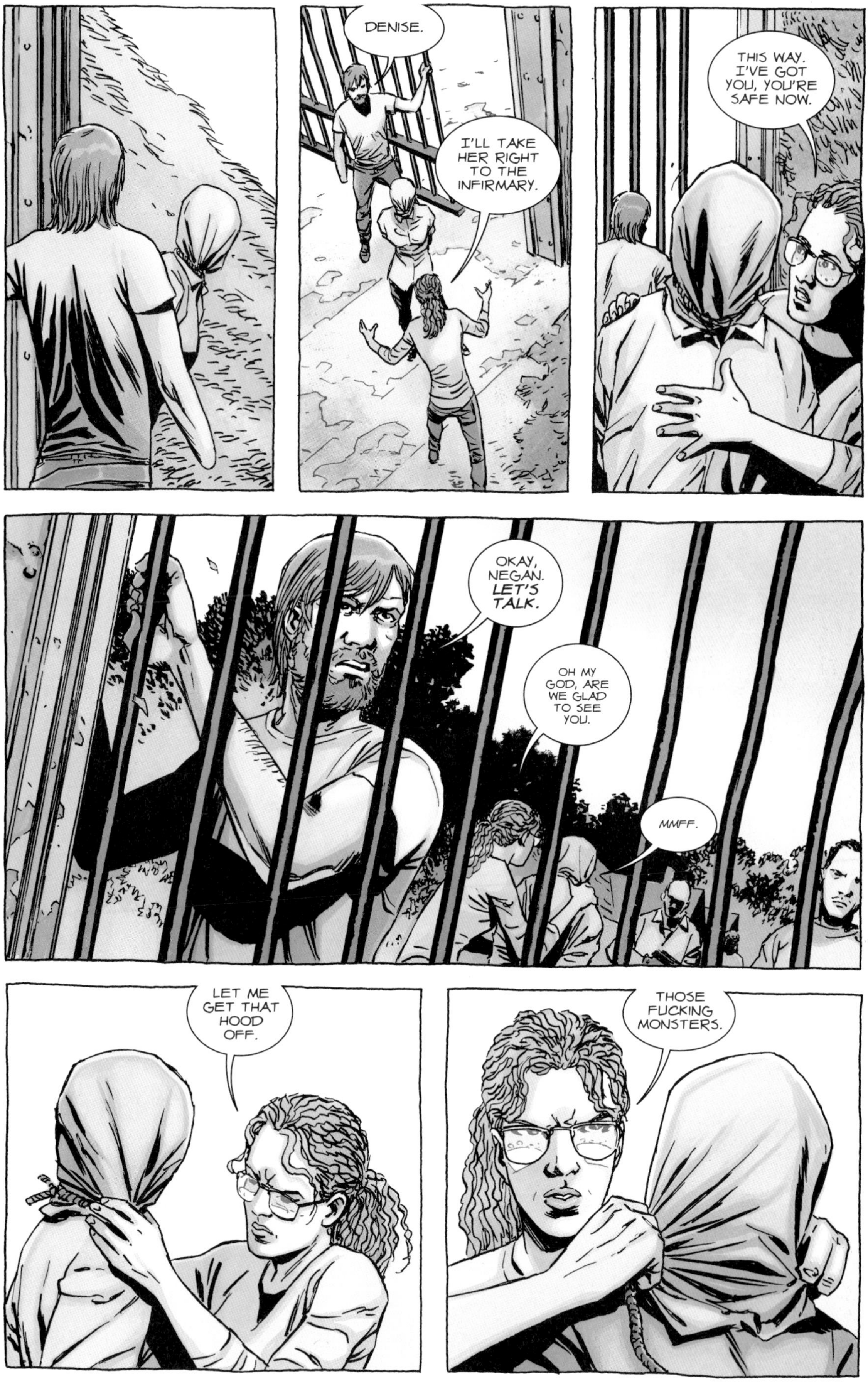
DENISE.
I'LL TAKE HER RIGHT TO THE INFIRMARY.
THIS WAY. I'VE GOT YOU, YOU'RE SAFE NOW.
OKAY, NEGAN. LET'S TALK.
OH MY GOD, ARE WE GLAD TO SEE YOU.
MMFF.
LET ME GET THAT HOOD OFF.
THOSE FUCKING MONSTERS.

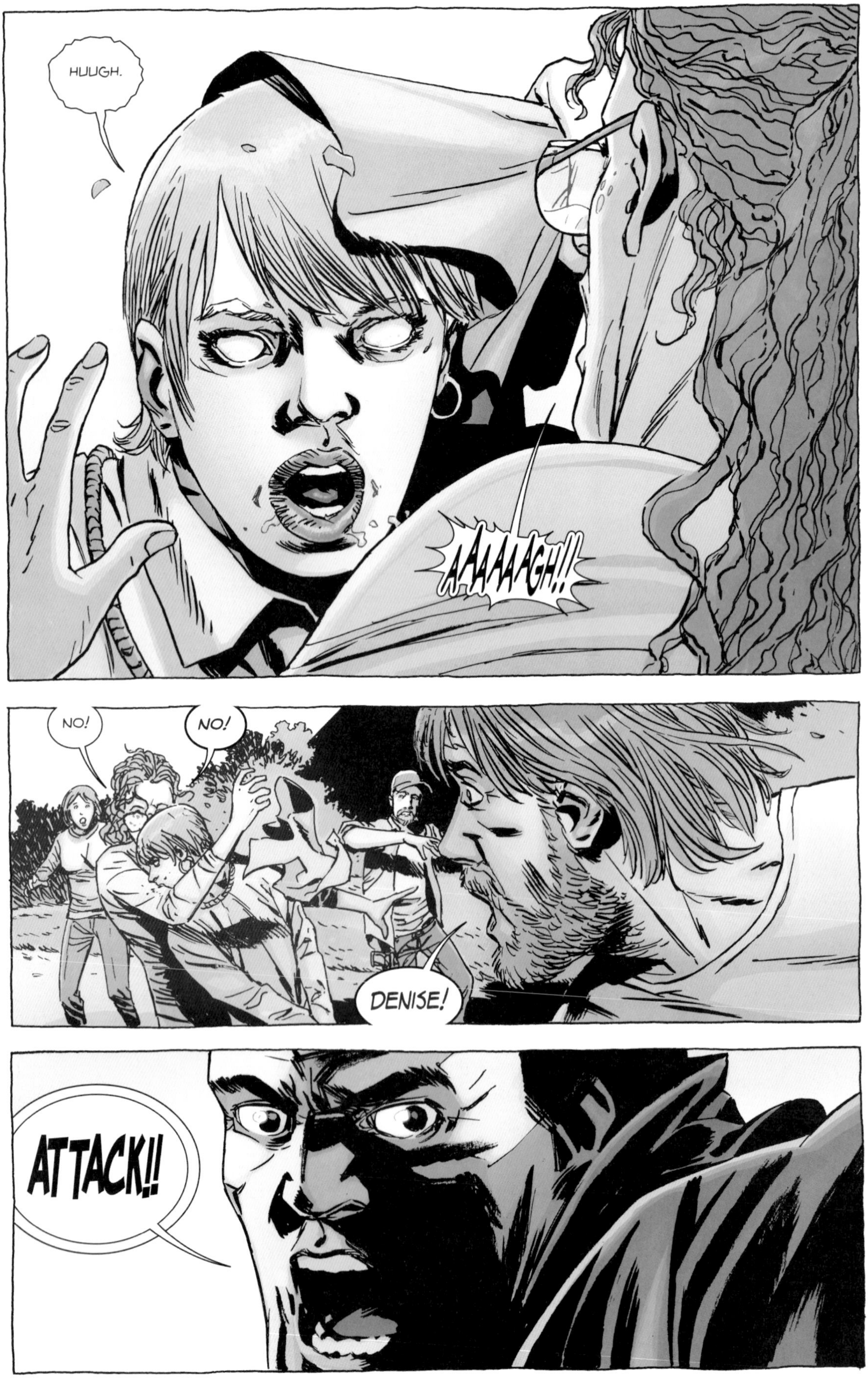
HUUGH.
AAAAAAGH!!
NO!
NO!
DENISE!
ATTACK!!

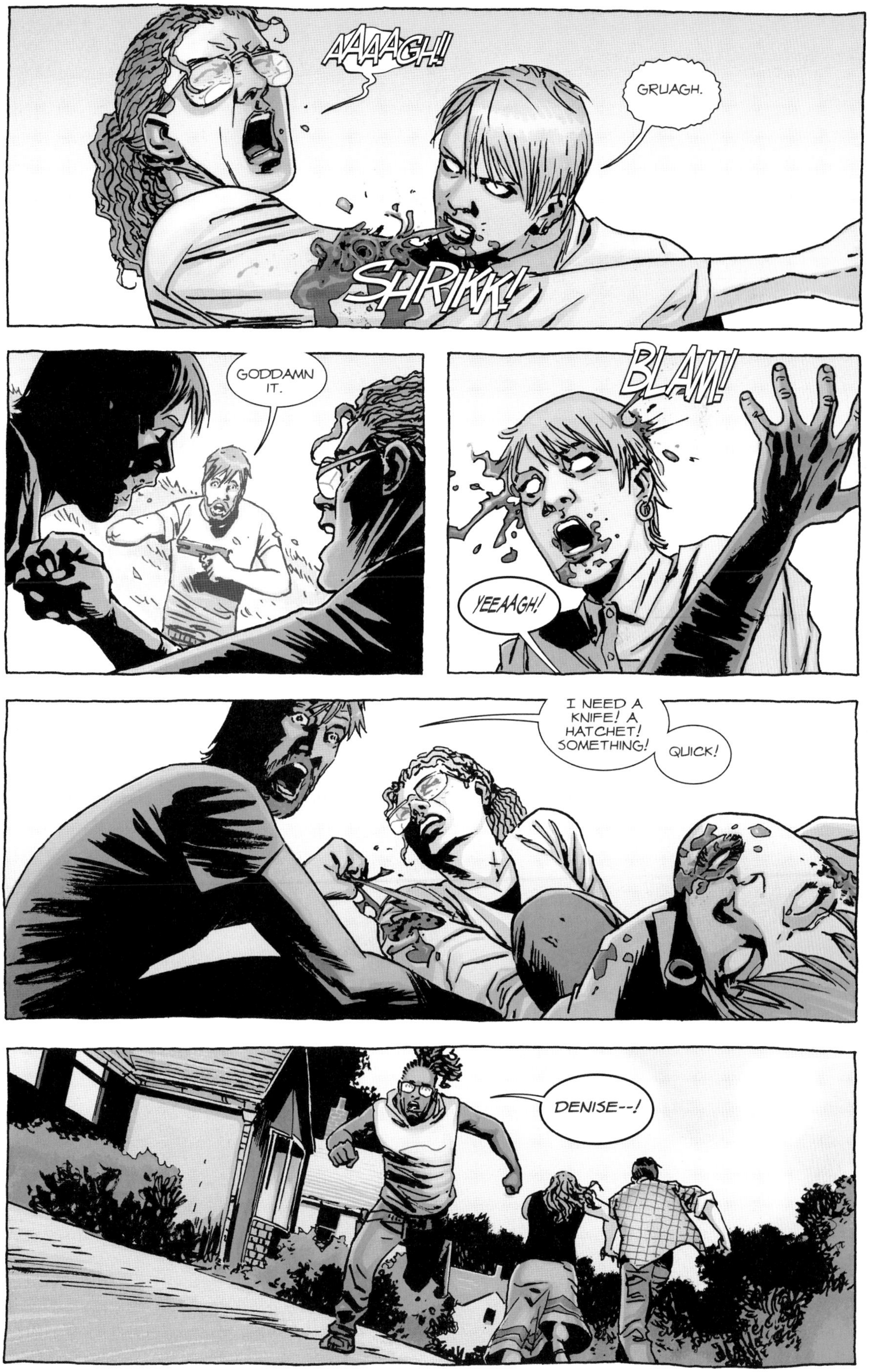
AAAAGH!
GRUAGH.
SHRIKK!
GODDAMN IT.
BLAM!
YEEAAGH!
I NEED A KNIFE! A HATCHET! SOMETHING!
QUICK!
DENISE--!

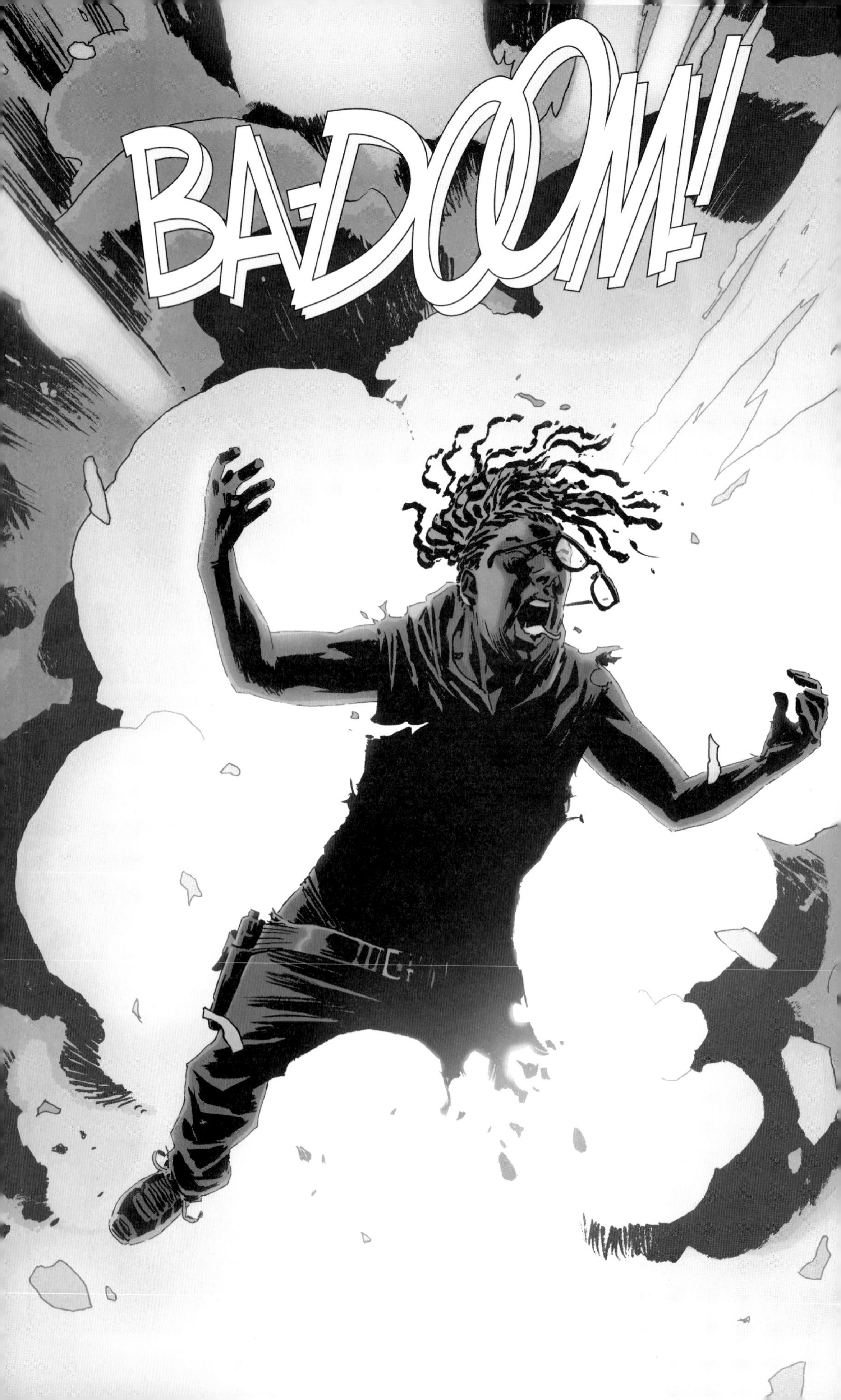
BA-DOOM!

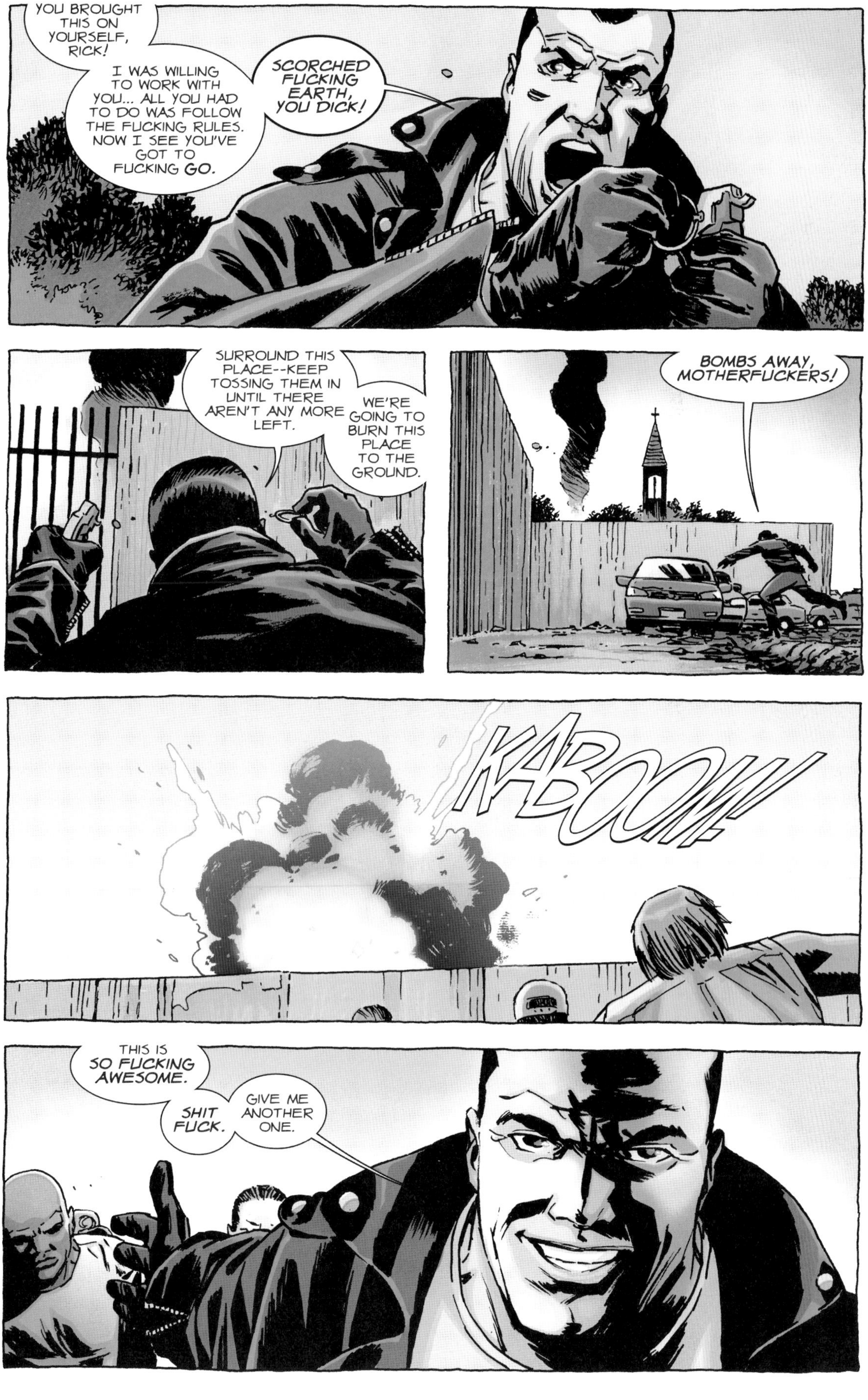
YOU BROUGHT THIS ON YOURSELF, RICK!
I WAS WILLING TO WORK WITH YOU... ALL YOU HAD TO DO WAS FOLLOW THE FUCKING RULES. NOW I SEE YOU'VE GOT TO FUCKING GO.
SCORCHED FUCKING EARTH, YOU DICK!
SURROUND THIS PLACE--KEEP TOSSING THEM IN UNTIL THERE AREN'T ANY MORE LEFT.
WE'RE GOING TO BURN THIS PLACE TO THE GROUND.
BOMBS AWAY, MOTHERFUCKERS!
KABOOM!
THIS IS SO FUCKING AWESOME.
SHIT FUCK.
GIVE ME ANOTHER ONE.

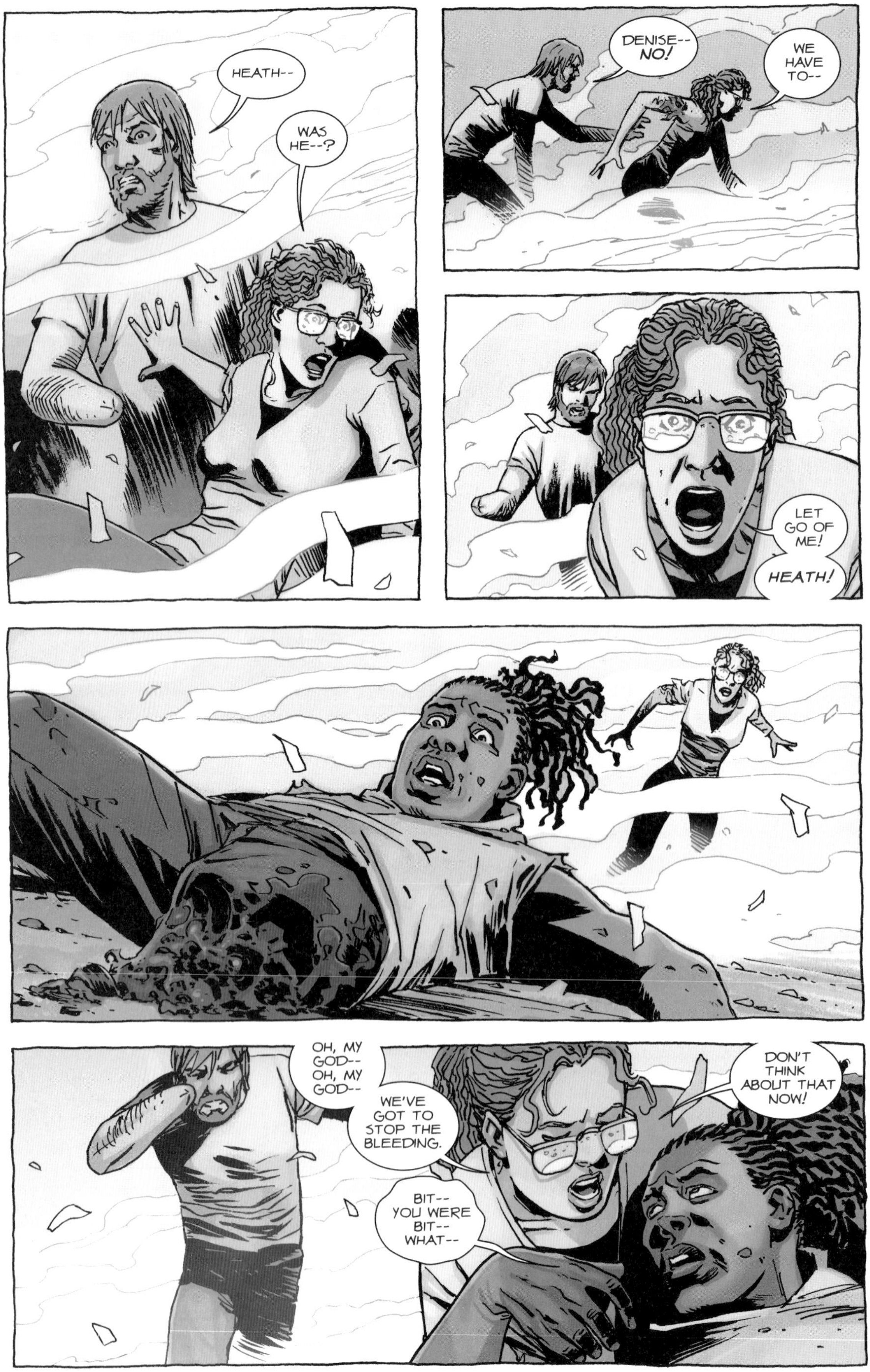
HEATH--
WAS HE--?
DENISE-- NO!
WE HAVE TO--
LET GO OF ME!
HEATH!
OH, MY GOD-- OH, MY GOD--
WE'VE GOT TO STOP THE BLEEDING.
DON'T THINK ABOUT THAT NOW!
BIT-- YOU WERE BIT-- WHAT--

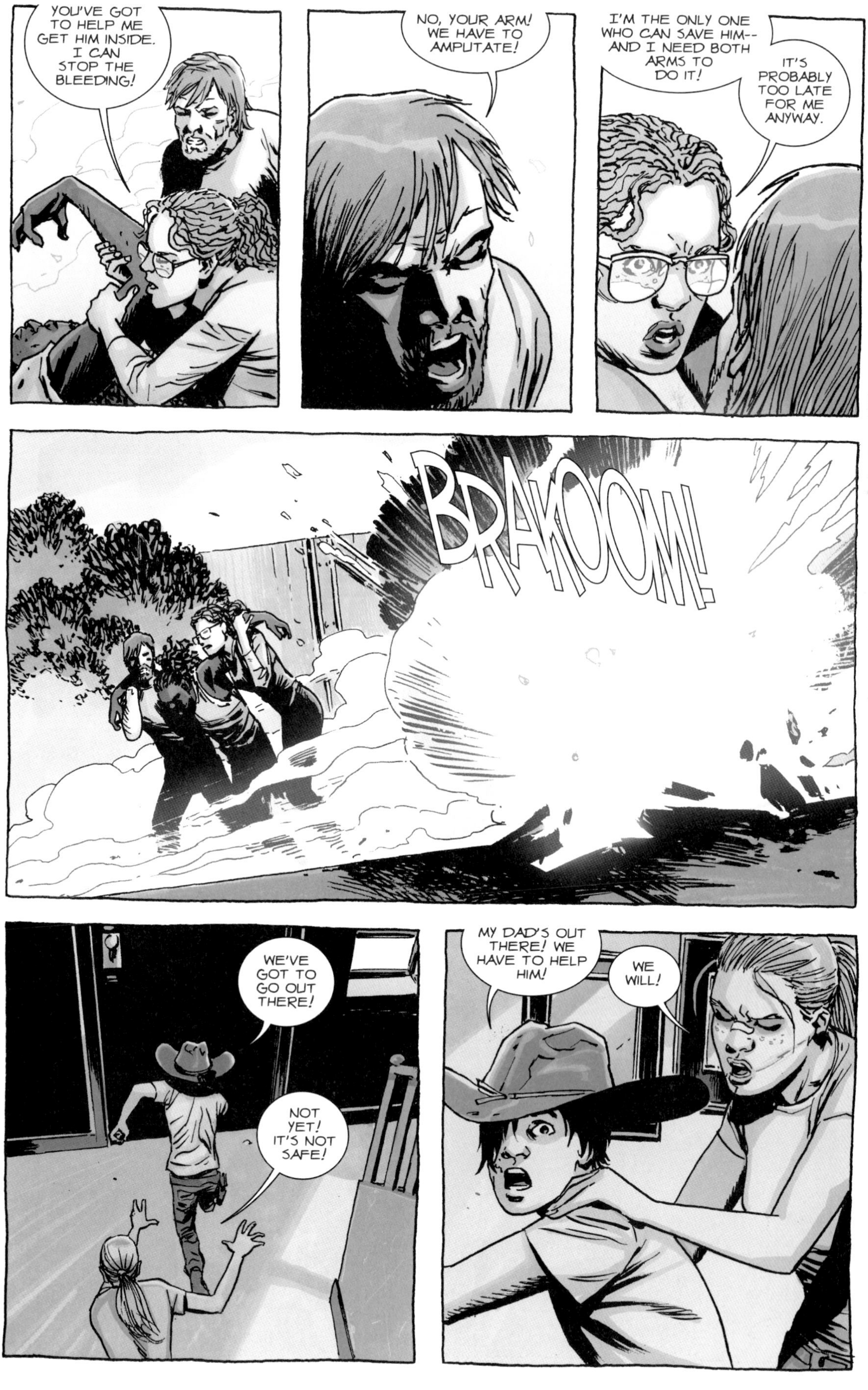
YOU'VE GOT TO HELP ME GET HIM INSIDE. I CAN STOP THE BLEEDING!
NO, YOUR ARM! WE HAVE TO AMPUTATE!
I'M THE ONLY ONE WHO CAN SAVE HIM-- AND I NEED BOTH ARMS TO DO IT!
IT'S PROBABLY TOO LATE FOR ME ANYWAY.
BRAKOOOM!
WE'VE GOT TO GO OUT THERE!
NOT YET! IT'S NOT SAFE!
MY DAD'S OUT THERE! WE HAVE TO HELP HIM!
WE WILL!

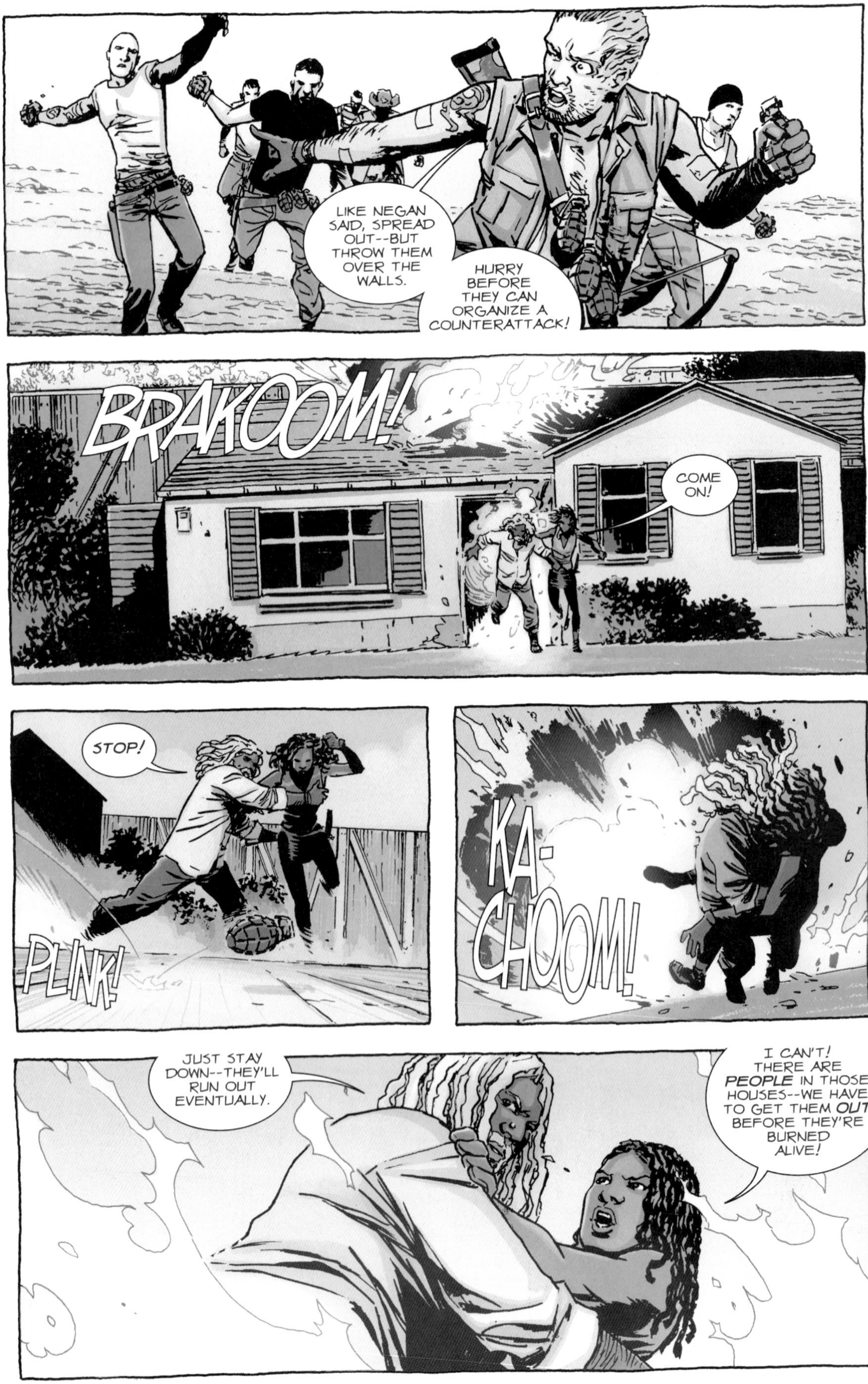
LIKE NEGAN SAID, SPREAD OUT--BUT THROW THEM OVER THE WALLS.
HURRY BEFORE THEY CAN ORGANIZE A COUNTERATTACK!
BRAKOOM!
COME ON!
STOP!
PLINK!
KA-CHOOM!
JUST STAY DOWN--THEY'LL RUN OUT EVENTUALLY.
I CAN'T! THERE ARE PEOPLE IN THOSE HOUSES--WE HAVE TO GET THEM OUT BEFORE THEY'RE BURNED ALIVE!

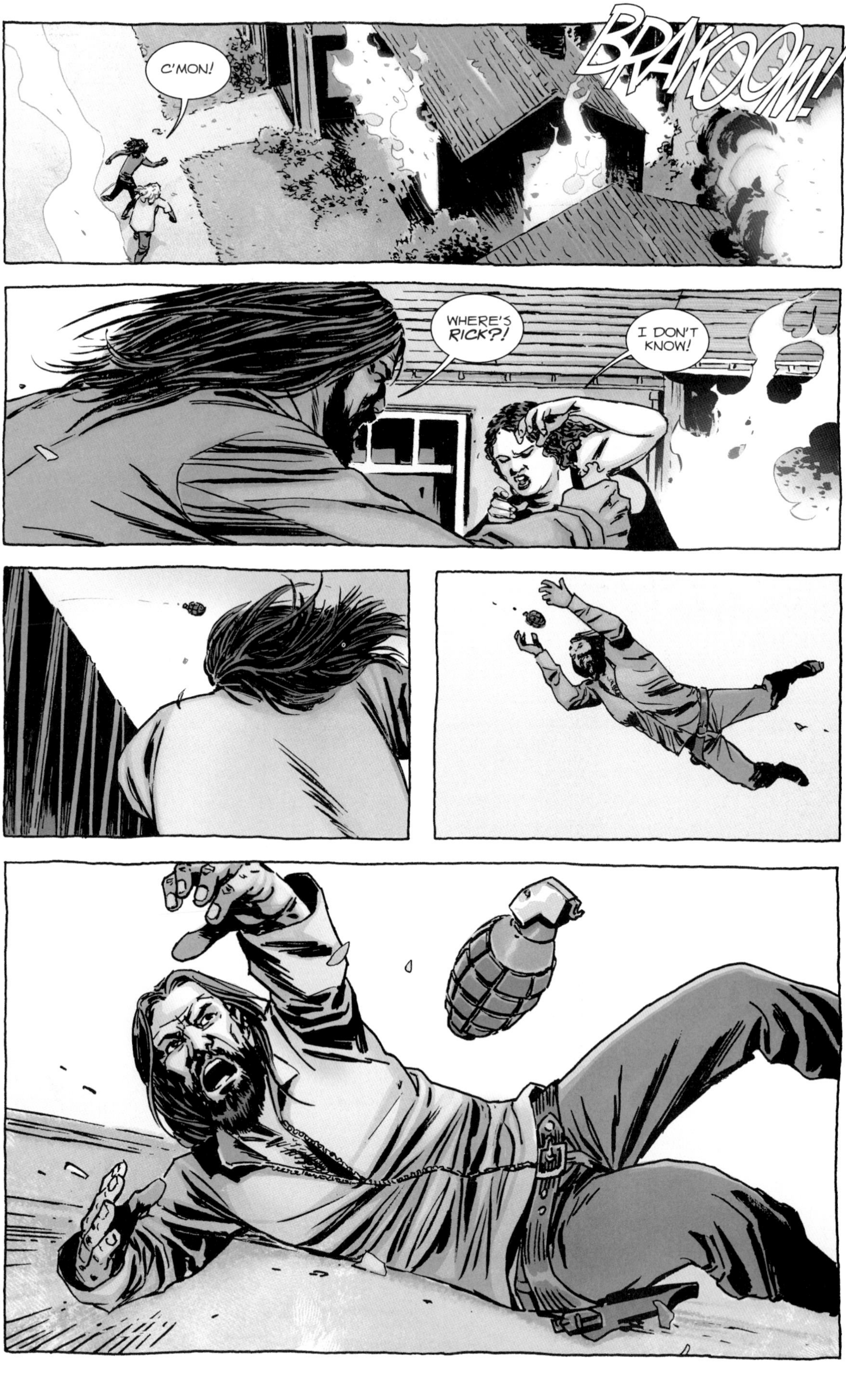
C'MON!
BRAKOOM!
WHERE'S RICK?!
I DON'T KNOW!

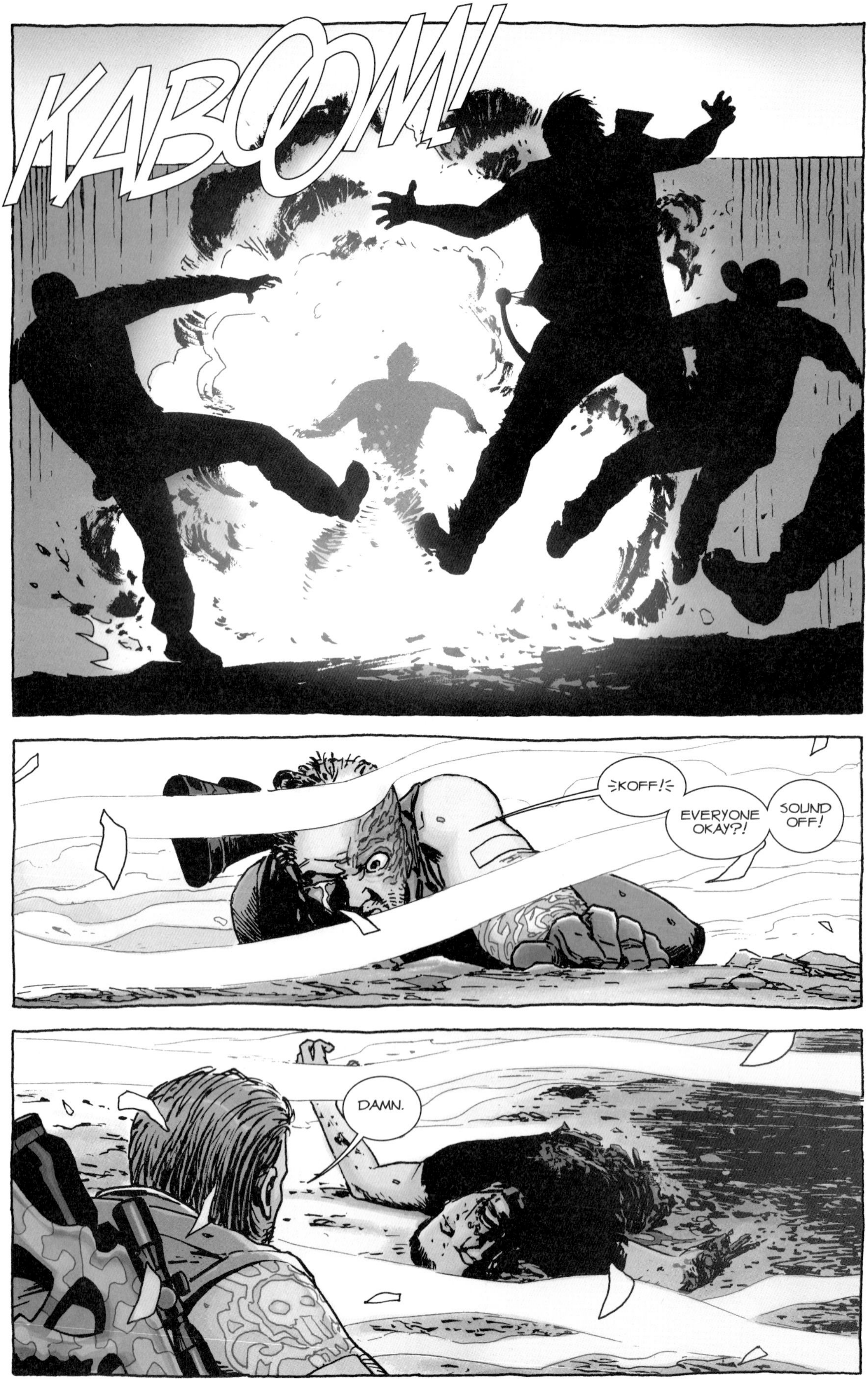
KABOOM!
KOFF!
EVERYONE OKAY?!
SOUND OFF!
DAMN.

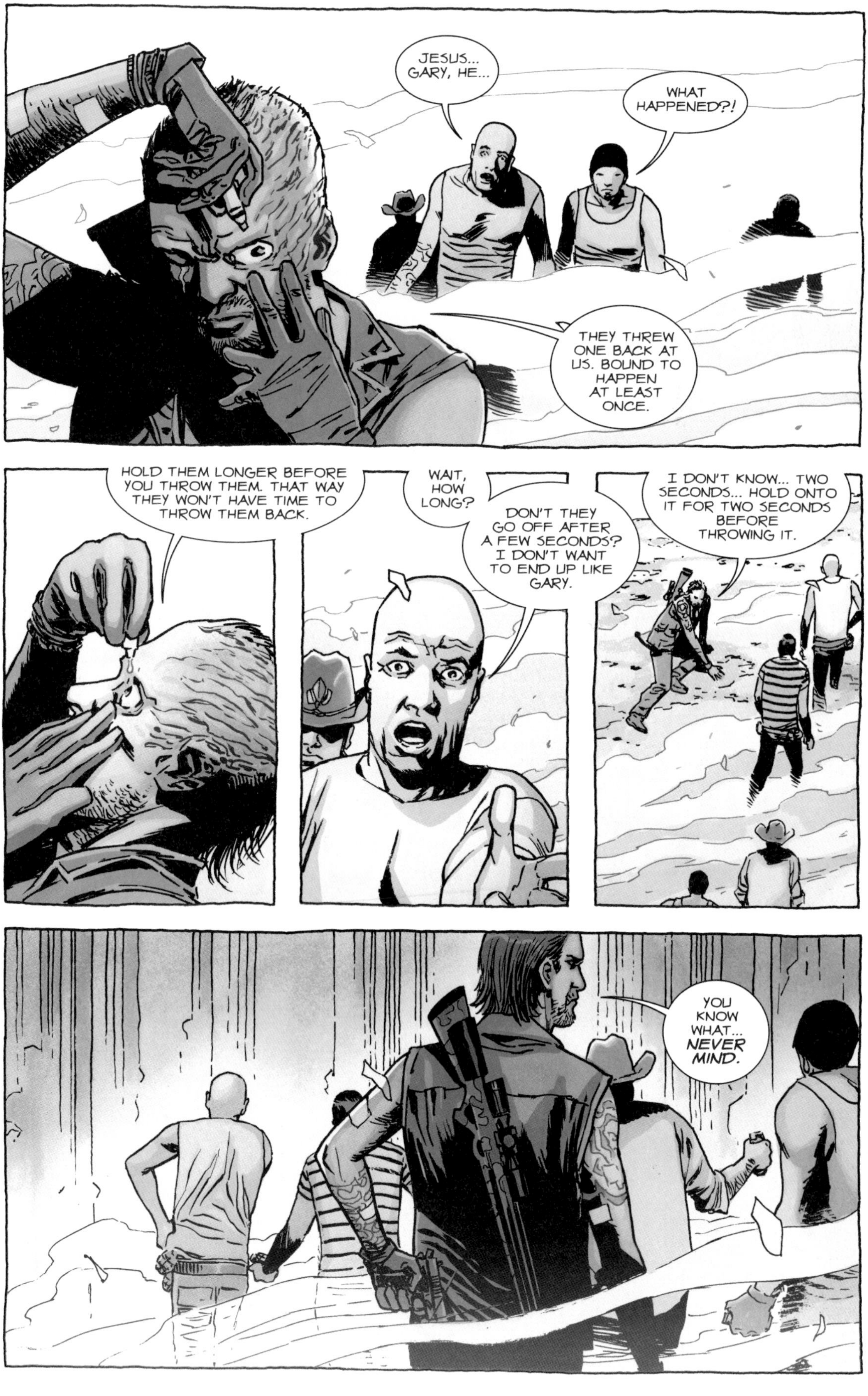
JESUS... GARY, HE...
WHAT HAPPENED?!
THEY THREW ONE BACK AT US. BOUND TO HAPPEN AT LEAST ONCE.
HOLD THEM LONGER BEFORE YOU THROW THEM. THAT WAY THEY WON'T HAVE TIME TO THROW THEM BACK.
WAIT, HOW LONG?
DON'T THEY GO OFF AFTER A FEW SECONDS? I DON'T WANT TO END UP LIKE GARY.
I DON'T KNOW... TWO SECONDS... HOLD ONTO IT FOR TWO SECONDS BEFORE THROWING IT.
YOU KNOW WHAT... *NEVER MIND.*

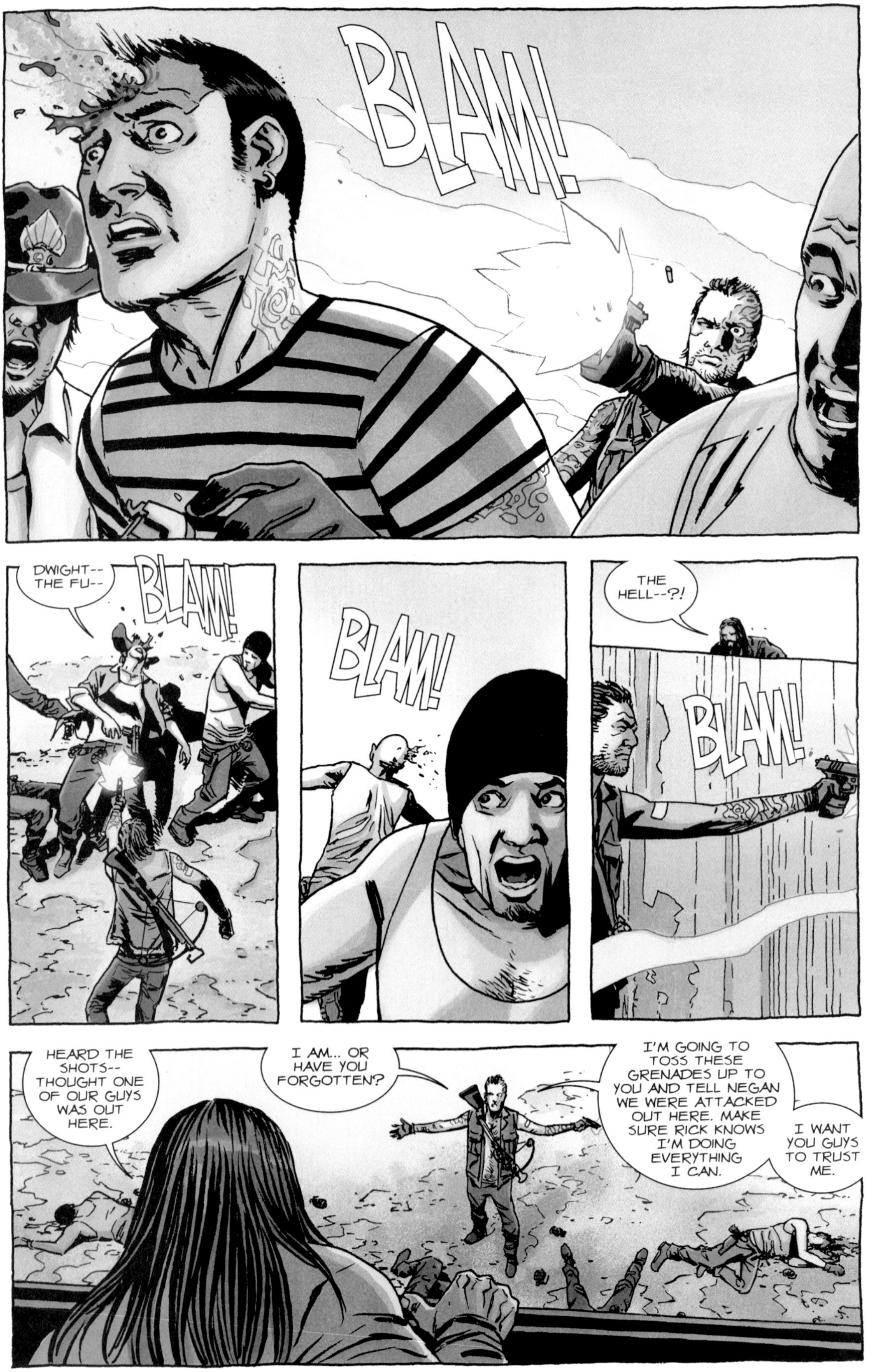
BLAM!
DWIGHT-- THE FU--
BLAM!
BLAM!
THE HELL--?!
BLAM!
HEARD THE SHOTS-- THOUGHT ONE OF OUR GUYS WAS OUT HERE.
I AM... OR HAVE YOU FORGOTTEN?
I'M GOING TO TOSS THESE GRENADES UP TO YOU AND TELL NEGAN WE WERE ATTACKED OUT HERE. MAKE SURE RICK KNOWS I'M DOING EVERYTHING I CAN.
I WANT YOU GUYS TO TRUST ME.

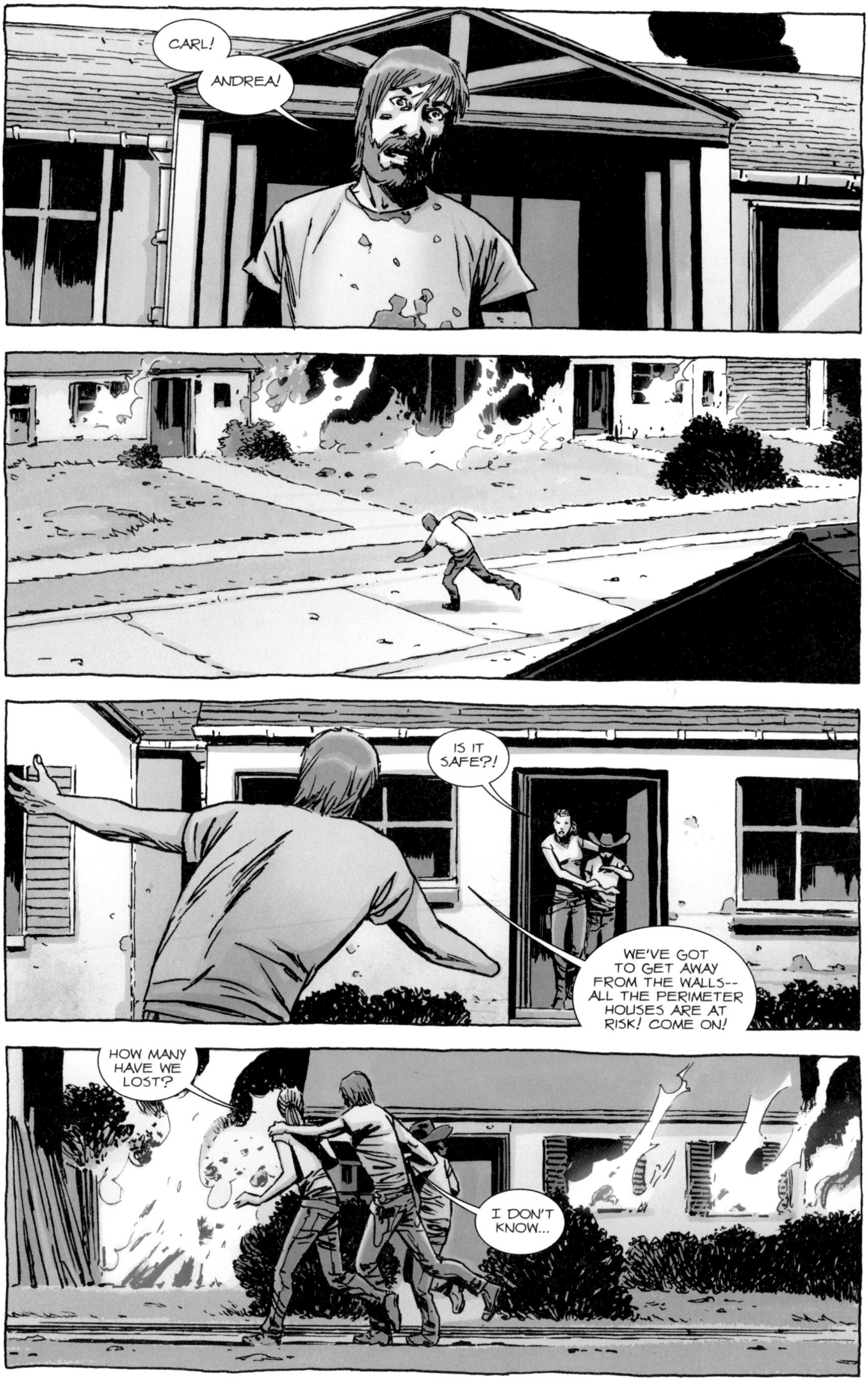
CARL!
ANDREA!
IS IT SAFE?!
WE'VE GOT TO GET AWAY FROM THE WALLS-- ALL THE PERIMETER HOUSES ARE AT RISK! COME ON!
HOW MANY HAVE WE LOST?
I DON'T KNOW...

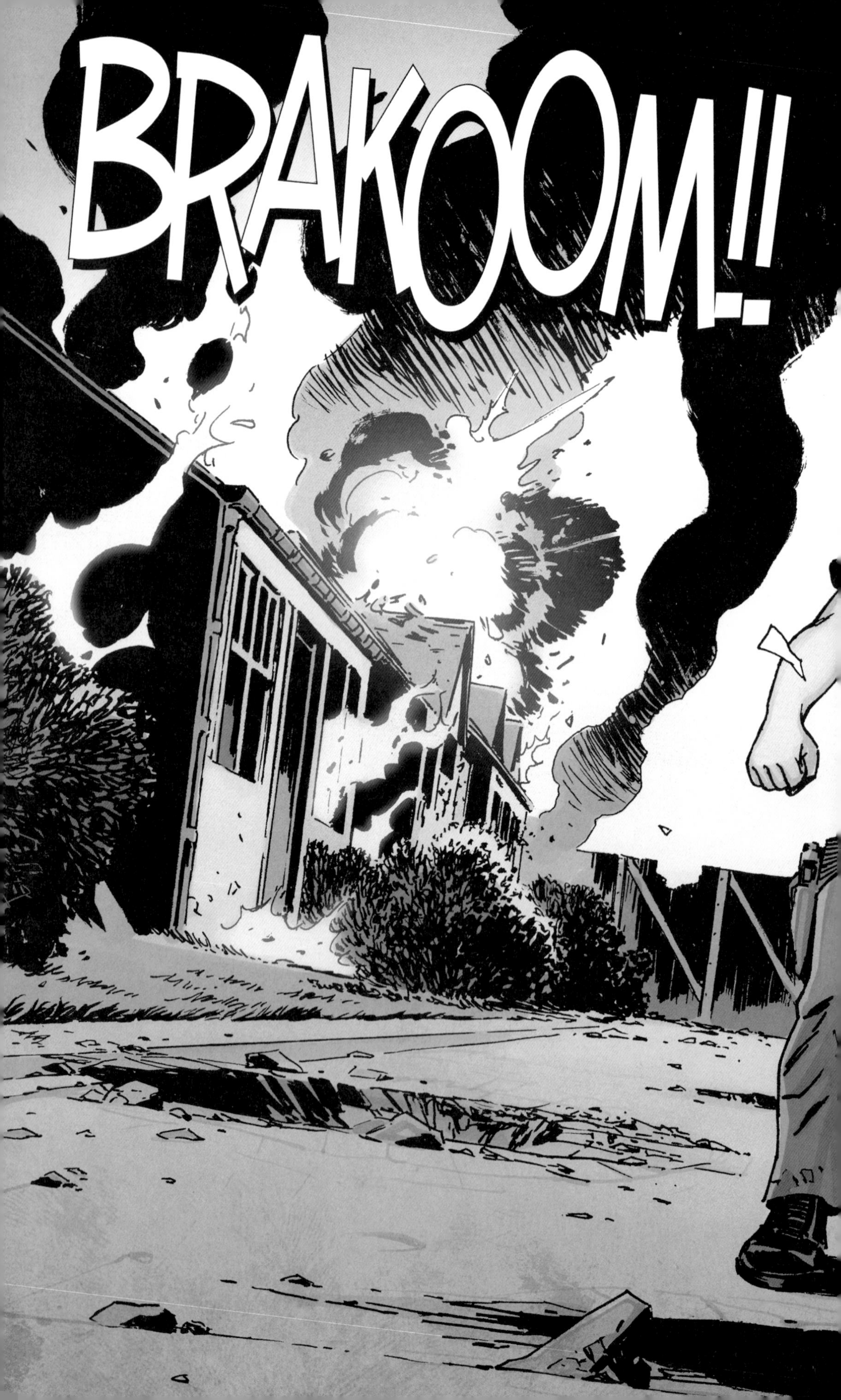
BRAKOOM!!

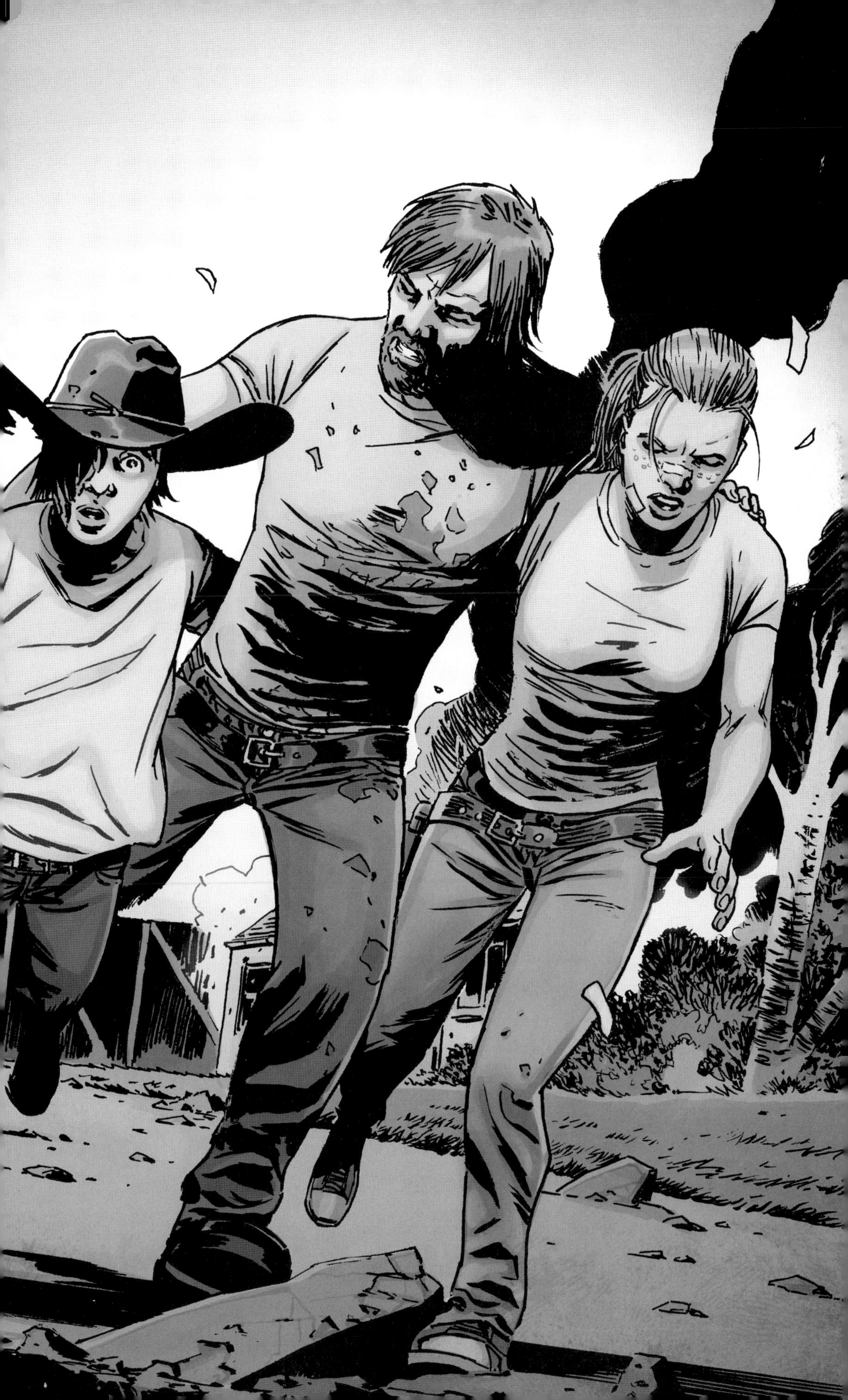

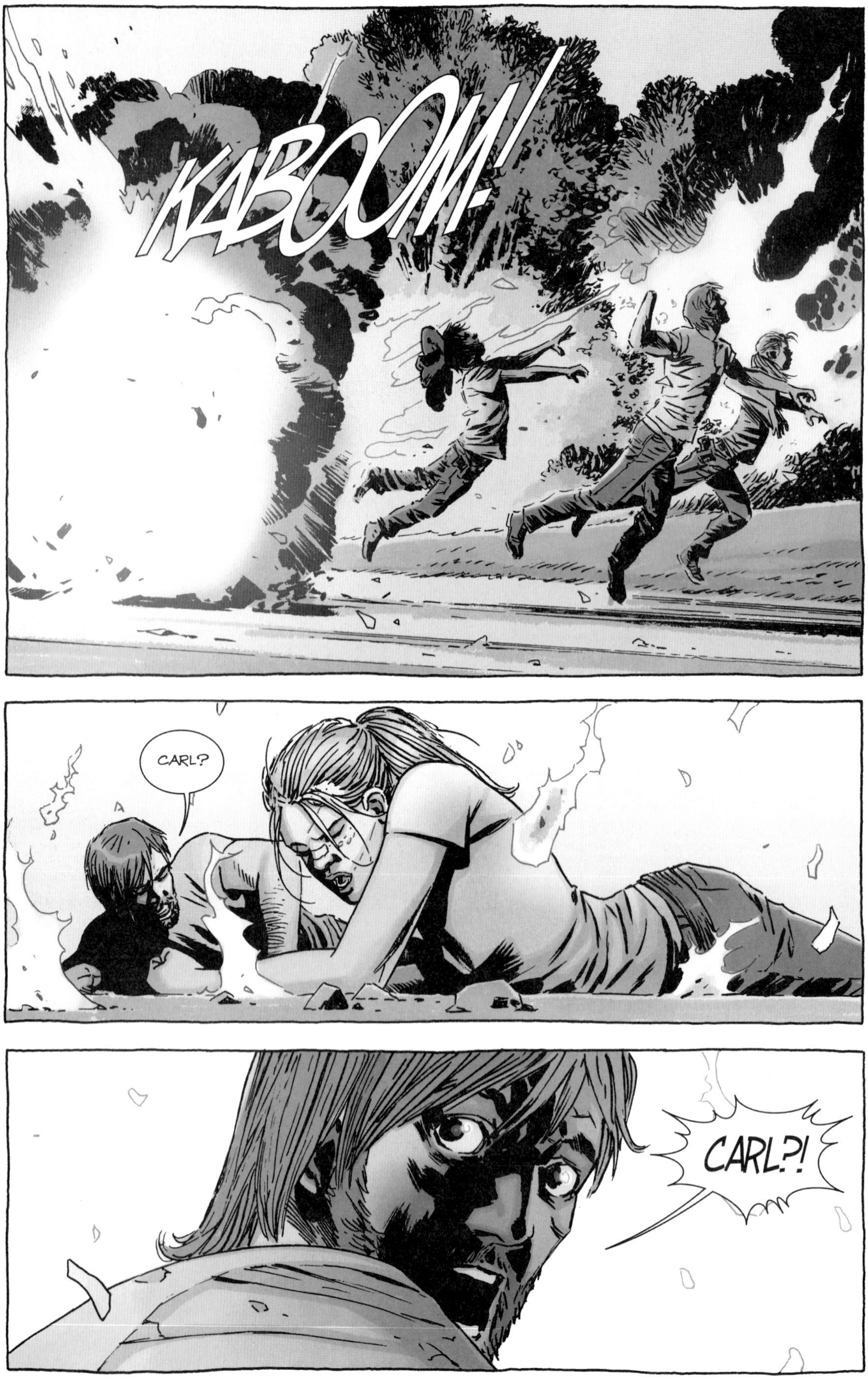
KABOOM!
CARL?
CARL?!

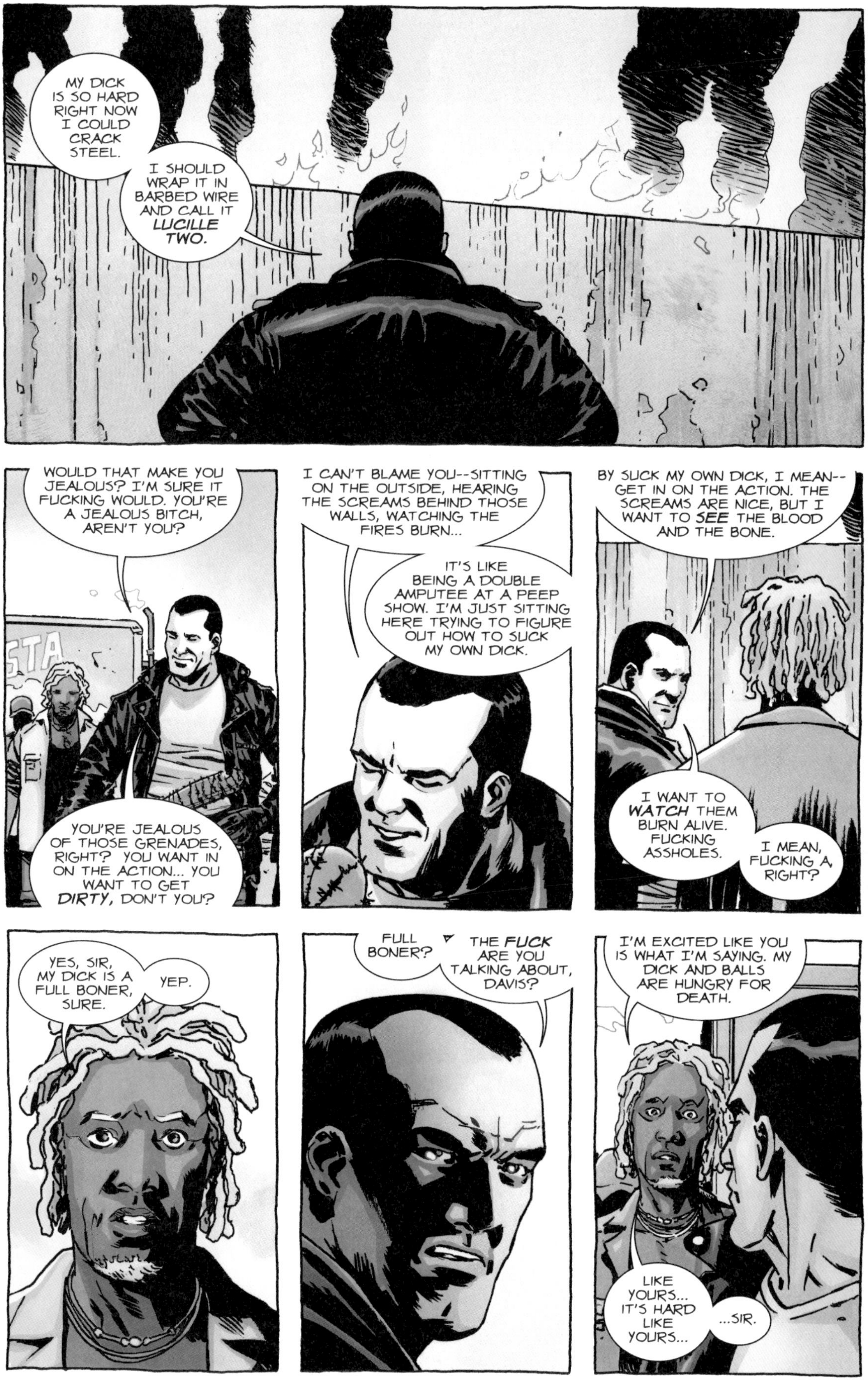
MY DICK IS SO HARD RIGHT NOW I COULD CRACK STEEL.
I SHOULD WRAP IT IN BARBED WIRE AND CALL IT LUCILLE TWO.
WOULD THAT MAKE YOU JEALOUS? I'M SURE IT FUCKING WOULD. YOU'RE A JEALOUS BITCH, AREN'T YOU?
YOU'RE JEALOUS OF THOSE GRENADES, RIGHT? YOU WANT IN ON THE ACTION... YOU WANT TO GET DIRTY, DON'T YOU?
I CAN'T BLAME YOU--SITTING ON THE OUTSIDE, HEARING THE SCREAMS BEHIND THOSE WALLS, WATCHING THE FIRES BURN...
IT'S LIKE BEING A DOUBLE AMPUTEE AT A PEEP SHOW. I'M JUST SITTING HERE TRYING TO FIGURE OUT HOW TO SUCK MY OWN DICK.
BY SUCK MY OWN DICK, I MEAN--GET IN ON THE ACTION. THE SCREAMS ARE NICE, BUT I WANT TO SEE THE BLOOD AND THE BONE.
I WANT TO WATCH THEM BURN ALIVE. FUCKING ASSHOLES.
I MEAN, FUCKING A, RIGHT?
YES, SIR, MY DICK IS A FULL BONER, SURE.
YEP.
FULL BONER?
THE FUCK ARE YOU TALKING ABOUT, DAVIS?
I'M EXCITED LIKE YOU IS WHAT I'M SAYING. MY DICK AND BALLS ARE HUNGRY FOR DEATH.
LIKE YOURS... IT'S HARD LIKE YOURS...
...SIR.

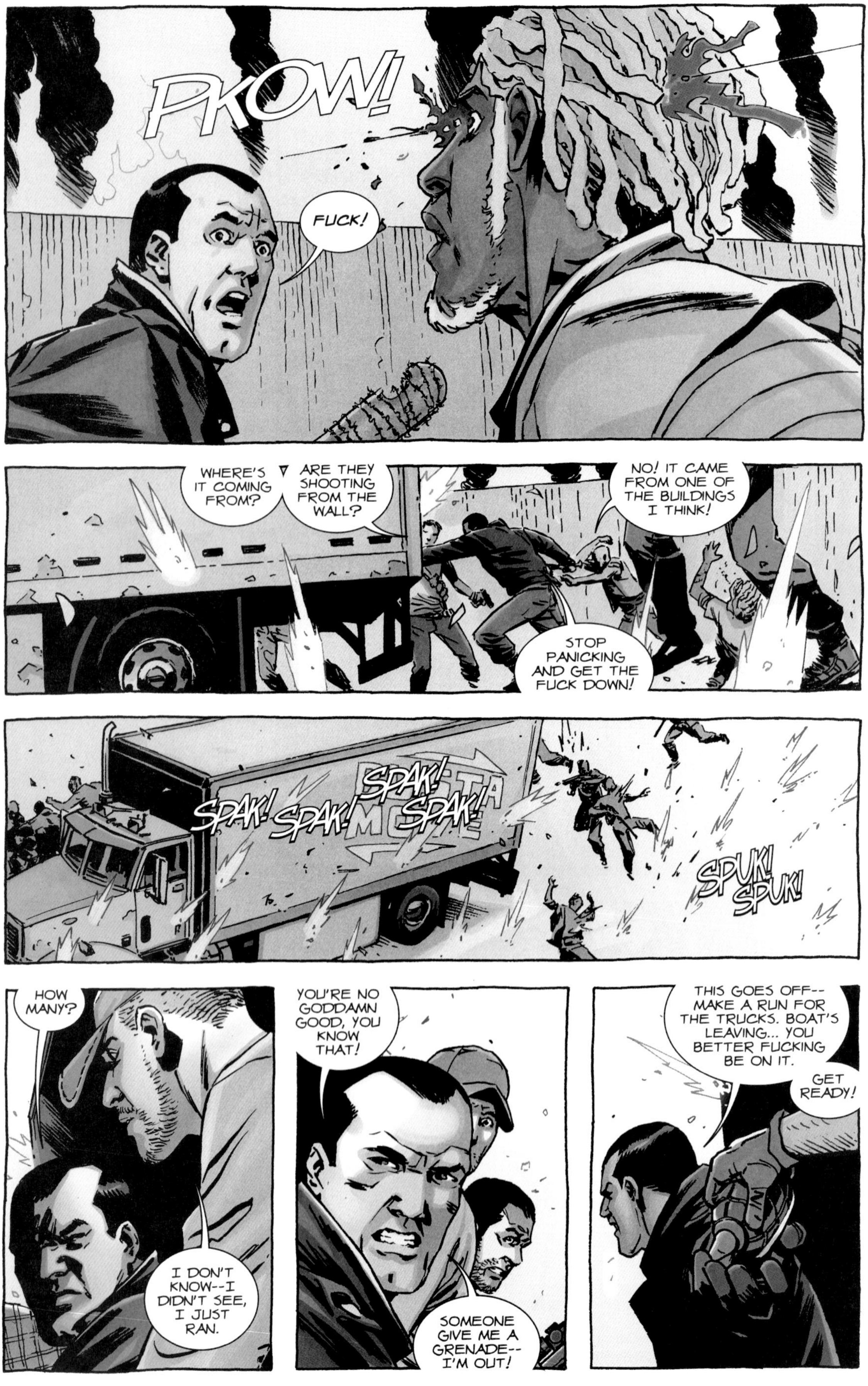
PKOW!
FUCK!
WHERE'S IT COMING FROM?
ARE THEY SHOOTING FROM THE WALL?
NO! IT CAME FROM ONE OF THE BUILDINGS I THINK!
STOP PANICKING AND GET THE FUCK DOWN!
SPAK! SPAK! SPAK! SPAK!
SPUK! SPUK!
HOW MANY?
I DON'T KNOW--I DIDN'T SEE, I JUST RAN.
YOU'RE NO GODDAMN GOOD, YOU KNOW THAT!
SOMEONE GIVE ME A GRENADE-- I'M OUT!
THIS GOES OFF-- MAKE A RUN FOR THE TRUCKS. BOAT'S LEAVING... YOU BETTER FUCKING BE ON IT.
GET READY!

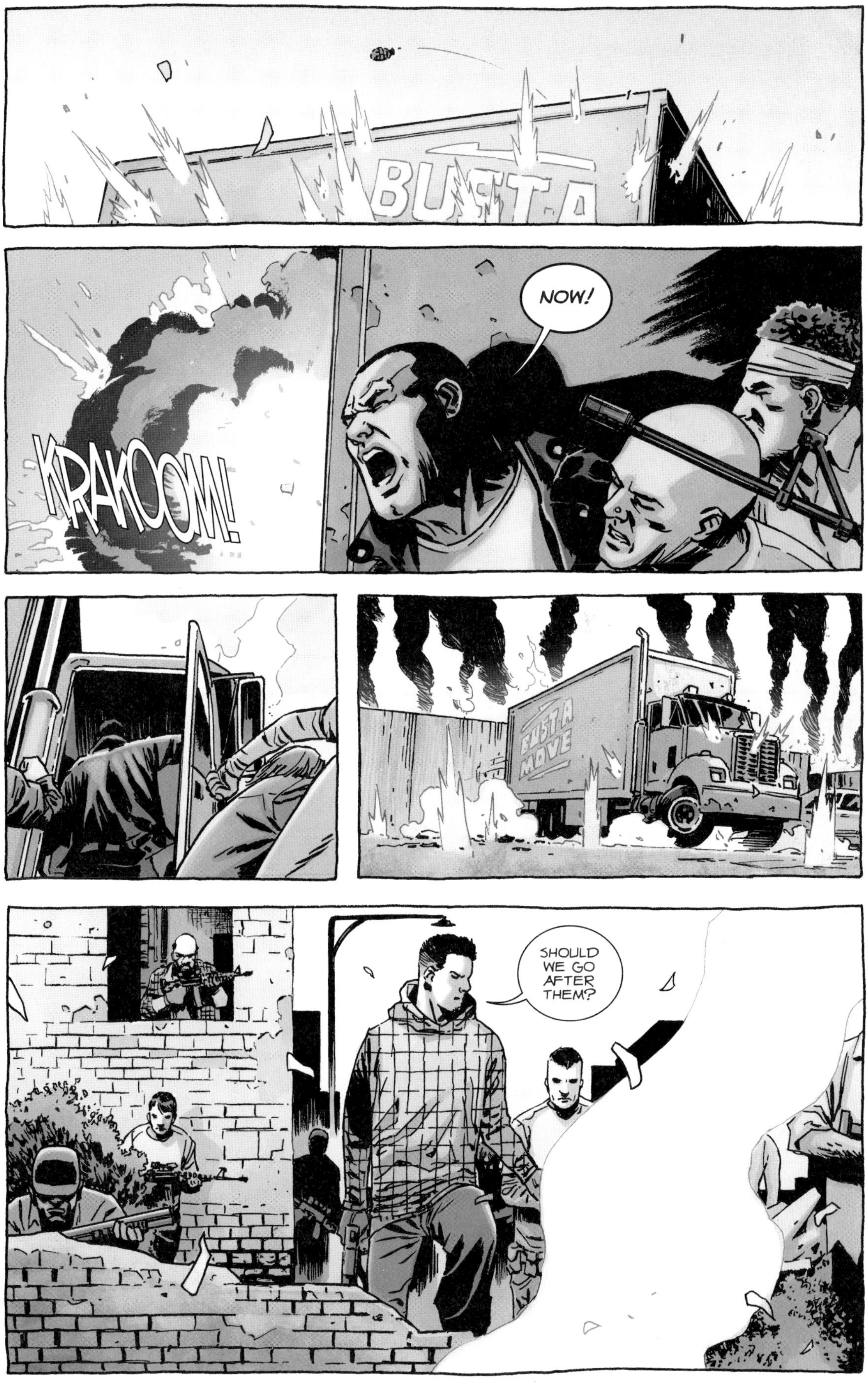
BUST-A
NOW!
KRAKOOM!
BUST-A MOVE
SHOULD WE GO AFTER THEM?

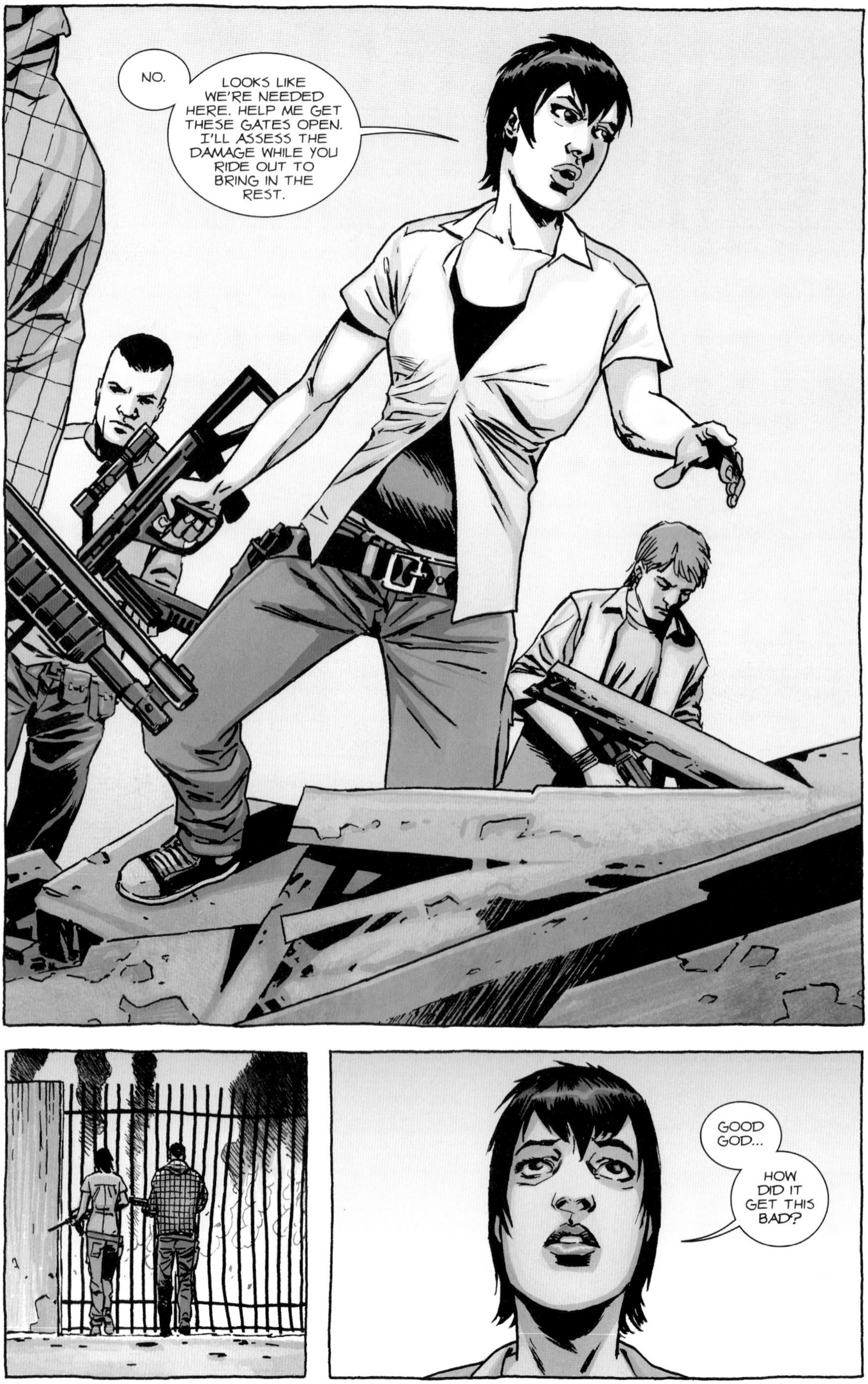
NO.
LOOKS LIKE WE'RE NEEDED HERE. HELP ME GET THESE GATES OPEN. I'LL ASSESS THE DAMAGE WHILE YOU RIDE OUT TO BRING IN THE REST.
GOOD GOD...
HOW DID IT GET THIS BAD?

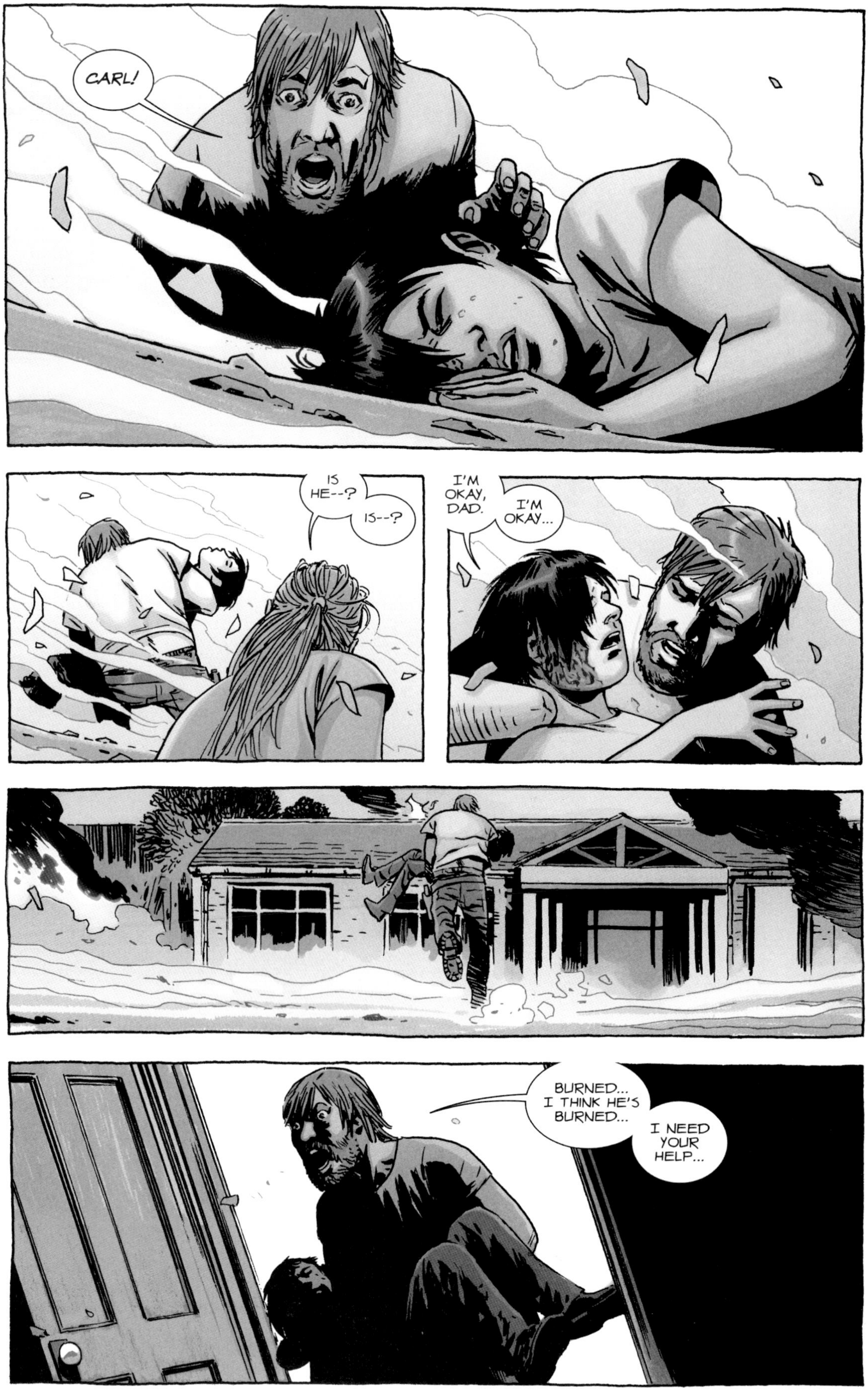
CARL!
IS HE--?
IS--?
I'M OKAY, DAD.
I'M OKAY...
BURNED... I THINK HE'S BURNED...
I NEED YOUR HELP...

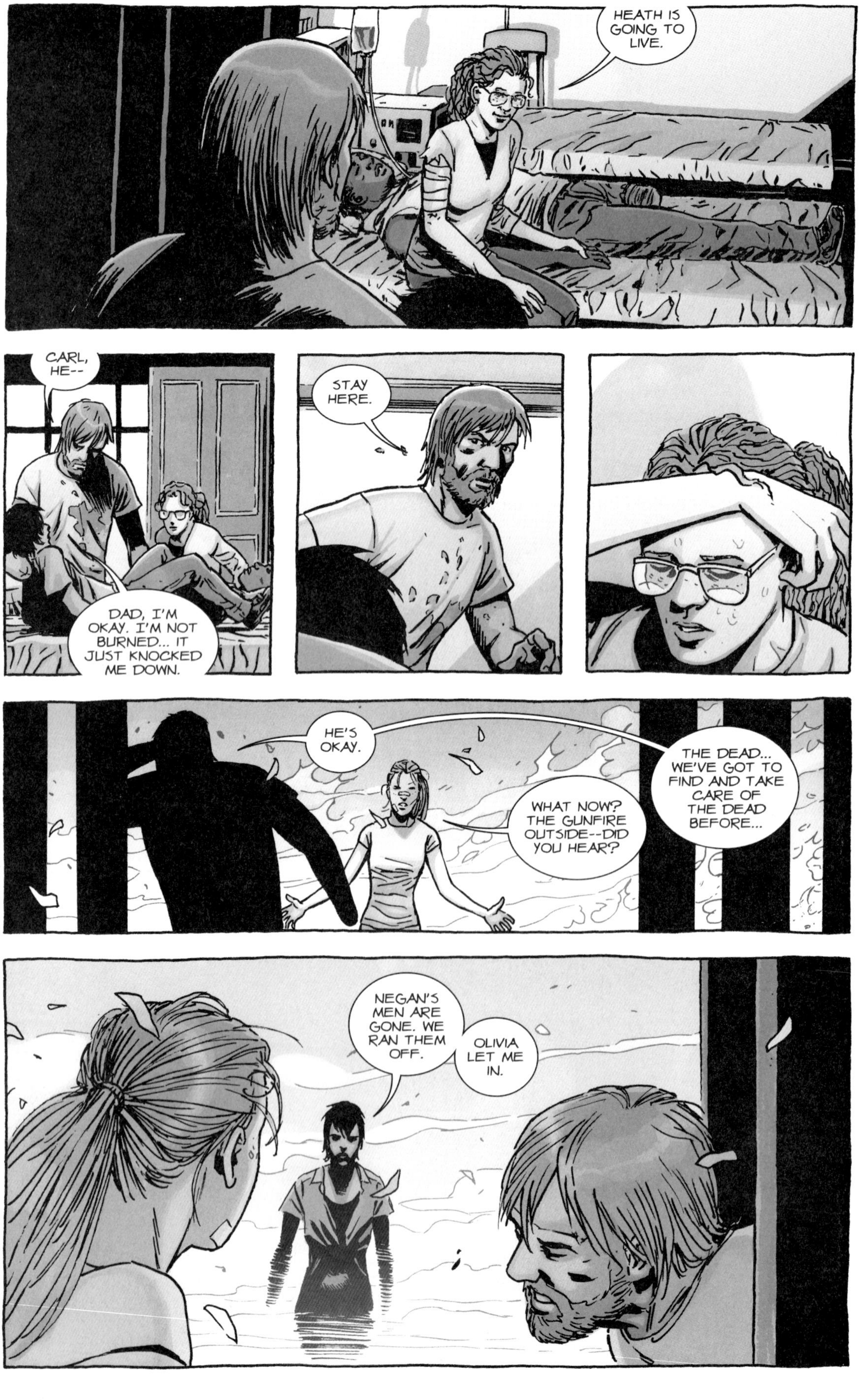
HEATH IS GOING TO LIVE.
CARL, HE--
DAD, I'M OKAY. I'M NOT BURNED... IT JUST KNOCKED ME DOWN.
STAY HERE.
HE'S OKAY.
THE DEAD... WE'VE GOT TO FIND AND TAKE CARE OF THE DEAD BEFORE...
WHAT NOW? THE GUNFIRE OUTSIDE--DID YOU HEAR?
NEGAN'S MEN ARE GONE. WE RAN THEM OFF.
OLIVIA LET ME IN.

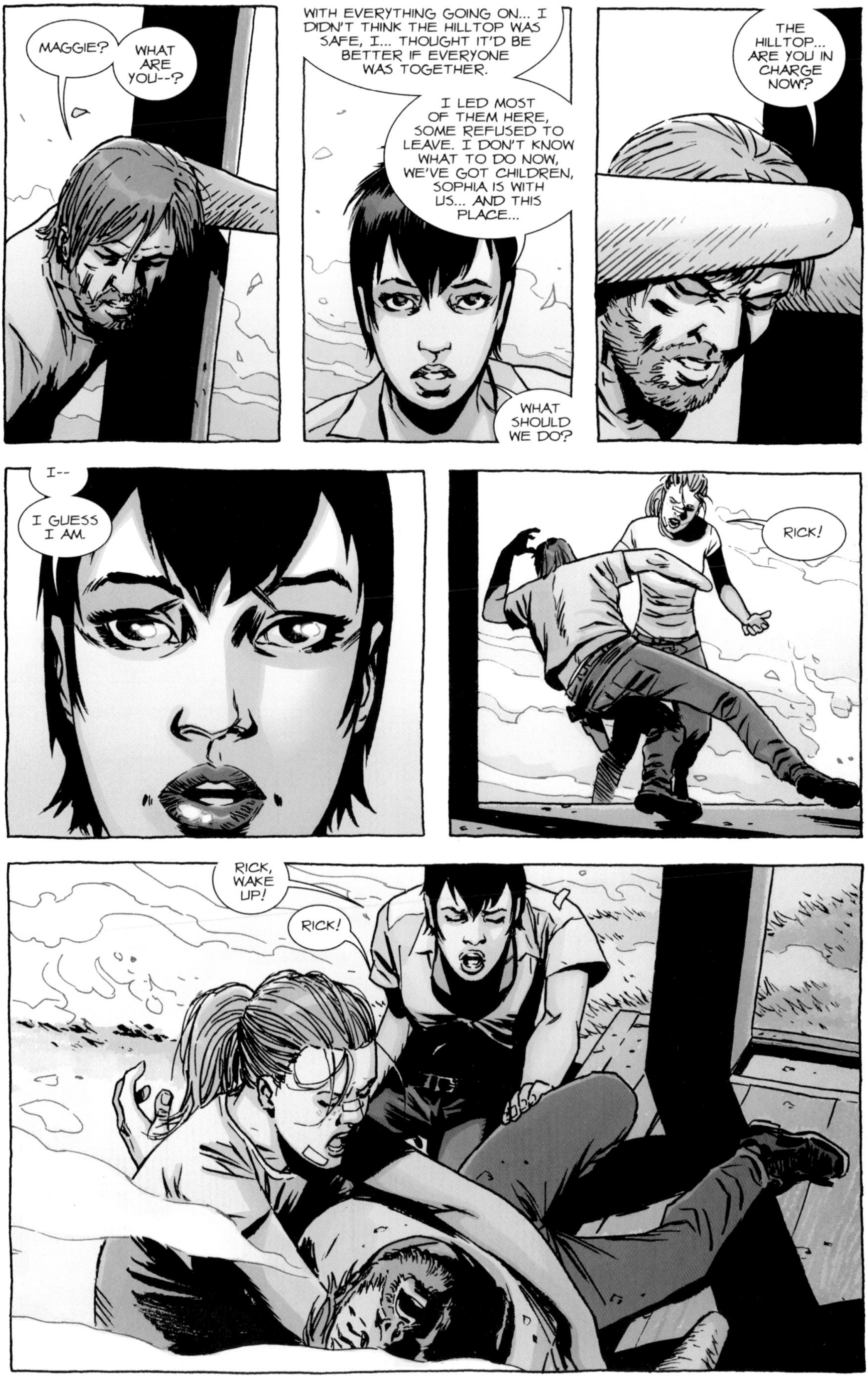
MAGGIE?
WHAT ARE YOU--?
WITH EVERYTHING GOING ON... I DIDN'T THINK THE HILLTOP WAS SAFE, I... THOUGHT IT'D BE BETTER IF EVERYONE WAS TOGETHER.
I LED MOST OF THEM HERE, SOME REFUSED TO LEAVE. I DON'T KNOW WHAT TO DO NOW, WE'VE GOT CHILDREN, SOPHIA IS WITH US... AND THIS PLACE...
WHAT SHOULD WE DO?
THE HILLTOP... ARE YOU IN CHARGE NOW?
I--
I GUESS I AM.
RICK!
RICK, WAKE UP!
RICK!

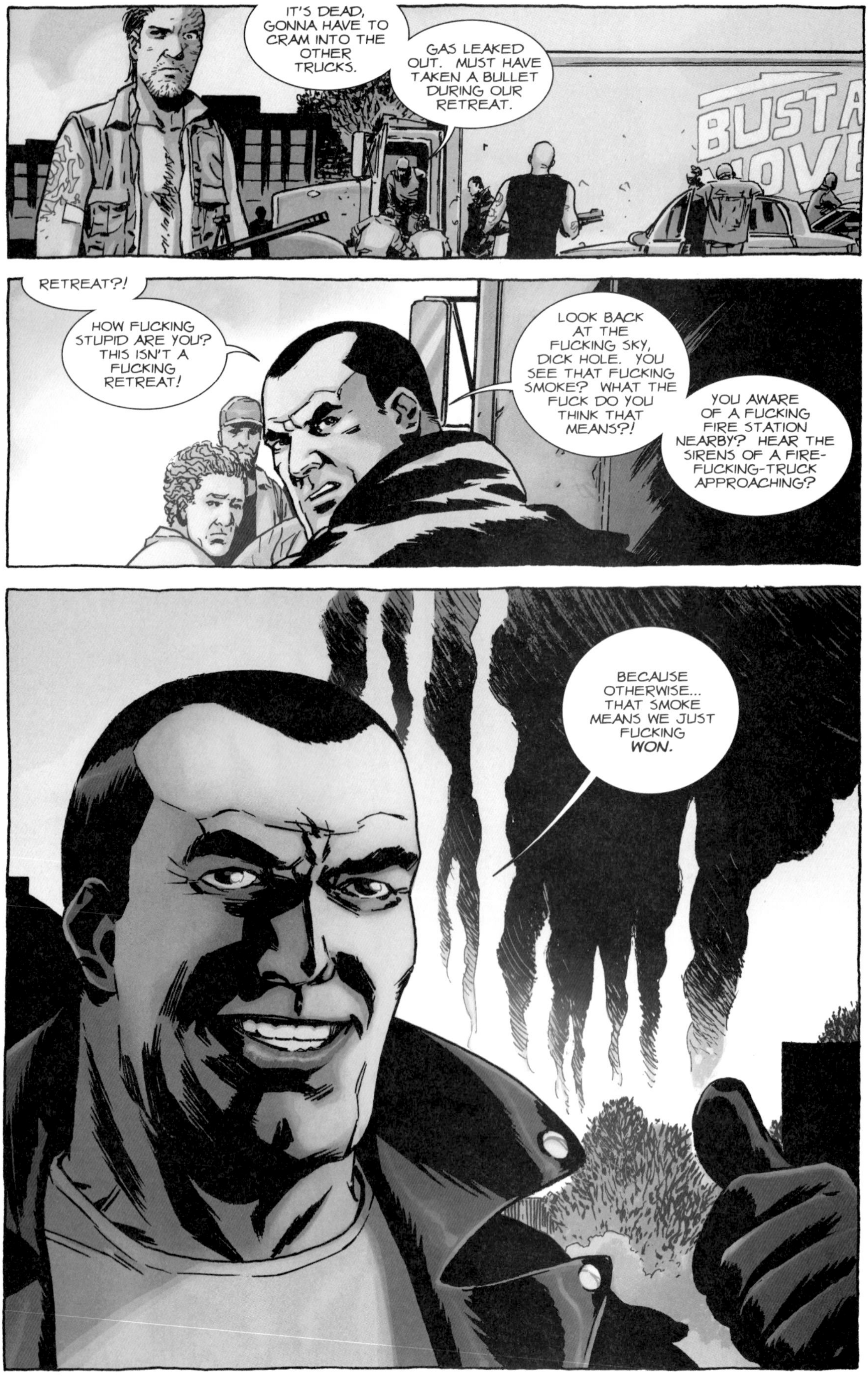
IT'S DEAD, GONNA HAVE TO CRAM INTO THE OTHER TRUCKS.
GAS LEAKED OUT. MUST HAVE TAKEN A BULLET DURING OUR RETREAT.
RETREAT?!
HOW FUCKING STUPID ARE YOU? THIS ISN'T A FUCKING RETREAT!
LOOK BACK AT THE FUCKING SKY, DICK HOLE. YOU SEE THAT FUCKING SMOKE? WHAT THE FUCK DO YOU THINK THAT MEANS?!
YOU AWARE OF A FUCKING FIRE STATION NEARBY? HEAR THE SIRENS OF A FIRE-FUCKING-TRUCK APPROACHING?
BECAUSE OTHERWISE... THAT SMOKE MEANS WE JUST FUCKING WON.

Chapter Twenty-One:
All Out War Part Two

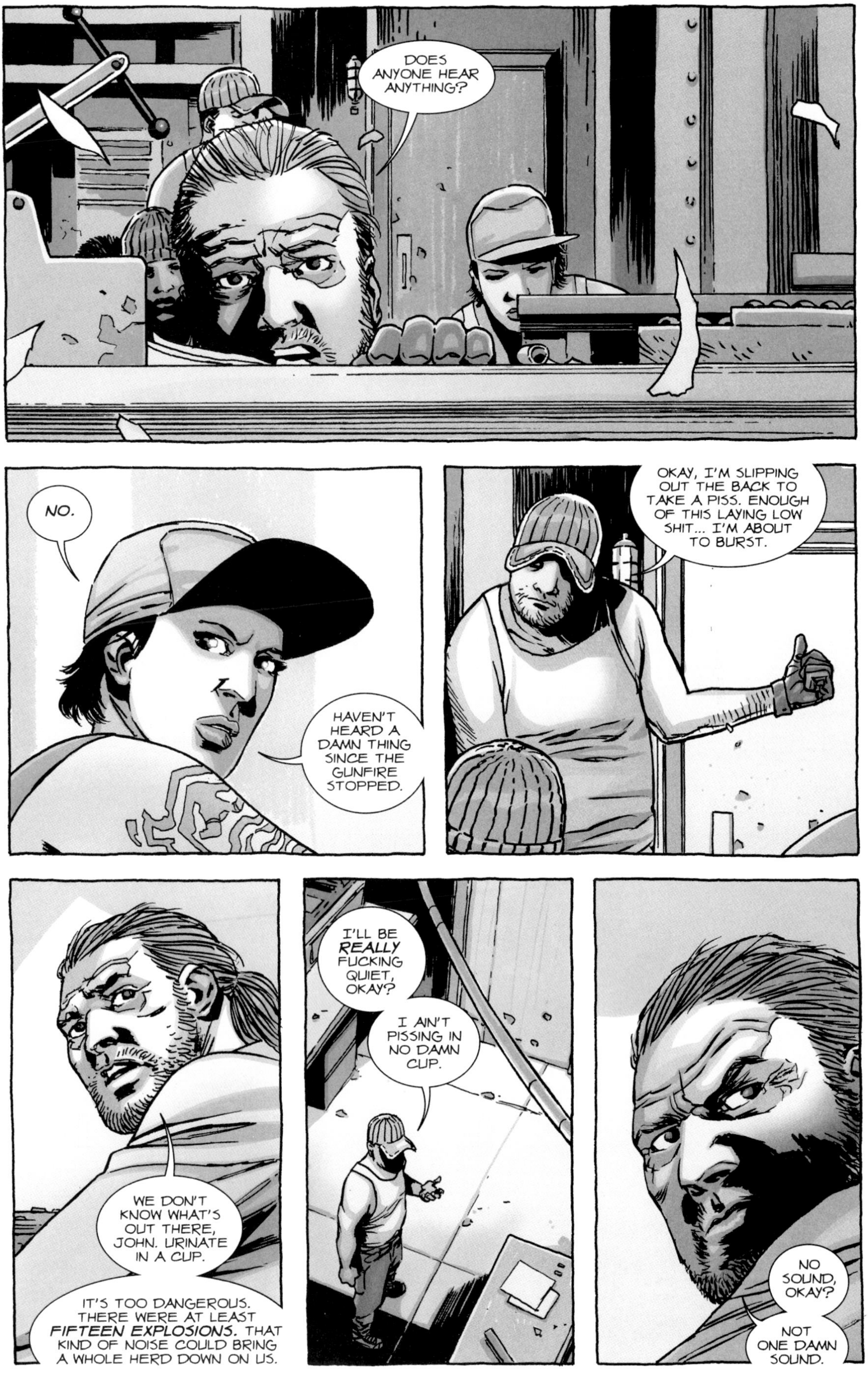

DOES ANYONE HEAR ANYTHING?
NO.
HAVEN'T HEARD A DAMN THING SINCE THE GUNFIRE STOPPED.
OKAY, I'M SLIPPING OUT THE BACK TO TAKE A PISS. ENOUGH OF THIS LAYING LOW SHIT... I'M ABOUT TO BURST.
WE DON'T KNOW WHAT'S OUT THERE, JOHN. URINATE IN A CUP.
IT'S TOO DANGEROUS. THERE WERE AT LEAST FIFTEEN EXPLOSIONS. THAT KIND OF NOISE COULD BRING A WHOLE HERD DOWN ON US.
I'LL BE REALLY FUCKING QUIET, OKAY?
I AIN'T PISSING IN NO DAMN CUP.
NO SOUND, OKAY?
NOT ONE DAMN SOUND.

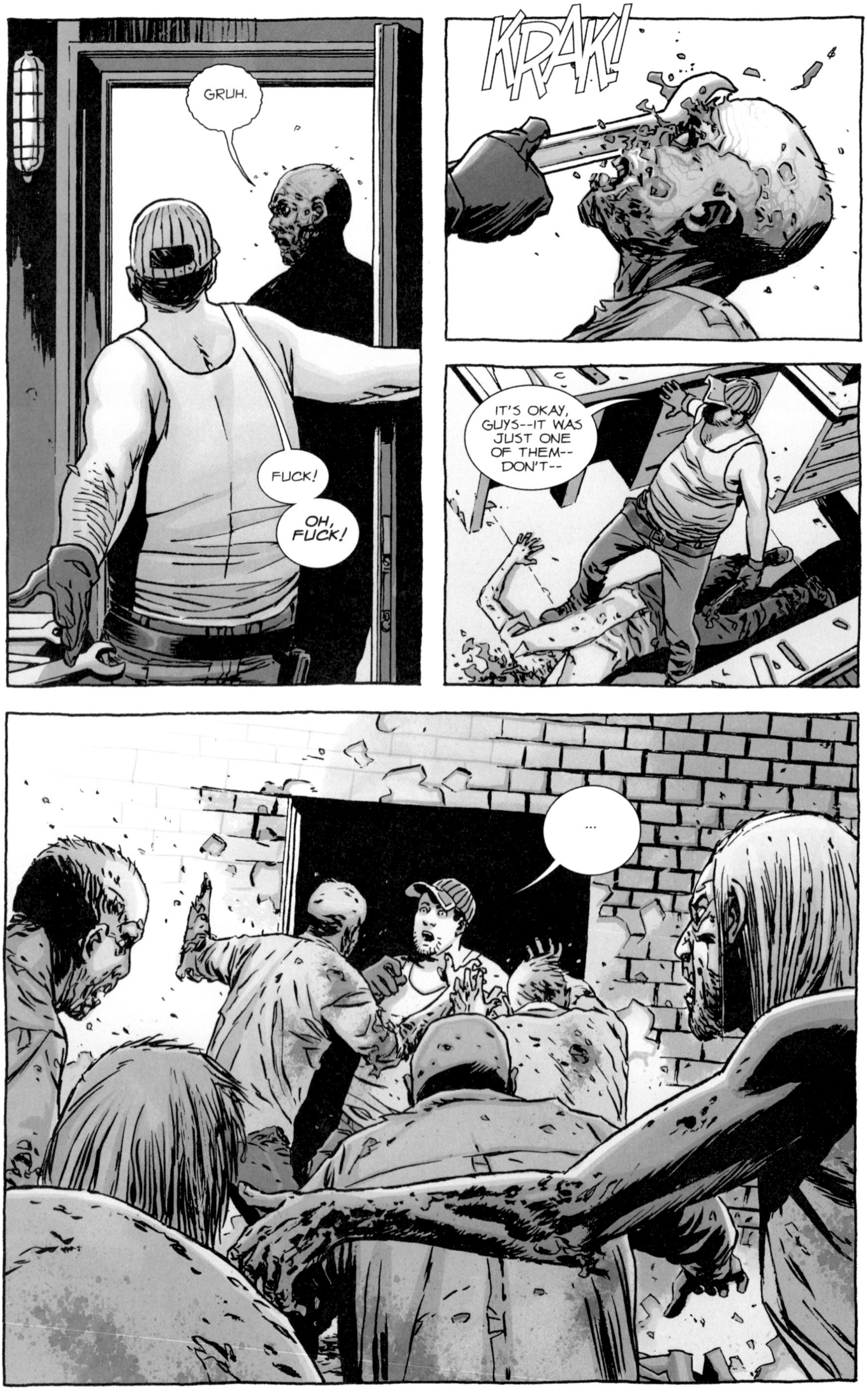
GRUH.
FUCK!
OH, FUCK!
KRAK!
IT'S OKAY, GUYS--IT WAS JUST ONE OF THEM-- DON'T--
...

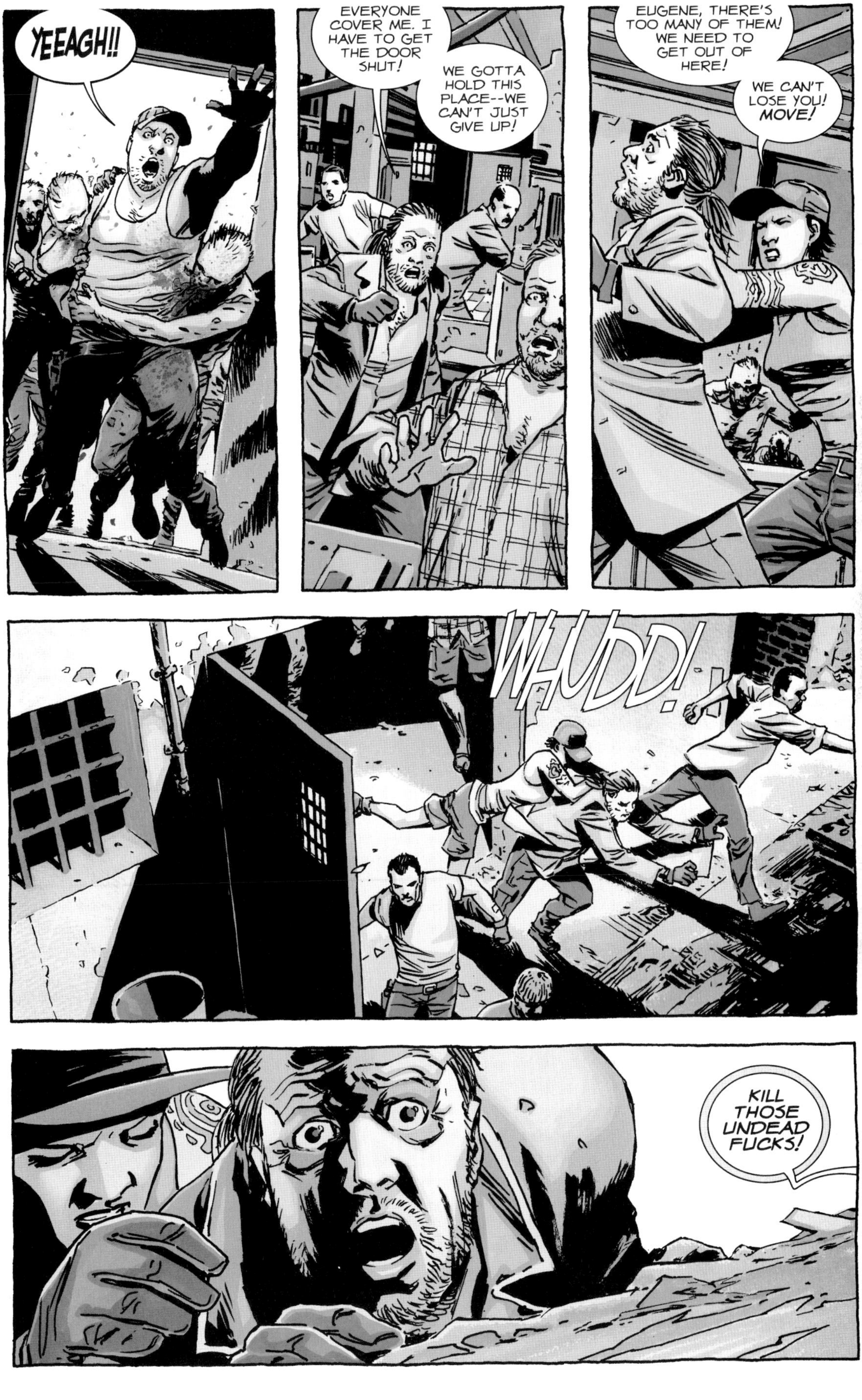
YEEAGH!!
EVERYONE COVER ME. I HAVE TO GET THE DOOR SHUT!
WE GOTTA HOLD THIS PLACE--WE CAN'T JUST GIVE UP!
EUGENE, THERE'S TOO MANY OF THEM! WE NEED TO GET OUT OF HERE!
WE CAN'T LOSE YOU! MOVE!
WHUDD!
KILL THOSE UNDEAD FUCKS!

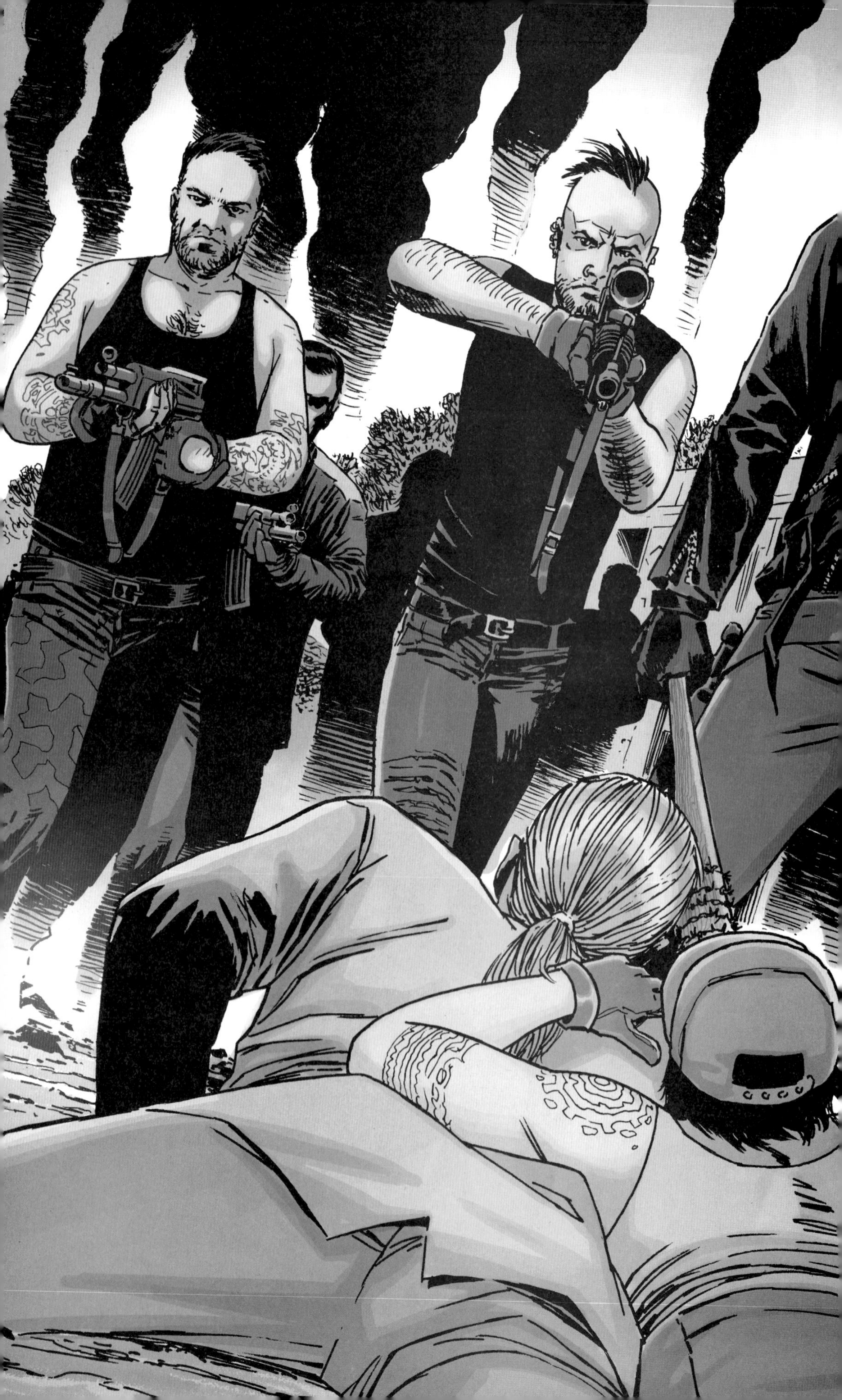

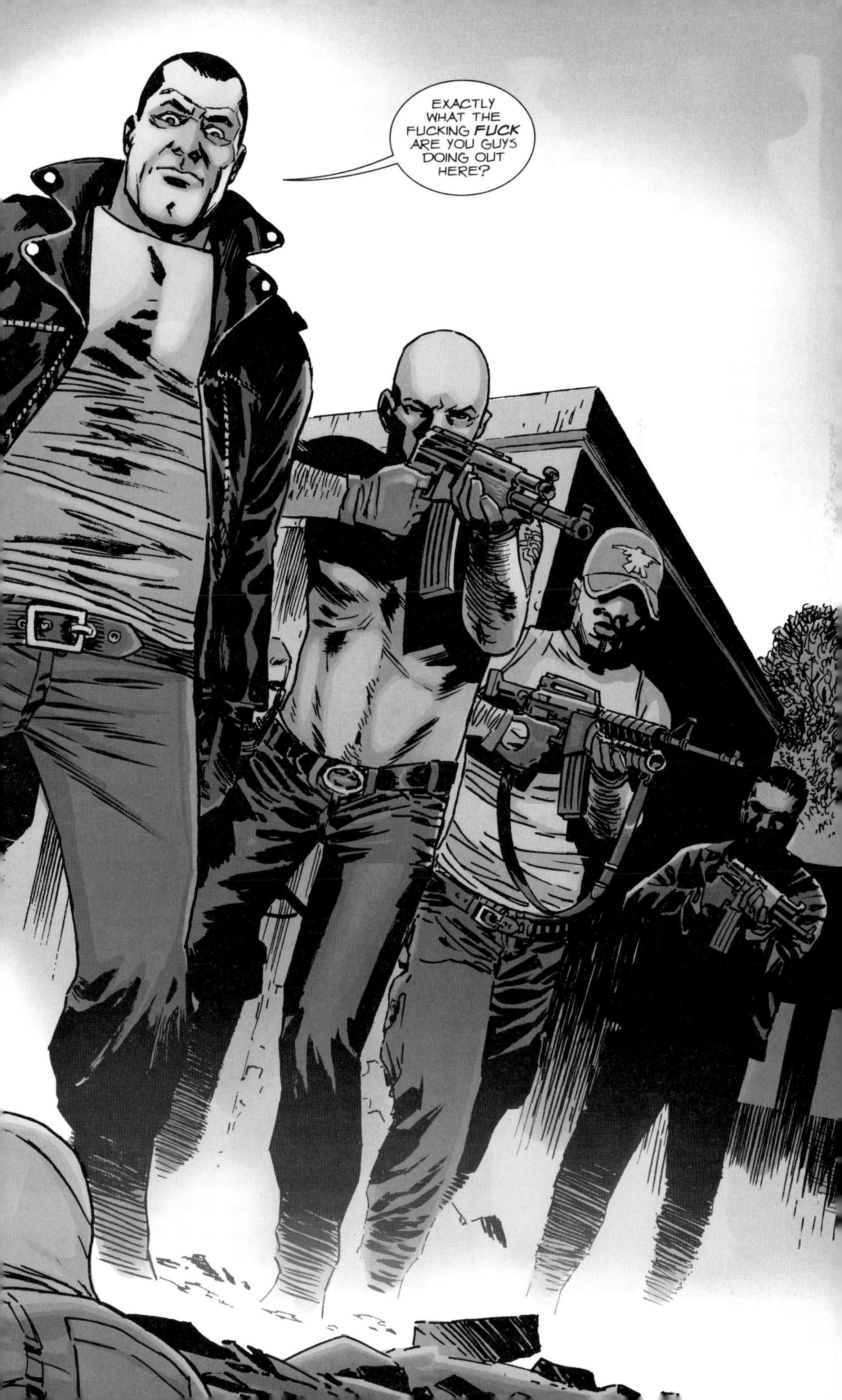
EXACTLY WHAT THE FUCKING FUCK ARE YOU GUYS DOING OUT HERE?

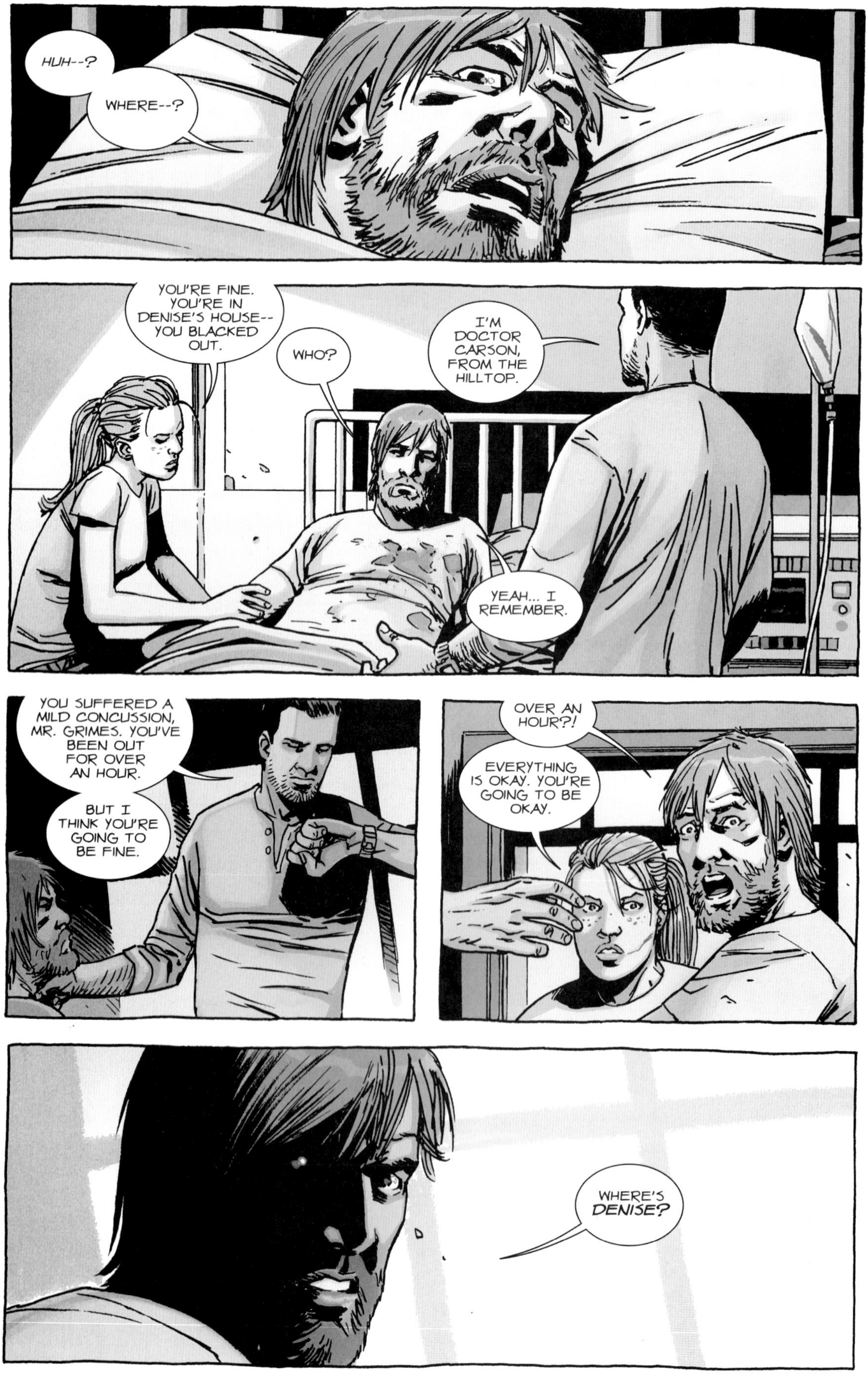

HUH--?
WHERE--?
YOU'RE FINE. YOU'RE IN DENISE'S HOUSE-- YOU BLACKED OUT.
WHO?
I'M DOCTOR CARSON, FROM THE HILLTOP.
YEAH... I REMEMBER.
YOU SUFFERED A MILD CONCUSSION, MR. GRIMES. YOU'VE BEEN OUT FOR OVER AN HOUR.
BUT I THINK YOU'RE GOING TO BE FINE.
OVER AN HOUR?!
EVERYTHING IS OKAY. YOU'RE GOING TO BE OKAY.
WHERE'S *DENISE?*

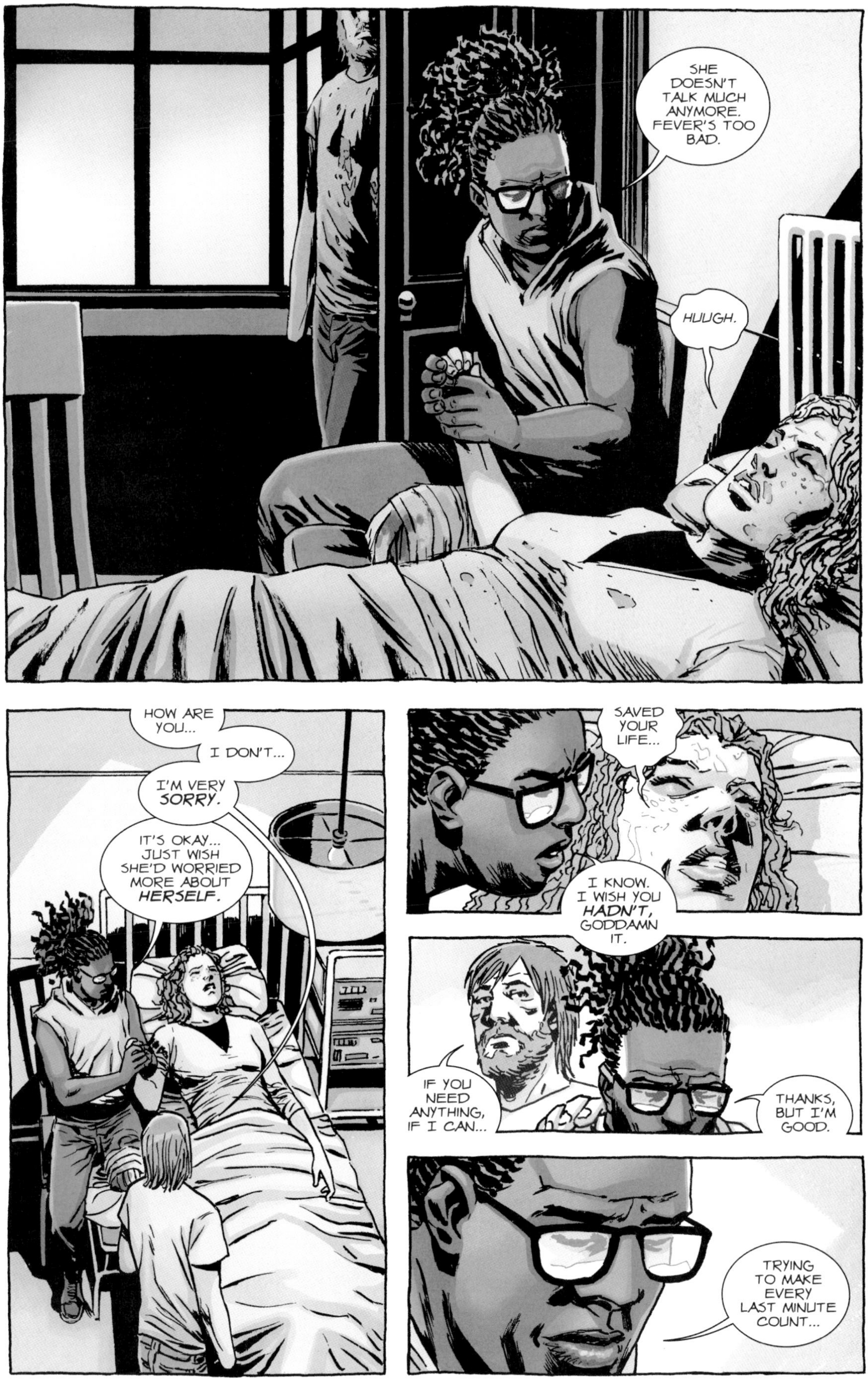
SHE DOESN'T TALK MUCH ANYMORE. FEVER'S TOO BAD.
HUUGH.
HOW ARE YOU...
I DON'T...
I'M VERY SORRY.
IT'S OKAY... JUST WISH SHE'D WORRIED MORE ABOUT HERSELF.
SAVED YOUR LIFE...
I KNOW. I WISH YOU HADN'T, GODDAMN IT.
IF YOU NEED ANYTHING, IF I CAN...
THANKS, BUT I'M GOOD.
TRYING TO MAKE EVERY LAST MINUTE COUNT...

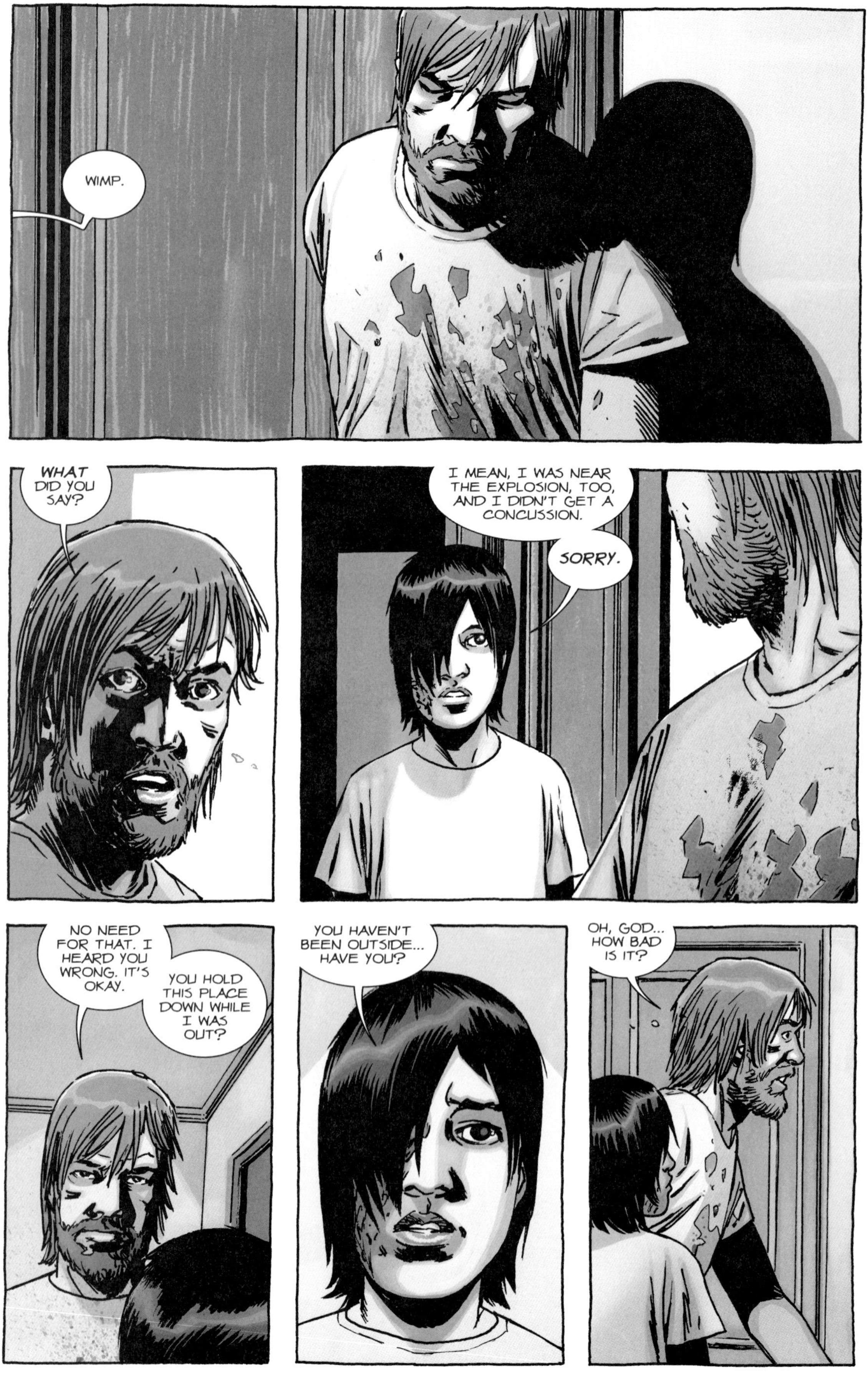
WIMP.
WHAT DID YOU SAY?
I MEAN, I WAS NEAR THE EXPLOSION, TOO, AND I DIDN'T GET A CONCUSSION.
SORRY.
NO NEED FOR THAT. I HEARD YOU WRONG. IT'S OKAY.
YOU HOLD THIS PLACE DOWN WHILE I WAS OUT?
YOU HAVEN'T BEEN OUTSIDE... HAVE YOU?
OH, GOD... HOW BAD IS IT?

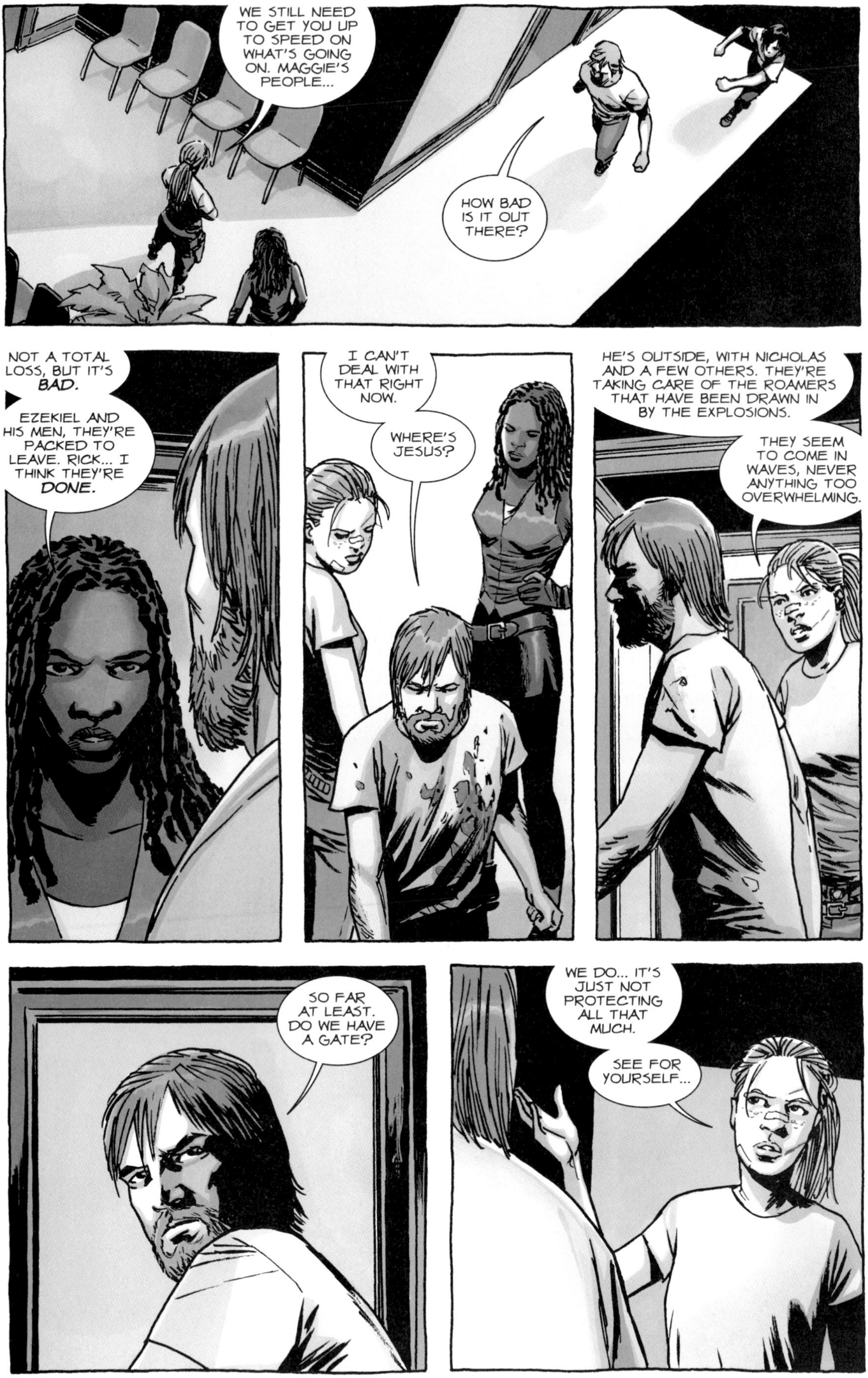
WE STILL NEED TO GET YOU UP TO SPEED ON WHAT'S GOING ON. MAGGIE'S PEOPLE...
HOW BAD IS IT OUT THERE?
NOT A TOTAL LOSS, BUT IT'S BAD.
EZEKIEL AND HIS MEN, THEY'RE PACKED TO LEAVE. RICK... I THINK THEY'RE DONE.
I CAN'T DEAL WITH THAT RIGHT NOW.
WHERE'S JESUS?
HE'S OUTSIDE, WITH NICHOLAS AND A FEW OTHERS. THEY'RE TAKING CARE OF THE ROAMERS THAT HAVE BEEN DRAWN IN BY THE EXPLOSIONS.
THEY SEEM TO COME IN WAVES, NEVER ANYTHING TOO OVERWHELMING.
SO FAR AT LEAST. DO WE HAVE A GATE?
WE DO... IT'S JUST NOT PROTECTING ALL THAT MUCH.
SEE FOR YOURSELF...

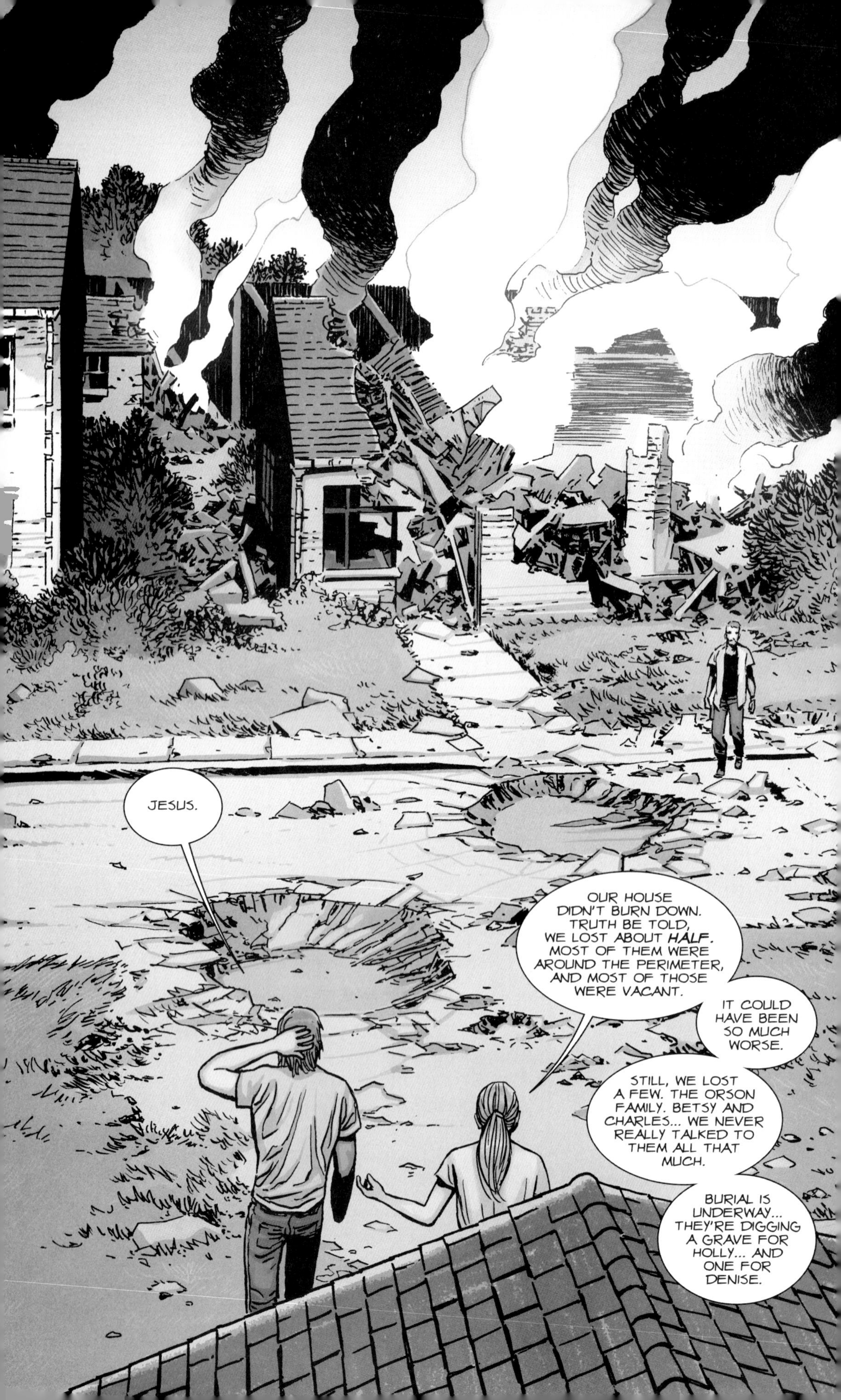
JESUS.
OUR HOUSE DIDN'T BURN DOWN. TRUTH BE TOLD, WE LOST ABOUT HALF. MOST OF THEM WERE AROUND THE PERIMETER, AND MOST OF THOSE WERE VACANT.
IT COULD HAVE BEEN SO MUCH WORSE.
STILL, WE LOST A FEW. THE ORSON FAMILY. BETSY AND CHARLES... WE NEVER REALLY TALKED TO THEM ALL THAT MUCH.
BURIAL IS UNDERWAY... THEY'RE DIGGING A GRAVE FOR HOLLY... AND ONE FOR DENISE.

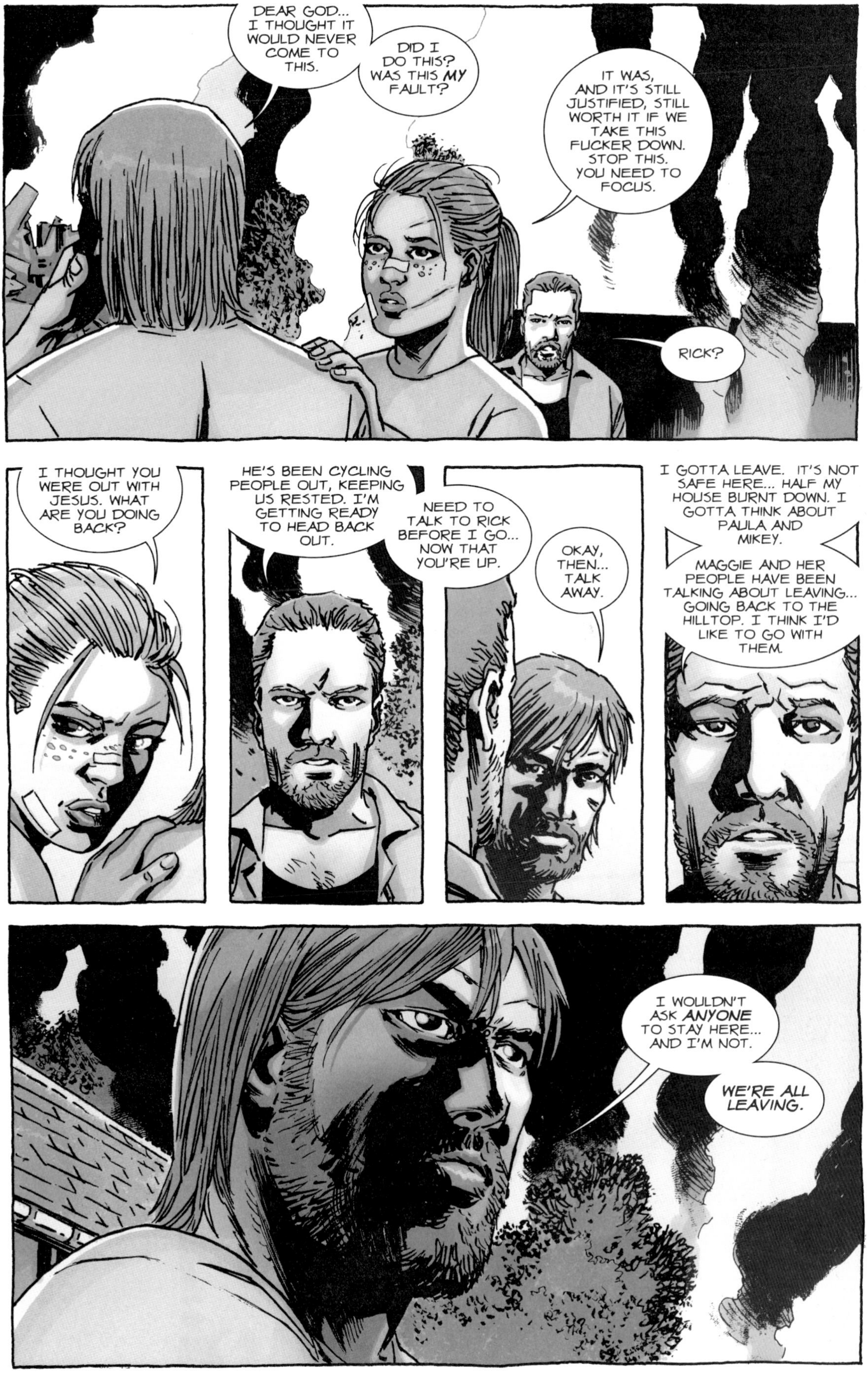
DEAR GOD... I THOUGHT IT WOULD NEVER COME TO THIS.
DID I DO THIS? WAS THIS *MY* FAULT?
IT WAS, AND IT'S STILL JUSTIFIED, STILL WORTH IT IF WE TAKE THIS FUCKER DOWN. STOP THIS. YOU NEED TO FOCUS.
RICK?
I THOUGHT YOU WERE OUT WITH JESUS. WHAT ARE YOU DOING BACK?
HE'S BEEN CYCLING PEOPLE OUT, KEEPING US RESTED. I'M GETTING READY TO HEAD BACK OUT.
NEED TO TALK TO RICK BEFORE I GO... NOW THAT YOU'RE UP.
OKAY, THEN... TALK AWAY.
I GOTTA LEAVE. IT'S NOT SAFE HERE... HALF MY HOUSE BURNT DOWN. I GOTTA THINK ABOUT PAULA AND MIKEY.
MAGGIE AND HER PEOPLE HAVE BEEN TALKING ABOUT LEAVING... GOING BACK TO THE HILLTOP. I THINK I'D LIKE TO GO WITH THEM.
I WOULDN'T ASK *ANYONE* TO STAY HERE... AND I'M NOT.
WE'RE ALL LEAVING.

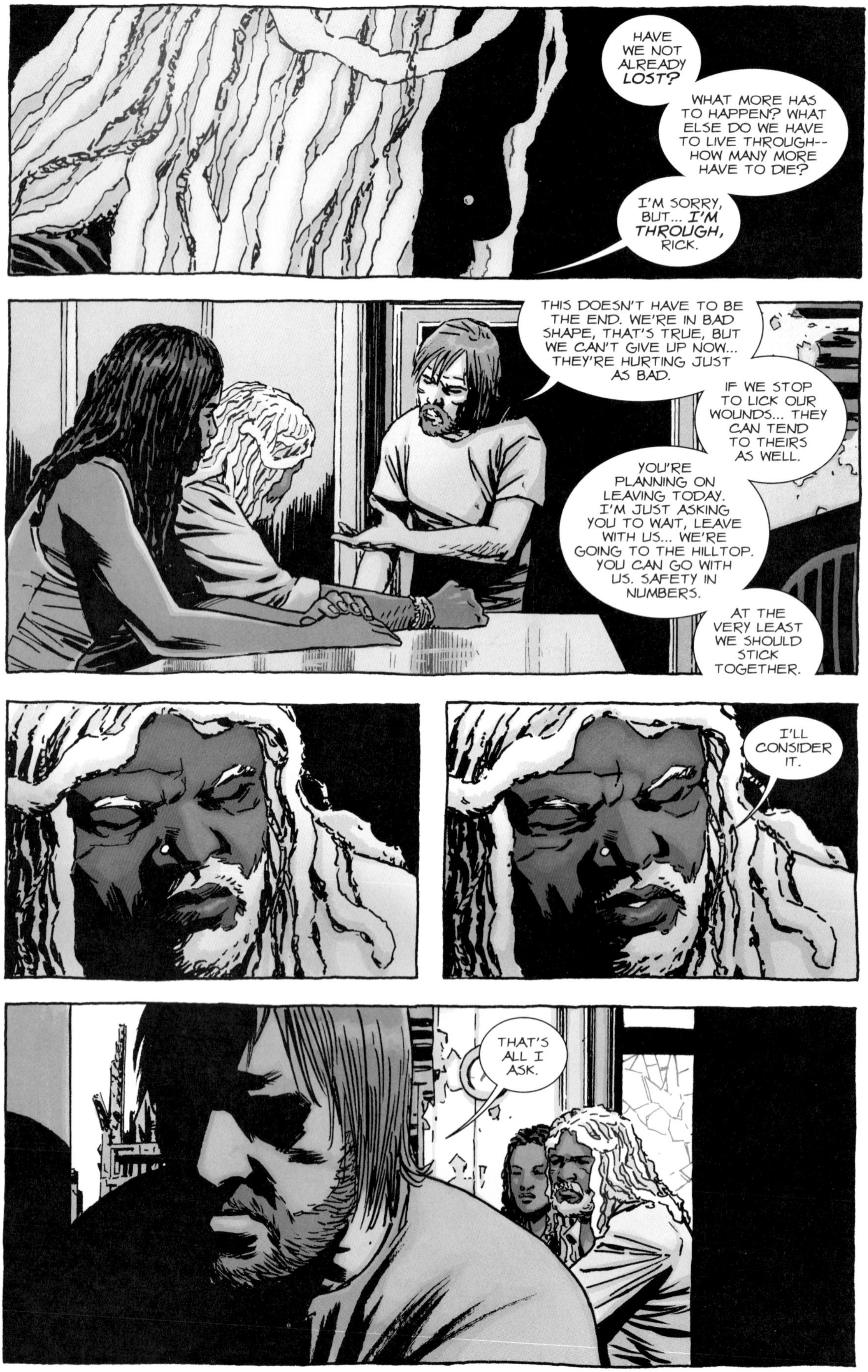
HAVE WE NOT ALREADY LOST?
WHAT MORE HAS TO HAPPEN? WHAT ELSE DO WE HAVE TO LIVE THROUGH-- HOW MANY MORE HAVE TO DIE?
I'M SORRY, BUT... I'M THROUGH, RICK.
THIS DOESN'T HAVE TO BE THE END. WE'RE IN BAD SHAPE, THAT'S TRUE, BUT WE CAN'T GIVE UP NOW... THEY'RE HURTING JUST AS BAD.
IF WE STOP TO LICK OUR WOUNDS... THEY CAN TEND TO THEIRS AS WELL.
YOU'RE PLANNING ON LEAVING TODAY. I'M JUST ASKING YOU TO WAIT, LEAVE WITH US... WE'RE GOING TO THE HILLTOP. YOU CAN GO WITH US. SAFETY IN NUMBERS.
AT THE VERY LEAST WE SHOULD STICK TOGETHER.
I'LL CONSIDER IT.
THAT'S ALL I ASK.

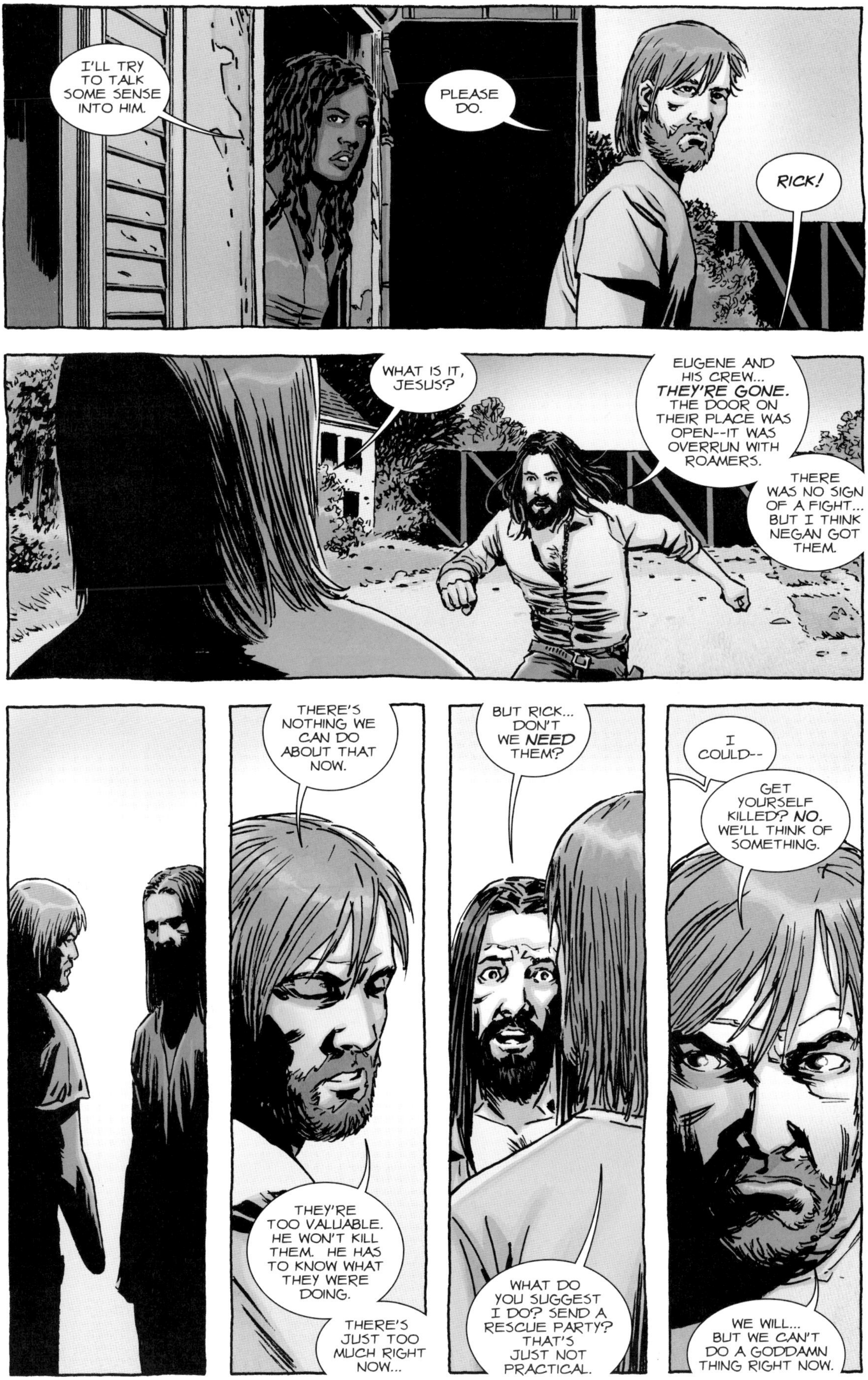

I'LL TRY TO TALK SOME SENSE INTO HIM.
PLEASE DO.
RICK!
WHAT IS IT, JESUS?
EUGENE AND HIS CREW... THEY'RE GONE. THE DOOR ON THEIR PLACE WAS OPEN--IT WAS OVERRUN WITH ROAMERS.
THERE WAS NO SIGN OF A FIGHT... BUT I THINK NEGAN GOT THEM.
THERE'S NOTHING WE CAN DO ABOUT THAT NOW.
THEY'RE TOO VALUABLE. HE WON'T KILL THEM. HE HAS TO KNOW WHAT THEY WERE DOING.
THERE'S JUST TOO MUCH RIGHT NOW...
BUT RICK... DON'T WE NEED THEM?
WHAT DO YOU SUGGEST I DO? SEND A RESCUE PARTY? THAT'S JUST NOT PRACTICAL.
I COULD--
GET YOURSELF KILLED? NO. WE'LL THINK OF SOMETHING.
WE WILL... BUT WE CAN'T DO A GODDAMN THING RIGHT NOW.

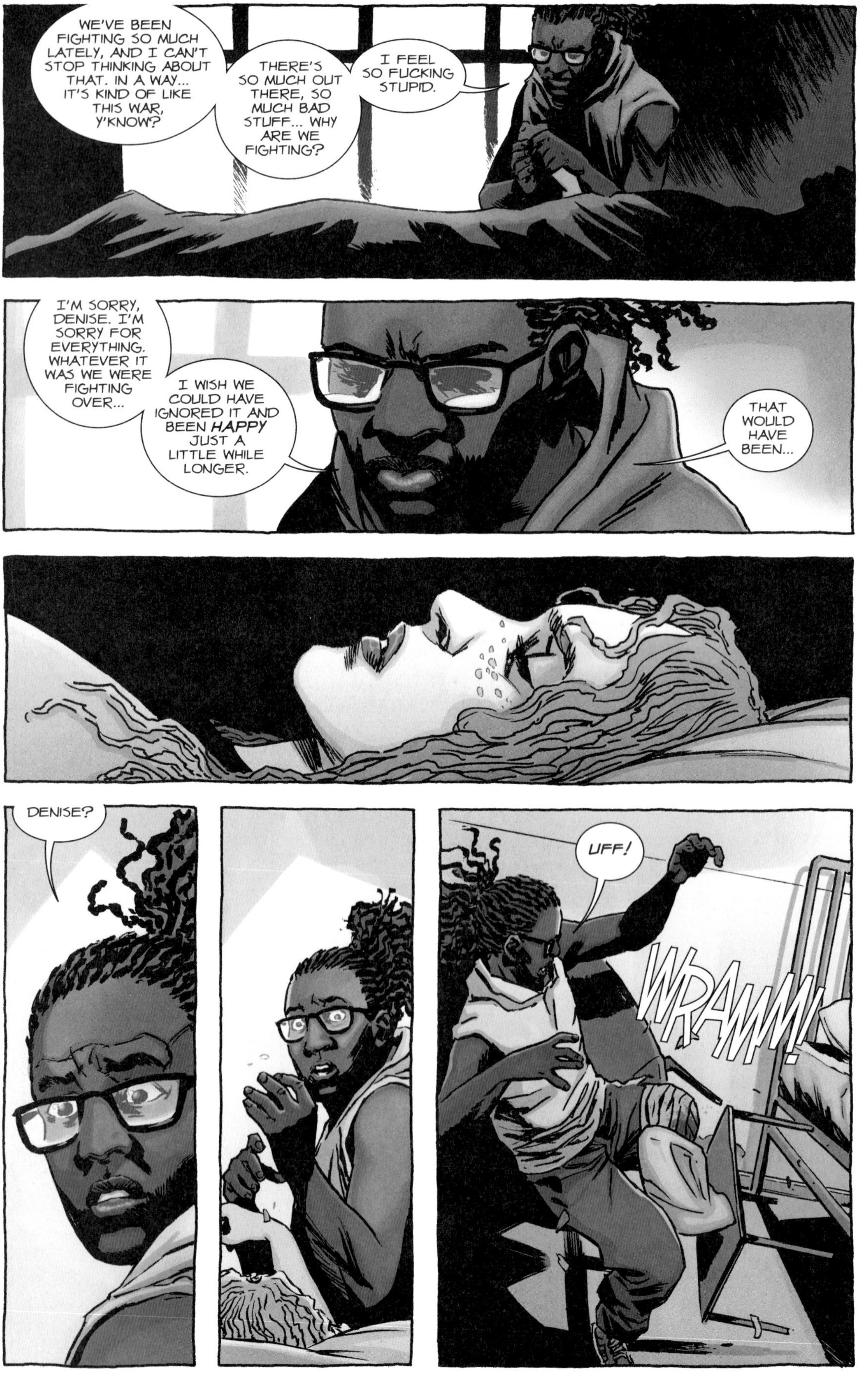
WE'VE BEEN FIGHTING SO MUCH LATELY, AND I CAN'T STOP THINKING ABOUT THAT. IN A WAY... IT'S KIND OF LIKE THIS WAR, Y'KNOW?
THERE'S SO MUCH OUT THERE, SO MUCH BAD STUFF... WHY ARE WE FIGHTING?
I FEEL SO FUCKING STUPID.
I'M SORRY, DENISE. I'M SORRY FOR EVERYTHING. WHATEVER IT WAS WE WERE FIGHTING OVER...
I WISH WE COULD HAVE IGNORED IT AND BEEN ***HAPPY*** JUST A LITTLE WHILE LONGER.
THAT WOULD HAVE BEEN...
DENISE?
UFF!
WRAMM!

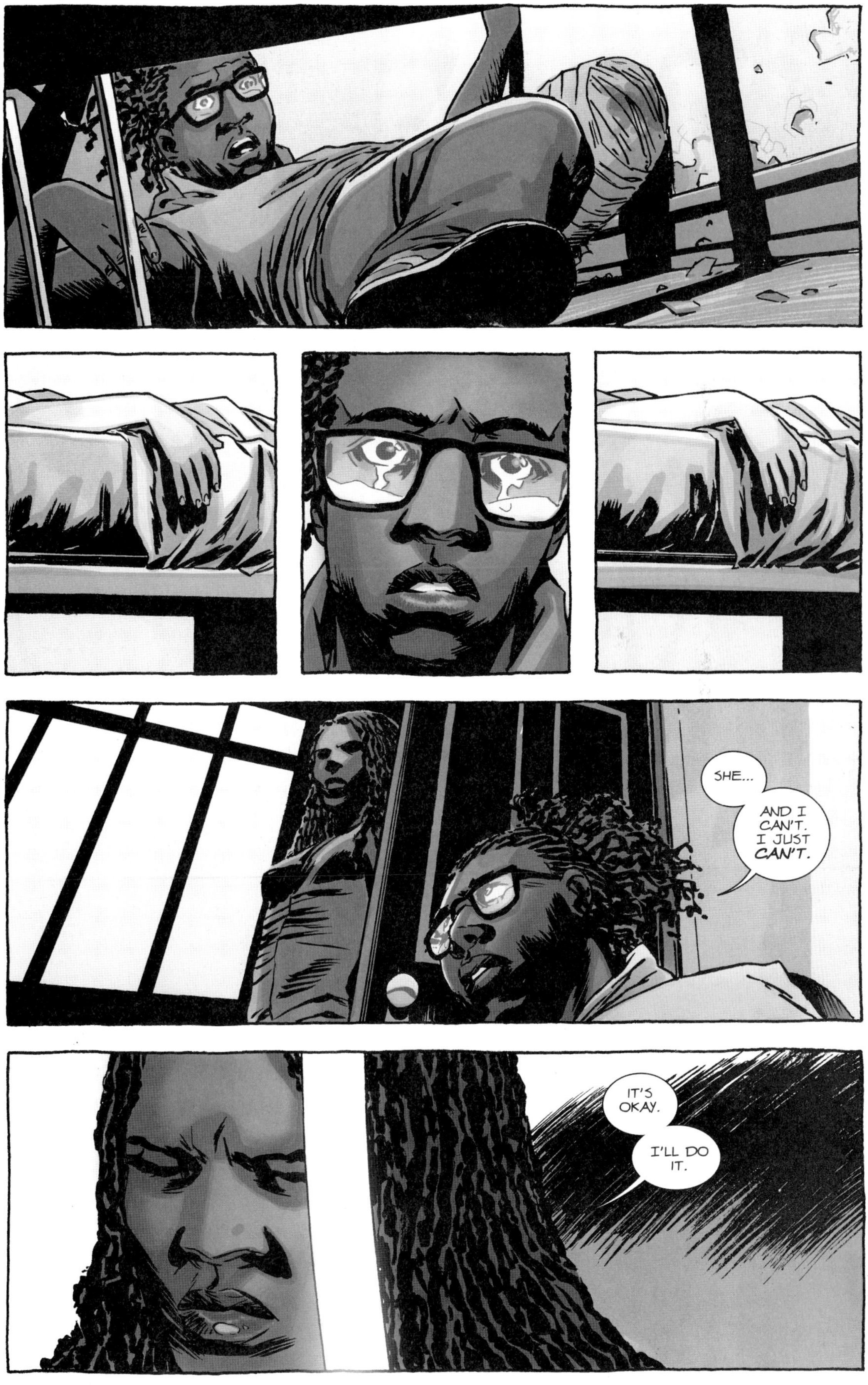
SHE...
AND I CAN'T. I JUST CAN'T.
IT'S OKAY.
I'LL DO IT.

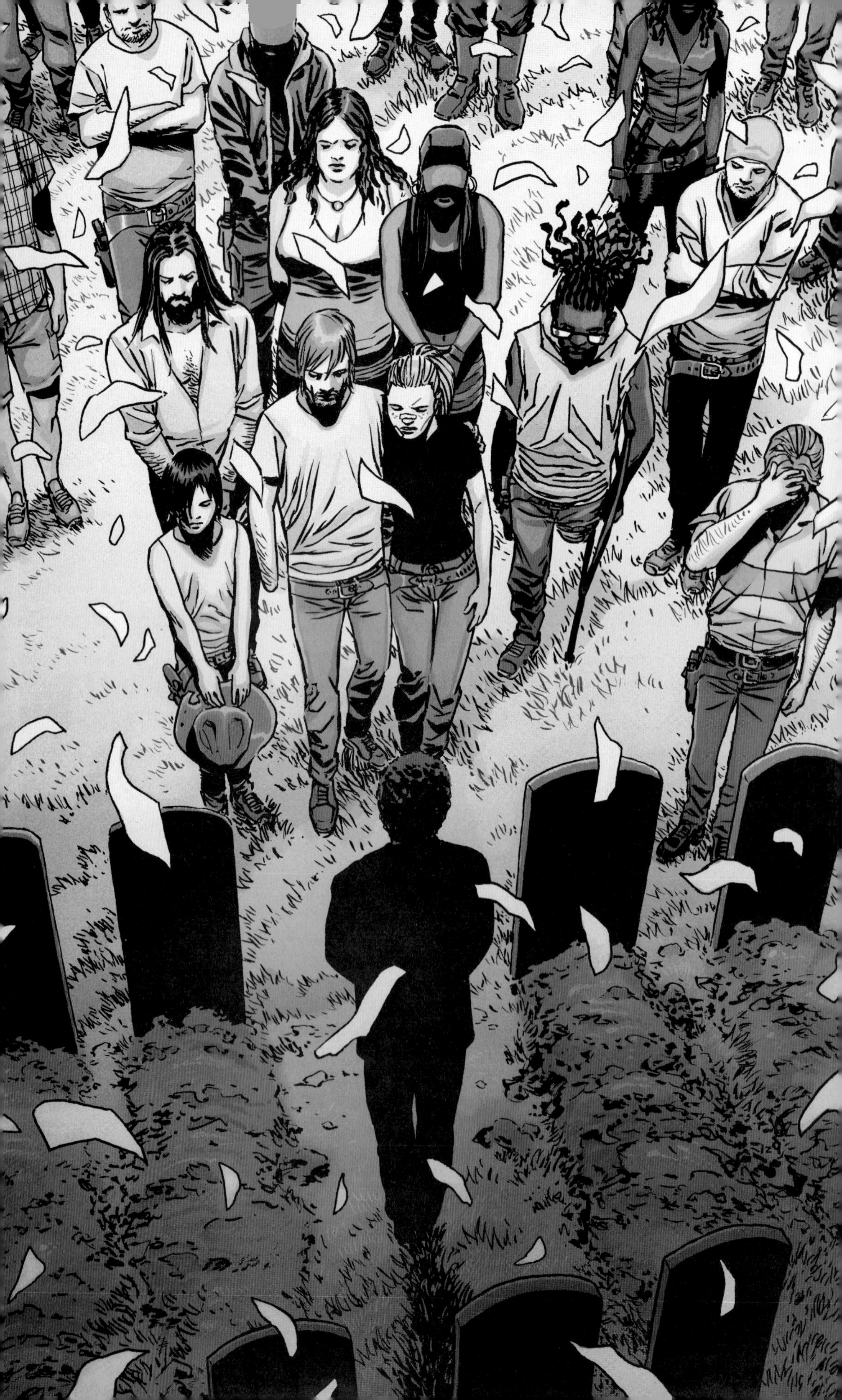

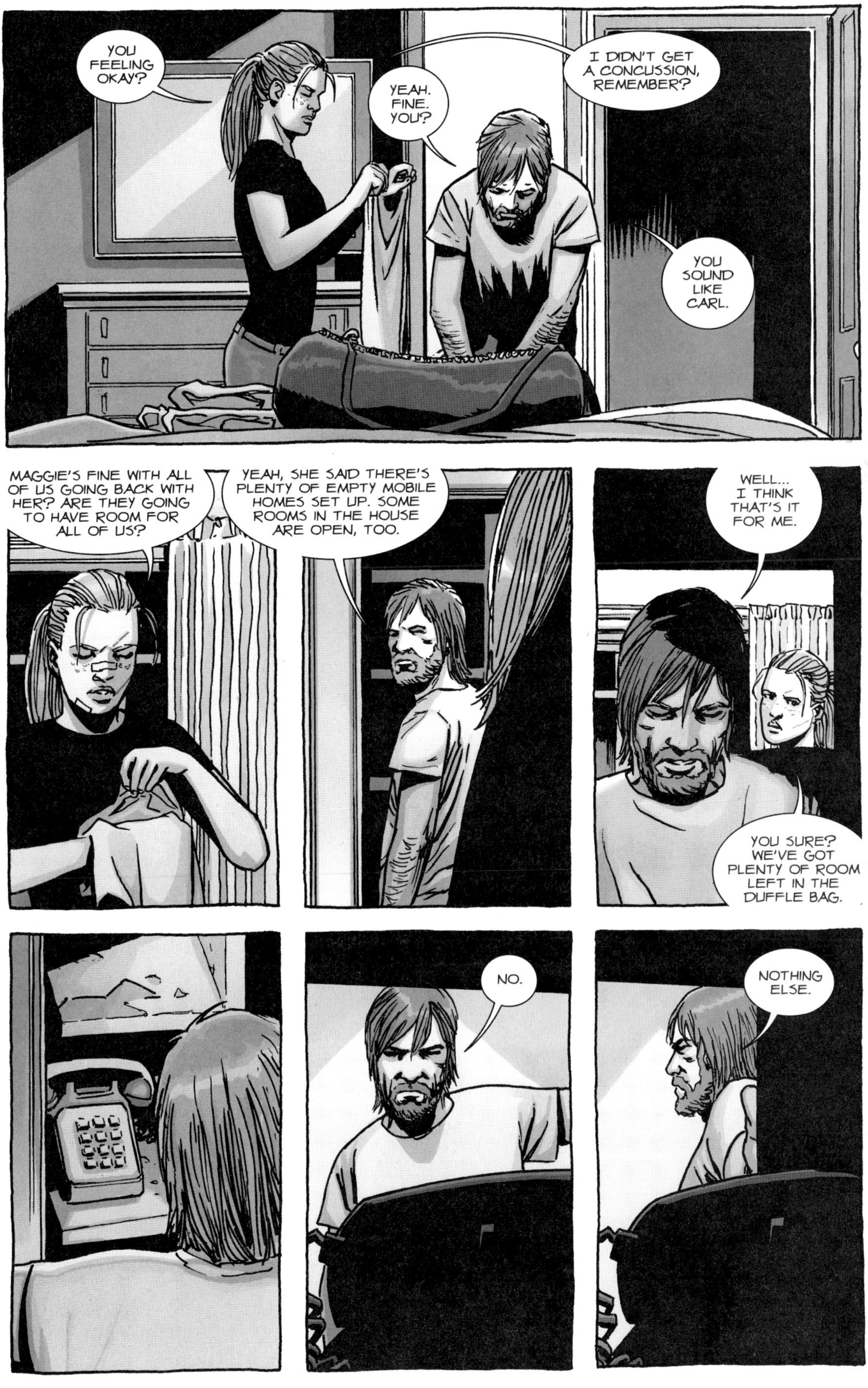
YOU FEELING OKAY?
YEAH. FINE. YOU?
I DIDN'T GET A CONCUSSION, REMEMBER?
YOU SOUND LIKE CARL.
MAGGIE'S FINE WITH ALL OF US GOING BACK WITH HER? ARE THEY GOING TO HAVE ROOM FOR ALL OF US?
YEAH, SHE SAID THERE'S PLENTY OF EMPTY MOBILE HOMES SET UP. SOME ROOMS IN THE HOUSE ARE OPEN, TOO.
WELL... I THINK THAT'S IT FOR ME.
YOU SURE? WE'VE GOT PLENTY OF ROOM LEFT IN THE DUFFLE BAG.
NO.
NOTHING ELSE.

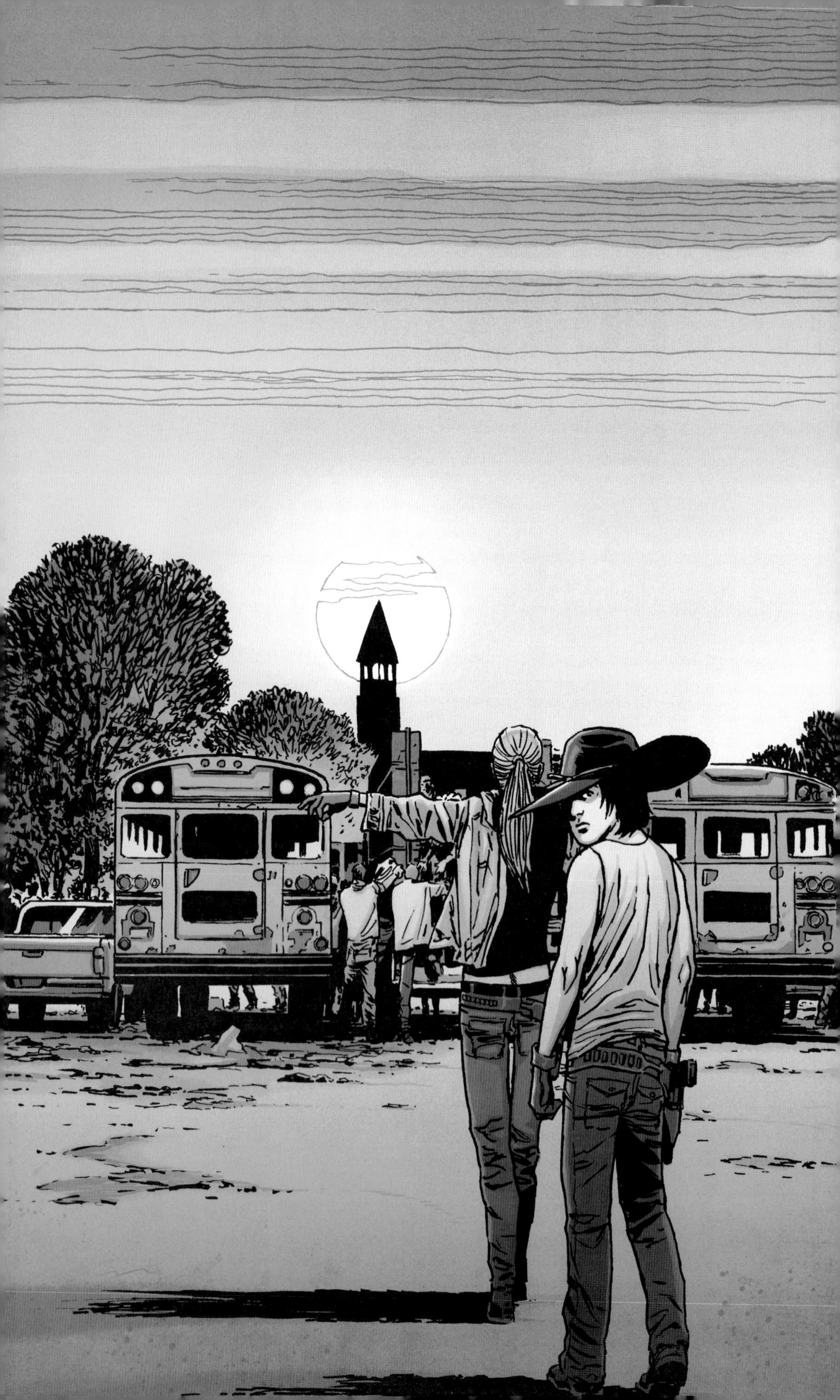

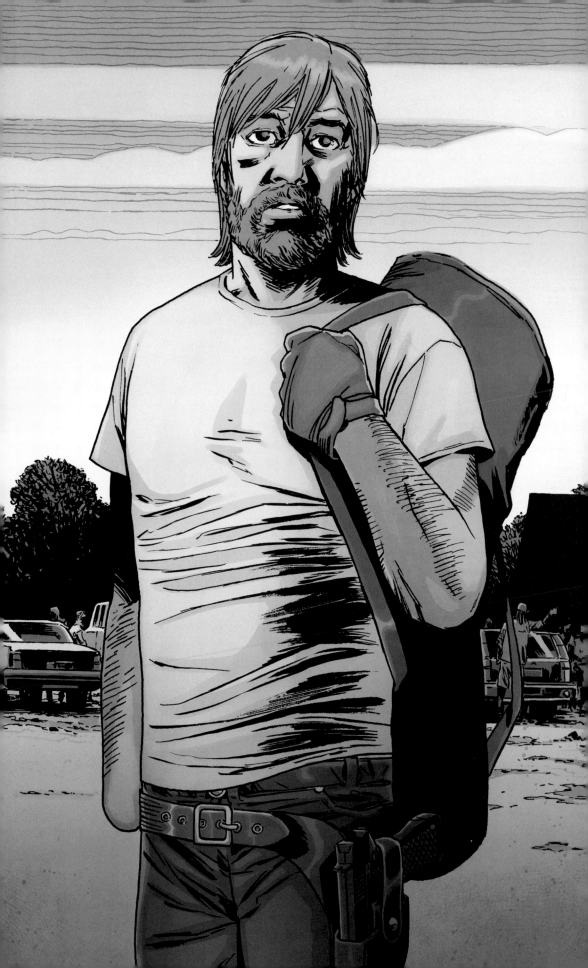

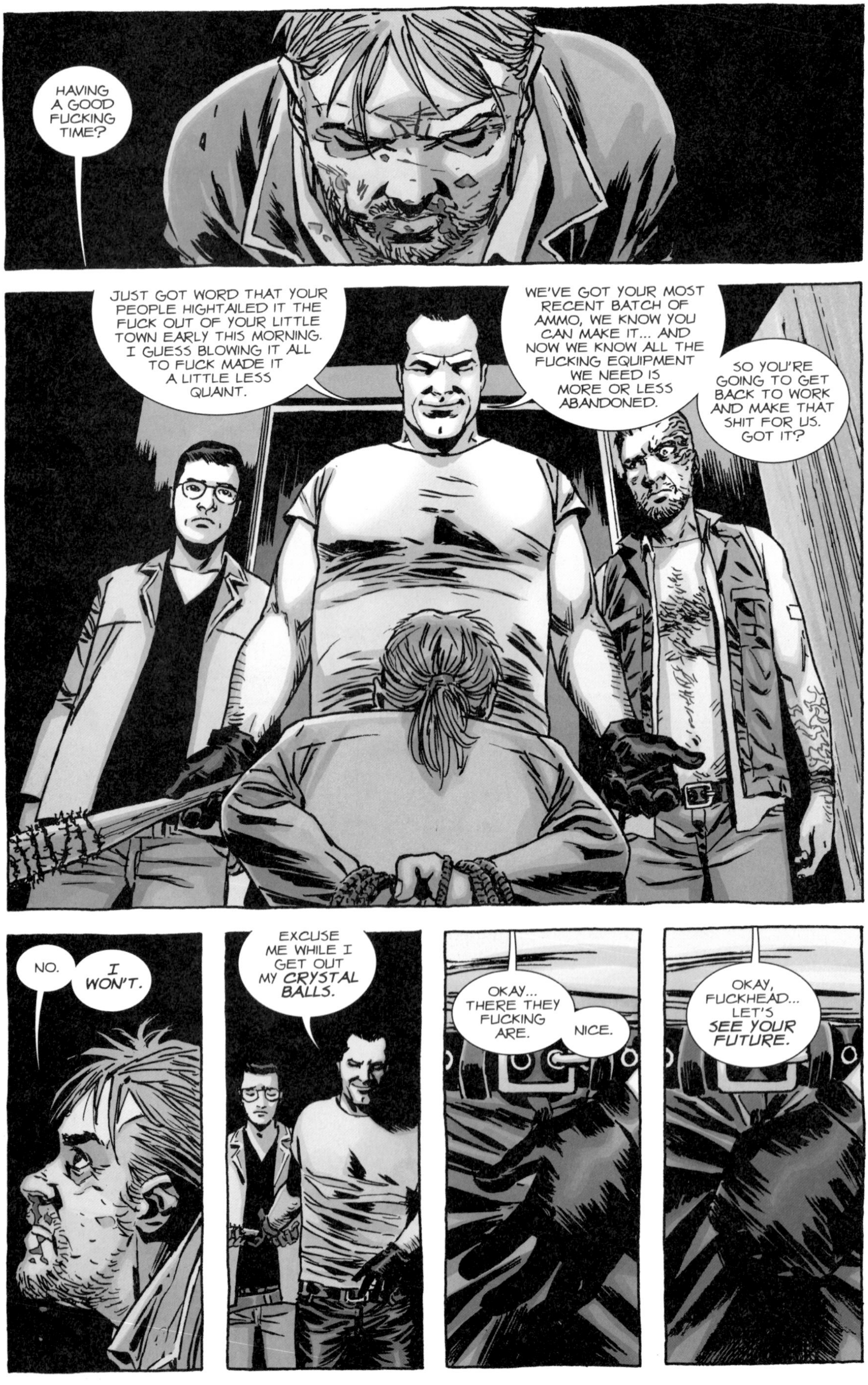
HAVING A GOOD FUCKING TIME?
JUST GOT WORD THAT YOUR PEOPLE HIGHTAILED IT THE FUCK OUT OF YOUR LITTLE TOWN EARLY THIS MORNING. I GUESS BLOWING IT ALL TO FUCK MADE IT A LITTLE LESS QUAINT.
WE'VE GOT YOUR MOST RECENT BATCH OF AMMO, WE KNOW YOU CAN MAKE IT... AND NOW WE KNOW ALL THE FUCKING EQUIPMENT WE NEED IS MORE OR LESS ABANDONED.
SO YOU'RE GOING TO GET BACK TO WORK AND MAKE THAT SHIT FOR US. GOT IT?
NO.
I WON'T.
EXCUSE ME WHILE I GET OUT MY CRYSTAL BALLS.
OKAY... THERE THEY FUCKING ARE.
NICE.
OKAY, FUCKHEAD... LET'S SEE YOUR FUTURE.

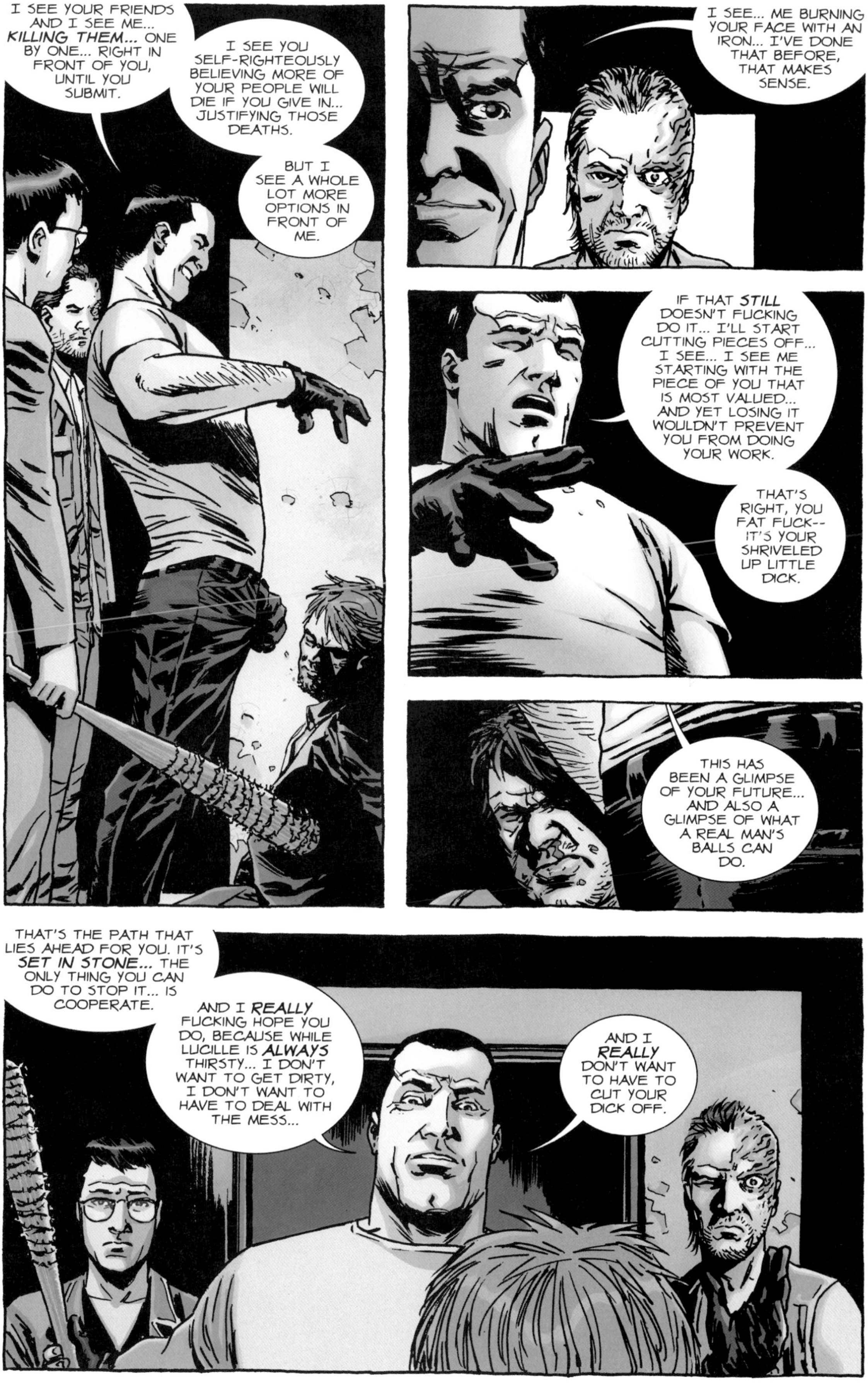
I SEE YOUR FRIENDS AND I SEE ME... KILLING THEM... ONE BY ONE... RIGHT IN FRONT OF YOU, UNTIL YOU SUBMIT.
I SEE YOU SELF-RIGHTEOUSLY BELIEVING MORE OF YOUR PEOPLE WILL DIE IF YOU GIVE IN... JUSTIFYING THOSE DEATHS.
BUT I SEE A WHOLE LOT MORE OPTIONS IN FRONT OF ME.
I SEE... ME BURNING YOUR FACE WITH AN IRON... I'VE DONE THAT BEFORE, THAT MAKES SENSE.
IF THAT STILL DOESN'T FUCKING DO IT... I'LL START CUTTING PIECES OFF... I SEE... I SEE ME STARTING WITH THE PIECE OF YOU THAT IS MOST VALUED... AND YET LOSING IT WOULDN'T PREVENT YOU FROM DOING YOUR WORK.
THAT'S RIGHT, YOU FAT FUCK-- IT'S YOUR SHRIVELED UP LITTLE DICK.
THIS HAS BEEN A GLIMPSE OF YOUR FUTURE... AND ALSO A GLIMPSE OF WHAT A REAL MAN'S BALLS CAN DO.
THAT'S THE PATH THAT LIES AHEAD FOR YOU. IT'S SET IN STONE... THE ONLY THING YOU CAN DO TO STOP IT... IS COOPERATE.
AND I REALLY FUCKING HOPE YOU DO, BECAUSE WHILE LUCILLE IS ALWAYS THIRSTY... I DON'T WANT TO GET DIRTY, I DON'T WANT TO HAVE TO DEAL WITH THE MESS...
AND I REALLY DON'T WANT TO HAVE TO CUT YOUR DICK OFF.

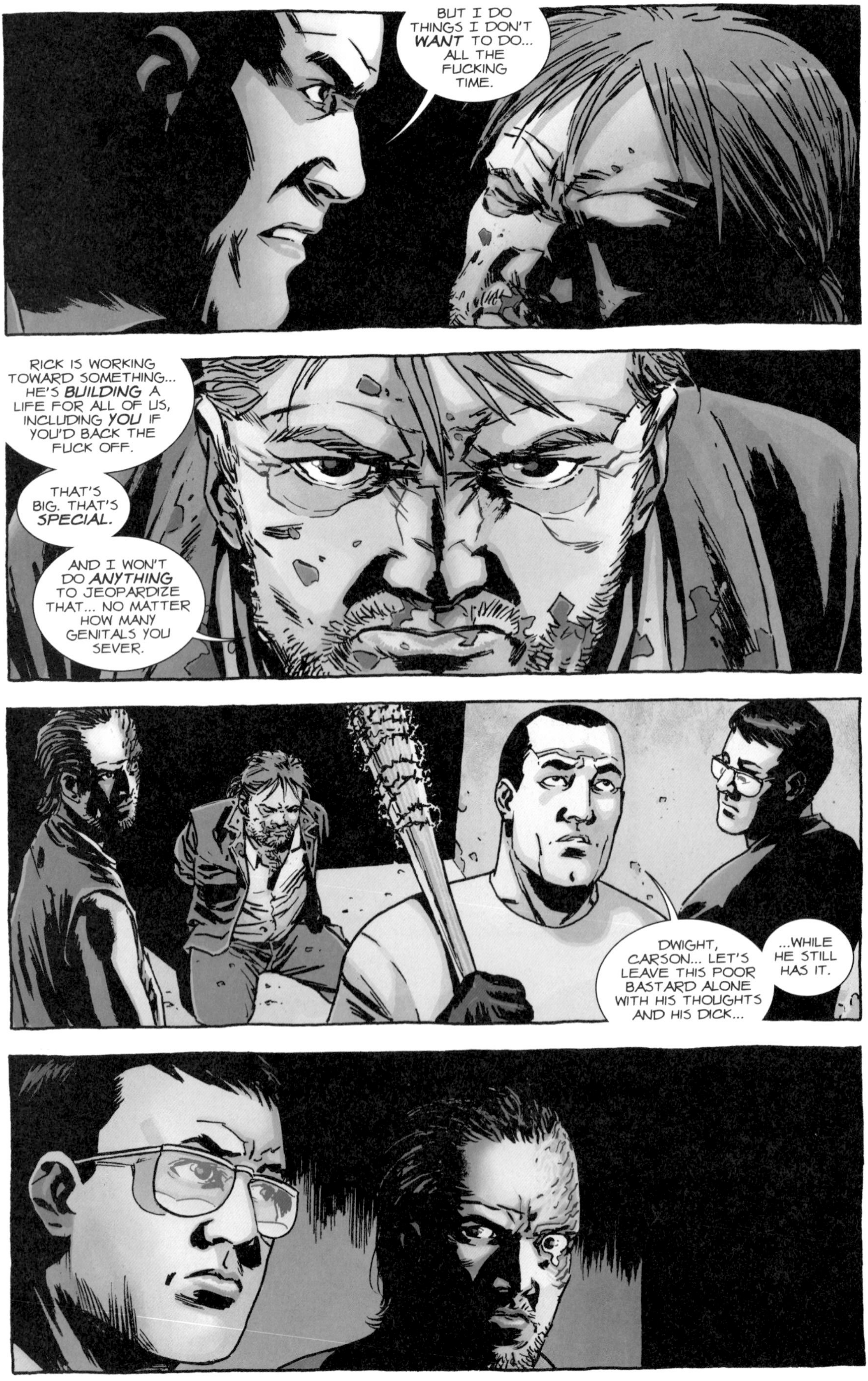

BUT I DO THINGS I DON'T WANT TO DO... ALL THE FUCKING TIME.
RICK IS WORKING TOWARD SOMETHING... HE'S BUILDING A LIFE FOR ALL OF US, INCLUDING YOU IF YOU'D BACK THE FUCK OFF.
THAT'S BIG. THAT'S SPECIAL.
AND I WON'T DO ANYTHING TO JEOPARDIZE THAT... NO MATTER HOW MANY GENITALS YOU SEVER.
DWIGHT, CARSON... LET'S LEAVE THIS POOR BASTARD ALONE WITH HIS THOUGHTS AND HIS DICK...
...WHILE HE STILL HAS IT.

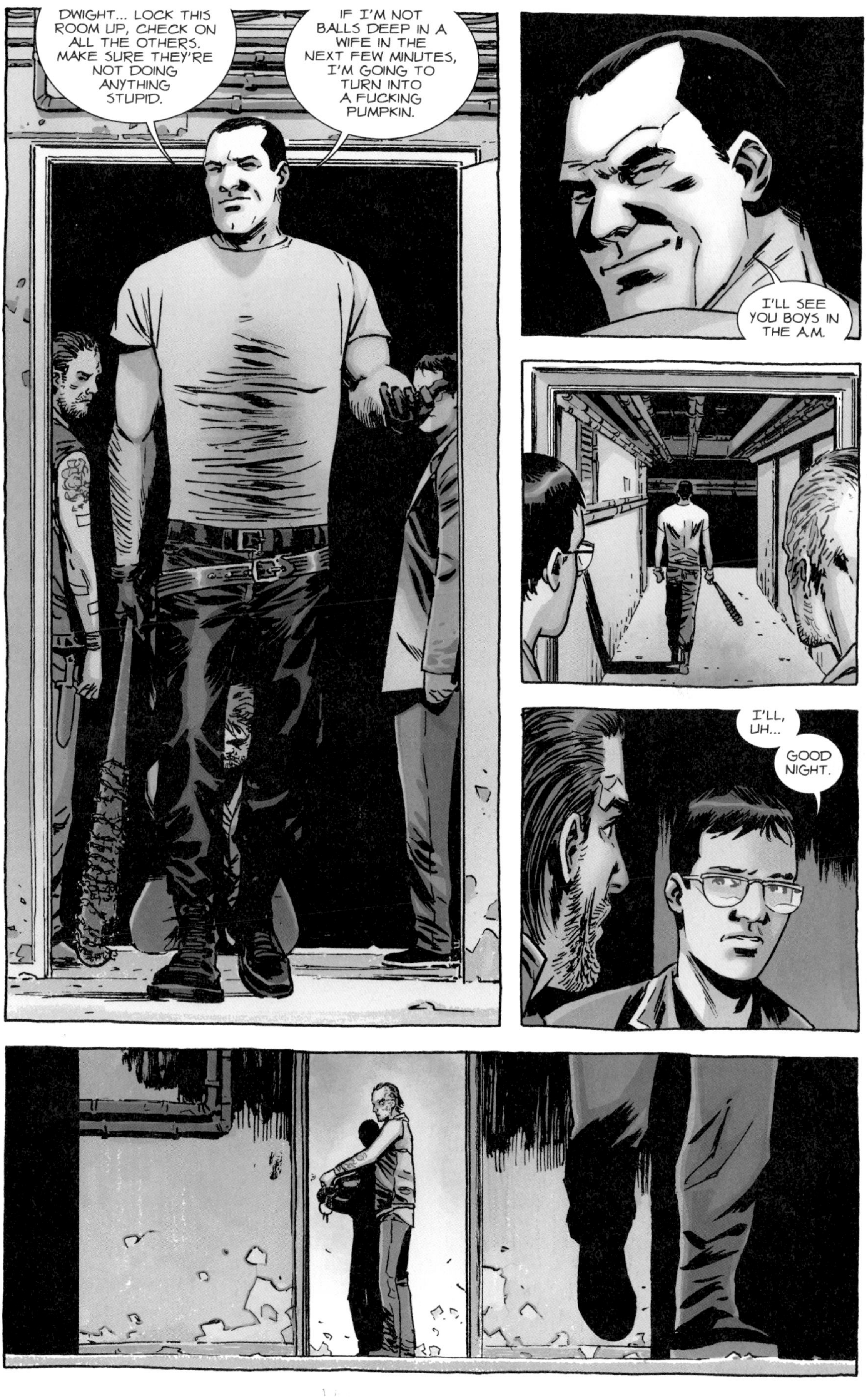
DWIGHT... LOCK THIS ROOM UP, CHECK ON ALL THE OTHERS. MAKE SURE THEY'RE NOT DOING ANYTHING STUPID.
IF I'M NOT BALLS DEEP IN A WIFE IN THE NEXT FEW MINUTES, I'M GOING TO TURN INTO A FUCKING PUMPKIN.
I'LL SEE YOU BOYS IN THE A.M.
I'LL, UH...
GOOD NIGHT.

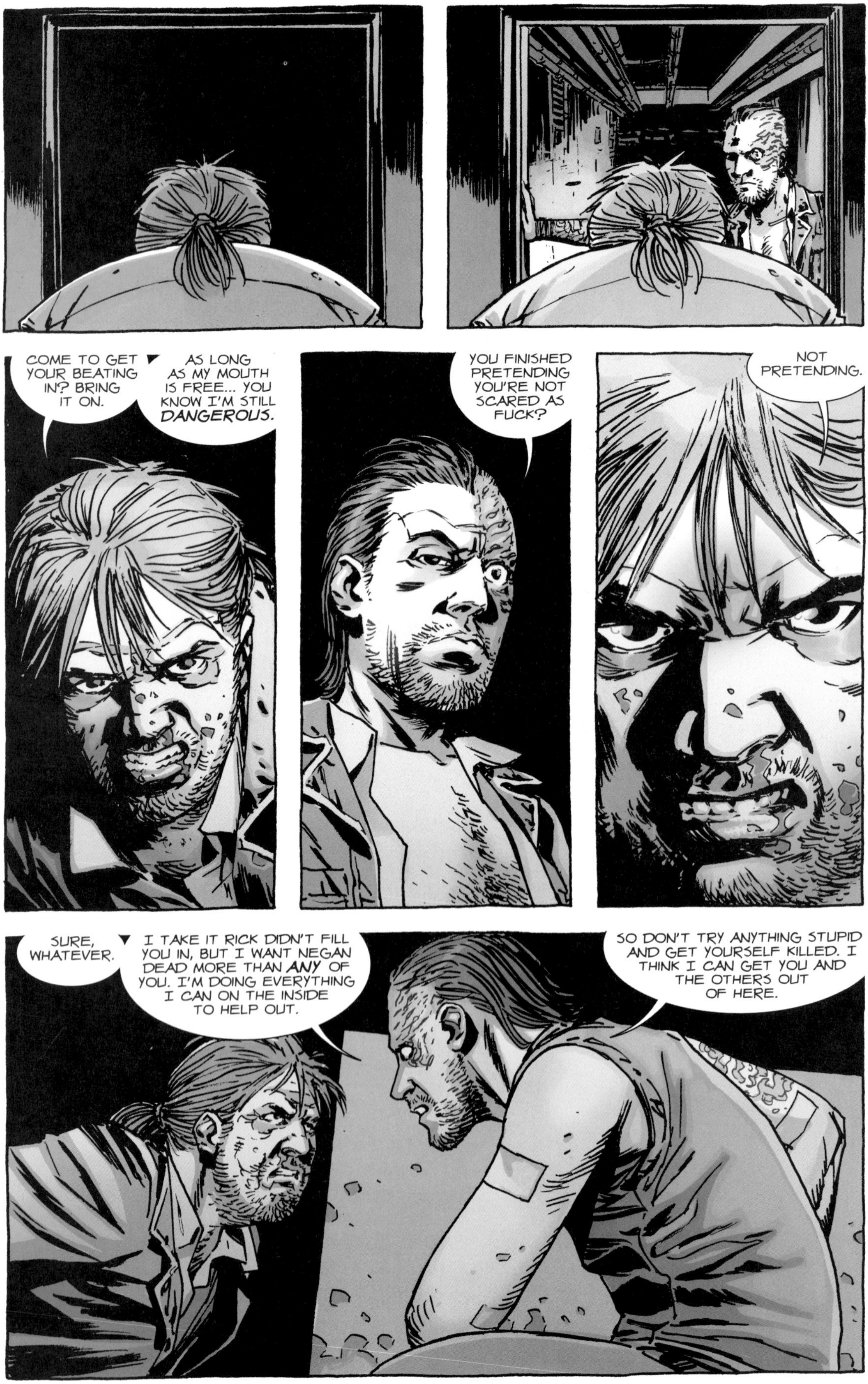
COME TO GET YOUR BEATING IN? BRING IT ON.
AS LONG AS MY MOUTH IS FREE... YOU KNOW I'M STILL *DANGEROUS.*
YOU FINISHED PRETENDING YOU'RE NOT SCARED AS FUCK?
NOT PRETENDING.
SURE, WHATEVER.
I TAKE IT RICK DIDN'T FILL YOU IN, BUT I WANT NEGAN DEAD MORE THAN *ANY* OF YOU. I'M DOING EVERYTHING I CAN ON THE INSIDE TO HELP OUT.
SO DON'T TRY ANYTHING STUPID AND GET YOURSELF KILLED. I THINK I CAN GET YOU AND THE OTHERS OUT OF HERE.

LIKE YOU DID WITH *HOLLY?*

I TRIED. THERE WASN'T AN OPPORTUNITY.

LIKE THERE ISN'T AN OPPORTUNITY TO SNEAK IN WHILE NEGAN IS ASLEEP AND PUT A KNIFE IN HIS EYE? IF YOU'D *REALLY* TURNED, THIS WOULD BE *OVER.*

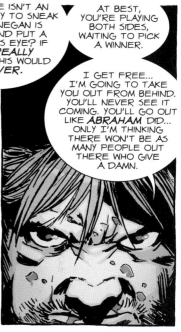

AT BEST, YOU'RE PLAYING BOTH SIDES, WAITING TO PICK A WINNER.

I GET FREE... I'M GOING TO TAKE YOU OUT FROM BEHIND. YOU'LL NEVER SEE IT COMING. YOU'LL GO OUT LIKE *ABRAHAM* DID... ONLY I'M THINKING THERE WON'T BE AS MANY PEOPLE OUT THERE WHO GIVE A DAMN.

I'M NOT TRYING TO SAY I'M A GOOD MAN, OR THAT I REGRET ANYTHING I'VE DONE OR THAT I'VE CHANGED. I'M SAYING I WANT WHAT *YOU* WANT-- *RIGHT NOW.*

I JUST WANTED TO GIVE YOU SOME REASSURANCE SO YOU DIDN'T PISS YOURSELF TOO MUCH.

TRUST ME, I GET A CHANCE TO PUT A KNIFE IN NEGAN'S EYE, I'LL FUCKING DO IT. I'D KILL THAT MOTHERFUCKER TODAY IF I DIDN'T THINK THESE PEOPLE WOULD TAKE MY HEAD FOR IT.

I'D--

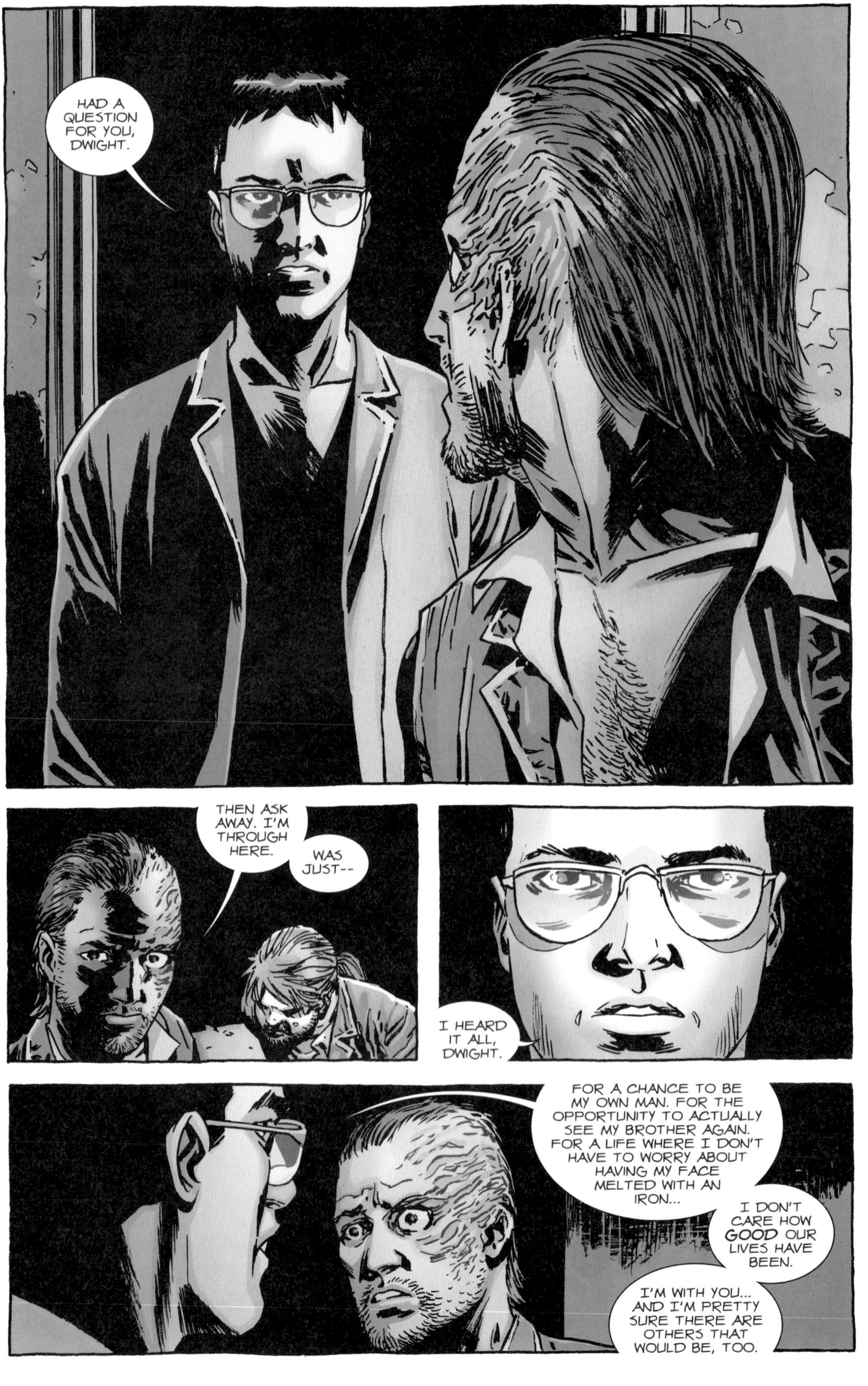
HAD A QUESTION FOR YOU, DWIGHT.
THEN ASK AWAY. I'M THROUGH HERE.
WAS JUST--
I HEARD IT ALL, DWIGHT.
FOR A CHANCE TO BE MY OWN MAN. FOR THE OPPORTUNITY TO ACTUALLY SEE MY BROTHER AGAIN. FOR A LIFE WHERE I DON'T HAVE TO WORRY ABOUT HAVING MY FACE MELTED WITH AN IRON...
I DON'T CARE HOW **GOOD** OUR LIVES HAVE BEEN.
I'M WITH YOU... AND I'M PRETTY SURE THERE ARE OTHERS THAT WOULD BE, TOO.

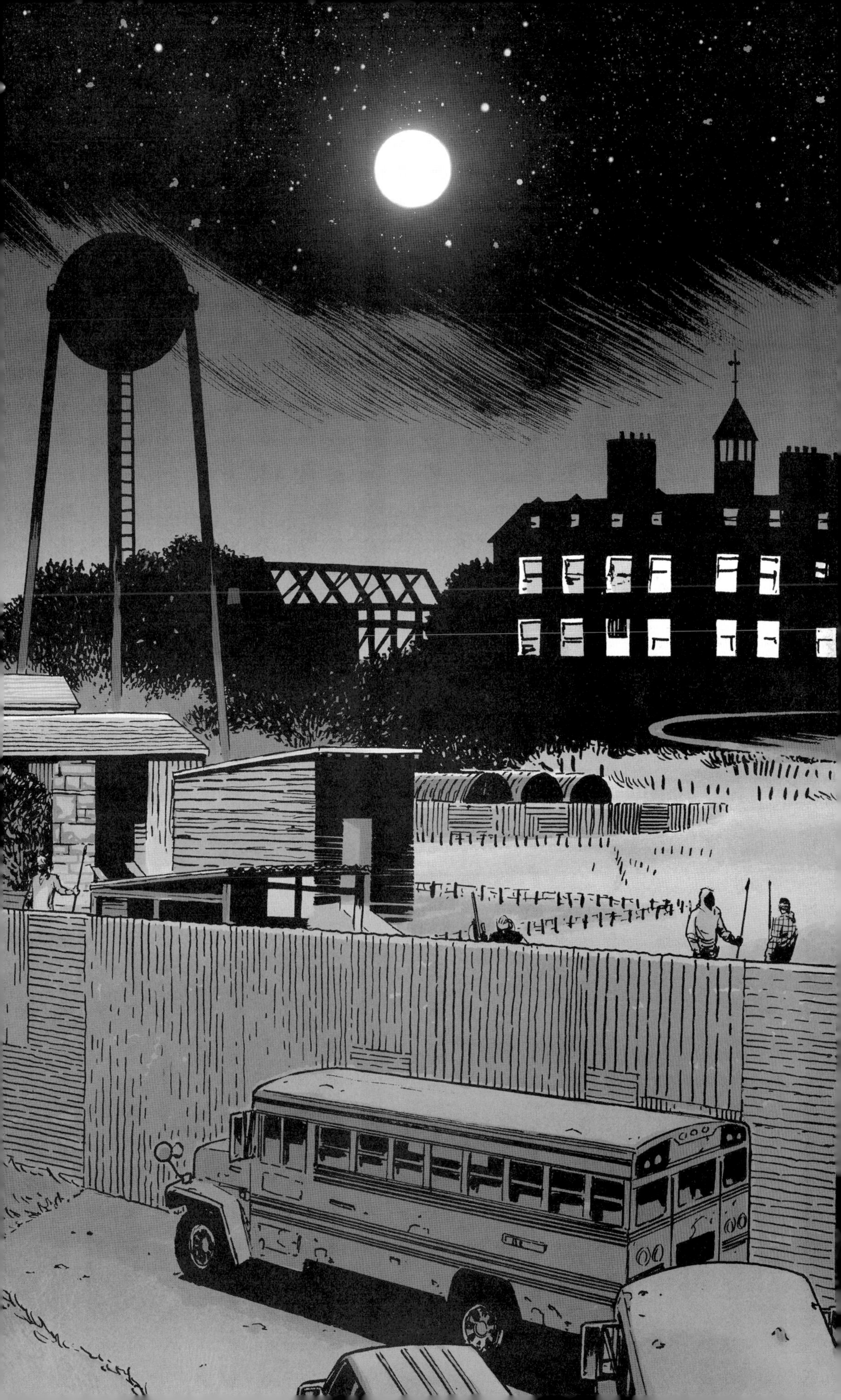

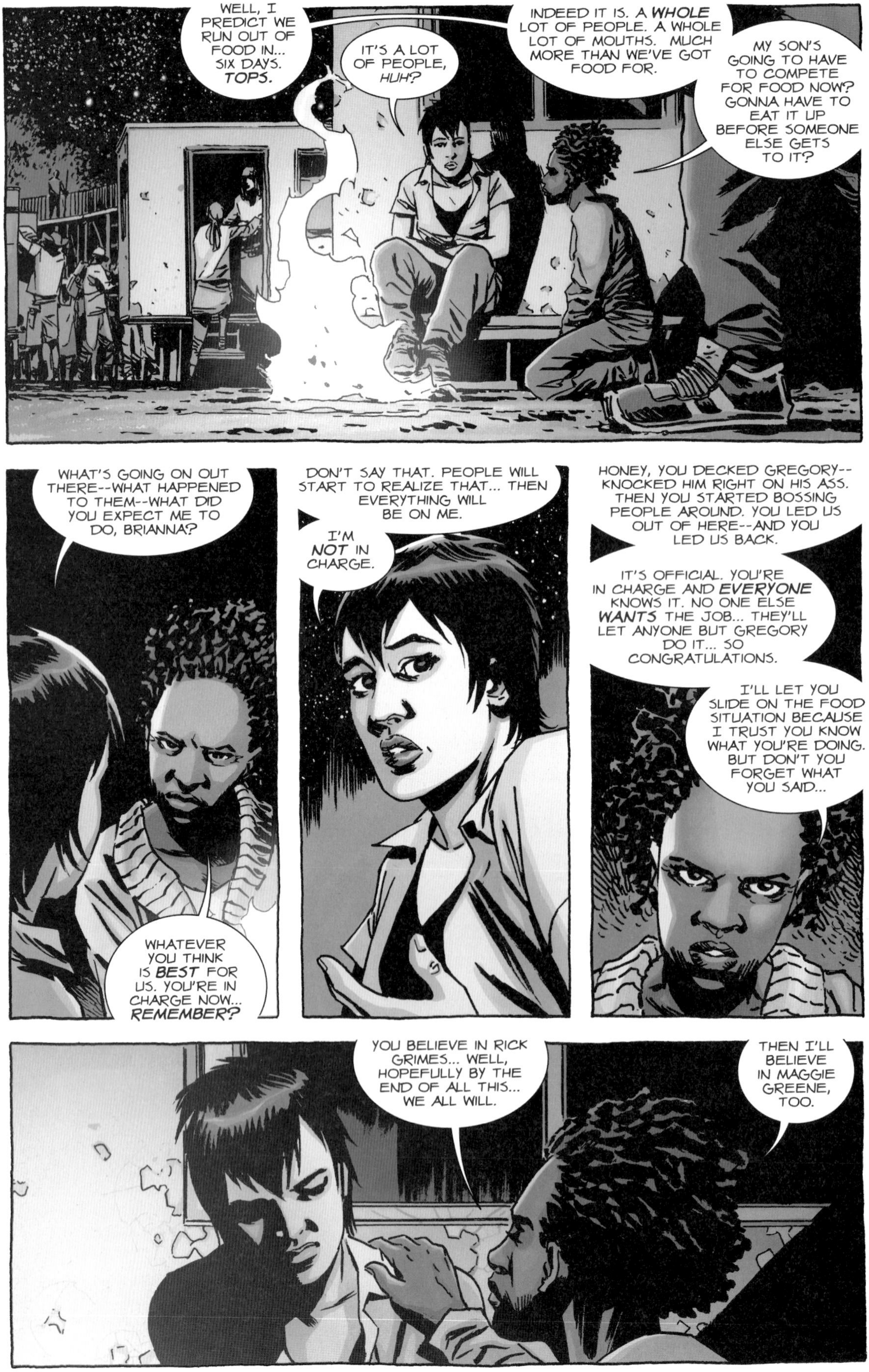
WELL, I PREDICT WE RUN OUT OF FOOD IN... SIX DAYS. TOPS.
IT'S A LOT OF PEOPLE, HUH?
INDEED IT IS. A WHOLE LOT OF PEOPLE. A WHOLE LOT OF MOUTHS. MUCH MORE THAN WE'VE GOT FOOD FOR.
MY SON'S GOING TO HAVE TO COMPETE FOR FOOD NOW? GONNA HAVE TO EAT IT UP BEFORE SOMEONE ELSE GETS TO IT?
WHAT'S GOING ON OUT THERE--WHAT HAPPENED TO THEM--WHAT DID YOU EXPECT ME TO DO, BRIANNA?
WHATEVER YOU THINK IS BEST FOR US. YOU'RE IN CHARGE NOW... REMEMBER?
I'M NOT IN CHARGE.
DON'T SAY THAT. PEOPLE WILL START TO REALIZE THAT... THEN EVERYTHING WILL BE ON ME.
HONEY, YOU DECKED GREGORY--KNOCKED HIM RIGHT ON HIS ASS. THEN YOU STARTED BOSSING PEOPLE AROUND. YOU LED US OUT OF HERE--AND YOU LED US BACK.
IT'S OFFICIAL. YOU'RE IN CHARGE AND EVERYONE KNOWS IT. NO ONE ELSE WANTS THE JOB... THEY'LL LET ANYONE BUT GREGORY DO IT... SO CONGRATULATIONS.
I'LL LET YOU SLIDE ON THE FOOD SITUATION BECAUSE I TRUST YOU KNOW WHAT YOU'RE DOING. BUT DON'T YOU FORGET WHAT YOU SAID...
YOU BELIEVE IN RICK GRIMES... WELL, HOPEFULLY BY THE END OF ALL THIS... WE ALL WILL.
THEN I'LL BELIEVE IN MAGGIE GREENE, TOO.

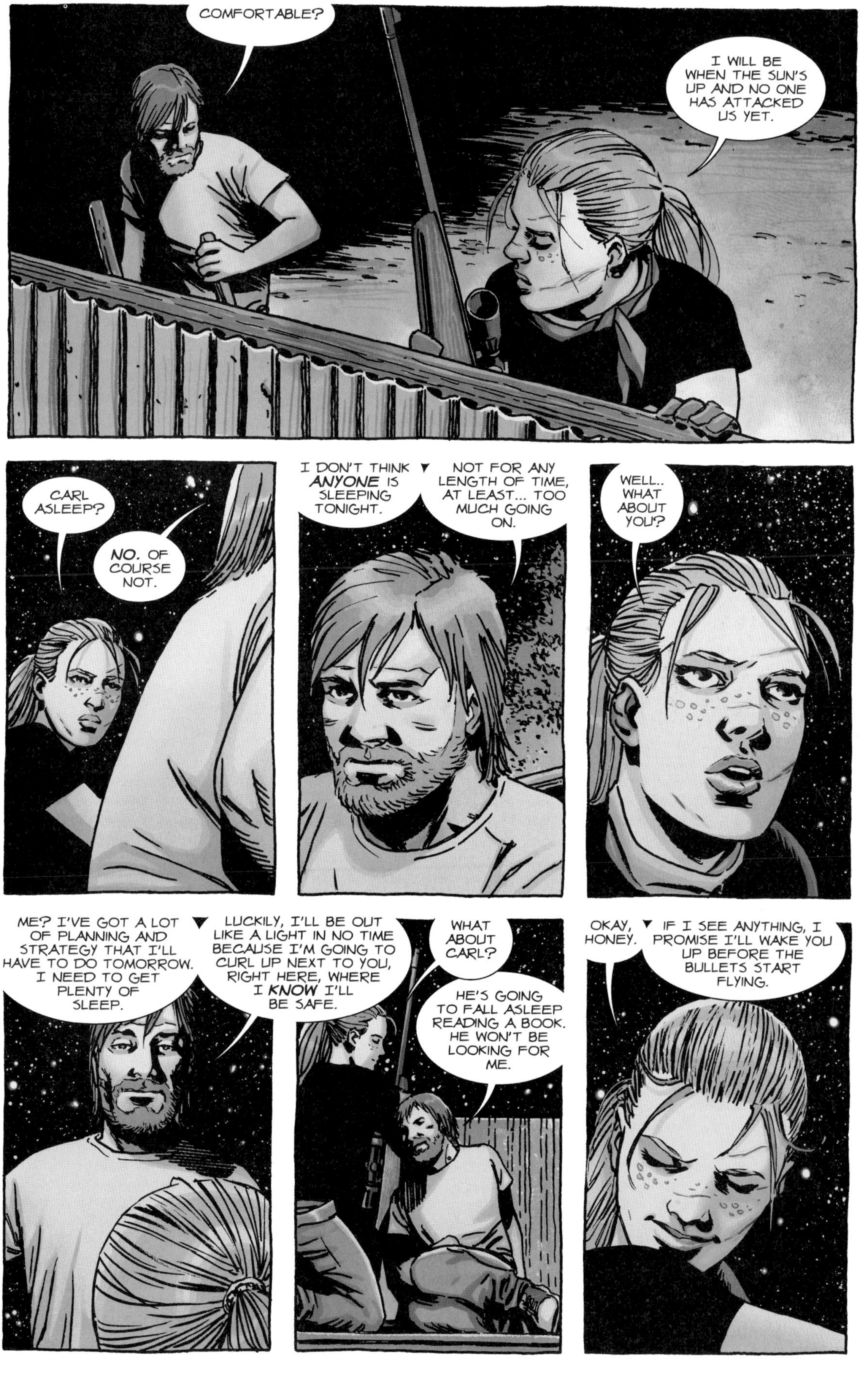
COMFORTABLE?
I WILL BE WHEN THE SUN'S UP AND NO ONE HAS ATTACKED US YET.
CARL ASLEEP?
NO. OF COURSE NOT.
I DON'T THINK ANYONE IS SLEEPING TONIGHT.
NOT FOR ANY LENGTH OF TIME, AT LEAST... TOO MUCH GOING ON.
WELL.. WHAT ABOUT YOU?
ME? I'VE GOT A LOT OF PLANNING AND STRATEGY THAT I'LL HAVE TO DO TOMORROW. I NEED TO GET PLENTY OF SLEEP.
LUCKILY, I'LL BE OUT LIKE A LIGHT IN NO TIME BECAUSE I'M GOING TO CURL UP NEXT TO YOU, RIGHT HERE, WHERE I KNOW I'LL BE SAFE.
WHAT ABOUT CARL?
HE'S GOING TO FALL ASLEEP READING A BOOK. HE WON'T BE LOOKING FOR ME.
OKAY, HONEY.
IF I SEE ANYTHING, I PROMISE I'LL WAKE YOU UP BEFORE THE BULLETS START FLYING.

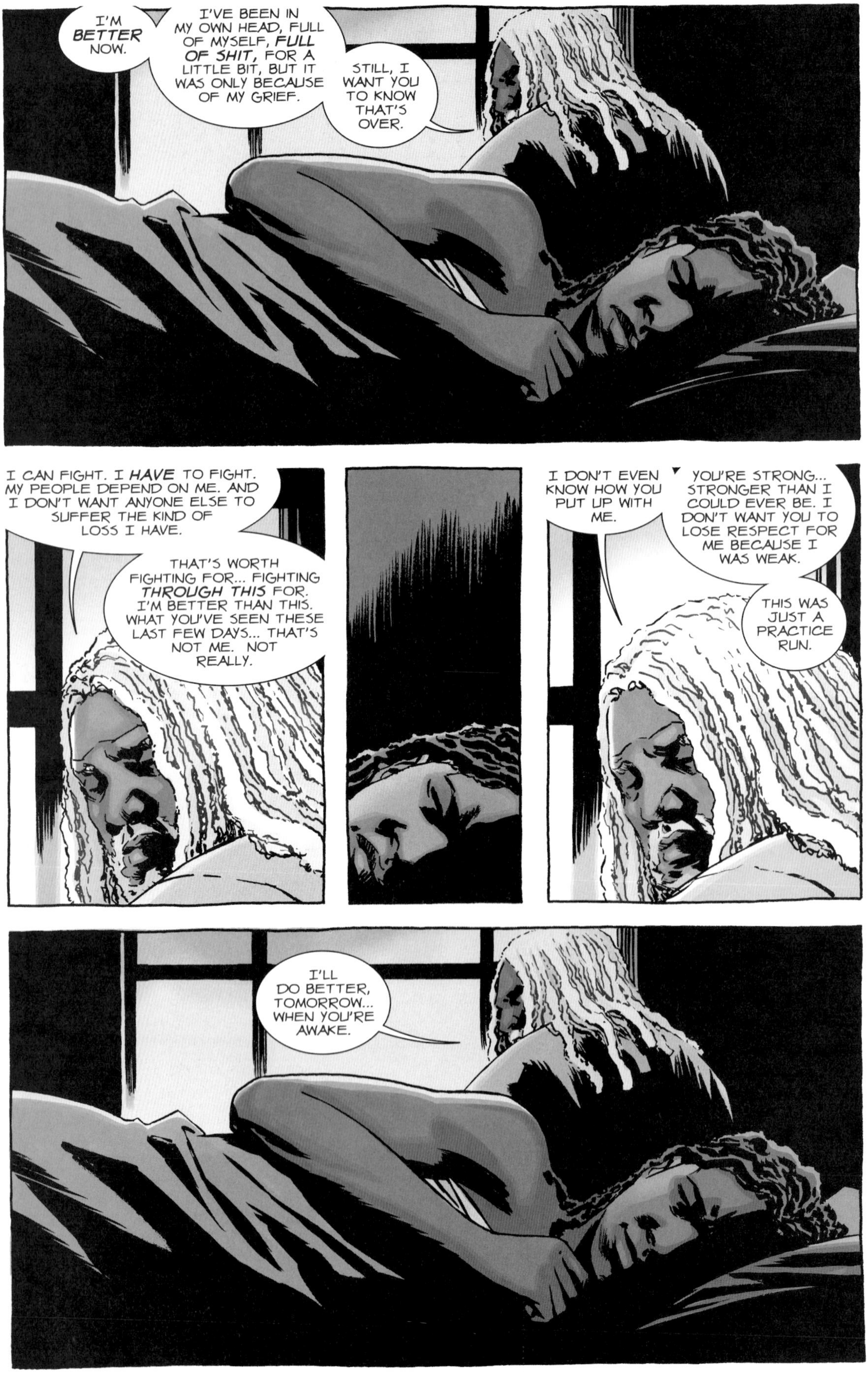
I'M BETTER NOW.
I'VE BEEN IN MY OWN HEAD, FULL OF MYSELF, FULL OF SHIT, FOR A LITTLE BIT, BUT IT WAS ONLY BECAUSE OF MY GRIEF.
STILL, I WANT YOU TO KNOW THAT'S OVER.
I CAN FIGHT. I HAVE TO FIGHT. MY PEOPLE DEPEND ON ME. AND I DON'T WANT ANYONE ELSE TO SUFFER THE KIND OF LOSS I HAVE.
THAT'S WORTH FIGHTING FOR... FIGHTING THROUGH THIS FOR. I'M BETTER THAN THIS. WHAT YOU'VE SEEN THESE LAST FEW DAYS... THAT'S NOT ME. NOT REALLY.
I DON'T EVEN KNOW HOW YOU PUT UP WITH ME.
YOU'RE STRONG... STRONGER THAN I COULD EVER BE. I DON'T WANT YOU TO LOSE RESPECT FOR ME BECAUSE I WAS WEAK.
THIS WAS JUST A PRACTICE RUN.
I'LL DO BETTER, TOMORROW... WHEN YOU'RE AWAKE.

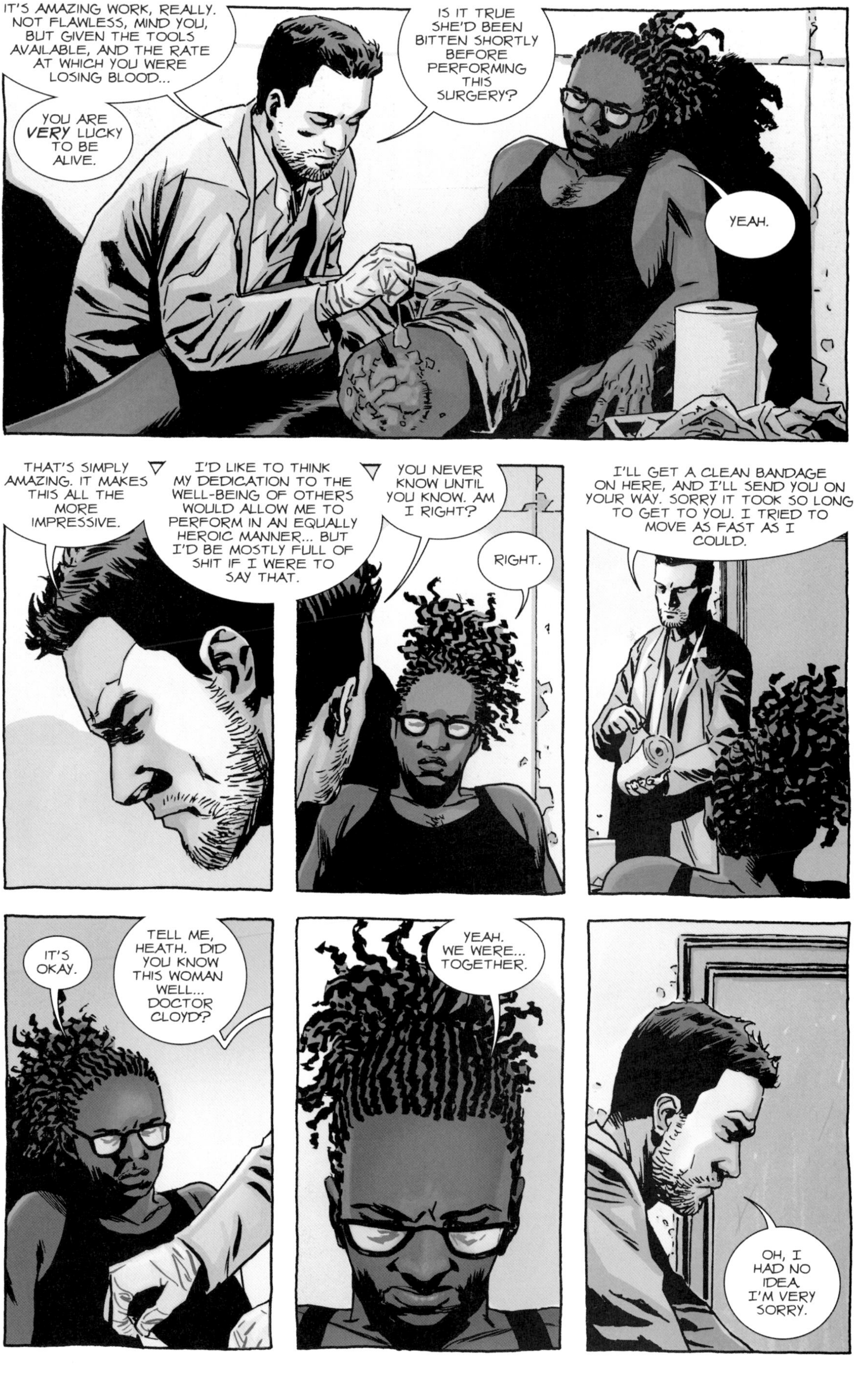
IT'S AMAZING WORK, REALLY. NOT FLAWLESS, MIND YOU, BUT GIVEN THE TOOLS AVAILABLE, AND THE RATE AT WHICH YOU WERE LOSING BLOOD...
YOU ARE VERY LUCKY TO BE ALIVE.
IS IT TRUE SHE'D BEEN BITTEN SHORTLY BEFORE PERFORMING THIS SURGERY?
YEAH.
THAT'S SIMPLY AMAZING. IT MAKES THIS ALL THE MORE IMPRESSIVE.
I'D LIKE TO THINK MY DEDICATION TO THE WELL-BEING OF OTHERS WOULD ALLOW ME TO PERFORM IN AN EQUALLY HEROIC MANNER... BUT I'D BE MOSTLY FULL OF SHIT IF I WERE TO SAY THAT.
YOU NEVER KNOW UNTIL YOU KNOW. AM I RIGHT?
RIGHT.
I'LL GET A CLEAN BANDAGE ON HERE, AND I'LL SEND YOU ON YOUR WAY. SORRY IT TOOK SO LONG TO GET TO YOU. I TRIED TO MOVE AS FAST AS I COULD.
IT'S OKAY.
TELL ME, HEATH. DID YOU KNOW THIS WOMAN WELL... DOCTOR CLOYD?
YEAH. WE WERE... TOGETHER.
OH, I HAD NO IDEA. I'M VERY SORRY.

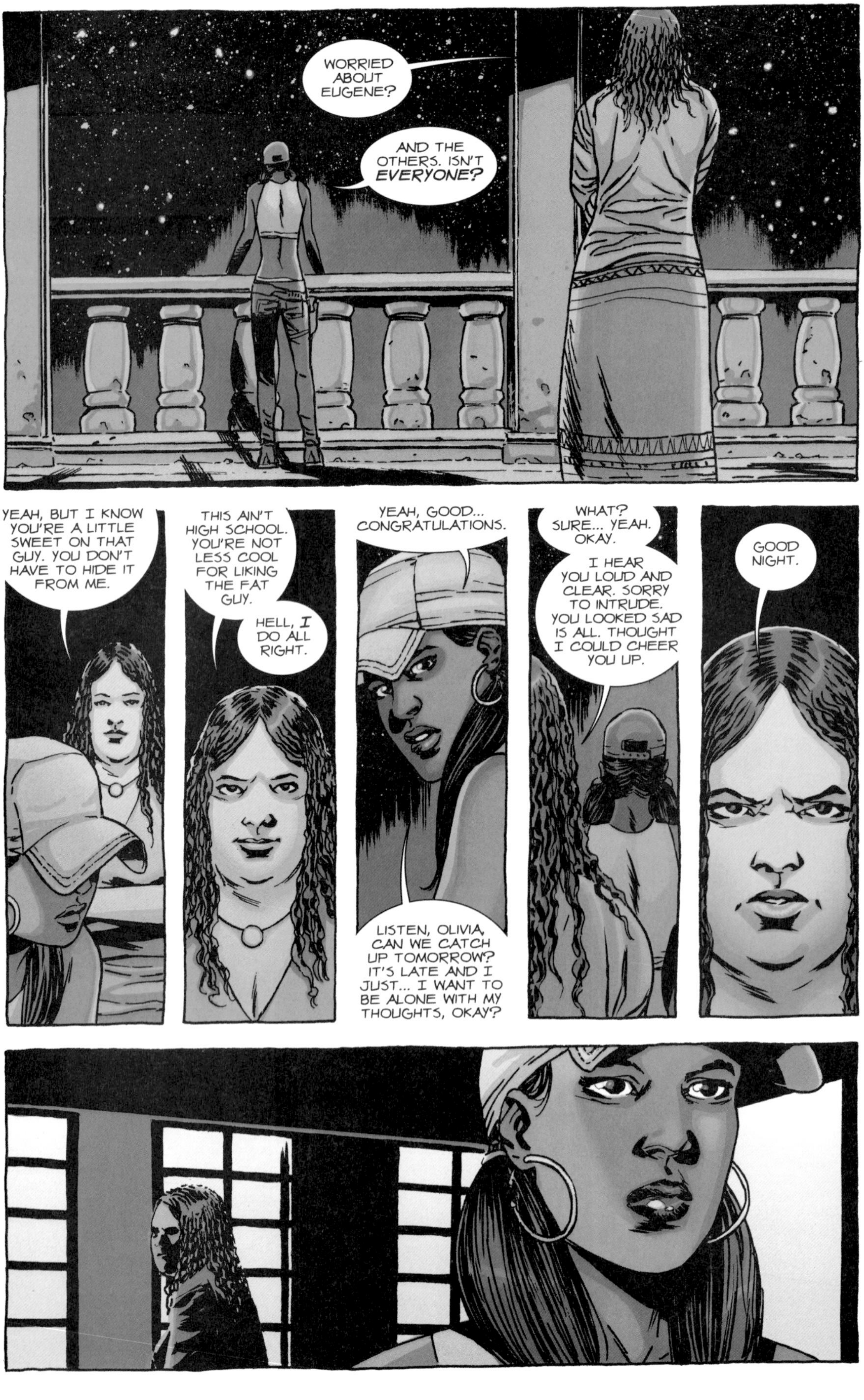
WORRIED ABOUT EUGENE?
AND THE OTHERS. ISN'T EVERYONE?
YEAH, BUT I KNOW YOU'RE A LITTLE SWEET ON THAT GUY. YOU DON'T HAVE TO HIDE IT FROM ME.
THIS AIN'T HIGH SCHOOL. YOU'RE NOT LESS COOL FOR LIKING THE FAT GUY.
HELL, I DO ALL RIGHT.
YEAH, GOOD... CONGRATULATIONS.
LISTEN, OLIVIA, CAN WE CATCH UP TOMORROW? IT'S LATE AND I JUST... I WANT TO BE ALONE WITH MY THOUGHTS, OKAY?
WHAT? SURE... YEAH. OKAY.
I HEAR YOU LOUD AND CLEAR. SORRY TO INTRUDE. YOU LOOKED SAD IS ALL. THOUGHT I COULD CHEER YOU UP.
GOOD NIGHT.

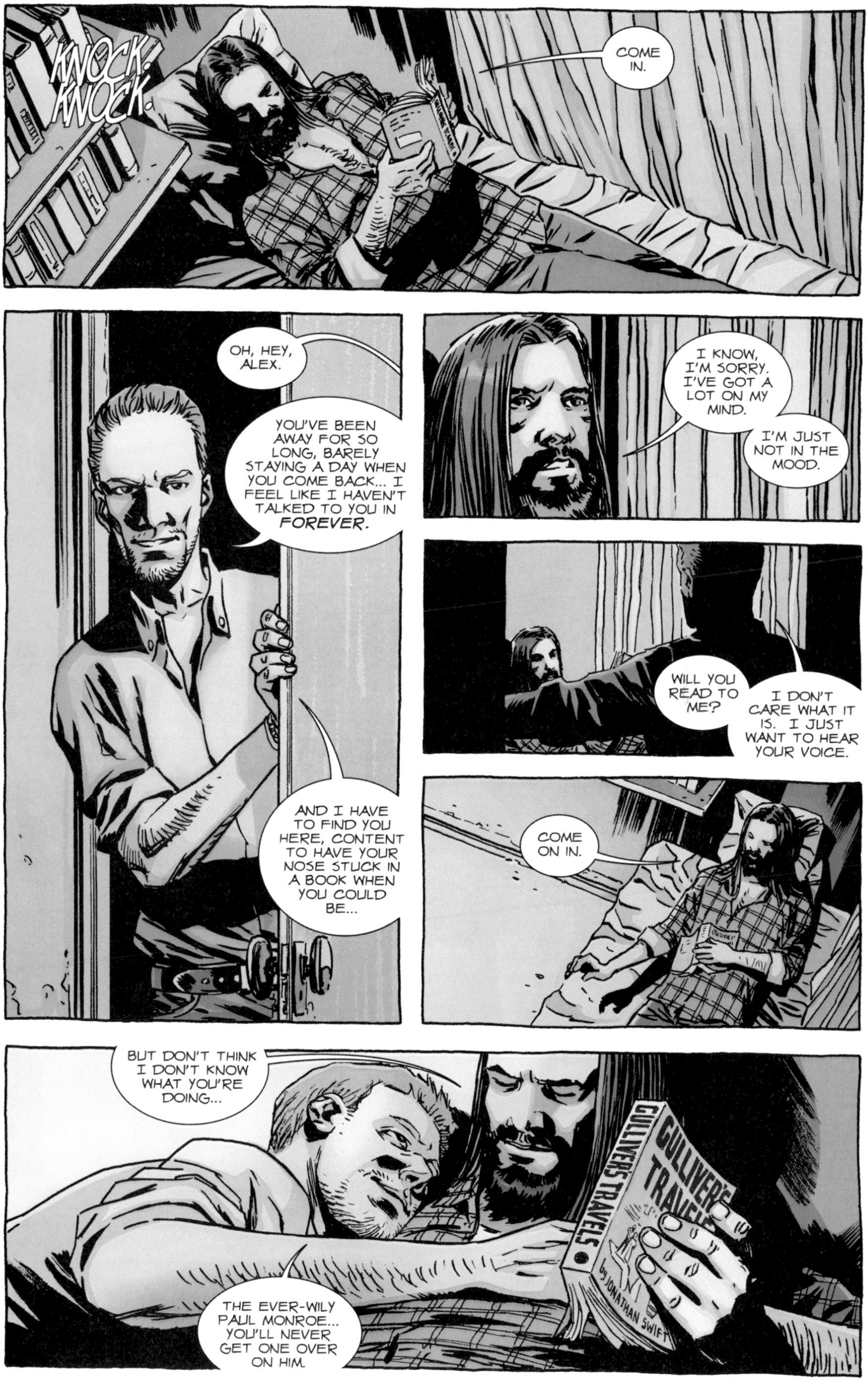
KNOCK KNOCK
COME IN.
OH, HEY, ALEX.
YOU'VE BEEN AWAY FOR SO LONG, BARELY STAYING A DAY WHEN YOU COME BACK... I FEEL LIKE I HAVEN'T TALKED TO YOU IN FOREVER.
AND I HAVE TO FIND YOU HERE, CONTENT TO HAVE YOUR NOSE STUCK IN A BOOK WHEN YOU COULD BE...
I KNOW, I'M SORRY. I'VE GOT A LOT ON MY MIND.
I'M JUST NOT IN THE MOOD.
WILL YOU READ TO ME?
I DON'T CARE WHAT IT IS. I JUST WANT TO HEAR YOUR VOICE.
COME ON IN.
BUT DON'T THINK I DON'T KNOW WHAT YOU'RE DOING...
THE EVER-WILY PAUL MONROE... YOU'LL NEVER GET ONE OVER ON HIM.
GULLIVER'S TRAVELS
by JONATHAN SWIFT

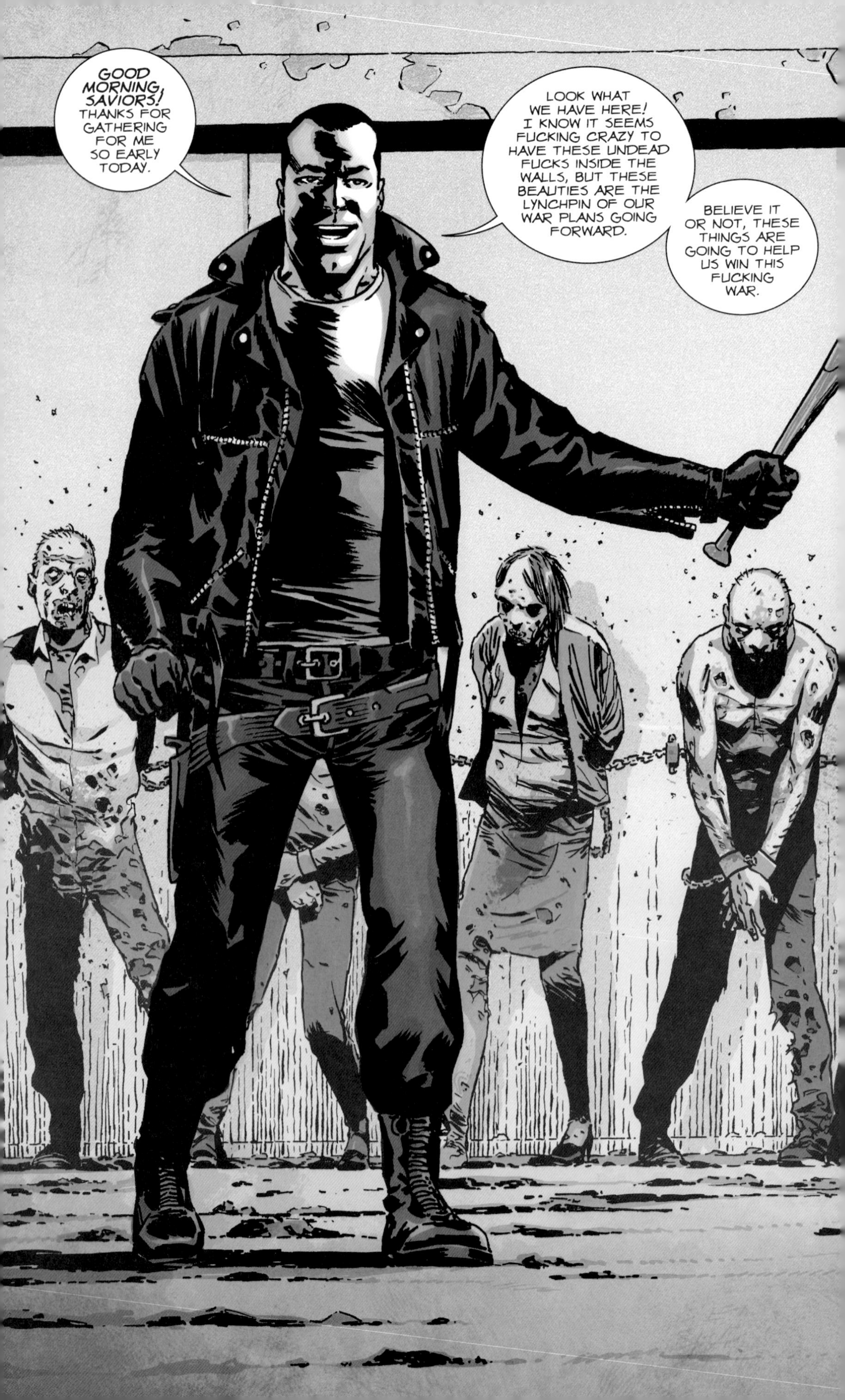
GOOD MORNING, SAVIORS! THANKS FOR GATHERING FOR ME SO EARLY TODAY.
LOOK WHAT WE HAVE HERE! I KNOW IT SEEMS FUCKING CRAZY TO HAVE THESE UNDEAD FUCKS INSIDE THE WALLS, BUT THESE BEAUTIES ARE THE LYNCHPIN OF OUR WAR PLANS GOING FORWARD.
BELIEVE IT OR NOT, THESE THINGS ARE GOING TO HELP US WIN THIS FUCKING WAR.

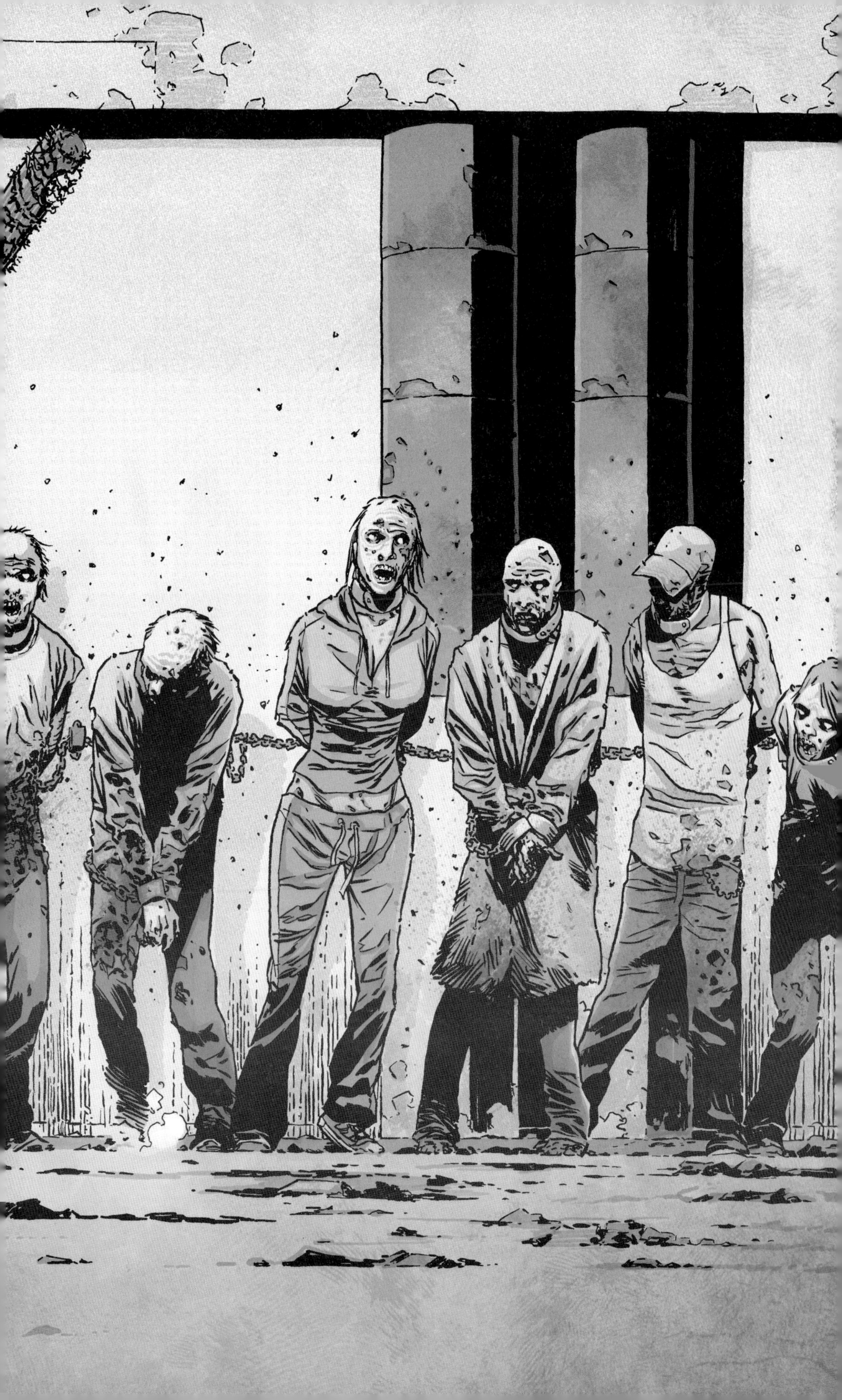

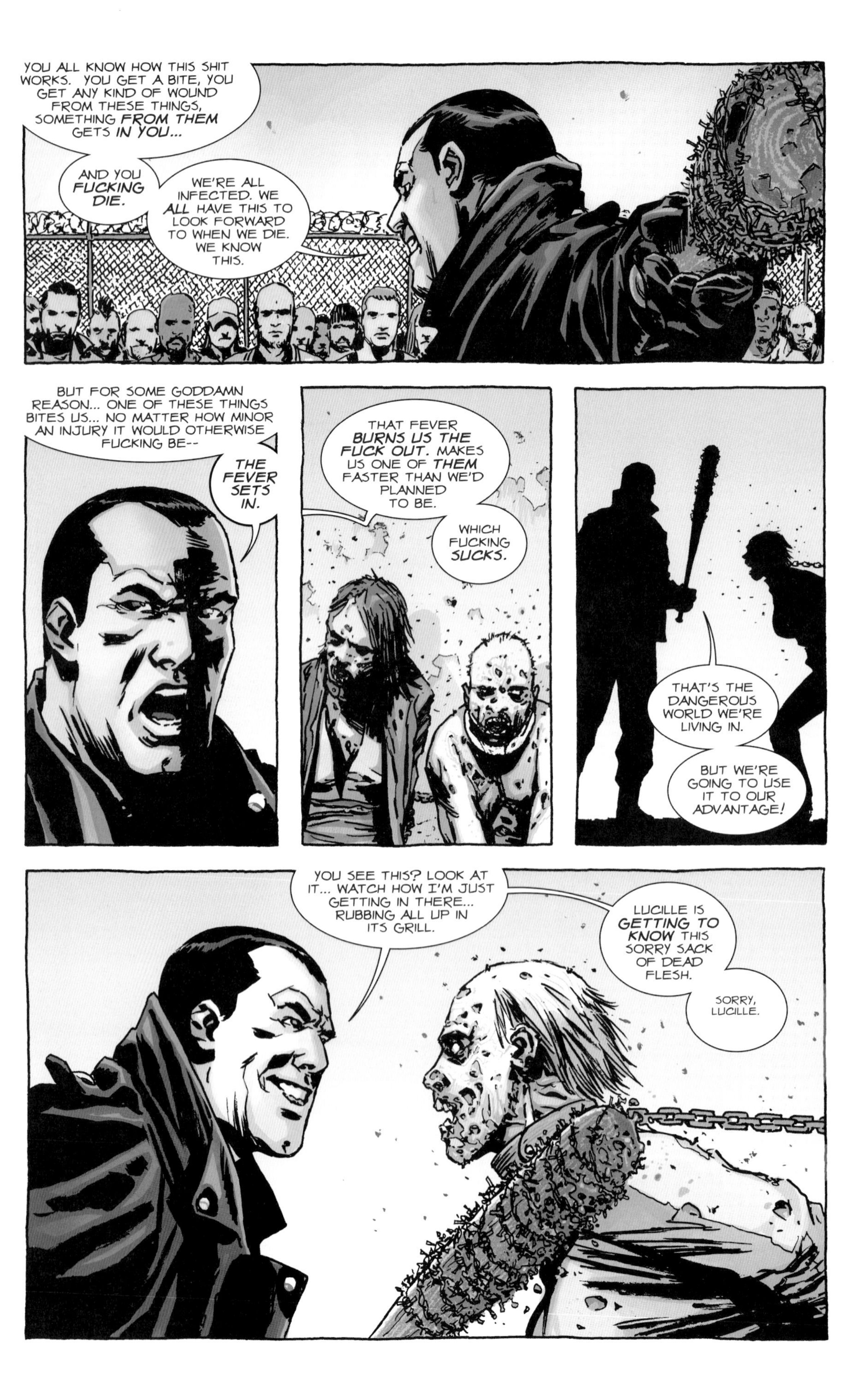
YOU ALL KNOW HOW THIS SHIT WORKS. YOU GET A BITE, YOU GET ANY KIND OF WOUND FROM THESE THINGS, SOMETHING FROM THEM GETS IN YOU...
AND YOU FUCKING DIE.
WE'RE ALL INFECTED. WE ALL HAVE THIS TO LOOK FORWARD TO WHEN WE DIE. WE KNOW THIS.
BUT FOR SOME GODDAMN REASON... ONE OF THESE THINGS BITES US... NO MATTER HOW MINOR AN INJURY IT WOULD OTHERWISE FUCKING BE--
THE FEVER SETS IN.
THAT FEVER BURNS US THE FUCK OUT. MAKES US ONE OF THEM FASTER THAN WE'D PLANNED TO BE.
WHICH FUCKING SUCKS.
THAT'S THE DANGEROUS WORLD WE'RE LIVING IN.
BUT WE'RE GOING TO USE IT TO OUR ADVANTAGE!
YOU SEE THIS? LOOK AT IT... WATCH HOW I'M JUST GETTING IN THERE... RUBBING ALL UP IN ITS GRILL.
LUCILLE IS GETTING TO KNOW THIS SORRY SACK OF DEAD FLESH.
SORRY, LUCILLE.

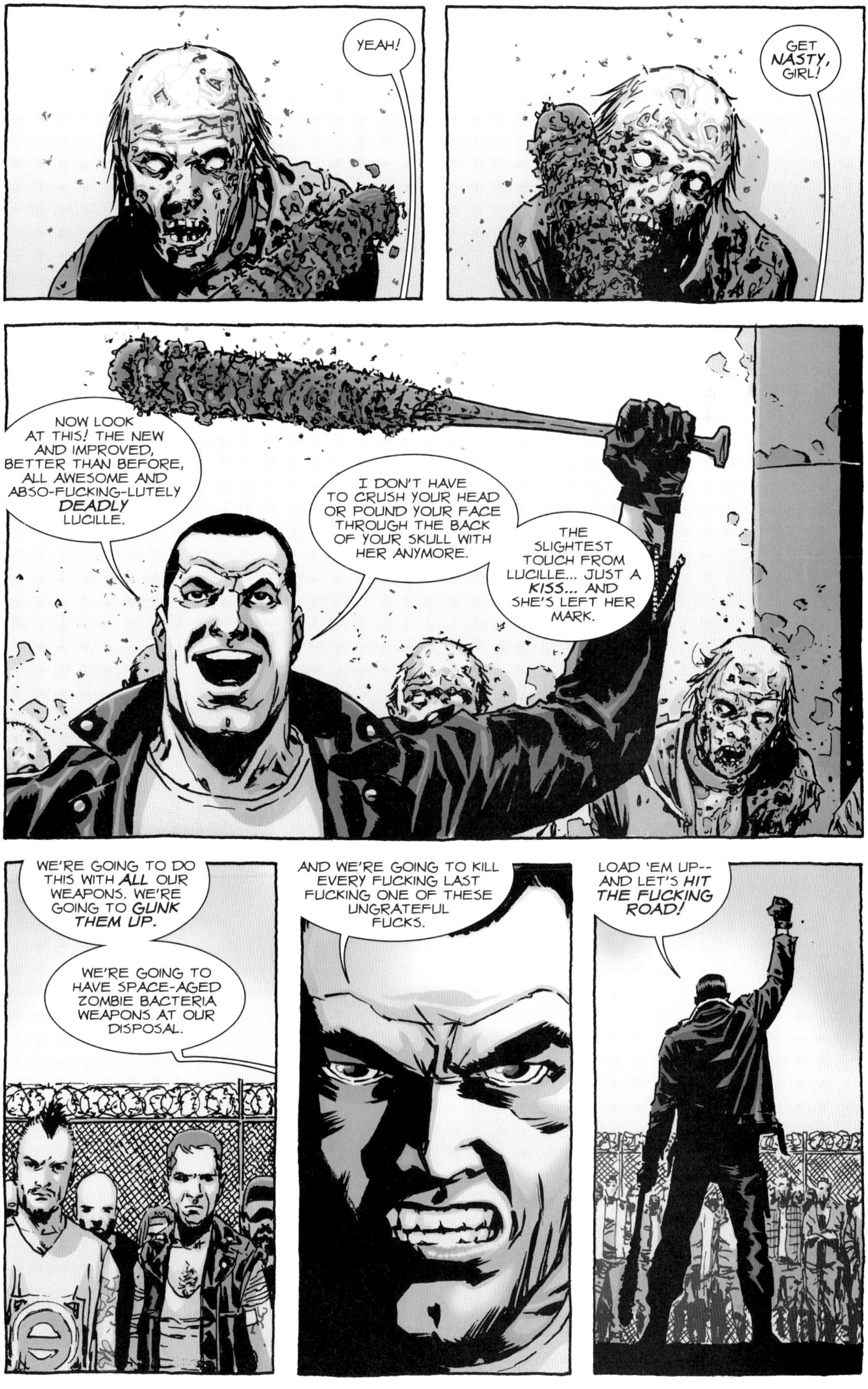
YEAH!
GET NASTY, GIRL!
NOW LOOK AT THIS! THE NEW AND IMPROVED, BETTER THAN BEFORE, ALL AWESOME AND ABSO-FUCKING-LUTELY DEADLY LUCILLE.
I DON'T HAVE TO CRUSH YOUR HEAD OR POUND YOUR FACE THROUGH THE BACK OF YOUR SKULL WITH HER ANYMORE.
THE SLIGHTEST TOUCH FROM LUCILLE... JUST A KISS... AND SHE'S LEFT HER MARK.
WE'RE GOING TO DO THIS WITH ALL OUR WEAPONS. WE'RE GOING TO GUNK THEM UP.
WE'RE GOING TO HAVE SPACE-AGED ZOMBIE BACTERIA WEAPONS AT OUR DISPOSAL.
AND WE'RE GOING TO KILL EVERY FUCKING LAST FUCKING ONE OF THESE UNGRATEFUL FUCKS.
LOAD 'EM UP-- AND LET'S HIT THE FUCKING ROAD!

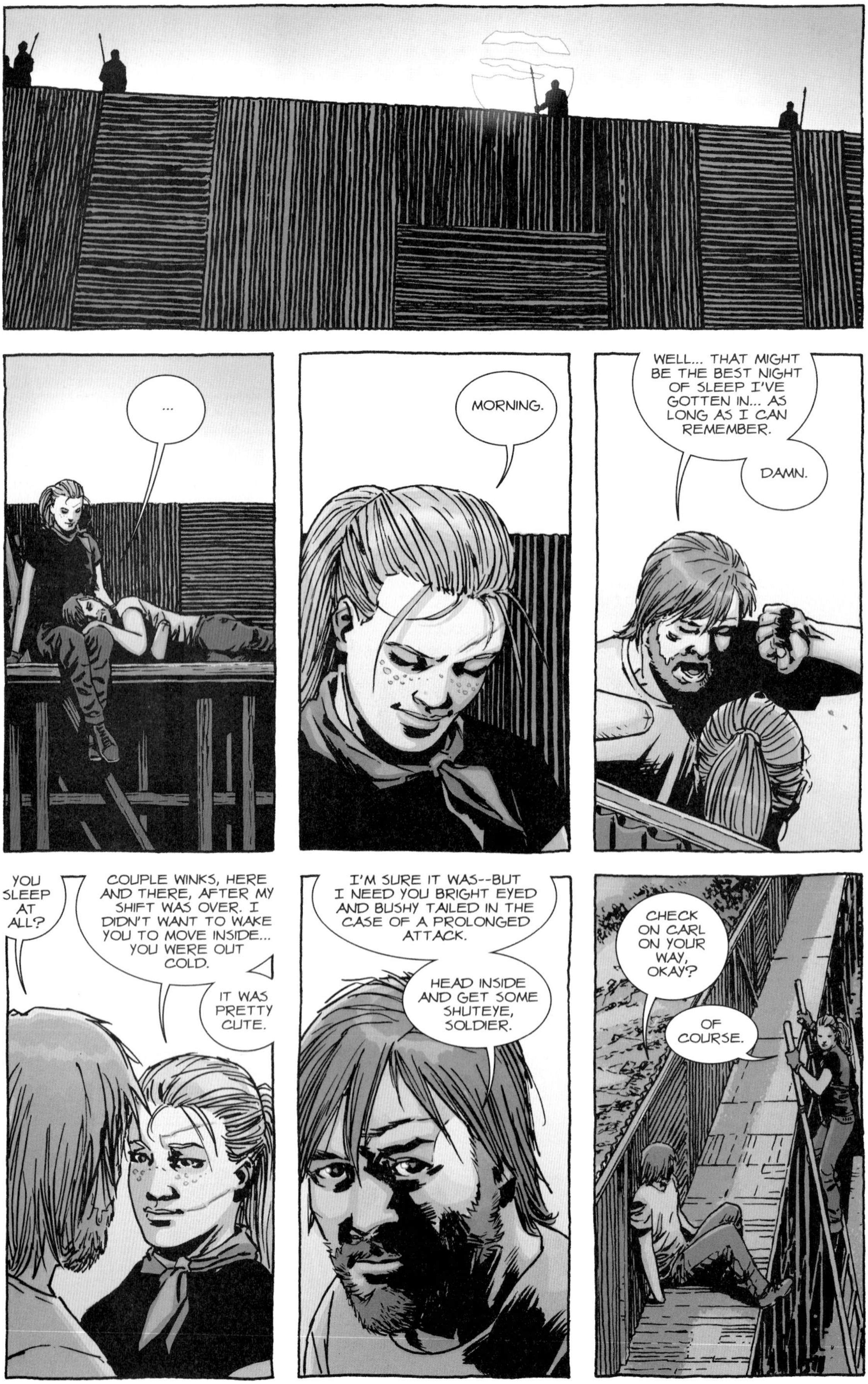
...
MORNING.
WELL... THAT MIGHT BE THE BEST NIGHT OF SLEEP I'VE GOTTEN IN... AS LONG AS I CAN REMEMBER.
DAMN.
YOU SLEEP AT ALL?
COUPLE WINKS, HERE AND THERE, AFTER MY SHIFT WAS OVER. I DIDN'T WANT TO WAKE YOU TO MOVE INSIDE... YOU WERE OUT COLD.
IT WAS PRETTY CUTE.
I'M SURE IT WAS--BUT I NEED YOU BRIGHT EYED AND BUSHY TAILED IN THE CASE OF A PROLONGED ATTACK.
HEAD INSIDE AND GET SOME SHUTEYE, SOLDIER.
CHECK ON CARL ON YOUR WAY, OKAY?
OF COURSE.

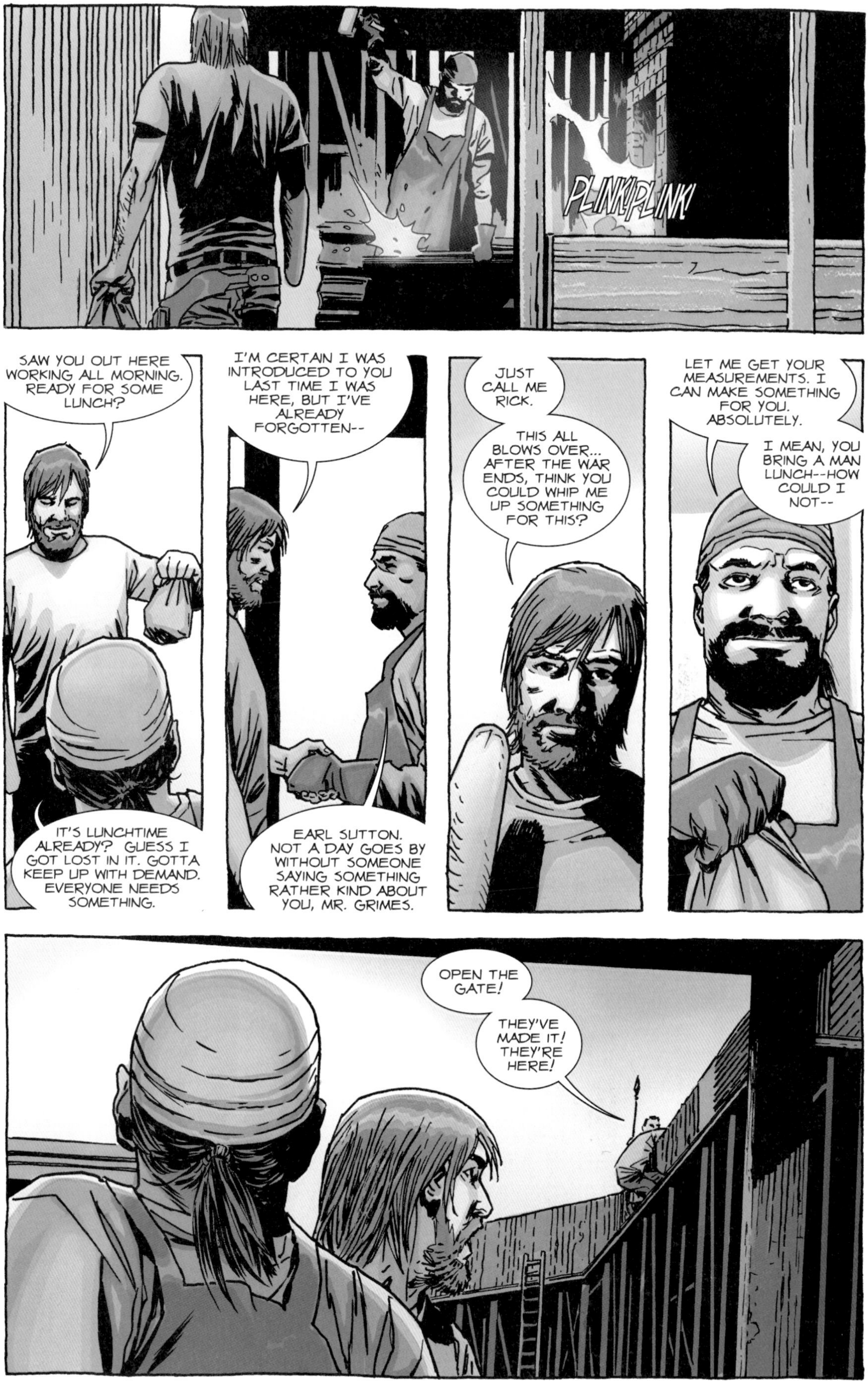
PLINK! PLINK!
SAW YOU OUT HERE WORKING ALL MORNING. READY FOR SOME LUNCH?
IT'S LUNCHTIME ALREADY? GUESS I GOT LOST IN IT. GOTTA KEEP UP WITH DEMAND. EVERYONE NEEDS SOMETHING.
I'M CERTAIN I WAS INTRODUCED TO YOU LAST TIME I WAS HERE, BUT I'VE ALREADY FORGOTTEN--
EARL SUTTON. NOT A DAY GOES BY WITHOUT SOMEONE SAYING SOMETHING RATHER KIND ABOUT YOU, MR. GRIMES.
JUST CALL ME RICK.
THIS ALL BLOWS OVER... AFTER THE WAR ENDS, THINK YOU COULD WHIP ME UP SOMETHING FOR THIS?
LET ME GET YOUR MEASUREMENTS. I CAN MAKE SOMETHING FOR YOU. ABSOLUTELY.
I MEAN, YOU BRING A MAN LUNCH--HOW COULD I NOT--
OPEN THE GATE!
THEY'VE MADE IT! THEY'RE HERE!

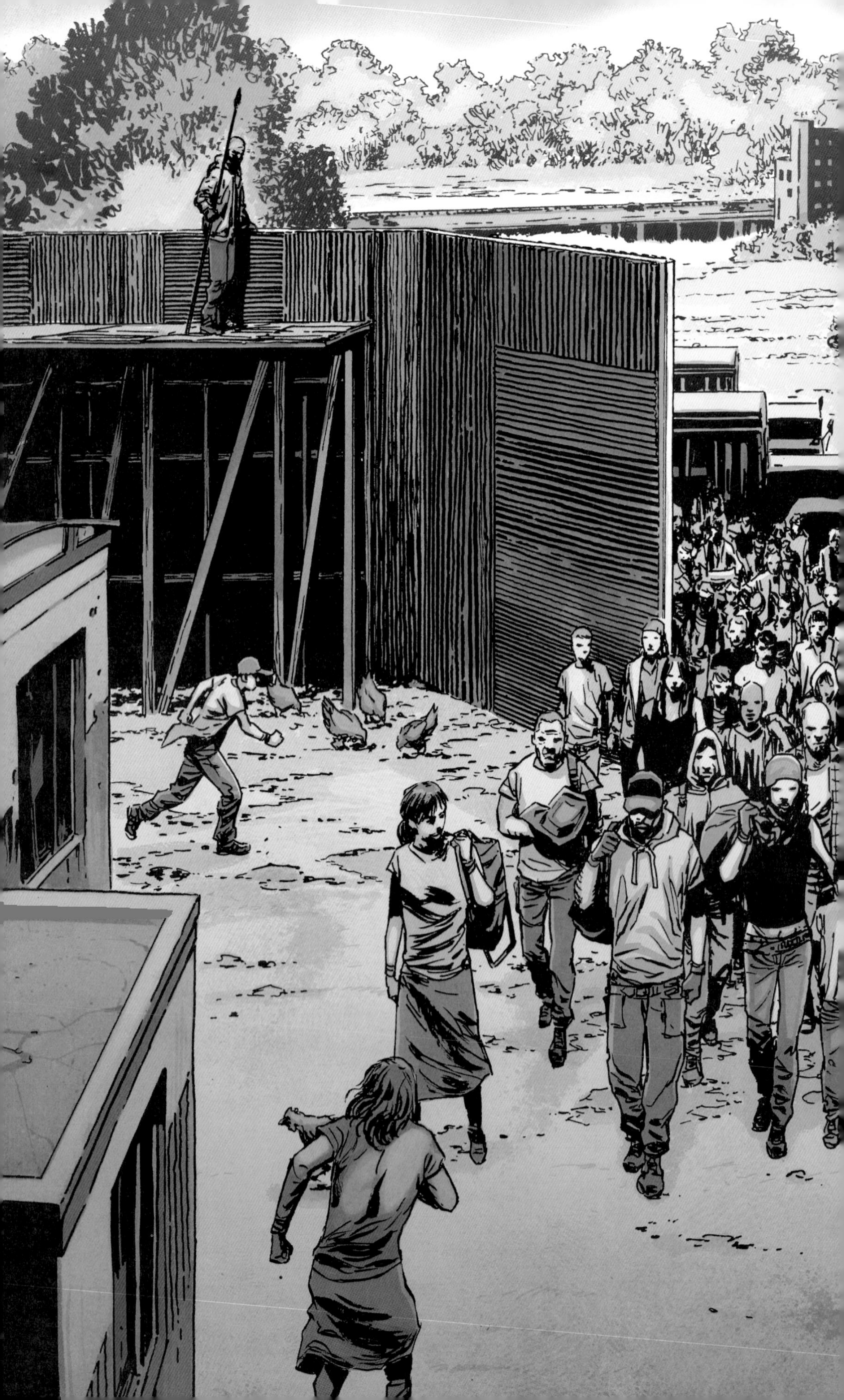

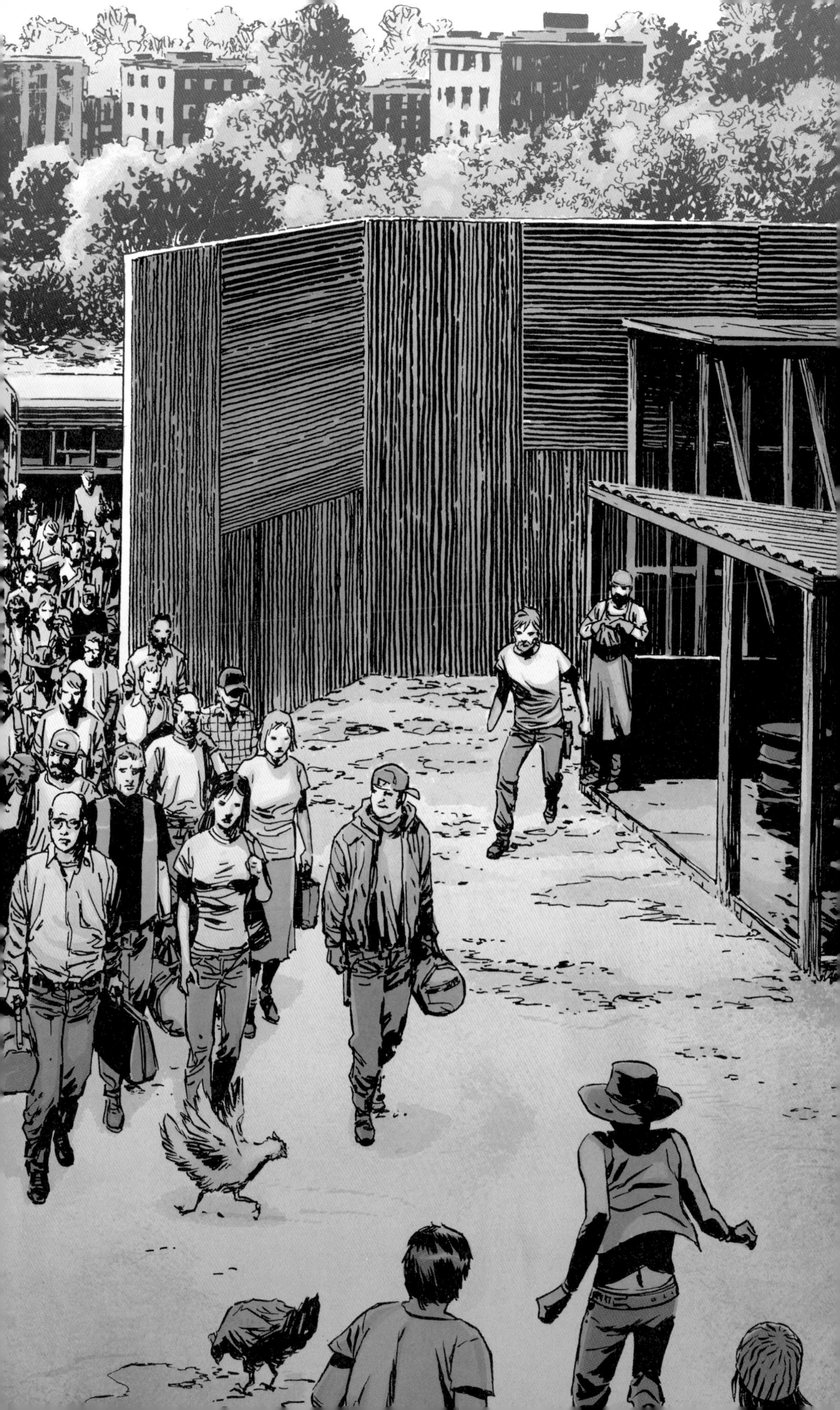

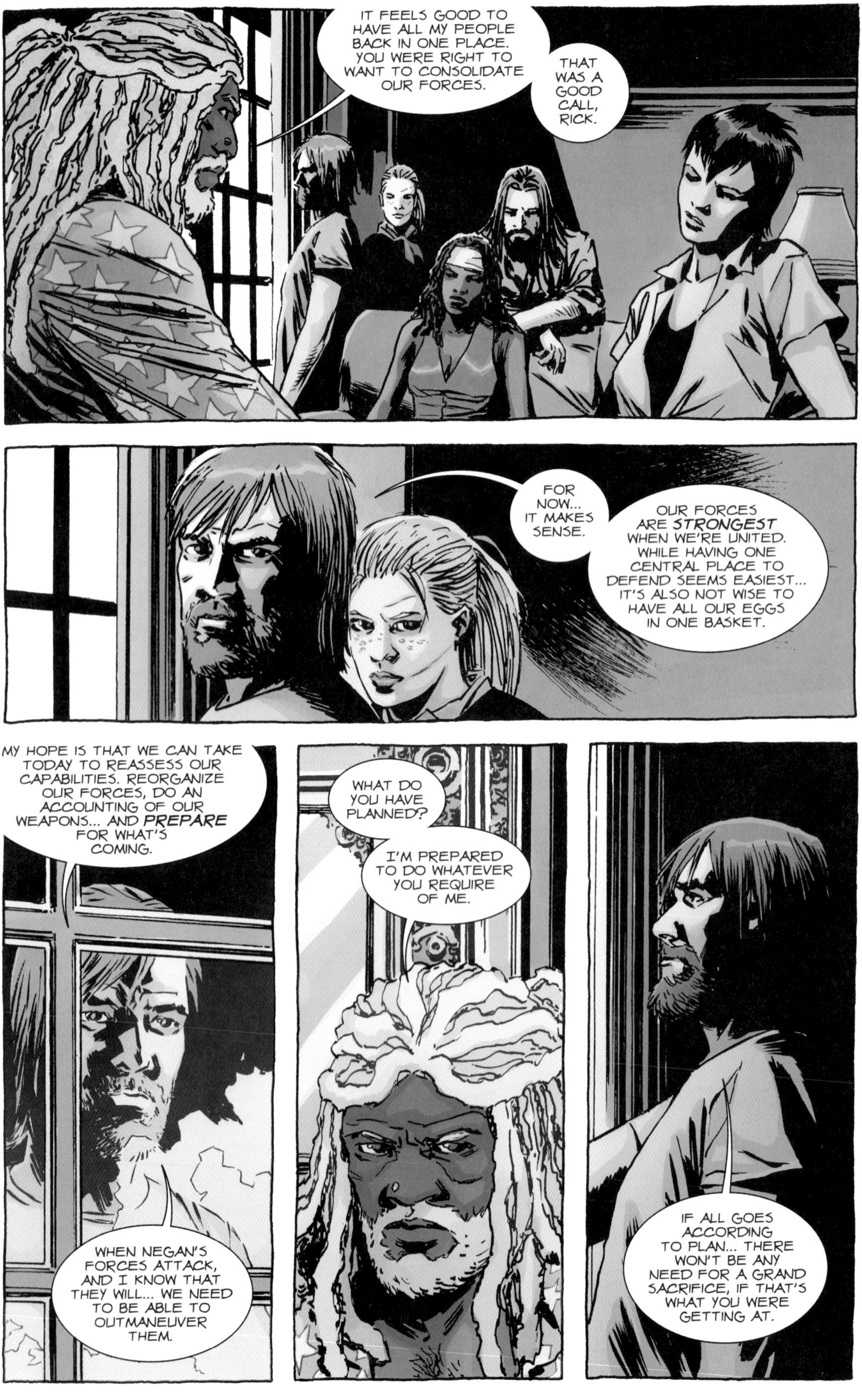
IT FEELS GOOD TO HAVE ALL MY PEOPLE BACK IN ONE PLACE. YOU WERE RIGHT TO WANT TO CONSOLIDATE OUR FORCES.
THAT WAS A GOOD CALL, RICK.
FOR NOW... IT MAKES SENSE.
OUR FORCES ARE STRONGEST WHEN WE'RE UNITED. WHILE HAVING ONE CENTRAL PLACE TO DEFEND SEEMS EASIEST... IT'S ALSO NOT WISE TO HAVE ALL OUR EGGS IN ONE BASKET.
MY HOPE IS THAT WE CAN TAKE TODAY TO REASSESS OUR CAPABILITIES. REORGANIZE OUR FORCES, DO AN ACCOUNTING OF OUR WEAPONS... AND PREPARE FOR WHAT'S COMING.
WHEN NEGAN'S FORCES ATTACK, AND I KNOW THAT THEY WILL... WE NEED TO BE ABLE TO OUTMANEUVER THEM.
WHAT DO YOU HAVE PLANNED?
I'M PREPARED TO DO WHATEVER YOU REQUIRE OF ME.
IF ALL GOES ACCORDING TO PLAN... THERE WON'T BE ANY NEED FOR A GRAND SACRIFICE, IF THAT'S WHAT YOU WERE GETTING AT.

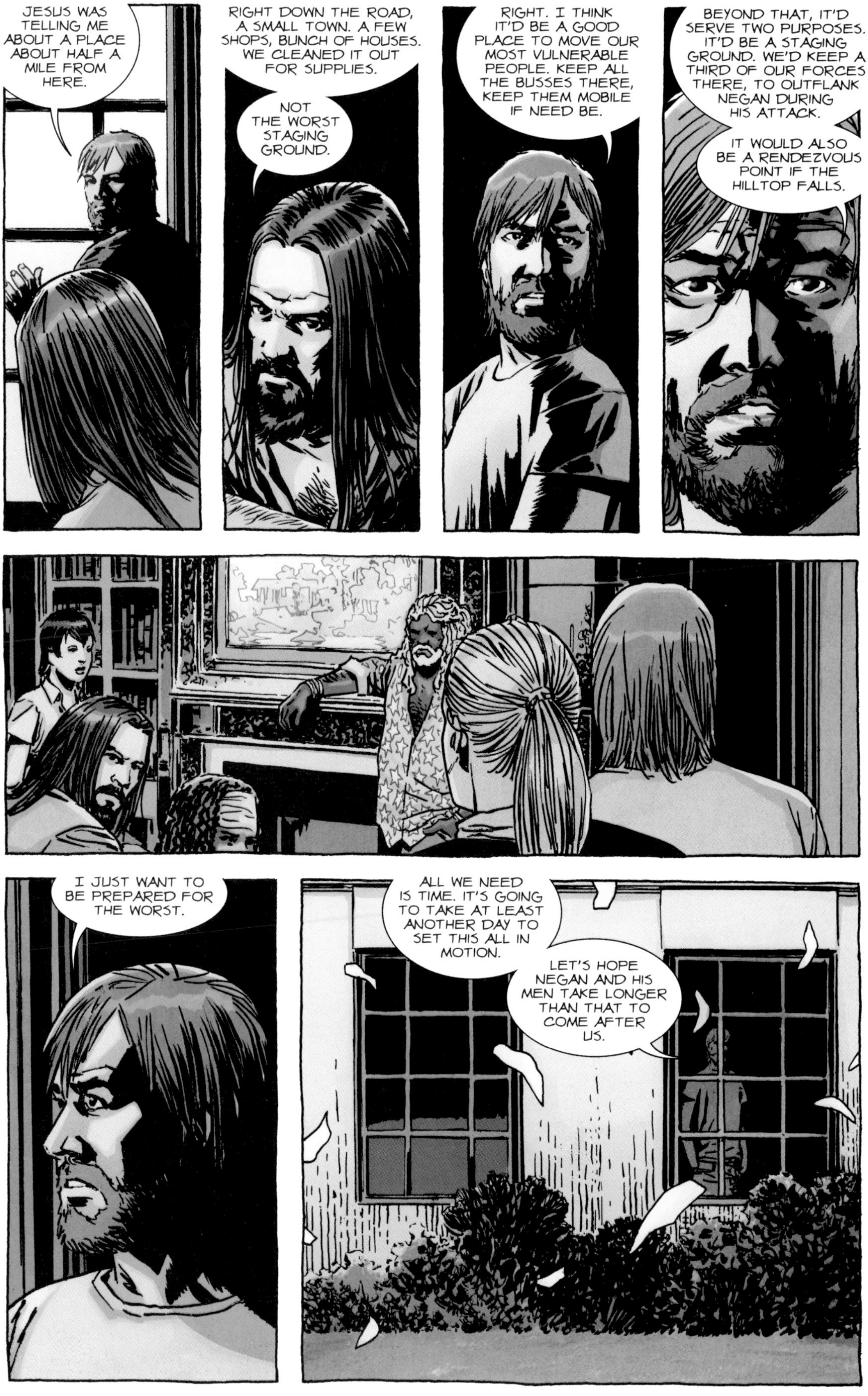
JESUS WAS TELLING ME ABOUT A PLACE ABOUT HALF A MILE FROM HERE.
RIGHT DOWN THE ROAD, A SMALL TOWN. A FEW SHOPS, BUNCH OF HOUSES. WE CLEANED IT OUT FOR SUPPLIES.
NOT THE WORST STAGING GROUND.
RIGHT. I THINK IT'D BE A GOOD PLACE TO MOVE OUR MOST VULNERABLE PEOPLE. KEEP ALL THE BUSSES THERE, KEEP THEM MOBILE IF NEED BE.
BEYOND THAT, IT'D SERVE TWO PURPOSES. IT'D BE A STAGING GROUND. WE'D KEEP A THIRD OF OUR FORCES THERE, TO OUTFLANK NEGAN DURING HIS ATTACK.
IT WOULD ALSO BE A RENDEZVOUS POINT IF THE HILLTOP FALLS.
I JUST WANT TO BE PREPARED FOR THE WORST.
ALL WE NEED IS TIME. IT'S GOING TO TAKE AT LEAST ANOTHER DAY TO SET THIS ALL IN MOTION.
LET'S HOPE NEGAN AND HIS MEN TAKE LONGER THAN THAT TO COME AFTER US.

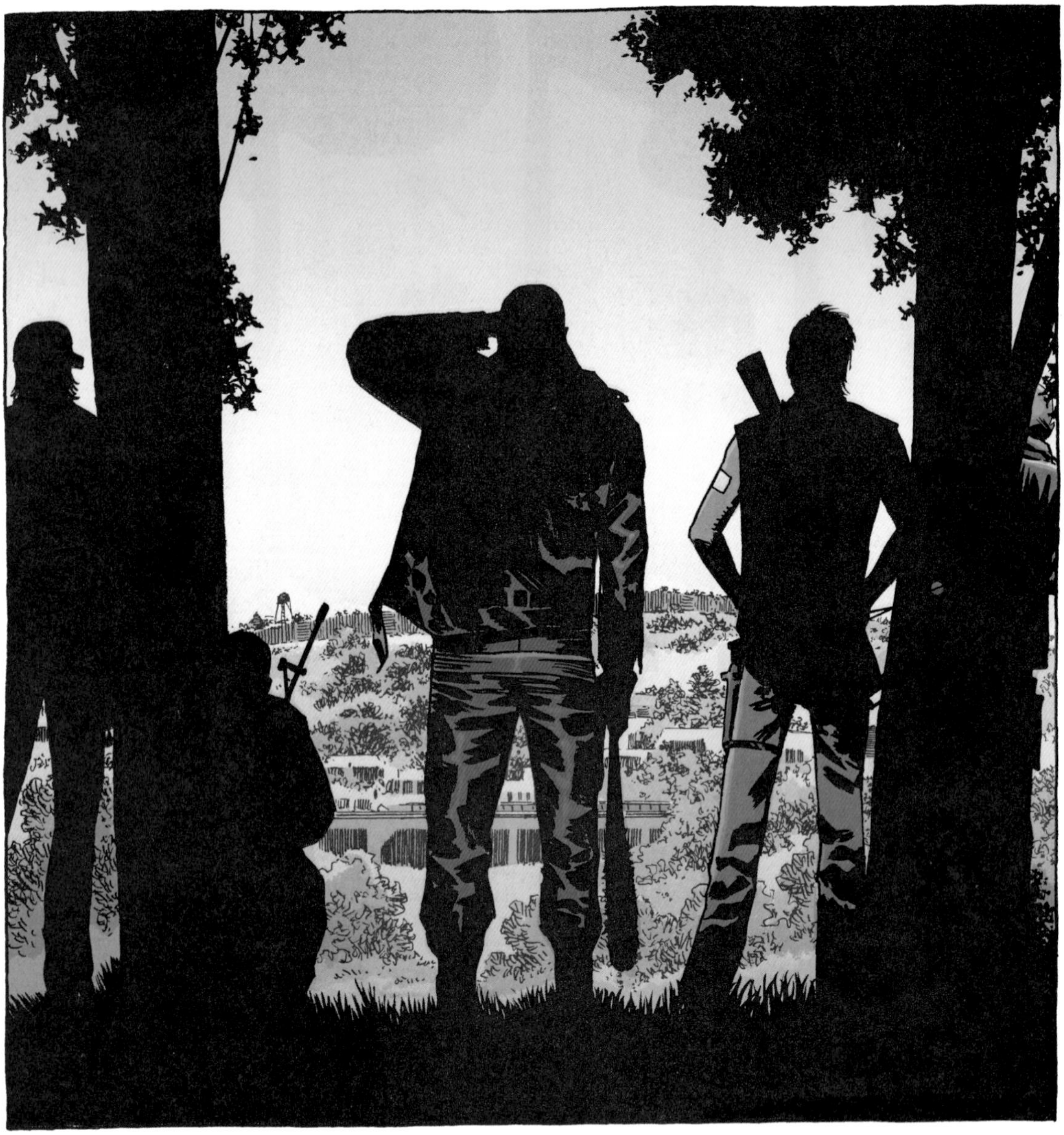

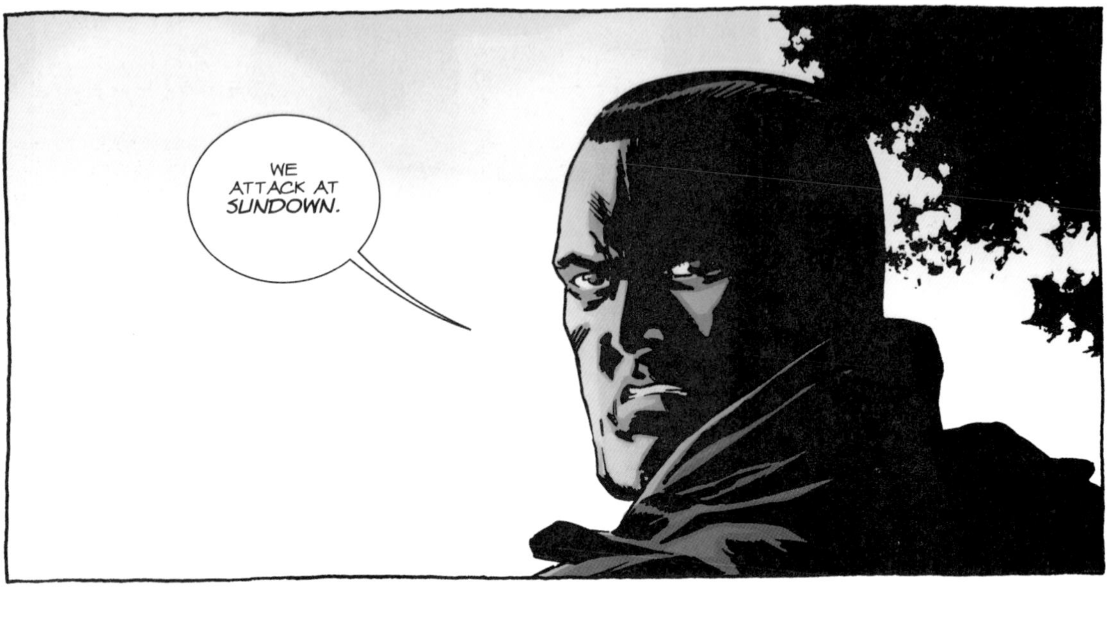
WE ATTACK AT SUNDOWN.

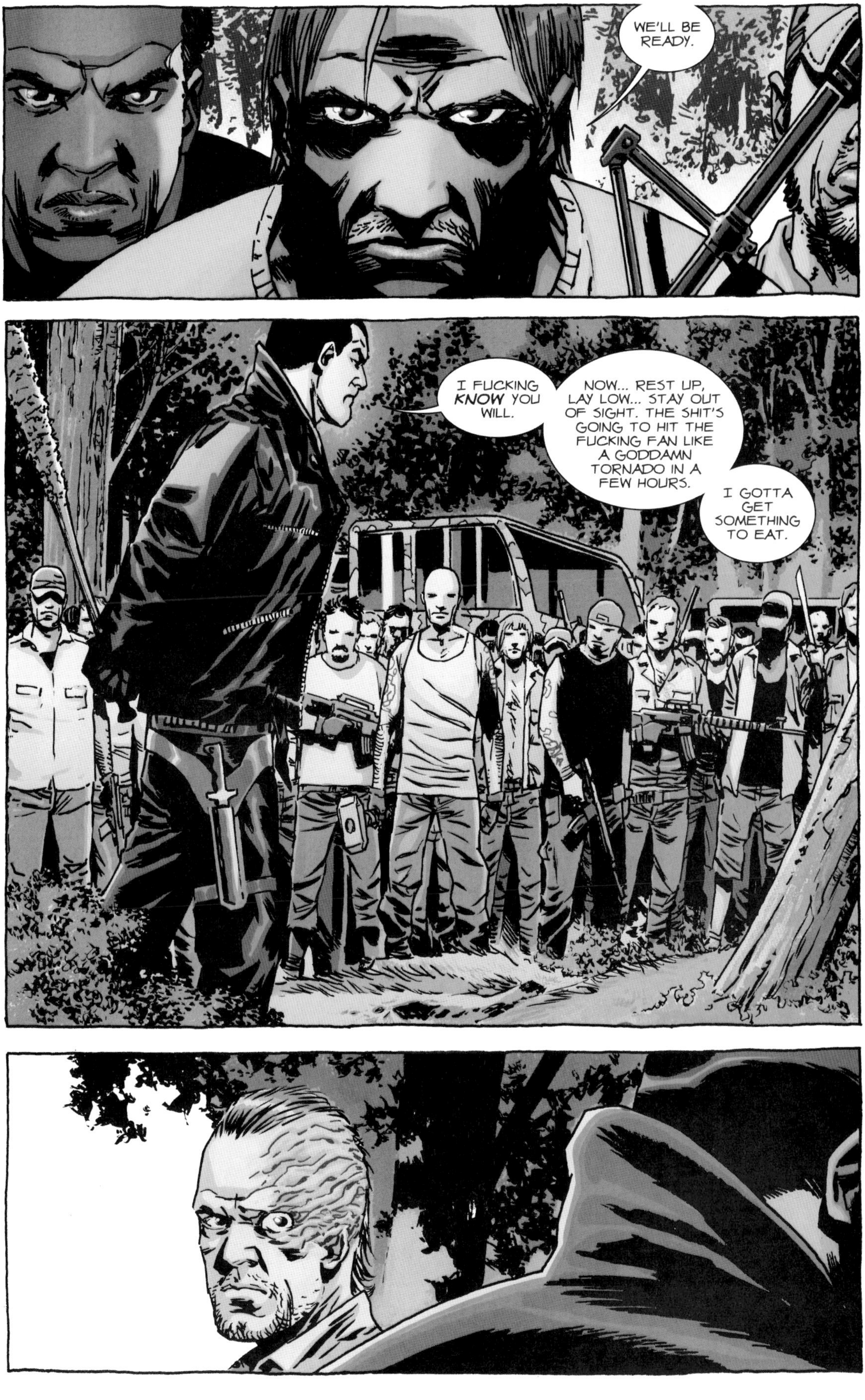
WE'LL BE READY.
I FUCKING KNOW YOU WILL.
NOW... REST UP, LAY LOW... STAY OUT OF SIGHT. THE SHIT'S GOING TO HIT THE FUCKING FAN LIKE A GODDAMN TORNADO IN A FEW HOURS.
I GOTTA GET SOMETHING TO EAT.

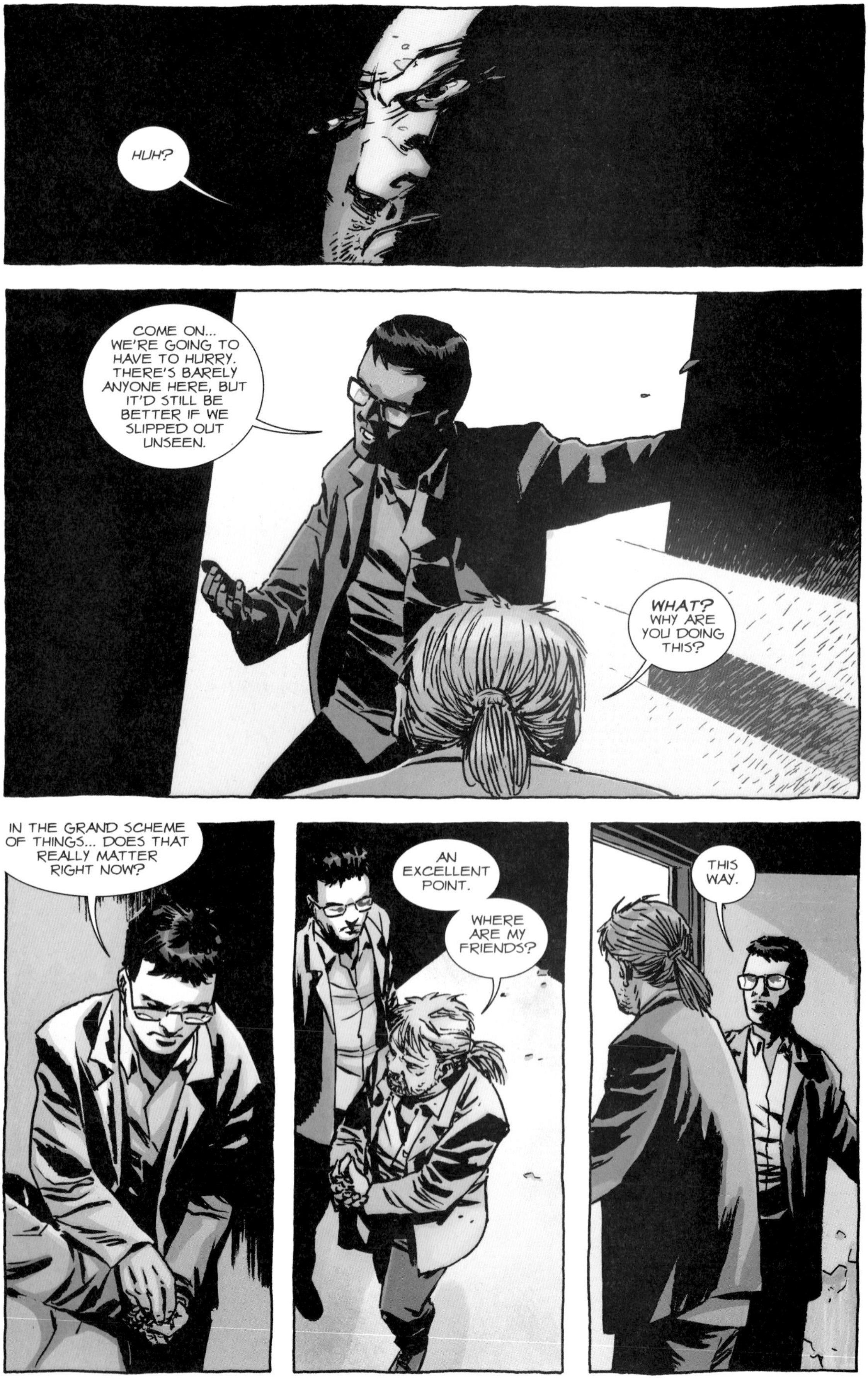
HUH?
COME ON... WE'RE GOING TO HAVE TO HURRY. THERE'S BARELY ANYONE HERE, BUT IT'D STILL BE BETTER IF WE SLIPPED OUT UNSEEN.
WHAT? WHY ARE YOU DOING THIS?
IN THE GRAND SCHEME OF THINGS... DOES THAT REALLY MATTER RIGHT NOW?
AN EXCELLENT POINT.
WHERE ARE MY FRIENDS?
THIS WAY.

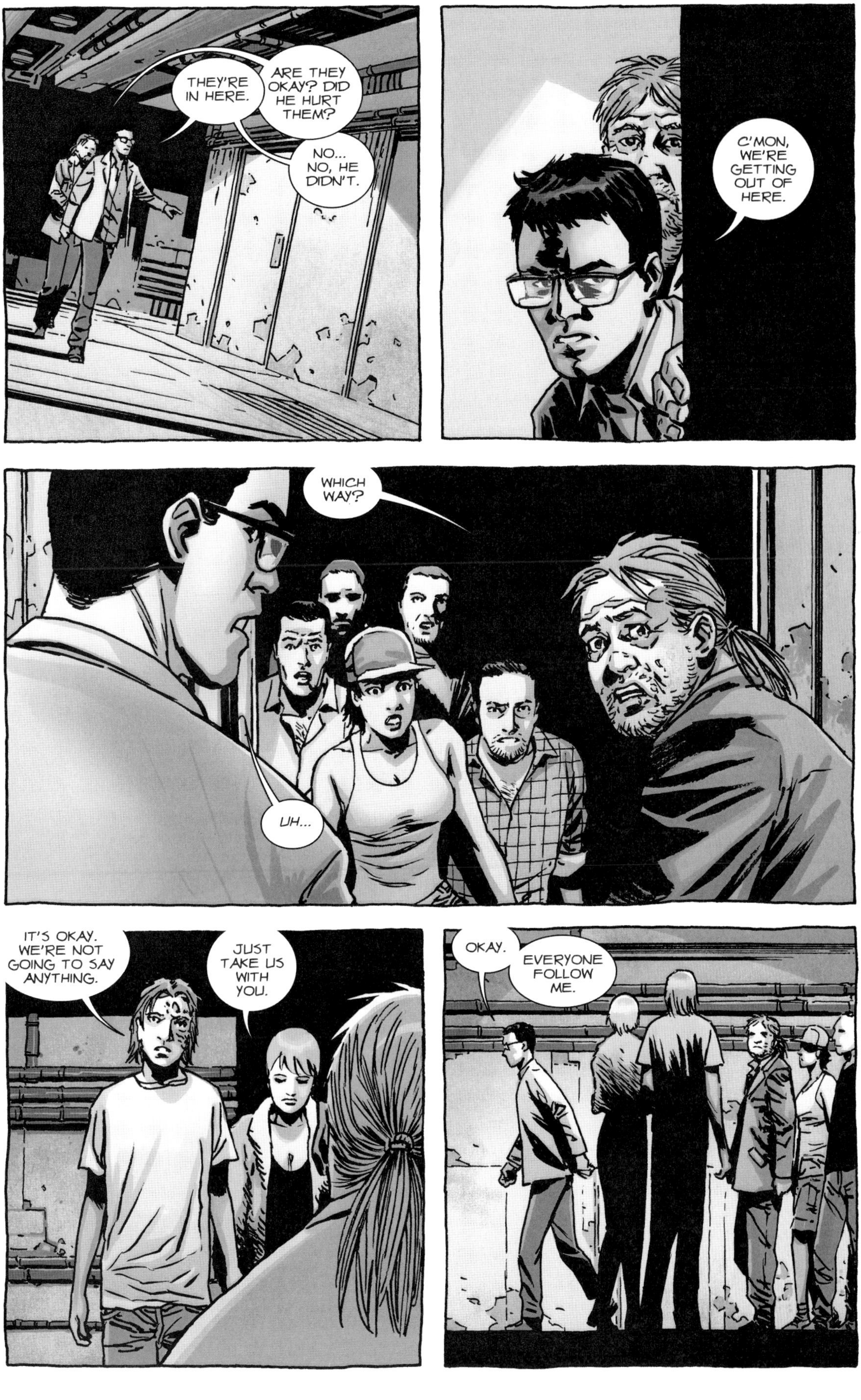
THEY'RE IN HERE.
ARE THEY OKAY? DID HE HURT THEM?
NO... NO, HE DIDN'T.
C'MON, WE'RE GETTING OUT OF HERE.
WHICH WAY?
UH...
IT'S OKAY. WE'RE NOT GOING TO SAY ANYTHING.
JUST TAKE US WITH YOU.
OKAY.
EVERYONE FOLLOW ME.

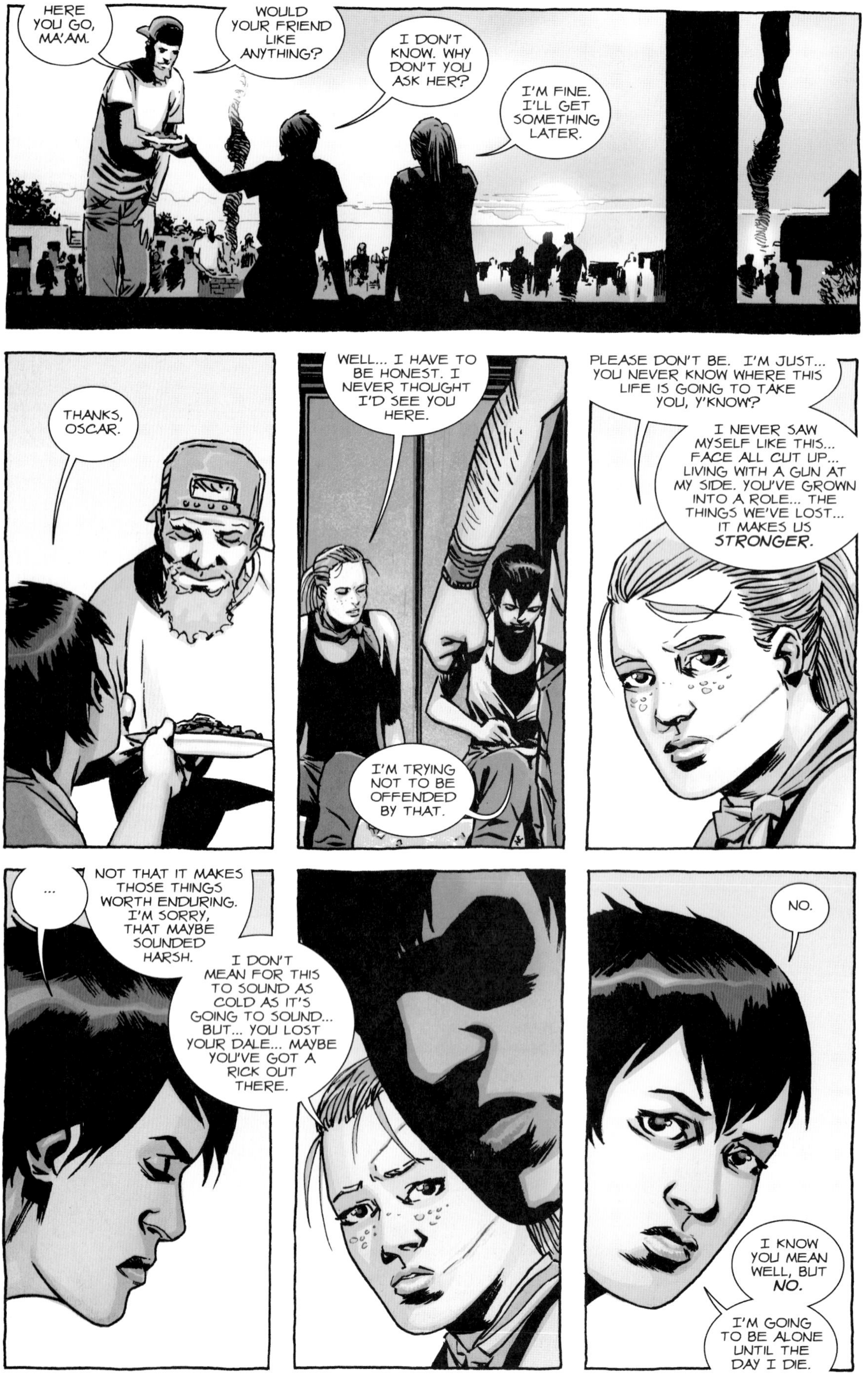
HERE YOU GO, MA'AM.
WOULD YOUR FRIEND LIKE ANYTHING?
I DON'T KNOW. WHY DON'T YOU ASK HER?
I'M FINE. I'LL GET SOMETHING LATER.
THANKS, OSCAR.
WELL... I HAVE TO BE HONEST. I NEVER THOUGHT I'D SEE YOU HERE.
I'M TRYING NOT TO BE OFFENDED BY THAT.
PLEASE DON'T BE. I'M JUST... YOU NEVER KNOW WHERE THIS LIFE IS GOING TO TAKE YOU, Y'KNOW?
I NEVER SAW MYSELF LIKE THIS... FACE ALL CUT UP... LIVING WITH A GUN AT MY SIDE. YOU'VE GROWN INTO A ROLE... THE THINGS WE'VE LOST... IT MAKES US STRONGER.
...
NOT THAT IT MAKES THOSE THINGS WORTH ENDURING. I'M SORRY, THAT MAYBE SOUNDED HARSH.
I DON'T MEAN FOR THIS TO SOUND AS COLD AS IT'S GOING TO SOUND... BUT... YOU LOST YOUR DALE... MAYBE YOU'VE GOT A RICK OUT THERE.
NO.
I KNOW YOU MEAN WELL, BUT NO.
I'M GOING TO BE ALONE UNTIL THE DAY I DIE.

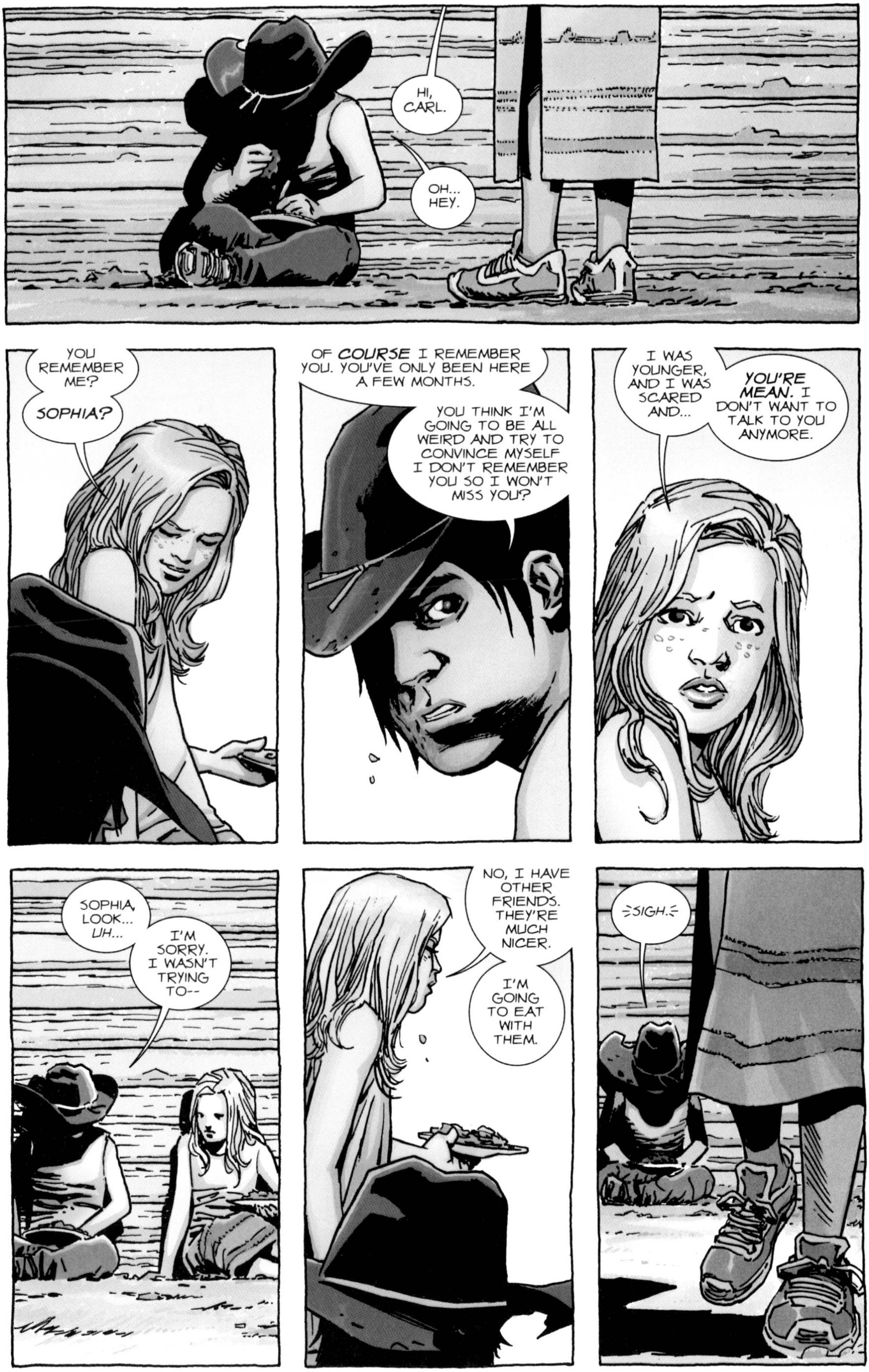
HI, CARL.
OH... HEY.
YOU REMEMBER ME?
SOPHIA?
OF COURSE I REMEMBER YOU. YOU'VE ONLY BEEN HERE A FEW MONTHS.
YOU THINK I'M GOING TO BE ALL WEIRD AND TRY TO CONVINCE MYSELF I DON'T REMEMBER YOU SO I WON'T MISS YOU?
I WAS YOUNGER, AND I WAS SCARED AND...
YOU'RE MEAN. I DON'T WANT TO TALK TO YOU ANYMORE.
SOPHIA, LOOK... UH...
I'M SORRY. I WASN'T TRYING TO--
NO, I HAVE OTHER FRIENDS. THEY'RE MUCH NICER.
I'M GOING TO EAT WITH THEM.
SIGH.

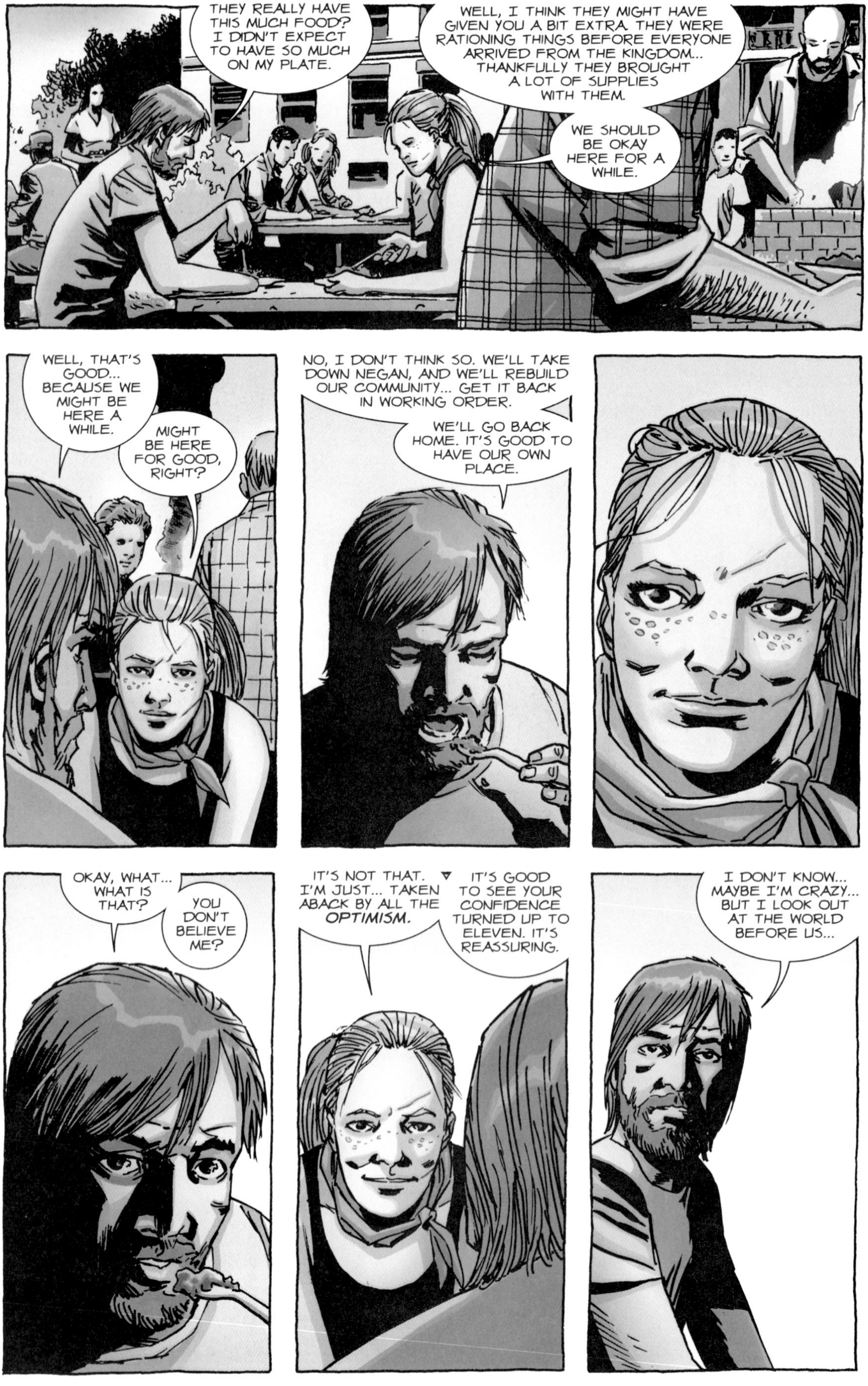
THEY REALLY HAVE THIS MUCH FOOD? I DIDN'T EXPECT TO HAVE SO MUCH ON MY PLATE.
WELL, I THINK THEY MIGHT HAVE GIVEN YOU A BIT EXTRA. THEY WERE RATIONING THINGS BEFORE EVERYONE ARRIVED FROM THE KINGDOM... THANKFULLY THEY BROUGHT A LOT OF SUPPLIES WITH THEM.
WE SHOULD BE OKAY HERE FOR A WHILE.
WELL, THAT'S GOOD... BECAUSE WE MIGHT BE HERE A WHILE.
MIGHT BE HERE FOR GOOD, RIGHT?
NO, I DON'T THINK SO. WE'LL TAKE DOWN NEGAN, AND WE'LL REBUILD OUR COMMUNITY... GET IT BACK IN WORKING ORDER.
WE'LL GO BACK HOME. IT'S GOOD TO HAVE OUR OWN PLACE.
OKAY, WHAT... WHAT IS THAT?
YOU DON'T BELIEVE ME?
IT'S NOT THAT. I'M JUST... TAKEN ABACK BY ALL THE *OPTIMISM.*
IT'S GOOD TO SEE YOUR CONFIDENCE TURNED UP TO ELEVEN. IT'S REASSURING.
I DON'T KNOW... MAYBE I'M CRAZY... BUT I LOOK OUT AT THE WORLD BEFORE US...

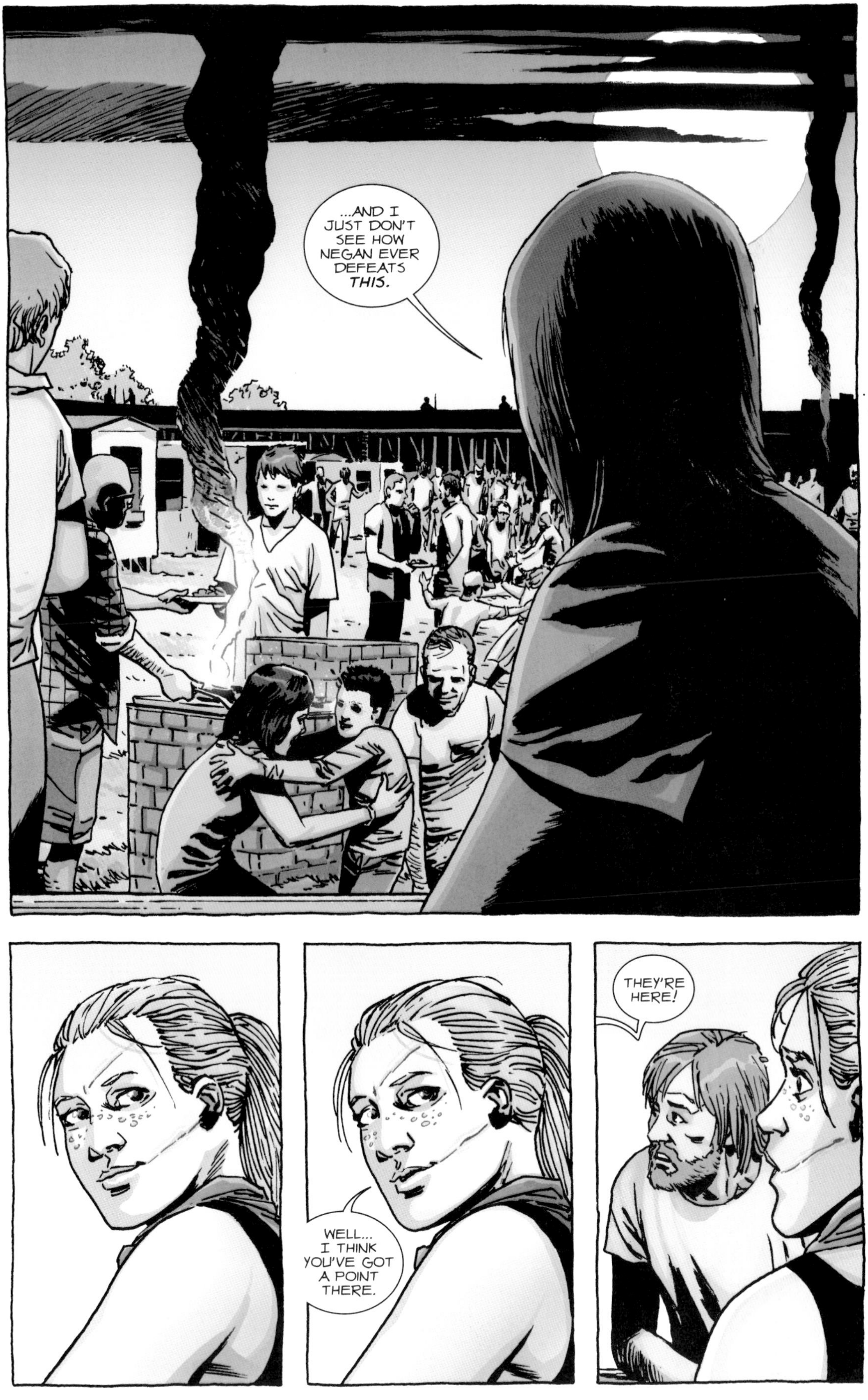
...AND I JUST DON'T SEE HOW NEGAN EVER DEFEATS THIS.
WELL... I THINK YOU'VE GOT A POINT THERE.
THEY'RE HERE!

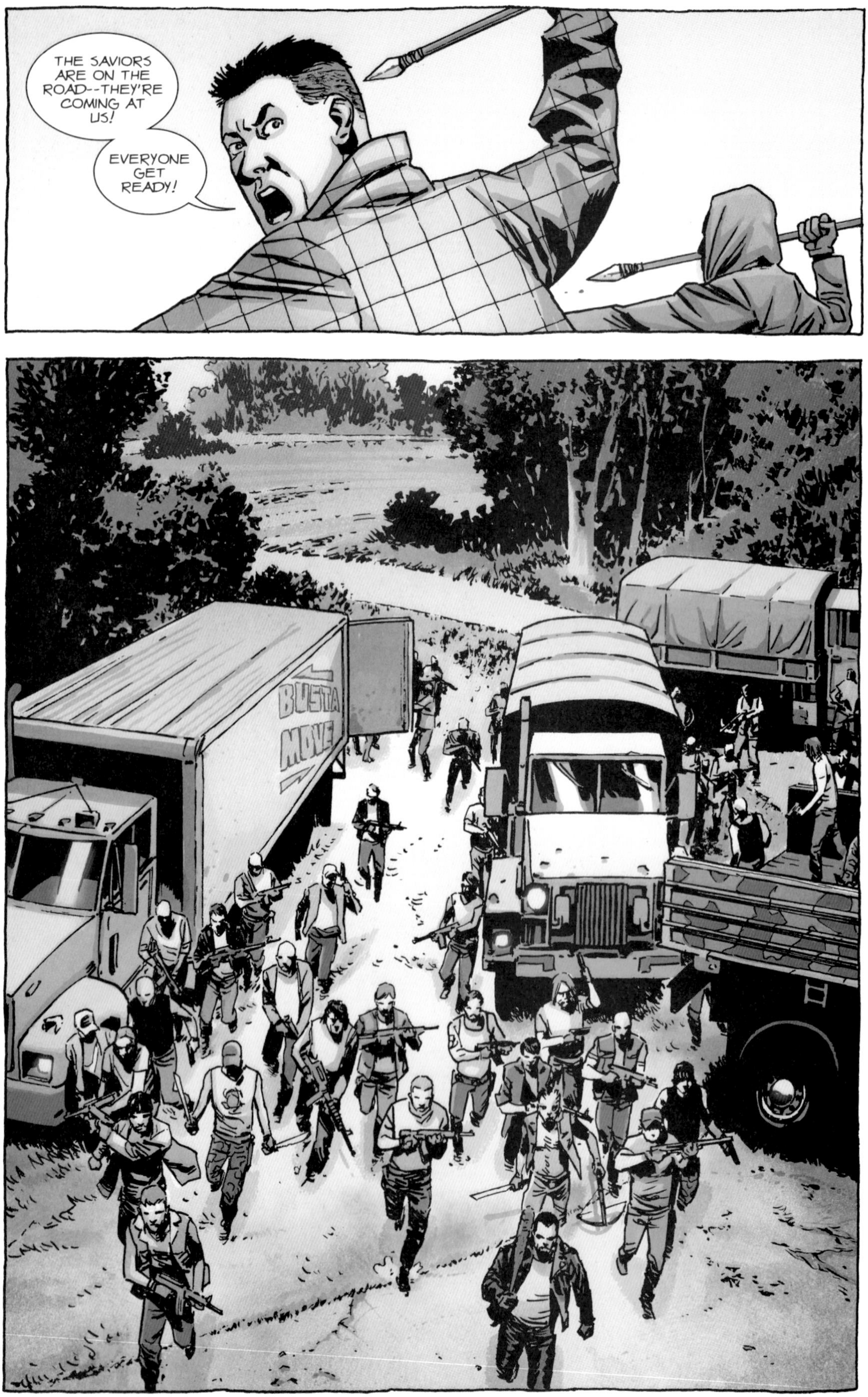
THE SAVIORS ARE ON THE ROAD--THEY'RE COMING AT US!
EVERYONE GET READY!
BUSTA MOVE

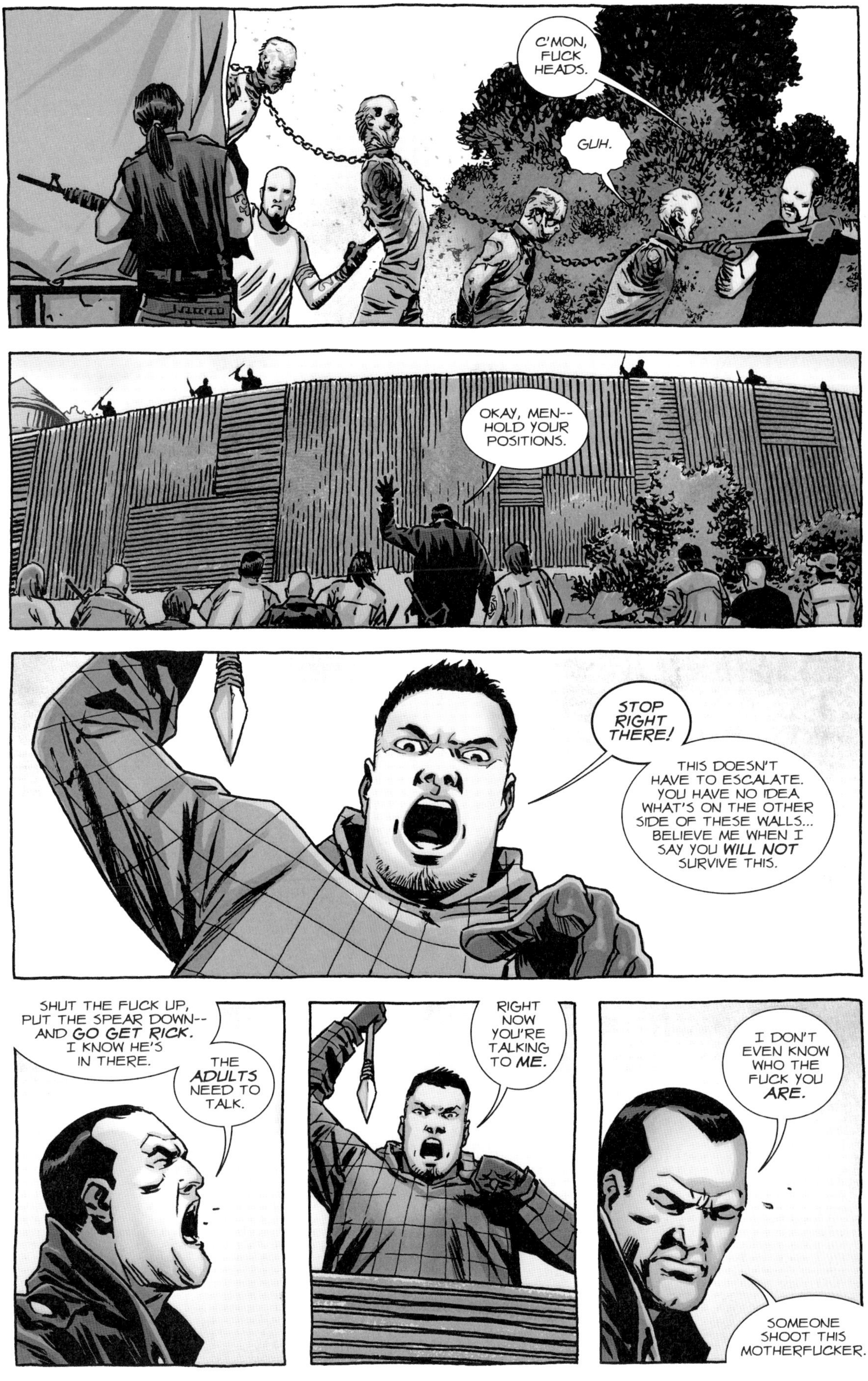
C'MON, FUCK HEADS.
GUH.
OKAY, MEN-- HOLD YOUR POSITIONS.
STOP RIGHT THERE!
THIS DOESN'T HAVE TO ESCALATE. YOU HAVE NO IDEA WHAT'S ON THE OTHER SIDE OF THESE WALLS... BELIEVE ME WHEN I SAY YOU WILL NOT SURVIVE THIS.
SHUT THE FUCK UP, PUT THE SPEAR DOWN-- AND GO GET RICK. I KNOW HE'S IN THERE.
THE ADULTS NEED TO TALK.
RIGHT NOW YOU'RE TALKING TO ME.
I DON'T EVEN KNOW WHO THE FUCK YOU ARE.
SOMEONE SHOOT THIS MOTHERFUCKER.

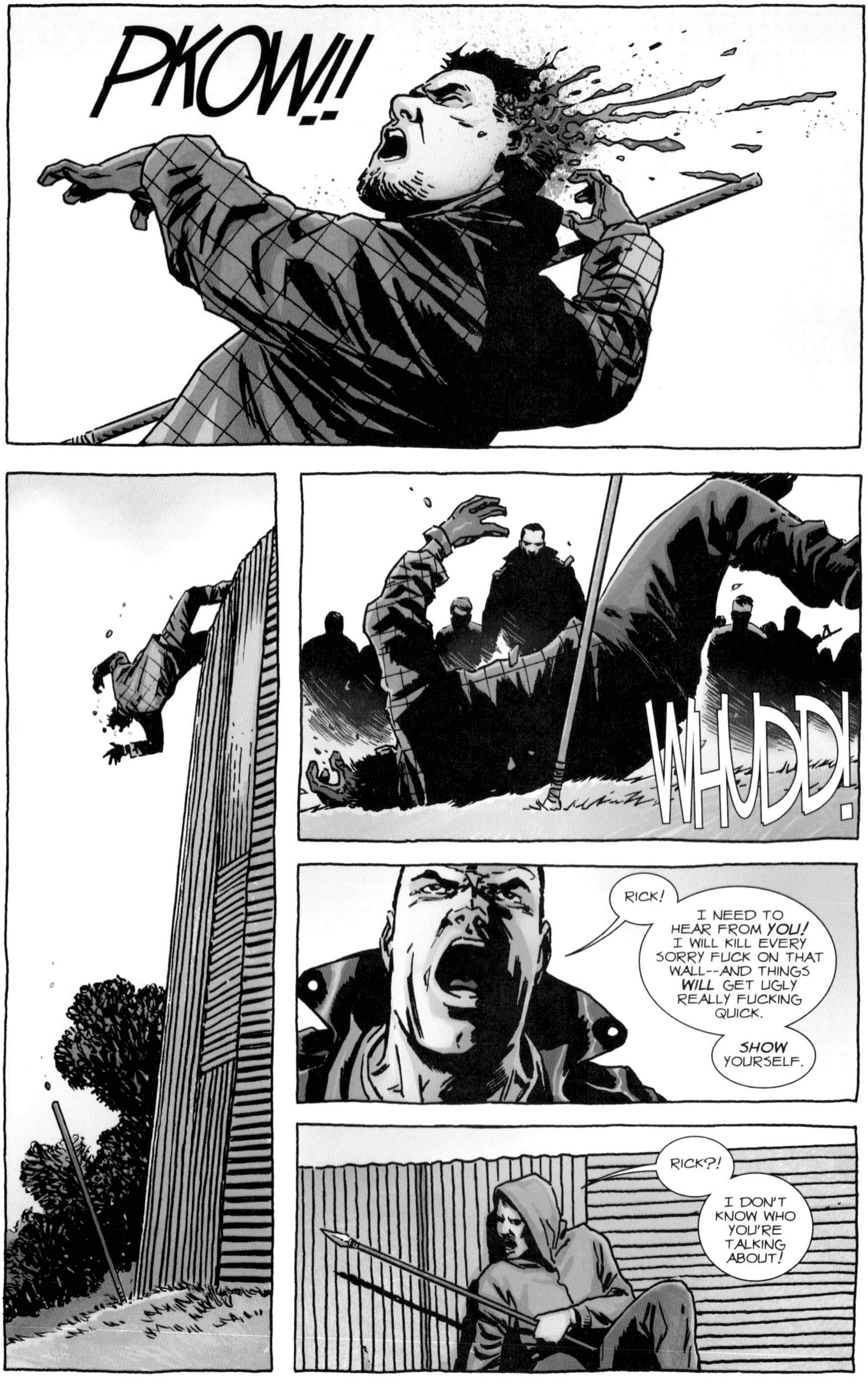
PKOW!!
WHUDD!
RICK!
I NEED TO HEAR FROM YOU! I WILL KILL EVERY SORRY FUCK ON THAT WALL--AND THINGS WILL GET UGLY REALLY FUCKING QUICK.
SHOW YOURSELF.
RICK?!
I DON'T KNOW WHO YOU'RE TALKING ABOUT!

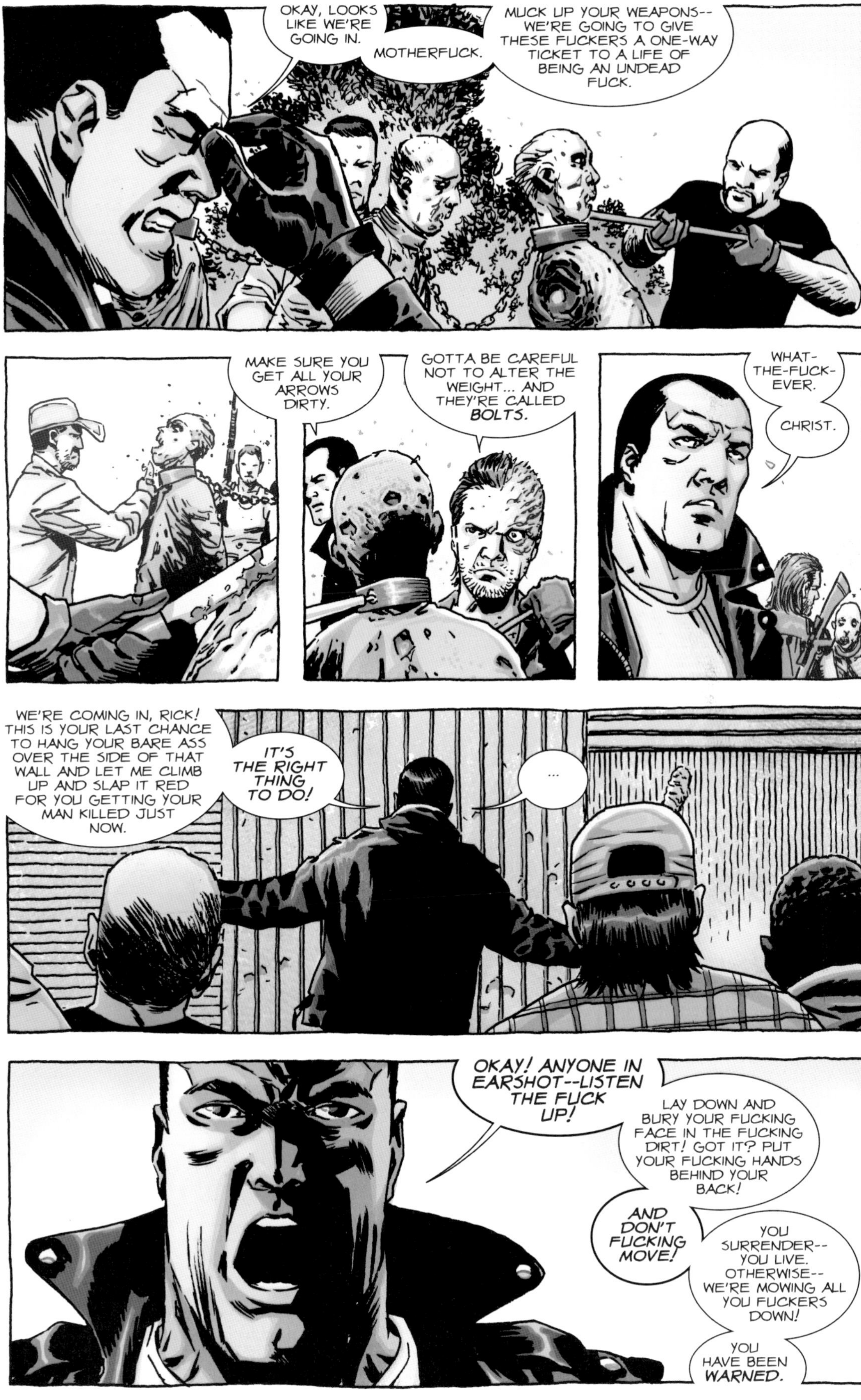
OKAY, LOOKS LIKE WE'RE GOING IN.
MOTHERFUCK.
MUCK UP YOUR WEAPONS-- WE'RE GOING TO GIVE THESE FUCKERS A ONE-WAY TICKET TO A LIFE OF BEING AN UNDEAD FUCK.
MAKE SURE YOU GET ALL YOUR ARROWS DIRTY.
GOTTA BE CAREFUL NOT TO ALTER THE WEIGHT... AND THEY'RE CALLED BOLTS.
WHAT-THE-FUCK-EVER.
CHRIST.
WE'RE COMING IN, RICK! THIS IS YOUR LAST CHANCE TO HANG YOUR BARE ASS OVER THE SIDE OF THAT WALL AND LET ME CLIMB UP AND SLAP IT RED FOR YOU GETTING YOUR MAN KILLED JUST NOW.
IT'S THE RIGHT THING TO DO!
...
OKAY! ANYONE IN EARSHOT--LISTEN THE FUCK UP!
LAY DOWN AND BURY YOUR FUCKING FACE IN THE FUCKING DIRT! GOT IT? PUT YOUR FUCKING HANDS BEHIND YOUR BACK!
AND DON'T FUCKING MOVE!
YOU SURRENDER-- YOU LIVE. OTHERWISE-- WE'RE MOWING ALL YOU FUCKERS DOWN!
YOU HAVE BEEN WARNED.

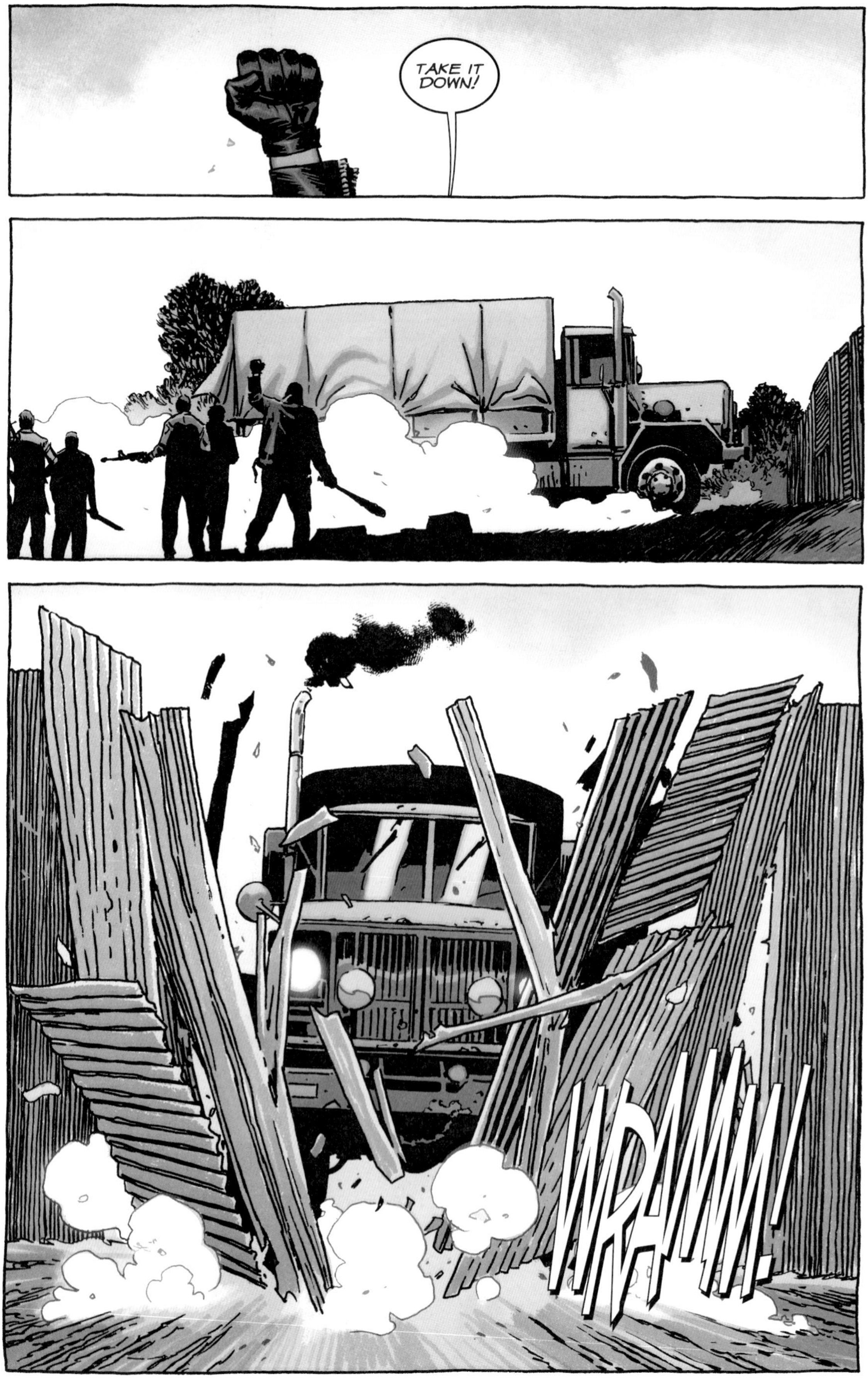
TAKE IT DOWN!
WRAMM!

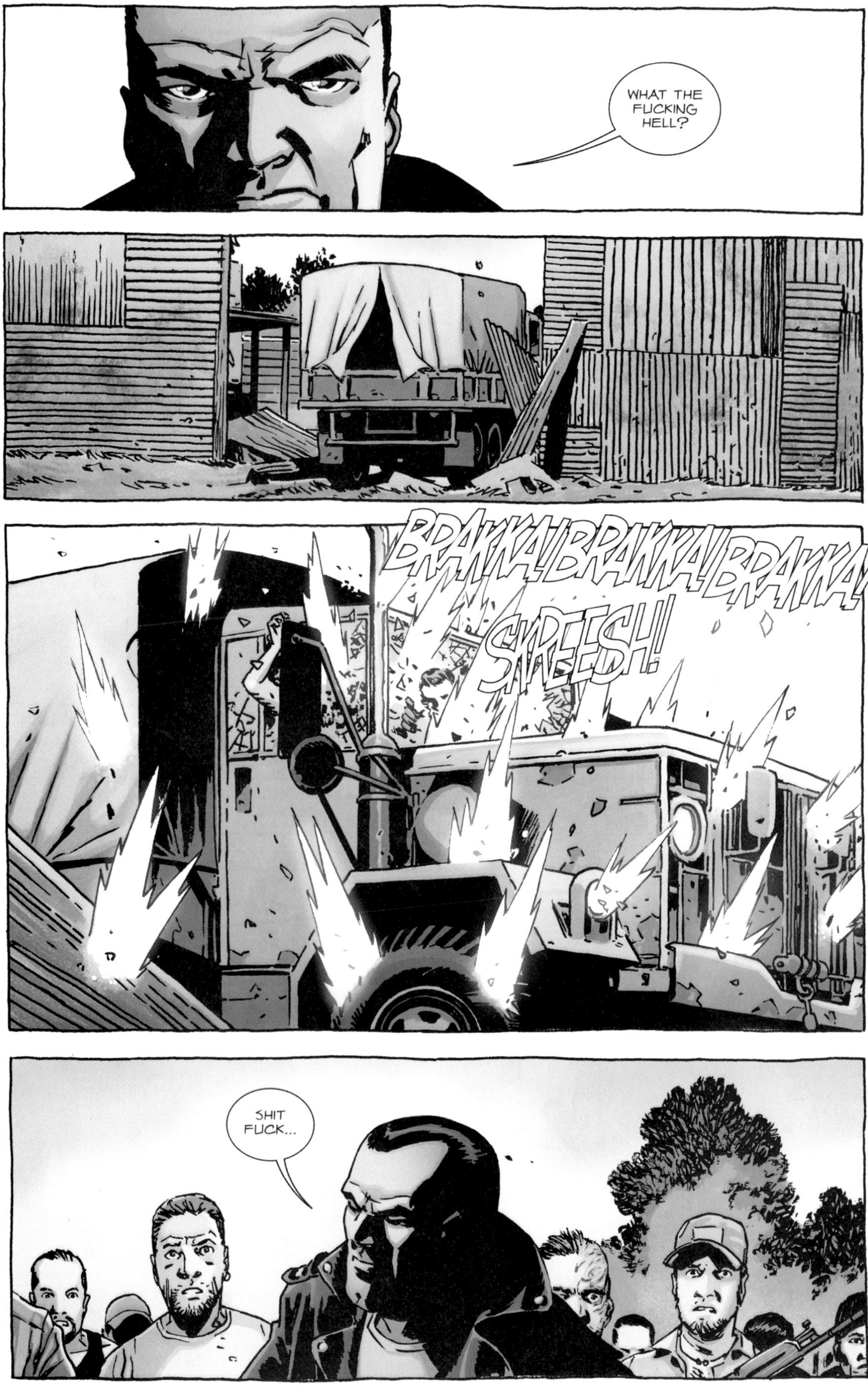
WHAT THE FUCKING HELL?
BRAKKA! BRAKKA! BRAKKA!
SKREEESH!
SHIT FUCK...

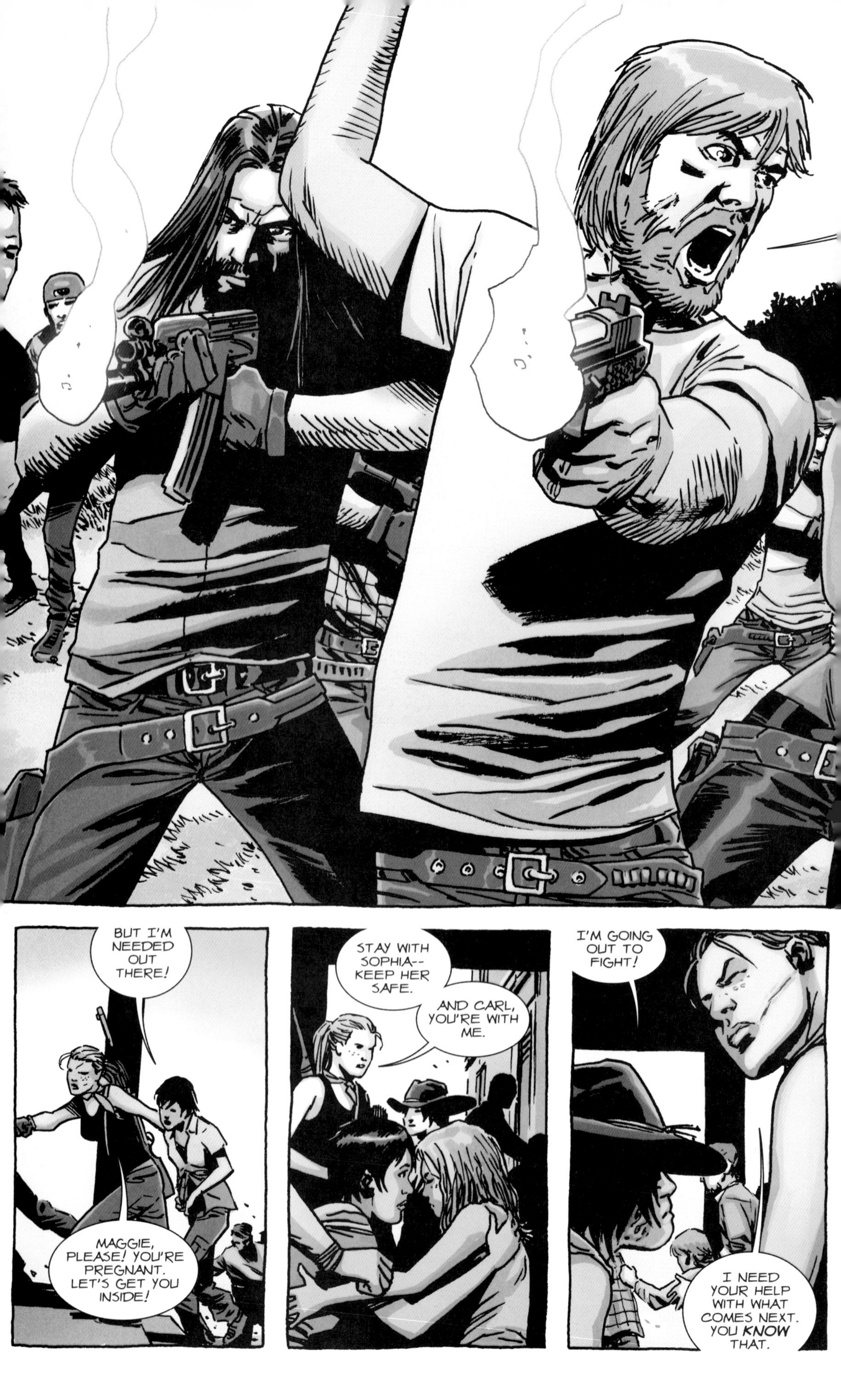
BUT I'M NEEDED OUT THERE!
MAGGIE, PLEASE! YOU'RE PREGNANT. LET'S GET YOU INSIDE!
STAY WITH SOPHIA-- KEEP HER SAFE.
AND CARL, YOU'RE WITH ME.
I'M GOING OUT TO FIGHT!
I NEED YOUR HELP WITH WHAT COMES NEXT. YOU KNOW THAT.

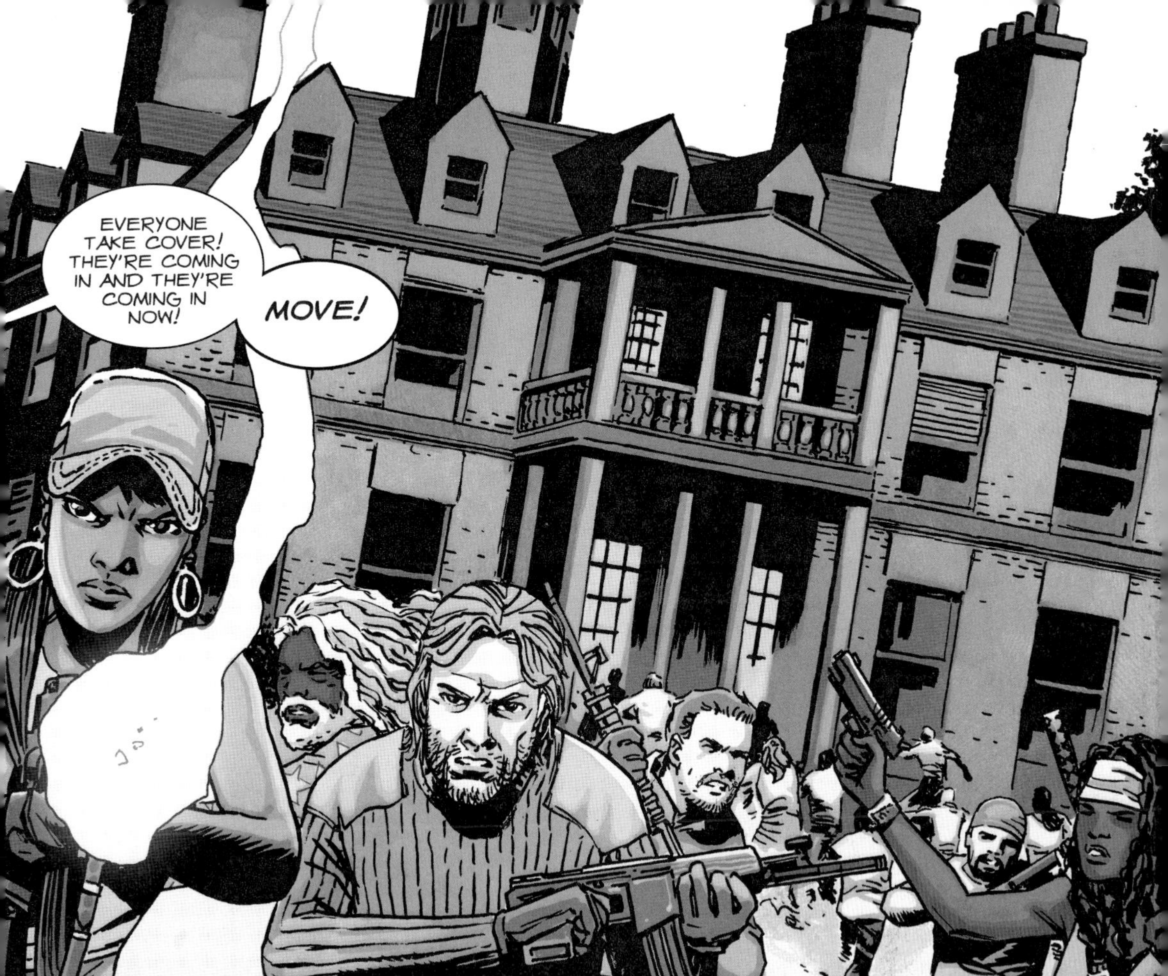
EVERYONE TAKE COVER! THEY'RE COMING IN AND THEY'RE COMING IN NOW!
MOVE!

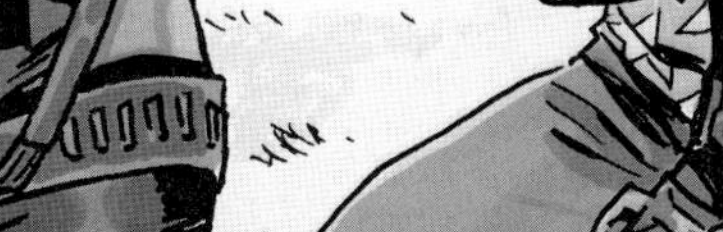
THIS ISN'T GOING TO GO DOWN LIKE LAST TIME. IT'S JUST NOT.
YOU'RE DAMN RIGHT.

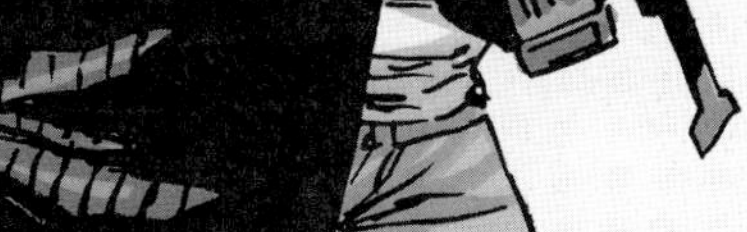
WHAT ARE THEY WAITING ON?!
COME AND GET US, YOU COWARDS!

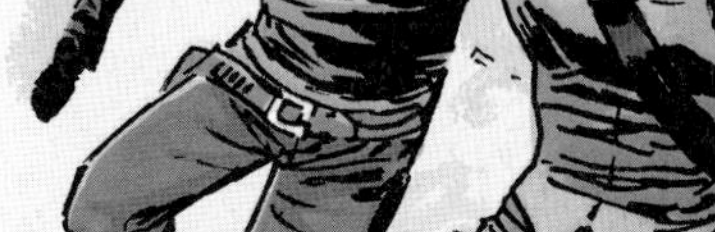
AARON, TAKE COVER!!

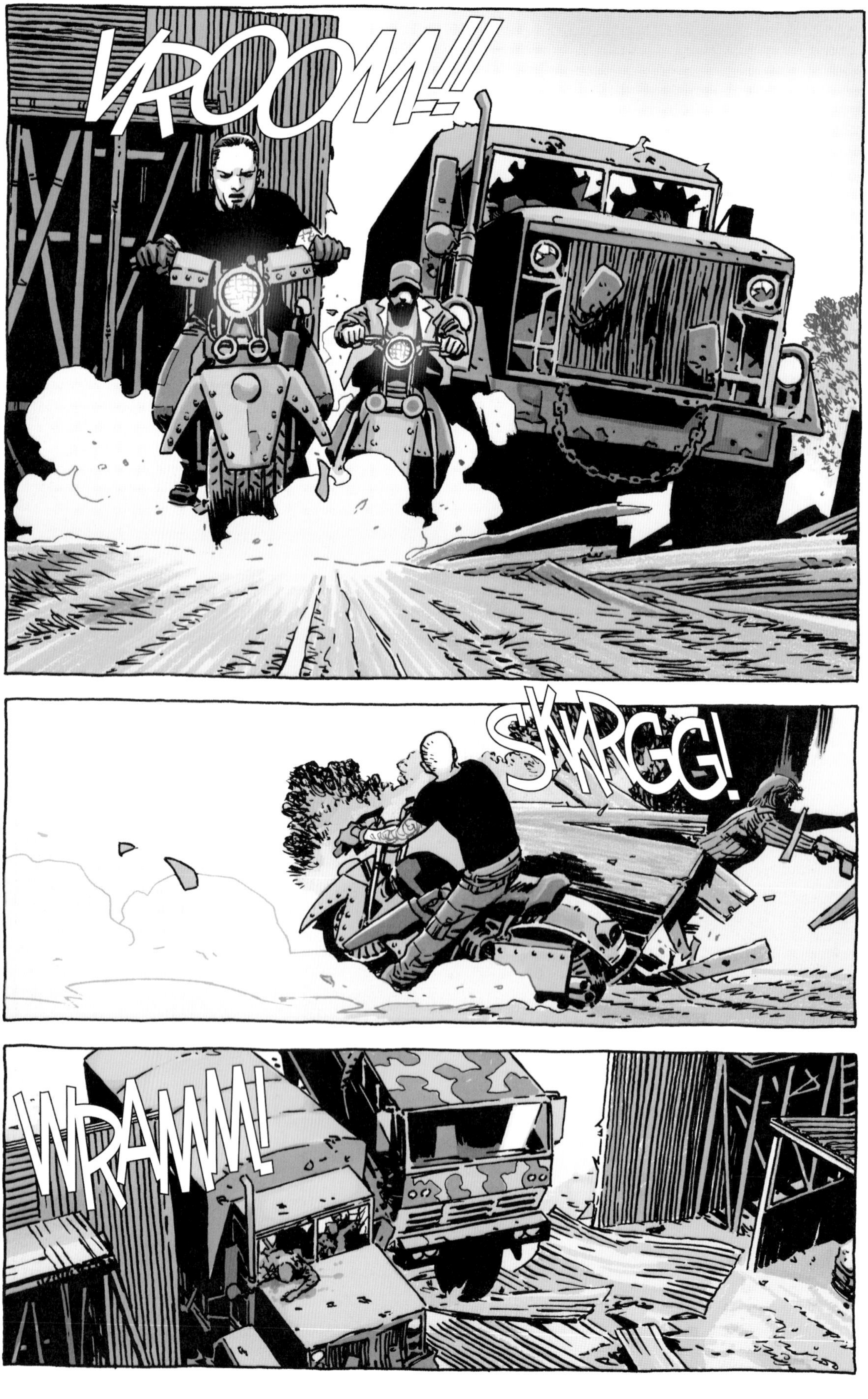
VROOM!!
SKRGG!
WRAMM!

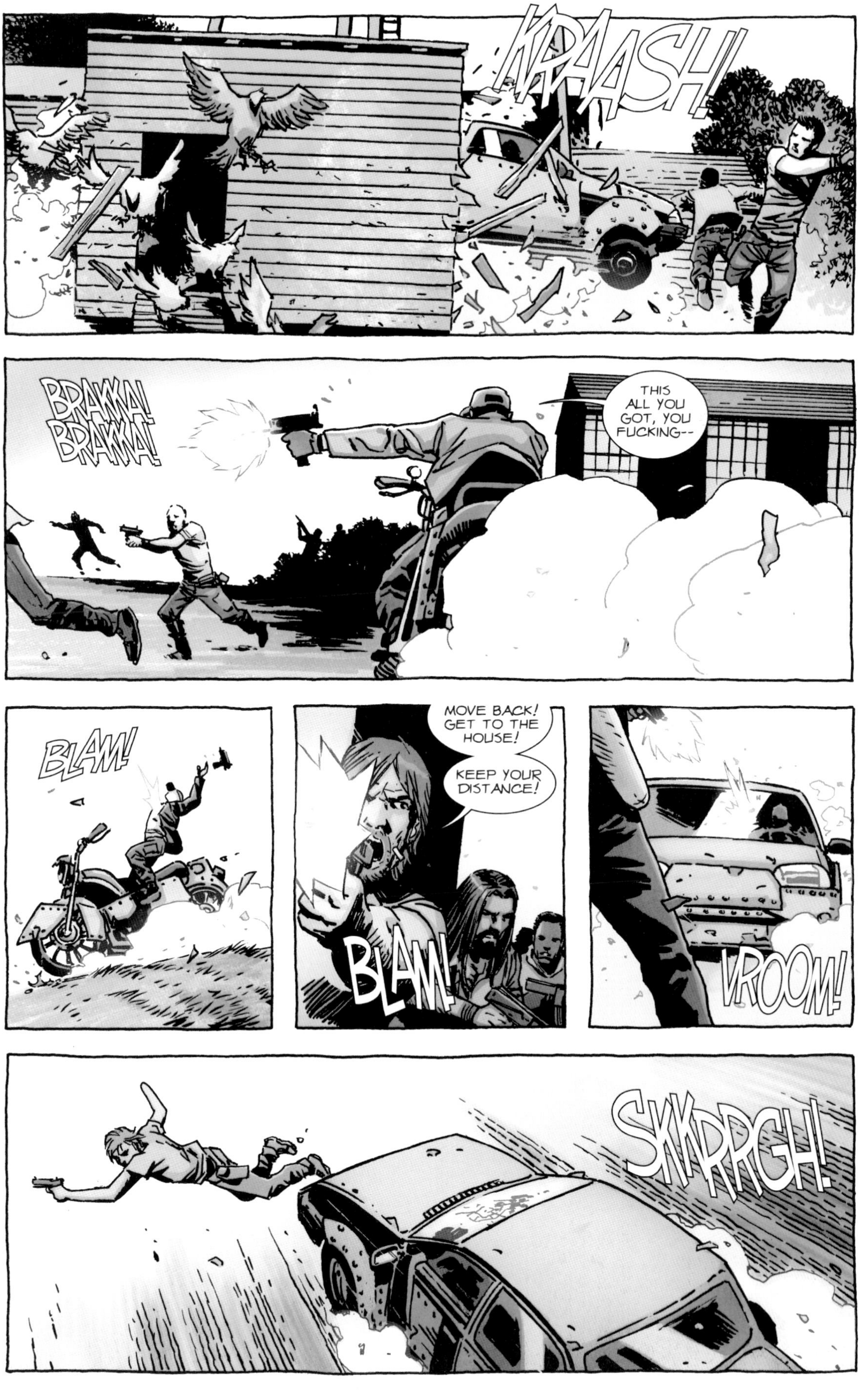
KRAASH!
BRAKKA! BRAKKA!
THIS ALL YOU GOT, YOU FUCKING--
BLAM!
MOVE BACK! GET TO THE HOUSE!
KEEP YOUR DISTANCE!
BLAM!
VROOM!
SKKRRGH!

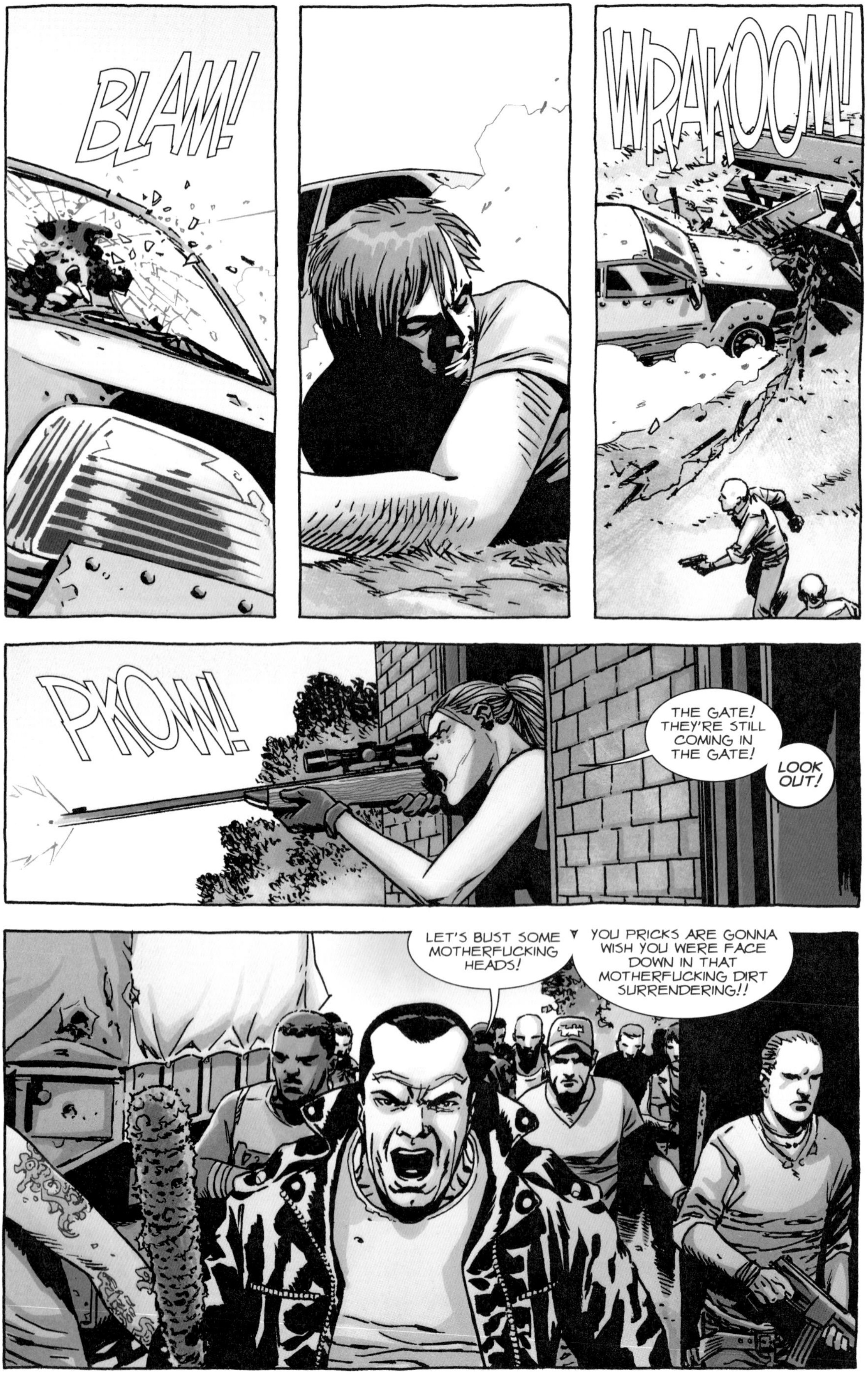
BLAM!
WRAKOOM!
PKOW!
THE GATE! THEY'RE STILL COMING IN THE GATE!
LOOK OUT!
LET'S BUST SOME MOTHERFUCKING HEADS!
YOU PRICKS ARE GONNA WISH YOU WERE FACE DOWN IN THAT MOTHERFUCKING DIRT SURRENDERING!!

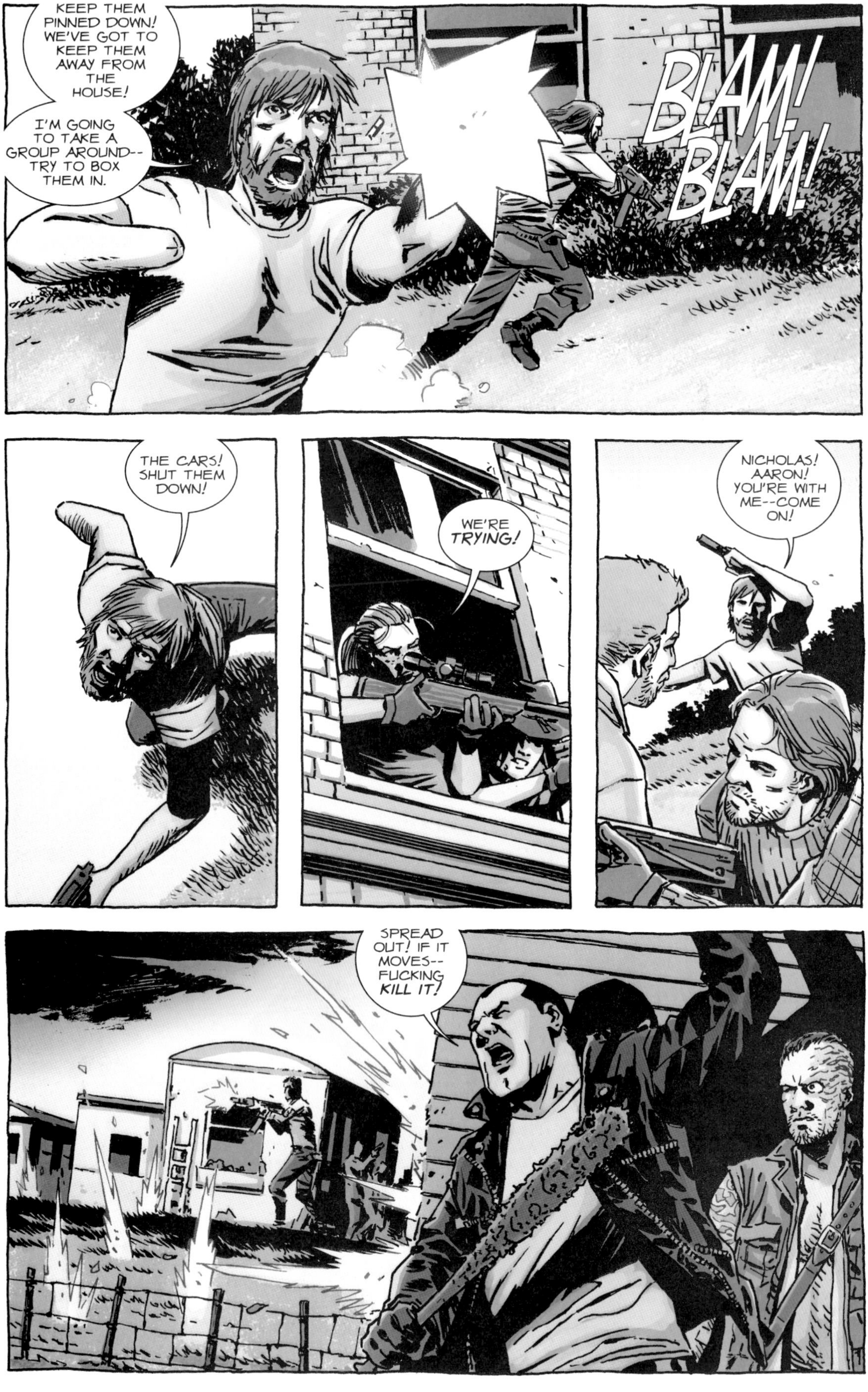
KEEP THEM PINNED DOWN! WE'VE GOT TO KEEP THEM AWAY FROM THE HOUSE!
I'M GOING TO TAKE A GROUP AROUND-- TRY TO BOX THEM IN.
BLAM! BLAM!
THE CARS! SHUT THEM DOWN!
WE'RE TRYING!
NICHOLAS! AARON! YOU'RE WITH ME--COME ON!
SPREAD OUT! IF IT MOVES-- FUCKING KILL IT!

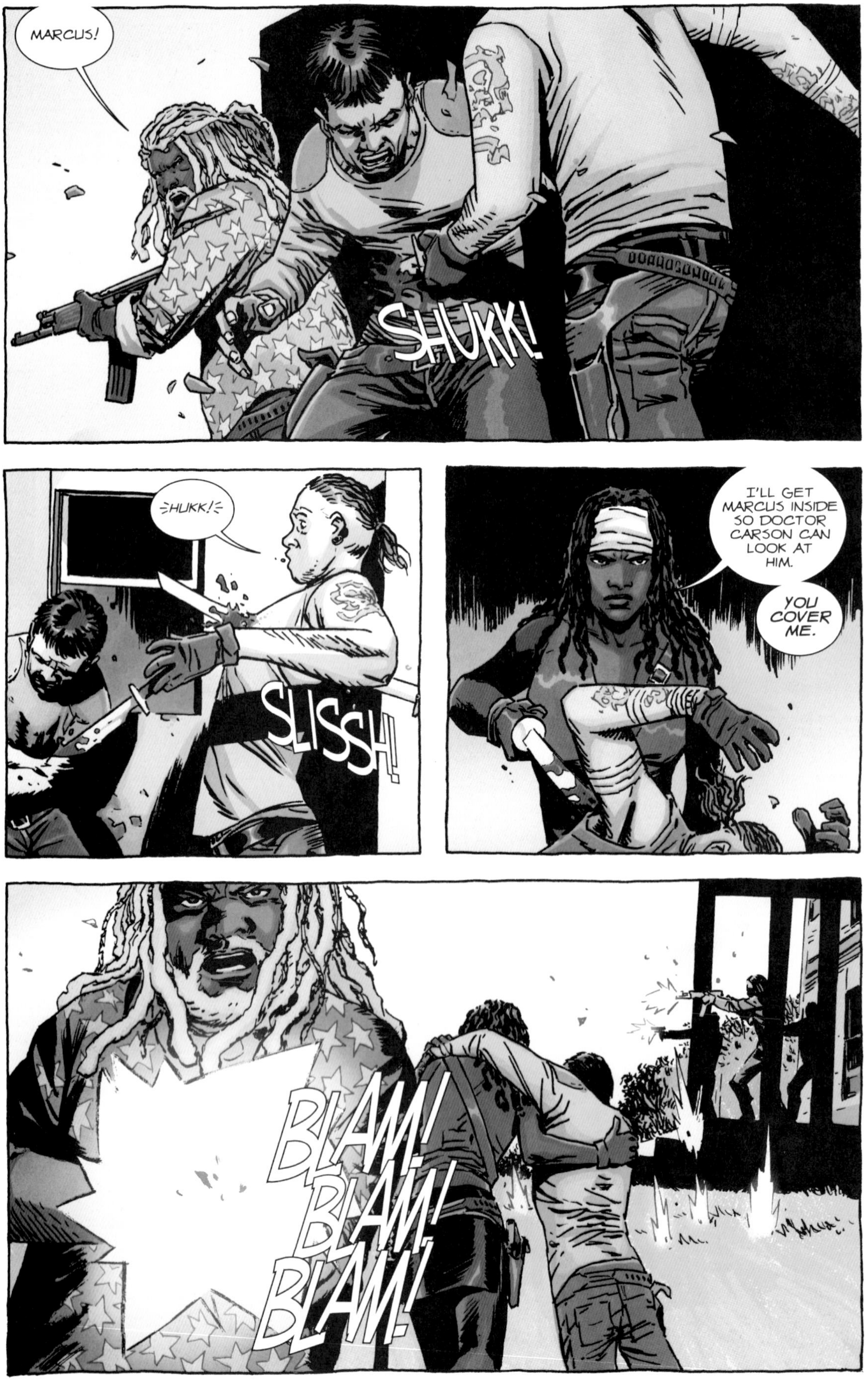
MARCUS!
SHUKK!
=HUKK!=
SLISSH!
I'LL GET MARCUS INSIDE SO DOCTOR CARSON CAN LOOK AT HIM.
YOU COVER ME.
BLAM! BLAM! BLAM!

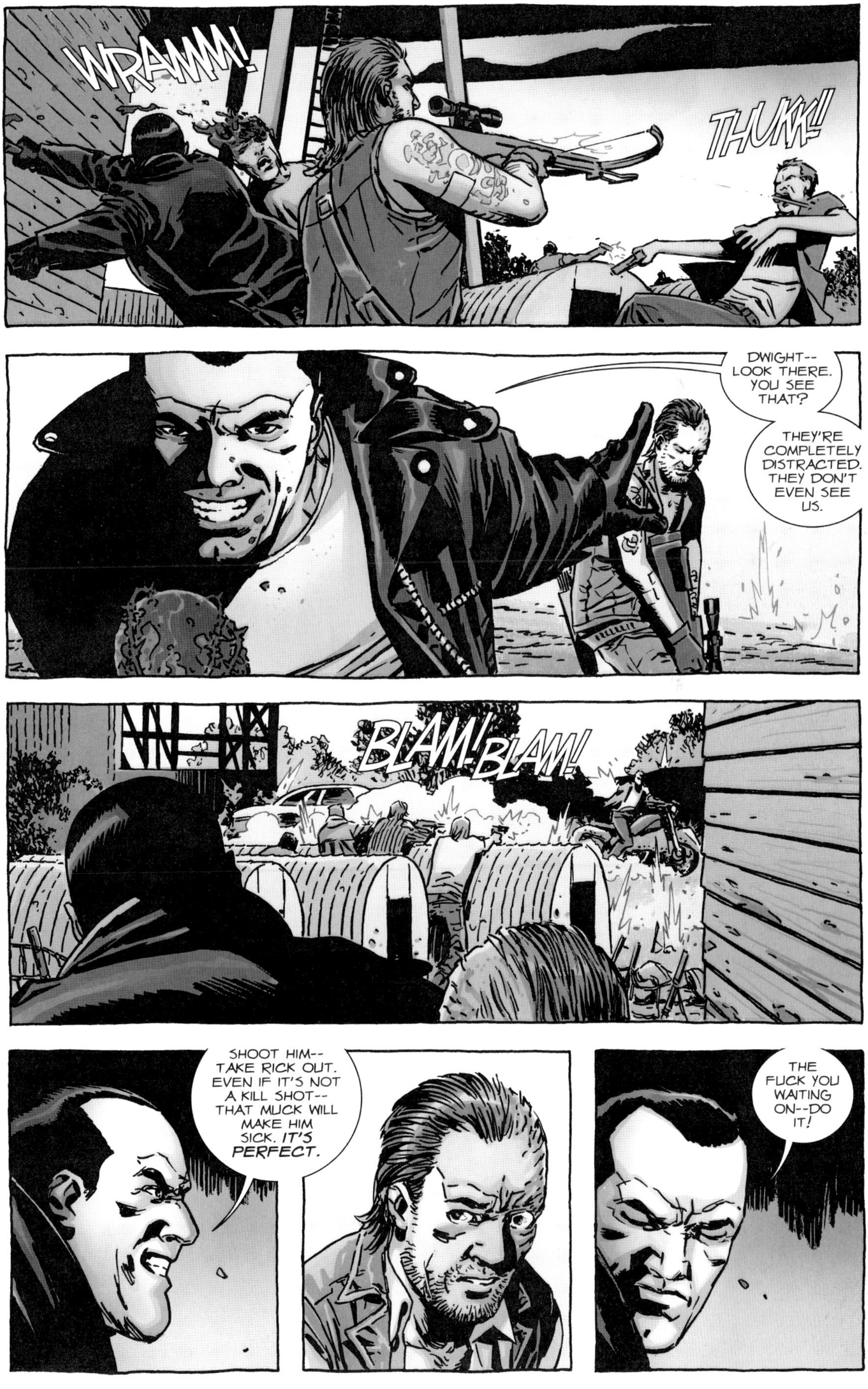
WRAMM!
THUKK!!
DWIGHT-- LOOK THERE. YOU SEE THAT?
THEY'RE COMPLETELY DISTRACTED. THEY DON'T EVEN SEE US.
BLAM! BLAM!
SHOOT HIM-- TAKE RICK OUT. EVEN IF IT'S NOT A KILL SHOT-- THAT MUCK WILL MAKE HIM SICK. *IT'S PERFECT.*
THE FUCK YOU WAITING ON--DO IT!

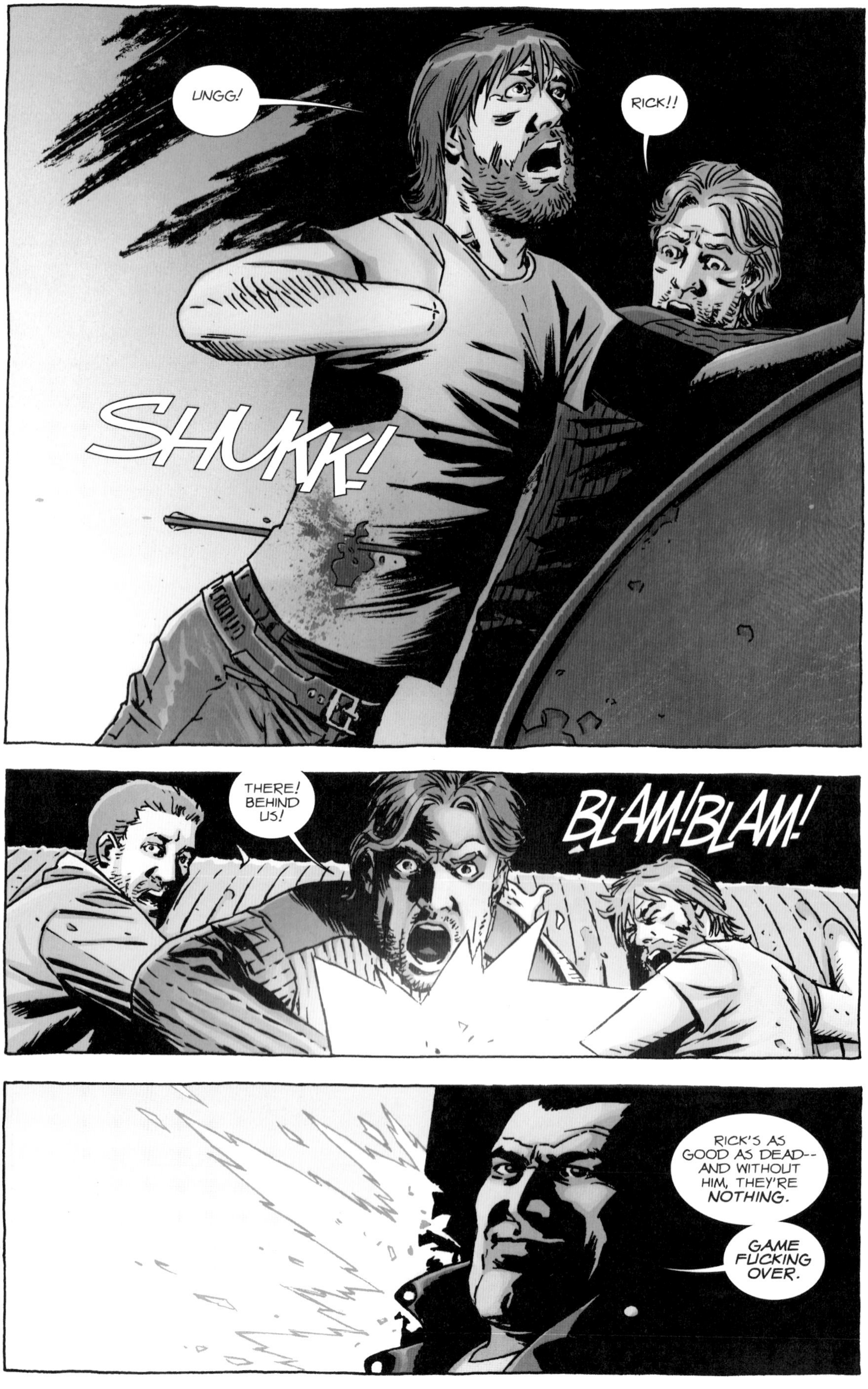
UNGG!
RICK!!
SHUKK!
THERE! BEHIND US!
BLAM! BLAM!
RICK'S AS GOOD AS DEAD-- AND WITHOUT HIM, THEY'RE NOTHING.
GAME FUCKING OVER.

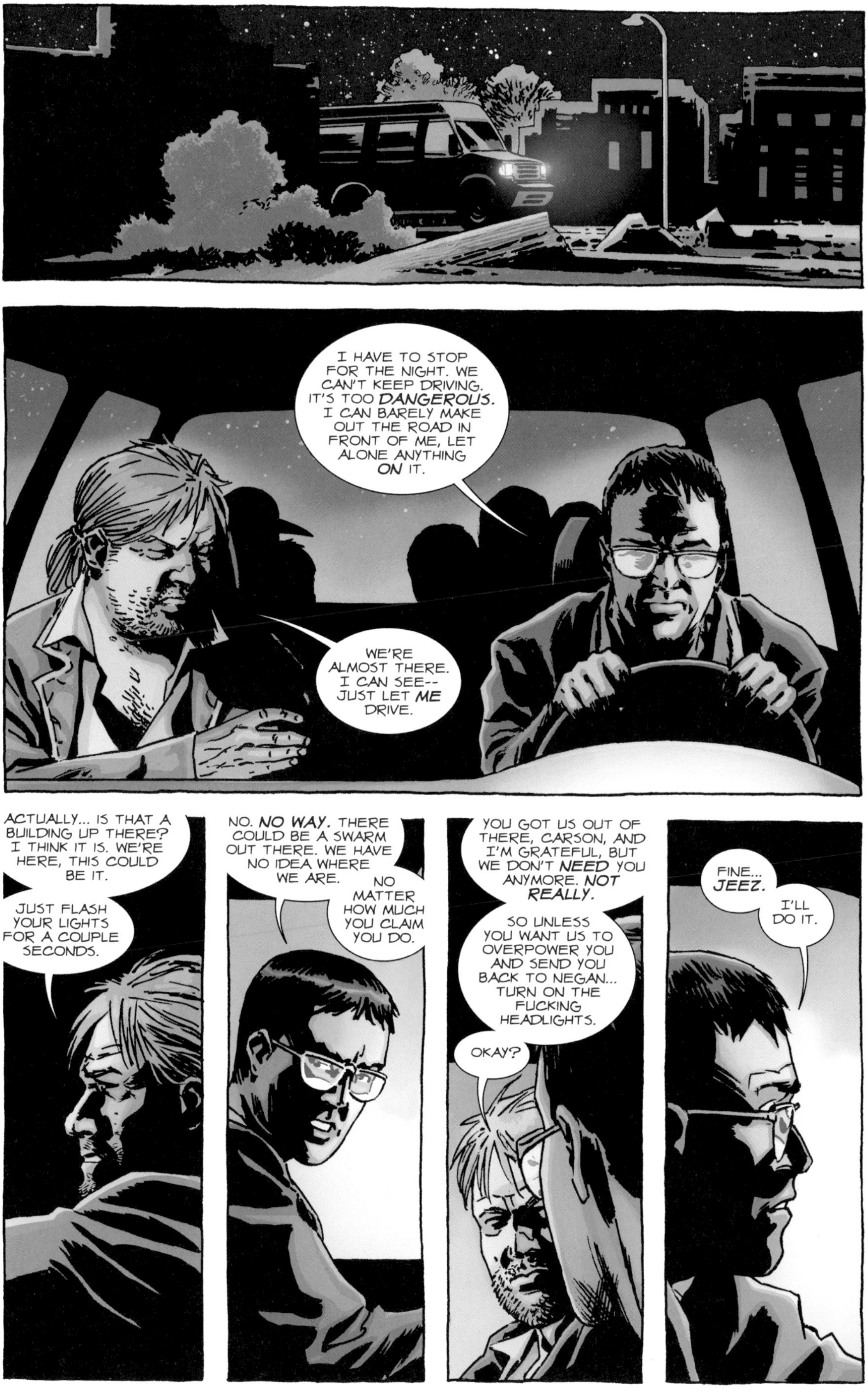

I HAVE TO STOP FOR THE NIGHT. WE CAN'T KEEP DRIVING. IT'S TOO DANGEROUS. I CAN BARELY MAKE OUT THE ROAD IN FRONT OF ME, LET ALONE ANYTHING ON IT.
WE'RE ALMOST THERE. I CAN SEE-- JUST LET ME DRIVE.
ACTUALLY... IS THAT A BUILDING UP THERE? I THINK IT IS. WE'RE HERE, THIS COULD BE IT.
JUST FLASH YOUR LIGHTS FOR A COUPLE SECONDS.
NO. NO WAY. THERE COULD BE A SWARM OUT THERE. WE HAVE NO IDEA WHERE WE ARE.
NO MATTER HOW MUCH YOU CLAIM YOU DO.
YOU GOT US OUT OF THERE, CARSON, AND I'M GRATEFUL, BUT WE DON'T NEED YOU ANYMORE. NOT REALLY.
SO UNLESS YOU WANT US TO OVERPOWER YOU AND SEND YOU BACK TO NEGAN... TURN ON THE FUCKING HEADLIGHTS.
OKAY?
FINE... JEEZ.
I'LL DO IT.

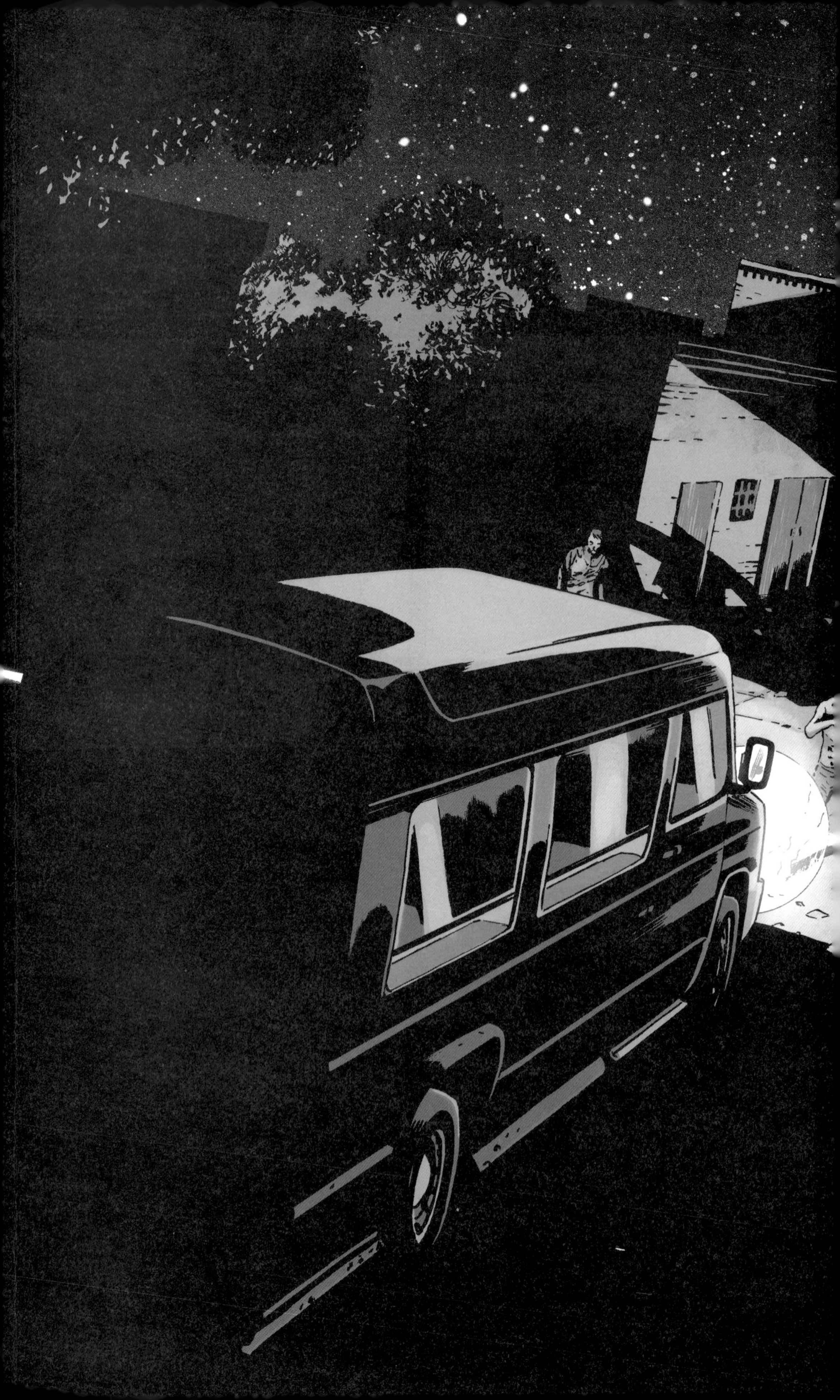

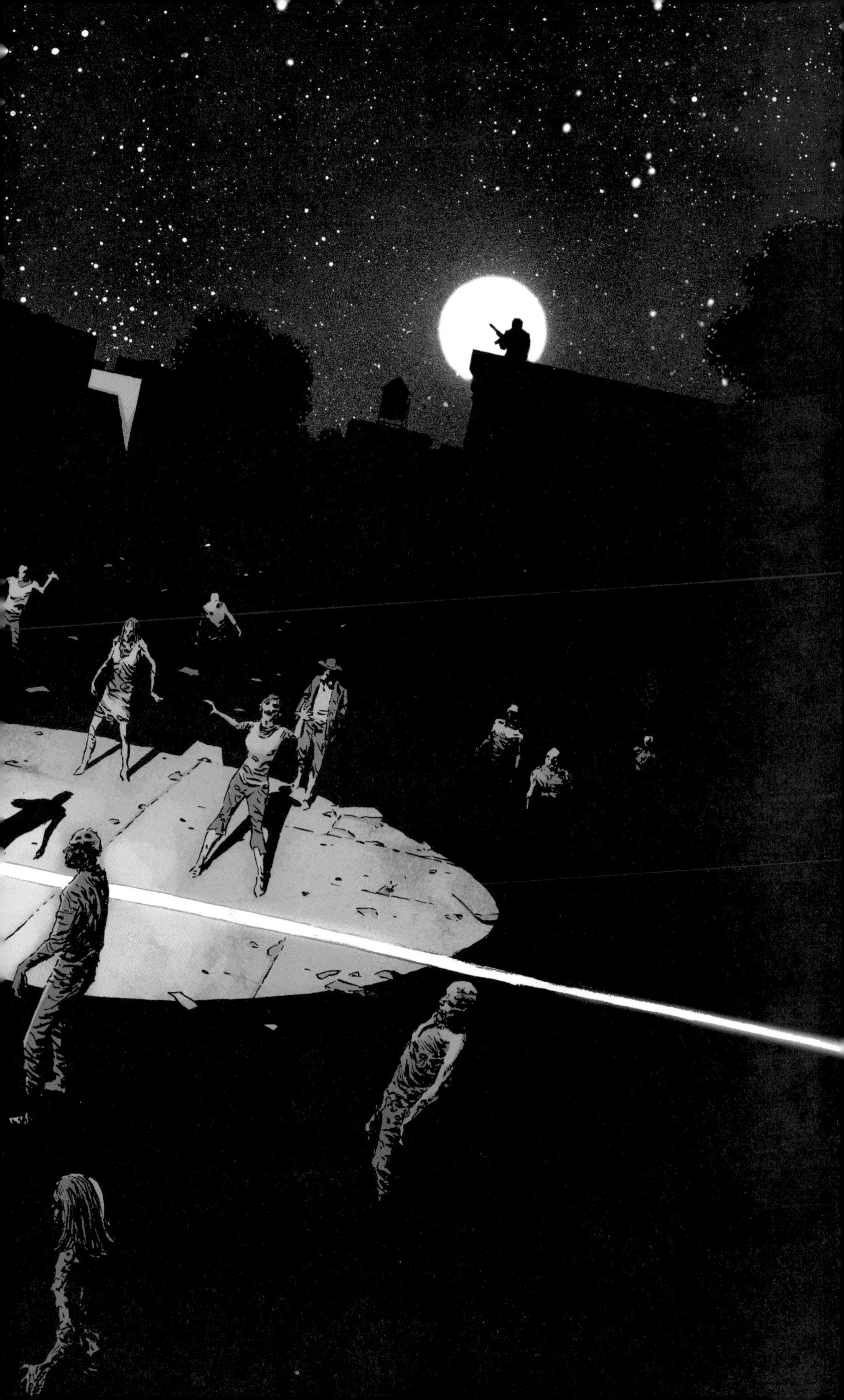

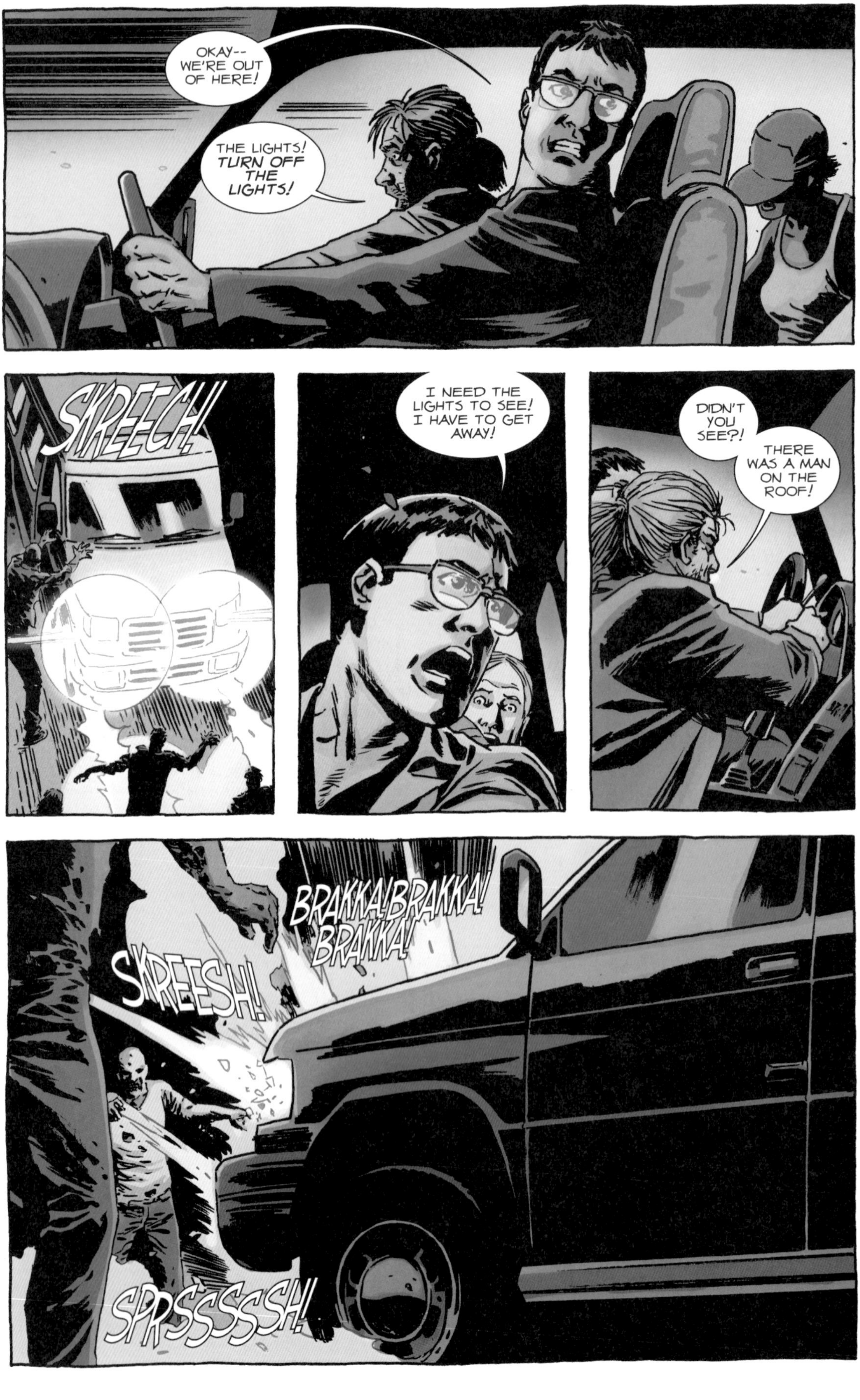
OKAY-- WE'RE OUT OF HERE!
THE LIGHTS! TURN OFF THE LIGHTS!
SKREECH!
I NEED THE LIGHTS TO SEE! I HAVE TO GET AWAY!
DIDN'T YOU SEE?!
THERE WAS A MAN ON THE ROOF!
BRAKKA! BRAKKA! BRAKKA!
SKREESH!
SPRSSSSSH!

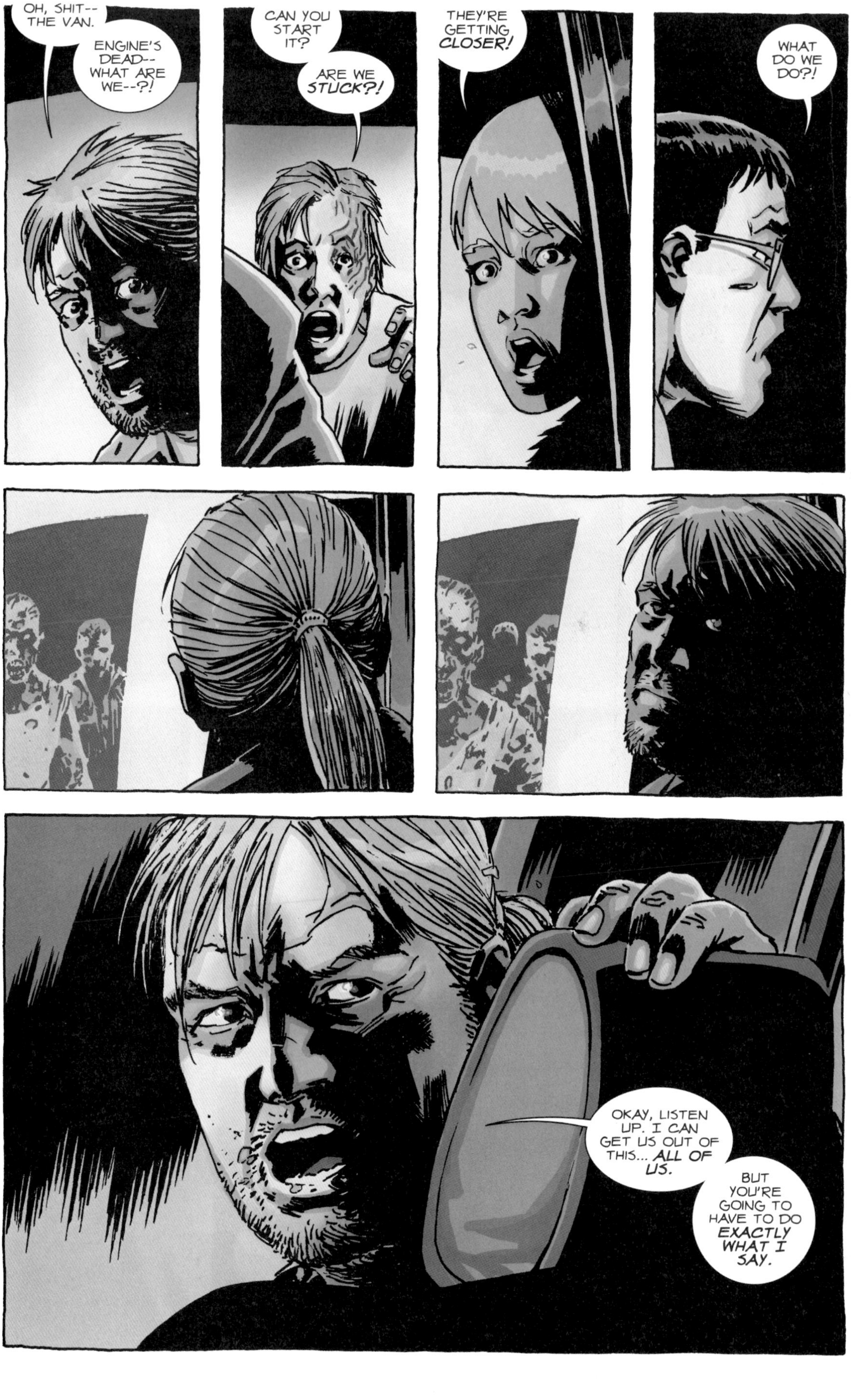

OH, SHIT-- THE VAN.
ENGINE'S DEAD-- WHAT ARE WE--?!
CAN YOU START IT?
ARE WE STUCK?!
THEY'RE GETTING CLOSER!
WHAT DO WE DO?!
OKAY, LISTEN UP. I CAN GET US OUT OF THIS... ALL OF US.
BUT YOU'RE GOING TO HAVE TO DO EXACTLY WHAT I SAY.

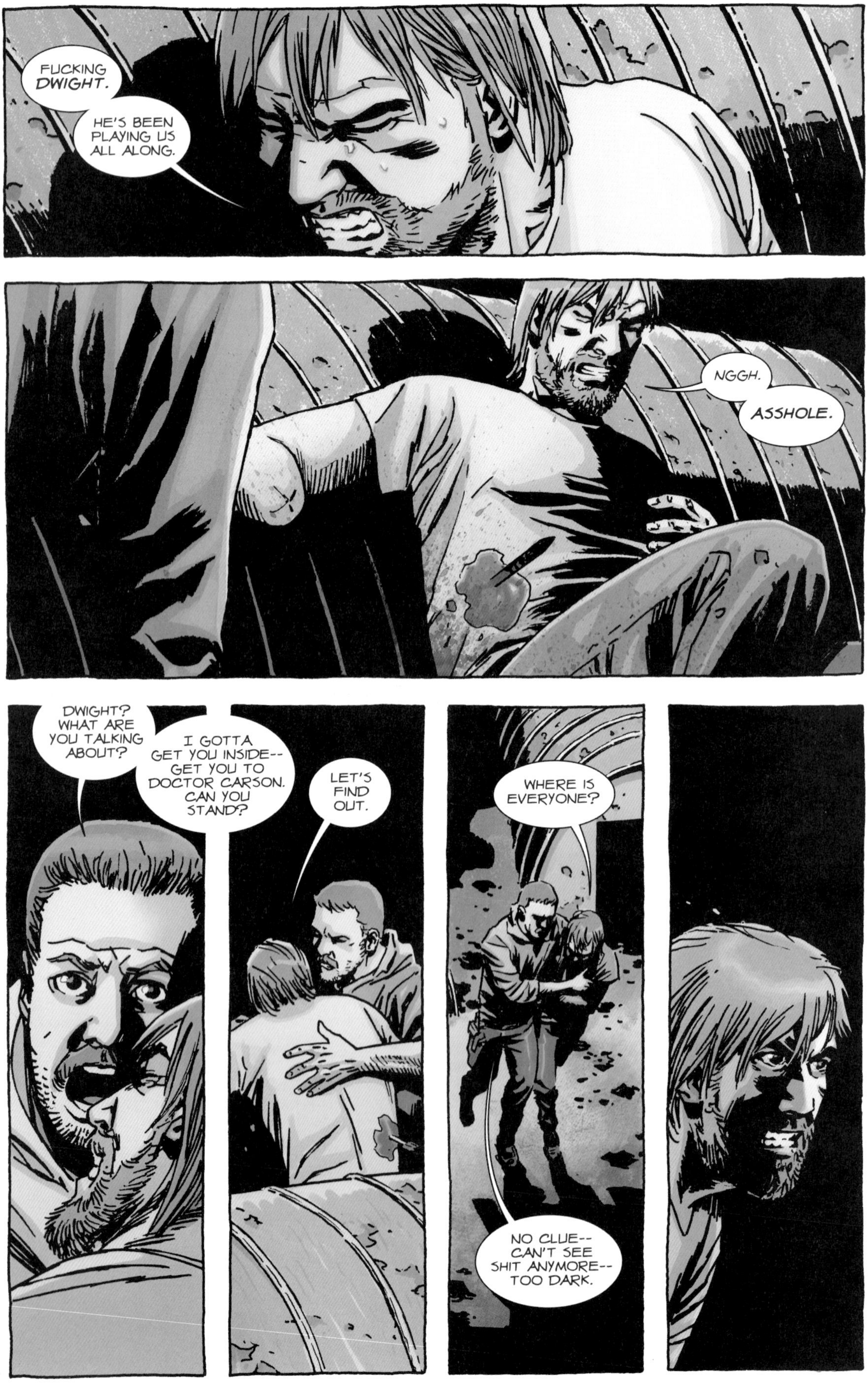
FUCKING DWIGHT.
HE'S BEEN PLAYING US ALL ALONG.
NGGH.
ASSHOLE.
DWIGHT? WHAT ARE YOU TALKING ABOUT?
I GOTTA GET YOU INSIDE-- GET YOU TO DOCTOR CARSON. CAN YOU STAND?
LET'S FIND OUT.
WHERE IS EVERYONE?
NO CLUE-- CAN'T SEE SHIT ANYMORE-- TOO DARK.

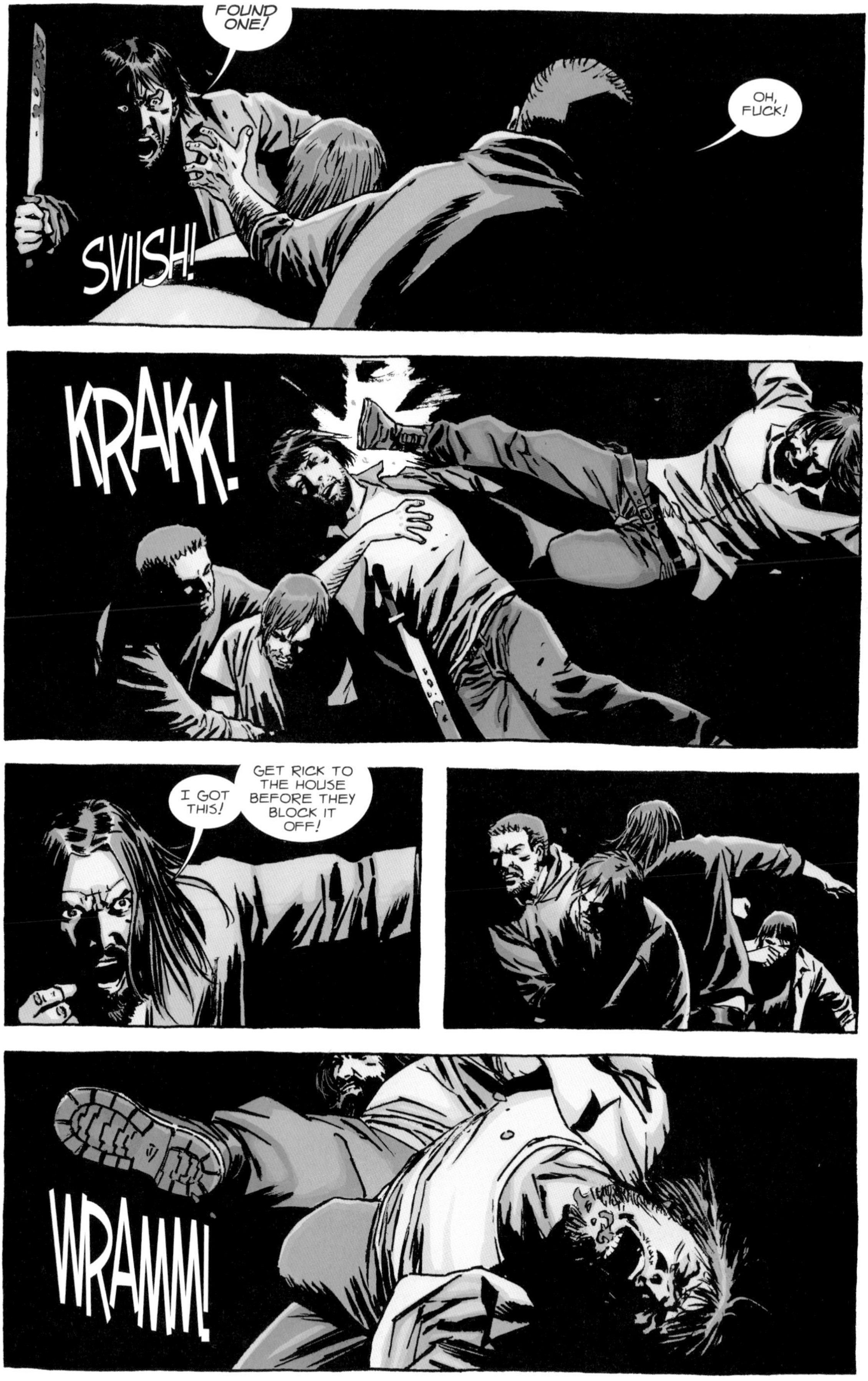
FOUND ONE!
OH, FUCK!
SVIISH!
KRAKK!
I GOT THIS!
GET RICK TO THE HOUSE BEFORE THEY BLOCK IT OFF!
WRAMM!

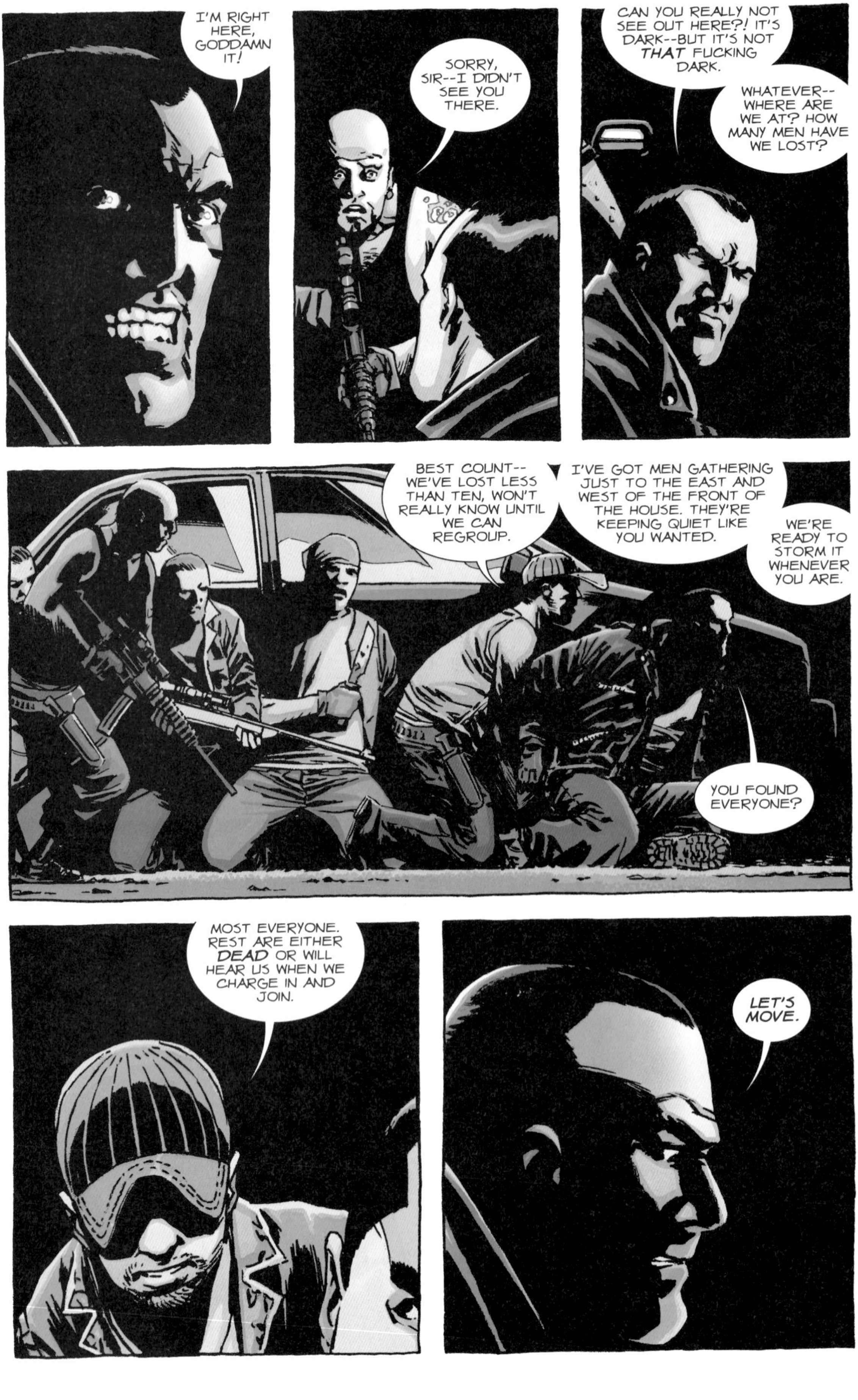
I'M RIGHT HERE, GODDAMN IT!
SORRY, SIR--I DIDN'T SEE YOU THERE.
CAN YOU REALLY NOT SEE OUT HERE?! IT'S DARK--BUT IT'S NOT THAT FUCKING DARK.
WHATEVER-- WHERE ARE WE AT? HOW MANY MEN HAVE WE LOST?
BEST COUNT-- WE'VE LOST LESS THAN TEN, WON'T REALLY KNOW UNTIL WE CAN REGROUP.
I'VE GOT MEN GATHERING JUST TO THE EAST AND WEST OF THE FRONT OF THE HOUSE. THEY'RE KEEPING QUIET LIKE YOU WANTED.
WE'RE READY TO STORM IT WHENEVER YOU ARE.
YOU FOUND EVERYONE?
MOST EVERYONE. REST ARE EITHER DEAD OR WILL HEAR US WHEN WE CHARGE IN AND JOIN.
LET'S MOVE.

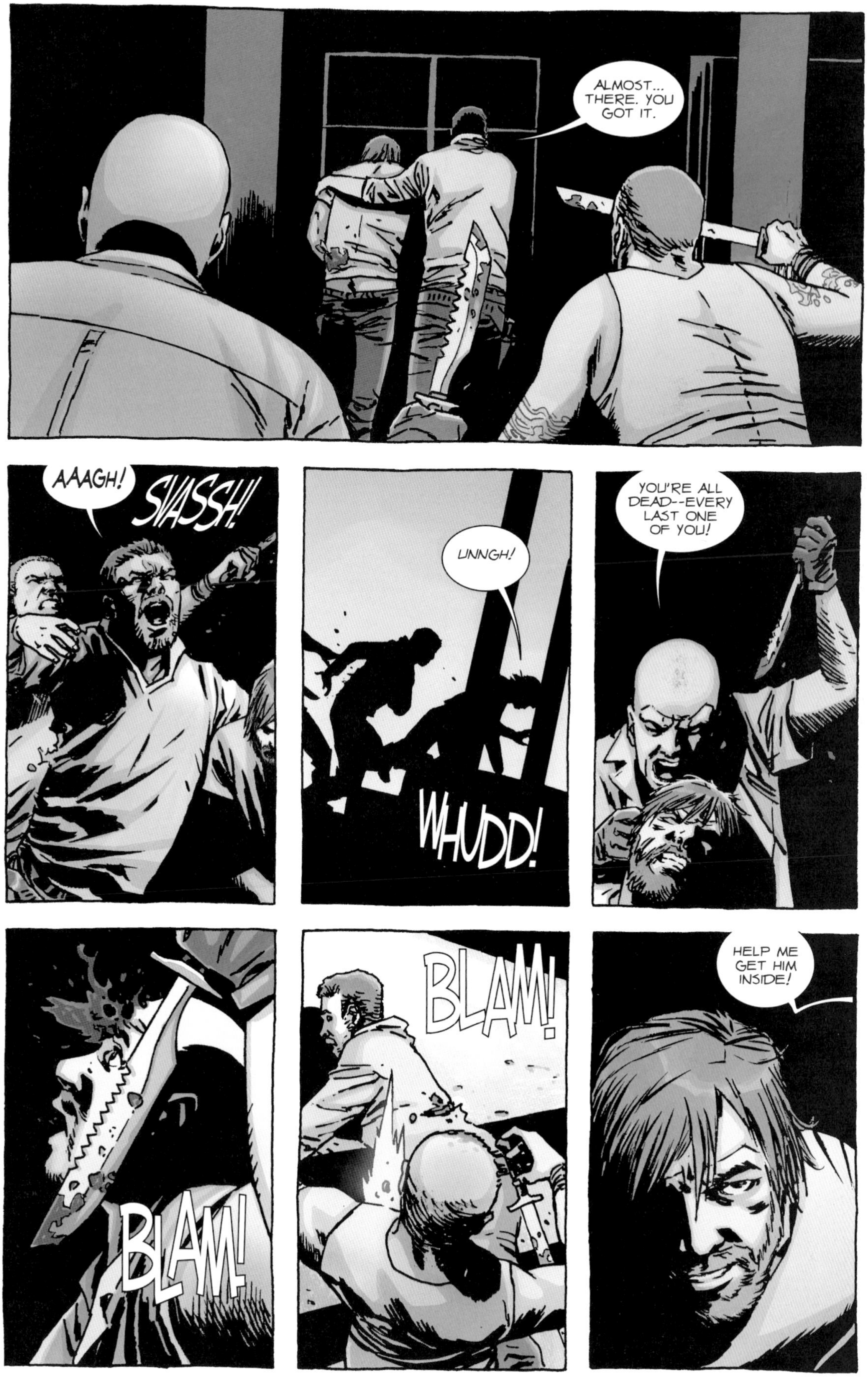
ALMOST... THERE. YOU GOT IT.
AAAGH!
SHASSH!
UNNGH!
WHUDD!
YOU'RE ALL DEAD--EVERY LAST ONE OF YOU!
BLAM!
BLAM!
HELP ME GET HIM INSIDE!

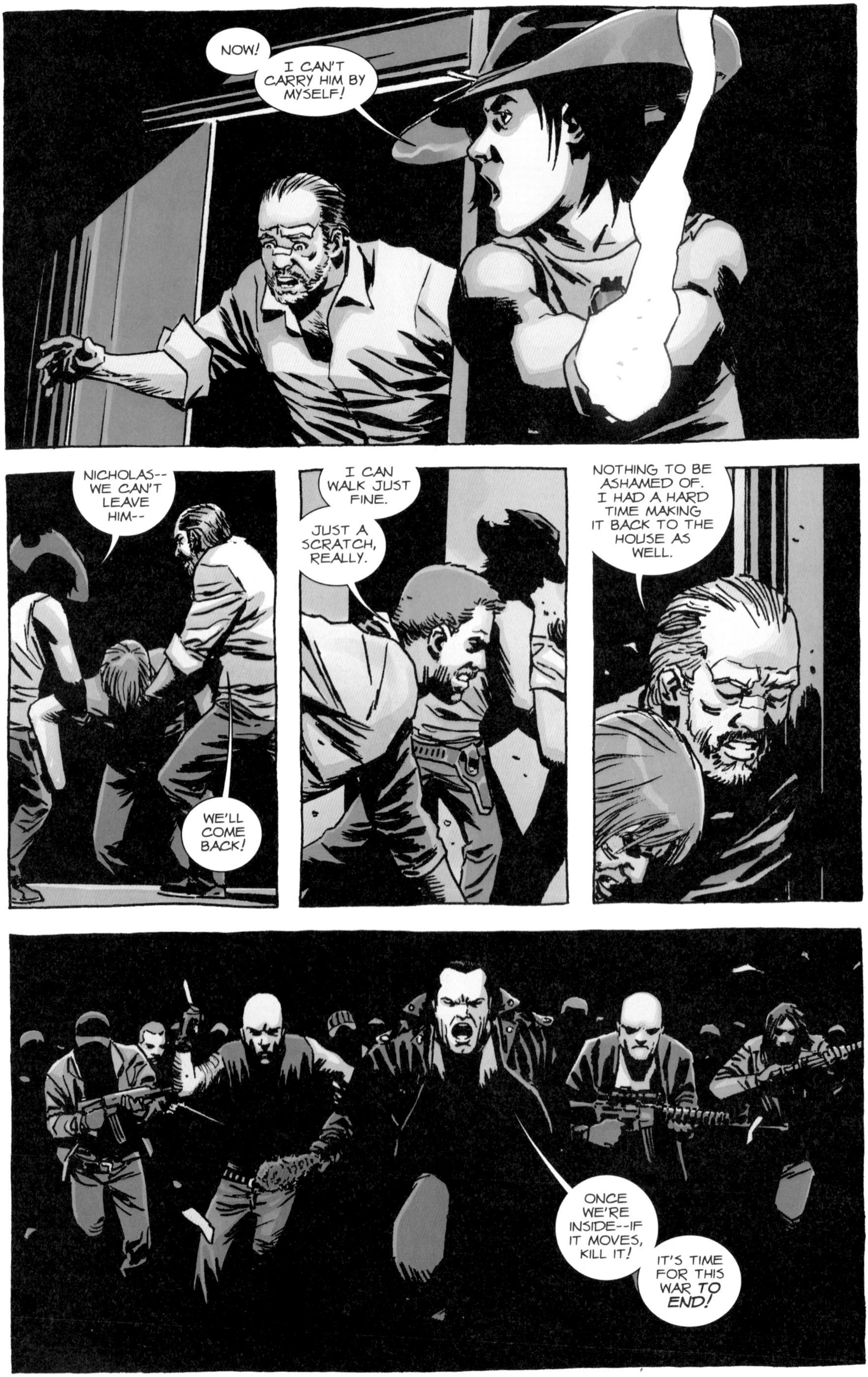

NOW!
I CAN'T CARRY HIM BY MYSELF!
NICHOLAS-- WE CAN'T LEAVE HIM--
WE'LL COME BACK!
I CAN WALK JUST FINE.
JUST A SCRATCH, REALLY.
NOTHING TO BE ASHAMED OF. I HAD A HARD TIME MAKING IT BACK TO THE HOUSE AS WELL.
ONCE WE'RE INSIDE--IF IT MOVES, KILL IT!
IT'S TIME FOR THIS WAR TO END!

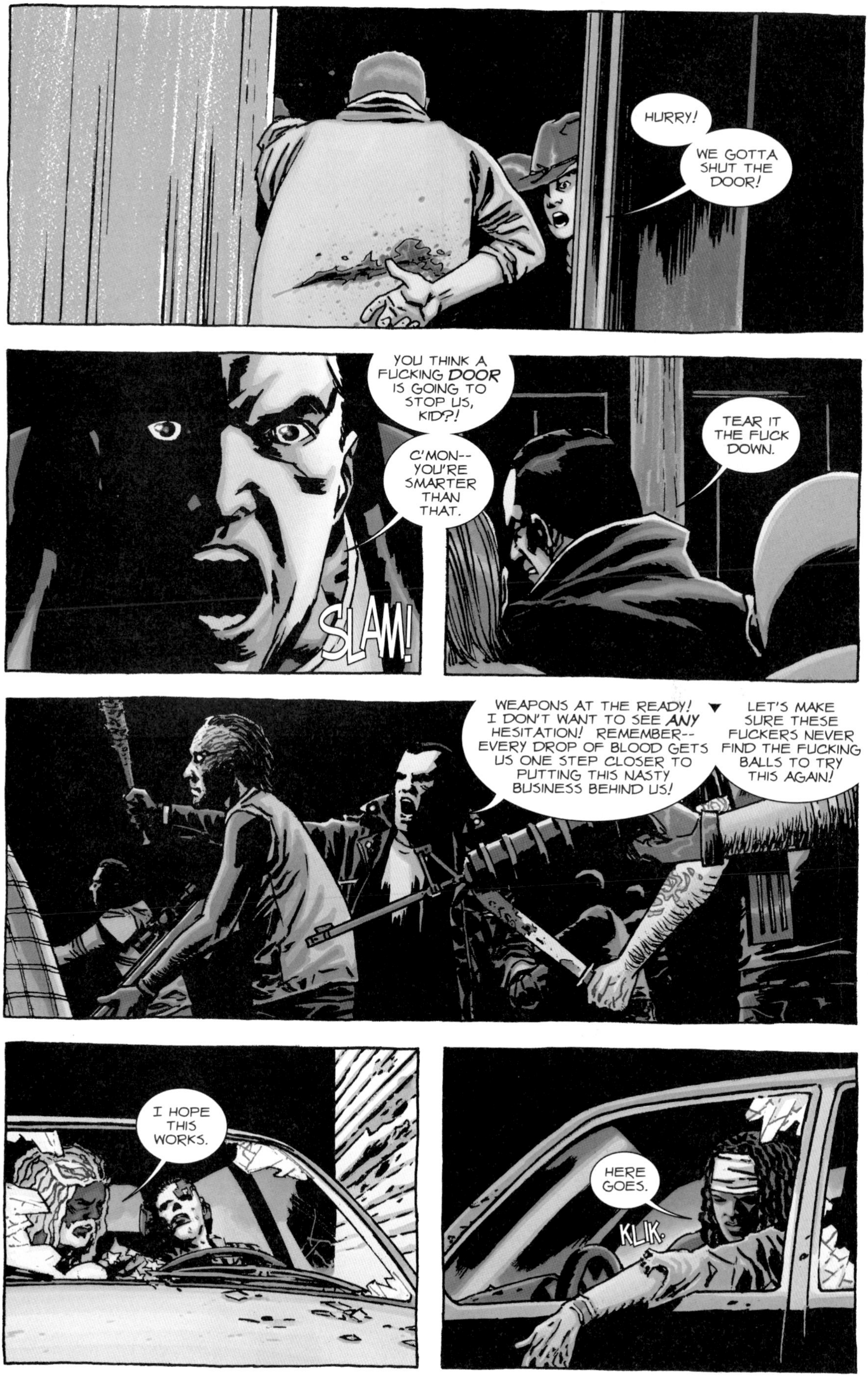
HURRY!
WE GOTTA SHUT THE DOOR!
YOU THINK A FUCKING DOOR IS GOING TO STOP US, KID?!
C'MON-- YOU'RE SMARTER THAN THAT.
SLAM!
TEAR IT THE FUCK DOWN.
WEAPONS AT THE READY! I DON'T WANT TO SEE ANY HESITATION! REMEMBER-- EVERY DROP OF BLOOD GETS US ONE STEP CLOSER TO PUTTING THIS NASTY BUSINESS BEHIND US!
LET'S MAKE SURE THESE FUCKERS NEVER FIND THE FUCKING BALLS TO TRY THIS AGAIN!
I HOPE THIS WORKS.
HERE GOES.
KLIK.

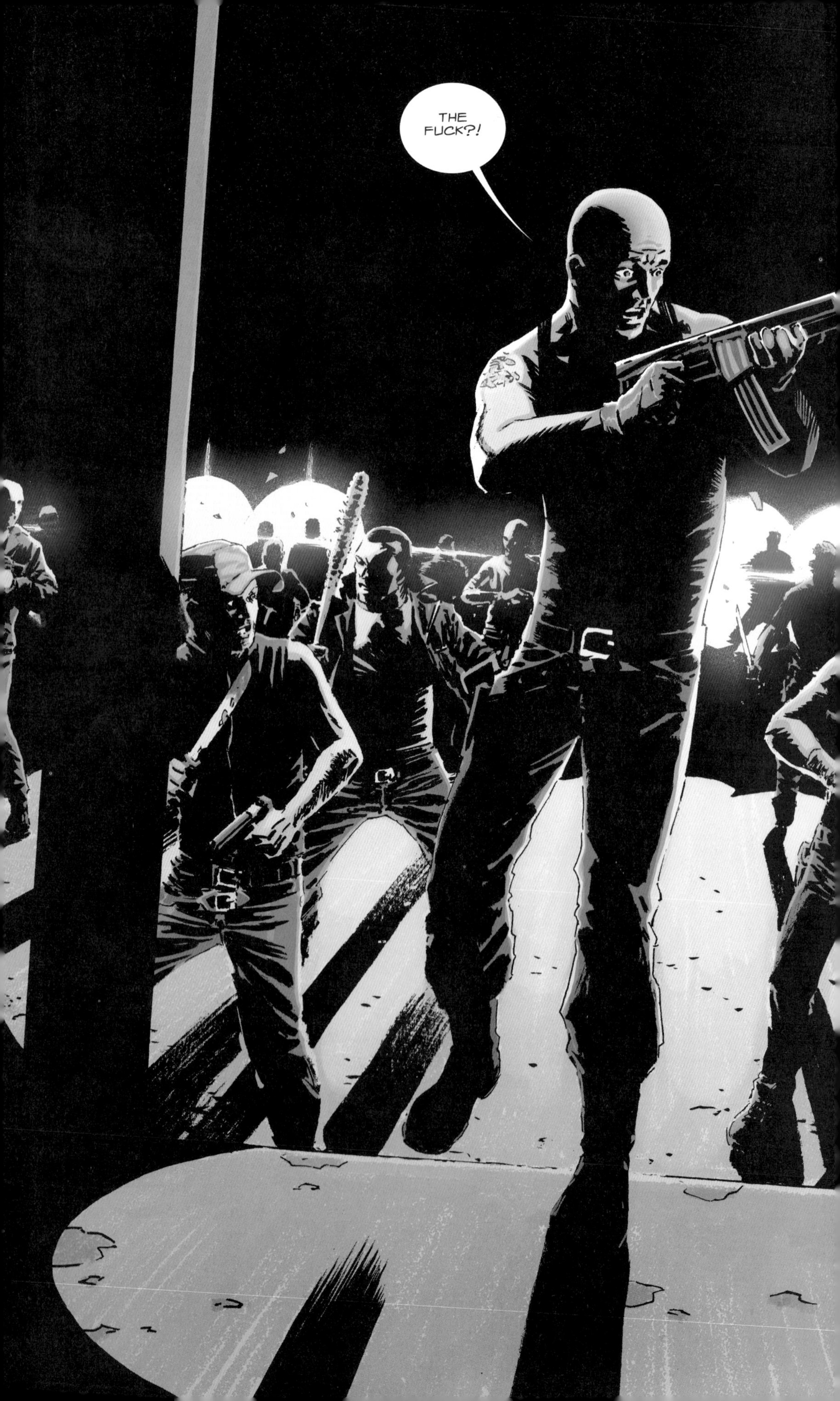
THE FUCK?!

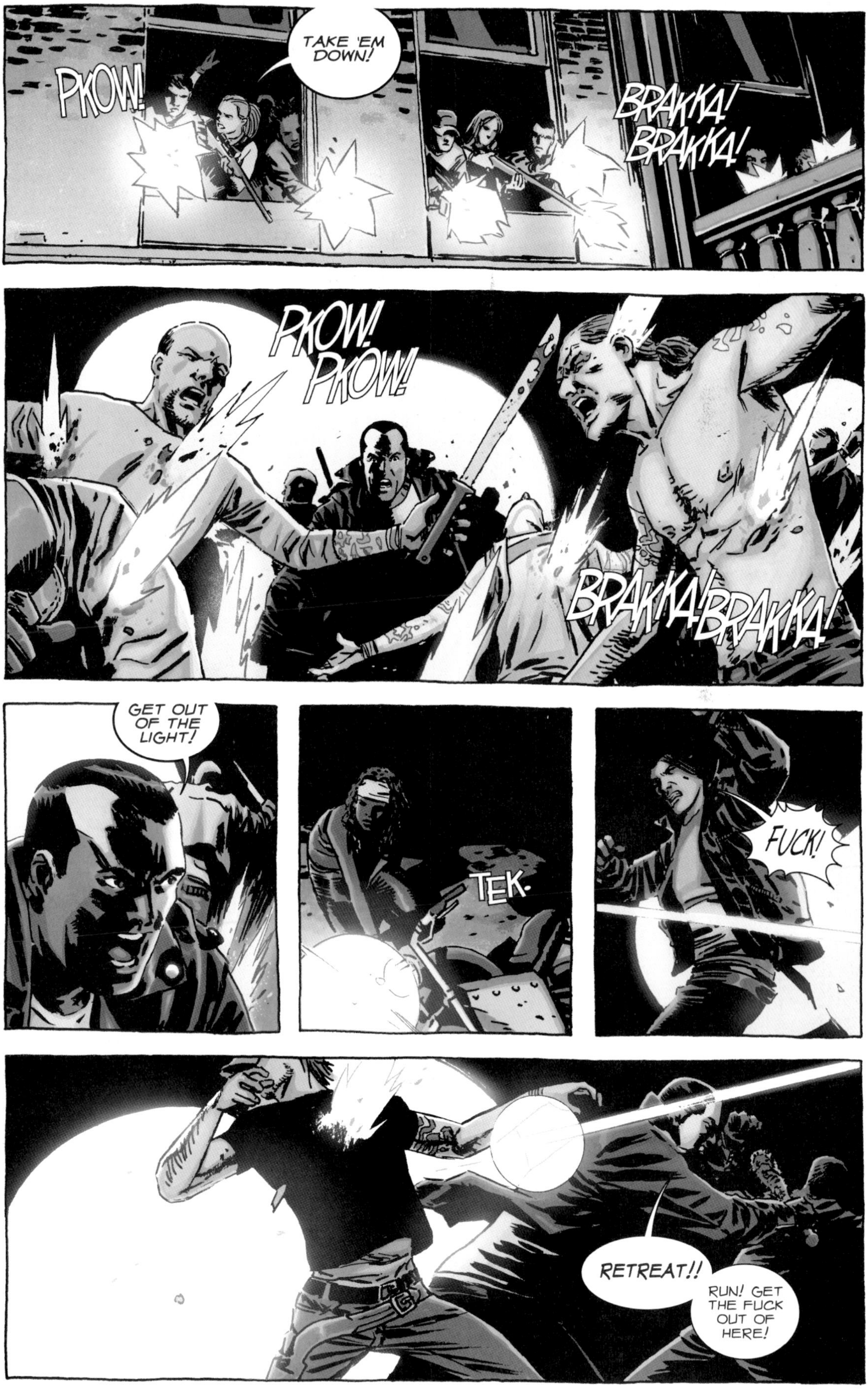
PKOW!
TAKE 'EM DOWN!
BRAKKA! BRAKKA!
PKOW! PKOW!
BRAKKA! BRAKKA!
GET OUT OF THE LIGHT!
TEK.
FUCK!
RETREAT!!
RUN! GET THE FUCK OUT OF HERE!

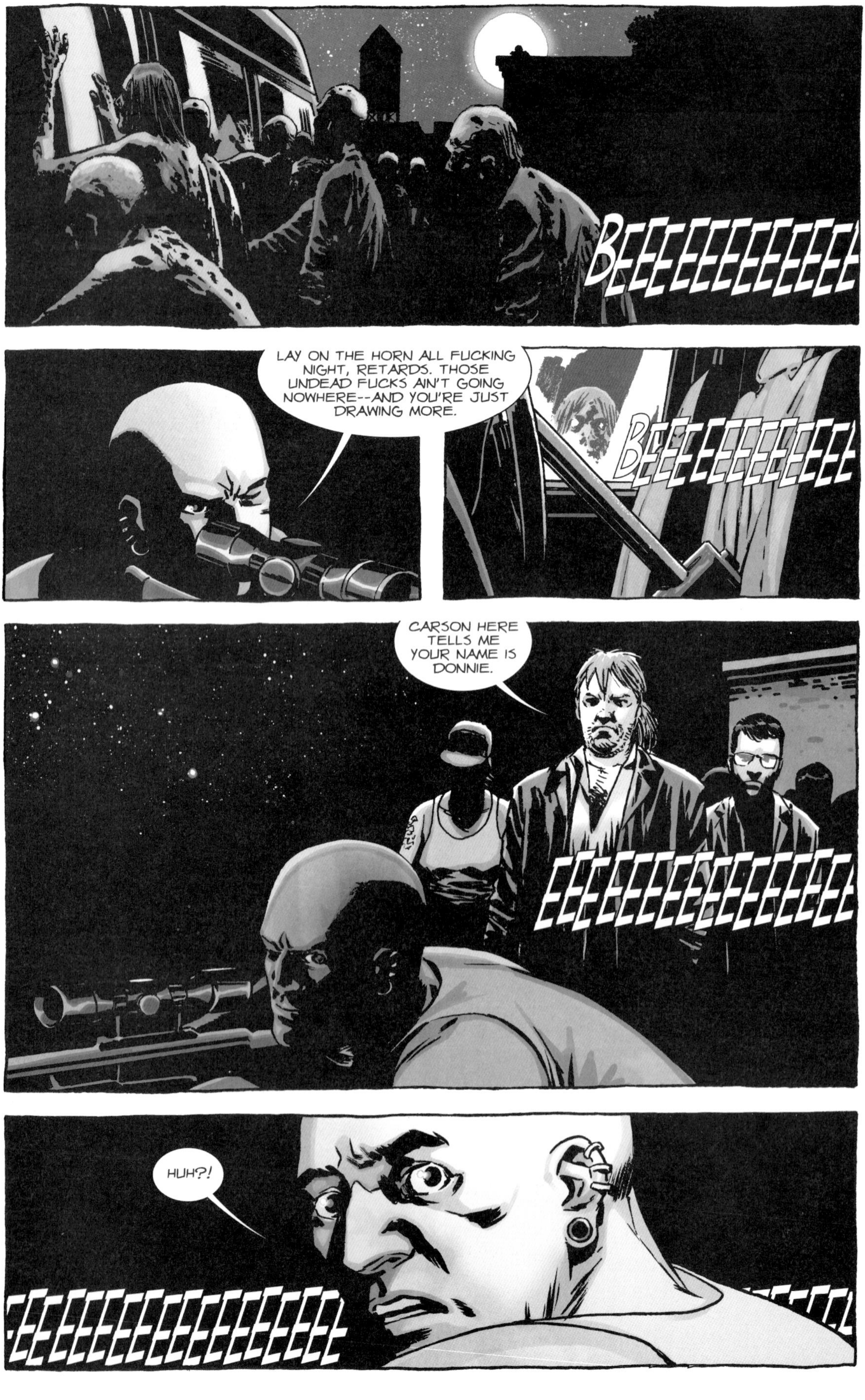
BEEEEEEEEEEEEE
LAY ON THE HORN ALL FUCKING NIGHT, RETARDS. THOSE UNDEAD FUCKS AIN'T GOING NOWHERE--AND YOU'RE JUST DRAWING MORE.
BEEEEEEEEEEEE
CARSON HERE TELLS ME YOUR NAME IS DONNIE.
EEEEEEEEEEEEEEEE
HUH?!
EEEEEEEEEEEEEEEEEEE
EEEEEEE

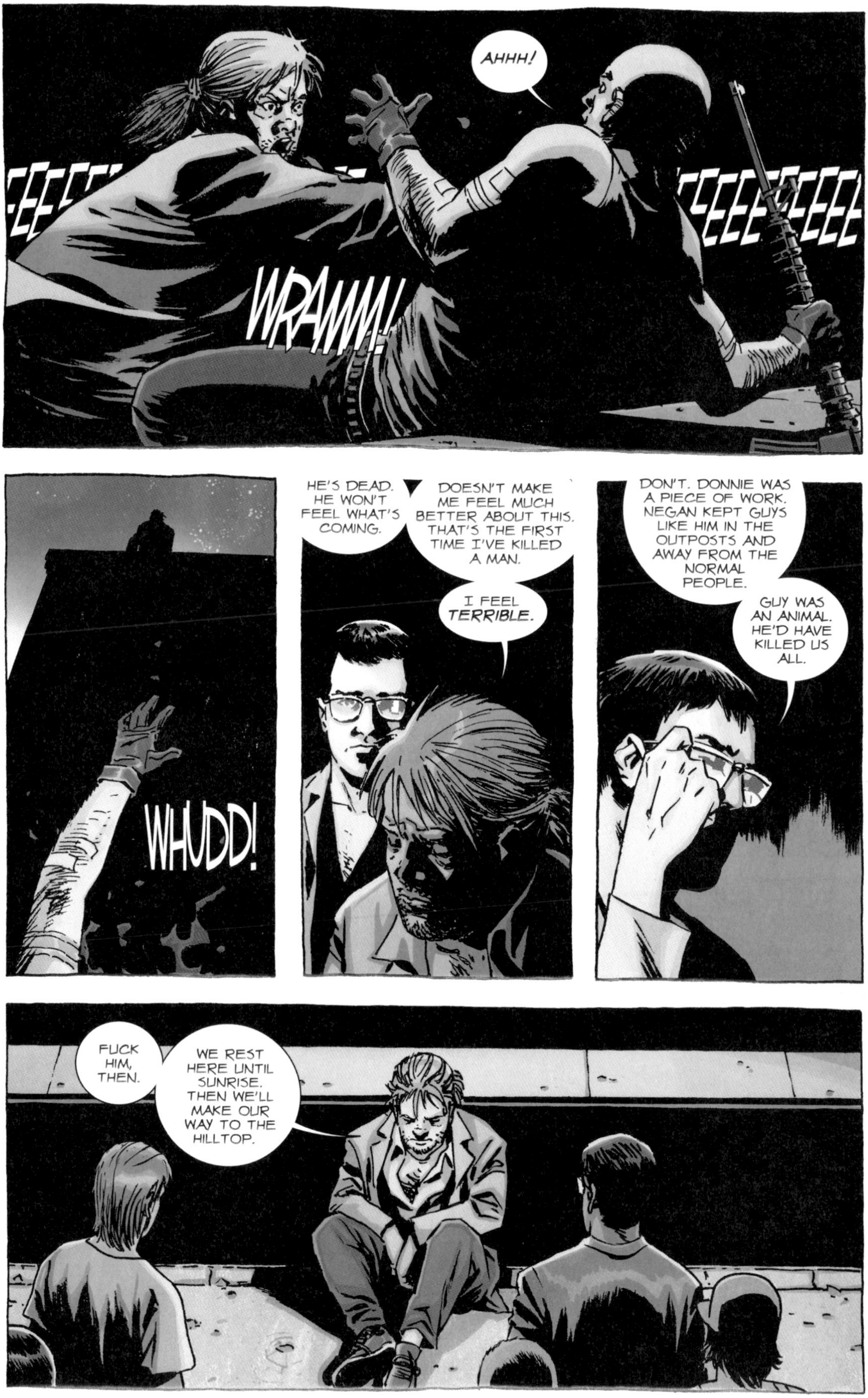
AHHH!
EEEEEE
EEEEEEEEEE
WRAMM!
WHUDD!
HE'S DEAD. HE WON'T FEEL WHAT'S COMING.
DOESN'T MAKE ME FEEL MUCH BETTER ABOUT THIS. THAT'S THE FIRST TIME I'VE KILLED A MAN.
I FEEL *TERRIBLE*.
DON'T. DONNIE WAS A PIECE OF WORK. NEGAN KEPT GUYS LIKE HIM IN THE OUTPOSTS AND AWAY FROM THE NORMAL PEOPLE.
GUY WAS AN ANIMAL. HE'D HAVE KILLED US ALL.
FUCK HIM, THEN.
WE REST HERE UNTIL SUNRISE. THEN WE'LL MAKE OUR WAY TO THE HILLTOP.

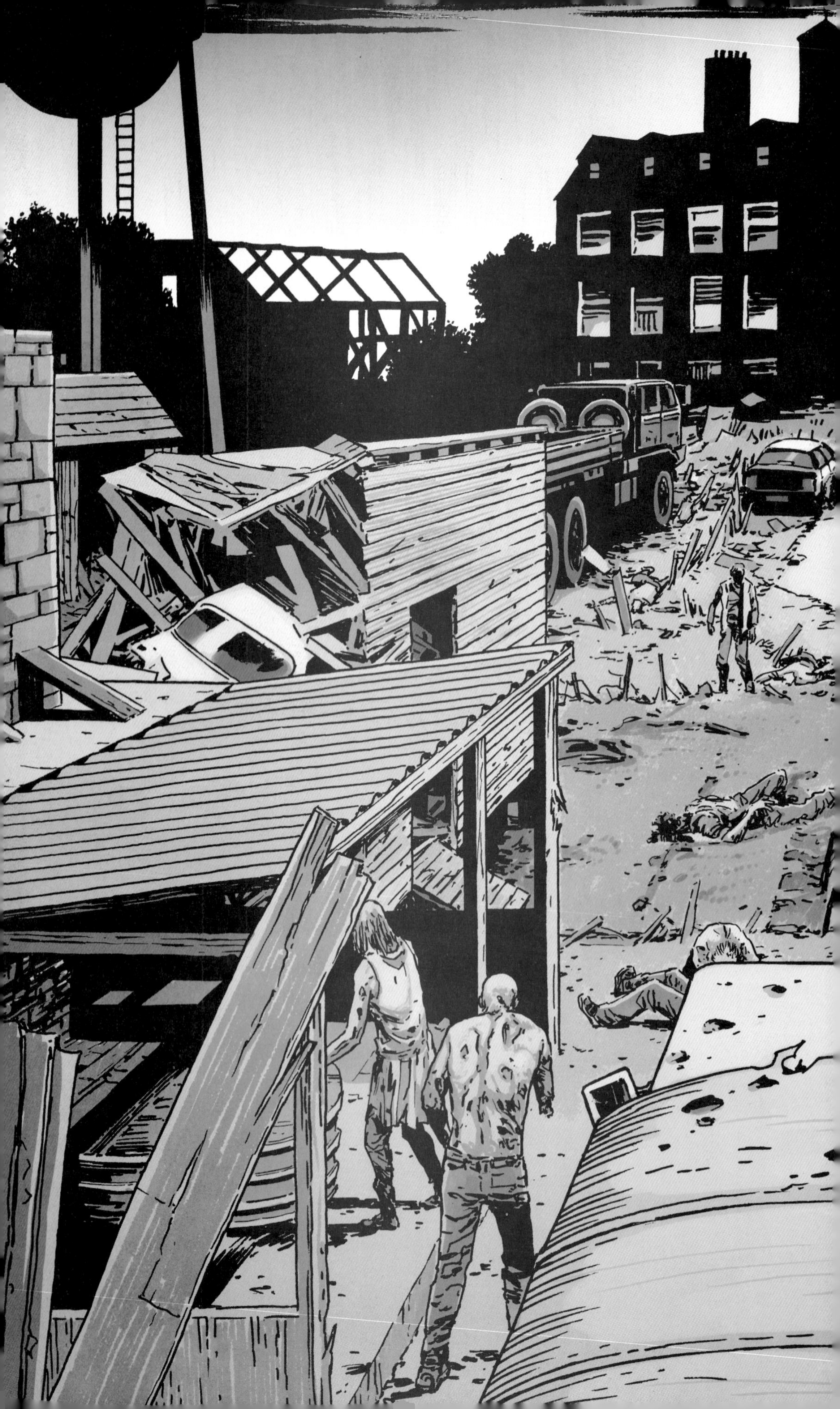

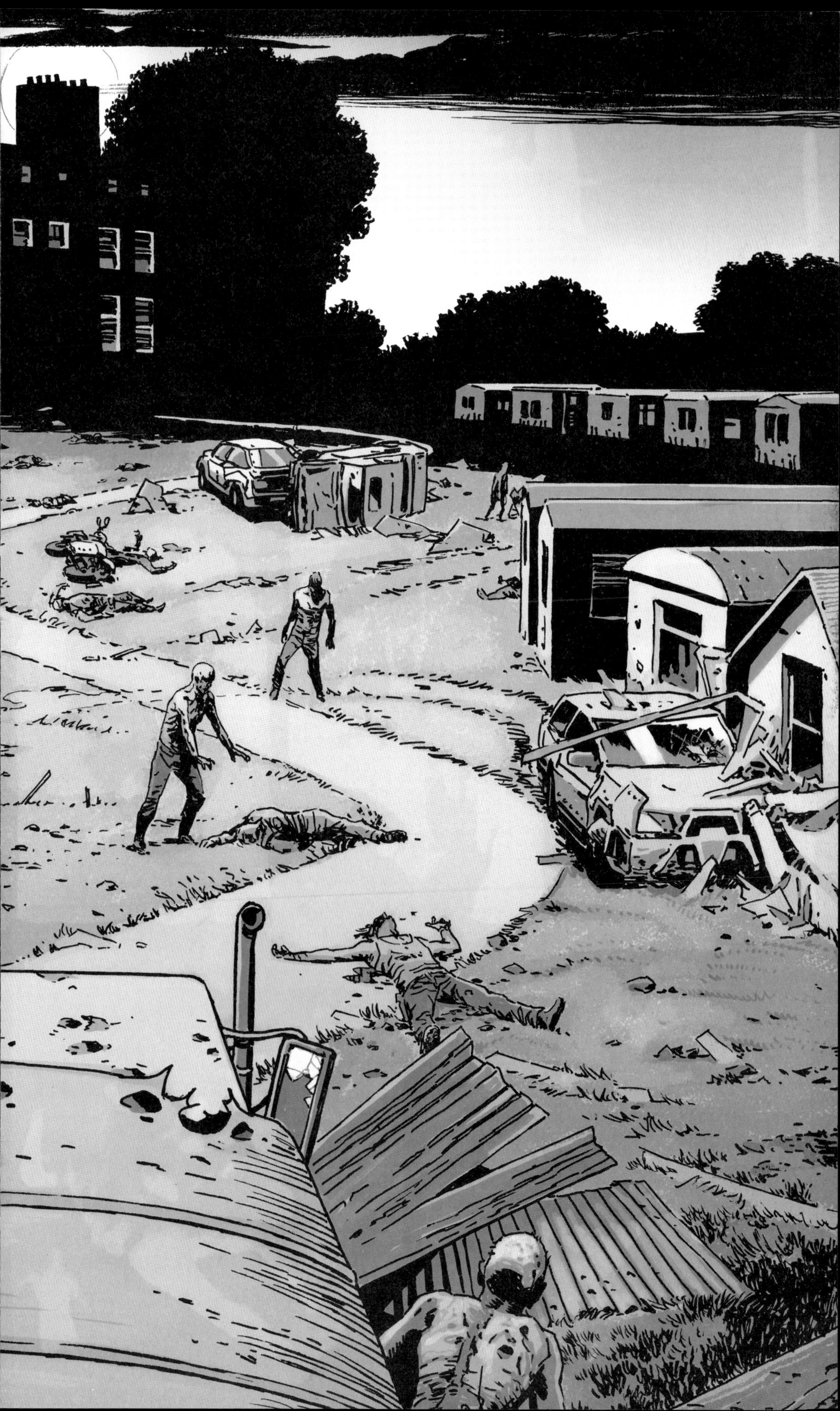

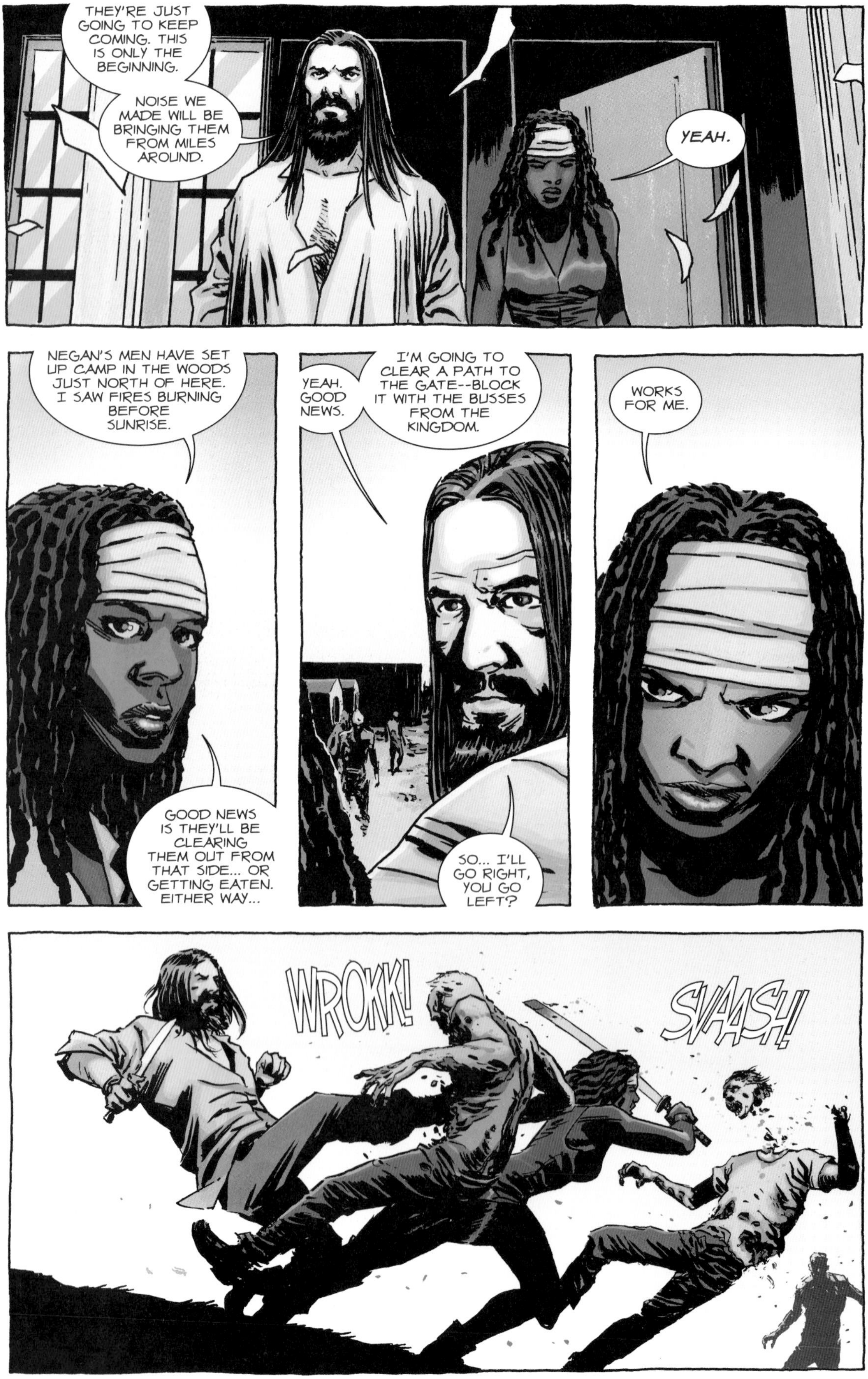
THEY'RE JUST GOING TO KEEP COMING. THIS IS ONLY THE BEGINNING.
NOISE WE MADE WILL BE BRINGING THEM FROM MILES AROUND.
YEAH.
NEGAN'S MEN HAVE SET UP CAMP IN THE WOODS JUST NORTH OF HERE. I SAW FIRES BURNING BEFORE SUNRISE.
GOOD NEWS IS THEY'LL BE CLEARING THEM OUT FROM THAT SIDE... OR GETTING EATEN. EITHER WAY...
YEAH. GOOD NEWS.
I'M GOING TO CLEAR A PATH TO THE GATE--BLOCK IT WITH THE BUSSES FROM THE KINGDOM.
SO... I'LL GO RIGHT, YOU GO LEFT?
WORKS FOR ME.
WROKK!
SVAASH!

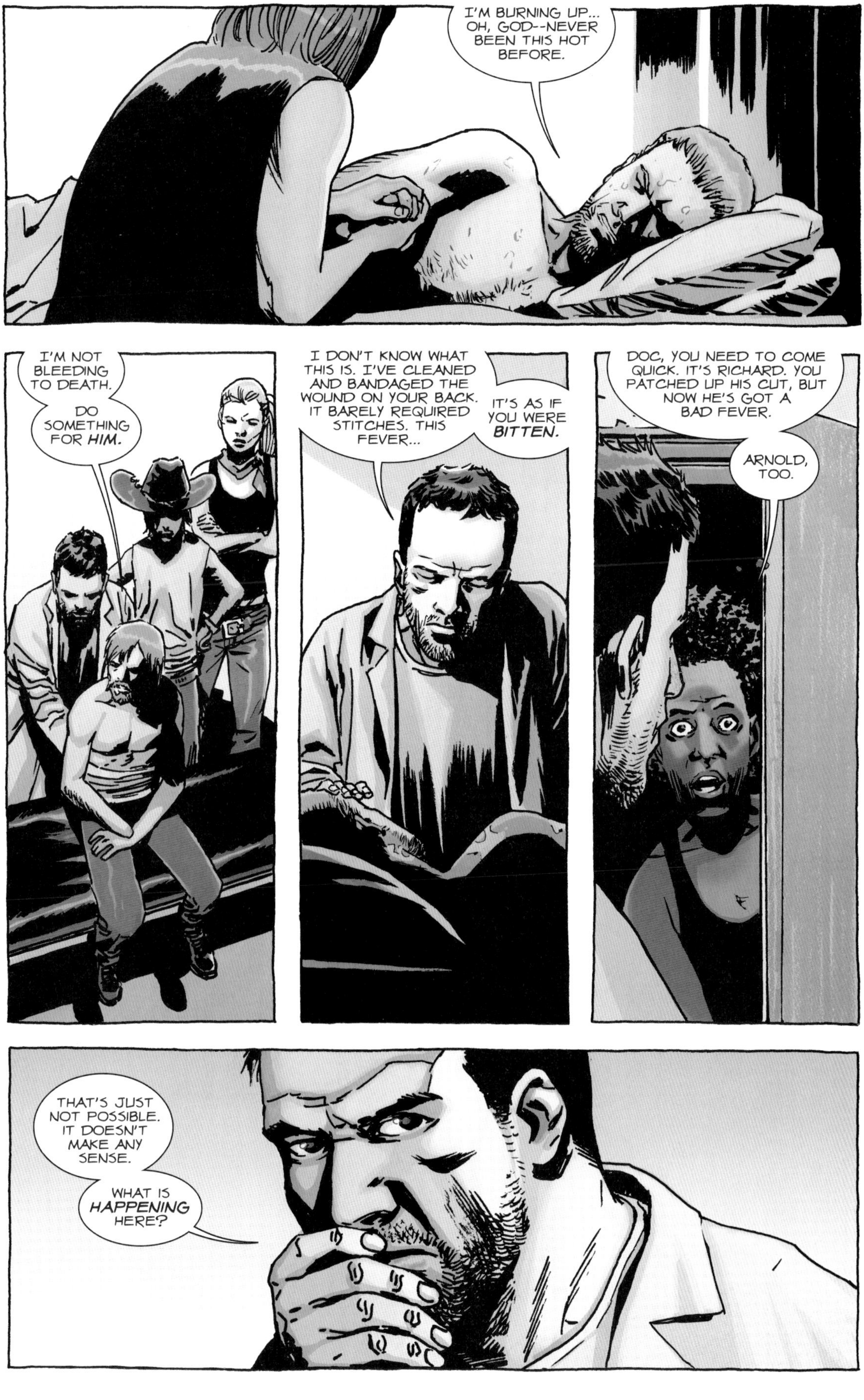
I'M BURNING UP... OH, GOD--NEVER BEEN THIS HOT BEFORE.
I'M NOT BLEEDING TO DEATH.
DO SOMETHING FOR HIM.
I DON'T KNOW WHAT THIS IS. I'VE CLEANED AND BANDAGED THE WOUND ON YOUR BACK. IT BARELY REQUIRED STITCHES. THIS FEVER...
IT'S AS IF YOU WERE BITTEN.
DOC, YOU NEED TO COME QUICK. IT'S RICHARD. YOU PATCHED UP HIS CUT, BUT NOW HE'S GOT A BAD FEVER.
ARNOLD, TOO.
THAT'S JUST NOT POSSIBLE. IT DOESN'T MAKE ANY SENSE.
WHAT IS HAPPENING HERE?

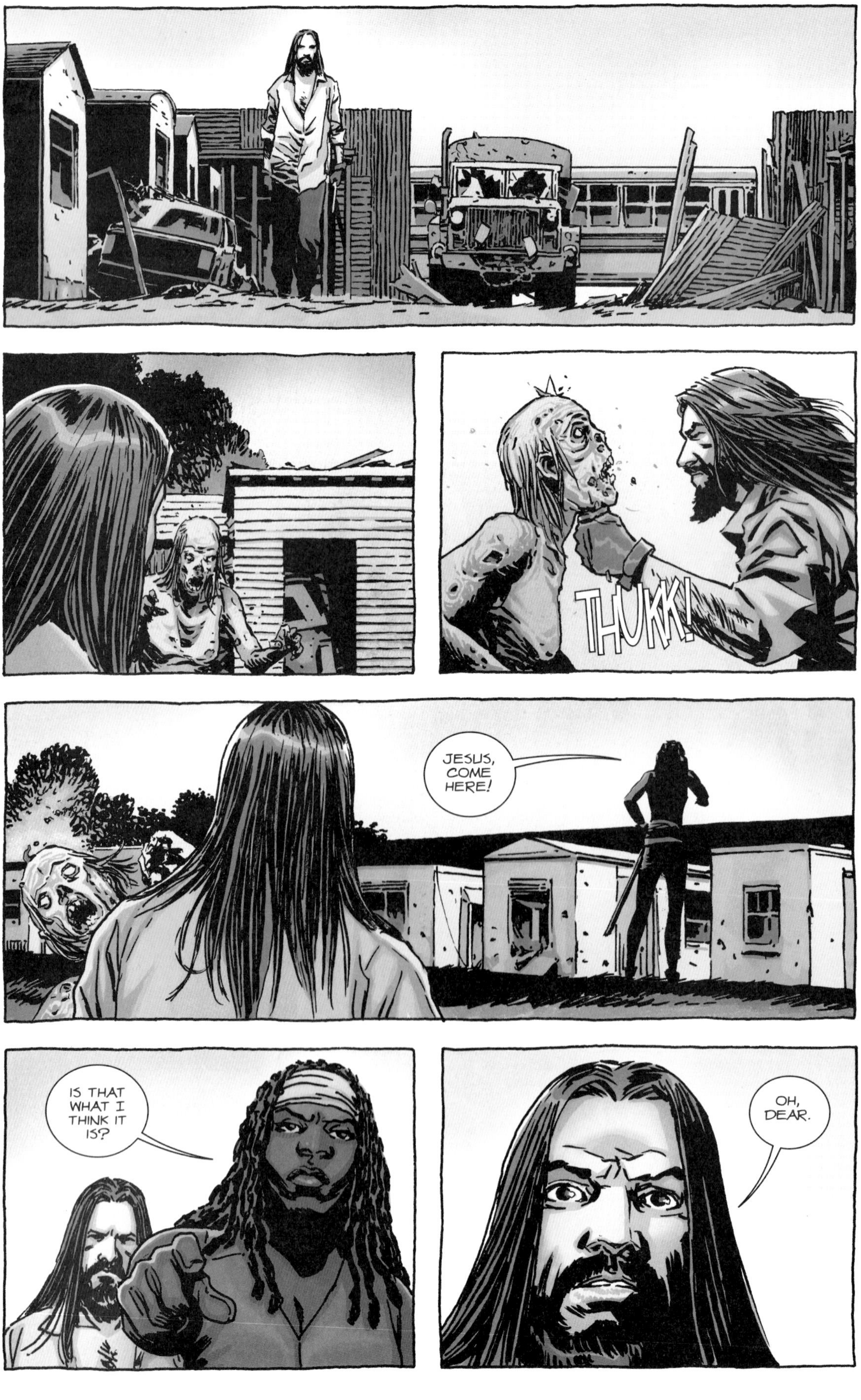
THUKK!
JESUS, COME HERE!
IS THAT WHAT I THINK IT IS?
OH, DEAR.

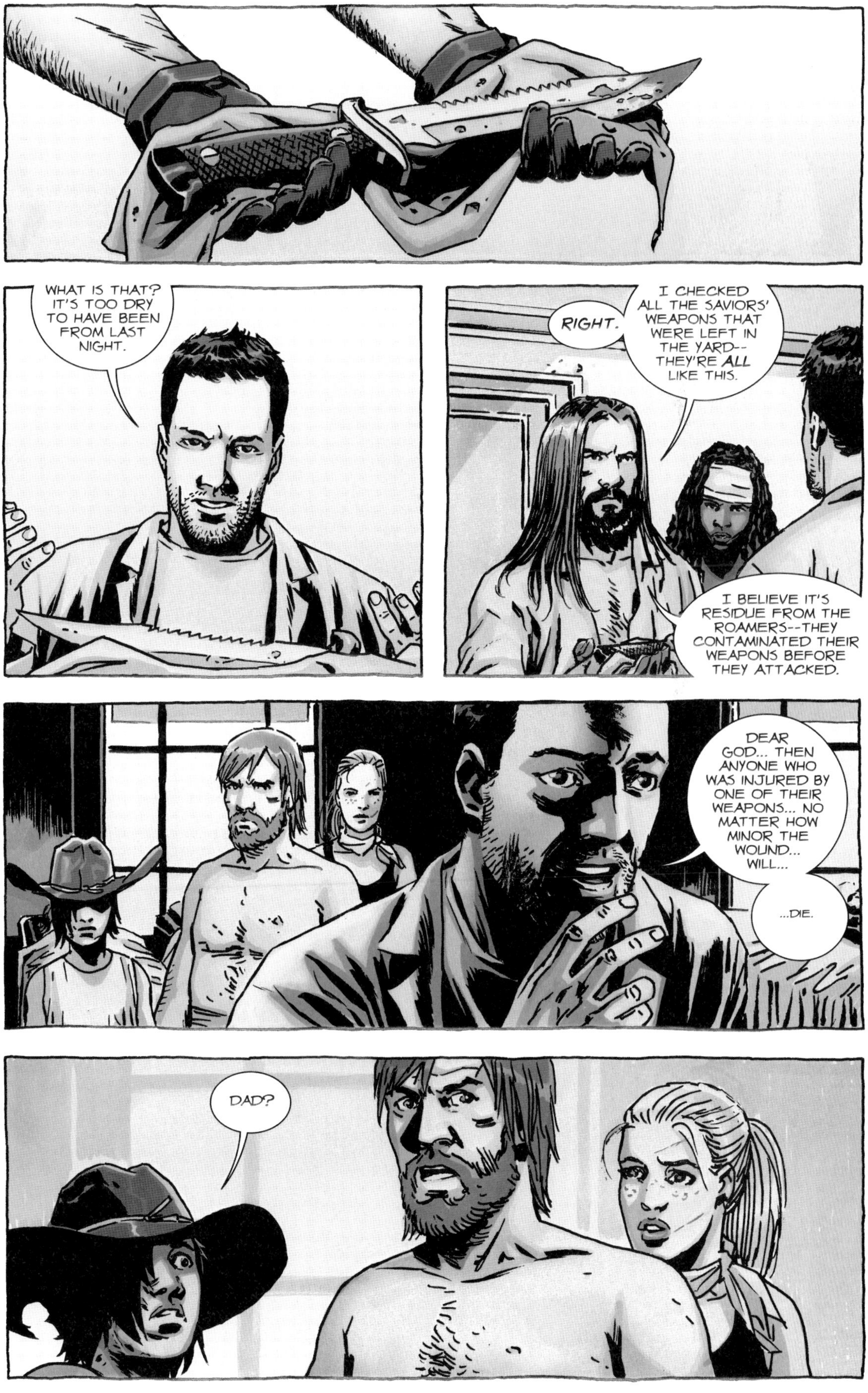
WHAT IS THAT? IT'S TOO DRY TO HAVE BEEN FROM LAST NIGHT.
RIGHT.
I CHECKED ALL THE SAVIORS' WEAPONS THAT WERE LEFT IN THE YARD-- THEY'RE ALL LIKE THIS.
I BELIEVE IT'S RESIDUE FROM THE ROAMERS--THEY CONTAMINATED THEIR WEAPONS BEFORE THEY ATTACKED.
DEAR GOD... THEN ANYONE WHO WAS INJURED BY ONE OF THEIR WEAPONS... NO MATTER HOW MINOR THE WOUND... WILL...
...DIE.
DAD?

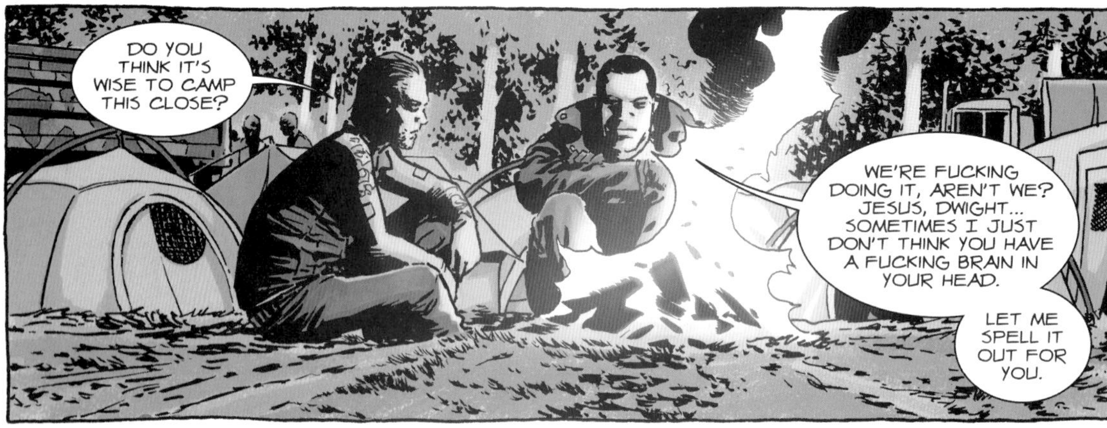
DO YOU THINK IT'S WISE TO CAMP THIS CLOSE?
WE'RE FUCKING DOING IT, AREN'T WE? JESUS, DWIGHT... SOMETIMES I JUST DON'T THINK YOU HAVE A FUCKING BRAIN IN YOUR HEAD.
LET ME SPELL IT OUT FOR YOU.

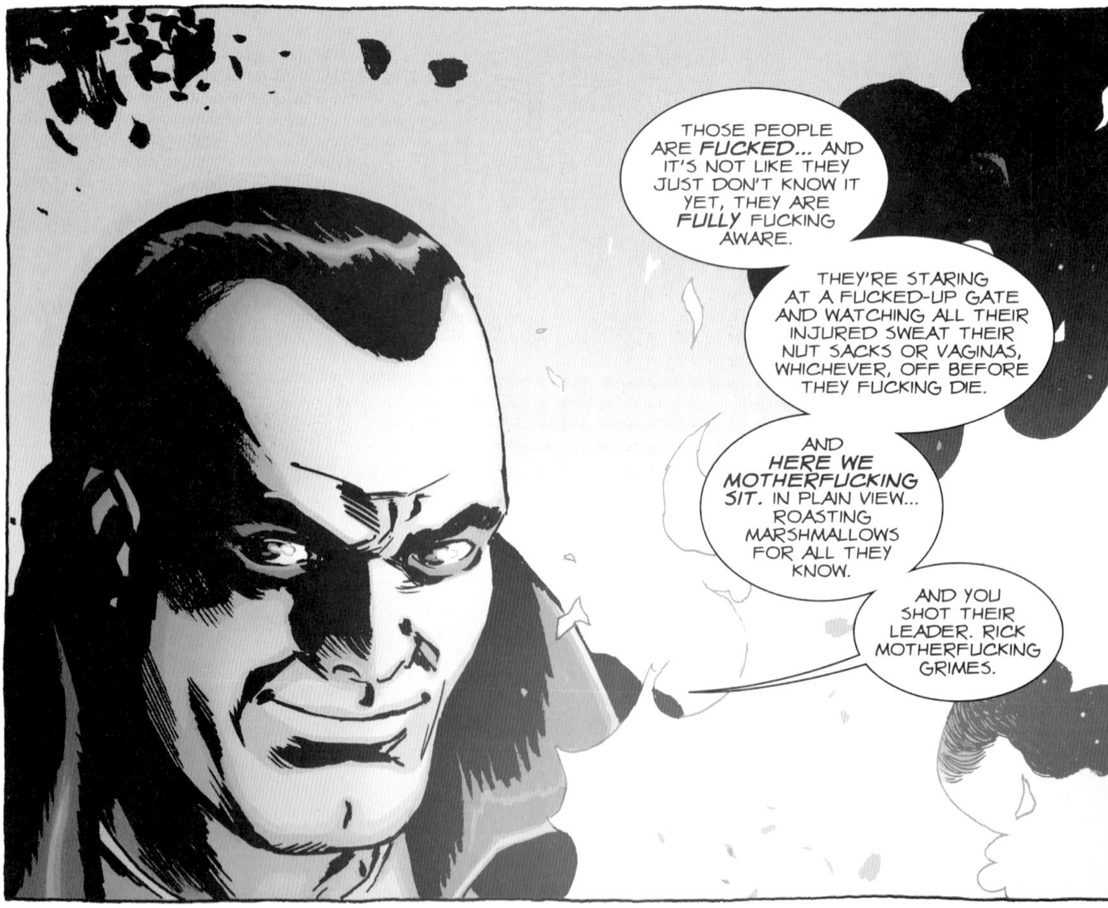
THOSE PEOPLE ARE FUCKED... AND IT'S NOT LIKE THEY JUST DON'T KNOW IT YET, THEY ARE FULLY FUCKING AWARE.
THEY'RE STARING AT A FUCKED-UP GATE AND WATCHING ALL THEIR INJURED SWEAT THEIR NUT SACKS OR VAGINAS, WHICHEVER, OFF BEFORE THEY FUCKING DIE.
AND HERE WE MOTHERFUCKING SIT. IN PLAIN VIEW... ROASTING MARSHMALLOWS FOR ALL THEY KNOW.
AND YOU SHOT THEIR LEADER. RICK MOTHERFUCKING GRIMES.

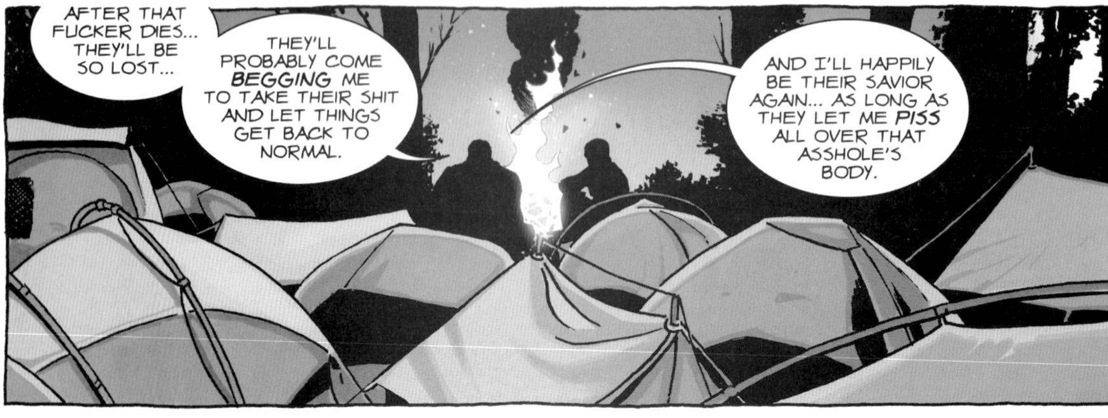
AFTER THAT FUCKER DIES... THEY'LL BE SO LOST...
THEY'LL PROBABLY COME BEGGING ME TO TAKE THEIR SHIT AND LET THINGS GET BACK TO NORMAL.
AND I'LL HAPPILY BE THEIR SAVIOR AGAIN... AS LONG AS THEY LET ME PISS ALL OVER THAT ASSHOLE'S BODY.

PISS ON HIM?!

YOU'RE *SERIOUS*, AREN'T YOU?

YOU COULD TRY *A LITTLE* HARDER TO HIDE YOUR DISDAIN FOR ME, DWIGHT. BUT I GET IT. WE'VE GOT A HISTORY...

...AND I'M TOO GODDAMN MOTHERFUCKING HAPPY ABOUT HOW WELL THINGS ARE GOING TO GET ANGRY WITH YOU.

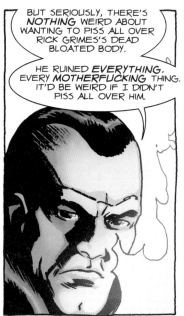

BUT SERIOUSLY, THERE'S *NOTHING* WEIRD ABOUT WANTING TO PISS ALL OVER RICK GRIMES'S DEAD BLOATED BODY.

HE RUINED *EVERYTHING*. EVERY *MOTHERFUCKING* THING. IT'D BE WEIRD IF I DIDN'T PISS ALL OVER HIM.

WISH I WAS THERE TO SEE HIM, SWEATING THROUGH HIS SHIRT... EYES SINKING BACK INTO HIS SKULL.

LITTLE CARL... CRYING HIS EXPOSED EYE SOCKET OUT--

SIR, GOT A REPORT FROM THE SCOUTS.

THERE'S A VEHICLE APPROACHING THE HILLTOP. THAT GUY YOU BROUGHT IN, THE BULLET MAKER... HE'S DRIVING.

AND, SIR... *CARSON* IS WITH HIM.

YOU KNOW WHAT? WHO FUCKING CARES?

WE'LL GET THEM BACK SOON ENOUGH.

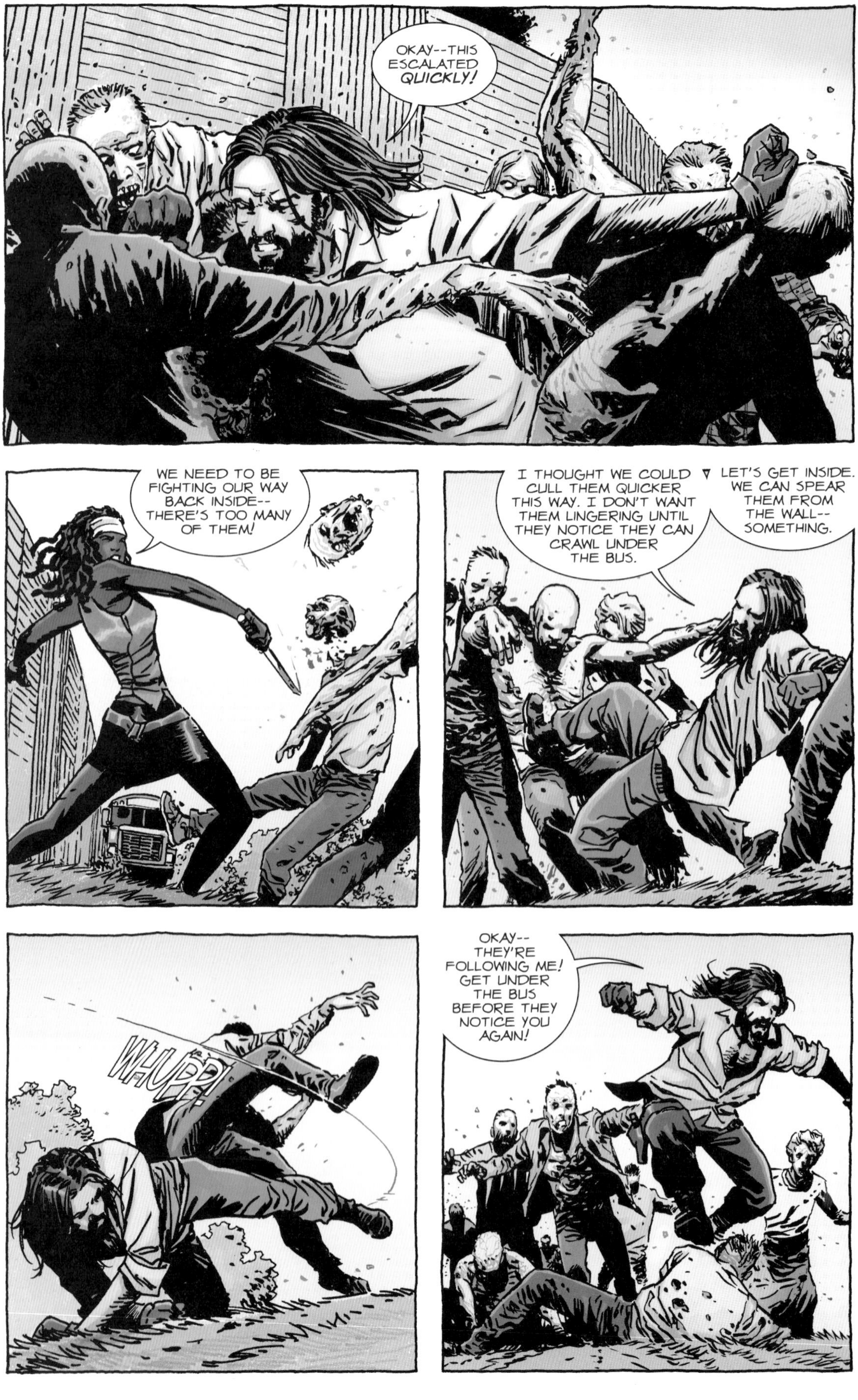
OKAY--THIS ESCALATED QUICKLY!
WE NEED TO BE FIGHTING OUR WAY BACK INSIDE-- THERE'S TOO MANY OF THEM!
I THOUGHT WE COULD CULL THEM QUICKER THIS WAY. I DON'T WANT THEM LINGERING UNTIL THEY NOTICE THEY CAN CRAWL UNDER THE BUS.
LET'S GET INSIDE. WE CAN SPEAR THEM FROM THE WALL-- SOMETHING.
WHUPP!
OKAY-- THEY'RE FOLLOWING ME! GET UNDER THE BUS BEFORE THEY NOTICE YOU AGAIN!

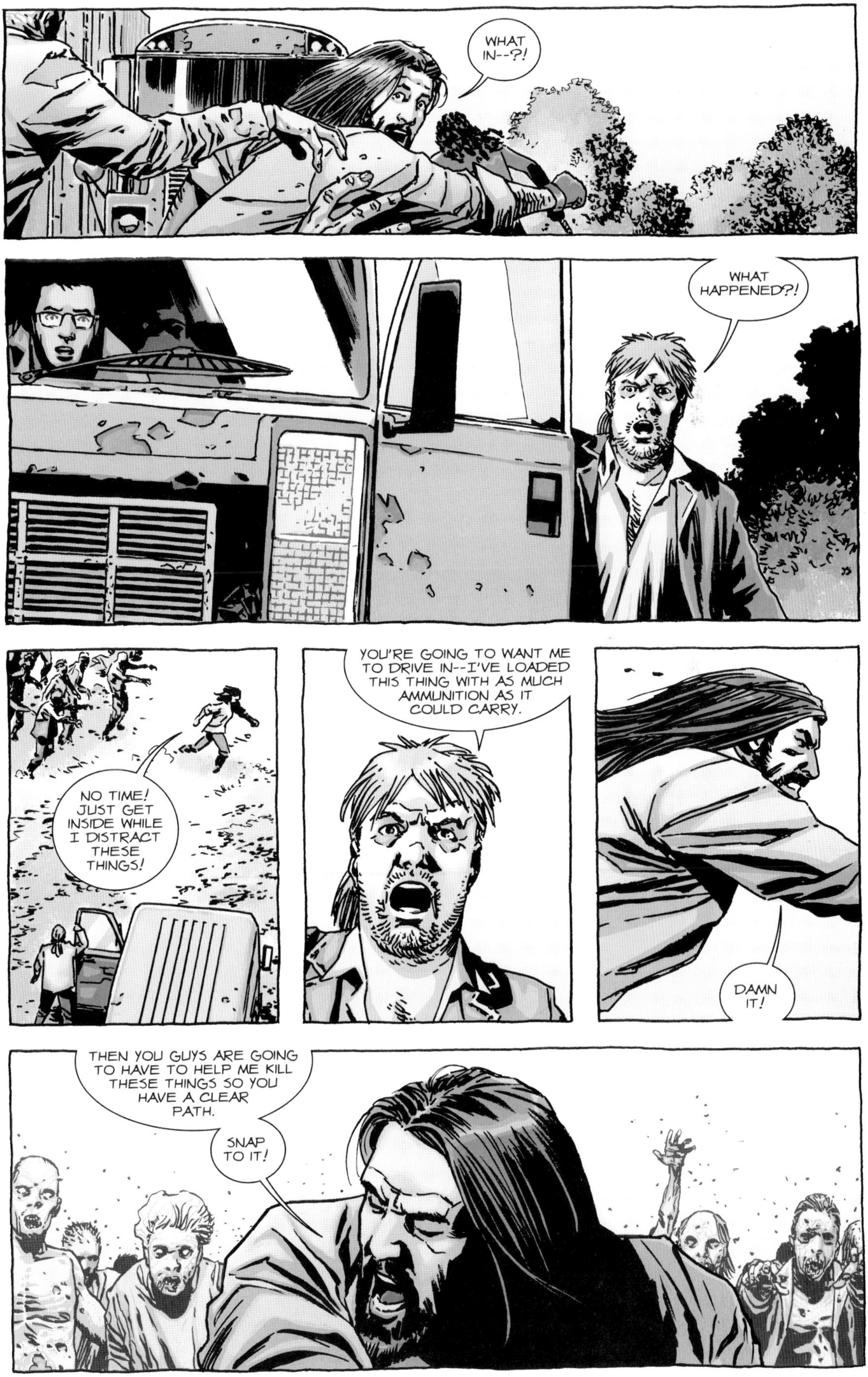
WHAT IN--?!
WHAT HAPPENED?!
NO TIME! JUST GET INSIDE WHILE I DISTRACT THESE THINGS!
YOU'RE GOING TO WANT ME TO DRIVE IN--I'VE LOADED THIS THING WITH AS MUCH AMMUNITION AS IT COULD CARRY.
DAMN IT!
THEN YOU GUYS ARE GOING TO HAVE TO HELP ME KILL THESE THINGS SO YOU HAVE A CLEAR PATH.
SNAP TO IT!

I DON'T WANT YOU TO SEE ME LIKE THIS.

PLEASE... PLEASE GO.

NICHOLAS, STOP. I SENT MIKEY OUT OF THE ROOM. WE NEED TO TALK ABOUT THIS. YOU...

YOU'RE GOING TO DIE...

I'M SORRY, PAULA. I LET YOU DOWN... I WON'T BE THERE FOR YOU ANYMORE.

I DON'T KNOW HOW... I'M SORRY.

DON'T BE. MIKEY AND I WILL BE OKAY. WE'LL GET BY. WE'VE BEEN GETTING BY EVER SINCE YOU GOT US TO ALEXANDRIA.

YOU DID THAT. YOU MADE US SURVIVE. YOU SAVED US, NICHOLAS.

...

I'M SO SCARED...

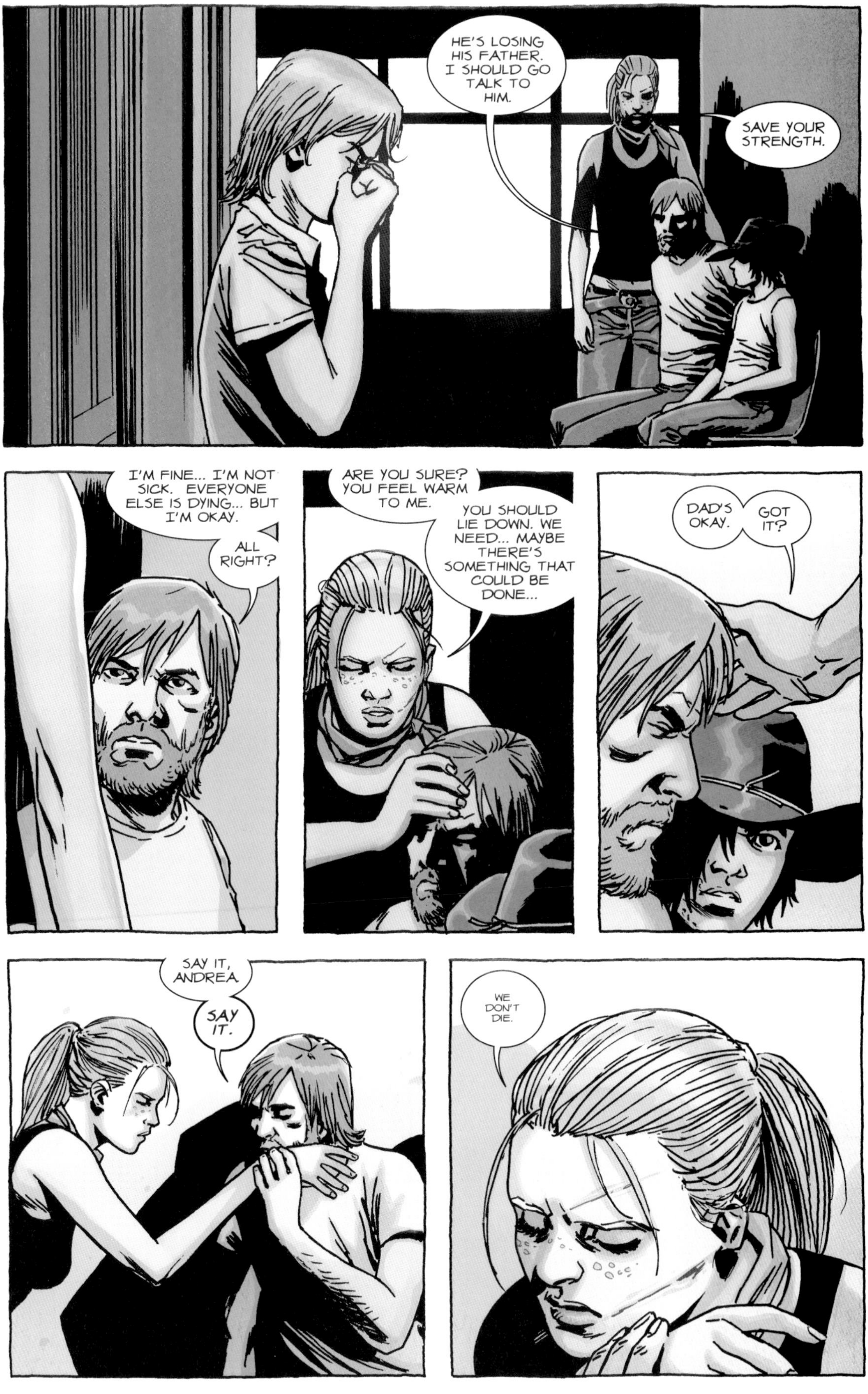
HE'S LOSING HIS FATHER. I SHOULD GO TALK TO HIM.
SAVE YOUR STRENGTH.
I'M FINE... I'M NOT SICK. EVERYONE ELSE IS DYING... BUT I'M OKAY.
ALL RIGHT?
ARE YOU SURE? YOU FEEL WARM TO ME.
YOU SHOULD LIE DOWN. WE NEED... MAYBE THERE'S SOMETHING THAT COULD BE DONE...
DAD'S OKAY.
GOT IT?
SAY IT, ANDREA.
SAY IT.
WE DON'T DIE.

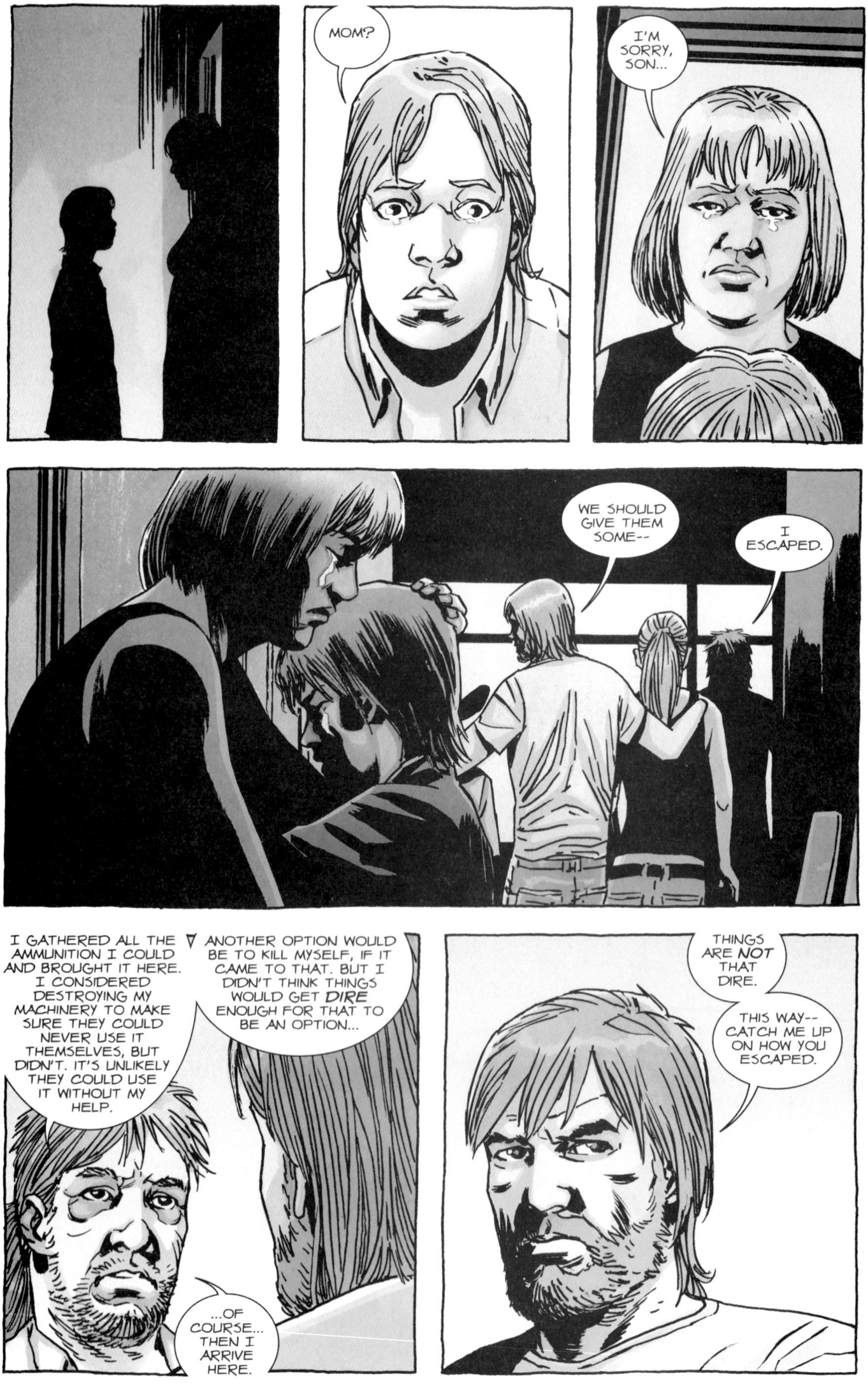
MOM?
I'M SORRY, SON...
WE SHOULD GIVE THEM SOME--
I ESCAPED.
I GATHERED ALL THE AMMUNITION I COULD AND BROUGHT IT HERE. I CONSIDERED DESTROYING MY MACHINERY TO MAKE SURE THEY COULD NEVER USE IT THEMSELVES, BUT DIDN'T. IT'S UNLIKELY THEY COULD USE IT WITHOUT MY HELP.
ANOTHER OPTION WOULD BE TO KILL MYSELF, IF IT CAME TO THAT. BUT I DIDN'T THINK THINGS WOULD GET DIRE ENOUGH FOR THAT TO BE AN OPTION...
...OF COURSE... THEN I ARRIVE HERE.
THINGS ARE NOT THAT DIRE.
THIS WAY-- CATCH ME UP ON HOW YOU ESCAPED.

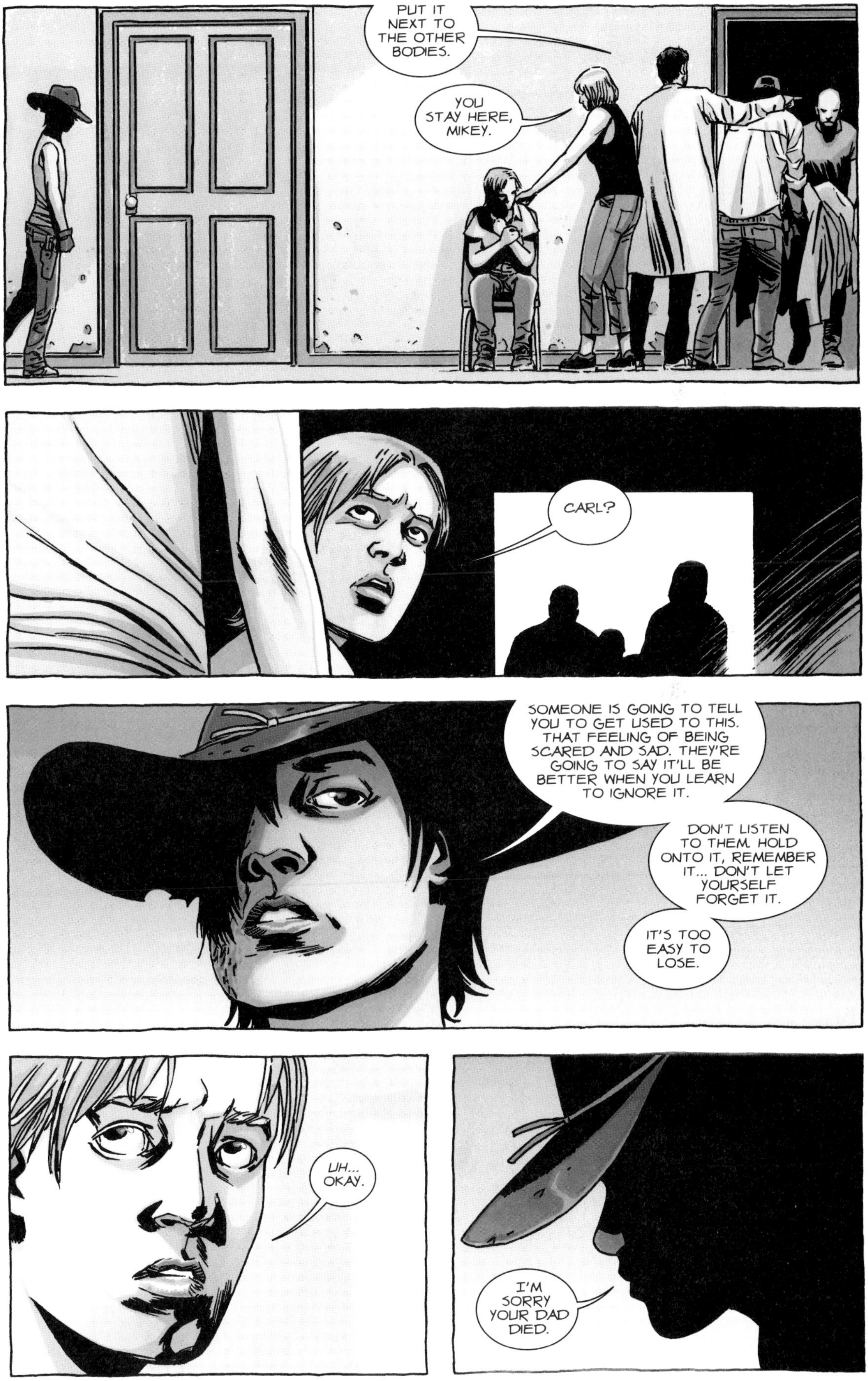
PUT IT NEXT TO THE OTHER BODIES.
YOU STAY HERE, MIKEY.
CARL?
SOMEONE IS GOING TO TELL YOU TO GET USED TO THIS. THAT FEELING OF BEING SCARED AND SAD. THEY'RE GOING TO SAY IT'LL BE BETTER WHEN YOU LEARN TO IGNORE IT.
DON'T LISTEN TO THEM. HOLD ONTO IT, REMEMBER IT... DON'T LET YOURSELF FORGET IT.
IT'S TOO EASY TO LOSE.
UH... OKAY.
I'M SORRY YOUR DAD DIED.

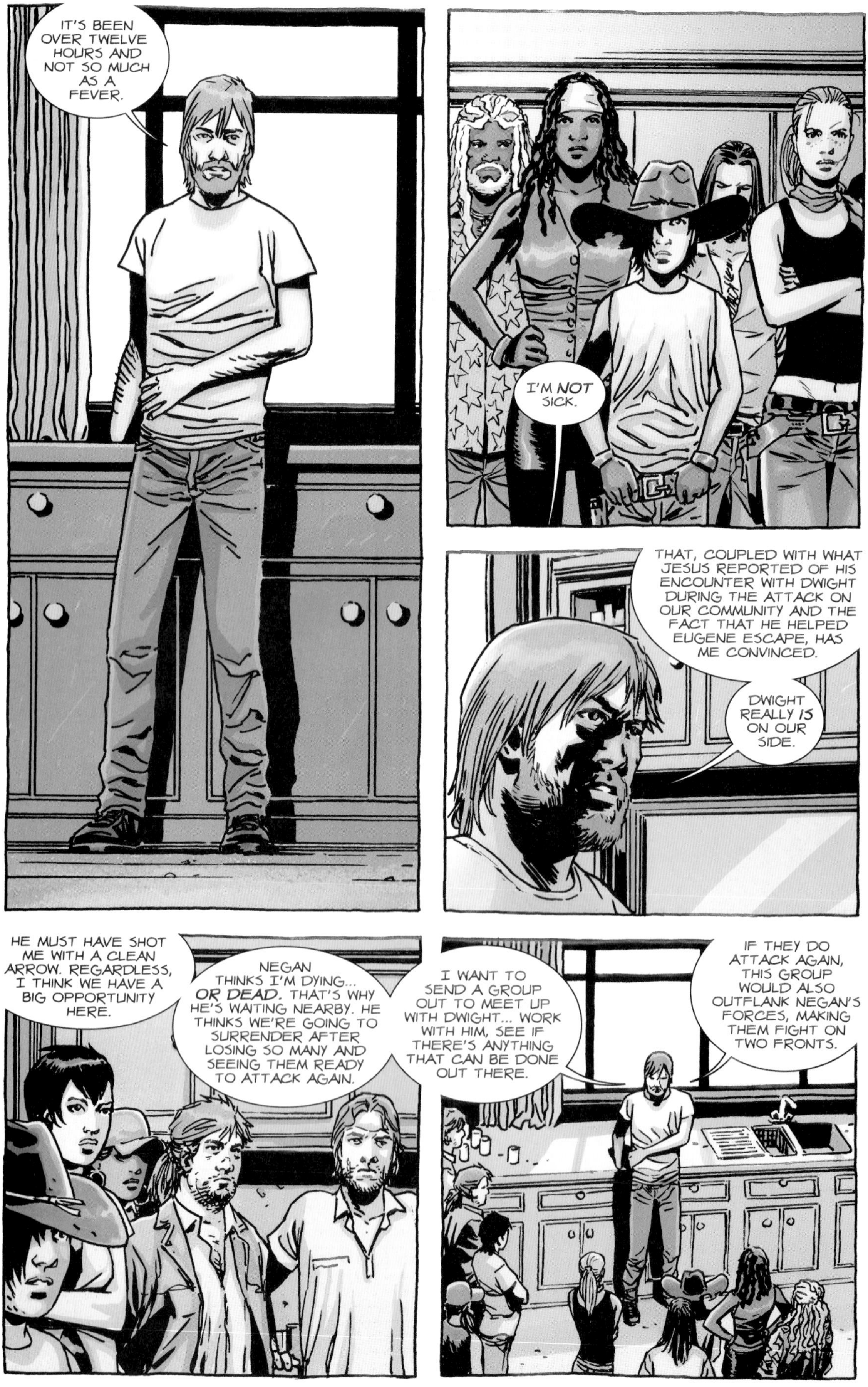
IT'S BEEN OVER TWELVE HOURS AND NOT SO MUCH AS A FEVER.
I'M NOT SICK.
THAT, COUPLED WITH WHAT JESUS REPORTED OF HIS ENCOUNTER WITH DWIGHT DURING THE ATTACK ON OUR COMMUNITY AND THE FACT THAT HE HELPED EUGENE ESCAPE, HAS ME CONVINCED.
DWIGHT REALLY IS ON OUR SIDE.
HE MUST HAVE SHOT ME WITH A CLEAN ARROW. REGARDLESS, I THINK WE HAVE A BIG OPPORTUNITY HERE.
NEGAN THINKS I'M DYING... OR DEAD. THAT'S WHY HE'S WAITING NEARBY. HE THINKS WE'RE GOING TO SURRENDER AFTER LOSING SO MANY AND SEEING THEM READY TO ATTACK AGAIN.
I WANT TO SEND A GROUP OUT TO MEET UP WITH DWIGHT... WORK WITH HIM, SEE IF THERE'S ANYTHING THAT CAN BE DONE OUT THERE.
IF THEY DO ATTACK AGAIN, THIS GROUP WOULD ALSO OUTFLANK NEGAN'S FORCES, MAKING THEM FIGHT ON TWO FRONTS.

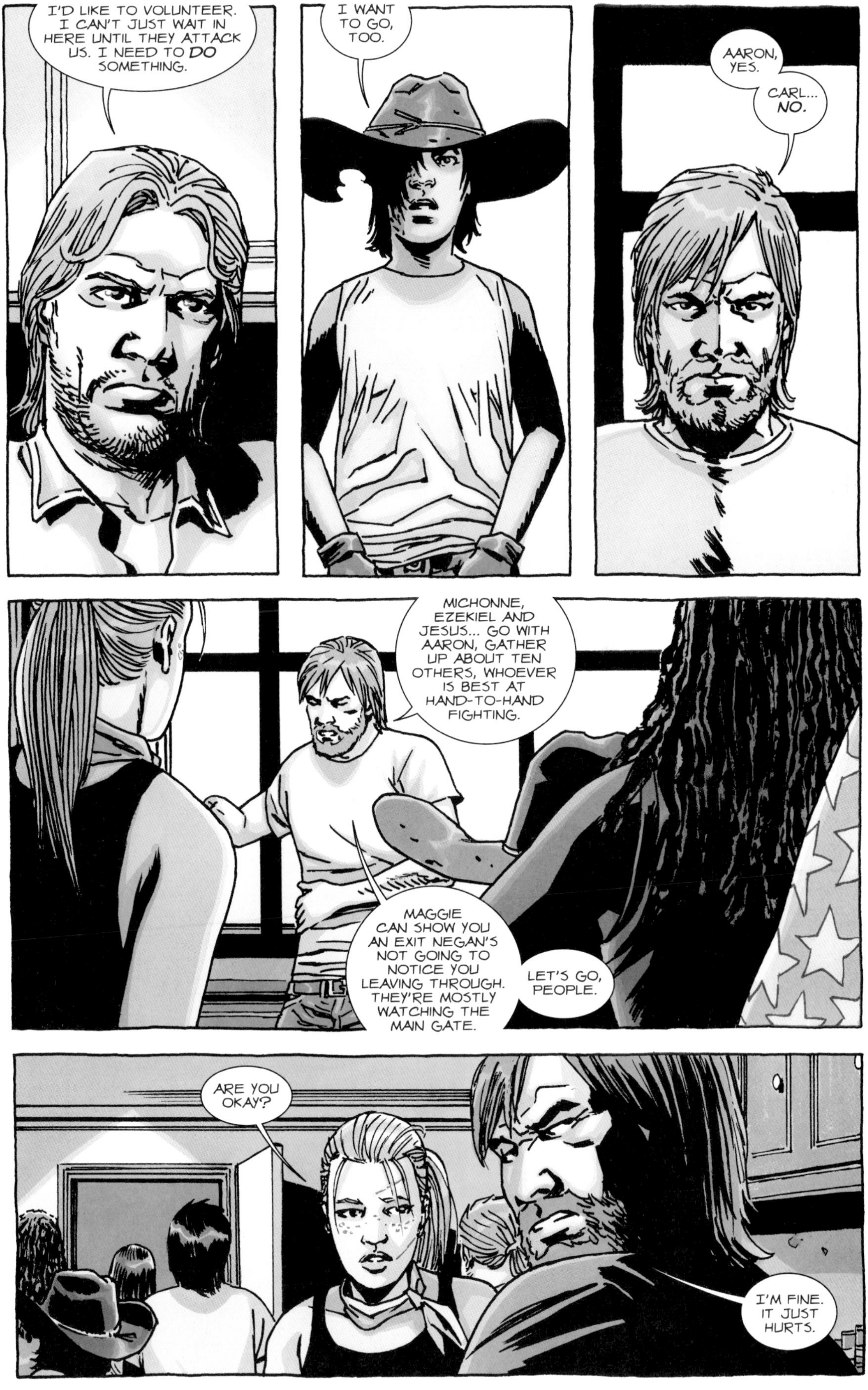

I'D LIKE TO VOLUNTEER. I CAN'T JUST WAIT IN HERE UNTIL THEY ATTACK US. I NEED TO DO SOMETHING.
I WANT TO GO, TOO.
AARON, YES.
CARL... NO.
MICHONNE, EZEKIEL AND JESUS... GO WITH AARON, GATHER UP ABOUT TEN OTHERS, WHOEVER IS BEST AT HAND-TO-HAND FIGHTING.
MAGGIE CAN SHOW YOU AN EXIT NEGAN'S NOT GOING TO NOTICE YOU LEAVING THROUGH. THEY'RE MOSTLY WATCHING THE MAIN GATE.
LET'S GO, PEOPLE.
ARE YOU OKAY?
I'M FINE. IT JUST HURTS.

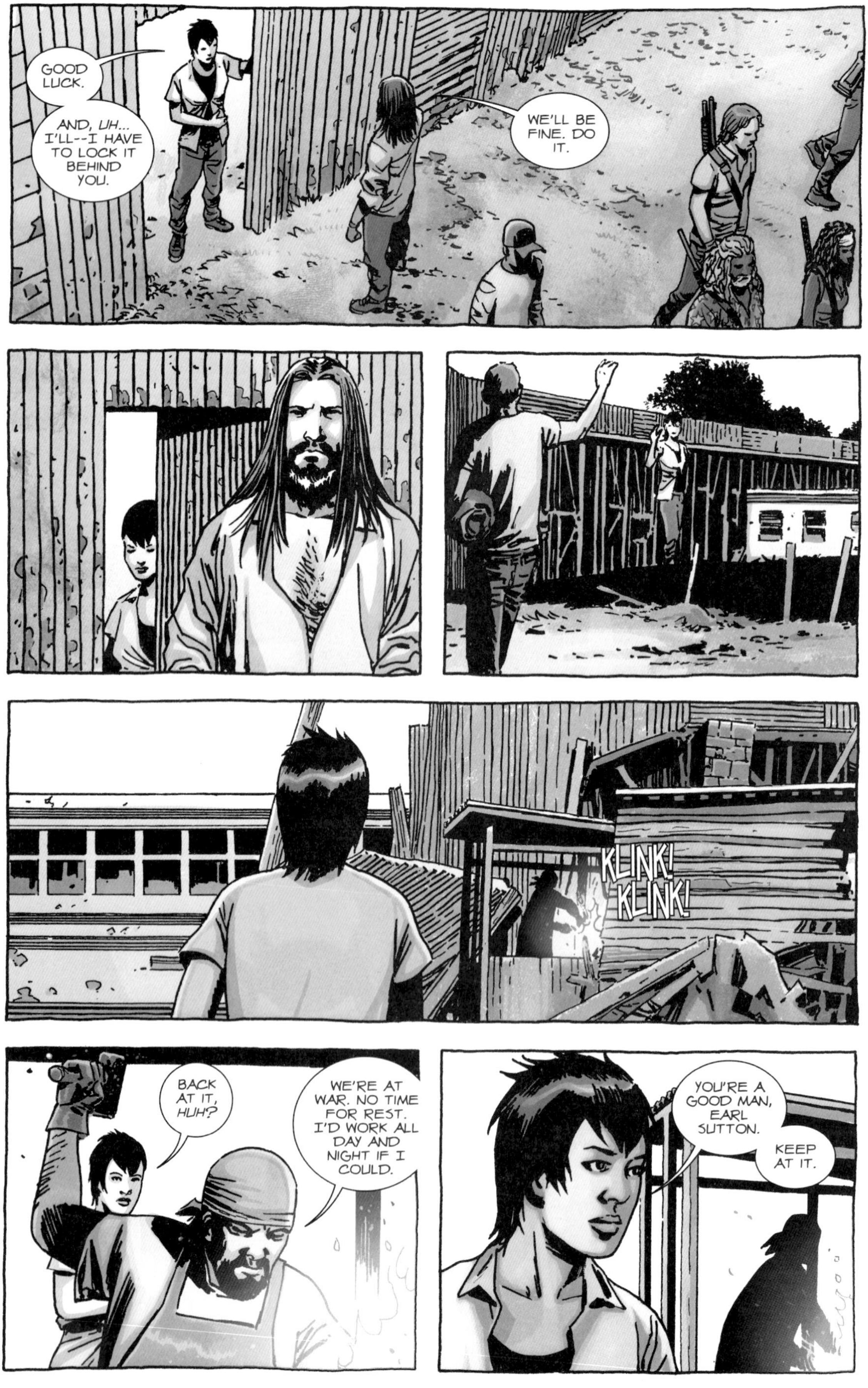
GOOD LUCK.
AND, UH... I'LL--I HAVE TO LOCK IT BEHIND YOU.
WE'LL BE FINE. DO IT.
KLINK! KLINK!
BACK AT IT, HUH?
WE'RE AT WAR. NO TIME FOR REST. I'D WORK ALL DAY AND NIGHT IF I COULD.
YOU'RE A GOOD MAN, EARL SUTTON.
KEEP AT IT.

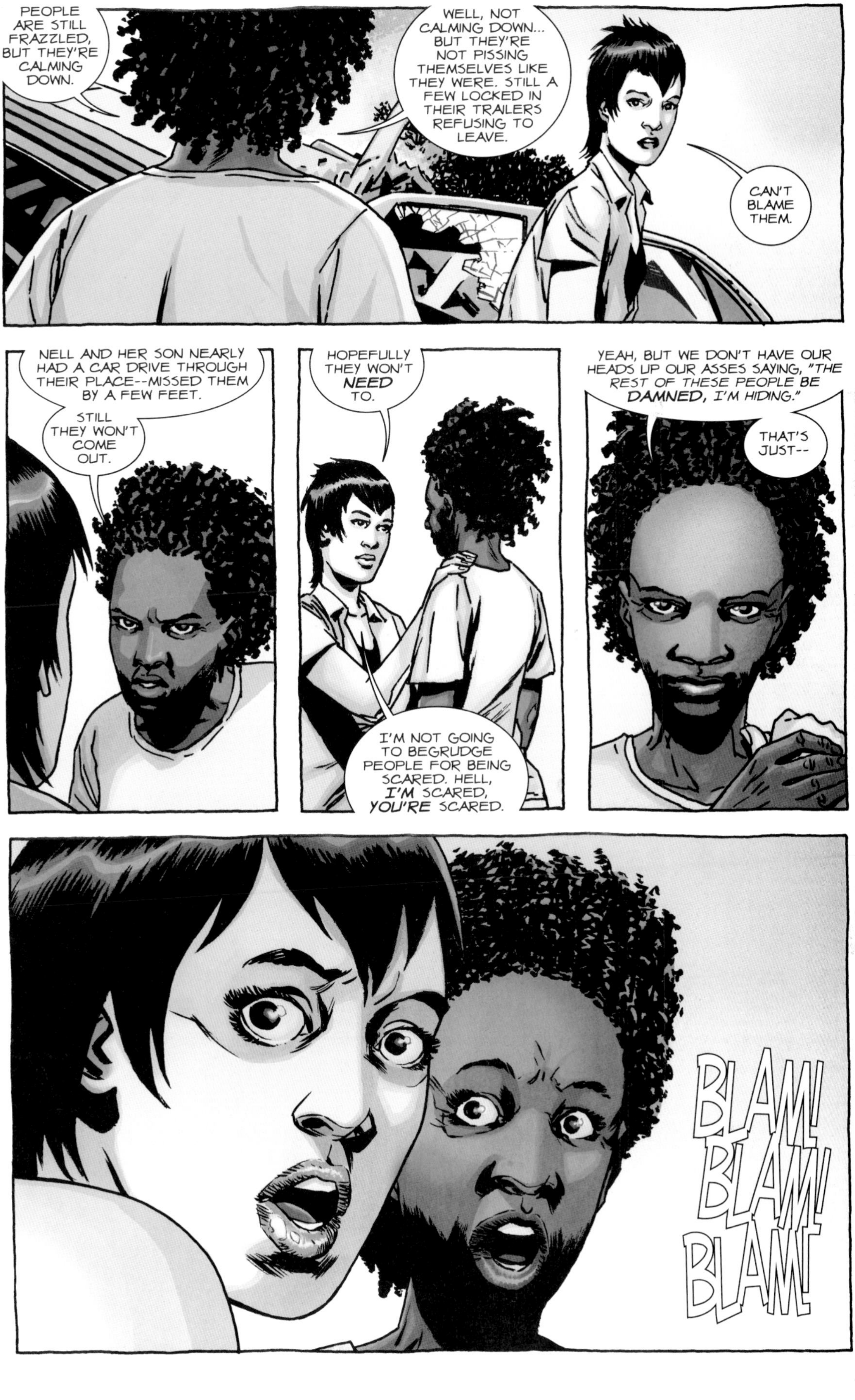
PEOPLE ARE STILL FRAZZLED, BUT THEY'RE CALMING DOWN.
WELL, NOT CALMING DOWN... BUT THEY'RE NOT PISSING THEMSELVES LIKE THEY WERE. STILL A FEW LOCKED IN THEIR TRAILERS REFUSING TO LEAVE.
CAN'T BLAME THEM.
NELL AND HER SON NEARLY HAD A CAR DRIVE THROUGH THEIR PLACE--MISSED THEM BY A FEW FEET.
STILL THEY WON'T COME OUT.
HOPEFULLY THEY WON'T NEED TO.
I'M NOT GOING TO BEGRUDGE PEOPLE FOR BEING SCARED. HELL, I'M SCARED, YOU'RE SCARED.
YEAH, BUT WE DON'T HAVE OUR HEADS UP OUR ASSES SAYING, "THE REST OF THESE PEOPLE BE DAMNED, I'M HIDING."
THAT'S JUST--
BLAM! BLAM! BLAM!

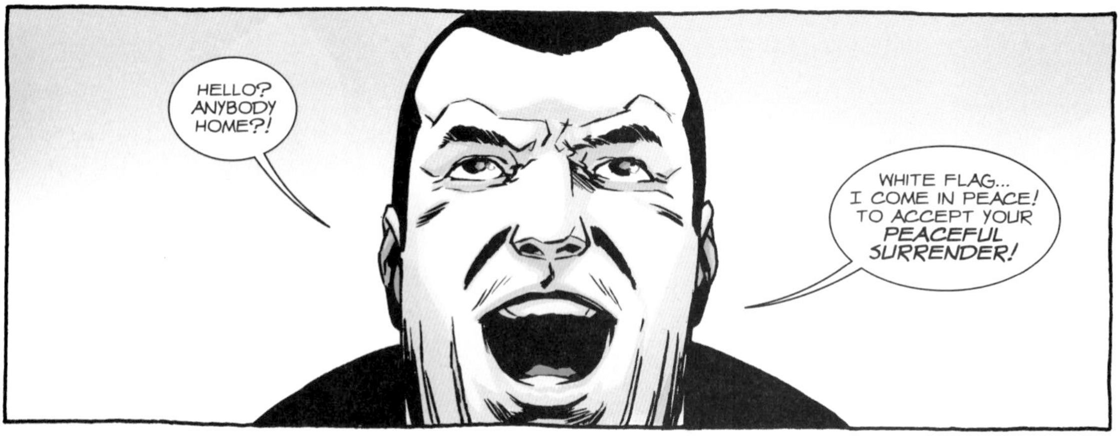
HELLO? ANYBODY HOME?!
WHITE FLAG... I COME IN PEACE! TO ACCEPT YOUR PEACEFUL SURRENDER!

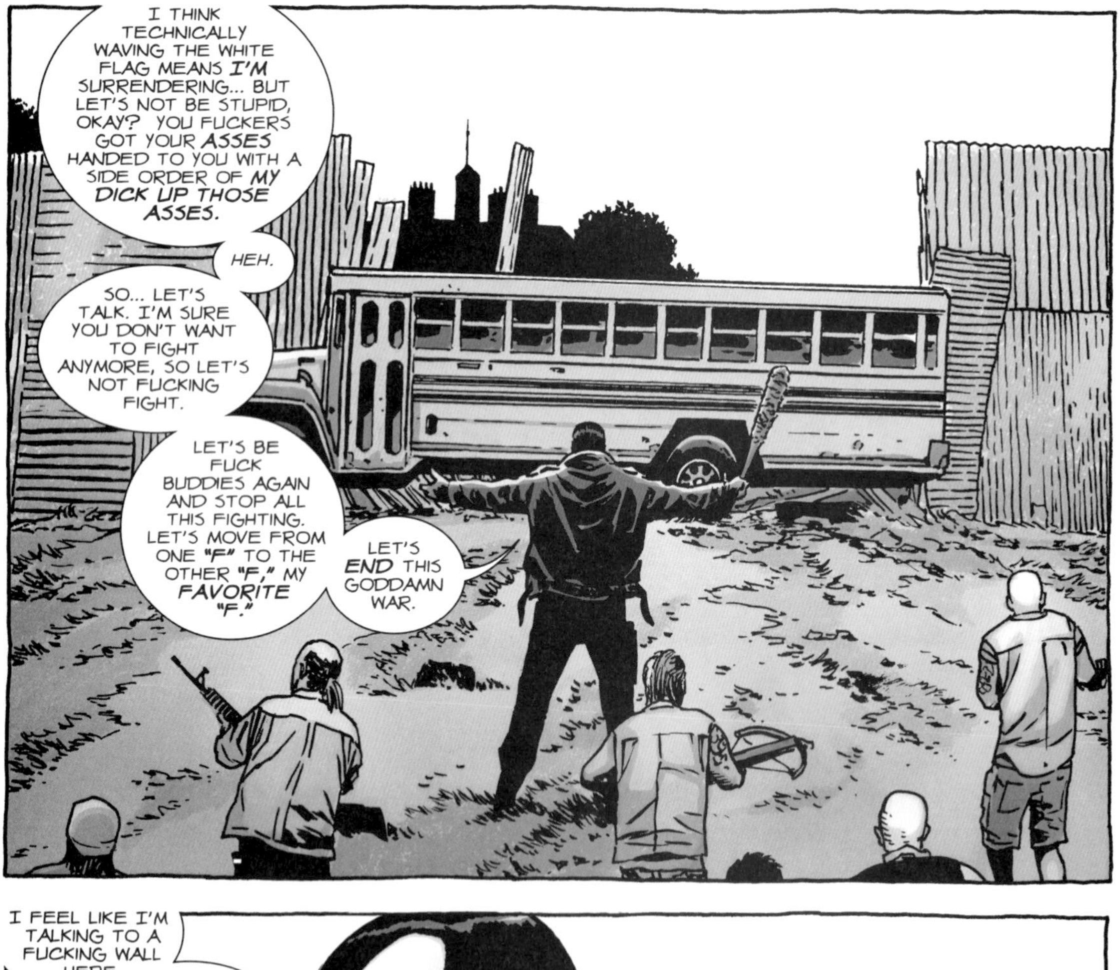
I THINK TECHNICALLY WAVING THE WHITE FLAG MEANS I'M SURRENDERING... BUT LET'S NOT BE STUPID, OKAY? YOU FUCKERS GOT YOUR ASSES HANDED TO YOU WITH A SIDE ORDER OF MY DICK UP THOSE ASSES.
HEH.
SO... LET'S TALK. I'M SURE YOU DON'T WANT TO FIGHT ANYMORE, SO LET'S NOT FUCKING FIGHT.
LET'S BE FUCK BUDDIES AGAIN AND STOP ALL THIS FIGHTING. LET'S MOVE FROM ONE "F" TO THE OTHER "F," MY FAVORITE "F."
LET'S END THIS GODDAMN WAR.

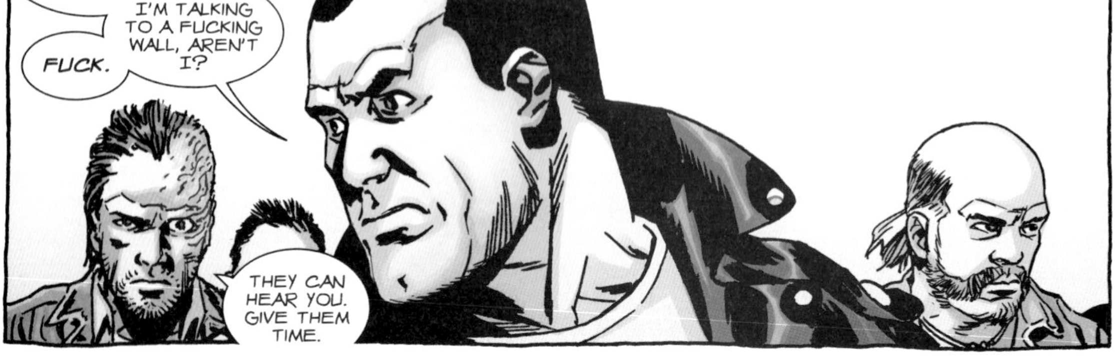
I FEEL LIKE I'M TALKING TO A FUCKING WALL HERE.
I'M TALKING TO A FUCKING WALL, AREN'T I?
FUCK.
THEY CAN HEAR YOU. GIVE THEM TIME.

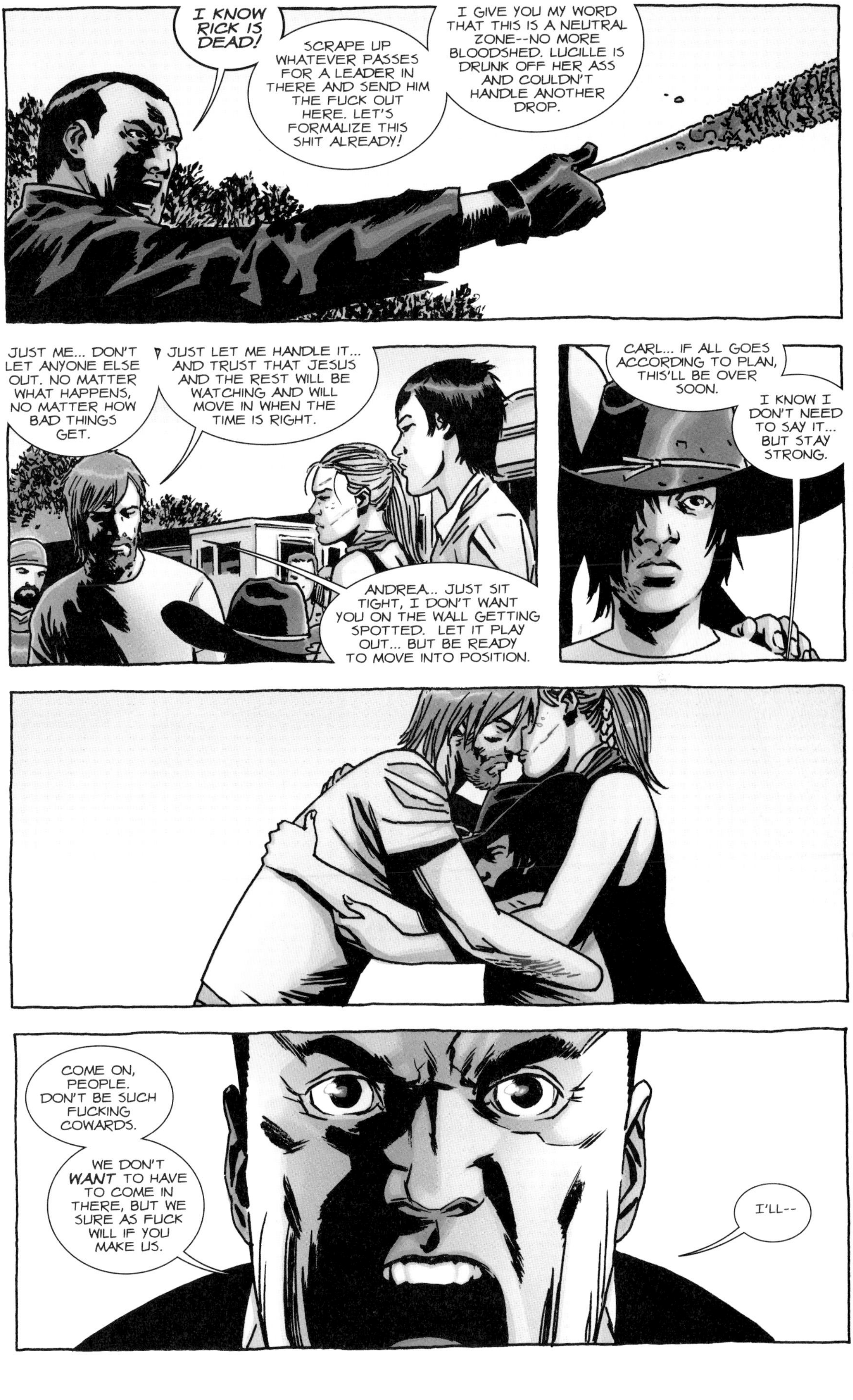
I KNOW RICK IS DEAD!
SCRAPE UP WHATEVER PASSES FOR A LEADER IN THERE AND SEND HIM THE FUCK OUT HERE. LET'S FORMALIZE THIS SHIT ALREADY!
I GIVE YOU MY WORD THAT THIS IS A NEUTRAL ZONE--NO MORE BLOODSHED. LUCILLE IS DRUNK OFF HER ASS AND COULDN'T HANDLE ANOTHER DROP.
JUST ME... DON'T LET ANYONE ELSE OUT. NO MATTER WHAT HAPPENS, NO MATTER HOW BAD THINGS GET.
JUST LET ME HANDLE IT... AND TRUST THAT JESUS AND THE REST WILL BE WATCHING AND WILL MOVE IN WHEN THE TIME IS RIGHT.
ANDREA.. JUST SIT TIGHT, I DON'T WANT YOU ON THE WALL GETTING SPOTTED. LET IT PLAY OUT... BUT BE READY TO MOVE INTO POSITION.
CARL... IF ALL GOES ACCORDING TO PLAN, THIS'LL BE OVER SOON.
I KNOW I DON'T NEED TO SAY IT... BUT STAY STRONG.
COME ON, PEOPLE. DON'T BE SUCH FUCKING COWARDS.
WE DON'T WANT TO HAVE TO COME IN THERE, BUT WE SURE AS FUCK WILL IF YOU MAKE US.
I'LL--

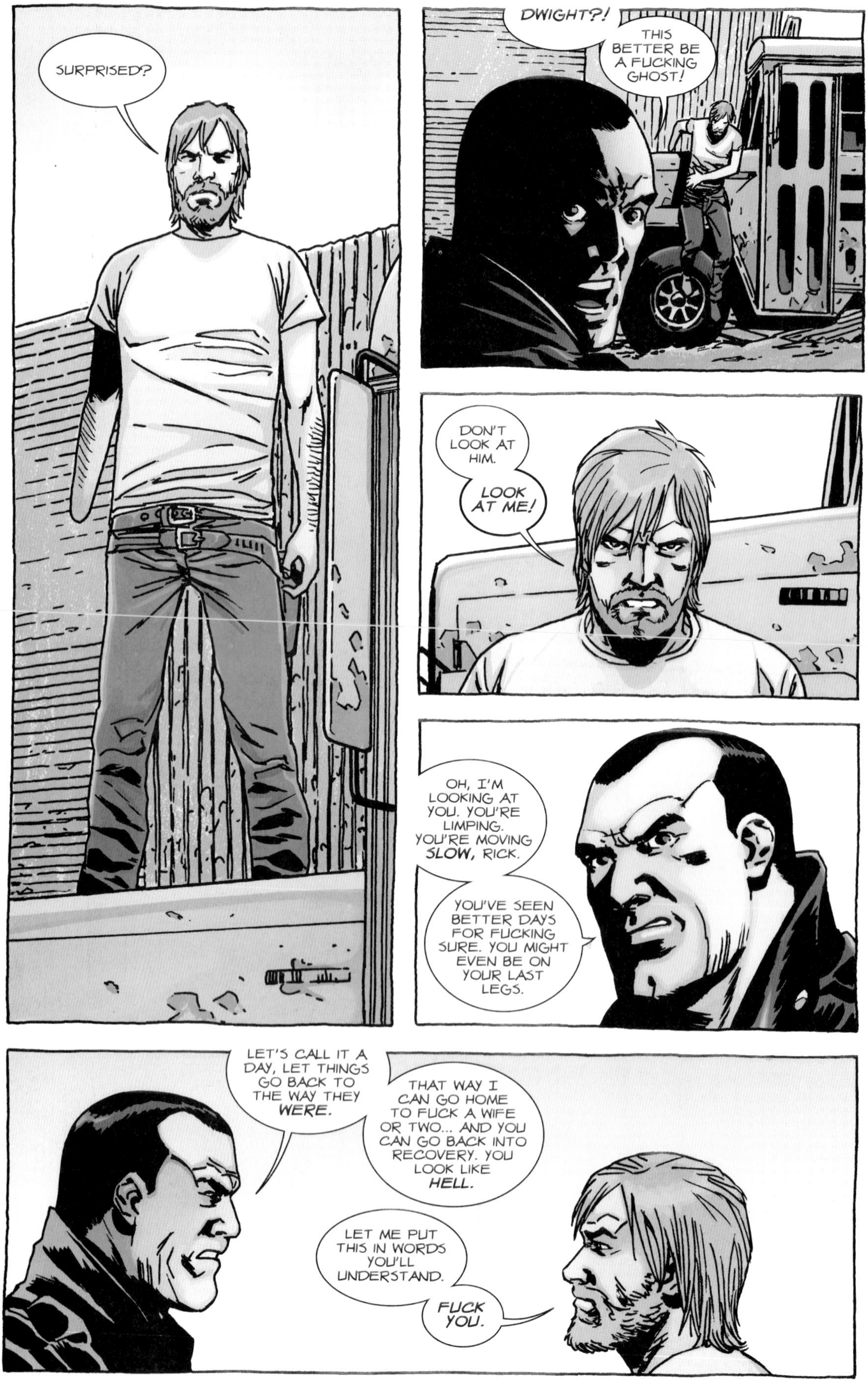
SURPRISED?
DWIGHT?!
THIS BETTER BE A FUCKING GHOST!
DON'T LOOK AT HIM.
LOOK AT ME!
OH, I'M LOOKING AT YOU. YOU'RE LIMPING. YOU'RE MOVING SLOW, RICK.
YOU'VE SEEN BETTER DAYS FOR FUCKING SURE. YOU MIGHT EVEN BE ON YOUR LAST LEGS.
LET'S CALL IT A DAY, LET THINGS GO BACK TO THE WAY THEY WERE.
THAT WAY I CAN GO HOME TO FUCK A WIFE OR TWO... AND YOU CAN GO BACK INTO RECOVERY. YOU LOOK LIKE HELL.
LET ME PUT THIS IN WORDS YOU'LL UNDERSTAND.
FUCK YOU.

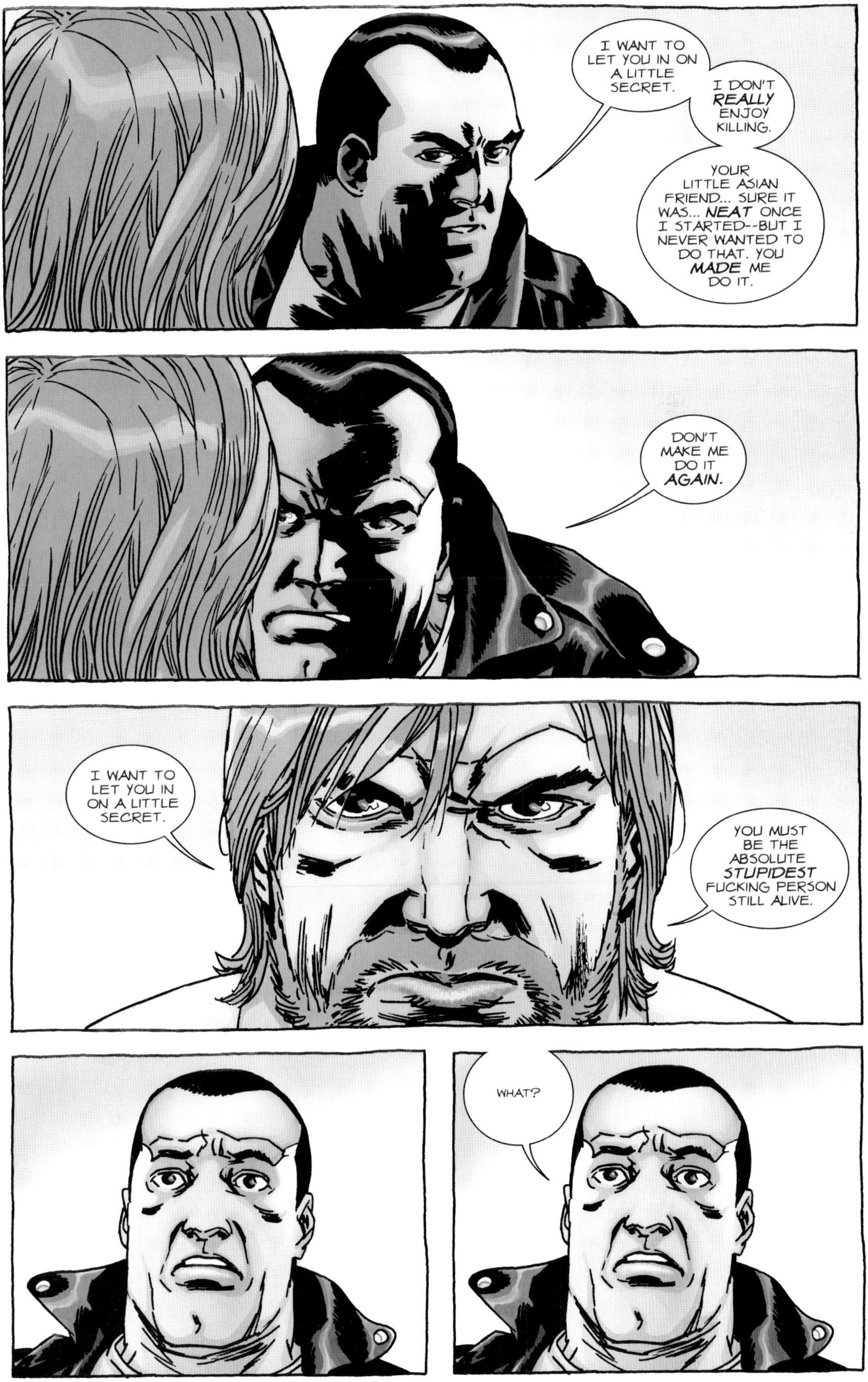
I WANT TO LET YOU IN ON A LITTLE SECRET.
I DON'T REALLY ENJOY KILLING.
YOUR LITTLE ASIAN FRIEND... SURE IT WAS... NEAT ONCE I STARTED--BUT I NEVER WANTED TO DO THAT. YOU MADE ME DO IT.
DON'T MAKE ME DO IT AGAIN.
I WANT TO LET YOU IN ON A LITTLE SECRET.
YOU MUST BE THE ABSOLUTE STUPIDEST FUCKING PERSON STILL ALIVE.
WHAT?

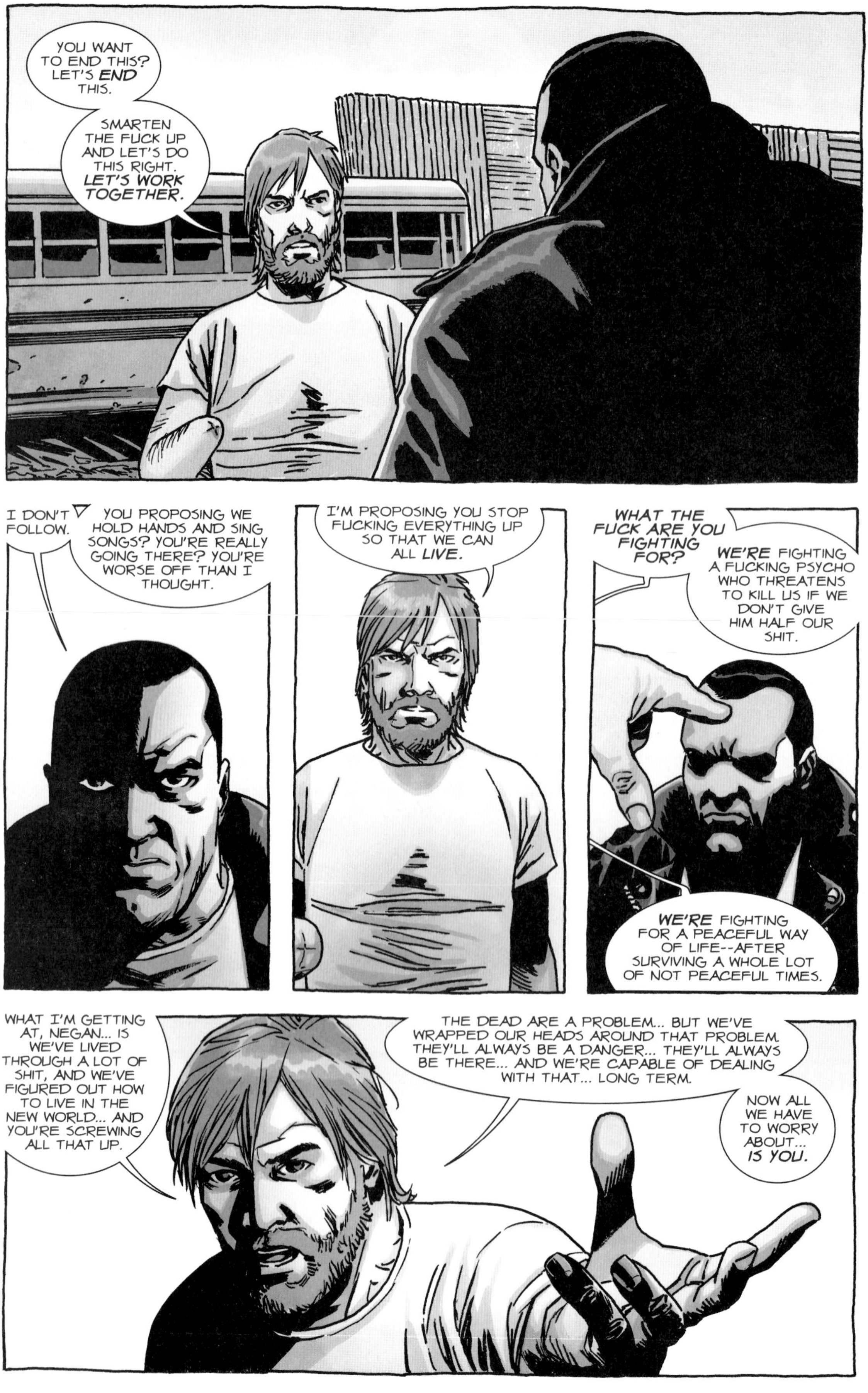
YOU WANT TO END THIS? LET'S END THIS.
SMARTEN THE FUCK UP AND LET'S DO THIS RIGHT. LET'S WORK TOGETHER.
I DON'T FOLLOW.
YOU PROPOSING WE HOLD HANDS AND SING SONGS? YOU'RE REALLY GOING THERE? YOU'RE WORSE OFF THAN I THOUGHT.
I'M PROPOSING YOU STOP FUCKING EVERYTHING UP SO THAT WE CAN ALL LIVE.
WHAT THE FUCK ARE YOU FIGHTING FOR?
WE'RE FIGHTING A FUCKING PSYCHO WHO THREATENS TO KILL US IF WE DON'T GIVE HIM HALF OUR SHIT.
WE'RE FIGHTING FOR A PEACEFUL WAY OF LIFE--AFTER SURVIVING A WHOLE LOT OF NOT PEACEFUL TIMES.
WHAT I'M GETTING AT, NEGAN... IS WE'VE LIVED THROUGH A LOT OF SHIT, AND WE'VE FIGURED OUT HOW TO LIVE IN THE NEW WORLD... AND YOU'RE SCREWING ALL THAT UP.
THE DEAD ARE A PROBLEM... BUT WE'VE WRAPPED OUR HEADS AROUND THAT PROBLEM. THEY'LL ALWAYS BE A DANGER... THEY'LL ALWAYS BE THERE... AND WE'RE CAPABLE OF DEALING WITH THAT... LONG TERM.
NOW ALL WE HAVE TO WORRY ABOUT... IS YOU.

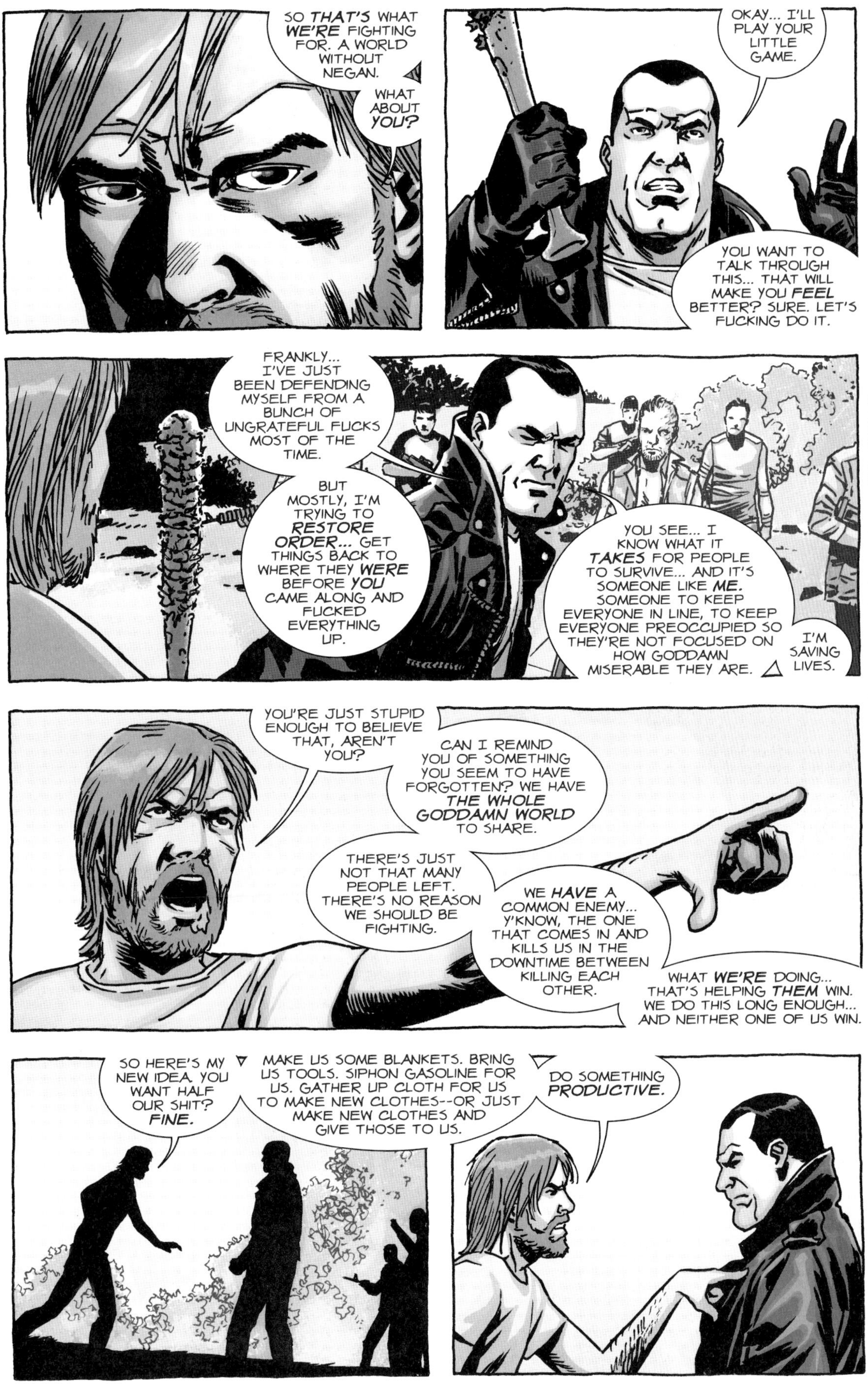

SO THAT'S WHAT WE'RE FIGHTING FOR. A WORLD WITHOUT NEGAN.
WHAT ABOUT YOU?
OKAY... I'LL PLAY YOUR LITTLE GAME.
YOU WANT TO TALK THROUGH THIS... THAT WILL MAKE YOU FEEL BETTER? SURE. LET'S FUCKING DO IT.
FRANKLY... I'VE JUST BEEN DEFENDING MYSELF FROM A BUNCH OF UNGRATEFUL FUCKS MOST OF THE TIME.
BUT MOSTLY, I'M TRYING TO RESTORE ORDER... GET THINGS BACK TO WHERE THEY WERE BEFORE YOU CAME ALONG AND FUCKED EVERYTHING UP.
YOU SEE... I KNOW WHAT IT TAKES FOR PEOPLE TO SURVIVE... AND IT'S SOMEONE LIKE ME. SOMEONE TO KEEP EVERYONE IN LINE, TO KEEP EVERYONE PREOCCUPIED SO THEY'RE NOT FOCUSED ON HOW GODDAMN MISERABLE THEY ARE.
I'M SAVING LIVES.
YOU'RE JUST STUPID ENOUGH TO BELIEVE THAT, AREN'T YOU?
CAN I REMIND YOU OF SOMETHING YOU SEEM TO HAVE FORGOTTEN? WE HAVE THE WHOLE GODDAMN WORLD TO SHARE.
THERE'S JUST NOT THAT MANY PEOPLE LEFT. THERE'S NO REASON WE SHOULD BE FIGHTING.
WE HAVE A COMMON ENEMY... Y'KNOW, THE ONE THAT COMES IN AND KILLS US IN THE DOWNTIME BETWEEN KILLING EACH OTHER.
WHAT WE'RE DOING... THAT'S HELPING THEM WIN. WE DO THIS LONG ENOUGH... AND NEITHER ONE OF US WIN.
SO HERE'S MY NEW IDEA. YOU WANT HALF OUR SHIT? FINE.
MAKE US SOME BLANKETS. BRING US TOOLS. SIPHON GASOLINE FOR US. GATHER UP CLOTH FOR US TO MAKE NEW CLOTHES--OR JUST MAKE NEW CLOTHES AND GIVE THOSE TO US.
DO SOMETHING PRODUCTIVE.

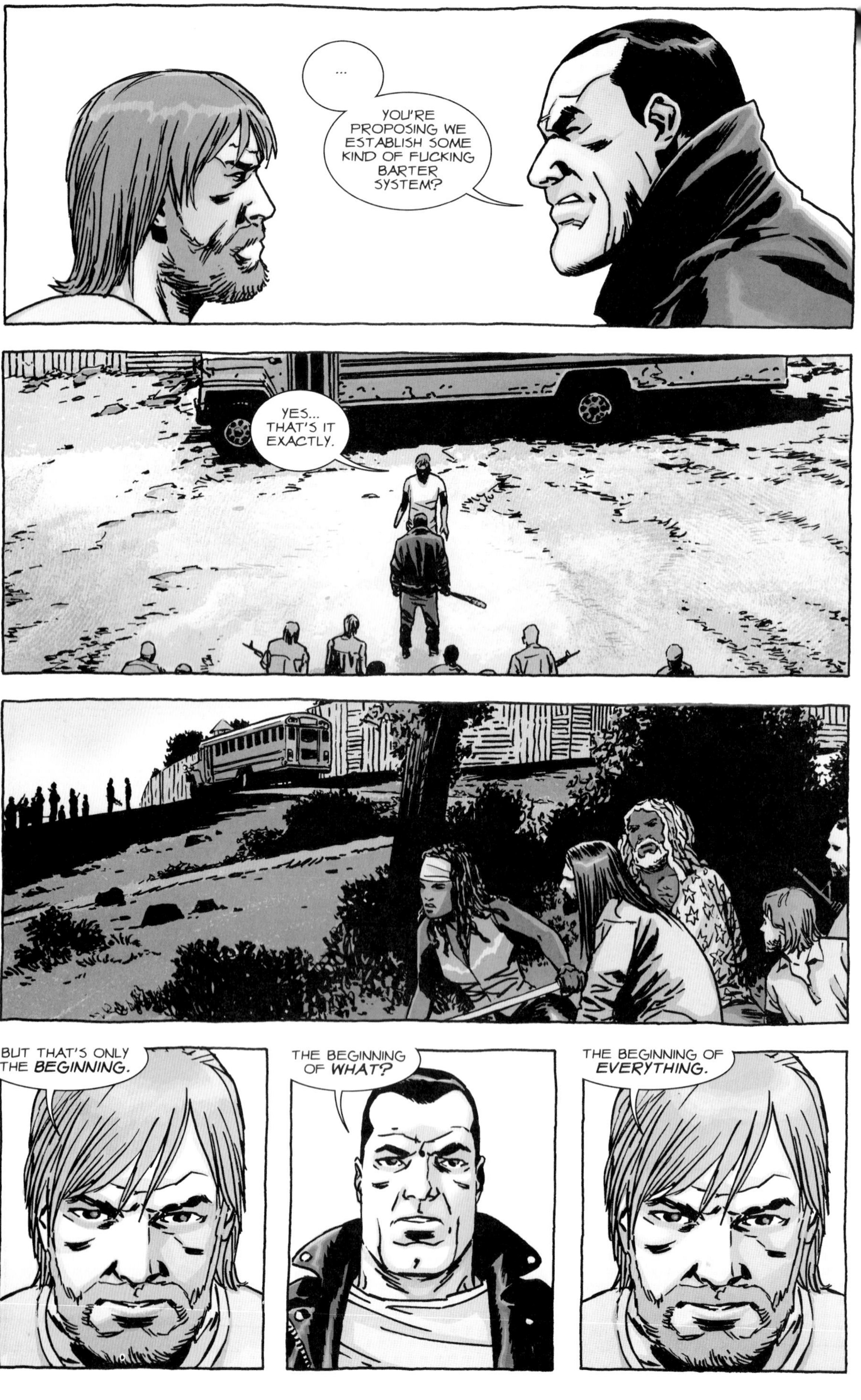
...
YOU'RE PROPOSING WE ESTABLISH SOME KIND OF FUCKING BARTER SYSTEM?
YES... THAT'S IT EXACTLY.
BUT THAT'S ONLY THE BEGINNING.
THE BEGINNING OF WHAT?
THE BEGINNING OF EVERYTHING.

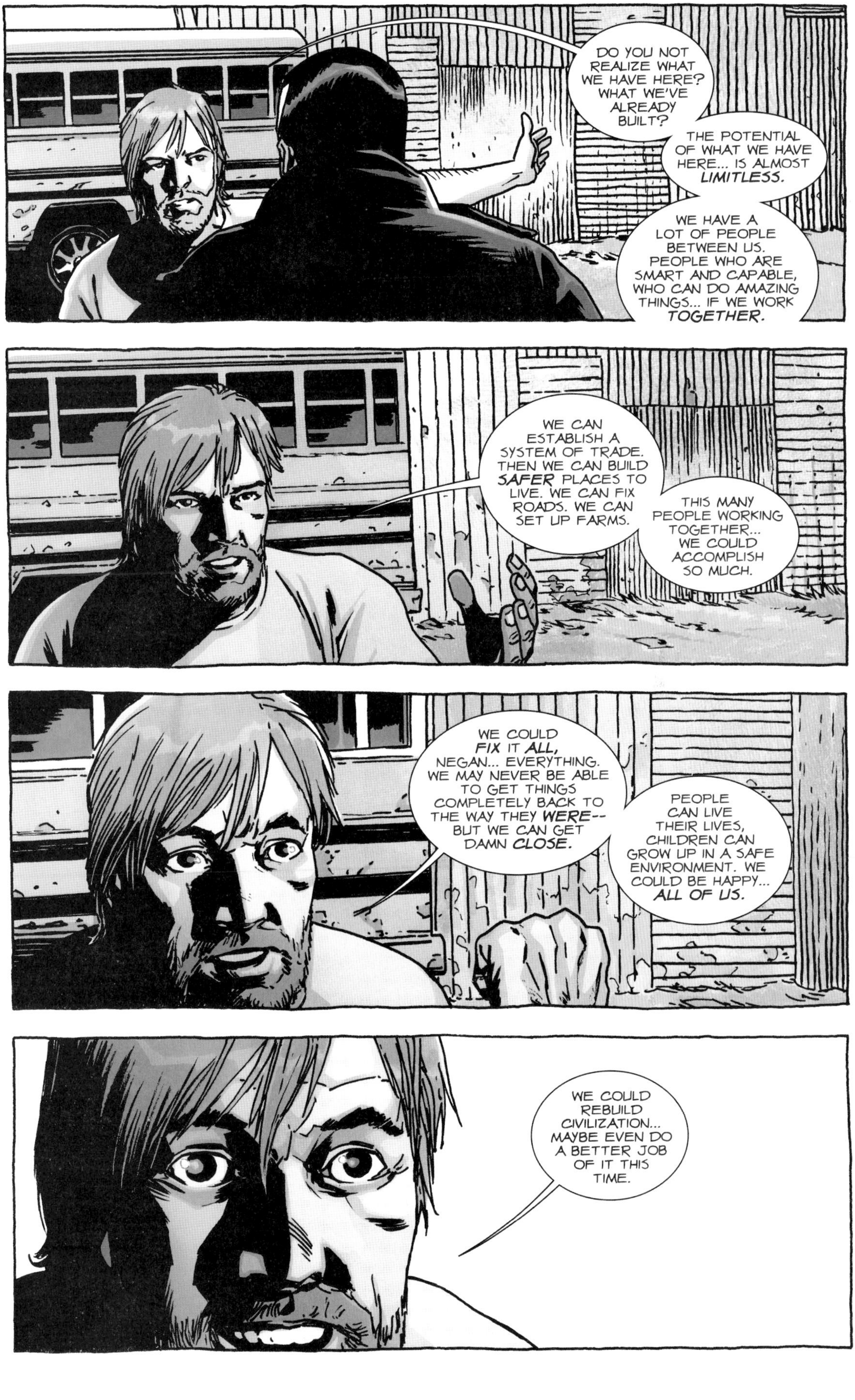
DO YOU NOT REALIZE WHAT WE HAVE HERE? WHAT WE'VE ALREADY BUILT?
THE POTENTIAL OF WHAT WE HAVE HERE... IS ALMOST LIMITLESS.
WE HAVE A LOT OF PEOPLE BETWEEN US. PEOPLE WHO ARE SMART AND CAPABLE, WHO CAN DO AMAZING THINGS... IF WE WORK TOGETHER.
WE CAN ESTABLISH A SYSTEM OF TRADE. THEN WE CAN BUILD SAFER PLACES TO LIVE. WE CAN FIX ROADS. WE CAN SET UP FARMS.
THIS MANY PEOPLE WORKING TOGETHER... WE COULD ACCOMPLISH SO MUCH.
WE COULD FIX IT ALL, NEGAN... EVERYTHING. WE MAY NEVER BE ABLE TO GET THINGS COMPLETELY BACK TO THE WAY THEY WERE-- BUT WE CAN GET DAMN CLOSE.
PEOPLE CAN LIVE THEIR LIVES, CHILDREN CAN GROW UP IN A SAFE ENVIRONMENT. WE COULD BE HAPPY... ALL OF US.
WE COULD REBUILD CIVILIZATION... MAYBE EVEN DO A BETTER JOB OF IT THIS TIME.

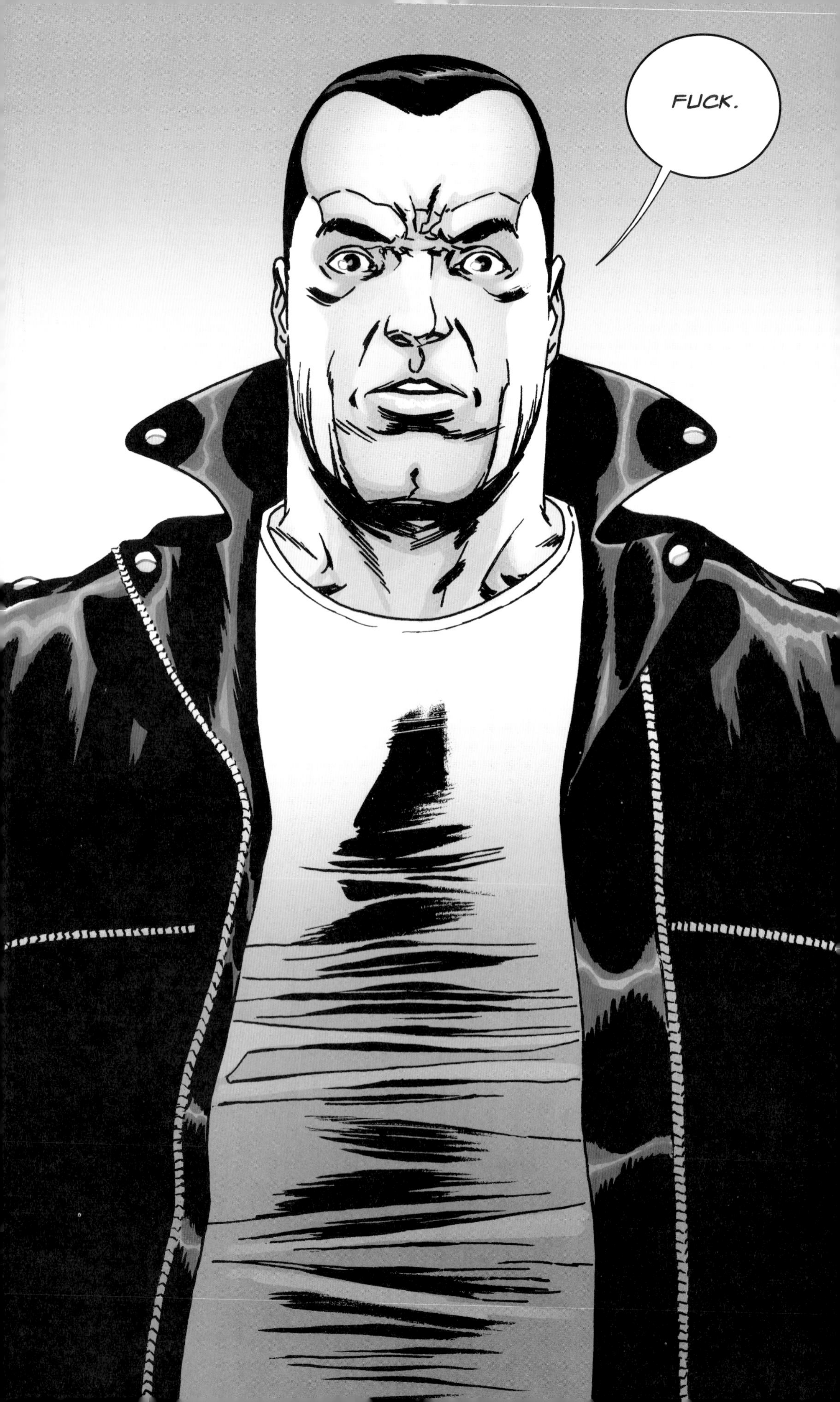
FUCK.

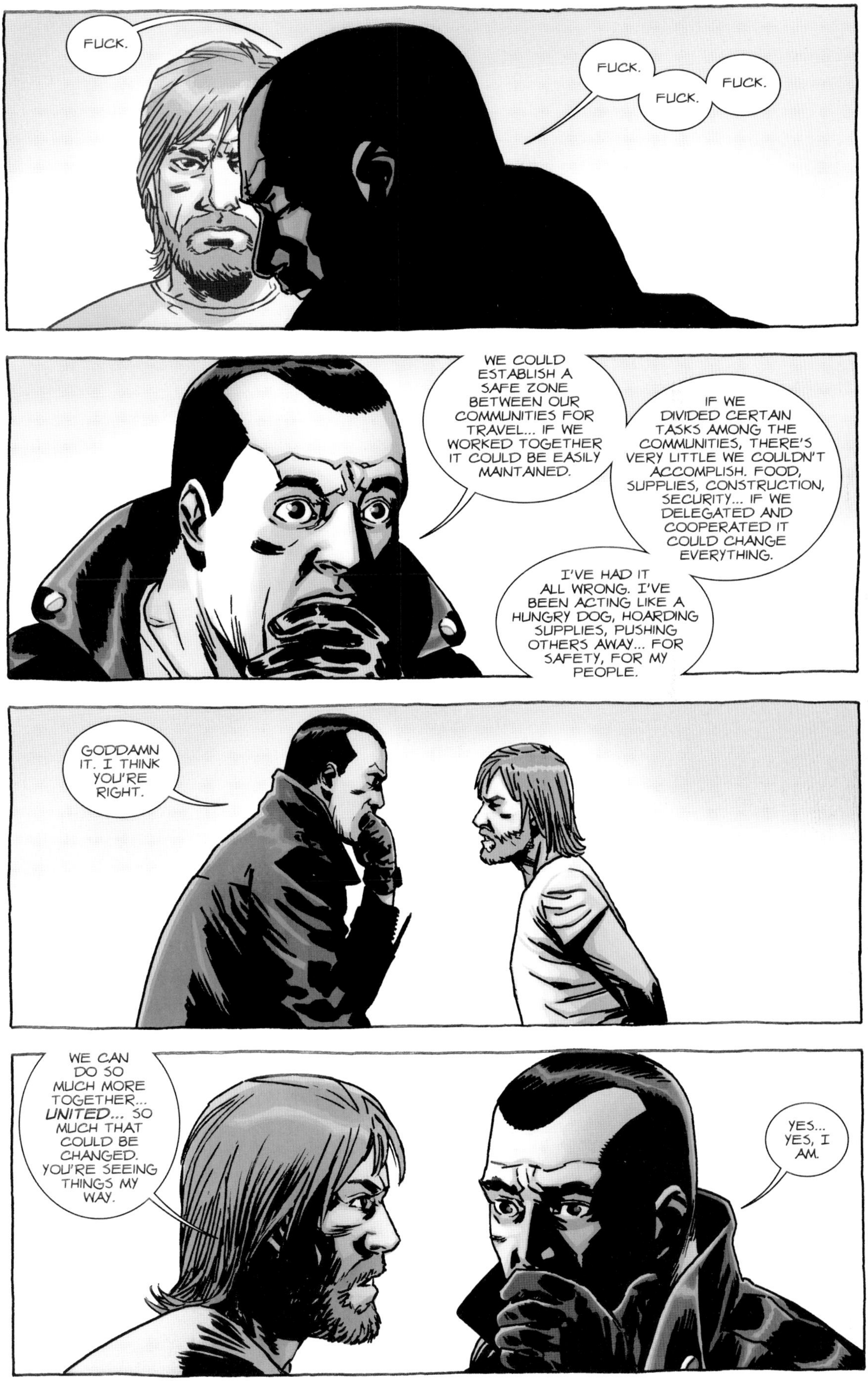

FUCK.
FUCK.
FUCK.
FUCK.
WE COULD ESTABLISH A SAFE ZONE BETWEEN OUR COMMUNITIES FOR TRAVEL... IF WE WORKED TOGETHER IT COULD BE EASILY MAINTAINED.
IF WE DIVIDED CERTAIN TASKS AMONG THE COMMUNITIES, THERE'S VERY LITTLE WE COULDN'T ACCOMPLISH. FOOD, SUPPLIES, CONSTRUCTION, SECURITY... IF WE DELEGATED AND COOPERATED IT COULD CHANGE EVERYTHING.
I'VE HAD IT ALL WRONG. I'VE BEEN ACTING LIKE A HUNGRY DOG, HOARDING SUPPLIES, PUSHING OTHERS AWAY... FOR SAFETY, FOR MY PEOPLE.
GODDAMN IT. I THINK YOU'RE RIGHT.
WE CAN DO SO MUCH MORE TOGETHER... *UNITED...* SO MUCH THAT COULD BE CHANGED. YOU'RE SEEING THINGS MY WAY.
YES... YES, I AM.

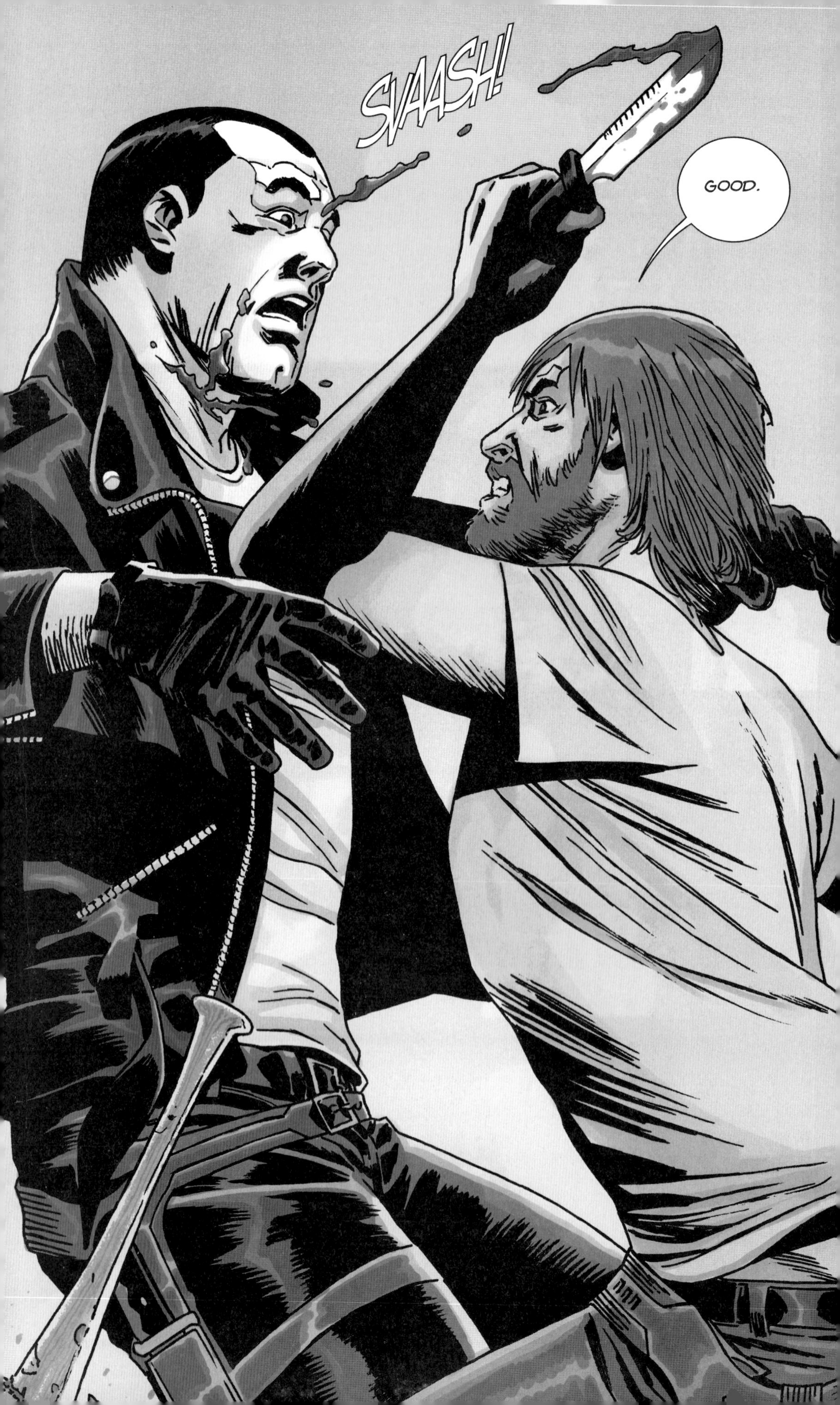
SVAASH!
GOOD.

=HUGK.=

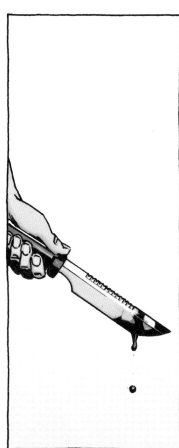

IT'S DONE! THIS WAR IS OVER!

WE HAVE A DOCTOR WHO CAN SAVE HIS LIFE!

SURRENDER AND ALLOW US TO TAKE HIM, AND WE WILL NOT ATTACK. YOU CAN APPOINT A NEW LEADER AND RETURN HOME.

DECIDE NOW BEFORE HE DIES!

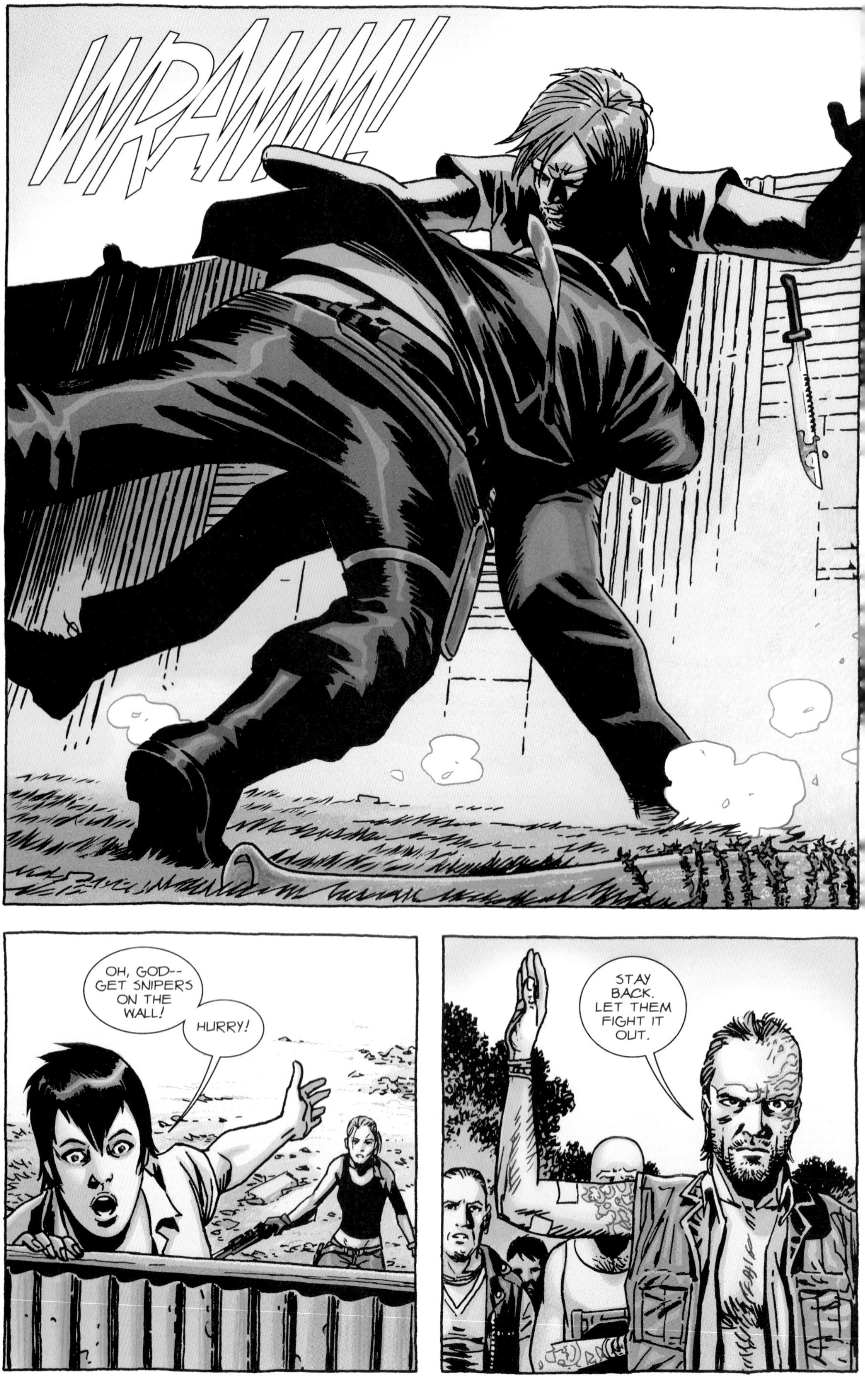
WRAMM!
OH, GOD-- GET SNIPERS ON THE WALL!
HURRY!
STAY BACK. LET THEM FIGHT IT OUT.

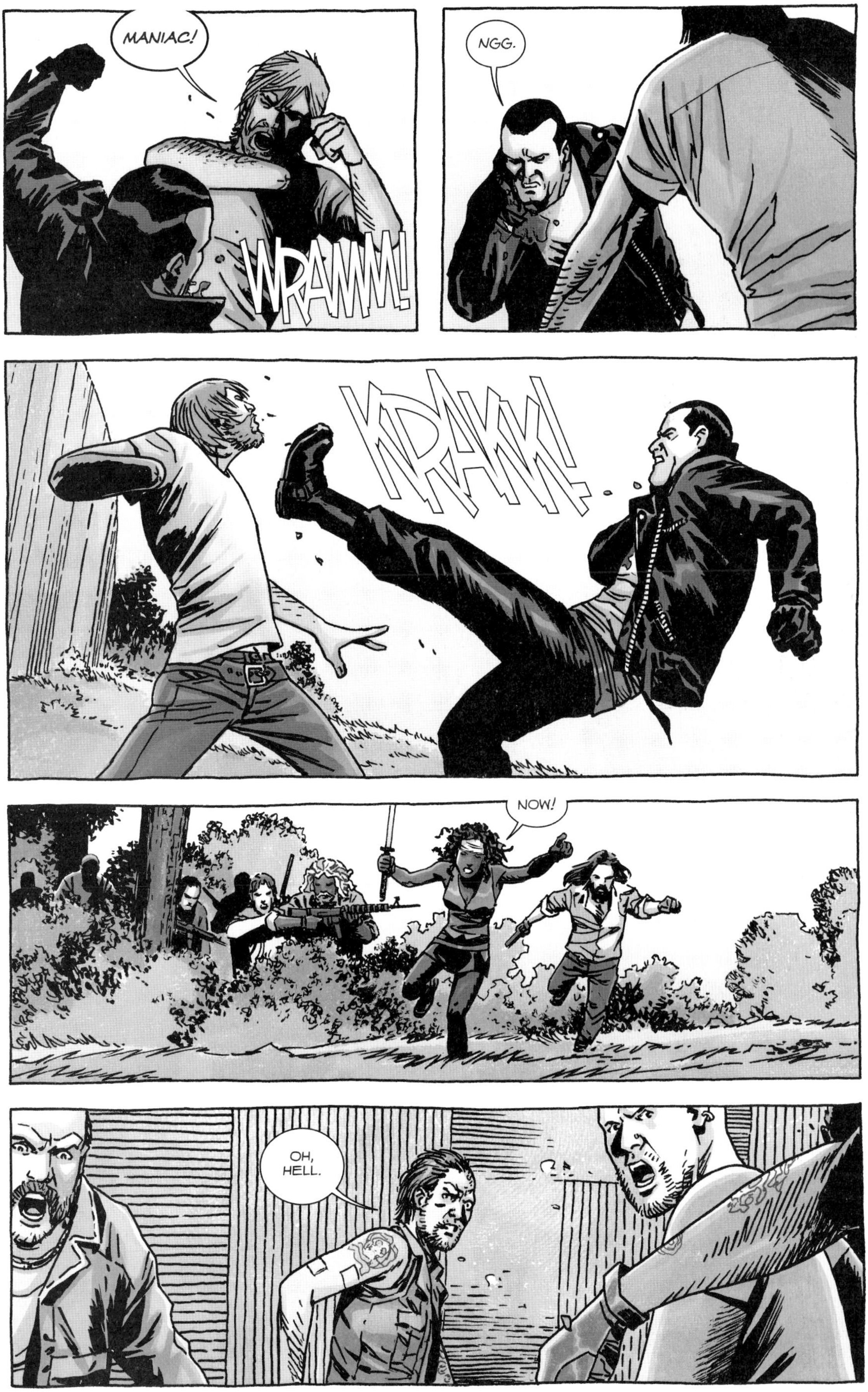
MANIAC!
WRAMM!
NGG.
KRAKK!
NOW!
OH, HELL.

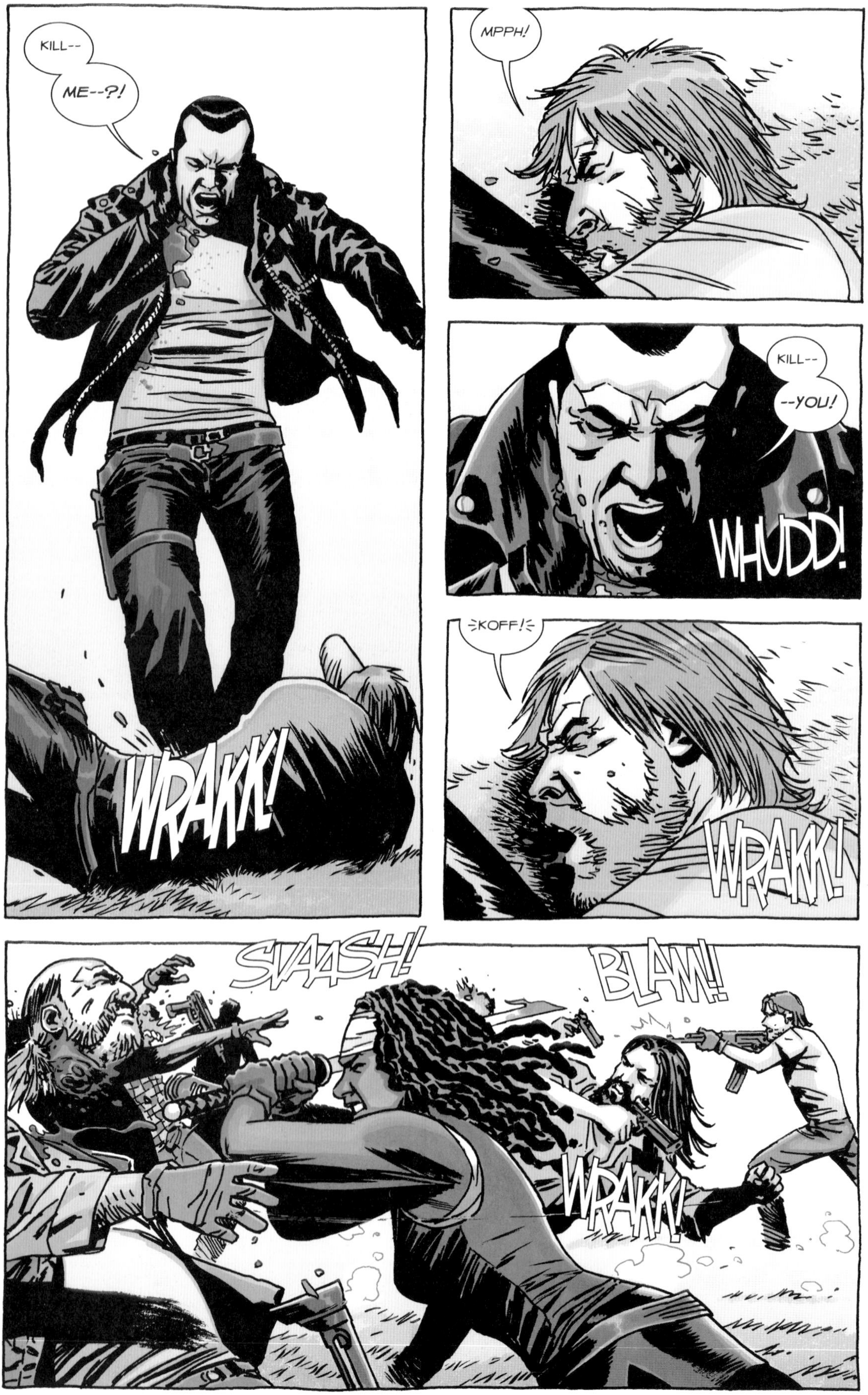
KILL--
ME--?!
WRAKK!
MPPH!
KILL--
--YOU!
WHUDD!
KOFF!
WRAKK!
SVAASH!
BLAM!
WRAKK!

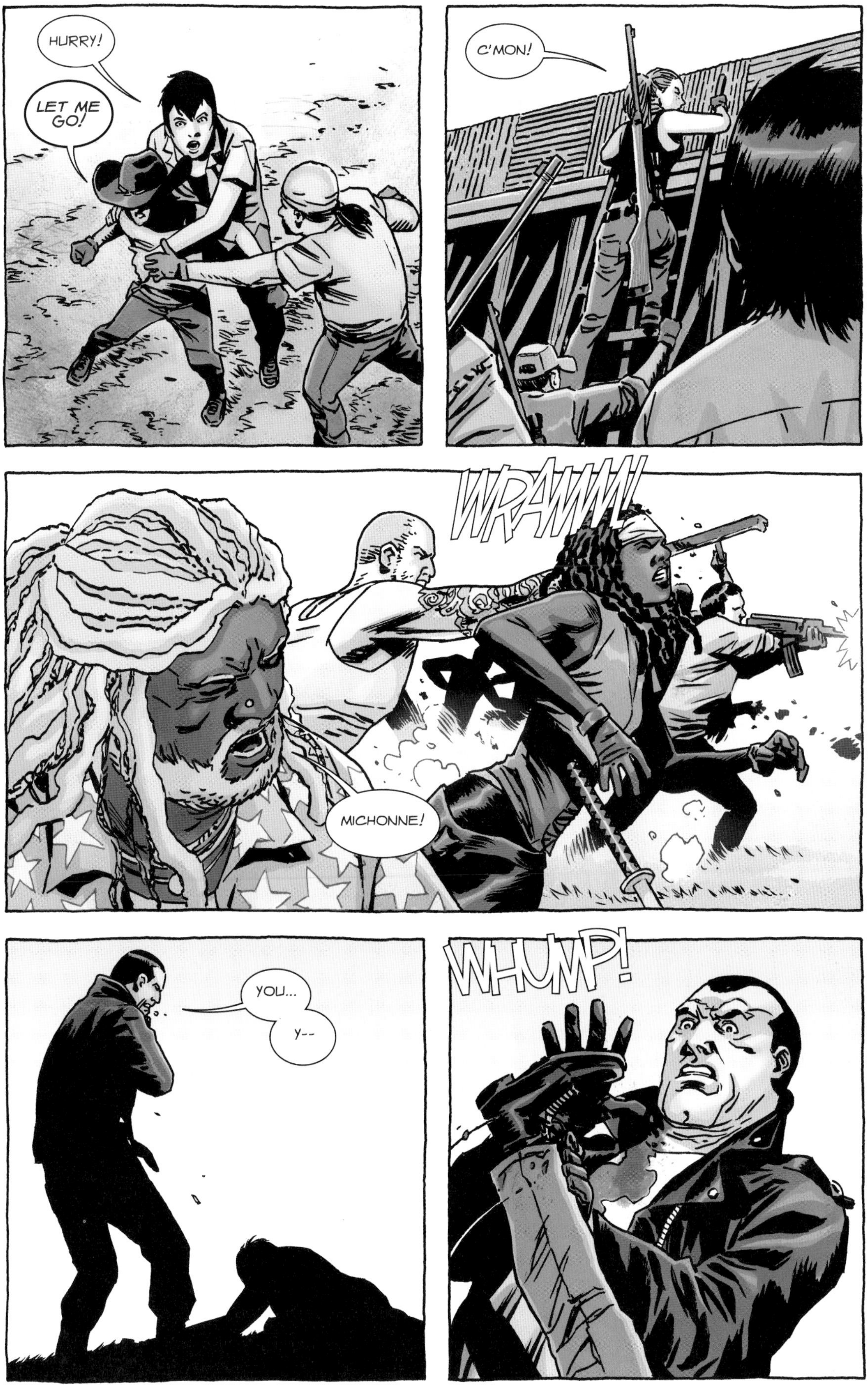
HURRY!
LET ME GO!
C'MON!
WRAMM!
MICHONNE!
YOU...
Y--
WHUMP!

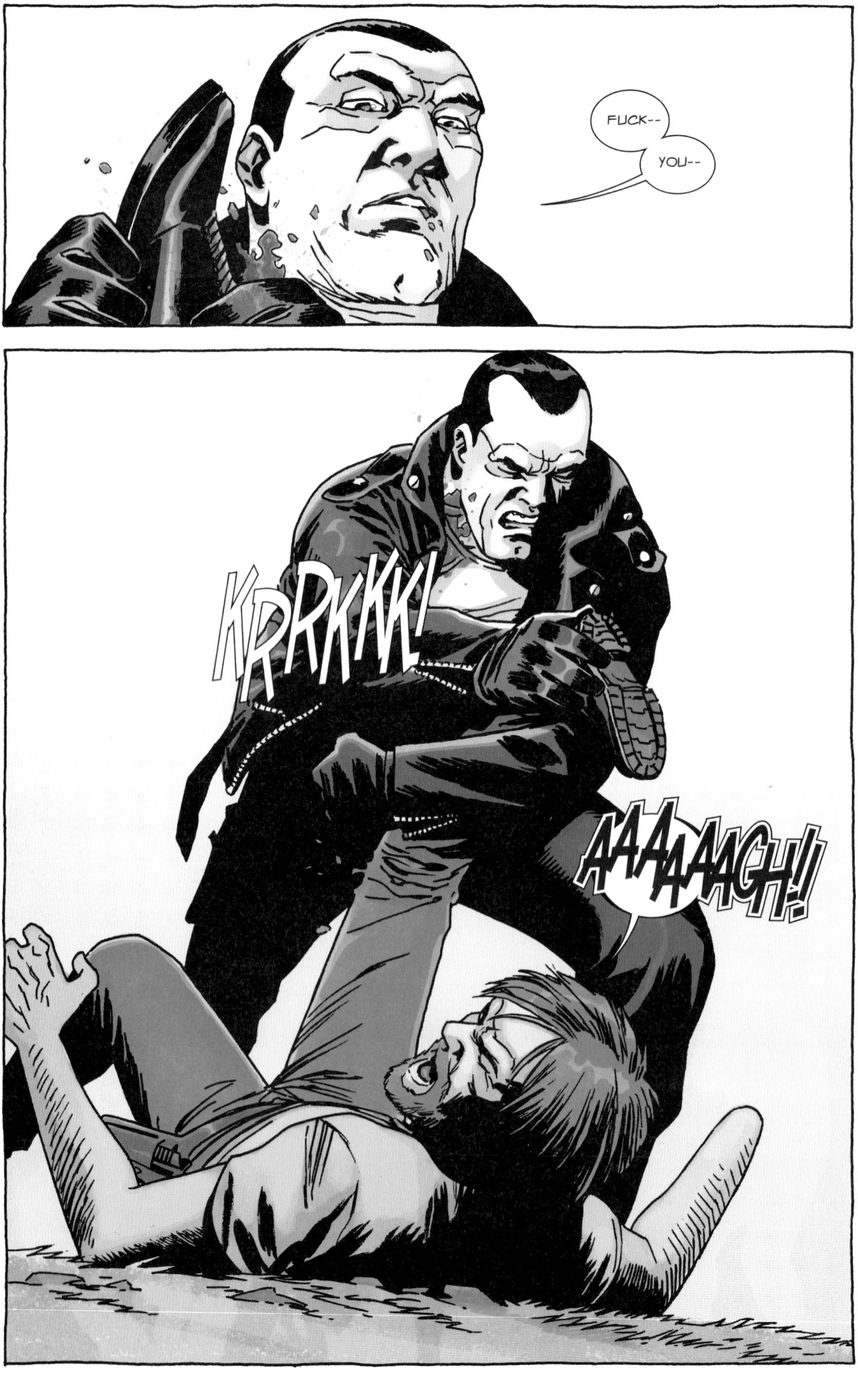
FUCK--
YOU--
KRRKKK!
AAAAAAGH!!

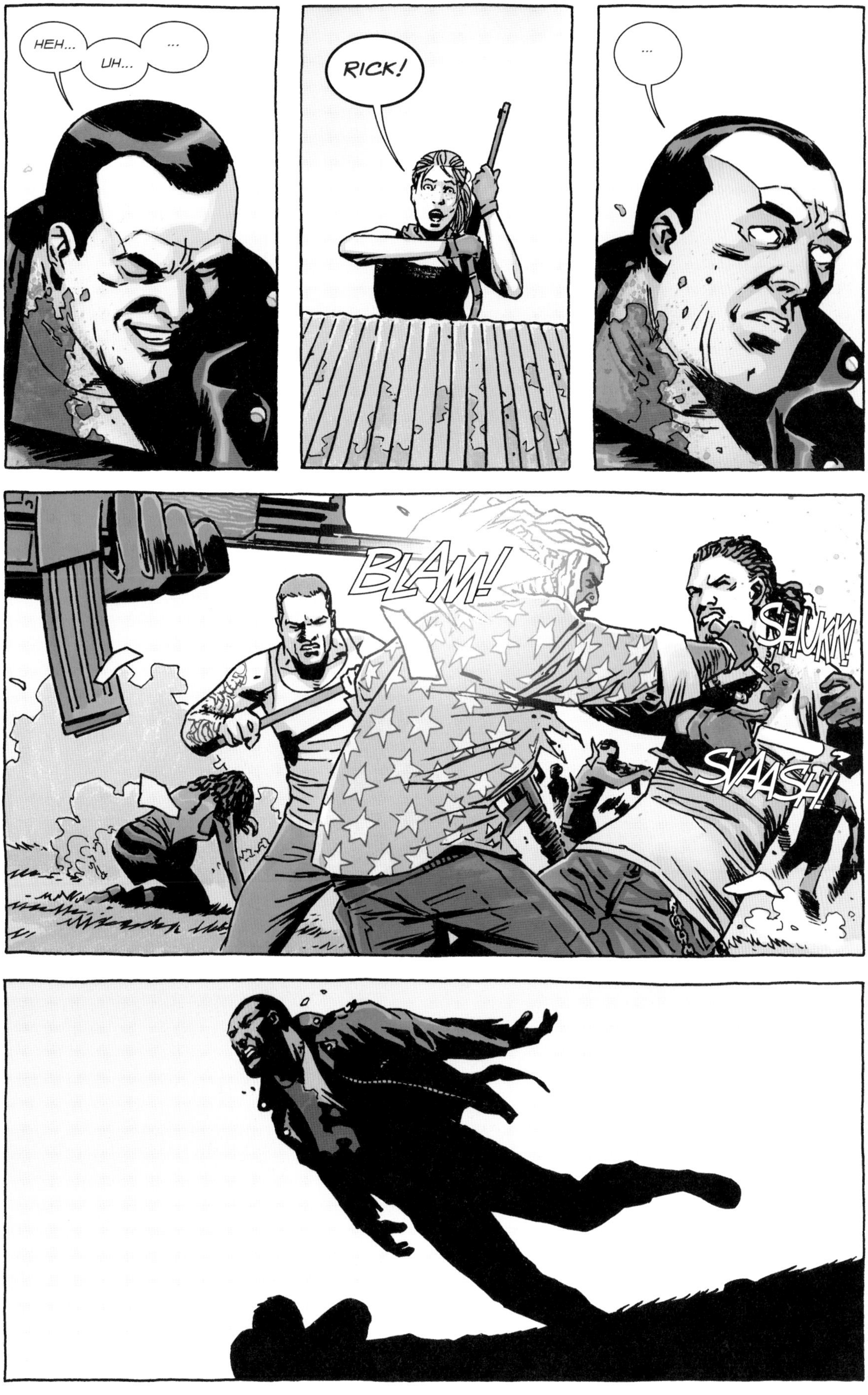
HEH...
UH...
...
RICK!
...
BLAM!
SHUKK!
SVAASH!

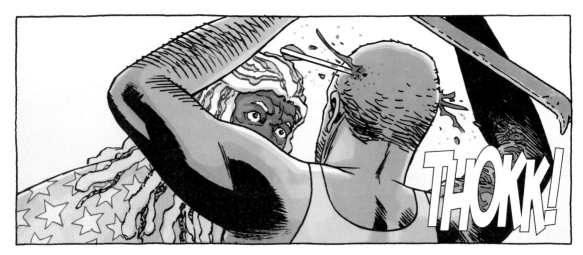

THOKK!

THANK YOU.

THE REST OF THE SAVIORS ARE COMING--THEY'VE SEEN THIS FIGHT AND THEY'RE ON THEIR WAY.

GET THAT BOLT OUT OF HIS HEAD BEFORE SOMEONE NOTICES.

WRAKK!

WHUDD!

CAN YOU STAND?

I PLAN ON DOING A WHOLE HELL OF A LOT MORE THAN THAT...

NNG.

DON'T GET ANY CLOSER!

I'M ON *YOUR* SIDE.

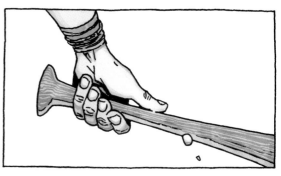

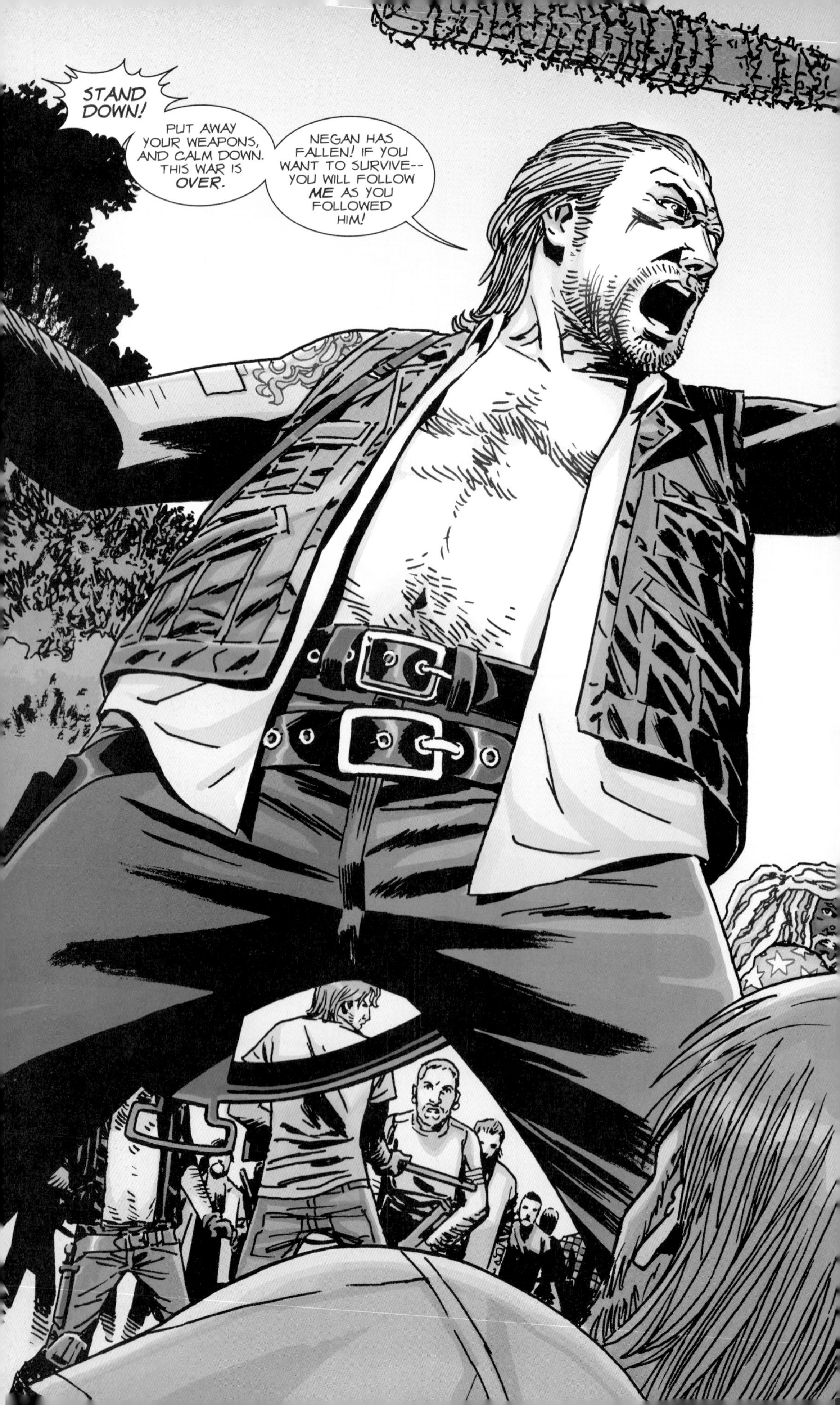
STAND DOWN!
PUT AWAY YOUR WEAPONS, AND CALM DOWN. THIS WAR IS OVER.
NEGAN HAS FALLEN! IF YOU WANT TO SURVIVE-- YOU WILL FOLLOW ME AS YOU FOLLOWED HIM!

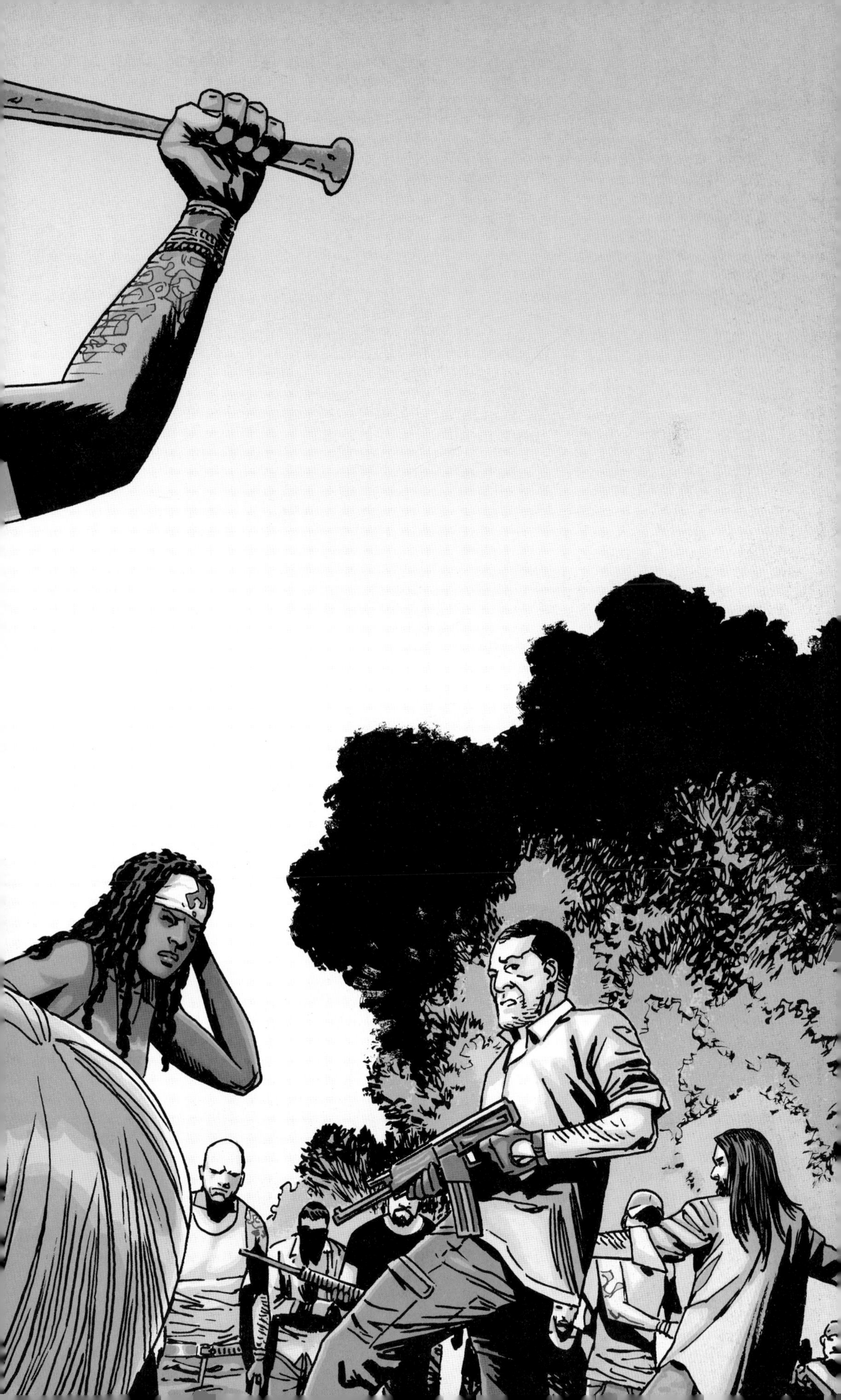

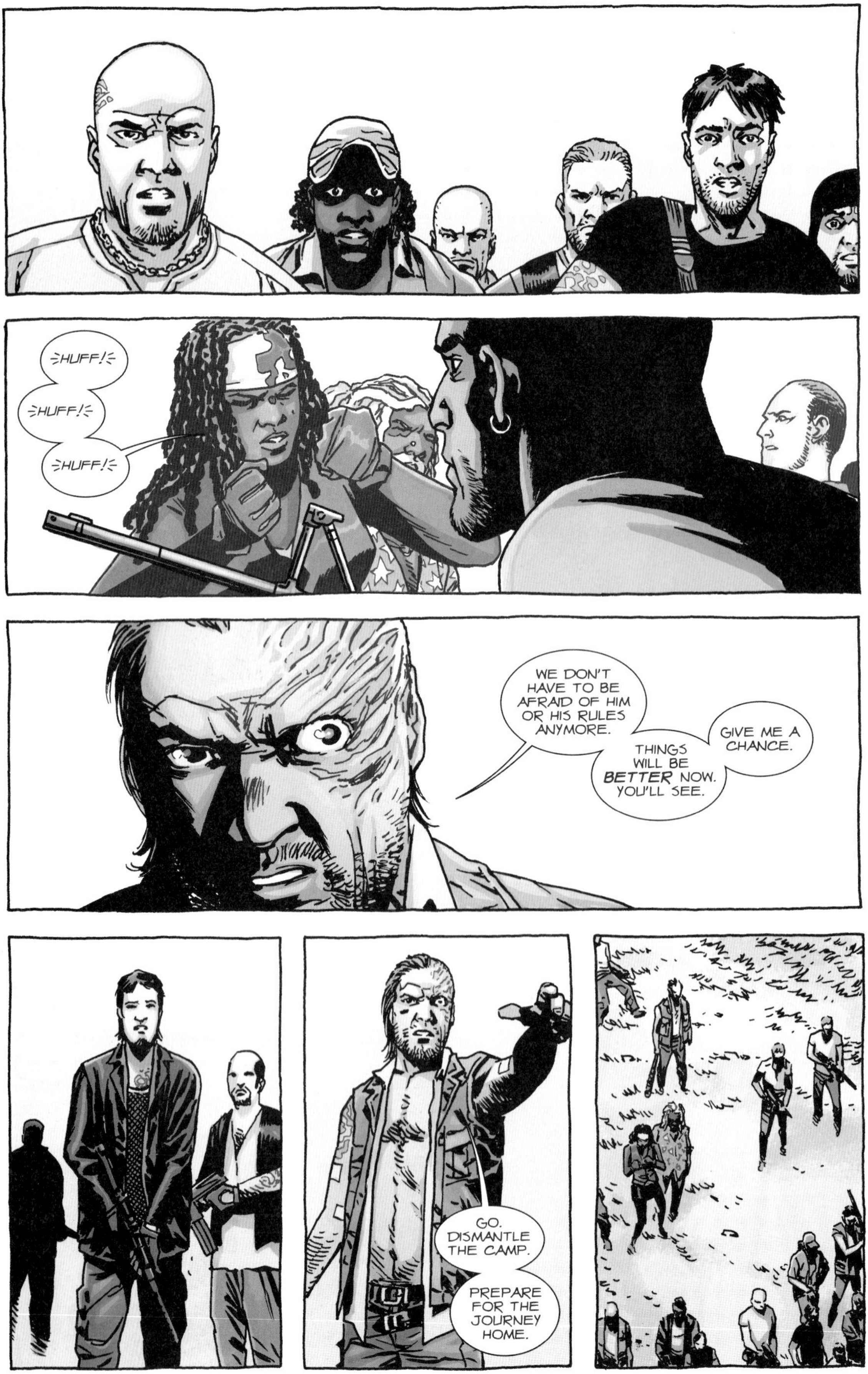
HUFF!
HUFF!
HUFF!
WE DON'T HAVE TO BE AFRAID OF HIM OR HIS RULES ANYMORE.
THINGS WILL BE BETTER NOW. YOU'LL SEE.
GIVE ME A CHANCE.
GO. DISMANTLE THE CAMP.
PREPARE FOR THE JOURNEY HOME.

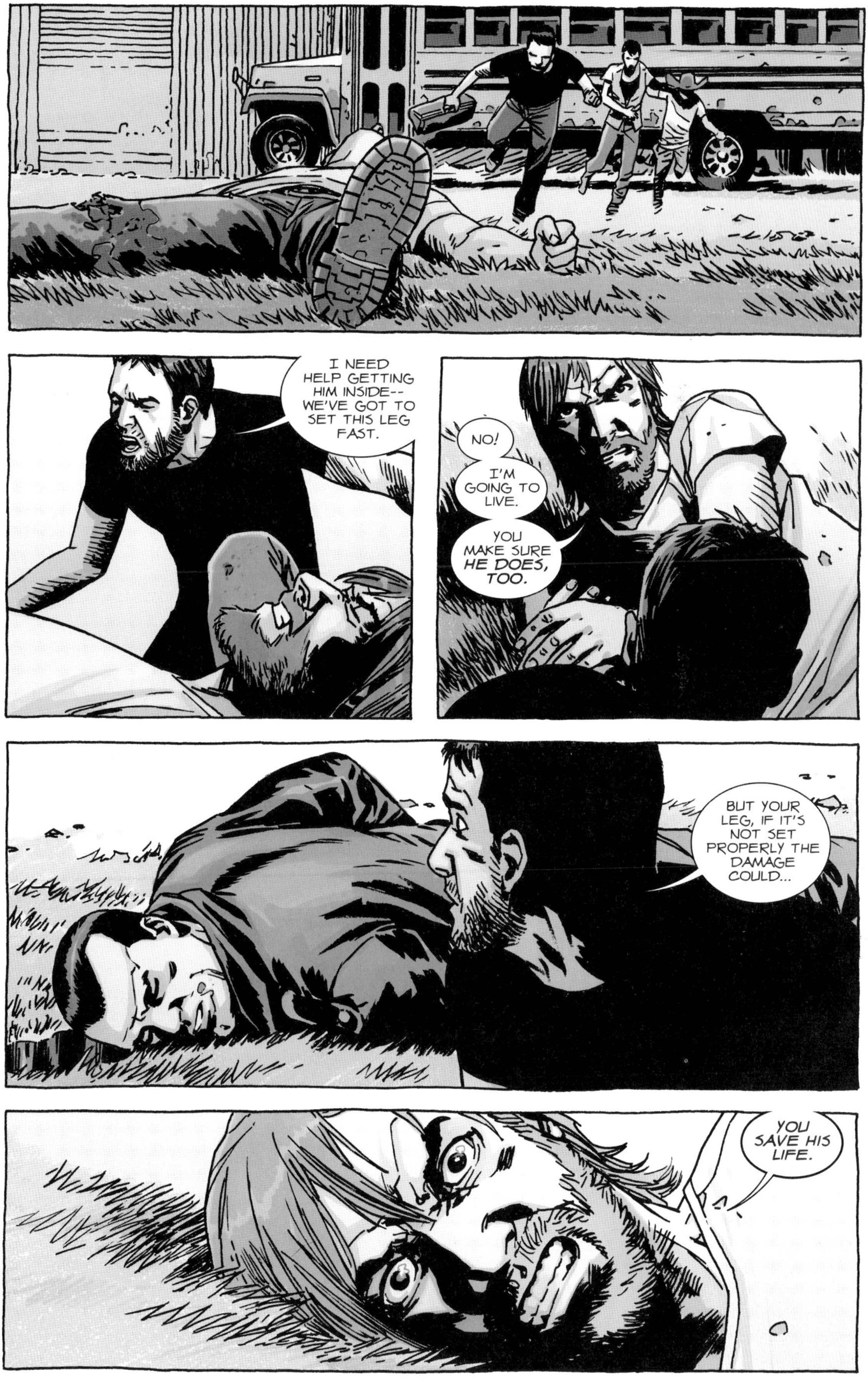
I NEED HELP GETTING HIM INSIDE-- WE'VE GOT TO SET THIS LEG FAST.
NO!
I'M GOING TO LIVE.
YOU MAKE SURE HE DOES, TOO.
BUT YOUR LEG, IF IT'S NOT SET PROPERLY THE DAMAGE COULD...
YOU SAVE HIS LIFE.

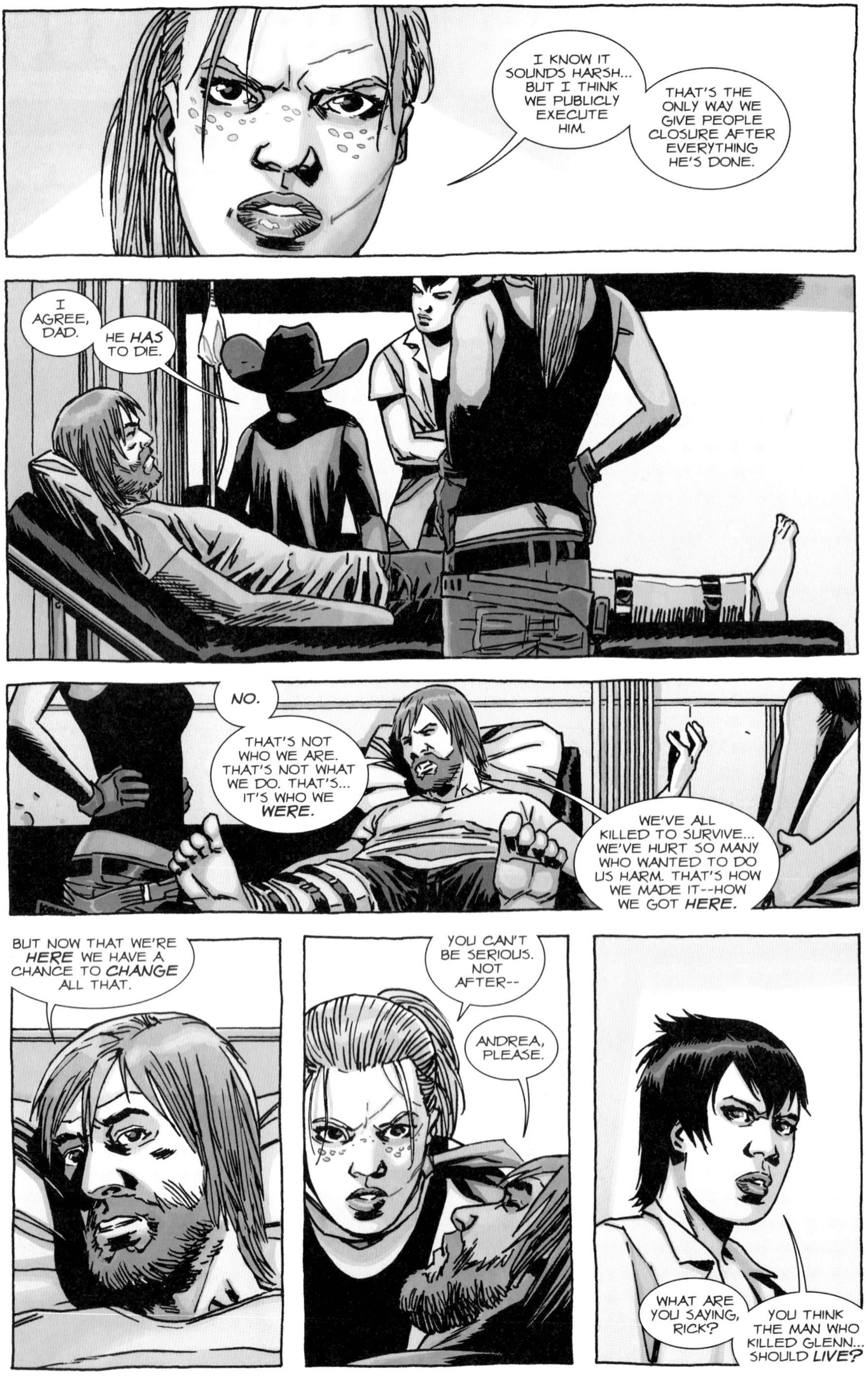

I KNOW IT SOUNDS HARSH... BUT I THINK WE PUBLICLY EXECUTE HIM.
THAT'S THE ONLY WAY WE GIVE PEOPLE CLOSURE AFTER EVERYTHING HE'S DONE.
I AGREE, DAD.
HE *HAS* TO DIE.
NO.
THAT'S NOT WHO WE ARE. THAT'S NOT WHAT WE DO. THAT'S... IT'S WHO WE *WERE.*
WE'VE ALL KILLED TO SURVIVE... WE'VE HURT SO MANY WHO WANTED TO DO US HARM. THAT'S HOW WE MADE IT--HOW WE GOT *HERE.*
BUT NOW THAT WE'RE *HERE* WE HAVE A CHANCE TO *CHANGE* ALL THAT.
YOU *CAN'T* BE SERIOUS. NOT AFTER--
ANDREA, PLEASE.
WHAT ARE YOU SAYING, RICK?
YOU THINK THE MAN WHO KILLED GLENN... SHOULD *LIVE?*

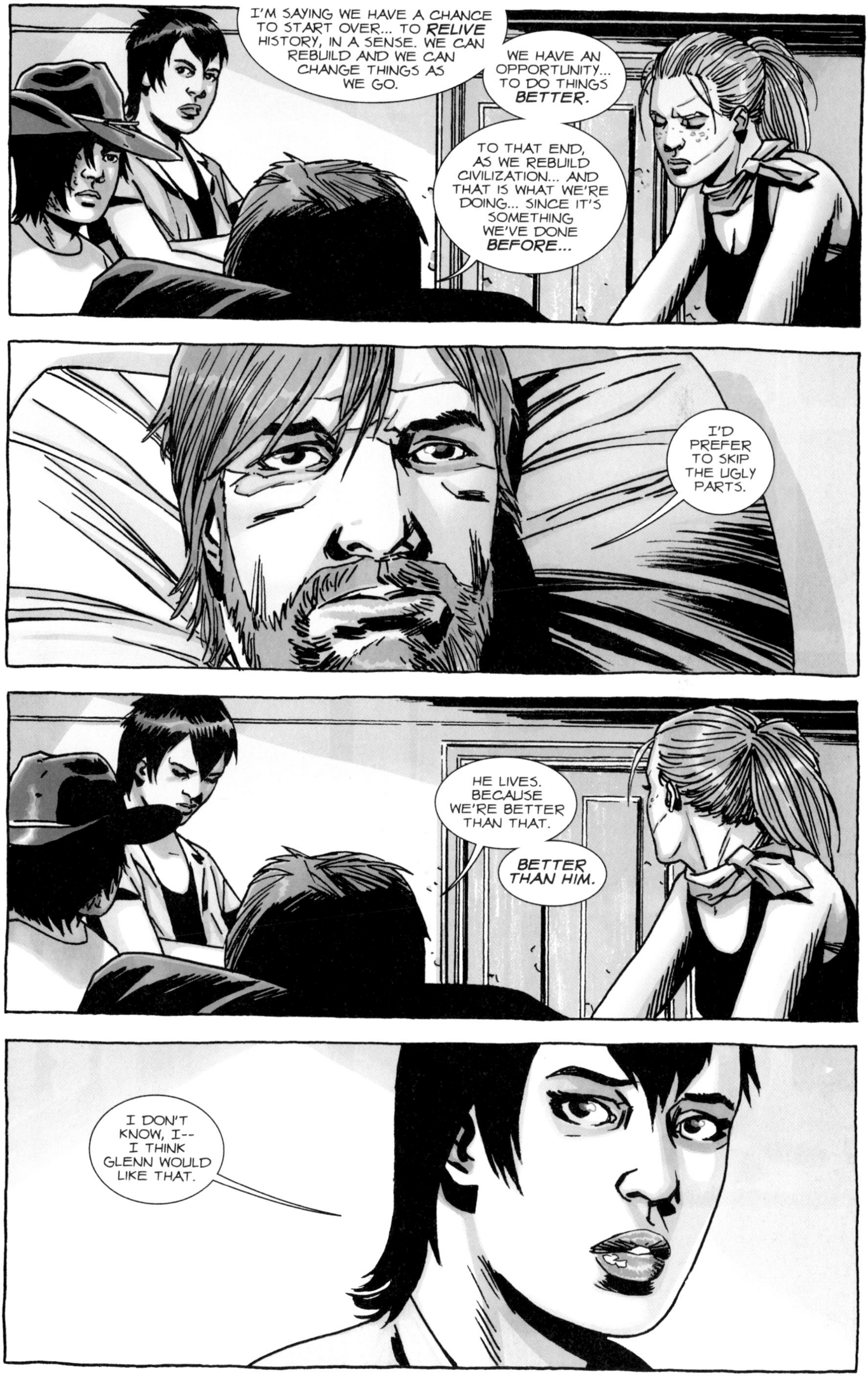
I'M SAYING WE HAVE A CHANCE TO START OVER... TO RELIVE HISTORY, IN A SENSE. WE CAN REBUILD AND WE CAN CHANGE THINGS AS WE GO.
WE HAVE AN OPPORTUNITY... TO DO THINGS BETTER.
TO THAT END, AS WE REBUILD CIVILIZATION... AND THAT IS WHAT WE'RE DOING... SINCE IT'S SOMETHING WE'VE DONE BEFORE...
I'D PREFER TO SKIP THE UGLY PARTS.
HE LIVES. BECAUSE WE'RE BETTER THAN THAT.
BETTER THAN HIM.
I DON'T KNOW, I-- I THINK GLENN WOULD LIKE THAT.

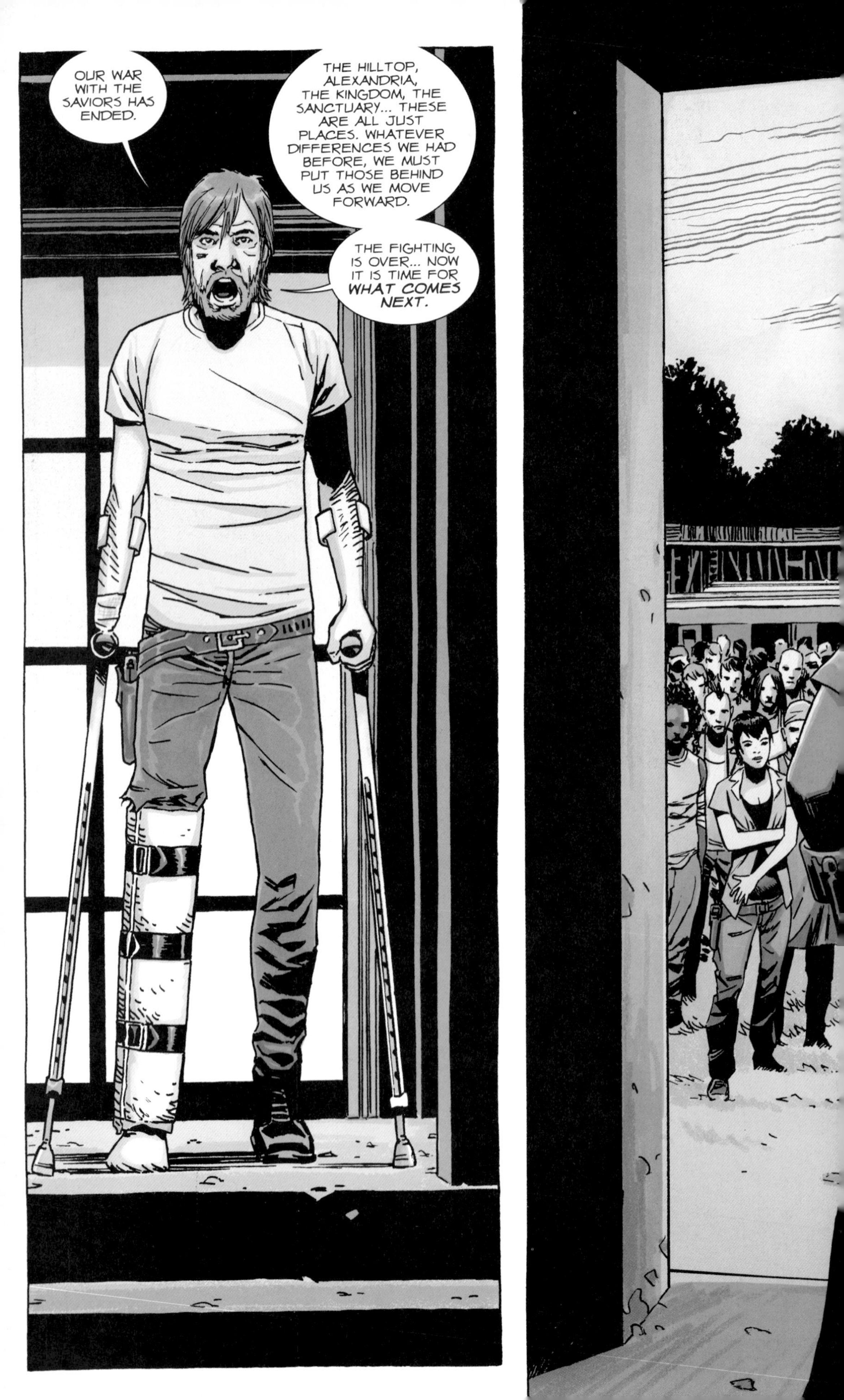
OUR WAR WITH THE SAVIORS HAS ENDED.
THE HILLTOP, ALEXANDRIA, THE KINGDOM, THE SANCTUARY... THESE ARE ALL JUST PLACES. WHATEVER DIFFERENCES WE HAD BEFORE, WE MUST PUT THOSE BEHIND US AS WE MOVE FORWARD.
THE FIGHTING IS OVER... NOW IT IS TIME FOR *WHAT COMES NEXT.*

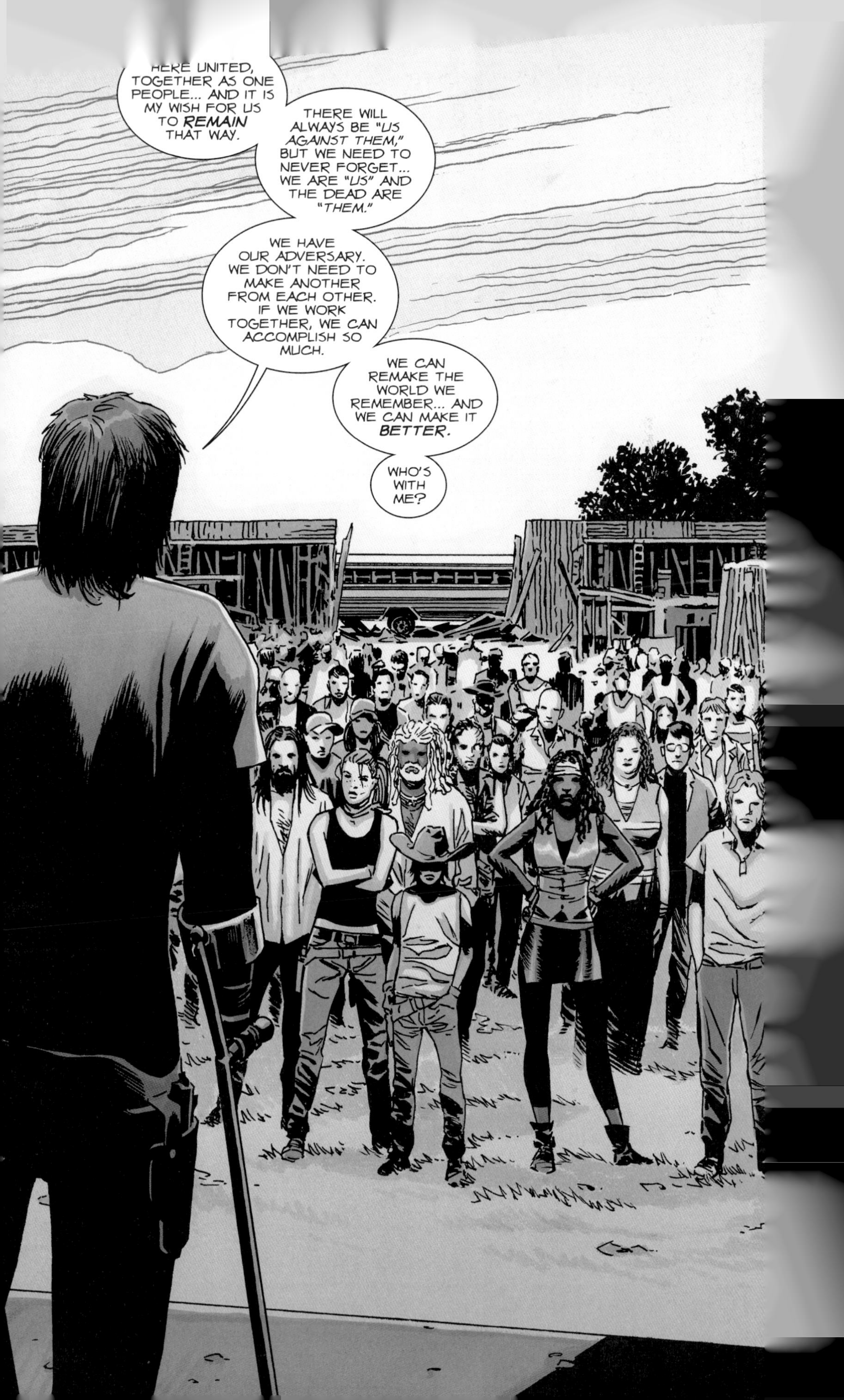
HERE UNITED, TOGETHER AS ONE PEOPLE... AND IT IS MY WISH FOR US TO *REMAIN* THAT WAY.
THERE WILL ALWAYS BE "*US AGAINST THEM,*" BUT WE NEED TO NEVER FORGET... WE ARE "*US*" AND THE DEAD ARE "*THEM.*"
WE HAVE OUR ADVERSARY. WE DON'T NEED TO MAKE ANOTHER FROM EACH OTHER. IF WE WORK TOGETHER, WE CAN ACCOMPLISH SO MUCH.
WE CAN REMAKE THE WORLD WE REMEMBER... AND WE CAN MAKE IT ***BETTER.***
WHO'S WITH ME?

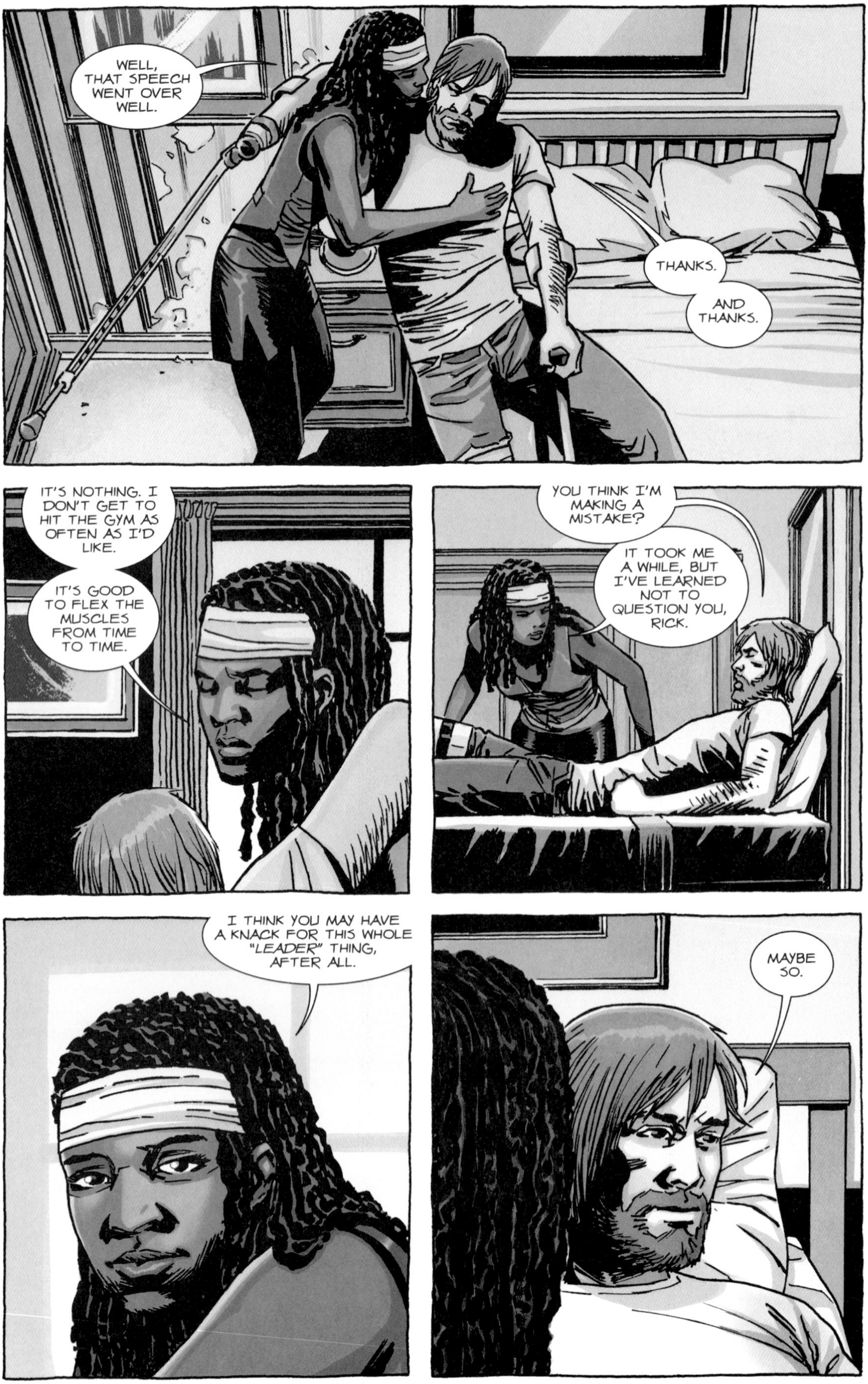
WELL, THAT SPEECH WENT OVER WELL.
THANKS.
AND THANKS.
IT'S NOTHING. I DON'T GET TO HIT THE GYM AS OFTEN AS I'D LIKE.
IT'S GOOD TO FLEX THE MUSCLES FROM TIME TO TIME.
YOU THINK I'M MAKING A MISTAKE?
IT TOOK ME A WHILE, BUT I'VE LEARNED NOT TO QUESTION YOU, RICK.
I THINK YOU MAY HAVE A KNACK FOR THIS WHOLE "LEADER" THING, AFTER ALL.
MAYBE SO.

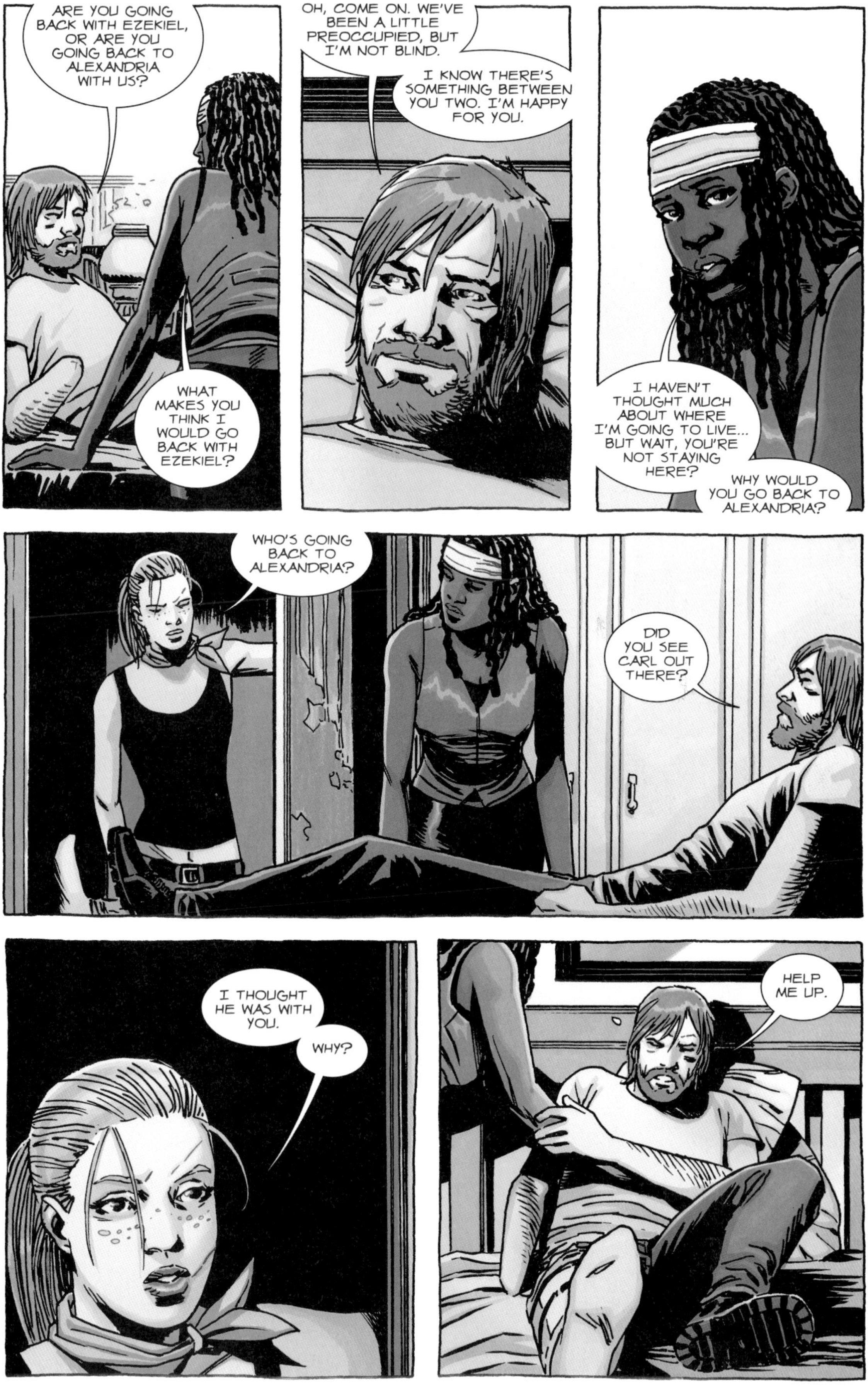
ARE YOU GOING BACK WITH EZEKIEL, OR ARE YOU GOING BACK TO ALEXANDRIA WITH US?
WHAT MAKES YOU THINK I WOULD GO BACK WITH EZEKIEL?
OH, COME ON. WE'VE BEEN A LITTLE PREOCCUPIED, BUT I'M NOT BLIND.
I KNOW THERE'S SOMETHING BETWEEN YOU TWO. I'M HAPPY FOR YOU.
I HAVEN'T THOUGHT MUCH ABOUT WHERE I'M GOING TO LIVE... BUT WAIT, YOU'RE NOT STAYING HERE?
WHY WOULD YOU GO BACK TO ALEXANDRIA?
WHO'S GOING BACK TO ALEXANDRIA?
DID YOU SEE CARL OUT THERE?
I THOUGHT HE WAS WITH YOU.
WHY?
HELP ME UP.

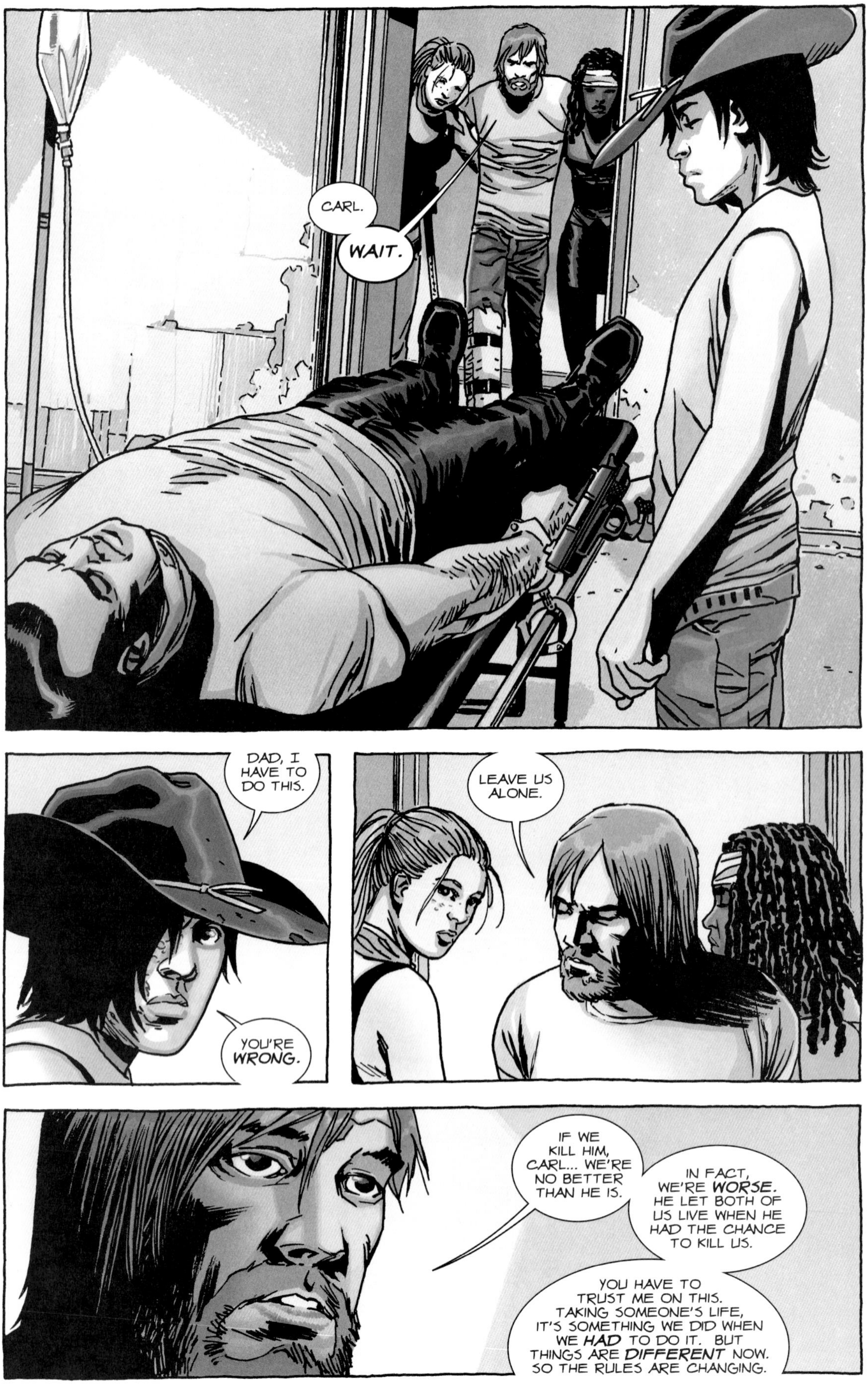
CARL.
WAIT.
DAD, I HAVE TO DO THIS.
YOU'RE WRONG.
LEAVE US ALONE.
IF WE KILL HIM, CARL... WE'RE NO BETTER THAN HE IS.
IN FACT, WE'RE WORSE. HE LET BOTH OF US LIVE WHEN HE HAD THE CHANCE TO KILL US.
YOU HAVE TO TRUST ME ON THIS. TAKING SOMEONE'S LIFE, IT'S SOMETHING WE DID WHEN WE HAD TO DO IT. BUT THINGS ARE DIFFERENT NOW. SO THE RULES ARE CHANGING.

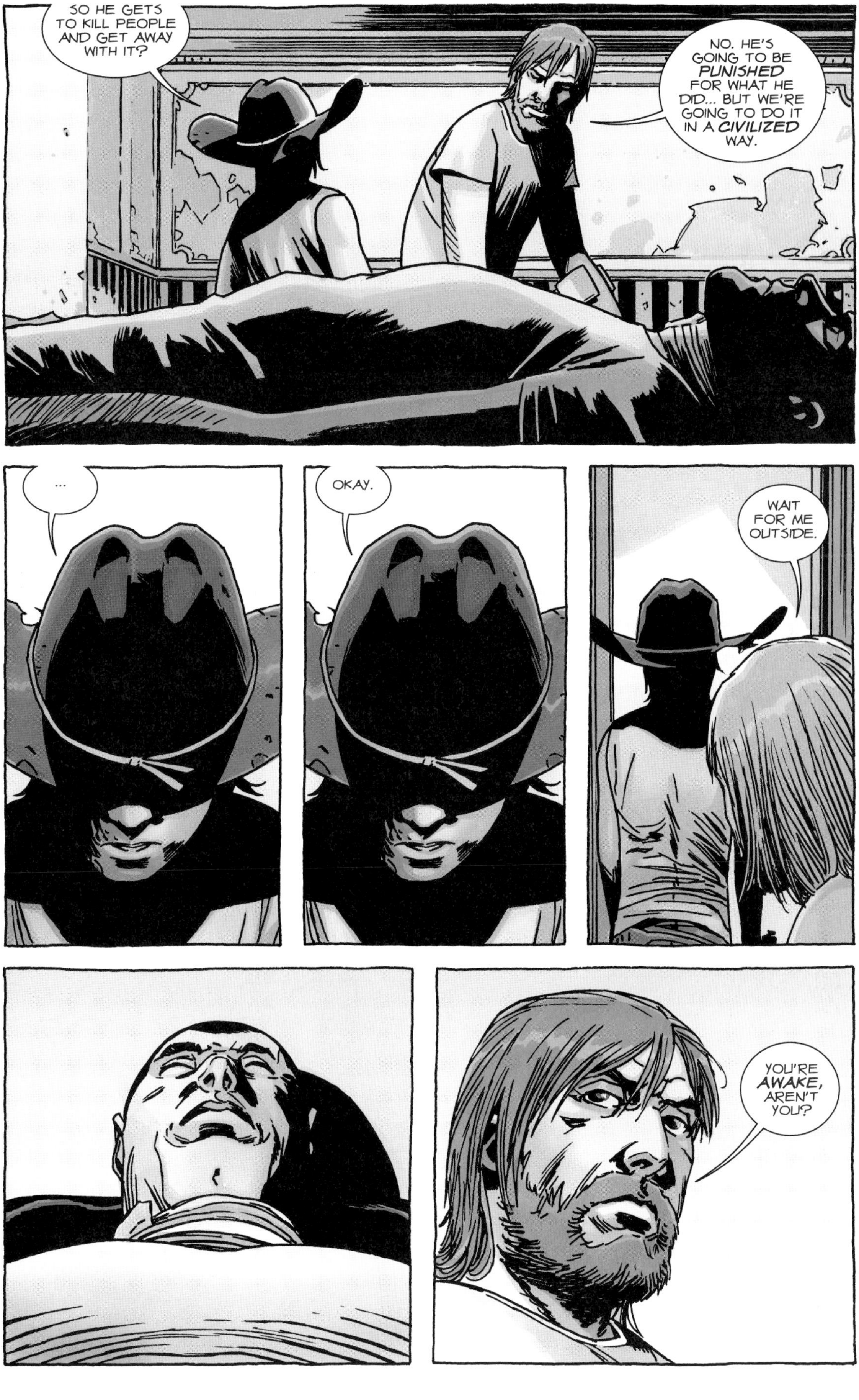
SO HE GETS TO KILL PEOPLE AND GET AWAY WITH IT?
NO. HE'S GOING TO BE PUNISHED FOR WHAT HE DID... BUT WE'RE GOING TO DO IT IN A CIVILIZED WAY.
...
OKAY.
WAIT FOR ME OUTSIDE.
YOU'RE AWAKE, AREN'T YOU?

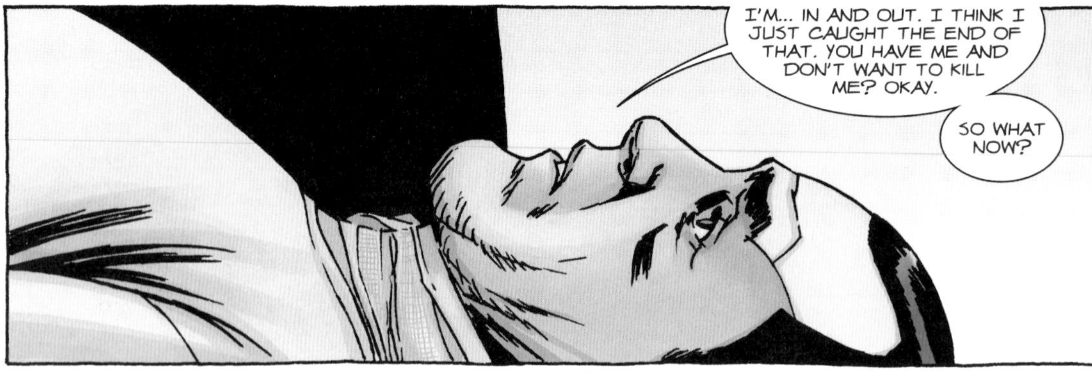
I'M... IN AND OUT. I THINK I JUST CAUGHT THE END OF THAT. YOU HAVE ME AND DON'T WANT TO KILL ME? OKAY.
SO WHAT NOW?

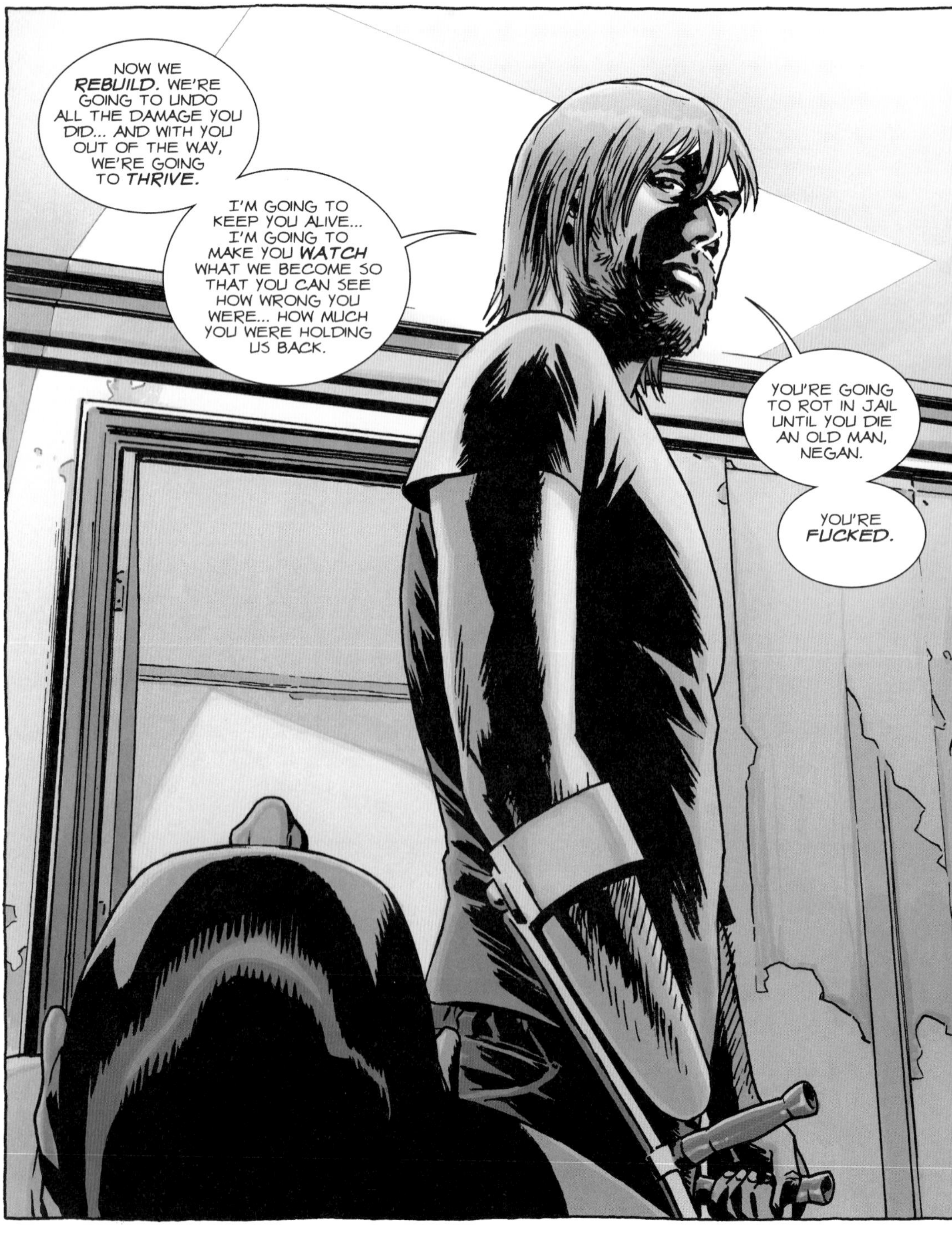
NOW WE **REBUILD.** WE'RE GOING TO UNDO ALL THE DAMAGE YOU DID... AND WITH YOU OUT OF THE WAY, WE'RE GOING TO ***THRIVE.***
I'M GOING TO KEEP YOU ALIVE... I'M GOING TO MAKE YOU **WATCH** WHAT WE BECOME SO THAT YOU CAN SEE HOW WRONG YOU WERE... HOW MUCH YOU WERE HOLDING US BACK.
YOU'RE GOING TO ROT IN JAIL UNTIL YOU DIE AN OLD MAN, NEGAN.
YOU'RE ***FUCKED.***

Chapter Twenty-Two: A New Beginning

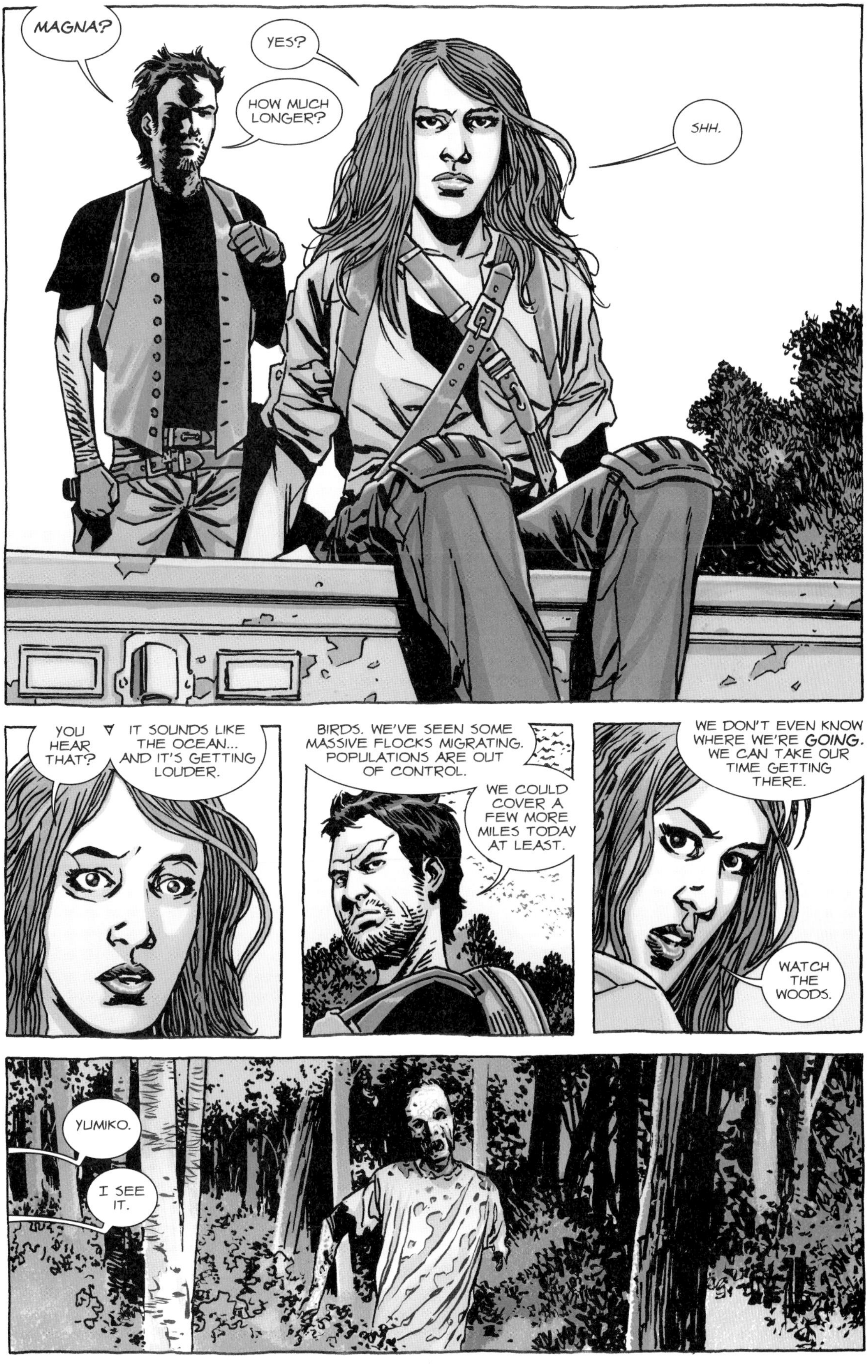
MAGNA?
YES?
HOW MUCH LONGER?
SHH.
YOU HEAR THAT?
IT SOUNDS LIKE THE OCEAN... AND IT'S GETTING LOUDER.
BIRDS. WE'VE SEEN SOME MASSIVE FLOCKS MIGRATING. POPULATIONS ARE OUT OF CONTROL.
WE COULD COVER A FEW MORE MILES TODAY AT LEAST.
WE DON'T EVEN KNOW WHERE WE'RE GOING. WE CAN TAKE OUR TIME GETTING THERE.
WATCH THE WOODS.
YUMIKO.
I SEE IT.

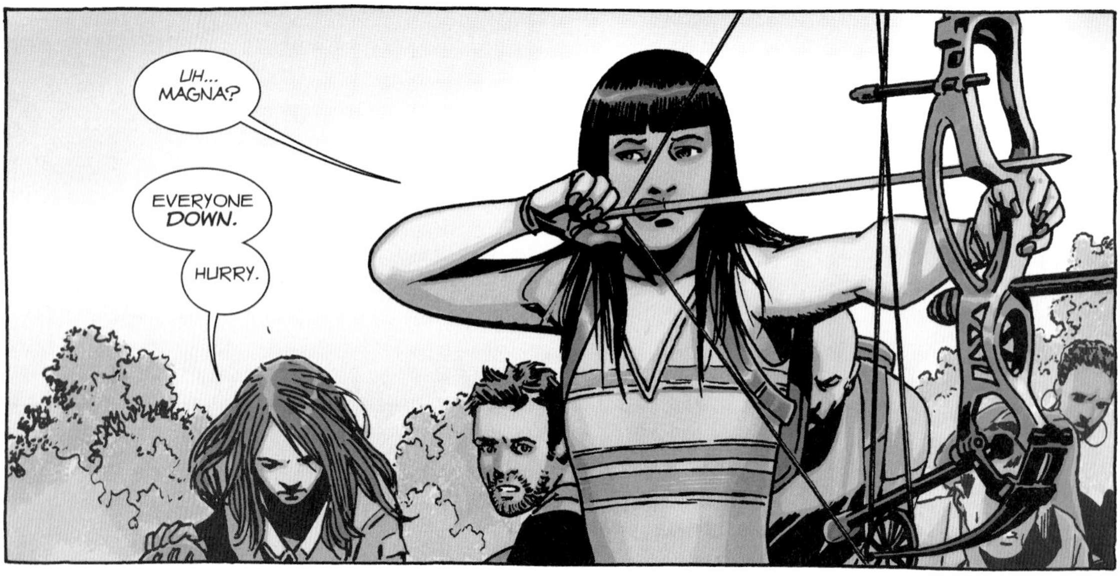
UH... MAGNA?
EVERYONE DOWN.
HURRY.

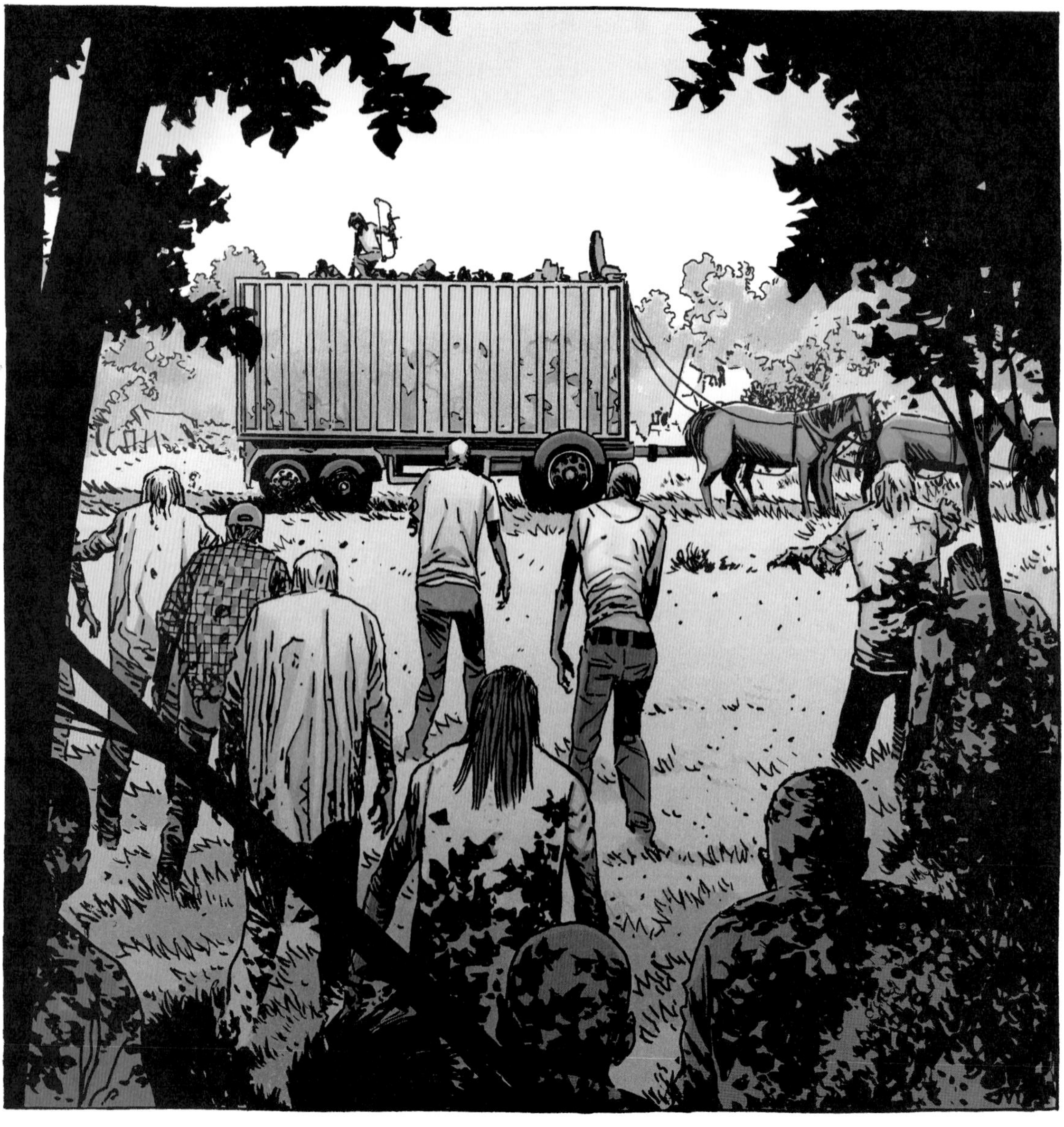

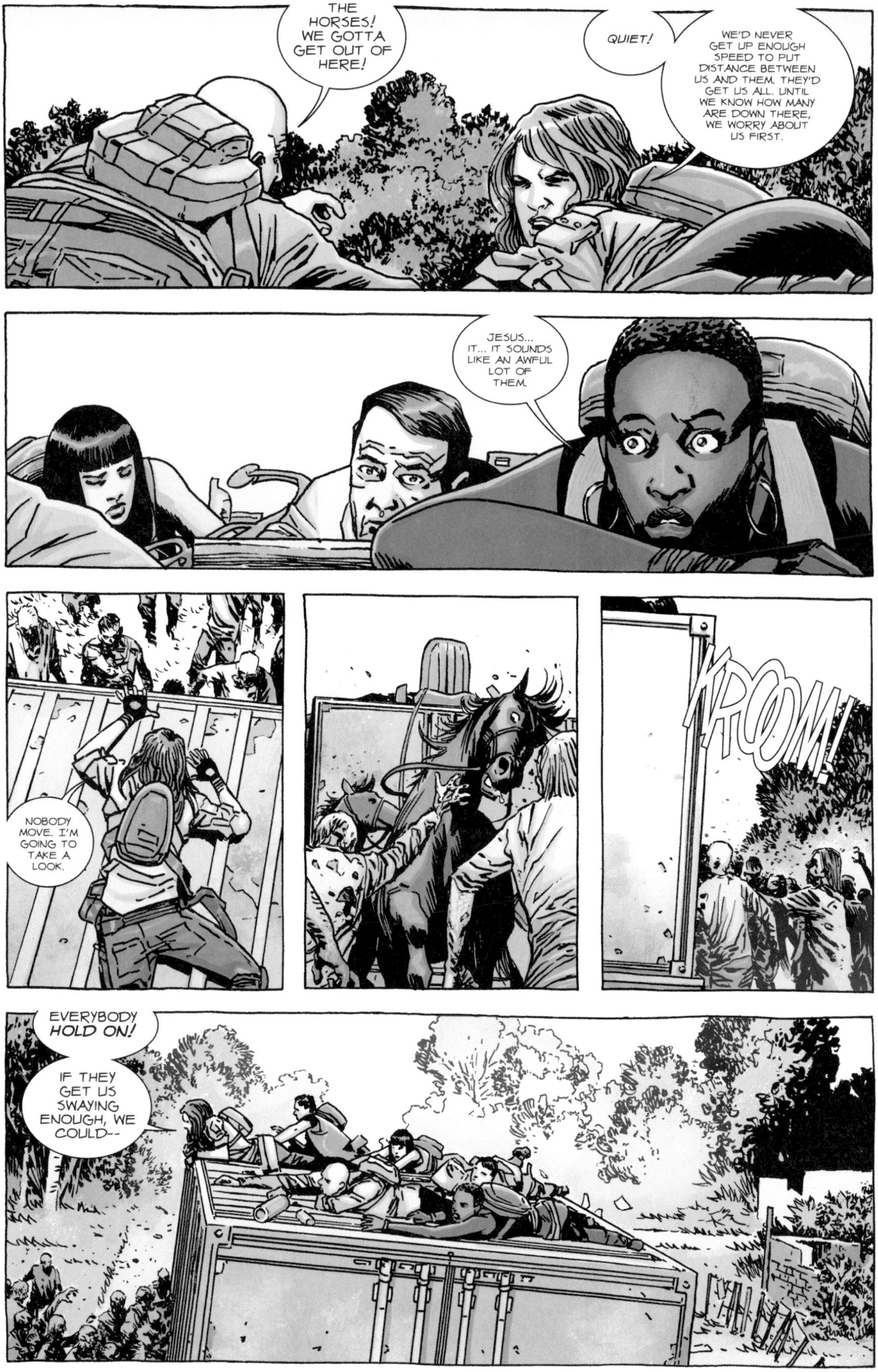
THE HORSES! WE GOTTA GET OUT OF HERE!
QUIET!
WE'D NEVER GET UP ENOUGH SPEED TO PUT DISTANCE BETWEEN US AND THEM. THEY'D GET US ALL. UNTIL WE KNOW HOW MANY ARE DOWN THERE, WE WORRY ABOUT US FIRST.
JESUS... IT... IT SOUNDS LIKE AN AWFUL LOT OF THEM.
NOBODY MOVE. I'M GOING TO TAKE A LOOK.
KROOM!
EVERYBODY HOLD ON!
IF THEY GET US SWAYING ENOUGH, WE COULD--

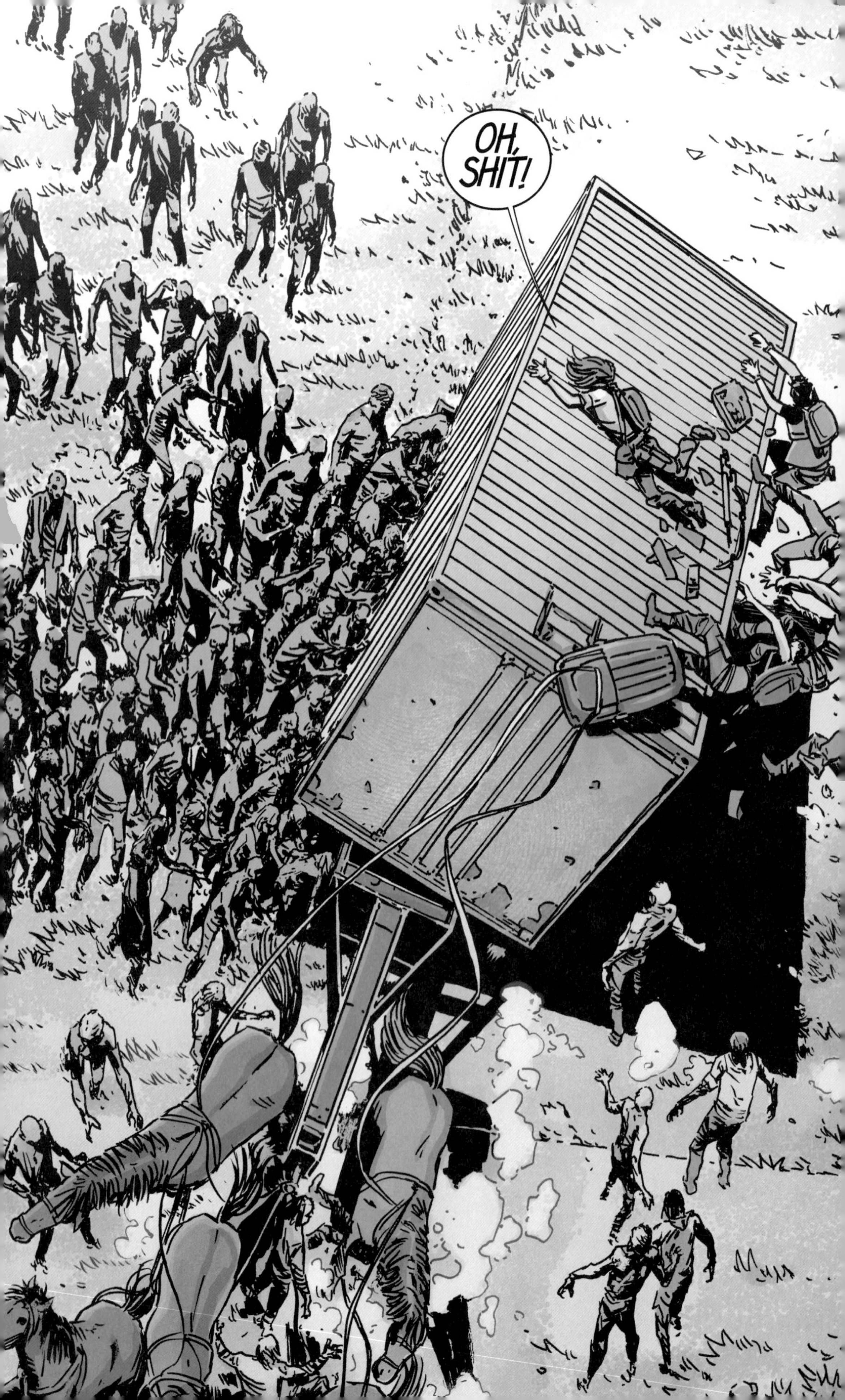
OH, SHIT!

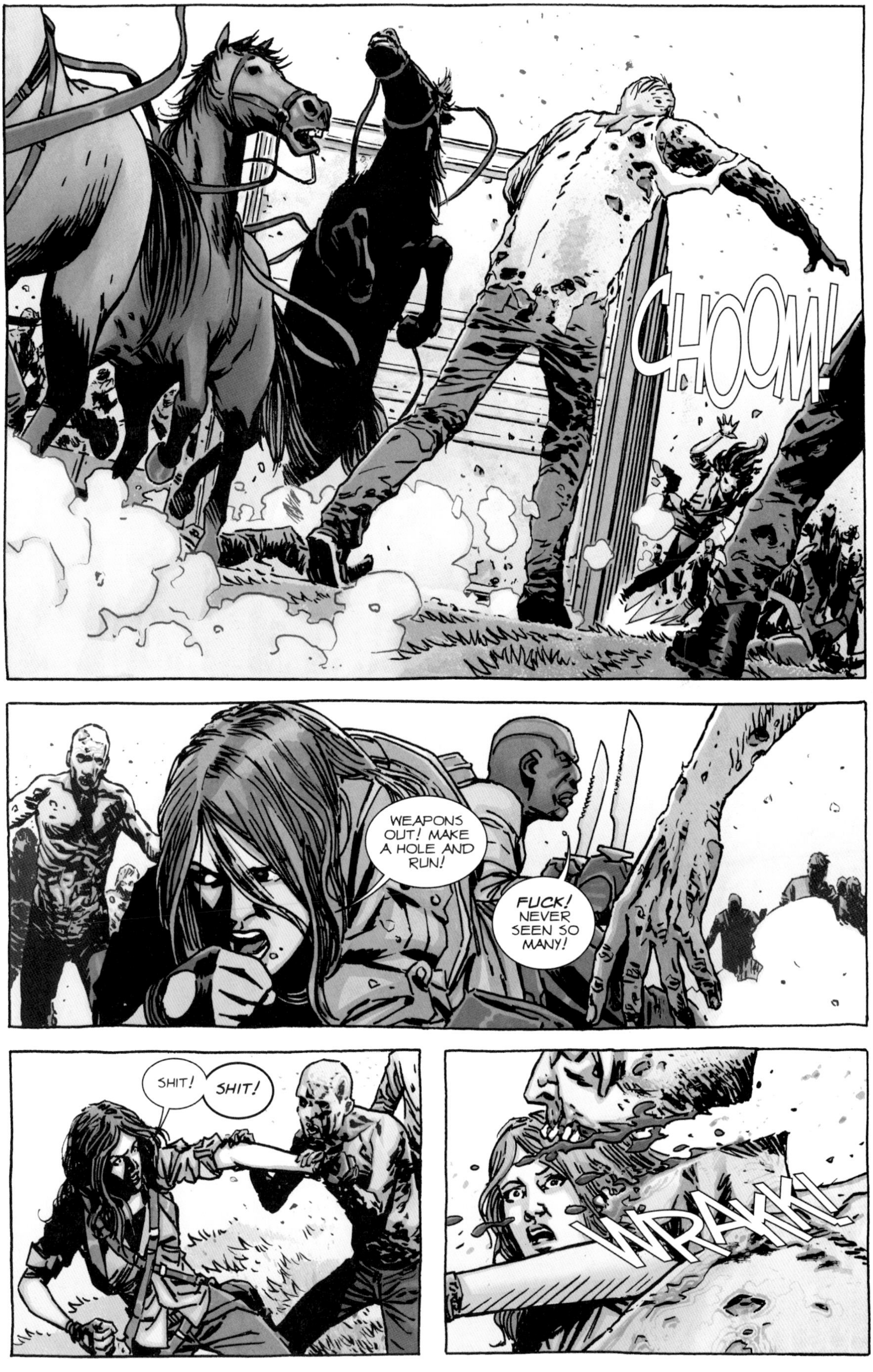
CHOOM!
WEAPONS OUT! MAKE A HOLE AND RUN!
FUCK! NEVER SEEN SO MANY!
SHIT!
SHIT!
WRAKK!

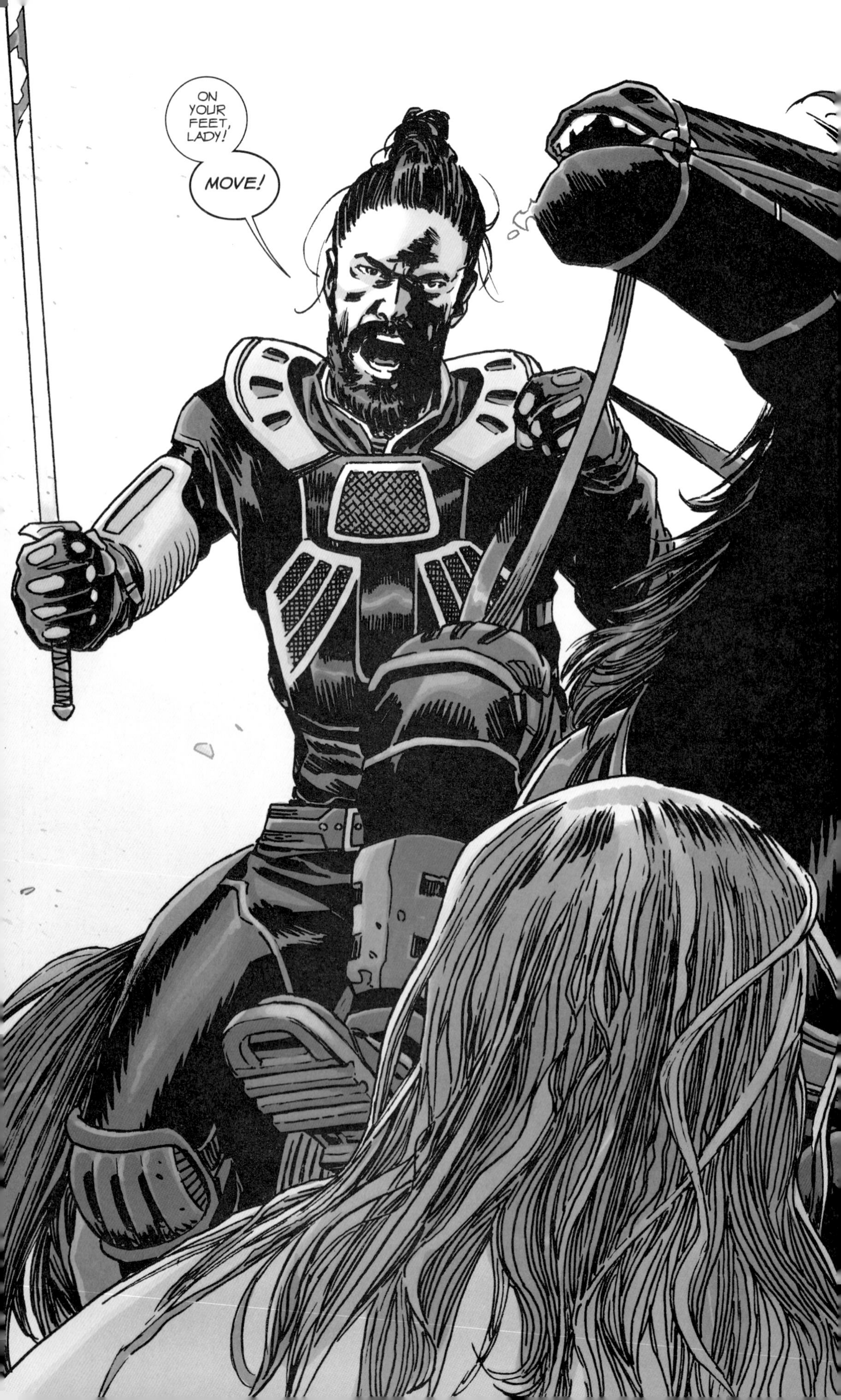
ON YOUR FEET, LADY!
MOVE!

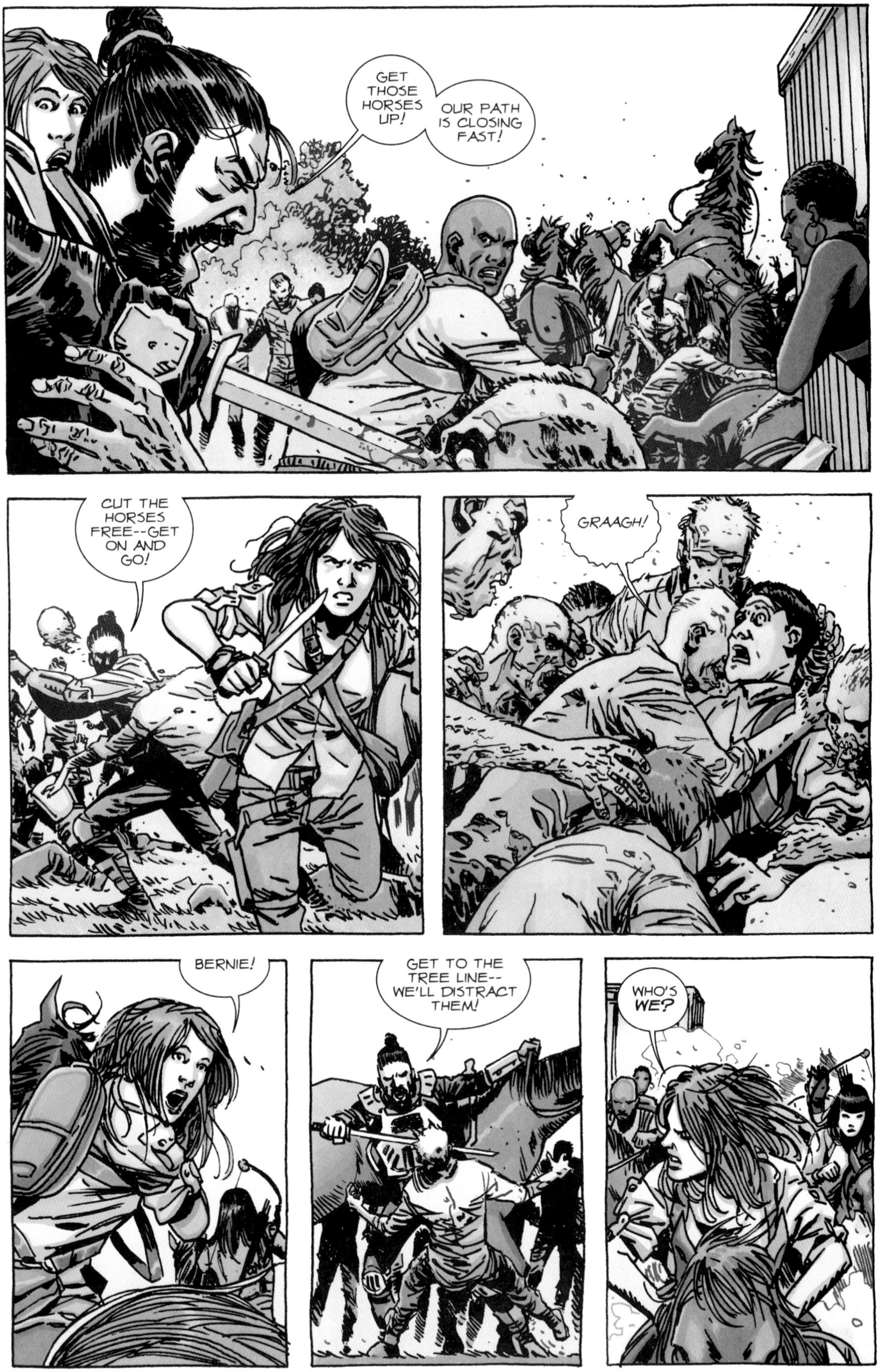
GET THOSE HORSES UP!
OUR PATH IS CLOSING FAST!
CUT THE HORSES FREE--GET ON AND GO!
GRAAGH!
BERNIE!
GET TO THE TREE LINE-- WE'LL DISTRACT THEM!
WHO'S **WE?**

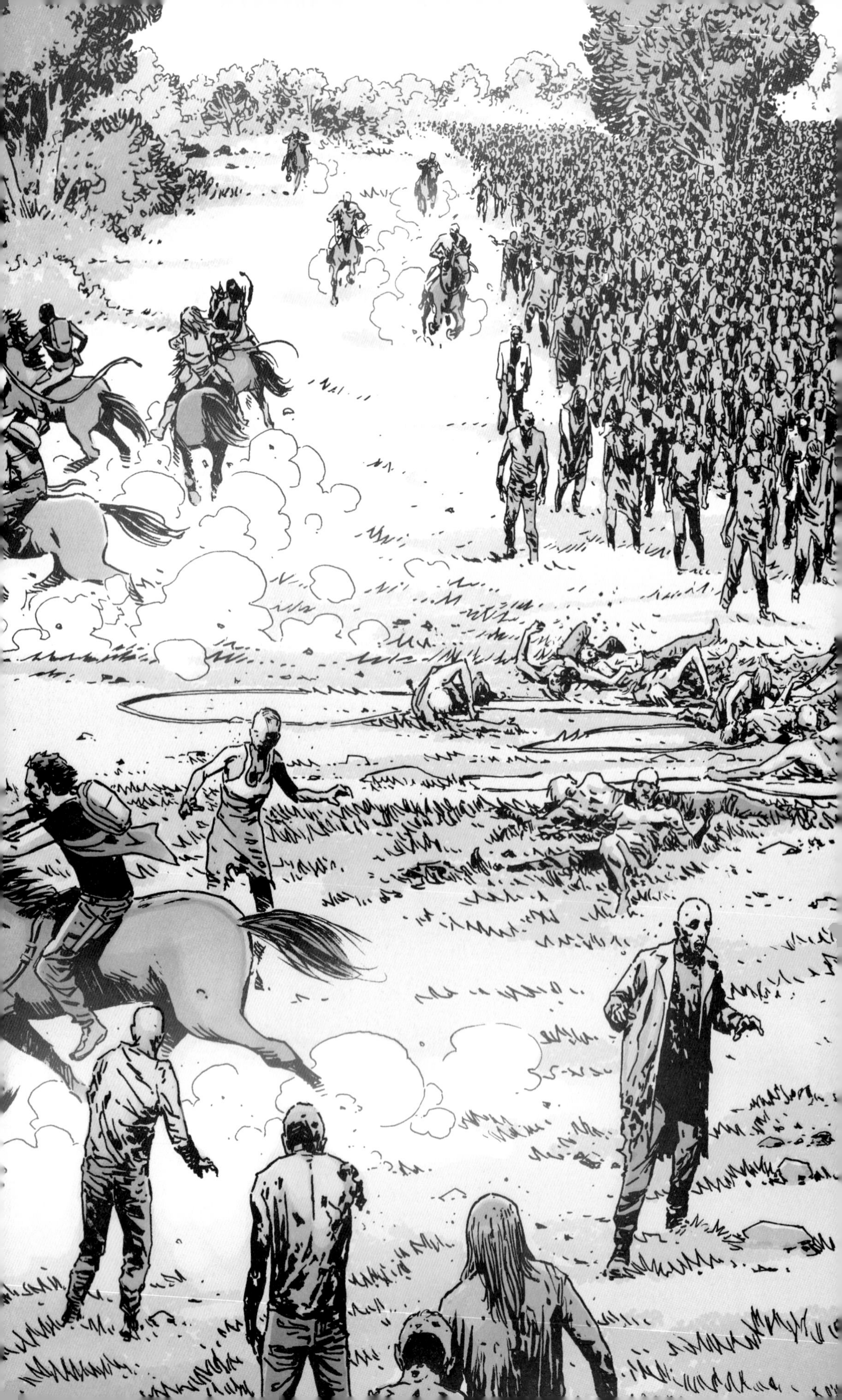

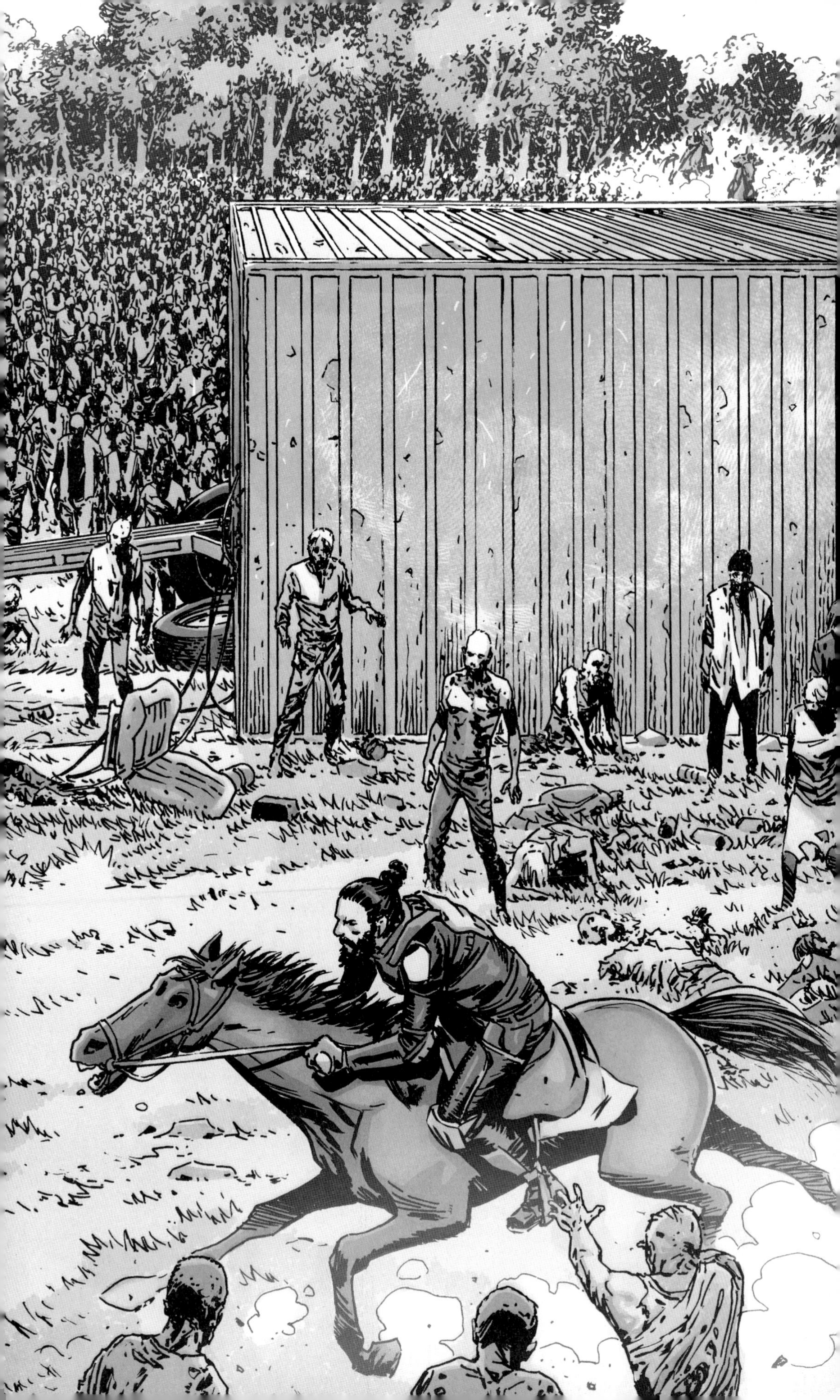

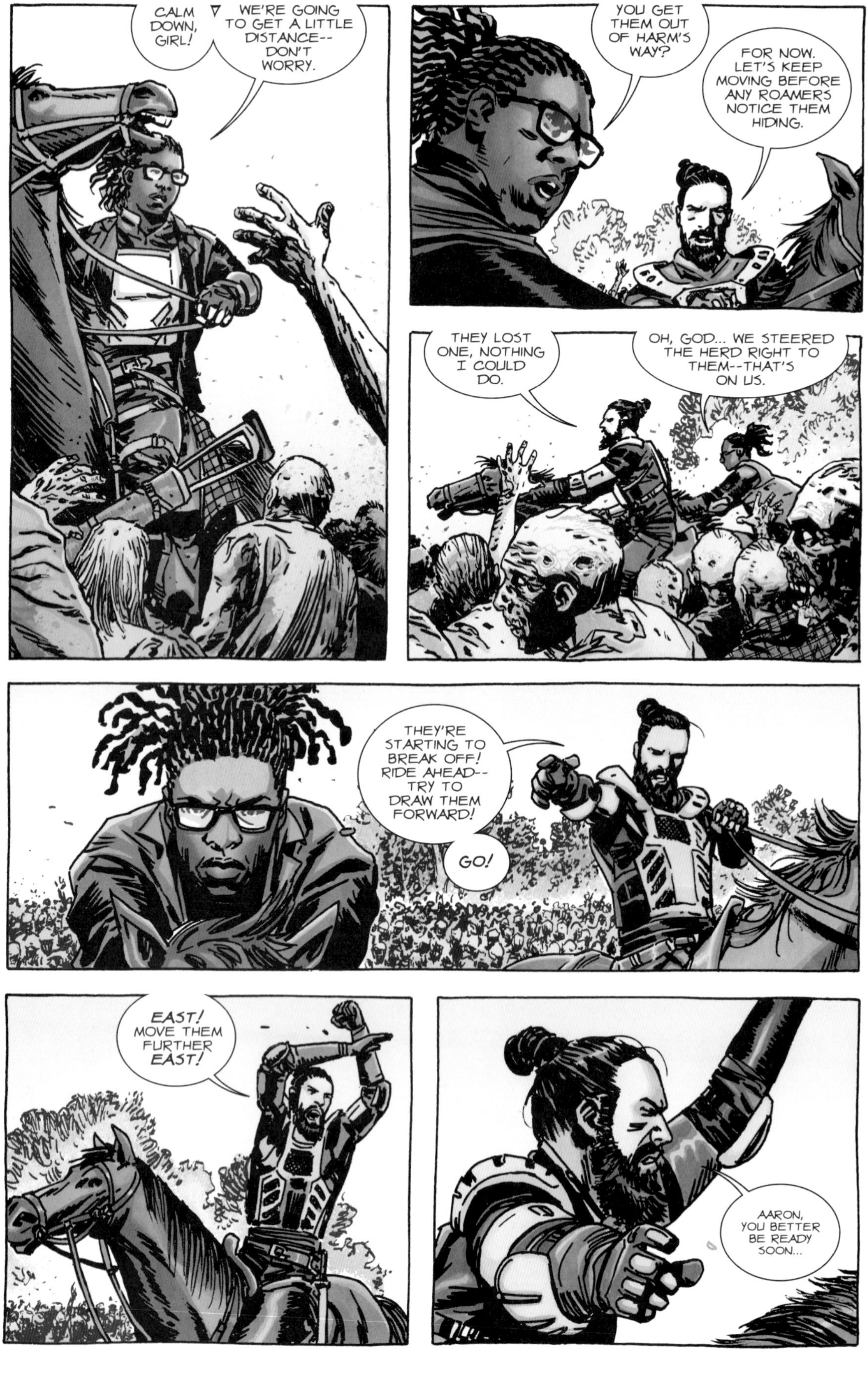
CALM DOWN, GIRL!
WE'RE GOING TO GET A LITTLE DISTANCE-- DON'T WORRY.
YOU GET THEM OUT OF HARM'S WAY?
FOR NOW. LET'S KEEP MOVING BEFORE ANY ROAMERS NOTICE THEM HIDING.
THEY LOST ONE, NOTHING I COULD DO.
OH, GOD... WE STEERED THE HERD RIGHT TO THEM--THAT'S ON US.
THEY'RE STARTING TO BREAK OFF! RIDE AHEAD-- TRY TO DRAW THEM FORWARD!
GO!
EAST! MOVE THEM FURTHER EAST!
AARON, YOU BETTER BE READY SOON...

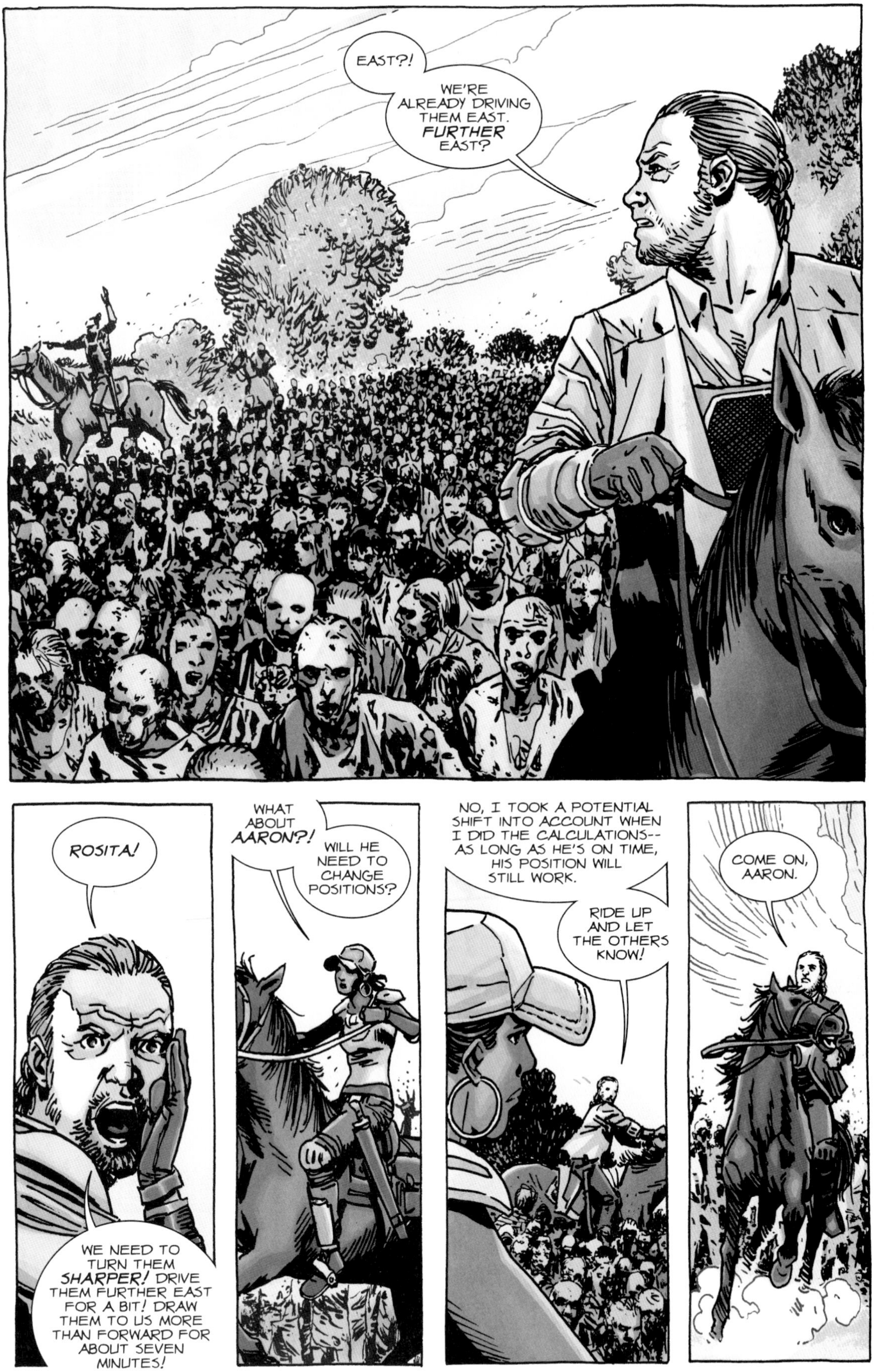
EAST?!
WE'RE ALREADY DRIVING THEM EAST. FURTHER EAST?
ROSITA!
WE NEED TO TURN THEM SHARPER! DRIVE THEM FURTHER EAST FOR A BIT! DRAW THEM TO US MORE THAN FORWARD FOR ABOUT SEVEN MINUTES!
WHAT ABOUT AARON?!
WILL HE NEED TO CHANGE POSITIONS?
NO, I TOOK A POTENTIAL SHIFT INTO ACCOUNT WHEN I DID THE CALCULATIONS-- AS LONG AS HE'S ON TIME, HIS POSITION WILL STILL WORK.
RIDE UP AND LET THE OTHERS KNOW!
COME ON, AARON.

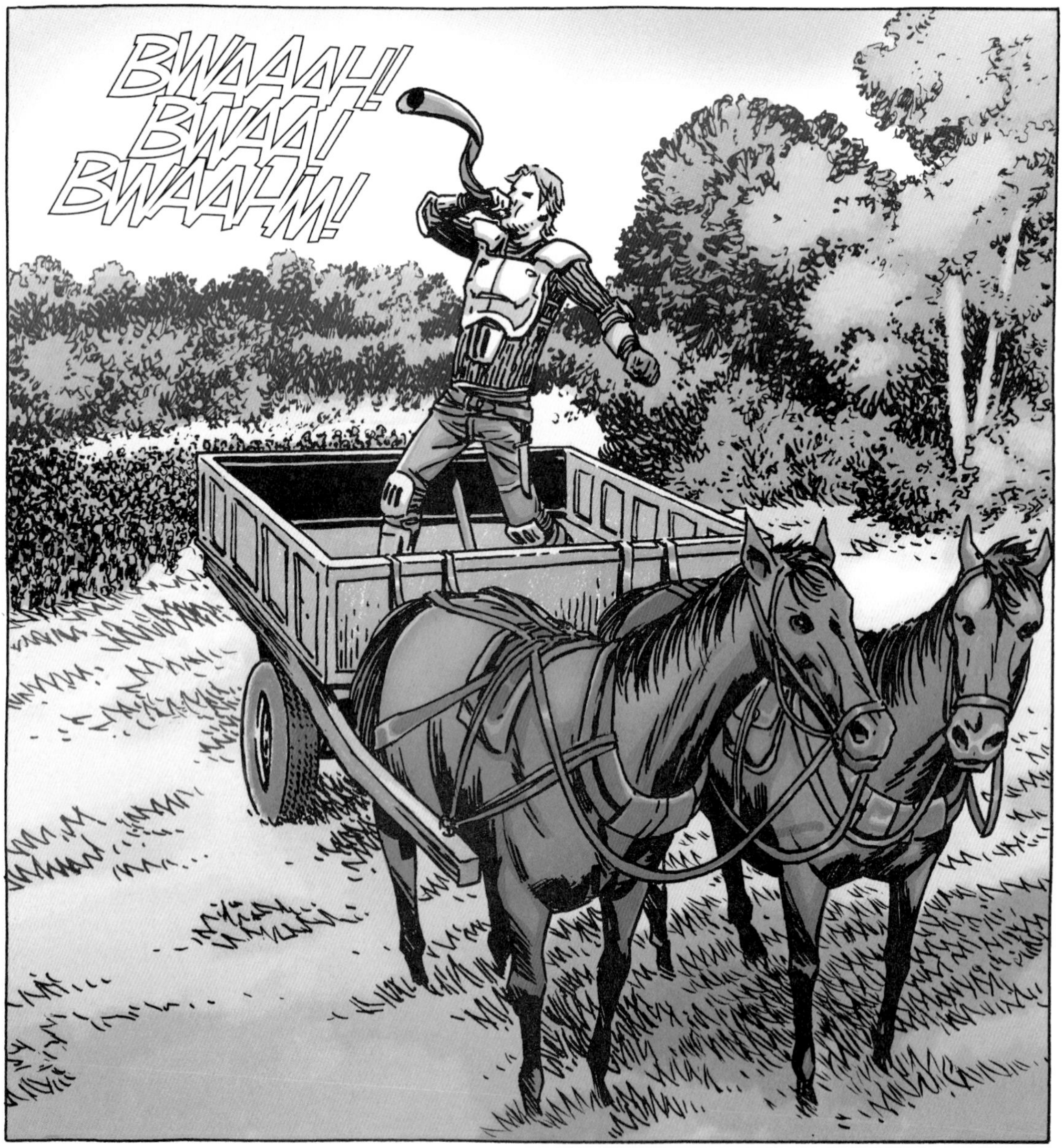
BWAAAH! BWAA! BWAAHM!

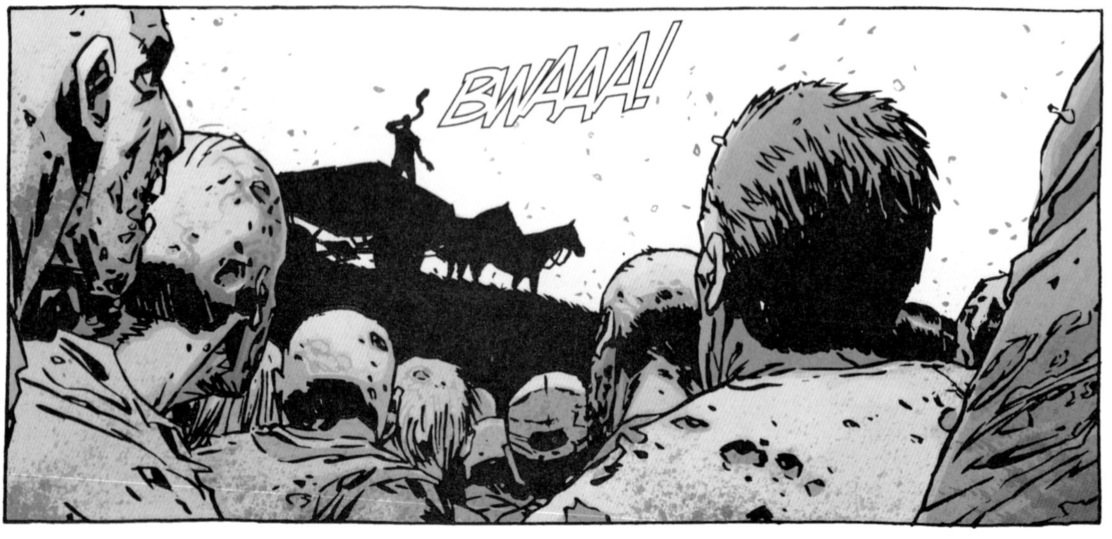
BWAAA!

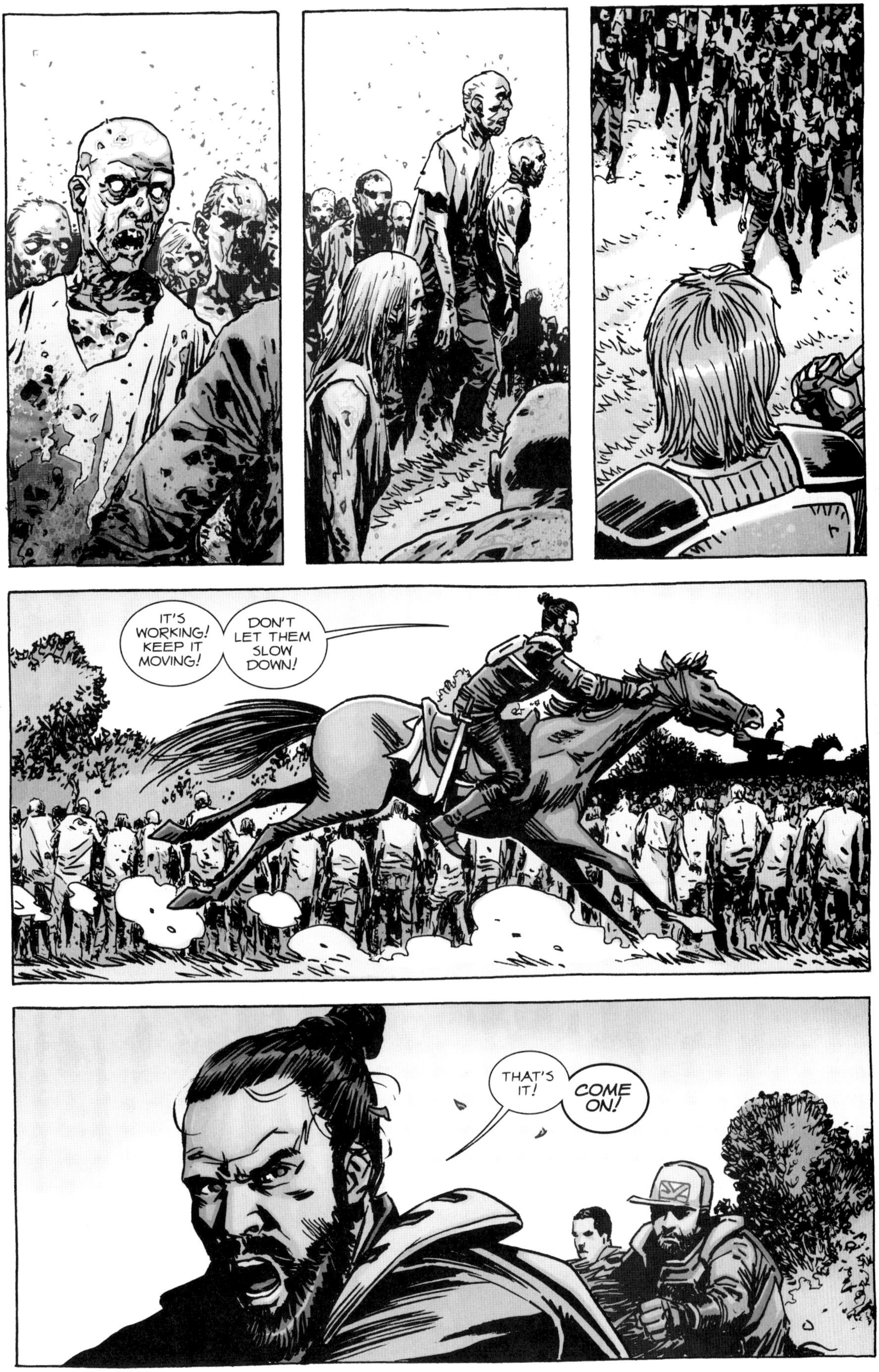
IT'S WORKING! KEEP IT MOVING!
DON'T LET THEM SLOW DOWN!
THAT'S IT!
COME ON!

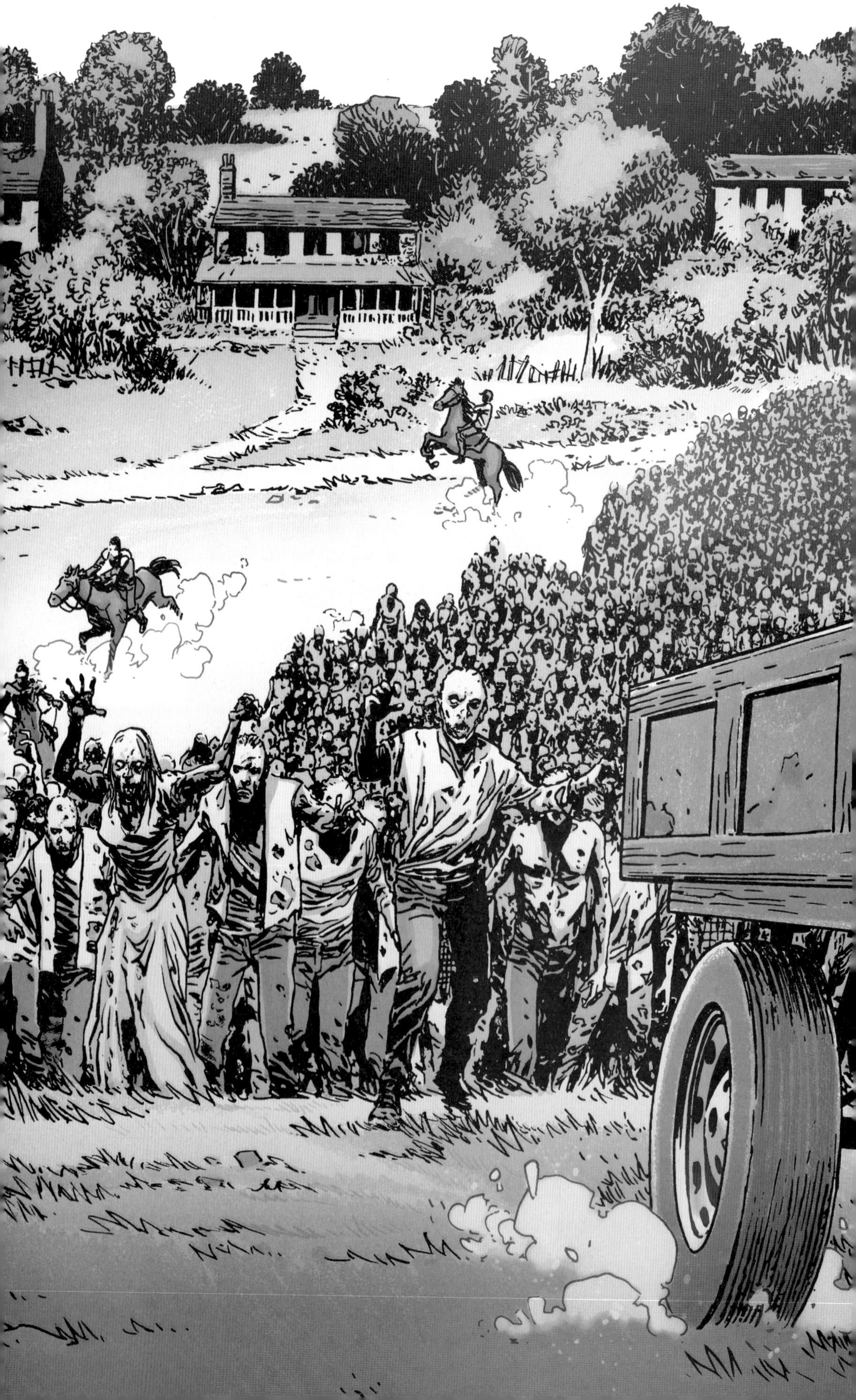

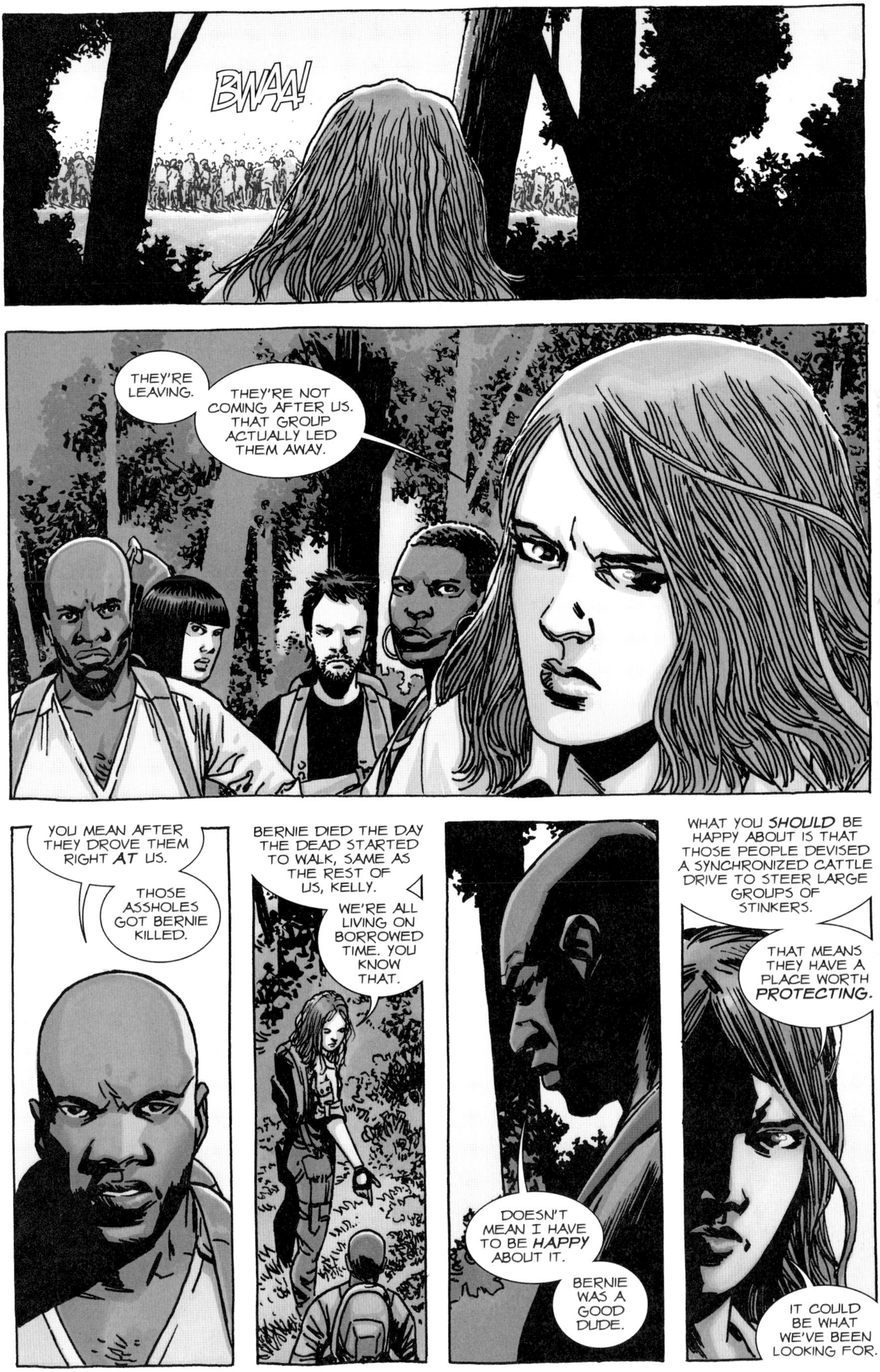
BWAA!
THEY'RE LEAVING.
THEY'RE NOT COMING AFTER US. THAT GROUP ACTUALLY LED THEM AWAY.
YOU MEAN AFTER THEY DROVE THEM RIGHT AT US.
THOSE ASSHOLES GOT BERNIE KILLED.
BERNIE DIED THE DAY THE DEAD STARTED TO WALK, SAME AS THE REST OF US, KELLY.
WE'RE ALL LIVING ON BORROWED TIME. YOU KNOW THAT.
DOESN'T MEAN I HAVE TO BE HAPPY ABOUT IT.
BERNIE WAS A GOOD DUDE.
WHAT YOU SHOULD BE HAPPY ABOUT IS THAT THOSE PEOPLE DEVISED A SYNCHRONIZED CATTLE DRIVE TO STEER LARGE GROUPS OF STINKERS.
THAT MEANS THEY HAVE A PLACE WORTH PROTECTING.
IT COULD BE WHAT WE'VE BEEN LOOKING FOR.

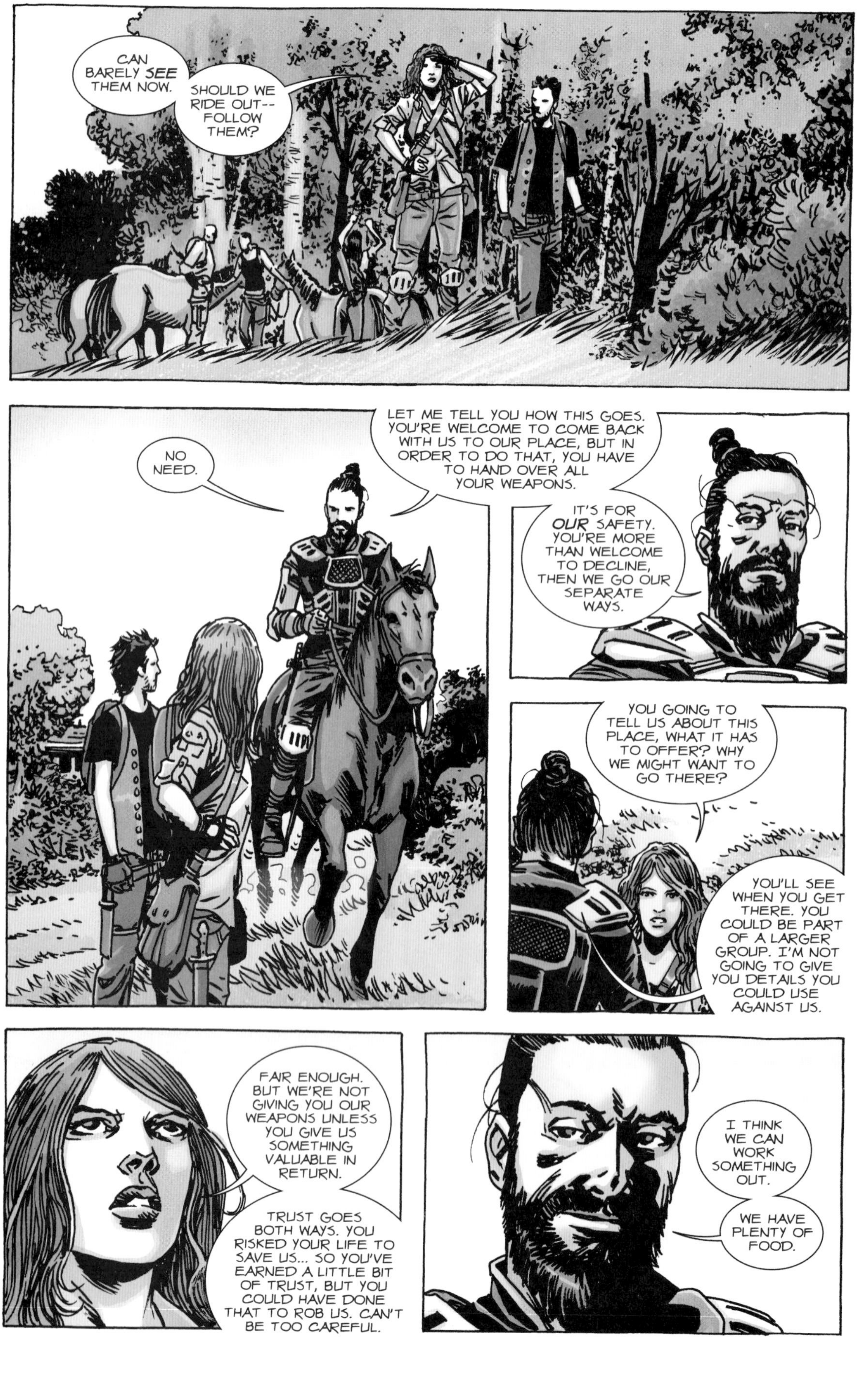
CAN BARELY SEE THEM NOW.
SHOULD WE RIDE OUT-- FOLLOW THEM?
NO NEED.
LET ME TELL YOU HOW THIS GOES. YOU'RE WELCOME TO COME BACK WITH US TO OUR PLACE, BUT IN ORDER TO DO THAT, YOU HAVE TO HAND OVER ALL YOUR WEAPONS.
IT'S FOR OUR SAFETY. YOU'RE MORE THAN WELCOME TO DECLINE, THEN WE GO OUR SEPARATE WAYS.
YOU GOING TO TELL US ABOUT THIS PLACE, WHAT IT HAS TO OFFER? WHY WE MIGHT WANT TO GO THERE?
YOU'LL SEE WHEN YOU GET THERE. YOU COULD BE PART OF A LARGER GROUP. I'M NOT GOING TO GIVE YOU DETAILS YOU COULD USE AGAINST US.
FAIR ENOUGH. BUT WE'RE NOT GIVING YOU OUR WEAPONS UNLESS YOU GIVE US SOMETHING VALUABLE IN RETURN.
TRUST GOES BOTH WAYS. YOU RISKED YOUR LIFE TO SAVE US... SO YOU'VE EARNED A LITTLE BIT OF TRUST, BUT YOU COULD HAVE DONE THAT TO ROB US. CAN'T BE TOO CAREFUL.
I THINK WE CAN WORK SOMETHING OUT.
WE HAVE PLENTY OF FOOD.

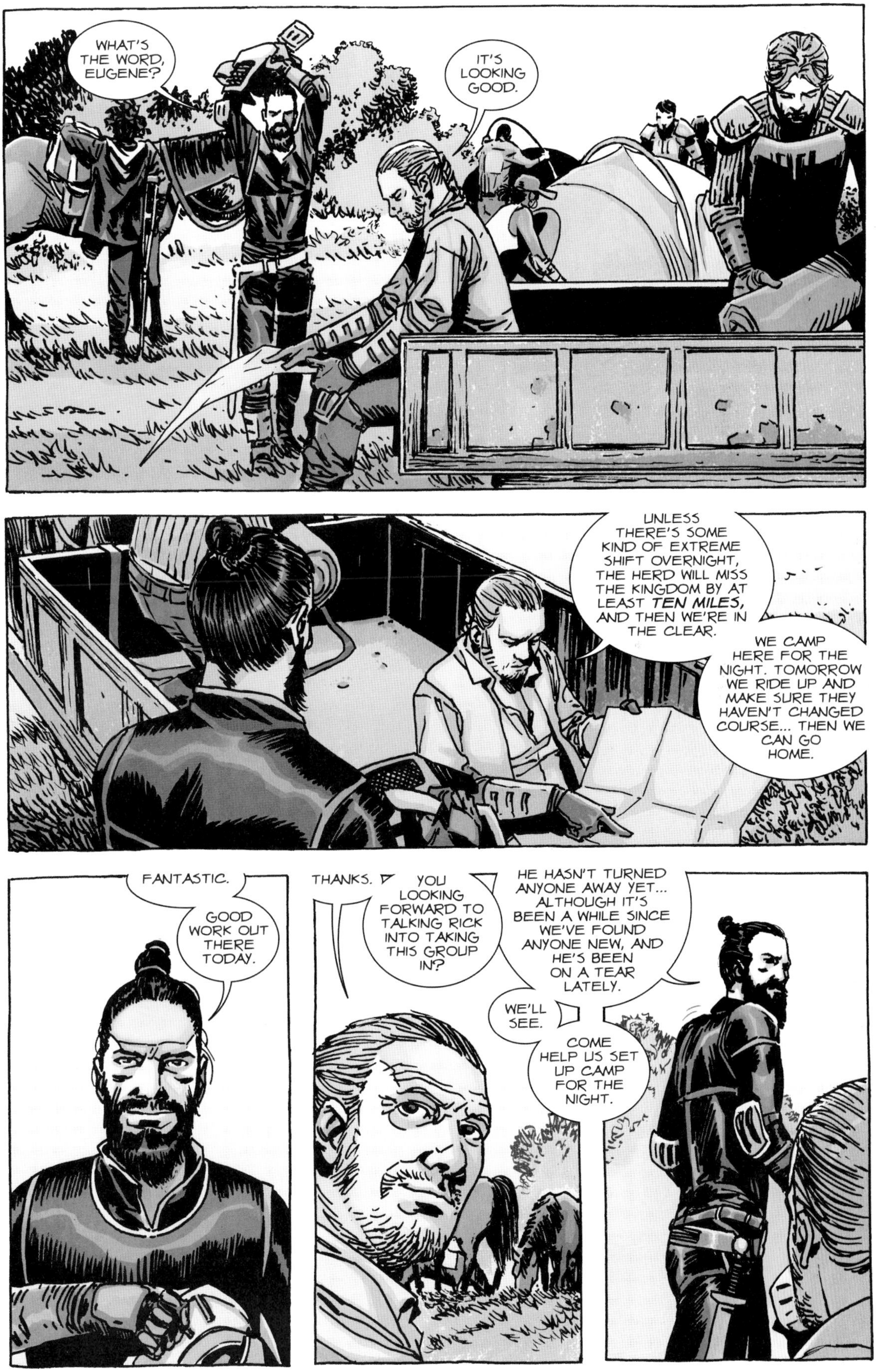
WHAT'S THE WORD, EUGENE?
IT'S LOOKING GOOD.
UNLESS THERE'S SOME KIND OF EXTREME SHIFT OVERNIGHT, THE HERD WILL MISS THE KINGDOM BY AT LEAST *TEN MILES,* AND THEN WE'RE IN THE CLEAR.
WE CAMP HERE FOR THE NIGHT. TOMORROW WE RIDE UP AND MAKE SURE THEY HAVEN'T CHANGED COURSE... THEN WE CAN GO HOME.
FANTASTIC.
GOOD WORK OUT THERE TODAY.
THANKS.
YOU LOOKING FORWARD TO TALKING RICK INTO TAKING THIS GROUP IN?
HE HASN'T TURNED ANYONE AWAY YET... ALTHOUGH IT'S BEEN A WHILE SINCE WE'VE FOUND ANYONE NEW, AND HE'S BEEN ON A TEAR LATELY.
WE'LL SEE.
COME HELP US SET UP CAMP FOR THE NIGHT.

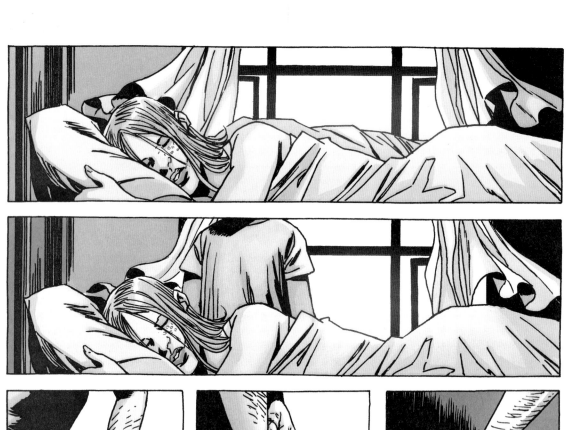

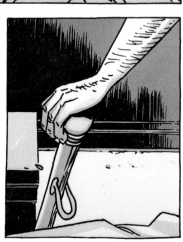

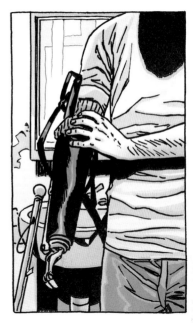

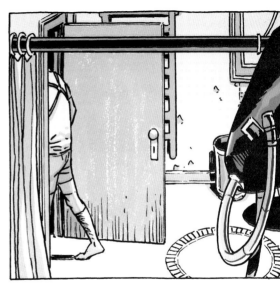

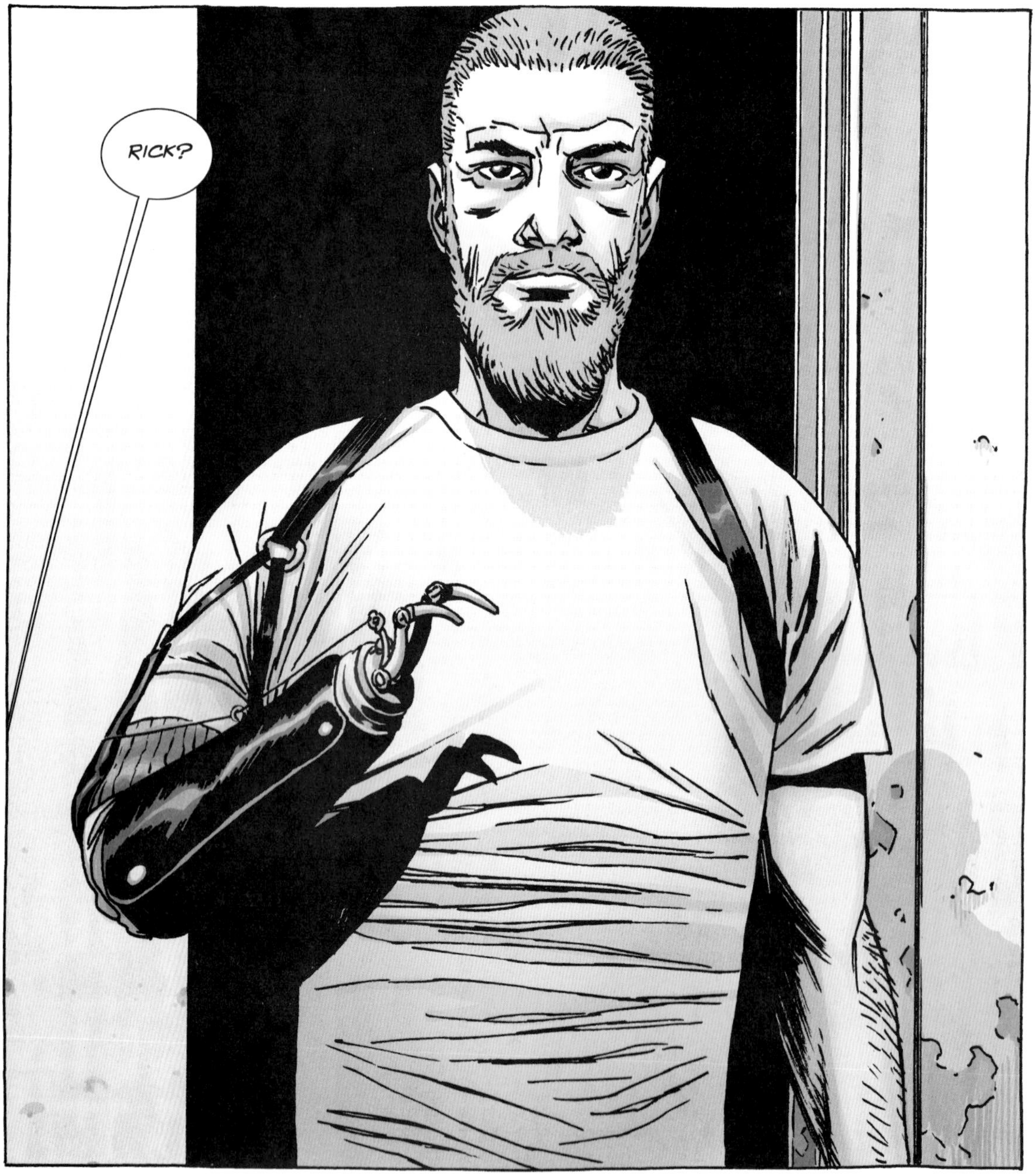
RICK?

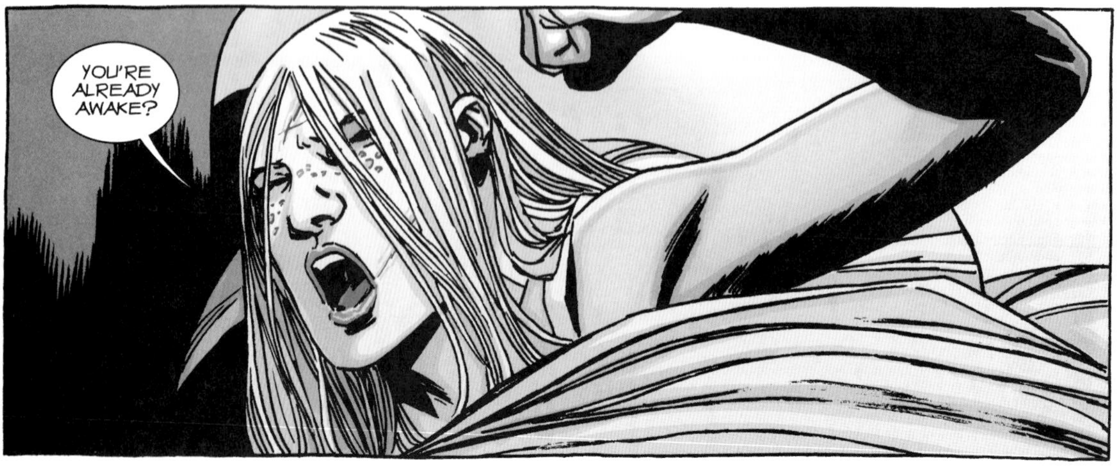
YOU'RE ALREADY AWAKE?

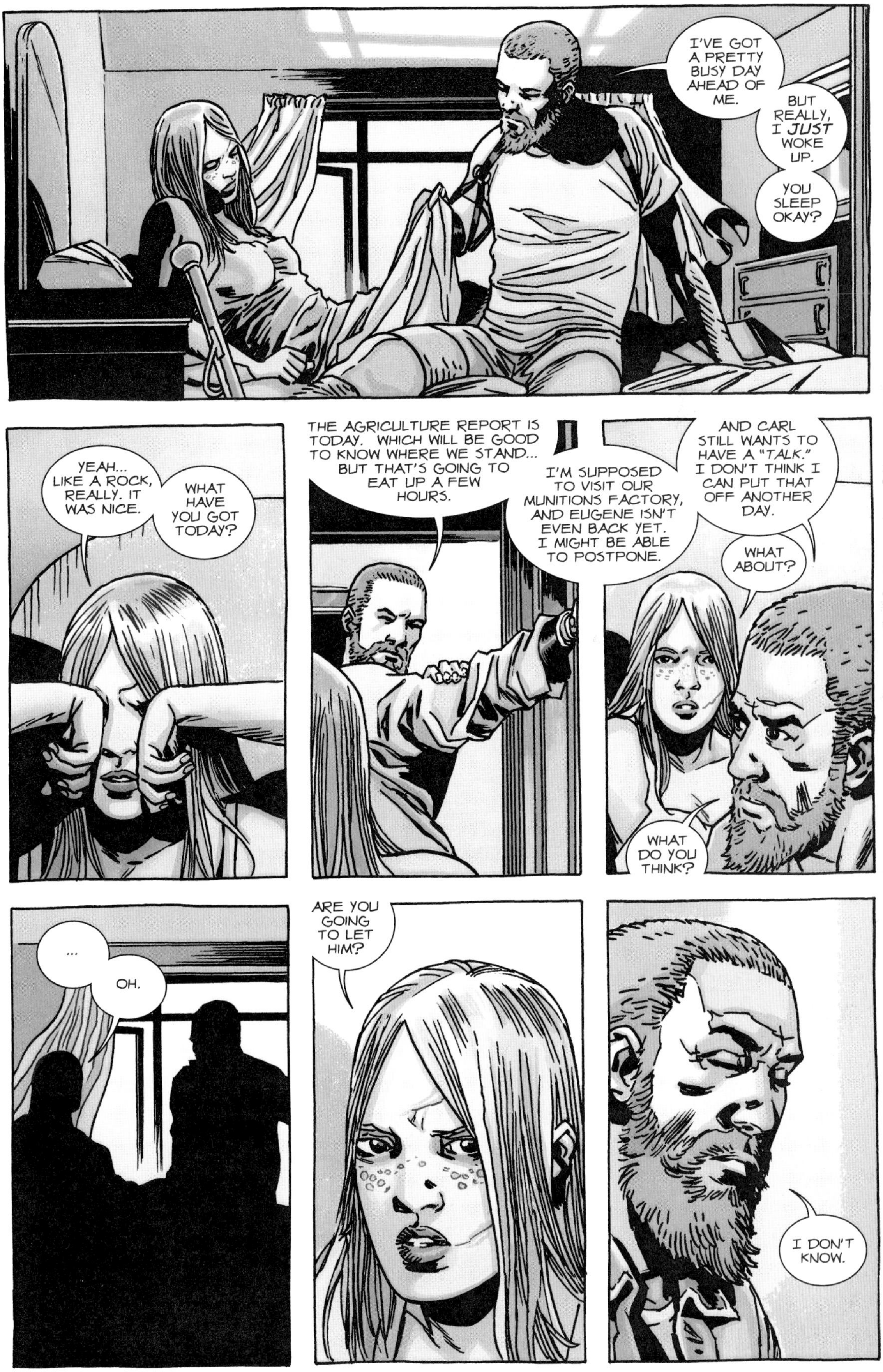
I'VE GOT A PRETTY BUSY DAY AHEAD OF ME.
BUT REALLY, I JUST WOKE UP.
YOU SLEEP OKAY?
YEAH... LIKE A ROCK, REALLY. IT WAS NICE.
WHAT HAVE YOU GOT TODAY?
THE AGRICULTURE REPORT IS TODAY. WHICH WILL BE GOOD TO KNOW WHERE WE STAND... BUT THAT'S GOING TO EAT UP A FEW HOURS.
I'M SUPPOSED TO VISIT OUR MUNITIONS FACTORY, AND EUGENE ISN'T EVEN BACK YET. I MIGHT BE ABLE TO POSTPONE.
AND CARL STILL WANTS TO HAVE A "TALK." I DON'T THINK I CAN PUT THAT OFF ANOTHER DAY.
WHAT ABOUT?
WHAT DO YOU THINK?
...
OH.
ARE YOU GOING TO LET HIM?
I DON'T KNOW.

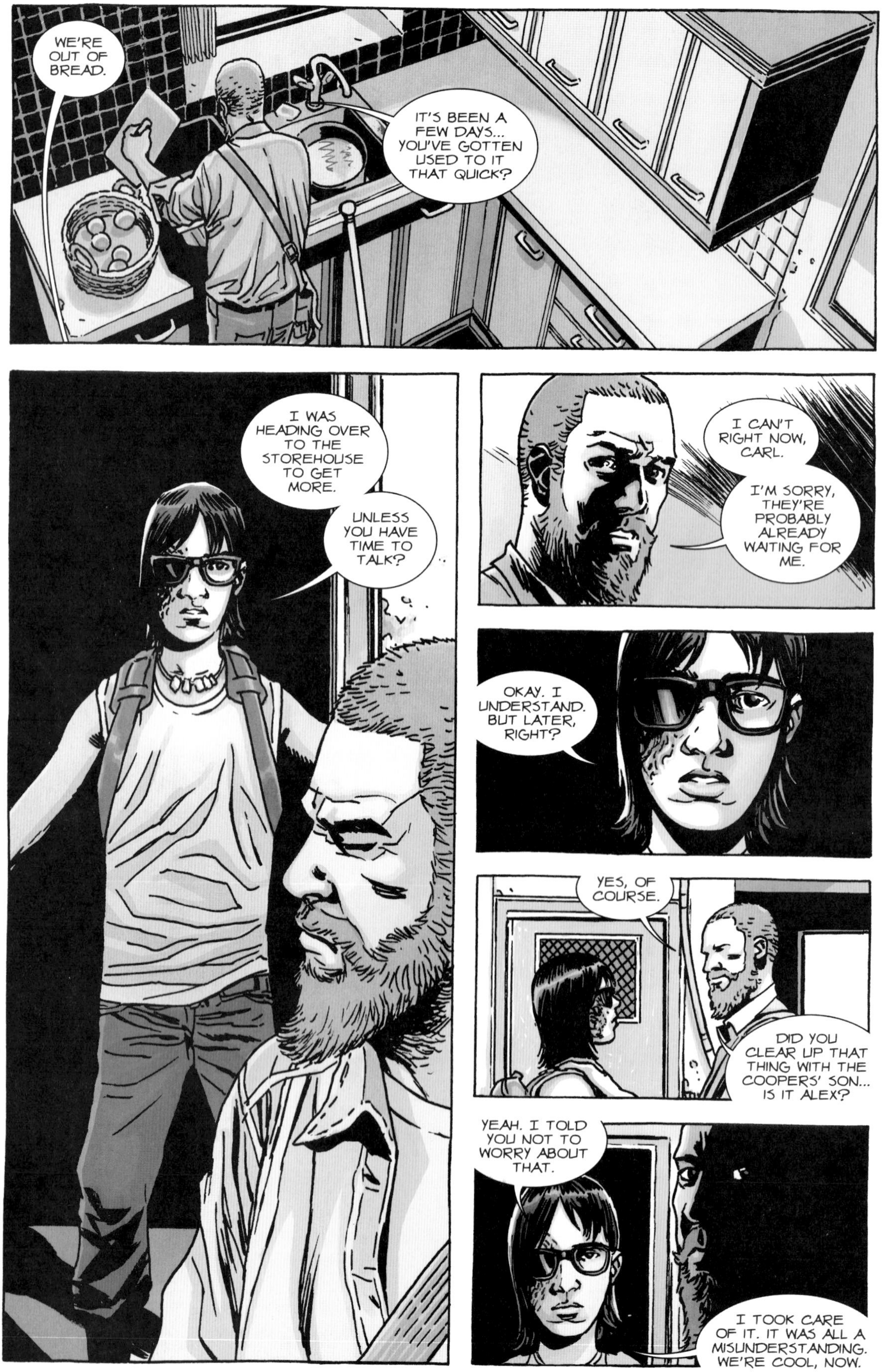
WE'RE OUT OF BREAD.
IT'S BEEN A FEW DAYS... YOU'VE GOTTEN USED TO IT THAT QUICK?
I WAS HEADING OVER TO THE STOREHOUSE TO GET MORE.
UNLESS YOU HAVE TIME TO TALK?
I CAN'T RIGHT NOW, CARL.
I'M SORRY, THEY'RE PROBABLY ALREADY WAITING FOR ME.
OKAY. I UNDERSTAND. BUT LATER, RIGHT?
YES, OF COURSE.
DID YOU CLEAR UP THAT THING WITH THE COOPERS' SON... IS IT ALEX?
YEAH. I TOLD YOU NOT TO WORRY ABOUT THAT.
I TOOK CARE OF IT. IT WAS ALL A MISUNDERSTANDING. WE'RE COOL, NOW.

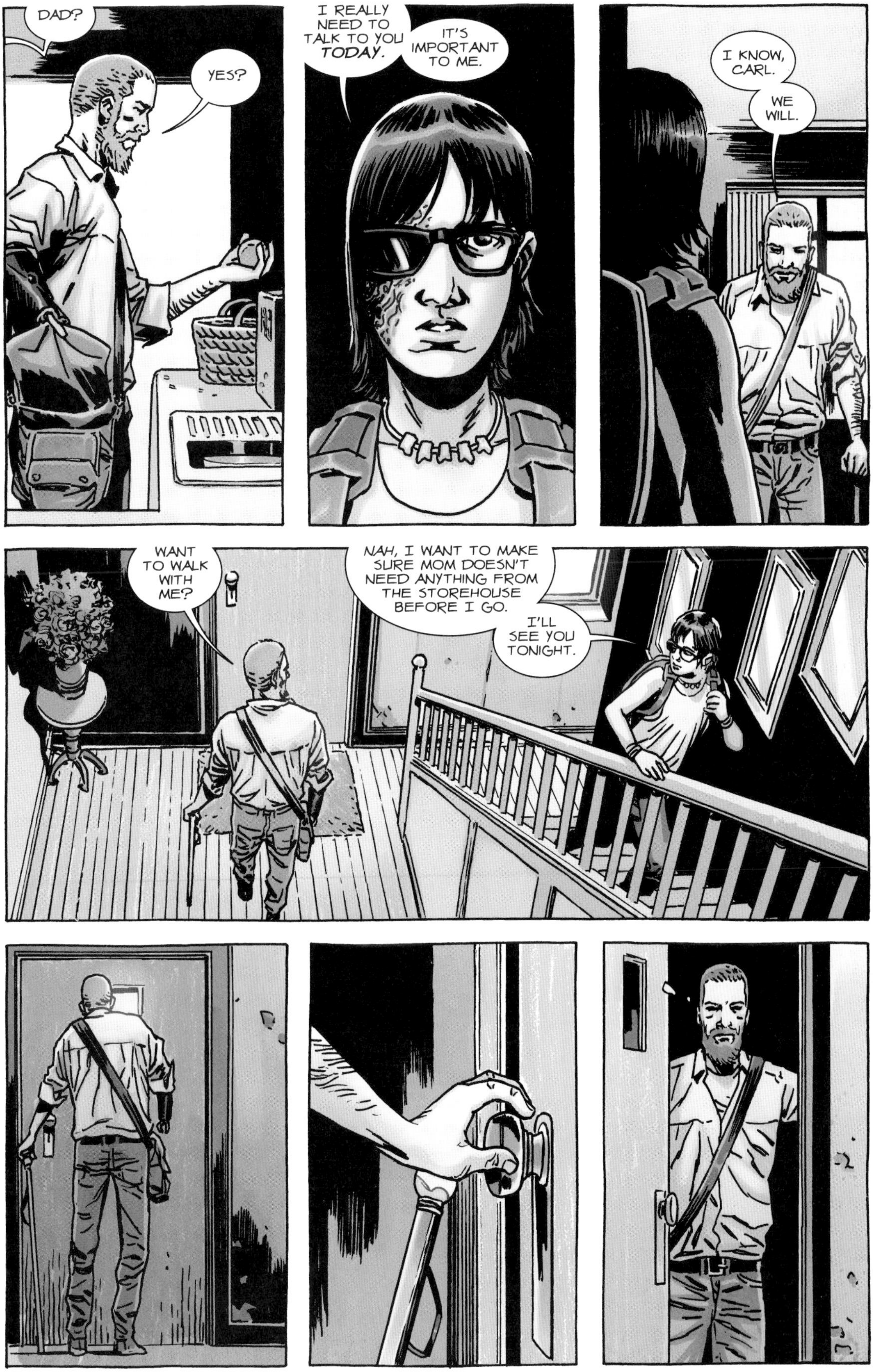
DAD?
YES?
I REALLY NEED TO TALK TO YOU *TODAY*.
IT'S IMPORTANT TO ME.
I KNOW, CARL.
WE WILL.
WANT TO WALK WITH ME?
NAH, I WANT TO MAKE SURE MOM DOESN'T NEED ANYTHING FROM THE STOREHOUSE BEFORE I GO.
I'LL SEE YOU TONIGHT.

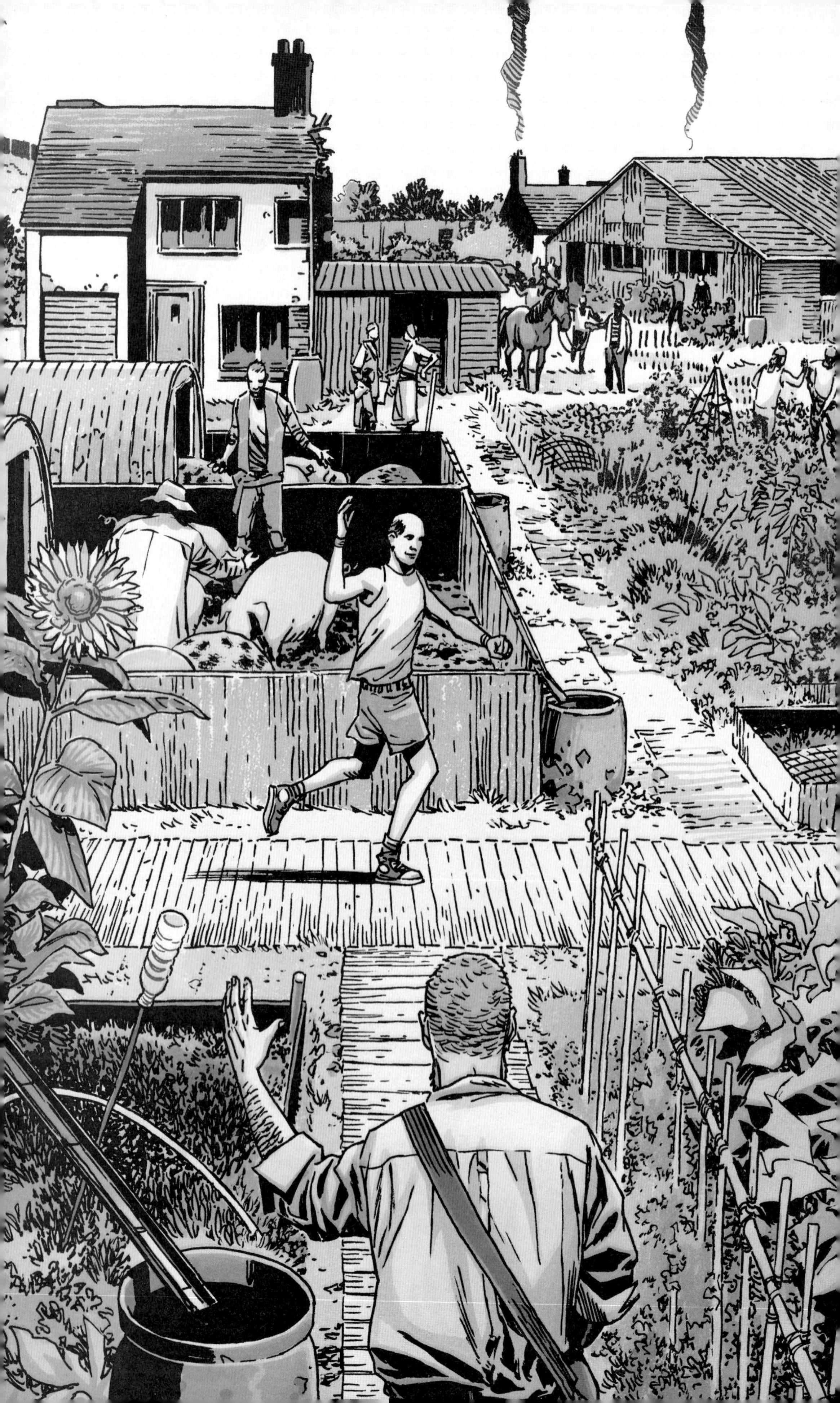

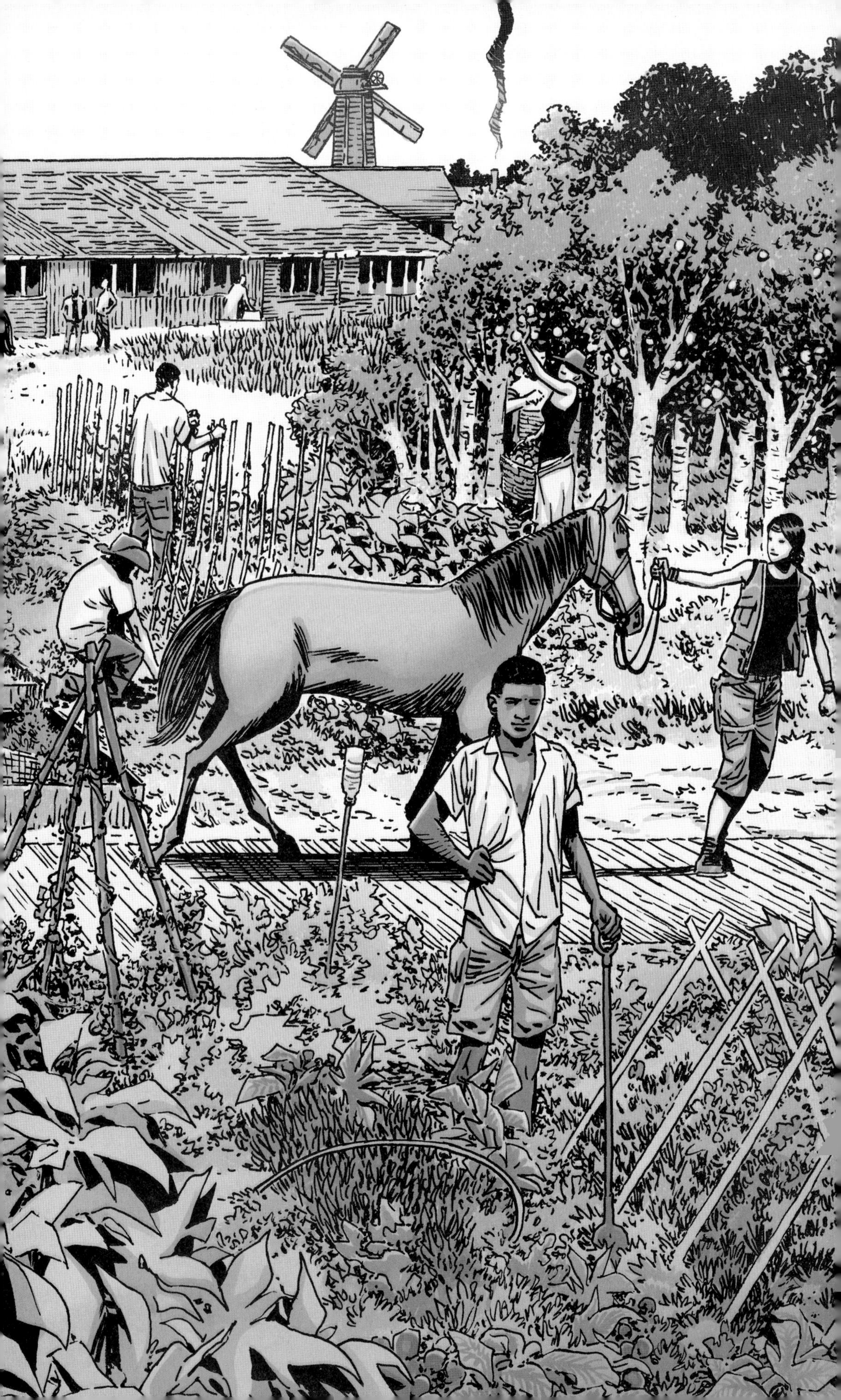

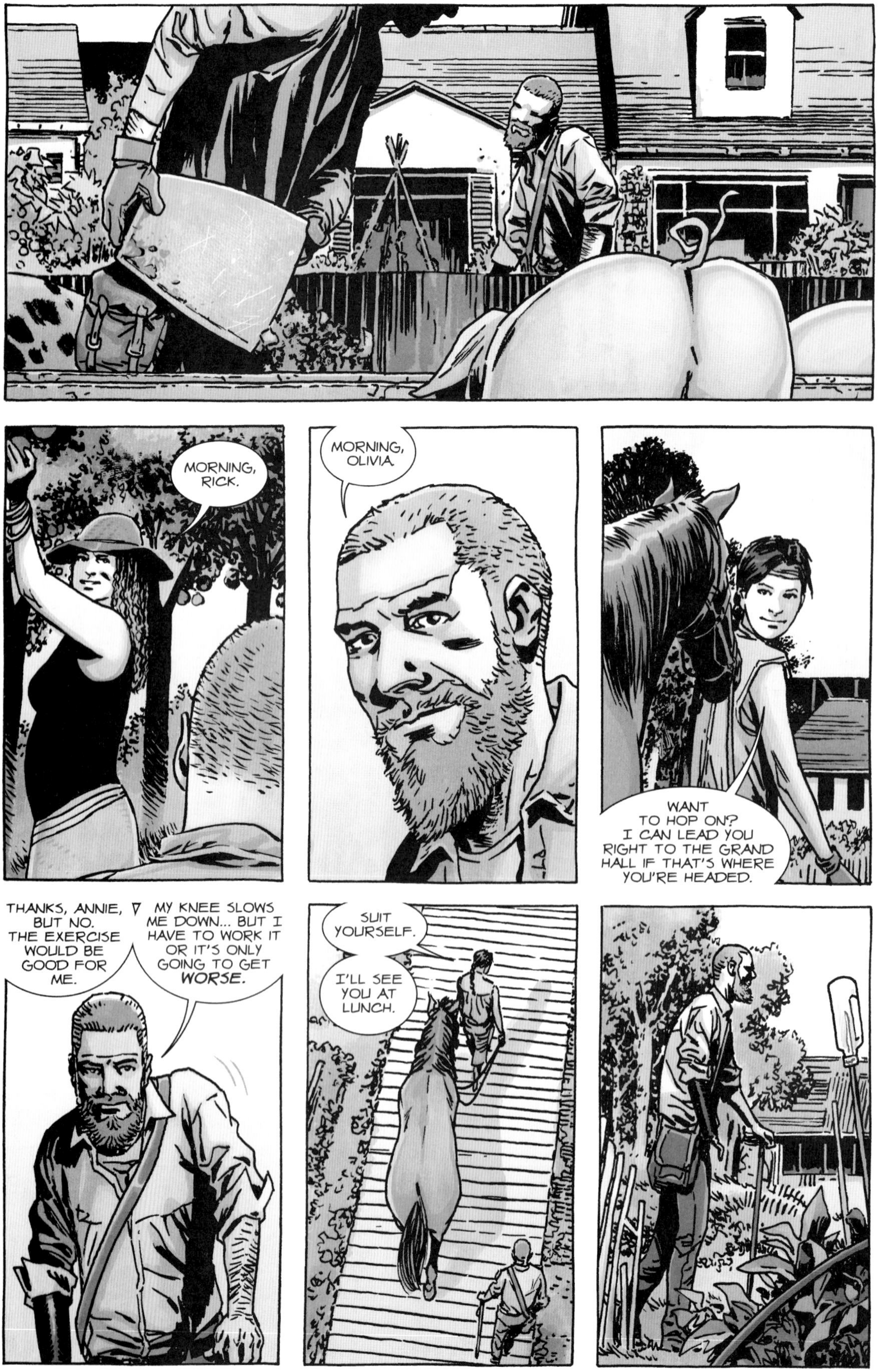
MORNING, RICK.
MORNING, OLIVIA.
WANT TO HOP ON? I CAN LEAD YOU RIGHT TO THE GRAND HALL IF THAT'S WHERE YOU'RE HEADED.
THANKS, ANNIE, BUT NO. THE EXERCISE WOULD BE GOOD FOR ME.
MY KNEE SLOWS ME DOWN... BUT I HAVE TO WORK IT OR IT'S ONLY GOING TO GET WORSE.
SUIT YOURSELF.
I'LL SEE YOU AT LUNCH.

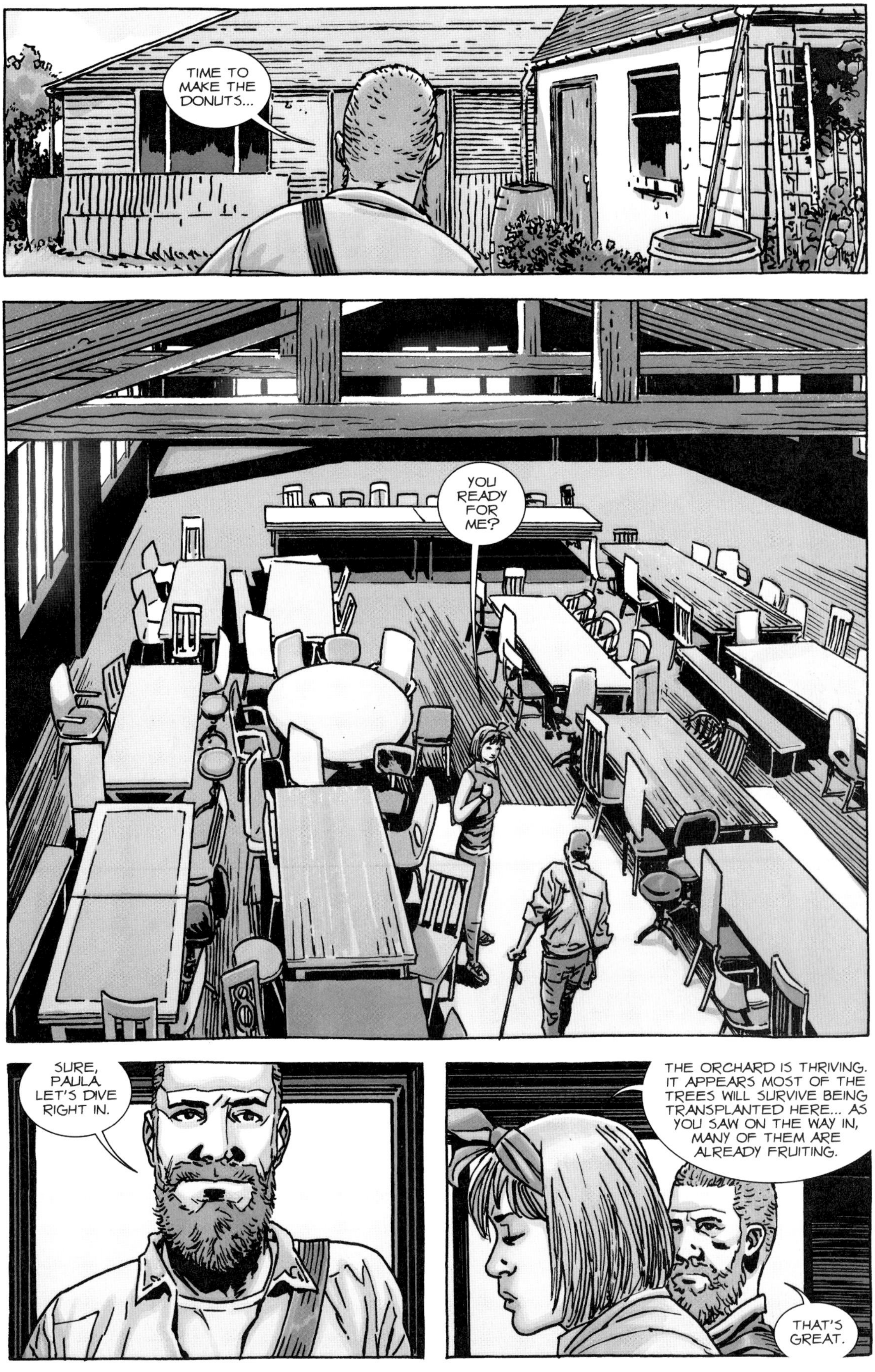
TIME TO MAKE THE DONUTS...
YOU READY FOR ME?
SURE, PAULA. LET'S DIVE RIGHT IN.
THE ORCHARD IS THRIVING. IT APPEARS MOST OF THE TREES WILL SURVIVE BEING TRANSPLANTED HERE... AS YOU SAW ON THE WAY IN, MANY OF THEM ARE ALREADY FRUITING.
THAT'S GREAT.

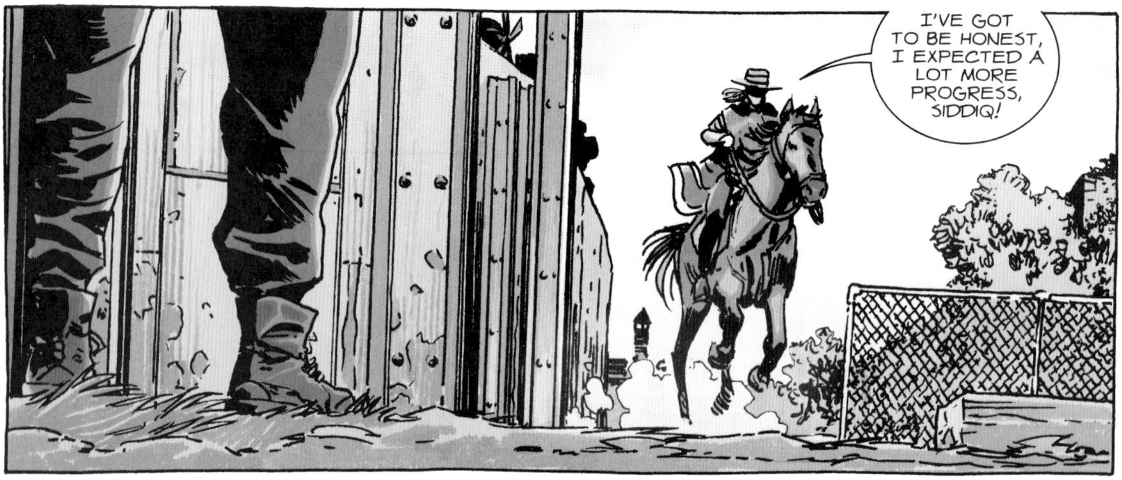
I'VE GOT TO BE HONEST, I EXPECTED A LOT MORE PROGRESS, SIDDIQ!

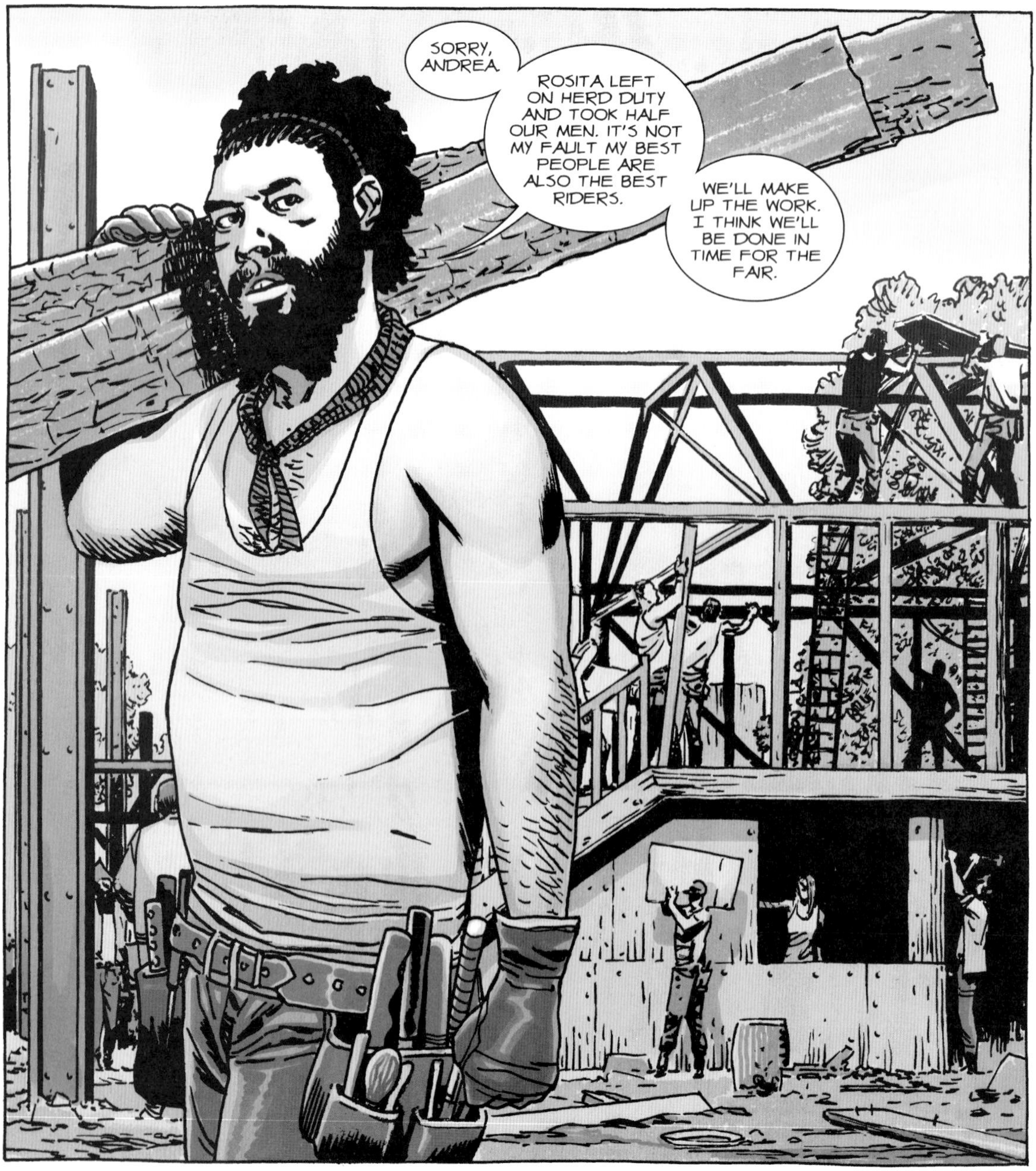
SORRY, ANDREA.
ROSITA LEFT ON HERD DUTY AND TOOK HALF OUR MEN. IT'S NOT MY FAULT MY BEST PEOPLE ARE ALSO THE BEST RIDERS.
WE'LL MAKE UP THE WORK. I THINK WE'LL BE DONE IN TIME FOR THE FAIR.

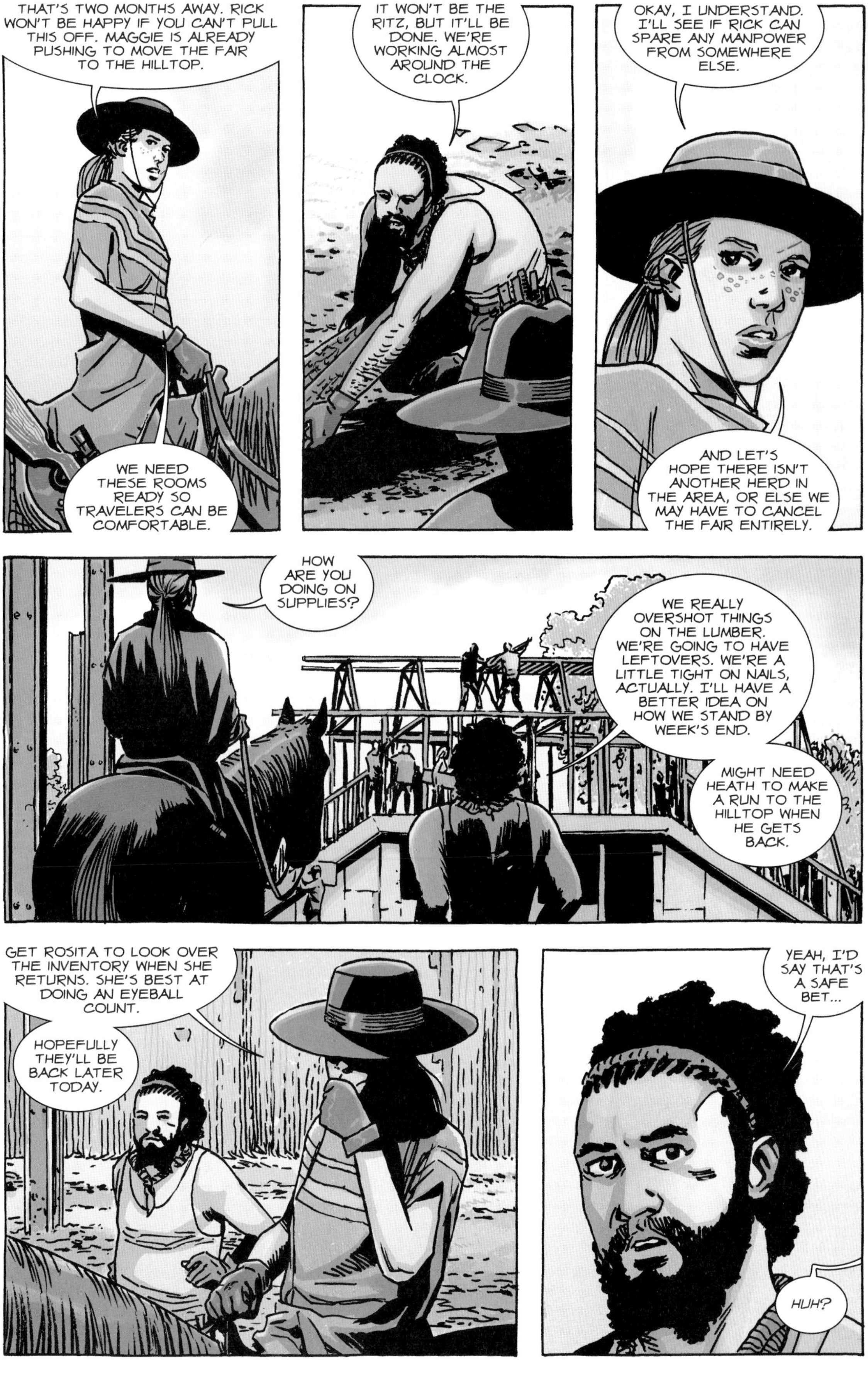
THAT'S TWO MONTHS AWAY. RICK WON'T BE HAPPY IF YOU CAN'T PULL THIS OFF. MAGGIE IS ALREADY PUSHING TO MOVE THE FAIR TO THE HILLTOP.
WE NEED THESE ROOMS READY SO TRAVELERS CAN BE COMFORTABLE.
IT WON'T BE THE RITZ, BUT IT'LL BE DONE. WE'RE WORKING ALMOST AROUND THE CLOCK.
OKAY, I UNDERSTAND. I'LL SEE IF RICK CAN SPARE ANY MANPOWER FROM SOMEWHERE ELSE.
AND LET'S HOPE THERE ISN'T ANOTHER HERD IN THE AREA, OR ELSE WE MAY HAVE TO CANCEL THE FAIR ENTIRELY.
HOW ARE YOU DOING ON SUPPLIES?
WE REALLY OVERSHOT THINGS ON THE LUMBER. WE'RE GOING TO HAVE LEFTOVERS. WE'RE A LITTLE TIGHT ON NAILS, ACTUALLY. I'LL HAVE A BETTER IDEA ON HOW WE STAND BY WEEK'S END.
MIGHT NEED HEATH TO MAKE A RUN TO THE HILLTOP WHEN HE GETS BACK.
GET ROSITA TO LOOK OVER THE INVENTORY WHEN SHE RETURNS. SHE'S BEST AT DOING AN EYEBALL COUNT.
HOPEFULLY THEY'LL BE BACK LATER TODAY.
YEAH, I'D SAY THAT'S A SAFE BET...
HUH?

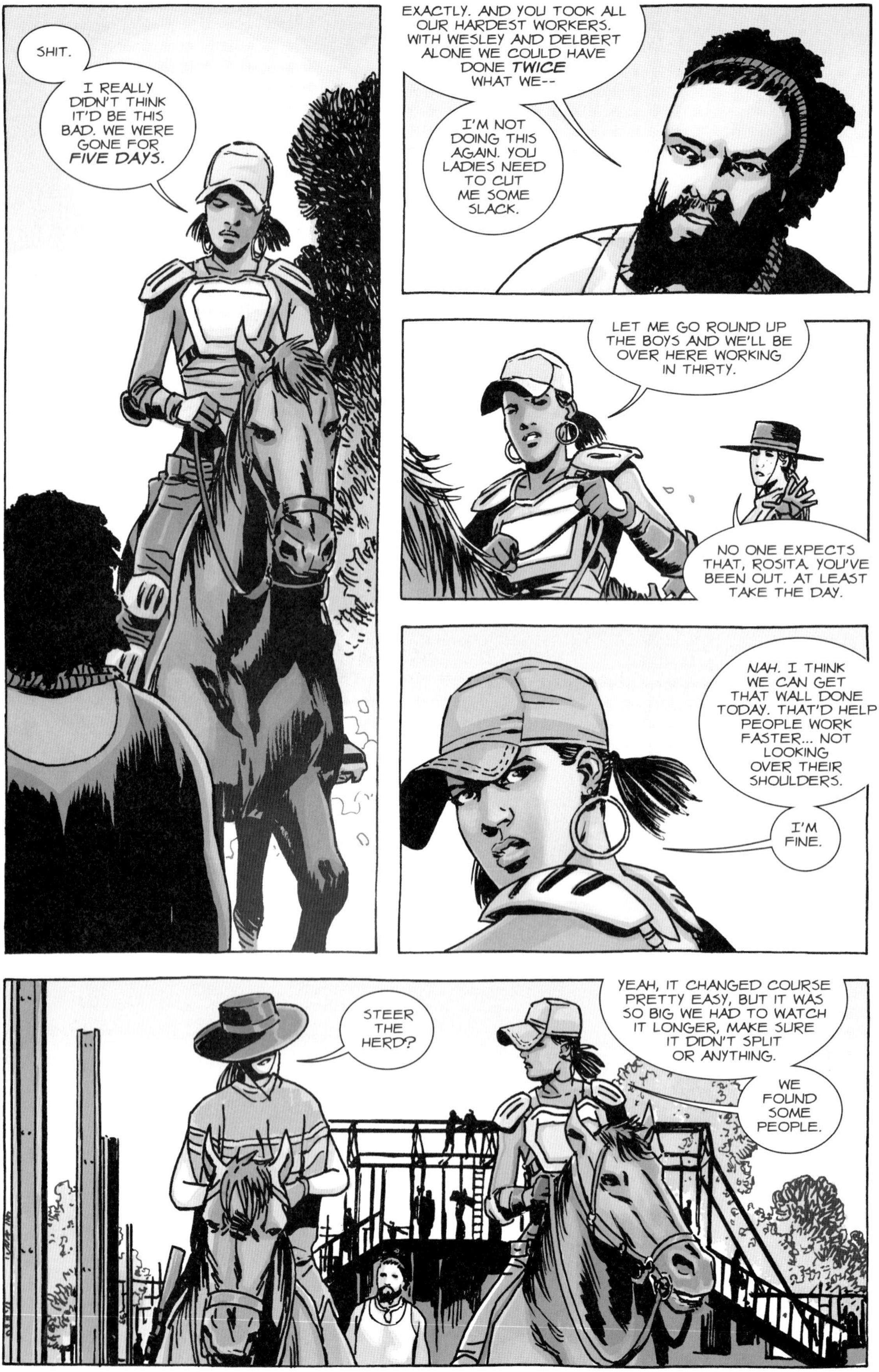
SHIT.
I REALLY DIDN'T THINK IT'D BE THIS BAD. WE WERE GONE FOR *FIVE DAYS.*
EXACTLY. AND YOU TOOK ALL OUR HARDEST WORKERS. WITH WESLEY AND DELBERT ALONE WE COULD HAVE DONE *TWICE* WHAT WE--
I'M NOT DOING THIS AGAIN. YOU LADIES NEED TO CUT ME SOME SLACK.
LET ME GO ROUND UP THE BOYS AND WE'LL BE OVER HERE WORKING IN THIRTY.
NO ONE EXPECTS THAT, ROSITA. YOU'VE BEEN OUT. AT LEAST TAKE THE DAY.
NAH. I THINK WE CAN GET THAT WALL DONE TODAY. THAT'D HELP PEOPLE WORK FASTER... NOT LOOKING OVER THEIR SHOULDERS.
I'M FINE.
STEER THE HERD?
YEAH, IT CHANGED COURSE PRETTY EASY, BUT IT WAS SO BIG WE HAD TO WATCH IT LONGER, MAKE SURE IT DIDN'T SPLIT OR ANYTHING.
WE FOUND SOME PEOPLE.

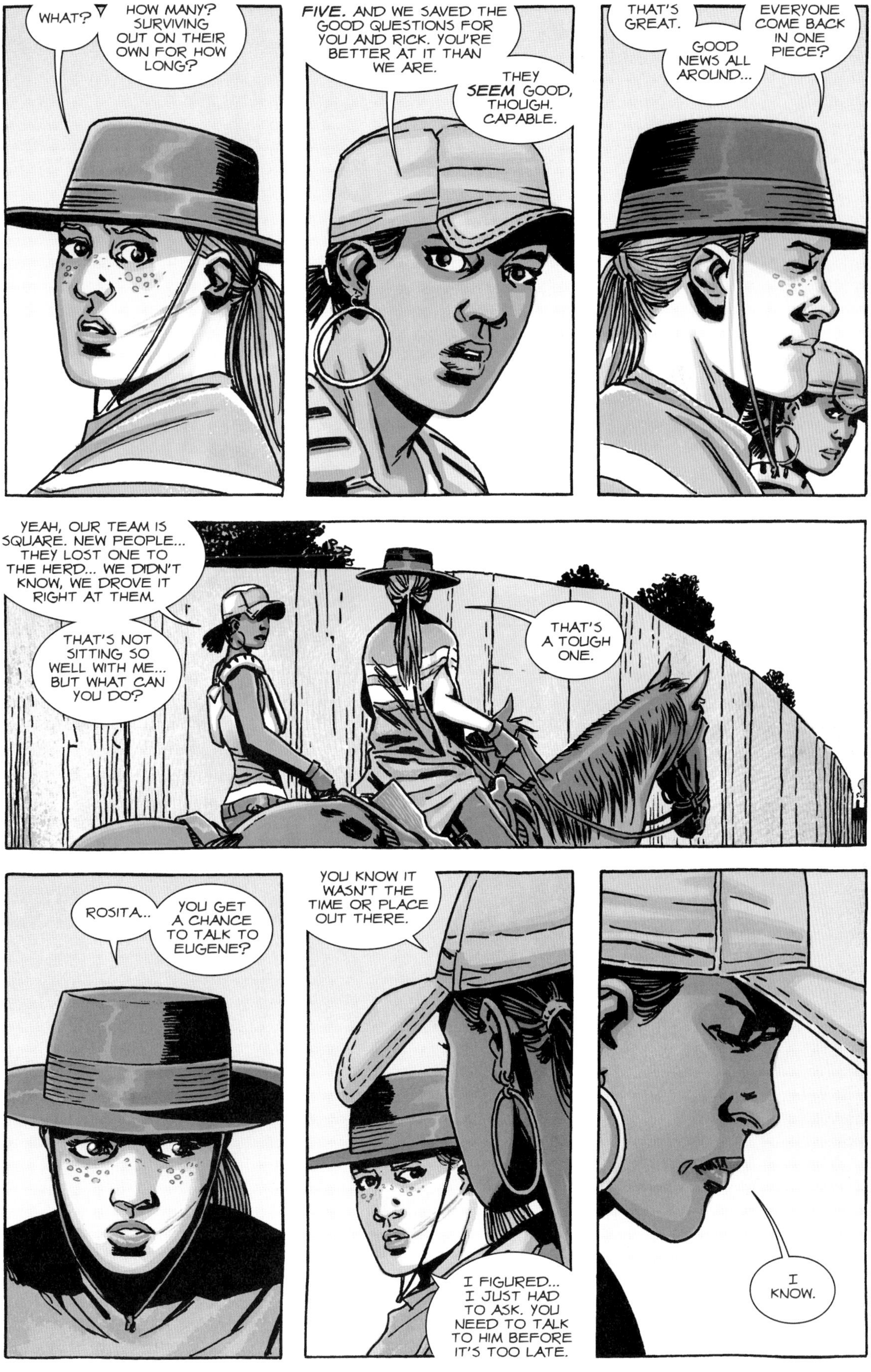
WHAT?
HOW MANY? SURVIVING OUT ON THEIR OWN FOR HOW LONG?
FIVE. AND WE SAVED THE GOOD QUESTIONS FOR YOU AND RICK. YOU'RE BETTER AT IT THAN WE ARE.
THEY SEEM GOOD, THOUGH. CAPABLE.
THAT'S GREAT.
GOOD NEWS ALL AROUND...
EVERYONE COME BACK IN ONE PIECE?
YEAH, OUR TEAM IS SQUARE. NEW PEOPLE... THEY LOST ONE TO THE HERD... WE DIDN'T KNOW, WE DROVE IT RIGHT AT THEM.
THAT'S NOT SITTING SO WELL WITH ME... BUT WHAT CAN YOU DO?
THAT'S A TOUGH ONE.
ROSITA...
YOU GET A CHANCE TO TALK TO EUGENE?
YOU KNOW IT WASN'T THE TIME OR PLACE OUT THERE.
I FIGURED... I JUST HAD TO ASK. YOU NEED TO TALK TO HIM BEFORE IT'S TOO LATE.
I KNOW.

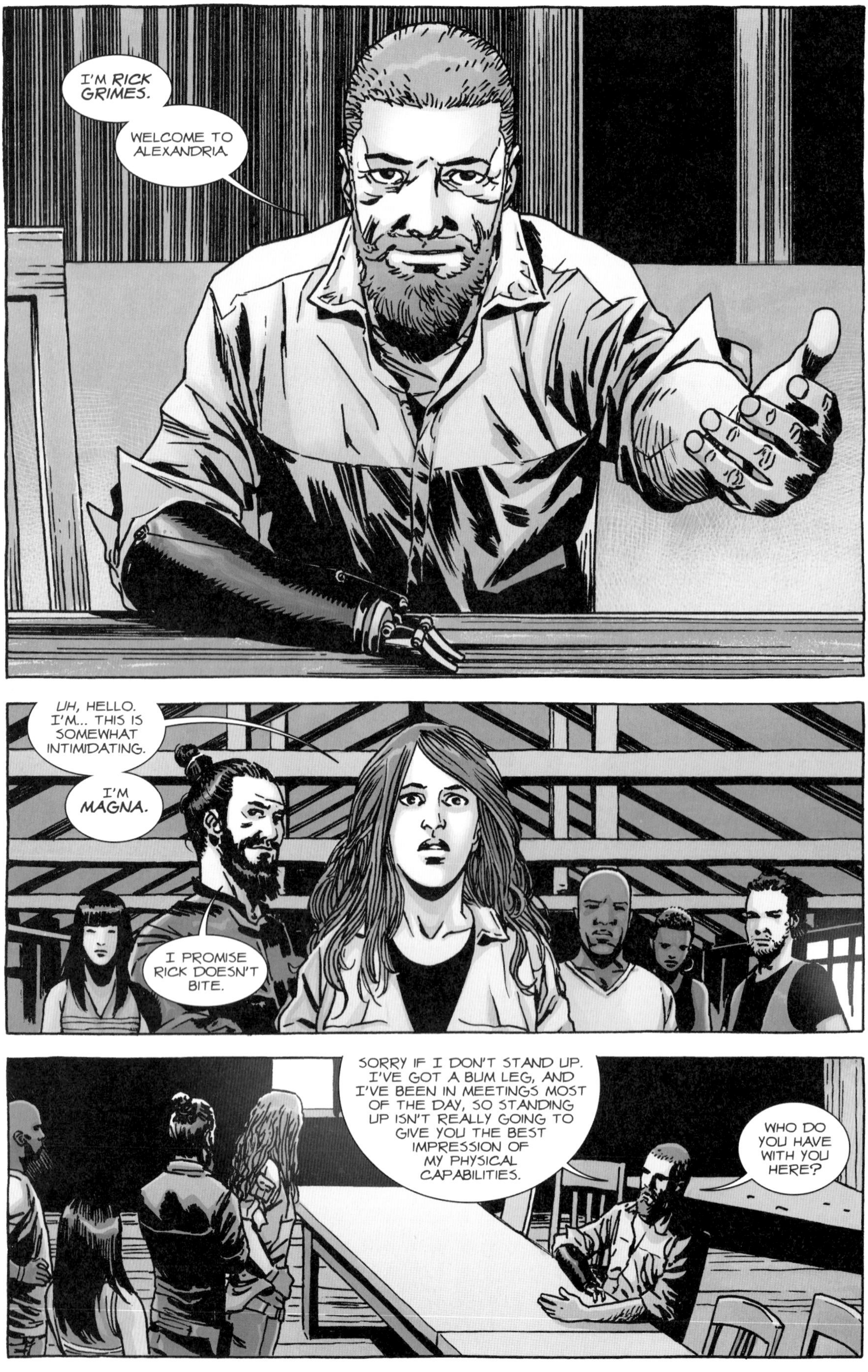
I'M RICK GRIMES.
WELCOME TO ALEXANDRIA.
UH, HELLO. I'M... THIS IS SOMEWHAT INTIMIDATING.
I'M MAGNA.
I PROMISE RICK DOESN'T BITE.
SORRY IF I DON'T STAND UP. I'VE GOT A BUM LEG, AND I'VE BEEN IN MEETINGS MOST OF THE DAY, SO STANDING UP ISN'T REALLY GOING TO GIVE YOU THE BEST IMPRESSION OF MY PHYSICAL CAPABILITIES.
WHO DO YOU HAVE WITH YOU HERE?

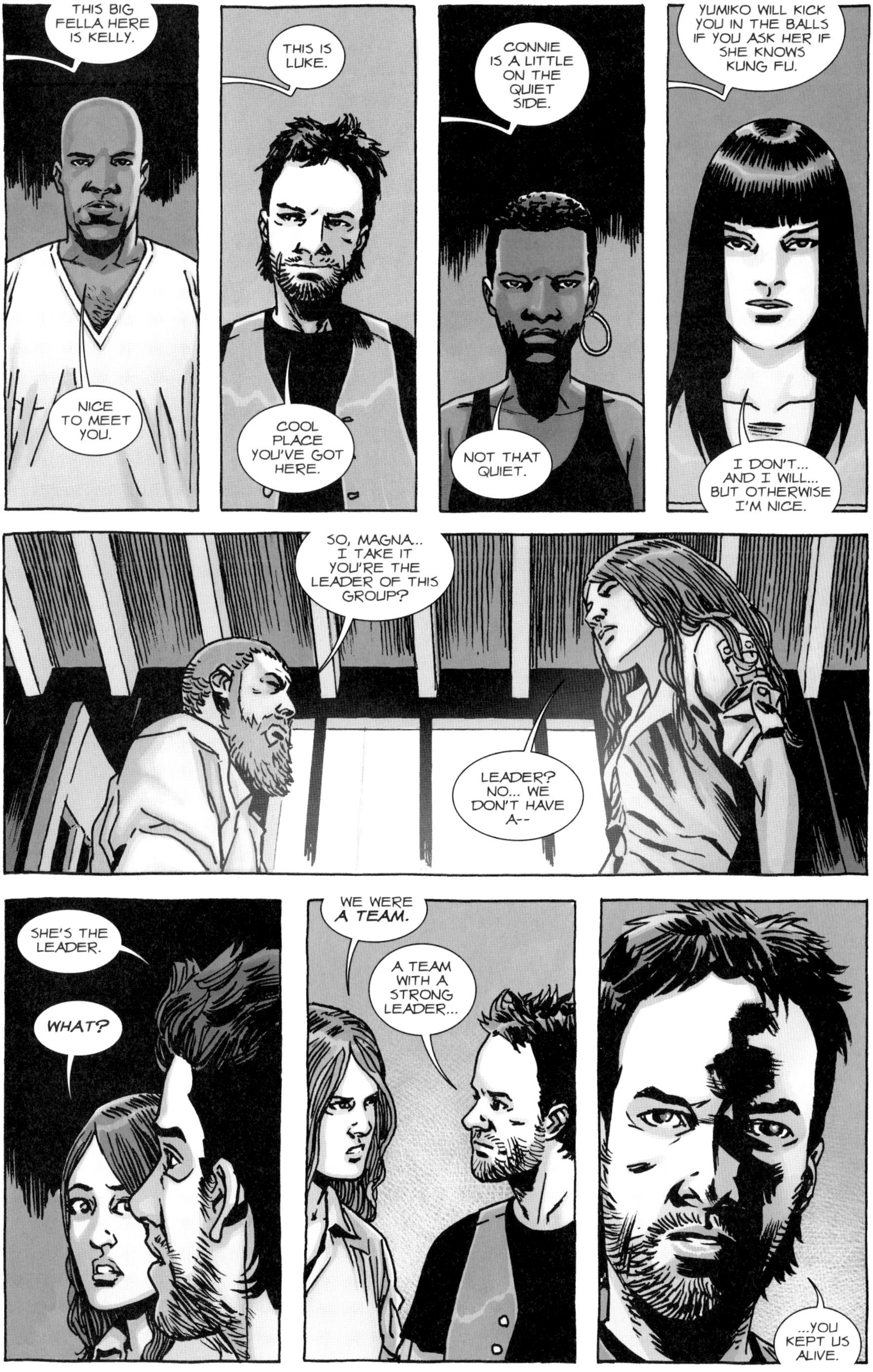

THIS BIG FELLA HERE IS KELLY.
NICE TO MEET YOU.
THIS IS LUKE.
COOL PLACE YOU'VE GOT HERE.
CONNIE IS A LITTLE ON THE QUIET SIDE.
NOT THAT QUIET.
YUMIKO WILL KICK YOU IN THE BALLS IF YOU ASK HER IF SHE KNOWS KUNG FU.
I DON'T... AND I WILL... BUT OTHERWISE I'M NICE.
SO, MAGNA.. I TAKE IT YOU'RE THE LEADER OF THIS GROUP?
LEADER? NO... WE DON'T HAVE A--
SHE'S THE LEADER.
WHAT?
WE WERE A TEAM.
A TEAM WITH A STRONG LEADER...
...YOU KEPT US ALIVE.

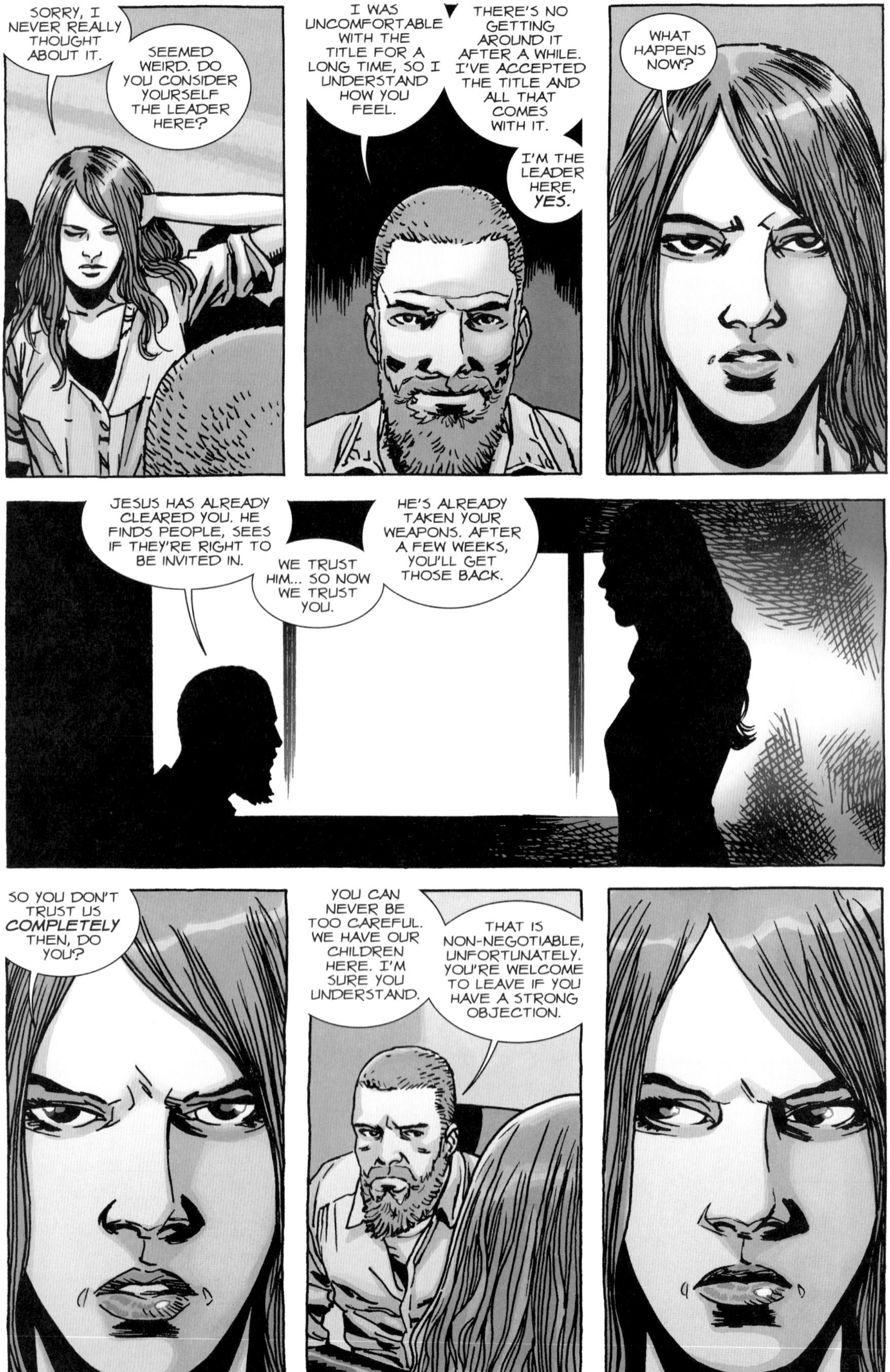
SORRY, I NEVER REALLY THOUGHT ABOUT IT.
SEEMED WEIRD. DO YOU CONSIDER YOURSELF THE LEADER HERE?
I WAS UNCOMFORTABLE WITH THE TITLE FOR A LONG TIME, SO I UNDERSTAND HOW YOU FEEL.
THERE'S NO GETTING AROUND IT AFTER A WHILE. I'VE ACCEPTED THE TITLE AND ALL THAT COMES WITH IT.
I'M THE LEADER HERE, YES.
WHAT HAPPENS NOW?
JESUS HAS ALREADY CLEARED YOU. HE FINDS PEOPLE, SEES IF THEY'RE RIGHT TO BE INVITED IN.
WE TRUST HIM... SO NOW WE TRUST YOU.
HE'S ALREADY TAKEN YOUR WEAPONS. AFTER A FEW WEEKS, YOU'LL GET THOSE BACK.
SO YOU DON'T TRUST US COMPLETELY THEN, DO YOU?
YOU CAN NEVER BE TOO CAREFUL. WE HAVE OUR CHILDREN HERE. I'M SURE YOU UNDERSTAND.
THAT IS NON-NEGOTIABLE, UNFORTUNATELY. YOU'RE WELCOME TO LEAVE IF YOU HAVE A STRONG OBJECTION.

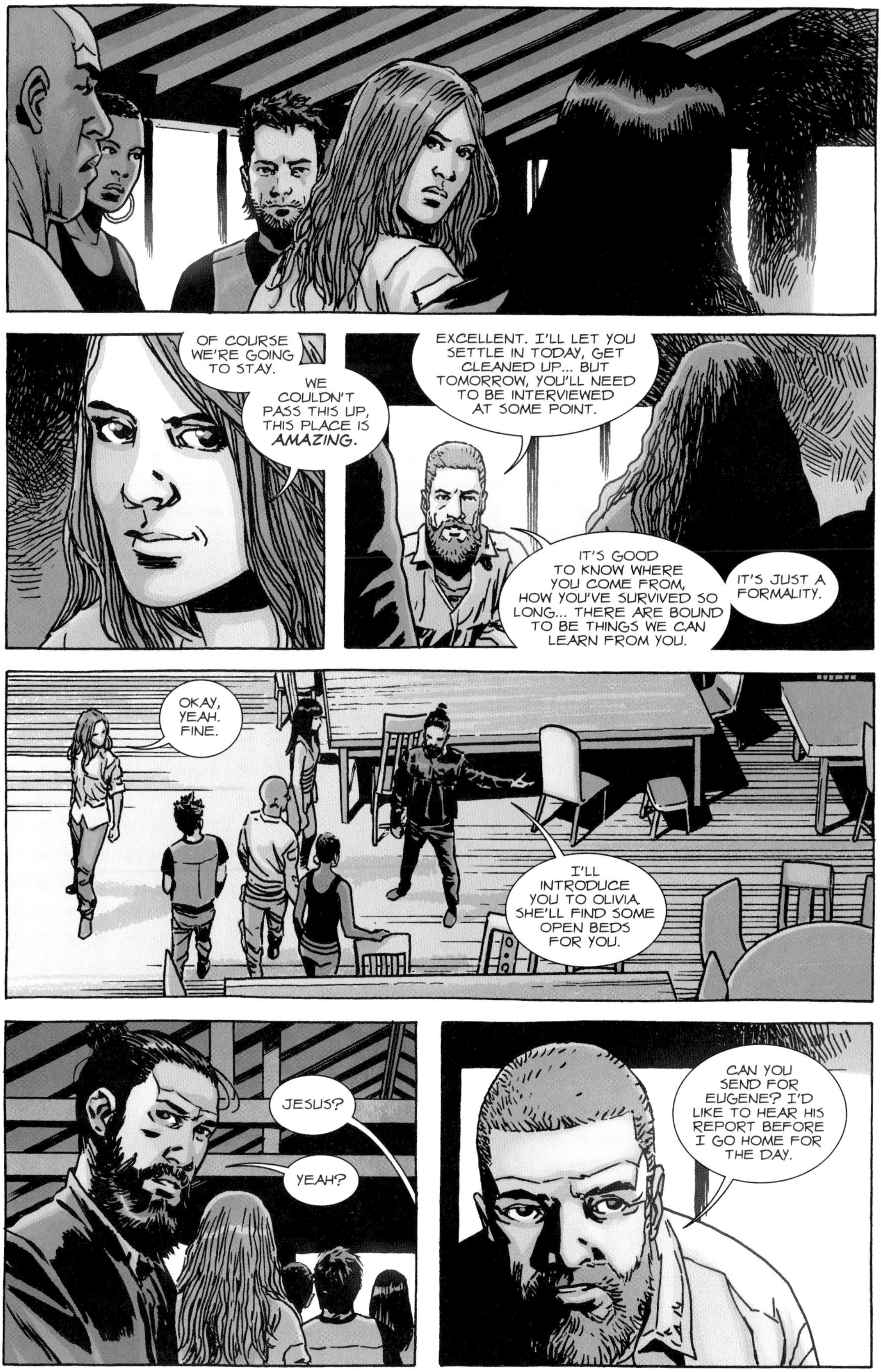
OF COURSE WE'RE GOING TO STAY.
WE COULDN'T PASS THIS UP, THIS PLACE IS AMAZING.
EXCELLENT. I'LL LET YOU SETTLE IN TODAY, GET CLEANED UP... BUT TOMORROW, YOU'LL NEED TO BE INTERVIEWED AT SOME POINT.
IT'S GOOD TO KNOW WHERE YOU COME FROM, HOW YOU'VE SURVIVED SO LONG... THERE ARE BOUND TO BE THINGS WE CAN LEARN FROM YOU.
IT'S JUST A FORMALITY.
OKAY, YEAH. FINE.
I'LL INTRODUCE YOU TO OLIVIA. SHE'LL FIND SOME OPEN BEDS FOR YOU.
JESUS?
YEAH?
CAN YOU SEND FOR EUGENE? I'D LIKE TO HEAR HIS REPORT BEFORE I GO HOME FOR THE DAY.

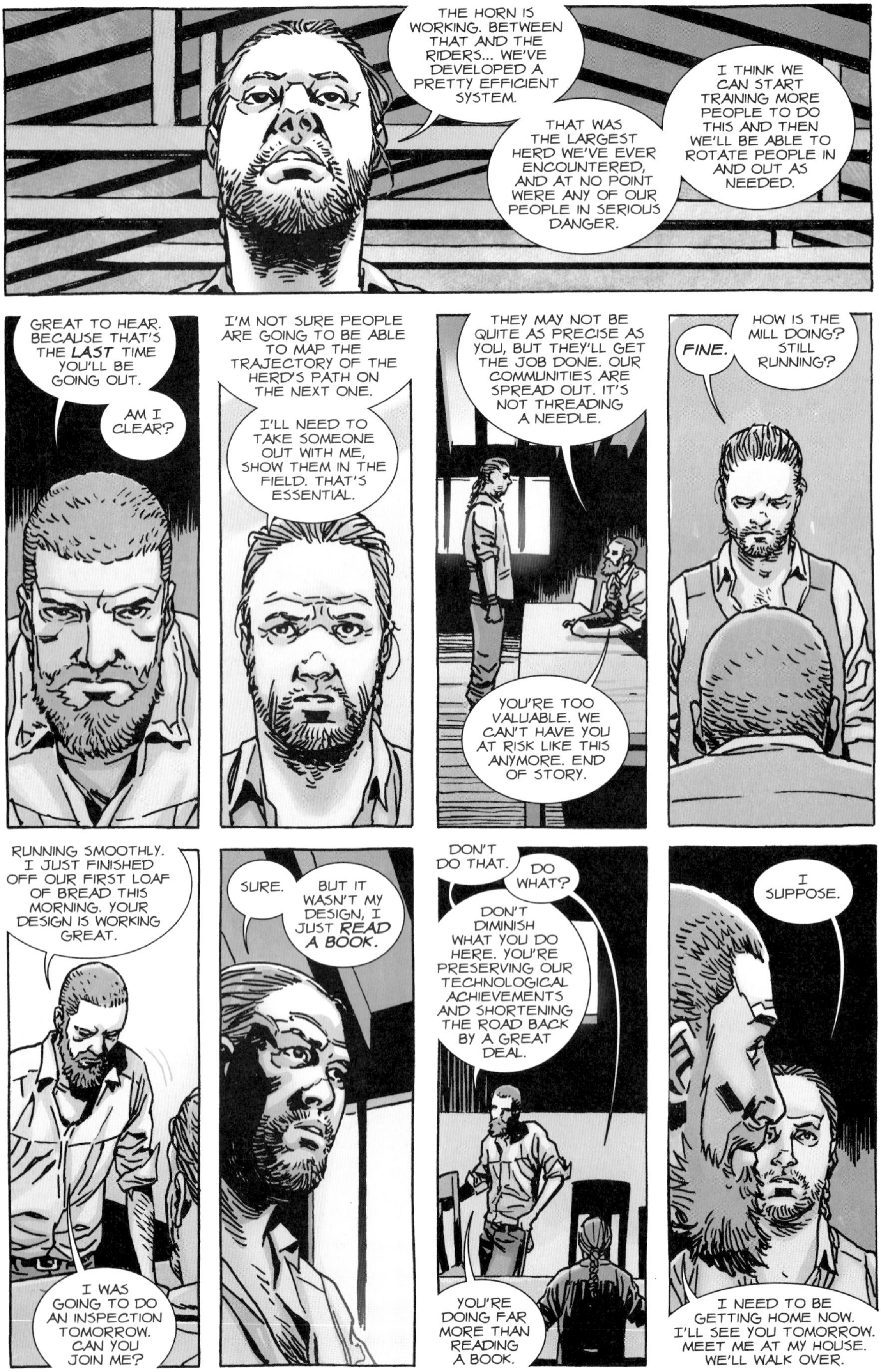
THE HORN IS WORKING. BETWEEN THAT AND THE RIDERS... WE'VE DEVELOPED A PRETTY EFFICIENT SYSTEM.
THAT WAS THE LARGEST HERD WE'VE EVER ENCOUNTERED, AND AT NO POINT WERE ANY OF OUR PEOPLE IN SERIOUS DANGER.
I THINK WE CAN START TRAINING MORE PEOPLE TO DO THIS AND THEN WE'LL BE ABLE TO ROTATE PEOPLE IN AND OUT AS NEEDED.
GREAT TO HEAR. BECAUSE THAT'S THE *LAST* TIME YOU'LL BE GOING OUT.
AM I CLEAR?
I'M NOT SURE PEOPLE ARE GOING TO BE ABLE TO MAP THE TRAJECTORY OF THE HERD'S PATH ON THE NEXT ONE.
I'LL NEED TO TAKE SOMEONE OUT WITH ME, SHOW THEM IN THE FIELD. THAT'S ESSENTIAL.
THEY MAY NOT BE QUITE AS PRECISE AS YOU, BUT THEY'LL GET THE JOB DONE. OUR COMMUNITIES ARE SPREAD OUT. IT'S NOT THREADING A NEEDLE.
YOU'RE TOO VALUABLE. WE CAN'T HAVE YOU AT RISK LIKE THIS ANYMORE. END OF STORY.
HOW IS THE MILL DOING? STILL RUNNING?
FINE.
RUNNING SMOOTHLY. I JUST FINISHED OFF OUR FIRST LOAF OF BREAD THIS MORNING. YOUR DESIGN IS WORKING GREAT.
I WAS GOING TO DO AN INSPECTION TOMORROW. CAN YOU JOIN ME?
SURE.
BUT IT WASN'T MY DESIGN, I JUST ***READ A BOOK.***
DON'T DO THAT.
DO WHAT?
DON'T DIMINISH WHAT YOU DO HERE. YOU'RE PRESERVING OUR TECHNOLOGICAL ACHIEVEMENTS AND SHORTENING THE ROAD BACK BY A GREAT DEAL.
YOU'RE DOING FAR MORE THAN READING A BOOK.
I SUPPOSE.
I NEED TO BE GETTING HOME NOW. I'LL SEE YOU TOMORROW. MEET ME AT MY HOUSE. WE'LL WALK OVER.

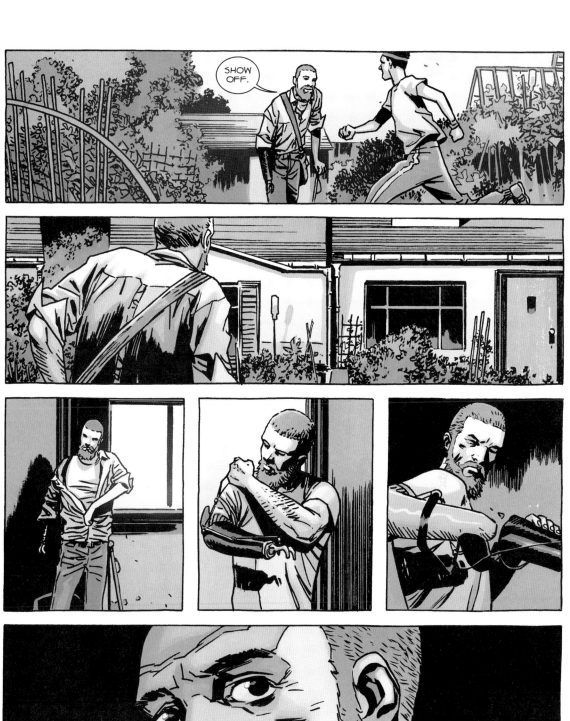

SHOW OFF.

CAN WE TALK NOW?

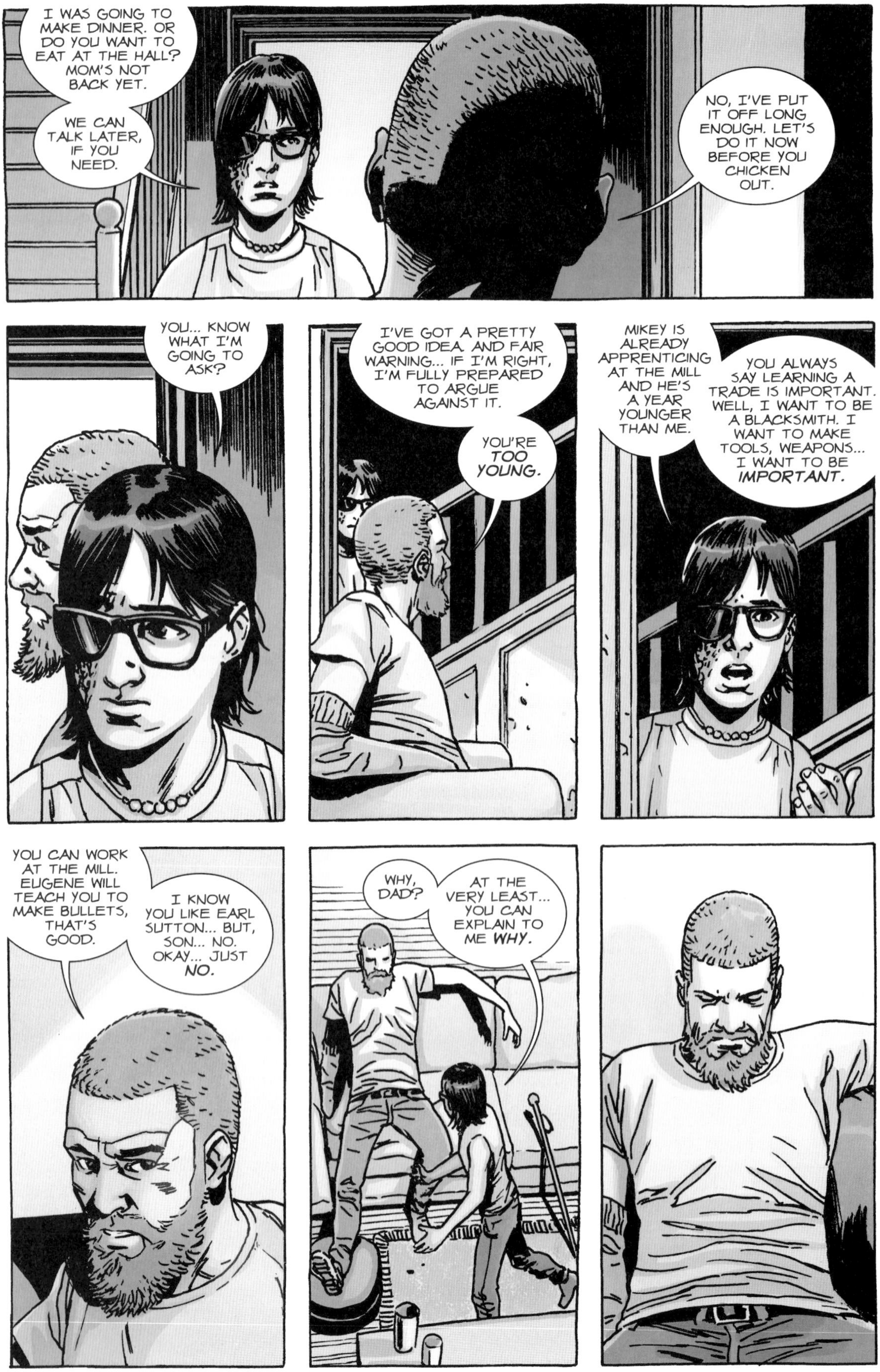
I WAS GOING TO MAKE DINNER. OR DO YOU WANT TO EAT AT THE HALL? MOM'S NOT BACK YET.
WE CAN TALK LATER, IF YOU NEED.
NO, I'VE PUT IT OFF LONG ENOUGH. LET'S DO IT NOW BEFORE YOU CHICKEN OUT.
YOU... KNOW WHAT I'M GOING TO ASK?
I'VE GOT A PRETTY GOOD IDEA AND FAIR WARNING... IF I'M RIGHT, I'M FULLY PREPARED TO ARGUE AGAINST IT.
YOU'RE TOO YOUNG.
MIKEY IS ALREADY APPRENTICING AT THE MILL AND HE'S A YEAR YOUNGER THAN ME.
YOU ALWAYS SAY LEARNING A TRADE IS IMPORTANT. WELL, I WANT TO BE A BLACKSMITH. I WANT TO MAKE TOOLS, WEAPONS... I WANT TO BE IMPORTANT.
YOU CAN WORK AT THE MILL. EUGENE WILL TEACH YOU TO MAKE BULLETS, THAT'S GOOD.
I KNOW YOU LIKE EARL SUTTON... BUT, SON... NO. OKAY... JUST NO.
WHY, DAD?
AT THE VERY LEAST... YOU CAN EXPLAIN TO ME WHY.

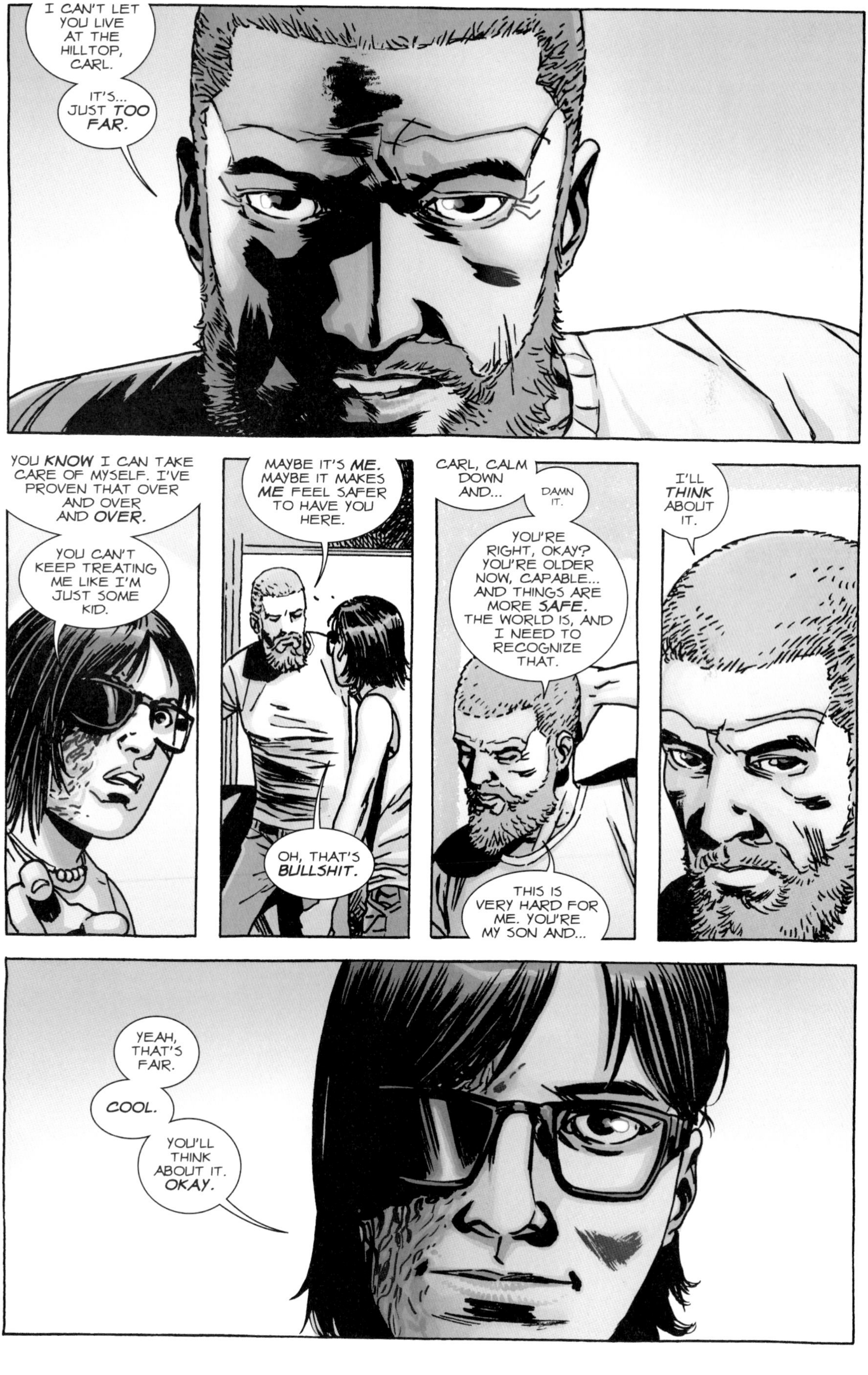
I CAN'T LET YOU LIVE AT THE HILLTOP, CARL.
IT'S... JUST TOO FAR.
YOU KNOW I CAN TAKE CARE OF MYSELF. I'VE PROVEN THAT OVER AND OVER AND OVER.
YOU CAN'T KEEP TREATING ME LIKE I'M JUST SOME KID.
MAYBE IT'S ME. MAYBE IT MAKES ME FEEL SAFER TO HAVE YOU HERE.
OH, THAT'S BULLSHIT.
CARL, CALM DOWN AND...
DAMN IT.
YOU'RE RIGHT, OKAY? YOU'RE OLDER NOW, CAPABLE... AND THINGS ARE MORE SAFE. THE WORLD IS, AND I NEED TO RECOGNIZE THAT.
THIS IS VERY HARD FOR ME. YOU'RE MY SON AND...
I'LL THINK ABOUT IT.
YEAH, THAT'S FAIR.
COOL.
YOU'LL THINK ABOUT IT. OKAY.

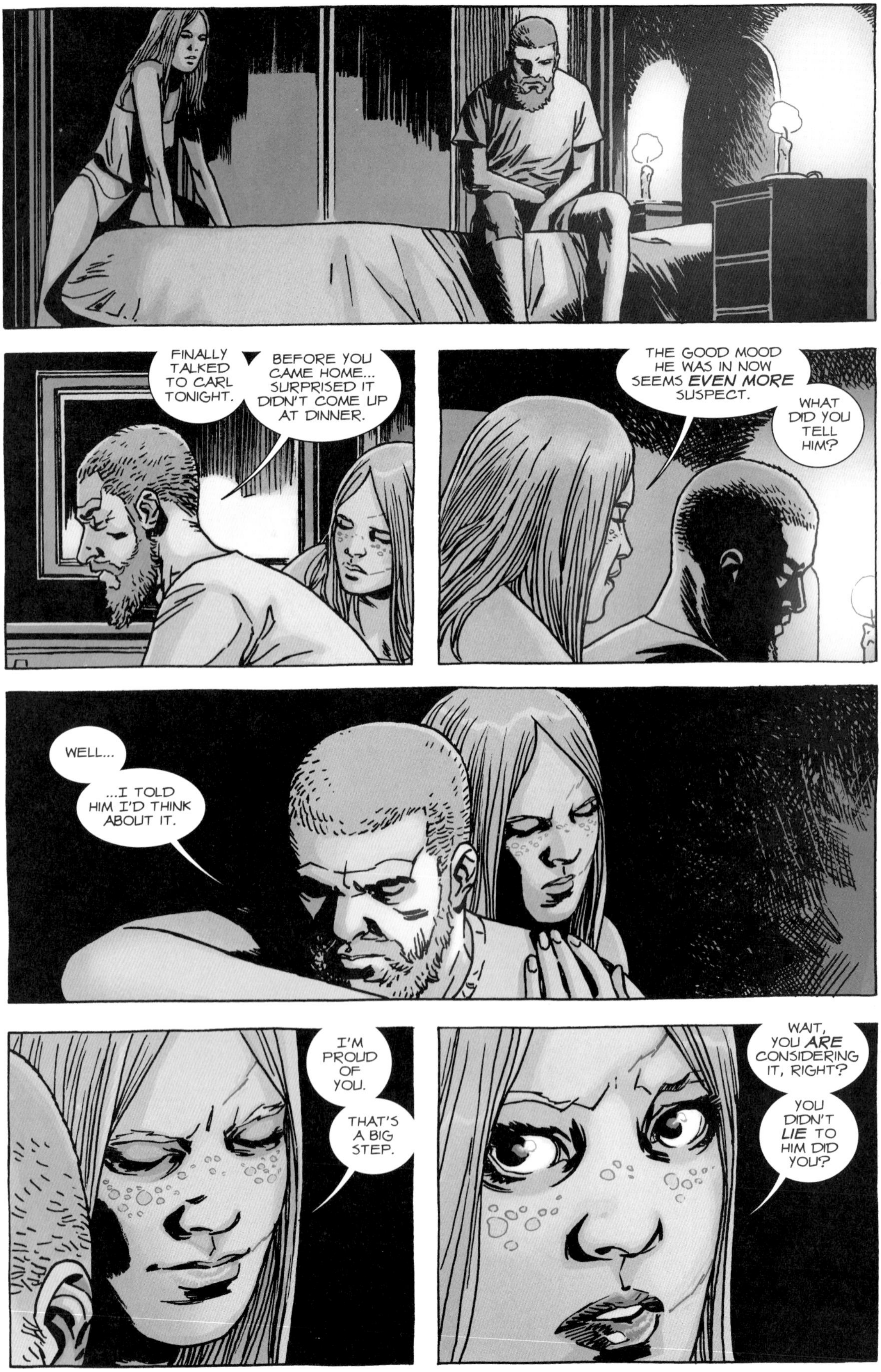
FINALLY TALKED TO CARL TONIGHT.
BEFORE YOU CAME HOME... SURPRISED IT DIDN'T COME UP AT DINNER.
THE GOOD MOOD HE WAS IN NOW SEEMS EVEN MORE SUSPECT.
WHAT DID YOU TELL HIM?
WELL...
...I TOLD HIM I'D THINK ABOUT IT.
I'M PROUD OF YOU.
THAT'S A BIG STEP.
WAIT, YOU ARE CONSIDERING IT, RIGHT?
YOU DIDN'T LIE TO HIM DID YOU?

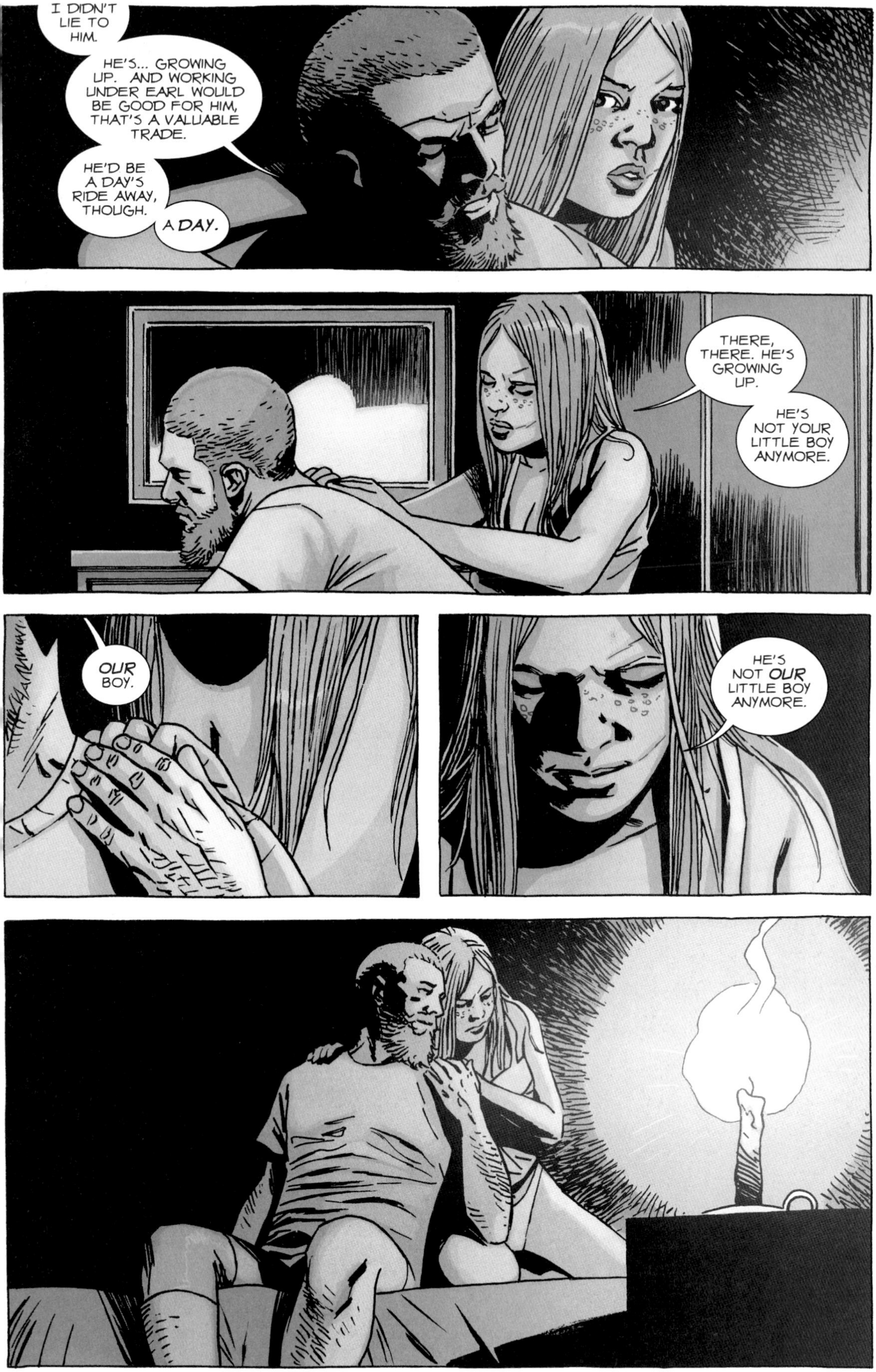
I DIDN'T LIE TO HIM.
HE'S... GROWING UP. AND WORKING UNDER EARL WOULD BE GOOD FOR HIM, THAT'S A VALUABLE TRADE.
HE'D BE A DAY'S RIDE AWAY, THOUGH.
A DAY.
THERE, THERE. HE'S GROWING UP.
HE'S NOT YOUR LITTLE BOY ANYMORE.
OUR BOY.
HE'S NOT OUR LITTLE BOY ANYMORE.

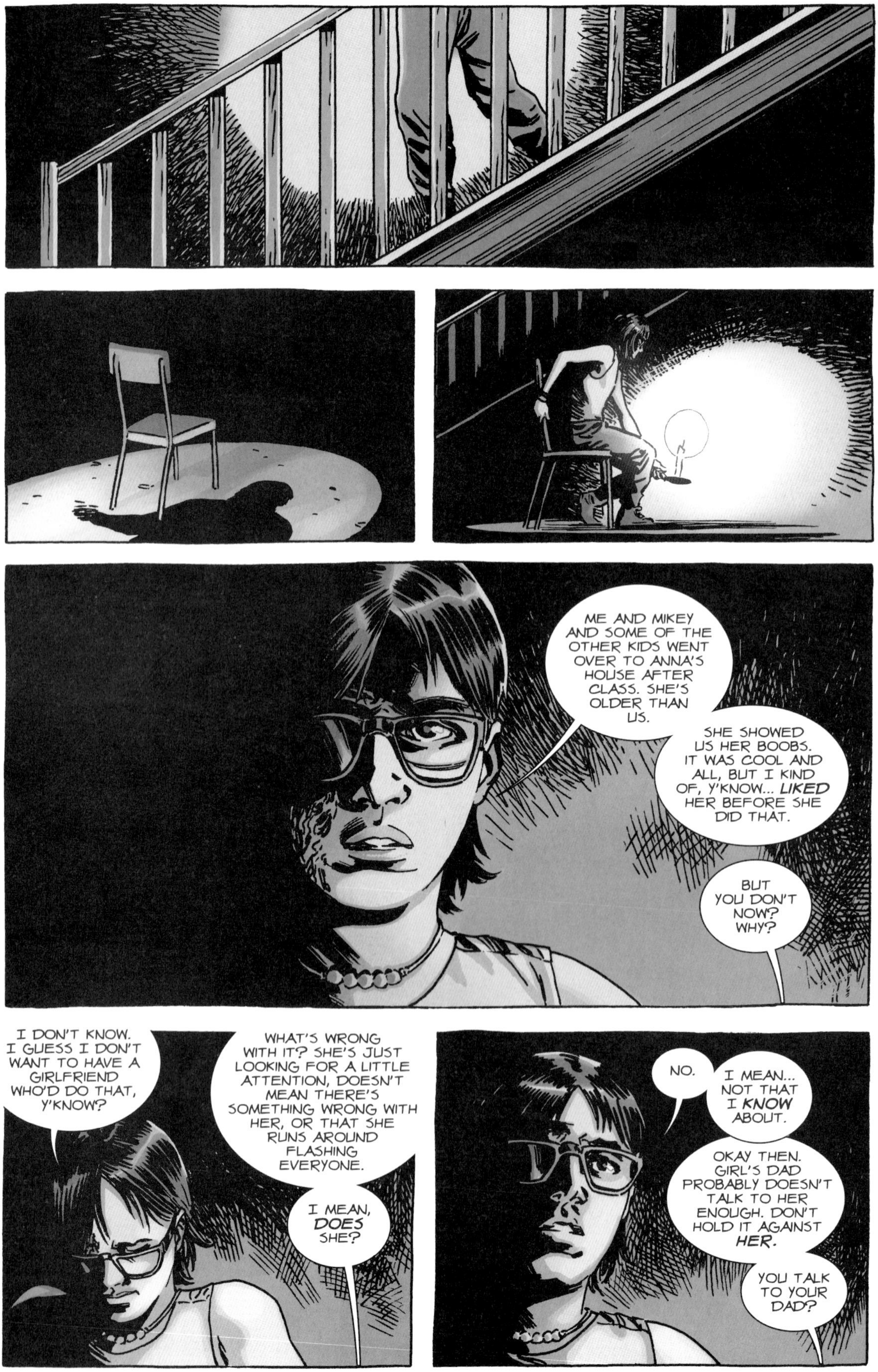

ME AND MIKEY AND SOME OF THE OTHER KIDS WENT OVER TO ANNA'S HOUSE AFTER CLASS. SHE'S OLDER THAN US.
SHE SHOWED US HER BOOBS. IT WAS COOL AND ALL, BUT I KIND OF, Y'KNOW... *LIKED* HER BEFORE SHE DID THAT.
BUT YOU DON'T NOW? WHY?
I DON'T KNOW. I GUESS I DON'T WANT TO HAVE A GIRLFRIEND WHO'D DO THAT, Y'KNOW?
WHAT'S WRONG WITH IT? SHE'S JUST LOOKING FOR A LITTLE ATTENTION, DOESN'T MEAN THERE'S SOMETHING WRONG WITH HER, OR THAT SHE RUNS AROUND FLASHING EVERYONE.
I MEAN, *DOES* SHE?
NO.
I MEAN... NOT THAT I *KNOW* ABOUT.
OKAY THEN. GIRL'S DAD PROBABLY DOESN'T TALK TO HER ENOUGH. DON'T HOLD IT AGAINST *HER.*
YOU TALK TO YOUR DAD?

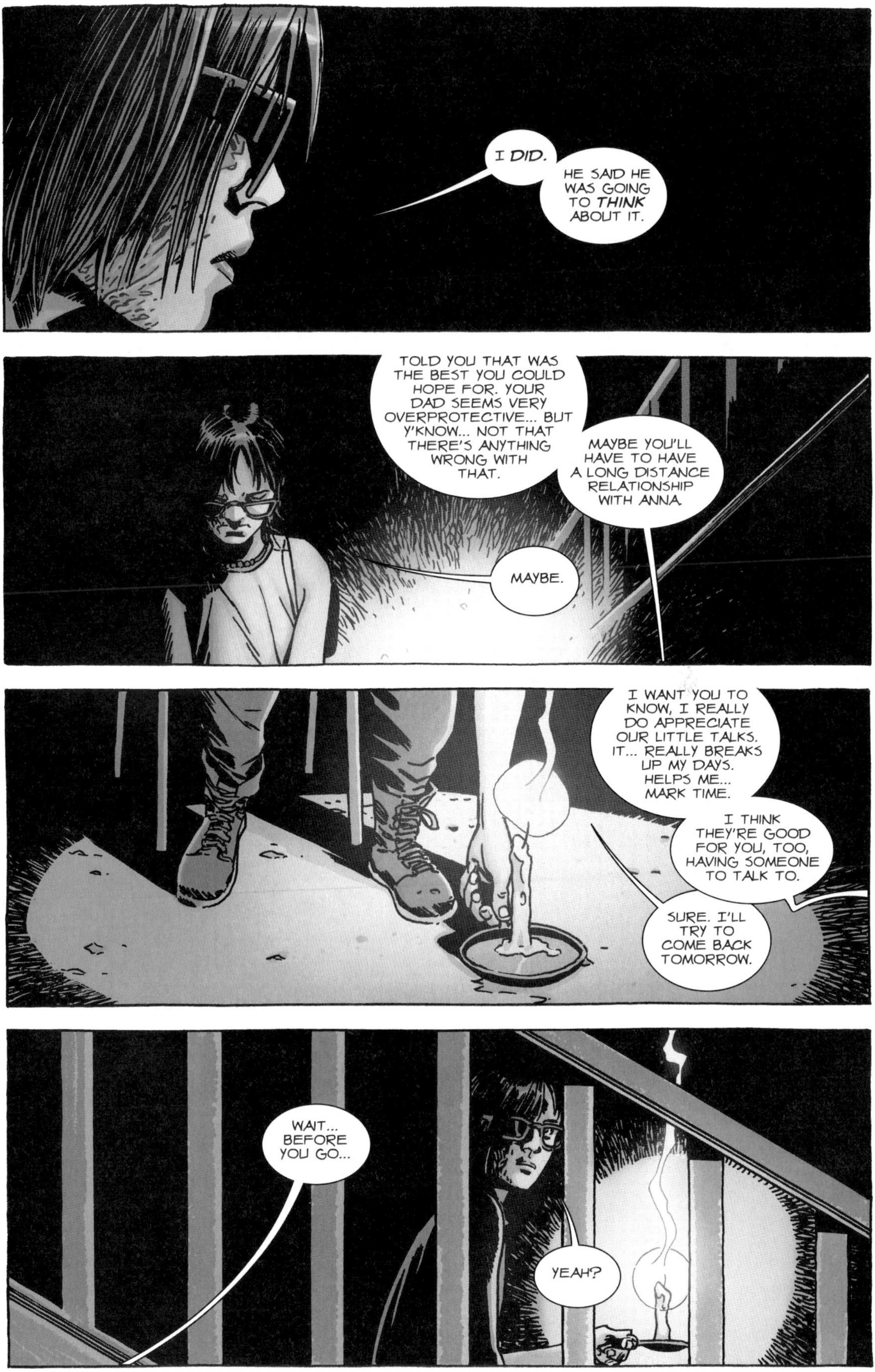

I *DID.*
HE SAID HE WAS GOING TO ***THINK*** ABOUT IT.
TOLD YOU THAT WAS THE BEST YOU COULD HOPE FOR. YOUR DAD SEEMS VERY OVERPROTECTIVE... BUT Y'KNOW... NOT THAT THERE'S ANYTHING WRONG WITH THAT.
MAYBE YOU'LL HAVE TO HAVE A LONG DISTANCE RELATIONSHIP WITH ANNA.
MAYBE.
I WANT YOU TO KNOW, I REALLY DO APPRECIATE OUR LITTLE TALKS. IT... REALLY BREAKS UP MY DAYS. HELPS ME... MARK TIME.
I THINK THEY'RE GOOD FOR YOU, TOO, HAVING SOMEONE TO TALK TO.
SURE. I'LL TRY TO COME BACK TOMORROW.
WAIT... BEFORE YOU GO...
YEAH?

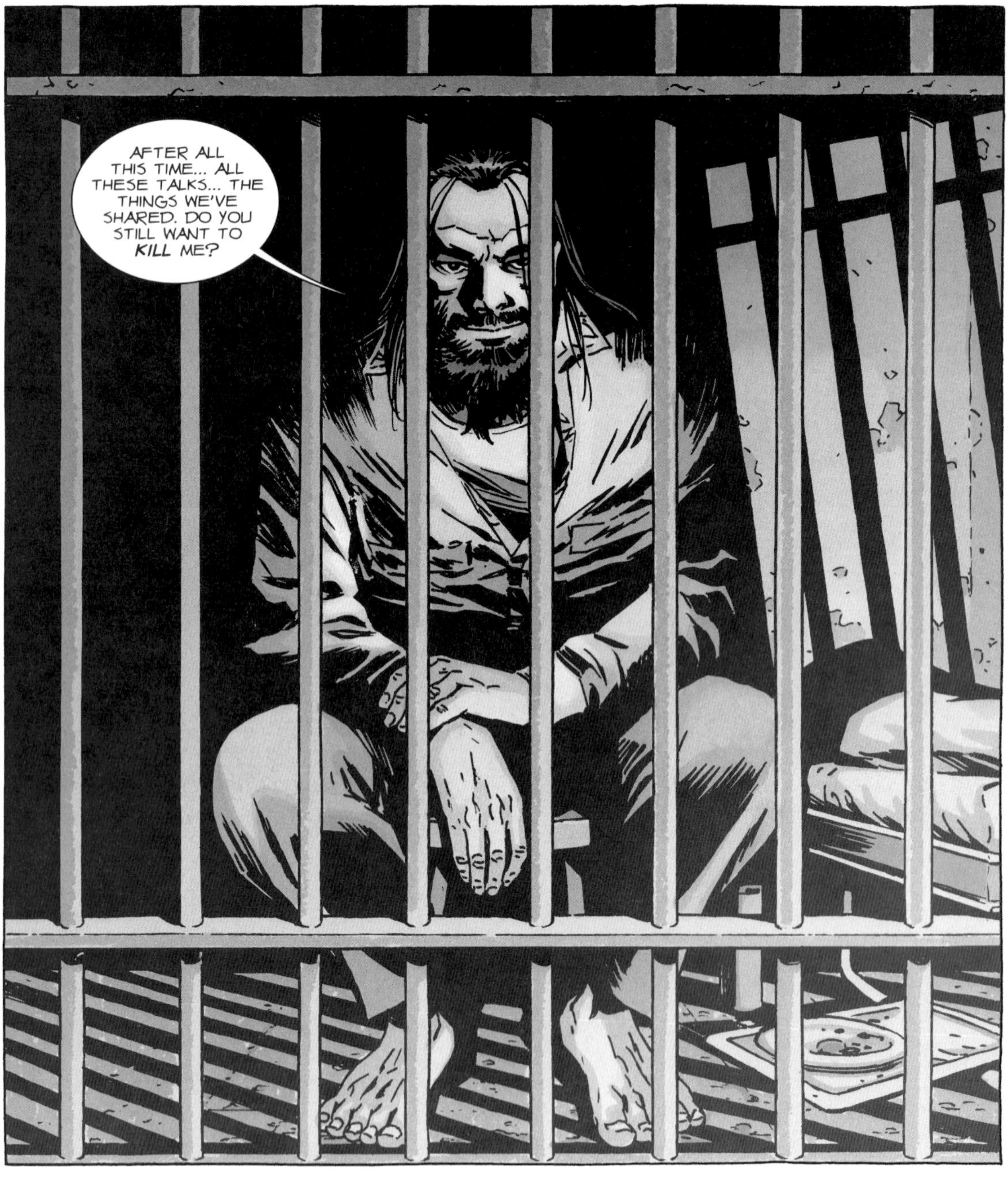
AFTER ALL THIS TIME... ALL THESE TALKS... THE THINGS WE'VE SHARED. DO YOU STILL WANT TO *KILL* ME?

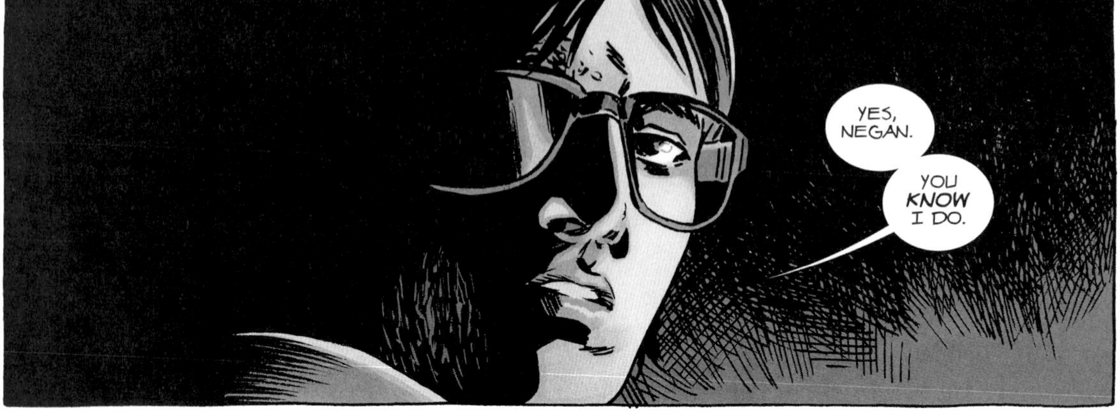
YES, NEGAN.
YOU *KNOW* I DO.

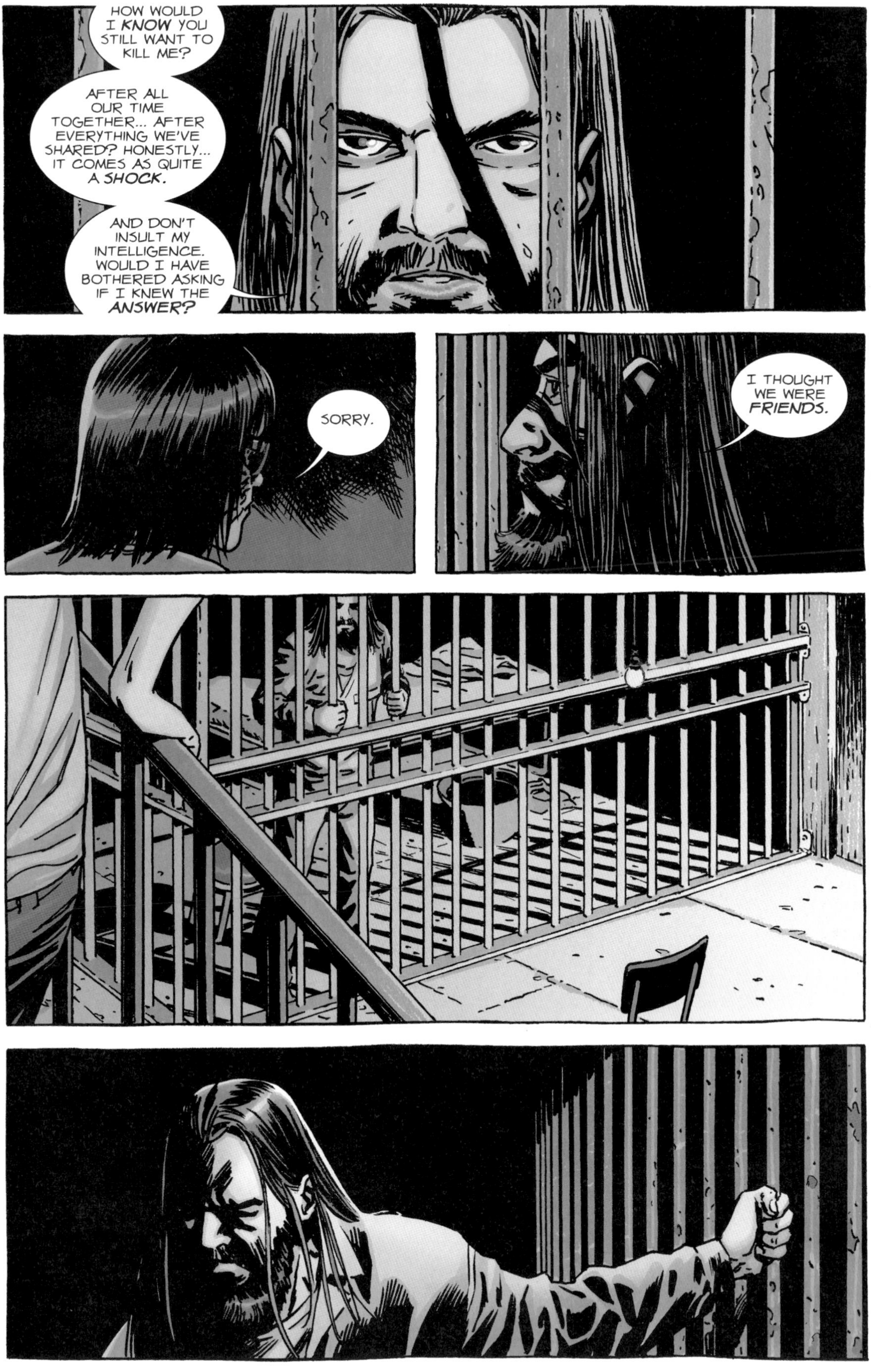
HOW WOULD I KNOW YOU STILL WANT TO KILL ME?
AFTER ALL OUR TIME TOGETHER... AFTER EVERYTHING WE'VE SHARED? HONESTLY... IT COMES AS QUITE A SHOCK.
AND DON'T INSULT MY INTELLIGENCE. WOULD I HAVE BOTHERED ASKING IF I KNEW THE ANSWER?
SORRY.
I THOUGHT WE WERE FRIENDS.

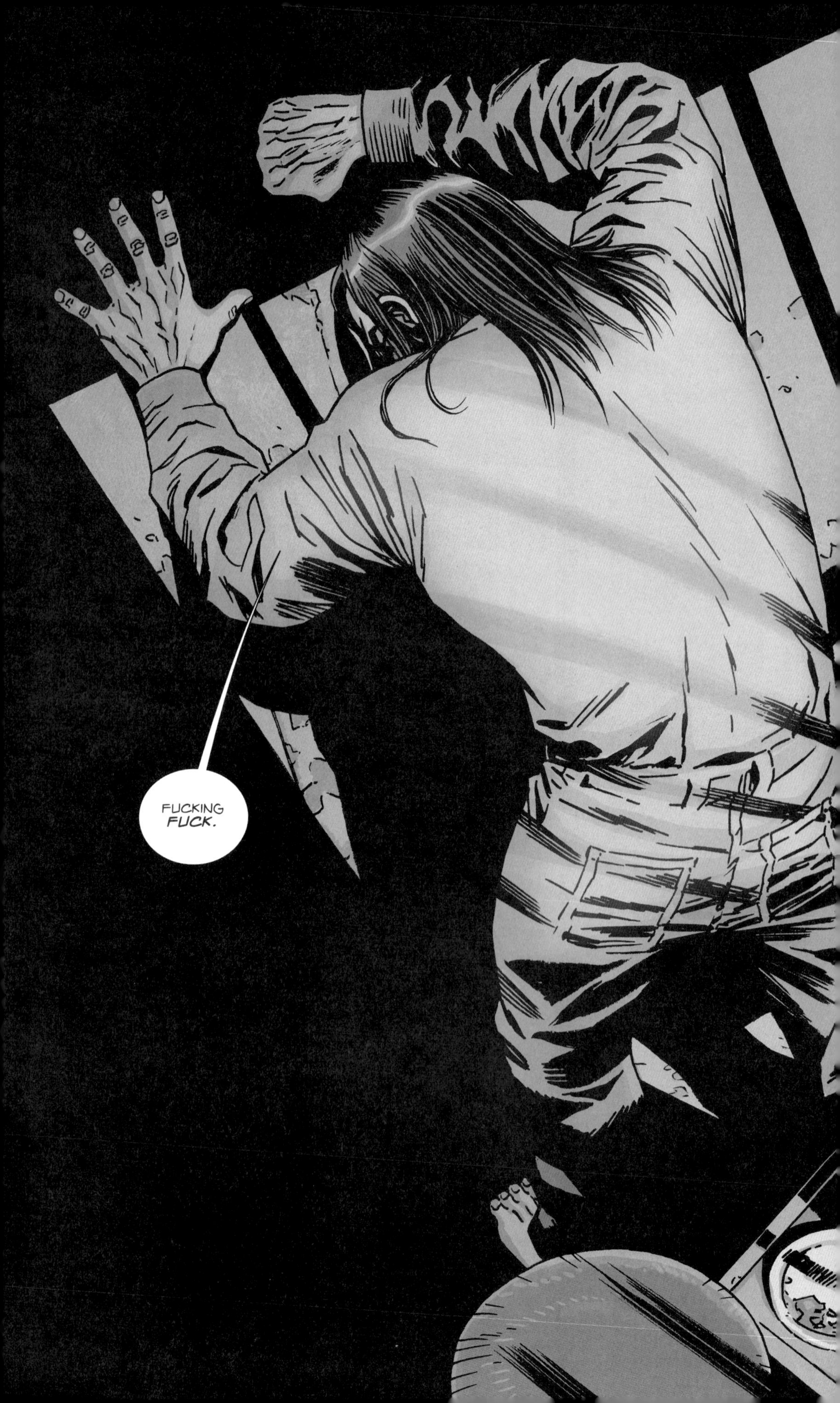
FUCKING FUCK.

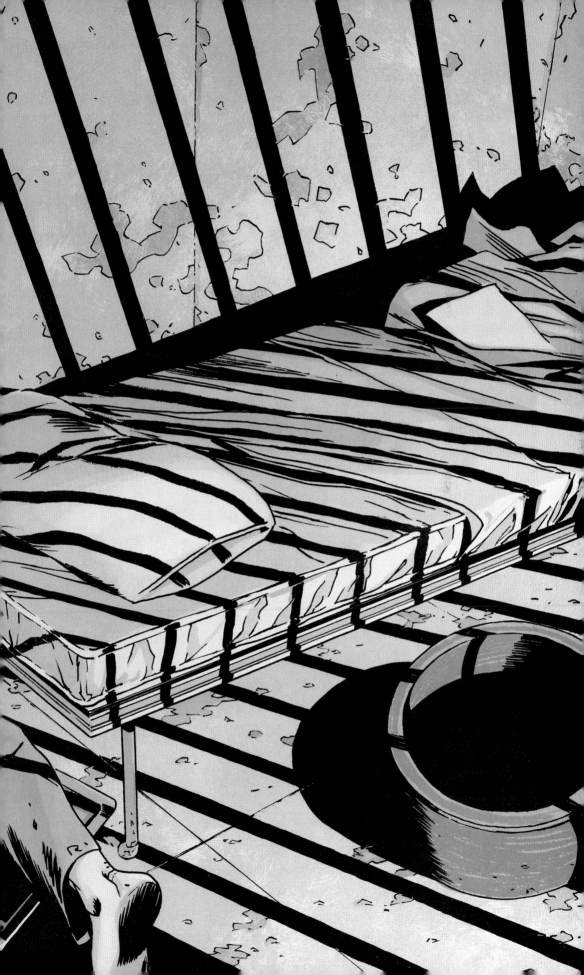

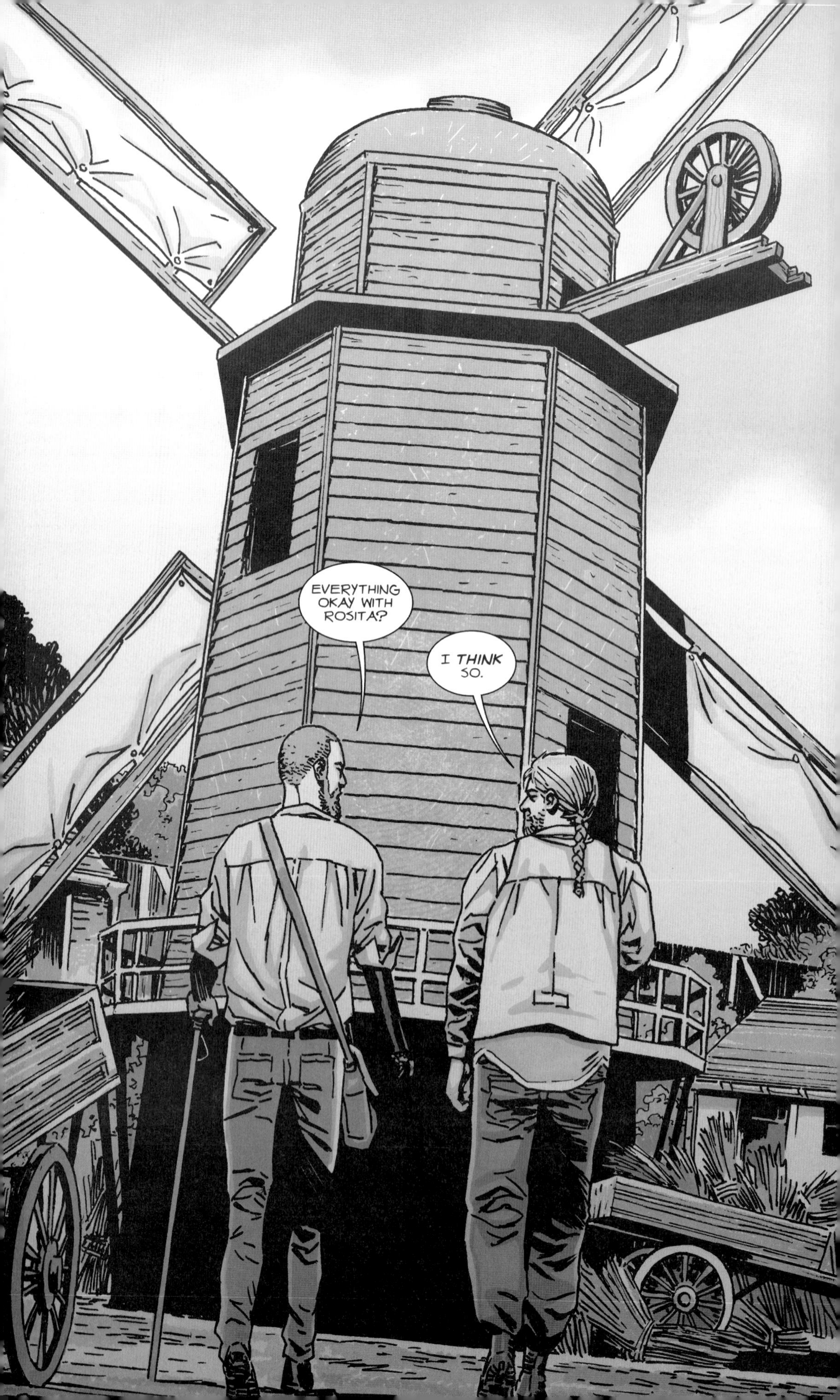
EVERYTHING OKAY WITH ROSITA?
I *THINK* SO.

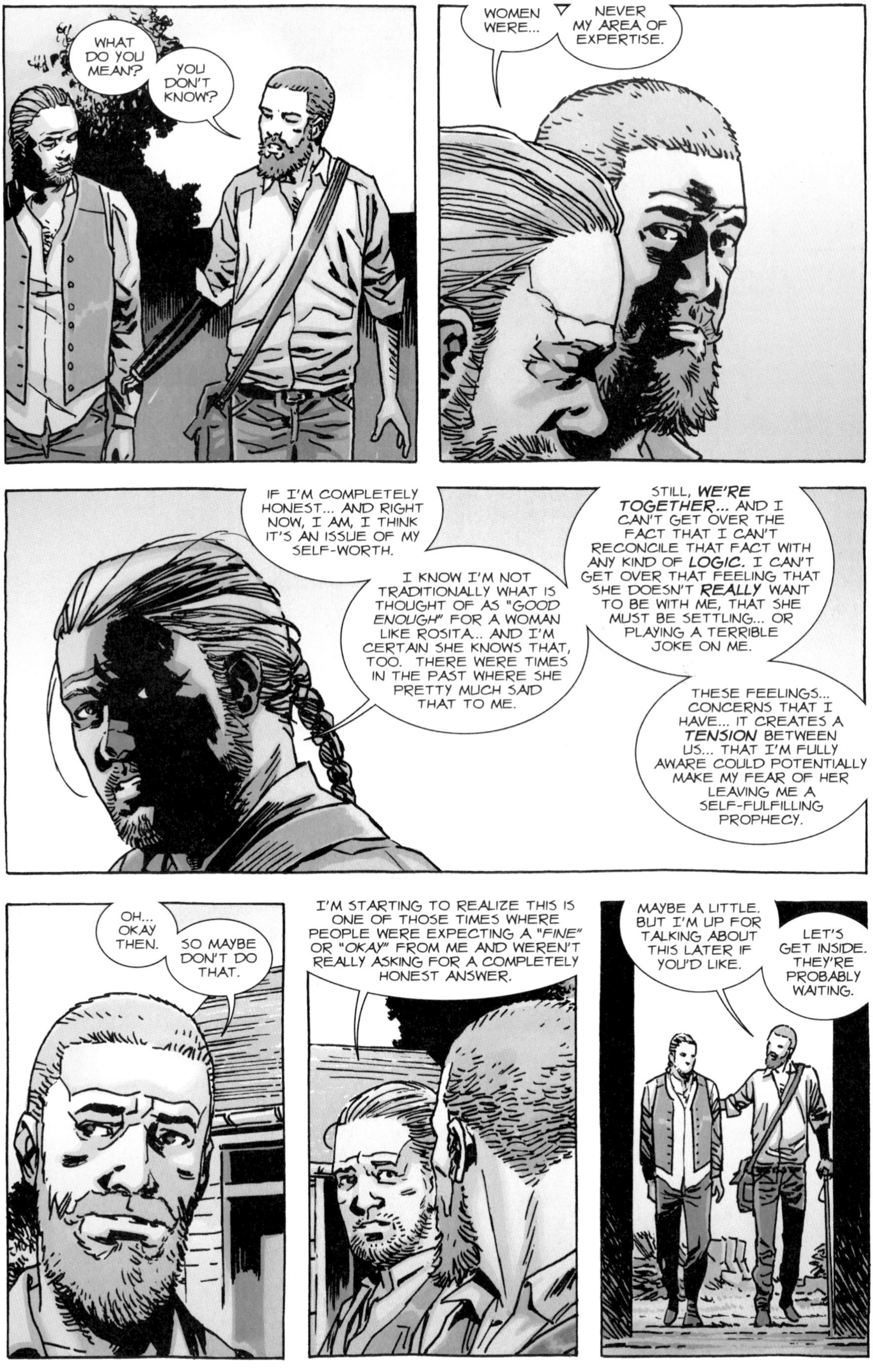
WHAT DO YOU MEAN?
YOU DON'T KNOW?
WOMEN WERE...
NEVER MY AREA OF EXPERTISE.
IF I'M COMPLETELY HONEST... AND RIGHT NOW, I AM, I THINK IT'S AN ISSUE OF MY SELF-WORTH.
I KNOW I'M NOT TRADITIONALLY WHAT IS THOUGHT OF AS "GOOD ENOUGH" FOR A WOMAN LIKE ROSITA... AND I'M CERTAIN SHE KNOWS THAT, TOO. THERE WERE TIMES IN THE PAST WHERE SHE PRETTY MUCH SAID THAT TO ME.
STILL, WE'RE TOGETHER... AND I CAN'T GET OVER THE FACT THAT I CAN'T RECONCILE THAT FACT WITH ANY KIND OF LOGIC. I CAN'T GET OVER THAT FEELING THAT SHE DOESN'T REALLY WANT TO BE WITH ME, THAT SHE MUST BE SETTLING... OR PLAYING A TERRIBLE JOKE ON ME.
THESE FEELINGS... CONCERNS THAT I HAVE... IT CREATES A TENSION BETWEEN US... THAT I'M FULLY AWARE COULD POTENTIALLY MAKE MY FEAR OF HER LEAVING ME A SELF-FULFILLING PROPHECY.
OH... OKAY THEN.
SO MAYBE DON'T DO THAT.
I'M STARTING TO REALIZE THIS IS ONE OF THOSE TIMES WHERE PEOPLE WERE EXPECTING A "FINE" OR "OKAY" FROM ME AND WEREN'T REALLY ASKING FOR A COMPLETELY HONEST ANSWER.
MAYBE A LITTLE. BUT I'M UP FOR TALKING ABOUT THIS LATER IF YOU'D LIKE.
LET'S GET INSIDE. THEY'RE PROBABLY WAITING.

HOW HAVE YOU SURVIVED?

I DON'T KNOW WHAT YOU MEAN. ARE YOU ASKING FOR SPECIFICS?

MOST EVERYONE IS DEAD. IF YOU'RE NOT, YOU DID SOMETHING *SPECIAL.* WE WANT TO KNOW WHAT THAT IS. MAYBE YOUR METHODS *CAN* BE ADDED TO OUR OWN TO MAKE US SAFER.

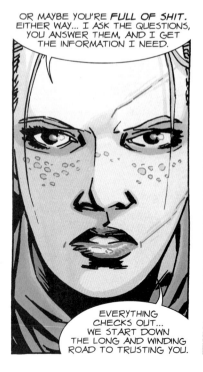

OR MAYBE YOU'RE *FULL OF SHIT.* EITHER WAY... I ASK THE QUESTIONS, YOU ANSWER THEM, AND I GET THE INFORMATION I NEED.

EVERYTHING CHECKS OUT... WE START DOWN THE LONG AND WINDING ROAD TO TRUSTING YOU.

WHAT ABOUT *US* TRUSTING *YOU?* THIS DOESN'T HELP THAT.

YOU TRUSTED US THE MINUTE YOU DECIDED COMING *HERE* WAS BETTER THAN BEING *OUT THERE.* YOU'RE RISKING NOTHING... WE'RE RISKING *EVERYTHING* BY BRINGING YOU IN.

YOU EARN *OUR* TRUST. DON'T LIKE THAT... WE'LL ESCORT YOU TO THE GATE.

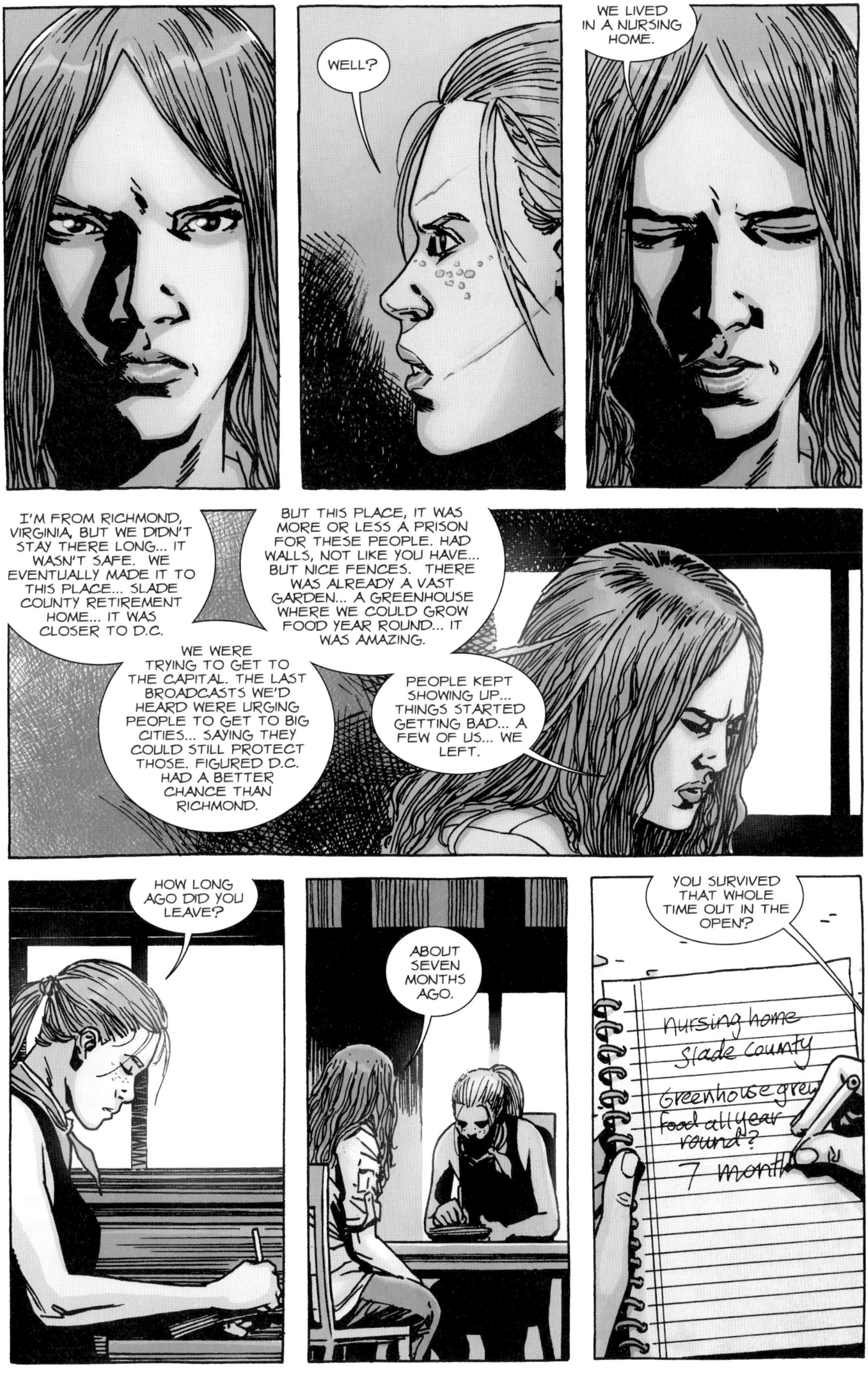
WELL?
WE LIVED IN A NURSING HOME.
I'M FROM RICHMOND, VIRGINIA, BUT WE DIDN'T STAY THERE LONG... IT WASN'T SAFE. WE EVENTUALLY MADE IT TO THIS PLACE... SLADE COUNTY RETIREMENT HOME... IT WAS CLOSER TO D.C.
WE WERE TRYING TO GET TO THE CAPITAL. THE LAST BROADCASTS WE'D HEARD WERE URGING PEOPLE TO GET TO BIG CITIES... SAYING THEY COULD STILL PROTECT THOSE. FIGURED D.C. HAD A BETTER CHANCE THAN RICHMOND.
BUT THIS PLACE, IT WAS MORE OR LESS A PRISON FOR THESE PEOPLE. HAD WALLS, NOT LIKE YOU HAVE... BUT NICE FENCES. THERE WAS ALREADY A VAST GARDEN... A GREENHOUSE WHERE WE COULD GROW FOOD YEAR ROUND... IT WAS AMAZING.
PEOPLE KEPT SHOWING UP... THINGS STARTED GETTING BAD... A FEW OF US... WE LEFT.
HOW LONG AGO DID YOU LEAVE?
ABOUT SEVEN MONTHS AGO.
YOU SURVIVED THAT WHOLE TIME OUT IN THE OPEN?
nursing home
Slade County
Greenhouse grew
food all year
round?
7 month

NOT ALL OF US. ABOUT *HALF*.

THE ONES YOU LOST. HOW'D THEY DIE?

HOW DO YOU THINK THEY DIED? CORPSES MADE THEM CORPSES.

THERE'S A WHOLE HELL OF A LOT MORE WAYS TO DIE.

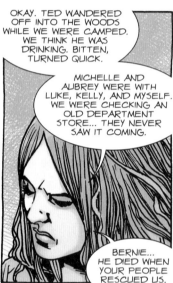

OKAY. TED WANDERED OFF INTO THE WOODS WHILE WE WERE CAMPED. WE THINK HE WAS DRINKING. BITTEN, TURNED QUICK.

MICHELLE AND AUBREY WERE WITH LUKE, KELLY, AND MYSELF. WE WERE CHECKING AN OLD DEPARTMENT STORE... THEY NEVER SAW IT COMING.

BERNIE... HE DIED WHEN YOUR PEOPLE RESCUED US.

I'M VERY SORRY.

HOW'D YOU LAST SO LONG OUT IN THE OPEN?

WE HAD A SYSTEM. WE KEPT OUR SUPPLIES IN A TRAILER, HAD IT HITCHED TO HORSES... WE SPENT MOST OF OUR TIME ON TOP OF IT, OUT OF REACH.

IT WAS LIKE OUR OWN MOBILE BUILDING.

HOW MANY *PEOPLE* DID YOU ENCOUNTER WHILE YOU WERE OUT THERE FOR SEVEN MONTHS?

NO PEOPLE.

Encountered NO PEOPLE

THE ENTIRE TIME?

UNTIL YOUR PEOPLE.

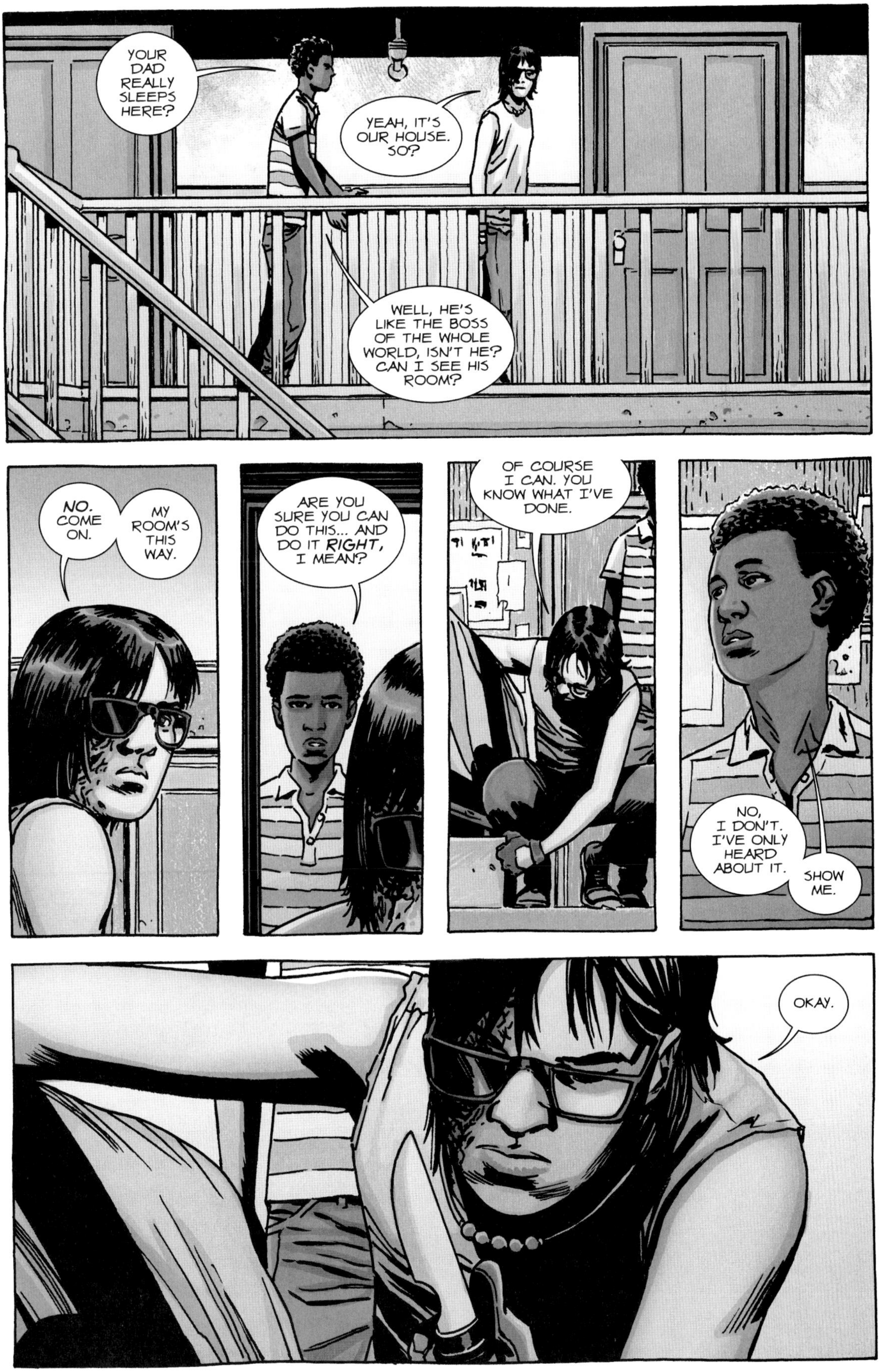
YOUR DAD REALLY SLEEPS HERE?
YEAH, IT'S OUR HOUSE. SO?
WELL, HE'S LIKE THE BOSS OF THE WHOLE WORLD, ISN'T HE? CAN I SEE HIS ROOM?
NO. COME ON.
MY ROOM'S THIS WAY.
ARE YOU SURE YOU CAN DO THIS... AND DO IT *RIGHT,* I MEAN?
OF COURSE I CAN. YOU KNOW WHAT I'VE DONE.
NO, I DON'T. I'VE ONLY HEARD ABOUT IT.
SHOW ME.
OKAY.

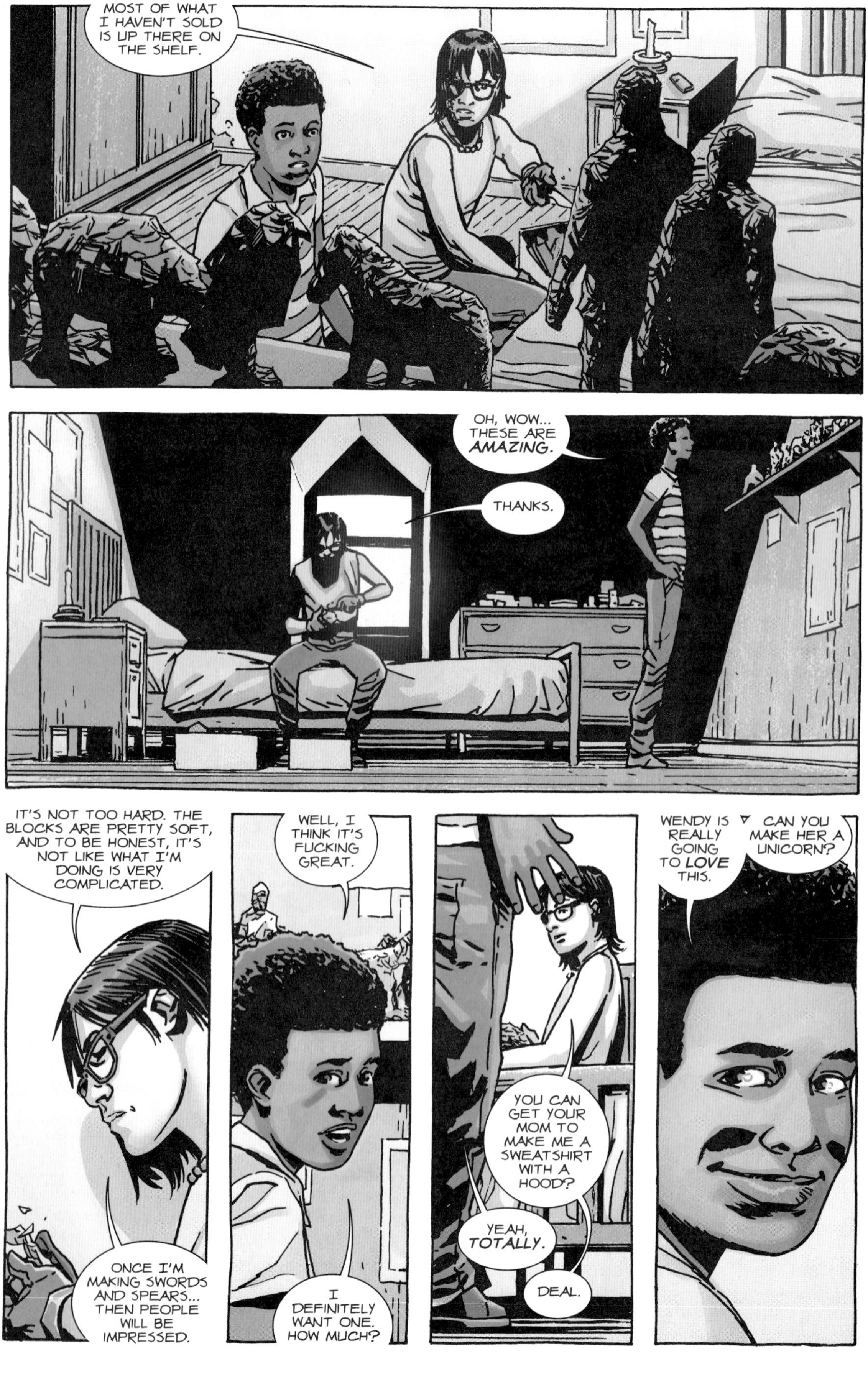
MOST OF WHAT I HAVEN'T SOLD IS UP THERE ON THE SHELF.
OH, WOW... THESE ARE *AMAZING.*
THANKS.
IT'S NOT TOO HARD. THE BLOCKS ARE PRETTY SOFT, AND TO BE HONEST, IT'S NOT LIKE WHAT I'M DOING IS VERY COMPLICATED.
ONCE I'M MAKING SWORDS AND SPEARS... THEN PEOPLE WILL BE IMPRESSED.
WELL, I THINK IT'S FUCKING GREAT.
I DEFINITELY WANT ONE. HOW MUCH?
YOU CAN GET YOUR MOM TO MAKE ME A SWEATSHIRT WITH A HOOD?
YEAH, *TOTALLY.*
DEAL.
WENDY IS REALLY GOING TO *LOVE* THIS.
CAN YOU MAKE HER A UNICORN?

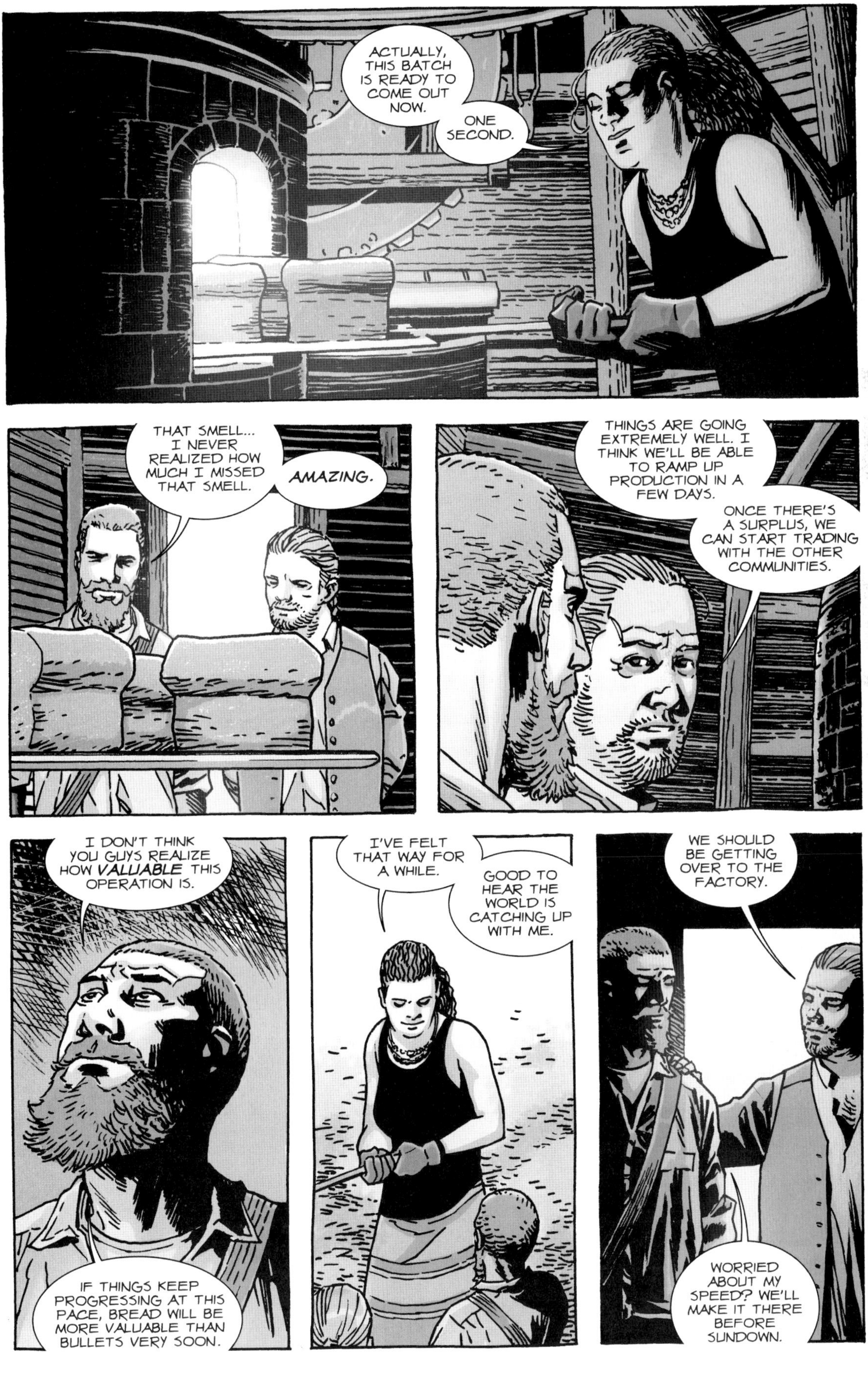
ACTUALLY, THIS BATCH IS READY TO COME OUT NOW.
ONE SECOND.
THAT SMELL... I NEVER REALIZED HOW MUCH I MISSED THAT SMELL.
AMAZING.
THINGS ARE GOING EXTREMELY WELL. I THINK WE'LL BE ABLE TO RAMP UP PRODUCTION IN A FEW DAYS.
ONCE THERE'S A SURPLUS, WE CAN START TRADING WITH THE OTHER COMMUNITIES.
I DON'T THINK YOU GUYS REALIZE HOW VALUABLE THIS OPERATION IS.
IF THINGS KEEP PROGRESSING AT THIS PACE, BREAD WILL BE MORE VALUABLE THAN BULLETS VERY SOON.
I'VE FELT THAT WAY FOR A WHILE.
GOOD TO HEAR THE WORLD IS CATCHING UP WITH ME.
WE SHOULD BE GETTING OVER TO THE FACTORY.
WORRIED ABOUT MY SPEED? WE'LL MAKE IT THERE BEFORE SUNDOWN.

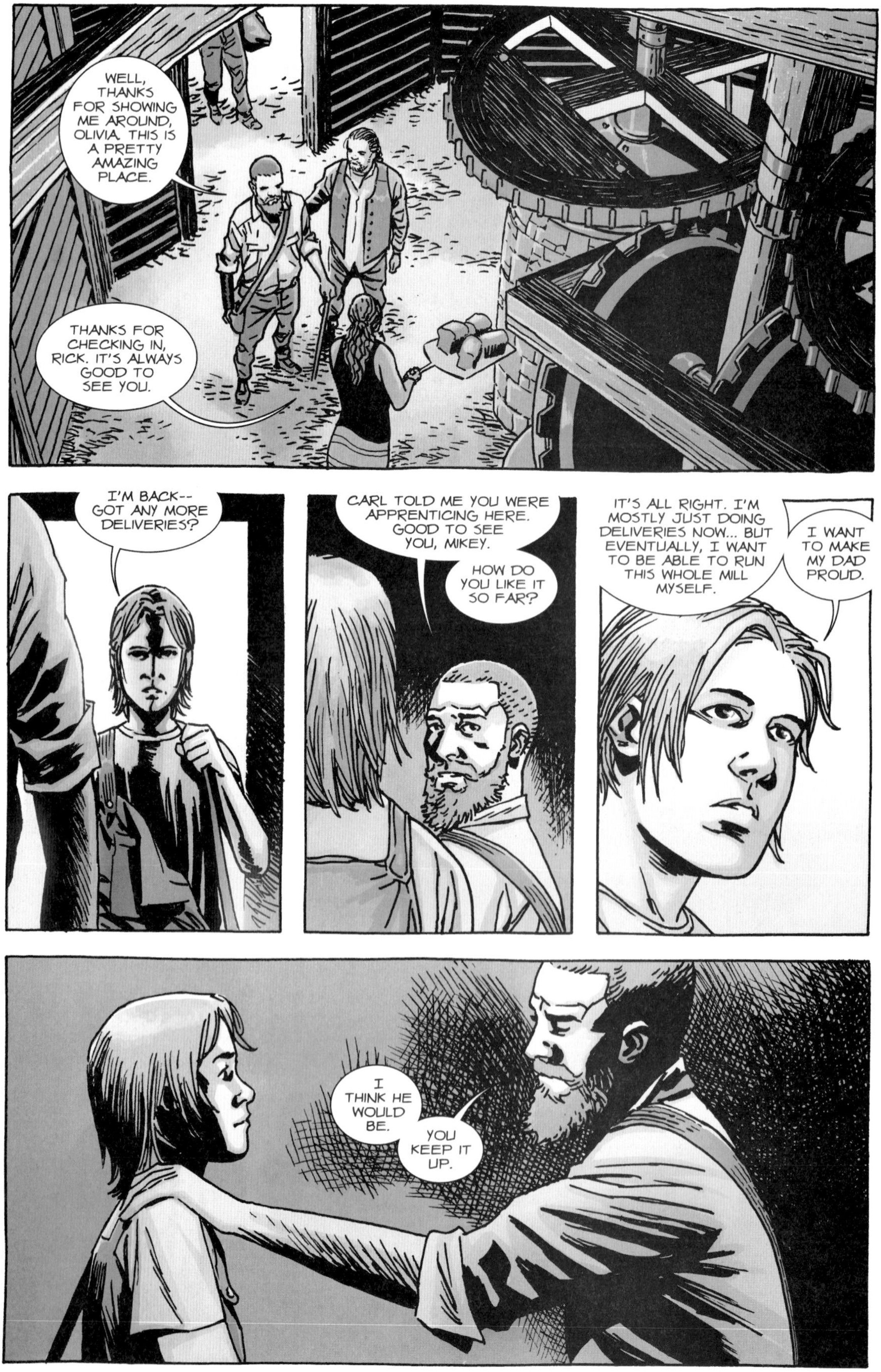
WELL, THANKS FOR SHOWING ME AROUND, OLIVIA. THIS IS A PRETTY AMAZING PLACE.
THANKS FOR CHECKING IN, RICK. IT'S ALWAYS GOOD TO SEE YOU.
I'M BACK-- GOT ANY MORE DELIVERIES?
CARL TOLD ME YOU WERE APPRENTICING HERE. GOOD TO SEE YOU, MIKEY.
HOW DO YOU LIKE IT SO FAR?
IT'S ALL RIGHT. I'M MOSTLY JUST DOING DELIVERIES NOW... BUT EVENTUALLY, I WANT TO BE ABLE TO RUN THIS WHOLE MILL MYSELF.
I WANT TO MAKE MY DAD PROUD.
I THINK HE WOULD BE.
YOU KEEP IT UP.

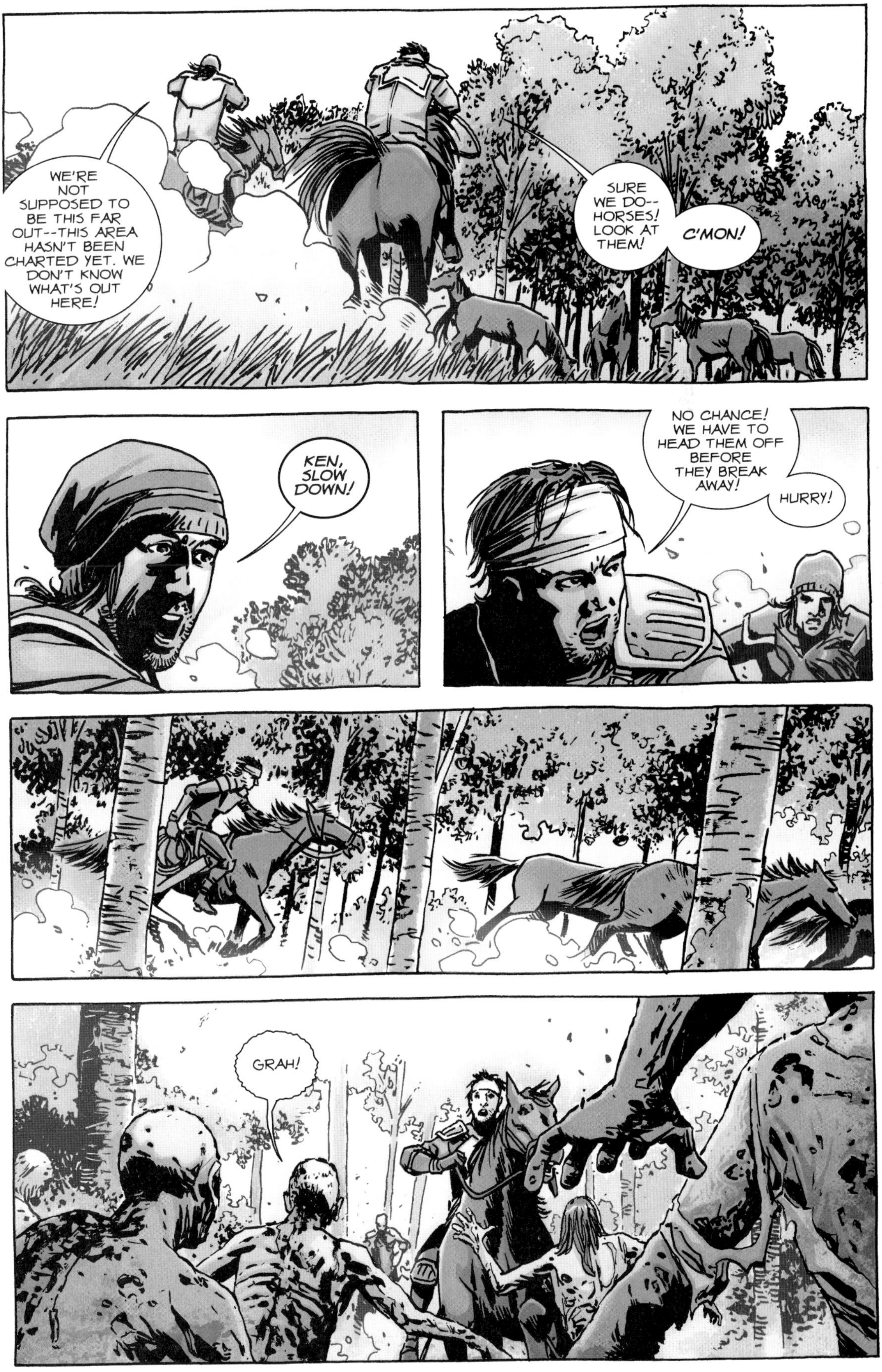

WE'RE NOT SUPPOSED TO BE THIS FAR OUT--THIS AREA HASN'T BEEN CHARTED YET. WE DON'T KNOW WHAT'S OUT HERE!
SURE WE DO-- HORSES! LOOK AT THEM!
C'MON!
KEN, SLOW DOWN!
NO CHANCE! WE HAVE TO HEAD THEM OFF BEFORE THEY BREAK AWAY!
HURRY!
GRAH!

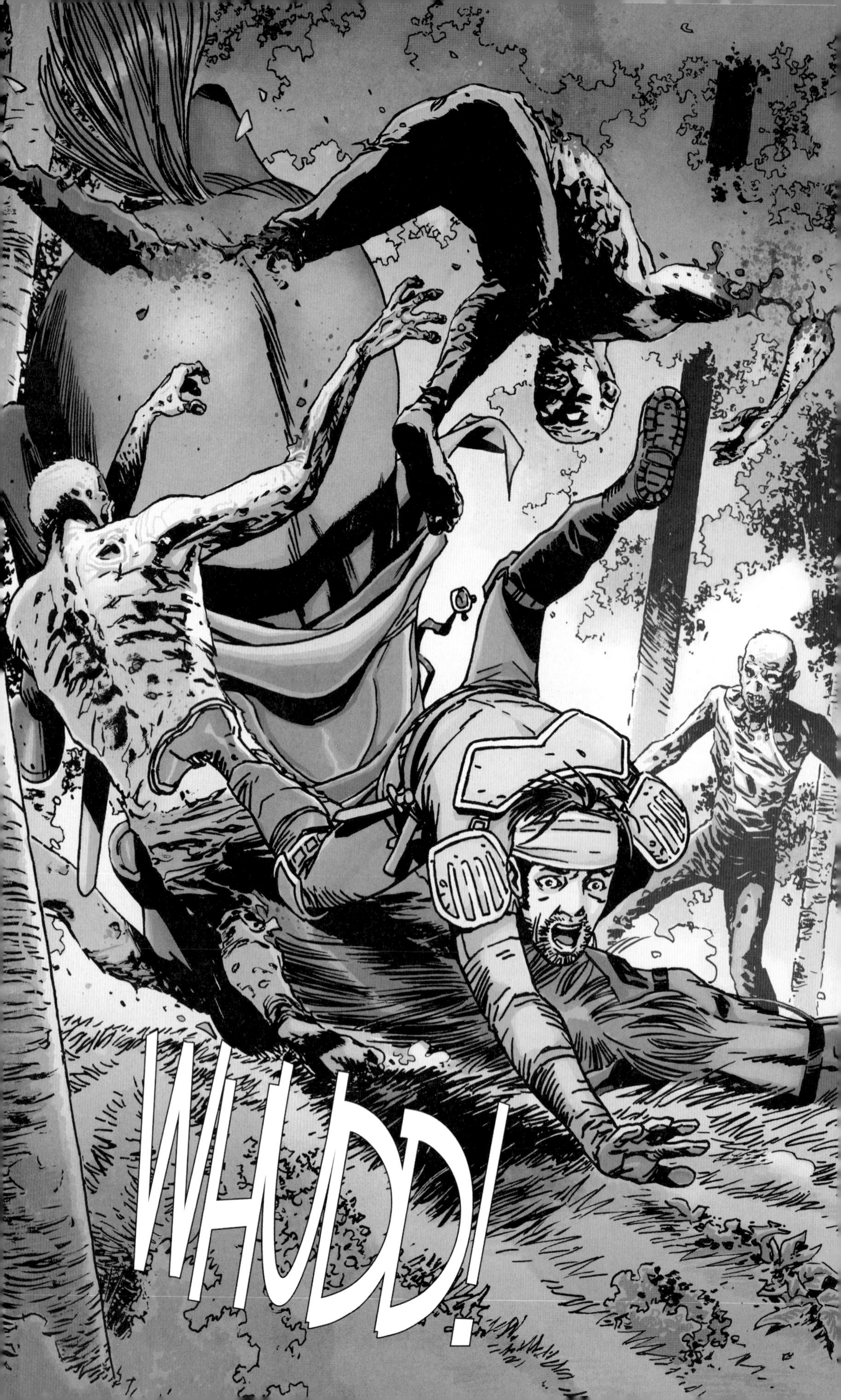
WHUDD!

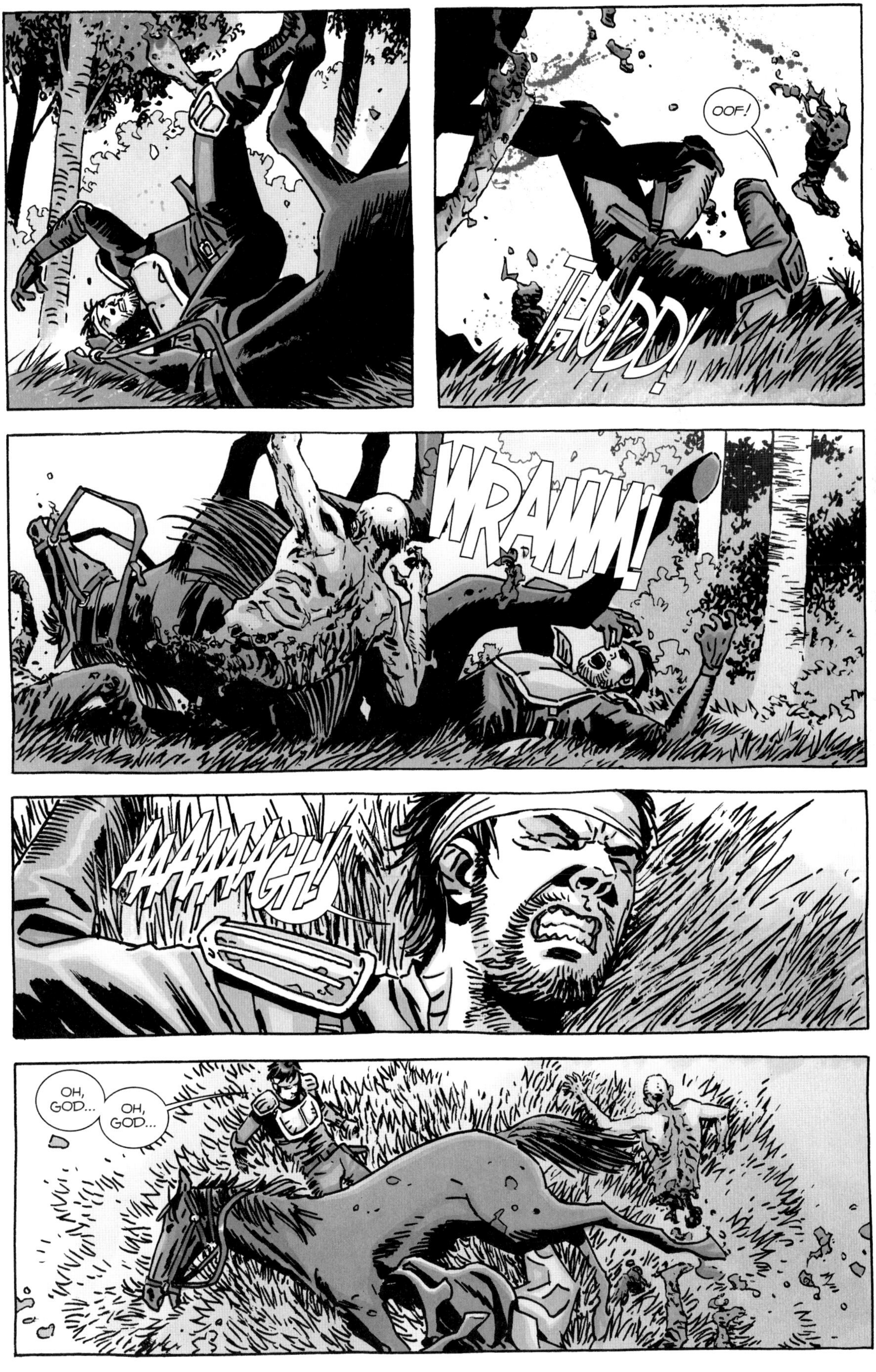
OOF!
THUDD!
WRAMM!
AAAAAAGH!
OH, GOD...
OH, GOD...

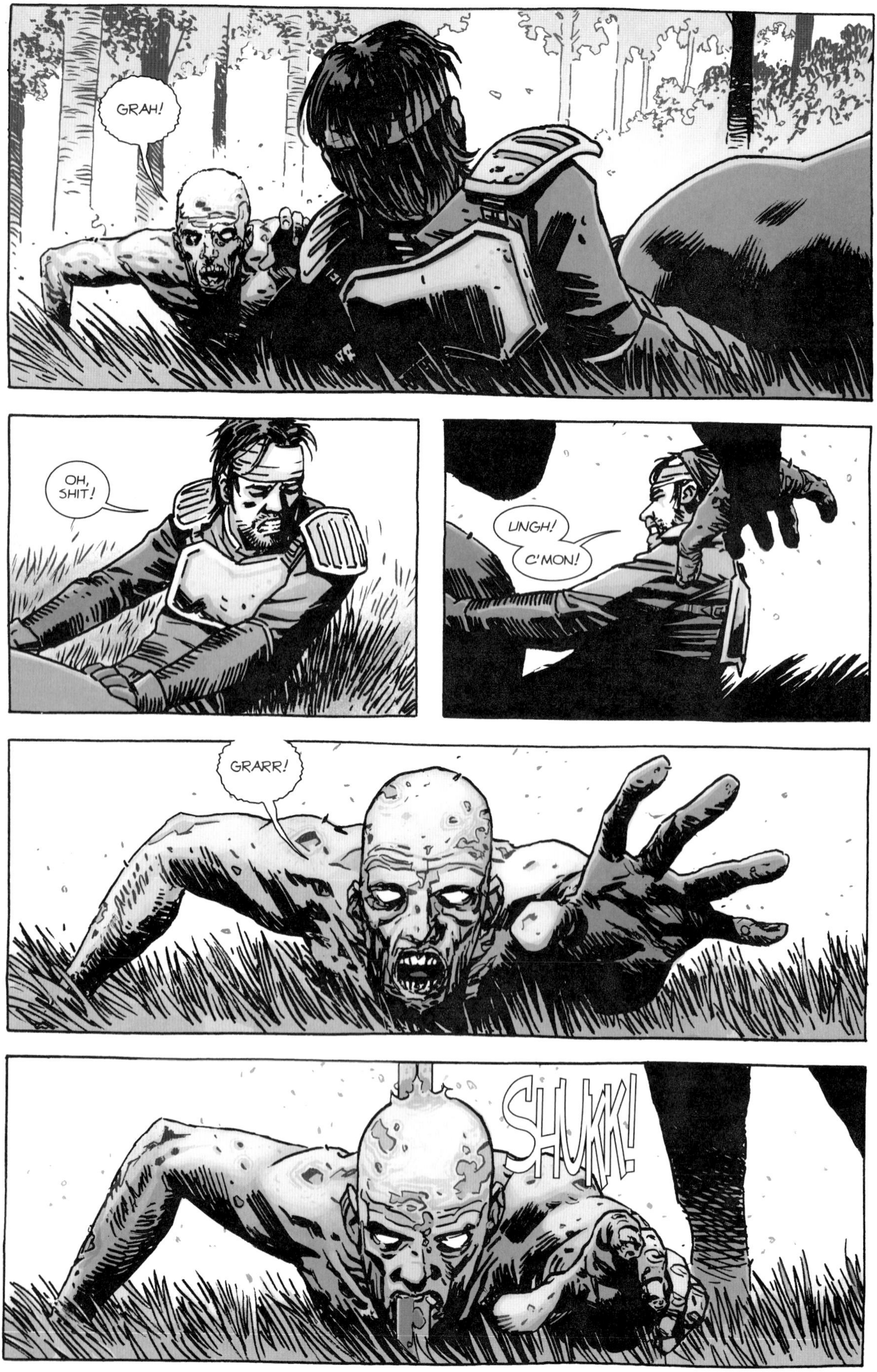
GRAH!
OH, SHIT!
UNGH!
C'MON!
GRARR!
SHUKK!

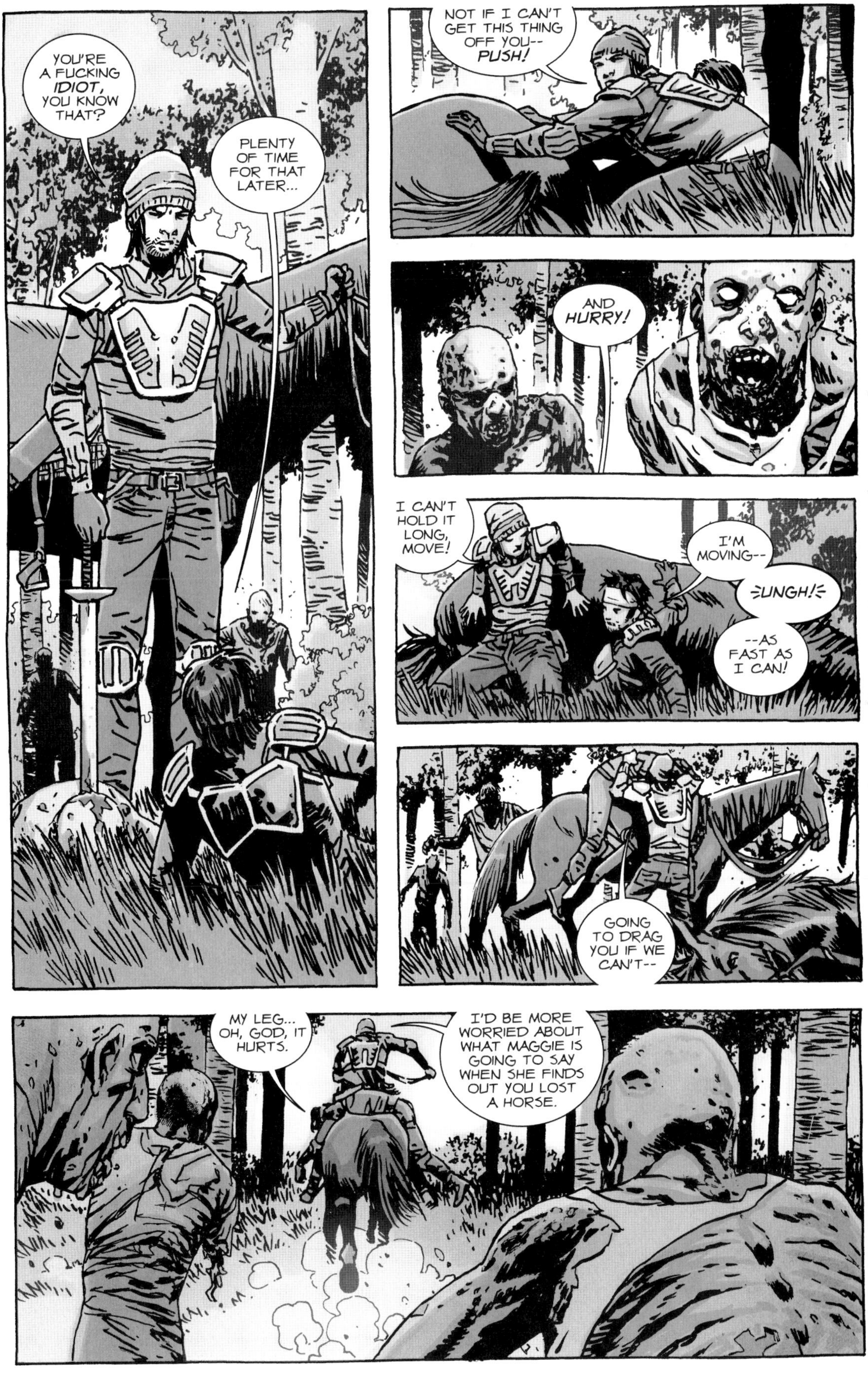
YOU'RE A FUCKING IDIOT, YOU KNOW THAT?
PLENTY OF TIME FOR THAT LATER...
NOT IF I CAN'T GET THIS THING OFF YOU-- PUSH!
AND HURRY!
I CAN'T HOLD IT LONG, MOVE!
I'M MOVING--
UNGH!
--AS FAST AS I CAN!
GOING TO DRAG YOU IF WE CAN'T--
MY LEG... OH, GOD, IT HURTS.
I'D BE MORE WORRIED ABOUT WHAT MAGGIE IS GOING TO SAY WHEN SHE FINDS OUT YOU LOST A HORSE.

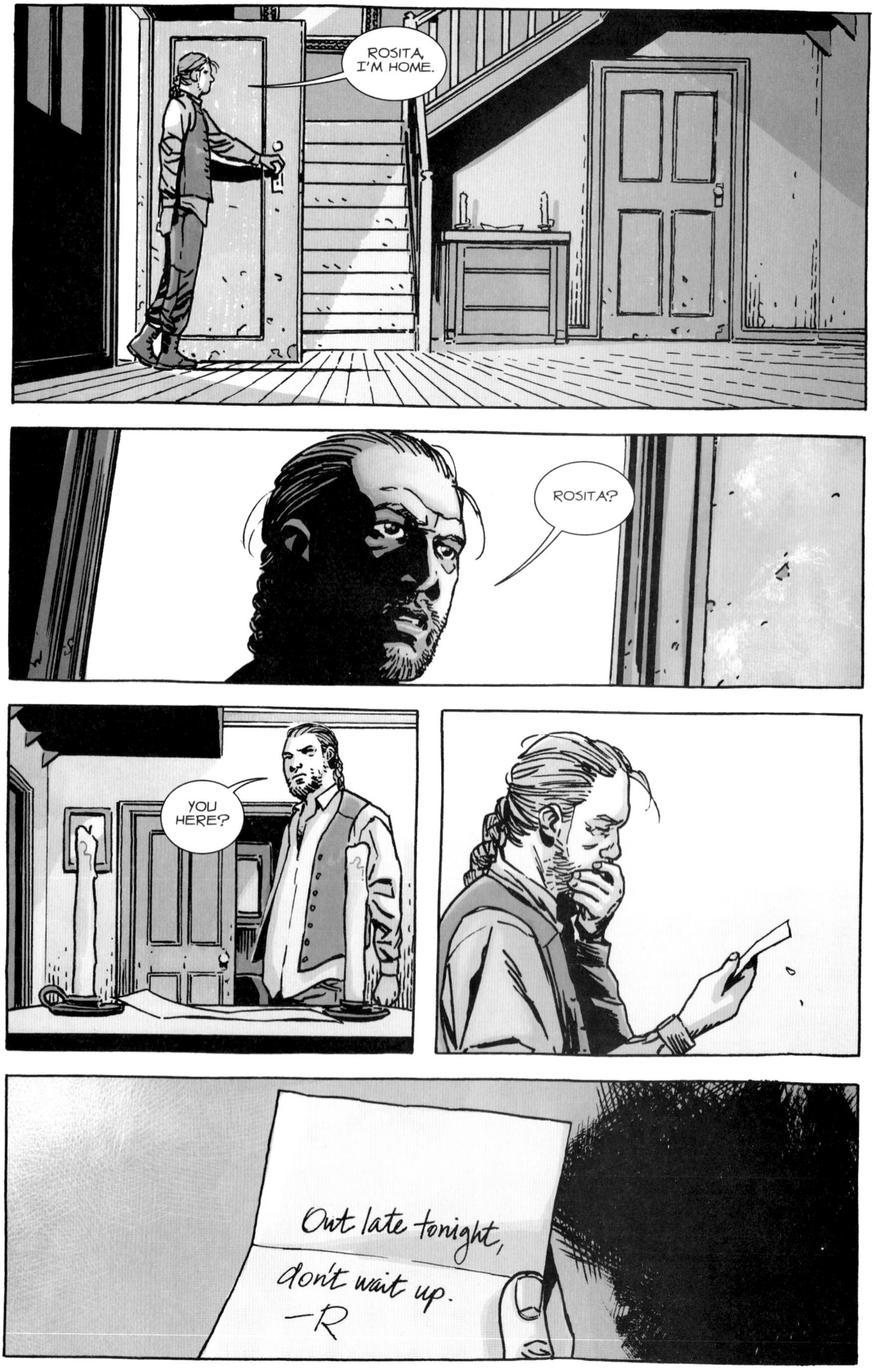

ROSITA, I'M HOME.
ROSITA?
YOU HERE?
Out late tonight, don't wait up. —R

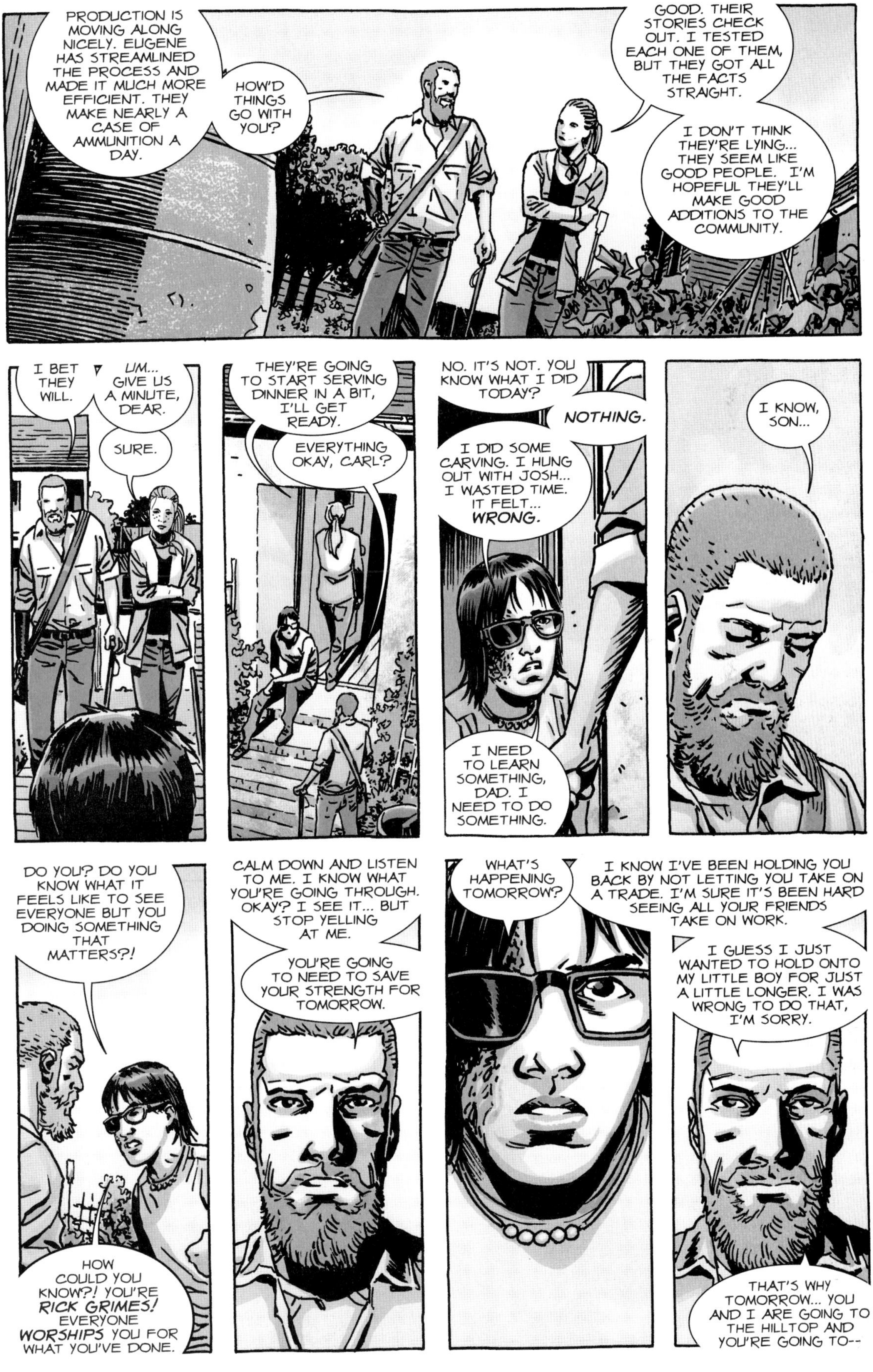
PRODUCTION IS MOVING ALONG NICELY. EUGENE HAS STREAMLINED THE PROCESS AND MADE IT MUCH MORE EFFICIENT. THEY MAKE NEARLY A CASE OF AMMUNITION A DAY.
HOW'D THINGS GO WITH YOU?
GOOD. THEIR STORIES CHECK OUT. I TESTED EACH ONE OF THEM, BUT THEY GOT ALL THE FACTS STRAIGHT.
I DON'T THINK THEY'RE LYING... THEY SEEM LIKE GOOD PEOPLE. I'M HOPEFUL THEY'LL MAKE GOOD ADDITIONS TO THE COMMUNITY.
I BET THEY WILL.
UM... GIVE US A MINUTE, DEAR.
SURE.
THEY'RE GOING TO START SERVING DINNER IN A BIT, I'LL GET READY.
EVERYTHING OKAY, CARL?
NO. IT'S NOT. YOU KNOW WHAT I DID TODAY?
NOTHING.
I DID SOME CARVING. I HUNG OUT WITH JOSH... I WASTED TIME. IT FELT... WRONG.
I NEED TO LEARN SOMETHING, DAD. I NEED TO DO SOMETHING.
I KNOW, SON...
DO YOU? DO YOU KNOW WHAT IT FEELS LIKE TO SEE EVERYONE BUT YOU DOING SOMETHING THAT MATTERS?!
HOW COULD YOU KNOW?! YOU'RE RICK GRIMES! EVERYONE WORSHIPS YOU FOR WHAT YOU'VE DONE.
CALM DOWN AND LISTEN TO ME. I KNOW WHAT YOU'RE GOING THROUGH. OKAY? I SEE IT... BUT STOP YELLING AT ME.
YOU'RE GOING TO NEED TO SAVE YOUR STRENGTH FOR TOMORROW.
WHAT'S HAPPENING TOMORROW?
I KNOW I'VE BEEN HOLDING YOU BACK BY NOT LETTING YOU TAKE ON A TRADE. I'M SURE IT'S BEEN HARD SEEING ALL YOUR FRIENDS TAKE ON WORK.
I GUESS I JUST WANTED TO HOLD ONTO MY LITTLE BOY FOR JUST A LITTLE LONGER. I WAS WRONG TO DO THAT, I'M SORRY.
THAT'S WHY TOMORROW... YOU AND I ARE GOING TO THE HILLTOP AND YOU'RE GOING TO--

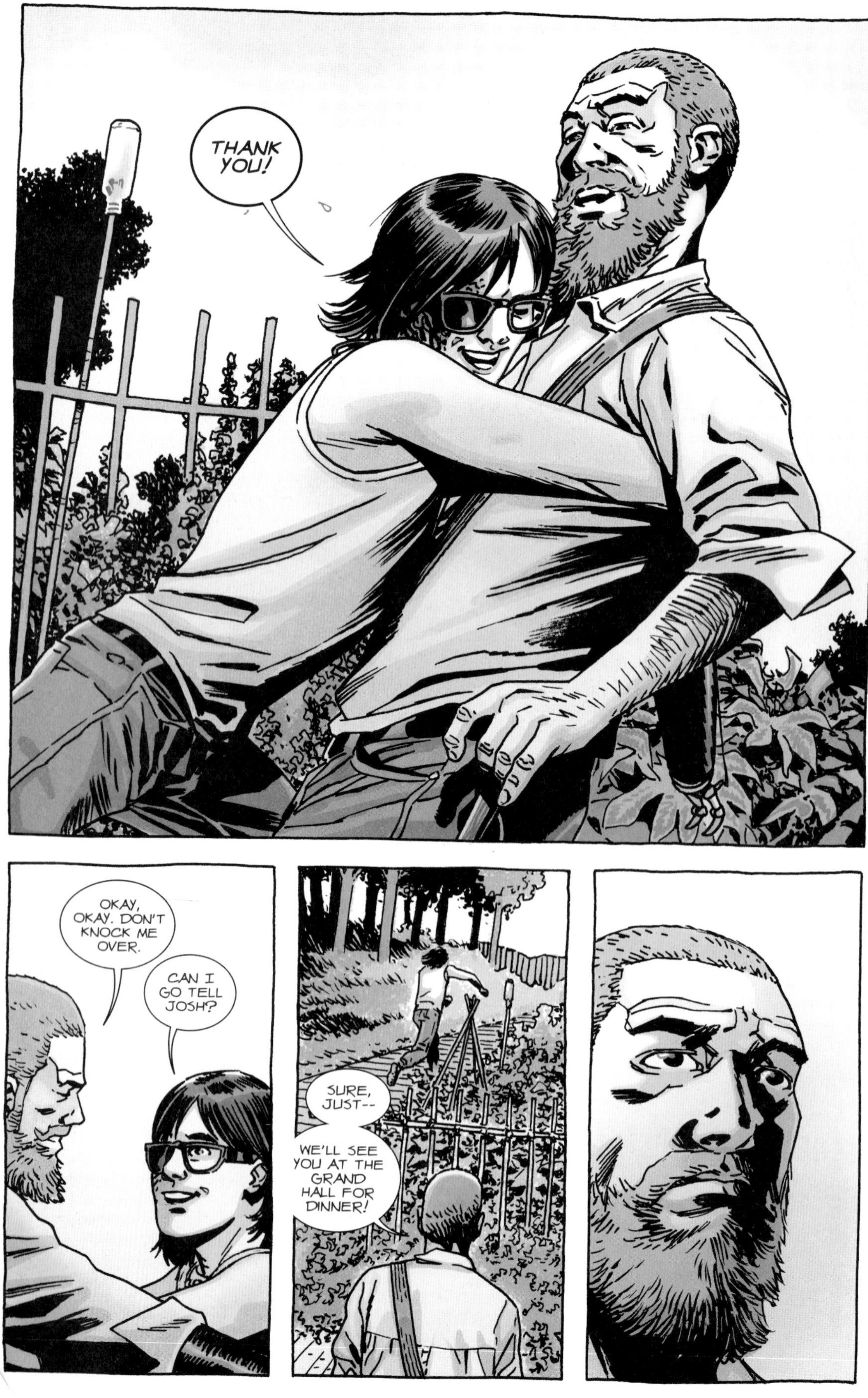
THANK YOU!
OKAY, OKAY. DON'T KNOCK ME OVER.
CAN I GO TELL JOSH?
SURE, JUST--
WE'LL SEE YOU AT THE GRAND HALL FOR DINNER!

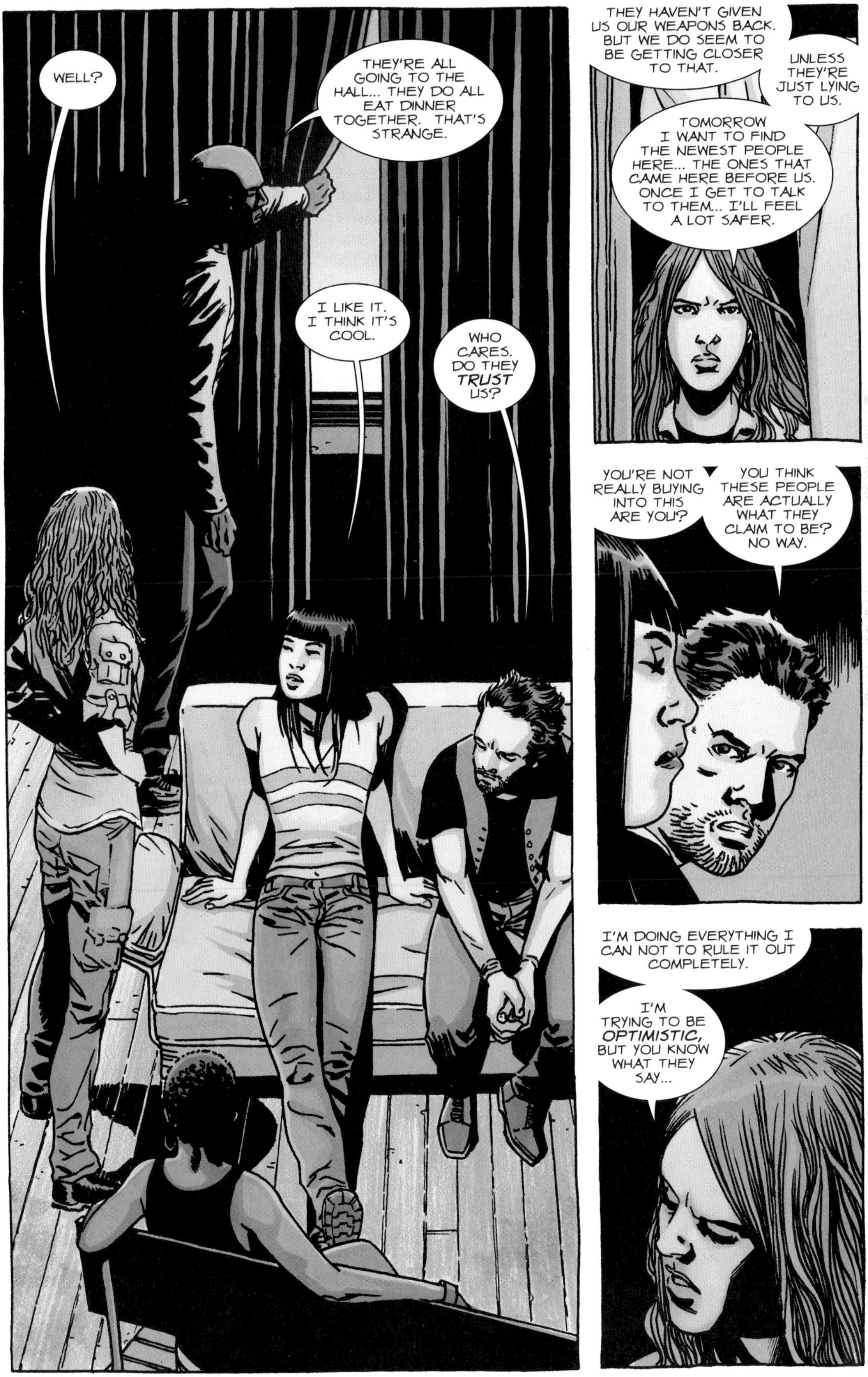
WELL?
THEY'RE ALL GOING TO THE HALL... THEY DO ALL EAT DINNER TOGETHER. THAT'S STRANGE.
I LIKE IT. I THINK IT'S COOL.
WHO CARES. DO THEY *TRUST* US?
THEY HAVEN'T GIVEN US OUR WEAPONS BACK. BUT WE DO SEEM TO BE GETTING CLOSER TO THAT.
UNLESS THEY'RE JUST LYING TO US.
TOMORROW I WANT TO FIND THE NEWEST PEOPLE HERE... THE ONES THAT CAME HERE BEFORE US. ONCE I GET TO TALK TO THEM... I'LL FEEL A LOT SAFER.
YOU'RE NOT REALLY BUYING INTO THIS ARE YOU?
YOU THINK THESE PEOPLE ARE ACTUALLY WHAT THEY CLAIM TO BE? NO WAY.
I'M DOING EVERYTHING I CAN NOT TO RULE IT OUT COMPLETELY.
I'M TRYING TO BE ***OPTIMISTIC,*** BUT YOU KNOW WHAT THEY SAY...

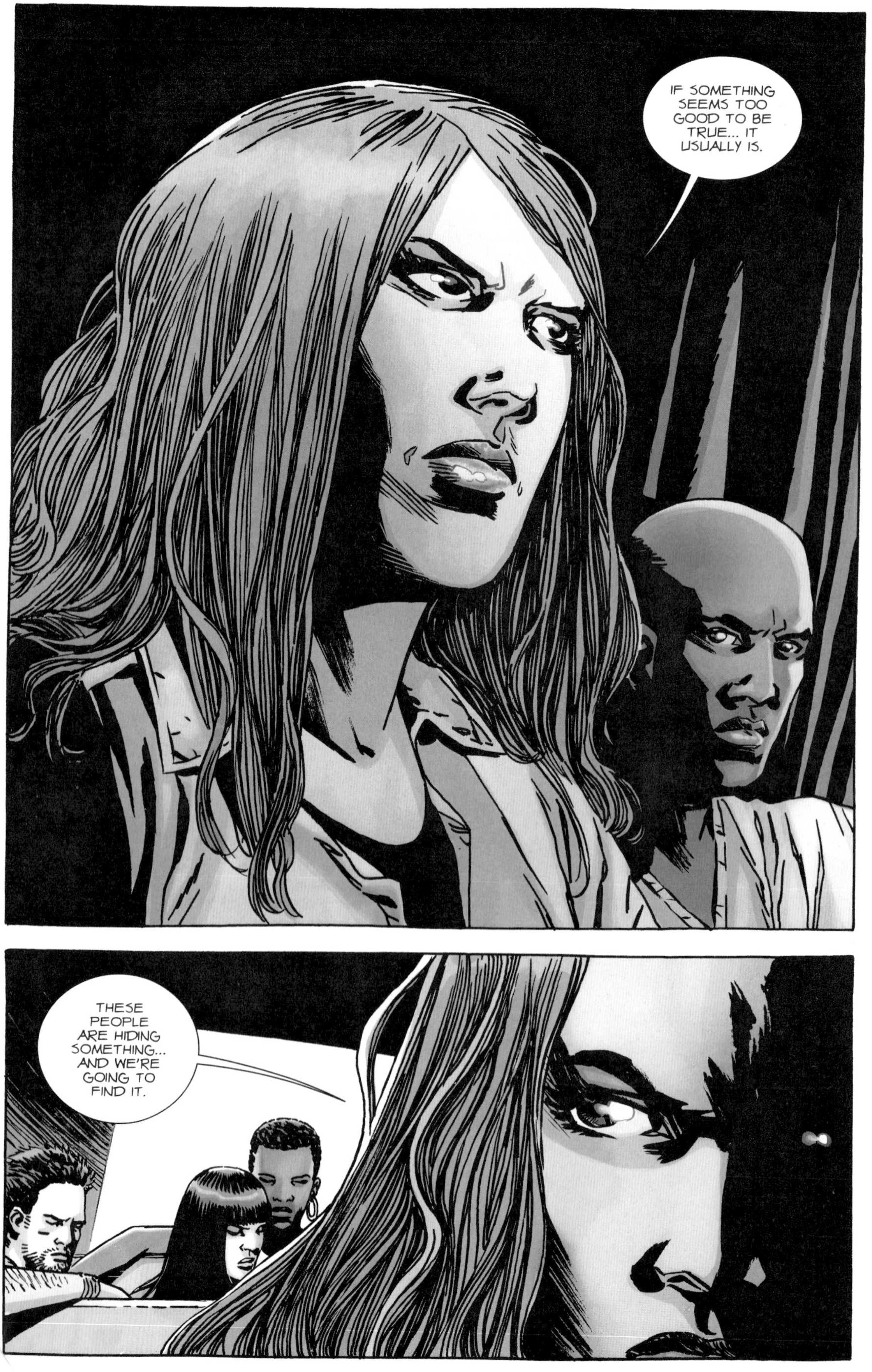
IF SOMETHING SEEMS TOO GOOD TO BE TRUE... IT USUALLY IS.
THESE PEOPLE ARE HIDING SOMETHING... AND WE'RE GOING TO FIND IT.

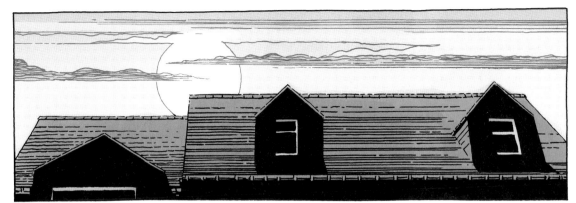

EVERYTHING OKAY?

NERVOUS?

NOT AT ALL.

I JUST... IT'S *WEIRD.* I NEVER THOUGHT I'D HAVE ENOUGH STUFF TO FILL *TWO* DUFFLE BAGS.

DON'T FEEL LIKE YOU HAVE TO TAKE *EVERYTHING.* IT'S NOT LIKE WE NEED THE ROOM.

AND IT MIGHT BE A WHILE, AND IT MIGHT WELL BE YOU VISITING WITH YOUR WIFE AND KIDS... BUT YOU'LL BE BACK.

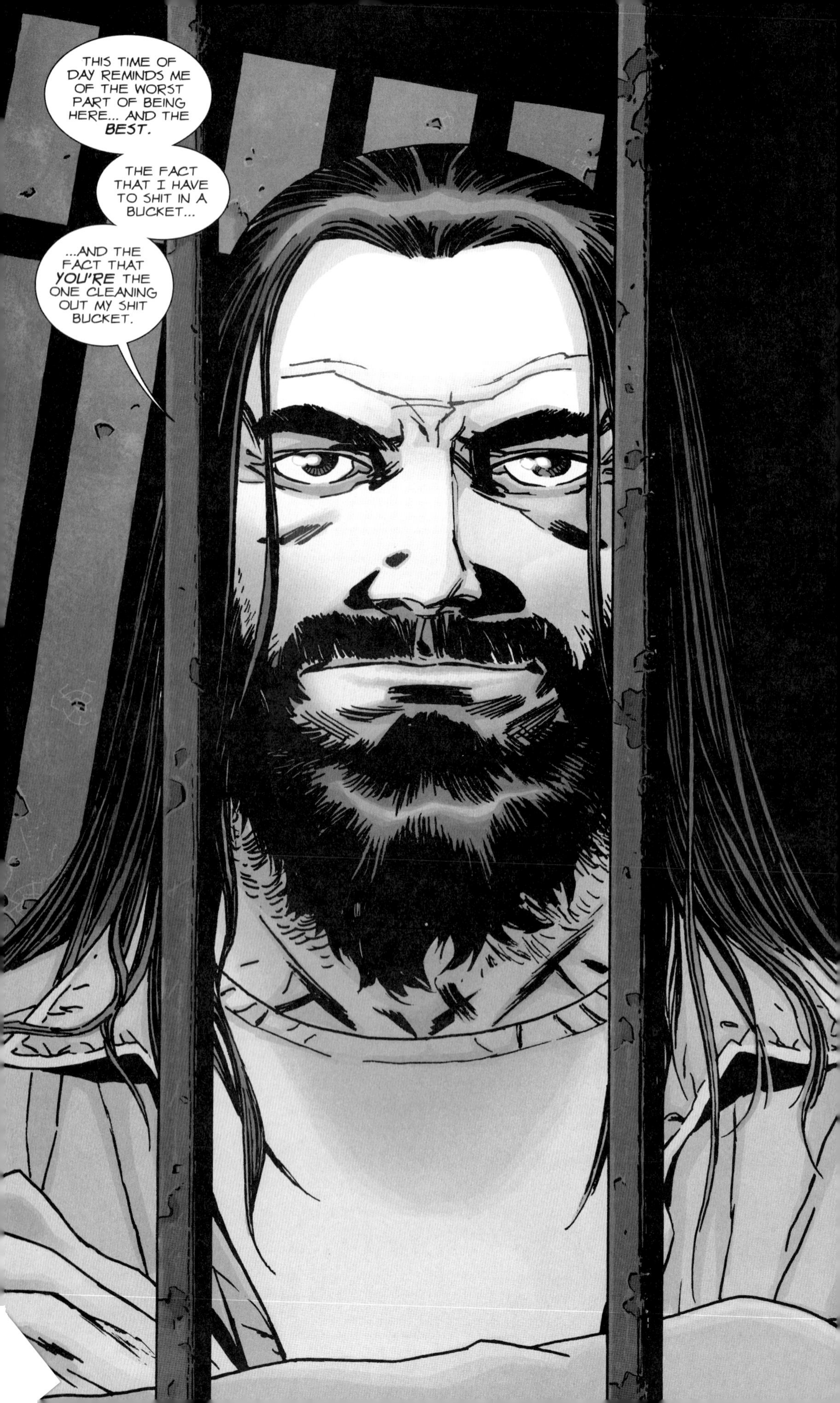
THIS TIME OF DAY REMINDS ME OF THE WORST PART OF BEING HERE... AND THE BEST.
THE FACT THAT I HAVE TO SHIT IN A BUCKET...
...AND THE FACT THAT YOU'RE THE ONE CLEANING OUT MY SHIT BUCKET.

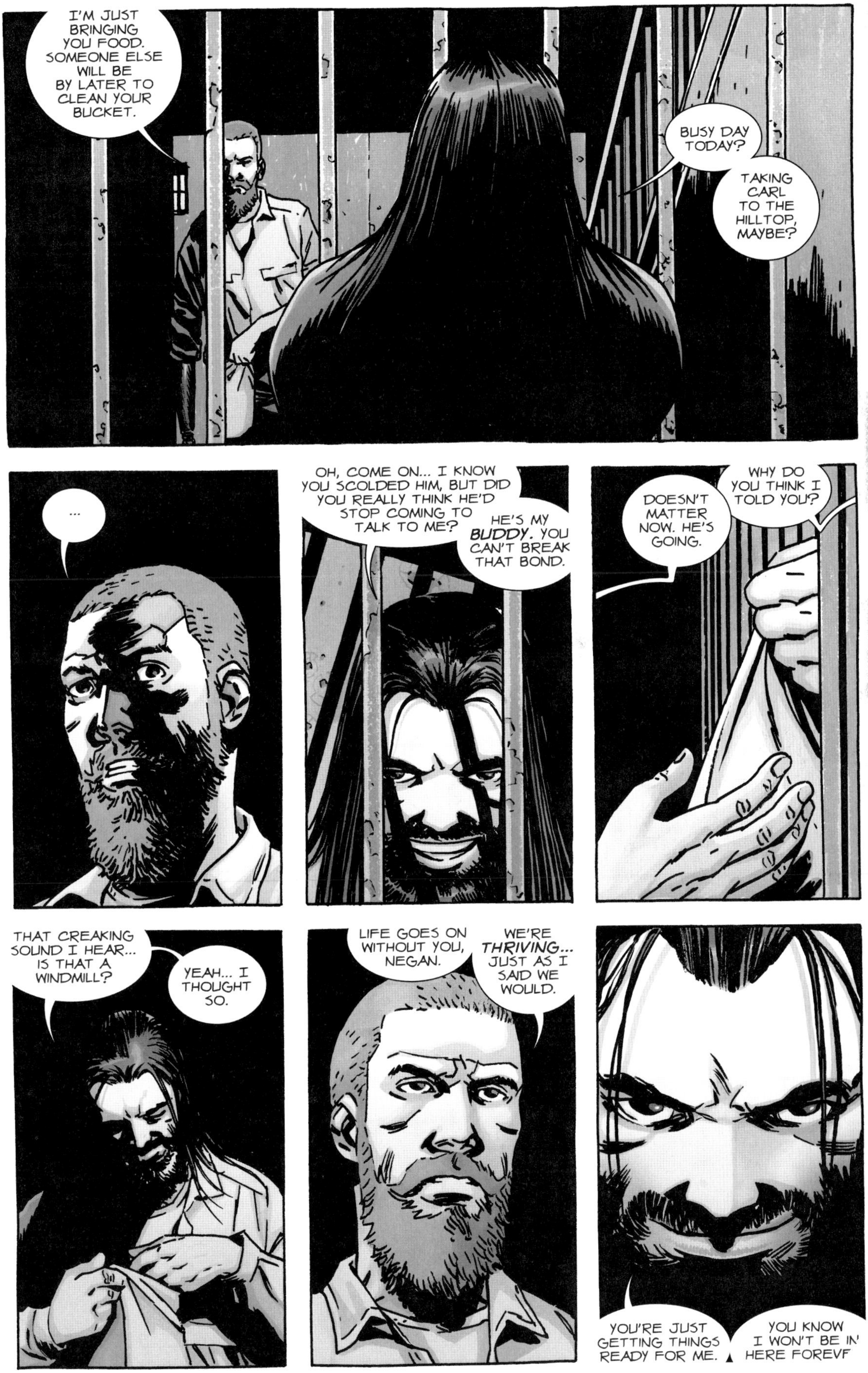
I'M JUST BRINGING YOU FOOD. SOMEONE ELSE WILL BE BY LATER TO CLEAN YOUR BUCKET.
BUSY DAY TODAY?
TAKING CARL TO THE HILLTOP, MAYBE?
...
OH, COME ON... I KNOW YOU SCOLDED HIM, BUT DID YOU REALLY THINK HE'D STOP COMING TO TALK TO ME?
HE'S MY BUDDY. YOU CAN'T BREAK THAT BOND.
DOESN'T MATTER NOW. HE'S GOING.
WHY DO YOU THINK I TOLD YOU?
THAT CREAKING SOUND I HEAR... IS THAT A WINDMILL?
YEAH... I THOUGHT SO.
LIFE GOES ON WITHOUT YOU, NEGAN.
WE'RE THRIVING... JUST AS I SAID WE WOULD.
YOU'RE JUST GETTING THINGS READY FOR ME.
YOU KNOW I WON'T BE IN HERE FOREVE

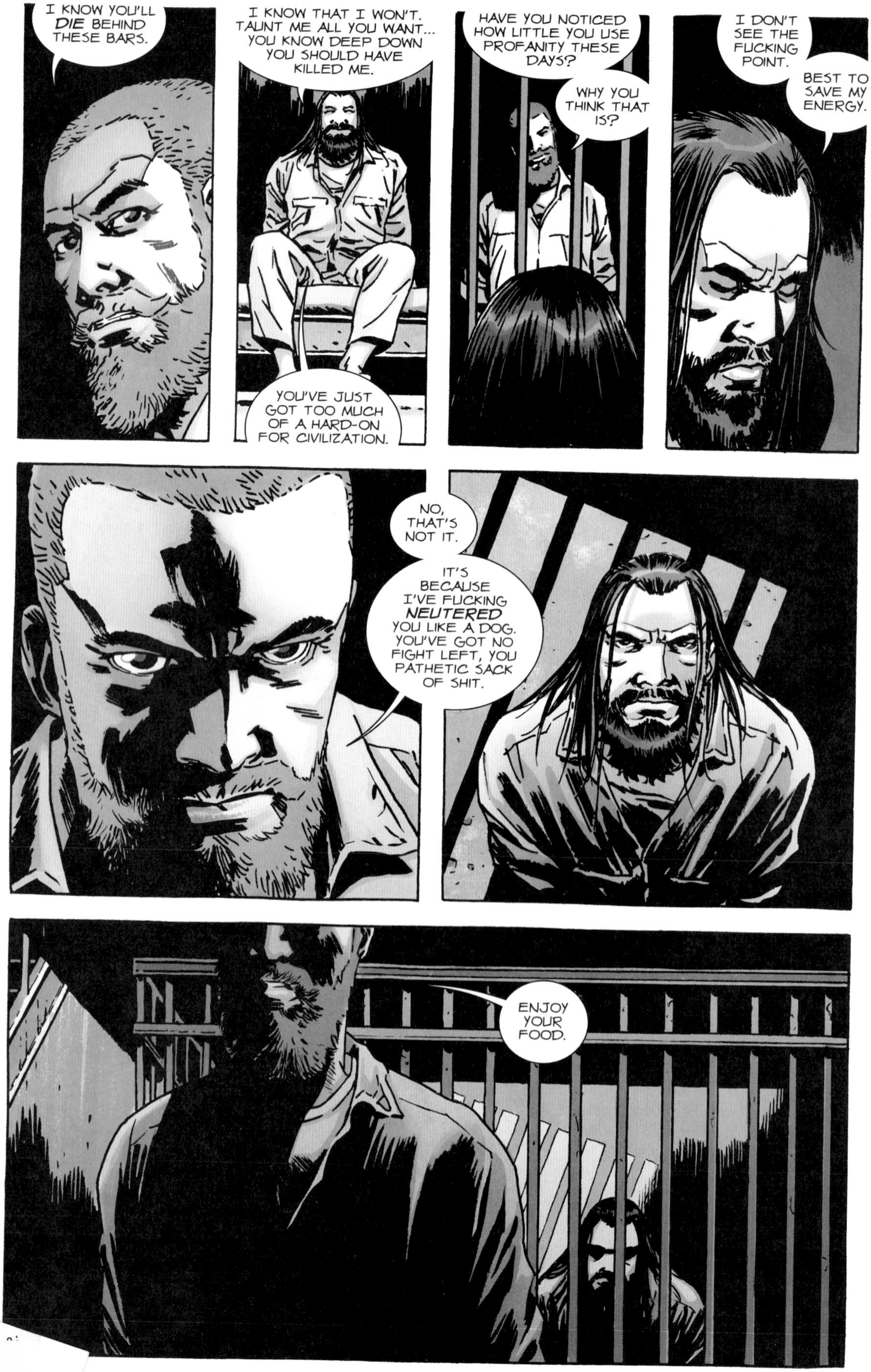
I KNOW YOU'LL DIE BEHIND THESE BARS.
I KNOW THAT I WON'T. TAUNT ME ALL YOU WANT... YOU KNOW DEEP DOWN YOU SHOULD HAVE KILLED ME.
YOU'VE JUST GOT TOO MUCH OF A HARD-ON FOR CIVILIZATION.
HAVE YOU NOTICED HOW LITTLE YOU USE PROFANITY THESE DAYS?
WHY YOU THINK THAT IS?
I DON'T SEE THE FUCKING POINT.
BEST TO SAVE MY ENERGY.
NO, THAT'S NOT IT.
IT'S BECAUSE I'VE FUCKING NEUTERED YOU LIKE A DOG. YOU'VE GOT NO FIGHT LEFT, YOU PATHETIC SACK OF SHIT.
ENJOY YOUR FOOD.

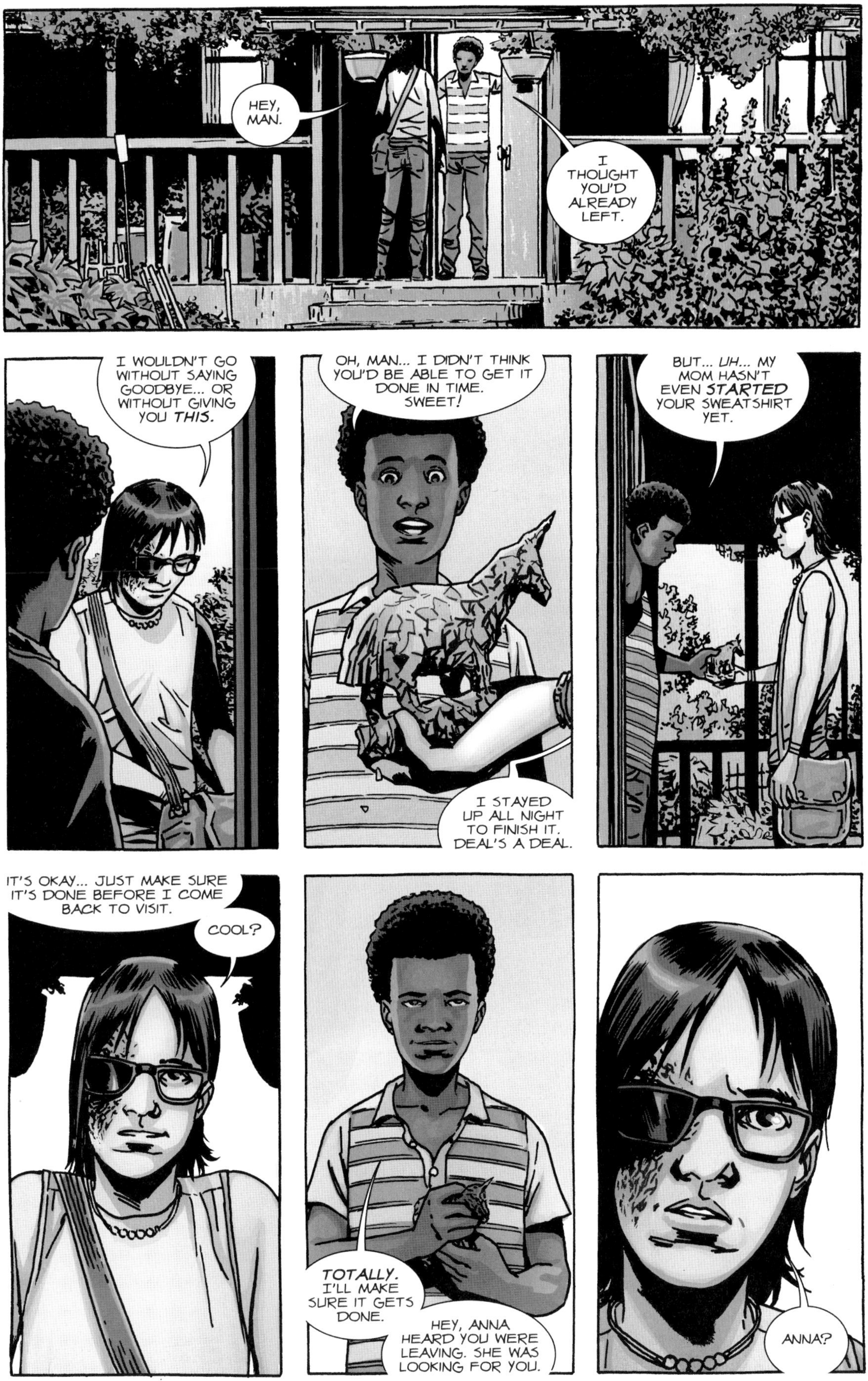
HEY, MAN.
I THOUGHT YOU'D ALREADY LEFT.
I WOULDN'T GO WITHOUT SAYING GOODBYE... OR WITHOUT GIVING YOU *THIS.*
OH, MAN... I DIDN'T THINK YOU'D BE ABLE TO GET IT DONE IN TIME. SWEET!
I STAYED UP ALL NIGHT TO FINISH IT. DEAL'S A DEAL.
BUT... *UH*... MY MOM HASN'T EVEN *STARTED* YOUR SWEATSHIRT YET.
IT'S OKAY... JUST MAKE SURE IT'S DONE BEFORE I COME BACK TO VISIT.
COOL?
TOTALLY. I'LL MAKE SURE IT GETS DONE.
HEY, ANNA HEARD YOU WERE LEAVING. SHE WAS LOOKING FOR YOU.
ANNA?

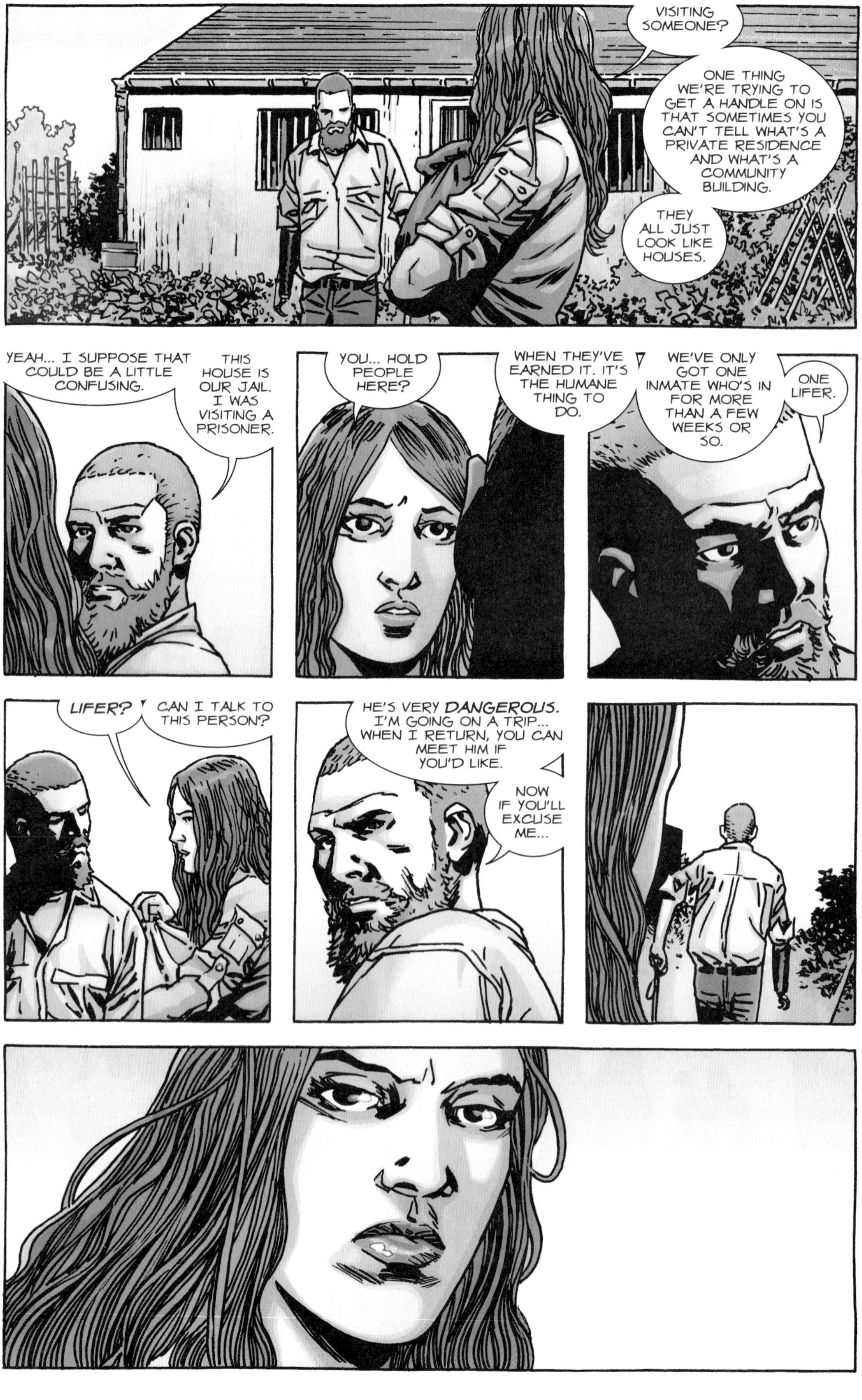
VISITING SOMEONE?
ONE THING WE'RE TRYING TO GET A HANDLE ON IS THAT SOMETIMES YOU CAN'T TELL WHAT'S A PRIVATE RESIDENCE AND WHAT'S A COMMUNITY BUILDING.
THEY ALL JUST LOOK LIKE HOUSES.
YEAH... I SUPPOSE THAT COULD BE A LITTLE CONFUSING.
THIS HOUSE IS OUR JAIL. I WAS VISITING A PRISONER.
YOU... HOLD PEOPLE HERE?
WHEN THEY'VE EARNED IT. IT'S THE HUMANE THING TO DO.
WE'VE ONLY GOT ONE INMATE WHO'S IN FOR MORE THAN A FEW WEEKS OR SO.
ONE LIFER.
LIFER?
CAN I TALK TO THIS PERSON?
HE'S VERY ***DANGEROUS.*** I'M GOING ON A TRIP... WHEN I RETURN, YOU CAN MEET HIM IF YOU'D LIKE.
NOW IF YOU'LL EXCUSE ME...

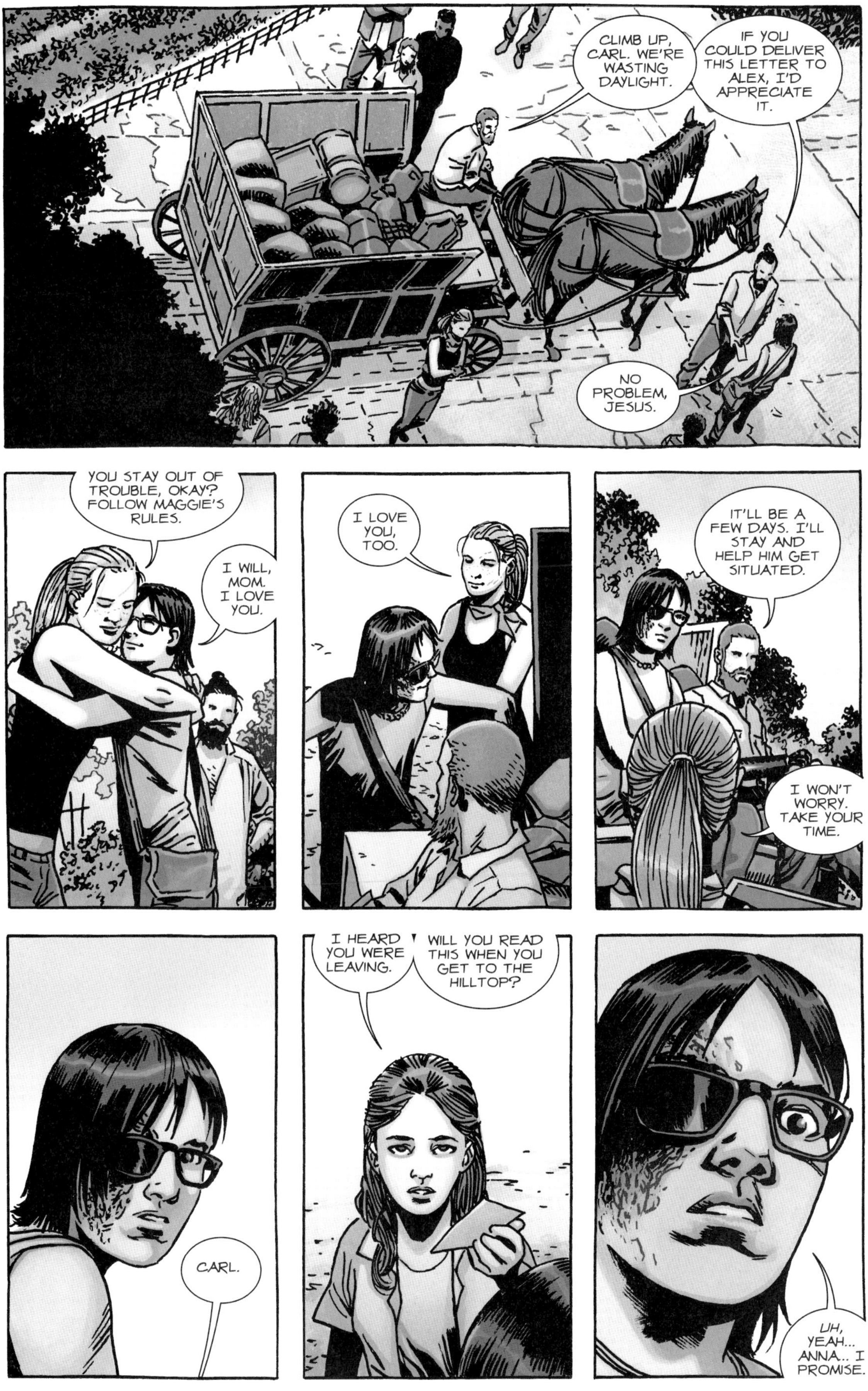
CLIMB UP, CARL. WE'RE WASTING DAYLIGHT.
IF YOU COULD DELIVER THIS LETTER TO ALEX, I'D APPRECIATE IT.
NO PROBLEM, JESUS.
YOU STAY OUT OF TROUBLE, OKAY? FOLLOW MAGGIE'S RULES.
I WILL, MOM. I LOVE YOU.
I LOVE YOU, TOO.
IT'LL BE A FEW DAYS. I'LL STAY AND HELP HIM GET SITUATED.
I WON'T WORRY. TAKE YOUR TIME.
CARL.
I HEARD YOU WERE LEAVING.
WILL YOU READ THIS WHEN YOU GET TO THE HILLTOP?
UH, YEAH... ANNA... I PROMISE.

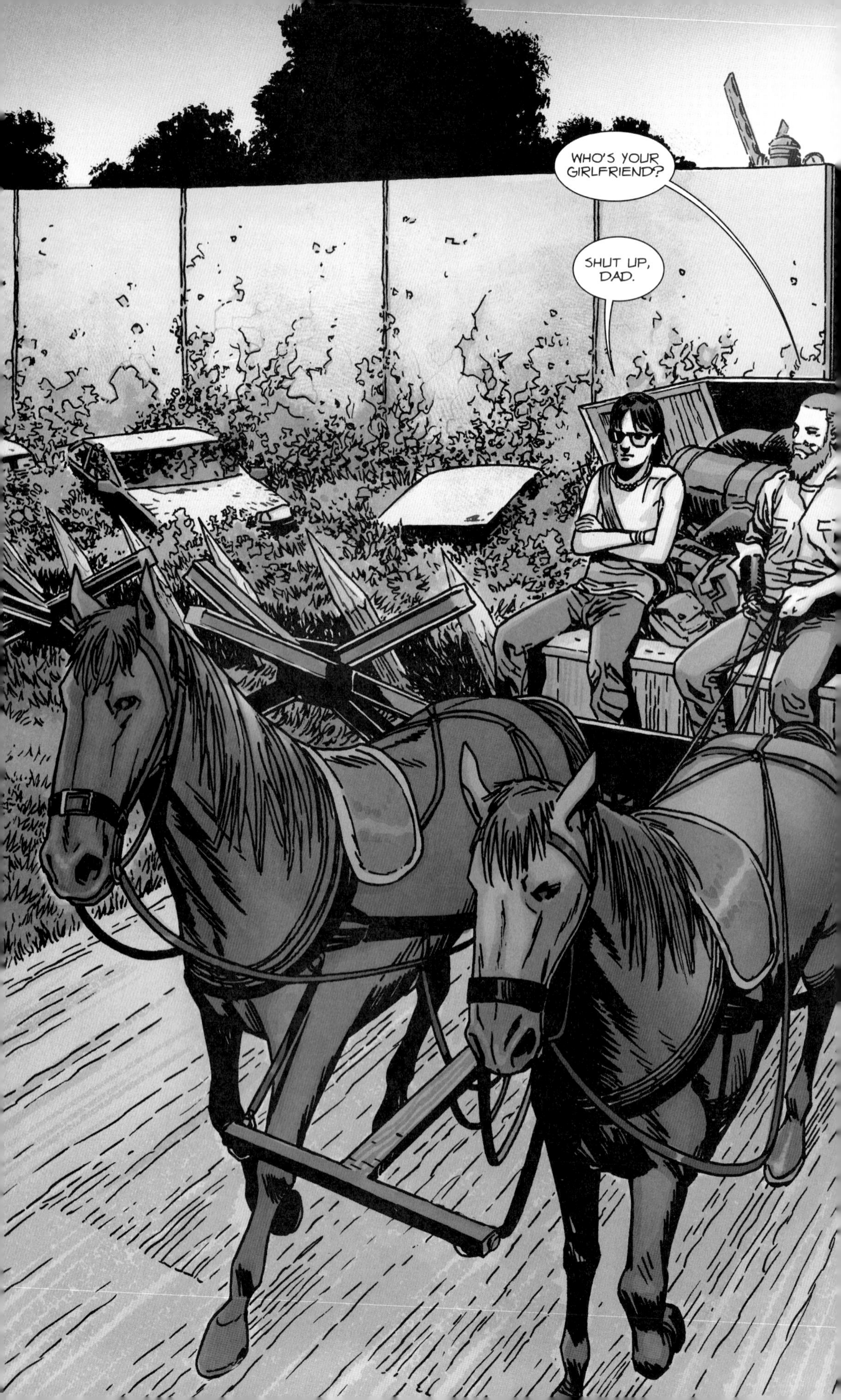
WHO'S YOUR GIRLFRIEND?
SHUT UP, DAD.

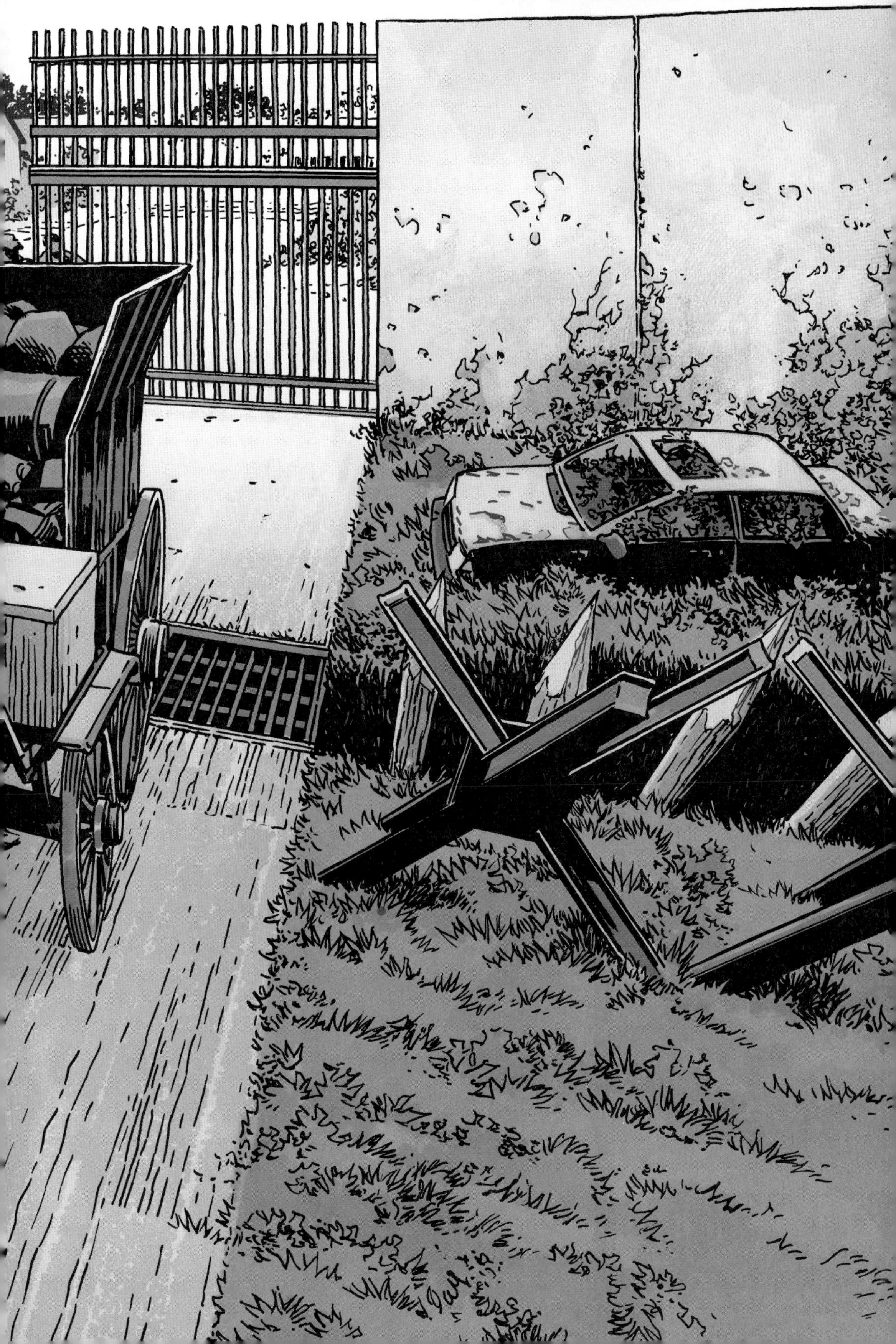

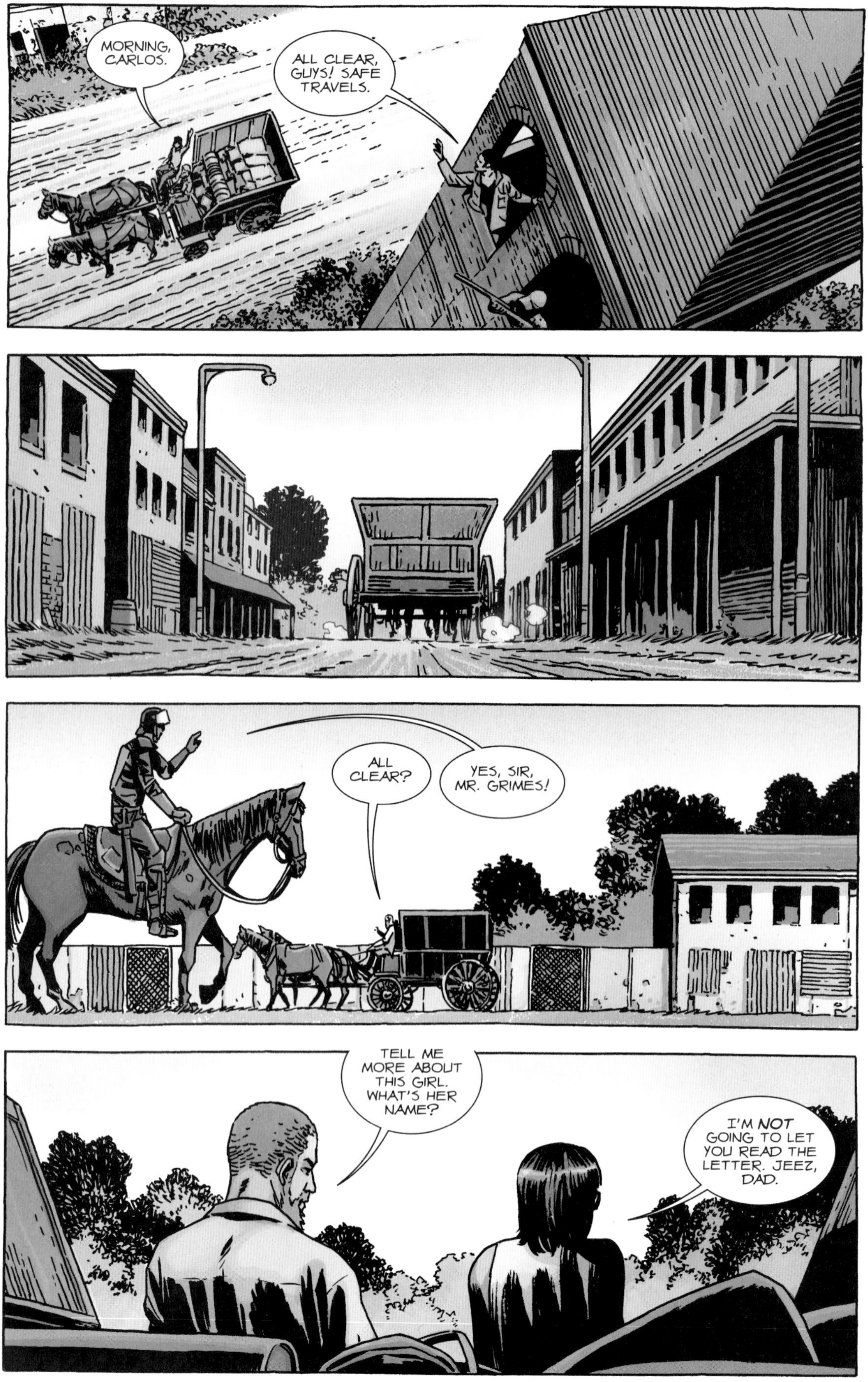
MORNING, CARLOS.
ALL CLEAR, GUYS! SAFE TRAVELS.
ALL CLEAR?
YES, SIR, MR. GRIMES!
TELL ME MORE ABOUT THIS GIRL. WHAT'S HER NAME?
I'M NOT GOING TO LET YOU READ THE LETTER. JEEZ, DAD.

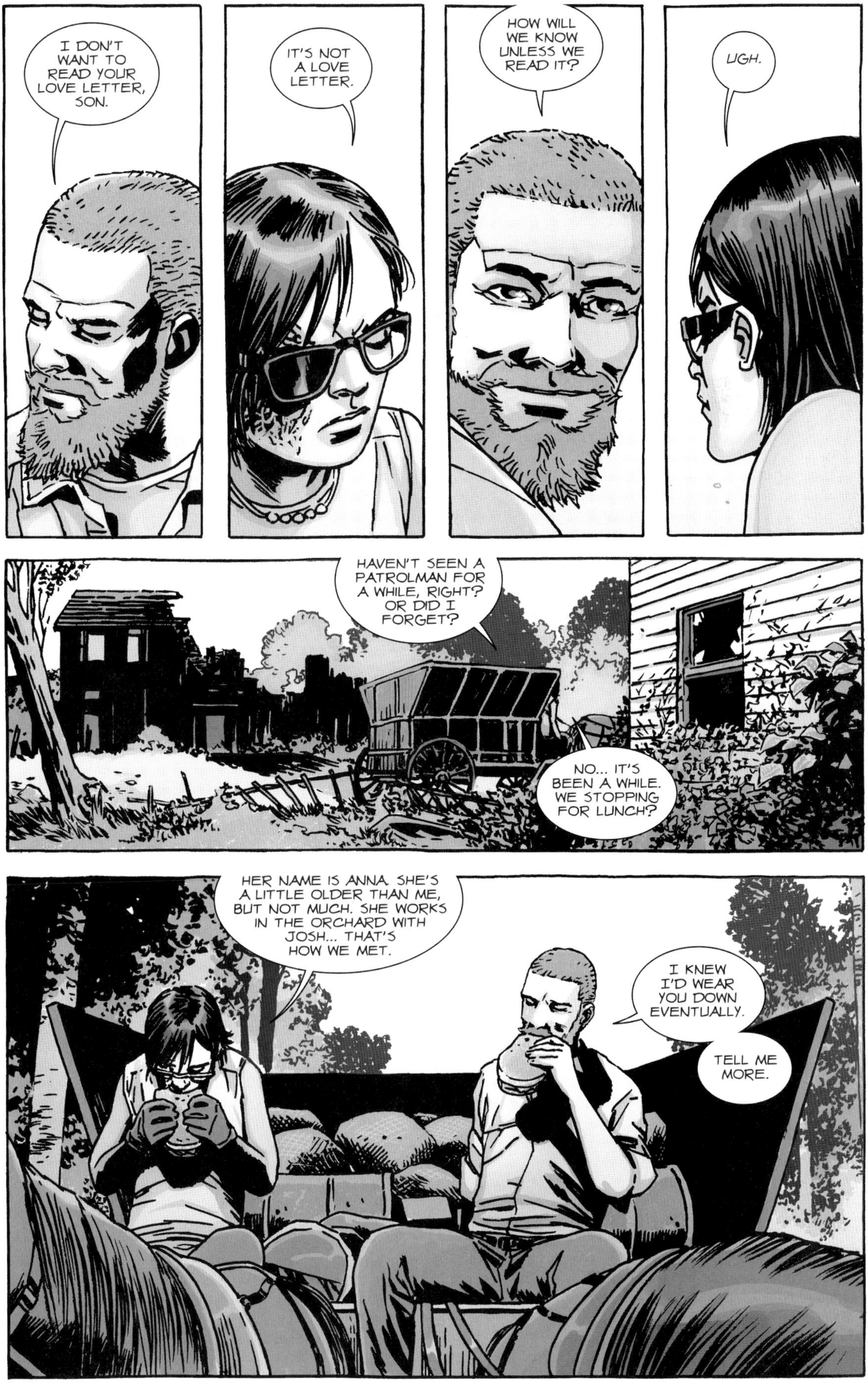

I DON'T WANT TO READ YOUR LOVE LETTER, SON.
IT'S NOT A LOVE LETTER.
HOW WILL WE KNOW UNLESS WE READ IT?
UGH.
HAVEN'T SEEN A PATROLMAN FOR A WHILE, RIGHT? OR DID I FORGET?
NO... IT'S BEEN A WHILE. WE STOPPING FOR LUNCH?
HER NAME IS ANNA. SHE'S A LITTLE OLDER THAN ME, BUT NOT MUCH. SHE WORKS IN THE ORCHARD WITH JOSH... THAT'S HOW WE MET.
I KNEW I'D WEAR YOU DOWN EVENTUALLY.
TELL ME MORE.

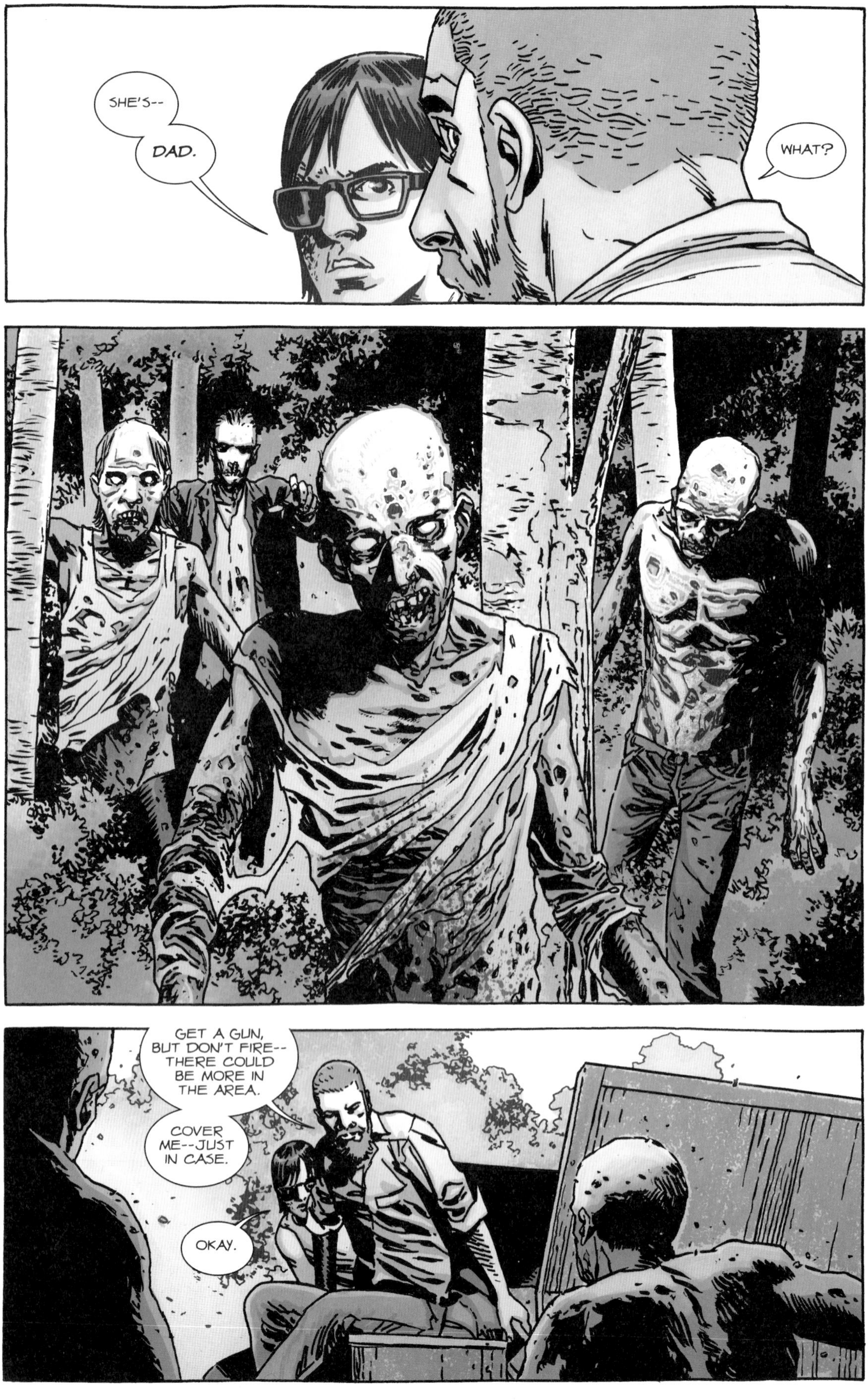
SHE'S--
DAD.
WHAT?
GET A GUN, BUT DON'T FIRE-- THERE COULD BE MORE IN THE AREA.
COVER ME--JUST IN CASE.
OKAY.

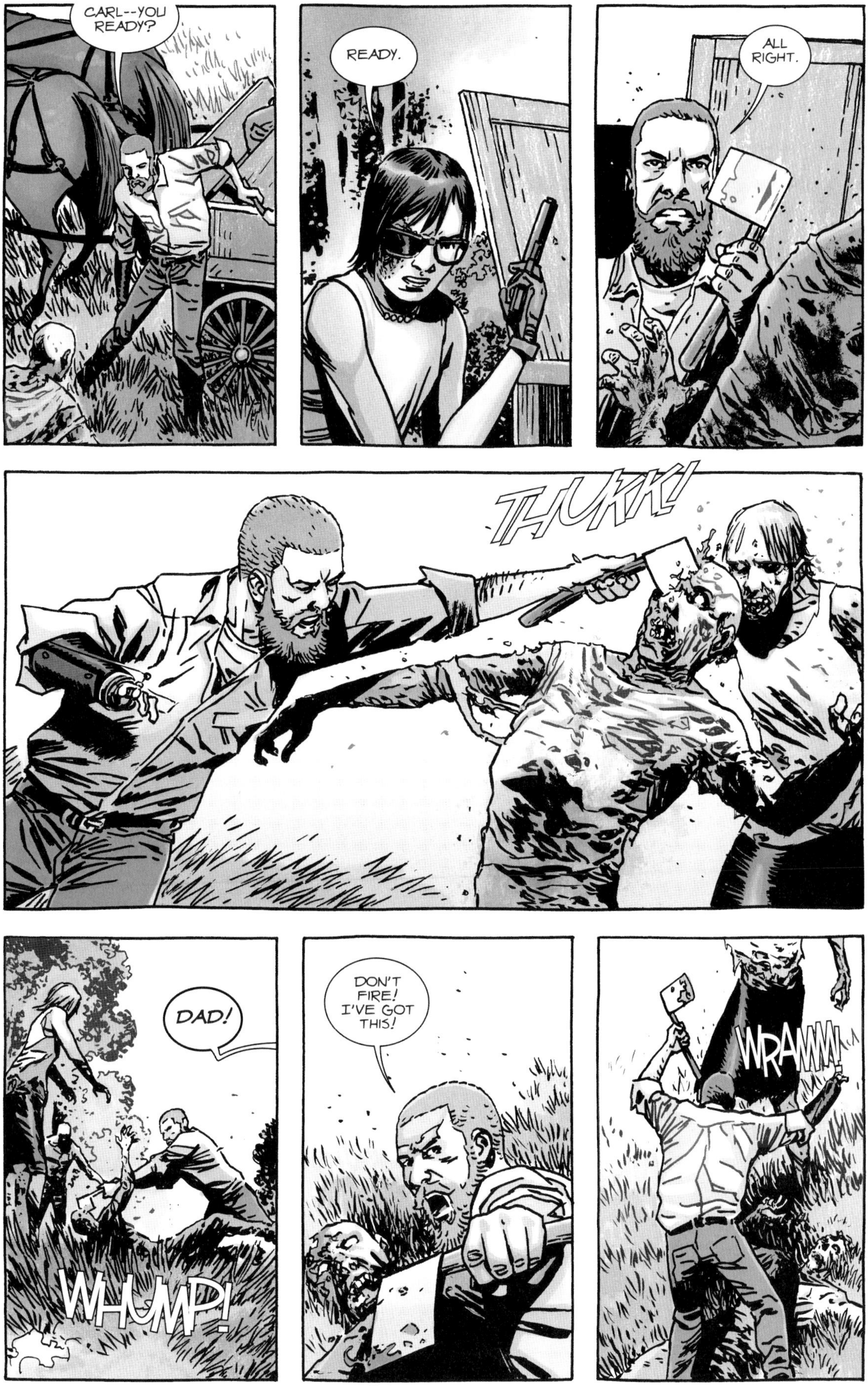
CARL--YOU READY?
READY.
ALL RIGHT.
THUKK!
DAD!
WHUMP!
DON'T FIRE! I'VE GOT THIS!
WRAMM!

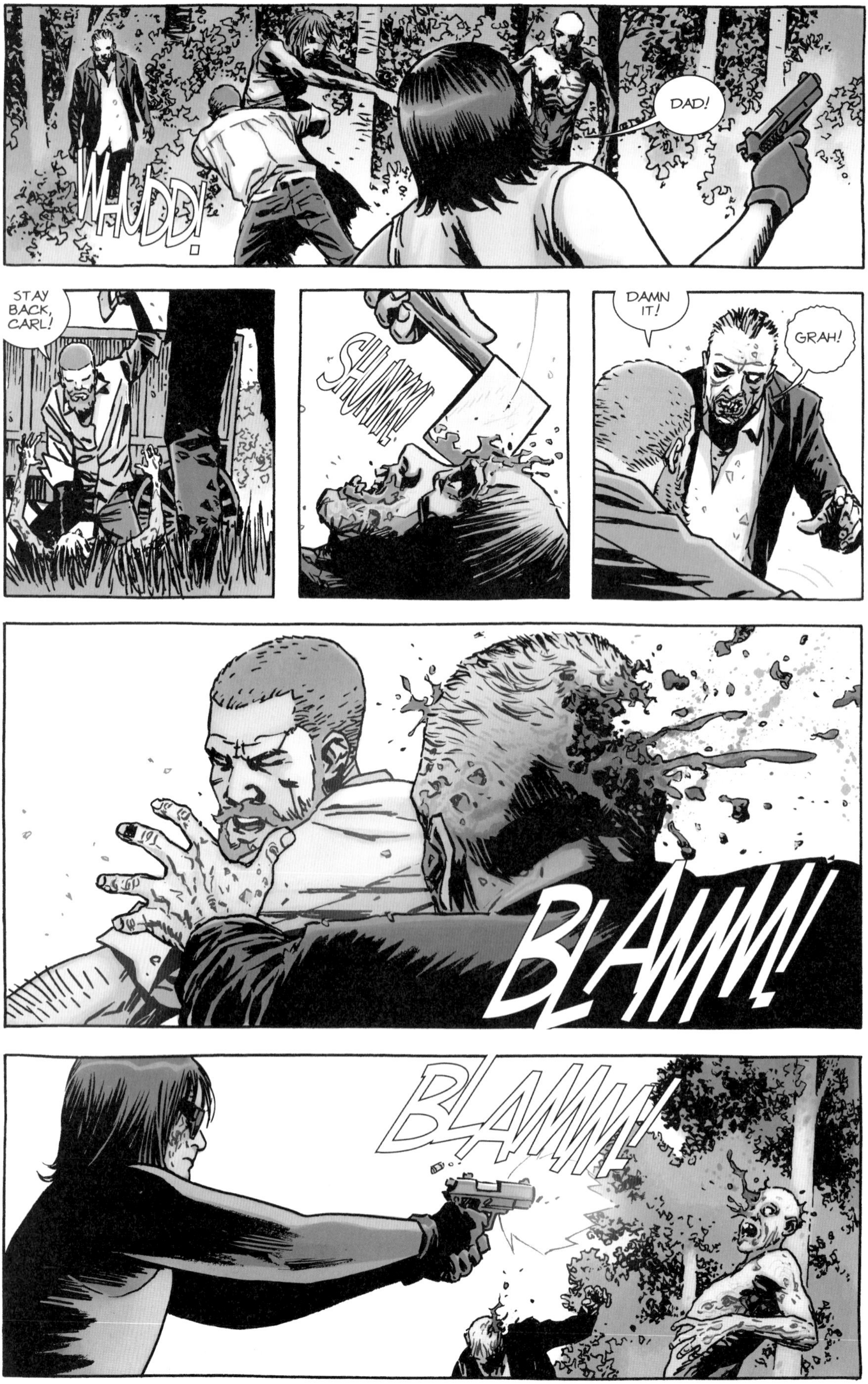
WHUDD!
DAD!
STAY BACK, CARL!
SHUNKK!
DAMN IT!
GRAH!
BLAMM!
BLAMM!

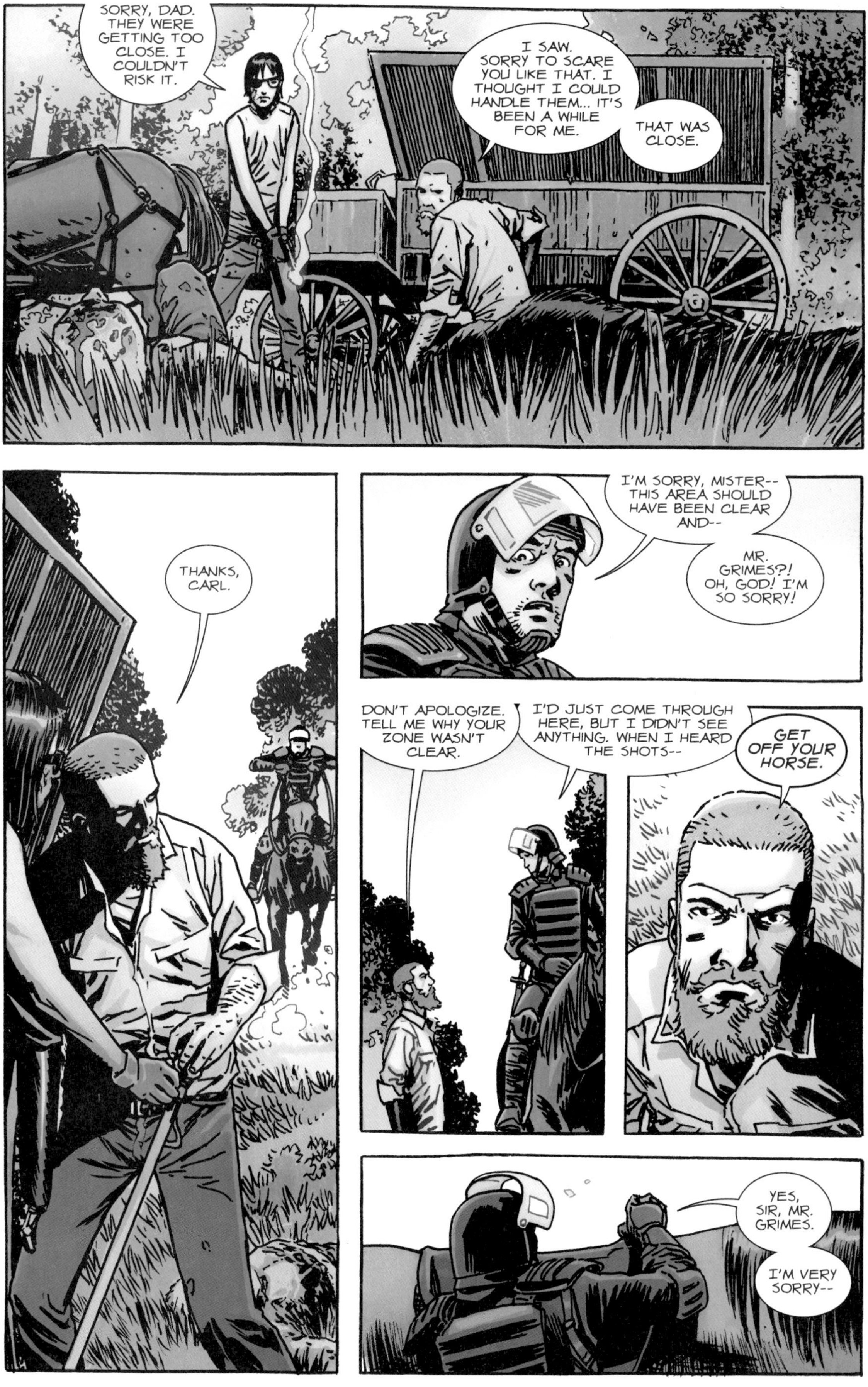
SORRY, DAD. THEY WERE GETTING TOO CLOSE. I COULDN'T RISK IT.
I SAW. SORRY TO SCARE YOU LIKE THAT. I THOUGHT I COULD HANDLE THEM... IT'S BEEN A WHILE FOR ME.
THAT WAS CLOSE.
THANKS, CARL.
I'M SORRY, MISTER-- THIS AREA SHOULD HAVE BEEN CLEAR AND--
MR. GRIMES?! OH, GOD! I'M SO SORRY!
DON'T APOLOGIZE. TELL ME WHY YOUR ZONE WASN'T CLEAR.
I'D JUST COME THROUGH HERE, BUT I DIDN'T SEE ANYTHING. WHEN I HEARD THE SHOTS--
GET OFF YOUR HORSE.
YES, SIR, MR. GRIMES.
I'M VERY SORRY--

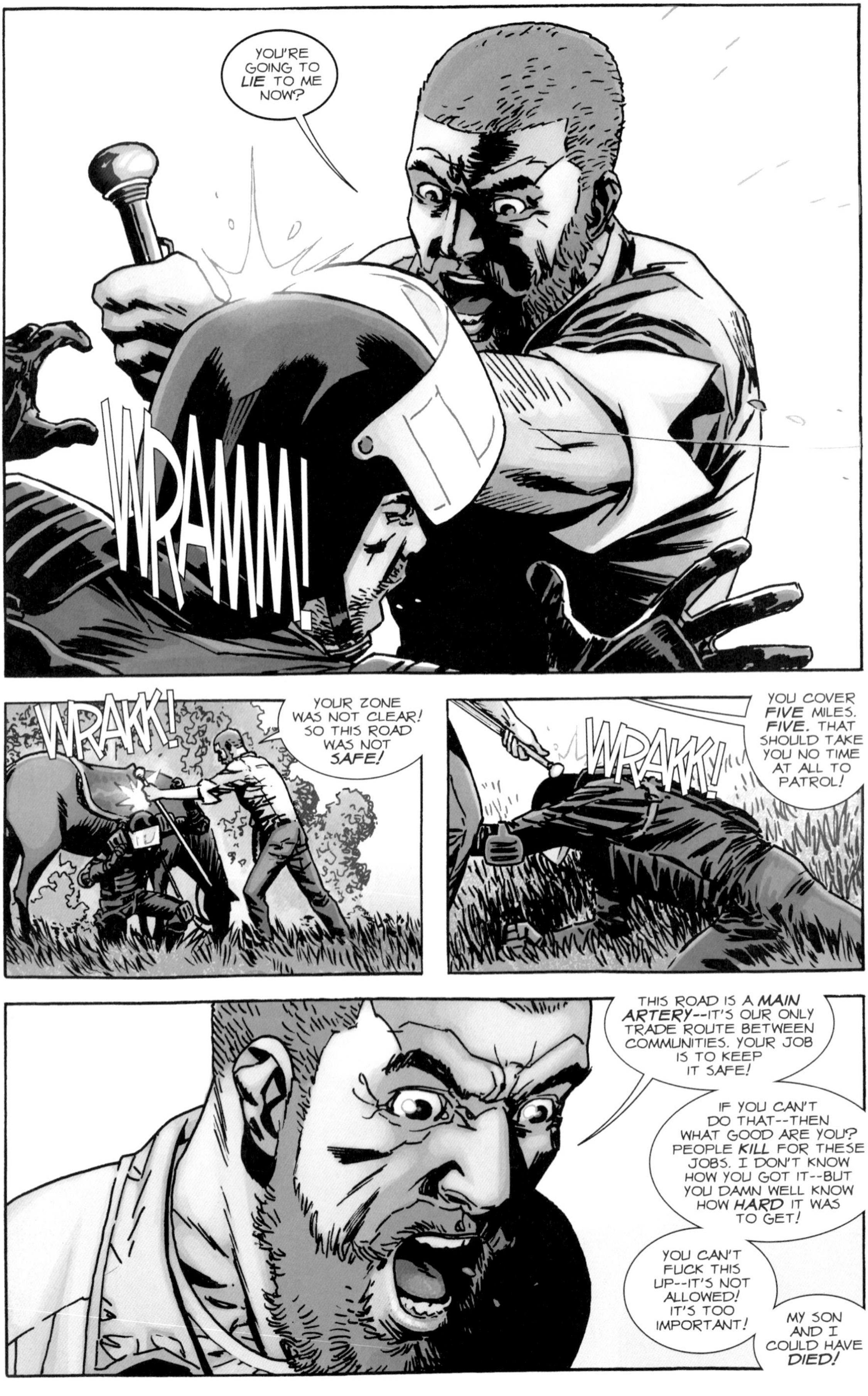

YOU'RE GOING TO LIE TO ME NOW?
WRAMM!
WRAKK!
YOUR ZONE WAS NOT CLEAR! SO THIS ROAD WAS NOT SAFE!
WRAKK!
YOU COVER FIVE MILES. FIVE. THAT SHOULD TAKE YOU NO TIME AT ALL TO PATROL!
THIS ROAD IS A MAIN ARTERY--IT'S OUR ONLY TRADE ROUTE BETWEEN COMMUNITIES. YOUR JOB IS TO KEEP IT SAFE!
IF YOU CAN'T DO THAT--THEN WHAT GOOD ARE YOU? PEOPLE KILL FOR THESE JOBS. I DON'T KNOW HOW YOU GOT IT--BUT YOU DAMN WELL KNOW HOW HARD IT WAS TO GET!
YOU CAN'T FUCK THIS UP--IT'S NOT ALLOWED! IT'S TOO IMPORTANT!
MY SON AND I COULD HAVE DIED!

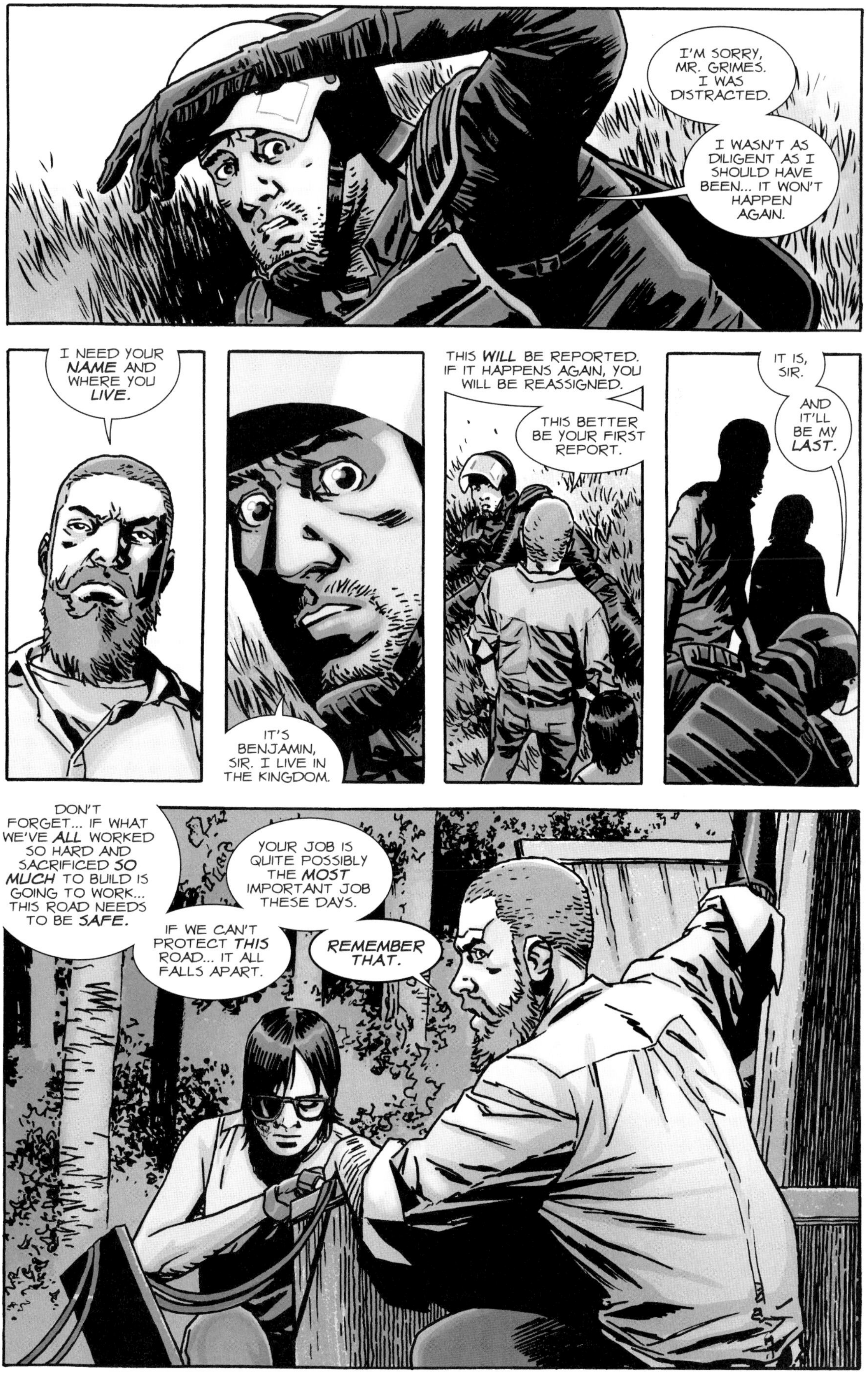

I'M SORRY, MR. GRIMES. I WAS DISTRACTED.
I WASN'T AS DILIGENT AS I SHOULD HAVE BEEN... IT WON'T HAPPEN AGAIN.
I NEED YOUR NAME AND WHERE YOU LIVE.
IT'S BENJAMIN, SIR. I LIVE IN THE KINGDOM.
THIS WILL BE REPORTED. IF IT HAPPENS AGAIN, YOU WILL BE REASSIGNED.
THIS BETTER BE YOUR FIRST REPORT.
IT IS, SIR.
AND IT'LL BE MY LAST.
DON'T FORGET... IF WHAT WE'VE ALL WORKED SO HARD AND SACRIFICED SO MUCH TO BUILD IS GOING TO WORK... THIS ROAD NEEDS TO BE SAFE.
IF WE CAN'T PROTECT THIS ROAD... IT ALL FALLS APART.
YOUR JOB IS QUITE POSSIBLY THE MOST IMPORTANT JOB THESE DAYS.
REMEMBER THAT.

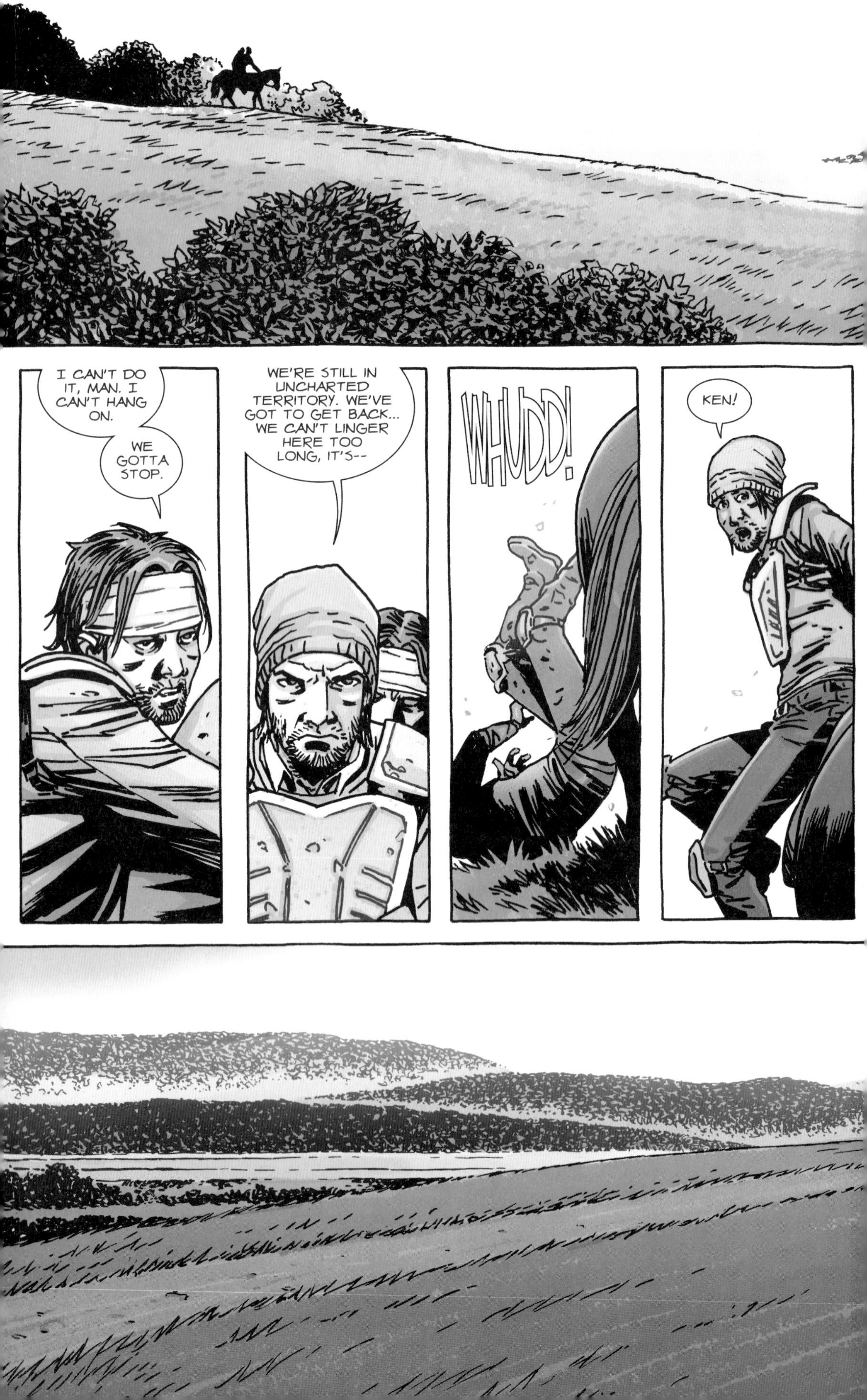
I CAN'T DO IT, MAN. I CAN'T HANG ON.
WE GOTTA STOP.
WE'RE STILL IN UNCHARTED TERRITORY. WE'VE GOT TO GET BACK... WE CAN'T LINGER HERE TOO LONG, IT'S--
WHUDD!
KEN!

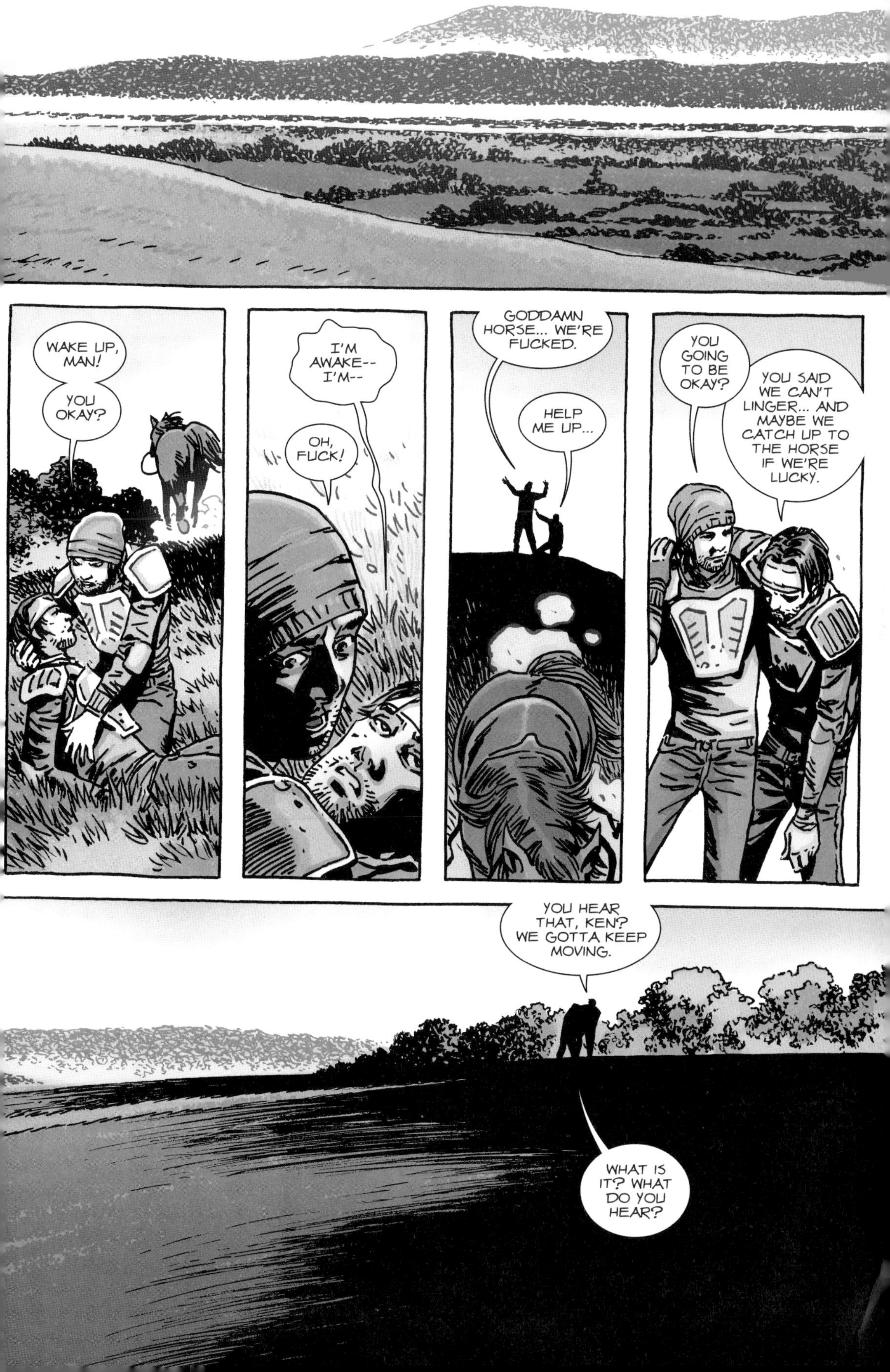
WAKE UP, MAN!
YOU OKAY?
I'M AWAKE-- I'M--
OH, FUCK!
GODDAMN HORSE... WE'RE FUCKED.
HELP ME UP...
YOU GOING TO BE OKAY?
YOU SAID WE CAN'T LINGER... AND MAYBE WE CATCH UP TO THE HORSE IF WE'RE LUCKY.
YOU HEAR THAT, KEN? WE GOTTA KEEP MOVING.
WHAT IS IT? WHAT DO YOU HEAR?

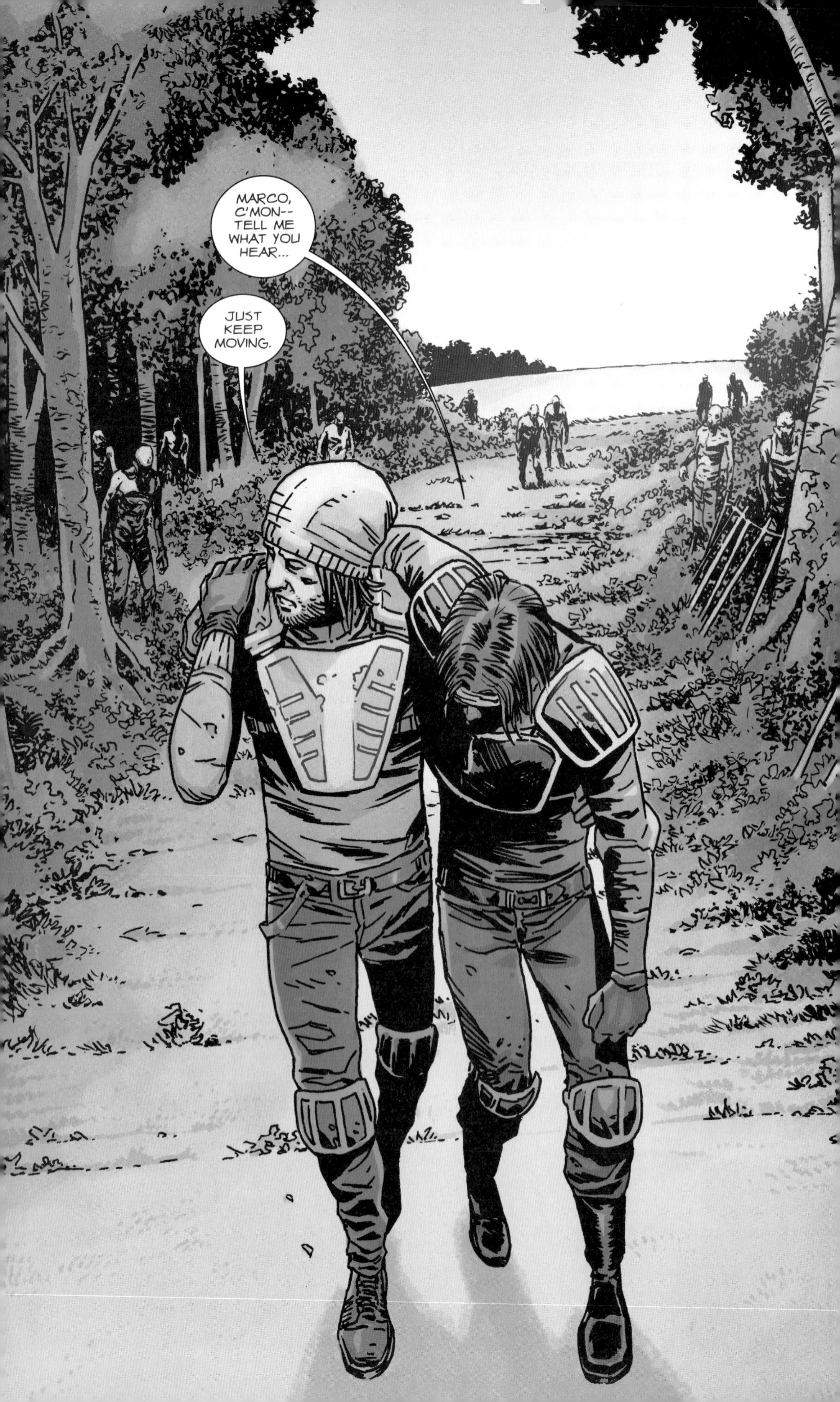
MARCO, C'MON-- TELL ME WHAT YOU HEAR...
JUST KEEP MOVING.

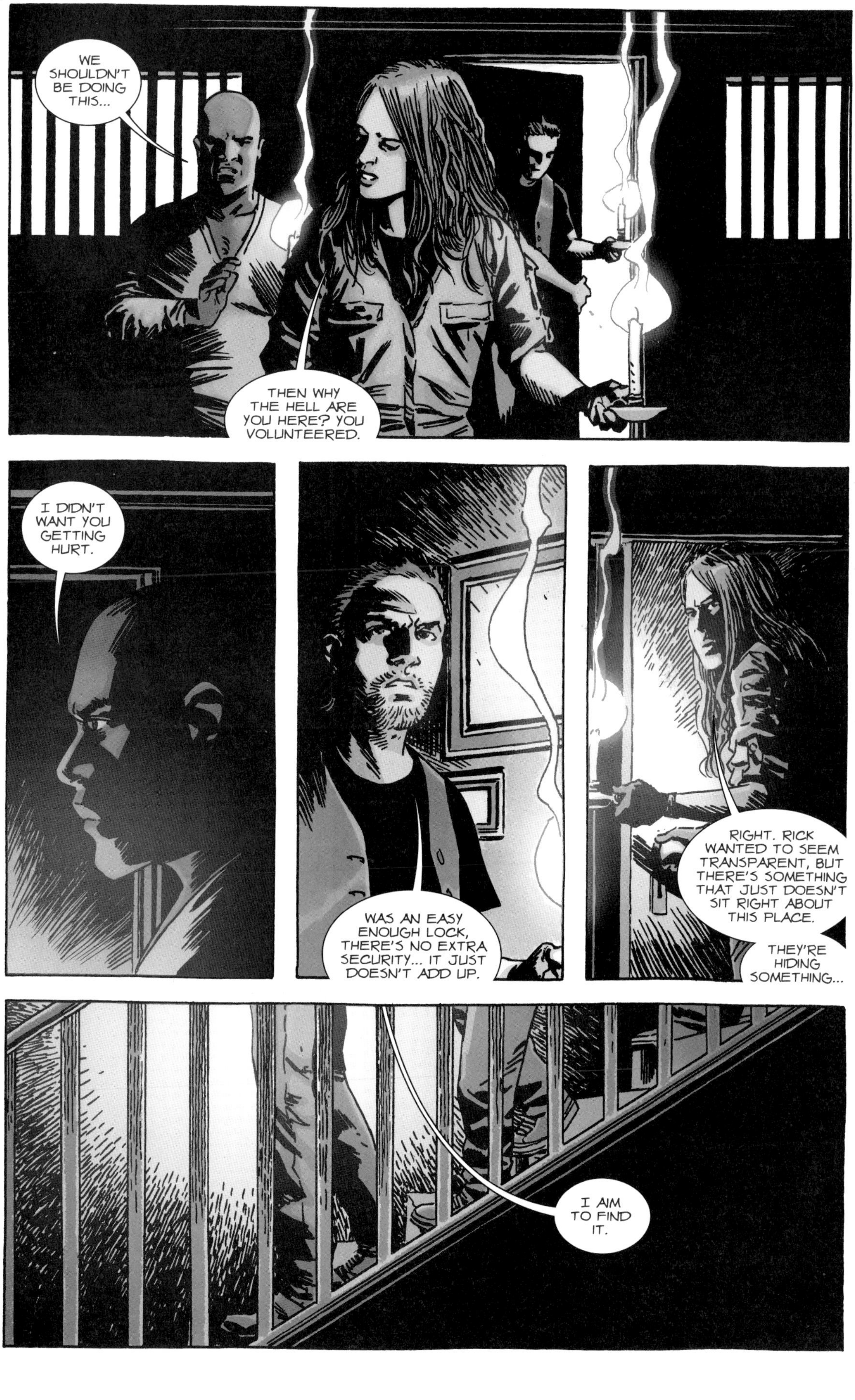
WE SHOULDN'T BE DOING THIS...
THEN WHY THE HELL ARE YOU HERE? YOU VOLUNTEERED.
I DIDN'T WANT YOU GETTING HURT.
WAS AN EASY ENOUGH LOCK, THERE'S NO EXTRA SECURITY... IT JUST DOESN'T ADD UP.
RIGHT. RICK WANTED TO SEEM TRANSPARENT, BUT THERE'S SOMETHING THAT JUST DOESN'T SIT RIGHT ABOUT THIS PLACE.
THEY'RE HIDING SOMETHING...
I AIM TO FIND IT.

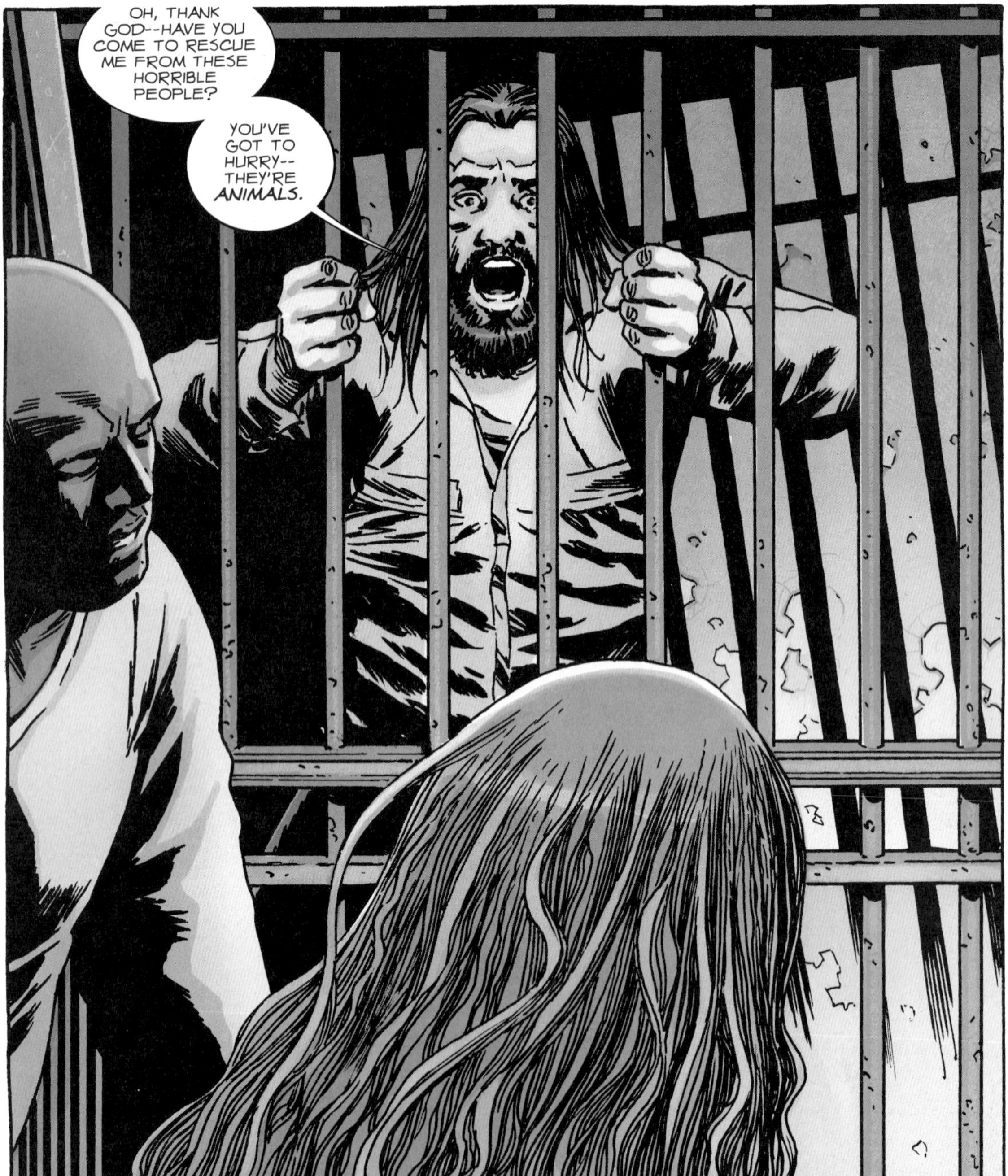
OH, THANK GOD--HAVE YOU COME TO RESCUE ME FROM THESE HORRIBLE PEOPLE?
YOU'VE GOT TO HURRY--THEY'RE *ANIMALS.*

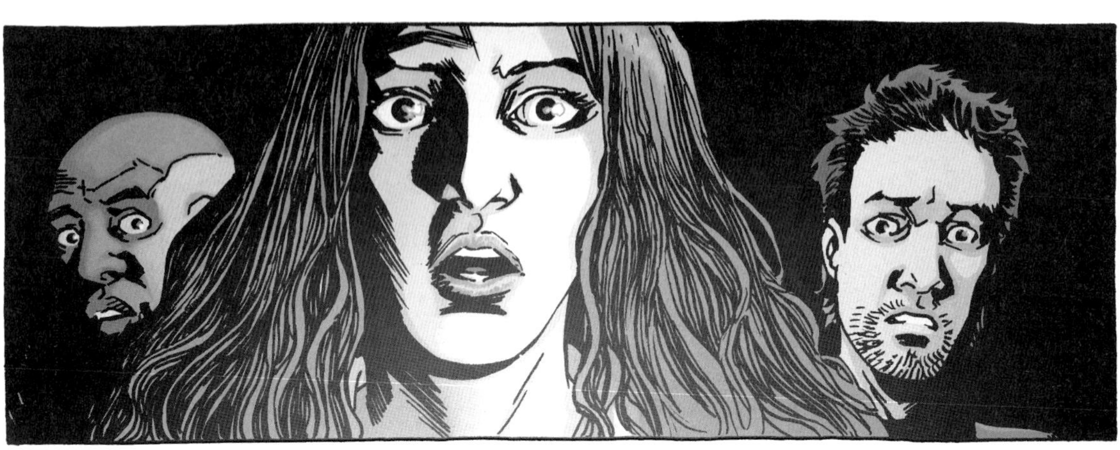

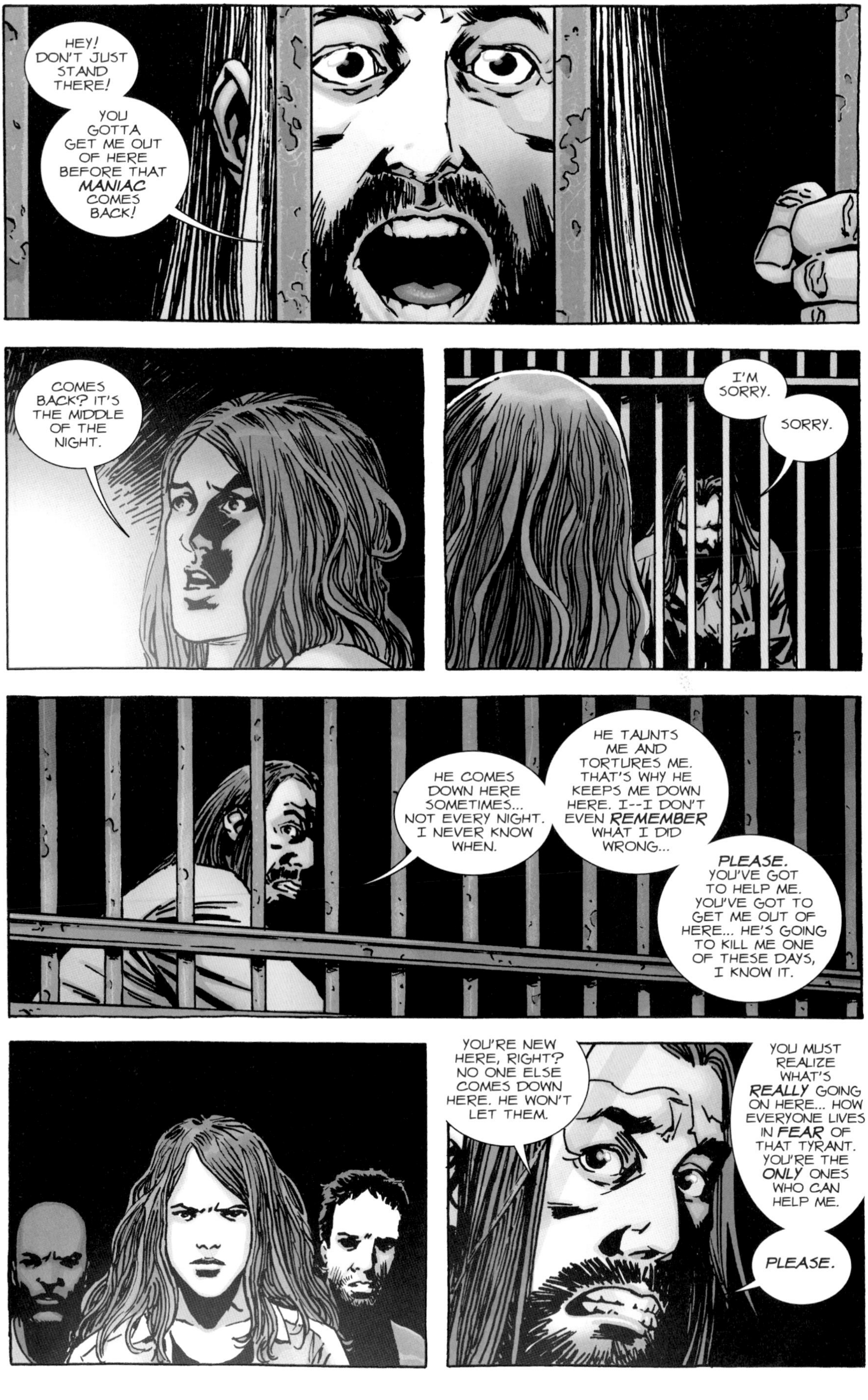
HEY! DON'T JUST STAND THERE!
YOU GOTTA GET ME OUT OF HERE BEFORE THAT MANIAC COMES BACK!
COMES BACK? IT'S THE MIDDLE OF THE NIGHT.
I'M SORRY.
SORRY.
HE COMES DOWN HERE SOMETIMES... NOT EVERY NIGHT. I NEVER KNOW WHEN.
HE TAUNTS ME AND TORTURES ME. THAT'S WHY HE KEEPS ME DOWN HERE. I--I DON'T EVEN REMEMBER WHAT I DID WRONG...
PLEASE. YOU'VE GOT TO HELP ME. YOU'VE GOT TO GET ME OUT OF HERE... HE'S GOING TO KILL ME ONE OF THESE DAYS, I KNOW IT.
YOU'RE NEW HERE, RIGHT? NO ONE ELSE COMES DOWN HERE. HE WON'T LET THEM.
YOU MUST REALIZE WHAT'S REALLY GOING ON HERE... HOW EVERYONE LIVES IN FEAR OF THAT TYRANT. YOU'RE THE ONLY ONES WHO CAN HELP ME.
PLEASE.

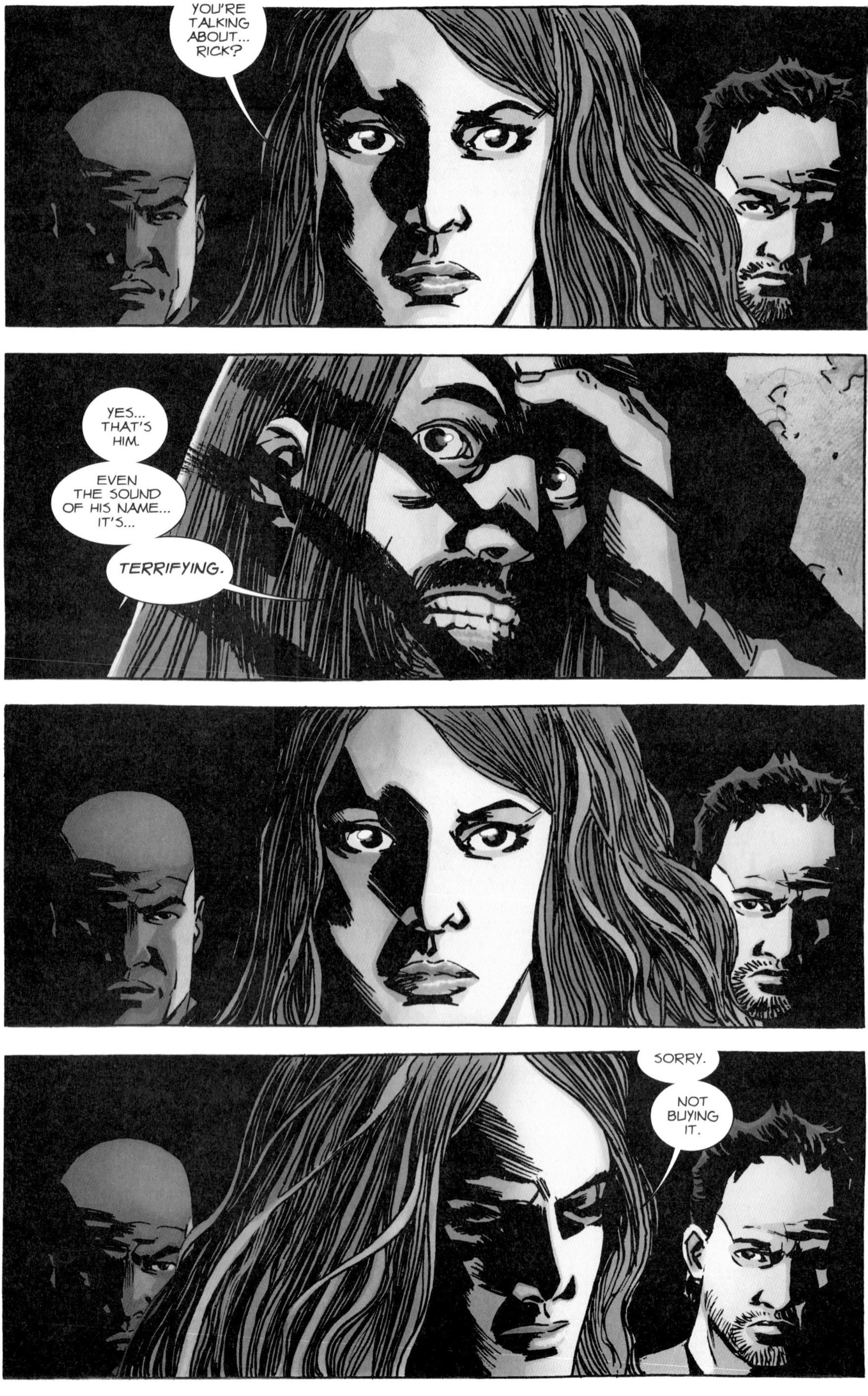
YOU'RE TALKING ABOUT... RICK?
YES... THAT'S HIM.
EVEN THE SOUND OF HIS NAME... IT'S...
TERRIFYING.
SORRY.
NOT BUYING IT.

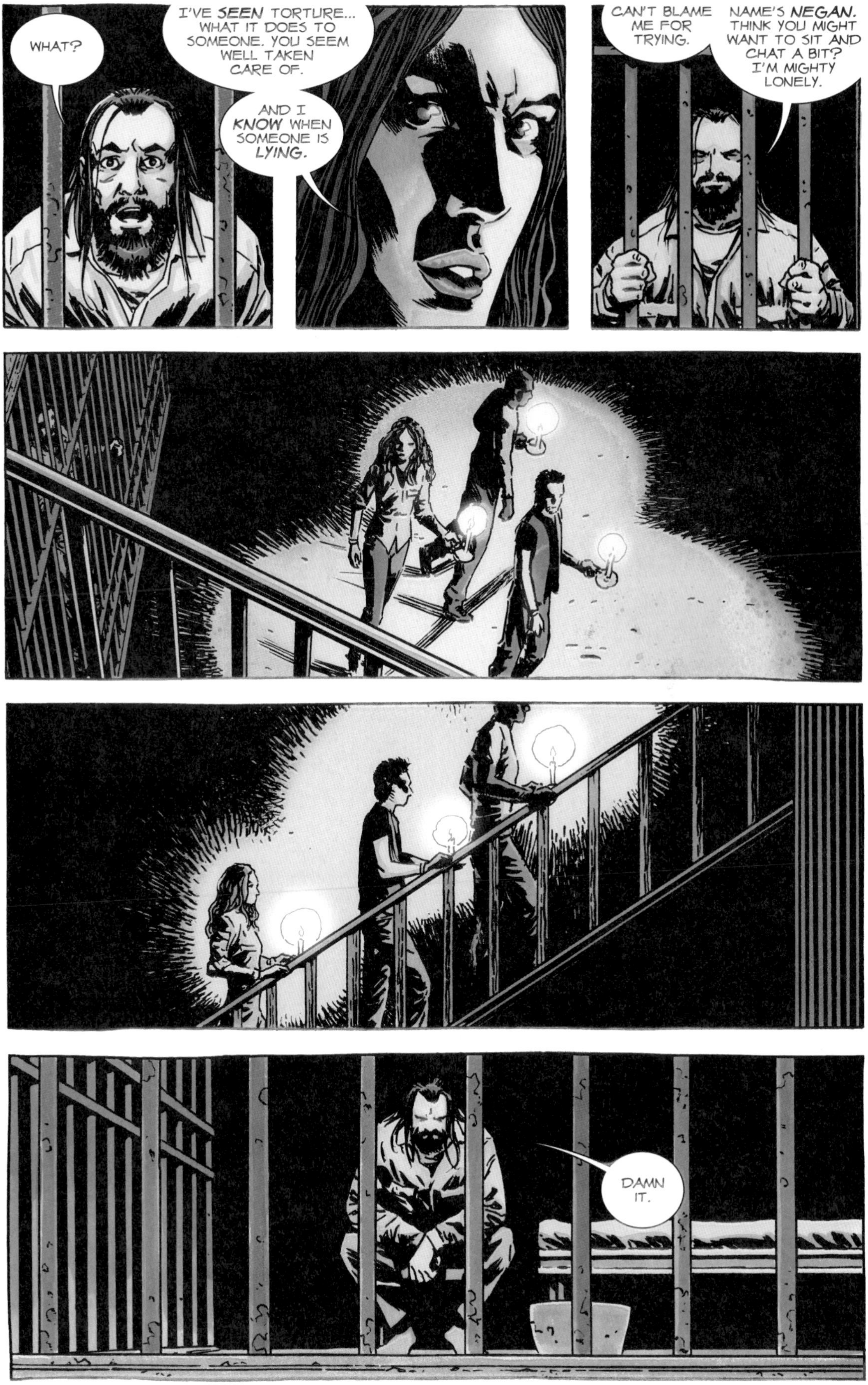
WHAT?
I'VE SEEN TORTURE... WHAT IT DOES TO SOMEONE. YOU SEEM WELL TAKEN CARE OF.
AND I KNOW WHEN SOMEONE IS LYING.
CAN'T BLAME ME FOR TRYING.
NAME'S NEGAN. THINK YOU MIGHT WANT TO SIT AND CHAT A BIT? I'M MIGHTY LONELY.
DAMN IT.

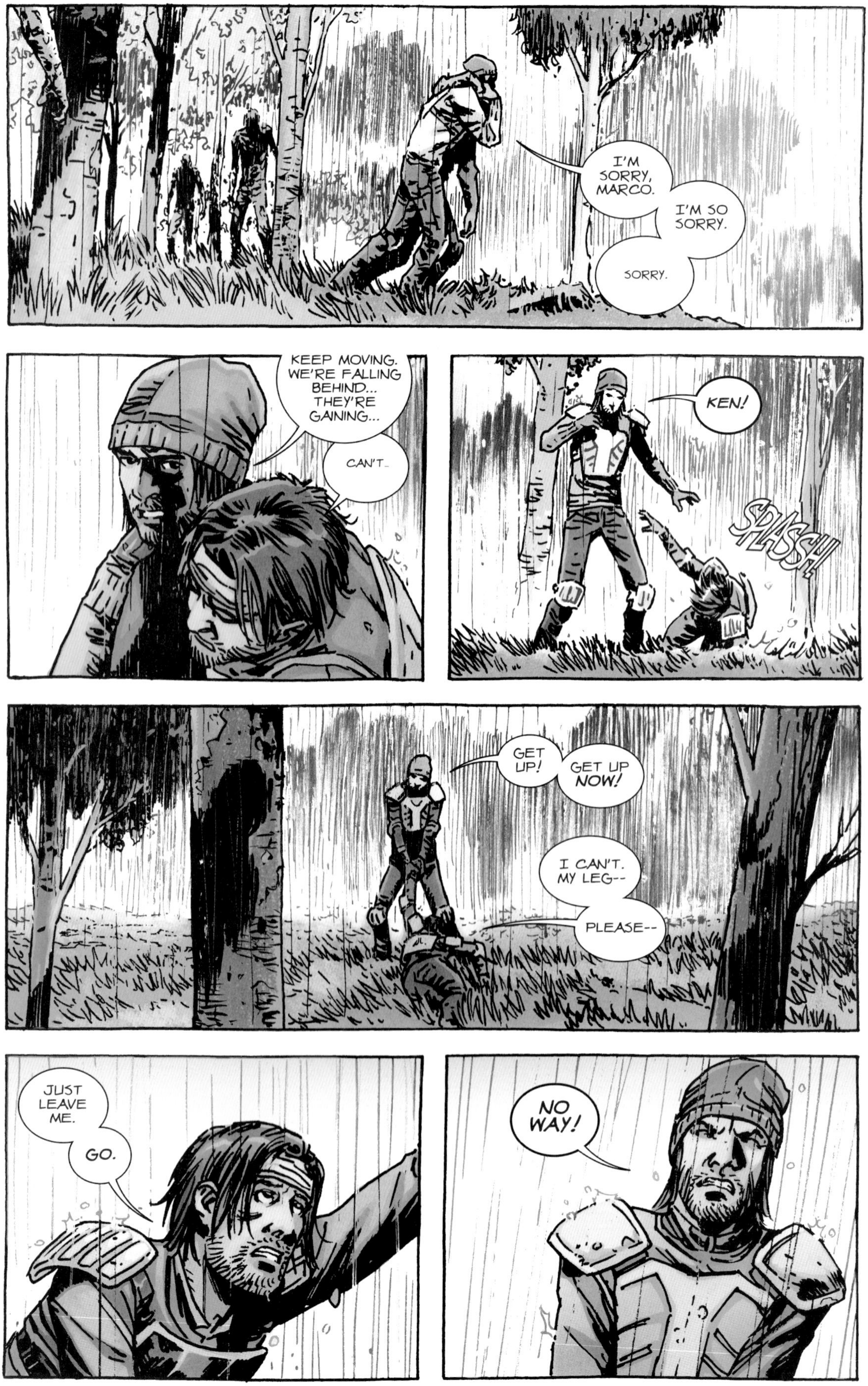
I'M SORRY, MARCO.
I'M SO SORRY.
SORRY.
KEEP MOVING. WE'RE FALLING BEHIND... THEY'RE GAINING...
CAN'T...
KEN!
SPLASSH!
GET UP!
GET UP NOW!
I CAN'T. MY LEG--
PLEASE--
JUST LEAVE ME.
GO.
NO WAY!

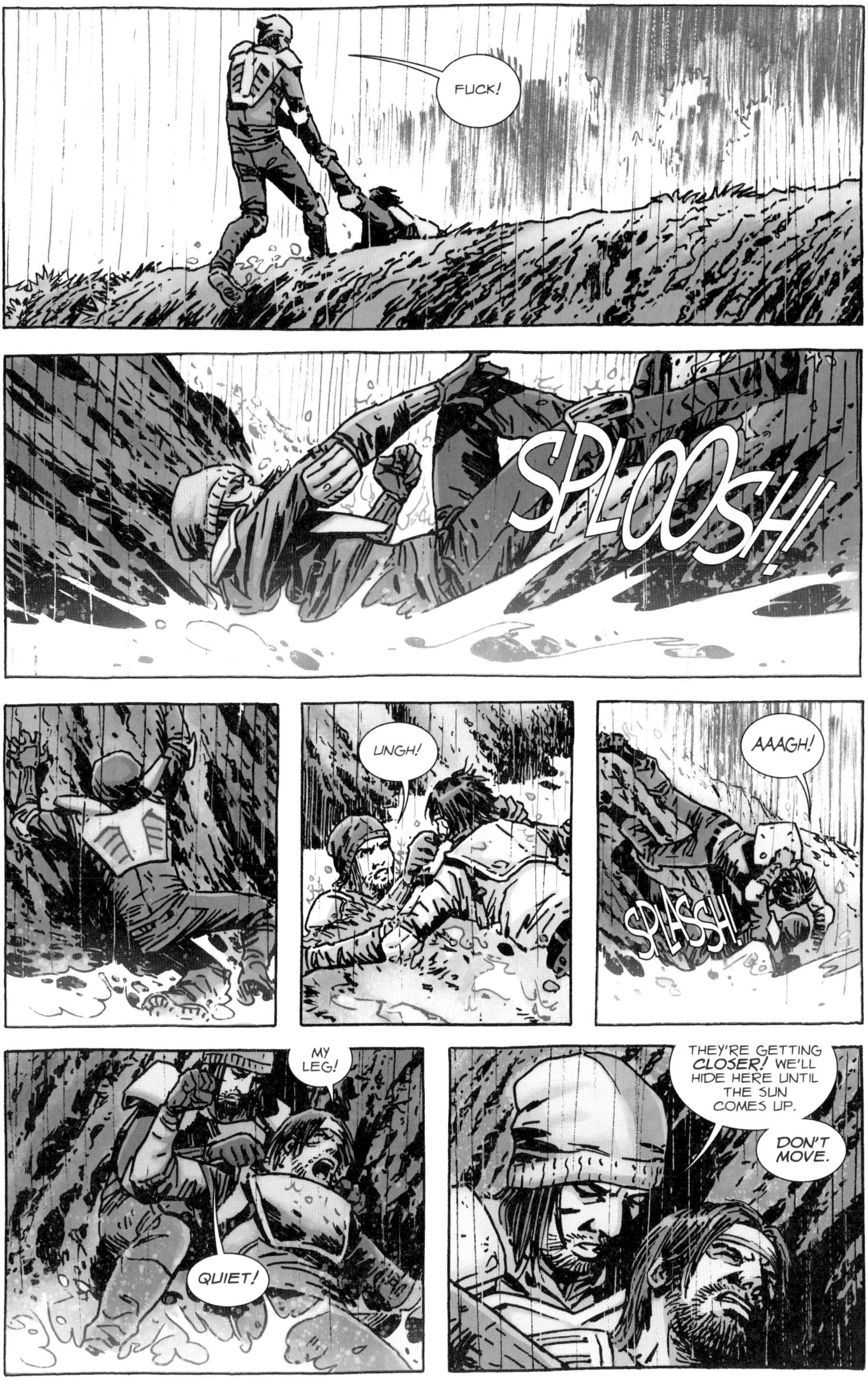
FUCK!
SPLOOSH!
UNGH!
AAAGH!
SPLASSH!
MY LEG!
QUIET!
THEY'RE GETTING CLOSER! WE'LL HIDE HERE UNTIL THE SUN COMES UP.
DON'T MOVE.

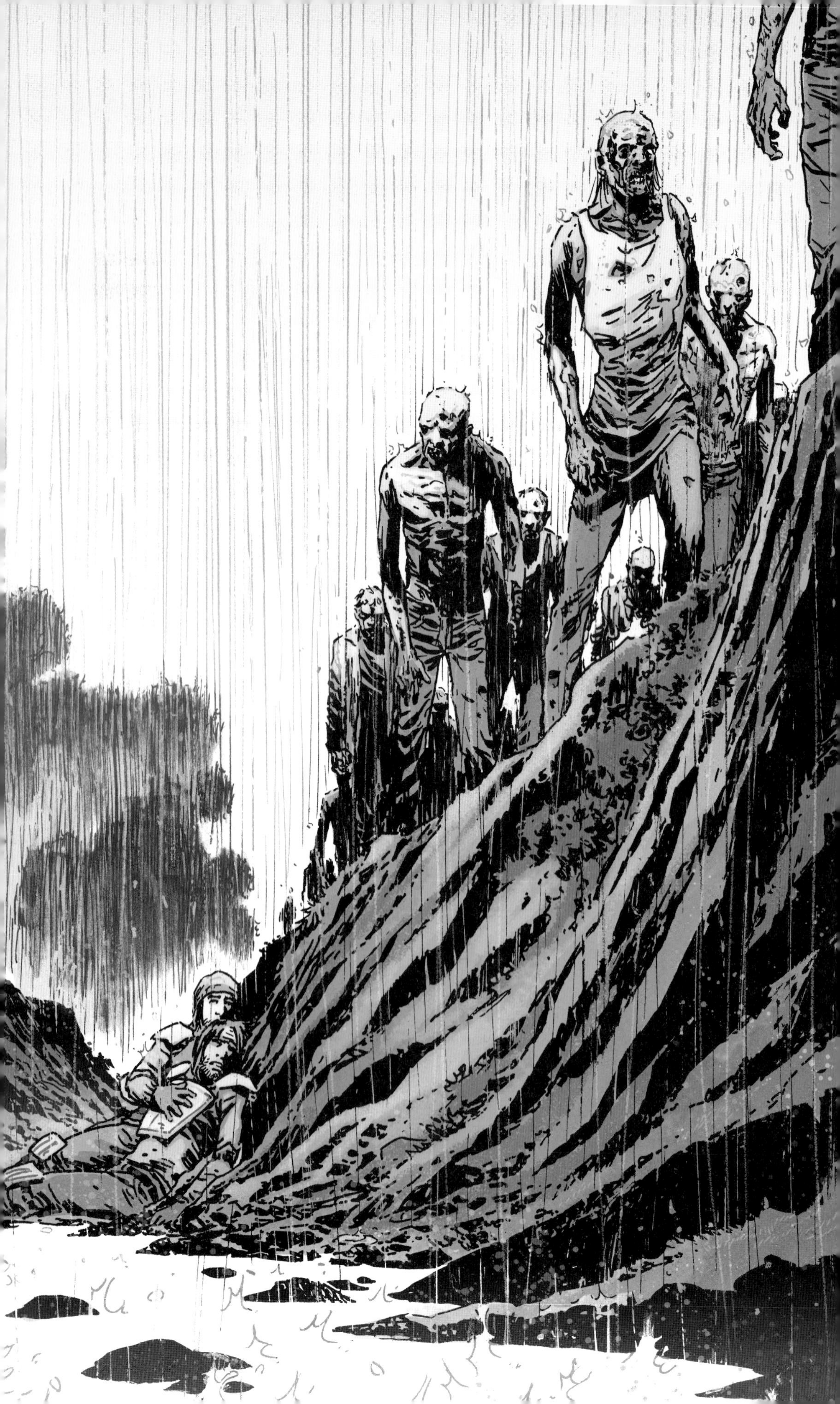

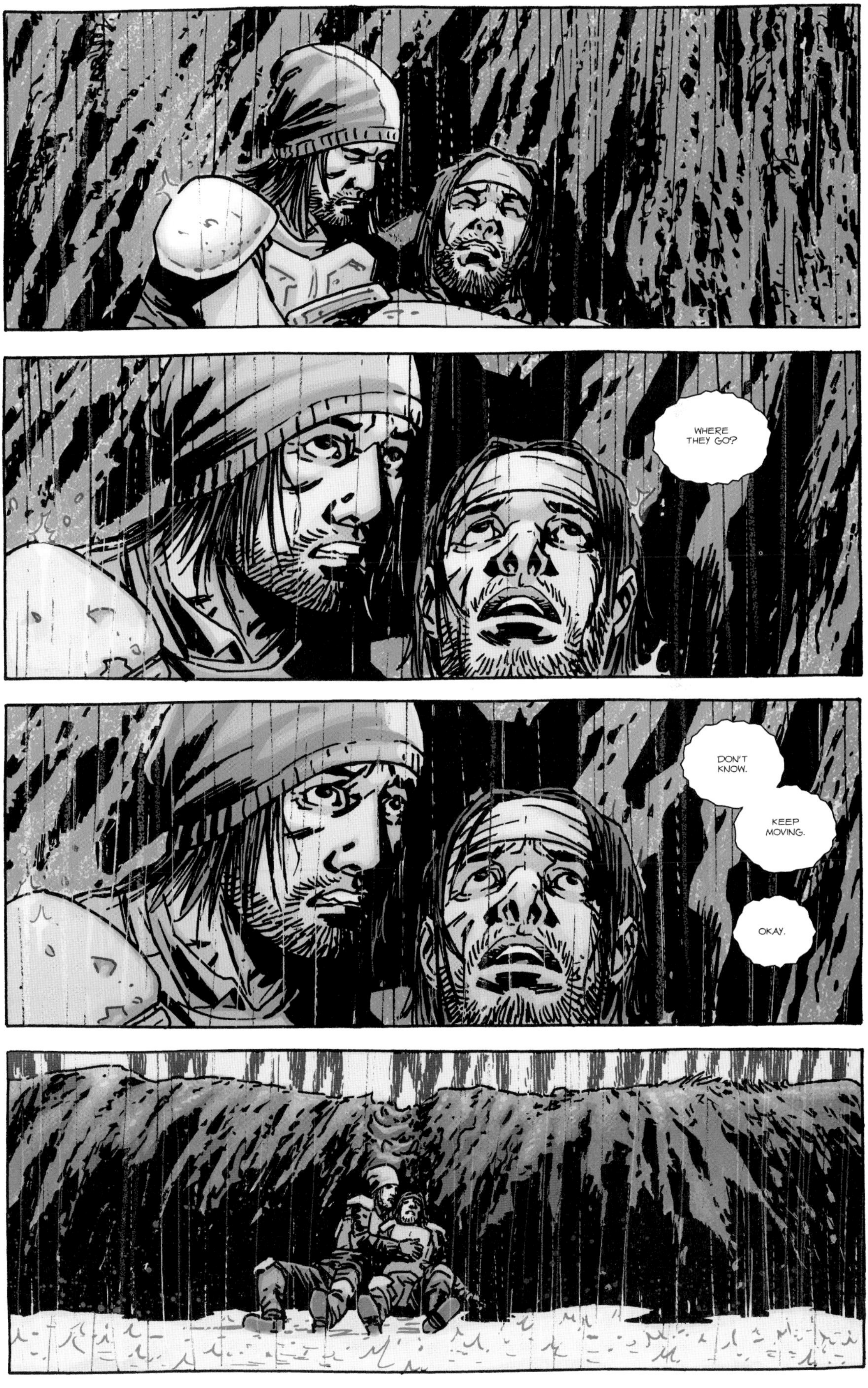
WHERE THEY GO?
DON'T KNOW.
KEEP MOVING.
OKAY.

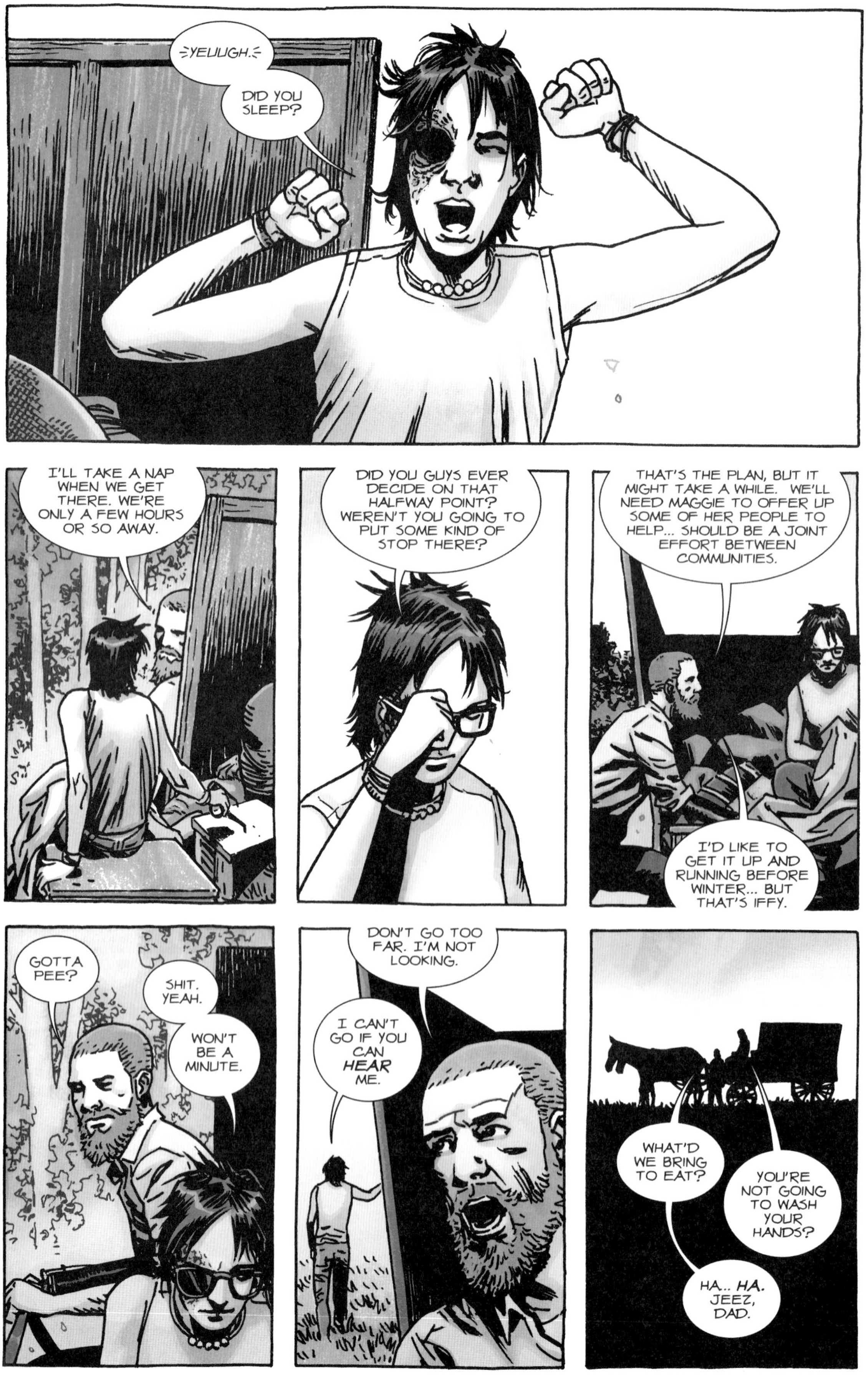
YEUUGH.
DID YOU SLEEP?
I'LL TAKE A NAP WHEN WE GET THERE. WE'RE ONLY A FEW HOURS OR SO AWAY.
DID YOU GUYS EVER DECIDE ON THAT HALFWAY POINT? WEREN'T YOU GOING TO PUT SOME KIND OF STOP THERE?
THAT'S THE PLAN, BUT IT MIGHT TAKE A WHILE. WE'LL NEED MAGGIE TO OFFER UP SOME OF HER PEOPLE TO HELP... SHOULD BE A JOINT EFFORT BETWEEN COMMUNITIES.
I'D LIKE TO GET IT UP AND RUNNING BEFORE WINTER... BUT THAT'S IFFY.
GOTTA PEE?
SHIT. YEAH.
WON'T BE A MINUTE.
DON'T GO TOO FAR. I'M NOT LOOKING.
I CAN'T GO IF YOU CAN **HEAR** ME.
WHAT'D WE BRING TO EAT?
YOU'RE NOT GOING TO WASH YOUR HANDS?
HA... **HA.** JEEZ, DAD.

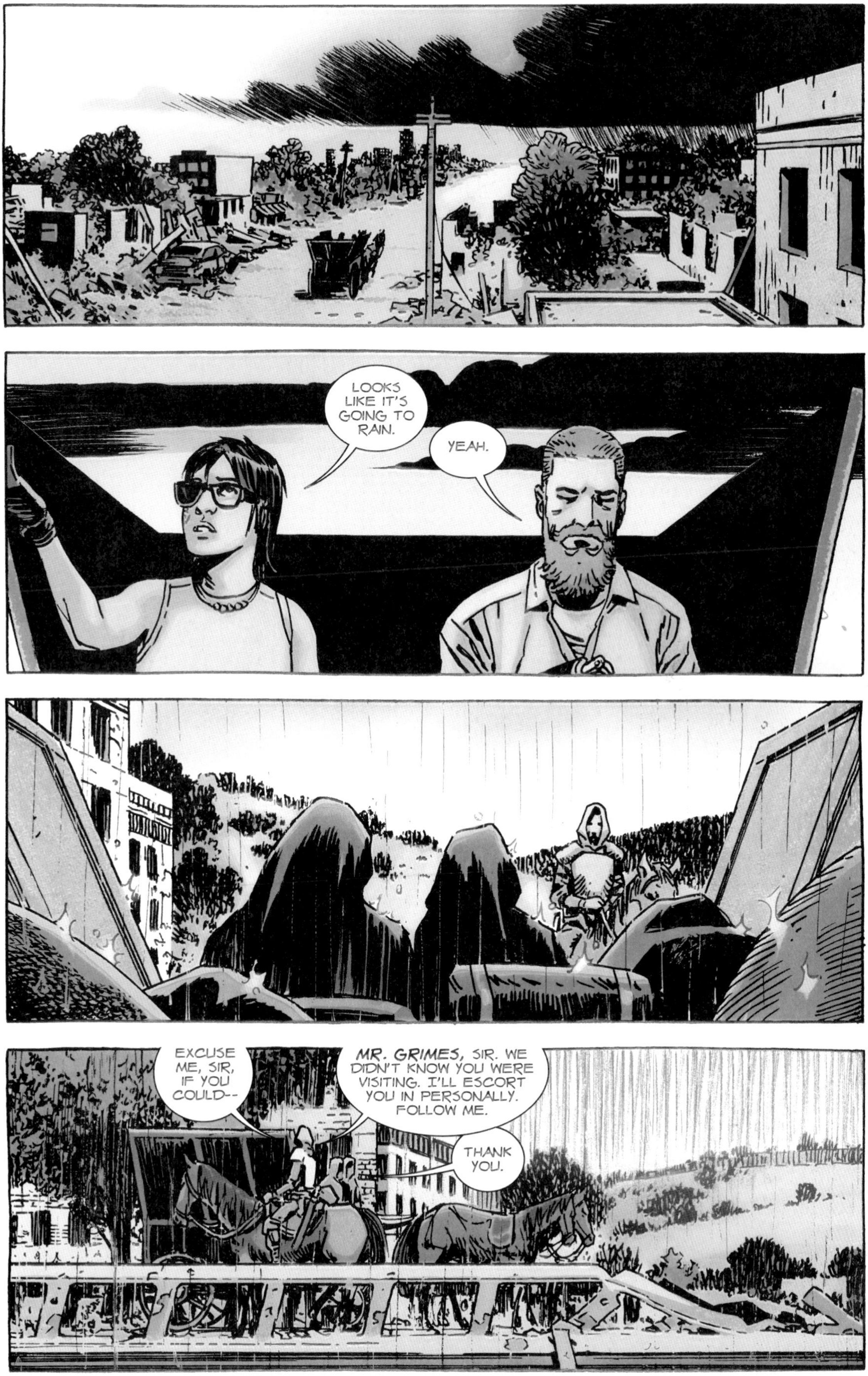
LOOKS LIKE IT'S GOING TO RAIN.
YEAH.
EXCUSE ME, SIR, IF YOU COULD--
MR. GRIMES, SIR. WE DIDN'T KNOW YOU WERE VISITING. I'LL ESCORT YOU IN PERSONALLY. FOLLOW ME.
THANK YOU.

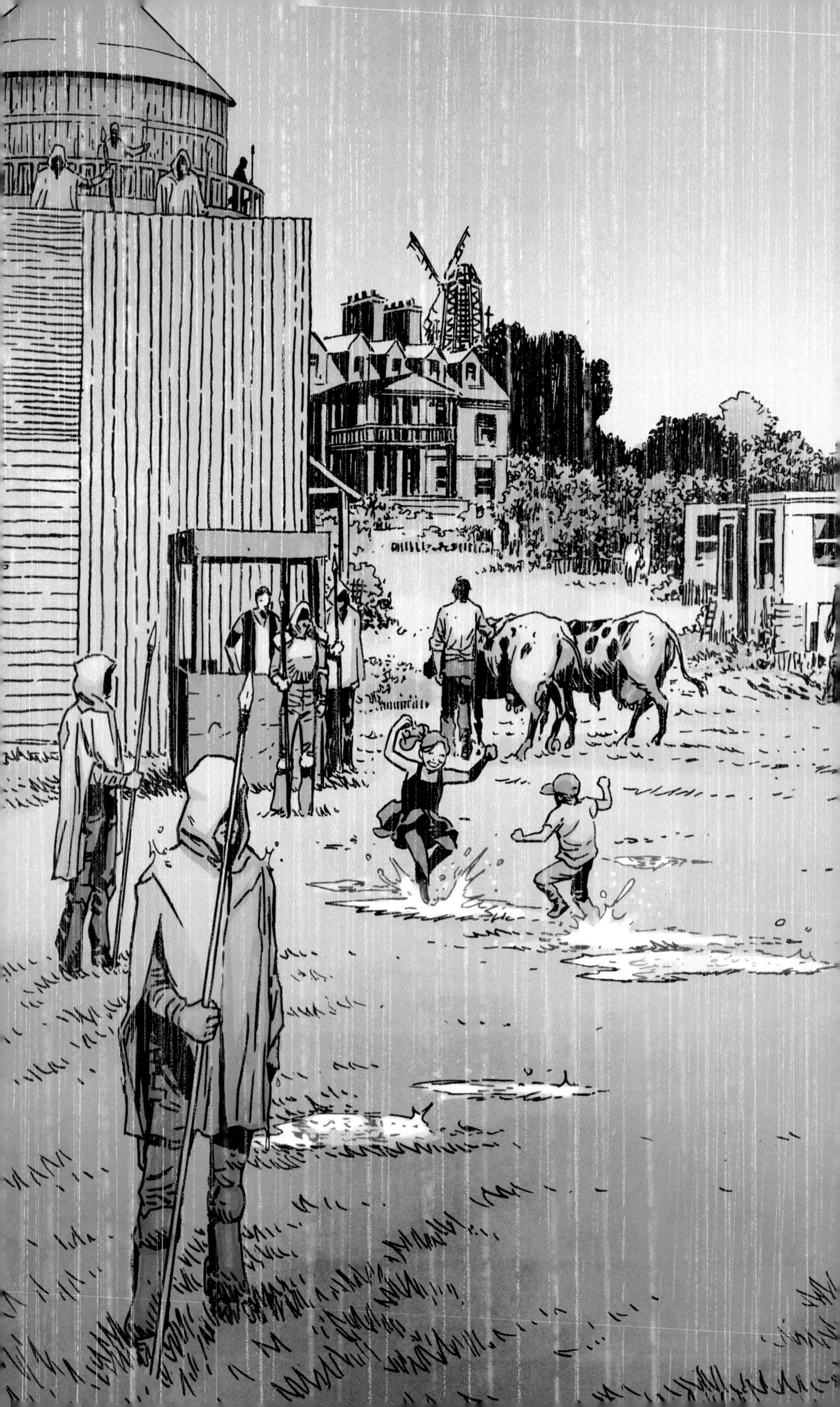

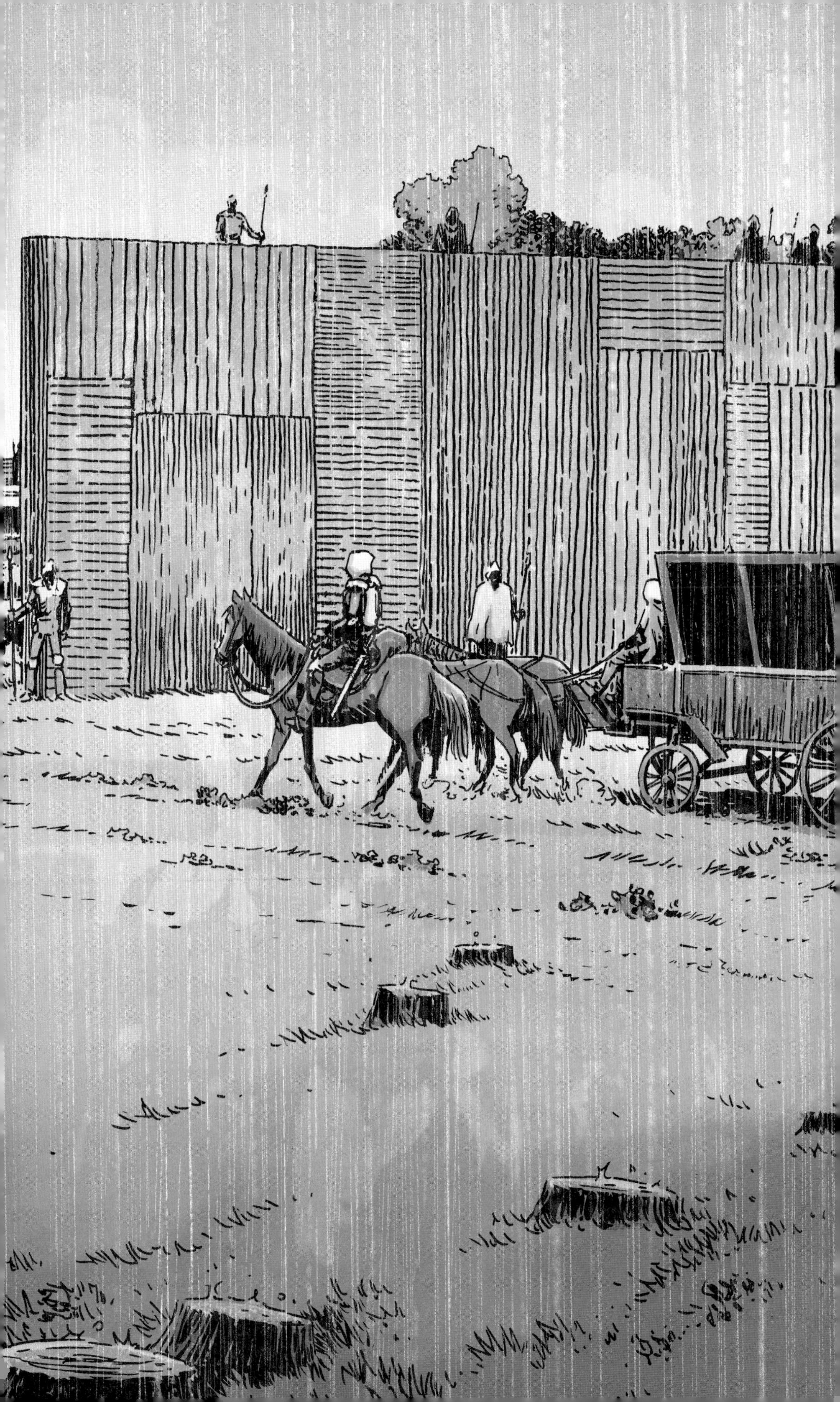

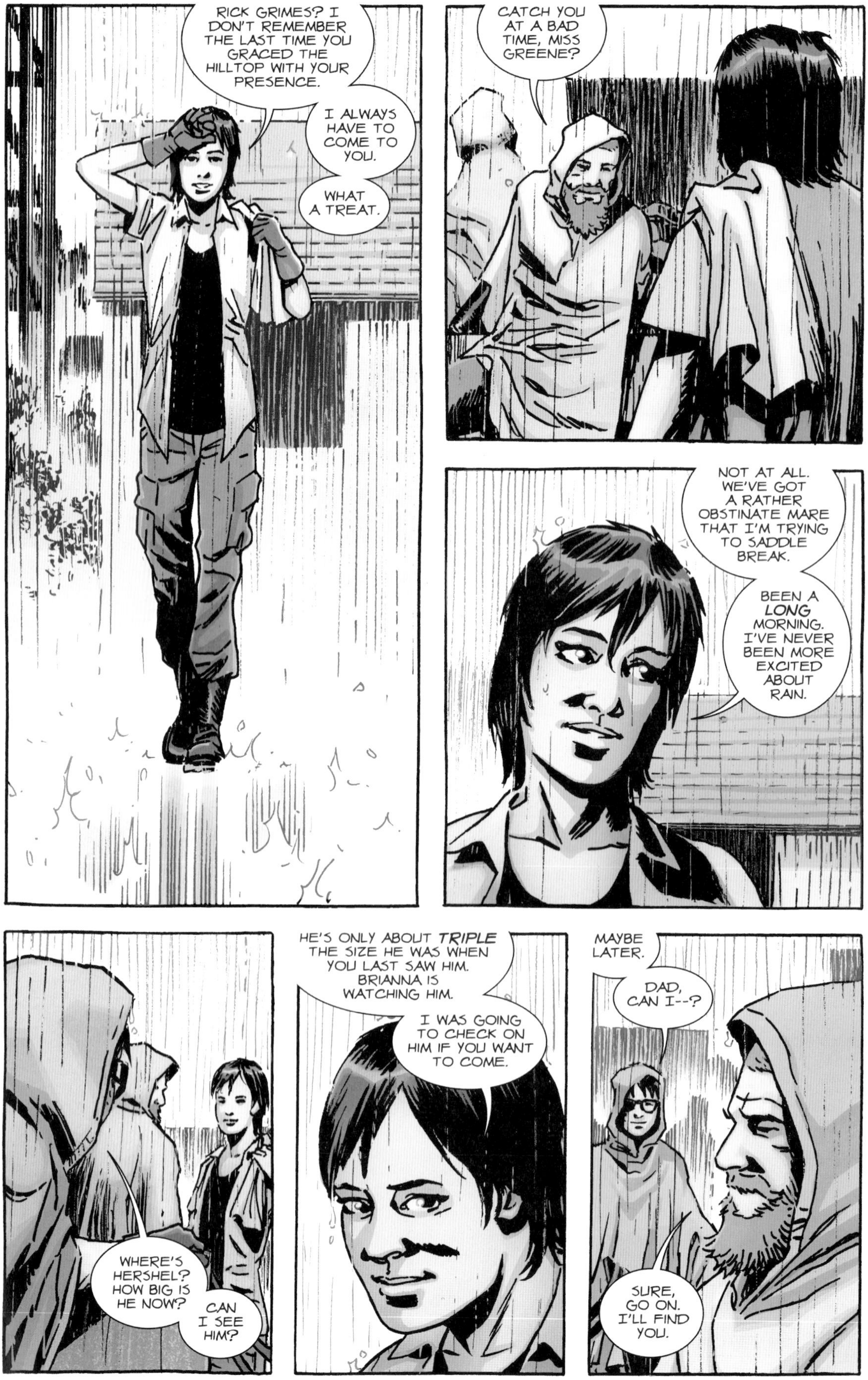

RICK GRIMES? I DON'T REMEMBER THE LAST TIME YOU GRACED THE HILLTOP WITH YOUR PRESENCE.
I ALWAYS HAVE TO COME TO YOU.
WHAT A TREAT.
CATCH YOU AT A BAD TIME, MISS GREENE?
NOT AT ALL. WE'VE GOT A RATHER OBSTINATE MARE THAT I'M TRYING TO SADDLE BREAK.
BEEN A *LONG* MORNING. I'VE NEVER BEEN MORE EXCITED ABOUT RAIN.
WHERE'S HERSHEL? HOW BIG IS HE NOW?
CAN I SEE HIM?
HE'S ONLY ABOUT *TRIPLE* THE SIZE HE WAS WHEN YOU LAST SAW HIM. BRIANNA IS WATCHING HIM.
I WAS GOING TO CHECK ON HIM IF YOU WANT TO COME.
DAD, CAN I--?
MAYBE LATER.
SURE, GO ON. I'LL FIND YOU.

WHY ARE YOU HERE?

CARL WANTS TO *LIVE* HERE, WORK WITH EARL. HE WANTS TO BECOME A BLACKSMITH.

THAT'S A GOOD TRADE FOR HIM. THAT'S *GREAT.*

WAIT-- SO YOU'RE MOVING HERE?

YOU KNOW I CAN'T DO THAT.

OH...

OH!

YEAH.

AND YOU'RE OKAY WITH THAT?

NOT EVEN A LITTLE BIT. I'M ACTUALLY DAMN NEAR *COMPLETELY* TERRIFIED.

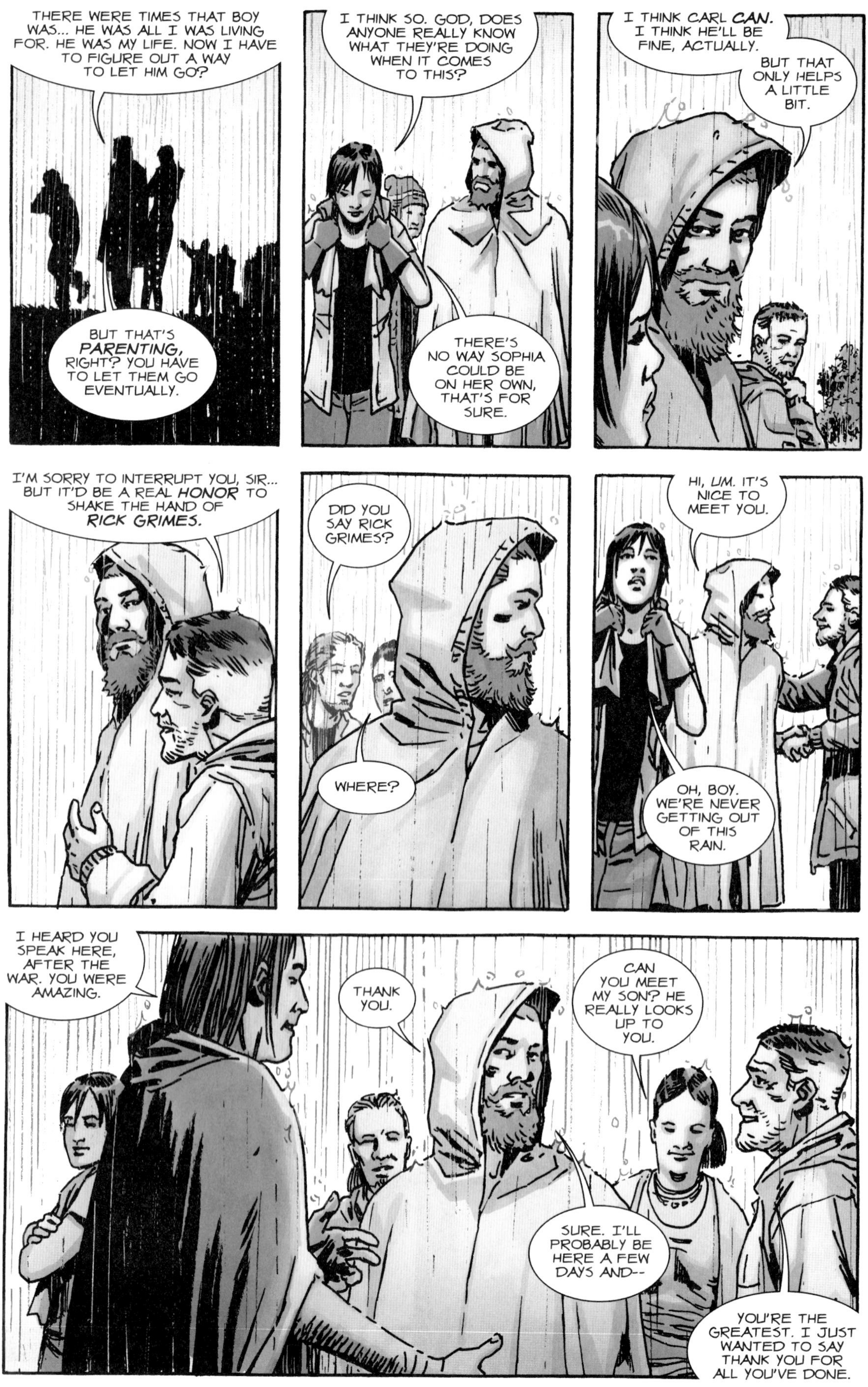
THERE WERE TIMES THAT BOY WAS... HE WAS ALL I WAS LIVING FOR. HE WAS MY LIFE. NOW I HAVE TO FIGURE OUT A WAY TO LET HIM GO?
BUT THAT'S PARENTING, RIGHT? YOU HAVE TO LET THEM GO EVENTUALLY.
I THINK SO. GOD, DOES ANYONE REALLY KNOW WHAT THEY'RE DOING WHEN IT COMES TO THIS?
THERE'S NO WAY SOPHIA COULD BE ON HER OWN, THAT'S FOR SURE.
I THINK CARL CAN. I THINK HE'LL BE FINE, ACTUALLY.
BUT THAT ONLY HELPS A LITTLE BIT.
I'M SORRY TO INTERRUPT YOU, SIR... BUT IT'D BE A REAL HONOR TO SHAKE THE HAND OF RICK GRIMES.
DID YOU SAY RICK GRIMES?
WHERE?
HI, UM. IT'S NICE TO MEET YOU.
OH, BOY. WE'RE NEVER GETTING OUT OF THIS RAIN.
I HEARD YOU SPEAK HERE, AFTER THE WAR. YOU WERE AMAZING.
THANK YOU.
CAN YOU MEET MY SON? HE REALLY LOOKS UP TO YOU.
SURE. I'LL PROBABLY BE HERE A FEW DAYS AND--
YOU'RE THE GREATEST. I JUST WANTED TO SAY THANK YOU FOR ALL YOU'VE DONE.

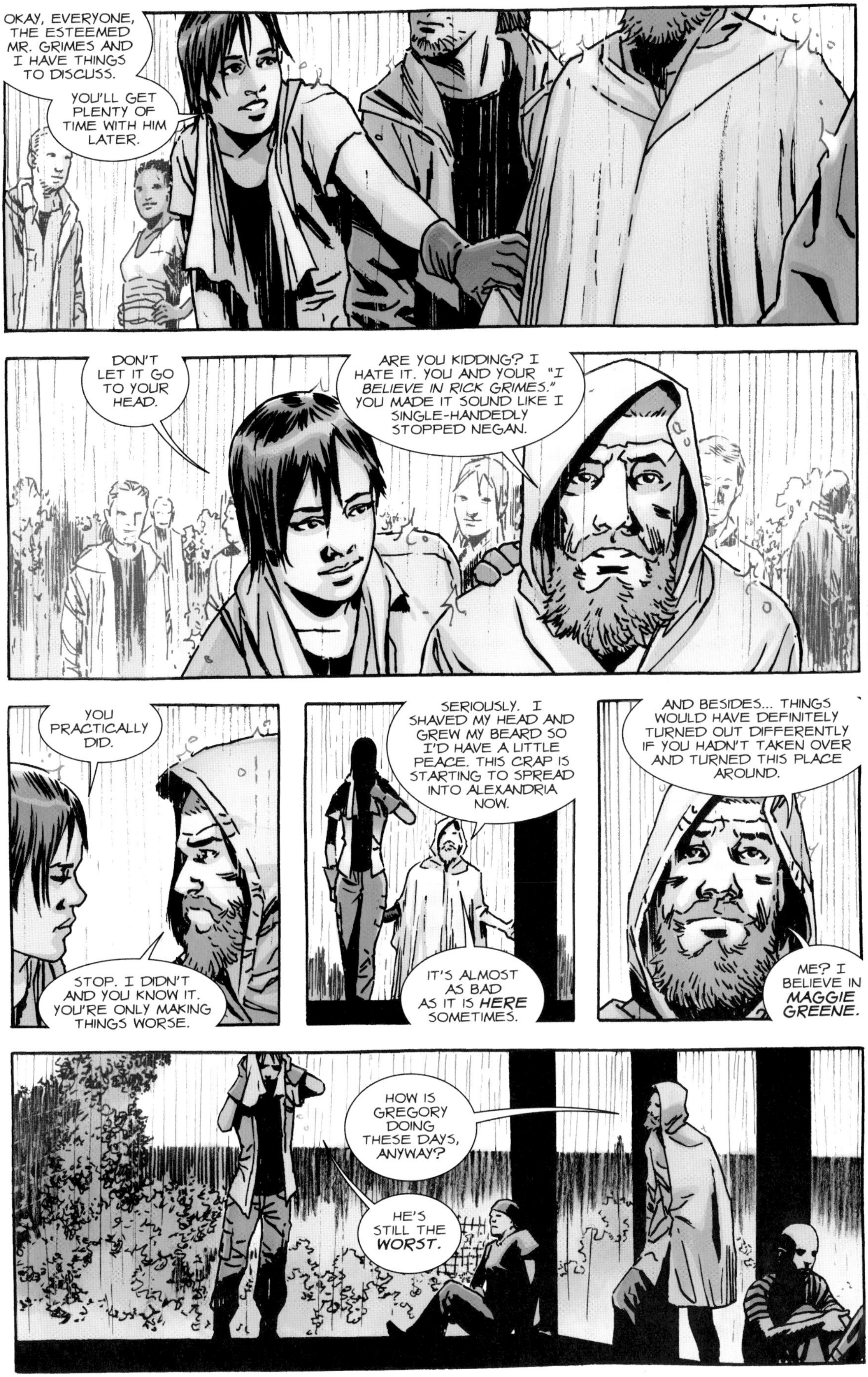
OKAY, EVERYONE, THE ESTEEMED MR. GRIMES AND I HAVE THINGS TO DISCUSS.
YOU'LL GET PLENTY OF TIME WITH HIM LATER.
DON'T LET IT GO TO YOUR HEAD.
ARE YOU KIDDING? I HATE IT. YOU AND YOUR "I *BELIEVE IN RICK GRIMES.*" YOU MADE IT SOUND LIKE I SINGLE-HANDEDLY STOPPED NEGAN.
YOU PRACTICALLY DID.
STOP. I DIDN'T AND YOU KNOW IT. YOU'RE ONLY MAKING THINGS WORSE.
SERIOUSLY. I SHAVED MY HEAD AND GREW MY BEARD SO I'D HAVE A LITTLE PEACE. THIS CRAP IS STARTING TO SPREAD INTO ALEXANDRIA NOW.
IT'S ALMOST AS BAD AS IT IS ***HERE*** SOMETIMES.
AND BESIDES... THINGS WOULD HAVE DEFINITELY TURNED OUT DIFFERENTLY IF YOU HADN'T TAKEN OVER AND TURNED THIS PLACE AROUND.
ME? I BELIEVE IN ***MAGGIE GREENE.***
HOW IS GREGORY DOING THESE DAYS, ANYWAY?
HE'S STILL THE ***WORST.***

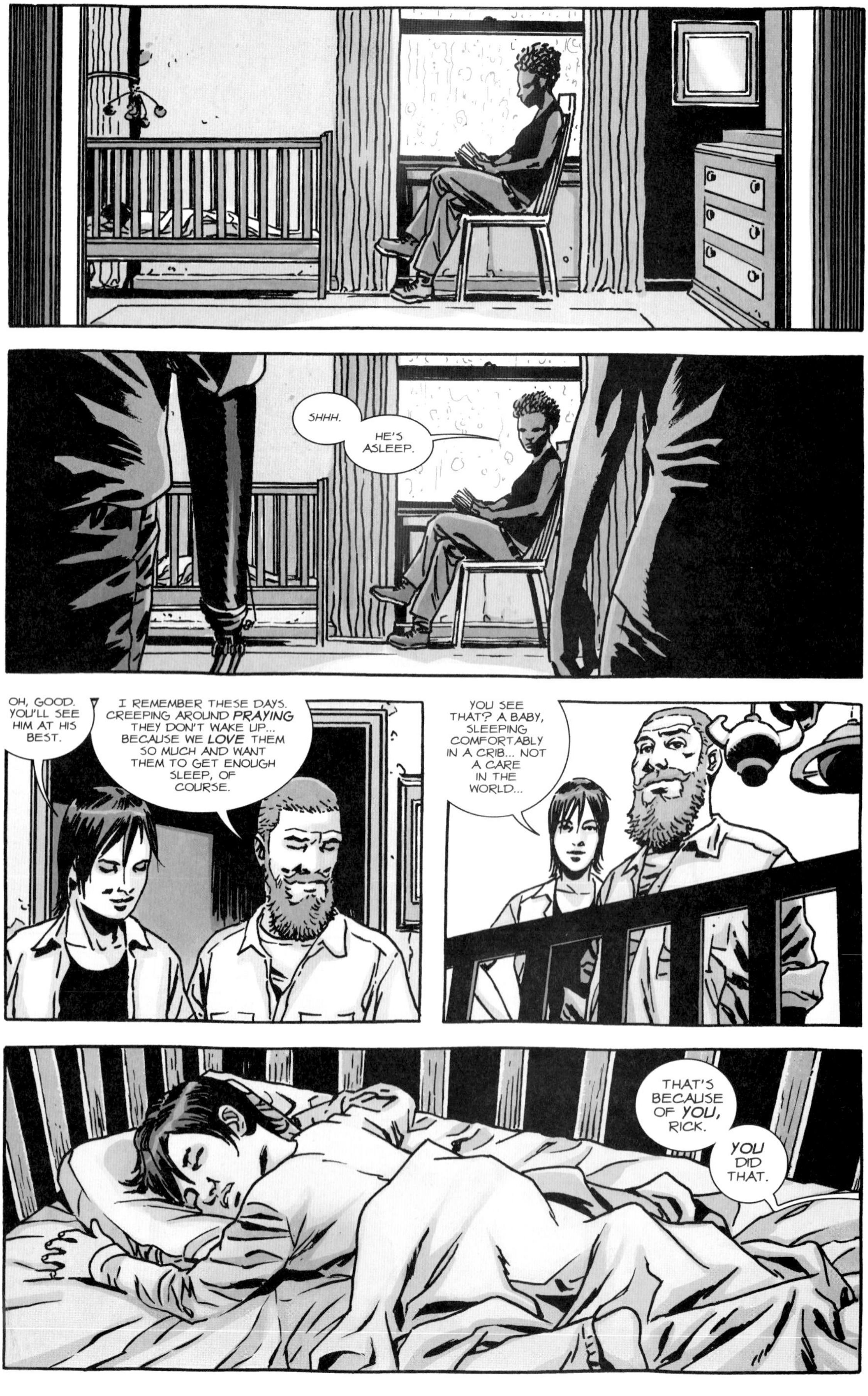

SHHH.
HE'S ASLEEP.
OH, GOOD. YOU'LL SEE HIM AT HIS BEST.
I REMEMBER THESE DAYS. CREEPING AROUND PRAYING THEY DON'T WAKE UP... BECAUSE WE LOVE THEM SO MUCH AND WANT THEM TO GET ENOUGH SLEEP, OF COURSE.
YOU SEE THAT? A BABY, SLEEPING COMFORTABLY IN A CRIB... NOT A CARE IN THE WORLD...
THAT'S BECAUSE OF YOU, RICK.
YOU DID THAT.

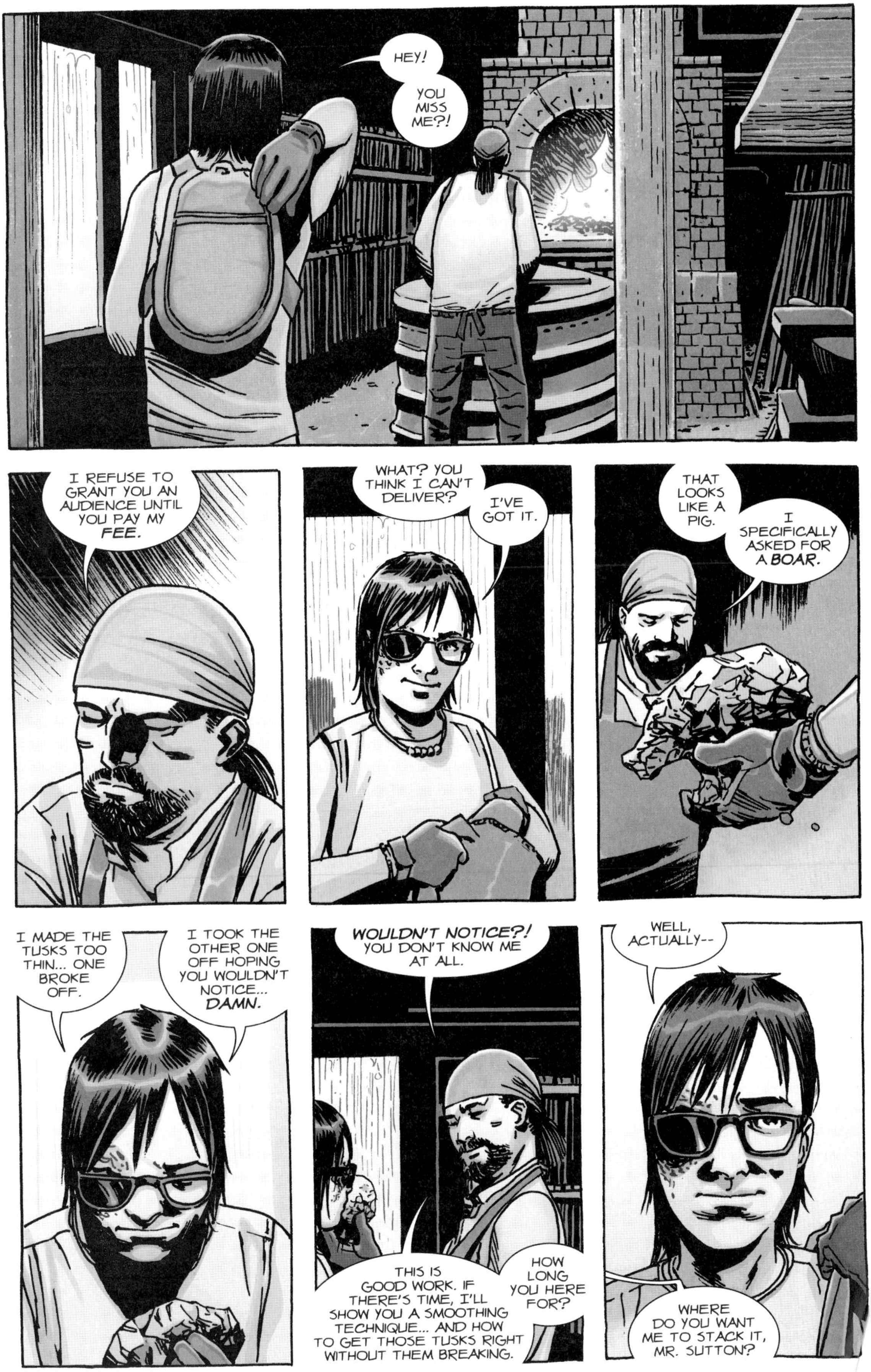
HEY!
YOU MISS ME?!
I REFUSE TO GRANT YOU AN AUDIENCE UNTIL YOU PAY MY FEE.
WHAT? YOU THINK I CAN'T DELIVER?
I'VE GOT IT.
THAT LOOKS LIKE A PIG.
I SPECIFICALLY ASKED FOR A BOAR.
I MADE THE TUSKS TOO THIN... ONE BROKE OFF.
I TOOK THE OTHER ONE OFF HOPING YOU WOULDN'T NOTICE... DAMN.
WOULDN'T NOTICE?! YOU DON'T KNOW ME AT ALL.
THIS IS GOOD WORK. IF THERE'S TIME, I'LL SHOW YOU A SMOOTHING TECHNIQUE... AND HOW TO GET THOSE TUSKS RIGHT WITHOUT THEM BREAKING.
HOW LONG YOU HERE FOR?
WELL, ACTUALLY--
WHERE DO YOU WANT ME TO STACK IT, MR. SUTTON?

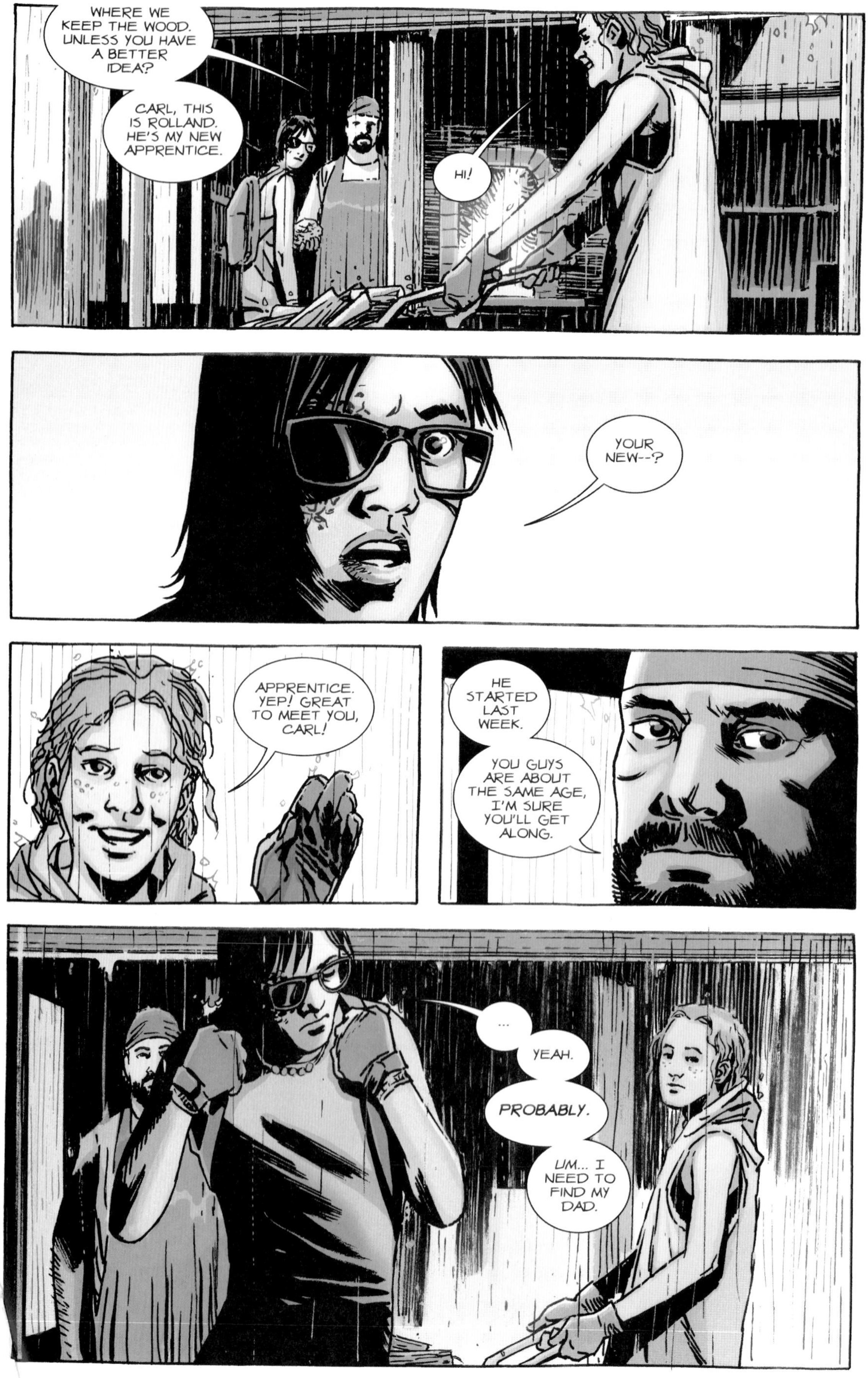
WHERE WE KEEP THE WOOD. UNLESS YOU HAVE A BETTER IDEA?
CARL, THIS IS ROLLAND. HE'S MY NEW APPRENTICE.
HI!
YOUR NEW--?
APPRENTICE. YEP! GREAT TO MEET YOU, CARL!
HE STARTED LAST WEEK.
YOU GUYS ARE ABOUT THE SAME AGE, I'M SURE YOU'LL GET ALONG.
...
YEAH.
PROBABLY.
UM... I NEED TO FIND MY DAD.

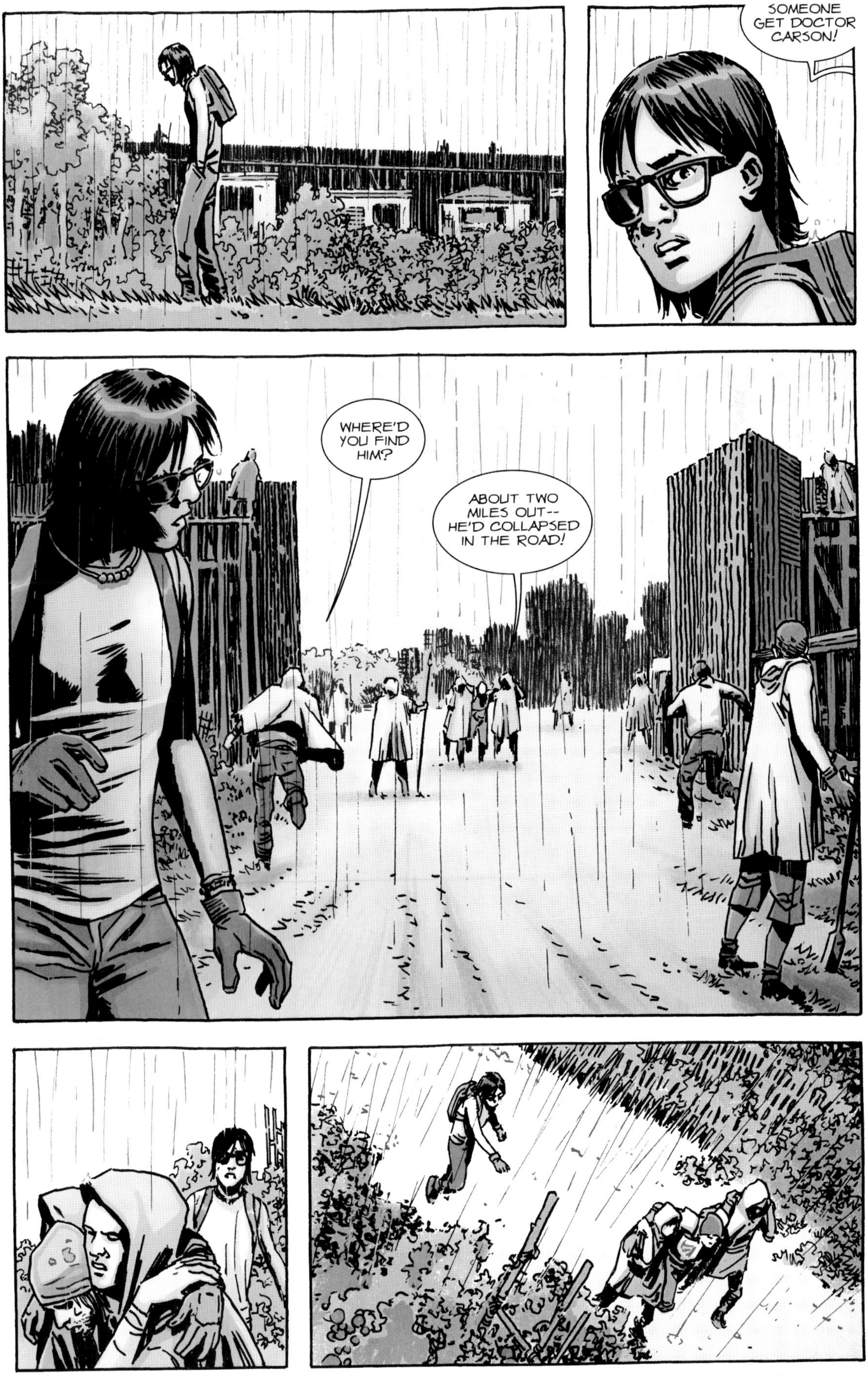
SOMEONE GET DOCTOR CARSON!
WHERE'D YOU FIND HIM?
ABOUT TWO MILES OUT-- HE'D COLLAPSED IN THE ROAD!

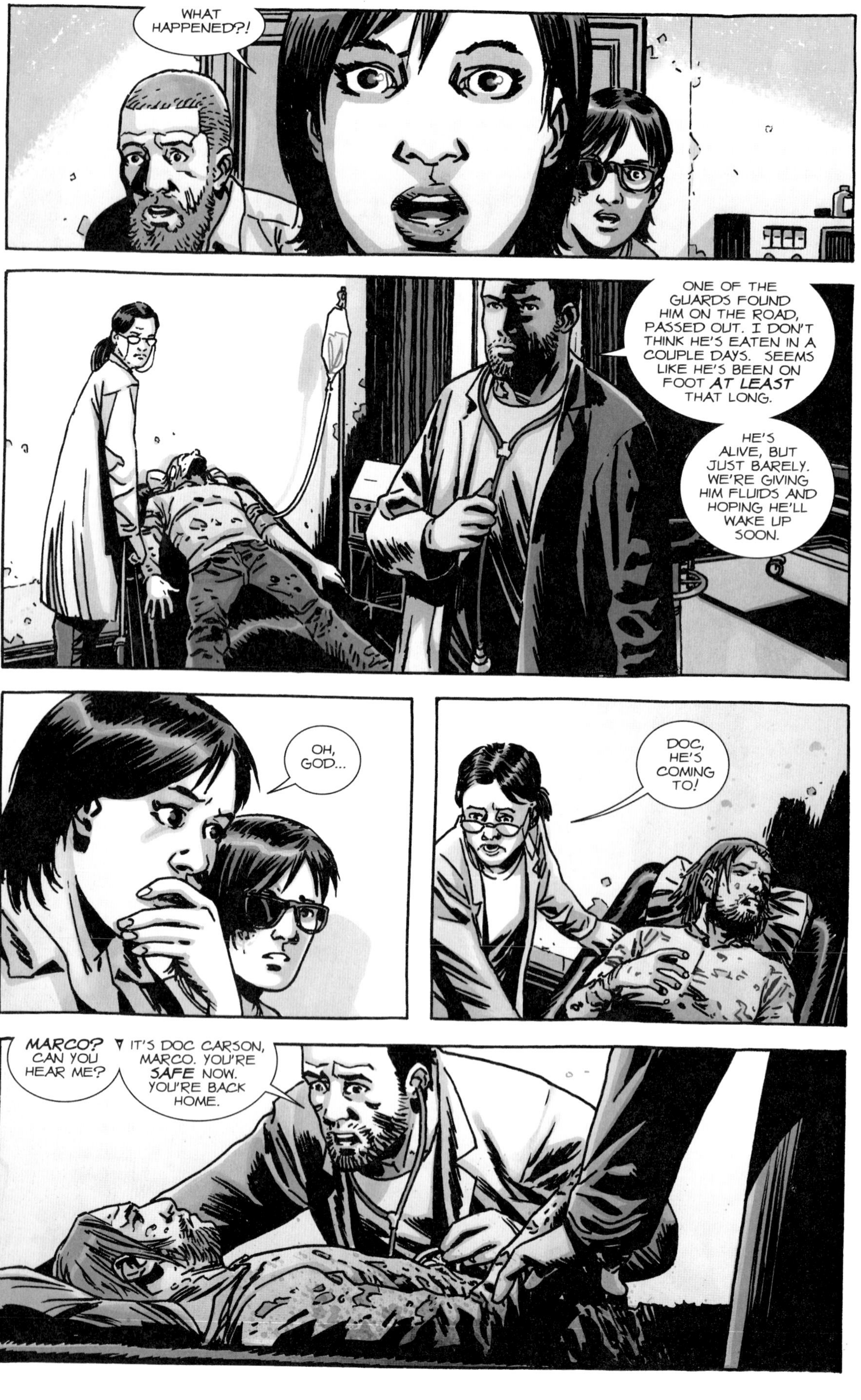
WHAT HAPPENED?!
ONE OF THE GUARDS FOUND HIM ON THE ROAD, PASSED OUT. I DON'T THINK HE'S EATEN IN A COUPLE DAYS. SEEMS LIKE HE'S BEEN ON FOOT AT LEAST THAT LONG.
HE'S ALIVE, BUT JUST BARELY. WE'RE GIVING HIM FLUIDS AND HOPING HE'LL WAKE UP SOON.
OH, GOD...
DOC, HE'S COMING TO!
MARCO? CAN YOU HEAR ME?
IT'S DOC CARSON, MARCO. YOU'RE SAFE NOW. YOU'RE BACK HOME.

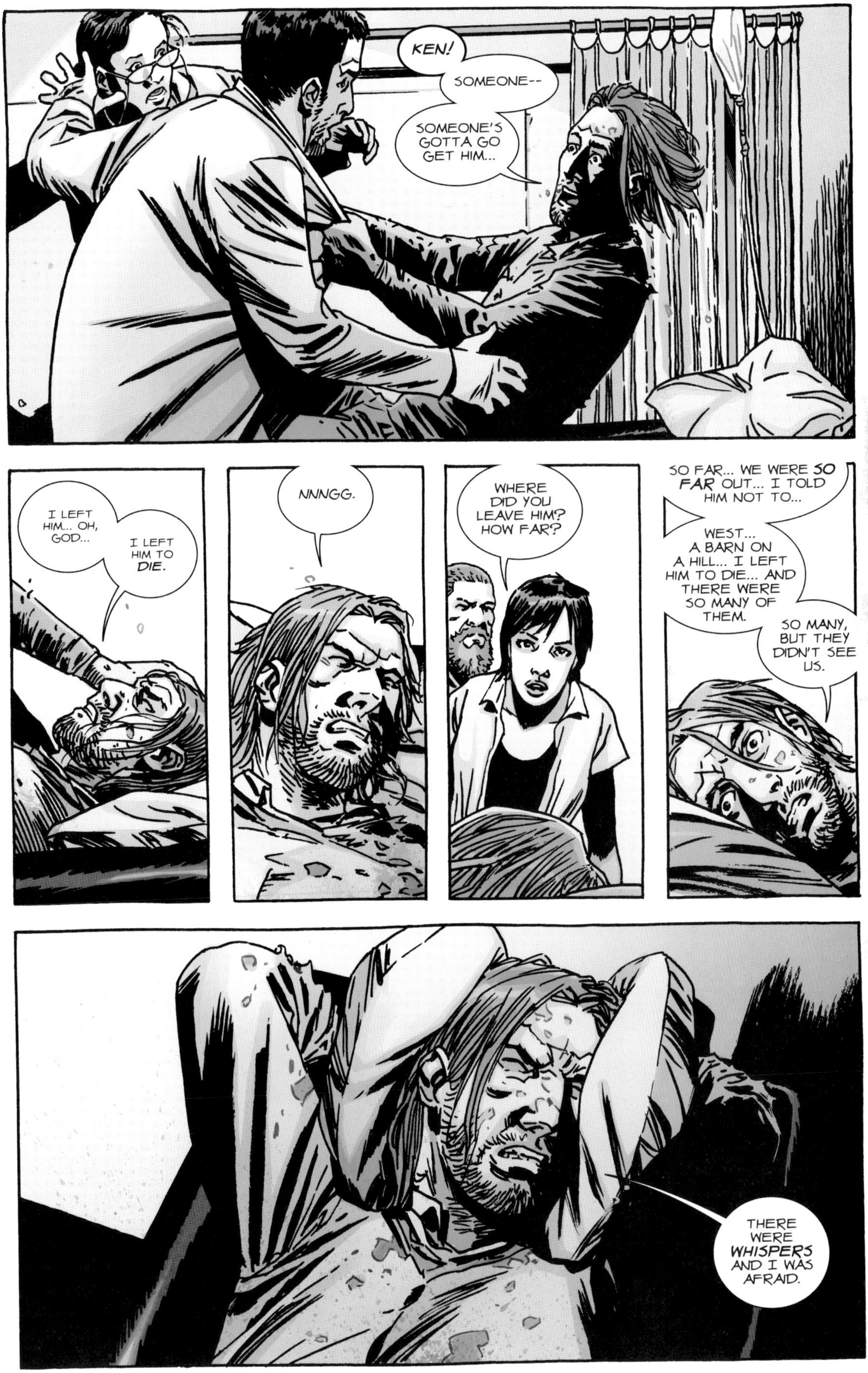
KEN!
SOMEONE--
SOMEONE'S GOTTA GO GET HIM...
I LEFT HIM... OH, GOD...
I LEFT HIM TO *DIE.*
NNNGG.
WHERE DID YOU LEAVE HIM? HOW FAR?
SO FAR... WE WERE *SO FAR* OUT... I TOLD HIM NOT TO...
WEST... A BARN ON A HILL... I LEFT HIM TO DIE... AND THERE WERE SO MANY OF THEM.
SO MANY, BUT THEY DIDN'T SEE US.
THERE WERE *WHISPERS* AND I WAS AFRAID.

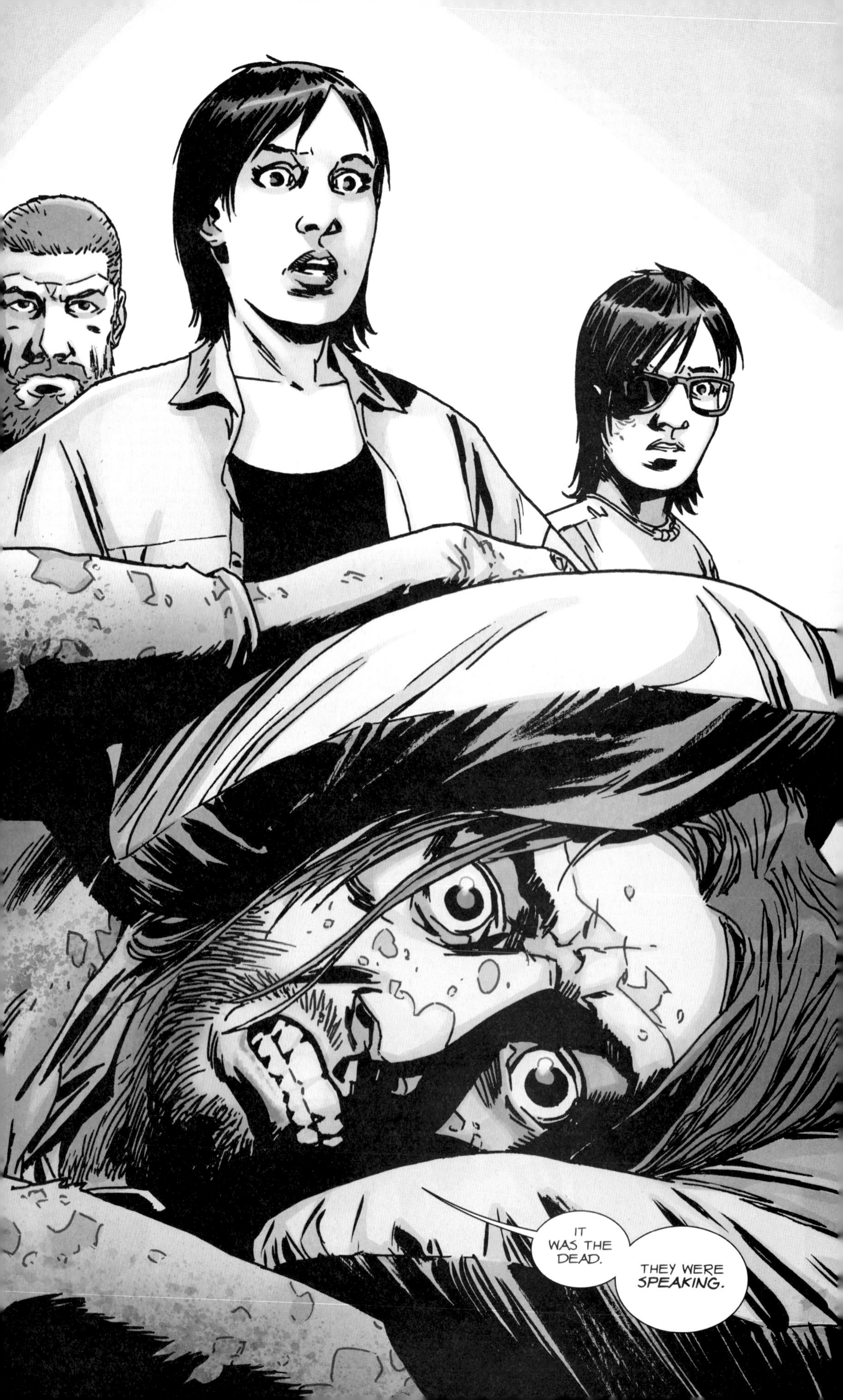
IT WAS THE DEAD.
THEY WERE SPEAKING.

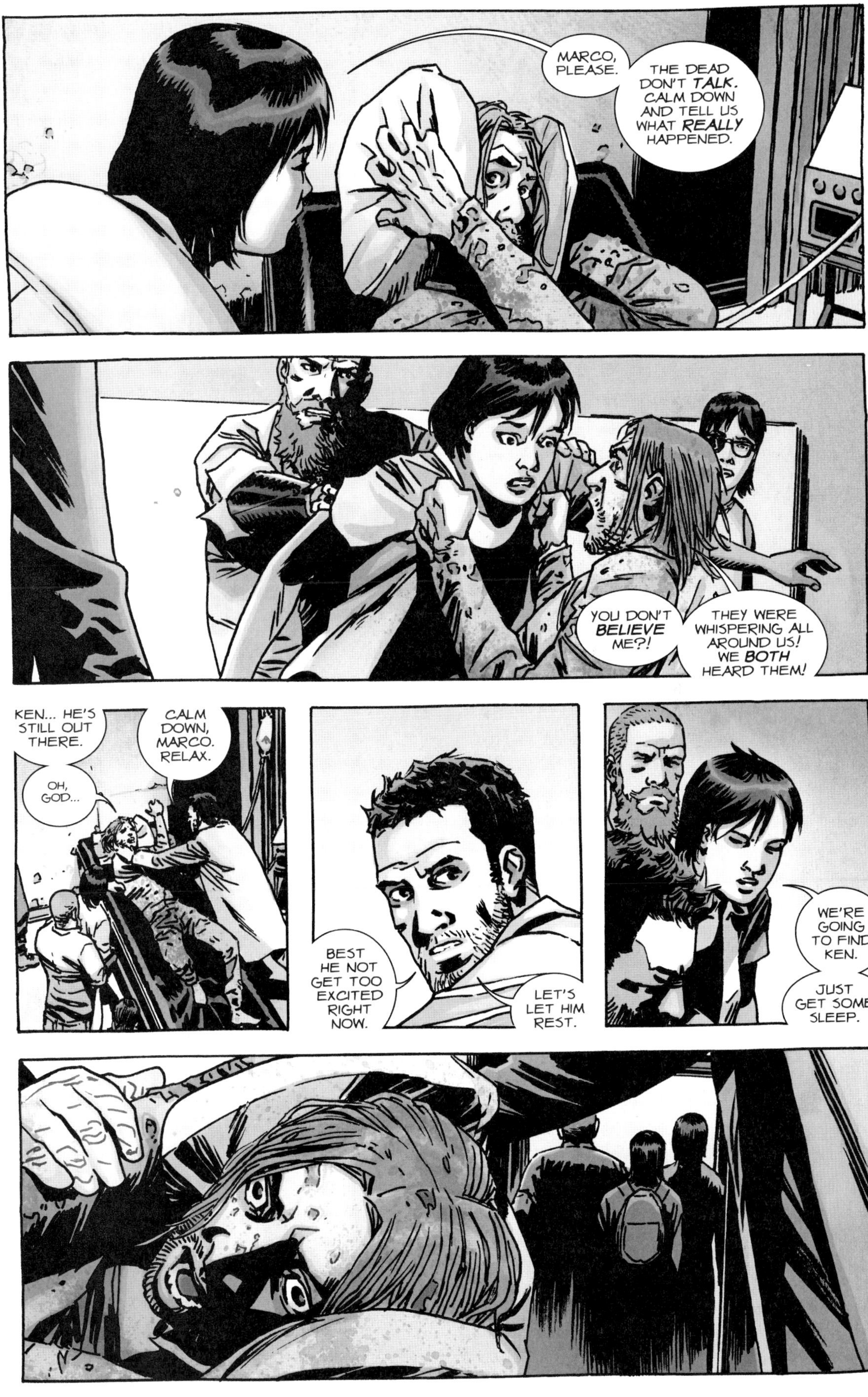
MARCO, PLEASE.
THE DEAD DON'T TALK. CALM DOWN AND TELL US WHAT REALLY HAPPENED.
YOU DON'T BELIEVE ME?!
THEY WERE WHISPERING ALL AROUND US! WE BOTH HEARD THEM!
KEN... HE'S STILL OUT THERE.
CALM DOWN, MARCO. RELAX.
OH, GOD...
BEST HE NOT GET TOO EXCITED RIGHT NOW.
LET'S LET HIM REST.
WE'RE GOING TO FIND KEN.
JUST GET SOME SLEEP.

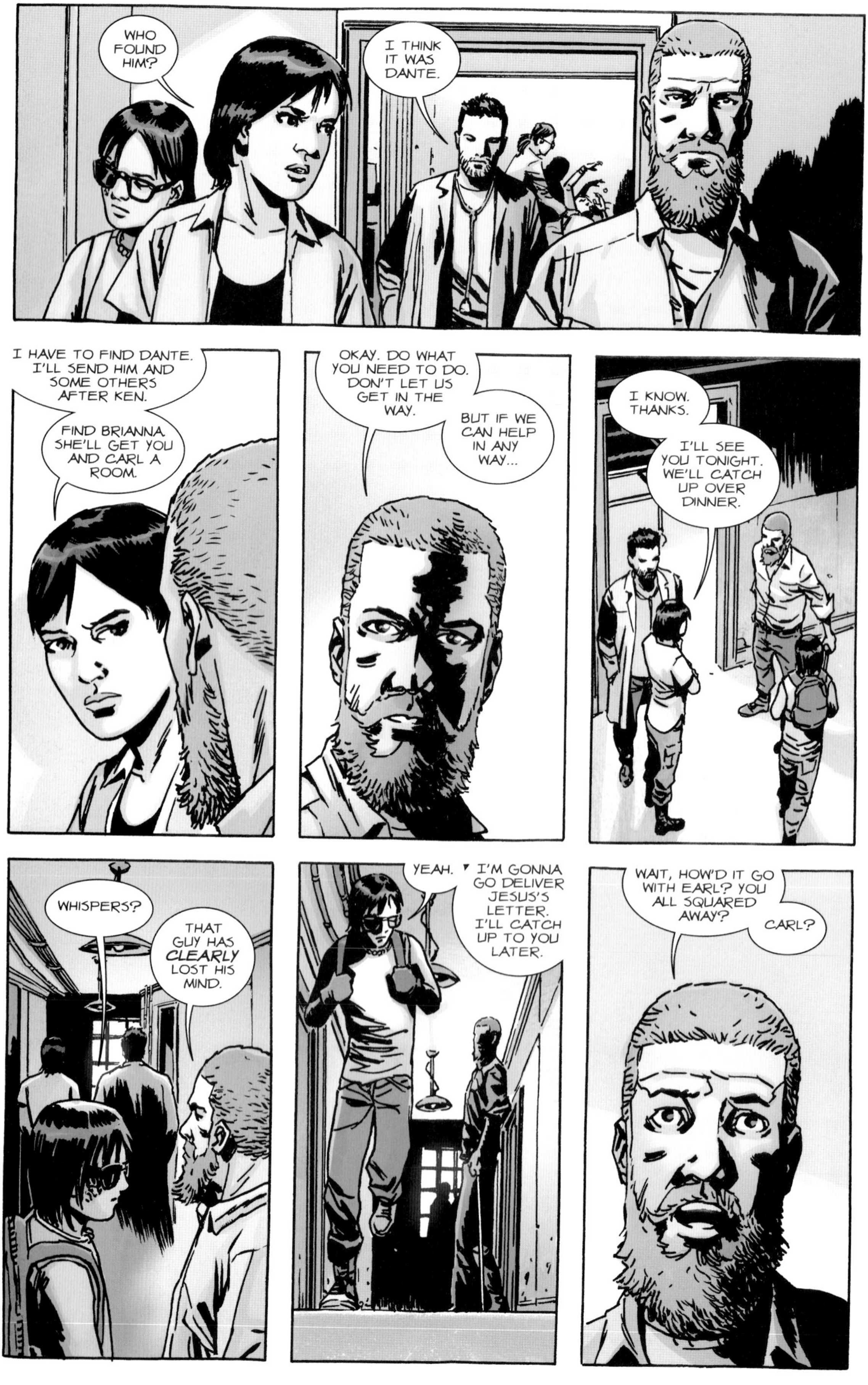
WHO FOUND HIM?
I THINK IT WAS DANTE.
I HAVE TO FIND DANTE. I'LL SEND HIM AND SOME OTHERS AFTER KEN.
FIND BRIANNA. SHE'LL GET YOU AND CARL A ROOM.
OKAY. DO WHAT YOU NEED TO DO. DON'T LET US GET IN THE WAY.
BUT IF WE CAN HELP IN ANY WAY...
I KNOW. THANKS.
I'LL SEE YOU TONIGHT. WE'LL CATCH UP OVER DINNER.
WHISPERS?
THAT GUY HAS CLEARLY LOST HIS MIND.
YEAH.
I'M GONNA GO DELIVER JESUS'S LETTER. I'LL CATCH UP TO YOU LATER.
WAIT, HOW'D IT GO WITH EARL? YOU ALL SQUARED AWAY?
CARL?

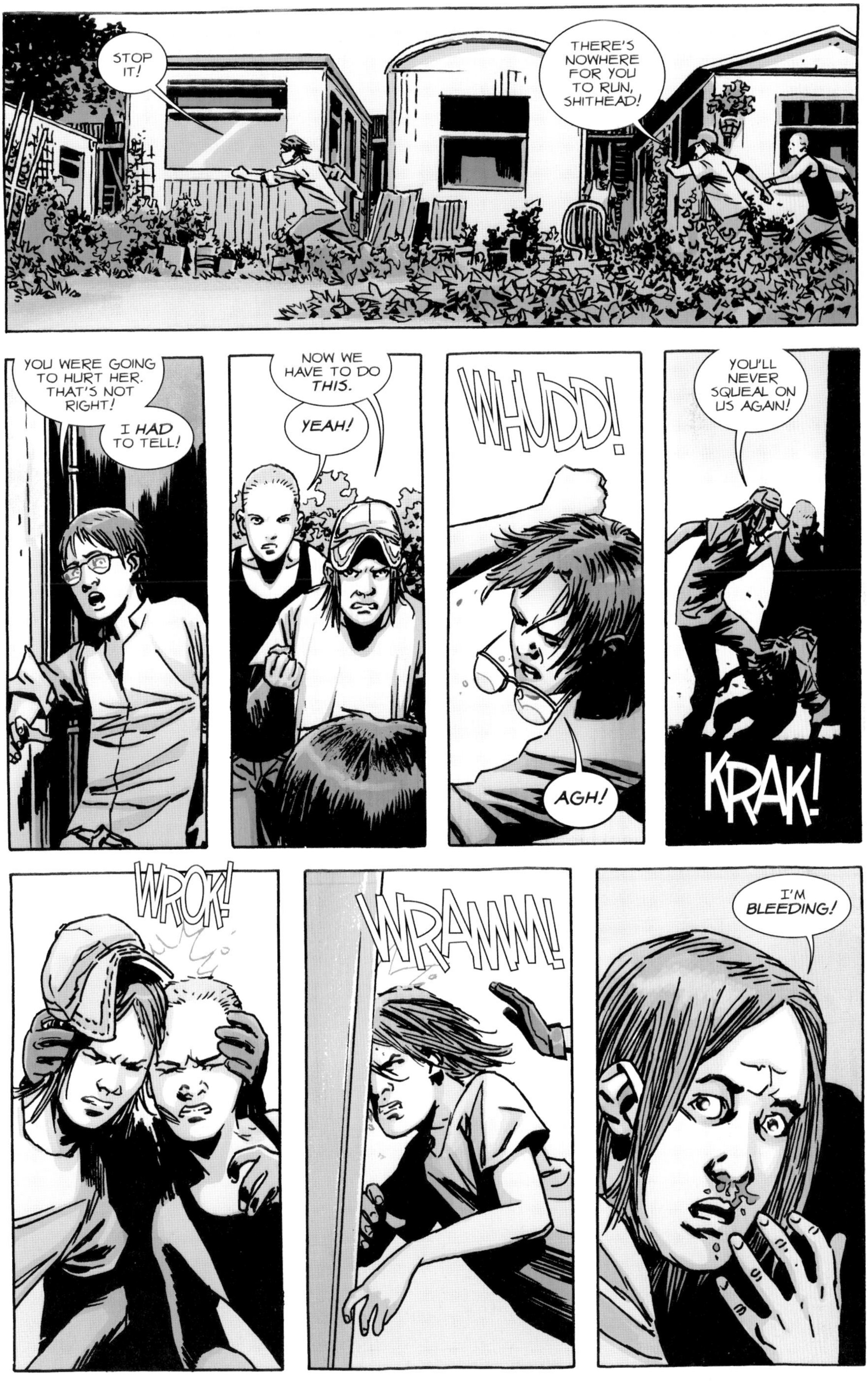
STOP IT!
THERE'S NOWHERE FOR YOU TO RUN, SHITHEAD!
YOU WERE GOING TO HURT HER. THAT'S NOT RIGHT!
I HAD TO TELL!
NOW WE HAVE TO DO THIS.
YEAH!
WHUDD!
AGH!
YOU'LL NEVER SQUEAL ON US AGAIN!
KRAK!
WROK!
WRAMM!
I'M BLEEDING!

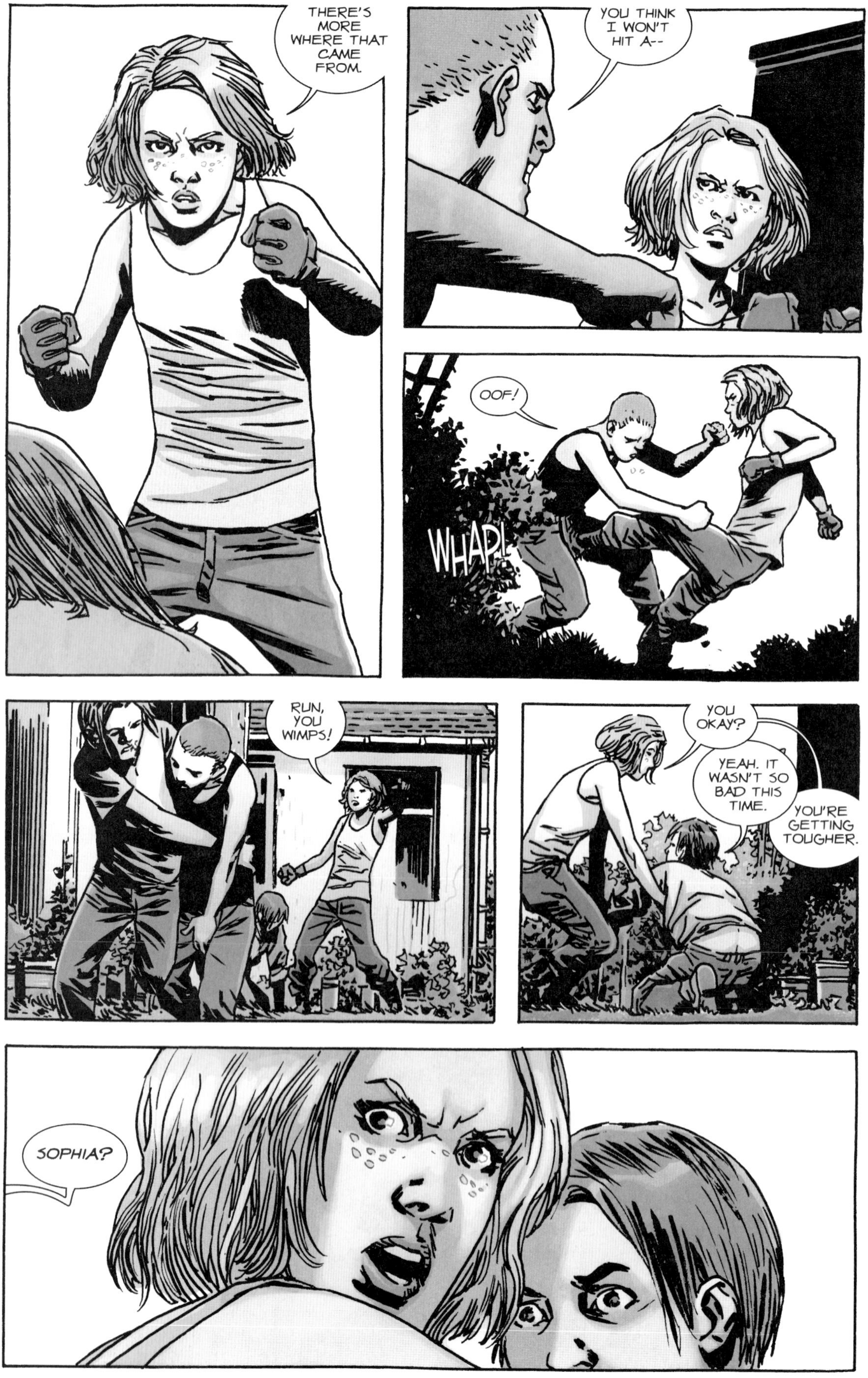
THERE'S MORE WHERE THAT CAME FROM.
YOU THINK I WON'T HIT A--
OOF!
WHAP!
RUN, YOU WIMPS!
YOU OKAY?
YEAH. IT WASN'T SO BAD THIS TIME.
YOU'RE GETTING TOUGHER.
SOPHIA?

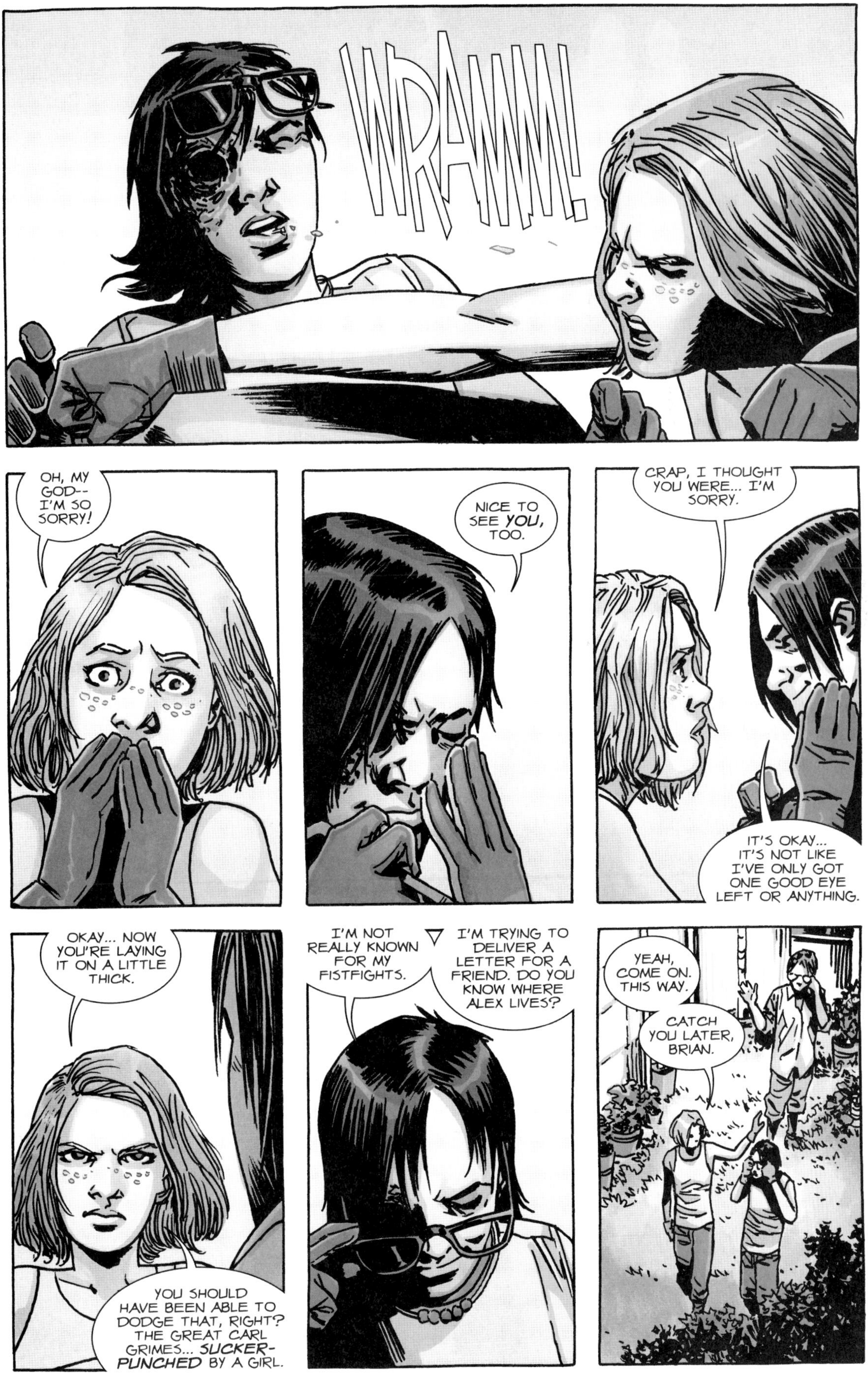
WRAMM!
OH, MY GOD-- I'M SO SORRY!
NICE TO SEE YOU, TOO.
CRAP, I THOUGHT YOU WERE... I'M SORRY.
IT'S OKAY... IT'S NOT LIKE I'VE ONLY GOT ONE GOOD EYE LEFT OR ANYTHING.
OKAY... NOW YOU'RE LAYING IT ON A LITTLE THICK.
YOU SHOULD HAVE BEEN ABLE TO DODGE THAT, RIGHT? THE GREAT CARL GRIMES... SUCKER-PUNCHED BY A GIRL.
I'M NOT REALLY KNOWN FOR MY FISTFIGHTS.
I'M TRYING TO DELIVER A LETTER FOR A FRIEND. DO YOU KNOW WHERE ALEX LIVES?
YEAH, COME ON. THIS WAY.
CATCH YOU LATER, BRIAN.

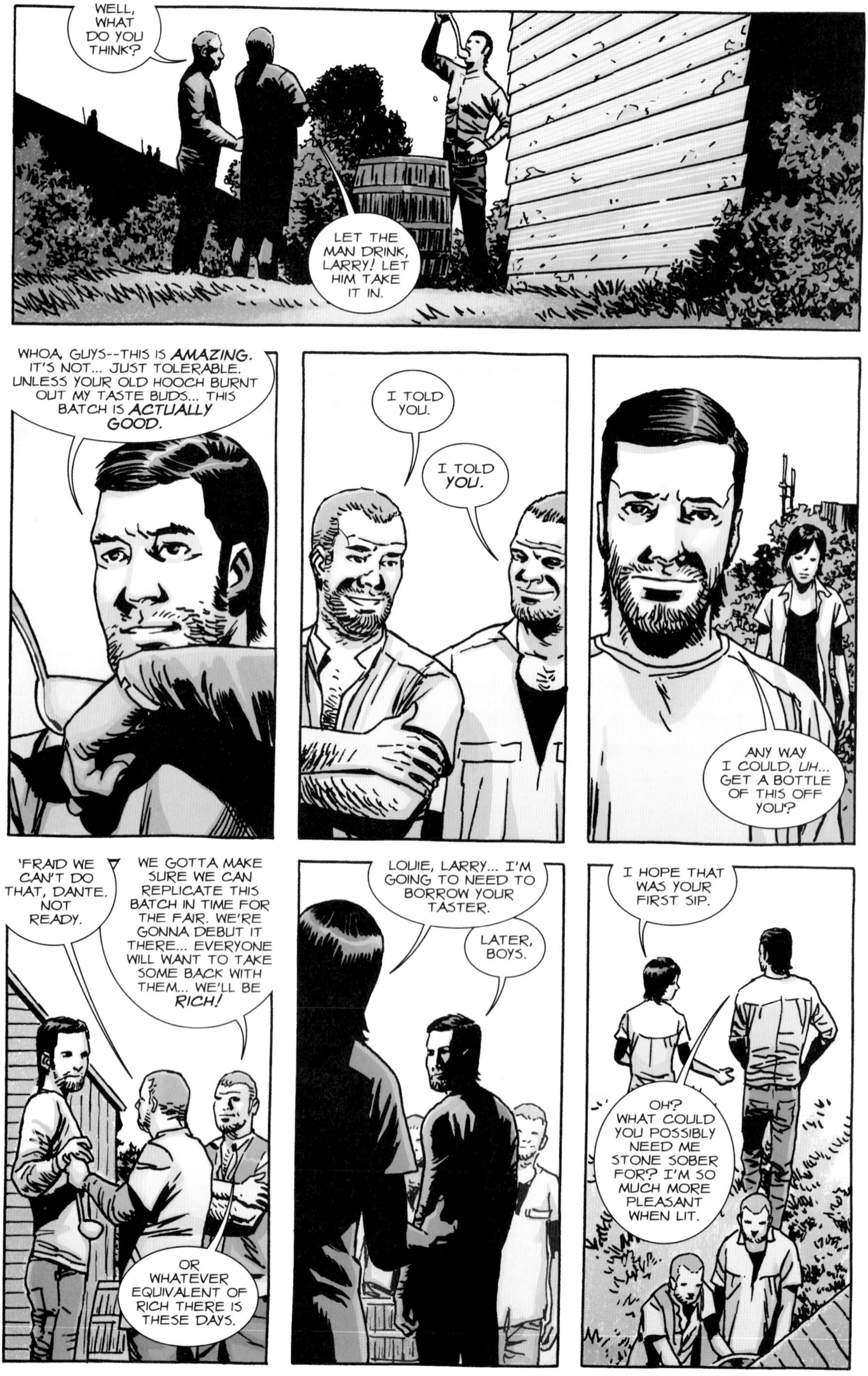
WELL, WHAT DO YOU THINK?
LET THE MAN DRINK, LARRY! LET HIM TAKE IT IN.
WHOA, GUYS--THIS IS AMAZING. IT'S NOT... JUST TOLERABLE. UNLESS YOUR OLD HOOCH BURNT OUT MY TASTE BUDS... THIS BATCH IS ACTUALLY GOOD.
I TOLD YOU.
I TOLD YOU.
ANY WAY I COULD, UH... GET A BOTTLE OF THIS OFF YOU?
'FRAID WE CAN'T DO THAT, DANTE. NOT READY.
WE GOTTA MAKE SURE WE CAN REPLICATE THIS BATCH IN TIME FOR THE FAIR. WE'RE GONNA DEBUT IT THERE... EVERYONE WILL WANT TO TAKE SOME BACK WITH THEM... WE'LL BE RICH!
OR WHATEVER EQUIVALENT OF RICH THERE IS THESE DAYS.
LOUIE, LARRY... I'M GOING TO NEED TO BORROW YOUR TASTER.
LATER, BOYS.
I HOPE THAT WAS YOUR FIRST SIP.
OH? WHAT COULD YOU POSSIBLY NEED ME STONE SOBER FOR? I'M SO MUCH MORE PLEASANT WHEN LIT.

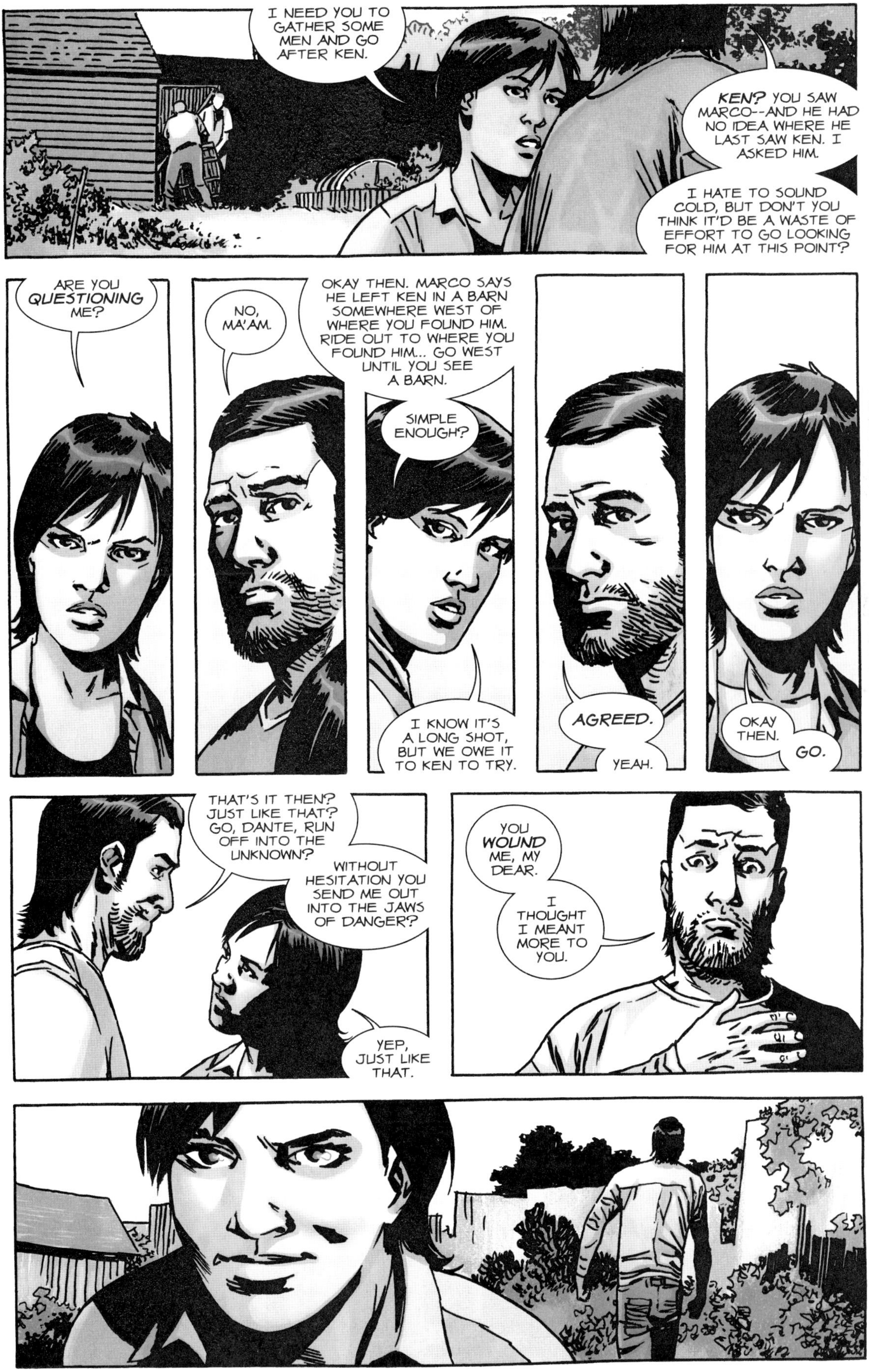
I NEED YOU TO GATHER SOME MEN AND GO AFTER KEN.
KEN? YOU SAW MARCO--AND HE HAD NO IDEA WHERE HE LAST SAW KEN. I ASKED HIM.
I HATE TO SOUND COLD, BUT DON'T YOU THINK IT'D BE A WASTE OF EFFORT TO GO LOOKING FOR HIM AT THIS POINT?
ARE YOU QUESTIONING ME?
NO, MA'AM.
OKAY THEN. MARCO SAYS HE LEFT KEN IN A BARN SOMEWHERE WEST OF WHERE YOU FOUND HIM. RIDE OUT TO WHERE YOU FOUND HIM... GO WEST UNTIL YOU SEE A BARN.
SIMPLE ENOUGH?
I KNOW IT'S A LONG SHOT, BUT WE OWE IT TO KEN TO TRY.
AGREED.
YEAH.
OKAY THEN.
GO.
THAT'S IT THEN? JUST LIKE THAT? GO, DANTE, RUN OFF INTO THE UNKNOWN?
WITHOUT HESITATION YOU SEND ME OUT INTO THE JAWS OF DANGER?
YEP, JUST LIKE THAT.
YOU WOUND ME, MY DEAR.
I THOUGHT I MEANT MORE TO YOU.

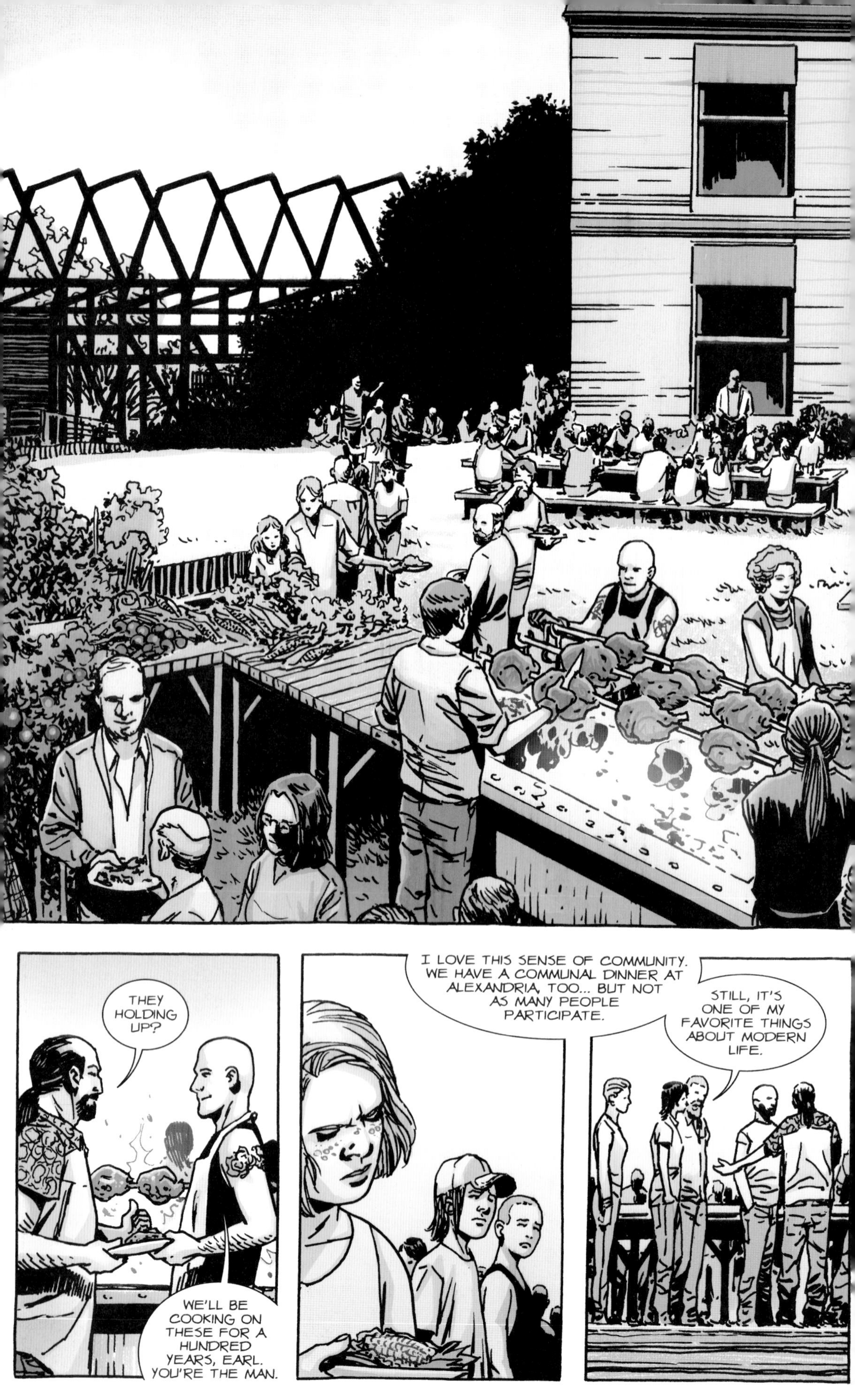
THEY HOLDING UP?
WE'LL BE COOKING ON THESE FOR A HUNDRED YEARS, EARL. YOU'RE THE MAN.
I LOVE THIS SENSE OF COMMUNITY. WE HAVE A COMMUNAL DINNER AT ALEXANDRIA, TOO... BUT NOT AS MANY PEOPLE PARTICIPATE.
STILL, IT'S ONE OF MY FAVORITE THINGS ABOUT MODERN LIFE.

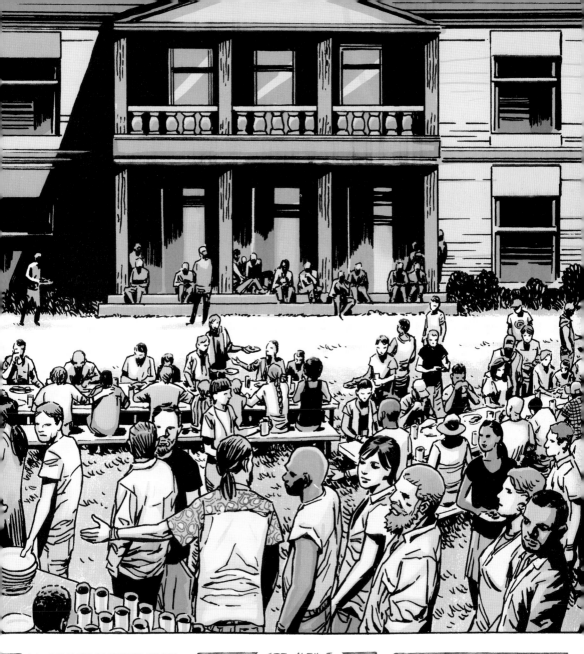

WE ONLY DO IT THREE TIMES A WEEK, BUT YEAH... IT'S NICE. IT'S GOOD TO SEE THE PEOPLE YOU LIVE WITH SO CLOSELY... SHARE A MEAL, GET TO *KNOW* THEM.

I STILL DON'T KNOW *EVERYONE* HERE. THAT BUGS ME, BUT I'LL GET THERE.

SEE, ALEX, I TOLD YOU HE CARED ABOUT YOU.

CARL?

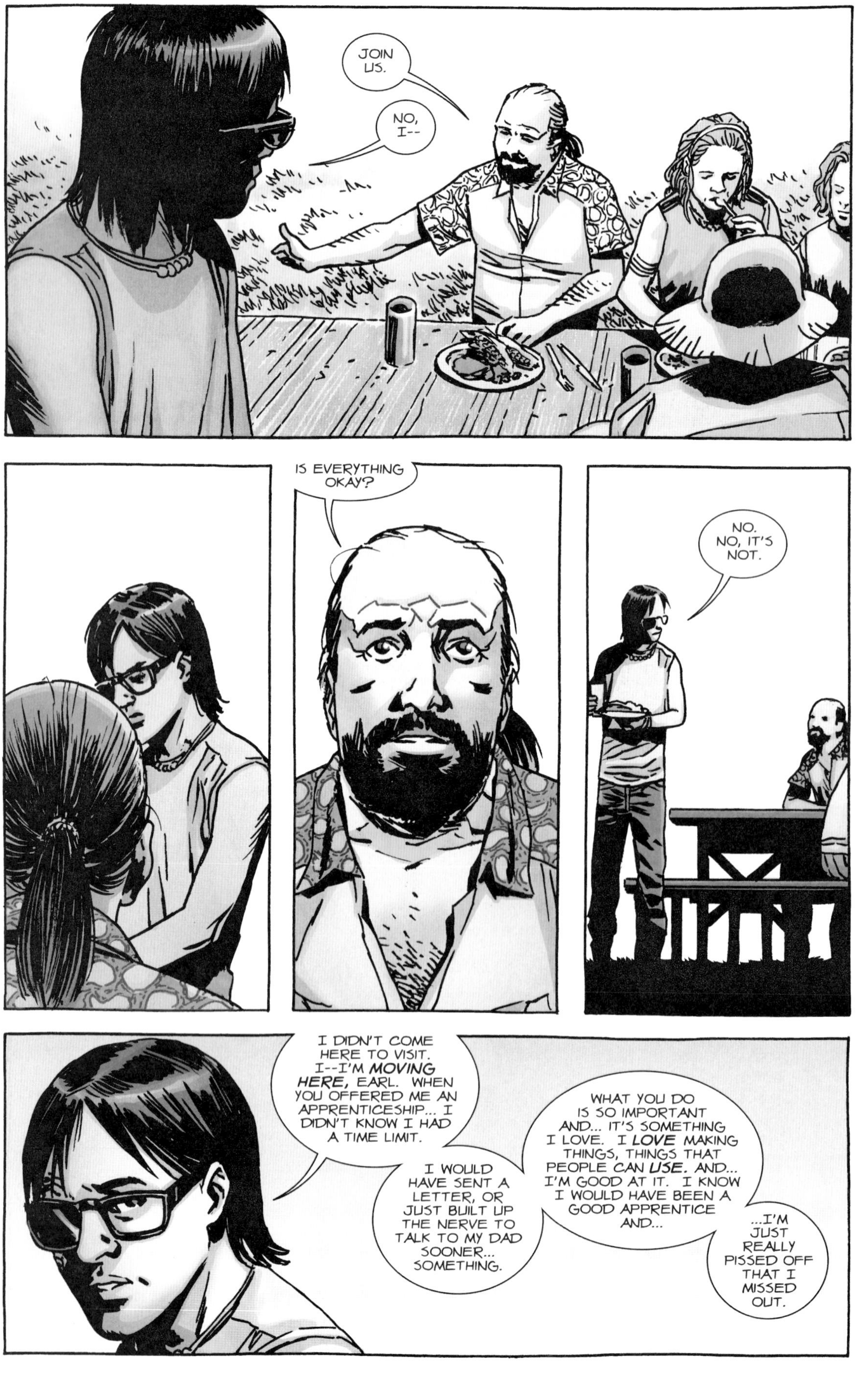
JOIN US.
NO, I--
IS EVERYTHING OKAY?
NO. NO, IT'S NOT.
I DIDN'T COME HERE TO VISIT. I--I'M MOVING HERE, EARL. WHEN YOU OFFERED ME AN APPRENTICESHIP... I DIDN'T KNOW I HAD A TIME LIMIT.
I WOULD HAVE SENT A LETTER, OR JUST BUILT UP THE NERVE TO TALK TO MY DAD SOONER... SOMETHING.
WHAT YOU DO IS SO IMPORTANT AND... IT'S SOMETHING I LOVE. I LOVE MAKING THINGS, THINGS THAT PEOPLE CAN USE. AND... I'M GOOD AT IT. I KNOW I WOULD HAVE BEEN A GOOD APPRENTICE AND...
...I'M JUST REALLY PISSED OFF THAT I MISSED OUT.

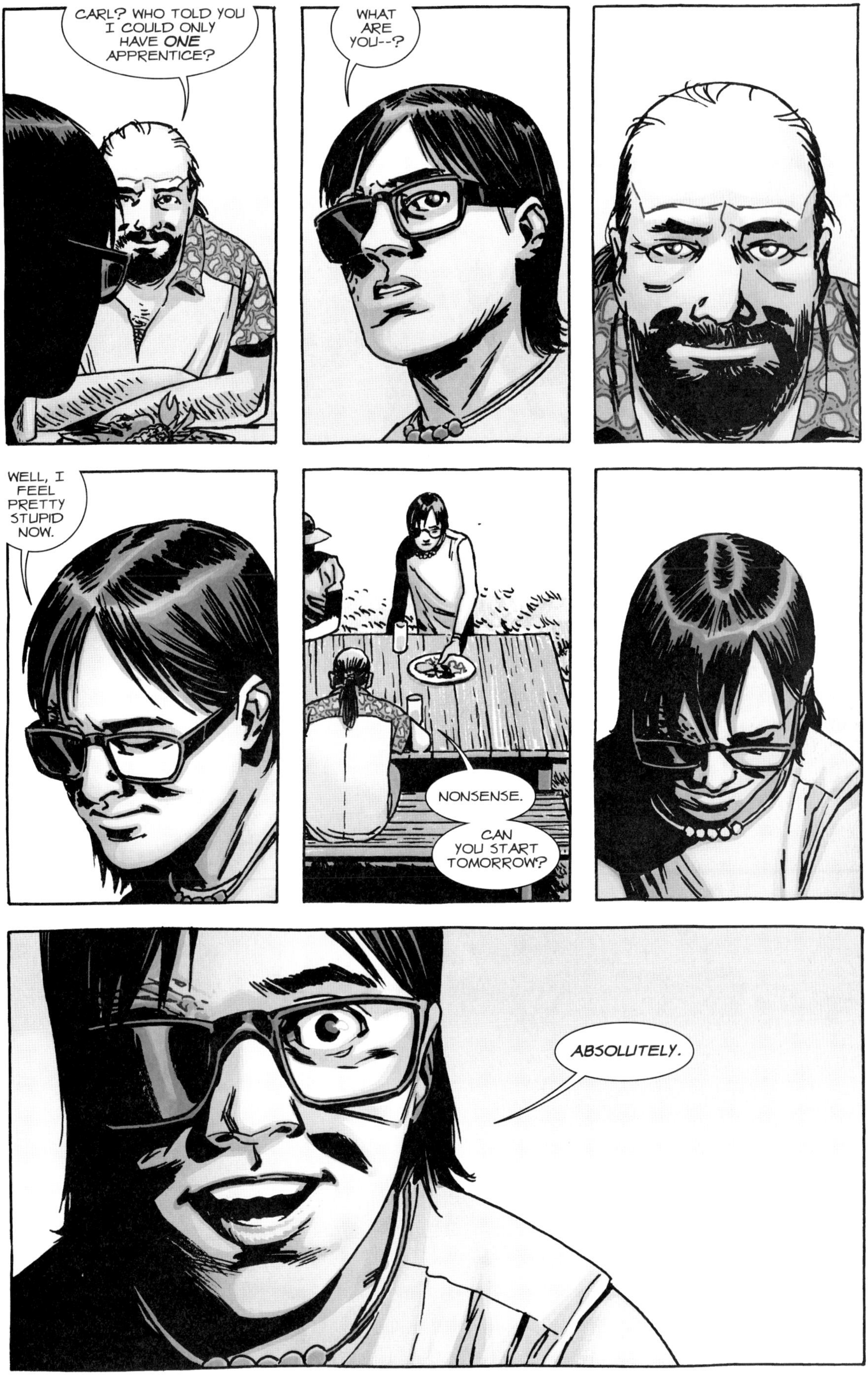
CARL? WHO TOLD YOU I COULD ONLY HAVE ONE APPRENTICE?
WHAT ARE YOU--?
WELL, I FEEL PRETTY STUPID NOW.
NONSENSE.
CAN YOU START TOMORROW?
ABSOLUTELY.

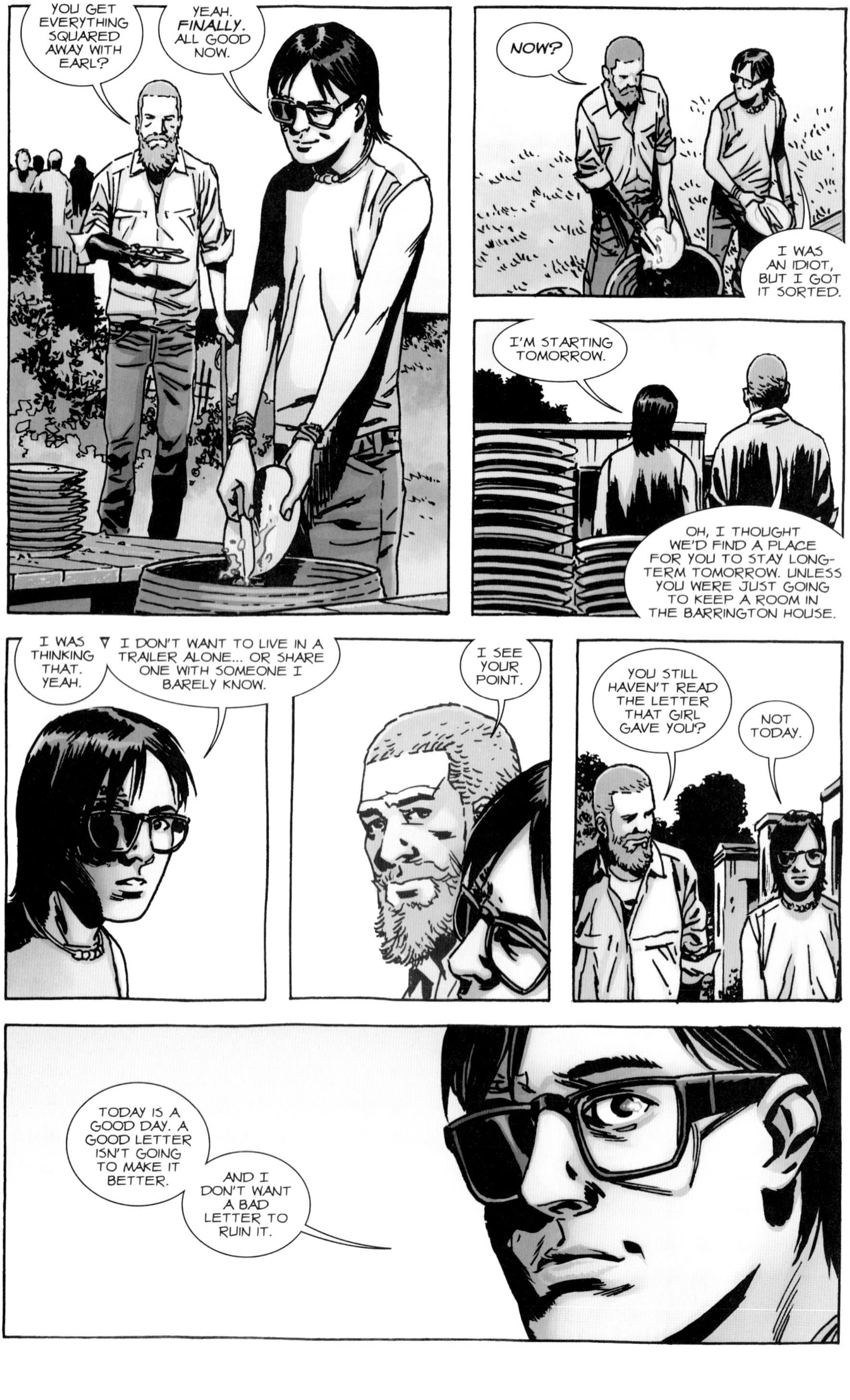
YOU GET EVERYTHING SQUARED AWAY WITH EARL?
YEAH. FINALLY. ALL GOOD NOW.
NOW?
I WAS AN IDIOT, BUT I GOT IT SORTED.
I'M STARTING TOMORROW.
OH, I THOUGHT WE'D FIND A PLACE FOR YOU TO STAY LONG-TERM TOMORROW. UNLESS YOU WERE JUST GOING TO KEEP A ROOM IN THE BARRINGTON HOUSE.
I WAS THINKING THAT. YEAH.
I DON'T WANT TO LIVE IN A TRAILER ALONE... OR SHARE ONE WITH SOMEONE I BARELY KNOW.
I SEE YOUR POINT.
YOU STILL HAVEN'T READ THE LETTER THAT GIRL GAVE YOU?
NOT TODAY.
TODAY IS A GOOD DAY. A GOOD LETTER ISN'T GOING TO MAKE IT BETTER.
AND I DON'T WANT A BAD LETTER TO RUIN IT.

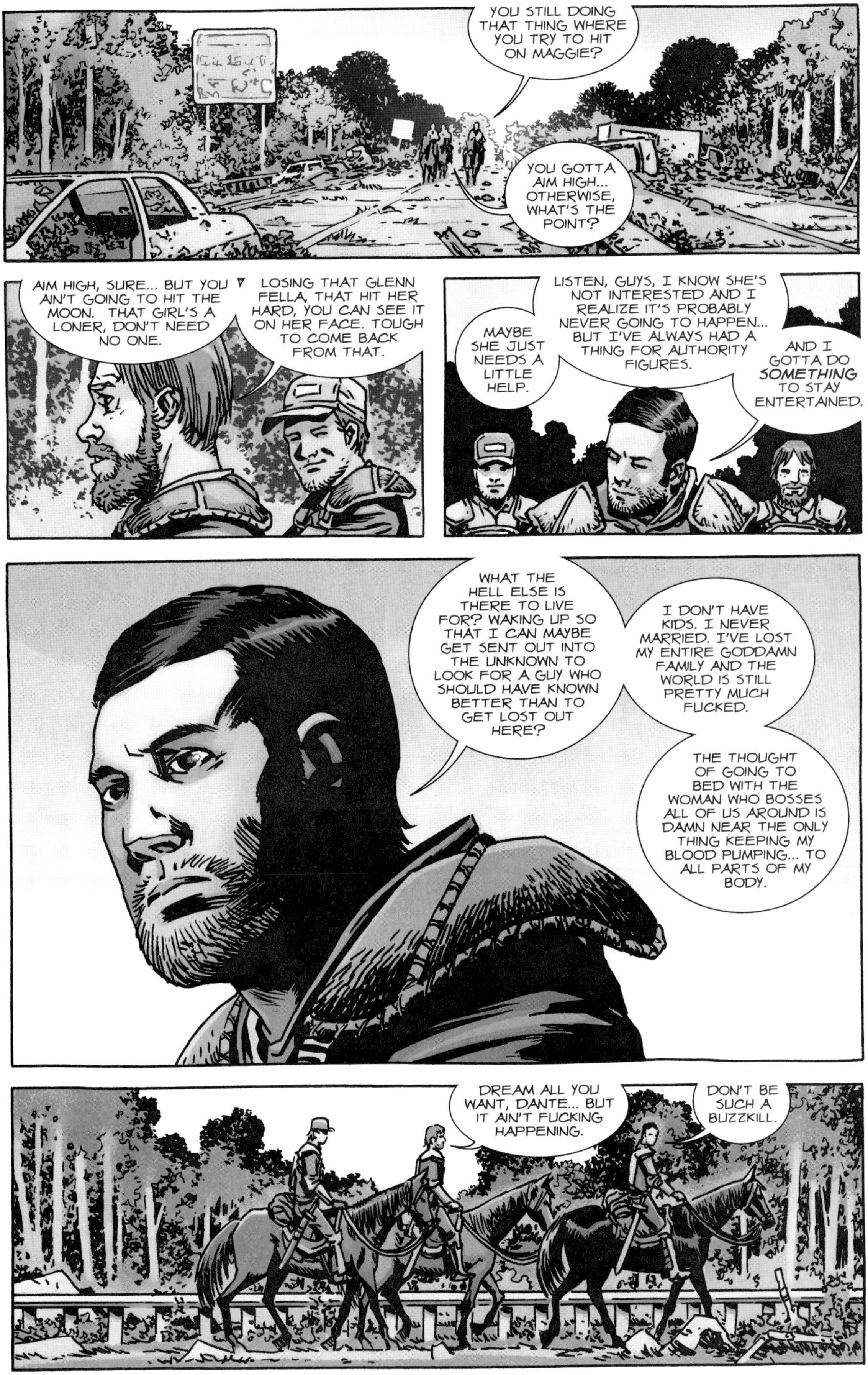
YOU STILL DOING THAT THING WHERE YOU TRY TO HIT ON MAGGIE?
YOU GOTTA AIM HIGH... OTHERWISE, WHAT'S THE POINT?
AIM HIGH, SURE... BUT YOU AIN'T GOING TO HIT THE MOON. THAT GIRL'S A LONER, DON'T NEED NO ONE.
LOSING THAT GLENN FELLA, THAT HIT HER HARD, YOU CAN SEE IT ON HER FACE. TOUGH TO COME BACK FROM THAT.
MAYBE SHE JUST NEEDS A LITTLE HELP.
LISTEN, GUYS, I KNOW SHE'S NOT INTERESTED AND I REALIZE IT'S PROBABLY NEVER GOING TO HAPPEN... BUT I'VE ALWAYS HAD A THING FOR AUTHORITY FIGURES.
AND I GOTTA DO *SOMETHING* TO STAY ENTERTAINED.
WHAT THE HELL ELSE IS THERE TO LIVE FOR? WAKING UP SO THAT I CAN MAYBE GET SENT OUT INTO THE UNKNOWN TO LOOK FOR A GUY WHO SHOULD HAVE KNOWN BETTER THAN TO GET LOST OUT HERE?
I DON'T HAVE KIDS. I NEVER MARRIED. I'VE LOST MY ENTIRE GODDAMN FAMILY AND THE WORLD IS STILL PRETTY MUCH FUCKED.
THE THOUGHT OF GOING TO BED WITH THE WOMAN WHO BOSSES ALL OF US AROUND IS DAMN NEAR THE ONLY THING KEEPING MY BLOOD PUMPING... TO ALL PARTS OF MY BODY.
DREAM ALL YOU WANT, DANTE... BUT IT AIN'T FUCKING HAPPENING.
DON'T BE SUCH A BUZZKILL.

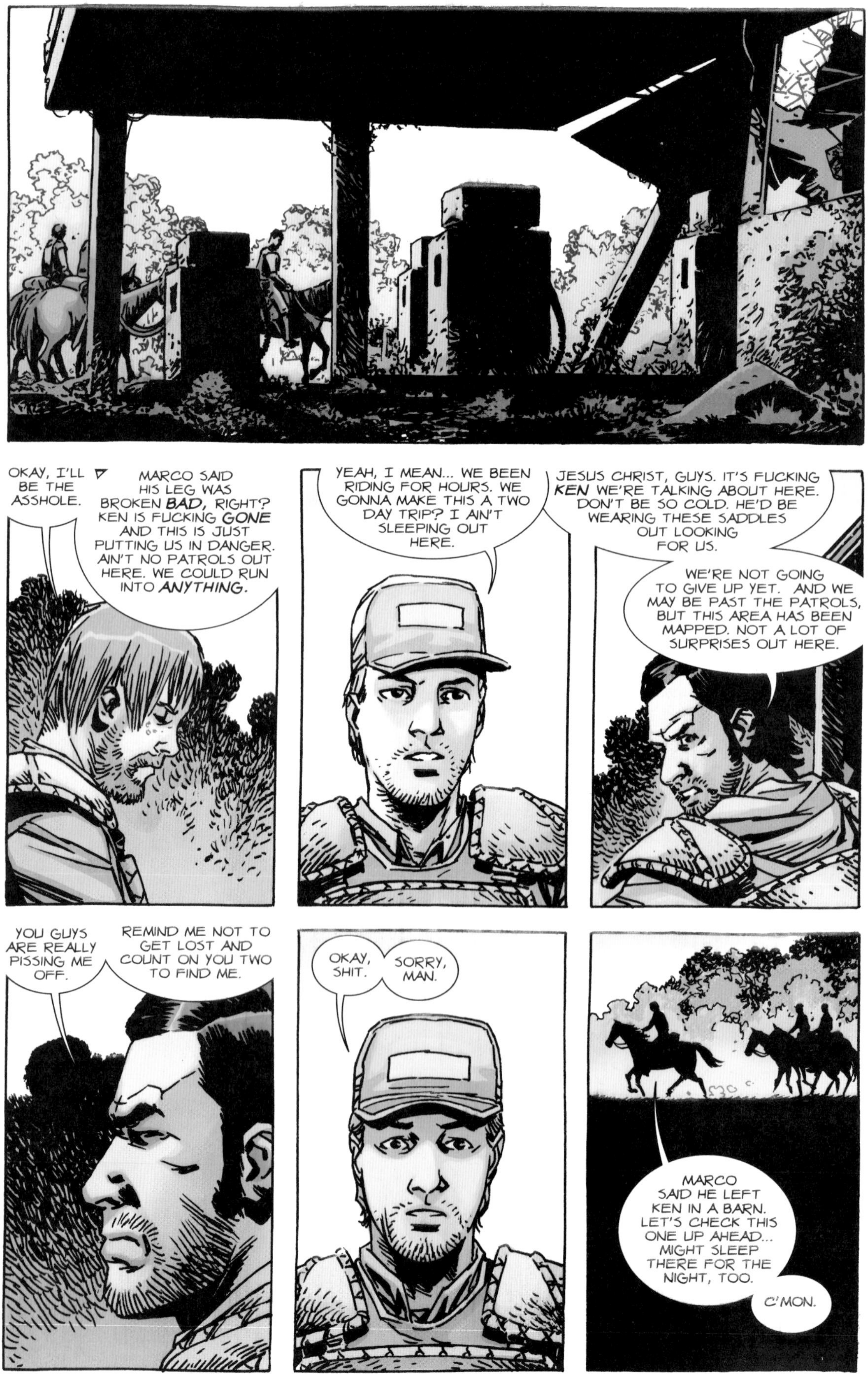
OKAY, I'LL BE THE ASSHOLE.
MARCO SAID HIS LEG WAS BROKEN BAD, RIGHT? KEN IS FUCKING GONE AND THIS IS JUST PUTTING US IN DANGER. AIN'T NO PATROLS OUT HERE. WE COULD RUN INTO ANYTHING.
YEAH, I MEAN... WE BEEN RIDING FOR HOURS. WE GONNA MAKE THIS A TWO DAY TRIP? I AIN'T SLEEPING OUT HERE.
JESUS CHRIST, GUYS. IT'S FUCKING KEN WE'RE TALKING ABOUT HERE. DON'T BE SO COLD. HE'D BE WEARING THESE SADDLES OUT LOOKING FOR US.
WE'RE NOT GOING TO GIVE UP YET. AND WE MAY BE PAST THE PATROLS, BUT THIS AREA HAS BEEN MAPPED. NOT A LOT OF SURPRISES OUT HERE.
YOU GUYS ARE REALLY PISSING ME OFF.
REMIND ME NOT TO GET LOST AND COUNT ON YOU TWO TO FIND ME.
OKAY, SHIT.
SORRY, MAN.
MARCO SAID HE LEFT KEN IN A BARN. LET'S CHECK THIS ONE UP AHEAD... MIGHT SLEEP THERE FOR THE NIGHT, TOO.
C'MON.

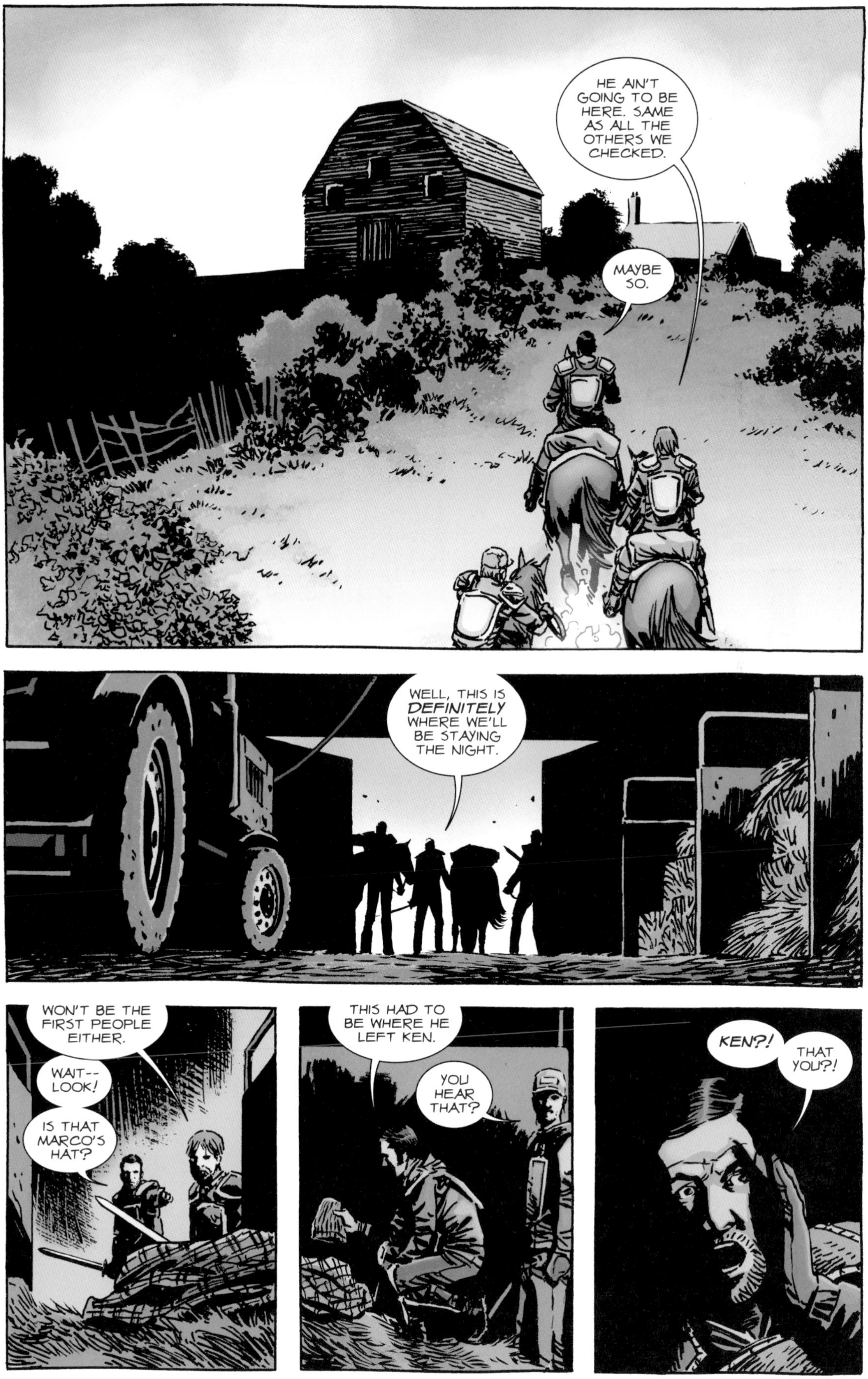
HE AIN'T GOING TO BE HERE. SAME AS ALL THE OTHERS WE CHECKED.
MAYBE SO.
WELL, THIS IS *DEFINITELY* WHERE WE'LL BE STAYING THE NIGHT.
WON'T BE THE FIRST PEOPLE EITHER.
WAIT-- LOOK!
IS THAT MARCO'S HAT?
THIS HAD TO BE WHERE HE LEFT KEN.
YOU HEAR THAT?
KEN?!
THAT YOU?!

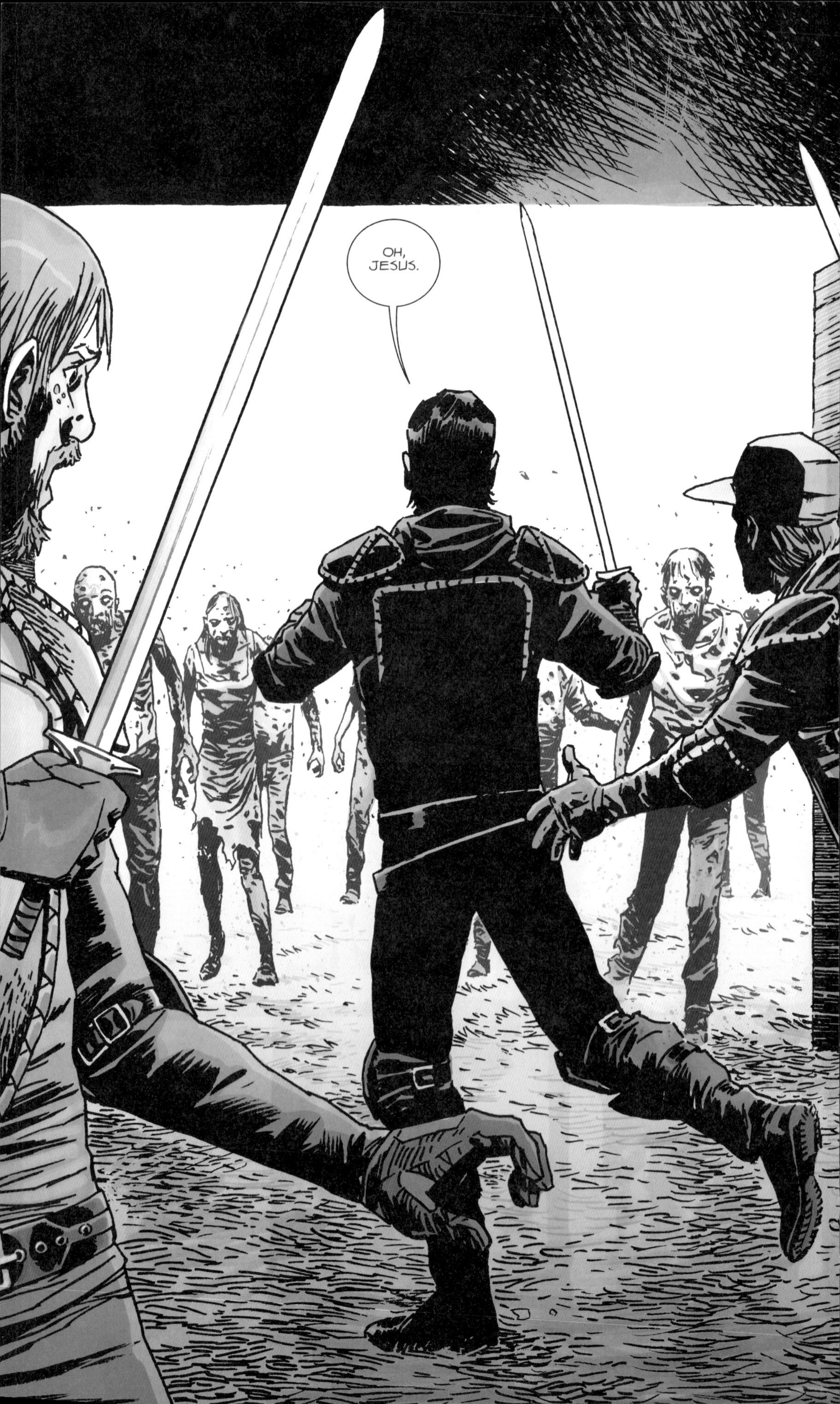
OH, JESUS.

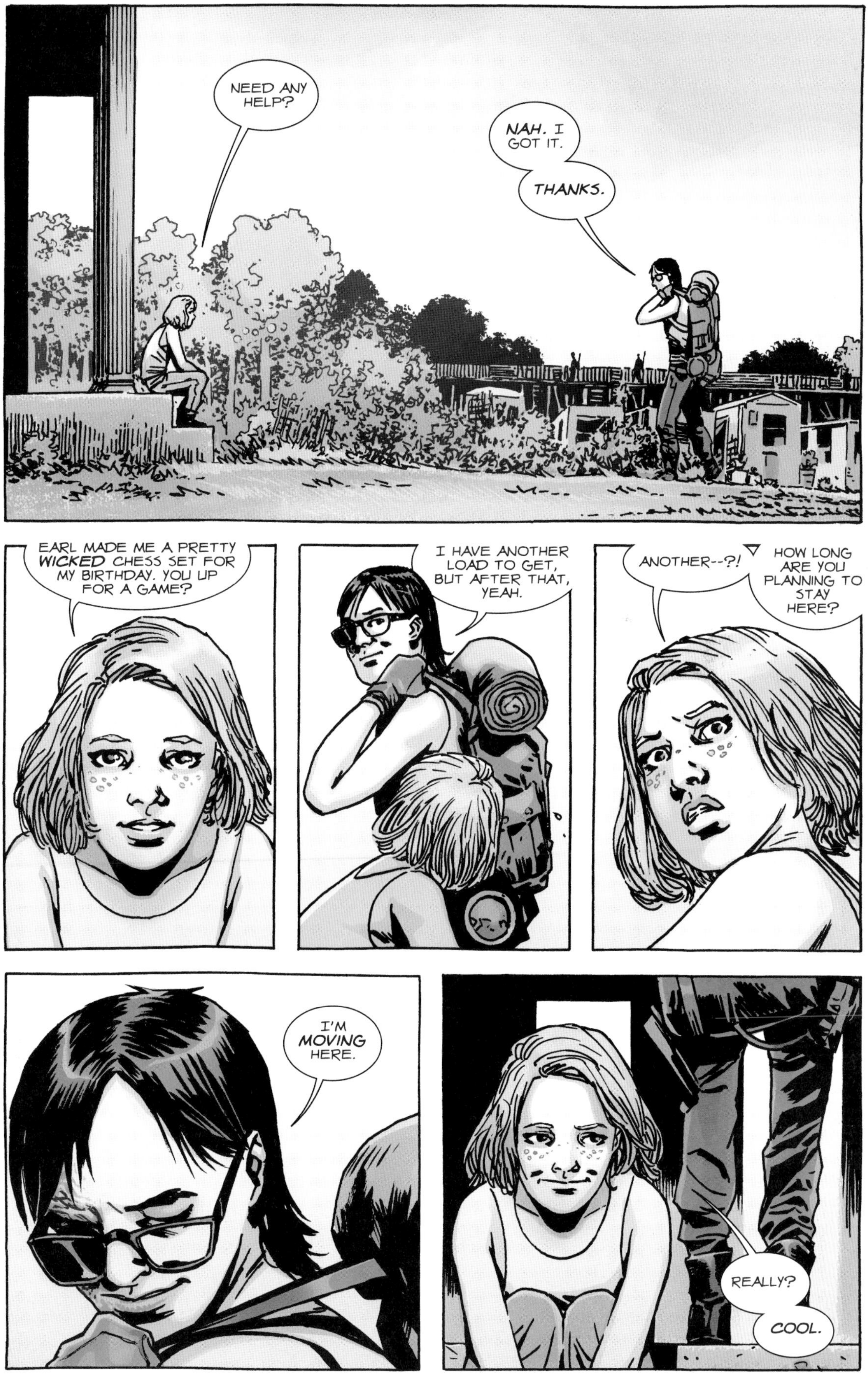
NEED ANY HELP?
NAH. I GOT IT.
THANKS.
EARL MADE ME A PRETTY WICKED CHESS SET FOR MY BIRTHDAY. YOU UP FOR A GAME?
I HAVE ANOTHER LOAD TO GET, BUT AFTER THAT, YEAH.
ANOTHER--?!
HOW LONG ARE YOU PLANNING TO STAY HERE?
I'M MOVING HERE.
REALLY?
COOL.

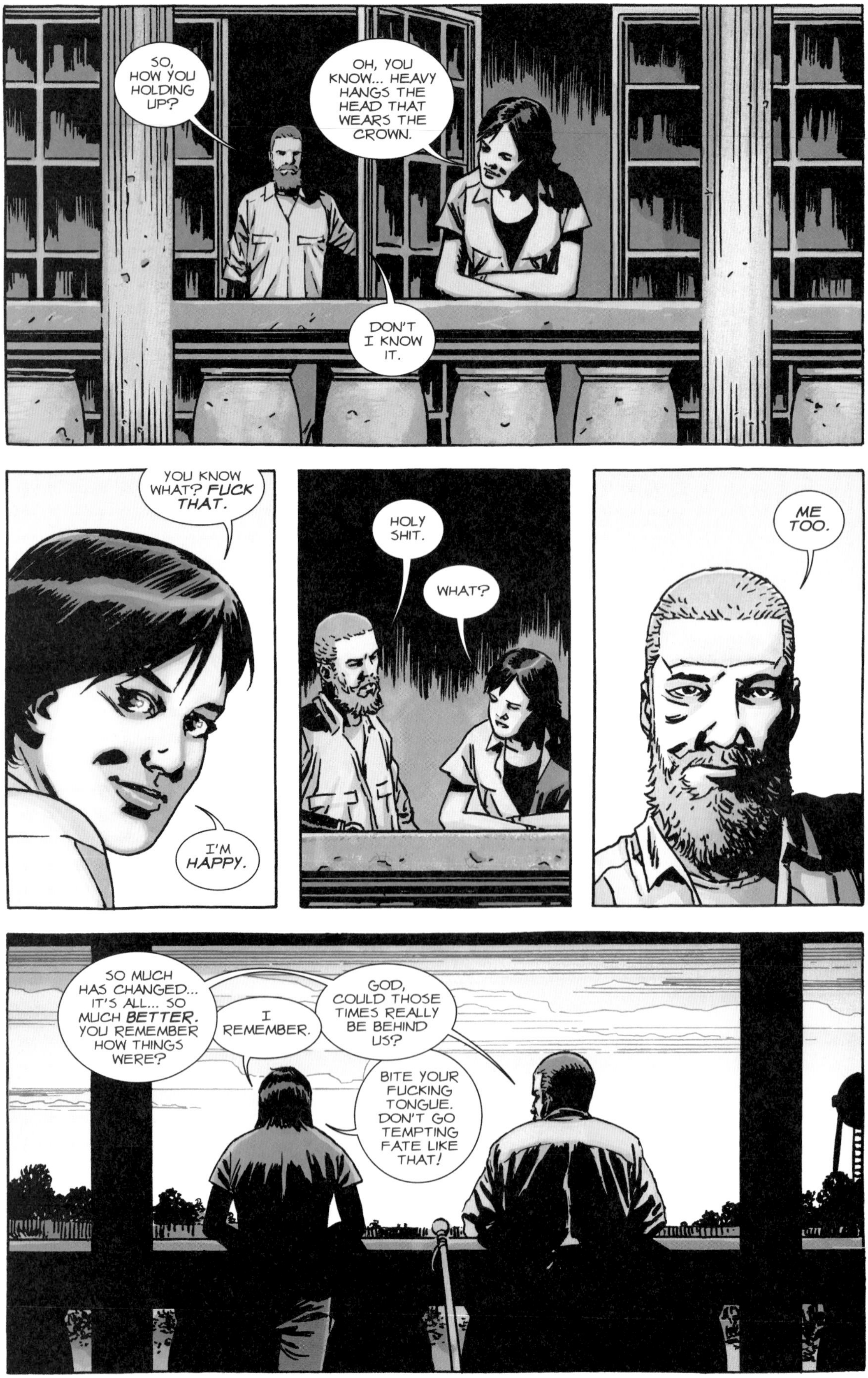
SO, HOW YOU HOLDING UP?
OH, YOU KNOW... HEAVY HANGS THE HEAD THAT WEARS THE CROWN.
DON'T I KNOW IT.
YOU KNOW WHAT? FUCK THAT.
I'M HAPPY.
HOLY SHIT.
WHAT?
ME TOO.
SO MUCH HAS CHANGED... IT'S ALL... SO MUCH BETTER. YOU REMEMBER HOW THINGS WERE?
I REMEMBER.
GOD, COULD THOSE TIMES REALLY BE BEHIND US?
BITE YOUR FUCKING TONGUE. DON'T GO TEMPTING FATE LIKE THAT!

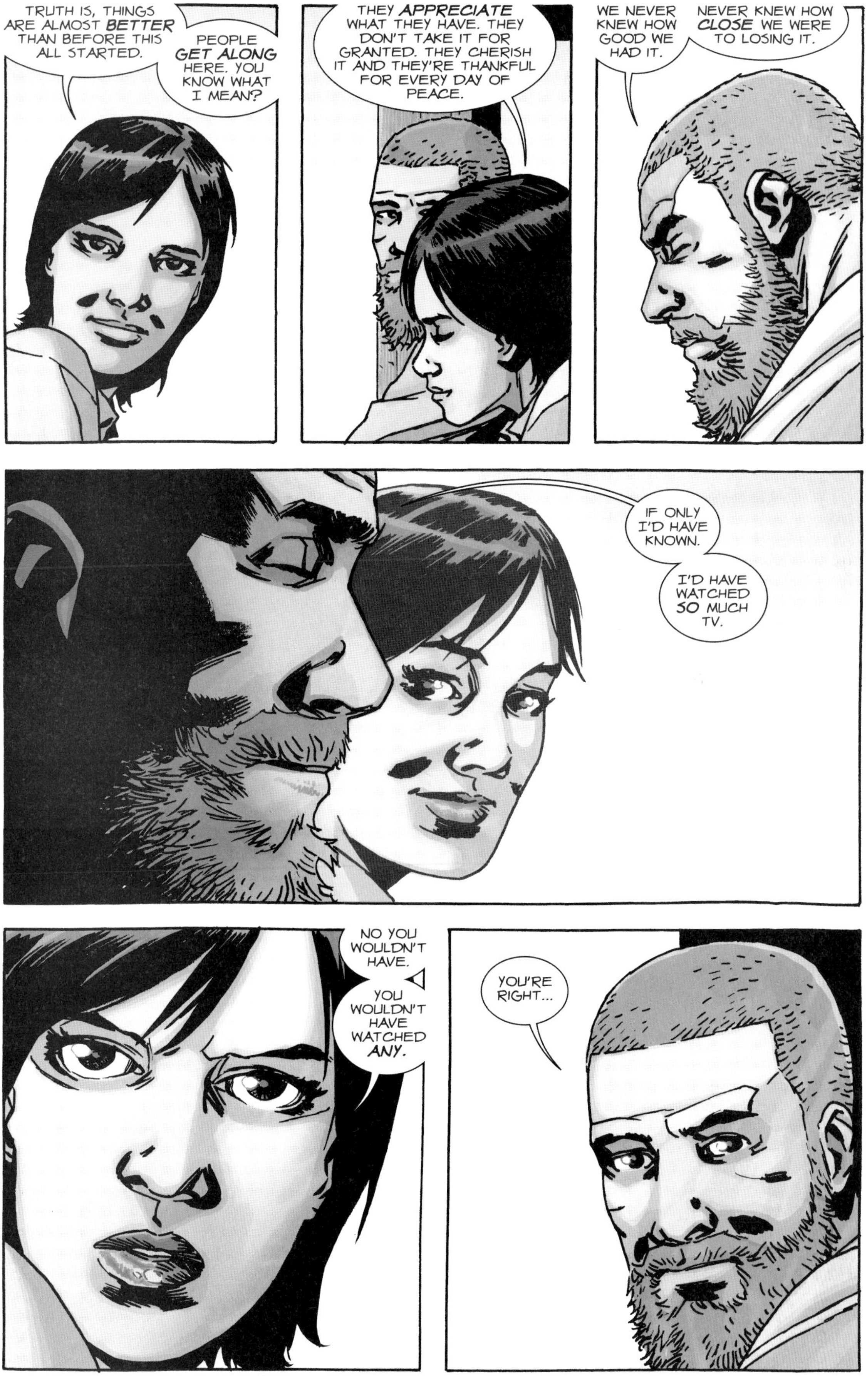
TRUTH IS, THINGS ARE ALMOST BETTER THAN BEFORE THIS ALL STARTED.
PEOPLE GET ALONG HERE. YOU KNOW WHAT I MEAN?
THEY APPRECIATE WHAT THEY HAVE. THEY DON'T TAKE IT FOR GRANTED. THEY CHERISH IT AND THEY'RE THANKFUL FOR EVERY DAY OF PEACE.
WE NEVER KNEW HOW GOOD WE HAD IT.
NEVER KNEW HOW CLOSE WE WERE TO LOSING IT.
IF ONLY I'D HAVE KNOWN.
I'D HAVE WATCHED SO MUCH TV.
NO YOU WOULDN'T HAVE.
YOU WOULDN'T HAVE WATCHED ANY.
YOU'RE RIGHT...

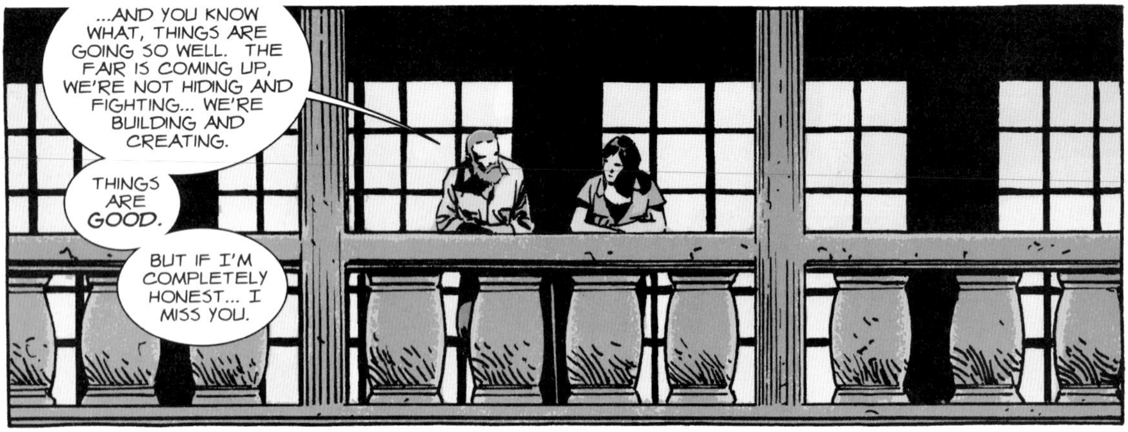
...AND YOU KNOW WHAT, THINGS ARE GOING SO WELL. THE FAIR IS COMING UP, WE'RE NOT HIDING AND FIGHTING... WE'RE BUILDING AND CREATING.
THINGS ARE GOOD.
BUT IF I'M COMPLETELY HONEST... I MISS YOU.

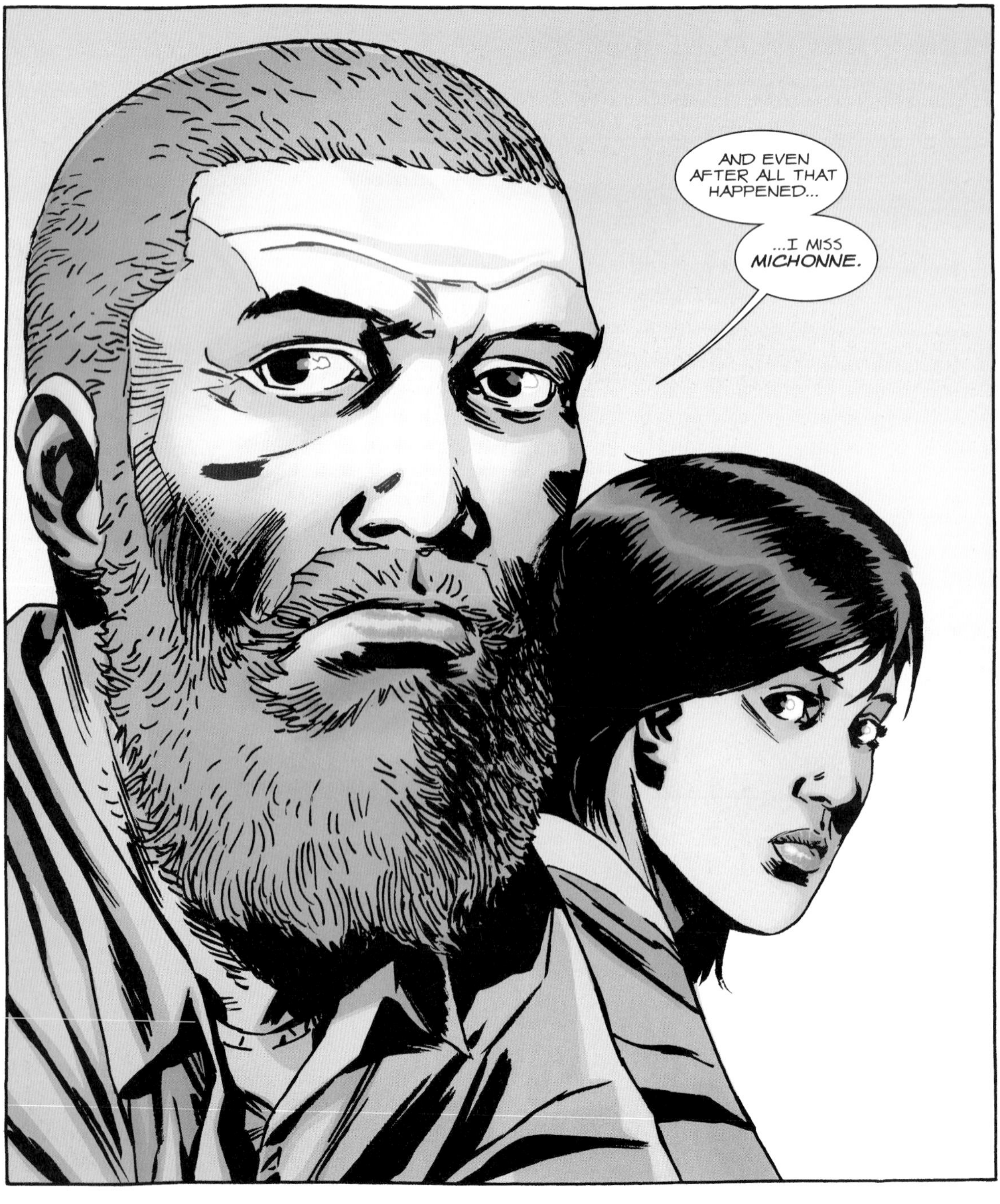
AND EVEN AFTER ALL THAT HAPPENED...
...I MISS MICHONNE.

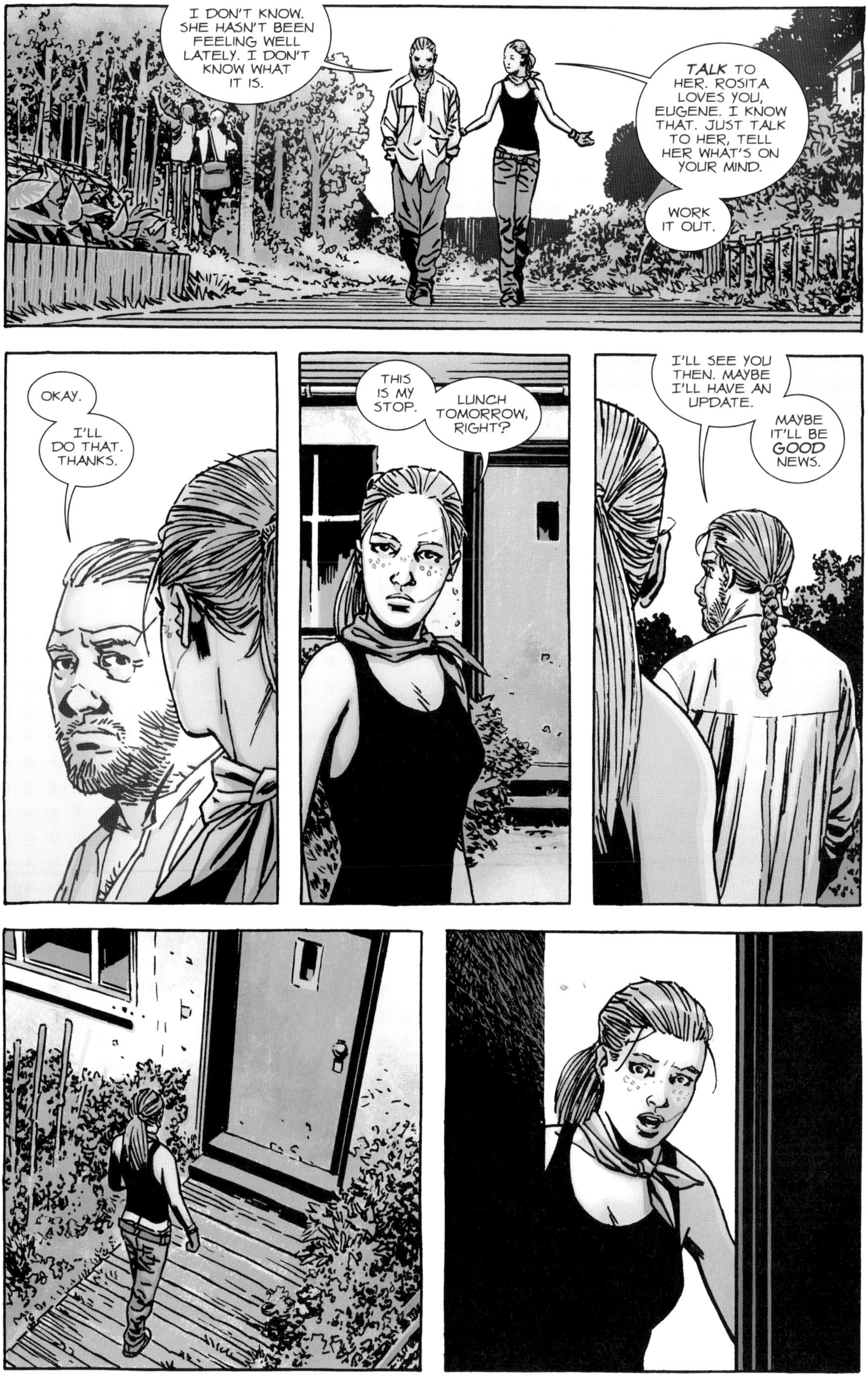
I DON'T KNOW. SHE HASN'T BEEN FEELING WELL LATELY. I DON'T KNOW WHAT IT IS.
TALK TO HER. ROSITA LOVES YOU, EUGENE. I KNOW THAT. JUST TALK TO HER, TELL HER WHAT'S ON YOUR MIND.
WORK IT OUT.
OKAY.
I'LL DO THAT. THANKS.
THIS IS MY STOP.
LUNCH TOMORROW, RIGHT?
I'LL SEE YOU THEN. MAYBE I'LL HAVE AN UPDATE.
MAYBE IT'LL BE GOOD NEWS.

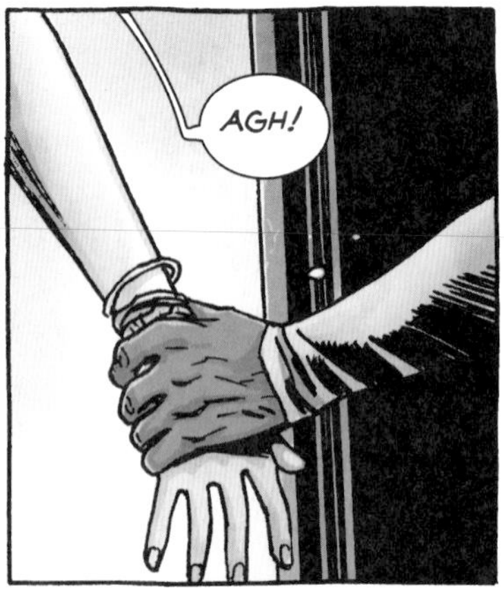
AGH!
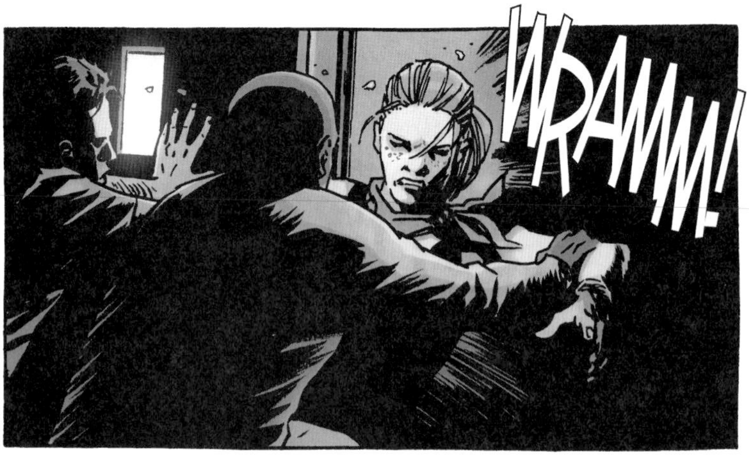
WRAMM!
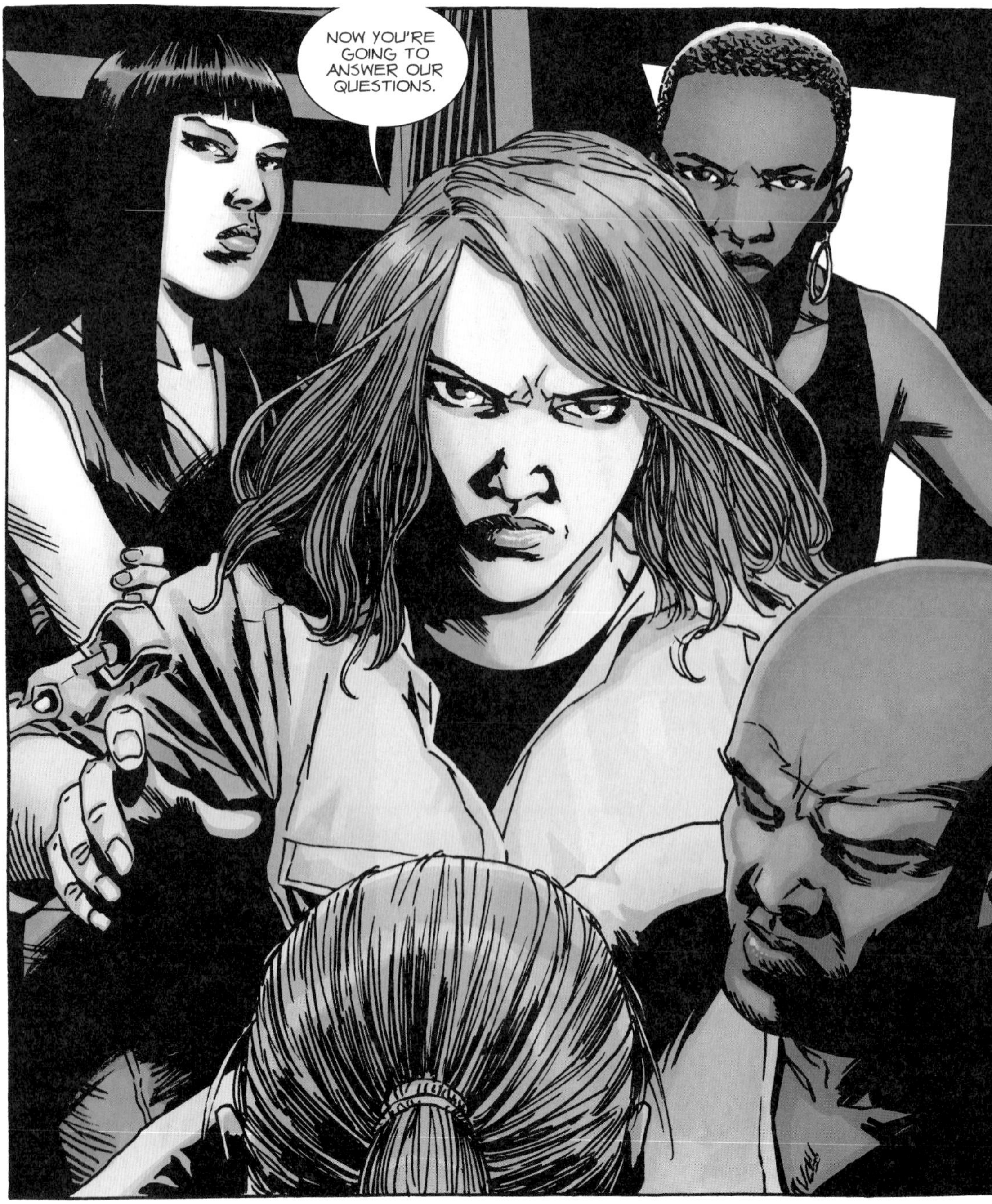
NOW YOU'RE GOING TO ANSWER OUR QUESTIONS.

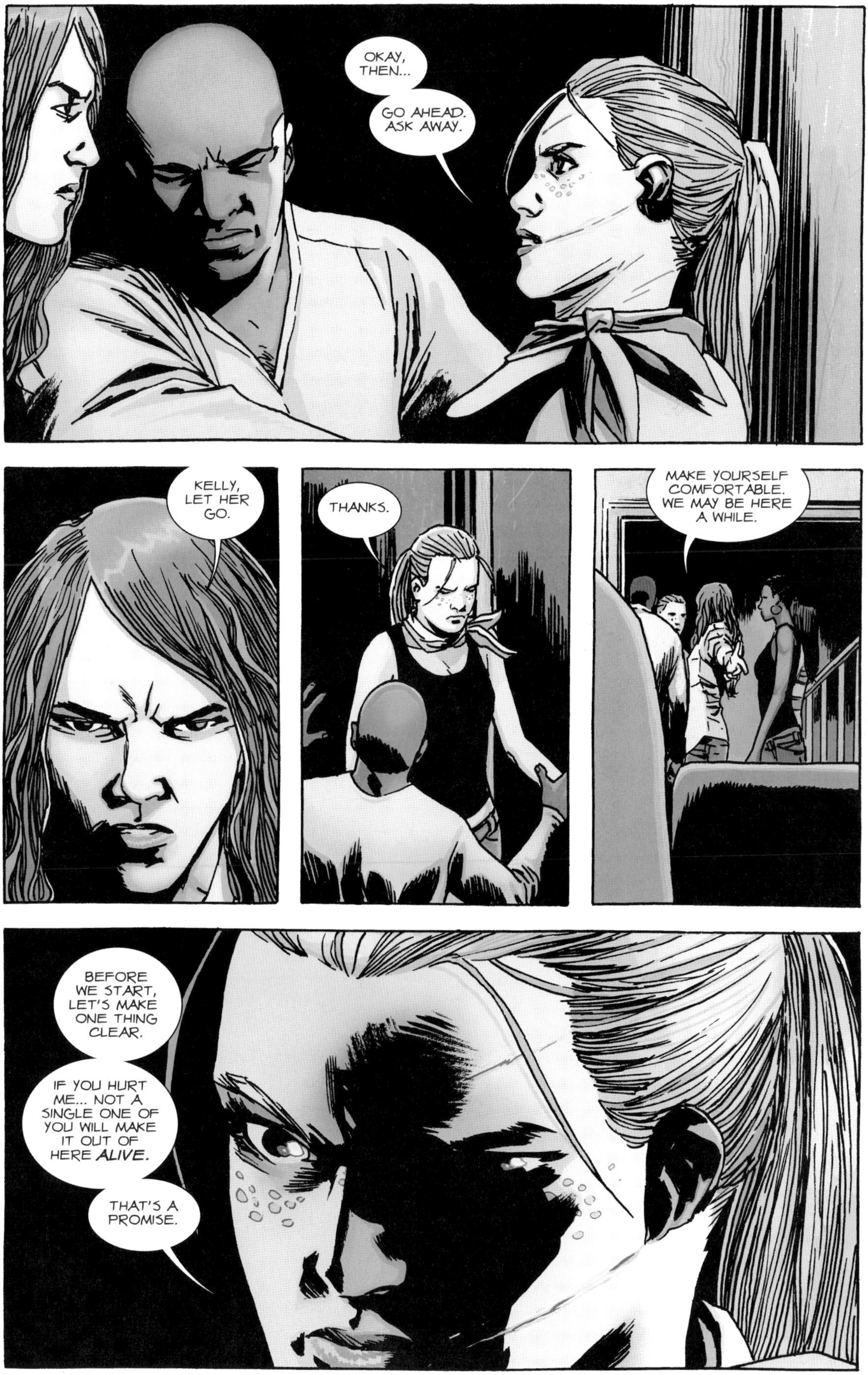
OKAY, THEN...
GO AHEAD. ASK AWAY.
KELLY, LET HER GO.
THANKS.
MAKE YOURSELF COMFORTABLE. WE MAY BE HERE A WHILE.
BEFORE WE START, LET'S MAKE ONE THING CLEAR.
IF YOU HURT ME... NOT A SINGLE ONE OF YOU WILL MAKE IT OUT OF HERE *ALIVE*.
THAT'S A PROMISE.

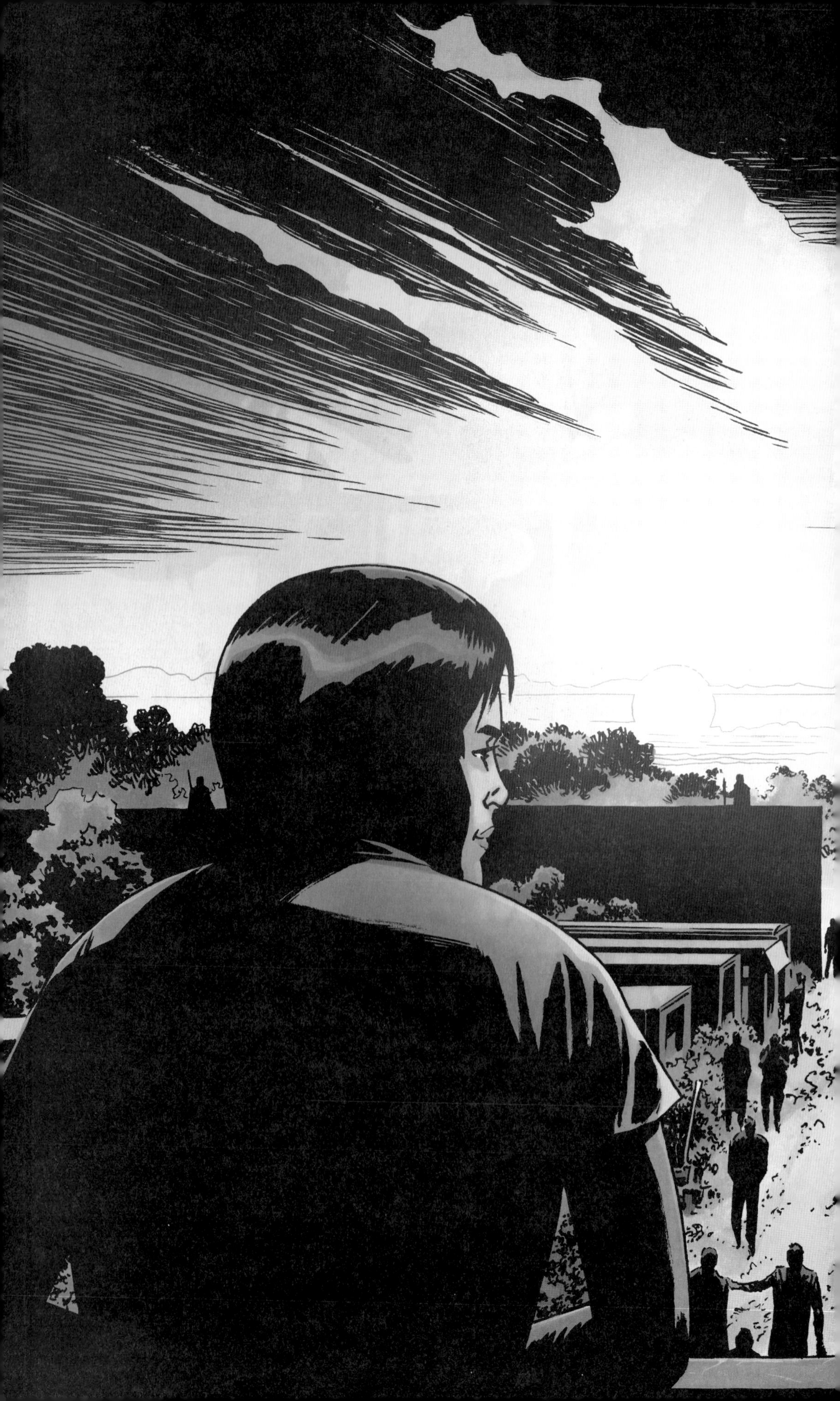

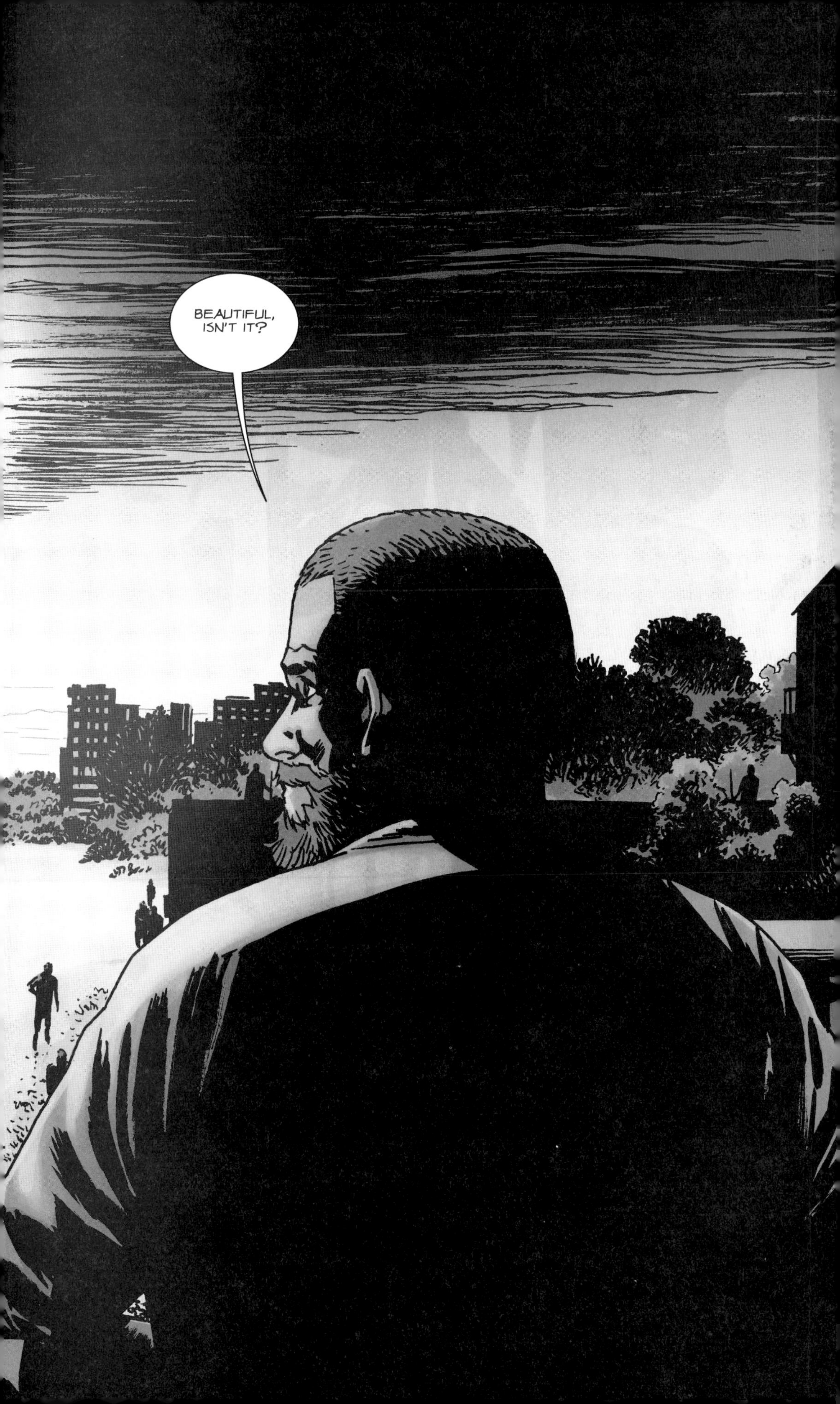
BEAUTIFUL, ISN'T IT?

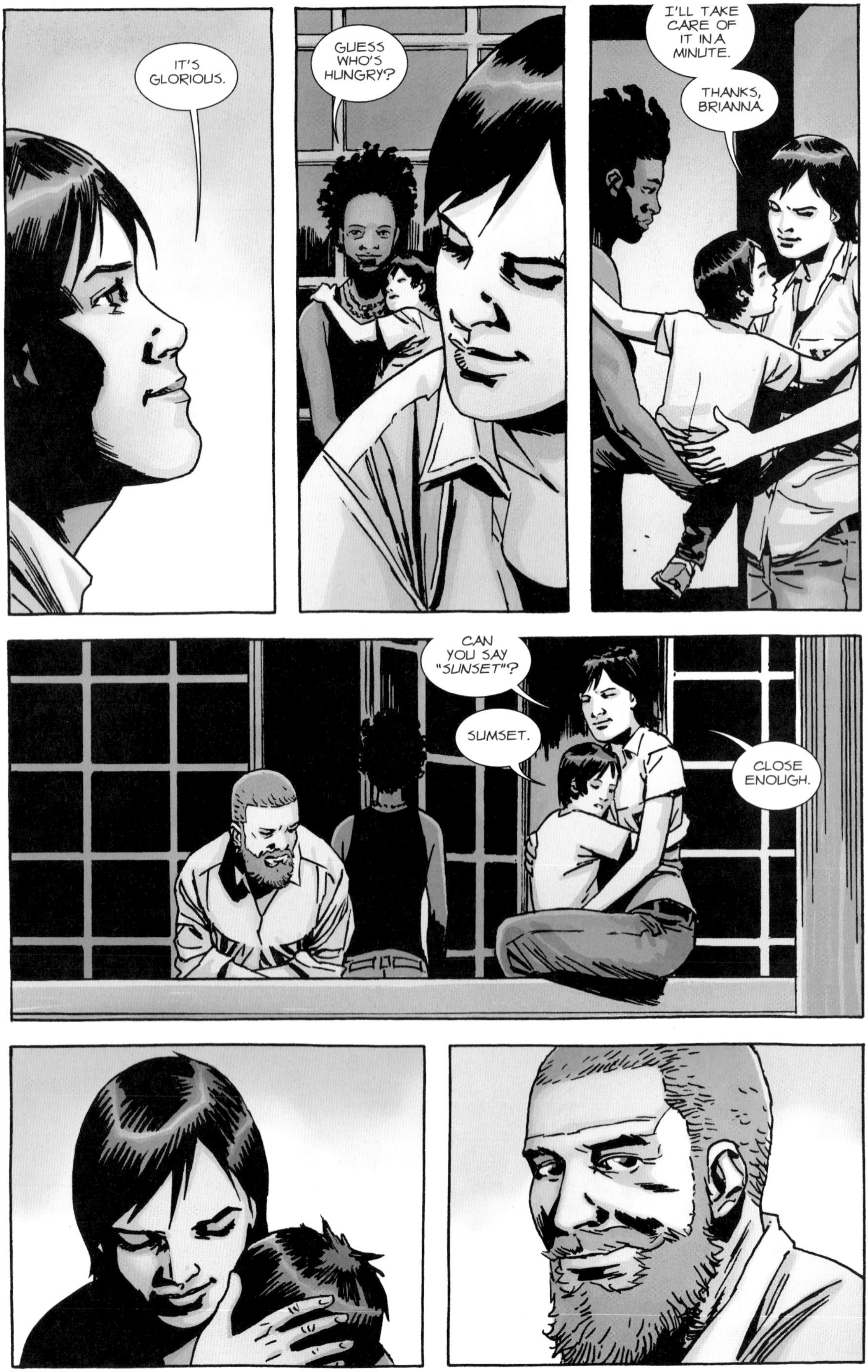
IT'S GLORIOUS.
GUESS WHO'S HUNGRY?
I'LL TAKE CARE OF IT IN A MINUTE.
THANKS, BRIANNA.
CAN YOU SAY "SUNSET"?
SUMSET.
CLOSE ENOUGH.

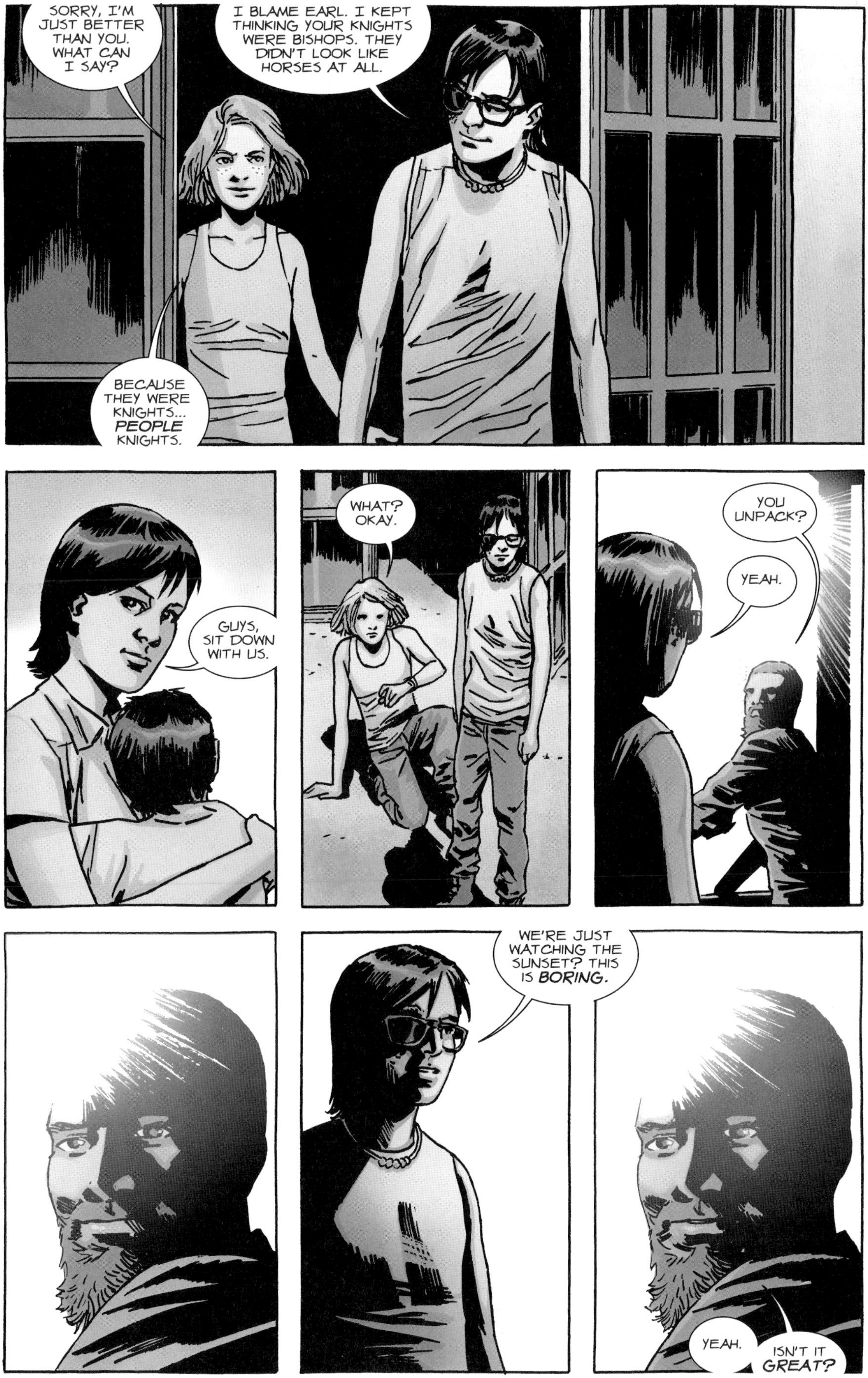

SORRY, I'M JUST BETTER THAN YOU. WHAT CAN I SAY?
I BLAME EARL. I KEPT THINKING YOUR KNIGHTS WERE BISHOPS. THEY DIDN'T LOOK LIKE HORSES AT ALL.
BECAUSE THEY WERE KNIGHTS... PEOPLE KNIGHTS.
GUYS, SIT DOWN WITH US.
WHAT? OKAY.
YOU UNPACK?
YEAH.
WE'RE JUST WATCHING THE SUNSET? THIS IS BORING.
YEAH.
ISN'T IT GREAT?

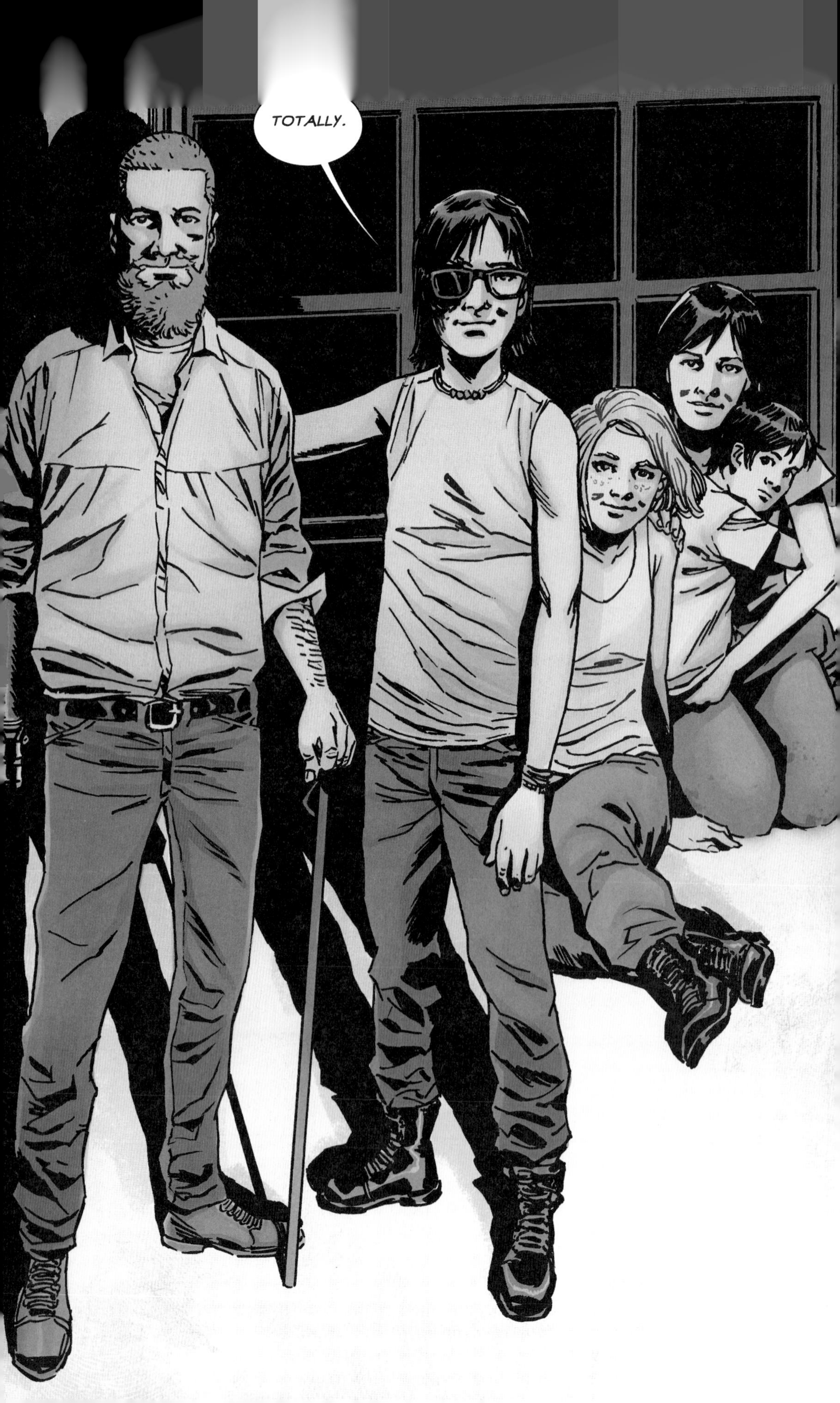
TOTALLY.

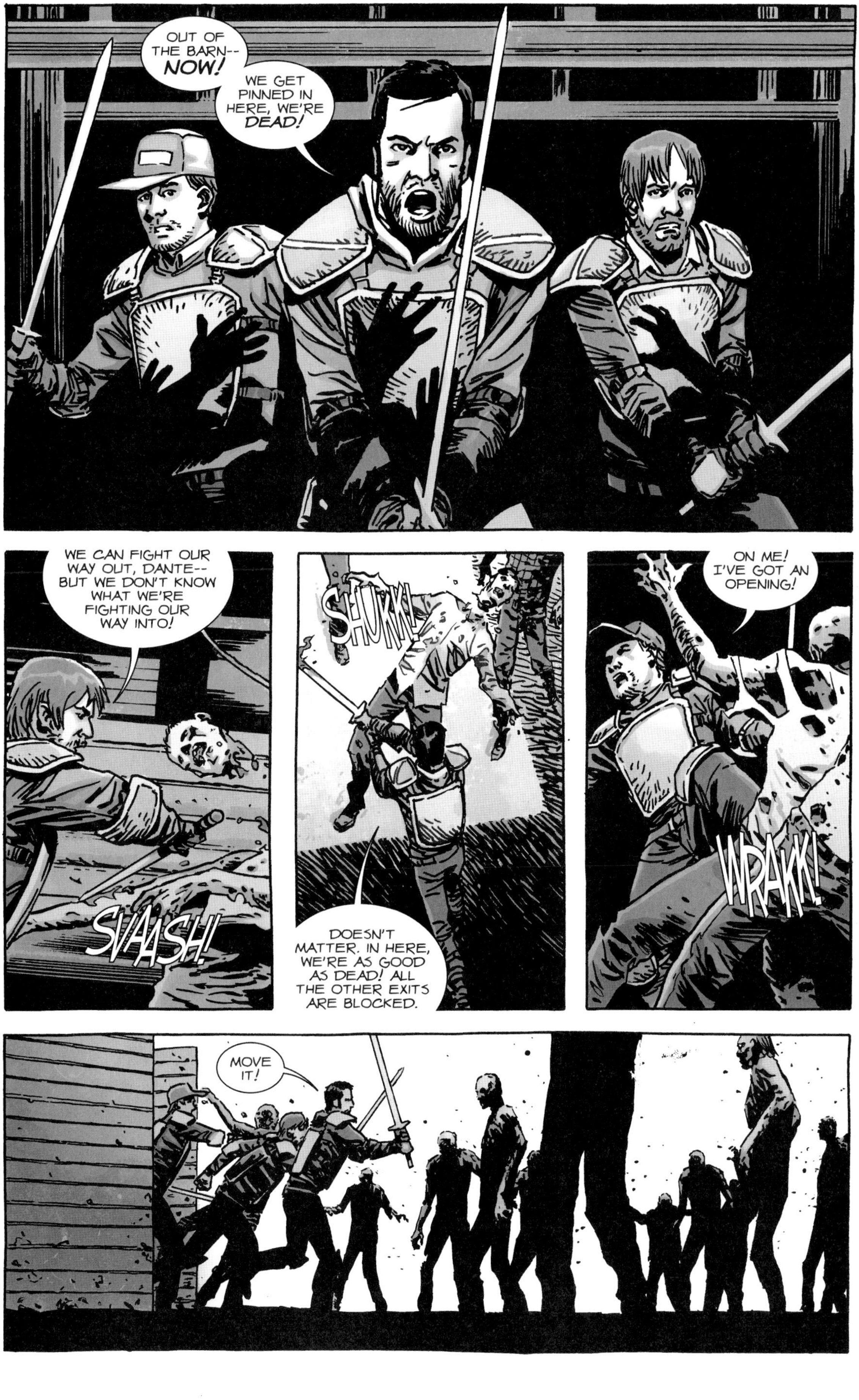
OUT OF THE BARN-- NOW!
WE GET PINNED IN HERE, WE'RE DEAD!
WE CAN FIGHT OUR WAY OUT, DANTE-- BUT WE DON'T KNOW WHAT WE'RE FIGHTING OUR WAY INTO!
SVAASH!
SHUKK!
DOESN'T MATTER. IN HERE, WE'RE AS GOOD AS DEAD! ALL THE OTHER EXITS ARE BLOCKED.
ON ME! I'VE GOT AN OPENING!
WRAKK!
MOVE IT!

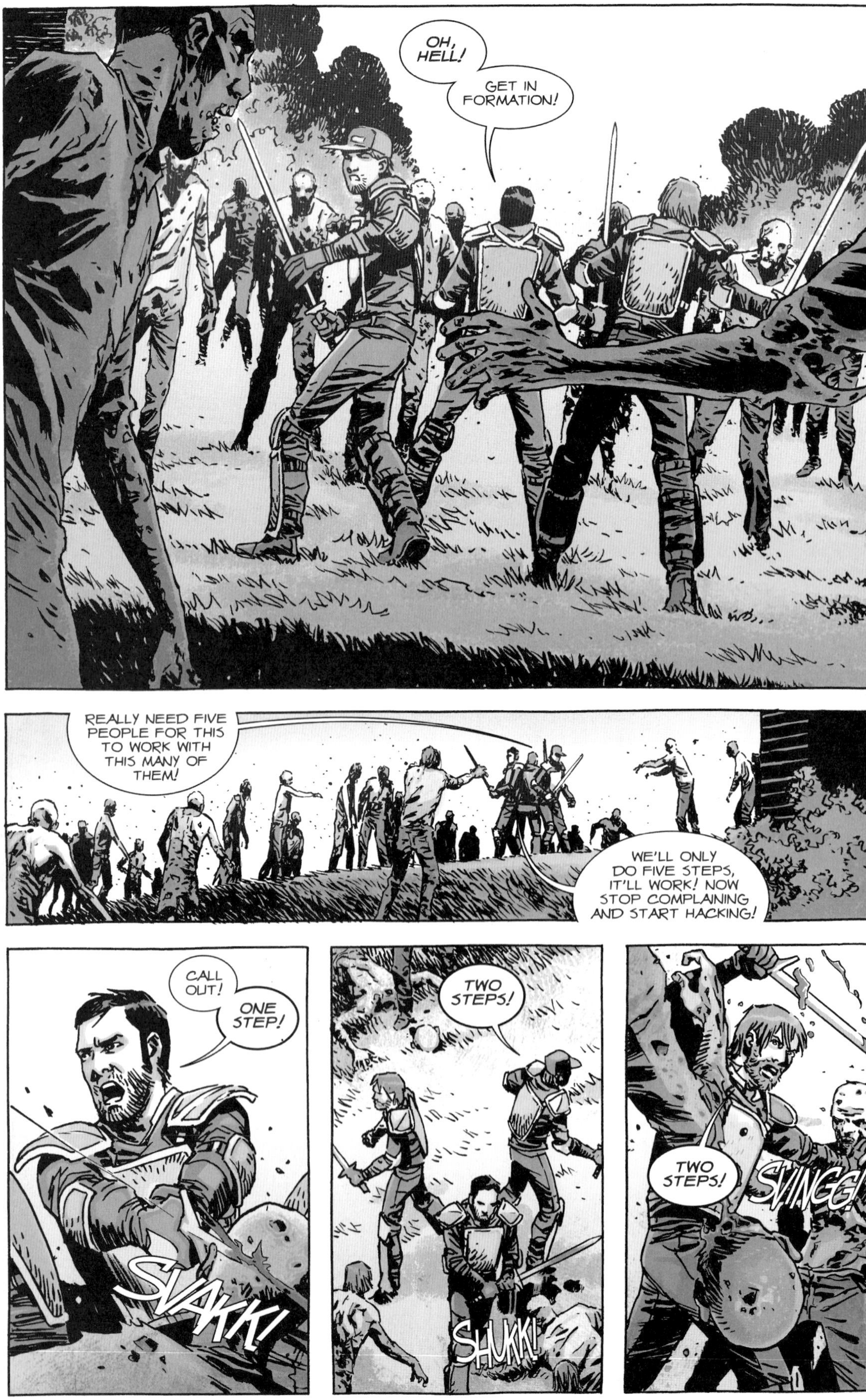

OH, HELL!
GET IN FORMATION!
REALLY NEED FIVE PEOPLE FOR THIS TO WORK WITH THIS MANY OF THEM!
WE'LL ONLY DO FIVE STEPS, IT'LL WORK! NOW STOP COMPLAINING AND START HACKING!
CALL OUT!
ONE STEP!
SVAKK!
TWO STEPS!
SHUKK!
TWO STEPS!
SVINGG!

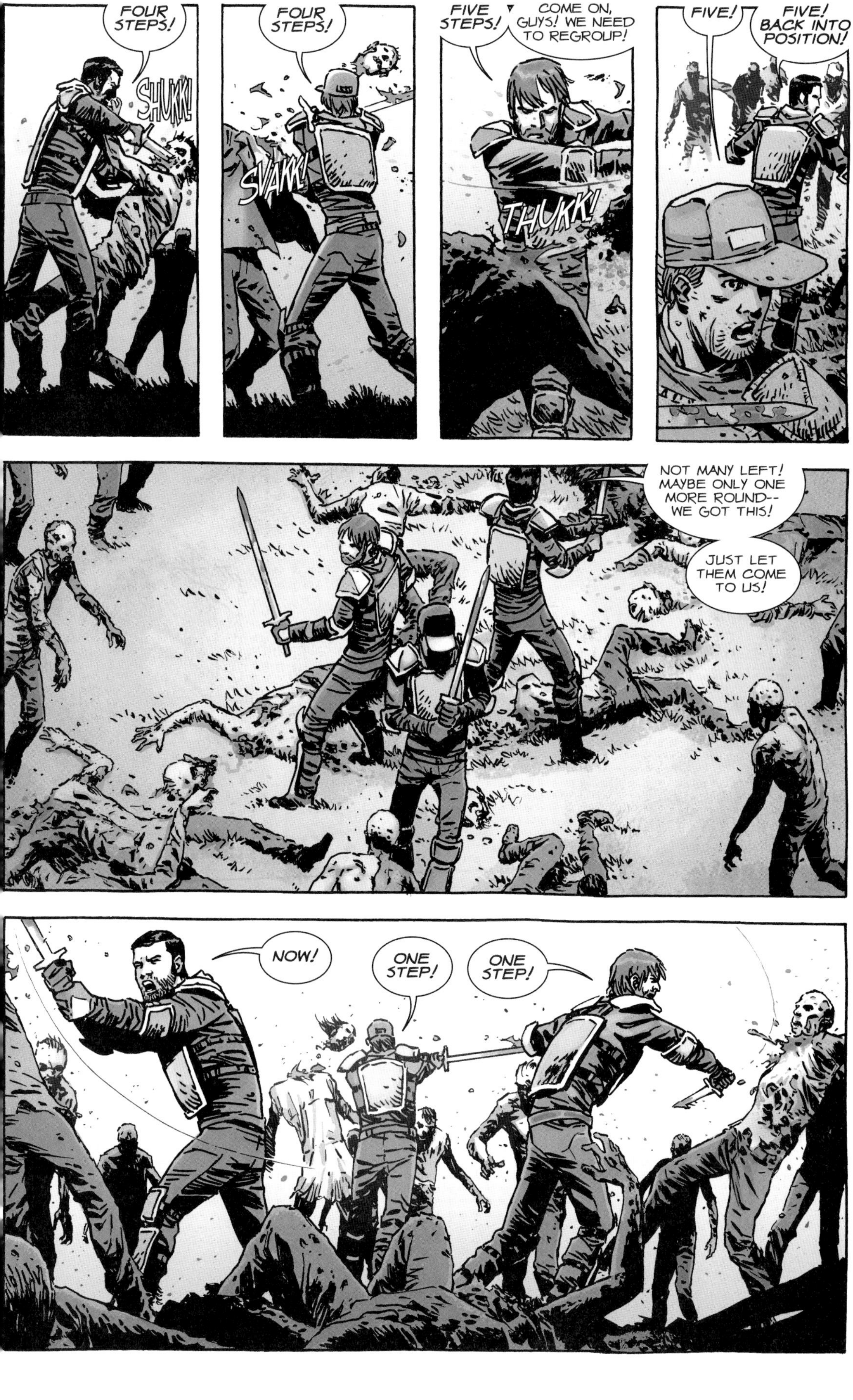
FOUR STEPS!
SHUKK!
FOUR STEPS!
SVAKK!
FIVE STEPS!
COME ON, GUYS! WE NEED TO REGROUP!
THUKK!
FIVE!
FIVE! BACK INTO POSITION!
NOT MANY LEFT! MAYBE ONLY ONE MORE ROUND-- WE GOT THIS!
JUST LET THEM COME TO US!
NOW!
ONE STEP!
ONE STEP!

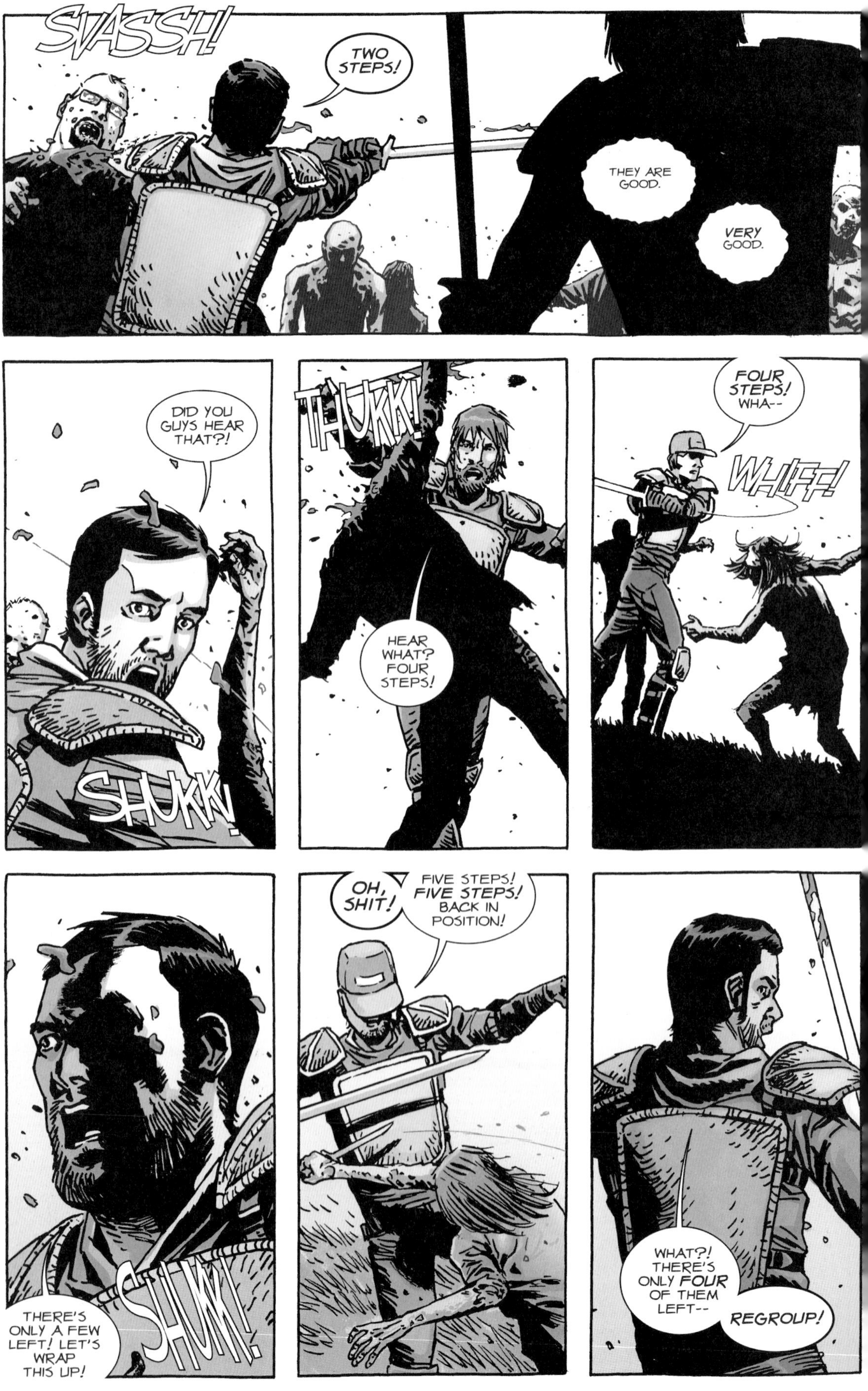
SVASSH!
TWO STEPS!
THEY ARE GOOD.
VERY GOOD.
DID YOU GUYS HEAR THAT?!
SHUKK!
THUKK!
HEAR WHAT? FOUR STEPS!
FOUR STEPS! WHA--
WHIFF!
SHUKK!
THERE'S ONLY A FEW LEFT! LET'S WRAP THIS UP!
OH, SHIT!
FIVE STEPS! FIVE STEPS! BACK IN POSITION!
WHAT?! THERE'S ONLY FOUR OF THEM LEFT--
REGROUP!

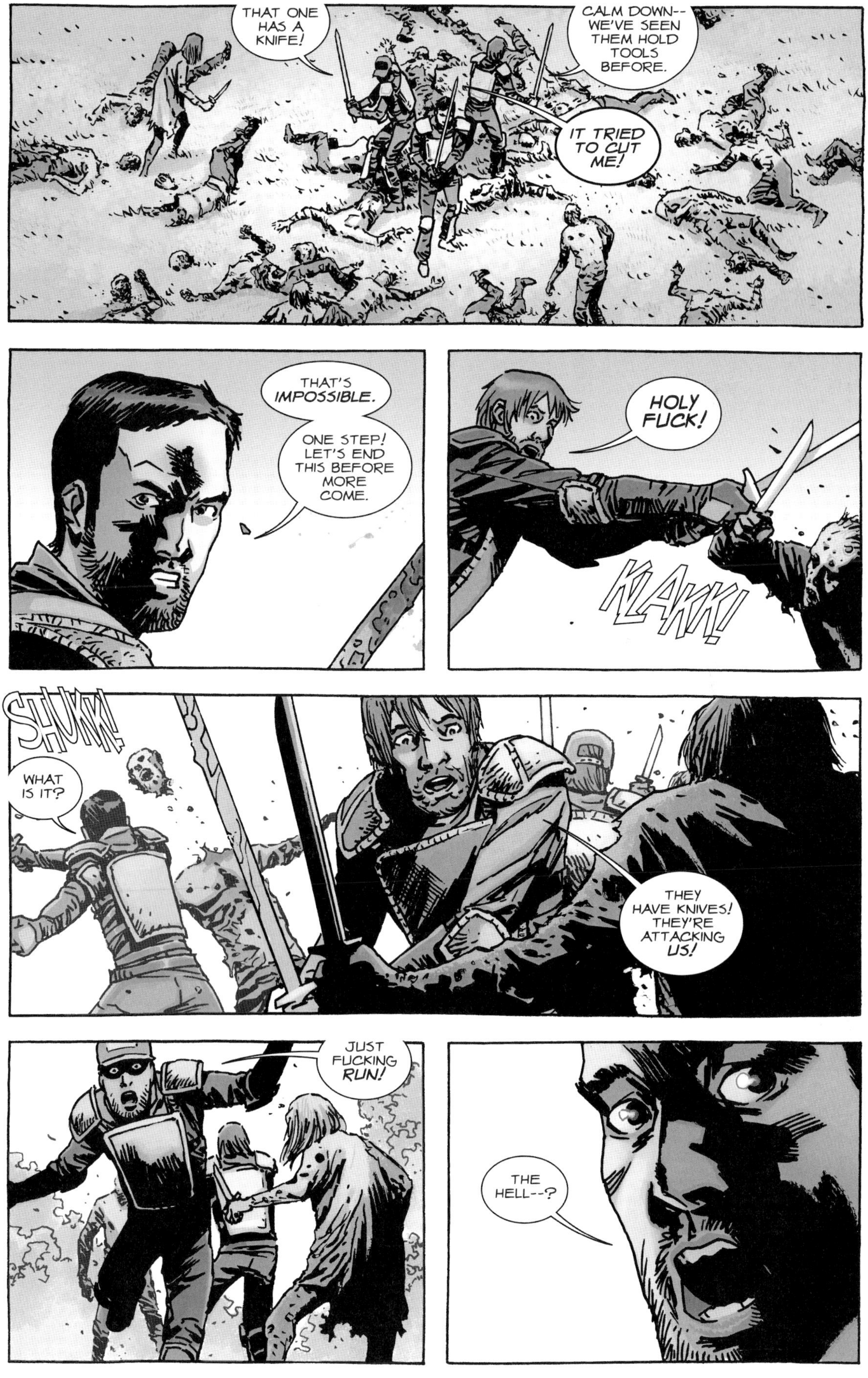
THAT ONE HAS A KNIFE!
CALM DOWN-- WE'VE SEEN THEM HOLD TOOLS BEFORE.
IT TRIED TO CUT ME!
THAT'S IMPOSSIBLE.
ONE STEP! LET'S END THIS BEFORE MORE COME.
HOLY FUCK!
KLAKK!
SHUKK!
WHAT IS IT?
THEY HAVE KNIVES! THEY'RE ATTACKING US!
JUST FUCKING RUN!
THE HELL--?

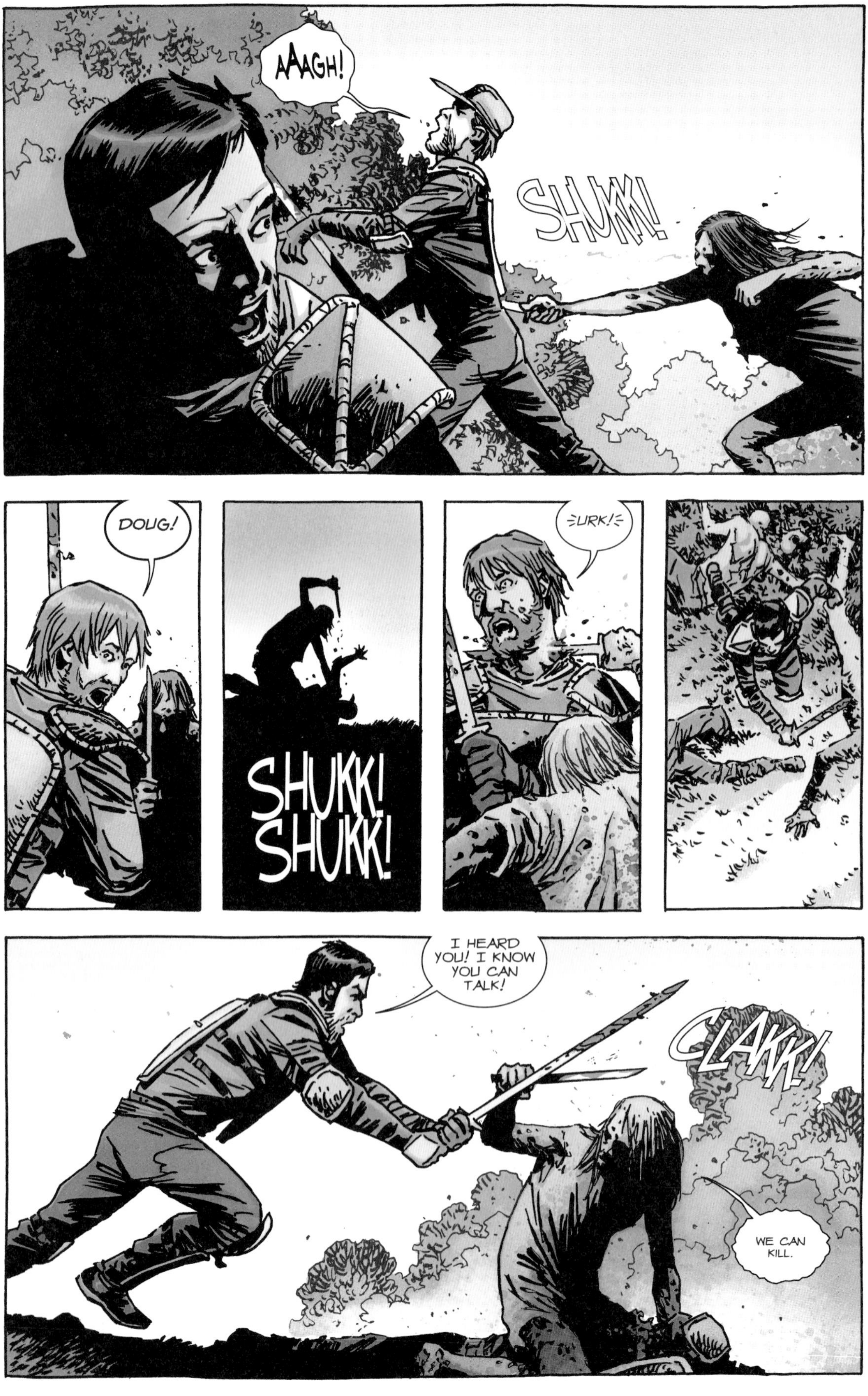

AAAGH!
SHUKK!
DOUG!
SHUKK! SHUKK!
URK!
I HEARD YOU! I KNOW YOU CAN TALK!
CLAKK!
WE CAN KILL.

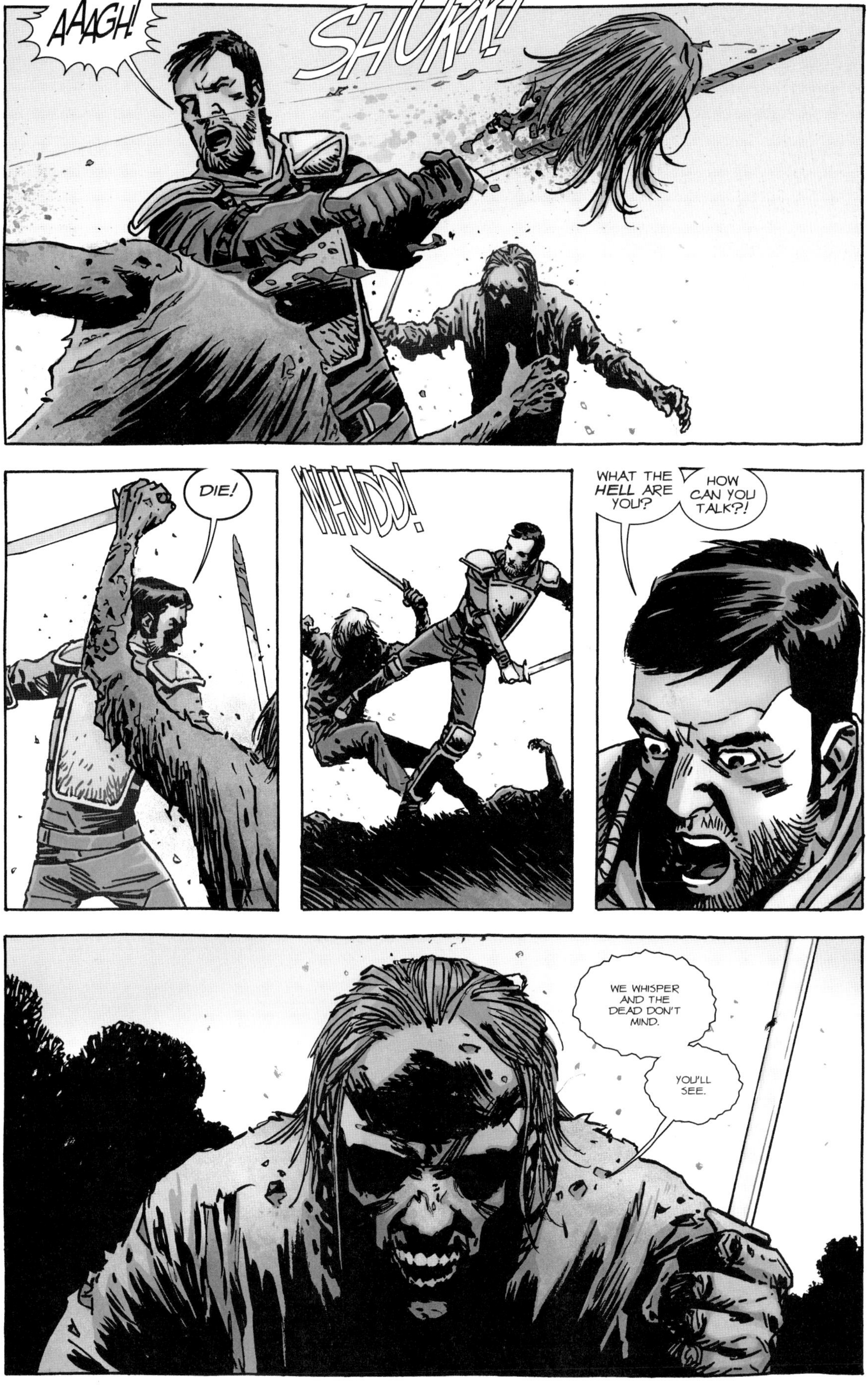

AAAGH!
SHUKK!
DIE!
WHUDD!
WHAT THE HELL ARE YOU?
HOW CAN YOU TALK?!
WE WHISPER AND THE DEAD DON'T MIND.
YOU'LL SEE.

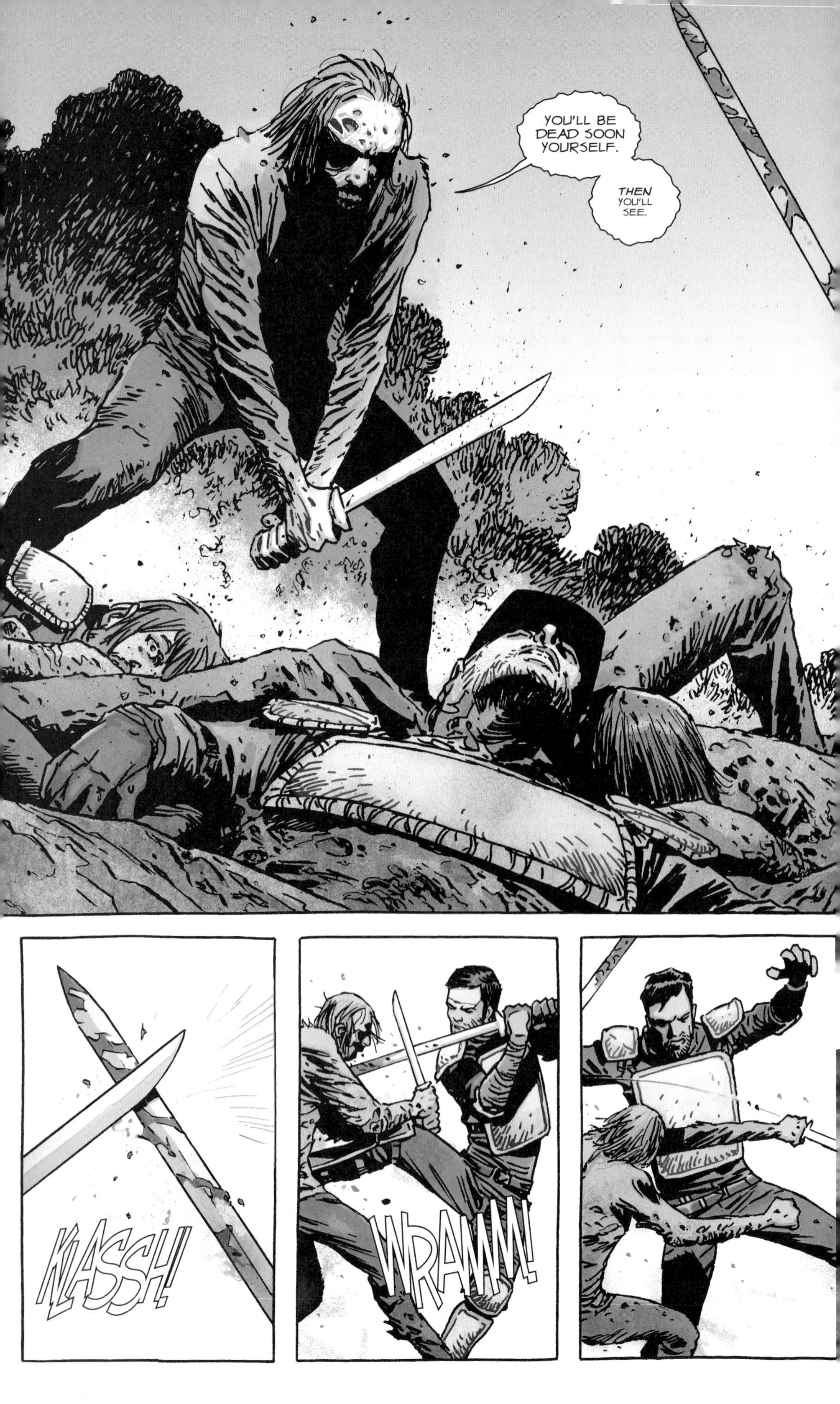
YOU'LL BE DEAD SOON YOURSELF.
THEN YOU'LL SEE.
KLASSH!
WRANNG!

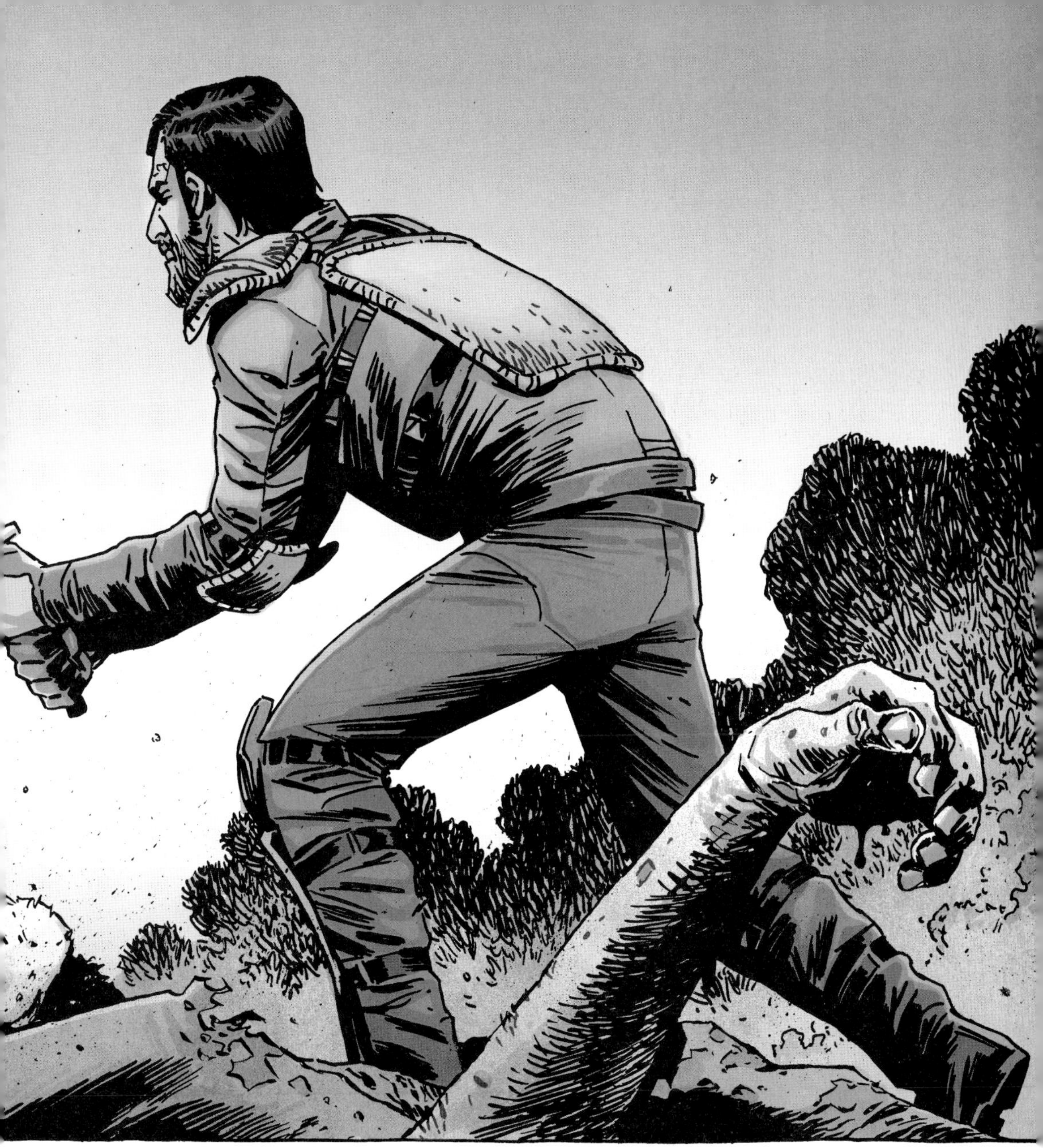

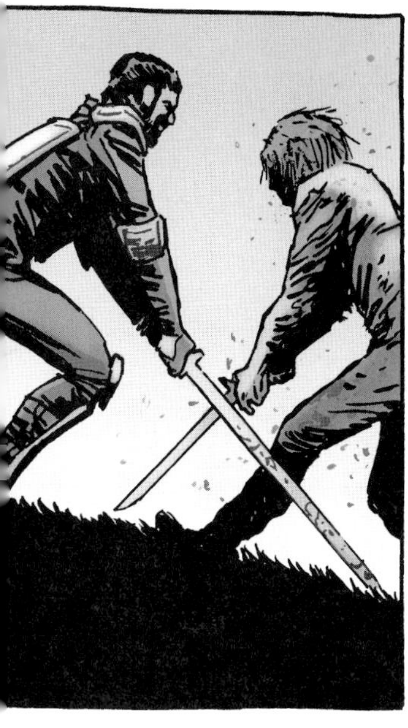

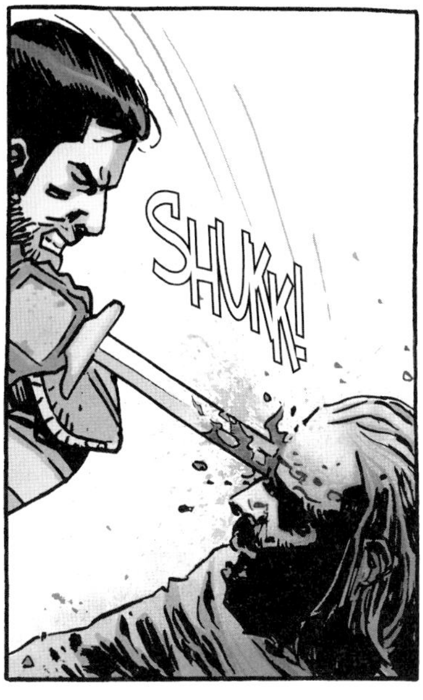
SHUKK!

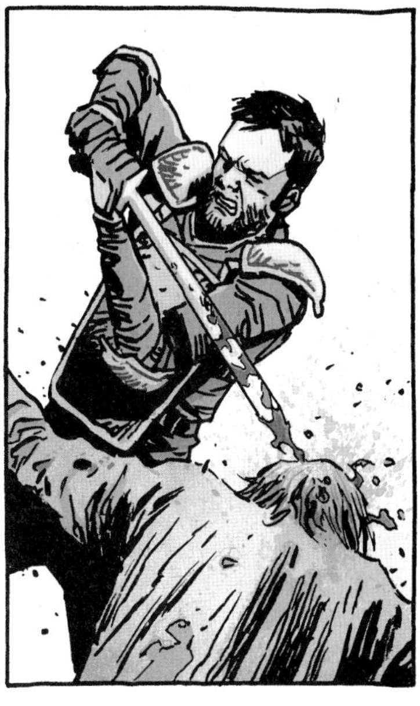

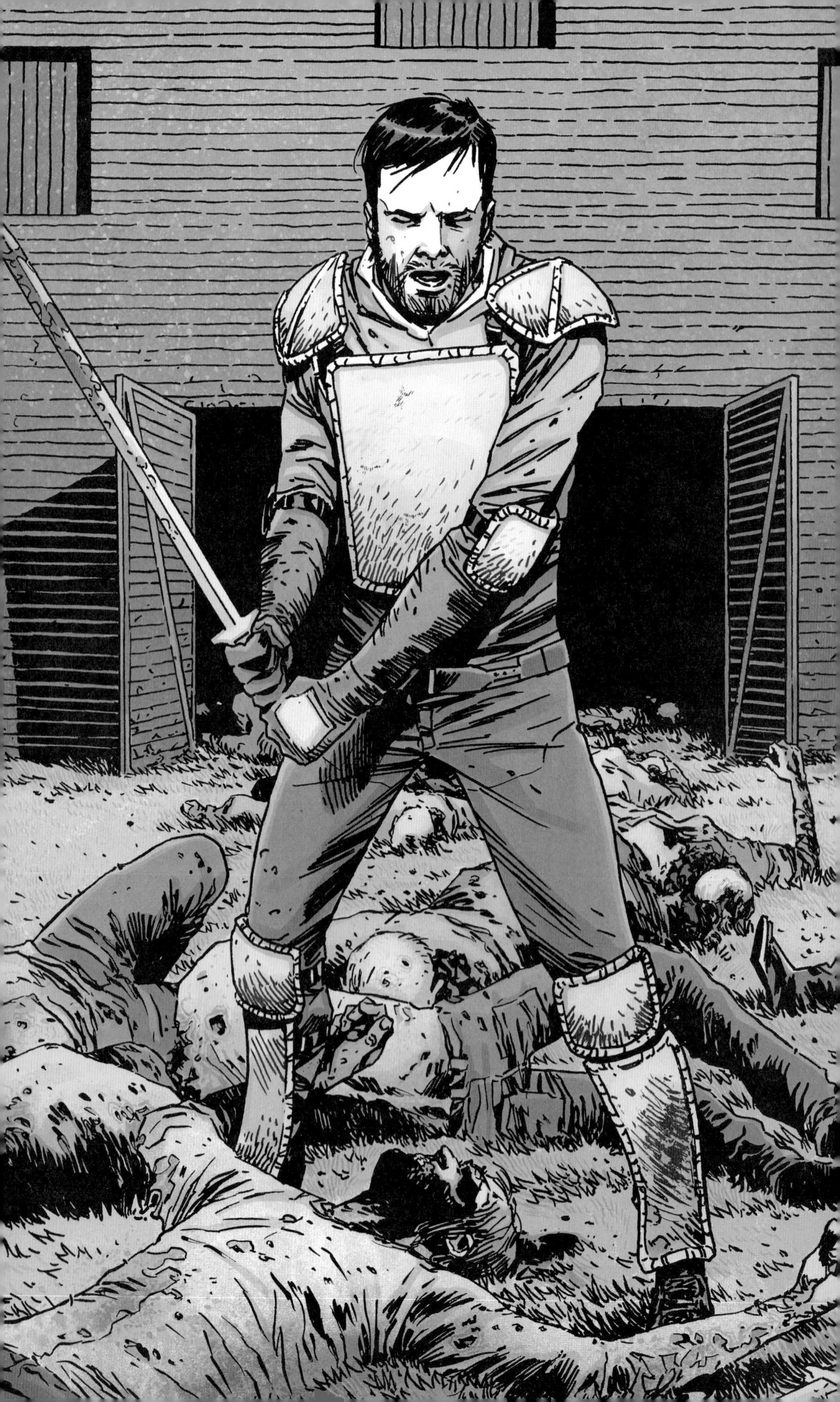

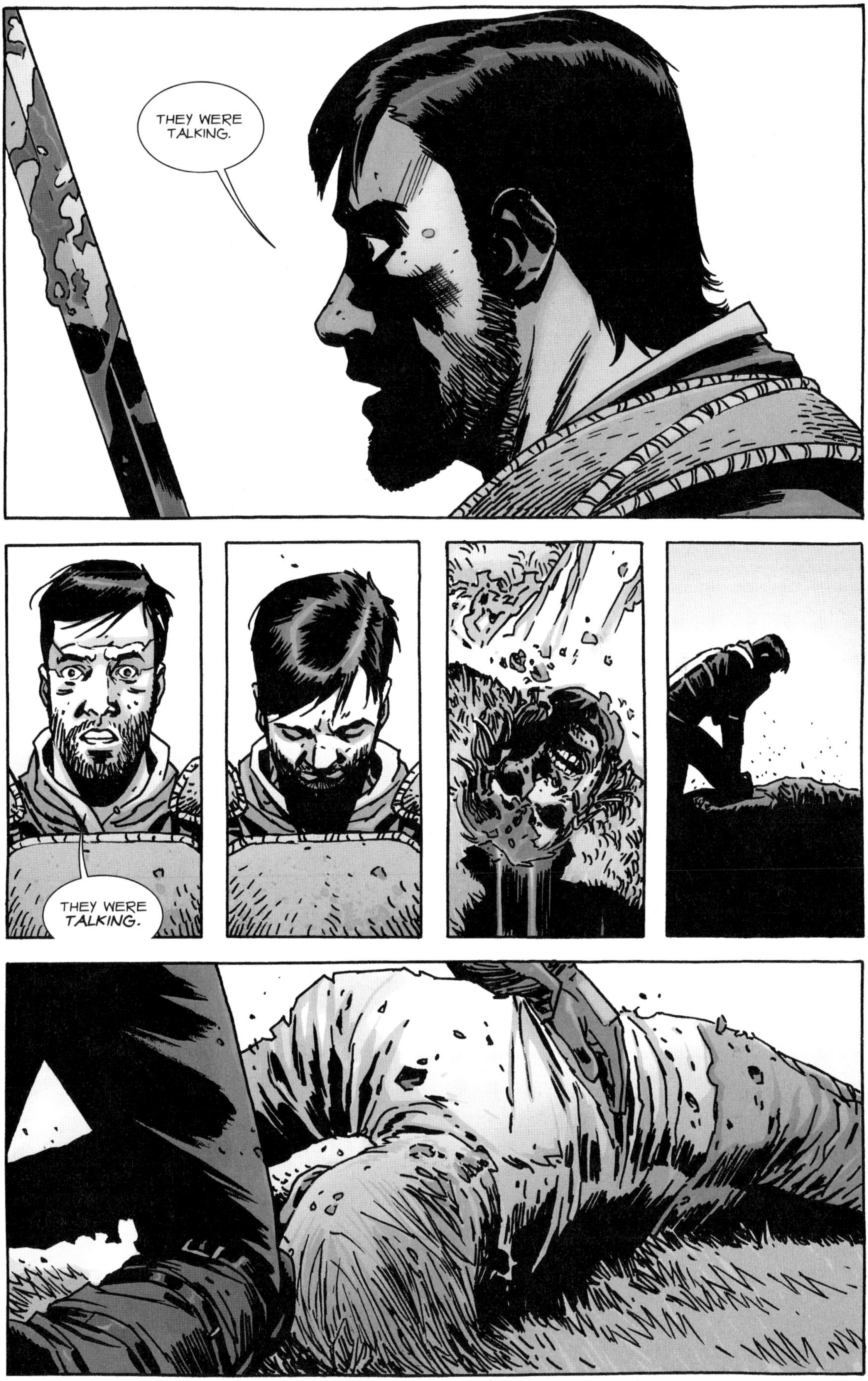
THEY WERE TALKING.
THEY WERE *TALKING.*

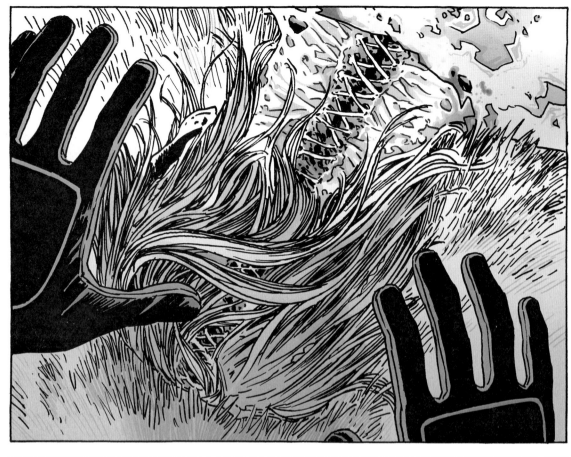

OH, MY
GOD...

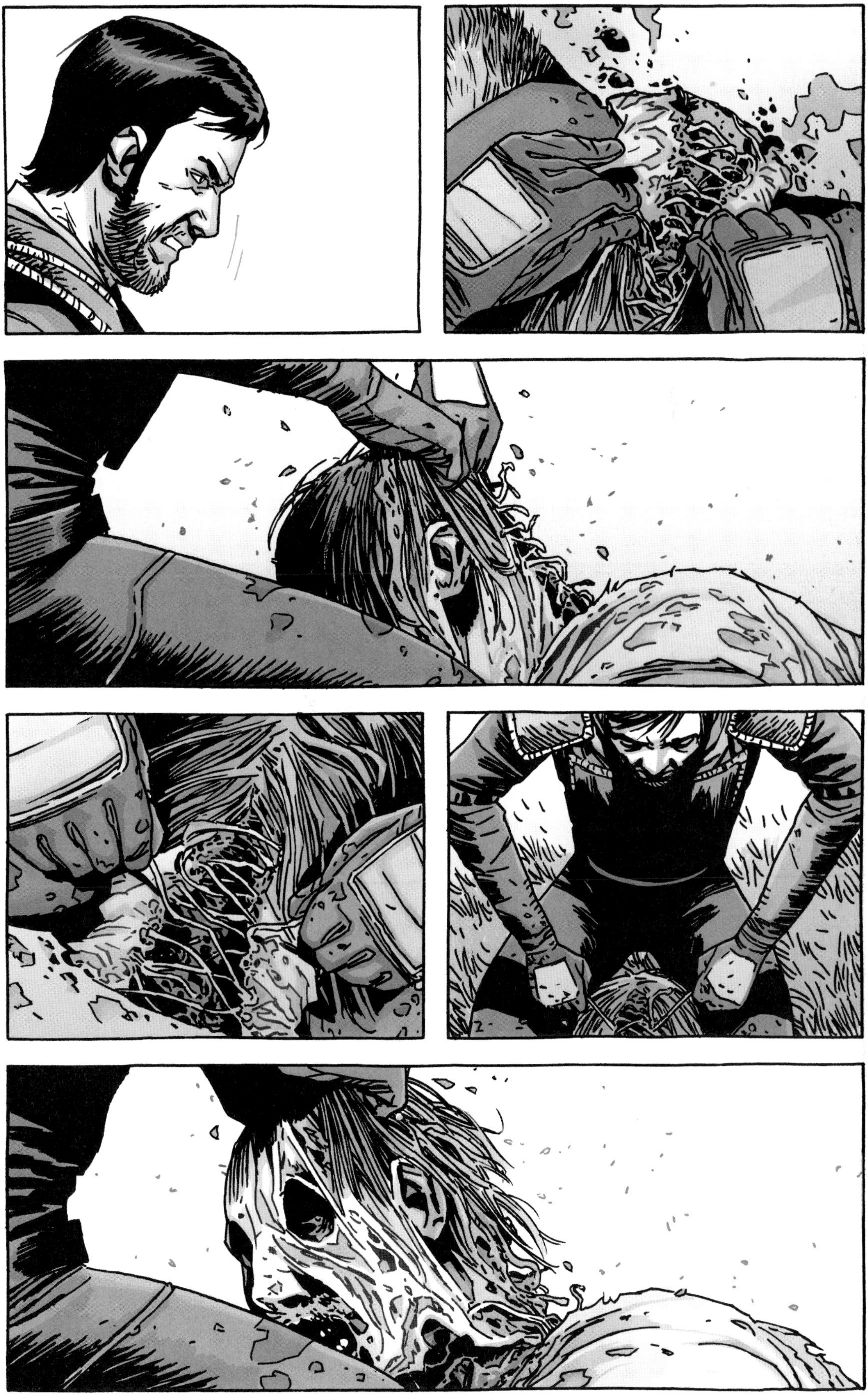

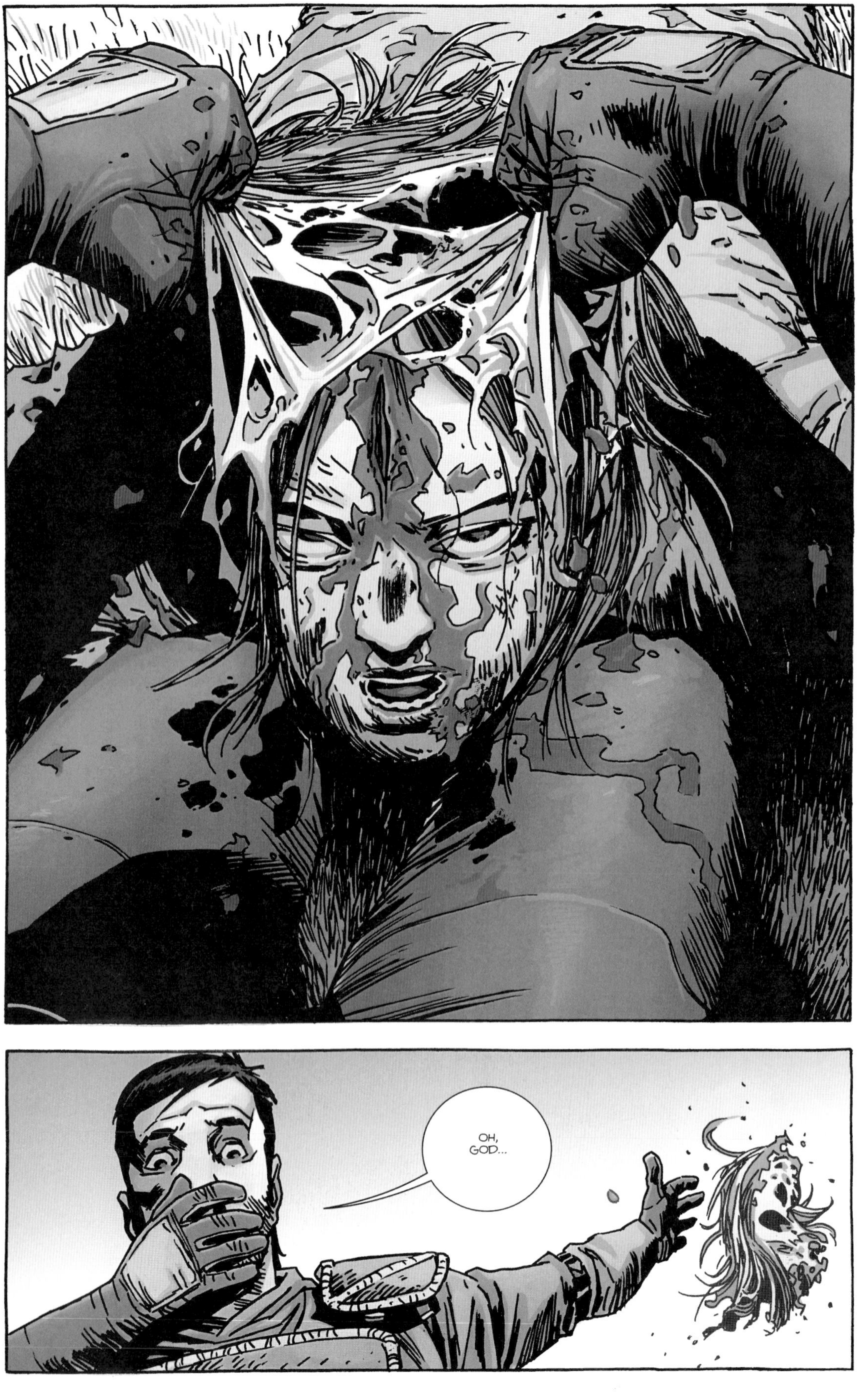
OH, GOD...

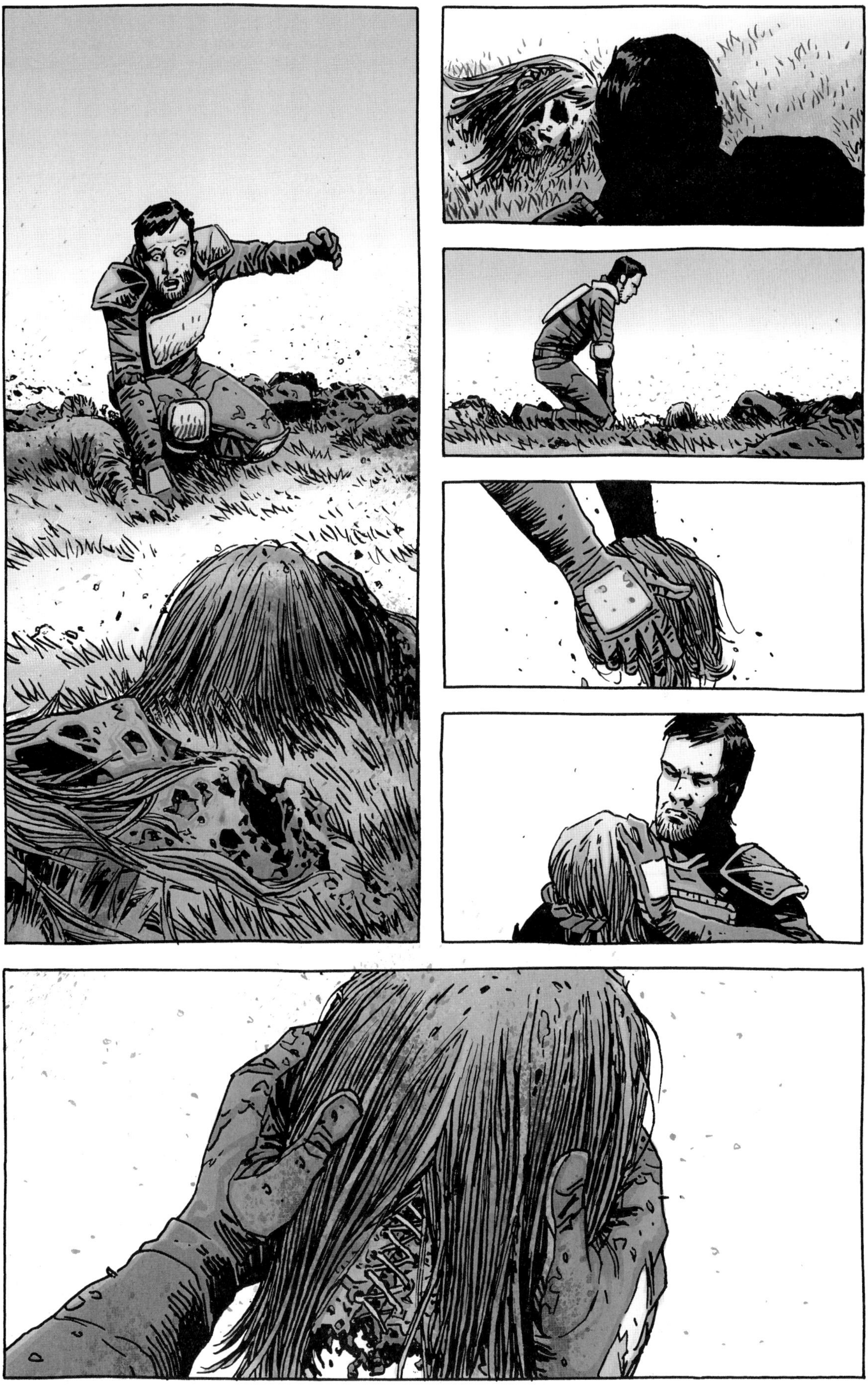

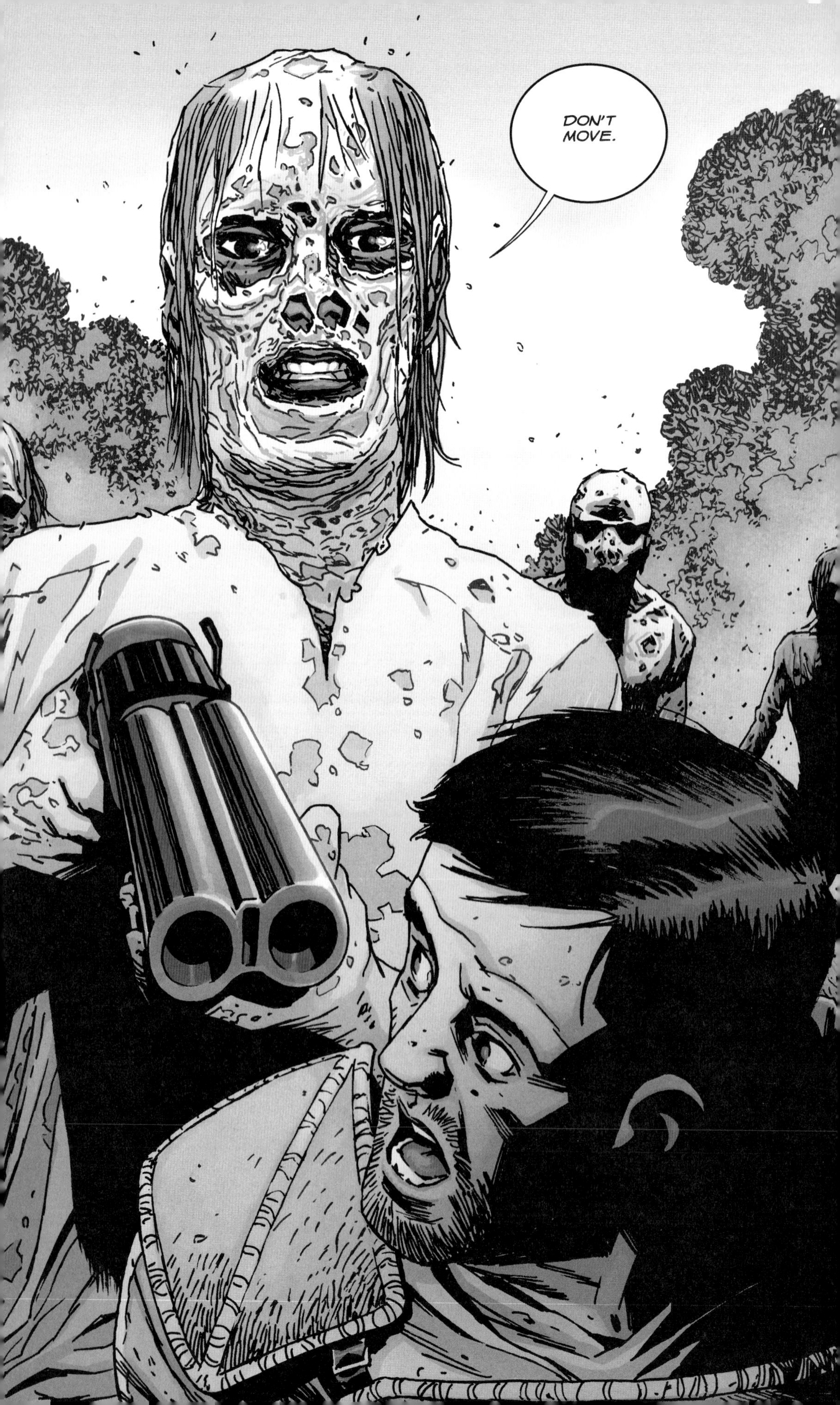
DON'T MOVE.

Chapter Twenty-Three:
Whispers Into Screams

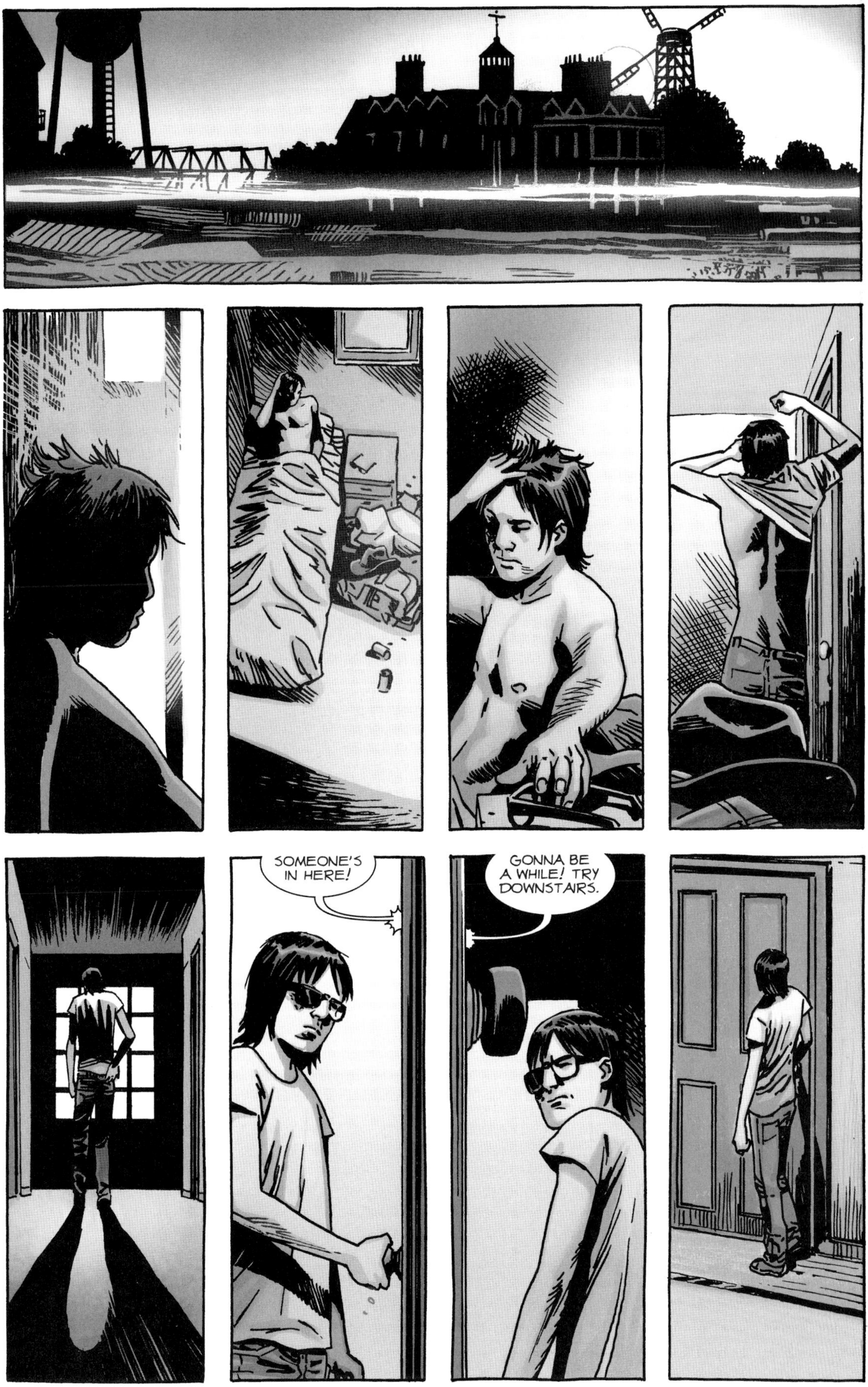
SOMEONE'S IN HERE!
GONNA BE A WHILE! TRY DOWNSTAIRS.

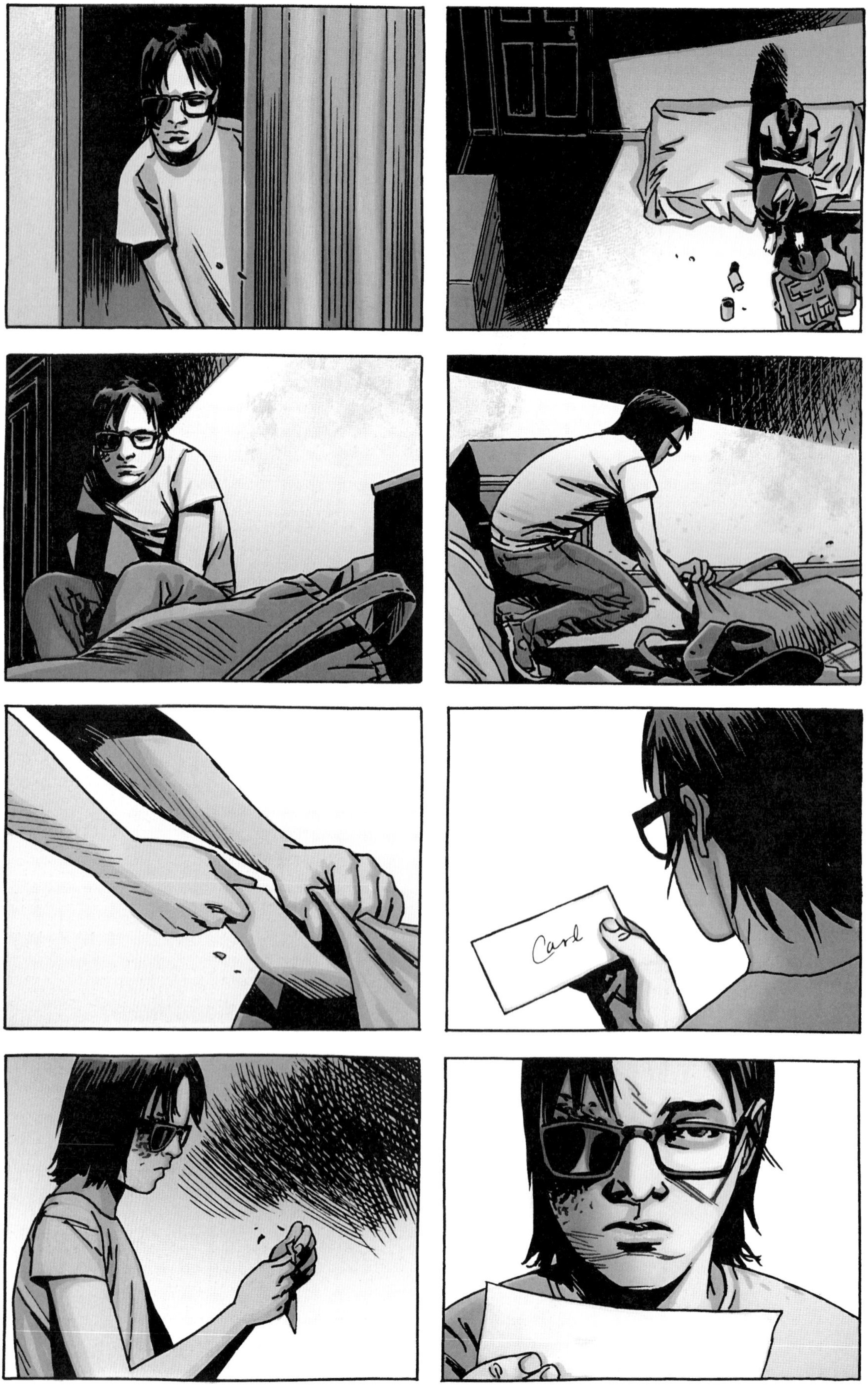
Carl

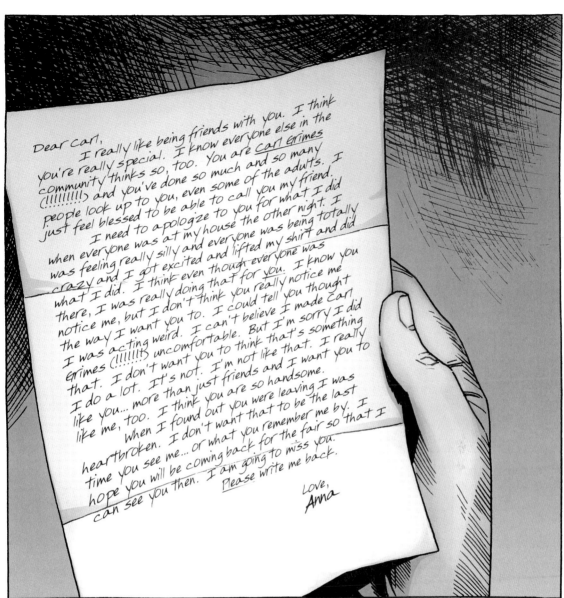

Dear Carl,
I really like being friends with you. I think you're really special. I know everyone else in the community thinks so, too. You are <u>Carl Grimes</u> (!!!!!!!!) and you've done so much and so many people look up to you, even some of the adults. I just feel blessed to be able to call you my friend.

I need to apologize to you for what I did when everyone was at my house the other night. I was feeling really silly and everyone was being totally <u>crazy</u> and I got excited and lifted my shirt and did what I did. I think even though everyone was there, I was really doing that for you. I know you notice me, but I don't think you really notice me the way I want you to. I could tell you thought I was acting weird. I can't believe I made Carl Grimes (!!!!!!!!) uncomfortable. But I'm sorry I did that. I don't want you to think that's something I do a lot. It's not. I'm not like that. I really like you... more than just friends and I want you to like me, too. I think you are so handsome.

When I found out you were leaving I was heartbroken. I don't want that to be the last time you see me... or what you remember me by. I hope you will be coming back for the fair so that I can see you then. I am going to miss you. <u>Please</u> write me back.

Love,
Anna

HE WAS SHOT IN THE FACE? AND HE SURVIVED?!

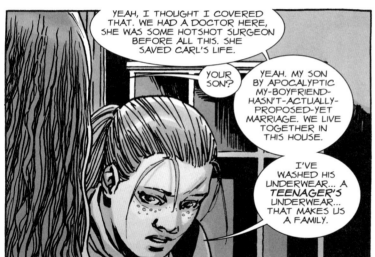

YEAH, I THOUGHT I COVERED THAT. WE HAD A DOCTOR HERE, SHE WAS SOME HOTSHOT SURGEON BEFORE ALL THIS. SHE SAVED CARL'S LIFE.

YOUR SON?

YEAH. MY SON BY APOCALYPTIC MY-BOYFRIEND-HASN'T-ACTUALLY-PROPOSED-YET MARRIAGE. WE LIVE TOGETHER IN THIS HOUSE.

I'VE WASHED HIS UNDERWEAR... A *TEENAGER'S* UNDERWEAR... THAT MAKES US A FAMILY.

THE GUY IN THE BASEMENT... THAT'S NEGAN, THEN? RICK ACTUALLY FOLLOWED THROUGH WITH THAT PLAN AFTER THE WAR?

YEAH. HE THOUGHT IT WOULD MAKE A STATEMENT... THE OLD WAYS ARE BACK... THAT KIND OF THING.

I DISAGREED... STILL DO, IF I'M HONEST. BUT I THINK IT WORKS. PEOPLE RECOGNIZE THERE'S A RULE OF LAW... AND PEOPLE LOOK UP TO RICK. THAT MOVE MORE THAN ANYTHING... THAT MADE HIM A LEADER.

I DON'T THINK HE REALLY ACCEPTED THAT ROLE UNTIL THEN.

WHAT HAPPENED TO THE REST OF THE SAVIORS?

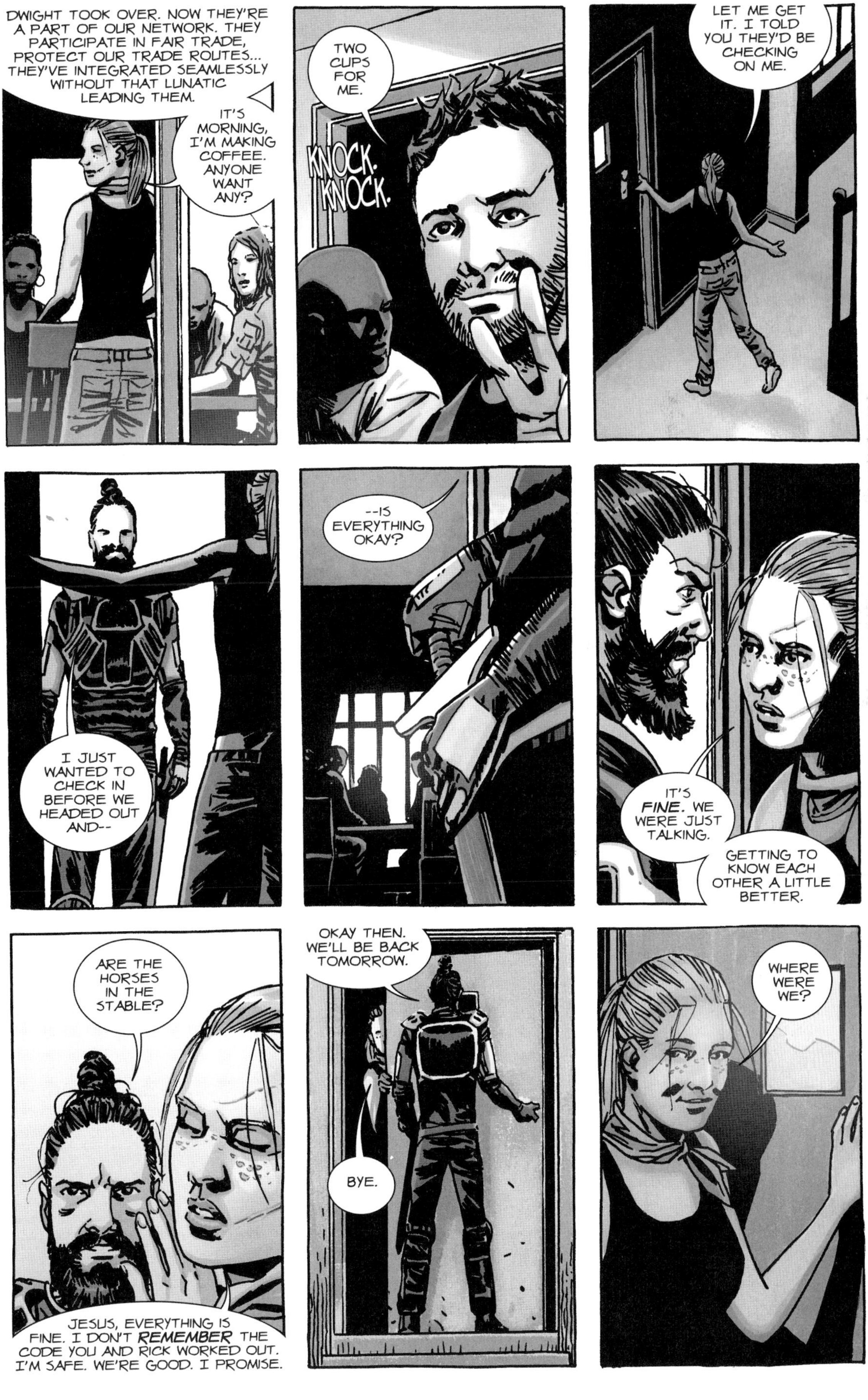
DWIGHT TOOK OVER. NOW THEY'RE A PART OF OUR NETWORK. THEY PARTICIPATE IN FAIR TRADE, PROTECT OUR TRADE ROUTES... THEY'VE INTEGRATED SEAMLESSLY WITHOUT THAT LUNATIC LEADING THEM.
IT'S MORNING, I'M MAKING COFFEE. ANYONE WANT ANY?
TWO CUPS FOR ME.
KNOCK. KNOCK.
LET ME GET IT. I TOLD YOU THEY'D BE CHECKING ON ME.
I JUST WANTED TO CHECK IN BEFORE WE HEADED OUT AND--
--IS EVERYTHING OKAY?
IT'S FINE. WE WERE JUST TALKING.
GETTING TO KNOW EACH OTHER A LITTLE BETTER.
ARE THE HORSES IN THE STABLE?
JESUS, EVERYTHING IS FINE. I DON'T REMEMBER THE CODE YOU AND RICK WORKED OUT. I'M SAFE. WE'RE GOOD. I PROMISE.
OKAY THEN. WE'LL BE BACK TOMORROW.
BYE.
WHERE WERE WE?

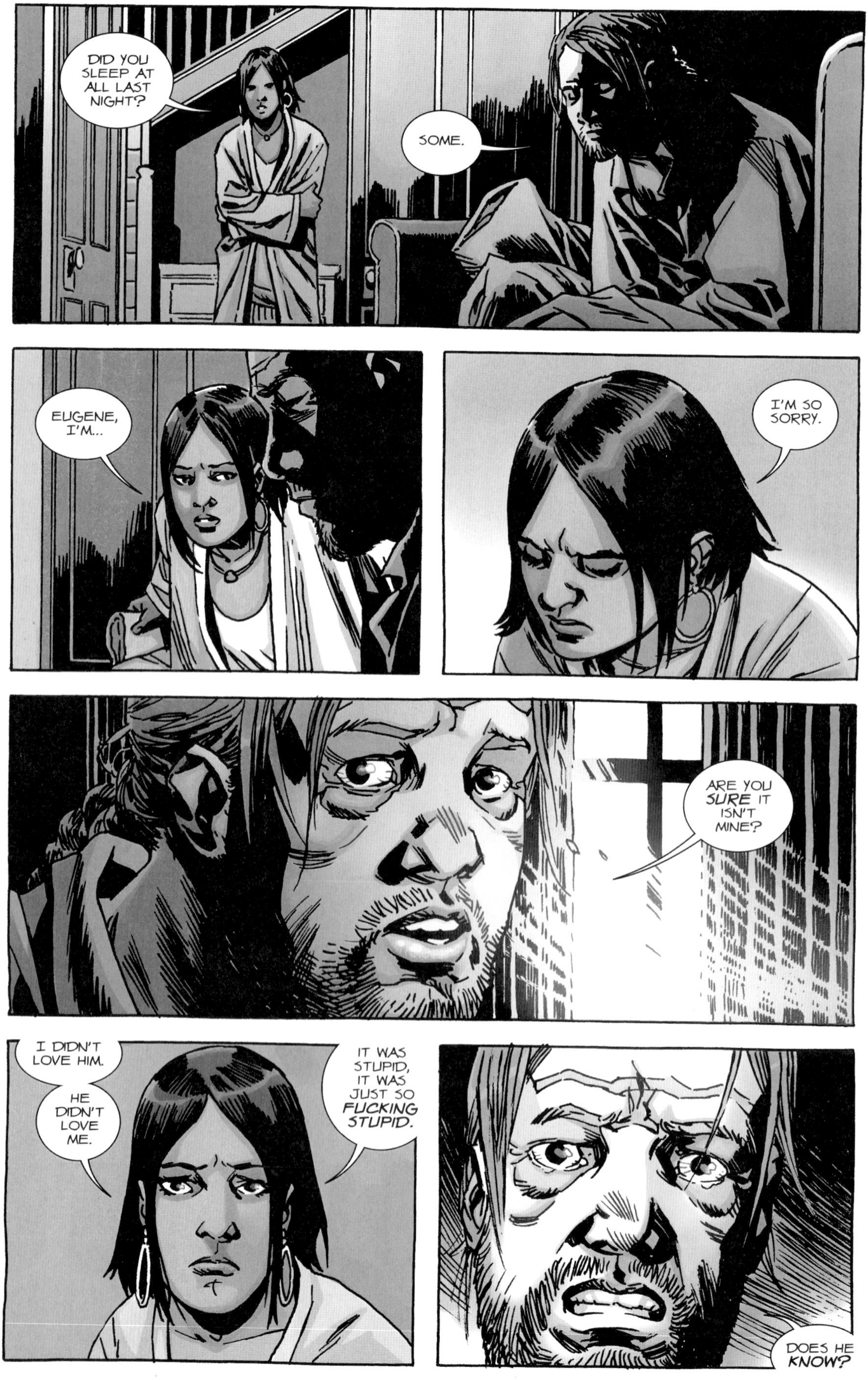
DID YOU SLEEP AT ALL LAST NIGHT?
SOME.
EUGENE, I'M...
I'M SO SORRY.
ARE YOU *SURE* IT ISN'T MINE?
I DIDN'T LOVE HIM.
HE DIDN'T LOVE ME.
IT WAS STUPID, IT WAS JUST SO *FUCKING STUPID*.
DOES HE *KNOW?*

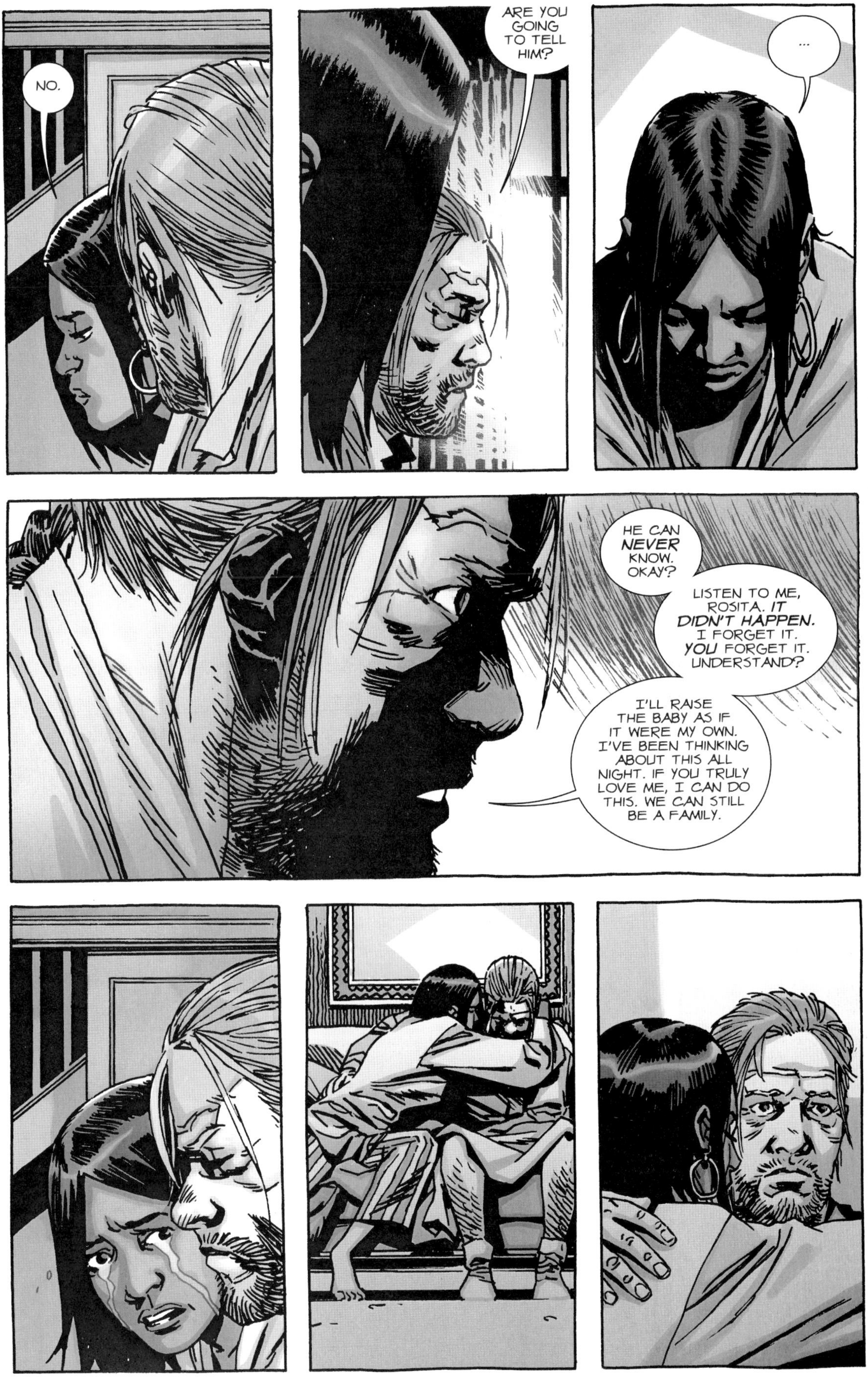
NO.
ARE YOU GOING TO TELL HIM?
...
HE CAN NEVER KNOW. OKAY?
LISTEN TO ME, ROSITA. IT DIDN'T HAPPEN. I FORGET IT. YOU FORGET IT. UNDERSTAND?
I'LL RAISE THE BABY AS IF IT WERE MY OWN. I'VE BEEN THINKING ABOUT THIS ALL NIGHT. IF YOU TRULY LOVE ME, I CAN DO THIS. WE CAN STILL BE A FAMILY.

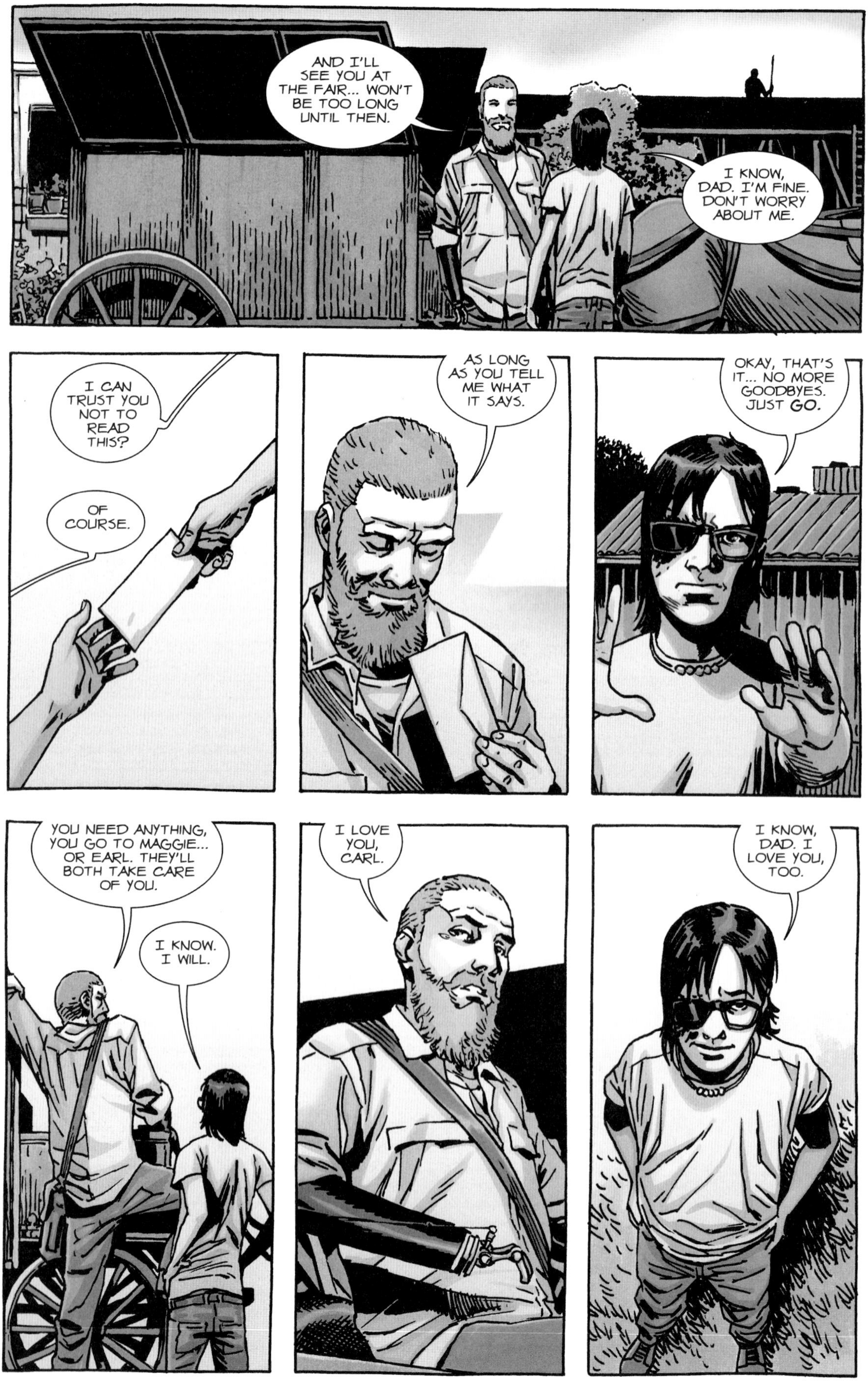
AND I'LL SEE YOU AT THE FAIR... WON'T BE TOO LONG UNTIL THEN.
I KNOW, DAD. I'M FINE. DON'T WORRY ABOUT ME.
I CAN TRUST YOU NOT TO READ THIS?
OF COURSE.
AS LONG AS YOU TELL ME WHAT IT SAYS.
OKAY, THAT'S IT... NO MORE GOODBYES. JUST GO.
YOU NEED ANYTHING, YOU GO TO MAGGIE... OR EARL. THEY'LL BOTH TAKE CARE OF YOU.
I KNOW. I WILL.
I LOVE YOU, CARL.
I KNOW, DAD. I LOVE YOU, TOO.

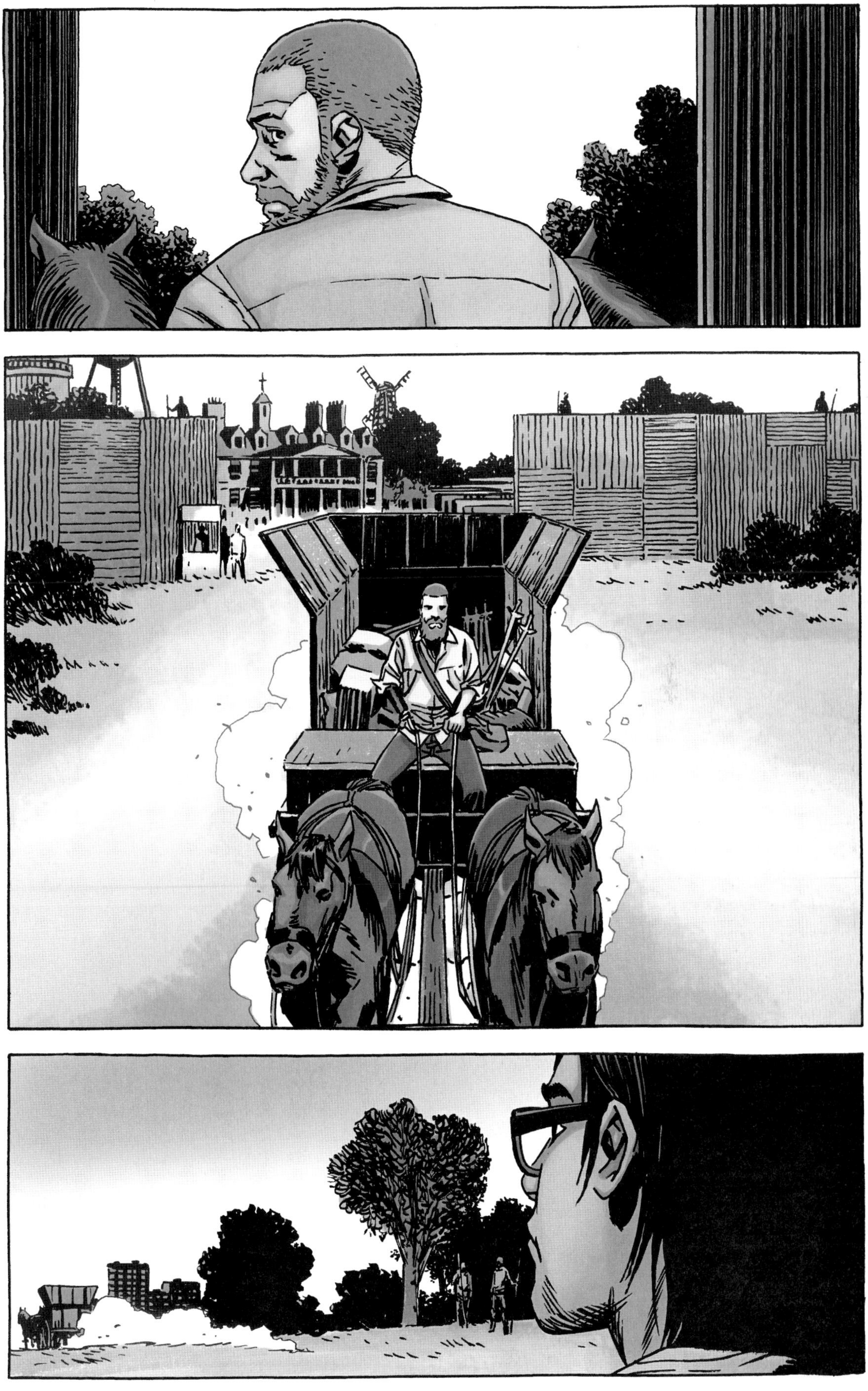

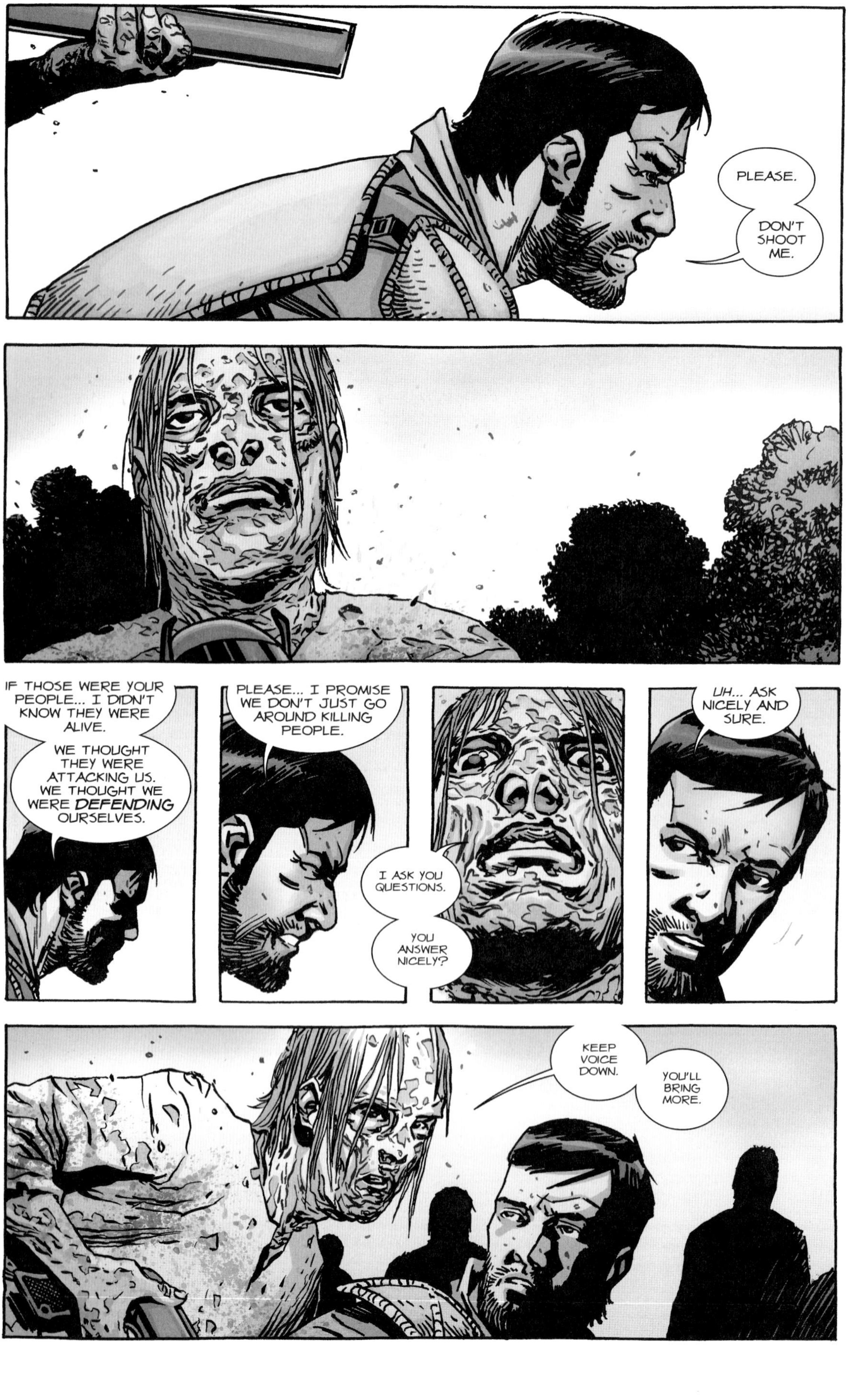
PLEASE.
DON'T SHOOT ME.
IF THOSE WERE YOUR PEOPLE... I DIDN'T KNOW THEY WERE ALIVE.
WE THOUGHT THEY WERE ATTACKING US. WE THOUGHT WE WERE *DEFENDING* OURSELVES.
PLEASE... I PROMISE WE DON'T JUST GO AROUND KILLING PEOPLE.
I ASK YOU QUESTIONS.
YOU ANSWER NICELY?
UH... ASK NICELY AND SURE.
KEEP VOICE DOWN.
YOU'LL BRING MORE.

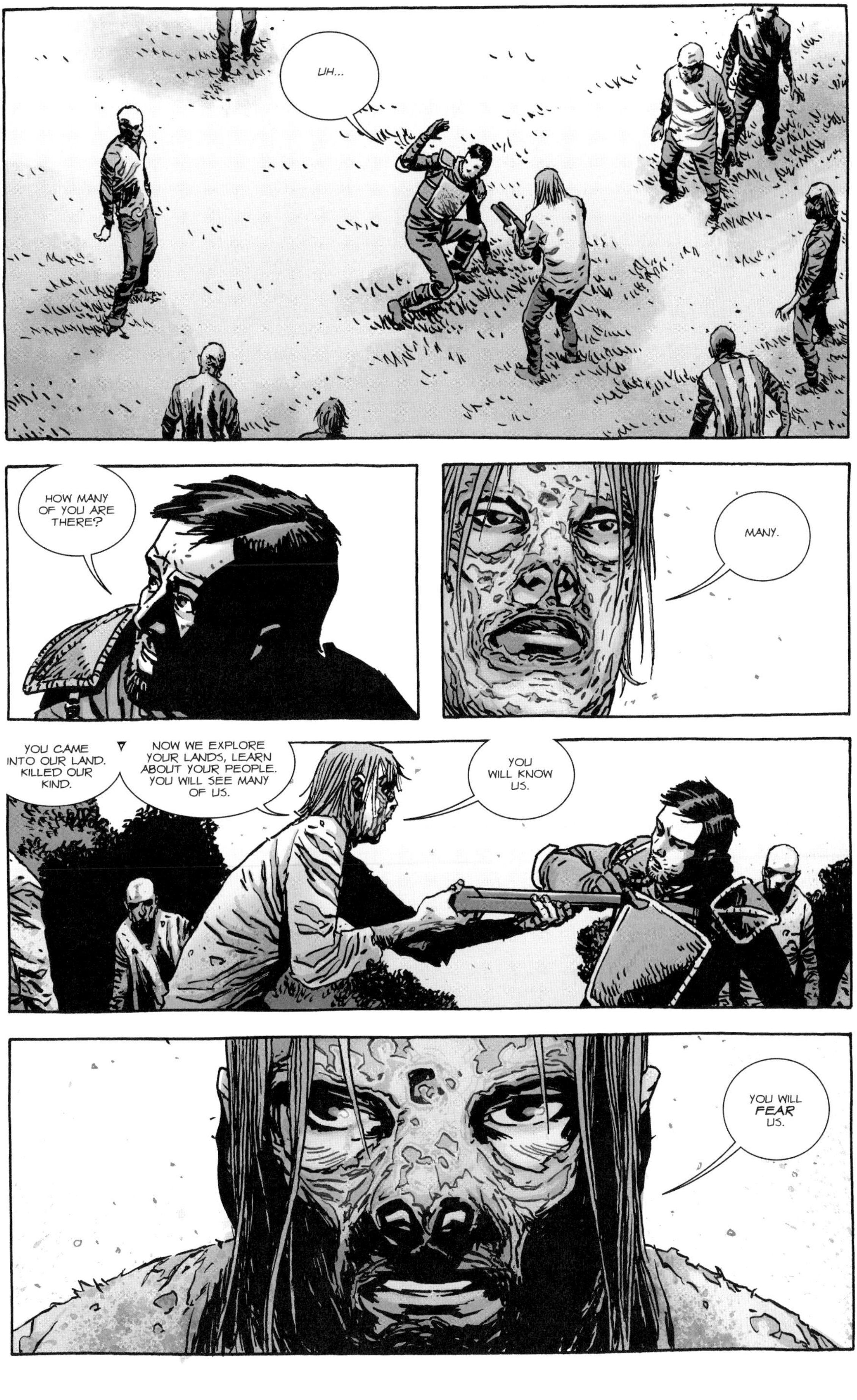
UH...
HOW MANY OF YOU ARE THERE?
MANY.
YOU CAME INTO OUR LAND. KILLED OUR KIND.
NOW WE EXPLORE YOUR LANDS, LEARN ABOUT YOUR PEOPLE. YOU WILL SEE MANY OF US.
YOU WILL KNOW US.
YOU WILL FEAR US.

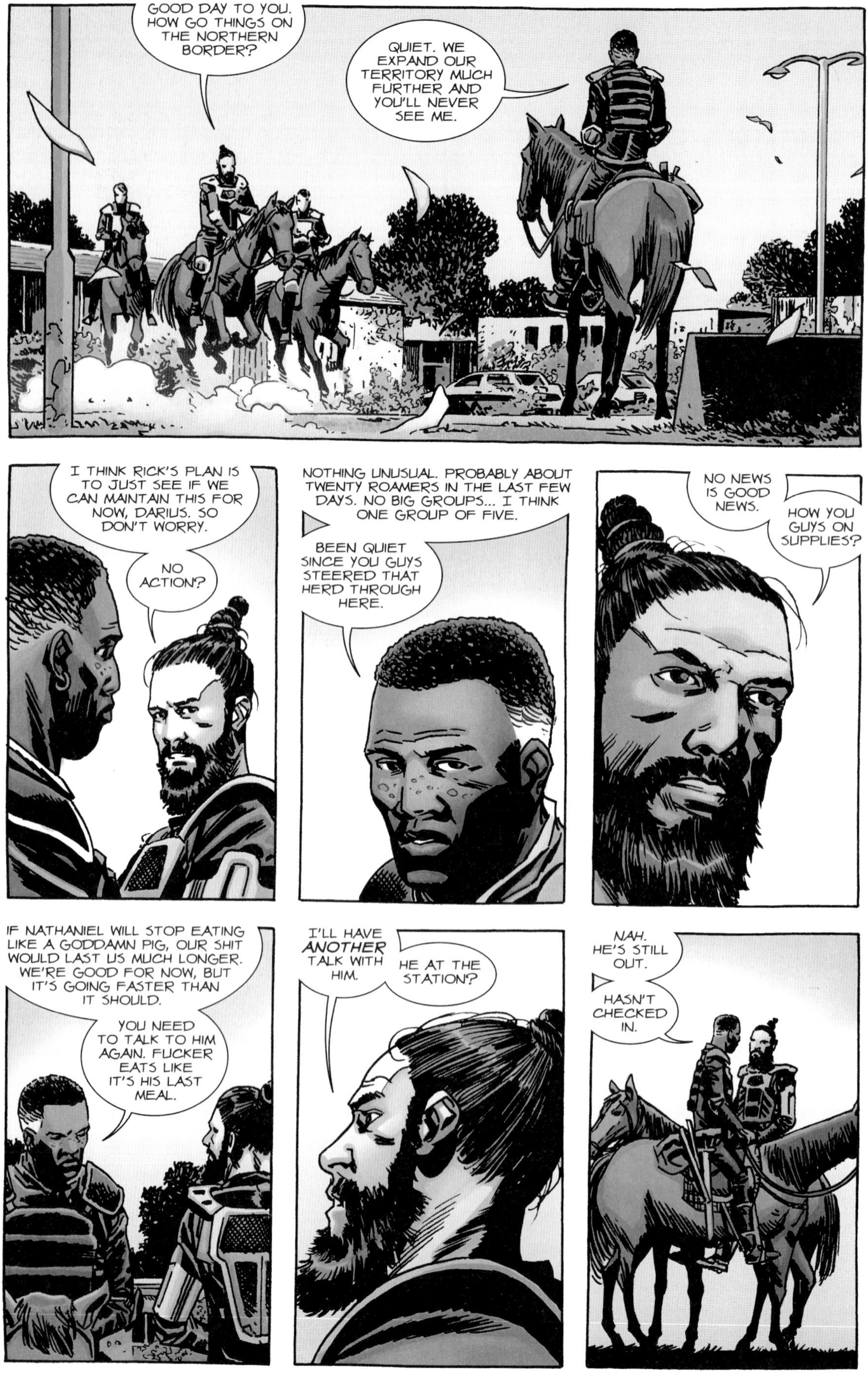
GOOD DAY TO YOU. HOW GO THINGS ON THE NORTHERN BORDER?
QUIET. WE EXPAND OUR TERRITORY MUCH FURTHER AND YOU'LL NEVER SEE ME.
I THINK RICK'S PLAN IS TO JUST SEE IF WE CAN MAINTAIN THIS FOR NOW, DARIUS. SO DON'T WORRY.
NO ACTION?
NOTHING UNUSUAL. PROBABLY ABOUT TWENTY ROAMERS IN THE LAST FEW DAYS. NO BIG GROUPS... I THINK ONE GROUP OF FIVE.
BEEN QUIET SINCE YOU GUYS STEERED THAT HERD THROUGH HERE.
NO NEWS IS GOOD NEWS.
HOW YOU GUYS ON SUPPLIES?
IF NATHANIEL WILL STOP EATING LIKE A GODDAMN PIG, OUR SHIT WOULD LAST US MUCH LONGER. WE'RE GOOD FOR NOW, BUT IT'S GOING FASTER THAN IT SHOULD.
YOU NEED TO TALK TO HIM AGAIN. FUCKER EATS LIKE IT'S HIS LAST MEAL.
I'LL HAVE ***ANOTHER*** TALK WITH HIM.
HE AT THE STATION?
NAH. HE'S STILL OUT.
HASN'T CHECKED IN.

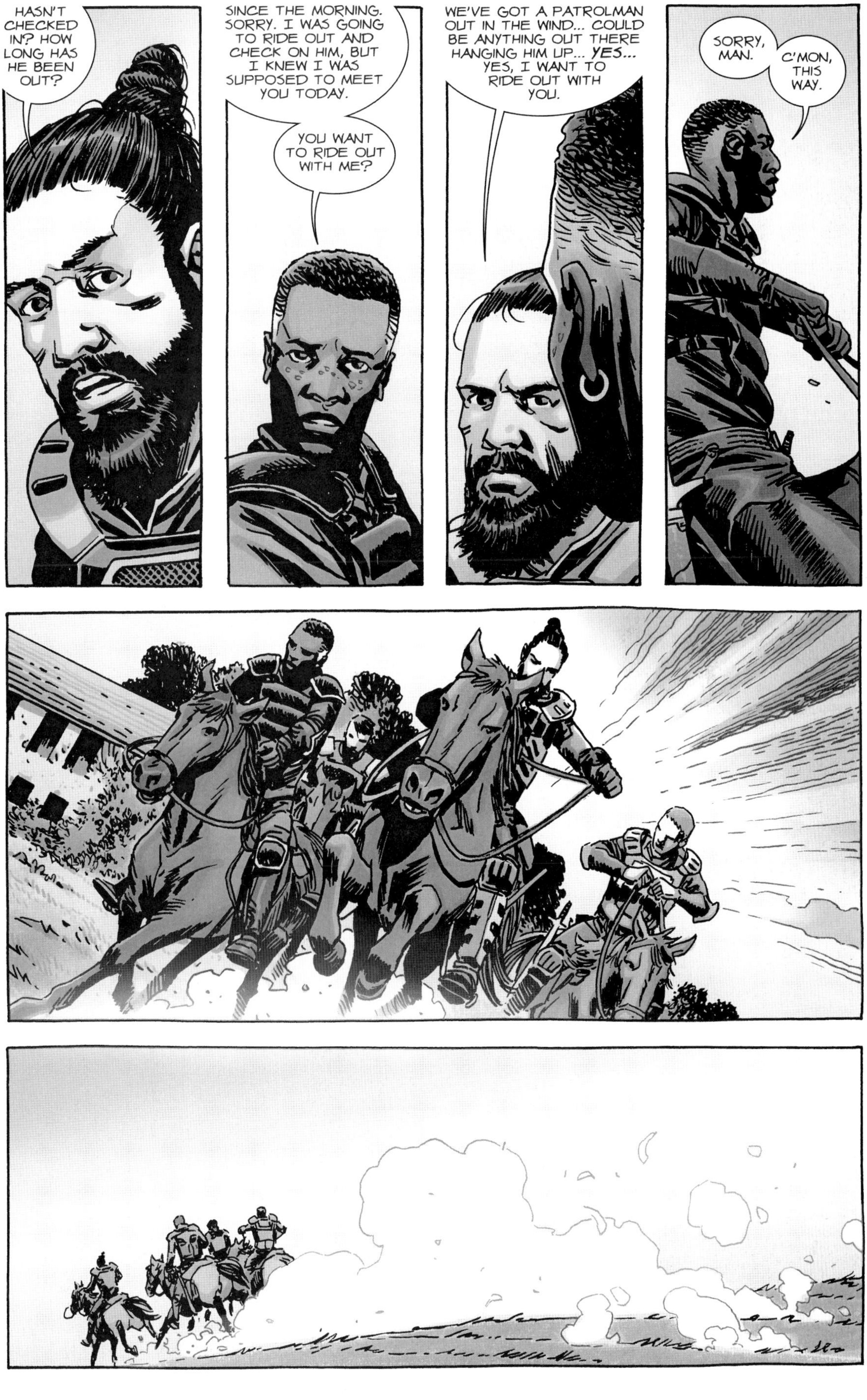
HASN'T CHECKED IN? HOW LONG HAS HE BEEN OUT?
SINCE THE MORNING. SORRY. I WAS GOING TO RIDE OUT AND CHECK ON HIM, BUT I KNEW I WAS SUPPOSED TO MEET YOU TODAY.
YOU WANT TO RIDE OUT WITH ME?
WE'VE GOT A PATROLMAN OUT IN THE WIND... COULD BE ANYTHING OUT THERE HANGING HIM UP... *YES...* YES, I WANT TO RIDE OUT WITH YOU.
SORRY, MAN.
C'MON, THIS WAY.

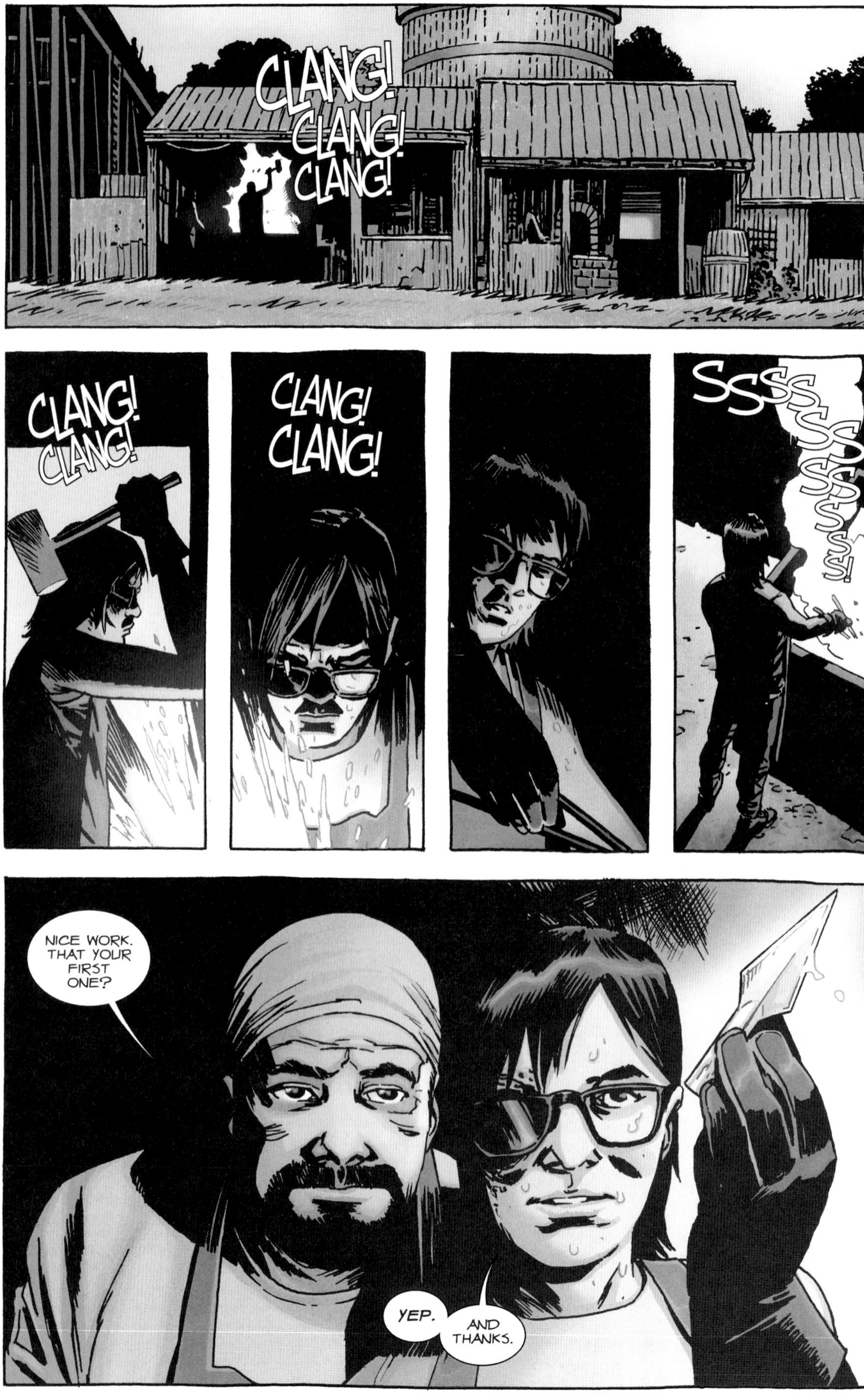
CLANG! CLANG! CLANG!
CLANG! CLANG!
CLANG! CLANG!
SSSSSSSSSSSSSS!
NICE WORK. THAT YOUR FIRST ONE?
YEP.
AND THANKS.

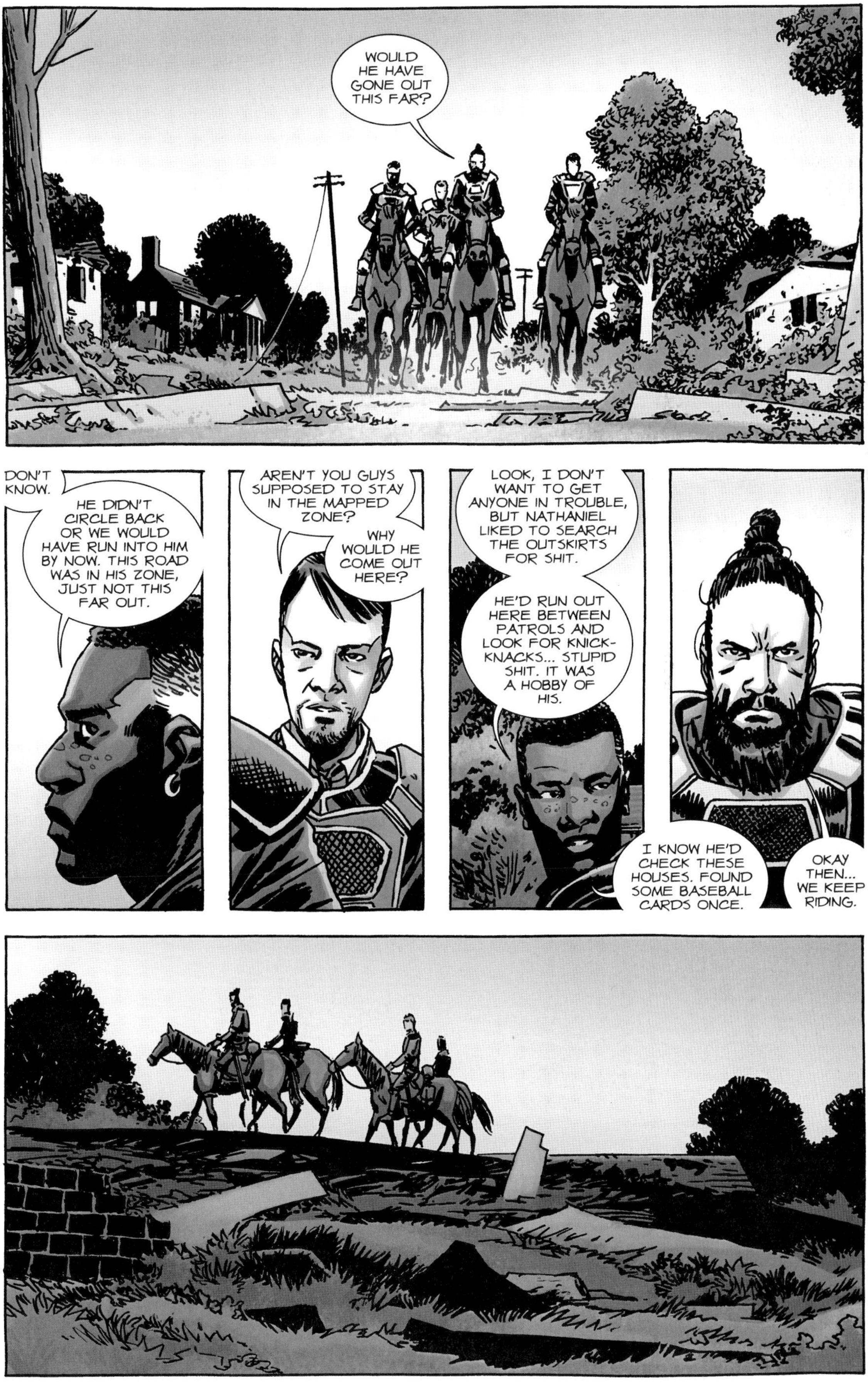
WOULD HE HAVE GONE OUT THIS FAR?
DON'T KNOW.
HE DIDN'T CIRCLE BACK OR WE WOULD HAVE RUN INTO HIM BY NOW. THIS ROAD WAS IN HIS ZONE, JUST NOT THIS FAR OUT.
AREN'T YOU GUYS SUPPOSED TO STAY IN THE MAPPED ZONE?
WHY WOULD HE COME OUT HERE?
LOOK, I DON'T WANT TO GET ANYONE IN TROUBLE, BUT NATHANIEL LIKED TO SEARCH THE OUTSKIRTS FOR SHIT.
HE'D RUN OUT HERE BETWEEN PATROLS AND LOOK FOR KNICK-KNACKS... STUPID SHIT. IT WAS A HOBBY OF HIS.
I KNOW HE'D CHECK THESE HOUSES. FOUND SOME BASEBALL CARDS ONCE.
OKAY THEN... WE KEEP RIDING.

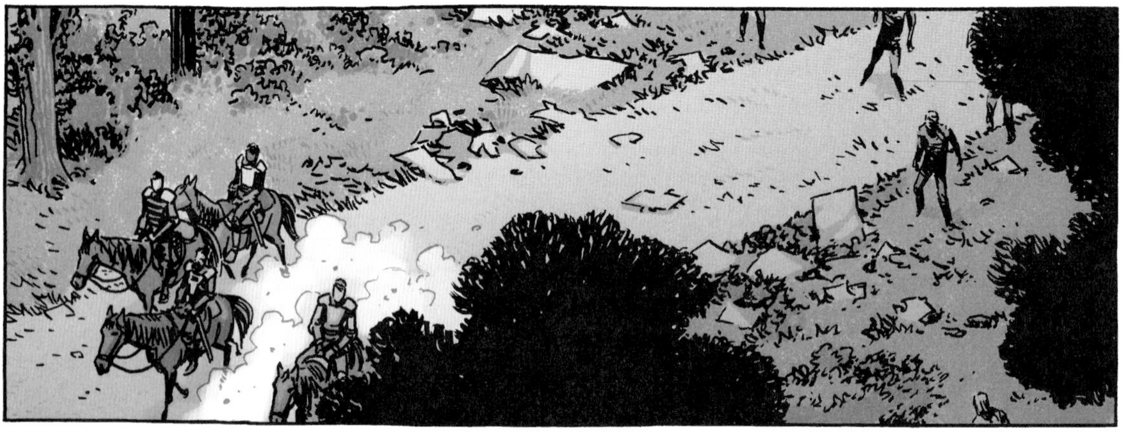

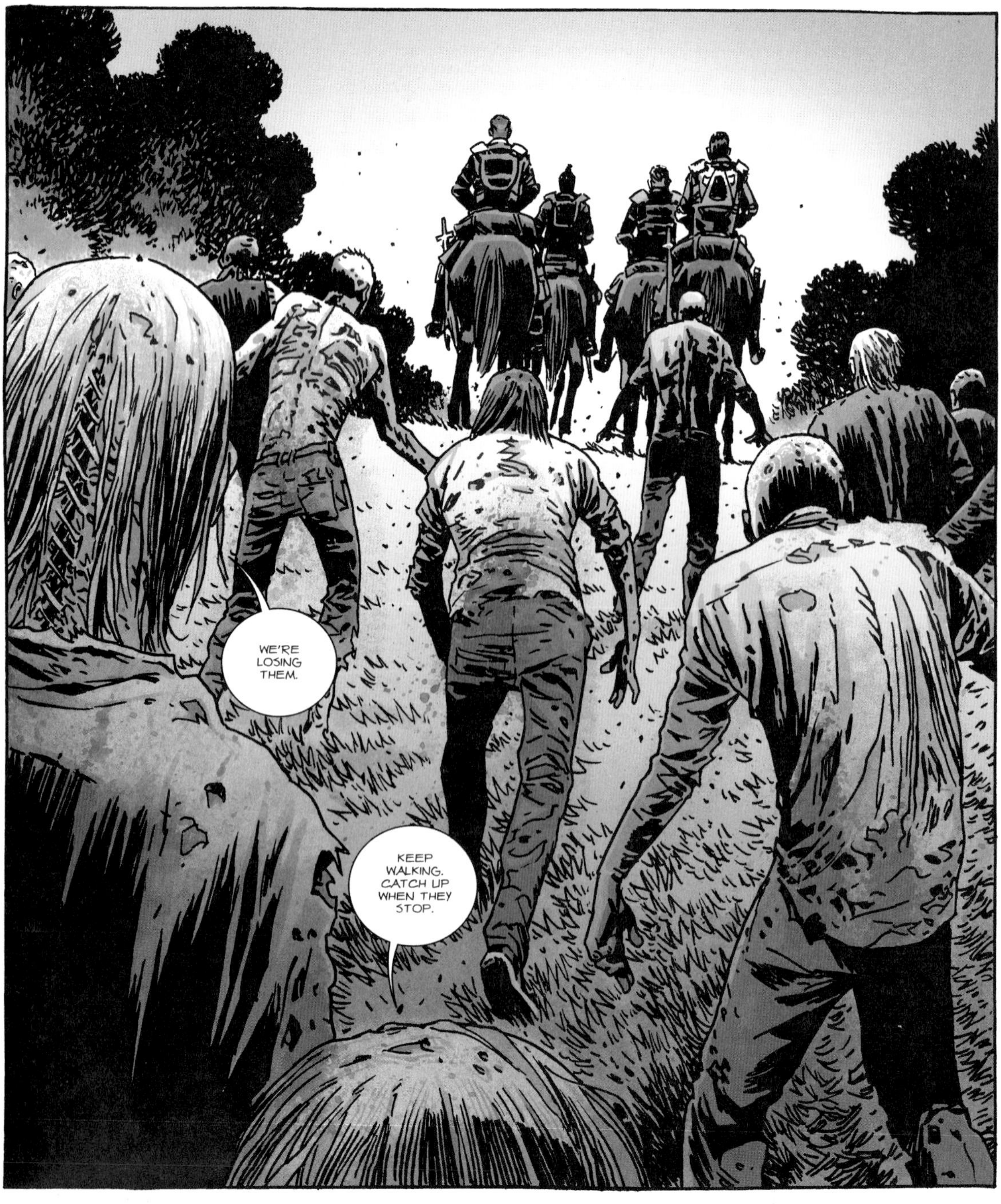
WE'RE LOSING THEM.
KEEP WALKING. CATCH UP WHEN THEY STOP.

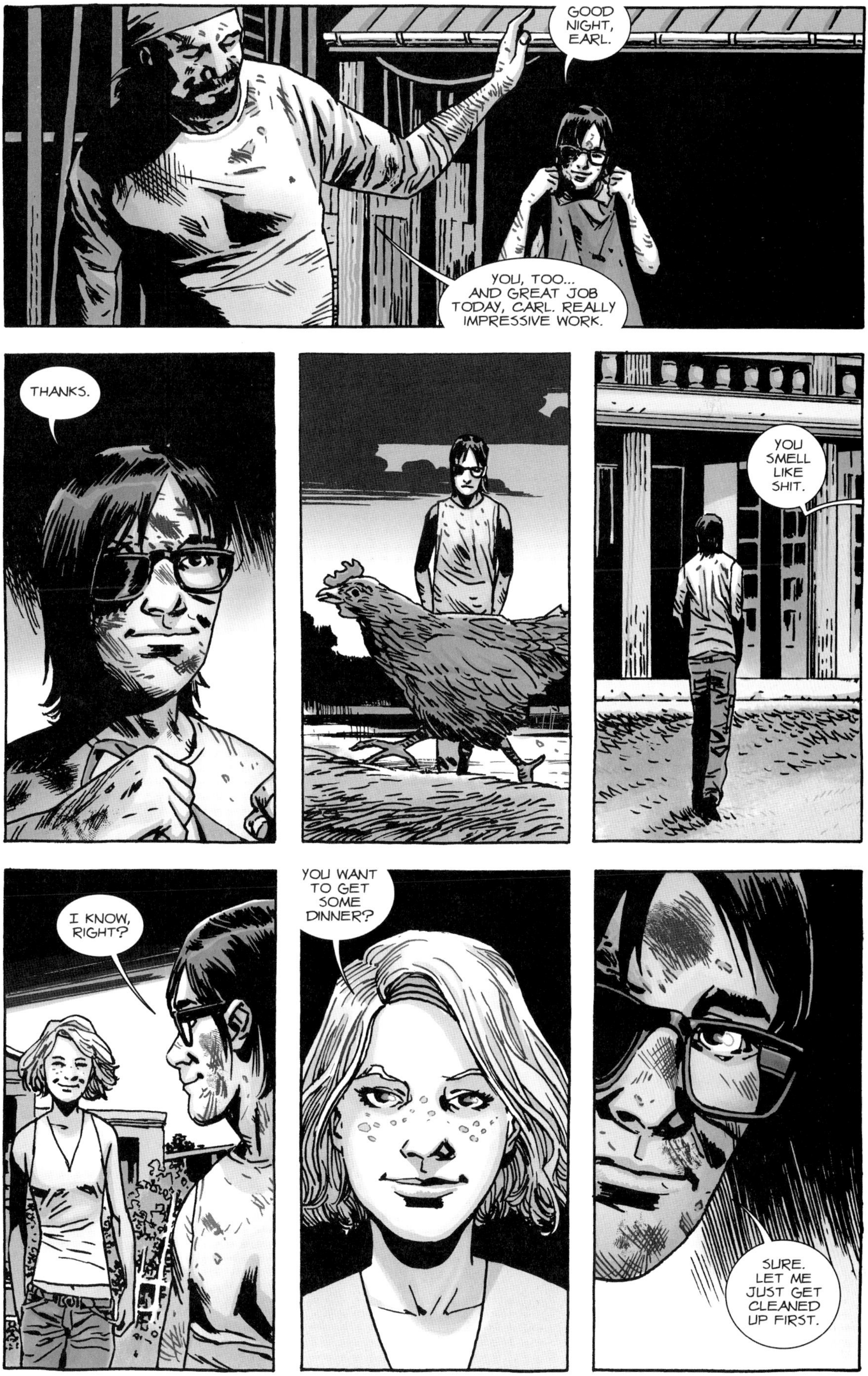
GOOD NIGHT, EARL.
YOU, TOO... AND GREAT JOB TODAY, CARL. REALLY IMPRESSIVE WORK.
THANKS.
YOU SMELL LIKE SHIT.
I KNOW, RIGHT?
YOU WANT TO GET SOME DINNER?
SURE. LET ME JUST GET CLEANED UP FIRST.

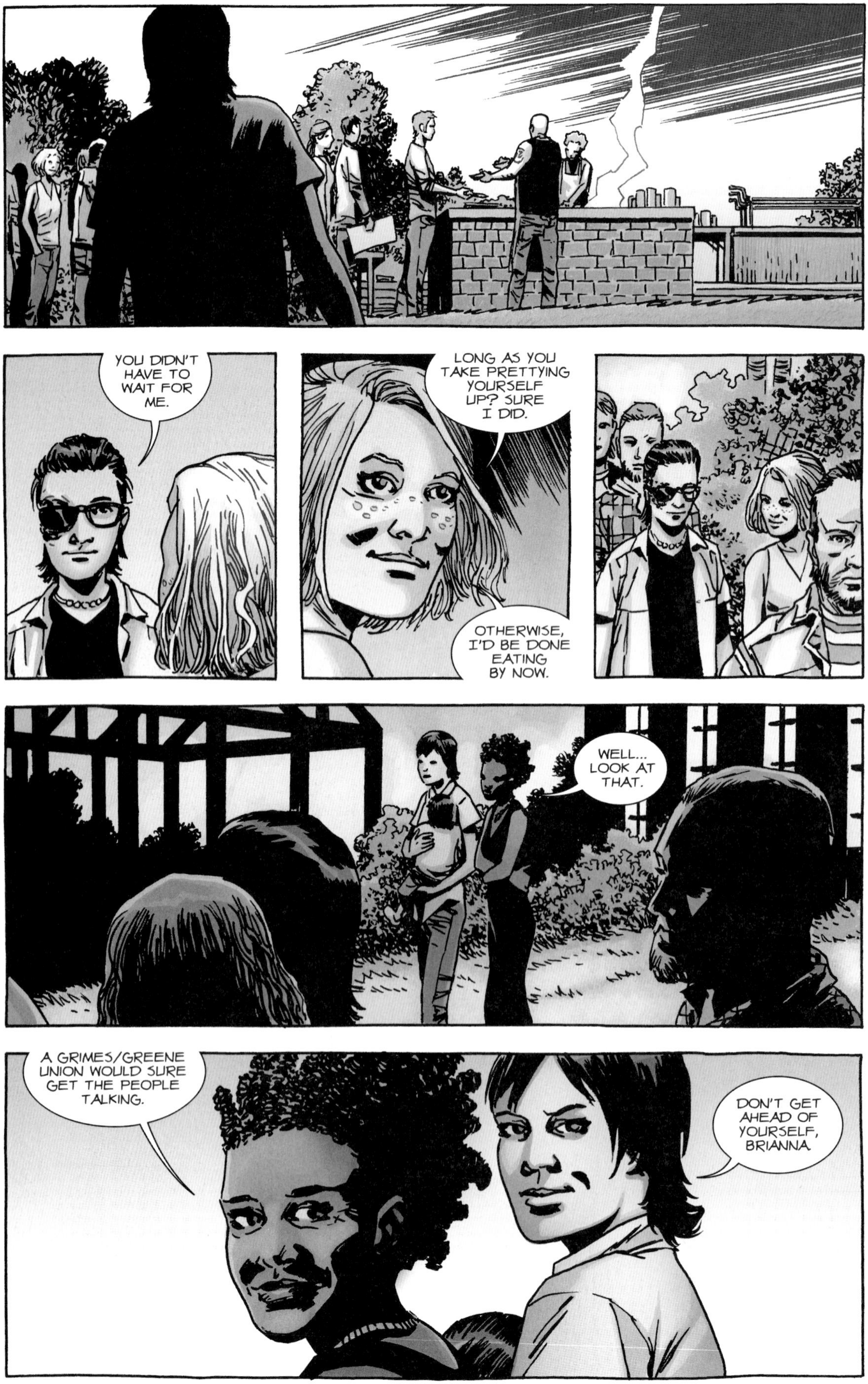
YOU DIDN'T HAVE TO WAIT FOR ME.
LONG AS YOU TAKE PRETTYING YOURSELF UP? SURE I DID.
OTHERWISE, I'D BE DONE EATING BY NOW.
WELL... LOOK AT THAT.
A GRIMES/GREENE UNION WOULD SURE GET THE PEOPLE TALKING.
DON'T GET AHEAD OF YOURSELF, BRIANNA.

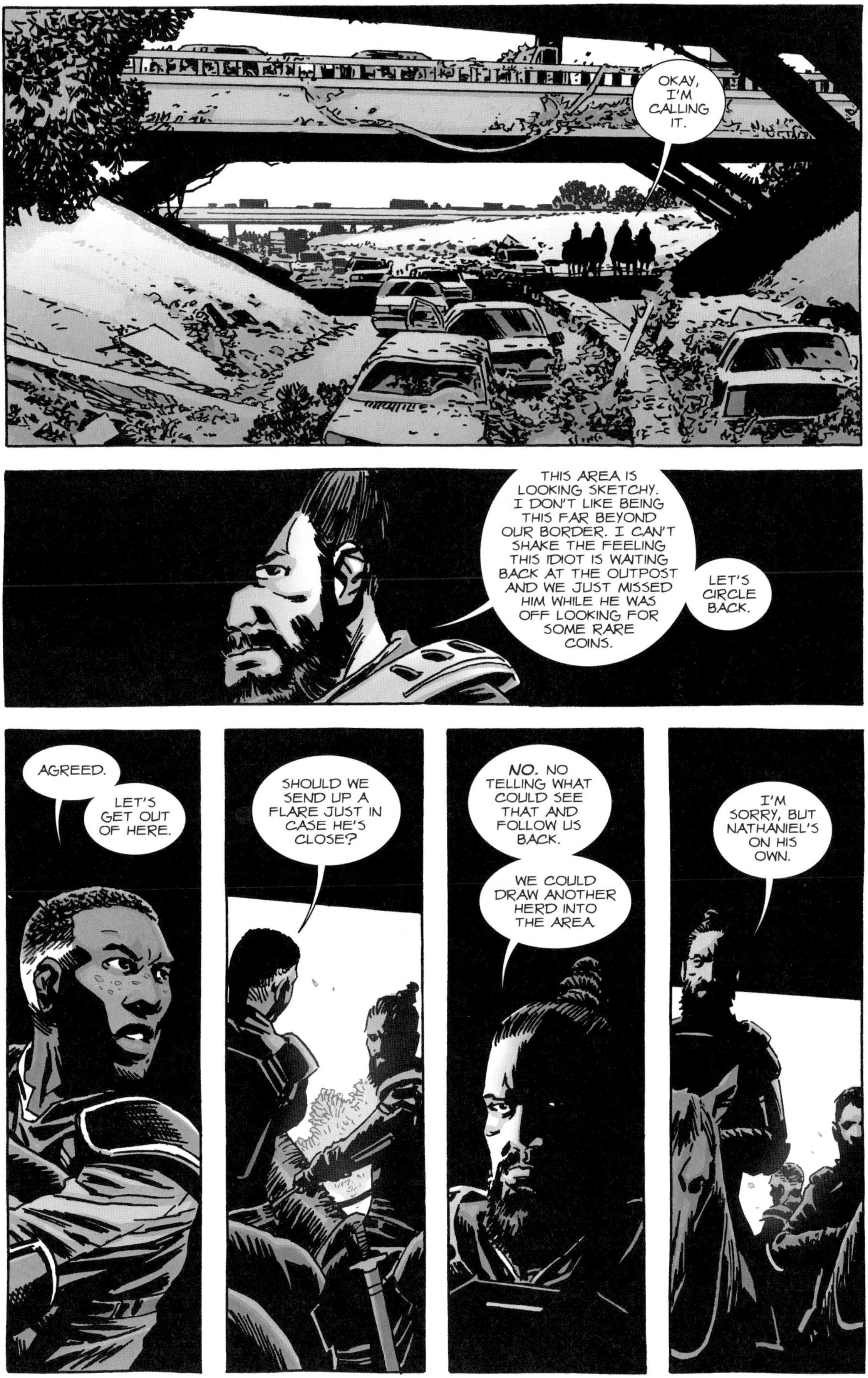
OKAY, I'M CALLING IT.
THIS AREA IS LOOKING SKETCHY. I DON'T LIKE BEING THIS FAR BEYOND OUR BORDER. I CAN'T SHAKE THE FEELING THIS IDIOT IS WAITING BACK AT THE OUTPOST AND WE JUST MISSED HIM WHILE HE WAS OFF LOOKING FOR SOME RARE COINS.
LET'S CIRCLE BACK.
AGREED.
LET'S GET OUT OF HERE.
SHOULD WE SEND UP A FLARE JUST IN CASE HE'S CLOSE?
NO. NO TELLING WHAT COULD SEE THAT AND FOLLOW US BACK.
WE COULD DRAW ANOTHER HERD INTO THE AREA.
I'M SORRY, BUT NATHANIEL'S ON HIS OWN.

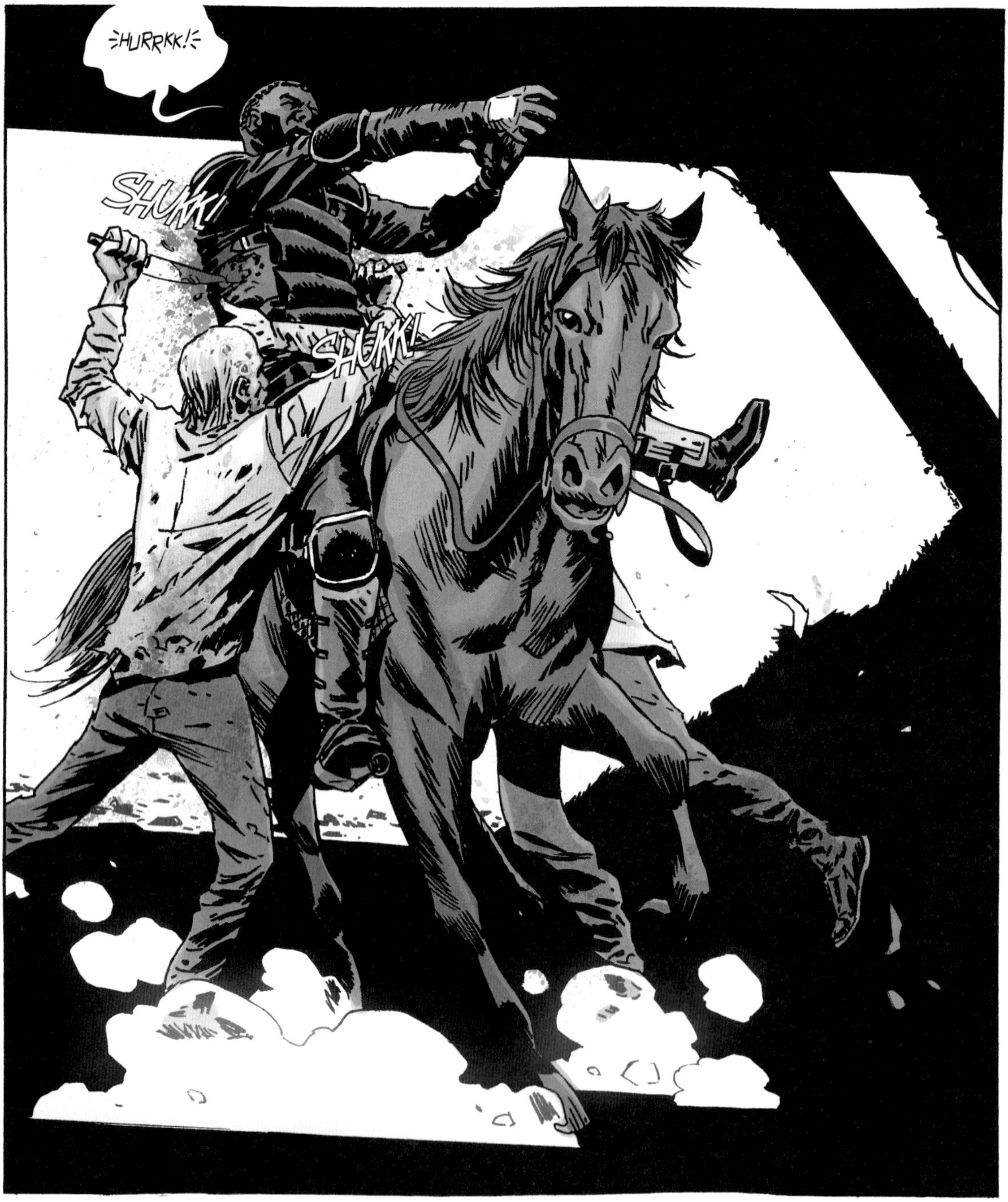

HURRKK!
SHUKK!
SHUKK!

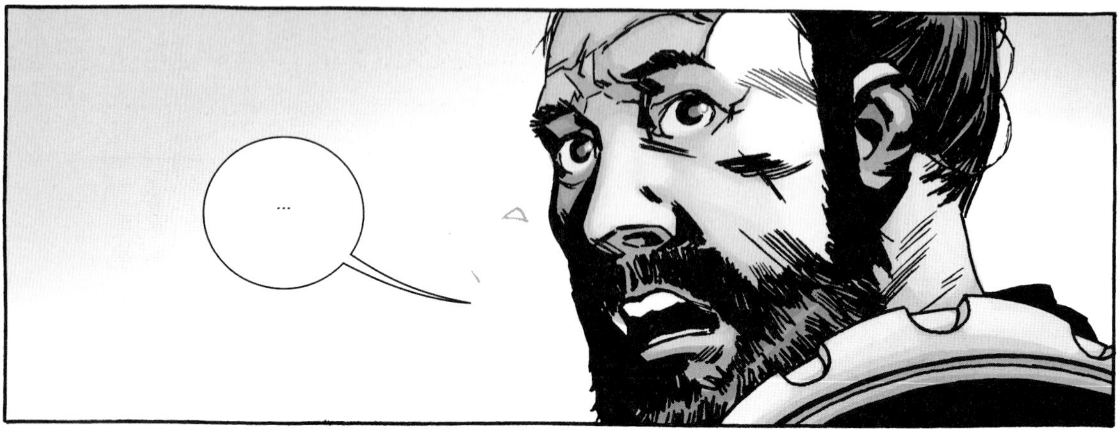

...

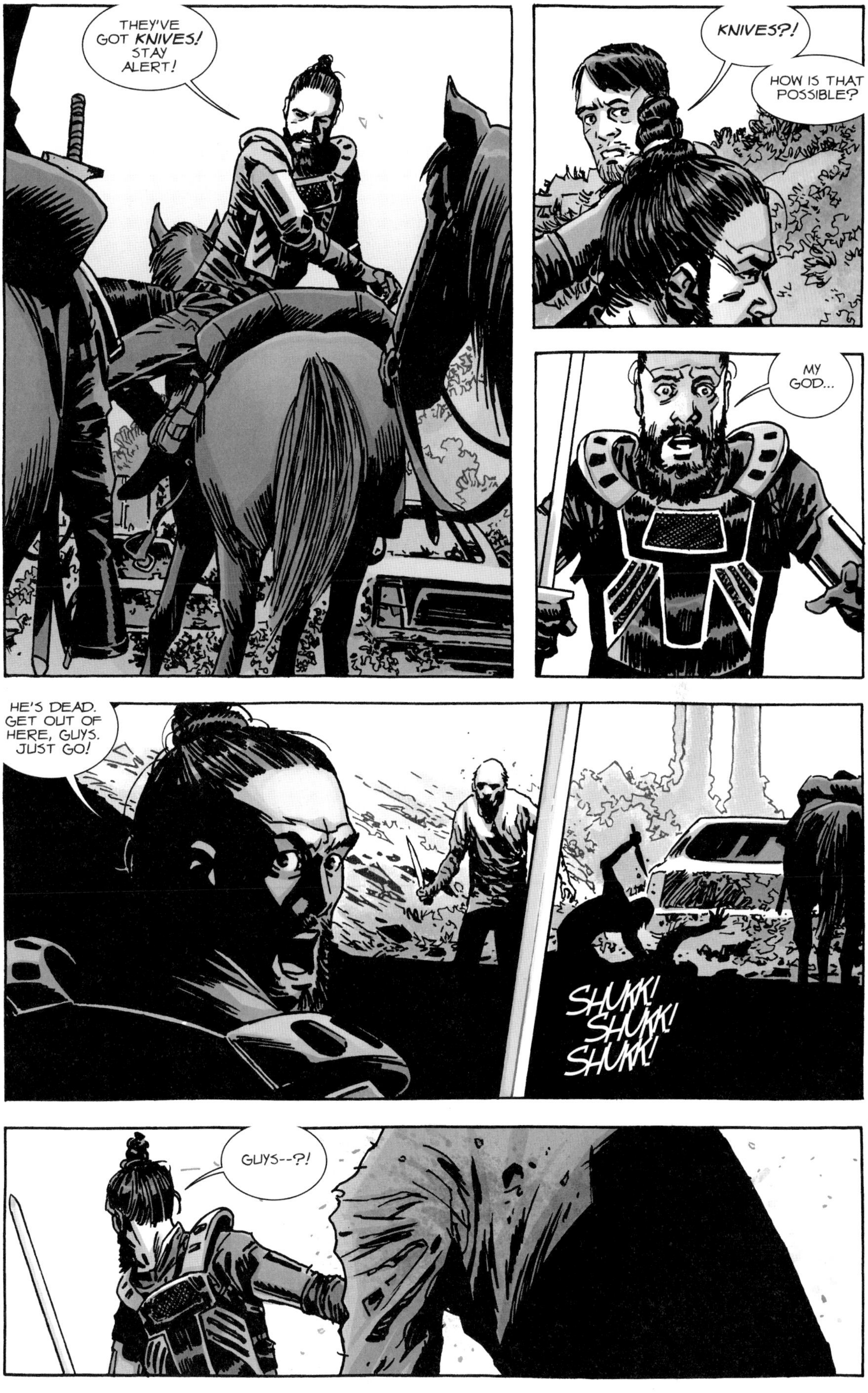
THEY'VE GOT KNIVES! STAY ALERT!
KNIVES?!
HOW IS THAT POSSIBLE?
MY GOD...
HE'S DEAD. GET OUT OF HERE, GUYS. JUST GO!
SHUKK! SHUKK! SHUKK!
GUYS--?!

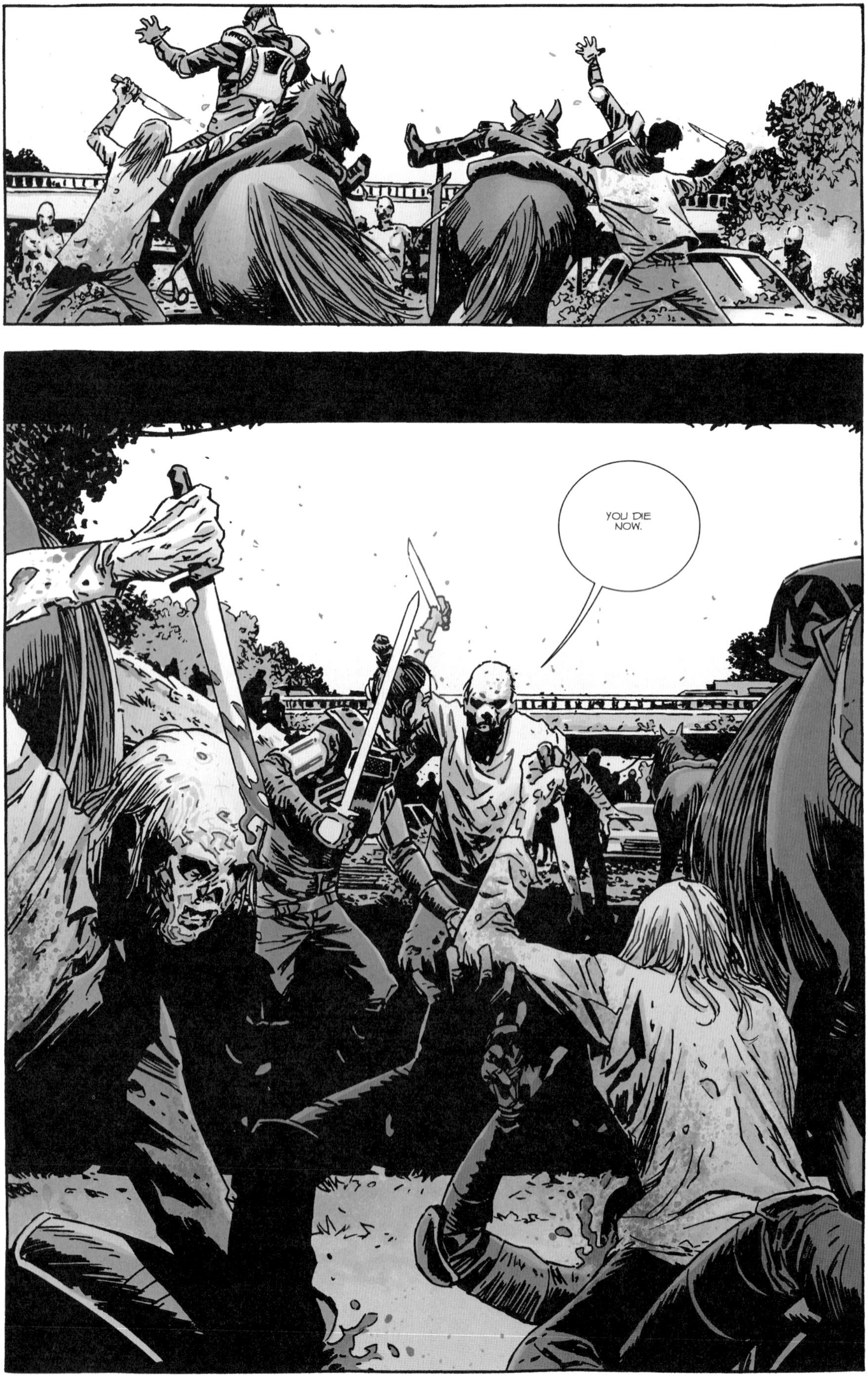
YOU DIE NOW.

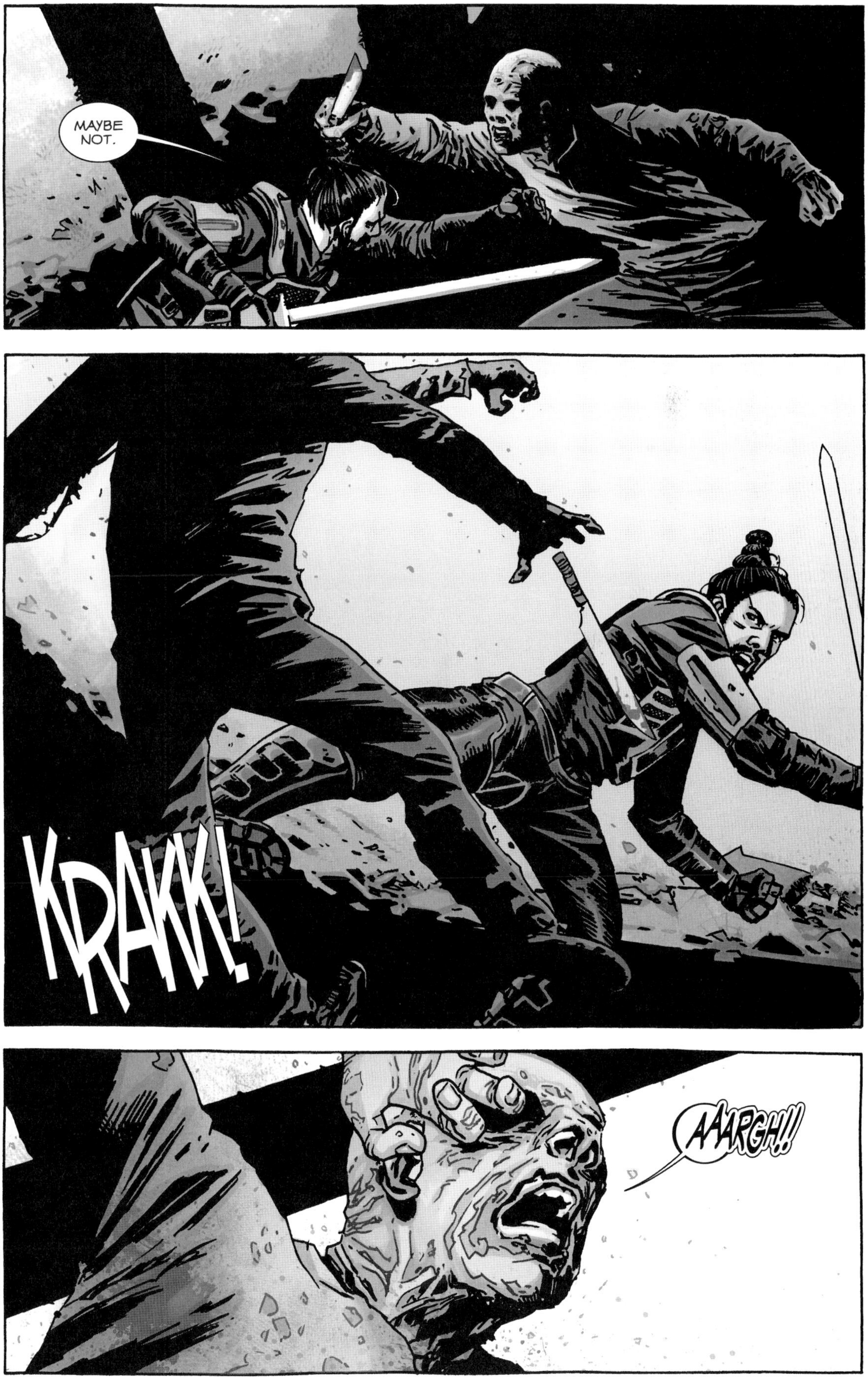
MAYBE NOT.
KRAKK!
AAARGH!!

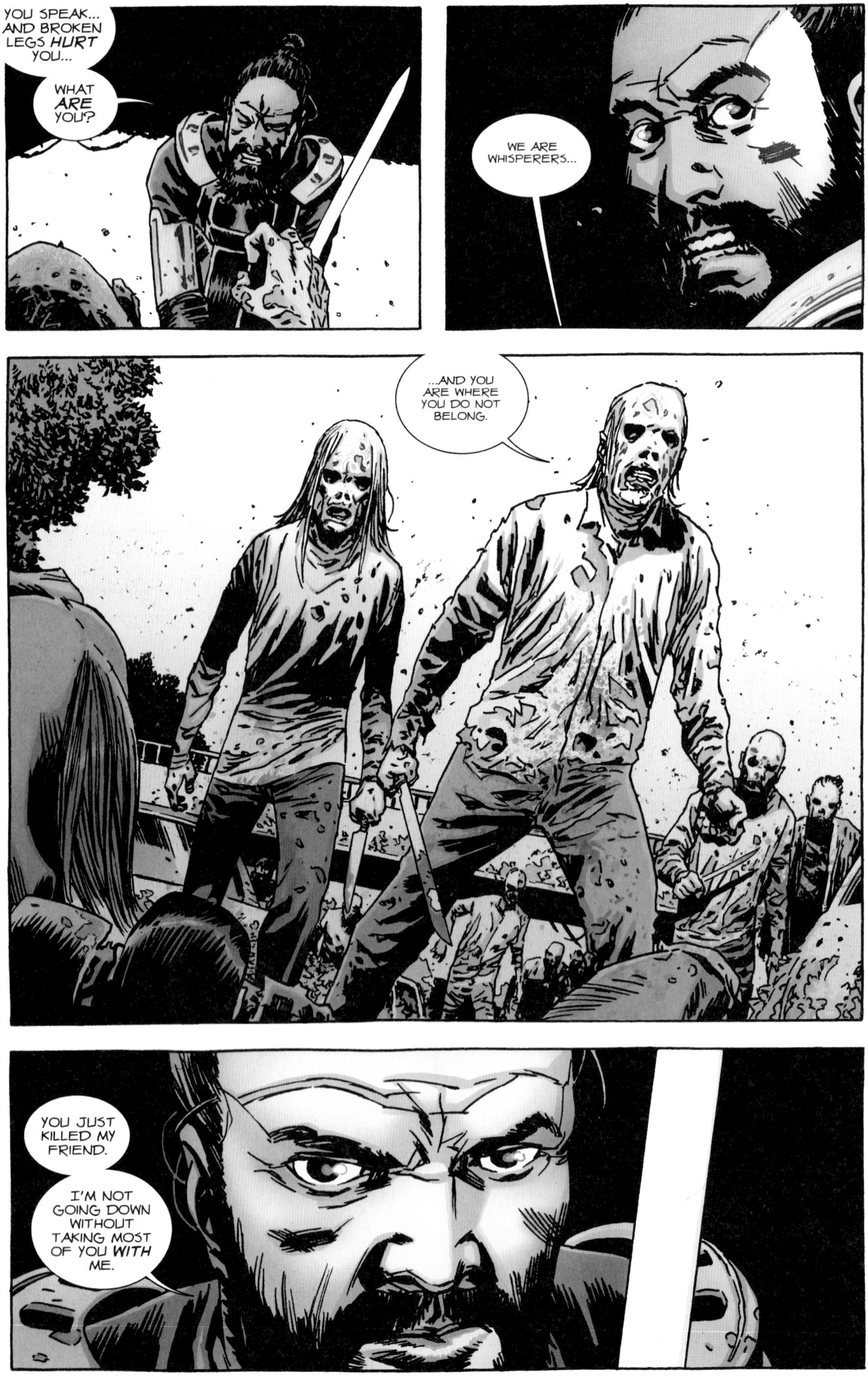
YOU SPEAK... AND BROKEN LEGS HURT YOU...
WHAT ARE YOU?
WE ARE WHISPERERS...
...AND YOU ARE WHERE YOU DO NOT BELONG.
YOU JUST KILLED MY FRIEND.
I'M NOT GOING DOWN WITHOUT TAKING MOST OF YOU WITH ME.

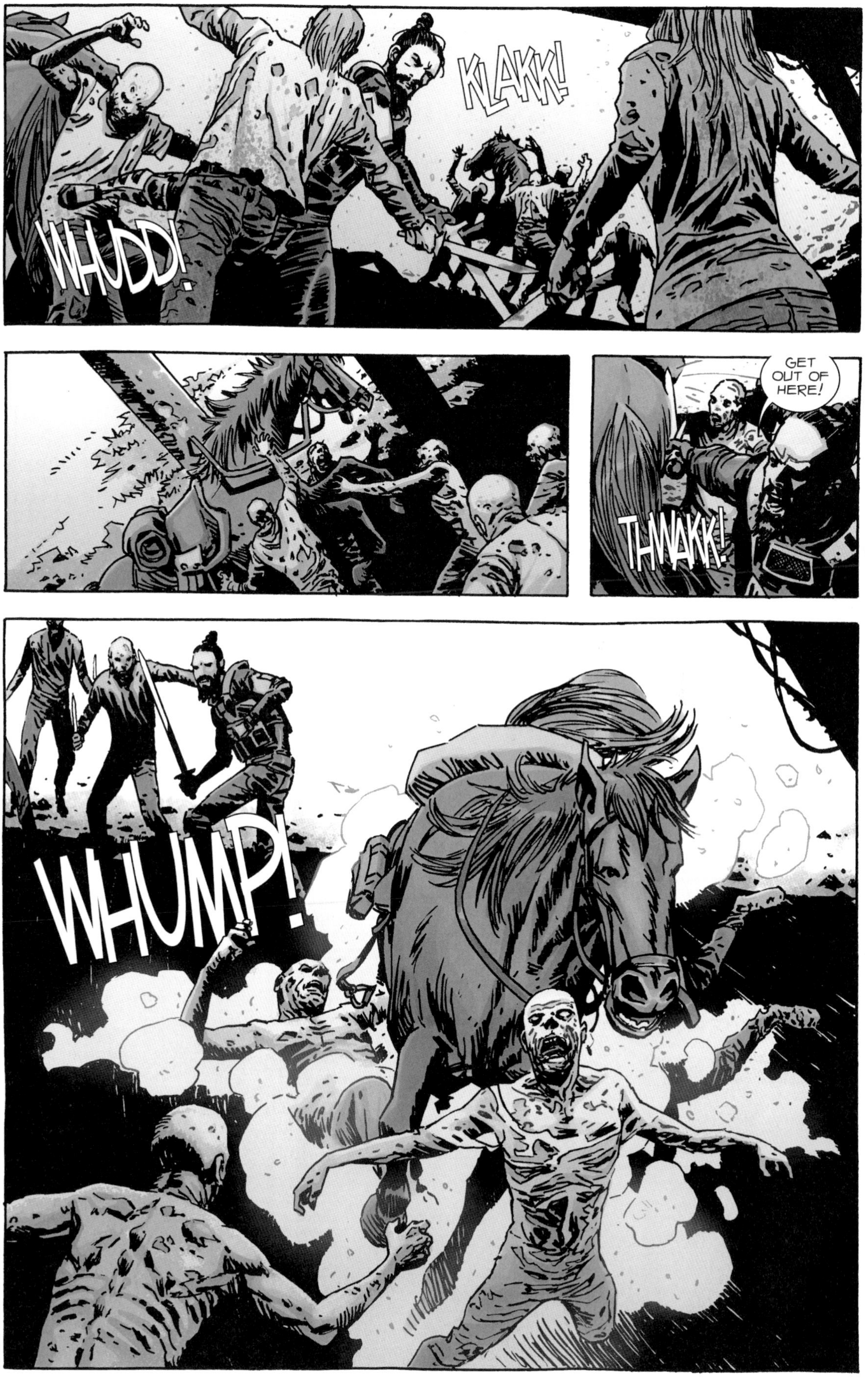
KLAKK!
WHUDD!
GET OUT OF HERE!
THWAKK!
WHUMP!

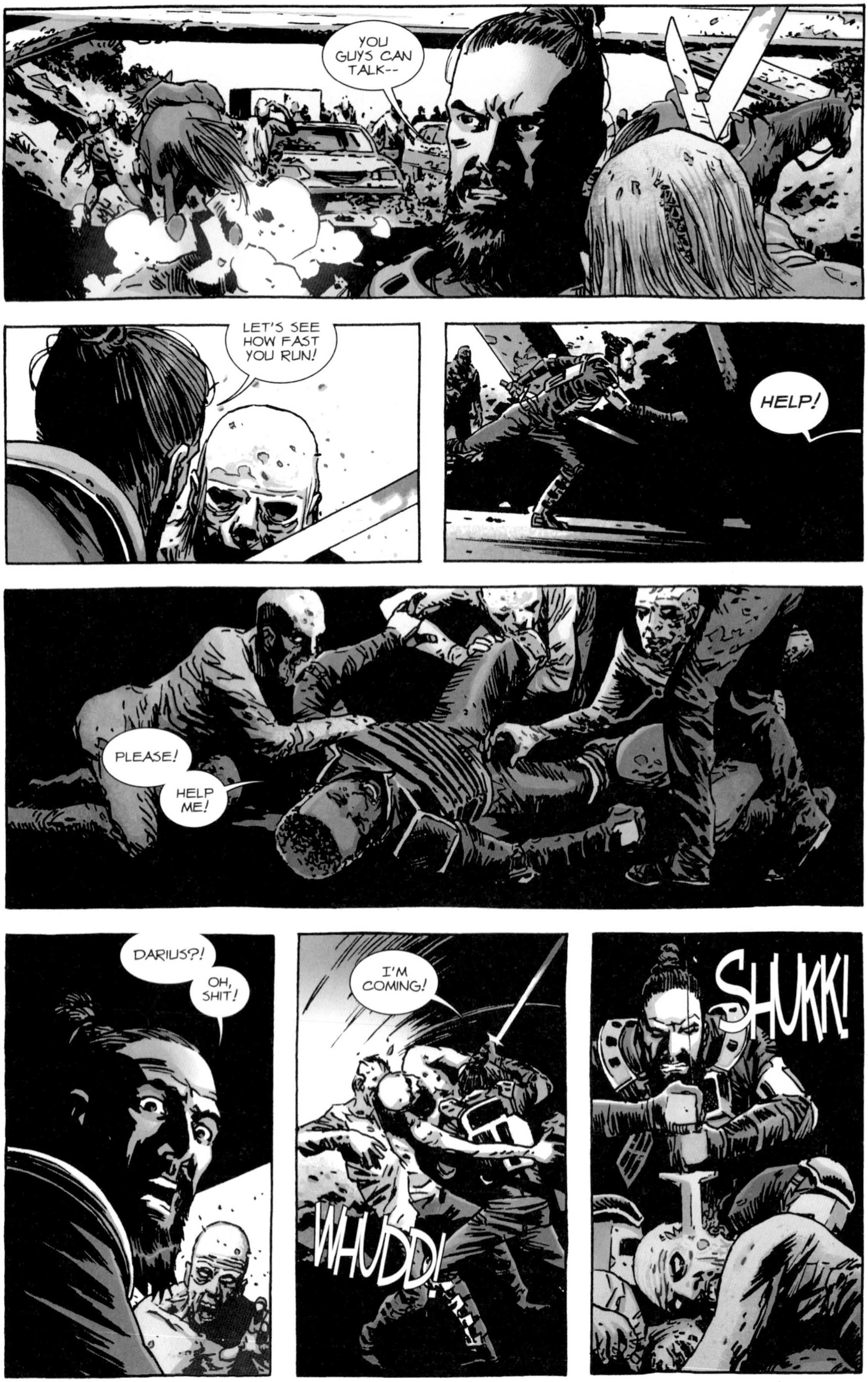
YOU GUYS CAN TALK--
LET'S SEE HOW FAST YOU RUN!
HELP!
PLEASE!
HELP ME!
DARIUS?!
OH, SHIT!
I'M COMING!
WHUDD!
SHUKK!

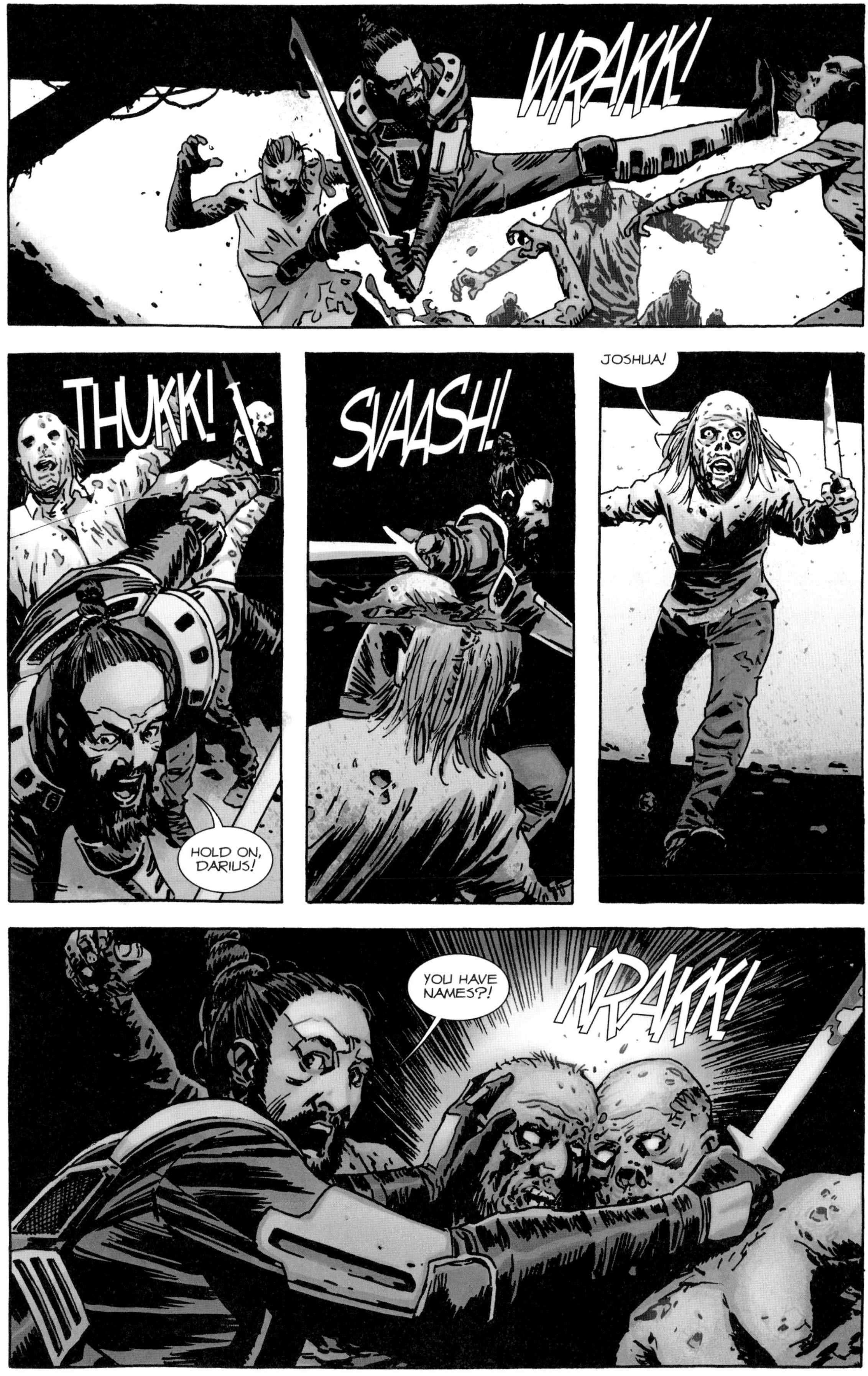
WRAKK!
THUKK!
HOLD ON, DARIUS!
SVAASH!
JOSHUA!
YOU HAVE NAMES?!
KRAKK!

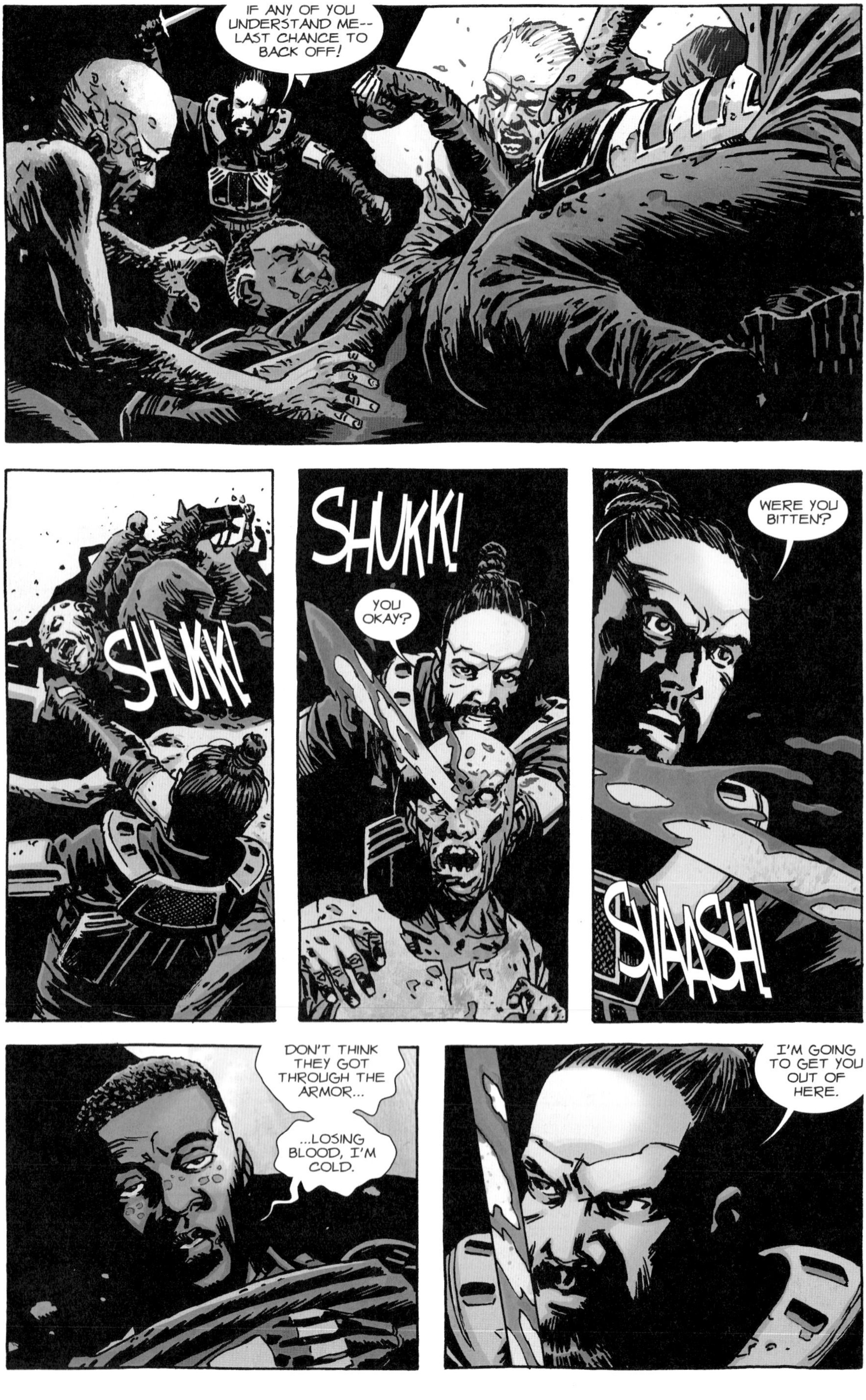
IF ANY OF YOU UNDERSTAND ME-- LAST CHANCE TO BACK OFF!
SHUKK!
SHUKK!
YOU OKAY?
WERE YOU BITTEN?
SWAASH!
DON'T THINK THEY GOT THROUGH THE ARMOR...
...LOSING BLOOD, I'M COLD.
I'M GOING TO GET YOU OUT OF HERE.

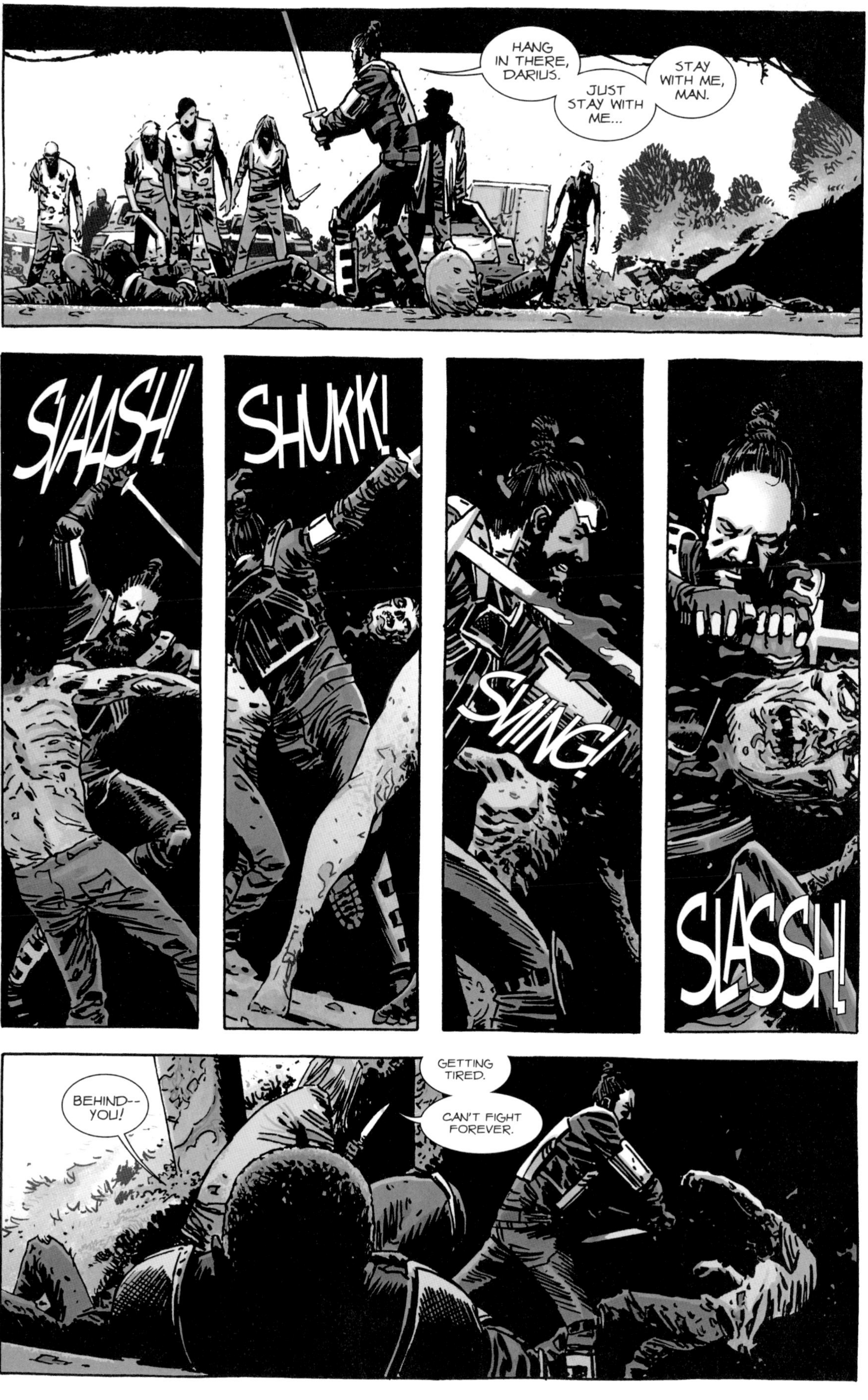
HANG IN THERE, DARIUS.
JUST STAY WITH ME...
STAY WITH ME, MAN.
SWAASH!
SHUKK!
SWING!
SLASSH!
BEHIND-- YOU!
GETTING TIRED.
CAN'T FIGHT FOREVER.

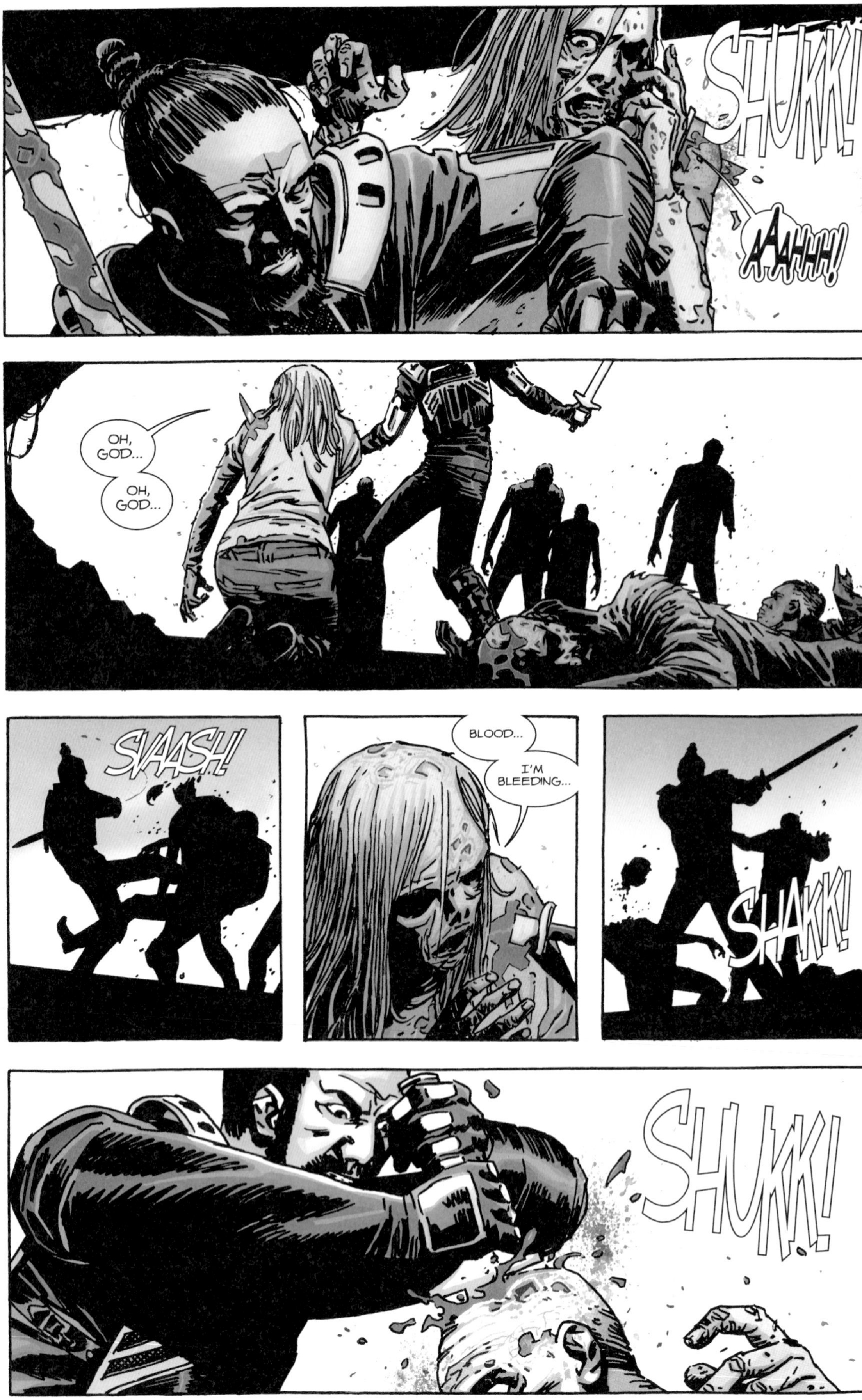
SHUKK!
AAAHHH!
OH, GOD...
OH, GOD...
SVAASH!
BLOOD...
I'M BLEEDING...
SHAKK!
SHUKK!

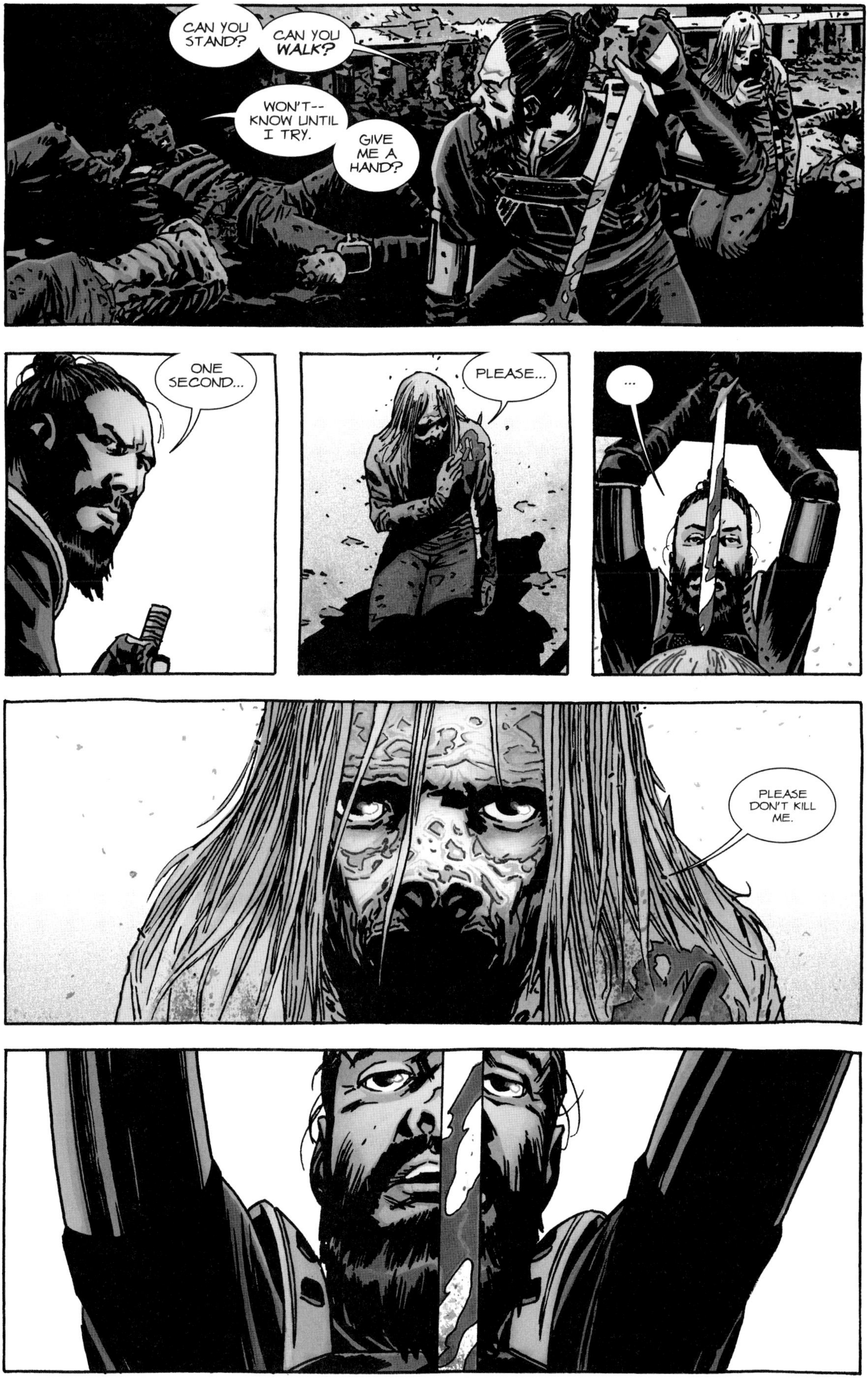
CAN YOU STAND?
CAN YOU WALK?
WON'T-- KNOW UNTIL I TRY.
GIVE ME A HAND?
ONE SECOND...
PLEASE...
...
PLEASE DON'T KILL ME.

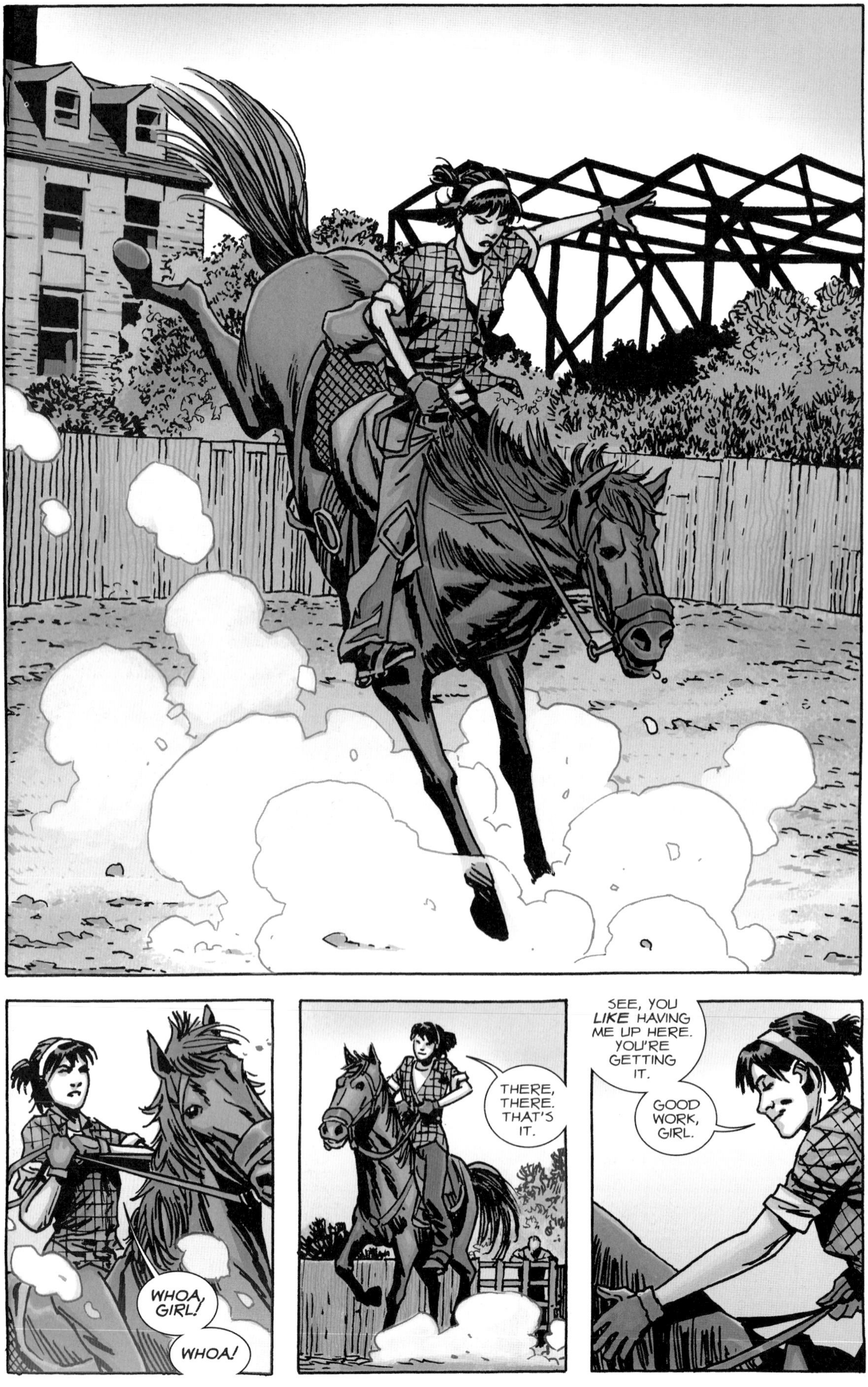
WHOA, GIRL!
WHOA!
THERE, THERE. THAT'S IT.
SEE, YOU **LIKE** HAVING ME UP HERE. YOU'RE GETTING IT.
GOOD WORK, GIRL.

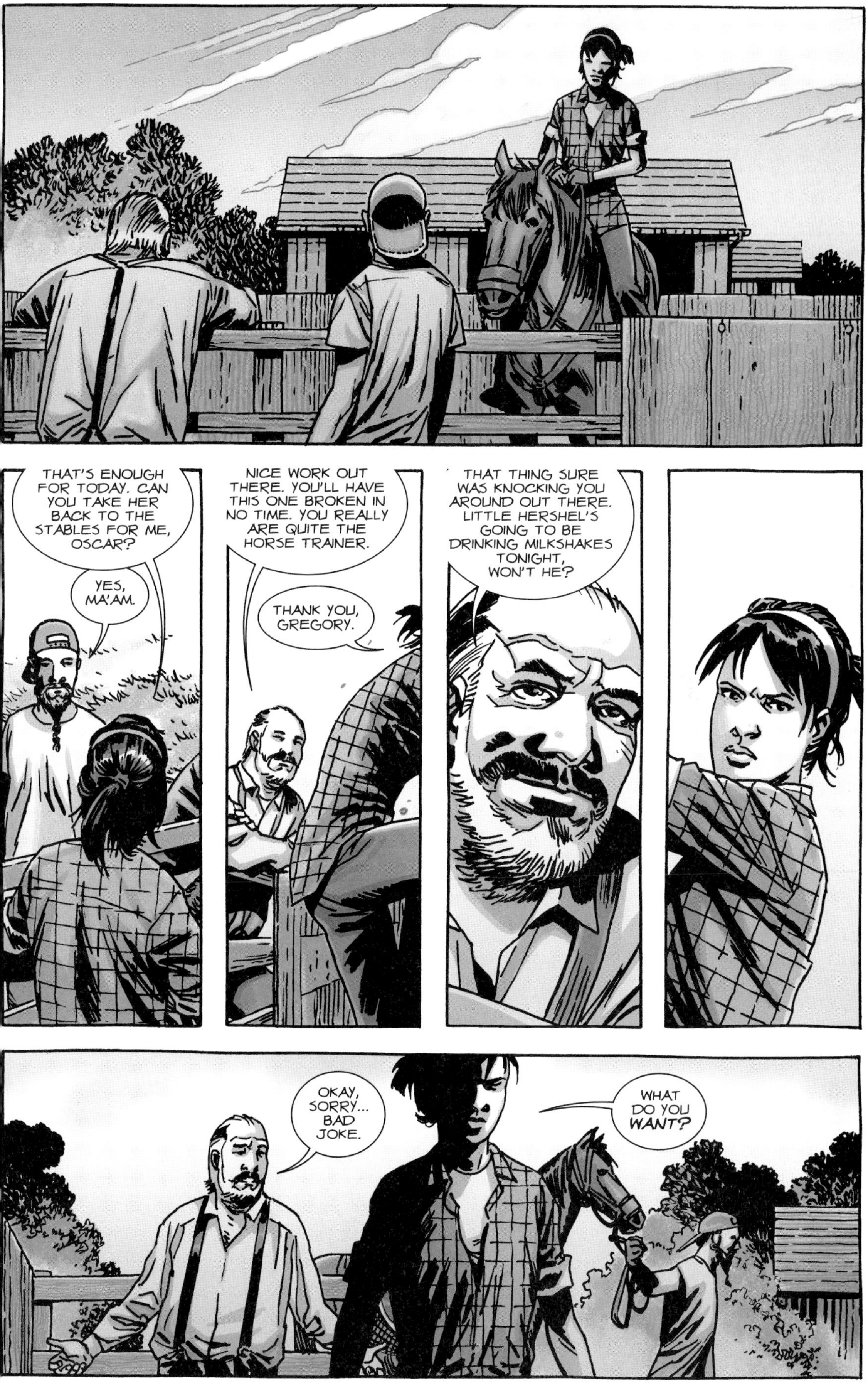
THAT'S ENOUGH FOR TODAY. CAN YOU TAKE HER BACK TO THE STABLES FOR ME, OSCAR?
YES, MA'AM.
NICE WORK OUT THERE. YOU'LL HAVE THIS ONE BROKEN IN NO TIME. YOU REALLY ARE QUITE THE HORSE TRAINER.
THANK YOU, GREGORY.
THAT THING SURE WAS KNOCKING YOU AROUND OUT THERE. LITTLE HERSHEL'S GOING TO BE DRINKING MILKSHAKES TONIGHT, WON'T HE?
OKAY, SORRY... BAD JOKE.
WHAT DO YOU WANT?

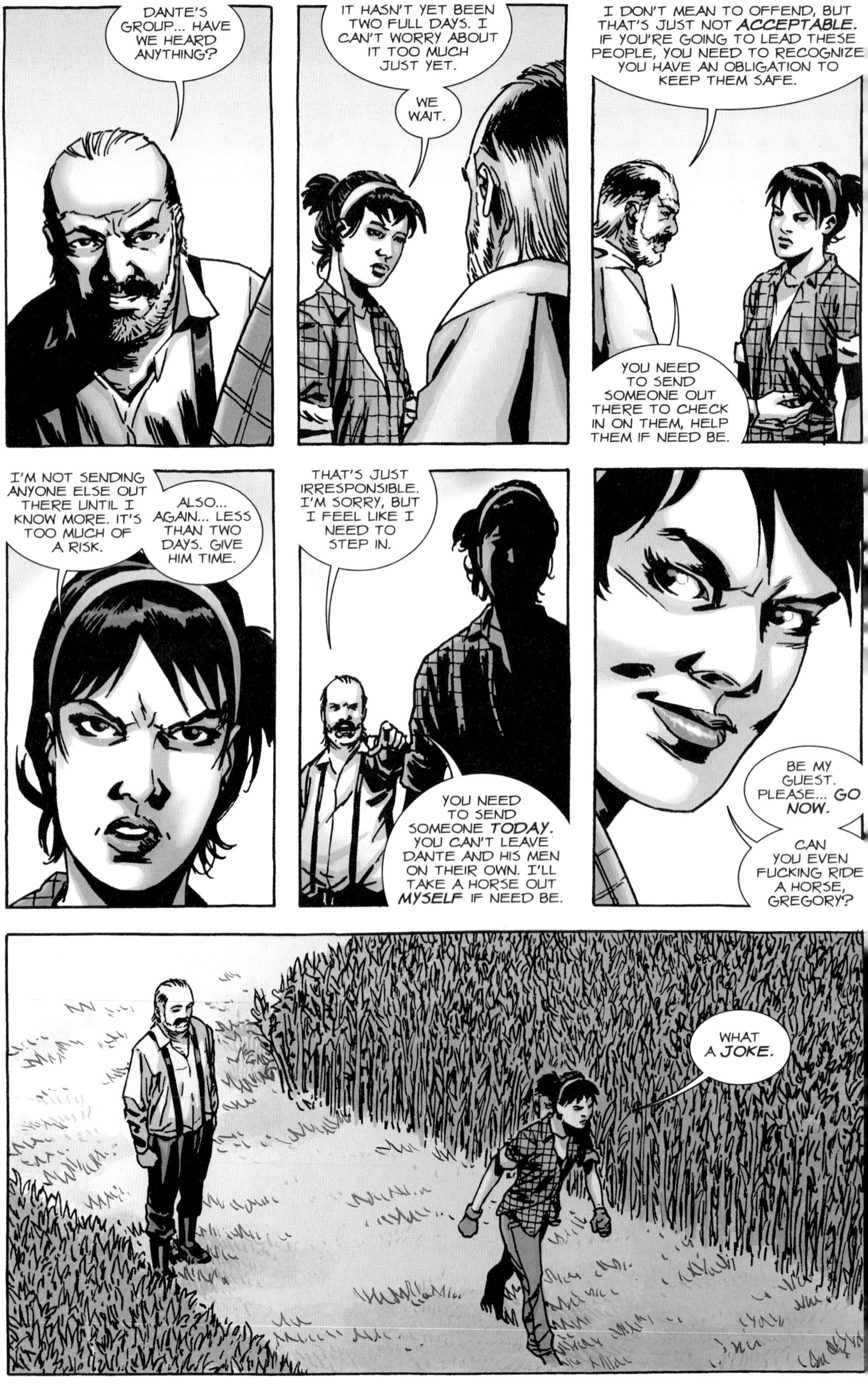
DANTE'S GROUP... HAVE WE HEARD ANYTHING?
IT HASN'T YET BEEN TWO FULL DAYS. I CAN'T WORRY ABOUT IT TOO MUCH JUST YET.
WE WAIT.
I DON'T MEAN TO OFFEND, BUT THAT'S JUST NOT ACCEPTABLE. IF YOU'RE GOING TO LEAD THESE PEOPLE, YOU NEED TO RECOGNIZE YOU HAVE AN OBLIGATION TO KEEP THEM SAFE.
YOU NEED TO SEND SOMEONE OUT THERE TO CHECK IN ON THEM, HELP THEM IF NEED BE.
I'M NOT SENDING ANYONE ELSE OUT THERE UNTIL I KNOW MORE. IT'S TOO MUCH OF A RISK.
ALSO... AGAIN... LESS THAN TWO DAYS. GIVE HIM TIME.
THAT'S JUST IRRESPONSIBLE. I'M SORRY, BUT I FEEL LIKE I NEED TO STEP IN.
YOU NEED TO SEND SOMEONE TODAY. YOU CAN'T LEAVE DANTE AND HIS MEN ON THEIR OWN. I'LL TAKE A HORSE OUT MYSELF IF NEED BE.
BE MY GUEST. PLEASE... GO NOW.
CAN YOU EVEN FUCKING RIDE A HORSE, GREGORY?
WHAT A JOKE.

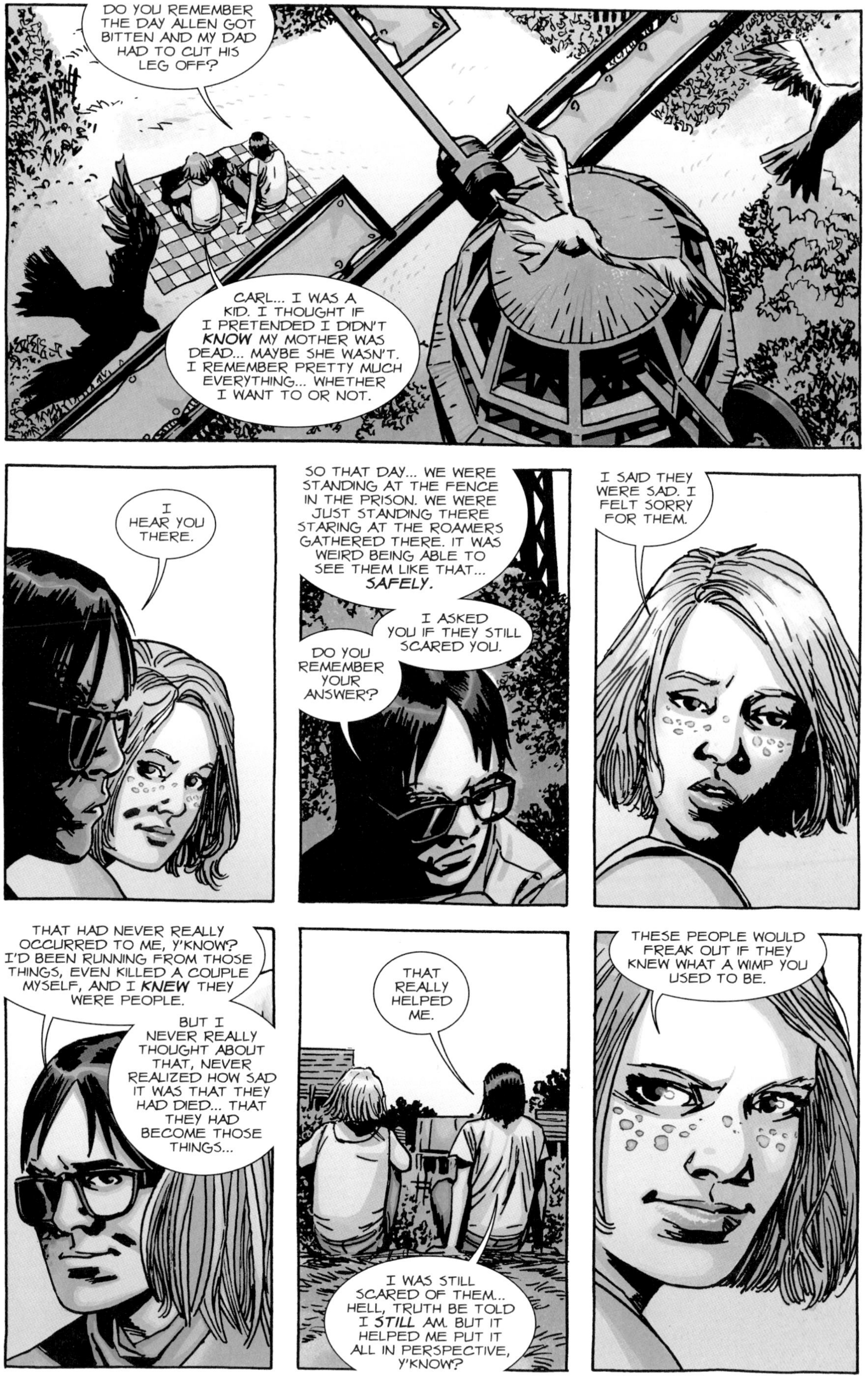
DO YOU REMEMBER THE DAY ALLEN GOT BITTEN AND MY DAD HAD TO CUT HIS LEG OFF?
CARL... I WAS A KID. I THOUGHT IF I PRETENDED I DIDN'T KNOW MY MOTHER WAS DEAD... MAYBE SHE WASN'T. I REMEMBER PRETTY MUCH EVERYTHING... WHETHER I WANT TO OR NOT.
I HEAR YOU THERE.
SO THAT DAY... WE WERE STANDING AT THE FENCE IN THE PRISON. WE WERE JUST STANDING THERE STARING AT THE ROAMERS GATHERED THERE. IT WAS WEIRD BEING ABLE TO SEE THEM LIKE THAT... SAFELY.
I ASKED YOU IF THEY STILL SCARED YOU.
DO YOU REMEMBER YOUR ANSWER?
I SAID THEY WERE SAD. I FELT SORRY FOR THEM.
THAT HAD NEVER REALLY OCCURRED TO ME, Y'KNOW? I'D BEEN RUNNING FROM THOSE THINGS, EVEN KILLED A COUPLE MYSELF, AND I KNEW THEY WERE PEOPLE.
BUT I NEVER REALLY THOUGHT ABOUT THAT, NEVER REALIZED HOW SAD IT WAS THAT THEY HAD DIED... THAT THEY HAD BECOME THOSE THINGS...
THAT REALLY HELPED ME.
I WAS STILL SCARED OF THEM... HELL, TRUTH BE TOLD I STILL AM. BUT IT HELPED ME PUT IT ALL IN PERSPECTIVE, Y'KNOW?
THESE PEOPLE WOULD FREAK OUT IF THEY KNEW WHAT A WIMP YOU USED TO BE.

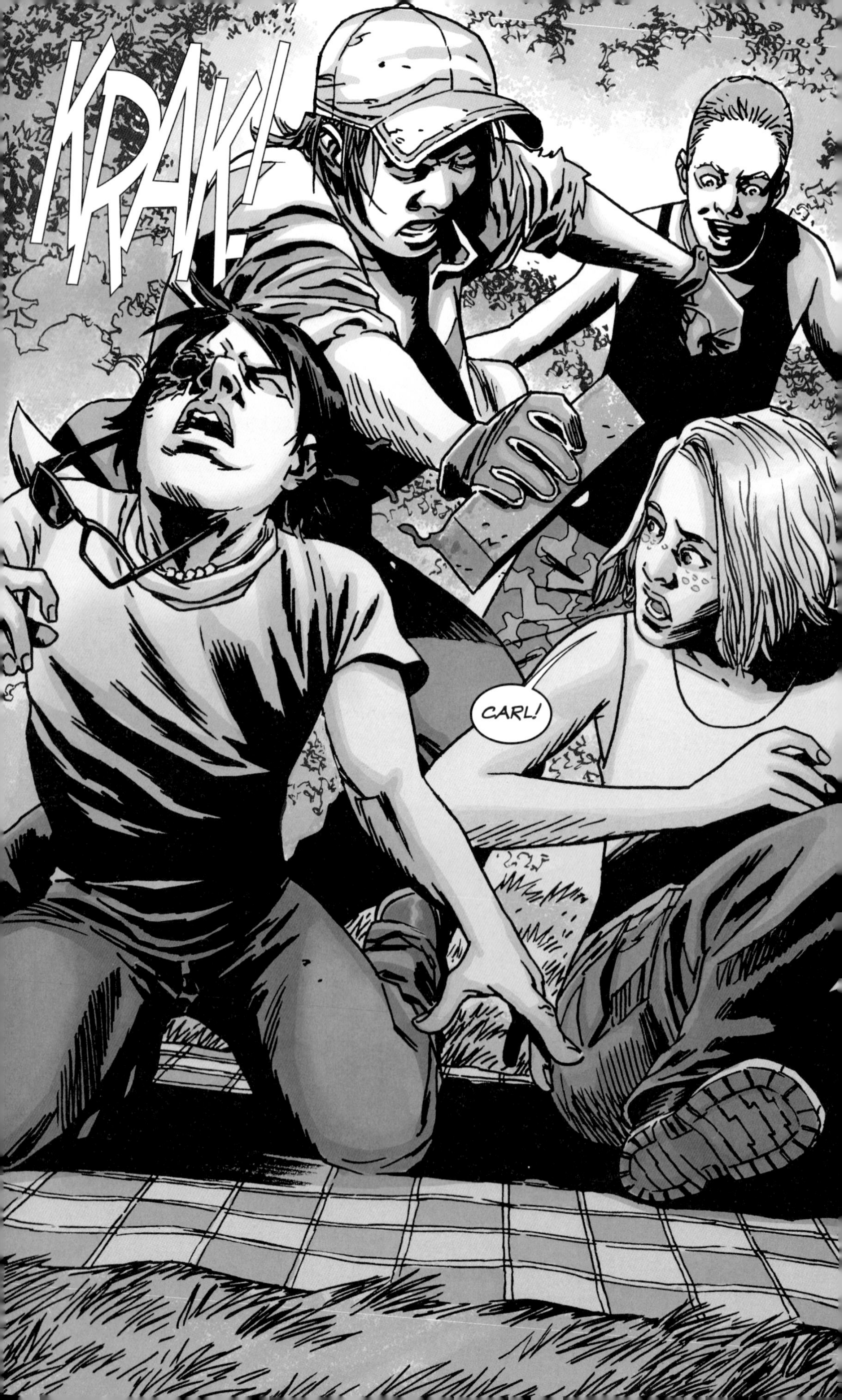
KRAK!
CARL!

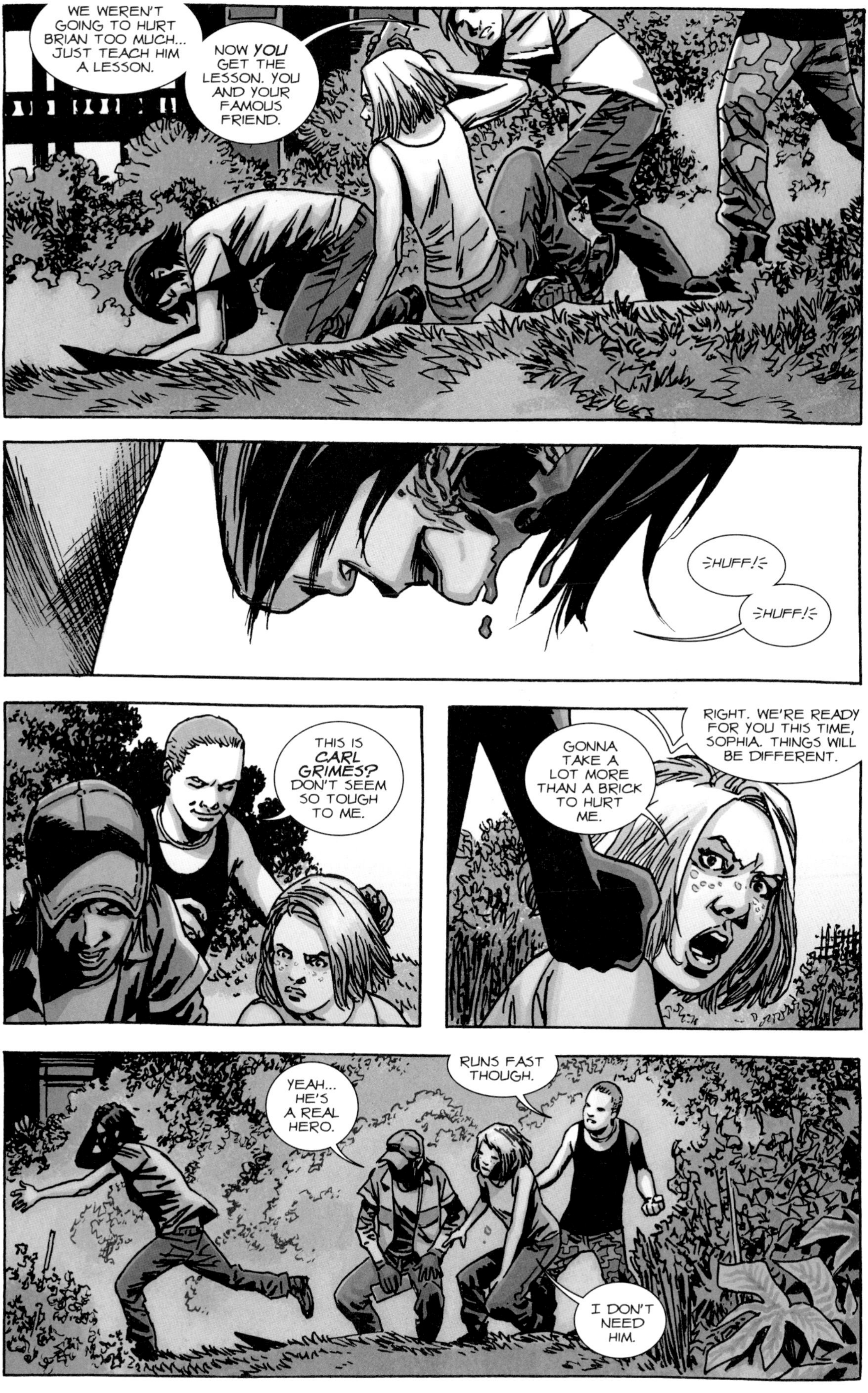
WE WEREN'T GOING TO HURT BRIAN TOO MUCH... JUST TEACH HIM A LESSON.
NOW YOU GET THE LESSON. YOU AND YOUR FAMOUS FRIEND.
HUFF!
HUFF!
THIS IS CARL GRIMES? DON'T SEEM SO TOUGH TO ME.
RIGHT. WE'RE READY FOR YOU THIS TIME, SOPHIA. THINGS WILL BE DIFFERENT.
GONNA TAKE A LOT MORE THAN A BRICK TO HURT ME.
YEAH... HE'S A REAL HERO.
RUNS FAST THOUGH.
I DON'T NEED HIM.

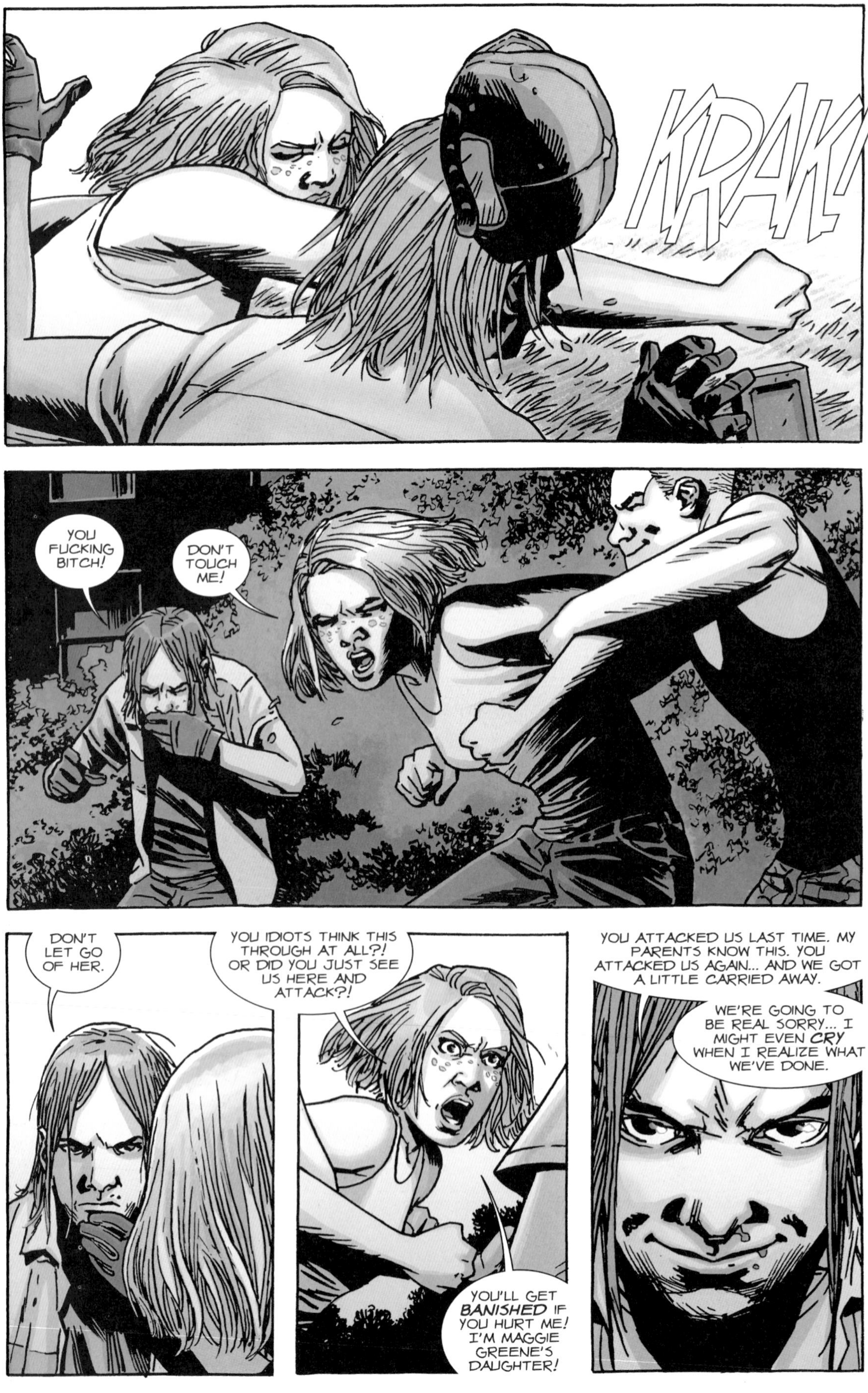
KRAAK!
YOU FUCKING BITCH!
DON'T TOUCH ME!
DON'T LET GO OF HER.
YOU IDIOTS THINK THIS THROUGH AT ALL?! OR DID YOU JUST SEE US HERE AND ATTACK?!
YOU'LL GET BANISHED IF YOU HURT ME! I'M MAGGIE GREENE'S DAUGHTER!
YOU ATTACKED US LAST TIME. MY PARENTS KNOW THIS. YOU ATTACKED US AGAIN... AND WE GOT A LITTLE CARRIED AWAY.
WE'RE GOING TO BE REAL SORRY... I MIGHT EVEN CRY WHEN I REALIZE WHAT WE'VE DONE.

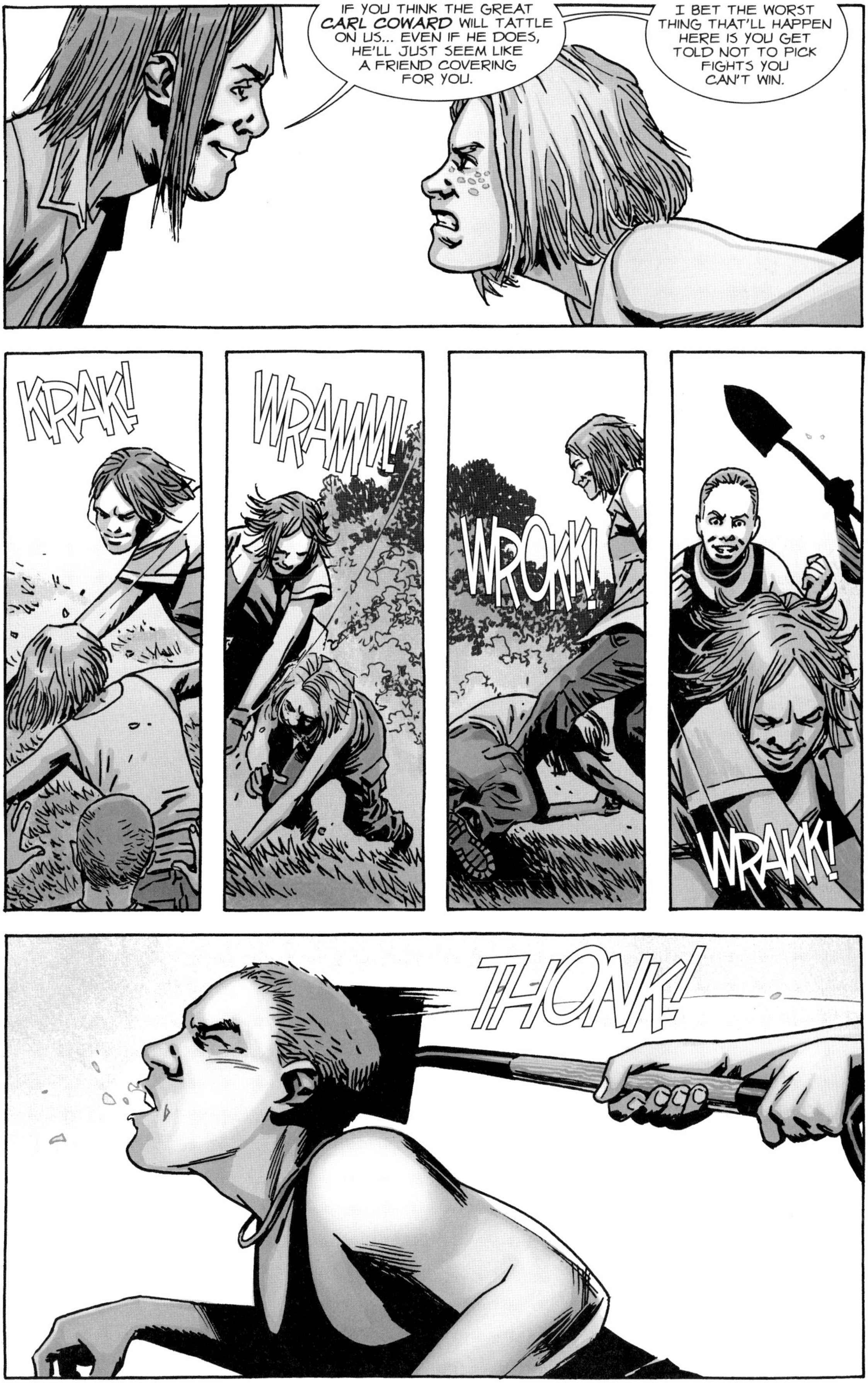
IF YOU THINK THE GREAT CARL COWARD WILL TATTLE ON US... EVEN IF HE DOES, HE'LL JUST SEEM LIKE A FRIEND COVERING FOR YOU.
I BET THE WORST THING THAT'LL HAPPEN HERE IS YOU GET TOLD NOT TO PICK FIGHTS YOU CAN'T WIN.
KRAK!
WRAMM!
WROKK!
WRAKK!
THONK!

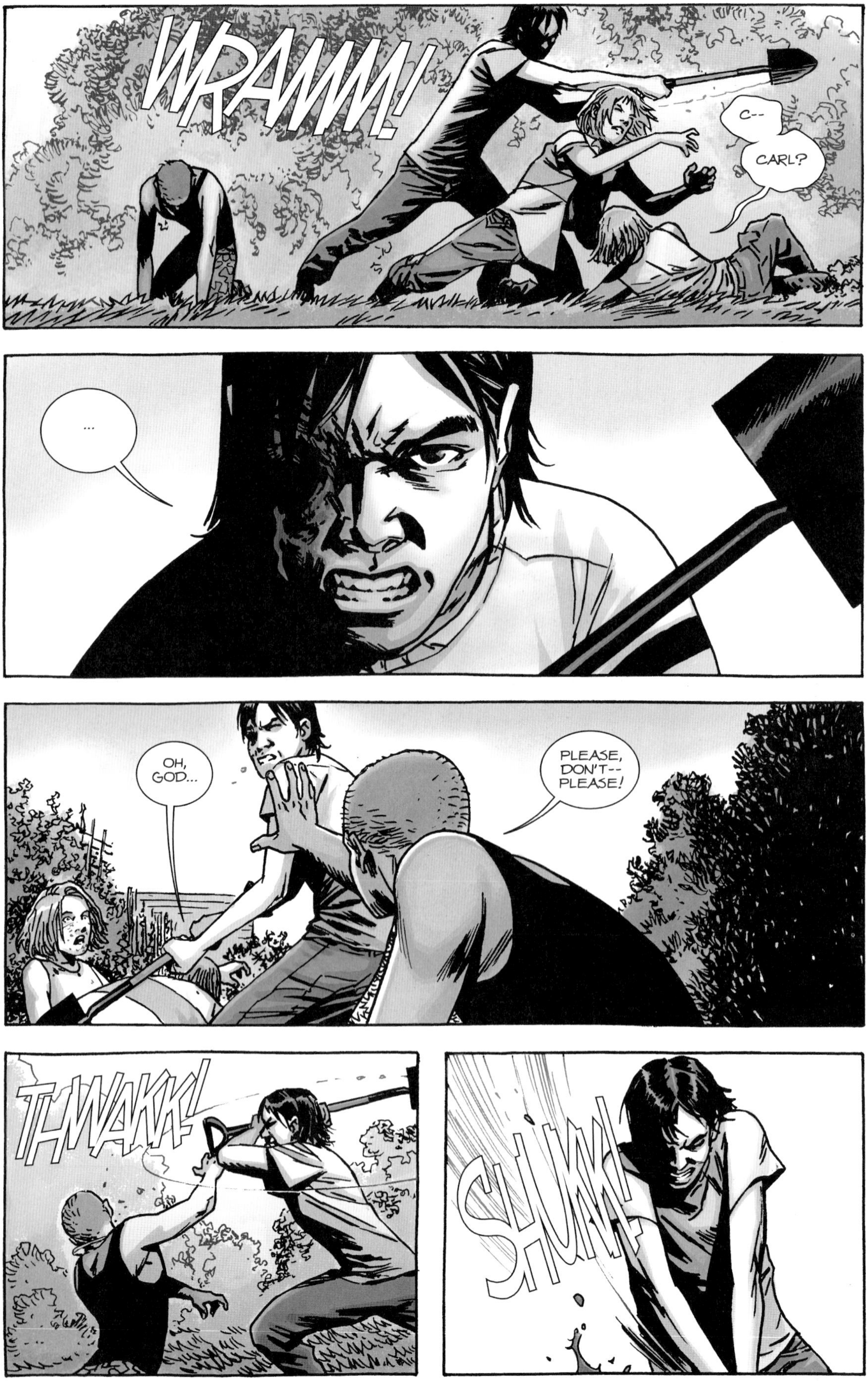
WRAMM!
C--
CARL?
...
OH, GOD...
PLEASE, DON'T-- PLEASE!
THWAKK!
SHUNK!

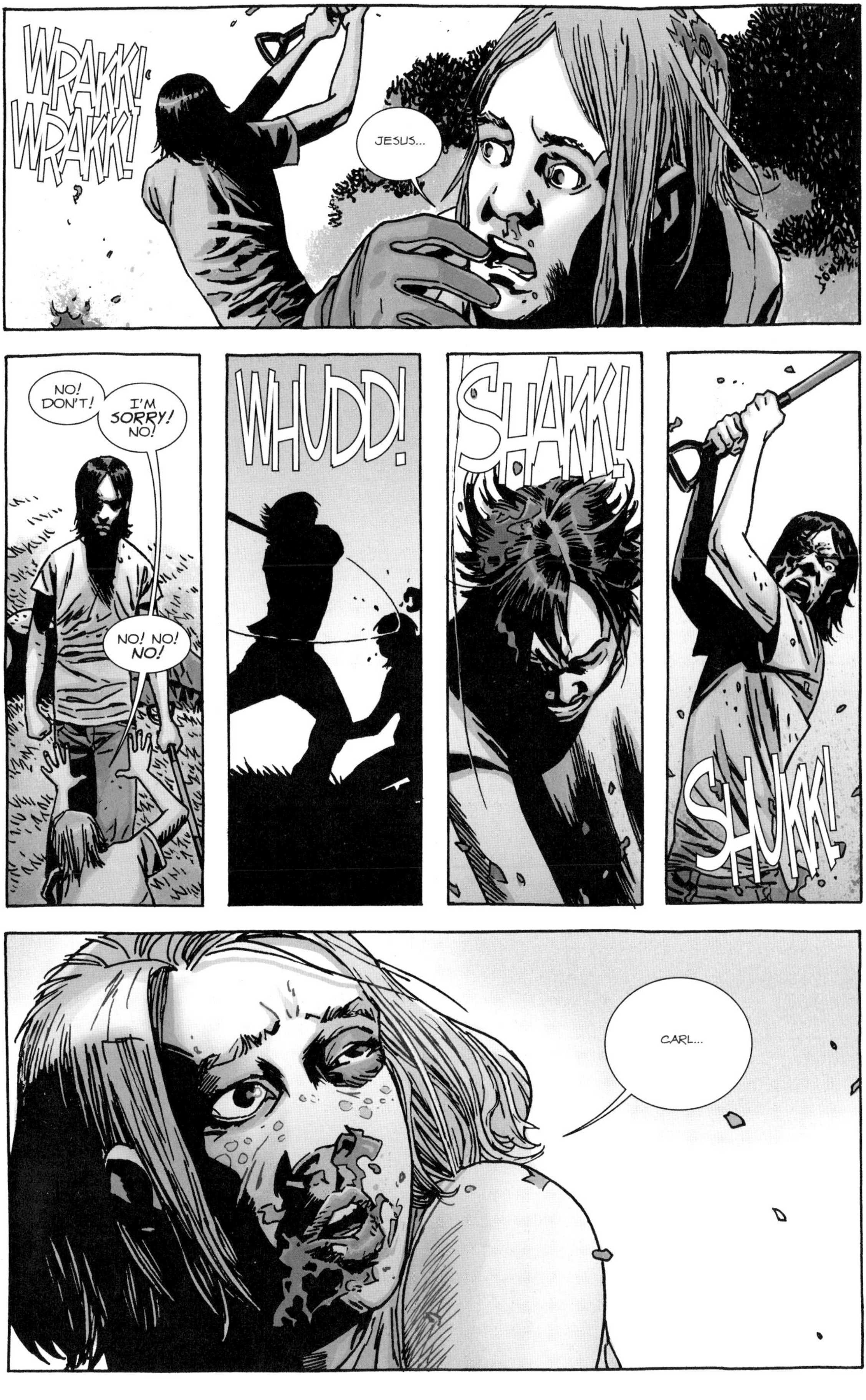
WRAKK! WRAKK!
JESUS...
NO! DON'T!
I'M SORRY! NO!
NO! NO! NO!
WHUDD!
SHAKK!
SHUKK!
CARL...

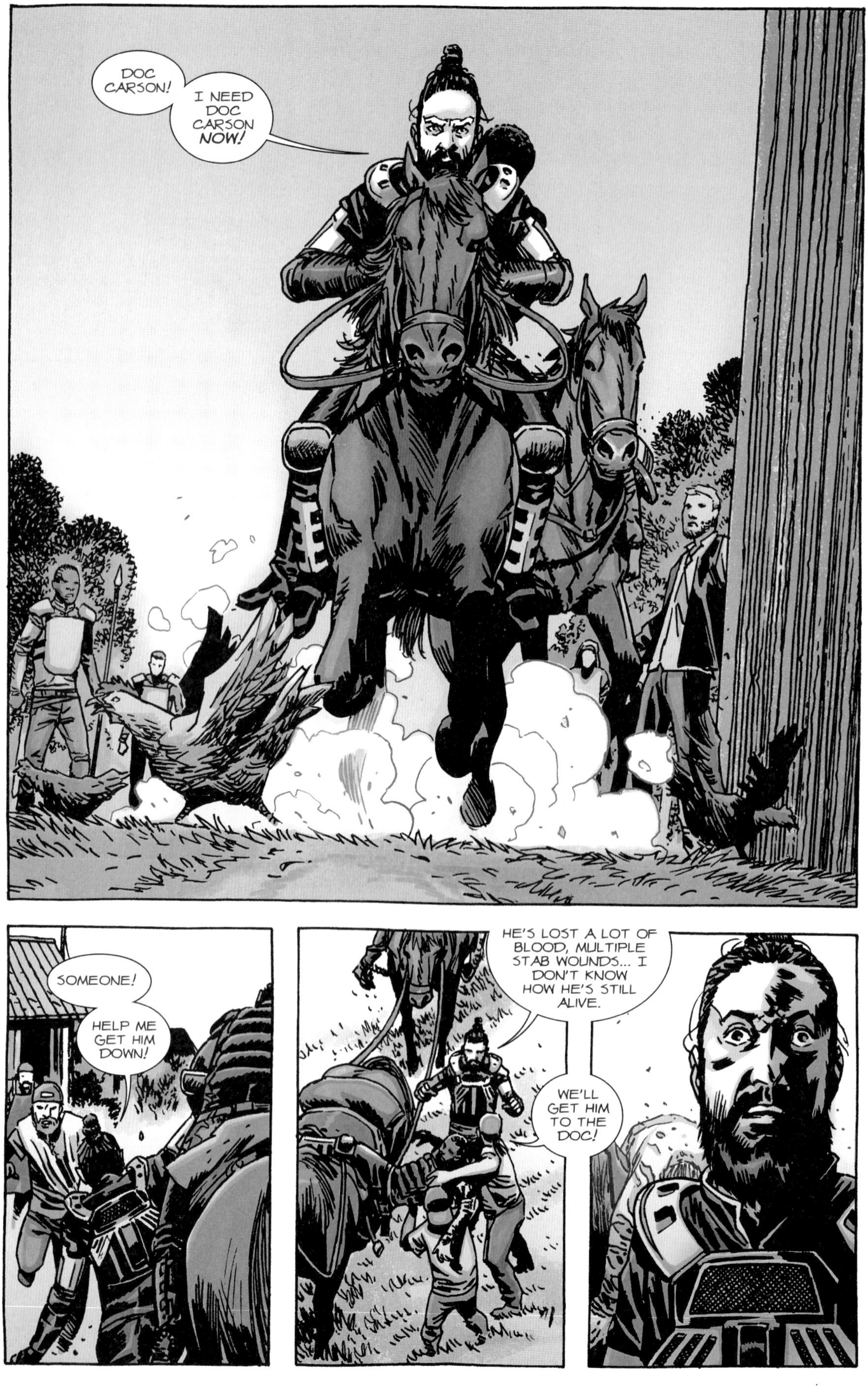
DOC CARSON!
I NEED DOC CARSON NOW!
SOMEONE!
HELP ME GET HIM DOWN!
HE'S LOST A LOT OF BLOOD, MULTIPLE STAB WOUNDS... I DON'T KNOW HOW HE'S STILL ALIVE.
WE'LL GET HIM TO THE DOC!

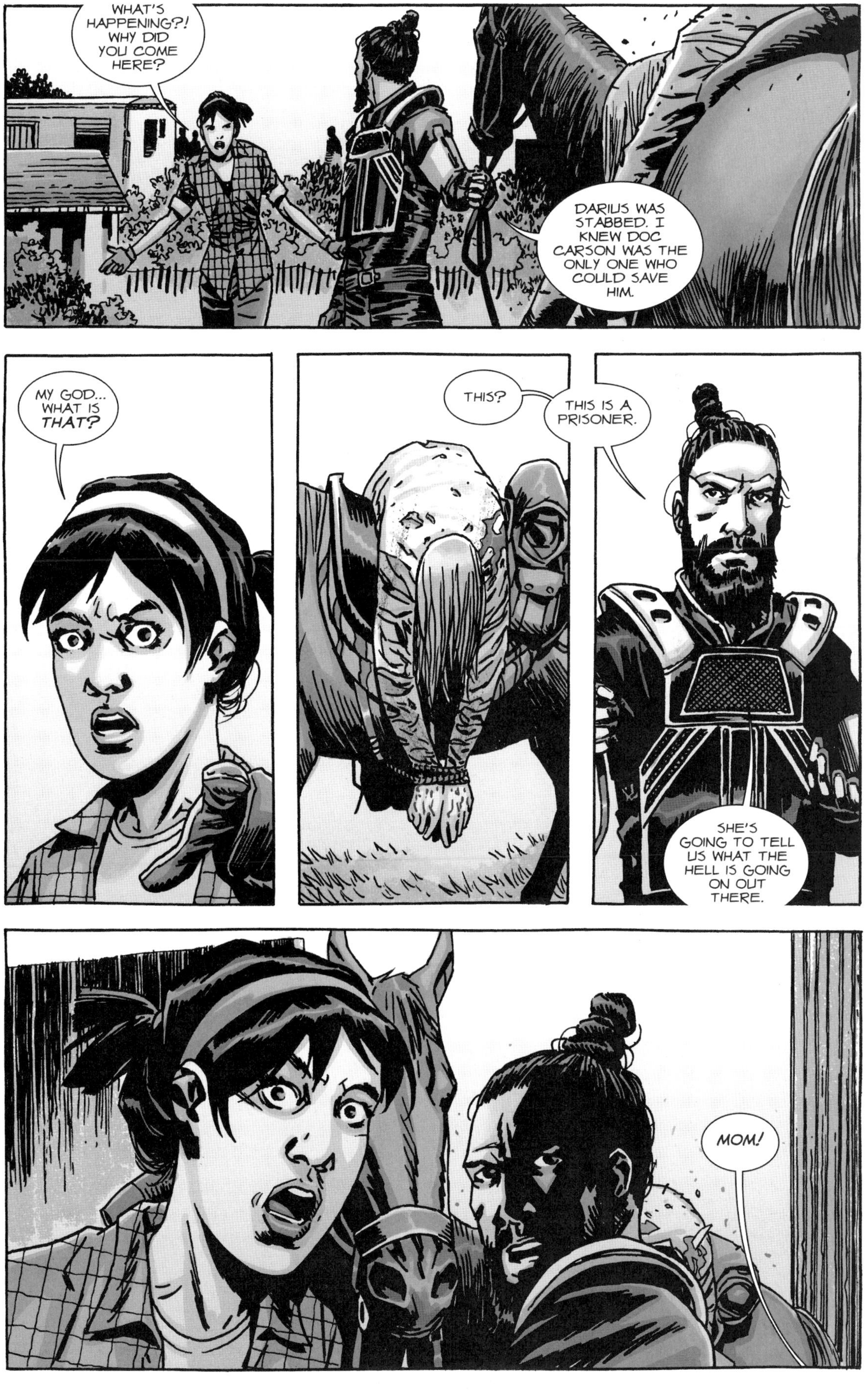
WHAT'S HAPPENING?! WHY DID YOU COME HERE?
DARIUS WAS STABBED. I KNEW DOC CARSON WAS THE ONLY ONE WHO COULD SAVE HIM.
MY GOD... WHAT IS *THAT?*
THIS?
THIS IS A PRISONER.
SHE'S GOING TO TELL US WHAT THE HELL IS GOING ON OUT THERE.
MOM!

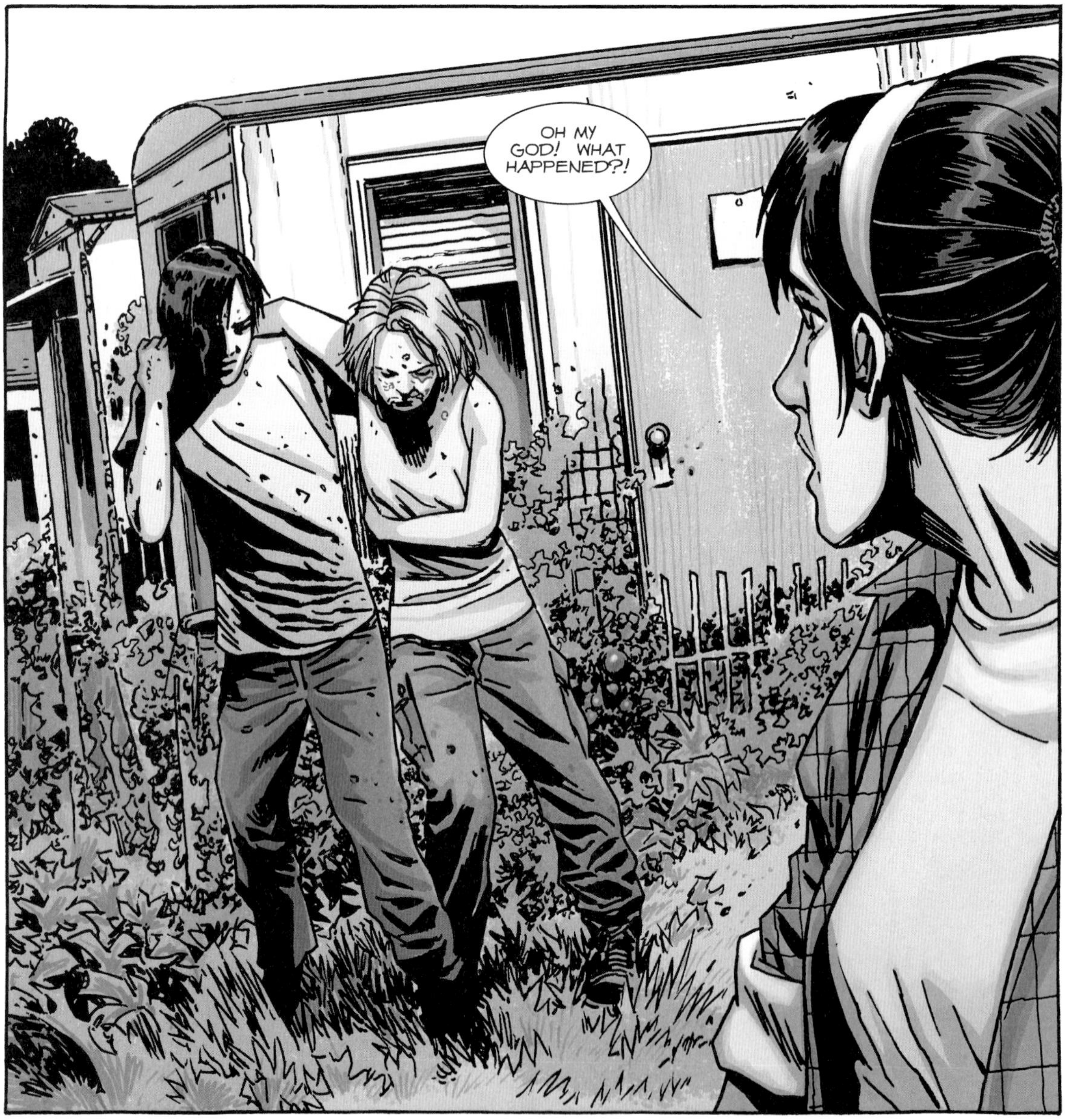
OH MY GOD! WHAT HAPPENED?!

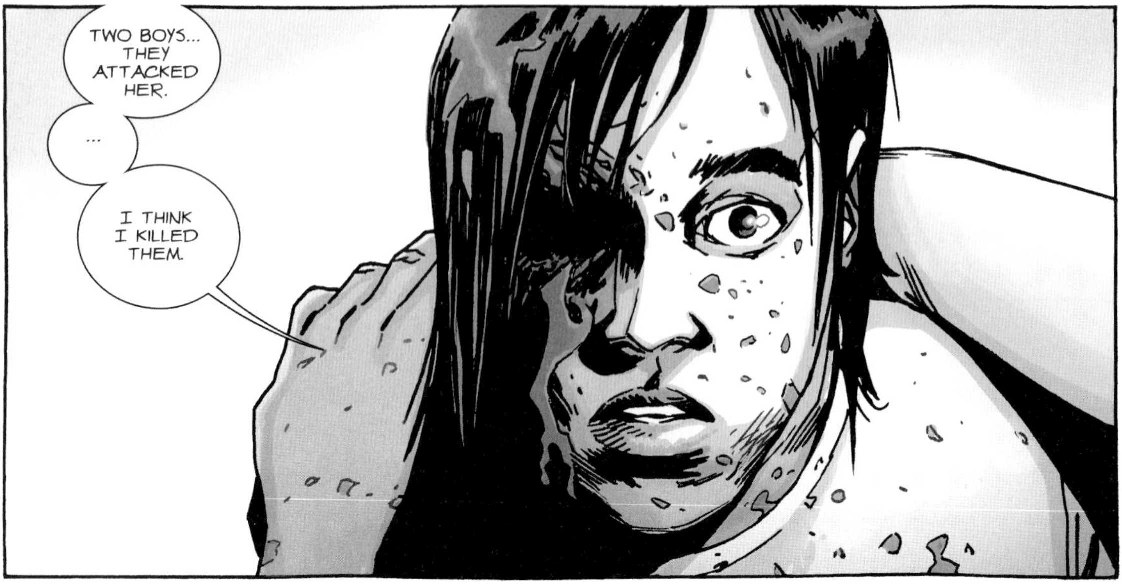
TWO BOYS... THEY ATTACKED HER.
...
I THINK I KILLED THEM.

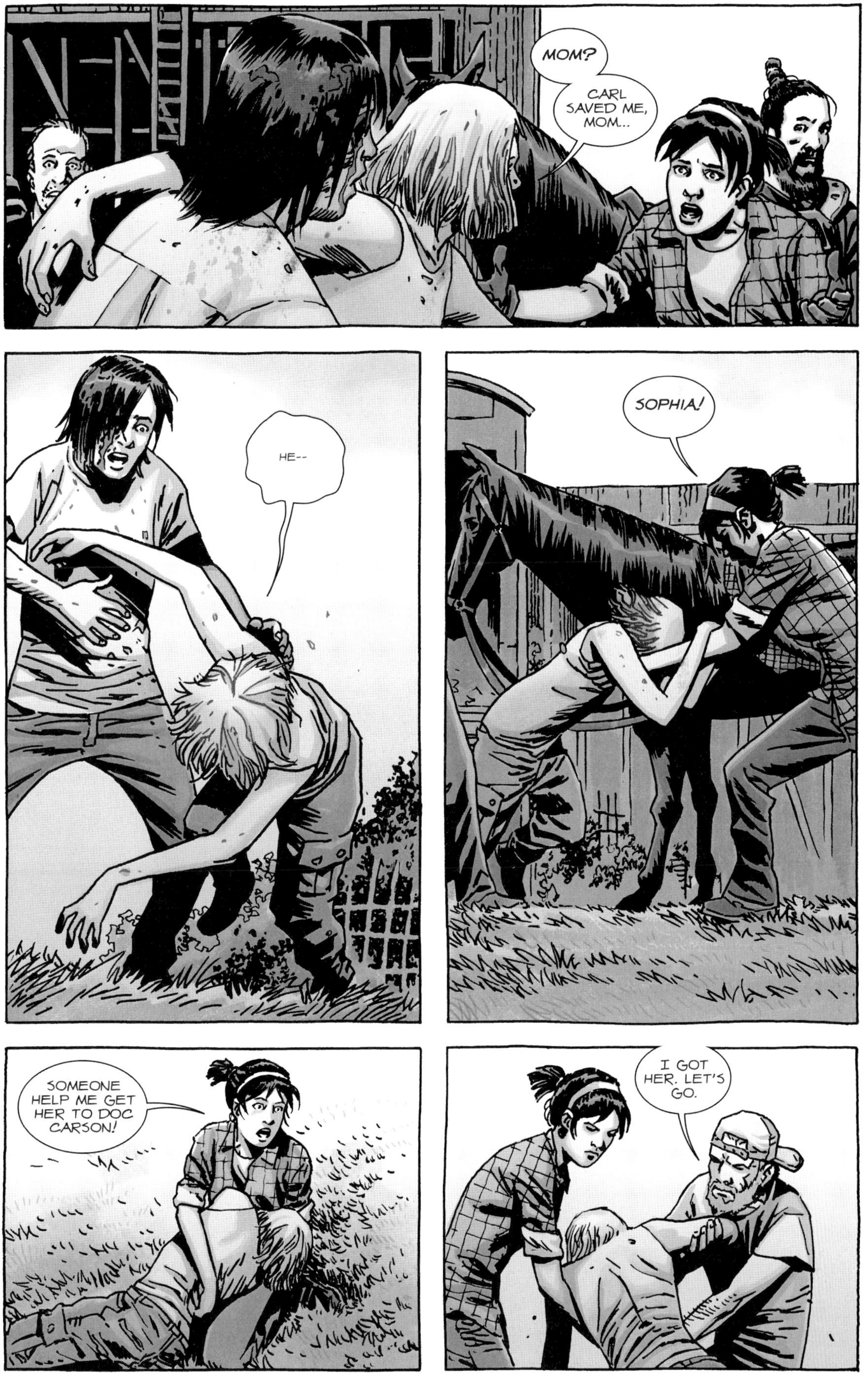
MOM?
CARL SAVED ME, MOM...
HE--
SOPHIA!
SOMEONE HELP ME GET HER TO DOC CARSON!
I GOT HER. LET'S GO.

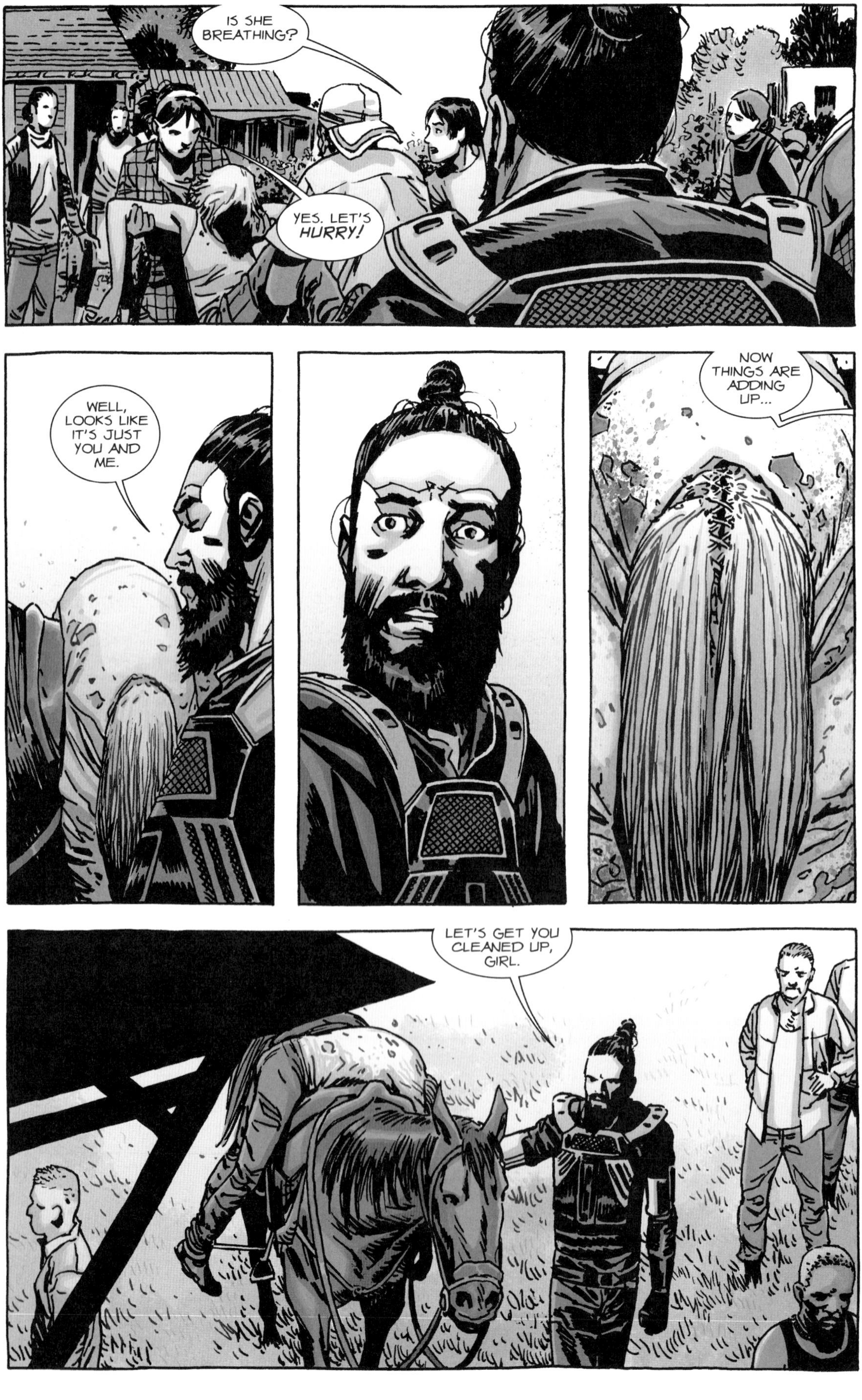
IS SHE BREATHING?
YES. LET'S *HURRY!*
WELL, LOOKS LIKE IT'S JUST YOU AND ME.
NOW THINGS ARE ADDING UP...
LET'S GET YOU CLEANED UP, GIRL.

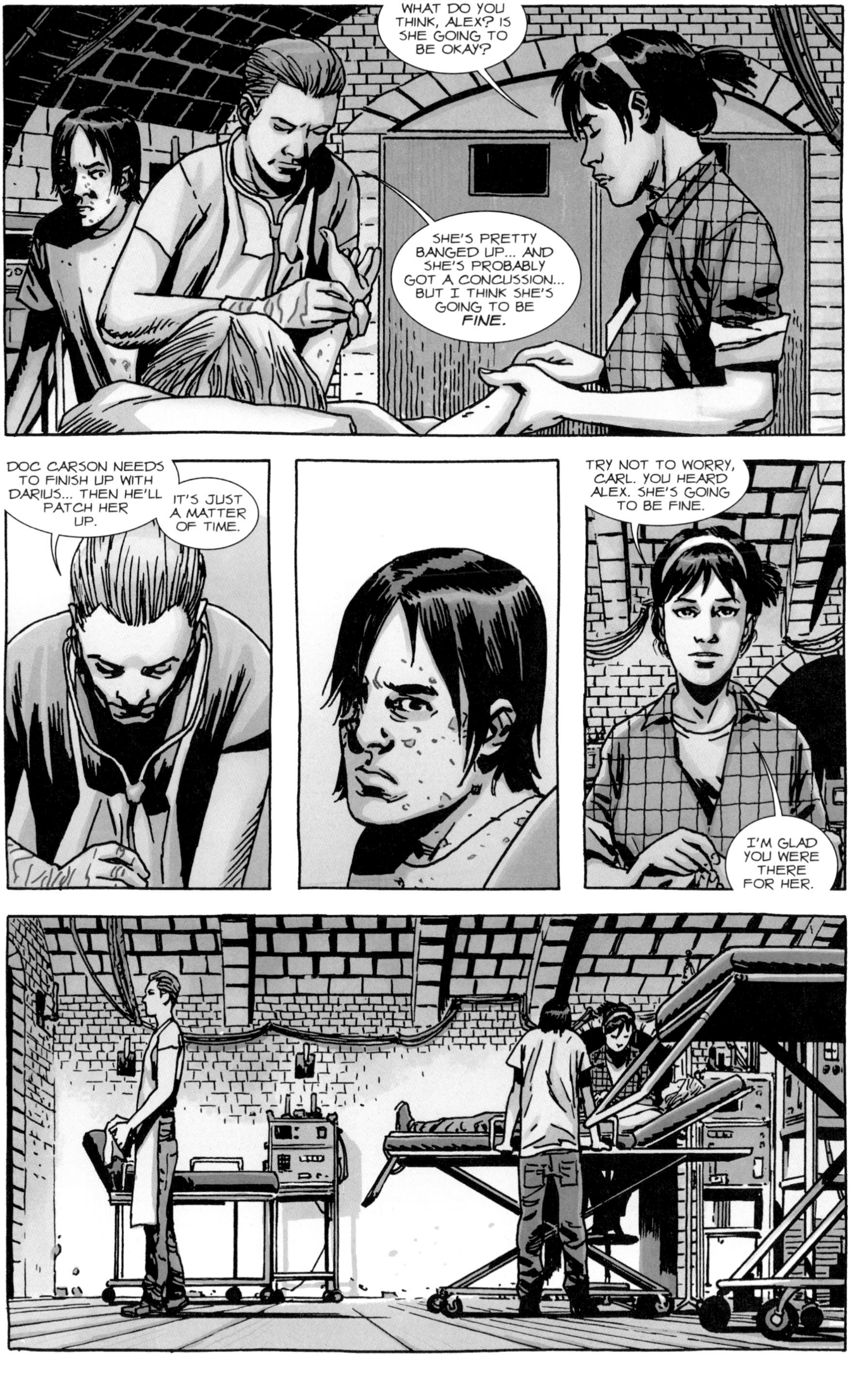
WHAT DO YOU THINK, ALEX? IS SHE GOING TO BE OKAY?
SHE'S PRETTY BANGED UP... AND SHE'S PROBABLY GOT A CONCUSSION... BUT I THINK SHE'S GOING TO BE *FINE.*
DOC CARSON NEEDS TO FINISH UP WITH DARIUS... THEN HE'LL PATCH HER UP.
IT'S JUST A MATTER OF TIME.
TRY NOT TO WORRY, CARL. YOU HEARD ALEX. SHE'S GOING TO BE FINE.
I'M GLAD YOU WERE THERE FOR HER.

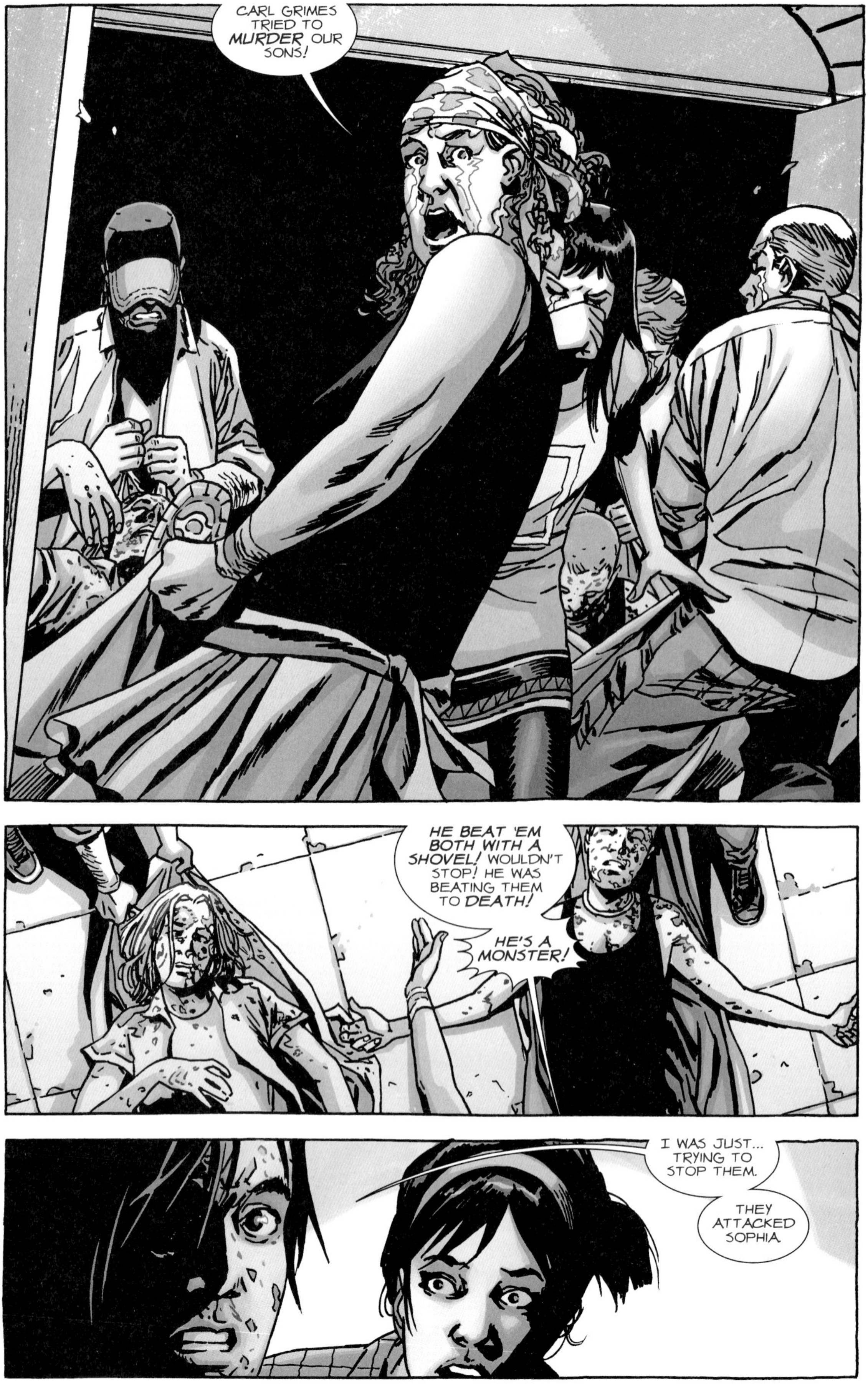
CARL GRIMES TRIED TO MURDER OUR SONS!
HE BEAT 'EM BOTH WITH A SHOVEL! WOULDN'T STOP! HE WAS BEATING THEM TO DEATH!
HE'S A MONSTER!
I WAS JUST... TRYING TO STOP THEM.
THEY ATTACKED SOPHIA.

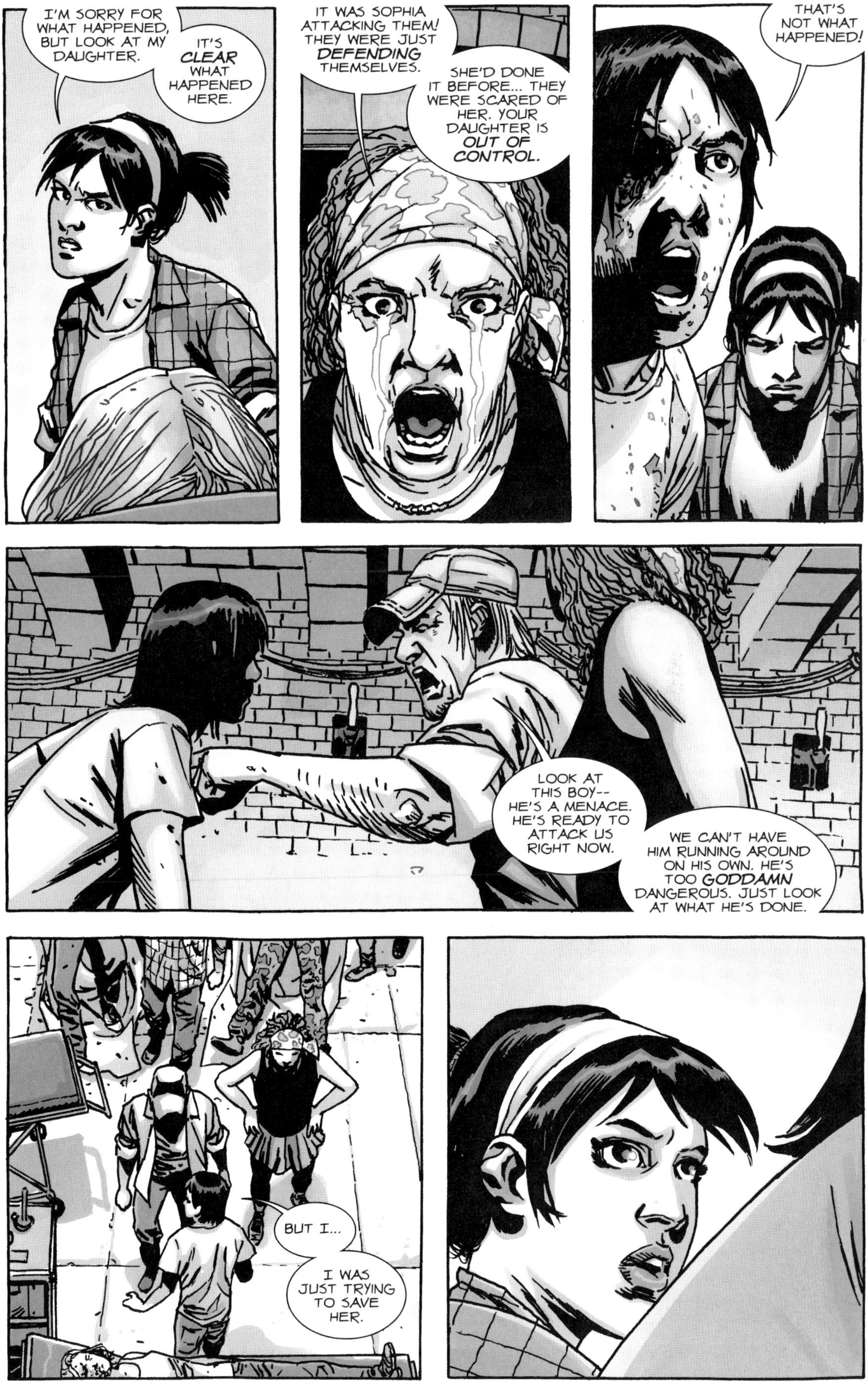
I'M SORRY FOR WHAT HAPPENED, BUT LOOK AT MY DAUGHTER.
IT'S CLEAR WHAT HAPPENED HERE.
IT WAS SOPHIA ATTACKING THEM! THEY WERE JUST DEFENDING THEMSELVES.
SHE'D DONE IT BEFORE... THEY WERE SCARED OF HER. YOUR DAUGHTER IS OUT OF CONTROL.
THAT'S NOT WHAT HAPPENED!
LOOK AT THIS BOY-- HE'S A MENACE. HE'S READY TO ATTACK US RIGHT NOW.
WE CAN'T HAVE HIM RUNNING AROUND ON HIS OWN. HE'S TOO GODDAMN DANGEROUS. JUST LOOK AT WHAT HE'S DONE.
BUT I...
I WAS JUST TRYING TO SAVE HER.

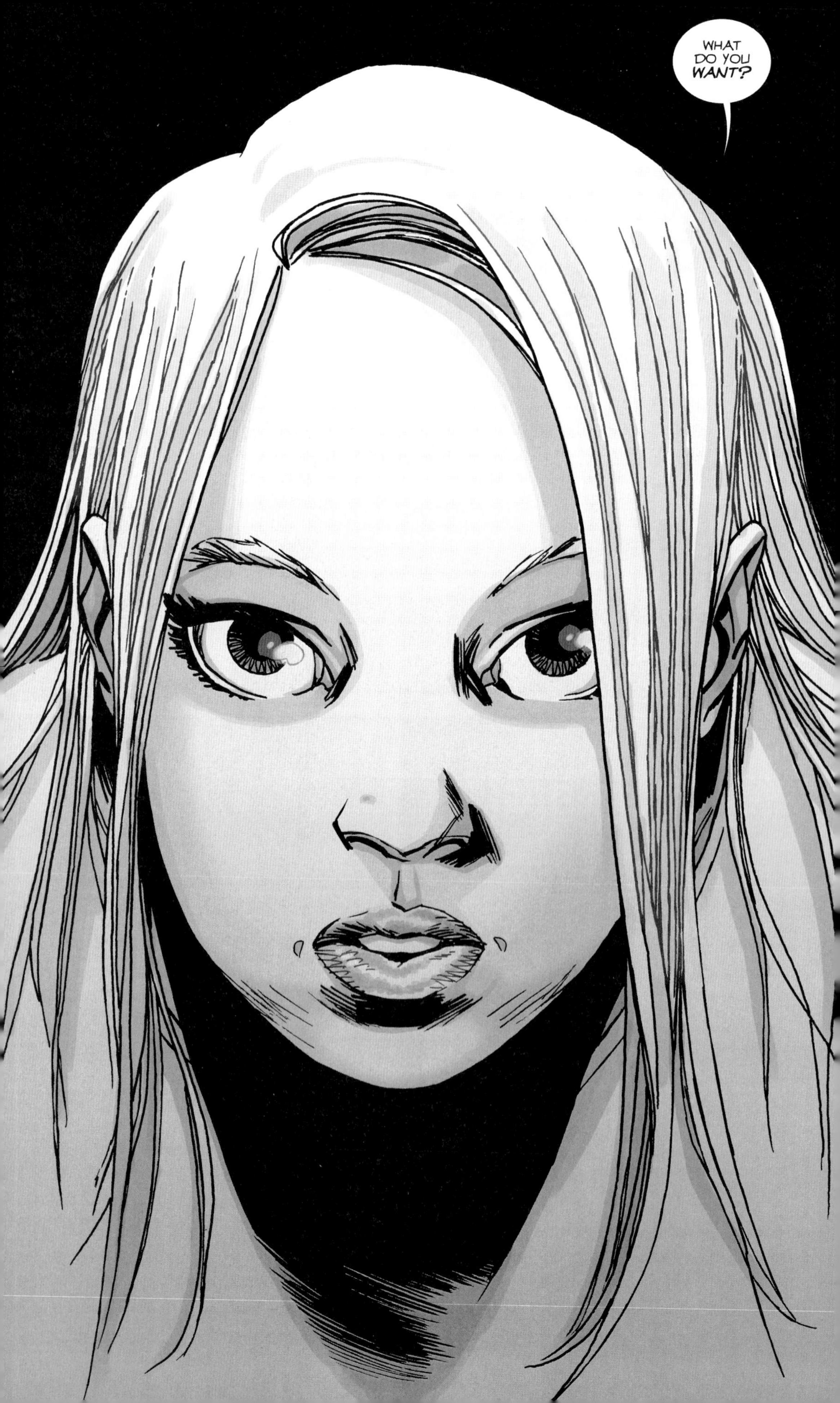
WHAT DO YOU WANT?

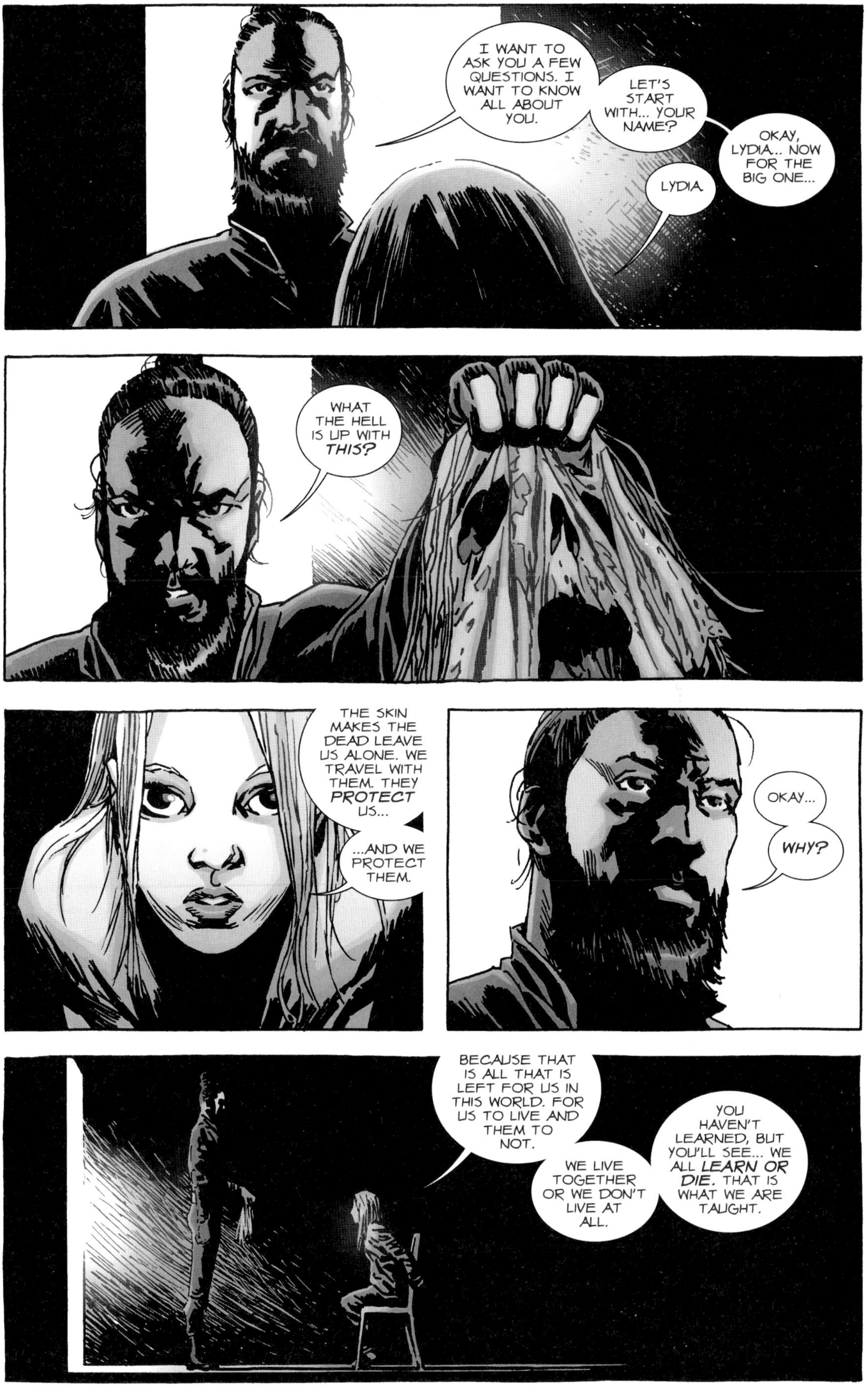
I WANT TO ASK YOU A FEW QUESTIONS. I WANT TO KNOW ALL ABOUT YOU.
LET'S START WITH... YOUR NAME?
LYDIA.
OKAY, LYDIA... NOW FOR THE BIG ONE...
WHAT THE HELL IS UP WITH *THIS?*
THE SKIN MAKES THE DEAD LEAVE US ALONE. WE TRAVEL WITH THEM. THEY *PROTECT* US...
...AND WE PROTECT THEM.
OKAY...
WHY?
BECAUSE THAT IS ALL THAT IS LEFT FOR US IN THIS WORLD. FOR US TO LIVE AND THEM TO NOT.
WE LIVE TOGETHER OR WE DON'T LIVE AT ALL.
YOU HAVEN'T LEARNED, BUT YOU'LL SEE... WE ALL *LEARN OR DIE.* THAT IS WHAT WE ARE TAUGHT.

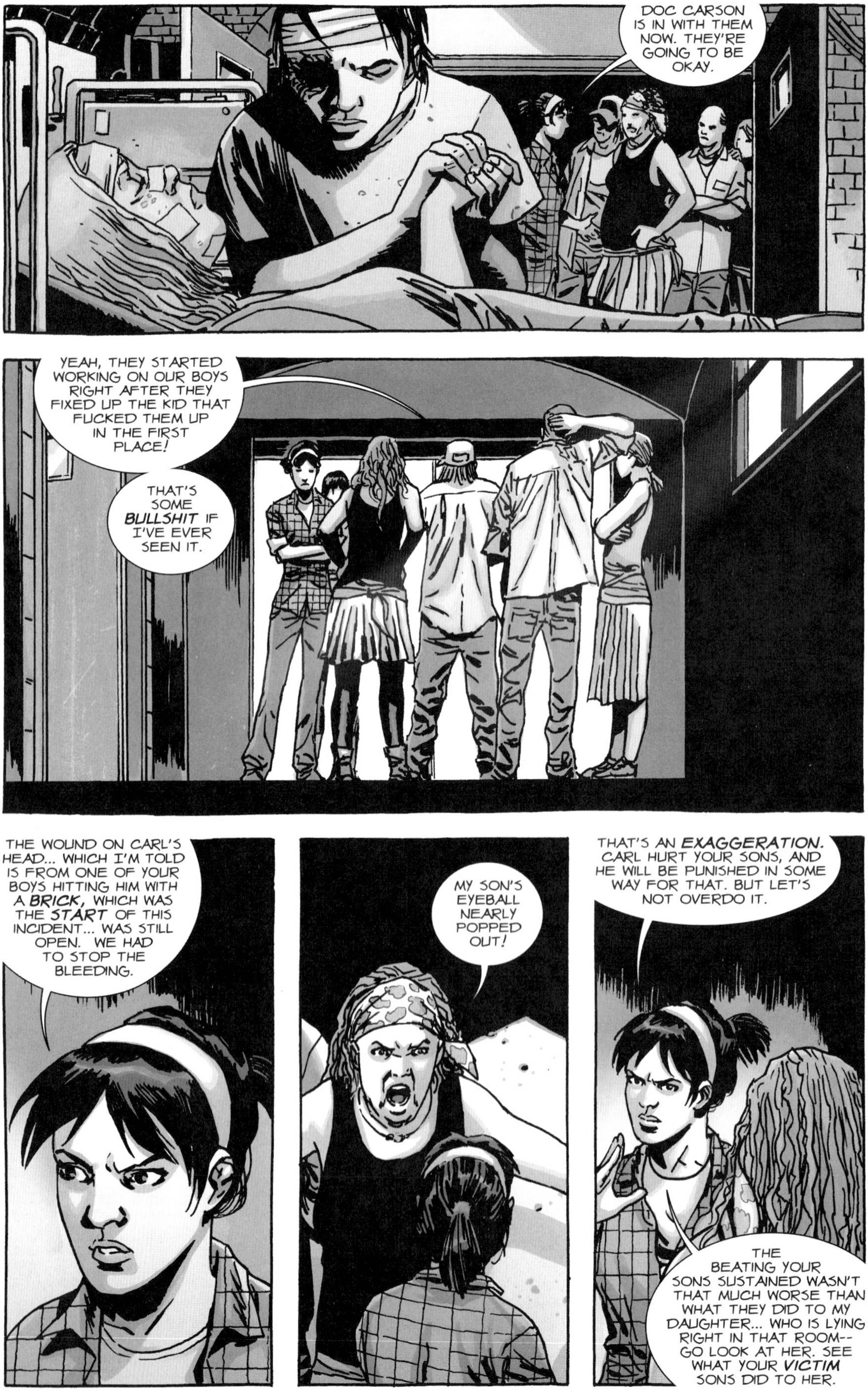
DOC CARSON IS IN WITH THEM NOW. THEY'RE GOING TO BE OKAY.
YEAH, THEY STARTED WORKING ON OUR BOYS RIGHT AFTER THEY FIXED UP THE KID THAT FUCKED THEM UP IN THE FIRST PLACE!
THAT'S SOME BULLSHIT IF I'VE EVER SEEN IT.
THE WOUND ON CARL'S HEAD... WHICH I'M TOLD IS FROM ONE OF YOUR BOYS HITTING HIM WITH A BRICK, WHICH WAS THE START OF THIS INCIDENT... WAS STILL OPEN. WE HAD TO STOP THE BLEEDING.
MY SON'S EYEBALL NEARLY POPPED OUT!
THAT'S AN EXAGGERATION. CARL HURT YOUR SONS, AND HE WILL BE PUNISHED IN SOME WAY FOR THAT. BUT LET'S NOT OVERDO IT.
THE BEATING YOUR SONS SUSTAINED WASN'T THAT MUCH WORSE THAN WHAT THEY DID TO MY DAUGHTER... WHO IS LYING RIGHT IN THAT ROOM-- GO LOOK AT HER. SEE WHAT YOUR VICTIM SONS DID TO HER.

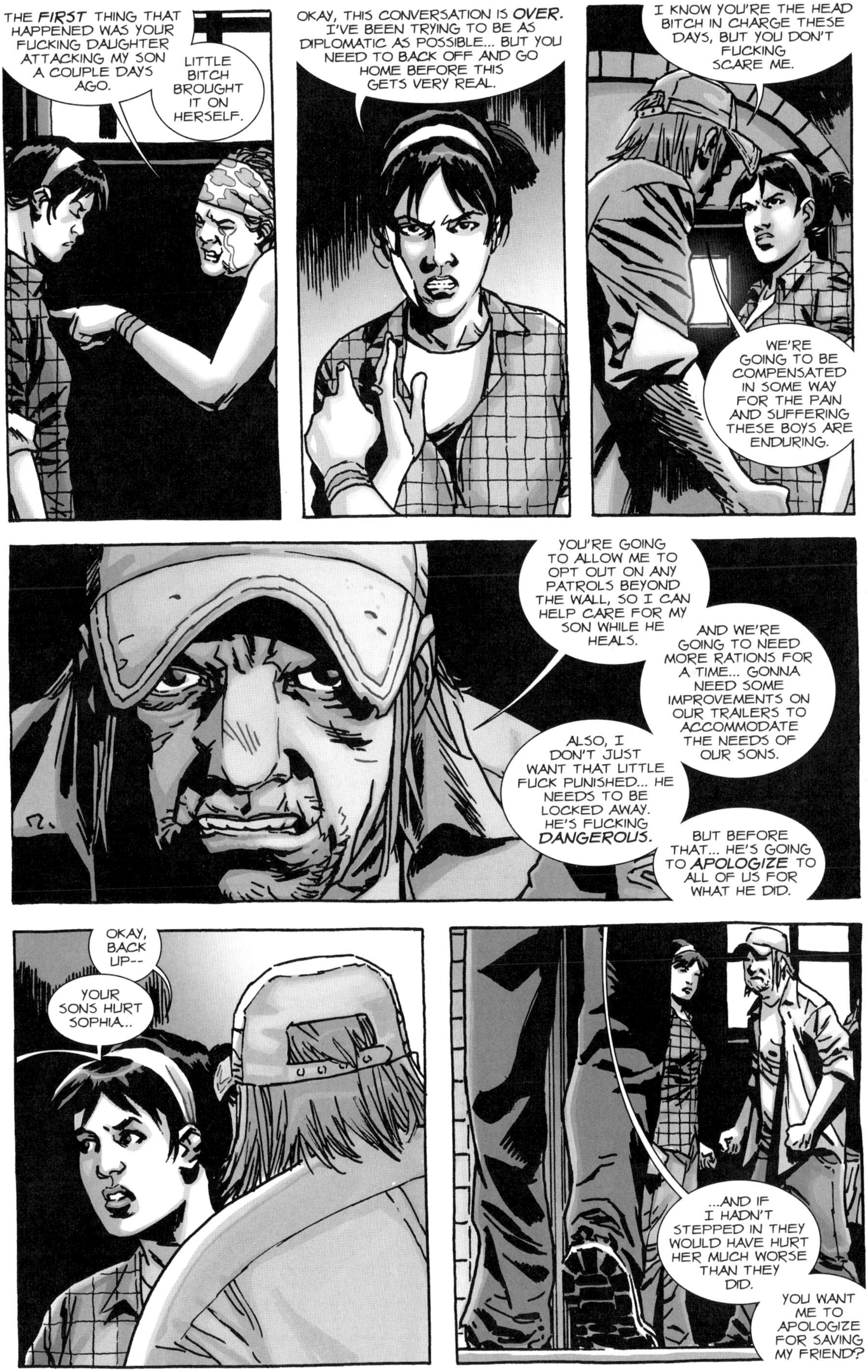
THE FIRST THING THAT HAPPENED WAS YOUR FUCKING DAUGHTER ATTACKING MY SON A COUPLE DAYS AGO.
LITTLE BITCH BROUGHT IT ON HERSELF.
OKAY, THIS CONVERSATION IS OVER. I'VE BEEN TRYING TO BE AS DIPLOMATIC AS POSSIBLE... BUT YOU NEED TO BACK OFF AND GO HOME BEFORE THIS GETS VERY REAL.
I KNOW YOU'RE THE HEAD BITCH IN CHARGE THESE DAYS, BUT YOU DON'T FUCKING SCARE ME.
WE'RE GOING TO BE COMPENSATED IN SOME WAY FOR THE PAIN AND SUFFERING THESE BOYS ARE ENDURING.
YOU'RE GOING TO ALLOW ME TO OPT OUT ON ANY PATROLS BEYOND THE WALL, SO I CAN HELP CARE FOR MY SON WHILE HE HEALS.
AND WE'RE GOING TO NEED MORE RATIONS FOR A TIME... GONNA NEED SOME IMPROVEMENTS ON OUR TRAILERS TO ACCOMMODATE THE NEEDS OF OUR SONS.
ALSO, I DON'T JUST WANT THAT LITTLE FUCK PUNISHED... HE NEEDS TO BE LOCKED AWAY. HE'S FUCKING DANGEROUS.
BUT BEFORE THAT... HE'S GOING TO APOLOGIZE TO ALL OF US FOR WHAT HE DID.
OKAY, BACK UP--
YOUR SONS HURT SOPHIA...
...AND IF I HADN'T STEPPED IN THEY WOULD HAVE HURT HER MUCH WORSE THAN THEY DID.
YOU WANT ME TO APOLOGIZE FOR SAVING MY FRIEND?

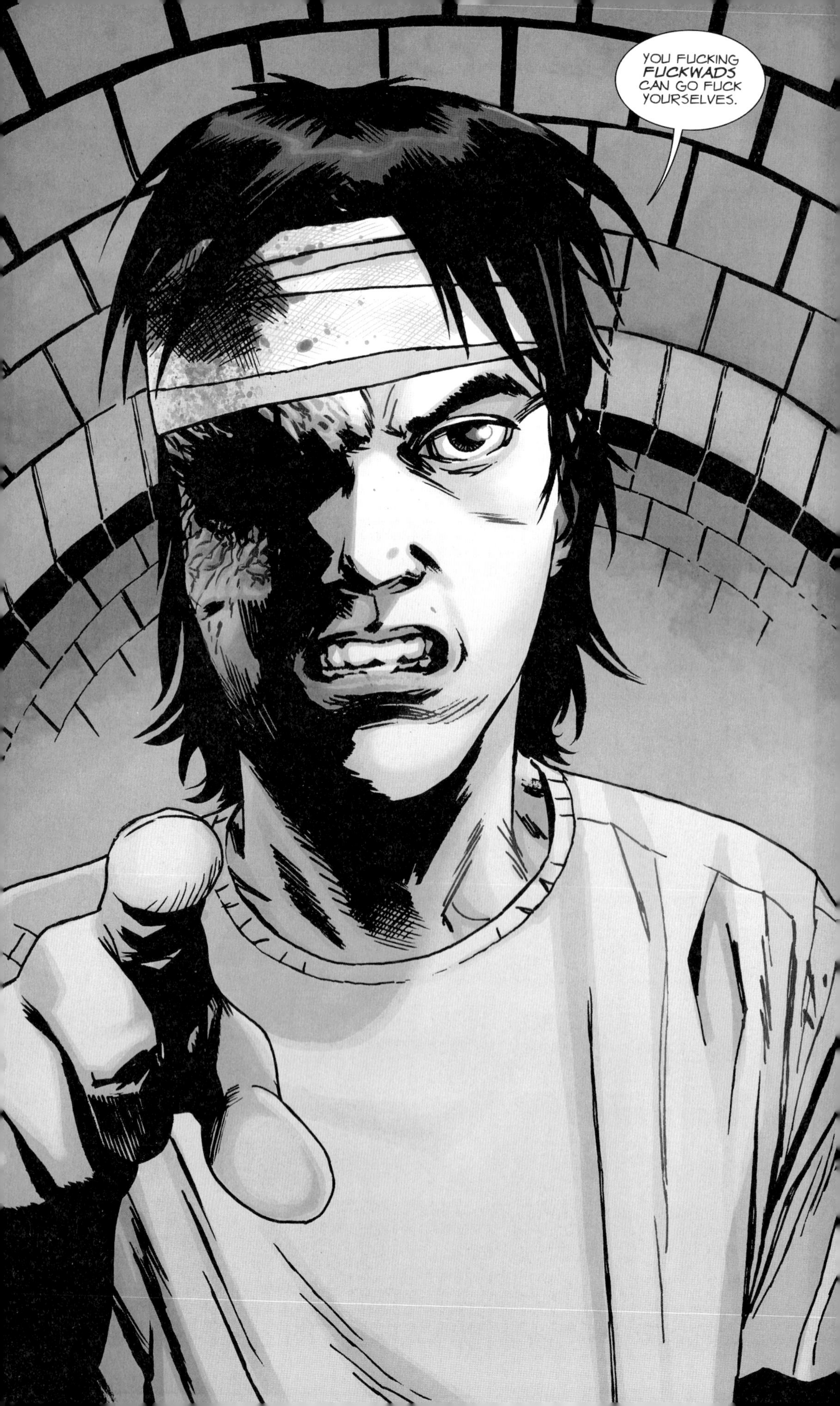
YOU FUCKING FUCKWADS CAN GO FUCK YOURSELVES.

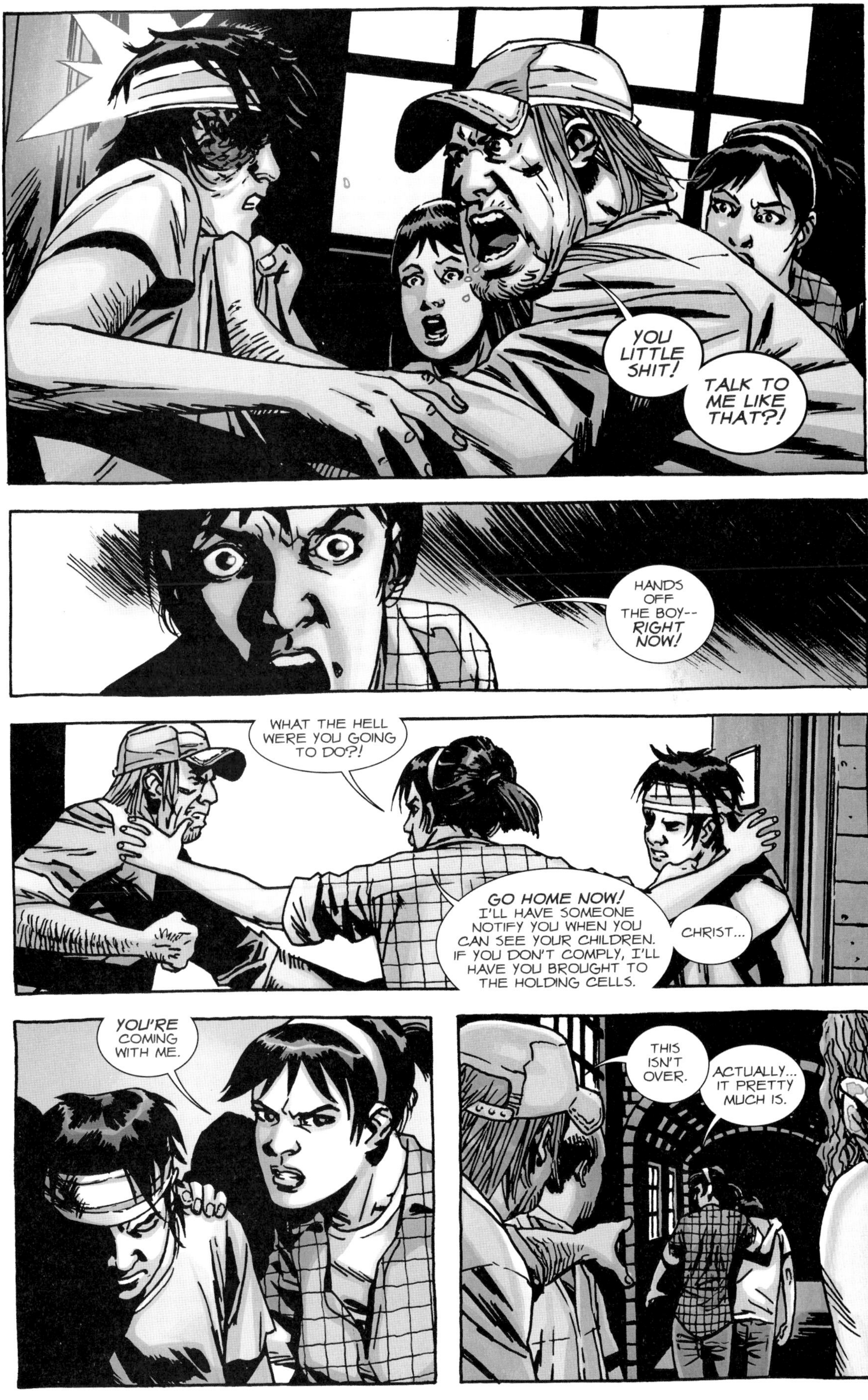
YOU LITTLE SHIT!
TALK TO ME LIKE THAT?!
HANDS OFF THE BOY-- RIGHT NOW!
WHAT THE HELL WERE YOU GOING TO DO?!
GO HOME NOW! I'LL HAVE SOMEONE NOTIFY YOU WHEN YOU CAN SEE YOUR CHILDREN. IF YOU DON'T COMPLY, I'LL HAVE YOU BROUGHT TO THE HOLDING CELLS.
CHRIST...
YOU'RE COMING WITH ME.
THIS ISN'T OVER.
ACTUALLY... IT PRETTY MUCH IS.

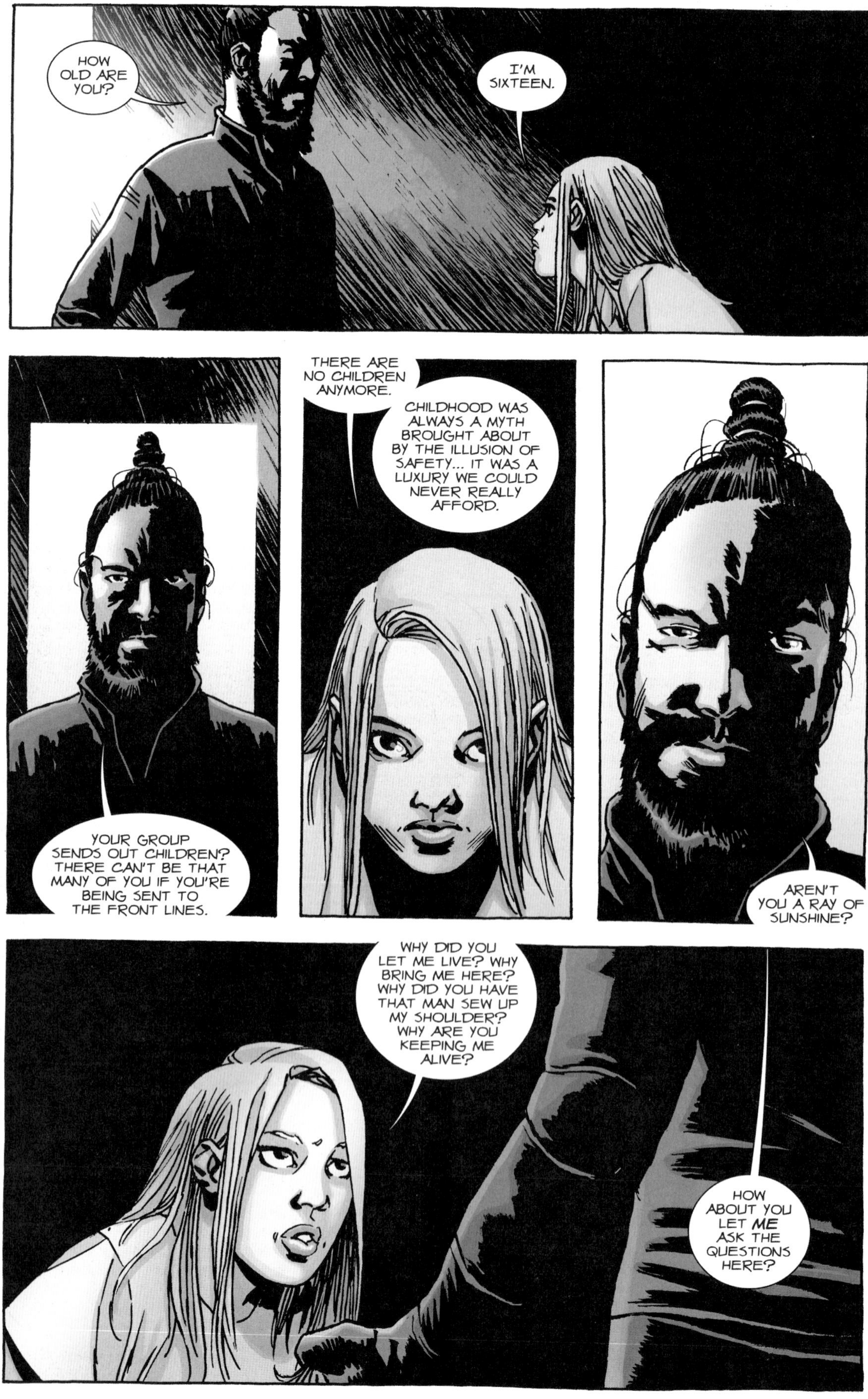
HOW OLD ARE YOU?
I'M SIXTEEN.
YOUR GROUP SENDS OUT CHILDREN? THERE CAN'T BE THAT MANY OF YOU IF YOU'RE BEING SENT TO THE FRONT LINES.
THERE ARE NO CHILDREN ANYMORE.
CHILDHOOD WAS ALWAYS A MYTH BROUGHT ABOUT BY THE ILLUSION OF SAFETY... IT WAS A LUXURY WE COULD NEVER REALLY AFFORD.
AREN'T YOU A RAY OF SUNSHINE?
WHY DID YOU LET ME LIVE? WHY BRING ME HERE? WHY DID YOU HAVE THAT MAN SEW UP MY SHOULDER? WHY ARE YOU KEEPING ME ALIVE?
HOW ABOUT YOU LET *ME* ASK THE QUESTIONS HERE?

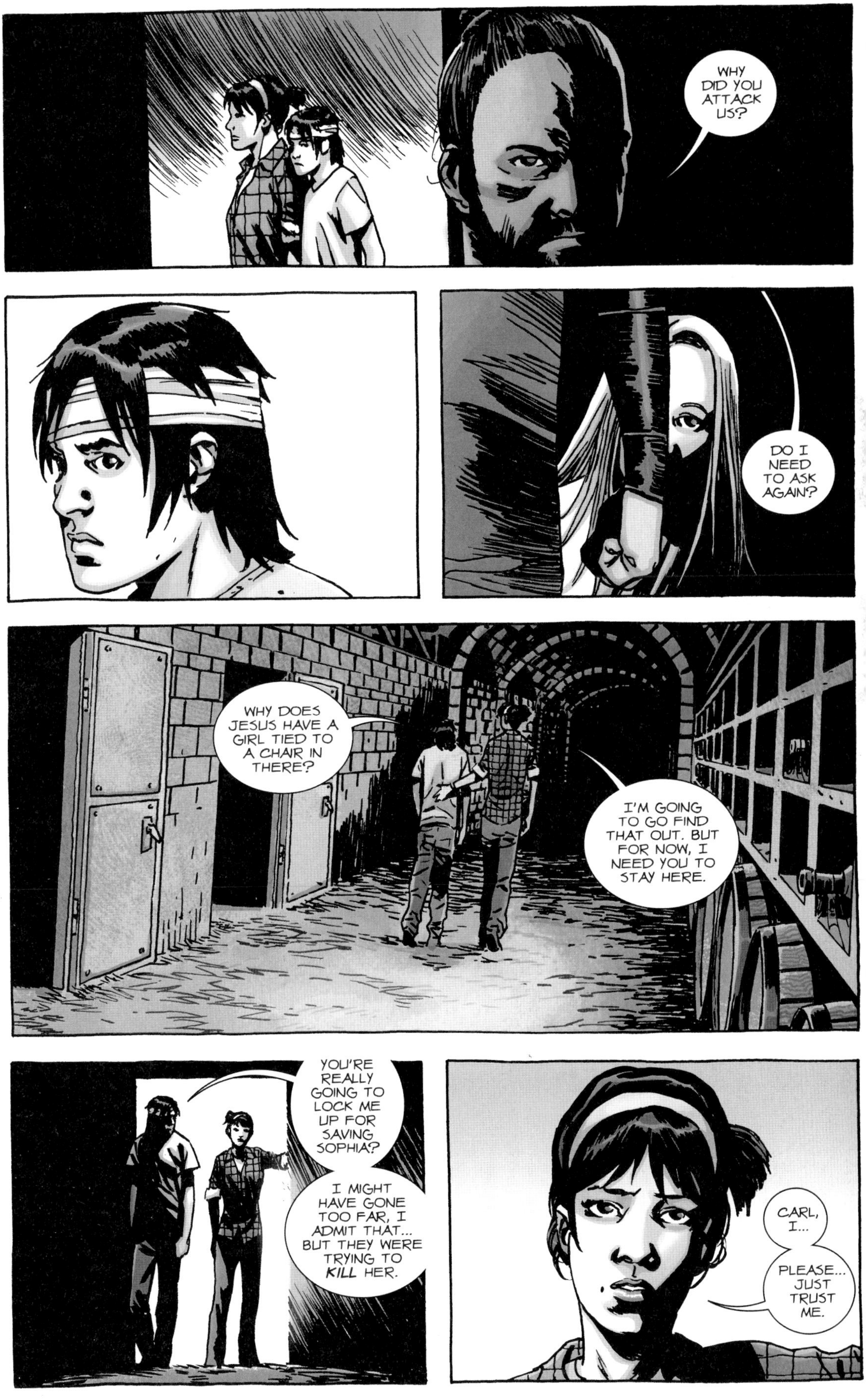
WHY DID YOU ATTACK US?
DO I NEED TO ASK AGAIN?
WHY DOES JESUS HAVE A GIRL TIED TO A CHAIR IN THERE?
I'M GOING TO GO FIND THAT OUT. BUT FOR NOW, I NEED YOU TO STAY HERE.
YOU'RE REALLY GOING TO LOCK ME UP FOR SAVING SOPHIA?
I MIGHT HAVE GONE TOO FAR, I ADMIT THAT... BUT THEY WERE TRYING TO *KILL* HER.
CARL, I...
PLEASE... JUST TRUST ME.

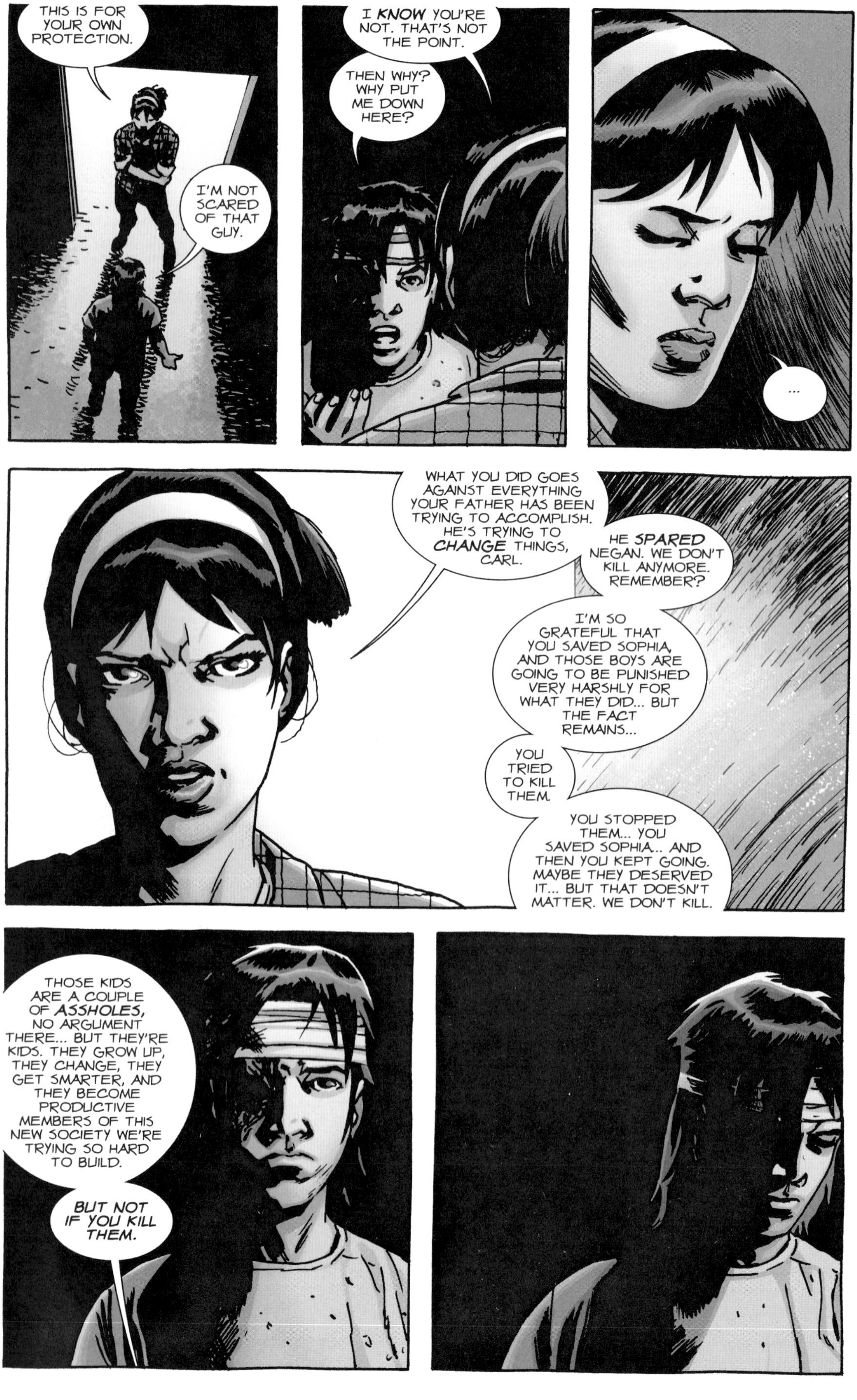
THIS IS FOR YOUR OWN PROTECTION.
I'M NOT SCARED OF THAT GUY.
I KNOW YOU'RE NOT. THAT'S NOT THE POINT.
THEN WHY? WHY PUT ME DOWN HERE?
...
WHAT YOU DID GOES AGAINST EVERYTHING YOUR FATHER HAS BEEN TRYING TO ACCOMPLISH. HE'S TRYING TO CHANGE THINGS, CARL.
HE SPARED NEGAN. WE DON'T KILL ANYMORE. REMEMBER?
I'M SO GRATEFUL THAT YOU SAVED SOPHIA, AND THOSE BOYS ARE GOING TO BE PUNISHED VERY HARSHLY FOR WHAT THEY DID... BUT THE FACT REMAINS...
YOU TRIED TO KILL THEM.
YOU STOPPED THEM... YOU SAVED SOPHIA... AND THEN YOU KEPT GOING. MAYBE THEY DESERVED IT... BUT THAT DOESN'T MATTER. WE DON'T KILL.
THOSE KIDS ARE A COUPLE OF ASSHOLES, NO ARGUMENT THERE... BUT THEY'RE KIDS. THEY GROW UP, THEY CHANGE, THEY GET SMARTER, AND THEY BECOME PRODUCTIVE MEMBERS OF THIS NEW SOCIETY WE'RE TRYING SO HARD TO BUILD.
BUT NOT IF YOU KILL THEM.

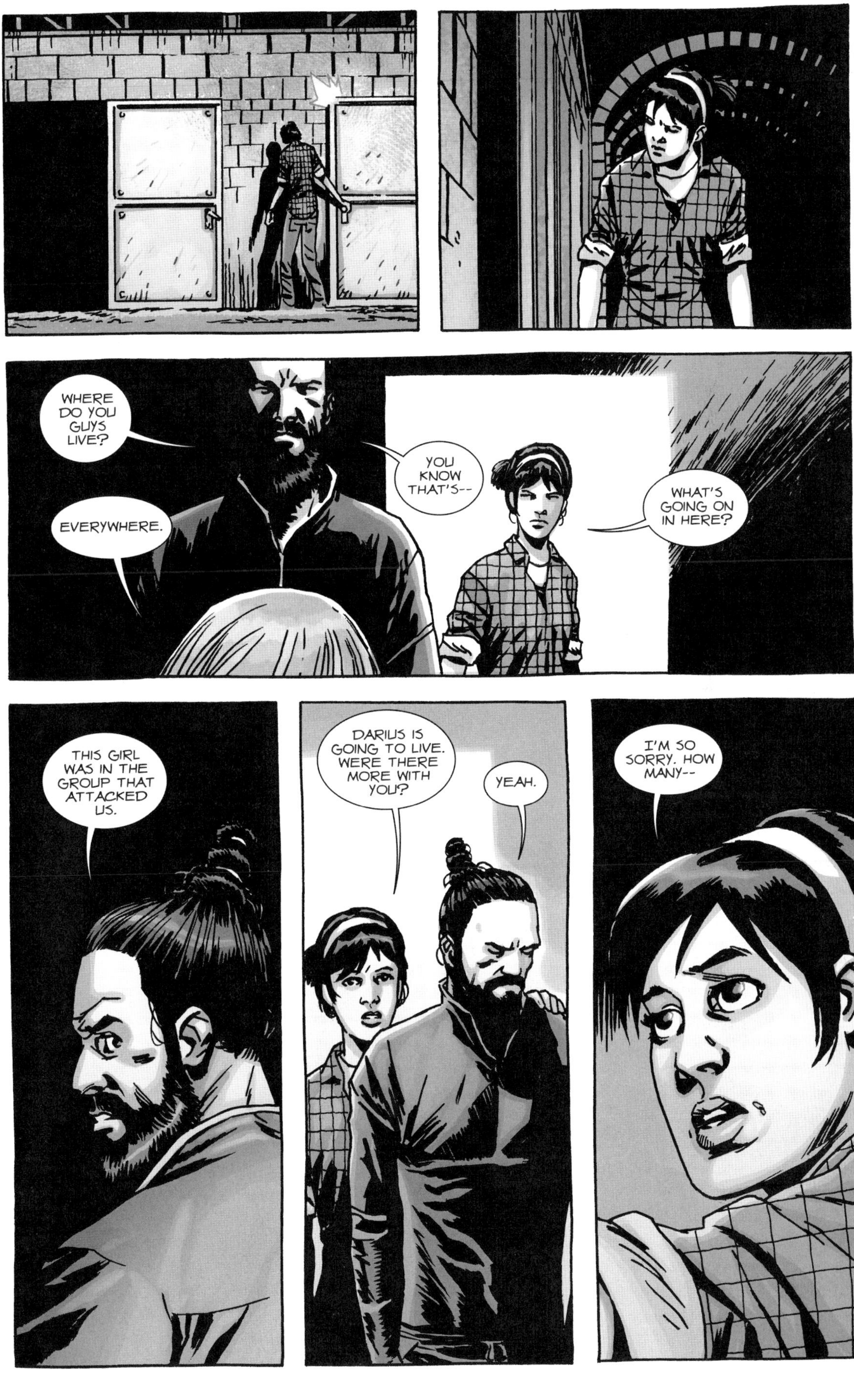
WHERE DO YOU GUYS LIVE?
EVERYWHERE.
YOU KNOW THAT'S--
WHAT'S GOING ON IN HERE?
THIS GIRL WAS IN THE GROUP THAT ATTACKED US.
DARIUS IS GOING TO LIVE. WERE THERE MORE WITH YOU?
YEAH.
I'M SO SORRY. HOW MANY--

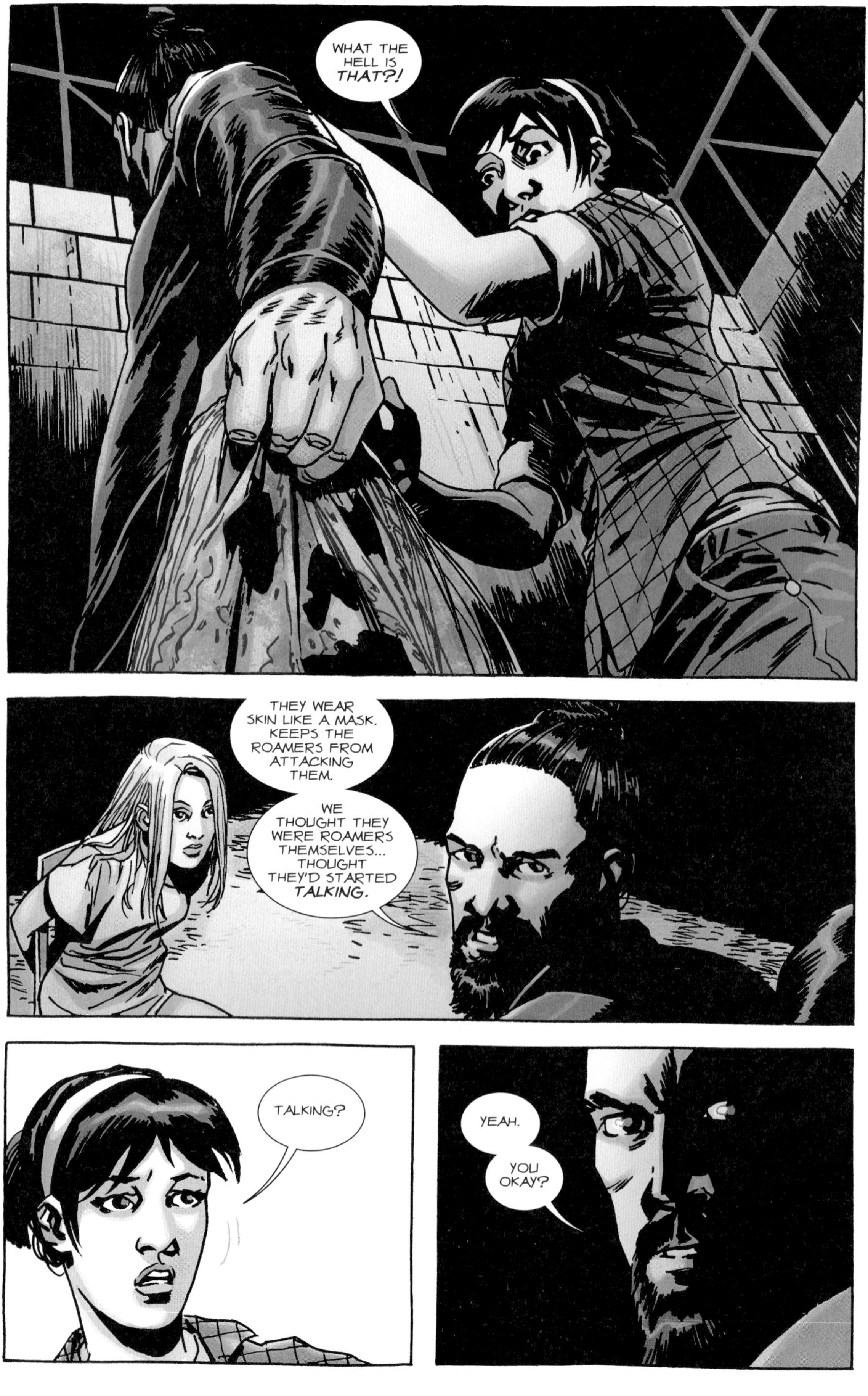
WHAT THE HELL IS *THAT?!*
THEY WEAR SKIN LIKE A MASK. KEEPS THE ROAMERS FROM ATTACKING THEM.
WE THOUGHT THEY WERE ROAMERS THEMSELVES... THOUGHT THEY'D STARTED *TALKING.*
TALKING?
YEAH.
YOU OKAY?

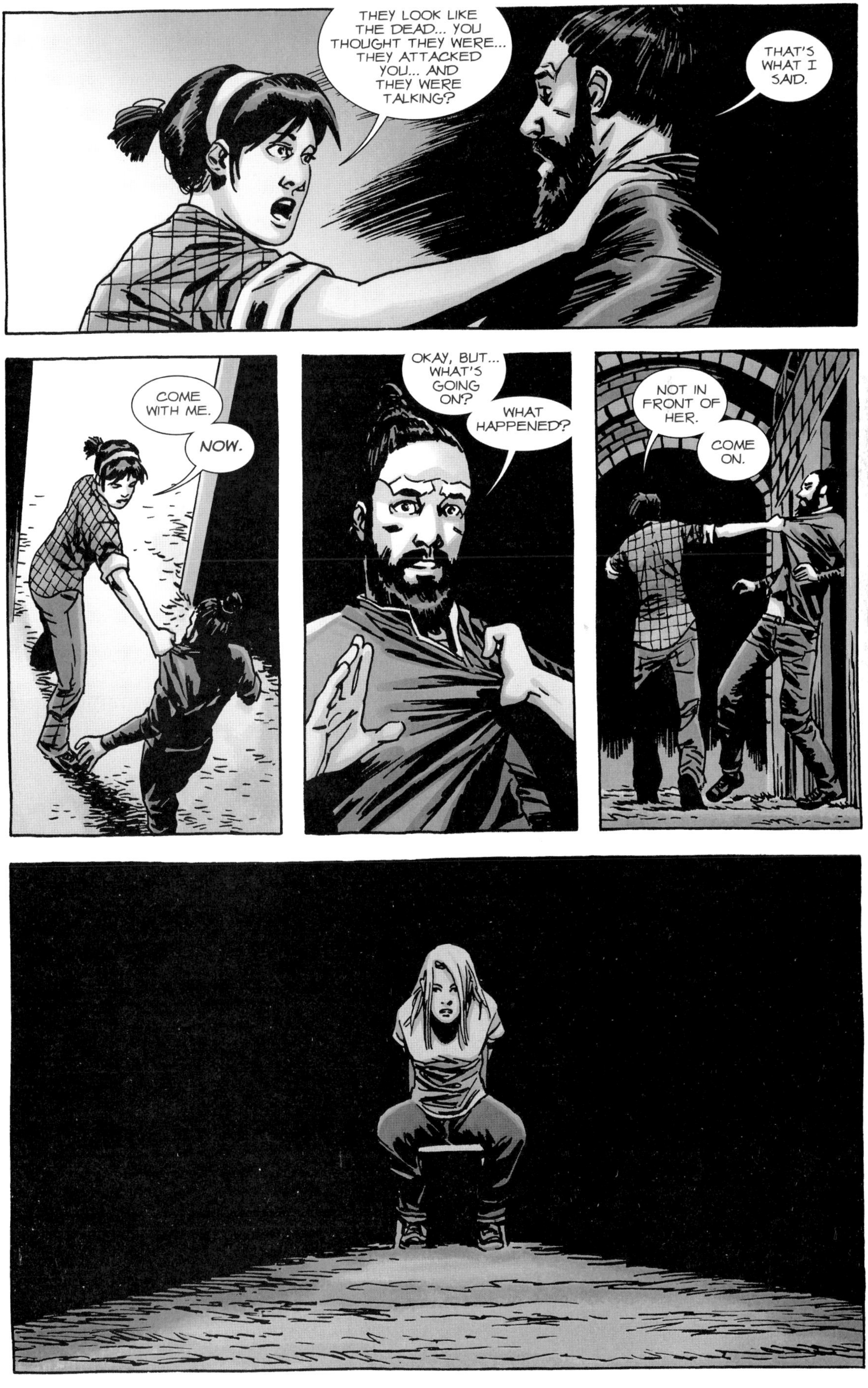
THEY LOOK LIKE THE DEAD... YOU THOUGHT THEY WERE... THEY ATTACKED YOU... AND THEY WERE TALKING?
THAT'S WHAT I SAID.
COME WITH ME.
NOW.
OKAY, BUT... WHAT'S GOING ON?
WHAT HAPPENED?
NOT IN FRONT OF HER.
COME ON.

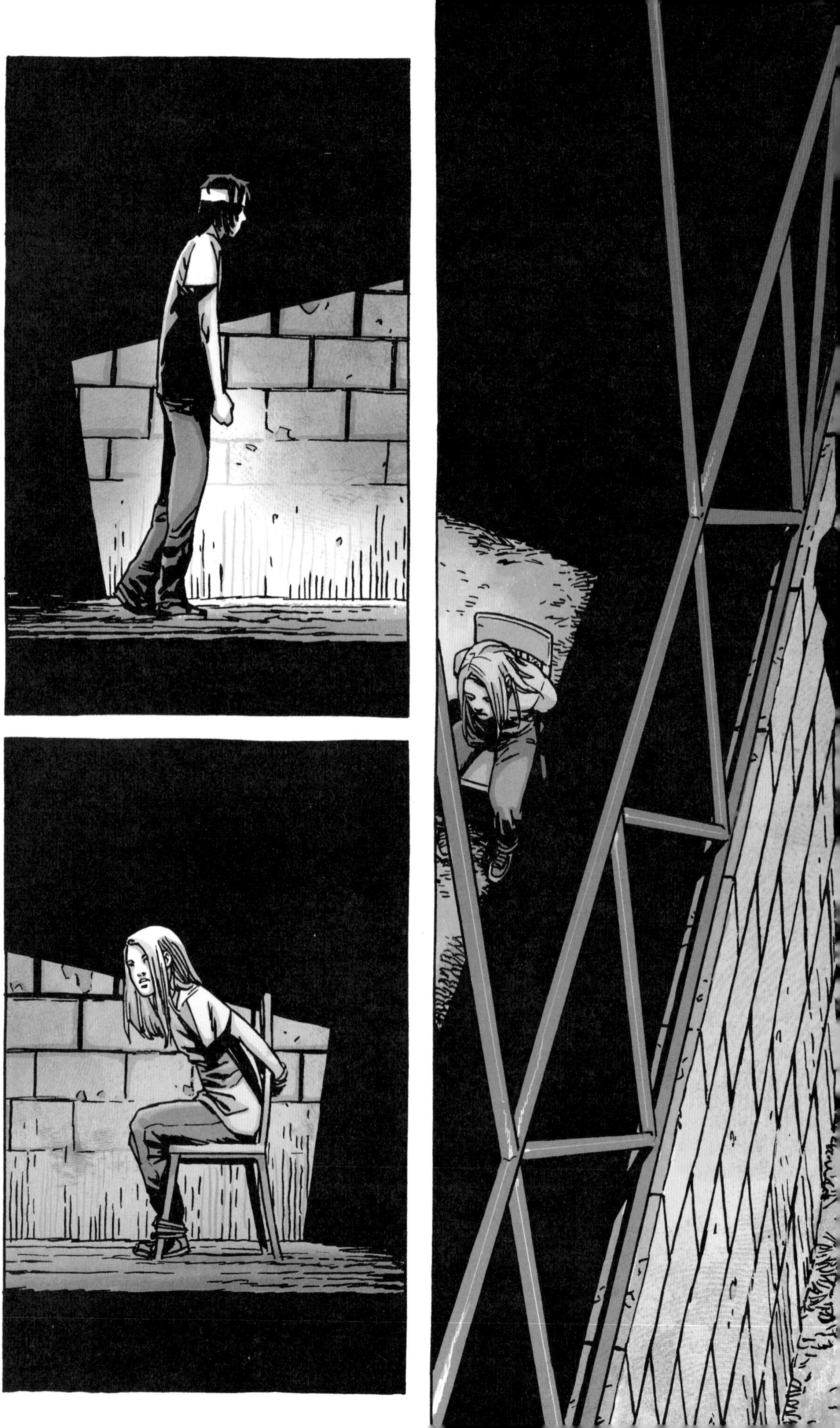

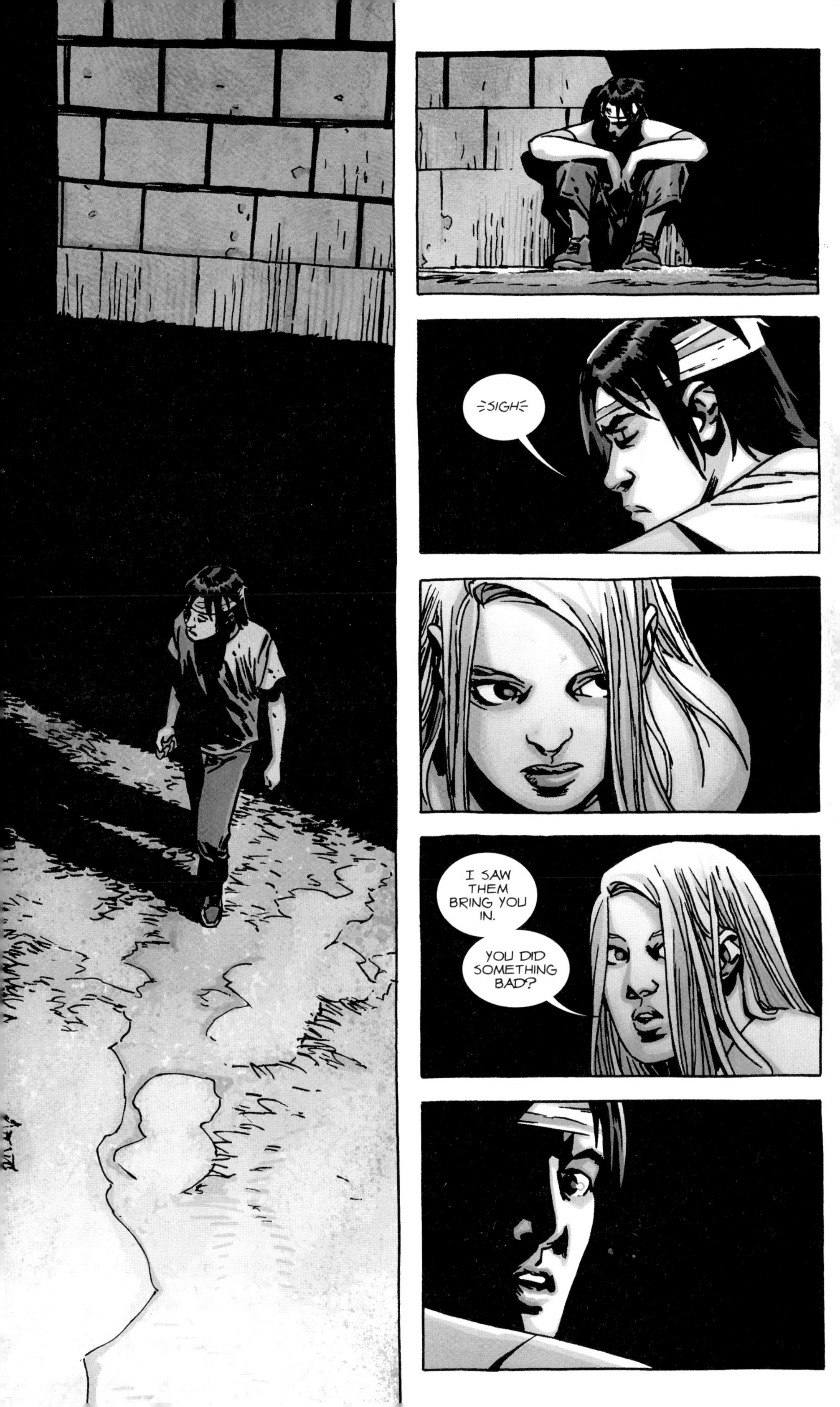

SIGH
I SAW THEM BRING YOU IN.
YOU DID SOMETHING BAD?

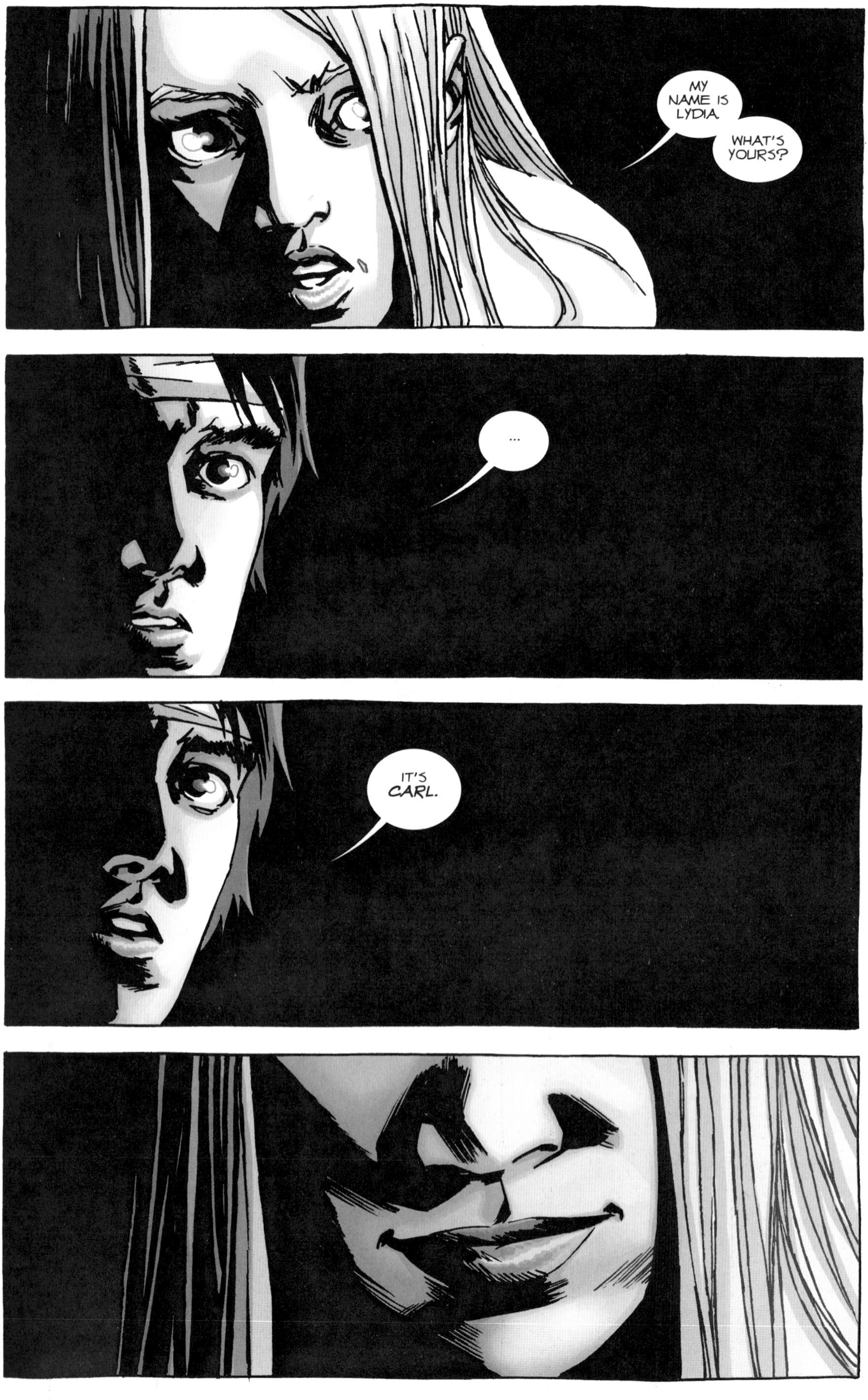
MY NAME IS LYDIA.
WHAT'S YOURS?
...
IT'S CARL.

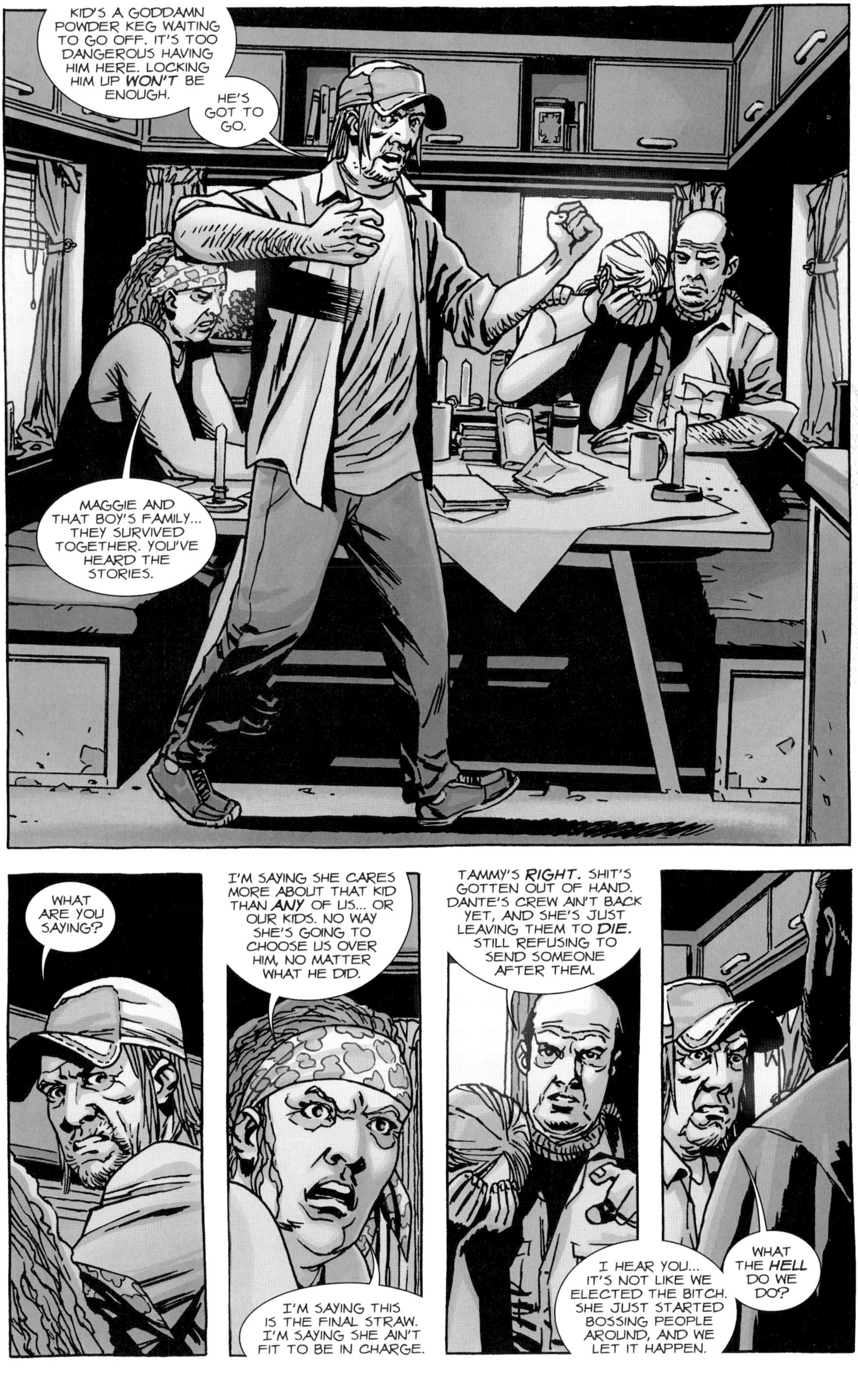
KID'S A GODDAMN POWDER KEG WAITING TO GO OFF. IT'S TOO DANGEROUS HAVING HIM HERE. LOCKING HIM UP WON'T BE ENOUGH.
HE'S GOT TO GO.
MAGGIE AND THAT BOY'S FAMILY... THEY SURVIVED TOGETHER. YOU'VE HEARD THE STORIES.
WHAT ARE YOU SAYING?
I'M SAYING SHE CARES MORE ABOUT THAT KID THAN ANY OF US... OR OUR KIDS. NO WAY SHE'S GOING TO CHOOSE US OVER HIM, NO MATTER WHAT HE DID.
I'M SAYING THIS IS THE FINAL STRAW. I'M SAYING SHE AIN'T FIT TO BE IN CHARGE.
TAMMY'S RIGHT. SHIT'S GOTTEN OUT OF HAND. DANTE'S CREW AIN'T BACK YET, AND SHE'S JUST LEAVING THEM TO DIE. STILL REFUSING TO SEND SOMEONE AFTER THEM.
I HEAR YOU... IT'S NOT LIKE WE ELECTED THE BITCH. SHE JUST STARTED BOSSING PEOPLE AROUND, AND WE LET IT HAPPEN.
WHAT THE HELL DO WE DO?

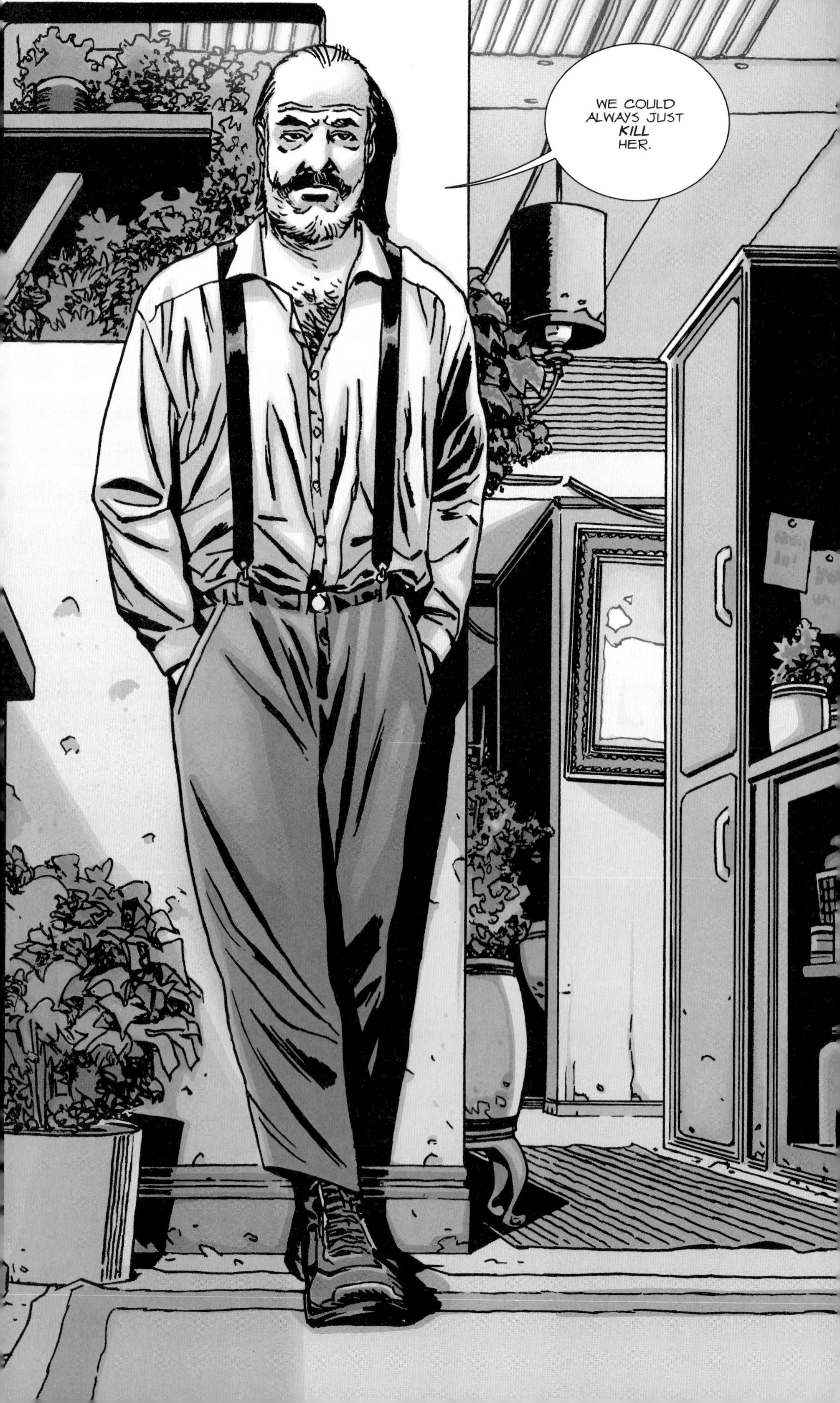
WE COULD ALWAYS JUST KILL HER.

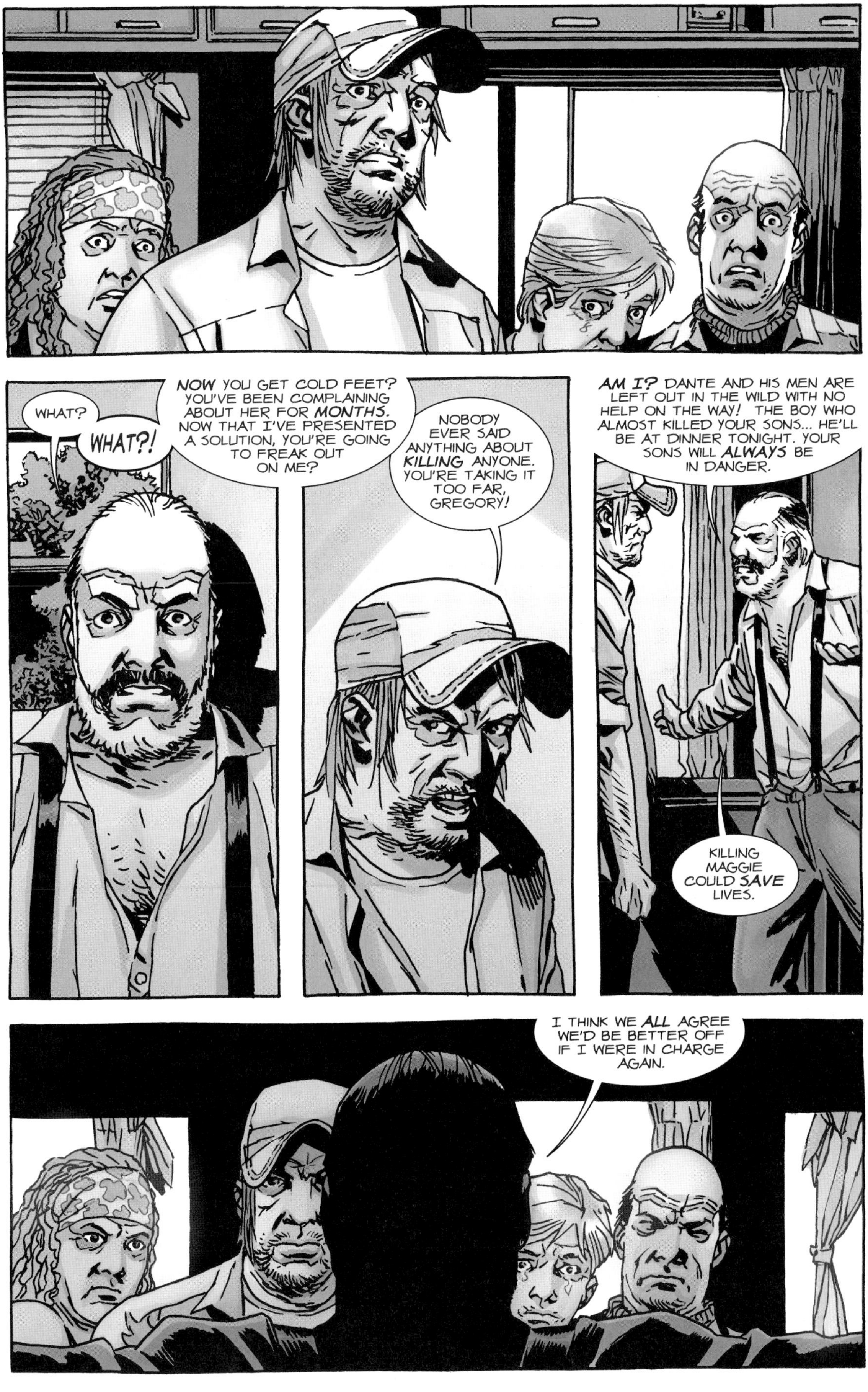

WHAT?
WHAT?!
NOW YOU GET COLD FEET? YOU'VE BEEN COMPLAINING ABOUT HER FOR MONTHS. NOW THAT I'VE PRESENTED A SOLUTION, YOU'RE GOING TO FREAK OUT ON ME?
NOBODY EVER SAID ANYTHING ABOUT KILLING ANYONE. YOU'RE TAKING IT TOO FAR, GREGORY!
AM I? DANTE AND HIS MEN ARE LEFT OUT IN THE WILD WITH NO HELP ON THE WAY! THE BOY WHO ALMOST KILLED YOUR SONS... HE'LL BE AT DINNER TONIGHT. YOUR SONS WILL ALWAYS BE IN DANGER.
KILLING MAGGIE COULD SAVE LIVES.
I THINK WE ALL AGREE WE'D BE BETTER OFF IF I WERE IN CHARGE AGAIN.

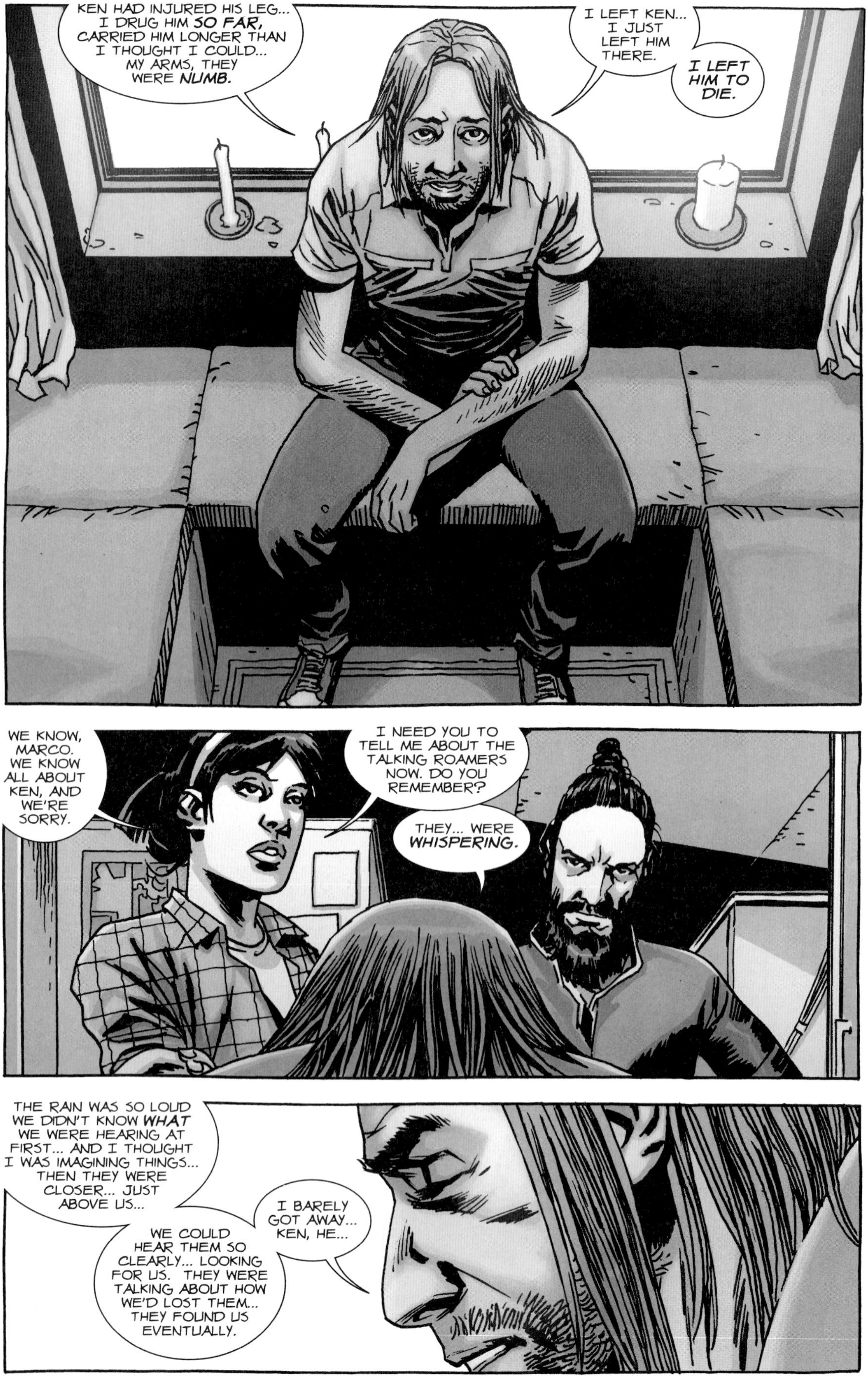
KEN HAD INJURED HIS LEG... I DRUG HIM SO FAR, CARRIED HIM LONGER THAN I THOUGHT I COULD... MY ARMS, THEY WERE NUMB.
I LEFT KEN... I JUST LEFT HIM THERE.
I LEFT HIM TO DIE.
WE KNOW, MARCO. WE KNOW ALL ABOUT KEN, AND WE'RE SORRY.
I NEED YOU TO TELL ME ABOUT THE TALKING ROAMERS NOW. DO YOU REMEMBER?
THEY... WERE WHISPERING.
THE RAIN WAS SO LOUD WE DIDN'T KNOW WHAT WE WERE HEARING AT FIRST... AND I THOUGHT I WAS IMAGINING THINGS... THEN THEY WERE CLOSER... JUST ABOVE US...
WE COULD HEAR THEM SO CLEARLY... LOOKING FOR US. THEY WERE TALKING ABOUT HOW WE'D LOST THEM... THEY FOUND US EVENTUALLY.
I BARELY GOT AWAY... KEN, HE...

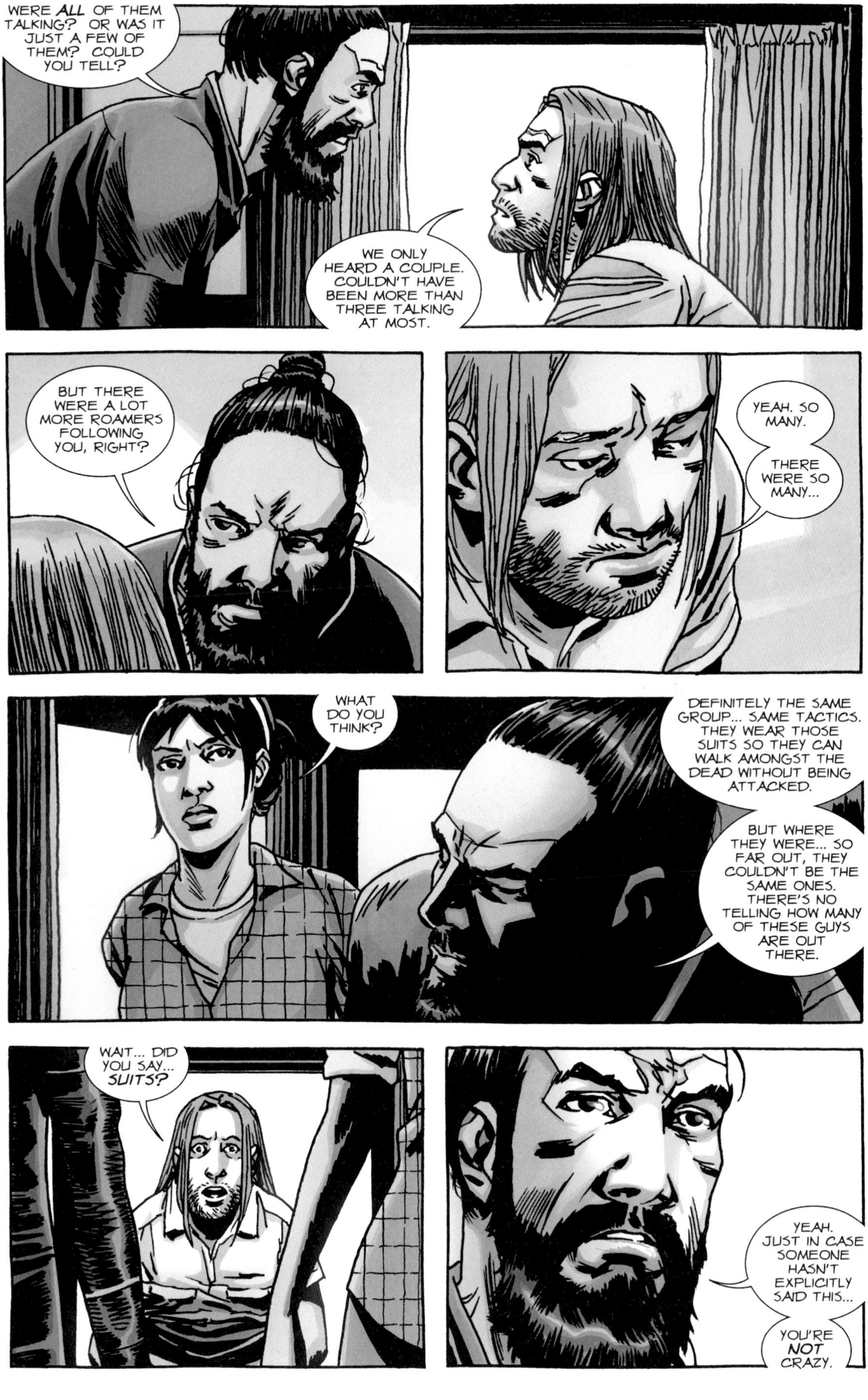

WERE ALL OF THEM TALKING? OR WAS IT JUST A FEW OF THEM? COULD YOU TELL?
WE ONLY HEARD A COUPLE. COULDN'T HAVE BEEN MORE THAN THREE TALKING AT MOST.
BUT THERE WERE A LOT MORE ROAMERS FOLLOWING YOU, RIGHT?
YEAH. SO MANY.
THERE WERE SO MANY...
WHAT DO YOU THINK?
DEFINITELY THE SAME GROUP... SAME TACTICS. THEY WEAR THOSE SUITS SO THEY CAN WALK AMONGST THE DEAD WITHOUT BEING ATTACKED.
BUT WHERE THEY WERE... SO FAR OUT, THEY COULDN'T BE THE SAME ONES. THERE'S NO TELLING HOW MANY OF THESE GUYS ARE OUT THERE.
WAIT... DID YOU SAY... SUITS?
YEAH. JUST IN CASE SOMEONE HASN'T EXPLICITLY SAID THIS...
YOU'RE NOT CRAZY.

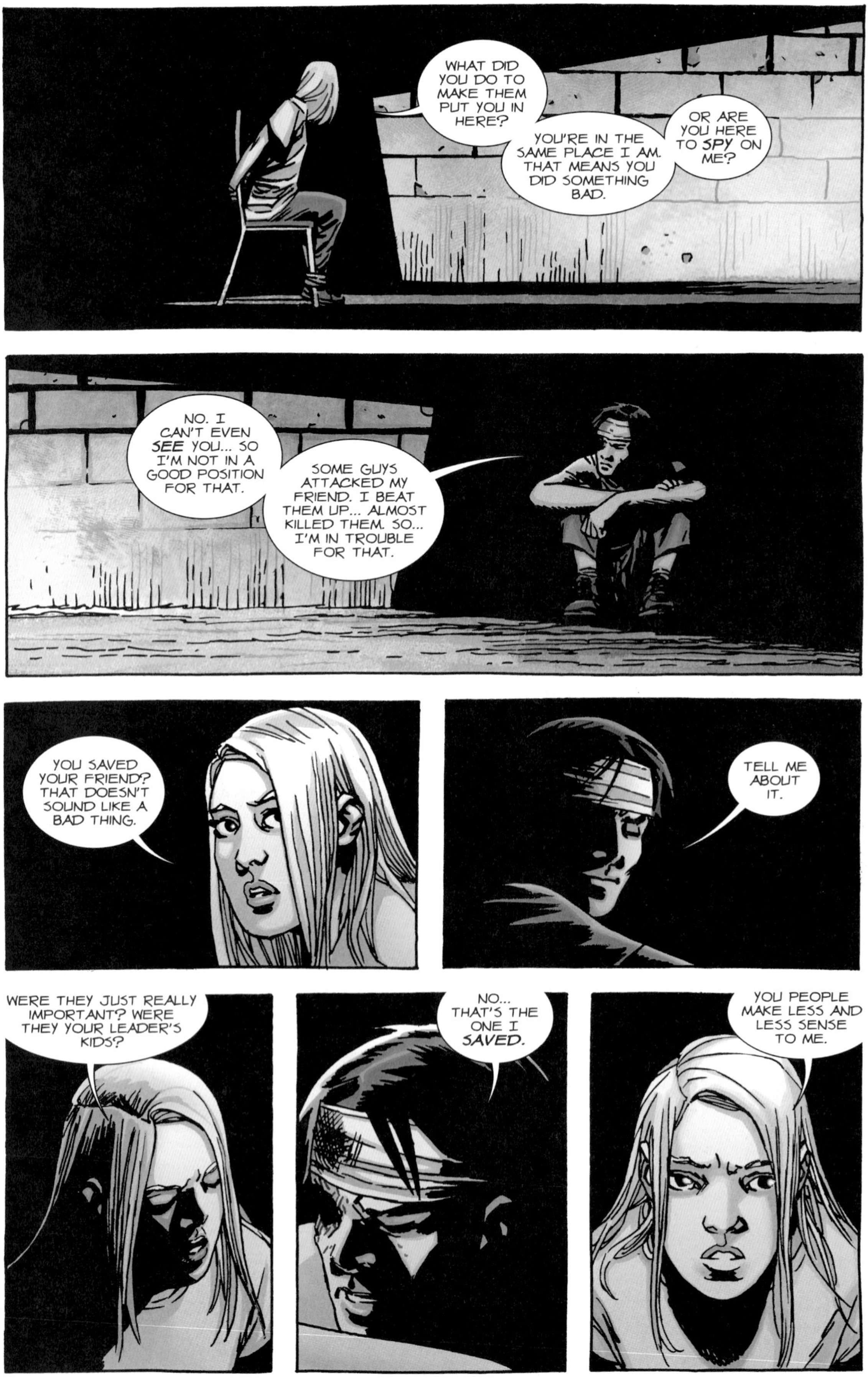
WHAT DID YOU DO TO MAKE THEM PUT YOU IN HERE?
YOU'RE IN THE SAME PLACE I AM. THAT MEANS YOU DID SOMETHING BAD.
OR ARE YOU HERE TO SPY ON ME?
NO. I CAN'T EVEN SEE YOU... SO I'M NOT IN A GOOD POSITION FOR THAT.
SOME GUYS ATTACKED MY FRIEND. I BEAT THEM UP... ALMOST KILLED THEM. SO... I'M IN TROUBLE FOR THAT.
YOU SAVED YOUR FRIEND? THAT DOESN'T SOUND LIKE A BAD THING.
TELL ME ABOUT IT.
WERE THEY JUST REALLY IMPORTANT? WERE THEY YOUR LEADER'S KIDS?
NO... THAT'S THE ONE I SAVED.
YOU PEOPLE MAKE LESS AND LESS SENSE TO ME.

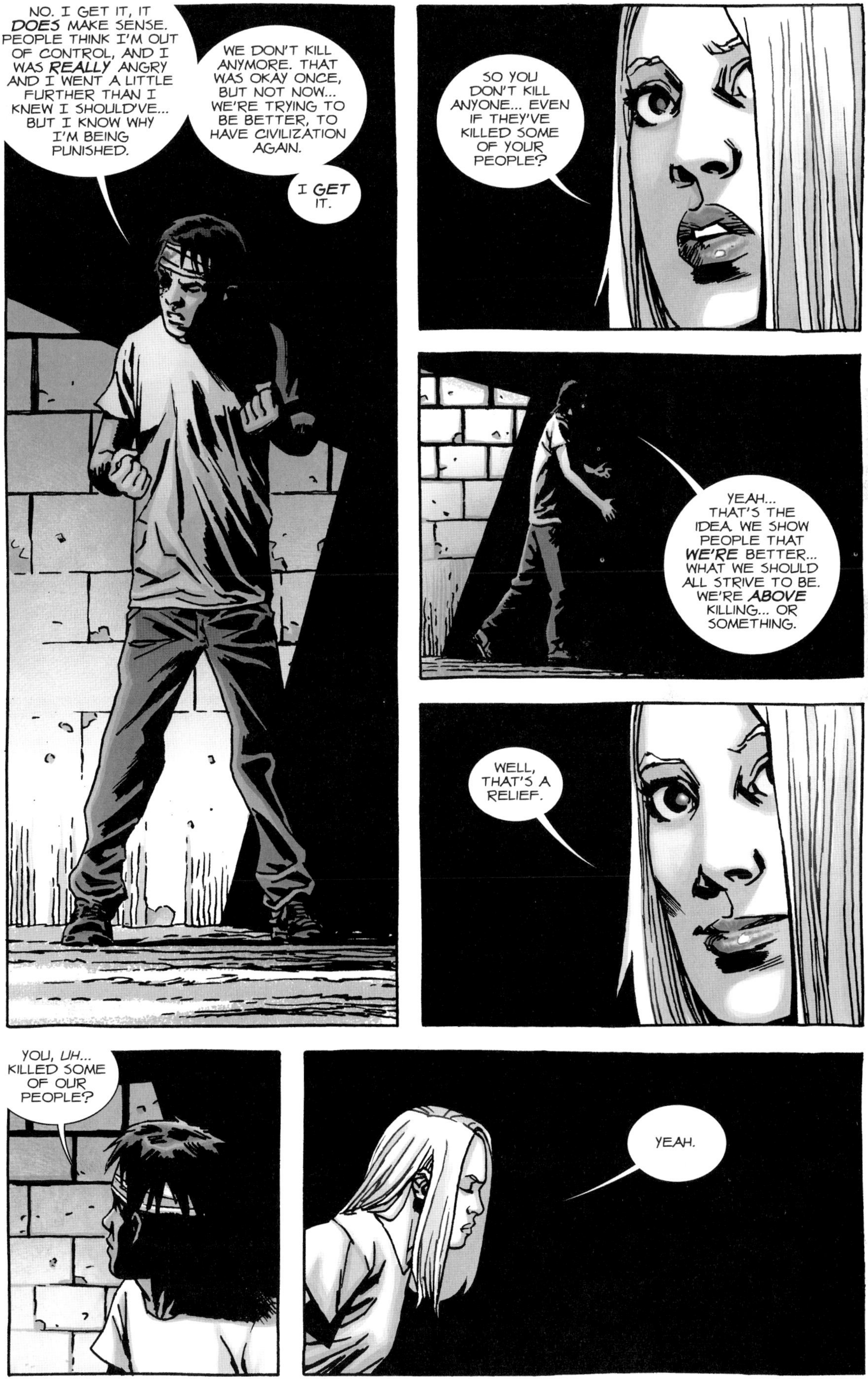
NO. I GET IT, IT DOES MAKE SENSE. PEOPLE THINK I'M OUT OF CONTROL, AND I WAS REALLY ANGRY AND I WENT A LITTLE FURTHER THAN I KNEW I SHOULD'VE... BUT I KNOW WHY I'M BEING PUNISHED.
WE DON'T KILL ANYMORE. THAT WAS OKAY ONCE, BUT NOT NOW... WE'RE TRYING TO BE BETTER, TO HAVE CIVILIZATION AGAIN.
I GET IT.
SO YOU DON'T KILL ANYONE... EVEN IF THEY'VE KILLED SOME OF YOUR PEOPLE?
YEAH... THAT'S THE IDEA. WE SHOW PEOPLE THAT WE'RE BETTER... WHAT WE SHOULD ALL STRIVE TO BE. WE'RE ABOVE KILLING... OR SOMETHING.
WELL, THAT'S A RELIEF.
YOU, UH... KILLED SOME OF OUR PEOPLE?
YEAH.

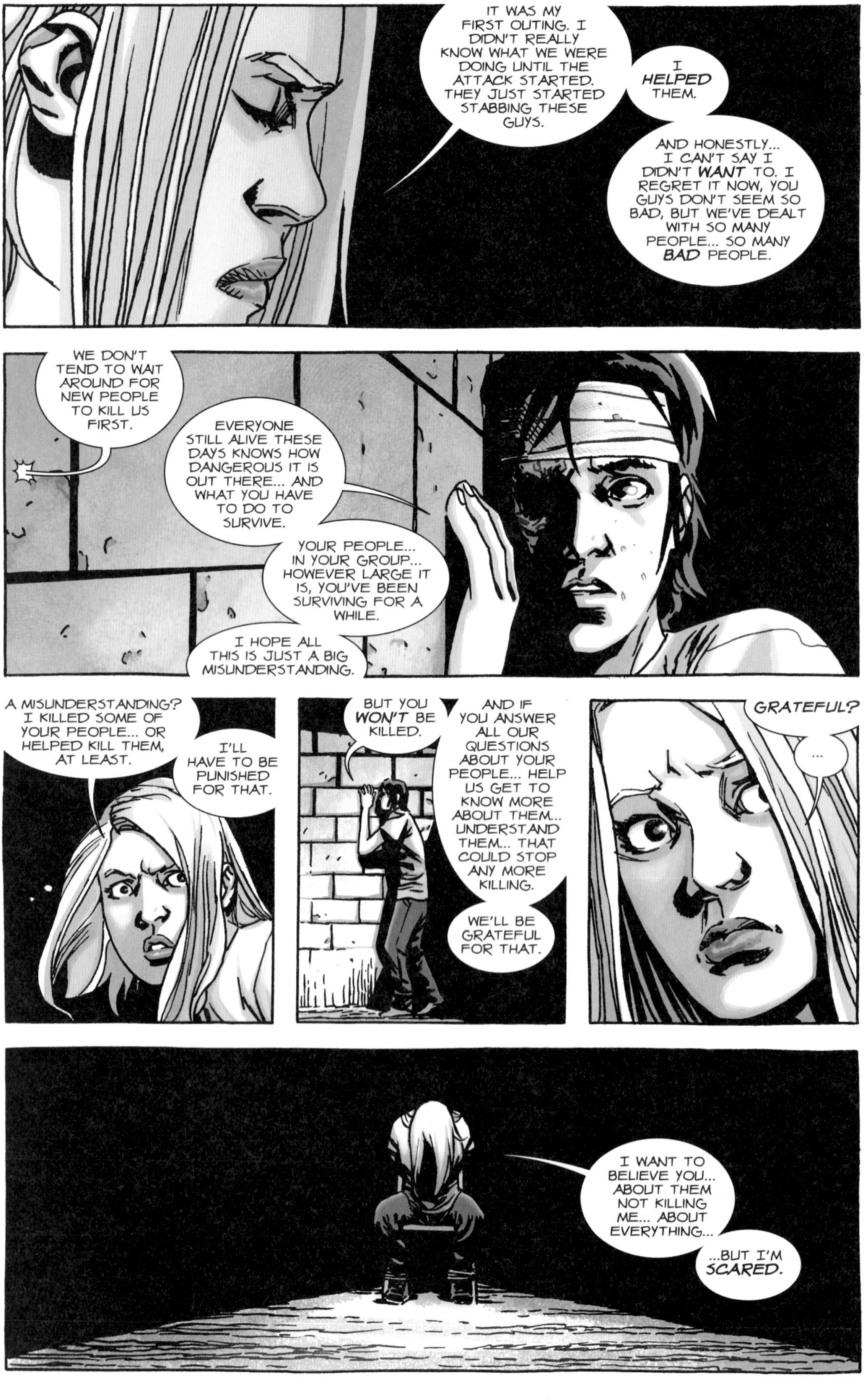
IT WAS MY FIRST OUTING. I DIDN'T REALLY KNOW WHAT WE WERE DOING UNTIL THE ATTACK STARTED. THEY JUST STARTED STABBING THESE GUYS.
I *HELPED* THEM.
AND HONESTLY... I CAN'T SAY I DIDN'T *WANT* TO. I REGRET IT NOW, YOU GUYS DON'T SEEM SO BAD, BUT WE'VE DEALT WITH SO MANY PEOPLE... SO MANY *BAD* PEOPLE.
WE DON'T TEND TO WAIT AROUND FOR NEW PEOPLE TO KILL US FIRST.
EVERYONE STILL ALIVE THESE DAYS KNOWS HOW DANGEROUS IT IS OUT THERE... AND WHAT YOU HAVE TO DO TO SURVIVE.
YOUR PEOPLE... IN YOUR GROUP... HOWEVER LARGE IT IS, YOU'VE BEEN SURVIVING FOR A WHILE.
I HOPE ALL THIS IS JUST A BIG MISUNDERSTANDING.
A MISUNDERSTANDING? I KILLED SOME OF YOUR PEOPLE... OR HELPED KILL THEM, AT LEAST.
I'LL HAVE TO BE PUNISHED FOR THAT.
BUT YOU *WON'T* BE KILLED.
AND IF YOU ANSWER ALL OUR QUESTIONS ABOUT YOUR PEOPLE... HELP US GET TO KNOW MORE ABOUT THEM... UNDERSTAND THEM... THAT COULD STOP ANY MORE KILLING.
WE'LL BE GRATEFUL FOR THAT.
GRATEFUL?
...
I WANT TO BELIEVE YOU... ABOUT THEM NOT KILLING ME... ABOUT EVERYTHING...
...BUT I'M *SCARED.*

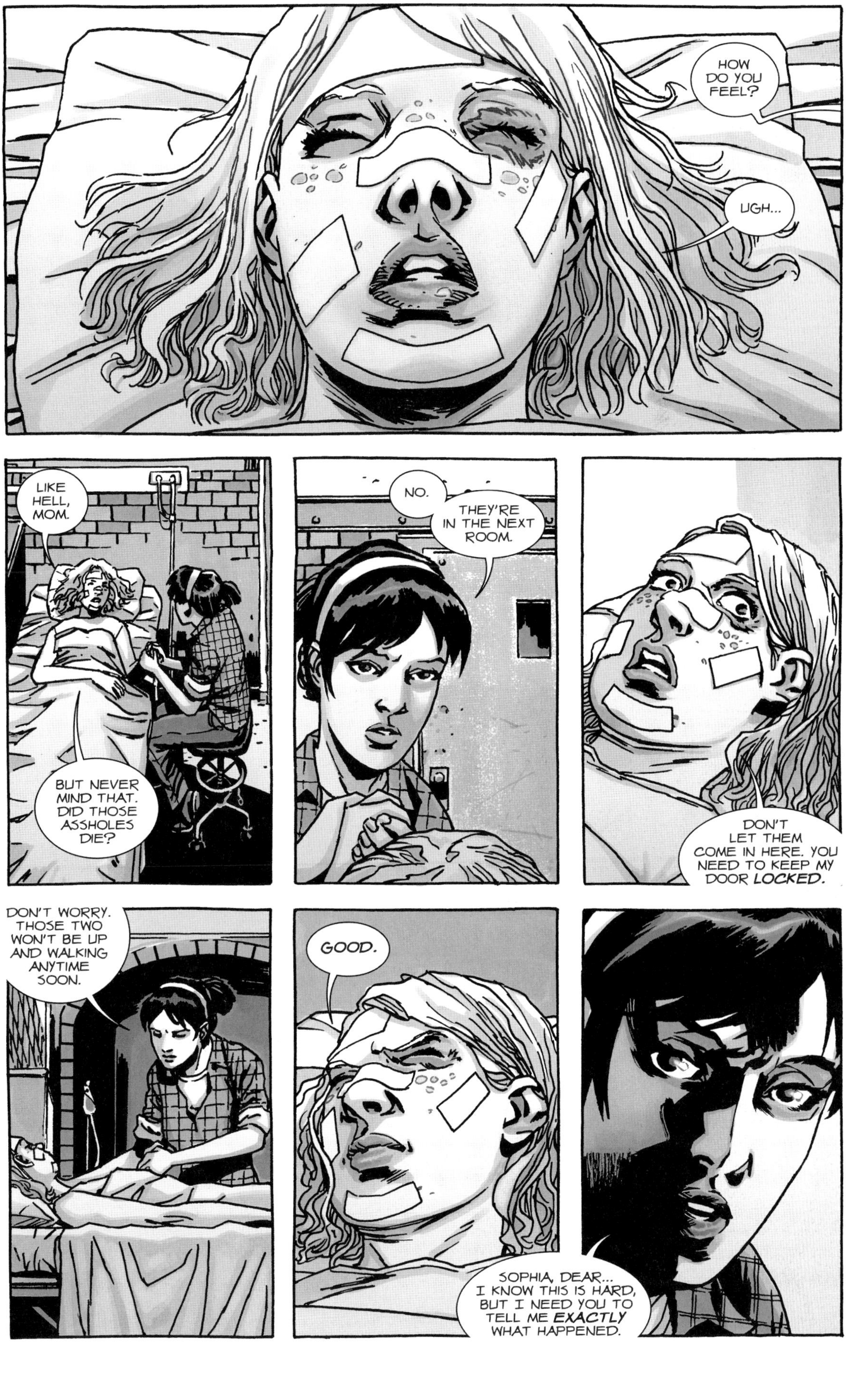
HOW DO YOU FEEL?
UGH...
LIKE HELL, MOM.
BUT NEVER MIND THAT. DID THOSE ASSHOLES DIE?
NO.
THEY'RE IN THE NEXT ROOM.
DON'T LET THEM COME IN HERE. YOU NEED TO KEEP MY DOOR *LOCKED.*
DON'T WORRY. THOSE TWO WON'T BE UP AND WALKING ANYTIME SOON.
GOOD.
SOPHIA, DEAR... I KNOW THIS IS HARD, BUT I NEED YOU TO TELL ME *EXACTLY* WHAT HAPPENED.

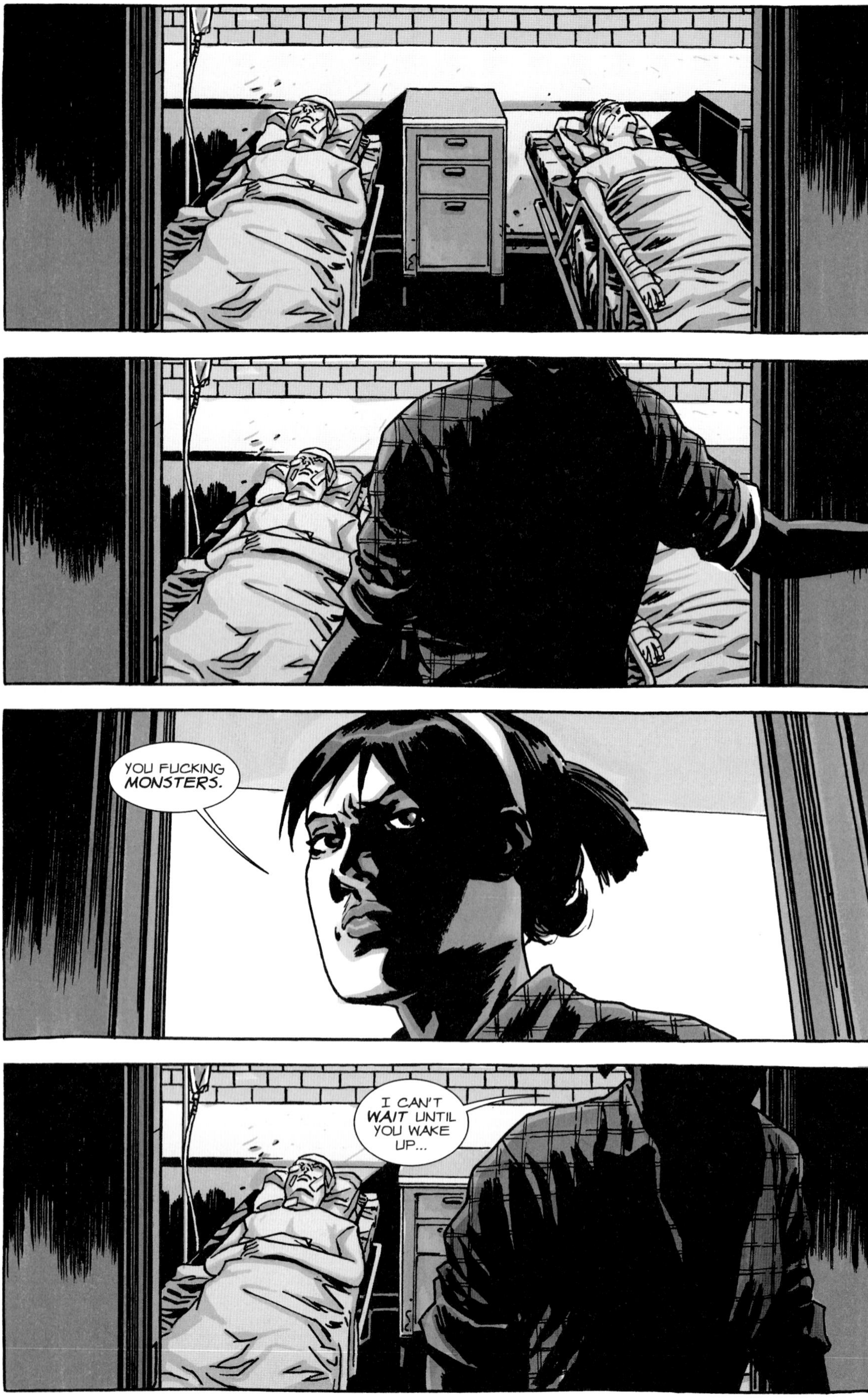
YOU FUCKING MONSTERS.
I CAN'T WAIT UNTIL YOU WAKE UP...

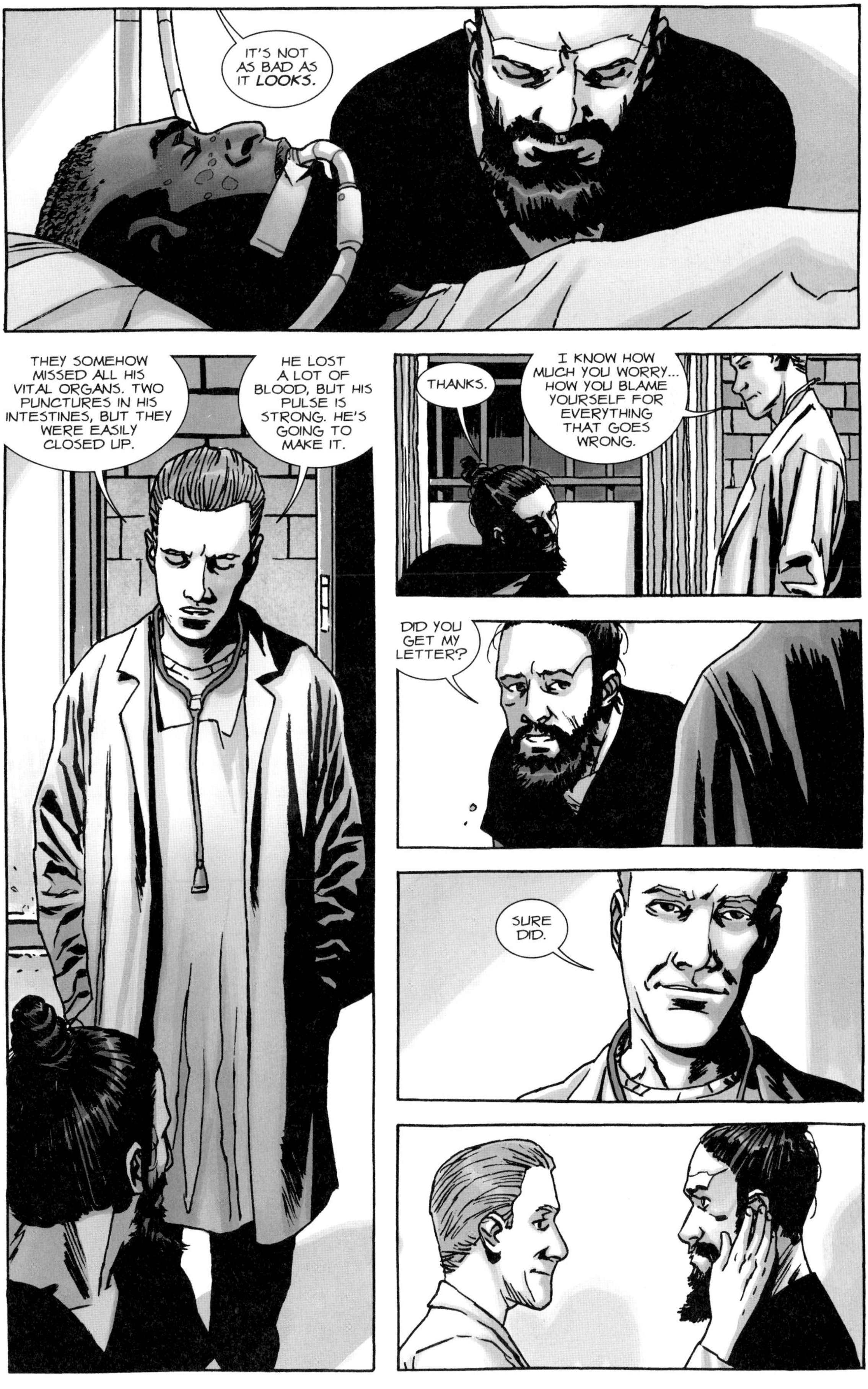
IT'S NOT AS BAD AS IT *LOOKS.*
THEY SOMEHOW MISSED ALL HIS VITAL ORGANS. TWO PUNCTURES IN HIS INTESTINES, BUT THEY WERE EASILY CLOSED UP.
HE LOST A LOT OF BLOOD, BUT HIS PULSE IS STRONG. HE'S GOING TO MAKE IT.
THANKS.
I KNOW HOW MUCH YOU WORRY... HOW YOU BLAME YOURSELF FOR EVERYTHING THAT GOES WRONG.
DID YOU GET MY LETTER?
SURE DID.

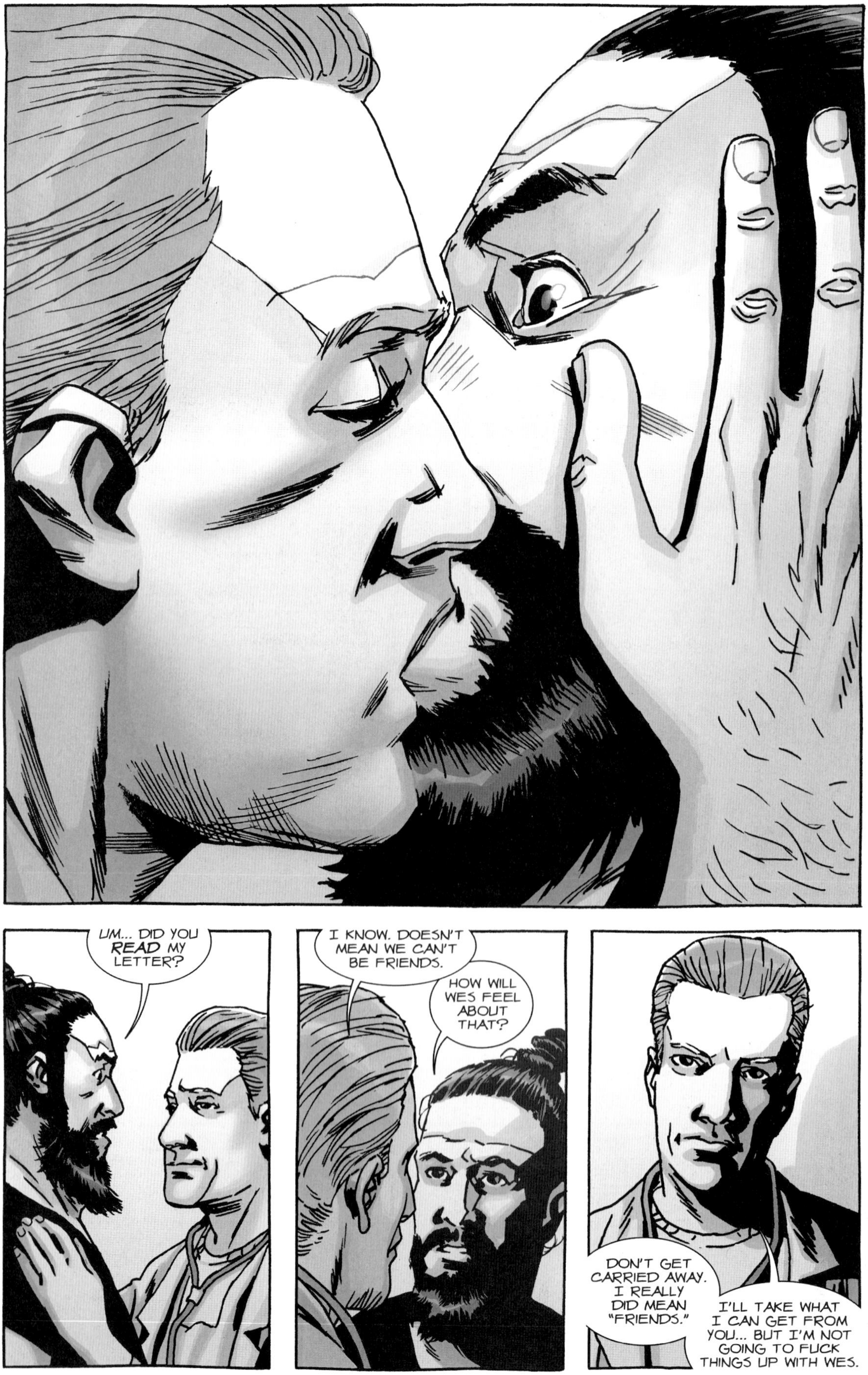
UM... DID YOU READ MY LETTER?
I KNOW. DOESN'T MEAN WE CAN'T BE FRIENDS.
HOW WILL WES FEEL ABOUT THAT?
DON'T GET CARRIED AWAY. I REALLY DID MEAN "FRIENDS."
I'LL TAKE WHAT I CAN GET FROM YOU... BUT I'M NOT GOING TO FUCK THINGS UP WITH WES.

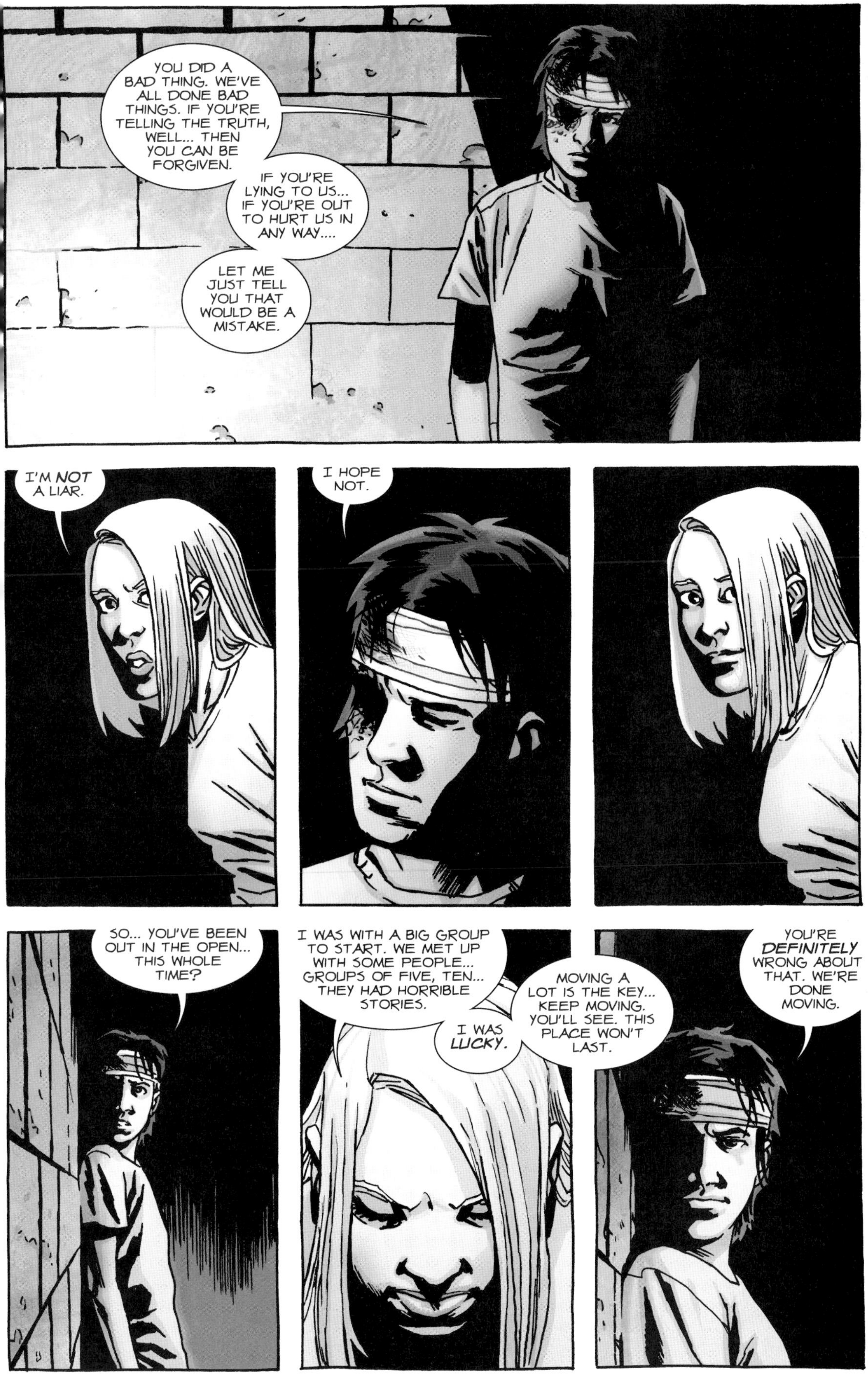
YOU DID A BAD THING. WE'VE ALL DONE BAD THINGS. IF YOU'RE TELLING THE TRUTH, WELL... THEN YOU CAN BE FORGIVEN.
IF YOU'RE LYING TO US... IF YOU'RE OUT TO HURT US IN ANY WAY....
LET ME JUST TELL YOU THAT WOULD BE A MISTAKE.
I'M NOT A LIAR.
I HOPE NOT.
SO... YOU'VE BEEN OUT IN THE OPEN... THIS WHOLE TIME?
I WAS WITH A BIG GROUP TO START. WE MET UP WITH SOME PEOPLE... GROUPS OF FIVE, TEN... THEY HAD HORRIBLE STORIES.
I WAS LUCKY.
MOVING A LOT IS THE KEY... KEEP MOVING. YOU'LL SEE. THIS PLACE WON'T LAST.
YOU'RE DEFINITELY WRONG ABOUT THAT. WE'RE DONE MOVING.

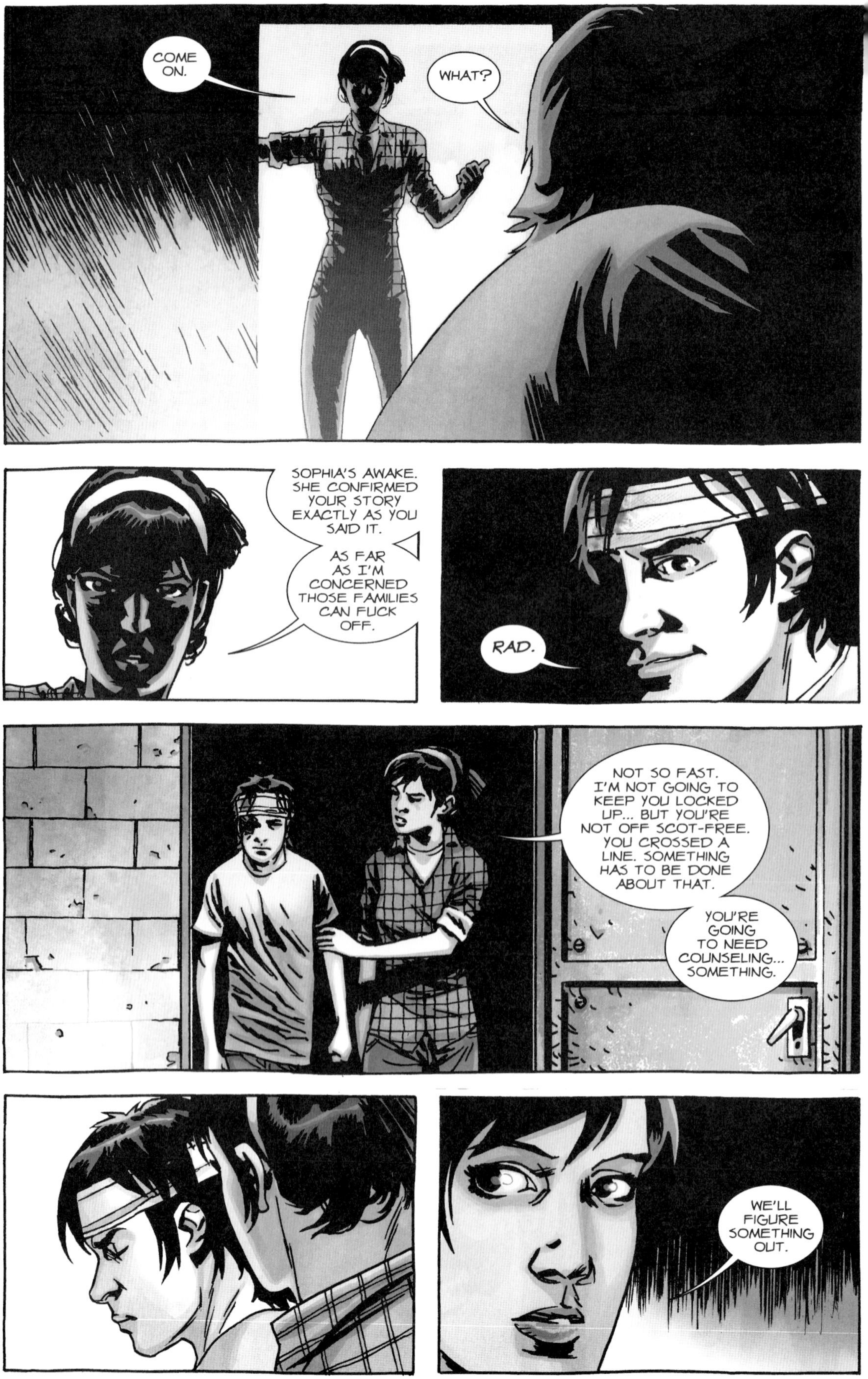
COME ON.
WHAT?
SOPHIA'S AWAKE. SHE CONFIRMED YOUR STORY EXACTLY AS YOU SAID IT.
AS FAR AS I'M CONCERNED THOSE FAMILIES CAN FUCK OFF.
RAD.
NOT SO FAST. I'M NOT GOING TO KEEP YOU LOCKED UP... BUT YOU'RE NOT OFF SCOT-FREE. YOU CROSSED A LINE. SOMETHING HAS TO BE DONE ABOUT THAT.
YOU'RE GOING TO NEED COUNSELING... SOMETHING.
WE'LL FIGURE SOMETHING OUT.

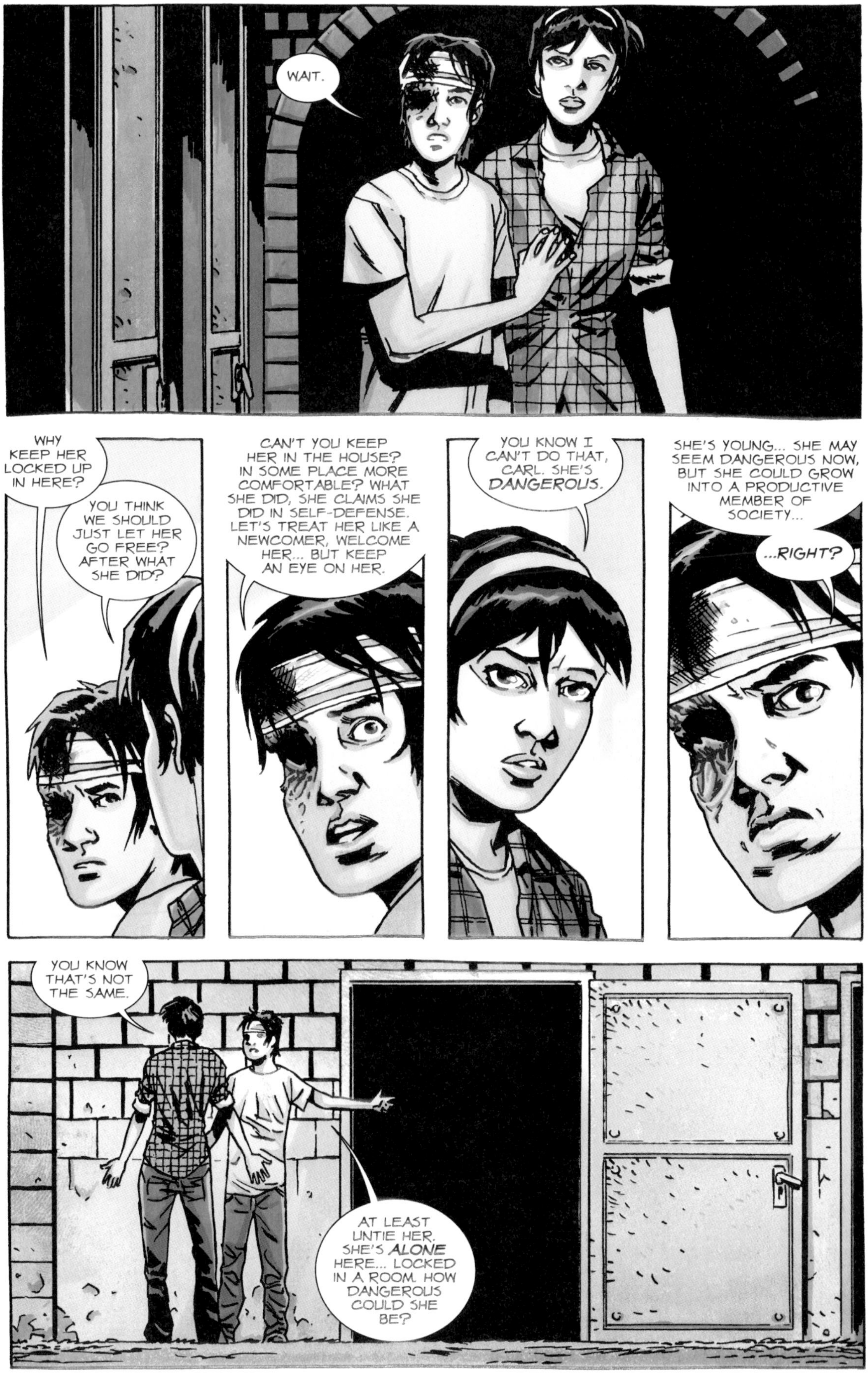
WAIT.
WHY KEEP HER LOCKED UP IN HERE?
YOU THINK WE SHOULD JUST LET HER GO FREE? AFTER WHAT SHE DID?
CAN'T YOU KEEP HER IN THE HOUSE? IN SOME PLACE MORE COMFORTABLE? WHAT SHE DID, SHE CLAIMS SHE DID IN SELF-DEFENSE. LET'S TREAT HER LIKE A NEWCOMER, WELCOME HER... BUT KEEP AN EYE ON HER.
YOU KNOW I CAN'T DO THAT, CARL. SHE'S *DANGEROUS.*
SHE'S YOUNG... SHE MAY SEEM DANGEROUS NOW, BUT SHE COULD GROW INTO A PRODUCTIVE MEMBER OF SOCIETY...
...*RIGHT?*
YOU KNOW THAT'S NOT THE SAME.
AT LEAST UNTIE HER. SHE'S *ALONE* HERE... LOCKED IN A ROOM. HOW DANGEROUS COULD SHE BE?

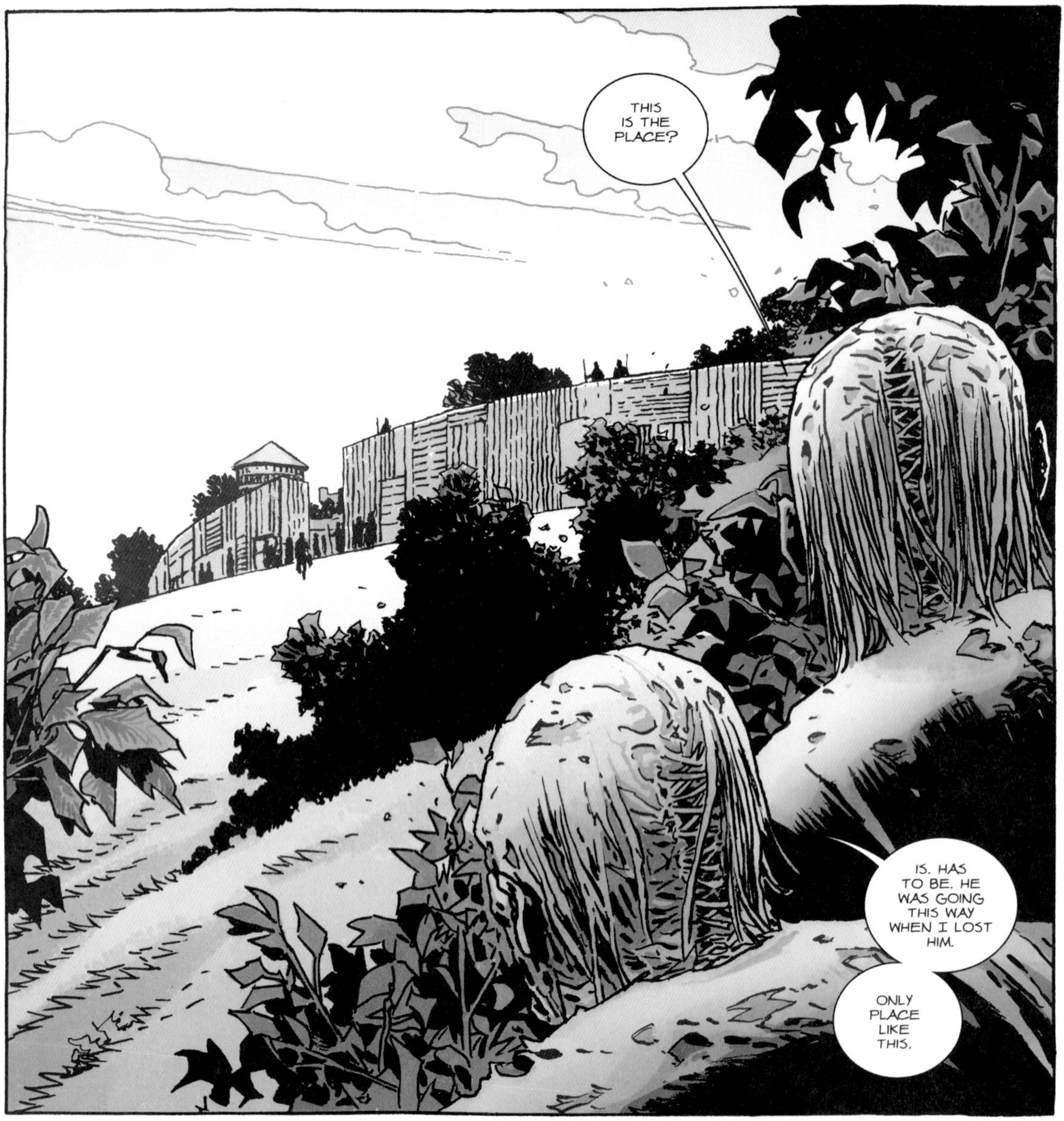
THIS IS THE PLACE?
IS. HAS TO BE. HE WAS GOING THIS WAY WHEN I LOST HIM.
ONLY PLACE LIKE THIS.

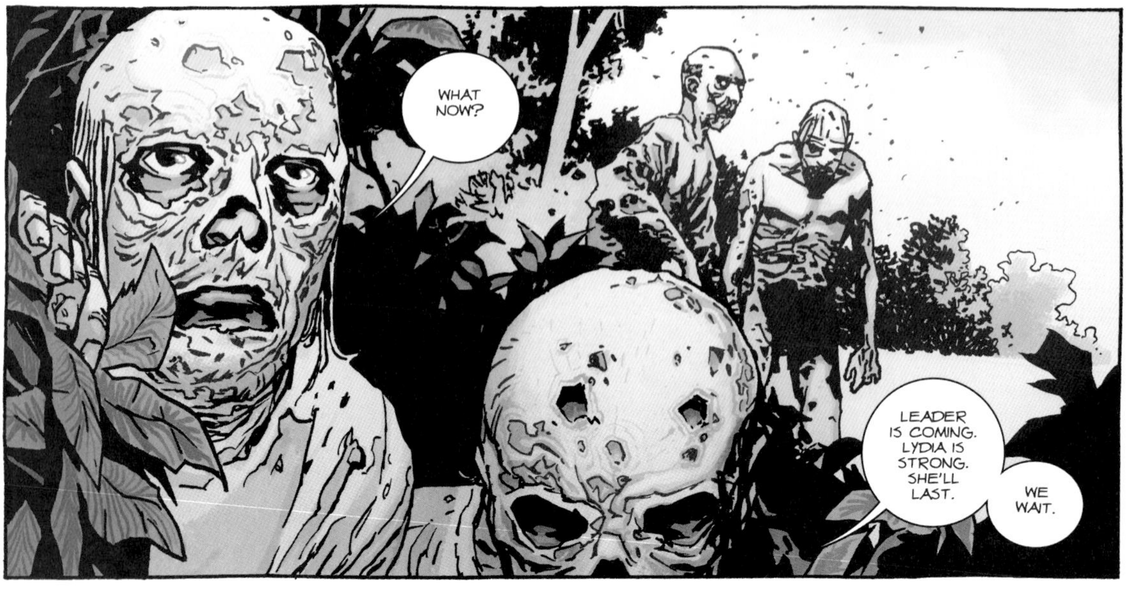
WHAT NOW?
LEADER IS COMING. LYDIA IS STRONG. SHE'LL LAST.
WE WAIT.

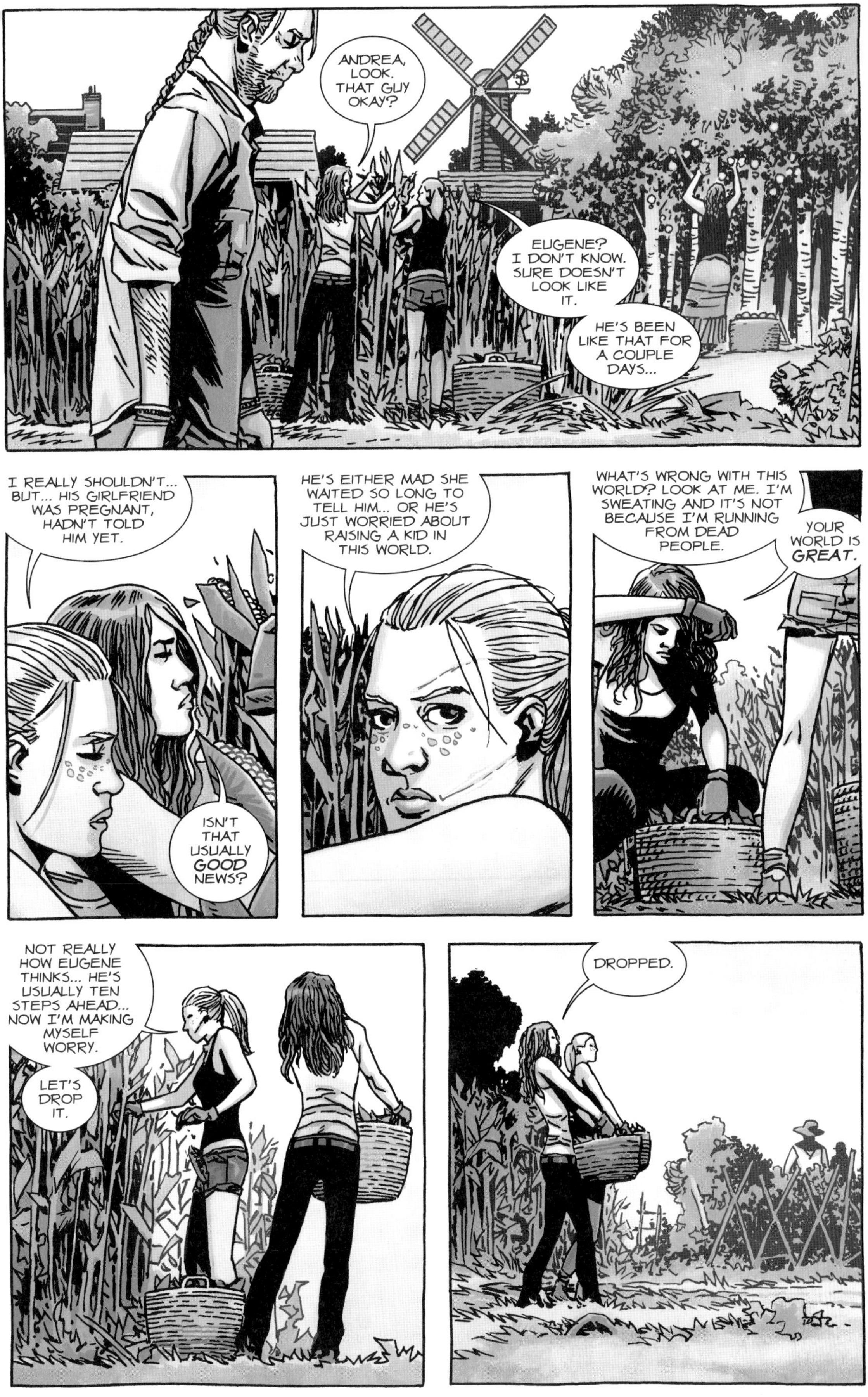
ANDREA, LOOK. THAT GUY OKAY?
EUGENE? I DON'T KNOW. SURE DOESN'T LOOK LIKE IT.
HE'S BEEN LIKE THAT FOR A COUPLE DAYS...
I REALLY SHOULDN'T... BUT... HIS GIRLFRIEND WAS PREGNANT, HADN'T TOLD HIM YET.
ISN'T THAT USUALLY GOOD NEWS?
HE'S EITHER MAD SHE WAITED SO LONG TO TELL HIM... OR HE'S JUST WORRIED ABOUT RAISING A KID IN THIS WORLD.
WHAT'S WRONG WITH THIS WORLD? LOOK AT ME. I'M SWEATING AND IT'S NOT BECAUSE I'M RUNNING FROM DEAD PEOPLE.
YOUR WORLD IS GREAT.
NOT REALLY HOW EUGENE THINKS... HE'S USUALLY TEN STEPS AHEAD... NOW I'M MAKING MYSELF WORRY.
LET'S DROP IT.
DROPPED.

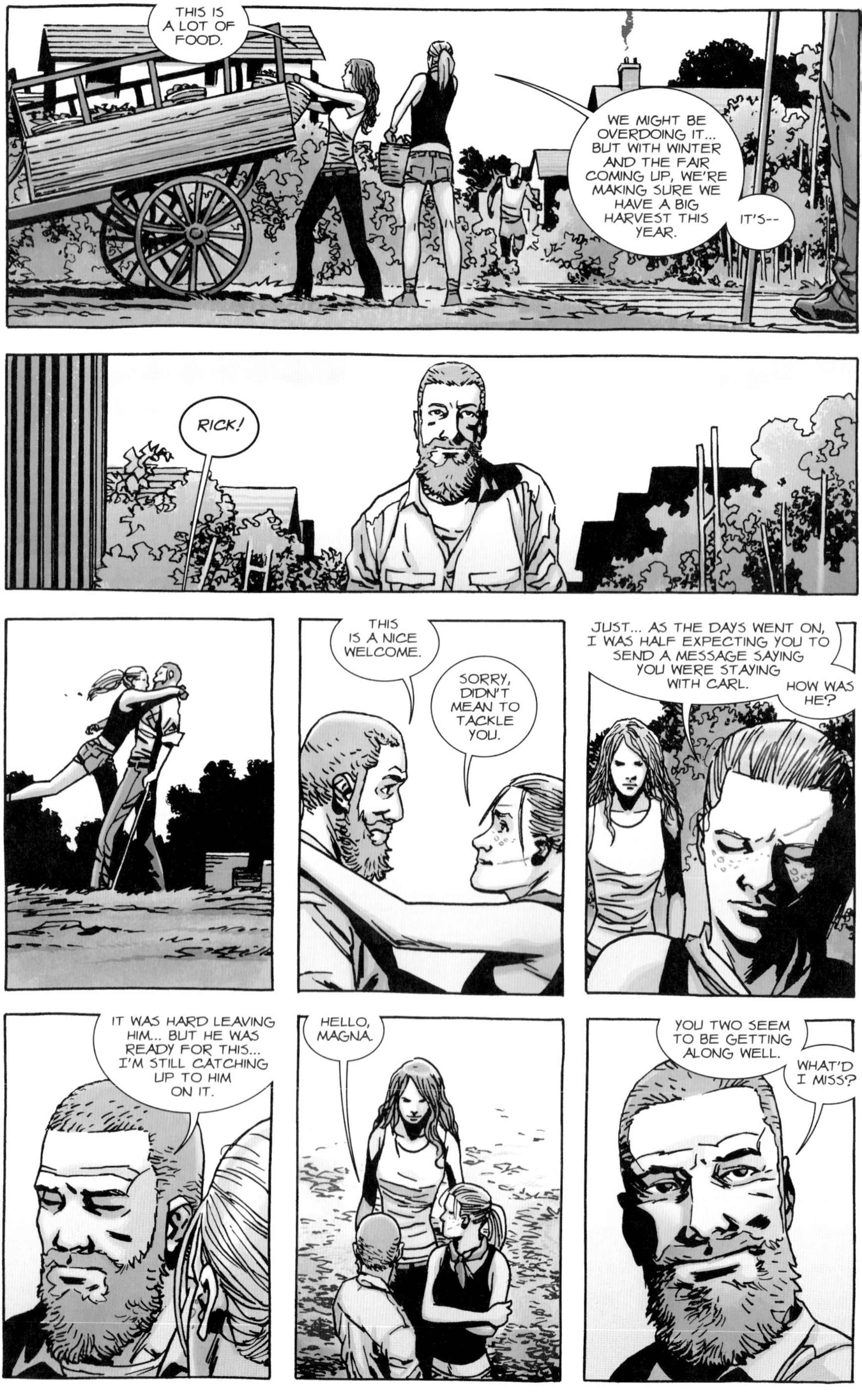
THIS IS A LOT OF FOOD.
WE MIGHT BE OVERDOING IT... BUT WITH WINTER AND THE FAIR COMING UP, WE'RE MAKING SURE WE HAVE A BIG HARVEST THIS YEAR.
IT'S--
RICK!
THIS IS A NICE WELCOME.
SORRY, DIDN'T MEAN TO TACKLE YOU.
JUST... AS THE DAYS WENT ON, I WAS HALF EXPECTING YOU TO SEND A MESSAGE SAYING YOU WERE STAYING WITH CARL.
HOW WAS HE?
IT WAS HARD LEAVING HIM... BUT HE WAS READY FOR THIS... I'M STILL CATCHING UP TO HIM ON IT.
HELLO, MAGNA.
YOU TWO SEEM TO BE GETTING ALONG WELL.
WHAT'D I MISS?

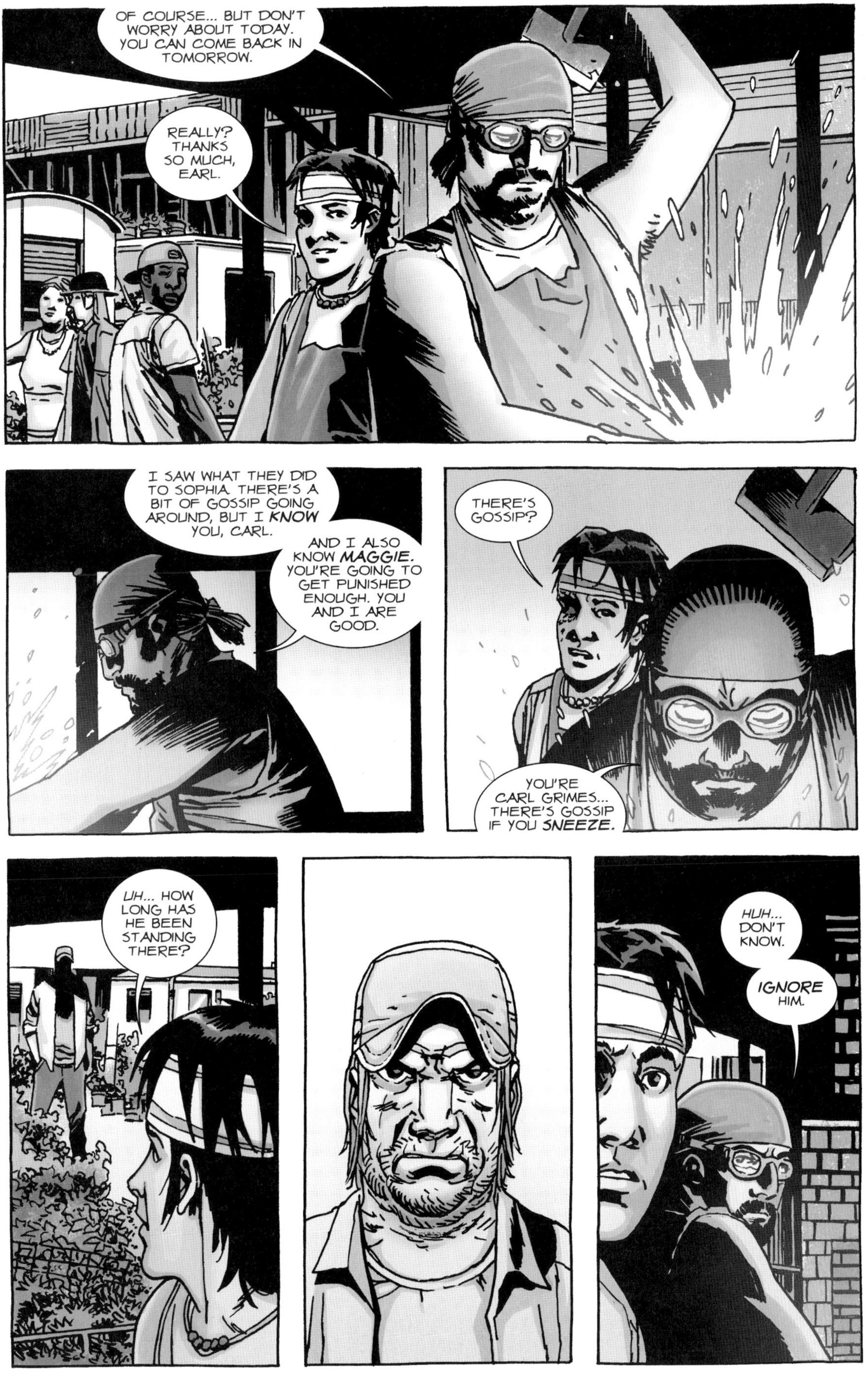
OF COURSE... BUT DON'T WORRY ABOUT TODAY. YOU CAN COME BACK IN TOMORROW.
REALLY? THANKS SO MUCH, EARL.
I SAW WHAT THEY DID TO SOPHIA. THERE'S A BIT OF GOSSIP GOING AROUND, BUT I KNOW YOU, CARL.
AND I ALSO KNOW MAGGIE. YOU'RE GOING TO GET PUNISHED ENOUGH. YOU AND I ARE GOOD.
THERE'S GOSSIP?
YOU'RE CARL GRIMES... THERE'S GOSSIP IF YOU SNEEZE.
UH... HOW LONG HAS HE BEEN STANDING THERE?
HUH... DON'T KNOW.
IGNORE HIM.

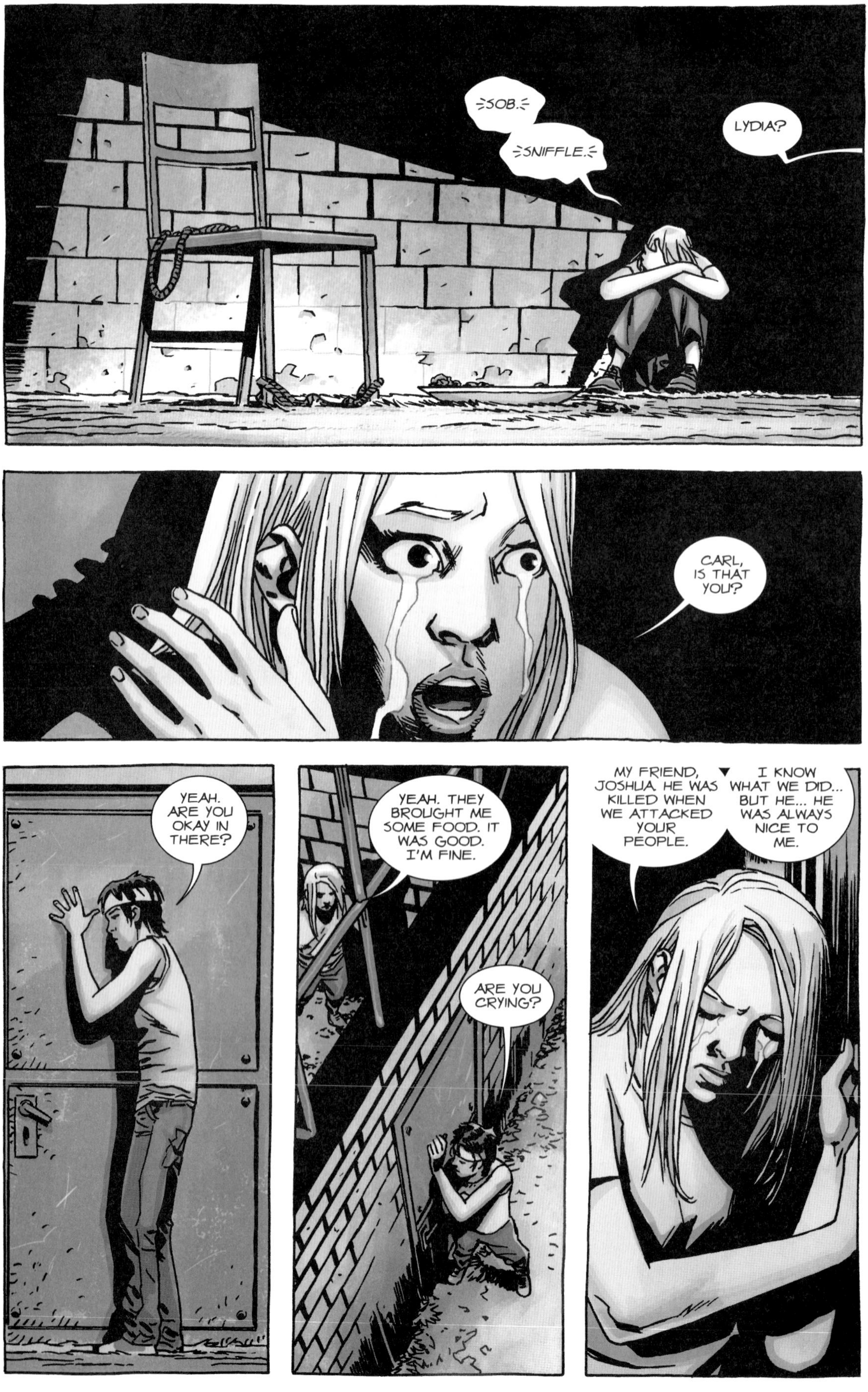
SOB.
SNIFFLE.
LYDIA?
CARL, IS THAT YOU?
YEAH. ARE YOU OKAY IN THERE?
YEAH. THEY BROUGHT ME SOME FOOD. IT WAS GOOD. I'M FINE.
ARE YOU CRYING?
MY FRIEND, JOSHUA. HE WAS KILLED WHEN WE ATTACKED YOUR PEOPLE.
I KNOW WHAT WE DID... BUT HE... HE WAS ALWAYS NICE TO ME.

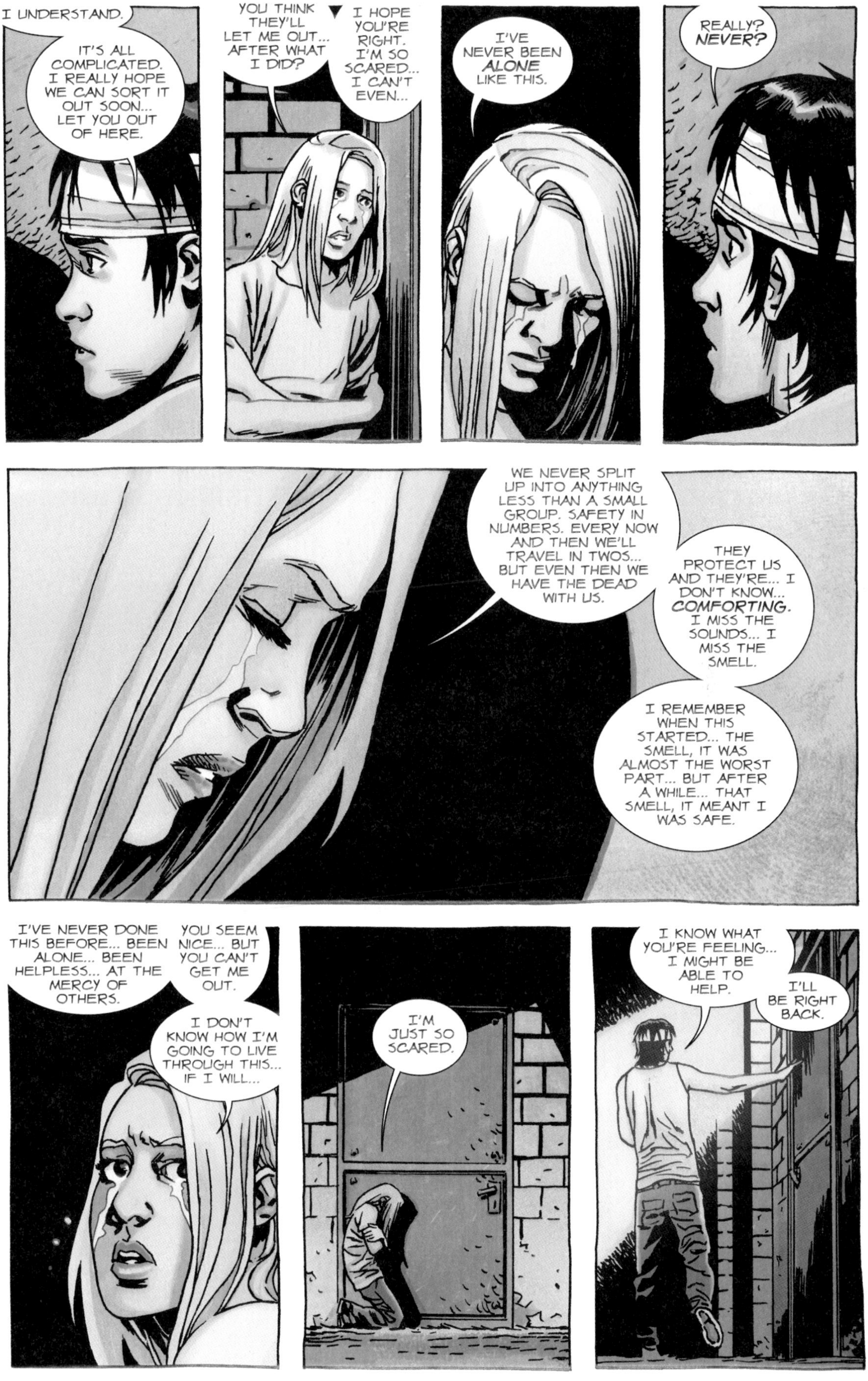
I UNDERSTAND.
IT'S ALL COMPLICATED. I REALLY HOPE WE CAN SORT IT OUT SOON... LET YOU OUT OF HERE.
YOU THINK THEY'LL LET ME OUT... AFTER WHAT I DID?
I HOPE YOU'RE RIGHT. I'M SO SCARED... I CAN'T EVEN...
I'VE NEVER BEEN ALONE LIKE THIS.
REALLY? NEVER?
WE NEVER SPLIT UP INTO ANYTHING LESS THAN A SMALL GROUP. SAFETY IN NUMBERS. EVERY NOW AND THEN WE'LL TRAVEL IN TWOS... BUT EVEN THEN WE HAVE THE DEAD WITH US.
THEY PROTECT US AND THEY'RE... I DON'T KNOW... COMFORTING. I MISS THE SOUNDS... I MISS THE SMELL.
I REMEMBER WHEN THIS STARTED... THE SMELL, IT WAS ALMOST THE WORST PART... BUT AFTER A WHILE... THAT SMELL, IT MEANT I WAS SAFE.
I'VE NEVER DONE THIS BEFORE... BEEN ALONE... BEEN HELPLESS... AT THE MERCY OF OTHERS.
YOU SEEM NICE... BUT YOU CAN'T GET ME OUT.
I DON'T KNOW HOW I'M GOING TO LIVE THROUGH THIS... IF I WILL...
I'M JUST SO SCARED.
I KNOW WHAT YOU'RE FEELING... I MIGHT BE ABLE TO HELP.
I'LL BE RIGHT BACK.

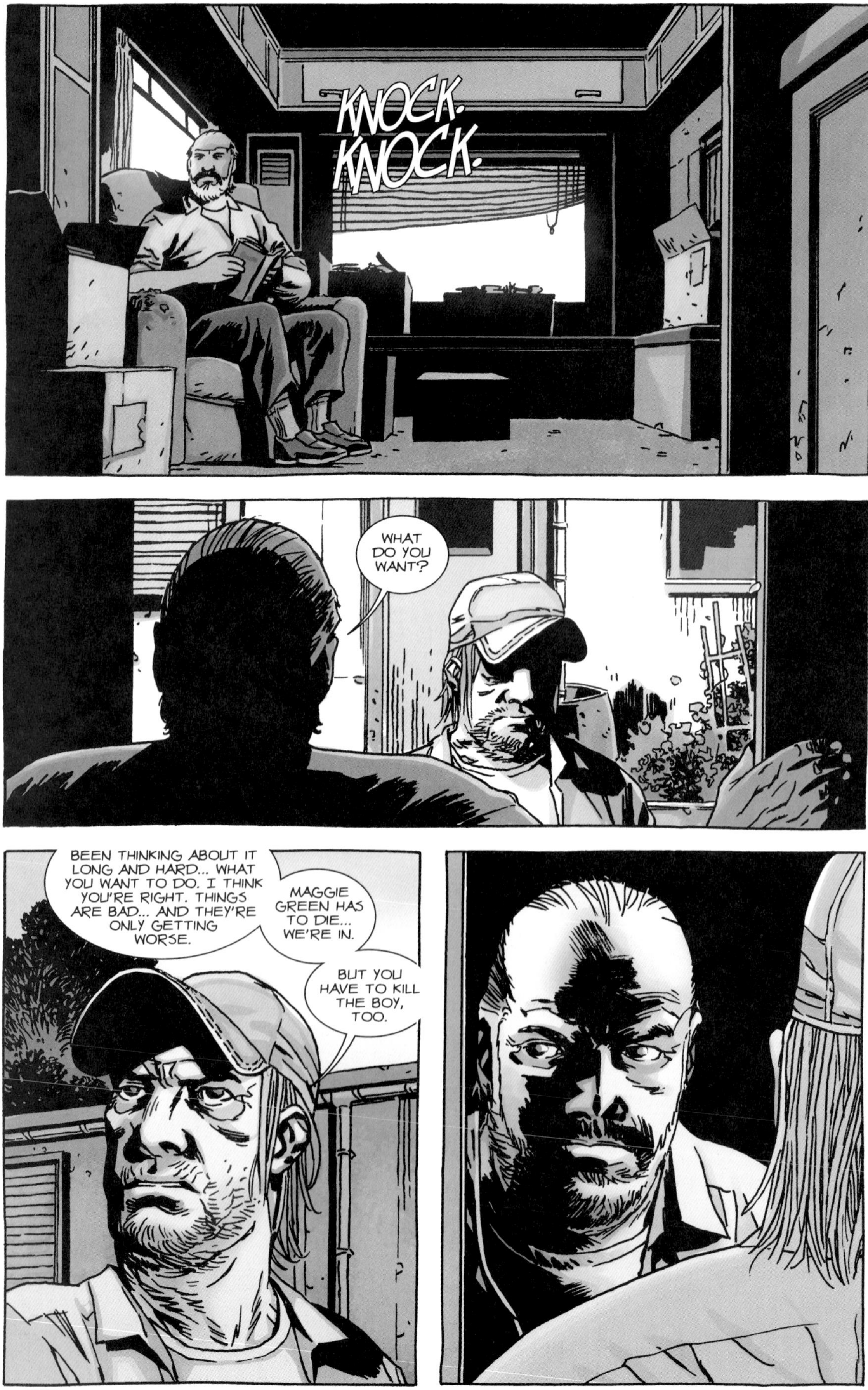
KNOCK. KNOCK.
WHAT DO YOU WANT?
BEEN THINKING ABOUT IT LONG AND HARD... WHAT YOU WANT TO DO. I THINK YOU'RE RIGHT. THINGS ARE BAD... AND THEY'RE ONLY GETTING WORSE.
MAGGIE GREEN HAS TO DIE... WE'RE IN.
BUT YOU HAVE TO KILL THE BOY, TOO.

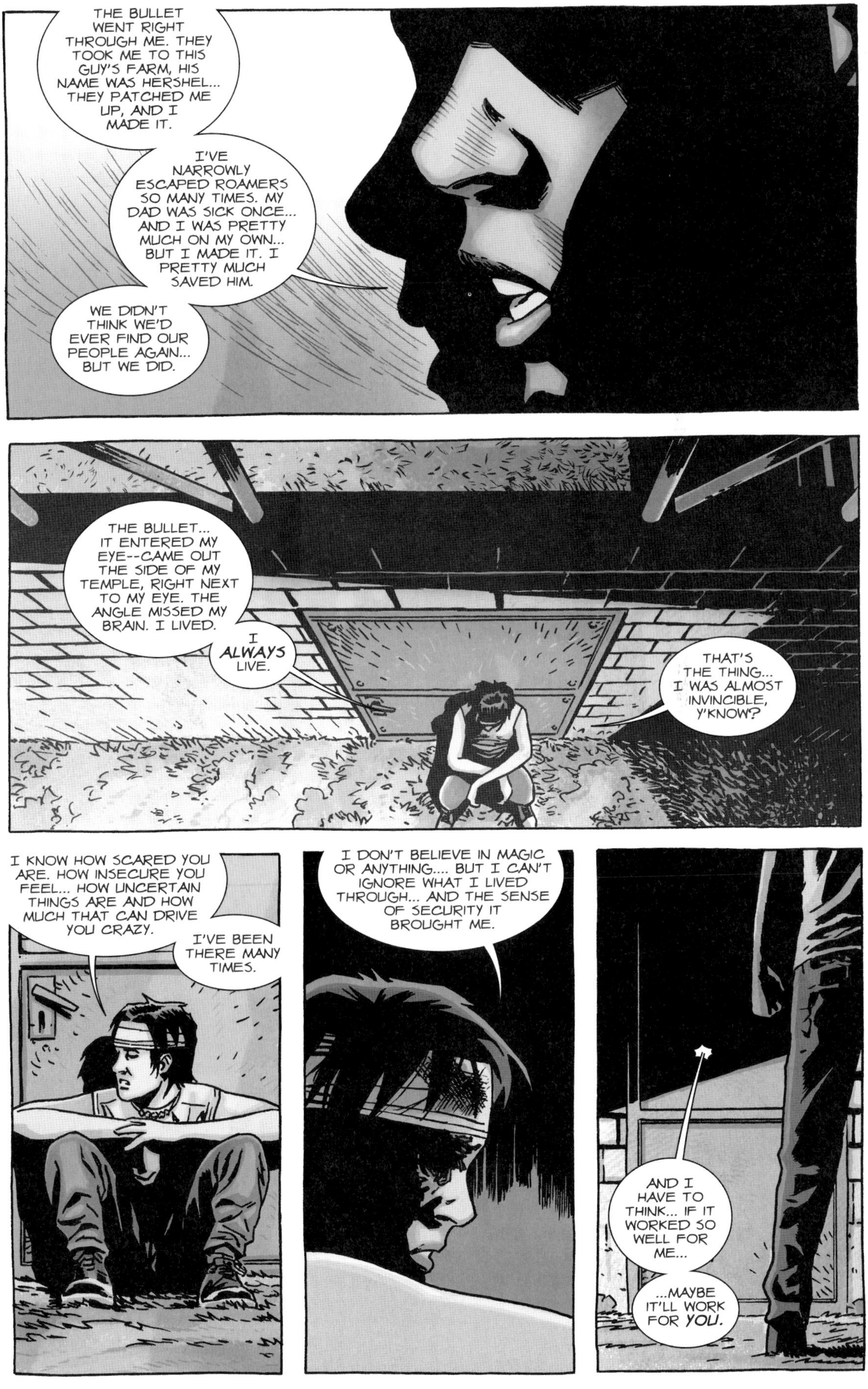
THE BULLET WENT RIGHT THROUGH ME. THEY TOOK ME TO THIS GUY'S FARM, HIS NAME WAS HERSHEL... THEY PATCHED ME UP, AND I MADE IT.
I'VE NARROWLY ESCAPED ROAMERS SO MANY TIMES. MY DAD WAS SICK ONCE... AND I WAS PRETTY MUCH ON MY OWN... BUT I MADE IT. I PRETTY MUCH SAVED HIM.
WE DIDN'T THINK WE'D EVER FIND OUR PEOPLE AGAIN... BUT WE DID.
THE BULLET... IT ENTERED MY EYE--CAME OUT THE SIDE OF MY TEMPLE, RIGHT NEXT TO MY EYE. THE ANGLE MISSED MY BRAIN. I LIVED.
I *ALWAYS* LIVE.
THAT'S THE THING... I WAS ALMOST INVINCIBLE, Y'KNOW?
I KNOW HOW SCARED YOU ARE. HOW INSECURE YOU FEEL... HOW UNCERTAIN THINGS ARE AND HOW MUCH THAT CAN DRIVE YOU CRAZY.
I'VE BEEN THERE MANY TIMES.
I DON'T BELIEVE IN MAGIC OR ANYTHING.... BUT I CAN'T IGNORE WHAT I LIVED THROUGH... AND THE SENSE OF SECURITY IT BROUGHT ME.
AND I HAVE TO THINK... IF IT WORKED SO WELL FOR ME...
...MAYBE IT'LL WORK FOR *YOU.*

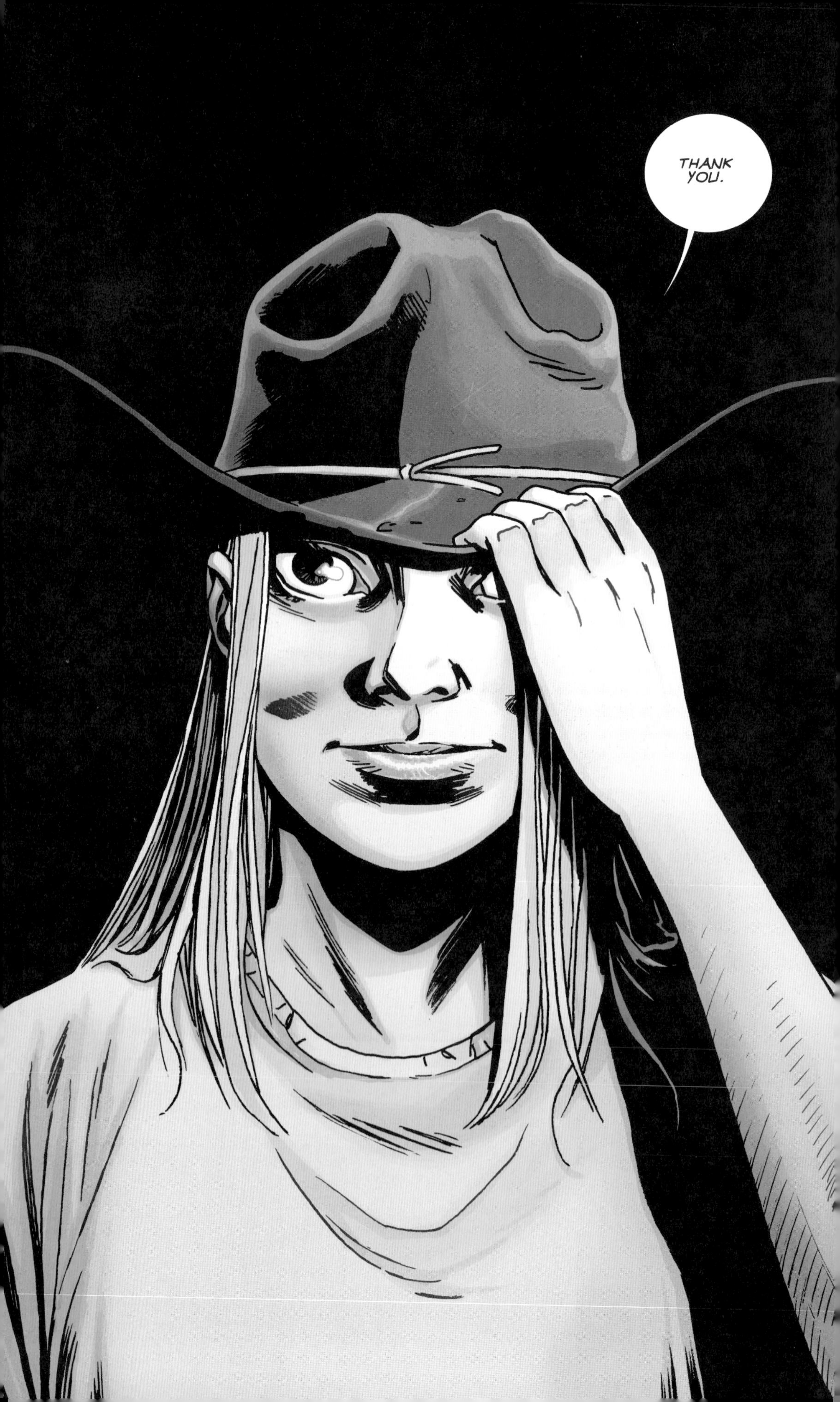
THANK YOU.

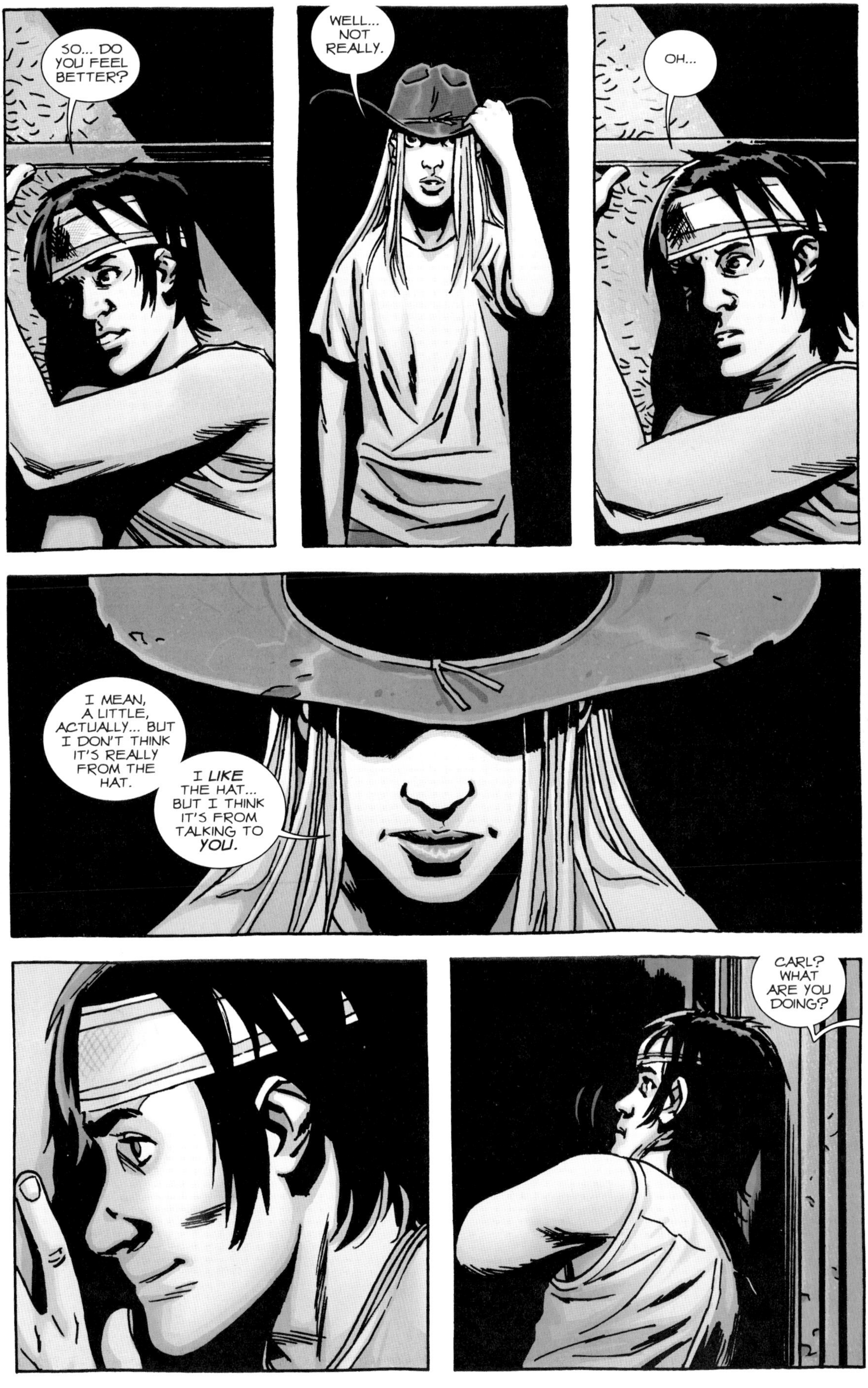
SO... DO YOU FEEL BETTER?
WELL... NOT REALLY.
OH...
I MEAN, A LITTLE, ACTUALLY... BUT I DON'T THINK IT'S REALLY FROM THE HAT.
I *LIKE* THE HAT... BUT I THINK IT'S FROM TALKING TO *YOU*.
CARL? WHAT ARE YOU DOING?

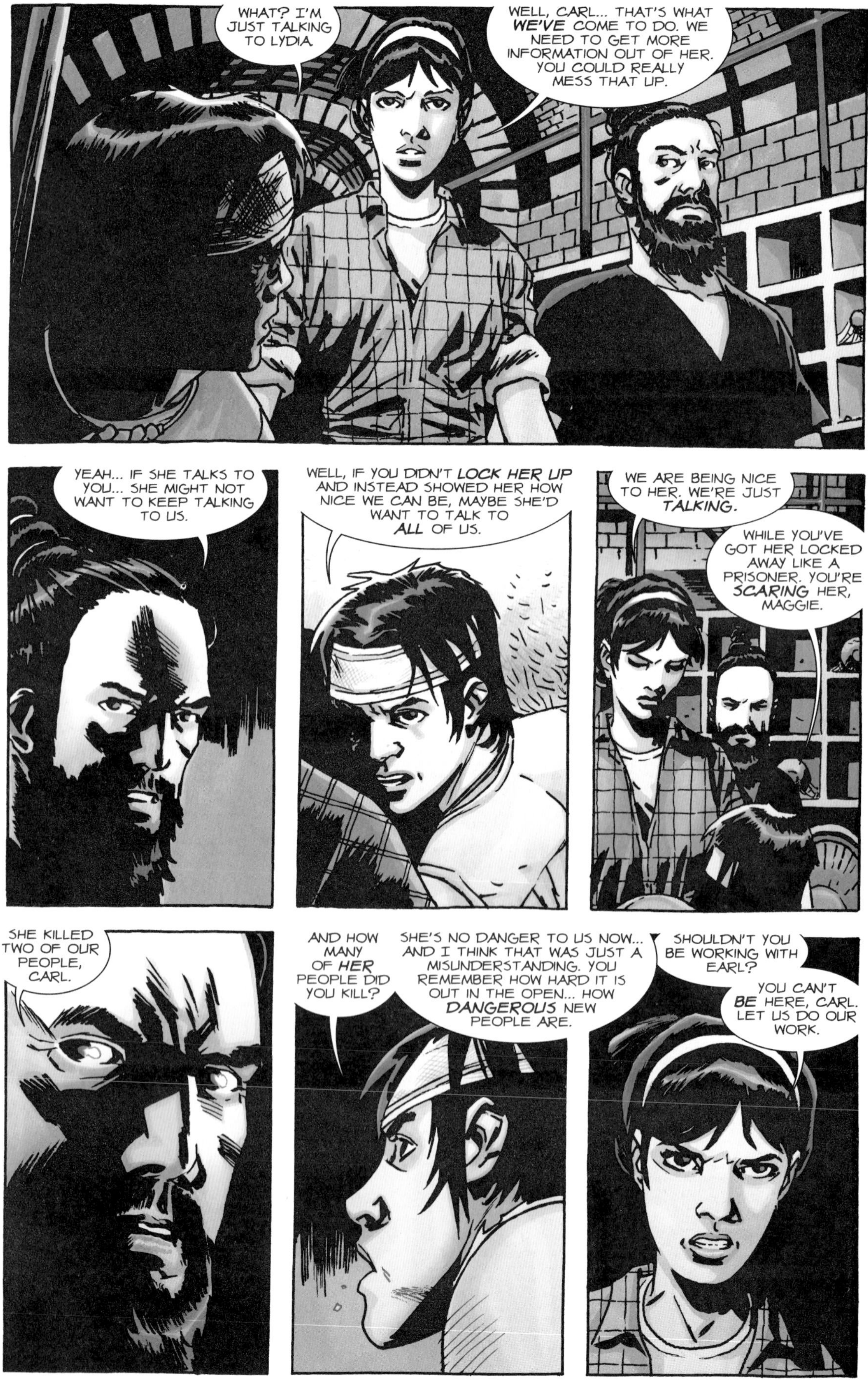
WHAT? I'M JUST TALKING TO LYDIA.
WELL, CARL... THAT'S WHAT WE'VE COME TO DO. WE NEED TO GET MORE INFORMATION OUT OF HER. YOU COULD REALLY MESS THAT UP.
YEAH... IF SHE TALKS TO YOU... SHE MIGHT NOT WANT TO KEEP TALKING TO US.
WELL, IF YOU DIDN'T LOCK HER UP AND INSTEAD SHOWED HER HOW NICE WE CAN BE, MAYBE SHE'D WANT TO TALK TO ALL OF US.
WE ARE BEING NICE TO HER. WE'RE JUST TALKING.
WHILE YOU'VE GOT HER LOCKED AWAY LIKE A PRISONER. YOU'RE SCARING HER, MAGGIE.
SHE KILLED TWO OF OUR PEOPLE, CARL.
AND HOW MANY OF HER PEOPLE DID YOU KILL?
SHE'S NO DANGER TO US NOW... AND I THINK THAT WAS JUST A MISUNDERSTANDING. YOU REMEMBER HOW HARD IT IS OUT IN THE OPEN... HOW DANGEROUS NEW PEOPLE ARE.
SHOULDN'T YOU BE WORKING WITH EARL?
YOU CAN'T BE HERE, CARL. LET US DO OUR WORK.

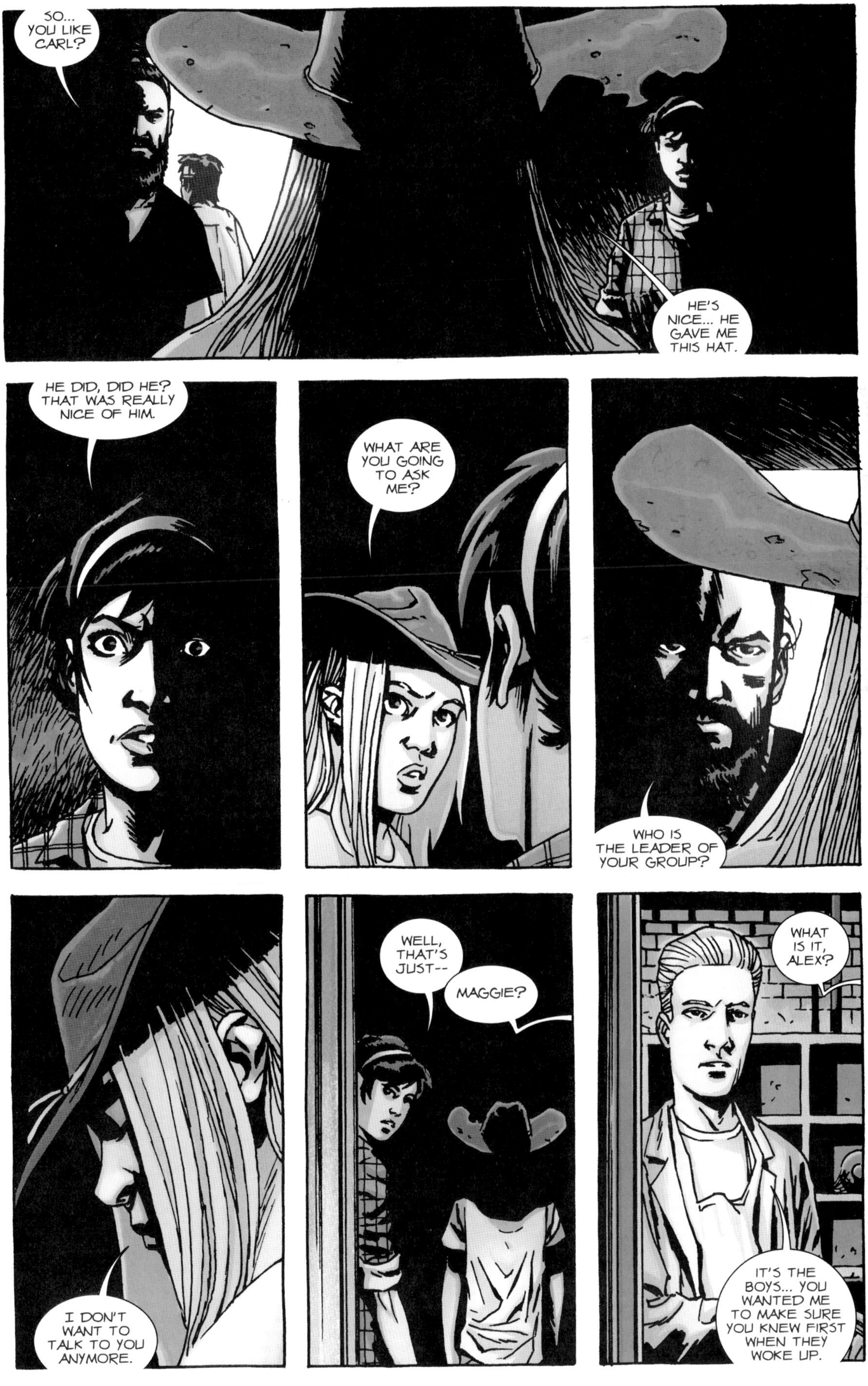

SO... YOU LIKE CARL?
HE'S NICE... HE GAVE ME THIS HAT.
HE DID, DID HE? THAT WAS REALLY NICE OF HIM.
WHAT ARE YOU GOING TO ASK ME?
WHO IS THE LEADER OF YOUR GROUP?
I DON'T WANT TO TALK TO YOU ANYMORE.
WELL, THAT'S JUST--
MAGGIE?
WHAT IS IT, ALEX?
IT'S THE BOYS... YOU WANTED ME TO MAKE SURE YOU KNEW FIRST WHEN THEY WOKE UP.

WHERE IS SHE?!

WHERE IS THAT *FUCKING* BITCH?!

SHE'S RIGHT HERE.

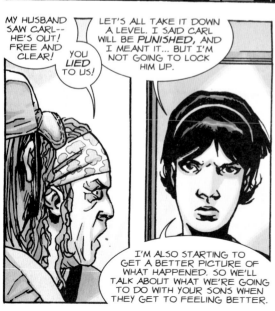

MY HUSBAND SAW CARL-- HE'S *OUT!* FREE AND CLEAR!

YOU *LIED* TO US!

LET'S ALL TAKE IT DOWN A LEVEL. I SAID CARL WILL BE *PUNISHED,* AND I MEANT IT... BUT I'M NOT GOING TO LOCK HIM UP.

I'M ALSO STARTING TO GET A BETTER PICTURE OF WHAT HAPPENED. SO WE'LL TALK ABOUT WHAT WE'RE GOING TO DO WITH YOUR SONS WHEN THEY GET TO FEELING BETTER.

WHAT THE *HELL* DOES THAT MEAN?

ARE YOU *FUCKING* JOKING? IS THAT A JOKE?! YOU CAN'T *FUCKING* BE SERIOUS!

I HONESTLY THINK IT'S TIME TO START DISCUSSING RELOCATION.

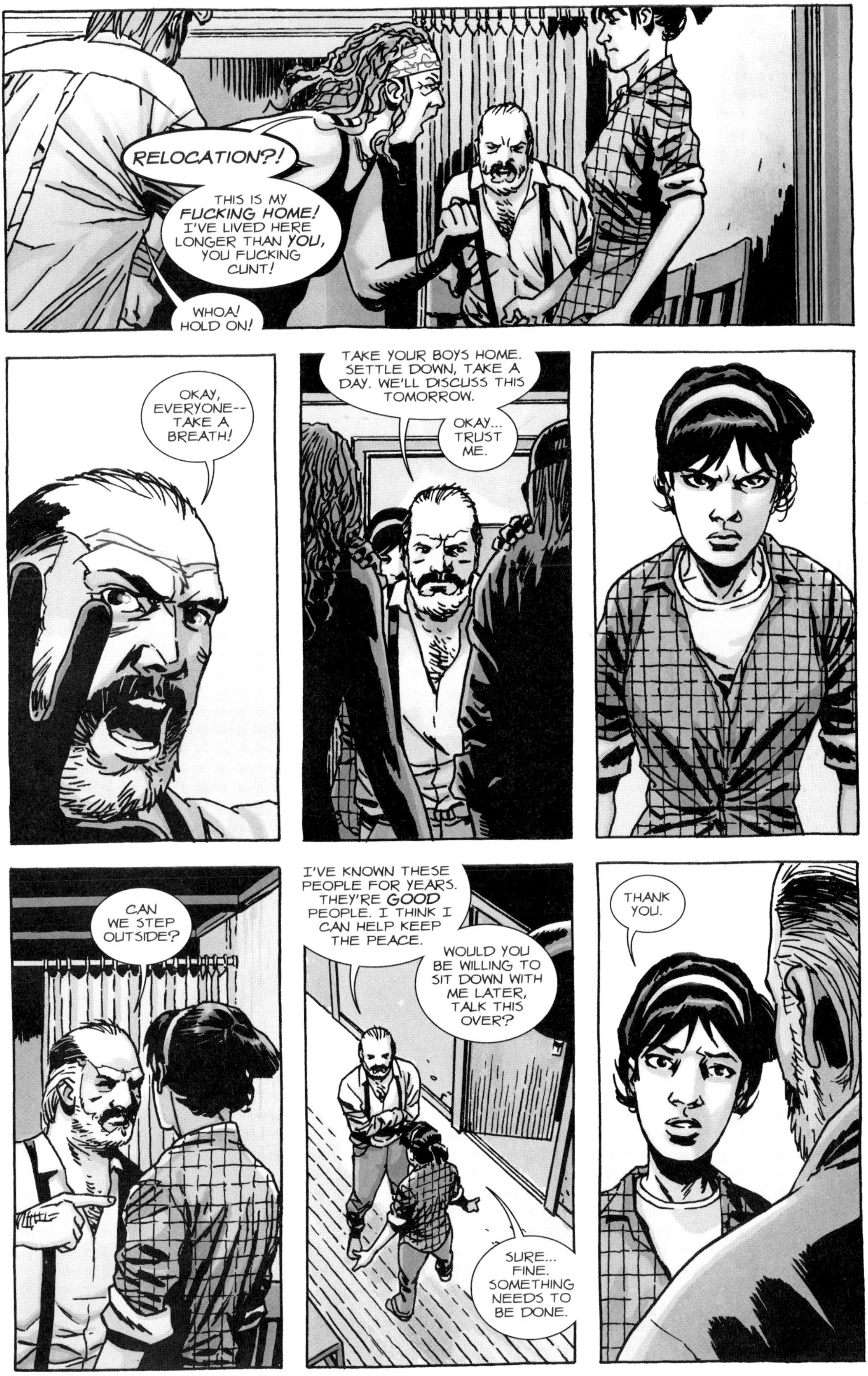
RELOCATION?!
THIS IS MY FUCKING HOME! I'VE LIVED HERE LONGER THAN YOU, YOU FUCKING CUNT!
WHOA! HOLD ON!
OKAY, EVERYONE-- TAKE A BREATH!
TAKE YOUR BOYS HOME. SETTLE DOWN, TAKE A DAY. WE'LL DISCUSS THIS TOMORROW.
OKAY... TRUST ME.
CAN WE STEP OUTSIDE?
I'VE KNOWN THESE PEOPLE FOR YEARS. THEY'RE GOOD PEOPLE. I THINK I CAN HELP KEEP THE PEACE.
WOULD YOU BE WILLING TO SIT DOWN WITH ME LATER, TALK THIS OVER?
SURE... FINE. SOMETHING NEEDS TO BE DONE.
THANK YOU.

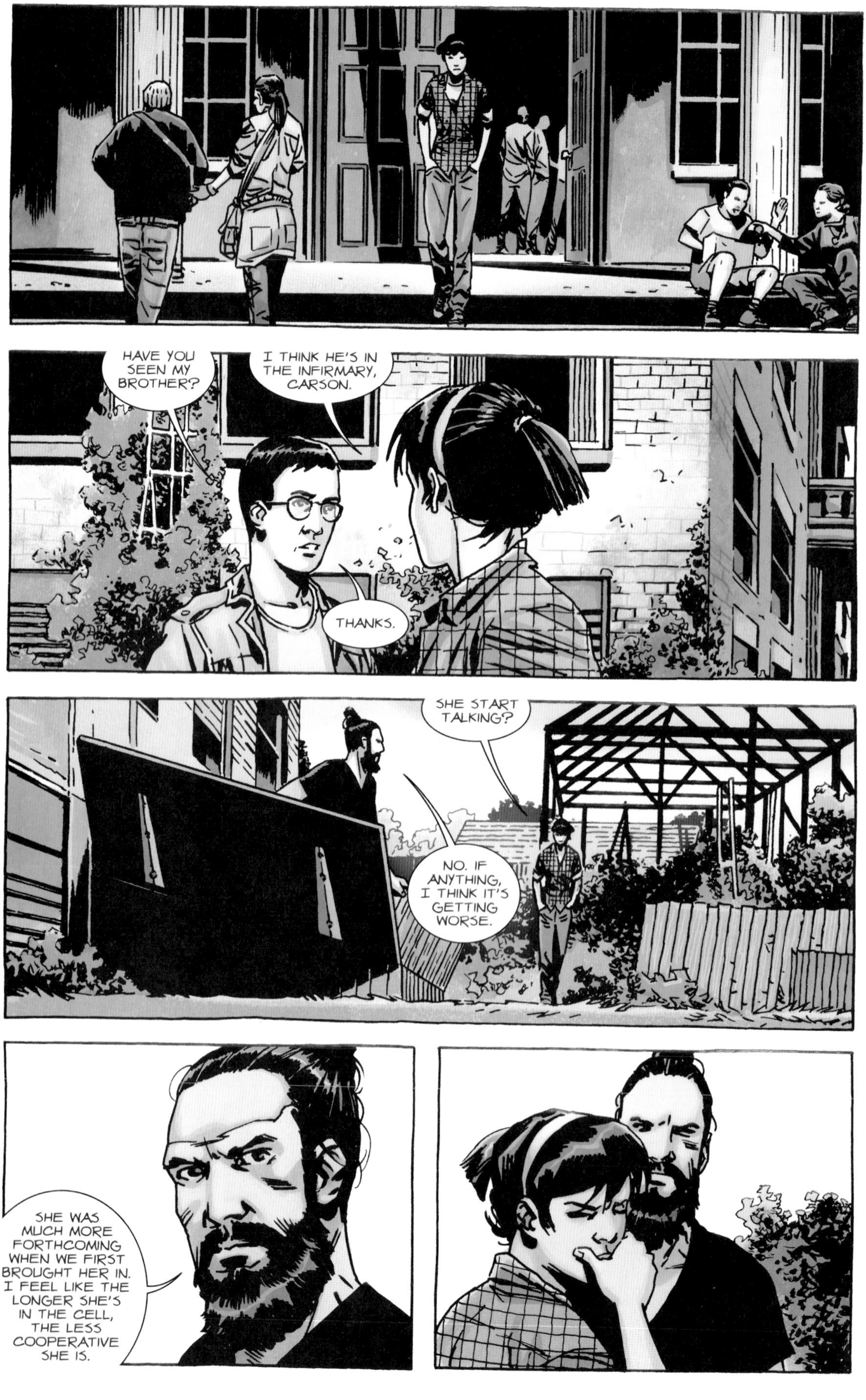
HAVE YOU SEEN MY BROTHER?
I THINK HE'S IN THE INFIRMARY, CARSON.
THANKS.
SHE START TALKING?
NO. IF ANYTHING, I THINK IT'S GETTING WORSE.
SHE WAS MUCH MORE FORTHCOMING WHEN WE FIRST BROUGHT HER IN. I FEEL LIKE THE LONGER SHE'S IN THE CELL, THE LESS COOPERATIVE SHE IS.

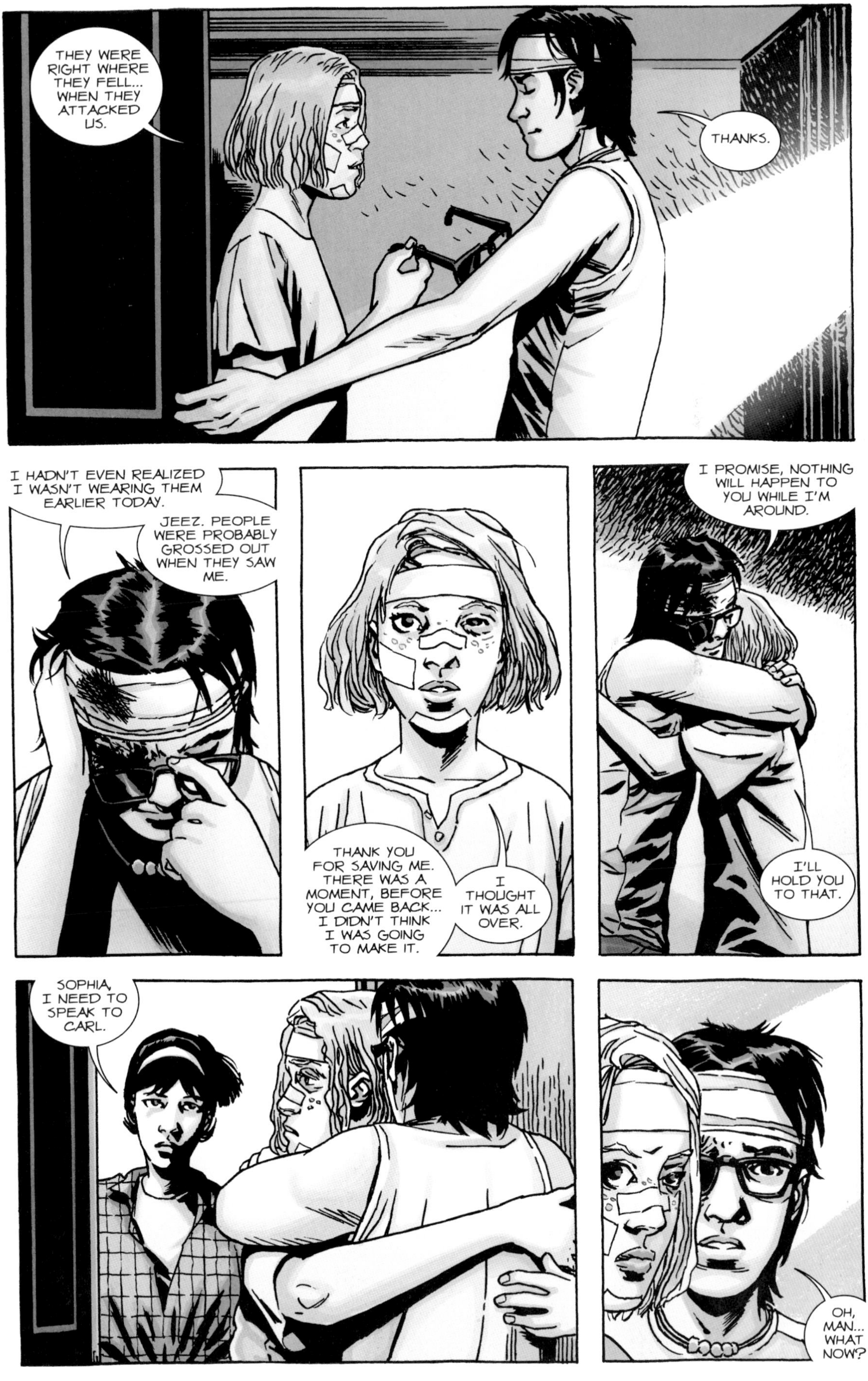
THEY WERE RIGHT WHERE THEY FELL... WHEN THEY ATTACKED US.
THANKS.
I HADN'T EVEN REALIZED I WASN'T WEARING THEM EARLIER TODAY.
JEEZ. PEOPLE WERE PROBABLY GROSSED OUT WHEN THEY SAW ME.
THANK YOU FOR SAVING ME. THERE WAS A MOMENT, BEFORE YOU CAME BACK... I DIDN'T THINK I WAS GOING TO MAKE IT.
I THOUGHT IT WAS ALL OVER.
I PROMISE, NOTHING WILL HAPPEN TO YOU WHILE I'M AROUND.
I'LL HOLD YOU TO THAT.
SOPHIA, I NEED TO SPEAK TO CARL.
OH, MAN... WHAT NOW?

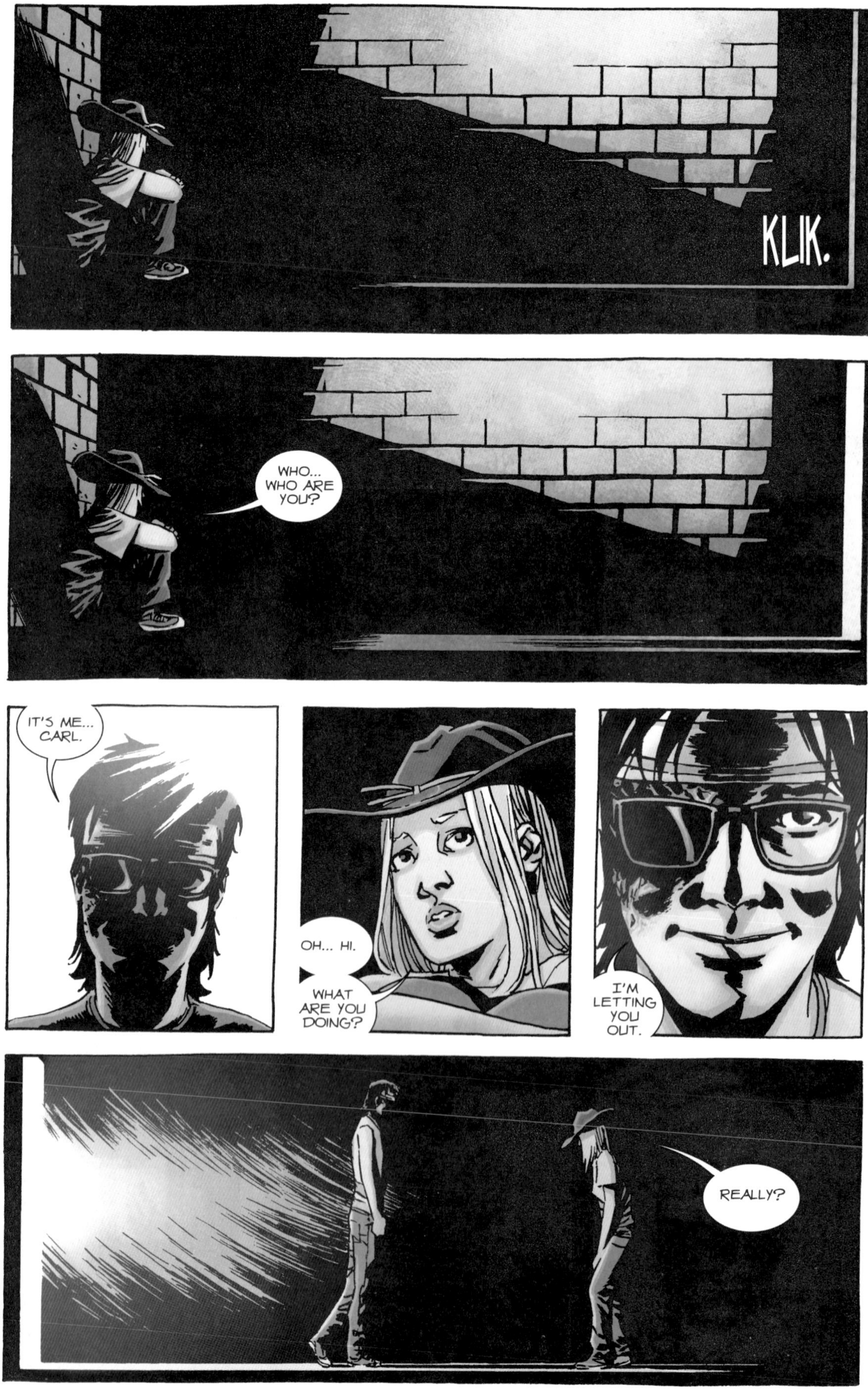
KLIK.
WHO... WHO ARE YOU?
IT'S ME... CARL.
OH... HI.
WHAT ARE YOU DOING?
I'M LETTING YOU OUT.
REALLY?

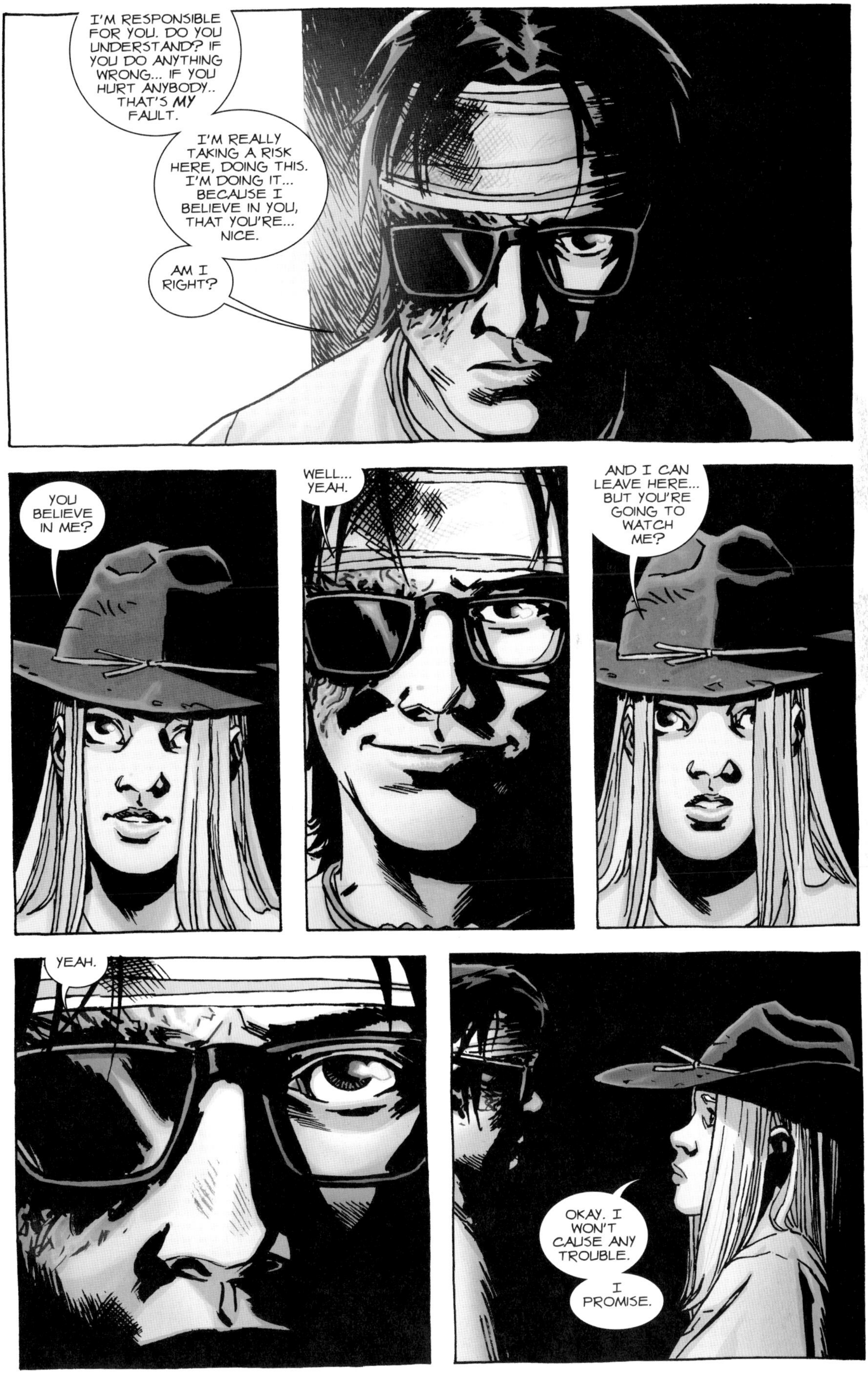
I'M RESPONSIBLE FOR YOU. DO YOU UNDERSTAND? IF YOU DO ANYTHING WRONG... IF YOU HURT ANYBODY.. THAT'S MY FAULT.
I'M REALLY TAKING A RISK HERE, DOING THIS. I'M DOING IT... BECAUSE I BELIEVE IN YOU, THAT YOU'RE... NICE.
AM I RIGHT?
YOU BELIEVE IN ME?
WELL... YEAH.
AND I CAN LEAVE HERE... BUT YOU'RE GOING TO WATCH ME?
YEAH.
OKAY. I WON'T CAUSE ANY TROUBLE.
I PROMISE.

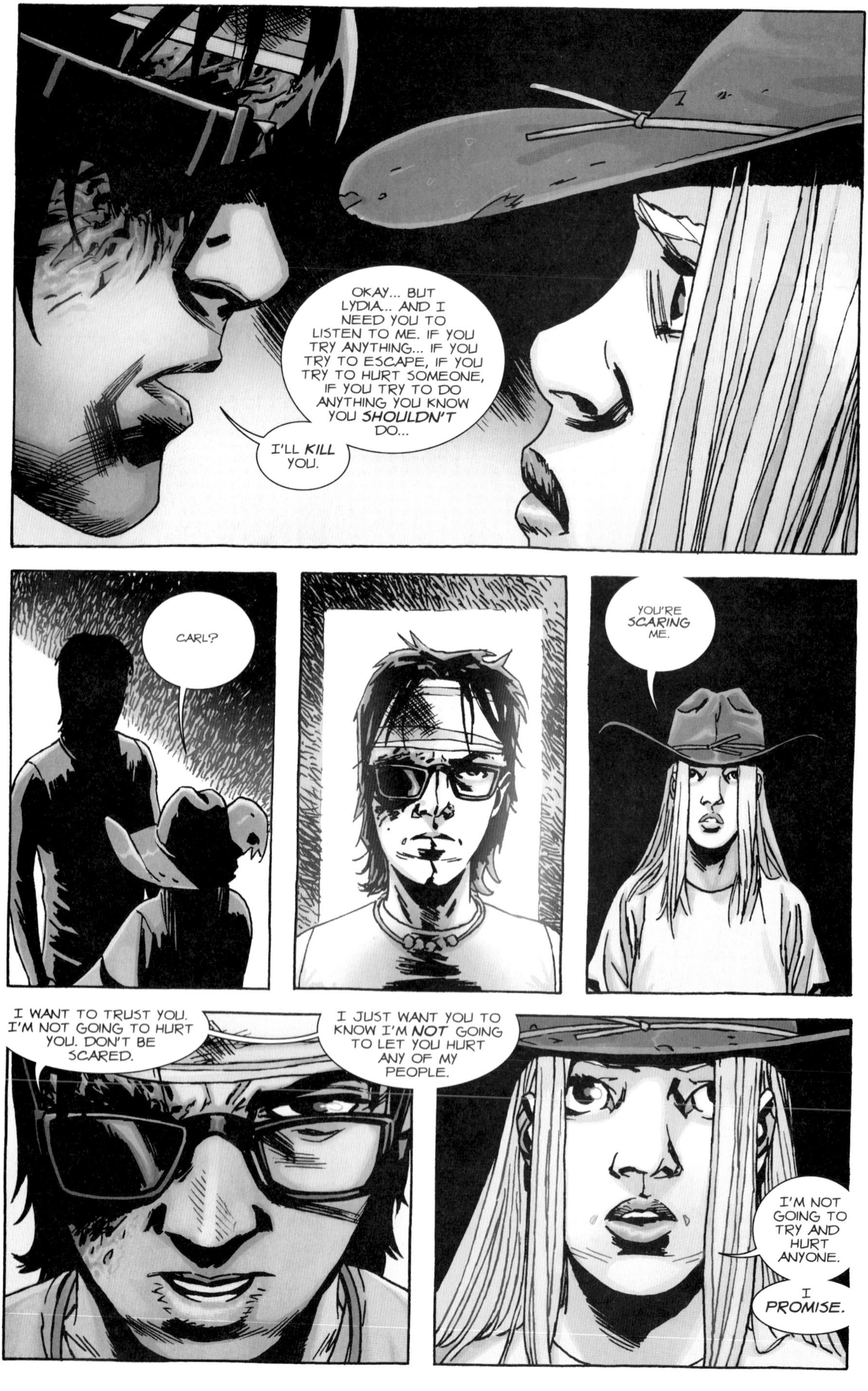
OKAY... BUT LYDIA... AND I NEED YOU TO LISTEN TO ME. IF YOU TRY ANYTHING... IF YOU TRY TO ESCAPE, IF YOU TRY TO HURT SOMEONE, IF YOU TRY TO DO ANYTHING YOU KNOW YOU SHOULDN'T DO...
I'LL KILL YOU.
CARL?
YOU'RE SCARING ME.
I WANT TO TRUST YOU. I'M NOT GOING TO HURT YOU. DON'T BE SCARED.
I JUST WANT YOU TO KNOW I'M NOT GOING TO LET YOU HURT ANY OF MY PEOPLE.
I'M NOT GOING TO TRY AND HURT ANYONE.
I PROMISE.

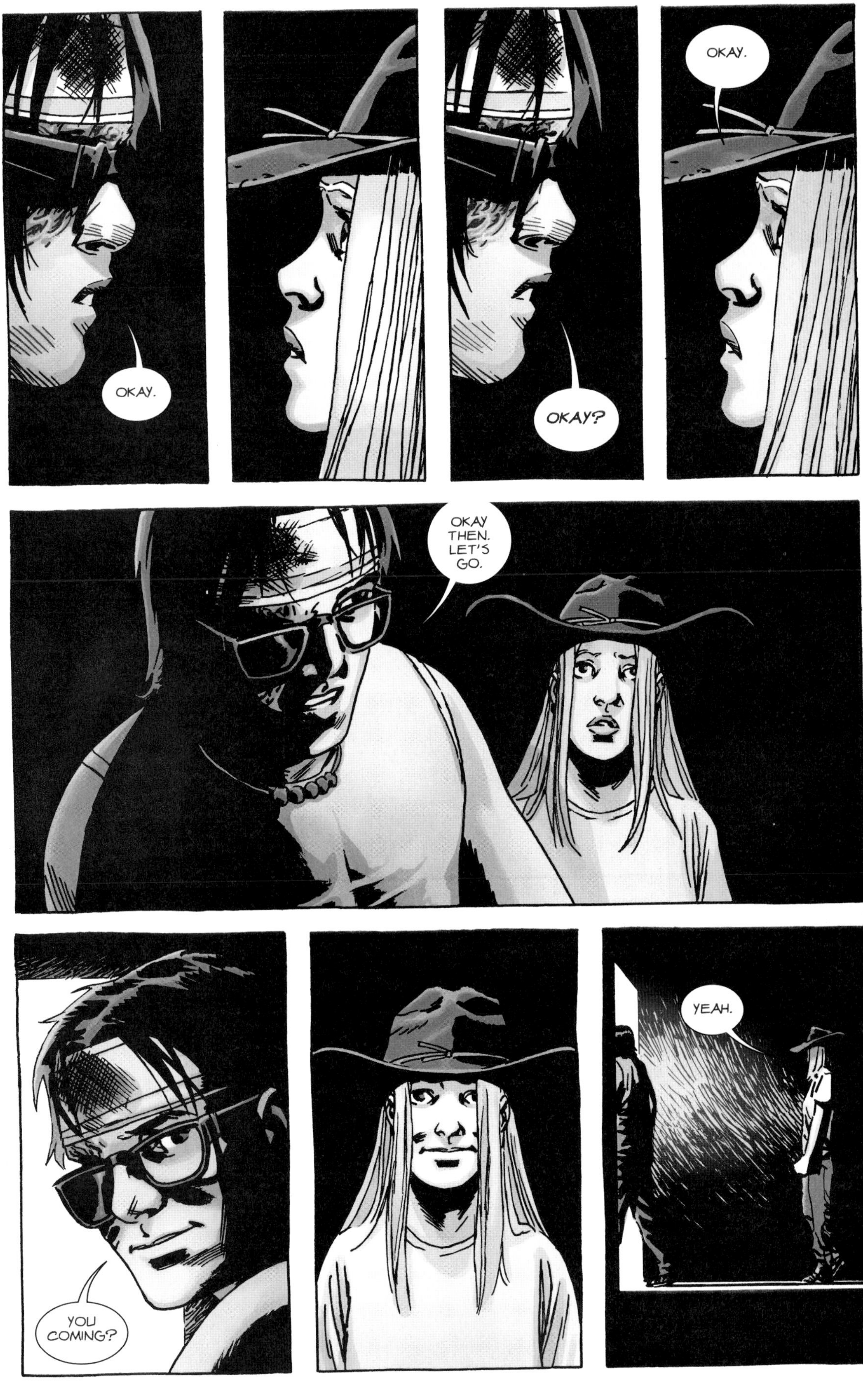

OKAY.
OKAY?
OKAY.
OKAY THEN. LET'S GO.
YOU COMING?
YEAH.

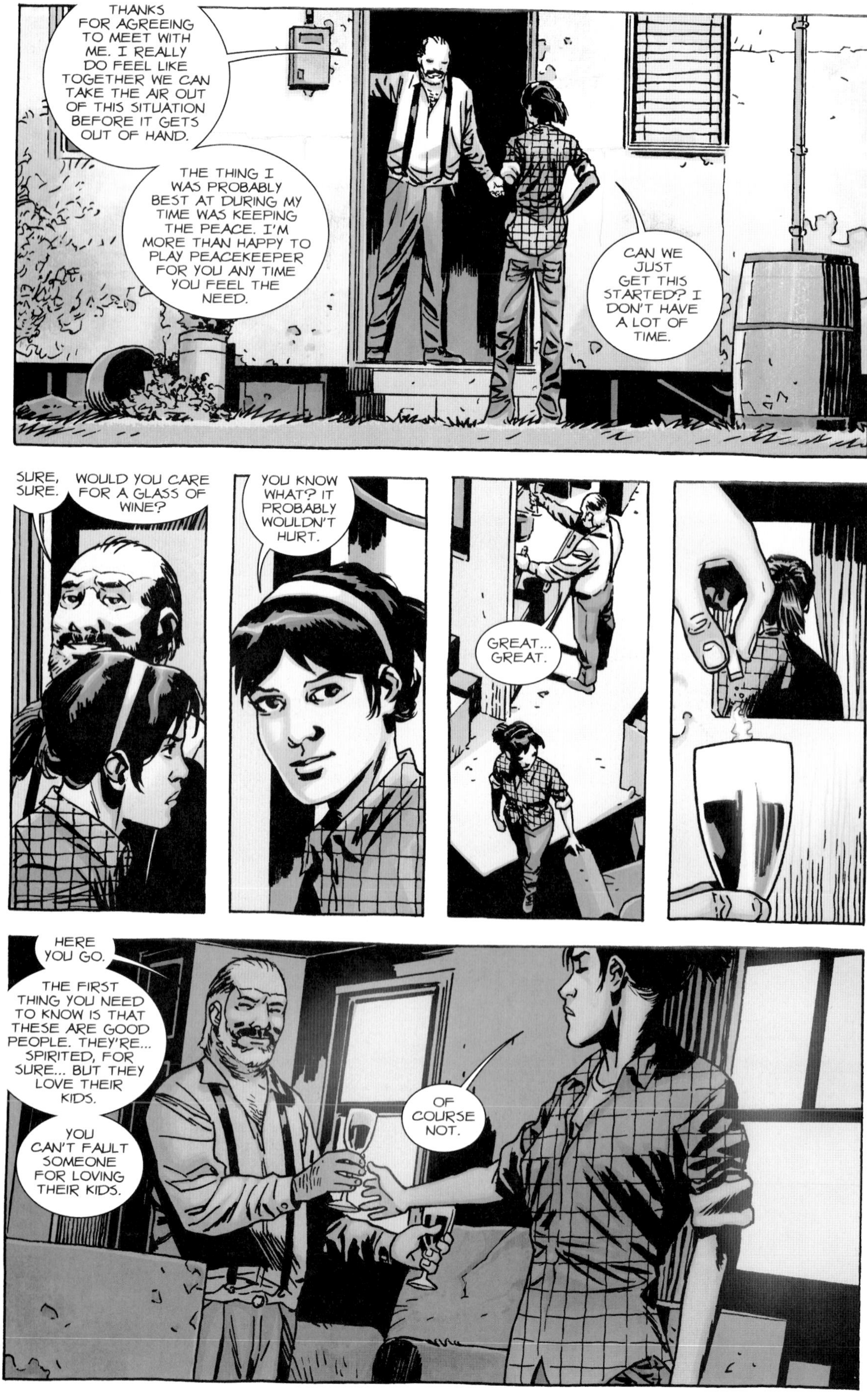
THANKS FOR AGREEING TO MEET WITH ME. I REALLY DO FEEL LIKE TOGETHER WE CAN TAKE THE AIR OUT OF THIS SITUATION BEFORE IT GETS OUT OF HAND.
THE THING I WAS PROBABLY BEST AT DURING MY TIME WAS KEEPING THE PEACE. I'M MORE THAN HAPPY TO PLAY PEACEKEEPER FOR YOU ANY TIME YOU FEEL THE NEED.
CAN WE JUST GET THIS STARTED? I DON'T HAVE A LOT OF TIME.
SURE, SURE.
WOULD YOU CARE FOR A GLASS OF WINE?
YOU KNOW WHAT? IT PROBABLY WOULDN'T HURT.
GREAT... GREAT.
HERE YOU GO.
THE FIRST THING YOU NEED TO KNOW IS THAT THESE ARE GOOD PEOPLE. THEY'RE... SPIRITED, FOR SURE... BUT THEY LOVE THEIR KIDS.
YOU CAN'T FAULT SOMEONE FOR LOVING THEIR KIDS.
OF COURSE NOT.

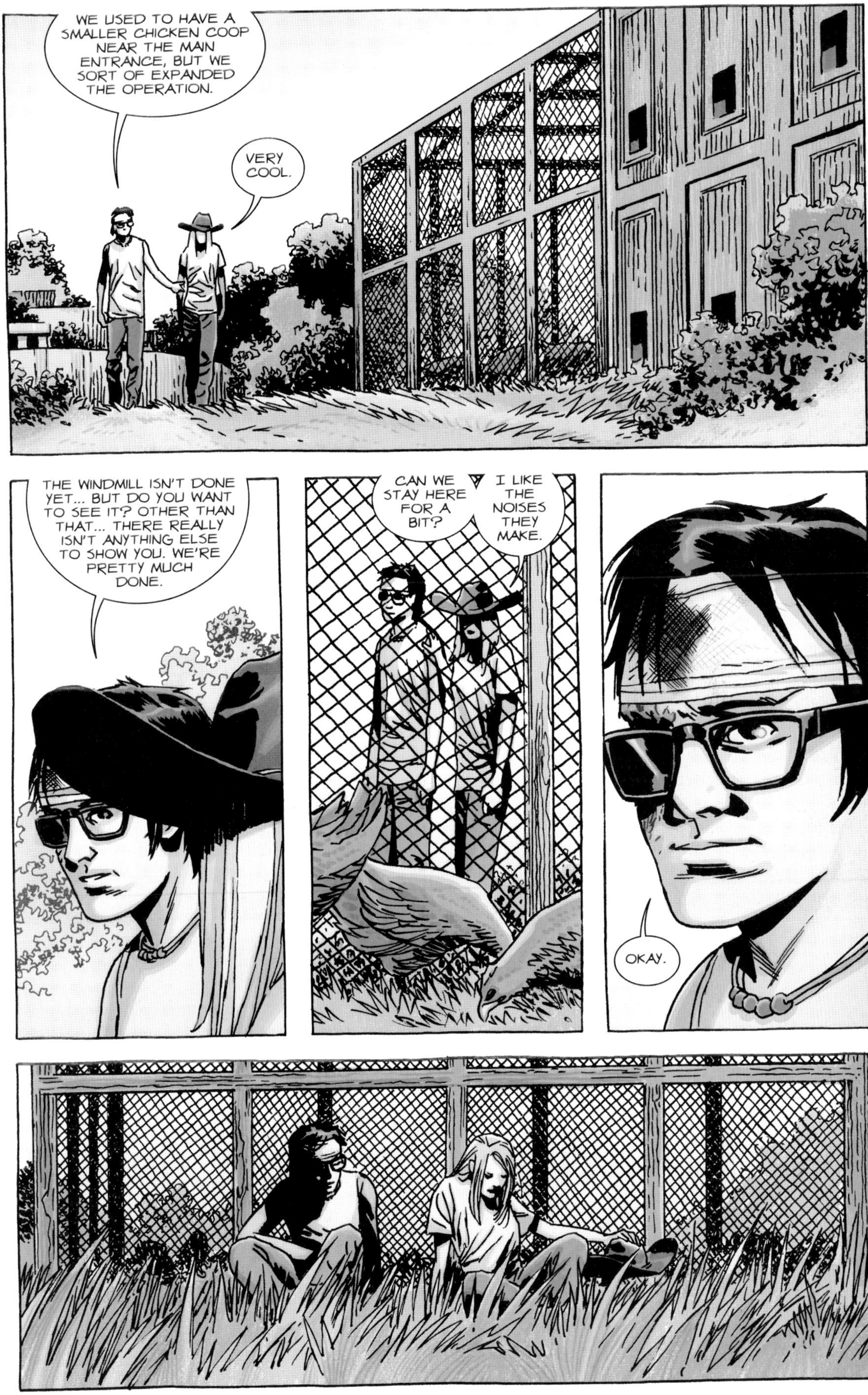
WE USED TO HAVE A SMALLER CHICKEN COOP NEAR THE MAIN ENTRANCE, BUT WE SORT OF EXPANDED THE OPERATION.
VERY COOL.
THE WINDMILL ISN'T DONE YET... BUT DO YOU WANT TO SEE IT? OTHER THAN THAT... THERE REALLY ISN'T ANYTHING ELSE TO SHOW YOU. WE'RE PRETTY MUCH DONE.
CAN WE STAY HERE FOR A BIT?
I LIKE THE NOISES THEY MAKE.
OKAY.

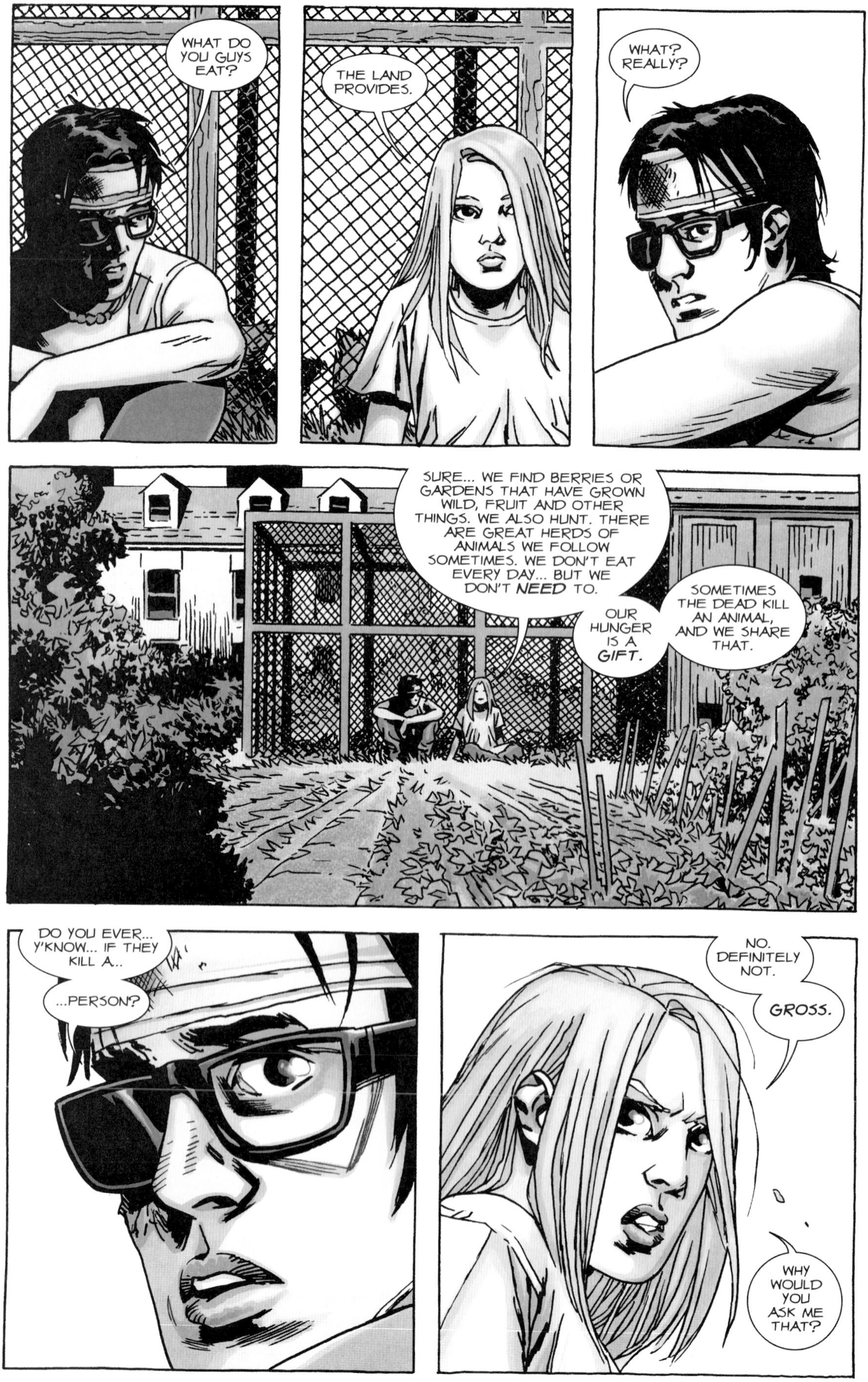
WHAT DO YOU GUYS EAT?
THE LAND PROVIDES.
WHAT? REALLY?
SURE... WE FIND BERRIES OR GARDENS THAT HAVE GROWN WILD, FRUIT AND OTHER THINGS. WE ALSO HUNT. THERE ARE GREAT HERDS OF ANIMALS WE FOLLOW SOMETIMES. WE DON'T EAT EVERY DAY... BUT WE DON'T NEED TO.
OUR HUNGER IS A GIFT.
SOMETIMES THE DEAD KILL AN ANIMAL, AND WE SHARE THAT.
DO YOU EVER... Y'KNOW... IF THEY KILL A..
...PERSON?
NO. DEFINITELY NOT.
GROSS.
WHY WOULD YOU ASK ME THAT?

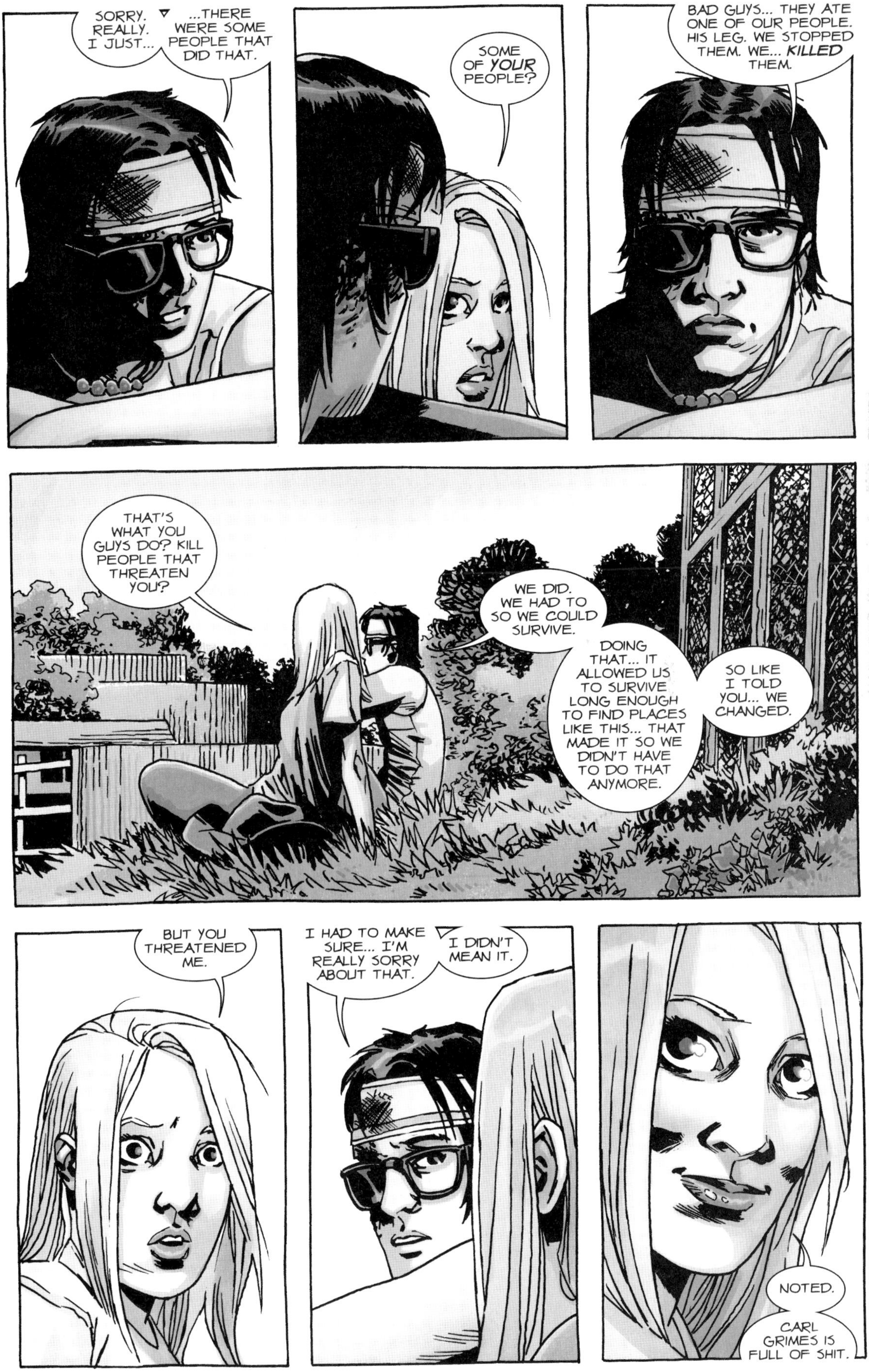

SORRY. REALLY. I JUST...
...THERE WERE SOME PEOPLE THAT DID THAT.
SOME OF *YOUR* PEOPLE?
BAD GUYS... THEY ATE ONE OF OUR PEOPLE. HIS LEG. WE STOPPED THEM. WE... *KILLED* THEM.
THAT'S WHAT YOU GUYS DO? KILL PEOPLE THAT THREATEN YOU?
WE DID. WE HAD TO SO WE COULD SURVIVE.
DOING THAT... IT ALLOWED US TO SURVIVE LONG ENOUGH TO FIND PLACES LIKE THIS... THAT MADE IT SO WE DIDN'T HAVE TO DO THAT ANYMORE.
SO LIKE I TOLD YOU... WE CHANGED.
BUT YOU THREATENED ME.
I HAD TO MAKE SURE... I'M REALLY SORRY ABOUT THAT.
I DIDN'T MEAN IT.
NOTED.
CARL GRIMES IS FULL OF SHIT.

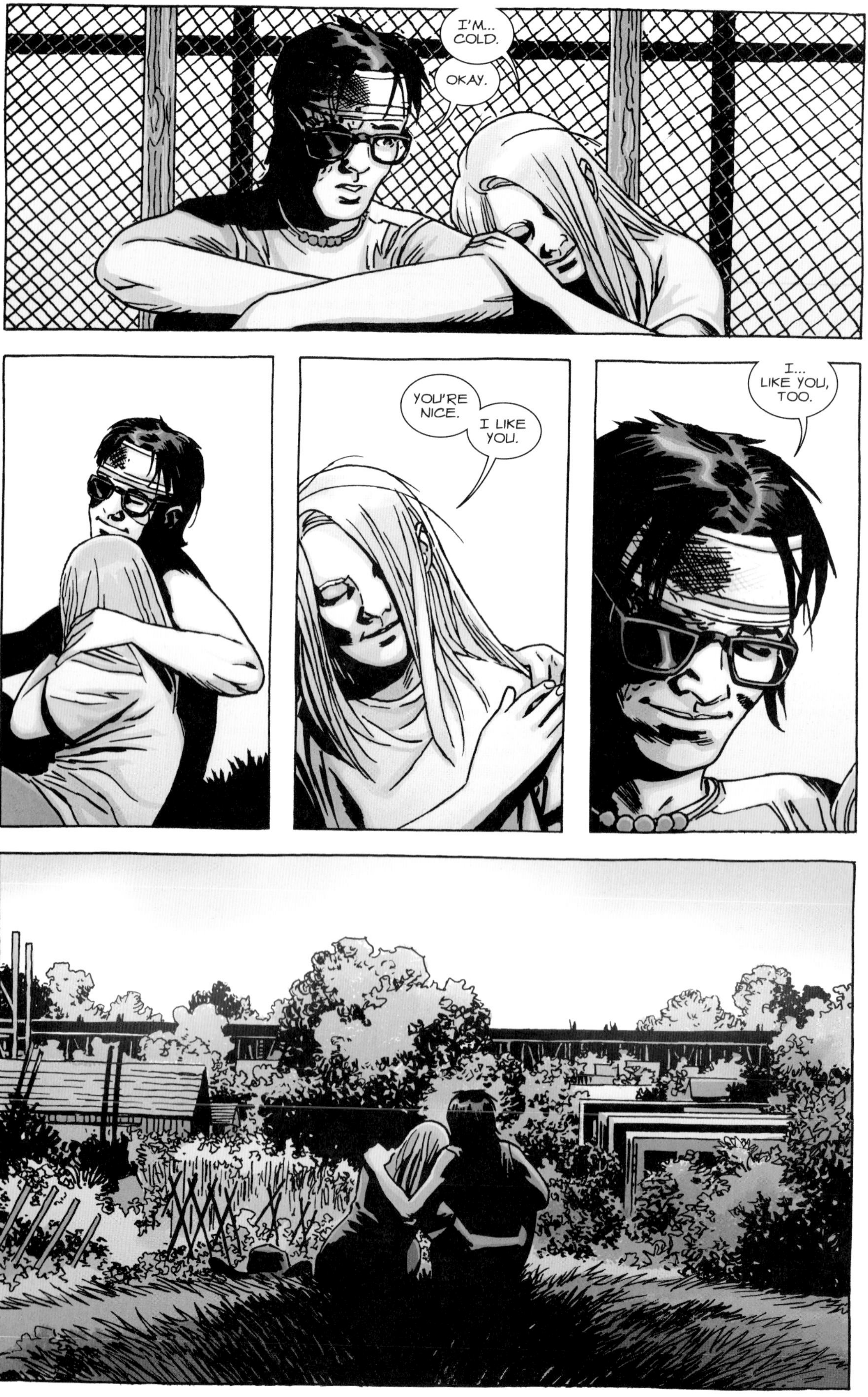
I'M... COLD.
OKAY.
YOU'RE NICE.
I LIKE YOU.
I... LIKE YOU, TOO.

I CAN TALK TO THEM ABOUT CARL. THEY'RE UPSET NOW, BUT THEY'LL SEE THINGS CLEARLY AFTER THEIR EMOTIONS CALM DOWN.

OF COURSE... BY THEN THINGS WILL HAVE TAKEN CARE OF THEMSELVES.

I'M SORRY, I CAN'T EVEN FOCUS... I'M JUST NOT FEELING WELL ALL OF A SUDDEN.

THE ROOM IS SPINNING.

YOU DON'T SAY?

HEH. THAT'S... ODD.

WHAT DID YOU DO?

YOU--

DID YOU FUCKING POISON ME?!

DID YOU--

GREAT, GET WORKED UP... IT'LL GO THROUGH YOUR SYSTEM FASTER.

I CAN TAKE IT.

IS IT TIME...?

IS IT OVER?

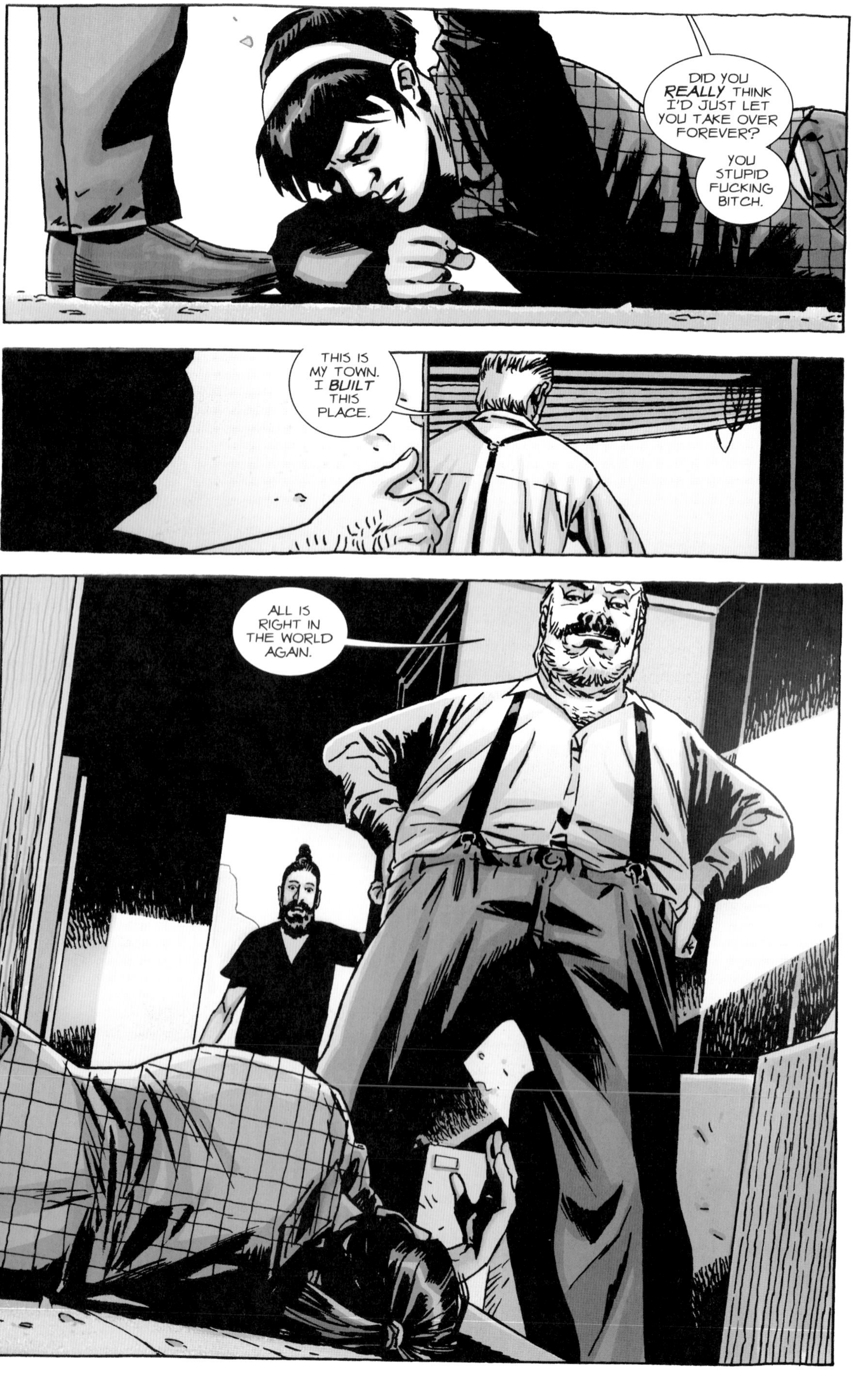
DID YOU REALLY THINK I'D JUST LET YOU TAKE OVER FOREVER?
YOU STUPID FUCKING BITCH.
THIS IS MY TOWN. I BUILT THIS PLACE.
ALL IS RIGHT IN THE WORLD AGAIN.

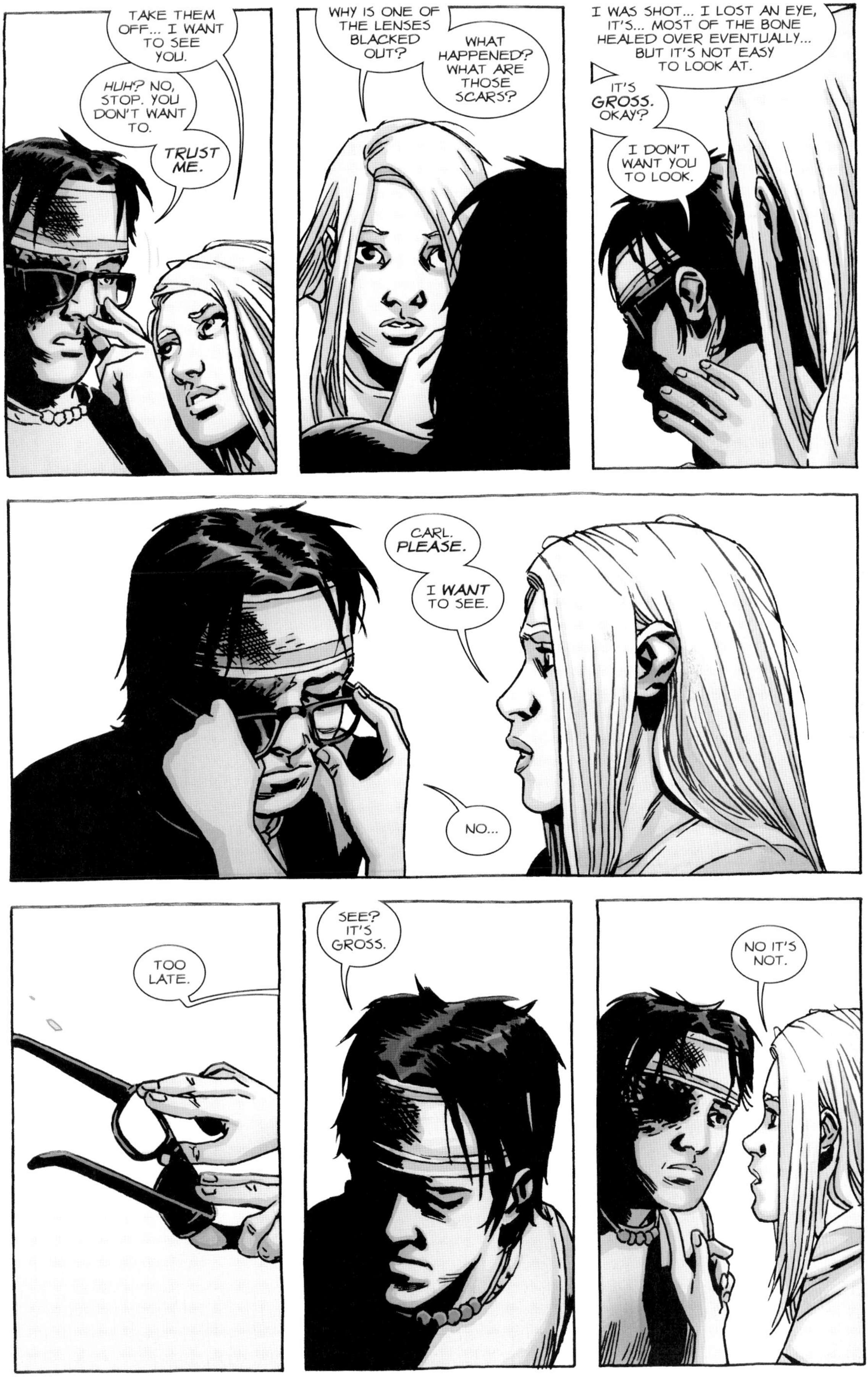
TAKE THEM OFF... I WANT TO SEE YOU.
HUH? NO, STOP. YOU DON'T WANT TO.
TRUST ME.
WHY IS ONE OF THE LENSES BLACKED OUT?
WHAT HAPPENED? WHAT ARE THOSE SCARS?
I WAS SHOT... I LOST AN EYE, IT'S... MOST OF THE BONE HEALED OVER EVENTUALLY... BUT IT'S NOT EASY TO LOOK AT.
IT'S GROSS. OKAY?
I DON'T WANT YOU TO LOOK.
CARL. PLEASE.
I WANT TO SEE.
NO...
TOO LATE.
SEE? IT'S GROSS.
NO IT'S NOT.

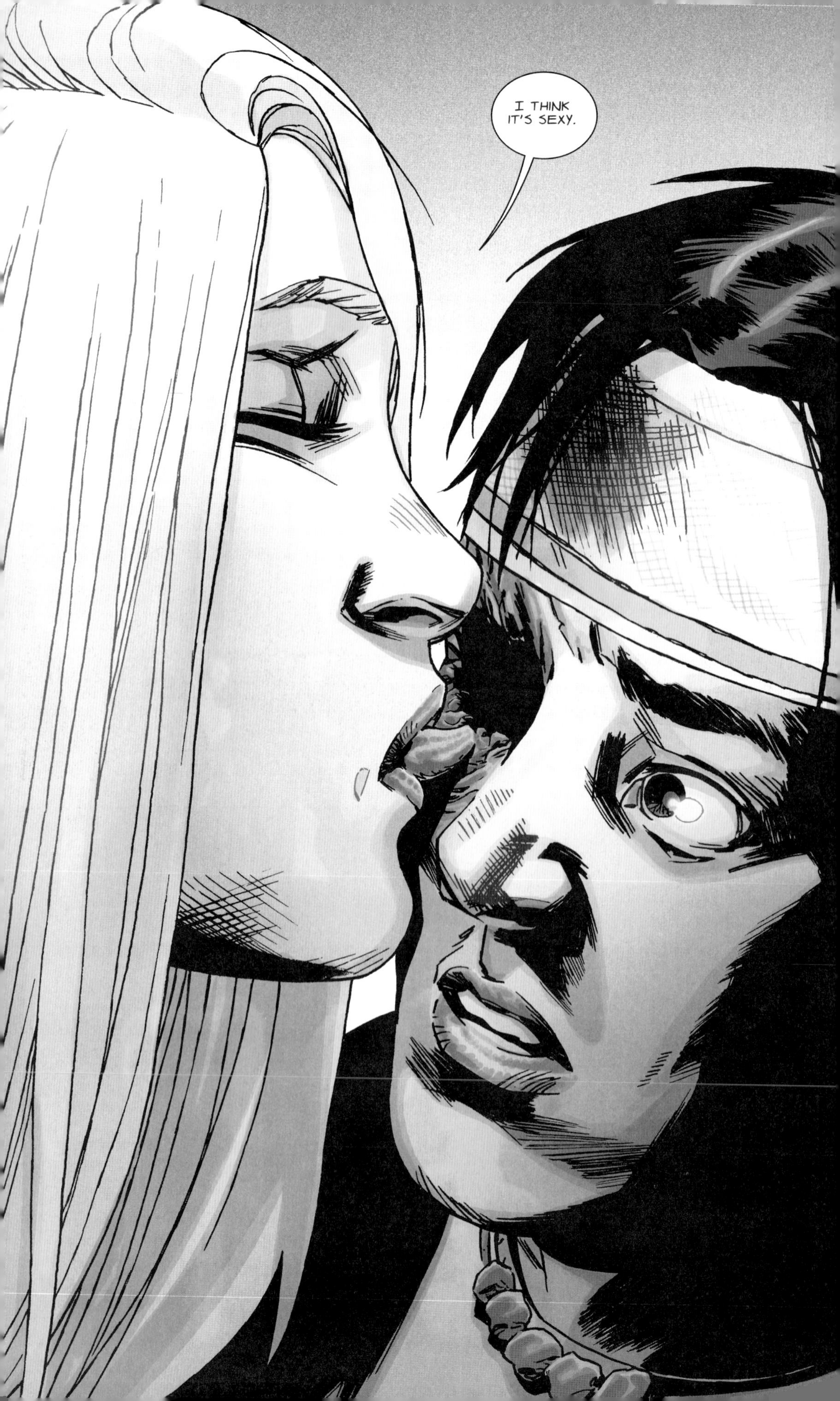
I THINK IT'S SEXY.

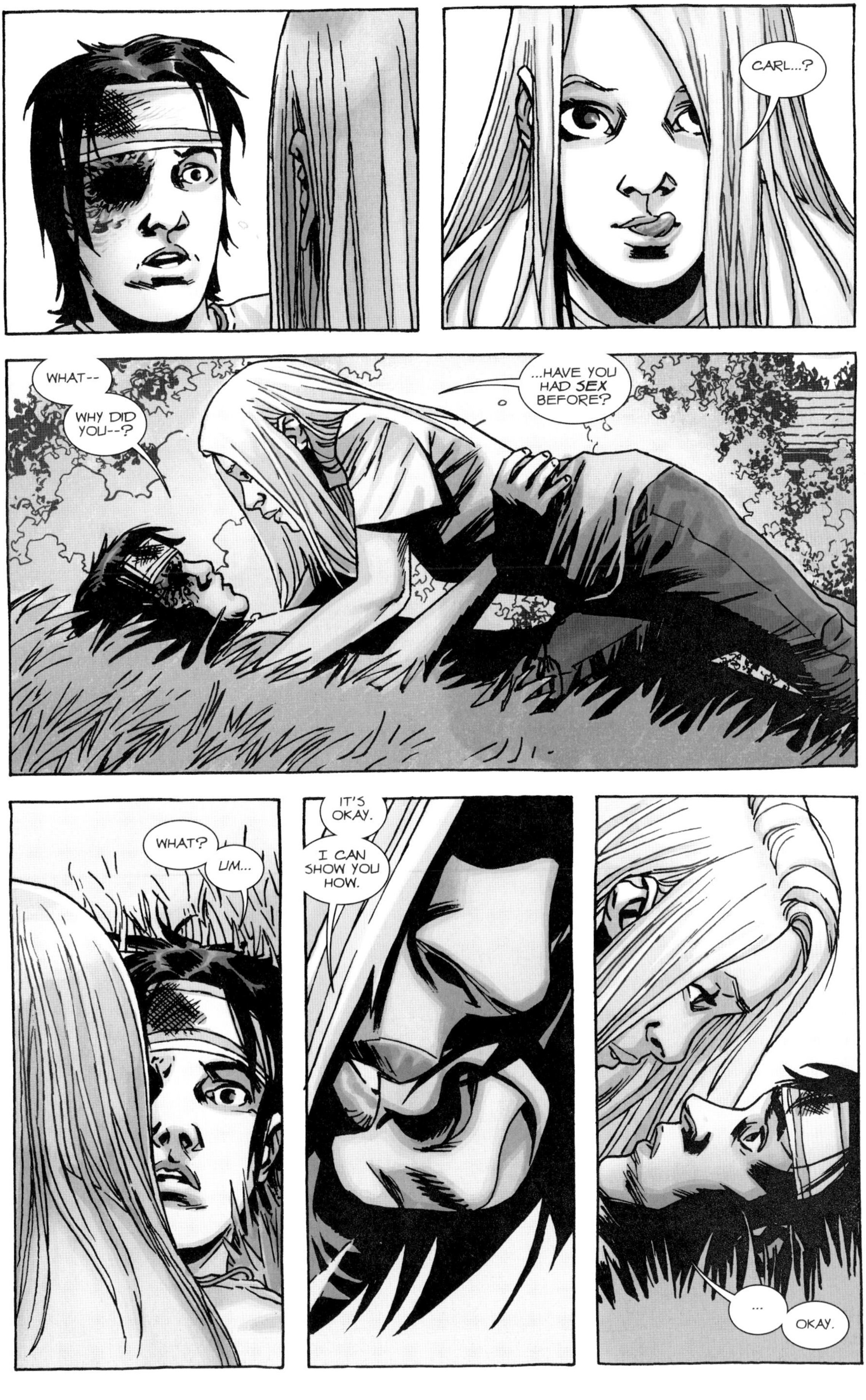
CARL...?
WHAT--
WHY DID YOU--?
...HAVE YOU HAD SEX BEFORE?
WHAT?
UM...
IT'S OKAY.
I CAN SHOW YOU HOW.
...
OKAY.

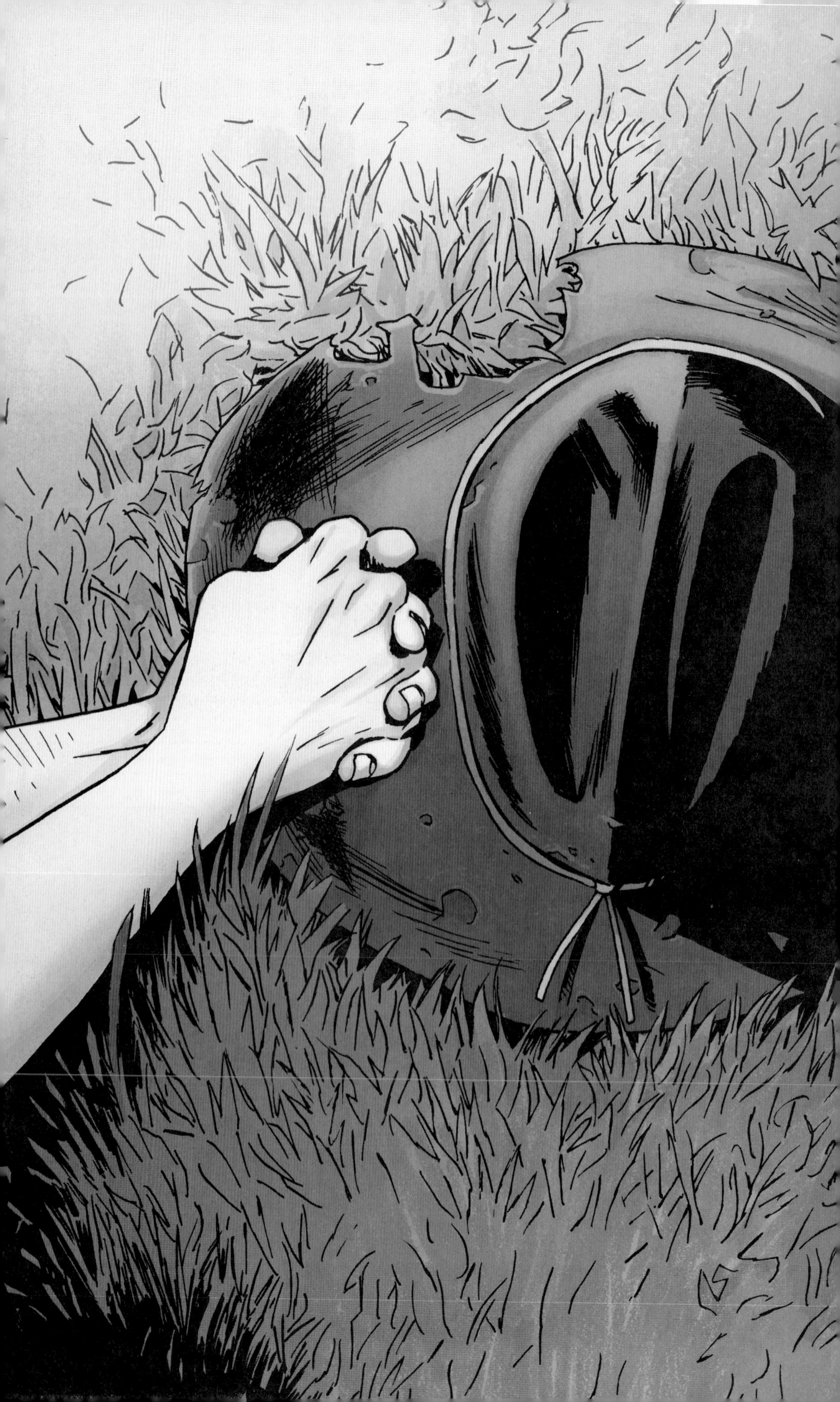

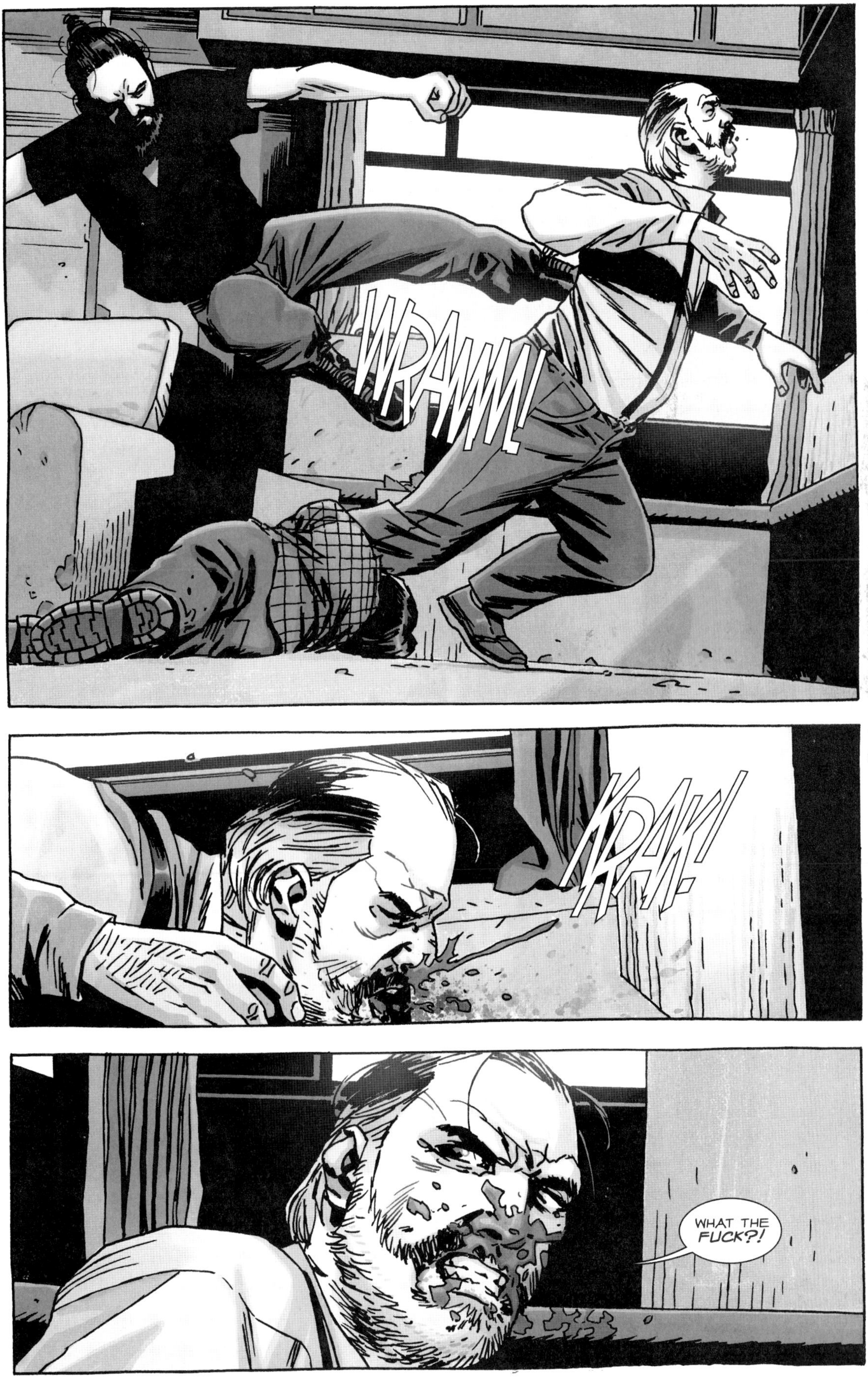
WRAMM!
KRAK!
WHAT THE FUCK?!

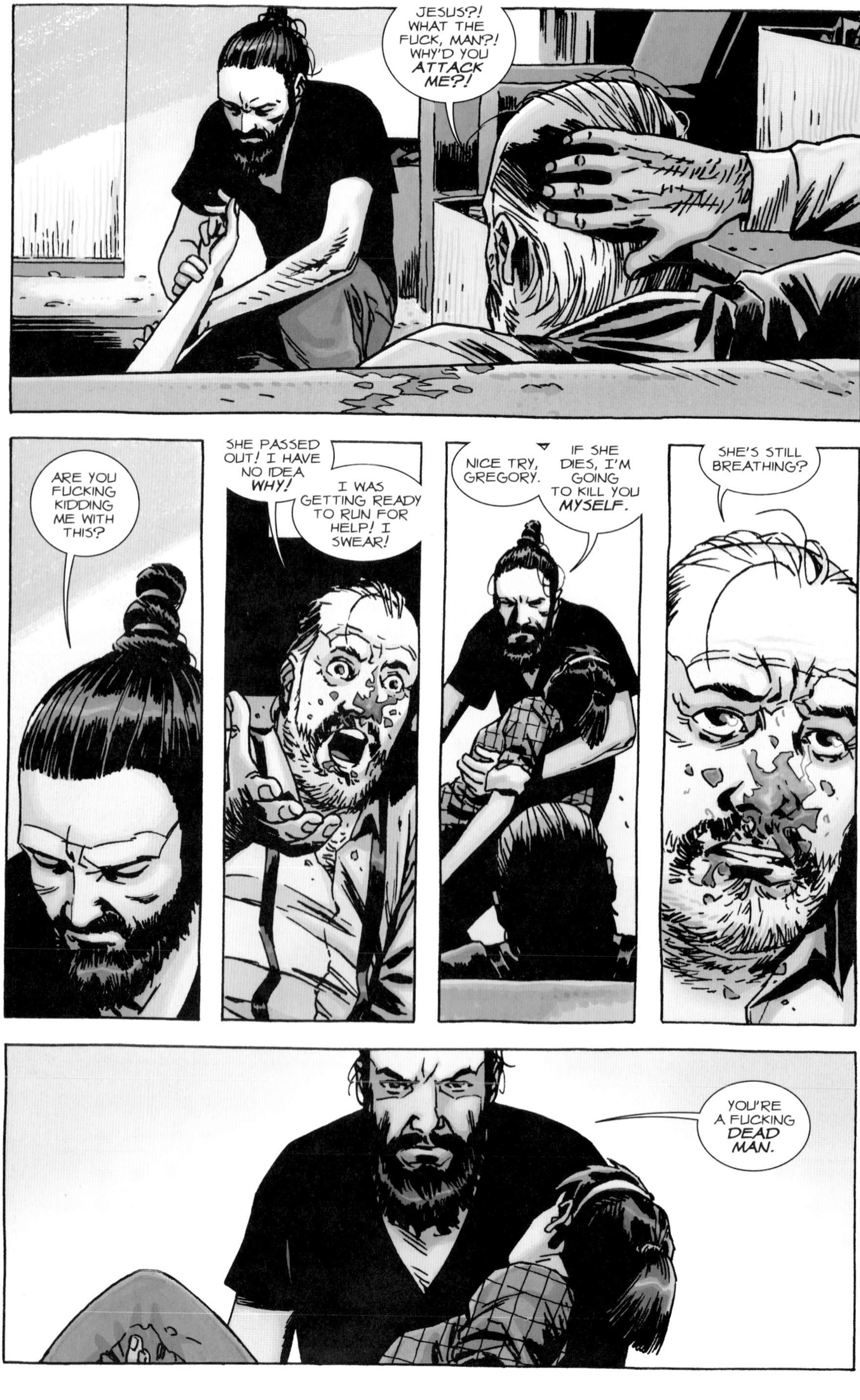
JESUS?! WHAT THE FUCK, MAN?! WHY'D YOU ATTACK ME?!
ARE YOU FUCKING KIDDING ME WITH THIS?
SHE PASSED OUT! I HAVE NO IDEA WHY!
I WAS GETTING READY TO RUN FOR HELP! I SWEAR!
NICE TRY, GREGORY.
IF SHE DIES, I'M GOING TO KILL YOU MYSELF.
SHE'S STILL BREATHING?
YOU'RE A FUCKING DEAD MAN.

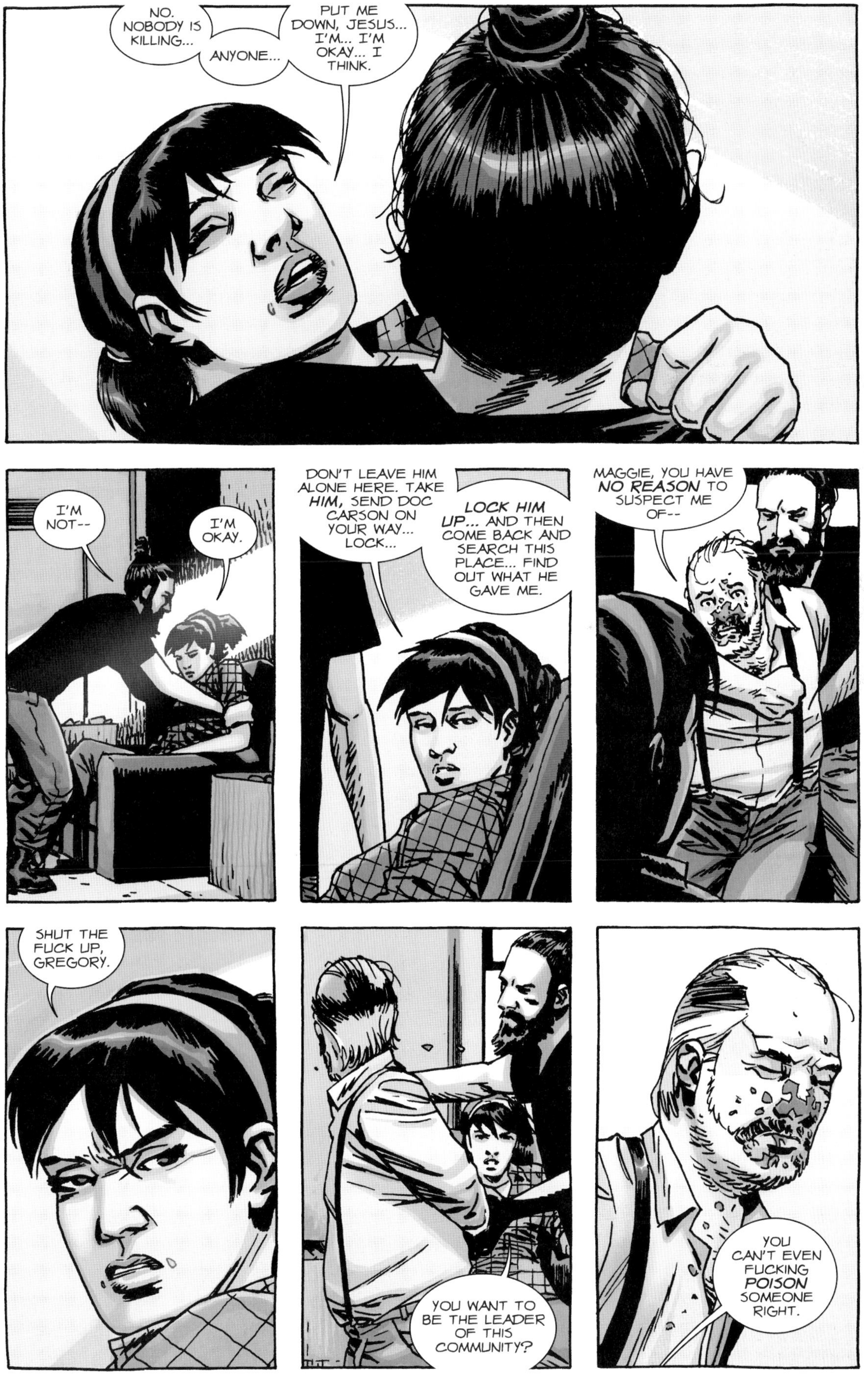
NO. NOBODY IS KILLING...
ANYONE...
PUT ME DOWN, JESUS... I'M... I'M OKAY... I THINK.
I'M NOT--
I'M OKAY.
DON'T LEAVE HIM ALONE HERE. TAKE *HIM,* SEND DOC CARSON ON YOUR WAY... LOCK...
LOCK HIM UP... AND THEN COME BACK AND SEARCH THIS PLACE... FIND OUT WHAT HE GAVE ME.
MAGGIE, YOU HAVE *NO REASON* TO SUSPECT ME OF--
SHUT THE FUCK UP, GREGORY.
YOU WANT TO BE THE LEADER OF THIS COMMUNITY?
YOU CAN'T EVEN FUCKING *POISON* SOMEONE RIGHT.

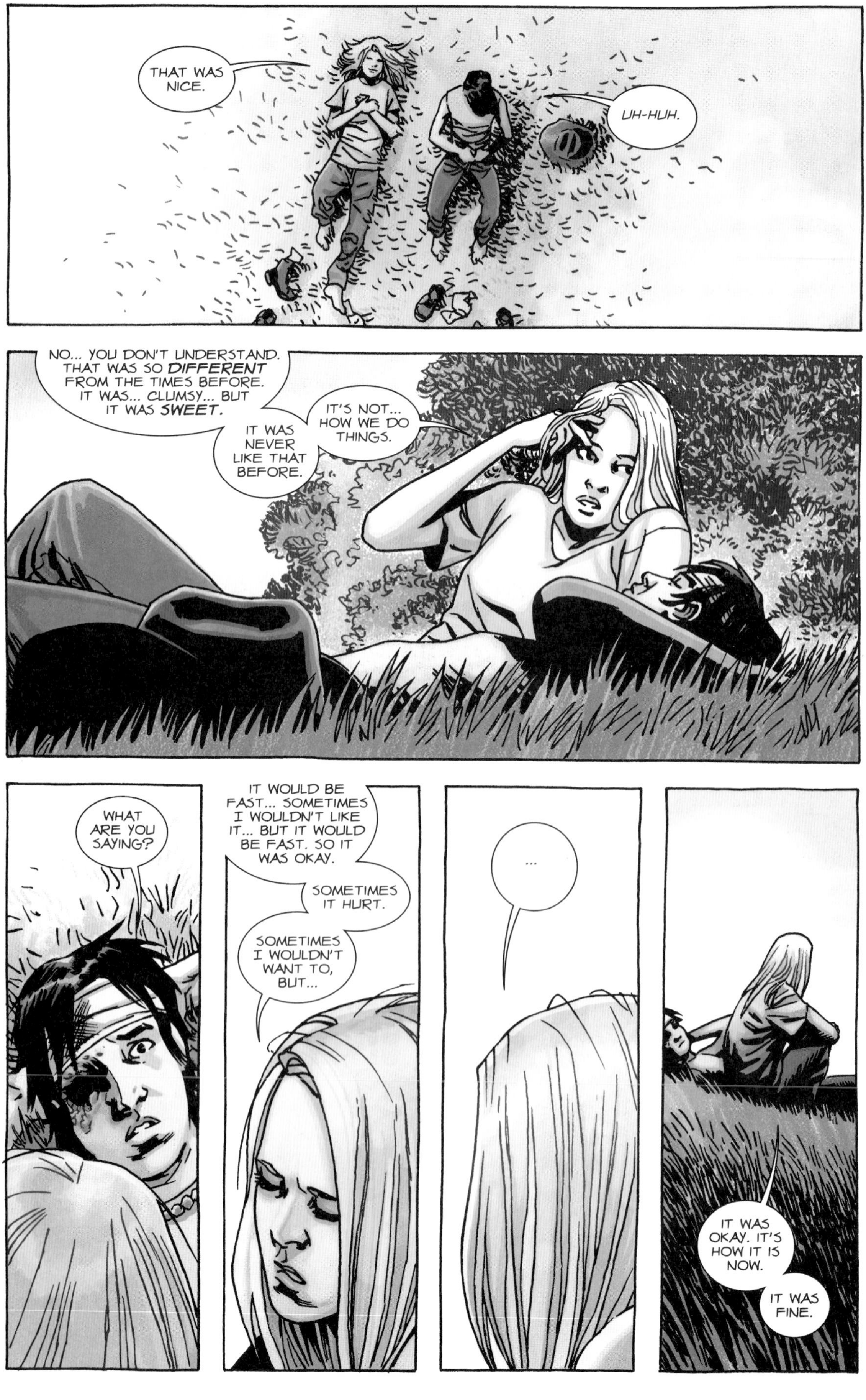
THAT WAS NICE.
UH-HUH.
NO... YOU DON'T UNDERSTAND. THAT WAS SO DIFFERENT FROM THE TIMES BEFORE. IT WAS... CLUMSY... BUT IT WAS SWEET.
IT WAS NEVER LIKE THAT BEFORE.
IT'S NOT... HOW WE DO THINGS.
WHAT ARE YOU SAYING?
IT WOULD BE FAST... SOMETIMES I WOULDN'T LIKE IT... BUT IT WOULD BE FAST. SO IT WAS OKAY.
SOMETIMES IT HURT.
SOMETIMES I WOULDN'T WANT TO, BUT...
...
IT WAS OKAY. IT'S HOW IT IS NOW.
IT WAS FINE.

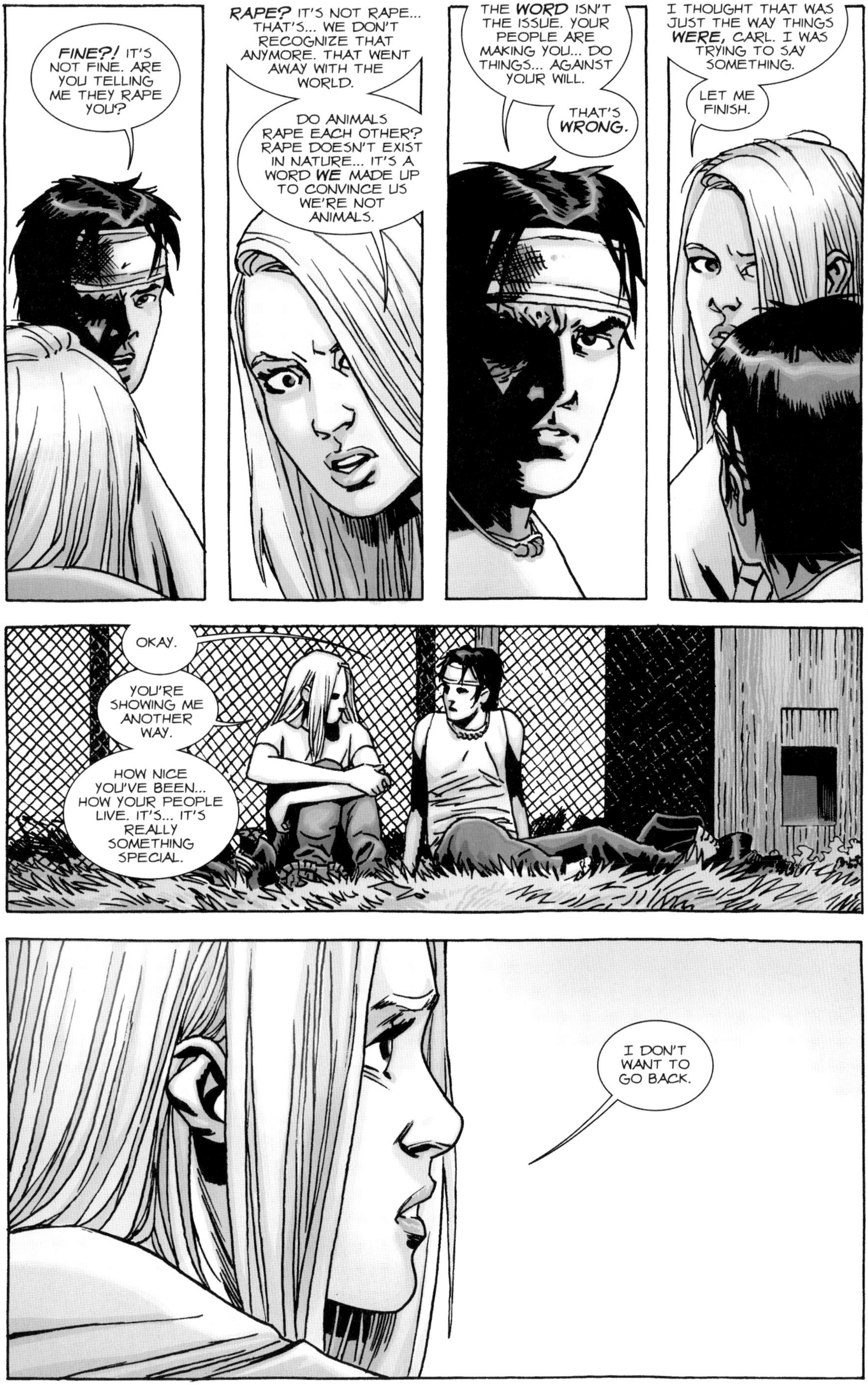
FINE?! IT'S NOT FINE. ARE YOU TELLING ME THEY RAPE YOU?
RAPE? IT'S NOT RAPE... THAT'S... WE DON'T RECOGNIZE THAT ANYMORE. THAT WENT AWAY WITH THE WORLD.
DO ANIMALS RAPE EACH OTHER? RAPE DOESN'T EXIST IN NATURE... IT'S A WORD WE MADE UP TO CONVINCE US WE'RE NOT ANIMALS.
THE WORD ISN'T THE ISSUE. YOUR PEOPLE ARE MAKING YOU... DO THINGS... AGAINST YOUR WILL.
THAT'S WRONG.
I THOUGHT THAT WAS JUST THE WAY THINGS WERE, CARL. I WAS TRYING TO SAY SOMETHING.
LET ME FINISH.
OKAY.
YOU'RE SHOWING ME ANOTHER WAY.
HOW NICE YOU'VE BEEN... HOW YOUR PEOPLE LIVE. IT'S... IT'S REALLY SOMETHING SPECIAL.
I DON'T WANT TO GO BACK.

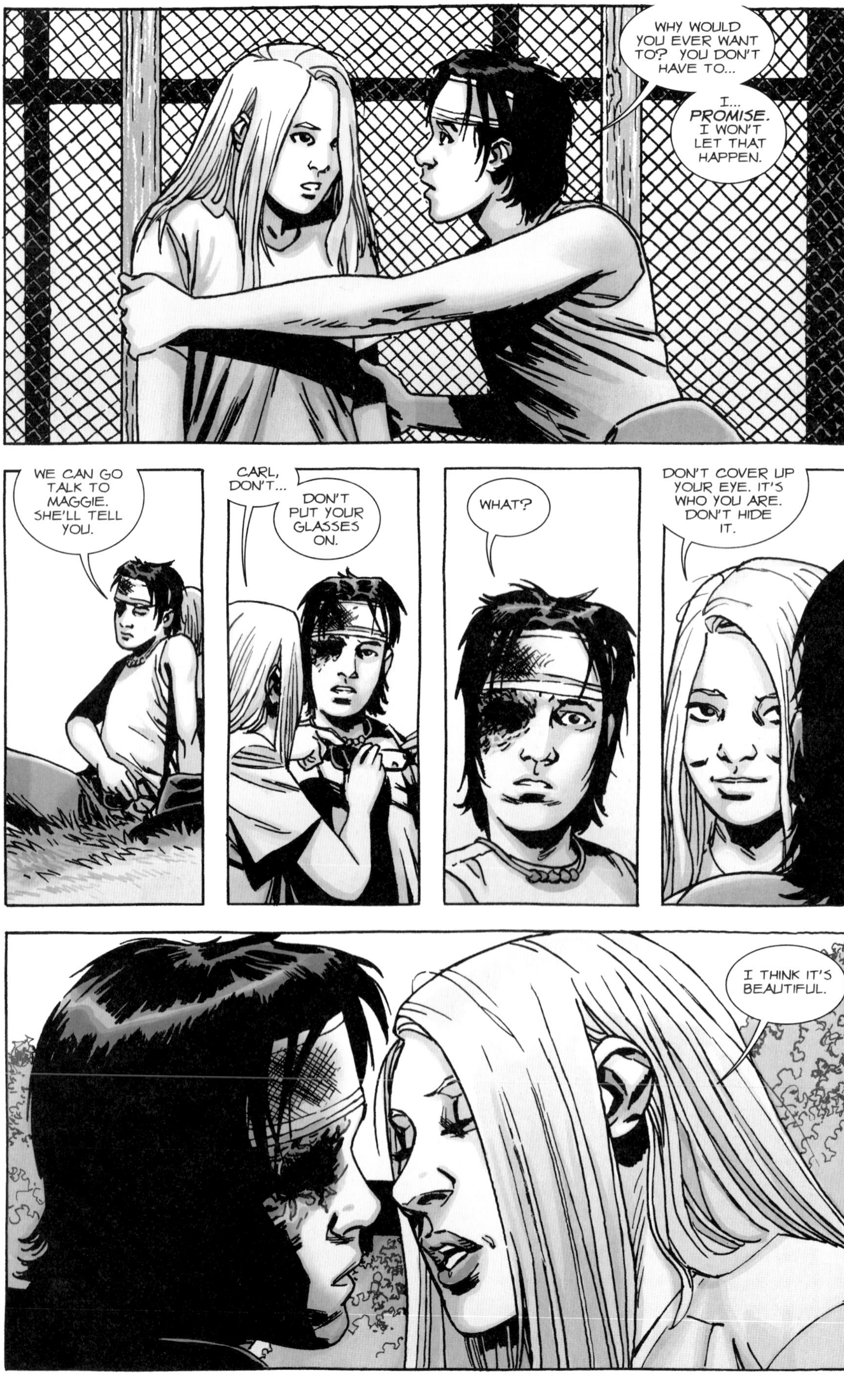
WHY WOULD YOU EVER WANT TO? YOU DON'T HAVE TO...
I... PROMISE. I WON'T LET THAT HAPPEN.
WE CAN GO TALK TO MAGGIE. SHE'LL TELL YOU.
CARL, DON'T...
DON'T PUT YOUR GLASSES ON.
WHAT?
DON'T COVER UP YOUR EYE. IT'S WHO YOU ARE. DON'T HIDE IT.
I THINK IT'S BEAUTIFUL.

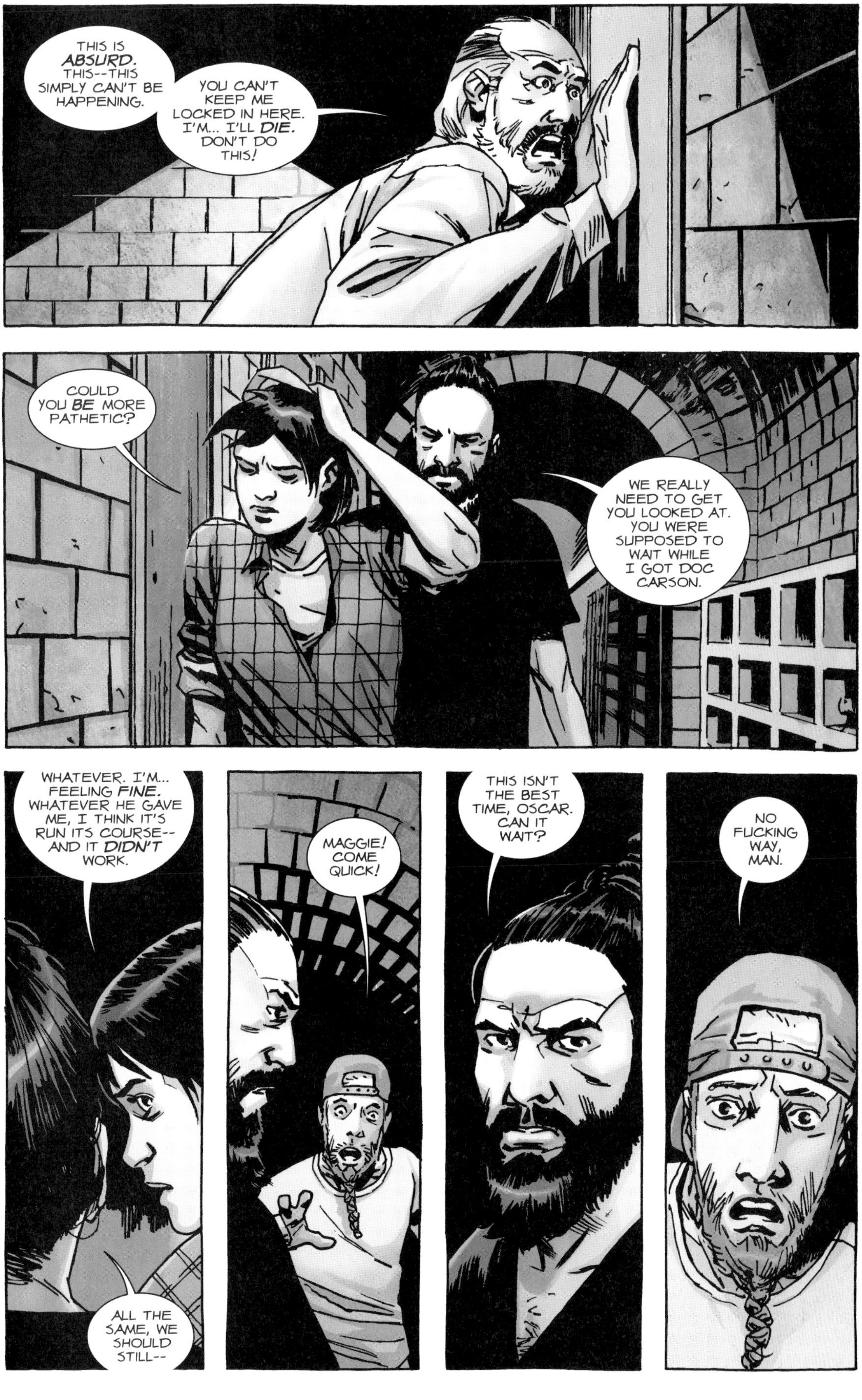
THIS IS ABSURD. THIS--THIS SIMPLY CAN'T BE HAPPENING.
YOU CAN'T KEEP ME LOCKED IN HERE. I'M... I'LL DIE. DON'T DO THIS!
COULD YOU BE MORE PATHETIC?
WE REALLY NEED TO GET YOU LOOKED AT. YOU WERE SUPPOSED TO WAIT WHILE I GOT DOC CARSON.
WHATEVER. I'M... FEELING FINE. WHATEVER HE GAVE ME, I THINK IT'S RUN ITS COURSE-- AND IT DIDN'T WORK.
ALL THE SAME, WE SHOULD STILL--
MAGGIE! COME QUICK!
THIS ISN'T THE BEST TIME, OSCAR. CAN IT WAIT?
NO FUCKING WAY, MAN.

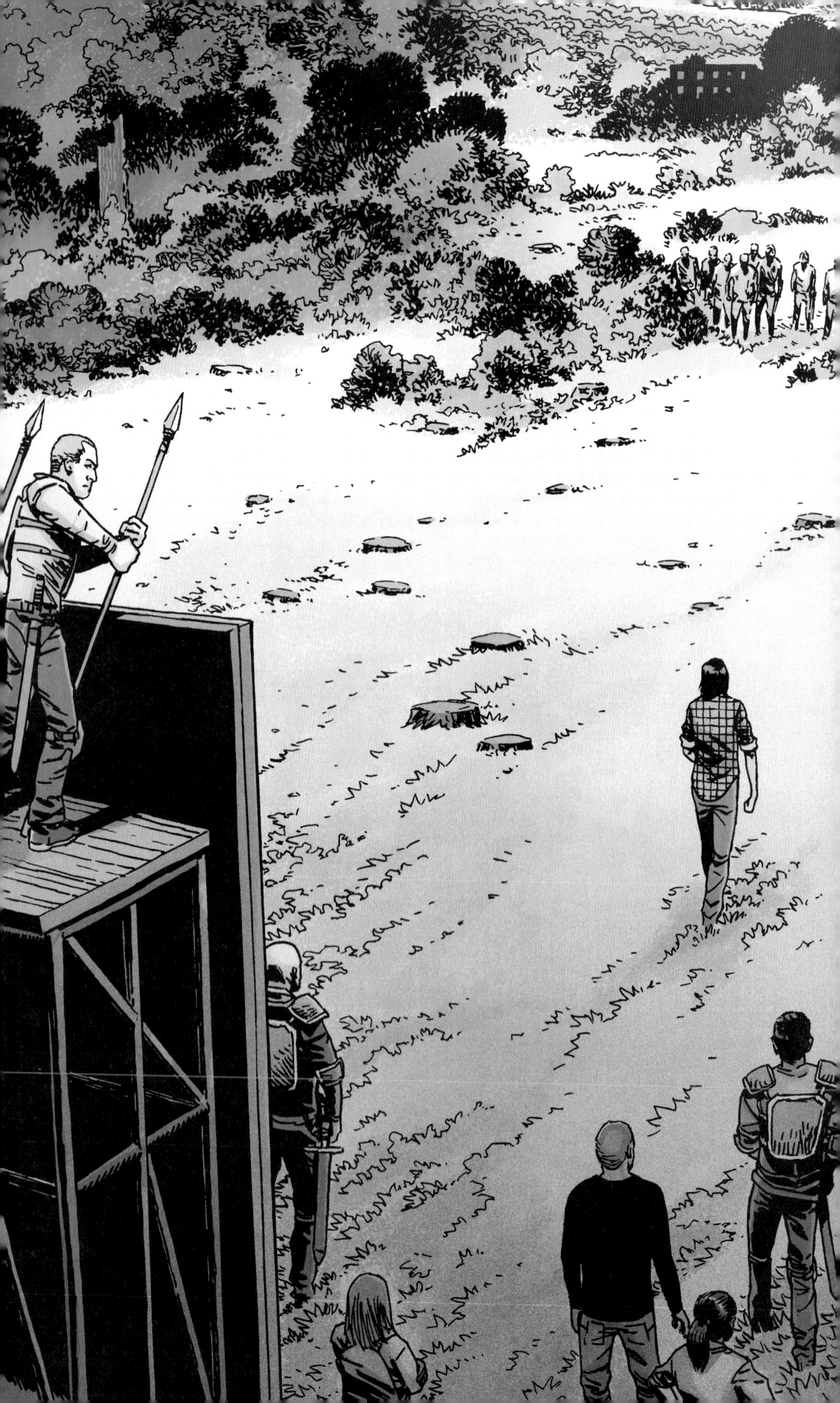

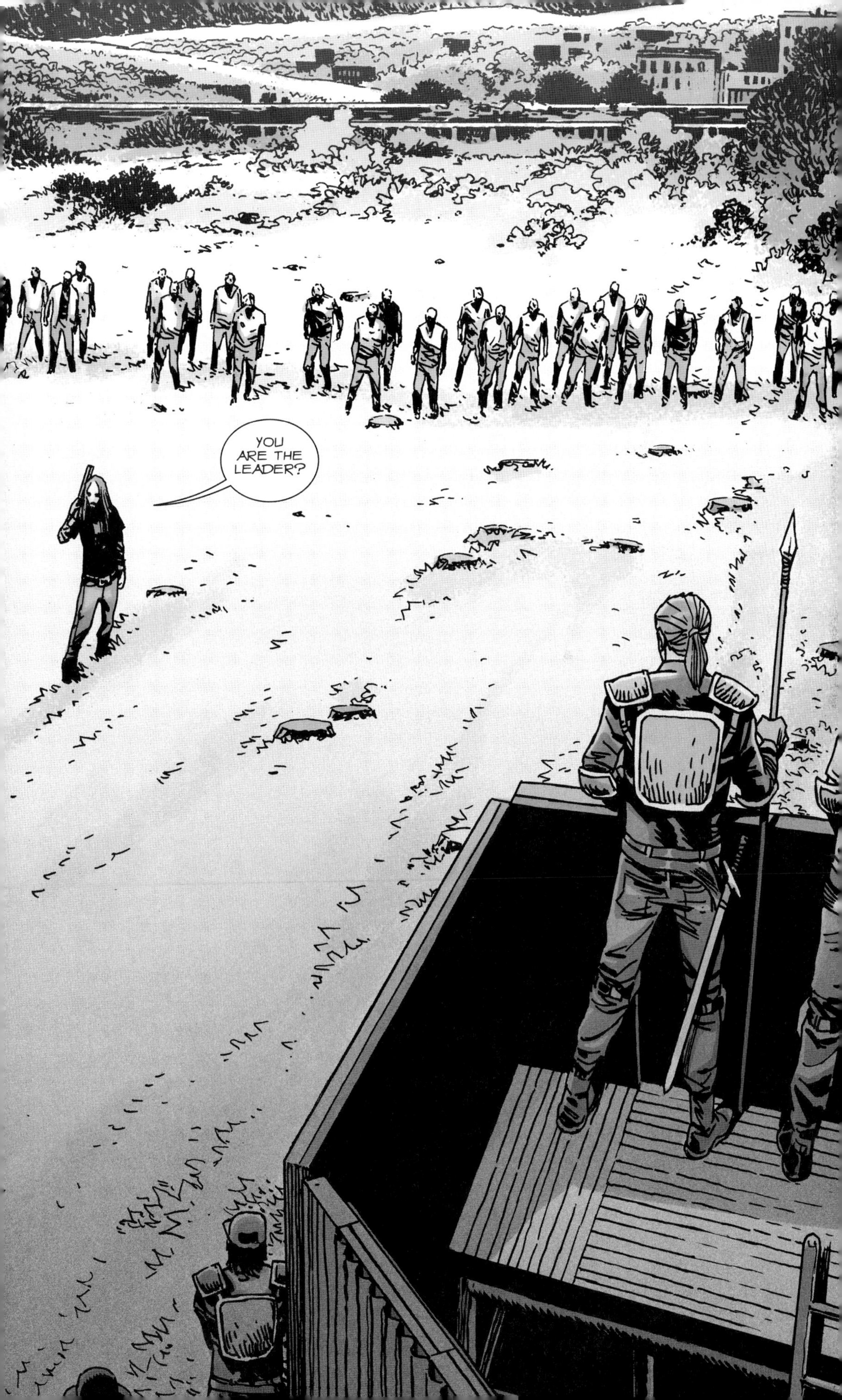
YOU ARE THE LEADER?

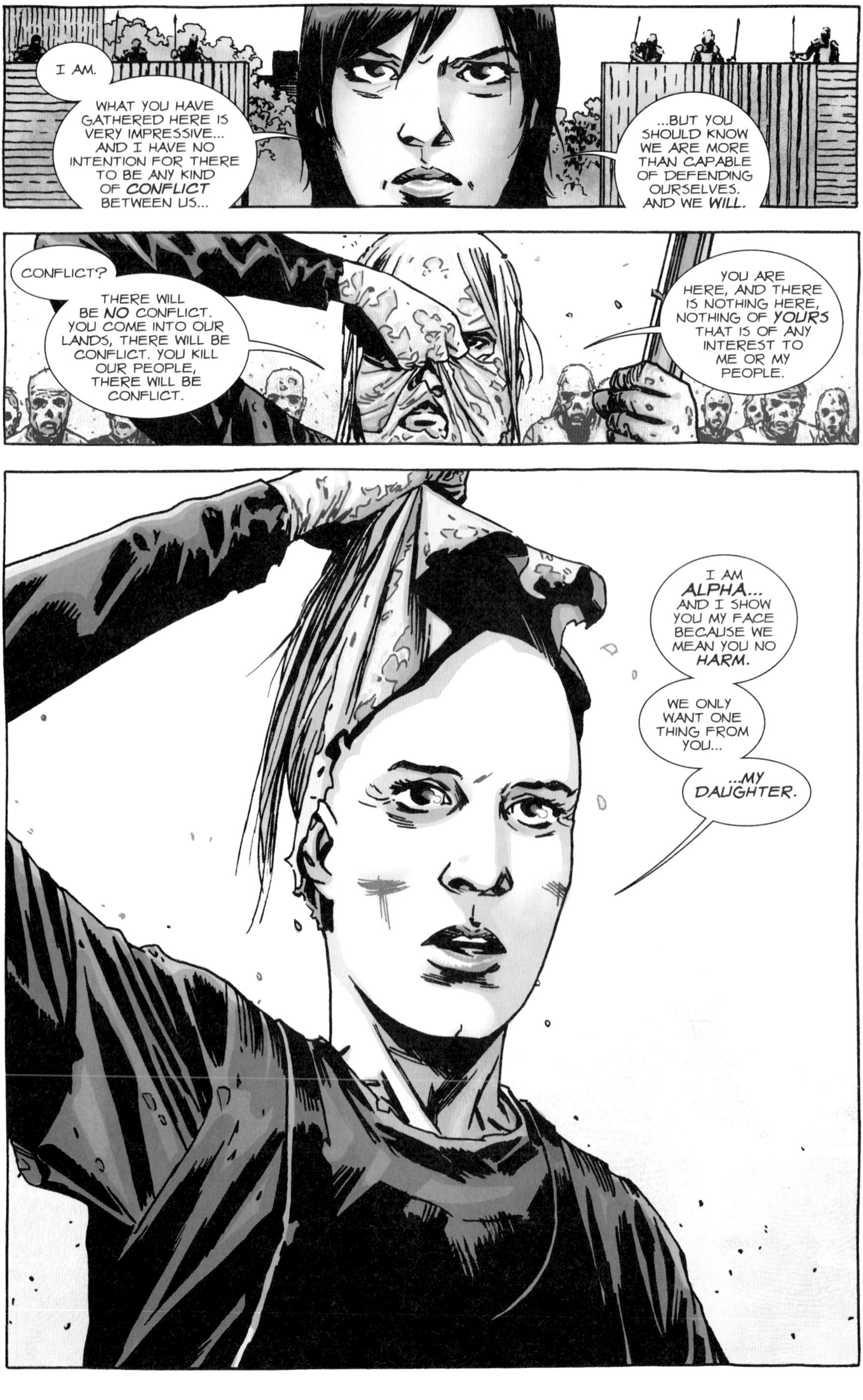
I AM.
WHAT YOU HAVE GATHERED HERE IS VERY IMPRESSIVE... AND I HAVE NO INTENTION FOR THERE TO BE ANY KIND OF CONFLICT BETWEEN US...
...BUT YOU SHOULD KNOW WE ARE MORE THAN CAPABLE OF DEFENDING OURSELVES. AND WE WILL.
CONFLICT?
THERE WILL BE NO CONFLICT. YOU COME INTO OUR LANDS, THERE WILL BE CONFLICT. YOU KILL OUR PEOPLE, THERE WILL BE CONFLICT.
YOU ARE HERE, AND THERE IS NOTHING HERE, NOTHING OF YOURS THAT IS OF ANY INTEREST TO ME OR MY PEOPLE.
I AM ALPHA... AND I SHOW YOU MY FACE BECAUSE WE MEAN YOU NO HARM.
WE ONLY WANT ONE THING FROM YOU...
...MY DAUGHTER.

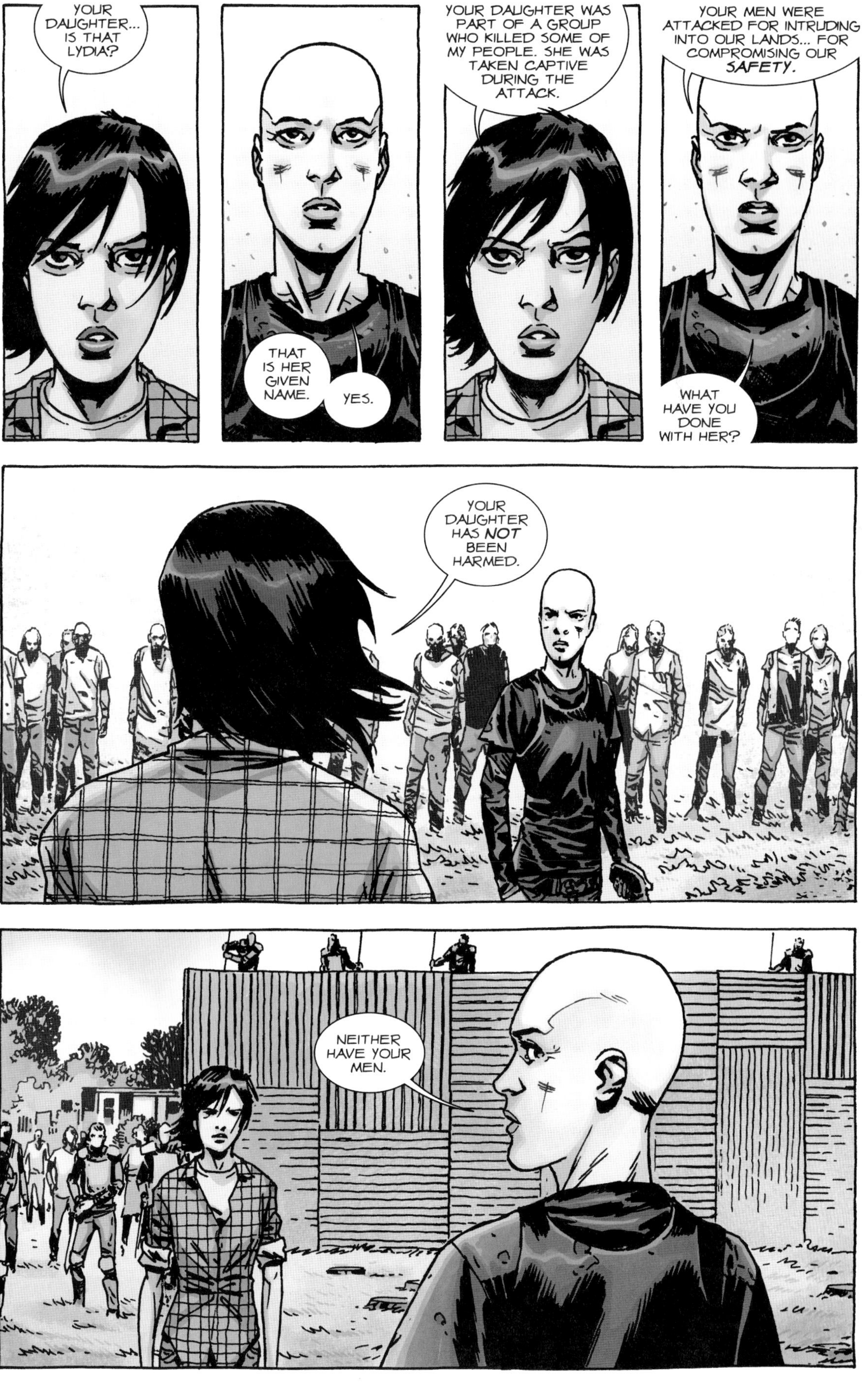
YOUR DAUGHTER... IS THAT LYDIA?
THAT IS HER GIVEN NAME.
YES.
YOUR DAUGHTER WAS PART OF A GROUP WHO KILLED SOME OF MY PEOPLE. SHE WAS TAKEN CAPTIVE DURING THE ATTACK.
YOUR MEN WERE ATTACKED FOR INTRUDING INTO OUR LANDS... FOR COMPROMISING OUR SAFETY.
WHAT HAVE YOU DONE WITH HER?
YOUR DAUGHTER HAS NOT BEEN HARMED.
NEITHER HAVE YOUR MEN.

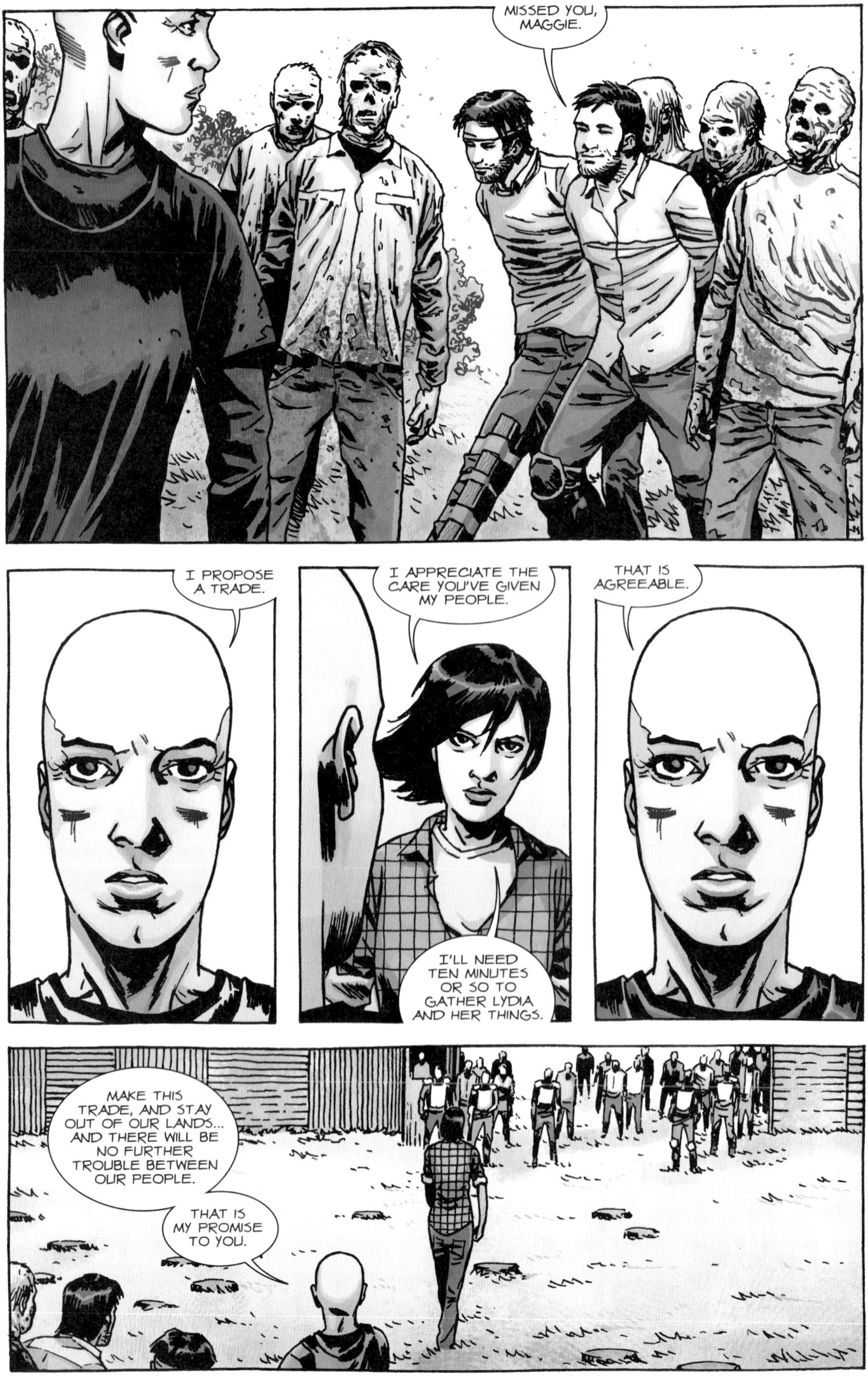
MISSED YOU, MAGGIE.
I PROPOSE A TRADE.
I APPRECIATE THE CARE YOU'VE GIVEN MY PEOPLE.
I'LL NEED TEN MINUTES OR SO TO GATHER LYDIA AND HER THINGS.
THAT IS AGREEABLE.
MAKE THIS TRADE, AND STAY OUT OF OUR LANDS... AND THERE WILL BE NO FURTHER TROUBLE BETWEEN OUR PEOPLE.
THAT IS MY PROMISE TO YOU.

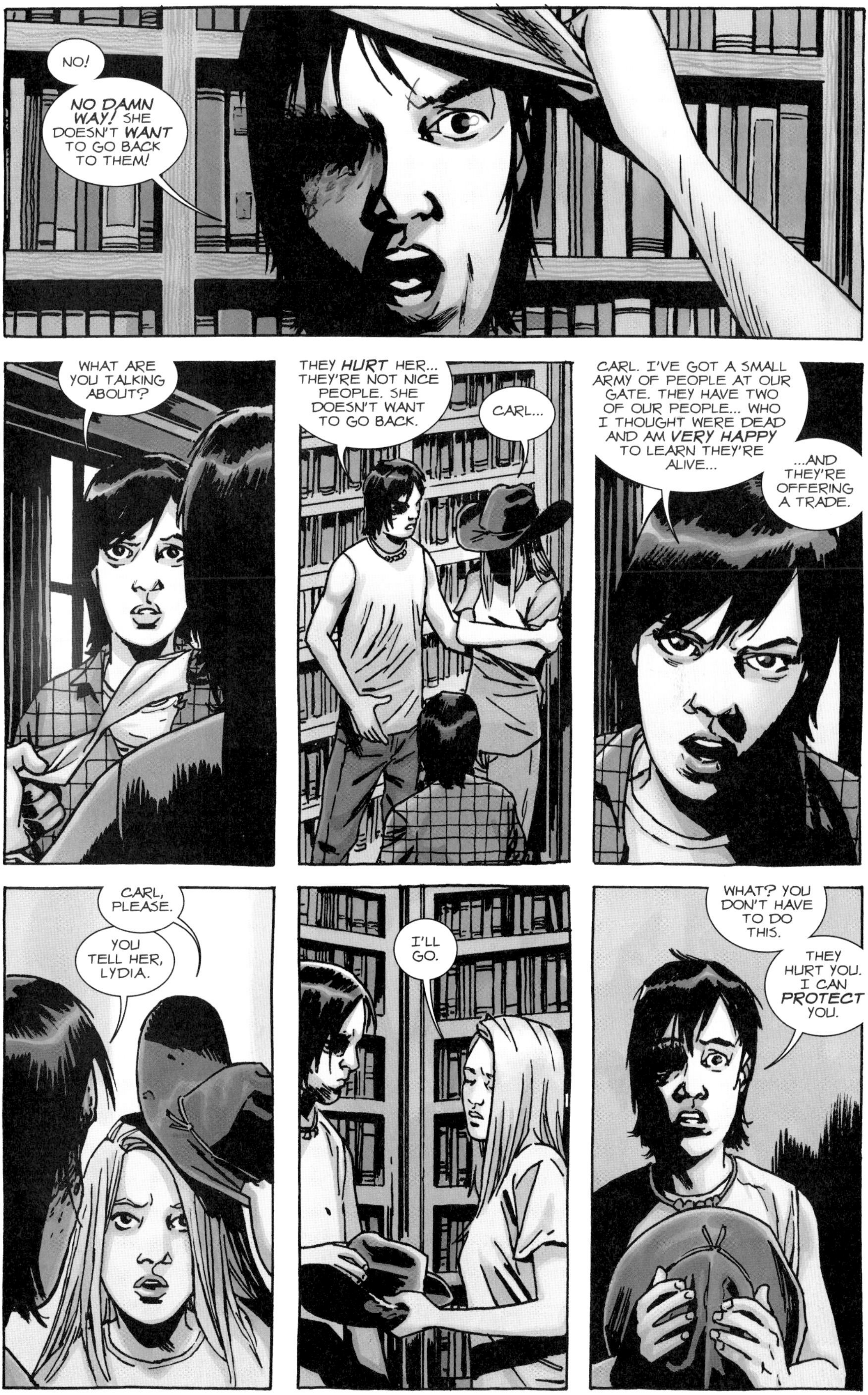
NO!
NO DAMN WAY! SHE DOESN'T WANT TO GO BACK TO THEM!
WHAT ARE YOU TALKING ABOUT?
THEY HURT HER... THEY'RE NOT NICE PEOPLE. SHE DOESN'T WANT TO GO BACK.
CARL...
CARL. I'VE GOT A SMALL ARMY OF PEOPLE AT OUR GATE. THEY HAVE TWO OF OUR PEOPLE... WHO I THOUGHT WERE DEAD AND AM VERY HAPPY TO LEARN THEY'RE ALIVE...
...AND THEY'RE OFFERING A TRADE.
CARL, PLEASE.
YOU TELL HER, LYDIA.
I'LL GO.
WHAT? YOU DON'T HAVE TO DO THIS.
THEY HURT YOU. I CAN PROTECT YOU.

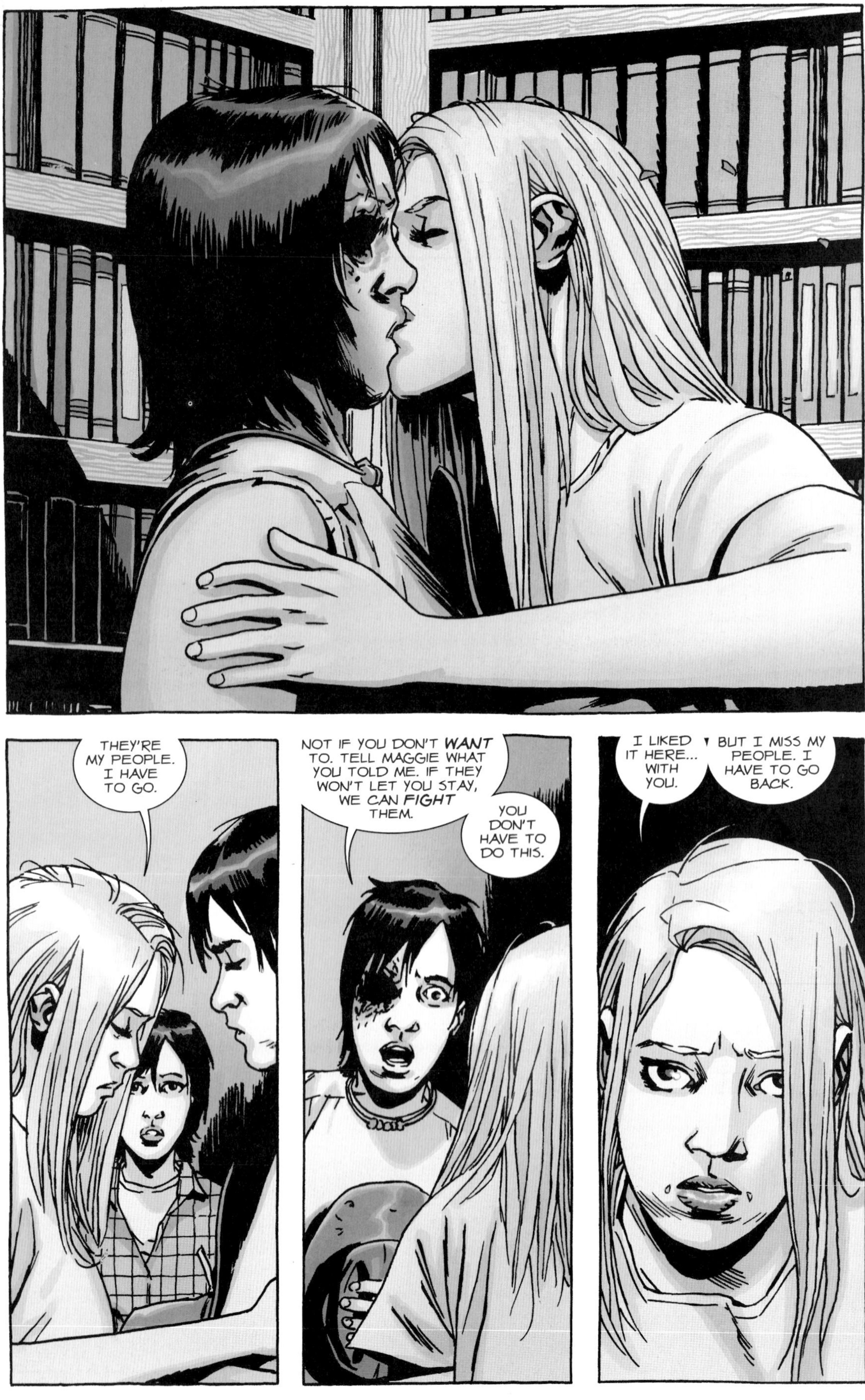
THEY'RE MY PEOPLE. I HAVE TO GO.
NOT IF YOU DON'T WANT TO. TELL MAGGIE WHAT YOU TOLD ME. IF THEY WON'T LET YOU STAY, WE CAN FIGHT THEM.
YOU DON'T HAVE TO DO THIS.
I LIKED IT HERE... WITH YOU.
BUT I MISS MY PEOPLE. I HAVE TO GO BACK.

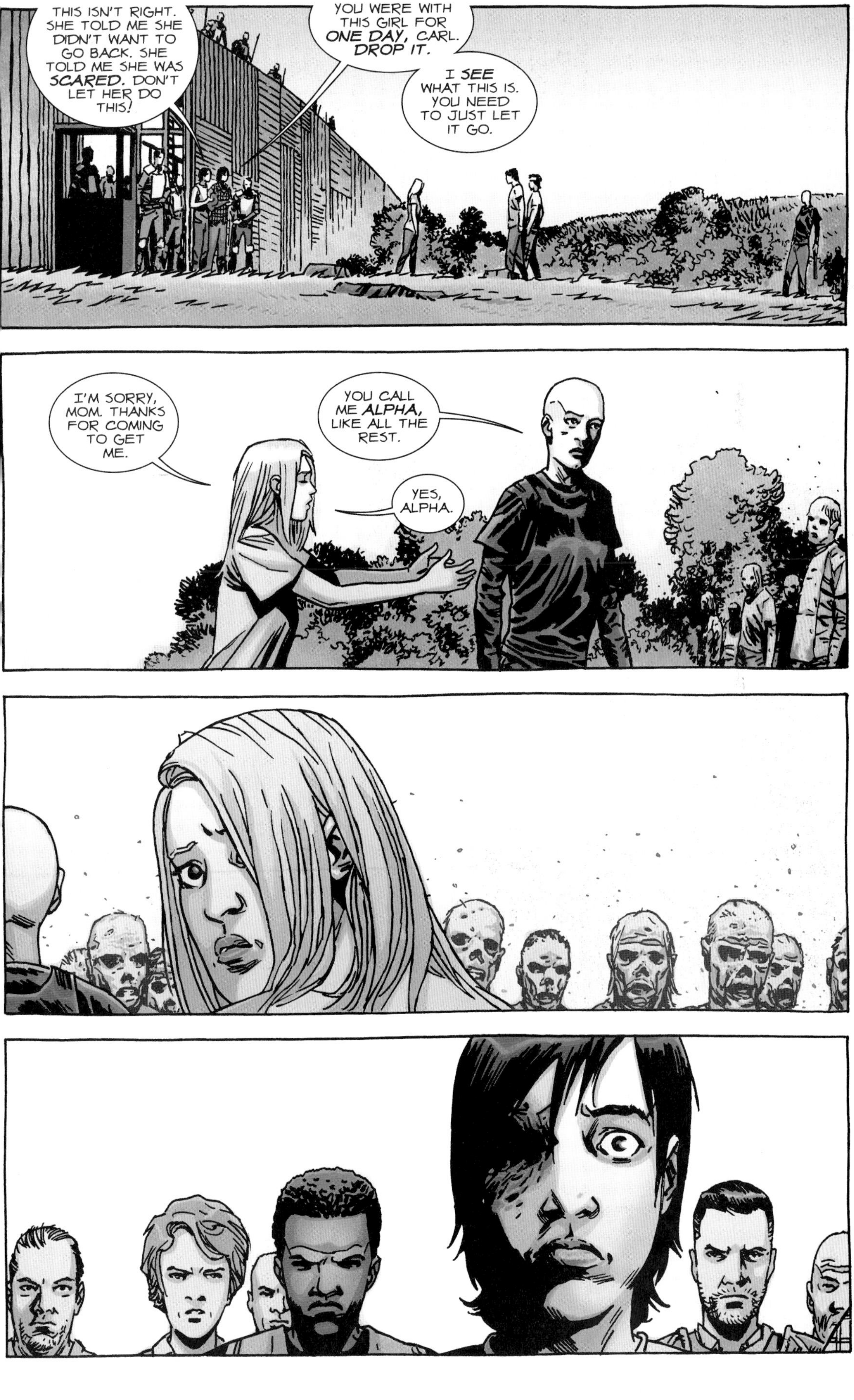
THIS ISN'T RIGHT. SHE TOLD ME SHE DIDN'T WANT TO GO BACK. SHE TOLD ME SHE WAS SCARED. DON'T LET HER DO THIS!
YOU WERE WITH THIS GIRL FOR ONE DAY, CARL. DROP IT.
I SEE WHAT THIS IS. YOU NEED TO JUST LET IT GO.
I'M SORRY, MOM. THANKS FOR COMING TO GET ME.
YOU CALL ME ALPHA, LIKE ALL THE REST.
YES, ALPHA.

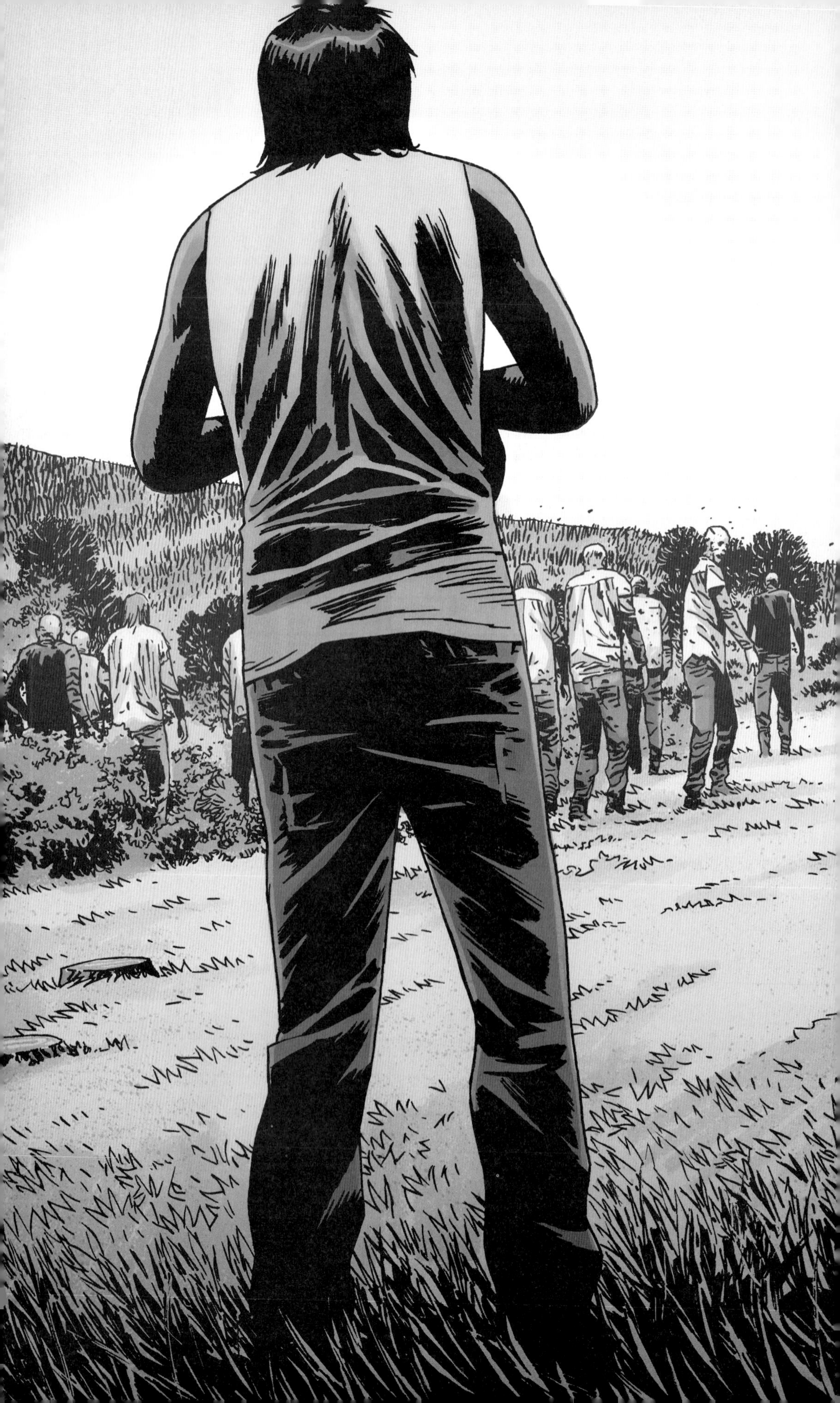

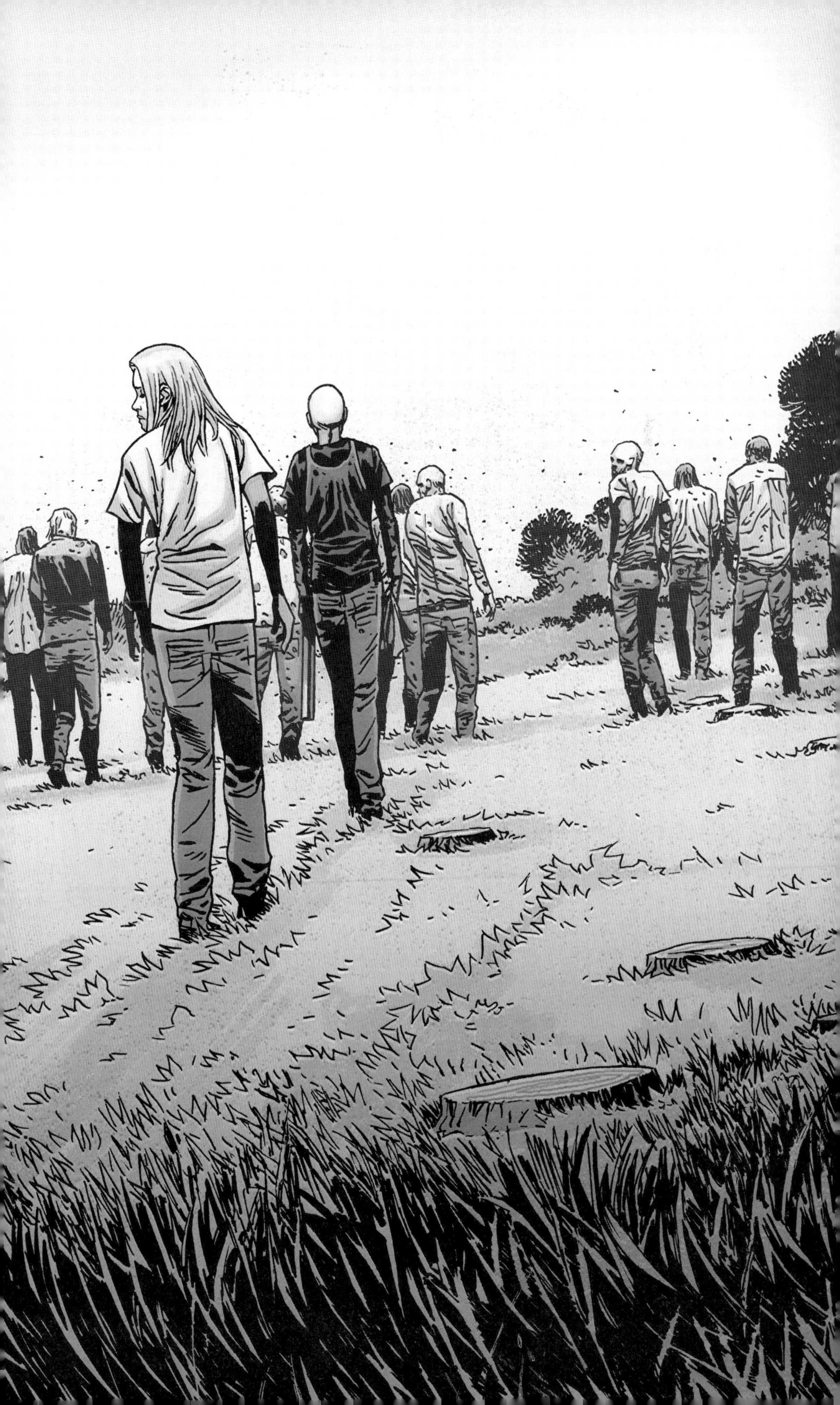

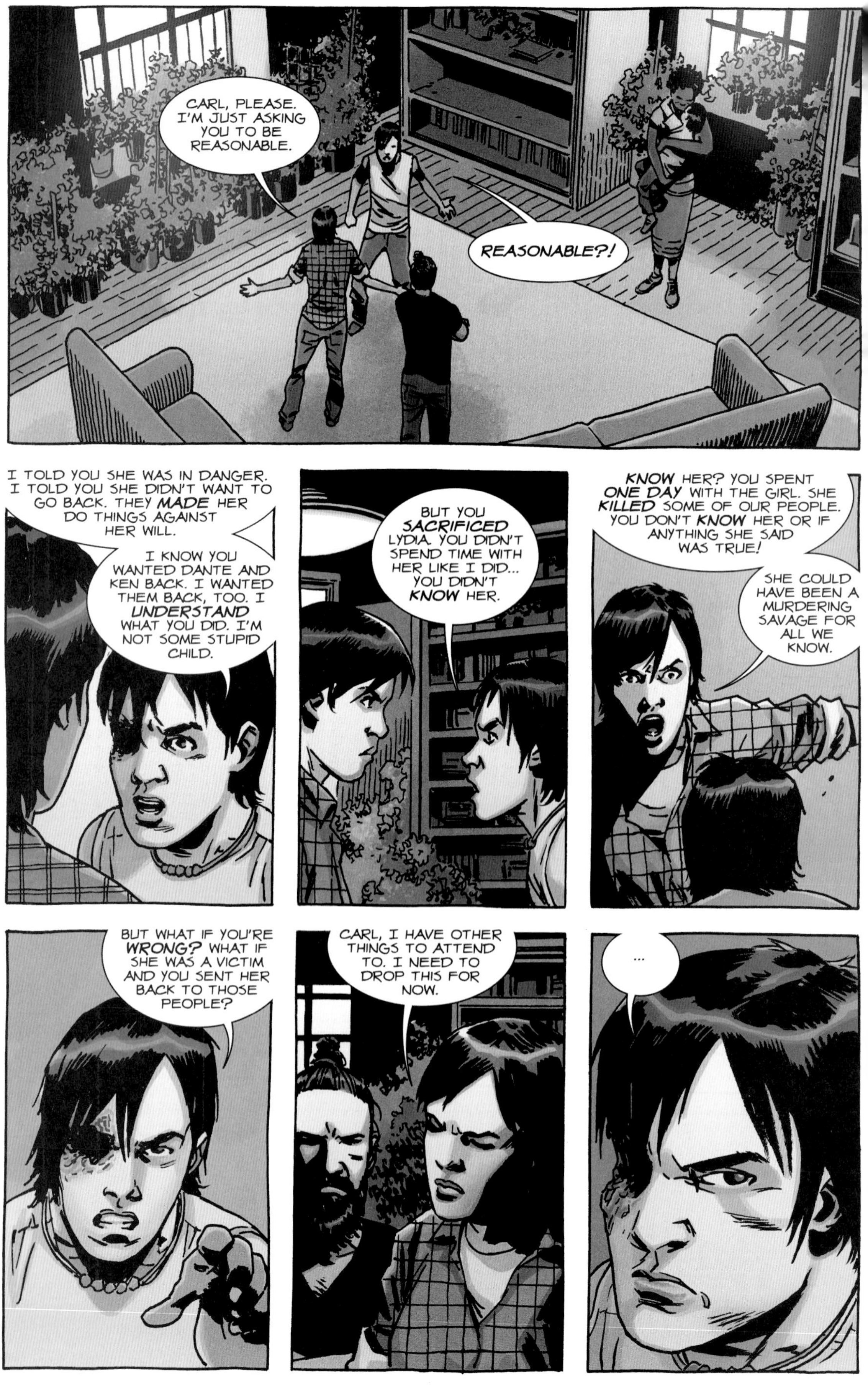
CARL, PLEASE. I'M JUST ASKING YOU TO BE REASONABLE.
REASONABLE?!
I TOLD YOU SHE WAS IN DANGER. I TOLD YOU SHE DIDN'T WANT TO GO BACK. THEY MADE HER DO THINGS AGAINST HER WILL.
I KNOW YOU WANTED DANTE AND KEN BACK. I WANTED THEM BACK, TOO. I UNDERSTAND WHAT YOU DID. I'M NOT SOME STUPID CHILD.
BUT YOU SACRIFICED LYDIA. YOU DIDN'T SPEND TIME WITH HER LIKE I DID... YOU DIDN'T KNOW HER.
KNOW HER? YOU SPENT ONE DAY WITH THE GIRL. SHE KILLED SOME OF OUR PEOPLE. YOU DON'T KNOW HER OR IF ANYTHING SHE SAID WAS TRUE!
SHE COULD HAVE BEEN A MURDERING SAVAGE FOR ALL WE KNOW.
BUT WHAT IF YOU'RE WRONG? WHAT IF SHE WAS A VICTIM AND YOU SENT HER BACK TO THOSE PEOPLE?
CARL, I HAVE OTHER THINGS TO ATTEND TO. I NEED TO DROP THIS FOR NOW.
...

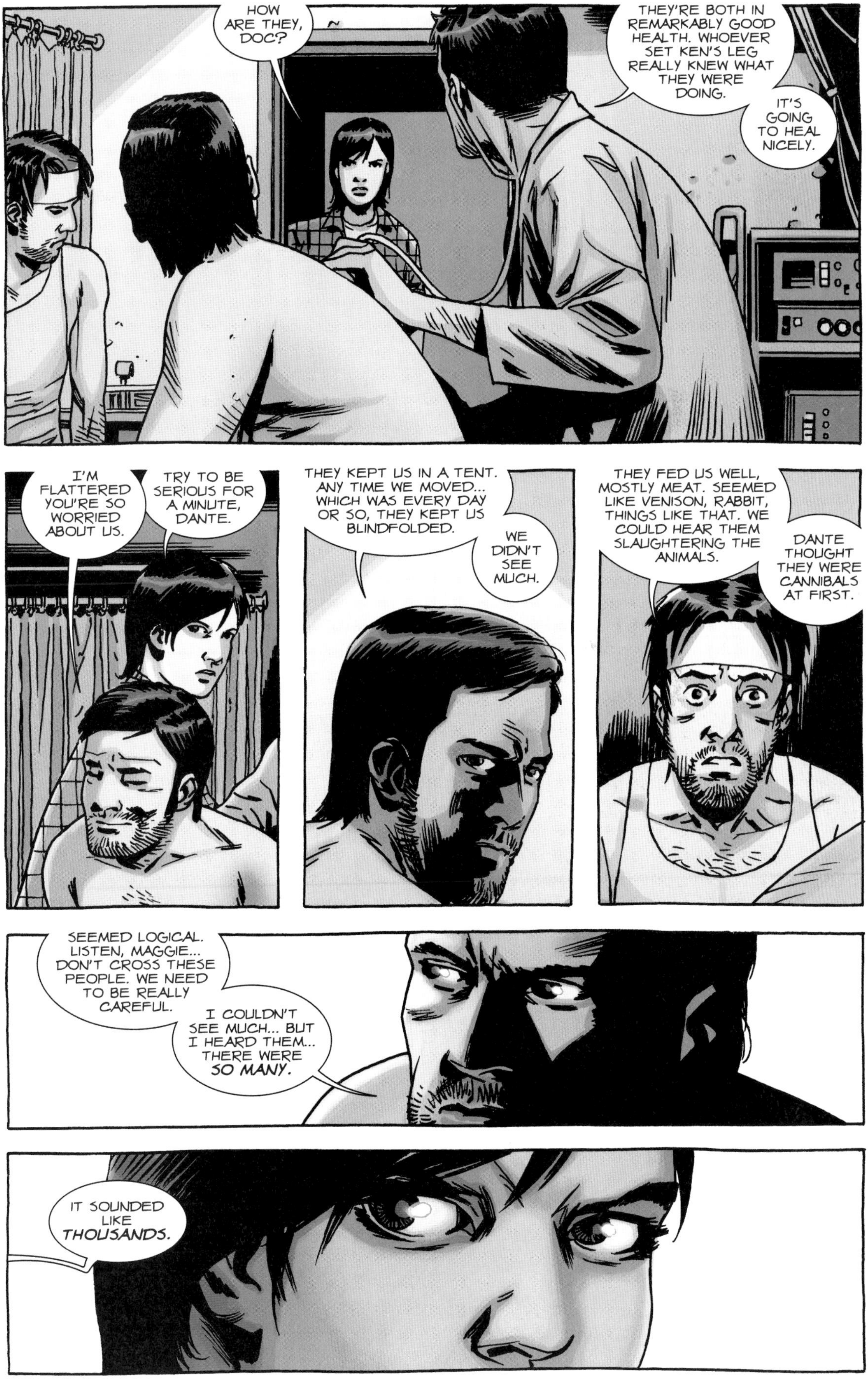
HOW ARE THEY, DOC?
THEY'RE BOTH IN REMARKABLY GOOD HEALTH. WHOEVER SET KEN'S LEG REALLY KNEW WHAT THEY WERE DOING.
IT'S GOING TO HEAL NICELY.
I'M FLATTERED YOU'RE SO WORRIED ABOUT US.
TRY TO BE SERIOUS FOR A MINUTE, DANTE.
THEY KEPT US IN A TENT. ANY TIME WE MOVED... WHICH WAS EVERY DAY OR SO, THEY KEPT US BLINDFOLDED.
WE DIDN'T SEE MUCH.
THEY FED US WELL, MOSTLY MEAT. SEEMED LIKE VENISON, RABBIT, THINGS LIKE THAT. WE COULD HEAR THEM SLAUGHTERING THE ANIMALS.
DANTE THOUGHT THEY WERE CANNIBALS AT FIRST.
SEEMED LOGICAL. LISTEN, MAGGIE... DON'T CROSS THESE PEOPLE. WE NEED TO BE REALLY CAREFUL.
I COULDN'T SEE MUCH... BUT I HEARD THEM... THERE WERE SO MANY.
IT SOUNDED LIKE THOUSANDS.

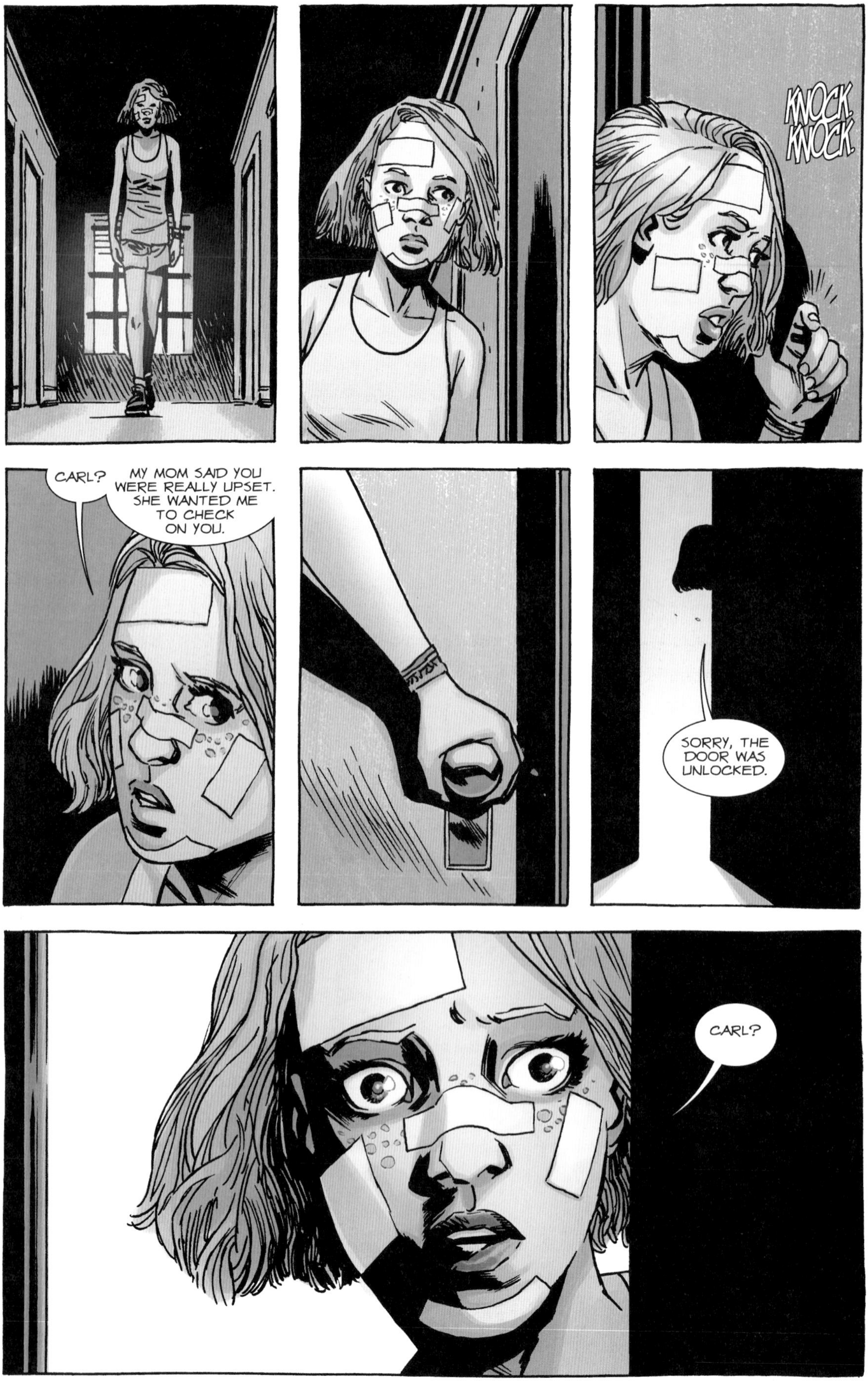
KNOCK KNOCK.
CARL?
MY MOM SAID YOU WERE REALLY UPSET. SHE WANTED ME TO CHECK ON YOU.
SORRY, THE DOOR WAS UNLOCKED.
CARL?

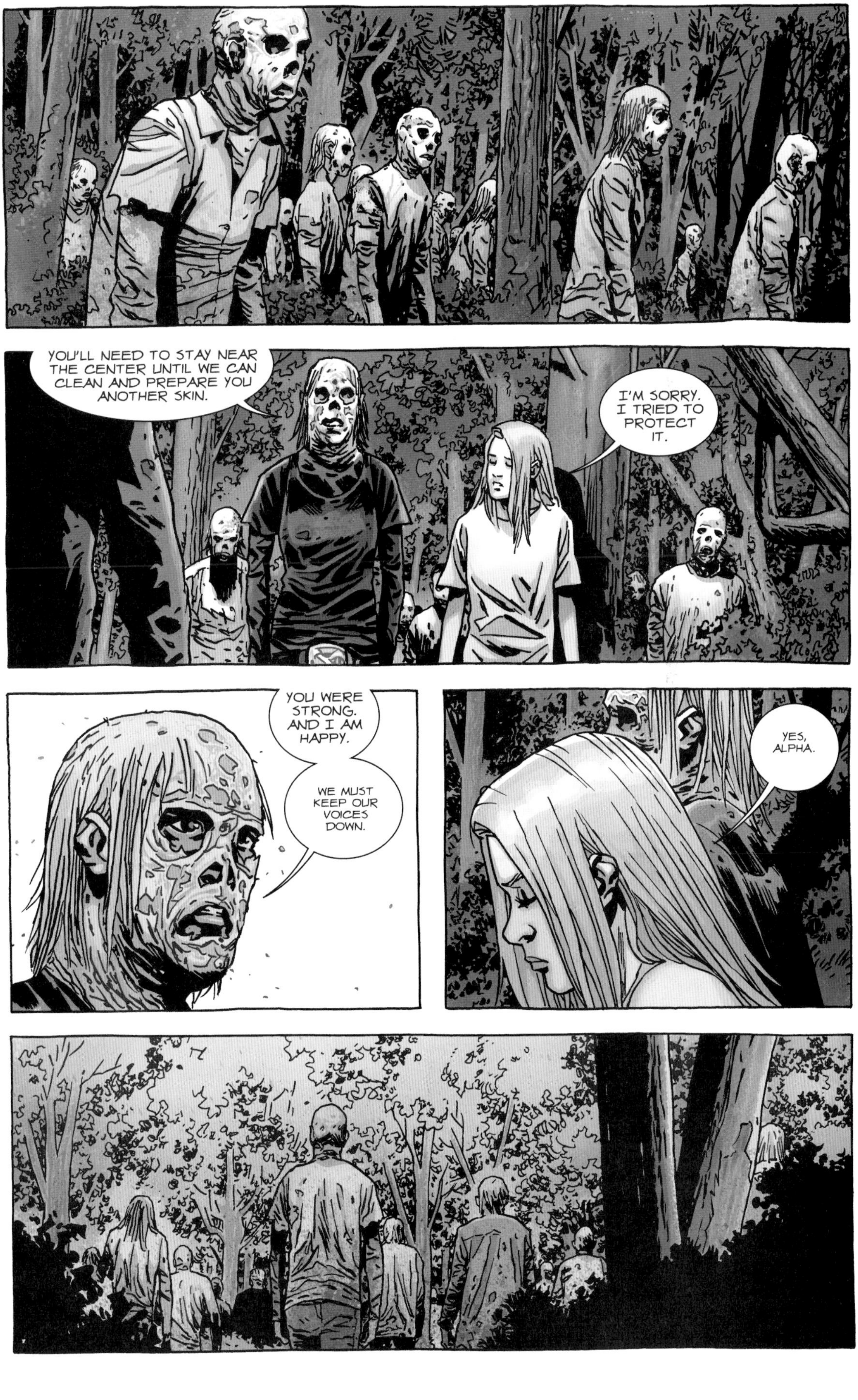
YOU'LL NEED TO STAY NEAR THE CENTER UNTIL WE CAN CLEAN AND PREPARE YOU ANOTHER SKIN.
I'M SORRY. I TRIED TO PROTECT IT.
YOU WERE STRONG. AND I AM HAPPY.
WE MUST KEEP OUR VOICES DOWN.
YES, ALPHA.

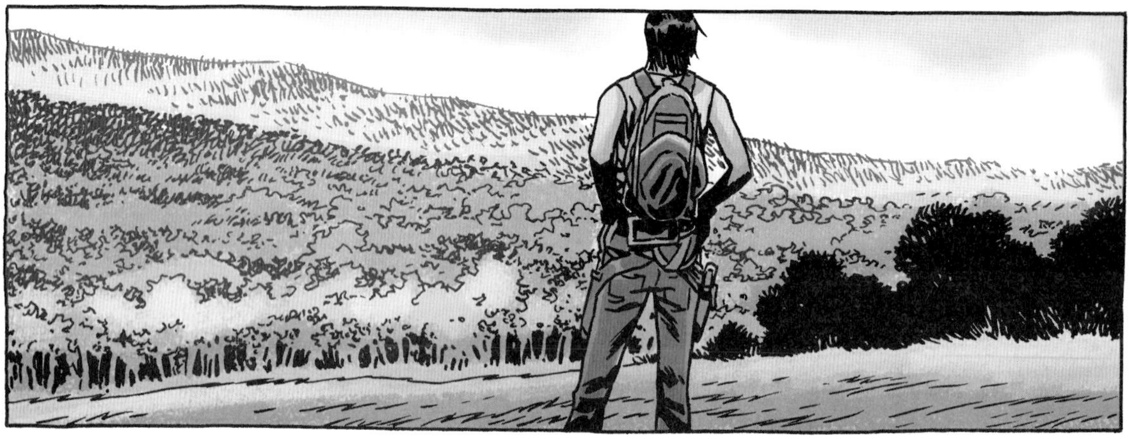

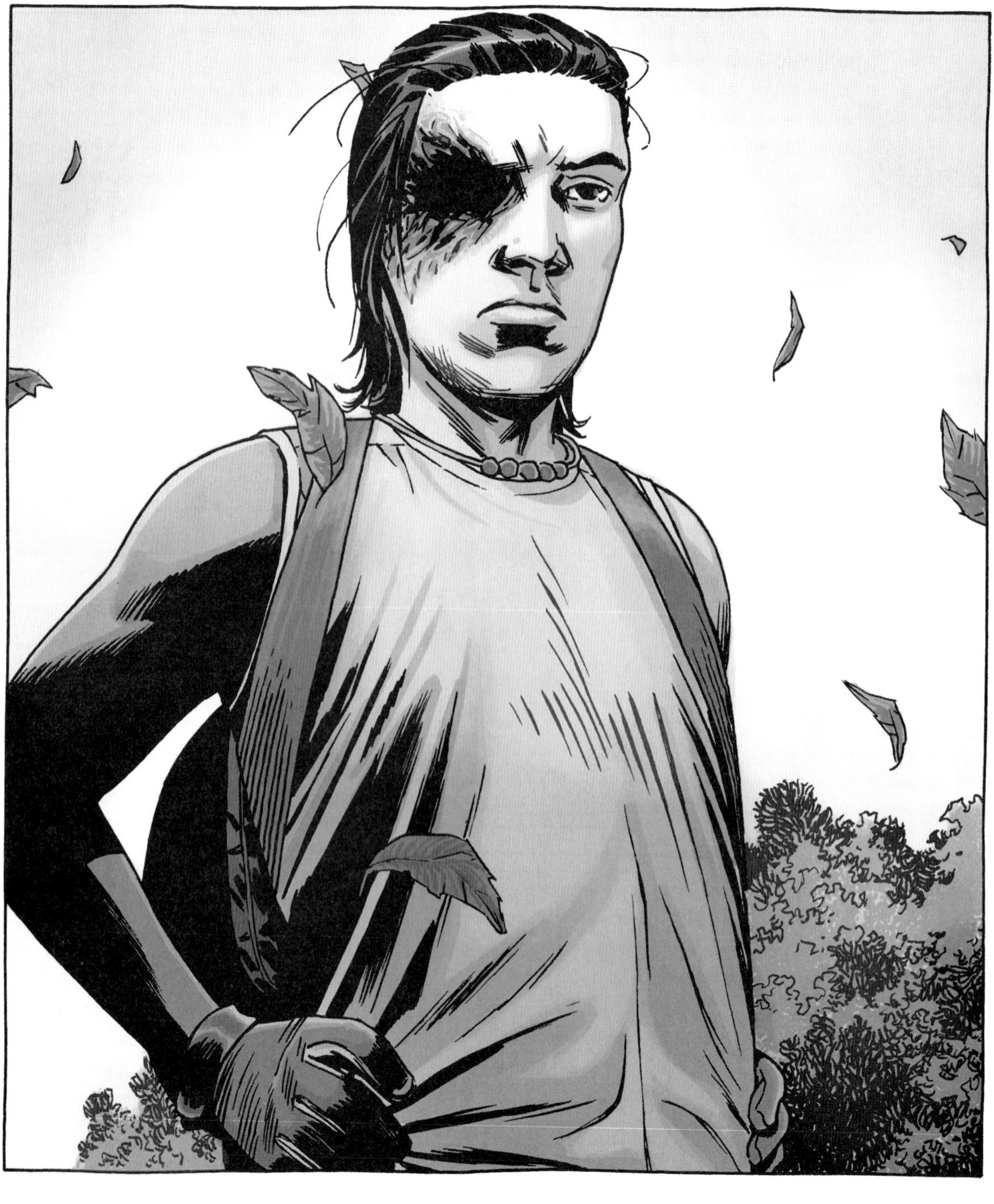

Chapter Twenty-Four:
Life and Death

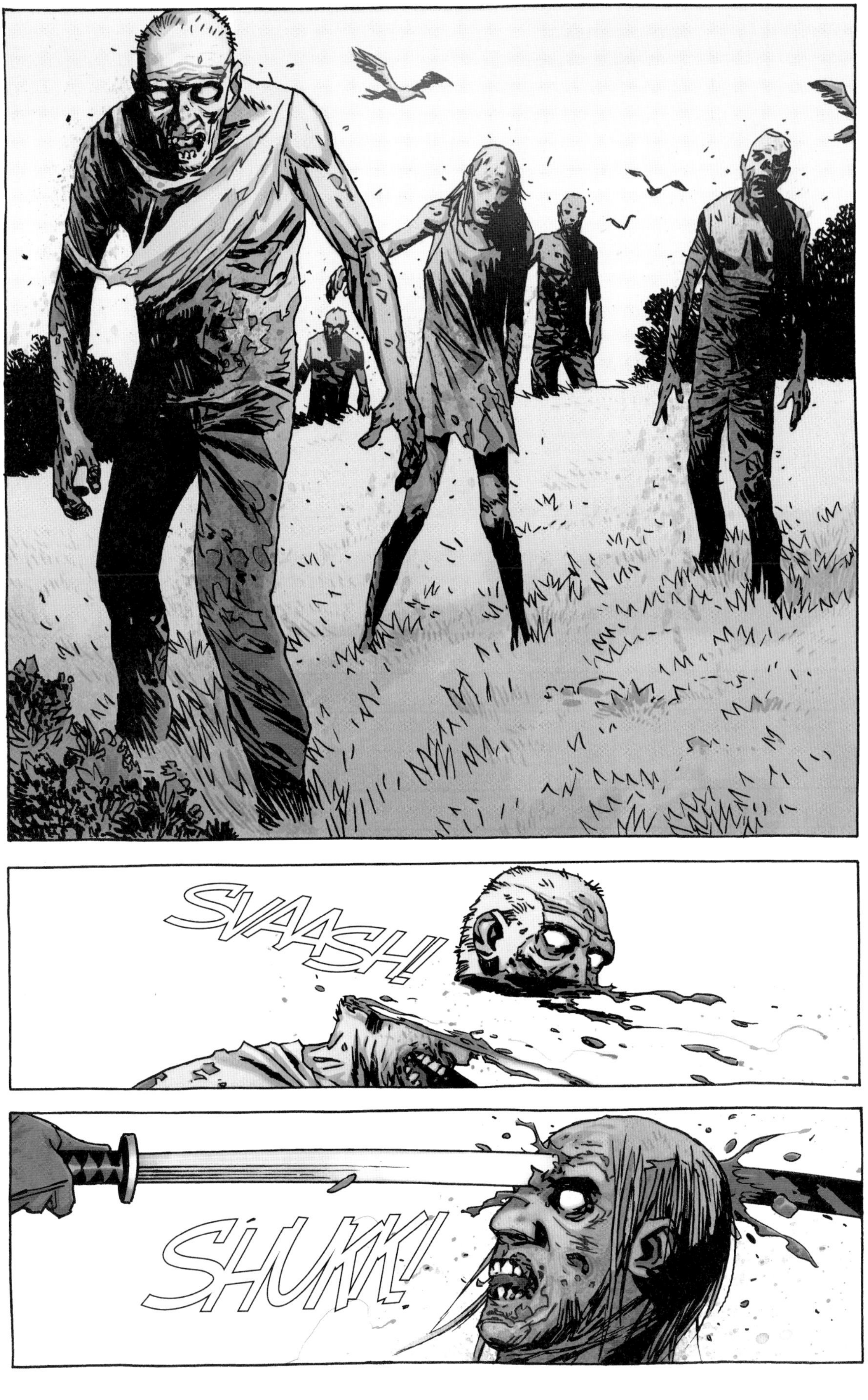
SVAASH!
SHUKK!

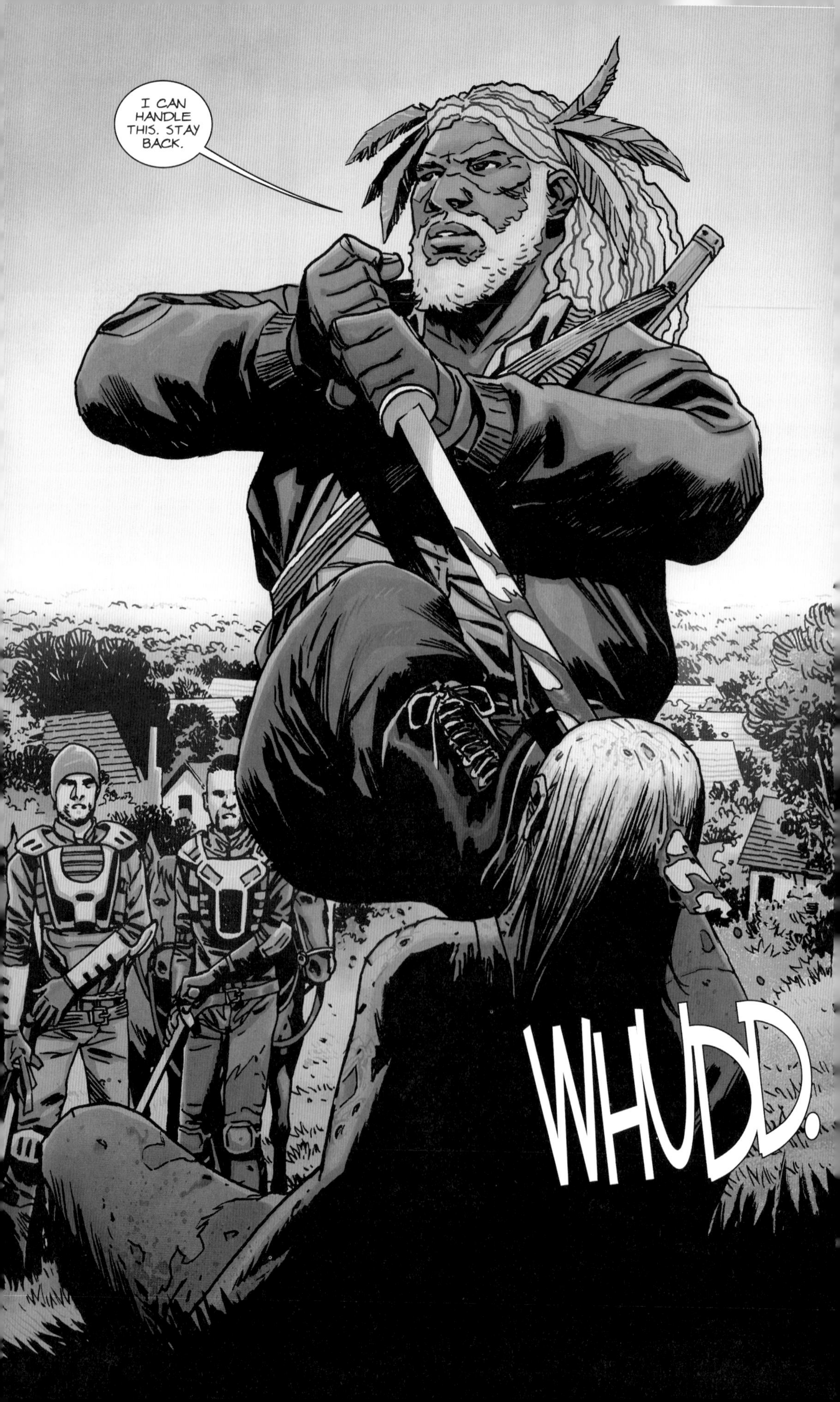
I CAN HANDLE THIS. STAY BACK.
WHUDD.

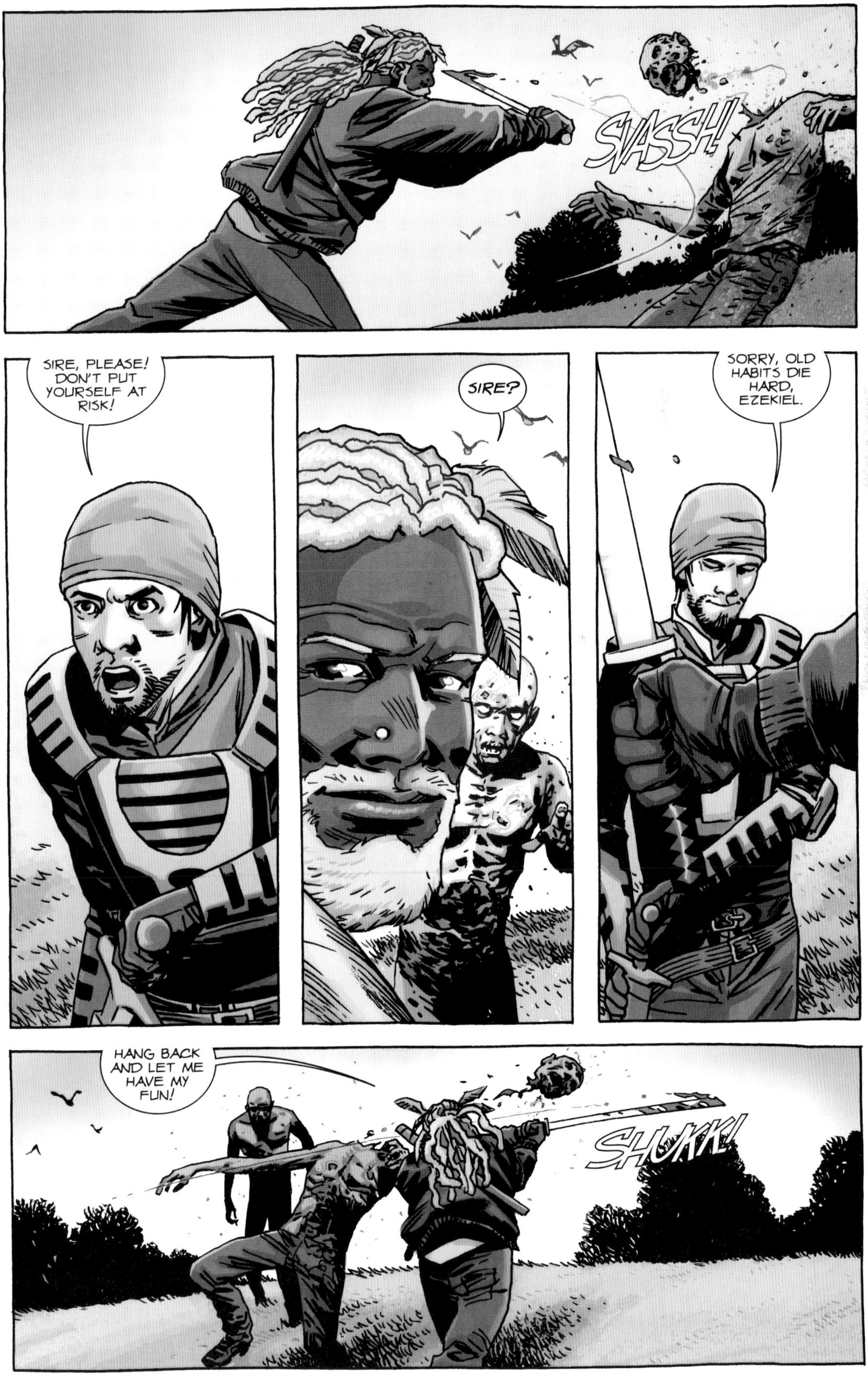
SVASSH!
SIRE, PLEASE! DON'T PUT YOURSELF AT RISK!
SIRE?
SORRY, OLD HABITS DIE HARD, EZEKIEL.
HANG BACK AND LET ME HAVE MY FUN!
SHUKK!

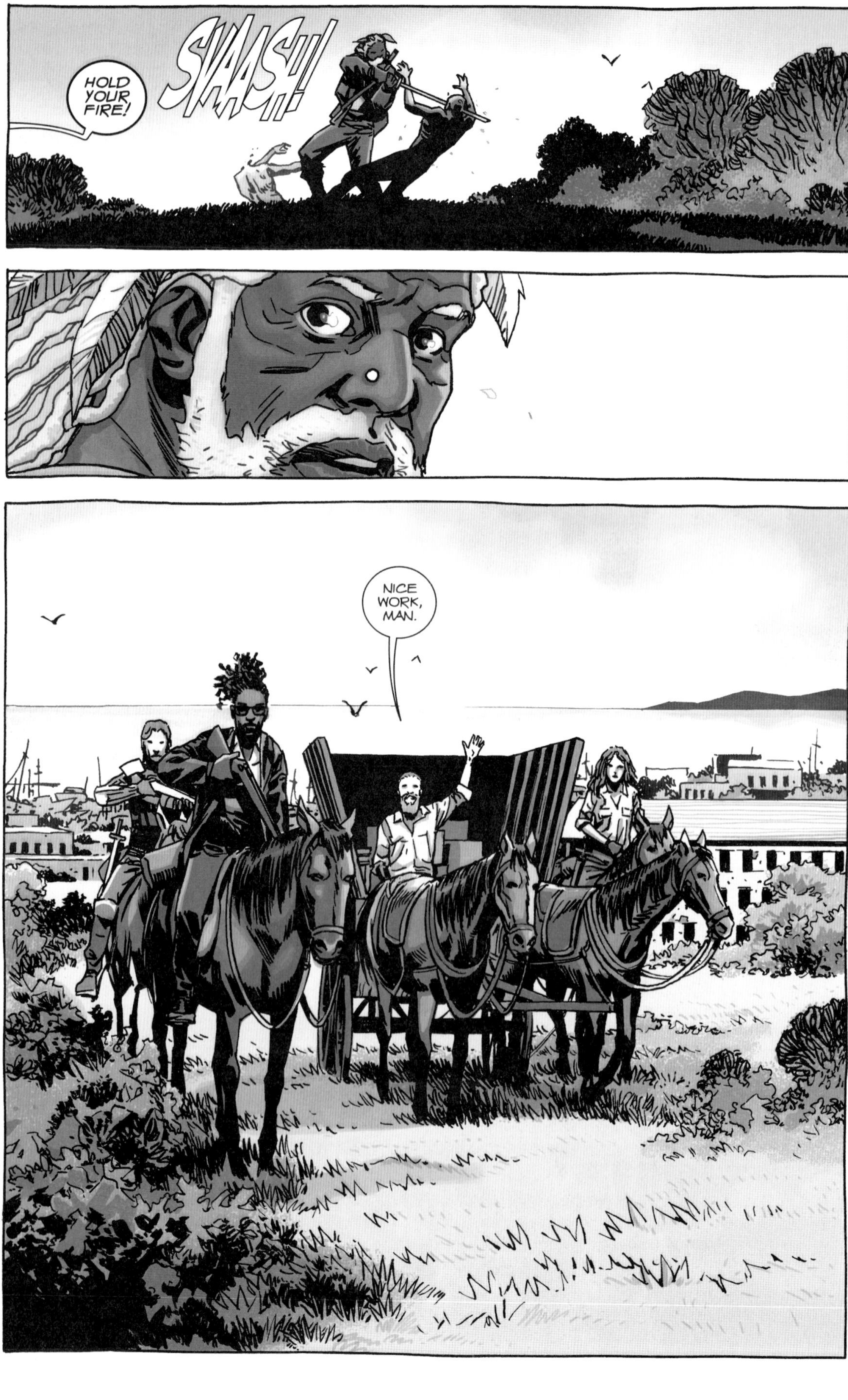
HOLD YOUR FIRE!
SVAASH!!
NICE WORK, MAN.

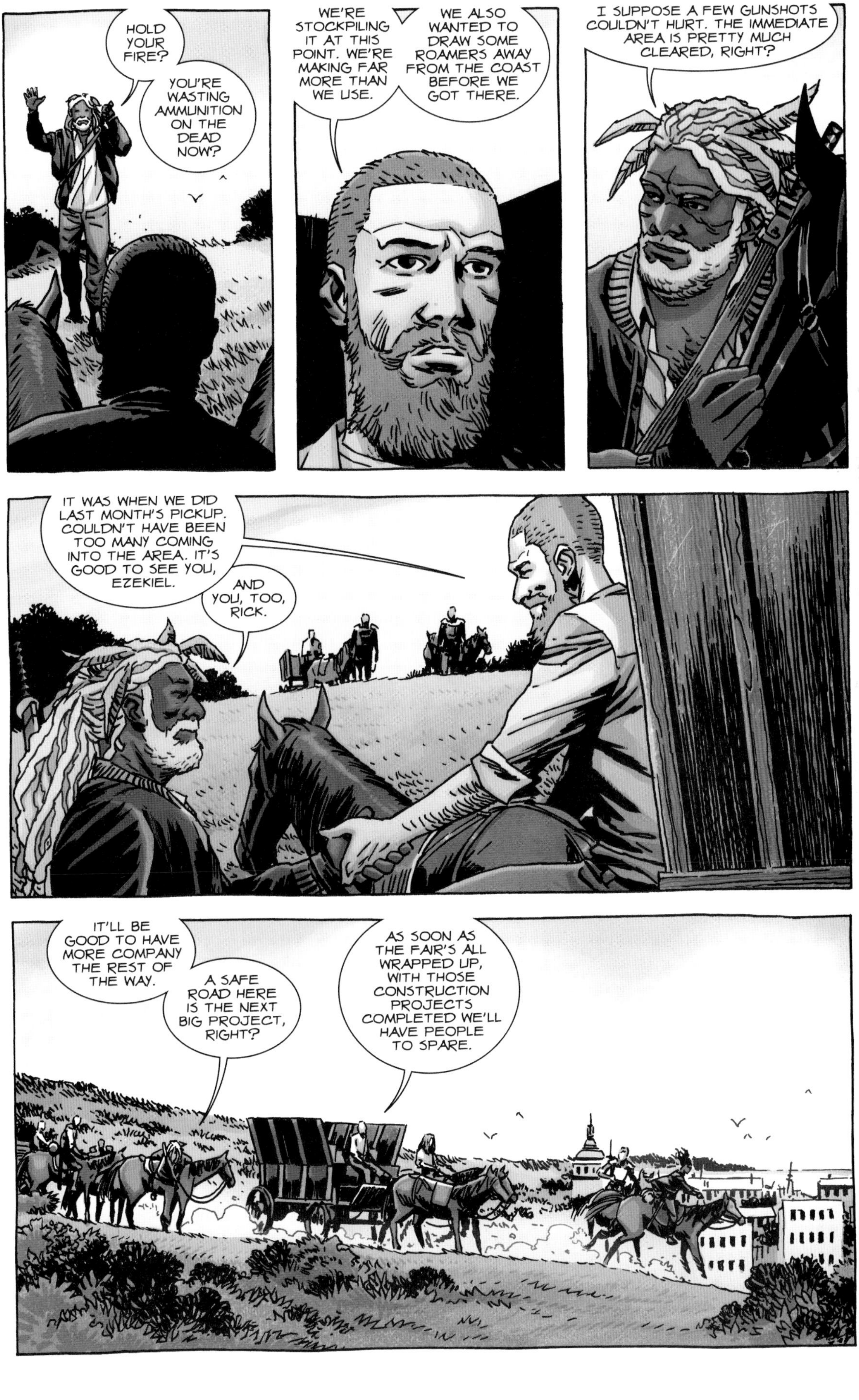
HOLD YOUR FIRE?
YOU'RE WASTING AMMUNITION ON THE DEAD NOW?
WE'RE STOCKPILING IT AT THIS POINT. WE'RE MAKING FAR MORE THAN WE USE.
WE ALSO WANTED TO DRAW SOME ROAMERS AWAY FROM THE COAST BEFORE WE GOT THERE.
I SUPPOSE A FEW GUNSHOTS COULDN'T HURT. THE IMMEDIATE AREA IS PRETTY MUCH CLEARED, RIGHT?
IT WAS WHEN WE DID LAST MONTH'S PICKUP. COULDN'T HAVE BEEN TOO MANY COMING INTO THE AREA. IT'S GOOD TO SEE YOU, EZEKIEL.
AND YOU, TOO, RICK.
IT'LL BE GOOD TO HAVE MORE COMPANY THE REST OF THE WAY.
A SAFE ROAD HERE IS THE NEXT BIG PROJECT, RIGHT?
AS SOON AS THE FAIR'S ALL WRAPPED UP, WITH THOSE CONSTRUCTION PROJECTS COMPLETED WE'LL HAVE PEOPLE TO SPARE.

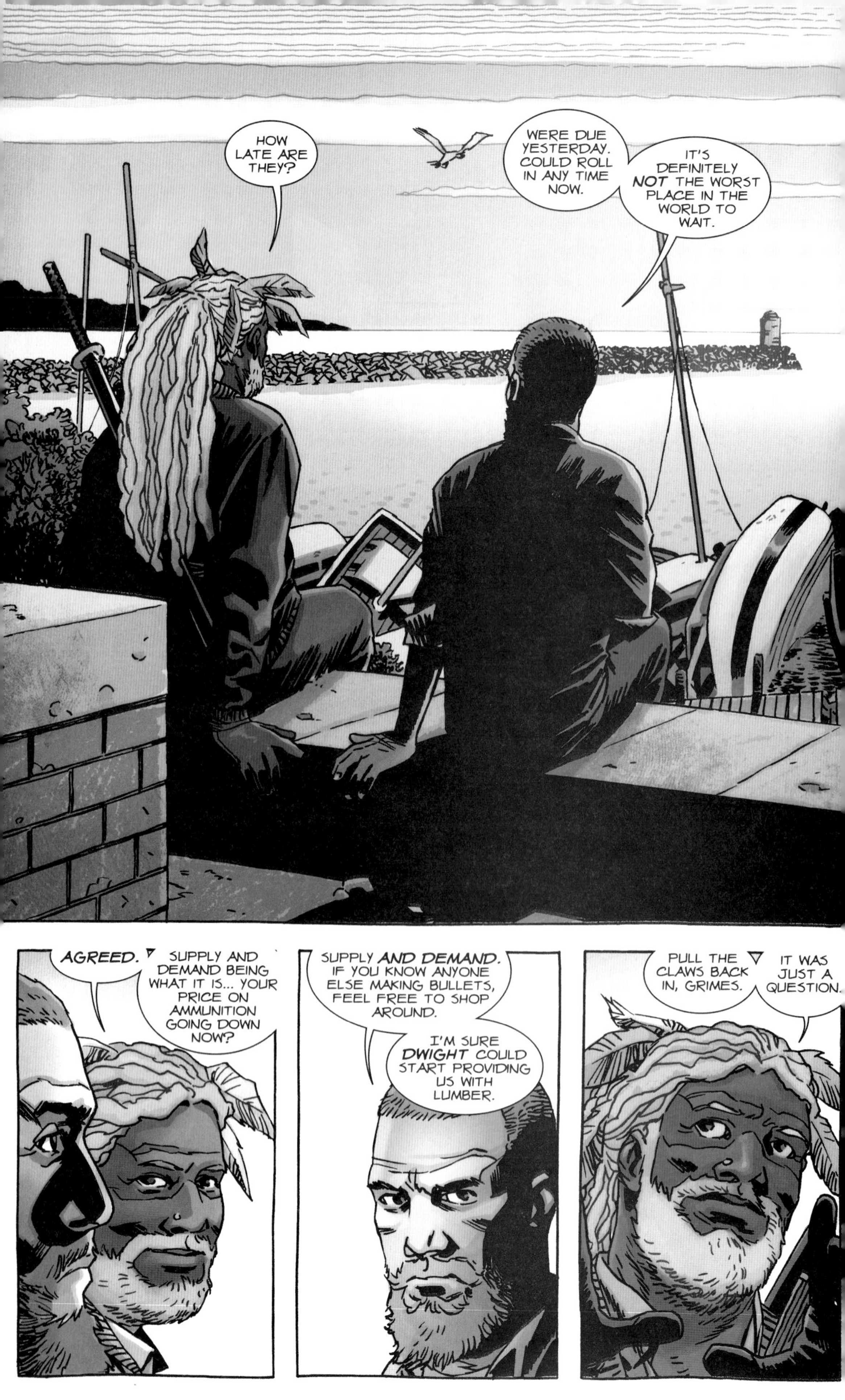
HOW LATE ARE THEY?
WERE DUE YESTERDAY. COULD ROLL IN ANY TIME NOW.
IT'S DEFINITELY NOT THE WORST PLACE IN THE WORLD TO WAIT.
AGREED.
SUPPLY AND DEMAND BEING WHAT IT IS... YOUR PRICE ON AMMUNITION GOING DOWN NOW?
SUPPLY AND DEMAND. IF YOU KNOW ANYONE ELSE MAKING BULLETS, FEEL FREE TO SHOP AROUND.
I'M SURE DWIGHT COULD START PROVIDING US WITH LUMBER.
PULL THE CLAWS BACK IN, GRIMES.
IT WAS JUST A QUESTION.

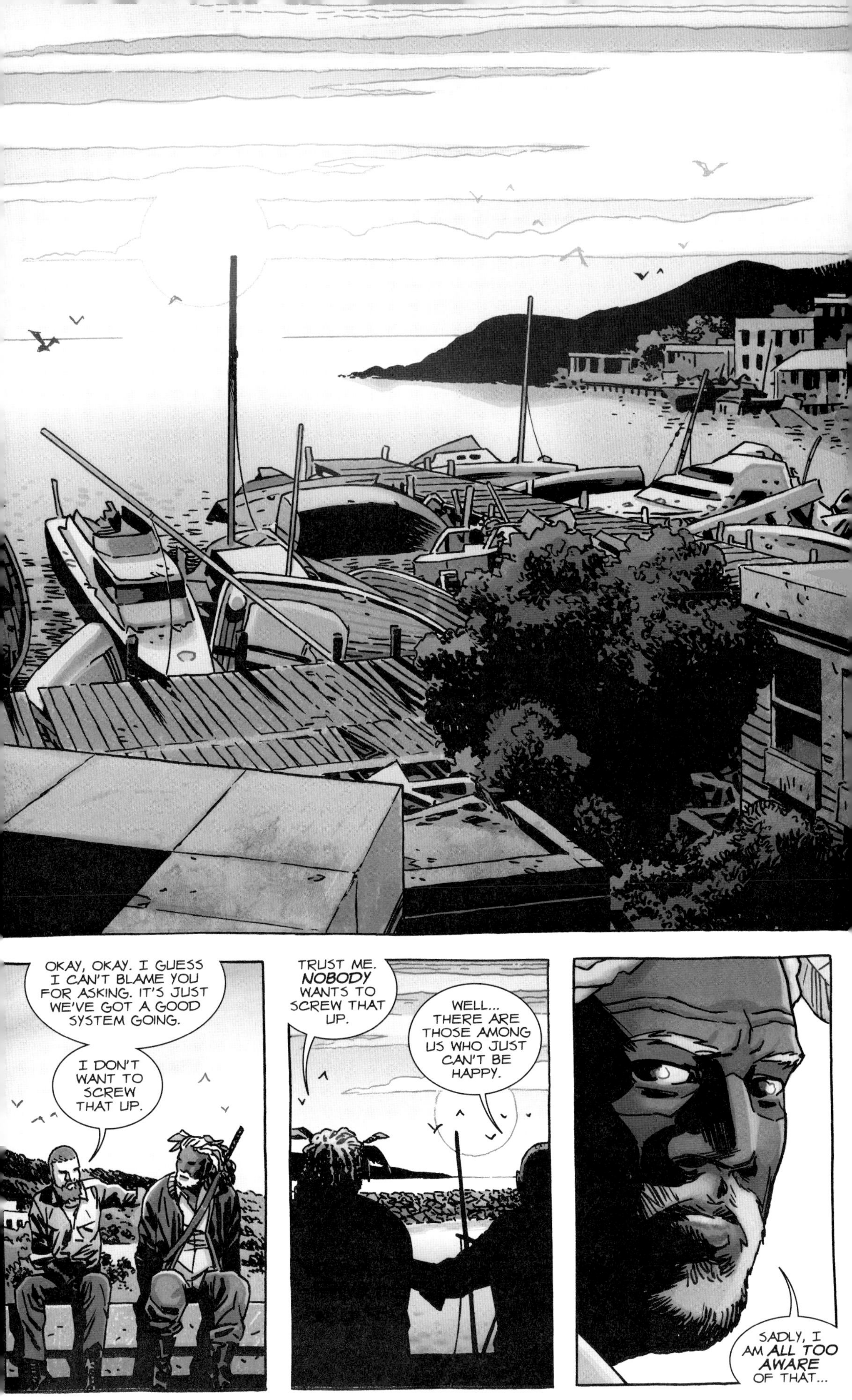
OKAY, OKAY. I GUESS I CAN'T BLAME YOU FOR ASKING. IT'S JUST WE'VE GOT A GOOD SYSTEM GOING.
I DON'T WANT TO SCREW THAT UP.
TRUST ME. NOBODY WANTS TO SCREW THAT UP.
WELL... THERE ARE THOSE AMONG US WHO JUST CAN'T BE HAPPY.
SADLY, I AM ALL TOO AWARE OF THAT...

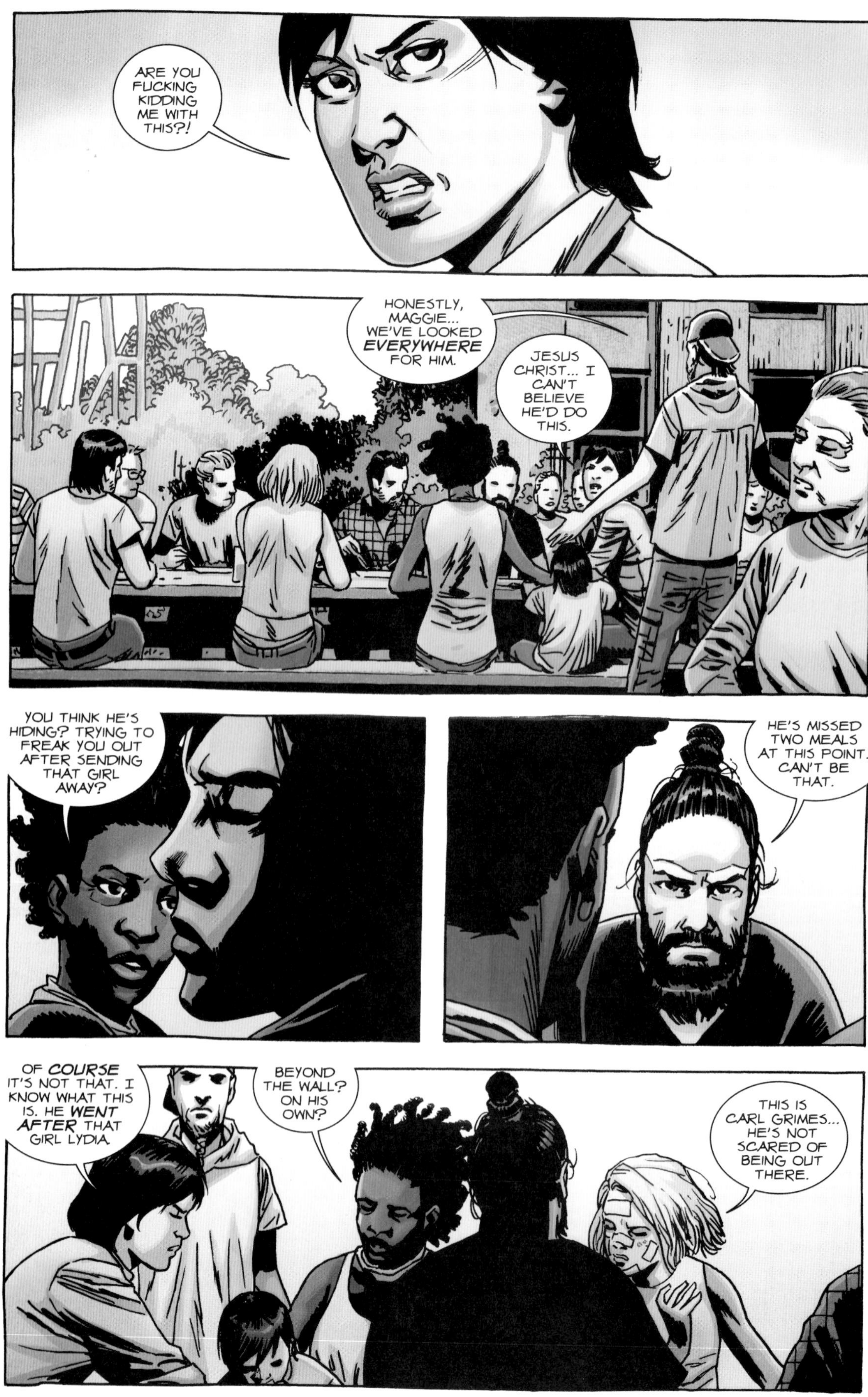
ARE YOU FUCKING KIDDING ME WITH THIS?!
HONESTLY, MAGGIE... WE'VE LOOKED **EVERYWHERE** FOR HIM.
JESUS CHRIST... I CAN'T BELIEVE HE'D DO THIS.
YOU THINK HE'S HIDING? TRYING TO FREAK YOU OUT AFTER SENDING THAT GIRL AWAY?
HE'S MISSED TWO MEALS AT THIS POINT. CAN'T BE THAT.
OF **COURSE** IT'S NOT THAT. I KNOW WHAT THIS IS. HE **WENT AFTER** THAT GIRL LYDIA.
BEYOND THE WALL? ON HIS OWN?
THIS IS CARL GRIMES... HE'S NOT SCARED OF BEING OUT THERE.

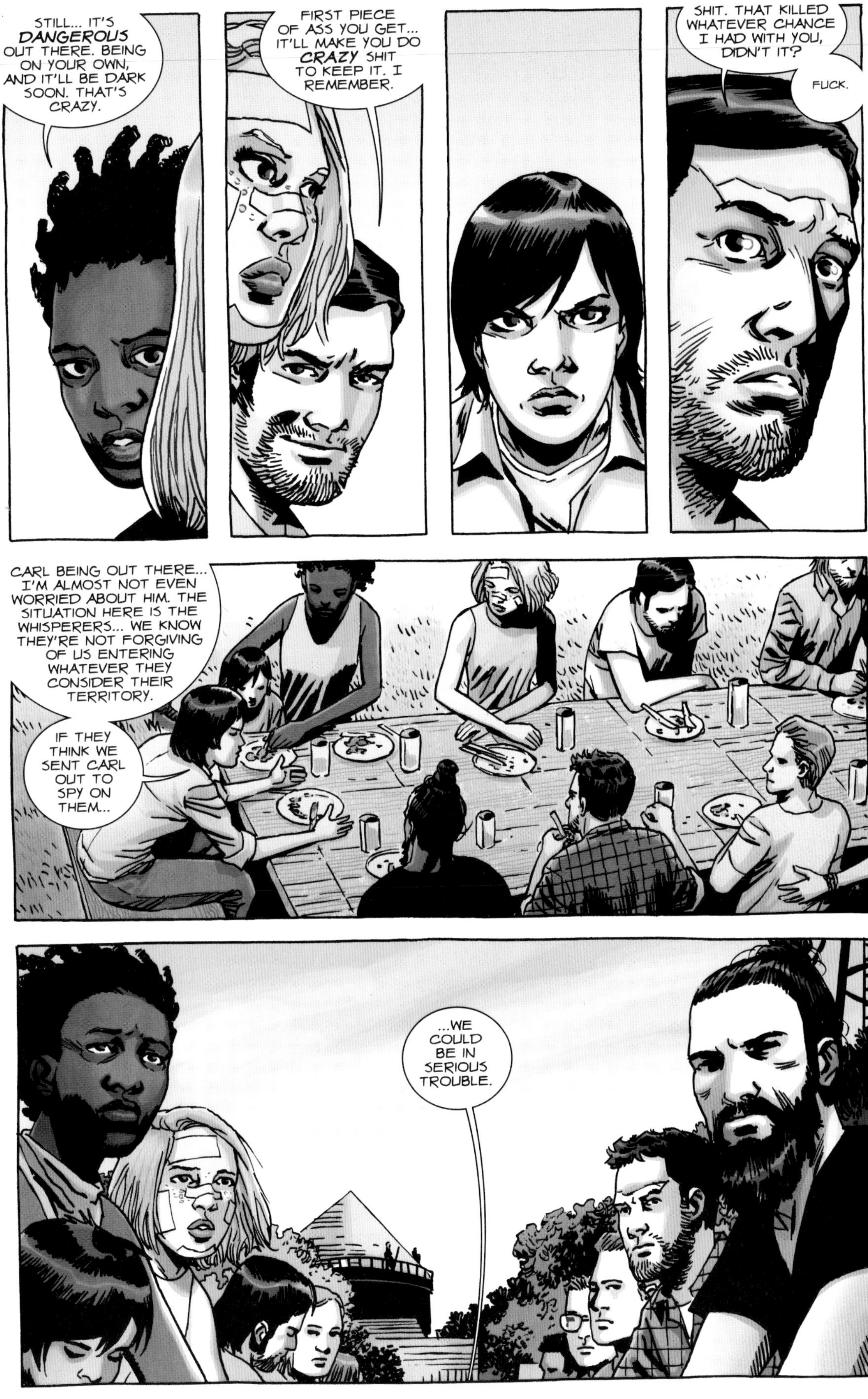
STILL... IT'S DANGEROUS OUT THERE. BEING ON YOUR OWN, AND IT'LL BE DARK SOON. THAT'S CRAZY.
FIRST PIECE OF ASS YOU GET... IT'LL MAKE YOU DO CRAZY SHIT TO KEEP IT. I REMEMBER.
SHIT. THAT KILLED WHATEVER CHANCE I HAD WITH YOU, DIDN'T IT?
FUCK.
CARL BEING OUT THERE... I'M ALMOST NOT EVEN WORRIED ABOUT HIM. THE SITUATION HERE IS THE WHISPERERS... WE KNOW THEY'RE NOT FORGIVING OF US ENTERING WHATEVER THEY CONSIDER THEIR TERRITORY.
IF THEY THINK WE SENT CARL OUT TO SPY ON THEM...
...WE COULD BE IN SERIOUS TROUBLE.

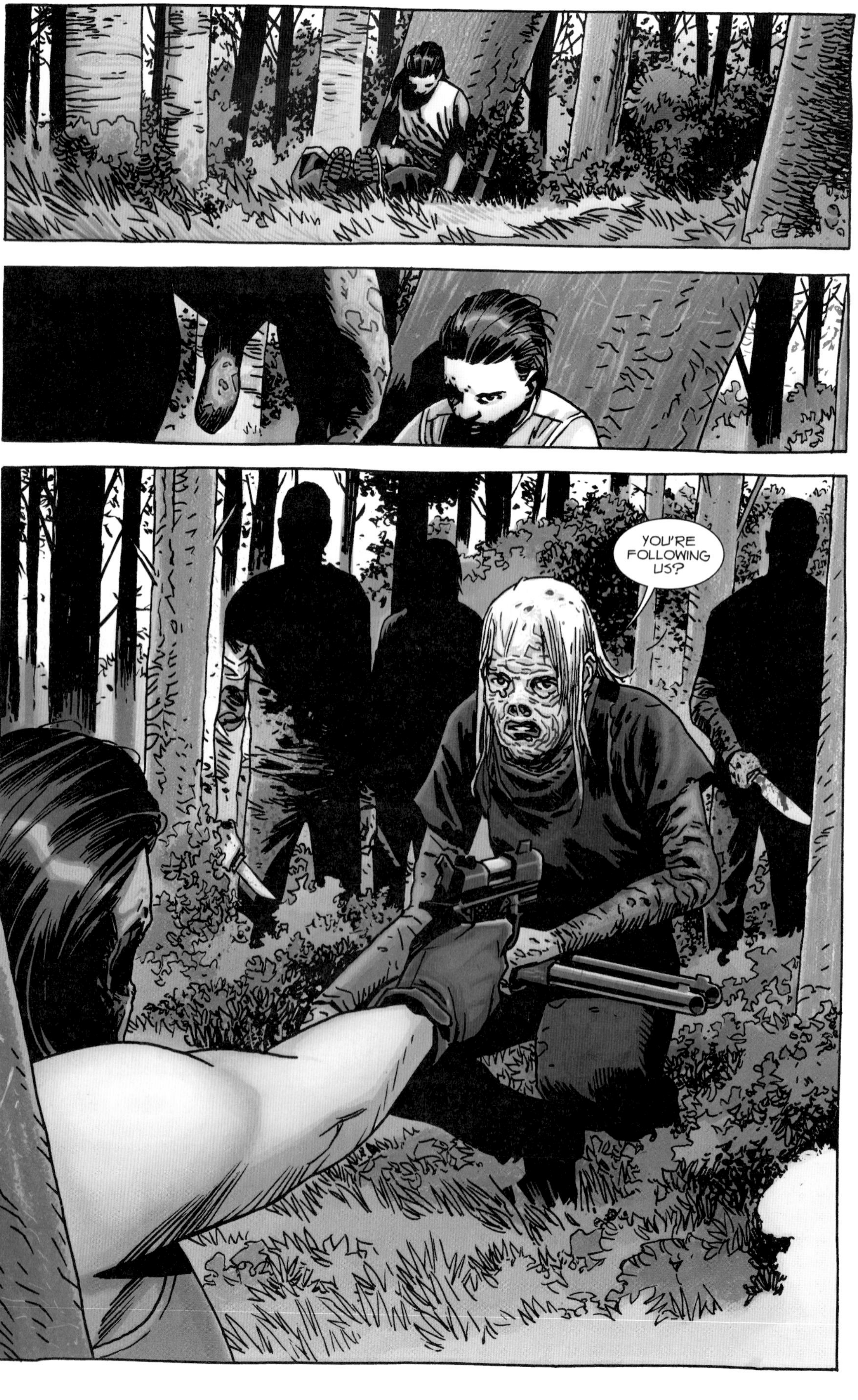
YOU'RE FOLLOWING US?

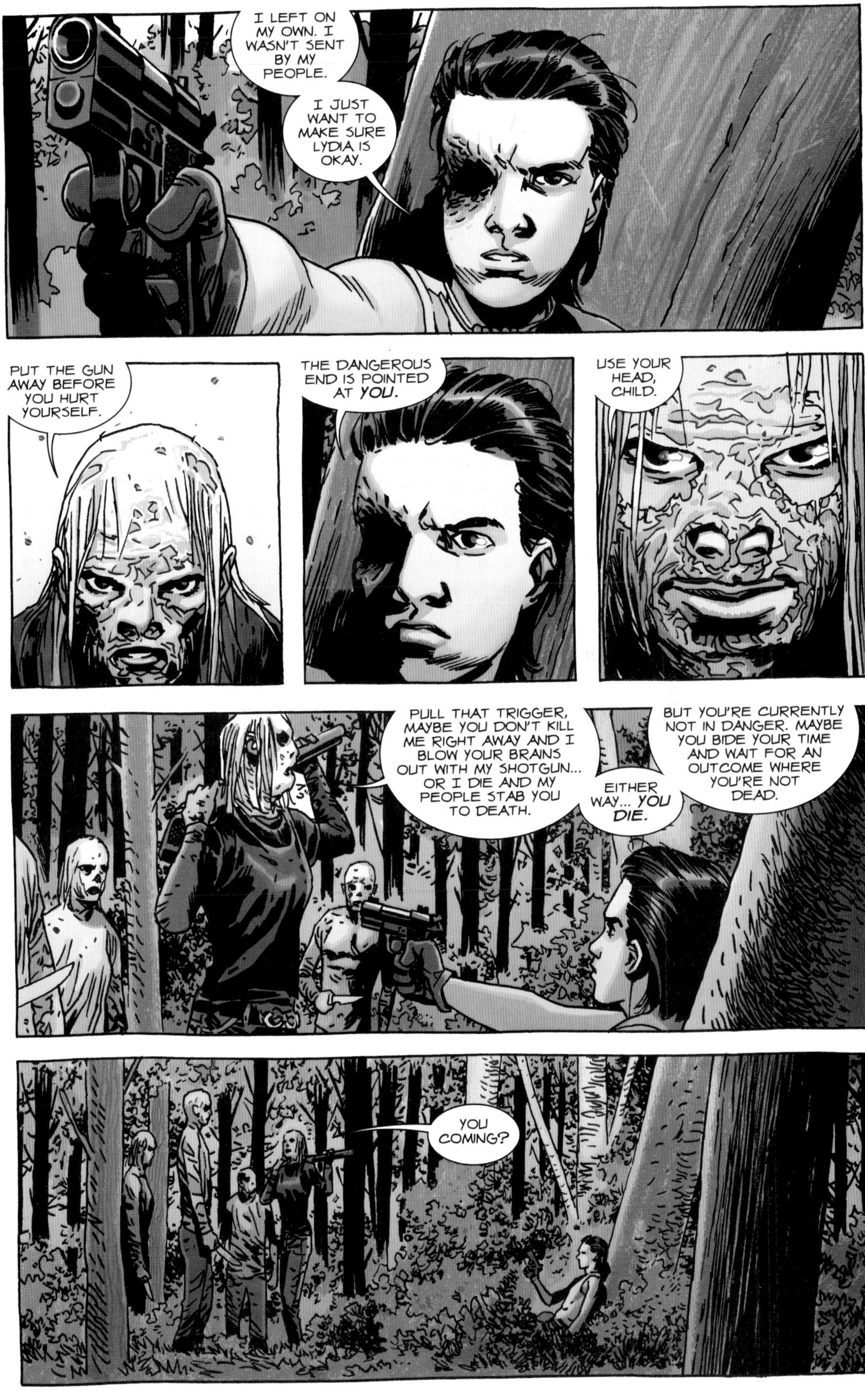
I LEFT ON MY OWN. I WASN'T SENT BY MY PEOPLE.
I JUST WANT TO MAKE SURE LYDIA IS OKAY.
PUT THE GUN AWAY BEFORE YOU HURT YOURSELF.
THE DANGEROUS END IS POINTED AT *YOU.*
USE YOUR HEAD, CHILD.
PULL THAT TRIGGER, MAYBE YOU DON'T KILL ME RIGHT AWAY AND I BLOW YOUR BRAINS OUT WITH MY SHOTGUN... OR I DIE AND MY PEOPLE STAB YOU TO DEATH.
EITHER WAY... *YOU DIE.*
BUT YOU'RE CURRENTLY NOT IN DANGER. MAYBE YOU BIDE YOUR TIME AND WAIT FOR AN OUTCOME WHERE YOU'RE NOT DEAD.
YOU COMING?

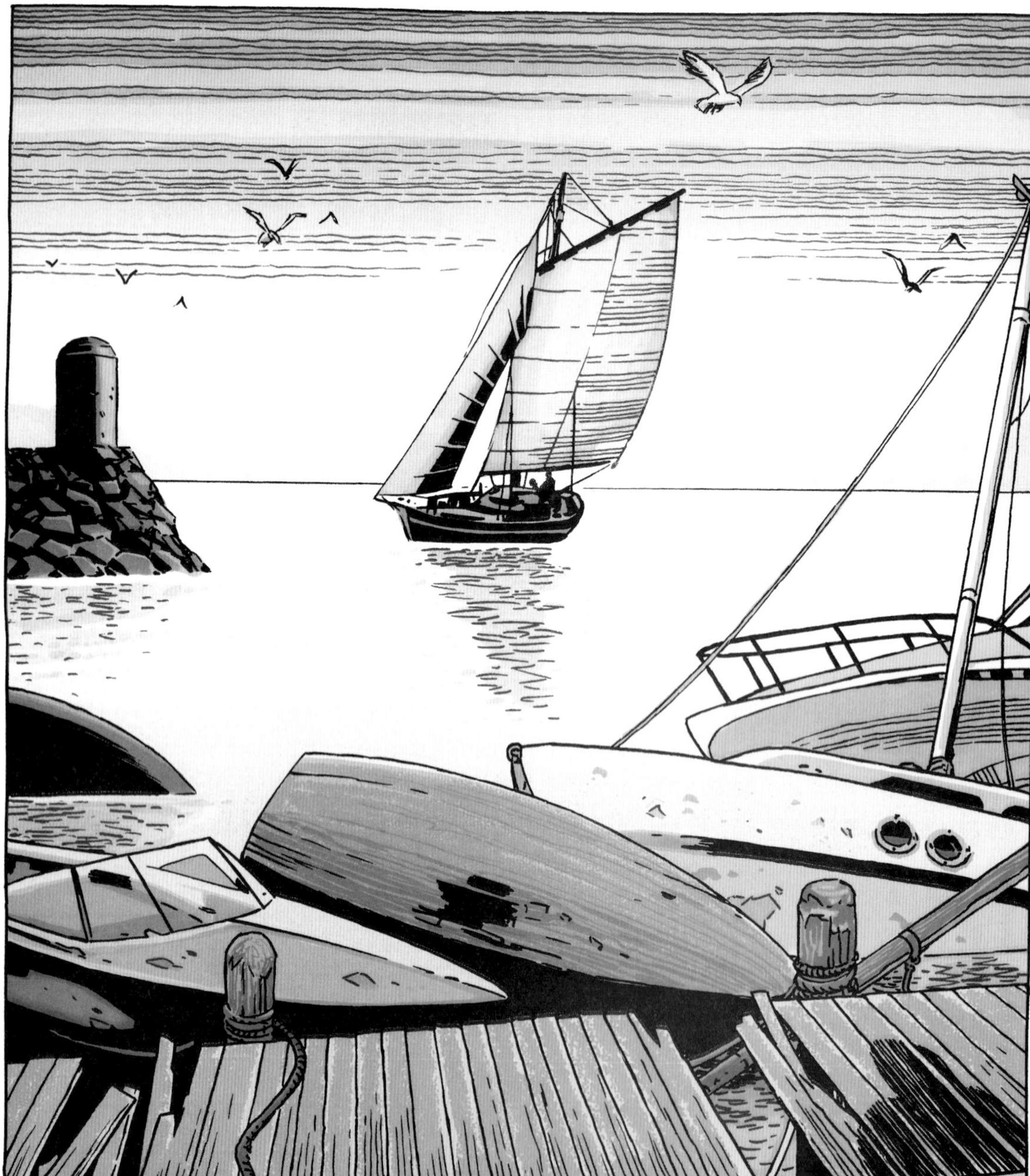

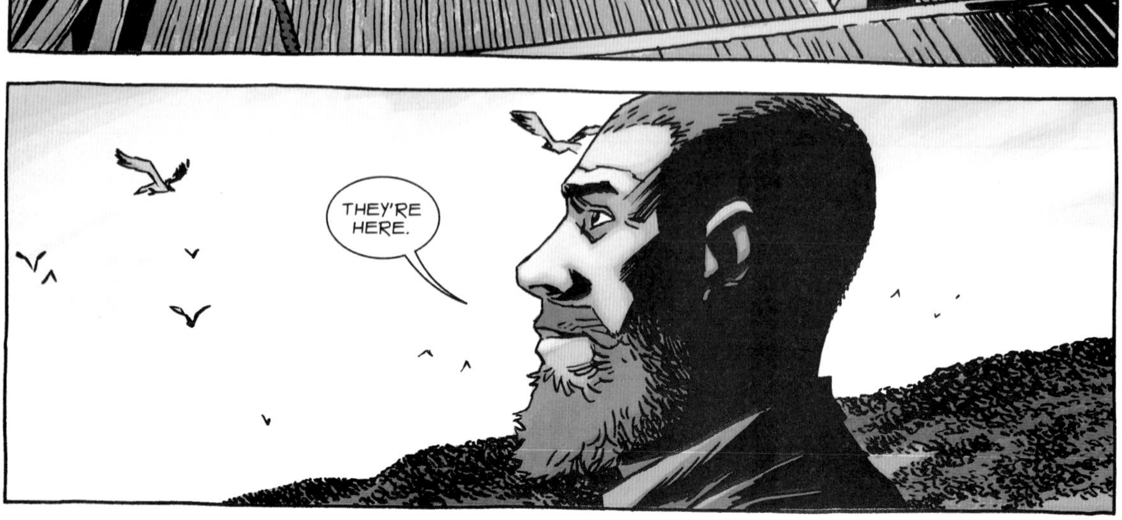
THEY'RE HERE.

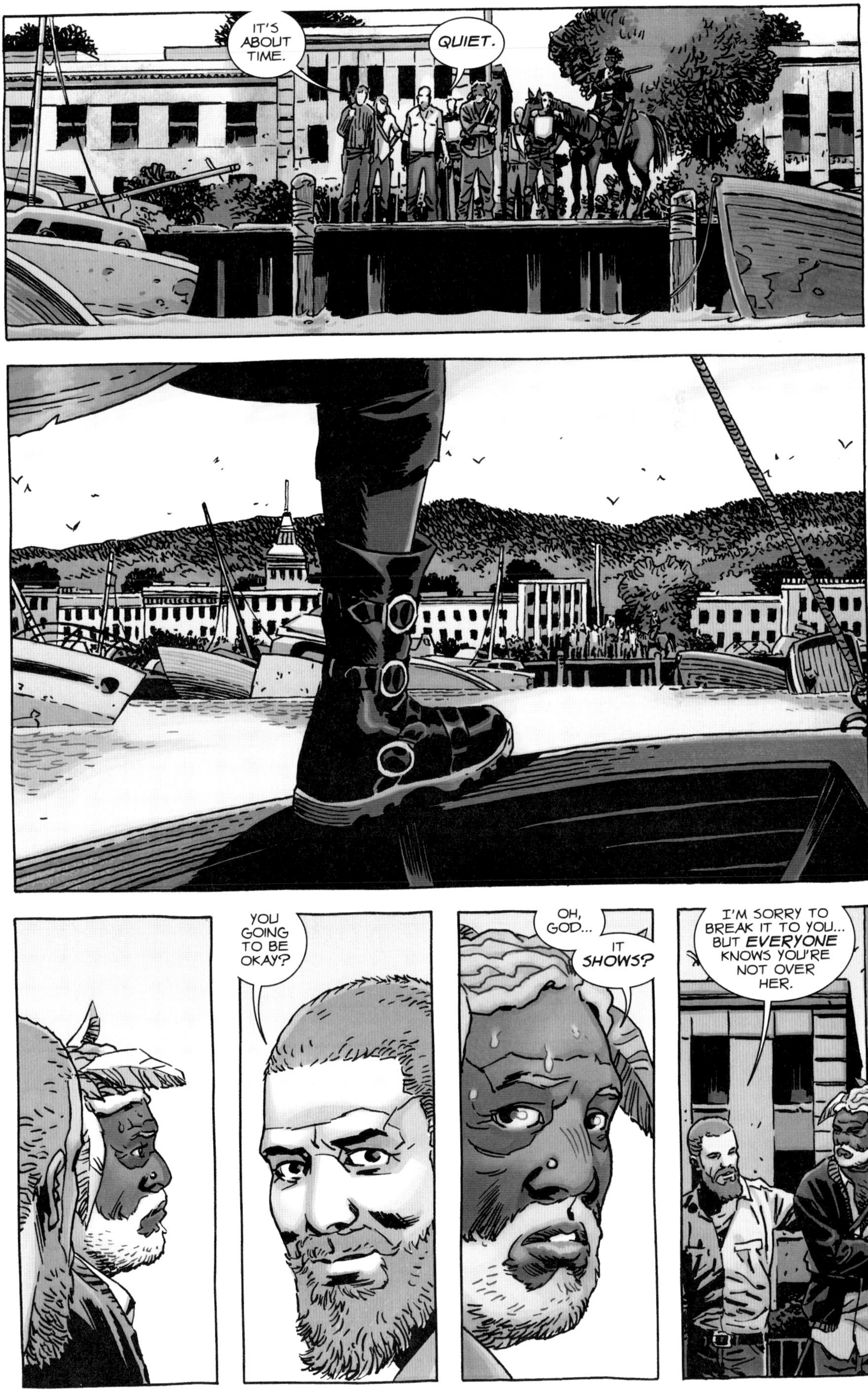
IT'S ABOUT TIME.
QUIET.
YOU GOING TO BE OKAY?
OH, GOD...
IT SHOWS?
I'M SORRY TO BREAK IT TO YOU... BUT EVERYONE KNOWS YOU'RE NOT OVER HER.

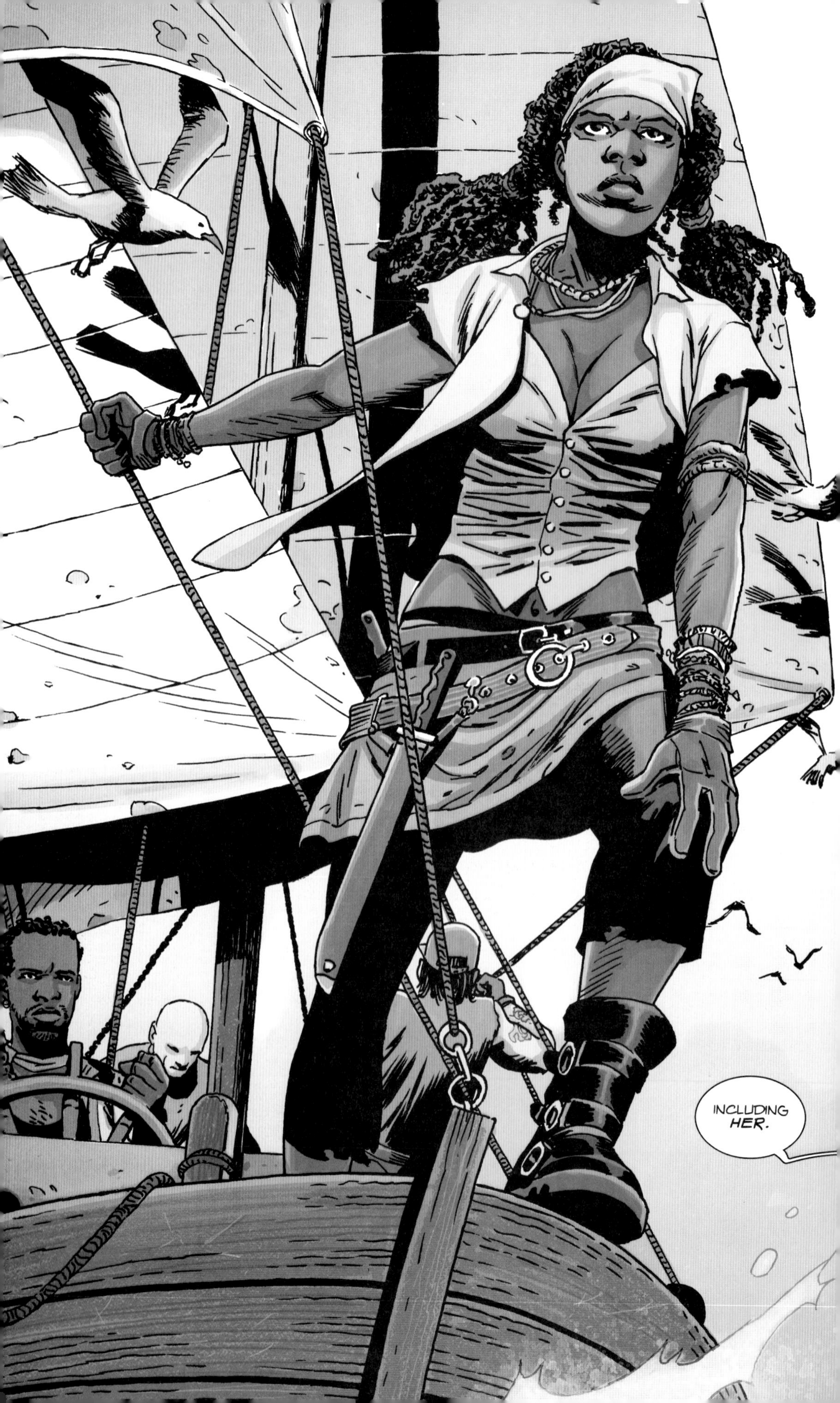
INCLUDING HER.

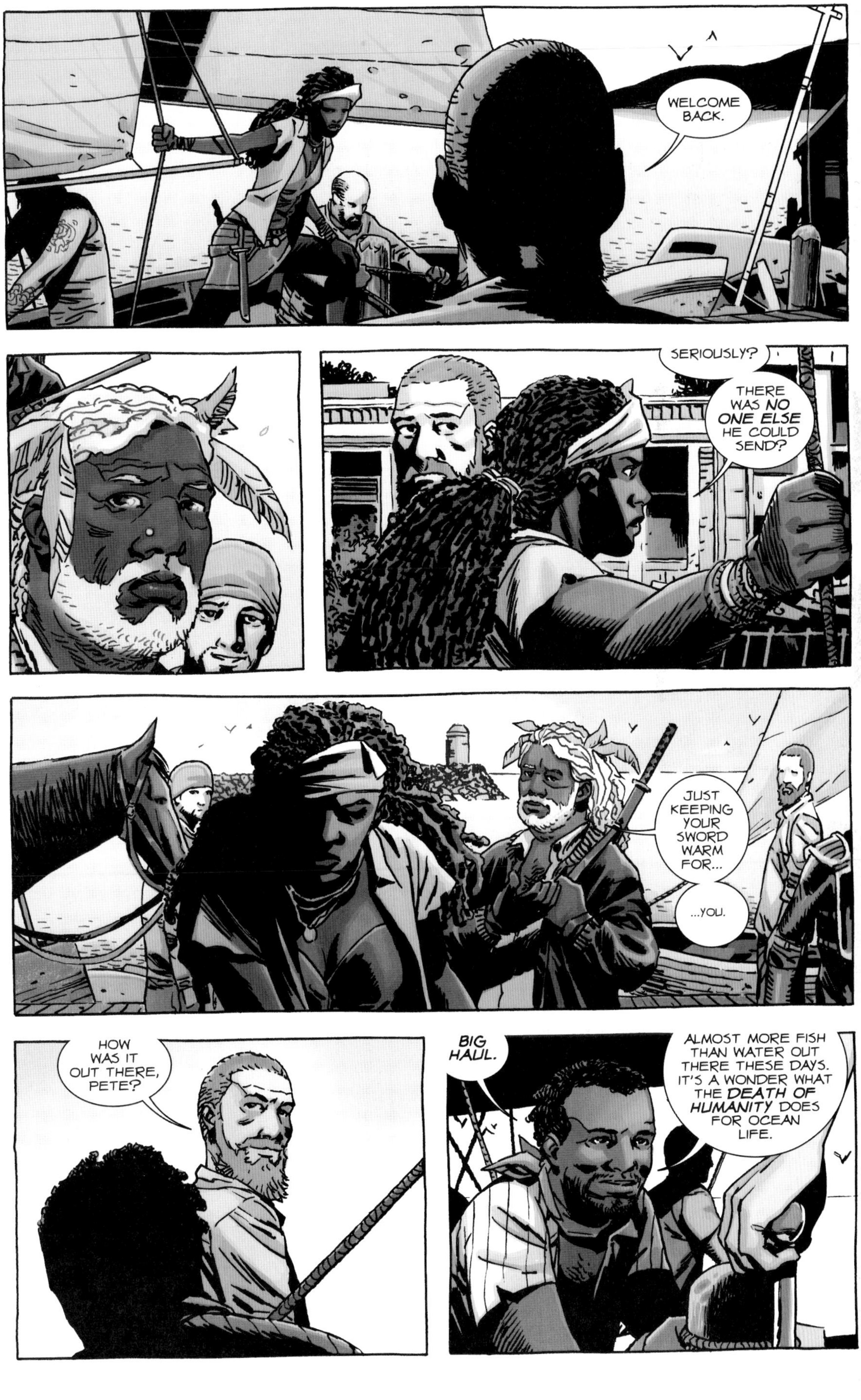
WELCOME BACK.
SERIOUSLY?
THERE WAS NO ONE ELSE HE COULD SEND?
JUST KEEPING YOUR SWORD WARM FOR...
...YOU.
HOW WAS IT OUT THERE, PETE?
BIG HAUL.
ALMOST MORE FISH THAN WATER OUT THERE THESE DAYS. IT'S A WONDER WHAT THE DEATH OF HUMANITY DOES FOR OCEAN LIFE.

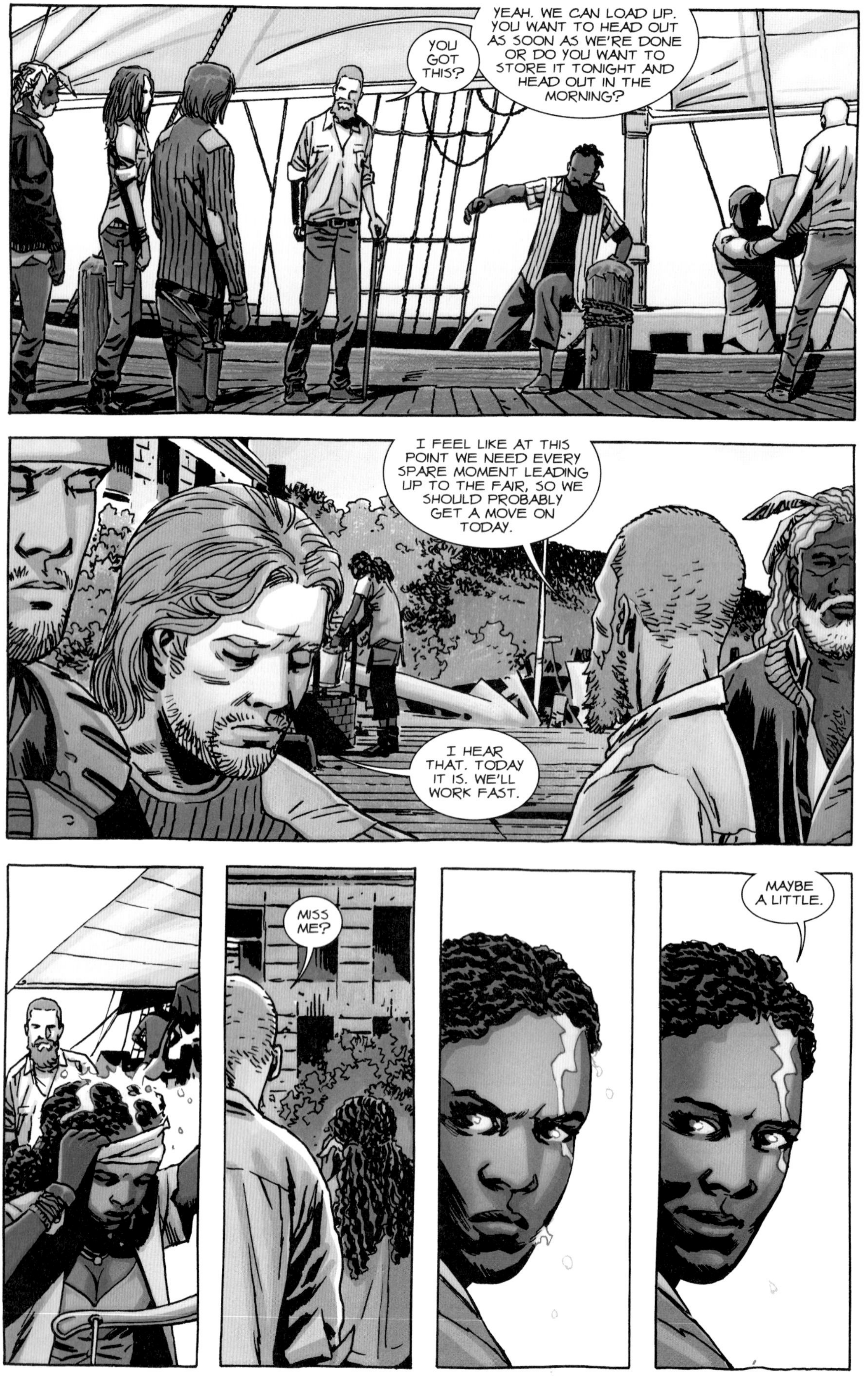
YOU GOT THIS?
YEAH. WE CAN LOAD UP. YOU WANT TO HEAD OUT AS SOON AS WE'RE DONE OR DO YOU WANT TO STORE IT TONIGHT AND HEAD OUT IN THE MORNING?
I FEEL LIKE AT THIS POINT WE NEED EVERY SPARE MOMENT LEADING UP TO THE FAIR, SO WE SHOULD PROBABLY GET A MOVE ON TODAY.
I HEAR THAT. TODAY IT IS. WE'LL WORK FAST.
MISS ME?
MAYBE A LITTLE.

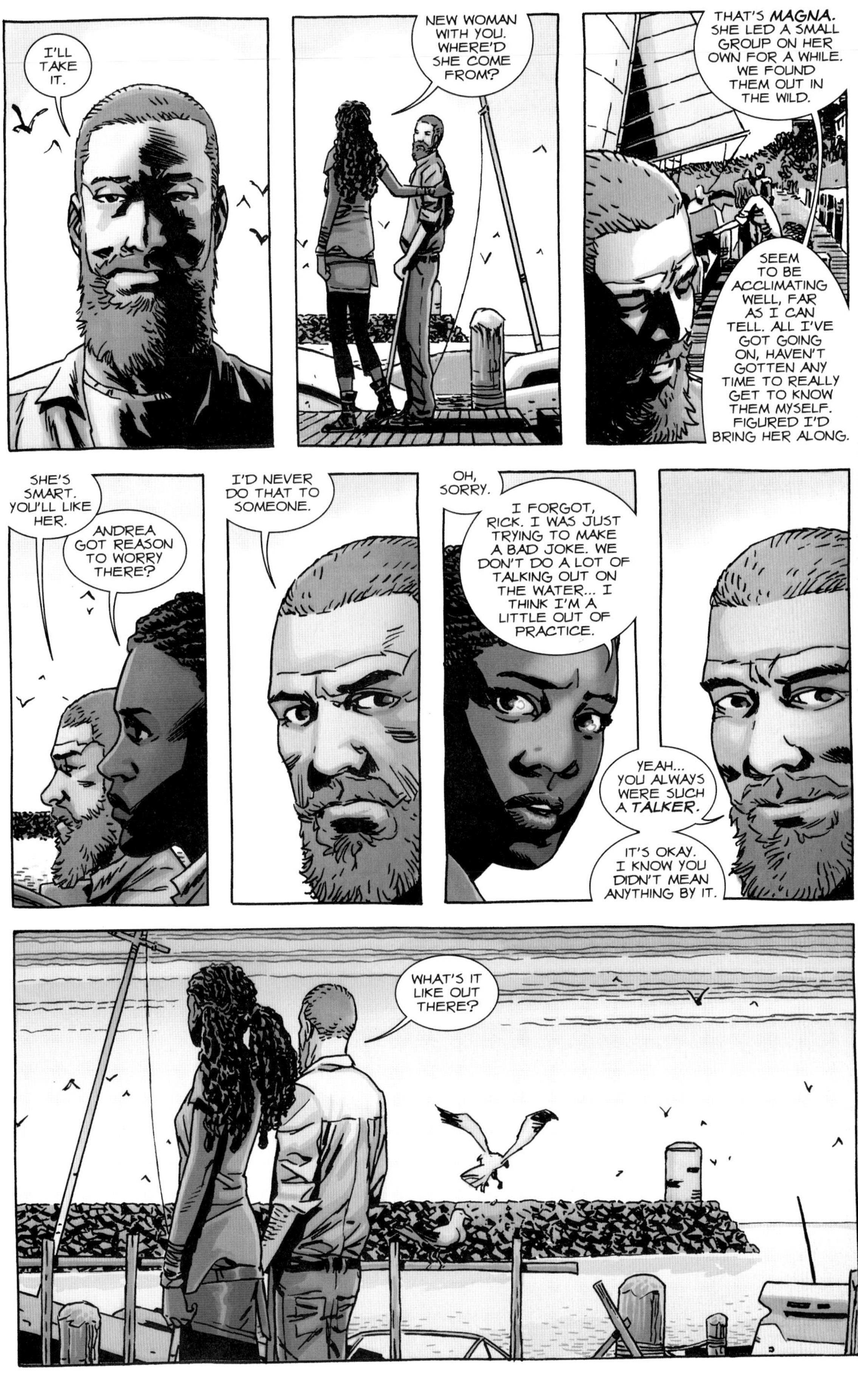

I'LL TAKE IT.
NEW WOMAN WITH YOU. WHERE'D SHE COME FROM?
THAT'S MAGNA. SHE LED A SMALL GROUP ON HER OWN FOR A WHILE. WE FOUND THEM OUT IN THE WILD.
SEEM TO BE ACCLIMATING WELL, FAR AS I CAN TELL. ALL I'VE GOT GOING ON, HAVEN'T GOTTEN ANY TIME TO REALLY GET TO KNOW THEM MYSELF. FIGURED I'D BRING HER ALONG.
SHE'S SMART. YOU'LL LIKE HER.
ANDREA GOT REASON TO WORRY THERE?
I'D NEVER DO THAT TO SOMEONE.
OH, SORRY.
I FORGOT, RICK. I WAS JUST TRYING TO MAKE A BAD JOKE. WE DON'T DO A LOT OF TALKING OUT ON THE WATER... I THINK I'M A LITTLE OUT OF PRACTICE.
YEAH... YOU ALWAYS WERE SUCH A TALKER.
IT'S OKAY. I KNOW YOU DIDN'T MEAN ANYTHING BY IT.
WHAT'S IT LIKE OUT THERE?

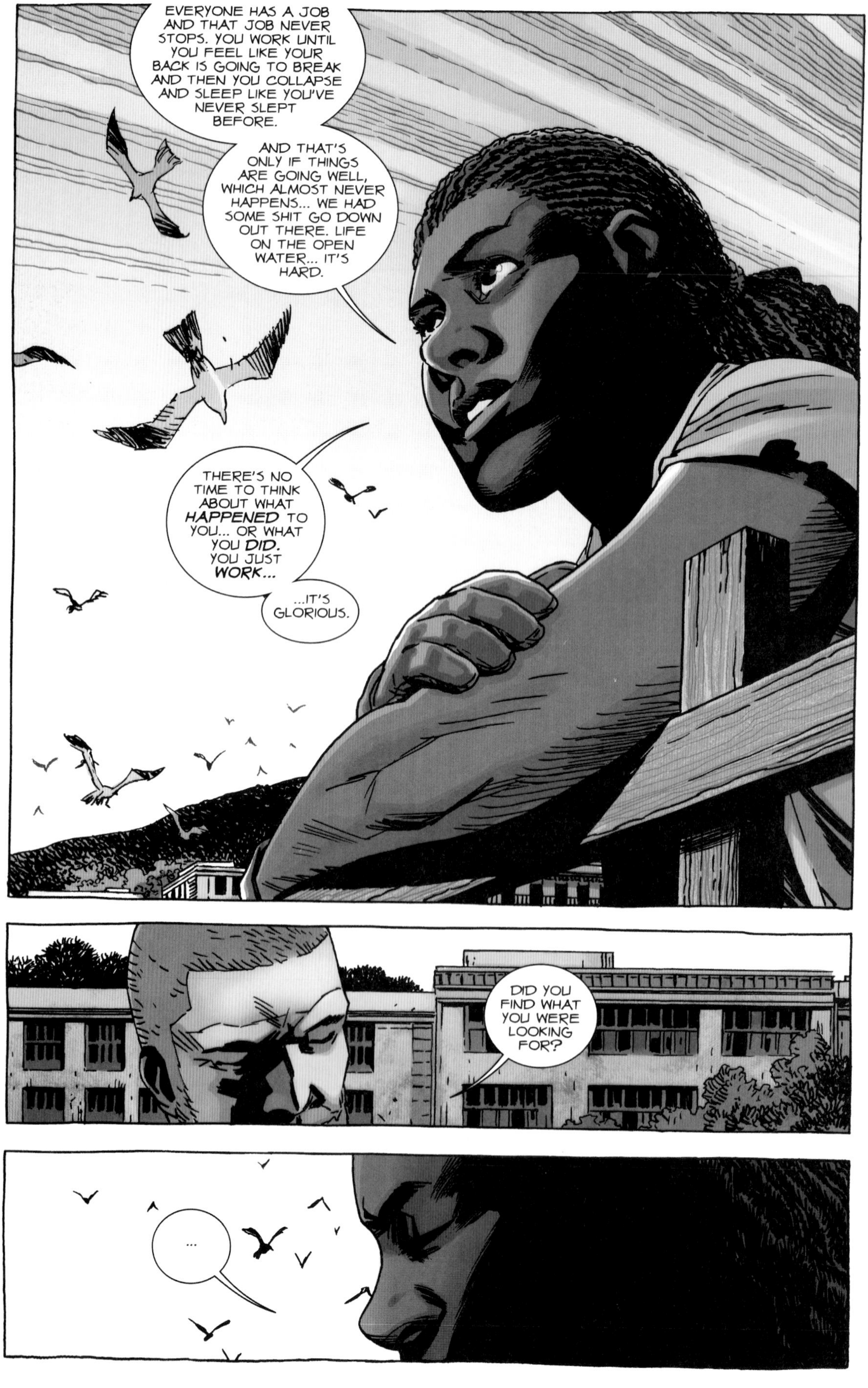
EVERYONE HAS A JOB AND THAT JOB NEVER STOPS. YOU WORK UNTIL YOU FEEL LIKE YOUR BACK IS GOING TO BREAK AND THEN YOU COLLAPSE AND SLEEP LIKE YOU'VE NEVER SLEPT BEFORE.
AND THAT'S ONLY IF THINGS ARE GOING WELL, WHICH ALMOST NEVER HAPPENS... WE HAD SOME SHIT GO DOWN OUT THERE. LIFE ON THE OPEN WATER... IT'S HARD.
THERE'S NO TIME TO THINK ABOUT WHAT ***HAPPENED*** TO YOU... OR WHAT YOU ***DID.*** YOU JUST ***WORK...***
...IT'S GLORIOUS.
DID YOU FIND WHAT YOU WERE LOOKING FOR?
...

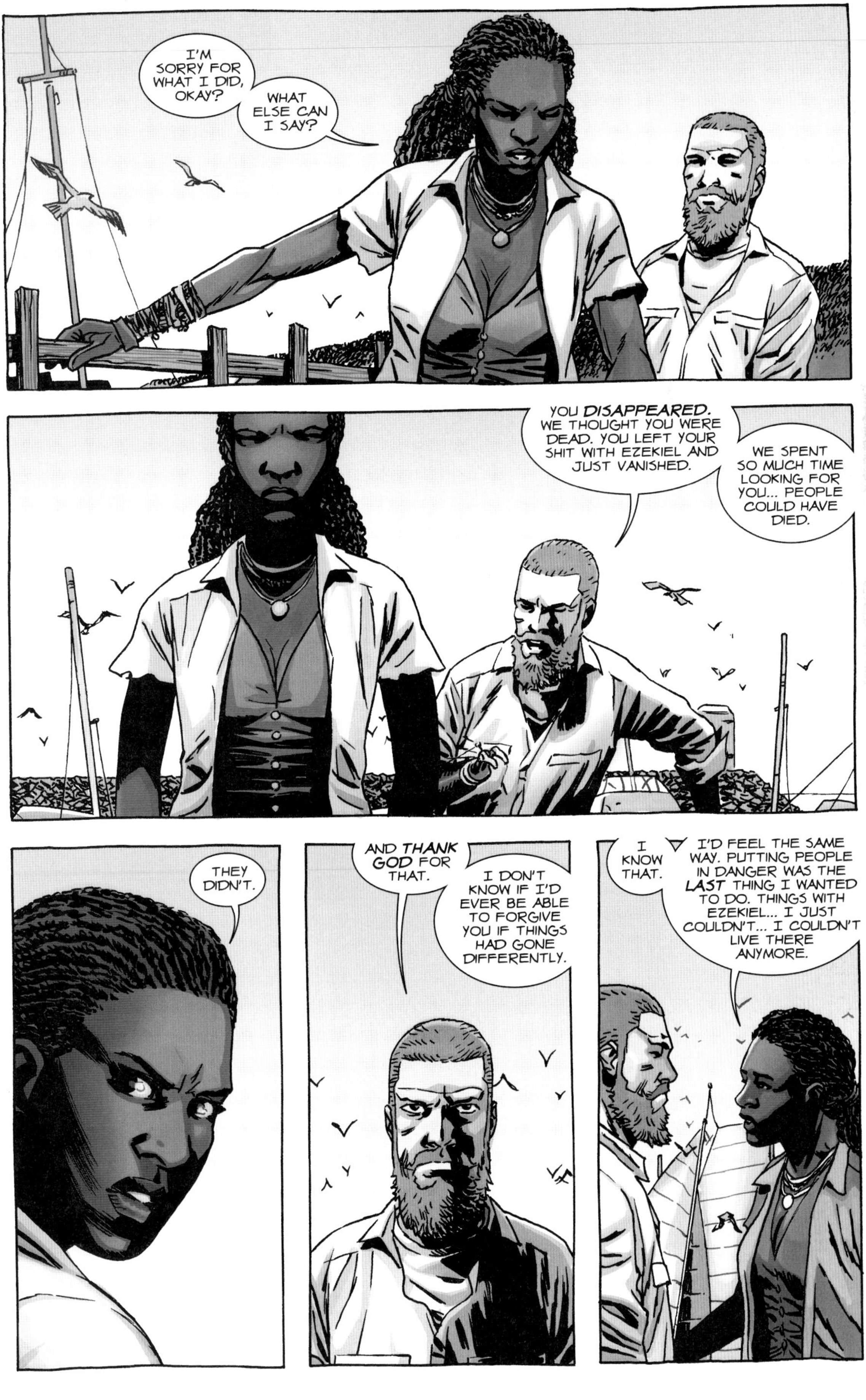
I'M SORRY FOR WHAT I DID, OKAY?
WHAT ELSE CAN I SAY?
YOU *DISAPPEARED.* WE THOUGHT YOU WERE DEAD. YOU LEFT YOUR SHIT WITH EZEKIEL AND JUST VANISHED.
WE SPENT SO MUCH TIME LOOKING FOR YOU... PEOPLE COULD HAVE DIED.
THEY DIDN'T.
AND *THANK GOD* FOR THAT.
I DON'T KNOW IF I'D EVER BE ABLE TO FORGIVE YOU IF THINGS HAD GONE DIFFERENTLY.
I KNOW THAT.
I'D FEEL THE SAME WAY. PUTTING PEOPLE IN DANGER WAS THE *LAST* THING I WANTED TO DO. THINGS WITH EZEKIEL... I JUST COULDN'T... I COULDN'T LIVE THERE ANYMORE.

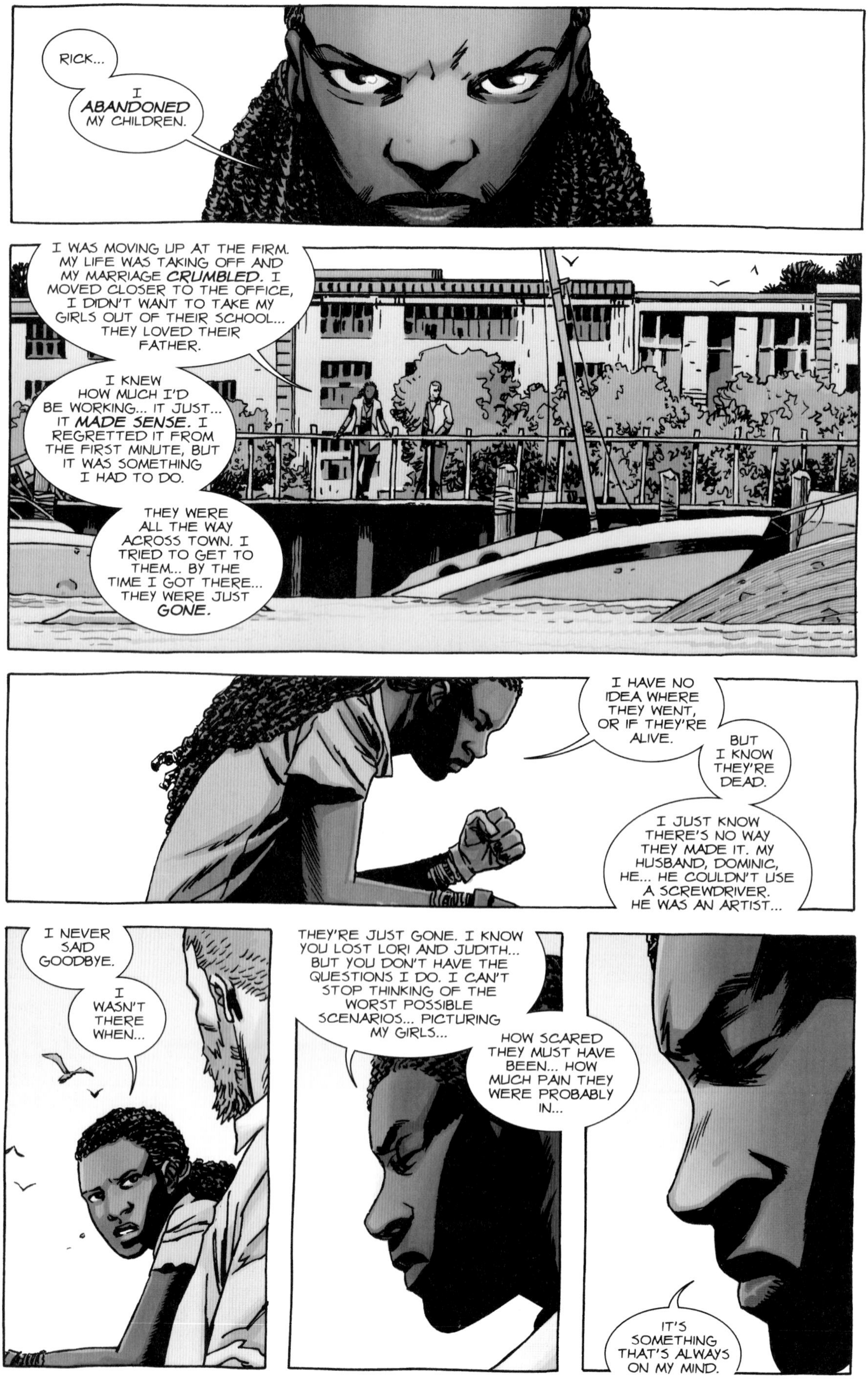
RICK...
I *ABANDONED* MY CHILDREN.
I WAS MOVING UP AT THE FIRM. MY LIFE WAS TAKING OFF AND MY MARRIAGE *CRUMBLED.* I MOVED CLOSER TO THE OFFICE, I DIDN'T WANT TO TAKE MY GIRLS OUT OF THEIR SCHOOL... THEY LOVED THEIR FATHER.
I KNEW HOW MUCH I'D BE WORKING... IT JUST... IT *MADE SENSE.* I REGRETTED IT FROM THE FIRST MINUTE, BUT IT WAS SOMETHING I HAD TO DO.
THEY WERE ALL THE WAY ACROSS TOWN. I TRIED TO GET TO THEM... BY THE TIME I GOT THERE... THEY WERE JUST *GONE.*
I HAVE NO IDEA WHERE THEY WENT, OR IF THEY'RE ALIVE.
BUT I KNOW THEY'RE DEAD.
I JUST KNOW THERE'S NO WAY THEY MADE IT. MY HUSBAND, DOMINIC, HE... HE COULDN'T USE A SCREWDRIVER. HE WAS AN ARTIST...
I NEVER SAID GOODBYE.
I WASN'T THERE WHEN...
THEY'RE JUST GONE. I KNOW YOU LOST LORI AND JUDITH... BUT YOU DON'T HAVE THE QUESTIONS I DO. I CAN'T STOP THINKING OF THE WORST POSSIBLE SCENARIOS... PICTURING MY GIRLS...
HOW SCARED THEY MUST HAVE BEEN... HOW MUCH PAIN THEY WERE PROBABLY IN...
IT'S SOMETHING THAT'S ALWAYS ON MY MIND.

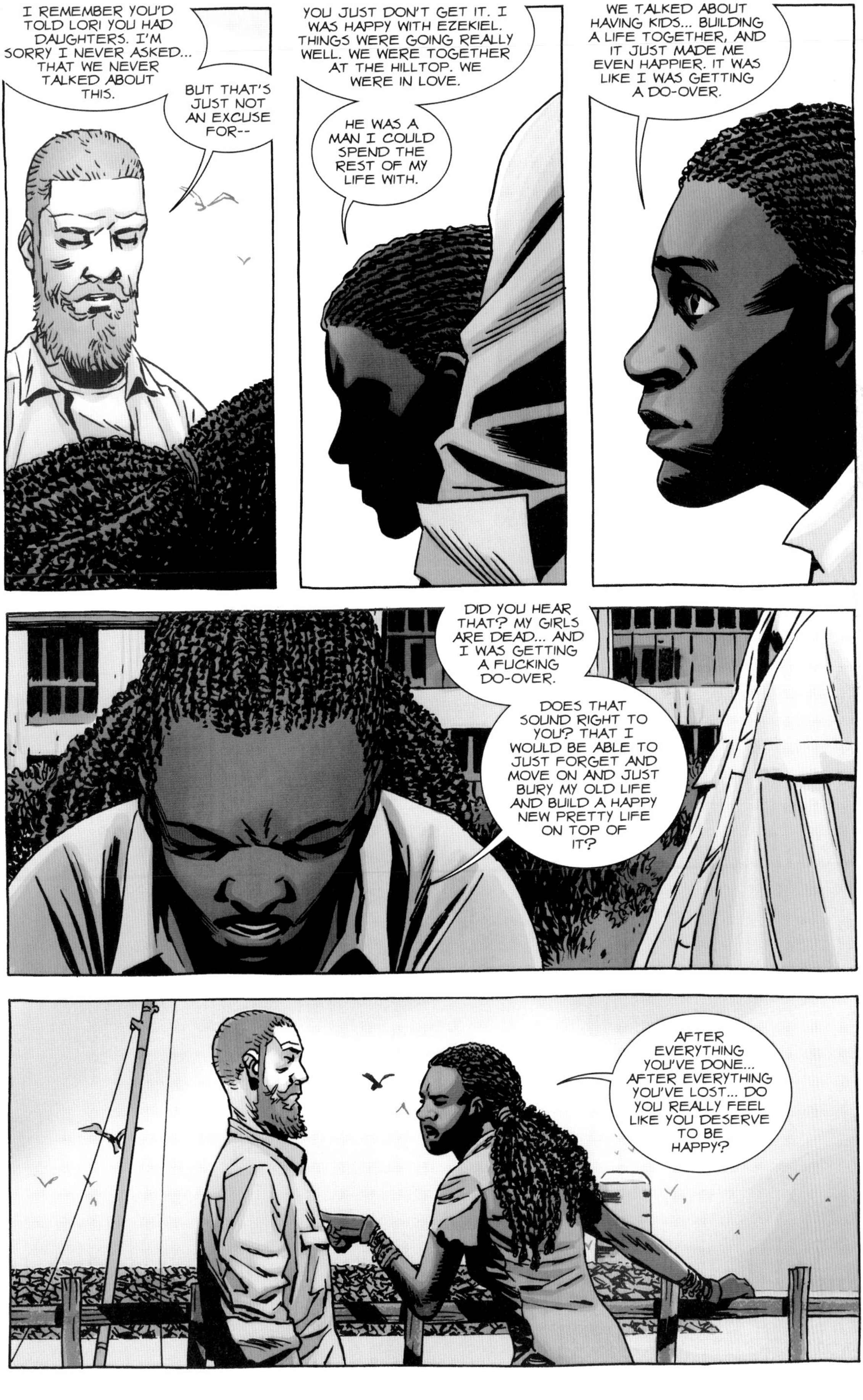
I REMEMBER YOU'D TOLD LORI YOU HAD DAUGHTERS. I'M SORRY I NEVER ASKED... THAT WE NEVER TALKED ABOUT THIS.
BUT THAT'S JUST NOT AN EXCUSE FOR--
YOU JUST DON'T GET IT. I WAS HAPPY WITH EZEKIEL. THINGS WERE GOING REALLY WELL. WE WERE TOGETHER AT THE HILLTOP. WE WERE IN LOVE.
HE WAS A MAN I COULD SPEND THE REST OF MY LIFE WITH.
WE TALKED ABOUT HAVING KIDS... BUILDING A LIFE TOGETHER, AND IT JUST MADE ME EVEN HAPPIER. IT WAS LIKE I WAS GETTING A DO-OVER.
DID YOU HEAR THAT? MY GIRLS ARE DEAD... AND I WAS GETTING A FUCKING DO-OVER.
DOES THAT SOUND RIGHT TO YOU? THAT I WOULD BE ABLE TO JUST FORGET AND MOVE ON AND JUST BURY MY OLD LIFE AND BUILD A HAPPY NEW PRETTY LIFE ON TOP OF IT?
AFTER EVERYTHING YOU'VE DONE... AFTER EVERYTHING YOU'VE LOST... DO YOU REALLY FEEL LIKE YOU DESERVE TO BE HAPPY?

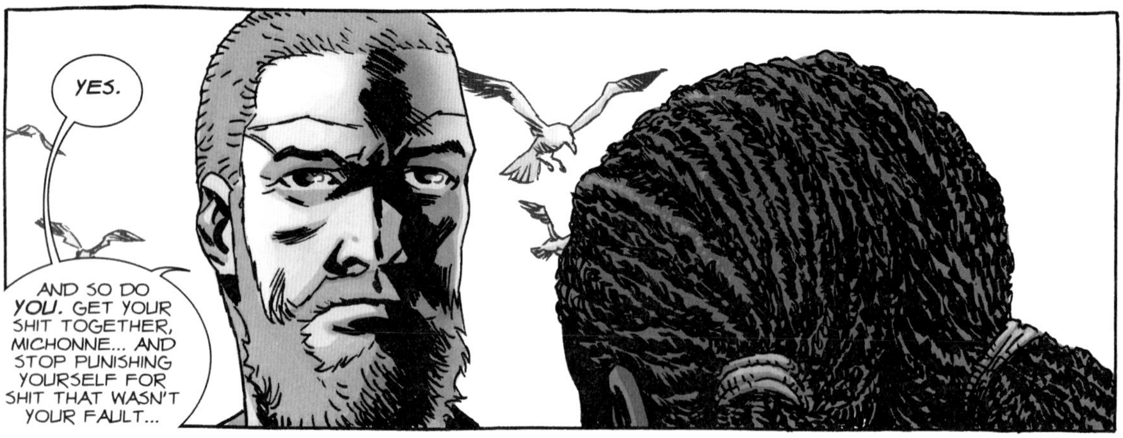
YES.
AND SO DO *YOU.* GET YOUR SHIT TOGETHER, MICHONNE... AND STOP PUNISHING YOURSELF FOR SHIT THAT WASN'T YOUR FAULT...

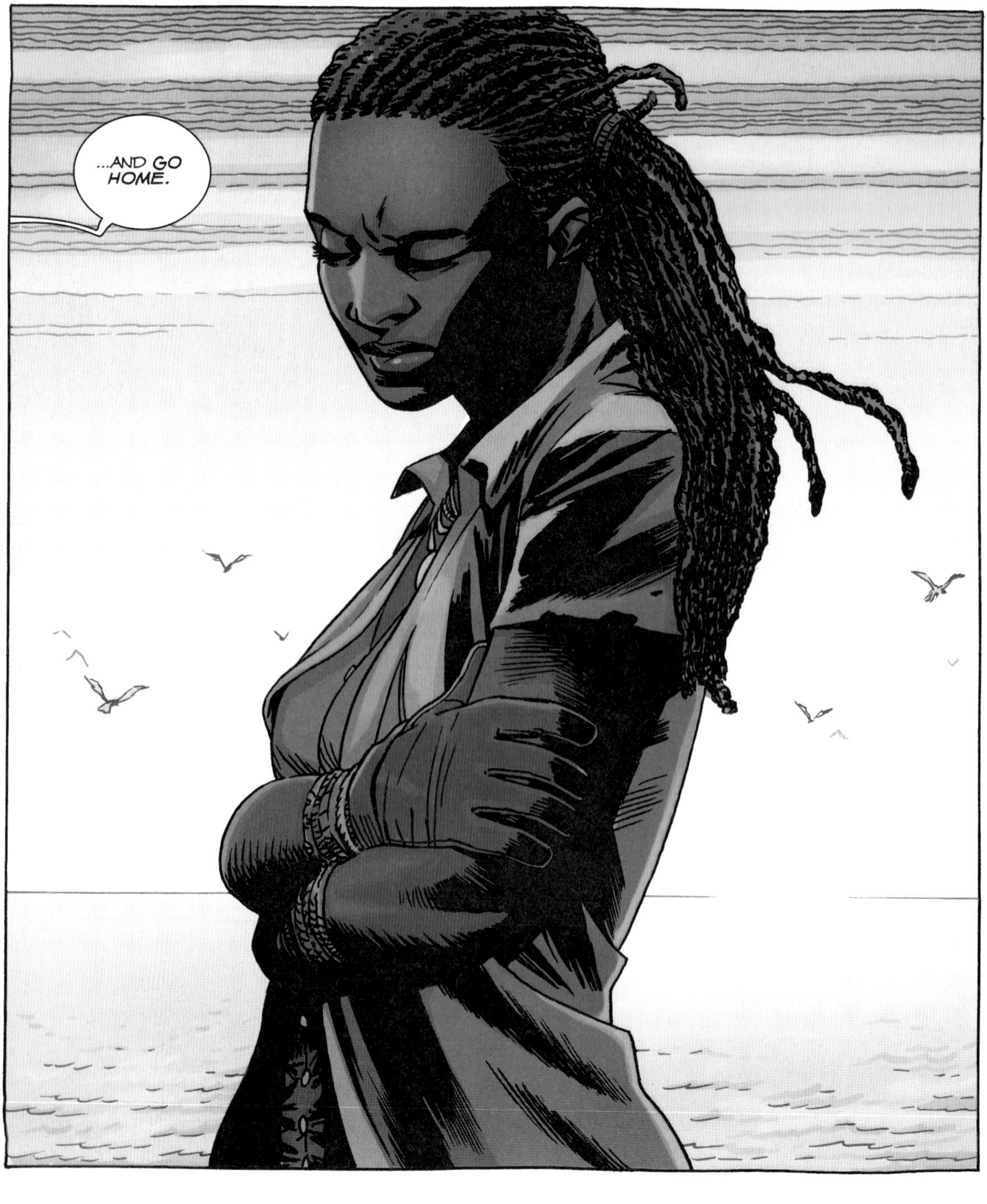
...AND *GO HOME.*

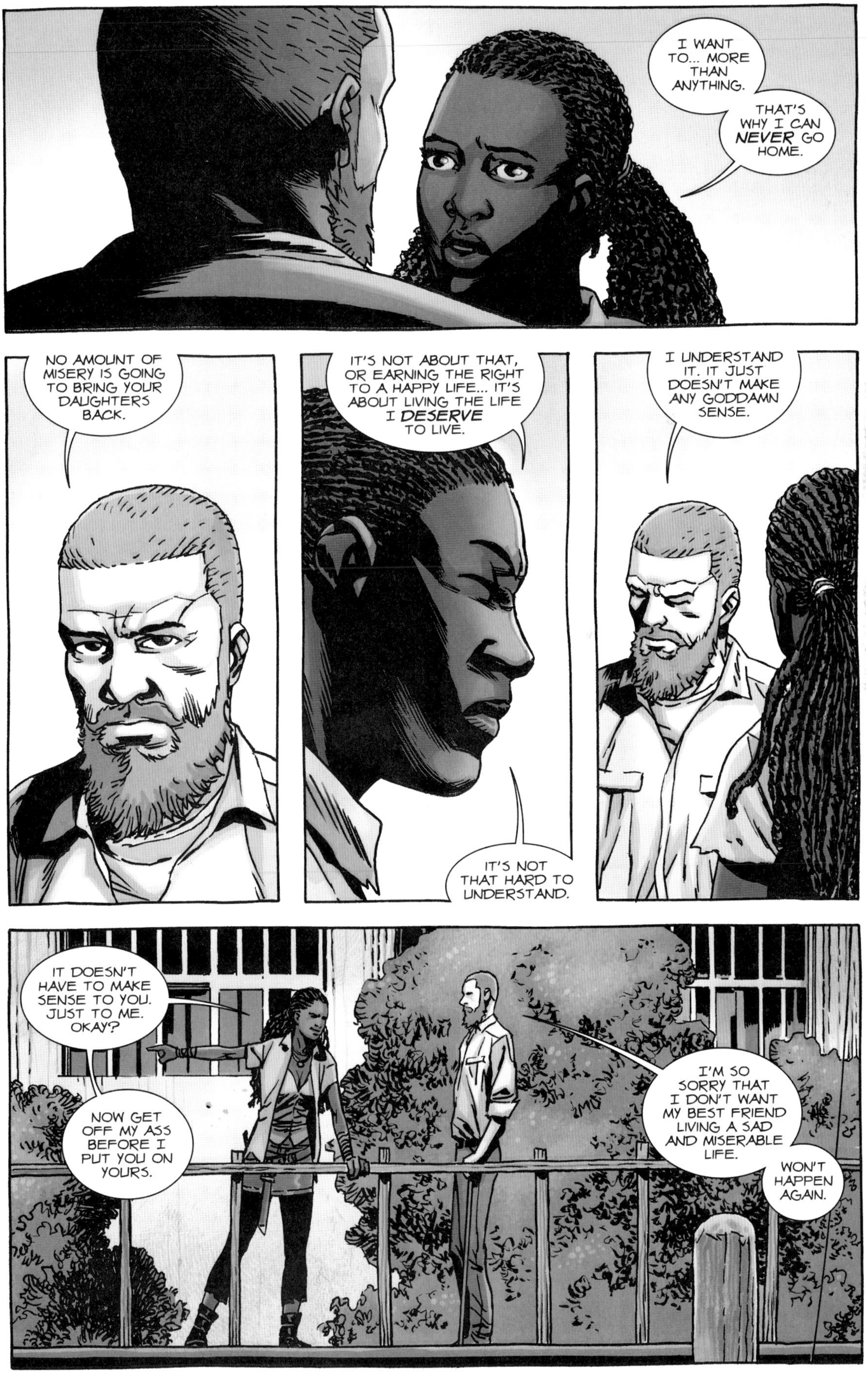

I WANT TO... MORE THAN ANYTHING.
THAT'S WHY I CAN *NEVER* GO HOME.
NO AMOUNT OF MISERY IS GOING TO BRING YOUR DAUGHTERS BACK.
IT'S NOT ABOUT THAT, OR EARNING THE RIGHT TO A HAPPY LIFE... IT'S ABOUT LIVING THE LIFE I *DESERVE* TO LIVE.
IT'S NOT THAT HARD TO UNDERSTAND.
I UNDERSTAND IT. IT JUST DOESN'T MAKE ANY GODDAMN SENSE.
IT DOESN'T HAVE TO MAKE SENSE TO YOU. JUST TO ME. OKAY?
NOW GET OFF MY ASS BEFORE I PUT YOU ON YOURS.
I'M SO SORRY THAT I DON'T WANT MY BEST FRIEND LIVING A SAD AND MISERABLE LIFE.
WON'T HAPPEN AGAIN.

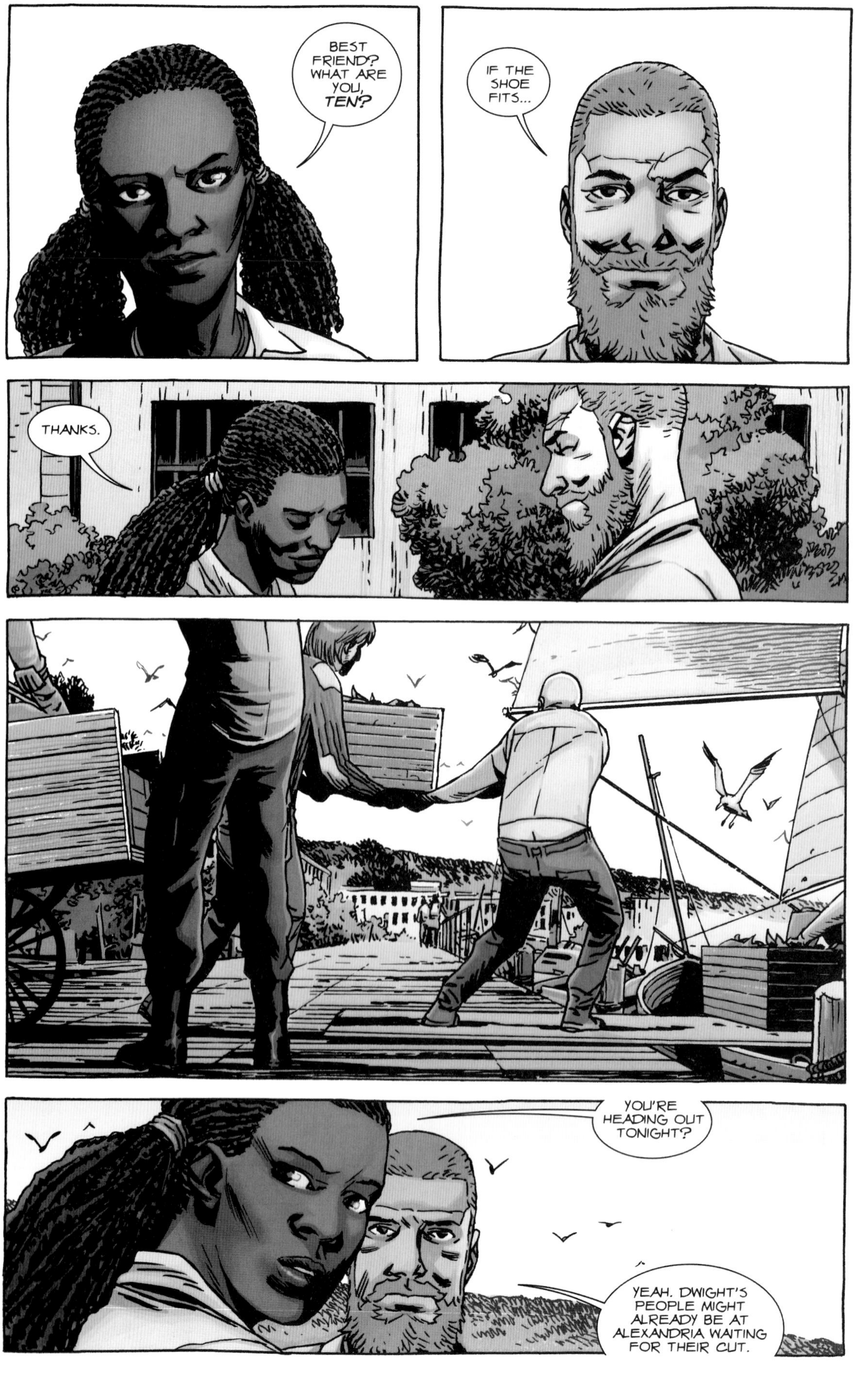
BEST FRIEND? WHAT ARE YOU, TEN?
IF THE SHOE FITS...
THANKS.
YOU'RE HEADING OUT TONIGHT?
YEAH. DWIGHT'S PEOPLE MIGHT ALREADY BE AT ALEXANDRIA WAITING FOR THEIR CUT.

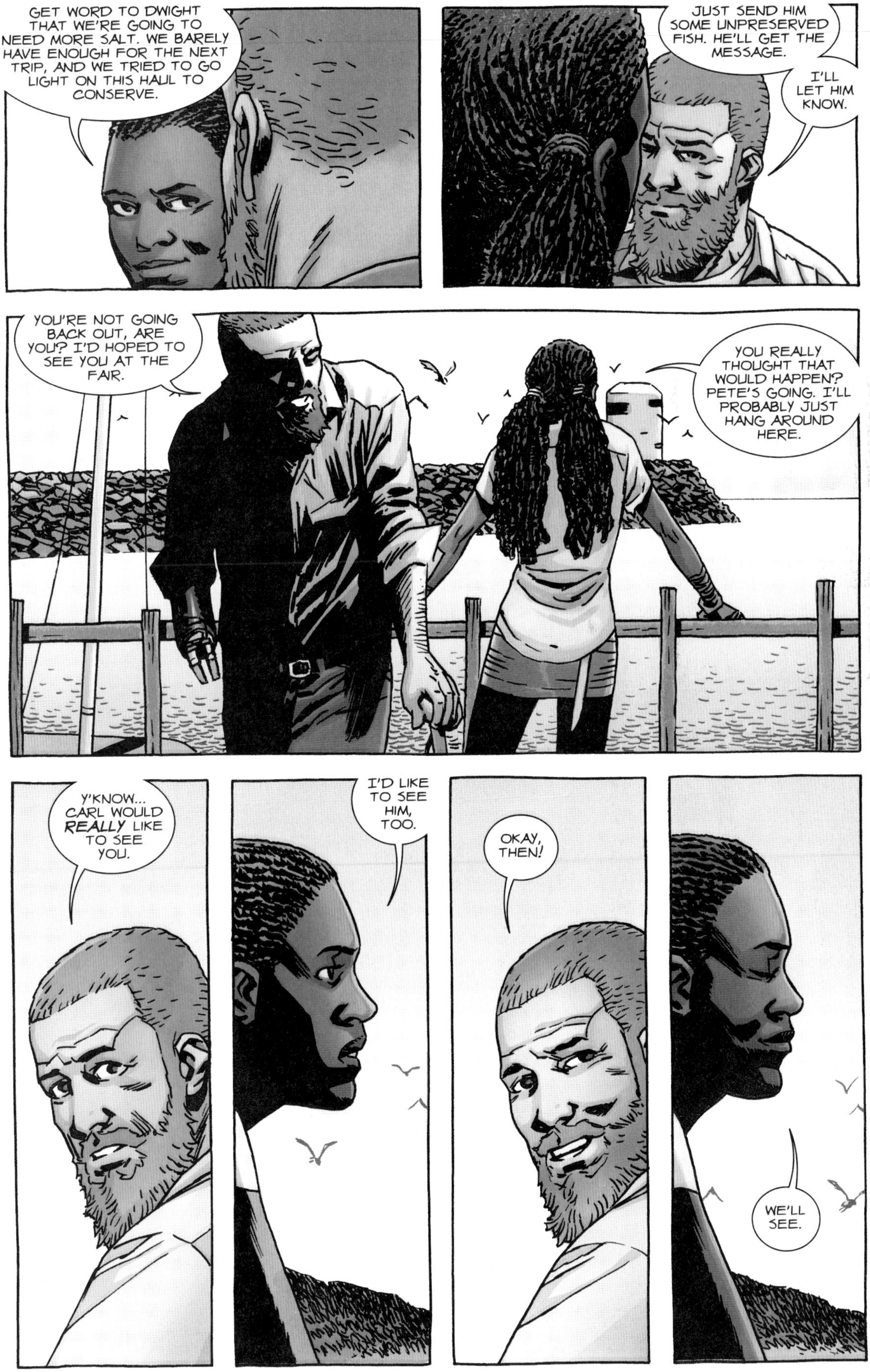
GET WORD TO DWIGHT THAT WE'RE GOING TO NEED MORE SALT. WE BARELY HAVE ENOUGH FOR THE NEXT TRIP, AND WE TRIED TO GO LIGHT ON THIS HAUL TO CONSERVE.
JUST SEND HIM SOME UNPRESERVED FISH. HE'LL GET THE MESSAGE.
I'LL LET HIM KNOW.
YOU'RE NOT GOING BACK OUT, ARE YOU? I'D HOPED TO SEE YOU AT THE FAIR.
YOU REALLY THOUGHT THAT WOULD HAPPEN? PETE'S GOING. I'LL PROBABLY JUST HANG AROUND HERE.
Y'KNOW... CARL WOULD REALLY LIKE TO SEE YOU.
I'D LIKE TO SEE HIM, TOO.
OKAY, THEN!
WE'LL SEE.

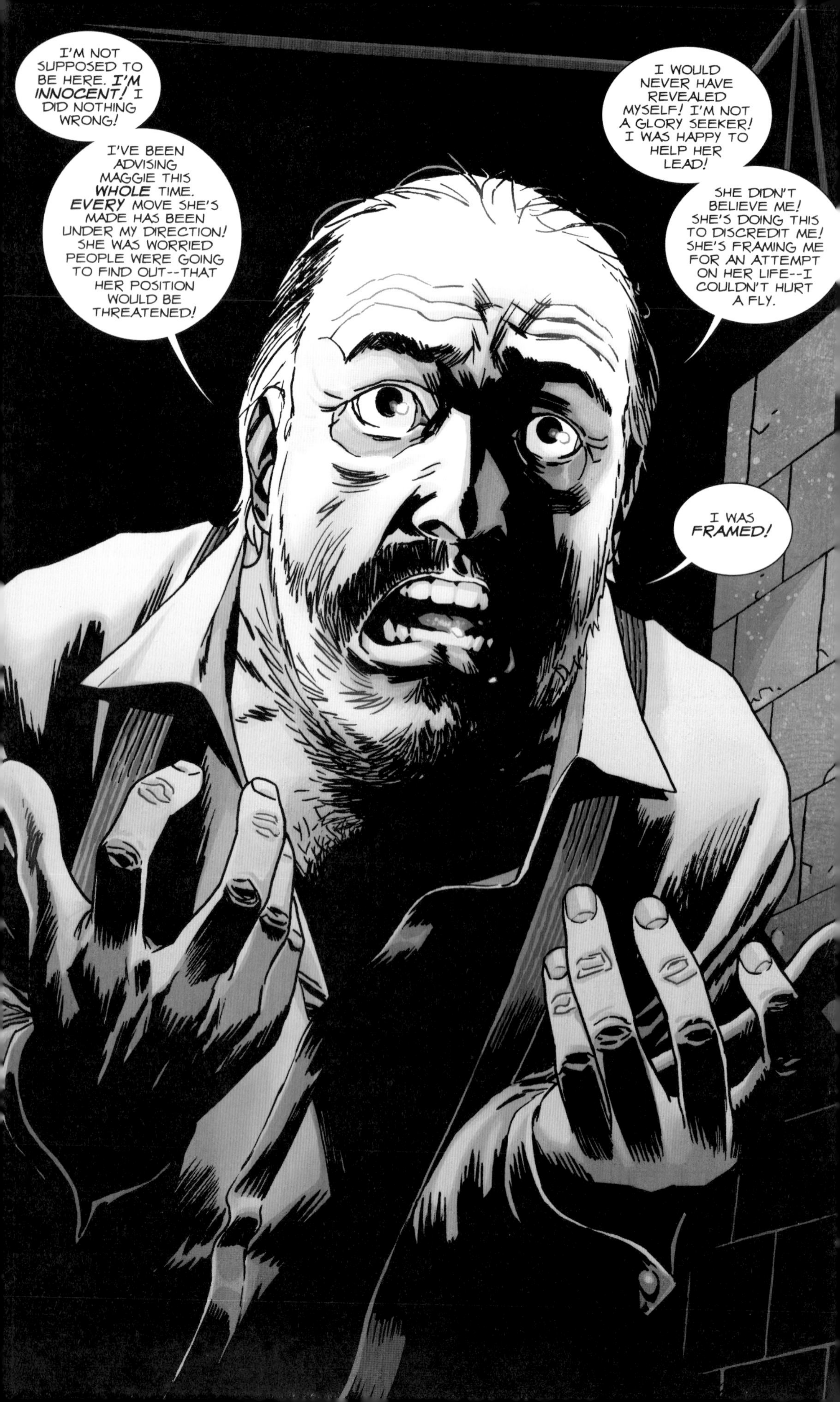
I'M NOT SUPPOSED TO BE HERE. *I'M INNOCENT!* I DID NOTHING WRONG!
I'VE BEEN ADVISING MAGGIE THIS **WHOLE** TIME. ***EVERY*** MOVE SHE'S MADE HAS BEEN UNDER MY DIRECTION! SHE WAS WORRIED PEOPLE WERE GOING TO FIND OUT--THAT HER POSITION WOULD BE THREATENED!
I WOULD NEVER HAVE REVEALED MYSELF! I'M NOT A GLORY SEEKER! I WAS HAPPY TO HELP HER LEAD!
SHE DIDN'T BELIEVE ME! SHE'S DOING THIS TO DISCREDIT ME! SHE'S FRAMING ME FOR AN ATTEMPT ON HER LIFE--I COULDN'T HURT A FLY.
I WAS *FRAMED!*

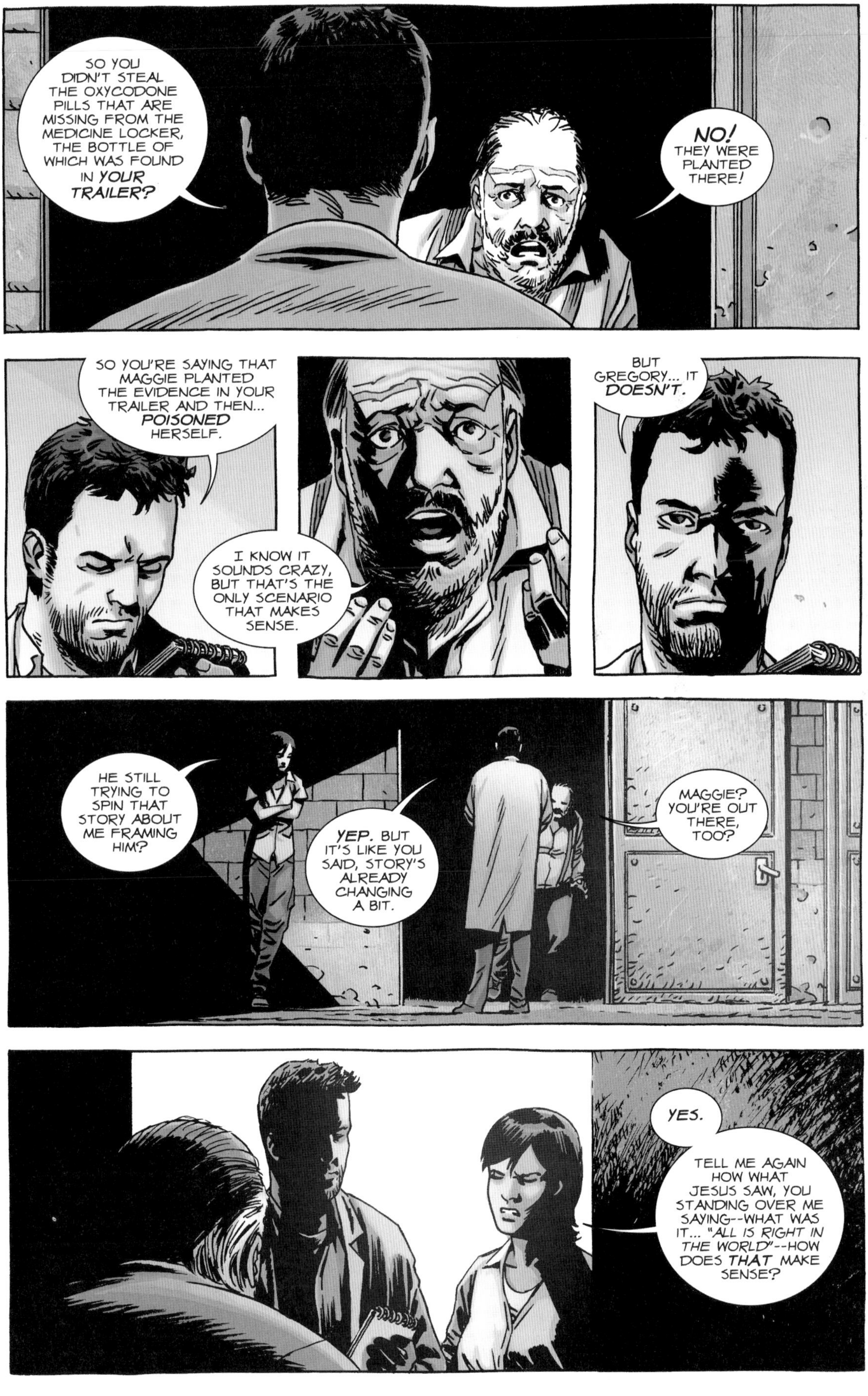

SO YOU DIDN'T STEAL THE OXYCODONE PILLS THAT ARE MISSING FROM THE MEDICINE LOCKER, THE BOTTLE OF WHICH WAS FOUND IN *YOUR TRAILER?*
NO! THEY WERE PLANTED THERE!
SO YOU'RE SAYING THAT MAGGIE PLANTED THE EVIDENCE IN YOUR TRAILER AND THEN... *POISONED* HERSELF.
I KNOW IT SOUNDS CRAZY, BUT THAT'S THE ONLY SCENARIO THAT MAKES SENSE.
BUT GREGORY... IT *DOESN'T.*
HE STILL TRYING TO SPIN THAT STORY ABOUT ME FRAMING HIM?
YEP. BUT IT'S LIKE YOU SAID, STORY'S ALREADY CHANGING A BIT.
MAGGIE? YOU'RE OUT THERE, TOO?
YES.
TELL ME AGAIN HOW WHAT JESUS SAW, YOU STANDING OVER ME SAYING--WHAT WAS IT... *"ALL IS RIGHT IN THE WORLD"*--HOW DOES *THAT* MAKE SENSE?

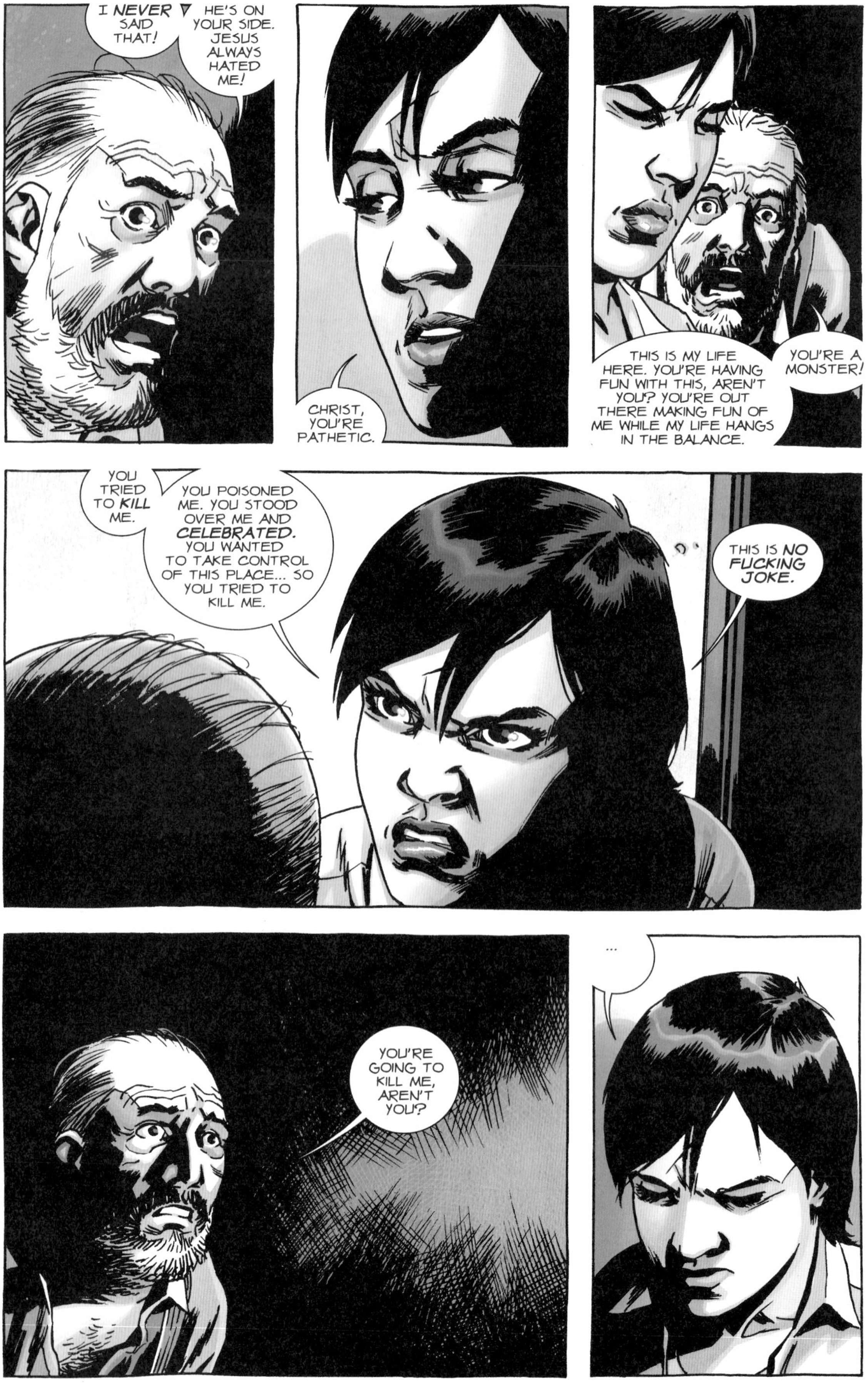
I NEVER SAID THAT!
HE'S ON YOUR SIDE. JESUS ALWAYS HATED ME!
CHRIST, YOU'RE PATHETIC.
THIS IS MY LIFE HERE. YOU'RE HAVING FUN WITH THIS, AREN'T YOU? YOU'RE OUT THERE MAKING FUN OF ME WHILE MY LIFE HANGS IN THE BALANCE.
YOU'RE A MONSTER!
YOU TRIED TO KILL ME.
YOU POISONED ME. YOU STOOD OVER ME AND CELEBRATED. YOU WANTED TO TAKE CONTROL OF THIS PLACE... SO YOU TRIED TO KILL ME.
THIS IS NO FUCKING JOKE.
YOU'RE GOING TO KILL ME, AREN'T YOU?
...

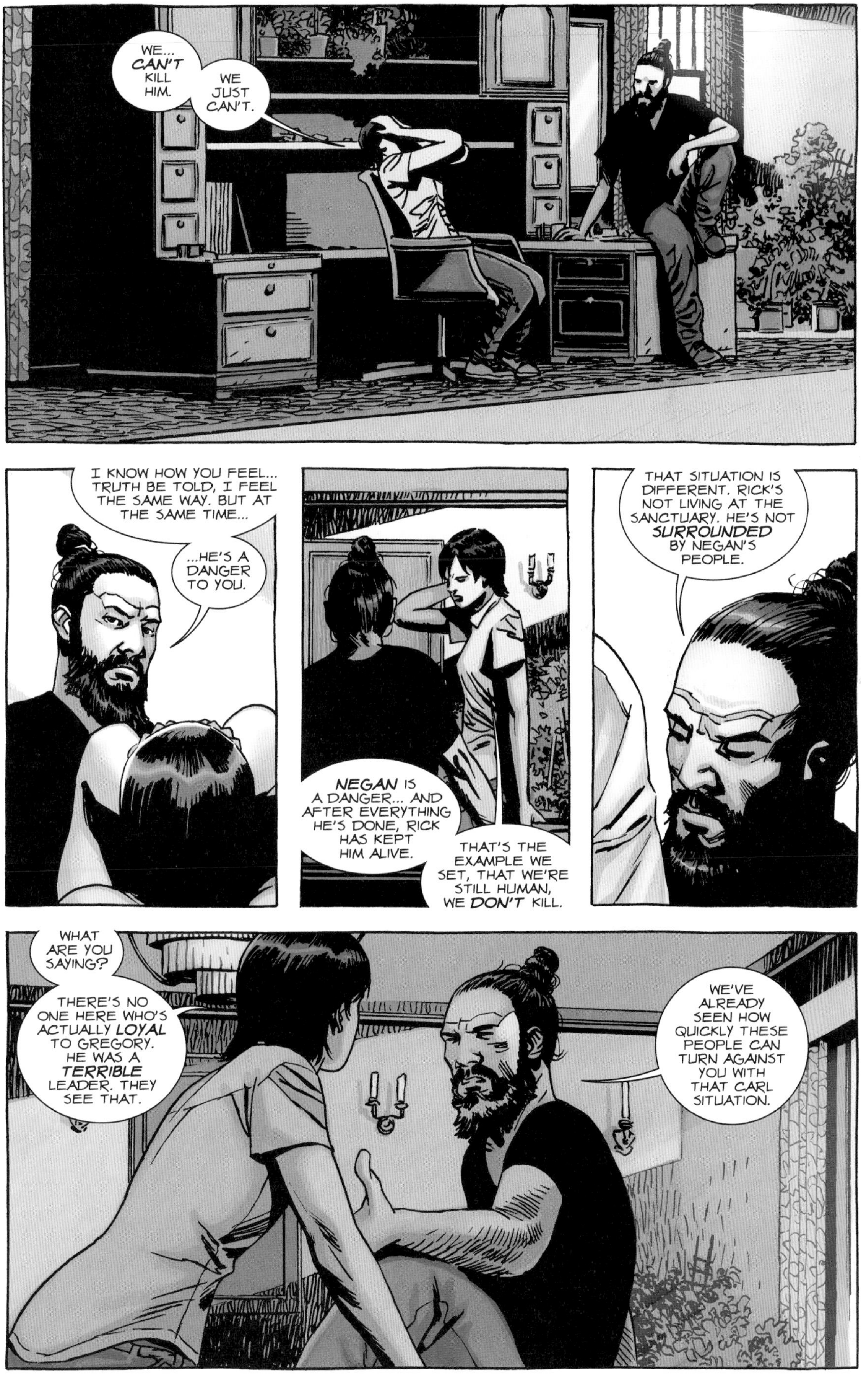
WE... CAN'T KILL HIM.
WE JUST CAN'T.
I KNOW HOW YOU FEEL... TRUTH BE TOLD, I FEEL THE SAME WAY. BUT AT THE SAME TIME...
...HE'S A DANGER TO YOU.
NEGAN IS A DANGER... AND AFTER EVERYTHING HE'S DONE, RICK HAS KEPT HIM ALIVE.
THAT'S THE EXAMPLE WE SET, THAT WE'RE STILL HUMAN, WE DON'T KILL.
THAT SITUATION IS DIFFERENT. RICK'S NOT LIVING AT THE SANCTUARY. HE'S NOT SURROUNDED BY NEGAN'S PEOPLE.
WHAT ARE YOU SAYING?
THERE'S NO ONE HERE WHO'S ACTUALLY LOYAL TO GREGORY. HE WAS A TERRIBLE LEADER. THEY SEE THAT.
WE'VE ALREADY SEEN HOW QUICKLY THESE PEOPLE CAN TURN AGAINST YOU WITH THAT CARL SITUATION.

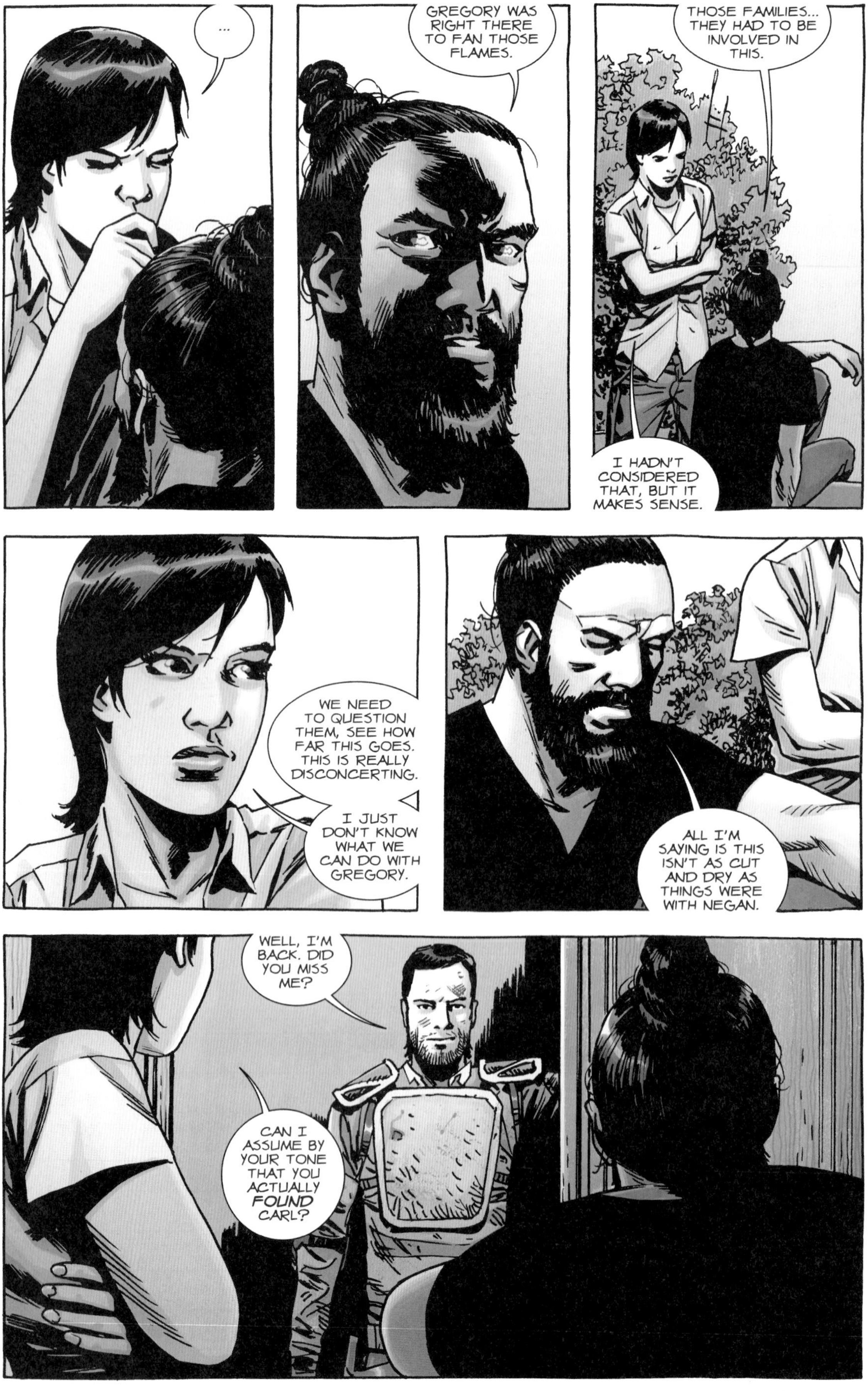
...
GREGORY WAS RIGHT THERE TO FAN THOSE FLAMES.
THOSE FAMILIES... THEY HAD TO BE INVOLVED IN THIS.
I HADN'T CONSIDERED THAT, BUT IT MAKES SENSE.
WE NEED TO QUESTION THEM, SEE HOW FAR THIS GOES. THIS IS REALLY DISCONCERTING.
I JUST DON'T KNOW WHAT WE CAN DO WITH GREGORY.
ALL I'M SAYING IS THIS ISN'T AS CUT AND DRY AS THINGS WERE WITH NEGAN.
WELL, I'M BACK. DID YOU MISS ME?
CAN I ASSUME BY YOUR TONE THAT YOU ACTUALLY FOUND CARL?

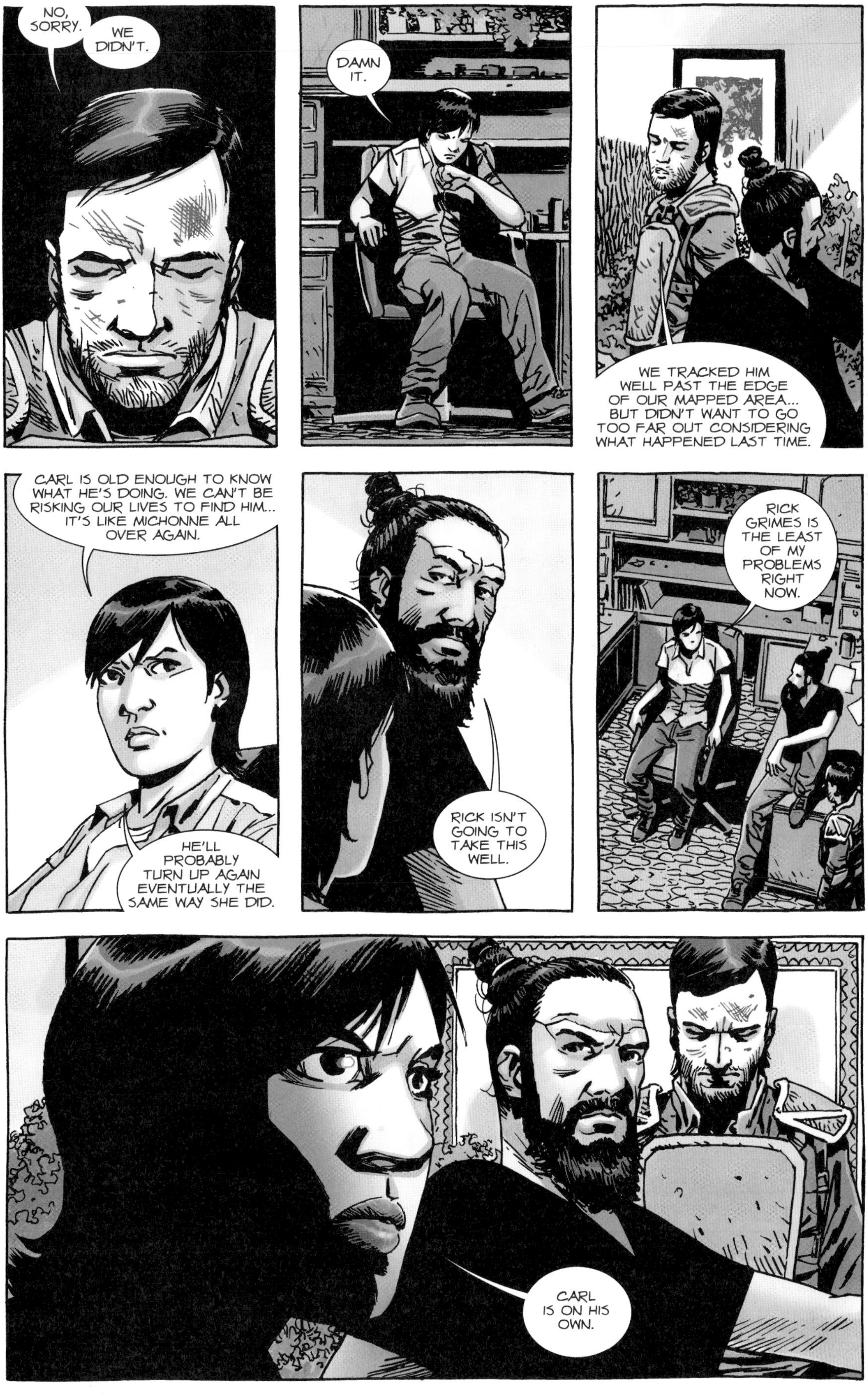
NO, SORRY.
WE DIDN'T.
DAMN IT.
WE TRACKED HIM WELL PAST THE EDGE OF OUR MAPPED AREA... BUT DIDN'T WANT TO GO TOO FAR OUT CONSIDERING WHAT HAPPENED LAST TIME.
CARL IS OLD ENOUGH TO KNOW WHAT HE'S DOING. WE CAN'T BE RISKING OUR LIVES TO FIND HIM... IT'S LIKE MICHONNE ALL OVER AGAIN.
HE'LL PROBABLY TURN UP AGAIN EVENTUALLY THE SAME WAY SHE DID.
RICK ISN'T GOING TO TAKE THIS WELL.
RICK GRIMES IS THE LEAST OF MY PROBLEMS RIGHT NOW.
CARL IS ON HIS OWN.

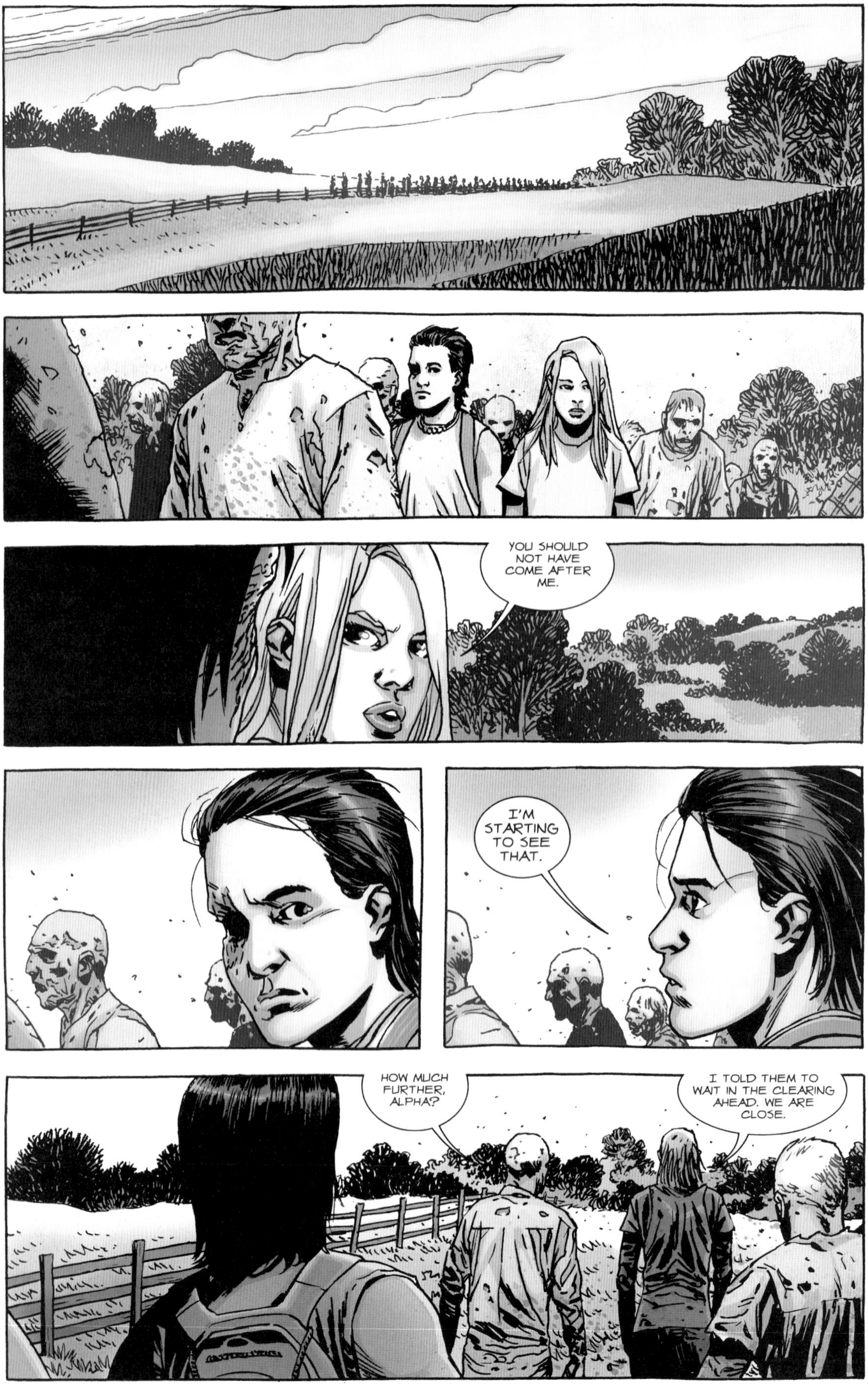
YOU SHOULD NOT HAVE COME AFTER ME.
I'M STARTING TO SEE THAT.
HOW MUCH FURTHER, ALPHA?
I TOLD THEM TO WAIT IN THE CLEARING AHEAD. WE ARE CLOSE.

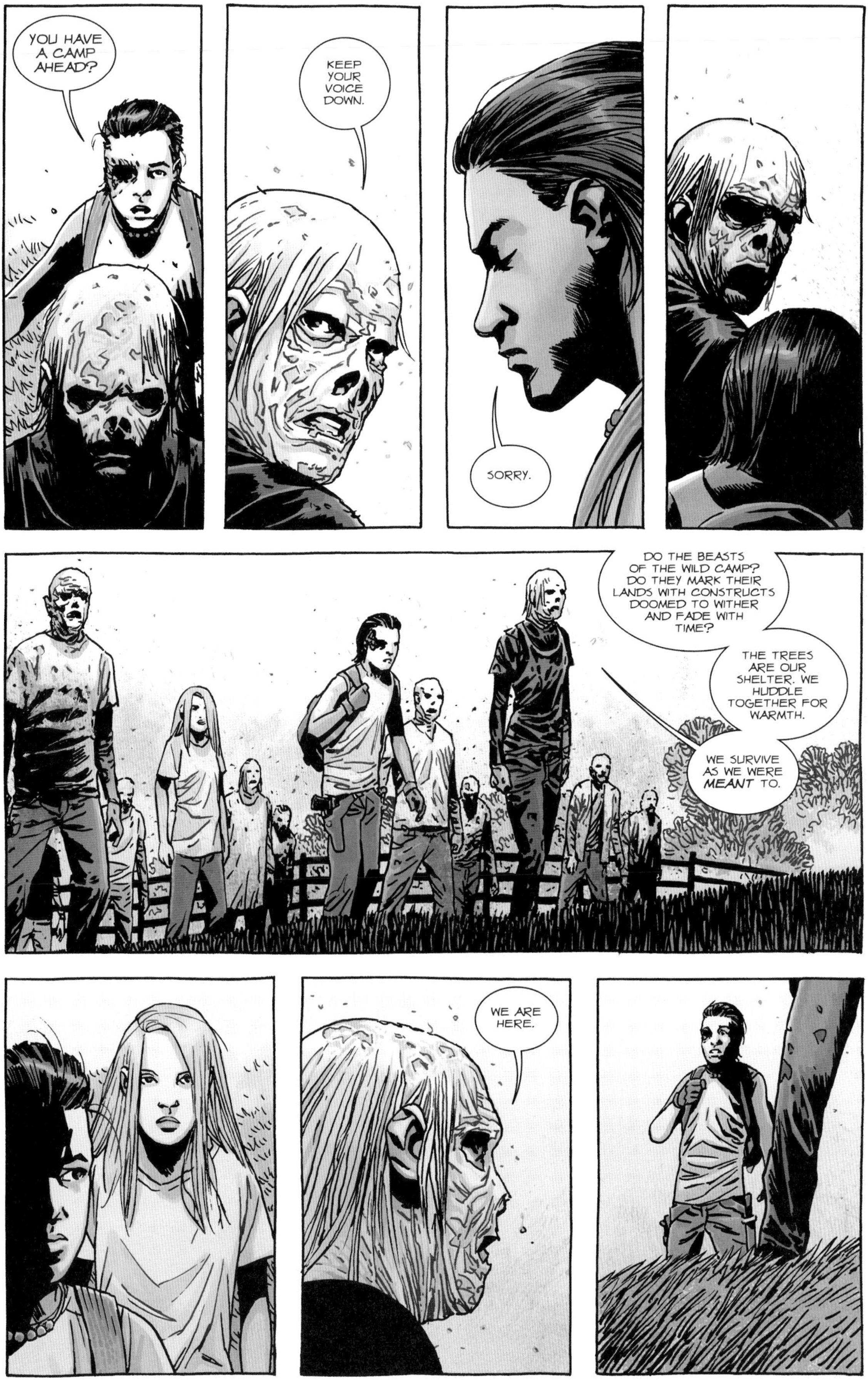

YOU HAVE A CAMP AHEAD?
KEEP YOUR VOICE DOWN.
SORRY.
DO THE BEASTS OF THE WILD CAMP? DO THEY MARK THEIR LANDS WITH CONSTRUCTS DOOMED TO WITHER AND FADE WITH TIME?
THE TREES ARE OUR SHELTER. WE HUDDLE TOGETHER FOR WARMTH.
WE SURVIVE AS WE WERE *MEANT* TO.
WE ARE HERE.

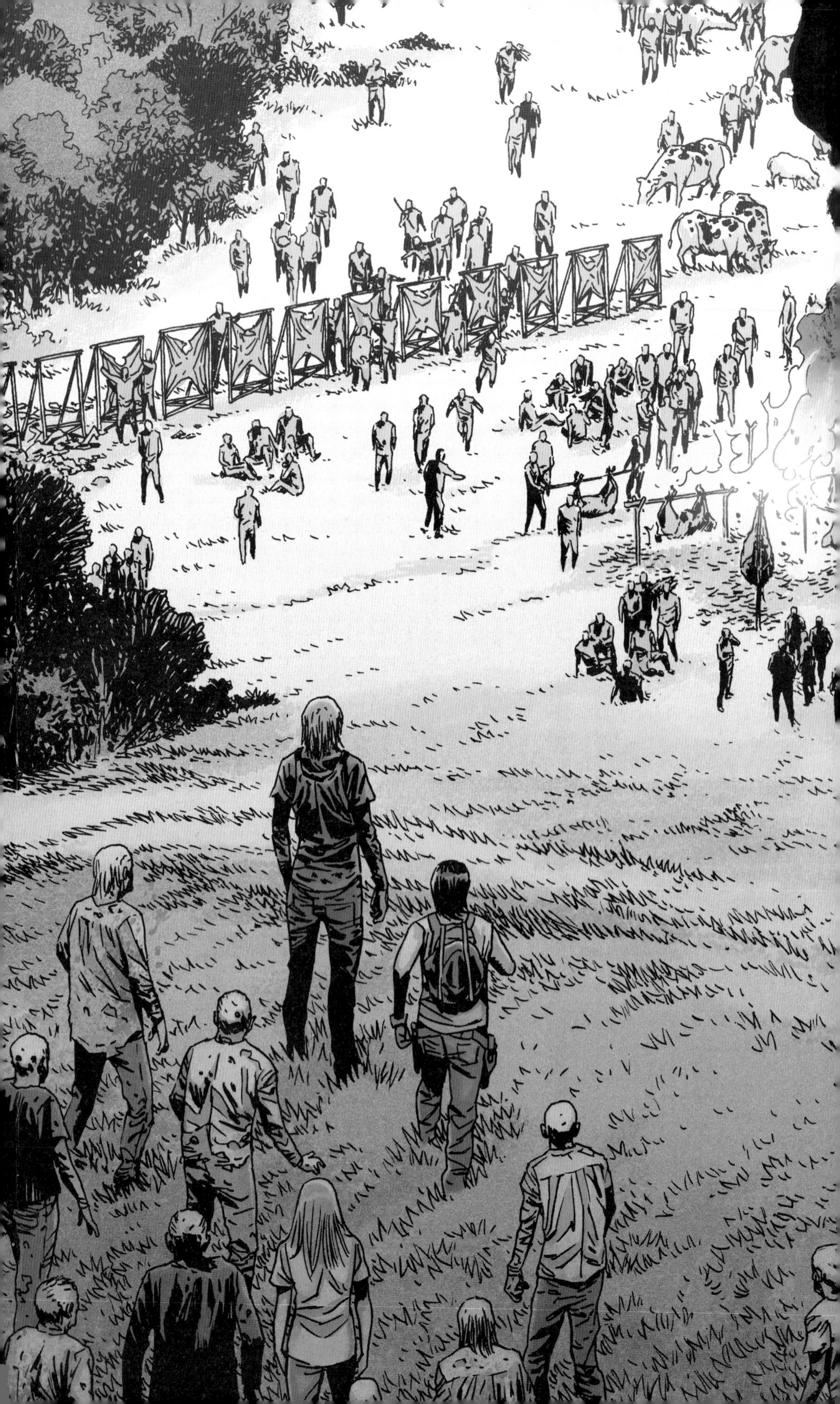

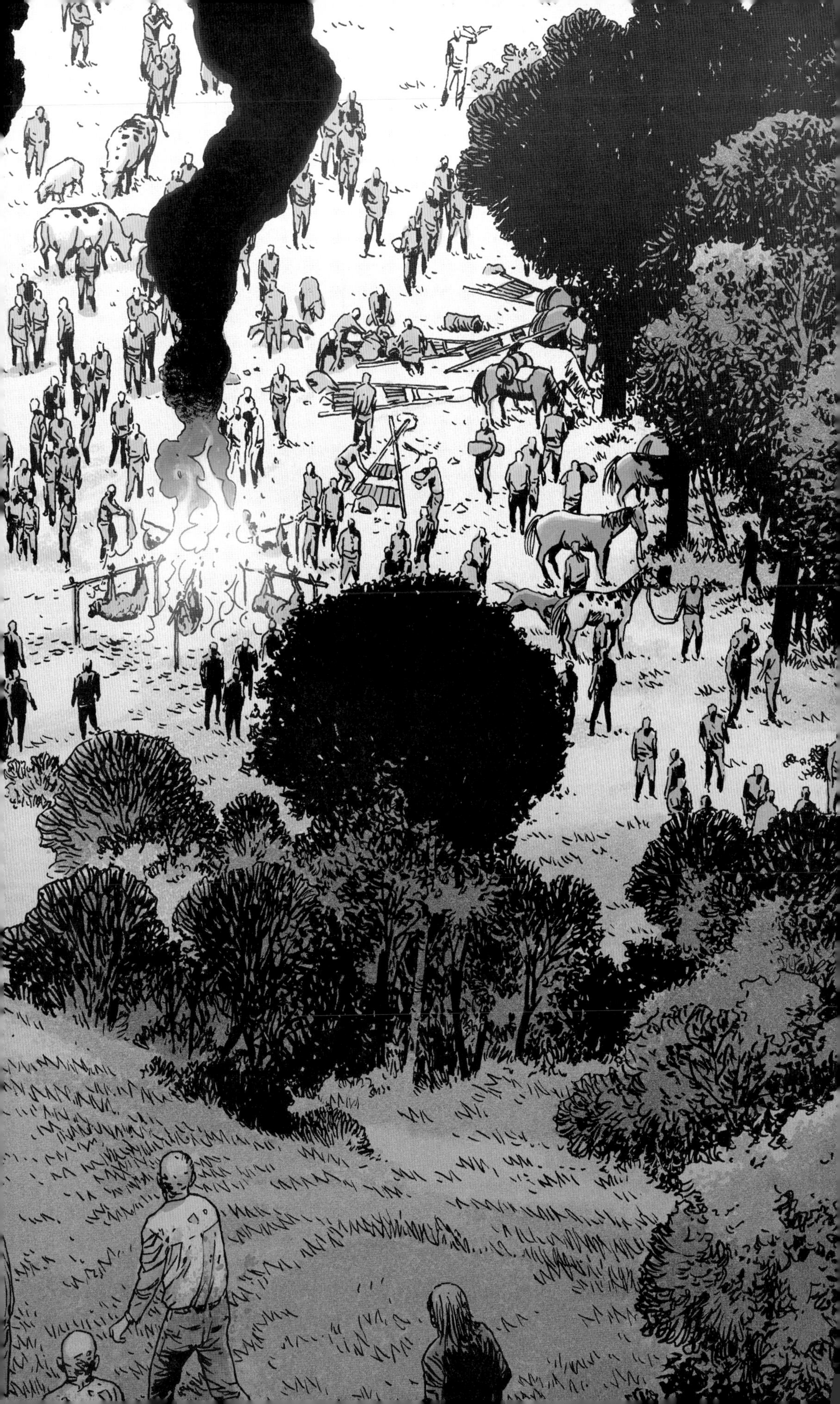

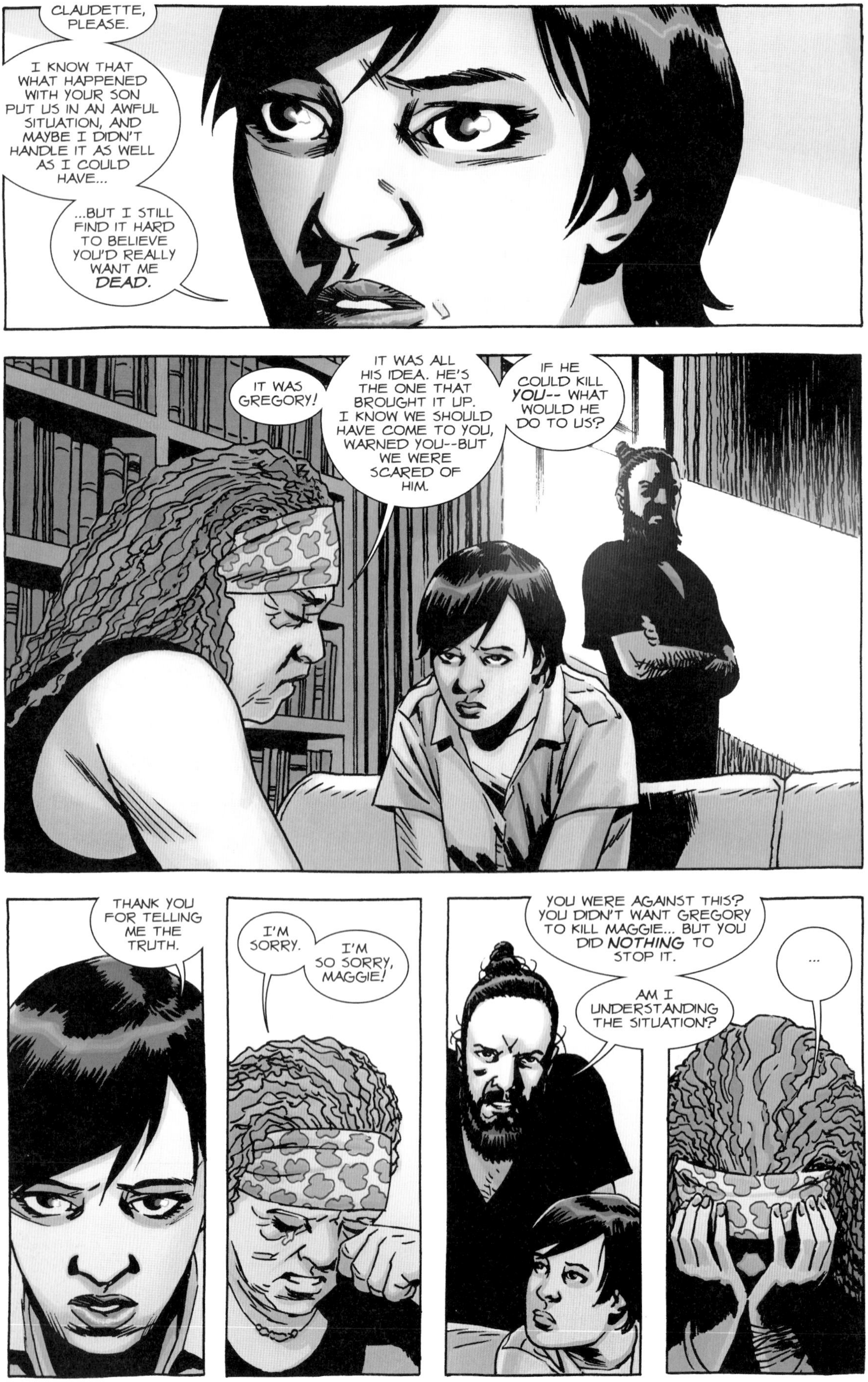
CLAUDETTE, PLEASE.
I KNOW THAT WHAT HAPPENED WITH YOUR SON PUT US IN AN AWFUL SITUATION, AND MAYBE I DIDN'T HANDLE IT AS WELL AS I COULD HAVE...
...BUT I STILL FIND IT HARD TO BELIEVE YOU'D REALLY WANT ME **DEAD.**
IT WAS GREGORY!
IT WAS ALL HIS IDEA. HE'S THE ONE THAT BROUGHT IT UP. I KNOW WE SHOULD HAVE COME TO YOU, WARNED YOU--BUT WE WERE SCARED OF HIM.
IF HE COULD KILL ***YOU--*** WHAT WOULD HE DO TO US?
THANK YOU FOR TELLING ME THE TRUTH.
I'M SORRY.
I'M SO SORRY, MAGGIE!
YOU WERE AGAINST THIS? YOU DIDN'T WANT GREGORY TO KILL MAGGIE... BUT YOU DID ***NOTHING*** TO STOP IT.
AM I UNDERSTANDING THE SITUATION?
...

I WAS *ANGRY.*
MY SON WAS HURT, YOU WERE ACTING LIKE IT WAS HIS FAULT. I THOUGHT I WAS GOING TO *LOSE* HIM.
SO... I WOULDN'T HAVE BEEN UPSET IF YOU'D DIED.
THAT SOUNDS *AWFUL.* NO.
WHAT I MEAN TO SAY IS IN THE MOMENT, AS ANGRY AS I WAS... I JUST WASN'T THINKING STRAIGHT.
I GET THAT WAY.
ALWAYS HAD A TEMPER.
AND YOUR HUSBAND, MORTON? AND THE HARLAN FAMILY?
THEY HAVE THE SAME TEMPER?
WELL...
GREGORY CAN BE REALLY PERSUASIVE.

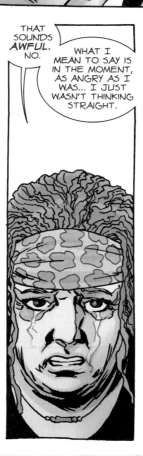

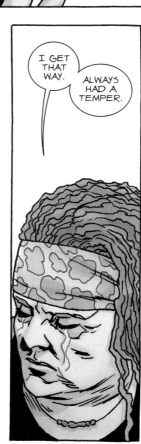

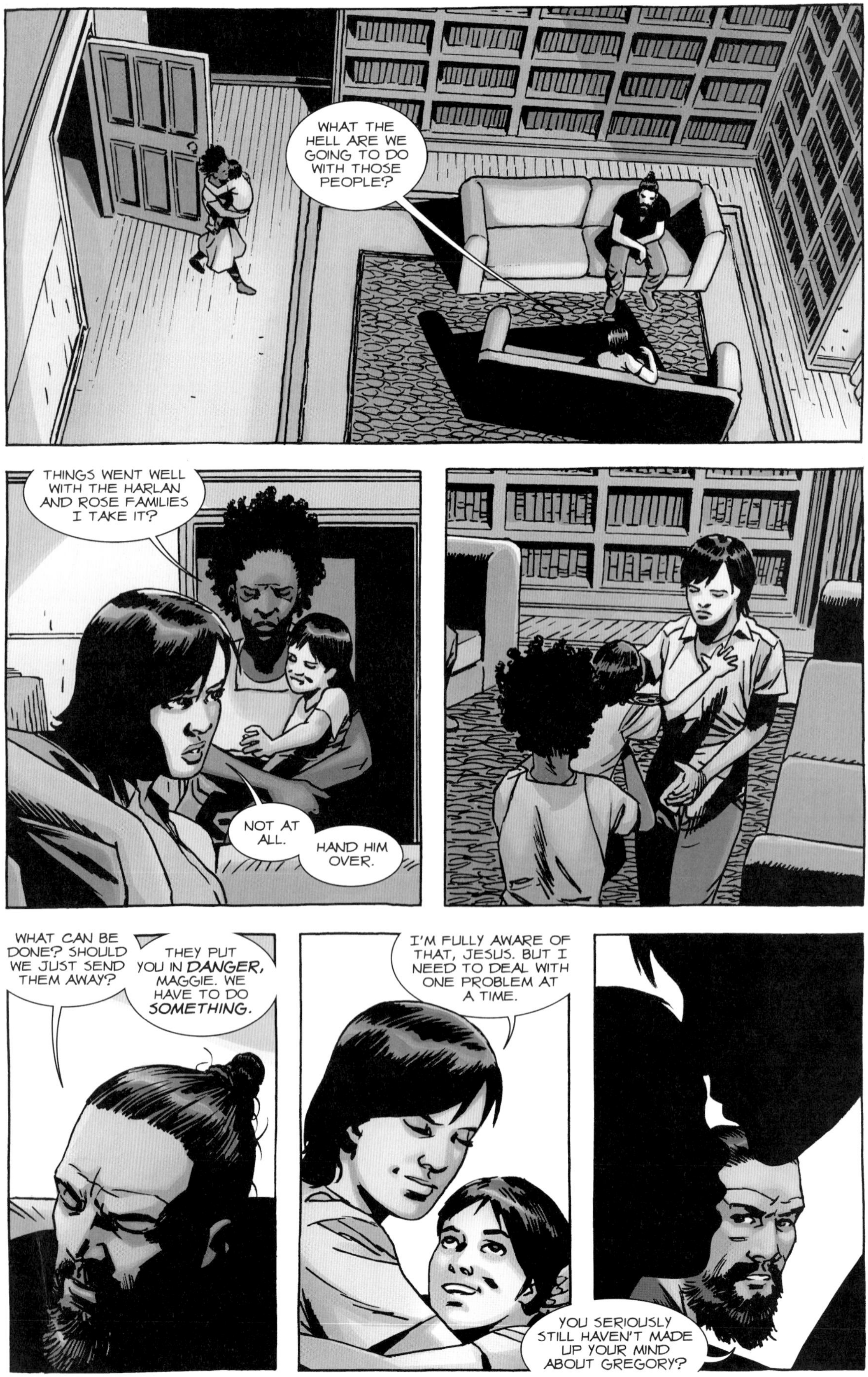
WHAT THE HELL ARE WE GOING TO DO WITH THOSE PEOPLE?
THINGS WENT WELL WITH THE HARLAN AND ROSE FAMILIES I TAKE IT?
NOT AT ALL.
HAND HIM OVER.
WHAT CAN BE DONE? SHOULD WE JUST SEND THEM AWAY?
THEY PUT YOU IN DANGER, MAGGIE. WE HAVE TO DO SOMETHING.
I'M FULLY AWARE OF THAT, JESUS. BUT I NEED TO DEAL WITH ONE PROBLEM AT A TIME.
YOU SERIOUSLY STILL HAVEN'T MADE UP YOUR MIND ABOUT GREGORY?

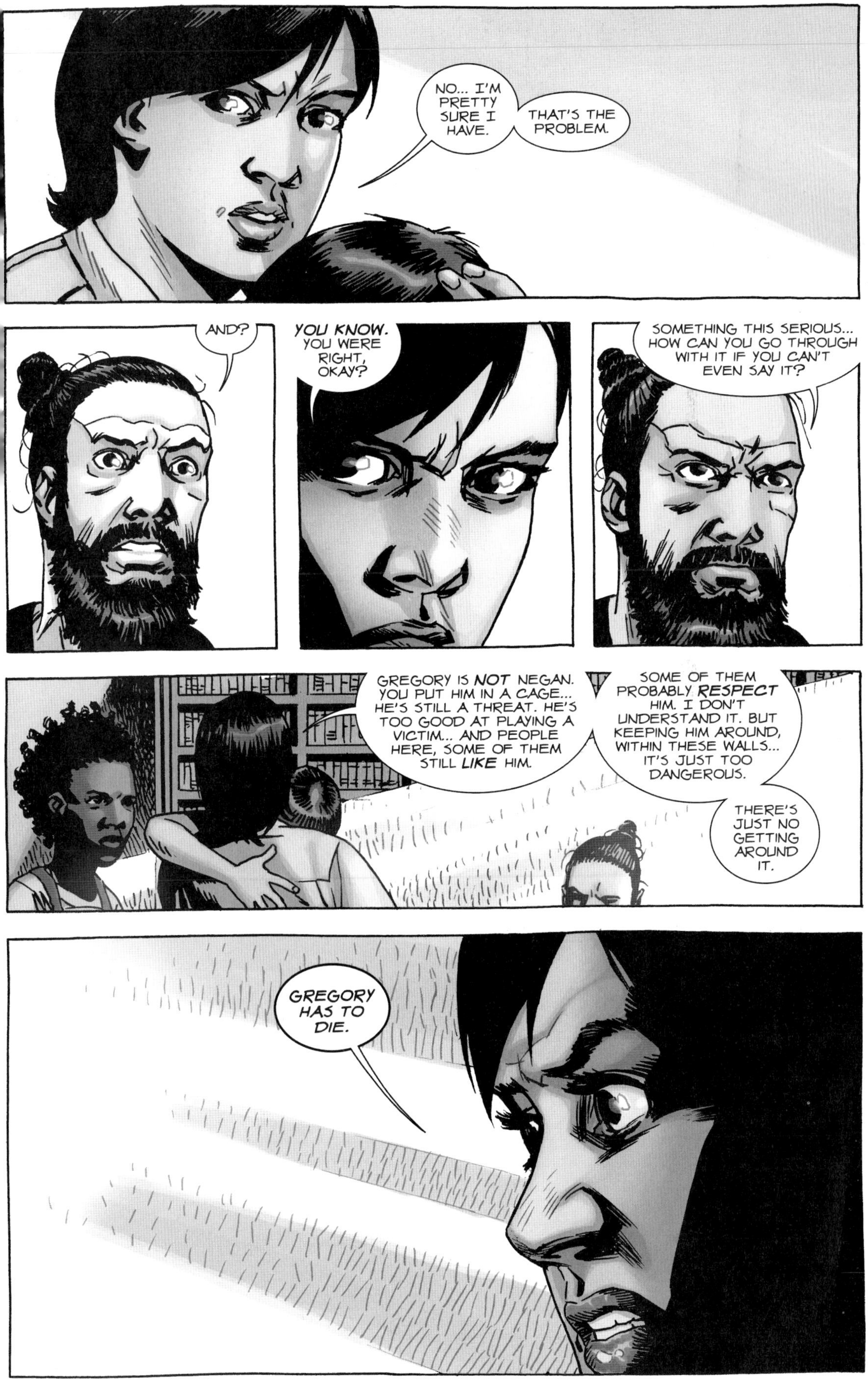

NO... I'M PRETTY SURE I HAVE.
THAT'S THE PROBLEM.
AND?
YOU KNOW. YOU WERE RIGHT, OKAY?
SOMETHING THIS SERIOUS... HOW CAN YOU GO THROUGH WITH IT IF YOU CAN'T EVEN SAY IT?
GREGORY IS NOT NEGAN. YOU PUT HIM IN A CAGE... HE'S STILL A THREAT. HE'S TOO GOOD AT PLAYING A VICTIM... AND PEOPLE HERE, SOME OF THEM STILL LIKE HIM.
SOME OF THEM PROBABLY RESPECT HIM. I DON'T UNDERSTAND IT. BUT KEEPING HIM AROUND, WITHIN THESE WALLS... IT'S JUST TOO DANGEROUS.
THERE'S JUST NO GETTING AROUND IT.
GREGORY HAS TO DIE.

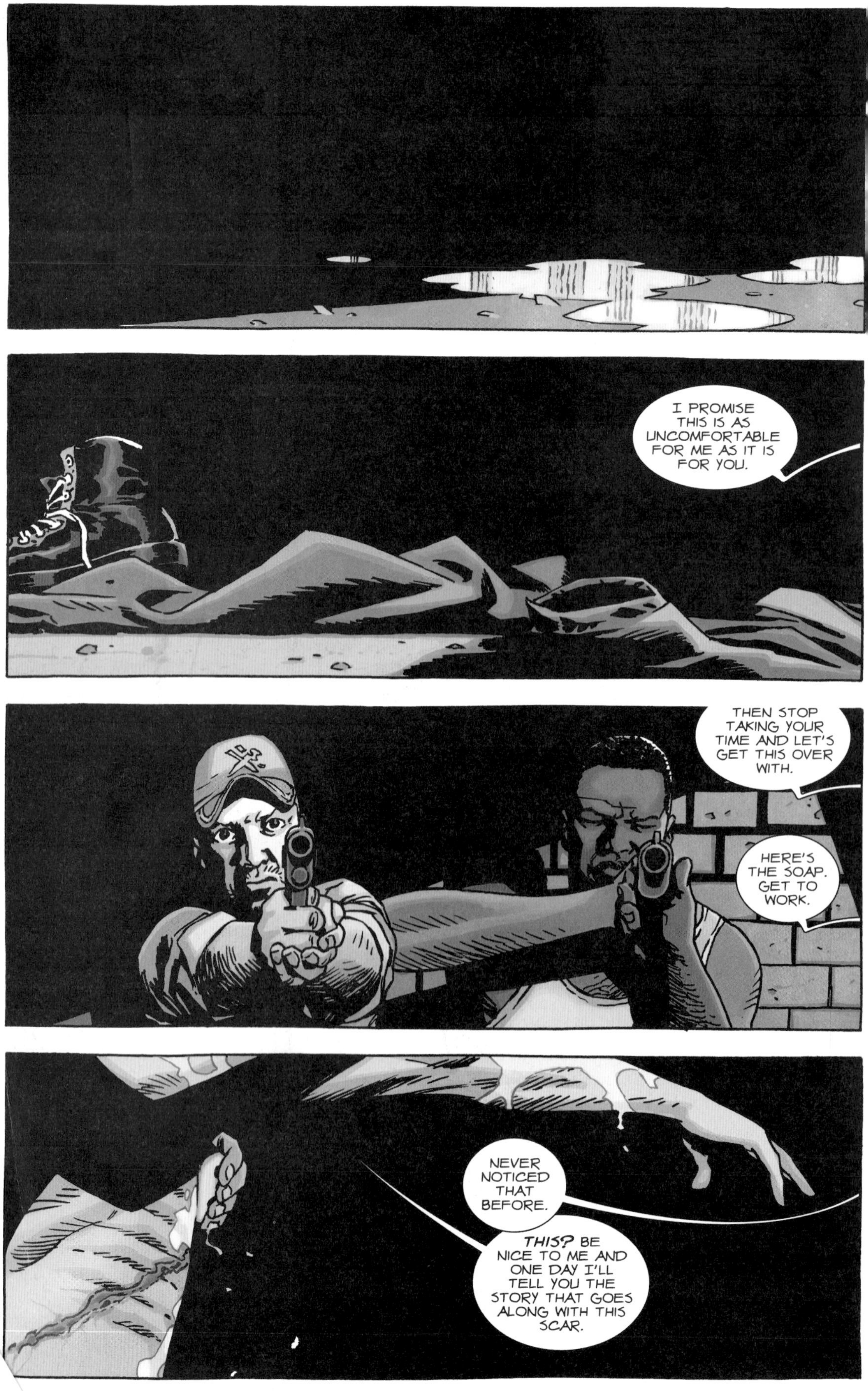
I PROMISE THIS IS AS UNCOMFORTABLE FOR ME AS IT IS FOR YOU.
THEN STOP TAKING YOUR TIME AND LET'S GET THIS OVER WITH.
HERE'S THE SOAP. GET TO WORK.
NEVER NOTICED THAT BEFORE.
THIS? BE NICE TO ME AND ONE DAY I'LL TELL YOU THE STORY THAT GOES ALONG WITH THIS SCAR.

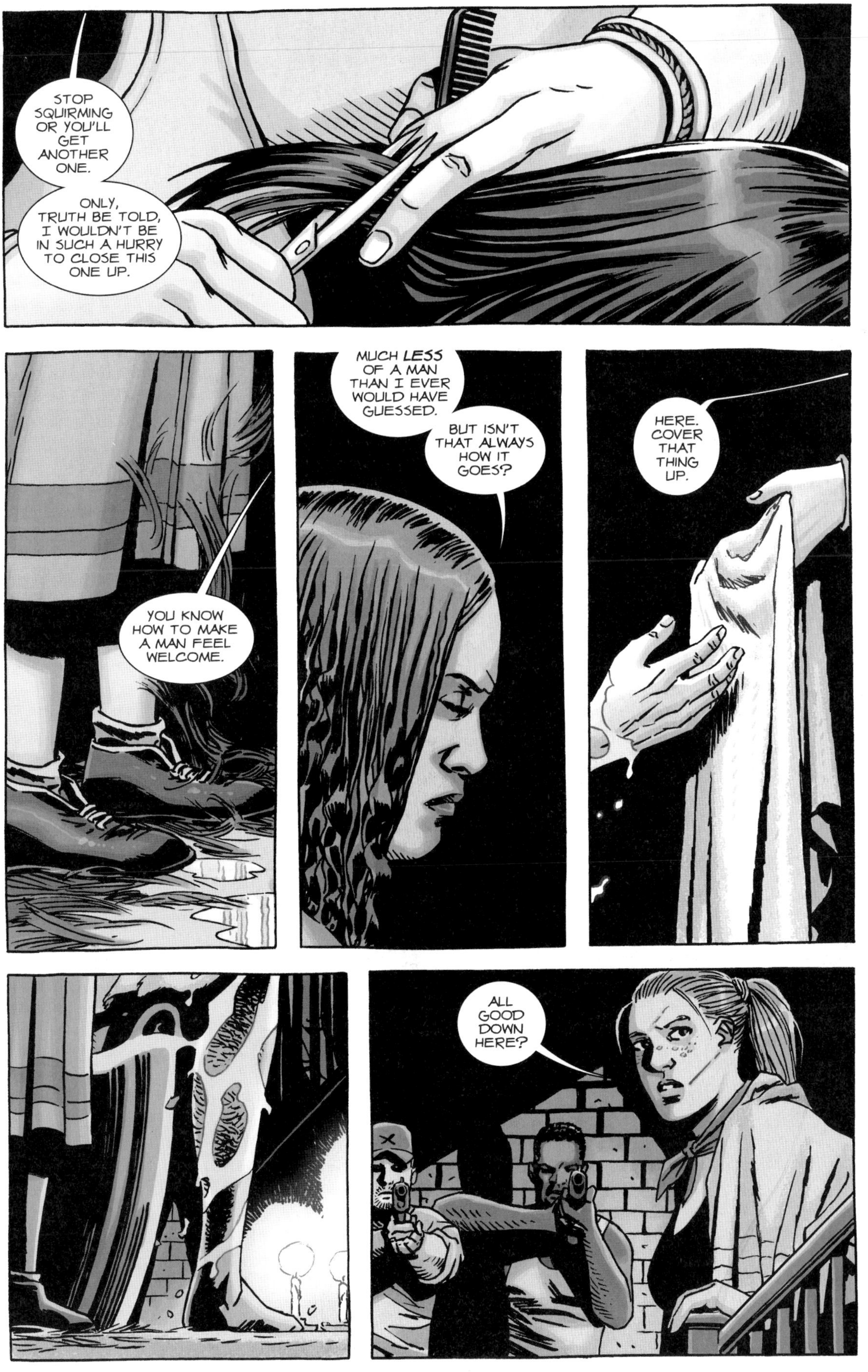
STOP SQUIRMING OR YOU'LL GET ANOTHER ONE.
ONLY, TRUTH BE TOLD, I WOULDN'T BE IN SUCH A HURRY TO CLOSE THIS ONE UP.
YOU KNOW HOW TO MAKE A MAN FEEL WELCOME.
MUCH LESS OF A MAN THAN I EVER WOULD HAVE GUESSED.
BUT ISN'T THAT ALWAYS HOW IT GOES?
HERE. COVER THAT THING UP.
ALL GOOD DOWN HERE?

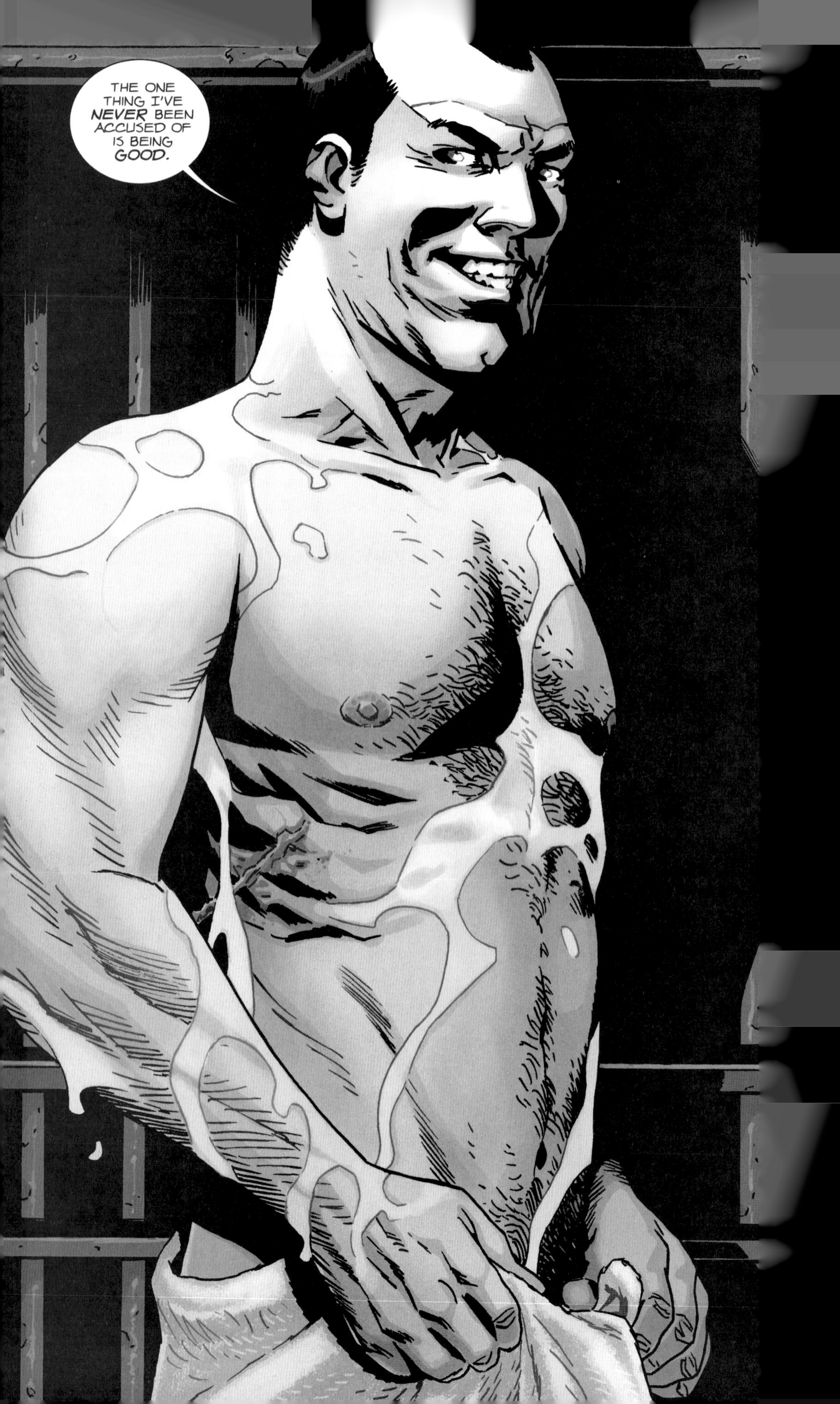
THE ONE THING I'VE NEVER BEEN ACCUSED OF IS BEING GOOD.

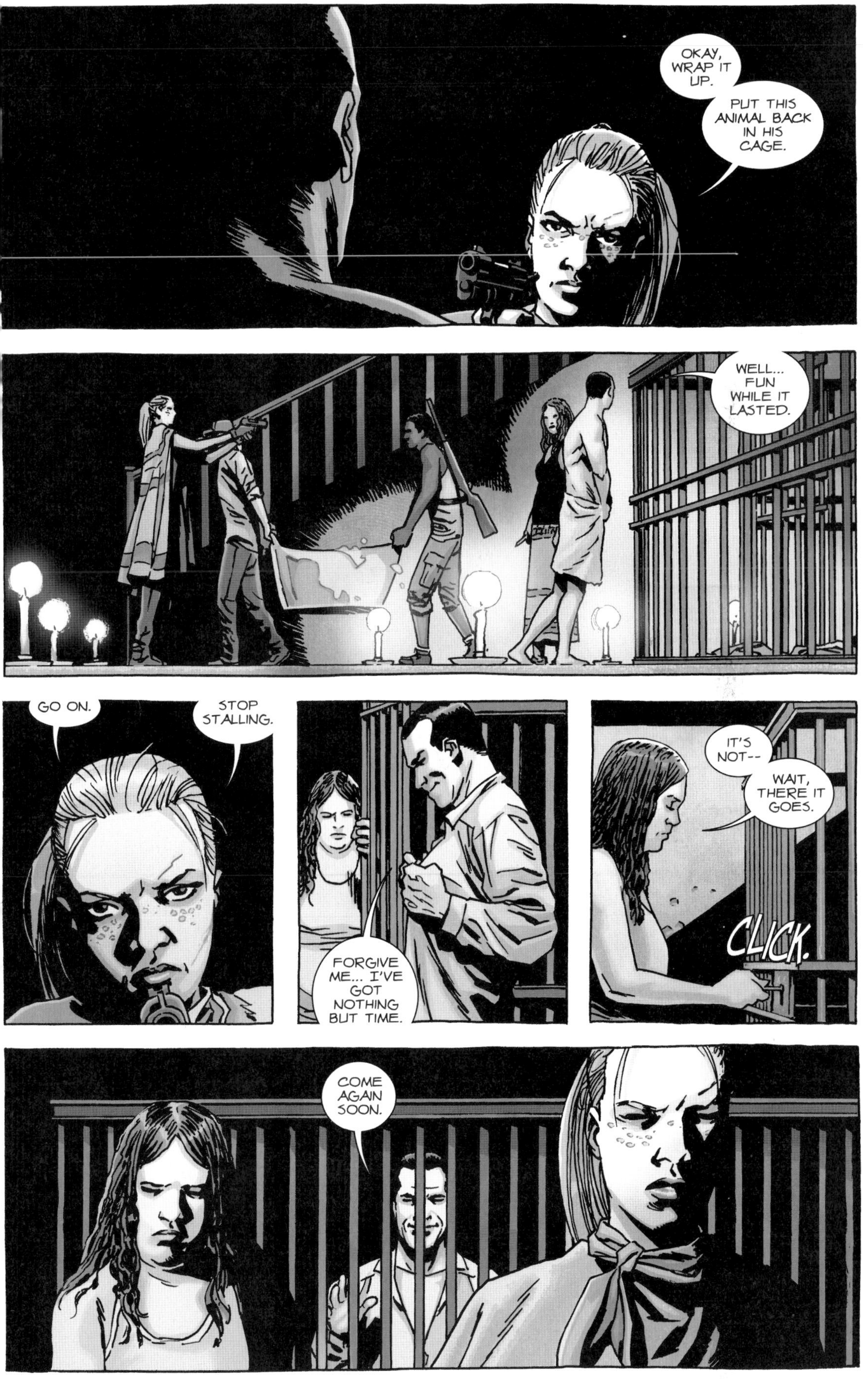
OKAY, WRAP IT UP.
PUT THIS ANIMAL BACK IN HIS CAGE.
WELL... FUN WHILE IT LASTED.
GO ON.
STOP STALLING.
FORGIVE ME... I'VE GOT NOTHING BUT TIME.
IT'S NOT--
WAIT, THERE IT GOES.
CLICK.
COME AGAIN SOON.

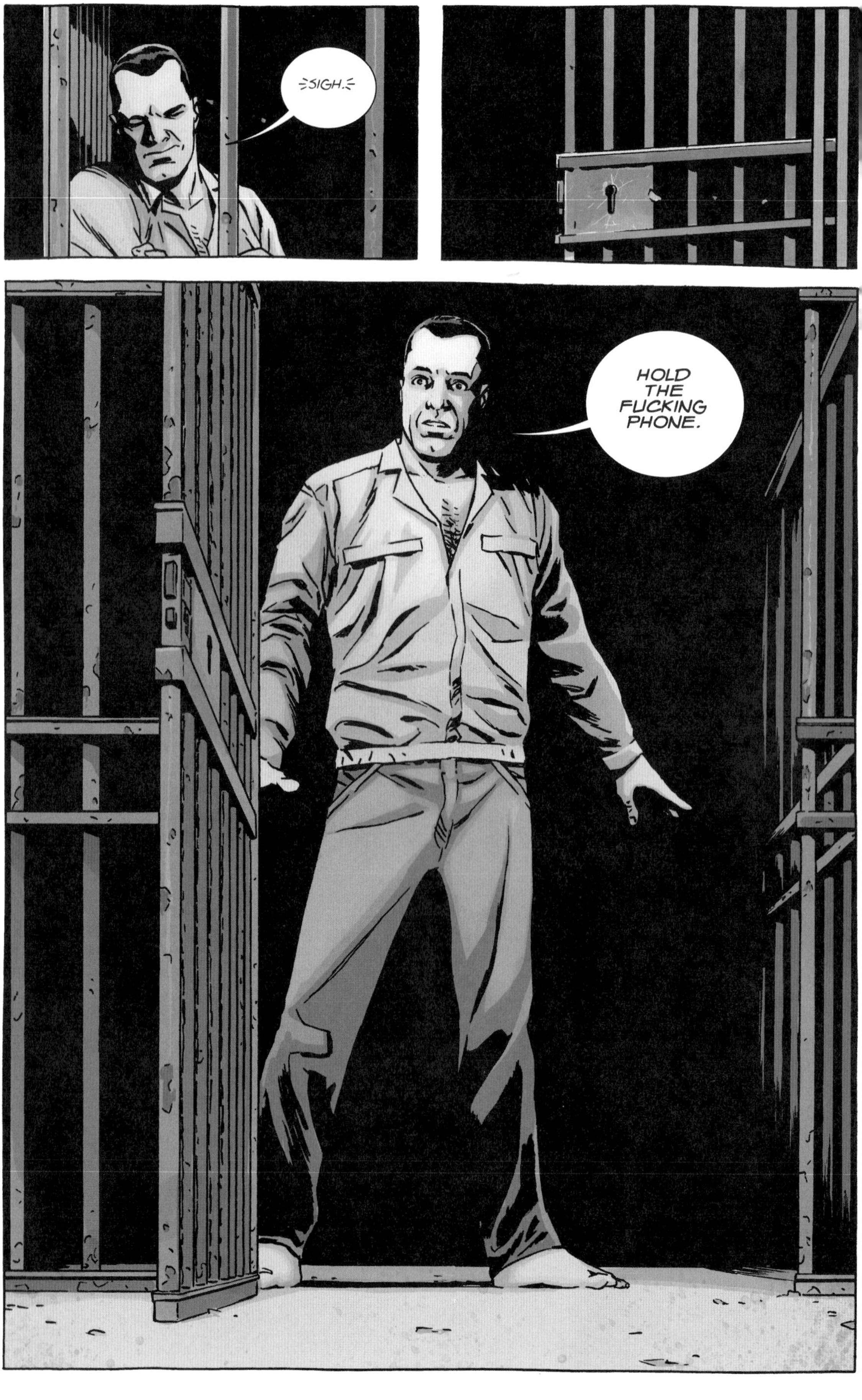
SIGH.
HOLD THE FUCKING PHONE.

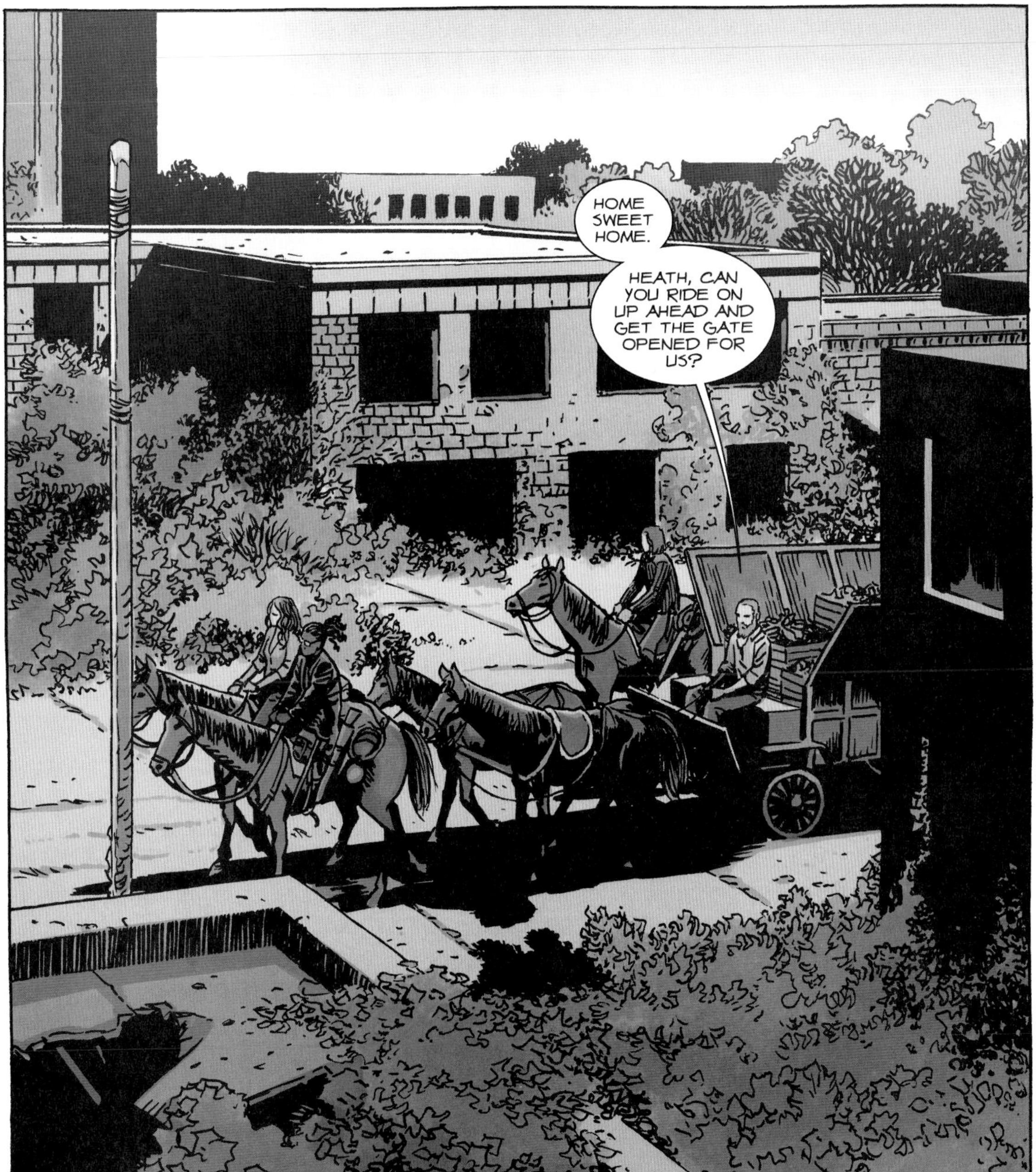
HOME SWEET HOME.
HEATH, CAN YOU RIDE ON UP AHEAD AND GET THE GATE OPENED FOR US?

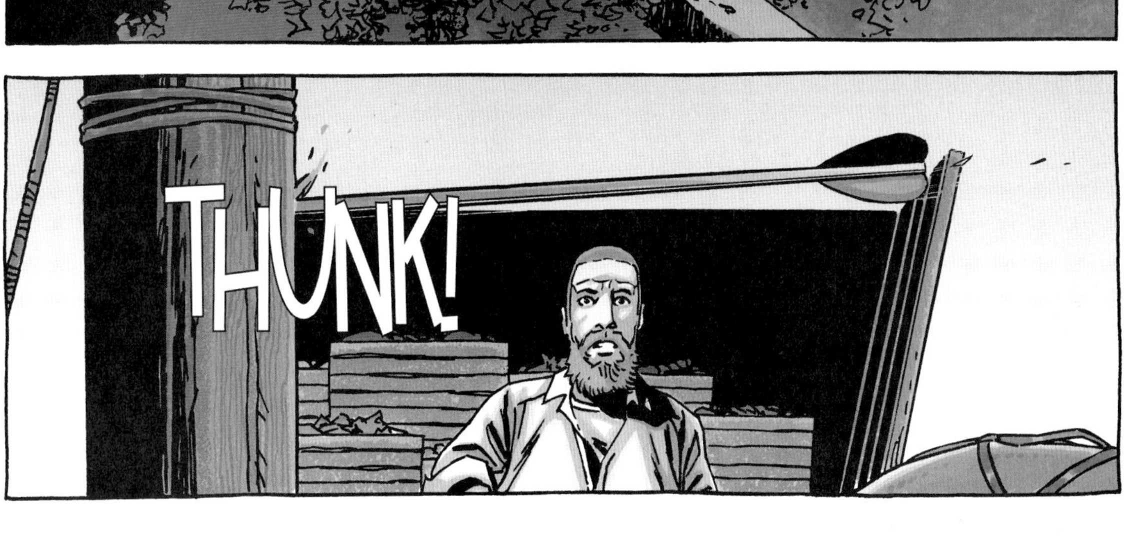
THUNK!

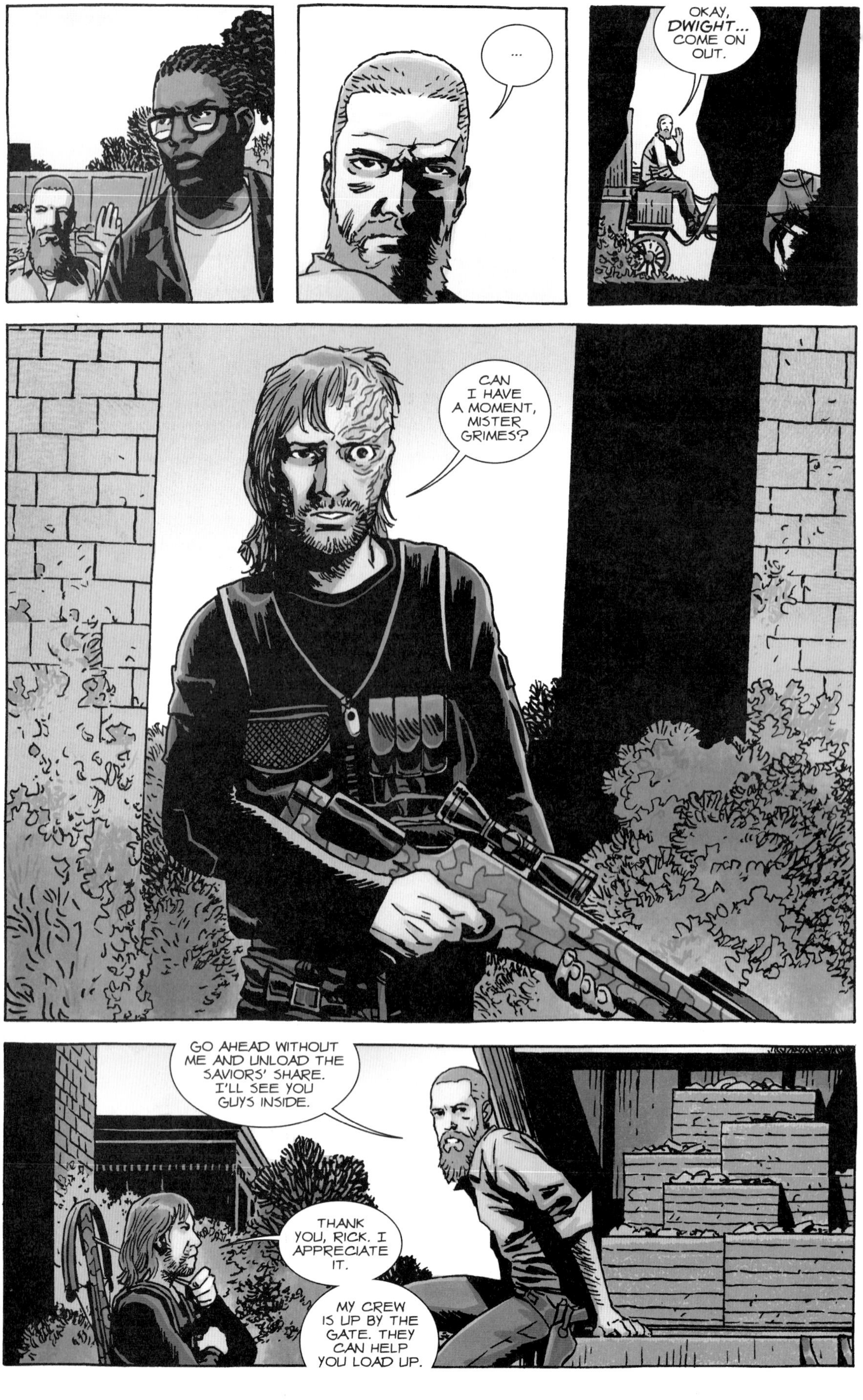
...
OKAY, DWIGHT... COME ON OUT.
CAN I HAVE A MOMENT, MISTER GRIMES?
GO AHEAD WITHOUT ME AND UNLOAD THE SAVIORS' SHARE. I'LL SEE YOU GUYS INSIDE.
THANK YOU, RICK. I APPRECIATE IT.
MY CREW IS UP BY THE GATE. THEY CAN HELP YOU LOAD UP.

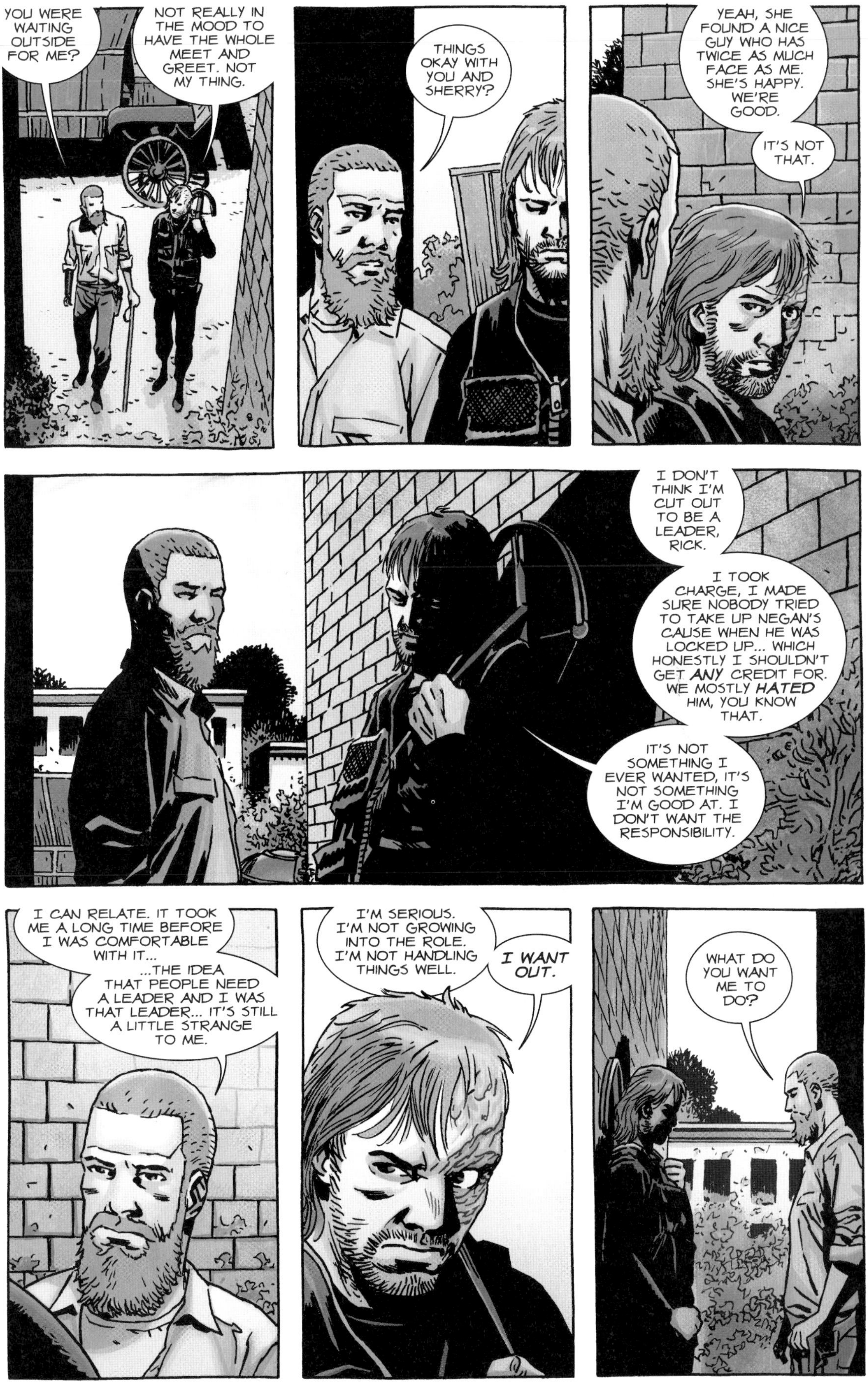
YOU WERE WAITING OUTSIDE FOR ME?
NOT REALLY IN THE MOOD TO HAVE THE WHOLE MEET AND GREET. NOT MY THING.
THINGS OKAY WITH YOU AND SHERRY?
YEAH, SHE FOUND A NICE GUY WHO HAS TWICE AS MUCH FACE AS ME. SHE'S HAPPY. WE'RE GOOD.
IT'S NOT THAT.
I DON'T THINK I'M CUT OUT TO BE A LEADER, RICK.
I TOOK CHARGE, I MADE SURE NOBODY TRIED TO TAKE UP NEGAN'S CAUSE WHEN HE WAS LOCKED UP... WHICH HONESTLY I SHOULDN'T GET ANY CREDIT FOR. WE MOSTLY HATED HIM, YOU KNOW THAT.
IT'S NOT SOMETHING I EVER WANTED, IT'S NOT SOMETHING I'M GOOD AT. I DON'T WANT THE RESPONSIBILITY.
I CAN RELATE. IT TOOK ME A LONG TIME BEFORE I WAS COMFORTABLE WITH IT...
...THE IDEA THAT PEOPLE NEED A LEADER AND I WAS THAT LEADER... IT'S STILL A LITTLE STRANGE TO ME.
I'M SERIOUS. I'M NOT GROWING INTO THE ROLE. I'M NOT HANDLING THINGS WELL.
I WANT OUT.
WHAT DO YOU WANT ME TO DO?

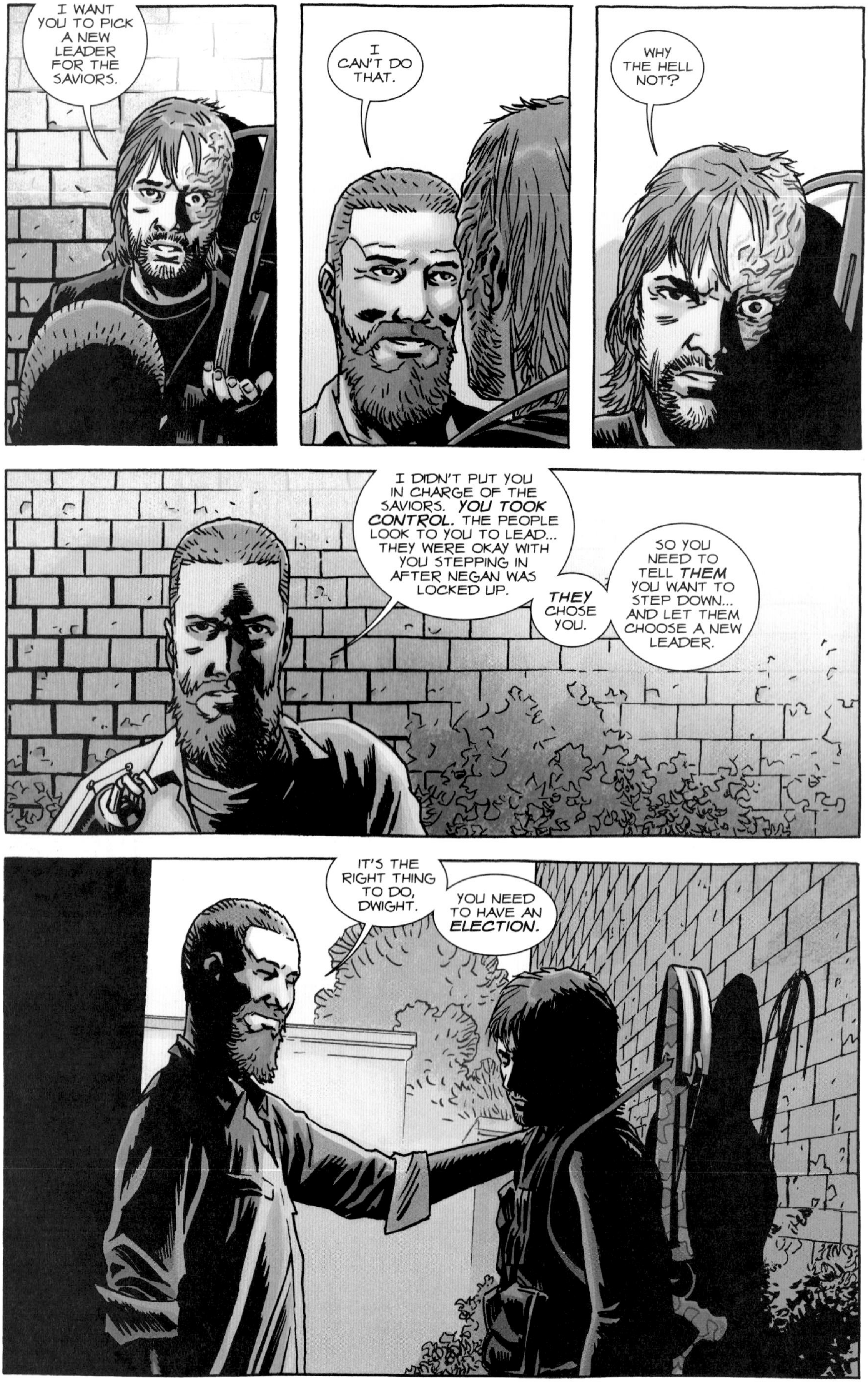
I WANT YOU TO PICK A NEW LEADER FOR THE SAVIORS.
I CAN'T DO THAT.
WHY THE HELL NOT?
I DIDN'T PUT YOU IN CHARGE OF THE SAVIORS. *YOU TOOK CONTROL.* THE PEOPLE LOOK TO YOU TO LEAD... THEY WERE OKAY WITH YOU STEPPING IN AFTER NEGAN WAS LOCKED UP.
THEY CHOSE YOU.
SO YOU NEED TO TELL *THEM* YOU WANT TO STEP DOWN... AND LET THEM CHOOSE A NEW LEADER.
IT'S THE RIGHT THING TO DO, DWIGHT.
YOU NEED TO HAVE AN *ELECTION.*

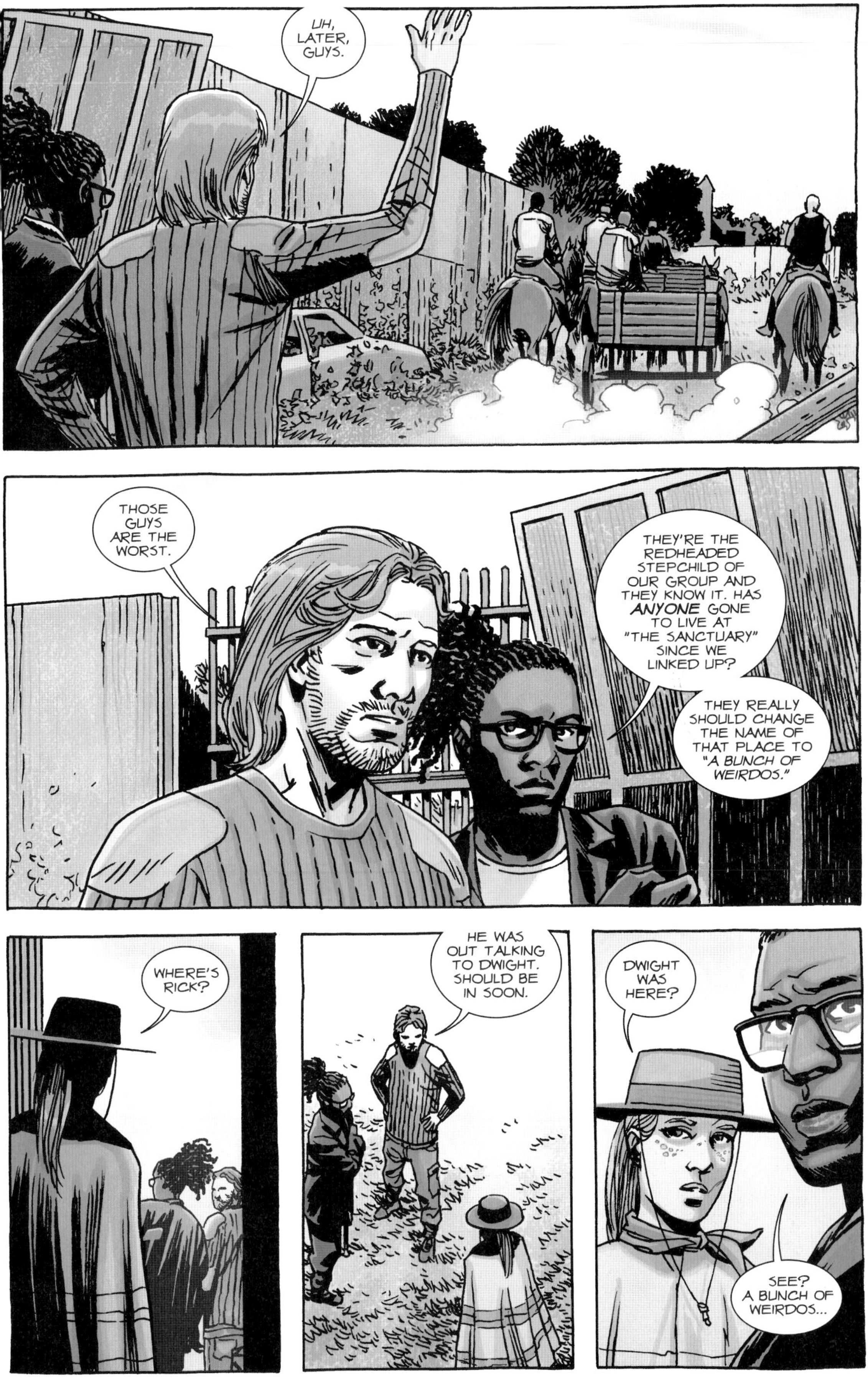
UH, LATER, GUYS.
THOSE GUYS ARE THE WORST.
THEY'RE THE REDHEADED STEPCHILD OF OUR GROUP AND THEY KNOW IT. HAS ANYONE GONE TO LIVE AT "THE SANCTUARY" SINCE WE LINKED UP?
THEY REALLY SHOULD CHANGE THE NAME OF THAT PLACE TO "A BUNCH OF WEIRDOS."
WHERE'S RICK?
HE WAS OUT TALKING TO DWIGHT. SHOULD BE IN SOON.
DWIGHT WAS HERE?
SEE? A BUNCH OF WEIRDOS...

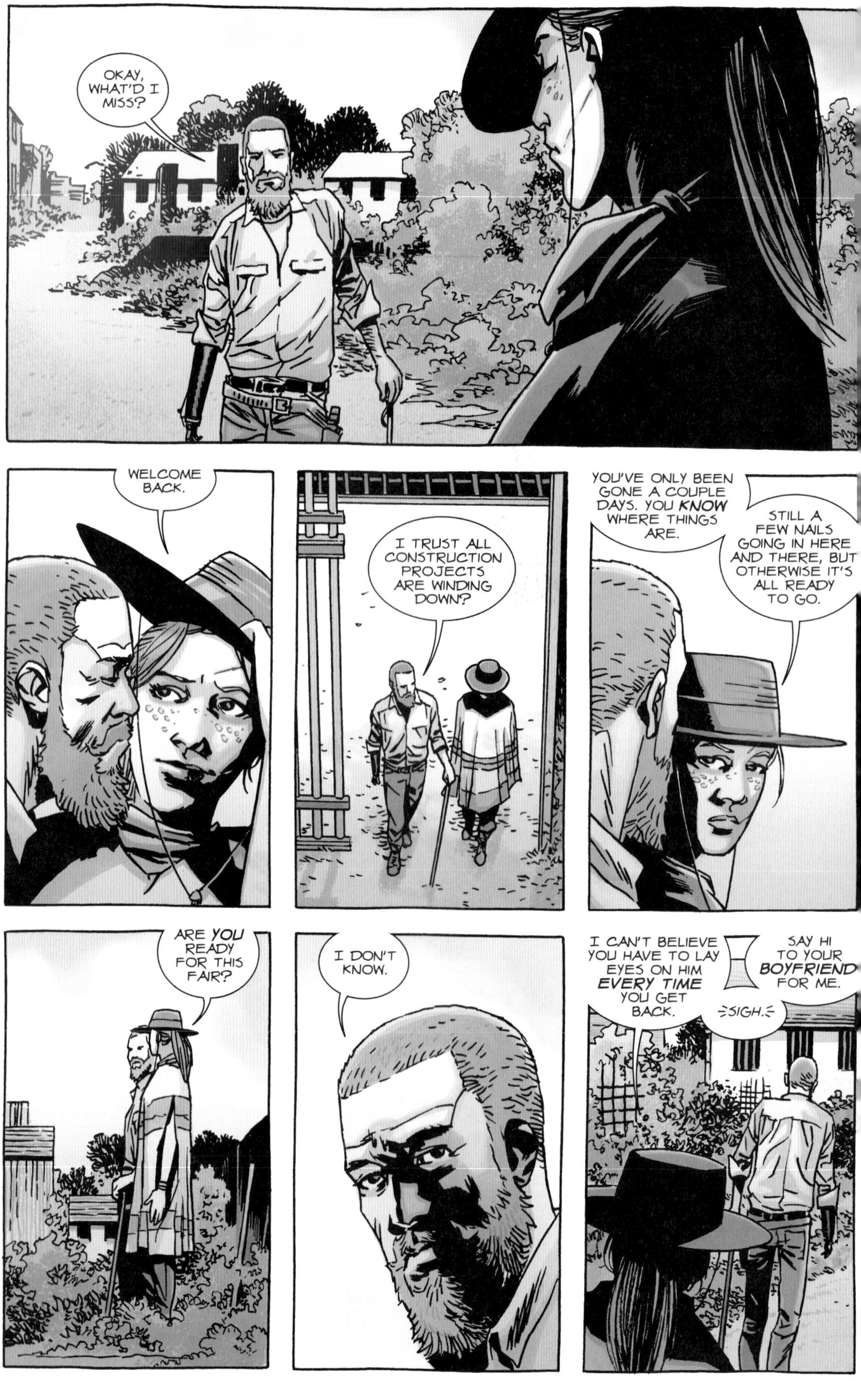
OKAY, WHAT'D I MISS?
WELCOME BACK.
I TRUST ALL CONSTRUCTION PROJECTS ARE WINDING DOWN?
YOU'VE ONLY BEEN GONE A COUPLE DAYS. YOU KNOW WHERE THINGS ARE.
STILL A FEW NAILS GOING IN HERE AND THERE, BUT OTHERWISE IT'S ALL READY TO GO.
ARE YOU READY FOR THIS FAIR?
I DON'T KNOW.
I CAN'T BELIEVE YOU HAVE TO LAY EYES ON HIM EVERY TIME YOU GET BACK.
SAY HI TO YOUR BOYFRIEND FOR ME.
SIGH.

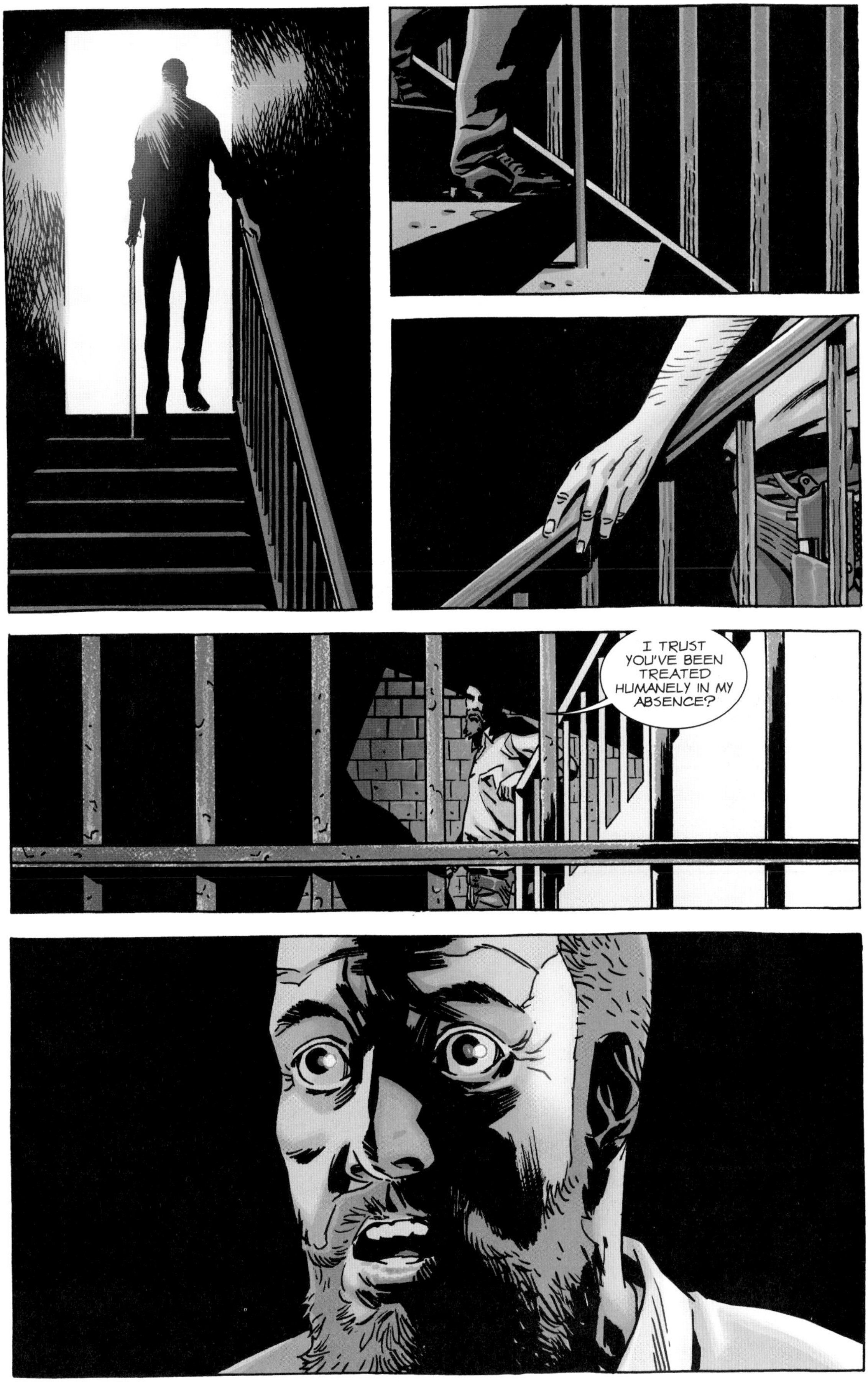
I TRUST YOU'VE BEEN TREATED HUMANELY IN MY ABSENCE?

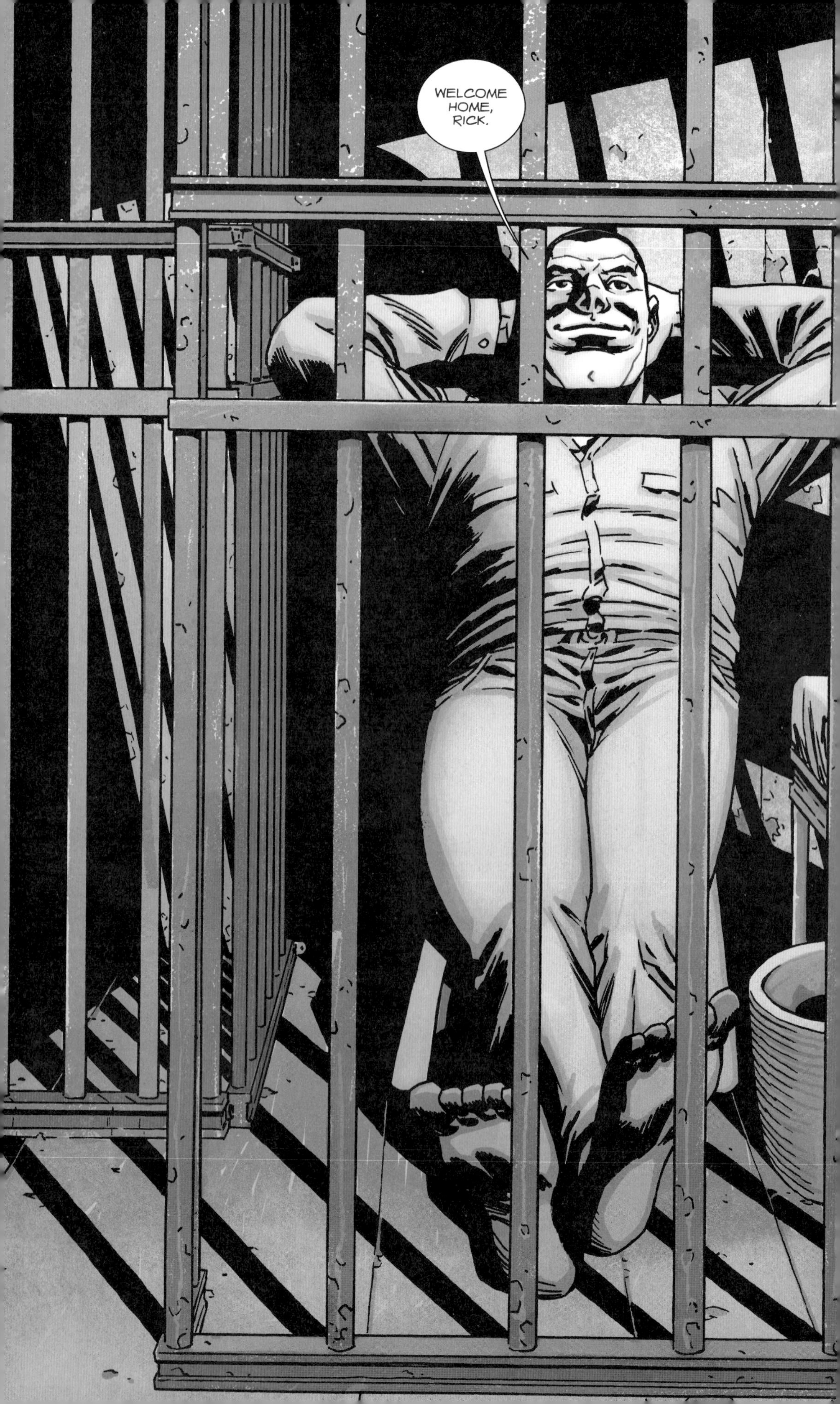
WELCOME HOME, RICK.

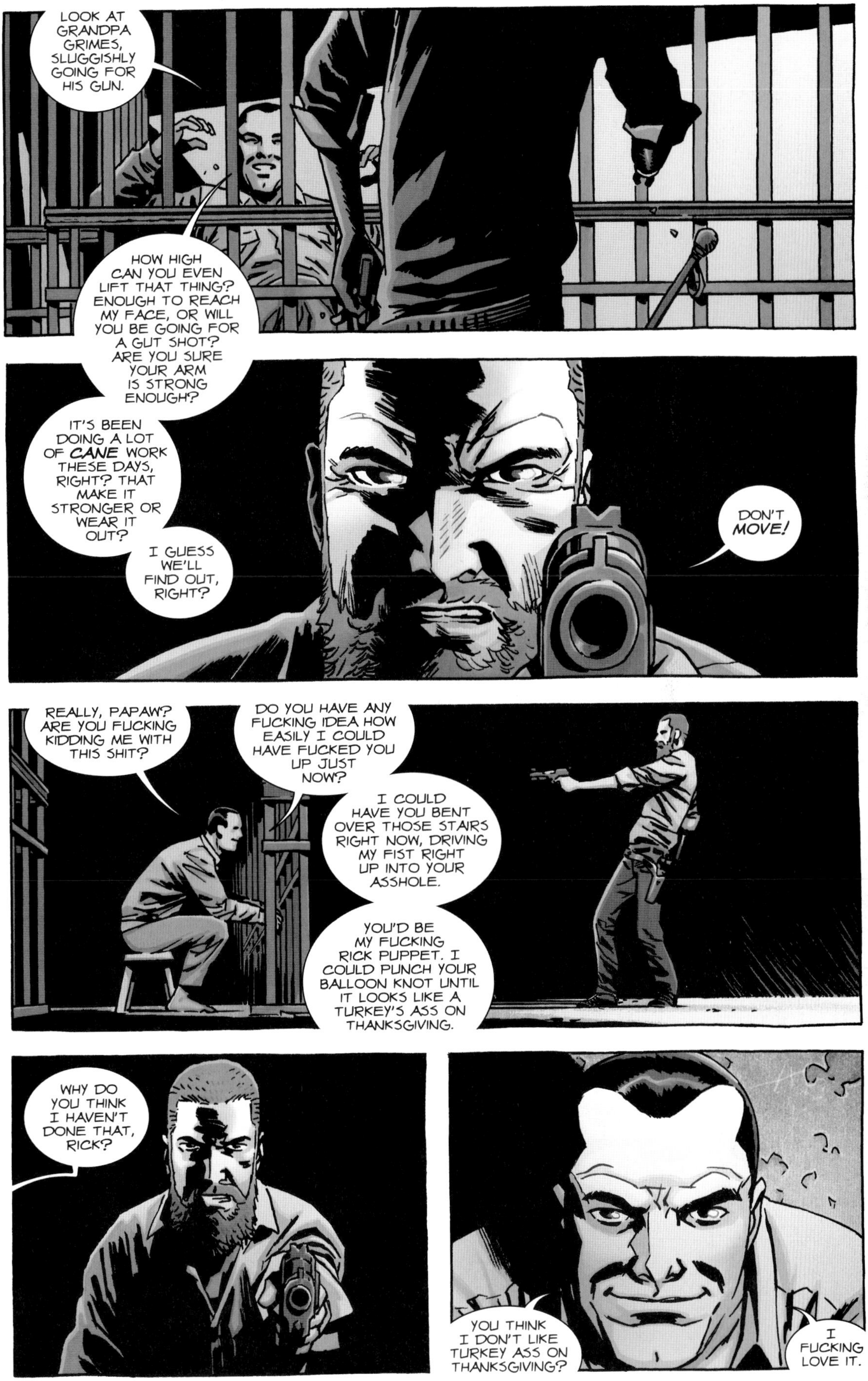
LOOK AT GRANDPA GRIMES, SLUGGISHLY GOING FOR HIS GUN.
HOW HIGH CAN YOU EVEN LIFT THAT THING? ENOUGH TO REACH MY FACE, OR WILL YOU BE GOING FOR A GUT SHOT? ARE YOU SURE YOUR ARM IS STRONG ENOUGH?
IT'S BEEN DOING A LOT OF CANE WORK THESE DAYS, RIGHT? THAT MAKE IT STRONGER OR WEAR IT OUT?
I GUESS WE'LL FIND OUT, RIGHT?
DON'T MOVE!
REALLY, PAPAW? ARE YOU FUCKING KIDDING ME WITH THIS SHIT?
DO YOU HAVE ANY FUCKING IDEA HOW EASILY I COULD HAVE FUCKED YOU UP JUST NOW?
I COULD HAVE YOU BENT OVER THOSE STAIRS RIGHT NOW, DRIVING MY FIST RIGHT UP INTO YOUR ASSHOLE.
YOU'D BE MY FUCKING RICK PUPPET. I COULD PUNCH YOUR BALLOON KNOT UNTIL IT LOOKS LIKE A TURKEY'S ASS ON THANKSGIVING.
WHY DO YOU THINK I HAVEN'T DONE THAT, RICK?
YOU THINK I DON'T LIKE TURKEY ASS ON THANKSGIVING?
I FUCKING LOVE IT.

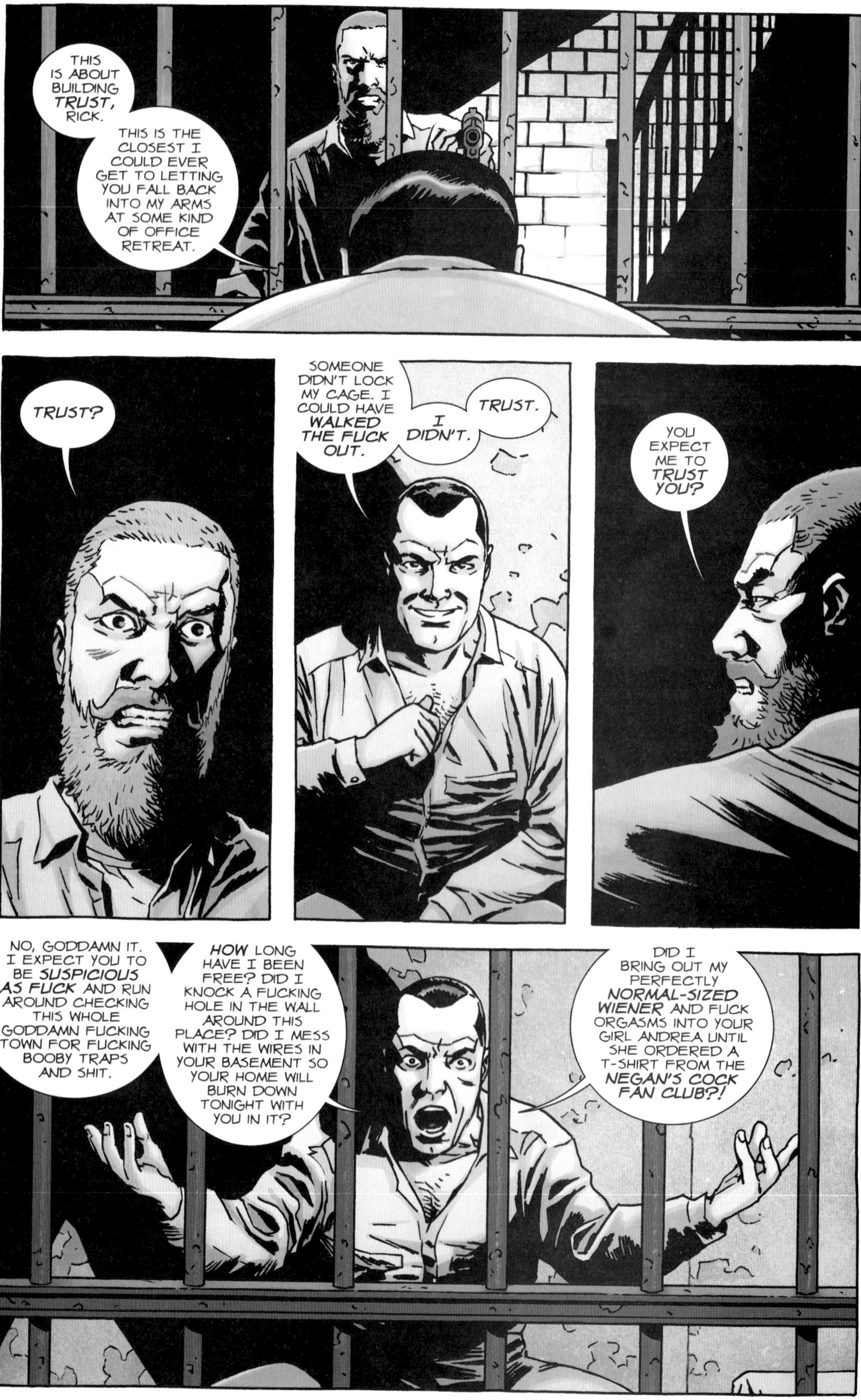
THIS IS ABOUT BUILDING TRUST, RICK.
THIS IS THE CLOSEST I COULD EVER GET TO LETTING YOU FALL BACK INTO MY ARMS AT SOME KIND OF OFFICE RETREAT.
TRUST?
SOMEONE DIDN'T LOCK MY CAGE. I COULD HAVE WALKED THE FUCK OUT.
I DIDN'T.
TRUST.
YOU EXPECT ME TO TRUST YOU?
NO, GODDAMN IT. I EXPECT YOU TO BE SUSPICIOUS AS FUCK AND RUN AROUND CHECKING THIS WHOLE GODDAMN FUCKING TOWN FOR FUCKING BOOBY TRAPS AND SHIT.
HOW LONG HAVE I BEEN FREE? DID I KNOCK A FUCKING HOLE IN THE WALL AROUND THIS PLACE? DID I MESS WITH THE WIRES IN YOUR BASEMENT SO YOUR HOME WILL BURN DOWN TONIGHT WITH YOU IN IT?
DID I BRING OUT MY PERFECTLY NORMAL-SIZED WIENER AND FUCK ORGASMS INTO YOUR GIRL ANDREA UNTIL SHE ORDERED A T-SHIRT FROM THE NEGAN'S COCK FAN CLUB?!

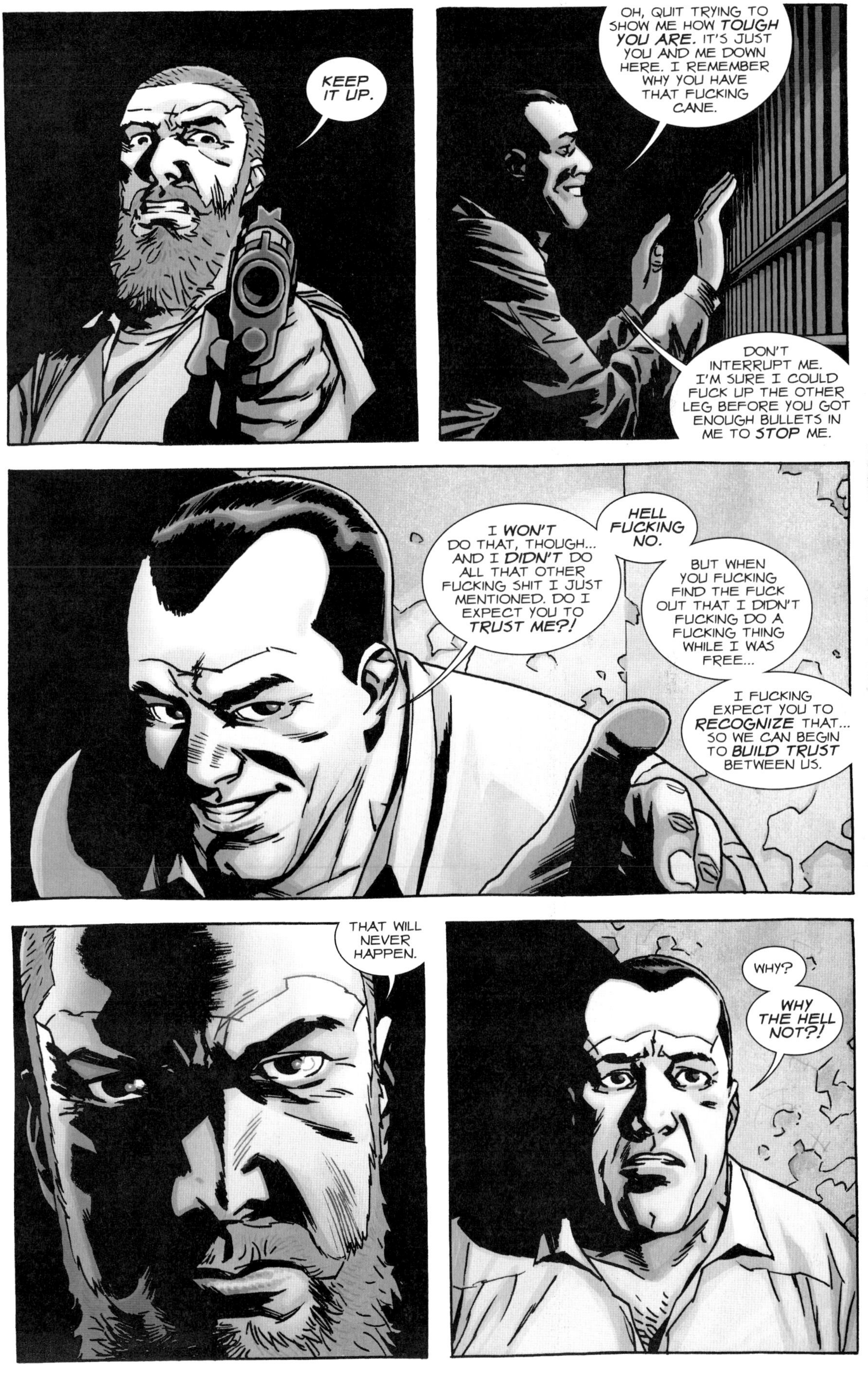
KEEP IT UP.
OH, QUIT TRYING TO SHOW ME HOW TOUGH YOU ARE. IT'S JUST YOU AND ME DOWN HERE. I REMEMBER WHY YOU HAVE THAT FUCKING CANE.
DON'T INTERRUPT ME. I'M SURE I COULD FUCK UP THE OTHER LEG BEFORE YOU GOT ENOUGH BULLETS IN ME TO STOP ME.
I WON'T DO THAT, THOUGH... AND I DIDN'T DO ALL THAT OTHER FUCKING SHIT I JUST MENTIONED. DO I EXPECT YOU TO TRUST ME?!
HELL FUCKING NO.
BUT WHEN YOU FUCKING FIND THE FUCK OUT THAT I DIDN'T FUCKING DO A FUCKING THING WHILE I WAS FREE...
I FUCKING EXPECT YOU TO RECOGNIZE THAT... SO WE CAN BEGIN TO BUILD TRUST BETWEEN US.
THAT WILL NEVER HAPPEN.
WHY?
WHY THE HELL NOT?!

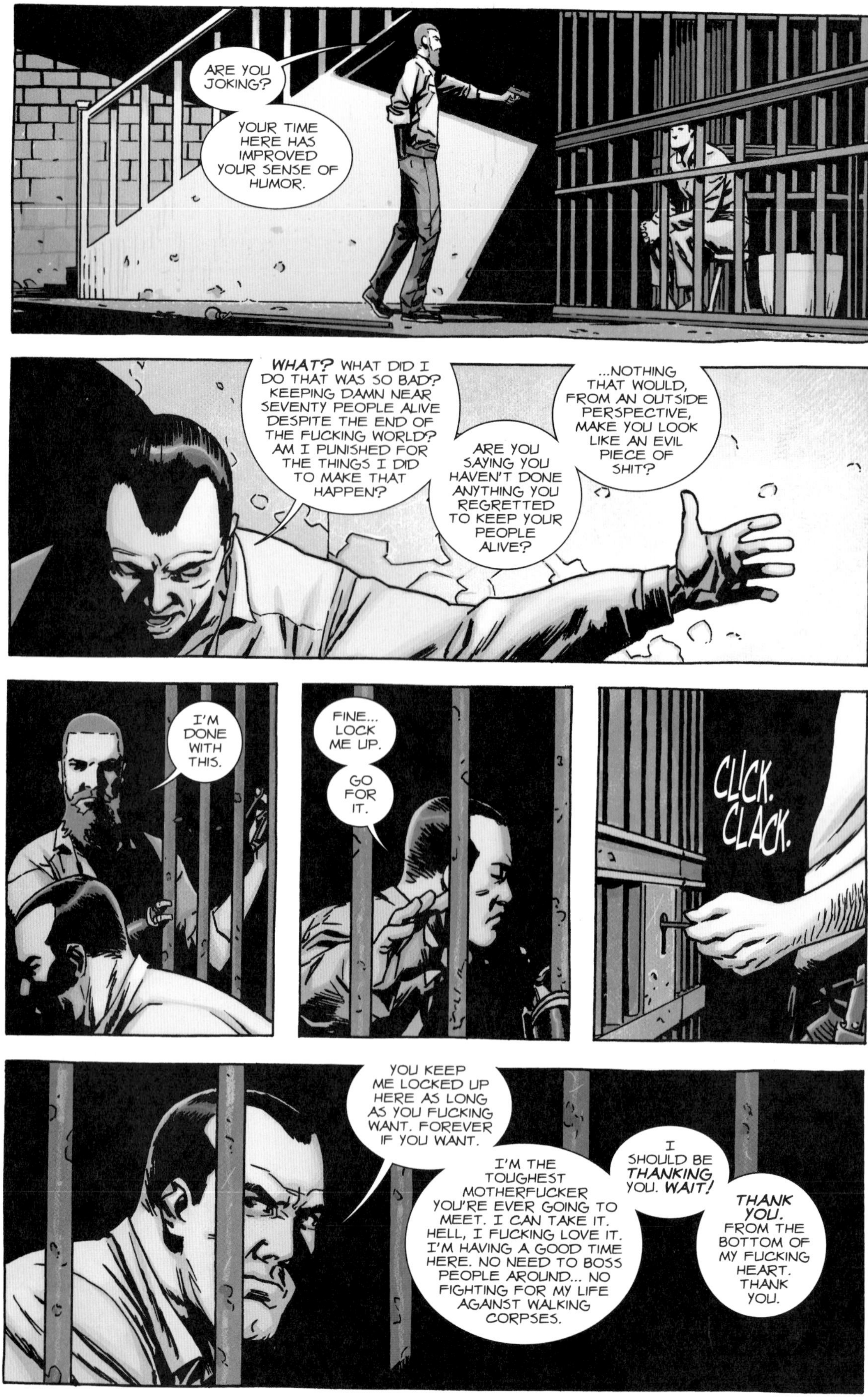
ARE YOU JOKING?
YOUR TIME HERE HAS IMPROVED YOUR SENSE OF HUMOR.
WHAT? WHAT DID I DO THAT WAS SO BAD? KEEPING DAMN NEAR SEVENTY PEOPLE ALIVE DESPITE THE END OF THE FUCKING WORLD? AM I PUNISHED FOR THE THINGS I DID TO MAKE THAT HAPPEN?
ARE YOU SAYING YOU HAVEN'T DONE ANYTHING YOU REGRETTED TO KEEP YOUR PEOPLE ALIVE?
...NOTHING THAT WOULD, FROM AN OUTSIDE PERSPECTIVE, MAKE YOU LOOK LIKE AN EVIL PIECE OF SHIT?
I'M DONE WITH THIS.
FINE... LOCK ME UP.
GO FOR IT.
CLICK. CLACK.
YOU KEEP ME LOCKED UP HERE AS LONG AS YOU FUCKING WANT. FOREVER IF YOU WANT.
I'M THE TOUGHEST MOTHERFUCKER YOU'RE EVER GOING TO MEET. I CAN TAKE IT. HELL, I FUCKING LOVE IT. I'M HAVING A GOOD TIME HERE. NO NEED TO BOSS PEOPLE AROUND... NO FIGHTING FOR MY LIFE AGAINST WALKING CORPSES.
I SHOULD BE THANKING YOU. WAIT!
THANK YOU. FROM THE BOTTOM OF MY FUCKING HEART. THANK YOU.

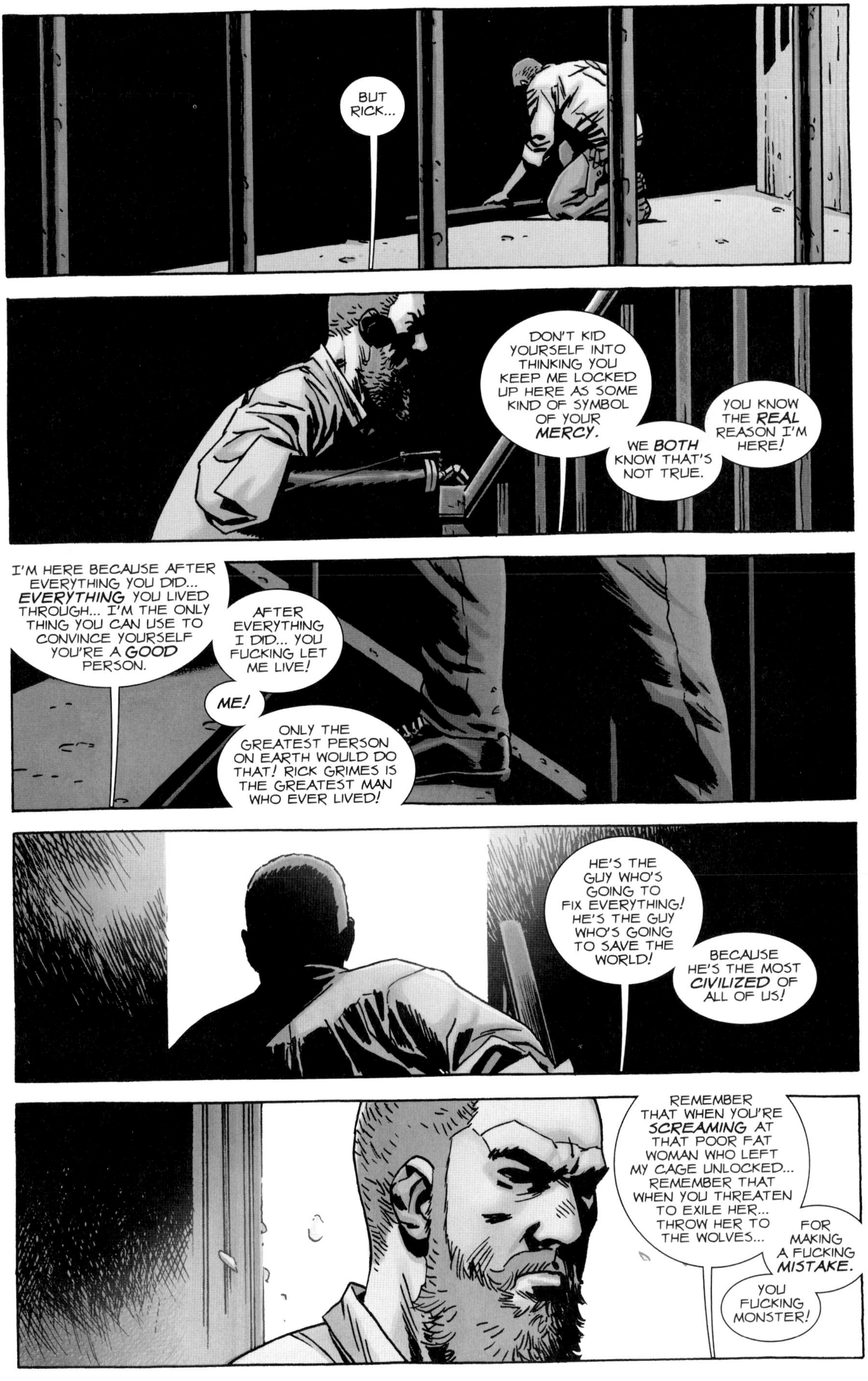
BUT RICK...
DON'T KID YOURSELF INTO THINKING YOU KEEP ME LOCKED UP HERE AS SOME KIND OF SYMBOL OF YOUR MERCY.
WE BOTH KNOW THAT'S NOT TRUE.
YOU KNOW THE REAL REASON I'M HERE!
I'M HERE BECAUSE AFTER EVERYTHING YOU DID... EVERYTHING YOU LIVED THROUGH... I'M THE ONLY THING YOU CAN USE TO CONVINCE YOURSELF YOU'RE A GOOD PERSON.
AFTER EVERYTHING I DID... YOU FUCKING LET ME LIVE!
ME!
ONLY THE GREATEST PERSON ON EARTH WOULD DO THAT! RICK GRIMES IS THE GREATEST MAN WHO EVER LIVED!
HE'S THE GUY WHO'S GOING TO FIX EVERYTHING! HE'S THE GUY WHO'S GOING TO SAVE THE WORLD!
BECAUSE HE'S THE MOST CIVILIZED OF ALL OF US!
REMEMBER THAT WHEN YOU'RE SCREAMING AT THAT POOR FAT WOMAN WHO LEFT MY CAGE UNLOCKED... REMEMBER THAT WHEN YOU THREATEN TO EXILE HER... THROW HER TO THE WOLVES...
FOR MAKING A FUCKING MISTAKE.
YOU FUCKING MONSTER!

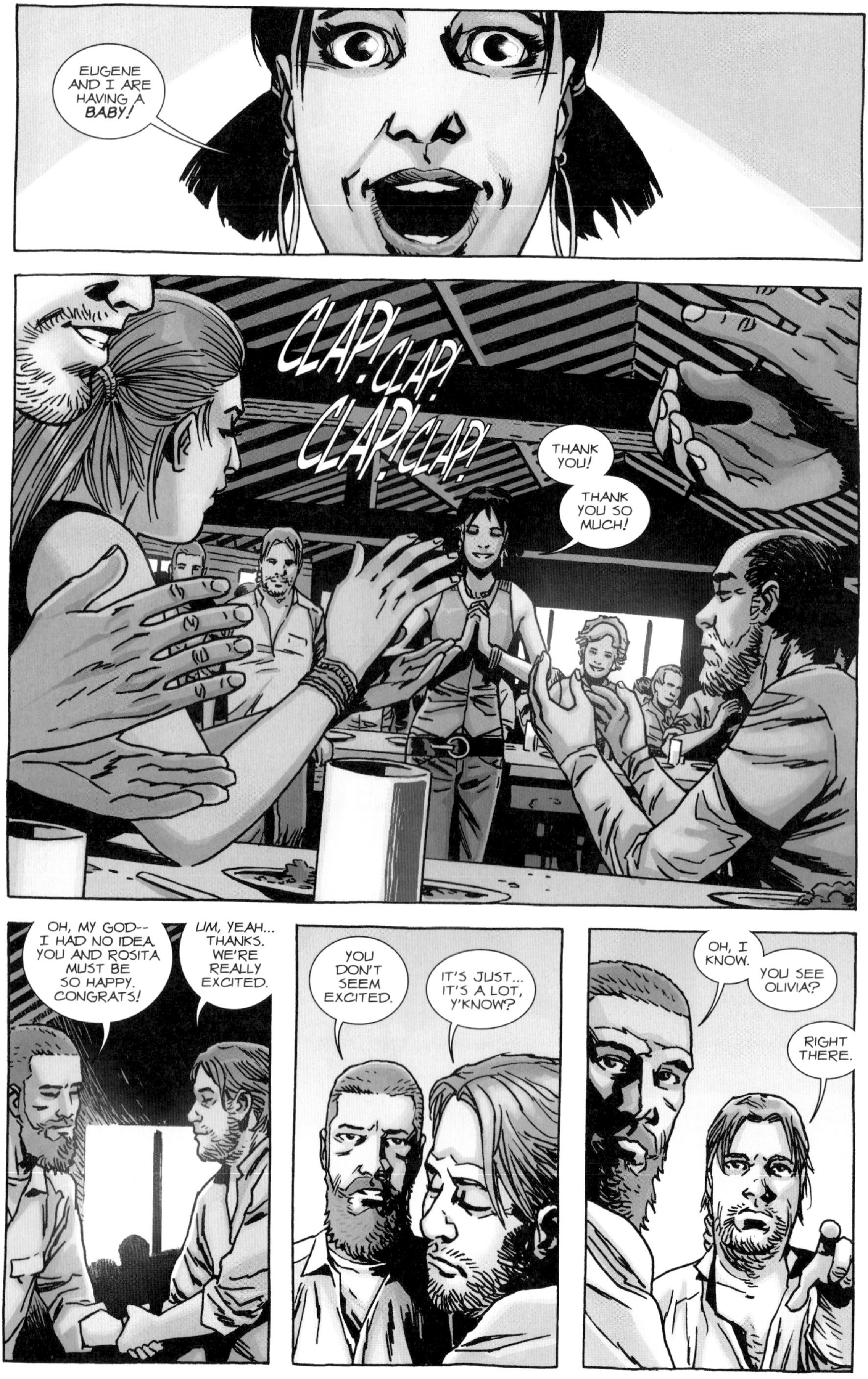

EUGENE AND I ARE HAVING A *BABY!*
CLAP! CLAP! CLAP! CLAP!
THANK YOU!
THANK YOU SO MUCH!
OH, MY GOD-- I HAD NO IDEA YOU AND ROSITA MUST BE SO HAPPY. CONGRATS!
UM, YEAH... THANKS. WE'RE REALLY EXCITED.
YOU DON'T SEEM EXCITED.
IT'S JUST... IT'S A LOT, Y'KNOW?
OH, I KNOW.
YOU SEE OLIVIA?
RIGHT THERE.

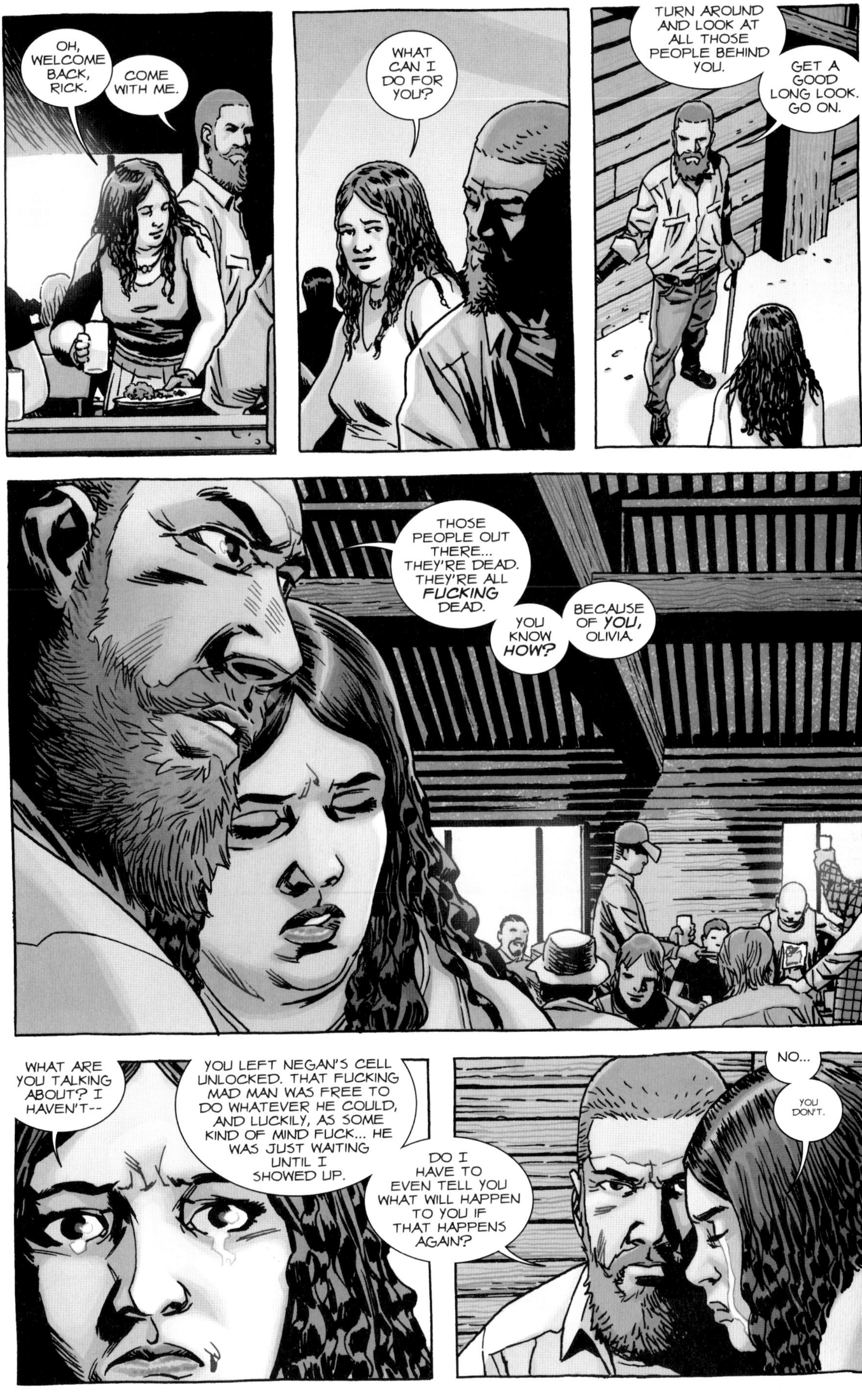
OH, WELCOME BACK, RICK.
COME WITH ME.
WHAT CAN I DO FOR YOU?
TURN AROUND AND LOOK AT ALL THOSE PEOPLE BEHIND YOU.
GET A GOOD LONG LOOK. GO ON.
THOSE PEOPLE OUT THERE... THEY'RE DEAD. THEY'RE ALL FUCKING DEAD.
YOU KNOW HOW?
BECAUSE OF YOU, OLIVIA.
WHAT ARE YOU TALKING ABOUT? I HAVEN'T--
YOU LEFT NEGAN'S CELL UNLOCKED. THAT FUCKING MAD MAN WAS FREE TO DO WHATEVER HE COULD, AND LUCKILY, AS SOME KIND OF MIND FUCK... HE WAS JUST WAITING UNTIL I SHOWED UP.
DO I HAVE TO EVEN TELL YOU WHAT WILL HAPPEN TO YOU IF THAT HAPPENS AGAIN?
NO...
YOU DON'T.

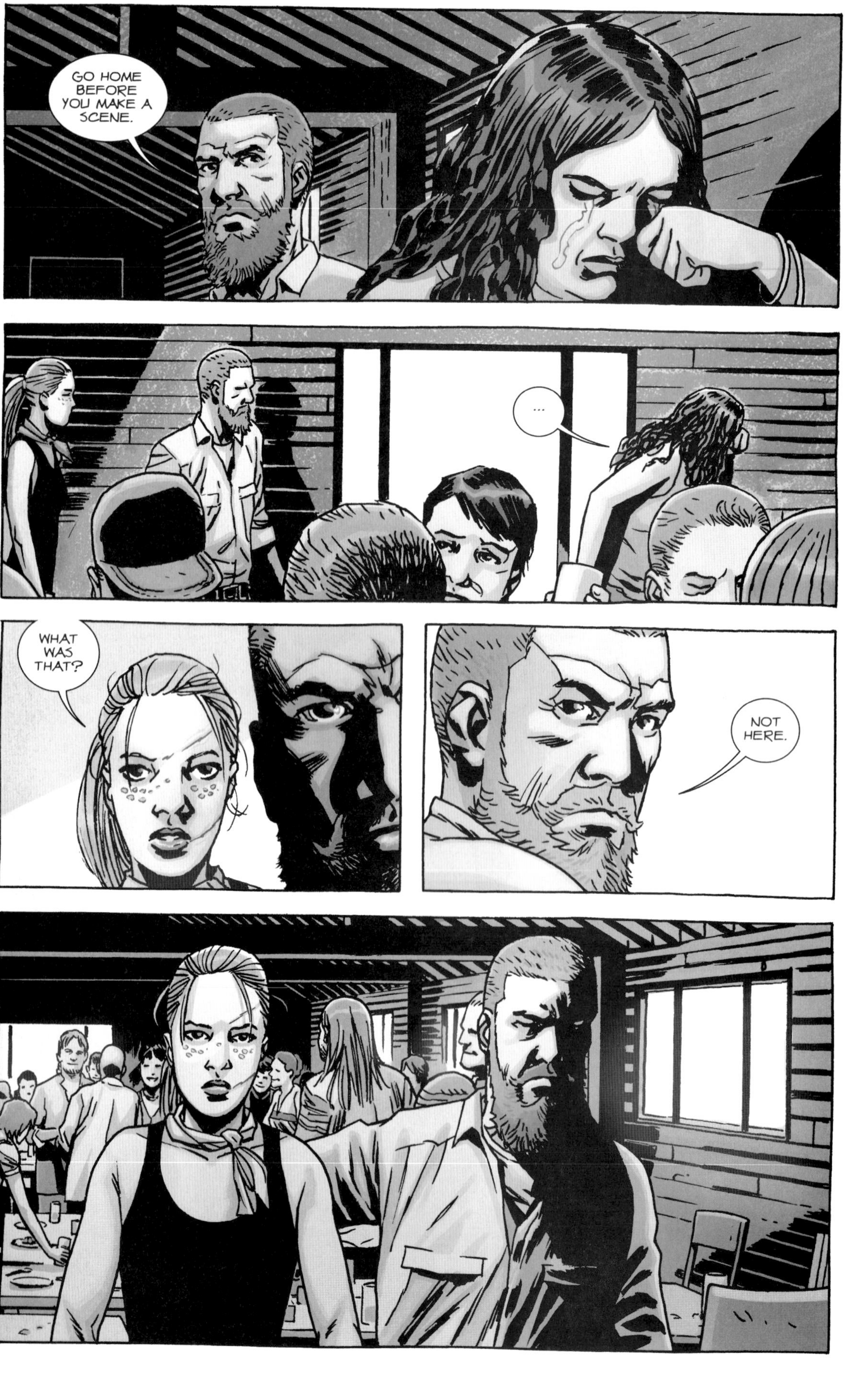
GO HOME BEFORE YOU MAKE A SCENE.
...
WHAT WAS THAT?
NOT HERE.

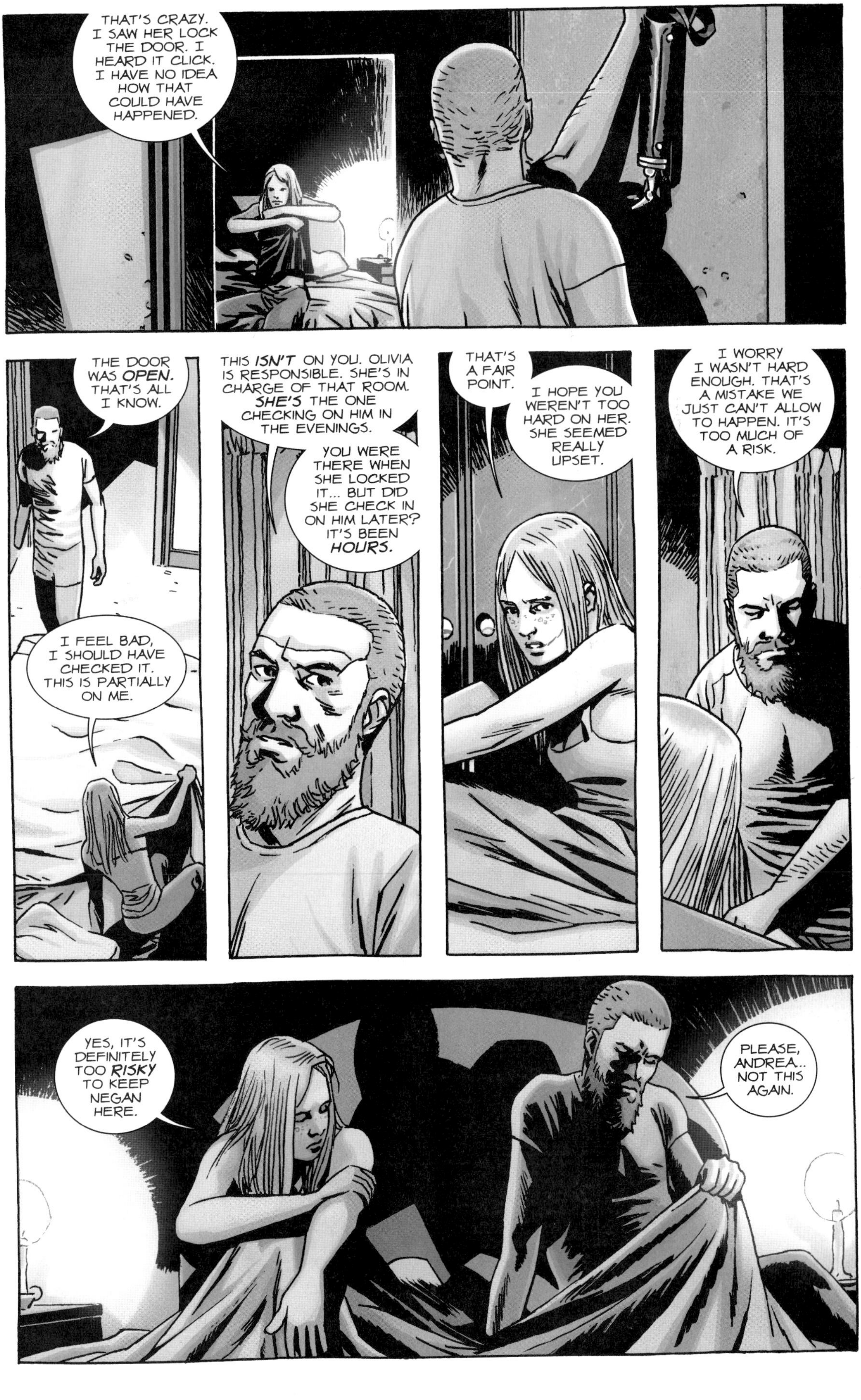
THAT'S CRAZY. I SAW HER LOCK THE DOOR. I HEARD IT CLICK. I HAVE NO IDEA HOW THAT COULD HAVE HAPPENED.
THE DOOR WAS OPEN. THAT'S ALL I KNOW.
I FEEL BAD, I SHOULD HAVE CHECKED IT. THIS IS PARTIALLY ON ME.
THIS ISN'T ON YOU. OLIVIA IS RESPONSIBLE. SHE'S IN CHARGE OF THAT ROOM. SHE'S THE ONE CHECKING ON HIM IN THE EVENINGS.
YOU WERE THERE WHEN SHE LOCKED IT... BUT DID SHE CHECK IN ON HIM LATER? IT'S BEEN HOURS.
THAT'S A FAIR POINT.
I HOPE YOU WEREN'T TOO HARD ON HER. SHE SEEMED REALLY UPSET.
I WORRY I WASN'T HARD ENOUGH. THAT'S A MISTAKE WE JUST CAN'T ALLOW TO HAPPEN. IT'S TOO MUCH OF A RISK.
YES, IT'S DEFINITELY TOO RISKY TO KEEP NEGAN HERE.
PLEASE, ANDREA.. NOT THIS AGAIN.

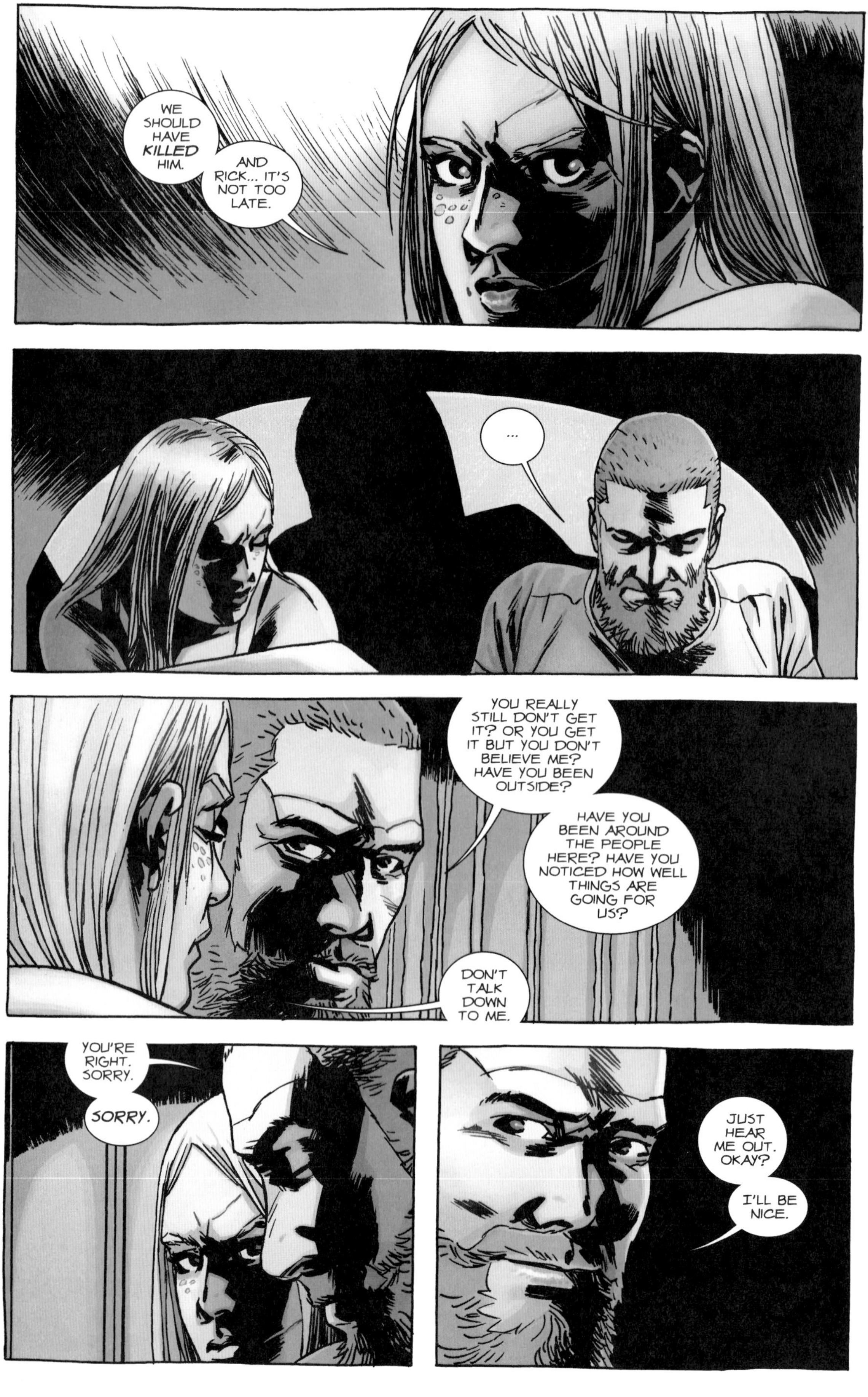

WE SHOULD HAVE KILLED HIM.
AND RICK... IT'S NOT TOO LATE.
...
YOU REALLY STILL DON'T GET IT? OR YOU GET IT BUT YOU DON'T BELIEVE ME? HAVE YOU BEEN OUTSIDE?
HAVE YOU BEEN AROUND THE PEOPLE HERE? HAVE YOU NOTICED HOW WELL THINGS ARE GOING FOR US?
DON'T TALK DOWN TO ME.
YOU'RE RIGHT. SORRY.
SORRY.
JUST HEAR ME OUT. OKAY?
I'LL BE NICE.

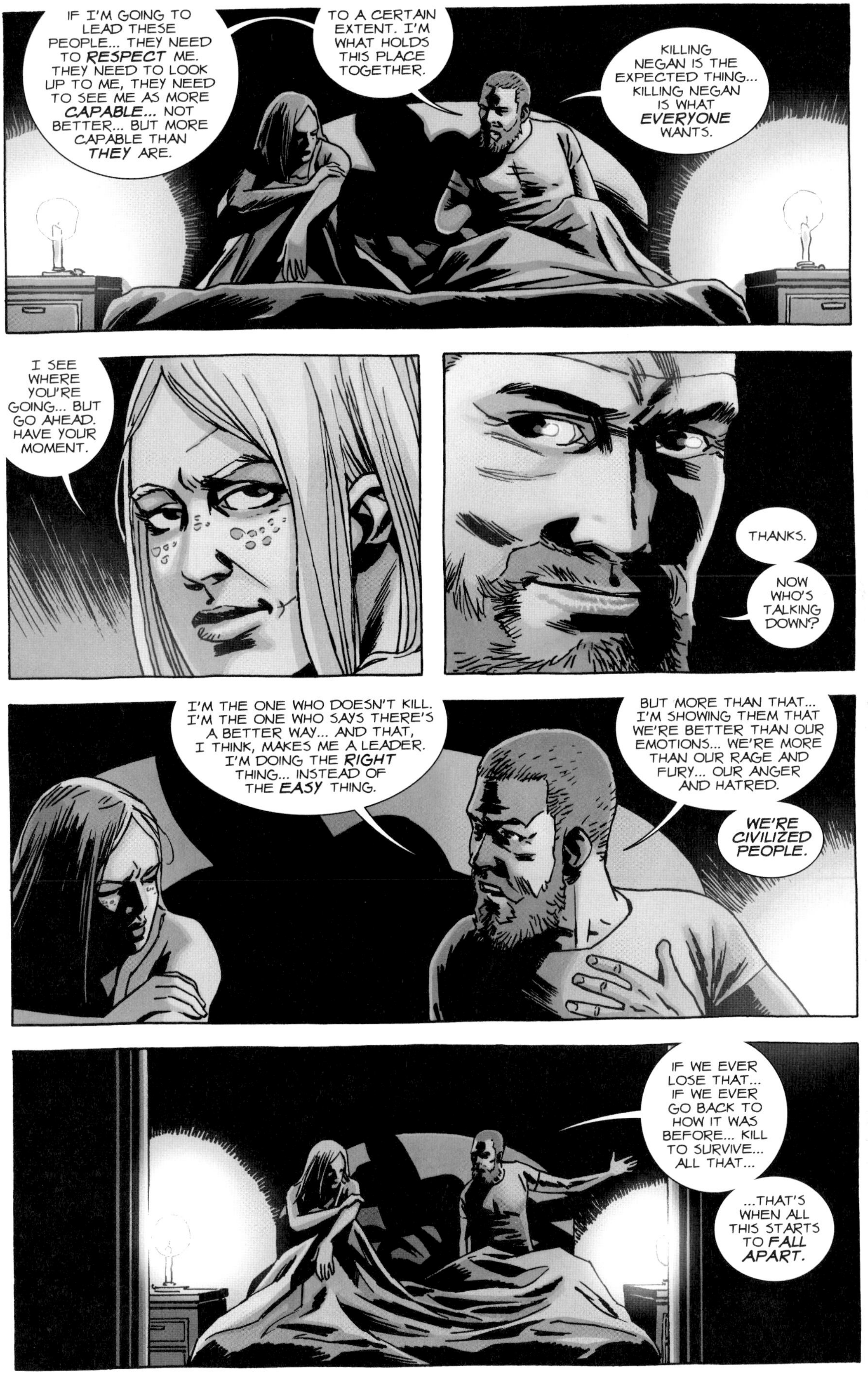
IF I'M GOING TO LEAD THESE PEOPLE... THEY NEED TO RESPECT ME. THEY NEED TO LOOK UP TO ME, THEY NEED TO SEE ME AS MORE CAPABLE... NOT BETTER... BUT MORE CAPABLE THAN THEY ARE.
TO A CERTAIN EXTENT. I'M WHAT HOLDS THIS PLACE TOGETHER.
KILLING NEGAN IS THE EXPECTED THING... KILLING NEGAN IS WHAT EVERYONE WANTS.
I SEE WHERE YOU'RE GOING... BUT GO AHEAD. HAVE YOUR MOMENT.
THANKS.
NOW WHO'S TALKING DOWN?
I'M THE ONE WHO DOESN'T KILL. I'M THE ONE WHO SAYS THERE'S A BETTER WAY... AND THAT, I THINK, MAKES ME A LEADER. I'M DOING THE RIGHT THING... INSTEAD OF THE EASY THING.
BUT MORE THAN THAT... I'M SHOWING THEM THAT WE'RE BETTER THAN OUR EMOTIONS... WE'RE MORE THAN OUR RAGE AND FURY... OUR ANGER AND HATRED.
WE'RE CIVILIZED PEOPLE.
IF WE EVER LOSE THAT... IF WE EVER GO BACK TO HOW IT WAS BEFORE... KILL TO SURVIVE... ALL THAT...
...THAT'S WHEN ALL THIS STARTS TO FALL APART.

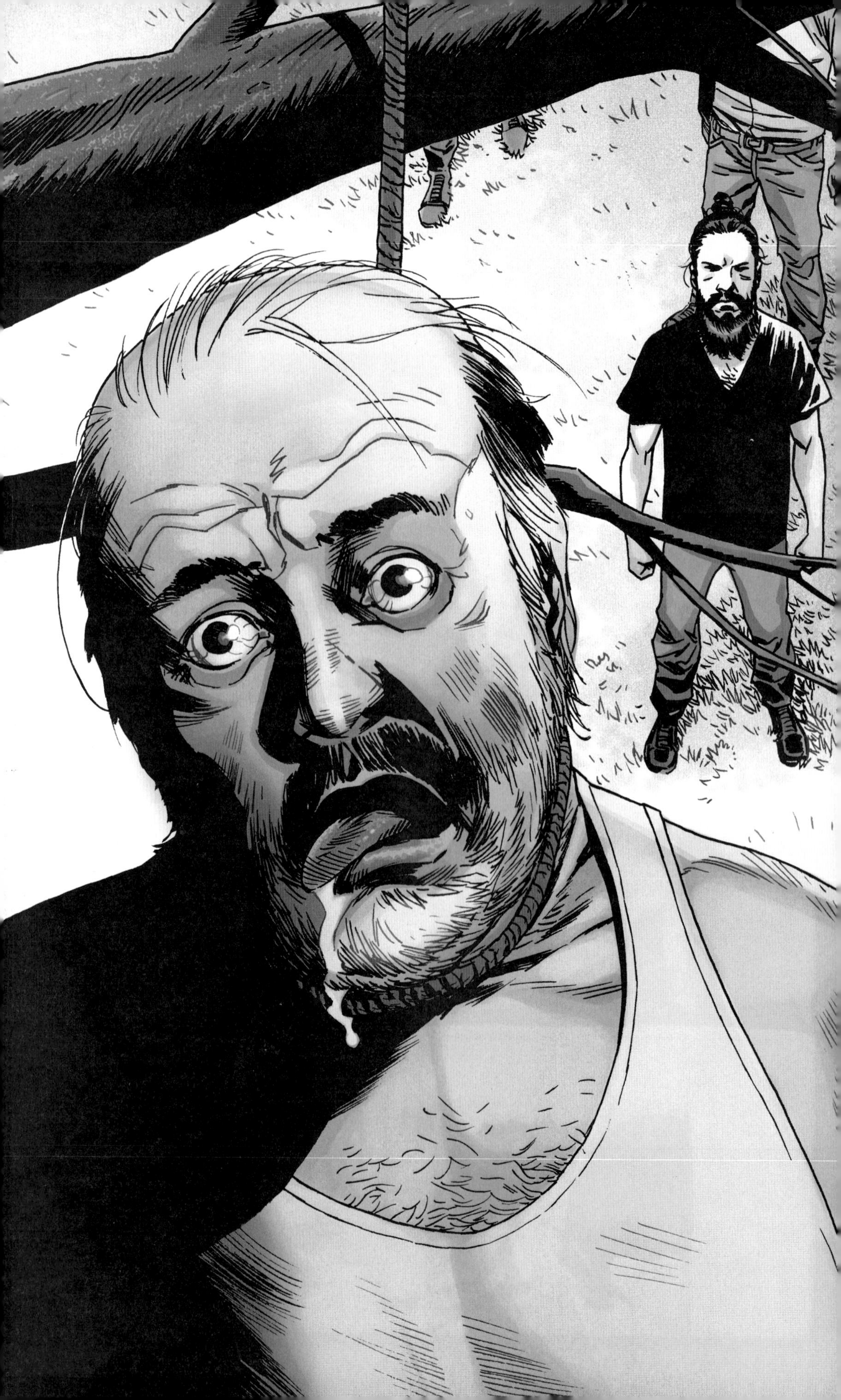

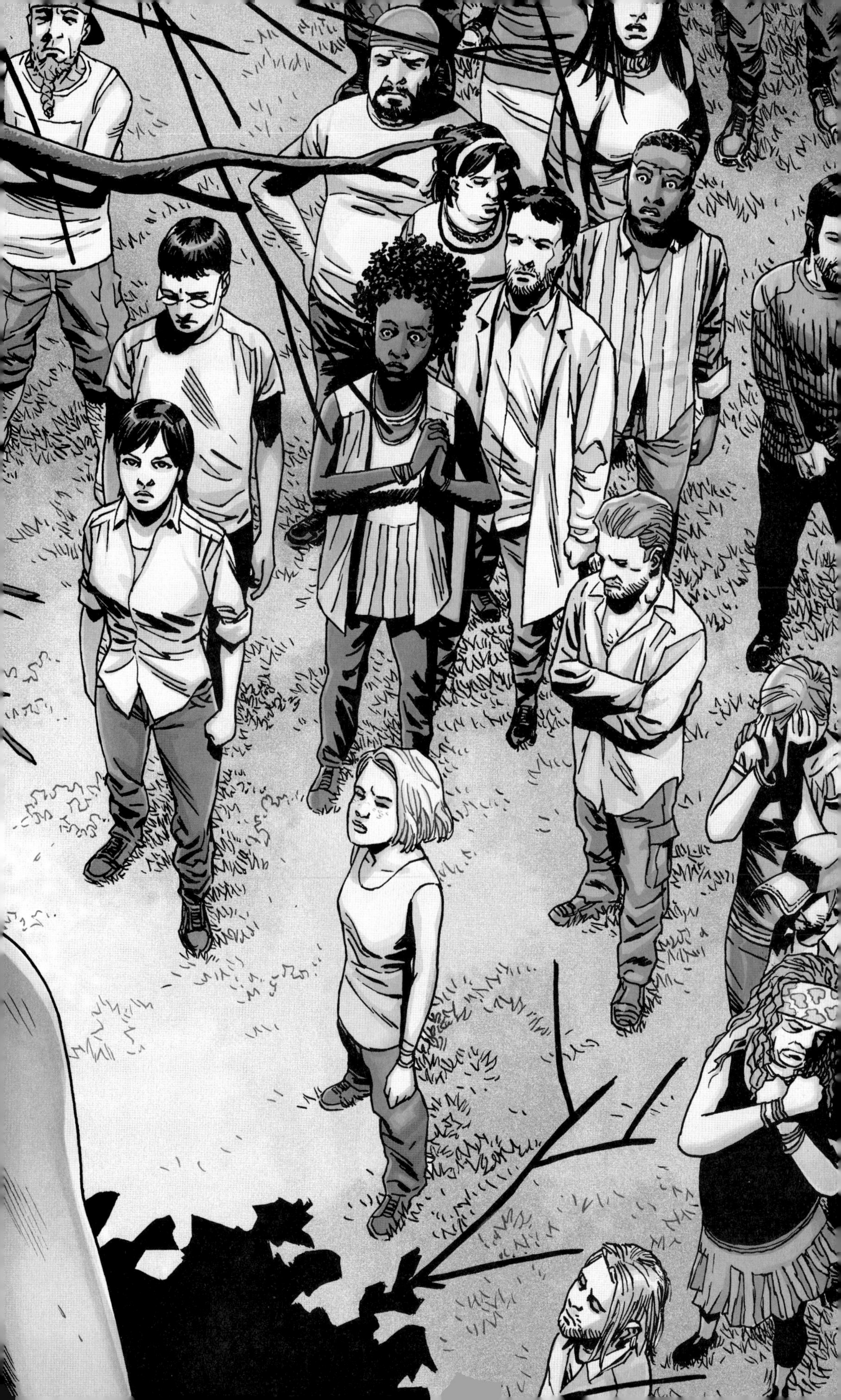

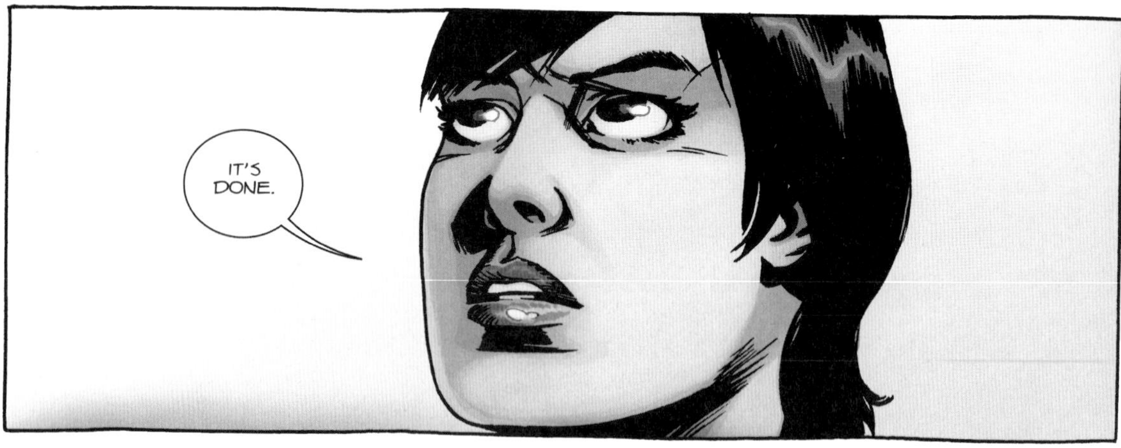
IT'S DONE.

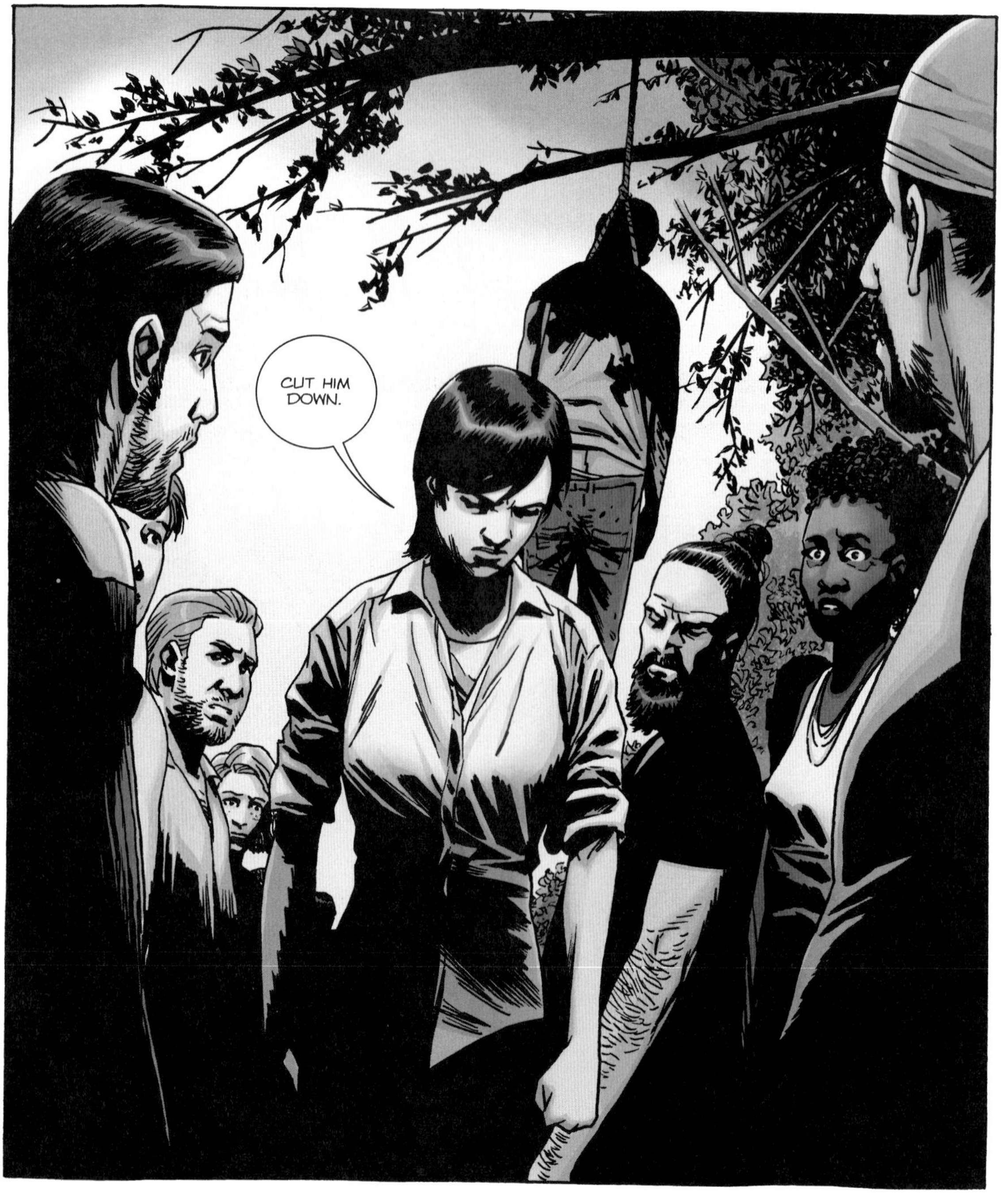
CUT HIM DOWN.

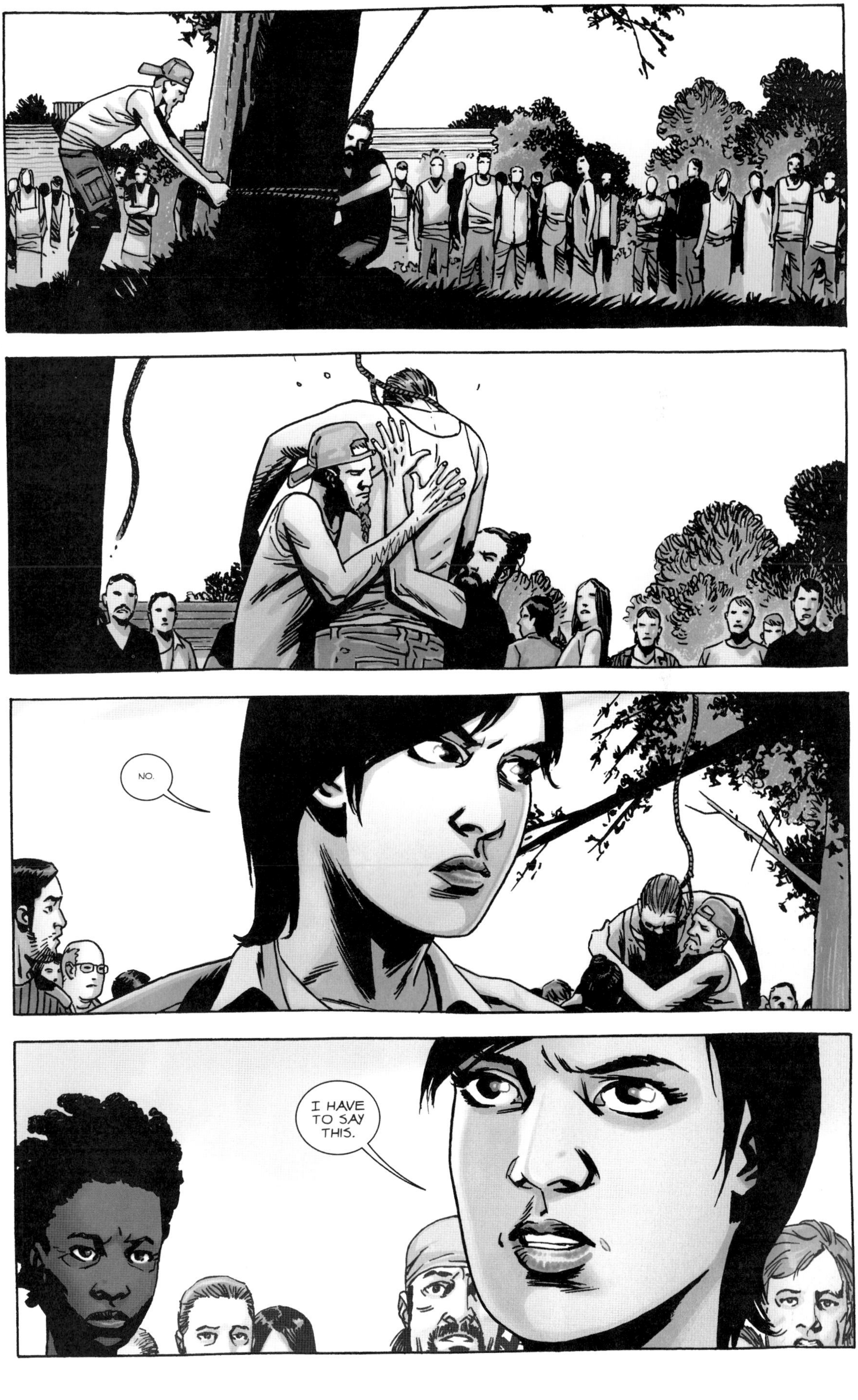
NO.
I HAVE TO SAY THIS.

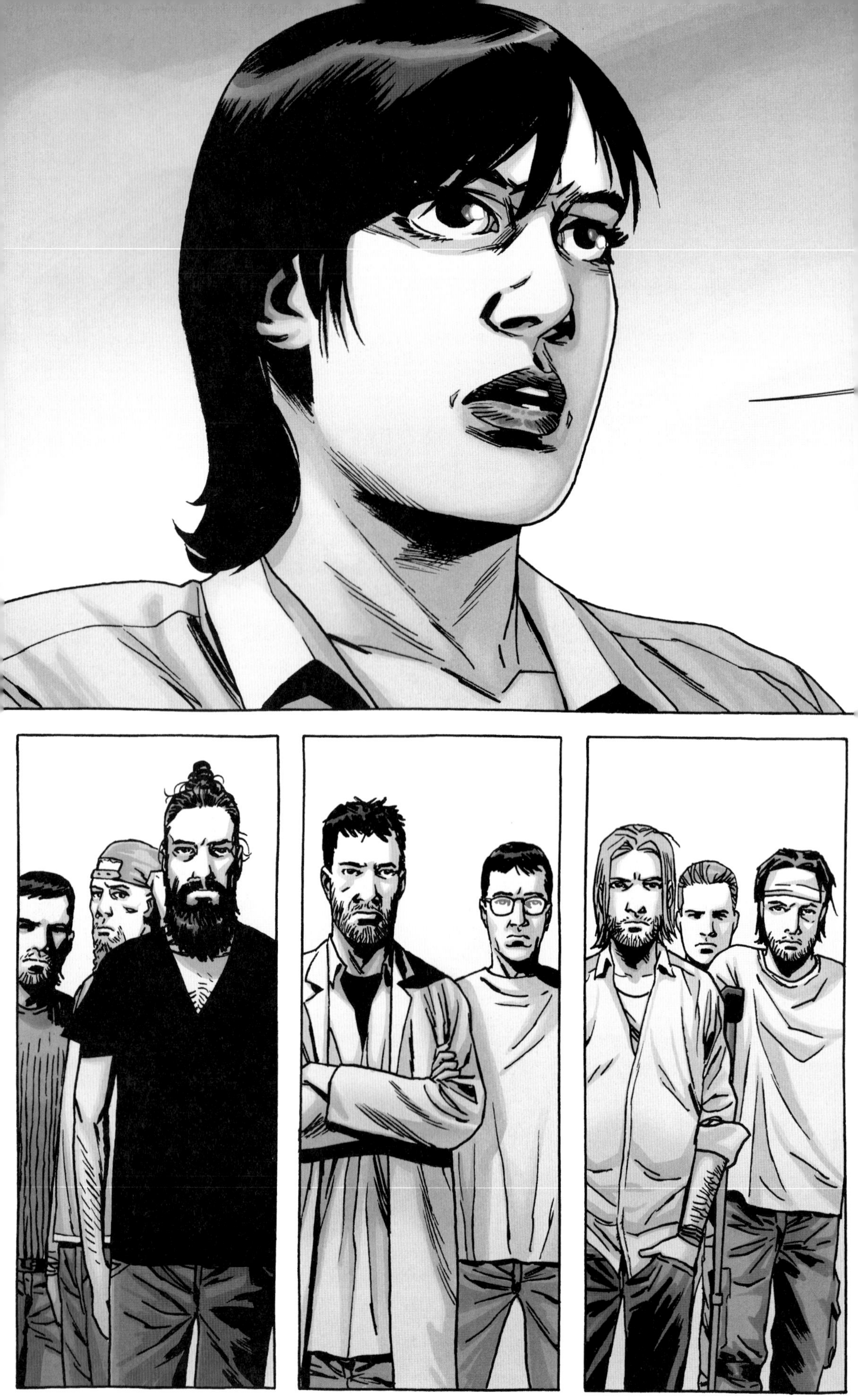

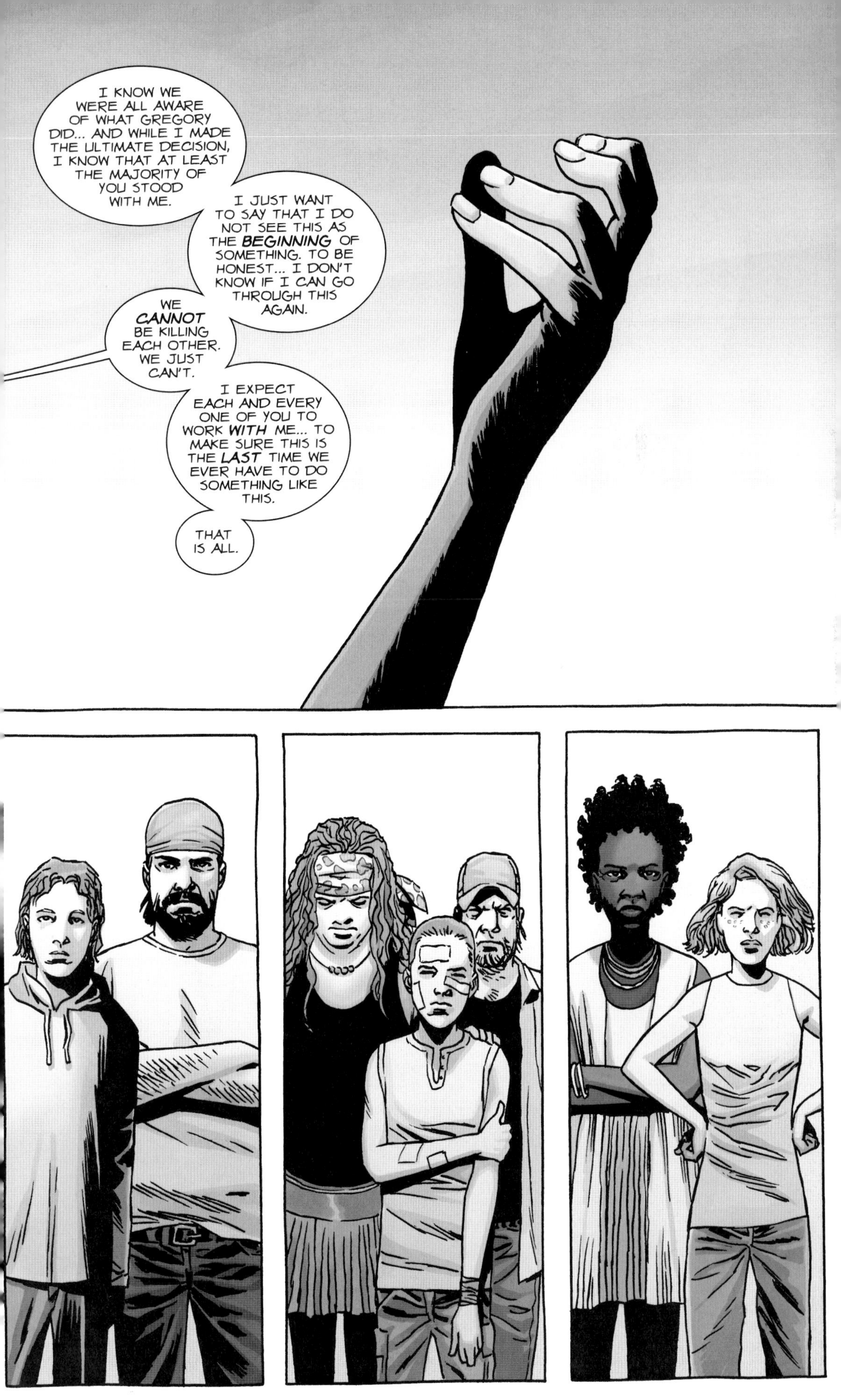
I KNOW WE WERE ALL AWARE OF WHAT GREGORY DID... AND WHILE I MADE THE ULTIMATE DECISION, I KNOW THAT AT LEAST THE MAJORITY OF YOU STOOD WITH ME.
I JUST WANT TO SAY THAT I DO NOT SEE THIS AS THE BEGINNING OF SOMETHING. TO BE HONEST... I DON'T KNOW IF I CAN GO THROUGH THIS AGAIN.
WE CANNOT BE KILLING EACH OTHER. WE JUST CAN'T.
I EXPECT EACH AND EVERY ONE OF YOU TO WORK WITH ME... TO MAKE SURE THIS IS THE LAST TIME WE EVER HAVE TO DO SOMETHING LIKE THIS.
THAT IS ALL.

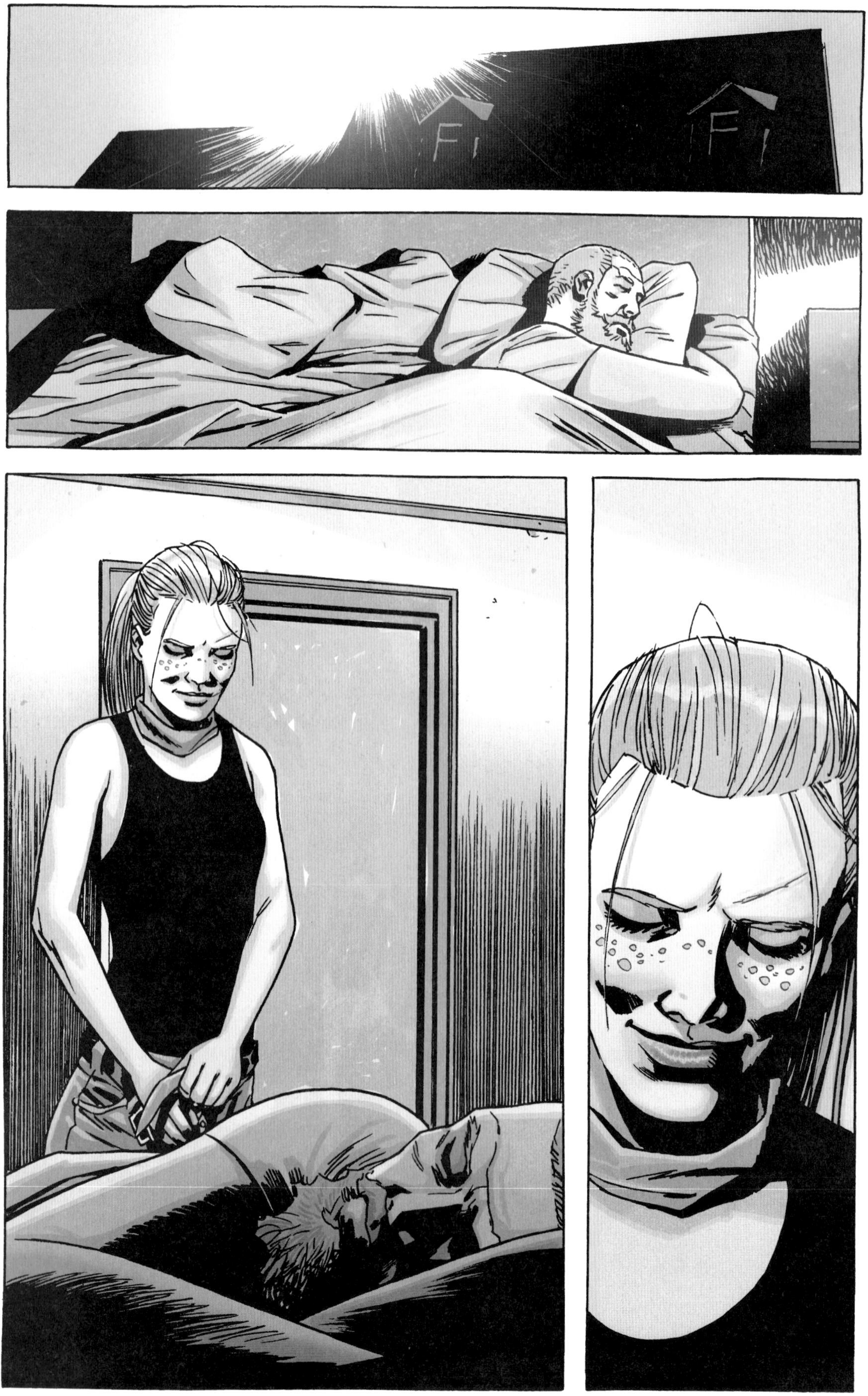

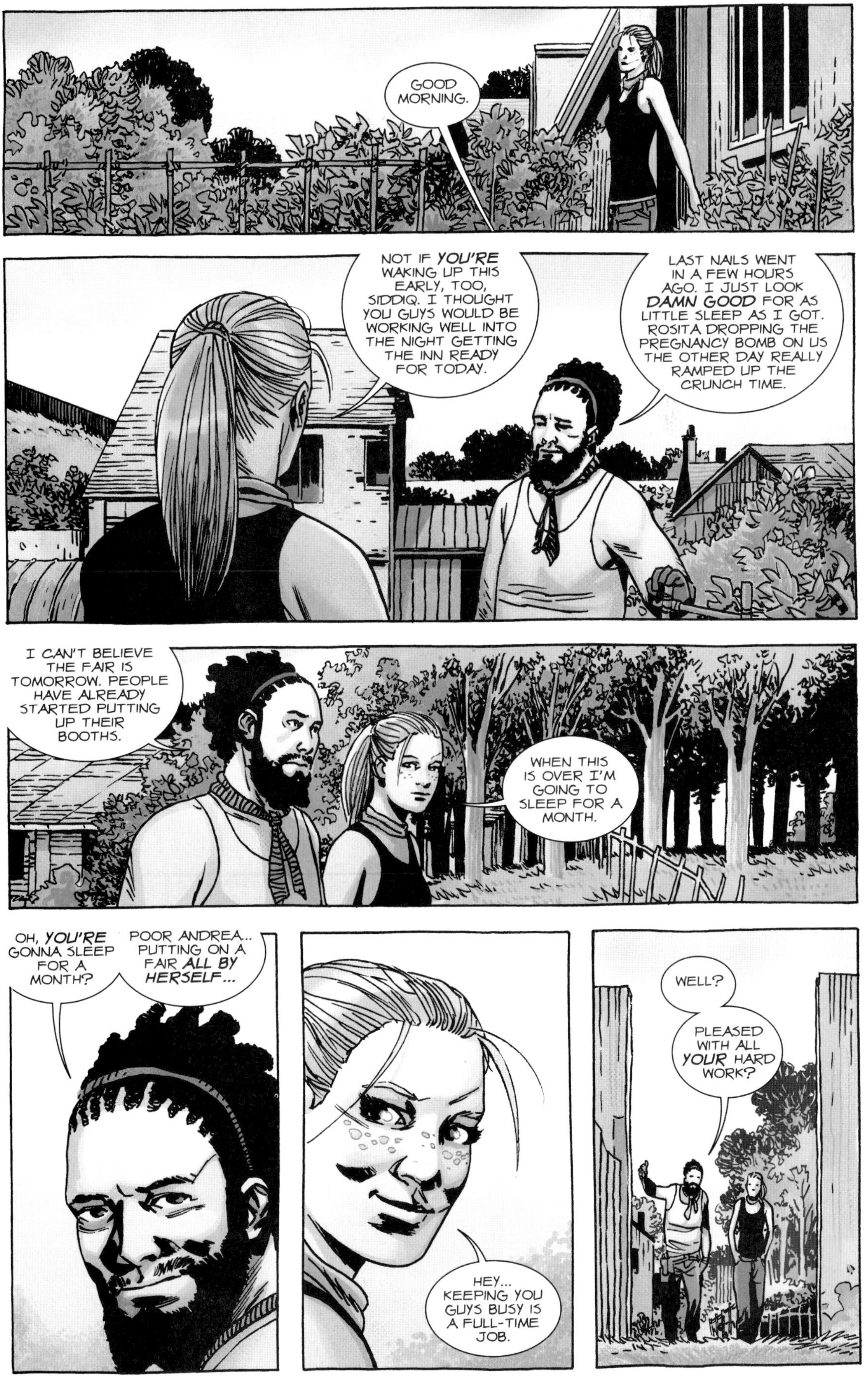
GOOD MORNING.
NOT IF YOU'RE WAKING UP THIS EARLY, TOO, SIDDIQ. I THOUGHT YOU GUYS WOULD BE WORKING WELL INTO THE NIGHT GETTING THE INN READY FOR TODAY.
LAST NAILS WENT IN A FEW HOURS AGO. I JUST LOOK DAMN GOOD FOR AS LITTLE SLEEP AS I GOT. ROSITA DROPPING THE PREGNANCY BOMB ON US THE OTHER DAY REALLY RAMPED UP THE CRUNCH TIME.
I CAN'T BELIEVE THE FAIR IS TOMORROW. PEOPLE HAVE ALREADY STARTED PUTTING UP THEIR BOOTHS.
WHEN THIS IS OVER I'M GOING TO SLEEP FOR A MONTH.
OH, YOU'RE GONNA SLEEP FOR A MONTH?
POOR ANDREA... PUTTING ON A FAIR ALL BY HERSELF...
HEY... KEEPING YOU GUYS BUSY IS A FULL-TIME JOB.
WELL?
PLEASED WITH ALL YOUR HARD WORK?

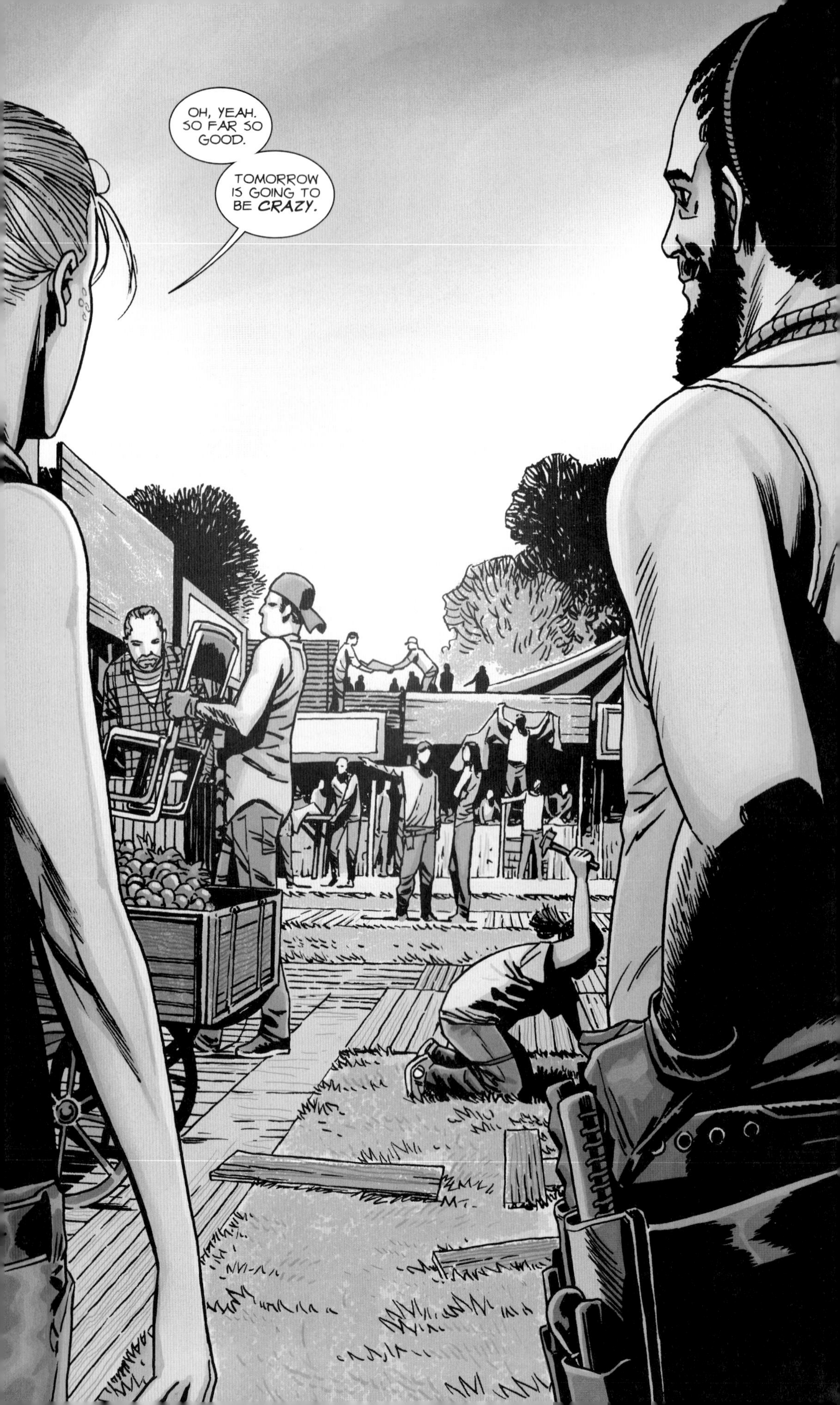
OH, YEAH. SO FAR SO GOOD.
TOMORROW IS GOING TO BE CRAZY.

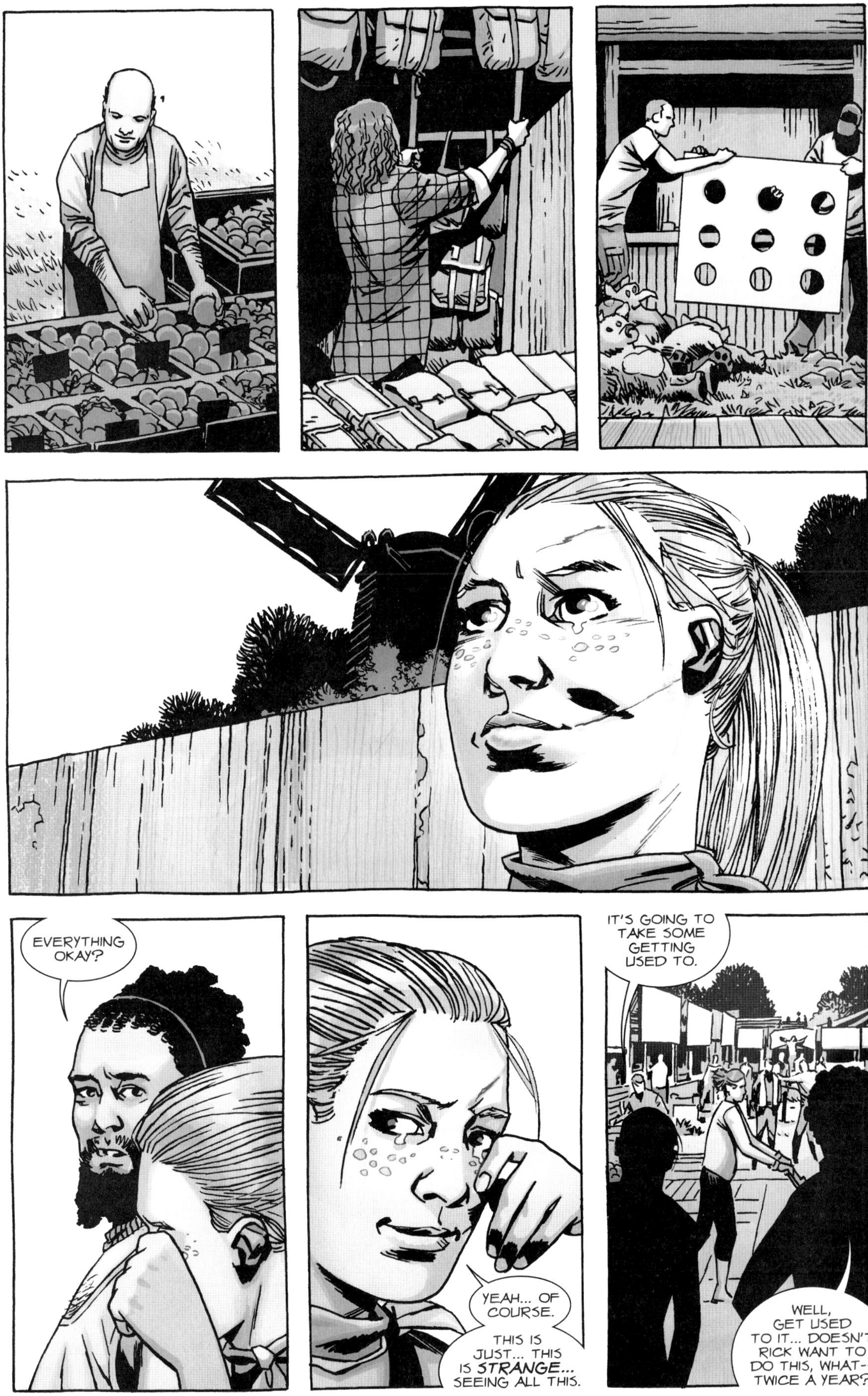
EVERYTHING OKAY?
YEAH... OF COURSE.
THIS IS JUST... THIS IS **STRANGE...** SEEING ALL THIS.
IT'S GOING TO TAKE SOME GETTING USED TO.
WELL, GET USED TO IT... DOESN'T RICK WANT TO DO THIS, WHAT-- TWICE A YEAR?

SHUKK!

SNISH!

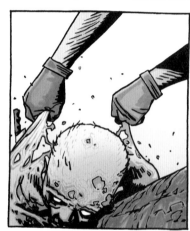

YOU LIKE IT, KID?

THIS CAN BE YOUR SKIN IF YOU'D LIKE.

IT'S ABOUT YOUR SIZE.

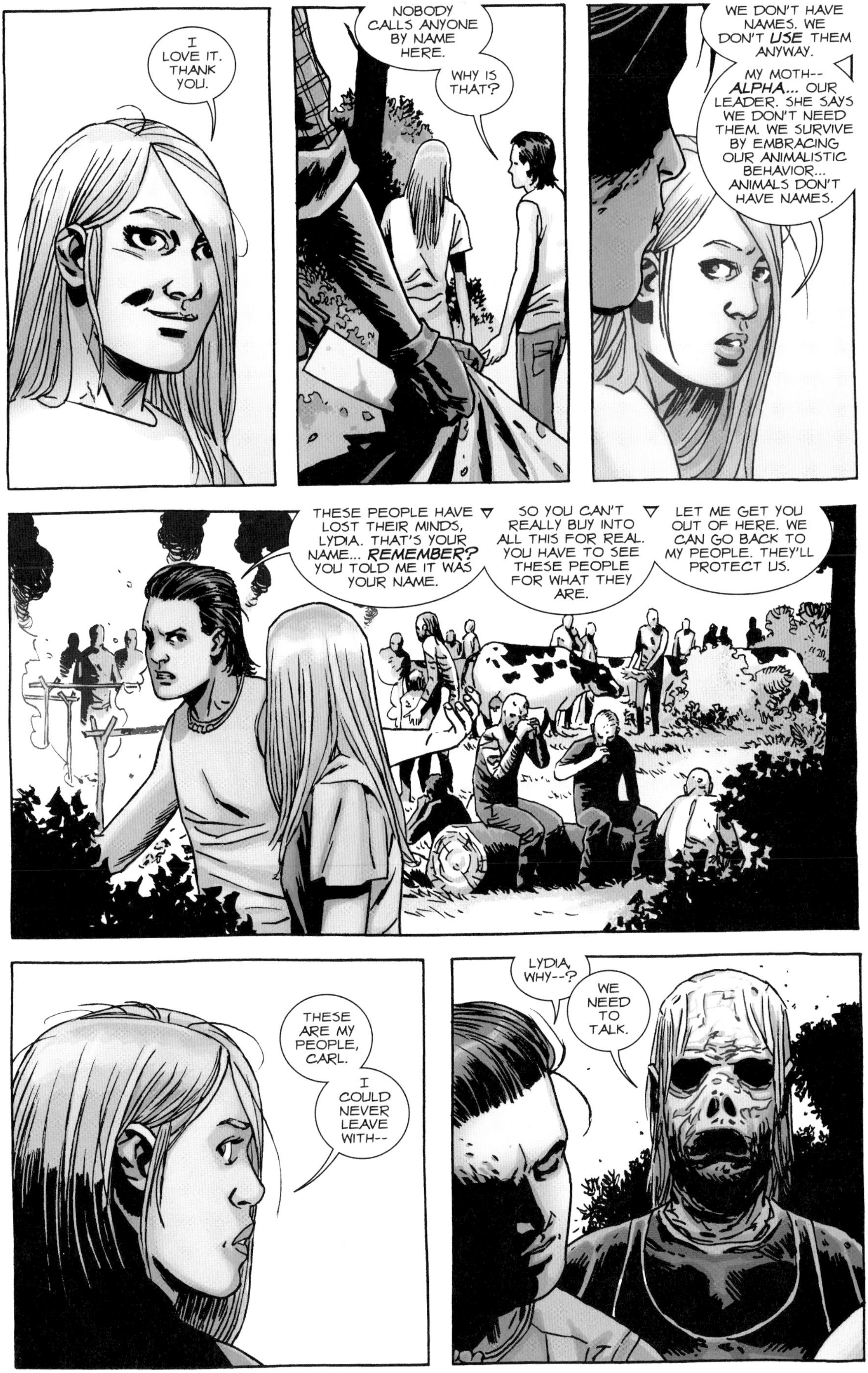

I LOVE IT. THANK YOU.
NOBODY CALLS ANYONE BY NAME HERE.
WHY IS THAT?
WE DON'T HAVE NAMES. WE DON'T *USE* THEM ANYWAY.
MY MOTH-- ***ALPHA...*** OUR LEADER. SHE SAYS WE DON'T NEED THEM. WE SURVIVE BY EMBRACING OUR ANIMALISTIC BEHAVIOR... ANIMALS DON'T HAVE NAMES.
THESE PEOPLE HAVE LOST THEIR MINDS, LYDIA. THAT'S YOUR NAME... ***REMEMBER?*** YOU TOLD ME IT WAS YOUR NAME.
SO YOU CAN'T REALLY BUY INTO ALL THIS FOR REAL. YOU HAVE TO SEE THESE PEOPLE FOR WHAT THEY ARE.
LET ME GET YOU OUT OF HERE. WE CAN GO BACK TO MY PEOPLE. THEY'LL PROTECT US.
THESE ARE MY PEOPLE, CARL.
I COULD NEVER LEAVE WITH--
LYDIA, WHY--?
WE NEED TO TALK.

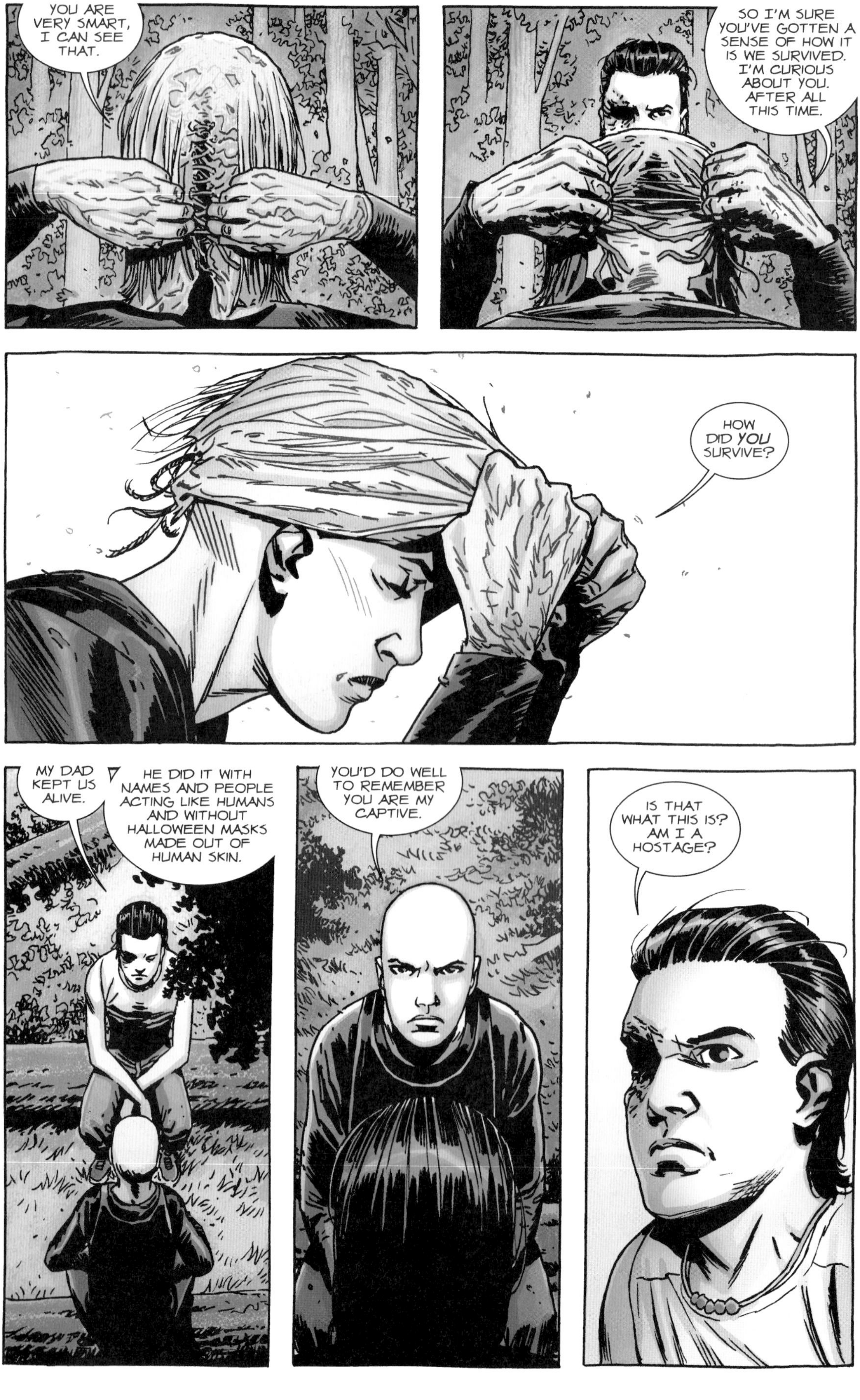
YOU ARE VERY SMART, I CAN SEE THAT.
SO I'M SURE YOU'VE GOTTEN A SENSE OF HOW IT IS WE SURVIVED. I'M CURIOUS ABOUT YOU. AFTER ALL THIS TIME.
HOW DID *YOU* SURVIVE?
MY DAD KEPT US ALIVE.
HE DID IT WITH NAMES AND PEOPLE ACTING LIKE HUMANS AND WITHOUT HALLOWEEN MASKS MADE OUT OF HUMAN SKIN.
YOU'D DO WELL TO REMEMBER YOU ARE MY CAPTIVE.
IS THAT WHAT THIS IS? AM I A HOSTAGE?

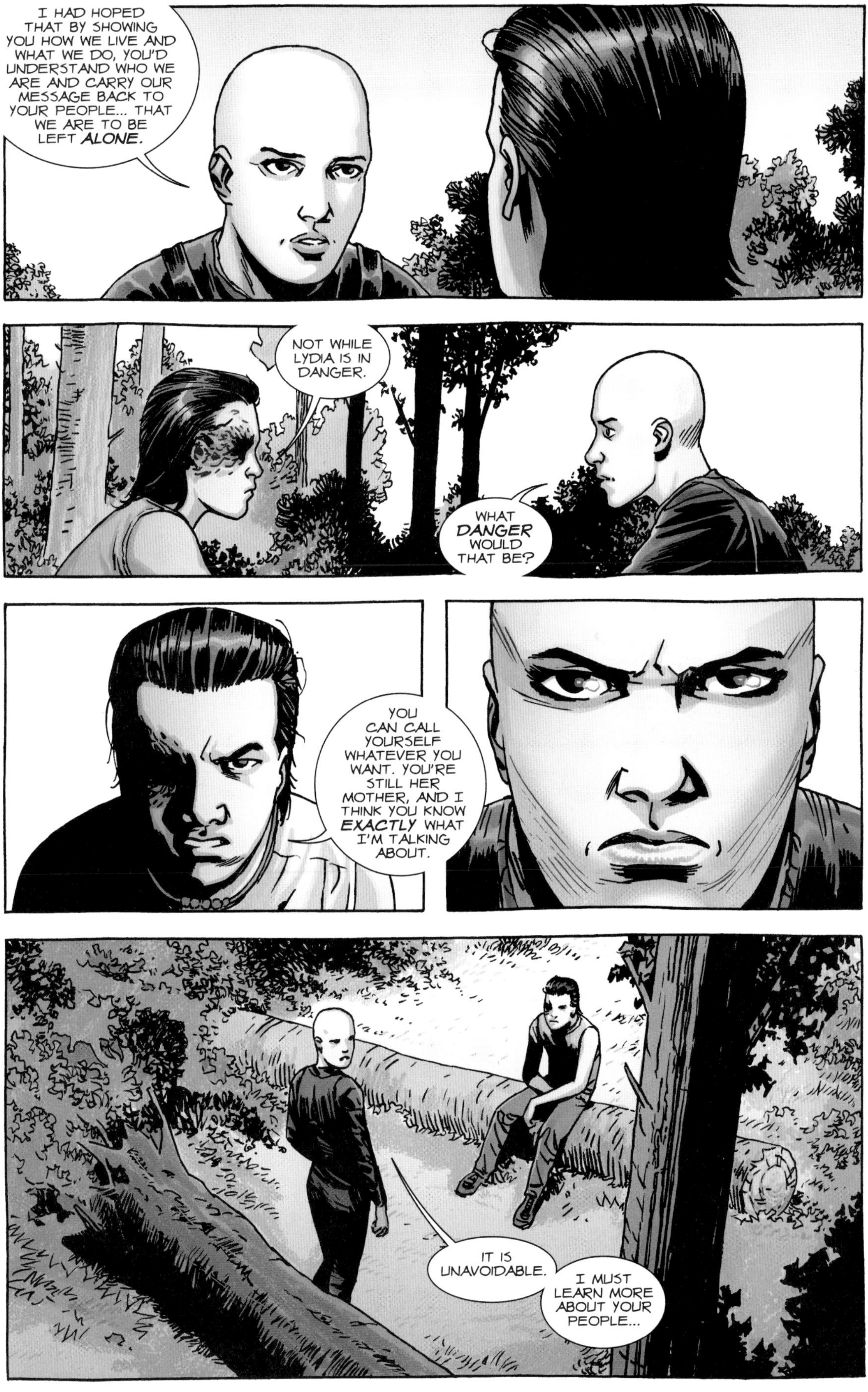
I HAD HOPED THAT BY SHOWING YOU HOW WE LIVE AND WHAT WE DO, YOU'D UNDERSTAND WHO WE ARE AND CARRY OUR MESSAGE BACK TO YOUR PEOPLE... THAT WE ARE TO BE LEFT ALONE.
NOT WHILE LYDIA IS IN DANGER.
WHAT DANGER WOULD THAT BE?
YOU CAN CALL YOURSELF WHATEVER YOU WANT. YOU'RE STILL HER MOTHER, AND I THINK YOU KNOW EXACTLY WHAT I'M TALKING ABOUT.
IT IS UNAVOIDABLE.
I MUST LEARN MORE ABOUT YOUR PEOPLE...

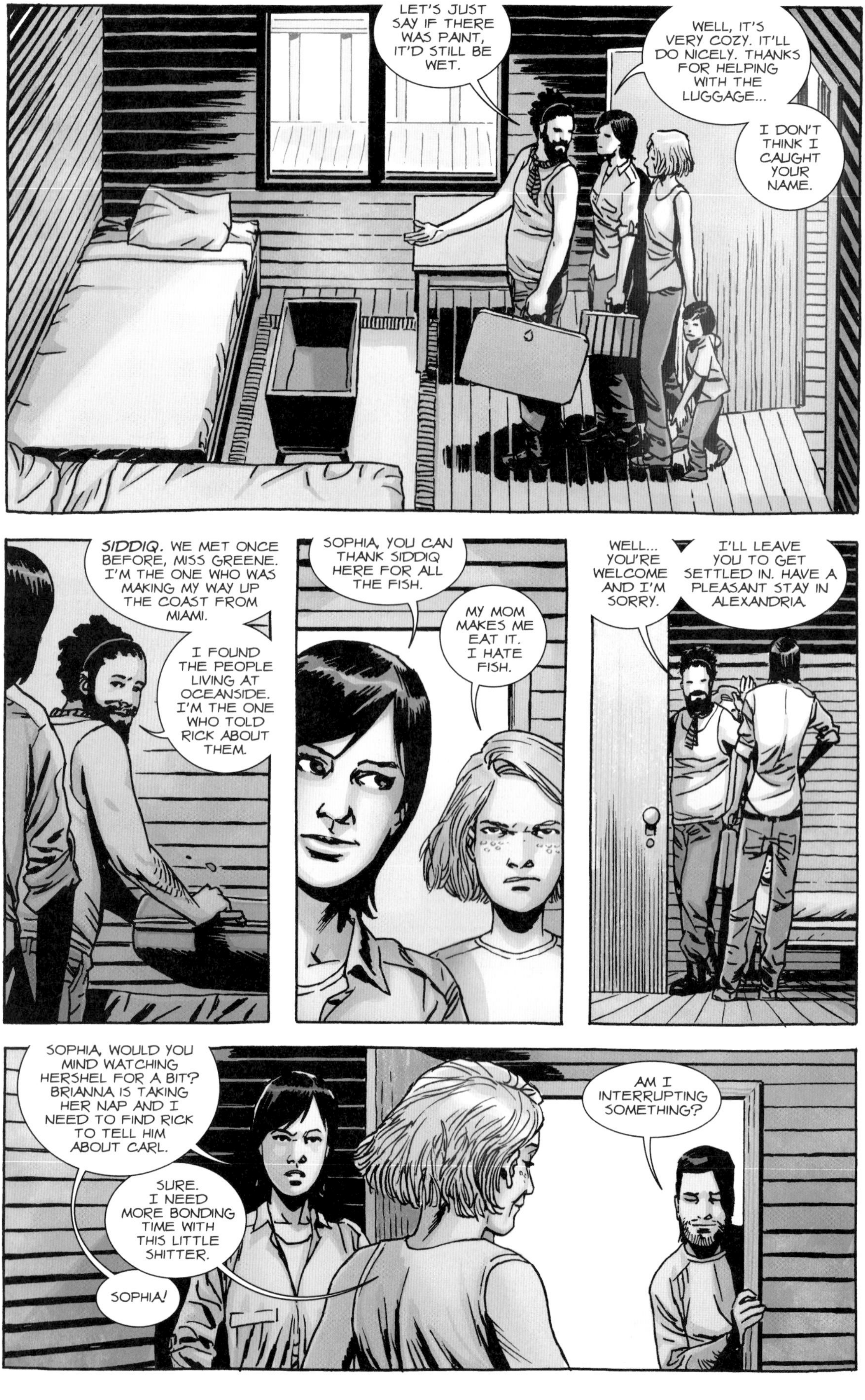
LET'S JUST SAY IF THERE WAS PAINT, IT'D STILL BE WET.
WELL, IT'S VERY COZY. IT'LL DO NICELY. THANKS FOR HELPING WITH THE LUGGAGE...
I DON'T THINK I CAUGHT YOUR NAME.
SIDDIQ. WE MET ONCE BEFORE, MISS GREENE. I'M THE ONE WHO WAS MAKING MY WAY UP THE COAST FROM MIAMI.
I FOUND THE PEOPLE LIVING AT OCEANSIDE. I'M THE ONE WHO TOLD RICK ABOUT THEM.
SOPHIA, YOU CAN THANK SIDDIQ HERE FOR ALL THE FISH.
MY MOM MAKES ME EAT IT. I HATE FISH.
WELL... YOU'RE WELCOME AND I'M SORRY.
I'LL LEAVE YOU TO GET SETTLED IN. HAVE A PLEASANT STAY IN ALEXANDRIA.
SOPHIA, WOULD YOU MIND WATCHING HERSHEL FOR A BIT? BRIANNA IS TAKING HER NAP AND I NEED TO FIND RICK TO TELL HIM ABOUT CARL.
SURE. I NEED MORE BONDING TIME WITH THIS LITTLE SHITTER.
SOPHIA!
AM I INTERRUPTING SOMETHING?

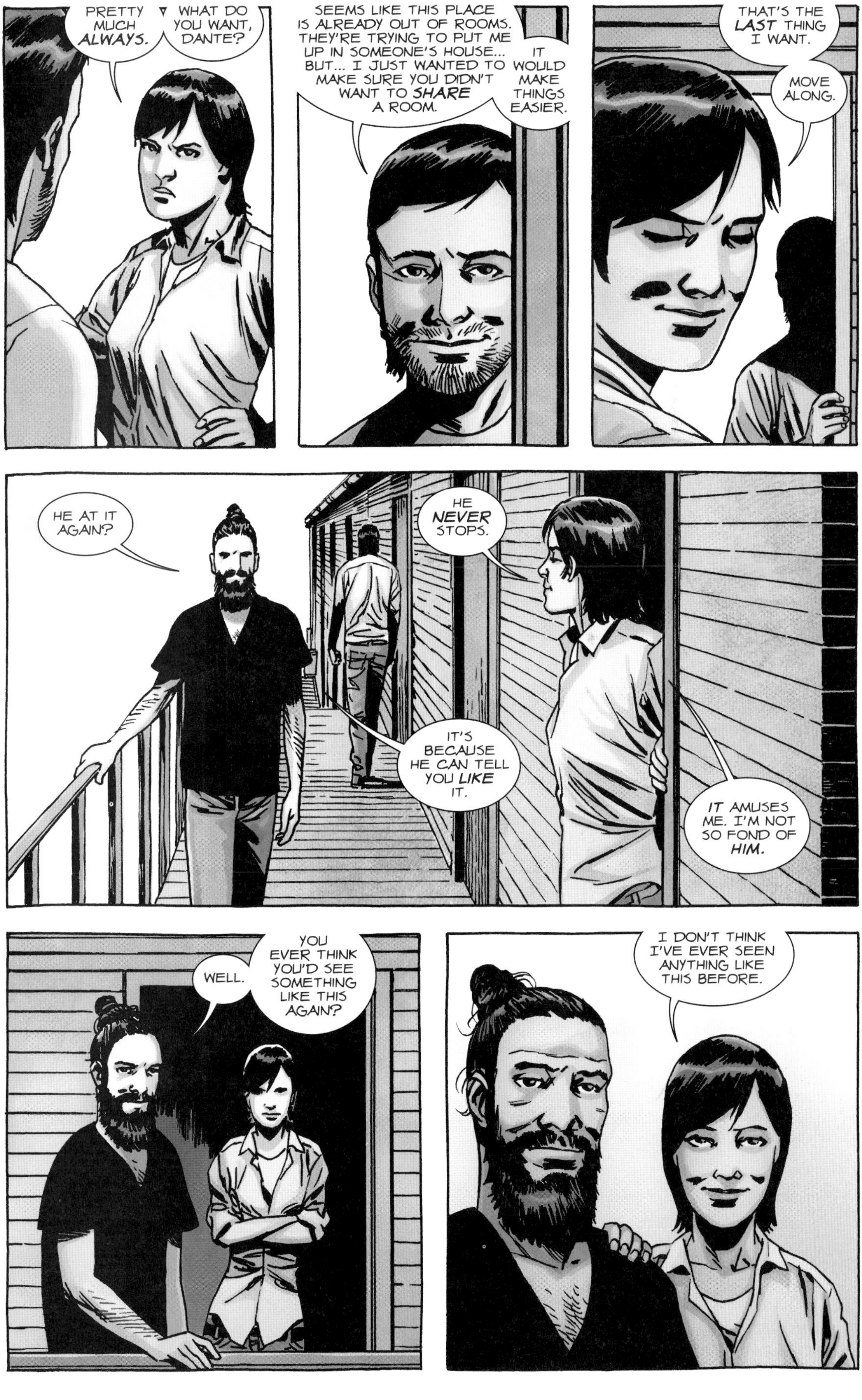
PRETTY MUCH ALWAYS.
WHAT DO YOU WANT, DANTE?
SEEMS LIKE THIS PLACE IS ALREADY OUT OF ROOMS. THEY'RE TRYING TO PUT ME UP IN SOMEONE'S HOUSE... BUT... I JUST WANTED TO MAKE SURE YOU DIDN'T WANT TO SHARE A ROOM.
IT WOULD MAKE THINGS EASIER.
THAT'S THE LAST THING I WANT.
MOVE ALONG.
HE AT IT AGAIN?
HE NEVER STOPS.
IT'S BECAUSE HE CAN TELL YOU LIKE IT.
IT AMUSES ME. I'M NOT SO FOND OF HIM.
WELL.
YOU EVER THINK YOU'D SEE SOMETHING LIKE THIS AGAIN?
I DON'T THINK I'VE EVER SEEN ANYTHING LIKE THIS BEFORE.

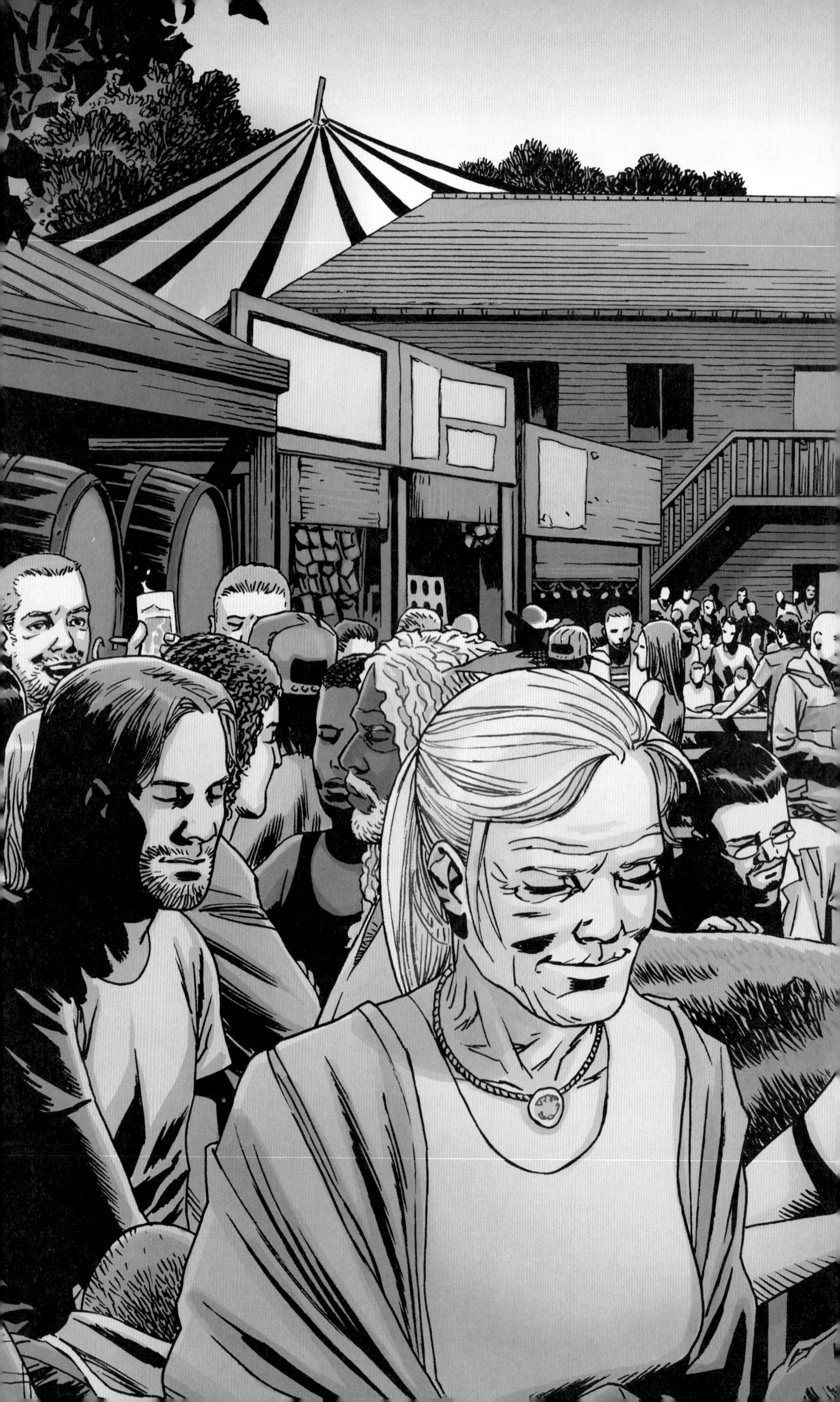

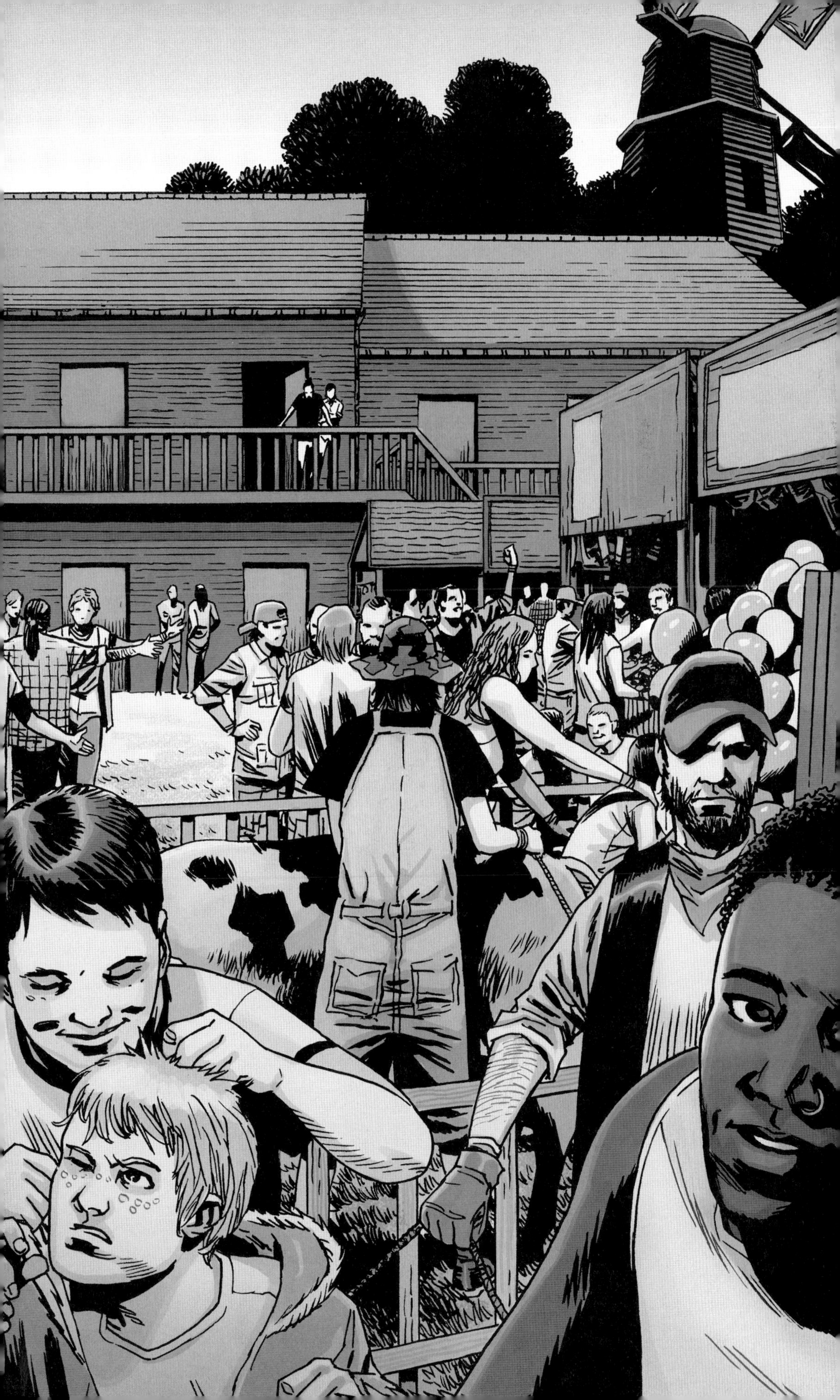

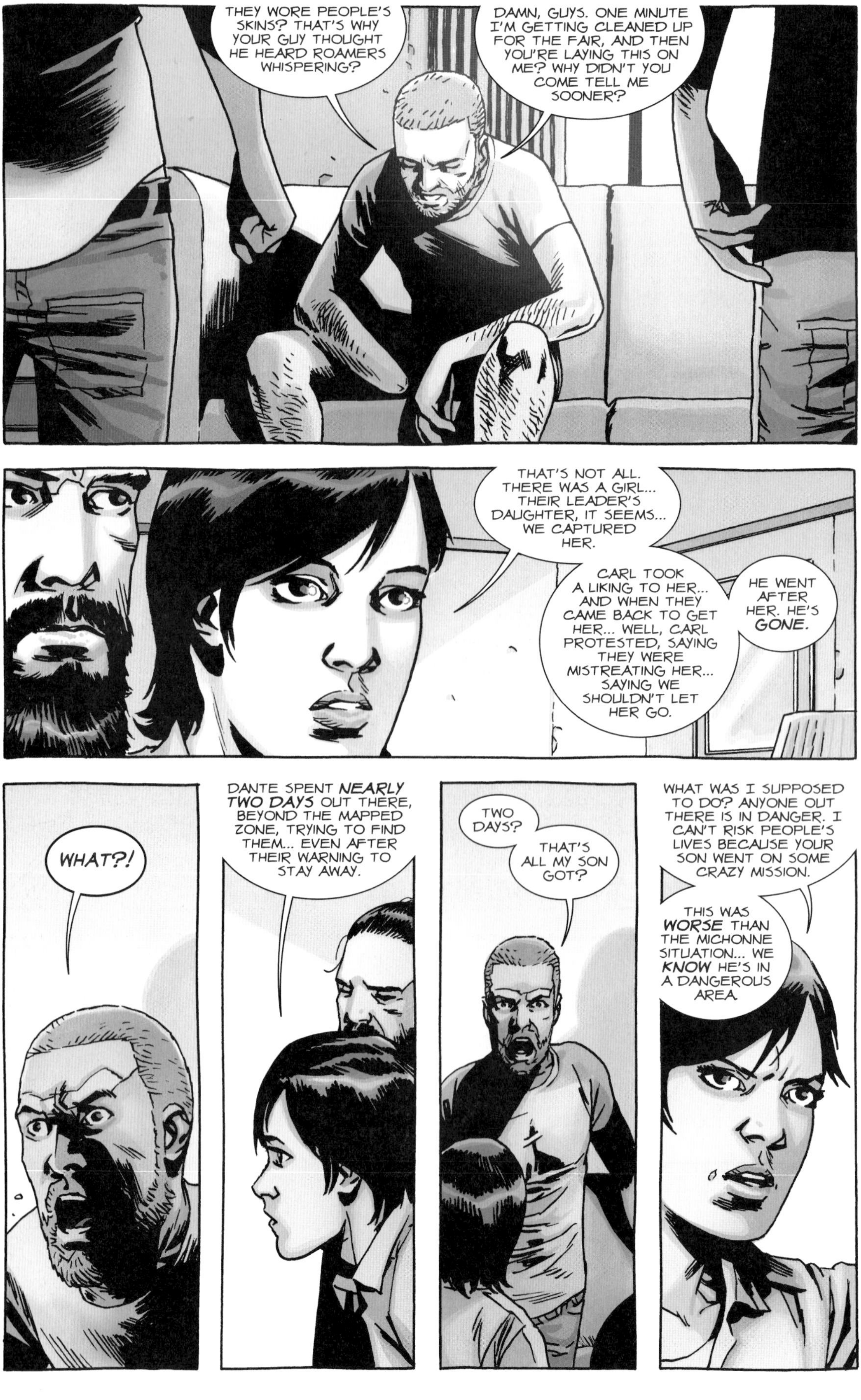
THEY WORE PEOPLE'S SKINS? THAT'S WHY YOUR GUY THOUGHT HE HEARD ROAMERS WHISPERING?
DAMN, GUYS. ONE MINUTE I'M GETTING CLEANED UP FOR THE FAIR, AND THEN YOU'RE LAYING THIS ON ME? WHY DIDN'T YOU COME TELL ME SOONER?
THAT'S NOT ALL. THERE WAS A GIRL... THEIR LEADER'S DAUGHTER, IT SEEMS... WE CAPTURED HER.
CARL TOOK A LIKING TO HER... AND WHEN THEY CAME BACK TO GET HER... WELL, CARL PROTESTED, SAYING THEY WERE MISTREATING HER... SAYING WE SHOULDN'T LET HER GO.
HE WENT AFTER HER. HE'S **GONE.**
WHAT?!
DANTE SPENT ***NEARLY TWO DAYS*** OUT THERE, BEYOND THE MAPPED ZONE, TRYING TO FIND THEM... EVEN AFTER THEIR WARNING TO STAY AWAY.
TWO DAYS?
THAT'S ALL MY SON GOT?
WHAT WAS I SUPPOSED TO DO? ANYONE OUT THERE IS IN DANGER. I CAN'T RISK PEOPLE'S LIVES BECAUSE YOUR SON WENT ON SOME CRAZY MISSION.
THIS WAS **WORSE** THAN THE MICHONNE SITUATION... WE **KNOW** HE'S IN A DANGEROUS AREA.

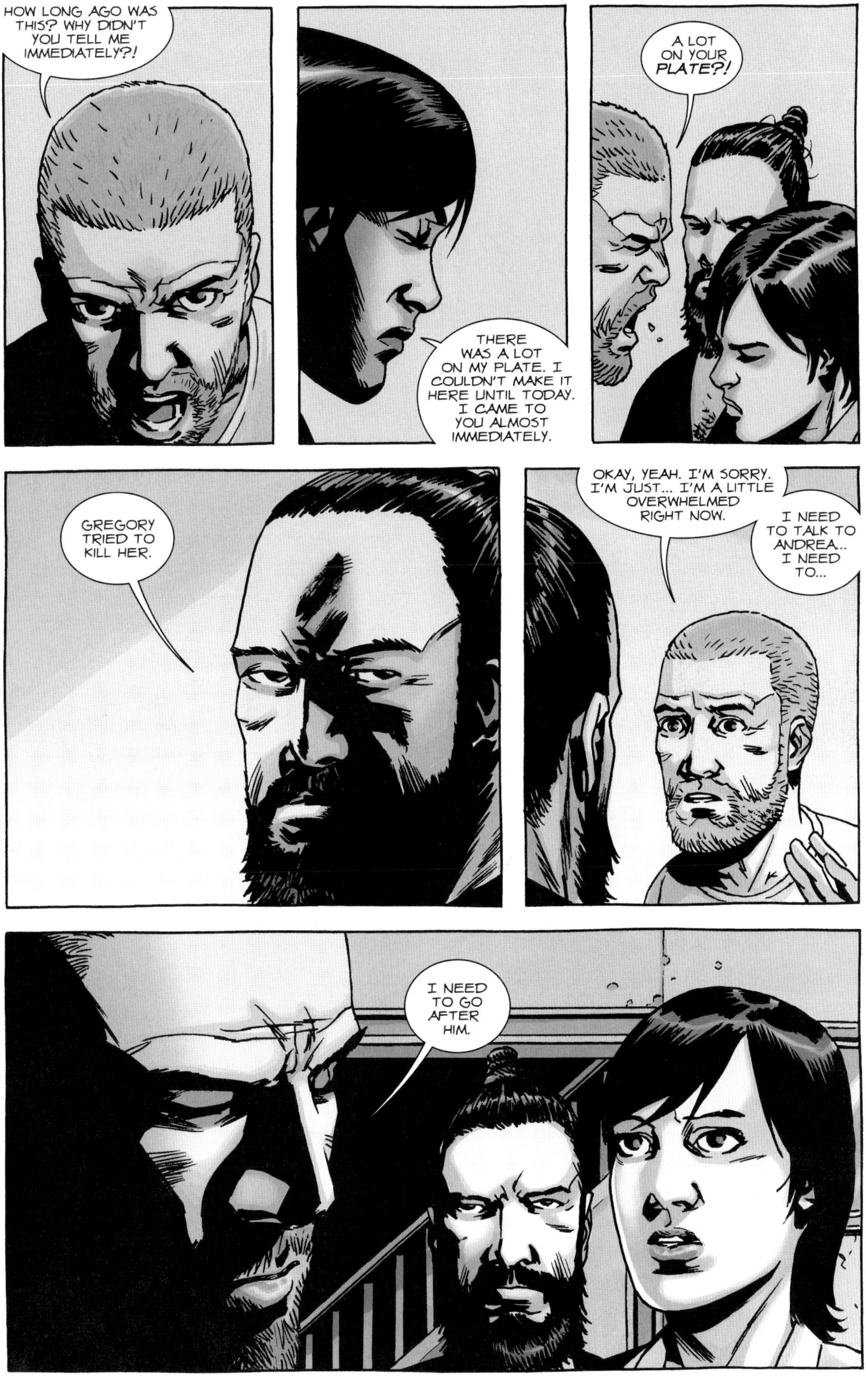
HOW LONG AGO WAS THIS? WHY DIDN'T YOU TELL ME IMMEDIATELY?!
THERE WAS A LOT ON MY PLATE. I COULDN'T MAKE IT HERE UNTIL TODAY. I CAME TO YOU ALMOST IMMEDIATELY.
A LOT ON YOUR *PLATE?!*
GREGORY TRIED TO KILL HER.
OKAY, YEAH. I'M SORRY. I'M JUST... I'M A LITTLE OVERWHELMED RIGHT NOW.
I NEED TO TALK TO ANDREA... I NEED TO...
I NEED TO GO AFTER HIM.

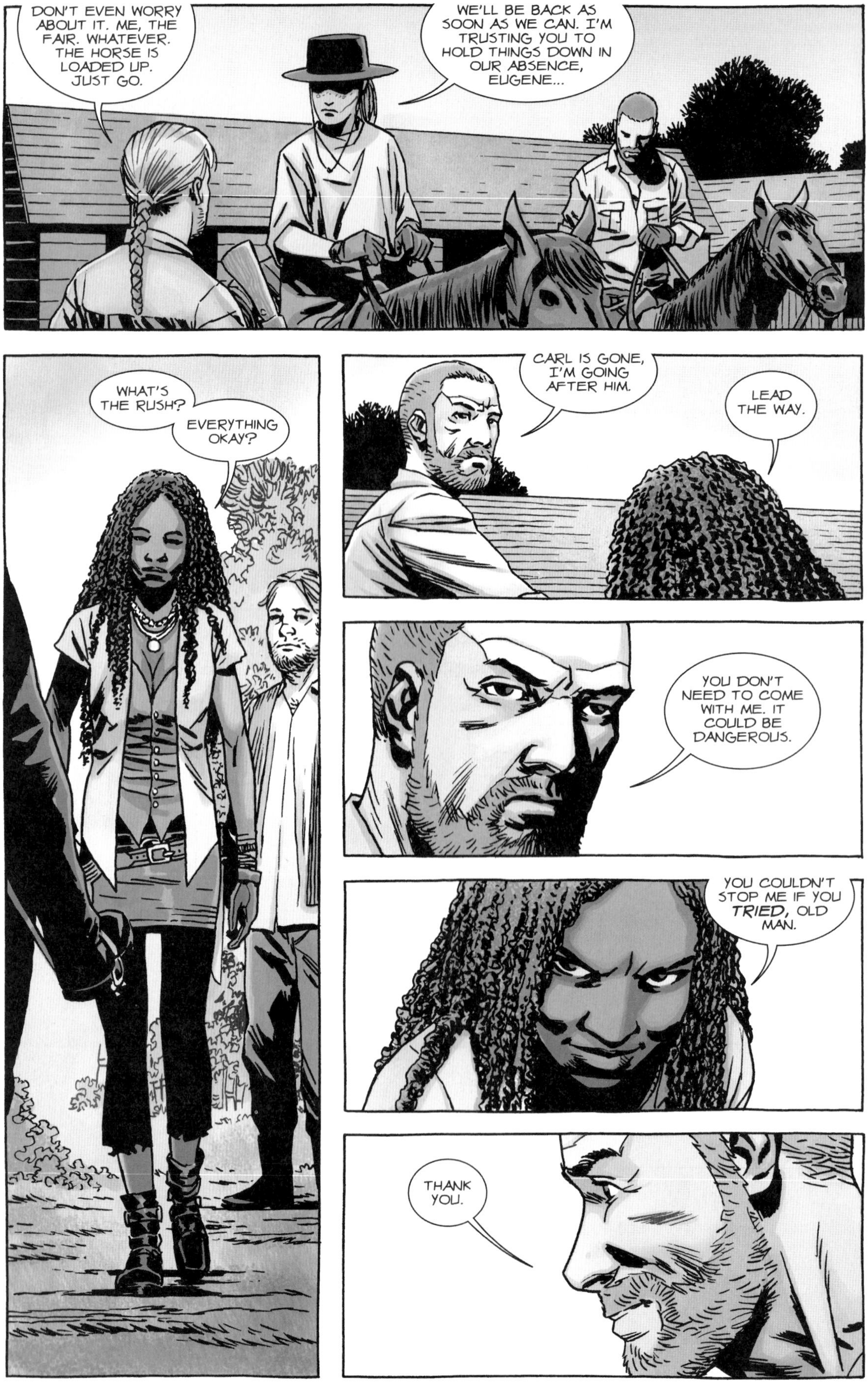
DON'T EVEN WORRY ABOUT IT. ME, THE FAIR. WHATEVER. THE HORSE IS LOADED UP. JUST GO.
WE'LL BE BACK AS SOON AS WE CAN. I'M TRUSTING YOU TO HOLD THINGS DOWN IN OUR ABSENCE, EUGENE...
WHAT'S THE RUSH?
EVERYTHING OKAY?
CARL IS GONE, I'M GOING AFTER HIM.
LEAD THE WAY.
YOU DON'T NEED TO COME WITH ME. IT COULD BE DANGEROUS.
YOU COULDN'T STOP ME IF YOU *TRIED,* OLD MAN.
THANK YOU.

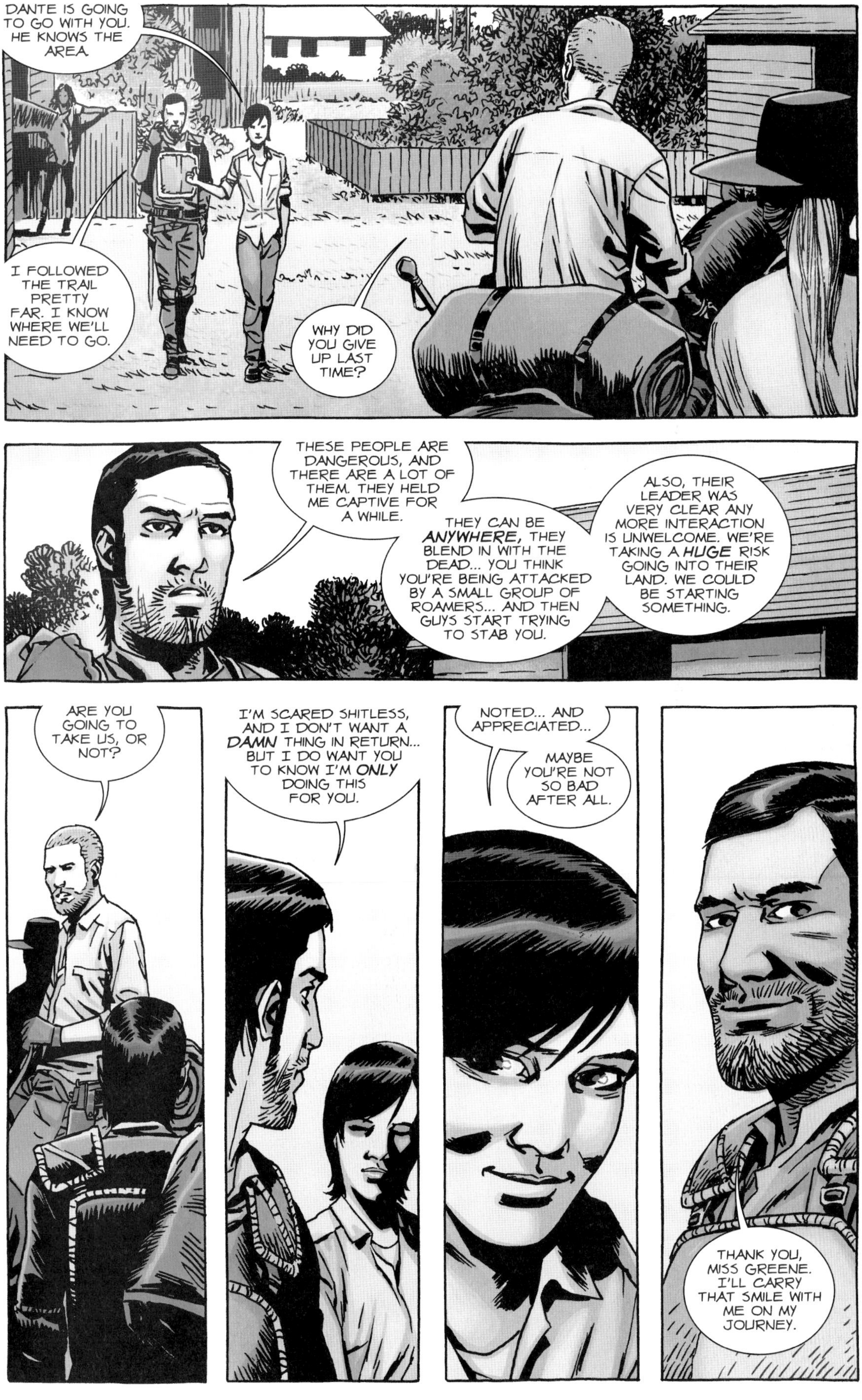
DANTE IS GOING TO GO WITH YOU. HE KNOWS THE AREA.
I FOLLOWED THE TRAIL PRETTY FAR. I KNOW WHERE WE'LL NEED TO GO.
WHY DID YOU GIVE UP LAST TIME?
THESE PEOPLE ARE DANGEROUS, AND THERE ARE A LOT OF THEM. THEY HELD ME CAPTIVE FOR A WHILE.
THEY CAN BE ANYWHERE, THEY BLEND IN WITH THE DEAD... YOU THINK YOU'RE BEING ATTACKED BY A SMALL GROUP OF ROAMERS... AND THEN GUYS START TRYING TO STAB YOU.
ALSO, THEIR LEADER WAS VERY CLEAR ANY MORE INTERACTION IS UNWELCOME. WE'RE TAKING A HUGE RISK GOING INTO THEIR LAND. WE COULD BE STARTING SOMETHING.
ARE YOU GOING TO TAKE US, OR NOT?
I'M SCARED SHITLESS, AND I DON'T WANT A DAMN THING IN RETURN... BUT I DO WANT YOU TO KNOW I'M ONLY DOING THIS FOR YOU.
NOTED... AND APPRECIATED...
MAYBE YOU'RE NOT SO BAD AFTER ALL.
THANK YOU, MISS GREENE. I'LL CARRY THAT SMILE WITH ME ON MY JOURNEY.

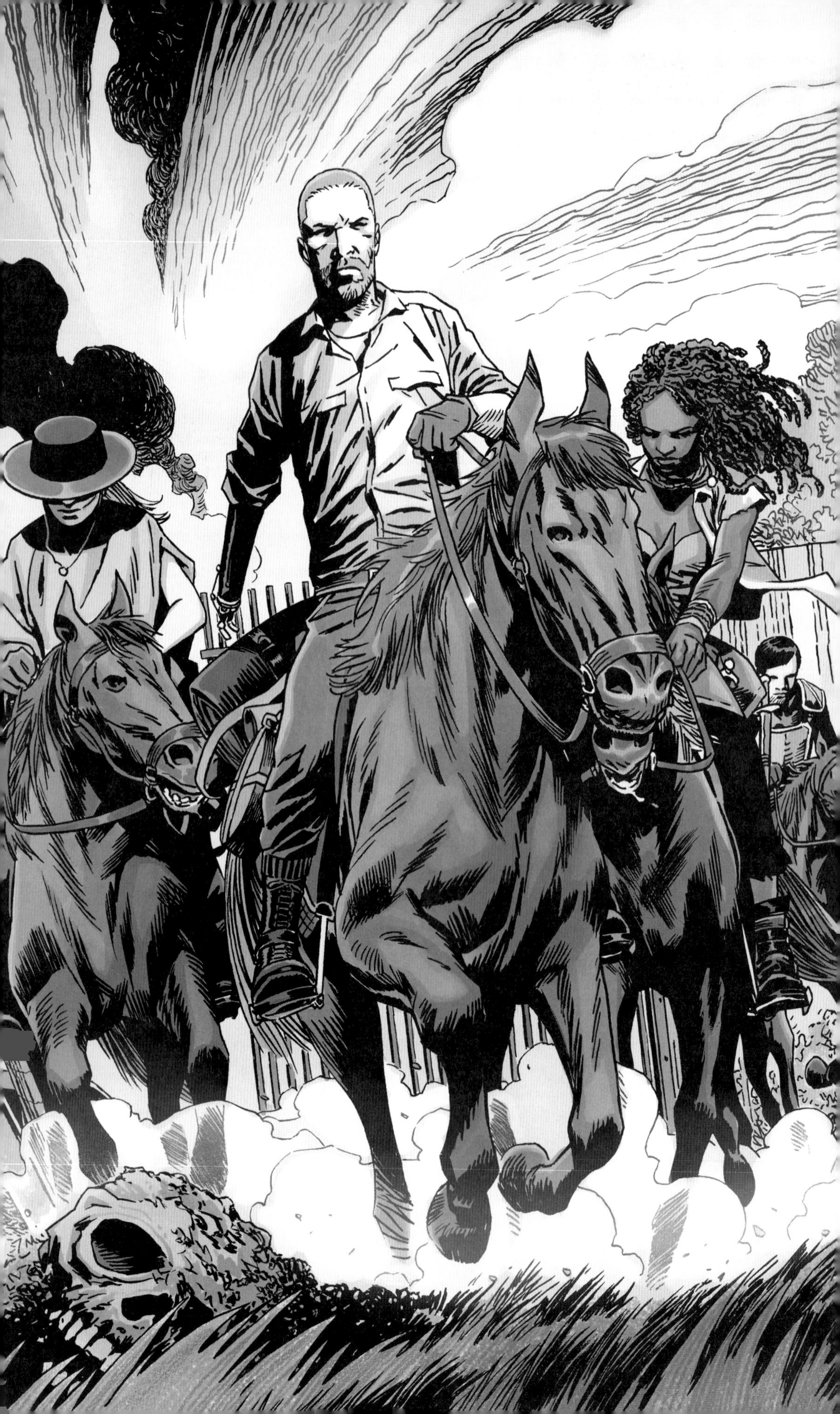

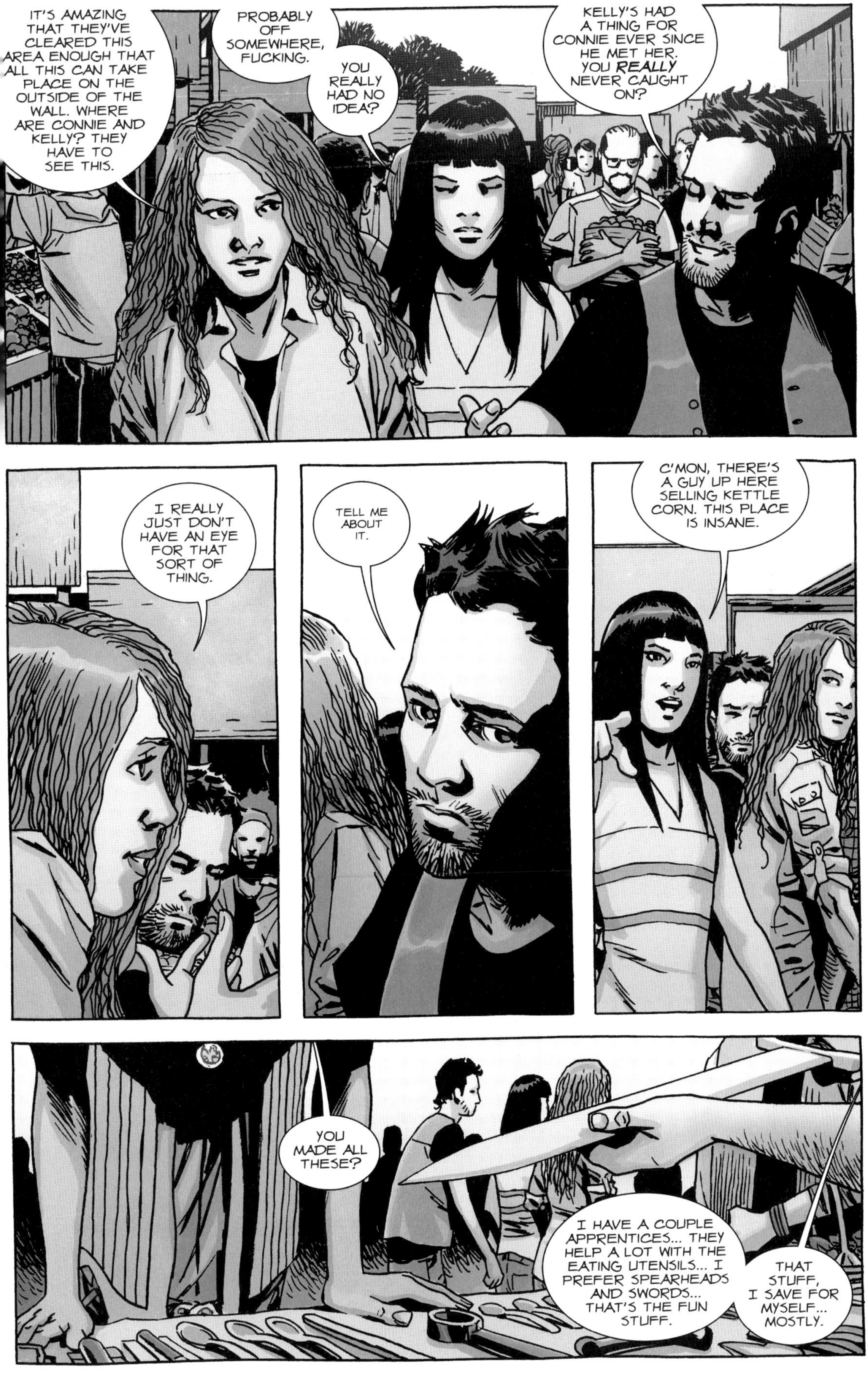
IT'S AMAZING THAT THEY'VE CLEARED THIS AREA ENOUGH THAT ALL THIS CAN TAKE PLACE ON THE OUTSIDE OF THE WALL. WHERE ARE CONNIE AND KELLY? THEY HAVE TO SEE THIS.
PROBABLY OFF SOMEWHERE, FUCKING.
YOU REALLY HAD NO IDEA?
KELLY'S HAD A THING FOR CONNIE EVER SINCE HE MET HER. YOU REALLY NEVER CAUGHT ON?
I REALLY JUST DON'T HAVE AN EYE FOR THAT SORT OF THING.
TELL ME ABOUT IT.
C'MON, THERE'S A GUY UP HERE SELLING KETTLE CORN. THIS PLACE IS INSANE.
YOU MADE ALL THESE?
I HAVE A COUPLE APPRENTICES... THEY HELP A LOT WITH THE EATING UTENSILS... I PREFER SPEARHEADS AND SWORDS... THAT'S THE FUN STUFF.
THAT STUFF, I SAVE FOR MYSELF... MOSTLY.

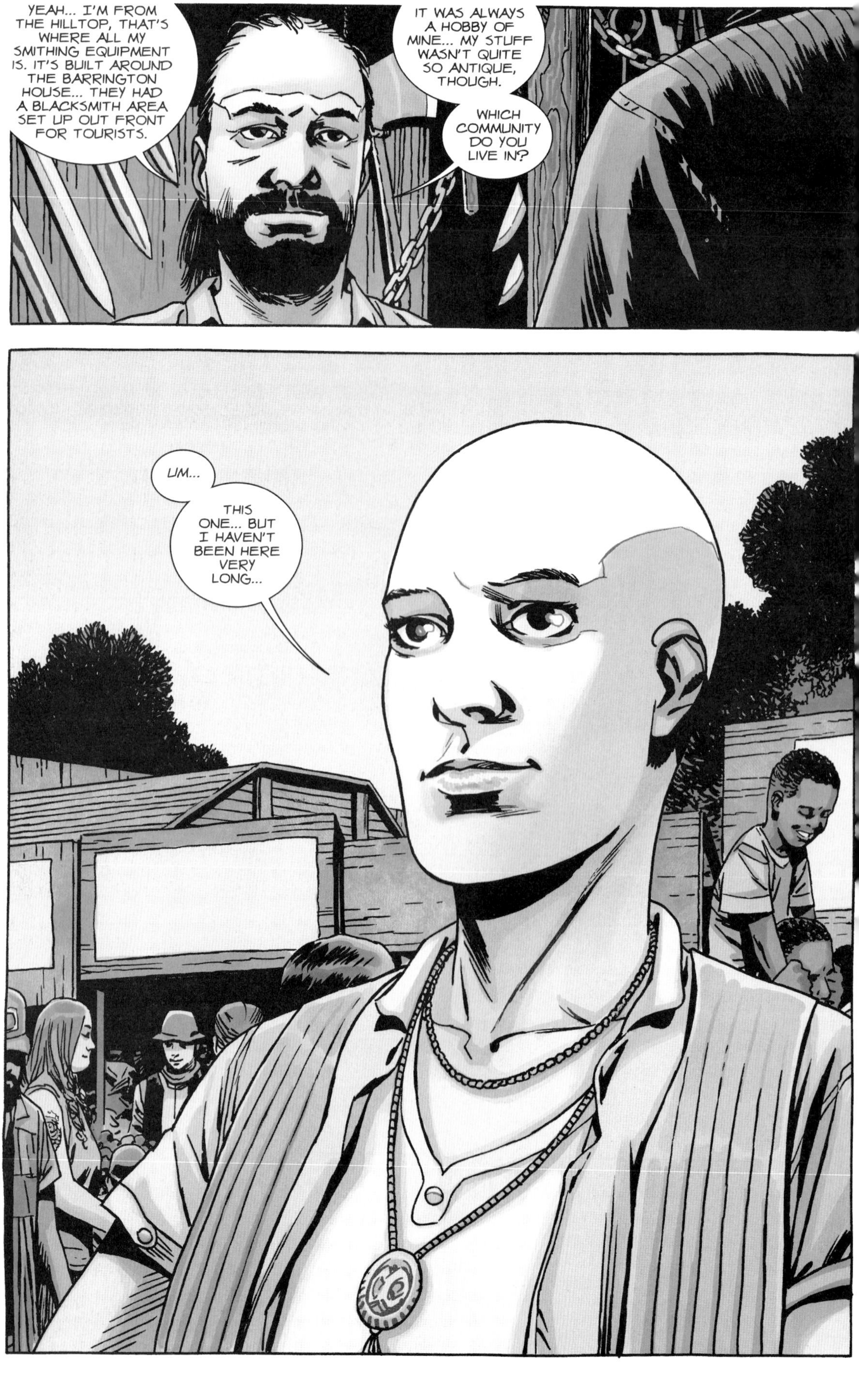

YEAH... I'M FROM THE HILLTOP, THAT'S WHERE ALL MY SMITHING EQUIPMENT IS. IT'S BUILT AROUND THE BARRINGTON HOUSE... THEY HAD A BLACKSMITH AREA SET UP OUT FRONT FOR TOURISTS.
IT WAS ALWAYS A HOBBY OF MINE... MY STUFF WASN'T QUITE SO ANTIQUE, THOUGH.
WHICH COMMUNITY DO YOU LIVE IN?
UM...
THIS ONE... BUT I HAVEN'T BEEN HERE VERY LONG...

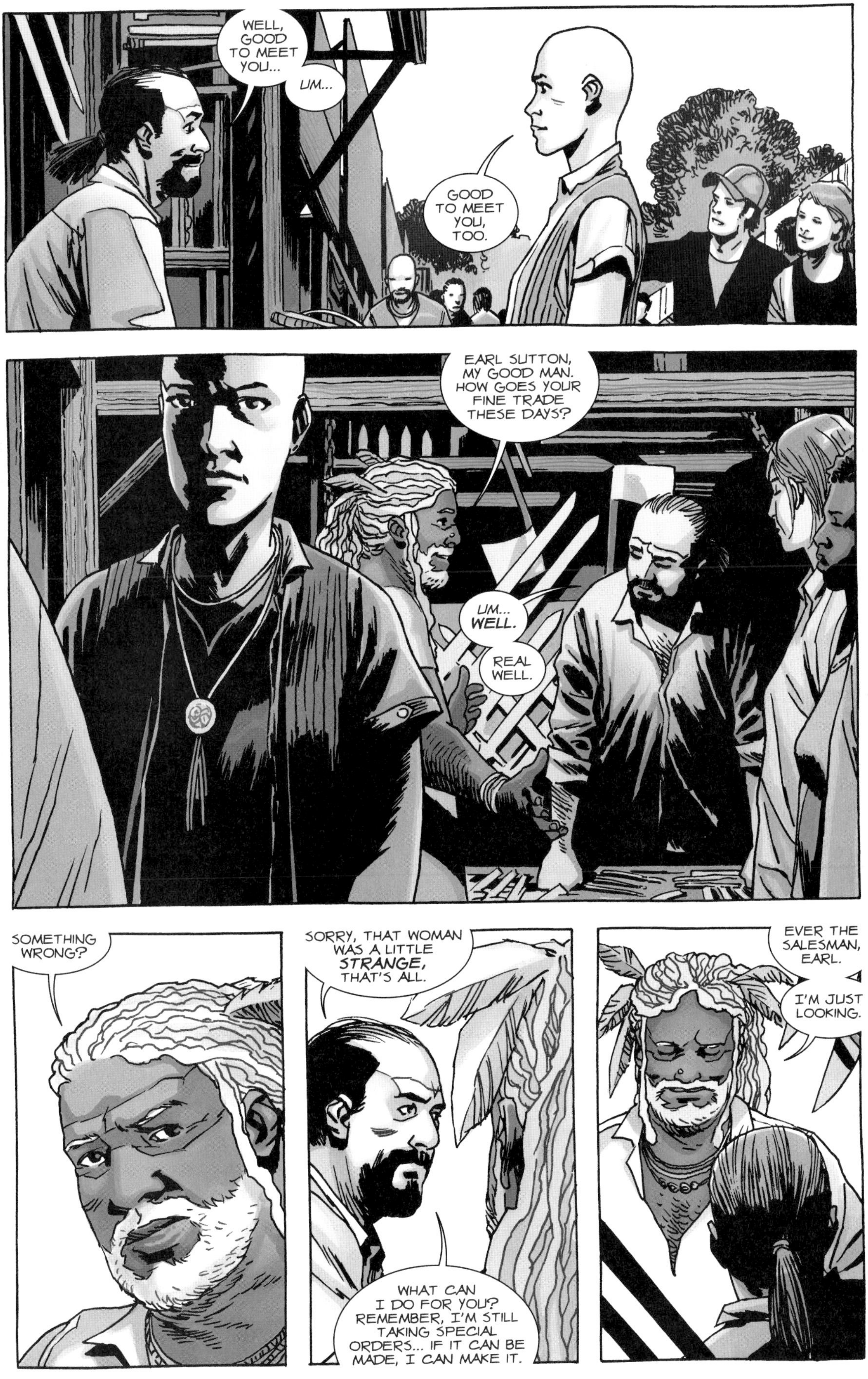
WELL, GOOD TO MEET YOU...
UM...
GOOD TO MEET YOU, TOO.
EARL SUTTON, MY GOOD MAN. HOW GOES YOUR FINE TRADE THESE DAYS?
UM... WELL.
REAL WELL.
SOMETHING WRONG?
SORRY, THAT WOMAN WAS A LITTLE STRANGE, THAT'S ALL.
WHAT CAN I DO FOR YOU? REMEMBER, I'M STILL TAKING SPECIAL ORDERS... IF IT CAN BE MADE, I CAN MAKE IT.
EVER THE SALESMAN, EARL.
I'M JUST LOOKING.

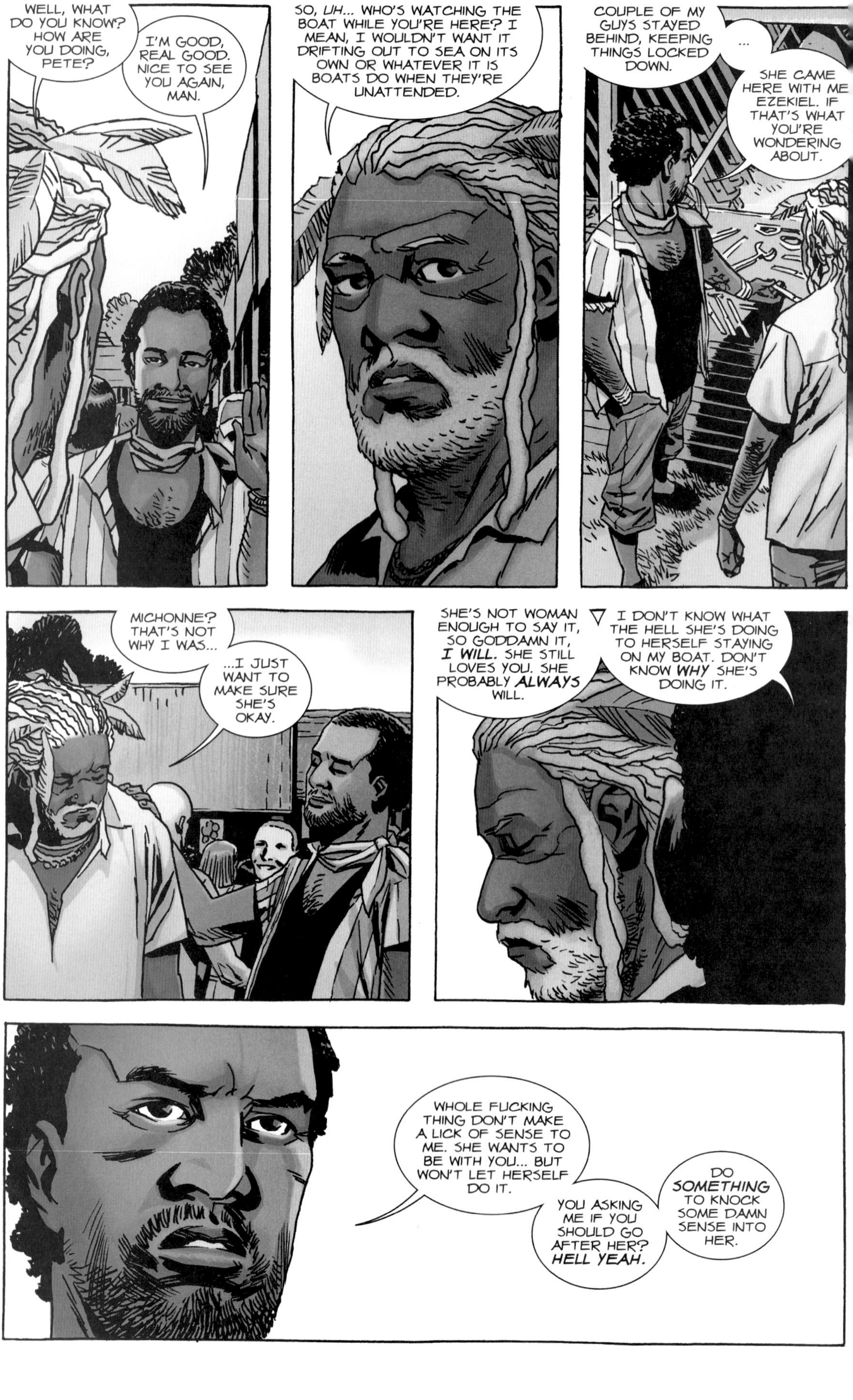
WELL, WHAT DO YOU KNOW? HOW ARE YOU DOING, PETE?
I'M GOOD, REAL GOOD. NICE TO SEE YOU AGAIN, MAN.
SO, *UH*... WHO'S WATCHING THE BOAT WHILE YOU'RE HERE? I MEAN, I WOULDN'T WANT IT DRIFTING OUT TO SEA ON ITS OWN OR WHATEVER IT IS BOATS DO WHEN THEY'RE UNATTENDED.
COUPLE OF MY GUYS STAYED BEHIND, KEEPING THINGS LOCKED DOWN.
...
SHE CAME HERE WITH ME EZEKIEL. IF THAT'S WHAT YOU'RE WONDERING ABOUT.
MICHONNE? THAT'S NOT WHY I WAS...
...I JUST WANT TO MAKE SURE SHE'S OKAY.
SHE'S NOT WOMAN ENOUGH TO SAY IT, SO GODDAMN IT, ***I WILL.*** SHE STILL LOVES YOU. SHE PROBABLY ***ALWAYS*** WILL.
I DON'T KNOW WHAT THE HELL SHE'S DOING TO HERSELF STAYING ON MY BOAT. DON'T KNOW ***WHY*** SHE'S DOING IT.
WHOLE FUCKING THING DON'T MAKE A LICK OF SENSE TO ME. SHE WANTS TO BE WITH YOU... BUT WON'T LET HERSELF DO IT.
YOU ASKING ME IF YOU SHOULD GO AFTER HER? ***HELL YEAH.***
DO ***SOMETHING*** TO KNOCK SOME DAMN SENSE INTO HER.

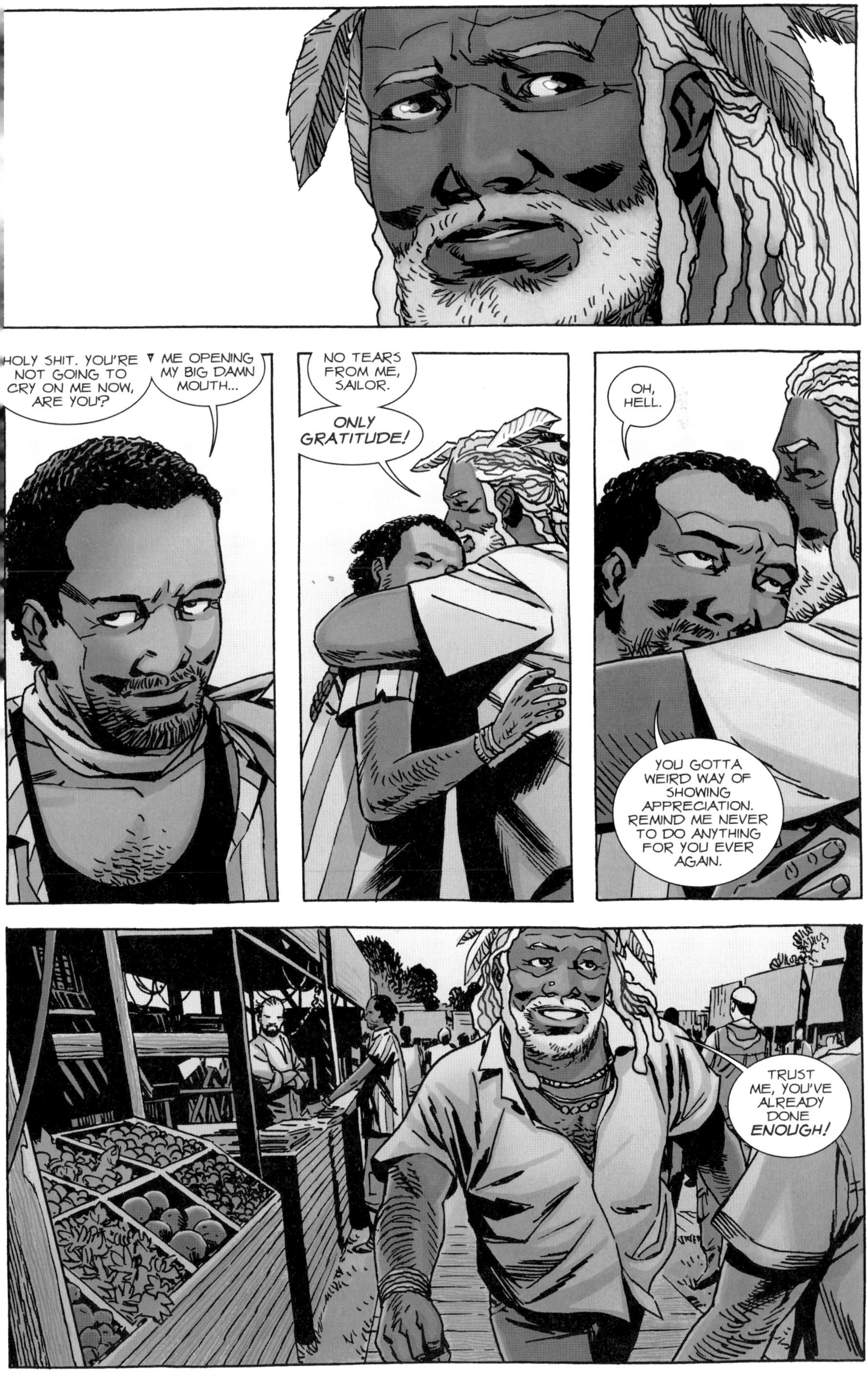
HOLY SHIT. YOU'RE NOT GOING TO CRY ON ME NOW, ARE YOU?
ME OPENING MY BIG DAMN MOUTH...
NO TEARS FROM ME, SAILOR.
ONLY GRATITUDE!
OH, HELL.
YOU GOTTA WEIRD WAY OF SHOWING APPRECIATION. REMIND ME NEVER TO DO ANYTHING FOR YOU EVER AGAIN.
TRUST ME, YOU'VE ALREADY DONE ENOUGH!

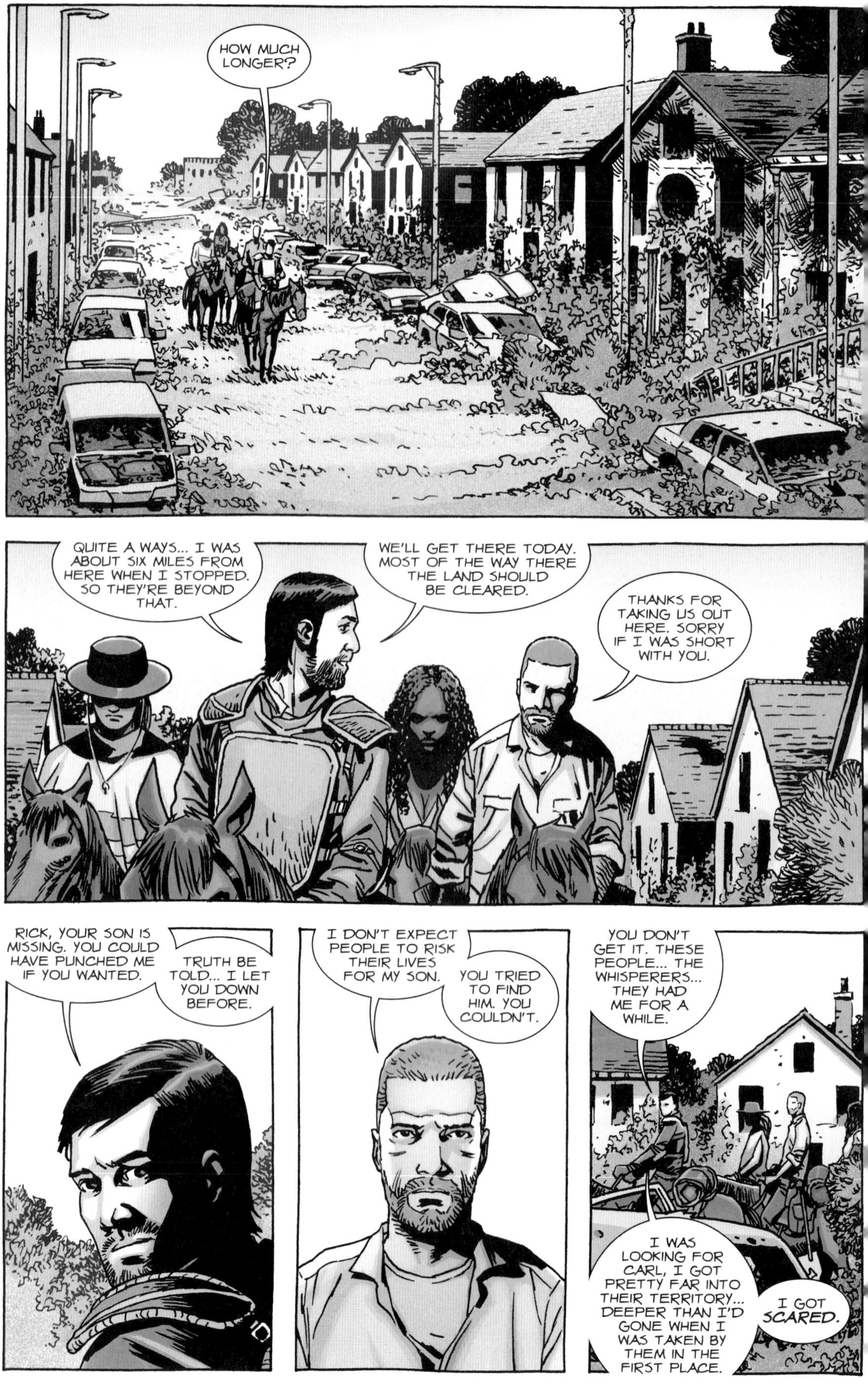
HOW MUCH LONGER?
QUITE A WAYS... I WAS ABOUT SIX MILES FROM HERE WHEN I STOPPED. SO THEY'RE BEYOND THAT.
WE'LL GET THERE TODAY. MOST OF THE WAY THERE THE LAND SHOULD BE CLEARED.
THANKS FOR TAKING US OUT HERE. SORRY IF I WAS SHORT WITH YOU.
RICK, YOUR SON IS MISSING. YOU COULD HAVE PUNCHED ME IF YOU WANTED.
TRUTH BE TOLD... I LET YOU DOWN BEFORE.
I DON'T EXPECT PEOPLE TO RISK THEIR LIVES FOR MY SON.
YOU TRIED TO FIND HIM. YOU COULDN'T.
YOU DON'T GET IT. THESE PEOPLE... THE WHISPERERS... THEY HAD ME FOR A WHILE.
I WAS LOOKING FOR CARL, I GOT PRETTY FAR INTO THEIR TERRITORY... DEEPER THAN I'D GONE WHEN I WAS TAKEN BY THEM IN THE FIRST PLACE.
I GOT SCARED.

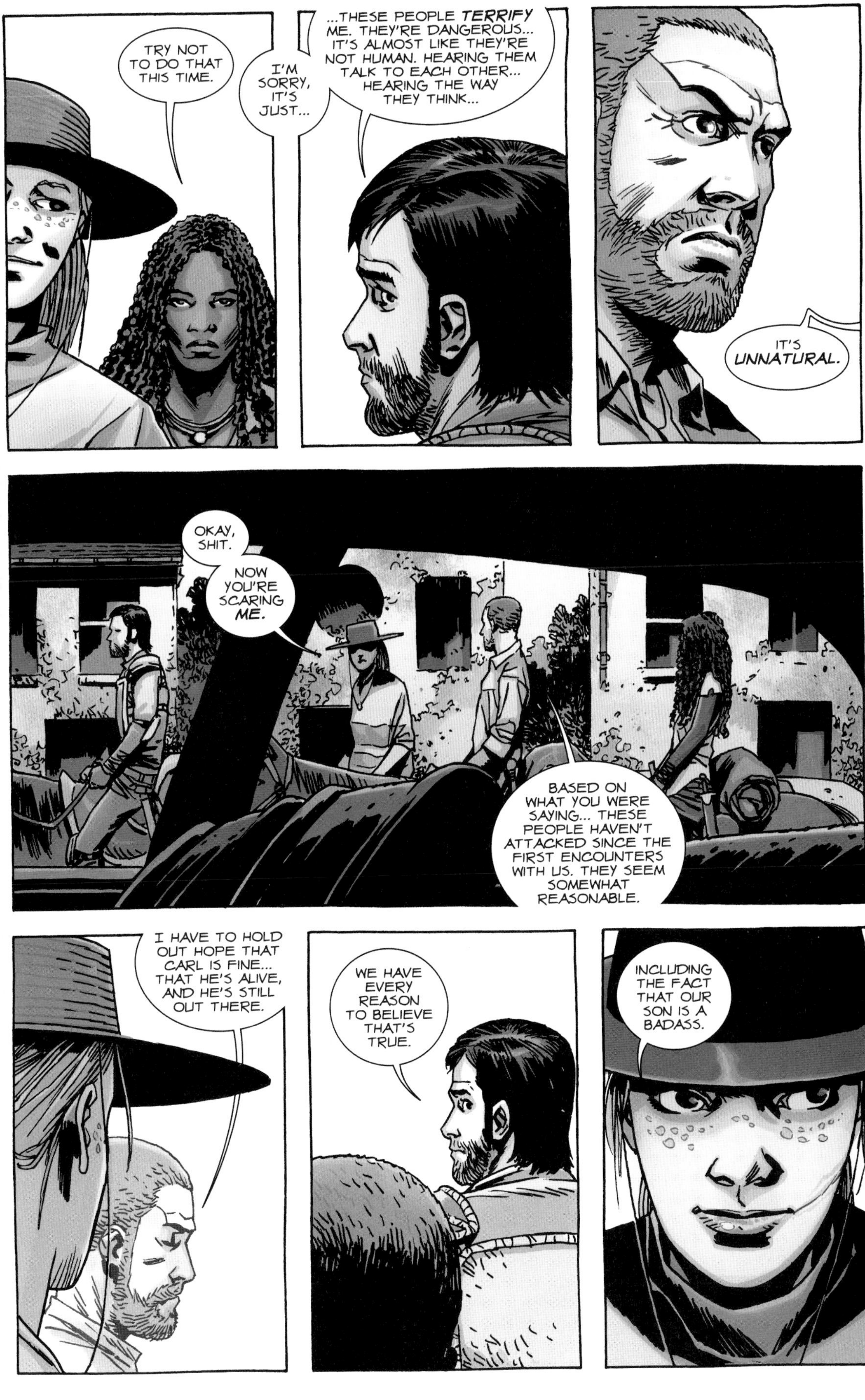

TRY NOT TO DO THAT THIS TIME.
I'M SORRY, IT'S JUST...
...THESE PEOPLE *TERRIFY* ME. THEY'RE DANGEROUS... IT'S ALMOST LIKE THEY'RE NOT HUMAN. HEARING THEM TALK TO EACH OTHER... HEARING THE WAY THEY THINK...
IT'S *UNNATURAL.*
OKAY, SHIT.
NOW YOU'RE SCARING *ME.*
BASED ON WHAT YOU WERE SAYING... THESE PEOPLE HAVEN'T ATTACKED SINCE THE FIRST ENCOUNTERS WITH US. THEY SEEM SOMEWHAT REASONABLE.
I HAVE TO HOLD OUT HOPE THAT CARL IS FINE... THAT HE'S ALIVE, AND HE'S STILL OUT THERE.
WE HAVE EVERY REASON TO BELIEVE THAT'S TRUE.
INCLUDING THE FACT THAT OUR SON IS A BADASS.

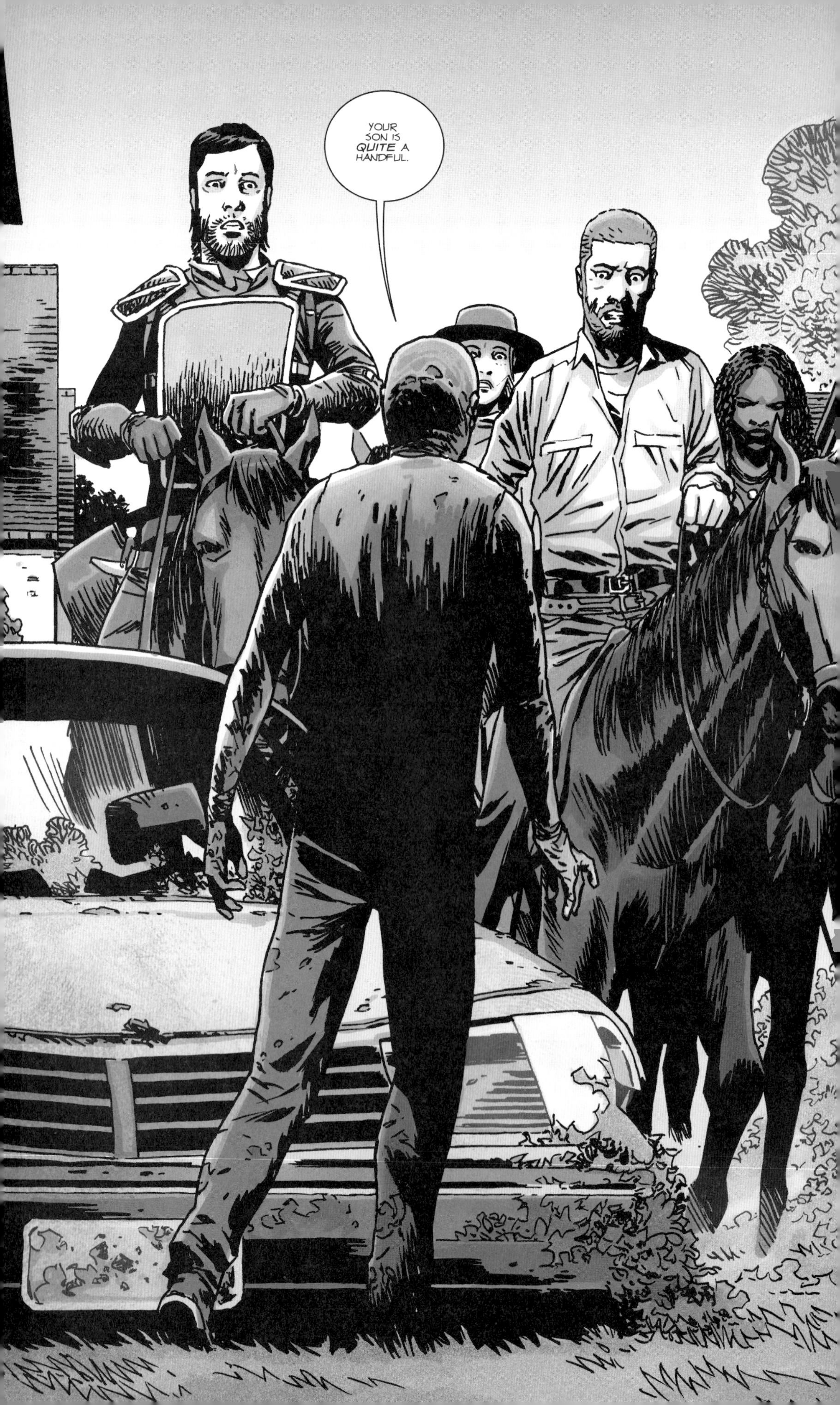
YOUR SON IS QUITE A HANDFUL.

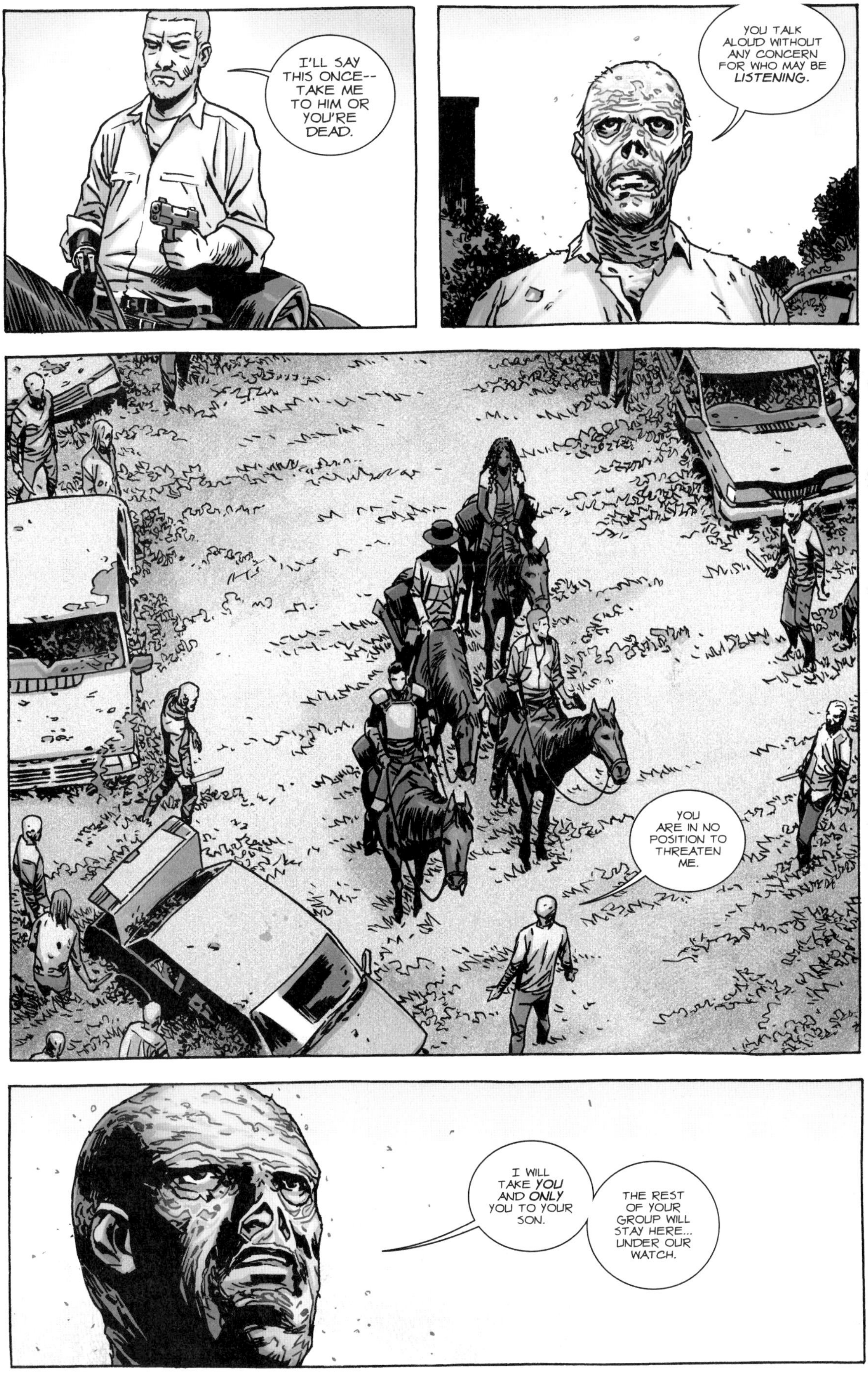
I'LL SAY THIS ONCE-- TAKE ME TO HIM OR YOU'RE DEAD.
YOU TALK ALOUD WITHOUT ANY CONCERN FOR WHO MAY BE *LISTENING.*
YOU ARE IN NO POSITION TO THREATEN ME.
I WILL TAKE *YOU* AND *ONLY* YOU TO YOUR SON.
THE REST OF YOUR GROUP WILL STAY HERE... UNDER OUR WATCH.

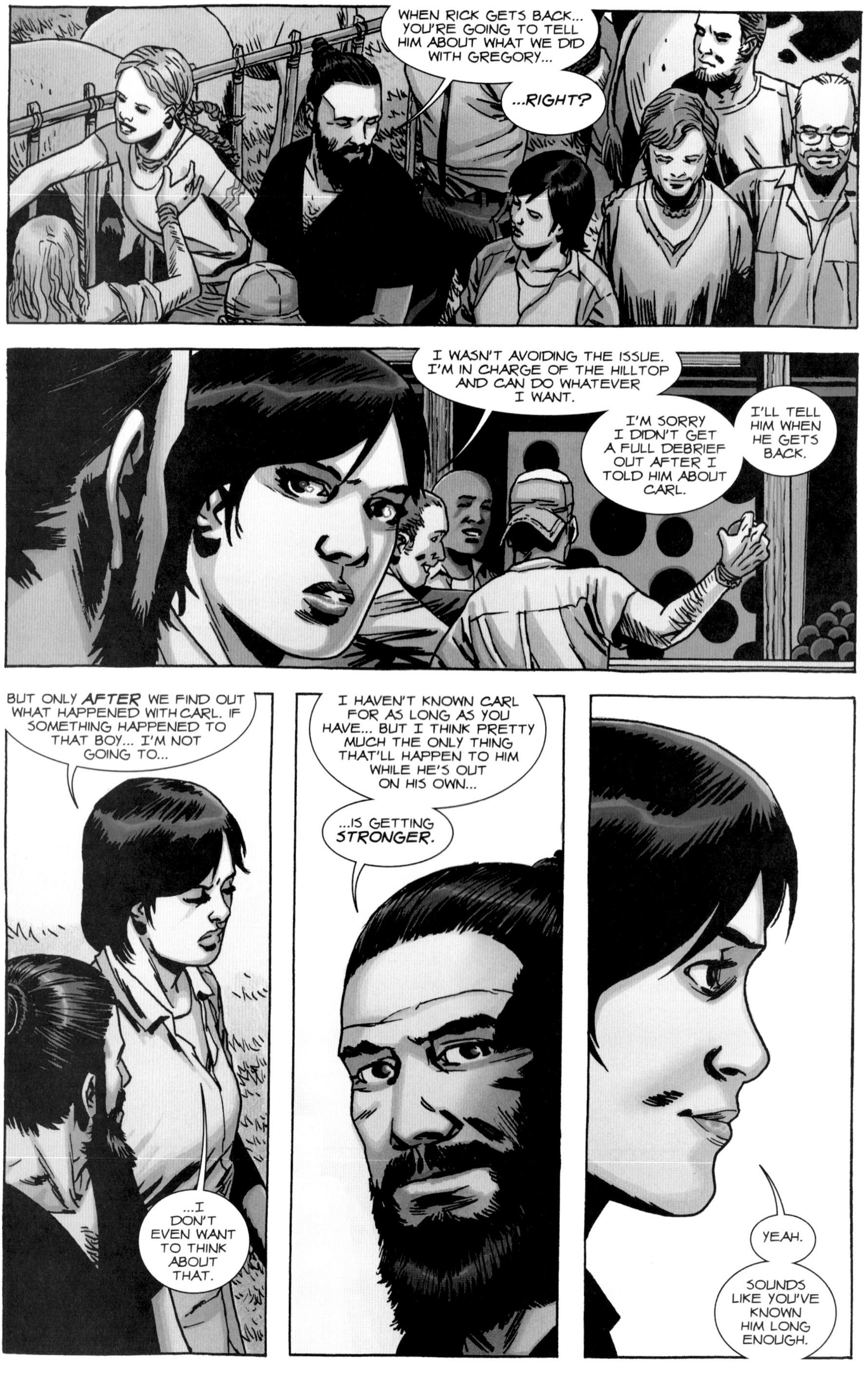
WHEN RICK GETS BACK... YOU'RE GOING TO TELL HIM ABOUT WHAT WE DID WITH GREGORY...
...RIGHT?
I WASN'T AVOIDING THE ISSUE. I'M IN CHARGE OF THE HILLTOP AND CAN DO WHATEVER I WANT.
I'M SORRY I DIDN'T GET A FULL DEBRIEF OUT AFTER I TOLD HIM ABOUT CARL.
I'LL TELL HIM WHEN HE GETS BACK.
BUT ONLY AFTER WE FIND OUT WHAT HAPPENED WITH CARL. IF SOMETHING HAPPENED TO THAT BOY... I'M NOT GOING TO...
...I DON'T EVEN WANT TO THINK ABOUT THAT.
I HAVEN'T KNOWN CARL FOR AS LONG AS YOU HAVE... BUT I THINK PRETTY MUCH THE ONLY THING THAT'LL HAPPEN TO HIM WHILE HE'S OUT ON HIS OWN...
...IS GETTING STRONGER.
YEAH.
SOUNDS LIKE YOU'VE KNOWN HIM LONG ENOUGH.

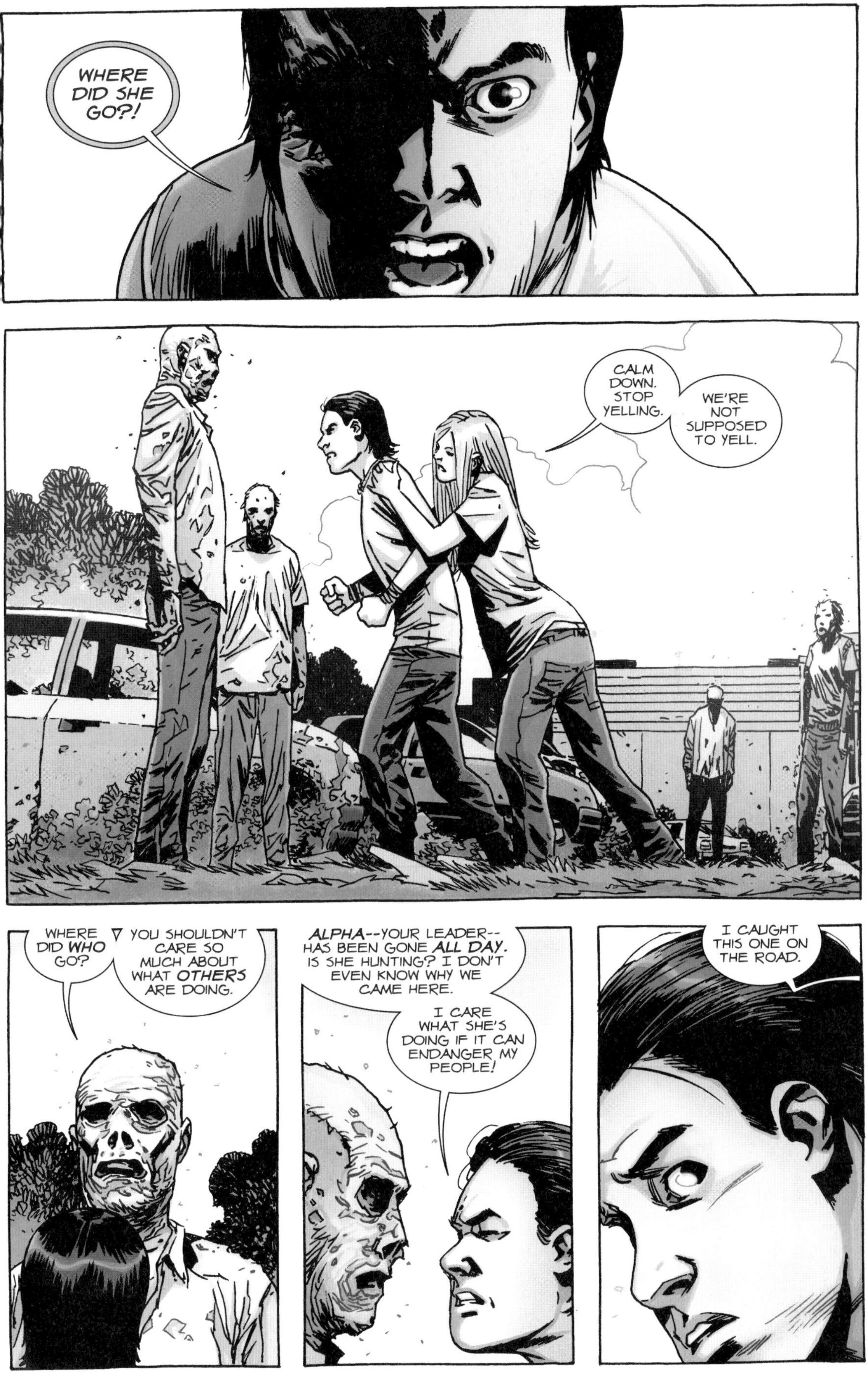
WHERE DID SHE GO?!
CALM DOWN. STOP YELLING.
WE'RE NOT SUPPOSED TO YELL.
WHERE DID WHO GO?
YOU SHOULDN'T CARE SO MUCH ABOUT WHAT OTHERS ARE DOING.
ALPHA--YOUR LEADER--HAS BEEN GONE ALL DAY. IS SHE HUNTING? I DON'T EVEN KNOW WHY WE CAME HERE.
I CARE WHAT SHE'S DOING IF IT CAN ENDANGER MY PEOPLE!
I CAUGHT THIS ONE ON THE ROAD.

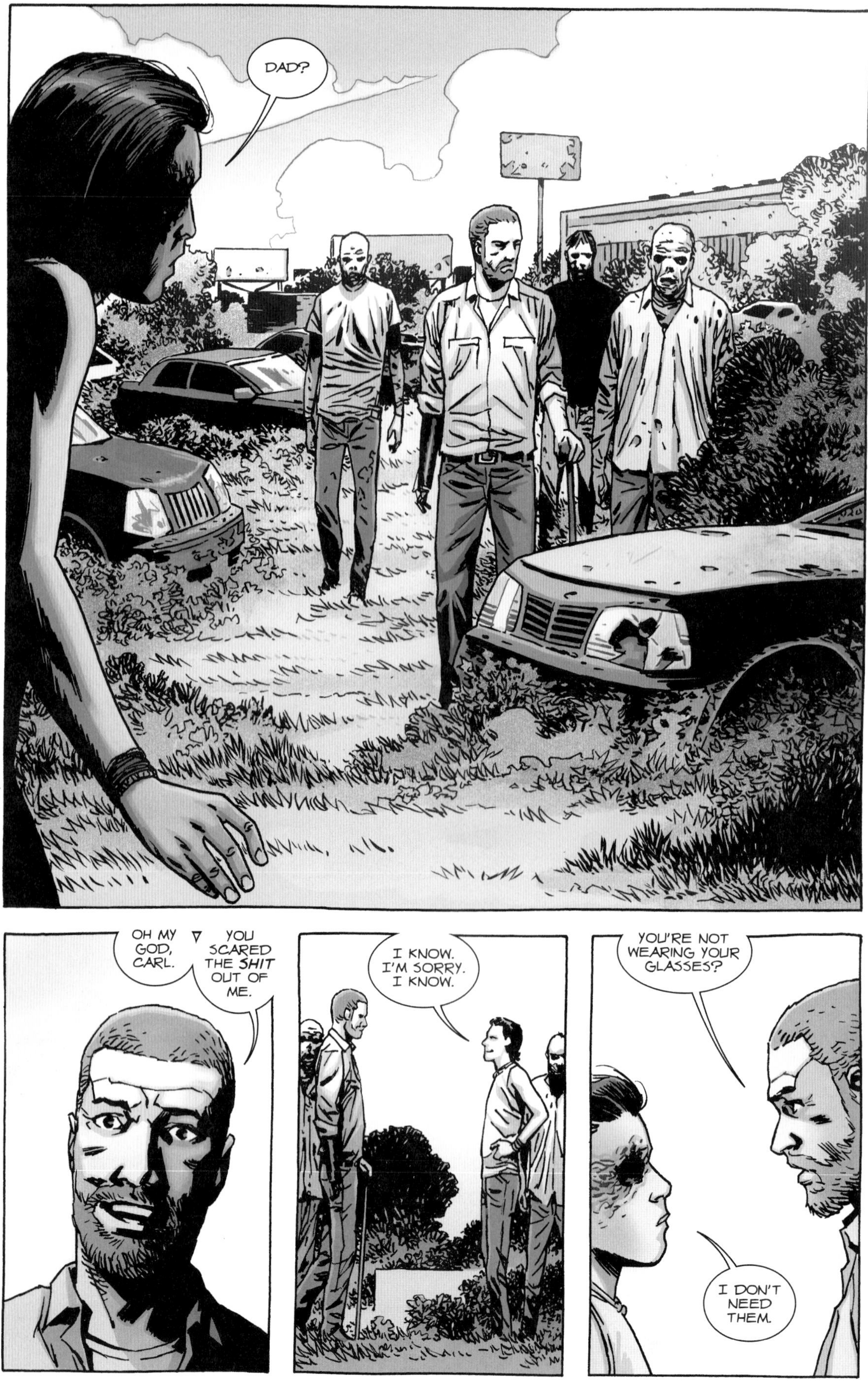
DAD?
OH MY GOD, CARL.
YOU SCARED THE *SHIT* OUT OF ME.
I KNOW. I'M SORRY. I KNOW.
YOU'RE NOT WEARING YOUR GLASSES?
I DON'T NEED THEM.

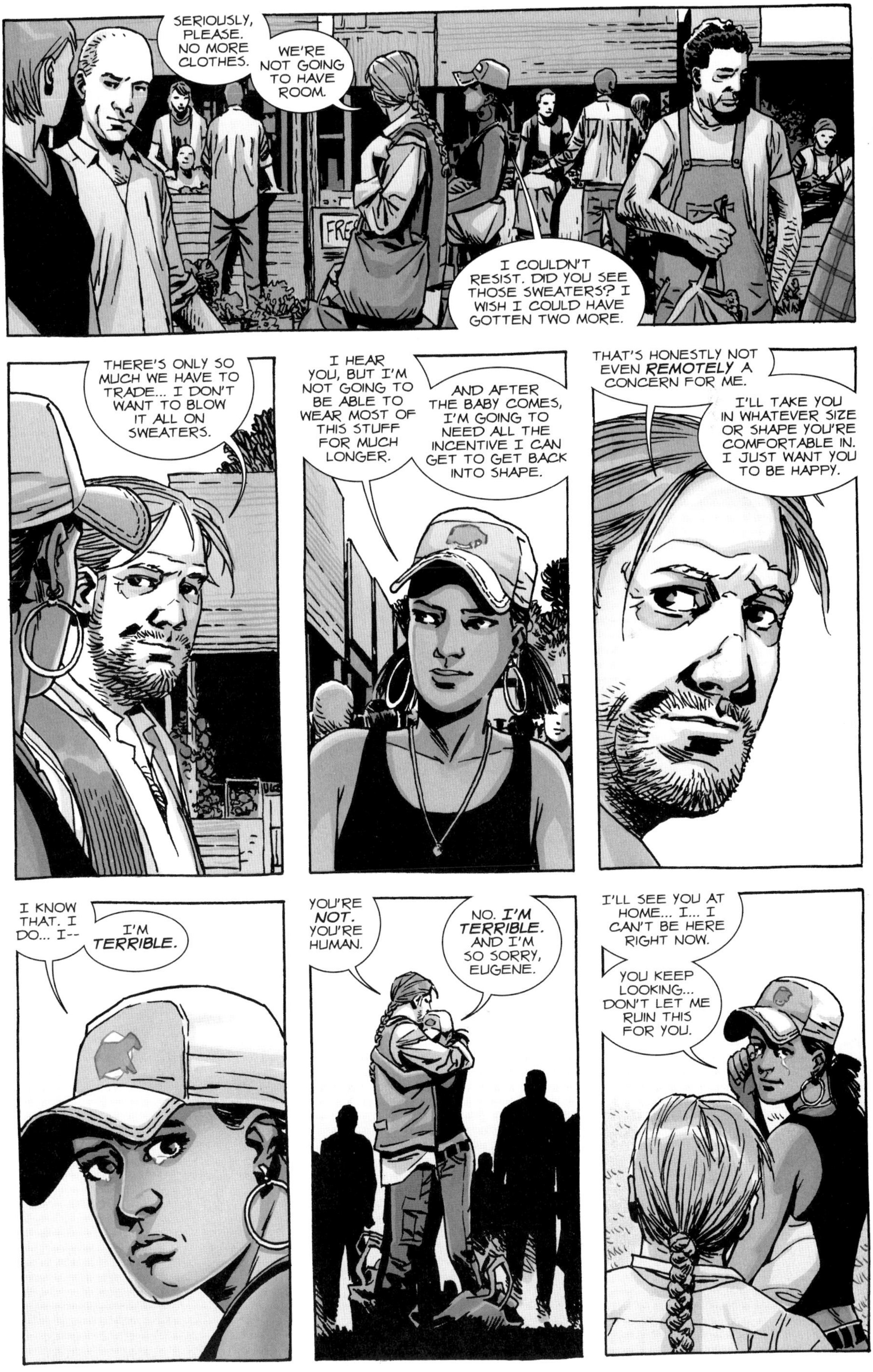
SERIOUSLY, PLEASE. NO MORE CLOTHES.
WE'RE NOT GOING TO HAVE ROOM.
FREE
I COULDN'T RESIST. DID YOU SEE THOSE SWEATERS? I WISH I COULD HAVE GOTTEN TWO MORE.
THERE'S ONLY SO MUCH WE HAVE TO TRADE... I DON'T WANT TO BLOW IT ALL ON SWEATERS.
I HEAR YOU, BUT I'M NOT GOING TO BE ABLE TO WEAR MOST OF THIS STUFF FOR MUCH LONGER.
AND AFTER THE BABY COMES, I'M GOING TO NEED ALL THE INCENTIVE I CAN GET TO GET BACK INTO SHAPE.
THAT'S HONESTLY NOT EVEN *REMOTELY* A CONCERN FOR ME.
I'LL TAKE YOU IN WHATEVER SIZE OR SHAPE YOU'RE COMFORTABLE IN. I JUST WANT YOU TO BE HAPPY.
I KNOW THAT. I DO... I--
I'M *TERRIBLE.*
YOU'RE *NOT.* YOU'RE HUMAN.
NO. *I'M TERRIBLE.* AND I'M SO SORRY, EUGENE.
I'LL SEE YOU AT HOME... I... I CAN'T BE HERE RIGHT NOW.
YOU KEEP LOOKING... DON'T LET ME RUIN THIS FOR YOU.

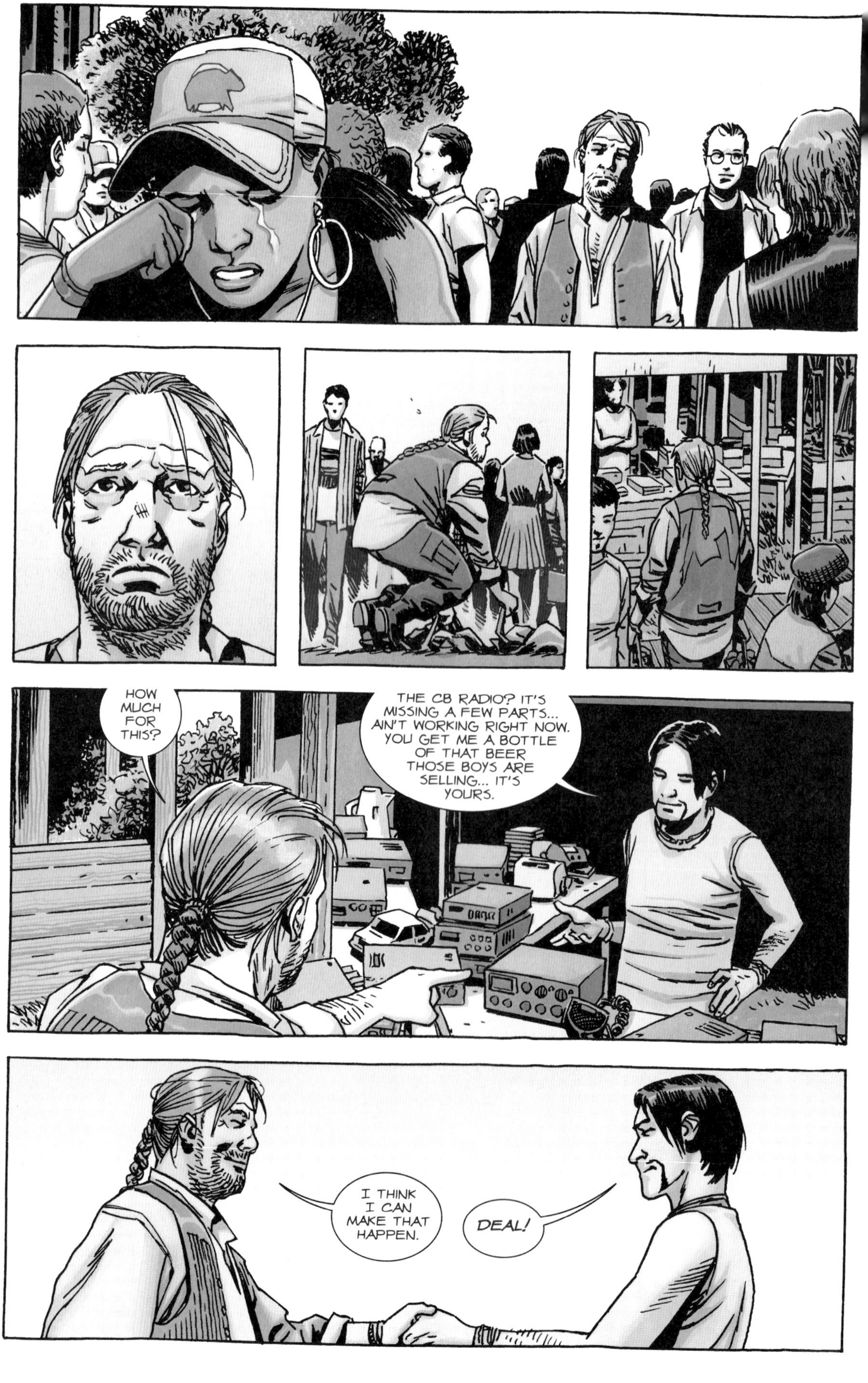
HOW MUCH FOR THIS?
THE CB RADIO? IT'S MISSING A FEW PARTS... AIN'T WORKING RIGHT NOW. YOU GET ME A BOTTLE OF THAT BEER THOSE BOYS ARE SELLING... IT'S YOURS.
I THINK I CAN MAKE THAT HAPPEN.
DEAL!

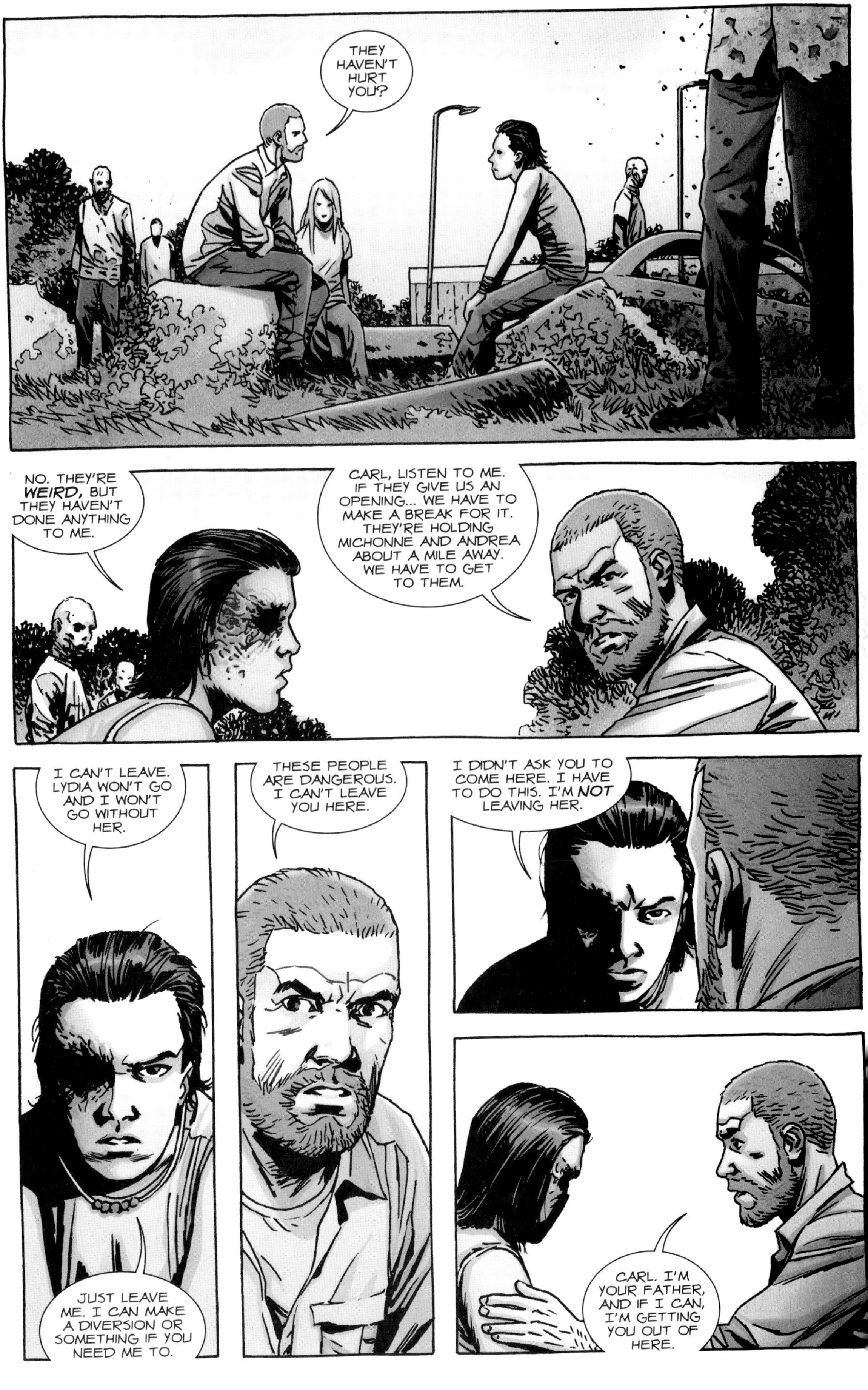
THEY HAVEN'T HURT YOU?
NO. THEY'RE *WEIRD,* BUT THEY HAVEN'T DONE ANYTHING TO ME.
CARL, LISTEN TO ME. IF THEY GIVE US AN OPENING... WE HAVE TO MAKE A BREAK FOR IT. THEY'RE HOLDING MICHONNE AND ANDREA ABOUT A MILE AWAY. WE HAVE TO GET TO THEM.
I CAN'T LEAVE. LYDIA WON'T GO AND I WON'T GO WITHOUT HER.
JUST LEAVE ME. I CAN MAKE A DIVERSION OR SOMETHING IF YOU NEED ME TO.
THESE PEOPLE ARE DANGEROUS. I CAN'T LEAVE YOU HERE.
I DIDN'T ASK YOU TO COME HERE. I HAVE TO DO THIS. I'M *NOT* LEAVING HER.
CARL. I'M YOUR FATHER, AND IF I CAN, I'M GETTING YOU OUT OF HERE.

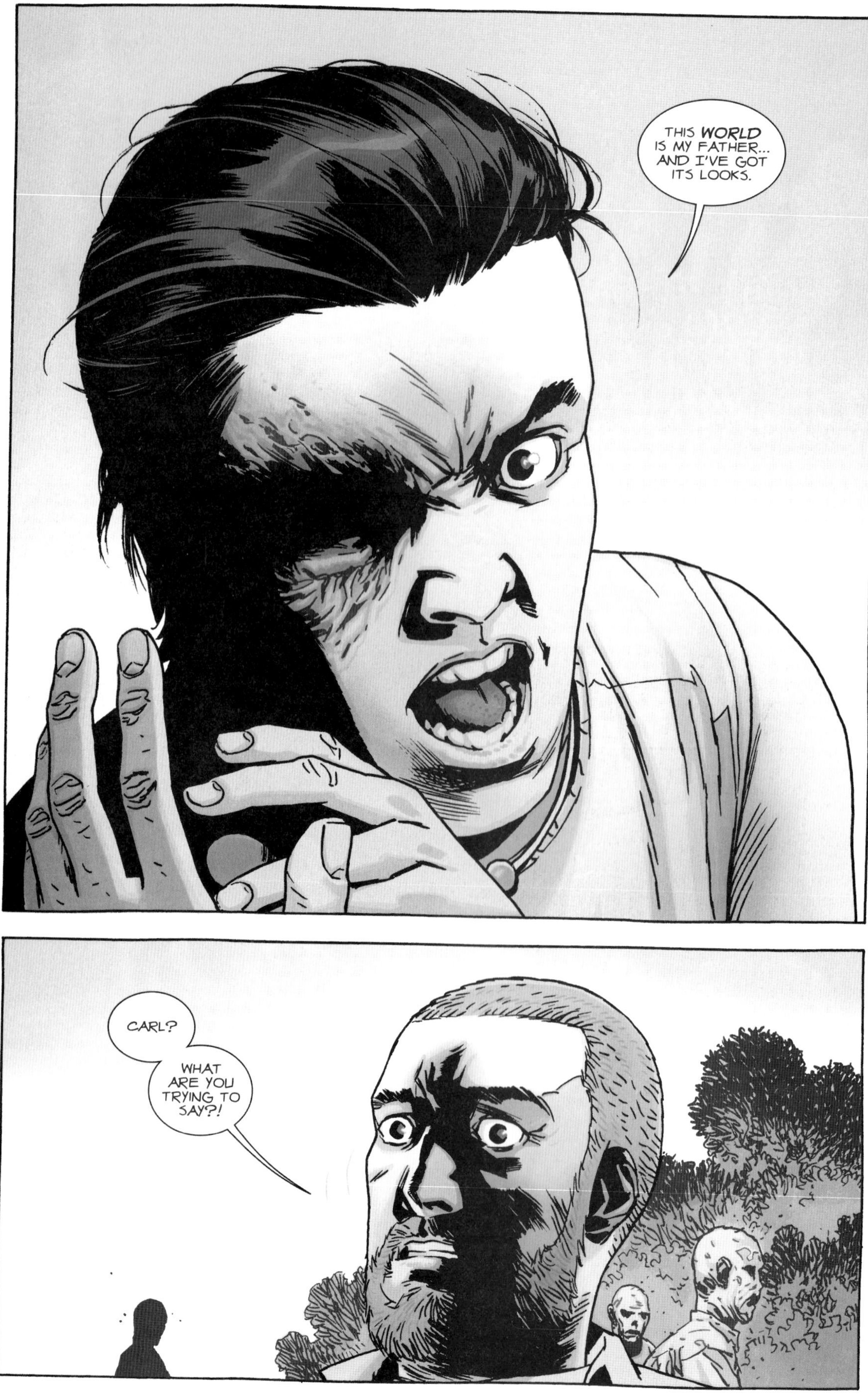
THIS WORLD IS MY FATHER... AND I'VE GOT ITS LOOKS.
CARL?
WHAT ARE YOU TRYING TO SAY?!

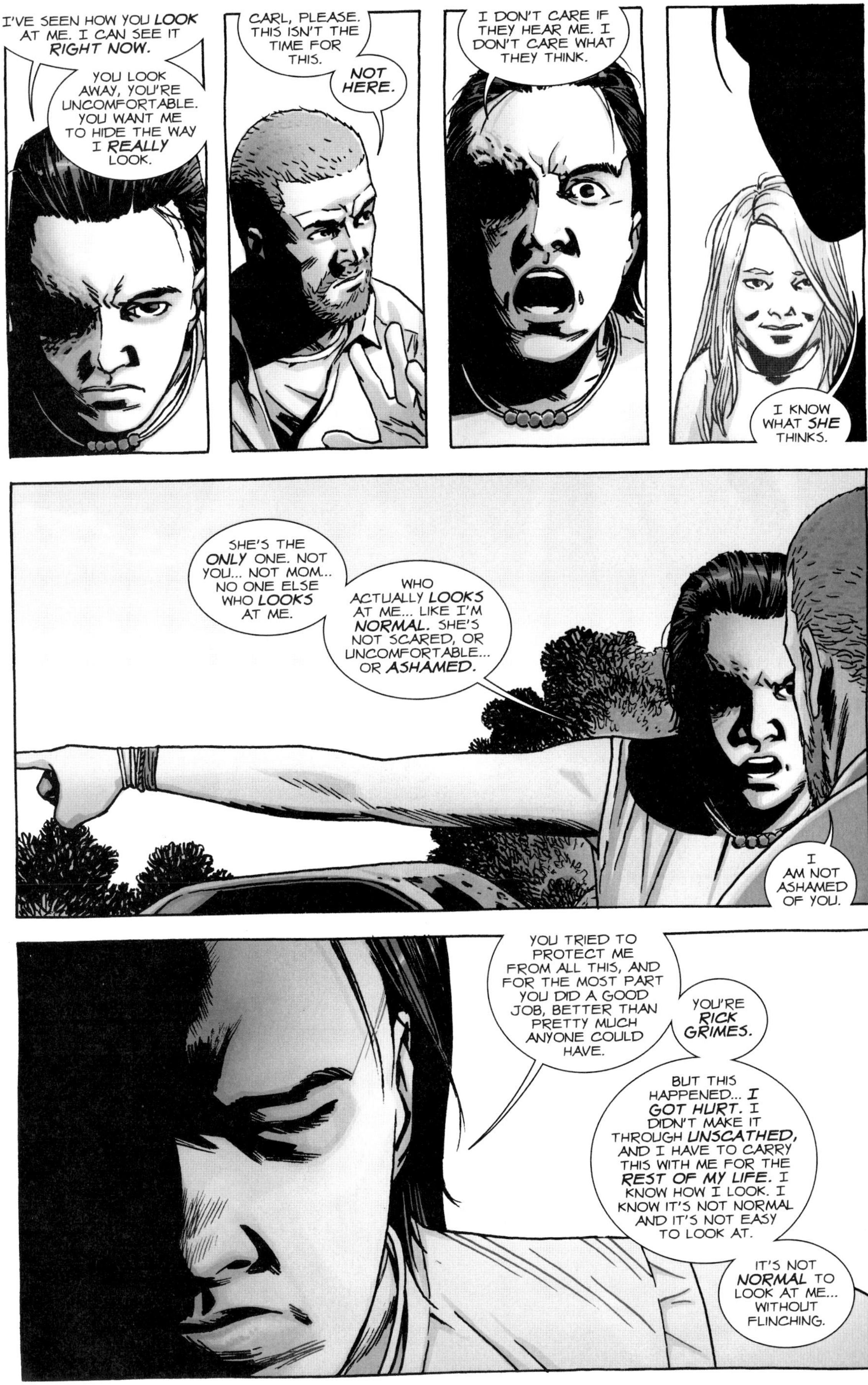

I'VE SEEN HOW YOU LOOK AT ME. I CAN SEE IT RIGHT NOW.
YOU LOOK AWAY, YOU'RE UNCOMFORTABLE. YOU WANT ME TO HIDE THE WAY I REALLY LOOK.
CARL, PLEASE. THIS ISN'T THE TIME FOR THIS.
NOT HERE.
I DON'T CARE IF THEY HEAR ME. I DON'T CARE WHAT THEY THINK.
I KNOW WHAT SHE THINKS.
SHE'S THE ONLY ONE. NOT YOU... NOT MOM... NO ONE ELSE WHO LOOKS AT ME.
WHO ACTUALLY LOOKS AT ME... LIKE I'M NORMAL. SHE'S NOT SCARED, OR UNCOMFORTABLE... OR ASHAMED.
I AM NOT ASHAMED OF YOU.
YOU TRIED TO PROTECT ME FROM ALL THIS, AND FOR THE MOST PART YOU DID A GOOD JOB, BETTER THAN PRETTY MUCH ANYONE COULD HAVE.
YOU'RE RICK GRIMES.
BUT THIS HAPPENED... I GOT HURT. I DIDN'T MAKE IT THROUGH UNSCATHED, AND I HAVE TO CARRY THIS WITH ME FOR THE REST OF MY LIFE. I KNOW HOW I LOOK. I KNOW IT'S NOT NORMAL AND IT'S NOT EASY TO LOOK AT.
IT'S NOT NORMAL TO LOOK AT ME... WITHOUT FLINCHING.

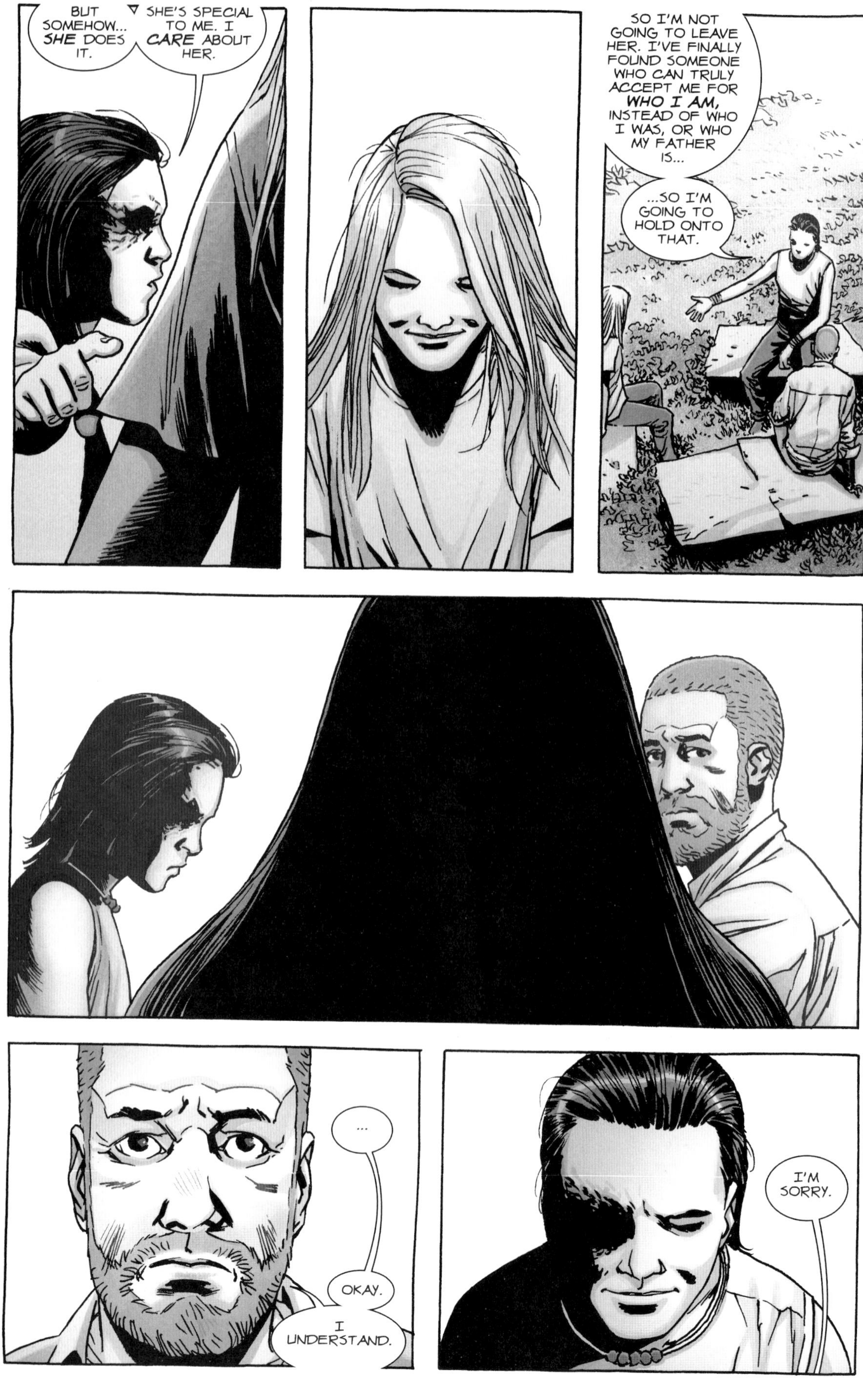
BUT SOMEHOW... SHE DOES IT.
SHE'S SPECIAL TO ME. I CARE ABOUT HER.
SO I'M NOT GOING TO LEAVE HER. I'VE FINALLY FOUND SOMEONE WHO CAN TRULY ACCEPT ME FOR WHO I AM, INSTEAD OF WHO I WAS, OR WHO MY FATHER IS...
...SO I'M GOING TO HOLD ONTO THAT.
...
OKAY.
I UNDERSTAND.
I'M SORRY.

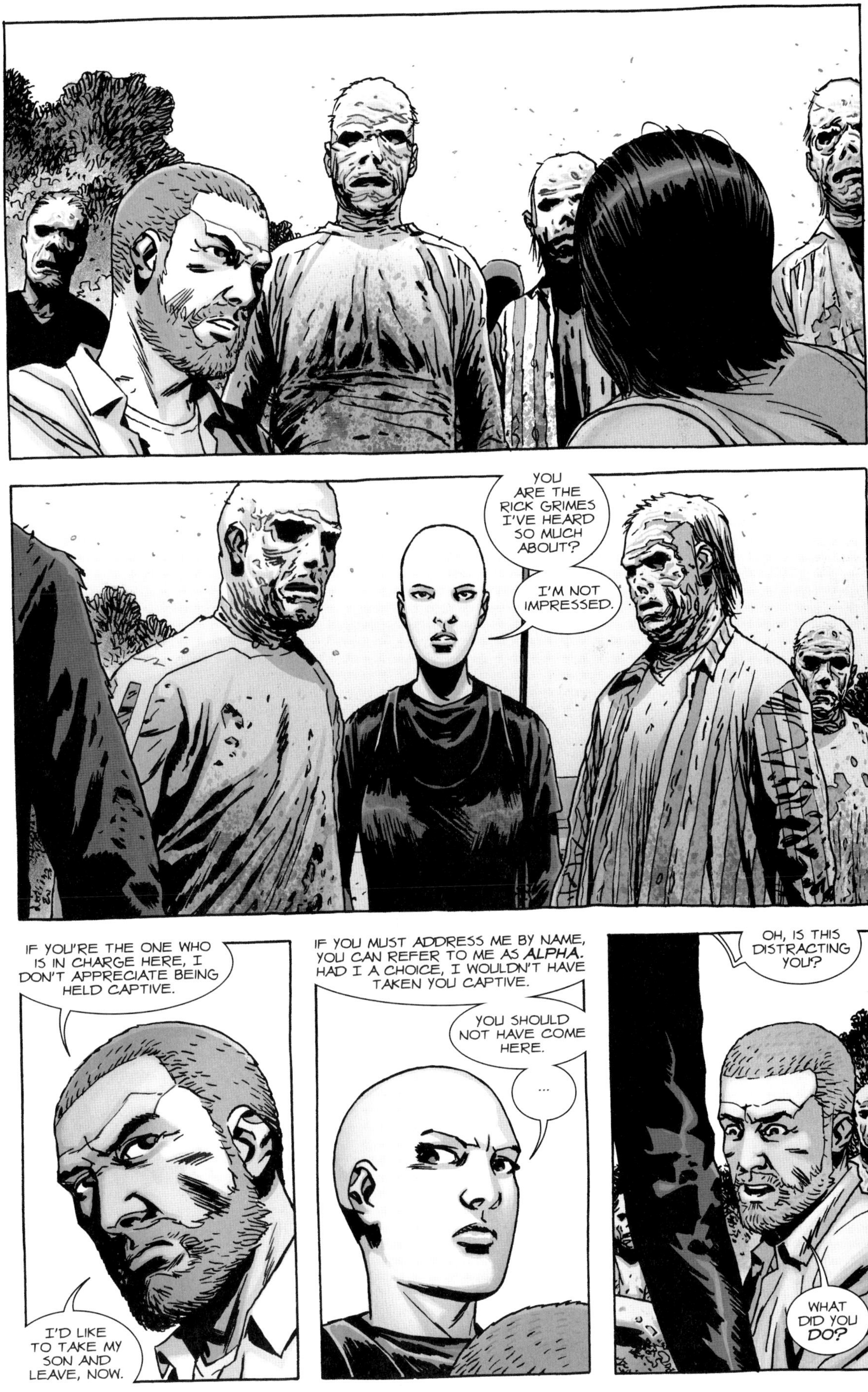
YOU ARE THE RICK GRIMES I'VE HEARD SO MUCH ABOUT?
I'M NOT IMPRESSED.
IF YOU'RE THE ONE WHO IS IN CHARGE HERE, I DON'T APPRECIATE BEING HELD CAPTIVE.
I'D LIKE TO TAKE MY SON AND LEAVE, NOW.
IF YOU MUST ADDRESS ME BY NAME, YOU CAN REFER TO ME AS ALPHA. HAD I A CHOICE, I WOULDN'T HAVE TAKEN YOU CAPTIVE.
YOU SHOULD NOT HAVE COME HERE.
...
OH, IS THIS DISTRACTING YOU?
WHAT DID YOU DO?

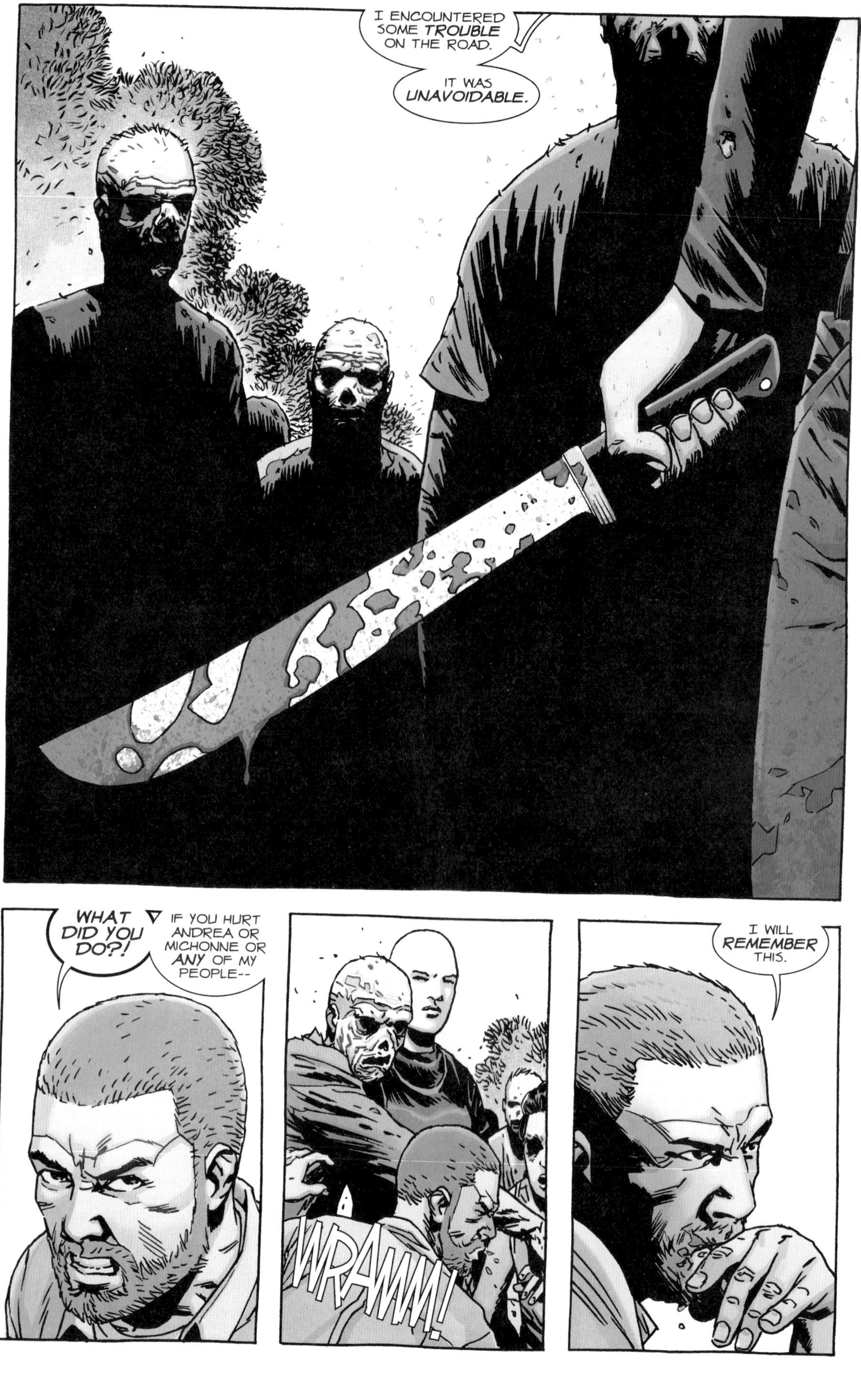
I ENCOUNTERED SOME TROUBLE ON THE ROAD.
IT WAS UNAVOIDABLE.
WHAT DID YOU DO?!
IF YOU HURT ANDREA OR MICHONNE OR ANY OF MY PEOPLE--
WRAMM!
I WILL REMEMBER THIS.

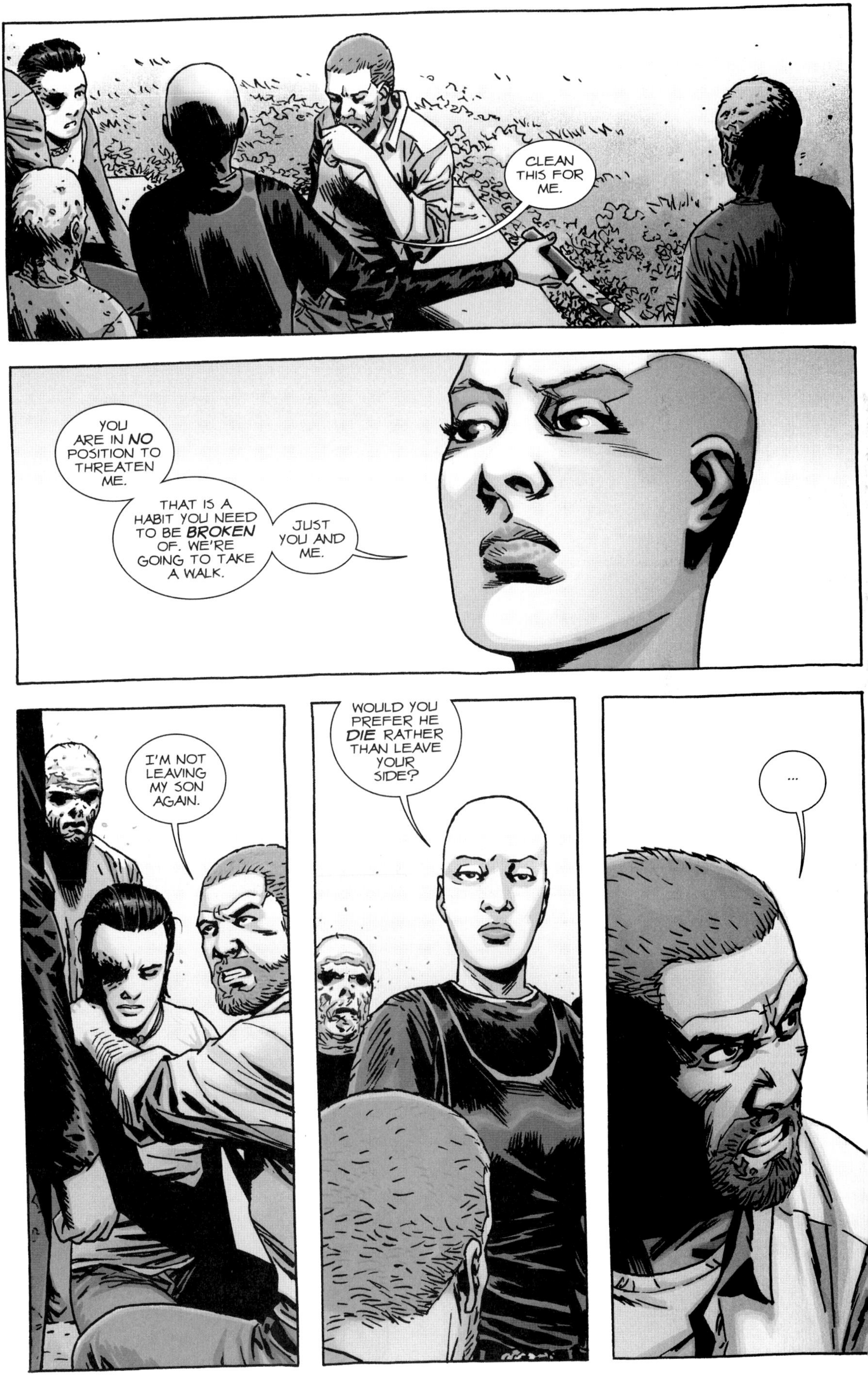
CLEAN THIS FOR ME.
YOU ARE IN NO POSITION TO THREATEN ME.
THAT IS A HABIT YOU NEED TO BE BROKEN OF. WE'RE GOING TO TAKE A WALK.
JUST YOU AND ME.
I'M NOT LEAVING MY SON AGAIN.
WOULD YOU PREFER HE DIE RATHER THAN LEAVE YOUR SIDE?
...

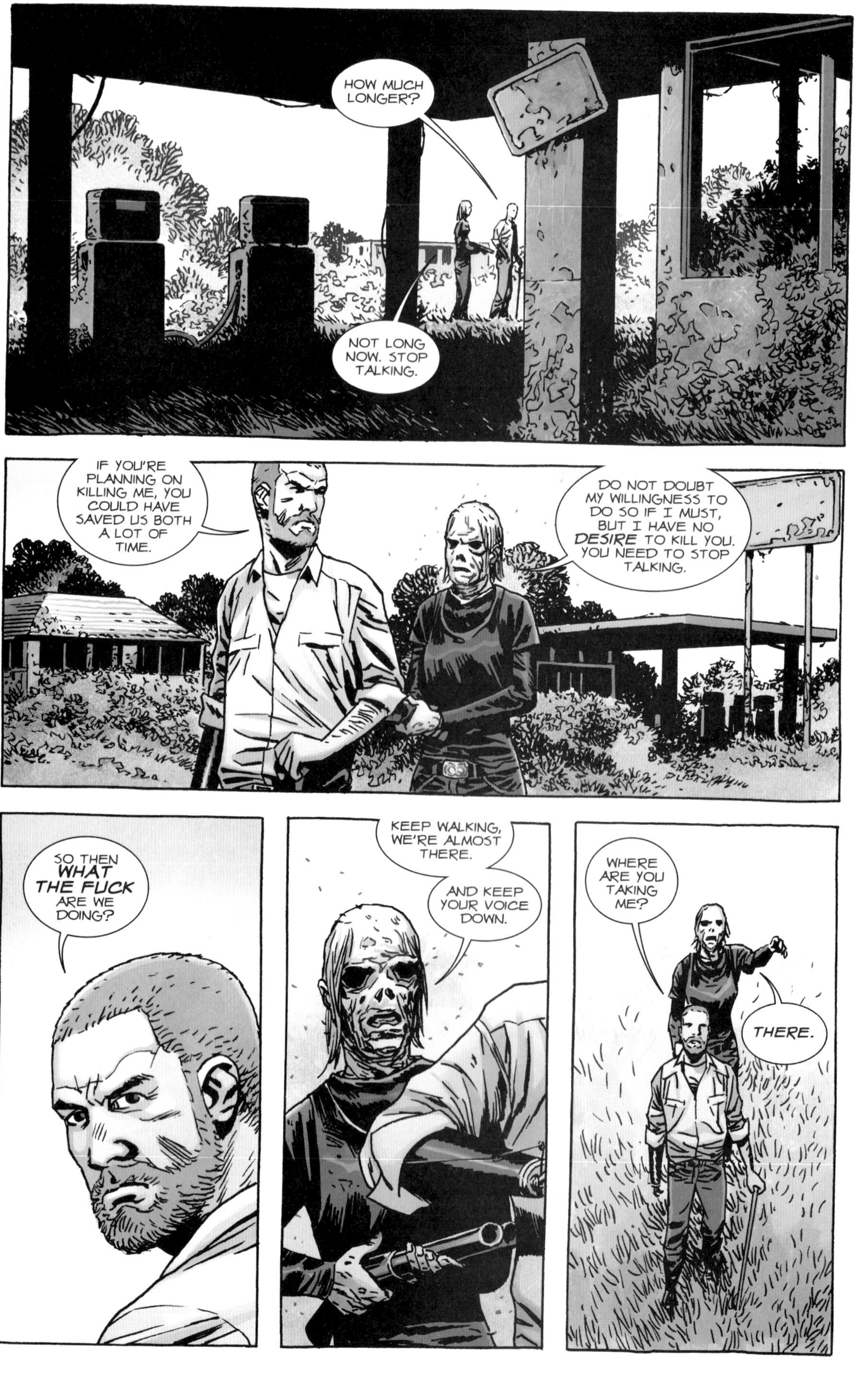
HOW MUCH LONGER?
NOT LONG NOW. STOP TALKING.
IF YOU'RE PLANNING ON KILLING ME, YOU COULD HAVE SAVED US BOTH A LOT OF TIME.
DO NOT DOUBT MY WILLINGNESS TO DO SO IF I MUST, BUT I HAVE NO DESIRE TO KILL YOU. YOU NEED TO STOP TALKING.
SO THEN WHAT THE FUCK ARE WE DOING?
KEEP WALKING, WE'RE ALMOST THERE.
AND KEEP YOUR VOICE DOWN.
WHERE ARE YOU TAKING ME?
THERE.

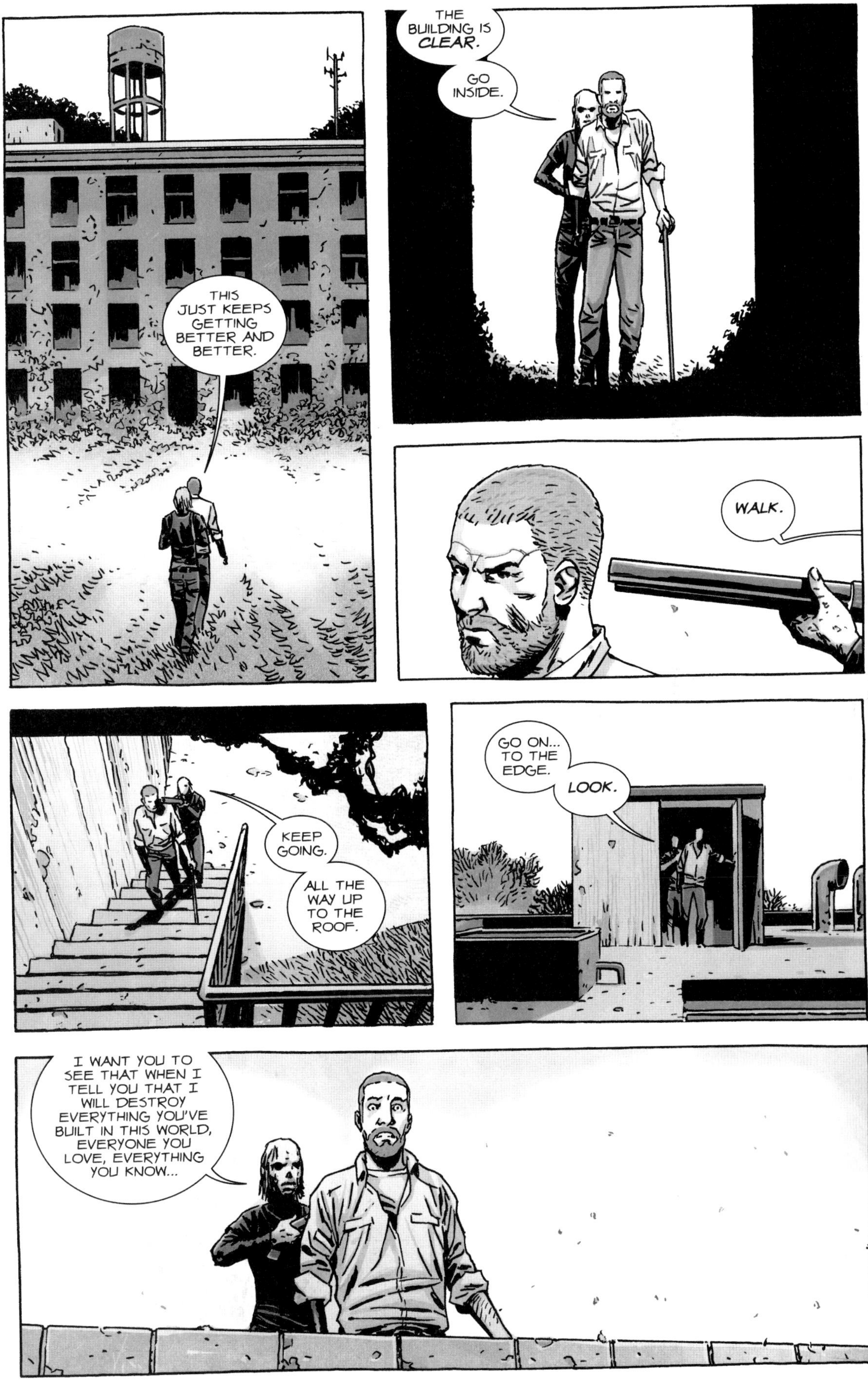
THIS JUST KEEPS GETTING BETTER AND BETTER.
THE BUILDING IS CLEAR.
GO INSIDE.
WALK.
KEEP GOING.
ALL THE WAY UP TO THE ROOF.
GO ON... TO THE EDGE.
LOOK.
I WANT YOU TO SEE THAT WHEN I TELL YOU THAT I WILL DESTROY EVERYTHING YOU'VE BUILT IN THIS WORLD, EVERYONE YOU LOVE, EVERYTHING YOU KNOW...

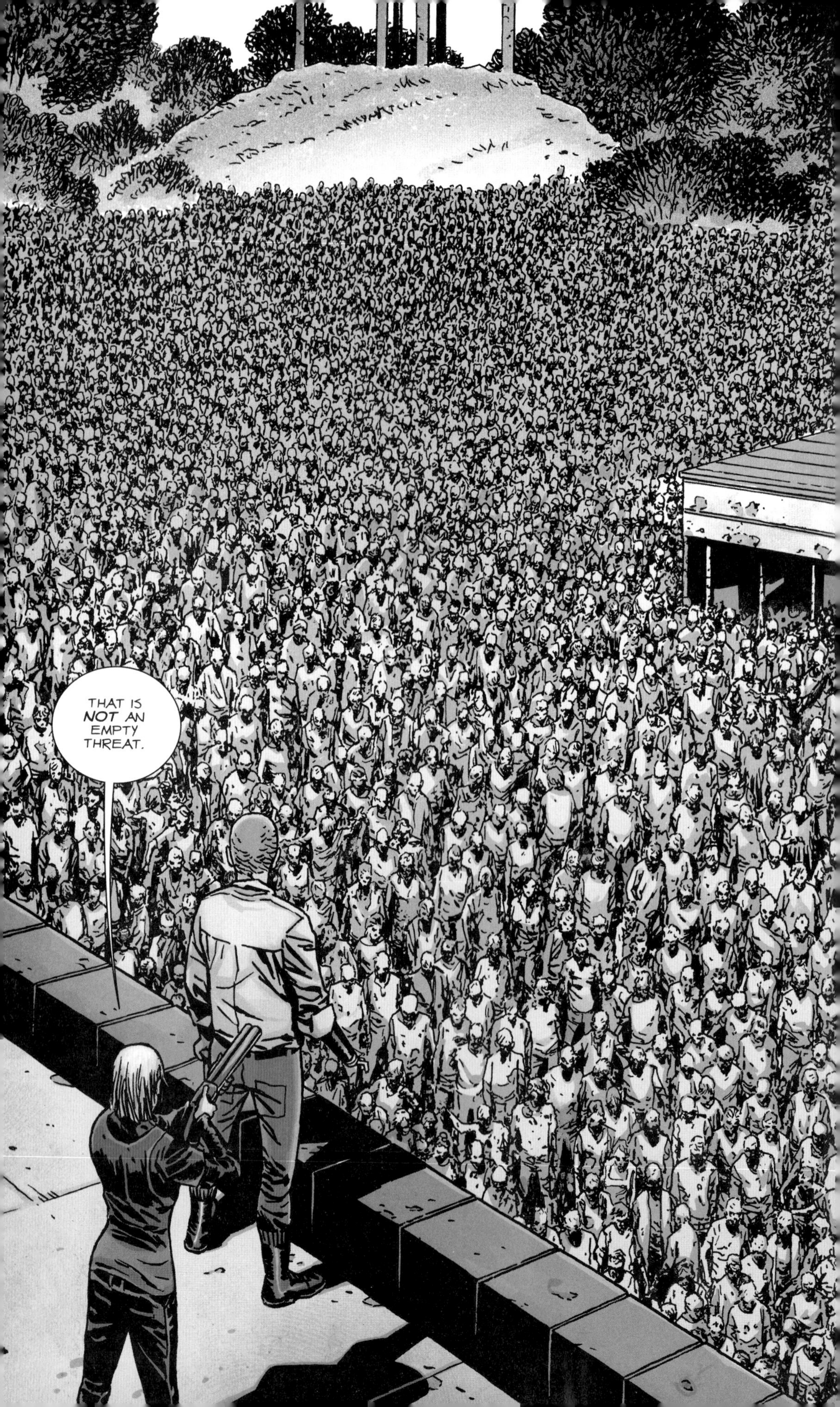
THAT IS NOT AN EMPTY THREAT.

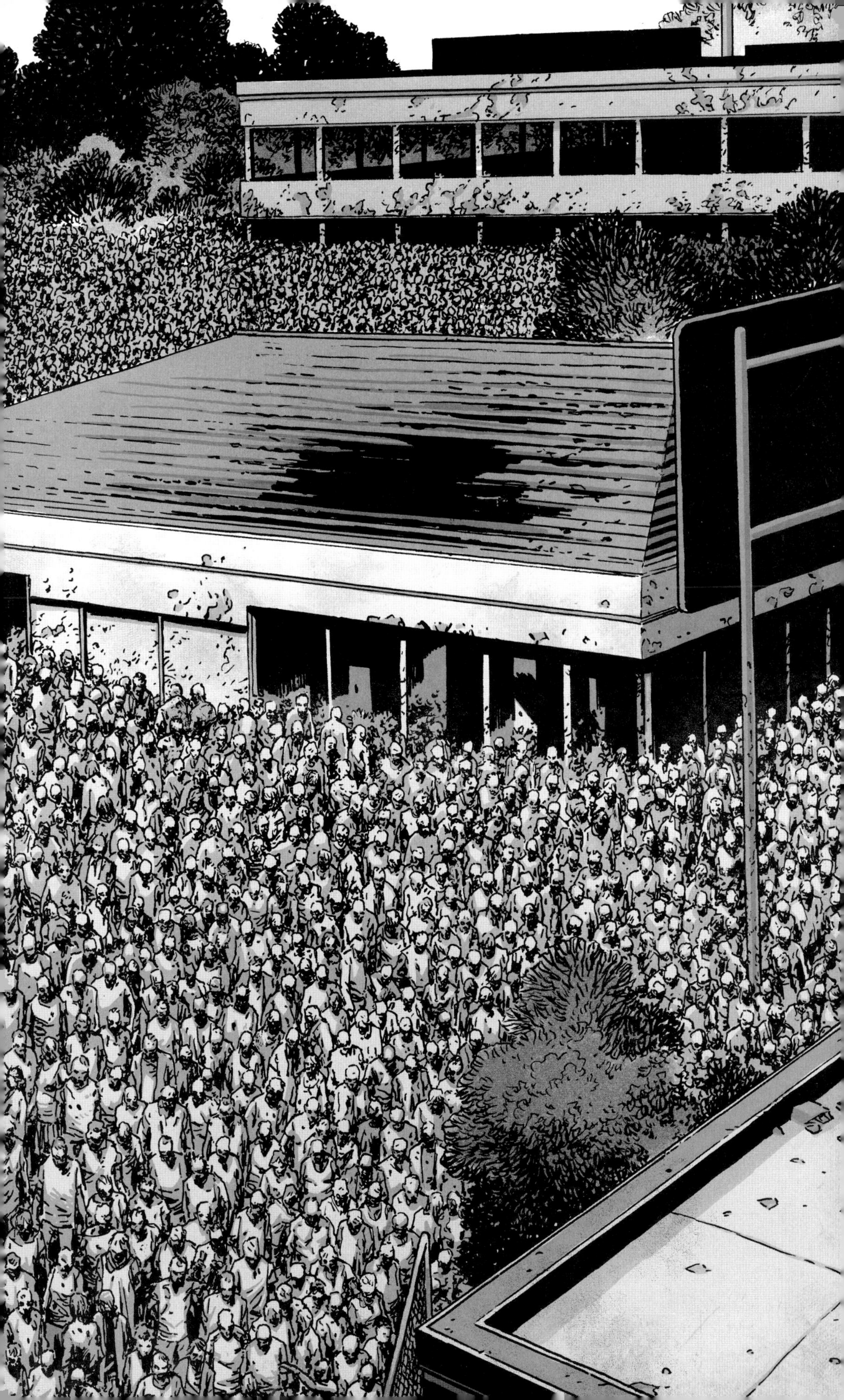

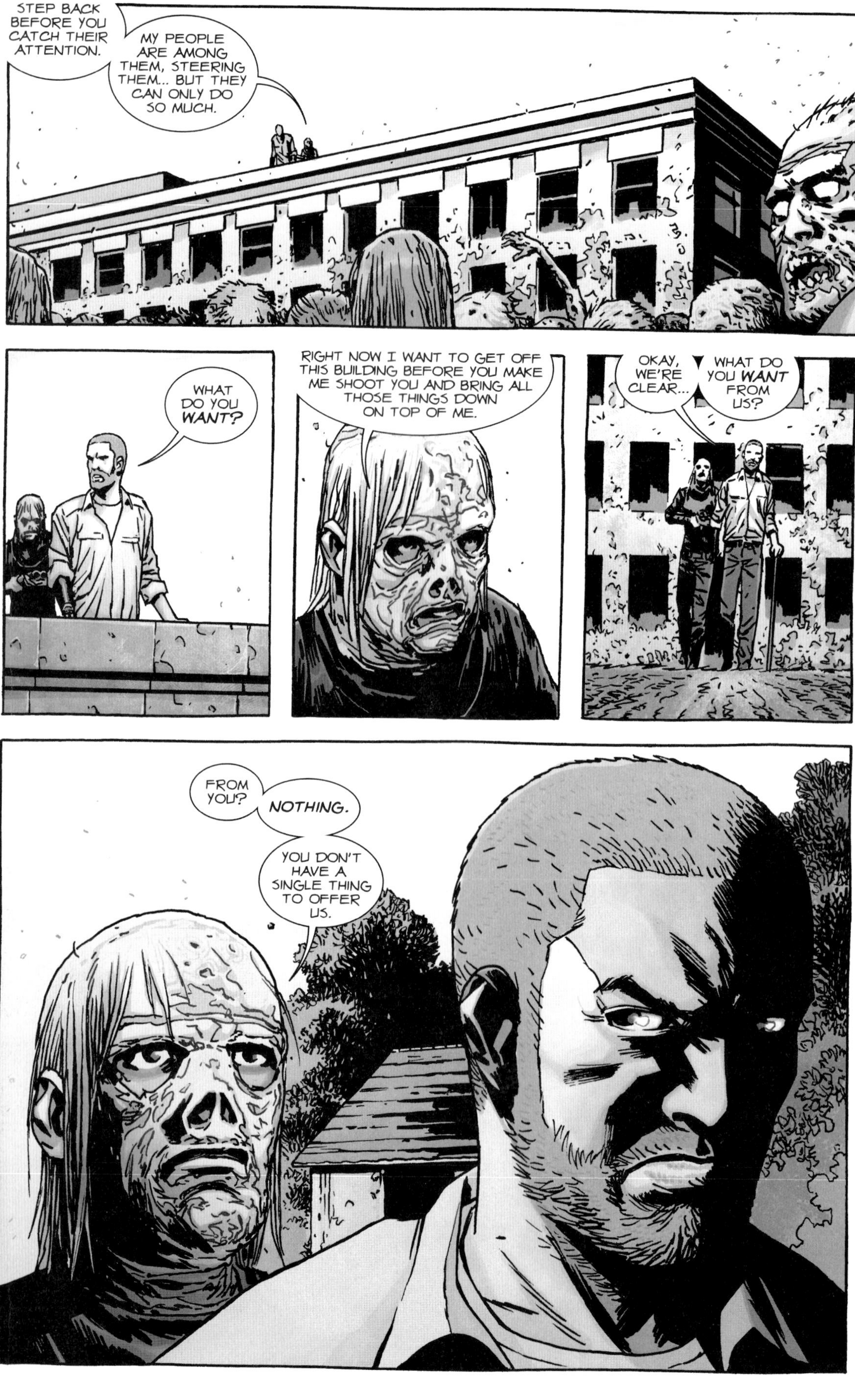
STEP BACK BEFORE YOU CATCH THEIR ATTENTION.
MY PEOPLE ARE AMONG THEM, STEERING THEM... BUT THEY CAN ONLY DO SO MUCH.
WHAT DO YOU WANT?
RIGHT NOW I WANT TO GET OFF THIS BUILDING BEFORE YOU MAKE ME SHOOT YOU AND BRING ALL THOSE THINGS DOWN ON TOP OF ME.
OKAY, WE'RE CLEAR...
WHAT DO YOU WANT FROM US?
FROM YOU?
NOTHING.
YOU DON'T HAVE A SINGLE THING TO OFFER US.

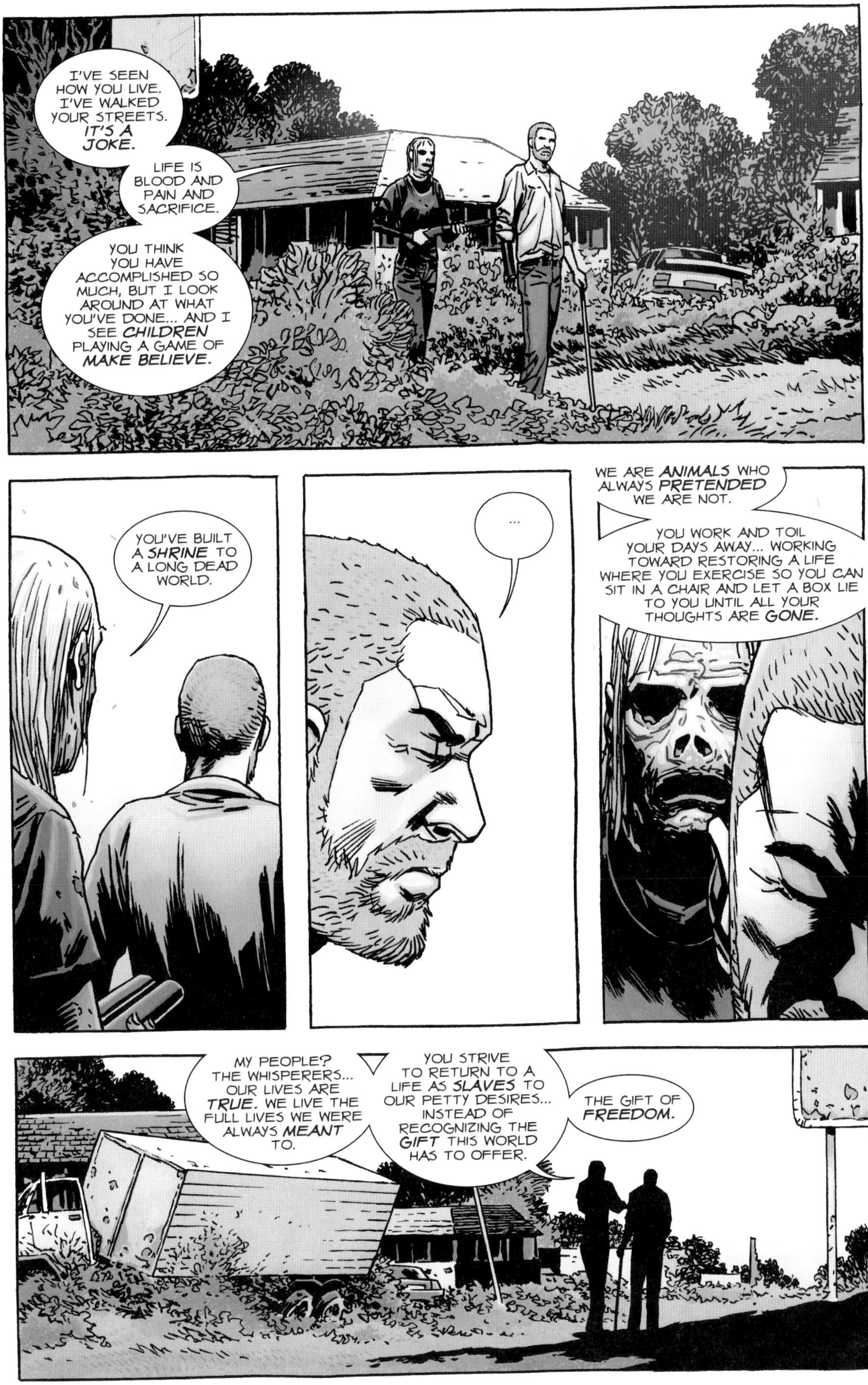

I'VE SEEN HOW YOU LIVE. I'VE WALKED YOUR STREETS. IT'S A JOKE.
LIFE IS BLOOD AND PAIN AND SACRIFICE.
YOU THINK YOU HAVE ACCOMPLISHED SO MUCH, BUT I LOOK AROUND AT WHAT YOU'VE DONE... AND I SEE CHILDREN PLAYING A GAME OF MAKE BELIEVE.
YOU'VE BUILT A SHRINE TO A LONG DEAD WORLD.
...
WE ARE ANIMALS WHO ALWAYS PRETENDED WE ARE NOT.
YOU WORK AND TOIL YOUR DAYS AWAY... WORKING TOWARD RESTORING A LIFE WHERE YOU EXERCISE SO YOU CAN SIT IN A CHAIR AND LET A BOX LIE TO YOU UNTIL ALL YOUR THOUGHTS ARE GONE.
MY PEOPLE? THE WHISPERERS... OUR LIVES ARE TRUE. WE LIVE THE FULL LIVES WE WERE ALWAYS MEANT TO.
YOU STRIVE TO RETURN TO A LIFE AS SLAVES TO OUR PETTY DESIRES... INSTEAD OF RECOGNIZING THE GIFT THIS WORLD HAS TO OFFER.
THE GIFT OF FREEDOM.

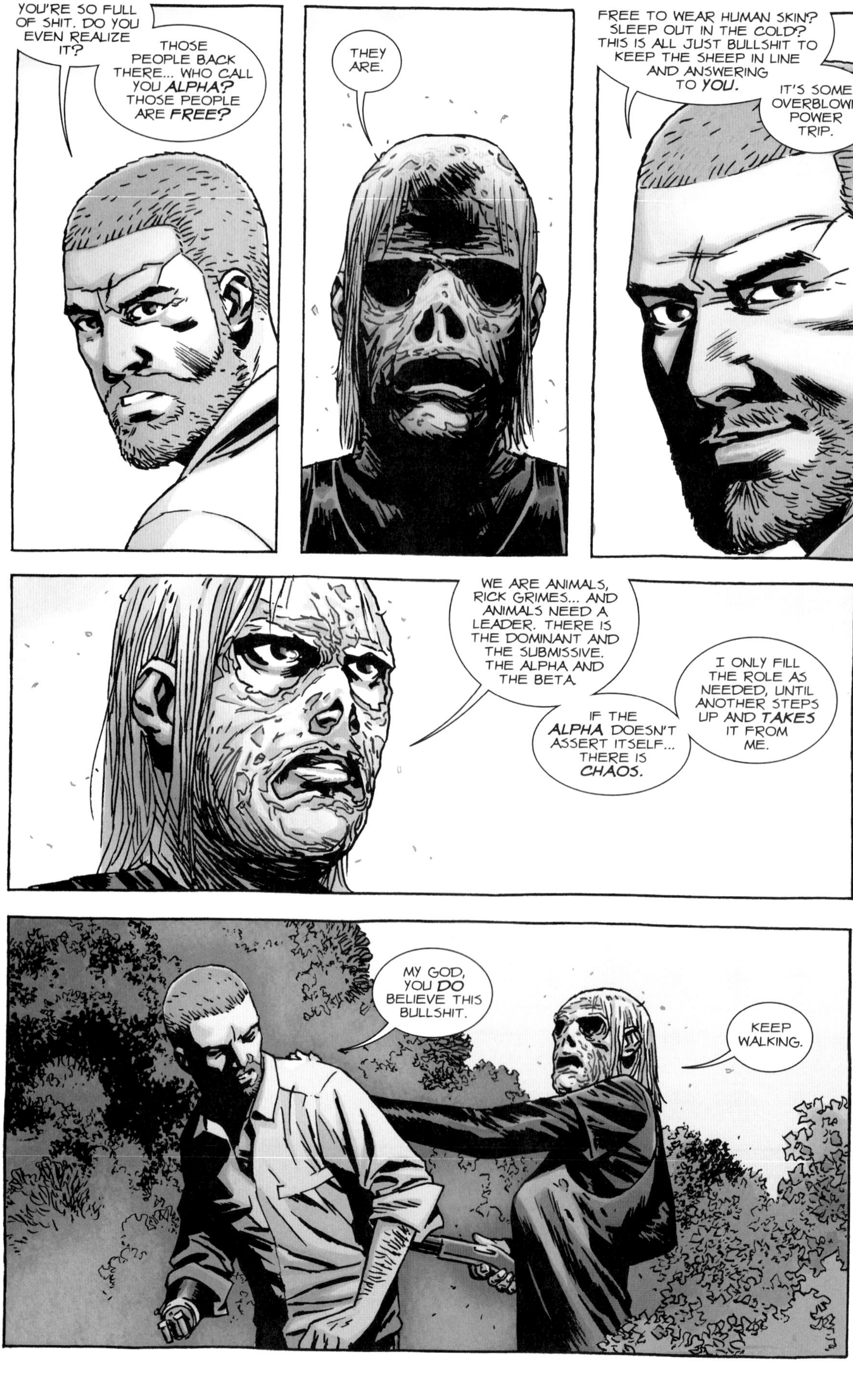
YOU'RE SO FULL OF SHIT. DO YOU EVEN REALIZE IT?
THOSE PEOPLE BACK THERE... WHO CALL YOU ALPHA? THOSE PEOPLE ARE FREE?
THEY ARE.
FREE TO WEAR HUMAN SKIN? SLEEP OUT IN THE COLD? THIS IS ALL JUST BULLSHIT TO KEEP THE SHEEP IN LINE AND ANSWERING TO YOU.
IT'S SOME OVERBLOWN POWER TRIP.
WE ARE ANIMALS, RICK GRIMES... AND ANIMALS NEED A LEADER. THERE IS THE DOMINANT AND THE SUBMISSIVE. THE ALPHA AND THE BETA.
IF THE ALPHA DOESN'T ASSERT ITSELF... THERE IS CHAOS.
I ONLY FILL THE ROLE AS NEEDED, UNTIL ANOTHER STEPS UP AND TAKES IT FROM ME.
MY GOD, YOU DO BELIEVE THIS BULLSHIT.
KEEP WALKING.

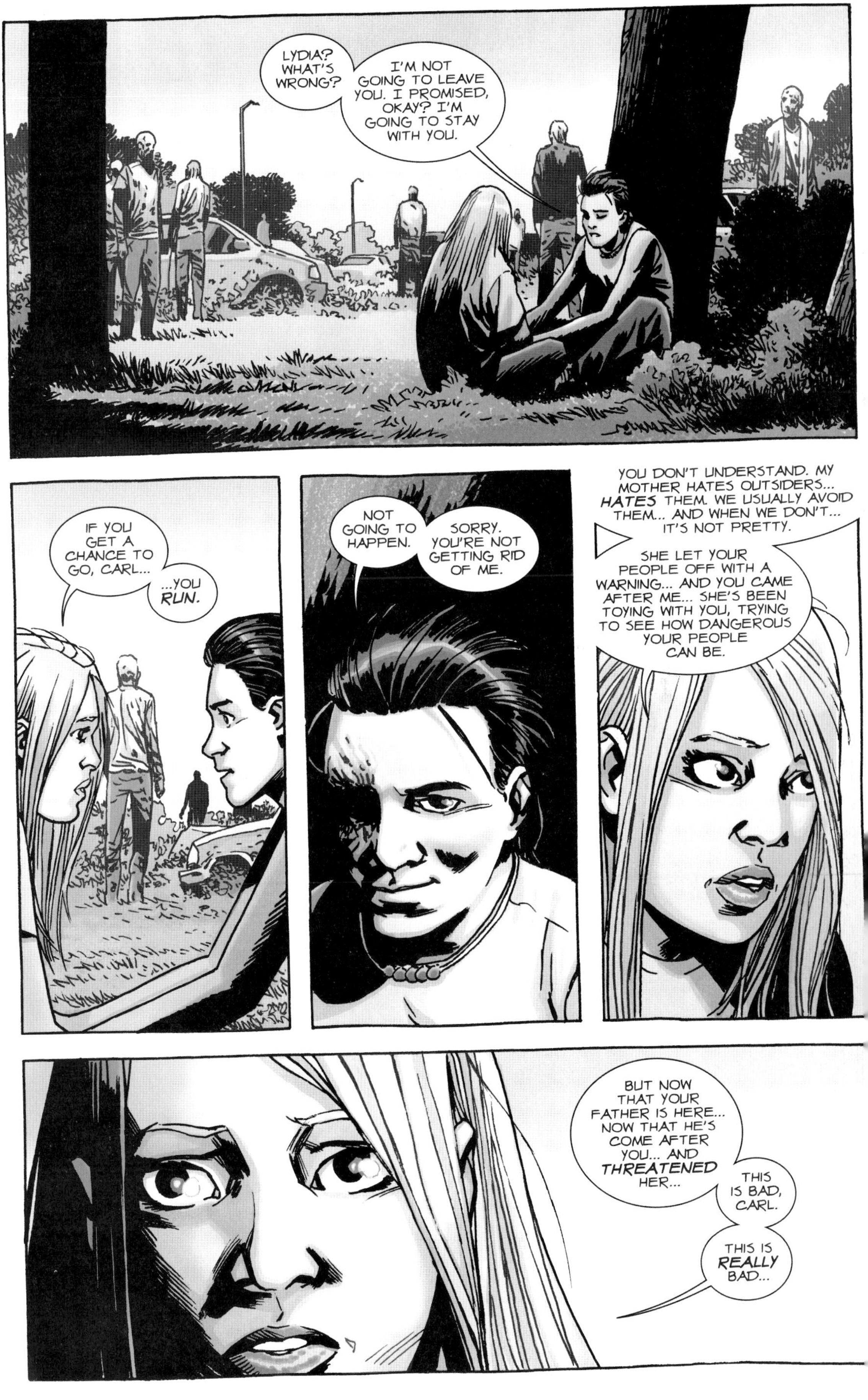
LYDIA? WHAT'S WRONG?
I'M NOT GOING TO LEAVE YOU. I PROMISED, OKAY? I'M GOING TO STAY WITH YOU.
IF YOU GET A CHANCE TO GO, CARL...
...YOU RUN.
NOT GOING TO HAPPEN.
SORRY. YOU'RE NOT GETTING RID OF ME.
YOU DON'T UNDERSTAND. MY MOTHER HATES OUTSIDERS... HATES THEM. WE USUALLY AVOID THEM... AND WHEN WE DON'T... IT'S NOT PRETTY.
SHE LET YOUR PEOPLE OFF WITH A WARNING... AND YOU CAME AFTER ME... SHE'S BEEN TOYING WITH YOU, TRYING TO SEE HOW DANGEROUS YOUR PEOPLE CAN BE.
BUT NOW THAT YOUR FATHER IS HERE... NOW THAT HE'S COME AFTER YOU... AND THREATENED HER...
THIS IS BAD, CARL.
THIS IS REALLY BAD...

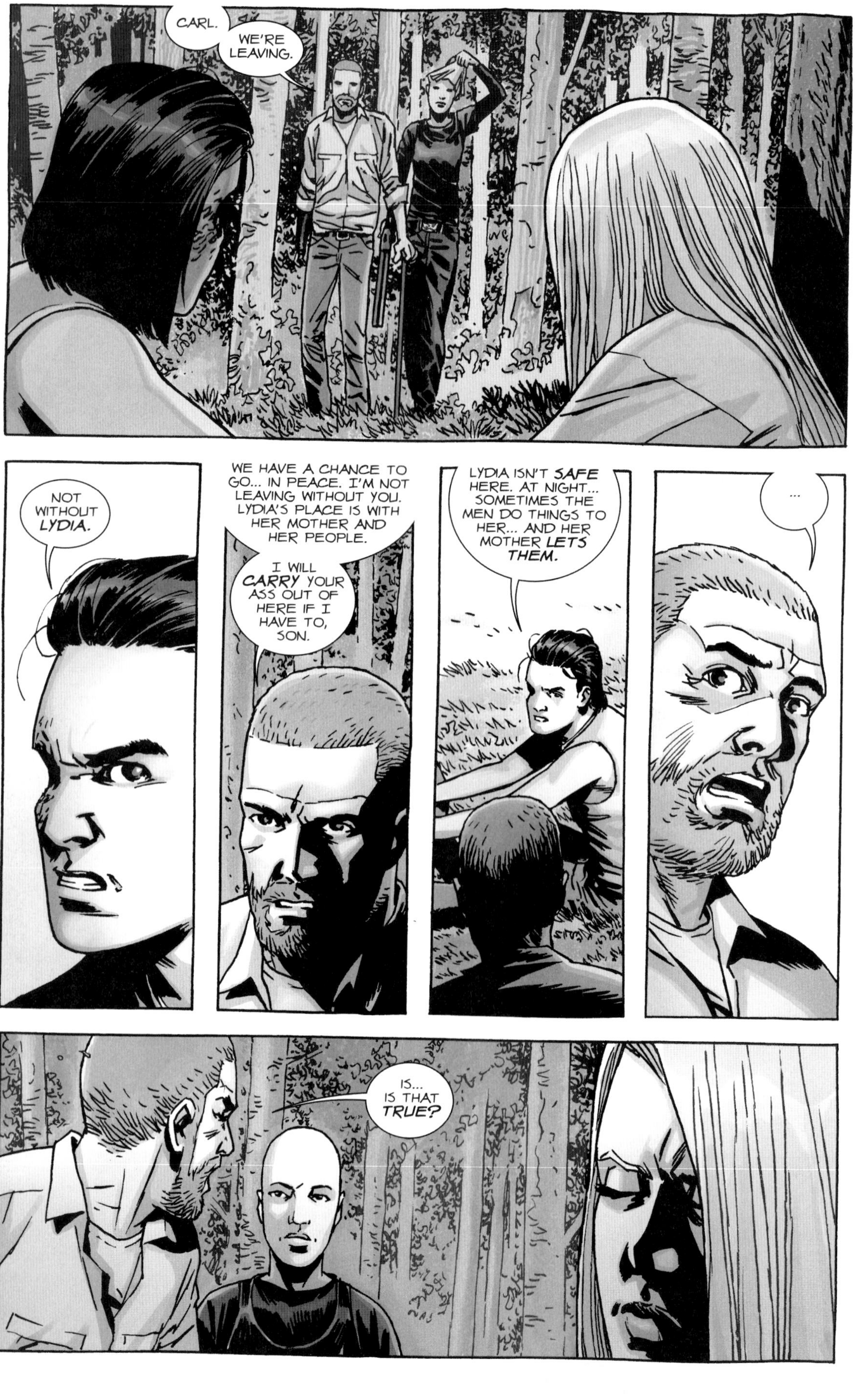
CARL.
WE'RE LEAVING.
NOT WITHOUT LYDIA.
WE HAVE A CHANCE TO GO... IN PEACE. I'M NOT LEAVING WITHOUT YOU. LYDIA'S PLACE IS WITH HER MOTHER AND HER PEOPLE.
I WILL CARRY YOUR ASS OUT OF HERE IF I HAVE TO, SON.
LYDIA ISN'T SAFE HERE. AT NIGHT... SOMETIMES THE MEN DO THINGS TO HER... AND HER MOTHER LETS THEM.
...
IS... IS THAT TRUE?

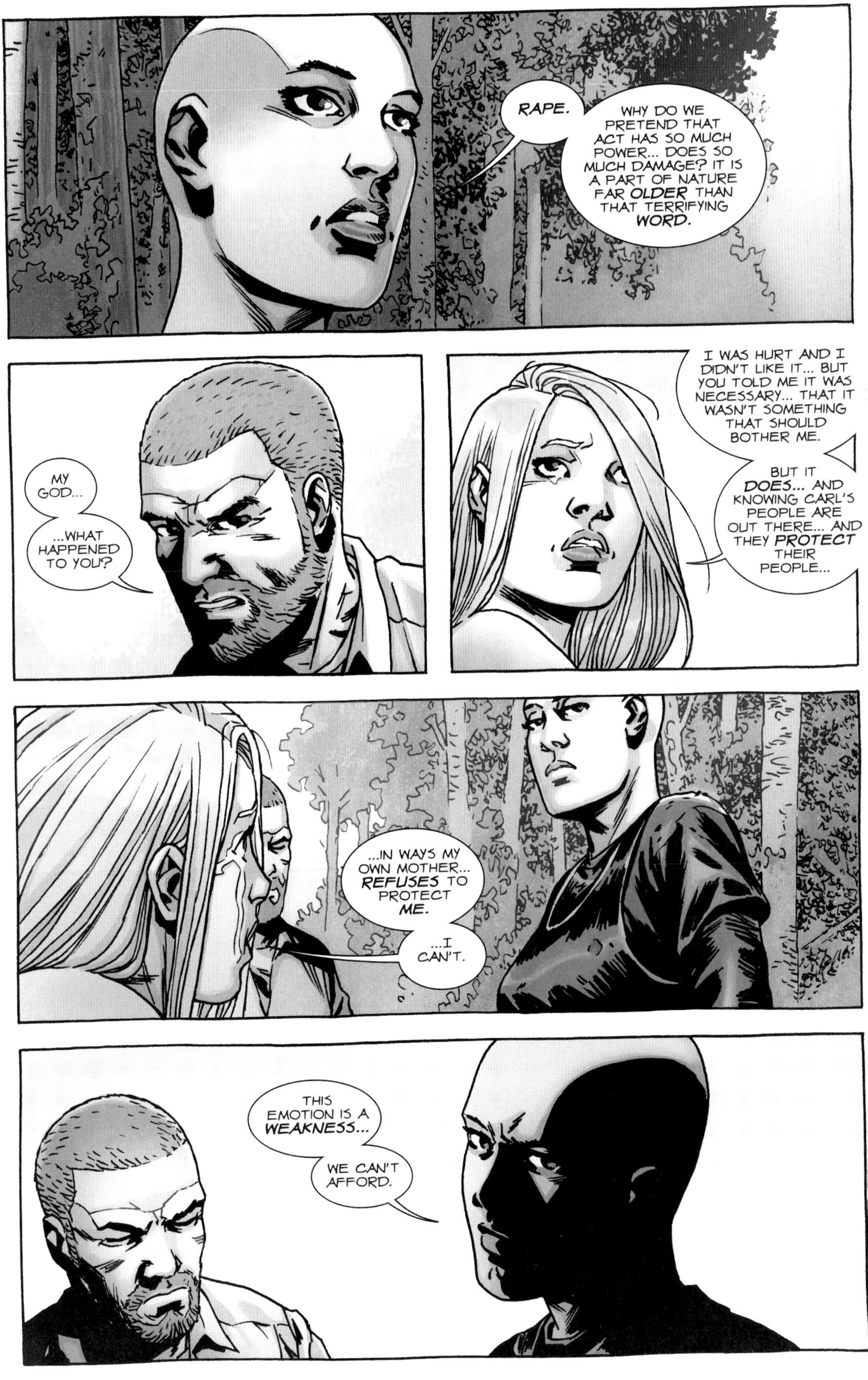
RAPE.
WHY DO WE PRETEND THAT ACT HAS SO MUCH POWER... DOES SO MUCH DAMAGE? IT IS A PART OF NATURE FAR OLDER THAN THAT TERRIFYING WORD.
MY GOD...
...WHAT HAPPENED TO YOU?
I WAS HURT AND I DIDN'T LIKE IT... BUT YOU TOLD ME IT WAS NECESSARY... THAT IT WASN'T SOMETHING THAT SHOULD BOTHER ME.
BUT IT DOES... AND KNOWING CARL'S PEOPLE ARE OUT THERE... AND THEY PROTECT THEIR PEOPLE...
...IN WAYS MY OWN MOTHER... REFUSES TO PROTECT ME.
...I CAN'T.
THIS EMOTION IS A WEAKNESS...
WE CAN'T AFFORD.

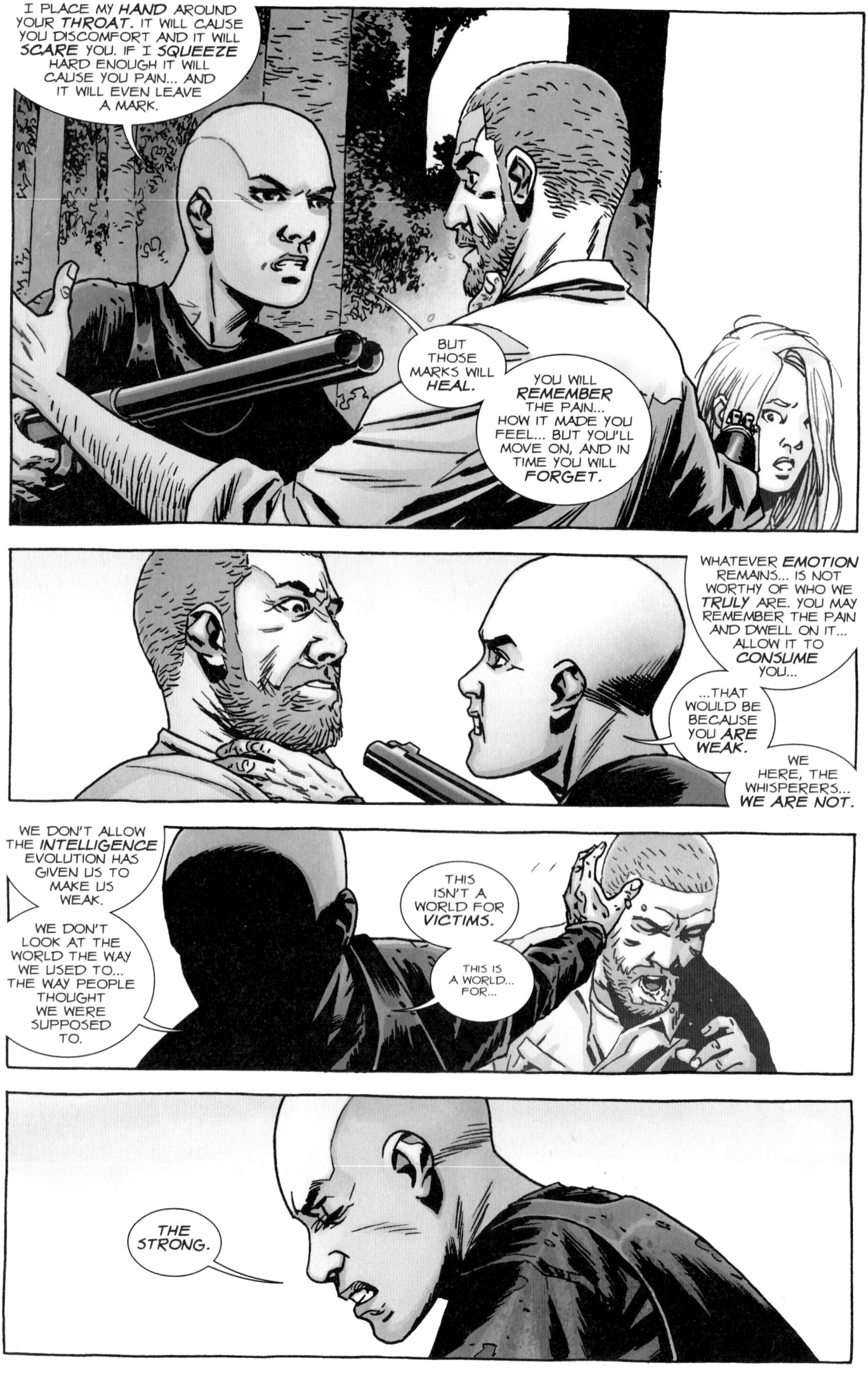
I PLACE MY HAND AROUND YOUR THROAT. IT WILL CAUSE YOU DISCOMFORT AND IT WILL SCARE YOU. IF I SQUEEZE HARD ENOUGH IT WILL CAUSE YOU PAIN... AND IT WILL EVEN LEAVE A MARK.
BUT THOSE MARKS WILL HEAL.
YOU WILL REMEMBER THE PAIN... HOW IT MADE YOU FEEL... BUT YOU'LL MOVE ON, AND IN TIME YOU WILL FORGET.
WHATEVER EMOTION REMAINS... IS NOT WORTHY OF WHO WE TRULY ARE. YOU MAY REMEMBER THE PAIN AND DWELL ON IT... ALLOW IT TO CONSUME YOU...
...THAT WOULD BE BECAUSE YOU ARE WEAK.
WE HERE, THE WHISPERERS... WE ARE NOT.
WE DON'T ALLOW THE INTELLIGENCE EVOLUTION HAS GIVEN US TO MAKE US WEAK.
WE DON'T LOOK AT THE WORLD THE WAY WE USED TO... THE WAY PEOPLE THOUGHT WE WERE SUPPOSED TO.
THIS ISN'T A WORLD FOR VICTIMS.
THIS IS A WORLD... FOR...
THE STRONG.

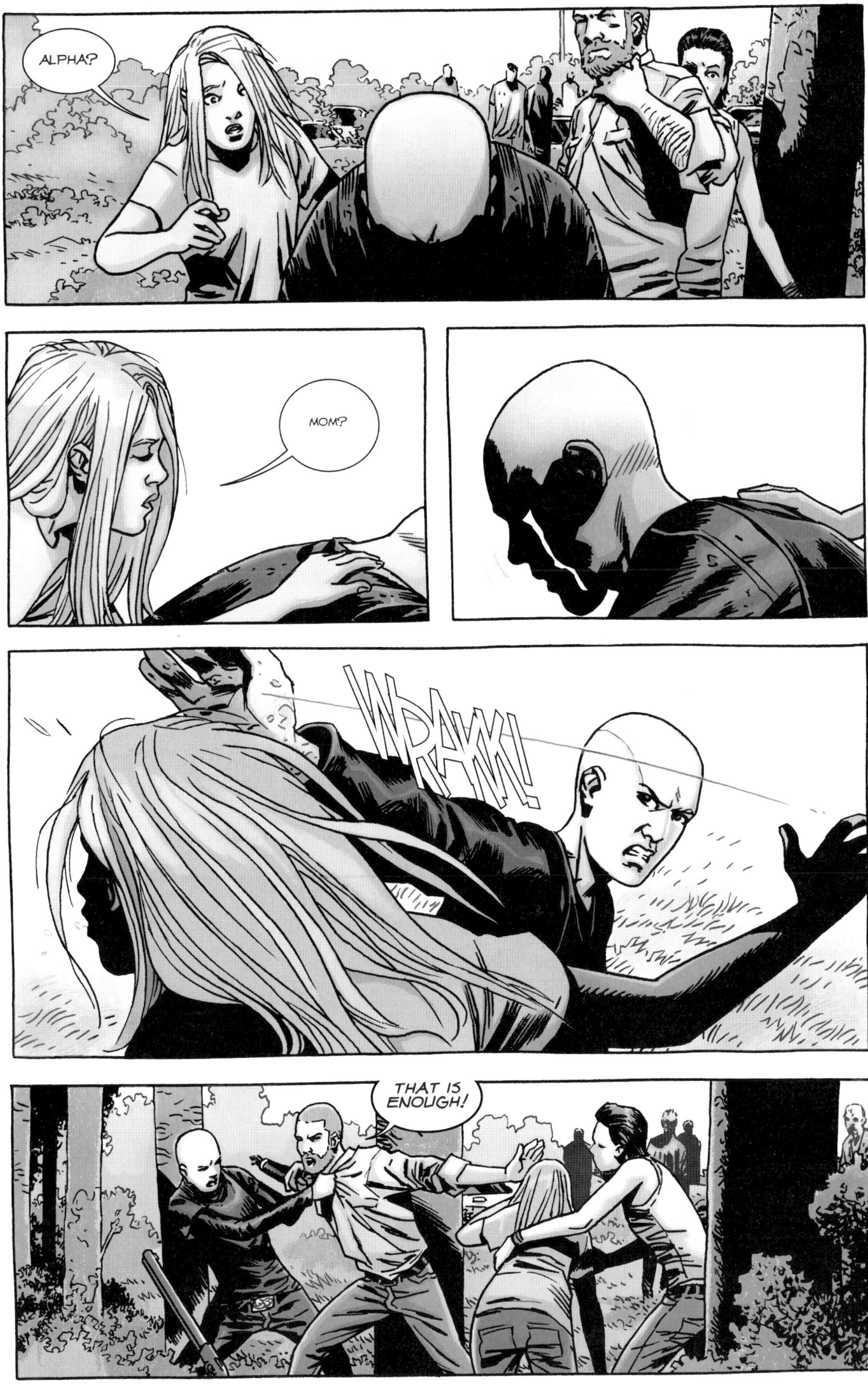
ALPHA?
MOM?
WRAKK!
THAT IS ENOUGH!

I CAN'T OFFER MY DAUGHTER THE LIFE SHE NEEDS. NOT *HERE*. NOT SAFELY.

BUT *YOU* CAN.

STAY BACK. I *DO NOT* NEED YOUR HELP.

YOU.

YOU DO NOT BELONG HERE. YOU ARE *WEAK* AND YOU LONG FOR THE OLD WAYS, THE BROKEN WAYS.

YOU BELONG WITH *THEM*.

BE GONE WITH YOU.

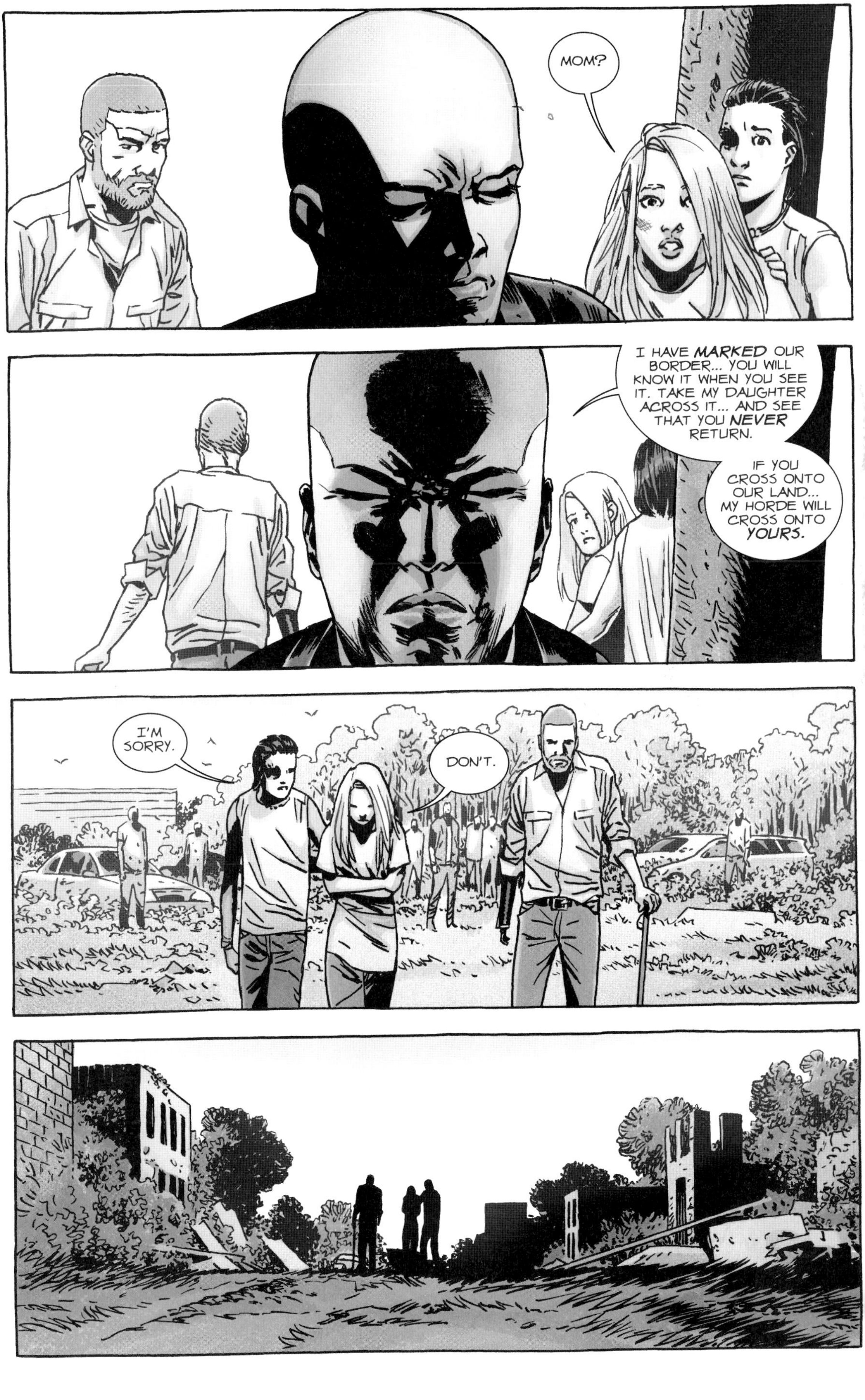
MOM?
I HAVE MARKED OUR BORDER... YOU WILL KNOW IT WHEN YOU SEE IT. TAKE MY DAUGHTER ACROSS IT... AND SEE THAT YOU NEVER RETURN.
IF YOU CROSS ONTO OUR LAND... MY HORDE WILL CROSS ONTO YOURS.
I'M SORRY.
DON'T.

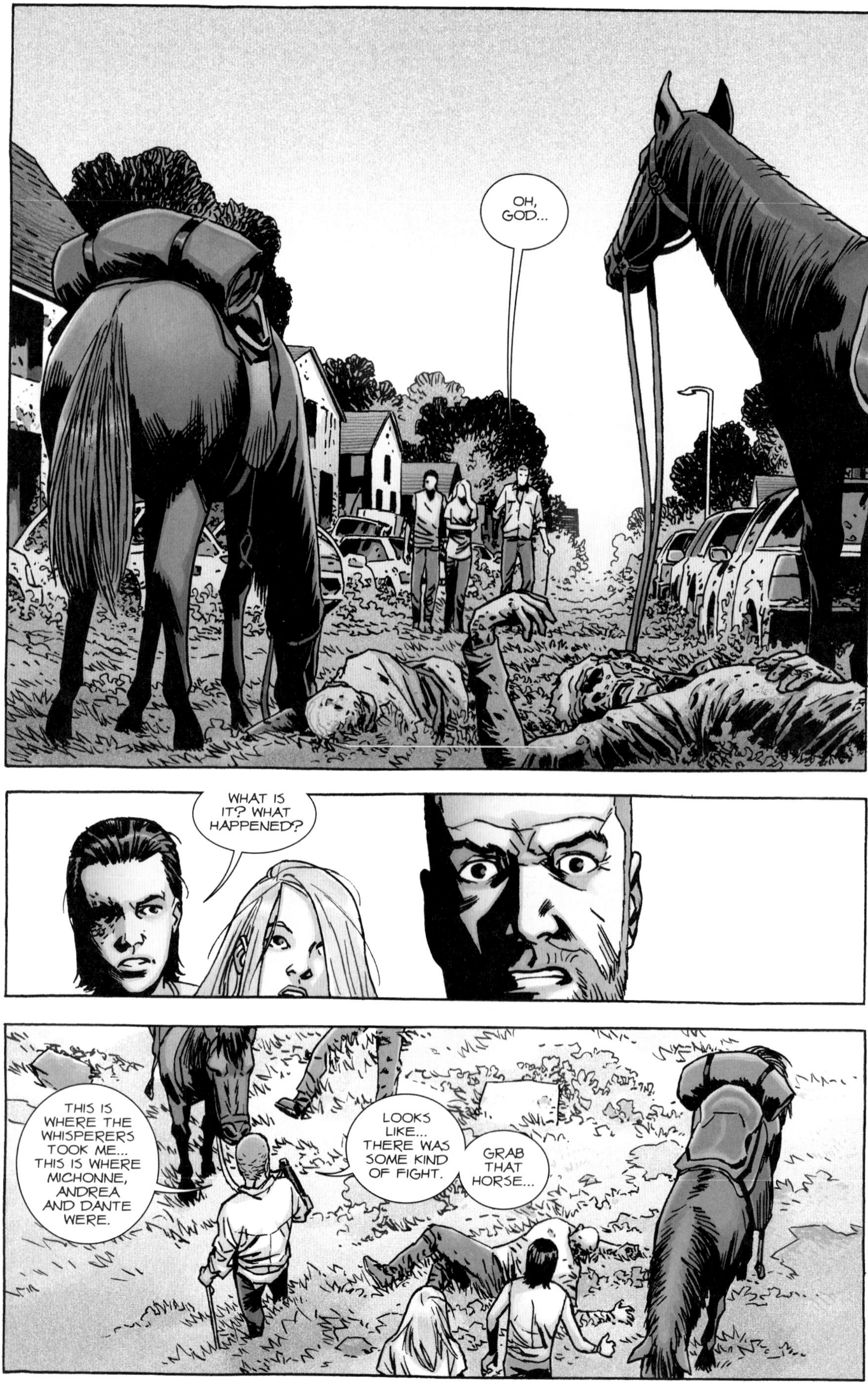
OH, GOD...
WHAT IS IT? WHAT HAPPENED?
THIS IS WHERE THE WHISPERERS TOOK ME... THIS IS WHERE MICHONNE, ANDREA AND DANTE WERE.
LOOKS LIKE... THERE WAS SOME KIND OF FIGHT.
GRAB THAT HORSE...

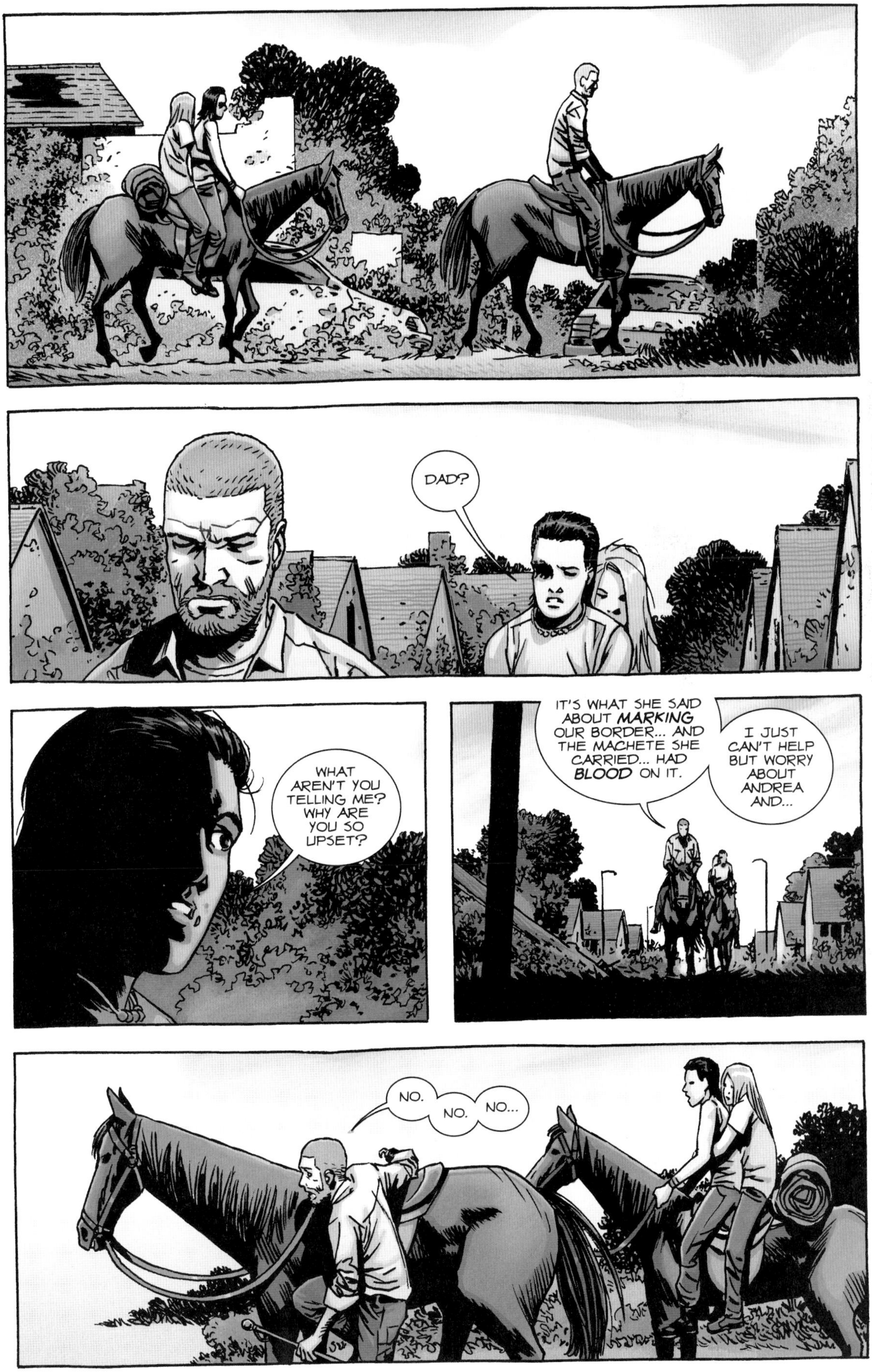
DAD?
WHAT AREN'T YOU TELLING ME? WHY ARE YOU SO UPSET?
IT'S WHAT SHE SAID ABOUT MARKING OUR BORDER... AND THE MACHETE SHE CARRIED... HAD BLOOD ON IT.
I JUST CAN'T HELP BUT WORRY ABOUT ANDREA AND...
NO.
NO.
NO...

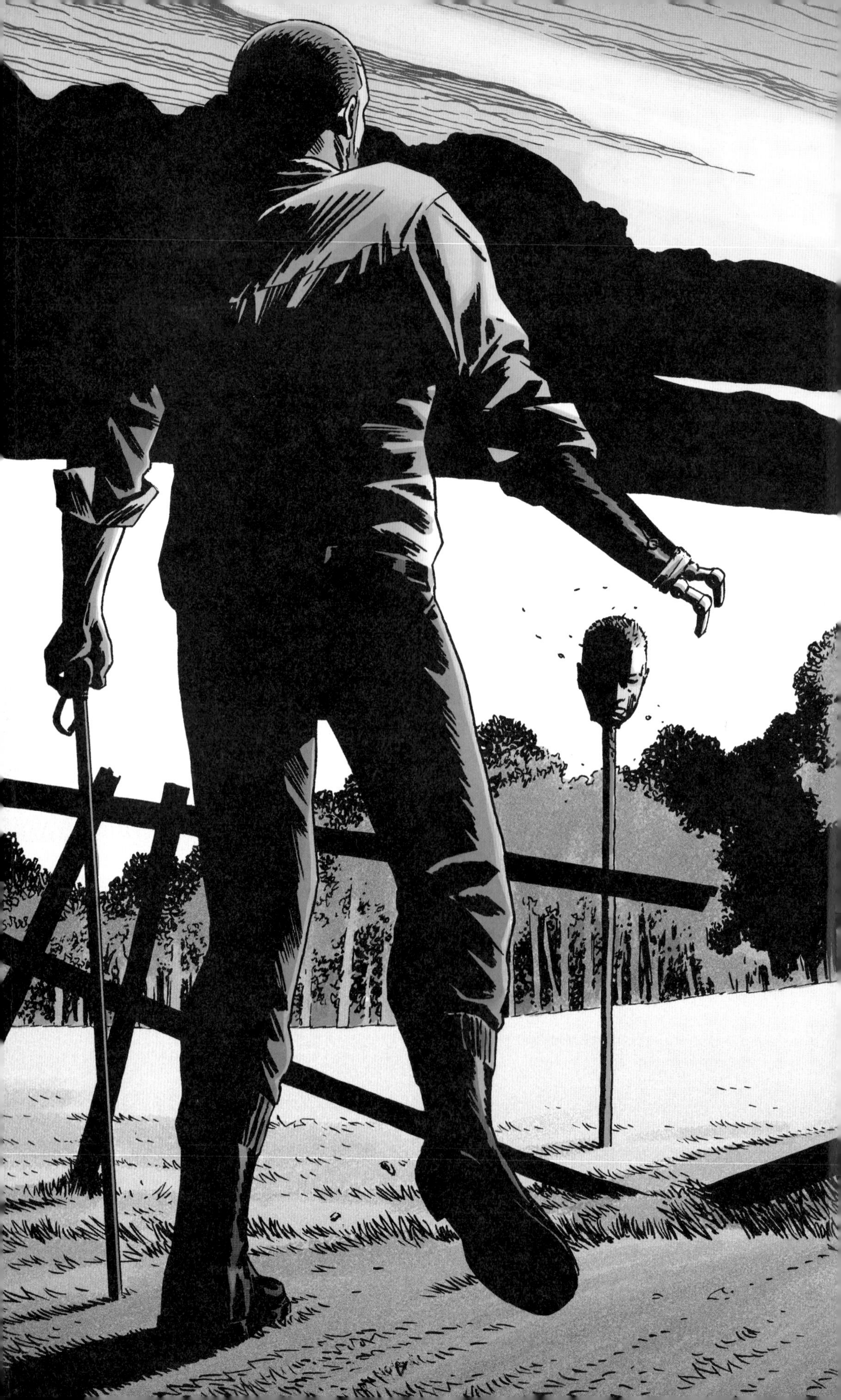

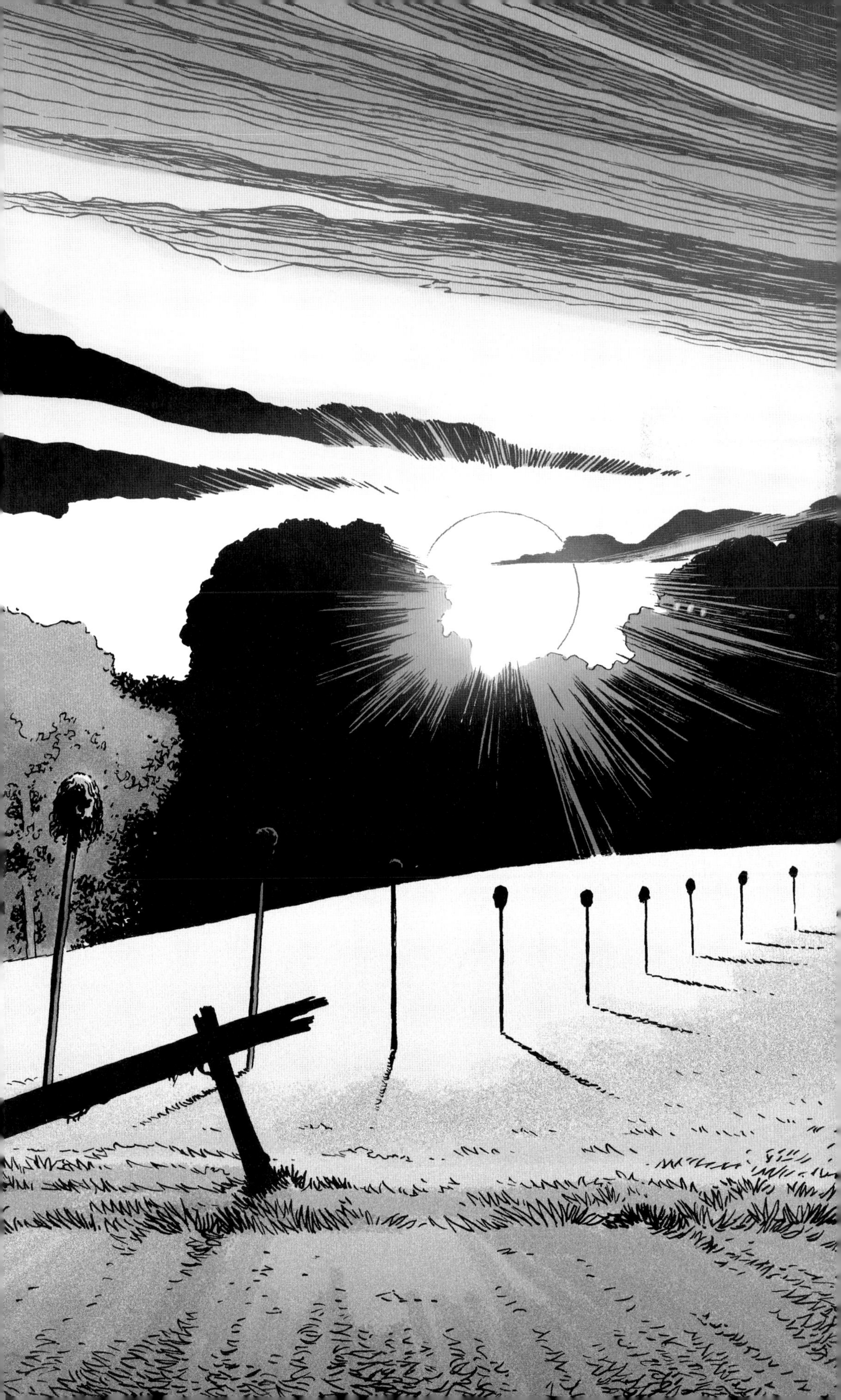

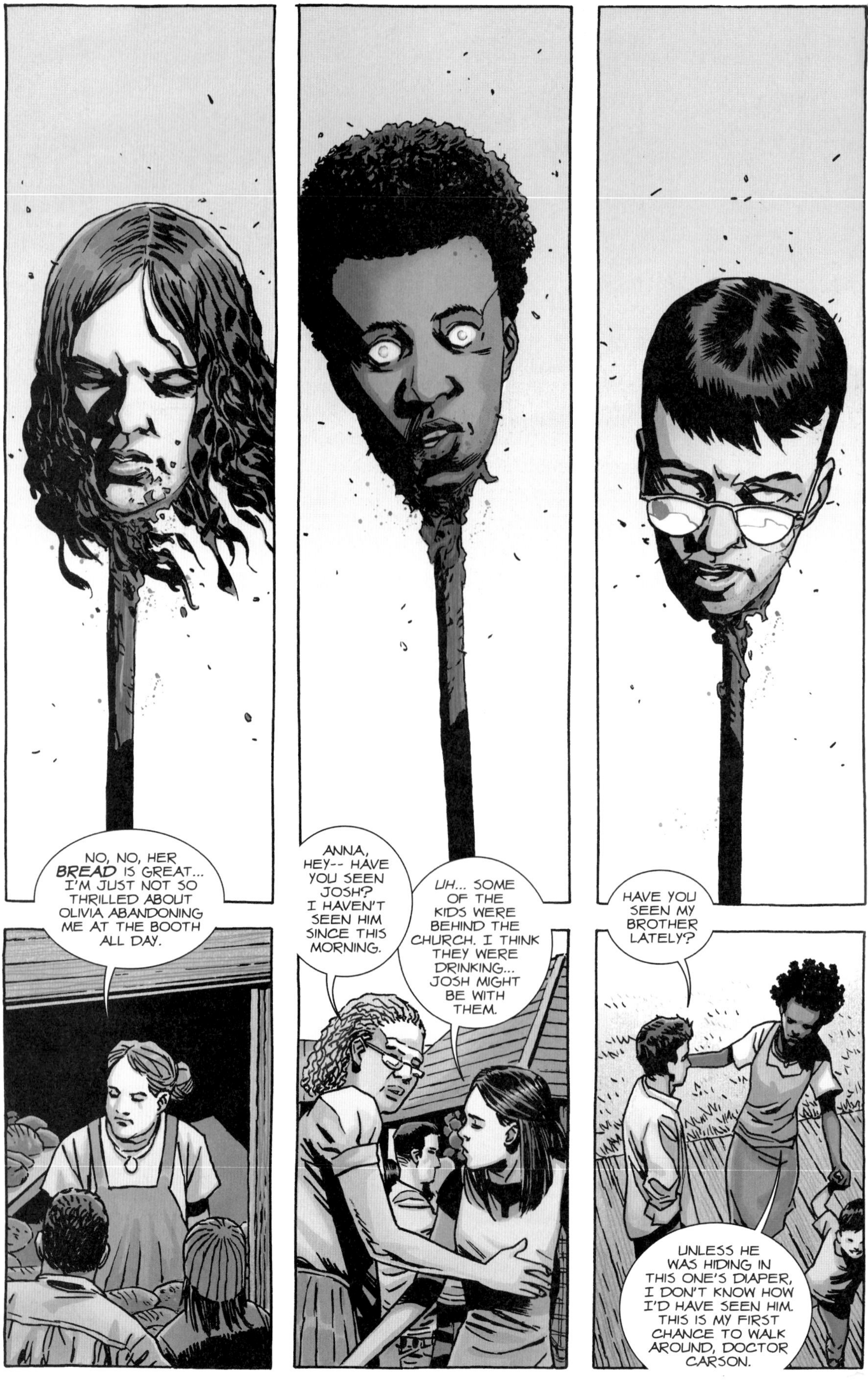
NO, NO, HER BREAD IS GREAT... I'M JUST NOT SO THRILLED ABOUT OLIVIA ABANDONING ME AT THE BOOTH ALL DAY.
ANNA, HEY-- HAVE YOU SEEN JOSH? I HAVEN'T SEEN HIM SINCE THIS MORNING.
UH... SOME OF THE KIDS WERE BEHIND THE CHURCH. I THINK THEY WERE DRINKING... JOSH MIGHT BE WITH THEM.
HAVE YOU SEEN MY BROTHER LATELY?
UNLESS HE WAS HIDING IN THIS ONE'S DIAPER, I DON'T KNOW HOW I'D HAVE SEEN HIM. THIS IS MY FIRST CHANCE TO WALK AROUND, DOCTOR CARSON.

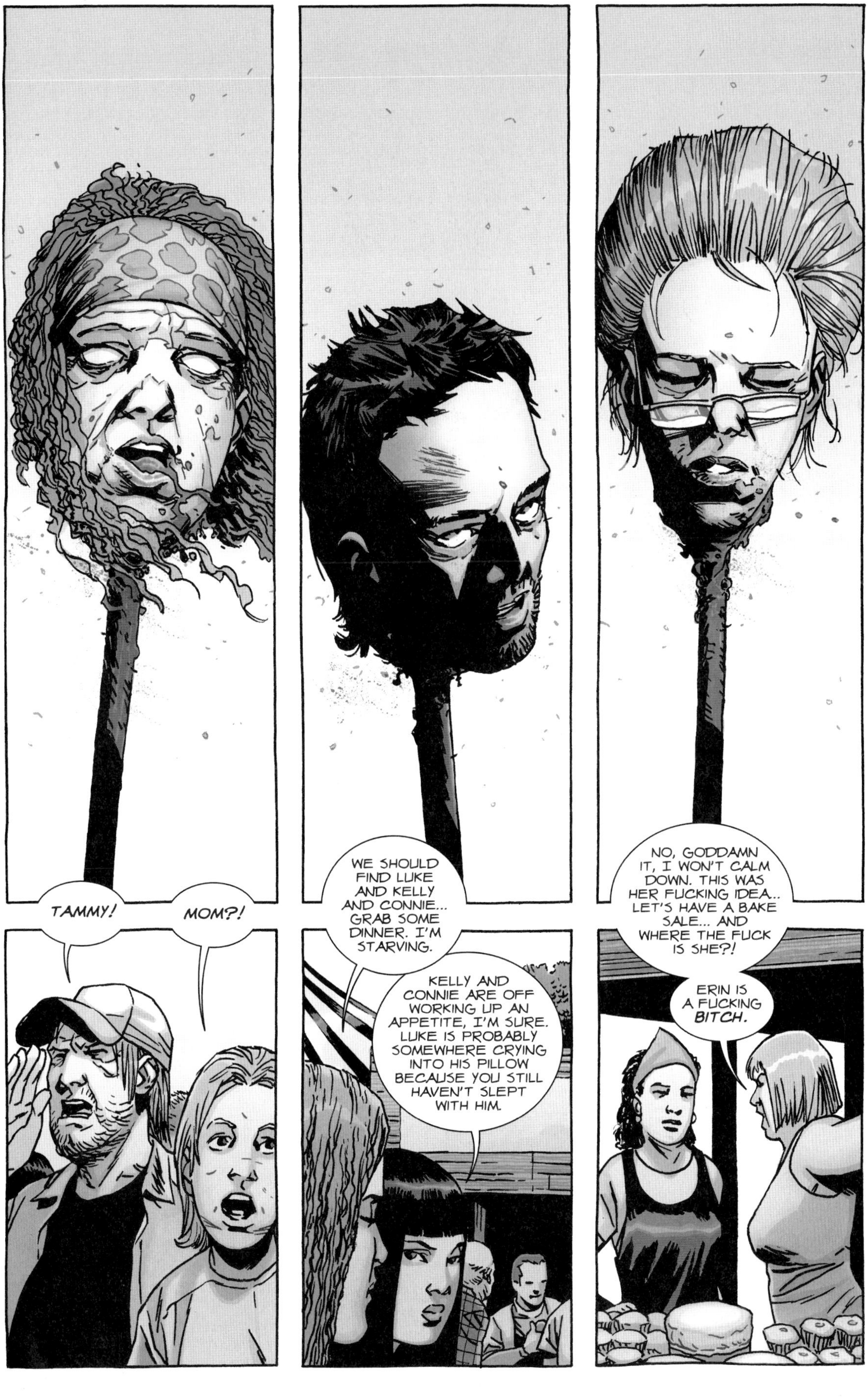
TAMMY!
MOM?!
WE SHOULD FIND LUKE AND KELLY AND CONNIE... GRAB SOME DINNER. I'M STARVING.
KELLY AND CONNIE ARE OFF WORKING UP AN APPETITE, I'M SURE. LUKE IS PROBABLY SOMEWHERE CRYING INTO HIS PILLOW BECAUSE YOU STILL HAVEN'T SLEPT WITH HIM.
NO, GODDAMN IT, I WON'T CALM DOWN. THIS WAS HER FUCKING IDEA.. LET'S HAVE A BAKE SALE... AND WHERE THE FUCK IS SHE?!
ERIN IS A FUCKING *BITCH.*

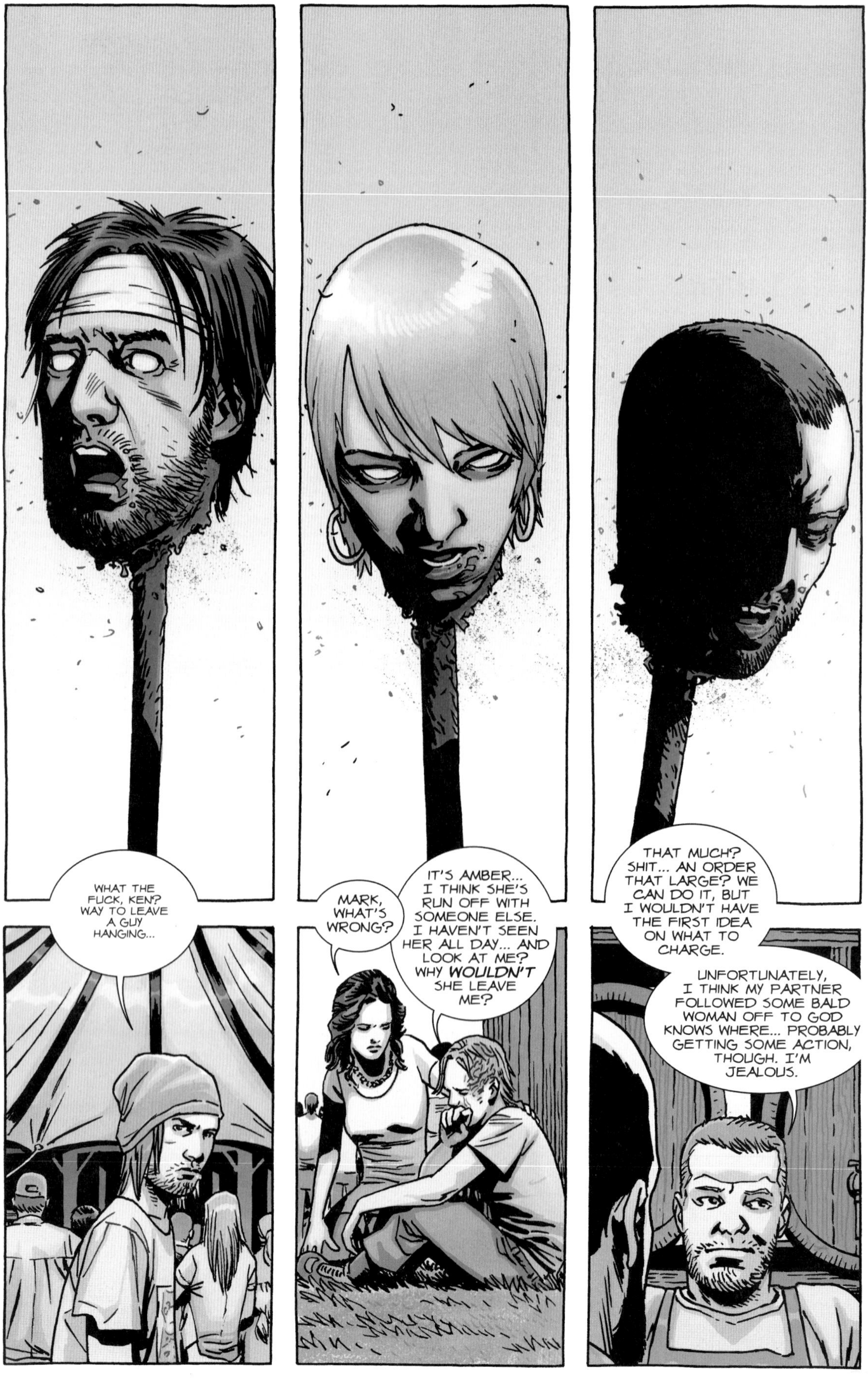
WHAT THE FUCK, KEN? WAY TO LEAVE A GUY HANGING...
MARK, WHAT'S WRONG?
IT'S AMBER... I THINK SHE'S RUN OFF WITH SOMEONE ELSE. I HAVEN'T SEEN HER ALL DAY... AND LOOK AT ME? WHY **WOULDN'T** SHE LEAVE ME?
THAT MUCH? SHIT... AN ORDER THAT LARGE? WE CAN DO IT, BUT I WOULDN'T HAVE THE FIRST IDEA ON WHAT TO CHARGE.
UNFORTUNATELY, I THINK MY PARTNER FOLLOWED SOME BALD WOMAN OFF TO GOD KNOWS WHERE... PROBABLY GETTING SOME ACTION, THOUGH. I'M JEALOUS.

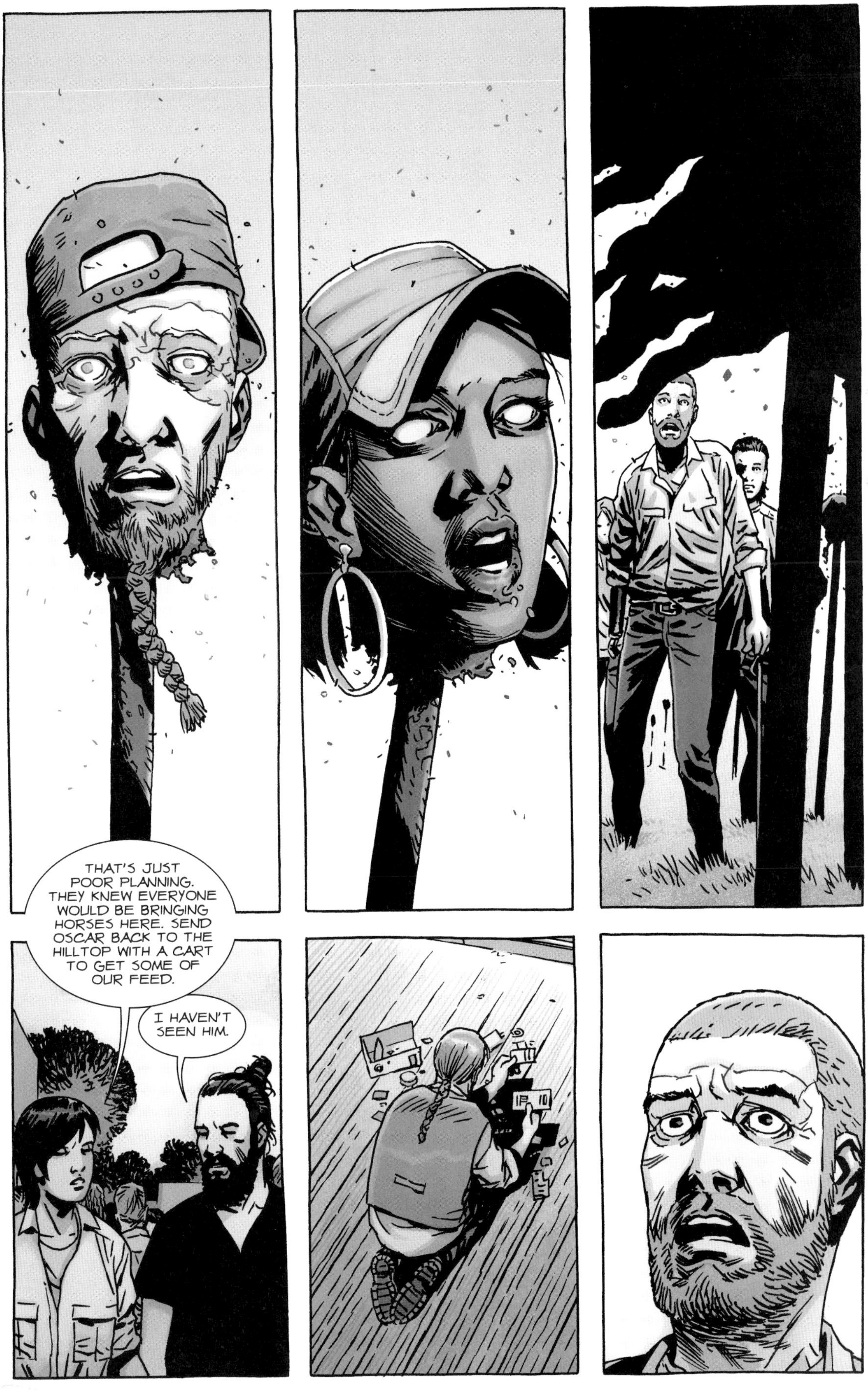
THAT'S JUST POOR PLANNING. THEY KNEW EVERYONE WOULD BE BRINGING HORSES HERE. SEND OSCAR BACK TO THE HILLTOP WITH A CART TO GET SOME OF OUR FEED.
I HAVEN'T SEEN HIM.

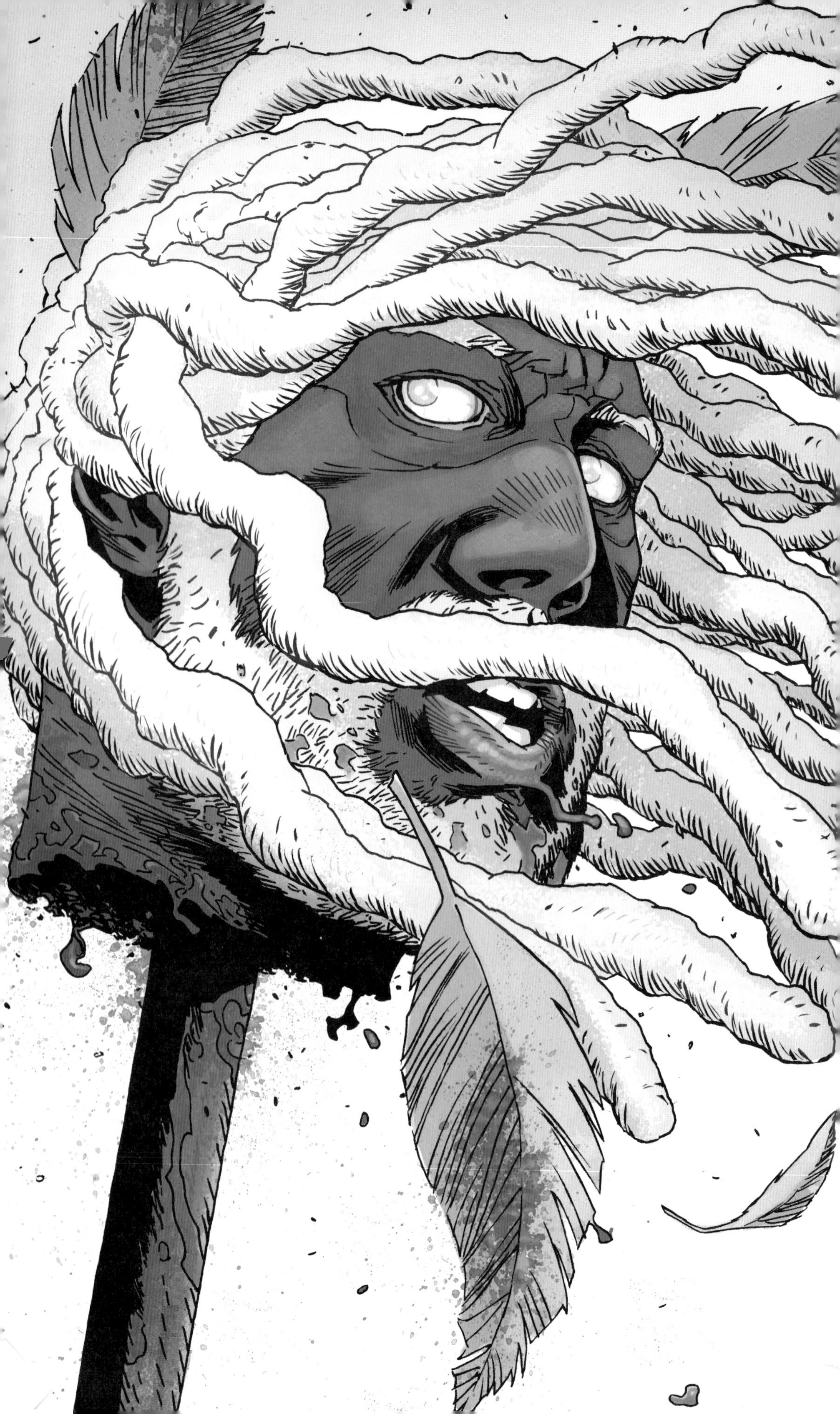

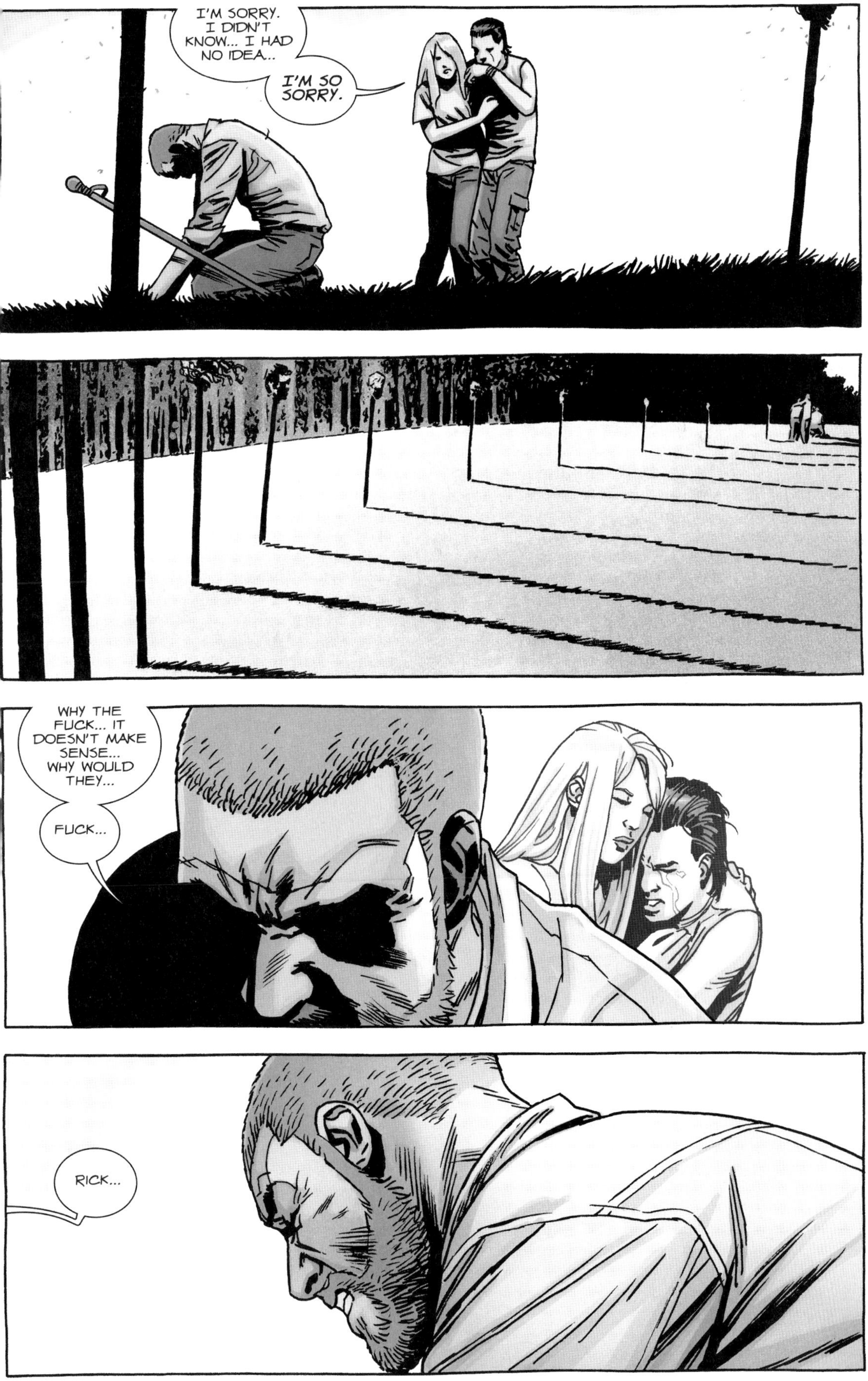
I'M SORRY. I DIDN'T KNOW... I HAD NO IDEA...
I'M SO SORRY.
WHY THE FUCK... IT DOESN'T MAKE SENSE... WHY WOULD THEY...
FUCK...
RICK...

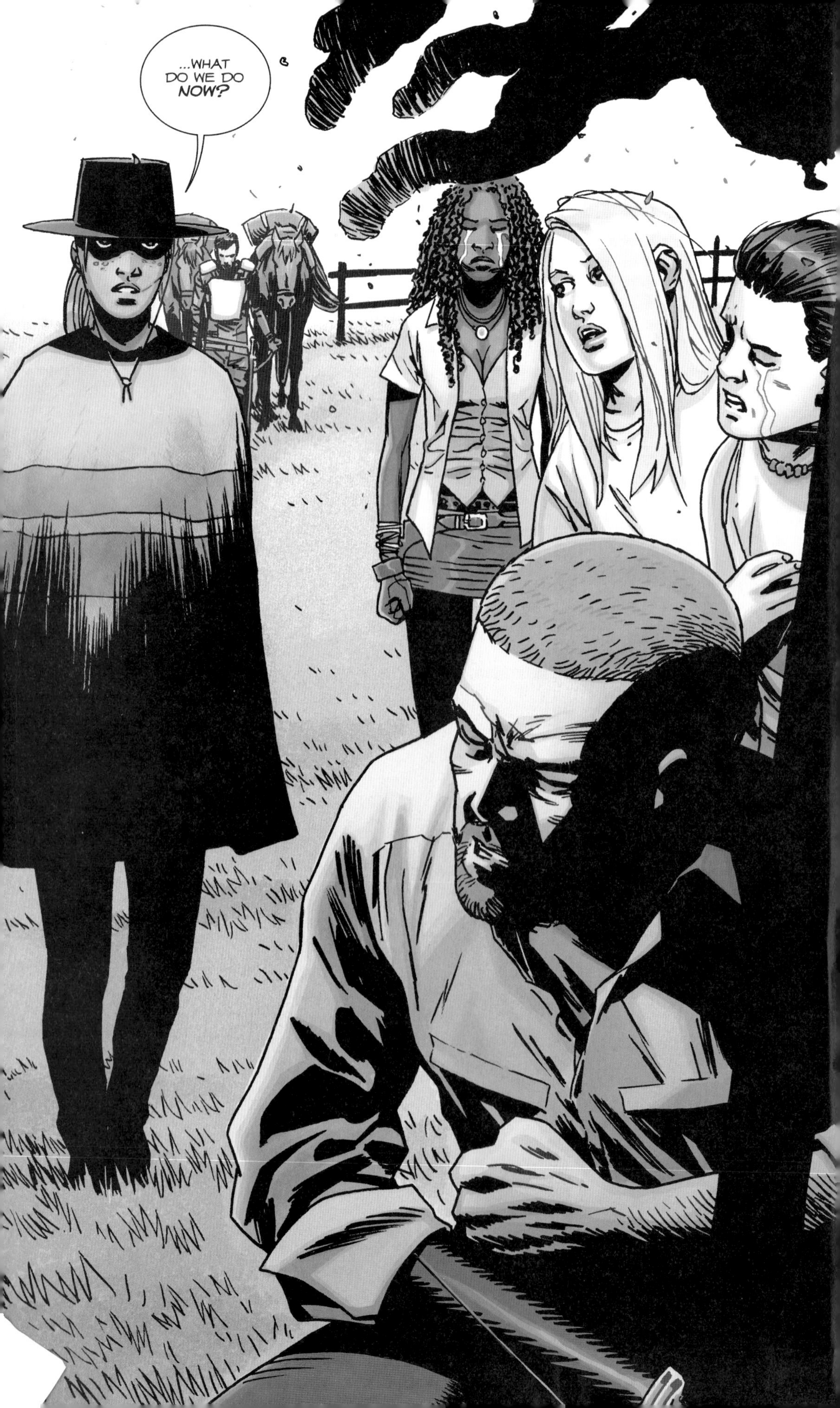
...WHAT DO WE DO NOW?

TO BE CONTINUED...

for more tales from ROBERT KIRKMAN and SKYBOUND

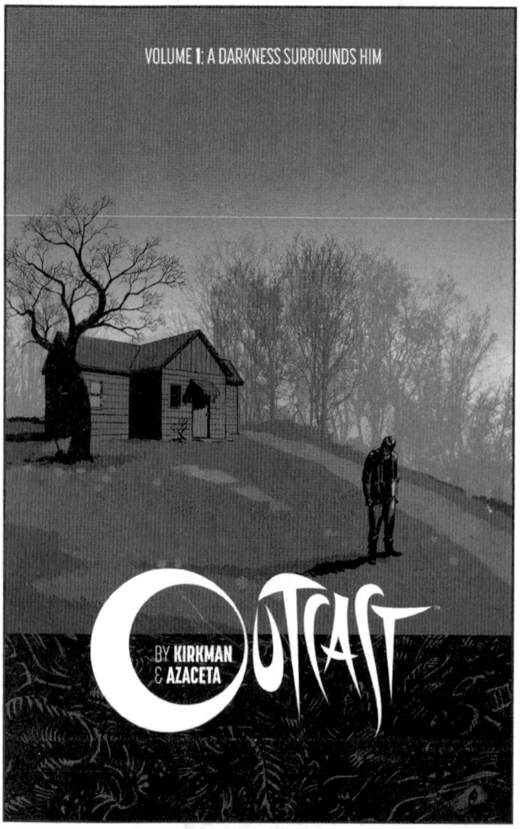
VOLUME 1: A DARKNESS SURROUNDS HIM
OUTCAST
BY KIRKMAN & AZACETA

VOL. 1: A DARKNESS SURROUNDS HIM TP
ISBN: 978-1-63215-053-0
$9.99

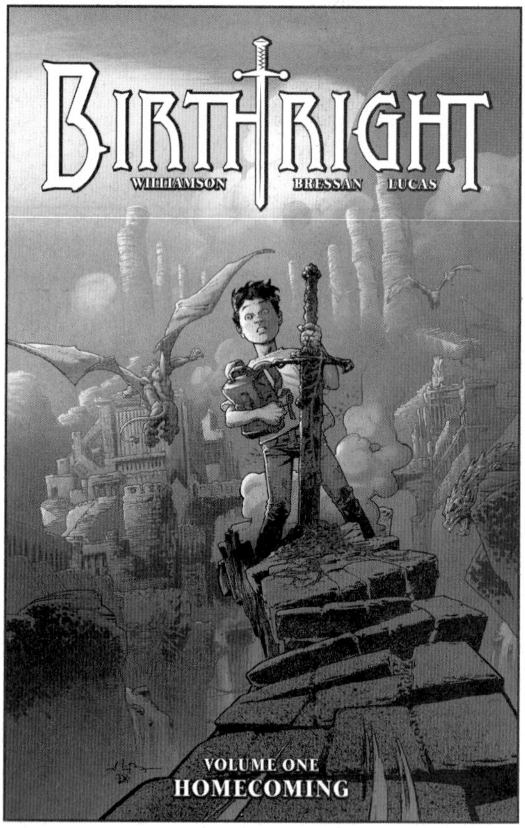
BIRTHRIGHT
WILLIAMSON BRESSAN LUCAS
VOLUME ONE
HOMECOMING

VOL. 1: HOMECOMING TP
ISBN: 978-1-63215-231-2
$9.99

VOL. 2: CALL TO ADVENTURE TP
ISBN: 978-1-63215-446-0
$12.99

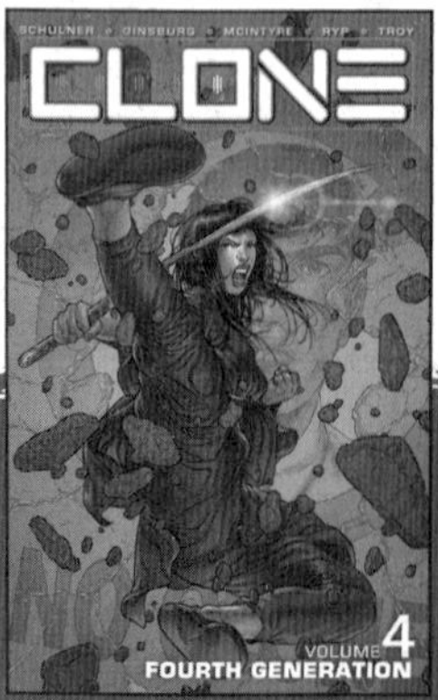
CLONE
VOLUME 4
FOURTH GENERATION

VOL. 1: FIRST GENERATION TP
ISBN: 978-1-60706-683-5
$12.99

VOL. 2: SECOND GENERATION TP
ISBN: 978-1-60706-830-3
$12.99

VOL. 3: THIRD GENERATION TP
ISBN: 978-1-60706-939-3
$12.99

VOL. 4: FOURTH GENERATION TP
ISBN: 978-1-63215-036-3
$12.99

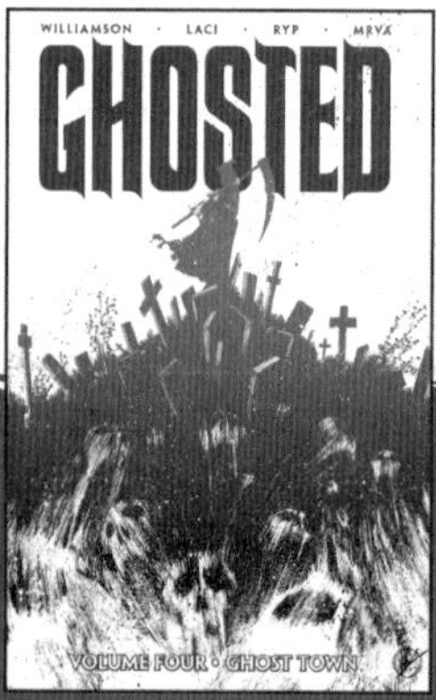
WILLIAMSON · LACI · RYP · MRVA
GHOSTED
VOLUME FOUR · GHOST TOWN

VOL. 1: HAUNTED HEIST TP
ISBN: 978-1-60706-836-5
$9.99

VOL. 2: BOOKS OF THE DEAD TP
ISBN: 978-1-63215-046-2
$12.99

VOL. 3: DEATH WISH TP
ISBN: 978-1-63215-051-6
$12.99

VOL. 4: GHOST TOWN TP
ISBN: 978-1-63215-317-3
$12.99

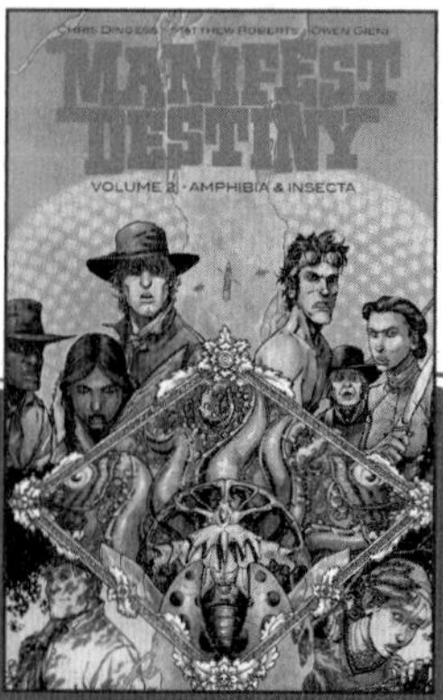
MANIFEST DESTINY
VOLUME 2 · AMPHIBIA & INSECTA

VOL. 1: FLORA & FAUNA TP
ISBN: 978-1-60706-982-9
$9.99

VOL. 2: AMPHIBIA & INSECTA TP
ISBN: 978-1-63215-052-3
$14.99

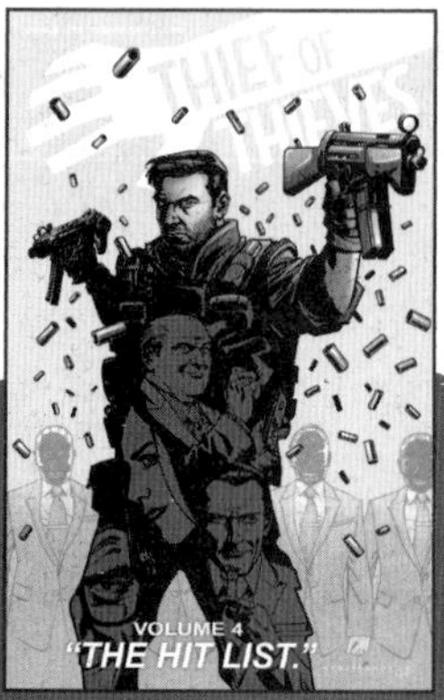
THIEF OF THIEVES
VOLUME 4
"THE HIT LIST."

VOL. 1: "I QUIT."
ISBN: 978-1-60706-592-0
$14.99

VOL. 2: "HELP ME."
ISBN: 978-1-60706-676-7
$14.99

VOL. 3: "VENICE."
ISBN: 978-1-60706-844-0
$14.99

VOL. 4: "THE HIT LIST."
ISBN: 978-1-63215-037-0
$14.99